Praise for the Rook & Rose Trilogy

"The characters are fun, the setting is magnificent, and the writing is smart and accessible." —*Los Angeles Review of Books*

"Lush, engrossing and full of mystery and dark magic...sure to please fantasy readers looking to dial up the intrigue....Jump in and get swept away." —*BookPage*

"Immersive.... A feast to savor slowly." —*BuzzFeed News*

"Utterly captivating. Carrick spins an exciting web of mystery, magic, and political treachery in a richly drawn and innovative world." —S. A. Chakraborty, author of *The City of Brass*

"A web of intrigue, magic, and the art of the con, this novel will catch hold of your dreams and keep you from sleeping." —Mary Robinette Kowal, author of *The Calculating Stars*

"Ushers you into the fascinating city of Nadežra, replete with complex politics, intricate magic, and mysteries that readers will be racing to unravel. Wonderfully immersive—I was unable to put it down." —Andrea Stewart, author of *The Bone Shard Daughter*

"For those who like their revenge plots served with the intrigue of *The Goblin Emperor*, the colonial conflict of *The City of Brass*, the panache of *Swordspoint*, and the richly detailed settings of Guy Gavriel Kay." —*Booklist* (starred review)

"An escape into a vast, enchanting world of danger, secret identities, and glittering prose." —Tasha Suri, author of *The Jasmine Throne*

"The richly layered city of Nadežra, combined with the deeply intertwined politics and rivalries of its residents, creates a perfect backdrop for the enchantment of Carrick's plot and characters. A fantastically twisty read."

—Fran Wilde, author of The Bone Universe trilogy

"An intricate, compelling dream of a book that kept me turning pages, with a world and characters that felt deeply real and plenty of riveting twists and turns. I loved it."

—Melissa Caruso, author of *The Tethered Mage*

"A tightly laced plot dripping with political intrigue. Carrick has built a strong foundation for things to come."

—*Publishers Weekly*

"This book was like nibbling my way through a box of gourmet chocolates curated just for Reader Me. A large box of gourmet chocolates."

—*Fantasy Literature*

"Has it all: complex, believable characters; a fast-moving, intricate plot; rich details of attire, cuisine, religion, and so much more, all of which lead the reader to believe that Nadežra exists in more than dreams. This novel starts off strong and only gets better."

—Jane Lindskold, author of The Firekeeper Saga

"A terrific heroine, intricate worldbuilding, and a bewitching combination of comedy-of-manners and action hooked me from the start and never let me go!" —Sherwood Smith, author of *Inda*

LABYRINTH'S
HEART

By M. A. Carrick

ROOK & ROSE

The Mask of Mirrors
The Liar's Knot
Labyrinth's Heart

LABYRINTH'S HEART

ROOK & ROSE:
BOOK THREE

M. A. CARRICK

orbit

orbitbooks.net

Copyright © 2023 by Bryn Neuenschwander and Alyc Helms
Excerpt from *The Phoenix King* copyright © 2021 by Aparna Verma
Excerpt from *The Jasad Heir* copyright © 2023 by Sara Hashem

Cover design by Lauren Panepinto
Cover illustration by Nekro
Cover copyright © 2023 by Hachette Book Group, Inc.
Map by Tim Paul
Author photograph by John Scalzi

Orbit
Hachette Book Group
1290 Avenue of the Americas
New York, NY 10104
orbitbooks.net

First Edition: August 2023
Simultaneously published in Great Britain by Orbit

Orbit is an imprint of Hachette Book Group.
The Orbit name and logo are trademarks of Little, Brown Book Group Limited.

The publisher is not responsible for websites (or their content) that are not owned by the publisher.

The Hachette Speakers Bureau provides a wide range of authors for speaking events. To find out more, go to hachettespeakersbureau.com or email HachetteSpeakers@hbgusa.com.

Orbit books may be purchased in bulk for business, educational, or promotional use. For information, please contact your local bookseller or the Hachette Book Group Special Markets Department at special.markets@hbgusa.com.

Library of Congress Cataloging-in-Publication Data
Names: Carrick, M. A., author.
Title: Labyrinth's heart / M.A. Carrick.
Description: First edition. | New York, NY : Orbit, 2023. | Series: Rook & Rose ; book 3
Identifiers: LCCN 2023000580 | ISBN 9780316539739 (trade paperback) |
    ISBN 9780316539753 (ebook)
Subjects: LCGFT: Fantasy fiction. | Novels.
Classification: LCC PS3603.A77443 L33 2023 | DDC 813/.6—dc23/eng/20230109
LC record available at https://lccn.loc.gov/2023000580

ISBNs: 9780316539739 (trade paperback), 9780316539753 (ebook)

Printed in the United States of America

LSC-C

Printing 1, 2023

For our families, both birth and found

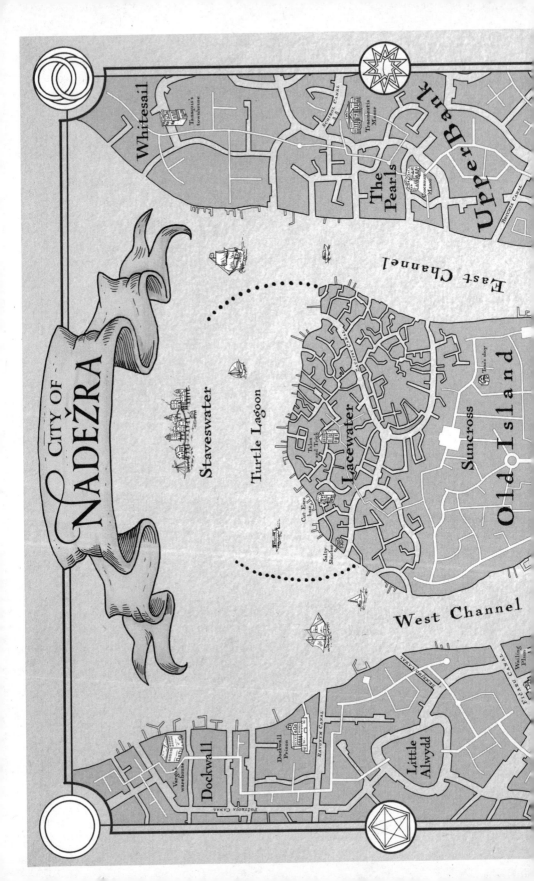

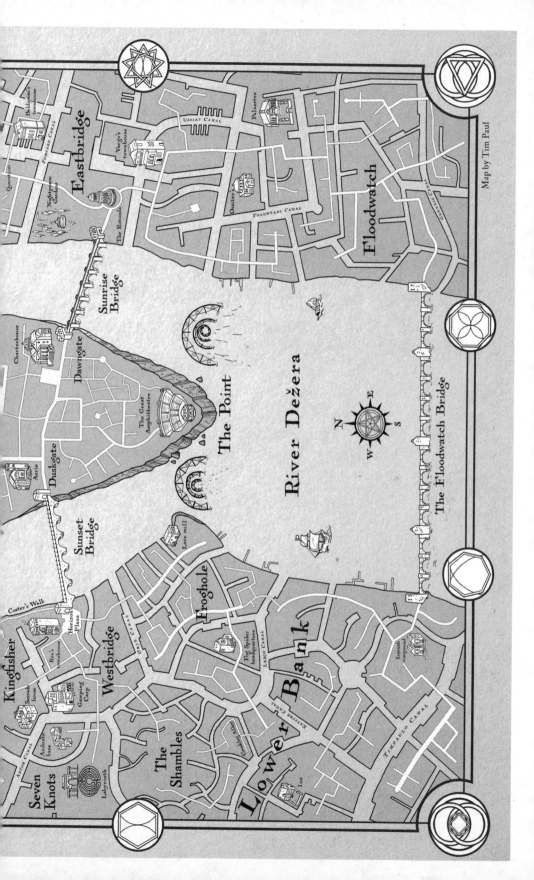

Dramatis Personae

Ren—aka Renata Viraudax, aka Arenza Lenskaya, a con artist

NOBILITY

House Acrenix

Eret Ghiscolo Acrenix—former head of House Acrenix, Caerulet in the Cinquerat (deceased)
Carinci Acrenix—his stepmother
Sibiliat Acrenix—his daughter and heir
Fadrin Acrenix—a cousin

House Coscanum

Faella Coscanum—sister of the head of house
Marvisal Coscanum—her grandniece
Bondiro Coscanum—her grandnephew

House Destaelio

Era Cibrial Destaelio—head of House Destaelio, Prasinet in the Cinquerat

House Extaquium

Eret Sureggio Extaquium—former head of House Extaquium (deceased)
Parma Extaquium—a cousin

House Fintenus

Eret Giuppero Fintenus—head of House Fintenus
Egliadas Fintenus—a cousin
Avaquis Fintenus—a cousin

House Indestor (disbanded)

Eret Mettore Indestor—former head of House Indestor, former Caerulet in the Cinquerat (deceased)

Mezzan Acrenicis—his son and heir, adopted into House Acrenix
Breccone Simendis Indestris—married in from House Simendis (deceased)

House Novrus

Eret Iascat Novrus—head of House Novrus, Argentet in the Cinquerat
Sostira Novrus—former house head and former Argentet

House Quientis

Eret Scaperto Quientis—head of House Quientis, Fulvet in the Cinquerat

House Simendis

Eret Utrinzi Simendis—head of House Simendis, Iridet in the Cinquerat

House Traementis

Era Donaia Traementis—head of House Traementis
Leato Traementis—her son (deceased)
Giuna Traementis—her daughter
Letilia Traementis—her former sister-in-law, originally called Lecilla
Tanaquis Fienola Traementatis—an astrologer and inscriptor working for
    Iridet
Meppe Traementatis—a cousin, formerly of House Indestor
Idaglio Minzialli Traementatis—a cousin
Nencoral Fintenus Traementatis—a cousin
Colbrin—a servant

House Vargo

Eret Derossi Vargo—crime lord and upstart nobleman
Alsius Acrenix, aka Master Peabody—a nobleman in a spider's body

DELTA GENTRY

Agniet Cercel—a former commander in the Vigil
Ludoghi Kaineto—a lieutenant in the Vigil
Rimbon Beldipassi—a rising success
Toneo Pattumo—Renata's former banker
Orrucio Amananto—a ubiquitous gentleman

THE STADNEM ANDUSKE

Koszar Yureski Andrejek—former leader of the Stadnem Anduske
Ustimir Hraleski Branek—his rival and new leader

Idusza Nadjulskaya Polojny—loyal to Andrejek
Dmatsos Krasnoski Očelen—loyal to Branek
Tserdev Krasnoskaya Očelen—his sister, head of the Crimson Eyes knot

VRASZENIANS

Grey Serrado—a duelist for House Traementis
Kolya (Jakoslav) Serrado—Grey's brother (deceased)
Alinka Serrado—Kolya's widow, an herbalist
Yvieny and Jagyi—their children
Jakoslav Szerado—father of Grey and Kolya
Laročja Szerado—mother of Jakoslav, an influential szorsa
Dalisva Mladoskaya Korzetsu—granddaughter of the Kiraly clan leader
Mevieny Plemaskaya Straveši—a blinded szorsa of the Dvornik
Zlatsa—Tanaquis's maid-of-all-work
Ivrina Lenskaya—Ren's mother, an outcast (deceased)

THE STREET

Nikory—one of Vargo's lieutenants
Pavlin Ranieri—Tess's sweetheart
Arkady Bones—boss of the biggest knot in the Shambles
Dvaran—keeper of the Gawping Carp
Oksana Ryvček—a duelist
Kasienka Ryvček—her niece
Stoček—a former aža dealer
Tess—Ren's sister
Sedge—Ren's brother
Simlin—a former Finger
Esmierka—a former Finger, now a thief in the Oyster Crackers
Ondrakja—former leader of the Fingers, also called Gammer Lindworm
   (deceased)

FOREIGNERS

Diomen—a Seterin inscriptor, leader of the Illius Praeteri (deceased)
Kaius Sifigno—aka Kaius Rex, aka the Tyrant, conqueror of Nadežra (deceased)
Varuni—sent to safeguard an investment in Vargo

The Rook—an outlaw

A Note on Pronunciation

Vraszenian uses a few special characters in its spelling: *č* is pronounced like *ch* in "chair," *š* like *sh* in "ship," and *ž* like the *z* in "azure." The combination *sz* is pronounced like the *s* in "soft," and *j* has the sound of *y*.

Liganti names and terms have the vowels of Italian or Spanish: a = ah, e = eh, i = ee, o = oh, u = oo. The letters *c* and *g* change before *e* and *i*, so Cercel = cher-CHELL and Giuna = JOO-nah; *ch* and *gh* are used to keep them unchanged, so Ghiscolo = gee-SCO-loh.

Seterin names share the same vowels as Liganti, but *c* and *g* are always hard, and the *ae* vowel combination sounds like the English word "eye."

The Story So Far

**(Or, this is their past, the good and the ill of it,
and that which is neither...)**

Ren infiltrated the noble House Traementis hoping to make a
better life for herself and her sister, Tess. Investigated by the Vigil
captain Grey Serrado, courted by the upstart crime lord Derossi
Vargo, and partnering with the hooded vigilante known as the
Rook—who was, in fact, Grey—she soon found herself caught up
in the lethal politics of Nadežra, when Mettore Indestor attempted
to destroy the Wellspring of Ažerais, the most holy site in all of
Vraszan.

When Leato, the Traementis heir, was killed in the magical disaster known as the Night of Hells, Ren—or rather, the Seterin noble-
woman "Renata Viraudax"—found herself adopted into House
Traementis as their new heir, but her successful con began to weigh
on her as her fondness for her adopted relatives grew. Trapped in
Renata's life, Ren sought escape in her Vraszenian persona, Arenza
Lenskaya. She tracked her friends from the radical Stadnem Anduske
group to the house of Grey Serrado's widowed sister-in-law,
Alinka...bringing her into dangerously intimate proximity with
Grey. Despite the risk that he might recognize Arenza as Renata,
she was reluctant to abandon the warmth growing between them.

In contrast, her relationship with Vargo grew colder. Having
learned that Vargo sold her out to Mettore Indestor, Ren began
to investigate him. As Renata, she accepted an invitation from the
astrologer Tanaquis Fienola to join a numinatrian mystery cult,
the Illius Praeteri—a cult Vargo showed particular interest in. As the
Black Rose, the mystical guise Ren created to save the wellspring

from destruction, she began to work alongside Vargo, hiding her distrust and hatred behind the Rose's mask.

The Black Rose was recruited by the ziemetse, the leaders of the Vraszenian clans, to oppose the new and more violent leadership of the Stadnem Anduske. With Vargo's aid, she captured a key target, and Vargo snared an enemy of his own: Dmatsos Očelen, brother to one of Vargo's most dangerous Lower Bank opponents. Unfortunately, Vargo's attempts to help the ousted leader of the Anduske, Koszar Andrejek, went wrong, and Andrejek was arrested. Even though a Praeteri ritual led Renata to openly turn against Vargo, vilifying him for his betrayal, Ren (as the Black Rose) had no choice but to team up with Vargo and the Rook to free Andrejek from the Dockwall Prison.

This tangle of relationships drew tight the night of a ball celebrating the adoption of Renata, Tanaquis, and others into House Traementis, when a letter from House Viraudax in Seteris arrived in Whitesail. Fearing it would expose her lies, Ren donned the Black Rose's mask to steal it, but she was caught by Vargo. To her surprise, he burned the letter without reading it, letting slip his regret that he had hurt Renata.

Their encounter saved Grey's life. That night, an ambush laid by Ghiscolo Acrenix caught and nearly killed the Rook. Ren was forced to temporarily don the Rook's costume in Grey's place, and in the aftermath, her only hope for saving him from the lethal curse draining his life was to take him to Vargo for aid. Vargo recognized the curse as the one used to assassinate Alsius Acrenix years ago—the same Alsius who became his spider companion, Master Peabody. At the risk of his own life, Vargo was able to save Grey from the curse.

With her identity revealed to both Vargo and Grey, Ren learned the deeper truth of Nadežra's problems. The Tricat-inscribed medallion she stole from her old mistress, Letilia, was one of a set of artifacts that used to belong to the Tyrant, Kaius Rex. It was the power of these medallions that the Rook fought against, and with Ren's help, Grey was closer to destroying them than any Rook before him. But after Vargo retrieved the lost Tricat from the realm of Ažerais's Dream, Tanaquis revealed what none of them had realized: The medallions called on the unholy and corrupting force of the Primordials.

And as dangerous as one medallion could be, the full set was worse. Ghiscolo Acrenix had a scheme to gather and join them together once more, giving himself the power Kaius Rex had used to conquer Vraszan. The trio successfully stopped him...but when the spirit of the Rook was willing to let Ghiscolo's ritual kill the medallion holders to destroy the malevolent artifacts, Grey defied that spirit to save Ren's life. In so doing, he broke the Rook, severing all connection to the spirit and its power.

Now Ren, Grey, and Vargo are each burdened with a medallion of their own. And they must find a way to destroy them before the Primordials corrupt their hearts...

LABYRINTH'S
HEART

Prologue

The world held three kinds of fear. There was the kind too strong to fight; if you were smart, you ran, hid until it passed you by. There was the kind you stood up and faced, because if you didn't, then you'd spend your whole life hiding.

And there was the kind you lived with. Because once it seeped into your bones, it never truly went away.

Grey knew he was supposed to enjoy the Festival of Veiled Waters. It was a time of celebration, from the Upper Bank to the Lower, when fog shrouded the city for a solid week, and everyone ran around in masks. There were singers and jugglers and plays about the fall of the Tyrant, and most people looked forward to it all winter.

But the week of unrelenting fog made him feel like someone might step out of it without warning, like he might vanish into it and never be seen again. His grandmother was Kiraly born and wed, but in Grey's mind she was as crafty as a Varadi spider, her influence and power stretching out like a sticky, entangling web. "We're safe," Kolya always said, when Grey shared that thought. "Two years we've been here; if she and Dodač were coming after us, they'd have done it by now."

Kolya didn't understand how deep the fear ran. He did everything he could to ease it, though, treating every trouble his little brother brought to their door with patient kindness—as when he returned to their Kingfisher lodging house on the first day of Veiled Waters and found Grey spattered with walnut dye, more of it seemingly on his hands than in Leato's once-golden hair. "When Eret Traementis sees you—" he groaned.

"It's a disguise!" Grey said, sticking his guilty hands behind his back. "So Leato can with us go around the Lower Bank."

"I want to see the performing monkeys," Leato said. "And the peddlers and the puppet shows and drink spiced chocolate and—"

Grey and Kolya couldn't afford half those things. Although House Traementis had given Kolya steady work, that only covered their lodgings and other necessities, not extravagances. The lift of Kolya's brow asked, *Is it Leato you invited, or his purse?*

The tiny shake of Grey's head answered that question. His friend might be a wealthy Liganti altan—not that he looked very rich or noble, with walnut dye staining head, hands, and half his borrowed clothes—but Grey wasn't hoping to sail a river of gold tonight.

He wanted someone with him, to chase away the fear brought by the fog. And he didn't want Kolya to carry that burden all night.

And Kolya nodded. Because even if he didn't understand, he never questioned. He just protected Grey, against any threat that might come.

With Leato at his side in a spare panel coat and paper mask, Grey could relax and enjoy the flash of bright clothes sweeping through swirls of mysterious fog, the real world seeming like a dream even in the off years when Ažerais's wellspring slumbered. Leato wanted to try *everything*: They feasted on toasted foxnuts, fried honey cakes, roasted crickets that crunched like embers and burned like fire. They shared a cup of spiced chocolate while watching a juggler catch and throw torches that burned away wisps of fog. That polished off, Grey dragged Leato into a Vraszenian dance, all stamps and claps, jostling shoulders and friendly mockery.

"Ugh, we've lost Kolya," Grey said once the dance shook them loose and they sat on the fringes, drinking great gulps of air and sweetened citron water. His brother leaned against a nearby barrel of millet beer, talking to an upriver girl. "Yesterday he met that one—Alinya, Gulinka, something like that—and an hour I had to stand there, listening to them flirt. Badly."

"Could be entertaining," Leato mused, laughing when Grey

slumped as though he'd been run through by that betrayal. "But that's a show we can watch any day. Let's go get our patterns read."

"*No.*"

Grey didn't even realize how cold and sharp it came out until Leato recoiled. With effort, he eased his voice. "At festivals like this, most likely they are frauds. Better ways there are to spend your money."

He could see Leato wanting to ask but swallowing it down. "Then what now?"

The bells rang third earth. Grey grimaced and said, "I would not have you in trouble with your family."

Leato tugged at his dyed hair. "I'll get a smack from Father no matter what time I get home. Might as well have all the fun I can first."

He said it so casually, as if a smack were nothing to fear. Pushing back his envy, Grey said, "Coster's Walk. You will like this, I think."

The embankment itself was full of slumming cuffs, but a troupe of Stretsko performed sword dances in Horizon Plaza every hour. To get there in time, Grey took back ways, dragging Leato through narrow alleys and across half-hidden bridges.

He went too fast, and the fog was too thick. Near the plaza, someone staggered backward out of an ostretta, directly into him.

"Watch it!" the other snarled, shoving Grey back. The light spilling from inside shone on an older Liganti boy, still in the gawky phase of growth, with straw-colored hair impeccably groomed behind his starred mask.

The boy's gaze flicked over Grey's panel coat and dark hair, and his lip bent in a sneer. "Oh, look. I stepped on a gnat."

Bow and apologize, Kolya always said. *It isn't worth the fight.* But it stuck in Grey's craw, when these cheese-eaters came to *his* side of the river. "Into me you ran," he said coldly. "On the Upper Bank are there no manners, that you apologize not?"

"What was that?" The boy cupped one hand to his ear, as two others followed him out of the ostretta. "All I heard was some buzzing."

Three of them together tipped the odds straight over to *bad*. When Grey tried to slip past, though, the boy shoved him back. "Where do you think you're going? Kneel and apologize."

Grey's heart drummed faster. He should have known better than to enjoy Veiled Waters. His grandmother wasn't the only threat hiding in the fog. And his brother—older, bigger—wasn't there.

"If anyone apologizes, it should be you." Leato stepped up to Grey's side, sounding every bit like the cuff he was.

The other boy only laughed. "A second one! Gnats always come in swarms. Shall we swat them?"

Pulling off his mask, Leato said, "Mezzan Indestor. It's me, Leato Traementis."

Grey's blood congealed in his veins. He knew that name. House Indestor held the Cinquerat's military seat: the foot inside the boot that kicked Vraszenians to the ground.

The flicker of surprise said Mezzan recognized Leato. But all too soon, the boy's sneer returned. "Dirty hair, dirty skin—no, you look like just another gnat. Don't you know it's illegal to impersonate nobility? I could take you to the Aerie right now. Wouldn't even have to bother Eret Traementis with this crime against his name." He grinned at his friends. "Assuming old Gianco could be dragged from the gambling tables long enough to care."

Grey recognized Leato's flinch all too well, the hurt of a bruise that never went away. Seeing it in his friend balled his hands into fists. "Leave him alone!"

Mezzan ignored him. Clamping one hand on Leato's shoulder in a gesture that looked friendly but bent Leato with pain, he said, "You should be more careful, Traementis. Don't want to court disease, keeping vermin around—your family's had enough bad luck already."

Bad luck. Words Grey had heard over and over again, for as long as he could remember, until they stuck like a splinter under scarred skin. The fear that his grandmother was right: that he was a curse, that he brought ill luck to everyone around him.

Snarling, Grey charged headfirst into Mezzan's stomach, ramming him against the wall. Leato tried to follow, but one of the other boys got him in a lock, pinning his arms. The third grabbed Grey—or tried to. Grey was weedy and fast and he didn't care if it hurt when he squirmed free, not if it meant he could plant his muddy shoe in Mezzan's pearls.

The third boy cursed. And unlike the others, he wore a sword.

Run, a voice in Grey's head said: Kolya, or his common sense. They sounded a lot alike.

But that would leave Leato at their mercy. Leato, who had stepped up to defend him like a brother.

As Mezzan curled on the ground, hands cupping his crotch, the third boy drew his blade and lunged. Grey retreated, skidding on the muddy cobblestones. Then again. But there was no room to keep withdrawing; he hit a stack of crates, rattling with empty bottles. Grinning, the boy circled his point in the air. "I think I'll carve a piece off you, to teach you a lesson."

Grey shucked out of his panel coat while the other boy was talking. When the lunge came, he whirled the cloth like a Ghusai veil-dancer to snag the sword.

It took the boy by surprise, yanking the weapon free of his grip. As it clattered to the ground, Grey thought, *Grab it*—but this was Nadežra. Here, the likes of him wasn't allowed a sword.

No laws against kicking it away, though. But before he could, a loop of rope fell, caught the boy around the middle, and hoisted him into the air.

Like a counterweight on a crane, a mass of fluttering black dropped into the street. Silver flashed, followed by two sharp smacks and two cries of pain. Leato stumbled free of his captor—then fell on his ass when he saw his rescuer. "Oh shit," he whispered.

Leaping forward, Grey planted himself in front of his friend, glaring up a length of steel into shadows without a face.

The Rook.

He felt none of the awe he'd heard in the voices of other kids on the street. Until he came to Nadežra, Grey hadn't even heard of the Rook. The outlaw wasn't a campfire tale, not like Constant Ivan and Clever Natalya.

But one thing he'd learned in the last two years: the Rook hated the nobility.

"Leave him alone," Grey said, flapping a hand behind his back. A futile gesture; Leato wouldn't run any more than Grey had.

"What do you think I'd do to him, little gutter cat? I came fishing for carp, not guppies." Stepping back, the Rook used the flat of his blade to herd the three larger boys into a clump. "The worst I might do is toss him into the river to grow some more. They don't *all* turn out poisoned." The glance the Rook gave Leato made Grey shiver.

Leato scrambled to his feet. "If you must do something to me, so be it. But let my friend go first."

"Such a pair you make," the Rook mused, eyeing them. "Almost a matched set—mismatched as you are."

"Better with a mismatched friend to stand than alone." Grey waited, tense and ready. Some fears you ran from, and some you faced. The Rook didn't scare him half so much as his grandmother, or his own cursed fate.

A smile glimmered inside that depthless hood. "You've got courage...but a lamentable lack of skill. With a proper teacher, you might do well."

Leato made a sudden, thoughtful noise. When Grey risked a glance, Leato whispered, "My teacher could train you. There's nobody better than Oksana Ryvček."

The Rook's barked laugh startled them both. "You, young Traementis, should watch what promises you make for other people. Now off with you both, before more trouble finds you."

With a flick of his blade, the Rook tossed Grey's panel coat back to him, only a little sliced by the Liganti boy's sword. Slinging a brotherly arm over his shoulders, Leato pulled him toward the light and sound of the plaza. In an awed whisper, he said, "What a night! I can't believe I survived the Rook!"

"Nor I," Grey said absently. His attention was all directed behind, at a figure shrouded in mystery, dragging three noble bullies to justice.

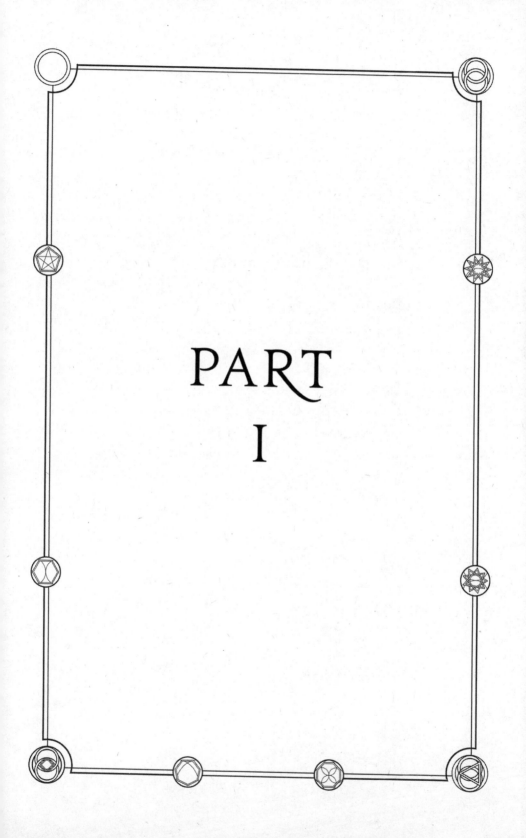

PART

I

1

The Welcoming Bowl

After so many years of desperation, misery, and loss, Donaia hardly knew what to do with happiness.

Or, for that matter, with dancing. "Rusty" did not begin to describe her skills: In the middle of a figure, she missed her cue to cast off and had to scramble out of the way of the pair of dancers hurtling up the set. Rather than find her place again, she ducked to the safety of the mingling crowd, chuckling at the thought of how Leato would tease her for abandoning her partner.

The laugh felt rusty, too. Memories of her lost son were everywhere, always... but she was trying to take joy in them instead of leaving her heart mired in sorrow. Giuna had come of age; guests had gathered at Ossiter's to celebrate her elevation as heir of House Traementis.

Looking through the atrium, one would never guess that a bare year ago, their house had been on the brink of financial and familial collapse. The tables groaned under the weight of pastries filled with stone fruit jam, soft cheeses rolled in dill and caraway, orange-glazed duck and spit-roasted boar fragrant with spices from all along the Dawn and Dusk Roads. Red wines poured from silver ewers carried by smiling servers, while bottles of white nestled into buckets chilled with numinatria.

But it was the people Donaia marveled at the most. Six months before, the silence of the Tricatium had almost swallowed the bare scattering of friends at Renata's adoption. Now that scattering had multiplied like silken scarves in a street performer's hands. Many delta families and all the noble houses had sent guests; even Octale Contorio was there, recently released from the Dockwall Prison and regaling a small audience with the poetry he'd written during his captivity.

Almost all the noble houses, she amended. Not a single member of House Acrenix was present—Faella Coscanum had made it clear they were no longer welcome in polite society. Without a word of explanation as to why...but given that Ghiscolo Acrenix was dead; his putative heir, Sibiliat, was at the family's bay villa "for her health"; and his adoptive mother, Carinci, had succeeded him as the head of their house, there was more than enough fodder for rumors. The most widespread held that Sibiliat had murdered her father— but if that were true, wouldn't the Cinquerat have put her on trial?

From the swirling, silken crowd came Scaperto Quientis, one fluted glass in each hand. "I wasn't certain if you would need fortification, or refreshment," he said, holding them both out.

Brushing flyaway wisps of hair from her face, Donaia reached for the chilled lemon water. "No wine for me tonight; I wouldn't want to put you through a repeat of our adoption ball. Nobody likes caring for a drunk."

"I didn't mind," Scaperto said, sipping the one she'd refused.

Despite the cool glass in her hand, warmth spread through Donaia. At first she hadn't been sure how to interpret Scaperto's kindness. But the days she spent at his villa had not only lessened the weight on her heart; they had cleared the fog from her eyes. While she wasn't quite ready for more than friendship, that shore was in sight. And she trusted that Scaperto would wait there until she arrived.

Meppe and Idaglio swung past, clumsy and laughing as the latter tried to teach his husband the steps. She was glad *they* were having fun. Tanaquis had fled as soon as etiquette allowed; lately she'd had her nose even deeper than usual in books and scrolls, pursuing some project she refused to discuss. Meanwhile, Nencoral looked none too pleased that the progression of the dance had forced her to join hands with Ucozzo Extaquium. Although his half sister Parma had retreated into mourning seclusion after Sureggio's suicide, the rest of their house was ready to go on indulging themselves as usual. Another bit of meat for the rumor-mongers to chew on, given the close timing of Sureggio's death and Ghiscolo's.

Donaia savored the lemon water and tried to banish those thoughts. *You're looking for trouble. Can't you just be happy?*

But how, with the curse on her house still unexplained and Ghiscolo's mysterious death hanging over them like Ninat's sickle?

And where that latter was concerned… "Have you had any luck prying information out of Faella?" When Scaperto shook his head, Donaia sighed. "Of all the times for that squawking seagull to close her beak."

"Era!" Scaperto feigned shock at her rudeness, but clinked his glass against hers. "Every time I try to draw her out, she just raises the question of who will fill the empty seat. If you won't take it, perhaps another from your house? Nothing in the law says Cinquerat members *have* to be the heads of their houses."

As if he meant any old relation, and not one in particular. A rush of amethyst silk and embroidered dragonflies swirled into view; the dance had brought her niece near. "Renata!"

Too late, she realized who Renata was partnered with. With a courtly bow, Derossi Vargo led her off the floor. The deep cobalt of his coat echoed the blue flash of Renata's dragonflies, complementing without matching, and Donaia worried that they'd planned it that way. Lately it was as if their previous falling-out had never happened. And Renata had mentioned wanting to speak with her tonight about an important matter: a conversation Donaia had avoided so far, dreading the possibility of having her worst suspicions confirmed.

The two promenaded over to Donaia and Scaperto as if they were still dancing, and Renata dropped into a curtsy as she arrived.

A year in Nadežra hadn't softened her crisp Seterin accent, but her tone was playful as she said, "You called?"

Donaia gestured with her lemon water. "Scaperto wants to toss you into Ninat's maw. Will you refuse him yourself, or shall I do so for you?"

That set him sputtering. "I meant no such thing! I only thought—"

"That two Caerulets have died in the past year, so why not recruit someone with incredible luck to replace them?"

The accusation carried an edge Donaia hadn't intended. But after losing so much to the curse on House Traementis, it didn't take much to make her worry. And she worried about Renata quite a lot.

Tanaquis wasn't the only one whose thoughts seemed to be elsewhere these days. Renata hadn't shirked her duties in the slightest, but she'd resisted Giuna's repeated suggestion that she could remain heir awhile longer. The girl seemed to swing between nestling into the warmth of House Traementis and holding herself aloof, as if she herself wasn't sure what she wanted. Or, perhaps, whether she could allow herself to have it.

By the sharpness of her laugh, Renata certainly didn't want what Scaperto was offering. "I'm afraid I'd be very ill-suited for Caerulet. I know nothing of military matters."

"Very few of us do," Donaia said. "Indestor had that seat for generations, and they granted hardly any charters outside their own control."

"House Coscanum holds one," Vargo mused, his kohl-lined eyes narrowing.

Scaperto cleared his throat. "Not even Faella can convince her brother to claim the seat. And I hope you won't take offense, Eret Vargo, that the Cinquerat is not considering you for it, either."

Donaia had forgotten that Vargo administered that charter on Coscanum's behalf. She expected a sharp reply, but he looked like he was suppressing a full-body shudder, one hand rising toward the hideous spider pin on his lapel. "That saves me having to find a polite way to say no."

Renata touched the watered silk of his sleeve, and Vargo flashed her an expression that was more grimace than smile. It seemed that seat's cursed reputation was enough to dampen even *his* ambition... for military power, at least. But Donaia didn't like the closeness—unspoken words, unreadable gestures—developing between the two.

Before Donaia could say anything, a small commotion at the door drew her attention. She'd rented the entirety of Ossiter's for tonight, only her guests permitted in, and one of the footmen was blocking a pair of people from entering.

"Excuse me," Donaia said, and hurried across the atrium.

"—servants' entrance, alongside the canal," the footman was saying, but he stopped as Donaia approached.

Grey Serrado snapped her a bow, as crisp as if he were still a Vigil captain. He wore the split-sided coat favored by duelists, a sword belted to his hip. At his side, Alinka looked practically Liganti in a surcoat of palest green. Apple blossoms picked out in cream and pink fluttered down the front from shoulder to hem, like she'd just come in from a springtime walk—Tess's work, and Donaia's gift for this special occasion.

Alinka's expression didn't match the carefree youth of her ensemble. She had one hand on her brother-in-law's sleeve, ready to retreat, but released him to curtsy to Donaia.

Stepping around the footman, Donaia took Alinka's arm in her own and gave the footman her most scathing look. "What do you think you're doing, interfering with my invited guests?"

The footman's bow was every bit as correct as Grey's. "My apologies, era. It was a misunderstanding."

As if he couldn't see they weren't dressed like servants. With a pointed sniff, Donaia led them past the footman and into the atrium. "I'm so glad you two could join us. Come, let's see where my daughter has gotten to."

She'd hardly spoken to Giuna all evening; with Sibiliat Acrenix and her dubious attentions removed from the field, quite a few prospective suitors were eager to parade themselves before the new heir.

Donaia couldn't find her now, until Alinka said softly, "There, by the planter."

Giuna was off to the side rather than dancing, letting Tess re-pin her hair. An effort she promptly undid by pulling free without warning so she could hug Grey. "You came!"

He returned the hug, then stepped back and bowed. "Of course, alta. We couldn't miss your celebration."

At heart, Giuna was still the girl who'd spent most of her childhood mewed up in the manor of a dwindling family, with very few people to call friend. She swatted his arm. "Why so formal? If anybody takes offense at you skipping the courtesies, I'll just have you duel them."

Giving him a long-term contract as their house duelist had been Renata's idea. They didn't need one nearly as badly as they had in past years—when they couldn't afford to hire one at all—but it was a kindness after he quit the Vigil. Donaia only wished she'd thought of it first. She still remembered the starveling boy who'd shown up on her doorstep with his older brother, begging for work. A nearly familial friendship had grown between him and Leato, despite the differences in their stations, and she felt more than a little affection for him herself.

Grey said mildly, "I'd prefer not to mar the night with swords. Good evening, Alta Renata."

Donaia hadn't noticed her niece approaching. Fortunately she'd rid herself of Vargo. Renata's nod to Grey was friendly, but nothing more; Donaia had a feeling she'd embarrassed them both by drunkenly shoving them together at the adoption ball. To Giuna, Renata said, "Orrucio Amananto was looking for you."

"Oh, *please* no," Giuna moaned. "Nothing against Orrucio—but if I don't rest, I'll collapse!"

"If the alta would take her seat again," Tess said, gesturing at an empty chair by the porcelain planter. "And *stay* there. Your hair still needs fixing; that should give you a moment to breathe."

Giuna plunked herself into the chair with obvious relief.

"Do you need Tess to see to your dress?" Donaia asked Alinka when she noticed the young woman tugging at the bodice of her surcoat. The gift had been a surprise, and while Tess had claimed confidence that she could take Alinka's measurements well enough from sight alone, Donaia still fretted.

"No, it's fine. You were very kind to have sent it," Alinka said in her soft, accented voice. "Only I'm...not accustomed to wearing such things."

"Ah, yes. I remember when Giuna and Leato were Yvie and Jagyi's age. I never had time for myself, either," Donaia said. Alinka merely gave a wan smile and murmured her agreement.

Clearing his throat, Grey said to Alinka, "Let me get you some wine. Era, altas, would any of you like some?"

All three of them waved the offer away, so he bowed and departed. In his absence, Renata drew Donaia to the side. "When everything is done tonight, we do need to talk."

So much for avoiding the news she feared. Donaia turned to watch the dancers, to mask the tightness of her smile. "It might need to wait until tomorrow, if this runs as late as it looks to. But you shouldn't waste time with me when you've admirers waiting. Eglia-das Fintenus was hoping to dance with you."

Renata's amusement looked strained as she said, "Matchmaking, are you?"

Trying to steer you anywhere other than Derossi Vargo. "It's an old woman's privilege and duty to try and pair the young off well. Especially since your mother isn't here, and likely wouldn't care even if she were." Letilia would be too busy trying to draw every eye to *herself*, married or not.

She hadn't even spoken the name. But like the tale of the sorcerer who appeared whenever someone said "Argolus," the high vault of the atrium rang with a voice that twenty-four years were not enough to scrub from Donaia's mind.

"My *darling* daughter! At last, we are reunited!"

Donaia went cold. *A nightmare. We've all been pulled into that dream realm again, and my worst nightmare is coming true.*

But no: She was awake. This was reality. Letilia Viraudacis—formerly

Lecilla Traementis—was posed with arms wide in the grand entrance of Ossiter's, in a gown so thick with multicolored embroidery that it strained the eye to follow.

A strangled sound came from Renata.

With a mouth gone dry in horror, Donaia whispered, "I think I need that wine."

Ossiter's, Eastbridge: Equilun 5

She's supposed to be in Seteris.

For one mad instant, a laugh almost forced its way past Ren's strangling horror. She'd told the lie so often, she'd started to believe it herself. But Letilia had never made it to Seteris after she ran away; she'd gotten stuck in Ganllech. Ren never dreamed that she might leave the comforts she'd arranged for herself there and come back to Nadežra.

Why is that Mask-damned woman here?

The musicians were still playing, but the dancers had straggled to a halt. Letilia swept past the footman trying to block her path as if the music were her fanfare and the dancers her audience. With a grand gesture, she spread the overly broad foreskirt of her surcoat: Seterin lines, but with a Ganllechyn flair tacked on. Literally. The multicolored embroidery, usually only hinted at on hidden plackets and underskirts, had been flipped to the outside instead. A menagerie of elongated hinds and hounds tangled down the front panel in an orgy of clashing colors. It drew every eye. It was impossible to look away.

Through the mental link that joined Alsius and Vargo, Ren heard Alsius's awed whisper. ::I understand now why embroidery is outlawed in Ganllech.::

His comment snapped Ren back to her senses. Did Letilia recognize—

"You've been gone from Seteris for *so long,*" Letilia cried as she drew near. "With nary a letter to tell me how you were faring. I simply *had* to take ship to visit you, poppet."

And then, before Ren could react in any way acceptable for Renata, Letilia was embracing her. But it was the kind of embrace Ondrakja used to give, the sort that was cover for fingers digging hard into her arms and a voice whispering venom in her ear. "Hello, Ren."

As if it had stopped, Ren's heart thudded painfully back into motion. Yes, Letilia knew exactly who she was.

"Letilia." Donaia's voice could have frozen the Dežera; her smile could have carved the ice into blocks. "Whatever are you doing in Nadežra? Having taken such pains to scrape our delta mud off your shoes, I can't imagine why you would set foot here again—even for your *beloved* daughter."

"The one you adopted out from under me, you mean?" Letilia didn't let go, but she transitioned the hold so they were side by side, Renata clamped there with one arm. "Really, Donaia, how *could* you."

"It was entirely Renata's choice. You haven't answered my question."

Ren could read the threat in the hand tightening on her arm. *Deal with this, or I will.* "Aunt Donaia, please. Let's not ruin Giuna's night with bickering."

"Giuna, yes! You've stolen away my daughter, Donaia. Perhaps I'll steal away yours. Where is she?" Letilia's gaze swept the nearby people, dismissing most of them without consideration. Tess had already ducked behind the planter, and the tension in Ren's gut eased by half a hair. Her sister had never been part of Letilia's household, but the woman might remember the Ganllechyn girl her maid used to spend so much time with.

Grey had stopped a short distance away, wineglass in hand. Ren met his gaze long enough to shake her head minutely: *Don't step in.* He knew how much of a disaster this was...but in Letilia's eyes, he would only be a filthy Vraszenian. Unless Donaia challenged Letilia to a duel, he had no grounds to intervene.

Giuna was Traementis in looks as well as name, easily spotted. Releasing Renata, Letilia dragged the frozen girl out of her chair and kissed both of her cheeks. "I'm your aunt Letilia, dear, though you've never met me."

" 'Aunt' is a term reserved for those in the register," Donaia said, pulling Giuna under her arm much as Letilia had done with Renata. "And this party is reserved for our *invited* guests."

Ren had performed this dance at Ondrakja's side too many times not to know her role…and the consequences if she failed to play it. "Surely we can host one more, when she's come all this way. How long have you been in Nadežra, Mother?" She had to force the familial term out of her mouth, and it tasted like rot.

Letilia affected a yawn. "Oh, I only just arrived today."

The pretense of exhaustion dropped away when she spotted Faella Coscanum, the old woman's face not remotely concealed by her fan. "That can't possibly be Alta Faella, can it? She doesn't look a day older than when I left! Renata, you simply *must* introduce me around. Or reintroduce, rather! I'm *so* eager to see all my old friends again."

Giuna silenced any protest from her mother with a touch to her arm. Although she looked like she'd swallowed a toad, Donaia said, "Yes, you're welcome to enjoy our party. I'm sure your friends haven't forgotten you."

Either Letilia didn't pick up on the veiled cut, or she didn't care. Ren was just as glad to separate the two before any blood was shed, and before Donaia could ask any questions Letilia didn't have an answer for. Because while clearly the woman had picked up the broad outlines of Ren's con, she couldn't possibly know every thread in the intricate tapestry of falsehood that was Renata Viraudax's life. Conversation with other people would be marginally safer.

With help, anyway. Dragging herself back into persona, Renata made a point of introducing Letilia with salient details: "my mother, come all the way from Endacium," or "my mother, wife of Ebarius Viraudax."

At least no one would wonder if the smile she troweled onto her face looked as fake as it felt. It was no secret that Renata harbored few warm feelings for her mother. And given how atrocious Letilia's attempt at a Seterin accent was—Lower Bank street performers would have drowned themselves in shame—any gritted teeth on Renata's part could be chalked up to that.

Letilia was in the midst of marveling over how many daughters Cibrial Destaelio had produced or adopted in the last twenty years when the crowd eddied and Renata caught a glimpse of Vargo leaning against one of the atrium columns. The nature of his bond meant he had to direct his thoughts to Alsius, perched on his lapel, but they were meant for Ren. ::If you need her taken care of, let me know.::

Vargo's notion of "taking care of" Letilia would probably end with her in the river, breathing optional. But there was no way for Ren to respond in kind and tell Vargo this wasn't a problem to be solved with murder.

She just wished she knew how it *could* be solved. What did Letilia want? How could Ren get her out of the city—and how quickly?

"Is that Scaperto Quientis? He and I used to be betrothed, you know. Renata, you simply *must* bring him over to speak with me."

Cibrial and her daughters had escaped while Renata was distracted. Scaperto talking to Letilia would be almost as bad as Donaia or Giuna; Renata didn't know how much of her story had been passed along to him. There were too many ways this could go wrong—too many opportunities for Letilia to make a mistake Renata couldn't plaster over.

"You must be so tired, though," Renata said, her voice dripping with concern. "Have you found a hotel yet? Why don't I take you there, and you and I can catch up on everything you've missed."

Letilia's gaze swept the atrium. Renata recognized that look all too well: a calculation of how many people were talking about her. Ren had made the same calculation at the Autumn Gloria, a year and a lifetime ago.

"As I recall, Ossiter's has private salons, doesn't it? I wouldn't mind resting for a bit." Patting the hand she had trapped under her arm, Letilia said, "Yes, poppet—come along and let's talk."

Ossiter's, Eastbridge: Equilun 5

Under any other circumstances, it would have been funny to watch Letilia's facade of merriment fall away like a discarded mask as soon as the door closed behind them. Ren didn't let her own guard down, though. Letilia might know perfectly well who she was, but keeping Renata's poise was important for the confrontation that was sure to follow.

So her words were still crisply Seterin as she said, "Why are you here?"

"You can quit with that ridiculous accent. How anyone believes *you're* Seterin is *beyond* my understanding." Sinking onto a lounging couch, Letilia stripped off her gloves and tossed them aside. "Ugh, I'd forgotten how confining these things are. I can't pick up *anything* without dropping it. Perhaps I'll start a fashion for glovelessness. Oh, stop gaping, girl. Fetch me some wine!"

It was like the past year hadn't happened. They might still have been in Ganllech, with Ren as Letilia's maid.

Ren gritted her teeth and picked up the carafe a servant had left on the table. Knuckling under galled, but most of the information she'd used to sell her con had been gleaned from the meandering monologues between Letilia's snapped orders. Still, she made a point of sipping from her own cup before handing the other to Letilia. "Do you want someone to overhear us and wonder at my voice?" Alsius was keeping watch outside, ready to warn her of eavesdroppers, but Letilia didn't need to know that. "I presume you don't intend to unmask me; otherwise you wouldn't have embraced me as your daughter."

"I'll unmask you in a heartbeat if it suits me," Letilia said, entirely predictably. But what followed was an unpleasant surprise. "And don't entertain any thoughts about getting rid of me. I've made arrangements for the truth to get out if I go missing for so much as a day."

"I'm not a murderer." The Seterin accent let Ren bite her words off very satisfyingly.

"You're Vraszenian, a liar, and a thief. How am I to know where your crimes end?" Letilia toyed with her wine, but her gaze didn't waver. "So long as you're no threat to me, though, I don't see any merit in exposing you—*if* you do as I say."

As though you've given me any choice. At least until I uncover these inconveniently prudent arrangements of yours.

Letilia might be canny enough to keep an eye on Ren, but she wouldn't know to watch for Grey. Or Vargo. Or Sedge. Or Tess. The line of people ready to help declaw Letilia would stretch out the door.

And so Ren forced herself into a curtsy. Not the elegant Seterin version, one hand sweeping up to the opposite shoulder; this was a servant's bob, a veil for her real intent. "What is it you're after?"

"The life you stole from me would be a start." Letilia lowered her voice to a hiss. "You ruined *everything* when you ran away! I took pity on you, gave good work to a foreign brat with no friends or prospects, but did you show me any sort of gratitude? No, you smeared your filthy hands all over my things and took whatever stuck to them. Including my *hen brooch!*"

She slammed her wine cup onto a side table, hard enough to splash her hand, then shook the droplets off like a slap. "Do you have any idea how jealous Prince Maredd is? He accused me of selling it, or giving it to some other lover! Everything started going wrong after that. It's been one disaster after another, until I had no choice but to come back to this mud pit of a city. All because you helped yourself to my jewels!"

Her jewels. Letilia's continuing rant sounded distant, muffled. Ren's pulse was louder, drumming a fast beat in her ears. *Tricat.*

The medallion. A piece of Kaius Rex's chain of office, broken when he died, its components divided up among his followers like dogs tearing apart a carcass. For generations House Traementis held the Tricat medallion, using its power to strengthen their position in Nadežra. Power drawn from A'ash, the Primordial of desire, one of the terrifying forces sealed outside the cosmos by the gods at the dawn of time.

Ren doubted Letilia had any idea what she'd stolen from her father, Crelitto. No more than Ren had known, the night she cleaned out Letilia's jewelry box, medallion and all, and ran. But that didn't matter.

Pain cracked across Ren's cheek. Letilia had just risen and slapped her. "You stupid gnat—you aren't even *listening* to me!"

Ren's street instincts had dulled. She didn't reflexively twist Letilia's arm behind her and slam the woman's face into the nearest wall. She only touched her cheek, distantly wondering how much of a mark the blow would leave.

"Here's what will happen," Letilia said, her tone sweet again, like icing over her anger. "You're going to take care of your darling mother. You'll pay for my hotel, my clothing, all the comforts I need...and you'll get me back into a register."

Disbelief shattered Ren's shock. "You want to rejoin House Traementis? A house you ran away from—now led by a woman you loathe, who loathes you in return?"

"I *want* the life I deserve. Even in Ganllech, there's been talk of House Traementis's change of fortunes, all due to their *wonderful* Seterin cousin. Imagine my surprise when I got here and discovered that cousin was my daughter, and that daughter was the Lacewater trash who used to scrub my pisspot. You should thank me for not spreading the truth from the Pearls to Floodwatch."

There was no way Letilia had discovered all of that tonight. She'd come to Ossiter's already aware of the situation, which meant she'd been in Nadežra for days, at least. Ren's allies would be able to track down where, and from that, what trap she'd set to reveal the truth.

Retrieving her wine, Letilia took a healthy swig. It left her lips wet and her cheeks flushed. "It doesn't have to be House Traementis. If you can't talk Donaia around, any noble house will do. And in return, I *won't* tell everyone you're a worthless Vraszenian *criminal*."

Or I could destroy you instead.

Ren didn't even have to do anything. Losing Tricat had clearly left Letilia cursed enough to turn her fortunes in Ganllech. Sooner or later, her own desires would be her downfall. It might take a while; Letilia had never worn the medallion that Ren had seen, disdaining the heavy piece of bronze as archaic and unfashionable. She'd only taken it to anger her father, and kept it as a trophy of her escape. But that wouldn't stop the curse from reaping her.

There was a faster path, though. If Donaia knew the curse on House Traementis could be laid at the feet of Letilia's petulant greed—that the death of her beloved son was, in a way, Letilia's fault...

For an instant Ren could *taste* it. The beautiful vengeance of seeing Letilia struck down, repaid at a stroke for years of misery and abuse.

Vengeance: an impulse associated with Tricat.

Her unsteady backward step had nothing to do with Letilia, and everything to do with the sudden recoil from that internal precipice. Letilia, however, smiled in triumph. "I see you're not completely mud-brained. You'll do what I say, girl, or I will see you—what's the idiom here, again?—*drowned in the Depths.*"

Ren's throat ached as she swallowed. For over a month she and the others had been seeking a way to destroy the medallions, without killing those who held them. So far they'd met with no luck. Until they did, Ren had to question every desire she had that fell under the auspices of Tricat. Even the ones she probably would have had anyway, she had to resist. Otherwise the Primordial's power would seep further into her soul. Changing her. Corrupting her.

I don't have to actually do it. Merely threatening Letilia might be enough to frighten her, familiar as she was with Donaia's temper.

But that would bring its own problems and complications. And if Ren frightened Letilia *too* much, the woman might bolt...and then the curse would destroy her. However deep Ren's revulsion of Letilia ran, her revulsion of Primordial power ran deeper. Nor was she alone in that. Tanaquis had purified everyone she could— all the Acrenix, the remaining survivors of the former House Indestor, Octale Contorio—because everyone agreed that letting a

Primordial's fury run free wasn't a good thing. Even among their enemies.

Which meant Letilia would need to be uncursed, too.

Ren's shoulders straightened. *So I wait.* Letilia wouldn't expose her yet; she needed Ren's assistance. That meant Ren had time to figure out a better way of dealing with her. And if at any point it seemed like Letilia was getting ready to use the knife she had at Ren's throat...

Then Ren could reveal her own knife, poised for use.

"I can pay some of your expenses, but there will be limits," Ren said, with calculated meekness. "I can't skim much off the accounts without being noticed; believe me, I've tried. And if Donaia revokes my access, I won't be able to cover so much as a bed in a Froghole flophouse."

No killing and no whoring. Her two rules. And now, *no embezzlement.*

Or was that, *nothing that would hurt the Traementis?* And could she trust that instinct? Tricat was also the numen of family. That might even be why Letilia wanted back into a house she'd cut herself out of a quarter century ago.

The show of obedience appeased Letilia. Huffing, she dropped back into her seat and crossed her arms. "Oh, fine. Once I'm in a register, I won't need your help anyway. But work fast, or I might grow bored and look for ways to entertain myself."

Ren hadn't forgotten the sort of entertainment Letilia enjoyed. She only waited, silent, until Letilia sighed and patted the chair next to her. "Have a seat, poppet. It's time you told your mama everything she needs to know about her life in Seteris."

Three Hands Join

Traementis Manor, the Pearls: Equilun 6

Even the Traementis kitchen's blackest, bitterest tea couldn't stop Renata's yawns the next morning.

Hardly anyone spoke. Last night Donaia had ranted herself dry, alternately exhuming Letilia's past crimes and assuring Renata, "Only say the word, and I'll ship her back to Seteris." She'd forgotten entirely that Renata had wanted to speak with her. Which was a relief, because Ren couldn't face the prospect of confessing her true identity right now. Not until she had a better grip on the situation with Letilia.

She yawned again. Giuna's spoon tinked too loudly against her teacup. Meppe and Idaglio were making their fourth doomed attempt to start a conversation when Colbrin entered and said, "Era, Alta Letilia Viraudacis is in the salon."

Like a trap springing shut, Donaia shot to her feet. "Now she has the nerve to show her face *here*? If she thinks she can come abuse my new family like she did the old, she's every bit as stupid as I remember. Don't trouble yourself, my dear; I'll deal with her."

Everyone wanted to deal with Letilia for Ren. Grey was ready to hood up and abduct Letilia; Vargo, according to Grey, had the same plan, sans hood. "Rook or Lower Bank rat," Grey had said in the early morning hours, as they sat together atop the roof of Traementis Manor, "one of us can remove that threat."

Ren wished it were that simple. Taking Letilia off the board was easy; the problem was whatever fail-safe she'd arranged. Until that was neutralized, they couldn't risk antagonizing her. Ren had talked Grey around, and he'd promised to talk to Vargo, Tess, and Sedge in turn. "We'll figure something out," he said, and sealed the promise with a kiss.

Now, Giuna caught her mother's sleeve before Donaia could storm out the door. "Perhaps it would be better if I handled her."

A muscle worked in Donaia's jaw, but she cupped Giuna's cheek in wordless thanks and sat back down.

Renata caught up with her cousin just outside the dining room. "Giuna, I need your help. Whatever else Letilia is now, she was once Traementis. If I was cursed, then likely she is as well."

Giuna had paused to tug on her gloves; with the second only halfway on, she caught a gasp behind her drooping fingers. "You're right. Oh, Lumen—yes. Whatever else we might say about your mother, she doesn't deserve *that*. How should we handle this, then?"

"I don't want to have to explain about the curse," Renata said. "But I need her to come to Whitesail with me. Anything you can do to help with that will be wonderful."

Letilia's lip curled in disdain when she saw that only the heir, not the head of the house, had come to greet her. But she was too canny to burn the ruins of a bridge she might need to rebuild; she was on her best behavior as she exchanged stiff greetings with Giuna and followed them into the parlour. Unfortunately, even her best behavior left something to be desired. Every compliment on the furnishings sounded like condescension; everything she said about her supposed life in Seteris turned into a boast.

Renata cut her off before the latter could lead into dangerous waters. "You met our other cousins last night, but I should introduce you to Tanaquis. I was thinking of visiting her in Whitesail this morning; why don't you come with me?"

"Whitesail? Oh, *definitely* not. I never go north of the Pearls. Unless it's to Seteris, of course!" Letilia's titter scraped like sandpaper.

Giuna pressed one hand to her chest and managed a very credible simper. "Oh, but Tanaquis is an inscriptor—the best in Nadežra! Iridet relies on her advice in *all* matters. Her birth charts are practically a *requirement* for anyone who wants to enter into a contract."

Or a register, Renata thought, wondering if Giuna had guessed Letilia's aim. Meanwhile Letilia huffed, arms crossed. "I don't see why I must go to Whitesail for that. I'll just send her the information."

"You could *try* that, but..." Giuna aped Letilia's habit of emphasizing every other word. Had she picked up that technique from Renata? "She refuses *so* many requests. It would be so *embarrassing* if it got out that she'd refused yours, like you were some stranger. I thought it might help for you to charm her in person." The suggestion faded with a wave of her hand. "But perhaps you'd rather send a letter."

Giuna's guileless innocence was worthy of Tess at her best—and it struck home with the precision of her needle. Letilia rose to her feet, but it was hard to loom over someone who smiled as if this were a friendly conversation.

"You think she'd refuse me?" Letilia demanded. Seizing Renata's arm, she dragged her to her feet. "Come along, poppet. I'd very much like to meet this cousin of ours."

Whitesail, Upper Bank: Equilun 6

By the time the sedan chairs set them down in Whitesail, an idea had coalesced in Ren's mind. She didn't *like* it—Letilia didn't deserve such generosity—but given her fears about the medallion's influence on her decisions, that might be a very good argument in favor of its merits.

"Ganllech was never your goal," she said, using one gloved hand to hold down wisps of hair the wind was trying to blow askew. "Seteris was. What if you could have that?"

Letilia eyed her with suspicion. "What do you mean?"

"I mean that I'm willing to set you up there. His Elegance, Iascat Novrus, has many contacts in Seteris. He's on good terms with Eret Vargo, and Eret Vargo owes me some rather large favors. I'll pay for your passage and a stipend. So long as you don't expose me, the stipend will continue."

"Last night you claimed you couldn't skim much from the accounts without Donaia noticing. Now you think you can support me in the style I require?"

Renata's smile didn't reach her eyes, and wasn't meant to. "Donaia may be a clutch-fist, but to get you out of her hair? She'll let me have whatever I ask for."

Letilia's gaze drifted, as if she were seeing Seteris rather than the shipping insurance office in front of her. *If I knew inscription*, Ren thought, *I could make her want it*. Tricat wasn't the numen best-suited to manipulating Letilia—Quarat would be better, feeding her greed—but the prospect was nauseatingly tempting anyway. She understood why Vargo and Alsius had flatly refused to learn the preparatory inscriptions needed to control people's desires with the medallions. Knowing would open the gate to doing.

She could only rely on Letilia's innate desire. Which flared briefly, as if she could already imagine herself at court in Seteris… but then died away. "I can't trust any promises you make," Letilia sniffed. "No, I'll remain in Nadežra, where I can keep an eye on you."

So we do this the hard way, Ren thought. Heading for the street that held Tanaquis's townhouse, she said, "Then let's not waste time."

For once, her cousin's disorganized household worked in her favor. Renata was able to leave Letilia in the parlour while she went upstairs to the garret, snatching a few precious moments to explain the situation.

She wasn't sure at first if Tanaquis was even attending to her words. The room was covered in numinatrian diagrams, the debris of multiple failed attempts to separate the medallions from their holders without any transfer to a new holder. Tanaquis and Alsius had hoped that would allow them to destroy the artifacts safely. With that hope now gone, she was pursuing different approaches, and Renata suspected the frown on Tanaquis's face meant she was mentally grappling with some tricky metaphysical problem.

But it turned out she was listening. "Yes, better not to tell her about the curse—don't want her asking where it came from. Will she sit still for the ritual?"

A creak on the stairs forestalled any reply. "What an *interesting* room!" Letilia said brightly as she came in, but her gaze was on Renata, not the garret with its skylights and star charts and prismatium circle in the floor. She clearly suspected Ren was plotting behind her back...and since the plot in question was for the woman's own good, that was more than a little infuriating.

"This is where Cousin Tanaquis does her best work," Renata said, ushering Letilia forward for introductions. "She's been pioneering all kinds of new methods—including something to cleanse one's chart of any baleful influences. Tanaquis, I know it's an imposition, but do you think you could spare a few moments for my mother?"

"Of course!" If the agreement sounded a touch too brittle and bright, that was only to be expected from someone whose life wasn't steeped in lies. "Alta Letilia, take your shoes off. Renata, could you draw three cards for me?"

Renata had brought her deck, but Tanaquis handed her a different one—a deck so new, the cards were still stiff and sharp-edged. She wasn't surprised that her cousin had acquired her own, and it meant Letilia was less apt to ask questions. Ren had forgotten to mention the pattern-related part of her lies last night.

Stepping to the side, Renata shuffled and drew three cards. Hare and Hound, The Face of Flame, and The Face of Roses. Adaptability, creativity, and health. Trying not to think of Letilia as the evil sorcerer in the story referenced by Hare and Hound and herself as Clever Natalya, she turned back to the room.

Letilia had utterly refused to sprawl on the floor making chalk birds, so Tanaquis was grumbling and setting up a more conventional numinat. When that was done, she placed the cards at equidistant points around Letilia, then said, "I'm closing the circle now." Her eyes narrowed as Letilia squirmed. "Remember, this outside figure is similar to an incendiary numinat. Too much movement will reduce you to ash."

"*What?!*"

Letilia's screech cut through the hum of energy as Tanaquis swiped her chalk to activate the numinat. But the warning served its purpose: She didn't twitch so much as a finger, even when the cleansing was done.

Which meant Tanaquis was able to step up behind her and snip off a bit of hair before Letilia realized what she was doing. That elicited a second screech, and Renata had to intervene. "It's part of her research, Mother. She did this for me as well, *and* for Donaia and Giuna. No harm will come from it." Tanaquis could use the hair to test whether the curse truly had been removed.

Letilia, fuming, demanded a mirror to check the damage to her coiffure. Tanaquis said vaguely that she thought her maid owned one, and that sent Letilia storming back downstairs. "I have one here," Tanaquis confided in Renata, gesturing at a trunk in the corner, "but—well. I see why you fled Seteris. Before you go, could I ask you to pattern me? With my deck, that is; I want to see whether using someone else's cards has any effect on the results."

Of course she did. Renata's vision of the szorsa who first helped Kaius Sifigno link the medallions into a chain had only intensified Tanaquis's interest in pattern. When numinatria had failed to sever the links between the medallions and their holders, Ren had tried in the dream, with no more success; the threads were too strong for her to break. Still, Tanaquis was convinced that if she just understood pattern better, she would find a way.

Unfortunately, her approach was very much that of a Liganti inscriptor, accustomed to clear rules and mathematical precision. "I don't think the deck has all that much influence," Renata said. "And testing the hair should tell you if the cards I drew worked."

"Yes, but—"

"I don't want my mother asking questions about me and pattern,"

Renata said quietly. "Not after she tried to burn the deck I found in Seteris." Another lie to brief Letilia on.

So many lies. How can she possibly remember them all?

Renata laid a hand on Tanaquis's arm before her cousin could protest. "Later, I promise. Right now, I have other problems to worry about."

Isla Čaprila, Eastbridge: Equilun 9

Grey took perverse pleasure in the harried look Vargo wore as he opened the door to his Eastbridge townhouse, his dark hair still rumpled with sleep. "You're early," Vargo said, in the half-irritable, half-confused tone of a man who was flat unconscious not long before.

"My apologies." Grey might not wear a hawk's uniform anymore, but he still offered a crisp bow. "I'm afraid it's my habit, in preference to being late."

He could hardly admit the truth, which was that he'd climbed out Renata's window just before dawn and had been skulking around the Upper Bank ever since. A foolish risk, spending the night with her like that...but now that Alinka and the children were home, and with Letilia clinging to Renata like a leech, he and Ren had to sneak time together when and how they could.

Besides, he enjoyed needling Vargo with the mask of the Very Proper Hawk. It was entertaining to watch the man bite back his first three replies.

The fourth was for him to wave Grey inside. "Then I guess you're also used to waiting. You know where the parlour is. I'll dress quickly."

It wasn't the first time Grey had been sent there to wait. Although he no longer had access to Vigil resources, he knew the Lower Bank well. So did Vargo, in his own underhanded way. The man they'd seen with the Ninat medallion had been well-dressed and had worn a sword—which might mean he was a gentleman—but some of the delta houses had their roots on the Lower Bank. There were also mercenaries, duelists, and plenty of places for a man to hide after he escaped a ritual meant to kill him. It made sense for Grey and Vargo to lead the search on that side of the river.

It also made for a great deal of awkwardness. Vargo didn't know that Grey no longer entertained visions of dropping him off a roof—that he'd had his chance, and passed it up. His behavior toward Grey was that of a man in the presence of one of the Vigil's attack dogs: Although it might not be savaging his leg *now*, that didn't mean it wouldn't, the moment it slipped its leash.

Vargo only left him waiting two bells before returning. His coat's indigo shade snubbed Liganti fashion, even as the tailoring cleaved to it as snugly as it clung to Vargo's frame. His damp hair had been finger-combed into place, the ends curling against his high collar. Dabbing a handkerchief against his freshly shaved cheek, he frowned at the streak of scarlet on the white cloth.

"If you keep taking the handkerchief away, the bleeding won't stop," Grey said in his best avuncular tone. "You need to apply continuous pressure."

"I know how to—" Vargo's teeth snapped shut on the rest of that response. The replacement came out through them. "Thank you. Your concern is appreciated."

Amusing though it was to make Vargo trot through the paces of courtesy, Grey had other reasons for arriving early. "I'm wondering if we should try a bolder approach in finding Ninat's holder. Print something in the broadsheets, asking after him in coded terms only he will understand."

"Wanted: Survivor of Event Nobody Talks About? Seeking Man in Possession of Lead Disc and Thoughts of Death? Show Us Yours; We'll Show You Ours?"

"I imagine that last would get many responses, but not the sort we're looking for."

Vargo sighed, balling up the handkerchief. "Iascat and I have discussed it, but we couldn't come up with an approach that avoided arousing interest we don't want. And besides, not much point in digging the man up before we've figured out how to destroy what he's got."

Tanaquis was working on the numinatrian side of that question; Ren was working on the pattern side. Too many problems, and no solutions to any of them yet.

That was a lie. They knew one way to find Ninat. Parma Extaquium had gone into ascetic seclusion; the suicide note she'd found along with Sureggio's Noctat medallion had sent her bolting for Utrinzi Simendis, who was only too happy to help her lock herself away from every sensuous desire she had. Noctat could draw Ninat to them, if they used the same eisar-based numinat Ghiscolo had employed in his damned ritual.

All they had to do was call on a *different* Primordial to do it. And that would never be an option.

"Any news from the Rook?" Vargo was preoccupied with a buttonhook, fastening his kid gloves at his wrists. A relief, since it meant he didn't see how Grey tensed.

The silence carried on too long, though. Vargo abandoned his buttons to study Grey with uncomfortable intensity. "No? That might be for the best. I think we can trust the Rook to do the right thing; I'm not so sure about the man under the hood."

"What makes you say that?" Grey asked. The question sounded stiff to his own ears, a shield over his guilt. There was no man under the hood anymore—or rather, there was *only* the man, and no Rook any longer.

And that was Grey's fault.

Vargo grimaced. "You weren't in the temple, but...He was willing to let everyone die to destroy the medallions. Willing to let Renata die. The Rook stopped him."

Grey choked on a bitter, ironic laugh. Swallowing it down felt like swallowing a blade. *It was the Rook who was willing to let them die. I broke him to prevent that.*

Snatching at the one topic that might knock Vargo off course, Grey asked, "Do you think that's what happened the night you lifted that curse from me? The man in the hood was more concerned with Beldipassi's medallion, so he left me to die?"

Now Vargo was the speechless one. Grey pressed his advantage. "Renata didn't spill your secret. I figured it had to be you or Tanaquis, and she wouldn't have dropped me on my doorstep in someone else's clothes."

"Blame Varuni for that," Vargo muttered.

"I'd rather not antagonize her. She made it clear she blames *me* for you killing yourself."

"She told you?" Groaning, Vargo rubbed his face. The nick from his razor hadn't just scabbed over; it was almost completely gone. Unnaturally fast. "The Isarnah are big on blood debts. A life pays for a life. She probably hoped that would settle our differences and save her the trouble of watching my back around you."

Shifting his weight, Vargo glanced toward the doorway like it was the Lumen's own light. "We should get moving."

"I was early. We have time." And Grey wasn't about to let him escape that easily. "So what do you think—are we even now?"

A brief flicker of contempt crossed Vargo's face. For Grey? Or for himself? "Don't go thinking it was more than an inconvenience for me. I'm harder to kill than most people." By way of demonstration, he tugged his collar down, baring the scar that raked his throat. "My life is bound to a...a spirit of sorts. It's why Tanaquis chose me to go into the realm of mind when Renata was ill; I had an anchor. Same thing let me lift the curse on you without any real danger. I knew I'd be fine."

Grey hadn't expected him to admit to Alsius's role. And while Vargo spoke with careless confidence, the hand that released his collar pressed briefly against his chest on the way back down. In the same place as his numinatrian brand—and the burn on Grey's own chest, from whatever started his heart beating again.

Even with an anchor to pull him back, dying was no small thing.

Vargo stalked toward the door. "The Night Moths are allies, not one of my knots. If we're late, they might decide they don't want a houseguest after all. We should go."

This time, Grey let him escape.

Nightpeace Gardens, Eastbridge: Equilun 9

After springing the Anduske from the Dockwall Prison, responsibility for hiding them had fallen to Vargo. The Lower Bank wasn't safe, so he'd struck a deal to put them in the last place the hawks would think to look: at the heart of the Upper Bank.

Nightpeace Gardens might be closed for the season, but Tiama Capenni herself let the two of them in via a side gate. "Follow that path around," she said, nodding at a dirt track not at all like the beautiful, sculpted areas open to the public. "And, Master Serrado, I'll have to ask you to surrender that weapon."

She made a small, mocking curtsy to Vargo as Serrado unbuckled his sword belt. "Your cane, too, Eret Vargo."

He wasn't at all surprised she knew about his concealed blade. With an equally mocking bow, he handed it over, then led Serrado down the dirt path.

::Should we be taking time for this?:: Alsius fretted. ::I know this Andrejek was helpful before, when you needed information on the Crimson Eyes, but we've learned all that's useful there. And we have bigger concerns.::

By which he meant the medallions. Vargo didn't disagree—but what else was he supposed to do while he waited for progress on that front? Tanaquis knew more about Primordials than the rest of them put together, while Alsius flat-out refused to learn any more on that topic than he had to. He was eager to assist with crafting a numinat to destroy the medallions, but not to grapple with the blasphemy of how Primordial power had come to be bound inside them to begin with. Vargo had, with great reluctance, gone pawing through the books of the late, unlamented Breccone Indestris, snagged at auction after the man's death; after all, he'd been a high-ranking member of the Illius Praeteri. If he'd owned any esoteric texts on heretical numinatria, though, he must have kept them somewhere other than his house. Maybe in Diomen's library, a cache none of them had been able to track down.

But he worried that Alsius's fretting was about more than just the medallions. For sixteen years the two of them had worked together to bring down Ghiscolo and the Praeteri. It had been Alsius's driving purpose, his reason to continue after he found himself trapped in the body of a spider.

Then they succeeded. And suddenly the driving purpose was gone.

Now they had the medallions instead, a blight Alsius was determined to wipe from the world. If all went well, though, soon that would be done with, too. What would they do then?

This wasn't the moment to have that conversation—though Vargo wasn't certain what a better moment would *be*. All he said was *Andrejek is interested in hamstringing Branek. Hamstringing Branek will take a club to the knees of my Lower Bank rivals. I'm all for destroying the medallions, but I'd rather not lose everything I built while we do that. So yes, we're taking time for this.*

Up ahead, Idusza Polojny sat under some trees, tossing pattern dice with a woman dressed like an ordinary laborer. Mažylo's Night Moths kept their own form of order in the gardens, regulating the night-pieces and the pickpockets who worked its grounds and protecting them against guests and the Vigil, but Tiama was pragmatic enough to put them to work weeding and hauling mulch in the off season.

Koszar Andrejek's safe house was a shed that ordinarily held groundskeeping supplies for the gardens. A narrow opening between wall and roof let in some fresh air, and the daylight filtering through was enough to see by. Someone had even brought a few chairs for visitors. It made the space cramped, but that was preferable to standing the whole time.

At least Andrejek was *capable* of standing now. He'd taken a hell of a beating after his arrest, and that on top of the one the Anduske traitors had given him during Veiled Waters. But Alinka, Serrado's sister by marriage, was a skilled herbalist, and Vargo had donated a few Quinat numinata to increase the effectiveness of her tinctures. With medicines and a safe place to rest, Andrejek was finally back to something like good health.

He greeted them both in Vraszenian. "Grey. Ča Vargo. Thank you for coming."

"If here you have called us," Serrado said in the same tongue, "then I suspect you have a plan at last."

Andrejek rubbed ruefully at the back of his neck. "'At last' is all too apt. Szorsa Arenza's cards advised me to be patient and wait, but I think not that she meant for it to be *this* long. Already Ča Vargo's gratitude must wear thin."

Serrado sat in one of the chairs like he was about to give a report to his former commander. It made Vargo want to lounge even more loosely than he would have otherwise. Everything Serrado did felt like a rebuke, and Vargo had never responded well to scolding.

But he kept his own Vraszenian polite as he said, "You bought a lot of hospitality with the information you gave me against Tserdev Očelen and her Crimson Eyes. And I'm still holding her brother, Dmatsos; so long as they can't find him, my leverage over her is secure. But I've had no news of Branek. Man's gone as thoroughly to ground as you have."

"Branek I must find, yes. The longer he controls the Anduske, the less it matters that his knot was not cut when he ousted me. But the more I hear of the strength he gathers, the more I realize I must look outward for aid." Andrejek laid his cane across his knees and ran one hand over the carved owl at its head. "Grey. After the Night of Hells, you worked with the ziemetse. Would you now be able to get a message to them?"

The *clan elders*? Judging by Serrado's twitch, he was as surprised as Vargo. "Able, yes. Should I? The ziemetse want your head almost as much as Branek does."

"This is why I ask you, rather than sending one of my own. But my ill future in the szorsa's pattern was The Mask of Ravens: the card for hatred and strife and division. I thought...perhaps not all divisions are unalterable fact."

He lifted one hand before either Vargo or Serrado could point out the risks. "It is likely they will hear me not, but if any you can find among the ziemetse who will speak with me—peaceably, under truce—then I wish to try."

Serrado ran one hand through his lengthening hair, as if that helped him put his thoughts in order. "Anoškin you are, so to the Anoškinič you must appeal. Otherwise you'll offend him. As for who might listen..."

His hand tensed subtly. Andrejek probably didn't see, but Vargo was starting to recognize the moods that ran beneath Serrado's mask. "The new Kiralič is known to be a fair man. And to be interested in pushing for more rights in Nadežra, rather than meekly accepting what the Cinquerat allows."

Andrejek brightened. "Yes, your own ziemič! Of course. With you at my side—"

"No," Serrado said. "That would help you not, I fear. The meeting I will arrange, but better if I am not there."

Vargo could guess why. More than once, he'd heard Vraszenians refer to Serrado as "the slip-knot captain," sneering at his willingness to cut his hair and grovel before his Liganti masters. A reputation like that wasn't easily shed.

And yet...as Andrejek said, Grey had worked with the ziemetse last year. So far as Vargo knew, that had gone well. At the time, though, the Kiraly had been without an elder, theirs having been killed during the Night of Hells. So maybe Serrado's current reluctance was more personal, a grudge with the new Kiralič.

Vargo could see Andrejek preparing to argue, and he cut in before the man could prod what might be a very sore spot. "Another there might be whose voice the ziemetse would listen to. I understand that the Black Rose has become quite the folk hero—and she's helped you in the past."

Alsius twitched under his collar. ::Oh dear. I hope he wasn't planning on asking Arenza to the meeting as well.::

If he was, Vargo thought, amused, *Ren will find a way out of it.*

Andrejek sat up like somebody had offered him a fresh honey

cake. "No love she has for Branek, certainly, and many favors has she done for the ziemetse. They say Ažerais speaks through her. Perhaps the ziemetse will listen. If you have a way of contacting her... think you that she would agree?"

"I know someone who can convince her to lend her support," Vargo said blandly. "But it'll still be up to you to convince the ziemetse there's any difference between you and Branek."

With a decisive tap of his cane, Andrejek said, "My best I will do to prove that I am the Face, and he the Mask."

Redgrass and Kingfisher, Lower Bank: Equilun 10

There was only one world in which it made sense for Sedge to play diplomat, and it was a world where the alternative was Varuni.

"Those two don't look nothing alike," the man in front of him said. He was the second-in-command of an off-charter mercenary company almost as well-known for banditry as it was for protecting traders; if the mercenaries weren't paid well enough, they could quickly become the bandits instead. Only the desperate sought out such companies.

The desperate, and those searching for them. "Yeah, we know," Sedge said, taking back the two sketches Vargo had provided. "You seen either of 'em?"

Around them, the stables bustled with outriders unsaddling their horses and guards bragging how they were going to spend their pay. This was farther west than Sedge had gone in his life, clear out on the edge of Nadežra where the butchers did their bloody work and people who wanted to avoid the city took lodgings. Varuni stood at his shoulder in stone-faced and silent intimidation, but her gaze was alive, searching the face of every man with a sword at his belt.

The lieutenant must be good at fighting, because he didn't have much intelligence to recommend him. "Thought you said it was only one you was looking for," he said, scratching a beard powdered dun with weeks of road dust.

Sedge was going to twist the paper into a garotte. "It *is* just one. Look, has anyone joined your company recently? Or paid to leave with one of your caravans?"

The lieutenant flipped the decira Sedge had given him. "Nothing like that. But the fellow on the right looks something like a man I met a few weeks back."

"Who? Where?" Sedge did his best to rein in his excitement. Looking too eager would label him an easy mark, and if he emptied their purse on excess bribes, Varuni would play knucklebones with his actual knuckles.

The coin rasped through the mercenary's beard as he scratched his chin with it. "Didn't take his name, just his money. Down at the Wailing Plum on Ship Street. Can't be sure it was your man; I was pickled in zrel. Oi, you! Who taught you to saddle a horse?" He was off to harangue one of his men before Sedge could ask more.

"Ship Street." Sedge met Varuni's eyes with rekindled hope. The lead was thinner than a single dog hair, but if they followed its scent... "That's Moon Harpy territory. They report anything?"

"No."

Not even that curt response could dampen Sedge's excitement. "Might be they en't asking the right people. Or the right people en't talking to them. We should check."

But Sedge's enthusiasm had fizzled by the time they'd walked the breadth of Kingfisher and spoken to everyone in the old gamblers' den on Ship Street. He ducked under the hanging sign of a split plum leaking juice, glowering at the two sketches sweaty and wind-crinkled in his hands. They really didn't look much alike: both were of men with large ears, but that was about where the resemblance ended. "You think there was some magic at work?" he asked Varuni as they walked. "Imbuing or numinatria or, hell, pattern—something that made it so people couldn't really see his face?"

She snorted. "No, people are just terrible at remembering that sort of thing. They *think* they remember, but they don't—not unless they're really paying attention. And sometimes not even then."

"This asshole's probably weeks gone," Sedge groaned. "He got compelled to walk into a secret temple, found himself there with four-fifths of the Cinquerat and the *Rook*, then watched Vargo smash Caerulet's head in with a brazier. If I were him, I'd be halfway to Xake by now." Sedge didn't even know where Xake was, but it sounded suitably far away.

"Might beat you there, if we don't find him."

Varuni sounding grim was normal. Varuni cracking jokes, now *that* unnerved Sedge. If he didn't know better, he'd say she sounded scared.

He tried for a laugh, but it was weak. "No need to cut and run just yet. Nadežra's survived a few centuries with these things floating around. Not like it'll get worse."

"Wonder if they thought the same, in the days before Fiavla fell." They parted around a cluster of canal scavengers going through salvage dug out of the Lower Bank muck. When they came back together, Varuni said, "You know, Fiavla sat on the best pass into Isarn?"

Sedge cast her a look, as surprised by her starting a conversation as he was by the geography lesson. "Guess I do now."

"Some of the Isarnah merchants got out before it got really bad. We have stories, passed down." Her jaw tightened, the sweat on her dark brow reflecting the light like silk. "A Primordial's influence can only ever get worse. Sometimes more quickly than anyone could imagine."

Ice ran down his back. *And Ren's holding one of those things.* Vargo, too, and Grey. He didn't want none of them within a thousand miles of this shit.

His forced laugh echoed hollow off the canal walk walls. "Well, we don't find this guy, maybe we *all* run off to another country."

How a grim look could come in so many shades, Sedge had no idea, but the one Varuni wore now seemed to be aimed a thousand miles south. "I'd rather not leave this kind of trouble behind me when I go home."

Another salvage pile loomed as they worked along the edge of Kingfisher to avoid Crimson Eye territory. Vargo had ordered his knots to clear the canals in preparation for the activation of the new river numinat. It was an order the local scavengers had taken advantage of, happily picking through piles for trash they could sell.

But the scavengers weren't the only ones clogging the canal walk. Beyond them, a gang of Vraszenians clustered under the deephanging eaves of an old courtyard house turned tenement. Red ribbons streamed through their braids like dripping blood, and their lashes were lined with kohl and crimson. Their carefree chatter quieted into silent menace as they noticed the intruders taking a stroll down their street.

"Speaking of trouble," Sedge muttered, slipping his hands inside his coat and around the hilts of the knives resting there. "En't this Moon Harpy territory? What's a bunch of Crimson Eyes doing this close to the border?"

"Things change," Varuni said, almost as softly as the clink of the chains dropping from her sleeves.

Sedge grunted. To the Crimson Eyes, Sedge himself was probably just another fist...but Varuni was well-known. Maybe enough so to be valuable as leverage.

"Fight or run?" he asked. He was good in a brawl, but he didn't relish the idea of ending the day bloody unless Varuni wanted it that way.

Then a clay bottle sailed through the air and shattered on the tenement's wall. The distracted Crimson Eyes shot to their feet, exclaiming in disgust, as the reek of piss washed over the other unpleasant scents of canal mulch and old sweat.

"Run," Varuni said, and they bolted back the way they'd come.

Sedge was only slightly surprised when they turned a corner and a pair of pity-rustlers beckoned them into an alley. They ducked behind a curtain of laundry just in time for a half dozen angry Crimson Eyes ripe with the stink of piss to charge past.

And he wasn't surprised at all when a familiar sparrow of a girl slid down from the roof a few moments later, a grin splitting her narrow cheeks and four puffy red claw marks crossing her brow. She led them through a laundry, the air thick with humidity from the vats and stinging with the scent of lye. The autumn air on the far side was sweet and crisp as fresh cider.

"Hah, I knew those pisspots was genius. Betcha we get more cats, we could sell 'em for profit. You two get any on you?" Arkady Bones leaned close enough to take a sniff of Sedge and Varuni. "Nope. Good thing. Once you're doused in cat piss, en't nothing getting that smell out of your clothes."

Given that she wore a new coat of piebald velvet in place of the patchwork one she'd favored before, Sedge suspected she'd learned this from experience. He knocked wrists with her, his knot charm against the wad filling out her sleeve. "Thanks for the distraction."

"That pot's been sloshing in my pocket all day waiting to get chucked. Figured I might as well save your ass so Chains could keep admiring it." Arkady's grin widened at Varuni's scowl. "Don't glare me to death! Might've found something for you. My kids heard some night-pieces talking about a big-eared guy with a nice sword holing up in a Lacewater flophouse. Could be they was just talking about his Noctat-given gifts, but…"

Odds were it would be like the Wailing Plum lead. But Sedge had already walked the length of Nadežra six times on this mission, and he would walk it six hundred times if that was what it took to end these medallions.

When he looked at Varuni, she gestured to a bridge that led east. "Lead the way."

The Pearls, Upper Bank: Equilun 15

Ren had plenty of practice at sneaking out of Traementis Manor via her suite's balcony. But not all of her business could be conducted at night, and these days, leaving the manor at normal hours meant acquiring an unwanted shadow.

That shadow wasn't even subtle about it. "I hear you know absolutely *everyone*," Letilia had said breezily. "Like mother, like

daughter! But it's been so terribly long since I was here. You absolutely *must* introduce me to your friends." The friendly arm she
looped through Ren's was, as usual, cover for her fingers digging in.

Ren knew what Letilia was doing: trying to ensure Ren had no
chance to hatch a conspiracy against her, while reestablishing social
connections. But all it truly meant was that Ren couldn't do the
things she wanted. Like slipping away to see Grey, or spending time at
Vargo's house just being herself. And it wore her patience to a thread.

Though on this particular occasion, she almost didn't mind.
"You remember Faella Coscanum, of course," she said to Letilia.
"She's invited me to tea—"

"Wonderful! I'll come along. Dear Faella was always *so* kind
to me."

Faella wasn't "always so kind" to anybody. But Ren had confidence that Faella expected Letilia to tag along, and she was curious
to see what the old woman had planned. Pulling herself properly
into Renata's head, she set out across the Pearls to Coscanum Manor.

The day was for intimate visits rather than social gatherings, so
the majordomo led them to an upstairs solar. Outside the open windows, the River Dežera stretched like a shining ribbon, with the
Old Island a stained cameo at its center.

Faella wasn't quite alone. Her grandnephew Bondiro sat with her
on the pale velvet couches, wearing a jonquil-striped coat somehow
comfortably rumpled despite careful pressing and tailoring. He did a
reasonable job of not looking bored with the small talk as he poured
tea. Renata might have been bored herself, if she weren't strung
tight with worry that Letilia would, despite coaching, make some
error in discussing her supposed life in Seteris. But Letilia's biggest
mistake was her continual attempt to do a Seterin accent, which
made Faella's eye twitch.

Eventually Bondiro said, "Alta Letilia, your daughter has such a
fine eye for art, she must have inherited it from you. If you wouldn't
mind, I have a collection of Seterin crossroads idols that I simply
must get your thoughts on."

He wasn't adroit enough to make it sound like anything other than a transparent attempt to get her to go with him, leaving Renata and Faella to their conversation. But Bondiro was also young, handsome, and unmarried, and Faella—who *was* that adroit—gave him the sort of indulgent smile one might expect from a fond great-aunt encouraging her grandnephew's courting.

Letilia took the bait. Once they were alone, Faella flicked her fan open and said, "He'll do a very good job of annoying her for the next few bells. I'm not about to let that tick dig into Coscanum flesh. Tell me, what plans do you have for shipping her back to Seteris?"

"I'm sure she'll tire of Nadežra soon enough," Renata said.

For all her skill at lying, she couldn't quite sell that line. Faella tsked. "If she's here, it's because something drove her back. Problems at home, I imagine. Has she shared those with you? No? Well, you're a clever girl; you'll winkle them out soon enough. In the meanwhile, we have business that is none of your mother's."

"Please tell me you've found the stranger."

Faella dashed her hopes with a sigh. "No—and it would help if any of us had taken a good enough look at the man to make a decent sketch. I suppose we were all distracted by Ghiscolo's attempt to murder us, though that's hardly an excuse. But I would know him if I saw him. You wouldn't *believe* the array of nobodies I've invited to my house, hoping to lay eyes on that man."

"Then what business did you have in mind?"

"Your own, my dear." Faella leaned forward, her eyes gleaming with delight. "Rumors have been hanging at your hem for months that you've a secret lover, but a *Vraszenian*? How shocking."

Renata's breath stopped.

"And it's more than just an affair of the body, isn't it?" Faella said, sounding not at all shocked. "The night your mother arrived, after you came out of that salon where the two of you talked...I saw where your eyes went. Oh, don't worry. You're far better at hiding such things than most—well, as long as you two aren't dancing. Your turn around the floor the night of the adoption ball was practically indecent. But when you were in trouble, it was Master Serrado your gaze went to."

Caught so badly off guard, Ren couldn't find words. "I—"

Faella patted her hand. "I'm not threatening you, girl. I'm offering my assistance. If you want to bring him out of the shadows to stand at your side...there might be a way."

Ren was still fumbling for coherence. What she'd thought was her private life had suddenly slammed into her masquerade, and all she could think was that Faella never offered her help for free. "In exchange for what?"

As though Renata had already agreed to her terms, Faella chose a puffed pastry filled with sweet cheese and took her time savoring it. After she'd swallowed, she said, "Marvisal's happiness."

Marvisal, whose best friend in Nadežra had been Sibiliat Acrenix. Marvisal, whose betrothed had been Mezzan Indestor—a man now damned twice over. Renata hadn't seen her at any social events for weeks.

"We're hardly friends," Renata said. "If she wants company—"

"She doesn't. In fact, she refuses to leave her room. Nor will she talk to me; believe me, I've tried." Faella's manner was polished smooth by decades of practice, but the noise of frustration she made sounded real. "She's cut herself off from society, and I'm the last person to understand that."

It was more than just a statement of personality. Faella had held the Illi-ten medallion since her youth. Tanaquis, in one of her conversations with Renata, had likened that numen to pattern. Illi, the None That Is Many, was the connection between all things: death and rebirth, ten and zero. And society, an influence that had seeped into Faella's very bones.

Yet it sounded like Marvisal, subject to that influence through the numinatria of their family register, was rejecting all connections. Renata said, "That's it? You simply want me to help Marvisal?"

Faella skewered her with a glare. "Don't sound so dubious. I never had much inclination to marry, and none for bearing children; I really don't understand the appeal. But I adore my Marvisal and Bondiro. I would snuff out the Lumen to make them happy."

Renata bowed her head in apology, and Faella went on in a

brighter tone. "As I said, you're a clever girl. Find out what Marvisal wants—help her, if you can—and I'll help you get your man. In fact, I'll make it so the city throws flowers in your honor."

"Forgive me for doubting again, Alta Faella, but I've seen the attitude toward Vraszenians here. What could overcome that?"

Faella pressed her palms together, looking almost as giddy as Tess confronted with a new bale of cloth. "*A story*, my dear."

She didn't keep Renata waiting for an explanation. "Tell me, did anyone ever hold the Trials of the Volti while you were in Endacium? There hasn't been one in Nadežra in decades...though I recall your mother tried to have them called for herself."

The name was faintly familiar, but Renata couldn't place it fast enough to cover for her ignorance. "I've never seen one, no. How do they work here?"

"It all depends on what virtues you want to test. The first trial is usually a dueling tournament; strength and courage are time-honored virtues, after all, and it makes for a good show. After that, it's up to you. Diponne Contorio had a maze cut into a rice field for his suitors. Watching all those women slosh around in the muddy water was entertaining, but the bugs were dreadful."

She leaned forward, putting one hand on Renata's knee. "But at the end... *nihil peto sed gratiam*. Or as my grandfather always phrased it when he told the tale, 'No favor do I ask but your favor.'"

That phrase allowed Renata to pin down the memory. It was an old piece of Seterin folklore, the story of how a humble shepherd had won the hand of a princess, in the days when Seteris was ruled by kings. She'd promised a boon to whoever passed her trials, and he'd asked only for permission to court her. Seterins and Liganti had made a tradition of it since, though not in Nadežra, not in Ren's lifetime.

"Just imagine the spectacle!" Faella said, when Renata still hesitated. "Don't you think we could use something to bring us together, after everything this city has been through lately? Those Anduske rebels, the Night of Hells, upheavals with Caerulet... ordinarily the trials would only be open to nobility and delta gentry, but for Master Serrado to enter, you'll have to open them to everyone. The

Lower Bank will love you for that. Especially if you offer secondary prizes at the earlier stages—money, charter administration contracts, clothing from that maid of yours. Whatever suits your fancy."

She was pushing a touch too hard, but not without effect. "You realize," Renata said, her thoughts gaining speed as she weighed the notion, "this will only help me if Master Serrado wins."

Faella wheezed a laugh. "Oh, my dear. People *assume* these trials aren't being played fair. Half the fun comes from trying to guess who the intended winner is! The other half comes from watching ambitious contenders try to upset those plans. But don't worry: With me arranging things, all will go according to your wishes."

The possibilities unfolded like a flower in Ren's mind. Dueling, Grey would have no difficulty with. And she could craft the other trials in his favor, give him hints and aid to ensure he won.

If she were still the heir of House Traementis, this would never work. But that was safely transferred to Giuna's hands now. And to Seterins, Vraszan was an exotic place, sitting at the heart of the trade routes that made up the Dawn and Dusk Roads. Alta Renata was known to frequent Vraszenian restaurants, to patronize Vraszenian merchants. This went a large step further...but the glamour and popularity she'd earned over the last year might be enough to buy such an audacious move.

A move she wanted so badly, she ached at the thought. Grey at her side, with no more sneaking about.

A burst of shrill laughter drifted through the open window, falling from above like broken glass. *Letilia*. If she thought for one moment Ren was putting personal concerns above her demands...

"I'll need to involve my mother," Renata said. She held up one gloved hand before Faella's smile could curdle into objection. "It's that or have her interfering at every turn."

"I suppose needs must—for Marvisal's sake." Faella sniffed. "I don't understand how you're related to that woman. You must take after your father."

It was possibly the highest compliment Faella had ever paid her. Let the old woman think Renata's smile was for that.

3

Jump at the Sun

Floodwatch, Upper Bank: Equilun 19

The Rook could go where Grey Serrado dared not—even if there was no Rook anymore, only Grey Serrado in a hood.

He tried to find a pearl of benefit in that as he and Ren sheltered behind a cow shed in southeastern Floodwatch, where the city petered out into the vegetable gardens and dairy farms that supplied Nadežra. The Rook was made to fight against the corruption of the medallions, and those instincts had always railed against being put to an unrelated purpose. If the Rook weren't broken, Grey would have had a difficult time coming here tonight, to a meeting where his job was to *help* two medallion-holding nobles mediate a dispute that had nothing to do with Kaius Rex.

Doesn't it, though? he thought, kneeling to tug open the mouth of his knapsack. The Stadnem Anduske fought to take Nadežra back from its Liganti overlords, and those overlords held it because of the Tyrant—with the help of the medallions. Just because tonight's meeting wouldn't get them any closer to destroying those artifacts didn't mean it wasn't an important step in picking apart that knot.

Assuming it went anything like well.

Ren helped him unpack the bag, draping items over her arms like a gentleman's valet. He was perfectly capable of getting dressed on his own, but her quiet presence was a balm, reminding him of what he'd saved by breaking the Rook.

He wasn't the only one who'd lost the Rook. It wouldn't answer to anyone. Ryvček had tried; Ren had tried; even Sedge had tried, hands trembling in awe as he donned the hood. It was nothing more than a piece of wool, silent and inert.

Which left Grey making use of the costume Fontimi had once worn to impersonate the Rook. Tess had made some improvements, imbuing it where she could to guard the wearer's identity, adding pins to ensure even the strongest wind couldn't tear the hood away. If it was a weak substitute for the real thing, she couldn't be blamed. Whatever had made the Rook went beyond normal imbuing or numinatria.

Ren reached around him to buckle his sword belt. Then lingered, fingers digging under the leather to pull him close. Her nose found the soft skin under his jaw, breathing in his scent. Coffee, probably; even out of the Vigil now, he found he still craved it. Leather and wool. Whatever she found, it pleased her. Her smile was soft against the stubble of a long day.

"That tickles," he said, stealing the smile away with a kiss.

Her grip tightened, and her breath came soft and fast and sweet. "Payback for what you took."

Stolen kisses, stolen moments. Fitting that he also had a stolen blade. The Rook couldn't be seen carrying Grey Serrado's sword. To get around that, they'd staged a confrontation last month, with Alta Renata wearing the Vicadrius-forged blade taken from Mezzan Indestor—a blade the Rook had once thrown into a canal. Doing his best impression of the voice the magic used to give him, Grey had declared that so fine a blade didn't belong in a cuff's hands, and they'd dueled. It had taken all his will to keep the flirtation at a reasonable level, especially when his disarm brought them body-to-body, her face mere inches from his.

That memory hummed through him, coiling low and hot—and then a sudden noise from the other side of the shed wall made Ren yelp and leap back. Grey fought the urge to laugh. "It's only the cow."

She gave the shed a deeply untrusting look. "Animals should not be so large."

There was so much of the world she hadn't seen. Nadežra, Ganllech, and the waters between: that was all Ren knew. Perhaps someday, once the medallions were destroyed, they could see more together. The broad, beautiful valley of the River Dežera; the mountains that ringed the edges of Vraszan. Forests thicker than the groomed stands in Nightpeace Gardens. Things Grey himself hadn't seen in years.

A strand of hair had escaped her coronet braid; he tucked it back behind her ear. Ren caught his hand and brushed her cheek against it. "Grey...I have an idea. Well, Faella Coscanum had it, but I think it could work. Although—now that I've started, I realize—no chance have I had to ask—"

She sent the words out in a rush. "Wish you to marry me?"

Her words caught him flat-footed, and he stood, staring, speechless. Fixing the Rook, or finding Ninat's holder, or destroying the medallions: Those were all topics he expected. Something about the Anduske, even. This...

Ill luck, his grandmother whispered in his head. *Since before you were born. You bring ill luck to everyone around you.* No one would marry a man cursed by the Masks.

Ren would. Ren didn't believe he was cursed.

He hadn't spoken. She dragged her gaze up, blushing. "If you wish it not..."

"I do." His voice was rough, and he cleared his throat. "Of course I do. But what of your life as Renata?" She'd said something about Faella. How did Faella figure into this?

She shook her head. "This is a plan to have both that and you. Faella has guessed about us—not who I am, but that I'm in love with you. And she suggested I stage the Trials of the Volti."

He listened as she outlined the idea. It was absurd, of course—but Faella was right; its absurdity might be its greatest strength. A romantic tale of a suitor overcoming all challenges and refusing all other rewards for the chance to win their beloved's heart...

"Stacking the deck for the intended victor is traditional," Ren said, grinning. "Already I have some thoughts."

Grey drew back in mock offense. "Believe you not that I can demonstrate my merit for real?"

One eyebrow arched. "Have you not called me Clever Natalya? Cheating is how she plays."

Not in the tale where Constant Ivan won her heart. For him, she'd been honest. But Grey had better reasons than folklore and pride for wanting to compete fairly. "If it's tradition to stack the deck, people will be on guard. I must win *despite* your intentions, and charm you with my victory. Otherwise..."

"Otherwise they will see me cheating to help a Vraszenian." Ren grimaced, and he could see her spinning and discarding different possibilities. Between the two of them—and wily old Faella—they might be able to cheat and not get caught. But Grey had confidence in his own skills.

That thought sent a thread of ice through his veins. Although he didn't carry the Quinat medallion on him, he was still bound to it. And excellence fell under Quinat's purview. *Is it feeding my desire to prove myself? Or would I feel this regardless?*

Ren cupped his face in her hands, her kiss scattering his thoughts. "Then you shall play fair. And we shall hope the plan works as intended."

They had no more time for side matters. Ren helped him pin the hood securely into place; he caught her hand as she drew away, stole a final kiss, lips brushing her bare fingers. Then, shifting his posture and mannerisms as best as he could, Grey went to be the Rook.

Floodwatch, Upper Bank: Equilun 19

"You going to tell me why we're getting our boots muddy over Vraszenian business?" Varuni asked as the carriage they were tailing passed the upper foot of the Floodwatch Bridge.

If he hadn't been so tense, Vargo wouldn't have jumped at Varuni's unexpected question. His plan for getting Koszar Andrejek and his followers safely to this meeting and back was a good one...at least, he hoped so. Anyone keeping an eye on Nightpeace Gardens would have seen Tiama Capenni—or someone dressed like her—board the carriage with her maid and a footman. Anyone who noticed it passing would see the Capenni coat of arms on the sides and think twice before hassling the occupant.

But he didn't trust much where Branek was concerned.

"Not out here in the open, I en't," Vargo said, lifting his sleeve as an ineffective ward against the stink of chickens and dung fires. *Everything all right up there?* he asked Alsius, standing sentry atop the carriage.

::All's quiet around us. I can't quite make out what Koszar and Idusza are saying; it's some southern dialect. I really must improve my Vraszenian.::

Varuni's chains clinked softly as she fiddled with them, a nervous gesture that was as unlike her as the ill-timed interrogation. "But there *is* a reason."

"What's going on?" Vargo asked, keeping his eye on the vegetable gardens around them. If Varuni was off her feed, *someone* needed to make sure the cabbages weren't going to attack.

"That's what I'm asking you," Varuni said, gesturing at the carriage ahead of them. "Tserdev's under control as long as we hold her brother, so why are you riling things up? You've gone well beyond the deal you made. That's not like you. Especially when you've got bigger issues. *Primordial*-sized ones."

Her voice faltered, and Vargo wrenched his neck looking for whatever threat she'd sensed, but there was nothing. Just the creak of the slow-moving carriage, the rush of the river, and the indignation of local livestock. Somewhere to the east, away from the river, a fox must be hassling a henhouse; muffled squawks of outrage, punctuated by the bleating of sheep, broke the stillness of the night.

Taking a deliberate breath, Vargo forced his fingers to relax around his sword cane. "There's nothing we *can* do about those bigger issues. Not until we find..." He waved toward the shadow of the Point, and by extension the temple beneath it. Where ten medallion holders had been drawn together, and one had escaped. "In the meanwhile, I'm helping with this because the Black Rose asked."

He hadn't told Varuni about the Black Rose. That was Ren's knot to untangle, the Black Rose, Arenza, Ren...Vargo had been trying to keep his promises to Varuni, trying to tell her what was going on instead of shutting her out, but some secrets weren't his to share.

This was why he avoided swearing knot oaths. They demanded a level of trust he wasn't certain he was capable of.

Varuni deserved answers, though. She'd just picked a damnably bad time to ask for them. "Let's just get through tonight," he said. "Tomorrow, I'll tell you what I can...or I'll tell you why I can't."

"You're only saying that so I don't toss you in the river on my way back to Isarn."

He shot a wary glance at the black water. Darkness hid the murk of farm runoff, but it couldn't hide the smell. "I'd rather you didn't."

::Vargo? We...have an unexpected problem,:: Alsius said, as the carriage slowed to a stop. The distant squawking of chickens had been replaced by the muffled jangle of bells and more bleating. Hip-high, ambulatory fleeces drifted across the road, engulfing the carriage like a low-lying cloud.

"Just what we needed," Vargo groaned into his palm. Varuni stifled a noise that from anyone else would have been a giggle.

The carriage door opened, and a black-braided head peered out. "Were you not meant to protect us from ambush?" Andrejek asked, his voice laced with humor.

"I didn't plan for sheep," Vargo said, coming forward and waving his sword cane at the beasts. They paid him about as much mind as Arkady's kids—which was to say, none at all. "We're almost there anyway. You up for walking the rest?" He held out a hand to steady Andrejek down from the carriage...

...and that was when the attack came.

Floodwatch, Upper Bank: Equilun 19

Once Grey had departed, Ren took out her own mask and ran the black lace over her fingers, thinking.

Even before the Rook was broken, Grey could only access echoes of the memories that lingered in the hood. He didn't know the specifics of how the vigilante had been made, only the general outlines. But it had been *made*—the different pieces crafted one by one, before something bound them together into a greater whole. Not like her own disguise, which she'd pulled from the dream, and which contained no imbuing or numinatria to assist her in her work.

But they shared this one aspect: When Ren drew on the mask, the rest of the Black Rose followed. As the hood had once done for the Rook.

Surely that similarity could guide them to repair the Rook... somehow.

Not tonight, though. Dalisva and Mevieny waited on the unpaved lane between the vegetable gardens. Ren made her footfalls audible so as not to startle the two of them. The blind szorsa, her empty eye sockets veiled with an embroidered cloth, heard her first; she tapped Dalisva's arm, and they both touched their hearts in respect as Ren approached. "Thank you both for agreeing to come," she said in the Black Rose's voice, melodious and Nadežran. "I suspect you two will be needed to keep the peace."

"The ziemetse come under truce," Dalisva said, sounding a little defensive. "They will not hurt Andrejek."

Mevieny's snort was more pragmatic. "Hurt, no. Toss overboard, perhaps. The current Anoškinič is...not a flexible man. And others blame *him* for Andrejek's misbehavior."

"We'll do what we can to soften him. Shall we?" Ren offered Mevieny her own arm.

Vargo's people had a cordon along the eastern bank, keeping

away anyone who might interfere with the meeting. Sedge grinned and knuckled his brow in a show of respect when he saw Ren—followed by a more serious show when Vargo came up behind, trailing Koszar and his bare handful of supporters.

"Problem?" Ren asked when she noticed Vargo's windblown hair and flushed cheeks, the crookedness of his neckcloth, as though someone had grabbed him by it.

::I should say so!:: Alsius huffed. ::This lack of a Caerulet is making all manner of ruffians think they can get away with—::

"Nothing we couldn't handle," Vargo said over the telepathic complaints. To Sedge he added, "Varuni's questioning the ones that are still conscious. We'll find out if Branek hired them."

That smoothed the worried furrow from Sedge's brow. "Dock's this way," he said, gesturing them toward the river.

With both moons dwindled to new, the brightest lights were the lamps edging the Floodwatch Bridge downriver, a string of gold beads across the Dežera's satin-dark throat. It meant Grey didn't need magic to be a shadow within a shadow, lounging against one of the posts used to tie up boats along the bank. He bowed to Ren, then said to Vargo, "You have people on the western side as well?"

"Of course," Vargo said, clearly miffed—though whether it was for the Rook questioning his precautions or getting past his cordon, Ren couldn't tell. "And here come our hosts."

Two more lights were drifting downriver, lamps at the bow and stern of an approaching barge. It was an ordinary cargo vessel, indistinguishable from the boats that brought rice and other staples into Nadežra. To Ren's eye, though, it wasn't carrying much in its hold; it rode too high in the water for that.

A whispered protest behind Ren was Idusza making a last-ditch argument that she should accompany Koszar on board. "If I return not," Koszar said, "then you must carry on our cause."

So he was prepared for this to go badly wrong. Ren vowed to get him off the barge if that happened—somehow. Despite Tanaquis's lessons, she could barely keep herself afloat, let alone someone else.

A lift of Vargo's ungloved hand sent his people back with Idusza, away from the immediate vicinity of the bank. He, Ren, and the Rook would form Koszar's entourage, with Dalisva and Mevieny as mediators. No other guards: the ziemetse had insisted. Ren couldn't blame them, however little she liked not having Sedge or Idusza or Varuni at her back.

They boarded the skiff tied up at the bank, and Vargo and Dalisva worked the oars to take them out to where the barge had dropped anchor.

Although the ziemetse had brought their own guards, those were courteous as they helped the visitors on board and directed them toward the cabin at the center of the deck. They didn't even object when the Rook said, "The sword stays with me."

They know they aren't his enemy, Ren thought. Grey had refused to attend as himself, but the Rook lent Koszar the legitimacy of his own crusade against Liganti control.

The interior of the cabin was much finer than the rest of the barge implied. The beds folded up against the walls, making room for cushions on the floor, each one richly embroidered. Numina-trian lightstones shone behind glass shields, deepening the shadows and whorls of the carvings that flowed over each beam and support. But luxurious or not, it was notably cramped once everyone was inside: six visitors, four guards, and the ziemetse who'd agreed to meet—the clan elders of the Anoškin and the Kiraly.

The last time Ren had seen the Anoškinič, at the Ceremony of the Accords, he'd been wearing the ghost owl mask of his clan. Tonight he wore an expression of disdain, which only deepened when Mevieny introduced Koszar with full formality, as Koszar Yureski Andrejek of the Anoškin. "Bold of you to claim clan and kureč," he said, interrupting, "with no shame for the disrepute you've brought upon us."

Koszar was unfazed. "Cast out I have not yet been. Until that changes, I will remember my people—though I confess, I have not valued that connection as I should. Too long have we allowed ourselves to be divided, fighting each other with one hand and the Cinquerat with the other."

"So now you join hands with such as these?" The Anoškinič gestured at Vargo with a contemptuous flick. "That man has the stamp of one whose blood mingles with the invaders."

Ren was glad of her mask, hiding her half-northern ancestry. Only as the Black Rose would she be heard by these people.

The Kiralič laid one hand on the arm of his fellow elder. "'That man' is Derossi Vargo, who saved the Wellspring of Ažerais during Veiled Waters. He has earned the right to speak here."

To Ren, the Rook murmured, "It's like the two of us weren't even there."

It earned him a bow of apology from the Kiralič. "No one disputes your presence. To us you gave the blasphemer Mettore Indestor; we have not forgotten."

"If I have the right to speak," Vargo said, "then I give my voice to Ča Andrejek. Whether you agree with him or not is up to you, but at least hear him out. And maybe we can sit while you do?"

Much of what Koszar said after they settled onto the cushions was old news to Ren: the truth of how Branek and the others had betrayed their leader, without first cutting their knots, and the increasing violence they'd engaged in since then. She couldn't tell how much of it the Anoškinič already knew; he sat so still, even the ribbons and knotwork charms braided into his hair didn't tremble. The Kiralič nodded along, though, with the expression of a man willing to be convinced.

When Koszar paused for breath, the Anoškinič said, "After the Night of Hells, when compensation we demanded, the Cinquerat cited *your* crimes as reason they should not make restitution. That you are less dangerous to us than Branek, I will grant—but that is a weak argument for supporting you."

Dalisva spoke up unexpectedly. "Please recall, elder, that the Rook and the Rose freed Ča Andrejek. One has fought the Liganti nobility as long as we have; the other to us is sent by Ažerais herself. Surely that must speak in his favor."

::It's like I wasn't even there,:: Ren heard Vargo say sardonically, over his mental link to Alsius.

::Didn't we want to remain—oh. You're peeved about the Liganti blood thing.::

::I don't remember my own parents, much less who fucked who a century ago. I'm *Nadežran*. Why do we matter less to the fate of this city?::

As Ren's heart squeezed with odd warmth, Koszar said, "I ask not that you support me. Our only hope is to work *together*—against Branek."

"Against our own?" the Anoškinič scoffed. "For you this is a different tune, Andrejek. Are not the invaders your enemy?"

Koszar pressed his hands palm-to-palm, as if to keep them from clenching into fists. "A szorsa recently laid The Mask of Ravens as my ill future. Rather than fighting the enemy who betrayed me, I seek to protect our people. And Branek threatens that directly."

The Kiralič leaned forward. "How?"

"The specifics I have not learned—not yet. Allies I still have among those who follow Branek, though, and they send me word. Others he gathers to him, not only from Nadežra, but from all of Vraszan. They hide themselves among those who prepare for the Great Dream...and I fear the reason for which he gathers them.

"A moment ago you spoke of the Night of Hells. We all remember the anger among our people after the old Kiralič died, after Szorsa Mevieny was blinded. To Branek's way of thinking, no better way there is to put them in motion against the Liganti than to light another fire of outrage."

By the expressions in the room, Ren wasn't the only one who saw what Koszar meant. She was just the first to give it voice, in a horrified whisper. "An attack against Vraszenians, during the Great Dream itself...he would profane even *that*?"

Not just the Great Dream. Every forty-nine years, the two moons waxed full on the same night, completing what Vraszenians called a Grand Cycle. The last one came long before Ren was born, but she knew that many saw the ending of a Grand Cycle as an omen for the decades to come.

Koszar's jaw clenched tight. "In Branek's heart, any blasphemy is justified, if in the end it brings freedom for our people."

"But who counts as 'our people'?" Ren said, over Vargo muttering similar words. "Plenty of Vraszenians in Nadežra don't follow clan ways. Those who have become untethered from their kretse. Those whose lineage is mixed beyond untangling." Like Grey. Like Vargo.

And like herself. She fought to keep the ache from her voice as she asked, "Are we not all Ažerais's children?"

Koszar bowed in acknowledgment. "The Black Rose echoes the szorsa's wisdom."

Ren couldn't tell if the muffled cough she heard was disguising Grey's laughter or Vargo's, but the dismissive snort came from the Anoškinič. "A child's wisdom—Face to the Stadnem Anduske's Mask. One would have us embrace our enemies; the other resists any compromise. Both lack an understanding of political nuance. The ziemetse protect our people's interests here—"

"The ziemetse protect their *own* interests here." Koszar slapped the deck, the frayed knot of his temper unraveling. "When with the Cinquerat you bargain, who benefits? Can you say honestly that it is those who *live* in Nadežra?"

"Peace," Mevieny said, raising her hands.

Such was the respect she commanded that even the Anoškinič subsided. In the quiet, Mevieny said, "Ča Andrejek. 'Alliance' is a word with no more substance than mist. And no force from outside can turn the Anduske from Branek back to you. What hope you to achieve here?"

He exhaled slowly, shoulders relaxing. "I have many hopes, Szorsa Mevieny. But your presence here gives life to one in particular. It is untrue that no outside force can return me to the leadership of the Anduske; there is one that could. Ažerais herself."

A puff of air escaped Vargo. "You're on speaking terms with a goddess?"

"Not me," Koszar said, looking at Mevieny. "But the speaker for the Ižranyi can oversee a judgment by ordeal."

Ren felt cold under her layers of leather and silk. She knew what Liganti judgment by ordeal looked like; it had featured in one of the plays she attended as Renata. The contesting parties were both required to walk "the path of the Lumen"—barefoot over a stretch of red-hot coals. She had no idea what form such a thing took in Vraszenian society. But the Black Rose, of all people, couldn't reveal her ignorance.

Vargo could. "How is that different from—" he started, when a sudden burst of shouting interrupted from outside the cabin.

Ren recognized the clash of metal, the sound of a scream. She was on her feet, moving for the door, and Vargo and the Rook just ahead of her, as the warning cry came too late.

"*River pirates!*"

River Dežera: Equilun 19

Vargo was perfectly happy to let the Rook go through the door first, in a low roll that carried him under the cudgel waiting there. As the attacker turned to follow the swirling black coat, Vargo got him in the back with a knife, then burst through onto the deck—a deck that now swarmed with utter chaos.

People seemed to be everywhere, and Vargo didn't need to see the color of their knots to guess what was happening. *Anduske. Stretsko. Branek.* While his Fog Spiders had dealt with what they thought was the main threat, another one had been waiting for them on the river.

The darkness shrouded half a dozen skiffs now surrounding the barge. Shouts drifted across the water from the Lower Bank, too, but Vargo didn't have time to worry about what might be happening there. A clump of river rats was climbing over the rail.

Vargo caught his knife hilt in his teeth and dug in his pockets for the clay pieces he'd stashed there. As the two half circles came together, he got the satisfaction of watching the rats blown backward off the boat, into the river.

It's more fun from this side, he told Alsius, shaking his hands to cool the sting from the explosion. Nothing in Diomen's notes had mentioned that. *Though next time I'll wear gloves.*

::Just make sure you don't point it in the wrong direction!::

Some of the pirates had turned to fish their dazed friends out of the river, but more poured over the side. Dropping the cracked numinat, Vargo reached for the second one he'd prepared, but his scorched fingers made him clumsy; he fumbled the pieces, and then someone came at him and there was no more time for numinatrian tricks. Only knifework, in close quarters, and in the dark it was hard to tell Vraszenian friend from Vraszenian foe.

Setting his back to the cabin gave him some protection and gave Peabody the chance to jump to the roof. *Anything?*

::The Rook's guarding the Black Rose at the bow. Oh my, those aren't Palaestra rules he's fighting by.::

Vargo ducked under a club meant for his head, came up knife first under the person's ribs. The heated blood stung the fresh burns on his fingers. Clubs—did that mean they were hoping to take prisoners, rather than slaughtering everyone?

He spied a flash of mist-pale clothing as the Anoškinič was dragged over the side, and a second flutter as Andrejek jumped after. The cry of pain that followed sounded more like Andrejek's bad knee giving out than anyone bleeding, and Vargo couldn't get to them to help anyway. To Alsius he snapped, *Any way out of here?*

::We're on a boat surrounded by boats. What sort of way were you hoping for?::

No exit strategy. Vargo should have insisted they hold the meeting somewhere *he* controlled. Although those tended to get raided a lot these days, too. *Should just stop having meetings.*

::Vargo, I see Branek! Lower Bank side, by the rail.::

He came himself?

Before Vargo could do anything with that, an arm circled his neck and jerked him back. The cold kiss of steel along the unscarred side of his throat suggested that taking Vargo prisoner was optional at best. He went still, and someone else wrenched his knife from him.

All around the barge, the chaos was dying down. There were

simply too many of Branek's people for the ziemetse's guards to fight them off, even with guests like the Rook to help. Someone had Ren's arms twisted up behind her in a painful joint lock, and the Rook knelt on the deck with no less than four blades pointed at him. Andrejek and the Anoškinič hadn't reappeared; for all Vargo knew, both were dead.

Branek strolled into the center of it all with a look of shit-eating satisfaction on his pox-scarred face.

His gaze swept over Vargo, the Black Rose, the Rook. The Kiralič, clutching his head as if he'd met one of those clubs too closely. Dalisva, also with a knife at her throat; even Mevieny had a guard. Blood stained the deck, and too many bodies lay unmoving.

Branek addressed the Rook first, in Liganti. "Lately you involve yourself in Vraszenian politics. Seem I like a chalk-faced noble to you?"

"Even someone like me needs variety every century or so," the Rook said, as if he weren't a breath away from being skewered. "And since you have a history of doing a nobleman's dirty work, it isn't far out of my way."

Branek scowled. "Then into the hold you will go, with the other prisoners."

Ren was the closest to the hatch. Her captor shoved her into the darkness below, followed by two of the ziemetse's people who were still breathing. Before anyone could prod the Rook to his feet, though, Branek stopped them and picked up the Rook's fallen sword. "But before you do . . . I have always wondered."

The tip of the sword reached out to flip back the Rook's hood. *Alsius!*

The spider wasn't close enough to bite Branek. But a scream went off in Vargo's ear and the hands holding him spasmed open, and that was distraction enough. He twisted free, lunged for Branek, wrenched the sword from his hand, and spun them both so that the rail was at Vargo's back.

Now *he* was the one with a blade at someone's throat, which he liked much better.

"If anyone's making the Rook strip at swordpoint," Vargo snapped with more bravado than he felt, "it'll be me. I owe him that."

Branek's wiry beard smelled of sweat and zrel, and he was taller and heavier than Vargo. The only thing keeping him still was the razor-sharp edge of the rapier against his neck.

Any other time, Vargo would take the cut and deal with the consequences. But Ren was below, and he'd promised the others his protection. If Branek died, they'd never get away.

A hostage standoff would suffice—he hoped. "Tell your people to—"

Vargo never got to finish that sentence. An explosion came from the hold. The boat shuddered, deck tilting precariously, and he and Branek went tumbling over the side.

River Dežera: Equilun 19

Ren didn't know which direction was up.

She hadn't had a specific plan when she scooped up the dropped pieces of Vargo's blasting numinat; they'd just seemed like they might be useful. And when she got shoved into the darkness of the hold, the use that came to mind was aiming them at the hull. It would make a distraction at least, which she hoped Grey and Vargo would be able to leverage—and if that actually opened a hole into the river, she figured she could swim out and come back aboard from an unexpected direction.

Instead the water that surged into the hold knocked her straight off her feet. Slammed against the hull, she had no time to find her bearings before it was over her head and the lone lamp snuffed out. The rushing pressure of water threw off any sense of up or down, left her spinning in a roaring void.

Hold your breath, go still, and you'll float upward, Tanaquis had said when teaching Renata to swim. But the hold was pitch black and it seemed like there was wood in every direction; she couldn't tell what was hull and what was deck and what was crate. Panic made her flail, bruising herself against unseen obstacles—and then she broke through into a pocket of air, gasping for blessed breath. But there was only a little space between her and the deck above, and it was shrinking fast, and in the blackness she couldn't tell where the hatch was that would lead to safety.

If there even was any safety to be had. By the shouts she could hear through the deck, the barge was sinking fast.

Ren searched with desperate hands, trying to find a way out, but there was nothing. In a moment her pocket of air would be gone. She screamed, knowing it was futile; no one up above was likely to hear it over everything else. Where was Grey? Where was Vargo? Were they still alive, or—

Don't think about that. Just get out.

Right before the pocket vanished, she sucked in as much air as she could and pushed off through the water, hoping to find a glimmer of light. Was that the hatch over there? Or was she hallucinating it, because the alternative was that she was trapped and about to die?

She didn't have enough air. Her lungs were burning, begging for a fresh breath she couldn't give them. This wasn't a nightmare she could wake from; it was real, it was inescapable, and she was going to *drown*—

A hand seized her arm, and pulled.

Floodwatch, Lower Bank: Equilun 19

Grey almost wept with relief when he broke the surface and Ren, held tight and safe in his arms, started coughing.

In the chaos that followed the explosion, his only thought had been to get below. But he'd forgotten that what he wore was only an imitation of the Rook's gear, without the numinatrian etching on the eye mask that would help him see in the darkness. He'd found himself in a hold rapidly filling with water, no light to guide him, and only the bone-deep terror that Ren would die to drive him forward. When his searching hand found an arm, he'd prayed for the Dežera's mercy that it was hers—that no one else was still in the hold, that he wasn't about to save the wrong person or leave someone else to die. And for the first time tonight, the Faces smiled upon him.

Swimming in the Rook's long coat was difficult, but it wasn't the first time he'd had to manage. Orienting himself by the lights of the Floodwatch Bridge, he struck out for the western bank, hoping Vargo's people hadn't been completely overrun there. All around him, others were doing the same, or else paddling toward the skiffs the attackers had used to board. He couldn't tell which, if any, were his allies.

His first priority was getting Ren onto land. Everything else he could deal with later.

The marsh-thick mud sucked at his boots as he dragged them both onto shore. Ren was on her hands and knees, coughing up spume; all Grey could do was rub her back and fight the urge to pull her close and never let go.

A fight he lost when she caught her breath enough to sink into his embrace. "You're all right. You're safe." He whispered words and kisses into her river-chilled braids. His hood cloaked them in dark warmth, closing out the world. "I would have dived to the bottom of the river to save you."

Her coughing resolved into words. "Never swimming again. *Fucking* river." And nothing about that was funny, but somehow they both were laughing.

He could have stayed there all night, but the cold would have forced them to move even if other circumstances hadn't. By the time he helped Ren to her feet, the area was relatively quiet. The skiffs had dispersed, and Grey didn't hear any fighting, but there were voices coming from the south, one recognizable as Vargo's. The two of them straightened themselves as much as possible—they couldn't do much about being soaking wet, but they could at least try to look more like legendary heroes than sodden kittens—and went to see what had happened.

At the sight of them, tension drained visibly from Vargo's shoulders. He bellowed, "Sedge! Got 'em. Call back the swimmers." A thunder of footsteps a half beat later was Sedge running back to see with his own eyes—then slamming to a halt as he forcibly restrained himself from hugging the Black Rose like the sister she was.

"Mask-damned bow lookout was paid off," Vargo rasped, raking his own wet hair out of his face. He'd shucked his coat, and the sopping lawn of his shirtsleeves clung to his arms. "With the moons new, and their oars muffled—the rats know how to be stealthy on the river. My people didn't see anything until it was too late."

"Koszar?" Ren said. "The others?"

Vargo jerked his chin toward a nearby shed. "He wrenched his bad knee getting the Anoškinič away, but compared to the last few messes he's fallen into, that's getting off lightly. Dalisva made it, too. But—" He kicked at the ground as if he wished Branek's head were there.

"The Kiralič," Grey said, his heart sinking.

"And the szorsa."

"Branek won't harm either of them," Ren said with more confidence than Grey felt. "This isn't something he can blame on the Liganti; hurting a clan elder and the current speaker for the Ižranyi will only turn people against him. They're hostages."

It was an improvement only by comparison. Grey should have insisted on better security—though what that would have looked like, he didn't know. Something that would have required the ziemetse to trust Andrejek more.

"Anyways, this is yours." Vargo picked something up off the ground and offered it hilt-first to the Rook: Ren's Vicadrius. "Wish I'd gotten more of Branek's blood on it, but I suppose it'd be bad luck to kill a man with the Rook's blade."

The blade that had come within a breath of unhooding Grey, until Vargo intervened.

You're not the Rook. You're just a man in a costume. Doesn't tonight prove it?

It took little effort to roughen his voice into an approximation of the Rook's as he accepted the sword. "You have my thanks. For this...and for your assistance."

"Thank my eight-legged friend; it was his doing." Vargo broke into a soft chuckle. "And he suggests that you take this as a lesson to be kinder to spiders."

Lower Bank: Equilun 19

Vargo's youth as a runner had mapped Nadežra into his bones. Some parts better than others, of course; few people sent messages from Froghole to the Pearls.

But the Lower Bank? That was his from Dockwall to Flood-watch, and always had been.

Two Cut Ears accompanied him as he made his way north, one of them in his shirtsleeves with his coat now on Vargo's back. Varuni had been reluctant to let him out of her sight, but the hit wasn't on him; it was Vraszenian business. Whatever trouble he had keeping his knots in line, nobody was on the hunt for him tonight. He'd be safe enough. The Kiralič and Szorsa Mevieny might not be, no matter what Ren had said.

So he left Varuni in charge of tracing their attackers and went back on foot, because like hell was he going to trust skiffers after this.

And because he always thought best on his feet.

He should be turning the night over in his mind, looking for what went wrong, how to control the damage that would come when the Lower Bank knots learned a Vraszenian elder had been taken on *Eret* Vargo's watch—as though he didn't have enough diffi-culty already, juggling the roles of cuff and crime lord.

But his thoughts kept slipping back to that moment on the deck of the barge, when the Rook was on his knees, mocking Branek as if it didn't matter that he might be unmasked.

Mocking...in a voice that niggled at the edges of familiarity.

Not the way it should have. Vargo had twisted his mind into tangles before, trying to identify the Rook's voice, but there was magic at work there. That voice always sounded like you *ought* to recognize it, but couldn't. This...this was different. Vargo couldn't place it, but he *knew* that voice.

Which meant something had gone wrong with the magic that hid the wearer's identity.

Or he's just a decoy. A false Rook in a costume.

::Eh?:: Alsius roused enough to mumble, a shift under Vargo's collar that was too familiar to tickle. Between delivering a full load of venom and cowering on Vargo's head as they splashed to safety, he was exhausted.

Just thinking. Go back to sleep.

The Sunset Bridge was empty save for the night hawks guarding it. They let Vargo and his fists pass without hassle, and the tightness in Vargo's shoulders eased as he left the Lower Bank.

He and Alsius had wondered before if the Rook was some kind of spirit, bound to a series of human bearers. If the magic was broken, he suspected he knew when it had happened: in the Praeteri temple, when the Rook let slip the chance to destroy the medallions in order to save Ren's life. He'd looked like he was fighting with himself then, and Vargo had assumed that was the spirit holding fast to its oath not to kill, in defiance of the person who carried it.

But now...

If anybody was willing to let Ren die, it wasn't the man who'd fought at her side tonight. Who'd dived headfirst into a flooding hold to rescue her when the barge started sinking and Ren was trapped below.

If I remove this hood, I'm just a man, the Rook had said as Vargo dangled from Sureggio Extaquium's rooftop.

A man who cared enough about Ren to set aside a calling two centuries old to save her. When she'd brushed off Vargo's interest in favor of a new lover, he'd assumed that was the Rook...and he might not be wrong. But might it not instead—also—be the man whose home Arenza Lenskaya had been visiting so often since midsummer?

They'd been in the same room before, the man and the Rook, but now that seemed almost like a bit of theatre. It was what Vargo would have done to throw off suspicion.

He stopped halfway to the Old Island. With the moonless sky above and the black river below, the only illumination came from the lightstones on the bridge. An illuminated path of Vargo's new life, from knot boss to noble.

There was something very wrong with the world, when it turned out Vargo was the only one *not* wearing a mask.

Alsius. Alsius! Vargo prodded his collar.

::What?::

He ignored the mental grumpiness. He needed the other half of his mind to confirm his suspicions. *I know this sounds crazy, but hear me out.*

I think Grey Serrado is the Rook.

4

Pouncing Cat

Ren expected nightmares of drowning when she went to sleep.

Instead she dreamed of the past again.

Not just Nadežra, smaller and lacking many familiar buildings. Sometimes it was different cities, in the broad plains of the Dežera valley, in the mountains that edged them. Or towns, or farms, an ocean of rice fields as far as she could see.

It wasn't a nightmare, not while she was in it. But every time Ren woke, a chill went down her spine.

Because she'd been having the dreams ever since she took Tricat back. And Tricat was associated with time.

The medallion was well-hidden in the false heel of a pair of winter boots, in a box with protective numinata inscribed on its inner sides. That should have limited its influence on her. The prospect that it could bleed through anyway...

Tess worried, she knew. They had to be cautious about what they said inside Traementis Manor, but Ren had told Tess about the dreams, and a glance and a touch on her shoulder in the morning said enough. Neither of them could do more than worry, except pray the medallions would be destroyed soon.

The last thing Ren wanted after one of those dreams was to deal with Letilia. But she had to tell the woman about the Trials of the Volti—and predictably, Letilia's first reaction was an attempted slap.

This time Ren stepped out of range. "You should be pleased, not angry. This is how we'll get what you want."

"What *I* want?" Letilia's brow twitched. "Do you expect me to suffer through some ridiculous challenge just for a chance to *beg* for readmission to House Traementis?"

Renata laughed. "Is that what you think this is for? However did you survive so long in Prince Maredd's court?"

They were in Renata's sitting room, which wasn't quite as elegant as it used to be, Ren having replaced one of the fine, delicate chairs with something plumper and more comfortable. She avoided that one now as she gestured for Letilia to sit: What she needed was not comfort, but poise.

Letilia huffed and dropped petulantly onto another chair, hard enough the legs squeaked in protest. Studying her, Ren sighed inwardly. Letilia had done a poor job of accepting the years as they came. If she could have had her way, time would have frozen when she was twenty-four, preserving her forever in that moment. She wasn't without beauty now, but she didn't understand—or didn't *want* to understand—how to let it grow and mature with the seasons of life.

Just like she didn't know how to work from the position she was in now, rather than the position she'd held as an exotic foreigner in an insular land. "At the moment," Renata said, "you're a hanger-on. Nadežra sees you as House Traementis's old scandal, come to stir up mud long dried. You're hoping they'll invite you to their parties— and they will, because they like no spice so well as scandal.

"But the Trials of the Volti will change that. It will be a grand event after a year of strife...and who will be orchestrating the show?"

"You," Letilia said spitefully.

Renata smiled. "No. *You.*"

Some of the affront bled out of Letilia as Renata went on. "Yes, the trials are for me. But *you* will be my sponsor. Don't worry; we'll have others to handle all the tedious organizational work, setting up the stands and so forth. You needn't trouble yourself with that." She didn't want Letilia anywhere near the logistics. "What everyone will see is Alta Letilia Viraudacis making her reentry to Nadežran society in grand style. You won't be hoping to attend *their* parties; *they'll* be hoping to attend *yours*."

Letilia was only somewhat mollified. "They're still trials in *your* honor. Not mine."

Adjusting her posture to mirror Letilia's, Renata cast another lure. "If this goes as I hope, there's a good chance it will end with my marriage. Donaia will dance with the moons in happiness to see me settled; she'll grant anything I ask...as will my new spouse." Let Letilia wonder what door that might open for her. "But would you want to cling to my surcoat like that, with all the other opportunities this will afford you?"

That would be the worst possible scenario, Letilia successfully joining another house and rooting herself so deeply in Nadežra that Ren couldn't dig her out. But right now, what Ren needed most was *time*. Vargo had found the ship Letilia arrived on, two weeks before she claimed. Tracing where she'd gone and who she'd visited was harder.

Letilia's mouth pursed in thought. Before any of it coalesced into words, the sitting room door swung open. "Renata," Tanaquis said, "I really need you to—oh." She blinked at Letilia. "You're busy. Well, it can't be helped. The stars have their own timing. The experiment I mentioned the other day—"

A moment of thought summoned the memory: Tanaquis wanted Renata to lay a pattern with a different deck, to see if that affected the results. It hardly seemed urgent, but letting Letilia chew on what Renata had said was better than pushing the matter any further right now. "Of course. I'm glad to help with your work."

Letilia hopped up like her chair had become red-hot. "Work?"

"More experimental numinatria," Renata said, hard and sweet as a honey stone. "Would you care to stay and observe?"

"No!" Giving Tanaquis a wide berth, Letilia paused at the door to frown at Renata. "We'll talk more when you're not dusting your gloves with chalk, poppet." Then she fled.

"There, that's dealt with." Tanaquis settled in Letilia's vacated chair. Then she rose just as quickly, pulling a deck from her surcoat pocket and setting it on the tea table before Renata, followed by a decira. "May I see the Face and not the Mask. Isn't that the proper incantation?"

"It is, yes." Renata eyed Tanaquis. Most people assumed she was oblivious to social nuance—and certainly there was truth to that—but sometimes, Renata suspected, that was a gambit to get away with bypassing the niceties. Tanaquis had disposed of Letilia quite neatly, just as she'd gotten the woman to sit still for an hour the last time they'd met. *Maybe I should ask her to take care of that problem.*

Perhaps when her cousin wasn't looking so agitated. It wasn't Tanaquis's usual distraction; instead of distant, her eyes were restless, flicking here and there. Renata removed her gloves, ready with an explanation if Tanaquis asked about the bruises left by her misadventure in Floodwatch. "Would you like me to try a seven-card wheel instead? Ever since the nameless szorsa showed it to me, I've been eager to try."

"No!" Smoothing back hair that seemed more frazzled than usual, Tanaquis said, "Consistency is key when experimenting. Introducing another difference would muddy the results."

She kept looking for pattern to be consistent, in all the wrong ways. But rather than argue, Renata shuffled the cards.

With her thoughts so full of Letilia, it wasn't until she began dealing the cards that she realized the significance of this moment. Tanaquis might think of it as an experiment, but it was also a *pattern*. And not a three-card line to address a problem, but the full pattern of someone's life.

Renata knew very little about her cousin. The last member of House Fienola; delta families rose and fell more often than the nobility did. Inscriptor and astrologer. Working for Iridet. Brilliant and boundlessly curious. A few personal quirks, like her tendency to disembowel dumplings before eating them. But almost nothing about Tanaquis's life, her old family, how her friendship with Donaia had formed. She simply didn't talk about herself: to Tanaquis, other things were far more interesting.

Pattern was as much about reading the client as the cards. To provide better guidance or to manipulate—the face and the mask of the szorsa. Feeling as if she was, for the first time, truly looking at Tanaquis, Renata said, "This is your past. The good and the ill of it, and that which is neither."

As soon as she turned over the ill card, she could guess why Tanaquis rarely spoke of the past. Three Hands Join, veiled. "When you see this," Renata said, "I imagine you think of Tricat."

Tanaquis's nod was tight and uncharacteristically silent. Renata said, "It's an apt association. This is the card of aid, and here I think it means your family. You grew up alone, didn't you?"

"House Fienola wasn't gone yet, and I was well cared for. Nannies, tutors—"

"That isn't what I mean."

"Why would I need more? I was brighter than my tutors anyway."

It was the answer of someone who had learned at an early age that those around her didn't care, so long as she fulfilled their expectations. Not abuse; just...indifference.

Tanaquis stroked her thumb across the seam on the opposing glove, where the stitches were starting to fray. "I did have one person, for a time. My uncle Bonavaito. My parents adopted him from House Ciagne when I was ten. But he was never a happy man, and he wound up killing himself." She inhaled deeply. "The veiled position means an ill interpretation, yes? I tried to help him. I failed."

"You were a child. You couldn't have been expected to save him."

"I know." The flat line of Tanaquis's mouth underscored the words. "That isn't guilt talking. His problems were beyond me to fix. I may have liked Uncle Bonavaito, but I resolved not to *be* like him."

Renata felt that resolve in the other end of the row, the card that showed what carried Tanaquis forward. "Ordinarily Storm Against Stone ought to mean physical force, because it's from the cut thread. But as you've so often complained, the cards are flexible in their interpretation—and to be quite honest, your determination to learn sometimes *feels* like a physical thing. It carried you to a point of decision." She tapped Two Roads Cross, in the center position. "But what that decision was...I'm afraid I don't know."

"Utrinzi," Tanaquis said. "He was the first to truly challenge me. To encourage me instead of humoring me."

Renata wasn't sure the card referred to that mentorship. But to her astonishment, Tanaquis's breath suddenly hitched, and a tear spilled down her cheek.

Only for an instant, before she dashed it away. "Oh, bother. Everything ends; Ninat is part of the Lumen's cycle. I should be used to that." Glaring at her dampened glove as though it had betrayed her, she said, "He fired me this morning. For my involvement with the Praeteri. I thought it was forgiven, but I suppose he just hadn't gotten around to it yet."

The cards suddenly faded into irrelevance. "Oh, Tanaquis—I'm so sorry—"

Her cousin brushed the sympathy aside. "I understand it's bad form to interrupt a reading. Please, go on."

Tanaquis wasn't the sort to cry on anyone else's shoulder, and Renata wasn't much good at offering comfort. The best she could do was to let this reading be the distraction Tanaquis clearly wanted— and hope it wouldn't dig too deeply into any more wounds. Turning over the next line, she said, "This is your present, the good and the ill of it, and that which is neither."

With what Tanaquis had just confessed, it wasn't hard to see the echo in the ill and ambiguous cards. The Liar's Knot, and Drowning Breath. She'd lost her mentor's trust; would others turn away from her, too?

"Lost trust can be regained," Renata said, thinking of herself and Vargo. "And fear can be a necessary reminder to be cautious." *To not play with eisar numinatria.* Tanaquis was far more sanguine about drawing on the power of the Primordials than any of the rest of them were comfortable with.

Yet they needed her knowledge. Without it, they would be completely lost.

Tanaquis nodded, but it didn't look like she was listening. "I'm allowed to continue researching how to deal with our current problem, but I'm forbidden to hire out my services as an inscriptor or astrologer. I'm not worried about the money—I have more than enough for my needs. But..." She shrank in on herself, looking small. Lost. "What am I supposed to do? If I'm denied my compass, my edge, and my chalk... is there any self left?"

"Of *course* there is." This time Renata was able to capture the other woman's hands in her own. "Tanaquis—cousin—you are more than simply your work. You have the Lumen's own light within you. And see, The Face of Ages, revealed: You still have your knowledge, your scholarship, the wisdom of the past."

"But compass, edge, chalk, self: All four are needed to know the cosmos. What I lost... Is there any way to get it back? To regain my—" She swallowed convulsively.

Her self. Praying an answer would lie within, Renata let go of Tanaquis to turn over the future line. The Mask of Mirrors, The Ember Adamant, and The Mask of Bones.

It wasn't like the twisted line of Grey's future—the pattern he'd warped with his own interference—but it drove the breath out of her anyway. The Ember Adamant: That card had been Grey's past, and the Rook's good future. A chance to fulfill his mandate once and for all, by destroying the medallions. The threads of Tanaquis's fate tangled with his, in the risk that they would fail. As they had *been* failing for the last two months.

She'd let the silence stretch too far. "That's secrets, yes?" Tanaquis said, pointing at The Mask of Mirrors. "Secrets and lies."

Renata nodded, dragging her gaze away from The Ember Adamant. "I don't know what secret it refers to. But the card is in the revealed position; the secret is one you *should* keep." The truth of Ren's identity? She'd wondered on occasion if she could share that with Tanaquis. But the woman was too prone to letting information slip when she was distracted.

Some hint of that doubt must have crept into her voice, because Tanaquis pinned her with a sharp gaze. "I can keep secrets. Despite what people think. I kept the Praeteri's, didn't I?" And in doing so, lost the trust of her mentor.

Renata studied the card's mirrored visage as if it would show her anything other than the wavy lines and warped half images of the reflection the artist had carved into the printing block. Whatever it referred to, it felt far bigger than the identity of one half-Vraszenian liar. "Not the Praeteri, but perhaps related to it. Like our current problem. Keeping the medallions secret may be necessary to ensure our success. The Ember Adamant, veiled, indicates a chance of failure in our duty. There are plenty in this city who would take that power for themselves if they knew of it. And then The Mask of Bones..."

"Is death."

Tanaquis didn't quite manage her usual matter-of-fact tone. "And endings more generally," Renata said hastily. "I think—hmm. It feels oddly tangled with The Ember Adamant. As if an ending isn't the same thing as success. I don't know."

She clamped her mouth shut on the rest. Because Tanaquis wasn't wrong: That card *did* mean death. And in its eyeless skull, Ren saw the possibility of Tanaquis's own demise.

It was the line the others had stepped back from, that day in the temple. They could have used the death of the holders to trigger the destruction of the medallions, accepting a mass sacrifice to rid the world of that poison.

But maybe ten people didn't have to die. Maybe only one did... if that one held all the medallions.

Every bone in Ren's body rejected that, and not because of the risk of a second Kaius Rex. She wasn't going to sacrifice her cousin for this. She wasn't going to sacrifice *anybody*. Grey had broken the Rook to avoid that, because the corruption of A'ash had already caused too much death and destruction. They would find another way.

By the press of Tanaquis's lips, she'd made the same calculation as

Ren. She'd vowed she wouldn't kill herself like her uncle had—but suicide and sacrifice weren't the same thing.

Renata didn't touch her again, but she leaned forward until she had Tanaquis's eyes on her. "I'll find the nameless szorsa," she said, soft and intense, as if she hadn't already tried and failed. "The spirit of a dead woman could also fulfill the meaning of The Mask of Bones. Don't assume the cards have only one significance, cousin."

"No, of course not." Tanaquis's answering smile didn't touch her eyes. "But it's good to prepare, just in case."

Isla Čaprila, Eastbridge: Equilun 21

"How'd you get rid of Letilia?" Vargo asked as he led Ren into the parlour. He hadn't seen her during daylight hours in weeks, thanks to her "mother" latching onto her tighter than a river leech.

Early-afternoon sun gleamed off the wood paneling like slow-dripping honey. He held up a bottle filled with brandywine the same mellow gold, but put it back when Ren shook her head. Tea it was, then. He activated the numinat to heat water as she said, "Tess agreed to divert her with dress fittings. I slipped out while she was covered in pinned muslin and couldn't follow." Ren's rueful grimace said she hated leaving her sister with that bag of weasels. But Letilia hadn't given any indication of remembering Tess, and Renata's association with the popular Ganllechyn clothier was too well-known to hide; trying would only cause suspicion.

"We'll pour one out to honor her sacrifice," Vargo said, measuring out a blend fragrant with cardamom and peppercorns. "What was so urgent you needed to see me alone?"

Ren's laugh held an odd, embarrassed tinge. "I have a favor to ask. And it's—well—personal."

"Quietly dumping Letilia in Owl's Fields?"

"I wish," she muttered, then drew a deep breath. "No, it's... oh, djek. There's no graceful approach to this. Recall you the conversation we had the night of the Extaquium lightning party? When I told you I wasn't available?"

If the mad suspicion that had mugged Vargo on the way back from Floodwatch had any truth to it... "I'm guessing that hasn't changed, or you wouldn't be so nervous. I'll put you out of your misery. Short of you asking me to feed the old man to a seagull, I'll probably say yes. He's napping right now, so you don't have to worry about him offering his opinions." At least, Alsius claimed to be napping. Since Ghiscolo's death, he swung between manic theories about designs for a destructive numinat and melancholy withdrawal, and it worried Vargo.

But at least it meant neither Vargo nor Ren had to suffer commentary on their sexual relationship—or rather, lack thereof.

Her tension broke into a wry grin. "Then will you pretend to be my secret lover so I can marry Grey Serrado?"

I was right.

Ren's smile only broadened as Vargo's silence stretched on. To keep her from guessing that more than just surprise had him tongue-tied, he rose and busied himself with pouring tea for them both, keeping his back to her until his thoughts settled. "I'll admit, that's not who I'd have guessed." He set a cup and saucer before her, then blew on his own to cool it.

"The Rook?" she said, arching an eyebrow. "Flirtations we have had, certainly. But immortal vigilantes with ancient missions make for poor company at the end of the day."

It was a neat dodge, and if Floodwatch hadn't planted suspicions in Vargo's head, he might have swallowed the misdirection. He didn't push: If Ren wanted him to know, she would have told him. "No wonder you've been spending so much time at the Serrado house... and you *did* beg me to save his life. But what do you need me for?"

The plan she outlined had all the audacity he would expect from two people who spent their nights chasing around the city in mask and hood. A public spectacle, a series of trials to win a favor from the famous Renata. "But if Grey wins," Ren said, "people will think he's the lover I've been hiding, and all this was merely a show to make him look legitimate."

"So you need someone *else* to pose as that lover. Somebody the crowd will cheer for him to beat." The one thing the cuffs disliked more than a Vraszenian nobody: a Nadežran *somebody*.

Ren didn't think like that, but the truth stung all the same. Masking that old twinge with a wry leer, Vargo said, "Makes sense; most people already assume we're fucking. I'm surprised Donaia hasn't clawed my bits to ribbons. Hope Serrado's not the jealous type; *he'd* prefer me at the bottom of the river."

Her nervousness melted like chocolate into something warm and gooey. "He wouldn't, you know."

Vargo did know. The Rook—*Grey*—had that chance and didn't take it. But that was a secret Ren wasn't sharing. It wasn't hers *to* share.

She leaned forward and touched his arm. "Helping me with this...No one else could do it. We will not forget that. And anything I can do in return—"

"You can stop right there. Of course I'll help. With all the other shit we have to deal with, it'll be fun to rile up the cuffs. We'll have you knotting wedding braids in each other's hair before year's end."

Patting her hand—a friend's touch, rather than a lover's caress—Vargo thought of the medallion sitting under a locked and warded floor panel upstairs. Sessat. Friendship. Camaraderie.

He gripped Ren's warm, gloveless fingers to drive away the chill.

Suncross, Old Island: Equilun 24

The shopfront on Drema Square was empty, holding only the scent ghosts of moths and mildew. The light seeping through the lamp smoke caking the windows danced with dust motes.

Pavlin sneezed. "At least the location is good?" he said, venturing inside with a sleeve raised to shield his nose.

Giuna remained in the doorway, less excited than she'd been when they left Traementis Manor. Tess had meant this to be an afternoon with Pavlin, for cleaning and maybe a few stolen kisses, but Giuna had said she wanted to help prepare the new shop and the tiny apartment above, and Tess could hardly refuse the alta.

"I know it's not much to look at now," Tess said to her, "but with a bit of work we can make it presentable enough for cuffs, yes?"

"Cuffs?" Giuna arched an amused brow—an expression stolen from Renata—and bravely stepped over the threshold.

Tess pressed cold fingers to burning cheeks. "Meaning no disrespect, alta." She shot a quelling look at Pavlin, who turned his laugh into a convincing sneeze.

"I'm not offended." Giuna stripped off her gloves and tucked them into the pocket of her surcoat—one of her older ones, rose grey and shapeless, from before Renata and Tess joined the household. Perhaps she *had* come prepared to clean. She scratched at the grime on the window, leaving a clean streak too narrow to see through. "And Master Ranieri's right about the location. I'm surprised it stood empty for so long."

No one had used it in years. Not since Ghiscolo Acrenix had someone carve out a passage into the Depths, allowing his Praeteri cultists to reach their temple without braving the rats and floods below.

Tess almost didn't care where the shop was—almost. What mattered was that it was *hers*. No more stitching in a back corner of someone else's house; she would be a respectable tradeswoman, with a sweetheart waiting upstairs at the end of the day.

It would mean spending less time with Ren. But the feeling that they were both trapped by her lies had started to fade. Ren and Tess could have something like normal lives at last...which was, after all, supposed to be the point of the whole con.

After they dealt with a few remaining problems. Like those Primordial-cursed medallions.

Rubbing the dirt from her finger, Giuna said abruptly, "Renata's mother. What are we going to do about her?"

Tess stifled a groan. Not a Primordial, but Letilia could be mistaken for one in dim light. So this was why Giuna insisted on coming to see the shop: so they could talk without risk of being overheard. "I suppose it's too much to hope there's room for her in the Dockwall Prison?" she asked with a wistful look at Pavlin.

He chuckled and slid an arm around her waist, tucking her neatly against his side. "If I'm made Caerulet, I'll make bothering your alta a crime. Until then, we need a different tactic."

"Boot her from Nadežra entirely," Giuna said, leaning against a wall with her arms crossed like a Lower Bank fist in a play.

Tess's heart thumped. "She's on guard for that, though. I heard her say—not that I was eavesdropping, mind you—"

Giuna snorted. "I know servants listen, Tess. And you're always guarding Renata's back. What did you hear?"

The best lies are crafted from the truth. Ren had taught her that, because it was true, and because Tess didn't have her sister's knack for weaving cloth out of nothing. Even now, her cheeks flushed again, and she just hoped Giuna would take it for embarrassment. "You remember that to-do over the letter from Eret Viraudax?"

"The one Eret Vargo destroyed. Yes."

Tess couldn't remember the specifics of what Ren had pretended the letter said, but she didn't have to. "Letilia's that vindictive, she'll ruin my alta's life if she gets thwarted here. She said she'd left a message somewhere, and if she goes missing, the message will be delivered and all those secrets will come out."

Giuna's brow knitted. "The secret that Renata isn't Eret Viraudax's daughter? I mean, not just that he didn't sire her, but that he never married Letilia. Would that truly ruin Renata's life?"

Tess had to improvise. "There might be more? Nobody knows a person's dirty laundry like their mother, after all. Whatever it is, it's enough to stay my alta's hand."

"I wish she trusted me better," Giuna muttered, picking at a loose thread on her sleeve. Then her shoulders straightened. "I understand being cowed by someone, though, and how hard it can be to come out from under that. If Renata won't act, we'll have to."

"I could ask around," Pavlin said. "Find out where she's been going, who she's been talking to, that sort of thing. Letilia's got no reason to pay attention to me."

Mother bless this man for being so smart. Tess had been trying to think how to ask him that very favor, without giving too much away. She squeezed Pavlin's hand in thanks as Giuna said, "I can ask around, too, in different corners. Letilia's been trying to renew all her old friendships, and some of them might gossip."

She bounced upright in a faint puff of dust. "You don't mind if I start now, do you?"

Tess had never expected her to do much cleaning here. Besides, the alta's departure would mean finally having time alone with Pavlin. "We'll sweep our dust out of the shop; you go sweep yours out of the city!"

As Giuna departed and Pavlin went to fill a bucket from the nearest pump, Tess stood in the middle of her shop, thinking.

Giuna searching; Pavlin searching; Vargo had put some of his people out as well. At this rate, Letilia didn't stand a chance.

But it would go easier if more of them could talk to each other.

When Pavlin came back in, Tess tugged the bucket out of his hands and set it down so she could wrap her arms around him and nestle her face against his chest. He buried his lips in her curls, breath warm and sending tingles across her scalp. He said, "I can clean tomorrow if you'd rather rest this afternoon. Might get started on asking around."

Like water filtered by a cleansing numinat, Tess's thoughts came clear. She hadn't asked Ren yet...but she knew her sister's mind, inside and out. And she knew Ren trusted her.

Steeling herself, Tess pulled out of Pavlin's embrace. "Actually, I need to tell you some things about my time in the Fingers. About my sister...and her time as Letilia's maid."

The Palaestra, Floodwatch: Equilun 27

"Ninat," Grey's opponent finally gasped, doubled over from the jab to the diaphragm that had ended their match.

Grey fought the urge to double over himself, exhausted after sparring all afternoon. Pointing his blade at the ground, he held out a gloved hand to help his opponent rise, thanking him for the match.

His courtesy earned him only a sour look as his fellow duelist stalked from the practice circle. At least this one didn't spit at his feet like the last one had.

Grey racked his practice blade and dragged a towel over his head and face, wishing he could shed the quilted jacket and mop down his entire body. Though the calendar said winter had come to Nadežra, the balmy air hung on him like a wet rag.

Dedicated duelists and charter mercenaries spent their days inside the ring of cold marble columns that marked the Palaestra proper. The cuffs who liked to carry swords preferred to take their practice in the surrounding gardens, where grassy paths and flowerbeds wound between the dueling rings and created space for admiring audiences.

Ninat's unknown holder had carried a sword. Whether he was a gentleman, a duelist, or some other commoner with the right to go armed, there was a chance he honed his skill at the Palaestra. Grey, cut off from Vigil resources, was haunting the place in the hopes he might appear.

He paid the price in sweat, and in challenges from people who took offense at House Traementis hiring a Vraszenian duelist with no reputation.

Deciding propriety could go hang, he tugged his sweaty gloves off and dunked his hands in a trough. The lukewarm water provided such relief that he seriously considered dunking his head as well.

"Are you done for the afternoon, or do you have one more in you?"

At that pleasant drawl, Grey's consideration shifted. Forget his head. Could he lift the trough to dump it on Vargo?

He blotted himself dry with insolent slowness before turning to greet the man. Vargo was dressed the part of a duelist, all too well. The leather gauntlets tucked into his belt were fresh from the tannery. His coat's seams and creases were pristine, the pale twill never snagged on a practice blade's pitted edge. Grey would bet Ren's Vicadrius that the embroidery at cuffs and collar were cooling numinata. Vargo would never let himself look sweaty and disheveled in public.

"You want to duel me?" Grey asked, letting his skeptical tone say what they both knew: Vargo wouldn't last a breath past the moment he said *Tuat*. "Why?"

"Surely you heard the news about Alta Renata's Trials of the Volti?" Vargo inspected the rack of practice weapons. "The first challenge is dueling. And I hear you're not bad at it."

"Good enough to know you'd do better with an earth-handed blade. All those are sun-handed."

Vargo paused. "So they are." A flush crept up his neck.

Grey went to another rack and pulled a weapon, but didn't hand it over. "Rumor says Eret Vargo could already get any boon he wanted from Alta Renata."

It was unspeakably peculiar, performing the duet of cooperative deception with Vargo. Grey knew perfectly well that Ren had recruited the man to help them, playing the role of the secret paramour doomed to lose to a noble-hearted upstart. But anyone listening had to hear the opening notes of that song.

Vargo shrugged. "Some things are harder to gain than others, and the approval of her house head is the hardest of all." He tugged on his gauntlets, then said, "Do you intend to enter the trials? You've been practicing so very hard. Worried you're not good enough?"

Staged banter gave way without warning to dull fury, but Grey couldn't say whether it was for Vargo or himself. *Or both.*

Because he *hadn't* been good enough. Branek's people had overwhelmed them at Floodwatch. Overwhelmed *him*. The Kiralič and Mevieny were captured—Ren had almost drowned—because Grey lost the fight.

Rationally, he knew they'd been wildly outnumbered. Even as the Rook, he might have ended up in the same position. But he'd been training like mad for weeks, honing his body into the finest tool he could, in a desperate attempt to make up for what he'd broken... and it still wasn't enough.

Worst of all was the fear lurking beneath that. Excellence: the domain of Quinat. How much of his self-doubt was the medallion feeding his drive to do better?

Grey threw the practice sword at Vargo too hard; it hit the man's chest and almost fell to the ground. Vargo's kohl-darkened eyes widened. "Let's see how you fare," Grey snapped. "If you can't land one touch on me in five passes...I get that fine coat of yours." It wouldn't fit—Grey was longer in the limbs and broader in the shoulders—but Tess could transfer the cooling numinata to one of his own coats.

"Should just hand it over now," Vargo muttered before taking a fair approximation of the opening stance. "Uniat."

"Tuat."

Grey tamped down the urge to disarm Vargo with his first attack. He could have done it easily—but was that just a desire to demonstrate his skill, his *power*? The other point of this theatre was to make it look like Vargo might stand a chance in the first trial. Grey wasn't certain how he expected to pass it on his own merit; the man was a fighter, but a rapier was too clean and elegant a weapon for the back-alley brawls he knew.

So Grey waited, letting Vargo make the opening move, a thrust from far too close range. Only after a few parries did he slap the sword from Vargo's hand. "First pass," he said. "Try again."

After a second disarm, he paused to correct Vargo's grip. The third pass ended in a stop-thrust to the man's ribs. "Your blade is longer than you think," Grey said. "*Use* that. It isn't just an overgrown knife."

Vargo paused, frowning oddly. "I didn't expect you to actually teach me. Given..."

That sentence couldn't go anywhere good, so he didn't finish it. Grey said, "Then why ask?"

"You looked like you were in a mood to beat someone up. And, well. I was here."

To take whatever punishment Grey wanted to deal out. Just like he had the night of the Traementis adoption ball, when Grey gut punched him in the shadows between two carriages. The night Vargo risked his life to save Grey's.

Offering advice had improved Grey's mood slightly, but now it soured again. "You're not the one I want to beat up. Other people shouldn't suffer for my mistakes."

Vargo winced at the verbal thrust, but he didn't cry Ninat. Instead he chewed briefly on his lip, then said, "How do you make it right, when you fail?"

"You can't," Grey said. To Vargo. To himself. "You just do better next time."

The blades came up again, but Grey finished the final two passes quickly and cleanly. "You can have the coat delivered to my lodgings," he said, bowing himself out of the ring. "I believe you know where they are."

Dockwall, Lower Bank: Equilun 29

From its rooftops, Nadežra looked serene. Just a quiet sea of tiles and chimneys, rippled by the lines of the streets and canals, and the distant glimmer of the Dežera. Up here, Ren couldn't see the problems and frustrations. Only the sleeping city, washed eldritch pale by the first quarter of Corillis.

She wished it could wash her own frustrations away.

Wherever Branek had taken himself and his prisoners after Floodwatch, it wasn't any of the usual places. Staveswater was closed to him, Prazode still angry over his niece's involvement with the Anduske. The Crimson Eyes' stronghold held nothing more than the usual collection of Tserdev's people. Branek hadn't even trumpeted his success in capturing the Kiralič; whatever he hoped to accomplish there, it wasn't a matter of public propaganda.

Maybe his real goal was to capture Mevieny. Koszar swore he hadn't shared his plan for judgment by ordeal with anyone prior to the meeting. But Branek might have other uses for the speaker for the Ižranyi.

Unfortunately, if Branek didn't want to advertise his achievement, the others couldn't, either. It would cause too much chaos if people knew Mevieny and the Kiralič were being held prisoner. Which meant Ren and her allies had to be circumspect in their searching.

Below them, the warehouse lanes slumbered. The only sounds were the lapping of water from the canals, the creak of boats in their berths, the distant ringing of a buoy. With a weary sigh, Grey sank onto the roof and tipped his head up. Tess's pins kept the replacement hood in place, but Corillis's light flowed over his features, highlighting his cheekbones, the sculpted line of his lip.

"I'm sorry you have to spend your birthday like this." He spoke in his own voice, not an approximation of the Rook's.

"In your company?" Ren said, light and teasing. "Believe me, searching Dockwall is an improvement on what came before."

"Your birthday dinner went badly?" He tugged her down to sit between his spread knees. They'd bantered as they searched, the Rook and the Black Rose, but it lacked its usual playfulness. He blamed himself: for the loss of the Rook, for the loss of his clan elder. His failures weighed heavily on him.

As Ren's challenges weighed on her. "Donaia invited Letilia."

Publicly, Renata's birthday was in Colbrilun, but the Traementis knew the truth. Donaia—in a fit of generosity as misplaced as it was dutiful—had concluded that she shouldn't exclude Renata's mother, thereby forcing Ren to sit through two excruciating hours of sniping conversation.

She expected some comment from Grey, but he was oddly quiet. Finally he said, "Szeren...still you have told Donaia not?"

About herself. About the truth. "Not until I've dealt with Letilia."

"Why?"

A straightforward question, softly delivered. Ren couldn't stop herself from stiffening, even though Grey, with his body wrapped around her, would feel it. But it was *Grey*: She didn't have to hide her tension from him. "The night of Giuna's party, I was going to tell her. Then Letilia appeared—"

"All the more reason to speak, I would think. Take that weapon from Letilia's hands."

"What if Donaia uses it herself? No longer is she cursed, but the Primordial influence lingers. Whether she exposes me or Letilia does, the result will be the same. What little hold I have over our fellow medallion holders will shatter."

His arms remained gentle, like he was holding a skittish cat. "Would that not have been true had you followed your original plan?"

It would. She hated him a little for noticing that, and simultaneously wanted to lean into him for comfort. One patient layer at a time, he was stripping away the deceptions she used to hide the truth...even from herself.

The night was quiet. Up on this roof, only Corillis and the stars were listening. And Grey, who would never turn from her.

"I am afraid," Ren whispered, her chin dropping. "That once I tell Donaia the truth, she will see me as no different from Letilia. That she will cast me aside. That they all will."

Like her mother's family had cast Ivrina aside. For them, a half-Liganti daughter was unacceptable; for Donaia, a half-Vraszenian niece would be the same. And then the family Ren had acquired, the pretense of belonging...all that would be torn away.

She didn't say that part, but she didn't have to. Grey knew. He tucked her against the warmth of his chest, and Ren wished briefly that she weren't in the Black Rose's guise, that he weren't costumed as the Rook. She wanted the elemental comfort of skin against skin, the freedom of shedding all her masks.

"The Traementis are not your only family, Szeren." Grey still spoke quietly, his voice as much felt as heard. "Perhaps this is the wrong moment to offer, but...your kin. Wish you to know them?"

Ren went still. Past the lump in her throat, she said, "My mother's koszenie was lost when Ondrakja disappeared." If Ren still had the shawl, the embroidery would have told her everything; instead, all she had were faded, untrustworthy memories of the few times she'd managed to slip it out from where Ivrina kept it folded away. Had the final stitches at one corner been blue, for the Varadi? Or perhaps green, for the Dvornik? Was the other side Kiraly grey, or Anoškin white? Which side marked the clan of Ivrina's birth?

Grey knew all of that. "There might be another way," he said. "If you dance the kanina."

The ceremony Vraszenians used to call up the spirits of their ancestors, the parts of their souls that remained in Ažerais's Dream. Mostly they danced it for special occasions: births, weddings, deaths. The ancestors didn't always appear, and it was never all of them; no one could control which ones came.

"My mother was cast out," she forced herself to say. "Why would they listen to me?"

"Some kretse are more forgiving than others, not passing those judgments on to the children. Your mother's might be one of them." Grey untangled himself from her and stood, holding out one hand. "The only way to know is to try. It need not be now, but it risks nothing to learn the steps."

Her rapid pulse had little to do with the exertions of the night. What if she danced, and no one answered?

Learn. Then you have the choice.

Ren took his hand and came to her feet. "Teach me."

She'd seen the dance performed many times—well, she'd glimpsed it. When she was very young, Ivrina had always hurried her away, and after her mother was gone it became only a painful reminder of what she couldn't have. The steps themselves were simple. The complexity came in the spinning, circling movements of the group as a whole... because like many Vraszenian traditions, the kanina was performed by the community, everyone from children barely old enough to walk to elders almost unable. Not by a single person.

We're a community of two, Ren told herself. *Will that be enough for my mother's people? When the other is no kin of theirs?*

A light touch on her jaw drew her from her thoughts. "Should I show you that again?" Grey asked, and Ren realized he was waiting. She'd missed her cue to switch to the three-soul-weave, the core figure that divided the segments of the dance like the chorus of a song.

She shook off her worries like water. "Walk it with me. We pass sunwise shoulder first?"

"Yes. It's easier when you do this full speed; your momentum should carry you naturally forward. But the dance gets faster as it goes. Soon the eldest step out and the children go spinning off. The rest keep going until they can't, and when everyone is exhausted..."

That was when the ancestors came. If they came at all.

Ren wasn't about to try it tonight. When she had the steps down, Grey pulled her close for a kiss. "Whatever happens—with the kanina, or with Donaia—you will be all right. Clever Natalya always manages."

"So long as she has her Constant Ivan."

He laughed softly, tracing the edge of her lace mask. "Shall I bring four horses to pull your caravan?"

It was one of the most well-known folktales: the challenge Clever Natalya set to choose the next leader of her kureč, with Constant Ivan gathering horses from the dawn and the dusk, the slopes of the mountains and the shore of the sea. Thinking of it, Ren's breath caught. "You already have."

Grey tilted his head in confusion. She said, "A shawl full of knives, like the white horse Natalya rode into battle. A kitten to help me sleep, like the red horse to lighten her burdens. A card that promised honesty, like the black horse that shared her secrets. And—" She hesitated, knowing this would brush close to pain. "And the hood when you needed me to be the Rook. Like the gold horse who worked at her side."

She wrapped his hand between hers and pressed lips to the thin leather glove, warmed by skin underneath. "To me, you truly are Constant Ivan."

His thumb traced the curve of her cheek. His eyes, unshielded by the false hood, glimmered with what could as easily be moonlight as tears.

Voice rough, he said, "In some versions of the tale, they danced before their wedding. Not the kanina. Have you heard of the osze-fon, the campfire dance?"

The phrase was distantly familiar, but it summoned up no images. When Ren shook her head, Grey's fond smile took on a wicked slant. "No surprise. It is not a dance for children."

Puzzled, she let him take her hands again. Grey said, "The osze-fon is the flicker of flame, the curl of smoke, the heat between lovers. It is a duel as much as a dance, taking and being taken. I move into your space, and you yield so you can slip into mine."

The basic step was easy; Ren picked it up quickly. "Good," Grey said. "Now we do it in the proper hold."

In one swift move, he pulled her flush against him. So *this* was why Ren's mother hadn't mentioned the oszefon...and why Grey claimed it wasn't for children. The proper hold meant that Grey's boot and knee slid between hers, his hand cupping hers against his chest. Ren had no alternative but to wind her free arm around his neck, fingers gliding across the wool of the hood, wishing they could nestle themselves in his hair.

"This is dancing?" she asked, her laughter breathless.

"The most intimate kind that still involves clothing," he mur-mured in her ear, like the ghost of a caress. Then he began to move.

It was nothing like the stiff Liganti dances she'd learned, or the wild energy of the kanina. Ren was exquisitely aware of Grey's body against hers, every shift of muscle and breath. Sometimes he moved at a slow drag, like pulling reluctantly from a kiss. Other times it was a staccato flash, pivots and flicks, igniting heat between them. "Every campfire throws sparks," he whispered.

Ren dipped one foot between his legs, a delicate invasion; then it was her turn to retreat—if anything could be called a retreat when they were in contact from shoulder to knee. They were two bodies moving as one, nothing existing beyond the circling movements of the dance.

At least, until they were interrupted by the whump of a bag thrown over the roof's lip, followed by the scuff of boots as the owner clambered after it.

The intruder was in his teens, in mismatched rags of black, with a pockmarked complexion and night-widened eyes. Too old to be a runner, but too young to make a good fist. His cry of surprise when he saw them got swallowed into something like a frog's croak. "Tyrant's nutsack, there's *two* of you now?"

His instinctive recoil would have sent him off the rooftop, if Grey hadn't lunged and caught him by his coat. The boy's hands flew up to protect his face. "I'll put it back! I didn't take much, but I'll return it all!"

Then, between parted fingers: "Wow. En't nobody gonna believe I got nabbed by the Rook."

Ren stifled a laugh. In the Black Rose's voice, she said, "I think that tadpole can go back in the water, don't you?"

"You're not my type of target," Grey agreed in the Rook's voice, tugging the boy to a safer footing. "Besides, I think Lady Rose and I have somewhere else to be."

She could read his meaning in his body, as if they were still entwined. *Somewhere more private, and more comfortable, than a Dock-wall warehouse roof.*

Together they vanished into the night, leaving the boy alone with his awe and his sack of stolen goods.

5

Sword in Hand

Grey had moved in with Alinka after Kolya died, because her herb-craft didn't bring in enough money to support her children on its own. Now that Donaia was paying for her services, Alinka didn't need him there anymore. And his duelist's stipend would cover a room in a lodging house for him.

The morning of Renata's first trial, he was on the verge of telling Alinka as much when she said, "I would ask a favor of you."

Had she come to the same conclusion he had? "Of course."

"Yvieny is seven." Alinka cast her gaze upward at the hammering of feet, coming distinctly through the floorboards. "She needs her koszenie."

She marked age the way it was done in Vraszan, with pregnancy counting as the first year of life. At the age of seven, children were supposed to receive their koszenie, the embroidered shawl that recorded a Vraszenian's lineage. By tradition, the mother stitched her side, and the father, his. A tradition not everyone followed—not everyone had enough skill with a needle—but Kolya would have.

"If only I had nagged Kolya to start the moment Yvie sprouted her milk teeth, and Jagyi too, so something of their father they might still have. Now, *you* are what they have of him." Alinka laid her hand over his on the table. "Will you help me with it?"

The question went through him like a hot spike. Her request made sense; if a parent was absent or unable, the next best thing was for a family member to step in. But how many times had Grey been kept away from ceremonies, his grandmother insisting that his presence would anger the deities? Stitching Yvieny's shawl would be tantamount to stitching that poison into her blood.

Alinka knew all of that. Yet her gaze was steady, and her hand, covering his, didn't move.

A knock came at the door before he could master his tongue enough to respond. Sighing, Alinka got up—and stiffened in surprise at the sight of the tall Liganti woman outside.

Grey leapt to his feet. "Meda Cercel."

"Serrado. How many times do I have to say the formalities aren't necessary?"

"You call me 'Serrado,'" he pointed out. "It feels odd to call you 'Agniet' in reply."

Her sigh was half laugh. "Fair. And I...well. May I come in?"

Alinka excused herself to quiet the children playing upstairs. Grey gestured his former commander to the table and offered tea, which she refused. Just as well—he needed to be at the Palaestra soon. But Cercel wouldn't have come all the way to Kingfisher without good reason; he could spare a moment.

"Congratulations on your new position," Cercel said once he sat. "Are you happy in it?"

Cautiously, Grey said, "So far, yes. I'm sorry I didn't take you up on the offer of finding me work as a mercenary—"

Cercel waved his apology aside. "That's not why I'm asking. Once the new Caerulet is installed, those who quit the Vigil in protest over that business with the Ordo Apis will be allowed back in. If they want. I'm here to ask if you would consider it."

A month ago he would have said no, easily and with pleasure. But now...

A Vigil officer had power a common duelist didn't. Like the power to track Letilia's movements and help Ren neutralize her.

Grey ran a hand through his hair, feeling a length it hadn't had in years. Almost long enough for a stubby braid. If he rejoined the Vigil, he would have to cut it again—and Ren would be sad. Not just for the hair itself, but for what the change would imply.

Sighing, he said, "I'm not certain there's any point. It would just be more of the same."

"What if it weren't more of the same?" Cercel asked, ignoring a childish shriek from upstairs. "I know that's a lot for you to imagine. But if the new Caerulet disbanded the Ordo Apis, reformed the Vigil, did all the things you and I both know are needed. Would you come back then?"

Grey made himself consider it, because without rank separating them, Cercel was a friend. In the end, though, his answer was unchanged. "I'd love to see that. But I don't have the fire to make it happen, not anymore. I'm sorry, Meda Cercel." He winced. "Agniet."

Cercel straightened her gloves, in a rare show of awkwardness. "About that. Keep this in your pocket until it's public, but...technically, as of this morning, I'm Alta Agniet Cercel Coscani."

Grey jolted like he'd broken an active numinat. "You're a member of House Coscanum now?"

"Adopted. Yes."

And that swiftly, the whole conversation came clear. "*You're* Caerulet."

Her mouth bent wryly. "Not yet, no. But if all goes well, I will be. There aren't many suitable candidates, so Alta Faella had the bright idea of ennobling somebody new to put forward. Please, no jokes about the seat being cursed."

It wasn't cursed—not anymore. The poison that used to infect the city's Caerulets was in Vargo's hands now. Which meant that, for the first time since Kaius Rex died, there was a chance of someone *not* trying to strangle Nadežra into their vision of order.

And if there was anyone Grey would trust in the military seat, it was his former commander.

Not least because she hadn't leaned on their friendship to get him to return. She'd presented it neutrally, letting him decide on the basis of his own feelings. "You're a good choice," he said, with complete sincerity. "And I wish you the best of luck."

"But you still won't return." Cercel sighed and stood. "I understand. It's a damn shame, though, Serrado. Maybe some of your former patrol will, at least."

"I'll talk to them," he promised. "And—if Pavlin rejoins—"

She nodded without hesitation. "Lieutenant. He deserves it."

Pavlin would need the higher pay if he ever wanted to set up his own household. With, for example, a certain Ganllechyn seamstress. The thought made Grey smile. "Thank you. Now if you'll pardon me..."

Cercel raised an eyebrow at the mask lying on the table. "Going somewhere? Perhaps to the Palaestra?"

"I hear there's to be dueling. A good way for a man to establish his reputation."

She clapped him on the shoulder. "You'll do well."

As he opened the door for her, he asked, "Do you know yet who you'll appoint as high commander?"

"I was thinking Serinval Isorran."

Grey's thoughtful nod stopped mid-dip. "House Isorran has some Vraszenian ancestry." Several generations back, and most people had forgotten, but Ryvček had mentioned it once.

Cercel smiled blandly. "Do they? I hadn't realized."

Laughing quietly, Grey gave her the bow due from a commoner to an alta—but not the title. "I look forward to seeing a new Vigil, Cercel. Meanwhile, I've got some duels to win."

The Palaestra, Floodwatch: Apilun 8

The first Trial of the Volti would have drawn a crowd and a makeshift market regardless of weather, but mild days and sunny skies meant people came out in droves. Wandering through the close-packed masses, Giuna regretted the sleeves of fine caprash wool tied onto her surcoat. They'd seemed like a good idea when she left Traementis Manor, but now her arms were prickly with sweat.

She wasn't the only one feeling the warmth. People had come out in Nadežran-style masks, imitating the heavier Seterin volti worn by the competitors, but most were using theirs as makeshift fans while browsing the stalls crammed in behind the spectator stands. A gaggle of children were staging mock duels with skewers of candied hawberry; their only face covering was sticky red syrup as they shouted bloodthirsty taunts. At the edge of the grounds, performers with painted faces worked the fringes of the crowd. The most popular featured blades to play up the draw of the day: knife juggling and throwing, blade dancing, sword-swallowing.

Giuna paused to watch a man with his head thrown back taking a length of steel easily as long as his forearm. Someone jostled her elbow and she turned, half expecting a sly comment about the performance that would make her blush and stammer . . . but it was only a stranger pushing past.

Why should it be anyone else? Leato was dead. Sibiliat was under house arrest, for reasons nobody would explain. Parma had disappeared from society, leaving Bondiro to mope and Egliadas with nobody to leaven his surly lack of humor. Renata was always busy, and besides, her aura of cool elegance made it hard to imagine her offering raunchy comments.

Who else did Giuna have, after a life lived mostly from the window of her bedchamber with a book in her lap? Her other friends were acquaintances at best, and had only become even that much after the Traementis fortunes were repaired.

Sighing, she removed her mask to ply it as a fan and continued on from the sword-swallower, alone.

Most of the Palaestra grounds were taken up by the dueling ring and the spectator stands, with the volti using the building itself as their staging area. Some already circulated through the crowd, recognizable by their full-faced masks. According to Renata, the tradition had its roots in the visored helmets worn by equites in Seteris, which allowed them to contend anonymously in tournaments. But in Nadežra, the plain helms of the archaic past had been transformed by local practice, and the competitors once identified by the emblems on their banners were instead named for their fantastical masks.

Like the fox-masked woman in front of the Palaestra's columns, arguing with Argentet's secretary.

"I told you, it was paid," the Fox Volto said with mounting irritation. "My aunt would not lie about such matters, nor such a mistake let slip." The spice of Vraszan flavored her tongue and gave her words bite.

"I can't find any record of entry payment," said the secretary, without opening the ledger at his elbow. Instead, he laid his hand across the table, palm up. The dueling tournament limited the field to those permitted to carry swords, but that included a certain number of commoners—and it seemed this man saw that as license to solicit bribes.

The Fox Volto huffed. "So it is incentive you need?"

His oily smile congealed when she smacked his hand aside. Her other hand landed on the hilt of her blade. "Perhaps instead my skill you need to see."

Rising from his seat, the secretary snapped, "You—"

"Ah, you've arrived!" Giuna leapt forward and caught the hand that rested on the sword. The woman's gauntlets hung from her belt, and the warmth of her hand through the fine cotton of Giuna's gloves felt like an imposition. But Giuna could hardly withdraw now. "What took you so long? Cousin Renata sent me to make certain you were settled."

After only a quicksilver moment of hesitation, the Fox Volto laughed softly and disengaged her hand from Giuna's—but only so she could twine their arms together. Sunlight caught fire in the woman's dark brown braids, casting an auburn halo of curling wisps around her head. "I owe her thanks. Especially when the messenger is as much a pearl as the mistress."

With no mask to hide behind, Giuna could only conceal her fluster with a frown. She turned to the gaping registrar. "I'm certain if you check again, you'll find my friend in the ledger." She let her smile sweeten, like hawberries hiding the skewer inside. "Or I can ask Eret Novrus to help, if you're having trouble. He'd hate for *any* of Alta Renata's volti to be turned away."

"No need, Alta Giuna. I...I must have overlooked it. Please." He shoved a competitor's badge at the woman like a Vraszenian propitiating the Masks.

"I'm sorry for that," Giuna said, leading the Fox Volto up the shallow steps into the Palaestra, now segmented into chambers by screens. "His Elegance has been trying to eradicate this sort of graft, but these things take time." She scanned the dim interior, looking for Iascat. If one registrant had been refused, there might be others.

The Fox Volto's smile was audible in her voice. "I can hardly complain when such a pretty defender stepped in to save me."

Giuna swallowed. Sibiliat had flirted, but her words had been a snake's, all twisting phrases and whispered innuendo that could mean anything—and that could be ignored when it became confusing. Giuna didn't know what to do with such charmingly blatant flirtation.

But she'd learned what to do with people who treated her heart like a game.

Untwining her arm, Giuna took a step back. "You can find your way from here. But a word of warning; you're wasting your time competing for Alta Renata's attention. She prefers men. *And* you're wasting your breath flirting with me. I prefer people who aren't using me to get to my cousin."

The laugh that followed was muffled by the mask, until the woman pushed it up, revealing skin brown enough to confirm that Vraszan was in her blood. She was still nipper-cheeked, maybe even as young as Giuna. And where Giuna expected to find mockery, the lopsided smile she flashed was wry and begged forgiveness. "I'm put in my place—though I can't promise I'll stop flirting. My aunt claims it's as necessary for those in our profession as water for fish. Though for such a brave protector as you, I could be happy to drown." A wink punctuated her contrition. "I promise I've no interest in the fair Renata. I compete to show my skill only, and perhaps earn some regard."

"Oh." Now Giuna felt foolish, and it was nobody's fault but her own. The young woman carried herself like a blade—bright flashing and spring-steel grace. Of course she was here to prove her mettle. Giuna scrambled for an apology and came out with "Your aunt?"

"Is well enough known that I hardly need to add to her renown by speaking her name. But *I* am Kasienka Ryvček." Bowing in the archaic manner favored by Vraszenian swordmasters, Kasienka lifted Giuna's gloved hand. From atop her head, the vixen mask laughed.

And instead of kissing Giuna's fingers, Kasienka turned her hand over and kissed the inside of her wrist, right where the short glove exposed the skin.

Struggling for breath that had gone the way of her wits, Giuna said, "I'm... Giuna. Traementis."

"I know," Kasienka said with another wink. Pulling her mask down, she added, "Perhaps today, I'll fight for *your* attention instead."

She certainly had it as she sauntered away, hips swaying a bit more than necessary. Giuna tugged her glove more tightly onto her hand as though that could stop her shiver. *What would Mother say?* Donaia might be happy to extend kindness to Grey and his family, but her heir flirting with Oksana Ryvček's niece would be a different matter.

So what? Giuna thought, suddenly fierce. *Why shouldn't I flirt with her?* Sibiliat had been of the right station in life, and see how that had turned out. And it wasn't as if Giuna was looking to marry. She just wanted to enjoy herself for once.

Resolving to cheer the Fox Volto on, she headed for the stands.

The Palaestra, Floodwatch: Apilun 8

In hindsight, perhaps Renata should have staged the first trial somewhere other than the Palaestra—somewhere with more space.

Faella was right, she thought, peering through the curtains at the back of the box where she would sit to watch the duels. *People are hungry for a spectacle.* Her field of view was limited, but the crowds packing the stands made her hope the carpenters they'd hired to build this temporary arena hadn't cut any corners. There had been problems with that in the past, stands collapsing under too much weight, people injured or even killed.

But Renata wasn't Crelitto Traementis, nor any of the other nobles who put profit above safety. And Faella, from whose coffers came much of the funding for this event, would hardly want it marred by tragedy. Not when she was clearly so keen for it to bring a bit of peace to the city.

"—but if they lose *two* duels in sequence, then it will come down to the points they've scored—"

Tanaquis's reminder to Letilia of how the duels would work had been going on for several minutes, and she still wasn't done. Renata hadn't really expected her to agree to handle the logistics; she'd made the request in what she thought was a vain bid to distract her cousin from the rift with Utrinzi. To her surprise, Tanaquis had eagerly accepted. Renata didn't want to set it up such that a volto had to win every single duel—too much chance for something to go wrong with Grey, Vargo, or both—and so Tanaquis, relishing the mathematical challenge, had instead designed a complex system to determine who would proceed to the second trial.

Too complex, in Renata's opinion. But it seemed to make Tanaquis happy.

And it irritated Letilia, who interrupted the explanation with a flap of a ring-heavy gloved hand and a dramatic yawn. "Take your numbers to Mede Beldipassi. Only the gamblers care." She nudged Renata aside with her hip, poking her pointed nose through the gap to survey the crowd, and thereby missed the way Tanaquis's fingers clenched around her pencil.

"If you don't explain the rules properly to the crowd, they won't—"

"The crowd didn't come for *rules*. They came to see blood,

sweat, and a bit of dash. A proper welcome for a prodigal daughter's return." Letilia patted Renata's arm, though clearly she was referring to herself. "I think it's just about time to give it to them. Wait back here until I introduce you, poppet."

"But—" Tanaquis's reach fell short of Letilia's draped sleeve as the woman swished through the curtain and out onto the announcer's dais.

"What odds would you give that she 'forgets' to call me forward?" Renata said, feeling guilty at the amusement she took from the murder sparking in Tanaquis's grey eyes.

"Even," Tanaquis grumbled. "Better an empty register than a mother like that."

If only it were that simple. Ren had been delighted when she got a position as Letilia's maid: Serving the influential mistress of one of Ganllech's many petty princes had seemed as far from her life as a Finger as she could get. Only with time had she come to realize the ways in which Letilia resembled Ondrakja. But in both cases, what was her alternative? Life on the street, without a protector. An empty register, to put it in Liganti terms, would have been the least of her worries.

Letilia hardly needed the amplification numinat scribed onto the dais. Her voice came through all too clearly, welcoming the crowd in terms that made it sound like they'd come to see *her.* But if that kept her docile long enough for Ren to work, it was a small price to pay—even if Ren stifled a grimace when Letilia started rambling in her terrible accent about who better to oversee a Seterin tradition than a woman who was *practically* Seterin herself?

If Renata had actually bet on Letilia leaving her out, though, she would have lost. At long last—and carefully avoiding the word "daughter"—Letilia proclaimed her in a voice they could probably hear in Whitesail, and Renata stepped through the curtain.

The stands were a riot of color, everyone turned out in their festival best. Not just nobility and gentry, either; Renata had reserved a portion of the tickets for Lower Bank attendees. Faella had promptly fenced them off in the worst seats, but they still made a grand show, panel coats and knotwork charms in abundance. A little gossip spread via Arkady had ensured Vraszenians knew Grey Serrado was among the volti, and he already had supporters.

Knowing the crowd's anticipation would soon dull, Renata kept her own speech short. Soon she declared, "My favor is not easily given, and I would see the ones who seek to win it. Call forth the volti!"

The crowd took up her cry. "The volti! The volti!"

And from the tent on the far side of the dueling grounds, a double line of masked figures emerged. They formed a glittering river of silk and velvet, jewels and beads and bright metal wire. The pale fabrics of Liganti fashion had been thrown aside as each attempted to outshine the others, not a dull hen to be found in the parade of peacocks. With their faces masked, they sparkled their way into anonymity: a gold sun; silver Corillis and copper Paumillis; beasts familiar and fantastical; shapes drawn from the numinata; and even a few masks inspired by pattern cards. Renata was surprised to see those, but perhaps she shouldn't have been. Alta Renata's interest in Vraszenian superstition had become widespread gossip.

After they'd paraded a circuit around the stands, waving and collecting thrown flowers and ribbons, the volti snaked into a single line. Letilia swept her hand down, and as one they dropped to their knees.

"Oh, I could do that all day," she murmured with a giddy giggle. Renata descended the stairs before Letilia decided to play puppet master with several score people bearing swords.

One by one the kneeling volti rose and introduced themselves, not by name, but by the devices of their masks. As Renata curtsied and wished each of them well, she wondered if one face in particular hid beneath a volto. There was a chance Ninat's holder would see the promised boon as a chance to win some kind of protection for himself.

If he had, Tanaquis would find out. Every competitor was required to unmask for her at the time of elimination.

As with their attire, each volto attempted to stand out from the crowd, with poems and gifts. The Fox Volto offered her a sleek dagger made for use rather than ornament; the Storm Volto gave Renata a glove—a move that received jeers from the crowd, who considered that joke played out. Vargo, in a shining prismatium mask whose polished surface almost evoked The Mask of Mirrors, presented her with a box of fine Vraszenian chocolates.

"But won't it melt in this sun?" Renata asked, smiling archly, as though her question and this whole exchange were extempore rather than scripted.

"Then the alta should enjoy them now. Allow me." Flipping tradition into the river, Vargo stood—angling to the side so that they could be seen from the stands—and took Renata's free hand. He peeled the glove down her arm slowly, to the scandalized gasps and delighted murmurs of the crowd.

He had reached her wrist when a third hand grabbed his arm and pulled it away.

"Is this how a volto shows respect?" asked the Raven Volto, his sober, storm-dark coat and feathered mask an inkblot that marked him out from the gaudy array. He stood opposite Vargo, the three of them clasping wrists like they were swearing oaths. Ren had an impulse to close the circle.

Vargo's chuckle was loud enough to carry. "You'd rather she dirty her glove?"

"Why should she, when another can take on such burdens for her?" Releasing his grip, the Raven Volto stripped off his gauntlet and plucked a confection from the open box. He held it before Renata's lips, letting her choose to close the last handspan of distance.

Knowing that nobody but the three of them was close enough to see it, Ren let her tongue flick out the tiniest bit to catch Grey's bare skin. It tasted of chocolate and spice, leather and salt.

Rubbing his empty fingers together as though pocketing a kiss, the Raven Volto lowered his arm and knelt. Vargo let out a shaky breath and a low curse that nearly had Ren breaking character with laughter, but he gathered himself enough to kneel as well.

She had to force herself to continue down the line with Renata's poise, giving all the volti time to present themselves, before clapping her hands and calling for the duels to begin.

The volti retired to their staging area, all except those who were up first. Renata took her seat in the box, now filled with the guests Letilia had invited to join them. People would circulate all day, but by dint of her social influence and involvement with the trials, Faella had first claim to the seat next to Renata's. She leaned in close when Renata sat down, her voice as sharp as the blades now flashing in the light. "A pretty show—but don't forget your side of the bargain. Marvisal still refuses to speak to me."

"She refuses to speak to anyone." Last week Renata had wasted an hour sitting outside Marvisal's closed door, trying and failing to coax the young woman into conversation.

"I don't understand that girl." Faella sniffed. "If she would just *tell* me what she wants, I would give it to her."

Underneath her serene facade, frustration roiled. Thanks to the Illi-ten medallion, Faella had rarely had to face not knowing what the people around her wanted. But was she stymied because she'd stopped using her medallion, or because Marvisal's desires were outside of Illi's purview?

Renata couldn't demand answers from Faella out in the open. And before she could do more than contemplate dragging the other woman somewhere more private, Letilia's shrill laugh pierced her skull.

"Oh, I'm sure we'll have some excitement before the end! You can *hardly* have this many duels and not expect some bloodshed. You know, I tried to persuade Renata to pit the volti against wild animals. It's *very* popular in Seteris, having them fight lions or bears. But she's too squeamish."

Renata entertained a brief vision of tipping Letilia over the railing into a boar pit. *Such a tragic accident. I mourn her loss.*

She distracted herself by watching the duels. Some competitors lost embarrassingly fast, but the Prismatium Volto wasn't one of them. Either Vargo had found a miracle sword imbued to make its wielder an expert swordsman—which wasn't even how imbuing worked, outside of tales—or he'd found some way to cheat. As long as he wasn't caught, she didn't particularly mind.

And it was a pleasure to watch Grey at work. He couldn't indulge in the Rook's panache, of course; she was surprised he'd even risked the raven mask. But he fought with an economy and elegance that held their own beauty, stretching out his duels just long enough to make for a good show, then finishing his opponents off with deft ease.

Keeping her eyes on Grey, though, meant she wasn't watching Letilia—which proved to be a mistake.

"Would you have fought for me like this, if my father had called three trials for my hand?" Letilia asked, fanning herself coyly with a mask of stiffened paper and swan feathers. Most of the time, it was easy to ignore her terrible flirting. But now her target was Scaperto Quientis.

"I'm afraid I lack skill with the blade," he replied politely, ramrod straight and focusing on the current bout like he'd spent a lifetime following the dueling world.

Letilia laughed as if he'd said something witty, leaning as close as the arms of their chairs allowed. "How lucky for you that you needed no ridiculous spectacle to win my favor."

"I thank Quarat every day for my good fortune," Scaperto said, his voice so flat that Renata nearly choked on her wine. His stiff posture broke as Letilia nudged even closer. "Is there something wrong with your chair, alta, that you feel the need to crawl into mine?"

"The sun is shifting; I must stay out of it. My daughter and I have to be careful. Our skin browns so easily, you know."

She favored Ren with a smile sweet as poison-laced almonds. The demand for assistance was clear, but Ren didn't know what Letilia expected her to do. Did she think she could revive some flame that never existed? Scaperto hadn't shed one tear over the breaking of that betrothal.

"Come sit beside me," Renata said, though the words were like pulling teeth. "I'm well in the shade."

Scaperto stood fast enough that his chair threatened to topple.

"And I see Mede Bagacci. I've been meaning to speak to him about dredging the Lower Bank canals—if you'll excuse me."

Letilia was too good at the game to let her scowl at his paper-thin excuse last for more than an instant. Then she smoothed it away and came to sit alongside Renata. Before she could speak, Renata said under her breath, "If you provoke Donaia by angling for Scaperto, you'll only make my task harder."

"He was mine before he was ever hers. And what's she going to do, marry into Quientis? She has her own register to worry about. Meanwhile, *I'm* only doing as you suggested, making use of this opportunity while you laze about. I'm beginning to question *why* I should keep my silence." Letilia brushed the feathers of her mask along her cheek, lips pursing in thought. "Wouldn't Scaperto be grateful to me, if I revealed the truth? Some of your crimes fall under Fulvet's jurisdiction."

This was a dangerous conversation to have in public. Letilia knew that, and was doing it to underscore her threat. Gritting her teeth, Renata rose to her feet. "Then come. My friend Parma wasn't able to make it today, but I see Ucozzo Extaquium in the stands. Let's invite him to join us."

The Palaestra, Floodwatch: Apilun 8

As with all things in life, money and rank bought privileges unavailable to other people. In the case of this tournament, they secured Vargo a private changing cubicle within the Palaestra. It was only a temporary shelter of four canvas walls open to the marble roof above, but it gave him a place to rest between bouts.

During bouts, too—since he wasn't the one fighting.

A single brief lesson with Grey Serrado wasn't remotely enough to make Vargo a contender in this trial. But since it wouldn't do Ren's plan any good for him to be ignominiously knocked out in his first duel, he'd hired a substitute: someone of the right build and, with the help of walnut dye, the right hair color to take his place. Rather than faking a scar on the other man's throat, which might peel off under the sweat of exertion, they both wore collars high enough to hide the mark. Now the "manservant" who'd accompanied him into the Palaestra was doing all the hard work, while Vargo hid away with bare face and hands, entertaining himself with a deck of cards.

A muffled cheer went up just as Vargo beat himself at sixes for the fourteenth time. ::That's the final point secured,:: Alsius said. ::You might have instructed him to be more sportsmanlike. He walked off without helping Manghisca out of the dust.::

I told him not to, Vargo thought, gathering the cards and tucking the deck away. *Manghisca shorted us on that last shipment of cochineal. People would expect me to hold a grudge.*

::Good thinking,:: Alsius said. ::He's accepted his victory token and is on his way back—oh no. Oh dear.::

Vargo sprang to his feet, but he couldn't just go charging out. *What's happened?*

::One of the arbiters just stopped him,:: Alsius said. ::I'm not close enough to hear what they're saying, but it doesn't look good.::

The spare mask Vargo had brought would hide his identity, but it wouldn't give him any grounds to intervene. He yanked the stiffened fabric over his face anyway, and by the time he left the curtained cubicle, he had an idea.

Alsius was thinking along similar lines. ::His Elegance is overseeing the replacement of the lemon water.::

Keeping his head low and his shoulders hunched like a servant busy with his work, Vargo swiped one of the discarded pitchers and sidled up to Iascat. "Eret Novrus, a word?"

Iascat's confused question died on parted lips when he met Vargo's eyes. Scowling, he dragged them both behind the nearest screen. "If you're going to cheat, you're supposed to stay hidden—not reveal your deception to the man *responsible for stopping such things.*"

"I meant to, but one of your arbiters is hassling my decoy."

"I won't ask how you know that." Running a hand through hair that looked its best when unartfully mussed, Iascat sighed. "I suppose you expect me to help."

His petulance should have made him seem surly, but all it did was draw attention to the soft fullness of his frowning lips. Vargo caught the lower one with his thumb. The drag of bare skin over soft flesh echoed the game Grey had played with Renata, minus the chocolate to lend it sweetness. "I'd be grateful if you would."

Iascat smacked his hand away. Not roughly, but Vargo flinched all the same. "Your gratitude is apparently all you're willing to give. At least to me."

Lifting his mask to better read what had crawled up Iascat's nose, Vargo said, "Are you...jealous?"

That pale skin flushed so easily. "I believed you when you said you weren't interested in emotional entanglements with anyone. But it seems Renata isn't just anyone."

Vargo sighed. They'd been meeting more often since Iascat took the Argentet seat, and not always to discuss the business with the medallions. He'd gotten to know Iascat very well.

Well enough to recognize how much he sounded like his aunt Sostira.

And well enough not to phrase it quite that bluntly. "You sure that's you talking, and not Tuat?"

As easily as Iascat's skin flushed, it also blanched. His hand flew to the vesica piscis brooch at his throat, the symbol of Argentet's office. "I...*Shit*." His brow hit Vargo's shoulder and rested there. "Can we pretend I didn't just make a fool of myself?"

"We can play whatever games you want. Later. If you get me through this trial." Vargo buried his hand in Iascat's hair and gently tugged his head up. "Renata's counting on me to court everyone's disapproval, so they'll rally to support the person she wants to win."

Iascat gave him a flat look. "It didn't occur to you that a *friend* might be able to help with that?'"

"Tuat's your weakness to guard against right now." Vargo grimaced. "Sessat's mine."

Tugging the mask back over Vargo's face, Iascat laid a finger across his paper lips. "Go back to your hiding place. I'll rescue your decoy."

The Palaestra, Floodwatch: Apilun 8

By the time his final duel ended, Grey wanted nothing more than to drain the entire jug of chilled lemon-mint water set out for the competitors. He was used to sparring, and the cooling numinata Tess had swapped from Vargo's coat to Grey's kept him from overheating completely, but fighting in a full-face mask...he felt like he'd dipped his head in a basin of sweat. His mouth, by contrast, was as parched as dry rice, craving a cool, tart drink.

He'd seen firsthand, though, what happened to those who gave in to that urge. If Vargo hadn't stopped him at the beginning of the day, Grey might have been one of them. "I don't recommend it," Vargo had said, nodding at the drinks laid out inside the Palaestra. "Saw someone adding to the jug, and I don't think it was honey." The competitors who'd bolted for the privy not long after gave miserable testimony to the wisdom of his warning.

A few stragglers were still fighting their last duels, but the staging area was crowded with volti bemoaning their losses or crowing victory. Some kept their masks on, but nearly everyone had shucked their coats and wore only wrinkled and sweat-limp shirtsleeves. Not even the numinata blowing air through the pavilion were enough to whisk away the funk of bodies after a day's exertion.

Still, the sweat and the smell couldn't dent Grey's good mood. While passing the first trial didn't require a volto to win *all* of their matches, if they wanted the crowd's favor, that was the bar they had to clear. And he'd done it with ease, despite the best efforts of others to thrash him in the ring. Some had targeted him because he was Vraszenian—his mask might cover his face, but not his hair or the back of his neck—but the real challenges came from the professional duelists, who saw him as Donaia's pet. After years without a house duelist, why would she hire a Vraszenian, unless it was out of pity? Grey's victories today had earned him not only a token for the next trial, but also—he hoped—a modicum of respect.

A foolish hope, he discovered as he headed for fresher air outside.

In the close-packed pavilion, the elbow that caught him under the ribs could be mistaken for an accident, but the kick to the back of his knee could not. Grey let himself drop, bringing his hands up to catch the foot aimed at his head. He almost took the woman down with him, but caution held him back. He'd been in this play before, countless times during his early days in the Vigil. If he retaliated, then when the dust settled, he would be the only one blamed.

By that same logic, his attackers couldn't keep it up for long without attracting notice. Grey let go of the woman and concentrated on shielding his head, leaving his ribs to fend for themselves.

Too late, he realized that left his pockets fair game for someone who wouldn't have lasted a bell working a Lower Bank crowd.

"What's going on here?"

Iascat Novrus truly had grown into his new position; his tone was authoritative enough that it snapped Grey to his feet. But with the pummeling he'd taken, could anyone blame him if he lurched into one of his attackers as he rose? The man wore a constellation mask, but Grey recognized him by the mole on the right side of his neck. He was a fellow duelist, Arran Licino. A skilled swordsman— he'd collected his victory token early on—and vocal about how *he* deserved the Traementis position more than a certain Lower Bank upstart.

"Apologies, Your Elegance," Licino said. "It's the crowds in here. The Raven Volto tripped."

Iascat's gaze found Grey. "Is this true?"

How many times had he been asked that question? The answer always had to be the same. "Yes, Your Elegance. I'm quite tired, and it made me clumsy."

Snorting a laugh, Licino let his friends lead him away. After a curious once-over, Iascat strode off as well. Grey was entertaining visions of the Rook paying the Licino townhouse a visit that night when a hand touched his elbow. This time reflexes took over: He caught the wrist and flipped it into a lock.

"Ow," Vargo said.

Grey let go like he'd grabbed a red-hot iron. "Sorry."

"My own fault," Vargo said, shaking the discomfort from his wrist. His prismatium volto reflected a distorted rainbow. "Check your pocket. I think one of them filched your victory token."

"They did. That was the whole point of attacking me. Well, that and teaching me a lesson."

Vargo's other hand held a glass of lemon-mint water. He looked at it and said, "I was coming to offer you this—it's fresh, and safe to drink—but we'd better go get your token back."

Even as he spoke, though, chimes began ringing, signaling the victorious duelists to present themselves outside for the closing ceremony.

A ceremony in which they would display their victory tokens, thus earning themselves a place in the next round.

"Shit. There's no time. Here." Vargo handed Grey the water and dug in the pocket of his waistcoat. Apparently *he'd* had time to change. In fact, he looked as fresh and crisp as someone who'd been lounging around all day... which Grey suspected was true, given how well the Prismatium Volto had done in his duels. Thrusting his token at Grey—a carved wooden disc bearing crossed swords—Vargo said, "Either way the plan is fucked, but better this way than the other."

Grey eyed the token like a trap. Not because he didn't trust Vargo, but because he didn't want to be grateful to him. And Vargo was right; it would ruin Ren's plan for him to be eliminated this early. If Grey accepted his help, though, he wouldn't have to show skills he'd prefer Vargo not know he possessed.

He saw you and the Rook in a room together. You're safe.

Shaking out the sleeve of his free hand, Grey let its contents drop into his palm: another carved wooden disc. "Thanks, but Licino seems to have misplaced his own."

The prismatium mask hid Vargo's expression, but not the wry

laugh that followed. "Guess you really are a gutter cat underneath those feathers."

Feathers. Did he mean the raven mask Grey wore now or the hawk's uniform he'd molted this past summer? Or...something else?

There wasn't time to ask. Draining the water—sweet and fresh and tart, as welcome as rain in summer—Grey said, "Let's go present ourselves to Alta Renata."

The Palaestra, Floodwatch: Apilun 8

With so many duelists competing, the first trial made for a long day. The crowds had thinned somewhat by the end, and Renata herself was more than ready to escape to a quiet room and a soft bed.

So far, though, all had gone according to plan. She hadn't gotten *everything* she hoped for out of the day; Tanaquis reported that Ninat's holder was nowhere among the losing duelists. But both the Raven Volto and the Prismatium Volto had won all their duels, ensuring themselves places in the second trial. If the latter had succeeded in part thanks to one opponent very obviously throwing a fight, that would only feed through the rumors: a nice little flourish Ren assumed had been Vargo's idea.

Except that when the successful volti lined up before her, she didn't see those two masks anywhere among them. They darted into the arena at the last moment, as if something had delayed them. Was that, too, part of the tale they were trying to sell? Or had something gone wrong?

Whatever had happened, it didn't interfere with the results. After Letilia had flattered the winning volti with praise for their skill and courage, she bid them present the fruits of their victory to Renata.

Tokens in hand, Renata took her place on the amplification numinat. Directing her words as much to the crowd as to the volti, she proclaimed, "In two weeks, we shall hold the second trial: a boat race through the canals of the Lower Bank!"

A ripple of dubious murmurs greeted that, subsiding when Renata raised her hands. "But I have no wish to expose anyone to the foulness of the water there." She laid the faintest stress on *any-one*, which did more to quiet the murmurs than mere gesture. "So I hope you'll permit me a small indulgence of self-congratulation. In *one* week's time, I invite you all to a grand celebration in Horizon Plaza. Eret Derossi Vargo is ready at last to fulfill the terms of the Traementis charter—to replace the West Channel cleansing numi-nat. The Dežera will run pure and clean once more!"

The noise this time was no ripple. A wave of cheers rose, crested, and showed no signs of ebbing. Pounding feet shook the stands, people hugging and flinging their masks in the air.

And if the jubilation came louder from the common stands than those of the cuffs, Ren didn't mind at all.

The Mask of Worms

Isla Traementis, the Pearls: Apilun 10

Donaia tore off her gloves the moment she entered Traementis Manor, slapping them onto the hall table rather than throwing them in Colbrin's face. He didn't deserve such treatment, but her fury demanded release.

"*Letilia,*" she snarled like it was the foulest curse, and his pinched brow smoothed into understanding. The *nerve* of that woman! Swooping down on her lunch meeting with Scaperto, peppering him with pointed questions about how he came to take the Fulvet seat from the Traementis, was it in recompense for their broken betrothal...

"Wouldn't it be a boon if I could get my hands on Fulvet," Letilia blithely said as he fled to the Charterhouse—and it was unclear if she meant the seat or the man.

It had taken all Donaia's self-control to remove herself from the ostretta without burning the place down. Now she said to Colbrin, "I'll be in my study. No interruptions."

Her new study was on the ground floor, a sunny room with a wall of windows overlooking the back garden and a door for Meatball to go in and out. Smaller and brighter than the cave her husband and generations of Traementis heads had used—where Meppe now worked his bookkeeping magic—it lightened her heart simply to be there.

Usually. Not today. Why did the steel of Renata's spine soften to wet paper in the face of her mother's demands? *You know the answer,* Donaia thought. Gianco had never been able to stand up to his father, Crelitto, either. Renata had to cross the sea to get out from under her mother's thumb, but now that thumb had followed her. And all the rest of Letilia, too. The woman was a curse wherever she went.

A curse.

Donaia stood utterly still, caught by her own sudden thought. The day Crelitto struck Letilia from the register, he'd made them all gather to watch it. All the members of House Traementis filling the manor's main hall, because in those days they were still large and powerful.

Was Letilia's departure the first drop in the flood of their decline?

She couldn't recall. Had Crelitto's brother Umattone died before or after Letilia left? They'd happened in quick succession, she knew, but this many years on, the precise timing escaped her.

The register would say.

The garden door creaked, Meatball nosing his way in. He thumped his head against Donaia's leg, but she didn't indulge his demand for petting. Nudging him out of the way, Donaia went to the new lockbox and removed its contents with care.

House Traementis's register was old and heavy. The oldest segments dated back to the time of Kaius Rex, though the imbued parchment still looked as new as the day of its making. Donaia spread it open on her desk, meaning to trace upward to the black Ninat over Umattone's name—and stopped again.

She knew what her register had looked like when the new members were added in Canilun, and it wasn't this. Every current name had a second Uniat scribed around it, the space between broken with tiny, complicated figures whose meaning she couldn't begin to parse.

Meatball whined a query as she rose to her feet. "Stay," Donaia said, and with the scroll in her arms, she went back out into the house.

When Donaia left for lunch, Tanaquis had been at the manor, in the room she used when she didn't want to go all the way back to Whitesail. She was still there now, and Renata with her, but Donaia ignored her niece as she dropped the scroll atop Tanaquis's papers and stabbed one finger at the mess of the current generation.

Tanaquis looked stricken—but not surprised. Donaia fought to keep her voice steady as she said, "You did this. Why?"

For some reason Tanaquis looked at Renata. Donaia did the same, searching Renata's hazel eyes. "Is this something to do with your mother?"

Renata pressed her lips together, then stood and took Donaia's stiff hands in her own. "No, not Letilia. It's...I'm sorry." Regret shadowed her gaze. "I've been trying to figure out how to tell you this, and I've let my uncertainty drag on too long. It has to do with the curse on House Traementis."

The old fear dug in, its claws never quite leaving Donaia's heart. "Are—are we cursed again?"

"*No*," Renata said firmly. "But Tanaquis and I have been investigating where the curse came from. We still don't know who's responsible...but we think we've found what was used to enact it. A numinatrian artifact, a profoundly malevolent one. Unfortunately, we can't simply leave it lying around; it's far too dangerous. I have it, but I was concerned that it might have an ill effect on the family. So I asked Tanaquis to make some alterations to the register to protect the rest of you."

Her gaze dropped to take in the scroll. "I'll admit, I didn't expect something quite so...extensive."

A malevolent artifact. Donaia had known Renata was still chasing the source of their curse, but she hadn't asked for details. Her own mourning had been a cocoon, shielding her from the guilt of letting others take on that burden. *I need to start paying more attention.*

Tanaquis was watching them silently. When Donaia looked at her, she said, "I have Iridet's permission to work on this matter. And the safety of House Traementis is one of my primary concerns. I promise, this has my full attention."

So quietly it was almost inaudible, Renata said, "The more I consider it, the more I wonder if it would be wiser to remove me from the register."

She tried to withdraw her hands, but Donaia tightened her grip. "Don't talk nonsense. I have my fill of that these days from *that* woman."

A mere touch wasn't comfort enough. She pulled Renata into a hug, murmuring into her niece's hair, "Even if you won't let me send your mother away, I can at least make sure you don't bear every burden on your own. If this artifact is so dangerous, then I'll take that danger on myself. I will not lose you."

Too, her heart whispered. From the way Renata flinched, she heard the unspoken echo.

When the girl pulled back, her eyes were limned with unshed tears. "No, this burden must remain mine. You're the head of this house; risking you means risking everyone. But..." She bit her lip. "You're certain?"

"That you're family? Yes," Donaia said. "We're Traementis. We don't give up on each other."

Kingfisher, Lower Bank: Apilun 10

"And I thought kneading dough was hard. My baking ancestors are burning for shame," Pavlin grumbled as Grey tied their borrowed splinter-boat up at a water stair. He stretched his shoulder, easing the strain of an afternoon of rowing and poling up and down the Lower Bank.

Grey did the same, though without the dramatic expression of suffering. "Vigil work will be easy by comparison. I'm grateful you took the time to help, though."

Pavlin would never have given his shoulder that comradely

nudge when Grey was his superior. "Of course I'd help. And not just because Tess has me wrapped around her thimbled finger." The winter sun was as bright as his grin. "You might not be pinning the hexagram back on, but you'll always be my captain."

A musty smell rose from the coats they'd shucked into the bottom of the boat. All their clothes smelled, spattered with splashes of algae-green canal water. Today had been good practice, even if Grey couldn't hope to be partnered with anyone so accommodating in the second trial.

"If you come back with me," Grey said, "Alinka can give you salve to ease the soreness." He would need some himself. Fit as he was, rowing was very different from dueling, and an activity he hadn't indulged in this much in years.

"Maybe something for blisters, too," Pavlin said, inspecting his palms.

Grey wasn't surprised to find a guest waiting at Alinka's house. The members of the Stadnem Anduske still had to be careful where they went, but Cercel's first action as Caerulet had been to disband the Ordo Apis, the special force Ghiscolo had created to hunt them down. Idusza perked up like a cat at the scent of fish when Grey came in; then her shoulders slumped. "The Faces have not smiled on you, I see."

"No luck," Grey admitted as Yvie ran shrieking across the room to hug his leg. He and Pavlin had used their rowing practice to sniff around the Lower Bank, hoping to glean hints of where Branek and his captives were holed up.

"Perhaps if we sought their blessing," Idusza said. "Offerings I have made, but we lack a szorsa's guidance. Not since Suilun have I seen Arenza."

Grey pried Yvie off his leg and tried to calculate how much was safe to say around his niece. She'd kept one major secret for them already, when Koszar was recuperating upstairs. But it wasn't fair to ask a child to carry adult burdens. "I spoke with Arenza myself, and she laid a three-card line. Our path is The Face of Stars: We must simply hope for a stroke of fortune." He'd spent the day giving fortune as many opportunities to strike him as possible, but the sky remained clear, and Grey's fortunes remained as luckless as they'd always been.

Grinding up a piece of brick tea, Alinka muttered, "Perhaps we would see her more if she were not given reason to stay away."

Idusza scowled; Pavlin shifted awkwardly toward the door. But Yvie wasn't old enough to know that some words were meant to be heard, not answered. "What reason?" she asked, far too loudly.

Alinka twitched guiltily. "Who can say? Come, alča. Go add more decorations to the front step; perhaps those will lure her to us." Catching up a bucket of colored chalk remnants Tanaquis had kindly—if unthinkingly—bestowed on the child, Alinka ushered her out onto the stoop.

But that wasn't the end of it. Once the door was closed behind Yvie, Alinka gave Grey a meaningful stare. "The first trial...That, I understood. As a duelist you must establish yourself, so the world sees you as more than Mistress Ryvček's apprentice or the grateful recipient of Era Traementis's charity. But now you borrow a boat and practice as if you mean to win the second trial, too. What hope you to gain from Alta Renata, when already you are the house duelist? Why have we seen nothing of Arenza?"

"Perhaps I should..." Pavlin took another step toward the door. "Ča Polojny, can I escort you to...somewhere?"

Snorting at the ill-concealed invitation to flee someone else's domestic squabble, Idusza rose and exchanged her house slippers for half boots. A shawl of faded rust with only the bleached remains of embroidery came up to cover her head. "Yes, to my friends I should take this lack of news. Alinka. Ča Serrado." Her polite farewell was its own condemnation. Arenza was a friend of hers, and she clearly didn't approve of any man toying with her heart.

Their departure left Grey alone with Alinka, and no more observers to hide behind. But what could he *say*? She was right to glare at him; from the outside, his behavior looked inexplicable. Alinka had been so glad when he found a sweetheart, but now here he was, chasing after an alta for reasons he refused to explain. Meanwhile he was betrothed, and she didn't even know it.

Ren's masquerade had always been a delicate balance. Letting others in on it might have improved her life, but it had made the dance significantly more difficult to maintain. And it meant that more people had to lie on her behalf.

Telling Alinka the truth would only widen that circle. Yet Grey couldn't imagine keeping it from her much longer.

The silence had stretched painfully long. "I promise, Arenza understands what I'm doing."

"Very nice for her. But I understand nothing."

"I know. Alinka, I—" Grey folded her into a hug. "She'll come visit. And she'll explain." Either with the truth, or with a deft lie. If anyone could come up with such a thing, it would be Ren.

But more and more, he didn't want her to.

Nor did he want to do it himself. "Sit down," Grey said. "I'll make tea... for you should know something about my own life." *And about the Rook.*

Hidden temple, Old Island: Apilun 11

Vargo was the only one in the underground temple when Renata strode in and announced, "I had to tell Donaia about Tricat. Not everything, of course—not its origin, nor about the other medallions, nor that it was losing this one that cursed the Traementis. I don't want her killing Letilia. But..."

He wasn't used to seeing her visibly uncertain. At last she said, "I haven't felt right, hiding the danger from her."

Vargo sat back on his heels, keeping his chalk-dusted hands clear of his dark trousers. She still maintained her Seterin accent when she wore Renata's mask, but more and more often, he found himself slipping into Lower Bank rhythms when they were alone together. "No secrets or debts between you, your enemies are my enemies. En't saying a family's the same as a knot, but similar principles, yeah? 'Cept nobody says it out loud when you join a family."

"Fortunate for me that they don't." Her wry laugh fell like golden leaves over a sinkhole of guilt.

They might have dispensed with secrets between themselves, but they still held many back from the world. Well, Ren did. Most of Vargo's major secrets had died with Ghiscolo, Diomen, and the Praeteri. Only Alsius remained, and practically everybody important knew about that now. As for his life, he'd never been anything to the world but belligerently himself. Ren, on the other hand, still had plenty to hide.

Tanaquis arrived soon enough after that Vargo knew she must have come with Renata and somehow gotten distracted halfway down the tunnel. Probably by the ward that kept intruders out—she still wanted to understand how that worked, and why triple clover knots let people pass through. "Oh, you've started," she said, hurrying over to examine the numinat Vargo had begun inscribing. "Let me see."

Today's work was their latest attempt to find the spirit of that nameless szorsa Ren had met in the dream. She'd tried taking aža here in the temple, but none of the glimpses it showed her were the one she wanted. Tanaquis had suggested the Tricat medallion might help, as it had before, only to recoil at the vehement refusal of the others.

Instead she'd taken a new tack. Her inspiration for today's numinat sprang from her mentor's obsession with music. "It's not the same as Tricat, which is embedded in time. The harmonic spheres *transcend* time," she'd explained, hoping to convince them to rig the cavern with wires that would turn the entire temple into a giant lyre. Eventually, she gave in to Vargo and Alsius's more reasonable suggestion of chalking out the figure for the harmonic spheres, an ever-widening path of seven overlapping circles. Combined with the figure Tanaquis had once used to send Vargo's spirit into the realm of mind, they hoped it would direct Ren to the szorsa.

::Do pay attention so you can give a thorough account when you return,:: Alsius implored Ren as Serrado arrived, a near echo of the instructions Tanaquis was giving her. ::Some people don't appreciate how wondrous an event it is, traveling through the realm of mind!::

Abandoning her to her fate, Vargo approached Serrado. Ren's excuse for inviting him had been that he was Vraszenian, and therefore knew more about Ažerais's Dream than any of them—the same reason Serrado had given back when they were trying to save Ren from sleeplessness. It made a good cover; if it weren't for his suspicions, Vargo would have bought it.

"I still don't understand why she needs to go in alone," Serrado muttered, as though the argument hadn't been settled several times over.

Really, they weren't being at all subtle—not if you knew where to look. Vargo would warn them, but watching their dance was one of the few amusements he had these days.

"More people going means more chance of someone getting lost." He felt bad the moment he said it, and the sour look Serrado gave him was like a thumb pressed to a bruise. "Besides, it's better for you to stand ready to retrieve her. Tanaquis and I will need to handle the numinatria."

Then Vargo raised his voice for everyone to hear. "By the way, am I the only one assuming that Faella used her medallion to put Cercel in the Caerulet seat?"

The chorus of "No" that answered him echoed melodiously from the temple's high ceiling.

"She's a good choice, though," Serrado said as the last of it faded. "Better than any other I can think of."

Renata nodded. "I doubt Faella used the medallion to control anyone's desires—I don't think she knows how. But she might very well have looked for someone who could get the support, not only of the Cinquerat, but of the city."

Social unity fell under Illi-ten's purview. Vargo growled low in his throat. "You know, if the medallions only helped people to act like selfish assholes, it would be easier to resist them. The problem is, they really *can* help, sometimes."

"Of course. There's nothing inherently wrong with desire, or any of the emotions that emanate from the Primordials." Tanaquis's declaration lacked her usual blithe confidence. The loss of Iridet's

respect and support had shaken her more than the fall of the Praeteri. "That's all Primordials are, really. Those concepts in their purest form."

::Lumen save us all, I am *not* wading through another apologist
debate,:: Alsius grumped. His admiration of Tanaquis's "innovative
mind" and "precise chalking" had soured in the face of her flirtation
with heresy.

"Perhaps you might have a word with Faella," Vargo said to
Renata, both of them fighting a smile at Alsius's pique. "After you
return safely, of course."

"That's hardly an incentive to come back."

He gave her an impudent wink as Tanaquis said, "While you're
at it, perhaps you could persuade Faella to talk to me about what
she saw during the ritual. I still only have reports from some of the
medallion holders; I'm lacking Sessat, Noctat, Ninat, and Illi-ten. It
isn't nearly enough."

"Not likely to get Noctat," Vargo muttered.

"I know!" Tanaquis huffed at Sureggio's rudeness, dying without
leaving a proper report. Vargo hadn't told her what he and Varuni
had discovered when they went to Extaquium Manor, intending to
remove that human stain from Nadežra, only to find themselves too
late. Whatever the man had seen in his temple vision inspired him
to end his life in an eleven-sided numinat. His note had said, *I surrender my soul to the purity of desire.*

Renata cleared her throat. "I've been meaning to ask... Vargo,
have you been having any peculiar dreams since you took a medallion? Sessat-related dreams?"

"Apart from the occasional nightmare of plague, I don't often
remember my dreams." And those he did were banal worries of
being trapped in a library full of blank books—probably bleed-
over from Alsius. "I take it you've been having Tricat nightmares,
Renata?"

She twisted her gloved hands in an uncharacteristic display of
nerves. "Not nightmares, exactly. Dreams of the past. And dreams
of the *Vraszenian* past, at that—some of them here in Nadežra, but

others elsewhere in Vraszan. At least, I assume it's Vraszan; I've never been farther inland than Floodwatch."

"Tricat dreams?" The brightness perking Tanaquis's tone was warning in itself. "How fascinating. Could you—"

"—give your report after we're finished here," Vargo said, placing chalk in Tanaquis's hand and turning her toward the numinat. "Perhaps your dreams can take you to wherever this nameless szorsa of yours waits."

Ažerais's Dream

The numinat that carried Ren's spirit into the dream felt a great deal like falling asleep. One moment she was sitting in the figure, listening to Tanaquis hum the seven-note melody she was supposed to use to return; then, without quite noticing the transition, she was somewhere else. A different version of the temple, with murals carved into the walls that flickered and changed in the corners of her eyes.

It wasn't quite right, though. While the place around her was recognizable as Ažerais's Dream, it was...too *precise*, Ren thought. Crystalline and hard.

The realm of mind, inscriptors called it. She'd always assumed it was the same thing as the dream—and it was. But the method she'd used to come here had left a sense of distance between her and the dream, like a pane of glass separated them. Nothing was quite immediate enough, quite *messy* enough. Like a dream described rather than experienced.

If she wanted to find the szorsa, she suspected she would have to break that glass.

Not with violence. Ren stretched her hands out, thinking. The dream was a place of instinct, intuition, the amorphous logic of symbols rather than the rational march of numbers. And what symbol did she have available to her that might draw her into the heart of the dream?

The Black Rose's disguise flowed up her arms, growing into gloves, sleeves, the overlapping layers of the body. The mask covered her face, first threading across her brow, then settling into the familiar veil of lace.

When that cleared from her vision, the dream felt *right*.

Ren smiled beneath the mask. She was in the dream...and for once she wasn't on ash, Tricat wasn't warping everything, there was nobody to rescue and nobody to flee. This was a dance where she was free to set the steps and call the tune. She could take a moment to simply enjoy its slipping, shifting beauty—to feel the half-caught sense of meaning around her, the same sense that came and went as she read pattern.

Only for a little while, of course. Who knew how much time it would take her to find the szorsa?

Assuming she could find the szorsa at all.

Ren had hoped the numinat might bring her directly to her target. Since her luck wasn't that good, she tried walking a labyrinth: first the usual complex path, swinging out as well as in, and then when that failed, the type she'd seen on the floor here, circuits that moved steadily inward. But when she got to the center...still nothing.

She bit her lip. The dream had given her a decira when she needed to pay for her pattern, and the lace mask when she called for it; could she make that work on purpose? Ren concentrated on her hand, and then there was weight in her palm, the familiar heft of her mother's deck.

The Face of Roses, Sleeping Waters, Ten Coins Sing. Ren's breath hissed between her teeth. She'd tried before, outside the dream, and gotten the exact same cards. And as before, apart from Sleeping Waters—the card of place, depicting the Point and its lost labyrinth, high above her head; she was in the right location—she couldn't read anything from them.

Because the szorsa wasn't just nameless. Being made Zevriz meant being severed from one's people...and from everything else. Pattern couldn't guide Ren, because that woman had been torn out of it. No threads led to her anymore.

But she was able to pattern me. That had to mean *some* kind of connection remained. Ren couldn't think how to find it, though. She would have to go back to the waking world and see if anyone else had an idea.

Then she hesitated.

There's more I could look for here than just her.

Connections. Kaius Rex and the szorsa had used the Uniat medallion to bind the others together into a chain. That chain had broken at his death; from the perspective of numinatria, only the pieces remained, nothing linking them into a whole.

But from the perspective of pattern, they couldn't *not* be connected. Their association with each other remained on a conceptual level, through their crafting and their history with the Tyrant. Could Ren use that to find the holder of Ninat?

She could try. And if it didn't work, she could try again with Parma, using the numinatrian harmony of Noctat with Ninat. Tanaquis would leap at the chance to combine those two traditions.

Ren was bound to her medallion, as the holder of Ninat was bound to his. And the medallions were connected to each other... so all she had to do was find the right thread, then follow it.

The threads glimmered into view as she looked for them, a shifting rainbow of strands. A moment of concentration settled them into colors she could sort: That silver one was her link to Grey; the blue one, Vargo. She avoided the putrescent purple one, shuddering. She'd strengthened her connection to the zlyzen, back when she rescued Vargo and the medallion from the dream—to what effect? She hadn't seen so much as a clawed limb of them since then. Not that she could really complain, but it worried her that nothing seemed to have come of it.

Tricat would be brown. There was more than one of those; one led to Tess and Sedge, another to the Traementis. She didn't see one for her mother, and a lump tightened Ren's throat. When Ivrina died, all Ren could afford was a pauper's pyre, burned with others in the Liganti tradition. Did that mean her mother's spirit was lost to the dream?

There. That, hidden beneath the rest, was the thread to the Tricat medallion. And strung through it, a dull tin line.

Uniat. The chain of office had been destroyed in the material world, but the idea of it still linked the medallions.

Plucking the tarnished wire, Ren followed it out of the temple. She expected to be led to Novrus Manor, since Tricat was most closely linked with Tuat. Instead, the wire turned sharply, leading her to the place where all paths converged in Nadežra.

The Point of the Old Island, with its Great Amphitheatre—and the wellspring within.

It was as full as if she'd stumbled into the middle of the Great Dream. Brightly painted stalls on the flat ground outside displayed wares and signs for services, tempting anyone who approached. Pilgrims dressed in their festival best milled around, waiting to sip from the waters of their goddess. The amphitheatre's crumbling top was crowned with dreamweaver nests, and the iridescent birds swooped over the crowd, the occasional fallen feather scrabbled over before someone claimed the prize. Such feathers promised good fortune for the seven years to come.

Yearning tugged Ren forward. Her mother's people might be here. And if she couldn't find a nameless szorsa or a faceless man, perhaps she could find *them*.

The mood inside the amphitheatre was reverently festive. A tune wended through the gathered people on the thrumming pulse of drums and feet. The glow of the wellspring washed the crowd with ghostly colors as they circled its rim.

Grey had taught her this dance, a version for two, on a rooftop mere weeks ago. The people here were performing the kanina to call their ancestors.

She had no kin to dance with. But surely here, of all places, she alone could be enough. Could find the answers she so desperately craved.

Her first step was wrong-footed, and she stumbled. A thread had tangled around her ankle, tripping her up. She kicked it free, but it clung as she entered the dance, catching her skirt, looping around her wrist, easily brushed off, but persistent as a puppy.

Ninat? She tried to look at the thread, but glancing down only made her collide with someone who grumbled in good-natured annoyance. Ren didn't want to abandon the dance for something unknown—something that might not even lead to any reward. Not when she was so close to finding her mother's family.

But that isn't why you came here. Duty dragged at her, irritating and unshakable. She was supposed to find the szorsa; failing that, she'd gone after Ninat's holder. Her unknown Vraszenian kin mattered only to her, not to anyone else. Not to Nadežra.

If she left, though, she might never have another chance.

Then so be it. Ren clenched her teeth and hardened her heart. Whoever her mother's kin were, they'd cast their daughter out. Even if she found them, what welcome would they give Ivrina's half-breed orphan?

The dull hurt of that thought was only partial armor against the tears as Ren stooped, heedless of the bodies slamming into her, and seized the thread. It led her through the crowd, bending first one way, then another; she crossed her own path more than once, in a looping knot that made her step over or under the thread as she passed. And as she followed it...

It's leading you nowhere. What you want is here. Family. Harmony. The answers to all your questions.

Cold spiked down Ren's back. The swirling bodies were a whirlpool, trying to drag her back into the dance. The drums sounded like thunder. Storm Against Stone: the winds that howled outside the Charterhouse on the Night of Hells, when Ren and Mevieny stood before the warped statues of the Cinquerat, and Ren sensed for the first time the Primordial power behind the medallions.

She'd followed Uniat's thread...and it lured her with the family she wanted, the answers she desired.

Straight into the grip of A'ash.

The whirlpool grew more violent, people's hands clawing her braid, skittering off the leather petal-plates of her disguise. Unable to catch her, they attacked the thread leading her out, trying to rip it from her grasp.

A sob tore from her throat as she clung tighter, drawing strength from the memory of the last time she'd climbed a rope to escape the claws of nightmare. Grey waited at the other end. Her friends must have realized something had gone wrong, and he'd come to save her again.

Planting her boots against the crumbling stone walls, she scrabbled up the line to where the dreamweavers built their nests. A hand reached down, and she caught it without thinking. Without question.

Only to blink in surprise when she saw the man hauling her to safety. He looked nothing like Grey: a few years older, at least, with the pale skin and sun-kissed hair of the north.

The original Rook? No. Even if the magic weren't broken, Ren had felt the memories and heard the stories from Grey. The original Rook had been a young woman—one with Vraszenian blood.

"Who...?" They both spoke at once, and the man's crooked smile broke into a laugh. Kneeling, he peered over the wall, into a pit of storms that roiled and flashed with lightning. There was no sign of the dancers now. "Ah, mistress. Quite a mess you fell into."

He peered up at her, hazel eyes catching the light. "But what most puzzles me is that your soul is whole. Szekani, čekani, dlakani. How managed you that?"

The man was speaking Vraszenian. With traces of a Seterin accent—but fluent Vraszenian, with knowledge of their beliefs as well. Ren should have answered his question, but what came out instead was "Who are *you*?"

"Gabrius," he said, standing and coiling the thread. "A humble inscriptor. One who wanted to understand better this place of your peoples...and wound up with all the time in eternity to study it. Have you a name I can use?"

She was still wearing the Black Rose's mask, but introducing herself that way felt pretentious. "Ren," she said. "What you pulled me out of..."

"An invasive pest." He spat into the cesspit. It wasn't the wellspring anymore; they were nowhere on the Point. "To contain it I've tried my best, but with so much seepage..."

Ren followed his gesture to the ring of nests and the birds crooning and preening. "The dreamweavers?"

"Is that how my circle appears to you? *Mirabile scitu*." Gabrius looked around again, as though wishing he could see whatever Ren did.

She rubbed her arms, like that could scrub away the clinging lure of her desires. "Know you what that 'pest' is?"

"Yes, and I'm guessing you know also. But name it not—that has a tendency to draw its attention." Gabrius gave her a sharp look. "Straight into its grasp you walked. What could possibly lead you to do that?"

She wasn't about to tell a Seterin stranger about the medallions, even if he had just rescued her. "I seek someone in the dream. The szekani of one who has died. But she is Zevriz... Know you what that means?"

"One whose connection has been cut." The grim slant of his brow said he also knew how important such connections were to Vraszenians. "Was she kin of yours, before?"

Ren couldn't suppress a bitter laugh, thinking of the promise she'd just walked away from. "Who can say? I know my own kin not, and hers are lost to time and severance. She..." Ren hesitated, weighing what she could and couldn't say. "This pest—she had a hand in bringing it here. I know not if she meant to, but I am hoping that if I find her, I can get rid of it at last."

"Finding one who cannot be found... now that would be a new challenge to pass the time."

The glint in his eyes reminded her of Tanaquis, the words of Alsius, but the graceful ease with which he hopped to the ground on the far side of the wall was unlike either of them. Following him, Ren landed in a twilight dream of Suncross Plaza, the sky burning from saffron to cobalt, the lamps hanging in the air like bubbles in thick honey. The buildings around her looked different, though: older, but newer at the same time.

"How long have you been here?" she asked.

His frown had a wry cast. "In this realm, time is fluid. Since before the pest, though. What you see is the Nadežra I knew in life."

"Went you south into Vraszan?"

"Briefly, but not far. Why?"

If he hadn't gone far, he couldn't have seen the things that appeared in her dreams, the cities and towns and fields. "It matters not. For the szorsa I should search."

"To your flesh you should return," he said firmly. "I object not to being trapped here—always there is more for me to learn—but you might not wish to join me. On your behalf I will search...though I know not how to tell you if I succeed."

She hesitated, suddenly wary. What if this was another Primordial trap?

It isn't what you want. She had no desire to cede her search into someone else's hands, or to go back to the waking world with nothing to show for her effort. Surely she could trust that.

As for future meetings, the thread was already there, formed when he led her out of the trap. It shimmered now with different colors, like aža, like Sebat, the numen most associated with inscription. Ren concentrated on it until she knew its feel. "With this, I can find you again."

He looped the thread thrice around his hand before giving her a salute of the sort she'd only seen in theatricals—historical productions where every gesture seemed artificial and archaic. "Until then, tread carefully, Ren. And be cautious of which threads you follow." So saying, he sauntered off into another Suncross, and another, until the haze of dreams between them was as impenetrable as a wall.

But the thread connecting them gave a playful tug. An assurance he was out there, somewhere.

The seven-note melody Tanaquis had been humming as Ren went into the dream was snagged in her mind like a fishhook. When Ren hummed it in reverse, a glittering peacock line appeared on the ground, bisecting the path of spheres that brought her here.

With a final pang of regret, Ren followed that line back to the waking world.

Hidden temple, Old Island: Apilun 11

Surfacing felt a great deal like waking from a dream, except that ordinarily Ren didn't wake to the avid faces of Tanaquis and Vargo hovering over her, waiting for a report.

Well, Vargo was mostly there as Alsius's sedan chair. "Any luck?" he asked, his voice a simple knife through the barrage of questions from Tanaquis and the spider.

She groaned and scrubbed at her face. "Not exactly. It'll be harder to find the szorsa than I realized—but I may have help in doing so. Believe it or not, I met a spirit in the dream. A Seterin man, an inscriptor. He said his name was Gabrius."

A heartbeat of silence greeted her statement. Then, out loud from Tanaquis and telepathically from Alsius: "Gabrius *Mirscellis*?!"

Renata recoiled from Tanaquis, but she couldn't stop Peabody from leaping onto her shoulder. "Er...he didn't say. Who is Gabrius Mirscellis?"

Vargo snorted. "Only the man whose work we cribbed from to design the numinat you're sitting in. Author of *Mundum Praeterire*? The first to investigate—never mind; neither of us cares. I used to have a bust of him in my office, until the Rook broke it. Thin nose, narrow jaw, looks like he's the only Seterin philosopher with a sense of humor?"

"He said he got caught in the dream," Renata said cautiously.

Alsius toppled from her shoulder into her lap. She caught him as Tanaquis said, "That sounds like him. How fascinating! He did get lost there when he was exiled to Nadežra."

::Exiled!:: Renata had to hold Alsius close to keep him from jumping at Tanaquis in defense of his hero. ::Vile propaganda spread by envious rivals. Anyone of sense knows he came here due to his interest in the realm of mind.::

"I thought he was fleeing gambling debts." Vargo grinned like a boy throwing pebbles to scatter pigeons. "Or an affair of the heart."

Unaware of Alsius's incoherent sputtering, Tanaquis said, "Whatever drove him here, he became curious about Ažerais's Dream. He was the first to speculate that it might be the same as the realm of mind."

"It is, and it isn't." Ren caught Grey's gaze. He was hanging back, trying to pretend he hadn't been worried. She risked a small smile, and his expression warmed with relief.

Shaking his head, Vargo retrieved the fuming Alsius. "Serrado, why don't you make certain Renata is recovered while Tanaquis and I clean up." His voice rose over twinned protests from his fellow inscriptors. "You can ask all the questions you want later. It's been almost three centuries. Mirscellis isn't going anywhere."

Flashing Vargo a look of wary gratitude, Grey knelt at Ren's side. His fingers brushed hers, as much as either of them dared when they had an audience. "You came back safely."

She swallowed, remembering the trap she'd fallen into, taking refuge in the warmth that grounded her. "I told you I would."

"I should know better than to doubt you." It was the respectful response of a commoner to an alta, but she could hear the words *Clever Natalya* echoing underneath. Then Grey's tone lightened. "A good thing, too; I don't think I can duel a dream on your behalf."

If anyone could, she believed it would be him. She let him help her to her feet, allowing her hand to linger a moment too long in his. Nobody was paying the slightest attention. Alsius had recovered from his pique and was arguing with Tanaquis, through a long-suffering Vargo, about whether *he* could be sent into the realm of mind to meet Mirscellis.

"Apparently he's an admirer," Renata murmured to Grey, amusement rising over the chill inside. "Just wait until I tell him the rest of it." About A'ash, and Mirscellis's efforts to contain that influence—and how she'd walked straight into its maw.

The chill returned, but holding it inside would help nothing. Squaring her shoulders, Renata said, "I'm ready to give my report."

River's Blessing

Westbridge, Lower Bank: Apilun 14

The wind blowing down the Dežera was as cool and crisp as the candied apple slices Tess was snacking on, but neither it nor the clouds dimmed the enthusiasm of the crowd flocking to the Lower Bank for the activation of Vargo's river numinat.

Or rather, flocking there for the festival. It was the Potter's Moon, when the Dežera's waters ran low enough for craftsmen to reach the thick, alluvial clay beneath the layers of silt; after weeks of hard, mud-mucking work, tradition called for people to drink from the first finished cups to celebrate the river's bounty. It was also a party for the volti who'd passed the first trial—and wherever there was food and entertainment, people would come.

Once, Tess would have been working the crowd as a pity-rustler, using her big eyes and quivering lip to charm coin out of people's purses, or distracting them while Ren made a lift. Now she strolled at Pavlin's side, stopping here and there at carts selling hot rice wine and cider. "Enough, enough!" she laughed when he tried to pass her a steaming cup, holding up her paper apple cone and her half-eaten capon leg. "If you're keeping my hands full so you can rob me later, I'll warn you I've nothing of value to take."

"Not true," Pavlin said, studying her with a discerning eye.

"There's at least one thing worth stealing."

He leaned in for a kiss. Tess ducked her head, but she could hardly swat him away with her hands full. Nor did she want to. Instead she crowded into him, hiding her glee against his shoulder and mumbling, "Ruffian. I should report you to the Vigil."

That shoulder was clad in fresh blue, the set of dress vigils she'd finished the night before. The steel of his new lieutenant's hexagram reflected the overcast sky. Pavlin was off duty, but Vigil officers were expected to attend public events in their uniforms, the better to remind people that no crimes could be hidden from the Aerie.

Her sweetheart was once more a hawk. In spring that discovery sent Tess into tears; in winter it had her crying with laughter. *How did this ever happen?*

"I'd be happy to accept the fair mistress's report," Pavlin said, too smooth and sure for her health to take. "But you'll need to show me what the thief absconded with."

Rising on her toes, Tess delivered her report to his cheek. "Do you think I'll ever get it back?"

"Perhaps I can bring it by your lodgings later?" Now Pavlin was the one blushing and ducking his head. "We should find Alta Giuna and tell her about Mede Pattumo."

Pavlin's flirting had clean driven his news from her head. Tess said, "We should get to the platform anyway—it's almost time."

She quickly finished off her apples and capon, washing them down with wine strong enough to sting her eyes. With the crowd parting for Pavlin's coat, they made their way toward the river.

An observation platform ran along the shore for the special guests. Its railing was lined with volti in their full-face masks, stars and willow trees and peacocks and flames, waving to the crowds below. Every so often someone tossed something up to them, and it wasn't always easy to tell the gifts from the signs of scorn. The lump of dung thrown at the Wave Volto was pretty clear, though; whoever he was, apparently he wasn't well-liked.

A few of Vargo's Fog Spiders guarded the steps, dressed clean for once, and they waved "Sedge's little sister" through with a smile for her and warning looks for Pavlin. The platform was far less crowded than the milling streets below, and most of its occupants were happy to ignore her. Tess ignored them in turn. Only a few wore coats or surcoats she'd sewn herself; the rest weren't worth her notice.

A crane towered above the layered numinata, angling over the river in a way Tess had a hard time believing was safe. Seven foci gleamed like stars, ready to be dropped into place. "There won't actually be much to see," Vargo had warned them beforehand. "Just the water gradually clearing." To which Ren, naturally, had said she would *provide* something to see.

Forty-nine trumpeters, seven times seven, blew a fanfare from atop the Great Amphitheatre as the foci rolled into their waiting slots. Fireworks went off a moment later, bright against the clouds. A barge, floating downriver from Floodwatch, passed through the gleaming structure with its own musicians aboard, picking up where the fanfare had left off with a jubilant song. It was all a great deal of expense—but not unnecessary, Tess thought as the crowds cheered in delight. The display told them House Traementis and House Vargo cared about this occasion enough to celebrate it: attention the Lower Bank rarely received.

To her surprise, Tess found herself tearing up. Renata might be a mask, but *this* was real. Ren and Vargo had made this happen: clean water for countless Nadežrans, after far too long without. Tess hadn't forgotten her days of trudging to the east side of the Old Island, or paying the water-carriers who filled their casks there and then carted it where it was needed. No one would have to do that again.

She wiped her eyes dry, and realized too late what had been obscured by the tears: an unfamiliar surcoat dyed with purple mallow and embroidered with jaundiced finches. By the time the wearer caught her arm and clamped her close like bosom friends, it was too late.

"If it isn't sweet little Tess," cooed Letilia. Her breath was hot and sharp as rice wine. "Who's made *such* a name for herself, creating clothes for my dear daughter. I *do* wonder where you acquired your skill. Everyone knows that such things are outlawed in Ganllech."

Pavlin edged closer, hand twitching as though he couldn't decide whether to pull Tess away or go for his sword. Grabbing that hand, Tess gave it a warning squeeze. It was safer to humor Letilia than to antagonize her.

But Tess didn't have Ren's skill for faking cordiality. "Is there something you needed, alta?"

"Oh, *many* things." Letilia's laugh trilled like she'd made the funniest jest. Tess gave her a close-lipped smile. "But your mistress is working on those. Perhaps you could encourage her to do so more quickly."

"I'm certain I don't know what you—"

"*After all,*" Letilia interrupted, loudly enough that Tess sucked in a breath, hoping nobody was paying attention. Letilia's smile widened, a shark sensing the blood of fear. "After all," she continued more quietly. "I only have one daughter...but I recall a maid of mine often shirked her duties to go visit her sister. A sister who later fled Ganllech for crimes against the princes."

Then, in a murmur that called up memories of Ondrakja: "Ren might be safe, but *you* are not. Not from the law in Ganllech, and certainly not for what you've abetted here. You should remind her of that before *someone* recognizes you."

Releasing her iron grip, Letilia flicked her fingers—the same gesture the princes of Ganllech used to send a criminal to be torn apart by hounds—and sauntered off.

Tess shivered in the cold wind licking down the Dežera. Not even Pavlin's arm was enough to warm her.

"It's an empty threat," she said, to reassure him as well as herself. At least she'd told him everything. If Letilia had hoped to set him against her, that thrust fell short. "She's getting desperate, is all. Nobody in Ganllech would give two penneths for one runaway seamstress." Not even one arrested for the blasphemy of stitch-witchery.

"I don't think it's Ganllech she was threatening you with." A furrow of concern cinched Pavlin's brow tighter than one of Vargo's waistcoats. "Renata's title gives her protections that you don't have. If Letilia wanted to cause trouble for you..."

"She'd have to expose Ren. And herself. She's not ready to do that yet, or she wouldn't be bothering with me." So there was no need to bother Ren with Letilia's empty threats. Bolstering herself with that thought, Tess straightened and searched the crowd. She spied Giuna hanging over the platform's rail to point at something in the river, bottom up and heels kicked high. A laughing woman in a fox volto pushed up to her brow held Giuna's hips to ensure she didn't topple tits-over-teacup into the mud below.

"Come on," she said, pulling him in her wake as she headed for Giuna. "It's past time the three of us trimmed Letilia's claws."

Eastbridge, Upper Bank: Apilun 16

"Alta Giuna! What an honor. Please, be seated. Would you like some coffee?"

"Tea, if you don't mind." Giuna smiled at Toneo Pattumo, settling into the chair he indicated. His office was surprisingly sparse, the sole painting depicting a ruined temple in the Seterin countryside. One might have taken it as mere austerity, the choice of a man who preferred simple surroundings...if there weren't visible marks on the walls where other pictures used to hang. And if one didn't know his reputation as a connoisseur of art.

Once the tea was made and sweetened to Giuna's liking, he took the chair behind the desk and said, "Is there some service House Pattumo can do for your family?"

"Oh, I hope so. My cousin Renata speaks highly of your services."

His teacup didn't quite hide the flicker of unease as he sipped. They both knew Pattumo had caused Renata a great deal of trouble in the days before her adoption, hounding her about problems with her letter of credit. Those debts were settled, but Renata had no reason to praise him.

Giuna set her cup into its saucer with an authoritative clink. "Some philosophers believe the world has an inherent balance. As fortunes rise in one place, they fall in another. For example, the Traementis fortunes have been climbing lately. Yours, on the other hand..."

He cleared his throat. "Alta Giuna, I—"

"Borrowed money from unfortunate sources. Money you would have been able to pay back...if your business partner Ebrigotto Attravi hadn't recently met with ignominious disgrace. Involvement with a heretical cult, I hear." A cult Pattumo himself had joined. That, like the identity of his Lower Bank creditors, had come from Vargo, by way of Tess. But Giuna was here because of what Lieutenant Ranieri had learned.

"Mede Pattumo," she said, before he could protest. "I'd love to repay your generosity to my cousin by helping you out of this inconvenient situation. House Traementis has just acquired the charter for assaying coinage; I think you'd be ideal for administering it."

A nervous flick of his tongue wet his lips. For all Giuna's sweet tone, he could tell there was a barb hidden inside. "However could I repay you for such an opportunity?"

At moments like this, Giuna could almost understand why Renata enjoyed navigating the Charterhouse. It wasn't nice to back Pattumo into a corner...but watching everything slot into place, neat as a puzzle? That, she could see the pleasure of.

"Alta Letilia," she said.

Pattumo flinched.

"Correct me if I'm wrong," Giuna went on, gentle and remorseless. "But I suspect she's given you something to hold on to for her. Knowing Letilia, she spun you some dreadful story about how she fears winding up facedown in a canal, the victim of Traementis cruelty. Mede Pattumo, do you believe I'm cruel?"

"No," he whispered.

"No. And I promise you, no one in my house—my mother

included—intends violence toward Letilia. But she's petty enough to ruin her own daughter's life if she doesn't get her way. So here's all I ask: Let me have what she gave you. Let me have it, and don't tell Letilia. Do that, and the administration contract is yours."

He fiddled with his teacup, rattling it against the saucer. "What if she asks to see it? She's done that once already."

The risk was real; the runners bringing messages from Letilia's hotel to Pattumo's door were how Lieutenant Ranieri had tracked this connection. *Life would be easier if Letilia were more stupid*, Giuna thought, sighing. "In that case..."

She wasn't nearly the innocent she used to be. In preparation for the heirship, Renata had described the underhanded tricks used to falsify deals.

"Loan it to me," she said. "I'll bring it back within two days." *Or something that looks like it, anyway.*

Pattumo rose and opened the strongbox in the corner of his office. The envelope was sealed with a wax-stamped numinat, a precaution Giuna trusted Vargo could circumvent easily enough. The looping, overembellished writing was familiar from the endless stream of notes Letilia sent to Traementis Manor. It read, *In the Event of My Disappearance.*

"I'll deliver the contract when I return this. *With* a clause stipulating your continued silence on the matter." Giuna curtsied, smiling. "It's a pleasure doing business, Mede Pattumo."

Kingfisher, Lower Bank: Apilun 19

Ren sat with Grey at the table in the Serrado house, waiting for Alinka to speak. She'd tried three times already, but each time the words had died on her tongue. She wasn't blinking enough, and the tea had long since gone cool between her motionless hands.

With every passing heartbeat of silence, the tension in Ren's heart wound tighter.

Finally the stillness cracked into a breathless laugh. "It is absurd. And it is the only thing that explains the absurdity of everything else." Alinka dragged her gaze up and met Ren's squarely. "He hopes to win the hand of Alta Renata...because *you* are Alta Renata."

The burning in Ren's eyes said she hadn't been blinking enough, either. "I am."

"And when first you came here—"

"That was no trick. For Koszar I searched, which led me to you. I was terrified when Captain Serrado walked through the door."

That drew another laugh from Alinka, this one less incredulous, though a moment later she shook her head again. "So this entire competition..."

"If I win, we will no longer have to hide," Grey said.

So far it was working. Everyone knew Vargo was the Prismatium Volto, and most assumed he was Renata's secret lover. Meanwhile, rumors were swirling about Vargo and Grey: The Rook had accused Vargo and Sostira Novrus of colluding in the Fiangiolli fire and the death of Kolya Serrado, but Grey Serrado had been seen visiting Vargo's townhouse. And hadn't Sostira's retirement been suspiciously abrupt? What was going on between those two?

Their rivalry was a perfect recipe for igniting interest in the trials. Knot boss versus ex-hawk; upstart cuff versus Kingfisher man. The Lower Bank wanted Grey to win. The Upper Bank wanted Vargo to lose. Beldipassi couldn't take bets fast enough.

Alinka made a frustrated sound. "You may not hide, but *she* will. Still she will be Alta Renata, instead of herself. And what am I to say to Era Traementis? Every Meralny I visit the manor. When I see Alta Renata there, am I simply to curtsy and pretend I know not? What of the *children*? Yesterday Yvie had her dolls throwing things at the 'cheese-eater' seducing her uncle away from Auntie Arenza. For you these lies may be easy, but for us they are not."

Ren groaned and buried her face in her hands. "I know. Alinka, I am so sorry. I never meant for things to become this tangled."

"Then untangle them." Cups and spoons clattered as Alinka's hand came down hard on the table. "Stop being Renata. Why keep this false life you have built? Would you not be more comfortable as yourself, among your own people?"

Three different responses tried to leap from Ren's throat at once. Each thwarted the others, leaving her mute. Grey voiced one of them on her behalf. "Alinka...I too would have to cut ties with the Traementis. Even if Donaia and the others recognize Arenza not, should Ren change one set of lies for another? Pretend she is a stranger to them?"

Gripping her tea like she meant to crack the cup, Alinka said, "I know to them you are grateful, because they helped you and Kolya when first you came to Nadežra. I myself am grateful; it is thanks to Era Traementis that I no longer worry how I will pay the next month's rent. Still, it is the only way Arenza can be herself."

She'd missed the message hidden in what Grey said. "But I am not Arenza," Ren said. "Not as you use that name. You think that with Vraszenians, I would be among my own people, but a lifetime I have of knowing that's not quite true. When to Nadežra I returned, the language was rusty in my mouth. Grey had to teach me to dance the kanina. What *real* Vraszenian needs such teaching, at my age?"

"I question you not—" Alinka began, stricken.

"I know you don't see me that way," Ren said, deliberately letting her phrasing be Liganti, even as her accent remained Vraszenian. "But others do. And meanwhile, would you have me abandon the Traementis? That life may have begun as a lie, but what I do as Renata is real—and it helps them. I'm their advocate in the Charterhouse, their influence among a dozen noble and delta houses. The river numinat charter was approved thanks to *Renata's* efforts."

Alinka opened her mouth like she wanted to respond, but Ren pushed onward, making herself say the next part before she could lose her nerve. "If they choose to throw me out, that is their decision, and I must find a way to live with it. But should I rip a hole in their register, just to simplify my own life?"

She knew the answer to that. It was right there, in what she'd said: *If they choose to throw me out.* The choice ought to be theirs.

No matter how much the prospect hurt. Maybe *especially* because it hurt. Donaia, Giuna, Tanaquis...she'd begun to think of them as real family. And she wanted nothing more than to keep that from changing.

Family. Stasis. Two desires the Tricat medallion would all too readily feed. Ren didn't blame a Primordial for making her want those things in the first place—but clinging to her lie, long after wisdom said to let it go?

An awkward silence had fallen. Alinka was staring at her tea; Grey's eyes were flicking between her and Ren. His gaze halted on Ren when she drew a deep breath and said, "I'll tell them. After the trials end, so Donaia can remove me quietly, should that be her decision." People would gossip far too much if she were disowned mid-trials. But afterward, if Grey won, there would be an easy explanation to hand.

Sensible logic that did nothing to dull the pain. But this was the hell she'd crafted for herself: She wanted too many things, and she couldn't have them all. To resist A'ash, she must stop thinking about her own desires, and start thinking about what other people needed.

But that's a desire, too, isn't it? The wish for them to be happy.

Bile rose in Ren's throat. She could chase her tail straight down into madness. Instead she clung to that promise. Not a desire, but a plan. *After the trials are done, I will tell Giuna and Donaia the truth.*

"More tea, I think," Grey said, stroking Ren's arm before reaching to collect Alinka's stone-cold cup. "I'll brew it, while the two of you get to know one another—for real."

The Point, Old Island: Apilun 22

The wind whipping across the Point threatened to tear Renata's hair from its careful arrangement. But standing atop the rim of the Great Amphitheatre, gazing over the Dežera, allowed her to feel for a moment like she was all alone, with nothing but the winter sky above and the waters far below.

To the south, she could see people gathering at the Floodwatch Bridge. Faella had suggested a footrace for this second trial—"Being fleet of foot is a traditional virtue, isn't it? And I imagine your man is good at that sort of thing, having run up and down the Lower Bank when he was still a hawk"—but Ren liked her idea better. Still a test of speed, but also a way to draw attention to the newly cleansed waters of the West Channel, and a private homage to the spirit of the Dežera. No one save her friends might recognize the Vraszenian impulse underlying her choice, but Ren took satisfaction in it.

And in the twist she'd added, both to send a message, and as insurance against trouble. This trial wouldn't only test speed; it would weigh a virtue she valued far more. The volti had to work in pairs, two to a boat, and no one would be considered to have completed the race if they reached the finish line alone.

She hoped that would shield Grey against interference. That it would still happen, she had no doubt; Faella had cackled over the obstacles inherent in sending the volti through the western canals, where the locals could both cheer on the spectacle and indulge in "Lower Bank tactics" to improve the chances of winning their side wagers. But at least Grey would have an ally with a vested interest in completing the race.

The tap of a cane on the stone recalled Renata to herself. She turned, one hand rising to keep her hair from her eyes, and discovered Faella had come to join her. Renata steadied the old woman as she attained the amphitheatre's rim.

"You could have let me wait in Duskgate," Faella grumbled. "The end is the interesting part, and these old bones can't rush down with the rest of you young folk."

"I asked you up here for a reason," Renata said. A quick glance showed her the others were staying back, out of the worst of the wind. They could speak here as privately as anywhere in Nadežra. "It's about Marvisal."

Faella's attention sharpened like a knife. "You've learned something?"

From a seven-card wheel—not that she could admit that to

Faella. Coffer and Key had said the main obstacle to Marvisal's happiness was the Illi-ten medallion. With the rest of the pattern giving Ren a lever, she'd been able to pry an answer out of Marvisal at last.

Renata asked, "How much do you truly value her happiness?"

The old woman's expression said she wasn't jabbing Renata with her cane only because she needed it to brace herself against the wind. "Are you questioning my love for my grandniece? I told you, I—"

"Would snuff out the Lumen to make her happy; yes, I remember. To be frank, that would be the easier path. I'm afraid what she wants requires something much more difficult: for you to give up what *you* want."

Faella's eyes narrowed. "Explain."

"It's no secret you've been grooming Marvisal to become your heir. The unspoken sixth Cinquerat seat, ruling polite society from her throne in the Pearls. But Marvisal's desires lie in quite another direction.

"Your grandniece has never loved that life the way you do, and her recent experiences with Mezzan and Sibiliat have quite soured her on it. What Marvisal wants, Alta Faella, is to leave all this behind. She wants to see the world—to travel to Seste Ligante, to Seteris, to Arthaburi or Ghus or anywhere that isn't *here*." Society might be the purview of Illi-ten... but the world was Illi-ten, too. That was how the Primordial influence seeping through the Coscanum register had manifested in Marvisal.

"Rubbish," Faella sniffed. "I didn't see—"

She cut herself short, but not soon enough. "Didn't see what?" Renata asked, her voice hardening. "Marvisal's desires, as shown to you by your medallion?"

The grinding of Faella's teeth couldn't possibly be audible over the wind, but Renata fancied she heard it. "Yes, all right; I used it on the girl, when she suddenly refused to talk to me. If she wanted the world, surely I would have seen that!"

Would she? Or had her own desires blinded her? "You've been using your medallion rather a lot, haven't you? Even after you learned what it is, and where its power comes from. You used it to secure the Caerulet seat for Agniet Cercel."

"You should thank me for that," Faella snapped. "I used it, yes—to find someone in this damned city who might have a prayer of keeping it from tearing apart. Given our recent history with Caerulets, isn't that a good thing? Oh, don't lift your nose like you smell something foul on your shoe. I want things to *endure*."

"Do you not understand the danger—"

"I've been marinating in that danger for most of my life." Faella jabbed her cane against the stone for emphasis. "You say the power in that thing corrupts the user; very well, I am corrupted. Stopping now will hardly change that. Meanwhile, this city lurches from one crisis to another. I am an old woman, Alta Renata, and I don't have much time left... but I intend to make sure my house and my homeland last after I'm gone.

"So yes. I used my medallion to find someone who could do a better job as Caerulet than her predecessors, for the sake of Nadežra; and then I scribed her into my register, for the sake of House Coscanum. It will make no real difference to the state of my soul, and you may well thank me for it later."

The speech left Renata briefly silent. She didn't know what she'd expected; something pettier, perhaps. Certainly not an argument she found difficult to refute. Cercel *would* be a good Caerulet—at least until Illi-ten's influence corrupted her, and hopefully the medallions would be long gone before that. Adoption was the only way to make her eligible.

But that was the insidious temptation of the medallions. Like a bad apple, they rotted even the good desires they touched.

The flag went up at Floodwatch Bridge, a fluttering white banner, bright in the winter sun. The volti were ready.

Faella wasn't done, though. Jabbing one finger at Renata's sternum, she said, "You owe me more than that, you know. Do you think I suggested this whole spectacle out of kindness toward you? Or even just to get your help with Marvisal?"

The rage numinat in the Praeteri temple. The delusion numinat in the prismatium workshop. Twice Ren had been influenced by Primordial power, and the memory made her sick. "You used your medallion *on me?*"

"I haven't bent your will, girl. I don't know how, and the one you hold protects you anyway. But I know better than to put all my goods in one boat. Our new Caerulet is one; you and that lover of yours are another. It showed me the two of you can help hold this city together, and it wasn't hard for me to guess how. A concession here and there, from the Upper Bank to the Lower, does a lot to soothe ill will."

Faella's smile did nothing to ease the sickness. This entire setup, the Trials of the Volti—she'd proposed it because of her *medallion*?

"I'll cancel the trials," Ren snapped.

"Don't be stupid," Faella scoffed. "The trials are merely an entertaining show. The only way to escape what I saw in you is to give up on any dream you have of calming Nadežra's troubles. Given the effort you've gone to this past year, I doubt you'll do that."

She was right. Ren couldn't walk away from this city and its problems. She'd decided that during Veiled Waters, when she went back to stop Mettore Indestor and Gammer Lindworm.

Faella nodded in satisfaction, as if she'd just scored a point in a duel. And in truth, she had. Petty anger at the revelation about Marvisal might have driven her to lash out...but that didn't make her wrong.

"I'm going to enjoy destroying your medallion," Ren growled. It barely came out in Renata's accent.

Turning toward the stairs, Faella cast one last thrust over her shoulder. "Remember the visions we all had in Ghiscolo's numinat? Mine showed me that even the light of the Lumen can't burn this stain away. It stays with you, Alta Renata. Even through death."

Then she was gone, puffing down the stairs. As if her departure had been a signal, everyone else came streaming upward, to join Renata at the top of the amphitheatre and watch the race begin.

Ren stood, frozen by more than the wind. *Even the light of the Lumen can't burn this stain away.*

Could Ažerais? Or would Ren, when she died, carry the taint of A'ash with her into the afterlife, into the dream, into the life that followed?

At least if anyone saw the tears stinging the corners of her eyes, she could blame the wind.

West Channel and Lower Bank: Apilun 22

When Grey realized Bondiro Coscanum was his partner, he nearly gave in to Ren's Clever Natalya instincts to cheat. Bondiro's laziness was as legendary as his height and long limbs—the latter two outweighing the former just enough for him to scrape through the dueling trial.

But if Grey were going to cheat, he should have done it before the pairs were drawn. As, it seemed, someone had already done. "Don't worry," Bondiro said, folding himself into the long, narrow boat like a stork in a sun mask. He'd brushed his eyelids with gold powder to match. Imbued, hopefully, or it would run into his eyes as soon as he began sweating. "Aunt Faella said she'd cut my accounts if I didn't do my best to help you."

So this wasn't chance. "I told Alta Renata I intend to win fairly."

"Did you tell my aunt? And what's more fair than me working my hands to blisters? Actually, that's entirely unfair. Point is, this isn't cheating. It's having someone at your back who won't sabotage you."

It was a moot point regardless; there was no changing things now. Grey stripped down to his shirtsleeves, settled himself, and readied his oars. Together they sculled out to the starting line, their boat's green-and-white flag snapping in the river breeze. All around them, the others were moving into position, some with more skill than others. He saw Vargo's prismatium volto shimmering nearby, and glanced reflexively at the man's partner.

Grey had seen those contemptuous eyes far too often for the wave-sculpted mask to disguise Lud Kaineto. For a brief moment, Grey felt sorry for Vargo.

When the starting firework went off, the murky waters churned into froth. In this first stretch, speed was the only arbiter: a straight shot down the Dežera, from the Floodwatch Bridge to the Orje Canal, just south of the Sunset Bridge.

Bondiro, to Grey's surprise, was a decent partner. He put his back into each stroke and kept a steady rhythm. They quickly outpaced the inexperienced rowers, one of a dozen craft slicing down the river's center, where the current added to their speed.

The yellow froth paled to clean white as they passed under the arch of the newly activated river numinat. Its shadow trailed a tingling caress across Grey's sweat-dewed skin—not just from chill, but from the power flowing along the prismatium lines. Although they weren't quite the first to reach the mouth of the canal, they weren't far behind, and with a drag of one oar, Grey angled them toward the Lower Bank.

The next leg was more about agility than speed—that, and knowledge of the Lower Bank canals. Tanaquis had designed a course that required them to pass through set checkpoints, forcing them deep into the maze of smaller waterways, but their path between those checkpoints was theirs to choose.

No doubt some competitors had bribed the checkpoint watchers. But Grey couldn't worry about that now.

Bondiro's long arms batted aside flotsam dumped into their path from a bridge overhead. "Your register is inked on pisspot papers!" he shouted at the crowd of delta youths in Terdenzi colors, flicking a moldy orange peel off his shoulder.

Grey was inured to having things thrown at him. He used his oar to fend off grasping hands trying to drag them back and tripped one interfering woman into the canal. The rest of the time, he was as much poling as rowing. It was impossible to say where they were compared to other competitors, but they'd passed the Westbridge checkpoint and the one on the edge of Seven Knots. They were headed into Kingfisher, where people knew and liked him, and they were doing well—

A lone reed along the waterway popped up with a splash. Too late, Grey realized it was a breathing reed, with someone at the bottom end. He got a brief glimpse of the face of Mede Attravi's eldest son—and then he was flying through the air.

The water he landed in was cleaner than it had been in years, but that was no consolation. The force that hit them must have come from a numinat, and he knew, even before he surfaced, what it would have done.

Their boat was half submerged, the hull cracked and leaking. It wouldn't take them to the end of the canal, much less the end of the race.

He'd lost.

Lower Bank: Apilun 22

Vargo figured he was in trouble the moment he realized he was paired with Lud Kaineto. *Is this some revenge from Carinci?* he wondered. She'd lain quiet since Ghiscolo died, apparently licking her wounds. But after the fall of the Praeteri, Kaineto had landed on his feet with House Destaelio, snagging a position as their duelist. He had no particular reason to help the hamstrung Acrenix.

Vargo appreciated Ren's design for the second challenge, though. Kaineto needed a partner if he wanted to advance to the third trial— though what he expected to win for himself there, the Masks alone knew. Renata would pick her teeth with him. Unfortunately, that meant that *Vargo* also had to work with *Kaineto*.

At least the arrogant little shit didn't argue when Vargo said they should hang behind the lead pack, to avoid the inevitable sabotage attempts waiting for the first boats to enter the canals. Which was true, though only part of the reason.

The rest paid off when they poled around a corner just in time to see the green-and-white-flagged boat ahead flip in an explosion of water and oars.

The resulting waves rocked Vargo's boat. He sank to a knee to steady the vessel and watched as Grey and the Coscanum idler discovered their hull too badly cracked to continue. Bondiro cursed and began splashing toward the nearest stair, but Grey remained low in the water. His hair streamed like river weeds, long enough that it no longer screamed "hawk," and dejection was written across every visible bit of him.

Kaineto was still poling forward, around the flipped boat. Leaning toward Grey, he called out in the sort of mock-friendly tone that got a man punched in the face, "I guess your Masks didn't have mercy!"

Vargo sighed.

And booted his partner over the side.

"Don't just float there," he said to Grey, shifting over to act as ballast while Kaineto flailed in the water. "We're falling behind."

The other man gripped the edge, but didn't pull himself up. "The rules—"

"Say it only counts if the boat crosses the line with two competitors aboard. They don't say it has to be the same two from the start. We're the embodiment of teamwork and cooperation! We're also wasting time."

The boat rocked dangerously as Grey hauled himself in. Vargo lifted his oar, ready to crack Kaineto across the knuckles if he tried the same; the delta shit thought the better of trying. "Come on," Vargo said, using his oar to renew their momentum. "I've got a shortcut."

"We still have to pass the checkpoints," Grey said, pushing them off the canal wall. "Unless you've bribed someone."

"Not the judges." Vargo's face felt like a steamed bun beneath his mask, but he was grinning. "The Moon Harpies. They control the Ship Street canal, and only open it for friends...which includes us. Should cut at least a bell off our trip."

He wasn't the only one who knew that way was usually impassable, so the canal leading toward it was empty. But as they poled up, the water gate that should have been standing open was closed.

"Problem, Mirka?" he called up to the woman straddling the gate.

Only belatedly did he realize she wore a charm around her wrist, not the boss's knot around her neck. Not Mirka, then, but her twin, Mileka—maybe. He could never quite be sure whether the woman he was dealing with was the Moon Harpies' boss, or her belligerent sister pulling an act.

"Mirka's off dealing with another Crimson Eyes attack," Mileka said, heels thumping the gate. "Seems they thought this'd be a good time to take another street, while we was all busy cheering you on."

She looked like she'd rather cheer Vargo on with a boot to his backside. He sighed and spared a glance back the way they'd come. The canal wasn't wide enough to turn the boat around, but they could pole backward easy enough.

Except they didn't have time for another delay. "What do you want?"

"I *want* a boss who cares that we're losing ground and people to those red-eyed flea barges, instead of one who'd rather play skiffer and eat cheese. Everyone knows you've got Tserdev's brother." Mileka rose to balance atop the gate. "Maybe you should send her a few pieces, to jog her memory."

Her suggestion would only lead to more problems—but explaining was a waste of Vargo's breath. Through clenched teeth, he ground out, "I'll deal with it."

"Swear on your oaths to us."

An empty price, easily paid. Vargo almost laughed. "I swear on my oaths to you."

His shoulders itched at Grey's hard stare. Ren knew Vargo held no such oaths; had she shared that knowledge with her lover?

Whether she had or not, Grey kept his opinions to himself, and Mileka nodded in acceptance of Vargo's word. At her shrill whistle, the water gate lifted, and they poled back into contention.

It was smooth skiffing to the Kingfisher checkpoint, but just past that they ran into another obstacle—almost literally. Vargo didn't know what had caused it—outside sabotage, interference between competitors, or just plain bad boating—but several craft had wedged themselves into a tangle up ahead, prows and sterns jammed against the canal walls, everyone too trapped to get out. The Fox Volto had leapt clear of the wreckage and stood on a bridge rail, laughing with the crowd at the predicament of her fellow competitors.

They were completely blocking the way.

Vargo wished he'd brought his own blasting numinat. Or that he'd thought to send Alsius to scout instead of leaving him with Ren, in case Letilia needed biting... but there was no way the spider could have kept ahead of them. He reviewed the map of Kingfisher in his head, trying to find a better route. Every path he could think of would put them massively behind.

Grey spoke for the first time since Ship Street, shoving their boat sideways in the channel. "This way!"

"There's no opening to get past—"

"We won't try." They were close enough to the wall for Grey to toss his oar onto the walkway. "If we portage across Čefor Square, we can get to the Lodry Canal. The rules don't say we have to go the whole way by water."

The rules didn't say it because trying to haul a boat through the streets and bridges of the Lower Bank was idiocy. *Slow* idiocy, with crowds in the way.

Vargo hadn't moved. Grey snapped in frustration, "I *know* Kingfisher!"

"Glad I didn't wear my good coat," Vargo muttered, hopping to the water stair and pulling the boat up until the hull scraped stone.

Canal water sloshed around Grey's calves as he pushed from the submerged part of the stair. "Once we're on the flat, we can hoist it—"

"Oi, Captain! Need some help with that?"

Vargo wasn't certain who in the crowd made the offer, but once they did, a chorus of voices joined in. Then hands, nudging him out of the way. With the aid of seven people who, judging by their shoulders, made their livelihoods hauling freight, the boat easily flipped up. Soon the whole parade was jogging in Grey's wake with shouts of "Make way, the captain's coming through!" and "Kingfisher's own's gonna win!"

The captain. Grey might have surrendered his Vigil hexagram, but it seemed his people still remembered one hawk fondly.

Vargo found himself grateful for Alsius's absence. If the old man were here, he'd be droning on about the life lesson to be learned from this: Vargo had to lie to his people for their cooperation. Kingfisher folk sprang to assist their captain without him needing to ask.

"Master of the Two Banks my ass," he grumbled as he followed along. A straight shot across the square brought them to a dead-end canal—one whose open end pointed right where they needed to go. The boat splashed back down and the wind of the cheering blew Grey and Vargo onward, toward Little Alwydd and the turn back into the river.

And, Vargo prayed, toward victory.

Duskgate, Old Island: Apilun 22

After the excitement of the early part of the trial, Renata got to the temporary pier set up along the Duskgate bank...and waited. She could hear shouting from the Lower Bank, but after the last of the boats lumbered around the corner into the Orje Canal, there was nothing to see.

It was almost easier to watch Letilia than to think about what Faella had said. Her supposed mother had declined either to oversee the start of the race in Floodwatch, or to join the others atop the Point; she preferred to wait in comfort at the end of the course, where she could gossip with her growing circle of acquaintances. Right now she stood with Avaquis Fintenus—an old friend of hers, or perhaps "hanger-on" might be a better word—and, more worryingly, Avaquis's head of house, Giuppero. Judging by the laughter and the way Giuppero kept casually touching Letilia's shoulder, that conversation was going all too well.

Renata's gloved hand tightened on her warmed honeymead, spiced to ward off the air's chill bite. Giuna had come through in grand style, winkling Letilia's accusations out of Mede Pattumo's hands. It hadn't been difficult for Ren to forge a new envelope filled with the lyrics to the bawdiest Vraszenian songs she knew; she used to handle Letilia's correspondence in Ganllech. The fail-safe was dealt with—but getting rid of the woman herself required Ren to wait until the third trial was done. Too many questions would arise if she returned to Seteris before the spectacle was over. If Letilia managed to secure herself a place in a Nadežran register before that...

"Tess. Isn't Avaquis Fintenus wearing one of your sleeved surcoats?" Renata murmured. Her gaze tracked the goldenrod sway of Avaquis's overskirts as she left Letilia's side to refill goblets for them both. In the absence of Ren, Letilia apparently was inclined to make anyone at her side into a maid to fetch and carry.

"The last one I'll be making for her, in this life or the next," Tess grumbled. "I'm not so desperate for custom these days that I need to compromise my principles for a woman that set on wearing yellow."

Renata couldn't see anything wrong with the ensemble, but she was wise enough not to argue with Tess. "I need an excuse to speak with her. Away from Letilia, but without looking suspicious."

Not even Tess's best pity-rustler pout could make her rescind her request, and Tess soon gave up trying. "The things I put up with..." she muttered, straightening her own servant's grey-and-white before wending through the crowd toward her mark.

She didn't bump into Avaquis herself; that was a beginner's mistake. But she was right on hand to help when poor Orrucio Amananto sent sticky honeymead streaming down Avaquis's generous bosom.

Tess led Avaquis off the pier and into an alcove created by a bricked-off alley, where they had a little shelter from prying eyes as she helped the woman blot the mess away. Renata followed a suitable beat later, with an air of mixed sympathy and anger. "Alta Avaquis, I am *so* sorry. Shall I send that Amananto fool home?"

Dabbing mournfully at the wool, Avaquis sighed. "It's too late. The damage is done." Her pout took on a calculated edge as her gaze slid sideways to Tess. "I suppose I'll need a replacement made. I hope you can help expedite that."

Tess had been spending too much time with Meatball and the puppies, judging from the whine she stifled at the back of her throat. Renata nudged her gently toward an escape. With luck, Avaquis would leave this conversation so offended, she wouldn't dare demand favors from Renata again.

"Of course," she said, pulling out her own handkerchief. "It's the least I can do after the way Mother treated you, back in the day. I didn't realize until I saw you together just now that you were the 'buzzing little bee' from her stories. You're much more gracious than I would be, forgiving her so readily."

Avaquis stiffened. "What do you mean? Letilia and I were friends. I might even call her cousin someday."

Renata was half guessing. Letilia *had* made reference to someone she called a bee; Avaquis often liked to wear yellow. She was also slightly younger than Letilia, and House Fintenus held no Cinquerat seat. That put Avaquis in precisely the right situation to hang around, convincing herself that the most fashionable young woman in Nadežra was her friend, while Letilia responded with her usual half-masked disdain.

Most people would be annoyed by the truth, no more. But Tess had flooded Ren's ear with gossip gleaned while fitting Avaquis's clothes: The Fintenus woman was both insecure, and vindictive enough to have fit in well among the old Traementis. By the way she stiffened, Renata's dart had hit its mark.

But best to press it deeper. "Oh, certainly," Renata said. "You know how Mother is—tongue like a stinger, until she wants something from someone. Then her words drip pure honey."

With perfect timing, Letilia's shrill laugh came from the temporary pier. She was standing now with Cibrial and one of the Destaelio daughters, the simpering flattery of her posture clear even from here. Renata tilted her head. "Looks like she might prefer a wealthier cousin than you."

Chin high, Avaquis smoothed her skirts of nonexistent wrinkles. "You know, people say that you must take after your father, not your mother." She spoke to Renata, but her gaze was fixed on Letilia. "How silly. I can see the resemblance quite clearly."

Sneer at me all you like, Renata thought as Avaquis stalked away. *As long as you don't adopt Letilia.*

But her satisfaction at putting that pebble into Avaquis's shoe soon faded to tension as she waited for the boats to make their way through the maze of the Lower Bank, silently cursing her own cleverness in designing this challenge.

And then it vanished entirely, when Letilia's hand closed on her arm.

The woman didn't even bother to be subtle as she dragged Renata off the pier. "What do you think you're doing?" Renata demanded, twisting to look back at the river. "The finishers will be arriving soon—"

Letilia ignored her objections. "You think you're *so* clever," she snapped, nails digging in as though she could pierce layers of wool and silk. The smile she kept on for any observers was jagged glass. "I don't know what you did to spike my efforts with Eret Fintenus— but *you're* the one who'll regret it if I miss my chance at a register."

Renata wondered what Avaquis had said, to make Giuppero pivot so fast. *Maybe I should have worked more subtly.* "I saw you talking with Cibrial," she said, improvising. "You'd hurt your chances with Destaelio if they thought—"

"Don't lie to me, *gnat!* And don't forget I can *destroy* you. Do you think a little humiliation is the worst I can do?"

The honeymead curdled in Renata's stomach. "Threatening violence? Not your usual style."

"Who said anything about violence? *I'm* not the criminal here. And before you start hiding behind the register place you *lied* to get into, I'm talking about your *charming* upbringing. Your filthy blood isn't the only reason you don't belong here." Letilia was barely moving her lips, so no one could try to read them, but it made her expression seem like an animal's snarl. "I wonder what the Cinquerat will do when they learn of your guilt in the amphitheatre business last year. After all, wasn't the person who so conveniently pointed her gloved finger at that Ondrakja charlatan once her best protégé? Her *pretty little Renyi.*"

Ren was glad she had her back to the pier, so no one could see her expression. *You wouldn't.*

This was Letilia. Of course she would. But there was no way she could make it stick, surely. Cercel, Scaperto—they knew Renata had helped stop Ondrakja. Neither of them would buy the tissue-thin pretense that Ren had only been turning on her coconspirator.

But that wouldn't matter. Even if she wasn't convicted in court, Letilia would have done more than enough damage. The people who'd suffered as a result of Indestor's fall would be only too glad to see Ren not merely fall, but float facedown in a canal. Surviving members of House Indestor, ones who hadn't landed on their feet as well as Meppe had. Former clients of that house, like Essunta, like Kaineto.

Donaia, whose son had died from the infighting between Ondrakja and Mettore. Even if she forgave Ren for lying her way into the Traementis, could she forgive *that*?

Ren had failed to mask her fear, and Letilia preened like a well-fed vulture. "Keep that in mind, since you're so clever. You have *far* more to lose than I do, poppet."

The wind carried Letilia's last words to Ren as she sailed past, back to the pier and the prying eyes there. "And stay away from my dealings with Cibrial."

Duskgate, Old Island: Apilun 22

After that, Ren wanted nothing more than to retreat from public view. Instead she had to be Renata, standing on the pier, waiting for her volti to return, pretending she neither saw nor heard Letilia flitting about.

It brought no comfort when a red-and-white-flagged boat emerged from the Semejno Canal downstream, implausibly early. "Galbiondi and Elpiscio aren't remotely subtle with their cheating," Faella sniffed, as if she hadn't been throwing her own poisoned barbs Renata's way not an hour before. "I wonder if that was even them in

Floodwatch, or if they've been sitting in Dockwall all this time in a second boat." But after that, nothing.

Until several more emerged in quick succession and began fighting their way upstream. The timing was crueler than Ren had intended: not only were the competitors rowing against the current, but the tide was going out. For those who hadn't paid off the checkpoint watchers, the hardest part came when they were the most tired.

And Renata, watching, prayed for some of them to give up. Nowhere in that cluster did she see the green-and-white flag of Grey's boat. But only the top eight finishers—the top four boats—would continue to the final challenge.

"Oh dear," Tess whispered, close enough that she could take Renata's gloved hand in her own and hide it in the mixed fall of their skirts. "Never you mind. For certain he's just around the corner."

As if this race were the biggest concern she had. But at the same time, it felt like the one bright hope currently within her grasp.

If it even was in her grasp. Ignoring the frontrunners, Renata kept her gaze fixed on the downriver shore and the last checkpoint Grey would have to pass before the sprint to the end. "I should have made certain," she murmured. *Why* had she let Grey convince her otherwise? Why, when everyone else was cheating, did *she* have to remain honest?

"What happens if he doesn't..." Tess swallowed the rest of the question, too late.

With an effort, Renata pulled coolness around her and disengaged from Tess's grip. Too many people were watching her reaction. Letilia was playing coy, as though she knew more than she did. Faella met Renata's gaze with a slow smirk.

Renata's false coolness chilled to real ice. Had Faella taken some revenge over what Ren said about Marvisal? Had she somehow signaled Bondiro to sabotage Grey, instead of helping?

If that were the case, she would *end* Faella. She would reawaken the Traementis reputation for vengeance by ripping House Coscanum apart. She would—

"Oh. Oh!" Tess flailed, then covered her mouth with both hands and a squeak.

Renata's gaze flicked back to the last checkpoint, but the straggler coming through bore an orange-and-black flag—no possibility of mistaking it for Grey's. Hope failing, her eyes dropped to the four boats closing in on the Sunset Bridge. They'd pulled close enough for her to make out the individual rowers.

Tess hadn't been looking into the distance. She'd been looking at the third-place finisher drawing up alongside the temporary pier—the one flying Vargo's blue-and-gold flag, which Ren, fixated on looking for green-and-white, had ignored.

Grey was slumped in the stern, chest heaving for breath, soaked from head to foot.

Murmurs spread across the pier like flames through the warrens of Lacewater, a wildfire of speculation Renata could only control by giving it voice. Loud enough to be heard, she said, "How strange to see the Prismatium Volto and the Raven Volto finish together! I would have expected your rivalry to keep you apart."

"Wasn't this a challenge of cooperation?" Vargo shouted back for the crowd's benefit.

His voice was rough with exertion and elation, but Grey's softer response was the one that snared the real attention. "It's a compromise I gladly make, when the alternative is losing Alta Renata's favor."

Greeting the third-place finishers first had done its job; she needed to congratulate the others as well. As she turned to do that, wisps of gossip reached her ears like river ghosts. *Derossi Vargo... Grey Serrado... killed his brother?...*

And, standing out among them: *Whatever he intends to ask for, he must want it very much.*

No doubt half of them expected Grey to ask her for vengeance or justice. They would be all the more surprised when the trials ended. But that was fine; she had two weeks to finish preparing that ground.

The fact that she would have that chance at all, she owed to Vargo.

She couldn't say it out loud. But as Vargo disembarked, windswept and river-soaked, she caught his gaze and knew she didn't have to.

Thank you.

8

The Friendly Fist

Lacewater, Old Island: Apilun 30

"So this is where my money's going," Ren muttered, eyeing the run-down building across from the Whistling Reed.

Not much of her money, by the looks of it, but that was hardly surprising. Letilia wasn't likely to arrange for a second room at her Eastbridge hotel for this, even if House Traementis was footing her bill. The lodging house—an *actual* lodging house, unlike the building the Fingers used to occupy—had the usual Lacewater patchwork of shutters in six different styles, plastered splotches where the walls had been repaired and repaired again, and pity-rustlers haunting its corners like spiders waiting for prey.

But for the people of the street, any room somebody else paid for was a good one.

"You sure about this?" Sedge asked, while Tess kept a wary eye out for pickpockets.

"No," Ren said, and went inside.

Once the shock of the confrontation with Letilia had faded, Ren's mind had gone to work on the woman's threat, calculating whether she needed to speed up her plans. That was when she'd recognized the clue Letilia had inadvertently let slip.

Her pretty little Renyi.

That Letilia had figured out Ren was one of Ondrakja's Fingers wasn't out of the question. Ren had never shared her life story with her employer—Letilia had never cared—but bits and pieces slipped out over the years, and Letilia was the sort to hoard any weapons she could find. That phrase was too specific, though. Only a few people these days would know it.

It seemed the letter stowed with Mede Pattumo was only *one* of the safeguards Letilia had in place.

After a minute of pounding and a muffled clink of bottles rolling, the door swung open on the scowl of her childhood nightmares.

"The fuck do— *You.*" Simlin hadn't so much grown up as out: broad shoulders, barrel chest, and hands as meaty as ham hocks. More than one Finger had been cowed into submission after a few blows from Ondrakja's favorite enforcer, Ren among them. He hadn't been allowed to touch her face, but there were many places on a child's body where bruises wouldn't show.

Ren retreated a half step. She'd thought herself prepared for this, with Tess and Sedge backing her up . . . but Ondrakja wasn't the only one who'd stamped an imprint of fear onto her heart.

And the threat Simlin posed now was far worse than a simple beating.

"Got the Tyrant's own wrinklies, knot-traitor," he said, slapping a sap against his thigh. Droop-lidded eyes flicked past her shoulder. "And the two of you, keeping loyal to a split-tongued viper. You know what happens when you trust a snake?"

He smiled, small and mean, at Ren. "You get *poisoned.*"

"Simlin." She forced her voice to remain steady. "We can talk out here, or we can talk in your room. Depends on how many neighbors you want knowing your business."

"The business where you've come to beat me bloody? People here pay to see that kind of sport. Might as well give 'em a show."

"Nobody's beating anyone today," Tess said coaxingly. "You know me; that isn't something I'd watch. Come now. I brought buns. Fresh, even, not day-old." Back in their Finger days, Sedge had defended Tess with his fists, and Ren with her clever tongue.

But they couldn't be around all the time, and she used to buy her way into Simlin's good graces with sweetness and food.

By the audible growl of his stomach, most of Letilia's money had gone for zrel instead. He snatched the bag from Tess and sneered, a scar in his lip giving it an extra twist. "Fine. Be interesting to get a peek at the dance Ondrakja's pet's been putting on for the cuffs."

Sedge preceded Ren into the room, a shield in case Simlin meant to spin around and slug her. In the past he might have, but now he just sprawled on the bed. With one heel, he hooked the stool that was the room's only other seating and kicked it under the frame, where no one could sit on it.

"Make yourselves comfortable," he said, his grin gummy white with half-chewed bun.

Abandoning the wisp-thin hope of diplomacy, Ren pulled her hand from Tess's. "Whatever Letilia's paying, I can offer more. If you leave Nadežra, I'll arrange a credit line with a banker. Anywhere you go, you'll have a nice life."

"And safety," Sedge growled. The two of them used to fight like starving dogs. He'd argued that Simlin couldn't write more than his name and would have a hard time revealing Ren's secrets without a tongue. But he'd grudgingly allowed they could try softer means first.

Jerking his chin at the knot bracelet Sedge proudly wore, Simlin said, "So, what? I take the money, or you come back with enough fists to silence me for good?" His own wrists were bare. The Stretsko hired him occasionally, but Sedge claimed Simlin never lasted long in any knot that took him. A leather thong around his neck, though, held a ratted tangle of green and purple threads. Ren had thrown her Fingers charm at Ondrakja's feet; years later, he still carried his.

At Sedge's shrug of acknowledgment, Simlin snorted. "You think anyone from Dockwall to Froghole would lift a finger if I told them they was protecting a knot-breaking traitor? I might not be sworn now, but I en't never broken my word. Or killed my boss."

That last was directed at Ren, who flinched. Simlin's expression got uglier. "You eeled out," he growled. "Ran away to Ganllech. 'Cause you knew what we would do if you stayed."

Running had always been the plan, even before Ren poisoned Ondrakja. But saying that wouldn't help.

Because he was right. She'd known exactly what the Fingers would do. Most would flee, hoping to find safety elsewhere; a few, like Simlin, would beat her bloody before they went. Like the Fog Spiders had beaten Sedge—and his crimes were far smaller.

"That's what you want," Ren whispered. She didn't need a Primordial's power to show her Simlin's desires. "You want revenge on me."

He spat. "Seems like justice from my end, but I en't some cuff, packaging ugly things up in pretty words. 'Swhat *you* do. 'Swhat you *are*. Ondrakja's pretty little Renyi." Simlin fished through the bottles rolling under his bed, shaking until one sloshed with dregs. He made a face when he took a pull. "Maybe I just want everyone to see the ugly you're hiding inside."

Pretty little Renyi. The ugly you're hiding inside.

Tess inhaled sharply. Sedge looked at her, then Simlin—then at Ren. "Oh, no," he breathed. "Fuck that."

Ren held up one hand. It trembled, but she couldn't stop that, and besides, Simlin would like seeing it. "Justice, then. If you have that...will you go?"

"Fuck *that*. Lacewater's home." He ran a tongue over his teeth, sucking loose the bits of bread stuck there. Then, carelessly, he said, "But I'll hold my tongue and leave you to your life. Figure Ondrakja would enjoy watching it, you pulling a big one over on those chalk-fuckers."

If he meant that as a compliment, it didn't quite land—but that might have been his intent anyway. Ren drew a deep breath. Before she could speak, though, Sedge stepped in front of her.

"*No way*," he snapped. "Ren, I en't letting this canal scum beat on you. What're you gonna say, when people want to know why Alta Renata's got a black eye?"

"En't she supposed to be a clever liar?" Simlin asked. Then he grinned, vicious as a shark. "Or, y'know. I could hit her somewhere softer."

Sedge had never heard Ondrakja say that. He'd already been left for dead when she made it clear that the next time Ren fucked up, she'd go after Tess.

The old Ren would have snatched out a knife and tried to stab Simlin. But living as a cuff had made her soft...and the people around her had made her better. Even if she could hear Vargo now, wondering why they weren't dealing with this problem in a more permanent fashion.

Tess had instinctively retreated. Ren turned and touched her shoulder, waiting until Tess met her eyes and nodded, before she addressed Sedge. "What he's asking for is fair."

The agony in Sedge's eyes cut like a blade. He'd always been her defender, not of her pretty face, but of *her*. What she was asking...it went against the core of who he was.

But it was her choice. Slow as a man ankle-deep in mud, he stepped out of her path, and she faced Simlin.

Who took his time sizing her up, savoring her fear. He even winked at Tess. "Guess they should have left you behind after all. Sure you don't want to step outside?"

"I'll stay," Tess whispered, taking Sedge's hand. For comfort... or to hold him back.

"You take this too far," Sedge said, a warning to Simlin and a reassurance to Ren, "and I'm stepping in. And you won't be stepping out of this room again."

"We'll see," Simlin said, and planted a fist in Ren's stomach.

She doubled over, retching. Simlin's voice was a distant buzz in her ear. "You spew on my floor, I'll make you lick it up." He shoved her upright while she was still gasping. The second punch landed high, striking her in the tit. Pain was a sharp-edged star radiating out from the point of impact, and instinct curled her arms to protect her body.

Pointlessly. The third punch landed with a meaty thud on her face, the one place Simlin had always been forbidden to damage. Cheek throbbing, she closed her eyes in preparation for a rain of blows, all the violence he'd never been allowed to unleash on her before.

Nothing followed.

She waited, trying not to cringe, sure he was just letting fear season the next strike. But then Simlin's voice came, dismissive and curt. "I'm done. Get the fuck out of here."

It took will to crack one eye open, lest that be the cue for him to lay into her again. When she did, though, she found that Simlin had gone back to the bed and was sitting with his elbows on his knees. "You en't worth more," he said, sounding tired.

She didn't know whether he meant that, or whether he'd decided that beating on her wasn't as satisfying as he'd hoped. Tess voiced the question she didn't dare speak. "And your word you won't do as Letilia wants?"

His laugh sounded like rocks grinding. "Still let her pay for my bed and my zrel, but I figure you don't want her knowing you got to me. She drags me out to expose you, well—" Simlin pressed fingers to his knuckles, hissing theatrically at the nonexistent damage her face had done to them. "You're just another chalk-face, and I'm gutter-spun trash. Might even be fun, ranting about all the great truths I seen on aža."

Ren exhaled slowly, her face pulsing with incipient swelling. She really would have a difficult time explaining that. But if a bruised cheek was the price of Simlin's silence, she would pay it.

And she believed he *would* keep quiet. This, not Letilia's plan, was what tradition said she deserved.

"Stoček isn't dealing anymore," she said, "but he knows who is. I'll make sure you get some aža."

She backed out the door, and Sedge and Tess followed silently, until they were in the street. Then they both hugged her. Ren returned the embraces, letting herself feel the pain, without and within.

Then she wiped her eyes and straightened. "It's done. Letilia's fangs have been pulled; now I can deal with *her.*"

"'Less she's got a third fail-safe in her pocket," Sedge reminded her. "But that's a worry for later. Right now, you need some cold meat for your face, and a drink for the rest of you. Come on. We're going to the Talon and Trick."

Lacewater, Old Island: Apilun 30

When Sedge and his sisters had stumbled across Stoček the day of Sedge's "birthday" at the Whistling Reed, the old aža dealer had looked as hard done as could be, cur-thin and nearly as mangy, several fingers shortened on one hand and the other gone completely.

A few months feasting on something other than zrel couldn't do nothing for the hands, but it had put more meat on Stoček's ribs and even done something for his hair. True to his word, Sedge had gotten the old man cleaned up and into a place his disreputable looks had value: the Talon and Trick, where slumming cuffs got just enough grime and tarnish to make the gambling parlour a thrill. Stoček couldn't deal cards or serve drinks one-handed, but sobered up, he had a keen eye and a knack for discouraging cheats with a friendly bump and a few sly words. It was the sort of soft touch needed in a place where you couldn't bounce your clientele without getting raided by hawks.

This early in the day, the nytsa parlour wasn't yet open for business. Stoček was alone at a table, wolfing down some noodles with hardly a pause for breath, when Sedge came in.

"Hey, Stoček," Sedge said, nerves twanging. *If word gets around . . .* But Stoček was trustworthy in his own way. "All right if we have a quiet drink with you?" And he gestured behind him, at Tess and Ren.

Stoček stared, a wad of noodles hanging out of his mouth. Coming here was a risk: the old aža seller weren't likely to connect Ren with Alta Renata, but he wouldn't have forgotten her. Nor how and why the Fingers fell apart.

But he also owed Sedge a favor. And Stoček weren't the sort to forget that, either.

The noodles slurped up into his mouth, a long tangle that took what felt like a whole bell to chew and swallow. By then he'd apparently made a decision, because the expression that appeared in the noodles' wake was a broad smile. "Little Ren!"

The knot in Sedge's gut loosened. *She always was one of his favorites.*

"Hello, Stoček." Ren came forward shyly. "I heard you were still around."

"Hello, hello!" Opening his coat with the padded hook strapped to his forearm, Stoček rooted through an inner pocket and came up with a familiar cone. Like his grin, it was only slightly crumpled. "Faces must have been telling me you'd come. Bought these this morning on impulse. What happened to *your* face?"

Unshed tears shone in Ren's eyes, bright as the candy she plucked from the cone. "You always had honey stones for me."

"I'll tell you a terrible secret, little Ren. They'd be for me, but my teeth ache when I eat them. So I enjoy watching you nippers eat them instead." He held out the cone for Tess, then for Sedge. "You too. Even if you en't been taking care of your sister like you should."

"Weren't my choice," Sedge muttered. He didn't feel like he deserved a honey stone, not after letting Simlin beat on Ren. Besides, he hadn't eaten one since before Ondrakja tried to kill him. Most fists didn't; they had to keep up a tough image.

But Stoček rattled the cone, and with nobody there to see but his sisters, Sedge popped the sweet candy into his mouth, savoring the half-forgotten taste.

"Sit, sit!" Stoček gestured them to the empty chairs—though it might only have been so he could go back to slurping noodles. Tess excused herself to the kitchen, where Sedge was willing to bet that whole cone Vargo had put in a cooling numinat for supplies. Ren perched on a chair and began chatting with Stoček, slipping back into their old teasing like no time had passed.

Tess came back with a chilled piece of mutton for Ren's face and beer for them all. Stoček took the latter, still chattering like an old gaffer, marveling at how Ren had grown and telling her all the ways Lacewater had changed. Sedge watched the tension melt out of his sister, her nodding and listening like she hadn't set foot on the Old Island in years.

But her manner brightened to real interest when Stoček mentioned some new people in the old Cut Ears' base. "*Who* is there?"

"Ah, don't mind me," Stoček said, after he'd downed the last of his noodle broth. "I'm just an old gossip who sees too much. It's folk you'd do better to stay away from; they won't bring you nothing but trouble. The Anduske gobble up sweet kids like they're honey stones. You stick with Sedge. He'll take care of you—no more black eyes." The eye he narrowed at Sedge said there'd be no more candy in Sedge's future, otherwise.

"Hey, en't my fault when she tells me *not* to take care of her!"

Ren laid her hand on Sedge's arm. "Worry not, Stoček. I have no interest in joining them."

Joining, no. But Sedge knew what Ren was thinking, even before she deftly brought the conversation to a swift close and the three of them left the Talon and Trick. Outside, Tess said, "Anduske. Branek's people, you think?"

"At least worth following up, yeah?" Sedge said to Ren.

She breathed out in a slow hiss. "If Stoček's right, it's a stroke of luck. And that's what we need, so...yes, we should look."

"Meaning me and you, or me and some other you?"

Ren shot him a wry look. "I think any other me would draw attention, yes?"

"I'll get word to Grey," Tess said, tugging her shawl higher. "Don't do anything foolish, you hear?"

"Never," Ren said, and they split.

The Cut Ears had abandoned their turf when Praeteri interference tore their knot apart. The survivors had taken refuge with Vargo on the Lower Bank, losing all their Lacewater territory. So far as Sedge knew, nobody controlled it these days; the evictions earlier in the year had really unsettled things.

A bit of careful loitering netted them enough glimpses of people Ren identified as Branek's to confirm that the dilapidated old house was occupied by Anduske. Sedge, craning his neck from the vantage of a nearby alley, nudged Ren with his elbow. "Hey. That look new to you?"

She had to climb onto a crate before she could see it. "The boards across the window? Very fresh. And very much like someone wants to make sure nobody leaves that room."

Sedge expelled a heavy breath. All of Lacewater held history for them, but this place more than most. Messing around with the Cut Ears had gotten them in trouble: Sedge almost murdered, his sisters almost murderers, and the two of them stuck in Ganllech for five miserable years. Smart choice would be to walk away.

But Sedge wasn't much known for his brains. "We try to figure out who's in there, we'll probably tip the Anduske off."

"So we gamble and hope calling nytsa doesn't give our opponent all the points?" Ren said, too light for her ease to be anything but a mask. She had to be warier of this place than Sedge was. Her next words confirmed it. "I'd rather not put you at risk."

"Who says I'm gonna be at risk?" Sedge grinned. For once, *he* was the one with a plan. "Seems to me, retaking their hideout is Cut Ears business."

Isla Čaprila, Eastbridge: Apilun 31

The old joke went, the four most terrifying words in a knot boss's world were one of his fists saying, "I got an idea."

"It's not...entirely unfeasible," Vargo said slowly, turning Sedge's pitch over in his mind to look for leaks. Varuni's grunt said she was not only in agreement, but guardedly impressed. Alsius's mental hum said the same. Only Ren, tension lines around her lips and fingers twisted in her skirts, betrayed reservation.

But she hadn't objected, and Vargo was certain that not even loyalty to Sedge would keep her from saying something if she'd spotted a flaw. Varuni knew the truth of her now; Ren could speak freely in front of everyone here. Whatever had her wound tight, it was more private than her identity.

Vargo had slept wrong the previous night, and even the

connection between his life and Alsius's didn't do much for a mere kinked neck. He pressed his fingers in like he could dig out the pain and rotated his head as he thought out loud. "Merapo doesn't have that big a crew these days. The Cut Ears lost plenty when that Praeteri numinat turned their old leader, and some of those who survived left for other knots. I don't know if it'll be enough. But I could loan him some people—"

Sedge cleared his throat, now looking as tense as Ren. "Actually...it'd work better if Merapo cut loose from you. Official. And public."

He was right to look tense. "The fuck makes you think I'd ever agree to that?" Vargo asked. Soft. Cordial. Because Sedge was a trusted fist and Ren's brother and Vargo probably shouldn't knife him—not without a chance to talk himself out of this hole.

The Cut Ears might be Old Island rather than Lower Bank, but they were still one of *his* knots. His grip was the only thing keeping the peace in the rookeries of Nadežra. A peace made more tenuous when word of Mileka's demands and the Moon Harpy deal got out. All his knots were on edge.

Ren's flat look said she recognized that tone of voice, and she thought he was being theatrical. Which he was, in a way: Vargo had spent years teaching his people to be afraid of that voice. But he wasn't doing it just for the hell of it, and he gave her a flat look right back.

She was unfazed. "Branek has half the Stretsko with him; we must assume he knows the Cut Ears joined you. If they do anything—if *any* of your knots do anything—he'll assume your hand is behind it. And he'll be right."

"So your answer is for me to let one of my knots cut free?" Vargo's fist tightened around nothing—the same nothing that tied the knots to him. "Sounds like sinking a boat over a few barnacles. I want the Kiralič and Mevieny back, but I en't dissolving my crews to get it."

::Vargo, take care. With that medallion influencing you—::

"This en't about Sessat," Vargo snapped. Ren could hear Alsius, and it wasn't like Sedge and Varuni weren't used to him talking to himself. "The answer would have been no from the moment I crawled out of Froghole. They're *mine*."

"Are they?" Ren asked quietly, an edge of challenge to her curiosity. "Forgive me...I know you're as loyal as any sworn boss, but to you they are not tied. And the people who make up the knots don't *belong* to you. That isn't how knots work."

She was right. Knots were friendship, not ownership. Not a Tyrant's rule.

Slumping forward like his strings had been cut, Vargo braced his elbows on his knees and scrubbed the frustration from his face. His thoughts felt like bugs under a turned cobblestone, scurrying from the light. "Look at it logically. Say Merapo and the others do cut knot—publicly enough for Branek to buy it. That means it's public enough for others to buy it. If I just let the Cut Ears walk, those others will start to think *they* can do the same without consequences. Pretty soon we're back to every corner of the Lower Bank being territory people knife each other over." The way it used to be, before Vargo's takeover began, fighting each other instead of banding together against their real enemies. No order, no structure, no—

Fuck. Maybe Sessat *was* influencing him.

But that didn't mean his fears weren't real. Merapo leaving would be the first trickle of water through a cracking dam.

Sedge blew out slowly. "Yeah, I know. But...how're you gonna stop that from happening anyway? Half your knots already want to pull loose, now that you're a cuff."

And that was the problem. Master of the Two Banks, Koszar Andrejek had once called him. But the more Vargo tried to bridge that divide, the more he felt stretched to snapping.

Becoming a cuff was a means to an end, not something he'd ever wanted for himself. But now that he had it, had tasted its power in the sweet, clear water of the West Channel...he wasn't about to take his foot off the Upper Bank just to keep the Lower.

Too bad Arkady Bones en't a few years older, he grumbled to Alsius. Only belatedly did he remember Ren could hear it, too, as her lips pressed down on a smile.

To Sedge he said, "I don't know. That, unfortunately, is the Lumen's own truth. But now the river numinat's up, I've got nothing but time on my hands. And apparently nothing to do but kick around here while you're off riling up Lacewater."

"Then you'll—"

"Tell Merapo I want borders settled before he cuts out. I get word of a turf battle over so much as a cobblestone, I'll drop our new Caerulet on the lot of them." His grin was more teeth than humor, but so be it. "She may not jump when a cuff snaps his fingers, but I know an ex-captain she listens to."

Lacewater, Old Island: Apilun 35

The warm weight of Sedge's hand on Ren's shoulder helped ground her. "It'll be all right," he murmured.

She wished she could believe that. But they'd been here before: the two of them lurking in an alley behind this tenement on a cold, misty afternoon, preparing for a job. They were older now, and she was masked as the Black Rose, but the years in between might as well have been a dream.

Or rather, a nightmare.

"Tide's out and the sky's clear. Why wouldn't it be all right?" Her false cheer was thin gauze over a ragged wound.

"Because last time it weren't," Sedge said bluntly.

Ren swallowed hard. "Sedge—"

"Don't. You din't know."

"I knew I was going further than I should. Further than I'd been told to." Ondrakja had sent Ren to steal back a pearl ring the Cut Ears had taken from her. But Ren, Tess, and Sedge were already preparing their escape from the Fingers, scraping what coin they could to build a life away from Ondrakja. When she'd seen a chance to take more...

She swallowed again, but the rock in her throat wouldn't go down. "I got greedy. And Ondrakja tried to kill you. Over *my* mistake."

"For the smartest of us, you sure do pack a lot of stupid between your ears." Sedge tweaked one of those ears lightly. "Blaming yourself, just like Ondrakja wanted. We was all tugging to get loose of her knot. So why're you still letting that thread tangle you up?"

Because she'd *hurt people.* Not even just Sedge: To Ren, the little statuette of An Mišennir Lagrek was just a bauble she could sell. To Yariček, the leader of the Cut Ears, it was the last thing he had of his father. He'd threatened war on the Fingers to get it back.

"I keep doing it." She didn't even realize she'd said that out loud until Sedge's hand tightened on her shoulder. "I keep putting people in danger. I keep hurting them. Because of my ambition." Like she'd hurt the Traementis. Sedge had survived; Leato hadn't.

"But now you're making it right."

He thought she was talking about the Kiralič and the failed meeting. He wasn't entirely wrong—and he was right about where her thoughts needed to be. Even as Ren drew a deep, steadying breath, shouts erupted from the next street over.

Sedge's plan was elegant in its simplicity. Branek had occupied the Cut Ears' old base? Then the knot should try to take it back. With their ties to Vargo publicly severed, it didn't look like a distraction, because it wasn't: Ren and Sedge were riding in the wake of a genuine bit of street warfare. It wasn't enough to get them directly into the building, but they didn't need that.

The tenement's narrow central hall shot like an arrow from front to back. To either side, the missing doors had been replaced by oxhide and cloth, or battered curtains of beads as gap-toothed as an old woman's gums. And because Lacewater loved a good brawl—so long as they could watch from the safety of windows or rooftops—the rooms were empty.

Mostly empty.

One of the curtains rattled as they approached, the only warning before a hip-high missile shot through and took Sedge out at the knees. He hit the wall with a grunt; the child landed on his ass with a hiccup of surprise.

It was a boy no older than Jagyi, and all set to start wailing when

Ren sank to one knee. "Oops!" she said, letting her laugh into her voice. "My friend wasn't watching where he was going. Sedge, tell this little fellow that you're sorry."

"He ran into *me*—" Sedge swallowed it down when Ren gave him a meaningful look. "Fine," he grumbled. "I'm sorry."

The boy wasn't even listening, staring open-mouthed at Ren. "You're the Black Rose! Gaf-gaf! Gaf-gaf! We're being burgled by the Black Rose!"

"Little we have for her to take," came a voice from inside the room, rough with pain and age. "Lemyi, get back in here and leave strangers to their business."

Unfortunately for him, Ren's business was in that room. When a second child peeked out, Ren let the girl add her weight to the boy's, both of them tugging her through the curtain.

Inside the windowless, cluttered room, an old man with a badly twisted leg sat on a stool, dandling an infant on his good knee while another crawled on a bit of worn canvas thrown over the splintered floorboards. At the sight of the Black Rose, the man's jaw dropped, but his hands remained firm on the child he held.

Extricating herself gently from the two holding her, Ren said, "Go on. Go to your gaffer."

The suspicion tightening the old man's gaze eased once Lemyi and the girl were safely peeking out from behind his chair. "You the cause of the fuss out there?" he asked, nodding toward the front.

"Just taking advantage of it," Ren said. "There's someone next door who needs rescuing. If you don't mind letting me through, grandfather, and letting my friend stay to keep watch, you'll have our thanks in the form of a solid meal for yourself and these children."

It was a better offer than money, which might have attracted attention. The old man pursed his lips and nodded. "I don't know what 'through' you mean, but well enough. Just go about your business quickly, or I'll make you change this one's nappies as a toll."

"My friend's good at that," Ren said, grinning, and went to the corner before Sedge could do more than glare.

Her amusement faded quickly. When she pulled the bed there

aside, her fingers found the outline of the hatch, irregularly shaped to conceal its presence. Lacewater was full of compartments and passages, used by smugglers to move goods and hide illicit business when the hawks came knocking. The important thing was, this one had openings into both this building...and the one next door.

The hatch opened with a creaking yawn on a darkness ready to swallow Ren whole. Her muscles tensed, refusing to move. *The last time I went in here...*

Behind her, the gaffer grumbled, "We'll be losing all the children in there now."

"Why don't you wait in the hall?" Sedge suggested. "Might be safer that way."

Ren heard him chivvy the gaffer and the kids past the curtain, but she couldn't turn to look. The darkness below held all her attention. A fen-rotted stench curled up from the opening, and the lamplight glinted off muddy water below. Low tide or not, Lacewater was always sinking into the muck.

Sedge's hand landed on her shoulder again. "I'll stay here with the lamp, in case you need to back out. Just make for the light, yeah?"

She laid her own hand over his, squeezed, let go. She couldn't back out. This was the only way in: Even with the Cut Ears attacking, Branek's people weren't dumb enough to leave their doors unguarded. And she was the only one who could fit through this passage.

Ren pulled off her mask. As much as she'd rather be the Black Rose right now, she didn't want that filth all over her disguise. Tucking the scrap of lace into the safety of her braid, she forced herself to drop into the fetid water below.

The lightstone she uncapped on her wrist revealed a mud-pocked undercroft of rotted wood pilings and worn numinata inscribed on crumbling masonry. Even at a crouch, she risked banging her head; she had to slosh her way forward on elbows and knees like some bloated fen salamander. She did her best to keep her wrist high and steady, the light casting a circle of dancing shadows around her.

Like zlyzen, twisting and crawling. The last time Ren came through here, she'd feared the monsters might be lurking. Now she *knew* they were real. Had watched them kill.

They're in the dream, she told herself, trying to slow her heart. *You haven't seen them in months. They're not here.*

But sometimes they crossed over.

Ren crawled faster.

Down here, it was hard to hear the shouting. How much longer would the distraction last? Could someone hear her coming? What if the hatch at the other end was nailed shut? She forced herself under a low beam, face almost in the water. On the far side there was more space, and when she touched the boards overhead, they lifted without protest.

If there'd been a guard in the room, they would've had ample opportunity to stab her. Ren hoisted herself out without so much as a preparatory glance, sloshing stinking runoff across the floor, and shut the hatch like a zlyzen was on her heels.

She wanted to stay there until her pulse slowed, but there wasn't time. Ren wiped her hands dry on a nearby sack—then stopped.

When she'd broken in before, this room was where the Cut Ears taught each other to fight. The bloodstains were probably still there, but now they were covered by bags of grain, barrels of water. And beyond them...stacks of crossbows and spears.

Koszar was right. Branek is preparing for violence.

The thought made her sick. But would he truly turn those weapons on his own people, just to motivate them against the Liganti?

Mevieny and the Kiralič might be able to tell her. But to free them, Ren needed help. She dragged the Black Rose's mask over her face, leather petals replacing her sopping, muck-smeared clothing, and crept out into the hall.

The Cut Ears' headquarters was tall and narrow, with a central stairwell that made defending the upper levels as easy as dropping rocks. Creeping up the steps, Ren kept her back to the outer wall to hide from anyone left to guard. If she and Sedge were right about the boarded-up window, her ultimate target was on the top floor...

but her first stop was just one flight up, a room with barred shutters that couldn't be opened from the outside.

Shutters the Anduske were smart enough to keep guarding.

There were distinct benefits to Grey having told Alinka the truth about the Rook—and to Ren being able to practice throwing at Vargo's house. A flick of her wrist sent a dart tipped with one of Alinka's imbued sedatives into the guard's neck. The yelp he got out wasn't loud enough to be heard over the chaos out front, and then Ren had a hand clamped over his mouth, her other hand twisting his arm into a lock until the dart took effect. When he slumped, she lowered him to the floor and unbarred the shutters.

Grey paused on the sill, the substitute Rook's hood doing nothing to disguise his grimace. He curled one arm around his lower face, coughing into his elbow. "Such an aromatic rose," he said, the words muffled by wool.

Primly, Ren said, "Even roses need fertilizer to grow strong."

"Is *that* what that is." He made up for his teasing by taking her hand without hesitation. "Up?"

"Up," she agreed.

There was a guard outside the room at the top, but Ren let Grey deal with that one. The scuffle was brief, and in its aftermath, she searched the man. He was smart enough not to keep the key on himself, but fool enough to store it atop the door frame. Not knowing if there would be one more threat waiting inside—or a different occupant than the ones they were hoping for—Ren eased the lock open as silently as she could. Then she hurled the door open and dove through, letting the Rook behind her serve as the taller, more obvious target.

It wasn't necessary. Only one person was inside: the Kiraly clan elder, sitting on a narrow cot and dealing out a well-worn set of cards.

Which flew everywhere when the door burst open, a shower of mismatched backs and poor inking. His yelp spun into a wry chuckle. "Have you practiced such dramatic entrances, or is it natural skill?"

"The blessings of Nem Zimat," Ren said wryly. There was nowhere in the room for anyone else to hide, guard or otherwise. "We've come to get you out—you and the szorsa both. Do you know where she is? In another room, perhaps?"

Her voice and manner made the urgency clear, but the Kiralič still took a moment to gather the scattered cards, knocking them straight. His furrowed brow said the answer to that question was complicated. "Mevieny has put her faith in Ažerais. She is no longer...quite...Branek's prisoner."

"Explanations can come later," the Rook said. "Our distraction won't last forever."

They were only halfway down the stairwell when voices began echoing up it. Ren had a brief view of faces staring up at them, like a ring of befuddled flowers; then Grey turned in a whirl of black coat. "Get the Kiralič out," he said. "I'll guard your retreat."

Would the Black Rose kiss the Rook? Not smelling like Ren did, she wouldn't. Instead she grinned, pushed the Kiralič toward the open window, and said, "Catch up when you can."

To the sound of ringing steel and the Rook's mocking laughter, they made their escape.

Isla Čaprila, Eastbridge: Apilun 35

Getting away was harder when Grey couldn't just pull the hood off and revert to ordinary clothes. But Ren and the others waiting to help her had to take a roundabout path in order to avoid leading any pursuers to Vargo's house, and with the Kiralič stuffed into a sedan chair—they couldn't trust the skiffers—they moved slower than he did. Grey arrived hard on their heels. Ren smelled better than before, and he wondered if she'd paused at a street pump to unmask and sluice herself off.

Vargo's shoulders eased visibly when he opened his kitchen door to them, but characteristically, he hid that relief behind a sardonic comment. "If I was the betting type, I'd be out a decira," he said as he led the Kiralič to the room at the back of the house. "Hurting you would have been stupid on Branek's part—but I didn't expect him to be sensible."

"It seems you bet on me returning, though," the Kiralič said, seeing the two who waited there with clenched hands and untouched tea. Koszar and the Anoškinič rose with the speed of relief, and the Kiralič touched his heart in greeting. "I will make offering in thanks to Šen Asarn Kryzet that you both escaped our ill-fated meeting."

"This one will have no knees left if he continues to leap about like he can fly," the Anoškinič muttered. With one toe he prodded the cane Koszar leaned on, but there was a warmth in his grumping that had been utterly absent before. If nothing else good had come of that disaster, Grey thought, at least Koszar's rescue of his ziemič had persuaded the man he wasn't entirely without virtue.

Injured knee notwithstanding, Koszar tried to lower himself to the floor. "Kiralič. Please believe, it was no intent of mine to lure you into danger—"

An impatient wave cut him off. "Get up. No ally of Branek are you; I heard enough to be sure of that. And more besides. Are we safe here?"

"Better be," Vargo muttered darkly, tugging the drapes shut. "Unlike that boat, I control this place."

Sorrow briefly shadowed the Kiralič's face. "The barge, yes. That was a gift from my wife, upon our wedding."

The bottom dropped out of Grey's stomach. The Kiralič's wife had been Kolya's master during his apprenticeship. Those fine carvings, now lost to the Dežera...had some been shaped by his brother's hand?

No one else would understand the stricken note in the Black Rose's voice. "My sincere regret for sinking it," she said—an apology to the Kiralič and Grey alike.

The Kiralič gestured it away. "Desperate times, and I cannot object when the Rose of Ažerais makes an offering to the Dežera."

Grey had reflexively drifted to the dimmest corner of the room, where the shadows supplemented those of his hood. He hoped the twinge of grief didn't show in his voice as he changed the subject. "You told us Szorsa Mevieny's not exactly a prisoner. She's sided with Branek, then? Is she the one who sold us out in Floodwatch?"

"Not at all," the Kiralič said hastily as the rest of them sat. "A great risk she takes, for the sake of us all. She has not forgotten Ča Andrejek's wish for judgment by ordeal. But to achieve that, first she must persuade Branek to listen to *her* wisdom, instead of…"

He trailed off for long enough that the Black Rose made a noise to prompt him. Sighing heavily, the Kiralič said, "You will hear eventually; no profit is there in hiding it. Branek has been taking advice from an elder szorsa of my own clan, one with much influence."

Swallowing fear like glass, Grey whispered, "Who?"

"Laročja Szerado." The Kiralič's braids swung as he turned to the Rook. "Perhaps you have memories of her? In two separate cycles, she has stood as speaker for the Ižranyi at the Ceremony of the Accords."

"I remember her." Not as the Rook, though. The Rook had no reason to feel cold nausea at her name. The Rook wouldn't wish he could dive out the window and remove himself from this business.

From Vargo came a soft intake of breath, and Grey tensed for him to ask. But it was Koszar who gave the question voice. "Szerado. The same kureč as the former hawk?"

"Unless the threads of his koszenie he has cut, yes," the Kiralič said. "But I know not the details of that family's business. It was none of mine." He smiled bitterly. "No matter what my wife used to say."

"And what does Szorsa Laročja say, that Branek is so willing to hear?" Grey asked. *What poison has she poured into his ears?*

The Kiralič's mouth hardened. "Whether the idea was hers or his, I cannot say, but she has him convinced it can work. He means to lure the Vigil away—by what means, he shared not. But when they are gone, his people will close off and barricade the bridges. They mean to take the Old Island."

"*Fuck me*," Vargo said, and then silence followed.

Rubbing at his eyes, the Kiralič said, "His plan is...unfortunately well thought out. Through his clan he has ties to the skiffers; they will guard the shores. In cellars and in the Depths he is stockpiling food, so they cannot easily be starved out. Already our people come for the Great Dream, for the end of the Grand Cycle. Before the mists rise, he will take and hold the island, and from there he will declare Vraszenian control of Nadežra."

It wouldn't be that simple. Taking the Old Island, perhaps—maybe even holding it for a time. Nadežra had a few warships, but none that could attack the Old Island; they were either ocean-going vessels that would run aground in the delta, or else riverboats too large to pass the Floodwatch Bridge. Their job was to defend against threats from the sea and the river, not from within. For that, Nadežra had usually relied on the Vigil. Cercel wouldn't order a massacre, the way Mettore or Ghiscolo would have done, but she wouldn't sit idle, either.

Even with the island in his hands, though, Branek would be far from victory. And the island didn't translate to control of Nadežra.

Those were the thoughts of a hawk, not a Rook. But Grey knew how to twist one to sound like the other. "If he tries it during sun hours, he'll have an entire Charterhouse full of Liganti hostages." Even a cleansing numinat wouldn't be enough to wash the blood from the Dežera then.

Koszar said, "And what of those on the island who have not come at his call? I understand now why Branek has brought in so many, but not all who live there care for his cause."

The Kiralič nodded grimly. "Even so. They plan to imprison *all* Liganti residents—and those who are, in Branek's eyes, too polluted by the blood of outsiders."

"Imprison." Ren's voice was a knife in the dark, sharp and quiet. "Somehow I doubt it will end there."

"With imprisonment it will begin," the Kiralič said. "But no, there it will not end. He...he expected me to rejoice in it. Our island, the place where Ažerais's children first gathered and saw her dream, purged of Liganti impurity."

Vargo's boot slid from his knee to strike hard against the floor. "As someone who's had his impurity dredged up from both sides of the river, I feel qualified to say 'fuck that.' We stop him. We *have* to."

"I doubt Branek can be turned from his path." Looking to Koszar, the Kiralič bowed his head. "But you wished to expose his oath-breaking and retake the Stadnem Anduske. If the support of the ziemetse you still desire, Prevomir and I will do what we can to secure it."

The Anoškinič scoffed, puffing up like the bird his clan was named for. "Speak for me, will you?"

"Yes, because you are a man of sense."

Scowling, the Anoškinič didn't argue. "It will not be easy. The Stretskojič I suspect gives support to Branek in secret, and the Varadič will look for opportunities to spin his own webs. But if it is as we fear... then we will get you what support we can."

The Mask of Bones

Isla Traementis, Old Island: Apilun 36

Traementis Manor still didn't feel entirely safe. To Ren, safety was home, and home was where she could be herself. By those standards, the closest thing she had was Vargo's townhouse.

But it was a good deal better than it had been, thanks also to Vargo. After she'd made a bitter comment about always fearing the servants overhearing or entering without warning, he'd presented her with two numinata: one that would chime when someone entered the sitting room, and one that would dampen sound, stretched across the canopy of her bed.

Impressively, he'd managed to explain the latter without so much as a salacious lift of his eyebrow.

Those two together meant that having Grey visit her at night was only somewhat foolish, rather than stupidly reckless. And Ren was willing to accept a bit of foolishness in exchange for the warmth of him at her back, the sight of his face in the morning. Grounding her once more in the present, after dreams of Vraszan's past.

Soon we will not have to hide.

She hoped. Only one trial remained, and while she had confidence Grey would win... would it be enough? Certainly there were people cheering him on, Lower Bank residents supporting one of their own, nobles eager to see someone—*anyone*—trip Vargo right before the finish line. But whatever the folklore behind the Trials of the Volti, Ren wondered if Faella's scheme was working. How would people react when Grey requested permission to court her? Would their support extend past that line?

Not just on the Upper Bank. Grey had been called a slip-knot before, when he was a hawk. He'd likely face that again, once he started courting a Traementis alta. They'd be together publicly, but it would still be a con, trying to sell the tale of their romance to the city.

And even if that worked... would it forever be tainted by its source? The method was Faella's idea, but her inspiration was Primordial.

"I can hear you thinking, Szeren," Grey murmured.

She'd told him what Faella said at the amphitheatre. Grey's thoughts were the same as hers: that their love for each other had nothing to do with a Primordial, and that they would benefit no one by abandoning the trials unfinished. But that wasn't the only weight on her mind.

The name the Kiralič had spoken. She and Grey hadn't discussed it the night before; he'd no sooner crept into her room than he sought comfort in her arms. And yet that comfort had not gone past kisses.

Perhaps Grey truly *could* hear her thoughts, because he turned on his side and touched his brow to her bare shoulder. "Yes, Laročja Szerado is kin to me. I wish we were not. She wishes it even more."

He almost never spoke of his family. What Ren guessed at came only from the shadows behind his words, and the one time he'd mentioned them directly. "Your... grandmother?"

"My nightmare," he said, simple and flat. "The reason Kolya stole me from our kureč, when I was only ten. Her and my father."

Grey had looked sick when he saw the bruises Simlin gave her. And there was a scar on his back, the long mark of a whip. She'd never asked him about it, assuming it had happened here in Nadežra. Carters and carriage drivers plied their whips against Vraszenians who didn't get out of the way fast enough. But the scar was an old one.

She'd never asked why they left, why Grey didn't use his patronymic. Now she stroked his hair and said, "They were cruel to you."

"Not without reason." Pressing into her hand in a fair imitation of Clever Natalya, who was dozing by his feet, he continued softly. "My grandmother...she is the reason I despise frauds. For years I watched her foretell doom for others, persuading them only she could avert it. Building a web of those dependent on her, in debt to her, as though she were Varadi. I think at times she believes her own lies. But once, in her cups..."

He fell silent, his body tensing against the confession. Ren stroked him again, kissed his brow. "You need not say it."

"Yes, I do. You have to know." His eyes closed. "When I was very small, my mother drowned herself in the river. She—she tried to drown me, too. Kolya saved me."

Ren's breath caught in her throat. Before she could find words, Grey went on. "She'd been sick in her heart ever since I was born. My grandmother's pattern said I was the cause—that my mother must give me up. She meant adoption into another kureč, ending our relationship...but my mother thought she was being kind. To her, The Mask of Bones could mean only one thing."

"You blame your grandmother for her death?"

"No. I mean—Alinka's told me this sickness can happen with women after childbirth. Usually only for a short while. Sometimes it lingers, though, or even grows worse. My grandmother, I think, made it worse. But after my mother died..."

His breath grew more ragged. "If I was the cause of my mother's sickness, my grandmother was convinced there must be a reason. And so she patterned *me*. It showed—she confessed this once, when she was very drunk; it is the only time the cards have spoken to her as clearly as a voice—I am cursed. I was *born* cursed."

"That's not true," Ren said, soft and firm. "I have laid your pattern, Grey. Nowhere in it saw I anything like that." A twisted future, yes, but he'd done that himself, trying to hide from her. No horror in his past. Nothing to blame a child for.

And yet they had blamed him. Dead-voiced, Grey said, "They

thought they could cleanse me of it. Help me atone. At first it was strict-ness only, but after Kolya went to his apprenticeship, they—they—"

He couldn't say it, and didn't have to. No embrace could ease that pain, but Ren tried anyway, folding Grey into her arms and hugging like she could drive the sorrow from him. His last words were muf-fled against her shoulder. "I *am* a curse. To everyone around me. My mother. Kolya."

I ruin whatever I touch. My grandmother was right. His words in the temple, after she stopped him from burning the Rook's hood.

"You are *not* a curse," she whispered fiercely. "Because of you, I am alive. Because of you, I am better than I was: happier, more honest, living for more than my own gain only. You have helped the people of this city. When I patterned you, I saw no evil. Trust me, if not yourself. Your grandmother was wrong."

Mere words. They couldn't erase the scars, visible or hidden. But he'd once thrown a rope to pull her from the pit of her own fears; she could only try to do the same now. To give him something to hold on to, now and forever.

She waited until his trembling stilled. Then she said, "Kolya was right to take you away from that. Would I be right to keep you from it now?"

Grey sighed and rolled onto his back, gaze caught in the drape of the canopy. "If only it were that simple. If my grandmother is help-ing Branek—"

"Then we deal with her by dealing with him."

Ren's mind reflexively went to work, tallying up what she needed to know, what vulnerabilities she might attack. Then she made herself stop. There would be time for that; right now, what mattered was the man beside her.

Wrapping herself around him again, she closed her eyes. Soon enough he would have to go; soon enough she would rise and be Renata and bring the Trials of the Volti to an end. And confess the truth of herself to Donaia. And deal with Letilia.

For now, she breathed in the warmth and the scent of him, and wished they could stay there forever.

The Point, Old Island: Apilun 36

In becoming a con artist, Ren had learned how to ride the jittering edge of her nerves. The breathless excitement and anxiety of a con in progress sharpened her thoughts, making her more aware of everything around her, every nuance and twitch of the people she manipulated.

But it was possible to overload that balance, and today, she clung to it by her fingernails.

On the one hand she had her guests, gathered at the Great Amphitheatre for the third and last of the Trials of the Volti. The field of competitors had narrowed to eight. They circulated through the crowd in their masks, though by now everyone knew who was still in the running. Renata had to walk a very delicate path, pretending not quite well enough to have no preference, masking her true hope with a little too much warmth shown to the Prismatium Volto.

A path she nearly fell off when Letilia's voice snagged her attention, like an old blister rubbed raw by new shoes.

"That's hardly fair, Mede Beldipassi. Wouldn't it skew the betting books if I shared a mother's insight? Though I will say that my *dear poppet* has shown a surprising inclination for the Lower Bank."

As though dispersed by Renata's glare, the crowd before the stage parted to reveal Letilia entertaining a circle of hangers-on, rich cuffs who laid large sums on small matters and called it sport. Letilia might be speaking to them, but she aimed her words at Renata like a cocked crossbow. "Didn't she live there for almost a year before she was adopted into my family's register? Perhaps she misses the smell."

The acoustics of the amphitheatre lifted the Raven Volto's soft reply far beyond the stage. "How can that be, when it's thanks to her efforts that the Lower Bank now smells as sweet as the Upper? We might more fairly shower Alta Renata with *our* favor, rather than begging for hers."

"I didn't act alone," Renata demurred, artfully touching the sleeve of the Prismatium Volto as though it were an unconscious gesture. "We owe as much thanks to Eret Vargo."

"He has my gratitude…but that's the limit of my generosity." The Raven Volto stepped within reach to catch and hold her fingers and her gaze alike. "I hope to make it the limit of yours."

The flutter in her belly as his lips warmed the thin silk between them had nothing to do with artifice. Her laugh was soft as thistle-down on the breeze. "I look forward to your efforts."

Her cluster of suitors dispersed quickly after that performance, but that only left her open to Letilia's approach. Stylized silver hounds chased gold egrets over the moss-green field of her surcoat—a vast improvement over the embroidery she'd worn on her arrival. Hoping to glean clues about any remaining fail-safes, Tess had bowed to Letilia's demand for a new ensemble. She'd sewn until her fingers resembled red pincushions and she was hunched like a Gan-llechyn stitch-witch of old just to get the embroidery done on time, and still learned nothing useful.

Did that mean there was nothing to find? Or had they missed one final trap?

Letilia clamped down on Renata's arm, a habit that was starting to make Ren flinch in apprehension. *Tonight*, she promised herself. Everything was in place. She had no doubt what Letilia's reaction would be when Renata granted Grey's request for courtship. In the wake of that, who would think it odd when Letilia chose to take ship back to Seteris? Especially since it would echo the way she'd fled over twenty years ago. The letter Ren had written in Letilia's handwriting, railing against her daughter's poor judgment, would catch any remaining doubts in its net.

And Letilia would get the life she'd always wanted—the life she'd refused, because she didn't trust Ren to give it to her. More than she deserved, but a small price to pay for peace.

"I do wish you'd worn something else tonight," Letilia said, eye-ing Renata's apricot surcoat and delicate golden river lilies with dis-taste. "We clash."

"You needn't be so tense. Haven't you done well out of this event? I hardly see you these days; you're too busy visiting new friends and old."

"*Friends* are not a *register*, and thanks to your foolish interference, I still lack one of those. Have you even *tried* to talk Donaia around? Or do you expect me to settle for House Vargo when that jumped-up piece of trash wins this farce?"

Stifling a snort at the thought of Letilia shackled by register to Vargo, Renata said, "I have every intention of speaking with Donaia once tonight's trial is over." She almost wished the conversation *would* be about Letilia, instead of about herself. About who she really was. Ren's imagination had spun out seventeen versions of that conversation, and far too many ended in Traementis vengeance.

Letilia clicked her tongue. "I'm getting tired of living in a hotel. I want my old rooms back in Traementis Manor. You'll see to it, yes?" She didn't even spare a glance for Renata, her gaze flicking over the crowd like a cook at market looking for the freshest catch...and settling on Scaperto Quientis. "Or I'll find better rooms elsewhere."

If that was a threat, Renata almost wished her luck. Few things enraged Donaia more than watching Letilia angle after Scaperto. For his part, he seemed to regard her as a barrel of black powder, stinking and liable to explode at any moment.

But she allowed Letilia to think the threat had landed, until the woman sailed back into the crowd. Then Renata blew out a long breath, trying to slow the rapid thud of her heart. Down in the city, the clock towers chimed ninth sun. *Time to get started.*

Everyone knew it, too. The crowd's noise dimmed to a whispering murmur as Letilia climbed the stage.

"My friends!" she proclaimed, spreading her arms wide. "Thank you *so* much for gathering here today. I'm delighted to welcome you all to the third and final Trial of the Volti. As you can see, servants are even now laying out food and drink for you in the box seats, and soon we'll have music for dancing. We must keep ourselves entertained *somehow*—as Renata, for some whimsical reason, has chosen a trial we can hardly even watch."

Her theatrical frown elicited a few boos from the crowd. *Blame Tanaquis*, Renata wanted to say. The initial seed idea she'd proposed had fired her cousin's creativity—but providing a spectacle for observers was the furthest thing from Tanaquis's mind.

The volti lined up on the stage, and Renata approached them, bearing a tray with eight sealed envelopes. Each was marked with a stylized drawing of the recipient's masks. "For the third trial," Letilia said as they took their envelopes, "Renata wishes to test your *cleverness*. Each envelope contains a clue that will lead you to a location on the Old Island. If you've puzzled it out correctly, you'll find in that place a second clue—a series of five in all, to prove your excellence.

"But beware! Though each of you begins with a different clue, as you proceed, you'll begin to encounter one another. Take too long in the solving, and you *may* find your opponents have beaten you to the next stage! And when it comes to the final one...then, my charming friends, there is only a single victor. Whoever reaches Alta Tanaquis and claims the victory token from her will return here— and win from Renata a boon of their choosing."

That was the script Renata had given her. But of course Letilia had to add a coda. "I *do* hope the volti will be safe, running hither and yon across the Old Island. But then, I suppose they all proved their strength in the first trial...and any who fail now are *clearly* unworthy of reward."

Renata couldn't tell whether it was deliberate or accidental that a sneer touched her lip when she looked at the Raven Volto and the woman in the willow mask. They were the only two commoners left in the pack. Had Letilia taken steps to sabotage them? She had no reason to do so, apart from sheer pettiness—but that might be enough.

If so, Ren had to trust Grey to overcome it. As hawk and as Rook, he'd dealt with far worse than Letilia. And the envelopes had come directly to Renata from Tanaquis; there was no way Letilia could have interfered with them. Ren doubted she could have imitated Tanaquis's scrawling handwriting, which might pose a bigger challenge to the volti than the riddling clues.

The volti had their envelopes. Letilia paused, letting the silence stretch out. Then she cried, "Begin!"

To the roar of the crowd, the volti ran for the exit.

Old Island: Apilun 36

To find the clue your path must bend
  Toward the place where all roads end.

::Dreadful poetry, but clearly referencing Ninat,:: Alsius said as Vargo folded his third clue and strode off through Suncross. Seeing him cut west, he added, ::Oh, you think?::

"It's the way Tanaquis would think, and that's what matters." Unlike the canal race, Vargo didn't have a crowd of spectators cheering and jeering him on; he took advantage of that to lift his prismatium mask and let the winds off the Dežera cool the accumulated sweat. "I think she's going easy on me."

Alsius huffed. ::Entirely unnecessary. She knows you have me to help you.::

"Your confidence that I could manage on my own is noted and appreciated," Vargo muttered as he reached the Duskgate at the foot of the Sunset Bridge. Even if the white envelope tucked between two of the disused gate's planks hadn't stood out like a banner, the Argentet lackey making sure no passerby swiped it would have given away the clue's location. Passing the lackey a decira, Vargo snatched out the envelope and broke the wax seal. At this rate, he'd be back at the amphitheatre before the sun set.

Three months of working with Tanaquis had made her handwriting easy to read.

Amid the walls of painted fear,
  You'll find your next clue hidden here.

The chill that passed through Vargo had nothing to do with the wind. He shoved the clue inside his coat and leaned against the gatehouse, sucking in breath after breath of fresh air.

When the first wave of *oh fuck no* had passed enough for him to speak, he said, "I take it back. Tanaquis hates me."

Alsius scuttled down Vargo's lapel like he meant to crawl inside and read the clue under the shadow of blue gabardine. ::Why? Is it difficult? Read it to me; I'm certain I can puzzle it out.::

"The Depths. She's sending us to the place Gammer Lindworm kept the children."

::Oh.:: Tucking his legs under like he did when he was trying to avoid the attention of seagulls, Alsius said, ::That's not *so* bad. Ondrakja's dead, after all.::

Not so bad? Vargo forced a laugh. "She kept zlyzen there, too. Remember?" His scars still pulled a bit when he twisted, making sure Vargo would never forget. Just like the nightmares he'd been fighting on and off since those monsters trapped him in the dream.

Alsius hadn't grown up with stories of the zlyzen. They didn't hold the same terror for him. ::But without her to call them, I'm sure it's fine. Come, we're wasting time! You may have beaten your opponent to this clue, but someone else may be headed into the Depths right now.:: Cunningly, he added, ::You don't want to go down there only to find you shouldn't have even bothered, do you?::

That prodded Vargo off the wall. *Ren and Grey. You're doing this for Ren and Grey.* Though the setup of the challenge made it damn hard for him to assist Serrado, or to watch for anyone sabotaging the man. After a moment's consideration, Vargo stuck the envelope back between the gate's panels, while the Argentet lackey looked surprised. If Serrado was on the same path as him now, the man would need that clue. And if it was someone else . . .

Then I only need to outrun that one when the zlyzen show up, Vargo thought mordantly, heading for the nearest river stair.

The tide was in his favor, though he wished he'd worn a scented mask as he picked his way along the river strand to the opening that led into the Depths. The prismatium one did him no good at all, and he let it hang from his neck as he peered into the tunnel opening. He hadn't thought to bring a light source—but he *had* brought a small inscription kit, on the chance that Tanaquis's puzzles would involve numinatria. A broken shard of plate washed up on the bank made an acceptable surface for inscribing a basic light numinat. Holding that like a shield, Vargo forced himself into the darkness.

The people he'd sent down here to wash the zlyzen blood off the walls must have missed traces. Or was that just his natural sense of dread, inspiring his skin to crawl right off his body? Every shifting shadow seemed to hold the unnatural angles of a zlyzen's limbs; every echoing scuff and drip was one of them creeping close. *If Ren weren't my friend, I'd be out of here so fast I'd leave my shoes behind.* But she was, and he pressed onward.

At least it was cooler down here. Vargo lifted his sleeve to his face, eyeing every midden and mulch pile to make sure it wasn't about to rise up and rake him with diseased claws. He was so busy shying from shadows that he failed to notice the other light source until he was almost upon it.

Turning a corner into a larger corridor, he came face-to-mask with Serrado.

"Pretty certain you're supposed to leave that on," Serrado said, his raven beak dipping toward the prismatium hanging around Vargo's neck.

"Oh no, I'm disqualified," Vargo drawled, not in the mood for Serrado's arid wit. "Guess I'll return to the surface like a *sane* person."

Serrado shuddered as he glanced behind himself. "I'm no happier being here than you are. Any sign of the clue yet?"

No veiled suspicion that Vargo might have already found and disposed of it. If Serrado had harbored any doubts about their plan, they'd drowned two weeks ago in a Lower Bank canal. And though he wasn't about to admit it, Vargo felt a lot more comfortable now that he had somebody bigger than a spider guarding his back.

"The burial niches, I suspect," he said. Where Gammer Lindworm had kept the children caged.

There was no attendant here, which meant they were in the wrong place—possible; that Tanaquis didn't think a nonpublic location needed a watcher—probable; or that the attendant had decided they weren't being paid enough for this shit, which Vargo considered extremely plausible. Especially as they approached the niches carved into the wall and the stench of the Depths grew chokingly foul.

But there was another white envelope resting between two of the bars Gammer Lindworm had installed. Vargo hung back, letting Serrado be the one to pick it up.

"'Pass beyond the unseen wall; take your prize, and win it all,'" Grey said. He arrived at the answer simultaneously with Vargo and Alsius. "The temple."

Where the Illius Praeteri had conducted their rites, and Kaius Rex before them. Vargo carried a triple clover charm all the time these days, because they'd been using the temple for their various experiments. He assumed Grey did the same, but if not, Vargo could hand over his own. "Let's go."

"Wait." Serrado pressed one hand over his mouth, gagging a little. "There's something else."

::Carrion,:: Alsius said uneasily, shifting on Vargo's shoulder. ::Something down here is dead.::

Serrado couldn't hear the spider, but he'd turned to look at the next niche along, raising his own lightstone. *Still a hawk*, Vargo thought with irritation. "We can come back later—"

Then Serrado reached out and turned over what Vargo had thought was a pile of cloth. A corpse rolled to face them . . . and with a jolt, Vargo recognized it.

"Fuck," he breathed. "That's Ninat."

The Depths, Old Island: Apilun 36

"Hold this." Shoving his lightstone into Vargo's free hand and tossing his mask aside so he could see properly, Grey dropped to his knees. There was no point checking for life; Grey had dealt with enough dead bodies to recognize this as one. The face was pallid as a fish belly, with the same flaccid sag, but nothing had started gnawing on it yet, nor had it sunk into rot. Days, then, instead of weeks or hours.

The limbs shifted like a puppet's, a fresh wash of rot rising up to choke Grey as he rooted through the dead man's clothes. *Ir Entrelke, let it be here. It has to be here.*

"Looks like he was hiding out," Vargo said. His own light was lifted to the niche above, where a few bottles and a knapsack were stashed. "I didn't even think to have anyone search the Depths."

"Nor did I." An understandable oversight, even if Grey was kicking himself for it now. The man hadn't looked like the sort to haunt the Depths. But in his fear, after what he'd seen, perhaps he'd never emerged from the tunnel. Perhaps he'd fled down, down, down...

A pouch slipped out of the man's coat and landed on the lip of the niche. Its thin velvet only muffled the dull clink of metal striking stone.

Relief and horror warred in Grey's heart. That had to be the Ninat medallion—and the timing couldn't be worse.

"Wait." Vargo's hand wrapped around Grey's wrist as he reached for the bag. The two lights in his other hand cast unsettling shadows up his face, but nothing could hide the conflict in his expression.

The Rook might be broken, but Grey still felt the old fury bubbling up, at all the people who didn't care who they hurt in their grab for any scrap of power. "We can't leave it here. Do *you* propose to take it instead?"

"Hell no. I'm already having enough problems with Sessat. It's only—" Vargo's grip tightened. Then he released Grey's wrist and stepped away. Not far; only to retrieve the raven mask Grey had dropped. "Neither of us should carry two."

Grey went perfectly still.

Vargo was still, too, not meeting his gaze. Tense. As if he feared what the response would be.

"How long have you known?"

Voice tight, Vargo said, "Suspected something after the meeting with the ziemetse. Been paying attention since then. I don't think anyone else is in a position to notice, but..." He shrugged one shoulder. "You and Ren. You're both damn good at lying, but I can see what's between you. Even when you're not being you."

Because the Rook is broken.

Grey couldn't afford guilt right now, nor self-recrimination for failing to hide the truth. Vargo was right; it wasn't safe for either of them to have two medallions. Neither was it safe to just leave Ninat here and hope no Depths scavenger came by and looted the body. The burial niches didn't see a lot of visitors, but that didn't make them secure.

"Tanaquis can take it," Grey said. "She's at the temple, with the victory token."

Vargo turned enough to offer him the volto. "You go. You've got a boon to win, and I can wail and gnash my teeth publicly later. I'll stay here and guard the thing—if you trust me."

There were as many layers to that comment as there were colors in Vargo's mask and tunnels in the Depths, and Grey didn't have the time to untangle them all.

But neither could he quite make himself say the words. He only said, "I'll need my lightstone."

Two steps away, he glanced over his shoulder and found Vargo uneasily settling as far from the niche and its stinking contents as he could. The memory of Yvie's recent artistic efforts on the front stoop flitted through his mind. "It's not a thread, but red chalk might work."

"Fuck you," Vargo grumbled—but he was already digging in his pockets as Grey hurried away.

He didn't need the Rook's memories to guide him through the tunnels, and only a healthy sense of caution kept him from breaking into a run. A sense of caution which frayed and broke as he drew closer, until he finally rounded a curve and found a well-lit area up ahead, just outside the ward protecting the entrance to the temple.

Someone else was there, in front of a board festooned with hundreds of numinatrian and knotwork charms. The Boar Volto— Mede Galbiondi—systematically grabbed one charm, tried the barrier, dropped it, and grabbed another, while Tanaquis watched from the far side.

Her amusement faded to something far tenser when Grey skid-
ded to a halt. "Are you all right?"

Deception had been drilled into his bones when he became the
Rook. He forced himself to glance at the clue tacked at the top of
the board, though he paid the words no heed; he had no doubt at
all that Tanaquis had stacked this deck for himself, Vargo, or both.
Ren might play honestly, at his request, but nobody else seemed to
feel so constrained. After a cursory glance at the board, he grabbed a
random charm and passed through the barrier, courtesy of the triple
clover knot in his pocket.

But he didn't take the victory token yet. In a murmur well-
hidden under the bellow of outrage from the Boar Volto, he said,
"We found the stranger. Vargo and I, in the burial niches. It's on
him, but—" Making his shudder convincing wasn't difficult. "I—I
was afraid to take it. I can't risk my family like that."

"Without a register to channel the energy, it wouldn't—" Tanaquis stopped herself mid-argument. "No, of course. And Vargo
shouldn't either, should he? Right, take this."

She shoved the victory token into his hands, then pushed past him,
through the unseen barrier. Following her, Grey said, "Is it safe—"

"I already scribed protections into the Traementis register," Tanaquis
said, while the Boar Volto stared at them both. "It will be enough. Go."
Not waiting for further argument, she darted off down the corridor.

Grey looked at the Boar Volto, whose gaze had fallen to the victory token he held. "Don't even think about it," Grey said in the
Rook's voice, and headed for the surface.

The Great Amphitheatre, Old Island: Apilun 36

The sun was nearing the horizon and Donaia was fighting off a
headache when excited shouting at the far side of the amphitheatre
heralded the return of the winning volto.

"Finally," she breathed. She didn't agree with Letilia on much, but it was purely cruel of Renata and Tanaquis to stage this last trial in a fashion that left the spectators with nothing to do but eat, drink, dance, and worry.

Though Donaia might be the only one doing that last. While no doubt all of Renata's volti wanted something from her, she'd feared from the start that her clever, persuasive niece had staged all of this in order to legitimize her relationship with Vargo. He might be a nobleman, but his title was less than a year old, and his boots and business remained firmly planted on the Lower Bank.

The cries got louder, and the musicians gave up. No one was dancing now anyway. Alinka rose onto her toes in a vain effort to see who'd won. The entry tunnel was clogged with people whose only business in this crowd was betting.

Please, let it not be Vargo. Would Donaia have no choice but to accept that man in Renata's life? Would she have to let her niece go, to be scribed into his lonely register of one?

Too many people were cheering and punching the air for that to be the result. The crowd finally parted, and Donaia's heart skipped a beat as she saw the victor.

The Raven Volto.

No one had openly confirmed the identities of the volti, but how could she not recognize that one? When she'd watched him grow from an abused little boy into the upright and honorable man he was now. She didn't need Alinka's yelp of delight to confirm it. And right then, floating on a cloud of breathless relief, Donaia was ready to give him a boon of her own in thanks.

Letilia was caught off guard. She'd been deep in conversation with a Cleoter cousin, and though she started to break that off so she could roll herself in Renata's reflected glory, her momentum faltered at the sight of the Raven Volto. Whether she cared enough to know his precise identity or not, she knew he was the only remaining Vraszenian competitor. With a flick of disgust, she gave up on returning to the stage, letting Renata stand alone to receive the victor.

He knelt before her, presenting in both hands the engraved silver disc of the final victory token. Renata took it and said, "Through my trials you have shown your strength and your courage, your speed and your fellowship, your cunning and your devotion. Remove your mask, Raven Volto, and ask what boon you will of me."

Grey's hair was rumpled and his face damp with sweat, but he still made a beautiful sight as he gazed up at Renata. And his voice was resonant with joy as he said, "*Nihil peto sed gratiam*. Like the humble shepherd in the tale, I ask no favor but your favor: your permission for me to court you."

Someone yelped. Someone else giggled. But mostly what Donaia heard was the mass rush of indrawn breath.

Including her own. Grey wanted to *court* Renata? But he was—

As if the river's winds had whipped away a fog, Donaia saw clearly at last. *He* was the lover Renata had been hiding, all this time. The distance she'd seen between them wasn't awkwardness or embarrassment; it was a mask over what they knew the city would condemn. Where Vargo fit into that picture, Donaia had no idea, but in this moment it hardly mattered. Renata's smile, too tenuous and bright to be anything but genuine, spoke the truth she'd been concealing for so long. *This* was what she wanted.

Gossip could go many ways. It all depended on which direction it was pushed, in the instant when everything balanced on the knife's edge.

No one blocked Donaia's path as she joined them on stage. Between the acoustics of the amphitheatre and the numinat under her feet, she didn't even have to raise her voice to be heard. "My niece's discernment and taste are known throughout Nadežra. I cannot say whether you will win her hand, when so many have tried and failed...but I want nothing more than to see Renata happy. If you can bring that to her, I will gladly open our register. I only wish my son were here to cheer you on, Master Serrado. You were ever like a brother to him."

Murmurs greeted that reminder of her loss. Part of Donaia was ashamed to be using Leato's death to squeeze sympathy out of blood-minded gossips, but she knew how he would have reacted to this turn of events. He would already be clapping Grey on the back, beaming fit to crack his own face in half. Just like Giuna was doing now, darting up to hug Renata, bouncing on her toes before throwing propriety to the wind and hugging Grey, too. And Donaia—

She didn't know how to feel. She felt too many things at once. Happiness, yes, because it was impossible to look at Renata and not realize that her niece had truly found what she wanted. Shock, because while the nobility might well take Vraszenians for lovers, *marrying* one was their least excusable scandal. Worry, because however well-orchestrated this entire display had been, there would still be knives poised for Renata's back...and Grey's as well.

But in this moment, what mattered was defending them both. And so Donaia warmly embraced Renata, then Grey, and tried not to think about the future.

Then she commanded the musicians to strike up a dancing tune and shooed the two lovers off to have a word on their own. Grey in particular looked impatient to escape for some private congratulations. Meanwhile, Donaia made a beeline for the nearest carafe of wine.

She found Letilia already there, glaring at her cup as though its contents had gone to vinegar. Donaia pivoted, but Letilia's voice caught her. "Happy to open your register, eh?" She slugged back the wine and poured herself another. "Open it for that *gnat*—but not for someone who has every right to be in it."

Letilia was drunk, they might attract an audience, and at the moment the Traementis duelist was otherwise occupied, but Donaia couldn't bite back her response. "What right? Your own father struck you from the register."

"For what crime?" Letilia's wine sloshed over to stain her glove as she spread her arms. Tears sparkled in her eyes; she'd always been able to call them up for dramatic effect. "What terrible thing did I do for you all to hate me? Leave home to follow my dreams? *That's* a disowning offense?"

On its own, no. But Crelitto's fury had lasted for years after Letilia's departure—all the way to his death. He'd never said why, only claimed to have his reasons.

Letilia was still talking, the venom thickening with every word. "You're no better than a Lower Bank night-piece, opening your doors for anyone who can bring you value, and everyone else can go fuck themselves. You like to *pretend* you care about family, but what welcome did I get when I returned? Not even my old rooms back."

"Those rooms are Giuna's now," Donaia said, casting around for anyone who could intervene and take Letilia away. Right now she would even recruit Scaperto, but he was busy talking to Cibrial, his back to her so he couldn't see her signal.

Letilia scoffed. "Then you could give me the heir's suite. I hear nobody's using it."

Leato's rooms. Fire and ice slammed through Donaia's bones, warring for supremacy. In one stride she was up in Letilia's face, grinding the words out through a throat gone as hard as stone. "You have only ever seen this family as a source of money and comfort. A thing to take from at your whim, and never give back to. But know this, Letilia: I will *burn* the Traementis register before I ever scribe you into it."

The woman staggered back a step, eyes going wide. For the smallest instant, Donaia wondered if she realized she'd finally gone too far.

But this was Letilia. She was incapable of that.

"Fine, then," Letilia said, biting off each word. "If that's how you're going to be, then you deserve what's coming."

Before Donaia could react, Letilia turned on her heel and strode through the milling crowd to the stage, into the center of the numinat. The breaking of glass echoed through the amphitheatre as she flung her wine cup to the ground and cried, "I have something to say!"

The Great Amphitheatre, Old Island: Apilun 36

"But having two medallions in the Traementis register—" Ren whispered.

Grey scrubbed a hand through his hair. They stood close together in the shadow of an entry arch, still in sight for propriety, but far enough away for privacy. "I know. But *someone* has to take it. Tanaquis thinks she's put in enough protections."

Remembering the marks festooning the register's clean lines, Ren thought Tanaquis might be right. *Hoped* she was. "It'll do for now, at least. I honestly don't know who else I'd trust to take it." She trusted Tess and Sedge, but she wouldn't inflict this on them. Ryvček, perhaps. But she wasn't here tonight, and they couldn't leave Ninat unclaimed.

Then Ren realized the crowd had gone quiet, the music limping off into silence.

And everyone was staring at her and Grey. Whispering to each other, some behind hands or fans, others openly.

No, not staring at them both. Just at *her.*

Letilia stood on the stage, cheeks flushed and arms akimbo, breathless with vindictive triumph.

Then Donaia hauled herself up to stand alongside Letilia. Her voice amplified by the numinat, she snapped, "What absolute horse-shit. You are a petty, jealous woman, and drunk besides—but this is too far, Letilia, even for you. Go home. Nobody of good taste wants you here, and nobody of good sense would believe such wild accusations."

How much had Letilia given away? How much had Ren missed? Ren couldn't drag her gaze from the woman, but the whispers of the crowd carried everything she needed to know. Everything she feared.

Vraszenian.

Con artist.

Liar.

She'd known that Grey's victory would anger Letilia. She'd thought she could use that to get rid of the woman. But she'd miscalculated: Instead it had driven Letilia straight over the edge of truth.

From nearby, a soft, hurt voice. Giuna's. "Renata..."

That broke the paralysis, and Ren wished it hadn't. Because

when she met Giuna's gaze, she saw that however much Donaia might condemn this as Letilia's drunken nonsense...Giuna knew it was possible.

A deep-seated reflex reached for something to say. Some way to spin this. That she wasn't Letilia's daughter would be difficult to refute, but the rest—so long as her makeup was on, nothing about her looked obviously Vraszenian—she could still try—

Maybe she could. Maybe, with enough effort, there was a way to salvage a few shreds of her masquerade.

But Ren was tired. And she'd sworn to reveal the truth once the trial was over.

The Masks, it seemed, were laughing at her.

She looked at Giuna and whispered, "I'm sorry."

The words were too soft to carry, but Donaia must have read the shape of them on Ren's lips. For one horrible moment, she was a frozen statue. Then she said in an unsteady voice, "You shouldn't have to apologize for your horrible mother. You—"

' "No. I mean..." Ren clamped her lips against the accent she'd adopted for over a year, the crisp syllables sitting like cut glass in her mouth. When she spoke again, it was with the fluid rhythm of the winding Dežera. "Tonight I meant to tell you. It is as she says. She is no mother of mine."

Dead silence. Not even a scandalized wave of whispers. Faella Coscanum stood with her jaw hanging loose, but Ren found no satisfaction in astonishing the city's most well-informed gossip.

Not when everything had fallen into dust.

"Get out," Donaia whispered. Even a birdcall would have been enough to drown it out, but with the numinat pitching her voice through the amphitheatre, it rang as clear as a shout. "Get out. And don't show your face to me again."

Grey's hand slipped into Ren's, the one solid thing in a world gone distant and faint. With him at her side, Ren walked through a crowd that parted around her like the Dežera around the Point. Down the aisle, out one of the amphitheatre's exits.

And out of Renata's life.

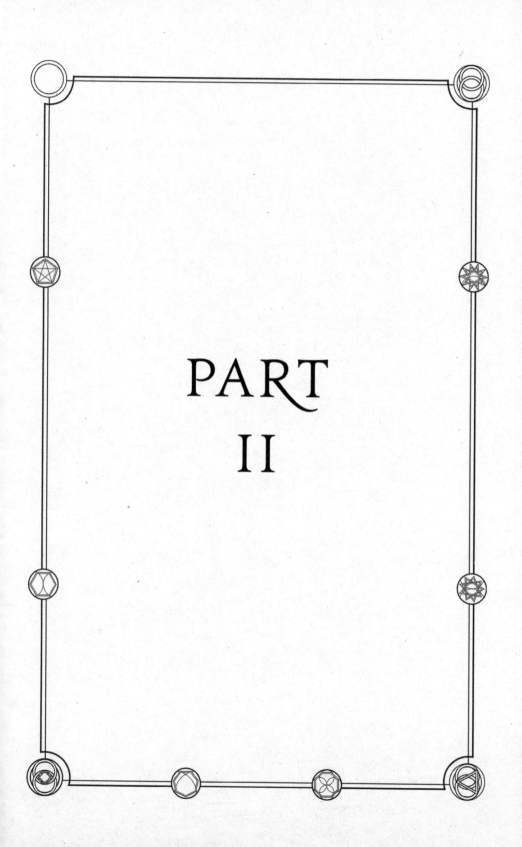

PART

II

10

One Poppy Weeps

Isla Čaprila, Eastbridge: Pavnilun 1

The next morning Ren lay in bed with Grey at her back, drifting on that peculiar, unreal wind of someone who went to bed too late, woke up too early, and couldn't fall back asleep. Or maybe it was the unreality of the same thing that disturbed her rest: the inescapable knowledge that Alta Renata was unmasked at last, her con exposed to the world.

Vargo had sworn fit to boil the Dežera when he found the two of them in the temple, too heartsore to decide what to do next. "If I'd been there—" he'd said, helplessly.

"You couldn't have done anything," Ren said, her own voice dull with shock. "And what you were doing mattered more." Standing guard over Ninat until Tanaquis could claim it. Ren supposed any concern over two medallions in one register was moot now. Tricat would be gone from the Traementis as soon as Donaia could unroll the parchment.

But Vargo hadn't found much comfort in that. And in his quest to do something, *anything* to help, he'd offered her the refuge of his own house. Grey didn't have his own lodgings yet—might never, if Donaia revoked his duelist contract—and it was better than crowding in with Alinka and the children, even if many poor Vraszenians lived their whole lives on top of one another.

Within the shock still hollowing Ren out, the emptiness of fear gnawed. How was she to pay for anything now? Not just lodgings but clothing, food, everything necessary for survival. Ren was licensed as an advocate for two more years—assuming Donaia couldn't revoke that, too—but who would hire a known con artist to represent them in the Charterhouse? And who would accept her petitions? She had no way to support herself, except by the old habits of grifting and theft. Habits half the city would know of when the morning broadsheets went out.

She wouldn't even be able to get work as a maid.

That thought made her whole body shake with something that wasn't a laugh. It roused Grey, whose arm tightened around her waist.

"I'm here," he said against the nape of her neck, his breath a warm comfort against the inner cold. Her fingers tangled with his, holding tight to him.

Though part of her said, *You should let go.* "I'll only bring you down with me," she whispered. Letilia's revelation would sour the sweet story they'd spun. A Vraszenian con artist and her Vraszenian lover, duping everyone and nearly getting away with it. It was disaster for them both.

"Then we fall together." He shifted, tugging at their joined hands until she rolled over and faced him, nose to nose and half buried under the heavy azure blanket. "When Clever Natalya faced evil sorcerers, Constant Ivan stayed true. Would you have me do less? We'll figure it out."

Maybe. But the part of her that was used to picking itself up off the ground just felt tired and broken. Like there wasn't any point in trying.

Muffled sounds came through the door that led from Vargo's bedroom to his study. The previous night he'd dragged his lounging couch into the other room, ceding his bed to them. Now it seemed he was awake, and trying not to wake anyone else.

Ren wanted to stay in bed forever, safe from the consequences of her actions. But her thoughts needled her like a burr in her stocking, and hiding wouldn't make anything better. She forced herself upright and said, "Perhaps food will help."

They had only their clothes from the previous night. But a pump and a warming numinat meant there was fresh hot water, washing away the cobwebs of sleep alongside the remnants of her makeup. After that, it felt almost fitting to don the tatters of Renata's identity. Ren left the heavy surcoat draped over a chair and followed Grey downstairs in nothing but a wrinkled underdress.

Tess's and Vargo's voices drifted out of the kitchen in a friendly squabble about the proper additions for tolatsy. Vargo was arguing for the spices and savories common in Vraszan, while Tess adamantly insisted on the superiority of the cream, honey, and dried fruit Ganllechyns used to make their boiled oats edible.

Ren's heart tightened, not entirely in pain. She hadn't lost everything.

Nobody brought up the events of the previous night when she came into the kitchen, for which Ren was profoundly grateful. Grey settled the breakfast debate with a declaration that they'd make both types, and soon Ren was ensconced in the sunlit room at the back of Vargo's house. In her hands was a bowl of proper tolatsy, and on the warming numinat was a smaller one sweetened in Ganllechyn style—"morning dessert," as Vargo termed it. A series of thumps in the alley behind turned out to be Sedge, who came in bearing a crate emitting a constant stream of protesting meows. "Your cat clawed me," he said accusingly as he lifted the lid, Clever Natalya springing free and bolting for cover.

Soft as the rice porridge was, Ren almost couldn't swallow her mouthful around the lump in her throat. With Grey's help, she'd broken into Traementis Manor the previous night...because as much as it hurt to do that, she couldn't risk someone else picking up the boots whose heel contained the medallion, even for the purpose of delivering them to her. But Clever Natalya had been off on her midnight prowls, and Ren couldn't afford to search for her—not when someone might notice the cat's disappearance.

She managed to whisper, "Thank you, Sedge." Putting the bowl down, she drummed her fingers to entice Clever Natalya onto her knee, then kept herself very busy petting the cat while everyone else got themselves settled.

"S'pose there en't no point in popping Letilia on a ship bound for Seteris now," Sedge said after the quiet went on too long with nobody breaking it. "Other than the pleasure it'll give us. Something to be said for that."

"Sedge!" Tess hissed, giving him an admonishing poke.

"What?" Sedge said. "It's what we was all thinking."

Ren coughed her throat clear. "Letilia is yesterday's problem. Now that Ninat has been found, we should focus on destroying the medallions."

New silence greeted her words. She dragged her gaze up and found everyone alternately looking at her, then exchanging glances with each other. "What?"

"Ren..." Tess took her hand. Gloveless. Ren wouldn't have to fuss with gloves anymore. "I'm not saying the medallions aren't important...but perhaps they aren't the *most* important thing right now. What about Donaia and Giuna?"

Something surged inside Ren, like a rat trying to claw its way out of her throat. "What can I say? I should have told them sooner; it would have hurt them less. Explanations now will sound like I'm trying to salvage my con. If I were them, I wouldn't listen to a word I say."

"Doesn't mean they don't deserve to hear it," Vargo said, poking at his tolatsy and studiously not looking at anyone. Grey, sitting next to Ren, inhaled softly. Vargo lifted his spoon, then let its contents goop back into his bowl. "If you're going to cut ties, do it because you want to. Not because you're afraid."

"I'm not—"

"Aren't you?" Vargo asked, meeting her gaze. He hadn't done more than throw on a morning robe yet; his eyes were bare of the kohl that usually lined them, giving him a softer, open look.

It cracked her open, and the first tear spilled. "All right, I am. What if I hurt them again? More than I already have. I might just make things worse." Not that she could fathom what "worse" might look like.

Nor could she bear everyone looking at her. When Clever Natalya *mrrp*ed in her lap, she ducked her head and let the next few tears fall on silky black fur.

A soft square of linen appeared in her hand—the one Grey carried for Yvie or Jagyi. He said, "I think worse might be leaving them with nothing but Letilia's explanation. They don't have to accept the truth from you...but don't you want to share it with them, for once?"

Not when the truth felt like a knife between her own ribs. Or— *No*, Ren thought. The knife was already there. This would be its removal. Which might end with her bleeding out; the metaphor wasn't comforting. But no matter what imagery she dressed it up in, they were right. Donaia and Giuna deserved an explanation from her.

She blotted her eyes and said, "A letter. If I show up at their door, odds are they'll turn me away. But a letter they can read when they choose. Or burn it. Whatever they prefer."

Tess brushed her hands briskly, like this was just another house-cleaning task. "Very good. Vargo, do you have paper?"

"Do I have—" He stared at her, spoon in hand as if he were fighting the urge to flick tolatsy in her direction. "Yes, I have paper. You can use my study, Ren; that way you'll have some peace and quiet."

She followed him upstairs to the study where, not that long ago, Vargo had saved Grey's life. Grey had told her last night, in their hurried conversation before everything fell apart, that Vargo knew about the Rook. She'd expected Grey to be wound wire-tight at that discovery, but he wasn't, and this morning the two of them were acting almost normal. Honesty: Sometimes it made things better. She clung to that thought as Vargo settled her into the desk chair and gave her paper, pen, blotter, ink.

After that, though, he still lingered. "I didn't want to bring this up around the others, because I didn't want you to feel pressured," he said. "But you can't stay here."

His words hit like a shock of cold water. She managed to say, "Of course. I'll leave once—"

"No, that's not..." The couch that served as his bed the previous night creaked as he dropped onto it. "I didn't mean you're not welcome. I mean that I doubt you *want* to stay here. But your old townhouse is still empty, and I've fixed up the broken windows. And Westbridge is much closer to Kingfisher."

"I can hardly afford—"

"Did I ask for payment? There's no debts between us."

The paper crimped under her fingers as she recognized the echo in his words. "We aren't knot-sworn."

"We could be."

His gaze was steady on hers again. Ren's hand trembled as she brushed loose strands of hair from her face. "Vargo...you hold Sessat. Even if you carry it not, it's still influencing you." Friendship and loyalty. *Damn* the medallions, and damn Kaius Rex.

He shrugged, a veil of carelessness over what lay beneath. "We were friends before I took Sessat. You already know all my secrets. You know me better than almost anyone, and..." Vargo rubbed distractedly at his chest, the brand hidden by layers of fabric. The sigil that bound his life and his spirit to Alsius. "That time wasn't exactly a choice. This is. And I'm not going to let some piece of numinatrian junk rule my life." He snorted. "I've already got a chatty spider doing that."

"But—" She had to force the words out. "I betrayed my knot. *Twice.* I poisoned Ondrakja, and I threw her to the zlyzen."

"You want to compare our sins? We'll need a few bottles of brandy and a lot more time." His crooked grin called up their drunken afternoon of truth-telling.

But then that grin gentled into something Vargo never showed the rest of the world. Vulnerability.

"Look," he said, soft as a shadow. "If you're saying no because you don't want to, I understand. You've got your blood siblings, and you'll be marrying Serrado. Maybe you don't want more ties. But if this is some 'for your own good' bullshit—or worse, 'I don't deserve it'—skip it. I *know* you. We know each other. And...that's a rare thing for me."

Ren felt like a sodden rag, leaking every time someone so much as touched her. But at least this time the tears stinging her eyes didn't spring from sorrow or fear. Because she knew exactly what Vargo meant: the breath-stealing sense of finding someone who could look at you—at *all* of you, sins and all—and still hold out their hand.

She rose from behind the desk and perched next to Vargo on the couch. Close enough to take one of the hands dangling loose between his knees and clasp it in her own. There didn't have to be a leader and followers; knot oaths were a ritual of friendship, a Vraszenian tradition long before they were adopted by Nadežran gangs.

"All our grudges are washed away," she said. Words she'd recited twice before...but she never meant them as sincerely as she did now. "Your secrets are mine, and mine are yours. Between us there will be no debts."

His voice was rough but his grip gentle as he repeated the oath. He released her hand—and then a shaky laugh as Ren impulsively threw her arms around him. She let go a moment later, but the feel of it stayed with her: a solidity she could trust.

"I en't no good at knotwork," he said, letting his diction slip. "And I din't exactly plan this in advance, so I don't have nothing prepared."

"You can ask Tess for cord." She laughed and wiped her eyes, glancing back at the desk. The blank paper and waiting pen didn't feel quite so frightening anymore. "I must write that letter anyway. But once that's done...I think you should bring out the aža."

Isla Traementis, the Pearls: Pavnilun 1

"—sent her man to collect her damned cat, but doesn't have the common decency to come here and give us an explanation! It's absurd, it's absolutely absurd—but you saw her reaction. You heard how she spoke at the end. She's Vraszenian! How is that even possible? A liar, all this time, living in our midst!"

Donaia's breath came fast and unsteady as she paced the room. Every time she dragged her voice down to a more reasonable level, it rose again. Well, so be it; not like the entire staff of Traementis Manor hadn't heard. The entire *city* had heard. More than a dozen people had helpfully delivered broadsheets to her door. She was the laughingstock of Nadežra.

Giuna sat curled into a tiny ball at the end of the couch, her shoes abandoned on the floor. Meatball, wedged under the side table, tracked Donaia with doleful eyes. Scaperto watched from the armchair, but his expression was unreadable. And Tanaquis sat at the desk, the heavy roll of the Traementis register unfurled before her, pen and ink at the ready. As soon as Donaia said the word, *Renata*—whoever she really was—would be struck from their ranks.

Scaperto cleared his throat. "Do you intend to bring charges against her?"

Donaia tripped over her own feet, catching herself on the back of the couch. "Charges? No! Why would I . . ."

Her fingers tightened on the padded backing, the chamois as soft as a daughter's cheek. Renata had sat there a year ago and talked Donaia out of sending her packing, using the promise of refilling the Traementis coffers, saving the Traementis reputation.

Taking vengeance against Traementis enemies.

Like true kin would. Like a daughter to replace the son she'd lost.

Donaia sagged as exhaustion washed through her. Giuna supported her mother until she could sink onto the cushions. Donaia said, "What could I charge her with? Making a fool of an old woman isn't a crime."

Lips flat, Scaperto glanced at Tanaquis's poised pen. Impersonating a noble *was* a crime. And once Renata was no longer in the register, she wouldn't be protected from her earlier lies.

So many lies! Layer upon layer, any crack in one patched with another. Tanaquis said thoughtfully, "It makes so much more sense now. If you stop to think about it."

The pattern cards. The slip about her birthday, when she'd been too ill to maintain her facade. The story of Letilia getting pregnant during Veiled Waters. The clues were there, if Donaia had only looked at them properly. But she hadn't, because Renata had so neatly lured her into biting the hook.

And because she hadn't acted alone.

"He investigated her," Donaia said, muffled by the hands she scrubbed over her face. "I had Grey look into her, at the beginning. No doubt he learned the truth—and she recruited him into her con. This whole time, they've been conspiring against me." That cut deeper than Renata's trickery. She'd known him since he was a boy. He'd been Leato's friend. She never would have expected him to be seduced by a pretty face.

But by a sharp mind? And Vraszenian blood? That mattered more to his people than registered bonds. Why wouldn't Grey side with one of his own?

Claws scrabbling on bare wood, Meatball dragged himself out from under the table and climbed into her lap—where he absolutely was not allowed, but Donaia had no heart to scold him. Draping herself over his back, she said into his fur, "No. No charges. Nadežra doesn't need more meat to chew on."

Scaperto relaxed, the mantle of Fulvet falling away to leave only the man. "Then what do you need from me? Shall I go talk to her?"

"And say what? Give her a chance to spin this all in her favor somehow?" Donaia couldn't conceive of what that might look like, but she knew all too well the persuasive power of Renata's silver tongue. In bargaining, one of the best maneuvers was to feign disinterest, luring the other party into offering more concessions. Renata had used that time and again, refusing adoption the first time Donaia offered, giving up the heir's position, suggesting she ought to leave the Traementis because of that cursed artifact.

Was that bargaining? a traitorous voice whispered, deep in Donaia's mind. *What concessions did she get in return?*

The regard of everyone significant in Nadežra, for one. Regard she could have spun into a better adoption, a prestigious marriage, even a seat on the Cinquerat.

But she'd refused those, too, instead putting together a convoluted ruse to marry her coconspirator.

Meatball whined softly as Donaia's fingers dug in, and she made herself ease off. Bile rose, bitter and acrid. "Isn't it ironic? Renata seems most like Letilia's daughter now that we've learned she isn't. The two of them deserve each other."

Giuna's hand touched hers. "I keep thinking that I should have listened to Sibiliat. She understood how Renata was playing us, if not why. She tried to warn me." At Donaia's protest, Giuna gripped her fingers. "I'm trying to keep my irritation that Sibiliat was right from clouding my judgment regarding Renata."

"And implying I shouldn't let my hatred of Letilia do the same?" Donaia asked, a wry note creeping in despite herself. When had her little girl grown into a wise woman?

A knock at the door interrupted Giuna's reply. Scaperto got up to answer it, revealing Colbrin. "My apologies, era," he said, bowing. In his gloved hands was a small tray with an envelope on it. "A letter has arrived from..."

He trailed off. How were they to refer to her now? Donaia didn't even know the liar's real name.

The thought of touching that envelope made every muscle tense, but she waved for Colbrin to come in. "Give it here. Let's see what she has to say for herself."

Suncross, Old Island: Pavnilun 3

Giuna's courage got her as far as exiting her sedan chair in Drema Square. Then, confronted with the freshly painted shop door, it failed her.

Just go inside, she told herself. *It's better than having to talk to Vargo. Or Mistress Serrado.* She at least knew Tess. Or thought she knew: Her mind still stuttered to a halt every time she remembered the months of deception.

She didn't even want to be out of the manor. It felt like everyone in Nadežra was laughing behind her back—or to her face. Donaia had cut off the money to Letilia, but even that feeble counterstrike could draw no blood; Letilia had already found fresh welcome as a guest of House Destaelio. From there, she was spreading tales far and wide.

At least Tess's shop was in Suncross, rather than the Upper Bank, like Giuna had once advocated for. The merchants here might be glancing sidelong at her, but none of them approached to deliver a witty, cutting remark.

Not yet, anyway. Giuna forced herself forward, across the plaza and through the door.

She'd never been in a proper dressmaker's shop before. At first the Traementis couldn't afford it; then they could, but they also had Tess. She knew, though, that the opening of any new establishment could be relied upon to attract curious explorers. Giuna expected to find the small interior crowded with bolts of fabric, sample garments, and people.

She found the first two, but not the third.

Tess rose from a cream-and-crimson settee striped with gold piping, a bright smile of greeting fizzling on her lips. She masked her disappointment with a subservient bob. "Alta Giuna. I didn't expect..."

"I apologize for barging in. I must have mistaken the date. I thought you'd opened already." She glanced at Pavlin, sorting notions on the counter. Notions Giuna had sorted into the wall of apothecary drawers just last week.

Make-work. When he'd expected to be busy charming customers and jotting down measurements.

"We're open," Tess said. Heaving a breath, she shouldered her sorrow and said with cheer as false as a fox's humility, "But it's early hours yet. I expect we'll be getting a rush soon."

It was seventh sun. Well past when even the nobility were out of their beds.

"What brings you here?" Tess pressed before Giuna could point out the obvious.

Fumbling for her purpose, Giuna said, "I, ah. A great many of Rena—of Ren's things are still at the manor." Her tongue tripped on the name. *Ren*, the closing signature on her letter had said. Still in Renata's elegant handwriting, but chopped down to what Giuna supposed might be the truth. "I know Master Sedge came and got the cat, but the rest... I'm not sure where to send it."

"We're at... She's at..." Tess's copper curls shook as she glanced toward the curtained workroom at the back of the shop. "Eret Vargo was kind enough to let her move back into the Westbridge townhouse."

The townhouse Giuna had helped them vacate. Where Ren and Tess had slept on the floor of the kitchen, until Giuna sent them a mattress.

Where Ren had sworn she was telling no more lies.

Giuna suspected her cheeks went redder than Tess's freckles. Before she could swallow the heat, Tess said in a rush, "I'm sorry. For my part in everything. It was a true pleasure, outfitting you. I hope someday you can forgive me enough to let me do it again." Her smile trembled. "I promise not to poke you with pins."

Ren's letter had made clear that while her supposed maid knew her scheme, all Tess wanted was a shop of her own. She'd tried to talk Ren into sharing the truth several times. Giuna wasn't quite certain she believed that; she'd seen how deep Tess's loyalty and support ran. But she *wanted* to believe it.

Clenching her fists in gloves Tess had made for her, Giuna said, "Is she here?"

Another glance at the curtain was answer enough. It twitched, and a stranger's face peered out.

A stranger's face, but familiar. And the hazel eyes were as dear as a sister's.

Or they had been.

Pavlin cleared his throat. "There's, uh. A private room in the back."

Giuna didn't want to have this conversation, not right now. But she couldn't just walk out—not when Renata, *Ren*, was right there.

"Thank you," she said curtly, and Ren faded out of her path as she swept through the curtain to the room beyond.

It held a small platform for the customer and several tuffets for sitting. Giuna perched on one; Ren shifted toward another, twitched, and reversed the half-finished bend of her knees. "Oh, sit," Giuna said wearily. "I'm not going to get a crick in my neck staring up at you."

Ren sat. Silence ensued. Giuna couldn't decide whether to be angry at that or not. She wanted her erstwhile cousin to say something, *anything*...and she also wasn't sure she wouldn't slap Ren for whatever she said.

One of them had to start. "I read your letter."

Ren's mouth worked for a moment before releasing a bitter laugh. "No idea you have how difficult it is to even speak. My voice still wants to be Renata with you."

Instead of herself. It was unutterably strange, hearing the thick, rolling sounds of a Vraszenian accent coming from that face. Giuna wanted to ask a million questions...but they were all different shapes for the same demand: for Ren's reassurance that they'd been more than marks to her. The letter said so, but what if that was another lie?

She should have rehearsed this, like when she'd told Sibiliat off. But why was it *her* responsibility to figure out the right words?

"Explain," she said curtly.

Ren blinked. "The voice, or—"

"*Yourself*," Giuna said. "I read your letter, but it was all about your life with us." Why she'd started the con—for money, pure and simple—and how that changed over time. How she should have told them sooner, and regretted that she hadn't. Nothing about herself. "I want to know who you really are...assuming I can even trust what you say."

Ren looked down at her hands, fiddling with a charm of interlaced blue-and-green cords around her wrist. "It won't justify what I did."

"I'm not looking for justification. I want to *understand*."

A slow, unsteady breath. Then Ren began to speak.

Giuna locked her hands and sat motionless through the litany: starting before Ren was born, her father a mystery and her mother an outcast, through the tumults of a Lacewater childhood. Gammer Lindworm, when she'd just been Ondrakja, the leader of a gang of thieves. Sedge's presumed death. Ganllech.

Ren paused, grimacing. "There is a lie I can drop at last. Letilia never made it to Seteris; House Viraudax is simply a name I chose at random. The letter Vargo destroyed in Whitesail presumably said they'd never heard of either of us."

At that Giuna almost spoke, but she bit down and let Ren continue.

Life in Ganllech, where Tess's skill with a needle saw her recruited into an illegal enterprise, making luxuries for the wealthy and powerful who flouted their ascetic laws in secret. Until Tess got arrested and Ren broke her out, the two of them fleeing back to Nadežra.

Here Ren stopped, looking helpless. "There—there is more. But, Giuna, some secrets I hold are not my own. I would have to get others' leave."

Giuna struck one hand against her knee. "More lies. More secrets. How can I know you're telling the truth about *that*? Every time I think I've pulled off the last mask, there's another underneath!"

"I'm the Black Rose."

Ren could have yanked the tuffet out from under Giuna, and it wouldn't have been as startling as this. She covered her face. If she didn't, she'd only end up laughing, and she couldn't do that right now. "Of course you are."

A breath of air stirred the curtain as she put her hands down, and Giuna half expected Tess and Pavlin to jump through and shout, *Surprise!* Part of her wished, with each increasingly absurd truth, that this was some aža dream. Like the one that...

"Did Leato know?"

Others words crowded behind the ones she could force out. *Did he find out your secret? Did you leave my brother to die?*

Did you kill him?

The hesitation answered her first question; the more it stretched out, the worse the others got. Then a soft rush of fabric as Ren slid from her tuffet to the floor in front of Giuna.

"It's my fault," she whispered, her elegant voice broken. "The whole Night of Hells. It happened because of me—because I was conceived on the Great Dream. Poison me with ash, and I go there in the flesh. And I dragged the others with me.

"Leato...if only I hadn't invited him to the Charterhouse. But I did, and he drank the ash, and we wound up in the nightmare. Yes, he found out the truth. He——" Ren's breath hitched, and whatever she would have said remained unspoken. "We tried to escape together. But Gammer Lindworm was waiting at the wellspring. With the zlyzen. If I hadn't let the Rook pull me out first—if I'd stayed—"

"Enough," Giuna choked through her own tears, recoiling not from Ren's guilt, but from her own. For even thinking Ren could do something like that. Yes, she'd lied. But as angry as she was at Ren, Giuna couldn't imagine her being so ruthless.

Soft. Naive. Standing, Giuna backed away from Ren's supplication. "I don't know what to believe. I don't know *how* to believe you."

Ren flinched like she'd been struck. Giuna hardened herself as much as she could. "All I know is that you hurt us. I understand that you tried to make up for it by helping. That you claim to be sorry— but I—" She spread her hands. Her *gloved* hands. For the first time, she realized Ren's were bare.

It didn't feel like intimacy between cousins. It felt like the most distancing thing in the world. Upper Bank and Lower. A sob lodged in Giuna's chest, as immovable as the Old Island cleaving the Dežera. "I don't know how to respond."

Ren's shoulders slumped. "And I know not what to say. Words cannot fix this. Perhaps nothing can."

That hurt more than anything. The idea that the bond they'd had was ruptured beyond repair. That once again, Giuna had lost family.

The silence was unbearable. Giuna pushed through the curtain, and neither Tess nor Pavlin said anything as she left.

Upper and Lower Bank: Pavnilun 4

The only warmth Grey received when he entered Traementis Manor was Meatball's eager, slobbery greeting. Even that was cut short at a sharp command from Donaia, one that made Grey flinch and Meatball whine in confusion before returning to lie at her feet.

Colbrin had shown him to her old study, the one she'd ceded to Meppe and his books. The high ceilings gave an impression of power, even as the dark wood made Grey feel like he was being crushed into submission.

And yet, the room wasn't cold as in years past. Heating numinata had replaced the old fireplace. Rich hangings from upriver Vraszan, shimmering with bronze and copper threads, warmed the wan sunlight streaming through the windows.

But nothing could warm the look Donaia fixed on him.

"We're not having this conversation here," Grey said, before she could set him down.

It broke the ice of her facade into cutting shards. "Consider yourself fortunate that we're conversing at all, Master Serrado."

This was Donaia's seat of power, steeped in two centuries of Traementis superiority. The curse of the medallions might be lifted, but places carried their own sort of gravity, wells for the memories gathered there. The Dežera was the thread stitching Vraszan together. Labyrinths were the cup that held his people's dreams. And the grounds of Traementis Manor were well-watered with the blood of vengeance against those who wronged their kin.

The words came out unplanned. "Leato always said it was impossible for us to talk as equals with the river between us."

Her flinch scraped her chair across bare wood. "That is *low*, using his name to win a point."

"Perhaps. Will you come?" He held out his hand.

She didn't take it. But she sailed past and called for Colbrin to summon a sedan chair.

Grey was well used to making the trek from Dawngate to Dusk-gate on foot. He was barely winded from his jog ahead of the sedan chair as they entered the tangle of streets on the edge between Seven Knots and Kingfisher and landed outside a run-down ostretta with a weathered wooden fish hanging from its eaves.

"The Gawping Carp?" Donaia raised a skeptical brow as she stepped out of the chair and took in their surroundings. Her gloved hand covered her nose, as though the scent of ginger, peppercorns, and other spices permeating the small plaza were unpleasant instead of merely unfamiliar.

"Leato and I often talked about bringing you here," Grey said, holding open the door. Actually, Leato had laughed at how wrong-footed and out of place his mother would be, but Grey had more faith in Donaia. She was nothing if not adaptable.

And she wasn't cruel by nature. All his hopes for this meeting hung on that.

Her clothes were plain by Upper Bank standards, just warm chocolate wool with an underdress of tea-dyed linen, but their quality still drew attention as Grey led her inside. Dvaran remembered Leato well enough to see the resemblance; he almost tipped over a pitcher of millet beer. But he said nothing as Grey led Donaia to a table—the same table he used to share with Kolya, and with Leato. A gesture from Grey brought that pitcher to their table, along with two cups and an expression that said Dvaran expected Donaia to knock the whole set to the floor in disgust.

She sat rigid until Dvaran had left. Then she said, "I hired you to *investigate* her. To tell me what I wasn't seeing."

"And I did. Everything I reported was true. I didn't know there was anything else to tell until after the Night of Hells. And by then..."

He'd struggled over it. Leato was dead; Renata was ill. The only thing keeping Donaia from collapse was her fierce need to protect what she could.

"You thought I couldn't handle it," Donaia whispered. "You thought I was too weak to know the truth."

"I wondered if the truth mattered. So often you and Leato told me that, for the Liganti, family isn't constrained by blood." He let the accusation of hypocrisy hover unspoken. "By then, you cared for Renata like family. And she cared for you the same."

"She *pretended* to."

"Is that what you believe? Or what you fear?" Grey held her gaze until the exuberant end to a round of nytsa in the far corner gave her reason to look away. "I'm not here to explain Ren's heart to you. Only to tell you that I've seen it, and I know her affection is no act."

Donaia swallowed hard. Then, in a sudden burst of motion, she poured herself a mug of beer and drained half in one go. He couldn't tell whether her grimace was for the taste, the turmoil within, or both.

Whichever it was, it left her voice unsteady. "Giuna came home from Tess's shop and spent the afternoon crying in her room. Nencoral is furious; she's been insisting Meppe go over all the books and find whatever Renata—whatever *Ren* did while she had custody of them. Tanaquis has come to the manor only once since the truth came out. That girl has torn a hole right through the middle of us, and I—I don't even know what to do about it."

The band of tension around Grey's chest eased. *This* was the Donaia he'd come to care for: not the vengeful Liganti noble out to make others pay for her humiliation, but the warmhearted, steel-spined woman who guarded her family's heart because it was her own.

He poured some beer for himself and curled his hands around the mug. "And what has Ren done, since she came into your lives? Ignoring the lie or the truth of her birth, what has she done to the Traementis?" *For* the Traementis.

Donaia pressed her lips together before answering, as if to make sure only the right words came out. "You're talking about our fortunes. And Indestor. And the curse. But—"

Dipping her chin low didn't hide the tear that fell to stain the table's battered surface. Almost inaudibly, she said, "Giuna told me. About the Night of Hells. About Leato's death."

Grey watched the elders at their nytsa game until his own tears eased enough to let him speak. Ren blamed herself...but wasn't Grey more at fault? She'd done everything she could to free Leato from that nightmare. He was the one who'd chosen to save the stranger in front of him before going back for his friend.

The urge to tell Donaia about the Rook choked him as thick as the tears. If it wouldn't just muddy things worse, he might have. It wasn't like the hood's demand for secrecy bound him anymore.

Instead he asked, "Do you think she's at fault?"

"Yes. And no." Donaia gave up on the pretense that she wasn't crying and swiped at her cheeks, salt staining her gloves. "I want to blame *someone*. I know Mettore and that Gammer Lindworm hag were responsible...but I didn't get to *do* anything about it. I only found out after they were dead, and it was too late for revenge."

Grey's jaw tensed, but Donaia went on before he could say anything. "You don't have to tell me that isn't fair. I know Ren didn't mean to get him killed—and now it at least makes sense, why she's always blamed herself. Why she's tried so hard to help us. She's trying to make up for his death."

No amount of help could ever do that, and they both knew it. But that wasn't how such scales got balanced. Grey said, "Because she *does* care. About you, and Giuna, and the Traementis."

Donaia drank more, as if to buy herself a delay before answering. When she put the cup down, it thunked hard against the wood. "Caring or not, how can we go on associating with her, now that everyone knows she's—"

"Vraszenian?"

It earned him a hard stare. "A con artist."

That was true. But they both knew it wasn't the whole truth. "Tell me honestly. If Ren truly had been a Seterin woman, or Liganti—still a con artist, still lying to you, but not Vraszenian— would you be this torn right now?"

It was a step too far, pushing Donaia when she felt herself the wronged party. She rose fast enough to jar the table, and Grey had to catch the pitcher before it canted over. "I have never... *never*," she spat, color high. "Didn't I treat you and your brother fairly? Wasn't I happy to accept you when you won the trial? I won't try to defend my fellow nobles, but I am *not* like them."

No, she wasn't like Mettore, trying to destroy the wellspring so Nadežra would no longer be a holy place for Vraszenians. She wasn't like the nobles who called his people "gnats" and passed laws to keep them poor. She'd helped him and Kolya, when they first came to the city.

But she didn't see the little points of friction. Giving clothes to Alinka—clothes in the *Liganti* style. The times when she said to Leato, "We aren't *Vraszenian*," as if that would be an awful fate. She'd given Kolya a job, because he was a desperate teenager with a traumatized younger brother in tow... but until Ren took charge of Traementis business, how many contracts had the house extended to Vraszenian merchants and artisans?

Donaia had gotten her voice under control. "I'm not certain what you hoped to prove by bringing me here, but I don't think there's anything more for us to say."

Smoothing her skirts, she pulled out her purse and marched to the counter, where she plunked down an entire forro. To the wide-eyed Dvaran she said, "Thank you for keeping my son out of trouble. Your beer is surprisingly palatable. If you would be so good as to have someone call me a chair?"

Grey waved Dvaran off before he could inform Donaia there was nobody to send. "I'll do it."

The crisp air outside was a relief, and the bearers who'd brought Donaia from the Upper Bank had wisely decided there was more money to be had in waiting to carry her back than trying to find a rich fare here. Donaia emerged a few moments later, her cheeks drained of their livid color. Grey wondered what Dvaran had said to her, in those few moments she'd remained behind.

"Be well, Era Traementis," he said, bowing. Which might not be the right thing to say, but formality was better than tongue-tied, heartsore silence.

When Donaia was gone, he went back into the Gawping Carp for another drink.

Isla Prišta, Westbridge: Pavnilun 5

Ren didn't need Tess to answer the door anymore. She was at her shop in Suncross anyway, working on a commission for a merchant who cared less about social politics than about getting an elegant waistcoat, and Grey was at Alinka's. When the knock came, Ren was the only one at home.

Being back in the Westbridge townhouse was unspeakably strange. Not because she was sleeping on the floor of the kitchen again; no, all the furniture was uncovered, and Vargo had supplied coal to tide them over until he could inscribe some numinata for the hearths. But this had been the one place in Nadežra where she could be herself, back when everyone but Tess and Sedge saw only the mask. Now she was herself, here and everywhere, and she opened her own door.

Tanaquis breezed inside without even a greeting. Rain beaded her dark hair and the sleeves of pewter wool that covered her from shoulder to glove-tip. "I've tracked down the identity of Ninat's former holder. It's much easier when you have the man in front of you—his corpse, anyway, and everything he had with him. His name was Stezze Chetoglio. I presume you don't want everyone in his register dying, so I'll need a nine-card pattern from you."

It didn't sound like the brusqueness of someone forced into Ren's unwelcome presence by business—more like Tanaquis's usual efficiency. But Ren hadn't seen her since before the third trial began, hadn't had any chance to speak to her about what happened.

Ren shut the door, sinking the front hall into dimness. "Tanaquis. Hello. I—I owe you an apology." And so much more...but her conversation with Giuna had proved that nothing could ever be enough.

Tanaquis clicked her tongue in annoyance. "You did waste my time, making me calculate a false birth chart. Maybe two, if you lied the second time as well—yes? Then you should give me the real date so I can do your chart properly. It'll bother me if I don't." She brushed the rain from her sleeves with brisk strokes. "Honestly, it explains so many oddities—like your skill with pattern. Is your parlour usable? Giuna said something about you sleeping on the floor."

Bemused, Ren led her into the parlour. Somehow a few short months of living at Traementis Manor left her half expecting someone to show up with tea. Making some would be a welcome distraction for her hands, but Tanaquis would get impatient. "You aren't angry?"

"Why, because you kept secrets? You're the one who drew The Mask of Mirrors for my pattern and told me that some secrets *ought* to be kept." Tanaquis settled herself on the couch. "You knew people wouldn't understand. I understand *that* very well."

Just as Tanaquis had known people wouldn't understand if she told them the Praeteri's eisar numinatria drew on Primordial power. The comparison made Ren's skin crawl. *Nothing I did is* that *bad. Is it?*

"Why you did it in the first place is beyond me," Tanaquis went on, "but it hardly matters. I'm mostly glad that it won't get in the way of our research anymore. Whatever knowledge you've been hiding, you can put it all on the table now. Along with cards, please—nine of them."

Letting out a laughing breath, Ren said, "Let me get my deck."

"No, use mine." Tanaquis pulled it out. "I'll need to take the cards with me, and it's better if you don't come. Mede Chetoglio thinks you have something to do with his cousin's death."

"What? Why? Think you that Stezze told them about Ghiscolo's ritual?"

Tanaquis examined her glove, then the edges of the deck. "No, it seems he fled afterward; no one in his house had seen him since Canilun. The evidence in the Depths suggests he'd been hiding there for some time. But he was found by some of your volti—on the night your true identity was revealed, no less. And everyone thinks the whole trial was rigged to begin with... I suppose they're not wrong."

"*You* rigged it," Ren said, seating herself across from Tanaquis. "No coincidence was it that you placed the victory token behind the ward. Very few could pass that test, and only two among the volti."

For a moment Tanaquis looked taken aback. Then she ducked her head. "All right, it's true. Though I thought it was Vargo you intended to win."

"He was the decoy." The deck was slightly damp from Tanaquis's glove, but not so much that Ren couldn't shuffle. "House Chetoglio...they trade primarily in spices. I wonder if they're poisoners. Ninat's influence will have bled into them somehow." Quaniet Scurezza must have had a source for the nuts she used to kill her entire family, though the Chetoglio weren't in the Praeteri. "Stezze I know nothing of."

"He was usually overseas on family business. That's why nobody recognized him."

Ren snorted despite herself. "Lucky for Ghiscolo that he was in town when the ritual began. Can you imagine us standing there for a month, waiting for Stezze to sail back?" She shuffled and dealt the cards, trying not to think about the oddity of laying a present and a future for a man who was dead. But a nine-card spread was appropriate for Ninat.

"Your Great Dream is coming up soon, isn't it?" Tanaquis said when she was done. "Clearly the wellspring is linked to how pattern works—maybe even the source of it all. I'll need to arrange to drink its waters; then maybe I'll finally understand."

Habit made Ren swallow down the response she wanted to make. Then she remembered she wasn't Renata anymore and could speak her mind. "Tanaquis, for my people there is no holier day. Many you will anger if you demand the right to sip from Ažerais's waters simply to satisfy your curiosity."

"Perhaps you could bring me a bottle—no? That's not how this works?" Tanaquis brooded. "I could understand *so much more*, though. And isn't that a good thing? A Liganti woman understanding your traditions?"

"You have more respect for them than many Liganti," Ren admitted, swallowing the addition of *though that's faint praise*. "But trust me when I say this is *not* the way. Argentet charges us for the right to visit, and entrance is limited. You would displace someone else."

Tanaquis perked up. "Then I'll talk to Iascat. And in the meanwhile, you and I can work together. I might be restricted from doing experimental numinatria, but technically this would be experimental... textilatria? What a terrible word. And it would be a welcome break from thinking about the medallions all the time. Alsius refuses to discuss the Primordial aspects of their power—Vargo says he degenerates into sputtering whenever I start speculating as to how they were made—and my own thoughts are going around in circles. New avenues. That's what I need!"

A smile as bright and fragile as blown glass accompanied her words. Ren remembered how badly Tanaquis had doubted herself after Iridet fired her—and now she held the Ninat medallion. The numen of endings, of the dissolution of the self back into the Lumen.

It was a desire that Tanaquis, with her endless curiosity to know the cosmos, would be particularly weak to. New beginnings might be her way of counteracting its draw. Ren bit down on the urge to ask if Tanaquis was taking appropriate precautions against the medallion. After all, Tanaquis had designed most of those precautions in the first place.

"I'll help however I can. But truly, I've told you most of what I know. Perhaps another szorsa you could consult—though the one I'm thinking of is... not available." They'd had no word of Mevieny apart from what the Kiralič said, nor even any hint of activity from Branek. Vargo had attempted to find out where the Anduske went after the Cut Ears took back their base, but with no luck. There was simply too much city for Branek to hide in while he plotted his next move. Unfortunately, Koszar's own next move relied on finding Mevieny: Judgment by ordeal used to be the special purview of the Ižranyi. With the clan gone, only their speaker could call an ordeal.

Ren gave Tanaquis the cards, and her cousin rose to go. "How inconvenient that you're over here in Westbridge; I'll waste so much time crossing the river. Perhaps Vargo has another townhouse I can rent. He's banned me from visiting him outside of daylight hours, did you know?"

Ren did know; Vargo had complained after Tanaquis knocked on his door at seventh earth for the third time in a week. "You can visit me at any time. The sooner we destroy the medallions, the better." She grimaced, thinking of Tricat hidden in the wine cellar, under the flagstone where she used to keep her pattern deck. Grey's Quinat was upstairs, as if distance between them might help. "At least we needn't worry about two medallions in one register, now."

Tanaquis waved this away. "Yes, protections around our names will be sufficient. There are some inherent challenges, given the resonance between Tricat and Ninat and the Traementis history with the former, but I don't expect any problems."

Not even Tanaquis could be *that* oblivious. "I meant now that I've been struck from the register. I presume you were able to uncurse the others with the original cards." She'd braced herself for the blow of the announcement, but Donaia hadn't even paid her the courtesy of informing her—not that she deserved such courtesy.

"Donaia considered it," Tanaquis said. "But she hasn't asked me to remove you."

That stole the breath from Ren's lungs. *I'm still in the register?* The scroll itself held very little significance for her; she hadn't grown up with that as the defining mark of family. But to Donaia, that *did* matter.

It wasn't forgiveness. It might only be that Donaia had decided not to strip Ren of the legal rights she'd gained, a tiny shred of protection in return for what she'd contributed.

But maybe forgiveness wasn't impossible.

"And I'm glad of it," Tanaquis said, sounding a little surprised. "What you saw when you patterned me...My original family was very different. But I like you, even with all those lies muddying the water. It would be a pity if you had to go away."

Ren swallowed. "I'll still be here, Tanaquis, whether a register joins us or not."

Tanaquis straightened, her quicksilver thoughts already moving on from such personal matters. "Come by my townhouse tomorrow. I want to know everything about you and pattern—now that it will be the truth."

11

The Face of Ages

The charm around Ren's wrist was interlinked coin knots in blue and green, and an odd warmth touched Grey's heart every time it peeked out her sleeve.

Vargo and Ren, bound by knot oath. Once he would have laughed at the idea; once he'd stood in the Seven Knots labyrinth and listened to the Black Rose swear vengeance against Vargo for his betrayal. But he couldn't deny that the man had become a true friend. And that was something Ren needed—not just right now, but in her life.

She wasn't the only one. *Neither of us should carry two.*

That moment in the Depths, Grey hadn't been able to spare much thought for Vargo's revelation. He'd been too busy worrying about Ninat. Then had come Letilia's strike, and he'd been busy taking care of Ren. Not until later had he been able to think about what to do with Vargo knowing, and by then the answer was clear: nothing.

The Rook would have been furious. But the Rook was broken. And time and time again, Vargo had acted to protect Grey. Saving his life. Helping in the trials. Keeping his secrets.

Not just about the Rook, but any other secrets Grey might have. In a brief visit to the Westbridge townhouse, Vargo had mentioned that the Kiralič was looking for him with questions about Laročja Szerado. "If you'd prefer, I can say I don't know where you are," Vargo offered. "Or I can arrange neutral ground."

"Here is fine," Grey said. "If my grandmother is working with Branek...yes. He and I should talk."

But it wasn't only the Kiralič who showed up. Grey did his best to ignore the assessing looks from Idusza and Koszar as he led them into the parlour, where Ren awaited them stiff-backed and ready to pour tea.

"Ažerais bless the road that brought you safely to us," she said, rising with Renata's grace even as she spoke the formal Vraszenian greeting.

Touching his hand to his brow, the Kiralič replied, "And the river that gives us life."

Some of the formality bled out of Ren's posture as she turned to the two Anduske, replaced by something Grey had seen far too much of lately: the guilty slump that awaited a blow. "Please believe...I regret abusing your trust."

Koszar took a seat, toying with the head of his cane. "When offered our knot, you refused. Is this why?" His wave took in Ren and the townhouse, all the parts that weren't the Arenza they'd known.

At Ren's nod, he expelled a hard breath. "No trust was abused. You gave no oath to share your secrets; you owe them not to us."

Idusza hadn't yet seated herself. She remained in the doorway, arms crossed, as if the room held a dead rat. "What of our first meeting? Was that truly Ažerais working through you, or only tricks to fool a simple woman?"

A fair question, but Grey's heart ached to see Ren hunch deeper, a turtle without her shell. "Tricks," she admitted. "I approached you because I wanted to know what Mezzan was doing."

"But I broke with Mezzan. And yet you remained."

"Yes," Ren murmured, not looking at Idusza. She'd braided her hair, along the sides of her head and joining at the back; one hand toyed with the tail now. "By then..."

By then she cared. As with the Traementis. Grey bit down on the urge to speak; his intervention wouldn't help.

Idusza sauntered over to loom above Ren. "When I realized *you* were the cheese-eater whose shrieking brought Mezzan low, I gave myself hiccups with laughing. And I thought, *this* is a woman I would drink with. You always seemed too mystical and untouchable before. No fun." A wry smile peeked through. She spat into her hand and held it for Ren to take. "Friends?"

The helpless relief in Ren's face as she looked up was like a rainstorm to break summer's heat. She spat in her palm and gripped Idusza's hand, and Grey tried not to visibly sag as the tension eased.

"We came not for this," the Kiralič said, only a little reproving. "We must speak of your grandmother, Gru—"

"Grey," he said before the Kiralič could resurrect a name he dearly wished he could bury. "I am called Grey now. And I know not what I can tell you about my grandmother. No words or news have I exchanged with my kin since Kolya and I left."

"I seek not news, but history." The Kiralič accepted the teacup Ren offered, gazing into its contents as if they might hold answers. "Szorsa Laročja...ordinarily it would not occur to me to question her wisdom. This path she guides Branek down, though..."

Ren passed Grey a teacup. It warmed away some of the coldness in his hands—some. "You think I might know why she's doing this."

The Kiralič grimaced, looking far older than his years. "My heart says the path they walk cannot be right. And yet."

The mirror surface of Grey's tea rippled until he set it down. The Kiralič was his own clan elder; he owed the man an honest answer. And he had no loyalty to a cruel old woman, nor had he ever hidden his disdain for the type of szorsa she exemplified.

But that disdain was the mere scratch of a thorn. The truth behind it was a cut to the bone.

A hand slipped into his, warm and dry, glove-free forevermore. Ren had finally embraced her past. He couldn't run from his.

"She told me the cards spoke truly to her only once," he said, hoping they wouldn't ask when. "Perhaps that has changed since I left. But before then, every pattern she read, *she* was the weaver. Always to serve her own ends, to bend others to her will."

Idusza made a small, satisfied noise, as if he'd only confirmed what she thought. The Kiralič shook his head. "For a szorsa to heed not the wisdom of Ažerais...worse, to never receive it, and instead present her own false guidance as truth...please believe, I question not your word. When your brother took you away, when Jakoslav found himself suddenly without sons, we knew something was fouler than we'd realized. Even so...convincing others will be difficult."

Grey squeezed Ren's hand—a question—and got an answering squeeze in turn. "Would the word of a true szorsa convince them? One conceived on the Great Dream, who with the turn of a card can change fates and lift curses, who has walked in Ažerais's Dream? Because you have one here."

The Kiralič eyed their clasped hands, brow rising in skepticism. "She admitted her skills were trickery."

"I trust the pattern she laid for me," Koszar said.

Ren gave him a fleeting, grateful smile. "I cannot pretend I have never used the cards to trick. But I also lay them true. Though whether any will heed me, who can say. After all, I am a known con artist...and only half-Vraszenian."

Her gaze challenged the Kiralič to deny that concern. Instead he did her the courtesy of nodding. "Yes. It casts doubt—all the more so when you lay your word against that of a respected szorsa."

One from a kureč that prized the purity of its blood. There were cousins in Grey's lineage who'd married outsiders—any kureč that traded along the Dawn and Dusk Roads did the same—but thanks to his grandmother, the children of those unions remained on the edges of the Szerado. She was proud to declare her ancestry entirely Vraszenian, right back to the fall of Fiavla.

Yet it was Ren, half-Vraszenian, who was the Black Rose.

Grey knew why she didn't fling that at the Kiralič. The Black Rose was a card up their sleeve, something they could possibly use against Branek; revealing her identity now would undercut its power. Ren merely said, "You may judge my skill for yourself. Shall I pattern you?"

The Kralič smiled. "Perhaps someday. But I would rather see what you advise for the situation."

"Very well." Cards in hand, she paused. "If you mind not...I would like to try a different spread. An older one, the seven-card wheel."

Grey didn't expect Koszar's sudden interest. "Where learned you that spread?"

"You've heard of such a thing?" the Kralič asked, frowning.

"The old szorsa in my kureč laid it sometimes, before..." Koszar swiped his eyes before the tears could fall. "Never have I known anyone else to lay cards like that. Learned you this from an Andrejek?"

Grey suspected Ren had suggested the wheel to flaunt her knowledge in the face of doubt. Now, having unexpectedly reminded Koszar of his lost kureč, she looked regretful. "I know not if she was Andrejek—I met her in the dream. She used it to pattern me, when I sought to right an imbalance there."

Fortunately, no one asked what the imbalance was. Eyebrows rising, the Kralič said, "I would very much like to see this spread."

Ren recited the prayers as she shuffled, invoking each clan ancestor in turn. Then she laid six cards in a ring, with a seventh in the center. "One card for each clan, in pairs to recall the twins. First come Meszaros and Stretsko: the Horse for what you have, resources and allies, and the Rat for what stands in your way, obstacles and enemies."

They all leaned forward as she turned over the first two cards. Touching the first, Ren glanced at Koszar. "The Mask of Hollows was the good of your own future. Here it returns, with the same meaning. The common people of Nadežra are not merely a prize to be seized; they can be allies. They *must* be allies, if you wish to succeed. If proof you seek that Branek's murderous plan is not the way, Kralič, here it is."

The ziemič looked neutral, but Grey suspected that masked wariness. It was almost too convenient, the card from Koszar's own pattern turning up first—but Grey had no doubt Ren had dealt honestly. This was Ažerais at work, not manipulation.

"For obstacles," Ren said, "The Face of Light. Almost a Liganti card, is it not? Rationality, logic, like their Lumen and numinatria. No surprise that they stand in the way."

And the medallions, too, Grey thought.

Ren went on. "But these cards go two and two, good and ill. Veiled, this speaks of logic's limitations. We cannot simply reason our way to better days; passions run high. But too high, and you may ruin your own hopes."

Or worse, think that passion and hope were good substitutes for pragmatism. Many attempts to retake the city had used those for fuel, but people couldn't eat passion, couldn't use hope as shelter or protection for their children. They were wildfires that scorched the earth. The medallions weren't the only reason Liganti rule had lasted so long.

Grey shook off such thoughts as Ren reached for the next two cards. "Owl and Spider, Anoškin and Varadi. The wisdom to remember, and the question to ask."

Two more Faces, of Crowns and of Weaving. Ren tapped the former. "The proper balance between ruler and subject. A thing Nadežra has not seen in centuries...but anarchy is no better. Has Branek any plan for what happens if he succeeds? It is not enough simply to take the island, or even the city; if you tear down the Cinquerat, in its place you must build something else. And The Face of Weaving..."

She was too disciplined to let any hint of smugness show. "The card of community," she said. "The question is, who is the community? Who belongs, and who does not?"

With his grandmother so fresh in his thoughts, Grey had to speak up. "I know not what cards Laročja has laid for Branek. If pattern gave her this one, though, she would use it to demand a purge of those who belong not."

Dull fury burned in his veins as he looked at the Kiralič. "But has Nadežra not always been a port, and the place where the Dawn and Dusk Roads meet? Always there have been others here. They, too, are part of the city."

"Peace," the Kiralič said softly. "Let your szorsa finish."

The next pair was Two Roads Cross and Storm Against Stone, for the Dvornik and the Kiraly. Grey was almost relieved they weren't Faces and Masks; after the first four, it would have been an unnerving sign of divine attention. "The Fox for your reward," Ren said. "A chance to act—to make a difference. And the Old Island is where roads meet. But the Raccoon for the risk you take..."

Grey suspected only he saw her minute shudder, because only he knew the cause. During the Night of Hells, that card—Storm Against Stone—had brought Ren into contact with an echo of A'ash. The overwhelming power of a Primordial.

But it could mean more than one thing at a time. "This will unleash terrible force," Ren said. "You cannot ride such power; in its rampage it will crush you. Take care lest this plunge all Vraszan back into war."

When no one responded, she said, "And the Dreamweaver, the hub on which all else turns."

Her fingers faltered as she turned over A Spiraling Fire. Two figures silhouetted before a campfire, closely embracing; dancing the oszefon, Grey imagined. It was the card of exertion, of passion, which perhaps echoed the warning from The Face of Light—but it seemed an odd choice.

Ren also frowned as she stared at it. "This...seems not right."

Her words made Grey tense. "As if someone interfered?" He didn't know who could have. No one else had touched the deck, and Ren wouldn't manipulate the cards. Not after what happened when Grey did that.

"No," Ren said, but she didn't sound certain. "It...I cannot explain it. This is not the right card, not the true hub. Yet I know not why."

It was the sort of show the frauds put on, making it seem like the querent's reading was divinely touched. But that usually led to a declaration of some wondrous meaning, and Ren only looked confused. Nor would she choose that route this time—not when she was trying to prove her gift was worth heeding.

"Perhaps it speaks to events we see not," the Kiralič said, watching Ren rather than the cards. "Or to Laročja's influence?"

Something flashed in her eyes, there and then gone. She swept up the cards. "I think not, but neither can I say what it is. Apologies. You wished to know if Ažerais speaks through me. This is the only answer I can give."

The Kiralič waited as she recited the closing prayer. Then he said, "Your willingness to admit doubt speaks well of you . . . though when it comes to convincing others, certainty would be of more use. I will think on what you've said, Szorsa Arenza."

For him to address her that way was a compliment, but Ren's smile was still brittle. "Call me Ren, Kiralič."

Grey held his questions until the others had left. Then he said, "That final card . . ."

She sighed, sagging against the closed door. "Truly, I know not. I wondered if it might signal Parma, with the Noctat medallion, but . . ." Ren shook her head, confused and annoyed. "This will bother me."

She only meant the confusing final card, the reading that felt incomplete, but her words sent a shiver of unease through Grey.

Ren had sensed A'ash on the Night of Hells, the storm battering against the stone of Ažerais's presence. She'd run afoul of the Primordial again when she ventured into the dream in search of the szorsa.

And Ren herself held Tricat. While also being connected, through her gift, to Ažerais.

What if the Primordial's influence was seeping through? What if the stone was crumbling in the face of the storm?

"We'll figure it out," he said, gathering Ren into his arms to keep them from shaking. And hoped that for once, *he* had the gift to tell the future true.

Lacewater, Old Island: Pavnilun 7

"So she's really dead?" Esmierka asked Tess over the rim of a chipped stoneware mug still bearing the potter's fingerprints. "En't coming back like bad zrel in the morning?"

The floor of the wharfside ostretta crunched with the broken remains of shells, the air redolent with brine and smoke. The Salty Shucker served the sort of fare they'd only dreamed of back in their Finger days, when the Lacewater shoreline was Cut Ears territory and off-limits to hungry little hands. When a runner brought Esmierka's lunch invitation to Tess's shop like they were both fine ladies, it amused Tess to suggest the dive clinging like a barnacle to the rim of Turtle Lagoon.

"Turned into a hag and ripped apart by zlyzen," Tess said, warming her wind-chapped hands around her own mug. In the deeper parts of winter, she mourned how the noble penchant for gloves meant common Nadežrans sneered at them as affectations, even when wearing them was only sensible.

Esmierka sat back and rubbed her belly, full of river mussels steamed in garlic and wine. "I'd buy you lunch every Tsapekny just to hear the tale again." Her smile stretched the burn scar Ondrakja had given her.

"I'd let you, just to tell it again." Tess's mug knocked against Esmierka's with a dull clunk. "I only wish I'd seen it firsthand."

"I'll just have to talk to the one who did."

Tess's gut rolled like she'd eaten a bad mussel. Esmierka hadn't mentioned Ren before. She'd assumed they were leaving that dog buried. Tucking her hands in her lap, she said softly, "I'm happy to strike palms and call friends with you, but if you mean to harm my sister..."

"Harm?" Esmierka spat onto the floor. "*That* for Ondrakja. Bitch burned my face just because I had the guts to cut myself out. She was never nice, but she got worse, long before she was Gammer Lindworm. Ren was just a kid, doing what she had to. Protecting herself—and protecting you. Fuck anybody who blames her for that."

Ren blames herself, Tess thought, remembering her sister standing there and letting Simlin hit her. But maybe that had finally leached the poison out of her heart, because Ren had a new knot charm on her wrist now.

"In fact—" Esmierka leaned forward, voice low. "Suilis is out now. Untied herself after that business with the Acrenix, left Nadežra with her brother. The Oyster Crackers could use more people. If Ren's hard up, I could talk the others around to letting her in. You too, if you're game for it. You go into houses for fittings and the like, right? You could feed us information. Suilis already told us everything there is to know about the Traementis, down to the color of their smalls, but there's more pickings in the Pearls than one noble house."

Giuna, standing inside the door of the Suncross shop, her lip trembling when Tess couldn't hold her gaze. The image had burned itself into Tess's mind, and it flared up again now.

Ren might have told the lie, but Tess had supported it.

"Steer clear of the Traementis," she said. "They have dogs. And if I learn even *one* of those has been poisoned or drugged, I'll be cracking oysters instead of mussels."

Esmierka cocked an eyebrow. "Is it only the dogs you're worried about, or their owners as well? I'd think you'd want payment for what happened."

"Only one I want to pay isn't part of the family anymore," Tess muttered. Then, as Esmierka's other brow went up, she added, "Letilia, not Ren."

Esmierka lounged back in her chair, smirking. "That can also be arranged."

Tess had only been speaking in jest. "But—"

"She's holed up with the Destaelio now, right? Hard house to get information on. Those daughters are fiercely loyal. Servants are well-paid. And the only place with more numinatrian defenses is

Simendis's manor—but only thing he's got is prudish opinions, and who'd steal those when he passes 'em out for free?"

Prudishness. Like the austerity laws in Ganllech—the ones their nobles flouted in secret.

"Forget the Destaelio for now," Tess said, an idea taking shape. "Can you find me a dog breeder?"

Esmierka huffed. "You want a mutt, I can get you one in the alley outside."

Tess swatted her arm. "His name's Rhuelt Glastyn. He bred two of his braches to Meatball—the Traementis dog. I don't know if he's in Nadežra anymore; he may have gone back to Ganllech." Donaia would know, but she'd never tell Tess.

"All right, you've got my curiosity." Esmierka leaned forward again. "What's important about a Ganllechyn dog breeder?"

"Nothing," Tess said. "But the dogs he breeds are fine hounds— princely. He talks to nobles. And I bet he'd have gossip on why a certain noblewoman fled Ganllech."

The Rotunda, Eastbridge: Pavnilun 9

Donaia would frankly have preferred to pull out her own toenails than go to House Coscanum's fete at the Rotunda. She knew what would happen: people whispering behind their gloves, casting sidelong looks at the members of House Traementis, then swanning up to offer some comment, sugar-sweet on top and poison underneath. *We hope the turn in Traementis fortunes doesn't prove as false as the woman who turned them,* or something as elegantly cruel.

But pulling out her toenails would do nothing for House Traementis's public image. And Donaia refused to add "cowardice" to "foolishness" in the list of barbs people could hurl her way. So she mustered the paltry ranks of House Traementis—minus Tanaquis, who never came to these things, and Nencoral, whom Donaia suspected would be resigning her place in the register as soon as

Fintenus accepted her back—and marched them to the Rotunda, where the Upper Bank had gathered to celebrate the elevation of Agniet Cercel Coscani to the Cinquerat.

It was a belated and clumsy event by Faella's standards, but the Traementis weren't the only ones humiliated by Ren's unmasking. Faella had shown the girl too much favor to escape the mud. But House Coscanum held a seat in the Cinquerat now, and this was a very pointed reminder that they were too influential to be snubbed.

"Orrucio's here, and Civrin Isorran," Giuna said, waving tentatively at them. Both were new acquaintances, made this past year as she came out of her shell—*as Renata coaxed her out*, Donaia thought sourly. "Do you mind if I go say hello?"

Civrin Isorran, whose mother was the Vigil's new high commander, under Alta Agniet. Those without the connections to approach the Coscanum were flocking to the Isorran instead. A school of razorteeth, and Giuna wanted to dive in.

"Do you need my permission?" Donaia snapped, then grimaced at Giuna's start. "I'm sorry. Go on. Idaglio, what do you think of the new mural?"

While Giuna flitted off to discover whether her friends would still talk to her, Idaglio and Meppe distracted Donaia with a critique of the rice fields and orchards painted along the band beneath the etched glass dome. A display of Era Destaelio's deep pockets and questionable taste, but there was no savor in mocking it. Even with Idaglio netting a few of his friends into the conversation, Donaia was all too aware of the whispers, the sidelong glances. *Damn that girl for putting us in this position.*

Then a hatefully familiar laugh echoed off the high vault of the dome.

"Oh, the *Rotunda*! I was *so* sad to have missed the Autumn Gloria this year. It really is one of the best events Nadežra has to offer. I have such delightful memories of this place—you know, one time my father paid for the entire stock of brocade a merchant brought from Plectia. All for me, and I gave bolts as gifts to my friends. You *must* remember that, Cibrial; yours was that lovely pale green with pomegranates."

Donaia remembered, if only because a silk faille of golden wheat sheaves that was supposed to become her wedding surcoat had wound up in Letilia's hands. The brat decided it made her look sallow, and left it as a feast for moths in the back of her wardrobe. Gut clenching like she'd drunk wine gone sour twenty-some years before, Donaia focused on the potted persimmon trees arching overhead and pretended she couldn't hear that spine-scraping voice moving closer. And closer.

Until something warm and sticky sloshed down her arm and dripped onto the bronze surcoat Tess had created for Renata's belated adoption ball.

"Oh, I'm *so* sorry. I didn't see you there," Letilia said, her smile as cloying as the mulled wine trickling into Donaia's glove. "Brown is such a dull color, you practically blend in with the walls."

"It's our family's tradition," Donaia snapped back. "But then, you never had much respect for that, did you?"

Letilia tittered into her glove, glancing at Cibrial as if inviting her to share the joke. A whole cluster of Destaelio cousins stood with them, sailing through the Rotunda like a cargo ship full of wealth. "How very rich, coming from the woman who sullied Traementis tradition by adopting a *Vraszenian*. But you didn't know, did you?"

And you played along with the lie. Donaia bit down before that response could escape. It was just asking for Letilia to lay a pitying hand on her arm and say she'd been trying to protect Donaia's family from humiliation.

"Not just a Vraszenian, but a *thief*," Letilia went on. "She stole all my jewelry when she fled, you know. Anything she left with you, I want back; those things are rightfully mine."

"The only thing I received from her was my mother's ring, which *you* stole when you abandoned your family." Flicking droplets of wine back at Letilia, Donaia said, "No wonder everyone believed you could be mother and daughter. One thief looks much like another."

Letilia hissed like an outraged goose. "You dare accuse *me*? Why, I have never been so insulted!"

Smooth as silk, Cibrial said, "You deserve satisfaction, Alta Letilia."

"A duel!" Letilia cried. "It's my right as a noblewoman! But whoever will stand on my behalf?"

"I'd be happy to offer the services of my duelist," Cibrial said. A wave of her hand brought a thin-faced, fair-haired man up to her side.

Theatrical outrage transformed to theatrical delight. "Mede Kaineto! Is it true you were the Wave Volto in the trials? I *so* enjoyed watching you defeat your dueling opponents. Very beautifully done, and so quick."

Kaineto bowed with one hand to his chest, in a bad mimicry of Seterin style. "I would have made it past the second trial, too, except the Raven Volto cheated—with that criminal's help. Now that we know the truth, I'm not surprised. But the entire city should be grateful to you for exposing those charlatans. My steel is yours."

They'd drawn an audience, and far too late, Donaia realized a confrontation must have been Letilia's plan. Before Leato's death, he'd borne steel for them. Then, at Renata's encouragement, it was Grey Serrado. It was still legally Grey; she hadn't broken his contract. But if she sent for him . . .

Letilia simpered, laying a hand over the one Kaineto had placed on his hilt. "It may stay sheathed today. It seems Era Traementis has no one willing to back her insult or defend her thievery."

"You're mistaken, Aunt Letilia," Giuna said, pushing through the crowd ringing them. Behind her came another girl, tall and lanky, with sun-burnished skin and dark hair triple-braided along the sides of her head.

Letilia looked ready to spit acid at the interruption. "Who's this?"

The tall girl bowed, dark eyes bright as though she found all of this vastly amusing. "Kasienka Ryvček."

A wave of murmurs swelled at the famous name attached to an unfamiliar face. Kasienka's crescent grin widened. "Yes, yes, everyone knows my aunt. My skill is not yet so sharp. But good enough, I hope, for Era Traementis?"

Donaia didn't have to hear the whispers to know what everyone would think. Why did Vraszenians keep popping up around her house like jack moles? Traementis was one of the oldest families. *Perhaps they've sunk too far into the mud*, the whispers said. *Perhaps they've forgotten their Liganti roots.*

A different voice drowned them out. *If Ren truly had been a Seterin woman, or Liganti, would you be this torn right now?*

That memory doused her ire like water over a sot's head. Donaia said, "Everyone knows and admires your aunt. I trust your blade to defend our name."

Like a song changing key, the excitement of a verbal spat gave way to the excitement of a public duel. Scaperto took charge, looking guilty for not having found Donaia faster. The open space at the center of the Rotunda made an ideal ring; before long, Kasienka and Kaineto faced each other with their coats shucked, swinging their arms to loosen the muscles. Donaia stood at the edge, twisting her sticky gloves into knots under her surcoat. To Giuna she whispered, "How do you know this girl?"

"We're—friends," Giuna murmured back. "We met at the dueling trial."

Before Donaia could ask more, the blades were out, the opening Uniat and Tuat exchanged, and the duel began.

Kasienka hardly seemed to be taking it seriously. "You know," she said, her sword flickering, "both the Liganti and Vraszenian styles have their strengths. For example, your straight-armed stance presents constant threat." She faded back, away from that threat. "On the other hand—"

Donaia couldn't quite see what happened. Kaineto's blade suddenly dipped, and he retreated in a hurry. "Against your stance, transport works well," Kasienka said, grinning.

"I'm not here for a lesson," Kaineto spat.

"Oh? I like learning from my opponents. From you, though, I think there is not much to learn. So if you have no interest, let us not waste our time." Kasienka made a careless-seeming thrust, much too distant to threaten Kaineto's body.

But he yelped, and his sword clattered to the marble floor.

"That's a disarm *and* first blood," Kasienka said, as red stained his white glove. "But I suppose I can only win once."

Giuna bounced on her toes. "Perhaps I should have mentioned," she said, loud enough for everyone to hear, "Mistress Ryvček was the Fox Volto in the first trial. I believe Mede Kaineto lost to her there, too."

Donaia shot her a dry look. In an undertone, she said, "Yes, perhaps you should have mentioned." *If only for the sake of my nerves.*

Scaperto examined Kaineto's hand and sent him off to be tended, then waved for Donaia and Letilia to join him at the center of the circle. With everyone poised for another bloodletting, Scaperto said, "I believe Alta Letilia owes House Traementis an apology. And House Destaelio owes one as well, on behalf of their guest."

Looking like she'd dined on mealy persimmons, Cibrial said, "Of course. My deepest apologies, Era Traementis."

Donaia expected Letilia to throw another tantrum—even relished the idea that she might, with everyone watching. But at a pointed stare from her host, Letilia only sniffed. "I suppose it was rash of me to accuse Donaia of theft. She's merely happy to call thieves kin." She leaned in close, but pitched her voice to be audible. "Or am I wrong, and you *have* struck that gnat from your register?"

And just like that, the whispers were back. Donaia should have known that a single victory wouldn't change the tide of gossip. Kasienka's steel might have defended them, but no one here had Renata's silver tongue.

She hated that the person she most depended on to defend her family was the one who'd put them into this mess.

"Come, Giuna," she said, straightening her back like an inscriptor's edge. "It's time we left."

Eastbridge, Upper Bank: Pavnilun 9

Giuna had come to the Rotunda hoping that after she'd performed her share of social niceties, she could slip away with Kasienka. She wasn't in the habit of hiding her activities from her mother—until recently, she'd had nothing *to* hide—but in the wake of Ren and Grey's betrayal, Donaia had gone back to old habits, holding her family close and strangers at arm's length. Giuna's stolen moments with Kasienka were bubbles of joy in what had become grim days, and she was reluctant to let Donaia's suspicions fall on her new friend.

Her *Vraszenian* friend.

But the duel and their subsequent grand exit from the Rotunda left no opening for escape. Giuna scarcely had time to duck behind a column for a brief goodbye. *"Thank you,"* she whispered fervently—and before Kasienka could respond with some clever quip, Giuna kissed her.

It was a brief, awkward thing. She managed to land off-center and too hard, her teeth knocking against her upper lip. "Oh. I'm sorry." *Dreadful.* She was absolutely dreadful at this.

Kasienka caught Giuna's elbow before she could flee. "To steal from me a first kiss, and then apologize? I should hope you're sorry for *that*, at least."

"That was never your first kiss," Giuna blurted, digging the hole she was in even deeper.

She expected laughter—Kasienka always seemed to be laughing—but all she saw was warmth and a curiously vulnerable fondness. Coaxing her closer, Kasienka said, "It was *our* first. Though—since I hardly had a chance to do my part—perhaps we might count this as the first instead?"

And the second, and the third, and the fourth, all *much* less dreadful, even if they ended far too quickly. After Giuna dragged herself off to join her family in the Traementis carriage, she kept her hand over her mouth, certain that her smile would give her away even if her reddened lips didn't.

The mood there was not nearly as light as her own, weighted down by Letilia's poison. As the carriage rolled across the cobblestones, the woman's accusations echoed in Giuna's memory, extinguishing all thoughts of romance. *Thief. Stole all my jewelry.*

"Mother," she asked slowly, "do you remember if Ghiscolo

Acrenix ever gave Letilia a gift? A numinatrian medallion cast in bronze?"

Donaia looked like she would have preferred uncomfortable silence to any conversation that touched on Letilia. "That wouldn't have been her style. Come to that, Ghiscolo wasn't her style, either." They rattled into one of the lanes leading northward from the plaza before she said, "Why?"

Meppe and Idaglio looked on curiously as Giuna began pecking through the half-truths and dropped hints from people who dismissed her as too young and naive to think for herself. "Letilia was asking after the jewels Ren stole. And I never told you—Sibiliat used to hound Renata about jewelry, especially numinatrian things. She said Letilia had an Acrenix family heirloom, a gift from her father, that she wanted back. She pretended it was an idle thing, but she hired people to break into the Westbridge townhouse and look for it when Renata couldn't sleep. And...do you remember the maid Suilis?"

"The one who quit without giving notice," Meppe offered.

Giuna nodded. "A few months ago—well, she kidnapped Tess."

That broke Donaia from her frozen posture. "*What?*"

"I should have told you," Giuna said in a rush. "Renata—Ren—she convinced me not to. Suilis was working for Sibiliat, trying to find that same medallion. Ren swore she didn't have it, but...but Ren lies."

"Like she breathes," Donaia muttered. "So Ren stole something she couldn't pawn—or wouldn't—and valuable enough that..."

She fell silent. "Mother?" Giuna prodded.

Barely audible over the clatter of wheels and creaking of carriage springs, Donaia whispered, "A malevolent numinatrian artifact."

"Well, numinatrian," Giuna said. "I don't know how malevolent it is."

"Renata and Tanaquis do," Donaia said, her whisper as grim as a winter freeze. "It's what was used to curse our house. Renata knows. She brought it *with* her."

Giuna knew that flush in her mother's cheeks, and it never boded well for those who'd wronged her. Before she could think of a way to divert or douse that spark of fury, Meppe spoke. "A curse? Is this what Cous—what Renat—what Ren was so frantic to have removed from me?" He worried Idaglio's hand in his own. "She said it had to do with the Indestor register being burned. Why would she curse me, then take me to Cousin Tanaquis to be cleansed?"

Confusion rippled Donaia's mask of anger. "*You* cursed? What? No, this was House Traementis, before your adoption. And—"

"And Ren herself," Giuna said.

"Yes. Ren was cursed, too." Donaia's tone had slowed, like the Dežera on a changing tide. "Even though she wasn't Traementis, nor any blood of Letilia's. Which means... that maggot-infested *eel carcass* of a woman!"

They all jumped when Donaia's fist connected with the side of the carriage. Cautiously, Giuna said, "Mother, what is it? What's going on?"

Donaia folded her gloved hands into a hard knot in her lap. The smile on her face held nothing of humor. "*Letilia* is the one who cursed our house all those years ago. And I intend to make her pay for it."

Hidden temple, Old Island: Pavnilun 12

"Before the others say anything," Vargo said when Ren and Grey arrived in the temple underneath the Point, "I have an idea to make things simpler. Well, sort of."

The exchange that followed was between the two of them alone, in a code no outsider could read: a tilt of Grey's brow, a wry smile and shrug from Ren, then both of them laughing quietly as Grey threaded their fingers into a woven whole. All Grey said after that was "I'm almost afraid to ask."

Couples, Vargo thought with a mental eye roll. Thank the Lumen he and Alsius weren't that annoying. He gestured toward Tanaquis, scribbling notes at the desk she'd dragged into the temple. "She and Alsius have approximately seven thousand and four questions they want to ask Mirscellis. *They* want to send Ren into the dream to ask those questions, with orders to bring back verbatim answers, after which I guarantee their list will only get longer."

"Do I detect the tone of a man who's been in that exact position?" Ren asked, grinning.

Alsius at least could hear Tanaquis for himself. But Ren wasn't wrong; Vargo's annoyance at having to play mouthpiece for the old man had prodded him to this idea. Life had been easier when everyone thought his lapel spider was a pin or a very unusual pet.

"I have an idea for how to talk to Mirscellis directly," Vargo said. "If Ren is willing to try."

Of course she was willing, even after she heard what he had in mind. Vargo knew a martyr's impulse when he saw one; Ren, still reeling with guilt over her con, would grasp at any opportunity to make up for it with something good. But he wasn't going to insult her by treating her willingness as insincere—and he wouldn't be suggesting this plan if he thought it would hurt her.

That didn't stop Grey from watching like the hawk he used to be as Ren settled into the numinat. He grumbled to Vargo, "Just promise me she's not going to come out of this with a Seterin inscriptor stuck in her head forever."

"Would I sentence another poor bastard to that fate?"

::Here now! I don't hear you complaining about the fine clothes and soft beds my instruction has brought you!:: Alsius said, hopping to his usual perch on Vargo's shoulder.

Ignoring Alsius, Vargo said to Ren, "Just concentrate on the connection you made with Mirscellis," and swiped his chalk to close the circle.

This numinat wasn't quite the same as the one Alsius had hoped would transfer his spirit into the body of a messenger boy, before accidentally winding up in the boy's spider instead. But the principle was similar, albeit temporary: Rather than sending Ren to talk to Mirscellis, they would bring Mirscellis to them.

In Ren's body.

She closed her eyes, and long moments passed. Vargo clasped his hands behind his back to hide their tension. "Should we have given her aža?" Grey asked, sotto voce.

"We can try that if this doesn't work," Vargo murmured back. Then Ren's head came up, blinking.

"What an odd feeling," she said.

Her accent sounded almost like Renata, and her posture had made a chameleon change. But not to Renata's crystalline poise; this was looser, and Vargo had the sudden, unsettling feeling that if he'd taken aža, he would have seen another face ghosting over her own.

Gabrius Mirscellis.

::It worked! It's him! Is it him?:: Alsius scuttled so far forward on Vargo's shoulder that he seemed about to leap into the numinat. Vargo took a step back. ::Ask him. Or I'll ask. Can you hear me, Master Mirscellis? You'll need to speak aloud; sadly, this connection with Ren only goes one way.::

One of Ren's hands rose, Mirscellis staring at it like he hadn't seen a hand in centuries. Then he touched his head, feeling along the line of the crown braid there. "Whose body am I in? Is this the young woman I met in the dream? Did she consent to this?"

Vargo liked him better for asking. "She did. And if you want to leave, we'll release you—"

::But we have so many questions!:: Alsius yelped.

Ren frowned—no, Mirscellis frowned. A different expression from the one Vargo knew so well. "Where is that voice coming from?"

::Me! It's coming from me!:: Alsius lifted his brightly colored abdomen and waved two legs in the air like he was signaling a lady spider. ::Altan Alsius Acrenix. Gracious, I hardly even know where to begin. I've read *all* your works, even *Mundum Praeterire*, which has become quite difficult to find. I suppose we should start at the beginning—not the *very* beginning, I mean, your childhood hardly matters, except I do want to discuss the time you led that student takeover of the Obrantum Agora, but for now let's focus on the experiments that stranded you in the realm of mind. Your notebook was lost, so we're not entirely sure what you were trying to accomplish with your journey. And how did you become trapped? Do you want out again? Is that even possible? I suppose if we found you a less-inhabited body to possess...::

Mirscellis looked taken aback. "I— No, I wouldn't want to claim anyone else's body. I *intended* to come back to my own. I'd planned my experiment very carefully, scheduling it before the Great Dream; I theorized that if I couldn't re-enter my flesh as intended, that event would let me cross back and hopefully restore myself by another route." His scowl had no bite; clearly the intervening centuries had worn the edges off his frustration. "Unfortunately, someone mistook my comatose state for death. They dismantled the numinat and moved my body, and—well. That was that."

His matter-of-fact tone made Vargo shudder. Alsius, meanwhile, was riding the wave of his own curiosity. ::The Great Dream? So you *did* come to Nadežra to explore how aspects of the Lumen manifest in Vraszan? That was a matter of great debate, you know, after your death. Sandetto claimed you'd started dabbling in blasphemies—but he was always jealous. Did you truly dump vinegar over his manuscript during an ostretta brawl?::

"His head. I would never destroy someone else's writings, no matter how spurious their—"

"All right!" Scooping Alsius into his palm before the spider decided to jump into the circle and damn the consequences, Vargo sent a desperate look to Tanaquis, who was madly scribbling notes.

"He asked about Sandetto, didn't he?" she said, amused. Then she nodded at their guest. "Master Mirscellis, I'm Tanaquis Fienola Traementatis. We're interested in whatever you can tell us about your explorations of the realm of mind. For example, when you first—"

"If I might," Vargo said, wishing he could scoop up Tanaquis as well. "Ren's doing us all a favor here, and we shouldn't press it further than we have to. Master Mirscellis, have you been able to find the szorsa she asked you to look for?"

Mirscellis was apparently more disciplined than either Alsius or Tanaquis, because he took the redirection without complaint. "I haven't. For which I owe her an apology. I suppose it was hubris to offer in the first place; I thought my mastery of the dream enough to find one szorsa's szekani, even if she *is* Zevriz. I was wrong."

Tanaquis leafed backward in her notebook. "But you found Ren—in the middle of a Primordial-influenced dream. I'm very curious how you managed that, and how you made this containment circle she described. I've met very few people who know how to invoke a Primordial's power, and even fewer who know anything about blocking it."

"Just why are you meddling with such things?" Mirscellis's voice cooled with suspicion.

Fortunately, it was Grey and not Tanaquis who answered. "Our only interest in Primordials is in ridding this city of them."

Mirscellis's tension eased. "I wish you luck. The gods themselves couldn't purge the Primordials entirely from the world—and who knows what it would look like if they had."

A world without desire, or rage, or fear. Fortunately, Grey kept talking before either Alsius or Tanaquis could snap up that philosophical bait. "Not in a cosmological sense. The Primordial of desire, the one you rescued Ren from, has an all too concrete presence here."

He gave an admirably succinct explanation of the medallions, with enough of a hawk's military tinge to keep everyone else quiet. Mirscellis rubbed Ren's jaw thoughtfully, as if feeling for stubble that wasn't there, and nodded when Grey was done. "That explains a *great* deal. I knew Nadežra had been conquered—I can enter the waking world at the Great Dream, and for several iterations there was no one there—and I knew that happened not long after the infection started. But I never knew the specifics. *Mirabile scitu.*"

Vargo said, "Ren had a vision of what Kaius Rex did. That's why she's trying to find the szorsa."

He related the story of Ren's vision, though he wasn't quite as successful as Grey at discouraging interruptions; Tanaquis kept quoting from her notes whenever he got a detail wrong. Mirscellis, meanwhile, looked like he wished he had his own notebook to scribble in. "I'd always wondered how Primordial influence managed to infest the dream. I didn't know it was possible to blend numinatria and pattern like that."

"More than possible!" Notes and pen forgotten, Tanaquis shifted forward in her chair. "I've even used pattern cards as foci for numinata—though it only works if Ren chooses them. Presumably other szorsas could achieve the same effect, though preliminary research suggests that not all of them can. And there are other applications. Like the numinat for destroying the wellspring, using the wellspring itself as a focus."

At Mirscellis's horrified blanch, Vargo said, "I dismantled it, and the people behind the attempt are dead."

"*Good*," Mirscellis said. "Ažerais's gift is not meant to be used that way. No more than we are meant to channel the power of the Lumen directly, rather than through its refractions. Nothing short of blasphemous—not to mention dangerous."

Alsius twitched in indignation. ::Are you implying Ažerais is on par with the *Lumen*?::

Mirscellis refused to be drawn into theological debate with a spider. He said, "What Ren saw might explain why you've had such difficulty destroying the things. Tell me, what can the medallions be used to do?"

Grey's body betrayed no hint of the tension that question must evoke in the man who was the Rook. "They allow the bearer to see what others want—colored by the numinat of the medallion they bear—and to force their will upon others to strengthen those desires. A bearer can also see who or what can be used to achieve their own desires."

"Tell me more about that last part." Mirscellis's gaze sharpened with interest, like a cat sighting prey.

Vargo said, "A medallion is the only way Mettore Indestor could've realized Ren could be used to destroy the wellspring. We don't think it told him outright that she was conceived on the Great Dream—just that she was helpful to his goals. But it was enough."

"That's what drew him to Arkady Bones as well. I was present when he first met her," Grey said. "Not even Arkady knows for certain when she was conceived or born, but Mettore knew the moment he set eyes on her that he could use her."

Mirscellis tried to rake Ren's fingers through her hair and snagged hard in the braids. His wince, though, was for something far more serious. "As I feared. If the creation of this chain drew the Primordial's power into the dream, then it stands to reason it also drew Ažerais's power into the medallions. Knowing how to gain one's desires is not within the purview of desire itself...but it *is* within the purview of a goddess of dreams and intuition."

Vargo's whispered curse was the only sound in the temple. Kaius Rex had waged decades of war and sparked centuries of unrest by taking the holy city of Vraszan for the Liganti. The Dežera would run with northern blood if Vraszenians thought he'd stolen their goddess's power to fuel his conquest.

We en't telling nobody *about this*, he thought forcefully at Alsius.

::No, my boy. Definitely not.::

For once Vargo was glad that Tanaquis's attention remained on matters metaphysical, rather than political. She said, "We do have a way to destroy the medallions. They're connected with their bearers' lives, in ways I suspect involve pattern as well as numinatria. If we destroy both bearers and artifacts together...but nobody wants to do that. Our next best alternative is to let one death do the job—with that one person holding all ten of the medallions." Her matter-of-fact tone left no doubt who she intended to take them all.

Grey's vehement refusal sounded more than a little like the Rook. "That's Ninat talking," Vargo added.

::*We* aren't affected by Ninat,:: Alsius mused. ::And we're more likely to survive the experience than another would be.::

We aren't killing ourselves for this, Vargo said. Not just for Alsius, but for Mirscellis, who'd drawn a sharp breath.

::So we'll do it to save one man out of guilt, but not for an entire city? Possibly more?::

"We had a ticking clock then. We don't now." Vargo hadn't

meant to say it out loud, and when Tanaquis and Grey turned confused looks on him, his scowl deepened. "Don't worry. I'm not the sacrificial type."

"Of course." Grey gave Vargo his blandest look. For the first time, it occurred to Vargo to wonder if that blandness was, in reality, Serrado being a smartass.

But Mirscellis was speaking. "I suspect you need to sever pattern's interference with the medallions before you can destroy them."

"Ren tried," Grey said, his frustration seeping through. "Of us all, she knows pattern the best. But she thinks she would need to be there bodily to make it happen, and the only method we have for doing that is..."

"Unacceptable," Vargo said flatly.

Mirscellis's thoughtful look deepened. "'Bodily' is the wrong term for my existence in the dream, and I don't want to go making more excessively confident promises I might not be able to keep. Still, it's possible I could help. You'll need the medallions in hand, though. All of them, I should think, with their bearers. And you'll need some substitution for the missing Uniat—tell me, Altan Alsius, Alta Tanaquis. Are you familiar with embodied numinatria?"

This time, interrupting the discussion would have been counterproductive. Vargo let Grey draw him aside, leaving the three chalkheads to swap citations. In a low voice, Grey said, "Do we need to worry about Tanaquis?"

"If you mean 'does she want to be the next Kaius Rex,' no," Vargo said. "She wants to understand the cosmos, not rule it. Though that's Ninat's domain, too." The boundary between the mundane and the infinite.

Grey looked only a little reassured. Vargo imagined the Rook's suspicions had soaked right down to the bone. "Look," Vargo said. "I wholeheartedly believe she's trying to destroy the medallions, if for no other reason than the sheer challenge. Is Ninat going to feed that desire? Of course. But it's like Simendis being an ascetic recluse. It helps us."

"That's boon and bane alike," Grey muttered. After that he said nothing, until Mirscellis was gone and Ren was back.

Vargo let Grey go to her first, but once the two of them had unclamped from each other, he eased forward. "You all right?"

Ren looked faintly surprised as she said, "Yes. It was...peculiar, but not unpleasant. I could not speak to him, but I felt his mind. Like a whirlwind of energy and light. Such curiosity—and such warmth." Her fingers curled unconsciously, as if around a hand that wasn't there.

"Could you hear our conversation?" Tanaquis asked, pen poised and ready.

Ren shook her head, and Grey patted her shoulder in ostentatious sympathy. "Get comfortable. This might take a while."

12

Coffer and Key

Seven Knots, Lower Bank: Pavnilun 14

Approaching the Seven Knots labyrinth, Ren fought the urge to touch her face. In the short time since her con had ended, she'd gotten used to walking around with her skin clean of cosmetics. Wearing Arenza's mask now made her itch, and not just physically. *I've learned to like honesty.*

But honesty wouldn't serve her now. Although Renata had been unmasked, Arenza hadn't yet. Sooner or later the truth would come out...but while the lie lasted, she would use it.

The square in front of the labyrinth was even busier than usual. Although Veiled Waters was nearly two months off, it was a Great Dream year; Vraszenians who could afford to flooded the city well in advance. Seven Knots was packed to bursting, every spare room rented, and the ones that weren't spare hosting twice as many as before. One enterprising fellow had renovated a traveling caravan to hold nothing but beds, and was boasting that twelve people could sleep in comfort. Looking at it, Ren believed the twelve, but not the comfort. She thought guiltily of the extra space in the Westbridge townhouse as she slipped through the crowd to the labyrinth.

The interior held not the usual throng of worshippers making offerings and artisans selling charms, but a flock of women in their finest clothes, from polished boots to embroidered sash belts and shawls. Ren tugged her own shawl closer as she searched for a familiar, blindfolded face. Though there had to be close to a hundred women present, nowhere did she see Mevieny.

The Kiralič had said she wasn't Branek's prisoner, but that didn't mean he would let her come here today. The purpose of this gathering was to choose who would represent the lost Ižranyi for the next seven years—the position Mevieny had held for the last cycle. Making that decision didn't require the current speaker to be present, though...and given that Branek likely wanted someone else in her place, he might well keep her away.

Which meant Ren had to fall back on her second, less appealing plan.

Her target wasn't difficult to find. After slipping what mills she could afford into the Faces and Masks on their pillars and walking the labyrinth path, it took questioning only one szorsa—a round-faced woman who didn't bother hiding her curiosity about this newcomer—to learn which cluster of women held Laročja Szerado.

Ren wasn't certain what she'd expected Grey's grandmother to look like. Some combination of Diomen and Gammer Lindworm, perhaps, a charismatic charlatan crossed with a nightmare hag. Laročja was neither. The braids of her silver hair held many knotted charms: a rose of Ažerais, a widow's wedding token, the seven-looped knot of a kureč's senior szorsa. The strands that escaped formed a halo as fine as spun floss. Weight had smoothed the wrinkles from her cheeks, making her seem younger than her years, but the crinkles around her eyes and mouth recalled as many smiles as frowns. She was smiling now, patting the hand of a woman around Ren's age.

"Never apologize for speaking truth," Laročja told her. "What Ažerais shows us, we have a duty to share, no matter how unpleasant the client finds it. To your kurenič my son will speak. No szorsa should be so disrespected."

Her son: Grey's father. Ren felt the weight of the throwing knives hidden in her shawl as she approached the small crowd. A tap on one woman's shoulder brought her around, creating an opening Ren could use to slip through. "Szorsa Laročja," she said as the young woman bowed herself away. "Could we privately speak?"

A few laughs escaped the press around Laročja. Swap the clothing and the language, and Ren might be some insignificant delta gentlewoman asking to speak privately with Faella Coscanum. Laročja's gaze dismissed Ren with familiar impatience. "I'm a busy woman, little one."

Ren touched her heart in a gesture of respect she didn't feel at all. "I come regarding the dreamweaver's lost fledgling."

In this crowd, she couldn't risk naming Koszar directly, only refer obliquely to the Anduske, the "children of the dreamweaver." But it was enough to make Laročja's gaze flick down to her shawl, eyes narrowing in calculation. "A moment," she said, not to Ren. Like a flock of starlings moving on, the crowd dispersed.

"You are the one advising the slip-knot owl," Laročja said when they were gone. The blue of her shrewd eyes was deeply familiar, but empty of the warmth Ren saw when she looked at Grey. "Think you it wise, twisting Ažerais's insights to suit your own ends?"

Only long practice at controlling her words kept Ren from calling the woman a hypocrite to her face. "I twist nothing, Szorsa Laročja. I tell him only what I see—though my experience is far less than yours."

"I advise you to leave that one to his fate. But I think not that you came for my wisdom." Stepping away from the nearest pillar—Ir Entrelke Nedje, the deity of luck; Ren doubted that was mere chance—Laročja gestured to a bench along the wall. "Let us talk. Though the men we aid are enemies, we need not be. That would be foolish and shortsighted."

Ren, sitting, wished the season gave her an excuse to cover her words with a fan. No doubt others were watching, hoping to read her lips as easily as they read the cards. "I hope you will aid me in ending the schism. It serves no one, least of all the Vraszenians of this city."

"You mean to turn the traitor over for justice?" One silvered brow rose in doubt. "For I know of no schism—only a few malcontents with a taste for cheese. The true children of the dreamweaver seek to remove the leech from their heart."

"Then no objection should you have to them submitting themselves to Ažerais's judgment, in the form of an ordeal."

The first eyebrow lift had been a measured act. The second shooting up to join it was not. "Only she who speaks for the Ižranyi may oversee such a thing."

"I'm sure you know where Szorsa Mevieny is."

"That honor she will not hold much longer."

The selection would take place today, but the handoff wouldn't occur until the Great Dream. By tradition, the lost clan's new speaker was the first to sip from the Wellspring of Ažerais. But by then, Branek would already have staged his rebellion. "We both know this cannot wait."

Laročja sniffed. "The young, always in a rush. I see no reason to hurry."

"You see no reason to prove that Branek is favored by Ažerais? For surely you have no doubt of that."

The pause said Laročja was giving the proposal serious thought. It should have been gratifying; instead it was the opposite. *She shouldn't be this easy to convince. What am I not seeing?*

Laročja clasped Ren's hand between her own. "Young as you are, you will not have attended this gathering before. Stay for the choosing, and afterward, we will talk."

Before Ren could reply, Laročja stood, brushed off her skirts, and strode into the sunlight blazing down on the labyrinth's path.

"My sisters," she called out to the assembled szorsas. The chattering faded almost immediately, everyone turning to look. "We come together to choose who will speak for the lost Ižranyi in the next cycle of our Lady's dream. But before that dream comes, our elders will again meet the Cinquerat in the Ceremony of the Accords. We all know of the horrors last year—horrors that robbed Mevieny Plemaskaya Straveši of her sight. Someone must take her place now, to finish out the cycle."

Djek, Ren thought, staring, as Laročja let sorrow drag her cheeks into a frown. "I have spoken for the Ižranyi before. I can do so again."

And make yourself the one who oversees the ordeal. Not just that: The szorsa who took the position during this Great Dream would lead their people into the new Grand Cycle. Even after she was replaced, her vision would influence the next forty-nine years.

Then a voice rang from the entrance, blessedly familiar. "Already you speak for me? The Ižranyi, I think, would be no more pleased than I."

Ren kept her gaze on Laročja, rather than turning with everyone else to look. She already knew Mevieny had arrived; what mattered was Laročja's reaction. Which was well-controlled...but not well enough to hide the flash of anger.

A girl Ren didn't know led the old szorsa forward, into the light of the labyrinth. A strip of pale gauze covered the empty sockets where Mevieny's eyes had been, but she stood proudly as she came to a halt. "If you win the support of our sisters and of pattern, then so be it, Laročja. But from me you will not take these final months."

Laročja's solicitous expression had the look of a well-practiced lie. "I thought only to lessen your burden. Surely you wish not to relive that night—nor to remind others of it. People whisper still that a curse lingers on all those touched by it."

Another woman spoke up. Ren instantly marked her as a syco-phant. "It has happened before that the Ižranyi's speaker dies before her cycle has ended. Then her successor is chosen early and takes her place. Why not cast our cards? If again Szorsa Mevieny prevails, then the matter is settled. If not..."

Clearly, she expected Laročja to win. Ren prayed she was wrong, because the suggestion was met with general acclaim, and the assembled szorsas all began to take out their decks.

Grey hadn't been able to tell her how the choosing was done; that wasn't for outsiders to know. Ren drifted toward the nearest szorsa. "I am new. What is the method?"

"Draw a card," the other woman murmured back, her own deck in hand. "Let its message guide to whom you give it."

The interior of the labyrinth whispered with traditional prayers and rustling cards. Most szorsas were giving an honest shuffle, but if the nature of the card chosen mattered, Ren had no doubt that at least some would rig their results.

Not all the cards began going to Mevieny or Laročja, though. Easily half a dozen other women appeared to have their own supporters, albeit fewer in number. "It is simply a vote?"

The young szorsa looked like she'd asked if the Dežera flowed out of the sea. "Of course not. With the cards they receive, they lay a pattern to show how they will guide our people in the coming cycle." She moved away, taking her card to Laročja.

Ren couldn't let Laročja administer the ordeal. She drew out her deck, then paused. *I could draw honestly . . . or I could send a message.*

Her mouth compressed into a fierce smile. *Mevieny may not use it—but message it shall be.* She shuffled her deck, making it look fair, but her fingers knew the shape of the one card ever so slightly different from the rest. Choice in hand, she headed for Mevieny.

One of the women who'd already gathered several votes was there, handing her small stack to Mevieny. A swift glance showed Ren someone else bringing her collected cards to Laročja. Candidates, it seemed, could throw their support behind each other.

Then it was her own turn. Ren stepped up and took Mevieny's hand, sliding her card into it. "The Constant Spirit," she said, since the blinded szorsa couldn't see its painted surface. "The card of the Meszaros. Not your clan, I know, but—"

Instead of taking the card, Mevieny seized her wrist. "Arenza?"

"Yes," she said reflexively—and then stopped.

She'd dealt with Mevieny as the Black Rose, but had the old woman ever met Arenza? Yes, Ren realized with dread. Once: on the Night of Hells, after Mevieny's eyes were torn out.

But Ren hadn't shared her name then. Mevieny shouldn't be able to connect those threads, to get from a familiar voice to the name of a persona she'd never met.

Unless she'd connected a lot more threads than that.

Mevieny's chin tilted to one side, ear angled toward Ren. "I hoped you remained at the side of old friends, but little news makes it to me these days."

Heart beating fast, Ren bent closer and murmured, "My old friend holds to his hope of an ordeal, but I fear I may have given Szorsa Laročja ideas instead. If she oversees it…" Ren couldn't see how many cards Laročja had compared to Mevieny, but if the final arbiter was not a tally but a pattern laid, then surely a practiced fraud had the advantage.

Another pair of szorsas approached, one offering a single card, the other a stack of four. Released from Mevieny's grip, Ren edged away. The Masks on the columns seemed to be laughing at her, for the ill luck she'd brought down on herself.

Until Mevieny caught the belled cuff of her sleeve. Then Ren knew they *were* laughing… because Mevieny pushed a stack of mismatched cards into her own hands.

"Ažerais has blessed this one," the old szorsa said, loud enough for others to hear. "Even with my eyes gone, I see it. If the time has come for me to step down, no more fit successor could I hope for."

Ren almost dropped the cards. *I can't speak for the Ižranyi!*

All eyes were on her, and Laročja's glare was pure poison. The other szorsas whispered to each other in surprise. All those who'd gathered votes were older, women who'd earned the respect of their peers. Ren was young and completely unknown.

Laročja sniffed, gathering her composure. "Your judgment has gone along with your sight, Mevieny. But so be it. Let those with cards lay what pattern they can."

One of her supporters spread her shawl across the grass so Laročja could kneel and lay the cards. Mevieny murmured in Ren's ear, "The layout is your choice, and the placement of the cards. The idea is not to read pattern but to shape it—to weave the fate of our people for the coming cycle."

Like szorsas were reputed to do in legend: not just interpreting Ažerais's Dream, but calling it into being. Like Ren had once pretended to do, making Sedge cough up worms to impress Idusza.

One woman had only five cards, and was arranging them into a three-card line on her own shawl. Laročja and the other were sorting their stacks for a full nine-card spread, though Laročja had far more to choose from.

Ren had more than enough—thirty-three cards in total. She knelt in the grass and spread her shawl out, then began flicking through the assemblage. Past, present, future. For the past, should she focus on the wounds Vraszan had suffered, the eras of its glory, or its legendary beginnings?

Then she stopped and flicked back through. *Did I really see . . .*

She had. And although it wasn't perfect, it came close enough that Ren knew what to do.

Laročja's voice rang out. "Let each woman show her vision."

The three-card line went first, then the other full pattern. When Laročja turned to Ren, her smile held the malicious expectation of failure. "And you, little one?"

Ren's hands were steady as she dealt the cards she'd chosen. Not a nine-card spread, but the seven of the wheel.

"This is an older layout, favored by the Anoškin," she said. "The wheel of the caravan that carries our people down their road. One card for each clan, with the Ižranyi the hub on which the wheel turns. I have not the Ižranyi clan card, of course; those are lost, their faces blanked and their name forgotten when the clan died. But I have done my best."

She turned over The Constant Spirit, The Friendly Fist, and The Silent Witness. The cards of the Meszaros, the Stretsko, and the Anoškin. Lacking The Kindly Spinner for the Varadi, she was forced to break the sequence with her best substitute, The Peacock's Web from the spinning thread, but she followed it with The Artful Gentleman and The Hidden Eye for the Dvornik and the Kiraly. Five out of the six remaining clan cards. And for the Ižranyi, she had chosen Labyrinth's Heart.

Ren sat up and said, "My vision for our people is the clans standing together in strength. And holding us together, the lost labyrinth that used to surround our Lady's wellspring."

Laročja shot to her feet with a speed that belied her age, boot catching her shawl and sending her own spread flying. Ignoring the gasps from onlookers, she snatched up The Constant Spirit and brandished it in Ren's face. "How got you this card?"

When Ren gave no answer, she turned her ire on the rest of the gathered szorsas. "*Who contributed this card?*"

"Laročja." Mevieny's hand came down hard on the older woman's shoulder, then felt down her arm to her wrist. Whatever she did there loosened Laročja's grip enough for Mevieny to take the card without damaging it. "Disrupting a pattern, touching another's cards without permission? Perhaps *you* are the one who's lost her senses."

Jerking out of Mevieny's hold, Laročja watched her return the card to Ren with an expression as cold as acid-etched steel. Then with a sob, she crumpled to the ground, hiding eyes Ren suspected were bone dry. "Forgive this sentimental old woman. It's only that I would know that card anywhere. It belonged to my precious daughter by marriage, given to me when she passed. Both have been lost for so long...to see the card now..."

Mevieny spoke before Ren could. "Grieved though I am for your loss, we are about the business of our people. Show your pattern, Laročja, and let this matter be settled."

Enough murmurs rose up in support to push Laročja back to her seat. Collecting her scattered cards, she laid them out with all the portentous oratory she could muster—and she had a few clan cards in there herself. Ren suspected she'd placed The Artful Gentleman in a veiled position as a dig at Mevieny, who was Dvornik.

But she'd undercut her own authority with that display over The Constant Spirit. And Ren pairing her clan cards with the old style of pattern had won more than a little admiration from those watching. When Mevieny called for those who had been swayed by pattern to change their vote, the woman who'd laid the three-card line passed her cards to Laročja. The one with the nine-card spread hesitated for a moment before handing her stack to Ren.

"Lucky for you that you have Ažerais's blessing," the woman said, soft enough that it would be only a murmur to other ears, "for you have made many enemies today. I hope only that you remember your friends in this next cycle."

Mevieny counted the cards, openly where others could see. Ren edged out Laročja by only three... but it was enough. Raising her voice, she cried, "Arenza Lenskaya shall succeed me!"

"At the Great Dream," Ren said loudly. "Not before."

Inwardly, she was cursing. *Djek.* How had she gotten herself into this? Everyone would want to know who she was, especially with no kureč name. Soon they would learn she was Grey Serrado's outcast, half-northern lover. She'd already been hanged on one side of the river; now she'd be hanged on the other.

But Mevieny would oversee the ordeal. Right now, Ren would take what victory she could get.

Hidden temple, Old Island: Pavnilun 15

If facing the gathered szorsas was daunting, stepping into the temple the next day took every bit of courage Ren could muster.

Cibrial spat audibly as Ren crossed the threshold. "I'm surprised you dare show your face here. Assuming that *is* your true face. Who knows how many masks a woman like you keeps at the ready?"

Most of the others were already there. Vargo she could trust, but Ren forced herself to meet the other gazes in turn: Cibrial contemptuous, Iascat wary, Parma disbelieving. Beldipassi looked like he wanted to poke her in the cheek with a finger, to make sure she was real. Utrinzi merely looked thoughtful, as if an unexpected shape had appeared in his numinat.

Faella was too dignified to actually spit, but the curl of her lip carried the same message. *Apologies for ruining your plans,* Ren thought, not feeling sorry at all. The medallions only showed what could be of use, not how. If Ren and Grey were going to help Nadežra, it would be by destroying this poison and stopping Branek, not by mollifying the Lower Bank with their romance.

Forcing a smile, Ren bent her knees in a mocking curtsy to the gathered nobles before turning to Tanaquis, busy at her desk. "What do you need us to do?"

With a swirl of green silk, Cibrial was in Ren's path, barring the way. "Before we do anything, shouldn't we reconsider *what* we're doing? We've been following the word of a con artist—a proven liar. Who's to say this isn't some new scheme of hers, to usurp our power and claim it for herself? My new guest has revealed some *interesting* things about how you came to hold Tricat. You stole one medallion before coming to Nadežra; maybe you came here to wrest the others from us!"

These things are the reason my land was overrun, you— But saying that would only reinforce Cibrial's argument. And just because Ren had been unmasked didn't mean she had to abandon all subtlety. "Happy you might be to accept the corruption of a Primordial, Your Charity, but I am not." The accent wasn't Renata's, but the scathing politeness was.

A sleeve swung as Cibrial gestured at Tanaquis. Its loose drape was Tess's work, Ren knew, and she had to fight the urge to tear it off and strangle the woman with it. By the time her flash of rage passed, she'd missed half of what Cibrial said.

"...times have we gathered to destroy them?" Cibrial was asking. "Always without success. Maybe they can't *be* destroyed. Maybe we ought to focus on learning to live with them, as safely as possible."

Nothing could have been better calculated to annoy Tanaquis. "Anything made can be destroyed," she snapped. "Especially now that we have Ninat."

The way Cibrial put her back to Ren would have been a duel-worthy insult to Renata. "I don't pretend to know more than you, Alta Tanaquis. But Utrinzi has said that Ninat also represents allowing old paths to end so that new ones might open. How much more time must we waste on a doomed endeavor? I, for one, tire of being called at the whim of scholars. Am I expected to make this my life's work when I have businesses to run and trade to oversee?"

::Whims?:: Alsius said, his outrage audible only to Vargo and Ren. ::The destruction of these abominations is our highest duty!::

Iascat stepped forward, hands up in placation. "Cibrial, I'm as busy as you are, but it's only a few hours here and there."

She sneered at him. "Says the man in bed with the con artist's accomplice. I may have loathed Sostira, but at least she had the wit to see when she was being manipulated."

Ren and Grey had talked about how this meeting might go, about how the support of a legendary enemy of the nobility like the Rook would only corrode her standing.

She wished now that she'd thought to have the same conversation with Vargo.

"I don't think—" he began.

Cibrial spoke over him. "Oh, Ghiscolo's *murderer* has opinions? I'm very interested to know the thoughts of a man who *somehow* has recently claimed both a title and a medallion."

Vargo's scar puckered with his scowl. "You'd rather I let him kill you? Because I can—"

"We are wandering far from the point." Utrinzi Simendis spoke so rarely that everyone fell silent at his interruption. He'd joined Tanaquis at the desk; now he held a piece of paper in his hands, still wet with ink. "So long as we cannot destroy the medallions, we must indeed accept the imperfect solution of trying to mitigate their influence. But that does not mean we should abandon all attempts to rid ourselves of corruption."

He held out the paper to Ren. "This is for you."

Mystified, she took it. The writing was hasty, but at the bottom was the seven-pointed star of Iridet's seal, marking it as a formal document.

Speaking to the room, he announced, "I have just issued her a contract to administer a charter I hold, for the destruction of these medallions. Should she fail to pursue this goal to the best of her ability, rest assured I will prosecute her. But the purgation of heresy falls under my authority as Iridet, and I require the cooperation of all—including my fellow Cinquerat members—in bringing that about."

The Rook's voice put a period to Cibrial's sputters. "I was wrong about you," he said to Utrinzi as he emerged from one of the back chambers, where he'd been hiding since before the others arrived. "I apologize for my assumptions during our first meeting. And my treatment of you."

"You should. I've yet to find a better procurer of instruments than Mistress Gredzyka, and she won't take my custom anymore."

Their odd exchange did nothing to steal the breath from Cibrial's argument. "You can't grant charters to common criminals!"

"Oh, shut it or we'll be here all day," Parma snapped, elbowing past her to join the others around the table. "She's still Traementatis, so Uncle Trinzi can slip her whatever he likes. And fuck keeping this thing any longer than I have to. Lumen, I miss sex so much."

Tutting at Parma's crudity, Faella laid a hand on Cibrial's shoulder. "Let's do what we came here to do, and see what results."

"Yes *please*," Beldipassi said timidly, from behind all the people who outranked him.

Tanaquis knew better than to make them wait while she spent hours on inscription. The figure was already chalked onto the floor, dizzyingly complex, with squares marked out for the subsidiary foci. "Ren, if you would?" Tanaquis said.

As she'd done at the labyrinth, Ren had chosen cards for each of the numina, doing her best—at Tanaquis's insistence—to look for points of connection between those forces and the concepts represented by pattern. She laid them around the numinat in sequence: The Face of Seeds, Orin and Orasz, Three Hands Join, The Face of Gold, The Face of Roses, The Liar's Knot, The Face of Light, A Spiraling Fire, The Mask of Bones, and The Face of Ages.

While Vargo distributed cups of aža-laced wine, Tanaquis said, "Ghiscolo's numinat would have worked, but at the cost of your lives. That's because each of us is bound to our medallion—so in order to destroy *those*, we would have to destroy *ourselves*. The goal today is to break that binding...with the help of Gabrius Mirscellis." She waited, but Utrinzi had already heard the plan, and no one else gasped in astonishment. "A very famous Seterin inscriptor," she said, sounding irritated.

"And the point of the aža?" Faella asked, making a face at her cup. "I haven't touched the stuff since that awful Night of Hells."

"This is aža, not ash," Vargo said, "and Mirscellis happens to be dead. His spirit is in the realm of mind—also known as Ažerais's Dream—so the aža should let you perceive him, and possibly also the connection he'll be cutting." He gave Faella an insolent smirk. "This way you can make sure he cuts the right thing. You don't want to find yourself severed from your house, do you?"

Vargo tossed his wine back like a dare. With a glare for his impudence, Faella did the same.

"Gather around the numinat," Tanaquis said, nudging Parma and Faella into position. "Hold hands; we have to re-create the missing Uniat ourselves."

Iascat took Ren's hand with an awkward twist of his mouth she thought was meant to be a smile. The others shuffled into place, with the last gap at Quarat, where Cibrial would have to join hands with Ren on one side and the Rook on the other. "This is absurd," she snapped.

"I thought you didn't want to waste any more time than you had to," Iascat said, with mild venom.

Grimacing like she was wading into an unclean canal, Cibrial joined them in the circle.

By the time the focus was in place, the outer circle closed, Ren felt the first prickles of aža's awareness. The taste of smoke lingered on the back of her tongue, and a quiet, shuffling music rang in her ears. She recognized it as dim echoes of the dance she'd escaped with Mirscellis's help, and her body tensed.

A squeeze on her left hand dragged her back. She gave Iascat a grateful smile.

The old carvings on the temple walls shifted and danced when she studied them, squinting through time's fog. Once this place had been used by the Praeteri; before them, by Kaius Rex. But what had it been before that?

A sheltered site in a Vraszenian city, buried beneath the wellspring. Who else would they worship here but Ažerais?

Ren's breath caught. Was that a true glimpse of the past, helped along by Tricat, or just a vision spun by aža? It made sense, though.

Pattern was bound into the medallions; Kaius and the nameless szorsa would have chosen this place to perform that binding for a reason.

Tanaquis's voice pulled her back to the present moment. "Call him."

Mirscellis. Gabrius. The thread shimmered into view when Ren looked for it. She couldn't touch it without letting go of Iascat and Cibrial—but what was a hand, really? Just an extension of the will. She knew him, far more deeply than their brief encounters should account for. That whirlwind of energy and light, the snapping fire of his intellect and the gentle glow of his concern for her well-being. Ren found herself hoping that when this was all over, the two of them could simply talk. He was what she'd pretended to be, a Seterin come to Nadežra; she wanted to know his tale.

But first they must free themselves. Ren breathed her will along the thread, and it glowed in response.

Oh good, it did work. Gabrius's voice rippled like water, but the Seterin accent was unmistakable. A moment later she saw him, flickering at first, then steady. A choked-off oath from Beldipassi said others could see him, too.

In the dream, his ghostly figure walked the perimeter of their circle, trailing one hand after him. *Not a bad Uniat*, he said. *Surprisingly strong. You're more united than I thought.*

United? After what Cibrial had said? But Ren wasn't about to argue with good news.

Gabrius brushed his spectral hands together and shot Ren a smile, which faded into a thoughtful frown. *He's never seen me properly*, Ren realized. She'd been the Black Rose when they met, and then he'd possessed her.

Only a moment of distraction; then he shook the frown away. *To unlace a boot, you start at the top. So—* He gave Faella a courtly, archaic bow. *Illi-ten, I believe. Allow me.*

With the care of a harpist, he plucked a single gold thread from among the many entwining Faella. A tug in both directions made Ren gasp and sway—and she wasn't the only one. "Careful!" Cibrial snapped.

This could be a problem, Gabrius murmured, peering at the thread more closely. Even from her poor vantage, Ren could see the dull tin woven through the gold. More, she could feel it yanking in her gut with every shift.

Tanaquis craned her neck at Faella. "So there *is* an Uniat thread, even though the chain itself was destroyed."

The carvings on the walls pulsed. Now the figures were detaching from them.

No: just one figure. One Ren knew.

"Behind you!" she shouted—too late.

The nameless szorsa lunged toward Gabrius, but her clawlike hands didn't strike his body. Instead they raked through the few threads that touched him, snapping them like cobwebs.

Gabrius cried out, his back arching. The entwined gold and tin strands slipped from his grasp, and boiling pain flooded through Ren.

The linkage of their hands broke. Faella clutched her head and reeled; next to Ren, Cibrial collapsed with a shriek. Before Ren could move, the szorsa shoved Gabrius backward—and he was gone.

The szorsa wasn't finished, though. She turned toward the rest of them, snarling. Ren cried out, "Zevriz! Stop! We mean you no harm!"

"No harm?" Gone was the quiet, sorrowful figure Ren had met before. This spirit was wild-eyed, her cascading braids whipping like angry snakes as she spun to face Ren. "You would break me! Snap me to pieces, worse than before, first body, then chain, now *this*!"

She spooled the tin thread between her hands, and with it came the strands connected to the other holders: gold, copper, silver. Ren's bronze wrapped around her chest like a constrictor, tightening until her bones creaked and she could barely draw air. "Stop. We aren't..."

"Zevriz. No right have you to claim *any* threads. Release them." Like Ren, the Rook spoke in Vraszenian.

The stranglehold eased, enough for Ren to suck in a deep breath. Around the circle, the other holders looked equally bad. Utrinzi clutched his chest, face grey and lips ashen. Vargo had fallen as if his feet were cut from under him; Tanaquis was curled in a ball, shivering like a sick kitten.

The Rook was one of the few still upright. The unnamed szorsa had released the skein and was tearing at her own clothes instead, where a single, gossamer-thin thread stretched from her to the Rook's coat.

To the hidden pocket where Grey kept the ruined hood.

"You," she whispered, but it wasn't an accusation. More like bewilderment—and hope. "I know what's in you. It isn't gone after all..."

With Cibrial on the floor, there was no one to block the glance Ren exchanged with Grey. Some connection between the szorsa and the Rook?

"You made me not," he said, cautiously. "I know that much. It was another, grieving and angry. But had you some part in it?"

"They came here." The szorsa turned, looking around the temple as if she didn't recognize it. "I hid them. I kept out the wrong ones. I thought...I thought I could..."

Kept out the wrong ones. The ward, the force that prevented people from entering the temple unless they had a triple clover charm. *She* was its source?

The szorsa reached out to the Rook, imploringly. "Give it back. Two threads make a stronger cord."

He exhaled in understanding. "Not *had* some part in it. You *became* part of it." His hand brushed down the front of his coat, like he was considering doing as the szorsa asked. Giving her the hood.

"Don't." Vargo hadn't regained his feet, but he reached out as though he could stop Grey. "Hers isn't the only spirit bound up in... that."

::How do you know?:: Alsius demanded.

::I'm on aža. And I know a bit about spirit bonds, don't I? Messing with Uniat called her here, and the thread to the Rook calmed her.:: Vargo's gaze met Ren's, his words for her as much as for the spider.

"Three parts to the soul," she whispered. There was a connection not only from the szorsa to the concealed hood, but from the hood to the tin thread of Uniat.

The medallions. The Rook's mission, from the earliest moment of his existence.

One part of the szorsa's soul, bound up in the medallions—in the Uniat that linked them together. One part bound up in the Rook, trying to fix her own mistake. And the third adrift in the dream, cut off from everything except the missing parts of herself.

Ren shifted back to Liganti and said, "Tanaquis. When the medallions were linked into a chain, it caught a piece of her in it. If we free her...that might be what we need to destroy them."

She prayed Tanaquis wouldn't start thinking out loud. So far they'd kept from the others the full story of Ren's Tricat vision, the fact that the szorsa had helped Kaius Sifigno forge his chain. Cibrial's Quarat vision had shown her that pattern was involved, but not how. Ren spoke obliquely, and hoped Tanaquis would understand.

Her cousin's mouth formed a silent, considering circle. Then Tanaquis said, "Yes. Though I have no idea how."

Or how to get her out of the Rook. Neither of those were problems they were likely to solve today. Ren faced the szorsa and spoke again in Vraszenian. "My word I give that we will aid you. Soon your spirit will be whole once more."

Hidden temple, Old Island: Pavnilun 15

There were a thousand questions after that, not least because Cibrial was deeply suspicious of Ren conducting a conversation in Vraszenian with a dead szorsa, and she didn't trust anything reported about what they'd said. When she finally left, arm in arm with Faella, it didn't take the insights of Tricat to know she would dig her heels in even harder after this.

But with the szorsa's appearance, Ren felt like she'd finally grasped a loose end in a tangled mass of string. The first step to unraveling it at last.

She expected another thousand questions from Tanaquis, but her cousin walked out without even demanding a report, mumbling something about wanting to consult her books at home. Possibly she wanted to get away from her erstwhile mentor and employer, who kept giving her disappointed frowns. Utrinzi frowned deeper when she abandoned him and Vargo to dismantle the numinat with a full bucket and stiff-bristled mops; by the time he left, he looked almost as irritated as Parma, trailing in his wake.

Quiet fell back over the temple, with only Ren, Vargo, Alsius, and Grey remaining. The last of whom pushed his hood back once everyone was gone and scrubbed his hands through his disheveled hair, sighing. "What of Mirscellis?"

The memory of those threads snapping reverberated through Ren's soul. All her vaunted skill with pattern, and she'd been helpless to protect him. "With his connections broken...he may now be like the szorsa." Adrift forever, after Ren dragged him into their problems. Could the szorsa help restore him? Not in her current state, Ren feared. Which meant—

She swallowed hard, dread lodging in her throat like a stone. "We may not be able to find him again."

::You *must*!:: Alsius crouched in the spot where Mirscellis had vanished, a bright spot of color on the damp-darkened floor. ::Whatever that mad spirit did to him—if this destroys him—::

At Ren's flinch, Vargo said, "He's survived the realm of mind a long time. I'm certain he's fine." His frown, though, said he was anything but. Scooping up the forlorn spider, he tucked Peabody under the warm shadows of his collar. "That szorsa...the description of your last meeting made her sound much less violent."

::Tricat's influence?:: Alsius said, shaky despite Vargo's assurances. ::That might explain it, if she was close to the heart of its presence. Tricat is stability, after all.::

Ren tried to find some stability in her own mind. Perhaps Tricat had shown Ren what that szorsa was like before she came apart.

Ordinarily a person's szekani was more of a shadow, rather than something coherent enough to read a pattern.

Then again, ordinarily the other parts of a person's soul didn't suffer the fate this one had.

Ren shared Alsius's comment with Grey, followed by her own thoughts, and Vargo nodded. "Yes. I'd like to know how exactly a soul gets ripped apart and stuffed into a hood and a set of Primordial medallions."

::We don't know that's what happened—::

"We don't know *what* happened." Vargo raked his hair back in frustration. "We're dealing with hidden history two centuries old, and—"

"I know," Grey said softly, turning the ruined hood over and over in his hands as though that history was written in its embroidery. "At least, some of it. Nothing about a szorsa. Well, not *this* szorsa. There was another..."

Ren heard Vargo bite down on the questions he wanted to ask. So did Grey, it seemed; he looked up and met Vargo's eyes. "The Rook is...sort of a spirit, and sort of a collection of spirits. It's a thing each bearer creates, imbuing our performance of the role. But I think it also contains the szekani of past bearers." He grimaced. "Not my own, I suspect. That was forced out when I defied it."

Alsius crept out from under Vargo's collar. ::Is he saying their souls don't go to their dream after they die? They dedicate themselves *that much* to their task?::

He sounded both awed and horrified, and Ren chose not to relay that comment as Grey went on. "I used to be able to touch on the memories of those past bearers when I wore the hood. But it was dangerous to give in too deeply—the more you *are* the Rook, the more you *become* the Rook—so I only know traces. There was a knot of people who swore to overthrow the Tyrant, here in this temple; they made the pieces of the Rook's disguise. A young woman was the first to play the role. And a szorsa did...something." A frustrated sound escaped him. "I don't know what."

With aža still spinning Ren's vision, she almost felt like she could *see* what Grey described. She'd never leaned on the little dream to guide her readings, the way some patterners did, but...

Her deck caught on the edge of her pocket as she pulled it out, undermining any dramatic effect the gesture might have had. "What if I tried to see?"

::Is that wise? Aža and medallions and whatever other strange influences linger here—should we take such risks for vague portents and ambiguous interpretations?::

"At this point, even vague portents are more than we have." Sweeping Tanaquis's scattered notes and equipment aside in a way that would get him scolded later, Vargo gestured to the desk.

Grey's touch on Ren's arm stopped her. "I doubt not your gift," he said, "but you told me that patterning the Rook left you feeling like you'd put your brain through a sausage grinder."

And even then, she still hadn't been able to see everything. Ren laid her hand over his. The leather of his gauntlets felt stiff and new, not the supple softness of the true Rook's guise. "I won't push. But shouldn't I *try*?"

"If she can get us answers instead of more questions," Vargo said, "I'm in favor of her trying."

Grey still hovered as Ren sat down and shuffled the cards. What layout should she use? What exactly was she trying to learn? Nine cards, she decided; it was the most complete pattern, the warp and weft of fate. And it felt...right.

Was that her instinct for pattern guiding her? Aža? Or the medallion in her pocket?

A chill washed through Ren as she dealt out the cards. Each one she turned over felt like an echo, the past reverberating into the present. For the lowest line, Sword in Hand, The Mask of Mirrors, Jump at the Sun. Cards that spoke to what happened before the Rook was made; their significance was a soft conversation in a neighboring room, real but not quite audible. The middle line, The Mask of Knives, Saffron and Salt, and—

Two cards in the central place. The Ember Adamant...but stuck to it, dealt at the same time, Sisters Victorious.

Ren's breath caught. "This is the pattern she laid. The pattern she *changed*." Like the szorsas selecting the speaker for the Ižranyi. Creating fate instead of merely reading it.

"Is that even possible?" A shadow fell across the paired cards as Vargo leaned in for a better view.

"Yes," Grey said, his voice as rough as a broken bone. "When a szorsa with the true gift lays the cards...I did it to myself. Trying to keep Ren from learning the truth, when she laid my pattern. It's how I broke the Rook."

Vargo shot upright. "I thought you did that to keep the Rook from killing her."

"Yes. But that happened because I interfered with my pattern. I cursed my own fate."

"Not a curse," Ren said. She couldn't look up at them; all her attention was on the cards, the last three above the ones that had changed. Pearl's Promise, The Mask of Chaos, The Face of Light. "They would have failed. The Tyrant's rule would have continued. She took Sisters Victorious out of the pattern in order to move the rest. Pearl's Promise would have been their ill future—no reward for all their effort. The Ember Adamant became their present, the burden of the Rook. Numinatria created him and imbuing gave him life, that woman surrendering herself completely to her role...but it was the changed pattern that made it possible." As a changed pattern had ended it.

::Which 'she'?:: Alsius dropped onto the desk and huddled, legs curling underneath him. ::Are you talking about this Zevriz one that attacked us, or the szorsa Master Serrado mentioned?::

Both. Ren was hardly breathing, as if that would break her tenuous connection. "A living szorsa laid the pattern, then changed it. But I think it worked because the one called Zevriz helped. Her spirit is in this place."

"Part of it, anyway." Vargo's sigh was a ghost ruffling Ren's hair. His shadow receded as he rounded the desk to stand near Peabody, one hand rubbing absently at his chest. "So what she did meant her soul got caught in the Rook? I wonder if she intended that."

Ren couldn't tell. Flicking through the remainder of her deck, she laid out the cards from Grey's pattern, alongside the one that made the Rook. Lark Aloft and The Mask of Nothing were meaningless; those were the cards he'd slipped into the top while she wasn't looking, and she set them aside now. Sword in Hand and The Ember Adamant were already in the Rook's pattern: commitment to a cause, an obligation to fulfill. Could she use one to patch the other? Or would that merely make things worse than ever?

::We can't just leave all those souls trapped. They have to return to the Lumen. Or Ažerais's Dream. Perhaps if we burned the hood?::

Vargo coughed. "I don't think that's a good idea. Remember 'smoosh'?"

Peabody's full-body shudder nearly toppled him off the desk. ::Ah. Perhaps we shouldn't be hasty.::

Grey's brow furrowed at the half of the conversation he could hear. "What idea?"

"Nothing you haven't already considered and discarded. Alsius is concerned about releasing the trapped souls to . . . wherever they're supposed to go."

Ren collected the cards of the two patterns and tapped them straight, trying to think. Trying to tease out what was insight, what was aža, and what was the medallion talking. She should have taken it out of her pocket before she began—but would she have understood as much without it?

And that's why you need to be afraid. Because you're asking yourself that question.

Unthinking habit had made her shuffle the small stack of cards. On pure impulse, Ren dealt three of them out in a line, faceup.

Three, like Tricat.

Or like the three parts of the soul.

She must have made some sound, because suddenly both Grey and Vargo were there. "What is it?" Grey asked.

"Advice for us to follow?" Vargo said.

"Not in the way you're thinking. It's *her*—the nameless szorsa." Ren couldn't pattern her directly, but following the few threads the woman still had, the hood and the medallions . . .

Her fingers hovered over the first card. "Pearl's Promise. The card they needed to move, so they would succeed in overthrowing the Tyrant. From the woven thread—as the szekani is that thread of the soul. Her szekani is the part of her *in the hood*. And The Face of Light." She shifted to the third card. "From the spinning thread."

::Like the Lumen?::

Ren nodded. "This is the card I associate most with numinatria. The spinning thread of the soul is the dlakani, which should pass on to reward or punishment. But instead, that is bound up with the medallions."

Grey inhaled. "And Sleeping Waters from the cut thread. The card of place—*this* place. But that would mean the part in the dream is her čekani. That's...not supposed to be there."

His flat tone belied his understatement. The čekani was the part that came back to the material world, to embodiment and to life, twining itself with a new szekani and dlakani in place of the old. It was in the wrong place—*all* the parts of her were in the wrong place. "I think she was not cut off from her people," Ren said. "Not in the usual way. She cut *herself* off, from shame, and the scattering of her soul means she cannot mend it."

Grey laid a hand on her right shoulder, a steadying grip against the vertigo of that thought. Strength that would hold her, when her own strength faltered.

And Vargo would keep thinking, when her own mind wanted to freeze in horror. "Remember Fadrin's vision?" he asked.

Fadrin had held Quinat during the ritual, and unlike Mezzan, he'd shared his vision with Tanaquis. It had shown him that for a time, Kaius was the master of the medallions, using their power without falling prey to it. But then a woman died, and after that, *they* mastered *him*. Transforming him into the Tyrant of legend, indulging his every terrible whim.

"We figured it meant the szorsa died," Vargo went on. "But we didn't know why. It makes sense now: She was his living Uniat, whether she wanted to be or not. She kept things in balance. But even dead, even with the physical chain destroyed, her soul still connects them." He brooded over it for a moment. "It's hard to destroy a soul. Maybe impossible."

"We *free* her," Ren said firmly. Not because she expected Vargo or Alsius to argue with her—much less Grey—but because she could already imagine what some of the other medallion holders might say. "We get her szekani out of the hood and her dlakani out of the chain, and we give her peace." She swept the cards together, murmuring a prayer. Then, shuddering, she pulled Tricat out of her pocket and slapped it onto the desk. A few inches of distance didn't protect her much, but at least she wasn't *carrying* it anymore. She couldn't wait to shove it back into its hiding spot.

"Nice words," Vargo said. "We still need a way to do it."

Ren had a notion, at least for the szekani. But she couldn't try it right now—not when the aža in her body was dulling to normalcy, the insights it granted fading like mist. Not without some careful thought first, and some offerings made to the Faces and the Masks.

But once that was done...

"The same way it became bound in the first place." She turned to Grey and Vargo, hoping her smile looked more confident than it felt. "I will change the Rook's pattern."

13

The Mask of Ravens

The problem with being trained by a perfectionist was that Vargo had picked up the same tendencies. He couldn't leave even the preliminary work of a major inscription in anyone else's hands. Which meant he wound up on his hands and knees in a canal-side warehouse in Dockwall while the day laborers moved pegs and string around, and Orostin pretended to be awake in the corner.

Sitting back on his heels, Vargo flexed his shoulders, wincing at the crackle of bones and sinew. This warehouse came courtesy of a charter from Fulvet—one Quientis might regret granting him now that everybody suspected Vargo of colluding with Ren. Vargo should have laid down some protective figures here a while ago, but he'd been too busy with the river numinat and the medallions. The numinata couldn't be inlaid until Vargo sketched them out, though, so here he was: coat shucked and sleeves rolled up, chalk dusting him almost as pale as a cheese-eater. Too late, he realized he'd exposed the knot of his oath with Ren, tied around his wrist, and he sneaked a quick glance at the dozing Orostin. Had the other man noticed?

::Ninat needs to be shifted slightly east. It's not balanced with Quarat,:: Alsius said from his spider's-eye view in the rafters as Vargo rolled his sleeves back down.

He was being exceptionally picky today. Not just today, either; ever since that disaster in the temple, when Mirscellis's spirit was driven away by the frenzied szorsa. Ren had tried to find him, without either hope or success. Pattern was about connections, those threads Ren saw, and Mirscellis had none anymore.

Neither had that missing piece of Ren's spirit, when the Night of Hells left her unable to sleep. But they'd had her body and the other parts of her spirit to help then. Vargo couldn't do anything for Mirscellis. Or for Ren or Alsius, each of them fearing the man was lost forever.

Except this: to grit his teeth and cooperate when Alsius criticized every tiny flaw in his inscription. Vargo checked the plans for the master numinat, with the various child numinata tucked along the elegant curve of the spira aurea: Quinat to protect against mold and vermin, Quarat to shield against misfortune like fire and flood, Ninat to prevent spoilage. Lowering the sketch, he peered at the tangle of chalked guidelines, like a game of skip-hop run amok.

Redrawing Ninat would keep him here until sunset. But the more precise his chalking now, the longer the protections would last. And it would make Alsius happier.

He briefly thought the creak as he stood up was his knees objecting to all that time on the floor. But Orostin went from apparent somnolence to on his feet in one breath, and a chilly breeze told Vargo the warehouse door had opened.

"You should be *between* Vargo and the door," Varuni said to Orostin, shutting it behind herself.

He grunted and slumped back. "En't like nobody could get at him here—not without me hearing noise from outside, first."

"Maybe, maybe not. But you're also responsible for stopping this asshole from slipping off without telling you."

"I haven't done that in a while," Vargo said, bracing against his own hip to crack his lower back. "Done in Floodwatch?" Her people had summoned her there for some kind of meeting, hence his being saddled with Orostin as a replacement.

Varuni glanced at the others. "Need to talk to you about that."

The warehouse's open interior left no space for private conversation. "You can have a break," Vargo told the day workers, and led Varuni to a far corner as they shuffled outside.

Alsius met them there, dropping onto Vargo's head. Usually that sort of antic would get at least an eyebrow twitch from Varuni, though Vargo had never determined if it was amusement or disgust. Now she didn't so much as blink. "What's wrong?" he asked.

She wasn't scowling at him, so he hadn't done anything to upset her. But something shifted under the stone of her facade. Something about their friendship, and her duty to her people.

She thinks of me as a friend?

A chill trailed down his spine like the tip of a knife. Varuni had always been unreadable. How was he reading her now? And not just her mood, but—

"I'm going home," Varuni said. "Back to Isarn."

"The fuck?" If there'd been a chair, Vargo would have dropped into it. He settled for bracing a chalky hand on the wall. "Did I piss someone off? You?" But she wasn't angry. Not at him, at least.

"You always piss me off." A smile glimmered, white teeth against dark skin like a falling star. Then it faded. "No. My family has less need of a smuggler now that Prasinet is relaxing the tariffs, and you have less need of a bodyguard now that you're protected by your title. Or so my mother's agent says. She wants me home."

"And what do you want?" Even as he asked, Vargo knew the answer. Varuni might keep a stoic countenance, but she cared deeply for her friends. Vargo, Sedge, a few others over the years. But she also felt the weight of duty, to her family and her people. A duty that was no longer in Nadežra.

He shouldn't *know* those things. Not from just looking at her.

"I haven't seen my family in years," Varuni said. "I've gained two siblings and ten cousins while I've been up here. And they want to reward me for our success. They invested in a smuggler, wound up with a nobleman." Another glimmer of a smile, but he could see the weight underneath. Her loyalty, pulling her in two directions.

And not just that. Fear—because as much as she might try to

hide it, this Primordial shit scared her. But Vargo felt like he saw that with different eyes. With normal ones.

Primordial shit. It must be the Sessat medallion showing him her conflict of loyalty. But he'd left it at home, safe behind imbued locks and layers of numinata.

Hadn't he?

As casually as he could, Vargo ran his hands down his waistcoat, like he was brushing away chalk. And felt it, a lump in the waist pocket that *shouldn't be there.*

Alsius, did you notice me picking up Sessat this morning? Maybe it was something else. A forgotten focus, an oversized forro.

::No. Why? You mean—you have it *on* you?::

Varuni peered at Vargo. "Are you all right?"

"Fine," he said reflexively. "Haven't eaten enough today. Orostin didn't think to remind me." Why the *fuck* had he picked up Sessat? Absentmindedly, like he might tuck a spare handkerchief into his pocket. But nobody should be half so casual around a Primordial artifact.

He forced himself to focus on Varuni. *Don't go—* The words almost leapt from his mouth. The idea of her leaving for Isarn was like the islet turning to mud under his feet. She gave his life stability, and damn it, she was a friend. Things Sessat liked. He'd thought, when he volunteered to take that medallion instead of Quinat, that he was picking the one he'd be less susceptible to.

He'd been a fool.

Give me a moment, Vargo said to Alsius, his heart beating far too fast. *One problem at a time.*

"Glad to be a success story," he said, scrambling for the thread of their conversation. Varuni had dodged his question about what she wanted; she hadn't made a decision. Maybe the right words could convince her to stay.

Maybe he didn't need words.

For a moment he couldn't breathe past the idea. He couldn't do it right here, right now; it required numinatrian preparation. But he could help Varuni make up her mind. He could keep from losing her. She was a friend, wasn't she? He had precious few of those. And she already wanted to stay. He wouldn't be making her do anything she didn't want.

A searing nip on his neck almost made him slap Peabody flat. The pain did its job, though; it broke Vargo from the Primordial spiral of his own thoughts. His heart pulsed like a battle drum. Use Sessat to fuck with Varuni's mind? That was the *last* thing a friend should do.

She was right to be afraid of this thing. And she was right to get away from him.

"When are you going?" Vargo asked, before Varuni could inquire into his sudden spasm. Small as it was, Alsius's nip still burned, and he leaned into that pain to keep his thoughts clear. "Sedge'll want to see you off. A few others that aren't terrified of you. Maybe a few that are, if you want to fuck with them one last time. We could have a party."

Her weight settled back, off the balls of her feet. "You don't need to worry about that. Plenty of other things keeping you busy."

"No, let me. Least I can do, after years of you keeping my uncooperative ass intact." Should he not say that? Fucking A'ash. Varuni had more than earned some reward, whatever a Primordial whispered in his ear. "Look, I'll be here a few hours more. Orostin's got my back; you go take care of your own business. We'll talk at home tonight."

Varuni's mouth bent in a frown, like she knew he was being weird about this but wasn't going to prod him as to why. "Let me talk to Orostin first."

While she did that, Vargo pretended to study his diagrams. *Alsius . . . I don't even remember picking it up. But it's in my pocket.*

He didn't add, *And that scares the liquid shit out of me,* but he didn't have to. Alsius crawled down to his shoulder. ::We should warn the others.::

Yeah. If I can't be trusted anymore . . .

::No, I meant the others may find themselves doing the same.::

That thought was even more nauseating. There was no way

Vargo could stay here, calmly scribing guidelines, with a piece of Primordial evil in his pocket. Earlier he'd been too wrapped up in his head to pay much attention to anyone around him, but now he looked at Orostin and saw that the man wanted to join some kind of legitimate organization—not the hawks, but maybe a mercenary company. Alsius wanted to restore Mirscellis, so they could discuss everything the man had ever written about numinatria and the underlying structure of the cosmos.

He had to get home and get this thing off him.

Varuni came back. "Put the fear of you into Orostin?" Vargo asked, with false lightness.

"Just confirming it was already there," she said, perfectly serious. "You and I will talk tonight."

Watching her leave, Vargo clenched his hands behind his back, to keep from reaching for the thing that could make her stay.

Froghole, Lower Bank: Pavnilun 19

The high-ceilinged ostretta the Fog Spiders claimed as their hole sucked up noise and boxed your ears with it till Sedge couldn't properly hear nothing. It only got worse the more people gathered. When everyone was shouting...

And *everyone* was shouting.

The cause lay scattered about the room, in cheap broadsheets crumpled up and stepped on and thrown. One of Ertzan Scrub's old loyalists had brought in the first copy, but others weren't far behind. They were all over the city, seemed like: little quarter pages announcing in bold type A KNOT OF LIES.

Beneath that, the knife to the ribs: the news that Derossi Vargo weren't sworn to the lieutenants who led his knots. Not any of 'em, and never had been.

Now every last damn Fog Spider was up in arms, demanding to know if it was true, demanding to know what they were going to do if it was, demanding that Nikory answer for this betrayal of knot oaths.

Your secrets are my secrets.

Sedge was getting tired of problems he couldn't solve by beating them up.

What he could do was drag out a crate for Nikory to stand on and bang a pewter flagon against the wall until the metal bent and people shut up...for all of two breaths, until Nikory admitted it was true.

After more shouting and banging, old Spitcrust Surz waved his copy of the broadsheet. "Why should we listen to you another moment? Scrub was our last true boss. Your loyalty's been bought and paid for, and it en't to us."

That called forth too many growls of agreement. This kind of mood got knot leaders overthrown. Sure, everyone here was tied to Nikory—but oaths didn't stop rebellions from happening.

Sedge didn't have another crate handy, so he settled for jumping onto a table, one boot skidding in spilled millet beer. "Show me how Nikory en't been loyal to us! What's a knot leader supposed to do, anyway? Protect his people, keep 'em safe, hit back at their enemies. When en't Nikory done that?"

He could have split his own tongue for letting that question slip, especially when someone shouted, "Din't we lose three people in the Dreamweaver Riots, running around on *Eret Vargo*'s orders?"

"Knocking heads and protecting what's ours," Nikory snapped back. "Like we would have done anyways."

"What about Hraček? And Yurdan! Vargo made him take ash, let him get shredded—"

"Don't you talk about Yurdan," Sedge snarled. Red rage pounded his skull at the memory of being helpless to protect one of his own. A rage Vargo had shared, for all he kept it behind a mask of calculation. "You don't know what shit you're spewing. I was there—"

A stamp from Nikory cut Sedge off, choking back his urge to play dentist with Surz's teeth. Nikory said, "Yurdan volunteered. And nobody here can say Vargo din't take vengeance for how they died. Or did you all forget how he earned that title you treat like piss in your mouths?" He let the silence hang for a moment before adding, "What else?"

Every complaint they brought, Nikory had an answer for, to the point where Sedge wondered if he'd expected this day to come. And after a bit, Nikory weren't the only one speaking in Vargo's defense. Newer people, like Lurets and Dneče—people who came to the Fog Spiders after Vargo's takeover.

After Vargo made the group better. Sedge had heard enough stories from fists like Old Piotr to know he wouldn't have wanted to go nowhere near their web before that.

"Look," Sedge said when the argument started going in circles. "Oaths matter, yeah. But they en't the only thing that matters, are they? You all know I was a Finger. Put my hands between Ondrakja's and swore the oaths. You know what she did? Beat me halfway to death, then cut me out and beat me nine-tenths the rest of the way."

The crowd around him was too close-packed for Sedge to spit without hitting somebody, but he made the noise. "Ask me who I'd rather follow, Vargo or that hag."

That got a few cheers and curses of support. Hardly enough to end the argument for good—nothing would manage that in an afternoon—but the shouting shrank to rumbles, and Sedge breathed out in relief. The threat to Nikory was past.

Vargo, though . . . he was still in a pit of trouble.

As Dneče rolled out the cask they usually saved for celebrations, Sedge sidled up to Nikory. "We en't the only knot having this conversation, you know."

They watched the mob break apart, Sedge noting the ones scowling the most, in case he needed to talk to them later, fist to fist. Nikory said, "I'll let Vargo know he might want to stay east of Dawngate for a while."

"What I want to know is," Sedge muttered, "who leaked this?" There were lots of suspects. Every one of Vargo's lieutenants knew they hadn't sworn any oaths with him, whatever their knots believed.

In a low voice, Nikory said, "I think it was me."

A strangled noise escaped Sedge. He stared at Nikory, and the man's shoulders hunched low. "You heard what Acrenix did to me?"

The Sessat medallion—though Nikory didn't know that was the cause. Ghiscolo had used it to poke Nikory's doubts about Vargo, getting him to sell out the meeting with Andrejek in Lacewater. "You told him about the oaths," Sedge said. "How there weren't none."

"Din't seem important at the time. But...yeah."

Ghiscolo was gone. But his people weren't. Maybe Sibiliat, sitting under house arrest out in the bay, had gotten her hands on a printing press. Maybe Carinci was getting revenge for her son's death.

Maybe it didn't matter. Just like Letilia spilling Ren's identity, the problem wasn't who said it.

The problem was, it was true.

"Maybe let me tell Vargo," Sedge said. Varuni was going to knit herself a cap from *somebody's* innards. Sedge just hoped it wasn't his.

Isla Prišta, Westbridge: Pavnilun 19

I will change the Rook's pattern.

Ren's words echoed in Grey's thoughts, like the tolling of the city's bells the night the Tyrant died. She had such confidence in her skills—and rightfully so. If anyone living could do it, she could.

But even for Ren, this was asking a lot.

She sat on the floor of the parlour with her entire deck spread around her. For the last two bells she'd been thinking out loud, debating the different kinds of pattern. "I remember a story where a szorsa cursed the lover who betrayed her," she mused, lying on her back and staring at the ceiling. "Some five-card arrangement. If I could invert that...But I know not how it is done."

Grey knew. If three cards made a thread, and nine, woven cloth, then a five-card crux was the shears that cut. Laročja used it to intimidate her enemies. Or to frighten her clients into paying for protection, pretending she was laying some other spread when her hands, "guided by Ažerais," mysteriously dealt five cards instead.

The memory choked him, and the words didn't come out. Ren sat up. "But this is not a curse. It is a—a reweaving."

"To free a spirit trapped in cloth," Grey said, sitting tailor-style across from her, tucked into a gap among the cards. She spoke Vraszenian more often since her unmasking, and he answered her in kind. "Though I know not how far textile metaphors will take us."

The smile she flashed at him didn't last. "Grey...have you considered what might happen if we succeed?"

"In destroying the medallions?" He blew out a slow breath. "I've tried."

"No, I mean..." She pushed cards out of the way so she could shift close enough to lay her hand on his knee. "When from the hood we free her. If her aid made the Rook, then losing her...We might never be able to fix him. There might not *be* a Rook any longer."

He'd already broken the Rook by refusing to let Ren die. If destruction was the only route to freeing another's soul—or possibly many...

"Then let him end." Grey touched The Laughing Crow. The card's meaning had nothing to do with the Rook, but the black bird always reminded Grey of him. "Once the medallions are destroyed, what purpose is left?"

"The Rook is more than that fight. Yes, for a single cause he was made—but you came with us to Floodwatch. You helped free Koszar from prison. Destroying the medallions will not fix all Nadežra's problems; still the city will need a champion when they are gone."

"As you said: *I'm* the one who came to Floodwatch. *I* chose to help in Dockwall. The city will have you, their Black Rose. And it will have me." He stroked her head, palm gliding over the braids she wore all the time now. "I'm not proposing to retire. But I can be enough. I can *make* myself enough."

"I never doubted that," Ren said. She bit her lip before adding gently, "But is it you who wants it...or Quinat?"

The bell clanging on the stoop interrupted any response Grey might give. Followed by pounding, and then a shrill voice as loud as a rooster's crow.

"Oi! Any of you lot at home? Stiff-britches? Freckles? Open up!"

"It appears Mistress Bones is paying a call," Grey said. He rested a hand on Ren's shoulder as he rose. "I'll let her in while you clean that up. Otherwise, she'll either demand a reading, or win your shirt from you in a game of sixes."

Ren's half-hearted laugh said they would return to their conversation once Arkady was gone, and it gnawed at Grey's heart as he went to answer the door. Was Ren right? Was the medallion affecting him more strongly than before?

Arkady barged in, knocking all those thoughts aside as she ricocheted off his hip into the wall. "You got problems," she said, shoving a wrinkled broadsheet into Grey's hands. "We *all* got problems now, thanks to that chalk-fucking friend of yours."

"Vargo? What's happened?" Ren popped into the hallway, deck in hand.

As Grey skimmed the smeared type, Arkady said, "Somebody decided to wave Vargo's smalls for everyone to see, is what. Now word is the knots are all riled up, looking for something to cut. I sent one of mine off to Eastbridge to warn him, but figured you'd want to know sooner than later."

"He isn't in Eastbridge," Ren said, stuffing the cards in her pocket and snatching the broadsheet from Grey. "He's in Dockwall, working on— Never mind. You're right. We have to warn him."

Dockwall, Lower Bank: Pavnilun 19

They were too late.

For one nauseating instant, Ren thought the body along the

canal was Vargo's. He'd been wearing plainer coats to the Lower Bank lately, so as not to catch attention; the bloodstained broadcloth could have been his. But the head had a balding patch, and shameful relief flooded through her when she realized it was Orostin.

"Fuck," Arkady said, toeing the body until it flopped over without the resistance of the living. "You think they went through his pockets before they dumped him?"

"Please don't check," Grey said, kneeling in the muck of the street to feel at Orostin's neck. Then under his nose. He shook his head and stood, grim eyes meeting Ren's.

She glanced up and down the empty walkway. Too empty for this time of afternoon. A pair of gloves lay on the flagstones, their knuckles bloody. Vargo's, still wet when she touched them. "Someone must have seen something."

"Sure they did." Arkady spat over her shoulder. "But you think they'll risk the local knot coming down on them?"

"I think I can be very convincing."

The quiet menace in Grey's words rocked Arkady back on her heels. Ren pushed through the open gate into the warehouse yard. She considered and discarded subtlety before calling out, "A forro for anyone who knows what happened outside!"

A head peeped out of the small building that housed the office. "You're that Alta Renata. The one that pulled one over on the cuffs?"

"Where's Vargo?"

The laborer edged out, gaze raking the yard. Grey and Arkady, following Ren in, didn't send him bolting for cover. "We was helping him with the work here. That Isarnah woman came to talk to him, and then he decided to leave early, but—" The man hunched defensively. "I en't paid to fight for him. Only to hold a peg while he walks circles with some chalk."

"How many? Did you recognize any of them? How badly was he hurt? Which way did they take him?" Grey rattled off questions like he was still in Vigil uniform. Ren fell back a step, keeping an eye on the gate—and saw a flash of color in the shadows.

"Alsius!" She rushed to the gap between the cobbles and the wall foundation, dropping to her knees where the little spider scuttled back and forth like a worried parent. With Vargo gone, she couldn't hear him. And she hadn't thought to bring the numinat that let him speak to her on his own.

But he was alive. And capable of walking, which meant Vargo must be, too—she hoped. Not just walking, but waving his legs like flags.

In a crack of the foundation, she spied the blue gleam of steel.

All the breath went out of her. *What the fuck is Sessat doing here?* Had Cibrial tried to remove the medallion from Vargo's untrustworthy hands?

Grey crouched beside her. "What are you—*djek*."

Ren shared her theory, and he shook his head. "It sounds more like a knot. Doesn't mean Cibrial couldn't have sent them, but—"

"But an angry knot is more likely." Vargo must have dropped the medallion to keep it from being found. Looking helplessly at it, Ren said, "One of us will have to take it. Or Arkady. Unless—"

The bright shape of Peabody splayed itself over the steel circle. Then he began laboriously nudging it out of the crack.

Despite everything, a touch of mordant humor crept into Grey's voice. "Do you think it counts if a spider has possession?"

If it did, then Vargo would be cursed. He hadn't used the medallion any more than he could avoid, so the curse ought to be light... but if one of his knots had taken him, he was in a situation where Sessat's impulses could very easily destroy him.

They had to find him. For so many reasons.

Ren was in Vraszenian clothing, including a paneled sash belt. She unlaced it and laid the fabric on the ground for Peabody to climb on, pushing the medallion; then she picked it up like a sling. When she looked at Grey, she got no preternatural insights. Either he had no desires related to Sessat, or Alsius was the medallion's holder, and she was just his sedan bearer.

Arkady leaned against the gate, watching like she'd stumbled on an awkward bit of street theatre. "En't even gonna ask. Guess I'll put my kids out and see if they hear anything, but dunno if I'll get much. The knots are gonna squabble over territory like gulls over day-old fish guts, soon as they realize there's nobody making 'em play nice. Wager the whole Lower Bank's about to go to shit."

"Hey!" the laborer called out as Ren turned to go. "What about that forro?"

Ren had only a few centiras on her. Thanks to Utrinzi, she had a source of income now, but the days of walking around with a fortune in her pocket were over. "Come to number four, Via Brelkoja, Isla Prišta in Westbridge," she called over her shoulder, tossing what coins she had his way. "You'll get paid. Right now, we have to rescue our friend."

Seven Knots, Lower Bank: Pavnilun 19

The bag over Vargo's head muffled sight and sound, and he went in and out of focus, but he was alert enough to notice when the language around him went from cant-spattered Lower Bank Liganti to city-flattened Vraszenian. Aware enough to smell the mix of sweat and spices, raw garlic and cooked rice, that said he was in Seven Knots. And canny enough to guess he'd been handed over to the Stretsko.

When the bag came off, he expected to see Branek. After all, the man's reach had extended beyond the Anduske to Stretsko knots along the Lower Bank, and he might well have figured out Vargo was involved with the Kiralič's rescue, despite the Cut Ears cutting loose. It turned out he'd guessed wrong, but Vargo recognized the deep-set eyes and strong brows of the woman leaning over him.

"Tserdev." He coughed out the dust-thickened phlegm clogging his throat. "How much did you pay for me?"

"Peace between the Stretsko and your *former* people until Veiled Waters has passed."

"Former?" He was halfway through a mental question to Alsius before he realized that if his thoughts were silent, it meant the old man was too far away to hear him. When the Roundabout Boys jumped them at the warehouse, Vargo barely had time to cast Sessat into the shadows of the gate before he was mobbed by his own fists. Alsius had protested strenuously at being ordered to stay behind and guard it, but he'd obeyed. At least Vargo could trust *that* loyalty.

He might have expected betrayal from the Moon Harpies or the Odd Alley Gang, both of them on the edge of Seven Knots and at war with Tserdev's people. The Roundabout Boys were a Dockwall crew—and mostly Nadežran, not Vraszenian. "What did you offer, to get them to turn?"

Laughter answered him. Kneeling close enough for spitting, Tserdev fished a crumpled broadsheet from her panel coat. Vargo only caught sight of the headline and a few random phrases before she crammed it into his mouth.

"How can someone betray a man who knows nothing of loyalty?" Standing, she waved to the fists looming behind her. "Search him."

Vargo spat out the ink-foul paper, pretending to be separate from his body as the men cut through his bindings and stripped him down. They were thorough—and not gentle—but they kept it impersonal. They removed his contraceptive numinat, and even found the tiny knife and packet of chalk powder he'd sewn into the band of his smallclothes.

The search got to his knot charm—the one he shared with Ren. "Don't you dare fucking cut that," Vargo growled.

"So *some* oaths you respect," Tserdev said. "Fortunate that your own people found this not." Taking the knife from her minion, she cut the cord and tossed the charm atop the pile.

Doesn't matter. Didn't cut it myself. Changes nothing. Vargo shook with the urge to rip the knife out of Tserdev's hands and do some cutting of his own.

"What's this?" Tserdev lifted one boot to nudge the brand over Vargo's chest.

"None of your fucking business," he snapped. A too-quick

answer would be taken for a lie. His breath hissed out when one of the fists yanked his head up by the hair, and the dull ache from his beating exploded like horses galloping through his skull.

Tserdev's smile was vicious. "Try again."

"Ow! Fine!" Marshaling his best *you're a fucking idiot who knows nothing about numinatria* expression, Vargo said, "It's an initiation brand. Like your knot bracelet. You heard about the cult Iridet cracked down on last autumn? This was the price of admission."

"What's it do?"

"Nothing—ow, *fuck!* Stop that." Vargo glared up at the fist yanking at his hair like the man was a rough lover. "Nothing *anymore.* Cult's disbanded, and all I got is this stupid scar."

"So to your own people you swear no oaths, but from the cuffs you'll accept this?" She spat, the gobbet striking Vargo's brand and oozing down his skin. "You deserve not the loyalty you've been given."

"What loyalty?" Vargo glanced around the shabby back room, as much as the grip on his hair would allow. Aside from his pile of clothing, there was only a thin pallet shoved against a wall, a bucket for night soil, and an oil lamp hanging from a hook by the door. He'd enjoyed nicer accommodations in Dockwall Prison.

Tserdev didn't give the obvious answer. Instead she crossed her arms and began pacing, like a cat without a tail to lash. "In Staveswater you and that Black Rose kidnapped my brother, so that to your will I would bend. For months I have searched, and *nothing.* I want him back." She stopped and gave Vargo a cruel smile. "Your knots know not where he is, but you do. And from you I will have my answers."

So this wasn't Anduske business. Tserdev was pursuing her own ends.

And it was obvious what methods she had in mind. Vargo stopped himself from rolling his eyes. "Let me guess. Splinters under the fingernails, crushing my balls, that sort of thing? I'll spare you the trouble. He's at the Isarnah trading house in Floodwatch."

Tserdev spat a dismissive noise like it was gristle between her teeth. "So quickly you answer my question?"

"Coward," muttered the man mauling his hair.

Vargo smiled like it was a compliment. "Ča Očelen, you and I are no longer at war. I took Dmatsos to keep you off my turf—but seems the Lower Bank decided they don't need me, so *I* don't need *him*. The Isarnah have your brother, and they'll trade him for me."

Tserdev caught his chin, nails digging into his skin. "Think you to trick me? Eret Vargo is so well-known for the webs he spins, he might as well call himself Varadi."

"But I'm not Varadi, am I? I'm Nadežran and a noble. I care about two things: business, and my own skin. Why suffer a beating to withhold information that could buy my freedom?"

The grip eased, Tserdev's heavy brows knitting over eyes glittering with the promise of retribution if this was a ruse. "Perhaps there is little left to trade. If my brother you have hurt—"

Vargo's barked laugh silenced the threat. "Again, where's the profit? Your brother has been treated well—a sight better than this." He couldn't move with Tserdev and the fists holding him, but his glance took in the grimy room and all his possessions stripped from him.

She sniffed an unamused laugh, but let him go. "We'll see what your foreign allies say. Until then . . . you are in *my* web now, Vargo. And I will make sure you stay there."

Floodwatch, Lower Bank: Pavnilun 21

The grey sky seemed low enough to touch, and a cold wind was knifing down the Dežera. Ren wanted to rub her arms for warmth, but the Black Rose couldn't show ordinary weakness. Instead she stood in a shadowed doorway and waited, hardly breathing, for Tserdev to arrive.

She'd expected tracing Vargo to be like following the target in a game of cup-and-shell—always assuming they didn't simply find his corpse in a canal. The speed with which a message arrived at the Isarnah compound in Floodwatch spoke of Vargo cutting a deal with his captor instead. A refreshingly straightforward trade: Vargo for Dmatsos Očelen.

The Isarnah were glad to hand Dmatsos over, but that was all they were willing to risk: no contingent of guards, no promise of retribution if the exchange failed. Which made more sense when Ren found out that Varuni had officially been recalled from her duties as Vargo's bodyguard, and was to be sent home to Isarn.

Varuni's comment on that had been succinct. "I'm not going anywhere until we get him back."

She waited outside the compound now, alongside Sedge and Nikory. The Fog Spiders hadn't sold Vargo out, but neither were they willing to offend Tserdev to get him back—especially not with Orostin dead. Those two were here as individuals, not as Fog Spiders. Ren, masked as the Black Rose, hid off to one side; Grey, hooded as the Rook, did the same on the opposite side.

The five of them, and no more. Ren's questionable status and Vargo's illegal past made her wary of seeking the Vigil's help, and Tserdev had refused to show if any cuffs got involved. Which meant that the group now approaching outnumbered them nearly three to one—*before* counting the men carrying five sedan chairs with their windows blacked out.

Varuni spoke first. "You try anything against us, and my people *will* intervene." Guards were watching from the top of the compound wall.

"There will be no need for such things so long as you hurt my brother not," Tserdev said. "Where is he?"

::Vargo's here,:: Alsius said to Ren, his mental voice shaking with relief. The numinat that let him communicate with her in Vargo's absence was on a barrel next to Varuni, weighted down with rocks. If Tserdev had shown up without her prisoner, Ren had wanted more than Alsius's silence to clue her in. ::Though...he's not talking. He's very disoriented. What have they done to him?::

Ren cursed her inability to answer him with her mind. Which chair was Vargo in? Tserdev had undoubtedly brought five precisely to keep them from trying to rush it.

The compound's gate opened. Varuni reached through and

pulled Dmatsos out, hands tied and feet hobbled with a short rope. "Unharmed, like I said. Now give me Vargo."

At a flick of Tserdev's hand, one of her fists dragged a body from a sedan chair, flopping it over his shoulder like a sack of laundry. Dirty, bloodstained laundry; Tserdev hadn't shown him a tenth the courtesy given to Dmatsos. Vargo's hair was stringy with grease and grit, falling over a bruised and swollen face, and mud was ground into his coat of blue broadcloth, like he'd been dragged through the streets by his boot.

::What did they do to him? Vargo? Vargo! Please tell me you're all right.::

::'Mm here. Stop yelling. Y'got Sessat safe?::

Ren fought the urge to sag with relief at that muzzy mental response. Alsius leapt off the barrel and skittered across the ground, leaving the numinat behind. But she could still hear him, through the connection with Vargo. ::Yes, you silly boy. Don't worry. We're going to get you safe as well. Then we can deal with curses and the like.::

Varuni stood impassive, letting her own scrutiny hide the fact that she was waiting for a warning from Ren. When none came, she nodded.

The fist put Vargo down and shoved him stumbling forward. Varuni cut the rope between Dmatsos's ankles and did the same. As the two men neared each other, though, the bright spot of Peabody slammed to a halt on the hard-packed ground.

::Wait. That's not right. Vargo, you're not hurt. *We're* not hurt. I'd feel it.::

::No. Drugged, maybe. Can't see where I am. Sedan chair? Fuck, gonna puke...::

Ren's blood froze. Her mouth didn't. "Varuni, it's a trick! They're swapping a fake!"

Floodwatch, Lower Bank: Pavnilun 21

The man Tserdev was trying to pass off as Vargo kept lurching toward the Isarnah compound. Everyone else went the other direction.

Grey had the longest legs, and he'd been poised to move since Tserdev appeared. That the woman loved her brother and wanted him back, Grey believed; that she was willing to let Vargo out of her own hands so easily, he didn't.

He outpaced the others, almost close enough to grab Dmatsos, but his eye was on a different prize. Vargo had to be in one of the other sedan chairs, a fallback if the fake was identified too soon. Which one, though?

Grey almost didn't notice the knife flung his way until it was too late to dodge. He swerved, and behind him Varuni spat a curse, but not in pain. The bearers had picked up the other four chairs and were bolting down different lanes. They'd dropped things on the ground, though—things vomiting smoke into the chill air, hiding their movements as they fled.

Djek. Can't see! The real Rook enhanced Grey's sight, but this substitute did nothing except hide his face. "I'll take the left!" he snapped, knowing the others were behind him, Ren and Varuni and Nikory and Sedge. Alsius might be able to figure out which chair Vargo was in, but not fast enough. They couldn't risk losing sight of any.

At least the sedan bearers were slowed by their burdens. One of the pursuers would catch the chair with Vargo in it. *And then what?* Grey thought, sprinting after his chosen target. They were outnumbered, and splitting up wouldn't help. But he couldn't think of anything better.

Tserdev's people would want to get to the river, to a friendly skiff. This lane bent parallel to the water, around a long set of grain warehouses, but Grey knew the doors to one of those warehouses lined up nicely, a shortcut he'd used before. He kicked his way through one—

There was no door on the opposite side. He'd gone into the wrong building. *I know my way around Floodwatch!* But he was used to relying on memories besides his own, all the echoes residing in the hood. Now there was only silence, and he'd gone the wrong way.

Cursing furiously, Grey lunged back out into the street. If he couldn't go through, he'd go over.

He leapt for the eaves, feeling grim satisfaction that at least he didn't need the Rook for *that*. Even without the lost gloves' improved grip, his muscles responded with smooth power, hauling him onto the low, flat roof. Crouching low, Grey ran across, looking for his quarry.

As expected, they were coming back his way, heading for the lane that led to the river. Grey timed his jump perfectly, crashing into the first guard and taking the man down amid the snap of broken bones. That surprise let him get the front chair bearer, dropping the carrying poles so the back bearer stumbled, and from there he spun to deal with the second guard, the weight of his whirling coat feeling almost like what he'd lost.

But any satisfaction died when he tore open the door of the sedan chair and found it empty apart from a heavy sack. No Vargo.

An explosive crack came from upriver. Grey pivoted and staggered as his knee screamed. He'd landed badly from that jump. Masks damn it all—*nothing* he did was working like it should!

That couldn't be allowed to stop him. Gritting his teeth, Grey threw an elbow into the throat of the last man standing and set off in a lurching run for the source of the noise.

He got there too late. A sedan chair lay on its side, its floor shattered, but the bearers and guards were nowhere in sight—much less any occupant the chair might have had. Following some bloody footprints, Grey found Nikory against a warehouse wall, dazed, but still breathing.

Vargo. The footprints had to be from Vargo, managing some numinatrian trick in an attempt to escape. But they petered out: Where was he now?

Gone.

Rage and frustration drove Grey's boot into the nearest wall. *Not enough. Never enough!* He'd joined the Vigil thinking it would give him a way to help Nadežra; he'd become the Rook thinking the same. Now he was neither hawk nor Rook, and on his own, he couldn't even help Vargo. When the other man needed him most, Grey failed.

He carried the ruined hood inside his coat, a talisman to spur him on. Grey dragged it out and glared at it, chest heaving with exertion and failure. *I can* make *myself enough*, he'd told Ren. It was a lie. *This* was what he needed: the true Rook, the spirit built up over centuries of effort. They couldn't let it be destroyed. There had to be a way to mend what Grey had broken, while still freeing what shouldn't remain trapped. He held the lock in his hands; he just needed the key.

Pounding footsteps made him drop the hood and reach for his sword. But it was only Varuni and the Black Rose, and the way they staggered to a halt told him they'd met with no more success than he.

Grey saw more than that. *Ren. She's the key.*

Then he realized his other hand was in another pocket, wrapped around the smooth curve of a metal disc.

Quinat. Just as Vargo had picked up Sessat without realizing, he'd brought Quinat with him. He'd gripped it in his hand, thinking about what he needed, what he *wanted*.

And A'ash had shown him the answer.

He snatched his hand back like the iron was red-hot as Ren knelt to examine Nikory. "Did you see—"

"No." *Yes.* "I got here too late."

Varuni stood like a statue, hands curled into fists with nowhere to strike. "We've lost him."

Floodwatch, Lower Bank: Pavnilun 21

"You're a wily fucker, I'll give you that," Tserdev said as she entered the room where Vargo's guards had stashed him after his failed escape attempt. A different room than before; this one lacked a cot and a closestool. It boasted a chair he suspected wasn't meant for him. And a lot of cobwebs.

The sole of Vargo's bare foot exploded with pain as Tserdev

kicked it. Sticky warmth followed, oozing past the wet scab of gummy blood and Lower Bank filth the kick had knocked loose. Vargo wondered if he should thank her for the abuse. With as fast as he healed, he'd prefer the muck to end up on the *outside*.

Not that he'd wanted to rip open his flesh on the splintered edge of an unpadded sedan chair seat, or run barefoot and bleeding down a Floodwatch alley. But they'd tied his hands and hobbled his ankles, thinking that was enough to keep him from running if the drugs wore off. It would have been, if Alsius hadn't drilled him so much on basic numinatrian sigils that he could—literally—scribe them with his toes.

Messy, but an explosive numinat didn't need to last longer than the blast, and Vargo didn't want anything strong enough to kill him. Just a little noise. A momentary delay. A loud-as-fuck chin-flick to the cosmos that might give his friends time to catch up.

Nails sharp as rat claws dug into Vargo's cheeks as Tserdev forced his chin up to meet her gaze. "Too bad for you that I'm wilier."

Too bad for him that he hadn't realized she brought decoy chairs. When he busted out, the only person in sight was an unconscious Nikory. With no other friends there, he could only run—badly. And get his bleeding ass caught—easily.

"What I want to know is, how are you even conscious? We drugged you enough to put out a Meszaros draft horse." The chair scraped as Tserdev dragged it closer. She drew a knife, examining her teeth in the blade's reflection. "Care to share?"

Given that it was the only thing that might get him out of this alive, *no*. "Did you get your brother back?"

"He has a few things to say to you about his time as your guest. Dmatsyi, you can come in."

Dmatsos's beard was overgrown and his coat and trousers sleep rumpled, but he hadn't suffered in his stay with the Isarnah. Vargo had been very clear about that. No point in making enemies through bad treatment.

A philosophy Tserdev and her brother didn't seem to follow. Vargo bit down on a scream as Dmatsos stomped on the fingers of his right hand. Then he realized there was no reason *not* to scream, and gave it full voice until it shredded his throat.

"Straighten them," Tserdev said. Dmatsos obeyed, drawing another series of cries from Vargo. Sweat dripped into his eyes, his mouth. Salty. And copper-flavored. He'd bitten through his lip.

Tserdev's knife prodded his throbbing hand. Vargo tried to pull away, falling still with a strangled whimper when the knife pierced the webbing between thumb and finger, pinning him in place.

"Can't tell from this," Tserdev muttered. "Maybe if we broke them enough to show bone?"

"Or we just make him tell us." Standing, Dmatsos wound up for a kick. It struck Vargo's side, hard enough to lift him off the ground—and rip his hand free of the pinning knife. Then another kick. Vargo tried to curl around it, to catch Dmatsos's leg so he couldn't draw back. Dmatsos shook him loose. "What's the trick? Everyone says you can walk away from anything. How?"

"Enough." Crouching, Tserdev yanked her knife free of the floorboards. She flipped the blade, dragging the tip over the scar at Vargo's brow, down the jagged line along his neck. With a flick, she opened the sweat-soaked collar of his shirt to lay steel over the mark seared into his chest. "I think there's one explanation only. Cult scar, you said? No longer works. Shall we test it?"

"No," Vargo whispered, helplessly—just as the blade slashed across the brand.

14

The Ember Adamant

Isla Prišta, Westbridge: Pavnilun 21

"You told me it was him!"

Ren had never heard Varuni raise her voice. Now it rang off the wood-paneled walls of the parlour, rounded by the Isarnah accent Varuni almost never let through. Vargo's stone-faced, stoic body-guard was in a perfect fury, and the brunt of it was directed at Ren.

"I thought it *was* him," she said, knowing the words were inade-quate. "Alsius said he was drugged—it was difficult to tell—"

A mental wail cut her off. Peabody hunched inward, a tiny, anguished spot of color on his fabric numinat. ::His fingers! Oh, Lumen—they're breaking his fingers—::

Ren swallowed down nausea. "We solve nothing, casting blame—"

Skirting the low tea table, Varuni stalked toward Ren. "Easy for you to say, when *you're* the one to blame."

"Here now!" Tess planted herself between them, cheeks flushed with fury. "Raise your hand to my sister, and I'll be putting my fist to your face." She shook one wind-chapped hand under Varuni's nose.

Pulling up like she'd been threatened by a pigeon, Varuni snorted. "That fist?"

"No. *That* fist." Tess jerked her chin toward Sedge, who'd come up to flank Ren, with Grey on the other side.

::We don't have time for this! He's... Ow! His ribs—::

Ren's knees wouldn't hold her anymore. She sank onto the couch, barely able to form words. "They'll kill him. Tserdev is vindictive. Now that she has her brother back... what reason has she to keep Vargo alive?"

Arkady hocked an unrepentant loogie into the hearth. "Money. Bargaining with the Fog Spiders, if they've stayed loyal. Leverage over that Anduske fellow Vargo's been helping. Or over *you*. Lots of things she can get out of him, besides blood."

Her pragmatic assessment helped ground Ren—until Alsius *screamed*.

She shot to her feet. "What is it? What are they doing?"

The spider didn't answer. He was writhing in the center of the numinat, legs flailing helplessly, but nothing came through the link. She could *see* his scream... but she couldn't hear it.

"What's wrong with him now?" Arkady asked, peering at the spider. "Seen roaches do that when you douse 'em with mint oil or salt water, but en't nobody touched him."

"They don't need to," Ren whispered. "His life is tied to Vargo's."

Sedge's hand at her back steadied her. "The spider's alive. Means Vargo en't dead, right? Maybe healing the spider'll help. Tess, you got any restoratives?"

"In the kitchen," Tess said, hurrying out of the room.

Ren didn't realize she'd been twisting the knot charm around her wrist tight enough to stop blood until Grey's touch coaxed her grip open. "You can't hear him anymore?" he asked. At a shake of her head, his gaze flicked to the numinat. "Perhaps there's another way to communicate."

By the time they'd cleared the tea table and chalked rough lettering across it, Tess had returned with a jar and a spoon for Alsius to sip medicine from. The spasms had passed, but he was still unsteady as he crawled across the table, tapping the letters he wanted.

His message was short and to the point. *Link cut.*

Ren swallowed hard. "Then he probably lacks your strength, too. Does that mean...you won't know what happens to him?" *Does it mean you won't know if he dies?*

Peabody began moving again. *Unsure. Help V.* Then he hopped, as if to underline his words.

Easy enough to say—but *how*? Sedge and Varuni were arguing, the latter demanding aid from the Fog Spiders, the former doubting their willingness, and Arkady insisting her kids could search. Grey drew Ren aside, where others couldn't overhear. "We need the Rook."

She pressed the heels of her hands to her forehead. "Can we afford the distraction right now? We know not how long Vargo will have value to Tserdev." And there were many ways to break a person, while keeping their value.

"It's not a distraction. I said before that I was enough on my own. I was wrong. And Vargo's paying the price."

Once, he wouldn't have cared. Might have even celebrated. Now the quietness of his voice couldn't mask the guilt, the fear, the pain. Ren gripped his hand in her own. "I'm not certain I *can* fix the Rook—"

"You can. I know it." The sick look in his eyes said he knew it because it *had* to be true. Because the alternative was unthinkable.

She couldn't disappoint him.

Ren raised her voice to cut across Sedge and Varuni. "Go, and let us know when you learn anything. We'll be in the temple, trying... something else."

"Something else?" Tess echoed, mingling doubt and hope.

Grey nodded. "Do me one favor. Send for Ryvček."

Hidden temple, Old Island: Pavnilun 21

"So this is what's in here," Ryvček said, twirling the triple clover knot charm around her finger as she entered the hidden temple. "Often I have wondered."

Ren said, "This is where the medallions were joined, and also I think where the Rook was made. We hope it will assist in mending him."

"And the Zevriz, she is here as well?" Ryvček peered into the shadows their lightstones didn't reach, as if the nameless szorsa might be lurking there.

"Caught in madness within Ažerais's Dream. She doesn't need you flirting with her," Grey said. The bag he dropped on the floor punctuated his disapproval. Unfair disapproval, Ren thought; Ryvček knew how serious their business was. But he burned with the need to set right what he had broken. Ren slid her palm down his arm, soothing as she did when Clever Natalya worked herself into a ball of bristling black fur.

Ryvček dismissed his surliness with a flick of her fingers. "As you say. I came to help; tell me what you need."

Ren reached into her pocket for her deck—and her fingers touched metal. *Masks have mercy.*

Alsius had told them about Vargo finding Sessat on him. Ren knew, with sick certainty, what was in her pocket, but she forced herself to draw it out anyway: the etched bronze disc of Tricat.

"I have no memory of picking it up," she whispered. *I didn't even notice it coloring my sight.*

Grey recoiled like she'd pulled out a viper, then buried his face behind his hands. "*Djek.* I'd hoped..."

"This is a new problem?" Ryvček kept her distance from them both.

Grey answered before Ren could. "Earlier, I also realized that my medallion was with me." His dragged his head up. "I've returned it to its hiding spot, but...it's how I know the Rook must be fixed. How I know Ren can do it."

The desperation she'd seen before made new and awful sense. "Grey—"

"You thought this was a good idea," he said, fiercely. "Before you knew why I suggested it. This is necessary. The Rook has defenses against the medallions that we have not. And—it's why I became the Rook, why I became a hawk. Because I wanted the power to change things, to make them better. I *know* Quinat feeds that—but does that make it wrong?"

The problem wasn't that his desire was wrong. It was that giving into one desire made the next that much harder to resist.

Ryvček tensed. "So these things you take up without knowing? That is..."

"Terrifying," Ren said, her mouth dry as dust. "I suspect it's a consequence of our last attempt to destroy them." Joining their hands together as a living Uniat. Mirscellis had intended to break the connections, but he'd failed; perhaps the effect had even been the opposite. And it had come at so high a cost.

In one convulsive move, Ren flung Tricat into the corner and scrubbed her hand down one leg as if that would cleanse it. *Not even death removes this stain. Faella told me that.* But one problem at a time. Ren forced herself to think about Grey's words, to evaluate them as rationally as she could.

He was right. They needed the Rook.

Ren reached into her pocket again and was relieved to find only cards there now. She said, "I will build the pattern from those laid before. The one that helped make him, the one I laid for the Rook, and the one I laid for you, Grey."

The tension he'd been carrying since the townhouse seeped away like foul blood from a wound. Pressing his brow to hers, he whispered, "Thank you. And I'm sorry."

A kiss brushed her cheek, cobweb-soft, before he turned away to mix a vial of aža with a measure of wine. Ren shared the cup that Grey drank from, but when he started to mix a third dose for Ryvček, she waved him to stop. "One of us should remain sober. And I'm not as necessary to this as you are."

"You give me too much credit," Grey said as Ren picked through her cards to find the ones she needed. "Ren will do most of the work."

"I hope he is not like this in bed," Ryvček said to Ren, startling a laugh from her.

Grey crowded his teacher away from the desk. "Must you always be like this?"

"Yes. Because this is how I am the Rook." Her smile glimmered like the silver threading through her hair, like the blade at her waist. Then Ryvček thrust a finger at Grey's chest. "You are a different Rook. Less fun. Too much brooding on rooftops, though I suppose that appeals to some. But both are needed here. With numinatria was the thread spun, and with pattern was the cloth woven, but what stitches the Rook into a whole is the person inside. The one who *becomes* him."

"Imbuing," Ren said. "A performance rather than a craft."

Grey blew out a slow breath. "Yes. Then...we *will* need this." He knelt and began pulling Fontimi's Rook costume from the bag.

Ren's fingers paused in their search at The Face of Balance, its visage divided between silver and gold. Not one she'd seen in any of those three readings...not one she'd *seen*. A faint twinge echoed in her temples, remembering the blinding headache that had gripped her when she patterned the Rook.

The central card. The one his defenses forced her to look away from. This was what she had missed: the card of law, order, and justice. She would have known in an instant that it was Grey.

With a rueful smile, she finished her search and laid the remainder of the deck aside.

Shuffling wasn't necessary, not when she would be selecting the cards. But she did one pass anyway, then one from Ryvček, followed by Grey. He pulled his gloves on after he was done, and after a moment's hesitation, drew the real hood over his head. "What now?"

"Now she does her business," Ryvček said. "And since you must be the Rook...*we* duel."

Old Island and Lower Bank: Pavnilun 21

Grey had dueled as the Rook. And he had dueled his teacher. Never both at once.

The quirk of Ryvček's mouth as she drew her blade said it was strange for her, too, but that didn't stop her from settling into a relaxed, cocky stance. "With no magic aid, are you certain you wish not to yield now?"

The tension coiling up Grey's spine had little patience for banter...but wasn't that part of the Rook? A part that lately he'd all but given up on. "Why? Uncertain you'll last past the first exchange? Don't worry. I'll go easy on your aged bones."

"Ha!" Ryvček didn't bother to test his defenses. Nor did she treat this as a light bit of sparring; her sword tip went straight for his face. Grey twitched aside rather than parrying and counter-lunged.

Ren ignored them both, sitting with a hand stuffed full of cards, like a sixes player who'd forgotten the rules. "The Laughing Crow," she said, but he wasn't sure if it was to them or herself. In aža's little dream, shouts became whispers, and the brush of a cat's paw could be heard across a room. "The card of communication."

"You're a talkative one," Ryvček agreed, snagging Grey's attention as she almost caught his blade in a bind. "Banter is one thing, but you share *secrets*. How many now know that you are the Rook? How many know of the medallions?"

Dueling while spun: not the sanest thing Grey had ever done. In that dark coat, it was easy to think of his teacher as the real Rook. The one he couldn't measure up to. "How many Rooks have gotten as far as I have?" he countered. He'd put her on the defensive; hopefully it wasn't a trap. "We've learned things none of my predecessors knew. Things we need, if we're to destroy the medallions at last."

It *was* a trap. Ryvček got him to overextend on a lunge, and only a quick twist saved him from a skewer through the arm. "Fine words. But can you back them up?"

"Those who stand beside you," Ren said, laying The Laughing Crow on the table.

"With the help of others, I can," Grey said. Then he got the bind Ryvček had missed, and a quick strike with his other hand knocked her sword from her hand.

Her eyes glimmered deep in her hood. She *was* the Rook now. *A* Rook, anyway. Grey was still costumed, but aža was showing him his teacher as his predecessor.

"Then why are you wasting time with me?" she said, stepping out of his path.

She was right. He couldn't properly be the Rook sitting around a disused temple under the Point, shadow sparring with himself. The Rook was made to be out in the world, taking action.

Uncapping the lightstone at his wrist, he ran out of the temple.

In the tunnels below, he followed sound and smell and the ever-downward slant into the Depths. Pressing against moss-slick stone, he skulked along with catlike tread. Just another blot of darkness in the ever-winding dark.

The Mask of Nothing, came Ren's whisper, trickling past him like water. A rat squeaked in response. *That which stands against you.*

The Depths stirred, murmurs of human refuse hunting for a safe place to sleep, screams of those trapped by rising waters. A dying woman, desperate enough to drink zlyzen blood. And underneath it all, Primordial poison seeping into the city's bones, until not even the great Dežera could wash it away.

He felt bars at his back before he heard the scuff of boot on stone.

"Traitor."

That wasn't Ren's voice. A man, unfamiliar—but memory stirred anyway. Grey wasn't surprised when the figure that appeared at the edge of his light wore the unrelieved black of another Rook. Glints shone around the man's gut, reflections off blood. The aža was showing him the one who'd died in the Depths.

Stained gloves clenched into fists. "You claim that hood, but you hold a medallion. You *use* it. How did we ever think one such as you was worthy?"

The medallions were a power the Rook shouldn't desire. Grey knew that, far too clearly...and when he touched his pocket, he felt a hateful weight inside. A hallucination brought on by the aža? Or had he not left it behind in Westbridge after all? He couldn't deny the other's accusation. He *had* used it—maybe not deliberately, maybe he hated himself for it, but even so. Just as the people he fought against had used their medallions.

But Grey wasn't like them. He wouldn't let himself be like them.

Was the niche at his side the one they'd found Ninat's holder in? Didn't matter. Grey drew out the Quinat medallion and hid it as deep in the niche as he could, then displayed his empty hand. "I can give it up."

The answering laugh held a wild edge. "So you claim. But you thought you'd put it down before."

"I will *continue* to put it down. To leave it where temptation cannot reach me, until we destroy them." His gaze slid toward the niche. Was he only imagining the dull glint of iron in the shadows? Had he already picked it up again? What guarantees could he give, when he couldn't even trust his own senses?

Thrusting his wrists toward the other Rook, he said, "Bind me."

After all, the Rook wasn't his enemy. A'ash was—and his own need for control.

Fears shrieked in his mind as the other Rook bound his wrists with a rope as red as blood. What if someone found the medallion before he could send an ally to secure it? And who *would* he send? It was safer in his own keeping—

The other one dragged him away by the rope. The old oath whispered in his mind, soothing the disarray of his thoughts. *Your secrets are my secrets; your debts, my debts.* The people who made the Rook had sworn themselves together as a knot. He could lean on their strength.

I remember that, Grey realized. The oath to end the Tyrant's reign, before the Rook was even a thought. It was a glimmer of light in his mind...and a literal glimmer ahead. He'd reached the mouth of the tunnel, the river rushing by outside. The other Rook was gone, and the only remnant of the rope was a red triple clover knot circling his wrist.

The cleansed river splashed around his boots as he emerged and hauled himself up the wall. Was it truly night already, or was that just what aža wanted him to see? And who did the hand belong to that grabbed his wrist and hauled him onto the solid ground of the Old Island? Perhaps there was no hand at all. Perhaps he was still in the hidden temple, grasping at visions while Ren laid out cards.

The wisdom you must remember. A ghost shadow swooped on down-silent wings, scattering pigeons in a burst of feathers and fury. In the fading echo of their screeching, Grey heard Ren's whisper: *The Mask of Chaos.*

The moons were wrong. Corillis should have been new, but it shone the silvered blue of a newly minted decira, painting the river walk in midnight hues. The hooded figure who'd dragged him to safety was a black silhouette, save for the sickle-thin curl of his lip. "Never fished in the river and pulled up a hawk," the Rook said. "Maybe I should throw you back."

"I'm no hawk." Grey yanked his arm free.

"That coat of yours looks blue by this light."

It did, and the breeches threatened to bleach into tan. Grey fought to keep them black—but that wasn't how aža worked. *I have to be the Rook. Dueling, creeping through the Depths . . .*

When the system is unjust, Ren said, *then justice must come from without.*

The hood Grey wore hid his grin, but he let the expression through anyway. "The better to learn their weaknesses. Want to go make some trouble?"

Like black-winged hunters, they descended on the Aerie and scattered the fat blue-feathered pigeons inside. Grey dueled three captains at once, while his counterpart lifted the master key from one of their belts. He cackled at their demands that he surrender himself.

"Has that ever worked?" he asked, bottlenecking the fight at the corridor to the holding cells. The creak of unoiled hinges told him he wouldn't be fighting alone for long. The turf battles between Vargo's former knots had filled the Aerie full to bursting. "When you order someone to give up, doesn't that only spur them to fight harder?"

As he'd fought harder. Every day, ground under the boots of his superior officers, he fought to fix the broken system, until he put the yoke on himself and thanked them for kicking him.

A laugh broke loose from a throat too long strangled. Free. He felt *free*.

He wasn't the only one. The slam of a door thrown open echoed down the corridor, the three swords against him dipping in shock.

"You might want to clear the path," Grey said, jumping aside as a rush of people descended on the doorway.

But one of the faces going by was familiar, known in the way people in dreams were known, even if never seen in life. Grey snagged the man by the arm and used the momentum to slam him into the wall. "You're one of Tserdev's Crimson Eyes, yes?" Grey said conversationally. "You and I should talk."

"As should we."

The crispness of the new voice almost brought Grey snapping to attention on reflex. He knew, before he turned, what he would see.

Cercel. Blade in hand, and still dressed as a commander, instead of as Caerulet. That alone suggested none of this was real, that he was back in the temple, hallucinating it all.

Be the Rook. He twisted the arm of the Crimson Eye behind his back and offered Cercel a courteous bow. "As much as I'd love to accept your invitation..."

"It wasn't an invitation."

"Come now. We both know the truth." Grey stepped closer, not afraid she would stab him. The Rook didn't fear. "You need me."

"For what? I'm trying to maintain order." Cercel's glance took in the busted door, the rainfall of paper and general chaos of the prison break. The air reeked of spilled coffee. "You're the opposite of order."

Yes, he was. Because he had to be. "When the day comes that the Vigil truly serves the people of Nadežra—when it's more than the shackles and the sword—then I won't be necessary. Until then... the Face needs its Mask."

He didn't know if he'd convinced her. But she didn't stop him as he shoved the Crimson Eye out the door.

In the shadows of a building, he stopped and pushed the man up against a wall. "Vargo. Where have your people taken him?"

"I en't telling you shit. Just 'cause you sprung me, you think I'll turn traitor?" The man horked back to spit, but choked on it when Grey spun him face-first into the bricks.

"I think two centuries is a long time to learn ways to make people talk," he whispered.

The man's lips moved, but his voice was Ren's. *The question you must ask. The Face of Balance.*

The counterpart to The Mask of Chaos. If the Face needed the Mask...wasn't the opposite also true?

"You're wasting your time," said another Rook from her perch in the eaves. One boot was hooked off the roof's edge, and blue string spanned her fingers in a game of dreamweaver's nest. The changing patterns as she hooked and looped and dropped and caught were hypnotic.

Grey shook his head, as if that would steady it against aža's spin. "He has information I need."

"Why?" Hook. "That fancy spider isn't our business." Loop. "The medallions are." Drop. "But you keep chasing roses and overturning dreamweaver nests." *Catch*: the thread became a net, falling on Grey and tangling him in its snare.

The Rook followed it, her landing cat soft. "You feel bound to them, because they saved your life. But we would have continued. We *have* to continue. Our purpose is to rid this place of that poison."

"Which poison?" Grey asked, trembling under the weight of memory, of another net. "The medallions? They're a tool—only one of many. You can't pull a single thread and not drag others with it. The Anduske exist because of Kaius Rex's invasion. The knots fight each other on the Lower Bank because of Liganti power on the Upper. Justice for Nadežra requires more than destroying a few bits of metal."

Like a breath of wind, Ren whispered, *What is justice?*

"You'll never rest," the Rook warned him.

Grey shrugged. "I never expected to."

At a tug from the Rook, the net unraveled into a single thread. She coiled it like knitter's yarn and handed it to Grey. Glancing over her shoulder to where the Crimson Eye no longer cowered, she said, "Sorry I lost your man for you."

"Rats are plentiful. I'll catch another." Casting the blue thread upward, Grey climbed to the place he'd always felt most at home, be he Rook or hawk or Kiraly raccoon.

The rooftops of the Lower Bank.

Where he caught sight of two figures running, one chasing the other, leaping the gaps of the streets.

Grey took off before he even identified the pursuer as another Rook. How many would he encounter? Every person who'd ever worn the hood? *The reward you gain,* Ren murmured in his ear. *Pearl's Promise.*

From the pattern that had made the Rook. The card they'd wanted to move, from the ill future—no reward for their efforts—to the good. He knew which Rook he was following, and he knew she would never catch her quarry on her own. It wasn't in the fate she'd twisted for herself. She was only the beginning of the thread that he'd cut short.

A wild leap took him over a narrow canal, more gutter than water. When the fleeing figure jinked aside to avoid Grey, that put him in the path of the other Rook. He swerved back, but Grey was too close. The rope snapped out like a herder's snare, and the stranger crashed hard onto the tiles.

The first Rook was upon him before he could even roll over, tearing at his clothes. When the man curled up like a snail to protect his softer parts, her claws turned into fists, raining blows down on him.

"Where is it? Someone must have it. I will tear apart every person in this city to find it . . . to end this . . ."

Her voice broke, young, weighted with sorrow like a body dumped in a canal. For two centuries, this was all she'd been. She'd made it so, and now she couldn't escape.

Pearl's Promise had become the good future, but that left The

Mask of Chaos as her ill. The Tyrant's single power broken into many, spreading disorder throughout Nadežra. And so this woman and all those who came after had continued to fight.

"Liatry." The name was on his tongue before he realized he knew it: aža speaking through him, Ažerais's memories longer than even a legendary vigilante's. He caught her wrists before she could strip her quarry down to his bones in search of something he didn't have. "You don't need to keep looking. We've found them. We're close."

The first Rook was rigid in his grip. "I failed. I thought Zmienka changing the cards would end it. We ended the Tyrant...but not the threat."

Zmienka. The nameless szorsa? No, the one Ren said had changed the Rook's pattern. Part of the knot sworn to take down Kaius Rex. One of a trio of women, the truth behind the legend of the three courtesans, played out every year on the Night of Bells.

"You haven't failed," Grey said. "*We* haven't. Can't you feel it?" Ren's hand, laying the cards, choosing their fate. She'd struggled on others, he thought, trying to decide what question the Rook needed to ask, what among her cards best represented the strengths he could bring to bear. But not this one. The position of reward, and the card of reward. It could never be anything else.

Liatry's voice was thin as a garotte wire. "Issena won't have died for nothing?"

He didn't need Ren's gift to feel those threads. The memories had drifted through him many times, in those moments when the hood reminded him why they fought. Two women had been Liatry's lovers: the szorsa who changed her pattern, and the Liganti noble whose death spurred that change.

"She hasn't died for nothing," he promised Liatry. "You ended the Tyrant. We'll end the rest together."

"Together," she echoed, gaze somewhere beyond the rooftops of Seven Knots. Ducking her head, she removed her hood—but only the hood. The disguise had begun as separate pieces, before she gave her life to knit them into one.

The woman beneath was young, with the mixed heritage of the Dawn and Dusk Roads stamped on her features. Nadežran to her bones. Pressing her hood into his hands, Liatry said, "You'll need this."

The wool tingled even through the leather of his gloves. *The Rook.* Not connected to him, to the hood on his head. Not anymore. But whole and unmarred and somehow lighter. Grey could return to the temple right now, and they would have done what they set out to do.

But...

Reeds Unbroken, whispered Ren.

The risk you take.

Liatry and her victim were gone. Grey stood alone, hood in his hands and doubt in his heart. Reeds Unbroken, the card of endurance. But he *had* broken.

From the street rose the high-pitched cries of children in fear. Two huddled back as three men swaggered forward. "En't your pitch no more," one of them sneered, shoving the nearest kid hard enough to knock her down.

"Oi!"

The shout brought that man around just in time to take a fist to the nuggets. The attacker dodged his outraged swipe, kicking out his knee. A fluttering coat of piebald velvet flickered to black and back again as the newcomer leapt between the men and the children. "Get going!"

And Grey felt a tug—the same tug Ryvček must have felt when she caught two boys facing off against Mezzan Indestor and his friends.

That one.

Someone who could be the Rook. Who would stand, outnumbered and outmassed, against people abusing their power...and who would fight dirty enough to win, flinging a handful of muck into the eyes of the first one who retaliated.

Hardly more than a child. Maybe not even. Grey had been that young when Ryvček took notice of him—but she hadn't laid the burden on him then. Not so soon.

One man knocked the defender down, and was rewarded with a boot to the ankle. He howled and staggered back, buying the kid time to get up and start running. Living to fight another day.

You're not broken until you agree you are. He couldn't tell if that was his own thought, or Ren's comforting voice.

His hand tightened on Liatry's hood. "I'm not done," he muttered. "And I'm not putting this on someone else. I'll see it through. I *have* to."

The hood wasn't in his hand. It was on his head, where it had been from the start. But now...now, again, *finally*, it was more than a piece of wool.

And Grey knew where to go.

The boots softened his landing as he dropped, the hood staying put without pins to hold it. The night unfolded itself to his eyes, sharper than natural vision. When he spoke, he heard the voice that wasn't his own. The voice of the Rook.

"Let her go," he said.

The hooded figure before him wasn't like the other Rooks he'd encountered. Those all showed the suggestion of a face—a smirk, a wink, a dash of panache that was as much a part of the Rook as his hood and his sword. This one was empty, a yawning darkness that was nothing and had nothing.

In his arms, slumped and sweating from her futile struggles, was the szorsa whose guilt had cut her off from her name, her people, and herself. Zevriz.

The Ember Adamant, came a voice from that darkness. Ren, with him even in this. *The hub on which all else turns.* The one card that was in all three readings: Grey's, the Rook's, and the one that made the Rook.

And in the pattern Laročja had laid for Grey, so many years ago. His ill future: a burden he couldn't bear, a debt he couldn't repay.

One card of three. It wasn't his entire future.

"I said, let her go."

"And let this go on forever?" His voice, the Rook's voice, echoed back to him. Or was he talking to himself? But he wasn't the one tightening his grip around a helpless woman's soul. "She began the whole thing, helping Kaius. Pull this thread, and it will all unravel. It's the easiest way. It might be the *only* way."

All around the square, shadows moved. People stepping out, black-clad from head to foot. The Rooks Grey had met, and others besides.

"We don't kill," Liatry said. "I swore it to Issena, before she died."

The other Rook—the spirit of the Rook—growled. "One death. *One death* can end all the rest."

"No." Grey drew his blade again. "I wouldn't let you kill before. And I won't let you destroy her soul now."

"None of us will." That was Ryvček, echoed by others all around.

And together they moved. A whirlwind of black coats, of blades flashing in the night. But it was *the Rook* they fought: the thing they'd created, each of them in their own way, the spirit who'd become greater than the mere humans that made him up. He moved faster than Grey could believe, dodging and weaving through the crowd of his bearers, the nameless szorsa still pinned with one arm.

He was stronger than any one of them. But not stronger than them all.

They herded him back, into a corner where two buildings met, with Rooks on the roof to stop him escaping upward. Grey advanced to the front and looked into the depthless darkness of the hood.

"Let her go," he repeated. Softly this time. "We've carried the burden of her mistake all this time. We don't have to carry it anymore."

With a sigh of relief, the Rook released the nameless szorsa and flowed like fog into Grey. Blinking like a dreamer waking from endless sleep, the szorsa released an unsteady breath. "I'm free?"

"We both are," Grey said. "We all are." The shades of other Rooks were fading—into the aža, into Ažerais's Dream. But even with their souls slipping loose, something remained. The thing they'd made, like a spirit born of Ažerais herself.

"Our Lady blesses you," the szorsa whispered, mouth and hand trembling.

"And she forgives you," Grey replied.

He meant to take her back to the Old Island, where another part of her tattered soul waited. But she faltered before they'd gone three paces, and he was forced to pull her onto his back. Walking as steadily and quietly as he could, he began heading for the river.

Partway there, the weight increased, and the half-conscious murmurs in his ear deepened to an abused baritone.

Dawn was rising. The szorsa was gone.

And Grey, hooded and armed as the true Rook, was emerging from Seven Knots with Derossi Vargo slung across his back.

The Face of Balance

Ren didn't know what Grey had said to Alinka. But after a fascinated Arkady arrived at the temple saying he was in Kingfisher with "what's left of Vargo," Ren and Ryvček hurried across the river to find Alinka bandaging wounds with no expression but clear-eyed determination. Whatever anger she held toward Vargo over her husband's death, it didn't stand in the way of helping an injured man.

And Vargo *was* injured, appallingly so. His face, his hands, his feet, his ribs; the worst was the bandage over his heart, mute testimony to the damaged numinat there. Peabody hunched above it like a helpless and miserable poultice.

Ren slumped on the floor against the wall, too exhausted to stand. Laying those cards...No pattern had ever drained her this badly. In the Seven Knots labyrinth she'd merely made choices; here she'd made those choices *matter*. Aža's Call had wanted to be the risk, the illusion of the Rook becoming reality, bearers losing themselves to his power. It had taken everything she had to lay down Reeds Unbroken instead, wondering all the while if that was an improvement, placing the burden on the backs of so many yet to come. As if the position of risk could ever be comforting and safe.

She would have sworn only minutes went by while she

considered the options, balancing what she hoped the Rook would be against the tension of his pattern. But when she looked up from the completed wheel, Ryvček told her hours had passed.

Hours in which Grey had done the impossible. Single-handed.

He looked like he wanted to collapse next to her. She'd only imbued a pattern; he'd imbued the *Rook*. But he remained on his feet as he drew Ryvček aside, away from Alinka. "I know not whether it was real or imagined, but in my journey... I thought I had Quinat with me." He'd stripped out of much of Fontimi's costume, gloves included; his knuckles whitened as his fists curled tight. "I—I gave it up. I *can't* be its holder. Not when I'm also..." Yvieny was asleep in a chair, but he left that sentence unfinished anyway.

"Assume for now it was real," Ryvček said. "Where think you that you left it?"

Grey's gaze was limp with gratitude. "You mean you..."

"Cannot let you take all the credit for dealing with this? Of course not." Her light tone belied the tension in her shoulders.

"If it isn't still in Westbridge, it's in the Depths. In one of the burial niches."

Where they'd found Stezze Chetoglio with Ninat. Where Gammer Lindworm had once lurked with Tricat. Ren had never liked any part of the Depths, but she was coming to loathe that bit.

Ryvček was already heading for the door. "Get your inscriptor friend ready. The other one, I mean."

Tanaquis. "We'll need a story to tell her," Ren said as Ryvček left. "Unless you are all right with her knowing."

Now Grey gave in to exhaustion, dropping into a graceless pile next to her. "*He* would prefer me not to. Not controlling me, just..."

Just that, Rook once more, he had to be cautious. The Laughing Crow stood with him, not The Face of Glass; he still wouldn't share his secrets freely.

Like iron to a lodestone, Grey's gaze slid back to Vargo. Alinka had washed away the blood, but nothing could erase the bruises mottling the man's body and face. "He'll need to be uncursed, too," Grey said. "Once he wakes up. Alinka, what remains to do?"

She was examining Vargo's shattered hand, swollen and discolored. "The bleeding has stopped. The papaver should keep him asleep, but in case not, hold him down while I set his fingers."

They both forced themselves up. Ren's arms felt like wet noodles, but she didn't need strength; she only needed to lean her body weight on Vargo's legs while Grey took his shoulders. The actual work was Alinka's, and Ren tried not to listen to the crunch.

Kingfisher, Lower Bank: Pavnilun 22

The first sensation marring the blissful sea Vargo floated in was the barest nibble. Just a small fish testing to see if this great lump was edible. But then came another, and another, until he was devoured bite by bite. Teeth raked along his fingers, sank into his chest, and stabbed into his lungs. Waves of pain crashed against his head in a relentless tide.

Dragging himself onto the shore of wakefulness, he opened his eyes to piercing light and the rounded face of a curious sea-maid. With her button nose only a breath away, all he could see was wind-wild hair and pond-water eyes. And a grin entirely too feral for comfort.

"The fuck are you?" he mumbled. Tserdev was recruiting them young.

But no. He wasn't with Tserdev anymore. The Rook...or many Rooks? Maybe that had been fever dreams.

Alsius?

Only silence answered.

"Fuck?" the feral child said. Her grin widened, like she'd been given a treasure immeasurable. "Fuck!" she shouted, then ran from the room, a shrieking trail of "fucks" bubbling up in her wake.

The face that replaced hers was older and careworn. "You're awake," the woman said in Vraszenian, then switched to accented Liganti. "Stay still. You have been badly beaten."

"Don't need you telling me that," Vargo mumbled. He wanted to answer in Vraszenian, to prove he could, but he wasn't sure which language came out. "Where's m' spider?"

A tickling sensation on his face loomed into an enormous shadow, eclipsing one eye. Vargo's other eye registered the woman shuddering, though she didn't look surprised. "Alsius," he whispered, a tear leaking out from beneath the spider. Here, and alive—but inaudible. Because Tserdev had slashed the numinat.

"My brand," he said, struggling to sit up as though he hadn't just been told—and agreed—not to. It was like being stabbed all over again, and he fell back onto the thin pallet beneath him. "Ow."

"If you insist on acting without thinking, be not surprised by consequences," she said, disapproving as only a parent could be. Jars rattled and clinked as she sorted through them.

"Story of my life," he muttered, gingerly herding Peabody so the spider rode the rise and fall of his chest. His right hand was swaddled in bandages and pulsed with a distant ache.

"I can't hear you," he said in response to the frantic leg-waving that usually accompanied information Alsius considered vital. As bad as the beatings had been for Vargo, how much more terrified must Alsius be, silenced like this?

"I need my brand healed. The one on my chest," he told the woman. "The rest doesn't matter. I'm earth-handed; if you bring me imbued medicines, I can improve them with a numinat."

But even then, how well would the mark heal? Tserdev hadn't exactly washed the wound afterward. How could it not scar? Flawing the numinat, such that it would never work again.

He clenched his eyes against tears, finger stroking to calm Alsius. "It'll be all right. We'll fix it." *Somehow.*

When he finally opened his eyes again, he found the woman watching him with an odd expression. "You know not where you are. Nor who I am."

Vraszenian. Healer. And treating Vargo's wounds...after *the Rook* rescued him.

Fuck.

"Ča Serrado." He tried to raise his bandaged hand to his brow in proper Vraszenian greeting and winced at the effort.

"Think you that gestures of respect will make this meeting easier?" she asked.

"I don't think anything could make this easier. On either of us." Vargo and Grey had reached a kind of peace—even friendship—despite their differences. He couldn't say the same of Kolya Serrado's widow.

Cupping his good hand around Peabody, he forced the words out. "I know it fixes nothing, but... I *am* sorry. For my part in your husband's death."

"You are right. It fixes nothing." She lifted the light bandage over his brand. Unstoppering a red clay jar, Alinka pressed a numinatrian seal onto it before dripping the contents over the slash. "Any healer will tell you a broken body cannot always return to what it was. Mended bones ache in cold weather; weak joints buckle under strain. Even wounds can reopen when a person eats poorly."

He watched the red-ragged line rather than her. Someone had pulled the skin together with fine stitches. He wished he could rip them out. "I'm not certain I follow this metaphor."

The breath she exhaled was like the wound: ragged, but holding together. "I know you meant not to kill him; I know you acted in pursuit of a greater cause. None of these bring him back. None erase the wound, any more than your regret does."

She smacked her hand abruptly against the table. "I would treat you regardless, Derossi Vargo, because I am a healer. But I know not if I can forgive you. Because of you, my children have no father. Because of you, my bed is cold. Great causes are no comfort in the face of that. If you wish to make it right, then in the future, *do better.*"

Color high, she folded a new bandage and placed it over the wound. "Touch this not. I will tell Grey and Ren that you are awake... assuming *they* are awake."

After she'd gone upstairs, Vargo expelled a hard breath—then winced as it pierced him like a blade of fire. "Let me guess," he said to Alsius, who'd gone still inside his cupped hand. Peabody's four largest eyes glittered in what Vargo took to be judgment. "You were warning me not to make an ass of myself. And now you're grumbling because I did. Tap once for yes."

A fuzzy leg tapped his palm with all the strength of a butterfly kiss. Then, after a pause, two quick taps.

"Not grumbling?" Another twinge in his chest, but this one couldn't be blamed on his ribs.

Before he could ask for clarification and much-needed comfort, two sets of footsteps sounded on the stairs. And if Vargo didn't have his expression under control by the time they arrived, he was ground too raw to care.

Ren looked like she wanted to hug him in relief, but couldn't find an unbruised spot to latch on to. She settled for gripping his wrist, gently enough not to rattle Alsius in his palm.

His *bare* wrist. "Din't cut knot myself," he mumbled, feeling like a boy who'd been caught filching market stall fruit. "That was Tserdev."

Her grip tightened like she meant to rebind their oaths with that alone. "You nearly died, and you think I give two mills for some knotted string?"

At his wince, she eased her hold. Tears glimmered, unfallen, as she said, "I'd make you a replacement every day if that would help you heal. When first I saw you, I thought..."

That I was a dead man. And he would have been, if not for... whatever Grey had done.

Vargo expected one of them to explain, but instead Ren said, "What *happened*? He was spun, and can tell me not. We aimed to fix the Rook so he could help you, but the helping was supposed to come later." The smile she shot Grey was full of fond recrimination.

"You're asking *me*?" Vargo said. "I was beat to Ninat and back. Though even that doesn't explain what I saw."

Grey cleared his throat. "I thought I was freeing the nameless szorsa from her bonds. I *did* free her. But—somehow I also grabbed you?"

"You, and about twenty other Rooks. I'd ask who you put in the costumes, except I don't think those were real people." Everything had been chaos and shouting, Tserdev losing her shit on an epic scale as Rooks seemed to emerge literally from the shadows.

The look Grey shot back at Ren was mixed bafflement, awe, and half-suppressed hilarity. "I'm afraid to find out what I did at the Aerie."

"Later," Ren said firmly, before Vargo could ask. "First, there are curses to deal with. Vargo, we found Alsius with Sessat, but—is it possible to uncurse yourself? Or must that be done by another?"

He hadn't expected to think about numinatria less than a bell after waking up, but he appreciated her concern. "I've worked with Tanaquis enough to understand the process. With cards from you and something to dull the pain, I don't see why I couldn't uncurse myself." A minor shift sent pain shooting up his arm. "Thank the Lumen it's not necessary. I may have, uh. Inscribed Alsius into my register."

After a moment's stillness, legs drummed his palm like a coxswain running ahead of a storm. Vargo tapped Alsius on the head. "Stop that. It tickles."

The expressions on the faces above him looked like comedic masks. Grey managed to say, "He's . . . in your *register.*"

As Vargo's father—but Vargo would rebreak his own hand before he admitted that, at least while lying flat on a table with no dignity to shelter behind. Bad enough that Alsius scrambled up his arm to nuzzle against the side of his neck, like the peacock spider equivalent of a hug. "Yes. So I'm fine. No curse removal needed."

"Unfortunately, there still is," Ren said. "In the course of mending the Rook, Grey gave up Quinat. Ryvček has it now, but that helps Grey not. I'll spin a story for Tanaquis; you must rest and heal."

"Not that I'm doubting you could, but . . ." *Every time you lie to your family, you cut out a piece of yourself.* Vargo hesitated over how to say what he meant. The silence in his head was distracting. How was this easier when he had a spider babbling suggestions at him? "Tanaquis is more perceptive than she lets on. And she might be examining everything you say these days. I can do it. I just need my kit."

And about a week on my back, he thought, but the familiar rejoinder never came. The silence hurt worse than Tserdev's knife.

Ren glanced at Grey, deferring to him. Grey held Vargo's gaze as he nodded. "Then we'll do that. Thank you."

Kingfisher, Lower Bank: Pavnilun 23

Grey's step felt lighter than it had in ages as he crossed the Sunset Bridge the next evening and headed for Kingfisher. As much as he regretted dropping the Primordial burden on Ryvček, he breathed easier not carrying it himself.

He regretted even more putting the burden of the curse's removal on Vargo's shoulders. The sheen of sweat on the other man's blanched face when he got up from inscribing the numinat said that broken ribs and chalking a floor made for a bad mix.

Now Vargo was on his way back to Eastbridge and his own physician, before Tserdev could find out where he'd vanished to and rain retributive fire on the one who sheltered him. Grey, meanwhile, was on his way to thank Alinka and apologize yet again. But when he opened the door, he found someone else at the table with her, cup of tea in hand.

"Grey." Koszar's smile carried a hint of tension. "With you I was hoping to speak."

"I'll make certain the children play quietly," Alinka said, hitching Jagyi onto her hip and herding a grumbling Yvieny upstairs.

"You're more likely to find me in Westbridge," Grey said, watching Koszar watch Alinka's departure. He bit back the urge to warn the revolutionary away from his marriage-sister. With as many leaks as his own boat had, he could hardly condemn another for sinking.

Pouring tea for himself, he sat. "But I'm here now. What need you from me?"

Koszar wasted no time with pleasantries. "Mevieny has done as we asked and called for Ažerais to judge us, through an ordeal. Branek has no choice but to agree."

"And?"

"And I want you at my side," Koszar said. "Whether Ažerais favors me or not, *someone* must speak out against Laročja. Perhaps Branek will listen not, but others may."

Grey's throat tightened enough that he almost couldn't swallow the tea. Once he'd forced it down, he said, "Koszar... it will be my word against hers."

"The word of her own grandson," Koszar said, soft and insistent. "There is none stronger."

"The word of a slip-knot. A man who cut his hair, altered his family name, and joined the Vigil." Waving at the world outside, Grey said, "They'll see me as you once did."

"If that were true, the Kiralič would not have asked for your opinion. You are better regarded than you believe, after this past year. People know you as an honest man. If you speak, those who need to hear will listen."

An honest man. Grey glared into the rippling mirror of his tea. If that were true, he'd admit why he had no intention of going anywhere near the ordeal, nor any other gathering his grandmother might attend. Vargo had relieved Grey of one curse, but no numinat could lift the one he'd been born under.

Instead he said, "Unless my grandmother speaks more loudly. Which she always does." He'd yelled himself hoarse as a boy, refusing to break beneath her words, or those of his father.

"I'll support you," Koszar said. "And Ren—"

"My half-Liganti lover? By now my grandmother will have learned the truth of her. A szorsa who cannot depend on her cards has other means of finding things out." He rubbed his hands over his face. "Koszar, I understand. But no. For me to stand up and denounce her... it would do no good."

No, he wasn't an honest man. The point wasn't whether his words would do any good. After all, he'd publicly quit the Vigil, expecting nothing to come of it except his own downfall. Denouncing Laročja was likewise the right thing to do, whether it had any effect or not.

But he couldn't. The mere thought sent sick fear writhing

through his gut. To face her, to look into those cold eyes, hidden in the mask of a kindly old woman—*You were born wrong; it's your fault she died...*

He was a good liar. His hands remained still, and his tea settled into a placid mirror.

The silence that answered him rang with Koszar's disappointment. But all the man said was "Then I suppose we must trust in Ažerais. And in Ren." He finished his tea and rose. "I will not trouble you with it again."

But he stopped at the door for a parting sally. "I will only remind you that however long and winding the Dežera's path, inevitably she finds her way to the sea. It is no different with blood and family."

Isla Čaprila, Eastbridge: Pavnilun 28

"I'll be *fine*," Vargo grumbled as Varuni passed through his study for the third time to make sure the windows were locked and the alarm numinata undamaged. "It's been a week, and Tserdev hasn't so much as thrown an egg at my windows. Probably too spooked by what happened. Still, I won't let anyone in but Ren and Tanaquis, and I'm not going anywhere like this."

He brushed his good hand down his morning robe, a patchwork of river blues. The silks snagged on his calluses, but the velvet was soft as a cat's purr. Usually Peabody would be tucked into the collar, a tickle against his cheek, but he'd wandered off shortly after Vargo dragged himself out of bed. With no voice to guide him, Vargo had no idea where the spider was hiding.

"Those promises are meaningless. You think I haven't learned that by now?" Varuni huffed a soft breath and twitched the thick curtains closed like the early spring sunlight was a threat to Vargo's safety. "I'll be back before first earth."

That familiar, decisive tone ate at him like acid. Vargo fiddled with his blotter paper, tearing off little pieces to roll into balls. When he'd been a boy and the bane of Alsius's days, he'd made a game out of flicking them at the spider instead of practicing numinatria.

No secrets between us. That oath was to Ren, not Varuni.

And that justification was a sack of shit.

"I don't want you to go." Damn it. He hadn't meant to say it like that, weighing her down with guilt. But his head was too muddled with the mix of papaver and stimulants that kept him something like functioning.

Varuni at least understood he didn't mean today's visit to Flood-watch. "Vargo...I have a duty to my family." The words were as solid and unwavering as Varuni herself. But so was the tension in her jaw, telling him her duty rested on an eroded foundation. It was knowledge he shouldn't have, and it tugged at him like sucking mud.

There was one way to make it easier for her. He didn't need to use a medallion. He already had her fear, his fear, and the truth.

"I thought about using Sessat on you. That day in Dockwall. I didn't want you to leave, and I could tell that part of you wanted to stay, and—"

"You did *what?*" She stumbled back a step, gaze flicking to the panel where the medallion lay hidden.

"*Thought* about it. I wouldn't do it." Vargo held up his hands, one splinted and the other shaking, to prove they were empty. "But...I *wanted* to."

He held silent and as still as pain allowed while she paced like a caged cat. "That's what these things do, right? They make you want to use them."

Vargo wished it was that simple. "They don't make anything that isn't already there. Which is why you should go. It's only getting worse, now that the chain has been strengthened." And it would *keep* getting worse, especially without Alsius acting as a tiny voice of reason.

He was glad he couldn't read Varuni's desires now, as her hands twitched like they wanted to pull off a net that wasn't there. "I— I have to go," she said at last, uncharacteristically rough. "They're expecting me."

"Go," Vargo said tiredly. He didn't ask if she would still be back before first earth.

Fortunately he wasn't left to brood for long. Ren showed up first, letting herself in and saying, "I'm surprised Tanaquis offered to come here."

Vargo was, too—but grateful. It meant he didn't have to haul his broken carcass up to Whitesail. "Might not want that maid of hers overhearing. Though this en't about the medallions." *For once.*

Ren didn't press for an explanation, saving Vargo from having to go through it twice. But they had a lengthy wait before Tanaquis showed up, more distracted than usual, her hair pulled into a single unwashed plait. "I hope this is important," she said, irritated. "I'm working on a figure of nested Tricats in a Ninat framework. I'm hoping it might let us pull the last piece of that woman's soul out of the chain. Though it would go much better if the chain *existed* for us to work with. But I can hardly get much done when I have to spend time traveling across the city."

"Coming here was your idea," Vargo reminded her. They'd scarcely seen so much as an ink stain of Tanaquis since Mirscellis's failed attempt to help. He was glad to know she'd gotten Ren's messages about the szorsa's soul and the piece that had been freed, but it would be nice if Tanaquis had *acknowledged* those messages. Or done anything to help them to try to get Mirscellis's spirit back. "As for whether it's important, well, depends on whether you want to find a new holder for Sessat after I kiss Ninat good night."

"I didn't bring my medallion. And why would you want to kiss it?" Her face cleared. "Oh, you mean dying. Why would you die?"

"Yes," Ren said, tone as dark as Tanaquis's had been bright. "Why *would* you die?"

"An exaggeration," Vargo said, hoping he could make it true. "But..."

Showing would be easier than telling. He tugged his robe open and peeled the bandage off his chest, hissing as the thin gauze pulled at the clots and fresh blood oozed free. "It's not healing. *I'm* not healing. Alsius is fine, but I'm like a bucket with a hole in the bottom."

That finally got Tanaquis's full attention. "Fascinating. Is the energy drain similar to what happens when an inscriptor imbues a numinat?" She came at him with an ink-blotched glove, blinking when Ren caught her wrist.

"I don't know," Vargo said. "I try to avoid imbuing numinata. Normally this goes in a cycle, energy flowing from me to him and back again. Only now the flow is one-way. Alsius based the design on some of Mirscellis's theories; Tanaquis, I'm hoping you might have ideas." What he really wanted was to ask Mirscellis himself. He'd tried an experimental numinat or two, as if those might succeed where pattern failed, but without Alsius to offer insights, he'd gotten nowhere.

Before anybody could suggest it, Vargo added, "I don't think making a new figure would work." Even if they could inscribe a numinat this complicated on a tiny spider body, there was no way to replicate the mad, muddled conditions of the night Alsius had inadvertently joined their lives in a desperate attempt to save his own.

Tapping her lip, Tanaquis said, "Can Alsius still feel anything from you? I'm curious if cutting the numinat severed the bond between you entirely, or if...hmmm. Ren, didn't you say a thread connected them, in the realm of mind?"

Vargo could translate the drawn-out nature of Ren's "yes"; she'd been significantly distracted by zlyzen both times she looked at it. "It makes sense," she said, fingers tracing an unseen line. "Any relationship is a connection; that one is stronger than most. I know not if what I saw is the same thing as the numinatrian link."

"But it *might* be. Isn't that why we asked Mirscellis to help with the medallions? Pity that szorsa interfered. Though her situation makes me wonder about imbuing numinata—what that would look like from a Vraszenian cosmological perspective. Also whether all souls are divisible, or whether that goes by ancestry, or faith. Heretical talk, I know, but Utrinzi isn't here to chide me for it." Tanaquis laughed, far too brittle. "Chiding. One time when I was a girl, I asked him about— Never mind; you don't want that story. But he got *so angry* with me. Did you know he can actually shout? He's always been too narrow-minded for his own good, never asking the next question. For him, the orthodoxy regarding death is enough."

She was rambling worse than usual, and Vargo didn't like the morbid turn it was taking. "*Tanaquis*. Ren. Do either of you have a suggestion to stop me metaphysically bleeding out?"

"I—" Ren looked helpless. "I can lay cards, see what they say. But I cannot apply it directly. A Brother Lost may be the card of wounds, but as a bandage it's not much use."

Tanaquis had come back to the point. "If I was looking for a purely numinatrian solution, I'd think in terms of the Lumen's cycle, passing through Ninat's gateway and returning to Illi to start anew." She perched on the edge of Vargo's desk and toyed with the pile of little paper balls, rolling them under her fingers as she theorized. "But if you're talking pattern..."

Vargo had never heard so pure a noise of frustration as the one Tanaquis made suddenly, and the balls jumped as she slammed her fist on the desk. "I still don't *understand*! No matter how much I read, no matter what questions I ask, I can't find how they fit together! I thought eisar would be the answer, but even *that* doesn't fit—imbuing isn't why the cards work as foci—pattern is pure *nonsense*, and yet it works! How can it work? Is the cosmos truly so disordered? There has to be some underlying structure, something I can't see—"

"*Tanaquis!*" Ren caught her cousin's gesticulating arms and held them tight. Vargo received Ren's worried glance and bounced it right back. Ninat: not just the numen of death and destruction, but also of seeing beyond the horizon, of apotheosis. For all her seeming unflappability, Tanaquis was profoundly vulnerable to that pressure.

Breathing heavily, she tried to reassert a semblance of control. "Forgive me. It's just—vexing. I believed the medallions were simple. But every time I think I have a way to deal with them, I find it will only produce some new problem. I may hold Ninat, but that doesn't mean I *want* people to die."

"Well, cheer up. If we don't fix this," Vargo said, jabbing a thumb at his damaged mark, "might be the shortest path to destroying the medallions will be giving them to *me*."

Tanaquis's frustration cracked into an inappropriate laugh, Ren taking on the burden of her frustration with a purse-lipped glare. But though Vargo waited for the voice that scolded him when he held his life too cheaply, all he heard was the buzzing silence of his own head.

Eastbridge, Upper Bank: Pavnilun 28

Ren had brought cosmetics to cover Vargo's injuries, on the presumption that he would accompany her tonight to the ordeal, in support of Koszar. Knowing what she did now, that was out of the question—and it was a mark of how drained Vargo must feel that he didn't press the point.

Unfortunately, the bell rang before she could convince him to rest. "Probably Tanaquis, back with a theory," Vargo said wearily.

But it wasn't. "Oh," Parma said when Ren opened the door, in the tone of one finding an unpleasant surprise on her shoe. "It's *you*."

Iascat laid a hand on her shoulder. "It's just as well, Parma. Ren, is Vargo in?"

For Parma to have left her defensive seclusion, this must be significant business. Ren led them to the morning room, where Vargo was eating a bowl of tolatsy with the dogged determination of a man with no appetite, but great need.

She'd forgotten to warn their unexpected visitors. Iascat took one look at Vargo and rushed to his side. "What the hell *happened* to him?"

The fact that he addressed the question to Ren said he knew Vargo to be an unreliable source when it came to his own injuries. "Lower Bank business," she said, not sure how much Vargo wanted to share.

Parma snorted. "So that's what Sibiliat's letter was hinting at. She said she'd make you pay. Thought she was talking Cinquerat politics—didn't figure she'd send someone to beat you up."

With dangerous mildness, Vargo said, "No, she destabilized the entire Lower Bank and started twelve knot wars at once. I suppose she thinks that's suitable compensation for me stopping her father from becoming the new Tyrant."

That quelled Parma. Iascat said, "We'll talk about that later... but it isn't why we're here." He smoothed the lay of his coat, as though checking his pockets after a run-in with a thief. "I've found myself picking up my medallion without meaning to—often realizing only *after* I've inadvertently used it. Parma and Utrinzi have as well."

"Fuck." Vargo started to rake his good hand through his hair, only to jerk away with a hiss when it touched his bruises. "Us too. I assume it's an unfortunate result of that ritual with the dead szorsa."

"Unfortunate, or deliberate?" Parma asked, gaze hard on Ren.

An echo of Renata's coolness frosted Ren's Vraszenian accent as she said, "Are you implying something, Alta Parma?"

"I'm outright saying it." Brushing aside Iascat's staying hand, Parma squared off against Ren. "We're all suddenly walking around with our medallions, making it easy for somebody to lift them. I don't like Cibrial enough to agree with her on the color of my own hair, but you suggested the ritual. And you aren't exactly famous for your honesty. *Alta Renata.*"

"What think you I wish to do?" Ren demanded. "Take all the medallions for myself? I want nothing more than to get this Mask-damned thing out of my life—get *all* of them out of *all* our lives."

Parma huffed. "So you claim. But you're working with the Rook, aren't you? Who just staged a one-man raid on the Aerie and broke a lot of prisoners out. Cibrial thinks this is all a plan the two of you hatched to destroy the nobility."

That's sounding like a better idea every day. Before Ren could suppress that bile enough to get other words past it, Iascat cleared his throat. "Cibrial and Faella are angling to get authority over this taken out of Utrinzi's hands. They've been scribing an edited version of the truth for Agniet and Scaperto, that you and the Rook are conspiring against the city."

"That's utter—" Vargo's attempt to rise was aborted by an insufficiently suppressed groan.

Worry flashed across Iascat's expression as Vargo sagged back onto the couch, but he only said, "I know. But they've used my relative newness and my connection to both of you to make me look biased. And Utrinzi has always had a reputation for being out of touch. If they can get Caerulet and Fulvet on their side..."

It wouldn't just be legal authority they'd lose, but access to several of the medallions. Ren's fingernails dug into her palms.

Dropping next to Vargo with an exhausted flumph, Parma said, "Look. I just want to get rid of this thing. And I don't mean giving it to someone else; I agree they need to be gone. After what my uncle did to himself..." She closed her eyes on a shudder. "But if you can't do it soon, we'll need some other way to stop Cibrial and Faella from taking them. They've already bent Beldipassi's flimsy spine to their will. They think it's just a matter of time and patience before they get me and Iascat."

Grey can talk to Cercel, Ren thought. But who would talk to Scaperto? Would another visit from the Black Rose sway him as easily as it had when Koszar was scheduled to be executed *de Ninate*?

None of that solved the actual problem. "We've freed one of the two trapped parts of the szorsa's soul," she told the others. "That leaves only her dlakani, in the chain."

"Great," Parma said. "How do Vraszenians get rid of this dala-whatever?"

Silence. Ren looked at Vargo, who was looking at her. He shrugged helplessly: Vraszenian religious practice was hardly his strong point. And Ren had only grown up on the fringes of that world.

Eyes rolling, Parma said, "What, you don't know your own people's funerary practices?"

"I couldn't afford a proper funeral for my mother," Ren snapped. "She was burned on a pauper's mass pyre."

Parma sank back like a chastened child, her round cheeks flushing splotchy red. Plucking at the lavender-threaded quilting of her thick surcoat, she said, "I was supposed to know that? The woman we all *thought* was your mother is jostling for a place at Cibrial's teat."

"So, we need more information on Vraszenian funeral rites," Iascat said, bodily inserting himself between Ren and Parma as though he feared someone might go for a knife. "Ren, if I stayed with Vargo, could you go talk to Master Serrado? Would he be willing to help?"

More than you know. "Certainly," Ren said. "I'll be seeing him tonight."

Seven Knots, Lower Bank: Pavnilun 28

I hope Koszar isn't making an enormous mistake.

A shiver crawled across Ren's shoulders as her group approached the night-shrouded Seven Knots labyrinth. Faith in Ažerais was one thing; staking the future of the Anduske on this ordeal was another. If Koszar failed, they would have no way to stop Branek except by passing word of the impending rebellion to Cercel...with all the bloodshed that would bring.

If Koszar fails, a little voice whispered, *won't that mean Branek is right?*

To shake off that thought, Ren looked up at the roof of the labyrinth. She couldn't see any shadows out of place, but she trusted the Rook was there. While Grey might not be able to face his grandmother as himself, the Rook could and would keep watch in case things went badly wrong.

And Ren expected them to go badly wrong. There were too many people present, and a disheartening number of people surrounded Branek along one side of the interior colonnade.

Idusza jerked her chin at a cluster gathered on the opposite side of the colonnade, by the Face and Mask for Nem Idalič Zimat. The stout older woman at their center glowered as though she'd been dragged out of bed for this nonsense. "Good—Nainev and her friends stand not with Branek. Ljunan said they might be ready to break. This bodes well."

Koszar's breath hissed through his teeth. "Better it would bode if the Black Rose joined us tonight."

Ren said nothing. What *could* she say? Koszar had begged her to accompany him. He didn't know the specifics of what had happened here at the labyrinth, but he knew she would be the next speaker for the Ižranyi. *You can have that, or the Black Rose. Which one do you want more?*

She'd chosen to come as herself. Unmasked, her face bare of the cosmetics she'd worn before, because by now Laročja would have learned the truth. There was no more point in lying.

Sure enough, the old woman stabbed a sharp-nailed finger toward Ren the moment she drew near. "That outsider," Laročja spat. "That half-breed. That *fraud*. In this labyrinth she stood and claimed the right to speak for the Ižranyi. She contaminates this sacred rite; no doubt all along her plan has been to manipulate it for the traitor's benefit."

"*I* will oversee the ordeal," Mevieny snapped, hand tightening on Dalisva's supporting arm. "A right *you* tried to wrest from me early. Szorsa Arenza only acknowledged what was already mine."

"She won with a stolen card!" Laročja proclaimed, playing to her audience rather than to Mevieny. The charms braided into her silver hair swayed as she turned to face the crowd, a reminder of her rank and authority. "My precious Meszaros clan card, taken from me years ago by a treacherous boy. The same cursed wretch who is now that one's lover!"

Mevieny scoffed. "Claim you that one card makes the difference? Of many threads is a pattern made. And our Lady weaves stronger than any one woman—be she girl or crone."

Before Laročja could find a response to that insinuation, Mevieny released Dalisva and clapped her hands. "For a purpose we have come, to discover whom—if anyone—Ažerais favors. Ustimir Hraleski Branek of the Stretsko, Koszar Yureski Andrejek of the Anoškin. Come, together let us seek the guidance of dream."

Dalisva mixed aža into a cup of yellow wine for the three of them to share. Then they circled the colonnade, one man on each side of Mevieny, guiding her steps. Branek made an ostentatious point of placing his offerings in the Faces and the Masks second, after Mevieny. Koszar, unruffled, went last. Either his serenity was a mask of its own, or his faith truly was steadfast.

When the offerings were done, the trio standing at the mouth of the path, Mevieny shook off their hands. With slow but sure-footed steps, she walked the labyrinth alone, following its twists and turns. *A lifetime of memories to guide her?* Ren wondered. *Or does she see with aža's sight?* The little dream transcended ordinary vision, but what it showed was fickle. Then again, the Seven Knots labyrinth had survived even the Tyrant. If anything on the Lower Bank had graven itself so deeply in Ažerais's Dream as to persist through the shifting images aža bestowed, it would be this place.

Ren had not made offerings of her own, but she still prayed. *May Koszar win. He has to win. Branek would drown us in blood.*

At the heart of the labyrinth, Mevieny dipped her fingers into the basin of water and touched them to her forehead. Then she turned to face the head of the path, and her voice rang full and rich. "Ustimir Hraleski Branek. Speak your grievance for Ažerais to hear."

Standing to one side of the path's entrance, Branek addressed the crowd. "I say that Andrejek has abandoned the ideals of the Anduske, the children of the dreamweaver. He is like The Face of Song, veiled: a facade of peace that fails to hide the trouble within. To the Cinquerat he would bow, rather than fight for the freedom of this city—while every day, our people suffer and bleed! To lead us, he is no longer fit...if he ever was."

Mevieny nodded in acknowledgment, while Ren wondered if Laročja had fed him that line about The Face of Song. "Koszar Yureski Andrejek. Speak your grievance for Ažerais to hear."

Koszar let a bitter smile touch his face. "No claim now that I cut my knot, Ustimir? At least you have respect enough not to lie before Ažerais." He tugged the knot from beneath his shirt collar: not a simple charm, but an interwoven mass inherited from all the Anduske leaders before him. "Here it is, uncut. To take power, Branek lied, condemning me for an act I committed not. *He* is the traitor—and no faith can you have in a man who has none."

On its own, it wasn't enough to turn people away from Branek. Perhaps if Koszar had been able to reveal the treachery months ago...but too much time had passed; his rival's grip had solidified. This was no longer simply about politics, though. It was about the judgment of Ažerais herself.

In theory. Ren bit her lips so hard, she feared they would bleed.

A strip of embroidered cloth already covered the gaps where Mevieny's eyes should have been. Still, she took out a length of violet silk and bound herself again. A symbolic gesture, but the symbol mattered: She would not see with her waking eyes. Only that which the dream showed her, in the name of the lost Ižranyi.

The clan both Branek and Andrejek claimed to honor. *If only the Ižranyi still lived*—a thing people said far too often, an invocation of an idealized past. A time long before the Tyrant, before Nadežra suffered under Liganti control.

Ren prayed to Ižranyi, ancestor of that lost clan. To Stretsko, Branek's holy founder. To Ažerais herself. *If Branek serves you not—if he serves Nadežra not—then stop him. Somehow. I beg you.*

"Ustimir Hraleski Branek of the Stretsko," Mevieny said. "By ordeal shall your claims and your heart be judged. Put your faith in Ažerais, and your path will be smooth beneath your feet."

Branek set his shoulders and began to walk.

He strode along the winding path like he wished he could bull across the grass and head straight for the center, blasphemous though that would be. With Nadežra he would do the same, crushing those who opposed him into blood and bone beneath his feet. It might be effective. It would also be a nightmare.

And nightmares answered him.

The torches that lit the labyrinth seemed to dim. The shadows of the colonnade lengthened, detached, scuttling down past the Faces and the Masks, spindle-limbed and hissing. Hairless hides, cracked like charred wood, shifted over raw bone and wiry muscle as the zlyzen swarmed.

Ren clapped both hands over her mouth to hold in her scream. She recoiled a step, grabbing at Idusza—and the other woman shot her an annoyed look. One finger, laid over Idusza's full lips, cautioned her to be quiet.

But she showed no hint of alarm. No one did... except for Branek.

His step faltered. In the silence of the labyrinth, Ren heard him draw an unsteady breath; then he forced himself onward. All around, the others watched, as if all they saw was the man submitting himself to ordeal.

Not the monsters who had come to test him.

Ren's hands stayed clamped over her mouth, but for a different reason now. *I can see them. I haven't taken aža. Why can I see them?*

Another night, another labyrinth. Atop the Point, in Ažerais's Dream. She'd gone to rescue Vargo from the zlyzen...and in exchange, she'd bound herself to them. Strengthening the connection formed when she swore herself into Ondrakja's blasphemous mockery of a knot.

As much as Ren loathed Branek, it was all she could do to keep herself from leaping forward when the zlyzen began attacking him. He'd taken aža, not ash, and so their claws passed harmlessly through his clothes and his flesh. But Branek couldn't control his flinches, his ragged gasps of fear. His progress along the path slowed.

And Ren couldn't control her memory. Vargo, crouching sick and afraid, holding the zlyzen at bay with nothing more than red chalk. Leato at the bottom of the empty wellspring, screaming. Dying.

"Leave me be!"

The shout was Branek's. The zlyzen chased him as he bolted from the path, but they stopped at the labyrinth's edge, slinking back and forth, crawling over each other and snapping at an audience that couldn't see them.

All around the colonnade, people were murmuring in shock. Abandoning the ordeal didn't necessarily mean Branek had lost, not when Andrejek had yet to walk. Ažerais might condemn them both. But it boded ill for him.

Ren, lowering her hands, risked a glance at Laročja. The older woman's expression was as unreadable as stone. But she stared straight ahead—not at Branek, gasping and huddled on the ground.

Mevieny must have seen it all, through aža's sight. Still, her voice was calm as she said, "Koszar Yureski Andrejek of the Anoškin. By ordeal shall your claims and your heart be judged. Put your faith in Ažerais, and your path will be smooth beneath your feet."

Koszar took a deep breath and laid his cane aside. Then he, too, began to walk.

And the zlyzen...

They lunged at him, all hissing growls and snapping fangs. But only from a distance: each time they pulled up short, like dogs on leashes, before belly-crawling away. Menacing, not attacking. Koszar's steady, uneven footfalls didn't falter as he traced the looping line of the path, swinging in and then out, doubling back upon itself in tight coils.

Until he reached the center of the labyrinth, where Mevieny waited. Then the snarling creatures faded like mist, leaving the courtyard quiet.

But before they went, Ren was horribly sure the leader of the zlyzen—the one who wore Ondrakja's old knot charm—turned and gave her a sharp-toothed grin.

Every part of her was cold. *I did this. I brought them here, because I wanted Branek stopped.*

Laročja was right. I tainted the ordeal.

She stood rigid as Koszar guided Mevieny out of the labyrinth, a straight line to the edge, leaving any ill luck behind. The speaker for the Ižranyi removed her violet blindfold and announced, "The ordeal is done. Ažerais has judged Ča Branek and Ča Andrejek, and all have seen the result. Ča Andrejek has her favor."

Ren tried to force words past the strangling tightness of her throat. Before she could, a woman cried out along the side of the labyrinth. "Look! In the mouth of Ir Entrelke!"

The deity of good fortune. With a trembling hand, the woman reached out and plucked a card from the opening where worshippers placed their offerings.

Ren knew that card. She'd seen the spreading wings of that ghost owl in the pattern Laročja laid, here in this same labyrinth: The Silent Witness, the clan card of the Anoškin.

Laročja moaned, staggering as if her knees had gone suddenly weak. Clasping her hands together, she said, "May the Faces and the Masks forgive my foolishness. This is the danger, when the loud voices of powerful men speak over the whispers of our Lady. But in the silence, at last I hear clearly. Ča Branek has lost his way; it is Ča Andrejek whom Ažerais means to lead us now!"

Regaining her strength, she faced Koszar and touched her heart. "Ča Andrejek, you have been wronged. But I will stand by you to make it right...and so will those who listen to me."

Cynicism cracked the ice around Ren's heart. *At least she didn't pull it from behind Koszar's ear.* It hardly mattered whether anyone else guessed that Laročja had planted her assistant with that card ahead of time, insurance against the possibility that Branek might fail the ordeal. The important thing was, she'd just thrown her allegiance publicly behind Andrejek. A threat, neatly wrapped in a concession: The Anduske might follow their leader, but Branek had gathered support from outside their ranks, too. Support Koszar would need, if he wanted to make real change happen in Nadežra.

Support Laročja could just as easily revoke as bestow.

Grey should have come like Koszar asked, Ren thought, fuming. Only he could expose Laročja for what she was: a fraud, a malicious liar who'd abused her grandson for years, who didn't deserve the respect and authority she'd been given. If he had the slightest concern for justice—

Sickness rose to gag her. *You know why Grey made the choice he did. And you know why you're angry at him.* Because the claws of A'ash were sinking ever deeper into her heart.

Mevieny's dry voice dragged her back to herself. "It seems Szorsa Laročja concurs with the judgment of the ordeal. What say you, Szorsa Arenza?"

What could she say? If she confessed—if Koszar's *half-Liganti advisor* confessed—that she might have inadvertently tainted the ordeal, she would be handing his enemies a knife to sink into his back.

Our Lady weaves stronger than any one woman, Mevieny had said. The blind szorsa stood serene, her hands wrapped in the purple silk that had hidden nothing from her. She couldn't meet Ren's gaze, but her manner had the same effect.

If the ordeal truly had been tainted, surely Ažerais would know. And their goddess had other ways to condemn Koszar, whatever the zlyzen did.

"Ča Branek's path is one of fear, violence, and failure," Ren said, forcing herself to speak with something like tranquility. "Always have I trusted Ča Andrejek to lead us to a better way. Tonight's events change that not."

"Then we are woven in agreement," Mevieny said. "Koszar Yureski Andrejek of the Anoškin, you are worthy in Ažerais's sight. You have broken no oaths, betrayed no trusts, and brought no shame to your kureč or clan." She couldn't outright reinstate Koszar's leadership of a dissident group, but she didn't need to. The message came through clearly.

As did Koszar's reply.

"Children of the dreamweaver," he declared, loud enough for all to hear. "As Szorsa Arenza said, Ča Branek's path was one of fear, violence, and failure. I will not lead you in such ways.

"But the path we walked was that of the labyrinth—like the sacred labyrinth that once marked the stone around our Lady's wellspring. A wellspring that has been outside our control for far too long."

The columns by the entrance held no Faces or Masks. Despite his bad knee, Koszar leapt onto the pedestal of one and wrapped his free hand around to hold himself in place, high enough for all to see. "Branek's goal is right, even if his methods are not. And so to you I pledge: We *will* take back what we have lost. But we will not with blood stain those pure waters. The Great Dream comes, and we must be ready to greet it—with the Old Island in *our* hands!"

The surge of cheering struck Ren like a blow. She faded into the shadow of a column, hoping her expression didn't show the depth of her shock. *I thought I was helping Koszar stop a rebellion.*

He hadn't even warned her. When had he made this decision? He must have been considering it well before tonight. But fear, violence, and failure: She'd handed Koszar the rhetoric herself.

And she couldn't deny he'd used it well. No tactic would bring *all* the Anduske to his side tonight; a few, Branek among them, were slipping out the back door of the labyrinth. A flash of light from the roof was the Rook signaling that he'd follow, in case they decided to protest the decision with violence. But they were the minority. The evidence of the ordeal, combined with Laročja's support and Koszar's declaration, meant that most of the Anduske were back in his camp, the divisions of the past year forgotten.

Ren looked at Dalisva, standing serene. Clearly *she'd* known this was coming. Which meant Koszar had probably been talking to the Kiralič, maybe other ziemetse as well. Did that mean they were ready to support him, not only against Branek, but against the Cinquerat itself?

She breathed out, trying to slow her heart. Trying to think clearly, if that was even possible anymore. *This isn't what I wanted. But is it what we need?*

The waters of the Dežera were rising. Soon the Wellspring of Ažerais would appear, ending not only this seven-year cycle, but a Grand Cycle. The beginning of a new age. If there was ever a time for Nadežra's rebirth, this was it.

Ren didn't want a rebellion. But she wanted what it might produce, so badly she could *taste* it.

Most importantly, she wasn't the only one who wanted it. All the cheering Anduske, the ziemetse willing to set differences aside for the chance at real change. Ren could see the place in the grass where she'd laid her vision of Nadežra's future: the clans coming together, with Labyrinth's Heart at their center. The promise of peace.

She didn't think she'd created this. But maybe she'd felt it coming.

And maybe it was time for a revolution.

16

The Face of Song

Isla Prišta, Westbridge: Pavnilun 30

"Andrejek did *what*?" Tess demanded, staring at Ren.

It was both like and unlike being back at Traementis Manor. Ren had to watch what she said at the townhouse, but not because she feared maids listening at keyholes; instead it was river rats she had to worry about. The shredding of Vargo's organization had left all the knots scrabbling over their territorial boundaries, and the resulting brawls had spilled over to innocent citizens—along with some not-so-innocent ones.

Arkady's territory had always overlapped that of other, older knots. Those knots had let it pass, because her kids were pity-rustlers and petty pickpockets, not any challenge to their control. When everybody grabbed for everything they could, though, the kids were the first to lose.

So they'd bolted for cover...into Ren's house.

Not all of them. Before she lost her place on the Upper Bank, she'd managed to get some of the most vulnerable into the households of adoptive families. Others had fled, or were old enough to earn places in adult knots. A few were dead in the canals. But Arkady had led much of the remainder straight to someone she knew had space for them, and a heart too soft to turn them away.

It meant Ren couldn't rant to Tess about Koszar's decision to go ahead with the rebellion, even though they were currently alone in the parlour. "I understand why," she said. "I even agree—I think. I only wish he had warned me." As if the leader of the Anduske had any obligation to consult with her. He didn't even know she was the Black Rose.

Tess said, "But . . . people will get hurt."

While Koszar wouldn't order a wholesale slaughter of the impure, some amount of bloodshed was inevitable. Ren's heart ached every time she imagined it. Yet what was the alternative? Let things continue as they were, with the Liganti controlling everything? With Vraszenians and common Nadežrans bleeding every day on the Old Island and the Lower Bank, metaphorically and literally?

And the deeper resentment, centuries old. This was a *Vraszenian* holy city. Filled with many other people, not just Liganti but Isarnah and Ganllechyns and more . . . but *theirs*. With the Great Dream coming, and the end of a Grand Cycle, how could they leave it in other hands?

Reasonable thoughts. But Tess caught her sleeve, and Ren realized that without thinking, she'd drifted toward the stairs. Toward the cellar, where her medallion was buried. How much could she help Koszar—how much could she help *Nadežra*—with just a little assistance from that disc of bronze?

The tug on her sleeve turned into a pinch. Ren laid her hand over Tess's with a wan smile of thanks. "We'll do what we can to protect people." *Without* Primordial aid.

"Right." Already Tess had taken the news and transformed it into bustle. She tucked her hair into her kerch as though she meant to set to work right that moment. "I'll need to move the shop's supplies. Else they'll get looted, sure as snapdragons. Little Alwydd should be safe. Vargo's old knots don't have a foothold there, and Old Mag has a passel of grandkids with too many muscles and not enough work. I'll just—"

"Oi!" Arkady's voice ripped through the house like a nicked razor. With so many children coming in and out, sitting on the porch or by the windows, Ren had no need for a bell anymore. "Got some cheese-eaters on the stoop says they know Re-*nah*-ta. They en't hawks or nothing. Want me to search 'em for weapons?"

It was probably Iascat and Parma again, coming to relay the newest trouble from Cibrial. "Faces and Masks, no," Ren murmured into her hand, then shouted back, "No, and not for purses, either. Bring them to the parlour."

"I'll make tea?" Tess said, but Ren caught her before she could leave.

"You're not my servant. Never were. And we owe no hospitality to—" Her words stoppered her throat in a frog's croak when she saw who was entering the room.

Donaia. And behind her, a tentative Giuna. Arkady and her kids lurked in the shadows of the hallway, eyeing the small gems sparkling on the cuffs and collars of the ladies' surcoats. Ren even caught the flash of a thumb knife palmed as soon as Arkady noticed her looking. A pointed glare sent the children scurrying and their leader skulking off.

"It isn't what it looks like!" Tess blurted when Donaia's gaze swung from Ren to Arkady and back.

"And what do you think it looks like?" Donaia asked.

"That...we're...setting up our own knot of child thieves?" Color rode high on Tess's cheeks. She pressed plump fingers to them. "We aren't."

"I didn't think you were," Donaia said. Her voice was cool, her gloved hands clasped tightly against a surcoat of brushed chocolate wool. From anyone else it might feel like a dismissal, but Ren was just relieved it wasn't outright condemnation.

"What...what brings you here?" she asked in a halting amalgam of Arenza's and Renata's voices. As when she'd met Giuna in Suncross, she didn't know who to be around these women.

"I'll fetch tea," Tess said and bolted, closing the door behind her.

At least trapping Ren like that made it difficult for her to slip downstairs to Tricat's hiding place. She forced her attention to her guests—if they *were* guests. "Have a seat. Just move Doomclaw not."

Arkady's ginger tom had taken over the most comfortable arm-chair and hadn't budged from it once that Ren had seen. In sleep he looked almost peaceable, but it was a bigger lie than any she'd ever told. The only creature he tolerated besides Arkady was Clever Natalya, who'd curled herself into a tiny inkblot between his paws.

At least Donaia didn't make them sit in awkward silence. Once she'd settled herself away from Doomclaw, she said, "Here is what I've pieced together. This 'malevolent numinatrian artifact' you and Tanaquis told me about may or may not have once belonged to the Acrenix, but it's connected to Ghiscolo's sudden death and Sibi-liat's house arrest. Letilia used it to curse my family when she fled Nadežra. Giuna told me she's been in Ganllech since then. At some point Letilia used it to curse you, and perhaps you found out; per-haps that's why you stole it and came back here. What I don't know is *why*. Were you hoping to get enough money to cleanse yourself? But you seemed surprised to discover we were cursed. And appar-ently Meppe was cursed at some point, too."

Donaia's hand tightened into a fist. "It almost fits together, but not quite. And I'm reluctant to take action against Letilia until I know the full extent of her crimes. I tried questioning Tanaquis, but we've hardly seen her since you were unmasked, and when I went to her townhouse, her maid blocked me at the door. Said she had orders not to let anyone in, not even by Cinquerat command. So I must come to you for answers."

Ren licked lips that had gone sandpaper dry. "You trust me to tell you the truth?"

"Yes." Donaia's gaze was level. She didn't say the rest: that if Ren lied now... then it truly *would* be over.

Doomclaw sighed and corkscrewed in his sleep, dislodging Nata-lya. She squeaked a protest and rearranged herself.

Ren raised her voice. "Arkady."

No sound came from behind the door, but she knew the girl was there. "Arkady, I need you to make sure no one overhears what we say. Yourself included."

Donaia's mouth thinned with doubt, but from behind the door

came a muffled voice. "You got it." And Ren trusted that Arkady would do as ordered.

Then she told Donaia everything.

It was easier to speak of Primordials than of her own lies and the pain they'd caused. Partway through, Giuna clamped her hands over her mouth, eyes as wide as an owl's. Donaia's expression was a brittle mask over whatever lay beneath. Ren kept her own gloveless hands folded in her lap, her posture as straight as Renata's, and talked steadily until she ran out of truth to give.

Well, almost ran out. Giuna unclamped her hands and whispered, "Does this have to do with you being the Black Rose?"

Donaia's head whipped around fast enough to unpin a tress of hair. Ren fought the urge to plant her face in her palm. "Not—not exactly."

Giuna flushed, realizing what she'd done. "Oh. Sorry. I— Wait!" This time she caught herself, the struggle visible; then she forged ahead anyway. "Grey is your sweetheart. And the Black Rose is... There are stories of her associating with..."

Why in the name of all the Masks did I choose clever people to con? She could have gone after Fintenus instead. Ren silenced Giuna's unvoiced question with a curt nod.

A full minute passed in perfect stillness, the only sound the rasping of Doomclaw's tongue as he groomed little Natalya with long sweeps that rocked her whole body.

Sighing, Donaia said, "I feel like Tanaquis, saying this, but... that all makes a great deal of sense. I'm only surprised you didn't use the Black Rose to frighten off Letilia."

"If only she were so easily frightened," Ren said. Not smiling, but feeling for the first time as though she could. All differences fell into the canal in the face of a mutual dislike.

"What was your plan for dealing with her?" Donaia held up a hand, forestalling a protest Ren had no intention of making. "Don't try to claim you didn't have one. I know you well enough for that."

"Seteris," Ren admitted. "I was going to send her there with money enough to make all her fondest dreams come true...and hope it would be too much hassle to return." Freed of Tricat's curse, Letilia's luck might be better than whatever drove her out of Ganllech.

Donaia huffed. "A kinder fate than I intend to give her. Whether she meant to hurt us or not—no, she *did* mean to hurt us. Just not to the degree she achieved. She deserves to be hurt in return."

"Does she?" Ren let the question hang until Donaia met her gaze. "Or is that what you *want*?"

She felt a little bad saying it, but only a little. Her own wish to strike buzzed in her throat like a caged hornet; the rebuke was as much for herself as for Donaia. The other woman's gloved hands, brushing the foreskirt of her surcoat straight, paused mid-stroke. A *brown* surcoat: Tricat's color, which Donaia wore often.

Her hands lifted as if she suddenly wanted no contact with her own clothing.

Giuna said, "Letilia is terrible, and I hate her for what she's done, but...she didn't know she was cursing us. She's already done her worst to Ren; maybe we should leave it at that."

"*She* won't leave it at that," Ren said. "Letilia has figured out that Tricat is important; she's trying to get it back." How much had Cibrial told her? Probably as little as possible.

Donaia smacked one hand against the arm of the couch she shared with Giuna. "Then we have to deal with her."

Ren hesitated. If she didn't ask, she couldn't receive the answer she dreaded. *You're more prepared to face Primordials than this?* Yes—but if she could brave the one, she could brave the other.

"When you say 'we,'" she said softly, "who do you mean?"

"Of course I mean..." Donaia sputtered to a stop, hand hanging in the air between them. It dropped to her lap with a whump. "How am I supposed to trust *anything* to do with family, knowing one of these cursed things had control of my mind?"

"Masks have mercy." This time Ren did give in to the urge to bury her face in her hands. "How think you *I* have felt, all this time?"

Donaia's answer came soft and weary. "I don't know how you've felt. Were we ever family to you?"

Ren sat up and found Donaia biting her lips together as if to hold back other words. Not angry ones—not even hurt, Ren thought. Just...lost. Uncertain. Looking for reassurance.

The same thing Ren craved.

"I—I know not how to...how to be family," she said. It felt like stretching a cramped muscle: painful, but good. "For Vraszenians, kinship is blood, but growing up, I had no kureč or clan. Only my mother. And after she died, Tess and Sedge—we swore to each other as siblings. Then...you."

She included Donaia and Giuna both in her admission. Tanaquis, with her curiosity and intellectual drive, had become a friend for sure, perhaps more. Meppe and Idaglio were nice enough. By the time Ren realized she saw Leato as more than a mark, it was too late. He had died and all she felt was guilt. But Donaia and Giuna had been with her through the worst of Storm Against Stone, as she'd been with them. That was all she'd ever known of family.

"I was afraid to tell you who I was. What I'd done." Her breath hitched with every word. "I didn't want to hurt you. I don't want to lose you. And the words I want you to trust most, you have lost all reason to believe."

It took everything she had to make herself meet Donaia's gaze. And what she saw there...

"Oh, *fuck* Primordials," Donaia said, and dragged her into a hug.

There would be salt stains on the shoulder of Donaia's surcoat later, but Ren suspected her aunt might shred her entire Tricat-colored wardrobe for dishrags. Once Ren had extricated herself from that hug and Giuna's that followed, she said, thick with the aftermath of tears, "If it helps, I grew closer to you *after* I lost Tricat. Not everything is Primordials." *Your own desires will destroy you*—that was how the curse worked. She certainly had wrecked herself fairly badly by caring for the Traementis. But the desire at least grew on its own, free of Primordial influence.

At a thump from the hallway, Donaia jerked and placed herself between Ren, Giuna, and the door. Arkady's voice rose up, audible even through the thick wood. "...told you five times already, she said nobody was to listen. So I en't letting *nobody* past."

Tess's response blazed a path through three languages, six impossible bedroom activities, and nine gruesome ways a person could become a corpse. In the gasping silence that followed, Arkady's soft whistle was clear as blown glass. "Damn, Freckles. You kiss your sweetheart with that mouth?"

"Yes. And he enjoys it. Now step aside, if you please."

The door opened, and Tess bustled in with a full tray and an expression as prim as a neatly tucked seam. "Sorry to have kept you waiting, but I don't think the tea's gone cold yet."

"No." Donaia's lips twitched. "But the cakes may have gotten a little scorched."

Tess weighed Ren with a swift glance as she set the tray down, taking in the marks left by tears. "Is there anything else you need, Ren?"

Two kinds of family in one room, and the knot charm around her wrist. She lacked only one thing.

"Yes," Ren said. "I need clothes to get married in."

Kingfisher, Lower Bank: Pavnilun 30

Yvieny wasn't playing on the stoop. That should have been Grey's warning. But after days of wrangling Arkady's kids in Westbridge and dealing with Koszar's pivot toward revolution, he saw the quiet as a promise of peaceful refuge.

When he stepped through the door, only cold shock kept him frozen in place, rather than fleeing.

"You said he visited rarely," Jakoslav Szerado said to Alinka. Lifting Jagyi off his knee, he set the boy on the floor. "I will take my leave. Go on, little bandit. Go to your mama."

At the gentle nudging, Jagyi's grip on his grandfather's panel coat firmed to toddler-backed steel. His face twisted up in a pout, and he sagged to the floor like he was Clever Natalya's caravan: immovable even with a team of four fine horses.

Grey found his voice, rough as unsanded wood. "What are you doing here?"

"Nothing. I meant not to intrude. I only wanted..." Jakoslav's water-pale eyes went like a lodestone to Jagyi, then Alinka. Yvieny crouched in the corner with her dolls, watching the adults with lips tight and eyes wide. "I came not to bring strife between you. I wished only to meet my daughter and grandchildren. I will go."

"Stay." Alinka pressed a hand to his shoulder, though Jakoslav had made no effort to rise. "We cannot send you away so soon."

Grey could and would—but this wasn't his house. He took the cup of tea Alinka thrust at him, but his knees refused to bend for him to sit. Instead he stood by the door, knowing it was awkward, unable to move. Just looking at his father made him feel small, like he was a ten-year-old boy again.

If he raises a hand to you, he'll learn how much has changed, he told himself. Just as he had at the labyrinth, looking down at the silvered head of his grandmother—but there he'd had the presence of the Rook to keep him strong. *And if he raises one to the children...*

Grey was suddenly and profoundly grateful that Ryvček held Quinat now. If he were still under its sway, he feared what he might have done.

He forced himself to sip the tea, and almost spat it out again. Not because it was bad; no, this was excellent tea, not the cheap brick sort that was all Alinka could afford. His gaze snapped to the hearth, to the beautifully painted box there, and Alinka smiled. "A gift from your father."

"It's nothing." Taking Jágyi's chubby hands in his, Jakoslav pressed the long blade of his nose to Jagyi's little mushroom. "I heard your mama's kureč comes from Zmadya upriver, and I thought she might miss the taste of home, so far from family."

Grey's hand trembled at the suggestion that he wasn't family, at the insinuation that he was neglecting Alinka and the children.

Alinka met his eyes and rolled her own, but that was scant bandage over a wound that had seeped blood his whole life. "Brother Grey takes very good care of us," she said.

From the corner came Yvieny's voice, soft but hinting at

belligerence. "Uncle Grey brings me honey stones. They're better than some yucky old tea."

It chased away some of Grey's gloom. Jagyi might be easily swayed, but at least he'd bought Yvieny's loyalty with years of sweets smuggled past Alinka's tolerant sighs.

"What is this 'Grey' nonsense?" Jakoslav asked. The thump of his bootheel on the wooden floor made Grey flinch. "Is his great-uncle Gruzdan's name not good enough for my son? You disrespect your family for a mere boy's grudge?"

A boy's grudge? Was that how his father remembered the years after Grey's mother died, before Kolya took him away? Was that how he managed to see himself as a good man and a wronged father?

"I remember those days differently," Grey said, as evenly as he could. With Kolya gone, if he didn't remember, who would?

Alinka could hardly miss the tension, but unfortunately, her instinct was to ease it with hospitality. "It's almost time for me to prepare lunch. Will you join us? Perhaps we can all share some happy tales of these past years. And Yvieny can show you the dolls Kolya made for her." Yvie let herself be herded forward, but she clutched her dolls protectively to her chest.

"I'd like that." Lifting Jagyi once more to his lap, Jakoslav held out a hand to Yvieny like he was coaxing a fawn. Grey found himself hoping for once that Yvie would give in to her penchant for biting. "Come, Yvie. Perhaps after lunch you can show me your koszenie, and I will tell you stories of your father's family."

"Yvie is only six," Grey said. "She hasn't yet been given her koszenie."

He deliberately counted it by Nadežran tradition, where the first year of life was the first year of age. His suspicion that Jakoslav had gathered plenty of information already was confirmed when his father said, "Nonsense. She was conceived during the Great Dream, which means she is seven. If her koszenie isn't done, I would be happy to embroider the paternal side. This old man has only time to occupy his hands."

"I've already started," Grey said, not mentioning that his efforts had only gone so far as to buy floss. Tess had promised to teach him, but so many other things kept them both occupied.

"Then little Jakoslav's. You wouldn't be so selfish as to deny me both." Jakoslav aimed his appeal at Alinka, as though he knew Grey would deny him anything and everything.

"Jagyi won't need his for years," Grey snapped. But he knew it for an error the moment the words came out of his mouth, even before Alinka flinched. He tried to moderate his voice, and knew he failed. "The boy has only just met you, Dodač."

The word slipped out, well-oiled by past habit. Few Vraszenian families these days were so formal as to use the old words for various relatives. But Jakoslav had always insisted on it, and even though Grey had sworn he would never call the man that again, his body remembered the blows that followed on the heels of disrespect.

That one word earned Grey his first smile of the day. His father's approving nod curdled like sour milk in Grey's gut. "You've shorn your hair and cut free of your name, but at least this place hasn't carved *all* manners from you."

After that, Grey could hardly shove his father out the door. Nor would he give Jakoslav the satisfaction of watching him flee. So he was forced to endure a meal with the man, listening to him make friendly, reasonable conversation with Alinka, well-greased with compliments toward the children.

No. Toward *Jagyi*. Yvie quietly sorted and resorted her dolls, ignored.

When the meal ended and Jakoslav finally left, Alinka closed the door and sagged against it, sighing. "Fear not, Grey. I haven't forgotten Kolya's stories, nor yours. Though…he is not as bad as I imagined."

Heat and cold washed through Grey in alternate waves. "He's very good at seeming not so bad. If he weren't, someone would have intervened long before Kolya took me away."

"Yes, yes." Alinka passed a hand over her brow. "Still…he deserves to know his grandchildren."

"If only that were all he wants." Grey fought to keep his voice low. Jagyi was asleep, and Yvieny had fled upstairs as soon as she was released from the table. He didn't want his nephew to wake, his niece to overhear this poison. "Alinka, my father has no heir."

That widened her eyes. "But—surely the Szerado are not without sons. There must be nephews, cousins, other male kin."

"There was a nephew, yes. But two years ago a horse threw him and he took a terrible blow to the head. The others aren't fit to lead—or at least my father considers them unfit." Grey had a lihosz cousin in Gursoven who would be ideal. That man's grandmother had been Isarnah, though, which meant Laročja would never accept him.

"But Jagyi is so young. It will be decades before he'd be suited to lead a kureč." Twisting the end of her sash belt in her hands, Alinka added, "Have you thought perhaps that his kindness to the children is to show he has changed—that he has regrets? Perhaps it is you he wishes to reconcile with."

And name as his heir. She didn't say it, but Grey had to laugh all the same. It was laugh or bleed, and the fact he could do the former came as a pleasant surprise. "The moons will set in the northern sea first." Even if his father considered it, Grey would never agree. Nor would his grandmother allow it. Not with the curse she'd found in his pattern, so many years ago.

With an effort, he pushed them from his mind. Taking Alinka's hands in his own, he said, "It matters not. My family is here, and family brought me here today. Ren and I have had enough of waiting. On the spring equinox, we will be married."

Alinka's shriek of delight pierced his gloom like sunlight. It roused Jagyi from his nap and brought Yvie dashing down the stairs, and their joy at his news was a reminder of what family could—and should—be.

Isla Traementis, the Pearls: Pavnilun 32

Few things gave Donaia more satisfaction than making someone she despised wait on her pleasure. When the person in question was Letilia, satisfaction grew to vindictive delight.

She did feel a slight tremor of guilt when she allowed the

bouncing pup at her heels to surge forward and greet their guest with dusty paws and slobbery tongue—but not for Letilia's sake. After the dog breeder gave her some pups from the litters Meatball sired, Colbrin had devoted much of his time to training them. It wasn't nice of Donaia to encourage such misbehavior...no matter how gratifying she found it right now.

"Dumpling. Down," she said, clicking her fingers.

The grey-brindled pup left off his excited leaps and trotted happily over to receive the morsel of dried mutton Donaia offered him. "Good boy," she said, giving a scruffle of encouragement as well.

Letilia shuddered and tried to scrape her composure back together. She'd never liked pets of any kind, seeing them as threats to her own dignity and skirts; Dumpling's enthusiasm had driven her into retreat between two chairs. Now, with him called off, she squared her shoulders and lifted her nose into the air. "I don't know *why* I did you the kindness of accepting your invitation; I should have made you come to me. I must be softhearted, giving you another chance, after everything you've done to me."

"What *I've* done to *you*?" Donaia's bark of laughter sent Dumpling under her skirts for shelter. All too aware of the lingering influence from the Tricat medallion, she'd intended to make this meeting brief and to the point...but surely anyone in her position would take a *little* time to relish their vengeance. "What did I ever do but bear your snubs in silence, while you did your best to turn our entire register against me? All your whinging to your father that I was a mere outer relation, that I should be grateful to be given meals and a bed—that with my mother gone, perhaps I should be struck out entirely? Gianco only wed me to protect me from you, you vicious little snipe."

"Yet here you stand as head of the house, with the rest of our family gone," Letilia hissed. "Apparently I was right to warn Father about the poison of outsiders."

Donaia lurched back a step, hand going to her gut as though Letilia's strike had been physical. *Poison*: the word Ren had used, over and over again, to describe the Primordial influence on their house.

Nothing in Letilia's manner said she knew what wound she'd just dug her thumb into. No, that was Traementis insularity talking, for all that she was Traementis no more. Tanaquis might have cleansed Letilia of the curse, but the influence of A'ash remained.

In *both* of them.

To keep herself from going for Letilia's throat, Donaia bent to extract Dumpling from her skirts. The pup was already getting too large to hide there, but the warmth of his barrel and the softness of his ears grounded her. She couldn't bring herself to be gentle with Letilia, not after the endless years of petty viciousness, the inability to care about anyone but herself. But she didn't have to fling that whole Primordial business in the other woman's face, either, revealing what was better kept secret.

She could get all the justice she needed out of Letilia's own situation.

"Yes," she said, fighting to keep her tone restrained. "I am head of House Traementis. And it's my duty to see to house business. I understand an offer was made to you on our behalf; I've invited you here to amend it."

That lanced the boil of Letilia's anger, deflating her into confusion. "What offer? Who made me an offer?"

"Ren. Your erstwhile...maid." She let the implication spool out, let Letilia draw the wrong conclusion.

Gloves straining over her knuckles, Letilia whispered, "You mean...you're willing to reinscribe me in the Traementis register?"

Donaia's satisfied smile rode roughshod over Letilia's incredulous one. "No, I'm referring to a different offer. More of a suggestion, really—that you leave Nadežra with funds to set yourself up somewhere else, and never return. Though I'm afraid the lack of prudence you showed in refusing that generous offer has cost you an opportunity, as any stipend is now off the table."

That brief, greedy hope hardened into scorn. "What game is this? You think you have the power to drive *me* out of this city? When you can barely show your *face* in public?"

As if she'd forgotten the thread of the conversation, Donaia glanced down at Dumpling. "This pup is the get of Lex Talionis, you know. We made arrangements earlier this year with a dog breeder, Rhuelt Glastyn—I don't suppose you met him while you were in Ganllech? I understand he's supplied dogs to many princely households...including that of Prince Maredd."

Letilia's face whitened beneath the powder. Voice barely louder than Dumpling's panting breaths, she whispered, "Has he."

"Indeed. Dog breeders mostly gossip about bloodlines, you know, but sometimes even that subject runs dry and they must find fresh meat. Like the news about Prince Maredd's mistress being stripped of the title he gave her and exiled from Ganllech, on pain of death. Something about a missing royal heirloom. A...hen brooch, I believe?"

Letilia had gone rigid, not quite hiding the panic that must be building inside. Letting the mask of casual conversation fall, Donaia said, "You do know that in Nadežra, impersonating a noble is a crime."

"A crime committed by that *gnat* you call a niece!"

"My niece, as you just pointed out, is a member in good standing of House Traementis. You, on the other hand, have no family willing to shelter you. Meanwhile, you've announced yourself as *Alta* Letilia Viraudacis, loudly and often. You've demanded a noble's right to have your honor defended in a duel. You've *threatened my family*, Letilia—and for that alone I would gladly see you drowned in the Depths." That, and ten thousand reasons beside. The years of constant, grating nastiness, before Letilia fled. The unwitting selfishness that had cursed House Traementis, reaping even Donaia's beloved son. For that, she could watch Letilia hang, and drink deep in celebration afterward.

But Leato wouldn't want his mother to go down that road.

"I will do you the courtesy of allowing you to leave Nadežra before I notify the Vigil. But if I see your face again, *Mistress Letilia*, be certain that my courtesy has reached an end." One hand signaled Dumpling to stay; with the other, Donaia opened the door. "And be eternally grateful that, thanks entirely to Ren, House Traementis no longer dines on vengeance."

She half expected bluster anyway, Letilia trying to play cards she didn't hold. Instead, white-faced, the woman walked out in silence, and Donaia shut the door behind her.

Alone, she slumped onto the couch. Dumpling sat at her feet, obedient but quivering; in contravention of all good principles of dog training, Donaia reached down and lifted him into her lap. A few moments later, voices came from the front hall: Tess and Giuna, chattering about what Giuna might wear to Ren's wedding. Another balm on Donaia's healing soul.

Smiling, she nudged Dumpling off her lap and went to join the conversation. Those two should know the fruit their efforts had borne. And she could ask Tess if Ren might like a dog of her own for a wedding gift.

Seven Knots, Lower Bank: Pavnilun 35

"Watch your head," Idusza said to Ren and Grey as she ducked under a beam bracing two sagging walls apart.

The Anduske headquarters were buried in the warren of Seven Knots, the path there deliberately confusing, making it harder for their enemies to reach them. If Ren had known the way, she might have spoken to Koszar sooner than this. The confrontation at the labyrinth hadn't taken Laročja out of the dance; she'd merely switched partners. The people she'd summoned from outside Nadežra to help make the rebellion a reality were a runaway caravan: Koszar could only grab the reins and do his best to steer it in a safe direction. But where else might Laročja drive him, without someone else to counter her influence?

Grey laid a reassuring hand on Ren's shoulder as Idusza knocked at the final door, and she flashed him a brief smile. She wished Vargo could have come with them, but he was still recovering—slowly. *Too* slowly, Ren feared. Not merely without his usual speed, lacking Alsius's life force to help him along; he was healing more slowly than an ordinary person. And though he hid it with makeup and sardonic wit, exhaustion hung over him like a shroud.

The door guard let them into a long series of rooms with their walls replaced by temporary divides of beaded curtains and lattice-work screens. Vraszenians clustered in every nook and alcove, the colors of every clan flashing in their braids. "These are all Anduske?" Ren whispered to Idusza. It didn't seem possible. Some of those they passed were lighter skinned, northern Vraszenians, with the lilt of Nadežra softening their tongues. Others were clearly from the south, one group dark enough to almost pass for Isarnah, and some of the accents were so thick she barely recognized the words as Vraszenian.

"No. Most have come for the Great Dream," Idusza said, clicking her tongue like many Nadežran natives did when the seven-year flood arrived in town. "They follow the tail of that old gutter cat."

Laročja. Seeing her people this deep in Koszar's sanctum worried Ren.

Then Idusza lifted a reed screen, and Ren saw that it wasn't only Laročja's supporters who'd gotten in.

Koszar sat in a circle of low camp stools with a cluster of people. Mevieny, Ren was glad to see... but the other two were Laročja, and a man whose resemblance meant he could only be Grey's father, Jakoslav Szerado.

Koszar levered himself up at the sight of the arrivals. "Szorsa, Grey, it's good to have you. As you can see, we are deep in planning."

"I imagine you have not much time," Ren said, hoping her dismay didn't show. She could hardly talk to Koszar about Laročja with the old woman right there. And it would look suspicious if she asked to speak with Koszar privately. "You intend still to begin before Veiled Waters?"

"We must." Koszar balanced with his cane as he sat. "It gives us hope of consolidating control before the Great Dream. I would not do as the Tyrant did, and deny our people access to our Lady's waters."

She wished she could persuade him to delay, but Koszar would want to know why, and she couldn't name the medallions as her reason. Couldn't even tell him for how long, not when they still hadn't figured out how to free the third part of the szorsa's soul from the Uniat chain. Grey had said there was no particular ceremony for sending the dlakani on its way, no kureč or clan to mourn a woman without name.

Grey himself was a tense pillar at Ren's side. She knew he'd encountered his father at Alinka's house; of course Jakoslav would be here as well. A sullen fire burned through Ren's veins when she remembered the stories Grey had told. The years of abuse, in the name of purifying an innocent child.

Now was not the time to drag that up. Neither Laročja nor Jakoslav looked at Grey, and Jakoslav cleared his throat pointedly. "Koszar. Regarding the Upper Bank—"

"What's this?" Ren asked, her attention snapping back. "I thought the plan was to control the Old Island."

"It is." Koszar held up a hand to forestall Jakoslav. "But even with the skiffers on our side, there are still the bridges to consider. The cuffs will retaliate, and their strength is greater than ours. We must occupy them with other worries."

"What other worries?" Grey asked. "Have you so many people that you would risk leaving them on the Upper Bank?"

"I will leave none of ours where they might face danger. But as I said, we have the skiffers. And the cuffs cannot watch the entire riverbank at once."

Raids. Like the Stretsko had done this past summer, the night they attacked Vargo's house. The nobles and delta gentry might play at boat racing, but the clan of the rat ruled the river. The clan of the soldier, whose thread was dyed with blood.

"If violence spills onto the banks," Ren said sharply, "where will it end? That you can take the Old Island, I believe; many who live there are sympathetic, or at least resent the cuffs as much as you do. But will you start a war? Have you the *means* to fight a war? Because if you attack the delta gentry and noble families where they live, you will have one."

Placing a steadying palm at her back, Grey said, "I know

something of Nadežra's military strength. Not only the Vigil, but the soldiers at our borders, who will turn inward if you give them reason. What hope you to accomplish with this?"

"Think not so ill of me," Koszar said, gesturing for them to sit. Ren forced herself to comply, despite the tension winding her tight. "Our plan is leverage, not bloodshed. And the ziemetse support it. Well, most of them."

Ren wondered if the holdout was the Varadič. Had the lack of that card in her stack at the labyrinth been prescient? Or had its absence influenced what was happening now?

Koszar was still talking. "The river they will blockade, cutting Nadežra off from the south. To the east and the west they'll interfere as they can with the Dawn and Dusk Roads. With no sea ships we cannot blockade the port, but while we make noise on the Old Island, Nadežra's trade will be choked on three sides of four—until the Cinquerat agrees to negotiate."

"They'll fight," Grey said, sounding more thoughtful than resistant. "The border forts won't sit quietly while you raid caravans. But on the river you have greater strength, and soldiers that fight your raiders east and west are soldiers that cannot be brought into Nadežra. It...is a good plan."

It *was* a good plan, and Ren dearly wished she knew who had suggested it. Was Laročja more reasonable than she thought? Was Branek or Jakoslav a canny strategist? Or was this from Koszar, or from the ziemetse? Too much was out of her control for her to breathe easy.

But this wasn't her rebellion. As Ren or Arenza, Renata or even the Black Rose, she was only one of many. She didn't envy Koszar trying to navigate so many shoals.

She could mark a few for him, though. "Delta family coffers are not so deep as the nobles'," she said. "Most have only a few sources of income, and much of it flows back into noble pockets. They will feel the bite first. But some have ancestors on both sides of the river; they would say they are Nadežran, not Liganti or Vraszenian. Get *them* on your side, and they will help you lean on the Cinquerat."

The rattle of cards shuffled and bridged was as polite an interruption as a cleared throat. Laročja drew a single card, frowned, then put it back into her deck.

Koszar's mouth pinched. "You have insight to offer, Szorsa Laročja?"

"What insight could I provide that would speak louder than one who has spent so much time among the Liganti? Who knows them so well, and shares their blood." Folding her hands over her deck, Laročja kept her eyes downcast. "Who has even bewitched a child of my own blood to turn against his—"

"Stop."

Grey's voice was soft, but sharp enough to cut Laročja's words short, and the hand at Ren's back clenched so tight it trembled.

For the briefest instant, Laročja's lips tightened like they were holding in a harsh reprimand. But she knew she had an audience; she merely said, "You see? This old woman will remain silent."

If only, Ren thought. And sure enough, Laročja spoke again before Koszar could move on. "If I give not my voice to these concerns, though, who will? I speak not for myself, but for Ažerais. And for Ažerais's children, who came here at our call to support a *Vraszenian* uprising."

"Ažerais speaks to me as well," Ren said, resisting the urge to add, *a good deal more clearly.* "Despite my northern blood."

Laročja laid one hand over her heart as though surprised. "Your *ancestry* is not what concerns the people, but your *allegiance*. Are you not written into a Liganti register? Bound more by ink than by blood? Many saw you come in here today; they will wonder where you go when you leave."

Ren stiffened. If Laročja meant to keep her prisoner here—

"Meaning no disrespect to an honored elder," Idusza said, braided head bowed. "But that is such utter horseshit, one might mistake you for a wagon mule."

Mevieny's hand found Idusza's shoulder with unerring accuracy. Her grip must have been harder than it looked, for Idusza bent under it. "And sometimes a rat can be mistaken for a cat, when it grows too big and bold. But Ča Polojny is not wrong about Szorsa Arenza's character. Much has she done to help our people in Nadežra. In quiet ways...but they speak louder than mistrustful whispers, Ča Szerado."

Only when Laročja's breath hissed between her teeth did Ren realize that last comment was addressed to her, rather than to Jakoslav. It was the polite way to address a Vraszenian—but not a szorsa.

Tugging her shoulder out of Mevieny's grip, Idusza said sullenly, "Not only quiet ways. She led us to the saltpeter for the amphitheatre bombing, and her cards helped us steal it."

Mevieny grimaced. "Of that...I was not aware." Her scowl landed to the left of Ren's head, but Ren knew it was for her all the same.

"*Peace,*" Koszar said, as much a warning as a plea. "Szorsa Laročja, for bringing these concerns to me, I thank you. But Szorsa Arenza has my full trust. She understands the need to keep our plans held close."

Ren went cold. She hadn't even thought that far—but she should have.

The Traementis. When Ren had made her confession to Donaia and Giuna, it had only been about the medallions, not anything to do with the Anduske. Not a deliberate omission; it simply hadn't been on her mind.

But she'd promised Donaia honesty.

And honesty now would cost the Anduske everything. If Donaia knew about the rebellion, there was no way she'd stay quiet. Whatever sympathy she had for Vraszenians, it didn't run deep enough to wash away the objections she would make about violence, about stepping outside the accepted channels for change. She would warn the Cinquerat. The Old Island would be lost, and all they'd gain would be another fifty years of retaliatory oppression.

If Ren kept this from her, though...it would be the end. Donaia couldn't take the betrayal of yet another secret, yet another lie. This fragile thing Ren had made with the Traementis, a new family born of ink rather than blood, would burn to dust.

No matter what Ren did, she would lose something. The Traementis, or a new Nadežra.

Grey's hand gripped her own. Laročja, seeing that, let a poisonous smile bloom.

The choice was no choice at all—and she wouldn't allow Laročja the satisfaction of knowing she bled inside. Ren said, "May An Lagrek damn me to the isolation of no name but Zevriz if I betray you, Koszar Yureski Andrejek."

Her oath made him straighten in surprise, but he knocked his cane against the floor before Laročja could speak. "Then the matter is settled, and this meeting is done. Though if you are willing, Grey, for you I have questions about the Vigil's likely response."

It was a dismissal to the rest of them, and Ren stood, trying not to shake. *Justice versus family. Whatever choice I make plays into Tricat's hands.* If she was sliding deeper into Primordial influence, though, at least she'd chosen the path that would benefit more people.

On sudden, panicked reflex, she checked all her pockets to make certain she hadn't brought the medallion. She hadn't noticed any particular insights into what other people wanted...but could she trust she wouldn't just chalk it up to her own skill?

Her pockets were empty, and then Mevieny caught her searching arm and tucked it close. "For *you* I have questions about your assistance to the Anduske."

Ren let herself be prodded away from Koszar and Grey, taking Mevieny to the far side of the reed screen. "I knew not what saltpeter even was used for when I helped Idusza steal it," she murmured back. "Much less what they planned for it."

"That is a relief—but not what I truly wished to speak of. Is anyone close enough to hear?"

They'd stopped in the corner farthest from the other clusters of revolutionaries. "No."

"Then this warning I give you. Only Dalisva and I know how much you are the chosen of Ažerais. For the rest...Laročja speaks truly when she says you are trusted not. That is as true among the ziemetse as among the Anduske. If news of this endeavor reaches

Liganti ears, it matters not whether you kept your oath to An Lagrek. Many will blame you. And they will seek retribution."

"Fear you any leak?" Ren asked softly.

Mevieny's breath huffed out. "In a group this large? Always. But—"

"Mevieny. *Ren*." Laročja's sweet voice made a point of omitting a szorsa's courteous title. "While the others chatter, I would speak with Ren alone."

"It's fine," Ren said, answering Mevieny's questioning squeeze with one of her own. Laročja's words couldn't wound Ren, and she didn't seem the sort to pull a knife. If she did, Ren had a shawl full of her own knives to answer with, courtesy of the grandson Laročja had spurned.

But the only daggers Laročja seemed inclined to cast Ren's way were of the glaring sort, and Ren tired of the contest. "As you have so kindly pointed out, I was not raised in a kureč, so my knowledge of proper manners toward elders is thin. If you have something to say, say it."

The hard edge sheared away, leaving a woman tired and concerned. The worst part was, it didn't look like a lie. "I fear I've angered you to the point where you will listen not, but still I must try. I failed our Kolya. I should have convinced my son to find the boys before it was too late . . . but Szerado men are so proud, it sometimes beggars all sense. Whatever else may be true of him, Gruzdan is the same."

His name is Grey. "Let me guess. This is prelude to you warning me he is cursed."

"So he told you. Even convinced you it is a lie, told by a wicked old witch. But here." Laročja lifted her deck, presenting a fan of cards to Ren. "Just one. Humor me, girl with Ažerais's gift."

Ren had seen countless tricks that began with a single-card draw, but Laročja didn't seem like she was preparing to astonish Ren with her sleight of hand. Sighing, she drew one.

The Face of Balance. The card of justice and order.

"You recognize this," Laročja said, watching her closely. "Not the card itself—it has special meaning for you."

"It means Grey," Ren said coolly. "When he was in the Vigil. I patterned him before he quit."

"Surely you saw more. A darkness that clings to his heels."

She hadn't even been able to look at The Face of Balance when it appeared in the Rook's spread. That had been defenses rising against her, though, nothing to do with Grey. *His* pattern had seized her throat until she almost couldn't breathe: his twisted future, brought about by him interfering with the cards. "What saw *you*, Laročja? What makes you so certain he is cursed?"

Ren suspected Laročja's shudder was deliberate—but not feigned. "A moment ago you swore by An Lagrek. The Mask of Unraveling was the heart of his pattern, telling me that with us he has never truly been woven. All across his spread, the Masks cursed him. In his past, The Mask of Worms, The Mask of Chaos; in his present, The Mask of Ravens. Where he goes, he brings conflict. His mother—"

"His mother was ill," Ren snapped. "She was ill, and your solution was to blame *her infant son*. That death is on your head, Laročja, and lucky you are that it wasn't two."

Now she saw the ugly truth behind Laročja's sweet mask, as the old woman went to ice. "You think that boy is The Face of Balance? No, girl—those are the hounds of justice at his heels. What crime Gruzdan committed in a past life, I know not, but he must pay for it. Yet always the price comes instead from the people nearest him. His mother is gone, and his brother. Would you condemn those sweet children to that? Would you condemn yourself?"

Ren lifted the card to fling it back at Laročja. The Face of Balance gazed at her: unsmiling, implacable. It was supposed to be the dlakani that received reward or punishment for its acts in life, not the part that was reborn...but was it possible Grey had carried some weight forward from a previous life? What could leave that kind of mark?

You know the answer to that. Faella had told her. And Laročja had seen it in Grey's own past, as The Mask of Worms.

The taint of a Primordial.

Ren was practiced in hiding her shock and horror, but Laročja hadn't earned her reputation as a gifted szorsa by relying on pattern's insight. She nodded as though all her claims had been confirmed. "Yes. You see it as I have. But the question remains—what will you *do* about it?"

Boots struck the floorboards hard enough to make her flinch, and then Grey was at Ren's side. He gave Laročja his shoulder, as though even her existence wasn't worthy of note. "I've told Koszar what I can. Are you ready to go?"

"More than," Ren said, shoving the card back at Laročja. "Come. Let us find fresher air to breathe."

17

Warp and Weft

Isla Prišta, Westbridge: Cyprilun 2

The townhouse's kitchen door was propped open when Vargo arrived by splinter-boat bearing several large ewers of the Heron of the South Wind's Vraszenian spiced chocolate. A decira was more than enough to buy the two skiffers' aid in carrying Vargo's wedding contribution inside.

"That will go cold," said the voice Vargo most dreaded, before his eyes even adjusted to the dim kitchen light. Alinka Serrado stood with her hands on her hips, frowning at the ewers steaming in the morning chill.

A tug on Vargo's peacock-hued waistcoat smoothed the creases obtained during his slumped journey from the Upper Bank. He hoped his mask of smiles and powder hid his exhaustion. Reaching past Alinka, he tilted one of the ewers and showed the red wax seal stamped underneath. "Warming numinat."

Alinka softened. "Thank you. This will help keep the children out of the wine." She gestured at three crates stacked in the corner.

Vargo's ribs creaked like the rotted hull of an old ship as he chuckled. "I see Era Traementis didn't stint on doing her part for the bride's family."

"I think the bottom one was already here?" Alinka frowned at the stack. "It has a House Extaquium stamp."

Shuddering, Vargo said, "Throw it in the canal. On second thought, don't. I went to a lot of effort to clean those waters."

"And grateful we are for it," Alinka said, with unexpected sincerity. Then she dug in her pocket and produced a clay bottle. "More of the tonic I gave you. But...it is not good for you to use so much."

"It wasn't good for Tserdev to work me over like that, either," Vargo said lightly. Alinka wasn't fooled; her concerned gaze flicked to his brow. To the old scar that cleaved it—which had started to crack and bleed like it was new.

"What she did was wrong. Here." Excavating her pocket again, Alinka pulled out a handful of odds: a sticky candy wrapped in paper, a handkerchief, a pretty green stone, an arm from someone's mutilated doll. And a small wooden box with waxy cream she reached out to dab on Vargo's brow.

"Uh." He looked at her finger, eyes crossed.

Alinka's skin was too dark to show a flush, but he read it in her sudden awkwardness. "Forgive me. You are no toddler. Here." Thrusting the box of unguent into his good hand, she swept the other trinkets back into her pocket and escaped upstairs.

It bought him a moment of privacy. He dabbed the salve onto his brow, then tucked it away. If he had more time later, he might unwind his neckcloth and see if it would do any good for the seeping scar on his throat.

Working one-handed was awkward, but Vargo managed to affix the numinat he'd prepared to the side of the clay bottle. A quick scratch with a stick of red ocher closed the line, and he downed the tonic before the numinat could burn out Alinka's imbuing.

It intensified the taste, too, and he stood gagging, pressing the back of one hand against his mouth. Peabody hopped onto the counter and drummed all eight legs at him. Bead-dark eyes gleamed like they were overflowing with tears and judgment.

"I know," Vargo muttered. "But the alternative is collapsing during their vows. You want that instead?"

No answer came, of course. He hadn't felt so alone since he was a child.

You're not alone. He had Ren, and with no reason to hide it anymore, a fresh charm around his wrist to prove it. He had other friends and allies.

He had the desperate hope they would find an answer to his problems, before it was too late.

Giddy shrieks and pounding feet above reminded Vargo that there were more children here than just Alinka's two nippers. He might not have any knots left to call his own, but he was still a master at commanding them. And besides, he had one more gift to deliver.

"Oi! Arkady Bones," he hollered, scooping up Peabody and stomping up the stairs. "Stop causing problems and get your knot together. You got work to do."

Isla Prišta, Westbridge: Cyprilun 2

Ren felt almost as unreal as she had after the Night of Hells left her sleepless. Somehow the impulsive decision to stop waiting and wed Grey had grown into an event with two dozen guests—*not* counting the kids Vargo had put to work, or the younger ones Old Mag was distracting with fire tales in an upstairs room.

"Hold still," Tess chided when she shifted in her seat. Ren's hair had to be loose for the start of the wedding, but that wasn't the same as leaving it untouched. Tess was combing elderflower-scented oil through it, trying to get every strand where she wanted. The mood was nothing like a maid to her mistress, and Ren smiled at Tess in the mirror.

Her sister swatted her when Ren reached for a necklace of interlocked crescent moons, a pre-wedding gift Giuna insisted she wear. By Liganti tradition, grey and silver were proper for a wedding—the colors of Tuat. To Vraszenians, though, those were Kiraly colors. Grey had looked magnificent in his panel coat when they'd gone to the Seven Knots labyrinth to make their offerings to the Faces and the Masks. Tess and Alinka had colluded to embellish the embroidery going up one side and down the other until the fabric was barely visible beneath the intricate, pearl-colored threads. But Ren, clanless, simply wore the finest Vraszenian clothing Tess had been able to provide on short notice. Her copper-threaded sash belt evoked the Traementis fondness for such shades without directly being Tricat's bronze.

The medallion itself was in the cellar, and Sedge was assigned to make sure Ren went nowhere near it, watching her like—"Not like a hawk," he'd said when she gave him that task. "Glad your man shed his feathers before you married him, or I'd have a problem." He'd raised a meaning-laden eyebrow at Tess, and she quickly steered the conversation toward matters unrelated to her choice in sweethearts.

At least Grey was free of Quinat now. Ren had done her best to push aside Laročja's conviction that some stain haunted him from a previous life, and her own flash of fear. Even if the old woman had found truth in her cards for once, it wasn't enough to drive Ren from Grey's side.

And she wasn't about to let thoughts of that malicious crone ruin her day. Lifting her chin, Ren fastened the necklace around her throat. She was Vraszenian *and* Liganti, after all, and didn't have to feel guilty about that.

When she was finally arranged to Tess's satisfaction, Ren stood for the last piece. She wasn't the first person to marry into a Vraszenian family from the outside, without a koszenie to wear. Tradition's answer for that was a piece of plain black silk. But Ren had chosen instead a private joke: the patterner's shawl the Rook had sent after ambushing her in the kitchen. Though she'd removed the knives for today: Bringing blades into a marriage invited strife.

Alinka tied the shawl around her hips and gave her a happily teary smile. "For your children's koszenie, we will need to invent a Traementis symbol."

Thanking the Faces for imbued cosmetics, Ren blotted away her own tears with one of the ample supply of handkerchiefs Tess had stuffed into her pocket. "A triple clover?"

From the gleam that sparked between Tess and Alinka, Ren suspected the two women liked the idea. "Later! Later," she said, laughing, before her wedding day turned into a stitching circle. "May I go downstairs now?"

"So ready to make my brother her husband," Alinka said, hands clasped over her heart.

Tess snickered. "Maybe she's just ready to have him unmake her bed."

Alinka met her, grin for grin. "Already he has seen to that!"

Ren fled before her blush burned away the powder on her cheeks.

Downstairs, she found the parlour and hall astonishingly full of people: Pavlin and Dvaran, Varuni and Iascat, Koszar and Idusza keeping a wary distance from Scaperto and Cercel, Yvieny and Arkady giggling in a corner in a way Ren hoped someone was keeping an eye on.

The Traementis contingent formed an awkward cluster off to the side, near the chair Doomclaw refused to relinquish. Nencoral had made good on her threat to return to House Fintenus, but Idaglio was discreetly dabbing at tears, while Meppe had Clever Natalya in the crook of one arm, making up for their separation with a lavish scratch under her chin. Even Tanaquis had come, though her distracted stare said that wherever her thoughts were, it wasn't this part of the cosmos. Ren diverted to join Grey in welcoming Dalisva, Mevieny, and the Kiralič as they arrived, but with that duty discharged, she went to her adoptive family.

Donaia's smile was tentative, but Giuna's beaming welcome brought summer in on a chilly spring day. "You look beautiful!" she cried, clasping Ren's hands in her own. At their twined fingers, covered and bare, she let slip a gasp of feigned shock. "But where are your gloves? Having sacrificed one to the Rook, did you cede the other to Grey so he wouldn't be jealous?"

"Stop being ridiculous. Of course a Vraszenian wouldn't wear gloves." Donaia batted Giuna's hands away, but only so she could capture Ren's in turn. "Though she's finally embraced our custom of sleeves," she added, winking.

Ren's laugh came naturally. Strange though it still felt, it was a delight to be herself with so many people. "It's far too cold to go without. And I have all the attention I need."

Donaia leaned in close. "I want you to know I didn't forget a gift; it's only that my original plan fell through. I was going to offer you a pup, but Tess tells me you're afraid of dogs? I never realized!"

"Meatball I've learned to tolerate," Ren said. "And the puppies are undeniably cute. But... actually. If a puppy you are willing to give, then I know Tess would love one."

"Oh." Donaia's conflicted expression quickly gave way to another smile. "Of course Tess should have one; she took such good care of Meatball. But in the meanwhile, I'll have to find another gift for you."

A cackling Arkady galloped past, bearing a shrieking Yvieny on her back, and followed by Jagyi toddling as fast as his chubby legs could manage.

"Perhaps I'll talk to Scaperto about allowing you and Grey some time at his bay villa," Donaia said dryly, patting Ren's shoulder with the long-suffering sympathy of a woman who'd raised children. "Now go. You have other guests to welcome. And Giuna tells me there's a warm Vraszenian drink I simply must try? One I *won't* regret in the morning?"

Leaving Giuna to introduce the Traementis to the glories of spiced chocolate, Ren continued circulating. Grey was doing the same, and every time she glanced across the room at him, she found him glancing back at her. Then they would laugh, and someone would notice and elbow one of them, and she felt like she would float away on the giddy joy of it all.

Until Vargo came up to her with Master Peabody on his shoulder and Sedge at his heels, the latter hiding something behind his back. Vargo's color was still bad and his kohl-rimmed eyes glittered like he had a fever, but he managed a reasonable smile. "I'm told gifts are usually given after the wedding's happened, but... you need this one before. Assuming Sedge and I got it right." His expression added, *Fuck, I hope we got it right.*

Sedge presented what he'd been hiding: a flat, beautifully carved box. He stood like a footman while Ren unfastened the latch and opened the box—

Revealing a neatly folded expanse of black silk, intricately embroidered in green and grey, white and blue, red and gold.

The colors smeared in Ren's vision, and her throat closed up. She could barely make her shaking hands lift the fabric from its case. *It cannot be—this is impossible—*

But the silk slid through her hands, and near the edge she found a place where it had been torn. Someone had repaired the damage with neat, tiny stitches, then replaced the embroidery that crossed the tear.

Ren knew that tear. She'd asked her mama what caused it; Ivrina had yanked her koszenie out of Ren's little hands and stuffed it back into the chest where she kept it hidden.

She was on the floor and didn't even know how she'd gotten there. Vargo crouched over her, worried. "Fuck. Maybe this was a bad idea. Is it the wrong one? After this many years, it was a long shot—"

"How?" Ren whispered, staring at him, at Sedge. Everyone else had stopped talking; they were crowding around, and Grey slipped through to kneel at her side. "How did you find it? Ondrakja claimed she had it, but..." All those years Ren tried to find her mother's lost koszenie, and Ondrakja had it all along. The final manipulation, a secret prize she would give back only once she had Ren's perfect loyalty. Instead Ren had poisoned her, and the koszenie was lost.

"Simlin," Sedge said, closing the box. "Got it from him that the Vigil sacked the lodging house after the Fingers broke apart. That led us to Gil Vasterbol, who holds the charter for selling confiscated goods. He's still got that big chest of hers—keeps stuff in it he wants locked up—so when we went to talk to him, he let me look for hidden compartments. When we found that in there..."

Vargo finished for him. "We thought there was at least a chance that it was the right one. I guess it is."

Ren barely heard the explanation, too busy passing her fingers along the embroidered lines like they held answers to her past, her mother's secrets and sorrows. Which, in a way, they did. But...

"I know not how to read it."

She looked at Grey as she spoke, but it was Alinka, worming her way into the growing tangle of people, who reached out. "May I?"

Letting go entirely would have taken more strength than Ren had, but she shifted her hold to let Alinka find the two corners and compare the stitches there. "Anoškin, for your mother's mother. The Čyrost kureč. But your mother was born into her father's kureč, the Volavka of the Dvornik." Alinka pointed at the trees of white and green embroidery that branched out before flowering into other patterns and colors, other kretse, other clans. Then she paused. "This is strange."

"What?" Ren fought the urge to pull the precious fabric away.

Alinka's brow knitted in puzzlement. "You claimed your mother was cast out. But at the corners, where the koszenie is tied around the wearer—they would have cut these threads. Cutting her off from her kin."

Like being cut out of a knot. Someone cast out would always be marked by the severed threads on their koszenie. Ren hadn't known, because Ivrina had never taught her the customs and code.

Confusion dried her tears as she studied the stitches. "I don't understand. Why would she lie? Why claim they wanted her not?"

Behind her, Grey drew a slow breath. "Perhaps she wanted to flee—just not enough to cut her own threads."

As he himself had done. But Mevieny's voice came through the press of people, soft and thoughtful. "The Volavka, I have heard of. I cannot swear that among them there is no badness; after all, who knows what happens out of sight? But their own daughter they would not cast out simply for bearing an outsider's child."

The Volavka. Ren finally had a name to put to the mass of people she'd imagined since childhood. Only they weren't what she'd imagined, traditionalists so fixated on purity that Ivrina's dalliance couldn't be forgiven. They might have even wanted her back.

They might want *Ren.*

It was too overwhelming to contemplate right now. Grey and Vargo helped Ren to her feet. "I'm sorry," Ren said to the guests. "I meant not to upset everyone."

"You're too smart to be that dumb," Sedge said, at the same time Vargo said, "Technically, it's our fault for upsetting you."

"Yes, in private might have been wiser." Alinka's scowl was worthy of Tess. Like a sister, which she soon would be. Ren had expected to gain a small family today, only a few twined threads. Instead she'd been given a whole tapestry.

Her gaze caught Grey's, his loose hair grown long enough to touch his shoulders. Just long enough to hold a braid. Waiting for her token to tie them together.

Ren brushed her cheeks dry and smiled. "No, this was a happy gift. The best gift. Here, help me." She fumbled at the knot of the Rook's apology shawl, and soon had it off.

Before Alinka could tie the koszenie around her hips, though, Tess darted in. "Wait! Dvornik? That's green, right?" With a yank and a twirl, she divested Ren of the copper sash belt and tossed it over her shoulder. "One hour! Give me till seventh sun, and I swear we'll do this proper!"

She ran upstairs, leaving Ren dishabille among her grinning wedding guests. Donaia broke the tableau by saying, "I think it's time we broke out the wine, don't you? Come, Scaperto."

Which gave Ren just enough privacy to bestow a rib-cracking hug on Sedge and a gentler one on Vargo. "Thank you," she whispered. "I know not what they will be—but now I can find answers."

Isla Prišta, Westbridge: Cyprilun 2

The lack of servants meant Donaia could escape into the half-basement kitchen to retrieve some bottles of wine.

"Are you all right?" Scaperto asked as he levered the top off a crate. "That business with the shawl...Ren could have other family out there."

Blood family, he didn't say. The kind Vraszenians held most dear.

Sighing, Donaia sagged against the table in the center of the kitchen. It was hard to imagine Ren sleeping on the floor here. And hard to think of her as Vraszenian, despite the evidence. "This whole business is difficult," she confessed. "I used to think the next family wedding I attended would be Leato's."

Scaperto left the wine and came to hold her hand. "I'm getting off easy by comparison. All I have to do is pretend I don't notice the fugitive radicals lurking in the corner." He hesitated, then said, "I helped them get out of the Dockwall Prison, you know. Well, I helped that Black Rose woman get them out."

Donaia swallowed the impulse to tell him that had been Ren. She'd told Scaperto a great deal of what Ren had shared with her, but only the parts that had to do with the city. What really happened to Ghiscolo, and the Primordial medallions behind it all. *My family*, she'd said incoherently, weeping into his shoulder. *All this time*. Poisoned by Tricat, and by A'ash. No wonder they'd clung to old Liganti ways, often marrying among themselves rather than bringing outsiders in. Gianco had been her second cousin.

"You're a good Fulvet," she said softly. "I never thought I'd say this...but I'm glad the office is in your hands, instead of ours. Yours are cleaner." So far as either of them knew, House Quientis had risen on its own merits; it had never held a medallion.

With his hand on hers, she felt his shudder. "It makes you question everything, doesn't it? Agniet, Iascat, and I are supposed to sit down with that Andrejek fellow, you know. Master Serrado's request, for his wedding: truce today, and diplomacy tomorrow, to see if we can find a peaceful path forward. Now that I know about those...things..." He trailed off, then shook his head. "I don't even know how to proceed."

"With the city's best interests at heart. Like you always do."

Scaperto huffed a quiet, rueful laugh. "Do you know what I thought, when I found out Ren was a Vraszenian imposter? After all the *what under the Lumen's light* and *how is that even possible* bits, I mean. I found myself thinking, no wonder she worked to calm the riots. To cleanse the West Channel. It makes so much more sense now." He drew his hand from Donaia's so he could rub it over his face. "What does my reaction say about *our* people?"

A burst of high-pitched giggles upstairs saved Donaia from having to find an answer. "I know the sound of children up to no good," she said dryly, pushing off the table. "If Mistress Serrado isn't careful, that imp will lead her daughter into bad ways. Let's go, or people will suspect we're up to something inappropriate down here."

Scaperto caught her before she could take more than a step. "Shame to waste perfectly good suspicion," he said. And Donaia, smiling, let him draw her in for a kiss.

Isla Prišta, Westbridge: Cyprilun 2

After making his sister cry in front of everyone, Sedge vowed not to fuck up his one job for the day: ensuring Ren didn't wander down to the cellar to stuff a Primordial artifact in her pocket. With this crowd here, he figured she was pretty safe, but no sense taking chances.

There was an armchair in a good spot by the parlour door, but that had been staked out by two cats curling around each other like the twin moons. Rather than risking his skin by disturbing Arkady's ugly yellow tom, he dragged up a spindle-thin chair with a hard seat and settled in for sentry duty.

"Shouldn't you be smiling at your sister's wedding? You look like a man who's eaten *a handful of worms*."

Idusza was drinking fine wine this time instead of cheap zrel, but her words took Sedge back to a Westbridge corner and a moment he'd been hoping she'd forgotten. His cheek throbbed in memory of her fist.

"Ah. Yeah." He eyed the glass in her hand warily. She was the sort of woman who'd break a bottle to knife a man. But probably not at a wedding? "Ren said you'd figured us out." She'd also said

Idusza had laughed. But maybe that good humor only extended to people who hadn't made swaggering asses of themselves.

He resisted the urge to scoot away as Idusza leaned against the wall, looming over him. "I've forgiven her. You, though—you nearly broke my hand."

"With my *face*." His jaw twinged in memory.

"It's a very punchable face," Idusza said... though the gaze that swept down his body suggested his face wasn't the only part that interested her. And possibly not for punching. Sedge shifted as far as he could without leaving his chair, searching the room for someone to rescue him.

"Too bad for you. That's my face to punch."

Someone *other* than Varuni. She'd been keeping an odd distance from Vargo today, but did she have to drift toward Sedge instead? He hunkered down as she came up on his other side, feeling like a mouse caught between two prowling cats. In the chair next to him, Arkady's demon-beast opened one yellow eye and yawned widely. Like Sedge needed reminding of how many teeth cats had.

"Not that I'm against it," he said as the silence grew tighter by the moment, "but can we at least agree that nobody gets to rearrange any of my parts until *after* my sister's married?"

Idusza swirled the wine in her glass. "I could agree to that," she said, raising a brow as though she'd asked Varuni a question.

"I don't share."

"Then I leave him to your mercy." Laughing, Idusza drained her glass. "This wine is terrible. I need more."

As she left to flirt with the decanter, Varuni turned her glare onto Sedge. He waved at Ren, deep in conversation with Dvaran. "I was just keeping watch over my sister," he said, feeling guilty without quite understanding why.

"Of course. Stay out of trouble." With something that might have been a smile, she sauntered off.

Leaving Sedge trading confused looks with the cat beside him. "What just happened?" he asked.

Doomclaw's only answer was to stretch his toes and curl once more around Clever Natalya.

Isla Prišta, Westbridge: Cyprilun 2

The women of Tess's illegal embroidery ring in Ganllech claimed there was no teaching someone how to imbue. Imbuing was the art and craft of *doing*. Explanations wrapped it in a hazy cloud of ambiguous wisdom, but none of that bestowed understanding. In her youth Tess couldn't make front nor back of it, no matter how often she tried. It made no sense.

Until one day, back bent over a chained snake knot for Prince Olyn's table runner, her confusion settled like mist on the moors. Her entire world became fingers and needle, silk thread and linen backing.

When she raised her head, her neck ached, the fire had burned down to coals, and most of the women were snoring on their pallets. Tess felt cored like an apple, and Mavvy Red nodded from her place by the hearth. "Now you've got the way of it," she said. Laid across Tess's lap, coiled at her feet, the embroidered snakes slithering along the runner gleamed like they'd been stitched with emeralds.

Now, years later and an ocean away, finding that place was as easy as slipping into a lover's warmth. The front panel of one of Ren's surcoats fit against the copper sash belt with only a bit of tucking needed. Tess's fingers flew and her needle flashed as she wove green and copper, gold and silver. Under that dance rose a slow-flowing river against a burnished sunset sky, gilded reeds rooted deeply along its bank. A long and gentle life that could withstand floods and drought, foul weather and fair. Her wish for her sister.

When Tess raised her head, blinking away bleariness, it was just like that first time: the finished sash bundled in her lap, and a feeling like she'd left something behind and couldn't recall what.

"You're incredible," Pavlin said, seated by the window and watching her with open-faced wonder.

Raising hot fingers to even hotter cheeks, Tess ducked from

his scrutiny. "It's just a bit of stitching. Nothing that'll save lives." Not like he was doing, helping change the Vigil in his crisp new lieutenant's coat. Or Ren and Grey, Vargo and Sedge. Now that Ren's secret was out, Tess wasn't even needed for the con. She loved her simple life. She preferred it. But sometimes..."Nothing that matters."

Pavlin tugged her to her feet. One by one, he kissed her needle-sore fingers. "Who decides what matters? Nobody needs spice cakes, but isn't the world a nicer place for them?" His dark gaze was so intense, she could become lost in it as easy as imbuing. "You do that. Make the world a nicer place. *My* world."

Then, while Tess tried to knit up her frayed thoughts, he blurted, "Marry me."

What? she wanted to blurt back, and *Now?* But what came out was a giddy "Yes!"

The breath of his surprise was like soft velvet on her fingertips. His smile curled against them. "Good."

She caught his laugh, her own bubbling up to join it, and then they were kissing, the embroidered sash crushed between them.

"No telling anyone," Tess said once they'd parted and set themselves to rights. She smoothed wrinkles from the sash and carefully folded it over her arm. "Not today. It's bad form."

"Of course not. But soon?" He twined his fingers with hers.

"As soon as I can make you a new coat. Sedge'll cry if I marry a man in a hawk's plumage." Grinning, Tess followed him downstairs to see her sister wed.

Isla Prišta, Westbridge: Cyprilun 2

Grey would have been happy to marry Ren in any colors at all. But when Tess reappeared with Ren's sash belt, now featuring river-green panels embroidered with shimmer-gold reeds of silk, it felt like turning over the final card in a szorsa's pattern. The koszenie Alinka tied around Ren's hips raised more questions than it answered, but they could pursue those later—together.

As the Kiralič led them to the cleared space in the parlour, though, Ryvček spoke up in her impudent drawl. "A moment. Fine enough to have Grey's clan leader perform the wedding on his own, when we knew not where Ren came from. But now I hear she is Dvornik! A daughter of the fox! As a fellow vixen, I insist on playing her family's part."

"Why should it be you?" Mevieny stood from the seat she'd claimed, fingers resting lightly on her cane. "Think yourself the only other fox skulking about? As close as you are to the groom, you're practically Kiraly. If any is to stand for Arenza's clan, it will be me."

Ryvček's gasp of outrage was exaggerated, her grin feral as she threaded past her audience to face her challenger directly. Her fingers brushed the back of Mevieny's hand. "Very well. If you want the honor so much . . . let us duel."

"I am no fool. I know your reputation, Oksana Mivriskaya Ryvček. But I have a counter-challenge." Flicking away the flirtatious touch, Mevieny laid her palm over Ryvček's cheek, thumb resting on her lower lip. "We'll kiss for it."

"She *does* know her reputation," Grey murmured to a snickering Ren as Ryvček dipped Mevieny in a dramatic embrace.

Once Mevieny was restored to her feet, Ryvček barked a fox's laugh. "I concede the victory! Szorsa Mevieny shall have this honor."

Taking Ren's hands in his own, Grey led her to stand before the ziemič and the szorsa. He'd had to tell her what to expect. Vraszenian weddings were often performed in public for the entire community to witness, but whenever Ren had drawn close to one, Ivrina had always hurried her daughter away.

First they shared a cup of aža, seven sips each, trading it back and forth with giddy smiles. Then the Kiralič spoke about each of their families. He negotiated those shoals with admirable diplomacy, given the sudden discovery of the uncut Volavka threads on Ivrina's koszenie, the presence of the Traementis, and the absence of Grey's immediate kin, who ordinarily would have been there.

By the time he gestured for them to braid the marriage tokens into each other's hair—the second ribbon now green for Ren's new-found Dvornik heritage—the aža was beginning to spin Grey's vision. With everyone assembled for the ceremony, he saw no hint of the brittle mask this parlour had once been over the truth of Ren's poverty and lies; instead the walls seemed a tapestry of many different threads, weaving and stitching themselves higher and warmer with every passing moment.

With a sure touch, Mevieny bound Grey's hand and Ren's together, weaving a narrow embroidered strip around them in a complex pattern. "May the Faces smile upon you always," she said, "and the Masks turn away."

With Ryvček smirking just past Mevieny's shoulder, reminding him of her recent performance, Grey couldn't let himself be outdone. The altered panel sash cinched Ren's waist small enough to let his fingertips meet at her back as he lifted her up, spun her around laughing, and dipped her low. Her laughter was like aža-laced wine, warm on her lips, sweet on his tongue, and intoxicating.

"I want to take you away *now*." Grey's whisper was cocooned by the fall of his hair, the lift of her arms over his shoulders. Their own little world, if only they could stay there.

Two kisses landed, one at each corner of his mouth. "Yvieny will cry if she cannot dance the kanina."

Sighing, Grey dragged himself upright, pulling Ren along with him. Ren. His *wife*.

But she was right. Marriage was about more than just two people. "Tie on your koszenie and truss up your skirts," he said, facing the room with a grin so broad his jaw ached. "Vraszenian or Liganti, join in our dance—our ancestors must hear that two threads have been tied!"

Cheers rattled the windows as Ryvček passed around aža-laced wine. Faithful to his duty, Sedge took none, but most others did. Mevieny reclaimed her seat and took up a round-framed drum and beater. Her initial *tick tick tick* against the frame gave everyone time to form a circle in the cleared space of the parlour. It was tight, but a kanina should be danced pressed shoulder to shoulder, until everyone moved as one.

The beat transitioned to the measured syncopation of wood on taut hide, the clop of horse hooves on the road, the murmur of the river over exposed rocks. Ren had already been swept from Grey's side. Giuna murmured stammering uncertainty as Grey caught her hands, and he grinned. "Even children learn this one. Come!"

They all danced, the Vraszenians with fluid joy, the Liganti with stiff unfamiliarity that gradually relaxed into the beat. Cercel had apparently attended a Vraszenian wedding before; she showed Iascat what to do. Dvaran had Donaia, the arm that lacked a hand behind her back, guiding her as the direction changed. Yvieny and Arkady were chaos whirling through their midst, reassuring the outsiders that it hardly mattered whether they got the steps right or not. Sedge had even coaxed Varuni away from the wall.

If this dance summoned ancestors, who would come? Not just Szerado, but Ren's unknown Volavka kin? Could the kanina call down Traementis from their Lumen? Grey would have asked Vargo, but neither of them had the air for it. The exertion had called a hectic flush to Vargo's cheeks, but despite that, his expression was one of bemused delight. He gave Grey a breathless grin when their gazes met, and a surge of warmth enveloped Grey's heart. That he could hope for Volavka at all—for Ren's people to see their dance and know of their union—was thanks in part to Vargo. Step by step, the man had woven himself into her life . . . and into Grey's as well.

The rhythm quickened, their bodies colliding and compressing like a bellows when the circle changed direction. Vargo stumbled, saved by Grey's arm around his waist. On his far side, Arkady and Yvieny had stopped their careening spin, Yvie's bright eyes fixed on some far point.

Her lips moved. Through the cacophony of laughter and drum, Grey couldn't hear what she said, but he read the word on the shape of her lips.

Papa?

Shock froze Grey in place. Yvie's joyous shriek pierced him to the core. *"Papa!"*

Kolya. Kolya stood there, at the edge of the room. And the person keeping Grey from falling to the floor was the man who'd killed him. The man Grey had been laughing with not a moment before.

Yvie dashed away before Grey could catch her, before he could remind her that when the ancestors came, it was only their szekani, a sight granted by aža's blessing. Wisps of memory and emotion, with no more substance than a breath. However much he might wish otherwise.

She reached the shade of her father—and he swept her into his arms.

Impossible. But there she was, with her little face buried against his neck. Alinka, pursuing her daughter, stopped just out of arm's reach; when Kolya reached out, she hardly seemed to breathe as she took his hand. But Kolya's translucent fingers wrapped around hers like flesh and blood.

"I can't stay," Kolya said, his voice holding the resonance Grey missed so badly, threaded through with a ghostly wind. "But called, I come."

That wind swept the laughter from the room. Grey would have dismissed this as an aža dream, if not for Yvieny babbling all the things her papa had missed, Alinka flinging her own arms around them both. Jagyi, ducking his head into his mother's skirts at the appearance of this soft-glowing stranger he barely remembered.

Grey couldn't find his tongue. Kolya's head tipped to one side, his slanted smile full of fondness and gentle mockery. "My little brother is wed. Will you let me meet my marriage-sister?"

That meant knowing where Ren was, and Grey couldn't drag his eyes from Kolya to search. But the crowd shifted and she was at his side, supporting him so Vargo didn't have to. The *strength* in her, as she helped him stumble toward his brother. Whatever shame Grey might feel for his own failings, he could never be anything but proud of Ren. Proud to introduce her to his only blood family that mattered.

"This is my wife, Arenza Lenskaya Volavka of the Dvornik." His faint stumble over the name Ren could now claim was nothing compared to how his voice faltered as he said to her, "This is my brother, Jakoslav Jakoski Szerado of the Kiraly."

Kolya balanced Yvieny on one hip so he could embrace Ren with the other arm. "Any woman who makes my troubled brother happy is a blessing."

Unspoken guilt weighed so heavily, Grey couldn't keep the words inside. "Kolya—the night you went to the warehouse—"

"I know." Kolya met his gaze seriously, but death hadn't erased the lines of laughter that fringed his eyes. "I *know*. Think you my brother could sneak around like that, and I wouldn't notice?"

It stole the breath from Grey. All this time, he'd assumed Kolya hadn't known he was the Rook. That when he'd warned Grey about the black powder hidden in the Fiangiolli warehouse, he'd only been warning his brother the hawk, not the legendary outlaw.

An outlaw who still hadn't been able to save him. A brother who had, somehow, without ever consciously deciding, forgiven Vargo for killing him.

How could he face Kolya, with the weight of that forgiveness on his conscience?

A translucent hand brushed past his new marriage braid to grasp his shoulder. "Glad I am that you have found peace. It brings *me* peace. That is no betrayal."

With a sob that shook his entire frame, Grey caught that hand and pressed it to his brow. When that soft contact wasn't enough, he leaned in, wrapping himself around Kolya and Yvie both. It was like embracing sunlight, warmth without substance. Already the sweat from the kanina was cooling, and Kolya was growing fainter. When they drew apart, Yvie had been passed to Grey's arms.

And Kolya's gaze had passed to Vargo.

The man stood silent and still like prey hoping to escape notice. The flush had drained from his cheeks, leaving them as waxen as putty. Peabody stood on his shoulder, legs and abdomen raised in purely ineffectual defense.

"And you," Kolya said, simply. Without accusation.

Vargo lifted his chin like a man accepting the gallows rope. "I'm not looking for peace. Too busy trying to make up for my mistakes."

"One need not close out the other. Perhaps you and my brother can help each other learn how." Hands to his heart, Kolya gave Vargo a formal bow. "Thank you for guarding his back when I could not."

The room was so quiet, even Vargo's tiny indrawn breath was audible.

Grey couldn't breathe at all.

Kolya touched Alinka's cheek, then bent to kiss her. "The dream fades. I must go."

Her trembling hand covered his. "I know."

"Be happy." His voice was only an echo now, his form dust in sunlight.

"I will try."

"We will meet again, when the road leads you home."

Alinka nodded, hand falling limp to her side. Kolya was gone. Into the emptiness, she whispered, "When the river meets the sea."

Isla Prišta, Westbridge: Cyprilun 2

Vargo didn't expect company after he stepped out of the gathering. Grey had his family to see to, and Ren had her guests; it was partly to make things easier for them that he slipped away.

He should have known better.

Ren found him sitting at the top of the stairs with a silent Peabody balancing on the back of his splinted hand. She was equally silent as she joined him, hip and shoulder warm against his, but in her case it was companionable. A presence, not an absence.

Vargo wiped his cheeks dry with the back of his good hand and tapped his temple. "It's too loud up here, without the old man to talk sense into me." When Peabody lifted up and down like a bouncing bean, Vargo stroked his fuzzy thorax. "Yeah, I know. I admitted it. Don't let it go to your head."

After a moment, she said softly, "Anger's easier to take, isn't it. You know what to do with that."

Fight back, most of the time. Other times, let it hit him like he deserved.

He didn't deserve what Kolya Serrado had said to him. Alinka Serrado's anger, yes. Her dead husband's forgiveness . . . no.

Vargo couldn't put that into words, and he didn't have to. He only gave a gentle bump of his wrist against Ren's, where the knot bracelet peeked out from the belled cuff of her shirt.

Then he tucked Peabody back into place and stood. Offering his arm, he said, "Come on. En't you supposed to be at a feast or something?"

"I am," Ren said, slipping a hand around his elbow. "And though I will understand if you leave, I would like you there."

He could hardly refuse. No one commented on his return; Grey only laid a warm hand on his shoulder. "Alinka took the children home," he said. "They need some time to breathe it in." But that still left a tableful of guests, and if the mood was a touch subdued, it soon livened up again into something like a wedding.

Happy though he was to be there, the effort left Vargo drained. Afterward he slumped onto the couch in the parlour as others took their leave, in some cases hurriedly—Tanaquis, bolting out the door like she had to catch a sudden idea before it escaped; in other cases gracefully—Donaia, with many blessings for the new couple's happiness; and in others, with salacious winks and offers of last-minute advice—Ryvček, her arm around Mevieny's waist in possibly unnecessary guidance. Pavlin went off to dispose of the last of Extaquium's wine, and Tess was clattering dishes down to the kitchen when Grey came in and found Vargo still there.

Vargo twitched upright. "Sorry, I'll head out. Just needed a moment to catch my breath."

"You shouldn't walk. I'll call you a chair."

"Won't be any safer. Half the sedan bearers around here are in with my old knots." So far they hadn't come for Vargo, but he'd rather not dangle his ass out for them. "Not certain I can trust anyone these days." He winced at how hollow and pathetic that sounded, and hoped Grey would mistake his reaction for pain.

"You trust Ren." Grey's gaze caught and held on the blue-and-green charm on Vargo's wrist. "You can trust me."

Vargo's laugh wasn't flecked with blood, but it felt like it should be. Kolya's appearance had torn away the old scab of guilt. "Just shows you're a better man than I am."

Grey sank onto a chair, looking pensive. "There was a time I would have said nothing could make me trust you. I thought you were out for nothing but your own profit and power—and that you didn't give a wet leech what you crushed on your way to those goals."

"You weren't wrong."

"Don't lie just to hurt yourself." Grey's gaze was steady. "You and Ren...you're two birds from one egg. You've both hurt people, trying to get what you want. Hurt them in ways you never intended, ways that can't be undone. But you've also taken care of them— sometimes without them even knowing. Ren with the Traementis. You with your knots."

"And they still tossed me to Tserdev." Vargo lifted his splinted hand. "Caring don't buy loyalty the way oaths do."

"Then would an oath convince you that you're better than the face you show to the world?"

Vargo's hand ached as he brought it down again. "You want to trade knot oaths with me, too?"

"I could. But it occurs to me that you owe me a brother."

Exhaustion must have muddled Vargo's thoughts; he was misunderstanding basic speech. "Eh?"

Grey tugged his shirt cuff back, exposing the inside of his wrist.

Even that took a moment to sink in. *Brother. Wrist.* Right, Vraszenians cut themselves and mingled their blood to make someone their—

"If this is a joke, it en't funny."

"I wouldn't joke about this. You saved my life, Vargo. You've guarded my back, protected my secrets—protected Ren's, too." A soft laugh escaped Grey, and he gestured at the room around them. At the house Vargo had given Ren and Grey when they needed refuge. "You probably don't even realize...among Vraszenians, it's a brother's job to arrange a place for a wedding."

Vargo reached out to Alsius with a mental wail—maybe the old man could explain this, 'cause he sure as hell couldn't—but it was like he'd said to Ren. He was alone in his head, and it was too noisy there to make sense of anything.

"You forgetting why it is I *owe* you a brother?" he asked, because apparently Alsius was the source of his manners as well as his sense.

Grey's hand held steady, the underside of his wrist soft and pale. Vulnerable. "I'm honoring what my brother said to us both. Peace can only be found in making peace between us."

I don't deserve peace—not from him, and not from you. But there was something gently implacable about Grey's manner. Insisting without words that yes, he did.

Just like Vargo had insisted to Ren that she deserved the trust of a knot, whatever lay in her past.

He tried to summon up a sardonic response, but all he managed was "I en't healing too well right now."

"We can wait if you—"

"No." Because if he waited, he'd talk himself out of this.

Grey had no blade, because he was still in his wedding clothes, but Tess had left her sewing basket on a chair. Vargo couldn't hold the thumb knife in his injured right hand, and he wanted the mark on his left wrist, alongside the knot he shared with Ren. Grey made the cuts for them both, then pressed their wrists together.

"I take you as kin," Vargo repeated after Grey. "With my name, I shield your children. With my body, I guard your spouse. With my heart, I protect yours." His tongue felt clumsy, and his voice shook. "As the Dežera connects the mountains to the sea, let our blood flow together, as brothers."

Wary of breaking the solemnity, he fell silent as Grey bound a handkerchief tight to his wrist. Vargo hoped the small cut would clot quickly.

But he could only hold his tongue for so long. "Pretty safe bet on your part. En't likely to marry or father brats, and my heart's a withered old thing."

Grey let out an aggravated groan. "You keep talking like that, and I—"

Whatever friendly threat he was about to make died at a sound from upstairs. A noise like a cry of alarm, cut short.

"*Ren*," Vargo said, and bolted for the door.

He was too tired and slow, even with his walking stick to support him, and Grey was taller. His new-sworn brother made it up the stairs faster, to the door of the bedroom. And inside...

Inside, a zlyzen had Ren cornered against a wall that was fading into mist.

"Sword," Vargo snapped, tossing his walking stick to Grey. In a flash he had it unsheathed and slicing toward the zlyzen.

"No!" Ren raised her arm as though she meant to block steel with flesh. Grey diverted the strike and caught hold of her instead. "It wants me to go with it."

Want looked a lot more like *force* from where Vargo was standing, but Tess was running up the stairs, Ren and Grey were fading into something Vargo suspected was Ažerais's Dream, and he had a choice to make.

No choice at all, really.

"We're following a zlyzen. Don't let anyone panic," he shouted at Tess. Then he lunged and caught Grey's bandaged wrist... and reality collapsed into a sinkhole of chaos.

18

Drowning Breath

She tried to hold on.

Through the veil that separated waking from dream, but not into any layer of imagined or remembered Nadežra; no, she spiraled further and deeper, past everything she knew, the only solid thing the grip on her arm. Grey, and behind him, Vargo, pulled on a journey they weren't meant to take.

She tried to hold on.

She failed.

He follows a twisted thread, into the past . . .

—he's a boy again, trapped between the bite of his grandmother's words and the lash of his father's belt. Wrong, wrong, seeping out of him like poisoned blood, staining the people around him. His mother's hands covered with it, shoving him under the river's flow to wash him clean, following behind to make sure he stays. He doesn't stay. Nature rejects him, spits him back to atone. Cursed child, stained, despised gutter cat. Only discipline can cleanse him. Lash, lash, lash go the belt and tongue until he's a curled and whimpering creature, neither fur nor mask to protect him. No mother or brother. Alone, left alone. *She* fears him, fears what she sees and doesn't understand. He sees it in her eyes. He runs, again and again, until someone steals him away—

...the thread winds on...

—steal through the streets, quick and quiet, stumbling through the night while farmers and fishermen sleep and hungry foxes watch with wary golden eyes. Bad luck follows in his wake, eggs with no yolk, milk curdling in the pail, nets full of eyeless fish. Ill omens, the villagers throw them out, but food is food and he is hungry and he roots through mangers and middens to fill his empty belly. Never stay, can't stay, or they'll find out he's the cause. If he's lucky they'll only chase him off, won't print their fear on his flesh, break his bones with their terror, hang charms to keep him away, *monster* not *starving child* only seeking to survive—

...the thread winds on...

—never survives, not for long, people flinch with fear from spiders. He sets his web in the wrong places, cast out, caught, crushed, even the kindly spinners don't want him. They leave him bound, struggling, in a web of red thread; tie it around your wrist, lay it around your bed, loop it around his throat, what do we do with him? Can't remove the curse, so remove the one that carries it. Saw at the ropes with broken glass, scuttle free before they find their nerve, slip away like the ghost they would make him—

...the thread winds on...

—ghost in an abandoned shack, silent hunter, eating mice, bats, nobody comes near but he hears them now, chanted prayers, sacred water, flaming brands, drive it out. This place is *empty*, why can't he stay he knows the answer he tastes their fear, he's twisted and wrong and no fire can burn him clean no water wash away the stain—

...the thread...

—bloodstained rocks on the ground around him, *it isn't even a rat it's a demon*, he's running but he can't run fast enough they're following they're screaming rock to the back of his knee he falls and the next strikes his head blood stains his sight crimson all he sees is terror—

...winds...

—horse terror thunder of hooves dust rising the storm clouds rushing toward him their hooves come down and he welcomes the end—

   ...on...

Vargo tried to keep hold of Grey's wrist. But the dream swirled like a turbulent current, yanking them apart, and when it stopped, he was in the middle of an empty lane.

Alone.

The lane was no place he recognized. It stretched out like driftwood: bleached as bone on the surface, a hollow air of weightlessness beneath. His boots scraped over paving stones as smooth as wet sand and as hard as brick. Houses and shops of weeping grey stone penned him in, their windows as empty as a corpse's eyes, lashed with planters of dead brambles. Mist lingered in the gutters instead of trash or sewage, until tattered by a breeze as soft as a whimper. The open doorways caught the breeze as it passed, and sang it back in a chorus of disharmony.

"Ren?" His shout was an anemic thing. "Grey?" Vargo reached for his collar, for the comfort of Alsius, and found the space there as empty as the place he'd landed.

They could be anywhere. The dream had as many layers as it had dreamers, and after that tumbling, spiraling journey, he couldn't even be sure they were in this empty city with him—though it sure felt like *something* was. The skin of his neck crawled like cold fingers were tickling it.

"Fuck," he muttered, putting his back to a wall. This whole place pulsed with a nightmarish cast Vargo hadn't felt since he'd last taken ash. What Mask-damned impulse had made him follow the others?

A bandaged cut, and the knot charm above it.

Vargo forced himself to think. He had the knot charm; he had the fresh cut; he had a numinat on his chest that wasn't healing right. For all the good any of those did. Vargo concentrated, trying to imagine threads coming out of them, but he lacked Ren's facility with the dream. Numinatria couldn't solve this for him, either; no inscription could point him in their direction, and unless he felt like calling on Primordials, no inscription could drag Alsius and Ren and Grey to his side.

But the nightmare was worse in one direction than others. There, where the clouds above gathered and roiled like a burgeoning scream.

A zlyzen had dragged Ren off. If she was anywhere, it was probably where things felt the most awful. Vargo's fingers curled against the wall, nails scraping like he was clinging to his last shred of good sense.

"Follow the fucking zlyzen," he growled. "Great idea." And, pushing off the wall, he headed toward the fear.

Ren stumbled to earth in a deserted street, with a lone zlyzen for company.

No Vargo. No Grey. She'd lost her grip on both in the transition to...whatever this place was.

"Where are they?" she demanded. Ren might be facing a monster from her childhood, dread might be radiating from her surroundings like everything was doused in zlyzen blood, but in that moment, her anger overwhelmed her fear. "Where did you send them?"

The zlyzen crouched low, like Meatball the one time Ren had seen him truly misbehave and be snapped at for it. The monster from her childhood looked...penitent.

Ren liked that even less than she liked the grin it had given her after the ordeal. It made her ill, acting like some kind of leader to the things that had killed Leato.

Hugging her own body, she glanced around as if Grey or Vargo might appear out of an alleyway. But there was no one, not even the shifting, half-seen shadows of the dream. The city was utterly empty.

She'd seen it before, though. Not this nightmare version; the living city, full of people. In the dreams she'd been having ever since—

Ever since I got Tricat back.

But she'd done more than one thing that night, hadn't she? She'd retrieved the medallion...and she'd strengthened her connection to the zlyzen. Which she'd thought had no effect until the ordeal. Clearly, she was wrong.

"You," she said, staring at the zlyzen. "*You've* been sending me those dreams. Why?"

It couldn't respond; she didn't think zlyzen were capable of speech. It only growled low in its throat, taking a few steps, looking over one wrong-jointed shoulder, waiting for her to follow.

"Not without the others," Ren said through her teeth. If they were in the dream, even some nightmarish zlyzen corner thereof, then she could make use of that. All she had to do was follow the—

She staggered, catching herself against a wall. Looking for the threads that bound her to Grey and Vargo was like looking into the pit of the empty wellspring where the zlyzen had torn Leato apart. A bottomless, snarling abyss, a place even Ažerais had forsaken.

Maybe the whine from the zlyzen was supposed to be comforting. But the creature was a piece of what she recoiled from, and the sound only made Ren shudder from head to foot.

"Why drag me here?" she demanded. "All this time, from me you have wanted something. What?"

By way of answer, the zlyzen walked a short distance, watching over its shoulder. Another whine.

It wanted her to follow it. Just as it had wanted her to follow it into the dream.

"Hello? Is anyone there?"

The sound of a human voice made Ren's heart leap. But it wasn't Grey or Vargo—and who else would be in this place? She pressed herself instinctively against the grit-crumbled wall, easing toward a corner.

This city had all the ups and downs Nadežra lacked. From Ren's vantage point she could see down a steep hillside into a square, where a man in a periwinkle coat was wandering aimlessly, shouting. "Where did you all go? I tried to hold on—"

A man in a *Liganti* coat, with hair like dark honey. And there was something nigglingly familiar about that voice...

She leapt onto a rooftop below, then to a balcony, then to the ground. She wasn't quiet; the man spun to look. And even though she'd never seen his face before, there was enough family resemblance to confirm her absurd hope.

"Ren! Oh, thank the Lumen you're safe—and look!" The skirts of his coat flared as he spun, displaying stylized numinata embroidered in cobalt and amethyst. "I'm human again!"

"*Alsius.*" Ren couldn't stop staring. "How—"

He laughed in delight. "You tell me! You're the expert in matters of dream, after all; I've never been bodily to the realm of mind. Look, I have *hands!*"

She caught them as he waved them in her face. "Alsius—where's Vargo?"

That dampened his giddy joy. "I don't know. We were separated and— Oh, Lumen's light shield us, it's one of those *creatures*..."

The zlyzen had followed her, crawling down a wall like it had crawled down a column during the ordeal. Alsius hid behind Ren, and she had the unsettling feeling he would have crawled under her hair if he could.

"We'll find them," Ren said, trying to sound more confident than she felt. "And we'll deal with whatever this thing wants. Then we'll get the *fuck* out of here."

The first splash of color was the last one Vargo wanted to see.

Blood.

Not much. Just a smear, like a bright flag draped across the edge of a public well. More on the paving stones, a copper-bright spatter trailing away from the well like escaped wishes.

"Ren? Grey?" he called. And out loud for once, "Alsius?"

The blood shimmered, all the brighter for the mist-dulled grey-ness around it.

"At least it's not zlyzen blood," Vargo muttered. It also wasn't leading in the direction of the worst fear. But that was only a theory, and this looked a lot like a sign, the first thing out of place he'd seen since arriving. Pulling out the two halves of the blasting numinat he'd taken to carrying at all times, he followed the blood.

The streets undulated up and down like a cast-off ribbon, past yards with empty chicken coops and milking pails, only broken eggshells and the stink of curdled milk suggesting they'd ever held anything but dust.

And more blood.

He found the first body wedged against the outside hearthwall of a house, hollow-bellied and starving thin, dead flesh blue from cold. Before Alsius, Vargo had lived on the streets, scuttling between squats, stealing food and warmth. Looking at that body was like looking at the future he'd managed to escape.

But the body wasn't his, and it wasn't Ren or Grey or Alsius. Shuddering, he went on, following the trail of blood.

To another body, young and rope-burned and bloody around the wrists, the cuts festered and foul. Vargo gagged on the smell, press-ing one sleeve to his nose to keep it out. *Zlyzen work?* But he knew all too well what it looked like when they tore someone apart. Only human cruelty looked like this.

Instinct yelled at Vargo to flee. He ignored it and kept going, and after the first two it wasn't a surprise to find a third corpse, this one the bloated, water-pale remains of a drowned girl. He was moving faster now, the speed necessary to overcome his common sense. Past a body lying amid the bloody rocks that had brought it down, past one trampled into unrecognizable pulp. He hadn't yet found a body he knew, but that charred lump up ahead looked like a dead zlyzen, and if their guide had died—

Then *everything* around him changed.

No more corpses. No more pulsating dread. No more *silence*; there were people all around, Vraszenians, going about the ordinary business of their lives. After what he'd just seen, the normality hit like a slap to the face.

Vargo stumbled, waving off concerned glances and flinching from helping hands. This was more than just illusion. They could touch him. Did that mean he would become the next corpse for the next fool to find?

His retreat brought him against the divided door of a tiny shrine crammed between two shops. The top half was propped open to make a window, the ledge over the bottom half wide enough for leaning.

And inside, watching him with curiosity, sat a szorsa.

She asked him a question, in a dialect so thick Vargo could only guess her meaning from the deck in her hands and the shawl over her shoulders. Did he want his pattern read? No—but in Ažerais's Dream, did he have a choice?

Then he noticed the tangle of a ribbon amid the free-fall tumble of her dark hair. Silver and green, and he *knew* those ribbons. Tess had picked them out herself, wanting only the best for—

"Ren?" he asked. But no, the braid was on the right side. If this was Ren, shouldn't it be the left?

The next question tripped inelegantly from his tongue. "Are you *Grey*?" It was a dream. Anything could happen.

The szorsa's brow furrowed at the name, like she was hearing a distant echo. "That naman...whi knawe ih that naman?"

The less he understood her words, the more certain he became. "You're Grey. You have his marriage knot." Vargo pocketed the blasting numinat and tugged his own hair to illustrate. "Remember? You got married?"

She let her hand drift up in mirror, gasping when her fingers found the braid. Pulling it forward, she examined the carved token, brow knitting in confusion. "Ih habbe nat an housbonde!"

Vargo reached for the szorsa, but she flinched back—as well she might, with a stranger trying to grab her. He put his hands up in a gesture of non-threat and tugged his cuff down to display the cloth bandaging his wrist. "We swore brotherhood, remember? You have one, too." Her loose sleeve had slipped down when she reached for her hair. "You, me, and Ren. She's my knot-mate, your wife. A zlyzen brought us here. Recognize *any* of this?"

Either she didn't, or the differences between his Vraszenian and hers were too great to surmount.

With a click of impatience, the szorsa shuffled her cards and drew one. The style was different from Ren's deck, but the constellation painted on it took an unmistakably human shape: The Face of Stars. Good luck, and the szorsa shrugged at Vargo as if to say, *Do what you will, stranger who speaks nonsense.*

"Right." Vargo hadn't come to the wedding intending to do numinatria, but these days he didn't go anywhere without supplies shoved into every conceivable hiding place. He pulled a brush, an ink vial, and a few imprinted wax foci from his pocket—then halted.

Whatever had seized Grey had affected his mind. Only the Primordials could do that, via their eisar. Vargo's thumb passed over the wax plug imprinted with the symbol for Celnis, the god most closely aligned to Uniat. The ordering of the chaotic self into awareness.

He'd never cared about the more religious aspects of numinatria; that was Alsius's game. Vargo only cared what it could do for him in the world of Lower Bank gang struggles and Upper Bank politics. But couldn't he imitate the way the Praeteri had imbued their blank foci, pouring himself into what he created?

Closing his eyes, he pressed the wax to his lips and prayed to the Lumen.

Celnis. Uniat. Self-awareness. Vargo had once told Ren he wasn't a complicated man. Just a frustrated one, because the world was a mess and didn't have to be. But even when he tried to carve out a bit of order, it led to chaos and unintended consequences. Like Alsius. Like Kolya Serrado.

His hand shook, breath shuddering out. He didn't want to think about Kolya. But...self-awareness didn't give two shits for your comfort.

Kolya's death had been only a vague regret at the time. Wrong place, wrong time, unintended, not his fault. The cost of doing business. Same with Alsius. Vargo hadn't chosen to help the old man any more than he'd chosen to harm him. In the early days he'd gone along with Alsius's plans because they brought food, a roof over his head, increasingly fine clothes on his back.

Was he any different from all those senseless, selfish people responsible for the chaos he despised? From his knots, tearing apart the Lower Bank because Vargo lied about swearing oaths instead of breaking them?

You and Ren... you're two birds from one egg, Grey had said. Hardened by the world, but a short drop away from cracking. Too willing to use people like tools; too wary of being used by others.

And yet, he'd tied himself to Ren. Mingled his blood with Grey's. Not because they were useful, but because he cared. And because *they* cared about *him*, as something more than a tool to discard as soon as its use ran out.

Those bonds didn't erase past wrongs, didn't transform him into a better person. But they gave him a reason to try again when it all went to shit. To look for people he could trust to help him drag the chaos kicking and screaming into a semblance of order.

They made it easier to accept their trust in *him*.

Breathing in his guilt, breathing out his fear, Vargo found a place of equilibrium. Of peace, if only for a moment.

He opened his eyes. The street remained busy, but the buzzing restlessness inside his skull had gone still. So often Vargo lived in his head, ignoring his body except when sex or pain dragged him into it, but for once he felt at home in his flesh. Uniat: the body as a whole.

The szorsa watched him warily as he reached across her counter. Her faint twitch didn't mar the line he drew, the soft bristles of his brush leaving behind a circle of cool ink, and she sat as still as a held breath when he pressed the Celnis focus, imbued by the Lumen's grace with self-awareness, to the center of her brow.

And then the szorsa was gone, and in her place was Grey.

He remembered.

Like the Rook's memories, fleeting shades he couldn't grasp in their entirety. But he *remembered*. Not just being himself, but the selves before that: life after life, reborn into one clan after another. Dvornik, Varadi, Ánoškin, Stretsko, Meszaros, a trail of ill fortune and violence.

Laročja had been right—and so very wrong. He *was* cursed... but less so with every life that passed. What he bore now was only a trace of the original weight.

And his suffering had *never* been the answer. Only the repulsed lashing out of people who couldn't see past their fear.

A hand waved in front of his eyes. "Grey? You with me?"

Grey blinked at Vargo. His tongue still held the flavor of a dialect not spoken in five hundred years, but his voice was his own as he said, "You brought me back. Thank you."

"Yeah, well." Vargo rocked back on his heels, hands twitching like he didn't know where to put them. "Just took an oath, din't I? Can't let Ren go from wed to widowed in a day. What was that? What is *this*?" He waved at the world around them, faded from colorful and crowded to a desolate wasteland in the space of a breath.

The buildings were the same, though. Grey opened the shrine's lower door and stepped into the abandoned street. "A dream." *Or a nightmare.* "Where's Ren? Why isn't she with you?"

"I blame the zlyzen." Vargo thumbed back in the direction he'd come from. "My original plan was to head for the worst fear, on the assumption that she's probably there."

It was an unfortunately logical assumption. Wishing he still had Vargo's cane sword, Grey said, "Then let's go find her."

Ren tried to shout for Grey and Vargo as she and Alsius followed the zlyzen, but it was hard. Every sound conjured the feeling that something was watching, that by making noise she was drawing the attention of a predator. Her voice kept withering in her throat. Alsius's delight had briefly made him ebullient enough to shrug off the creeping dread, but soon it settled in. She heard the tremor every time he called Vargo's name, and she held tightly to his hand as they walked.

Not a living thing, not rat nor fly nor carrion crow, disturbed the bleached stillness. The gardens they passed were all dead branches and no leaves. Just when Ren was ready to plant her feet and demand—what? That the zlyzen somehow manifest the ability to talk and explain itself?—the street they were climbing became a staircase, then flattened out into a broad plaza.

With Grey and Vargo at the far side.

Zlyzen forgotten, Ren dashed across the plaza to Grey's waiting arms. Their marriage tokens tangled as she pressed her cheek to his. "Thank the Faces. How found you this place?"

"Vargo's idea. Head to wherever felt like the biggest danger." Grey's reply was a chuff of strained laughter against her ear.

"Blame me not." She pulled away. "We only just arrived ourselves. The zlyzen led us here."

"Us?" Vargo asked. All his attention had been for her, but now he looked up and past.

Just in time to keep his balance as Alsius crashed in, arms flinging around him in a relieved embrace. "Never do that again to me, my boy!"

After weeks of Vargo's ashen complexion, it was a relief to see color flood his cheeks. His good hand came up to touch Alsius's back like he expected the dream to yank the man away at any moment. "How—how are you—" Then, sputtering, he pulled back. "Wait. Weren't you old when we met?"

Alsius's sputters sounded very much like Vargo's. "I wasn't old; I was exactly this age! You were simply a brat. With bad manners and a worse memor—urk!"

The words cut off as Vargo's arms tightened around him. The cloth of Alsius's coat muffled Vargo's reply, but it still came through. "It's good to hear your yammering, old man."

Old man. Ren had been thinking of him as sixty, but he was in his midthirties at most. He'd been trapped as a spider nearly half as long as he'd been human.

This time Alsius was the one to draw back. "I've been thinking while we looked for you. Alta Ren—or Szorsa Arenza, perhaps I should say—can you help my boy? We're in a place of dream; can you...?" He gestured toward Vargo. Toward the faint lump of the bandage beneath Vargo's shirt.

The connection between them. Tanaquis had wondered if Ren would be able to mend it—but Ren, shivering, remembered what had happened when she tried to see the threads linking her to other people.

Vargo, drained and gaunt. Alsius, the picture of human-shaped health. How much longer could Vargo survive the imbalance between them?

She stepped forward, hesitant. "I...will try. But first you must tell me what you wish done."

Vargo stared at her. "Thought that would be obvious. We want you to fix it. What part of me metaphysically bleeding out did you miss?"

The part where I laid a line for this problem, and the third card was Hundred Lanterns Rise. The card of release, and where their path ended. But before that came Warp and Weft—the union between their two spirits—and for the path to follow, The Face of Balance.

Whatever their connection had grown into, it had begun as a crime: Alsius trying to take over Vargo's body for his own survival. If she was to renew it, this time they had to *choose* that path.

When she said so, Vargo looked at Alsius. Wetness gleamed at the edges of his eyes. "Spider or not, he's the only father I've ever had. Worst days of my life have been these past ones, not being able to talk to him. So, yes. I want it...if he does."

Alsius sniffled audibly. "My boy. You're a better son than I deserve."

Vargo tugged the collar of his shirt open, and Grey helped him peel the bandage loose. Ren laid one hand on his seeping mark, the other on the same spot on Alsius. Drawing a deep breath, she thought, *You don't have to look. Only to mend.*

Father and son. A thread of love and support, even though it began in the desperate moment when Alsius looked into the face of his own death—

Her breath wavered. That was the horror of this place, trying to seep in. The zlyzen had stood a little distance off while the four of them reunited, but now she felt its gaze on her. The skin between her shoulder blades crawled.

They aren't choosing out of fear. There it began, but they have passed through that shadow. To each other, they are a source of comfort. Strengthening each other not only in body but in heart. The shelter Ren herself had lost when her mother died, leaving her alone.

She remembered her own fear. Let it wash into *her*, not the connection. Every other bit of her was cold, but her hands were warm as she drew them together, feeling the thread, until at last her fingers met.

It shone briefly in her vision, the strong thread of family, untouched by the nightmare around them. Then it vanished from view.

Ren sagged against Grey. Alsius cupped his hands over his chest as if he held something precious. Gasping like it was his first breath in days, Vargo clawed his shirt out of the way. His skin was unmarred, the lines of the numinat restored. His laugh was as unsteady as Jagyi at a run. "Tanaquis will lose her *mind* that she wasn't here to see that."

"Do *I* have one now?" Alsius struggled with the complicated knot of his neckcloth.

Slinging an arm over his shoulders, Vargo said, "If it's in the same place as Peabody's, might want to check the other end, old man."

"Perhaps you can examine the content of your trousers later," Grey said. "There's an unnervingly patient zlyzen glaring at us."

It had moved, pacing over to crouch by the entrance to the labyrinth. Ren didn't want to look in that direction: It was like looking down the throat of ash itself, made with zlyzen blood. But the creature had brought her here for a reason. She doubted it would let her leave until that reason was fulfilled.

Wetting her lips, she said, "We must go."

Entering the labyrinth was like plunging into the Dežera in winter. She shuddered from head to foot at the sense of wrongness. The interior felt more than merely deserted; it felt *desecrated*. The stones of the path were broken and heaved out of place, the column shrines shrouded in plain fabric, the carved figures no more than half-seen ghosts beneath the cloth. As though this corner of the dream had to be hidden from the gaze of the deities themselves.

The zlyzen paced across the labyrinth's path—ill luck, walking inward that way; as if such a creature cared—to a center of blackened ground and stones like sun-bleached bone. The sides of the enameled basin there were bubbled and cracked. Ren shivered, as though all the heat had been drawn from the world.

"What nightmare is this?" she whispered.

The zlyzen only clawed at the basin's rim.

Ren couldn't make offerings to the hidden Faces and Masks. Instead she walked a circuit of the colonnade, praying briefly at each column for the safety of herself and her companions. Then, with the others trailing in her wake, she walked the broken path itself. There was no serenity to be found this time, no feeling of purification. Ren focused on the sound of her footfalls to stave off the horror that bled in with each breath.

At the center, the basin was dry. Its curve cradled only a soft mound of ashes.

Ren looked to the others, but they were as mystified as she—and all crowded to one side, as far from the zlyzen as they could get.

Reflexively, Ren reached for her pocket. But there was no reason for her to carry her pattern deck on her wedding day. She didn't dare try to dream one into existence, either, not with this place trying to taint her. But Grey knew that gesture, and he handed her a stack of cards. "These...I found them here."

She'd handled pattern cards countless times. Even with the differences in paper, her fingers knew the heft of a deck that was slightly too full. Riffling through, Ren saw The Artful Gentleman, The Silent Witness—*all* the clan cards save for the Ižranyi, adding to the sixty of an ordinary deck.

Ren prayed to the ancestors and shuffled, the rattle too loud in this silent place. Tiny spires of ash wafted up, and she reflexively twitched away, not wanting to touch those soft grey motes. Nine cards, or seven? What exactly was she trying to pattern, anyway— this place? Those ashes? She made up her mind to deal nine, but when she knelt to lay them out, last-minute hesitancy stayed her hand. This deck held the clan cards; seven it would be.

"The Horse for what you have," she said, turning over Hundred Lanterns Rise.

What they had was ashes: a sacrifice. Whatever the contents of the basin represented, it was a desperate plea for mercy. When Ren relayed that, Vargo muttered, "I don't think it worked."

"Maybe it did," Ren said uncertainly. "This position is meant to be positive." But the pattern Ivrina had dealt on the Night of Hells was warped to ill, even the good positions. Ren had been poisoned with ash that night. It was likely pure accident, the drug called ash and the ashes here—but who had named the drug? Gammer Lindworm? Mettore Indestor? Breccone Indestris? They'd never found out.

She turned over the next card, and her skin turned to ice.

Sleeping Waters. The card of place.

"I know where we are."

"The realm of mind—or rather, Ažerais's Dream," Alsius said, peering at the card's depiction of the Point, crowned with its beautiful, lost labyrinth. "But this is no reflection of Nadežra."

"No," Grey whispered, before Ren could. "It's Fiavla."

A noise pierced the silence between them, so low it scraped the edge of hearing. The zlyzen, growling. Not from anger or fear, but from excitement.

Grey turned to look at the desecrated labyrinth, his eyes wide and lost. "What you saw me as, Vargo—what you drew me from— that is where it began. The ill fortune that's hounded me from life to life...it is because once, centuries ago, I was a szorsa of the Ižranyi."

Ren's breath caught. *The Mask of Worms.* Showing up in her patterns, again and again, as the corruption of a Primordial. What Laročja had seen in her grandson...

He'd been Ižranyi. Before Fiavla fell.

When Fiavla fell.

"How do we get out of here?" Vargo asked, his voice far too controlled. "*Now.*"

"To leave a pattern half read is bad luck," Ren whispered.

"To stay in a Primordial-cursed city might be just a touch worse, *wouldn't you say?*" He pitched high on the last words. Vargo might have personal reasons to fear the zlyzen, but everyone from the tip to the tail of the Dežera had heard horror stories of fools who tested the boundaries of Fiavla, even to this day.

Her hands moved faster as she turned over the third card. "The Owl, for the wisdom you must remember."

Coffer and Key, the card of objects. "What they burned," Ren said, looking up at the basin. "To stop the destruction... what sacrifice might earn that mercy?"

A whole clan, destroyed. But like the corruption of A'ash spreading through a numinatrian register, the destruction *only* struck those bearing the Ižranyi name. It hadn't spilled out to everyone of that blood. If it had, all Vraszan would have died; centuries of marriages meant that practically everyone had ancestors in every clan. Ren likely had Ižranyi forebears herself, though too many generations had passed for it to be recorded in the branching strands of Ivrina's embroidery.

Grey answered, staring at the ashes. "Their koszenie. They—*we*—burned our own koszenie, to destroy the bonds of kinship. To keep the chaos from spreading."

Blasphemy. Desecration. Sacrilege. The labyrinth reeked of it. No wonder they had shrouded the Faces and the Masks: to hide the shame of their deeds.

The zlyzen's faint growl gained strength and fervor. It bellycrawled forward to lip at the toe of Grey's boot. Teeth like jagged obsidian left pale scratches along the leather, and he flinched back.

Ren hurried onward. Ten Coins Sing, the card of generosity; the position of the Spider was the question they must ask, and they had already answered it. The blasphemy of the Ižranyi had been for the sake of others. "You—your people—acted for the good of all," Ren said to Grey, fiercely. "Without your sacrifice, how many more would have died?"

His gaze was bleak. "Yet that crime I carried through many lives, in all three parts of my soul. I *saw* those lives, Ren. I was—never welcome. Always feared, always treated like a monster. Less so with each life, but still... for what we did, we were damned." He swallowed. "I still am."

Pattern itself gave Ren the counter she needed. "The Hidden Eye," she said, lifting the fifth card for Grey to see. "The reward you earn: your own clan card. As you said, with each life it is less. The poison Laročja saw was your past. Not your present, and not your future."

Vargo made a noise that wasn't a laugh. "No, that's a different poison and a different Primordial. But why does that zlyzen care? Why has it been stalking Ren like a starving mutt?"

The Hidden Eye had occupied the position of the Fox. For the Raccoon, the clan animal of the Kiraly, Ren turned over Labyrinth's Heart. "The card of stillness for the risk we take," Ren murmured, looking at it. "But I think... that is not what it means."

She heard an indignant huff from Alsius, the vocal equivalent to his mental snort. His numinatrian-trained mind still disliked the slipperiness of pattern, the way one meaning could be bent to another. "Sleeping Waters cannot be in two places at once, and already it has been used," Ren said, pointing at the second card. "So instead I have a different labyrinth—to indicate the one that stands atop the Point. There is danger to the wellspring."

"Another damned numinat, then?" Vargo growled. "Breccone en't around to make it. Some clever new idea of Branek's?"

Ren shook her head. "I know not. We ourselves may put it in danger somehow. Not directly, but as a consequence of what we do here." Perhaps by bringing the stain of a second Primordial back with them. The skin of her back hadn't stopped crawling since they arrived, but now it crawled harder.

That left only the central card, for the Ižranyi. The hub on which all else turned.

Sisters Victorious. The card of courage.

Ren's breath fell out of her in a sigh of understanding. "What is courage...but the overcoming of fear?"

The zlyzen hadn't retreated far. Her dread of it had waned; surrounded by this defiled labyrinth, the creature hardly seemed as bad. Now it came forward and, with a hesitant muzzle, nudged at the koszenie still tied around her hips.

Months of dreams, not just of Fiavla but of other places. Market towns, fishing villages. Parts of Vraszan she'd never seen, and centuries old.

Dreams given to her by the zlyzen.

Hardly believing her own daring, Ren reached out and took that charred, twisted head in her hands. "What do you get when dreams and fear combine?" she whispered. "You get a creature of nightmare."

She looked up once more at Alsius, at Vargo. At Grey, who had been Ižranyi; Grey, who in life after life had been feared. Hated. Treated like a monster.

"The zlyzen," she said. "The zlyzen are what remain of the Ižranyi."

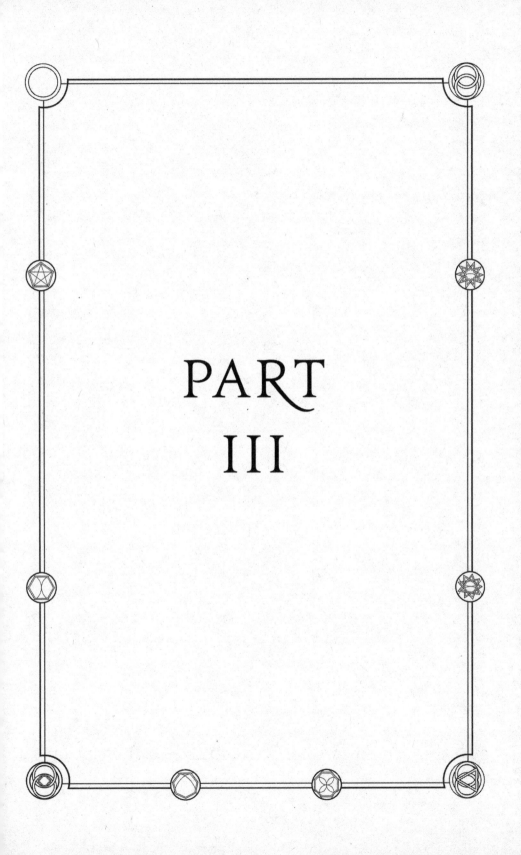

PART

III

The Mask of Knives

Tess hadn't heard anything from Ren for four days, but she still crossed to the Upper Bank to update the Traementis on the lack of news. "A burden shared is a burden halved," she told Donaia when the woman fussed over her wasted trip, and left Traementis Manor with a lighter heart, as though the adage were the literal truth.

But her steps dragged as she dwelt on the unshared part of her burden: that a zlyzen had taken Ren and the others. She'd blundered her way through a lie about numinatria and the realm of mind rather than make Donaia relive Leato's death. After the Night of Hells, the corpses had surfaced from the dream into the waking world. If the worst happened now, would they even find a body to burn?

Don't think about that. Tess wrapped her striped woolen more tightly against a chill both within and without. *Ren will be all right. And Grey and Vargo, too.* Nobody knew Ažerais's Dream like her sister.

She edged around a barrel-filled cart stopped in the middle of the Sunrise Bridge. A Vraszenian fellow was leaning over the bridge's rail—had the carters lost something over the edge? If so, she didn't envy whoever might dive in after it; the twilight wind was bitterly sharp. Tess still had a long walk to Westbridge. To the house Sedge hardly dared leave with a medallion in the wine cellar and a gaggle of children that needed looking after whether they thought so or not. To the fading hope that she'd glance into the parlour and find Ren had returned, safe and—

Sudden force hammered Tess to the cobblestones.

Her ears rang as she pushed herself to her knees, wondering what had happened. When she touched her chin, her fingers came away bloody. As if from a great distance, she heard people shouting and screaming. Twisting to look behind her, Tess saw a great plume of black smoke rising from where the cart had been.

Lacewater-raised instinct said that whatever had just happened, she didn't want to be anywhere near it. Tess regained her feet and stumbled in the other direction, past people staggering upright and demanding explanations. A group of angry cuffs stormed by, masked for a night of drinking and calling for a hawk to bring order.

No hawk came swooping down. And as Tess ran for the Sunset Bridge, it became clear there weren't any hawks *to* come. Only more and more people with braided hair and clan colors, carrying cudgels and knives, beating drums and singing fierce Vraszenian songs.

The Anduske. Andrejek's uprising. *But Ren's not back yet*, Tess thought, the explosion still scrambling her thoughts. How could they start their rebellion when Ren was lost?

A foolish thought. Almost as foolish as thinking she could escape to the Lower Bank. By the time she got to Duskgate, the wind had shredded the second plume of smoke, but shouting and chaos told her the same thing had happened here. Of course they wouldn't take out only one bridge.

A skiff, then. But as Tess ran north to follow the shore, she knew it was futile. Weren't half the skiffers Stretsko? There were boats on the water, to be sure, but none taking passengers. Instead they were forming a cordon around the island, or swarming other vessels, shoving their oarsmen into the river. Fists wearing the knot of Tserdev Očelen's Crimson Eyes knocked down anybody attempting to get to an unattended boat.

Tess's mouth was dry. *Think. You've been through this before.* It wasn't a riot, not yet; the people around her—those not displaying clan emblems—were mostly confused and frightened, not angry. That could change fast, though. A man wearing the Anduske knot was standing atop a crate, shouting in Vraszenian. Tess didn't speak it well enough to understand everything, but she got the gist: declaring the Old Island was in Vraszenian hands, calling for others to join the cause, and for them to seize hold of any...

Any Liganti.

She veered down an alley before the man's eye could fall on her. Ganllechyn wasn't Liganti, but how many would know or care when they saw a pale face? Right now the crowd and confusion were her best protection; she had to find shelter before those ran out. Tess dragged her woolen over her head and ducked her chin low. The stripes were like a banner, but better that than her copper-bright hair.

"Oi!"

The shout could have been directed at anyone, but rabbit fear said it was aimed at *her.* Tess turned a corner and hurried faster, only to hear heavy boots following. A second "Oi!" and now there was no mistaking it; the man was after her. Tess reached for her scissors—pitiful protection—and now he was right behind her, saying, "Oi, *Tess—*"

Simlin barely jerked out of range as she swung around with the scissors. "Fucking pisspot hell, Tess!"

"You stay back!" She waved her scissors. "I've shucked an Oyster Cracker for putting his hands on me. Don't think I won't poke holes in you, too!"

Simlin backed up a step. "Save it for someone who means you harm. There's enough of 'em around here."

"And you're not one?" Something crashed down the alley. A woman screamed. Tess glanced away long enough that Simlin could have easily torn the scissors from her hand.

He only said, "I en't. And I know we en't knotted no more, but we was once, and you weren't a blade-tongued bitch like Ren. If you don't want my help, though, good luck with those scissors of yours." He strode back down the alley, away from the scream that had become many, voices raised in a confusing tangle of languages.

"Wait," Tess called, keeping her scissors at the ready. Simlin slowed enough for her to catch up. "Where are you going?"

"Not back to my flop. Place was swarming with assholes come in from upriver. Figure they're in on this." He stopped where the alley spat out onto a narrow canal walk.

Tess's flight had taken her deep into Lacewater; they weren't far from Lifost Square. "Think we can get to the Talon and Trick? Vargo protected his business and property during the Dreamweaver Riots. They'll have been ready for this."

"And they'll just let us in?" Simlin said, but he turned in the right direction.

"As long as someone there recognizes me," Tess said, following behind like thread trailing a needle.

She knew better than to try the front door, with the crowd milling around the square. But nobody answered her knock at the side entrance, not even when it turned to pounding, or invoking Vargo's name. Not until she cried, "Please, Stoček knows me."

Then the door cracked. So did Tess's hope, when the face peering out was a stranger's. A woman. And Vraszenian. "Anyone can say they know Vargo. How know you the other?"

"He used to give us honey stones as children."

"Sounds like him." Dark eyes flicked from Tess's covered hair, to her bleeding chin, to Simlin hulking behind her. "You'll bring trouble on us all if you keep shouting in the alley. Get in here."

The door cracked farther, enough to let them squeeze through. The woman closed and bolted it behind them, and Simlin helped her drag a heavy cask to block it.

Empty of laughing cuffs and their glittering masks and coats, the gambling parlour slumped like a laborer after a hard day. A creak from the staircase had Tess clutching her woolen shawl tighter, but it was only Stoček, grim-faced and dour as she'd never seen him.

A grimness that lightened when he spotted her. "Tess? That racket was you? And hey, isn't that pouty little Simlin?"

"Not little no more," Simlin grumbled.

"Still pouty, though." Stoček tried to pinch his cheek between a thumb and a finger-stub, but Simlin dodged like it was Tess's scissors.

Tess sagged against the cask and said, "We didn't know where to go." Stoček wasn't safety the way Ren and Sedge were, but he wouldn't toss her to the street.

Grabbing a cloth from an abandoned table, Stoček nudged her chin up with his padded hook and blotted away the blood. Tess hissed at the sting of zrel, but helped Stoček bind a clean cloth around her head without complaint.

"Little rabbit," he said, hook flicking one of the bandage ends. Tess blinked back tears.

Simlin swiped the zrel and knocked back a slug. "So what—we just sit here and hope nobody else comes knocking?"

The woman's jaw tightened when Stoček looked at her. "We've no more room," she said.

With the Talon and Trick standing empty, she must mean something else. Stoček confirmed Tess's suspicion when he said, "Room in the bilge still. She can take my place down there."

"That's one. We have two more now."

"I can stay up here," Simlin said. "Nobody gonna mistake me for a Lig. I'll say Stoček's my grandda."

"Gaffer, you mean," Stoček said, and Simlin grunted.

Tess's jaw ached as she watched the conversation bounce between them. "I didn't mean to bring trouble."

"You didn't," Stoček said, with a glare at the woman. "Everyone knows the cuffs come to the Talon and Trick. Only a matter of time before someone comes looking for hostages."

"So you'll say you sent them away?"

"Masks willing, they'll believe it." Grasping her elbow, the woman led Tess to a room shielded by a beaded curtain. Inside was a table covered by a szorsa's shawl, with bowls for offerings to the Face and the Mask. The woman pushed the table aside and pried up a hidden trapdoor. "Down you go. Make no noise, or all of us will pay the price."

Any thought Tess had of arguing or asking more questions died at a new pounding and a voice shouting in Vraszenian, "Open up!"

Stinking water, just an inch or two deep, splashed around her as she went through the trapdoor. The space beneath the floor was barely tall enough for a person on her hands and knees, and when the entrance banged shut, the only light came from tiny cracks between the floorboards. In the moments before darkness closed in, she'd seen several other people, their fine clothes incongruous in that place.

Tess tried to edge away from the trapdoor, but the others were too closely packed. A woman hissed, "Stop! You'll bring those gnats down upon us!"

Biting back her retort, Tess forced herself still. The water sloshed quiet, and then she heard something grinding away from the front door.

The trio upstairs put on a good performance, even Simlin. Why had they barred the door? Because they'd be fools not to. They'd lived through riots before. Was anyone else here? No, the chalk-faces all bolted when the trouble began. Were they sure of that? Yes, very sure. Would they object to the Anduske searching?

Tess almost stopped breathing when boots clomped across the floor, as if they'd hear it above their own noise. From the banging, they were smart enough to search for hidden compartments; Lace-water was riddled with them. If they found this one, Tess would be the first person they grabbed. Could she buy any safety by saying she knew Andrejek? Would they even listen?

The bilge wasn't the only hidey-hole, it seemed. Screams from upstairs made Tess hunch like a terrified rabbit: Liganti voices pro-testing their treatment, threatening retribution, cutting off with the unmistakable sound of violence. Stoček's voice—"Here now, no need for that"—and then a cry from the old man, and a rough shout from Simlin.

Tess clapped both hands over her mouth. They stank of moss and fouled river water, and she fought the urge to gag.

The Anduske left. Time passed with only breathing to measure it; the rebels must have targeted the temples to stop the bells from being used as signals. Pavlin had mentioned once that Seterins had a code for passing messages in wartime, which every officer of the Vigil was expected to know.

Pavlin. He'd be worried if she went missing. Sedge would tear up both banks to find her. Giuna might help him. She had to get to safety, or at least get word to them.

Not even her hands were enough to stop her shriek when the trapdoor swung open and light flooded in.

"Had to see to Stoček first," the woman said. Her cheek was swollen. "The hatch I can leave open, but if you come out, they'll see the water if they come back."

They'll come back, the tension in the woman's shoulders said. Them, or someone else.

"Simlin?" she whispered. Maybe he was tending Stoček. She hoped he was tending Stoček.

But that wasn't what Simlin would do.

The woman's flat, bloodless lips were a worse confirmation than any words. Tess squeezed her eyes shut. She'd never much liked Simlin...but he wasn't all bad. He'd shown that at the last.

"We can't stay here," said the cuff crouched next to Tess, his voice high with impending panic. She'd seen him before, hanging on Giuna at events. An Amananto boy. "There might be spiders! Or rats!"

"Rats and spiders up there, too," muttered someone farther back.

Tess opened her eyes to see the szorsa's lip curl. "You prefer the streets, go with my blessing. There is a back way out. But past that door, you will be on your own."

A spark of hope kindled in Tess's chest. Only a tiny one; there was still a lot of island between her and safety.

Her...and the others. She couldn't abandon these people here, hiding in terror and stagnant water. Even if she was tempted to leave behind the one who'd called Vraszenians "gnats."

"I know a safe place," she said. With a nod toward the szorsa, she added, "One that won't bring more trouble on you. If Stoček can walk, we'll take him with us. But getting there won't be easy."

"Where?" the Amananto boy asked, clutching her arm.

If Tess couldn't get off the Old Island, the next best thing was to put herself somewhere her friends would think to look for her. Because they *would* come, sure as the moons would rise.

"Someplace dry," Tess said. "Protected by magic, too." What if someone had looted her shop? She'd already removed most of the valuables, but people took the oddest things.

She glanced up at the szorsa. "I'll need some triple clover knots."

Eastbridge, Upper Bank: Cyprilun 10

With most of the Upper Bank's sedan chair bearers conscripted for other duties and the few remaining chairs reserved for Cinquerat use only, Donaia had two choices for getting to their temporary head-quarters: break out the Traementis carriage, or walk. The habit of frugality, not yet shed, made her walk.

It meant she saw very clearly the effects the takeover of the Old Island had already had on her city. Prasinet, understandably distrust-ful of what might happen to any cargo unloaded into Dockwall, had directed all shipping to empty its holds into Whitesail. Which rap-idly overflowed—those warehouses couldn't handle everything—so that spilled over into neighboring districts, the Pearls included. *Cibrial made sure we get the* high-class *cargo*, Donaia thought sourly, watching a cart laden with wine casks lumber over one of the few bridges in the Pearls wide enough to take it.

Storage would only be a problem for a while, though. Forces from some of the Vraszenian city-states were blockading the Dežera upriver and harassing caravans along the Dawn and Dusk Roads. The ships that came into Nadežra were used to selling their cargo, then loading up again with goods to take north. If Nadežra had nothing to offer, soon they would stop coming.

Don't borrow future trouble, she told herself. *We have plenty to keep us busy right now.*

The prospect of violence hung over the city like a fog. It had already begun; those escapees who'd managed to swim the East and West Channels before the cordon tightened said the rebels had taken control of the Charterhouse, killing the evening guards. The Aerie still stood, the last anyone heard, but a false rumor that the Anduske would bomb the bridge at Floodwatch had drawn the bulk of the Vigil's forces there just before the takeover. Then they'd blown spans out of the Sunrise and Sunset Bridges instead, cutting off the Old Island entirely.

Donaia shivered as she reached Eastbridge, and not because of the Dežera's chill wind. Structures rose along the bank, facing the Old Island: trebuchets, with piles of stone around them ready to be hurled, and numinatrian engines of war.

None had yet seen use. Donaia unashamedly muttered a prayer of thanks that Ghiscolo Acrenix wasn't still Caerulet, or worse yet, Mettore Indestor. Neither of them would have held back from an immediate assault on the Old Island, bloodshed be damned. Agniet Cercel Coscani would at least give diplomacy a chance to work.

Or she was just buying time. The Vigil weren't sufficient to storm the island, and Agniet couldn't afford to draw their military forces away from the borders. Not with the neighboring city-states ready to pounce at the first sign of inattention. That meant hiring merce-naries, as they'd done in previous wars, but this rebellion had taken the Cinquerat enough by surprise that all they had right now were a few local companies usually contracted to guard caravans.

Donaia shouldn't have let her thoughts stray in that direction. *Some* people must have known this was coming. She was terribly, terribly afraid that two of them were Ren and Grey.

But she was even more afraid of what had happened to them. Eight days, and no sign of either. Nor of Vargo, whom Tess had said went with them. Into the dream, for what purpose Donaia could hardly imagine. Eight days since the wedding, four days since the city went to hell, and Donaia didn't know if she would ever see her niece again.

She came at last to Rivershore Plaza, with the Rotunda's dome gleaming at its eastern end. Limping a little from a blister—Donaia had been elated when she could finally buy herself new shoes, only to find them less comfortable than the old pairs molded to every knob of her feet—she pushed through the chaos outside the Rotunda to the chaos within.

A fabric canopy painted with an enormous numinat stretched across the mouth of the dome, keeping the noise to an acceptably dull roar. The shops below had been emptied to make offices for the displaced Cinquerat, and clerks dashed this way and that, the papers they carried lacking even the usual leather folders to protect them. There were no statues to proclaim the mottoes of the Cinquerat seats—*I speak for all; I counsel all; I support all; I defend all; I pray for all*—but the open center of the Rotunda held the usual constellation of five desks, and the usual secretaries to direct traffic, looking no more harassed than usual.

Donaia ignored them. Bypassing the desks, she pushed through the crowd to the shop at the back of the Rotunda, which was not so much the Cinquerat's audience chamber as their war room.

Another numinat on the door muffled sound as it closed behind her. Empty shelves within mocked the gathered leaders, a reminder of the room's prior purpose. The sales counter had been transformed into a strategy table. A map of Nadežra spread across it, the Old Island dominating the center, with the Upper and Lower Banks stretching down its sides. The Cinquerat stood around it, listening to Cercel.

"We'll need cover for the removal crews," she said, tapping the Point with a rod. "If the rebels realize what we're doing, they could easily station archers here and rain Primordial hell on both sides of the channel."

"And risk damaging the river numinata?" Scaperto asked. His gesture took in two filigree half masks, repurposed to represent the structures spanning the East and West Channels. Small boat markers flocked alongside them.

Cercel sighed. She was younger than Donaia, but the few months she'd been Caerulet weighed on her like years. "If they realize the river numinata are our goal, they might risk it to stop us."

"They would be right to do so," snapped Utrinzi Simendis. His people were busy inscribing weapons and providing aid, but his emergence from self-imposed isolation to attend this meeting told Donaia how serious it was. "Destroying the river numinata is an act of madness. The effects will harm this city far more than a scuffle with a few radicals."

"Destroying the *what*?" Donaia snapped. The table shook when her hand came down on it. "House Traementis holds the charter for one of those numinata, and we have *not* given our consent."

"Not destroying." Scaperto righted a few of the toppled markers, conspicuously not meeting her glare. "Removing the foci to temporarily disable them."

Flapping like an angry gull, Utrinzi said, "Which will destroy the East Channel numinat! An inscriptor *died* to create that work. You can't simply reactivate it when you please!"

"So we'll replace it. Vargo managed it; so can we." Scaperto reluctantly raised his gaze to Donaia's, heavy with regret—but also with resolve. "The Cinquerat is invoking the public good clause in your charter. House Traementis has no say in this. We're informing you as a courtesy."

"But—" She felt like someone had pulled the ground out from under her. They'd summoned her here for *this*? "Won't that leave the whole city with nothing but filthy water?" The Lower Bank had relied for years on peddlers who carted water from the clean East Channel. With both sides fouled...

Iascat said, "We're making plans for emergency supplies of clean water. There are wells outside the city, and Iridet's people can make smaller cleansing numinata."

"Supplies that will be distributed to *both* banks, for as long as we can hold Floodwatch," Scaperto hastened to add. "I wouldn't countenance this if they weren't."

It still wouldn't be enough. Not with less than a month to the Great Dream, and Vraszenians flooding the city in anticipation. Donaia didn't side with the Liganti who assumed they were all radicals and insurrectionists in need of containment, but insufficient supply might guarantee further insurrection.

Cibrial's mouth pinched with cynicism. "Assuming we can get our hands on enough barrels. Rimbon Beldipassi has bought up all the available stock. I would accuse him of espionage, but he started doing it *before* Agniet had this idea."

"And whose fault is that?" Iascat said sharply. "If you hadn't encouraged him..."

It produced a brief silence, during which Cercel looked confused and Scaperto abruptly looked sick. Donaia arrived at understanding a beat after he did. *Those light-forsaken medallions.* She already had the unpleasant suspicion Cibrial was using hers to manage the city's financial affairs in the face of this crisis; things on that front were going too smoothly to be explicable otherwise. And Faella Cosca-num seemed to be everywhere these days, talking to everyone, keeping the delta gentry in line. Beldipassi's sudden investment in barrels might be driven by the same Primordial inspiration.

Cibrial glared at Iascat. "To think I'd regret the day Sostira was gone, replaced by a *boy* without the guts to do what's needed. Don't go throwing stones at me; at least I'm trying to hold this city together."

"In the short term. Some of us have an eye toward the longer term and larger threats." Iascat's riposte earned a harrumph and a nod from Utrinzi.

Cercel, possibly the only person present who didn't know what they were talking about, dragged them back on topic. "This matter falls under Caerulet and Fulvet, and with Prasinet's support, we are in three-fifths agreement. This meeting isn't for discussion; it's to inform you of our plans."

A clerk scurried in and shoved a folded missive into Cibrial's hands. She cursed sulfurously when she read it. "Those damned rebels have started burning the deeds for Old Island property and writing their own, giving the land and buildings to the *shopkeepers*—to secure their support, I imagine. I need to deal with this. We're done here."

She stormed toward the door, which opened to reveal Faella waiting on the other side. Even with the renewed wave of noise,

Donaia heard Cibrial's muttered comment as they stalked away together. "That Fienola woman could end this in a bell, if she'd just answer her damn door."

Tanaquis. According to Ren, she held the Ninat medallion: death and endings. Donaia hugged herself to forestall a shudder, grateful that Tanaquis was more interested in the cosmos than in the conflicts of the everyday world. Unlike most of the medallion holders, she had the skill to employ hers to its full and devastating effect.

She'd been holed up in her townhouse since the wedding, though, refusing all callers. When she left Westbridge, she'd been muttering something about Vraszenian souls not properly moving through the Lumen's cycle—but with the air of one inspired, not her usual grumbling complaints. Donaia could only hope her epiphany had something to do with destroying the medallions.

Scaperto touched Donaia's arm, recalling her to herself. "I know this is hard, and I'm sorry we have to be so high-handed. But cutting off clean water to the island puts pressure on them to capitulate. It's our best bet for ending the rebellion without bloodshed."

No, the deaths would come more slowly, as unclean water spread disease. At the same time, Scaperto wasn't wrong. There was no way out of this conflict that wouldn't cause suffering.

She could only do her best to mitigate it. Squaring her shoulders, Donaia said, "I'll go have a talk with Mede Beldipassi."

Eastbridge, Upper Bank: Cyprilun 10

Chill water swirled around Sedge's bare knees and rolled trousers as he waded out past a decayed jetty on the Froghole shore. The usual lights along the riverbanks had been snuffed, and clouds veiled Corillis and Paumillis. To the south, a bright line marked the bridge at Floodwatch; north of him, the Sunset Bridge was a broken line. Between the two, everything was darkness and rushing sound.

And somewhere in that darkness, his sister needed him.

He hadn't been there when the zlyzen got Ren. No, he'd gone off like a damn fool to drink with Varuni and spent the night learning that not all her impulses toward him were violent. And he hadn't been there when the bridges blew, with Tess caught somewhere between the Pearls and safety. He couldn't go into the dream after Ren, but he *could* find Tess.

She was on the island. She had to be.

Sedge took a deep breath and dove in.

The cold threatened to drive the air from his lungs. He'd learned to swim because it was useful for Vargo's smuggling work, but never in snow-melted spring flood. Sedge hadn't gone three strokes when he started wondering if this was a mistake. His balls were trying to crawl inside his body for protection, and his feet were already numb. On the far shore there would be rebels, who could hear him coming even if they couldn't see. Rebels, and worse: People said they'd seen zlyzen patrolling the waterfront, as if defending the island.

He didn't try to fight the current, flowing fast with the rising flood behind it. Instead he let it carry him downstream toward the cleansing numinat, focusing on angling across toward Lacewater. Praying all the while that he'd make it before the current swept him past the Old Island entirely. Years ago a farmer had found his infant self among the riverside sedge; he didn't want his corpse to wind up there, too.

The water hadn't yet stopped stinking when the clang of metal on metal made him thrash defensively. The sound came from above, though. He glanced up as he passed through the cleansing numinat's skin-deep buzz and saw faint, shielded lights dancing above like pearl ghosts. Was it Andrejek or the Cinquerat that had stationed people on the numinat?

Distraction cost him valuable paddling time. The suddenly clean waters were sweeping him toward the piers of the broken Sunset Bridge, and he weren't anywhere near the island yet.

Trying to get over faster made too much noise. A strong lightstone beam suddenly blazed across the water. That gave Sedge enough warning to duck under, and a moment later he heard a muffled splash, far too close for comfort. He flailed under the surface, trying to sense which way the current was taking him, trying to go a bit rightward from that. How far north had he traveled? How much of the island was left for him to catch?

He came up gasping and saw the shore sliding by, buffered by the sandbags Fulvet had placed against flooding. Not quite within reach, but he pushed for them, hands slipping on the wet, rounded burlap. He was running out of sandbags when he finally managed to wedge his hand into a gap and pull himself to a halt.

His relief was short-lived. A rock thudded into his arm; cursing, Sedge flailed for a new hold. "I en't your enemy!"

Whoever was up above didn't give a shit. More rocks struck him; a shard of tile cut his scalp. Sedge tried to haul himself enough onto the sandbags to curl up and protect his head.

Then someone grabbed his arm—his *bad* arm. And he hadn't worn the brace Tess made for him, because it would interfere with swimming.

Sedge's arm came out of its socket with a familiar, meaty sound. He howled with pain as the defender hauled him over the sandbags and onto the pavers above. A boot thudded into his ribs, washing agony through him, and Sedge didn't know what words were coming out of his mouth. He'd prepared a speech, something to convince the Anduske he wasn't a threat, but all the words were gone—

"Stop that, you fool!" someone shouted in Vraszenian. "Andrejek's orders; Cinquerat spies should be brought in for questioning."

"I en't a spy," Sedge mumbled, but nobody was listening to him. "Idusza Polojny—I got news for her." Only the news that Ren and Grey and Vargo were still missing, but these people didn't have to know that.

"What of the one who knifed Orsoly?" another voice snapped. "We cannot take the risk. Better to be safe—"

In Sedge's ear, a voice whispered, "*Keep quiet.*"

That was just enough warning for him to bite down on a scream as someone dragged him backward, into a narrow alley. "Up," the new voice said. "While they're distracted. Wait for me by the Plešy Bridge."

Sedge staggered to his feet. In the dim light, he could barely make out the hooded figure at his side. He choked on the name that wanted to burst out. "G—"

"*Go*," the Rook said, and Sedge went.

Behind him he heard a burst of alarmed cries and a mocking laugh. He wanted desperately to look back, but made himself lurch forward on feet he couldn't feel, past broken windows and boarded-up doors, until the tiny Plešy Bridge came into view. Then he wedged himself into its shadows and waited, panting.

By the time the Rook returned, Sedge's trousers were half frozen to his legs. But he'd had plenty of time to think about that voice. "You en't the real Rook," he said harshly, prying himself upright.

The Rook eased back the hood enough to let in a touch of light, revealing Oksana Ryvček. "An older vintage," she said dryly. "Come. Or I'll have rescued you for nothing."

He didn't realize until after she'd led him to a cellar room that his feet were bleeding, cut by glass from the shattered windows. Ryvček attended to his shoulder first, dragging it back into place with experienced hands, before picking shards out of his soles and wrapping them tight. "Only spies, fools, and the desperate come here," she said when she was done. "I know which I am. You?"

"Desperate," Sedge said grimly. "I'm looking for Tess."

Ryvček must be wearing the costume Grey had used. It looked good enough to send a thrill through him, despite everything—and she'd dealt so easily with those guards. *An older vintage*, she'd said, and he knew Grey had once trained with her. Was she the Rook before him? Her fingers snagged on a frayed braid when she ran a hand over her head. "Turns out your other sister has the courage of the first, when need calls."

Sedge almost grabbed her. "You know where Tess is? She's alive?"

"Alive, and doing what she can. Andrejek blew the bridges early—or *someone* on his side did. They were supposed to go at midnight, when few northerners would be here. Instead many were caught. In prison Andrejek keeps them, the ones lucky enough to be brought to him, but even that is far from safe. Tess is helping a few hide."

Relief melted Sedge into a puddle. Tess was alive. And—not safe, but he weren't surprised Tess couldn't just keep her head down. "You've gotta take me to her."

The sardonic arch of Ryvček's brow halted him. "Sopping wet, with slashed feet, and without coat or shoes? You're Nadežran enough to avoid trouble, but not looking like that. Give me time to find you clothing. Not that you have much choice; you know not where she is."

Sedge scoffed. If the rebels were going after outsiders, Tess would head for the safest place available. And there was one place better than any other. "I'll bet you the boots I left behind that she's in the temple. But I'll wait for that coat."

Eastbridge, Upper Bank: Cyprilun 12

Giuna wished she had someone, *anyone* for company as she slipped into an Eastbridge alley. No one had heard from Tess since the Old Island fell to the rebels; Giuna feared she was trapped there. Even *hoped* she was—because all the alternatives were worse.

But there was no one to go with Giuna. Lieutenant Ranieri was devoting every moment not swallowed by his duties guarding water distribution on the Lower Bank to looking for Tess. Sedge had gone missing, doing the same. She would have asked Kasienka, but the other girl was off on business for her aunt and hadn't come by the manor in days. Giuna couldn't even bring Meatball. Donaia would ask why she was taking him, and Giuna didn't want her mother to know what she was doing.

So she was on her own as she stripped off her gloves, faced the door at the back of the Eastbridge Quaratium, and rapped on the wood.

No answer came, not after the first knock, nor the second or third. *Maybe they're all out*, Giuna thought. *Or they moved after we found them.*

When she tested the latch, the door swung open.

"Hello?" she called up the stairwell, hating how timid she sounded. "I'm looking for Esmi—Mistress Esmierka." She didn't know the woman's family name. She didn't know if the woman *had* a family name. Neither Tess nor Sedge seemed to.

Giuna ventured up the steps. "I'm sorry for the intrusion. If it weren't important, I wouldn't be here." The staircase opened into the room she'd seen before, still decorated with the mismatched trophies of the Oyster Crackers, the most successful knot of thieves on the Upper Bank. They hadn't moved on; they just weren't home. "Hello?"

The reply came in the form of an arm around her throat and the cold kiss of steel against her skin. "What part of our last meeting made you think you got an invitation here, *alta*?"

"I know I don't." Nerves made Giuna want to swallow, but she was terrified she'd cut herself if she did. The voice was Esmierka's, though: one mercy from the Vraszenian Masks. "I'm sorry. I—I came to ask a favor of you."

Esmierka released her. The knife stayed out as the thief circled to face her. "The likes of you, asking a favor from the likes of me, at a time like this. That's almost as rich as you are."

Her cynicism was understandable. Esmierka had a Vraszenian name and some of the blood, though her accent was purely Nadežran. "The favor will help you, too," Giuna said, discarding all opening pleasantries. "My plan is to cut Cibrial Destaelio off at the knees."

The burn scar made Esmierka's expression hard to read, but her abrupt stillness said plenty. After a moment she dropped into a chair. "As opening cards go, that one's at least interesting."

Giuna remained standing, like a supplicant. Little tricks she'd picked up from Ren, who'd taught her that honest persuasion was a kissing cousin to dishonest manipulation. "Are we alone?"

Esmierka nodded.

"I mean it," Giuna insisted. "If we aren't, this could be incredibly dangerous to *everyone*. The rest of your knot included."

The other woman's brows rose, but she said, "Truly, we're alone."

Giuna had to trust it was the truth. "Do you remember the bronze medallion Suilis was looking for? The one she thought Ren had?" At a second nod, Giuna said, "Her Charity has one very much like it, except cast in copper and etched with Quarat. I need someone to steal it. And you're the only thief I can ask."

Esmierka's bark of laughter was entirely deserved. "What about your cousin?"

"Ren's missing. Nobody's seen her for days."

That snuffed the amusement like a pinched candle. "Tess neither. Her man came asking. Think they're in the same place?"

"I don't think so. But I don't know." Everything felt like it had spun out of Giuna's control. No sign of Grey and Vargo, either, unless the rumors about sightings of the Rook on the Old Island were true. Tess missing. Sedge missing. Tanaquis wasn't opening her door to anybody, even when Giuna stood outside pleading for an hour. And Donaia was busy trying to keep the barge that was Nadežra from steering itself straight onto a shoal. Giuna couldn't do anything about any of it.

Except this piece. *She's using her medallion, I'm sure of it*, Donaia had said. *Faella, too.* When Giuna went to talk to Iridet, she'd found Parma at his house. Parma said she could take care of Faella; that left Cibrial in Giuna's hands.

Esmierka spun the knife around her fingers. "Two of 'em, now. Why do these medallions matter so damned much? There's lots of numinatria in this city."

Giuna wasn't about to give the whole story to someone who hadn't yet agreed to help, but she could share part of it. "They're what Kaius Rex used to conquer Vraszan."

The knife spun free and clunked to the floor.

"So," Esmierka said, her voice flat. "You're a typical cuff after all. You want me to steal this thing and give it to you."

"*No*," Giuna flung back, shuddering down to her bones. "I want you to hide it—hide it where nobody else can find it, not even your knot-mates. These things are *evil*, Esmierka; they're evil and dangerous and I'm asking you to take a terrible risk by stealing one. But we need to destroy them, and I don't trust Cibrial to cooperate."

Esmierka stood slowly, not taking her gaze from Giuna's. "Tess said you're not much of a liar, but this... You truly want to undercut your own Cinquerat, in the middle of a war, because you think these things are *that* bad."

"If we're relying on them to keep control of this city," Giuna said, her voice trembling, "then we're no better than the Tyrant."

That got a short, sharp nod. Then Esmierka spat into the palm of her hand.

Giuna's gloves were still in her pocket. She spat in her own hand and met Esmierka's grip, palm-to-palm.

"If I'm keeping my crew in the dark," Esmierka said, "I'll need someone else's help finding where she keeps it."

Giuna sighed. "By 'someone else,' I suppose you mean me."

Scar twisting with her glee, Esmierka said, "Suppose so. Welcome to the Oyster Crackers, Alta Giuna Traementis."

Hidden temple, Old Island: Cyprilun 13

Even though Tess knew the temple was warded against intruders, she still tensed up every time she heard footsteps approaching. There was always the chance that someone had let slip the secret of how to get in, or that someone wearing a triple clover charm just happened to try the barrier. Enough people had come onto the Old Island for the rebellion that some might not even know there *was* a barrier. And she could only imagine what the rebels would do if they found her collection of refugees hiding in a temple that used to belong to Kaius Rex.

Stoček hurried over to the entrance, as if he'd be much of a defense should an enemy come through. Tess followed, carrying the chair leg that was her makeshift club. But it was only Sedge, hauling a small cask of water.

"All I could get," Sedge said at Tess's disheartened look. "What

Andrejek's passing out is the water they'd set aside for putting out fires—they filled their barrels before the numinata got destroyed. But there en't much left."

Tess licked lips that already felt far too dry. The temple made a good shelter, but a bad place to wait out a siege. The only food or water they had was what Sedge could scrounge outside. The Amananto boy, Orrucio, claimed to know a little bit of inscription; he'd been trying to make a cleansing numinat using supplies left behind in the temple. So far, no success.

"We'll make it last," Stoček said. But Tess knew that no amount of thrift would stretch that cask very far.

An answer came from the tunnel, Ryvček's voice deepened and stripped of its usual accent. "No, drink up. Because tonight you're getting out of here."

Tess's heart leapt as the Rook's hooded silhouette appeared behind Sedge. "You've got a way off the island?" How, she couldn't imagine. But Ryvček had all the Rook's resourcefulness, even without his magic to help.

"I told you I would. But you'd better move fast, because the longer we wait, the more likely it is that somebody finds the boat."

Dust burned in Tess's throat as she looked at Sedge's cask, but her conscience held her back. If they were leaving, then someone else should have the clean water.

She was about to say so when the numinata lighting the temple flickered and dimmed.

Footsteps echoed from everywhere and nowhere, mixed with cries of alarm from the refugees. A chill spread across Tess's skin, slow, crawling horror that made her cringe from the shadows. Except there was nowhere to go but more shadows, and a smell like worms broken free of overturned earth.

"Zlyzen," Sedge rasped, arm coming around Tess like he would protect her.

But then the light flickered back like it had only been the shadow of a passing gull. Around the temple, the refugees cowered in confusion.

And at the center of the room stood Ren, Grey, and Vargo.

Seven as One

Hidden temple, Old Island: Cyprilun 13

Stepping out of the dream felt like stepping from a boat onto solid land. After the creeping, corrupted horror of Fiavla, suddenly everything was bewilderingly normal.

Ren tried to hold on to Alsius as they passed through—tried to hold on to him *as Alsius*, the man rather than the spider. Hadn't she once drawn the Black Rose's mask out of nothingness into reality? But that had been when the amphitheatre numinat was fraying the boundary between the two realms; in the absence of that, her control had limits. The threads of him slipped through her fingers, and when the temple solidified, he was a spider once more.

At least he was there, and Grey and Vargo with him, everyone safe and whole.

So focused was she on that, she didn't see her siblings until they barreled into her with hugs and glad cries.

While Ren was still giving reassurances and a garbled account of where they'd been to Sedge and Tess, Vargo took in the stares of the wide-eyed people around the fringes of the room. "You turned Kaius Rex's temple into a nytsa parlour?" he drawled. "Just how long have we been gone?"

"Eleven days!" Tess cried, dabbing Ren's tears and then her own with her sleeve.

Ren flinched at the number. Eleven days: the time it took for Fiavla to fall and the Ižranyi to become... what they'd become. She didn't dare assume it was coincidence.

"You're here just in time to make my life difficult." That came from a familiar hooded figure. "I was about to get these people off the island."

After so much time dealing with both versions, Ren could tell the genuine Rook from the false, Fontimi's old costume and the hood Tess had imbued. Without that, though, she would have never known it was Ryvček.

"What mean you, 'get these people off the island'?" Grey said. "What's happening?"

Sedge looked awkward. "So, while you were gone... Andrejek went through with it. Old Island's under Vraszenian control. Not just the Anduske; seems like half the continent came downriver to help retake Nadežra."

That prompted a garbled account in the other direction, Tess and Sedge explaining what Ren had missed—the bridges down, the river running foul, zlyzen tearing into the swimmers Caerulet had sent to infiltrate the island by night. *This* was more like expecting solid ground, only to fall down an unnoticed step. It hadn't felt like eleven days passed in the dream—it hadn't felt like *one* day—but suddenly she jolted into a world changed irrevocably from the one she'd left.

"Andrejek and his advisors are meeting with the Cinquerat," Sedge finished. "At the Sunrise Bridge gap, so they can't throw more than words at each other. While they're all busy, we're gonna get these people to safety."

The people in question were all northerners. Orrucio Amananto gave Ren an awkward wave.

She pressed her fingers into her eyes. *I was supposed to be here. I was supposed to help mitigate Laročja's influence.*

It wasn't too late. "They're meeting now?" she asked. Sedge nodded. "Then I may still be able to do something. The rest of you go; I will head to the Sunrise Bridge."

Grey caught her wrist. "We're going together."

She wanted to say yes. As Rook or as Grey, she wanted him by her side. But Laročja would be with Koszar, and besides… "You need to make certain my unwanted possession is secure," she murmured in Vraszenian.

"And I need to do something about the river numinata. Might skin whichever shortsighted imbecile made that call," Vargo growled. "If we end up with an outbreak of the bloody flux, might be I'll skin the lot of them and save Andrejek the effort."

Sedge crossed his arms and looked his most menacing. "I'll keep her safe. En't needed out there, and things here are rough."

Ren wasn't about to argue. "I'll join you when I can," she promised Grey. If Koszar was meeting diplomatically with the Cinquerat, then some amount of contact with the banks must be possible.

Reluctance was clear in every line of Grey's body. But he knew as well as she did that they would be more effective if they divided their efforts. He traced one finger down the ribbons braiding the wedding token into her hair: a reminder that they were now joined, in the world as well as in their hearts.

Brow pressed to hers and lips separated only by breath, Grey murmured, "I suppose it was too much to ask for a single night to enjoy it before everything came crashing down."

"All the more reason to keep yourself safe until we can," she whispered back, tugging his token to stress her warning.

"Heed your own advice, Szeren," he said, and kissed her to ensure his word was the last on the matter.

But the world couldn't wait for long. Reluctantly, Ren let him go, hugged Tess farewell, and gripped Vargo's knot-bound wrist. And then they were gone.

She was still in her wedding clothes, koszenie and all. After a moment's hesitation, she stripped that off and tied it under her skirt instead. Although the threads might not be cut, that didn't give her the right to claim Volavka connections, not when she hadn't even met her mother's kin.

As she finished smoothing her skirt, movement caught her eye.

The zlyzen that had taken her to Fiavla was there, slinking through a shadow. Ren swallowed hard. Even knowing what the creature was, fear and horror still tainted her pity. Whatever the zlyzen had been through, they'd also torn Leato apart.

Ignoring the creature, Ren drew a deep breath and said to Sedge, "Guess it's up to us to stop a war."

Dawngate, Old Island: Cyprilun 13

Before Ren left, diplomacy between the Anduske and the Cinquerat was supposed to take the form of a quiet meeting with Scaperto, Iascat, and Cercel on one side, Koszar and a few of his people on the other. She didn't know if that meeting had occurred in her absence, but the image was replaced by a new reality: two groups shouting across the fractured span of the Sunrise Bridge, with the sludge-brown Dežera passing below. The Liganti had the benefit of numinatria amplifying their demands—along with every petty disagreement muttered between them. The Vraszenians made do with speaking trumpets.

It wasn't just them, either. Crowds had gathered to watch and hear what they could, on both sides of the river. This wasn't like the Dreamweaver Riots, with furious Vraszenians against flights of hawks with dogs, but Ren felt no safer. People looked at her and Sedge as they worked their way forward, and she could feel those gazes weighing her appearance and his. Her Vraszenian finery earned her north-touched features a pass, but he collected an increasing number of scowls and curses.

Finally they broke through to the line of guards holding people back. At the sight of Ren, the guards' reflexive move to grab her stuttered to a halt.

She leapt on that opening. "I am Arenza—" What name should she add to that? None at all; that wasn't where her authority lay. "By the szorsas of the clans I was chosen to speak for the Ižranyi in the next cycle. I have a right and an obligation to be at this meeting. Let me pass."

A man wearing dull Meszaros browns scoffed. "Convenient that you're showing up now, Arenza of no clan. Where were you this past week and more?"

"In Ažerais's Dream, receiving insight from our goddess," Ren shot back. It wasn't even a lie. "Think you that you understand her wisdom better than I?"

Idusza shoved her way past the guard. "I know this one—and that brother of hers. Let them pass." She grabbed Ren, dragging her toward Andrejek's group. "You have Ola Tlegu's own timing, coming now, after all that has happened."

"It seemed only a few hours," Ren murmured back, studying the people at Koszar's side. Mevieny and Dalisva were nowhere to be seen. But Laročja was there, watching Ren's approach with hard eyes and a death-stiff smile.

On the far side of the bridge, Cibrial's sails were full with the wind of outrage. "—expect us to do what, relocate every Liganti currently living in this city? And I'd almost *like* to see you try to take over our trade agreements, just to place bets on how long it would take them to collapse. But you underestimate your bargaining power, Master Andrejek, if you think your control of that island is enough to bring the Cinquerat to its knees. I say we adjourn this waste of time. We'll see what tune you're singing after a week of drinking from your beloved Dežera."

Ren's heart leapt to see Donaia standing with the Cinquerat delegation. Her aunt clutched Scaperto's arm when she spotted Ren, the other hand pressing her heart. Though Donaia couldn't outshout Cibrial, her lips formed words Ren could make out: *Grey? The others?* Ren nodded, and Donaia sagged with visible relief.

It was the only relief to be had. Koszar snapped back, "Polluting this whole city to preserve your power is evidence of why you deserve it not. How will your own people feel, reduced to begging at your feet for clean water? And we control more than just this island—tell me, how fare those trade agreements you're so concerned with?" Then someone touched his arm, and he turned and saw Ren.

He handed off his speaking trumpet and swapped his cane to his left hand so he could touch his brow in respectful greeting. "Thank the Faces you're back safely. I regret we could not wait for your return, but the Great Dream approaches. Our people *must* have free access to our Lady's wellspring. I have promised it."

Ren wondered how he meant to keep his promise if the Cinquerat refused to deal with him. Already she regretted rushing here. A successful con relied on knowing the mark and the stage, and negotiations were no different. From Cibrial's words, she could guess that he'd demanded the Cinquerat cede Nadežra in its entirety: an opening gambit intended to soften them to more-balanced demands. Whose idea had that been—his, or Laročja's? If Ren had been here, she would have advised him to start at a less extreme point.

Now she was fighting a rearguard action. "Too much force will break a reed," Ren said. Empty words of clichéd wisdom, buying herself time to come up with better ones, but Koszar had never met a metaphor he didn't like.

"You have advice on how to bend our enemies?" Koszar asked. "You know them best."

"Yes." Laročja raised her voice, turning a private greeting into a public play. "Are you not one of them? Arenza Lenskaya *Traementatis.*"

The wind over the river whipped her words to the other delegation. Donaia stepped forward, hands balling into fists. "You have the *gall* to chide my niece for her choice of family?" she shouted back, the numinat magnifying her reply. "Breathtaking arrogance from a harridan whose abuse drove her own grandsons to this city, just to escape her!"

If Ren could have leapt across the shattered gap to push Donaia's words back into her mouth, she would have. Laročja grinned like a shark scenting prey. "Her Liganti aunt defends her! If this girl wishes to join the negotiations, on the other side of the bridge she should be. Among us she has no standing—only a title she won by theft and deceit. A title whose responsibilities she abandoned as soon as they suited her not. *I* stand with Ča Andrejek, as the voice of the lost Ižranyi. This slip-knot has no place here!"

The answer surged in Ren's throat. *I've* found *the lost Ižranyi, you fraud. If I asked, one of them would probably tear you apart!*

But her last shred of self-control kept her teeth clenched shut. She'd already misstepped, rushing into this confrontation without taking time to prepare. Both sides were looking at her with contempt, the Cinquerat because she stood with Koszar, the rebels because of her Liganti ties. The truth about the zlyzen was too horrifying; revealing it here would only add to the chaos—if anyone even believed her.

She had to wait. Bide her time, regain her footing, plan her next move. Be the calculating manipulator once more, for the good of Nadežra and everyone in it.

Her posture was Renata's cool assurance, even if her accent wasn't. "When all shout, none listen. If you regard me as an advisor, Ča Andrejek, then with Idusza I will go until you are ready to speak. If I am reviled as a spy, then I submit myself to her custody." She reached for Idusza, leaving it ambiguous whether she meant to take the other woman's hands, or offer her own wrists to be tied. "But there are things I must tell you, and things that must be done... or these bridges you've destroyed will never be mended."

The Depths, Old Island: Cyprilun 13

"You've got to admit there's some irony in *you* doing this," Vargo murmured to Ryvček as she led them through the tunnels. She might not be wearing the real hood, but she'd steeped herself in its impulses for years.

"Pragmatism," she answered, equally soft. "So far Andrejek has restrained his more bloodthirsty allies, but no sense waving more fresh meat than necessary. And if his grip fails, it will only drive support to the more bloodthirsty nobles."

She cast a glance over her shoulder. "Besides…half these people are shopkeepers. Not noble, not even delta gentry. Not all Liganti are cuffs, much less the target of my mandate. But some among the rebels don't make that distinction."

Vargo expected a comment from Alsius, but there was only silence as the Rook stopped and dragged a sack into the light. "Put these on," she said, passing wads of black cloth to the refugees. "If the shore watchers see light heads, they'll shoot. These will confuse them long enough for us to get away."

She sounded more confident than Vargo felt. The cloth turned out to be coats and hoods, stitched with flimsy spangles, the dye bleeding black smudges on whatever skin or fabric it touched. Rook costumes, and cheap ones. Vargo swallowed a snort.

"How many tailors did you rob for these?" Grey asked as Tess helped the Amananto boy squeeze into a too-small coat. The unmistakable noise of a ripping seam made her click her tongue in annoyance.

"Only three." The Rook bowed with a swirl of black wool and more than a little mockery. "I'm a popular costume."

The mob of mismatched Rooks forming in the dim tunnel looked more like a street farce than the terrifying night of Vargo's rescue from Tserdev. Ryvček might be right, though; the rumors flying about that night might buy them the hesitation they needed.

"Where's ours?" Vargo asked. The peacock-blue brocade of the coat he'd worn to the wedding wasn't suitable for a vigilante.

"Guests who fail to notify the host of their attendance have to fend for themselves." Ryvček tossed one last bundle to the tunnel's floor. "This was for Sedge. You two can fight over it."

Any hope that Grey had the real thing tucked away died when the other man shook his head. "Take it," Grey said. "I'll manage."

Lowering his voice, Vargo said, "You've got more experience with this shit than I do."

"And you look less Vraszenian than I do. We don't have time to argue. Put it on."

Ryvček shook her head at Grey while Vargo, swearing inwardly, stripped out of his coat and shoved himself into the stupid costume. "Caught so unprepared? I'm disappointed. Well, if you take a crossbow bolt between the eyes, maybe you'll learn a valuable lesson."

"Duck?"

Grey's flat tone and Ryvček's snort were a poignant reminder of Vargo's relationship with his own mentor. *You still there, old man? Tell me you can hear me.* If what Ren did in the dream had faded...

The response was small and subdued, like the spider body tucking itself deep under Vargo's borrowed collar, but it made him sag in relief. ::I'm here. Just...thinking.::

Not exciting intellectual thoughts about the realm of mind, not with that tone. As Ryvček led them onward, a graceful black swan capping a file of awkward cygnets, Vargo thought back, *It was hard, not hearing you. All those times I swore I'd give somebody's left arm to have my head to myself again—I take it back. I was worried. But we made it through; Ren fixed us.* He could still use a week of sleep, but he no longer felt like there was a hole in his heart, draining the life out of him. The aches of broken bones and bruised muscles were already fading.

Something tickled Vargo's cheek, Peabody venturing out. ::What you said in the dream...Truly, you think of me as a father?::

Think, nothing. It's official. Laid it out in the register. With a ward around Vargo's own name to protect Alsius from Sessat.

Peabody quivered with emotions too strong for a spider's small body to contain. ::I—::

Dull pain thudded through Vargo as the woman behind him swatted Peabody off his shoulder, followed by a second thud as the spider hit the wall. Vargo dove to catch him before he could tumble into the sloshing stream.

"The fuck is your problem?" he snarled, glaring up at the woman.

"Sp-spider!" she shrieked.

"Yeah, I know!"

Ryvček's hissed "Shut! Up!" came too late. From a branching passage came a shout, demanding to know who was there.

They were completely unprepared for a confrontation. Ryvček

was armed, but Grey, still in his wedding clothes, had only one of the decorative swords she'd stolen along with the costumes. Beyond that, it was all useless shopkeepers and delta pups. As Alsius scrambled onto his sleeve, Vargo fumbled in his waistcoat pocket for the blasting numinat he hadn't used in Fiavla. In this tunnel, it ought to work quite nicely...but if they needed more than one, they were fucked.

Then the darkness shifted up ahead—writhed—melted into a trio of living, wrong-jointed shadows.

Vargo froze. He didn't doubt Ren that the zlyzen were the surviving Ižranyi—if you could call it survival when they'd become horrible monsters. That didn't change the fact that they were *monsters*, and whatever kinship they felt toward Ren, he doubted it extended to anybody else—

Grey stepped forward.

All the moisture in Vargo's mouth dried to dust. Ren hadn't said it outright, but Vargo had caught the look in Grey's eyes when she said the creature that dragged them into Fiavla was Ižranyi. And hadn't Vargo seen it, following the trail of dead bodies from Grey's previous lives? A charred lump that looked like a dead zlyzen.

Looked like...or *had been*.

Grey didn't speak. Only stood, unmoving, his back to the whimpering tangle of Liganti.

Then the zlyzen darted away, toward the approaching sound. A moment later, there were screams.

Of terror rather than pain—at least Vargo hoped so. There were people he would gladly set zlyzen on, but random Vraszenian rebels weren't on that list. And Grey wasn't the killing sort.

But he'd just sent them off like a pack of well-trained hunting dogs.

Grey's eyes were wide enough to show the whites when Vargo came up to his side. "I remember it now," he said, barely audible. "I remember being...*that*."

The last, bleeding scrap of hope that Vargo's new-sworn brother hadn't once been *a fucking zlyzen* died. Then its corpse got booted out of his head by Ryvček's hand slamming into his shoulders. "*Go!*"

They were in the lowest passages now, filling with the rising tide, and there was light up ahead, an exit to one of the river's channels. There they found the centerpiece of Ryvček's plan: a splinter-boat, just narrow enough to fit into the tunnel. "We can't wait for the distraction I arranged," Ryvček snapped, pushing the refugees into the boat. "This will have to suffice."

Which meant the shore guards would still be alert. Even with Rook hoods hiding pale heads and stories of Rook flocks to introduce confusion, the boat would be an easy target—especially while it floundered up to speed under the disorganized rowing of people more used to paying skiffers.

"Give Serrado your oar. I need your back," Vargo said to Amananto. He didn't remember if the boy had been in the canal races, but he trusted Grey's strong arms.

With the young man's back as an unsteady desk, Vargo used a pencil stub to dig a Tricat into the wax of his two-part blasting numinat. Time and stasis. He didn't need a big explosion. He needed something longer-lasting and more contained.

The boat shoved out into the river, blindingly bright after so long in the dark. Shouts came immediately from up above; how long before arrows followed? Vargo folded himself over the stern, trying to reach the water, and had a vision of taking a bolt to the ass.

"Everyone, hang on," he shouted. And to Amananto, more quietly: "Don't let me fall overboard."

Then he clapped the two sides of the numinat together, slotting the focus into place.

Only Amananto's grip on Vargo's hips kept him from staying behind when their boat bucked straight out of the water. Timbers groaned in protest as they splashed down; the boat was made for the Dežera's muddy current, not the swells of the open sea. Vargo almost lost his hold on the numinat. The power flaring out of it churned the murky water to yellow foam.

But they were unquestionably *moving*, and the fast-receding shouts from the island's shore reached them better than the accompanying arrows. Despite everything, Vargo cackled with glee as

Grey did his best to steer the boat toward a landing on the Lower Bank.

His cackling faded when water began swirling around his boots. Pretty soon the race wasn't between arrows and escapees, but between the river and reaching safety. By the time they got to a stair, the boat was wallowing, succumbing to its wounds.

Vargo's cheap coat slapped against his knees, a dragging weight as he crawled from the river, the last in a line of sopping Rooks. He stank of dead fish, but the knowledge that he'd be shivering harder in only waistcoat and shirtsleeves kept him from throwing it off. *Not what that was designed for, eh?* he thought at Alsius. *But it worked.*

Then, with horror, he realized Peabody wasn't with him. "Alsius!" He splashed back the way he'd come, searching the thigh-deep water. If the spider had fallen into the river—

::It's all right, my boy. I'm on the island.::

What? Why?

::You'll be able to communicate better with Ren if I stay. My turn to play messenger boy, I suppose.::

The humor sounded forced. *Why didn't you tell me you were plan-ning that?*

::Because by the time I thought of it, you were getting ready to shoot that boat between the moons. I didn't want to distract you. Go; I'll be fine.::

He hated the thought of leaving Alsius behind, but their explosive flight had drawn attention from the hawks patrolling the Lower Bank. Catching Grey's conflicted grimace, Vargo echoed Alsius's own words. "Go. You need to make sure everything's secure at the townhouse. Fancy cuff, en't I? I'll take care of matters here."

Ryvček had already disappeared into the shadows. With a nod of thanks, Grey caught Tess's arm and did the same. Vargo straightened his stinking coat and waved the hawks down with a cheery hand. "Eret Vargo. Yes, I know we're all dressed as the Rook; don't you just hate it when everyone else picks the same Night of Bells cos-tume as you? These people need shelter. I'm invoking my right to the Vigil's assistance." For however much longer that right existed.

Between them, the Anduske and the Cinquerat had done a fine job of fucking things up while he was gone. Who knew what would still be standing when the dust settled? If Vargo had been in charge of the revolution, it wouldn't have begun until his victory was already assured.

Which might have meant another fifty years with nothing happening. The choice wasn't in his hands.

And since he couldn't take back those eleven days and stop what Andrejek had started, the only alternative was to hope the Nadežra that emerged on the other side was preferable to the one they went in with.

No. Not hope. Following a woman with a captain's hexagram pin, Vargo thought, *I'll make sure of it.*

Dawngate, Old Island: Cyprilun 13

Ren and Sedge were left to twiddle their thumbs in the entry hall of the Charterhouse for at least an hour before Koszar showed up. It gave her plenty of opportunity to study the defaced statues, and the new mottoes painted in below the old: *I deceive all. I manipulate all. I bribe all. I kill all. I damn all.* The words the statues had spoken on the Night of Hells.

Ren shuddered. Had Mevieny told someone? Had the reports filed with Tanaquis gotten out? Or were those nightmarish phrases echoing through other people's dreams?

She forced herself to look away, gaze settling on the next bench over . . . where a familiar splotch of color waited just outside swatting distance. "Alsius?" she whispered.

He scuttled up to perch on her knee. If he was talking, she couldn't hear him; she hadn't thought to bring the numinat from the temple. But they'd come up with some stopgaps over the past weeks of silence.

"Have they made it safely?" she whispered, slumping with relief when he waved his forelimbs once for yes. "You came back?" No. "Chose to stay?" Yes. "I imagine Vargo loved that."

...No.

She covered her laugh.

Peabody hid when Koszar entered, his cane clacking against the stone. "A boat just flew through the air from Duskgate to Westbridge, filled with Rooks," he said. "Most of whom seem to have been Liganti. Know you anything of this?"

Sedge answered for her as smoothly as he would have in their Finger days. "En't there been stories of the Rook all over the island? Seems to me it's probably his doing."

"Like you getting *onto* the island?" Koszar asked, raising an eyebrow at Sedge. "A report I had of someone matching your description swimming across three nights ago—but he vanished, apparently with the Rook's help."

"Sounds like a good trade to me," Sedge said nonchalantly, lounging back on the bench. "Pack of useless Ligs for one expert fist."

The amusement that bent Koszar's mouth had a sour cast, but he didn't press the point. "If your sister's safety I pledge, may I speak with her alone? Thank you." He gestured for her to follow him. Ren waited until his back was turned to slip Peabody into her pocket.

They went to Fulvet's office, which showed little evidence of mayhem. To Ren's relief, they truly were alone once Koszar closed the door behind them. He sank into Scaperto's large, padded chair with a relieved sigh and propped his cane against the desk. His leg must be paining him, she realized. He likely ran out of Alinka's imbued medicines after the occupation began.

"I'm sorry," she said, before Koszar could speak. "For barging into that meeting—I acted without thinking. And for not being here before."

"Where *went* you? From your sister we had a mad tale about zlyzen kidnapping you into—" Koszar stopped, searching her expression. "It wasn't a tale."

Ren rubbed her face. "I wasn't kidnapped, but...yes. Could I have been here to help you, I would have. Koszar, what was that madness at the bridge? You must know the Cinquerat will not cede the whole city without a fight!"

"Certainly I know. But if they are tensed to keep the whole together, they may relax when we let them have a portion." Koszar waved at a map of the city that hung on Fulvet's wall, the river sparkling like crushed lapis, the buildings and banks picked out in shining gold. "Against the Upper Bank Elsivin the Red broke herself, trying to claim it for her own. I have learned from her mistake. Let them have it; we will keep the rest."

Dividing the city in two. "Or in fifty years a lesson you will be for your successor, as Elsivin was for you. Draw lines on a map all you wish; people are not so easily divided. Have you forgotten your pattern, the meaning I read in The Mask of Hollows? Or have you placed your trust in a different szorsa?"

Koszar's expression hardened. "I have ideas of my own, Ren, and you have not been here. But I cannot disregard Laročja's counsel—not when half my forces came here at *her* word. If too timidly I act, they will abandon me. Or worse, overthrow me. How think you this rebellion will proceed then? Leaving the Upper Bank in Liganti hands may be a temporary solution, but better that than no solution at all."

"A solution that breeds more ill will is worst of all," Ren snapped.

Tense silence gripped the room. Ren broke it by sighing and spreading her hands on Scaperto's desk. "We fight each other instead of the Cinquerat."

"That is how Vraszan fell," Koszar agreed, sagging back. "After the loss of the Ižranyi, the city-states were less unified than before. By the time they recognized the scope of the Tyrant's threat, it was too late."

The Ižranyi. So often invoked at moments like these, when Vraszenians lamented the divisions among them. "Koszar, the Ižranyi are not all lost. A fragment of the clan survives. This is the revelation I went seeking."

If his leg could have borne it, he probably would have been on his feet. "How? Where?"

"You will like it not," Ren warned him.

By the time she was done explaining, she doubted any force could have helped Koszar stand. Into the hand braced over his mouth, he said, "The zlyzen...they have been defending the island. The stories say they cannot stay past dawn, yet for days they have been here. Even in daylight."

Ren's skin prickled with unease. The ordeal, with the zlyzen striking at Branek but leaving Koszar untouched. She was certain now that *had* been her work, all unwitting. When she'd prayed to Ižranyi for Branek's failure and Koszar's success, she'd called them. Was their defense of the island the same? But how could they remain here, when before they could not?

The kanina. A dance to call the ancestors—including twisted ancestors who'd burned their own koszenie to protect the rest from Fiavla's fall. In the moment before Kolya's appearance, she'd thought she glimpsed a wrong-shaped shadow in the corner. Was she responsible for both? His unexpected solidity, and zlyzen remaining in the waking world, rather than fading with the dawn?

Rather than share that horrifying thought with Koszar, she said, "For now you must keep this secret. I want to help them, and there must be a way to use this to our benefit—but my lesson I have learned. I will not act until I have thought." Not until she was prepared to confront Laročja. There *had* to be a way to pry her off the board, while aligning her supporters solidly behind Koszar and the Anduske.

He nodded, and Ren traced the wood grain on the surface of Fulvet's desk, thinking. "Koszar...know you that I was the woman seen in the dream? On the Night of Hells. When I met Dalisva and Mevieny."

"That was you?" His disbelieving snort was almost a laugh. "Is there a pot in this city to which you've added no salt? I trust you, Ren...but is it any wonder others question where your loyalty lies, when so many lies you have told?"

I deceive all. The twisted inscription under Argentet's statue. And it gave her an idea.

Ren said, "My loyalty lies with those who call this city home. What if, instead of tearing our home apart and leaving it to bleed, there was a way to stitch it together? Instead of mimicking the Liganti by drowning out all voices but our own, letting all voices speak?"

"Even if the Liganti agreed, know you how hard it is to get our people to accept new ways?" Elbows planted on the desk, Koszar buried his head once more in his hands. "I wasted reams of ink and paper trying to make it happen."

"Not new ways. *Old* ways."

That got his attention. "Mevieny and I saw *seven* statues in the Charterhouse that night," Ren said. "You know Nadežra's history better than I; was it not always ruled by a council? But of seven, rather than five."

Koszar said slowly, "Yes. One representative for each clan. But you are suggesting—"

"That it represent the Nadežra we have today," Ren said. "Vraszenian, and Liganti, and those who are neither—only citizens of this city."

In her pocket, Peabody twitched. She could only imagine the questions Alsius wanted to ask, the objections he wanted to raise. Koszar sat back, his gaze lost in details. He said distantly, "I would need to seed the suggestion so it comes from other mouths than yours. If you said the Dežera runs north, Laročja's faction would agree it flows south. But...it is worth consideration. Think you the Cinquerat would accept a weakening of their power?"

"I think they are tensed to keep the whole together," she said, throwing his words back at him. "This at least offers them a portion to hold."

And if they could destroy the medallions...then for the first time in two centuries, the balance of that power might be fair.

Koszar retrieved his cane. "Look frustrated when you leave, as if our conversation went poorly."

Grinning, Ren stood and offered him a pert, Seterin-style curtsy. "I can manage that."

Isla Prišta, Westbridge: Cyprilun 13

The door to the townhouse didn't open when Grey tried it. He could lift the latch, but something held the door shut.

From behind the thick panels came a shout: "Piss off! En't none of you getting in here, 'cept over our juicy, rotting corpses!"

Tess had shed her Rook costume; Ryvček had stripped down to nondescript black breeches and shirt. A swift glance said they were no more enlightened than he. Of course not: They'd been on the island.

The voice was that of a child. One of Arkady's lot, though Grey couldn't remember who. "It's me, Grey," he said through the door.

"En't falling for your tricks, neither!"

"You could just..." He pounded the door frame in frustration. "Didn't anyone think to make a peephole?"

"So you can poke out our peepers? We en't stupid. Give us the passphrase or get crusted."

Tess nudged Grey aside before he could kick the door. "Doom-claw's real name is Constable Fuzzybritches."

There was a moment of silence. Then scraping as something heavy gouged grooves into the hall flooring. "How did you know the passphrase?" Grey asked.

"I don't." Tess winked, and the door creaked open.

A boy scowled and beckoned with one scrawny arm. "Well, get in here! Before somebody sees our guard is down!"

There was no one on the street except ordinary residents, but the three of them hurried inside, past the kids and the cabinet they'd hauled back from the door. Through the opening to the parlour, Grey saw other furniture had been tipped up to block the windows. "Are you worried the Old Island situation will spill over?"

"Naw." That was Arkady, giving the front hall a suspicious peer before advancing. "Some shitlicker broke in a few days ago. I figured him for a thief—and he sure didn't expect the welcome he got." Snickers came from the kids, but Arkady wasn't laughing. "Only, after that somebody came around and said we was squatting here. Tried to get the Vigil to drive us out, but that man of Tess's been keeping them off. Still, we been bottling our piss in case they come back." She waved at a stockpile of wine bottles by the door, wedding trash they hadn't had a chance to dispose of.

Fear gutted Grey as he raced downstairs. They'd filled the wine cellar with junk to cover up the flagstone that hid Tricat, but Arkady and her gang had ransacked the room for barricade material. Or was that someone else's work, searching for Tricat? The flagstone was in place, but he couldn't trust it. He waited an endless moment while Tess shooed off the onlookers before he pried it up.

Since the containment numinata he'd devised seemed not to be much use, Vargo had instead taken inspiration from his own adventures retrieving Tricat from the dream and scribed one that held the medallion down like a magnet. The silk pouch they'd placed the medallion in was still there. Grey dared not touch it, not even to check its contents, but a lump the right size and shape showed through. No sign of disturbance. He put the flagstone back and slumped, exhaling slowly.

Tess had been consulting with Arkady in the hallway. "She said Pavlin's running the water station on the border of Kingfisher and Westbridge."

"Go," Grey said. He recognized the yearning in her posture; it was the same yearning he felt, to be with the one he loved.

Her curls were too lank and matted to bounce with her nod. "Might be he knows who was trying to get in."

"I'll reinforce Arkady's defenses." Grey pressed fingers into his brow to ward off a headache. "But all the people who might be seeking it have the power to force their way. It can't stay here."

Tess bit her lip. Because while what Grey said was true, with Ren trapped on the Old Island, there weren't many who could take it without cursing her. He might be married to her, but he wasn't in the Traementis register.

Once Tess was gone, Grey found Ryvček at the kitchen door, helping the kids improve a booby trap that would swing a wine bottle into the skull of any intruder. "Safe?" she asked, and when Grey nodded, she said, "Good. I should see to my own."

He wondered where she kept Quinat, and wrestled with whether he should ask. Before he made up his mind, pounding came from the front door, intermingled with the jangling of the bell. Grey had retrieved his sword; now he bared the steel as the two of them raced upstairs.

A familiar voice came through the door. "Ren! I've figured it out! That dance at your wedding gave me the idea, though I had to work out how to redirect the energy into— Oh, no one ever cares about explanations, never mind—just let me in!"

Grey sheathed his sword and seized the cabinet himself, not waiting for the kids. If Tanaquis meant what he hoped...

She pushed inside without a single question about where he'd been. "Why did you put a cabinet in the front hall? Never mind. We'll need to do this in the temple, but—"

He cut her off by the expedient of a hand over her mouth, suspecting that in Tanaquis's current state of distraction, nothing else would suffice. "Not here," he said, nodding at the children. "Come with me. Arkady, *nobody* listens in."

"Got it!" Arkady said, and stationed herself at the bottom of the staircase like she would bite anyone who tried to get by. Anyone except Ryvček, who gave her a look that said *try it* and walked right past.

"Where's Ren?" Tanaquis asked, brow furrowing as Grey steered her upstairs. The study was equally disheveled—Arkady and her kids had been thorough—but it had a door they could close behind them. "I don't want to have to repeat myself."

Ryvček leaned against the door, clearly listening for anybody who might get past Arkady. They'd already fed Tanaquis a story about the Rook passing Quinat off to a safer holder—it wasn't even false, though it was seriously incomplete—so she didn't give Ryvček a second look. Grey righted a chair, saying, "Ren's still on the island. When we came out of the dream, we were in the temple."

"You were in the dream? Why? Has Ren been talking to that szorsa's spirit again?"

Had Tanaquis really failed to notice their disappearance? Had nobody told her after the fact? Apparently so. Grey weighed the benefits of explaining their journey to Fiavla against the likelihood that Tanaquis would become irreparably distracted, and decided it wasn't worth it. "You've figured out how to destroy the medallions?"

"Yes!" Confusion vanished in the fire of her delight. "We don't even have to kill anyone, because she's already dead. We put the medallions in a modified funerary numinat, and then we give *her* a funeral. Send her soul to the Lumen. It'll be like pulling a thread and having a whole seam come undone." Tanaquis waved a sleeve at him. Now that he looked, he could tell it had been pulled off, then reattached with stitches so bad they would embarrass even Arkady.

"Her? Meaning the Zevriz szorsa?" Tanaquis hadn't sat in the chair; Grey almost sank into it himself. "You want to send her to the *Lumen*? She's Vraszenian."

Tanaquis merely blinked, as if this were irrelevant.

He gritted his teeth. "We don't go to the Lumen."

She brushed the reminder aside. "Clearly. And if you had proper funeral rituals, we might be able to do this your way." Tanaquis raked gloveless fingers through her hair, so oily they left furrows. "But Vraszenian rituals require family members, or those koszenie shawls, and we don't have either. So that's no use. If we can send her to the Lumen, at least she returns to *some* kind of cycle."

"No." Grey set his sword gently on the desk so he wouldn't be tempted to use it. "Figure out another way."

Tanaquis shrugged. "There *is* another way. We've had it for ages. Kill all the holders and send ourselves to the Lumen, or give all the medallions to one person and kill *them*. Their soul takes the Primordial energy out of the world, and all our problems are solved. But no one wanted to do that. My way harms nobody, and it helps a trapped spirit move on!"

Ryvček shifted off the door and spoke quietly. "Will she not be reborn into corruption? Our dream perhaps can purify a soul, or at least divide its poison. But your Lumen cannot remove this stain."

That earned her an impatient chop of Tanaquis's hand. "Not the Lumen, no. *Living.* It may take her soul lifetimes, but it will recover."

"What?" The weight on Grey's heart lessened by a hair. "Faella told Ren it stays with you through death."

"Yes, because it's living that cleanses your soul. Not the purifying tribulations of the numina." Tanaquis clicked her tongue. "Faella told me that herself, from her vision during Ghiscolo's ritual. She should have known better."

No doubt she *had* known better, and had given Ren a half-truth out of spite. Grey sagged against the desk. *Living. Living burns it off.* As he had lived through life after life, clan after clan.

Laročja was wrong. He wasn't atoning for a crime. He was purging the last traces of the Primordial stain that had blighted his soul, five hundred years ago.

"Can we move along?" Tanaquis asked, twitching. "I've been working on this for so long—now that we have an answer in hand..."

Whatever relief Grey had found for himself, it didn't ease his reservations about the szorsa. "You want to tear a woman's *soul* away from her people. Send her to an unfamiliar afterlife—and how will she be reborn? Among strangers? We *can't* condemn her to that." He directed his plea to Ryvček. She might be city-born Vraszenian, but surely she understood.

And his teacher nodded. But what she said was "Think you the choice should be ours?"

The Zevriz szorsa had cut herself from her name, from her people, out of shame for what she'd done. What if that shame drove her to cut herself from Ažerais as well? Assuming they could even make her broken spirit understand the cost.

But Ryvček was right. They shouldn't make that choice for her.

Heart heavy, Grey said, "I'll get word to Ren." She would hate this option as much as he did...but maybe she could find a better way. "And I'll start looking for a way to smuggle a group of nobles *onto* the Old Island."

21

The Mask of Ashes

Even with most routes across the river closed off by the conflict, gossip spread remarkably fast. A Vigil report said Grey Serrado and Derossi Vargo had rescued a group of Liganti shopkeepers from the Old Island, and it seemed like the whole Upper Bank knew about it a bell later.

As soon as she heard, Giuna set off on foot to Eastbridge. The report hadn't mentioned Ren, but Vargo might be able to tell her what under the Lumen's light had happened between the wedding and now.

She was right, though she had to pick the explanation out of his sulfurous curses toward whatever idiot had deactivated the river numinata. "It wasn't Mother's decision," she assured him seven times over, worried that his fury might spill onto the wrong target. "The Cinquerat did it without asking."

"Of course they did," Vargo said darkly, and went back to cursing.

Giuna had only just managed to extract the full tale when more people arrived. "Tess!" she yelped, throwing her arms around the other woman. "I'm so glad you're all right! First Ren gone, and then you disappeared, too—we didn't know if you'd gone after her—"

Tess patted her shoulder. "No, I was on the island when the bridges blew. Ren's still there—"

"Mother said she saw her at the bridge. But why—"

Their questions and explanations tumbled over one another like anxious puppies seeking comfort. Tess wasn't alone, either; Pavlin had brought not just her across the guarded Floodwatch Bridge, but Grey and Oksana Ryvček. And, to Giuna's absolute surprise, Tanaquis.

Tess soon hurried off with Pavlin to tell Donaia what she could. Giuna turned to her cousin, demanding, "Where have you *been*? You might as well have vanished with Ren, for all we've seen of you."

Tanaquis was sitting with one hand pressed to her heart, staring at the wall. At Giuna's question, she blinked awake. "What?"

"She's been helping us," Grey said. "And thanks to her, we may have a plan at last."

Giuna could hardly understand half of what followed, especially once Vargo started asking Tanaquis questions about numinatria. But she understood enough to anticipate the objections he raised at the end. "It might work, magically speaking. The pragmatics are a different matter. Getting everybody onto the island..." He rubbed his brow. "Hell, that's the *easy* part. First we have to convince Cibrial and Faella to stop sucking at the Primordial teat."

"Grey and I have swords," said Ryvček, with a sharp smile. "Not to mention the Rook. The three of us can prod them into cooperation—or pry loose what they hold."

"But—" Giuna said, before catching herself. Ren must not have told Ryvček she'd guessed the Rook's identity. *Oh, the piles of secrets!* Would anything ever sweep them entirely away?

Then again, she was holding a secret of her own.

Nerves made her fiddle with a loose thread on her surcoat as she said, "You won't have to do that. At least, I hope not. I've got someone I trust in the Oyster Crackers working to retrieve Quarat, and Parma's made arrangements for Illi-ten. Mede Beldipassi's still in question, but I've seen shoals that were more stable—and besides,

Mother blasted him with the Lumen's own fire recently. I suspect he'll go along with what the Rook tells him."

When silence greeted her news, she looked up. Tanaquis was distracted again, and the other three were all too self-controlled to openly gape, but the silence itself measured their surprise. Giuna swallowed. "I hope I didn't overstep?"

Ryvček broke their tableau with a bark of laughter. "Blood be damned; no question that you're Ren's cousin. Well has she mentored you, Alta Giuna."

It shouldn't have felt like high praise. But it was.

Then Tanaquis deflated the mood. "If Ren is trapped on the island, who's going to retrieve Tricat? It would be a shame if she isn't the one to destroy it. I wouldn't have known pattern held any substance at all if it weren't for her." Her eyes gleamed like those of a fever victim.

Giuna's throat clogged with loathing. Everything Ren had said about the medallions, the ongoing horror she saw in her mother every time Donaia realized how thoroughly Tricat had poisoned their house, the ways Cibrial and Faella were using that power to keep Nadežra in their grip... Giuna wanted to crawl right out of her skin to get away from her own thoughts.

But if she understood how these things worked, there were only a few possible answers. And only one she could accept.

"I'll take it."

Grey understood first. Before he could object, Giuna said, "That way it stays in the register, right? So Ren won't be cursed, and I can give it back to her for your ritual. I won't have it for very long." Even a heartbeat was too long. But if this helped them get rid of it forever, she'd take the risk.

"It isn't just you," Vargo said. "If you take Tricat, its influence, however small, will spread through your register. Ren's warded, but you're not."

"I think we're all warded. Right?" Giuna looked to Tanaquis for confirmation. Her cousin nodded hesitantly. "Mother told me. There's marks around *all* the names."

Vargo snorted. "Chalk one up for overkill."

That didn't assuage Grey's worries. "Your mother would never agree," he said, gently, the fond worry in his eyes reminding Giuna of Leato.

But Leato always begged forgiveness instead of asking permission. "I won't tell her. Mother would take it herself, to spare me—but she grew up under Tricat's influence. She's far too vulnerable. I was born after Letilia stole the medallion. I'm the safest choice."

"She's right," Tanaquis said. "Well, Idaglio would be safe. And Nencoral—wait, she left, didn't she? And Meppe...hmmm. I wonder if there would be any interesting aftereffects from House Indestor, given the resonance between Tricat and—"

"You and I can discuss that later," Vargo said smoothly. "I have to go to the Lower Bank anyway, to keep in touch with Alsius and let Ren know the plan. I'll take Alta Giuna to retrieve it—assuming she doesn't mind my company."

Grey exhaled his objections unspoken. "As much as I dislike involving more people...this isn't a problem we can solve without help." It ended on a wry snort. "Which is true of everything in Nadežra these days. Go; we'll see to the rest."

It wasn't until Giuna and Vargo were out the door that she recalled Carinci Acrenix at the Theatre Agnasce, months ago, saying, *I'll ask that you not gossip about my son.*

"Vargo," she said, "who's Alsius?"

He eyed her, then groaned. "I'll explain on the way."

Westbridge, Lower Bank: Cyprilun 13

Shortly before everything went to hell, Vargo had acquired an ostretta on Coster's Walk in Westbridge. It was closed for renovations—he hoped it would still be *standing* for renovations when the dust settled—but that meant it was empty when he crept inside at sunset and headed for a window overlooking the river.

You there, old man?

::Aren't you going to call me 'Father' now? It would be more respectful.::

Vargo leaned against the wall, grinning in relief. *I've gone, what, sixteen years without being respectful? Don't see no reason to start.*

::Ren's listening.::

Your point?

Vargo spotted the bright copper and green of Ren's wedding sash on a short landing jetty. A cluster of Vraszenians patrolling the shore walk watched her warily, but didn't hassle her.

Pushing the window open, Vargo settled in the casement, one boot propped against the frame, the other swinging free over the edge. *Looks like the Anduske haven't given Ren too much trouble. You're both safe?*

::For now. But Caerulet's strategy with the river numinata is distressingly effective. They've gone through most of the clean water they had stored.::

In the long pause that followed, Vargo could only watch the movement of Ren's hands and wonder what she was saying that Alsius refused to pass on. Finally Ren's arms crossed, and Alsius sighed. ::People are starting to get sick. And there have been some scuffles over water distribution.::

Scuffles. Alsius could be dramatic, except when he was deliberately obfuscating. *You mean riots.*

::Nothing on the scale of last spring.::

Not yet. But the longer this went on... *Well, this doesn't solve the water problem, but it will help on other fronts. Tanaquis thinks she has a workable plan at last.*

Predictably, his account of the plan perked Alsius up immeasurably. At this distance Vargo couldn't see the bouncing dot that was Peabody—hopefully Alsius retained enough sense to avoid being seen by others—but it came through in the excited mental replies, his lament that he couldn't personally examine Tanaquis's design. *Ren all right with this?* Vargo asked, when Alsius paused to regroup. *Grey accepted on the grounds that the szorsa be allowed to choose, but...*

He wished he could hear her reply directly. After a moment, Alsius said, ::She says her mother, Ivrina, was cremated Liganti-style. She believes—I apologize, Ren; I will use your precise words—she *chooses* to believe that this does not cut a person's soul off from Ažerais.::

It wasn't an issue Vargo had ever given much thought to; theology was more Alsius's field. But he hoped for Ren's sake that she was right.

Rather than say that, he added, *Mind you, we still have to get onto the island. I'm open to any bright ideas.*

Another pause. ::Ren believes she can arrange something with Koszar. She also wants to know how on earth you persuaded Cibrial and Faella to play along.::

We didn't. Giuna and Parma have been busy while we were away. They won't move until we're ready to head for the island—we don't want to tip our hand—but we're done waiting for that pair to cooperate. Vargo picked at a bit of peeling paint. His broken hand was mending fast, as if making up for lost time. *When we take their medallions, the curse will hit their families, hard.*

::The worst effects shouldn't manifest immediately,:: Alsius said. ::We'll do something about it after the medallions are gone—presuming the destruction doesn't solve that problem for us.::

Vargo huffed a humorless laugh. *Sure, normally it takes a while. But it's quicker and worse the more you use your medallion, right? Those two have dived headfirst into the Primordial sea, trying to keep Nadežra under their control.* He didn't think they were using Quarat and Illiten to influence anyone's desires, but only because neither of them was inscriptor enough to know how.

He liberated a strip of paint, steeling himself for the next part of this conversation. *Giuna's at the townhouse right now . . . collecting Tricat.*

Silence.

Alsius?

::Ren hasn't said anything yet.::

Vargo watched her across the brown waters of the river, and saw the moment her shoulders sagged. A few breaths later, Alsius said, ::She accepts the necessity, though neither of us is pleased. Giuna is . . . a sweet girl.::

She would still be a sweet girl when this was over. Because Vargo wasn't going to let that medallion stay in her keeping one heartbeat longer than it had to.

The burnished bronze light of sunset was fading, sinking both Ren and the river into shadow. The patrols along the bank were lighting lanterns. Vargo said, *I'll keep working on an alternate plan in case Koszar doesn't come through.*

It seemed Ren had been speaking in the pause. Alsius said, ::Before you go, Ren has a favor to ask. Can you contrive a way to get something small and lightweight to us? She needs one more thing from the townhouse.::

Duskgate, Old Island: Cyprilun 15

"For your own safety this is," Andrejek said, loud enough to be heard well beyond where Sedge stood. Laročja's supporters were gathered on the quay, to make certain Sedge really left. "And to respect our debts to Ča Vargo, for the aid he's given our cause."

"Yeah. Thanks," Sedge grumbled as he boarded the scow set to take him across to the Lower Bank. He didn't have to fake the worried look he cast toward Ren. He hated leaving her here alone, especially since isolating her played right into Laročja's hands.

Even if Ren was the one who'd manipulated Laročja into insisting that he leave. It was all part of the plan, she assured him.

Sometimes, being Ren's brother gave him headaches *and* ulcers.

"Just don't dump me halfway 'cross," he told the rowers, casting a wary glance at the murky water. "Don't fancy taking a bath in piss."

Not that he was worried with this particular pair. They might have left the Leek Street Cutters to take up the fight for the Vraszenians of Nadežra, but he'd known Smuna and Ladnej since they were ickle, gap-grinning runners. No longer tied didn't mean all loyalty was gone.

That was why he'd suggested them, when Ren insisted she needed him to leave the island.

"You let her get hurt," Sedge said to Andrejek, nodding meaningfully at Ren, "and you and I are gonna have our *own* war." That was for the crowd, too...but he meant every word.

Andrejek nodded, and Smuna pushed off.

The scow was a nice one, fresh lacquered and not leaking even a little. Much better than the one sunk after the Dockwall prison break. "We should make *you* row," Ladnej said as she set to work with her oar.

"Sure, if you want to go in circles," Sedge muttered, sitting in the bow with his back to the rowers and the Old Island so nobody could see his face. "But if you help me with something, I'll be your bilge boy for a week."

Silence, except for the splashing strokes. Then: "What you need?"

"Boss—I mean, Vargo—he's got a package for Ren. Don't worry; it's little. Just pass it to her when nobody's looking."

He didn't need to turn around to see the look they gave each other. Sedge almost added, *and don't peek,* but bit it back. That would only guarantee they *did* peek.

Smuna asked, "How's he gonna get it to us without anybody seeing? Cinquerat's got guards on the bank. They en't gonna let him ship something back across with us."

"Vargo will have a plan," Sedge said, with complete confidence and absolutely no clue.

"How little?" Ladnej asked. She'd always been the more world-wise of the two. "If it's poison, I'm dumping it in the channel."

Sedge chewed down his flash of fear. Just what they needed, Ažerais's gift swept out to sea. "No poison. Nothing that'll hurt anyone. Just a message, and Vargo's got no other way to get it to her. No way he trusts."

He leaned into the implication of that. *Vargo's trusting you.*

Once, that trust was as good as a gold forro. But seemed everything on the Lower Bank lost value one day. Hopefully, a debt from Vargo at least was still worth *something.*

They hadn't responded. Sedge finally twisted in his seat and found Smuna studying the gleaming brass of the oar lock and the shining lacquer of the boat's rail. She said, "Suppose it couldn't hurt, helping out the boss again."

Not even *one last time*. Grinning, Sedge turned back to face the rapidly approaching bank—

And fell off his bench as a crossbow bolt thudded into the scow's pretty rail. A bolt, Sedge realized a moment later, with a tiny, wax-coated parcel stuck to the shaft.

"*This* was Vargo's plan?" Smuna hissed.

"Ah..." A glance at the bank revealed Vargo, Varuni, and a squad of hawks screeching blame at each other for the misfired bolt. Tess's man Pavlin was among them, sheepishly taking the brunt of it. "Guess so."

The scow jerked with the force of Ladnej yanking the bolt free of the wood. Sedge didn't have time to steady himself before she shoved him into the water. "You owe me another scow, fucker!" she shouted at Vargo as Smuna hastily turned them about and began rowing hard for the Old Island.

Lips pressed tight to avoid swallowing murky water, Sedge swam for shore. Varuni, bless her, kept to her usual silent judgment. Vargo greeted him with a smirk. "Good to have you back."

Sedge spread his dripping, stinking arms. "Keep smiling like that," he promised, as sweetly as Ren might, "and I'll thank you with a hug."

Dawngate, Old Island: Cyprilun 15

Judging by the look Smuna gave Ren—and the time that elapsed between their return and the wax-coated packet being palmed to her—they'd opened Vargo's delivery. Ren had known the risk, and taken it anyway.

Because she wasn't at all sure that she could manage another private conversation with Koszar. After that first time, Laročja had been haunting him closer than his own shadow, making sure Ren had no chance to interfere.

The Black Rose was a different matter.

She was just another shadow in the night as she spider-walked a ledge outside the Charterhouse. Climbing into Fulvet's office through his window, she had an abrupt, powerful yearning for the Rook at her side. This kind of thing was more fun with company.

She was sitting tailor-style on the desk, playing dreamweaver's nest, when Koszar came through the door. The half dozen advisors who'd been at the Sunrise Bridge negotiation clogged the hallway behind him.

And at his shoulder stood Laročja.

Djek, Ren thought, even as she dropped her thumbs and twisted her hands to make a rose out of string. In Liganti she said, "Ča Andrejek. We must speak. Alone."

Calculation flashed across Laročja's face, replaced a moment later by insincere awe. "The Black Rose! Of you I have heard many tales. A spirit sent by our Lady herself...That is what people say, at least."

"People tell many stories about me," Ren agreed, giving Laročja a knife-sharp smile. Still in Liganti, with the Black Rose's Nadežran accent, though Laročja had spoken in Vraszenian.

Awe turned into artful puzzlement. "But your voice. I heard it said—I believed it not—how odd, that the hand of Ažerais should speak thus."

"Why is it odd? The Wellspring of Ažerais sits at the heart of Nadežra. Many who venerate her sound like I do." The truth was that Ren didn't dare speak Vraszenian in front of Laročja or Koszar. Her ease with the language had improved enormously, but not so much that she trusted her ability to disguise her voice in it.

"All the more reason to regain the purity we had before the Liganti corruption." Laročja spread her hands, head low in feigned humility. "But I am an old woman, with only road dust in my wrinkles and hope for a free Nadežra in my heart. What know I of such things?"

Ren untangled the string and looped it around her wrist. "Road dust, hmmm. I'd expect anyone who speaks proudly of that to be aware of how often her people intermarry along the Dawn and Dusk Roads."

"Mingling bloodlines abroad is different." Laročja's smile hardened. "Our holy city should not be polluted."

Behind Koszar, still in the hallway, several of his advisors shifted uncomfortably. *Thank you for taking the bait*, Ren thought. Nobody liked hearing their family called "polluted," and the odds that they had kin abroad were high.

Sliding off the desk, she said, "Do you also embrace such views, Ča Andrejek? Perhaps I wasted my time in coming here. Ažerais disdains closed minds and closed hearts."

"Wait," Koszar said, before Ren could take more than a step toward the window. "Lady Rose, my mind and heart are open to your counsel. The rest of you, leave us." His grip on Laročja's arm was firm as he guided her across the threshold and closed the door.

Giving Ren a lopsided smile, he limped to one of the chairs Scaperto kept for visitors. "May I sit?"

"By all means." Ren didn't join him. Grey had said once, *The Rook doesn't do anything so ordinary as sit in a chair.* The Black Rose should be the same. But she leaned against the desk, her manner casual, until Koszar was settled. Then she said, "I have a favor to ask. And I'll warn you now that it's a big one."

"You saved my life, Lady Rose. Anything I can do, I will."

She smiled with better cheer than she felt. "Excellent. I need you to allow a group of people onto the Old Island and off it again. With no interference, and no questions."

He gaped. Ren added, "You have my word that this is no attempt to undermine your rebellion. In fact, what I'm doing will make it easier to achieve your goals."

"But—"

She watched his protest snag on *no questions*. Koszar's grip tightened on the head of his cane, as if he dearly wished to get up and pace, but couldn't. Muscles tensed in his jaw, releasing only enough for him to say, "You ask a great deal."

"I know. I wouldn't if it weren't important."

His head bent. Then, softly, he said, "You ask a great deal for someone I know not."

Before she could respond, he went on. "Lady Rose, you saved our sacred wellspring, and you saved me. But at other times... Where were you when this rebellion began? When I faced Branek in the ordeal? Nothing have I seen of you since the Kiralič was rescued— yet in Floodwatch you appeared, when Derossi Vargo needed aid. If you are Ažerais's servant, if you are the protector of Nadežra... why is what we do here of so little importance to you?"

His plaintive query cut deep. *I've been at your side*, Ren thought. But not recently, and he didn't know about the other times.

How could she convince him to trust her? She couldn't admit who the people were; they'd have far too much value as hostages. She couldn't tell him their purpose, not when Primordial magic was involved. She didn't even have the deck of cards Grey had given her in the dream—and that was more Arenza's tactic, anyway, not the Black Rose's.

So let Arenza persuade him.

"You know not what I *have* been doing." Ren slipped into Vraszenian, into the tone and cadence he'd come to expect from another. "You know not that I *have* been helping. And would have been here... had I not been walking in Ažerais's Dream."

Silence. Koszar couldn't seem to find his voice.

Ren didn't dare take off her mask. Fulvet's door was imbued against eavesdropping, but it was also unlocked; anyone could walk in. She hoped the admission would be proof enough. "For some time Mevieny has known. Dalisva, too. I would prefer you keep my secret, as they have."

"But..." He stared, as if trying to see through the black lace mask. "How?"

"During the last Veiled Waters, Ažerais blessed me with this guise so I could stop Mettore Indestor from destroying the wellspring. I cannot say I understand her purpose in doing so, but I have tried to honor it. I honor it still when I ask this favor of you."

Koszar let out a slow, wavering breath. Then inhaled, and let out another. "If Laročja knew the truth—djek. The Black Rose, half-Liganti. She might drop dead of apoplexy."

Would save us all some headaches if she did. "Can you do what I need? Time is extremely pressing."

He thumped his cane and pushed to his feet. "If two days more you can wait, then the Night of Bells. We're arranging a celebration—such as we can, under the conditions. All eyes will be elsewhere."

The Night of Bells. When the Tyrant had died, and his chain of office was broken.

Koszar would ask the reason if he saw the smile that wanted to break through. Ren only said, "Two nights from now. So be it."

Eastbridge, Upper Bank: Cyprilun 17

Only four days off the Old Island, and Tess found herself in the soup again—this time by her own choice.

Her feet ached and lower back was kinked from standing on the hard marble floor of a Rotunda annex. Five chairs had been dragged in, probably from nearby townhouses. Mismatched but comfortable, except for the one supporting Utrinzi Simendis's bony ass; he seemed to thrive on discomfort. Though if that was what it took for him to resist the lure of his medallion, Tess could only cheer him on.

She only faced four Cinquerat members, though. Cercel had abandoned her chair once it became clear Tess had little information of value to Caerulet; she had bigger fires to put out than one Ganllechyn seamstress with questionable loyalties.

Cibrial Destaelio, perching on the edge of her chair as though it was padded with needles, clearly did not agree.

"You claim you had *no* foreknowledge of this violent attack on our city?" she drawled, in the disbelieving tone of someone who'd already decided the answer.

That didn't stop Tess from disappointing her. "I didn't, Your Charity." She turned to the other three members of the tribunal, appealing to logic since she lacked much skill for lying. "Would I have been on the Sunrise Bridge when it blew if I knew what they were about?"

"Perhaps you were on that bridge precisely *because* you knew," Cibrial said. "Perhaps you were working with them. We know your accomplice and former mistress has been. You expect us to believe that gnat told you nothing?"

"As she's said multiple times," Scaperto Quientis cut in, tapping his knee impatiently. "I doubt her answer will change just because you harp on it. May we return to more-useful matters?"

His interruption was a kindness, and perhaps a response to the rising color in Tess's cheeks. Much more of Cibrial's vile talk against her sister, and Tess might be tempted to feed the woman a good old Lacewater lunch: a generous helping of her fist, served with a side of Cibrial's own bloody teeth.

"Yes, please," Iascat Novrus said. "Or the rebels will have won the city before we learn anything of use." Between them, Fulvet and Argentet had been doing a good job of goading Prasinet into digressions. Which was helpful, since Tess could hardly concentrate on what she was here to do when she was arguing for Ren's innocence—and her own.

She has the Quarat medallion on her, I'm sure of it, Giuna had cried in frustration the morning after Tess escaped the Old Island aboard a raft of Rooks. *She's using it too often to keep it elsewhere.*

But Esmierka couldn't spot it, and with only one chance to make the lift—her scar was too recognizable to allow for another—they couldn't risk being wrong.

So like the helpful fool she was, Tess offered to present herself to the Cinquerat to answer questions about her time on the occupied Old Island. If anyone could spot a hidden medallion in the broken drape of a skirt or a strange misalignment of tailoring, she could.

She'd hoped her own efforts to save a gaggle of gentry would protect her from accusations of treason. She failed to account for Cibrial Destaelio's fury at Ren and everyone connected to her.

Fulvet won't let you land in prison, she told herself, wiping her sweating palms dry on her skirts and focusing her attention on the fall of Cibrial's surcoat. Though Tess had created ensembles for several of the Destaelio daughters, she'd never outfitted the house head herself. Cibrial still favored older styles, shapeless dresses stiffened with reed and whalebone. The cornucopia of falling fruit embroidered on it was picked out in gold. Or threads that shimmered like it, anyway—Tess would eat her own apron if they were truly gold. The stitching was so thick, it almost obliterated the background of verdant green velveteen; with real gold, Cibrial wouldn't be able to stand for the weight.

How was she supposed to puzzle out the location of one thumb-sized medallion by sight alone, when Cibrial wore the contents of an entire coffer spilling down the front and back of her surcoat?

Something Iascat said must have snapped the last thread of Cibrial's patience. She stood with barely a rustle. "This entire endeavor is a pointless waste of my time; you're all too much in that liar's thrall to do anything to stop her. If you'll excuse me, I'm returning to Whitesail, where I can do some good."

Tess's pulse leapt. Cibrial was leaving, and taking with her what might be their last chance to steal Quarat.

Before Tess could think better of it, she lunged forward and caught Cibrial's trailing sleeve. "Your Charity must forgive me for not giving adequate answers. It's just... I was so distracted by this embroidery. Who did the imbuing? It's so good, I could almost mistake the fiber for real byssus!" As she babbled, she tugged and pulled, testing the weight and drape of Cibrial's clothing for anything out of place.

Yanking the cloth free of Tess's groping hands, Cibrial snapped, "It *is* real byssus, you charlatan! You think I'd waste money on false goods?"

"Is... is that what you were told?" Tess cringed under that glare, honestly cowed. Still, she got the rest of her insult out. "Well, you must know better than I what's real, and what's only gilt imbued to fool an easy mark."

Cibrial shoved her so hard that Tess's aching back collided with the unforgiving marble of a Rotunda column. Then she was sailing away, with a frothy wake of daughters trailing behind.

But Tess didn't need to follow to do her part. Calling on old signals from her days working for Ondrakja, she trailed two fingers down her side to tap a spot just southwest of her sitbone. A spot corresponding to a particularly juicy pomegranate on Cibrial's surcoat.

Near the entrance, a temporary clerk with a burn scar blazoned across her face stumbled into Cibrial's path in an explosion of fallen papers and apologies.

"Bravely done," Iascat murmured, helping Tess to her feet.

Leaning into his support, Tess said, "Now let's hope Parma manages her part."

Eastbridge, Upper Bank: Cyprilun 17

Holding the black hood in his hands, Grey wondered if this would be the last time.

His mind kept helpfully listing all the ways tonight could go wrong. Esmierka might not manage to steal Quarat; whatever Parma had in mind might not secure Illi-ten. Beldipassi might lose his nerve, or someone else succumb to the temptation of keeping their medallion. Koszar could take them all prisoner the moment they reached the Old Island. The ritual itself could fail.

But if it succeeded...

Then the city will still need a Rook. He was about more than just the medallions, now. Grey and Ren had seen to that.

He drew the hood over his head.

It wasn't quite like before. The disguise still flowed around him, coat and boots and the sword at his hip. But now being the Rook was a conscious choice: a performance, not a force threatening to take him over. The spirit was still there, two centuries' worth of memories, and it rose around him like fog as Grey thought, *I am the*

Rook. The black-hooded figure glimpsed in alleys and on rooftops, undercutting the powerful, helping those in need. Always with a hint of danger and a touch of panache.

When he pivoted, the skirts of his coat flared satisfyingly. Grinning to himself, the Rook sped across the quiet street and vaulted the garden wall.

Everything was where he'd left it. Mede Beldipassi's flightiness served a use tonight; after he stopped hiding at the Gawping Carp, he'd taken another house much closer to the trading nexus of Whitesail. Leaving this one in Eastbridge empty.

Whether Koszar upheld his end of the bargain or not, nobody could simply ask Cercel to relax her guard and let them across the East Channel. Those guards had to be distracted instead.

The Rook touched a tiny incendiary numinat to the bundled fuses stretched along the path.

Then back over the garden wall, down the street, moving with the swift silence only the Rook's true disguise could bring. He was well away by the time the fireworks started, booms and flares of light erupting from Beldipassi's garden. From a distance, it could easily be mistaken for an attack.

He arrived at the mouth of the Pomcaro Canal to find Vargo and Ryvček loading their cloaked and masked crowd into a skiff. "*Fireworks?*" Vargo said, gaping like the Rook had just made the most inappropriate joke he'd ever heard.

"Of course." The skiff rocked as the Rook pushed them off. The onyx-dark river sparked with reflected flashes of ruby and citrine, sapphire and emerald. "It's the Night of Bells. It's traditional to celebrate."

Hidden temple, Old Island: Cyprilun 17

Ren couldn't keep herself from pacing. How much longer until the others arrived? Was it already past time, and something had gone wrong?

::I can't hear Vargo yet,:: Alsius said when she stopped to peer again into the darkness of the passage. ::I'll let you know the moment I do.::

She had no doubt, if only because the spider was nearly as twitchy as she was. He sat in the middle of the communication numinat, but he kept skittering restlessly within its confines.

Until he hunkered down and spoke in a voice so soft she might have imagined it. ::Before he gets here, there's something I wanted to ask you.::

Gabrius, Ren thought. Alsius had taken the disappearance of Mirscellis's spirit as hard as she had, in his own way. And now they were back in the temple, where she'd stood by and let the nameless szorsa snap Gabrius's connections. She still didn't know how to mend that damage—but in truth, she'd given it little thought lately. Too many other things had crowded it from her mind.

She was still racking her brain for some useful idea when Alsius said, ::It's about what you saw in the realm of mind. That is, *me*.::

Ren knelt by the numinat. "Yes?"

With his legs tucked under him and his abdomen low, Alsius looked almost as small as a regular king peacock spider. ::I find myself wondering... you've pulled things into reality before. Could you do so again?::

Alsius's human form. Ren sighed. "I...honestly don't know. Yes, I created the Black Rose. But—I tried, when we stepped back across. To hold on to you in that shape. I failed."

His response attempted to be casual, but the way he hunkered even lower showed the lie. ::Ah well. It was just a foolish fancy.::

"Not foolish," Ren said, aching inside. "And I can try again. If there will ever be a time when such things are possible, it will be during the Great Dream." The wellspring granted true dreams, insight that went far beyond the glimpses offered by pattern. It might show her how to do this. Perhaps even how to help Gabrius—she couldn't let his light be lost forever.

::You'll have more to worry about that night than an old man like me. Oh! They're coming!:: Alsius sprang so high, he jumped out of the numinat. He scurried back in while Vargo reported that they'd made the crossing without difficulty.

Even with the stream of mental conversation to reassure her, Ren didn't relax until the group filed into the temple, cloaked and masked in case someone spotted them along the way. Esmierka's scarred face she expected, once they began to unmask, but that lanky figure next to Parma—

"*Bondiro?*" Ren murmured to Giuna as she took Tricat. "*That's* how Parma got Illi-ten away from Faella?"

Giuna's giggle was a relief. As though a few days with the medallion could have tarnished her shine. "She told him the sooner these were destroyed, the sooner they could get back to their old fun."

The Rook had slipped around the crowd to stand at Ren's side. "Guess even the laziest man will act with the proper motivation," he said. Then, amusement fading from his voice: "Let's get started."

Hidden temple, Old Island: Cyprilun 17

The numinat stretched across the floor, an echo of the blasphemous one Ghiscolo and Diomen created in their bid to restore the Tyrant's power.

This one, however, would end it forever.

Creating it went quicker than the Rook could have hoped for. With three of Nadežra's best inscriptors there, he had a chance to see true mastery at work—when he wasn't prowling the shadows and adjoining chambers, restless as a cat searching for prey. Even knowing they'd gathered to destroy the medallions, some part of him twitched at being so close to those blasphemous artifacts, at working *with* the people who held them.

"Should've brought snacks," Bondiro mumbled, and Giuna smacked him. Apart from that, silence reigned.

Until Tanaquis stood and dusted off her hands, looking more excited and alive than the Rook had ever seen her. "We're ready to begin."

It wasn't precisely a funeral. There were no relatives to bid farewell to the deceased, no pallbearers to carry the body to the terminus of the spiral. But there *was* a body, after a fashion: a chain of new-forged tin Tanaquis had brought. She laid a black cloth over it with as much formality as a mourner veiling a corpse.

Grey couldn't say what he wanted to; it was *his* concern, not the Rook's. But if Tanaquis had forgotten—

"The szorsa must agree," Ren said. "We will not by force send her to the Lumen."

I'm going to kiss that woman the moment we're back home.

Tanaquis nodded impatiently. "Yes, yes. But first we have to call her. Join hands, everyone."

It was easier this time, without Cibrial and Faella. Esmierka grinned unrepentantly at Ren and Ryvček as they clasped palms. *I pray it works*, the Rook thought. It hadn't occurred to him until now that replacing three links in the chain—his own included—might affect the living Uniat. How much was it tied to the holders, and how much to their medallions?

His concern vanished as soon as it formed. The moment Bondiro took Beldipassi's hand, closing the circle, the szorsa faded into view.

She crouched on the outside spiral, surrounded by overturned cards like fallen leaves. No amount of sweeping her hands across the ground would collect them; no sooner did she touch the paper than it tumbled away, as if blown by a wind.

"Zevriz," the Rook said softly, wary of invoking the ire and violence of her last appearance.

But the spirit who looked up at him was drained of such passion. The return of her szekani had steadied her. Only one piece was still missing, flickering in a circle around them like heat lightning. The last part of her soul, caught in Kaius's Uniat chain.

"Apologies, dream-seeker," the szorsa said. "Your pattern I cannot read. No bowls have I to collect offerings for the Faces and the Masks; no cards have I to consult."

The numinat wasn't active yet. He ducked under Ren's and Esmierka's hands and knelt by the szorsa. "It's all right," he said in

Vraszenian. "I've come not to ask for a pattern. I've come to give you a choice. If you wish it, you can be free...though it carries a price."

"All pearls have a price," she whispered. She caught a card at last, but her tears washed the colors away, leaving it blank.

Then his words registered. "Free?"

"Your soul will pass on. But not according to the rituals of your people. We think your freedom, and the destruction of the medallions, will require numinatria."

She dropped the blank card and clenched her hands. "I swear to you, I knew not what he intended. Perhaps even *he* intended it not, when he began. We thought only of what we might achieve—what might come from the joining of traditions."

Just like Tanaquis did. It was hard to imagine Kaius Sifigno as something other than the Conqueror and the Tyrant...but there would have been a point in his life before those things. Gently, the Rook said, "I condemn you not."

"Our Lady might." More cards bled white as her tears fell. "Our Lady does. See how she rejects me?"

It was her own guilt that severed her from her kin; he suspected the blank cards had the same cause. If Ažerais didn't abandon the Ižranyi for burning their koszenie—if she didn't abandon *him*—he had to believe she wouldn't abandon this lost daughter. "Not to Ažerais will you go, but to the Lumen."

"Ah." The tension ran from her like ink, leaving only the stain of exhaustion behind. "Better that light than living in shadows. What must I do?"

She was Zevriz, and dead two hundred years. He couldn't offer to find her kin and tell them of her passing, couldn't dance the kanina for her. All he could do was guide her to the center of the numinat, where the tin chain lay covered by its black veil.

"May the Lumen light your road back home," he said, exiting the numinat. At Tanaquis's instruction, he set the focus in place, then stepped out and closed the circle.

Heat flared, the dust in the air burning out in a bright flash like a firework, the veil burning quick as paper, the tin melting into a puddle. But the flames didn't touch the szorsa. Only a sun-fierce brightness that overwhelmed the Rook's enhanced sight, making Grey's eyes water and leaving spots in his vision when he looked away. On the other side of that light, Tanaquis sang the traditional hymn to Anaxnus, the Liganti god of death, in an uneven mezzo.

The air rang like a bell, like the bells on the night of the Tyrant's death. The medallion holders' hands parted, each person stepping back. As if he'd taken aža, the Rook saw that the tin-dull thread binding them had burned away.

"Uniat has been destroyed," he said, voice almost as unsteady as Tanaquis's singing. Two hundred years, and this was, at last, the beginning of the end.

No. The beginning of the end was over there, between Bondiro and Iascat. The Rook moved to stand in front of Illi-zero. "Mede Rimbon Beldipassi. Cast off that which shackles you to your desires."

Beldipassi hesitated. But it was in Illi-zero's nature to fall from its holder's hand, each new beginning a mere transient spark. The Rook bowed him forward, and he tossed his gold medallion into the burning numinat.

The air rang a second time.

"Eret Iascat Novrus, cast off that which shackles you to your desires."

The air in the temple had thickened, the space around Iascat swirling with the desires that tempted him. A shadow of Vargo—but the man's back was turned away. Iascat, like Sostira Novrus, craved the sort of love where souls met in complement, and he would never get it from that source. Other things, yes, good in their own way, but not the tender warmth that Grey shared with Ren.

And Iascat knew it. Straightening his shoulders, he stepped forward and surrendered his silver to the flames.

A third chime, and Ren. "Alta Arenza Lenskaya Traementatis, cast off that which shackles you to your desires."

He didn't need visions to know what Ren wanted. That gaping void within her had filled, though—with Tess and Sedge, with the

Traementis, maybe even with the Volavka. With her bonds to Grey and Vargo, giving her a different warmth to complement that of kin.

"You have enough," he murmured in Vraszenian.

Ren's gaze went past him to where Giuna stood breathless and rigid, outside their circle. Giuna, who'd risked Primordial taint to help her.

"Yes," Ren said. "I do." And bronze, too, burned.

The Oyster Cracker cracked a grin when he stood before her. "Isn't this a lucky day, meeting the Rook! An old friend of mine knew you—or so he claimed. Not certain how I'm supposed to give up this bauble, though." Her fingers curled hard around copper Quarat. "I'm a thief. Luck's something I need, and wealth is why I need it."

Fortune and bounty, Quarat's domain, swirling around her like a dance. But if it was a dance, then Esmierka was the dancer. "Is it the prize you love, or is it the chase?"

Her smile faltered, then came back rueful and true. "Fair. And really, I can do without this sudden craving for kids and a womb to cook 'em in." She chucked the medallion into the numinat, and the Rook turned to the next in the circle.

His predecessor. His teacher. His mentor.

Ryvček had made herself the best at everything she set her hand to. As a duelist she was unmatched; as the Rook, she'd been everything Grey aspired to. Yet it was *Grey* who'd brought them to this point, to the fulfillment of the Rook's mandate at last.

That impulse to excellence bent all too easily into competition, into the need to surpass those around her.

"It's never been about any one of us," he whispered, his voice going no farther than her ears. "It's about all of us, together. Without you, I would fail."

She managed a grin, wry and only a little sick from what she held. "Forget it not." With a flourish, she rid herself of Quinat.

"Fuck me," Vargo said when the Rook turned to him, scrubbing his face with his free hand. The other clutched Sessat close like a gut wound. He'd removed his gloves to inscribe the numinat, and his knuckles shone white against the blue of his coat. "I know. I *know.* I'm trying."

When they'd agreed to take the medallions, they thought Grey was a safer pairing for Quinat's drive for excellence and power, Vargo for Sessat's order and camaraderie. And it was true, after a fashion: Those things aligned with their better urges, rather than their worst failings.

But even good desires gave A'ash a foothold in their spirits. And now the Rook was asking Vargo to let go of those things that made him more than a ruthless bastard, climbing over everyone in his path. All around Vargo, the things he'd built were crumbling: his network of knots, the elite among whom he'd clawed his way to stand. He wasn't just gripping Sessat; in the vision that surrounded him, he was holding desperately to what remained.

The Rook didn't dare touch the medallion. But Grey tugged his glove down, baring the skin beneath. The cut, mostly healed now, yet still visible.

He gripped Vargo's forearm, pressing wrist to wrist. Scar to scar. In Vraszenian, knowing the only ones who spoke it weren't a threat, he said, "You won't lose everything. Trust us, and let go."

Some of the tension bled out of Vargo. And steel went onto the pyre.

The ringing no longer faded between destructions. It built each time, resonating in Grey's bones, making his teeth ache. Dust sifted down, as though the Point itself felt the press of building power. He hurried on to Utrinzi Simendis, who stood with his eyes closed. Surrounded in darkness. The protective cocoon of seclusion he'd woven around himself, trying to stay safe—even as that, too, fed Sebat's Primordial desire. At this point he couldn't even see that escape had become possible.

Unshielding the lightstone on his wrist, the Rook shone its light directly into Utrinzi's face. The other man flinched and awoke.

"It's time," the Rook said, and led him out of the darkness of solitude. The scintillating flash of burning prismatium bathed them all in rainbow light.

Parma also stood with her eyes closed, in a mimicry of Utrinzi's isolation, her breathing slow and even. The dream around her remained strangely empty of the fleshly visions the Rook expected. She cracked an eye when his boots scuffed the stone in front of her, but not even that marred her aura of serenity.

"Is it time?" she said over the tolling bells. At his nod, she sagged in relief. "Thank the Tyrant's rotting nutsack. Which I'd honestly rather hold than this diseased thing." She dusted her hands after casting her cinnabar medallion into the flames, muttering, "Can't believe that meditation shit actually worked. Don't you *dare* tell Utrinzi." As though he weren't standing right beside her, fighting a proud smile.

Two more to go. The Rook ached with eagerness, with the urge to see this *done*, his mandate fulfilled, victorious at last. They were unbinding the medallions' power, one numen at a time, but he had a dreadful feeling that power wasn't dissipating. Instead it built like an unseen thundercloud, raising every hair on his body.

No way out but through. "Alta Tanaquis Fienola Traementatis. Cast off that which shackles you to your desires."

It should have been easy. Destruction was Ninat's domain; if any of the ten would hasten its own end, surely this would be it.

But the moment he looked at Tanaquis, he knew he'd miscalculated.

A transcendent light had come upon her, and all around her spun the beautiful dance of the cosmos. Not just numinatria's geometric perfection, but pattern's threads weaving through it all, binding things together. The deeper truths Tanaquis had always craved. Some of Ninat's past holders had been assassins, and certainly she'd never flinched from death . . . but that wasn't what gripped her tight. Tanaquis wanted to *understand*.

And A'ash promised to give her that.

"Tanaquis," he shouted, over the cascading knell of the air. "Tanaquis! You must accept that there are things which lie beyond you!"

She gave no sign that she even heard.

The stone of the temple trembled beneath his feet. Primordial power surged, like water about to break over a dam. He was certain now: If they stopped, if they even hesitated too long, that unbound power would drown them all. The legend of Fiavla's fall would fade in the face of a new cataclysm. And Tanaquis...she *wanted*, too badly to give it up.

He could barely see, his vision blurring as the air shook. He was out of time.

The Rook seized Tanaquis by the wrist, trying to shake the medallion loose. He'd kick the damn thing in if he had to, and worry about curses later. He only succeeded in hauling her off balance. She stumbled forward, both of them within brushing distance of the circle. The stone beneath his boots was cracking open. What would happen if those cracks reached the numinat?

He couldn't let this go on—and she wouldn't let Ninat go.

She didn't even react as he shoved her hand into the flames.

The stench of roasted flesh washed through the room as the Rook hauled Tanaquis back. The medallion was gone...and so was her hand, burned away in an instant by the pyre. Her arm ended in a cauterized stump.

Giuna screamed. Tanaquis's face had gone chalk white, her eyes now firmly fixed on this world, on the Rook. He didn't have time to apologize; he didn't have time for anything. Only Illi-ten remained.

"Altan Bondiro Coscanum. Cast off—"

"Yes! Right!"

Gold flashed as the last medallion sailed through the air. The Rook had a heartbeat of praying that his aim was true...

Then it landed in the flames.

And the terrible mounting toll of that Primordial bell *stopped.* Like a thread snapping, the tension broke. The fires roared high— then died down to nothingness.

Leaving an empty numinat behind.

22

The Mask of Unraveling

Hidden temple, Old Island: Cyprilun 17

Ren had never felt so *free*.

It was as if she'd been struggling under a terrible weight, one she'd been carrying so long she hardly remembered it was there. Then she set it down, and suddenly she felt as if she could leap the Dežera without trying.

For an instant she floated... then came back to where she was, and what had happened.

"*Tanaquis!*" She lunged toward her cousin. Tanaquis sat on the floor, staring, not even clutching the charred stump where her hand had been. Livid red marks flowed along her throat and face, branching like a tree. Her remaining hand pressed over her heart, as if trying to keep it in place.

Giuna followed Ren, supporting Tanaquis, tears streaming down her face. *A physician*, Ren thought, the ice of her horror warring with that beautiful feeling of lightness. *She needs a physician.* None of them knew what to do for this, and just because shock gripped Tanaquis too tight for her to scream didn't mean she wasn't in agony.

In her peripheral vision she saw the others moving, Vargo deactivating the numinat, Ryvček wiping her brow, Bondiro folding himself to fit in Parma's embrace. "Making everyone my puppet'd be too much work anyways," he mumbled into her shoulder.

And Grey. Like iron to a lodestone, he drew Ren's gaze. As always, the magic of the hood cloaked his face in shadow...but the sheer looseness of his body spoke the magnitude of his relief.

He came and crouched at her side. "I'm so sorry. I—I had to do it."

"There was no time and less choice," Ren said, torn between sorrow and joy. The medallions were *gone*. After two hundred years, the Rook had succeeded. Nadežra was free of that poison at last. However horrifying the price...it was worth it.

"Is she—"

A soft gasp from Tanaquis silenced him, the hand clutching her heart spasming as her pain-hazed gaze snapped back to the present. "I did it."

Ren gripped her cousin's shoulder, trying not to look at the charred flesh below it. "You did. We all did."

Giuna flinched from the Rook. She knew it was Grey under the hood...but maybe that made it worse. A faceless stranger mutilating her cousin would have been easier than someone she knew and cared for. Helping Tanaquis to her feet, she said, "We need to get her out of here."

"I'll help. I know a bit about burns." Esmierka tugged loose the ribbons that tied Giuna's billowing sleeve to her surcoat bodice and wrapped the cambric around the nightmare of cracking char and seeping fluid. Then she lifted Tanaquis's arm over her shoulders, her height helping to elevate it. Ren doubted it was an accident that Esmierka placed herself between the injured woman and the Rook.

Ryvček took charge, getting everyone to cloak and mask again and leading them from the temple. The dank air of the tunnels was a comparative pleasure, because at least it didn't smell like burned flesh. In silence they filed along, following Ryvček's lightstone, with Ren, Vargo, and the Rook bringing up the rear.

Until they neared the barrier, and suddenly the line stopped.

Ren heard Ryvček say, "I thought the deal was that you'd allow us to come and go unhindered."

"Unhindered, but not unwatched. And we know who's beneath those masks."

Koszar's voice washed the exhaustion from Ren like a splash of icy water. When she pushed her way through the crowd, she was drearily unsurprised to find Laročja standing with Koszar and a small cluster of others, blending smugness and fury into a seamless whole. "As I feared," the old woman said, dripping relish rather than regret. "With her Liganti friends this slip-knot conspires in secret. And to what end?"

"To destroy the last remnants of the Tyrant's power," Ren snapped. "A power your enemies have been using against you. Heard you that noise just now, like the tolling of the Night of Bells? That was its destruction, at our hands." Fortunately, no one with her was likely to let slip the word "Primordial"—though her heart ached to think of what had silenced Tanaquis.

Laročja's lip curled in disbelief, but Koszar drew a sharp breath. More quietly, Ren said, "Koszar, to the Black Rose you gave your word. Keep it now. Let us pass."

His cane tapped a rapid tattoo, the only sound in the tunnel. Ren wondered how Laročja had discovered them; she had no doubt the old woman was behind it. Koszar wouldn't have pried. But now that he knew what she'd hidden from him, he couldn't simply ignore it. Not when the group before him included five nobles and two members of the Cinquerat itself.

Koszar bowed his head, and Ren thought, *He can't even meet my eyes as he betrays me.*

"I cannot," he said.

"Your word is nothing?" Ren fought and failed to keep her voice steady.

He shook his head. "Knot oaths I have also sworn—an oath you were once offered and refused. Would you have me break those instead? If by breaking my word to one person, I can save the lives of many and end this conflict sooner..." He flipped his hand as though weighing the balance. "That burden I must bear."

Ren couldn't even blame it on Laročja. The old woman might have pried into their secrets tonight, but Koszar was the one speaking now, with the voice of a commander at war.

The silken whisper of a drawn blade drew attention to Ryvček. "Lives you will still lose, if you force us to fight past you."

"I doubt not the threat some here pose," Koszar said, not bothering to remind her of his own threat. He had numbers, and an entire island under his control. They would feel the pain of a fight more than he would. And they would lose.

"So we stay here," Ren said, nodding at the tunnel behind her. "You have not the secret of passing this barrier."

"A hostage under siege is still a hostage. How much food and water have you?"

None at all—and then a horrible realization seized Ren. The nameless szorsa had been the source of that ward... but now she was gone. Which likely meant the only thing preventing Koszar from walking across that line was his assumption that the ward remained. A single rebel poking at it out of curiosity would leave them with no defenses at all.

That wasn't Ren's most pressing concern, though. The soft moan behind her was Tanaquis, emerging from her daze into the burning pain of her injury.

Could Ren at least trust Koszar to see her cousin tended to? The rest... She didn't know what to do. She had the Black Rose's mask with her, but retreating to the temple and coming back in that guise wouldn't change anything. Koszar already knew who the Rose was, and Ažerais herself wouldn't move Laročja.

Tanaquis had to come first. Everything else later.

As she drew breath, Iascat pulled off his mask and stepped forward. "I will stay," he said, "if you let the rest go."

Tension cropped Koszar's laugh short. "Why should I settle for one, when I can have many?"

"Because one on his own will negotiate with you in good faith to find a satisfactory end to this war. One among many will not."

"Empty Liganti words," Laročja scoffed. "When with the

Cinquerat our people negotiated before, what came of it? A yearly ritual of submission and humiliation."

Iascat offered her a shallow bow. "Then that's the first point we can discuss: an end to the Ceremony of the Accords. Perhaps to be replaced with something better, should all go well. I imagine you also want to discuss the Great Dream, and the ruinous price my predecessors have charged for access. All of these things are possible . . . if you let the others go."

Koszar was considering it, Ren could see. His gaze flicked past Iascat, searching the rest of the group. With an unsteady hand, Utrinzi unmasked as well. "I—I suppose that I—"

"Should go back to the Upper Bank," Iascat said, smiling the unspoken offer away. "I'm sticking you with the worse job, Utrinzi; you've got to explain to the rest of the Cinquerat what I'm doing and why."

Because who else would they believe? Not Ren, nor any of the people connected to her, Giuna and Vargo included. The strongest alternatives were Parma and Tanaquis. The latter was in no state for politics, and the former looked like Ren had felt when facing a leap off the Floodwatch Bridge.

"We want clean water again," Koszar said. "Before we discuss anything."

Utrinzi's fingers curled as though searching for something to strangle. "The foci were removed against my recommendation. And unfortunately, we can't simply put them back—"

"There's no easy fix for the East Channel numinat," Vargo said, eeling through the crowd to stand at Iascat's side. "But let us go— and guarantee Argentet's safety—and I'll make restoring the *West* Channel numinat my first priority."

The Upper Bank would be furious, but Koszar's wry smile suggested their anger held some appeal. When Laročja made a sound that heralded a new objection, he quelled her with a look, then stepped to the side with the tiniest of bows. "Very well. Follow us, Eret Novrus; we'll take you to the Charterhouse. The rest of you may go."

Isla Traementis, the Pearls: Cyprilun 18

It was past dawn, the light streaming into the hallway a delicate pearl pink, when Donaia was roused from her front hall vigil by noise outside. She yanked open the door before the bell could ring.

"At least you're not climbing in through the windows," she said— then choked on the words. It wasn't just Giuna on the stoop, but Tanaquis carried by Bondiro Coscanum and an earthwise woman who looked no better than a ruffian.

And Ren.

Donaia couldn't stop herself from hauling the girl in for a hug. "Thank the Lumen you're safely off that island."

Giuna was hurrying past, leading the others to the parlour. Belatedly, Donaia registered the harrowed look on Giuna's face, the livid marks spidering up Tanaquis's throat. "What's going on?"

"Vargo's sending a doctor," Ren said. "Tanaquis—she—"

Following them into the parlour, Donaia saw what she'd missed before, in her relief at Ren's safe return. Tanaquis's right sleeve ended in charred horror . . . and so did the arm inside.

Donaia's shriek brought the servants running. Within moments it seemed like all Traementis Manor was awake, and helpless to do much in the face of such appalling injury. Vargo's physician, when he showed up, banished them all while he tended to her wound. Bondiro and the stranger took their leave; Donaia retreated to her study with the girls, where Colbrin had a pot of fortifying tea waiting.

"What happened?" she whispered, blotting the sweat from her brow. "How—how could that . . . ?"

"We destroyed the medallions."

That was all Ren got out before a sob jerked through her. Donaia pulled her into another hug, and Giuna nestled in like the little chick she'd always be in her mother's heart. Donaia stroked the hair of both, trembling in relief. "I heard the bells last night, but I thought...Oh, you brilliant girls. You truly did it? That poison's gone from our house? From our *city*?"

They stood together for a long time before finally separating and pouring the tea. Gone were the days when Meatball obeyed his training to stay off the furniture, but Donaia found she needed his weight sprawled across her lap, his warm ruff and wiry hair under her fingers as the girls told her how Tanaquis had come to be injured—and how that injury had bought their freedom from Primordial hell.

"House Destaelio will be cursed now," Ren said, gripping her teacup like that and pragmatic concerns were the only things keeping her grounded. "Not Coscanum, though; we *think* the destruction will have freed those of us who gave our medallions to the fire. Though we need to be sure. Tanaquis—Tanaquis was going to verify it for us."

"I'll speak to His Worship," Donaia said.

Silence fell. Giuna had kicked off her shoes and sat with her knees bent under her skirt, tea cradled to her chest. Ren was dressed in wedding clothes that looked much worse for wear. Ren herself didn't look much better. The last time Donaia had seen her so wan and red-eyed had been during that time of hellish sleeplessness.

She hadn't yet said what happened while she was gone, but Donaia didn't think that was secrecy at work; there was just too much to say at once. But even thinking of that made a new question bubble up—one she hadn't been able to ask before now.

"Would you have told me, if you hadn't disappeared?" At the furrow of Ren's unvoiced confusion, Donaia said, "This Vraszenian uprising. Were you planning to warn me? Did you know this was going to happen?"

After all, Koszar Andrejek had been at Ren's wedding. At Grey's insistence, he'd tried to sit down with Cercel, Iascat, and Scaperto. Only after that failed had the Anduske destroyed the bridges.

Ren had promised honesty, and Donaia wanted to believe it. But a splinter of distrust remained in her heart, that not even release from Primordial influence could dislodge. If Ren knew...

"Yes, I knew," Ren said. Her eyes were soft, and full of regret—but not repentance. "No. I was not going to tell you."

Part of Donaia knew it must be coming. And yet the admission drove the air from her.

"I *couldn't*," Ren went on, voice strained. "For them to succeed, they needed surprise. You would have felt obligated to tell the Cinquerat. And they *have* to succeed."

"You want our home in chaos?"

"I want it *cleansed*! Not as Laročja would do, purging everyone not pure enough for her—but Liganti power here has stood on a foundation of those Mask-damned medallions for two hundred years. It isn't enough to pull those out; we need more. We need changes in the laws, my people permitted a voice."

My people. And she spoke with a Vraszenian accent—with her natural accent.

Meatball whined. Donaia forced her hands to relax. "I know there are problems. But the way to address them is through diplomacy. Not through bombing the bridges, trapping people on the Old Island as hostages. Not through chaos and bloodshed."

"We've *tried* diplomacy. Koszar told me how the meeting went. They refused to recognize him as a legitimate representative of Vraszenians in Nadežra."

"Because he's a criminal seditionist—"

"Nor will they recognize the ziemetse, because they're foreign powers. So no one has the authority to speak for Vraszenians here, and even the most reasonable people in the Cinquerat take that as reason to leave things as they are."

This wasn't the conversation Donaia wanted to have with her niece, not with everything they'd been through. But having started, they couldn't simply stop. "Ren, can you be certain this isn't Tricat influencing you? Vengeance for your mother's death, for your own suffering...I know what it's like to want someone to pay."

Ren met her gaze, unflinching. "Tricat is justice, too. And yes, perhaps I was influenced. But that's why I'm glad this rebellion isn't mine to lead. Koszar Andrejek, Idusza Polojny, the Kiraly clan elder... never have they touched Primordial power. Think you that so many people fight for this simply because *I* want it? I could not stop it if I tried."

"But you didn't try. You didn't even warn me. You promised me honesty, and then you put your family in danger, without so much as a *thought* for us!"

Despite everything Donaia knew, she didn't believe it was calculation that put such anguish into Ren's expression. "I could not sleep for thinking of it. I knew this was more secrecy, more dishonesty, after I'd promised you truth. But... this matters more." She flinched from her own words. At Giuna's soft exhalation, some understanding passed between them—an understanding that left Donaia outside.

Ren's final words were barely audible. "I *couldn't* put personal promises above that. No matter how much it hurt you."

The silence that followed was the horrible, echoing rift of everything that separated them. Upper Bank from Lower. Liganti from Vraszenian. Rich from poor. Donaia had thought family ties might bridge that chasm, but...

Setting aside her teacup, Giuna rose and sat next to Ren. One hand sought out her cousin's and gripped it tight.

"I understand," Giuna said, meeting Ren's tear-edged gaze. "And you're right. This matters more. What we have stands on a rotten foundation. We've got to tear it out and build a better one—together."

Her last words were aimed not at Ren, but at Donaia. "Leato would have agreed."

Giuna's soft observation hit like a slap. Donaia recoiled, mouth opening to defend herself.

But over the rush of blood to her ears and cheeks, she heard the words of that barman at the Gawping Carp, all the sharper for the lack of judgment in them.

Your son was a good kid. I expected better of his mother.

If Leato were still here...

Donaia looked at Ren, and she didn't see the masterful manipulator, the con artist who'd fooled her and all of Nadežra time and time again. She saw the motherless young woman who'd sat across from her in Westbridge and confessed that she didn't know how to be family. A young woman who'd taken countless blows from life, but kept reaching for ways to make things better. To help others. Even when the cost to herself was high.

All the fight bled out of Donaia. Every argument her mind raised, every protest about how this problem should have been handled, failed in the face of one simple truth: She'd rather admit she was wrong than be at odds with her family.

She heaved Meatball off her lap, ignoring his whine, and knelt in front of the two young women, taking their free hands in her own.

"You're right," she said. "Both of you. And since Leato isn't here...I'll try to make him proud."

Kingfisher, Lower Bank: Cyprilun 18

Grey wanted nothing more than to go with Ren to Traementis Manor. Not because he thought he was needed there or could do anything to help, but simply so he wouldn't have to leave Ren's side. They hadn't had a single quiet moment together since the wedding: Instead it had been zlyzen, Fiavla, the Old Island.

Destroying the medallions. His fingers still remembered the feel of Tanaquis's arm in his grip, the shock of her hand going into the flames and nothing coming out. If he hadn't done it, though, they might not be free now, the poison gone at last.

But others needed to know, too. That miraculous news was poised on Grey's tongue when he entered Alinka's house.

It died when he found his father sitting at the table, a square of black silk in front of him and a needle in his hand.

"I need more blue, for your great-grandmother." Jakoslav wasn't talking to Grey; he spoke to Jagyi in his lap, stubby fingers knotted up in tangles of floss. "She was Varadi. Can you find me blue, little bandit?"

He didn't even acknowledge Grey's arrival. Swallowing down the unpleasant jolt, Grey said, "Where's Alinka?"

"Good boy." Jakoslav took the thread Jagyi offered him, ruffling his dandelion-fluff curls. Only then did he look up at Grey. Redness rimmed his eyes, as though he'd been drinking. "Upstairs. Sleeping. You leave that poor girl to run herself ragged, after she's had such a shock."

Grey leaned against the door. "She told you what happened with the kanina."

"*I should have been there.*" Jakoslav pitched his voice low, but the curl of his lip and the tension in his arms were too reminiscent of Grey's childhood. Only the distance of years and iron control kept him from flinching. "What evil have I done, that you would deprive me of seeing my son?"

Not drink, then, but the ragged remains of tears. And anger. That was how it had always gone, after Grey's mother died: grief for Noeri transmuted to anger at the one blamed for her loss.

"Tell me truthfully," Grey said. For Jagyi's sake he tried to keep his voice casual, but it was like trying to hold back the Dežera. "Would you have come and wished good fortune to me, marrying a *half-breed*?"

"So as usual, the fault is mine. For my efforts to protect this family, I must be robbed of its joys."

You can't even pretend *you would have been happy for us.* Grey wouldn't have believed it anyway. But once again, in Jakoslav's mind, he and Laročja were the innocent victims of a cursed son.

If Laročja hadn't been a fraud—if she could have seen clearly what lay in Grey's past—how different might everything have been?

Asking that question was asking for pain.

"If the son's a thief, look to the father." Refusing to be cowed, Grey pushed off the door and approached the table, catching the corner of the silk. Jakoslav had already embroidered the first lines, silver for the Szerado, warm chestnut brown for Noeri's Meszaros kin. "I told you I'd make Jagyi's koszenie."

"Yet here it lay, untouched. While you yourself were nowhere to be found. Alinka needs family she can rely on."

"She *has* family she can rely on. What she needs not is family that wishes only to use her." Seeing how Jagyi had gone silent, his floss-tangled hands limp in his lap, Grey leashed his anger. He plucked his nephew from the trap of Jakoslav's arms and set him on the stairs. "Go wake your mother, Jagyi. Tell her I'm home and your grand-father is leaving."

They watched Jagyi hoist his slow way up, each step a hurdle to be mounted. At least Jakoslav waited for the door to close before rounding on Grey. "You make decisions that should be left to his mother."

"Alinka tolerates your presence because she's kind. But she knows what Kolya would have wanted."

"So you ruin *her* life, as you ruined his?"

Without warning, the rage slipped its leash. Grey slammed his hand onto the table, looming over his seated father. The hood was tucked safely away, but he didn't need it to play this role. He wasn't a frightened, abused child anymore. And he would make Jakoslav see that.

"You cannot face it, can you?" he said, his voice suddenly and chillingly conversational. "That your own fear and cruelty ruined everything. That your mother's so-called guidance convinced your wife her only choice was to take her life and mine. That your attempt to beat the ill fortune out of me did nothing but harm. That Kolya was so horrified by what he found when he returned from his apprenticeship, *he* chose to take us both away from you. That your own hand has snapped the threads of this family."

"No threads have I cut. Nor have you, for all your disrespect." Shoving the chair back, Jakoslav rose to meet Grey's anger. Age had rounded his chest like a barrel, but in other ways he seemed diminished. No, Grey had just grown. Tall enough to meet him eye-to-eye; confident enough to make the choice Kolya had always left in his hands.

His koszenie was folded inside his shirt, where it wouldn't be damaged. Grey drew it out now, the memory of what the Ižranyi had done dragging at his spirit like a lead weight.

The burning of their koszenie had been blasphemy. But it was a reminder that sometimes, to protect others, to protect oneself, to get rid of old poison . . . a binding must be severed.

Snatching a thumb knife from the tangle of embroidery floss, Grey slipped it under the silver stitches marking him as Szerado—

And cut them.

Jakoslav cried out, hands reaching too late. For all his cruelty, he'd never cast Grey out. He'd even overruled Laročja when the old woman suggested sending Grey to be adopted by another kureč— because in the end, Jakoslav couldn't let go of his own blood. Even if that was selfish pride rather than love, it mattered to him.

Now he staggered backward. "You—you—"

"You have no sons, Jakoslav Jakoski Szerado. One is dead, and the other you drove away." He'd expected it to feel like opening a vein, bleeding himself dry of everything that made him Vraszenian. Instead it felt like the medallions being destroyed at last. Not without cost . . . but worth it all the same.

A creak dragged Grey's attention from his speechless father. Alinka stood on the stairs, hair mussed and pillow creases on her cheek, but composed and calm. "In light of this," she said coolly, "I must ask you to leave, Ča Szerado."

To Jakoslav.

The old man sputtered. "Me? *He* is the one who severed our thread. Who cast himself out of this family."

"He did." Descending the last few steps, she stood at Grey's side, hand slipping into his. Clammy cold, but firm in its grip. "My sympathy you have for what you've lost . . . but Grey is my kin. Which makes you kin no more."

Grey tightened his hand on hers, not caring if his relief showed.

Jakoslav's rage rose in familiar defense. "Your son—"

"Is not yours to take, as replacement for what you've lost. Better a small family than one that would treat him so." Alinka stood tall, unafraid of Jakoslav's curled fists. "I said you should leave, Ča Szerado. I will not ask again."

Grey let go of Alinka so he could step forward. Jakoslav retreated, fumbling for the door. He couldn't seem to find the latch, until Grey reached past him to open it.

Into the ear of the man who had been his father, he murmured, "Get over your Mask-damned obsession with blood purity and call Oramir from Gursoven to be your heir. Then, should the kanina call Kolya from the dream again, you'll be able to look him in the eye."

The door opened. Jakoslav stumbled out. And Grey closed it on him forever.

Isla Traementis, the Pearls: Cyprilun 18

Tanaquis wasn't the first person Ren had seen lose a hand. The Fingers were thieves; one of the punishments for thievery was amputation. Some of the magistrates held back from sentencing children to that fate, but not all.

Sitting by her cousin's bedside, she felt simultaneously like she was back in Lacewater, and a world away from the slums of her childhood. Unlike the Fingers, unlike most people outside the Upper Bank, Tanaquis had received the best care possible. The physician had cleaned the stump and stretched a flap of skin over its raw end; he was confident it would heal well, and he'd left behind restoratives and imbued ointments. Tanaquis wouldn't have to fear infection, much less starvation in a gutter.

But she was sun-handed. Ren had seen how fragile Tanaquis became after Iridet fired her, when she was barred from performing inscription except to deal with the medallions. Now she wouldn't be able to perform it at all.

If she's denied her compass, her edge, and her chalk . . . is there any self left?

Ren scrubbed a tear away. This wasn't the end. Tanaquis was strong. She'd made thoughtful, approving noises when she heard how Alsius made Vargo practice inscription with both hands and even, on a basic level, with his feet. She could learn to use her other hand. They would all help her.

That didn't make the loss any less horrifying.

And so Ren sat her vigil praying to the Lumen and Šen Asarn alike that her cousin would recover, until a rustling brought her head up. Tanaquis shifted in bed—and then her eyes opened.

Ren leaned forward, ready to still her if necessary. "Try not to sit up. You've been dosed with papaver."

"Water," Tanaquis said, in a desiccated whisper.

Ren gave it to her in little sips, until Tanaquis coughed. Then she set the glass aside. "Tanaquis... recall you what happened? In the temple?"

Her cousin's eyes glittered before she turned away, exposing the branching marks on her neck and face. The doctor had promised they weren't painful. He'd seen such marks as a result of numina-trian accidents; they would fade with time. The sight still made Ren want to look away.

"The medallions," Tanaquis whispered.

"Yes." Ren inhaled, steeling herself. "Everyone else gave theirs to the fire. You... The Rook had to force you. And your hand—"

A tiny nod saved her from having to say it. "I know."

Ren waited, but no outburst came. Either emotion hadn't yet made its way through the haze, or Tanaquis hadn't yet absorbed the consequences of her loss. Ren wasn't about to shove them in her face.

One thing, however, couldn't be left until later. "Vargo's exam-ined the others, and none of them are cursed." House Destaelio was, their medallion taken from them by theft, but not Esmierka. "You having held on to yours... there's a risk you may be."

"I'm not."

Tanaquis spoke with simple certainty. Ren's lips pressed together. "You can't be sure of that." And she'd held Ninat. Tanaquis might have vowed not to end her own life like her uncle had, but after the loss of her hand...

Her cousin turned back. That glassy-eyed look was unnerving, like Tanaquis was seeing past her into some other realm. Not the visions of aža, but whatever papaver showed her. After a moment, Tanaquis said, "I designed the numinat that verified the presence of a curse. I designed the numinat that removes the curse. I designed the numinat to destroy the medallions. Who in this city knows more about Primordial power than I? And I tell you, I'm not cursed."

Ren regretted having raised the issue at all as Tanaquis sagged deeper into her pillow. But her cousin's certainty came as a relief. It was true; Tanaquis knew more about these matters than anyone. If she was sure, Ren could trust that.

It eased some of the fear, though far from all. The rest would have to wait for the days to come. "Then sleep," she said, "and heal."

She meant it to be reassuring. Instead it broke the barrier that had held back her own tears. "Masks have mercy," Ren whispered. "Tanaquis—I'm so sorry—"

"There's nothing for you to be sorry about," Tanaquis said, her eyes drifting shut. "I promise."

Isla Čaprila, Eastbridge: Cyprilun 18

Given that they'd just destroyed blasphemous Primordial artifacts, Vargo expected Alsius to fill his head with chatter as they wearily made their way home. Prayers of thanks to the Lumen, after-the-fact evaluation of the numinat, theological speculation about what would happen to the szorsa's soul, horror over what Tanaquis had suffered—all of the above and more, in a never-ending flood of giddily analytical relief.

Instead he got silence.

The emptiness of the house only drove that in harder. He hadn't seen Varuni since they delivered the Black Rose's mask via crossbow bolt; for all he knew, her people had already sent her home to Isarn. He ought to send a message to ask, but all he really wanted to do was strip down, scrub himself from head to foot, and fall asleep, possibly without getting out of the tub first.

There would be no relaxation, though, with that echoing silence in his head. To break it, Vargo said out loud, "You all right, old man? I thought you'd be dancing with the moons."

::Oh. Yes, of course. Naturally I'm pleased.::

Instead of his usual rounds making certain no vermin had invaded their bedroom, Alsius tucked himself into the curling scrollwork of Vargo's headboard. Watchful and quiet. Pensive.

"Out with it. What's going on?" Vargo gave up his dreams of a scrub-down and settled onto the bed. The knobs and divots of the headboard pressed unevenly into his back.

After a pause long enough that Vargo started to nod off, Alsius said softly, ::I'm tired.::

"We both are. I know there's more to do, with the uprising and the river numinat, but I think we're allowed a half day's rest."

::No. I mean... It was terrible, being cut off from you. Voiceless. So *helpless*. And then, in the realm of mind, I was myself again, and I'd forgotten. How do you forget what it's like to be human?:: The shadows stirred. Something soft brushed past Vargo's cheek, and then Peabody settled on his chest, lighter than the lump constricting Vargo's throat.

Past that lump, Vargo said, "Are you sorry you came back?"

Alsius didn't answer directly. ::I sometimes worried about how I would occupy myself after we took down Ghiscolo and the Praeteri. But then there were the medallions to deal with. They had to be destroyed, and I'm glad I was there for that, even if what happened to poor Tanaquis was awful.:: His shiver was as light as a butterfly's kiss. ::Now this rebellion, and the river numinat again. I know it's all important, but....::

"You're tired." Of being stuck in this life. Of being stuck as a spider.

Maybe even of being stuck with Vargo.

Not that, he thought, where Alsius couldn't hear. The bruised part of himself that expected others to turn away was healing, and he knew Alsius's joy at being scribed in as his father hadn't been feigned. But... for sixteen years, the old man had only one person to talk to. Now he had two—but maybe that only drove home how tightly his circumstances constrained him.

"Ren can find a solution," he said, clutching at a thin strand. "She made the Black Rose out of nothing. Maybe she can— I don't know. Make you a new body."

Alsius sagged flat, the spider equivalent of a sigh. ::I asked. But some things, I fear, are beyond even her.::

The doorbell ringing felt like a reprieve. Vargo couldn't marshal the right words to comfort Alsius, not with exhaustion numbing his thoughts. He didn't much want to entertain guests, either—but it might be Ren, or Grey. Groaning, he heaved himself off the bed, Alsius coming along for the ride, and went downstairs.

Fadrin Acrenix was on his front step.

"The *fuck*?" The words sprang from Vargo's mouth before he could stop them.

Fadrin stepped aside and jerked his thumb. A plain-sided carriage stood at the foot of the steps, its open door revealing Carinci Acrenix. Her expression a stony mask, she called out, "You can join me in here, or Fadrin can bring me inside."

No fucking way was he getting into an Acrenix carriage. Vargo jerked his own thumb at Fadrin, then waited while the other man carried Carinci up the steps and into his parlour. A trembling warmth at the back of his neck was Alsius, hiding from the woman who had been his mother.

She settled herself with dignity, straightening her skirts and gloves. Vargo hovered, wondering if he should skip the intervening steps and just draw a knife. Months since Ghiscolo had died—since Vargo killed him—and not a word from Carinci. Had it upset her at all? Ghiscolo was born to a contract wife; Carinci adopted him only after Alsius died. Vargo had no idea if there had ever been any love there. He had no idea what to expect from Carinci at all.

When her appearance was tidied to her satisfaction, Carinci drew her own verbal knife. "For months I was something Faella Coscanum couldn't scrape off her shoe fast enough, and then this morning she shows up at my door. Are you trying to pick up where

Ghiscolo left off? Fancy yourself a better Tyrant than he would have
been?"

"A saner one, at the very least." Without a trapped szorsa to act
as his chain, Ghiscolo had tumbled into power-madness far quicker.
"But if you mean to imply I'm trying to gather more medallions in
my own hands, you're laughably off mark."

"Am I? And yet you haven't asked why Faella came to me."

Vargo's indifferent sprawl concealed his tension. "I assume
because her Illi-ten medallion went missing. She can stop looking.
It's been destroyed. All of them have."

Carinci went as rigid as a statue. Hesitantly, Alsius asked, ::Are
you certain it's wise to tell her?::

*Wiser than leaving her searching for them. What can she do? They're
gone.*

A decorative bowl flew past Vargo's head, smashing into the wall
and leaving a star of porcelain dust on the wood. Carinci's grip on
her chair's arms was white-knuckled like she'd launch herself next.

"You! How could you let this happen?" she hissed. Her gaze was
set not on Vargo's face, but on his shoulder.

::She—she knows I'm here?::

Ghiscolo had figured it out, that his half brother was somehow
stuck in the body of a spider. Perhaps he'd told Carinci, or Sibiliat
had. It didn't matter. The point was, she *knew.*

"Face me," Carinci snapped. One bony hand gestured imperiously at Vargo. "You. Tell me what he says. It's long past time my
son and I talked."

Vargo felt the tremor as the bright blot of Peabody crept into
view. ::I'm listening, Mother.::

Feeling half like a fool, half like a protective son, Vargo parroted
Alsius's words.

"And? Answer my question, boy. How could you let our family
come to this?"

::*Ghiscolo* is the one who brought us to this. He's the one who
sought the power of Primordials. He's the one who was going to kill
most of the Cinquerat—and Faella, too! He's the one who killed *me*.::

Vargo's voice wavered on those last words. Ghiscolo might have given the order, and Diomen created the numinat for the cursed cloak, but Vargo had delivered it.

Carinci sniffed. "Clearly, he didn't kill you thoroughly enough."

::...Mother?::

That whisper was a plea Vargo didn't—couldn't—repeat. Instead he sat up straight and asked for himself: "What exactly do you mean by that?"

Any one of his fists would have known by his tone to choose their next words with great care. Even Fadrin shifted in discomfort. Carinci's lip curled like she'd stepped barefoot on a slug. "I knew from early on that this useless son of mine had his head too firmly up the Lumen's ass to properly use the power granted to our family line. He probably would have colluded with that fool Utrinzi to destroy it all the sooner. I told his father he would make a terrible heir. Ghiscolo at least understood how to lead House Acrenix."

Vargo stilled. "You told Ghiscolo to have Alsius murdered?"

"The idea was his. But I certainly didn't stop him."

In one swift move Vargo was on his feet, fist raised, Carinci's age and infirmity be damned. Fadrin caught his wrist before he could strike. For a brief moment they strained against each other; Fadrin had bigger muscles, but Vargo had six ways to break the deadlock, each one increasingly vicious. He transferred his murderous glare to the Acrenix cousin, and Fadrin dropped his wrist like he was holding hot iron.

Vargo spat at Carinci, the spittle striking her cheek. "You should have died alongside your precious heir. And your register should have been burned like Indestor's. Get the *fuck* out of my house."

Fadrin obeyed without waiting for Carinci's response. Vargo didn't follow, certain he would kick them both down the stairs if he did. Carefully picking up the pieces of broken bowl, he waited for Alsius to speak.

He was sweeping up the last splinters with a hand brush when it came. ::I'm glad you didn't strike her.::

Vargo wasn't. Why should her condition or her age protect that woman from the consequences of her abject cruelty? "You're better than that whole fucking family."

::Am I? You're forgetting how I tried to save my life. What landed me in this body in the first place. Perhaps this is the punishment I deserve.::

Every response Vargo could think of was too barbed. He sank onto the bottom step of the staircase, head in his hands. "You *would* have dedicated your life to destroying them. She was afraid because she knew you were a better person than Ghiscolo. And I'm proud that we got the chance to prove it." He tried to channel his sincerity through the link, even though it had never worked that way before. Ren had remade it for them; maybe it worked that way now.

But it didn't. Or it wasn't enough.

::I . . . I'm sorry. I need some time to think.:: Hopping away, Peabody scuttled up the banister.

His weight was tiny, but with it gone, Vargo's shoulders sagged. He should get up, clean up, sleep, but his body felt too heavy to move.

He didn't know how long he sat there before the doorbell rang again. Vargo rose to his feet, half hoping it was Fadrin and Carinci come back to let him have another go.

Instead it was Grey, recoiling when Vargo yanked the door open.

"Now's *really* a bad time," Vargo snapped.

"I can see that," Grey said, taking in his appearance. "Do you want to talk about it?"

There was a bottle of zrel dangling from Grey's left hand, and he looked about as ragged as Vargo felt. Vargo weighed the question, passed a weary hand over his face, and swung the door wider for his brother to enter. "I suspect we both do. Come on in—and get that zrel open."

The Face of Weaving

Floodwatch, Lower Bank: Cyprilun 23

Waiting in line to cross the guarded Floodwatch Bridge, Ren shielded her eyes with one hand to study the crane rising over the deactivated West Channel numinat. True to his word, Vargo had moved to get it repaired as soon as possible, aided by Koszar granting the release of some of his Liganti hostages.

Even for Vargo's design, though, repair was easier said than done. The original setup had relied on slotting all seven foci into place simultaneously; placing them one at a time risked cracking the whole structure. The mechanism for the activation having long since been dismantled, his workers had to build a new one before the water would flow clean again.

Still, it was an encouraging sign of progress. Iascat on his own was proving a more effective diplomat than the whole Cinquerat shouting across a broken bridge—helped in part by the sudden chaos in Whitesail. Without her medallion, Cibrial's control over the foreign merchants had disintegrated like cheap paper in the rain; worse for her, several creditors had called in their loans before Vargo and Utrinzi could remove her curse. The pressure was on for some kind of compromise to be reached.

Assuming Koszar didn't lose control of his own people first.

Rumor said his decision to let Ren and the others go had put a rift between him and Laročja—and therefore between the Anduske who followed him, and the newcomers who followed *her*. If that rift grew too wide, it could threaten everything they'd achieved so far. But Ren had no way to intervene there, and she hadn't yet figured out a way for the Black Rose to help, either.

By comparison, her purpose today felt frivolous. Having got hold of one end of a thread, though, she couldn't stop until she unraveled the whole thing.

The preparation hadn't even been difficult. A few questions in knowledgeable ears; an afternoon spent gossiping with some gammers only too happy to talk. It was enough to net her some names and a destination.

In western Floodwatch she turned north. Past one of the distribution points for clean water; past clusters of Vraszenians muttering about the approach of Veiled Waters. That was another fire waiting to break out: If people started to believe they wouldn't get access to the Old Island in time for the Great Dream, the Lower Bank might see another riot. The last time they'd been denied their holy festival had been under the rule of the Tyrant, and no one had forgotten.

Worrisome thoughts—yet almost preferable to the ones trying to sink their claws into her mind. It was ridiculous that she'd faced down Gammer Lindworm, survived the nightmare of Fiavla, and helped rid the world of a Primordial poison, but *this* was what made her afraid: a Floodwatch inn rented out from cellar to ceiling by three kretse.

She stepped through its gate into a yard filled with painted caravans, pickets of horses, and Vraszenians everywhere she looked. Exchanging news, striking deals, beating out dusty blankets; behind the open stable door, two youths had concealed themselves not quite well enough to hide their clumsy kisses.

Ren's heart beat loud enough that she could barely hear any of it. Only momentum carried her across the yard, toward the inn door, where a boy on the cusp of adolescence lounged with the unspeakable boredom of that age. A roll of cinnamon bark dangled from his teeth, the end dark and gummy from chewing.

"Can you help me?" Ren asked in Vraszenian, touching the end of her braid for comfort. Her mouth was dry. She should have stopped for some of that water. Or brought Grey. But no—she had to do this herself. She had to know.

The boy looked up, his boredom only faintly cut by curiosity. Ren made herself say, "I'm looking for the Volavka."

"Yeah." The boy's flat look asked, *And?*

Her information-gathering said there was a Volavka man named Lenismir; shortened for a patronymic, that would become Lenskaya. But was he the one she sought? "I would speak with an elder of that kureč."

The boy dragged the stick from his teeth, sucking spittle off the end. "Elders are usually busy." His bored eyes drifted to the purse stitched into Ren's sash.

A centira quickly palmed, and the boy rose from his slouch. "What name?" he asked, leading her through the inn's common room to an alcove whose sheltering curtain was tied open. "Ai, Ama. City stitch looking to talk trade."

The woman there quickly finished pinning a braid back into place and stood—then stopped. The braid, insufficiently fixed, slipped free to dangle over her right shoulder as she stared.

She looks like me, Ren thought, even as the woman whispered, "*Ivrina?*"

"Arenza." The name dropped from her numb lips, barely audible.

The woman's mirror fell to the floor in a clatter of bronze. She pushed past the boy, hands coming up to frame Ren's cheeks. Warm and road-worn, chafed red across the knuckles. Her face held the same warmth, a deeper shade than Ren's and spattered with dark spots.

Spattered with tears now, too. "Arenza? You're...you're Ivrina's girl. You must be." A sob hiccuped free; then Ren was swept into a hug, tears dampening her shoulder.

It was one thing to see the koszenie, its threads uncut. This was confirmation. *They didn't cast her out.*

But then...why? Why had Ivrina tried so hard to make certain Ren would never find her kin?

The woman pulled back to say, "I am Tsvetsa. Your mother's sister. Ivrina—is she—"

Ren shook her head before the woman—her *aunt*—could force the rest of the question out. "Many years ago."

Tsvetsa's chin dipped to her chest. Her voice shook as she said, "Alenši, fetch your grandfather."

His mother's reaction sparked more alacrity than Ren's coin had. Once he'd darted off, Tsvetsa's grip eased. She smoothed the bunched cotton of Ren's sleeves, an unspoken apology. "How came you to find us? Why came you not before?"

How to answer that question? The explanation was a lifetime long. "I knew not who you were. My mother—she never told me. And her koszenie..."

Before she could say more, an older man appeared, led by Alenši. Apparently the boy had conveyed some portion of what was going on, because while the man touched the wall for support at the sight of Ren, he didn't collapse. "It's true. Oh, child...you have the stamp of your mother." Tears spilled down his cheeks. "My poor, lost Ivrina."

"She named her Arenza," Tsvetsa said.

Vraszenian tradition named the eldest son after his paternal grandfather, the eldest daughter after her maternal grandmother—Lenismir's wife. Alenši caught the older man before he could falter completely. The boy's sullen glare said he blamed Ren. "She could be lying. Planning to cheat us somehow. Isn't Arenza the name of that—"

"Alenši!" The boy flinched at the smack of Tsvetsa's hand on the table. "See to your cousins. Keep them out of trouble."

Once he'd slunk away like a scolded cat, Tsvetsa tugged Ren to sit. "Forgive him. He's at that age."

Lenismir caught Ren's wrist across the table, his own fingers gnarled and knobbed like brown roots, but holding tight. "You must tell us everything."

"I hardly know what to tell," Ren said, her voice unsteady. "I grew up thinking you had cast my mother out. Because of me."

"*Never,*" he said, fierce and sure.

It stole her breath again. The gossips said the Volavka weren't like that... but one had only to look at the Szerado to know that public and private weren't always the same. She'd come here hoping, not knowing.

They'd wanted Ivrina. They wanted *Ren.*

Tsvetsa said, "Ivrina left *us.* She— Oh, Masks have mercy. Because of you, yes, but not any fault of yours."

Ren's hands were clasped so tightly her knuckles ached. "Tell me."

"She was gifted, my sister. Meant to become a great szorsa." Tsvetsa settled into a worn cadence of a kureč's memory-keeper, only her fretful touches on Lenismir's sleeve giving away that she was telling their own story. "We're not a wealthy kureč, as you see, but we paid well for her to drink from the wellspring. To have from Ažerais a true vision."

"The price was too high," Lenismir muttered. Ren didn't think he was speaking of Argentet's fees.

"We couldn't have known," Tsvetsa said. "The vision your mother had... for months she shared it not with us. But anyone could see it left her unsettled."

"Me." Ren forced the word out. She could see the pattern taking shape, inevitable and true. Hadn't something similar happened to Grey? "There was something wrong with me."

"Not wrong!" Tsvetsa reached across to grasp her wrist, mirroring her father. "But the cards Ivrina laid, when she knew she was bearing..."

Lenismir said, "She became convinced that if ever her child danced the kanina, a great terror she would bring into the world."

It was so unexpected that it cut through the tension and pain. Dancing the kanina—that would explain why Ivrina lied, why she kept her koszenie hidden. If Ren didn't know her kin and thought they wouldn't want her, she had no reason to seek them out. But what would Ivrina have done when Ren was grown and ready to—

To marry.

Dancing the kanina with Grey. Pulling Kolya into the world;

that was no great terror. But neither was he a mere shade. He'd been solid enough to touch.

And something else had come. Something that stayed, long after dawn should have banished it back to the dream. Something indeed born of terror.

The zlyzen.

"She was right," Ren whispered, her wrists slipping free. Right—but unable to see the whole of the weave, even guided by Ažerais. Ren touched the token braided into her hair. "When I danced at my wedding... It is a story for later. I know not why, though. It cannot be only that I was conceived on the Great Dream."

"I refuse to believe my granddaughter is the source of some great evil." Lenismir spat to the side. "No, if there's blame, it belongs to that Mask-damned spirit who seduced her."

"That was no seduction, Papa." Tsvetsa's eye roll was worthy of her son, and probably where he learned it. "Think you Ivrina's head was so easy to turn?"

Their words burned through the fog in Ren's mind. "Spirit? What spirit? I thought—the way I look—was my father not Liganti?"

"Seterin," Tsvetsa said. "At least, once he was. Ivrina claimed he was a philosopher, one whose spirit became lost in the dream."

Had Ren not been sitting, she would have fallen down. The last piece of the pattern wasn't a mere card; it was the stroke of chalk that activated a numinat. "You're saying my father *is Gabrius Mirscellis?*"

Over Lenismir's well-worn mutters, Tsvetsa said, "Yes, that was the name. She said he walked this world during the Great Dream—that at the next cycle she would seek him. To see if he could keep us all safe. We looked for her then, and the next as well, but..."

But Ivrina's house had burned mere months before the Great Dream—taking with it nearly everything she and Ren owned. She could barely afford food, let alone entrance to the amphitheatre. And by the cycle after that, Ivrina was dead.

Gabrius. That bright, energetic spirit, with hazel eyes like Ren's own, so long caught in the dream that he moved in it like his natural home. What would happen when a man like that sired a child?

Ren had found her father. And then she'd lost him, all his connections snapped, before she had a chance to realize what they meant.

Lenismir was weeping again. "All this time...Where were you? What became of my Ivri?"

Her throat closing with tears—for Lenismir, for Gabrius, for herself—Ren said, "A happy tale it is not."

"We are Vraszenian," Tsvetsa said. Her uneven smile included Ren in that statement. "Sad words are better than silent weeping."

Ren took a deep breath. "Very well." And she told the tale.

Floodwatch, Lower Bank: Cyprilun 25

This should have been Ren's life, Grey thought, following his wife into Floodwatch with the rest of their group. *A loving kureč, not the hardship of Lacewater.* And yet, that hardship and everything that followed it had brought her to him, just as his own troubles had brought him to her. How was one supposed to weigh those things against each other, the suffering and the joy?

Hearing music up ahead, he smiled wryly to himself. *You make a song out of it.* Like Vraszenians had been doing for ages uncounted.

The inn the Volavka shared with two other kretse was blazing with colored lanterns, and the melody spiraled up to the twilight sky like smoke. To celebrate the return of a lost daughter, they'd spared no effort. That the daughter was half-Seterin, a registered noblewoman of Nadežra, and a famous—or infamous—szorsa slated to be the next speaker for the Ižranyi only seemed to delight them all the more.

"She's here!" shouted a wiry beanpole of a boy with sly amber eyes and a girl Yvie's age on his shoulders. "Arenza Lenskaya Volavka, who comes with you, and what bring you from your travels?"

It was an old road greeting. Demanding gifts was rude, but travel spoils were different when kin met kin. After Ren said she wanted her family to meet the Volavka, Grey had warned the others what to expect, so they wouldn't arrive empty-handed.

Tess, predictably, brought fabric: a caravan blanket quilted out of rich brown silks, river-sleek satins, and cat-soft velvets. Sedge, equally predictably, brought alcohol: Grey had talked him up from zrel, so instead it was a bottle of chrysanthemum wine. Pavlin brought baked goods—but his introduction ran aground on an unexpected shoal. "I'm not family yet," he said, "but Tess and I are to be married, so—"

"You're *what?*"

That burst from Grey and Ren in tandem. Tess and Pavlin gaped; then Tess clapped both hands over her mouth. "Oh, Crone chide me for a fool...We never told you." Cheeks flaming, she shifted her hands to her hips. "Well, it was your wedding day! We didn't want to distract! And then you were gone, and—"

Ren cut the explanation short with a hug. "Bright news would have been no distraction," she said into Tess's curls, as Grey clapped Pavlin into his own embrace and Sedge muttered something not at all angry about damned hawks. "I'm so glad for you both."

The Volavka waited patiently through the congratulations, one road-worn gammer already on her third tear-soaked handker-chief. Recalling them to their purpose, Grey stepped forward, self-consciously touching his stubby wedding braid. "I am Grey, Ren's husband. Once threads bound me to kureč and clan, but no longer."

Thus far Lenismir had been accepting the gifts, but now two men took his place. The first was the Volavka kurenič, and the second—to Grey's shock—was the Dvornik clan elder. "Kiraly's loss is Dvornik's gain," the latter said, quoting a well-known fable about foxes raising raccoon kits as their own.

The kureč leader nodded. "Indeed. You are welcome among us, as Grey Noeski Volavka."

The sound of his mother's name taking the place of his father's made Grey's throat tighten with welcome tears. Then a snicker came from the sentry boy. "Just proves, better to be a chicken thief than a gutter cat—ow!" He smoothed the hair ruffled by Tsvetsa's gentle smack. "I meant it nicely!"

That released the tightness enough for Grey to chuckle. "It seems Ren is not the only Volavka with Ažerais's gift." Picking up the cage he'd carried all the way from Eastbridge, he flipped up the cloth cover.

The fat hen inside squawked with displeasure. She didn't know or care that she was the traditional gift from a husband to his wife's family; she just knew her nice dark shelter had suddenly gotten very bright. Grey let the cloth drop again. "Not stolen. But given in the hope that to you new wealth comes every day." The hen was duly handed over to Lenismir.

Alinka followed with her expected gift of healing tisanes, and Yvie's unexpected offering of her Elsivin doll. Lenismir examined it with the gravity of a man who'd raised many children and grandchildren, then returned it, saying, "I must count on you to keep brave Elsivin safe in your hands, and her dreams safe in your heart."

Once Yvie had solemnly accepted this charge, Grey sent Vargo forward with a none-too-gentle nudge. His brother had given five flavors of excuses not to join them, most of them having to do with Alinka's comfort. All of them foiled when Ren tapped his wrist— the knot bracelet and the pale scar beneath—and reminded him he was doubly bound.

"I'm Vargo. No relation to the Varadi, whatever the rumors might say." He brushed empty hands along the nap of his sueded coat, an uncharacteristic admission of nerves. "And I'm afraid my gift's still at the wainwright's waiting for the finishing touches. Figured these two might have opinions on their new caravan. Even if the rest of the family's more likely to use it once you return to the road."

Leave it to Vargo to keep his gift secret, then offer one more extravagant than appropriate. And yet, Grey's heart surged with gratitude and warmth. Never mind the exclamations from the Volavka, embarrassment and approval and one gaffer shaking his head over the young these days; Ren's shining eyes said the words Grey couldn't voice. Vargo had given them a *home.* Just as he'd done with the Westbridge townhouse: a home for each half of their lives.

Fitting, then, that after the excitement died down, Giuna was last to step forward. Donaia had declined to come tonight—not out of reluctance, Grey thought, but out of awareness that her presence would make an already awkward meeting that much stiffer. Her daughter would serve as the first, tentative embassy from the Traementis to the Volavka.

Giuna tugged her gloves until they came off. Bare-handed, she said, "I'm Giuna Traementis. Ren's cousin by register. I was told spices were a good gift, so I've brought that." She passed over a small coffer containing the traditional saffron and salt. "But I wanted to do more if I could. I don't know how matters will go, with the negotiations and all. But if the usual vouchers are distributed for the Great Dream this year, House Traementis will happily give ours to the Volavka."

The musicians in the courtyard were still playing, and Flood-watch had its usual noise, but a blanket of silence fell over the court-yard entrance. The Volavka knew Ren had been adopted into a noble house... but it was one thing to know, and another entirely to have Giuna standing before them offering what, in a more just world, would have been theirs by right.

The Dvornič settled the matter with a few short words. "You are welcome among us, Giuna Traementis," he said, and she exhaled visibly.

It didn't make the situation any less strange, a Liganti noble-woman joining this Vraszenian celebration. But it was a cautious strangeness, not a hostile one. And looking at the mixed group Ren had brought—Pavlin, Sedge, and Vargo Nadežran, Tess with her red Ganllechyn hair—Grey thought, *This is who she is. If they want her, they must have those who come with her.*

The Volavka kurenič bade them enter, and twilight faded into boisterous night, with Ren being introduced to every Volavka who hadn't met her yet: countless cousins and aunties and uncles, every-body wanting the story of her. They'd heard rumors about the con artist who pulled one over on the Liganti, but had never dreamed that con artist was one of *theirs*. She was well on her way toward becoming the new Clever Natalya—and, Grey thought with amusement, they didn't even know about the Black Rose.

As far as he was concerned, the celebration was a feast for a starving heart. Even as a child, he'd never truly been welcomed, and having cut his threads a mere week before, it was disorienting to suddenly be woven into a family that bore him no ill will at all. He found it easier to help the others, teaching Giuna the steps of a dance, guiding Tess toward some gammers she could talk embroidery with, warning Pavlin away from a dish that carried a heavy dose of Isarnah peppers and passing it to Sedge instead. Vargo needed little help: He already had his head bent with several road-worn elders, trade talk drifting from them like campfire smoke. Grey fully expected at least three deals by dawn.

He assumed he'd barely see Ren the rest of the night, but after a while she came and perched beside him on a traveling chest. Strands of hair had slipped free of her braids, edging her face like lace. Eyes wide, she said, "Masks have mercy. Once I had almost no family; now I need a chart to track them."

Not just the extended numbers of the Volavka, he suspected, but the Traementis as well, overlapping like the figure inscriptors called a vesica piscis. Vraszenians in one circle, Liganti in another, and Ren in the sliver between. Plus Tess and Sedge; normally the oath they'd sworn would have been witnessed by Ren's kurenič, but he seemed willing to accept it after the fact. Plus Grey, and through him, Vargo.

And Mirscellis, Grey thought. Ren had wanted to rescue his spirit anyway; she felt she owed it to him, after dragging him into their problems. Now that she knew the truth, nothing would stop her, even if the task was impossible.

Not tonight, though. Ren leaned against him, sighing. "How is this done when Vraszenians marry outsiders along the Dawn and Dusk Roads? Who belongs to whose family?"

"It's complicated," Grey said. "And it depends on the people in question."

He put one arm around her shoulders, and she nestled in close. "Can it even work to be both?" she asked. "Volavka and Traementis?"

In Nadežra, the answer was usually no. By law, no one linked to Ren by marriage or blood counted as Traementis, not unless they were inscribed in the register. Grey didn't even have the status of a contract husband. They hadn't had time to figure out what to do about that.

But in Nadežra, noble families didn't usually adopt Vraszenians. Mixing had happened, countless times in the last two hundred years, but very little of it enjoyed legal recognition.

Grey kissed the top of her head and gazed out at the celebration for the Volavka's daughter, an alta of the Upper Bank. "Perhaps now, it can."

The Dvorničn approached them, and they both rose to their feet. "Thank you for your kindness to Giuna," Ren said, twitching as if reflex wanted to offer Renata's Seterin curtsy.

A smile flickered at the corner of the Dvorničn's mouth. "Thank me for more in a moment—or not, perhaps. With Miškir I have been speaking."

The use of the Kiraličn's given name was a pointed reminder of who they were talking to. The clan elders weren't rulers; they governed none of the city-states to the south. Nevertheless, they held a great deal of power and authority in Vraszan.

Like an actress changing masks, the newfound daughter became the political tactician. "About the negotiations."

"About Laročja Szerado," the Dvorničn said. "Little could we do for you before; thanks to her, all know that your only standing among us is a position dubiously won. Without kin, without kurečn, without clan…"

Things Ren now had. Grey inhaled, wondering if the Dvorničn aimed where he thought.

An elaborate fox-knot charm swung from the hand the Dvorničn extended. "Speak on my behalf," he said.

Grey's pulse leapt. In the eyes of the Cinquerat, the ziemetse were foreign powers; they officially couldn't negotiate on behalf of Nadežrans. So the clan elders had unofficially chosen representatives: Vraszenians born and raised in the city, with no formal rank, but with a voice in Koszar's councils.

Ren didn't take the charm yet. "How would you have me speak?"

"As Ažerais guides you," the Dvornič said. "And I pray you speak louder than a certain carrion crow."

Dislodging Laročja would take more than words. But Ren accepted the charm, her fingers curling around its silken twists. "One way or another, I will."

Floodwatch, Lower Bank: Cyprilun 25

After nearly two hours of too many hugs and back claps and not enough wine to make them welcome, Vargo escaped the raucous Volavka reunion. The location in Floodwatch gave him a ready excuse; it was scarcely a bell's walk from the inn to the Isarnah compound.

And it was long past time he visited. Varuni might be a woman of few words, but there was a difference between silence and avoidance.

She hadn't gone home to Isarn while Vargo was off touring the Primordial-haunted nightmare of Fiavla. Instead she'd been in Floodwatch, leaning on the Isarnah ambassador to support the Vraszenian rebellion. She must have annoyed someone, because the ambassador's secretary led Vargo to the courtyard where Varuni was training without bothering to warn her of her visitor.

Veiled Waters was perhaps a week off, so the mists breathed out by the river were purely the product of nature, but that didn't lessen the chill that rode with them. Despite the weather, Varuni had changed into the clothes favored south of the mountains that cleaved Vraszan from Isarn: a sleeveless cotton tunic, formfitting and wax-resist dyed in deep purples and greens, with voluminous white trousers full through the hips and gathered tight around the calf.

Her gaze flicked briefly to him, but she didn't stop, making her slow, staccato way across the courtyard. Her chain flashed as it spun, changing direction whenever she whipped it around her elbow, her leg, her neck. The only sounds were the rattle of steel and Varuni's steady breathing.

On her return, she didn't stop at the transition from packed dirt to stone-paved walkway. The chain swept closer and closer to Vargo's face until he felt each pass like a lover's breath.

With a final twist of her elbow, Varuni caught the end, flipped the chain, and caught it again so it folded neatly in her hand. No danger to Vargo.

Unless she decided to punch him.

She didn't make any move for it, though. "That bell sound everybody heard," she said, pulling a towel from a hook on the wall and wiping away sweat. "Was that the end of it?"

"Yeah," Vargo said warily. He hadn't forgotten that in their last real conversation, he'd confessed to almost using Sessat on her.

Nor had she. "You got anything to say to me?"

"I shouldn't have thought about using a medallion to make you stay."

"And?"

And? *Oh. Right.* "And I shouldn't have leaned on your fear of that to make you leave."

"No. You shouldn't have," she said.

And *then* she punched him.

Later, after he was seated on the walkway with his back against the rail, the blood from his nose sopped up by her sweaty towel, she sank onto her haunches before him. "Guess you're back to healing quicker than a drunk denying he's soused," she said, ignoring his hiss when she pulled the towel away to examine her work.

"Yeah, after we came back from...Wait. You didn't know?" Vargo demanded, gingerly testing his sore nose. A beat later, he caught her sly, close-lipped grin. "Oh, fuck you."

"I prefer to be the one doing the fucking," she said, which was more about her relationship with Sedge than he really wanted to know. She spared him the torment of dwelling on that by asking, "You still being poisoned by anything?"

She deserved his honesty. "Poison like this doesn't go away easy. Might take lifetimes before I'm clean. But...it can't hurt anyone else. *I* can't hurt anyone else. At least, not that way."

Varuni nodded. Then she said, "I'm still going home."

He was braced for it; his shoulders didn't slump. "Understood."

The silence lasted just long enough to make him reach for more words, but there were none he felt comfortable using. Then Varuni snorted. "I'm going home for a *visit*. I'll be back in autumn. Try not to get killed before then."

"That was a *test*?"

Varuni punched his shoulder, a tap compared to what she'd inflicted on his nose. "And you passed. Congratulations. As your reward, you get to help me find gifts to take back to my family. I have a *lot* of cousins."

Isla Traementis, the Pearls: Cyprilun 26

A welcome spate of rain began falling as Ren hurried up the steps of Traementis Manor with Grey and Vargo at her heels. Although Scaperto had arranged carefully supervised water deliveries to the Old Island as part of the negotiations, even a brief rain would improve the situation there.

Shaking off the droplets that had beaded on her surcoat, she asked Colbrin, "Is Donaia here?"

"In her study, alta." Colbrin's behavior toward her hadn't changed in the aftermath of the revelations; so long as she was a registered member of the Traementis—and not hurting Donaia—his manners remained impeccable. But he had a touch of Vraszenian ancestry, Ren knew, and she wondered sometimes what thoughts flowed behind his courteous, disciplined mask.

Donaia's thoughts were much easier to read. Her warm welcome for Grey cooled to closed-lip cordiality when Vargo entered, though she didn't reach immediately for her gloves. "I didn't expect you two would bring company. Eret Vargo. You appear in good health."

::I don't understand. Why does she still dislike you?::

::It's the game we play, old man.:: Vargo seemed more amused than offended. Taking Donaia's bare fingers in his own, sheathed in grey sueded leather, he bowed with all the elegance that wasn't his birthright. "Kept so by the ill wishes of my enemies—isn't that the saying, Era Traementis?"

Her lips pressing flat on an unwanted smile, she buried her reclaimed hand under her new surcoat of soft rose twill. "What brings all three of you to me?"

Ren sank into a chair. Her mind reached reflexively for graceful ways to phrase the news, but these days, Donaia preferred blunt honesty. "I found out who my father is. And even by the standards of my life, it's..."

::Complicated,:: Alsius said, and Vargo echoed it with a twitch of his mouth.

Donaia's gaze flicked between them. "Politically complicated?"

"Metaphysically." Ren pressed her fingers to her brow. "Have you heard of the Seterin philosopher Gabrius Mirscellis?"

"I recognize the name."

"Over two hundred years ago, he came to Nadežra and got his spirit lost in Ažerais's Dream. But during the Great Dream, he can manifest—thoroughly enough that apparently he can sire a child."

For a moment, Donaia was perfectly still. Then laughter escaped her in a bark worthy of Meatball. Then more, until she was bent over her knees and gasping for breath. "Completely inappropriate. I apologize," she said between wheezes, waving away Grey's offer of assistance. "It's only...no wonder you developed a habit of lying. Who would believe the truth?"

Certainly the lies were sometimes more comfortable. Ren kept remembering the pain she'd given Lenismir and Tsvetsa by telling them about her life, and her mother's. She might be about to upset Donaia, too. "We've been in contact with his spirit, before I knew he was my father—I'll explain later, if you wish. The problem is that all connections to him in the dream have been severed. So now we have no way of finding him."

"Unless we make one," Vargo said. "That's where my inscription services come in."

Ren would have preferred it to be Tanaquis. Vargo didn't have her cousin's admiration for Mirscellis, nor her fascination with pattern. But with her injury, Tanaquis was in no shape for inscription—nor in any mood for company. She'd retreated to her townhouse at the first opportunity, over Donaia's fierce objections. It worried Ren, too, leaving Tanaquis on her own with only her maid, Zlatsa, to tend such an awful wound. She wasn't even sure they were in Whitesail; no one had answered the door when she knocked.

Or perhaps that door was closed only to *her*.

The silence had stretched out long enough for Donaia to fill in what hadn't been said. "You want this Mirscellis added to the Traementis register."

"As my father. Yes." Ren fidgeted with the cherry-piped edging of her surcoat. She'd donned Liganti attire and gloves for this visit; if she intended to accept her Seterin father, it seemed only right to acknowledge her northern heritage. "I know not if he'd wish it. I doubt he even knows he has a child. But all our other efforts to find him have failed. Once we restore him, he can make his own decision."

Donaia tipped her forehead onto her fingertips. "You know I don't do this lightly. Scribing someone in makes them *family*."

Like the scar on Ren's wrist—and the ones Grey and Vargo shared. Ren said, "If you would prefer we not—"

"This isn't about what I prefer. It's about what you des—" Donaia caught on the word, smiled ruefully, and said, "What you want. If it matters to you that he's your sire, then it matters to me. But if this is just a pragmatic way of solving a problem..."

Then they could do it by other means. Add him to Vargo's register—Alsius had suggested it already—or ignore the fact that Fulvet regulated such things and make a new one.

Ren thought about Gabrius, that sense she'd had of his spirit when the numinat called him into her body so he could speak to the others. Was it only that experience which made him feel so familiar, so fond? Would she have cared so much when his threads were severed, if that possession hadn't forged an odd bond between them?

The question was ultimately pointless. Whatever the road they'd traveled, this was where she stood now. From the moment Gabrius pulled her from a Primordial trap, she'd liked him. And yes, it mattered to her that he was her blood—spectral though that blood might be. She was Vraszenian enough for that to carry weight.

"He's a good man," Ren said quietly. "Whether he cares that I am his daughter, I cannot say. But...I care that he is my father."

Donaia rose and retrieved a scroll case from the lockbox behind her desk. The wood grain was rich and well-oiled, the bands and fixtures shining Tricat bronze. She frowned at them as she opened the case and unfurled the heavy scroll. "I hope you don't mind working here," Donaia said to Vargo. "I'd rather not send our register out like a rug in need of cleaning."

He flourished his straightedge. "I can perform anywhere, Era Traementis."

The innuendo in his voice deepened her frown, but she stepped aside and let him begin.

Grey poured Ren a cup of tea and laced it with aža while Vargo marveled at the extent of the protections Tanaquis had inscribed and Ren tried not to think of her cousin. As she drank the tea, Donaia settled on the couch next to her. "How did matters go with the Volavka? Giuna said everyone was kind, but she's picked up Leato's penchant for coddling me."

"I won't pretend there was *no* awkwardness, but..." Ren squeezed her aunt's hand, glove against skin. "I'd like you to meet them."

Donaia patted her arm. "And I will. Though with the way things are right now, who knows when that might be possible."

An oblique way of saying what they both dreaded: The longer negotiations between the Cinquerat and the Stadnem Anduske went on, the closer they came to the Great Dream without a resolution, the likelier it was for everything to collapse.

Vargo's work took no longer than the aža. By the time he finished, Ren was beginning to see into the dream.

She'd never looked at a register while spun. The crisp lines of the numinatria became a beautiful tapestry, colored all the warm tones of Tricat. Even death didn't cut them; family remained family after they were gone. Tanaquis's protections were a delicate net, filtering the strands running from her name to Donaia, Giuna, Tanaquis, all the Traementis—and others besides, branching out from the register's surface.

And a new thread, tenuous but present. The connection to Mirscellis.

When Ren concentrated on it, on the thought of Gabrius as her father, it sang like a plucked harp string, that single note resonating off the others into complex harmony. Heart aching, Ren thought, *If only Tanaquis were here to see.* The ways threads and people wove together into family, notes and melodies becoming songs. She was trying to craft how she would describe this to her cousin later when the thread suddenly brightened...and then Gabrius was there, stumbling to his knees on the carpet before her.

For a moment he gasped for air, as if surfacing from the river. Then he looked up, and his eyes widened.

So it was not merely my imagination. Your face... mirabile scitu. *I know you. Or—that is—you look like—*

"Ivrina Lenskaya Volavka," Ren said softly. "You met her at the Great Dream, many years ago."

One pale finger traced the line that linked them. *I remember her. She and I...* A faint blush tinged his translucent features. *I suppose what we did has become obvious. You're her daughter?*

Obvious—but he still didn't dare make the claim. "And yours."

His chin tucked like a penitent, but then his gaze flicked up to meet hers. *What of Ivrina?*

"She died. Years ago."

To everyone else, she was talking to thin air. They were speaking Vraszenian, which Donaia didn't understand, but she would know the cadences of grief. Her hand tightened on Ren's. Alsius had left Vargo's shoulder and was hovering near the focus of her gaze, as if sheer willpower could show him what she saw.

"I only learned of our connection recently," Ren said. "When I found the Volavka for myself."

Is that how . . . Gabrius touched the thread, and she felt the resonance in her bones.

"No. A Seterin connection for a Seterin father." She waved at the desk, at the rainbow array of threads spun by ink and parchment. "You're now in my family's register as Altan Gabrius Mirscellis Traementatis. Should you wish it."

He rocked back in surprise, gaze darting to the desk. What did he see, looking from the dream into the waking world? Was it the same tapestry to his eyes?

For once, *she* was the one thinking too metaphysically. Gabrius said, *You're an* alta? *How came that to be?*

It startled a laugh from her. They'd met when she was masked as the Black Rose; then he'd possessed her—and wasn't *that* a profoundly strange thought, in hindsight—then he'd seen her briefly when he tried to help them break Uniat's chain. Long enough to recognize a familiar cast in her features, but with no chance to learn who she was. What life she'd led.

Ren turned to Donaia, blinking past the dream layers of weariness and sorrow until she perceived the woman underneath, as strong and resilient as a river reed. Reeds Unbroken: She didn't need her deck to know that was Donaia's card. In Liganti Ren said, "Can we have fresh tea brought in? I have much to tell him while the aža lasts."

"Of course." Donaia stood, brushing off her skirts. "We'll—"

The door burst open to admit Scaperto Quientis. Anger flushed his cheeks, and the iron-dulled gold of his hair was in disarray. "Those damned Anduske go too far. Donaia, you won't believe—"

He stopped when he spied Ren and Vargo. "You two. If that boy ends up mutilated, I'm holding *you* responsible."

Ren shot to her feet. "Which boy?"

He answered her, but the weight of his scowl was on Vargo. "Which one do you think?"

"Iascat," Vargo said, his compass falling to the floor with a dull thunk. Grey reached out to steady him.

Scaperto hurled a crumpled wad of paper at Vargo. "That

patterner of theirs says her cards prove he's only stalling, making promises he has no intention of keeping, while we bring up soldiers to cut them all down. I won't deny that Caerulet has continued with military preparations, just in case—"

"But Iascat's negotiating in good faith," Ren said as Grey stooped to pick up the wad. She knew him well enough to believe that—and knew Laročja well enough, too.

"What have they threatened to do?" Vargo's quiet anger brushed over Ren's skin like spiderwebs, leaving a cold shiver in its wake. He'd declared his restoration of the West Channel numinat contingent on Iascat's safety, but he'd hardly stop the repairs when they were so close to done. Which gave Laročja leverage.

Grey smoothed the paper flat on the desk. In a controlled voice, he said, "Argentet's traditional punishment for lies and sedition. A split tongue."

"At least he'll survive it." For all the dismissal in Vargo's words, his flat tone said that if they went through with this, someone would regret it. "When and where?"

Vargo's solution would be bloody. The only question was whether Ren could find a better one. Looking at her, Grey said, "They're making a public example of him. Ninth sun, in Suncross Plaza."

That didn't give them much time—which, no doubt, was by design. Ren calculated. She'd still be aža-spun, but not so much that she couldn't function, especially with Grey to lead her.

She'd almost forgotten Gabrius. He stood, drawing her eye. *You are needed elsewhere.* A bow forestalled any apology she might have made. *Go. Now that I know . . . we will have many opportunities to speak again.*

She hoped that was true. As Gabrius faded deeper into the dream, she said, "The Dvornič made me his representative. I can get onto the island. Possibly you two as well—" That was to Grey and Vargo, who'd helped the Anduske in the past. But Donaia and Scaperto were out of the question.

"I'll make my own preparations," Scaperto said. It didn't sound like they'd be much less bloody than Vargo's. He was fond of Iascat, in an avuncular way.

"Do nothing rash," Ren pleaded. "Once we get there..."

What, then? A daring rescue by the Black Rose? That would only save Iascat, not fix the underlying problem.

"Once we get there," Ren said, her voice darkening, "we'll deal with Laročja."

Suncross, Old Island: Cyprilun 26

To facilitate negotiations, a single plank now spanned the gap in the Sunrise Bridge. The Faces smiled on Ren; the Anduske guarding it recognized both Grey and Vargo, and they didn't question the fox-knot charm Ren shoved at them. Then it was a run through the streets of Dawngate to Suncross Plaza, with an all-too-familiar voice shouting through a speaking horn up ahead.

Between them and that was a wall of bodies. "I'll find another way," Vargo muttered, and then he was gone. His "other way," Ren suspected, would involve knives, numinatria, or both. These days, he always had a few of those blasting numinata stuffed into his pockets.

She had to stop it from going that far. Not because she faulted Vargo, but because if things started down that path, there would be no stopping. If Iascat was maimed, the Cinquerat would retaliate; if the Cinquerat retaliated, it would be outright war.

They might be too late already.

Both Grey and Ren had plenty of practice at slipping through crowds, and at fighting dirty when slipping ceased to be enough. They left angry protests in their wake, but they managed to break through into the open space at the center.

Where Ren found Iascat chained to the plaza's flogging post with a placard around his neck proclaiming, *I deceive all*. Aža layered him with the shades of countless people who'd suffered in this place, bleeding for crimes great and small, or just for making the wrong cuff angry. But blinking through those, Ren saw that Iascat didn't seem to be wounded yet, and the pliers and knives on the table before him were clean.

And Koszar stood between Iascat and Laročja's men, cane raised in defense.

"So quickly you turn against me?" he demanded. His words were addressed not only to Laročja, but to the supporters flanking her. They wore the knotted charms of kureč leaders, and they outnumbered the ones wavering at the edges of the standoff. Idusza stood in the grip of a thick-armed man, though his broken and bloody nose said it hadn't gone easy for him. "At the labyrinth in Seven Knots, you proclaimed that our Lady guided you to support me. Which was false: your words then, or your words now?"

Then his gaze fell on Ren—and so did Laročja's.

Threads stretched around the old woman like a spider's web, but she was no kindly spinner, dancing with grace along their strands. Her step, as she came forward, landed with unfeeling force on the connections that wreathed her. "Yes, Ča Andrejek, speak to us of that night in Seven Knots. When the very demons that profane our Lady's dream rose to your aid—called, no doubt, by this kinless slipknot!" Her hand rose to point dramatically at Ren.

So much for that idea. Ren hadn't been sure whether she or Grey could do anything to call the zlyzen, but to try it now would only strengthen Laročja's net.

Like she'd done at the bridge, she'd rushed in without preparation. But what other choice did Ren have? Iascat was watching her with mute hope; Vargo was nowhere to be seen. Koszar was about to lose control of this rebellion. Striking Laročja would make her a martyr, but merely denouncing her would have all the effect of a pebble in the Dežera.

Ren had the Black Rose's mask with her. But before she could play that final card, Grey caught her wrist and kept it from plunging into her pocket.

He spoke to Laročja, but loud enough for all to hear. "So quick you have always been to speak poison against those with no defense or shield from you. Poison so potent, it drove your daughter by marriage to her death, drove your grandsons far from the kureč of their birth. How many others have you forced into misery, too frightened and cowed to speak out?"

Grey turned to gesture at the watching crowd. It wasn't the Rook's polished theatricality; Ren could feel his hand shaking on her wrist. Still, he went on. "And now this liberation, this glorious chance to finally regain Nadežra for our people—to certain failure you would drive it, all because you insist on *shouting* over Ažerais's voice instead of *listening*."

His voice, too, had begun to shake—but with passion, not fear. He drew a settling breath and shook his head. "No more. This woman you would silence has kin, and a name to speak from. She is Arenza Lenskaya Volavka of the Dvornik."

Ren had seen where his thrust was aimed. When he dragged her hand high, what she held was not the mask of the Black Rose. That would only distract everyone from the true problem here, Laročja's arrogance and her lies. Instead, the mist-tinged afternoon light caught on the green threads of the complex knot given to her by her new ziemič: the emblem of her right to speak on his behalf.

"A fool might refuse to heed one conceived on the Great Dream, touched by Ažerais herself," Grey said, strong now and sure. "A fool might refuse to heed one chosen in fair judgment by your fellow szorsas. But beyond foolishness it would be, heeding not the words of one recognized by the Dvornič himself. Will you shout over the voice of an entire clan? Will any here who wear a fox's colors and bear the Dvornik name stand for such an insult?"

"If to her he entrusted his token, it's the fox who's been made the fool!" Laročja snapped. Those around her in Dvornik green, who'd shifted with discomfort or surprise when Grey revealed Ren's token, bristled with indignation at being called fools...by a *Kiraly*, no less. Dvornik's twin, and his constant rival.

Realizing her misstep, Laročja rushed to speak before someone else could shout her down again. "So proudly you declare her names, but have you not forgotten one? *Traementatis*. This woman, Liganti by blood and by register, has profaned the purity of our rituals by seizing the right to speak for the Ižranyi! A szorsa she calls herself, while with her foreign arts she summons monsters! Ažerais *spits* upon her—and I call upon pattern itself to condemn her!"

Without shuffling, without prayers, Laročja drew a card and threw it to the ground in the direction of the dawn.

A hush fell. Not for the card—Ren could barely make out The Mask of Fools from only a few paces away—but for the words and gesture.

The calling of a curse.

Laročja snarled, "From the farthest edge of dawn, Ži Babša sees you. The Mask of Fools: As you listen not to the wisdom of your elders, so may you and those who stand at your side grow deaf in old age." Another card, this one to the west. "To the farthest end of dusk, the twin moons see you. Orin and Orasz: As you are two-faced in your dealings, so may the tears of sorrow cleave your cheeks and drown those who follow your lead."

Empty words, vague threats: a fraud's stock in trade. Ren would have laughed, save that those around her had already stepped back. *They* believed in Laročja's power. Only Grey remained at her side, his grip on her hand just short of pain. And Vargo, hidden somewhere in the crowd.

A third card, to the south. "From the waters' birth, your ancestors see you. Sword in Hand: May the swords of those who oppose you find a home in your heart, and the swords of those who support you break in their hands."

Ren caught her frown before it could crease her brow. That one came without an invocation of her sins, as if Laročja couldn't think of how to connect them. Yet the other szorsa wasn't even looking at the cards she threw; she already knew what they were.

She'd planned this scene, and she'd stacked the deck accordingly—but not for Ren. Her curse had probably been intended for Koszar; Laročja was altering it on the wing.

And it was reaching its climax. "To the Dežera's final rest,

Ažerais sees you. Sleeping Waters: May you and yours forever be denied our Lady's blessings." Stepping out of the scissored cross of the four cards, Laročja threw down the fifth and last card. "The final judgment of the Faces and the Masks upon you—"

She gasped and clutched her remaining deck to her chest. Her whisper carried in the sunset hush. "The Mask of Bones. *Death*."

How many times had Laročja done this before? But there was nothing to fear from a fraudulent szorsa. Aža still spun Ren's vision; no threads bound the pattern Laročja had laid, much less connected the cards to their target.

Ren allowed a heartbeat to pass. Then she spoke, boredom dripping from her tone like melted ice. "Are you finished scaring people and making mock of our deities?"

At her side, Grey stifled a laugh.

She gave him a squeeze before letting go and stepping up to the table set before Iascat. A sweep of one hand knocked the implements of torture to the ground; a sweep of the other spread her deck in a smooth fan.

Ren faced Laročja. "Let the Faces and the Masks judge us both. We will see who ends up cursed."

She didn't even have to search her deck. The cards practically slid into her hands, The Face of Glass and The Mask of Mirrors. And thanks to Laročja, now she knew how to use them. "From the farthest edge of dawn, let Hlai Oslit Rvarin judge our truths and our lies."

When she threw them both in the air, they fluttered down in separate directions. The Face of Glass at Ren's feet, and The Mask of Mirrors at Laročja's. Ren smiled, as sharp as broken glass. "For your falsehoods and manipulation, you stand judged. Let none ever again believe a word you say."

Laročja spat. "*You* are the liar, and all here know it. You came to save your Liganti master!"

Another pair: The Face of Stars and The Mask of Night. "To the farthest end of dusk, let Ir Entrelke Nedje judge which szorsa has served them well."

A gust of wind carried The Mask of Night past Laročja to land behind her. For the first time since Ren began, people started murmuring. "For your perversion of pattern, you stand judged," Ren said. "Let the eyes that refused to see become a warning to those who look."

"She wastes our time! Clear this slip-knot from our path, and let the prisoner be punished!"

But no one was listening to Laročja. They were all staring, aghast. Because while she looked about, gesturing imperiously at her followers...swirling pitch had seeped into her eyes, dyeing them the unrelieved black of a starless night.

When Ren had shaped pattern to restore the Rook, she'd done so with intention. Now she hardly felt like it was her hand turning the cards. Their course was laid out like the river, divine power flowing through her.

The Face of Crowns and The Mask of Knives. "From the waters' birth, let Dov Szarit Rožny judge who leads these people well." Ren wasn't even surprised anymore when the cards parted in midair. Every word, every action, was inevitable. Pattern did not so much predict the future as see where the present could lead, and this path had only one end. "For your malicious guidance, you stand judged. Let the mark of your authority be taken from you."

And Laročja's hair began to fall.

Silver strands drifted like rain to the ground, taking with them everything braided within: her wedding token, a rose of Ažerais knot, the charm that marked her as the senior szorsa of her kureč. Laročja's hands flew to her head, but she couldn't stop the cascade; within moments, her scalp was as bare as an egg.

She didn't shriek condemnations anymore. For the first time, Ren thought, she believed in what was happening.

But Ren wasn't done.

"To the Dežera's final rest, let Šen Asarn Kryzet judge who brings health or sickness to this city." The Mask of Worms had shown up in her patterns before, indicating the Primordial corruption of the medallions...but there was more than one kind of poison. The Face of Roses drifted down before Ren, while its counterpart completed the bracket around Laročja.

The worms Sedge vomited, those long months ago when Ren set out to win Idusza's trust, were palmed into his mouth. Laročja's hands were nowhere near her face when she doubled up and retched worms onto the cobblestones.

Ren swayed, the world spinning so fast there could have been a riot around her and she wouldn't have seen. The only fixed points were the cards. It needed one more...and though her heart ached, she knew which one she must choose.

And what she must do.

The Constant Spirit. The card of the Meszaros. Ren raised it high. "From your daughter by marriage you had this card, a gift to the szorsa of her new kureč. But you lack even the wisdom to see where your limits lie...and that lack killed Noeri Evriskaya Szerado. In the name of the ancestors, and for the destruction you have wrought, I revoke the gifts you have been given."

Ren tore the card in half—

—and Laročja's scattered deck began to burn.

The old woman's shriek was an animal thing. She tried to save the flaming cards; when that failed, she lunged at Ren, night-shot eyes wild, hands twisted into claws. Only Ren's stumble of exhaustion saved her face from being gouged. Grey caught her; Koszar's cane caught Laročja, its end jabbing into her gut. While Grey gently lowered Ren to the ground, others dragged the spitting, howling old woman back.

Ren tried to see who, whether it was only the ones who'd backed Koszar or whether Laročja's supporters had turned. But a dagged sleeve, its edges embroidered in red thread, eclipsed her view and blotted the exhausted sweat from Ren's brow. It belonged to Idusza, blood between her teeth and smile fierce as a rat's, kneeling over Ren where she lay across Grey's lap. "Say what you like," Idusza said. "Never will you convince me *that* was a hoax."

"It wasn't." Ren let her head fall back, meeting Grey's concerned blue gaze. "Your mother's card. I—"

"I know. Thank you. No longer can she profane Ažerais to hurt others." He closed his eyes, and she thought he murmured a prayer of gratitude.

Ren struggled to sit up. She'd thrown everything she had into discrediting Laročja. Was it enough? "Iascat. Is he..."

Idusza looked up and twitched in surprise. "Gone while we were distracted. The chains are empty."

A breath of a laugh seeped from Ren. "Vargo. Good."

She wanted to say more. To stand up and speak in support of Koszar; to use whatever credit she'd gained to push the tide in a useful direction. But she'd poured herself empty. She didn't even protest as Grey scooped her up and carried her home.

The Living Dream

Several hours of listening to nobles squabble like gulls over a soggy bun had given Vargo a headache that not even his renewed connection to Alsius could banish.

Almost makes you want to burn our register and move back to Froghole, doesn't it? he thought at Alsius. The old man had roused himself for the rescue of Iascat and the mad escape across the Sunrise Bridge gap, but in the days of diplomatic haggling that followed, he'd sunk back into his doldrums.

A mood that wasn't improved by the meeting Iascat had begged Vargo to attend.

::Those were better times,:: Alsius agreed wistfully, as Cibrial Destaelio picked apart yet another trade concession Iascat and Andrejek had hammered out between them.

"Forget the minutiae," Faella Coscanum said, pinching her snoozing nephew to wakefulness. Apparently Bondiro's punishment for stealing the medallion was having to attend these meetings. "The entire premise is laughable. Abolish the Cinquerat and replace it with a pack of foreigners? The Old Island can wash away before I'll agree to that nonsense."

With a sound more groan than sigh, Iascat said, "That's not what we're proposing. The Setterat is a redistribution for a more equitable division of power: two Liganti representatives, two Vraszenians, and three Nadežrans of mixed background. Your Mercy, if Caerulet's house member can't resist clouding this discussion with silt, I request that you remove her."

Cercel's lips flattened like she dearly wished she could. "We're overlooking the core problem. How can we accept any design for peace from people who used violence to force it? If we bend now, we'll invite more chaos in the future. Let them surrender their position and turn over their leaders; *then* we can settle terms."

"You know that won't happen, Agniet," Scaperto growled. "Asking them to give up every bit of leverage they have, with only the promise that we'll play nice afterward? *I* wouldn't trust that. Would you?"

Vargo could feel the frustration rising off Ren like heat from an oven. She'd achieved a miracle both figurative and literal, removing Laročja from the board; her blatant display of power had put her into bed for two days and rallied the entire rebellion behind Koszar. With that wind in his sails, he'd brought his side around to a remarkably sane compromise—one that recognized the mixed nature of Nadežra and made sure no one would be left without a voice.

It was far from perfect, of course. How were these representatives to be chosen? How could they make sure no group came to dominate the council later on, without forcing everyone into rigid divisions between Liganti, Vraszenian, and Nadežran? Not to mention all the smaller details tucked in alongside the big one, like the repeal of certain regulations that kept Vraszenians in poverty and robbed of influence. Nobody was under any illusions that the agreement would solve all the city's problems in one go, and a scant few of the objections raised so far today had actually managed to improve it.

But none of that would matter if they couldn't get the cuffs to support it.

Shouldn't have let everybody else in here, Vargo thought sourly as Era Cleoter started enumerating, yet again, the supposed dangers of allowing Staveswater to be recognized as a formal city district, rather than an eyesore the Liganti could smash whenever they pleased. *Hard enough to get five people to agree, without letting the entire Upper Bank stick their oars in.*

He'd directed the thought at Alsius, which meant Ren could overhear it. "If they weren't here," she murmured, nodding at Era Cleoter, Faella, and the other attendees without Cinquerat seats, "we wouldn't be, either."

Vargo's drifting gaze caught on Carinci Acrenix, a sullen Fadrin at her shoulder. So far, Carinci hadn't said much. Her scornful sniffs and swallowed tuts were more than enough to communicate her displeasure.

Fuck her, Vargo thought, keeping that bit of simmering rage to himself. She couldn't have squashed Alsius flatter if she'd stepped on him. Even if her cruelty was the result of a life under the Quinat medallion, Vargo couldn't forgive her. The Primordial only fed desires that were already there, and Carinci, it seemed, loved power more than her own son.

Fifteen years spent taking down Ghiscolo, and this was what they had to show for it. Carinci in charge of House Acrenix, and the Cinquerat still mired in mud. He'd held more real power—and been able to get more shit done—when he'd been the boss of the Lower Bank.

You're still that same man.

::What?:: Alsius said, suddenly alert, and Ren shot Vargo a worried look. Apparently he'd let that thought slip.

If Pearls politics en't working, time for some Froghole practicality, Vargo replied. He stood, cutting off an argument between Cibrial Destaelio and Tastral Cleoter about lading fees nobody had been trying to claim.

The look Iascat shot him was half-grateful, half-pleading. His voice courteous, he said, "You have something to add, Eret Vargo?"

"Yeah. You're empty-skulled idiots if you refuse this."

That caught their attention. All those bickering nobles straightened as if somebody had jammed a rod up their collective asses. Ren muffled a laugh behind her gloved hand.

"This is a good solution," Vargo said, slipping between chairs until he stood at the center of the Rotunda, before the Cinquerat's makeshift thrones. "A fair deal. Better than I expected, honestly, and the best you're going to get. Toss it, and you'll find out what a bad deal looks like."

Carinci sniffed. "I see weakness runs in your register," she said, as cloyingly sweet as poison hidden in Extaquium wine.

"I see impotent griping is all that remains in yours," Vargo snapped back. "I'll lay this for you plain. Half of you already know Kaius Rex used the power of a Primordial to conquer this place, and that the noble houses have been leaning on that power ever since. Well, it's gone now; you can't rely on it to prop you up anymore. And if you don't accept the *very good deal* Argentet has managed to broker for you, I'll tell the entire city your secret. Let's see how they feel about their leaders controlling their minds and slowly poisoning their everlasting souls."

The half of the room that hadn't known about that murmured in shock and confusion. Scaperto had gone rigid; Donaia's mouth hardened in grim acceptance of Vargo's point. Iascat looked like he was torn between kissing Vargo and ripping his own hair out.

Cibrial, predictably, shot to her feet. "That's sedition," she snarled.

"Call it what you like, Your Charity." He gave her a mocking bow. "I notice you didn't mind accepting my help in getting your family uncursed, after we liberated the Primordial artifact you refused to surrender. But honestly, I don't give a wet leech what you think. I've got a printing press all set up, ready to paper this city with the secrets you've tried so hard to keep." His second bow, to Iascat, was more ironic than mocking. "Somehow I don't think His Elegance will be in a rush to prosecute me."

::When did we set up a printing press?::

It's a good thing I'm the face of this operation, old man. You're a shit liar.

Ren didn't even bother to hide her amusement. Alsius huffed, ::Just remember whose brains got you out of Froghole to begin with.::

No, I won't ever forget that. Vargo gently patted Peabody. His fond smile bloomed into a full smirk when Cibrial gave a tiny shriek and recoiled from the spider peeking out from under his collar.

"Your threats won't work on me," said the cadaver-thin head of Fintenus. "I've had nothing to do with any supposed Primordial artifacts."

If he thought bringing down the current Cinquerat meant the wheel would turn in his favor, Vargo was only too happy to smash him under the rim. "Oh, I wouldn't specify which noble families were involved. Let people draw their own conclusions."

When nobody else dared protest, Vargo approached the desk where Iascat had laid out the draft of the treaty. "You know, I think you might be right. Peaceful negotiation *can* be effective," he said. Taking the pen Iascat offered him, he signed his name with a flourish.

They still argued, of course. If they didn't, he would have had to look outside to see if the Dežera was flowing backward.

But in the end, they signed.

The Point, Old Island: Cyprilun 33

How Dalisva could talk cheerfully while darting up the path to the Great Amphitheatre, Ren didn't know. She herself couldn't spare breath for anything other than trudging along, eyes on the rocky slope. The confrontation with Laročja wasn't the first time she'd imbued a pattern, but it was the first time she truly understood how imbuing a numinat could kill someone. All she had to do was imagine that outpouring continuing without end.

Vargo caught her when she stumbled, and Ren smiled at him. "I'm fine," she murmured. "We're almost there."

Grey had reached the top a step after Dalisva, and Ren leaned gratefully against him while the other woman spoke. "We'll be stringing a rope down the path to separate the people coming up from those going down, and you can see they're already building fences to channel the crowd entering the amphitheatre. We've based the lottery size on Argentet's figures for past attendance—though this being the end of a Grand Cycle, we've scaled up as much as we dare."

The lottery was an unfortunate necessity. If the Wellspring of Ažerais manifested in the middle of an open field, it might be possible to let in everyone who wanted to drink from it, but here atop the Point, there simply wasn't space. They had to limit the crowd somehow—and this year, at long last, control over that was in Vraszenian hands.

The fact that Vraszenians would therefore catch the brunt of any dissatisfaction wasn't lost on Ren. But dissatisfaction was inevitable, and she preferred this to Liganti extortion any day.

Dalisva was still talking. "An hour before sundown, the first pilgrims will be allowed into the amphitheatre, but the labyrinth path we'll keep clear for you and the ziemetse to walk when the wellspring appears. Have you appropriate clothing?" She cast a skeptical eye at Ren's outfit—the same attire she'd worn for her wedding, now cleaned and mended. But what was fitting for a street szorsa was as inadequate for the incoming speaker for the Ižranyi as nettle cloth would be for a Liganti alta.

"I'll manage something," Ren said, offering a mental apology to Tess and her poor, overtaxed fingers.

"You need a mask of dreamweaver feathers. I'll arrange it." Waving for Ren and the others to follow, Dalisva led them through one of the tunnels that pierced the stands. Her voice echoed off the walls as she said, "In one of the noble boxes you'll wait with the ziemetse until the procession begins. Traditionally, Ižranyi fills her cup last, but drinks first."

The amphitheatre opened up around them. Someone had laid markers on the stage, tracing the labyrinth pilgrims would walk. It reminded Ren of the blasphemous numinat painted in dreamweaver blood the previous year...but this was its holy opposite, an echo of the sacred site the Tyrant had torn down.

A cluster of people stood nearby, talking. She knew the Kiralič and the Dvornič, of course, and the Anoškinič she remembered from a few months previously. The other three she'd seen during the Ceremony of the Accords last year, but she could identify them only by their coats and colors.

She hesitated on the threshold, nerves sapping her strength. This past year she'd danced with and lied to many important people... but these were her *elders*. How could she—a half-blooded con artist who couldn't even name her kureč a month ago—stand among them?

As if Grey could hear Laročja's denunciations echoing in Ren's head, he nudged her forward. Dalisva said, "They're looking forward to meeting you, speaker-to-be."

It wasn't just the ziemetse, Ren saw as she came onto the stage. Koszar and Idusza were there, too, along with Mevieny. The process by which Setterat members would be chosen was still being hammered out, but rumor had Mevieny as the leading contender for the religious seat.

Koszar, by contrast, would hold no seat at all. That had been one of the conditions the Cinquerat demanded: that the radical who led the rebellion not be rewarded with further power.

Ren touched her brow in respect to the ziemetse, and tried not to twitch when they responded in kind. "Speaker-to-be," the Dvornič said. He looked like a fox well-fed with chickens; his decision to support her against Laročja had added considerably to the prestige of his clan. "Consider this a rehearsal for the Great Dream. Embarrassing it would be, if we stumbled over each other before our gathered people."

His wink didn't reassure Ren. But then, she had other reasons to be nervous. Only hours of rehearsing what she intended to say gave her the confidence to stop Dalisva from marshaling them to their starting points for the procession. "Before we begin," Ren said, "news I have that I must share with you all as the coming speaker for the Ižranyi. News *about* the Ižranyi."

Koszar straightened, his eyes widening. When she met his gaze, he nodded encouragement. Ren said, "Always we have believed that when Fiavla fell, the Ižranyi died with it. But recently, in Ažerais's Dream, I learned this is not quite true. Some Ižranyi are not lost. Some of them... became the zlyzen."

Stares all around, as if she'd told them the Dežera flowed with zrel instead of water. It was too absurd to sink in immediately. Before the initial disbelief could curdle into horror, Ren said, "We must help them. Too long have their souls been trapped. If for the Ižranyi I am to speak, then no other words can I give you."

Then she told them the story. Not the entire truth; Grey had agreed that unless it became necessary, nobody else needed to know the "great sacrifice" made to save the other clans was the blasphemy of burning their koszenie. But she related enough to cut through the questions they would have asked, to bypass the protestations that she must have somehow become hideously confused. The Ižranyi of beloved memory, trapped as *zlyzen*. How could she suggest such a thing?

"For us they have fought," Koszar said when she was done. "On the Old Island, they worked in the shadows of our people to free Nadežra. We owe them at least as much, to free their spirits of this curse."

Ren might have overleapt the others' doubts, but that just brought her more rapidly to their revulsion. "Surely this curse is a sign of great wrongs," the sour-faced Varadič said. "The judgment of the Faces and the Masks upon them. Who are we to counter the will of Ažerais?" He spoke to the other ziemetse, but chanced a side-long glance at Ren, no doubt thinking of Laročja's recent fate.

Grey answered him, admirably steady. "A curse it is—but one they took upon themselves to save the rest of our people. And one they *can* be freed of. As I was: The dream showed me I was once Ižranyi, twisted into the form of a zlyzen and later killed. So I lived and died, and was reborn."

Into the shocked silence that followed Grey's confession, the Kiralič said, "The ill fortune your grandmother claimed to see..."

"Was one I'd paid off, over many lifetimes. I would spare the others that undeserved debt."

The Varadič still looked doubtful that it was undeserved, but Mevieny stretched out one hand until Ren took it in her own. To the ziemetse, Mevieny said tartly, "One moment you call her speaker-to-be; the next, you question her words. Had I come with this tale to you, what would you say? If we can heal a great wrong, we must." She huffed a quiet laugh. "It seems to be a year for such things."

Ren squeezed her hand in thanks as the Anoškinič said, "Speaker-to-be, I doubt not that Ažerais has blessed you. But can even *your* gift cleanse them?"

"My gift, no," Ren said. "But there is another way."

As with the Traementis register, she would have preferred Tanaquis's aid. Though she had the greatest respect for Vargo's and Alsius's skills, neither of them quite had her cousin's brilliance, her ability to stretch the bounds of what numinatria could do. And Tanaquis adored this kind of thing, a chance to explore the place where different traditions met. The loss of her hand might prevent her from performing the inscription herself, but her mind would have leapt on this challenge like a starving alley cat.

But Ren still hadn't seen or heard from her cousin, nor had Donaia. Zlatsa, Tanaquis's maid, turned away all callers with sullen assurances that her mistress was well but didn't want company. If it hadn't been for the light in the garret window at night, Ren might have wondered if Tanaquis had left Nadežra entirely. As it was, she'd given serious thought to climbing in through that window, law and courtesy be damned.

What stayed her hand was the fear that Tanaquis had withdrawn because she blamed them all for her loss. That she didn't *want* to see them—not now, and maybe not ever.

Vargo edged forward, but the Stretskojič sneered before he could even speak. "You'd have us accept solutions from an inscriptor? An ambitious man who values no oaths and, from reports, has extended his own life using profane magics—not much different from Kaius Rex—"

"Excuse me? I have *much* finer discernment in my vices." At Ren's not-so-surreptitious kick to his ankle, Vargo sighed. "I also have experience removing similar curses using a numinat with a pattern card as a focus. So it would be a mix of traditions. Rather like me."

That last was half buried under renewed mutters from the ziemetse. "Wish you our blessing for this?" the Meszarič asked, his light voice freighted with doubt.

"More than your blessing," Grey said. "Ižranyi was sister to Meszaros and all the others. To free the souls of her people, we need the clans—and you represent them. For this ritual, we must have your aid."

A chop of the Meszarič's hand killed that idea. "I will not give it. Where the spirits of our people are concerned, only our own ways will I trust. There is no place here for Liganti figures."

"Pattern alone can't do this," Vargo said. His frustration was boiling close to the surface, and so was Ren's: Everything they tried to do, someone stood in the way. They'd kicked down or leapt over one obstacle after another, but new ones sprang up like weeds. "We didn't even think *numinatria* could do it, until Tanaquis Fienola figured out—"

As the voices rose in argument, Ren groaned and pressed the heels of her palms to her forehead. She wasn't rested enough for this debate; she'd hoped the awe of what she'd done to Laročja would carry her through.

Her gaze fell upon the labyrinth path marked on the amphitheatre stage.

"Wait," she said.

Apparently the awe was enough to make them listen, because the argument died down immediately. "A labyrinth path," she said.

Grey touched her shoulder. "What are you thinking?"

"That Tanaquis said once— Look." With renewed energy, Ren darted to its edge and began pointing. "As the path wraps, see how it creates layers? Count them, from center to edge."

"Seven," Vargo said. "Sebat. Purification."

"We walk the labyrinth to purify ourselves of ill fortune. It may not be a numinat as the Liganti construct it, but Tanaquis thought it might hold power nonetheless." Along with knotwork charms and Ganllechyn stitchery. Seterins and Liganti embroidered numinata into their clothing; such a figure had killed Alsius and almost done Grey in as well. Was this that much different?

She heard Alsius's objections before Vargo shared them. ::What focus would it have—the bowl of water at the center? And there's no enclosing figure to activate it!::

"But we walk the path," Ren said. "As Diomen did. *Performing* the figure, instead of inscribing it."

"Prayer can be a form of imbuing," Grey whispered. They shared a look between them. A braid of three traditions, together stronger than any one on its own.

The Anoškinič had his head bowed toward Andrejek, so close that salt tangled with pepper. Drawing away from that conference, he said, "The ghost owl's role is to remember the past and protect it in the present, just as the speaker's place is to advocate for the...apparently not-so-lost Ižranyi. I am in agreement with Szorsa Arenza that we must purify them of this curse and return them to our Lady's cycle—but not here. The wellspring appears for a single night only, and our people have waited too long."

Vargo snorted to Alsius. ::Not to mention that asking them to wait in line while we deal with nightmare monsters might not go over well.::

"The Seven Knots labyrinth," the Dvornič suggested, his quick support warming Ren. True, there might be political benefit in backing her, but there were risks as well. "And before the Great Dream. Better to send lost souls on at the end of a cycle, rather than start a new one with mourning and death."

One by one, the others fell into line—the Varadič last and most grudgingly. When they had all agreed, Ren said, "Seven Knots, then. And may the Ižranyi find release at last."

The Depths, Old Island: Cyprilun 34

With the river rising and Veiled Waters swiftly approaching, the usual passages Grey used to enter the Depths as the Rook were no longer safe. And someone in Koszar's faction had discovered the ward to the old temple no longer protected it, so now the clans did. The discovery of a forgotten place once holy to Ažerais, underneath the old labyrinth, was almost as exciting for his people as the retaking of Nadežra.

That was how people were starting to speak of it, even with the concessions made for the Liganti to have some voice in the new council. Nadežra was a Vraszenian city once more. People were flooding downriver more swiftly than the waters to celebrate a victory they'd had little part in.

The lightstone strapped to Grey's wrist cast bouncing shadows along the uneven stone walls, emphasizing the perpetual slickness. Dirty water from puddles in the lower reaches spattered Grey's boots up to his ankles. Ren was busy wrangling the ziemetse and details of the ritual; Vargo had hesitated for all of a heartbeat at the prospect of again entering the zlyzen- and disease-fouled Depths, before declaring that even blood brotherhood had its limits and Ren probably needed his help. When Grey had grumpily called him a coward, Vargo accepted the title with pride.

So it was Grey's footsteps alone, echoing in counterpoint to the sound of dripping water. With no other notion of how to track his quarry, he followed the cold dread pooling like stagnant river water in his gut.

He'd always feared and loathed the zlyzen. After that journey to the dream of Fiavla, it was worse instead of better. He didn't want to accept that he'd once crawled alongside them, wrong jointed and foul. That he'd fed on dreams. Maybe killed people.

You've killed people as a hawk.

But that was different. Wasn't it?

Heedless of the damp stone, he braced one hand against the wall and closed his eyes. *They were human, once. They deserve to pass on to Ažerais's grace.* He was living evidence of that. A small, shameful part of him had considered that killing the zlyzen would also release them—but to lifetimes of slow purification, working off the stain while those around them struck out or flinched away. Better to cleanse them now, and let their souls be reborn freely. So they wouldn't suffer like he had. So they wouldn't suffer like they were doing now.

So they can't kill again.

Opening his eyes didn't banish the memory of Leato's body, the blood-wet shreds of his sparkling Rook costume covered by Pavlin's coat. Grey couldn't undo the choice he'd made that night, dragging Ren up before going back for Leato. He couldn't even bring himself to regret it, knowing Pavlin's coat could have been Ren's shroud. But it was hard not to hate himself a little for that lack of regret. Even harder not to hate the zlyzen, who were only acting under Ondrakja's control.

That was what Grey told himself, forcing one foot in front of the other as he ventured farther into the Depths.

His route took him toward the old cages where Ondrakja had trapped children and fed their dreams to the zlyzen. The actual passages leading there were blocked by floodwaters, murky mirrors of black glass that Grey's eyes avoided for fear of what he might see.

Instead he crouched at the lip of one of the pools and placed his palm flat against the surface. During the ordeal, the zlyzen had come in answer to Ren's prayers. They'd also come when he desperately needed something to distract the patrol in the Depths so the Rook-costumed refugees could escape. Her connection to them was the thread she'd spun in the dream; his was something else.

Grey called with the part of his soul he'd always feared existed, no matter how much of a fraud he knew Laročja to be. Called with the last, fading remnants of a curse that hung off him like wisps of fog, soon to be banished by the morning light.

The water shifted, a smooth carbuncle rising like a shell encasing the shape underneath. Then the shroud broke, water flattening the corpse grass hair and sheeting down the elongated muzzle of a zlyzen. It dripped from the creature's fangs, spattering the bare back of Grey's hand. Another rose, and another, the zlyzen surfacing from the underground pool like clicking beetles from a burrow.

Every instinct in his body screamed *run*. The Primordial that destroyed the Ižranyi was fear, and knowing that didn't do anything to reduce its scrape along his nerves. So many in one place, and he was alone, in the dark, with nothing but hope and a sword to defend himself—

The head of one dipped low. He thought it might be the one that had appeared in Westbridge, the one that took them into the dream. A leader, inasmuch as they had one.

Except now that leader was bowing to *him*.

Grey remained perfectly still. Breathing through his fear, his horror, his revulsion. *This is what Laročja felt when she looked at your pattern.* But how different would things have been if she could have seen past that, to compassion?

He had to be better than she was. Had to look the zlyzen in the eye. Had to accept that among them were the ones who'd killed Leato, tearing apart a man he could have called brother. He'd forgiven Vargo for Kolya's death; these creatures—these *people*— deserved his mercy, too.

The fear didn't leave. It wouldn't, not until the Ižranyi were purified and released. But he breathed until it settled onto his shoulders like a cloak, until he could carry its weight.

Until he could reach out and touch the twisted shoulder of the Ižranyi in front of him, and think of it in those terms. A person he was touching, not a monster.

Then he said, "Come with me. It's time for you to be free."

Seven Knots, Lower Bank: Cyprilun 34

From where she stood in the plaza outside the Seven Knots labyrinth, Ren could only see the fireworks as bright spots through the fog. In a display of both excellent and abysmal timing, the lottery to choose who would enter the amphitheatre for the Great Dream had fallen on the first night of Veiled Waters, when the mist rose from the river and would not dissipate for a week. But Argentet had provided fireworks to mark the occasion, and so they were duly set off, even if their glow was muffled. Perhaps the people gathered at the amphitheatre for the lottery could see them, the Point lifting them above the murk.

Ren felt a little bad for abandoning Dalisva and Mevieny to handle the lottery themselves. As the incoming speaker, she probably ought to be there. But once the Stretskojič suggested that the event would create an ideal opportunity to sneak the zlyzen into Seven Knots, she knew she was needed more elsewhere.

Just as Grey was needed, to find and guide the zlyzen to the labyrinth where the ziemetse waited. Just as Vargo and Arkady were needed, to clear the streets so some poor soul didn't wander down the wrong alley at the wrong time and trip over a pack of walking nightmares. "We're the red thread what keeps everybody else safe," Arkady had told her kids, handing out thread labyrinths, and they trusted her enough to follow that lead.

A soft light warmed the fog drifting across the plaza, lower and gentler than the blooms of color in the sky. Ignoring the pockets of shadow that could be mistaken for mist if not for the low, hissed greetings, Ren met Grey in the middle of the square.

"Any difficulty?" she asked, withdrawing from a too-brief embrace.

His hand lingered in her hair, brushing dampness from her braids. "No. I cannot tell if I'm unnerved because that bodes ill, or just due to the company."

Her gaze followed his gesture. No mistaking the shadows now for anything but what they were. Zlyzen, skulking like a pack of cadaverous hounds. "Is this all of them?"

"I think so," Grey said, though they had no way of confirming it. "I think they know what we intend. I think they welcome an end to their suffering, and hope for a return to Ažerais's grace."

I hope we can give it to them. Her suggestion of using a labyrinth was an untested theory. For all she knew, it would corrupt the sacred space and leave the zlyzen untouched. The confidence she'd felt at the amphitheatre was thinner and more tenuous in the darkness and the fog, with zlyzen all around.

Or that was just the fear they exuded, making her imagination spin dreadful scenarios. Ren swallowed and said, "Let's bring them inside."

The ziemetse were all elders of their clans, regardless of their age. They wouldn't have held those positions if they couldn't maintain an air of dignity in the face of provocation. Still, several retreated an involuntary step when Ren and Grey entered the labyrinth, the zlyzen at their heels.

The Meszarič, demonstrating the true spirit of his clan, showed no such hesitation. He was short and slight compared to the born men leading the other clans, but he held his chin high as he stepped forward. To Ren he said, "If along the path you will guide us, szorsa, then I am ready to lead these who were once our kin."

Grey's memories from their journey to Fiavla had given them a map. Six lifetimes he had lived, each washing away some of the corruption staining his spirit. To release the zlyzen, they would try the same, starting with the eldest of Ažerais's children.

Ren had already made her offerings to the Faces and Masks. Now she dug under the drape of her mother's koszenie to retrieve her cards. As she set her foot on the path, her lips moved with the first prayer. The rasp of shuffled cards sounded loud in the hush of the labyrinth.

Back and forth, following the looping, ever-turning way. It took concentration to shuffle while walking, but her training in card tricks and false shuffles stood her in oddly good stead. She even paced it correctly, reciting the final prayer as she arrived at the center. "Ižranyi, favored daughter of Ažerais, bless me with your insight, that I may honor my ancestors and the wisdom of those who have gone before."

His deep breath visible even from across the labyrinth, the Meszarič began to walk—and the zlyzen followed.

They were numerous enough to trail out in a long line behind the ziemič. This was the first time Ren had been able to count them, though, and her heart ached at the sight of how few they truly were. Less than a hundred. Where had the rest gone? Some zlyzen had no doubt died, like Grey, like the one Ondrakja killed. But five hundred years ago, the Ižranyi would have numbered in the tens of thousands. More, even. Only a few became zlyzen; the rest were lost even to the dream. Would purifying these survivors also save them?

She didn't know. Still, the reminder of how much had been lost helped her hold steady as the Meszarič reached the center, trailing fear in his wake. Deck in hand, Ren dealt a card onto the wide, flat edge of the bowl at the labyrinth's heart.

It almost tipped into the water as her hand shook. The Constant Spirit: the card she'd torn up to bring Laročja down. It shouldn't have been in her deck; the halves had blown away in Suncross, her sacrifice to the Faces and the Masks. Yet here it was, whole once more.

The Meszarič cleared his throat, dragging Ren's attention back to the moment. She gestured at the card on the shining silver rim. "Honest and enduring, the children of Meszaros are a constant spirit in memory and deed. Will you reclaim kinship with these, Ažerais's lost children, and grant them forgiveness on her behalf?"

It was a delicate weave of words and implications. The corruption of Fiavla's fall needed to be cleansed...but if she left the secret blasphemy of the burned koszenie unaddressed—if they let those threads remain severed—then the spirits of the lost Ižranyi might end up like the nameless szorsa, untethered and wandering.

The clan of the horse was constant, but not necessarily clever. Hearing nothing worrisome in Ren's words, the Meszarič said, "I will." He dipped his hand into the bowl of water. One by one, the zlyzen approached, and he touched his finger to their foreheads as they passed.

As each was anointed, the zlyzen crossed straight over the twisting pathways of the labyrinth, leaving their sins and troubles behind. Ren hoped it was not her imagination that, as they passed the far edge, their torn skin smoothed, their twisted limbs straightened, and the miasma of curdled fear eased, like the lifting of a horse's yoke after a long day.

The Stretskojič looked like he retained serious doubts, but he wasn't about to let his Meszaros counterpart upstage him. When the last of the zlyzen had reached the colonnade, he began the walk anew, leading them along the path. And Ren, waiting for them, dealt a second card.

This time it was more than a mere gift, restoring what she had sacrificed. The zlyzen crossed freely over the barrier between waking and dream; it seemed they blurred it for those around them, too. The Friendly Fist had never been in Ren's deck, but what she dealt onto the bowl's rim was the card of the Stretsko.

No terrible bell shivered the air as the cycle continued. Instead the atmosphere lightened with each pass, as if the sun were rising in this flame-lit space. One by one the ziemetse led the zlyzen along the labyrinth; one by one Ren dealt cards that were nowhere in her deck, The Silent Witness, The Kindly Spinner, The Artful Gentleman, The Hidden Eye. The clan elders acknowledged the zlyzen as their lost kin, and every time the creatures crossed the labyrinth path, they left a little more of their inhumanity behind.

Until it came to Grey. Who'd walked that road before them, purifying himself through one life after another.

The figures that followed him walked upright now. Still hunched, heads bowed, translucent as though the more human they became, the less they belonged in the waking world. Ren's cheeks were damp, and it wasn't from the dense fog spilling through the labyrinth's open roof. But she couldn't dry her face; already she held her cards in the folds of her skirts to keep the dew from them.

Grey's fingers brushed the tears away when he came before her. "I'm here, Szeren," he said, his voice for her alone. "Though lifetimes it's taken me to find my luck again."

A suppressed laugh caught her chest like a hiccup. She pressed her cheek into his palm, briefly, before turning to the bowl to deal the last card. If the pattern held, it would be one that hadn't existed since Fiavla's fall. Her fingers slipped on her deck, numb with fear that here, at the last moment, the dream would fail her. That they might release the zlyzen, but the card wiped from the world would remain lost forever.

A soft intake of breath from Grey drew her attention down to the bowl.

The water was as still as glass, but something lay in its depths. Color rippled around it like inks bleeding into fog. Hand shaking, Ren reached in and closed her fingers around a piece of stiffened paper.

It came out as dry as her throat, as clear as if newly painted—and real.

"The Living Dream," Ren whispered, reading the name from the scrolled panel at the bottom. Was that what it had always been called? Or was this a new card, a new dream to take the place of the old?

She might never know the answer to that question, but she knew what the card meant. "Our Lady's most profound blessing. Ižranyi and her gift were the threads that wove seven clans into one people. Ažerais's lost children, of your nightmare you have been cleansed. Will you tie your threads to ours once more?"

As insubstantial as they looked, the people who had once been zlyzen were solid enough for Grey to touch. Dipping his hand into the water, he anointed each one in turn, and sent them out with his own murmured blessing. They were individuals now, male and female, young and old, the chance survivors of unspeakable horror. Ren's vision blurred as they went, and she thought at first that her tears were responsible for what she saw.

But it was no delusion. The Ižranyi didn't fade into the dream. When they reached the colonnade, they stood clean—human—*solid*. Spirit transformed into flesh.

Naked flesh. The Meszarič was the first to respond, jolting out of his shock to strip off his panel coat and wrap it around the woman nearest to him. An older woman, sagging dark skin striped with paler lines across her belly from bearing children, her hair shot with white. When his panel coat touched her shoulders, she broke into sobs, dragging the Meszarič to his knees as she fell. He wrapped his arms around her, breathing prayers as he wept.

Others were kneeling, crying, burying faces in shaking hands as though unready to face the world they'd returned to. After a frozen moment, the rest of the ziemetse followed the Meszarič's lead, shedding panel coats and vests and even shirts. But there were only six of them, outnumbered by the Ižranyi gathered beneath the watching Faces and Masks.

"Grey," Ren whispered, not certain what she wanted to say. What she *could* say. They'd expected to send these spirits on to rebirth, like they had with the nameless szorsa. Not...*this*.

His blue eyes mirrored her shock and wonder. And the smile he gave her, the smile that was only for her, she reflected back at him. Her husband. Her love. The thread she happily wound around her heart, with whom all things seemed possible.

Grey kissed her, pressing his lips to her brow. Then his fingers touched the same spot, cool with the water from the bowl. Ren did the same, blessing him as he'd blessed her.

The clan cards were still there, balanced on the rim. And in her other hand, The Living Dream. It was as real as the Ižranyi.

"We must help them," Grey said. And Ren, gathering up her cards with a whisper of thanks, followed him to welcome the clan that was no longer lost.

25

The Peacock's Web

Isla Čaprila, Eastbridge: Fellun 4

"Are you certain you're not the one leaving for Isarn?" Iascat asked as Vargo navigated around the trunks that had sprung up throughout his parlour like mushrooms. Either Varuni had enough cousins to form her own Vraszenian clan, or they expected a *lot* of gifts. He'd let her use his house as a temporary depot, and she was milking his guilt for all it was worth.

With the other seating taken over by sacks of Lumen only knew what, Vargo was left to squeeze onto the couch next to Iascat. Anticipating this, he'd only prepared one bowl of tolatsy for them to share. A *big* bowl. They'd worked up an appetite the previous evening.

"Gotta admit, the thought's tempting," he said, passing the bowl and a second spoon to Iascat.

"Then I'll have to tempt you to stay," Iascat said, leaning forward. He might prefer his tea cloying, but Vargo didn't mind the sweetness that lingered on his lips afterward.

He pulled away, though, before they could fall too deeply into distraction. "We should get dressed. Interruptions will be here soon."

"If you insist. But I'm stealing this robe," Iascat said, smoothing a hand over the river-blue patchwork of silks Vargo had tossed to him when they woke.

Vargo laughed and swiped a chunk of seared pork before Iascat could scoop it up. "See, this is why you wouldn't last a day on the Lower Bank. A good thief doesn't warn their mark."

"Oh? And what would you know about Lower Bank thieves, *Eret* Vargo?"

He must have caught Vargo's flinch, a bruise as tender as the ones Iascat had left on his skin. Too bad Vargo couldn't heal spiritual hurts like he did physical ones. Grin fading, Iascat said, "Sorry."

"For speaking the truth? You're not the one who sold me out." That had been Sibiliat, with Carinci's help. But he'd left himself open for it, knowing all the while that somebody could plant a knife there.

They ate quietly after that, and parted sooner than Vargo might have preferred. When Varuni arrived with a wagon and two Isarnah porters, she led them inside to take stock of her haul; Vargo bade Iascat farewell and then lingered on his stoop, watching the mist of Veiled Waters swirl in his wake.

He should have known better than to stake himself out like a target dummy for the Masks. No sooner had the fog swallowed Iascat's sedan chair than it coughed up two new figures, drawing close enough to resolve into Nikory and Sedge.

But only the two of them. No other Fog Spiders slipped out of their namesake weather. Not a drub-gang then, come to teach their former boss a painful lesson.

::What do they want?:: Alsius grumbled. It was the first he'd spoken all morning. If not for the familiar lump shifting the set of his collar, Vargo might not have known he was even there.

Nikory winced when Vargo echoed the question aloud, complete with Alsius's surly intonation. "Knot bosses want to talk to you. Figured you'd trust the message from us more'n someone else."

He was half-right. "You, I trust. The rest of that lot can drink piss," Vargo said, luxuriating in pettiness like a warm bath. "If anyone wants to speak to me, they know where to find me. My Dockwall warehouse, for example."

Where he'd been jumped by the Roundabout Boys. Where

Orostin died defending him because nobody in his knots gave Vargo the courtesy of a warning before they turned on him.

Nikory flinched. Sedge looked like he would speak, but his mouth clamped oyster-tight when Varuni emerged from the house to stand silent at Vargo's side.

"*We* didn't sell you out," Nikory said. "We tried to help with the swap for Dmatsos."

"You two did. The rest of them threw me in the gutter like I wasn't even worth selling at a remnants stall." Years of habit, of hiding his heart like the deepest currents of the Dežera, kept Vargo's tone as bright and sleek as a knife's blade.

::I didn't realize you were so angry.::

Neither did I. He'd been too busy to think about it, what with trapped spirits and Primordial medallions and a revolution cleaving his city in half. But the hurt Iascat had accidentally brushed against wasn't just a bruise. It was an open wound. "I'm not walking into another trap. If they've something to say, they can come to *me*."

"It en't a trap. And I think you'll want to hear this." Sedge finally spoke up as Vargo turned away. The only voice from his old knots Vargo was willing to take a risk for. Not because of oaths never actually sworn, but for two that were. Vargo touched his wrist, the knotted cord of his oath with Ren, the faint scar of his oath with Grey. He trusted them, and they trusted Sedge.

Vargo gave Varuni a rueful, twisted smile. "You up for protecting my ass one more time?"

Froghole, Lower Bank: Fellun 4

It ends where it started, Vargo thought with grim amusement as Nikory led him to the old lace mill in Froghole.

He'd refitted the place since Ondrakja and Breccone Indestris used it to make ash out of zlyzen blood, and by day it almost looked respectable. The bird shit had been scoured off, the rot-pitted floorboards replaced. Not even the memory of that blasphemous numinat remained. It could hardly be called the same building—no more than Vargo was the same boy who hid here after his life was bound to a Liganti noble trapped inside a spider.

::Stop being so morbid. They won't hurt you. They can't. Not with me here.::

Vargo was inclined to argue—by nature, Alsius would say—but he couldn't afford the distraction when he entered the wide-open warehouse and saw too big a crowd for his comfort. Knotted cords were everywhere, on wrists, around necks. Pinned to coats or braided like wedding tokens into hair. And every color: the sapphire blue of the Fog Spiders, the crimson and cream of the Odd Alley Gang. No Roundabout Boys—and a good thing, too, because Vargo would have walked right back out if they dared show—but Moon Harpies, Leek Street Cutters, and even Blackrabbit Drifters all the way down from Dockwall. A score of people, easy, many of them former seconds of his old bosses—names he didn't know attached to faces he recognized. The bosses he'd worked with before had the most dour expressions, like they'd just as soon see Vargo floating in the Dežera as walking into the lace mill.

A clank from his other side said Varuni already had her chain whips out in case. But Vargo knew the look of people who wanted something from him. He stepped forward, as though daring one of them to throw the first punch. "You've got something to say to me? Then say it."

"I'll start," said Mirka, the head of the Moon Harpies. Mileka stood beside her, hair hacked short and bowed head not enough to hide her swollen nose and cut lip. Given the knot boss's sharp grin and blood-scabbed knuckles, Vargo assumed Mirka had won whatever disagreement her twin had raised about coming here. "Things've gone to shit since we... Well, it en't cutting knot if there was no knot to cut, but you know what I mean."

Quiet as the mist of Veiled Waters descending, the other bosses murmured their grudging agreement.

"And now, with this new treaty, gonna be a lot more'n just rats moving in on our turf," grumbled the new boss of the Odd Alley Gang. Their patch bumped up against Tserdev's, and had always been one of the bloodiest of Vargo's holdings.

"Gutter cats, chicken thieves," spat a woman with the recognizable fur cap of the Blackrabbit Drifters. "Whole swarm of vermin looking to take what's ours."

Nikory huffed, crossing his arms. "Let 'em try. Fog Spiders will be as close as any Varadi gets to taking over the Lower Bank."

::We just ended one possible war; now we're saddled with another. Lovely.:: Alsius sounded tired. Resigned. Like he often did these days.

I don't think so. Vargo rubbed idly at his chest, a vain attempt to soothe a hurt that wasn't his. Every eye in the room snapped to his hand. More than a few awed whispers followed. It seemed his time with Tserdev had done more good for his reputation than bad.

"Sounds like a problem that isn't mine anymore," Vargo said. He suspected he saw the shape of what they wanted, but he was going to make them ask, rather than giving them the satisfaction of his guess.

"Could be," said Odd Alley's new boss. "We got agreement from the fists, and any boss that en't in has been cut out."

Nikory lifted a shoulder when Vargo cast him a surprised glance. "Told 'em I weren't bringing you here if they was just going to waste your time."

::But everything's finally settled down,:: Alsius whined. ::Is this a headache we really want again?::

Most of our investments are on the Lower Bank. Might be a headache worth taking. Vargo hadn't worn gloves, but he toyed with the lace edging of his cuffs, a subtle reminder of why they'd given him the boot. "And what do you want from me?"

"What we should have had before. You take the aža, you take the oath. You make yourself one of us instead of keeping apart." One man was talking, but every person in the room nodded—except Sedge, massaging his brow, and Varuni, whose lips were flat against what Vargo suspected was a laugh.

Having no such reservations, Vargo chuckled dryly. "Tie myself to a dozen different horses? That's asking to be ripped apart. You want a boss that crazy, talk to Arkady Bones."

"Told you this was a waste of breath," muttered Mileka. Definitely the one who'd given him trouble on the canal during the boat races. "Cuffs en't got loyalty to nobody."

The temptation to lift his sleeve and show off the knot charm around his wrist rose and ebbed without breaking. Vargo said, "En't my loyalty you want, is it? It's my ability to keep the peace and make you money. Don't need oaths for that. I just need charters. And with Fulvet having to repair the East Channel numinat so the cuffs aren't drinking their own piss-water, I've got the leverage to get them."

"Fulvet?" Mileka scoffed. "Don't militia charters come from Caerulet?"

"Right. Because what the rookeries need is *more* blood in the streets." Under Vargo's steady stare, her shoulders curled in like scorched paper. "A Fulvet charter sets the boundaries of your patches, then has you doing what you're doing already: keeping people safe, seeing after the nippers without family to do it for 'em, getting the sick what they need so we don't come down plague-ridden, finding a squat for everyone so they en't clogging our gutters. Only with a Fulvet charter, the hawks can't hassle you, and you get *paid.*"

That was only part of what his knots did, of course. They also smuggled goods, made sure local merchants dealt fairly and didn't get run out by newcomers, ran gambling dens and other enterprises on the more illicit side of the line. Pulling any of that muck up into the light would require negotiation with other seats, Prasinet in particular. But he'd start with Fulvet and see how far that got him—and how many of his knots were tired enough of street war that legitimacy looked good.

They sent Vargo outside with Sedge and Varuni to cool his heels while they debated his counteroffer. The rise and fall of voices behind the repaired walls made it sound like the lace mill had been invaded by seagulls again.

"Hope your sister will advocate for me in this," he said to Sedge. "Fulvet trusts her more. Which hurts, since of the two of us, I'm the one that *en't* juggling masks and names like a street performer."

They were all three laughing when the lace mill door opened and Nikory stepped out with Mirka.

"They want agreement from Fulvet that he'll consider the charters before they agree to anything," Nikory said, "but the truce should keep things quiet until then."

At a nudge of his elbow, Mirka grimaced and said, "And to show we mean to play fair, I've got something to confess. It's old news, but maybe you can still make use of it. It's about that man you were looking for, Stezze Chetoglio. The one who turned up as a corpse in the Depths."

Seven Knots, Lower Bank: Fellun 4

The streets around Grey were full of uninhibited revelry. The previous year's Veiled Waters had been marred by blasphemy and riots; as if to make up for it, this year was bestowing on Nadežra the end of the Cinquerat. Here on the Lower Bank, nobody mourned its imminent passing. Soon enough that would give way to cynicism and complaints, Grey knew—the new Setterat would hardly be an instant cure for all the city's ills—but for the time being, people just wanted to celebrate. They ran through the streets in fantastical masks, everything from the clan animals to branching trees to the divine Faces and Masks themselves, drunken, singing, laughing whenever they collided at a fog-shrouded corner. A woman in a sea-crested mask circled Grey with a dancing step, crying, "Bright dreams to you in the coming cycle!" When she swooped in for a kiss, he let her have a good one. It was hard not to be exuberant, with so many of his burdens lifted.

Duty, unfortunately, dragged him away from the boisterous chaos. Grey didn't know who the ziemetse had bribed, blackmailed, or beaten to obtain lodgings for the reborn Ižranyi, but something of the sort must have happened; even though the city was leaking at the seams with revolutionaries come for an uprising and pilgrims come for the Great Dream, the ziemetse had somehow freed up an entire section of a courtyard house at the western edge of Seven Knots.

It was still tight quarters, the former zlyzen sleeping in close ranks on the floor for lack of sufficient beds. They didn't seem to mind, though. Released from five centuries of cursed existence, reborn into a world unlike the one they remembered, they flinched from everything. Their behavior reminded Grey of prisoners the Vigil locked into solitary cells for days or weeks on end. Only their clan-mates were familiar, a source of comfort.

He wondered how much they remembered of their time as zlyzen, but didn't ask. He didn't really want to know.

Communication was difficult enough anyway. Ren might be speaker-to-be for the Ižranyi, but Grey had unofficially become the speaker *to* them. The memories regained in the dream gave his tongue and ears just enough familiarity with their speech to get by—better than anyone else could, at least. Most people could barely understand anything the Ižranyi said, let alone respond.

The residents of the house's other sections had a bonfire going on the courtyard flagstones, banishing the mist within the gates; musicians were playing an oszefon tune, couples dancing around the flames. Seeing them, Grey promised himself that before long, he and Ren would have a proper dance. Then, sighing, he knocked on the Ižranyi door.

Szorsa Olena had taken up residence in the topmost room of the three-story building. Middle-aged and rimasz, she'd led that desperate sacrifice in the Fiavla labyrinth, burning their koszenie to stop the spreading terror of the Primordial. With their clan elder long gone, she was the closest thing the Ižranyi had to a leader.

Six others were with her when Grey reached the top of the stairs. He'd learned all their names, determined to overwrite his memories of the zlyzen with those of people. The six came from five different kretse; the two from the same kureč weren't close cousins. Broken threads, all of them. It was one thing for the ziemetse to acknowledge the Ižranyi as lost kin, but another thing entirely to weave them back into the fabric of Vraszenian life. Would the surviving lineages be restored from those individual roots? How many had been lost forever?

The question Grey brought today was smaller, and hopefully easy to address. Shaping the formal greeting to unfamiliar vowels, he said, "Ažerais blesse the weye that hyder broght thee sauf and sounde unto me."

Olena waved the others off, though they didn't leave the room. So far as Grey knew, none of the Ižranyi had been alone since their transformation. Not moving from her high-backed chair, she said, "By thy contenaunce, so as it semed me, thou bryngest muche matere for to speken of here."

He did have matters to speak of, though it took him a painfully long time to stumble through them, guessing at how to adjust his words for Ižranyi pronunciation, sometimes running aground entirely when the word used five hundred years ago had a completely different modern equivalent. That happened especially with Liganti terms that had seeped into the Vraszenian spoken in Nadežra.

The news he brought today, though, required few such words. People must be told the Ižranyi were back; the ideal time to do that was during the Great Dream, when the wonder of the night and the significance of a Grand Cycle ending could justify many miracles.

When he finished relating this to Olena, he said, "Al the ziemetse made forward also that thy folk sholde habban leve for to drynke of the welle-spryng."

Instead of looking delighted at the prospect, she recoiled. "That honour we deserve nought. Through oure folye, al this wrak was y-wroght. Of oure Lady grace, othere folks be moore worthy."

Grey's Rook-honed instincts sharpened. The destruction of the Ižranyi was centuries ago and a long road away... but the cause had never been revealed. Fiavla had been one of three city-states consolidating power over its neighbors, with all the enemies that brought. In the aftermath of its fall, people had pointed fingers in every direction: at Fiavla's rivals, at discontented client cities under its sway, at foreign powers with no desire to face a more unified Vraszan.

But Olena claimed the disaster was because of their folly. Maybe someone in Fiavla had entertained the same ambitions as the Tyrant, by way of a different Primordial, and their attempt to become a conqueror went wrong.

When Grey asked, Olena went silent, and he wasn't sure at first if she'd failed to understand his words. Then she lifted her head and called out, "Dmitri."

He was one of the oldest Ižranyi, a man whose shoulders remained stooped even after losing his twisted zlyzen posture. He came and sat on a stool by Olena's chair, and she said something too rapid for Grey to follow.

Dmitri blanched. Grey, regretting having asked, said, "Thou nedest nat tellen that tale."

"Ih moste," Dmitri said, bleakly. "Lest som othere wight that thilke mysded again wolde doon."

Olena had enough skill with languages to bend her speech a little toward modern sounds; Dmitri lacked that, and many teeth besides. She had to repeat his words for Grey, more slowly and clearly. "Stoones rounde ther were, and ech of them y-corven was with signes of that namelesse thing demonyak—"

Stones instead of medallions, but the mention of Primordials— what she called nameless—brought a familiar chill all the same. "Som wight used them?"

Listening to Dmitri's reply, Olena shook her head. "No. Nothyng good cometh of that namelesse thing demonyak, for it bodeth noght but daungers. The wiseste of Fiavla bad that they be brogth to destruccioun. But thir wisdom fulfild nothyng of swich entente. It unbond al the wikkednesse withinne the stoones, and unbounde, that wikkednesse overwheyld us al."

Drowning in Primordial power. Grey remembered all too well the atmosphere in the temple as the medallions went one by one into the fire. The air around him, tolling like a terrible bell. The feeling that by destroying the medallions, they were setting something loose—that if they didn't finish, it would fly beyond control. But they *had* finished. "Hadde ye ech of them? And som al-hole endured…" He could imagine all too well what would have happened had they left one medallion intact.

"Elleven stones," Olena said, on the heels of Dmitri's reply. "Lik to the custume of the north. Al were destroyed. So was oure kyth and kinn."

Grey's mind spun, snatching at points of difference. Medallions instead of stones; perhaps they'd been made by different means. The Primordial of desire instead of fear. The nameless szorsa as a living Uniat, her soul remaining trapped even after she died. Maybe she'd taken that unbound power with her into death.

But they'd sent her soul on *before* they destroyed the medallions. Before he felt that mounting pressure.

We did it the right way, he told himself uneasily. *The people in Fiavla wouldn't have used numinatria. Tanaquis's method was safer— that's all.* The fact that Nadežra hadn't dissolved into a maelstrom of unchecked desires was proof of their success. Eleven days of nightmare terror preceded Fiavla's fall. More than three weeks had passed since the destruction of the medallions.

Still, he'd feel better after he shared this with Ren and Vargo. They could assure him there was nothing to fear, no devastation like Fiavla's in their future.

Olena was watching him sharply. "Ye drede daunger in Nadežra. Ih swere, we wol doon nought for to dreden."

"I know you mean us no harm," Grey said, forgetting to say it in her dialect. He shoved himself to his feet. "But I must go."

Isla Traementis, the Pearls: Fellun 4

"Apologies, alta," Colbrin said as he let Ren in. "Era Traementis and Alta Giuna have not yet returned from Extaquium Manor, though I expect them shortly."

Ren stifled a laugh. Parma was celebrating her return to society with a party every single day of Veiled Waters. For today she'd gotten her hands on a small cleansing numinat, and had invited everyone to pour the last of her uncle's abominable wine through it. If Ren hadn't been so busy preparing for the Great Dream, she would have been there herself. But she'd only just collected her finished sash belt from Tess, adorned with shimmering, iridescent dreamweaver feathers. She wanted to show it off to her aunt and cousin before going home to rehearse her part one last time.

"That's all right," she said to Colbrin. "I can—"

From the direction of the service area she heard a voice, accented with Vraszenian and raised in strident fury. "Tell who you like; I care not! I am done. Not a day more will I work in that house!"

"My apologies," Colbrin said, moving to close the servants' door. "It is no problem with Traementis Manor, I assure you. Alta Tanaquis's maid is here."

Ren stopped him with one outstretched hand. Zlatsa hardly ever spoke, much less in such a passion. And she rarely ventured from Tanaquis's townhouse unless it was her day off. "I'd like to speak with her."

If she'd been raised an alta, she would have asked Colbrin to bring Zlatsa to her. Instead she went downstairs, to the servants' dining room, and found Zlatsa haranguing a helpless-looking footman.

"—owed my wages for the entirety of Cyprilun, and be glad I demand nothing for these first days of Fellun." Spying Ren, Zlatsa shoved past the footman and planted herself in Ren's path. "Your cousin is not well."

Guilt surged in Ren's throat. *I should have broken in.* "Has the wound become infected?"

Zlatsa shuddered. "Her *head* is infected—with what, I know not. All day and all night she spends in her workshop, scribbling, muttering. Then today she left, and I came straight here. I am done. Her oddities I mind not, but this is something else."

The guilt chilled to fear. For Tanaquis's behavior to put off the phlegmatic Zlatsa, it must be extreme indeed. "Where did she go?"

"Who knows? Her words are as much a tangle as her workshop, nothing more than ravings."

Ren hadn't given her coat to Colbrin. Curling one hand around Zlatsa's arm, she said, "You still have the key, yes? Show me."

Whitesail, Upper Bank: Fellun 4

It was worse than Ren had imagined.

Tanaquis and her workshop always displayed a certain untidiness, but now it looked like a great storm had swept through the space. Cups of coffee going fuzzy with mold decorated the windowsill, next to untouched plates of food. Books and papers were everywhere, not just on tables but on the floor, chalky footprints showing where she'd stepped on them. Her scrawled handwriting had degenerated into a tangle of ink—did that predate her injury, or had she done it with her off hand? The bits drawn on the walls had to be from earlier: sketches of numinata, of labyrinths, both the complex layout used for religion and the simpler back-and-forth shape Kaius and the nameless szorsa had used in binding the medallions.

Zlatsa spat a curse when Ren picked up a small metal framework, the poured cast of a numinat. "I should have known something was wrong when she got that one marked on her. Tattoos are for sailors, not inscriptors."

Ren spun. "Tanaquis got a tattoo? When? Where?"

"While you were missing. Right here, over her heart." Zlatsa thumped her own chest. "Numinata should not be marked on the body. It's not safe. Even *I* know that."

Vargo and Alsius had numinata on their bodies, linking their souls. Had Tanaquis taken the idea from them? But for what purpose? If she'd done it while Ren was missing, then it happened long before they destroyed the medallions and she lost her hand.

And she'd kept it secret.

The Mask of Mirrors, Ren thought, sick with guilt. When she patterned Tanaquis, she'd told her cousin there was a secret she must keep. But this wasn't it. Whatever Tanaquis was hiding, it was a dangerous cancer, not a truth in need of guarding.

Careful not to step on any floor-chalked lines, Ren picked her way toward the worktable on the far side of the room. Perhaps there were notes legible enough to take to Vargo. Or she could drag him here.

Ren stopped before she got to the table. In a clear patch of floor lay a scatter of pattern cards, all faceup and too evenly spaced to be accidental. Too many for a seven-card wheel, and they followed the dusty chalk outline of a spiral instead of a true circle.

Mouth dry with dread, Ren bent to examine them. The Mask of Fools; Sisters Victorious; Three Hands Join; The Face of Crowns; The Face of Glass; Two Roads Cross; The Face of Balance; Four Petals Fall; Storm Against Stone; Aža's Call; The Face of Flame.

Eleven cards. And underneath the final one, at the tail end of the spiral, a symbol she'd only seen etched into the Tyrant's medallions.

The sigil for A'ash.

Tanaquis didn't give up her medallion. The Rook had to force it from her. Ren felt sick. Had that caused this madness? Or was it something else—something to do with that tattoo?

Zlatsa was still in the doorway. She wasn't a fair target for Ren's fear and fury, but they wouldn't stay caged. "Why said you nothing before now? Why send us away when we came to make sure she was well?"

She expected Zlatsa to snap back. Instead the other woman looked shaken. "I *tried*, but the words would not come. A hundred times I meant to go fetch you. But then... always I would do something else. Eat lunch, take a nap. Telling myself, I can leave afterward."

Until Tanaquis vanished. And whatever eisar numinatria she was using to control Zlatsa lost their effect.

"It is not your fault," Ren said, past the panic clawing her heart. "And thank you for coming to us instead of fleeing. I'll see to it that you're paid. But will you do one more thing for me? Send runners for Eret Vargo and Grey Serrado. Tell them they must come at once."

Whitesail, Upper Bank: Fellun 4

With Zlatsa gone, Ren searched the townhouse for more hints of what had driven Tanaquis to this state, or where she'd gone. She found her answers mostly in absences: the sturdy boots Tanaquis preferred were missing, as was the coat with many pockets that Tess had made for her at the start of winter. Her inscriptor's satchel hung from its hook by the door, useless to Tanaquis without her sunwise hand.

Ren was pacing the entry hall when a pounding came at the door. It opened on Vargo, breathing hard like he'd run the entire way, cheeks flushed and hair swept off his brow, slick with mist or sweat or both.

"Tanaquis! You—oh." He shook off his surprise and strode past her, making for the stairs. "Good. Saves me having to look for you. Where's Tanaquis?"

"You got my message not?" Ren chased him up the stairs. "I sent one to your house."

"Came straight from Extaquium Manor. I may have ruined Parma's party."

What has Parma to do with anything? Ren opened her mouth to ask, but a second knock pulled her back to the door. As she let Grey in, Vargo's yell came from above. "What the *fuck* happened here?"

They took the stairs two at a time. "Tanaquis has vanished," Ren said. Breathless from her climb, she related in quick gasps what Zlatsa had said—including the numinat Tanaquis had placed on herself.

Vargo picked up the metal figure and blanched. "I don't think she tattooed it. Not unless the tattooist was also an inscriptor. I think she heated this up and *burned* it into herself."

Even the thought made Ren flinch. "What's it *for*?"

::It's a conduit,:: Alsius said, his mental voice faint. ::Not unlike the one I placed on Vargo all those years ago. It's meant to draw energy into her. And...I think it's related to the numinat she designed. The one that destroyed the medallions.::

Ren could barely make herself echo that for Grey. When she did, he went ashen. "With Szorsa Olena I was just speaking. She—she made it sound like destroying the medallions should have released their power into the world. That was how Fiavla fell."

Vargo's voice was strangled. "Those marks on her afterward. It wasn't just that she touched the numinat. Tanaquis drew the energy *into herself.*"

Zlatsa, constantly giving in to other urges besides the one to walk out the door. It was the kind of thing someone with a medallion could do, without need of a numinat...but the medallions were gone.

The power they held was not.

But Tanaquis wasn't Kaius Rex. Whatever had happened to her cousin, Ren didn't believe this was some mad bid to dominate the world. "Could she have known?" Ren asked. "That we would destroy ourselves if we destroyed the medallions? She kept saying someone had to die—she was willing to *be* the one to die—"

Papers snowed the air as Vargo slapped them off the table. "Of course she fucking was. Got news from my old knots. One of 'em had Chetoglio—that delta cuff that had Ninat—stashed away in the attic of the Wailing Plum. They didn't tell me, 'cause they was looking to use him as leverage against me. But here's the interesting part: According to them, he din't have the medallion long. Found it back in Canilun, on the floor of a sedan chair he hired in Eastbridge. Not far from my house."

The floor of a *sedan chair*? That made no sense. But Grey saw what Ren, still reeling, didn't. "You think Tanaquis had it before that? She ditched it when she learned of Ghiscolo's plans?"

Who could give up a medallion like that? No one—except, perhaps, the one who held Ninat. Death, and endings...

...and transcendence. The ability to see beyond the horizon, into the deepest mysteries of the cosmos.

"She wished us not to know," Ren whispered. Tanaquis, who

learned at an early age that she could rely only on herself. Who'd been scolded by her mentor when she showed interest in heretical ideas. Whose family had died out...but then she was welcomed into a new one. A family whose register she'd defaced with protections on every living name, additions to close Ren and Tricat off from everyone else. Additions that masked the need to protect them against herself, too—herself and Ninat.

Vargo kept talking right over her whisper. "—said he wandered right out of the bolt-hole in the middle of the afternoon, like he was in a trance. Like something was *controlling* him."

The way Diomen and Ghiscolo had controlled the medallion holders. Ren's hand found Grey's, but even his warm grip wasn't enough to steady her. "That's why you went to speak with Parma."

"Noctat could call Ninat to itself," Vargo said. "Parma's just been going where we pointed her, so she didn't think much of it when Tanaquis asked for her help with another ritual. Even knew it was eisar-based, but she didn't mind hiding the attempt from Simendis; if it meant getting rid of these things sooner, she thought that was a fair trade. But she claimed it didn't work."

"Or Tanaquis had Chetoglio stopped before he arrived." Grey's voice sounded more like the Rook's, low and grim.

Stopped. How had his body wound up in the Depths, right where Tanaquis's riddles led Vargo and Grey? If she'd shown up with Ninat in hand, they would have had questions. Instead the two men found it under circumstances where neither of them could risk taking it. She might have even guessed why Grey couldn't.

Ren was hiding from the rest of that thought. From the possibility that Tanaquis's hands were stained, not just with ink, but with blood.

It seemed impossible. But if Tanaquis had held Ninat before Ghiscolo's ritual and abandoned it to protect that secret, giving it up would have left her cursed, doomed to be destroyed by her own Ninat-related desires. And Tanaquis had hounded Ren with that new pattern deck of hers, asking for a nine-card spread, as the life she'd built slowly crumbled around her. Had she tried the removal first with a pattern she laid herself, and met with no success?

Vargo prowled the room like an anxious tomcat, taking in the chalk lines. "Apart from being a blasphemous atrocity, does this look familiar?" He'd stopped at the spiral of pattern cards, tilting his head for another perspective.

Alsius answered. ::The amphitheatre numinat?::

"Breccone Indestris was a mediocre inscriptor. I never understood how he came up with that one. Or the numinat to make ash."

"But—" Ren's tongue was lead in her mouth. "She helped us *stop* that."

"Right. *After* she realized that pattern was more than just Vraszenian superstition, and that destroying the wellspring would be a shortsighted waste."

Grey released Ren's hand, but only so his arm could go around her shoulders. The szorsa in her wanted to trace the threads; the con artist in her wanted to figure out how the game had been played, and why.

But the member of House Traementis, the woman who had become Tanaquis's cousin and friend, was too heartsick to do anything but stand frozen.

Besides, all of it, the how and the when and the why, mattered less than what came next. Swallowing hard, Ren said, "More than anything, Tanaquis wants to *understand*. How the cosmos works. How pattern and numinatria fit together."

"Tomorrow night comes the Great Dream," Grey said. "If pattern she seeks to understand . . . the source of it all is the wellspring."

"She'll be there," Ren said softly. Would it be enough for Tanaquis to witness the Great Dream? To drink from Ažerais's waters, experiencing the insight they bestowed?

With the power of the medallions flowing through her, Ren feared it would not.

Vargo's expression was that of a man who was all too accustomed to putting necessity above friendship. "Yes, she'll be there. And so will we."

26

Labyrinth's Heart

The Great Amphitheatre, Old Island: Fellun 5

A sea of mist lapped against the stone foundation of the amphitheatre, the Point rising above Veiled Waters' fogs to kiss a sky painted jewel-bright by the setting sun. On the opposite horizon, the twin moons of Orin and Orasz rose to supplant it, dripping gold like fresh-minted forri. It was a rare meeting of siblings, brother and sister promenading together before spinning off to dance through the heavens apart.

On such a night as this, their light joined with that of Ažerais, and her seven children were conceived. On such a night as this, the Vraszenian people were born.

The Great Amphitheatre was packed with people: mostly Vraszenians, and many of those pilgrims from outside the city, but among them a good scattering of mixed-blood Nadežrans who honored Ažerais. Part of the stands held the first segment of the long line waiting to drink from the wellspring, trailing out an exit and across the Point. The rest held onlookers, families waiting to welcome their kin who came bearing true dreams, and even a few Liganti who'd paid to see the event.

It was a far cry from the night Ren and Grey had attempted to con Nadežra into approving of their marriage. But Faella hadn't been entirely wrong, even if she'd missed the mark on *how* her assistance could bear fruit. They'd indeed been part of bringing peace to Nadežra—along with many other people.

Grey adjusted the hang of his panel coat. The silvered embroidery Tess had added for his wedding remained an unfamiliar texture under his nervous fingers. It was the finest coat he'd ever worn—and carefully cleaned after his adventures in Fiavla and the Depths—but it paled like the stars at dawn against the finery of the ziemetse. Their panel coats were entire tapestries of silk thread, each one imbued so the landscapes and creatures they depicted almost seemed alive.

Ordinarily he would have no business standing among them. *Ren* had a place here, as speaker for the Ižranyi—though she'd almost insulted Dalisva when she refused a dreamweaver mask. All the ziemetse wore masks that evoked their clan animals, and szorsas were permitted dreamweaver feathers on theirs. Ren braided the feathers into her hair and had Tess work some onto her sash belt instead. Her mask, though, was the prismatium one Vargo had bought, what seemed like a lifetime ago.

Grey was the one in a dreamweaver mask. Olena had insisted, when she agreed that she and two other Ižranyi would accompany him tonight. He tried not to think about what that might imply as the sun touched the horizon, and together with Ren and that trio, he strode out onto the amphitheatre's stage.

The waiting crowd expected Ren, after all the stories that had circulated, but to the clans outside the city, Grey was a nonentity. The three behind him were even more unknown, and a confused murmur passed through the crowd when he stepped into the amplification numinat.

Grey wasn't like Ren, used to baring his face and performing for all to hear. He was more comfortable with his hood and the Rook's shadows. But Olena insisted, and the ziemetse agreed, and now an entire amphitheatre full of people were wondering who the hell he was. They only wanted the sun to set, the wellspring to appear.

Fighting the urge to clear his throat, Grey spoke.

"Five hundred years ago, our people suffered an unspeakable

wound. A terrifying force tore through the city of Fiavla and all the members of the Ižranyi clan. Eleven days later, when the chaos died down, they were gone."

He didn't quite have silence. People were shifting, murmuring to each other. Asking why he would evoke such horror at so sacred a moment.

Grey might not be used to doing this unhooded...but he knew how to play to a crowd.

"Or so we thought."

A ripple of sound that died away to stillness.

"A remnant of the Ižranyi survived," Grey went on. "Trapped deep within Ažerais's Dream, held captive by the zlyzen, they slept away the centuries. Until Arenza Lenskaya Traementatis Volavka, a szorsa of the Dvornik and speaker for the Ižranyi, found them. Together with the help of the ziemetse, we have returned them to the world."

A politic tale, woven of equal parts truth and lies. Ren had been the one to suggest it. "If everyone knows they *were* the zlyzen," she'd said, the night the Ižranyi were restored, "the fear of that will haunt them until the last one passes away—perhaps even after. But the zlyzen are no more. Say instead that by those creatures they were held captive, and when at last they were freed, the zlyzen vanished. Those who need to will know what happened."

Grey gestured, and the trio behind him stepped forward. Olena, Dmitri, and the youngest of the Ižranyi, a fifteen-year-old girl named Svetlana, who'd been preparing to make the pilgrimage to Nadežra in her first life. Grey could see them fighting not to cringe from the countless eyes upon them, not to retreat into the shadows they'd called home for so long.

"A bare sixty have returned to us." It was probably coincidence, the survivors numbering the same as the cards in the core of a pattern deck, but Grey wasn't above squeezing the symbolism for sympathy. "Three braved this changed world to join us here today. Let us praise the Faces for the kindness they have shown, and give thanks to the Masks for withdrawing their wrath. The clans are seven once more!"

An unsettled murmur greeted his words. Just as when the

ziemetse had heard, people were more surprised and confused than anything else. The Ižranyi, returned to the world? It sounded wonderful—and also impossible. Especially when Grey had no more to show for it than three Vraszenians standing awkwardly at his side. They were simply people, like any other. If the crowd had been there to see their transformation...but then the crowd would have seen the nightmare that preceded it.

Whispers rippled through the amphitheatre as one by one, the ziemetse embraced the three Ižranyi, offering their own prayers of thanks. The Kiralič finally broke the odd tension of the moment, casting his voice up into the stands. "How happy my clan is to be the youngest no longer!" A scattering of laughter greeted his words, probably from other Kiraly. But the true reaction...that would take longer to come. Grey only hoped it would be the warm embrace of a family restored, not the hostility of a world that preferred the Ižranyi as a golden, untouchable memory.

For now, Mevieny took her place in the amplification numinat. "The Grand Cycle ends; a new one begins. What better omen than this for the next seven times seven years? In the future, for themselves will the Ižranyi speak once more. But as Arenza Lenskaya Traementatis Volavka helped bring this miracle about, one last time we shall hand off the honor of being the first to drink from our Lady's cup."

The sun was sinking below the horizon now, traveling the Dusk Road into night. As Mevieny presented a silver chalice to Ren, the last sliver of light slipped away, and the gold-burnished sky flashed green.

Light answered it from below, iridescing from the stage of the amphitheatre, as the Wellspring of Ažerais flowed into the waking world.

The Great Amphitheatre, Old Island: Fellun 5

Ren had seen the wellspring in many forms. Mist-veiled radiance when she rescued Vargo from the zlyzen; a pulsating wound of poisoned light when Mettore tried to destroy it. The dry, empty scar of the Night of Hells.

Manifested as it should be, it took her breath away.

The light was a gentle caress along her skin, whispering of dreams. It shimmered through all the colors of a dreamweaver's feathers, cool as water, entrancing as fire. All the traditions of her people had their roots here, in this miraculous moment, when the veil parted and something impossible became real.

Her fear of what Tanaquis might be planning was a mouse's squeak drowned by the wonder flooding through her. For a moment she wasn't sure her legs would hold; it was fortunate she didn't have to move first. That honor went to the Meszarič, who walked the labyrinth path with a measured, steady tread, to fill his cup in the shifting waters. Then the Stretskojič, and all the other ziemetse in the order their founders were born. Ižranyi, youngest and most favored daughter of Ažerais, came last.

Ren's hands trembled as she dipped her silver chalice into the wellspring. But she didn't spill a drop as she lifted it high.

"Ages past, led by their sister Ižranyi, our ancestors came to this place, a rocky stone caught in the spreading skirts of the Dežera. Here they prayed, and here their mother gave them her most sacred gift: a wellspring of her waters, which bring the insight of pattern into the world. Tonight, we drink in thanks, and accept the true dreams Ažerais bestows upon us."

The silver was a silken kiss against her lip. The liquid it held was cool as a shiver and electrifying as a stormfront, rippling down her nerves and warming every part of her. Unlike with aža, there was no delay; her senses bloomed open like a flower, and Ren saw all the hidden connections of the world.

A great, intricate tapestry, weaving all her people together. Strong ropes from the ziemetse to the members of their clans; delicate threads from person to person, binding sister to brother, lover to lover, friend to friend. More threads spinning outward, through the whole fabric of Nadežra, of Vraszan, of the world. The sheer beauty of it brought tears to Ren's eyes. *None of us are separate. None of us are alone.*

Seven guards ringed the wellspring as she and the ziemetse stepped back to let the masked pilgrims approach. But three others would go before the rest of the line: the three Ižranyi, who had reluctantly agreed to accept that honor.

As Grey coaxed them forward, Ren turned from the crowd. The insight flooding her knew what she would find even before she saw it.

Instead of the light-beaded choker of Floodwatch Bridge to the south, she faced a down-soft blanket of fog. The pinks and golds of sunset were rapidly giving way to the deeper blues and violets of night, chased silver by the rising moons. And a straight-backed figure sat on the edge of the stage, his booted feet dangling over mist that looked solid, but was no more of this world than he.

Mirscellis. Gabrius. Father. All true names, but she wasn't sure which one to use. The Volavka she was coming to know; he remained all but a stranger to her.

"I hoped you might be here," Ren said, drawing off her mask and perching next to him.

His smile, like his eyes, was familiar. She'd seen it in a mirror often enough to know it. Ren had always thought of herself as looking like her mother, and she wasn't wrong; the resemblance was strong enough for Tsvetsa to have recognized her on sight. But some details came from her father.

"As though I would miss it," he said, shifting to face her, one boot braced on the stage, the other still hanging over the mist. "I'm relieved to find you safe. And that boy you were worried about? Did you make it in time?"

So much had happened since she last saw him, it took her a moment to recall what crisis had interrupted their meeting. "Iascat. Yes. He helped broker peace for this city."

"I thought the arrangements looked different this year." He glanced at her sash belt, worked through with dreamweaver feathers, then over his shoulder at the line wending its way through the amphitheatre. The pilgrims looked stately, distance masking their excitement. "I think you have other duties than entertaining me."

"Yes." She was meant to draw a card for any pilgrim who drank from the wellspring. They were waiting for her. Ren took a dragging step away. She'd hoped to see Gabrius, but now that she had, she couldn't say what she wanted. "Perhaps we can speak later. Before dawn."

"Or after. I suspect you'll always be able to find me with aža. But there's something I'd like that only tonight allows." He opened his arms, lowering them when she didn't move. "Ah. You might not want a father...but perhaps at least a friend?"

She hadn't even realized what invitation he was offering. Hesitantly, Ren stepped forward and let him hug her.

This is what I should have had. A father to take her in his arms: warmth and affection when Ivrina was alive, shelter when she was gone. But the strange circumstances of her life had made that impossible.

Here, now, she had this. And Ren's own arms came up to hug her father back.

"Go," he said, tears thickening his voice as he released her. "My daughter."

The Great Amphitheatre, Old Island: Fellun 5

Vargo prowled the lowest tier of the amphitheatre, close enough to the milling grounds to make out faces, but elevated enough to see over the crowd. For once he wished it weren't such a firm Nadežran tradition to wear masks at festivals. How was he supposed to recognize Tanaquis?

Look for the woman missing a hand.

He shuddered, curling his own hand tight. The sad truth was that looking at arms would only narrow the field, not catch her out. The decision to shift access to the Great Dream from expensive tickets to a cheap lottery had opened the event to many who wouldn't have been able to afford it before...including the sorts of Nadežrans on whom the Cinquerat's notion of justice fell most heavily.

Still, the people they'd stationed everywhere knew to look for that. Tess, Pavlin, and a contingent hired by House Traementis were in Whitesail, in case Tanaquis returned to her house. The Cut Ears were loitering near the base of the path up the Point; Iascat's guards, managing the line outside the amphitheatre, were requiring everyone to lift their masks before they entered. This afternoon they'd conducted a thorough search of the chambers below the amphitheatre, blocking all of them off. Unless Tanaquis had figured out a numinat that could let her fly, they should see her coming.

Vargo lifted his own spiderweb, crystal-dewed mask long enough to wipe his face dry. *No sign of her yet*, he thought at Alsius—and by proxy at Ren, though he wasn't sure if she heard. She sat at the back of the stage, outside the labyrinth's path, but he could barely see her past the crowd waiting to have a card drawn by the infamous szorsa. *Anything on your end?*

::None of the warning flares have gone up. I wonder if I should have gone with Varuni and the Fog Spiders to the temple. If Tanaquis went there after all, they have no way to signal us. I could—:: He cut off abruptly.

Alsius? Alsius! Vargo elbowed his way past a family of delta cuffs come to watch the spectacle even if they couldn't drink. When it looked like one might take his rush as an opportunity for belligerence, Vargo let an inch of steel slide free of his new sword cane. "Don't give me a reason," he growled.

Face crumbling into pale chalk, the man scrambled out of Vargo's way.

What's happened, old man? Where is she?

::Sorry, sorry! It's not Tanaquis. Gabrius is here. I'm explaining the situation. Keep looking.::

The wash of panic drained away, leaving behind irritation. How was it Alsius could talk privately to Mirscellis? Squelching the reaction that tried to rise, Vargo made another pass through the stands. And another. Every thought he sent to Alsius was brushed aside with a dismissive ::Nothing yet.::

The moons were high, Vargo's feet aching and his nerves as frayed as a retired fist's charm, when he gave in to frustration. *We missed something, I know it*, he said to Alsius. *Maybe I should check the temple, if you're too occupied.* Tanaquis might be putting the finishing touches on a numinat there.

He wished the scar he shared with Grey gave them a way to communicate, but his brother was nearly as busy as Ren: Half the people in the amphitheatre, including some who weren't in line for the wellspring, were trying to mob the Ižranyi. Vargo pitied the three who'd agreed to show up. Now that the initial confusion had worn off, they were a miracle and a sideshow, all in one. The only question was whether the gawkers who thought they were the divine personified on earth would outnumber the doubters who questioned the story they'd been fed. He hoped nobody's true dream tonight showed them the part about the zlyzen.

::Vargo, I— No, never mind. Now isn't the time; I don't want to distract you.::

Alsius's sober tone brought Vargo up short. *What do you mean?*

::My conversation with Gabrius. You and I must talk later. Before the night ends.::

Meaning before the Great Dream ended. Shifting his gaze from the grounds, Vargo searched the stands. Alsius had perched on the top wall so he could watch both sides. The spider was too small to see, but Mirscellis stood on the rim like a misplaced statue. *Spit it out. Otherwise I'll be more distracted, wondering.*

After a pause as long as the Dežera, Alsius said quietly, ::My boy... I'm not needed here anymore. My revenge is done; the medallions have been destroyed. You have people now. Ren, and Grey, and that Novrus boy, and your knots, and—and I'm tired of being a spider. Of having only two people I can speak to. Of not having *hands*.::

Heat flashed through Vargo, leaving a chill colder than winter in its wake. He steadied himself against the barrier to the next tier. "You want to leave me?"

Oblivious to Vargo's spoken whisper, Alsius continued laying out his reasons. ::I'm in no rush to return to the Lumen, but ever since I met Gabrius—since our bond was damaged—since I got to be myself again in Fiavla, I've wondered if there might be another option. And Gabrius thinks it's possible. To move on without any harm to you. But it would have to be done tonight, before the wellspring fades back into the dream.::

You're just bringing this up now? Vargo turned his glare on the wellspring, as though its shimmering radiance were to blame for the tightness in his chest, the tremor shaking him loose from his moorings. *Don't you think we should make certain there still* is *a wellspring in the morning before we—*

His nails scraped stone as he clutched the barrier, leaning over it as though a handspan closer could change what he'd just spotted: a shift in the line shuffling toward the wellspring. People who'd won a precious chance at the sacred waters, shifting aside without complaint for a minnow-thin form crossing the path, clothed and masked in unrelieved black.

They'd underestimated her.

Yes, they had guards stationed everywhere, with descriptions and accurate sketches and strict orders not to let Tanaquis anywhere near the wellspring. But she held the unleashed power of A'ash. It would tell her where to go, the exact moment to move, to get what she wanted without interference. It would help her shift people out of her way, leaning on their desires to pause or step forward or turn to speak with a friend.

For all Vargo knew, it had just leaned on *him.* Making him argue with Alsius when he most needed to stay alert.

And now Tanaquis had a clear path to the wellspring.

With voice and with mind, Vargo yelled, *"Ren!"*

The Great Amphitheatre, Old Island: Fellun 5

True dreams. That was what the wellspring granted—and Ren, conceived on the Great Dream, born to a szorsa mother and a father whose spirit had walked in dreams for two hundred years, was drowning in them.

Card after card she drew for the pilgrims, and each one carried a whole tale. Dawn and Dusk: This woman would have great fortune on her next trade journey, but only if she left soon. The Face of Seeds: Far to the south, that man's daughter was being born this very night. Grief for a lost lover, guilt over an unconfessed theft, a feud that could be resolved with an apology to the right person. Pattern was the connections between things; now Ren saw *everything*, the way those threads could be plucked and tied and released.

She wanted a moment to herself. A moment to breathe and absorb the torrent of knowledge, the way everything she looked at evoked more. A moment to stop and *think*, to apply these insights to the problem of her cousin, because buried in all the rest of it were things she needed to know. But she was like the Ižranyi, overrun by everyone who wanted a moment of her time, a little of her reflected blessing. The crowd around that trio was growing thicker, Grey calling out in futility for a little patience and peace.

Labyrinth's Heart. The card of stillness, of patience. The card that had, in Fiavla, warned her that by helping the zlyzen, they might put the wellspring in danger.

The crowd. Shoving forward, their voices increasingly shrill, until three of the guards ringing the wellspring stepped away to intervene before the press could break into chaos. Because all those people wanted nothing more than to speak with the Ižranyi, to touch them, to verify the miracle for themselves.

They *wanted.*

::*Ren!*::

Vargo's shout plucked a thread. It vibrated like the note of a harp, off-key, tuned too sharp—a thread woven of gold and silver and prismatium and lead.

Ren reached for it, too late and targeting the wrong thing. The crowd was the distraction, drawing the guards away. Making an opening for the black-clad figure of Tanaquis.

Who stood poised on the edge of the wellspring—

—and then, smooth as an otter, dove in.

The world changed.

On the Night of Hells, its fabric had shredded out from underneath Ren, dumping her into Ažerais's Dream. Now it pulsed like the skin of a drum. The crowd surged around her, almost like a dance.

A dance with the power to reach into the dream.

"Mama?" Ren whispered, watching Ivrina's shadow flicker and take form in the moonlight. Not lost to the Lumen. She was there, just out of reach. But Ren knew how to bring her forth.

As she'd brought the zlyzen forth. As she'd brought Kolya.

She couldn't make the body Alsius wanted. He wasn't her ancestor. But Ivrina *was*.

"I can fly!" proclaimed the eagle-masked man who'd been waiting for a card. Laughing with joy, he ran to the back of the stage, to the edge of the Point dropping off into a cloudy sea, and leapt with arms flung wide.

Ren let him go. Her feet knew the dance, stamping it out to the pulsating shouts of the crowd. Grey had taught her the steps. She didn't need anyone to dance it with, not even the Volavka. She was touched by Ažerais. She was enough, all on her own.

Mama. I'm coming. You will live again.

"Fight me!" a man shouted, brandishing his fists. "I'm the strongest in Vraszan—the strongest in the world! Against any comer, I will prove my might!"

Fool, Grey thought. But he was used to fools. As a hawk he'd broken up countless pointless fights; as the Rook he'd taken down plenty who thought themselves his match. He had nothing to prove.

But he had people to save.

"I'm Ižranyi, see?" A woman in a mask of camellia blooms waved her koszenie at the cringing Olena. "In my heart I've always known it! My father said my grandmother hundreds of years ago was Ižranyi—I'm one of you!"

"Take me with you!" a man cried, pushing past her. "Among the children of Ažerais, you are the most blessed! Everything wrong in my life, you can make right!"

They shoved forward, forgetting even the wellspring, while the Ižranyi shrank back farther and farther. Behind them someone knocked a Liganti man to the ground, roaring that Nadežra would be pure once more...but Grey knew where his duty lay. He'd *been* Ižranyi. He'd been a zlyzen. He'd helped bring them back, and now they looked to him as a leader.

I can protect them. I can save them.

We will not be lost again!

The challenge wasn't in finding chalk, or a chop for the focus. Vargo had everything he needed in his inscriptor's satchel. The problem lay in finding a large enough space safe from people running through it.

He'd had to reposition and restart his numinat twice thanks to some asshole under the delusion that he was the greatest actor of all time. Vargo had kicked the man to the base of the stage, and now the numinat was taking shape by the back wall, not far from the shrieking crowd mobbing the Ižranyi. The noise didn't bother him, so long as nobody stepped on his work.

"I have my compass, my edge, my chalk, myself," he chanted over and over as he freehanded the most important numinat of his life. Alsius didn't want to leave; Alsius only wanted a *body*. A normal existence. A reason to stay in Nadežra, at Vargo's side. Ren couldn't give that to him—but Vargo could, if he just made his brain shut up for once in his life and let instinct guide his chalk.

It was the easiest inscription he'd ever done. He moved like the old man had moved, that night so many years ago in a darkened study, trading one life for another.

Vargo had been frightened then, and reluctant. Unwilling to surrender what he had.

He gave it happily now.

Ren could work miracles. She'd done it before. But she danced, wild and fast, and still Ivrina wasn't there. It wasn't enough.

Because I must be more than just myself. The way she'd felt that night in the fall, when she and Grey had investigated the prismatium workshop. Only it hadn't been them; it was the Black Rose and the Rook.

The Black Rose, born of nothing more than a dream. Why else would Ažerais have given that to Ren, if not for her to weave another, more precious dream into reality?

The lace mask was in her pocket. Ren drew it out, drew it down over her face—

And everything solidified with a jolt.

Light whirled out of the wellspring in a dizzying storm. Not the poisoned sickness of last year's ash-tainted numinat; this was different. The true dreams of the wellspring had been twisted into something else, blazing outward through the city.

Delusions. The belief that anything was possible—if you wanted it badly enough.

Tanaquis!

There was no sign of Ren's cousin. Only the wellspring, pulsing with an unholy blend of A'ash and Ažerais.

But sheltered by the mask of the Black Rose, Ren's mind was clear. It wasn't too late to stop this. Whatever Tanaquis was doing, she hadn't finished it yet.

And that meant Ren could still stop *her.*

The crowd battered at Grey, straining to get at the Ižranyi huddling behind him. He didn't want to hurt anyone—but did he have another choice?

His heel caught on something, and he nearly fell. Mevieny's

cane, the szorsa herself nowhere to be found. Grey snatched it up; with his sheathed sword in his other hand, he used them as bars to shove people back. To the Ižranyi he yelled, "Gooth thee to the bak! Ih kepe the gate!"

It opened a big enough gap for them to flee. A gap through which Grey could see the Black Rose of Ažerais bloom into being, black leather petals and silver bladed thorns and red lips that were *his* to kiss.

Lust seized his gut and twisted tight, before easing into warmth. He didn't need to chase her. They were already each other's.

But the Rose ought to have her Rook.

Grey shoved through the crowd, breaking through into open air. He dropped the cane so he could pull out the hood—and nearly stumbled over some fool crouched in his path.

A fool he'd had to save before. A fool he had to save again. Vargo, kneeling in the center of a numinat . . . and slicing just above the scar of their brotherhood to ink a focus.

He's imbuing it. The man's rapt attention, not acknowledging Grey tripping over him, made that obvious. Whatever Vargo was doing, he was about to give his own life to make it happen.

The Rook could save him. As he'd saved countless others before.

Unfolding the soft black wool, its edge intricately stitched with numinatria, Grey dropped the hood over Vargo's head.

Vargo fell on his ass as something enveloped his mind and chased away the fog of delusion.

Scowling at a world brighter than daylight, at the unrelieved black that had replaced the watered emerald of his coat, he scrambled to his feet. The unwelcome weight of the foreign presence steadied him, like ballast in a narrow-hulled skiff.

::What is *that*?:: Alsius's voice was creaky with confusion, and Vargo got the distinct impression that the third presence imposing itself on them was profoundly dubious about sharing a mind with not one but *two* noblemen.

We're the Rook, Vargo thought, clamping a hand around his wrist to stop the blood pulsing out of the slice he'd just carved across his inner forearm. An incredulous giggle escaped him; he swallowed the ones jockeying to follow. *And Tanaquis jumped into the wellspring. Hold on.*

He seized Grey, leaning into the Rook's strength and instincts to pin the other man against the back wall of the stage. Grey's shirt ripped open easily enough, but Vargo couldn't release him to get to his inscriptor's satchel.

"No compass, no edge, no chalk," he muttered with grim humor, another voice layering over his own until even he couldn't recognize it. "Leastways I still got myself."

In the nightmare of Fiavla, he'd used Uniat and the sigil for Celnis to call Grey back to himself. Without ink and brush, Vargo made do with what he had: the seeping cut on his wrist. Yanking apart the Rook's sleeve and glove, he dug a finger into the gash and carefully wrote out the sigil, then drew a simple circle around it, for the self-awareness of Uniat.

That protection wouldn't last for long. But maybe it was good that it wouldn't, because Vargo was pretty sure he'd just imbued it.

Grey's voice came, unsteady but clear. "I don't think you're supposed to be my successor."

"Definitely *not*," Vargo said, his heartfelt sentiment echoed by the spirit wrapped around him. "But thanks for snapping me out of it." The numinat he'd been inscribing...it would never have created a body. That wasn't what numinatria was *for*. But for a moment, he'd believed it.

Believed it enough to die for it.

Because the wellspring was spitting out madness like a viper. The entire amphitheatre was in chaos; for all Vargo knew, the entire city was. What was Tanaquis trying to do?

A figure all in black was silhouetted against the coruscating light. Not Tanaquis this time: Vargo would know Ren anywhere, no matter what guise she wore.

"Come on," he growled, and dragged Grey off the wall.

Ren stood balanced at the edge of the wellspring.

She'd always known it was more than a mere pool of water. It was the greatest blessing of the Vraszenian people; it was the holiest site of Ažerais; it was the source of pattern's power. Drinking from it gave true dreams, an insight into all the connections that bound the world together.

It was a *conduit*. The means by which Ažerais's power entered the world.

And if it could channel that...it could channel the power of A'ash instead. Unleashing the Primordial of desire, not just in a brief cataclysm, but in an ongoing flood.

Ren couldn't see any shadow that might be Tanaquis in the shimmering, brilliant light. To find her cousin—to stop her, before it was too late—Ren would have to follow.

As she swayed toward the pulsing waters, someone caught her wrist.

"Thought you weren't much of a swimmer," the Rook said.

Even as he spoke, Grey came up on her other side and took her hand more gently. "Still you think, Szeren, that you must do things alone. You know better now."

The Rook on one side; Grey on the other, with a numinat on his chest that looked like it had been fingerpainted in blood. It wasn't Ryvček in the hood. "*Vargo?*"

"Explanations later," Grey said with a trace of humor. "Saving Nadežra now."

"We making an annual event of this?" the Rook muttered. *Vargo*: Even true dreams couldn't wrap Ren's mind around that.

There was no time to argue. Not if she wanted to stop Tanaquis. Ren swallowed, whispering, "I know not what we'll find inside. I know not if we'll come out again."

The Rook shrugged Vargo's shrug. "En't letting you go alone." And Grey, lifting her hand, kissed her fingers.

Together, the three of them leapt into light.

Ažerais—

Lady—

Goddess of my people—

—I know what you are.

Ren floated in a place without ground, enveloped by waters that were not water. What flowed past her in dizzying, twisted streams was Ažerais's power, laced with the overwhelming desires of A'ash... and with something else Ren recognized.

The force she'd sensed that night in the prismatium workshop, standing in the Praeteri numinat that made her forget she was anything other than the Black Rose. A numinat that called on the Primordial of delusion.

That called on Ažerais.

They were the same. Not Mask and Face, but Primordial and goddess. One the relentless, elemental, destructive force that would overtake and annihilate everything if given the chance; the other transmuted, like steel to prismatium, into a power humans could draw on safely. Through pattern, through aža, through the wellspring. Not delusion, but *intuition*. Seeing connections where they truly lay, rather than imagining them where they lay not.

Perhaps this was what the ancients had reached for when they made artifacts like the medallions. But those were a failure. The Wellspring of Ažerais was success.

A success the raw hunger of A'ash threatened to destroy. It was unraveling the conduit, releasing the unfiltered, delusional energy of Ažerais's Primordial self. They had to stop this, had to find Tanaquis, and Ren knew where to look—or perhaps she made it true. Here, perhaps, there was no difference.

Labyrinth's Heart. The card of stillness, the eye at the center of the storm. The path to the source from which Ažerais came.

A purifying path, seven layers deep. It was a serene current, tracing loops of intuition through the turbulence of delusion and desire.

Ren flowed along it, pulling the others after her, praying this would be enough to protect them. Vargo had the Rook, but he wasn't its true bearer. Grey was, but he didn't have the hood. Then again, did that matter? Like her lace-patterned mask, the hood was merely a vessel to hold the connection.

She wanted to stop and explore that idea, the relationship between the nodes where pattern's threads crossed and the physical manifestations that represented them. Understanding was there, just out of reach. If she gave it a moment—

The current swept her forward, into the labyrinth's heart. Where Tanaquis stood, seeking the answers to all those questions and more.

She was a sucking vortex of chaos, eating away at the pocket of stillness. From head to foot she was clothed in black, Ninat's color, but the collar of her shirt was pulled aside to expose the numinat burned over her heart. Power rose from it like clouds of smoke, like a snake's coils. It concentrated in a mass where her right hand had been, gloving her arm like sleek eelskin—and somehow that writhing, Primordial mass held a knife.

Vargo's experience recognized her intent faster than Ren's Ažerais-given insight. "Don't let her cut the lines!"

And the Rook answered.

From behind Tanaquis he came, defying the strictures of distance and direction. His gloved hand closed around the smoke-like shape of her wrist; the tip of her knife gouged a line across her chest as he wrenched her arm away, but the bloody track didn't touch the numinat. Razor filaments of Primordial chaos struck out, shattering like ice against the Rook's coat. He'd been made to stand against Kaius Rex, against the power of the medallions. A'ash could not harm him.

Vargo stood at Ren's side, no longer hooded. Grey...Grey held Tanaquis pinned. Here, it was the connections that mattered, not the objects themselves. Grey *was* the Rook. He'd made himself so.

Though he'd stopped Tanaquis from destroying her numinat, the stillness continued to shred and shrink. She wailed like an inhuman thing. "Let me go! It isn't enough—I see what Ažerais is—but I have to see what lies *beyond*! Imbuing, pattern, numinatria, there's something that unifies them all, something that holds all those pieces in the palm of its hand, something—"

"Something Primordial," the Rook growled, tightening his grip.

Even now, even here, Tanaquis brightened. "Yes! Unleashing it in the temple would have created a second Fiavla. I didn't want that to happen. But now, with this conduit, I can bring A'ash fully into the world. We'll see things no one has seen since the dawn of time!"

Vargo spat a curse. "And when did you get that idea—before or after you drew the power of a Primordial into yourself? You're smarter than that, Tanaquis. You know what A'ash wants—what *any* Primordial wants. To pour unfettered through the world. It's using your desires to serve its own ends."

"And you'll destroy the conduit," Ren said, desperately. "Tanaquis, look around you; already it unravels this place. A'ash will come through, but not safely. Not as Ažerais does."

And they would lose Ažerais in the process. All that remained would be the Primordial of delusion. No more pattern, no more Great Dream. An end to everything that defined the Vraszenian people.

Tanaquis attempted to twist free, but no amount of desire to escape could break the Rook's hold. Half to her, half to the others, he said, "Tell me how we stop this."

Around them, the stillness heaved, trying to tear apart. "We pull her out," Ren said, gesturing at the path behind her.

"It won't solve the problem," Vargo said. "She's still got A'ash in her."

"People outside are going mad," Ren snapped. "Even dying. If we pull her out, time at least we will gain."

"Time isn't what we need." Vargo's voice didn't carry the hard edge Ren expected. In his gaze, she saw compassion. But also resolution.

And she knew what he would say.

"We cannot kill her," Ren breathed.

The arm the Rook held across Tanaquis's chest shifted toward her throat. "Would that work? If she dies with that numinat intact, this ends?"

Vargo's gaze flicked to the hooded figure. "Yes. Like we could have done with the medallions. If her life ends, her soul will take the power with her. Out of this world. No second Fiavla."

"We *cannot*," Ren repeated. To the Rook and to Grey—because unlike that time in the temple, there was no longer a conflict between the two. "You wouldn't before, when it was me." But he loved her. He didn't love Tanaquis.

Regret shadowed his voice without softening it. "There were other options then, and no immediate danger if we didn't act." His hood jerked to the chaos closing in around them. "We don't have time now to find the perfect solution."

He was right—and she still couldn't accept it. Couldn't stand there and let her cousin die.

"It's all right." Tanaquis sagged in the Rook's arms. "I was willing to die before, to destroy the medallions. Before A'ash showed me that more was possible. But this way . . . this way, at least my soul will get to go beyond. Past the limitations of the Lumen."

To dwell forever with a Primordial.

Ren couldn't let that happen.

"Tanaquis." Ren ventured a step forward, just out of reach of the swirling chaos of A'ash. "Tanaquis, *you* can fix this. All you must do is let go." Like she hadn't before, with the medallions. Like the Rook had forced on her, against her will. "Right now, you can see how to get anything you want. Is this truly what you desire? If you unleash A'ash here, the wellspring you will destroy, and pattern with it. Think you that you understand everything now? Ažerais is only the beginning. There is so much more. You can protect it; you can end this safely, simply by wanting to. And you can *live*."

"Ninat is the gateway." Tanaquis's lips were grey ash, her whisper barely stirring the embers of her usual bright-eyed passion. "We reach understanding through death."

"Perfect understanding isn't ever achieved," Vargo said. His words sounded very much like Alsius, though Ren couldn't hear the older man's voice. "The journey through the Lumen is a *cycle*. If A'ash uses your desires to lure you off that path, you're walking away from everything you've dedicated yourself to. Away from the world itself, and all that remains to know."

It wasn't enough. They were fighting Tanaquis on her own ground, on the logic and symbolism of numinatria. But they stood in the very source of pattern—and what was pattern but the connections between things? Not just glimpsing their existence, but the creation and severance of those bonds. Ren had done that again and again over the last year, her understanding and control growing with every trial she faced.

That was the tool best fitted to her hand.

The thread from Ren to Tanaquis was there: Tricat's warm brown, laced with the faint iridescence of Sebat, the inscriptor's numen. But it was fraying, thinning down to the last, fragile strands.

She wouldn't force it to strengthen. Not against her cousin's will. Instead, Ren let spill the tears she'd been holding back. "Please, Tanaquis. You're the first Liganti I've known to actually care about pattern. To look at what my people have, to look at what I do, and see its value."

"But it annoys you every time I try to understand, because I don't understand already. You don't think I *can*." The thread frayed further, strands snapping one, two, three.

All the times Tanaquis's high-handed explanations had grated on Ren's heart. All the times she'd tried to make pattern fit into numinatrian clothing. The memories threatened to choke Ren silent. She forced herself past them. "I was wrong. Because of our conversations, I've come to understand more than I ever did before. You challenged me to look deeper. Leave me not to ask these questions by myself, when we can learn so much more together. We *have* learned so much together. Were you truly more content when it was you alone?"

The smile on Tanaquis's face was bitter and sad. "I'm still alone. I always have been."

Even in House Traementis. Even working for Iridet. She'd said it herself, when Ren patterned her: Why would she need help? Not because she didn't, but because she'd learned at a young age that no one would give it to her. If she wanted answers, *she* had to find them. Others would only get angry at her incessant questions. Or they'd grow bored or impatient, interrupting her so they could move along to what *they* considered important.

As Ren herself had done, more than once. All of them had.

She drew off the Black Rose's mask. In her other hand, a card took shape: The Mask of Unraveling. The card of solitude... of self-reliance... of loneliness.

Every Face had its Mask; every Mask had its Face. Just as the numina could be turned against their sunwise or earthwise spins, double meanings layered into one.

Tanaquis didn't merely want to understand. She wanted to be *understood*.

Ren turned the card around. On the reverse side, instead of the familiar triangle of spindle and shuttle and shears, it showed The Face of Weaving. "Tanaquis... if you leave. If you die. Then I'll lose my chance to know you. To truly become your cousin and your friend."

The broken strands of their fraying thread stretched, yearning toward each other. Breath hitching, Tanaquis said, "You won't like it. The things I've done..."

Chetoglio's death. Her involvement with Mettore Indestor. They'd already guessed at some of it; Ren knew there would be more.

The card vanished, leaving only her open, reaching hand. "We've all done things we should not have. Things we regret. I want the story behind them, before I decide. Will you let me have that chance?"

Tanaquis stared at Ren's hand like it was a foreign thing, beyond understanding. "That part of me burned away."

In spirit as well as in flesh. "But Ninat's flames lead to new birth. Have you not told me that, so many times? If you go beyond, Tanaquis, you will never return. I will lose you forever. Please... let this be a beginning, not only an end."

The Rook loosened his grip at Ren's nod, though he tensed again as Tanaquis reached out with the chaos she'd wrapped around herself to replace her missing hand. She stopped a breath away from touching Ren's fingers. "I don't see how I can...Oh." A spark flared amid the ashes, a tiny smile touching her lips. "Like invoking eisar. I can imbue it."

She opened her hand, fingers unfurling like a blossoming flower. The chaos giving it shape unraveled and reformed, becoming a perfect cabochon focus, etched with the sigil of A'ash.

Then she threw it. Out of the sanctuary of the labyrinth's heart, past the boundary where delusion transformed into intuition. Delusion was a thing outside reality...and that was where the Primordials dwelt.

Ren drew in a deep, shuddering breath, then stretched her arms wide. From the wellspring she had drunk, before A'ash began tearing it apart; she knew how this place should feel.

She expected a tremendous outpouring of effort, like when she'd cursed Laročja. Instead it was as easy as releasing a held breath. All around them, the damaged fabric of the conduit wove itself back together, and the riverine flow eased into a steady, unpolluted stream.

The Rook released Tanaquis. In his place, Ren wrapped her arm around her cousin's shoulders. And Vargo, sagging in relief, said, "Wellspring en't going to stay open forever. Let's go home."

27

Pearl's Promise

The Labyrinth of Nadežra, Old Island: Fellun 5

At the last moment before they stepped through into the world, as Ren put the mask of the Black Rose back on, Grey dragged the Rook's hood off his head. How many people had been lucid enough to pay attention, he didn't know...but anyone who'd seen him going into the wellspring needed to see him come out again.

He had enough wit left to think that far ahead. Not enough to realize he should have put it back on Vargo—not until it was too late.

Might be for the best, he thought in resigned amusement. *I don't think either of them enjoyed the exp—*

And then his thought stopped dead, because they weren't in the amphitheatre.

Atop the Point, yes, with the sea of fog spreading below them. The night they left, yes, because the twin moons were nearing the horizon, both still shining full. But where the Great Amphitheatre had been—the stage, the stone-tiered seats, the entire massive edifice Kaius Rex used to try to destroy the wellspring...

Graceful columns rose all around, each side bearing a finely carved Face or Mask. Within their embrace, a path wound across the mossy ground, its line traced by wooden markers sculpted with the clan animals.

The Labyrinth of Nadežra. Destroyed two hundred years ago—but Vraszenians had never stopped mourning its loss. On this night, at the end of a Grand Cycle and the beginning of a new one, with the return of the city to Vraszenian rule, the return of the Ižranyi fresh in everyone's mind, and the power of desire and dreams spilling through the city . . . they'd wanted it back.

And it had come.

The crowd atop the Point had thinned—or perhaps it only seemed that way, without the walls of the Tyrant penning them in. But Grey wasn't the only person stunned into silence. Along the great colonnade, reverent petitioners gaped up at the open sky, or knelt and pressed their brows to the mist-damp paving stones. One old man with tears funneling down his care-wrinkled cheeks lifted a trembling hand to place an offering in the mouth of An Mišennir. The Face of Weaving; the deity of community.

Grey turned to Ren, but he couldn't bring himself to break the reverent hush that hung like cool mist in the labyrinth. Her lips were parted in awe, the iridescing light of the wellspring casting shades of sapphire, emerald, and amethyst across the lace rose petals engraving her cheeks.

"Lady Rose!" someone cried, before he could warn or hide her. That call was the first pebble in an avalanche of cries, of people jostling closer and calling for answers, for explanations, for her blessing.

Despite everything she'd been through, Ren snapped visibly into persona. "Is this how we comport ourselves when offered the grace of Ažerais?" she called—not in the Black Rose's voice, but in her own accented Liganti. "Is this proper behavior for this place? This night?"

The growing uproar quieted, and she nodded. "Give your thanks to Ažerais for this miracle. See to those harmed during its birthing. And let me speak with the ziemetse."

Her words carried enough authority to make people fall back. The clan elders were in one of the box seats on the right side of the stage, some looking disoriented, others embarrassed by whatever they'd done. Grey was relieved to see the three Ižranyi among them. *Poor souls. First one Primordial, now another. It might have been better had we let them stay away.*

Before he could go to them, there was one matter more pressing. In a low voice, Grey said to Ren, "What do we do with Tanaquis?"

Her cousin was leaning against Ren as if almost too tired to stand. But however wounded and exhausted she might be... Tanaquis still had things to answer for. To the ziemetse, to the Cinquerat, to the people of Nadežra.

Ren's arm tightened around Tanaquis's shoulders. "She comes with us. Whatever happens next, it will be after we've all had a chance to think. Not in the heat of the moment."

Nodding, Grey followed her to the gathered clan elders.

The Labyrinth of Nadežra, Old Island: Fellun 5

Vargo dragged behind the others until he could sidestep into the shadow of a column. They didn't need an outsider mucking around in Vraszenian issues, and now that disaster had been averted, he had a conversation to finish.

Ren would be an unwilling eavesdropper, but he couldn't wait. *Alsius?*

::Thank the Lumen you're safe! It was like before, when you went into the realm of mind; I could sense you, but not hear you. What happened?::

A small body landed on Vargo's head and scuttled down to his shoulder. That tiny weight was a heavy stone on Vargo's chest. *Ren saved the world with talking.*

::I suppose if anyone could...::

Alsius's pause invited a laugh. Vargo couldn't dredge one up.

::What I mentioned—before everything devolved into madness—::

"You should go," Vargo said out loud. The words sliced his throat worse than the glass bottle that left him scarred, but what he had to say was for Alsius alone. "I don't want you to. I'll never want you to. But this is about what you need, not what I want."

Ren's plea to let go had been aimed at Tanaquis. Vargo was only caught in the blast.

But it didn't make what she'd said any less true.

After a moment, Alsius bumped gently against Vargo's neck. ::My boy. I wish more than you can know that I had arms right now to put around you. I know this isn't easy; we've been through too much for it to be easy. But I've taught you...::

A ragged laugh pulled free. "Everything you know?"

::Hardly! Enough for you to find me, though, in the realm of mind. We'll still be connected—tonight proves that—though it won't be the same.::

Never the same. Not the constant stream of exasperated, affectionate chiding in his mind. Not a gaudy little weight beneath his collar, faceted eyes peeking out from the shadows. Not there for the best and the worst of everything Vargo went through.

"You'll have a host of new stories and ideas to pester me with whenever you come back." Nobody was paying attention to him, but Vargo still ducked his head to hide that he was blotting his cheeks dry with his sleeve. "I'll try to keep everything we've built from crumbling into dust."

::As though Nadežra could do anything but improve under your hand,:: Alsius said, and somehow the raw pride in that affirmation made the floodwaters rise. Vargo banged his head gently against the column, wet eyes on the cut crystal clarity of the stars. They were set in a sky of black velvet, but he imagined he saw a hint of blue rising at the eastern edge.

Clearing his throat, he said, "Not much time left if you need the wellspring. And we'll have to get past the guards."

"I can help with that."

The soft reply was Ren's, delivered in her own voice. When Vargo turned, wiping his eyes, he found her no longer masked as the Black Rose, with Grey at her side. By the compassion on her face, she'd heard enough to understand.

Spiders couldn't cry, especially not in their minds, but Alsius still managed to sound clogged as he said, ::Oh, good. I was hoping to make my farewell to you.::

She offered him Alta Renata's Seterin curtsy, one hand sweeping up to the opposite shoulder. "Altan Alsius, it has been an honor."

And together they went to the wellspring, once more glowing with serene light, as the last of the pilgrims—those who'd neither had their chance sooner, nor fled during the chaos—drank from its waters. One of the guards was missing, but someone else had taken the man's place: a figure Vargo recognized from the bust that once stood in his office.

"Altan Gabrius," Vargo said with a crispness rivaling Renata at her cuffiest. He might let Alsius go, but he didn't have to like the man taking him away. "Say farewell to your ears. They're about to be talked off."

::Here now!:: A fuzzy leg whacked Vargo's jaw. ::I only speak when I have something worthwhile to say!::

Out of respect for the moment, the twitching at the corners of Mirscellis's mouth didn't bloom into a full grin. But a veil of amusement crept over his words as he said, "Which I'm sure is quite often."

Then he turned to Vargo and bowed. "I hope we'll come to know one another better over time. From what Alsius has said of you, I suspect we could have many interesting conversations. I'll try to end them before you throw anything at me."

A little of the tightness eased in Vargo's chest. If Alsius had to leave, at least he'd be safe with Ren's spectral father.

I guess this is goodbye.

::No. What are Vraszenians fond of saying? We will meet again when the road leads me home.::

When the river meets the sea, he thought back, because he couldn't make the words come. Scooping Peabody from his shoulder, he struggled for *any* words before finally managing to ask Mirscellis, "So...how does this work? Should I just...fling him in?"

::Don't you dare!:: Alsius squeaked. ::I knew you were spending too much time with that defenestrating lout.::

Mirscellis said, "If Ren lowers him in, I should be able to separate his spirit from that body."

The sky was noticeably lighter now. The last push of pilgrims vying for a taste of the waters was starting to crowd too close. Ren hugged Mirscellis tight, and through the fog of sorrow over Vargo's heart, he realized that she, too, was saying goodbye to her father.

With a hand steadier than it had any right to be, Vargo passed Peabody over to Ren, and stepped back.

Unlike Tanaquis, Mirscellis didn't dive in. He just stepped forward and dissolved into light. Then Ren knelt and, with a whispered farewell, lowered Peabody toward the water's glowing surface.

Just...promise me you won't return to the Lumen without letting me know.

Ren paused just above the lapping waters. Alsius raised Peabody's forelegs and colorful abdomen in salute. ::I won't go until you do, my boy.::

He wouldn't. He couldn't. But the promise encompassed more than just the binding of their lives. It was a reminder that, even separated, they walked this cycle together.

At Vargo's nod, Ren's hands dipped into the light. And when she removed them, the spider cupped there lay still, the colorful marks on his abdomen bleached away.

Hidden temple, Old Island: Fellun 6

Tess had near worn the hems off her skirt with pacing when noise finally came down the tunnel to the hidden temple. Ignoring Sedge's caution and Pavlin's restraining hand, she flung herself at Ren the moment she emerged. Caught between giddy relief and frazzled exasperation, Tess could only squeeze and squeeze harder, breathing in the warm comfort of a sister safely home.

"Mother and Crone, I'm that tempted to sew a sleeveless casing and stitch you up in it for all the Veiled Waters to come," she whispered into Ren's cheek.

"Sedate me while you're at it," Ren said, with a tired huff of laughter. "Just to be sure."

Pulling back, Tess worked off the rest of her worry by patting down Ren's Vraszenian finery like a hen pecking at her chick. "I only arrived a bit ago—took me forever to find a skiffer to bring me up from Whitesail—but Sedge says things got strange for a bit before they settled down. You found Tanaquis in time? Is she..."

The sobering of Ren's expression didn't look like grief, and Tess breathed out the last of her tension. "Locked up until we can decide what to do with her. But she backed down before it was too late. She had no desire to hurt anyone."

Desire or no, she'd certainly managed a fair bit of that. Sitting with Pavlin in the Whitesail townhouse, Tess had been outside the spreading fog of chaos, but fringes of it brushed against them in their rush to the Old Island. She'd gotten off lightly, compared to some others: For a few moments, the urgency to find her brother and sister had unraveled and she'd embraced Pavlin...and the extremely unlikely chance that they could overcome certain physical facts to make a child.

A yearning they'd set aside to discuss later, after the delusion faded and they hurried to make certain it wasn't a temporary reprieve.

Without dislodging Tess's limpet-cling, Sedge made his own quick check to confirm Ren had come to no harm. "What about the others?"

"Grey's gone to see to Alinka and the children. Vargo—"

Ren's eyes gleamed wet as she drew back from the embrace. "Alsius is gone," she said softly. "Not dead; with my father he chose to go into the dream. So he can be himself again. Vargo is distracting himself with politics."

Tess groaned, sinking against Pavlin's chest and hiding her face in her hands. "With the peace so fragile, this had to happen. Are we facing another riot? Revolution? How bad will it be?" Practicality of the whole business aside, wouldn't it have been a kind of madness, she and Pavlin bringing a child into a world this unsettled?

Ren drew Tess's hands down. She'd always been more willing to face troubles than hide from them. "I think not. Enough Vraszenians were there, with enough desire to reclaim what was once ours. The amphitheatre is gone. The labyrinth stands once more in its place, drawn whole from the dream. The ziemetse say it is a miracle from Ažerais. It may be enough to keep the peace intact."

If the ziemetse believed that, Tess suspected it was only because Ren had convinced them of it. She squeezed her sister's hands in thanks. "And you? How are you?"

Seven different moods chased each other across Ren's face. Worry and relief and exhaustion and wonder and more, like even her layered identities weren't enough to contain everything she felt.

"I am well," Ren said at last, half smiling as if she couldn't quite believe the words. "And I would like to sleep for a week."

Owl's Fields, Upper Bank: Fellun 9

Ren had never visited Utrinzi Simendis's house. There was a Simendis Manor closer to the river, but he dwelt in a smaller structure on the eastern outskirts of Nadežra, where he could have the solitude he desired.

Though he'd had an unusual number of houseguests in the last year. First Parma, living in ascetic seclusion to protect herself against Noctat; now Tanaquis, living under house arrest.

"It's my fault," he said wearily when he let Ren in, four days after the Great Dream. "When she was young, Tanaquis asked me questions about numinatria beyond Illi, about the Primordials. I thought the stern lecture I delivered would teach her not to dabble in such blasphemies. Instead it taught her she couldn't trust me with the secret of the medallion her uncle left behind after his suicide. All that time she had Ninat, and I didn't see it—not even as her family dwindled down to one."

Not from a curse, but from Ninat's lethal energy filtering

through their register. They weren't the first, either; a few bells digging through Fulvet's records showed that House Ciagne had suffered the same fate, until their last survivor, Bonavaito, was adopted into Fienola—and brought that fatal force with him.

Tanaquis hadn't let that mistake repeat itself. She'd protected the Traementis, placing wards around all the names to hide the fact that what she was containing was her own dangerous association.

One of the many points the Cinquerat was arguing over in their final days of authority, trying to decide what to do with Tanaquis. She'd protected the Traementis; she'd protected the city, absorbing a power that would otherwise have made Nadežra a second Fiavla. She'd also willfully ignored the kidnapping of children for the creation of ash, committed blasphemy and murder, and helped Mettore's attempt to destroy the Wellspring of Ažerais.

"You're not to blame," Ren said heavily. "Or many of us are. We didn't see the signs." Because they hadn't really looked. They'd taken Tanaquis for granted.

Utrinzi escorted Ren to a small study bare of books but full of strange stringed instruments. In a plain surcoat and underdress of moss-green linen, her hair tidy and her brow dry despite the humid warmth that followed Veiled Waters, Tanaquis looked better than she had since long before the Great Dream. Sleepless bruises no longer darkened the skin around her eyes...but those eyes also no longer sparked with the excitement of inquiry.

Without a second hand to steady it, the pot trembled when she poured the tea.

"I'm renouncing my membership in House Traementis," Tanaquis said, before Ren could speak. "To protect you from any consequences for my actions, but also to save Donaia any conflict she might feel over removing me. It will be several lifetimes before she's able to burn away Tricat's influence, and I don't want her struggling over which aspect is stronger in her, family or vengeance."

Ren swallowed her surprise. Tanaquis might not always be alert to social nuances, but that didn't mean she didn't understand Donaia in her own way. The revelation of Tanaquis's actions had cut deep into Donaia's heart—a heart that had taken too many such blows already. That her dear friend had designed the numinat to create ash, thus indirectly leading to Leato's death...Donaia had recused herself from all the debates over how to address Tanaquis's crimes, rather than face that impossible struggle.

Instead Ren said, "You realize that will strip you of your legal protections. You'll be an ordinary commoner."

"And more likely to be executed. I know." Tanaquis grimaced. "And I know what you'll say. I don't...*want* to die. Not like my uncle did, in the end."

"He had Ninat before you."

There was no humor or pleasure in Tanaquis's smile. "He thought it was what protected Kaius Rex against death. Which it was, in a way; the Tyrant didn't want to die, and so the medallions guided him. But Uncle Bonavaito thought it was a good luck charm. When he finally realized it was responsible for the death of his own family, for the Fienola dying off, he killed himself in shame."

She took a deep breath and straightened. "That was never how Ninat affected me, though. And I didn't intend to be a murderer, either—though I realize I became one. If the Cinquerat decides death is what I deserve, so be it."

Ren wanted to take Tanaquis's good hand, but she knew it wouldn't be welcome. Wrapping her fingers around the teacup, she said, "Your death would serve no cause but retribution. Which some people want; I won't pretend otherwise. But we've had enough of that in this city. I'm arguing for other solutions—ones that might create some good, in the wake of the bad." Her advocate's license had unexpected application, giving her the right to represent House Traementis in the Cinquerat's debates.

"I only wish they'd decide already." Tanaquis hugged herself, looking small. Her tea steamed forgotten at her knee. "It's the not knowing that makes it hard. And the waiting, with nothing to *do*. I'm not even allowed pen and ink to record what happened."

The cruelest punishment of all. Forbidding Tanaquis the free use of her mind. A room empty of books, of paper, of pen. She'd lost her hand; she had nothing with which to hurt anyone...but people were still afraid.

And it wasn't quite true she couldn't hurt anyone. Utrinzi had left them alone, and Ren doubted he would eavesdrop, but she lowered her voice all the same. "Tanaquis. When we were in the wellspring—what I said about Ažerais—"

"Yes. It makes sense. Explains so much, really. The Primordial of delusion, refined and brought into the world as intuition. As pattern." Absently, Tanaquis lifted her tea to drink, then winced at the heat.

"Have you told anyone?" Ren asked. Then: "You *cannot* tell anyone."

Tanaquis cocked her head, the light of connections being made bringing life back to her eyes. "I remember. You laid The Mask of Mirrors for me. A secret I must keep...I thought it meant the secret I was already keeping." She grimaced, the same face she'd made when she sipped the tea. "You know, pattern would be taken more seriously by scholars if it bothered to be more specific."

For once, the deprecation of pattern made Ren smile instead of fume. Tanaquis's training had started with the clean lines and clear logic of numinatria; that would always be her intellectual home. "I care not if scholars take it seriously. Only that *you* do."

The grimace softened. "I'm sorry I almost ruined it. Twice. The first time, Mettore proposed it to me as a puzzle: Could the wellspring be destroyed? I'd never even given it thought before, and once I did..." The teacup clinked back into its saucer, too hard. "Destruction. It was more tempting than I expected. Yet I was so sure I was in control of what I held, that self-awareness could protect me from its influence. Delusion of a different sort—the ordinary kind."

"I understand," Ren said. "But in the end, you acted to protect it. Twice." First when she'd sent Vargo to dismantle the wellspring numinat, and again when she relinquished the power of A'ash.

Ren meant it when she added, "I forgive you."

Tanaquis didn't acknowledge the words. "Of course I won't tell anyone. I presume the others have promised the same. I want to learn more about it, but..."

That brief flare of life faded. *But no one will let you,* Ren thought. Questions of that sort had already led Tanaquis to the brink of destruction once.

"Whatever the Cinquerat decides, your mind burns too brightly to be smothered." Ren braved reaching out. Not taking Tanaquis's hand, but offering hers like she had before. "And I meant what I said that night: I want to understand you, too."

Tanaquis looked at the outstretched hand, then put her own in it, with the air of someone stepping off a bridge into the river. "I hope you get the chance."

Isla Traementis, the Pearls: Fellun 12

One of the many benefits of having a dog was that Donaia could blame her nervous fidgeting on the animal's misbehavior. Or she could if Meatball weren't a panting lump thanks to the first hot day of the season, barely raising his head when Ren, Grey, and Vargo were shown into her parlour.

While Colbrin hurried off to fetch Meppe and Idaglio, Giuna fussed with the tea and Donaia gloved her twitching fingers in Meatball's thick ruff. Once everyone was settled, she cut off Meppe's attempt at small talk to say, "You've brought news."

News she still wasn't certain she wanted to hear. Half her heart ached for Tanaquis. One of the only friends Donaia could claim in foul times and fair, who'd never let on that she struggled with her own worries and loneliness.

The other half burned cold with fury. Because if it weren't for Tanaquis, Leato would be here to gentle her desire for vengeance.

Ren sat close to her. "The Cinquerat passed sentence today. Tanaquis will not be executed."

Idaglio hugged Meppe, and Donaia let go of Meatball long

enough to wipe away a tear. "Thank the Lumen." Even at her angriest, she hadn't been able to see anything in Tanaquis's death but more pain.

Giuna was a warm bolster of support at Donaia's side. "Then what's to become of her?"

A tinge of Vigil efficiency crept into Grey's response, though his accent remained Vraszenian. "Tanaquis's personal possessions—her house, her library, and so forth—will be confiscated and sold. To House Chetoglio a portion of the money will be paid, in reparation for Stezze's death."

It wouldn't make them whole. Nothing could. Donaia wasn't surprised when Vargo added, "Utrinzi passed up any share of the money. Tanaquis may have used her medallion to nudge Breccone into killing himself, but the man wasn't of Simendis anymore. With no Indestor left to claim reparations, and in light of Breccone's own crimes..." He shrugged.

"To the Ižranyi will the rest of the money be given," Grey said. "Our elders have agreed they need it the most, since they have no homes or lives to go back to."

"But that's just money," Donaia said. There had to be more. "What of Tanaquis herself?"

Ren let out a slow sigh. "Indentured servitude. For her crimes against the wellspring, the elders have decided she will serve Szorsa Olena in whatever capacity she requires for the next seven years."

It was unexpected enough to crack some of Donaia's worry. Indentured servitude had been common after the conquest of Vraszan; any number of Liganti settlers had come to Nadežra on those terms, working off the cost of their passage after their arrival. The practice had largely fallen out of use, though. Which member of the Cinquerat had suggested reviving it? Donaia suspected Utrinzi; it was kinder than execution, and he'd always had a fondness for his disciple.

Servitude to the Ižranyi szorsa...Donaia couldn't begin to guess what this Szorsa Olena would ask of Tanaquis. But after five hundred years out of the world, the Ižranyi would certainly need people to help them.

The other question eating at her heart wasn't one she wanted to ask in front of everyone. Thankfully, Vargo stood, the iridescent violet skirts of his coat catching the sunlight streaming in through the windows. "I believe Tanaquis hasn't been stricken from your register yet. If you'd prefer not to involve others in private matters, I'm willing to make the necessary adjustments."

That offer, from a man she'd treated with chill civility at the best of times, startled a choked laugh from Donaia. "Thank you, Eret Vargo. I suspect you're one of the few who can undo the tangled mess she made of it."

He bowed. "Then if I might make use of your study? Altan Meppe, Altan Idaglio, perhaps you can show me the way."

At a prod from his husband, Meppe blurted, "Of course!" and scurried ahead of Vargo. Idaglio gently shut the door on his way out.

"And what of you?" Donaia said to Ren before the click of the latch faded. "Now that you've found your mother's kin and your place among your people...what do you wish to do?"

Ren was too alert not to understand what that question meant. And it seemed she'd healed enough inside not to read into that question a blow that wasn't coming. "I understand there are some legal complexities around claiming membership in both a kureč and a register. But *someone* must be the first to do it, and once the members of the Setterat are chosen, they can determine how to untangle those threads."

Donaia, by contrast, had still been afraid. *I shouldn't have been. I know her heart.* Yes, for Vraszenians, the only true family was that of blood...but Ren wasn't only Vraszenian. She stood with one foot on each bank—and if she had her way, that idiom would cease to have meaning. Nadežra would become a strong fabric, not two fragments badly stitched together.

Now you're thinking in their metaphors. It brought a smile to Donaia's face as she said, "If your Volavka kin don't object, then you know I'm glad to keep you. But what of you, Grey?"

He straightened, head tilted in surprise. "Ask you if I wish to become Traementatis?" he asked, accent thickening to a depth she hadn't heard from him since he was a boy.

"You and Ren are wed, and I won't have anyone think we insult you by keeping you only as a contract husband." Her primness softened at a poke from Giuna. "And you have long been like family. Though I don't know if it matters to you, ratifying it in this manner."

Leaning forward to catch her hand in his, Grey said, "It matters that you asked."

The touch felt strange. Neither of them was gloved. His hands were rougher than Leato's had been, with calluses from more than just a sword. His grip was warm and firm, though, and she squeezed back just as tightly. "But the answer is no?"

"I hope there will be more unions like ours, and that they will have the same chance. But if I were made an altan..."

She felt his shudder through his grip, and laughed a little tearily at his rejection of that notion. "So you'll rewrite this city around yourselves, to make room for others to live in new ways. I knew you were daring, but the courage that takes is something else entirely."

Meatball nosed at their hands, wet tongue coming out in an exploratory lick. Grey laughed and let go of Donaia to scratch behind the dog's ears. "Old waters grow tedious. We must find new currents to sail."

Donaia watched as he wiped his hand dry and smiled at Ren. The Rook and the Black Rose: What an odd pair of people had wandered into her life.

But she wouldn't trade them for anyone.

Isla Čaprila, Eastbridge: Fellun 14

Apart from a chatty spider, Vargo had lived alone since he was a boy. In the early years, "home" was whatever squat he could talk his way into, or scrape together the mills for, or squeeze between the walls of when words and mills were lacking. But after he got himself spirit-bonded to an angry cuff, things changed. One of Alsius's first demands had been proper shelter at night, and one of the first things he'd done was help Vargo get it.

That came in handy when Vargo developed the habit of talking to himself. Now he wandered around his Eastbridge townhouse, truly alone, and he kept having the impulse to speak.

But there was no one there to hear.

Iascat had extended an open invitation to provide any distraction Vargo needed, but accepted with patient understanding when that invitation was declined for now. Not that Vargo didn't want sex, or even companionship, but...

"No, you'd rather rattle around in an empty house like a maudlin ass," he muttered to himself. "You en't alone, and you know it." It wasn't only Iascat's company he'd turned from. Ren and Grey were just a skiff ride away. The Fog Spiders offered him his office back if he'd reinscribe the cooling and airing numinata in their head-quarters. Varuni had promised to return before winter snows closed the passes from Isarn. He could even scratch together a numinat and contact Alsius if the solitude became unbearable, dragging his father away from whatever realm of mind adventures he was having with his numinatrian idol.

Still, the house felt...dead, without that gaudy little lump and that haughty mental voice.

The jangle of the bell was a welcome cacophony. Vargo hurried downstairs in his dressing gown and stocking feet, almost hoping for a new crisis to distract him.

A hope that was answered, after a fashion, in the form of a scrawny girl in a piebald velvet coat that looked like a poor, stained cousin of Vargo's.

"Mistress Bones. I assume you've come with a message?" It was unexpected—usually she sent one of her kids—but maybe it was of a delicate nature.

She at least had the decency to scrape her boots on the land-ing before clomping into his foyer uninvited. "Naw." Arkady barely gave him a look as she spoke, instead studying her surroundings like she was planning a break-in. Vargo might need to make his defensive numinata less lethal when he reinforced them, lest he end up with dead nippers on the landing. "It's more of what you might call a 'business proposition.'"

Or perhaps he'd remove the numinata entirely. It might be less painful to just let her rob him outright. Praying to the Lumen for the survival of his carpets, Vargo led her up to his study.

"What sort of business proposition?" he asked, leaning on his desk rather than sitting behind it like the sort of cuff who thought the Lumen shone out his ass.

After a circuit of the room—she was checking out his window locks; didn't even bother hiding it!—Arkady settled before him with feet planted and arms crossed. "Hear you've been telling your knots you can get 'em administration rights for Fulvet charters. Making 'em official-like, setting borders and paying them to take care of their turf. I want in."

Vargo hid his wince. Working out the maps had been a nightmare, and three different knots had already staked out territory in the Shambles. He hadn't even gotten Quientis to buy into the plan yet, though with Ren backing it, the poor bastard would fold like wet paper. But Vargo nodded as though he hadn't already promised away Arkady's patch. "Are you certain your kids could fulfill the administration duties? You'd be expected to—"

"Don't want the ones you're passing out to the others. I'm already fulfilling the *doodies*." She snorted, as though he needed more than the emphasis to recognize the pun. "Fulvet does the orphanages, right? Figure I'm doing as much as any of those nipper-nabbers, and better'n most. Shouldn't I get paid for it?"

Fulvet wanted to tear down the current orphanage system and replace it entirely, though whether he would get the chance was a very open question. The plan for the Setterat called for the civil seat to be allocated to a commoner, and Vargo didn't see Quientis giving up his charter of nobility to keep it.

Which was actually a pity. Though Vargo would never admit it to the man's face, Scaperto Quientis was a surprisingly decent Fulvet.

Just like Arkady's point was surprisingly solid. Too bad her age and Lower Bank background worked against her. Even if Vargo could scrape an allowance for the latter, there was no way Quientis or his successor would accept the former.

Unfortunately. Because if anyone could pull off administering such a charter on wits and bravado alone, it was Arkady Bones. Facing her was like looking into a distorted mirror.

Although...

Where once Alsius's squawks of outrage and dire predictions of failure would have filled Vargo's head, there was only quiet. His voice felt like a thing separate from him as he said, "Charter administration might be more than I can manage. But would you consider a counteroffer? I don't have an heir."

"Eh?" Arkady tilted her head, even whacked her ear a few times. "What's that got to do with me?"

"As heir to House Vargo, you'd have an allowance, and patronage rights. You could petition for your own charter and pick your own administrator. We might even be able to hire House Traementis's advocate."

Rising on her toes, Arkady sniffed his face. "You drunk?"

"I assure you, I'm completely sober. And serious. Don't you know I have a reputation for assimilating my rivals?" If this one agreed, he wouldn't be rattling around in silence anymore. And just thinking about Alsius's reaction when he learned about his new granddaughter made warmth blossom in Vargo's chest.

She snorted. "Yeah, right. Me, Alta Arkady Vargi or Vargitatis or whatever—"

"Vargonis." *Maybe I should have taken the chance to swap it for something fancier.* Or not. He'd done that once already as a kid, bestowing on himself the grandest-sounding name he could think of: *Derossi.* He didn't need *two* stupid names to regret.

Arkady's expression narrowed into a stink eye of suspicion. With the air of one testing, she said, "That mean I move in here? And Doomclaw. I en't leaving him behind. And you'll teach me that number magic? I wanna blow things up like you do."

Instead of regretting his impulsive offer, Vargo grinned. "I en't teaching you to blow up nothing till I'm sure it won't be *my* ass getting blown."

Arkady's cackle was a terrifying thing. She spun in place, making her tattered coat flare, then spat into her hand and held it out. As Vargo spat in his own and gripped her tight, she said, "Guess I can agree to that, old man."

Old man. Somewhere, he was sure, Alsius was laughing.

Kingfisher, Lower Bank: Fellun 19

The sun had long since set, but Alinka's courtyard glowed with light from lanterns of dyed paper, oil lamps of cut tin filigree, and numinatrian lightstones shielded by glass. The shifting colors vied with the koszenie of the gathered guests and the iridescent dreamweaver feathers braided into their hair or pinned to their collars. Or, in the case of Yvieny, Jagyi, and a few of the younger Volavka children, tucked safely away until the feathers weren't in danger of being chewed on or pulled apart by curious, sticky fingers.

It was tradition, Olena had told Ren—through Grey, but Ren was getting better at parsing out the archaic language on her own—that every Ižranyi wore such a feather to mark their lineage, even when their koszenie was put away. Ren still felt like *she* was going to ruin her feather...but her new status meant she had to wear it.

"How can you be her apprentice!" Tsvetsa had exclaimed, when she heard the arrangement Ren had made. "You, conceived on the Great Dream, sired by a spirit *in* the dream—the Black Rose of Ažerais herself! You are no one's apprentice!"

That last secret had slipped out in the aftermath of the events at the amphitheatre. Too many people had seen Ren put on the lace mask and transform into the Black Rose for her to pretend it wasn't true. And they'd seen something else, too: the Black Rose going into the wellspring with Grey and the Rook at her side...and coming out with Grey and *Vargo*.

Grey had laughed himself to collapse when he realized people now thought Vargo was the Rook. It wasn't just what happened at the wellspring; rumors had spread about the strange mass of Rooks that flocked to rescue him from Tserdev, and the daring escape from the Old Island. Vargo himself had merely looked resigned. "My heart to protect yours," he muttered, echoing the words of their brotherhood oath. "En't the worst thing people have ever called me."

Touching her feather as she watched the Volavka mill about the courtyard, Ren didn't at all mind being Olena's apprentice. The last formal instruction she'd had was from her mother, years ago; as the ordeal at the labyrinth and the choosing of the Ižranyi speaker had shown, there were countless traditions Ren didn't know. And Olena was the only szorsa accustomed to working with all the clan cards—cards that were now a part of Ren's deck, including The Living Dream.

A hush fell over the gathering when Grey entered, followed by the Ižranyi. Not just a few representatives, but all of them, skulking and cringing in a manner too reminiscent of the zlyzen for Ren's comfort. It would be a long time, if not a lifetime, before the horror of Fiavla and the following centuries ceased to weigh them down.

"Poor dears," Tess whispered, twisting her hands in her skirt as though she wished she could reach out to the skittish Ižranyi. "Strange to think I was ever afraid of them."

Sedge grunted. He'd actually seen and fought the zlyzen. But all he said was "Maybe we should have done this in the daytime."

"Most of them still can't handle bright light," Ren said, and went to talk to the Dvornič and her grandfather Lenismir, who were gossiping together like old gaffers.

The Dvornič sighed theatrically at Ren. "Such a short time I was able to claim you and your husband as our own . . . alas, other things come before my pride."

"I would have been glad to stay," Ren said with absolute sincerity. She'd called herself Dvornik many times before—when she wasn't calling herself Meszaros or Varadi or Anoškin. Always lies, told to suit the con of the moment. She'd had less than a month to be Dvornik in truth.

But the Ižranyi were too few and too scarred to fend for themselves in a changed world. They needed Ren, the Black Rose of Ažerais, to train as their szorsa. And they needed a clan elder who could mediate between them and the city they now lived in—someone who could speak both to them and to Nadežra.

They needed Grey to be their Ižranjič.

Ren might be Traementis and Volavka both, but no one could lead one clan while belonging to another. When she'd tearfully confessed to her grandfather that she and Grey had to leave her kureč, so soon after joining their ranks, he'd hugged her tight and proposed a better way. The Ižranyi needed more than two people to hold them steady and teach them how to walk in this strange new world. And so some of the Volavka would remain Dvornik...but others, those most closely tied to Ren, would follow their lost daughter onto a new road.

Lenismir took Ren's hand in his own and held it tight, as if to squeeze out any remaining guilt. "Blood is a river with many branches. We abandon not our Dvornik ancestry in joining now with the Ižranyi."

"Nor will we forget our cousins just because the river has swept them downstream," the Dvornič said. He dipped his chin toward the tense Ižranyi. "But a kindness it would be to begin, I think."

Ren had sworn kinship to Tess and Sedge in a grubby corner of the Lacewater labyrinth, hurrying through the words before someone kicked them out; Grey and Vargo had made their bond in her parlour. Heart mattered more than the trappings of ceremony. So while adoptions were supposed to be grand affairs, conducted in a labyrinth with offerings to the Faces and the Masks and everyone invited to witness, for the sake of the Ižranyi they kept it simple.

And they kept it short. By Vraszenian tradition, no ritual had been needed for Ren to become Volavka; she already was one, by virtue of her mother. By virtue of the marks on their wrists, so were Tess and Sedge; by virtue of his marriage to Ren and his severance from the Szerado, so was Grey. Alinka formed the bond for her children, mingling her blood with that of Lenismir. Then it only needed three: Grey, Ren, and Lenismir exchanging oaths with Olena, bringing all the others, born and bound, along with them.

Ren wondered if even that was too much, with the Ižranyi—the *original* Ižranyi—shrinking back from their new cousins. But then the music started up, and people began dancing, and she saw some of the uneasiness bleed out of the former zlyzen. In a city where so much was new and strange, this was familiar: a melody they knew, steps they could follow. Joy they could share in.

Grey had spent three finger-mincing days with Tess finishing Yvie's koszenie, but it was worth it to see her stamping and spinning her way through the kanina, taking hands with everyone. Jagyi was passed from hip to shoulder to back and hip again, the Ižranyi clinging to him as long as the dance allowed, his smile and giggles and wisp-wild curls drawing out their fear like poison from a wound.

Like the fear that had once lived in Ren's own heart. Now she had her Volavka kin at her side, knowing her for who she was, and welcoming her into their ranks. She had the Ižranyi, rescued at last from their torment. Would the kanina call forth their ancestors, those who'd died before the fall of Fiavla? Could it bring back those who didn't survive to become zlyzen, those whose souls were said to be lost even to the dream?

She didn't know. But as she danced, she lost all sense of time, all sense of the world beyond the whirling bodies around her. Thought dissolved, and she gave herself wholly over to the performance.

And at the edge of a courtyard, a vision took shape. A familiar face, because she'd seen one so much like it in the mirror, every time she disguised herself to look fully Vraszenian.

Ren whirled herself out of the dance, and went to embrace her mother.

Epilogue

Victory wore many faces.

It looked like the restored labyrinth atop the Point, columns lifting gracefully to the sky where once the amphitheatre had hunched in ugly reminder of the Tyrant's reign. Even as workers began clearing away the ruined East Channel numinat, the feet of worshippers tracing the seven-layered path revealed a secret lost to time: that once the labyrinth had been not only a place of faith and pilgrimage, but a way of cleansing the Dežera's divided waters. With the growth of the city, both methods would be necessary, but it brought some much-needed relief to the Upper Bank.

Victory looked like Tess and Pavlin's wedding, which filled Little Alwydd to bursting not only with all those closest to Tess, but with Ganllechyn nans like Old Mag, Tess's newly acquired Vraszenian cousins, some of her more open-minded customers—Donaia escorted by Scaperto, Giuna by Kasienka—and a burn-scarred Upper Bank thief who could outdrink, though not outflirt, Oksana Ryvček. Everyone sang and ate and drank and danced, and no one got hurt, no monsters appeared.

Victory looked like the different parts of the city gathering to select who would represent them. In the final agreement, the cultural and crafting seats went to Liganti residents, the economic and religious seats to Vraszenians, and the civil, military, and diplomatic seats to Nadežrans of mixed heritage. Mevieny won Albet, the new religious seat; Scaperto took Caeset, overseeing the guilds. Iascat held on to the cultural seat, now called Viridet for its new association with Dvornik green, though he openly admitted he'd rather step down once the transition between Cinquerat and Setterat was more secure.

As for Ren and Vargo...

"Welcome!" Dvaran said as the two of them followed Grey into the Gawping Carp. "I've been to *your* house; 'bout time you came to mine."

"Actually," Ren said, grinning, "I was here once before. During the riots, when you were kind enough to loan Alta Renata a Vraszenian shawl before she went into Seven Knots."

It pulled him up short. "So you were. I—ah—what do I call you?"

Vargo swept a grand bow, like he was a herald announcing her at a ball. "You have the honor of addressing Her Serenity, Alta Szorsa Renata Arenza Lenskaya Mirscellis Traementatis Volavka, formerly of the Dvornik, now of the newly restored Ižranyi, Black Rose of Ažerais, and Ostrinet of the Setterat."

Ren smacked his shoulder with the back of her hand.

"Call her Ren," Vargo added.

"Call *him* Your Grace." Ren's purr was as sweet as honey-soaked cream and vengeance. "Dvaran, Grey mentioned you had some opinions to share with the new civil seat? Well, here he is."

Dvaran needed no encouragement. He trapped Vargo with a hand on his arm and a litany of improvements that could be made to the disposal of waste, while Ren was dragged into a nytsa game with the old gaffers, one hand for every name she had. She played fair, and lost almost every round.

"That was cruel," Vargo grumbled once he'd escaped, joining Ren and Grey at a back table with a fresh pitcher of autumn brew and a third cup. They'd already run through most of the pitcher on the table, and Ren was feeling the warmth of bad drink and good friends.

"Get used to it," she said, amused. "You're the one who decided to relinquish your ennoblement charter and put yourself up for Auret."

Vargo knocked back a gulp of beer and said, "Well, Scaperto

wasn't going to do it. And the only thing worse than doing it myself would be watching somebody else botch the job." Wiping foam from his lip, he set the mug down. "Though Arkady won't let me hear the end of it. 'You mean I don't get to be Alta Arkady Bonis Vargonis?'"

His imitation of her voice was uncannily good. Grey poured him more beer. "Careful, or she'll jump ship for a better prospect."

"It en't half a joke," Vargo grumbled. But he was smiling as he said it.

Ren sank back in her chair and nursed her drink as the conversation ranged from Dvaran's wished-for improvements to the Ižranyi's new housing to whether the mark on the table looked like a raccoon poling a skiff—a debate that only got more impassioned as the level in the pitcher got lower. Eventually the two men swayed unsteadily to the bar to insist Dvaran adjudicate, leaving Ren to guard the table by herself.

But not alone. Not anymore. She had a kureč and a clan now, as well as a register and a house. Friends, family—more names than she knew what to do with—love and the safety she hadn't known she craved when she returned to Nadežra. A future she could face without need of a mask.

Truly, a favored daughter of Ažerais.

~Illi~

Acknowledgments

What do you say when you reach the end of a path this long and grueling?

You thank the people who helped you along the way.

We've been thanking them at the end of each book, of course, but gratitude can survive a little repetition. Adrienne Lipoma, Kyle Niedzwiecki, Wendy Shaffer, and Emily Dare continue to be patient, supportive, and even (dare we say it) enthusiastic about this six-hundred-thousand-word digression from some humble gaming roots. To that set we must add the members of our Carrickmacross Discord, aka the Screaming Peaches, who have bonded over Discord's most terrifying "welcome" GIF and provided us with a wonderful community as we wrestle this kraken of a plot to its conclusion. The Wailing Plum is for you.

For this particular book, one bit of research assistance stands out. After Marie had the masochistic idea of representing the archaic speech of the Ižranyi with Middle English, she knew right away that she wasn't going to be able to make that happen with only a dictionary and a reference grammar to help. A PhD candidate in the English department at Harvard University stepped into the breach: Ahmed Seif, who went above and beyond mechanical translation of the original dialogue, navigating the multiple dialects of Middle English to find options that would balance accuracy against something approaching comprehensibility for the modern reader. If you still have difficulty with the Ižranyi speech, blame Marie for having this idea in the first place; she freely admits it's her fault.

When it comes to the publishing front...do you realize how

many people it takes to make a book happen? Even we authors sometimes lose sight of the number, but we've done our best this time around to collect the full list. On the editorial side, our glorious and indefatigable editor Priyanka Krishnan is joined by Jenni Hill, Tiana Coven, and Tim Holman; on the publicity and marketing side, Alex Lencicki, Ellen Wright, Angela Man, Paola Crespo, Natassja Haught, and Nazia Khatun; on the managing editorial side, Bryn A. McDonald shepherded this whole thing through the transition from laptop to bookshelf. Our gorgeous covers are brought to you by Lauren Panepinto, Stephanie A. Hess, and the wonderful artist Nekro. Nikki Massoud has done a tremendous job with all the shifting accents of the audiobooks—we apologize (again) for the Middle English!—with Tom Mis and Caitlin Davies bringing her work to all our listeners. And we must also thank our tireless agents, Eddie Schneider and Paul Stevens, with Cameron McClure coming in on the home stretch to help carry us through to the conclusion.

Thank you all for coming with us on this journey. May we meet again when the road leads you home, when the river meets the sea.

Glossary

advocate: An individual licensed to conduct business within the Charterhouse, usually on behalf of a noble house.

alta/altan: The titles used for nobility who are not the heads of houses.

Argentet: One of the five seats in the Cinquerat, addressed as "Your Elegance." Argentet oversees the cultural affairs of the city, including theatres, festivals, and censorship of written materials.

aža: A drug made from powdered seeds. Although it is commonly spoken of as a hallucinogen, Vraszenians believe that aža allows them to see into Ažerais's Dream.

Ažerais's Dream: This place, called "the realm of mind" by inscriptors, is a many-layered reflection of the waking world, both as it was in the past, and as it may be metaphorically expressed in the present.

Ča: A title used when addressing a Vraszenian.

Caerulet: One of the five seats in the Cinquerat, addressed as "Your Mercy." Caerulet oversees the military affairs of the city, including prisons, fortifications, and the Vigil.

Ceremony of the Accords: A ritual commemorating the signing of the peace agreement that ended the war between the city-states of Vraszan and Nadežra, leaving the latter in the control of its Liganti nobility. The ceremony involves the ziemetse and the members of the Cinquerat, and takes place each year during the Night of Bells.

Charterhouse: The seat of Nadežra's government, where the Cinquerat offices are located.

Cinquerat: The five-member council that has been the ruling body of Nadežra since the death of the Tyrant. Each seat has its own sphere of responsibility. See *Argentet, Fulvet, Prasinet, Caerulet*, and *Iridet*.

clan: Vraszenians are traditionally divided into seven clans: the Anoškin, the Dvornik, the Ižranyi, the Kiraly, the Meszaros, the Stretsko, and the Varadi. The Ižranyi have been extinct for centuries, following a supernatural calamity. Each clan consists of multiple kretse.

era/eret: The titles used for the heads of noble houses.

Faces and Masks: In Vraszenian religion, the divine duality common to many faiths is seen as being contained within single deities, each of which has a benevolent aspect (the Face) and a malevolent one (the Mask).

Festival of Veiled Waters: A yearly festival occurring during the springtime in Nadežra, when fog covers the city for approximately a week.

Fulvet: One of the five seats in the Cinquerat, addressed as "Your Grace." Fulvet oversees the civic affairs of the city, including land ownership, public works, and the judiciary.

The Great Dream: A sacred event for Vraszenians, during which the Wellspring of Ažerais manifests in the waking world. It occurs once every seven years, during the Festival of Veiled Waters.

Illi: The numen associated with both 0 and 10 in numinatria. It represents beginnings, endings, eternity, the soul, and the inscriptor's self.

imbuing: A form of craft-based magic that has the effect of making objects function more effectively: an imbued blade cuts better and doesn't dull or rust, while an imbued cloak may be warmer, more waterproof, or more concealing. It is also possible, though more difficult, to imbue a performance.

inscriptor: A practitioner of numinatria.

Iridet: One of the five seats in the Cinquerat, addressed as "Your Worship." Iridet oversees the religious affairs of the city, including temples, numinatria, and the pilgrimage of the Great Dream.

Kaius Sifigno / Kaius Rex: See *The Tyrant*.

kanina: The "ancestor dance" of the Vraszenians, used on special occasions such as births, marriages, and deaths. When performed well enough, it has the power to call up the spirits of the dancers' ancestors from Ažerais's Dream.

knot: A term derived from Vraszenian custom for a street gang in Nadežra. Members mark their allegiance with a knotwork charm, though they are not required to wear or display it openly.

koszenie: A Vraszenian shawl that records an individual's maternal and paternal ancestry in the pattern of its embroidery. It is usually worn only for special occasions, including when performing the kanina.

kretse: (sing. kureč) A Vraszenian lineage, a subdivision of a clan. The third part of a traditional Vraszenian name marks the kureč an individual belongs to.

lihoše: (sing. lihosz) The Vraszenian term for a person born female, but taking on a male role so as to be able to lead his people. Lihoše patronymics end in the plural and gender-neutral "-ske." Their counter-parts are the rimaše, born male but taking on a female role so as to become szorsas.

meda/mede: The titles used for members of delta houses.

The Night of Bells: A yearly festival commemorating the death of the Tyrant. It includes the Ceremony of the Accords.

Ninat: The numen associated with 9 in numinatria. It represents death, release, completion, apotheosis, and the boundary between the mundane and the infinite.

Noctat: The numen associated with 8 in numinatria. It represents sensation, sexuality, procreation, honesty, salvation, and repentance.

numina: (sing. numen) The numina are a series of numbers, 0–10, that are used in numinatria to channel magical power. They consist of Illi (which is both 0 and 10), Uniat, Tuat, Tricat, Quarat, Quinat, Sessat, Sebat, Noctat, and Ninat. Each numen has its own particular resonance with concepts such as family or death, as well as associated gods, colors, metals, geometric figures, and so forth.

numinatria: A form of magic based on sacred geometry. A work of numinatria is called a numinat (pl. numinata). Numinatria works by channeling power from the ultimate godhead, the Lumen, which manifests in the numina. In order to function, a numinat must have a focus, through which it draws on the power of the Lumen; most foci feature the name of a god, written in the ancient Enthaxn script.

pattern: In Vraszenian culture, "pattern" is a term for fate and the interconnectedness of things. It is seen as a gift from the ancestral goddess Ažerais, and can be understood through the interpretation of a pattern deck.

pattern deck: A deck currently consisting of sixty cards in three suits, called threads. The spinning thread represents the "inner self" (the mind and spirit), the woven thread represents the "outer self" (social relationships), and the cut thread represents the "physical self" (the body and the material world). Each thread contains both unaligned and aspect cards, the latter of which allude to the most important Faces and Masks in Vraszenian religion.

Prasinet: One of the five seats in the Cinquerat, addressed as "Your Charity." Prasinet oversees the economic affairs of the city, including taxation, trade routes, and guilds.

prismatium: An iridescent metal created through the use of numinatria, and associated with Sebat.

Quarat: The numen associated with 4 in numinatria. It represents nature, nourishment, growth, wealth, and luck.

Quinat: The numen associated with 5 in numinatria. It represents power, excellence, leadership, healing, and renewal.

rimaše: (sing. rimasz) The Vraszenian term for a person born male, but taking on a female role to act as a szorsa. Rimaše patronymics end in the plural and gender-neutral "-ske." Their counterparts are the lihoše, born female but taking on male roles to lead their people.

Sebat: The numen associated with 7 in numinatria. It represents craftsmanship, purity, seclusion, transformation, and perfection in imperfection.

Sessat: The numen associated with 6 in numinatria. It represents order, stasis, institutions, simplicity, and friendship.

soul: In Vraszenian cosmology, the soul has three parts: the dlakani or "personal" soul, the szekani or "knotted" soul, and the čekani or "bodily" soul. After death, the dlakani goes to paradise or hell, the szekani lives on in Ažerais's Dream, and the čekani reincarnates. In Liganti cosmology, the soul ascends through the numina to the Lumen, then descends once more to reincarnate.

sun/earth: Contrasting terms used for many purposes in Liganti culture. The sun hours run from 6 a.m. to 6 p.m.; the earth hours run from 6 p.m. to 6 a.m. Sun-handed is right-handed, and earth-handed is left-handed. Sunwise and earthwise mean clockwise and counterclockwise, or when referring to people, a man born female or a woman born male.

szorsa: A reader of a pattern deck.

Tricat: The numen associated with 3 in numinatria. It represents stability, family, community, completion, rigidity, and reconciliation.

Tuat: The numen associated with 2 in numinatria. It represents the other, duality, communication, connection, opposition, and the inscriptor's edge.

The Tyrant: Kaius Sifigno, also called Kaius Rex. He was a Liganti commander who conquered all of Vraszan, but according to legend his further spread was stopped by him succumbing to his various desires. Reputed to be unkillable, the Tyrant was supposedly brought down by venereal disease. His death is celebrated on the Night of Bells.

Uniat: The numen associated with 1 in numinatria. It represents the body, self-awareness, enlightenment, containment, and the inscriptor's chalk.

The Vigil: The primary force of law and order within Nadežra, nicknamed "hawks" after their emblem. Separate from the city-state's army, the Vigil polices the city itself, under the leadership of a high commander who answers to Caerulet. Their headquarters is the Aerie.

Vraszan: The name of the region and loose confederation of city-states of which Nadežra was formerly a part.

Wellspring of Ažerais: The holy site around which the city of Nadežra was founded. The wellspring exists within Ažerais's Dream, and manifests in the waking world only during the Great Dream. Drinking its waters grants a true understanding of pattern.

ziemetse: (sing. ziemič) The leaders of the Vraszenian clans, also referred to as "clan elders." Each has a title taken from the name of their clan: the Anoškinič, Dvornič, Kiralič, Meszarič, Stretskojič, Varadič, and (formerly) Ižranjič.

extras

orbit

meet the author

John Scalzi

M. A. Carrick is the joint pen name of Marie Brennan (author of the Memoirs of Lady Trent) and Alyc Helms (author of the Adventures of Mr. Mystic). The two met in 2000 on an archaeological dig in Wales and Ireland, including a stint in the town of Carrickmacross, and have built their friendship through two decades of anthropology, writing, and gaming. They live in the San Francisco Bay Area.

Find out more about M. A. Carrick and other Orbit authors by registering for the free monthly newsletter at orbitbooks.net.

if you enjoyed
LABYRINTH'S HEART

look out for

THE PHOENIX KING

The Ravence Trilogy: Book One

by

Aparna Verma

In a kingdom where flames hold magic and the desert hides secrets, an ancient prophecy comes for an assassin, a princess, and a king. But none are ready to face destiny—and the choices they make could burn the world.

For Elena Aadya Ravence, fire is yearning. She longs to feel worthy of her Phoenix god, of her ancestors who transformed the barren dunes of Sayon into a thriving kingdom. But though she knows the ways and wiles of the desert better than she knows her own skin, the secrets of the Eternal Fire elude her. And without them, she'll never be accepted as queen.

For Leo Malhari Ravence, fire is control. He is not ready to give up his crown—there's still too much work to be done to ensure his legacy remains untarnished, his family protected. But power comes with a price, and he'll wage war with the heavens themselves to keep from paying it.

For Yassen Knight, fire is redemption. He dreams of shedding his past as one of Sayon's most deadly assassins, of laying to rest the ghosts of those he has lost. If joining the court of flame and serving the royal Ravence family—the very people he once swore to eliminate—will earn him that, he'll do it no matter what they ask of him.

But the Phoenix watches over all, and the fire has a will of its own. It will come for all three, will come for Sayon itself . . . and they must either find a way to withstand the blaze or burn to ash.

CHAPTER 1

Yassen

The king said to his people, "We are the chosen."
And the people responded, "Chosen by whom?"

—from chapter 37 of *The Great History of Sayon*

To be forgiven, one must be burned. That's what the Ravani said. They were fanatics and fire worshippers, but they were his people. And he would finally be returning home.

Yassen held on to the railing of the hoverboat as it skimmed over the waves. He held on with his left arm, his right limp by his side. Around him, the world was dark, but the horizon began to purple with the faint glimmers of dawn. Soon, the sun would rise, and the twin moons of Sayon would lie down to rest. Soon, he would arrive at Rysanti, the Brass City. And soon, he would find his way back to the desert that had forsaken him.

Yassen withdrew a holopod from his jacket and pressed it open with his thumb. A small holo materialized with a message:

Look for the bull.

He closed the holo, the smell of salt and brine filling his lungs.

The bull. It was nothing close to the Phoenix of Ravence, but then again, Samson liked to be subtle. Yassen wondered if he would be at the port to greet him.

A large wave tossed the boat, but Yassen did not lose his balance. Weeks at sea and suns of combat had taught him how to keep his ground. A cool wind licked his sleeve, and he felt a whisper of pain skitter down his right wrist. He grimaced. His skin was already beginning to redden.

After the Arohassin had pulled him half-conscious from the sea, Yassen had thought, in the delirium of pain, that he would be free. If not in this life, then in death. But the Arohassin had yanked him back from the brink. Treated his burns and saved his arm. Said that he was lucky to be alive while whispering among themselves when they thought he could not hear: "Yassen Knight is no longer of use."

Yassen pulled down his sleeve. It was no matter. He was used to running.

As the hoverboat neared the harbor, the fog along the coastline began to evaporate. Slowly, Yassen saw the tall spires of the Brass City cut through the grey heavens. Skyscrapers of slate and steel from the mines of Sona glimmered in the early dawn as hover-trains weaved through the air, carrying the day laborers. Neon lights flickered within the metal jungle, and a silver bridge snaked through the entire city, connecting the outer rings to the wealthy, affluent center. Yassen squinted as the sun crested the horizon. Suddenly, its light hit the harbor, and the Brass City shone with a blinding intensity.

Yassen quickly clipped on his visor, a fiber sheath that covered his entire face. He closed his eyes for a moment, allowing them to readjust before opening them again. The city stared back at him in subdued colors.

Queen Rydia, one of the first queens of Jantar, had wanted to ward off Enuu, the evil eye, so she had fashioned her port city out of unforgiving metal. If Yassen wasn't careful, the brass could blind him.

The other passengers came up to deck, pulling on half visors that covered their eyes. Yassen tightened his visor and wrapped a scarf around his neck. Most people could not recognize him—none of the passengers even knew of his name—but he could not take any chances. Samson had made it clear that he wanted no one to know of this meeting.

The hoverboat came to rest beside the platform, and Yassen disembarked with the rest of the passengers. Even in the early hours, the port was busy. On the other dock, soldiers barked out orders as fresh immigrants stumbled off a colony boat. Judging from the coiled silver bracelets on their wrists, Yassen guessed they were Sesharian refugees. They shuffled forward on the adjoining dock toward military buses. Some carried luggage; others had nothing save the clothes they wore. They all donned half visors and walked with a resigned grace of a people weary of their fate.

Native Jantari, in their lightning suits and golden bracelets, kept a healthy distance from the immigrants. They stayed on the brass homeland and receiving docks where merchants stationed their carts. Unlike most of the city, the carts were made of pale driftwood, but the vendors still wore half visors as they handled their wares. Yassen could already hear a merchant hawking satchels of vermilion tea while another shouted about a new delivery of mirrors from Cyleon that had a 90 percent accuracy of predicting one's romantic future. Yassen shook his head. Only in Jantar.

Floating lanterns guided Yassen and the passengers to the glass-encased immigration office. Yassen slid his holopod into the port while a grim-faced attendant flicked something from his purple nails.

"Name?" he intoned.

"Cassian Newman," Yassen said.

"Country of residence?"

"Nbru."

The attendant waved his hand. "Take off your visor, please."

Yassen unclipped his visor and saw shock register across the attendant's face as he took in Yassen's white, colorless eyes.

"Are you Jantari?" the attendant asked, surprised.

"No," Yassen responded gruffly and clipped his visor back on. "My father was."

"Hmph." The attendant looked at his holopod and then back at him. "Purpose of your visit?"

Yassen paused. The attendant peered at him, and for one wild moment, Yassen wondered if he should turn away, jump back on the boat, and go wherever the sea pushed him. But then a coldness slithered down his right elbow, and he gripped his arm.

"To visit some old friends," Yassen said.

The attendant snorted, but when the holopod slid back out, Yassen saw the burning insignia of a mohanti, a winged ox, on its surface.

"Welcome to the Kingdom of Jantar," the attendant said and waved him through.

Yassen stepped through the glass immigration office and into Rysanti. He breathed in the sharp salt air, intermingled with spices both foreign and familiar. A storm had passed through recently, leaving puddles in its wake. A woman ahead of Yassen slipped on a wet plank and a merchant reached out to steady her. Yassen pushed past them, keeping his head down. Out of the corner of his eye, he saw the merchant swipe the woman's holopod and hide it in his jacket. Yassen smothered a laugh.

As he wandered toward the homeland dock, he scanned the faces in the crowd. The time was nearly two past the sun's breath. Samson and his men should have been here by now.

He came to the bridge connecting the receiving and homeland docks. At the other end of the bridge was a lonely tea stall, held together by worn planks—but the large holosign snagged his attention.

WARM YOUR TIRED BONES FROM YOUR PASSAGE AT SEA! FRESH
HOT LEMON CAKES AND RAVANI TEA SERVED DAILY! it read.

It was the word *Ravani* that sent a jolt through Yassen. Home—
the one he longed for but knew he was no longer welcome in.

Yassen drew up to the tea stall. Three large hourglasses hissed
and steamed. Tea leaves floated along their bottoms, slowly steep-
ing, as a heavyset Sesharian woman flipped them in timed intervals. On her hand, Yassen spotted a tattoo of a bull.

The same mark Samson had asked him to look for.

When the woman met Yassen's eyes, she twirled the hourglass
once more before drying her hands on the towel around her wide
waist.

"Whatcha want?" she asked in a river-hoarse voice.

"One tea and cake, please," Yassen said.

"You're lucky. I just got a fresh batch of leaves from my connect.
Straight from the canyons of Ravence."

"Exactly why I want one," he said and placed his holopod in the
counter insert. Yassen tapped it twice.

"Keep the change," he added.

She nodded and turned back to the giant hourglasses.

The brass beneath Yassen's feet grew warmer in the yawning
day. Across the docks, more boats pulled in, carrying immigrant
laborers and tourists. Yassen adjusted his visor, making sure it was
fully in place, as the woman simultaneously flipped the hourglass
and slid off its cap. In one fluid motion, the hot tea arced through
the air and fell into the cup in her hand. She slid it across the
counter.

"Mind the sleeve, the tea's hot," she said. "And here's your cake."

Yassen grabbed the cake box and lifted his cup in thanks. As he
moved away from the stall, he scratched the plastic sleeve around
the cup.

Slowly, a message burned through:

Look underneath the dock of fortunes.

He almost smiled. Clearly, Samson had not forgotten Yassen's
love of tea.

Yassen looked within the box and saw that there was no cake but something sharp, metallic. He reached inside and held it up. Made of silver, the insignia was smaller than his palm and etched in what seemed to be the shape of a teardrop. Yassen held it closer. No, it was more feather than teardrop.

He threw the sleeve and box into a bin, slid the silver into his pocket, and continued down the dock. The commerce section stretched on, a mile of storefronts welcoming him into the great nation of Jantar. Yassen sipped his tea, watching. A few paces down was a stall marketing tales of ruin and fortune. Like the tea stall, it too was old and decrepit, with a painting of a woman reading palms painted across its front. He was beginning to recognize a pattern—and patterns were dangerous. Samson was getting lazy in his mansion.

Three guards stood along the edge of the platform beside the stall. One was dressed in a captain's royal blue, the other two in the plain black of officers. All three wore helmet visors, their pulse guns strapped to their sides. They were laughing at some joke when the captain looked up and frowned at Yassen.

"You there," he said imperiously.

Yassen slowly lowered his cup. The dock was full of carts and merchants. If he ran now, the guards could catch him.

"Yes, you, with the full face," the captain called out, tapping his visor. "Come here!"

"Is there a problem?" Yassen asked as he approached.

"No full visors allowed on the dock, except for the guard," the captain said.

"I didn't know it was a crime to wear a full visor," Yassen said. His voice was cool, perhaps a bit too nonchalant because the captain slapped the cup out of Yassen's hand. The spilled tea hissed against the metal planks.

"New rules," the captain said. "Only guards can wear full visors. Everybody else has to go half."

His subordinates snickered. "Looks like he's fresh off the boat, Cap. You got to cut it up for him," one said.

651

Behind his visor, Yassen frowned. He glanced at the merchant leaning against the fortunes stall. The man wore a bored expression, as if the interaction before him was nothing new. But then the merchant bent forward, pressing his hands to the counter, and Yassen saw the sign of the bull tattooed there.

Samson's men were watching.

"All right," Yassen said. He would give them a show. Prove that he wasn't as useless as the whispers told.

He unclipped his visor as the guards watched. "But you owe me another cup of tea."

And then Yassen flung his arm out and rammed the visor against the captain's face. The man stumbled back with a groan. The other two leapt forward, but Yassen was quicker; he swung around and gave four quick jabs, two each on the back, and the officers seized and sank to their knees in temporary paralysis.

"Blast him!" the captain cried, reaching for his gun. Yassen pivoted behind him, his hand flashing out to unclip the captain's helmet visor.

The captain whipped around, raising his gun... but then sunlight hit the planks before him, and the brass threw off its unforgiving light. Blinded, the captain fired.

The air screeched.

The pulse whizzed past Yassen's right ear, tearing through the upper beams of a storefront. Immediately, merchants took cover. Someone screamed as the crowd on both docks began to run. Yassen swiftly vanished into the chaotic fray, letting the crowd push him toward the dock's edge, and then he dove into the sea.

The cold water shocked him, and for a moment, Yassen floundered. His muscles clenched. And then he was coughing, swimming, and he surfaced beneath the dock. He willed himself to be still as footsteps thundered overhead and soldiers and guards barked out orders. Yassen caught glimpses of the captain in the spaces between the planks.

"All hells! Where did he go?" the captain yelled at the merchant manning the stall of wild tales.

The merchant shrugged. "He's long gone."

Yassen sank deeper into the water as the captain walked overhead, his subordinates wobbling behind. Something buzzed beneath him, and he could see the faint outlines of a dark shape in the depths. Slowly, Yassen began to swim away—but the dark shape remained stationary. He waited for the guards to pass and then sank beneath the surface.

A submersible, the size of one passenger.

Look underneath the dock of fortunes, indeed.

Samson, that bastard.

Yassen swam toward the sub. He placed his hand on the imprint panel of the hull, and then the sub buzzed again and rose to the surface.

The cockpit was small, with barely enough room for him to stretch his legs, but he sighed and sank back just the same. The glass slid smoothly closed and rudders whined to life. The panel board lit up before him and bathed him in a pale blue light.

A note was there. Handwritten. How rare, and so like Samson.

See you at the palace, it said, and before Yassen could question *which* palace, the sub was off.

if you enjoyed
LABYRINTH'S HEART

look out for

THE JASAD HEIR
The Scorched Throne:
Book One

by

Sara Hashem

In this Egyptian-inspired debut fantasy, a fugitive queen strikes a deadly bargain with her greatest enemy and finds herself embroiled in a complex game that could resurrect her scorched kingdom or leave it in ashes forever.

Ten years ago, the kingdom of Jasad burned. Its magic was outlawed; its royal family murdered down to the last child. At least, that's what Sylvia wants people to believe.

The lost Heir of Jasad, Sylvia never wants to be found. She can't think about how Nizahl's armies laid waste to her kingdom and continue to hunt its people—not if she wants to stay alive. But when Arin, the Nizahl Heir,

*tracks a group of Jasadi rebels to her village, staying one
step ahead of death gets trickier.*

*In a moment of anger, Sylvia's magic is exposed, capturing
Arin's attention. Now, to save her life, Sylvia will have to make
a deal with her greatest enemy. If she helps him lure the rebels,
she'll escape persecution.*

*A deadly game begins. Sylvia can't let Arin discover her identity even
as hatred shifts into something more. Soon, Sylvia will have to choose
between the life she wants and the one she left behind. The scorched
kingdom is rising, and it needs a queen.*

CHAPTER ONE

Two things stood between me and a good night's sleep, and I was
allowed to kill only one of them.

I tromped through Hirun River's mossy banks, squinting for movement. The grime, the late hours—I had expected those. Every apprentice in the village dealt with them. I just hadn't expected the frogs.

"Say your farewells, you pointless pests," I called. The frogs had
developed a defensive strategy they put into action any time I came
close. First, the watch guard belched an alarm. The others would
fling themselves into the river. Finally, the brave watch guard
hopped for his life. An effort as admirable as it was futile.

Dirt was caked deep beneath my fingernails. Moonlight filtered
through a canopy of skeletal trees, and for a moment, my hand
looked like a different one. A hand much more manicured, a little
weaker. Niphran's hands. Hands that could wield an axe alongside

656

the burliest woodcutter, weave a storm of curls into delicate braids, drive spears into the maws of monsters. For the first few years of my life, before grief over my father's assassination spread through Niphran like rot, before her sanity collapsed on itself, there wasn't anything my mother's hands could not do.

Oh, if she could see me now. Covered in filth and outwitted by croaking river roaches.

Hirun exhaled its opaque mist, breathing life into the winter bones of Essam Woods. I cleaned my hands in the river and firmly cast aside thoughts of the dead.

A frenzied croak sounded behind a tree root. I darted forward, scooping up the kicking watch guard. Ah, but it was never the brave who escaped. I brought him close to my face. "Your friends are chasing crickets, and you're here. Were they worth it?"

I dropped the limp frog into the bucket and sighed. Ten more to go, which meant another round of running in circles and hoping mud wouldn't spill through the hole in my right boot. The fact that Rory was a renowned chemist didn't impress me, nor did this coveted apprenticeship. What kept me from tossing the bucket and going to Raya's keep, where a warm meal and a comfortable bed awaited me, was a debt of convenience.

Rory didn't ask questions. When I appeared on his doorstep five years ago, drenched in blood and shaking, Rory had tended to my wounds and taken me to Raya's. He rescued a fifteen-year-old orphan with no history or background from a life of vagrancy.

The sudden snap of a branch drew my muscles tight. I reached into my pocket and wrapped my fingers around the hilt of my dagger. Given the Nizahl soldiers' predilection for randomly searching us, I usually carried my blade strapped in my boot, but I'd used it to cut my foot out of a family of tangled ferns and left it in my pocket.

A quick scan of the shivering branches revealed nothing. I tried not to let my eyes linger in the empty pockets of black between the trees. I had seen too much horror manifest out of the dark to ever trust its stillness.

My gaze moved to the place it dreaded most—the row of trees behind me, each scored with identical, chillingly precise black marks. The symbol of a raven spreading its wings had been carved into the trees circling Mahair's border. In the muck of the woods, these ravens remained pristine. Crossing the raven-marked trees without permission was an offense punishable by imprisonment or worse. In the lower villages, where the kingdom's leaders were already primed to turn a blind eye to the liberties taken by Nizahl soldiers, worse was usually just the beginning.

I tucked my dagger into my pocket and walked right to the edge of the perimeter. I traced one raven's outstretched wing with my thumbnail. I would have traded all the frogs in my bucket to be brave enough to scrape my nails over the symbol, to gouge it off. Maybe that same burst of bravery would see my dagger cutting a line in the bark, disfiguring the symbols of Nizahl's power. It wasn't walls or swords keeping us penned in like animals, but a simple carving. Another kingdom's power billowing over us like poisoned air, controlling everything it touched.

I glanced at the watch guard in my bucket and lowered my hand. Bravery wasn't worth the cost. Or the splinters.

A thick layer of frost coated the road leading back to Mahair. I pulled my hood nearly to my nose as soon as I crossed the wall separating Mahair from Essam Woods. I veered into an alley, winding my way to Rory's shop instead of risking the exposed—and regularly patrolled—main road. Darkness cloaked me as soon as I stepped into the alley. I placed a stabilizing hand on the wall and let the pungent odor of manure guide my feet forward. A cat hissed from beneath a stack of crates, hunching protectively over the half-eaten carcass of a rat.

"I already had supper, but thank you for the offer," I whispered, leaping out of reach of her claws.

Twenty minutes later, I clunked the full bucket at Rory's feet. "I demand a renegotiation of my wages."

Rory didn't look up from his list. "Demand away. I'll be over there."

He disappeared into the back room. I scowled, contemplating following him past the curtain and maiming him with frog corpses. The smell of mud and mildew had permanently seeped into my skin. The least he could do was pay extra for the soap I needed to mask it.

I arranged the poultices, sealing each jar carefully before placing it inside the basket. One of the rare times I'd found myself on the wrong side of Rory's temper was after I had forgotten to seal the ointments before sending them off with Yuli's boy. I learned as much about the spread of disease that day as I did about Rory's staunch ethics.

Rory returned. "Off with you already. Get some sleep. I do not want the sight of your face to scare off my patrons tomorrow." He prodded in the bucket, turning over a few of the frogs. Age weathered Rory's narrow brown face. His long fingers were constantly stained in the color of his latest tonic, and a permanent groove sat between his bushy brows. I called it his "rage stage," because I could always gauge his level of fury by the number of furrows forming above his nose. Despite an old injury to his hip, his slenderness was not a sign of fragility. On the rare occasions when Rory smiled, it was clear he had been handsome in his youth. "If I find that you've layered the bottom with dirt again, I'm poisoning your tea."

He pushed a haphazardly wrapped bundle into my arms. "Here."

Bewildered, I turned the package over. "For me?"

He waved his cane around the empty shop. "Are you touched in the head, child?"

I carefully peeled the fabric back, half expecting it to explode in my face, and exposed a pair of beautiful golden gloves. Softer than a dove's wing, they probably cost more than anything I could buy for myself. I lifted one reverently. "Rory, this is too much."

I only barely stopped myself from putting them on. I laid them gingerly on the counter and hurried to scrub off my stained hands. There were no clean cloths left, so I wiped my hands on Rory's tunic and earned a swat to the ear.

The fit of the gloves was perfect. Soft and supple, yielding with the flex of my fingers.

I lifted my hands to the lantern for closer inspection. These would certainly fetch a pretty price at market. Not that I'd sell them right away, of course. Rory liked pretending he had the emotional depth of a spoon, but he would be hurt if I bartered his gift a mere day later. Markets weren't hard to find in Omal. The lower villages were always in need of food and supplies. Trading among themselves was easier than begging for scraps from the palace.

The old man smiled briefly. "Happy birthday, Sylvia."

Sylvia. My first and favorite lie. I pressed my hands together. "A consolation gift for the spinster?" Not once in five years had Rory failed to remember my fabricated birth date.

"I should hardly think spinsterhood's threshold as low as twenty years."

In truth, I was halfway to twenty-one. Another lie.

"You are as old as time itself. The ages below one hundred must all look the same to you."

He jabbed me with his cane. "It is past the hour for spinsters to be about."

I left the shop in higher spirits. I pulled my cloak tight around my shoulders, knotting the hood beneath my chin. I had one more task to complete before I could finally reunite with my bed, and it meant delving deeper into the silent village. These were the hours when the mind ran free, when hollow masonry became the whispers of hungry shaiateen and the scratch of scuttling vermin the sounds of the restless dead.

I knew how sinuously fear cobbled shadows into gruesome shapes. I hadn't slept a full night's length in long years, and there were days when I trusted nothing beyond the breath in my chest and the earth beneath my feet. The difference between the villagers and me was that I knew the names of my monsters. I knew what they would look like if they found me, and I didn't have to imagine what kind of fate I would meet.

Mahair was a tiny village, but its history was long. Its children would know the tales shared from their mothers and fathers and grandparents. Superstition kept Mahair alive, long after time had turned a new page on its inhabitants.

It also kept me in business.

Instead of turning right toward Raya's keep, I ducked into the vagrant road. Bits of honey-soaked dough and grease marked the spot where the halawany's daughters snacked between errands, sitting on the concrete stoop of their parents' dessert shop. Dodging the dogs nosing at the grease, I checked for anyone who might report my movements back to Rory.

We had made a tradition of forgiving each other, Rory and me. Should he find out I was treating Omalians under his name, peddling pointless concoctions to those superstitious enough to buy them—well, I doubted Rory could forgive such a transgression. The "cures" I mucked together for my patrons were harmless. Crushed herbs and altered liquors. Most of the time, the ailments they were intended to ward off were more ridiculous than anything I could fit in a bottle.

The home I sought was ten minutes' walk past Raya's keep. Too close for comfort. Water dripped from the edge of the sagging roof, where a bare clothesline stretched from hook to hook. A pair of undergarments had fluttered to the ground. I kicked them out of sight. Raya taught me years ago how to hide undergarments on the clothesline by clipping them behind a larger piece of clothing. I hadn't understood the need for so much stealth. I still didn't. But time was a limited resource tonight, and I wouldn't waste it soothing an Omalian's embarrassment that I now had definitive proof they wore undergarments.

The door flew open. "Sylvia, thank goodness," Zeinab said. "She's worse today."

I tapped my mud-encrusted boots against the lip of the door and stepped inside.

"Where is she?"

I followed Zeinab to the last room in the short hall. A wave of incense wafted over us when she opened the door. I fanned the white haze hanging in the air. A wizened old woman rocked back and forth on the floor, and bloody tracks lined her arms where nails had gouged deep. Zeinab closed the door, maintaining a safe distance. Tears swam in her large hazel eyes. "I tried to give her a bath, and she did *this*." Zeinab pushed up the sleeve of her abaya, exposing a myriad of red scratch marks.

"Right." I laid my bag down on the table. "I will call you when I've finished."

Subduing the old woman with a tonic took little effort. I moved behind her and hooked an arm around her neck. She tore at my sleeve, mouth falling open to gasp. I dumped the tonic down her throat and loosened my stranglehold enough for her to swallow. Once certain she wouldn't spit it out, I let her go and adjusted my sleeve. She spat at my heels and bared teeth bloody from where she'd torn her lip.

It took minutes. My talents, dubious as they were, lay in efficient and fleeting deception. At the door, I let Zeinab slip a few coins into my cloak's pocket and pretended to be surprised. I would never understand Omalians and their feigned modesty. "Remember—"

Zeinab bobbed her head impatiently. "Yes, yes, I won't speak a word of this. It has been years, Sylvia. If the chemist ever finds out, it will not be from me."

She was quite self-assured for a woman who never bothered to ask what was in the tonic I regularly poured down her mother's throat. I returned Zeinab's wave distractedly and moved my dagger into the same pocket as the coins. Puddles of foul-smelling rain rippled in the pocked dirt road. Most of the homes on the street could more accurately be described as hovels, their thatched roofs shivering above walls joined together with mud and uneven patches of brick. I dodged a line of green mule manure, its waterlogged, grassy smell stinging my nose.

Did Omal's upper towns have excrement in their streets?

Zeinab's neighbor had scattered chicken feathers outside her door to showcase their good fortune to their neighbors. Their daughter had married a merchant from Dawar, and her dowry had earned them enough to eat chicken all month. From now on, the finest clothes would furnish her body. The choicest meats and hardest-grown vegetables for her plate. She'd never need to dodge mule droppings in Mahair again.

I turned the corner, absently counting the coins in my pocket, and rammed into a body.

I stumbled, catching myself against a pile of cracked clay bricks. The Nizahl soldier didn't budge beyond a tightening of his frown.

"Identify yourself."

Heavy wings of panic unfurled in my throat. Though our movements around town weren't constrained by an official curfew, not many risked a late-night stroll. The Nizahl soldiers usually patrolled in pairs, which meant this man's partner was probably harassing someone else on the other side of the village.

I smothered the panic, snapping its fluttering limbs. Panic was a plague. Its sole purpose was to spread until it tore through every thought, every instinct.

I immediately lowered my eyes. Holding a Nizahl soldier's gaze invited nothing but trouble. "My name is Sylvia. I live in Raya's keep and apprentice for the chemist Rory. I apologize for startling you. An elderly woman urgently needed care, and my employer is indisposed."

From the lines on his face, the soldier was somewhere in his late forties. If he had been an Omalian patrolman, his age would have signified little. But Nizahl soldiers tended to die young and bloody. For this man to survive long enough to see the lines of his forehead wrinkle, he was either a deadly adversary or a coward.

"What is your father's name?"

"I am a ward in Raya's keep," I repeated. He must be new to Mahair. Everyone knew Raya's house of orphans on the hill. "I have no mother or father."

He didn't belabor the issue. "Have you witnessed activity that might lead to the capture of a Jasadi?" Even though it was a standard question from the soldiers, intended to encourage vigilance toward any signs of magic, I inwardly flinched. The most recent arrest of a Jasadi had happened in our neighboring village a mere month ago. From the whispers, I'd surmised a girl reported seeing her friend fix a crack in her floorboard with a wave of her hand. I had overheard all manner of praise showered on the girl for her bravery in turning in the fifteen-year-old. Praise and jealousy—they couldn't wait for their own opportunities to be heroes.

"I have not." I hadn't seen another Jasadi in five years.

He pursed his lips. "The name of the elderly woman?"

"Aya, but her daughter Zeinab is her caretaker. I could direct you to them if you'd like." Zeinab was crafty. She would have a lie prepared for a moment like this.

"No need." He waved a hand over his shoulder. "On your way. Stay off the vagrant road."

One benefit of the older Nizahl soldiers—they had less inclination for the bluster and interrogation tactics of their younger counterparts. I tipped my head in gratitude and sped past him.

Follow us:

/orbitbooksUS

/orbitbooks

/orbitbooks

Join our mailing list
to receive alerts on our
latest releases and deals.

orbitbooks.net

Enter our monthly
giveaway for the chance
to win some epic prizes.

orbitloot.com

AMERICAN STUDIES

AN ANNOTATED BIBLIOGRAPHY

VOLUME I

AMERICAN STUDIES

AN ANNOTATED BIBLIOGRAPHY

VOLUME I

Edited by

JACK SALZMAN
Director, Columbia Center for American Culture Studies

on behalf of

THE AMERICAN STUDIES ASSOCIATION

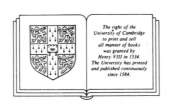

The right of the
University of Cambridge
to print and sell
all manner of books
was granted by
Henry VIII in 1534.
The University has printed
and published continuously
since 1584.

CAMBRIDGE UNIVERSITY PRESS

CAMBRIDGE

LONDON NEW YORK NEW ROCHELLE

MELBOURNE SYDNEY

Published by the Press Syndicate of the University of Cambridge
The Pitt Building, Trumpington Street, Cambridge CB2 1RP
32 East 57th Street, New York, NY 10022, USA
10 Stamford Road, Oakleigh, Melbourne 3166, Australia

First published 1986

Printed in the United States of America

ISBN 0-521-26686-6 Vol. I
ISBN 0-521-32555-2 Set of three volumes

Library of Congress Cataloging-in-Publication Data

American studies.

    Includes indexes.
    1. United States--Civilization--Bibliography.
I. Salzman, Jack. II. American Studies Association.
Z1361.C6A436 1986 [E169.1]   016.973   86-17164
ISBN 0-521-32555-2 (set)

CONTENTS

INTRODUCTION

In the Spring of 1978, the American Studies Association entered
into an agreement with the United States Information Agency (USIA)--then
called the International Communications Agency (ICA)--to prepare a bibliography which would "provide foreign nationals with a reasonably comprehensive and authoritative list of sources of information concerning this
country." The project was coordinated by Murray G. Murphey, with Luther
S. Leudtke serving as Editorial Consultant. The Bibliography was divided
into ten sections, with a separate editor for each section: Art and Architecture was edited by Kenneth Ames; Economic History by Louis Galambos;
Political Science by W. Phillips Shively; Science and Technology by Thomas
P. Hughes; Literature, Language, and Journalism by Harrison T. Meserole;
Sociology and Psychology by Peter I. Rose; International Relations by
Frederick W. Frey; History by William H. Goetzmann; Popular Culture by
Larry Landrum; Anthropology and Folklore by Anthony F. C. Wallace. In
some sections only books were listed; others contained both books and
articles. In all, a little more than 3,100 items were annotated. American
Studies: An Annotated Bibliography of Works on the Civilization of the
United States was published in four volumes in 1982.

The following year the American Studies Association obtained rights
to the bibliography. The Association's Special Projects Committee decided
to publish the work in this country, but only after the bibliography had
been revised and brought up to date. At that point I was asked by the
Association to undertake the revision, and on behalf of the Center for
American Culture Studies at Columbia University I agreed to do so. Shortly
thereafter, Cambridge University Press expressed interest in publishing
a substantially reworked version of the original bibliography and an agreement was entered into by the Press and the ASA.

American Studies: An Annotated Bibliography is, in fact, considerably more than a revision or a reworking of the annotated bibliography

vii

published in 1982. It is, essentially, a totally new work, with more

than twice the number of previous entries. Sections on Music and Religion

appear here for the first time; other sections have been reorganized;

almost all the annotations have been rewritten; articles have not been

included. In addition, books which are primarily theoretical or methodo-

logical have been excluded; so, too, have biographies, unless they have

an important cultural framework. It is indeed this cultural emphasis

that has been the guiding principle in our selection process for all books.

Because this work has been conceived as a permanent reference guide rather

than a guide for the purchasing of books, ISBN numbers have not been

included, reprint information has been excluded, and the annotations are

non-evaluative. The prefaces to each section introduce the reader to

the basic bibliographic resources necessary to doing research in that

particular discipline. The Index, which is divided into three categories--

Author, Title, and Subject--will provide the means of locating a book

being sought. What has been produced here, then, is an annotated biblio-

graphy of books written during this century through 1983 that fall into

eleven distinct fields of American Studies.

*   *   *   *   *

Although this Bibliography has been prepared under the auspices

of the American Studies Association, in actuality the Association assumed

little responsibility for the completion of the work. Some members of

the Association--Michael H. Cowan, Hamilton Cravens, William Ferris, Philip

Gleason, Myron Lounsbury, Karal Ann Marling, James McCutcheon, Bernard

Mergen, Lillian Miller, Lawrence E. Mintz, John Raeburn, Eric J. Sandeen,

Albert Stone, and Norman Yetman, for example--were most helpful and coopera-

tive.

But finally the publication of the bibliography is the result of

two and a half years of arduous work on the part of the staff of the Center

for American Culture Studies. With extraordinary skill and dedication,
the Center's staff undertook the work left undone by others. Many staff
members are acknowledged in the list of contributors which follows this
introduction; in particular, however, the efforts of John Davis, Lucy
Rinehart, and Jay Sullivan, who undertook the coordination of the sections
devoted to Art and Architecture, Music, and Psychology, respectively,
need to be recognized. In addition, for their help and support, I would
like to formally express my gratitude to Linda Ainsworth, Elizabeth Auran,
David Austin, Paul Bongiorno, Chris Castiglia, Daniel J. Cohen, Douglas
E. Fiske, Lisa Freihofner, Kathy Gaffney, Jeanne Gottschalk, Lucy Hitchcock,
Kevin Keenan, Donna Kerfoot, Bette Kirschstein, Francesca Kobylarz, Paul
Kwartler, Elizabeth Langdon, Paul Mah, Andrea Masters, Marianne Noble,
Nancy Nystul, John S. Peters, Michael Phillips, Thomas Pitoniak, Susan
Rogers, Mark Rothman, Linda C. Salzman, Lydia Sam-Lamb, Michael Shoop,
Laurance Sopala, Abbas Shah, Nancy Stula, Emily Wright, Margaret Vandenburg,
and Richard Wollman.

Other members of the Columbia University community were exceptionally
generous with their time and help, none more so than Quentin Anderson,
Marcellus Blount, Andrew Delbanco, Michael Denning, Mary Dobbie, Ann
Douglas, Eric Foner, Robert J. Gallione, Joy Hayton, Carl Hovde, Eleanor
Johnson, Karl Kroeber, Patricia Nealon, Richard Sacks, James P. Shenton,
G. Thomas Tanselle, and Alden T. Vaughan.

At the same time, it is a pleasure for me to thank Janice Bradley,
Allan M. Brandt, Kathy Evertz, Frances K. Foster, Eugene T. Murphey, Kate
Roberts, Jennifer Scalora, and Tracy Smith, for proofreading and checking
parts of the manuscript. Anne Goldstein somehow managed to persevere
and typed the entire manuscript, while Stephen Zietz undertook the difficult task of coordinating the Index. Andrew Brown of Cambridge University
Press once again gave us all the support we could have asked of him.

Finally, the efforts of three people must be singled out. Cameron
Bardrick read and reread the entire manuscript and saved us from making

innumerable mistakes. Paul McNeil, friend and colleague, deserves all

the accolades one can bestow on him; but for him the bibliography would

never have been completed. And, above all, Cecily endured my own obsessive

needs to see the project to completion and stayed with me despite it all.

To them, and all the people at the Center, no need to ever say again,

"Bibliography Nears Completion." Here it is, done at last.

Jack Salzman
Columbia University

ANTHROPOLOGY AND FOLKLORE

Michael Cowan
James Deutsch
Eugene Murphy
Kate Riley

ART AND ARCHITECTURE

John Davis
James Deutsch
F. Jack Hurley
Michael Knies, Jr.
Gary O'Conner
Julia Plant
Irwin Richman
Robert Thompson

HISTORY

Doran Ben-Atar
Tyler G. Anbinder
Brian Abrams
Regina Bannan
Lawson Bowling
Gail Farr Casterline
Clarke A. Chambers
Joseph DePlasco
Gary M Fink
Timothy Gilfoyle
Fred Grittner
Maureen A. Harp
Tatiana M. Holway
Dwight W. Hoover
John Howe
Faith Jaycox
Thomas Jorge
Steven C. Kottsy
Chris Levenduski
Jeffrey Levin
Jonathan Margolis
Nathaniel Margolis
Isaac McDaniel, O.S.B.
Castle McLaughlin
Marjorie McLellan
Paul M. McNeil
Michael Meranze
Pamela Mittlefehldt
Keith Morton
John Recchuiti
John C. Rodrigue
Ellen Salzman
Eric J. Sandeen

Thomas J. Schlereth
Michael Sugrue
Karen P. Ward
Deborah Welch
Gretchen Wendt
Steve Wiley
Patrick Williams
Emily Wright
Gayle Graham Yates

LITERATURE

Meryl B. Altman
Nat Austern
Cameron Bardrick
Robert E. Clark
Mary V. Dearborn
Laura Henigman
Eric Lott
Paul M. McNeil
Geraldine Murphy
Jane Remus
Lucy Rinehart
Clare Rossini
Mark Sherman
J. Jordon Sullivan
Jay Williams

MUSIC

Dwight Andrews
Paul Bongiorno
Mark Booth
William E. Grant
Sue Hart
Timothy Lubin
Jay Mechling
Robert Oliveri
Lucy Rinehart
Thomas J. Slater
Gordon Tapper
Barbara L. Tischler

POLITICAL SCIENCE

John Kilduff
Daniel L. Manheim
Isaac McDaniel, O.S.B.
D. Geoffrey Peck
Katharine Tehranian
Florindo Volpacchio

POPULAR CULTURE

Michael Barton
David Cantor
Benjamin DeMott
Kathleen Diffley
Patricia Francis
Scot Geunter
Gena Giobbi
Eric Haralson
Melissa Hilbish
John Hyman
Carol Kearney
Myron Lounsbury
Kevin M. Mace
Daniel L. Manheim
Ronald Miller
Lawrence E. Mintz
Marsha A. Mullin
Thomas J. Schlereth
Gregory S. Sojka
Nancy Struna
Steven Tischler
Don B. Wilmeth
Steve J. Wurtzler

PSYCHOLOGY

J. Jordan Sullivan

RELIGION

James R. Wetzel

SCIENCE AND TECHNOLOGY

Hamilton Cravens
Mary V. Dearborn
Gregory A. Sanford

SOCIOLOGY

Mary P. Corcoran
Kenneth Robert John
Danquing Ruan
Norman P. Yetman

INDEXERS

Michael Bereza
Karen Dobrusky
Christian-Albrecht Golub
Stephen J. Zietz

ANTHROPOLOGY AND FOLKLORE

Outside the well-developed fields of folklore and Native American studies, there exists no comprehensive or systematic reference guide to scholarship and primary sources relevant to anthropological perspectives on the U.S. In the Subject Catalog of the Library of Congress, for example, the heading "Anthropology, United States" almost exclusively yields works on American Indians; other relevant aspects of American culture must be gleaned laboriously from dozens of other subject headings from "Acculturation" and "Americanization" to "National Characteristics" and "Rites and Ceremonies." This situation in part reflects the complex interpenetration of contemporary anthropology and history, sociology, psychology, linguistics, and other fields. Perhaps more importantly, it reflects the fact that, until relatively recently, only a handful of professional anthropologists have considered U.S. society as a whole as an appropriate field of investigation. No single journal, for example, devotes itself primarily to a holistic anthropological understanding of the U.S. To the extent that such an understanding has begun slowly to emerge, it has been primarily Americanists in other disciplines who have attempted, with varying degrees of rigor, to apply various anthropological concepts and methods to their own fields of specialization. The brief comments below are intended primarily to help such Americanists explore this relatively uncharted territory.

With some effort, a number of general reference guides can be made of use to Americanists. Margo L. Smith and Yvonne Damien, eds., <u>Anthropological Bibliographies</u>: <u>A Selected Guide</u> (South Salem, N.Y.: Redgrave, 1981), includes several hundred bibliographies dealing with the U.S.; most of these deal with American Indians, but a number deal with other American ethnic and regional groups. The sections on "Anthropology and Ethnology" and "Folklore and Popular Customs" in Eugene P. Sheehy, comp., <u>Guide to Reference Books</u>, 9th ed. (Chicago: American Library Association,

1976) and Supplement (1980), are also good starting points. The "Anthropology" section in Lee Ash, ed., Subject Collections: A Guide to Special Book Collections and Subject Emphases as Reported by University, College, Public, and Special Libraries in the United States and Canada, 5th ed. (New York: Bowker, 1978), focuses almost entirely on American Indian holdings in specific institutions, but relevant institutional holdings on other aspects of American culture are listed under specific places and ethnic groups and under such headings as "United States—Social Life and Customs." The subject index of Brigitte T. Darnay, ed., Directory of Special Libraries and Information Centers, 8th ed., 2 vols. (Detroit: Gale Research, 1983), can be used in a similar fashion, as can American Doctoral Dissertations (1957-), Masters Abstracts (1962-), and David R. McDonald, Masters' Theses in Anthropology (New Haven, Conn.: HRAF Press, 1977). Similar strategies will yield relevant sources from the most comprehensive listing of anthropological journals, Serial Publications in Anthropology, eds., F. X. Grollig and Sol Tax, 2nd ed. (South Salem, N.Y.: Redgrave, 1982); from the unannotated listings of articles in the annual Anthropological Index to Current Periodicals in the Museum of Mankind Library (1963-; formerly the Anthropological Index to the Royal Anthropological Institute Library), the annual International Bibliography of Social and Cultural Anthropology (1955-), and the annual Anthropological Literature: An Index to Periodical Articles and Essays (1979-); and from the annual Abstracts in Anthropology (1970-). Probably more directly useful as a guide to anthropologically-oriented articles on recent and contemporary American society are Volume I of The Combined Retrospective Index Set to Journals in Sociology, 1895-1974 (Washington, D.C.: Carrollton Press, 1978), and the subject index of the Cumulative Index Issue of Sociological Abstracts (1953-). Use of the annual subject index to America: History and Life (1963-) can also yield relevant materials, particularly if one goes beyond listings under "Anthropology" and "Ethno-

4

graphy" to such categories as "American Character," "Rites and Ceremonies," and "Myths and Symbols."

One other important general source is worth mentioning. The Human Relations Area Files contain intricately cross-referenced information on some 300 past and present cultures in the world, including many American Indian and ethnic groups. The best entry point is Robert O. Lagace, Nature and Use of the HRAF Files: A Research and Teaching Guide (New Haven, Conn.: HRAF Press, 1974). The Files are in effect a series of interlocking reference volumes. George P. Murdock, et al., Outline of Cultural Materials, 5th rev. ed. (New Haven, Conn.: HRAF Press, 1982), presents the detailed cross-referenced subject and trait classification system of the Files. Murdock's Outline of World Cultures, 6th rev. ed. (New Haven, Conn.: HRAD Press, 1983) presents a detailed place index. Using these two volumes in tandem, one can find relevant works on the U.S. in the periodically updated heart of the Files: Raoul Naroll and Donald Morrison, eds., Index to the Human Relations Area Files, 8 vols. (New Haven, Conn.: HRAF Press, 1972), and Joan Steffens, ed., Supplement 1, 8 vols. (New Haven, Conn.: HRAF Press, 1979).

Although no comprehensive bibliographical guide exists that focuses primarily on the anthropological examination of mainstream American society, a useful, if quite selective, start can be found in Donald A. Messerschmidt, ed., Anthropologists at Home in North America: Methods and Issues in the Study of One's Own Society (New York: Cambridge University Press, 1981), pp. 281-99, which lists about 500 books and articles. Also useful, although uneven, is Conrad P. Kottak, Researching American Culture: A Guide for Student Anthropologists (Ann Arbor: University of Michigan Press, 1982). Among the more specialized bibliographical guides, the following are representative examples of those of potential anthropological relevance: William C. Miller, A Comprehensive Bibliography for the Study of American Minorities, 2 vols. (New York: New York University Press, 1976); G. Carter Bentley, Ethnicity and Nationality: A Bibliographic

5

Guide (Seattle: University of Washington Press, 1981); Dell Hymes, ed.,
Language in Culture and Society (New York: Harper & Row, 1964), pp. 711-
49; and some of the bibliographies attached to essays in M. Thomas Inge,
ed., Handbook of American Popular Culture, 3 vols. (Westport, Conn.:
Greenwood Press, 1978-81).

In the field of Native American studies, at least (as reflected
in many of the works cited above), the massive amounts of published and
unpublished materials on Native Americans in the U.S. have stimulated
a large number of highly useful reference guides. Three excellent introductions to these guides and to the field as a whole have recently been
published: William Hodge, A Bibliography of Contemporary North American
Indians (New York: Interland, 1976); Arlene B. Hirschfelder, et al.,
Guide to Research on North American Indians (Chicago: American Library
Association, 1983); and Margaret L. Haas, Indians of North America:
Methods and Sources for Library Research (Hamden, Conn.: Library Professional Publications, 1983). Extensive manuscript holdings on Native Americans can be found in the National Union Catalog of Manuscript Collections
(1959-) and Edward Hill, Guide to Records in the National Archives of
the United States Relating to American Indians (Washington, D.C.: General
Services Administration, 1981). By far the most comprehensive bibliography
of published works is George P. Murdock and Timothy J. O'Leary, Ethnographic Bibliography of North America, 2nd ed., 5 vols. (New Haven, Conn.:
HRAF Press, 1975), which includes 40,000 listings of books and articles.
Dissertation references can be found in Frederick J. Dockstader, comp.,
The American Indian in Graduate Studies: A Bibliography of Theses and
Dissertations, 2nd ed. (New York: Museum of the American Indian, 1973)
and Supplement (1974), and in Gifford S. Nickerson, Native North Americans
in Doctoral Dissertations: A Classified and Indexed Research Bibliography
(Monticello, Ill.: Council of Planning Libraries, 1977). Dwight L. Smith,
ed., Indians of the United States and Canada: A Bibliography, 2 vols.
(Santa Barbara, Calif.: ABC-Clio, 1974, 1983), is based on the holdings

6

of America: History and Life and contains abstracts of nearly 5,000 articles published between 1954 and 1982. Examples of the numerous more specialized useful guides are James P. Kandy, ed., Native American Periodicals and Newspapers, 1828-1982, comp. Maureen E. Hady (Westport, Conn.: Greenwood Press, 1984), Judith C. Ullom, Folklore of the North American Indians: An Annotated Bibliography (Washington, D.C.: Library of Congress, 1969), and two major series of specialized bibliographies, one published by the Newberry Library Center for the History of the American Indian, the other by Scarecrow Press. In pursuing these rich resources for anthropological perspectives on Native Americans, one should be constantly reminded of their equal importance to students of history, social, economic, and political organization, and artistic expression.

Anthropological study of the United States, as of other societies, unavoidably involves the study of material culture. For Americanists, the amount of materials from the national and pre-national past, let alone from contemporary life, is so immense and diverse as to defy classification. Important suggestions toward a collection and classification strategy can be found in Frederick L. Rath, Jr. and Merrilyn Rogers O'Connell, eds., A Bibliography on Historical Organization Practices, 5 vols. (Nashville, Tenn.: American Association for State and Local History, 1975-80), esp. Vol. 4, Documentation of Collections. Rich displays of artifacts, organized usually on other anthropological lines, can be found in the numerous local, state, regional, and national museums throughout the U.S. as well as at organized historical sites and in the collections of private organizations. A helpful guide to these facilities is The Official Museum Directory, an annual published by the American Association of Museums. Among more specialized guides are Ormond Loomis, Sources on Folk Museums and Living Historical Farms (Bloomington: Folklore Forum, 1977); L. R. Wynar and L. Buttlar, Guide to Ethnic Museums, Libraries, and Archives in the United States (Kent, Ohio: School of Library Science, 1978); Simon Brascoupe, ed., Directory of North American Indian Museums and Cultural Centers, 1981 (Niagara Falls, N.Y.: North American Indian Museums Association, 1980); and Arnold L. Markowitz, Historic Preservation: A Guide to Information Sources (Detroit, Mich.: Gale Research, 1980). The best bibliographical source to date for the study of material culture in the U.S., as well as the most useful introduction to the field, is Thomas J. Schlereth, ed., Material Culture Studies in America (Nashville, Tenn.: American Association for State and Local History, 1982).

Fieldwork has also been central to anthropological examination of American life. However, although numerous monographs and articles on the methods and problems of fieldwork in the U.S. are in print, drawn from anthropology, sociology, linguistics, and other fields, no comprehensive bibliography on the subject yet exists. A sampling of recent writing on fieldwork can be found in the bibliography of William B. Shaffir, et al., eds., Fieldwork Experience: Qualitative Approaches to Social Research (New York: St. Martin's Press, 1980), pp. 311-22, and in the notes to Robert A. Georges and Michael O. Jones, People Studying People: The Human Element in Fieldwork (Berkeley: University of California Press, 1980).

*   *   *   *   *

Any discussion of major library and archival resources in the fields of American folklore and folklife must begin with the Library of Congress. Not only do the general collections at the Library of Congress contain the majority of works published on these topics, but the Library's Archive of Folk Culture constitutes the oldest and largest resource of its kind in the U.S.

Founded in 1928 as the Archive of American Folk-Song, the Archive of Folk Culture today is still primarily a resource for American folk music and ethnomusicology, controlling more than 28,000 hours of recording. But in recent years as its scope has expanded, and in cooperation with other units at the Library of Congress—including the American Folklife Center, the Prints and Photographs Division, and the Manuscript Division—

the Archive of Folk Culture should be able to provide the researcher with information and resources on nearly any aspect of folklore and folklife.

Aside from the Library of Congress, the major centers of folklore study generally are associated with universities—notably Indiana University, the University of Pennsylvania, U.C.L.A., and the University of Texas—where folklore doctorates are awarded. Not associated with an academic program, but highly important nonetheless, is the John G. White Department of Folklore at the Cleveland Public Library. A photographic reproduction of the catalogue cards for this collection has been published as Catalog of Folklore, Folklife, and Folk Songs, 3 vols. (1964; 2nd ed. Boston: G. K. Hall, 1978).

To locate other major archival resources, one should consult the most recent directory (issued periodically by the Archive of Folk Culture) entitled "Folklife and Ethnomusicology Archives and Related Collections in the United States and Canada." For a more selective list of American folklore archives, see the chapter on "Using a Folklore Archive" by Janet Langlois and Philip LaRonge in the Handbook of American Folklore, edited by Richard M. Dorson (Bloomington: Indiana University Press, 1983).

The Archive of Folk Culture also has published some 200 bibliographies and finding aids covering specialized areas and subjects in the fields of folklore, folk music, and ethnomusicology. An inventory of these bibliographies and lists is available at no charge from the Archive of Folk Culture, Library of Congress, Washington, D.C. 20540.

An especially good overview of bibliographical resources is the article on "American Folklore Bibliography" by Richard M. Dorson in American Studies International 16 (Autumn 1977), 23-37. The bibliographical notes included at the end of Dorson's American Folklore (Chicago: University of Chicago Press, 1959) are also extremely useful in identifying paths for future research. These notes were revised and updated when the text was reprinted in 1977. Detailed bibliographical notes are similarly found at the conclusion of each chapter in Jan Harold Brunvand's

9

The Study of American Folklore: An Introduction (1968; 2nd ed. New York:
Norton, 1978).

Three other bibliographical essays that should not be overlooked
are: Richard Bauman and Roger D. Abrahams, "American Folklore and American
Studies," American Quarterly, 28 (Bibliography Issue 1976), 360-77; Simon
J. Bronner, "'Visible Proofs': Material Culture Study in American Folk-
loristics," American Quarterly, 35 (Bibliography Issue, 1983), 316-38;
and Robert Wildhaber, "A Bibliographical Introduction to American Folklife," New York Folklore Quarterly, 21 (December 1965), 259-302.

Another good guide is "Bibliographies and Indexes in American Folklore Research" by Angela J. Maniak in the Handbook of American Folklore
(1983). Although there is no need to duplicate that essay here, several
items (including some not mentioned by Maniak) deserve special recognition.

By far the most comprehensive folklore bibliography is Charles
Haywood's A Bibliography of North American Folklore and Folksong, 2 vols.
(1951; 2nd ed. New York: Dover Books, 1961). Unfortunately, the second
edition is little more than a reprinting of the first. So, essentially,
the Haywood bibliography cuts off around 1948-49. Supplementing Haywood
is American Folklore: A Bibliography, 1950-1974 (Metuchen, N.J.: Scarecrow Press, 1977) by Cathleen C. Flanagan and John T. Flanagan. Some
3,500 books and articles are listed here, but the coverage is limited
to verbal folklore only.

Turning to folklore bibliographies that cover more specialized topics,
the following may be useful.

For black folk culture, see John F. Szwed and Roger D. Abrahams,
Afro-American Folk Culture: An Annotated Bibliography of Materials from
North, Central and South America and the West Indies, 2 vols. (Philadelphia:
Institute for the Study of Human Issues, 1978). Volume 1 deals with North
America.

For Chicano culture, see Michael Heisley, An Annotated Bibliography
of Chicano Folklore from the Southwestern United States. (Los Angeles:

Center for the Study of Comparative Folklore and Mythology at U.C.L.A.,
1977).

For women, see Francis A. de Caro, Women and Folklore: A Bibliographic Survey (Westport, Conn.: Greenwood Press, 1983).

For films and videotapes, see the two volumes compiled by the Center
for Southern Folklore: American Folklore Films and Videotapes: An Index
(Memphis, Tenn.: Center for Southern Folklore, 1976) and American Folklore
Films and Videotapes: A Catalog (New York: Bowker, 1982).

For material folk culture, see Simon J. Bronner, A Critical Biblio-
graphy of American Folk Art (Bloomington: Indiana University Folklore
Publications Group, 1978); Linda Campbell Franklin, Antiques and Collec-
tibles: A Bibliography of Works in English, 16th Century to 1976 (Metuchen,
N.J.: Scarecrow Press, 1978); and Susan Sink, Traditional Crafts and
Craftsmanship in America: A Selected Bibliography (Washington, D.C.:
American Folklife Center, Library of Congress, 1983).

Since the early 20th century, folklorists have been working to collect and classify the universe of folk materials. One of the earliest
of these compilations is The Types of the Folktale: A Classification
and Bibliography, first published in 1910 by the Finnish folklorist, Antti
Aarne, and then translated and greatly expanded by Stith Thompson, Rev.
ed. (Helsinki: FF Communications, 1961). In this volume, each of some
2,000 folktales, mostly from Indo-European sources, is assigned a number
with the key elements and tale variants described.

The basic units of folklore are known as motifs. In the Motif Index
of Folk-Literature: A Classification of Narrative Elements in Folktales,
Ballads, Myths, Fables, Mediaeval Romances, Exempla, Fabliaux, Jest-Books
and Local Legends, 6 vols., Rev. ed. (Bloomington: Indiana University
Press, 1955-58), Stith Thompson has identified, catalogued, and cross-
indexed thousands of motifs (or "narrative elements") from cultures
around the world. Thompson's sources, all of which are identified through

bibliographic references under each motif, include not only folktales, but also many other forms of folk narrative.

For English-language folktales and motifs, see Ernest W. Baughman's Type and Motif-Index of the Folktales of England and North America (The Hague: Mouton, 1966). Baughman examines 371 tale types, with 1,652 variants, and 1,211 whole-number motifs, with 11,431 variants, in order to determine what relationships exist between folklore from the British Isles and folklore from North America.

The proverb is another form of oral folklore for which useful compilations and catalogues exist to aid the researcher. Early American Proverbs and Proverbial Phrases (Cambridge, Mass.: Harvard University Press, 1977), by Bartlett Jere Whiting, identifies the proverbs and proverbial phrases found in a variety of sources (including diaries, memoirs, books of travel, sermons, and polemical papers) from the first decade of the 17th century to 1820. An earlier volume, A Dictionary of American Proverbs and Proverbial Phrases, 1820-1880 (Cambridge, Mass.: Harvard University Press, 1958), by Archer Taylor and Bartlett Jere Whiting, extends the coverage from 1820 to 1880, though its source materials are literary (the writings of American authors) only.

A similar collection, focusing on a particular genre of folklore, is Popular Beliefs and Superstitions: A Compendium of American Folklore, 3 vols. (Boston: G. K. Hall, 1981), by Wayland Hand, Anna Cosetta, and Sondra B. Thiederman. Some 36,000 items are included, divided into a variety of subject categories.

Covering many different genres, but focusing in a comprehensive way on a single geographic area, is The Frank C. Brown Collection of North Carolina Folklore, 7 vols. (Durham, N.C.: Duke University Press, 1952-64). Here may be found: games and rhymes, beliefs and superstitions, riddles and proverbs, ballads and folksongs, and more.

One last reference work, the Standard Dictionary of Folklore, Mythology, and Legend, 2 vols. Rev. ed. (New York: Funk & Wagnalls, 1972), edited by Maria Leach and Jerome Fried, is a good starting point for useful definitions and other basic information. The contributors include some of the foremost authorities in the field of folklore.

Over the years, annual bibliographies of folklore were compiled in two folklore journals. The most extensive of these are the bibliographies that appeared annually in Southern Folklore Quarterly, beginning in 1938 (for the year 1937) through 1973 (for 1972). For the years 1973, 1974, and 1975, the annual bibliographies did not appear in the journal, but were published separately in book form under the auspices of the Indiana University Folklore Institute.

The other series of annual folklore bibliographies appeared as supplements to the Journal of American Folklore (the official publication of the American Folklore Society), beginning in 1955 (for the year 1954) through 1963 (for 1962). From 1963 until 1975, the American Folklore Society tried a new format for its annual bibliography, publishing the Abstracts of Folklore Studies as a separate periodical.

Currently, the only annual bibliography of folklore materials is that which is part of the MLA International Bibliography, published each year by the Modern Language Association of America.

For locating articles published in the major folklore journals, several cumulative indexes are available. See especially: Tristram P. Coffin, An Analytical Index to the Journal of American Folklore (Philadelphia: American Folklore Society, 1958), covering the journal's first seventy years, from 1888 to 1957; James T. Bratcher, Analytical Index to the Publications of the Texas Folklore Society, Volumes 1-36 (Dallas, Texas: Southern Methodist University Press, 1973), covering the years 1916 to 1972; Joan Ruman Perkal, Western Folklore and California Folklore Quarterly: Twenty-Five Year Index (Berkeley: University of California Press, 1969), covering the years 1942 to 1966; Alice Morrison Mordoh's "Analytical Index to the Journal of the Folklore Institute, Vols. 1-15," which appeared in volume 18 (1981), pp. 157-273; and Judith E. Fryer,

25 Year Index to Pennsylvania Folklife (Collegeville: Pennsylvania Folk-life Society, 1980), covering the years 1949 to 1976.

Finally, to identify pertinent theses and dissertations published from 1869 to 1968, an essential source is Alan Dundes, Folklore Theses and Dissertations in the United States (Austin: University of Texas Press, 1976).

Michael Cowan
University of California, Santa Cruz

James Deutsch
George Washington University

I.   BACKGROUND

A-F 1. ARENSBERG, CONRAD M. and SOLON T. KIMBALL. Culture and Community.
New York: Harcourt, Brace, 1965. 349 pp.
This book develops an anthropological approach to complex society and
culture by isolating a unit of analysis which provides a key to the organization of the society as a whole. Community, according to Arensberg and
Kimball, is the form in which "culture finds its enduring and characteristic pattern." Part I outlines definitions and methods; Part II presents
a typology of American communities and subcultures; Part III concentrates
on the institutional basis of American community structure; and Part IV
concentrates on the study of the community in process.

A-F 2. AVEDON, ELLIOTT M. and BRIAN SUTTON-SMITH, eds. The Study of Games.
New York: Wiley, 1971. 530 pp.
Avedon and Sutton-Smith approach the study of games through history, anthropology, and folklore. Games are presented as a general phenomenon, but
most of the examples are drawn from American or Western European contexts.
Many previously published articles are brought together to illustrate
the forms and functions of games. The editors provide introductions to
each of the thirteen sections, and include topical bibliographies in the
text.

A-F 3. BASSO, KEITH and HENRY A. SELBY, eds. Meaning in Anthropology.
Albuquerque: University of New Mexico Press, 1977. 255 pp.
The nine theoretical articles in this collection investigate cultural
meanings and symbolism. Among the essays included are Harold W.
Scheffler's critique of David Schneider's work on American kinship, Roy
D'Andrade's article on Euro-American beliefs about disease, David
Schneider's theoretical discussion of the nature of culture, and Susan
Ervin-Tripp's sociolinguistic discussion of speech acts. The essays focus
on meaning not with the intent to define the concept, but rather to use
it as a "conceptual rallying point" for symbolic anthropologists and sociolinguists exploring new conceptualizations of culture and cultural analyses.

A-F 4. BENEDICT, RUTH. Patterns of Culture. New York: Houghton Mifflin,
1934. 291 pp.
Viewing culture as "personality writ large," Benedict develops the idea
that each culture elaborates human potentialities in a unique way by
reinforcing certain personality types. Three cultures are discussed in
detail: the Apollonian Zunis of New Mexico are described as approaching
life cautiously without exploring "disruptive psychological states"; the
Kwakiutl of British Columbia are characterized as Dionysians who attempt
to break through the boundaries of the senses to another order of existence;
and the behavior patterns of the Dobuans of Melanesia are classified by
Benedict as "paranoid."

A-F 5. DE LAGUNA, FREDERICA, ed. Selected Papers from the American Anthro-
pologist, 1888-1920. Evanston, Ill.: Row, Peterson, 1960. 930 pp.
STOCKING, GEORGE W., Jr., ed. Selected Papers from the American
Anthropologist, 1921-1940. Washington, D.C.: American Anthropological Association, 1976. 485 pp. MURPHY, ROBERT F., ed.
Selected Papers from the American Anthropologist, 1940-1970.
Washington, D.C.: American Anthropological Association, 1976.
424 pp.
These three volumes reprint articles from the major general anthropological
journal. Few articles deal with U.S. mainstream culture but many are
about American Indians. Introductions by the editors outline the interests
and concerns of American anthropologists in such areas as archaeology,

linguistics, and physical anthropology, as well as cultural and social anthropology.

A-F 6. **HALL, EDWARD T.** Beyond Culture. Garden City, N.Y.: Anchor Press, 1976. 256 pp.
This discussion of the way culture influences behavior, perception, and thought is based theoretically on a generalized version of the Sapir-Whorf hypothesis. Hall's purpose is to make Americans aware of the pervasiveness of culture and how it can affect their behavior in the international community. He uses examples of cross-cultural contact to expose American cultural values and attitudes in action.

A-F 7. **HALL, EDWARD T.** The Silent Language. Garden City, N.Y.: Doubleday, 1973. 240 pp.
Hall explains the anthropological concept of culture for both a general and a scholarly audience, stressing the importance of non-verbal aspects of culture to cross-cultural understanding. He begins with the premise that culture is a communication system in which messages are conveyed on formal, informal, and technical levels. He then defines ten primary message systems which he considers basic to culture: interaction, association, subsistence, bisexuality, territoriality, temporality, learning, play, defense, and technology.

A-F 8. **HARRIS, MARVIN.** The Rise of Anthropological Theory: A History of Theories of Culture. New York: Crowell, 1968. 806 pp.
This is a survey of the intellectual development of cultural anthropology, evaluated in terms of Harris's own theory of cultural materialism, in which technological and economic factors are emphasized as the bases of cultural change and evolution. Harris organizes his material chronologically and focuses on such figures in the discipline as Boas, Kroeber, and Lowie.

A-F 9. **HINSLEY, CURTIS M.,** Jr. Savages and Scientists: The Smithsonian Institution and the Development of American Anthropology 1846-1916. Washington, D.C.: Smithsonian Institution Press, 1981. 319 pp.
This history of the growth of anthropology between the Civil War and W.W. I is also an examination of the culture that produced it. Industrialization and the disintegration of face-to-face society, Hinsley argues, brought on a need to regroup. Similarly, urban poverty spawned idealistic responses such as the supposedly objective science of Evolutionism and the movement to merge American Indian and European Enlightenment philosophies to create an ideal and homogeneous society. The optimism that gave birth to the Smithsonian Institution was slowly undermined over the second half of the century by the specter of subjectivity and by the increased activity of individualist researchers whose resentment toward centralized government regulation produced the Boasian era of autonomous, university-based research.

A-F 10. **HONIGMANN, JOHN J.,** ed. Handbook of Social and Cultural Anthropology. Chicago: Rand McNally, 1973. 129 pp.
The twenty-eight original articles in this volume constitute an introduction to contemporary cultural anthropology. Each author describes the intellectual background to his or her specialization and reviews current work. Some of the areas relevant to American culture include the history of anthropology, the historical approach in anthropology, cognitive anthropology, sociolinguistics, the study of narrative, economic anthropology, political anthropology, the anthropology of law, the study of pluralism, urban anthropology, medical anthropology, psychological anthropology, and the anthropology of education.

16

A-F 11. HSU, FRANCIS L. K. The Study of Literate Civilizations. New York:
         Holt, Rinehart & Winston, 1969. 123 pp.
This is a guide to the anthropological study of large-scale literate societies. Hsu summarizes the goals and methodology of both national character
studies and studies of more limited subjects and communities. He also
proposes two methodological approaches to the study of literate civilizations.

A-F 12. HYMES, DELL, ed. Reinventing Anthropology. New York: Pantheon
         Books, 1973. 470 pp.
This self-proclaimed "antitextbook" is a collection of sixteen essays
which contend that cultural anthropology has forsaken its early goals
and has become mired in academe. The authors of the essays propose to
"reinvent" anthropology and redirect it in a way more sensitive to social
issues. Half of the papers deal specifically with the application of
anthropology to U.S. culture, and much attention is focused on the political implications of cultural anthropology.

A-F 13. KARDINER, ABRAM. The Psychological Frontiers of Society. New
         York: Columbia University Press, 1943. 475 pp.
This is a study of personality and culture. Principles of psychodynamics
are applied to several societies to test the functionalist theoretical
position that social institutions are interrelated. The societies studied
are the Comanche; the Alorese in the South Pacific; and the community
of Plainville, U.S.A.

A-F 14. KLUCKHOLN, FLORENCE ROCKWOOD and FRED L. STRODBECK. Variations
         in Value Orientations. Evanston, Ill.: Row, Peterson, 1961.
         437 pp.
In this study of five cultures—Zuni, Navajo, Spanish-American, Texan
homesteader, and Mormon—in the Rimrock, New Mexico area, measures of
value orientation and dimensions of contrasts were devised, applied, and
analyzed qualitatively and quantitatively. The authors argue that conformity to and deviation from social and cultural systems can be better
analyzed in terms of dominant and variant values than in terms of dominant
values alone.

A-F 15. MEAD, MARGARET and MURIEL BROWN. The Wagon and the Star: A Study
         in American Community Initiative. Chicago: Rand McNally, 1967.
         223 pp.
In analyzing patterns of organized voluntary action, the authors discuss
the concepts of community and leadership as specifically manifested in
the U.S. Brief case studies of the National Association for Retarded
Children, Ruritan National, the National Congress of Parents and Teachers,
and the National Traveler's Aid Association are presented. Mead and Brown
argue that government programs cannot have a meaningful effect without
initial voluntary community organization.

A-F 16. MEAD, MARGARET and RUTH L. BUNZEL, eds. The Golden Age of American
         Anthropology. New York: Braziller, 1960. 630 pp.
This volume contains a selection of the writings of individuals who influenced American anthropology during its formative period (1880-1920).
Mead and Bunzel have included the writings of explorers and other observers
of the period who prepared the way for the development of anthropology
in America. A presentation is also made of the research sponsored by
the Smithsonian Institution and the Bureau of American Ethnology, the
two institutions which dominated American anthropology until approximately
1900. The role of private museums, especially the American Museum of
Natural History, is discussed. The majority of the writings in the first
sections are descriptive, and deal with the collection and ordering of
information about American Indian cultures. The final two sections consist
of theoretical writings by anthropologists of the early 20th century which

provide a historical perspective for the descriptive writings and subsequent developments in the field. The editors provide headnotes for each section and each author.

A-F 17. MEAD, MARGARET and RHODA METRAUX, eds. The Study of Culture at a Distance. Chicago: University of Chicago Press, 1953. 480 pp.
Mead and Metraux's manual describes strategies, objectives, and methods for the study of national character, and their applications. It also provides background information which establishes the place of national character studies in the anthropological literature. A bibliography of national character studies and studies of personality and culture is included.

A-F 18. MESSERSCHMIDT, DONALD A., ed. Anthropologists at Home in North America: Methods and Issues in the Study of One's Own Society. New York: Cambridge University Press, 1981. 310 pp.
This book is a collection of fourteen case studies done in the U.S. and Canada by both graduate students and professionals on such subjects as a San Francisco co-op, an Arizona mining town, a state insurance regulation commission, elderly residents of San Diego center-city hotels, and the Saskatchewan Cultural Ecology Research Program. An introductory essay examines how research at home now tends to be issue-oriented, and another analyzes the debate over the value of this method of ethnography.

A-F 19. NAROLL, RAOUL and RONALD COHEN, eds. A Handbook of Method in Cultural Anthropology. Garden City, N.Y.: Natural History Press, 1970. 1017 pp.
A collection of forty-nine articles by forty-seven authors, this book is an introduction to contemporary cultural anthropological research. The work is organized into seven sections: a general introduction to methodology and epistemology in anthropological generalization, a section on the broad problems that anthropology addresses in descriptive and historical studies, an extensive consideration of the fieldwork process, models of ethnographic description and analysis, and three sections on cross-cultural comparison in anthropology. The editors emphasize the importance of the use of cross-cultural data to generate and test hypotheses about human culture.

A-F 20. OPLER, MARVIN K., ed. Culture and Mental Health: Cross Cultural Studies. New York: Macmillan, 1959. 533 pp.
Views on mental health and mental illness in societies in North and South America, Oceania, Asia, and Africa are presented in the twenty-three papers collected in this volume. Problems of mental health in the U.S. are given special attention. In particular, mental illness among minority groups—American Indians, blacks, Irish, Italians, Jews, and Spanish-Americans—is examined. The contributions put American concepts of mental health into a cross-cultural perspective.

A-F 21. POWDERMAKER, HORTENSE. Stranger and Friend: The Way of an Anthropologist. New York: Norton, 1966. 315 pp.
In this account of her anthropological career, Powdermaker describes her education and her four fieldwork experiences: at Lesu in Melanesia, Indianola in Mississippi, Hollywood, and Zambia. She gives detailed descriptions of the field situations in which she worked and describes her attitude toward her work in various areas. The book is intended as an anthropological investigation of the participant observation method itself: "a case history of how an anthropologist lives, works and learns; how he thinks and feels in the field." The sections on Mississippi and Hollywood offer an ethnographic perspective on cultural patterns in the U.S.

18

A-F 22. REDFIELD, ROBERT. The Little Community. Chicago: University
of Chicago Press, 1960. 182 pp.
Redfield introduced the community study perspective into anthropology.
In this work he describes the "little community" as a unit of culture
study which is small, homogeneous, distinctive, and self-sufficient.
He sees it as a cultural configuration which arose with the development
of complex civilizations. The Little Community provides the conceptual
framework for many of the subsequent studies of communities in the U.S.

A-F 23. VOGET, FRED W. The History of Ethnology. New York: Holt, Rinehart
& Winston, 1975. 879 pp.
Voget traces the intellectual history of cultural anthropology from the
earliest indications of systematic interest in other cultures to the present. The book is organized into four parts. The first part describes
early developments from Greco-Roman, Renaissance, and Arabic intellectual
traditions. The second part looks at the period from 1725 to 1890, when
the major intellectual view, Developmentalism, held that humanity was
advancing toward a perfect social state. The third part, "Structuralism,"
deals with the varieties of structural-functionalist, cultural historicist,
and culture and personality schools of anthropology, including discussions
of economic, legal and political anthropology, cultural ecology, and acculturation and applied anthropology studies. A final overview points to
historical patterns of change in the discipline and prospects for the
future of a discipline increasingly integrated with other fields.

II. GENERAL AND COMPARATIVE STUDIES

A-F 24. ARENS, W. and SUSAN P. MONTAGUE, eds. The American Dimension:
Cultural Myths and Social Realities. Port Washington, N.Y.:
Alfred, 1976. 221 pp.
In this collection of short, original articles, the authors apply the
theoretical positions of Claude Levi-Strauss and Clifford Geertz to studies
of the symbolic basis of American culture. The book is divided into two
parts. The first concentrates on the symbolic analysis of forms of entertainment, such as television, movies, literature, and sports. The second
concentrates on social interaction in diverse settings.

A-F 25. ASHCRAFT, NORMAN and ALBERT E. SCHEFLEN. People Space: The Making
and Breaking of Human Boundaries. Garden City, N.Y.: Anchor
Press, 1976. 185 pp.
Ashcraft and Scheflen discuss territoriality as a principle of human interaction. Moving from personal and interpersonal territoriality to the
expression of territoriality in the landscape and in architecture, the
authors consider the implications of territoriality in American culture
for regional development. The work also contains a number of observations
about urban and regional planning.

A-F 26. AYABE, TSUNEO, ed. Ethnicity and Cultural Pluralism in the United
States: A Report of Field Research in the U.S.A. (1976). Fukuoka,
Japan: Kyushu University Press, 1978. 365 pp.
Five of the seven separate studies of American communities in this col-
lection are reports by Japanese anthropologists on fieldwork they con-
ducted in the U.S. The topics of the papers are: The Ethnicity of Polish
Americans and Its Political Mobilization; The Social and Cultural Char-
acteristics of Spanish- and Mexican-Americans and the Chicano Movement;
A Human Ecology of Mushroom Production and Polyethnic Contact in Southern
Chester County, Pennsylvania; a Study of Cultural Content of Kin Gatherings

Among Black Americans; The Ethnic Heritage of the Italian Americans in the United States and Their Community Life; Jewish Communities in Western Massachusetts; and Jewish Ethnicity Viewed from the Analysis of Their Organizations.

A-F 27. BENEDICT, BURTON. The Anthropology of World's Fairs: San Francisco's Panama Pacific International Exposition of 1915. Berkeley, Calif.: Scolar Press, 1983. 175 pp.
This book was written in conjunction with an exhibit at the Lowie Museum of Anthropology, University of California, Berkeley, in which artifacts from the 1915 World's Fair were displayed. Focusing on the San Francisco exposition, the five essays present a history of World's Fairs from the first in London in 1851 to the one in Tokyo in 1970. The spatial and social arrangements, and material inventions and innovations represented reorganizations in the way nations and other groups sought to glorify themselves. In addition to those by Benedict, essays are provided by M. Miriam Dobkin, Grey Brechin, Elizabeth N. Armstrong, and George A. Starr.

A-F 28. BENNETT, JOHN W. Northern Plainsmen: Adaptive Strategy and Agrarian Life. Chicago: Aldine, 1969. 252 pp.
This book is a study of four groups representing four ways of life in a rural region in Southwestern Saskatchewan: ranchers, farmers, Hutterite Colonists, and Cree Indians. Although set in Canada, the description is representative of social and economic adaptations made in the Northern Plains at large. The ways that the Canadian regions differ from what would be found south of the border in the U.S. are noted, and Bennett's use of ecological adaptation as his major frame of reference makes his approach widely applicable to the U.S. After the region and the cultures are described generally, each group is discussed individually. The way that each group perceives itself in relation to the other groups is described. In a final overview, agrarian development and change are analyzed in terms of cooperation and competition, both regionally and in the context of the larger society.

A-F 29. BENNETT, JOHN W., ed. The New Ethnicity: Perspectives from Ethnology. St. Paul, Minn.: West, 1975. 334 pp.
These eighteen articles, eleven of which are studies of the U.S., discuss ethnicity in complex societies. The papers are arranged by Bennett to illustrate four themes in the study of ethnicity: (1) ethnicity as identity; the search for self and the definition of group boundaries; (2) ethnicity as a set of strategies for acquiring the resources one needs to survive and consume at desired levels; (3) ethnicity as one of the distinctive characteristics of nations; and (4) ethnicity as structurally related to class structures. Individual studies focus on mainstream groups and minorities, and on small groups and large sociopolitical units.

A-F 30. BOAS, FRANZ. Anthropology and Modern Life. 1928; Rev. ed. New York: Norton, 1932. 255 pp.
Boas discusses ways in which anthropological knowledge can be applied to problems in "modern life." Concerned primarily with the implications of the concept of race for European and American industrialized civilization, Boas stresses the position that all races are equivalent in mental capacity and discusses the great influence that culture has on individuals. The anthropological perspective, Boas contends, can aid in the necessary process of integrating ever larger groups of peoples in ways that respect traditional patterns while responding to the inevitable frictions of progress.

A-F 31. BODLEY, JOHN H. Anthropology and Contemporary Human Problems. Menlo Park, Calif.: Cummings, 1976. 246 pp.
Bodley discusses large-scale human problems attributable to the development of civilizations. Considering such problems as the threat of nuclear war, resource depletion, and unchecked population growth, he compares contemporary civilizations with small-scale societies to assess the effect of widespread industrial and military growth. Most of Bodley's examples are taken from the U.S., although he discusses the problems in global terms.

A-F 32. COLLINS, THOMAS W., ed. Cities in a Larger Context. Athens: University of Georgia Press, 1980. 152 pp.
This collection of essays treats urban anthropology from the perspective of an open system in which boundaries are permeated by linkages with the national and international arena; "city" is rejected as too arbitrary a unit of study. Specific subjects include: economic change and school segregation in Memphis, Tennessee; the Scottish roots of Southern Protestant ceremonial gatherings; migratory theory examined ethno-historically in Illinois, Texas, and Georgia; and the future of cities, independent of nation-states, acting as connecting nodes for multinational enterprise.

A-F 33. DEETZ, JAMES. In Small Things Forgotten: The Archeology of Early American Life. Garden City, N.Y.: Anchor Press, 1977. 184 pp.
This book discusses the sources of data, types of research, and potential contributions of historical archeology. Deetz is primarily interested in the ways that material products of human activity can be interpreted to gain an understanding of the cultural patterns of early America and the lifeways of common people in the past. He illustrates his argument with archeological analyses of early American earthenware, gravestones, New England architecture, and an excavation of a site near Plymouth, Massachusetts.

A-F 34. FELDMAN, SAUL D. and JERALD W. THIELBAR, eds. Life Styles: Diversity in American Society. Boston: Little, Brown, 1972. 383 pp.
The selections in this book, dating from 1922 to 1971, discuss U.S. national character, ideological variation, class structure, ethnic groups and social deviance. Ranging in approach from theoretical and analytic to documentary and narrative, the book attempts to show that unity crosscuts the diversity of U.S. lifestyles. The readings are taken from both academic and popular literature.

A-F 35. GARRETSON, LUCY R. American Culture: An Anthropological Perspective. Dubuque, Iowa: William C. Brown, 1976. 58 pp.
In this anthropological analysis of American culture, Garretson attempts to illuminate the underlying value structure of U.S. culture rather than to deal with statistical variations or technological facts. She stresses ideal values and social forms that are central to culture, and applies a simple "rationality" model to explain the transformation of social forms and values from a "natural state" into the idealized American Dream. Socialization in terms of family structure, schooling, and the work ethic also is discussed. Several case studies are introduced, and some of the conflicts between actual and ideal forms are mentioned.

A-F 36. GASTIL, RAYMOND D. Cultural Regions of the United States. Seattle: University of Washington Press, 1975. 366 pp.
Gastil presents a cultural-geographical overview of the U.S., organizing his material according to a basic premise that cultural regions can be defined "primarily by variations in the cultures of the peoples that dominated the first settlement and the cultural traits developed by these people in the formative period." Gastil defines and describes thirteen

cultural regions, ranging from such distinct localities as the New York
Metropolitan region to such broadly defined areas as the Mormon region.
Basic cultural traits such as religion and dialect are discussed in terms
of regional variation, and the distribution of several social indicators
is examined.

A-F 37. GERLACH, LUTHER P. and VIRGINIA H. HIME. Lifeway Leap: The
Dynamics of Change in America. Minneapolis: University of Minnesota Press, 1973. 332 pp.
The authors attempt to interpret for a general audience the evolutionary
and revolutionary changes taking place in American life. Surveys, public
media, and studies of social, political, and religious movements are used
to explain and examine cultural change in the U.S. Such change is explored
by analyzing the differences and interrelations between revolution and
evolution, by investigating the relevant contributions of systems theory,
and by analyzing recent popular American movements. Finally, an attempt
is made to present these changes in an evolutionary perspective.

A-F 38. GOFFMAN, ERVING. Frame Analysis: An Essay on the Organization
of Experience. New York: Harper & Row, 1974. 586 pp.
In this work, Goffman elaborates his ideas on the organization of experience in everyday life. He is interested in the ways that "situations"
are defined, particularly the "frames," or basic elements, out of which
situations are built by an actor. Starting with the primary frameworks
of a culture, Goffman shows how frames and situations are redefined and
manipulated in the course of ongoing activities, and "laminated" to create
situations. His purpose is to show how experience is ordered from the
point of view of the actor rather than that of society. The bulk of his
examples are drawn from writings on American culture, especially newspaper
accounts.

A-F 39. GOFFMAN, ERVING. Interaction Ritual: Essays on Face-to-Face
Behavior. Chicago: Aldine, 1967. 267 pp.
These six essays deal with the syntactical relations among the acts of
individuals in a group. Goffman examines from several points of view
the cultural roles which guide and direct interpersonal behavior. "On
Face Work" is a discussion of the ways individuals maintain an image of
self during social encounters. "The Nature of Deference and Demeanor"
investigates the Durkheimian notion of the religious symbol as it is used
in the definition of the self. Three short essays--"Embarrassment and
Social Organization," "Alienation from Interaction," and "Mental Symptoms
and the Public Order"--deal with specific topics in the study of social
interaction. In the longest essay, "Where the Action Is," Goffman applies
his analysis of face-to-face behavior to the study of gambling.

A-F 40. GOFFMAN, ERVING. The Presentation of Self in Everyday Life. Woodstock, N.Y.: Overlook Press, 1973. 259 pp.
In this work, which explores face-to-face interaction in social situations,
Goffman argues that all social situations involve impression management,
whereby a "tacit agreement is maintained between performers and audience
to act as if a given degree of opposition and of accord existed between
them." Drawing from sociological, ethnographic, and literary examples,
Goffman describes how social interaction can be organized in terms of
participants, roles, and regions, and manipulated by the actors. While
concentrating on American society, Goffman punctuates his work with examples from other societies and provides a setting for understanding American
culture within a wider perspective.

A-F 41. GOFFMAN, ERVING. Relations in Public: Microstudies of the Public
          Order. New York: Basic Books, 1971. 396 pp.
Relations in Public is a collection of six essays on face-to-face interaction which characterizes the world as a potentially dangerous place,
and stresses the idea of social order. Taking much of his terminology
and descriptive orientation from ethnology, Goffman describes and interprets the ways in which individuals in European and American society analyze the potential threat of a situation. Sampling situations which can
be made to seem more or less threatening, Goffman shows how clever
criminals and comedians create an appearance of normality which can then
be manipulated to their own ends.

A-F 42. GOFFMAN, ERVING. Stigma: Notes on the Management of Spoiled
          Identity. Englewood Cliffs, N.J.: Prentice-Hall, 1963. 147 pp.
Goffman defines "stigma" as an attribute of a person which is deeply discrediting when related to a negative stereotype. He discusses the idea
of stigma in terms of social identity (the "social information an individual communicates about himself") and uses the concept to discuss the
social identities of mental patients, as well as the nature of social
identity in American life.

A-F 43. GOFFMAN, ERVING. Strategic Interaction. Philadelphia: University
          of Pennsylvania Press, 1971. 145 pp.
In two essays, "Expression Games" and "Strategic Interaction," Goffman
explores the game-like aspects of social interaction. The former investigates the individual's capacity to acquire, reveal, and conceal information. The latter develops ideas about the ways in which individuals
have to decide among alternatives for behavior in a given situation.
The basic approach is similar to Goffman's other work in that face-to-
face interaction is used as the unit of analysis for the study of social
structure, and the presentation follows his usual style of selecting examples of situations from a wide range of sources, from the European Anti-
Heretical Inquisition to techniques of surveillance in intelligence work.

A-F 44. GOODMAN, MARY ELLEN. Race Awareness in Young Children. 1964;
          Rev. ed. New York: Collier Books, 1970. 280 pp.
Goodman studied the racial preferences of four- and five-year-old nursery
school children in the Boston area in the 1940s. Sampling fifty-seven
black and forty-six white children, she determined whether the children
showed racial "In-group Preference" or "Out-group Preference." Statistically, 26% of the black children showed an In-group Preference, compared
with 92% of the white children. The study was influential in the 1954
Supreme Court decision (Brown vs. Board of Education) concerning racial
integration in schools.

A-F 45. GOVER, GEOFFREY. The American People: A Study in National Char-
          acter. 1948; Rev. ed. New York: Norton, 1964. 246 pp.
This is a psychocultural account of those features of American culture
which influence the thought, speech, and action of individual Americans.
The book is based on several years of formal and informal anthropological
and psychological research in the U.S. by Gover, and is organized around
the primary psychological determinants Gover perceived in American socialization. Foremost among these is the distrust of authority and the importance of the mother in the American family. Gover also discusses American
attitudes toward socialization (especially the concept of "sissy"), personality, the material world, success, social hierarchy, and ethnocentrism.

A-F 46. HARRIS, JANET C. and ROBERTA J. PARK, eds. Play, Games and Sports
        in Cultural Contexts. Champaign, Ill.: Human Kinetics, 1983.
        521 pp.
These essays from several disciplines survey the role of sports and play
cross-culturally. They are organized into five sections: (1) games seen
as socio-cultural symbols, (2) games functioning ritually as statements
about the social order, (3) the role of play in psychological terms, (4)
the socializing effect of game-playing, and (5) the borrowing of games
between ethnic groups as a mechanism of acculturation, as well as the
role of sports in preserving ethnic diversity when played in a culturally
pluralistic setting.

A-F 47. HENRY, JULES. Culture Against Man. New York: Random House, 1965.
        495 pp.
This is, as the author claims in the introduction, "not an objective
description of America, but rather a passionate ethnography." From a critical viewpoint, Henry focuses on several areas which seem to him to be
central. He looks at the economic aspects of American culture and criticizes the notion of dynamic obsolescence created through technology and
advertising which he calls the Pecuniary Philosophy. He discusses American
processes of socialization, especially in the family, grammar school,
and high school, and illustrates his views with a case study of the families of psychotic children. The final section of the book, on "human
obsolescence," presents studies of two mental hospitals and a nursing
home.

A-F 48. HICKS, GEORGE L. and PHILIP E. LEIS, eds. Ethnic Encounters:
        Identities and Contexts. North Scituate, Mass.: Duxbury Press,
        1977. 289 pp.
Six of the fourteen articles in this collection are studies of groups
in the U.S. Their subjects are Haitian immigrants in American politics;
cultural adaptations made by Catawaba and Monhegan Indians; American tech-
nicians on an Ecuadorian sugar plantation; ethnic revitalization in the
U.S.; ethnic relations in a New England town; and ethnicity in a Fourth
of July Committee in a Rhode Island town. By approaching ethnicity in
a comparative framework, the editors intend to demonstrate the value of
ethnicity as a tool of analysis in the study of social interaction in
plural societies. They deemphasize ethnicity as such in favor of focusing
on "the uses of ethnic identity in the conduct of social relations."

A-F 49. HODGE, WILLIAM H. The First Americans: Then and Now. New York:
        Holt, Rinehart & Winston, 1981. 551 pp.
This book surveys thirteen Native American groups from nine cultural areas:
Micmac, Oneida, Menominee (Northeast/Woodland), East Cherokee (Southeast),
Northern Cheyenne (Plains), Navajo, Hopi, Papago (Southwest), Pomo (Cali-
fornia), Klamath, Kwakiutl (Northwest Coast), Hare (Subarctic), Eskimo
(Arctic). It portrays their pre-contact culture, then examines their
present adaptations to contemporary life, and concludes with an exploration
of Native Americans in their urban context.

A-F 50. HSU, FRANCIS L. K. Americans and Chinese: Purpose and Fulfillment
        in Great Civilizations. 1953; Rev. ed. Garden City, N.Y.:
        New York Historical Press, 1970. 493 pp.
In this revised edition of his 1953 national character study, American
and Chinese: Two Ways of Life, Hsu describes and compares Chinese and
American cultures, using each as a means to understand the other. The
basic difference, according to Hsu, lies in the fact that Americans are
individual-oriented and Chinese are situation-oriented. This theme is
explored in terms of politics, law, religion, art, education, and many
other aspects of culture.

A-F 51. JORGENSEN, JOSEPH G. and MARCELLO TRUZZI. Anthropology and American Life. Englewood Cliffs, N.J.: Prentice-Hall, 1974. 524 pp.
This is a collection of twenty-nine previously published articles. The book is organized around general topics in anthropological research such as kinship, language, religion, education, occupation, deviance, recreation, subcultures, and social change. The editors tend to emphasize diversity in American culture. For example, the two articles about religion are concerned with occultists and a group that uses LSD, while more traditional forms of religion in the U.S. are not considered. The selections in the other sections are more representative of mainstream American culture.

A-F 52. KIM, CHOONG SOON. An Asian Anthropologist in the South: Field Experiences with Blacks, Indians, and Whites. Knoxville: University of Tennessee Press, 1977. 155 pp.
The author, a native Korean, documents his experiences as an anthropological field worker in Georgia, Tennessee, and Mississippi. Kim provides insights into American culture by describing personal encounters from his fieldwork. The work is an account of the personal development of an anthropologist rather than a report of the results of his research. The particular fieldwork projects in which Kim was involved were a study of woodpulp workers in Georgia and investigations among the Choctaw Indians in Tennessee and Mississippi.

A-F 53. KLUCKHOHN, CLYDE. Mirror for Man: The Relations of Anthropology to Modern Life. New York: Whittlesey House, 1949. 313 pp.
Kluckhohn's introduction to anthropology, written for a general audience, includes descriptions of the various sub-disciplines of anthropology, and a chapter in which he analyzes American culture in terms of characteristics, patterns, values, and assumptions. Kluckhohn proposes that the outstanding features of American culture are consciousness of diversity of cultural origins, emphasis on technology and wealth, the frontier spirit, trust in science and education and indifference to religion, unusual personal insecurity, and concern over discrepancies between theory and practice in the culture. He also offers some proposals about future directions in American culture.

A-F 54. LEE, DOROTHY. Freedom and Culture. Englewood Cliffs, N.J.: Prentice-Hall, 1959. 179 pp.
Lee brings together fifteen of her previously published essays which examine, from several perspectives, the relationship of the individual to culture. While only a few of the essays are about U.S. culture, Lee compares data gathered during research on a number of small-scale societies with life in the U.S. The author takes the position that culture is composed of a series of codes through which physical reality is transformed to experienced reality. From this perspective, she looks at religion, creativity, language, values, responsibility, and symbols. Basic American values are examined throughout the book.

A-F 55. LIGHTMAN, ALLAN J. and JOAN R. CHALLINOR. Kin and Communities: Families in America. Washington, D.C.: Smithsonian Institution Press, 1979. 335 pp.
These essays from the Smithsonian's Sixth International Symposium represent a cross-disciplinary approach to "roots." The topics include: monogamy among non-humans and, cross-culturally, among humans; Native American pre-history; family myth creation as in the case of the dynastic Adams family; the family life cycles produced by the Great Depression; aging in black families; the position of women in a frontier Saskatchewan community; the roles of family and government in caring for the insane in antebellum Massachusetts; and a comparative analysis of Chinese and American families. The symposium included discussions of the methodology of family and community research and of the future of the American family.

25

A-F 56. **MEAD, MARGARET.** Male and Female: A Study of the Sexes in a Changing World. New York: Morrow, 1949. 477 pp.
Mead draws on her field research experiences to discuss the roles of men
and women in modern American society. She discusses the ways that children
and adults in small-scale and large-scale societies learn to act properly
as males or females. In her discussion Mead provides multiple examples
of similarities and differences in the ways different cultures define
and maintain male and female role relationships. She argues for the recognition of the capabilities of both sexes. This book was written for a
general audience as an anthropologist's response to the problem of sex
discrimination in American life.

A-F 57. **MORLAND, J. KENNETH,** ed. The Not So Solid South: Anthropological
Studies in a Regional Subculture. Athens: University of Georgia
Press, 1971. 143 pp.
The thirteen papers in this volume cover a wide variety of topics and
illustrate the position that the Southern U.S. should not be considered
a uniform culture area. All of the papers focus on relatively small groups
which are specialized occupationally, regionally, or culturally. None
of the papers deals with "mainstream" Southern culture although there
is an assumption that a mainstream culture exists. Topics include, among
others, a black healing cult, techniques for making illegal "moonshine"
whiskey, criminals' tactics for eluding capture by hounds, and Irish "gypsies."

A-F 58. **NOEL-HUME, IVOR.** Here Lies Virginia: An Archaeologist's View
of Colonial Life and History. New York: Knopf, 1963. 316 pp.
Noel-Hume discusses the relationship of historical archeology to documentary history by describing the ways in which historical archeology
has contributed to understanding the history of the state of Virginia.
His presentation is organized around three topics: archeological sites,
the relationship of documents to artifacts, and the areas of Colonial
activity which have been revealed most clearly by archeology. The Roanoke
Colony, the Jamestown Colony, and the reconstructed town of Colonial
Williamsburg are given special attention.

A-F 59. **NOEL-HUME, IVOR.** Historical Archaeology. New York: Knopf, 1969.
355 pp.
This is a general survey of the methodology of historical archeology.
Noel-Hume gives a brief background to the specialization of historical
archeology and describes the methods used to amass, record, and preserve
data. The author describes both general archeological excavation techniques and those techniques which are particularly important to historical
archeology, such as the use of historical documents. The book contains
an annotated bibliography of references on historical artifacts, the methodology of historical archeology, and American history.

A-F 60. **NORBECK, EDWARD** and **CLAIR FARRER,** eds. Forms of Play of Native
North Americans: 1977 Proceedings of the American Ethnological
Society. St. Paul, Minn.: West, 1979. 290 pp.
These nineteen papers analyze forms of play aesthetically, ritually, eth-
nically, and historically within political and social frameworks. Some
are cross-cultural (staying within Native American bounds) and some address
such specific cultural phenomena as Ojibwa conjuring, Pueblo clowning,
North Alaskan children's knife tales, and stick and ball games in the
Southwest.

A-F 61. PERIN, CONSTANCE. Everything in Its Place: Social Order and Land Use in America. Princeton, N.J.: Princeton University Press, 1977. 291 pp.
To this study, based on intensive interviews with twenty individuals involved in residential land-use planning in Houston and Philadelphia, Perin brings a theoretical perspective drawn from semiotics and symbolic anthropology. The author combines experience in residential land-use planning with an analysis of the symbolic system of housing developers and planners, and attempts to determine the assumptions which guide the actions of the producers and consumers of suburban housing. In her discussion, Perin considers the cultural, sociological, and economic factors which influence the decisions made by developers and residents of various types of housing. These include presumed differences between renters and home-owners, American ideas about social categories, and theories of metropolitan developers concerning potential markets and resources.

A-F 62. PETTITT, GEORGE A. Prisoners of Culture. New York: Scribner, 1970. 291 pp.
Taking a broad view, Pettitt discusses U.S. culture in light of evidence from human evolution, from small-scale societies, and from psychology. Pettitt is concerned with the problems he sees in contemporary U.S. culture—for example, juvenile delinquency, anomie, unemployment, and over-mechanization—and offers suggestions for their resolution.

A-F 63. SAFA, HELEN ICKEN and GLORIA LEVITAS, eds. Social Problems in Corporate America. New York: Harper & Row, 1975. 519 pp.
Drawing on papers originally published in the journal Transaction/Society between 1968 and 1973, Safa and Levitas offer an anthropological perspective on social problems in the U.S. The majority of the papers were written by social scientists other than anthropologists, but the editors provide commentary which puts the papers in an anthropological framework. The sixty-two papers are organized into eight sections: The Urban Crisis, Poverty and Social Inequality, Racism and Repression, Violence, Crime and Punishment, The Changing Economy, Changing Life Styles, and The Burden of Responsibility. The editors advance the view that diversity is an important feature of society rather than evidence of deviance and pathology.

A-F 64. SCHNEIDER, DAVID M. American Kinship: A Cultural Account. Englewood Cliffs, N.J.: Prentice-Hall, 1968. 117 pp.
In this book on kinship as a symbolic system, Schneider analyzes how Americans define the category of "relative," and how cultural distinctions are made within that category. His work is based on a sample of middle-class informants from Chicago. Taking a structuralist position, he argues that the central symbol of the American kinship system is sexual intercourse between a husband and wife. Through this symbol, fundamental contradictions in American culture between nature and law, and nature and human kind, are resolved.

A-F 65. SIEBER, R. TIMOTHY and ANDREW J. GORDON, eds. Children and Their Organizations: Investigations in American Culture. Boston: G. K. Hall, 1981. 250 pp.
Each essay in this collection takes as its subject an organization and its effects on the children or teen-agers involved (for example, sex role socialization in rural Southern education, an "unconventional" youth center, a Texas summer camp for girls, and an army basic combat training camp as the location of an initiation ritual). However, the attempt was to avoid a "community study" approach to modern institutions, and the authors have tended more toward a child development and social psychology methodology.

A-F 66. **SOUTH, STANLEY.** Method and Theory in Historical Archeology.
         New York: Academic Press, 1977. 345 pp.
South applies the current archeological methods of quantitative data gathering, hypothesis testing, and quantitative analysis of data from historic
sites of archeology. Three artifact patterns are discussed: the Brunswick,
North Carolina refuse disposal pattern, the Carolina artifact pattern,
and the Frontier artifact pattern. Through qualitative measures and statistical tests of hypotheses, interpretations are made about the behaviors
and cultural patterns represented by these artifact assemblages.

A-F 67. **SPICER, EDWARD H.**, ed. Ethnic Medicine in the South West. Tucson:
         University of Arizona Press, 1977. 291 pp.
In this volume, four medical anthropologists present descriptive analyses
of the traditional medical beliefs and practices of four major Southwestern
U.S. ethnic groups: blacks, Mexican-Americans, Yaqui Indians and Anglo-
Americans. In his introduction, Spicer synopsizes the similarities and
differences of these "parallel medical traditions" and "popular medicines,"
and emphasizes the interpretation of healing practices with the cultural
(especially religious), historical, socioeconomic, and environmental
aspects of these different ethnic groups.

A-F 68. **SPICER, EDWARD H.** and **RAYMOND H. THOMSON**, eds. Plural Society
         in the South-West. New York: Interbook, 1972. 367 pp.
The theme of these nine original articles from a 1970 conference is cultural diversity in the American Southwest, which here includes the area
from Northern Mexico through California, Nevada, Utah, Colorado, Oklahoma,
and Texas. Topics covered by the articles are a description of Southwestern cultural pluralism and its implications for a general understanding
of cultural diversity, an ethnohistorical approach to the Northern Mexican
culture area, Mormon theology and identity, the modern political organization and political awareness of the Navajo and the Hopi, cultural processes among the Mexicans in the Southwest, and historical and comparative
comments on Southwestern cultural pluralism. The book expands the research
begun by the Harvard Values Project (see A-F 73).

A-F 69. **SPINDLER, GEORGE** and **LOUISE SPINDLER**, eds. Urban Anthropology
         in the United States: Four Cases. New York: Holt, Rinehart
         & Winston, 1978. 504 pp.
The Spindlers have compiled four studies from the "Case Studies in Cultural
Anthropology" series published by Holt, Rinehart and Winston: Chicano
Prisoners by Theodore Davidson, Lifelines by Joyce Aschenbrenner, The
Portland Longshoremen by William Pilcher (see A-F 131), and Fun City by
Jerry Jacobs. This volume is intended for use in general, applied, and
urban anthropology courses as well as courses in urbanization, moderniza-
tion, and American culture and society. The editors include short biblio-
graphies relevant to the subject matter of each case study.

A-F 70. **SPRADLEY, JAMES P.** and **DAVID McCURDY,** eds. The Cultural Experience:
         Ethnography in Complex Society. Palo Alto, Calif.: Social Sci-
         ence Research Associates, 1972. 246 pp.
The editors' purpose for compiling cultural anthropological fieldwork
done by their undergraduate students is to show other anthropologists
that student fieldwork can be fruitful, rather than to offer an incisive
analysis of American life. Each of the twelve papers approaches a specific
aspect of American culture through the methodology of ethnoscience. Among
the subjects of study are a jewelry store, a junior high school, a third
grade class, a car theft ring, airline stewardesses, and an elementary
school recess.

A-F 71. STEIN, HOWARD F. and ROBERT F. HILL. The Ethnic Imperative:
Examining the White Ethnic Movement. University Park: Pennsylvania State University Press, 1977. 308 pp.
In this psychocultural analysis Stein and Hill argue that the New White
Ethnic Movement is a "salve for modern wounds of violated and vulnerable
identities." They regard the movement not as a return to a traditional
way of life but as an attempt by the American middle class to isolate
itself psychologically from unfulfilled ambitions. The authors use an
historical framework to show how the meanings of ethnicity have changed
through American history, and how such events as the assassinations of
John Kennedy, Martin Luther King, Jr., and especially Robert Kennedy have
set the stage for the current movement toward segmentation in American
society. They feel strongly that the New White Ethnic movement is a dangerous, pathological phenomenon, and that it runs counter to the possibilities
for equality in America.

A-F 72. TEFFT, STANTON K., ed. Secrecy: A Cross-Cultural Perspective.
New York: Human Sciences Press, 1980. 351 pp.
These fourteen essays represent a multi-disciplinary analysis of the issues
of secrecy and privacy--the former referring to information relevant to
but kept from the public, the latter to an individual's concealment of
personal information. The essays proceed from the supposition that privacy
and secrecy are important aspects of all social relationships, and explore
the use and function of both in interpersonal, interfamily, interorgani-
zational and international contexts. Owing to the cross-cultural and,
to a lesser extent, historical orientation of the essays, the volume lends
itself to considerations of what constitutes legitimate and illegitimate
uses of secrecy. Specifically U.S. subjects (the police, the Ku Klux
Klan, Taos Pueblo, multi-national corporations) are represented in the
collection.

A-F 73. VOGT, EVON Z. and ETHEL M. ALBERT, eds. People of Rimrock: A
Study of Values in Five Cultures. Cambridge, Mass.: Harvard
University Press, 1966. 342 pp.
Nine essays by different authors summarize the results of the Comparative
Study of Values in Five Cultures project of the Laboratory of Social Rela-
tions, Harvard University. The findings from studies of Zuni, Navajo,
Spanish-American, Texan homesteader, and Mormon cultures of the Rimrock,
New Mexico area elucidate problems in defining the concept of values.
Chapters deal with intercultural relations, learning of values, kinship
systems, ecology and economy, politics, religion, and expressive activities.
Although each topic uses data from all of the cultures, interpretations
differ according to the theoretical approaches applied.

A-F 74. WARNER, W. LLOYD. American Life: Dream and Reality. Chicago:
University of Chicago Press, 1953. 292 pp.
Warner's summary of the character of American society draws heavily on
his earlier work in the Yankee City Series and his studies of business
and the mass media. He stresses social status and role, social class
and caste, and Durkheimian concepts of collective representations and
social solidarity, with a major emphasis on ways of maintaining the structure of caste and class.

A-F 75. WEAVER, THOMAS, ed. To See Ourselves: Anthropology and Modern
Social Issues. Glenville, Ill.: Scott, Foresman, 1973.
485 pp.
The eighty-nine abridged selections in this book deal with the responsibility of anthropology toward contemporary social problems. The articles
are divided into nine sections: The Social Responsibilities of the Anthropologist; The Myth of the Melting Pot; Anthropology and the Third World;
Race and Racism; Poverty and Culture; Schooling; Violence; Environment;

and Anthropology and Intervention. Each section has an introductory and a concluding article by the section editor, and the relevance of each selection is explained in a short paragraph. There is a balance between theoretical and ethnographic selections.

A-F 76. WILLIAMS, JOHN E. and J. KENNETH MORLAND. Race, Color, and the Young Child. Chapel Hill: University of North Carolina Press, 1976. 360 pp.

This book is an investigation of the development of race concepts in young children in the U.S. The authors review concepts of race and color, discuss the cultural factors which influence the learning of attitudes toward race and color, and suggest biological factors, such as a tendency to prefer lightness over darkness, which might operate in the learning of cultural differences. Two psychological tests were administered to children (preschool to grade four) to measure racial and color perceptions. The authors found a preference for the color white over black in both Afro-American and Euro-American children. They also found that racial classification ability increased as children grew older. On these bases they propose a developmental theory of color and racial bias.

A-F 77. WILLIAMS, PETER W. Popular Religion in America: Symbolic Change and the Modernization Process in Historical Perspective. Englewood Cliffs, N.J.: Prentice-Hall, 1980.. 244 pp.

Williams has arranged his discussion of religions at the margins of modern organized religion in four parts: (1) the evolution of traditional Native-American and Afro-American religions in the present-day context, (2) Judaic and Catholic folk tradition, (3) the fundamentalist and evangelical outcroppings of Protestantism, and (4) "Post-modern, Post-Puritan Religion in Mass Society" from California sects to "UFOism." He sees modernization and urbanization as forces directed toward dissolving "the ancient linkage between symbolic expression and communities united by those symbols."

A-F 78. ZELINSKY, WILBUR. The Cultural Geography of the United States. Englewood Cliffs, N.J.: Prentice-Hall, 1973. 164 pp.

Blending theory and factual detail, Zelinsky offers a sketch of U.S. culture in relation to the land. In the first part, he discusses the historical and cultural factors which characterize the U.S., and combines data from anthropology, sociology, history, and geography to explicate the American ethos. The second part of the book stresses the geographical dimensions of cultural variation across America. An annotated bibliography of books and articles relating to the cultural geography of the U.S. is included.

III.   ETHNOGRAPHIC STUDIES

A-F 79. ALCANTARA, RUBEN R. Sakada: Filipino Adaptation in Hawaii. Washington, D.C.: University Press of America, 1981. 190 pp.

Sakadas were the Filipinos recruited to Hawaii to work the sugar plantations from 1906 to 1946. Focusing on one Sakada community in Oahu, and using the sugar companies' documents and the workers' life histories, Alcantara has reconstructed a picture of the changing life goals and strategies of three generations of Sakadas.

A-F 80. BECKER, HOWARD SAUL, BLANCHE GEER, and EVERETT C. HUGHES. Making the Grade: The Academic Side of College Life. New York: Wiley, 1968. 150 pp.
Using participant-observation fieldwork and applying the concept of symbolic interaction, Becker, Geer, and Hughes present the college social system from the perspective of the students at the University of Kansas. The students operate in a complex social system dominated by the faculty and administration, who assume that learning is determined by individual ability and initiative, with grades as the major reward. Students seek to counter the system of subjugation by "deviant" collective activities.

A-F 81. BENNETT, JOHN W. Hutterian Brethren: The Agricultural Economy and Social Organization of a Communal People. Stanford, Calif.: Stanford University Press, 1967. 298 pp.
Bennett describes the social and economic organization of six Hutterite colonies in Southwestern Saskatchewan. He offers a description of the Hutterites' adaptation to the Northern Plains environment and the internal social and economic organization of the colonies. Although the colonies are in Canada, the communal cultural system of these groups is comparable to that of other colonies within the U.S.

A-F 82. BOHANNAN, PAUL, ed. Divorce and After. Garden City, N.Y.: Doubleday, 1970. 301 pp.
This collection of eleven articles considers anthropological, sociological, psychological, medical, and legal questions about divorce in the U.S. The book is organized into five parts: recent trends in U.S. divorce patterns; the process of divorce; the aftermath of divorce; divorce in other cultures; and divorce law reform. Other topics covered include: the incidence of post-marital coitus among widows and divorcees; the structural anomalies in the American family system which create problems in post-marital social arrangements; the presence of networks among divorced and remarried individuals which resemble pseudo-kinship structures; and examples of divorce in Swedish, Eskimo, and Kanauri cultures.

A-F 83. BURROWS, EDWIN G. Hawaiian Americans: An Account of the Mingling of Japanese, Chinese, Polynesian, and American Cultures. New Haven, Conn.: Yale University Press, 1947. 228 pp.
This book was written shortly after W.W. II when the stresses undergone during the war by Japanese-Americans and other Asian-American groups became a matter of social concern. Burrows describes how the acculturation of these Pacific groups was related to the growth of the prestige of American culture and how the Hawaiian-Americans reacted to that growth through aggression, withdrawal, and cooperation.

A-F 84. CASSELL, JOAN. A Group Called Women: Sisterhood and Symbolism in the Feminist Movement. New York: McKay, 1977. 240 pp.
This book is organized into two parts. The first part is an informal social-psychological analysis of the recruitment of women into the women's movement. This section includes a discussion of the symbolic interaction whereby a woman's image of herself changes as she comes to perceive herself as a member of a group called women. The second part is a structural examination of the women's movement as a social movement unified by a dominant symbolic form: the opposition between "the woman's way" and "the way men do things." Central to this opposition is the idea of leadership. Since formal leadership is seen as an aspect of the men's way, its presence leads to a conflict between what Cassell calls radical egalitarianism—which perceives differences in ability to be hierarchical—and individual self-realization.

A-F 85. CASTILE, GEORGE PIERRE and GILBERT KUSHNER, eds. Persistent Peoples: Cultural Enclaves in Perspective. Tucson: University of Arizona Press, 1981. 274 pp.

These essays deal with ethnic minorities in America, including blacks, Mormons, Amish, Hutterites, and Shakers. The authors' position is that the locus of group identity is a set of shared symbols, which may change over time along with behavior without altering the members' sense of belonging. Also emphasized is the idea that although groups can be internally heterogeneous ethnicity will persist if social mechanisms, either generated from within or externally imposed, create a situation of enclavement, a form of "enslavement," or some intermingling of the two.

A-F 86. CAUDILL, WILLIAM. The Psychiatric Hospital as a Small Society. Cambridge, Mass.: Harvard University Press, 1958. 406 pp.

This is a social anthropological study of a psychiatric hospital. Caudill combines three closely related studies which are based on different data collection techniques. The first study was based on daily observations of interaction at all levels of activity in the hospital. The second used photographs of hospital activities as eliciting devices in discussions with staff and patients. The final study focused on the interaction among staff in daily administrative conferences. Combining the results of these studies, Caudill concludes that the hospital can be described as a small society in which particular patterns of interaction, largely determined by historical circumstances and administrative policy, strongly affect the achievement of the stated goals of the hospital.

A-F 87. CAVAN, SHERRI. Hippies of the Haight. St. Louis, Mo.: New Critics Press, 1972. 205 pp.

Cavan uses data collected during nine years of residence in the Haight-Ashbury district of San Francisco to address the problem of the relationship between belief and practice. The ideological beliefs held by members of this society are examined in their relation to practical affairs. She describes the development in the 1960s of the Haight-Ashbury hippie neighborhood and the hippie ideology. The author describes the hippies' way of life in terms of their categories for behavior, and focuses on their sanctioned options for behavior. In applying the data to her central problem, Cavan is most interested in the "disjunction between the members' ideological interpretation of what 'life should be' and the actual events they encounter."

A-F 88. CAVAN, SHERRI. Liquor License: An Ethnography of Bar Behavior. Chicago: Aldine, 1966. 246 pp.

Using participant-observation methods, Cavan describes the manner in which behavior is structured in a "bar" from the point of view of the patron. She discusses types of bars and characteristic features of behavior in each type. The description concentrates on seating and spatial distribution, internal movement, and face-to-face interaction. The influence of Erving Goffman's work is acknowledged by the author and reflected in the analysis.

A-F 89. CLARK, MARGARET and BARBARA GALLATIN ANDERSON. Culture and Aging: An Anthropological Study of Older Americans. Springfield, Ill.: Thomas, 1967. 478 pp.

This is an applied anthropological study of the social position of the aged in American society. The study is based on a survey of 435 elderly people in San Francisco, randomly selected from a larger sample, in which such factors as socioeconomic status, place of birth, and whether or not the individual was institutionalized were considered. The authors examine the participation of the elderly in the larger society. The major finding is that American cultural values grant self-esteem to those who are independent, but that in old age physical survival requires assistance. The authors recommend that an attempt be made to change the attitudes of Americans so that people are prepared for the dependency of old age.

A-F 90. COHEN, DAVID STEVEN. The Ramapo Mountain People. New Brunswick, N.J.: Rutgers University Press, 1974. 285 pp.
This is an account of the history, culture, and folklore of a group of descendants of Dutch and black pioneers in three communities in the Ramapo Mountains along the New York-New Jersey border. These people have remained culturally and socially distinct since the 17th century. Cohen traces the history of their settlements and documents the migration of the principal families of the group. He shows that the generally accepted history of the Ramapo mountain people--that they are descendants of Hessian deserters from the Revolutionary War and West Indian prostitutes--is wrong, and that these communities were established by black pioneers in the early 19th century. The author provides sketches of the history and character of the three current communities and describes cultural factors such as kinship, racial identity, and religion. He also offers examples of the folklore currently shared by the Ramapo mountain people.

A-F 91. DANER, FRANCINE JEANNE. The American Children of Krsna: A Study of the Hare Krsna Movement. New York: Holt, Rinehart & Winston, 1976. 117 pp.
This ethnography concentrates on those features of the International Society of Krsna (Krishna) Consciousness which make it appealing to American youth. Daner describes the Hare Krsna movement as a revitalization movement. The author's premise is that the structural and ideological models presented to youth by mainstream American culture produce confusion about identity. She contends that young people immerse themselves in the all-encompassing institution of the International Society for Krsna Consciousness temples in order to alleviate their identity confusion and personal alienation. She also gives a short description of the history, ideology, and ritual practices of the Hare Krsna movement. The core of the book is a series of life histories of devotees, showing how they all had been struggling to "find out who they were."

A-F 92. DOBYNS, HENRY F. Spanish Colonial Tucson: A Demographic History. Tucson: University of Arizona Press, 1976. 256 pp.
Dobyns's work is a history of Spanish Colonial activities in Tucson and their effects on the population of the surrounding Piman Indians. He structures his work around the two major sources of documentation for the period: the records of the Roman Catholic Mission and those of the military. He traces the expansion and development of Tucson from a tiny Indian settlement to a substantial town at the time of Mexican Independence in 1821. The author shows that the American Indian population in Tucson was maintained by the immigration of people from the countryside, leading to general depopulation of the surrounding area.

A-F 93. DOUGLASS, WILLIAM A. and JON BILBAO. Amerikanuak: Basques in the New World. Reno: University of Nevada Press, 1975. 519 pp.
Douglass and Bilbao trace the history of Basques in North and South America over a period of nearly 500 years. The first part of the book deals with the early history of the Basques in Europe and their role in the Spanish colonization of the New World. Later sections are devoted to the development of the role of Basques as shepherds in both South and North America. Most of the book discusses the historical and cultural position of Basques in the Western U.S. as sheepmen and as a distinct ethnic group. Throughout the book attention is given to the means by which Basques have maintained a distinct ethnic identity.

A-F 94. GALLAHER, ART, Jr. Plainville Fifteen Years Later. New York:
         Columbia University Press, 1961. 301 pp.
Gallaher's reappraisal of "Plainville" (see A-F 161) is a complete community study in itself. He both documents the changes which have taken
place since Carl Withers's original study and provides a portrait of a
Midwestern community in the mid-1950s. The author describes the community
setting, economy, social organization, religion, and status rank system.
He notes three major changes from Withers's findings. Rather than being
isolated and resistant to change, the community has welcomed increased
communication with the outside world. The rigid class system described
by Withers has been supplanted by a social continuum along which individuals move according to achievement. Finally, farmers have become much
more capitalistic in their view toward land.

A-F 95. GALLIMORE, RONALD, JOHN WHITEHORN BOGGS, and CATHIE JORDAN. Cul-
         ture, Behavior, and Education: A Study of Hawaiian-Americans.
         Beverly Hills, Calif.: Sage, 1974. 287 pp.
This study combines psychiatric and ethnographic procedures to produce
a cultural account of Hawaiian-American family structure as well as an
"interface" study of the behavior of minority students in classrooms.
In a five-year study in a small community in Oahu, Hawaii, observations
of natural situations were combined with structured interviews, surveys,
and experimental classroom situations. The results are an ethnographic
description of the Hawaiian-American socialization system in the first part
of the book and a report of the interface analysis in the second part.
The authors conclude that the Hawaiian-American children are behaving
in culturally consistent and coherent ways which are inappropriate in
an American classroom context. They argue that the conflicts which lead
to the categorization of the Hawaiian-American children as retarded or
deviant stem from a lack of understanding of the cultural context of their
behavior.

A-F 96. GOFFMAN, ERVING. Asylums: Essays on the Social Situation of
         Mental Patients and Other Inmates. Garden City, N.Y.: Anchor
         Press, 1961. 386 pp.
In the first essay of this collection, Goffman defines "total institutions"
as those settings, such as mental institutions, prisons, army camps, old
age homes, and monasteries, that are all-encompassing for an individual
and that erect barriers to social intercourse with the outside. The subsequent papers explore themes introduced in the first essay. "The Moral
Career of a Mental Patient" and "The Underlife of a Public Institution"
consider the effects of life in a mental hospital on a patient, detailing
the changes demanded of a patient and the means by which patients respond
to those demands. The final paper concentrates on the ways medical practitioners interact with mental patients.

A-F 97. GOLDSCHMIDT, WALTER. As You Sow: Three Studies in the Social
         Consequences of Agribusiness. New York: Harcourt, Brace, 1947.
         288 pp.
Three farming communities in California's Central Valley, selected to
be representative of industrial agriculture, were studied between 1940
and 1944. Industrial agriculture is characterized by intensive cultivation,
high per-acre and per-farm capital investment, high specialization in
single crops on individual farms, highly mechanized operations, and large
requirements of wage labor hired on an impersonal basis. Goldschmidt
argues that industrialization leads to urbanization of rural culture with
urban social arrangements and value systems entering the rural communities.
He makes a number of recommendations about how this process can be
managed--primarily, through the unionization of farm laborers.

A-F 98. GROPPER, RENA C. Gypsies in the City: Culture Patterns and
          Survival. Princeton, N.J.: Darwin Press, 1975. 235 pp.
Gropper describes Gypsy culture in a general, non-localized way. The
book proceeds according to a standard ethnographic format, discussing
the history, economy, religion, politics, life-cycle, and (briefly) social
boundary maintenance of the Gypsies. Throughout her observations Gropper
pays particular attention to the Gypsies' ability to maintain their cultural identity despite 500 years of often intense pressure to assimilate
to the societies within which they have lived. This interest in the processes of culture change is central to the final chapter: "Choice Taking:
A New Theory."

A-F 99. GUBRIUM, JABER F. Living and Dying at Murray Manor. New York:
          St. Martin's Press, 1975. 221 pp.
In this work, based on a period of fieldwork, Gubrium shows how the people
who live and work in a nursing home come to define it as a place composed
of many smaller places. After describing the setting, he discusses the
ways in which people in the three principal social categories of the home--
clients, floor staff, and administrative staff--organize their behavior
and structure their perceptions in carrying out their roles. The author
shows how the differences in behavior and perceptions among these three
social categories lead to conflicts, how these conflicts arise, how they
may be resolved or circumvented, and how they may not be perceived at
all.

A-F 100. HALL, ROBERT L. and CAROL B. STACK, eds. Holding on to the Land
           and the Lord: Kinship, Ritual, and Tenure and Social Policy
           in the Rural South. Athens: University of Georgia Press, 1982.
           164 pp.
Despite the traditional values of cooperation which act as a protective
buffer, rural Southern communities cannot, according to the editors, remain
isolated and unaffected by the world of industrial competition. These
essays illustrate this theme through eleven community studies focusing
on three areas: religion, the articulation of kinship and local politics, and the struggle between traditional land tenure rights and U.S.
social policy. The studies are set in Mississippi, Alabama, Kentucky,
South Carolina, North Carolina, and Florida.

A-F 101. HAYANO, DAVID M. Poker Faces: The Life and Work of Professional
           Card Players. Berkeley: University of California Press, 1982.
           205 pp.
As a poker-player first, then an anthropologist, Hayano has written a
work that takes the form of an "auto-ethnography." The cardroom in Gardens,
California is his field of study. Though he examines it more descriptively
and anecdotally than through any systematic analytic method, much of his
information is that of the privileged insider, and by sifting it with
sociopsychological theory he transmits the poker-player's sense of a separate society and "other world" mentality.

A-F 102. HEILMAN, SAMUEL C. Synagogue Life: A Study of Symbolic Inter-
           action. Chicago: University of Chicago Press, 1973. 306 pp.
Synagogue Life combines ethnography with Erving Goffman's dramaturgical
perspective in a study of an American Orthodox Jewish congregation.
Heilman argues that the central position of the synagogue (or shul) in
the community is maintained through mutual obligations which serve to
strengthen social bonds, as well as through the dilemma of traditionalism
versus modernity facing these Orthodox Jews. He regards the movements
toward modernity by the members as a means of maintaining social bonds
within the congregation, as these members find themselves stigmatized
simultaneously by two groups: the mainstream of the contemporary world,
which does not accept Orthodoxy, and the traditional Orthodox community,
which does not accept modernity.

A-F 103. **HEIZER, ROBERT F.** and **ALAN F. ALMQUIST.** The Other Californians: Prejudice and Discrimination Under Spain, Mexico, and the United States to 1920. Berkeley: University of California Press, 1971. 278 pp.

Heizer and Almquist describe the prejudicial attitudes and discriminatory acts of Anglos toward the major non-European ethnic groups in California-- Indians, Mexicans, Chinese, Japanese, and blacks--in the period from 1770 to 1920. The attitudes and acts are documented by quotations from original documents and the inclusion of longer documents in an appendix.

A-F 104. **HICKS, GEORGE L.** Appalachian Valley. New York: Holt, Rinehart & Winston, 1976. 112 pp.

Hicks describes a rural Appalachian culture with particular attention to its distinctiveness and the changes which have taken place in the area since W.W. II. He outlines the history of the settlement of the valley and discusses the institutions and cultural orientations which characterize this community. Kinship, sex roles, the value of land, the structure of the community, the importance of stores as hubs of communication, and relations with outsiders are all discussed. The major changes that have taken place as a result of increased contact with outside society through increased mobility and widened communication are explored throughout the book.

A-F 105. **HORWITZ, RICHARD P.** Anthropology Toward History: Culture and Work in a 19th Century Maine Town. Middletown, Conn.: Wesleyan University Press, 1978. 197 pp.

The theoretical and methodological approach of ethnoscience is applied to historical data from a small, rural Maine town in the early 19th century in an attempt to produce a psychologically valid categorization of occupational and social types in the community. Horwitz's analysis consists of producing taxonomies of occupations such as "farmer," "farm hand," and "mechanic," and discussing the resulting definitions. Besides the community values highlighted by his study, Horwitz explores the diachronic dimension suggested by his data: the changing values and standards for "perceiving, believing, evaluating and acting" in the industrializing Northeast of 1820-1850.

A-F 106. **HOSTETLER, JOHN A.** Amish Society. 1963; Rev. ed. Baltimore, Md.: Johns Hopkins University Press, 1980. 414 pp.

This is an ethnography of the Amish, a major agrarian religious group who trace their roots to the Anabaptist movement in Europe in the 17th century. Established longest in an area of Southeastern Pennsylvania, they have adhered to a fundamentalist interpretation of Christianity which sets them apart from the surrounding American society, and has led them to resist technological changes in farming and stylistic changes in dress. Hostetler's concern is with the ways the Amish have maintained their way of life in the context of modern American society. He uses Redfield's (A-F 22) model of the "little community" to explain the status of Amish society. He also describes the conflicts, the resolution of conflicts, and the technological and symbolic accommodations made with the larger society.

A-F 107. **HOSTETLER, JOHN A.** Hutterite Society. Baltimore, Md.: Johns Hopkins University Press, 1974. 403 pp.

Concentrating on three colonies, one in Montana and two in Canada, Hostetler describes, historically and ethnographically, the development and structure of the oldest and most viable North American communal society. His presentation of Hutterite history and migrations focuses on the ways that modern Hutterites have incorporated the past into the present. The ethnography is descriptive and sympathetic, with some discussion of psychological testing and mental illness, but limited consideration of causes

36

or cultural factors. The book incorporates and updates work presented in an earlier publication, The Hutterites in North America (A-F 108).

A-F 108.   HOSTETLER, JOHN A. and GERTRUDE ENDERS HUNTINGTON. The Hutterites in North America. New York: Holt, Rinehart & Winston, 1967. 119 pp.

This ethnography of a communal religious group living in the Great Plains of the U.S. and Canada describes the way in which the Hutterites have been able to continue successfully in the face of pressures to assimilate. The book is meant to be descriptive of the patterns of organization of the communal colonies and is organized by category: world view, social patterns, economic patterns, life cycle, and outside pressures. Sociali- zation is the major theme of the book, and each section considers practices, institutions, and behaviors as ways of preparing individuals to become members of the communal society and reinforcing the organization of the society.

A-F 109.   HOWARD, ALAN. Ain't No Big Thing: Coping Strategies in a Hawaiian-American Community. Honolulu: University of Hawaii Press, 1974. 311 pp.

Howard combines ethnography with social-psychological testing to charac- terize cultural norms and their variations in a modern Hawaiian-American homestead community. Beginning with a study of socialization patterns, he constructs a social learning model which is used to explain modal behav- ior patterns. Variations in the modal behaviors are called "coping strate- gies" and "tactics," which he describes as having to do with interpersonal confrontation, risk-taking, withstanding illness, and child-rearing. In the final part of the book the Hawaiian and Anglo-American cultural concepts are compared and the future of Hawaiian-American ethnicity is discussed in terms of strategy options.

A-F 110.   HOWELL, JOSEPH T. Hard Living on Clay Street: Portraits of Blue Collar Families. Garden City, N.Y.: Anchor Press, 1973. 381 pp.

This book is a description of the life of urban working-class families who, as Howell says, "live hard." The account takes the form of a narra- tive of the day-to-day life of the families with whom the author worked as a participant-observer. Howell presents two families in detail and uses a number of others as examples of the distinctive aspects of hard living: heavy drinking, marital instability, emotional toughness, politi- cal alienation, rootlessness, present-time orientation, and a strong sense of individualism. The work combines decriptions with interpretation.

A-F 111.   HRABA, JOSEPH. American Ethnicity. Itasca, Ill.: Peacock, 1979. 386 pp.

Hraba analyzes three schools of thought on the subject of American ethnicity—assimilationism, ethnic pluralism, and ethnic conflict theory— at the same time as he discusses racism at the psychological level. He proposes a synthesis of these approaches and focuses on several ethnic groups: American Indians, Mexican Americans, black Americans, and Asian Americans. He suggests there are two possible paths for ethnic groups— perpetuation or disintegration—depending on the dominant society's pres- sures and the ethnic group's choice of political and economic adaptive strategies.

A-F 112.   IANNI, FRANCIS A. J. with ELIZABETH REUSS-IANNI. A Family Busi- ness: Kinship and Social Control in Organized Crime. New York: Russell Sage, 1972. 199 pp.

This book examines the social structure and culture-historical basis of an Italian-American organized crime family. Using data collected through participant-observation fieldwork, the Iannis provide a description of

37

the social system and rules of conduct of the "Lupollo" family. They also investigate the historical roots of criminal organizations in Southern Italy, and the way that these organizations were transplanted to the U.S. The authors dispute the claim that there is a nationwide conspiracy of Italian-American crime families. They argue that each of the families operates independently, with a common understanding of rules of conduct.

A-F 113. KIEFER, CHRISTIE W. Changing Cultures, Changing Lives: An Ethnographic Study of Three Generations of Japanese Americans. San Francisco: Jossey-Bass, 1974. 260 pp.
This is a treatment of the process of culture change in the Japanese-American community in San Francisco. There are three organizing themes to the book: personality development, acculturation, and history. Kiefer used participant-observation, formal interviews, and the administration of psychological diagnostic tests to gather her data, and stresses the role of the individual in the process of culture change. The book is both an ethnography and a theoretical statement.

A-F 114. KIMBALL, SOLON T. and MARION PEARSALL. The Talladega Story: A Study in Community Process. University: University of Alabama Press, 1954. 259 pp.
Kimball and Pearsall describe the process of community action in an analysis of a community-initiated study in the city of Talladega, Alabama, in 1951-1952. The social scientists did not participate in the study of the town; rather, they studied the course of the project in order to understand the structures and values of the community. The report contains general statements about American communities and about Talladega itself. Particular aspects of the self-study, such as an attempt to have fluoride introduced into the city's water system, are discussed in detail to show how community action was organized.

A-F 115. KUTSCHE, PAUL and JOHN R. VAN NESS. Canones: Values, Crisis, and Survival in a Northern New Mexico Village. Albuquerque: University of New Mexico Press, 1981. 244 pp.
Using culture and personality theory and cultural ecology in this study of a small, isolated Hispanic village, Kutsche and Van Ness reconstruct its history and discuss its present state (much of it persistently Spanish-Mexican in form). The authors assess the viability and efficacy of cultural values in facing change through their analysis of a 1966 community rebellion against the U.S. government's attempt to close down the community's one-room schoolhouse and bus the children six miles away.

A-F 116. LA BARRE, WESTON. They Shall Take Up Serpents: Psychology of the Southern Snake-Handling Cult. Minneapolis: University of Minnesota Press, 1962. 208 pp.
La Barre offers a psychological description of an aberrant Protestant sect in the South whose most striking feature is the proclamation of faith through the handling of poisonous snakes. He describes the history of the cult in the American South and a typical religious service. He then reviews the literature on snake symbolism cross-culturally, drawing examples from Africa, North America, and the Ancient Near East. La Barre's evidence shows that snakes can be interpreted as phallic symbols in most cultures in which they have a high symbolic value. A detailed psychological analysis of a leader of the cult in Florida attempts to explain why this psychopathic behavior provides emotional satisfaction to him and to the cult members. The author portrays the snake cult as an outlet for the sexual repression of the leader and the members as well as a means of fulfilling emotional needs for people whose social position offers limited opportunities for entertainment, psychological release, and personal satisfaction.

A-F 117. LAWRENCE, ELIZABETH ATWOOD. Rodeo: An Anthropologist Looks
at the Wild and the Tame. Chicago: University of Chicago Press,
1982. 288 pp.
This interpretive study takes rodeo as its ritual text, a symbolic con-
veyance and perpetuator of the ethos of the cowboy. As the working ranch
embodied the frontier drive to conquer the wilderness, the rodeo represents
the ongoing effort to dominate nature. Relationships between man and
man, between man and animal (especially horses), and between man and land
are "dramatically delineated, categorized, and manipulated" in the rodeo
ring. Lawrence examines rodeo as both cultural display and social contest.

A-F 118. LEWIS, HYLAN. Blackways of Kent. Chapel Hill: University of
North Carolina Press, 1955. 337 pp.
Lewis describes the culture of the black community of a moderate-sized
Southern Piedmont town. Participant-observation fieldwork was conducted
between 1947 and 1949 as part of a general study of the town of "Kent"
(see the companion volumes; A-F 125 and A-F 136). In presenting his material, Lewis relies on extended quotation from his field notes. He breaks
down his material into such major cultural categories as material culture
complexes, family, economics, religion, socialization, relations with
the government, social organization, and orientations and values. The
black society of Kent is found to share the general values and goals of
American culture in general, with transformation and differential emphasis
of some of these resulting from an adaptive response to the realities
of the local situation.

A-F 119. LUEBKE, FREDERICK C. Ethnicity on the Great Plains. Lincoln:
University of Nebraska Press, 1980. 237 pp.
This interdisciplinary treatment of the influx, impact, and adaptations
of ethnic groups from Texas to Saskatchewan includes essays on: the Westward movement of Eastern Indians; Plains Indians' Treaty Councils; Volga
Germans from the Russian steppes; Swedish migration to the Dakota frontier;
an Amish community; religion among Texas Germans; Hungarian folk religion
in Saskatchewan; Czech-Americans; agricultural change in Nebraska; Czech
farmers and Mexican laborers in Texas. Taken as a whole, the book delineates ethnic differences in assimilation, cultural and religious affairs,
economic activities, political affairs, demography, and linguistic change.

A-F 120. LUNDSGAARDE, HENRY P. Murder in Space City: A Cultural Analysis
of Houston Homicide Patterns. New York: Oxford University
Press, 1977. 269 pp.
Lundsgaarde analyzes murder as a cultural phenomenon by investigating
the attitudes that are associated with the high murder rate of Houston,
Texas. He shows how killing is classified culturally by examining the
relationships between killers and victims, circumstances of killings,
police investigation procedures, and court procedures for dealing with
killers. The author finds that tacit cultural rules and values influence
how a killer is categorized by the social and legal system. Thus, a killer
who is a friend or relative of the victim is less likely to be punished
than one who is a stranger to the victim. Lundsgaarde uses a quantitative
analysis of the police records of 200 killings that took place in Houston
in 1969 to illustrate his argument.

A-F 121. MacCANNELL, DEAN. The Tourist: A New Theory of the Leisure
Class. New York: Schocken Books, 1976. 214 pp.
MacCannell applies a semiotic approach to the phenomenon of sightseeing
in modern society. He offers a sociological study of tourists, and he
attempts to illuminate the interaction between tourists and modern civilization. His examples are international but concentrate primarily on U.S.
tourism. The author argues that tourist attractions develop from the
interaction of tourists, sights, and markers. Markers are the social

and cultural conventions by which significance is attached to sights, and by which sights are differentiated from less famous or less authentic places.

A-F 122. MATTHEWS, ELMORA MESSER. Neighbor and Kin: Life in a Tennessee Ridge Community. Nashville, Tenn.: Vanderbilt University Press, 1966. 178 pp.
Matthews is concerned with the kin-based organization and patterns of social stratification in a rural farming community in the hills of Tennessee. She applies anthropological and sociological concepts of community to the area, which consists of two named localities inhabited by a total of sixty families who have been intermarrying since 1786. Her concentration is on what she describes as the "so-so" way of life—a community orientation in which an effort is made to distribute equally the resources available to the community rather than concentrating on the individual acquisition of resources. The author shows how this egalitarian ethos is achieved and how it can break down, producing high levels of violence in the community.

A-F 123. MINER, HORACE. Culture and Agriculture: An Anthropological Study of a Corn Belt County. Ann Arbor: University of Michigan Press, 1949. 96 pp.
This general ethnographic study of an Iowa county was conducted in 1939 for the U.S. Department of Agriculture to assess the successes and failures of New Deal farm policy. Topics examined are settlement history, types of farming, farm life, and cultural reactions to social action. The study was conducted at a time when farm life was changing through increased mechanization (50.7% of the farmers had tractors), electrification (47% had electricity in their homes), and communication (85% had radios).

A-F 124. MITCHELL, WILLIAM E. Mispokhe: A Study of New York City Jewish Family Clubs. The Hague: Mouton, 1978. 262 pp.
Mitchell describes a type of social group, the family club, which has arisen among Eastern European Jewish immigrants and their descendants. In these kin-based family clubs, descendants of one of the founders can claim membership. The author explains the origin of family clubs as a conscious effort to counteract the disruptive effects of immigration, industrialization, and urbanization on the extended family structure of the immigrants. Family clubs are discussed in terms of contemporary anthropological kinship theory as an example of the forms that traditional kinship structures can take in a modern industrialized and urbanized society.

A-F 125. MORLAND, JOHN KENNETH. Millways of Kent. Chapel Hill: University of North Carolina Press, 1958. 291 pp.
Written as part of a collaborative effort (see A-F 118 and A-F 136) to study the Piedmont community of "Kent," Morland's book gives an ethnographic description of the mill workers in the town. Strictly descriptive, this account follows a standard ethnographic pattern of presenting setting, economic life, family life, socialization, religion, recreation, social structure, and personality. The work gives a description of the mill workers' lives, and shows how the group is segregated from the other two major subcultures of the community—the townspeople and the blacks—and how all three groups maintain these cultural boundaries.

A-F 126. NASH, DENNISON. A Community in Limbo: An Anthropological Study of an American Community Abroad. Bloomington: Indiana University Press, 1970. 230 pp.
Nash studies the problems of adaptation of an American community in Spain, made up primarily of businessmen and their families and distributed through a section of one city. The community does not have the support of a large system of American institutions such as would be found on an American

military base. The author attempts to show how these Americans face the anxiety and anomie of being strangers in another society.

A-F 127. **NEWTON, ESTHER.** Mother Camp: Female Impersonators in America. Englewood Cliffs, N.J.: Prentice-Hall, 1972. 136 pp.
Female impersonators who perform on stage before both homosexual and non-homosexual audiences, and who have long been the most visible of homo-sexuals, are the subject of this book. Newton describes types of female impersonators, types of performers, role models, and homosexual bars, and delineates the life of these men in terms of their cultural values and categories. The study shows how homosexuals have been stigmatized in the U.S.

A-F 128. **ORBACH, MICHAEL K.** Hunters, Seamen, and Entrepreneurs: The Tuna Seinermen of San Diego. Berkeley: University of California Press, 1978. 304 pp.
Orbach spent two years living in a fishing community on land and five months at sea working as a crew member on two different boats to collect the data for this study. His ethnography examines the life of the fisher-men at sea and in port, although most of the attention is devoted to the former. The aspects on which the author concentrates are the boats, the seining process, decision-making at sea, communication and information management in the seining process, conflicts and conflict management, recruitment of crews, alliance among crews, the economics of the industry, implications of international law, and the social structure and organi-zation among fishermen at sea.

A-F 129. **PARTRIDGE, WILLIAM L.** The Hippie Ghetto: The Natural History of a Subculture. New York: Holt, Rinehart & Winston, 1973. 88 pp.
Partridge describes his work as a participant-observer in a small hippie ghetto in a university town in Florida. He argues that the styles of life which are labeled as "hippie" are too diverse to permit a single characterization of the hippie way of life, but also takes the position that "counter-culture" is not the best description of the hippie life-style, since so much of the hippie orientation rests on the basic tenets of American culture. The author believes that the hippie movement resem-bles a revitalization movement, and he also applies Van Gennup and Turner's approach to rites of passage to portray hippie ghetto life as a rite of passage into a subculture.

A-F 130. **PEARSALL, MARION.** Little Smokey Ridge: The Natural History of a Southern Appalachian Neighborhood. University: University of Alabama Press, 1959. 205 pp.
Pearsall describes the setting, the history of settlement, the economy, the contacts outside the local area, the social and supernatural value systems, and the experiences with the outside world of an isolated mountain neighborhood. He presents the ridge people's values in their own terms, and shows how these values are in conflict with those of the mainstream culture, especially in terms of time schedules and individualism. As a result, he sees the "frontier" orientations of the Little Smokey Ridge inhabitants as anachronistic and poorly adapted to the present conditions in which they are living.

A-F 131. **PILCHER, WILLIAM W.** The Portland Longshoremen: A Dispersed Urban Community. New York: Holt, Rinehart & Winston, 1972. 128 pp.
This ethnography of a specialized occupation deals with the community of longshoremen in Portland, Oregon. The author, before being trained as an anthropologist, worked for ten years as a longshoreman in Portland and is therefore able to present an intimate picture of the community.

The first part of the book deals with the history of the longshoremen's union and with the specialized knowledge required to do the job. The second part of the book describes the longshoremen in terms of the larger community, showing that while there is not a residential community of longshoremen, they share a common identity which Pilcher uses to define a community.

A-F 132. POWDERMAKER, HORTENSE. Hollywood, the Dream Factory: An Anthropologist Looks at the Movie-Makers. Boston: Little, Brown, 1951. 342 pp.
The purpose of Powdermaker's study is to explain how the social system underlying the motion picture industry influences the movies. She examines occupational categories in the movie industry; producers, writers, directors, and actors were interviewed and the part that each plays in the making of movies is explained. She is especially concerned with the psychological profiles of individuals in each of the categories and stresses the underlying values and attitudes on which movies are based.

A-F 133. REYNOLDS, DAVID K. and NORMAN L. FARBERO. Suicide: Inside and Out. Berkeley: University of California Press, 1976. 226 pp.
The purpose of the research reported here was to improve the understanding of the mental ward as experienced by the patient. Using the technique of "experiential research," Reynolds posed as a severely depressed suicidal patient in a psychiatric ward. The major part of the book is Reynolds's account of his experience in the ward, including his reflections on the ethical implications of posing as a patient. Further information comes from a study of the structure of professional care at another hospital. The authors conclude that for suicide deterrence, a "humanized" atmosphere that builds self-esteem is most helpful.

A-F 134. RUBEL, PAULA G. The Kalmyk Mongols: A Study of Continuity and Change. Bloomington: Indiana University Press, 1967. 282 pp.
Using structured and unstructured interviews and participant-observation fieldwork, Rubel describes the process of acculturation in a Kalmyk Mongol immigrant community in New Jersey. Emphasizing the way in which the traditional social and cultural systems of the Kalmyks have been maintained, the author gives special attention to the social organization of the Kalmyks rather than to their language and their Lamaist Buddhist religion. She includes a description of the history and the migrations of the Kalmyks, documenting their demography and social organization at the time of her study. The most extended analysis is devoted to the major expressions of Kalmyk identity—the annual ceremony of Tsagan Sar and marriage—where patterns of acculturation may be seen most clearly. In her conclusion, Rubel describes some of the factors which promote or inhibit change in the Kalmyk Mongol community.

A-A 135. RUBIN, ISRAEL. Setmar: An Island in the City. Chicago: Times Books, 1972. 272 pp.
This is a study of an "ultra-Orthodox" and militantly anti-Zionist Hassidic Jewish community in Brooklyn, New York. Rubin shows how the people of this community have maintained their distinctiveness through an analysis of their major social institutions—religion, kinship, education, and economics—and discusses these institutions in terms of their contribution to the autonomy of the community from the surrounding city.

A-F 136. RUBIN, MORTON. Plantation County. Chapel Hill: University of North Carolina Press, 1951. 235 pp.
Rubin uses a community study approach to describe the culture of a county in the Southern U.S. Participant-observation fieldwork was conducted in 1947-1948 as part of a large-scale study of the culture of the South (see A-F 118 and A-F 125 for other publications from this study). The

42

economic system of the county—plantations, small independent farms, and factories—is described in some detail; special attention is directed to the operation of the plantations with tenant farmers and laborers; and the social structure of the area is described in terms of racial castes and social classes. Chapters are devoted to belief systems and to the life cycle. The general orientation of the plantation culture is described in terms of three major themes: mastery of the land, conformity with the word of God, and "ideal" stratification of mankind.

A-F 137. **SALISBURY, RICHARD R.** Structures of Custodial Care: An Anthropological Study of a State Mental Hospital. Berkeley: University of California Press, 1962. 138 pp.
Salisbury offers an ethnographic account of two wards in a state mental hospital for long-term mental patients, concentrating on the socially defined positions of doctor, attendant, and patient. After describing the system of relationships, the author shows how the system is maintained and argues that this social system impedes the patients' progress out of the wards.

A-F 138. **SCHWARTZ, GARY.** Youth Culture: An Anthropological Approach. Reading, Mass.: Addison-Wesley, 1972. 47 pp.
Schwartz provides an anthropological assessment of the youth and counter-culture movements of the 1960s and 1970s. He argues that the ambiguous position of adolescents in cosmopolitan industrial cultures, where there is not a sharp distinction between adult and non-adult, has led to the development of the youth subculture with its own symbolic system of meanings. The author supports his argument with an extensive review of the literature on youth rather than with fieldwork.

A-F 139. **SEELEY, JOHN R., R. ALEXANDER SIM,** and **ELIZABETH W. LOOSLEY.** Crestwood Heights: A Study of the Culture of Suburban Life. Toronto: University of Toronto Press, 1956. 505 pp.
Crestwood Heights is the product of a five-year study made in the early 1950s. Although the actual setting of this book is a suburb of Toronto, Canada, the authors argue that with some allowances for Canadian and British influences the study is representative of U.S. suburban life and values. Although it provides an ethnographic description, the primary orientation of the study is toward education and mental health, and much of the work was carried out in schools. The researchers adopted what they describe as an activist and therapeutic approach to their work: they describe contradictions that they found in the culture of Crestwood Heights, and suggest possible implications of their research for the resolution of these contradictions.

A-F 140. **SMITH, VALENE L.,** ed. Hosts and Guests: The Anthropology of Tourism. Philadelphia: University of Pennsylvania Press, 1977. 254 pp.
The articles in this collection discuss, from various perspectives and in various contexts, some of the anthropological questions which arise from the growth of tourism. The principal question has to do with the effect of tourists and tourism on local communities and cultures. Tourists from a number of industrialized nations are considered, but many of the generalizations apply to Americans. A general typology of tourism is proposed and used throughout the book. The typology distinguishes the goals, numbers, and impacts of tourists, who range from explorers, whose impact is typically small, to charter tourists, whose requirements usually have a major impact on the local culture. In most of these studies the local culture is the unit of analysis, and the tourists become a generalized category seen from the point of view of the local people.

A-F 141. SPRADLEY, JAMES P. You Owe Yourself a Drunk: An Ethnography
          of Urban Nomads. Boston: Little, Brown, 1970. 301 pp.
Urban nomads, more commonly known as "bums," are the subject of this study.
Spradley employs the technique of componential analysis—in which the
relationships between a set of words are made explicit through the use
of taxonomies and paradigms—to portray the life of the Seattle nomads.
He describes in detail their life in jail, the ways bums make their money,
and the relations of the urban nomads to each other and to those in the
"straight" world.

A-F 142. SPRADLEY, JAMES P. and BRENDA J. MANN. The Cocktail Waitress:
          Woman's Work in a Man's World. New York: Wiley, 1975.
          154 pp.
This ethnographic description of a particular social position has several
objectives. In addition to describing the cultural context of the cocktail
waitresses in a single Midwestern bar, Spradley and Mann argue the fruitfulness of anthropological fieldwork for the study of mainstream U.S.
culture, and give their ethnography a female rather than a male emphasis.
The authors present an account of the things that a cocktail waitress
needs to know to perform adequately in this social position. Their analysis consists primarily of a taxonomic semantic analysis of terms used
to describe patrons or types of activities.

A-F 143. SROLE, LEO, THOMAS S. LANGNER, STANLEY T. MICHAEL, PRICE
          KIRKPATRICK, MARVIN K. OPLER, AND THOMAS A. C. RENNIE. Mental
          Health in the Metropolis: The Midtown Manhattan Study. 1962;
          Rev. ed. New York: New York University Press, 1978. 553 pp.
This interdisciplinary study, carried out in the 1950s, was an attempt
to combine psychiatric and sociological variables in the study of a large
(170,000 people) neighborhood in the New York borough of Manhattan. Mental
health was correlated with sociological and demographic variables such
as socioeconomic class, age, length of time in the U.S., and religious
background. The adult population of the neighborhood was surveyed and
psychiatric evaluations were based on the results of the survey. The
revised edition of the book contains five new chapters and two new appendices in which Srole reflects on the impact of the project and responds
to criticism of the study.

A-F 144. SUDNOW, DAVID. Passing On: The Social Organization of Dying.
          Englewood Cliffs, N.J.: Prentice-Hall, 1967. 176 pp.
Sudnow discusses the concepts of "death" and "dying" as they are used
in the occupational setting of two large hospitals. Most of the data
comes from a large hospital with lower-income patients. The author concentrates on the way that their conceptions of death and dying influence
the behavior of the hospital staff in relation to the social organization
of the hospital. A hospital serving an upper-middle-class community in
the Midwest provides comparisons of the ways that the dead and dying are
treated in the two settings. There is a short section on the way that
doctors convey the news of death to relatives and the way that the relatives react to a death.

A-F 145. SUGARMAN, BARRY. Daytop Village: A Therapeutic Community.
          New York: Holt, Rinehart & Winston, 1974. 134 pp.
Daytop Village is a therapeutic residential community for the rehabilitation of drug addicts which is staffed by ex-addicts and applies a communal and familistic concept to rehabilitation. Sugarman studied Daytop
Village from 1968-1970, and describes its organization, philosophy, social
controls, and encounter-group therapy sessions. He concludes the book
with a description of an internal administrative conflict that severely
disrupted Daytop Village's operation.

A-F 146. SUTHERLAND, ANNE. Gypsies: The Hidden Americans. New York:
          Free Press, 1975. 330 pp.
Sutherland has produced a social anthropological study of a group of Rom,
or Gypsies, living in California. Concentrating on the social, political,
and economic organization of the Rom, she applies concepts of symbolic
purity and pollution to explain how they maintain social boundaries which
keep them separate from the surrounding society. She describes the norms
and values by which the Rom have adapted to the American social system
and have adopted welfare, theft, and fraud as legitimate means of competition with the Gaje, or non-Gypsies.

A-F 147. THEODORATUS, ROBERT JAMES. A Greek Community in America: Tacoma,
          Washington. Sacramento, Calif.: Sacramento Anthropological
          Society, Sacramento State College, 1971. 234 pp.
The strong ties that the Greek immigrants in Tacoma have with Greece is
the major concern of this study, which shows how these ties influence
the rate and course of acculturation and assimilation. Theodoratus focuses
on the institutional structure of the community, describing the function
of the family, the church, school, coffeehouses, and mutual aid societies.
Although the author gives little attention to the place of the Greek-
American community in U.S. society at large, he is able to point out some
of the factors which influence the acculturation of an immigrant group.

A-F 148. VOGT, EVON Z. Modern Homesteaders: The Life of a Twentieth-
          Century Frontier Community. Cambridge, Mass.: Harvard Univer-
          sity Press, 1955. 252 pp.
This book is concerned with a community of Texas farmers who established
the town of "Homestead" in Western New Mexico. After an introduction
to the theoretical, historical, geographic, demographic, and economic
context of the study, Vogt organizes his presentation around a set of
primary "value orientations" of the Homestead community. These include
the hope of mastery over nature, future-time orientation, orientation
to success, achievement of time for leisure, individualism, and an ideology
of status hierarchy in relationships with other groups. Vogt concludes
that the stress on individualism goes against the unity of the community,
promoting an atomistic social organization rather than a town.

A-F 149. VOGT, EVON Z. and RAY HYMAN. Water Witching U.S.A. Chicago:
          University of Chicago Press, 1959. 248 pp.
Vogt and Hyman present the results of a cultural anthropological and psychological inquiry into the techniques for finding water termed water witching,
or dowsing. Data come from a survey of county agricultural extension
agents, reviews of literature, and personal observation. They examine
the reliability of water witching, the causes of the movement of the dowsing rod, the character of the people who perform water witching, and the
factors which lead people to consult a dowser. They conclude that the
probability of finding water by dowsing is not significantly better than
chance and that the behavior of the rod is the result of involuntary muscle
action in conjunction with ground surface cues and suggestions to the
dowser. They explain the persistence of water witching in the U.S. by
relating it to similar behaviors found in other cultures, especially in
Malinowski's description of deep sea and lagoon fishing in the Trobriand
Islands, in which magical behavior is associated with deep sea fishing,
which entails greater risk than lagoon fishing. The authors see well-
digging as a high-risk activity where there is little assurance of success,
and the dowser as providing a culturally appropriate reinforcement to
the risk.

A-F 150. WAGNER, JON, ed. Sex Roles in Contemporary American Communes.
Bloomington: Indiana University Press, 1982. 241 pp.
This selection of six ethnographic studies of gender relations in American
communes appears to document a trend toward male dominance despite ideologies of equality and cooperation. The oppression ranges from institutionalized and regularized (for instance, the polygyny of Black Hebrew
Israelites or the Utah Levites' rules for women to wear uniforms), to
the loosely imposed, different-but-not-inferior division of labor schema
at The Farm which denies women public power. Almost all the communes
were formed by charismatic "spiritual" male leaders. No synthetic analysis
is offered for this patriarchal patterning.

A-F 151. WARNER, W. LLOYD. Democracy in Jonesville: A Study in Quality
and Equality. New York: Harper, 1949. 319 pp.
Jonesville, a fictitious name for a Midwestern city, is studied in a manner
very similar to that used in Yankee City (A-F 154). The problem addressed
is the way in which the American ideal of "equal common men" is resolved
in light of the reality of social inequality, and of upward and downward
social mobility. The study emphasizes the impact of W.W. II on the city,
and resulting insights into Jonesville's social structure.

A-F 152. WARNER, W. LLOYD. The Family of God: A Symbolic Study of Christian Life in America. New Haven, Conn.: Yale University Press,
1961. 451 pp.
This is an edited revision of Warner's The Living and the Dead (A-F 153).
The first two chapters of this book are new. The first chapter offers
additional information on symbolism in family life, and the second introduces comparative material from non-Western societies. The remainder
of the book has been changed only minimally.

A-F 153. WARNER, W. LLOYD. The Living and the Dead: A Study of the Symbolic Life of Americans. New Haven, Conn.: Yale University
Press, 1959. 528 pp.
Warner examines the major symbols of Yankee City. Political, historical,
social, and religious symbols are discussed from a theoretical perspective
which examines the role of symbols in human life and action. Following
Durkheim, symbols are seen as related to the maintenance of the moral
order, and as part of a biological system of adaptation. Many examples
are presented to support Warner's theory of symbolism.

A-F 154. WARNER, W. LLOYD, ed. Yankee City. New Haven, Conn.: Yale
University Press, 1963. 432 pp.
This abridgement includes the major points of the five-volume Yankee City
Series (A-F 153; 155-158) with some reorganization. Much of the material
on religion and symbolic structures, as presented in The Family of God
(A-F 152), is excluded from this book. This work is organized into three
parts. Part I describes the institutional system and the social class
system of the city, combined with some information on symbolic structures
supporting the social systems. Part II deals with the factory system.
Part III presents material on the social position of ethnic groups in
Yankee City.

A-F 155. WARNER, W. LLOYD and J. O. LOW. The Social System of the Modern
Factory: The Strike, a Social Analysis. New Haven, Conn.:
Yale University Press, 1947. 245 pp.
This volume in the Yankee City Series describes the industrial aspects
of Yankee City, concentrating on factory workers. By tracing the historical development of Yankee City industrialization, including the changes
brought about by W.W. I and the Great Depression, the authors show a strike
in the shoe industry to be a result of the changing position of the workers
in the community social status hierarchy as brought about by increasing
mechanization of the factory.

A-F 156. WARNER, W. LLOYD and PAUL S. LUNT. The Social Life of a Modern
          Community. New Haven, Conn.: Yale University Press, 1941.
          460 pp.
In the first volume of the Yankee City Series, Warner and Lunt provide
background information to the series, discuss its theoretical and methodological orientation, and give a general summary of the social structure
of "Yankee City"—the fictitious name for a moderate-sized city in New
England. The authors' general objective is to apply the principles of
social anthropology to a community in a modern industrial society. They
use a structural-functionalist approach to anthropology which focuses
on social institutions and emphasizes the relationships between institutions. The basic variable used to organize the data in this and the other
Yankee City volumes is social class. In this volume the basic social
structure of Yankee City is presented and the relation of economics,
religion, politics, and intellectual activity to social class is delineated.

A-F 157. WARNER, W. LLOYD and PAUL S. LUNT. The Status System of a Modern
          Community. New Haven, Conn.: Yale University Press, 1942.
          246 pp.
Warner and Lunt describe the social system of Yankee City in terms of
six social classes, seven social structures, and eighty-nine status positions. A large proportion of the book is devoted to tables that show
how each ethnic group fits into the status system and how status positions
are related to one another. The seven kinds of social structures isolated
by Warner and Lunt are family, clique, association, economy, school, church,
and politics. The eighty-nine status positions are derived from the combination of classes and social positions.

A-F 158. WARNER, W. LLOYD and LEO SROLE. The Social Systems of American
          Ethnic Groups. New Haven, Conn.: Yale University Press, 1948.
          318 pp.
This volume of the Yankee City Series focuses on the ways in which recent
immigrants adapt to the American social system. Using the six-class model
of the American social system, the authors describe a process of adaptation
in which "each group enters at the bottom of the social heap (lower-lower
class) and through the several generations makes its desperate climb
upward." According to this model, the earlier arrivals will be higher
in the social heap than the later ones. The authors present their argument
through a discussion of the ethnic groups in the community and by looking
in detail at particular cultural and social systems such as a family,
church, language, education, and associations. By so doing, they attempt
to document how social and cultural change takes place.

A-F 159. WEISS, MELFORD S. Valley City: A Chinese Community in America.
          Cambridge, Mass.: Schenkman, 1974. 269 pp.
This ethnography is concerned with the history, demography, social organization, and community organization of a Chinese community in California.
Weiss is most interested in presenting the patterns of assimilation and
acculturation of the people in this community. He outlines the history
of Chinese immigration to Valley City (a fictitious name) and discusses
the social organization of overseas Chinese in comparison with Chinese
Americans. The core of the presentation is the functional description
of three subcultural categories of the community: traditionalists, modernists, and activists. Weiss describes each of these categories in detail
and in isolation.

A-F 160. WEPPNER, ROBERT S., ed. Street Ethnography: Selected Studies
          of Crime and Drug Use in Natural Settings. Beverly Hills, Calif.:
          Sage, 1977. 288 pp.
These ten original papers are concerned with ethnographic descriptions
of lifestyles associated with marginal occupations such as prostitution,
thievery, alcoholism, and drug addiction. All but one of the studies
describe research done in the U.S. The authors present descriptive data
along with the theoretical and ethical implications of their work.

A-F 161. WEST, JAMES (Carl Withers). Plainville, U.S.A. New York: Colum-
          bia University Press, 1945. 238 pp.
Plainville is an anthropological community study done in the U.S., in
which West writes a sympathetic and comprehensive ethnography of a Midwestern rural farming community. West focuses on the social structure
in terms of institutional organizations, class structure, and the life
cycle.

A-F 162. WHYTE, WILLIAM FOOTE. Street Corner Society: The Social Struc-
          ture of an Urban Slum. Chicago: University of Chicago Press,
          1955. 364 pp.
In this study of an Italian slum neighborhood, Whyte describes the social
organization of the neighborhood by concentrating on an important type
of neighborhood group: the men's corner societies and clubs. He shows
how two major forces in the neighborhood, racketeering and politics, are
related to and depend on support from the men's cliques. His major goal
is to provide a description of the community which will aid in the resolution of the poverty and discrimination that the members of the neighborhood must endure.

A-F 163. WOLF, DEBORAH GOLEMAN. The Lesbian Community. Berkeley: Uni-
          versity of California Press, 1979. 196 pp.
In this ethnography of a lesbian community in Berkeley, California, studied
between 1972 and 1974, Wolf attempts both to affirm the positive lifestyle
available to gays in America and to present "a model for small, self-
sustaining urban communities of the future, whatever the affectional preference of their members." She notes incongruities between ideal and actual
behavior and is especially interested in the conscious mechanisms developed
for synthesizing the two. She then concludes that separatism is sometimes
a necessity for any minority attempting to engender corporate activity
aimed at creating a sense of self-worth for the individual.

A-F 164. WONG, BERNARD P. Chinatown: Economic Adaptation and Ethnic
          Identity of the Chinese. New York: Holt, Rinehart & Winston,
          1982. 110 pp.
In this community study, Wong addresses traditional Chinese symbols and
behavior, family structure, local businesses and social service agencies,
relations between subgroups which arrived in different periods and for
different reasons, and the new issue of "ethnic power." He is interested
in the way the social structure functions and what strategies it offers
for integrating newcomers into American society.

A-F 165. WROBEL, PAUL. Our Way: Family, Parish, and Neighborhood in
          a Polish-American Community. Notre Dame, Ind.: University
          of Notre Dame Press, 1979. 192 pp.
This study of a working class Polish-American community in Detroit in
the early 1970s examines the ways in which the Catholic parish creates
a framework of social activities which establishes a coherent ethnic group
identity. Using a participant-observer approach as teacher in the parish
grade school, Wrobel was able to gain access into the otherwise closed-
off, extremely private domain of the people's everyday lives, winning
sufficient trust to conduct more intensive formal interviews.

IV. BLACK AMERICANS

A-F 166. ASCHENBRENNER, JOYCE. Lifelines: Black Families in Chicago.
         New York: Holt, Rinehart & Winston, 1975. 146 pp.
This ethnography focuses on the families and kinship relationships of
ten people in Chicago's black community. Aschenbrenner questions the
idea that the black family is an unsuccessful adaptation of mainstream
norms and values under conditions of poverty. By presenting individual
accounts of the kinship networks of each of ten individuals, the author
shows the families in this community to be centered on an extended family,
with consanguineal ties given greater importance than marriage ties, and
with a major emphasis placed on the mother-daughter relationship. The
author concludes by characterizing the family pattern as rich, complex,
and functional.

A-F 167. BAUGH, JOHN. Black Street Speech. Austin: University of Texas
         Press, 1983. 149 pp.
In this book, Baugh examines one facet of black American culture: black
street speech. The author interviewed blacks in several cities across
the U.S. The same adults were repeatedly interviewed under different
social circumstances. These interviews document Baugh's observation that
there are several styles of street speech, and that people adopt the style
of speech that suits their social situation.

A-F 168. BELL, MICHAEL. The World from Brown's Lounge. Chicago: Uni-
         versity of Chicago Press, 1983. 191 pp.
This book provides a description of a specific segment of black life in
America: the culture of the black middle-class. Bell chose to do his
fieldwork in the informal atmosphere of a black bar in West Philadelphia.
This book is an ethnographic study of middle-class black Americans at
play. Bell, although white, became a part of the community in Brown's
Lounge. Through participant observation, Bell studied the manner in which
the daily life and style of a black bar reflects the values of the black
community.

A-F 169. BETHAL, ELIZABETH R. Promiseland: A Century of Life in a Negro
         Community. Philadelphia: Temple University Press, 1981.
         329 pp.
Promised Land is a black community located in South Carolina. Bethal's
purpose in doing this study was to research the types of coping mechanisms
used by the inhabitants of this community since its birth in 1870. From
research and observations on the internal structure of Promised Land,
Bethal presents a case study of black community members who have adopted
unique strategies to cope with their status as second-class citizens.

A-F 170. CLARK, THOMAS. Blacks in Suburbs. New Brunswick, N.J.: Rutgers
         University Center for Urban Policy Research, 1979. 127 pp.
The purpose of this book is to study the recent rapid movement of black
Americans to the suburbs. Clark investigates the suburbanization process
in several metropolitan areas. He examines the socioeconomic backgrounds
of the different types of black families that migrate to the suburbs.
His investigation indicates that black suburbanization is not a monophonic
process, rather that the patterns of migration are very complex.

A-F 171. CROCKETT, NORMAN. The Black Towns. Lawrence: Regents Press
         of Kansas, 1979. 239 pp.
Crockett made a study of five black towns located across the U.S. As
used in this book, the term "black town" refers to an isolated community
containing a mostly black population. Studying these communities gave

49

Crockett the opportunity to observe black attitudes about American life and the impact of isolation on individuals and groups. This study focuses on the formation, growth, and failures of black towns located in Kansas, Mississippi, and Oklahoma.

A-F 172. DAVIS, ALLISON and JOHN DOLLARD. Children of Bondage: The Personality Development of Negro Youth in the Urban South. Washington, D.C.: American Council on Education, 1940. 299 pp.
Organizing their presentation around W. L. Warner's concept of the U.S. class and caste structure (see A-F 157), Davis and Dollard discuss the personality development of eight black children, aged twelve to sixteen, in New Orleans, Louisiana, and Natchez, Mississippi. One upper-class, three middle-class, and four lower-class children were selected for detailed presentation out of a group of over 100 children. The life history of each of the eight children is presented, and their personality development is analyzed in terms of Freudian and, especially, behaviorist psychological perspectives.

A-F 173. DAVIS, ALLISON, BURLEIGH B. GARDNER, and MARY B. GARDNER. Deep South: A Social Anthropological Study of Caste and Class. Chicago: University of Chicago Press, 1941. 558 pp.
This study, conducted under the direction of W. Lloyd Warner, applies Warner's model of caste and class to a small city in the South. Basing their study on participant-observation fieldwork in both the white and black sections of a city, the authors describe the social and economic structures of the city. Caste is defined here on the basis of the regulation of sexual access and the social position of the offspring of a cross-caste sexual relationship. The economic system is used as a detailed example of the operation of the caste and class system in the community.

A-F 174. DAVIS, GEORGE and GREGG WATSON. Black Life in Corporate America: Swimming in the Mainstream. Garden City, N.Y.: Anchor Press, 1982. 204 pp.
This study, which is based on personal interviews, considers the entry of blacks into the managerial class and their adaptation to corporate life. The authors find that, though a superficial amity prevails, avoidance and defensiveness characterize white colleagues' treatment of racial issues raised by blacks. Davis and Watson address the struggle to integrate the managerial strategy and the more recent presence of black women in executive ranks.

A-F 175. FOLB, EDITH A. Runnin' Down Some Lines: The Language and Culture of Black Teenagers. Cambridge, Mass.: Harvard University Press, 1980. 260 pp.
This sociolinguistic study focuses on the vernacular vocabulary used by black teenagers who reside in Los Angeles' south-central inner city. It is Folb's premise that studying a group's idiomatic usage of vocabulary in a social context will reveal a great deal about the concerns, values, and beliefs of the group members. Folb analyzes approximately 1,100 terms and phrases of a group of black teenagers in order to understand the way in which vocabulary is a manifestation of cultural environment.

A-F 176. FREIDLAND, WILLIAM H. and DOROTHY NELKIN. Migrant: Agricultural Workers in America's Northeast. New York: Holt, Rinehart & Winston, 1971. 281 pp.
This is an ethnography of the migrant farm workers who move from Florida to the Northeastern states each summer as they follow the fruit and vegetable harvests. The data were collected by students who lived as migrants for several weeks in different migrant camps throughout the Northeast. On the basis of the impressionistic accounts of the student fieldworkers, the authors describe the migrants' life as disorganized and unpredictable and as one which traps workers into a system of dependency.

A-F 177. GLASGOW, DOUGLAS G. The Black Underclass: Poverty, Unemployment, and Entrapment of Ghetto Youth. San Francisco: Jossey-Bass, 1980. 206 pp.

This study examines the impact of mainstream institutional practices and market dynamics on a group of young black males from Watts, Los Angeles. Glasgow's purpose in writing this book is twofold. First, he wants to show what unemployment can do to the ambitions of black youths. And second, he attempts to identify some of the major patterns that entrap blacks in an underclass status. Glasgow seeks to do more than pinpoint the problems of black youth; he also investigates policies that can reverse the growth of a black underclass.

A-F 178. GWALTNEY, JOHN LANGSTON. Drylongso: A Self-Portrait of Black America. New York: Random House, 1980. 287 pp.

This book is the product of a field study conducted by Gwaltney in several Northeastern urban black communities. Drylongso is a portrait of poor black communities, a compilation of narratives contributed by the author's relatives, friends, and acquaintances. Gwaltney's goal is to produce an authentic representation of black culture; he intended this book as a vehicle for black people to express their own view of their way of life.

A-F 179. HANNERZ, ULF. Soulside: Inquiries into Ghetto Culture and Community. New York: Columbia University Press, 1969. 236 pp.

In analysis of black ghetto culture, which combines participant observation fieldwork with a review of recent interpretations of black ghetto life, Hannerz describes a black community in Washington, D.C. He is especially concerned with the position of men in the ghetto culture and divides the male social system—on the basis of value orientations—into four categories: mainstreamers, swingers, street families, and street men. The street men, whom he associates with the subjects of Elliot Liebow's study (A-F 186), are the major subjects of his description. Ritual insults, which have been seen as pathological, are interpreted in terms of ghetto cultural values, rules, and male role model expectations. The various types of conjugal arrangements found in the ghetto are also described. Finally, the author compares his description of the ghetto to a larger picture of mainstream culture to demonstrate differences and similarities.

A-F 180. HERSKOVITS, MELVILLE J. The Myth of the Negro Past. New York: Harper, 1941. 374 pp.

In this early publication about Afro-America by an American anthropologist, Herskovits makes a case against the once widely held position that Africans who came to the New World lost their African cultural identity. Using ethnohistorical methods and data, he argues against the supposed passivity, lack of intelligence, hopeless diversity, and cultural backwardness that were alleged to have accelerated the loss of African culture in the New World. Comparing contemporary ethnographic data from the U.S., the Caribbean and South America with that of West Africa, Herskovits posits a number of New World cultural patterns (in social organization, religion, language and art) which could be traced directly to African antecedents.

A-F 181. HIPPLER, ARTHUR E. Hunter's Point: A Black Ghetto. New York: Basic Books, 1974. 237 pp.

Taking a psychological view toward the structure of this black community in San Francisco, Hippler argues that the major factor shaping the lives of the people in Hunter's Point is the social emasculation of the men and the resulting conflicts in interpersonal relations. The family structure and the life cycle are described using a matrifocal model, and case studies of several families, with their responses to a psychological diagnostic test, are included. Hippler's approach differs from that of most anthropological studies of black communities, stressing the emotional factor in social organization, and concluding that the community is dysfunctional and contains many unresolved conflicts.

A-F 182. IANNI, FRANCIS A. J. Black Mafia: Ethnic Succession in Organized
Crime. New York: Simon & Schuster, 1974. 255 pp.
Using observations and interview data collected by black and Puerto Rican
ex-convicts, Ianni describes the structure and function of organized crime
in black and Puerto Rican ghettos. Claiming that there has been a succession of ethnic groups who have held major control of organized crime
in the U.S., he argues that blacks are now succeeding the Italians, who
were preceded by Jews and by the Irish. Ianni describes networks of black
and Puerto Rican criminals to show how they have become a part of the
organized crime network. Organized crime is viewed as a functional part
of the American social system, complexly interrelated with ethnicity and
politics, "with its own symbols . . . logic . . . beliefs . . . and means
of transmitting these systematically from one generation to the next."

A-F 183. KEISER, R. LINCOLN. The Vice Lords: Warriors of the Streets.
New York: Holt, Rinehart & Winston, 1969. 83 pp.
Keiser's ethnography depicts the social and cultural organization of a
gang of black youths in Chicago in 1966. He shows from the insider's
point of view how the group is organized—concentrating on social structures, contexts of interaction, and ideology—and includes a lengthy autobiographical chapter by a former member of the gang. The book conveys
the way individuals perceive their options and structure their actions
according to a set of cultural rules and categories.

A-F 184. KENNEDY, THEODORE. You Gotta Deal with It: Black Family Relations in a Southern Community. New York: Oxford University
Press, 1980. 277 pp.
Although You Gotta Deal with It is primarily a personal account of
Kennedy's hardships and survival techniques during his one year of fieldwork
in a Southern community, the book offers insights into black American
family relations. Using community members' own words, Kennedy attempts
to make his reformulation of "the black family" accessible to a lay audience. His analysis of four extended families demonstrates that the Southern black family is not maladaptive, but is a stable viable structure.

A-F 185. KUNKEL, PETER and SARA SUE KENNARD. Sprout Spring: A Black
Community. New York: Holt, Rinehart & Winston, 1971. 99 pp.
This short ethnography, based on fieldwork done from 1964 to 1968,
describes a small stable black community in a city of 25,000 located in the
Ozark Mountains. Kunkel and Kennard describe the community in terms of
types of families, types of non-kin groups, and the relationships of various social positions, such as husband-wife, parent-child, and siblings.
They illustrate their account with many detailed descriptions of individuals and families and their strategies for surviving in the face of low-
key discrimination. This work was carried out when integration was a
major issue in the South and the authors describe how the individuals
in this particular community coped with the change.

A-F 186. LIEBOW, ELLIOT. Tally's Corner: A Study of Negro Streetcorner
Men. Boston: Little, Brown, 1966. 260 pp.
Liebow provides a detailed description of a small, informal group of poor
black men centered on a streetcorner of a Washington, D.C., ghetto. The
author makes it clear that the men of Tally's Corner have aspirations
equivalent to those of the mainstream culture which, for a variety of
reasons, they have not been able to fulfill. He records the interactions
of these men with each other and with others to illustrate their poverty,
then describes the expectations of employers and employees which lead
to the chronic job failure among these men, and finally characterizes
their behavior as it varies with different social positions, such as father,
husband, friend, and lover.

A-F 187. MANDELBAUM, DAVID G. Soldier Groups and Negro Soldiers. Berkeley
University of California Press, 1952. 142 pp.
Mandelbaum reviews sociological, psychological, anthropological, and military literature to show why racially integrated military units exhibit
better performance than segregated ones. The basic argument is that each
soldier is a member of a primary group--a small, face-to-face group to
which he has responsibility and on which he is dependent. Effective
leaders take advantage of and identify with this primary group because
"American infantry men in combat will usually fight only in the presence
of . . . others in the primary group." The performance of segregated
black military units is impaired because these units tend to interpret
unpleasantness and misfortune in terms of racial discrimination. Integrated units, however, benefit from the power of the primary groups, and
the interdependence among the men leads to an increase in their morale.

A-F 188. MORGAN, KATHRYN. Children of Strangers: The Stories of a Black
Family. Philadelphia: Temple University Press, 1980. 116 pp.
In Children of Strangers, Morgan has written down the oral tradition of
her own family. These "Caddy legends," as the author affectionately refers
to them, were named after the author's great-grandmother. Morgan interweaves these legends with her family history in order to show how they
have served, over the past four generations, as "buffers" against racism
for the members of her family.

A-F 189. PARKER, SEYMOUR and ROBERT J. KLEINER. Mental Illness in the
Urban Negro Community. New York: Free Press, 1966. 408 pp.
The authors find that levels of aspiration, when correlated with the means
for achieving goals, provide an index for predicting frequency of mental
illness. In a study conducted among blacks in Philadelphia they found
that native Philadelphians show a higher rate of mental illness than
migrants from the Southern U.S.

A-F 190. POWDERMAKER, HORTENSE. After Freedom: A Cultural Study in the
Deep South. New York: Viking Press, 1939. 408 pp.
Powdermaker conducted an ethnographic study of a small town in Mississippi
in which she concentrated on the social relationships between blacks and
whites from the blacks' point of view. She examined the changes in attitudes toward racial inequality in the different generations of black people
in the town, finding that the older generations maintained a stance of
inferiority when dealing with whites, while the younger generation dealt
with the situation of anti-black prejudice by avoiding contact with whites.

A-F 191. ROHRER, JOHN H. and MUNRO S. EDMONSON. The Eighth Generation:
Cultures and Personalities of New Orleans Negroes. New York:
Harper, 1964. 346 pp.
This is a reappraisal, after twenty years, of the individuals studied by
Davis and Dollard in Children of Bondage (A-F 172). The authors located
ninety of the 107 people studied as teenagers in the original study, interviewed forty-seven of them, and studied twenty intensively. The life
histories, and the authors' psychological and psychiatric analyses, of
nine of these individuals are presented in detail in this book. The
authors discuss the major events and other factors which have affected
the personalities of these individuals. Topics selected for detailed
inquiry include segregation, W.W. II, matriarchy, and family influences.

A-F 192. STACK, CAROL B. All Our Kin: Strategies for Survival in a Black
Community. New York: Harper & Row, 1974. 175 pp.
All Our Kin is an ethnographic study of the social and economic networks
through which poor black people in a Midwestern city structure their lives.
In a book based on three years of participant-observation fieldwork in
the ghetto, Stack concentrates on the adaptive strategies individuals

use to cope with poverty and racism. Rather than employing a mainstream
conception of family, Stack uses households as her basic unit of analysis,
and describes the networks of cooperation in which goods, labor, and child-
rearing duties are shared in the community. She also describes the strategies by which the people in these networks maximize their limited options.
The structures and strategies so described are shown to be rational
responses to harsh conditions.

A-F 193. STAPLES, ROBERT. The World of Black Singles. Westport, Conn.:
          Greenwood Press, 1981. 259 pp.
The purpose of this study is to investigate the black single life-style
and the formation of a black singles world. The study is confined to
college-educated blacks between the ages of twenty-five and forty-five.
Arguing from his interviews with 100 people in the San Francisco area
and his review of 400 questionnaires distributed in cities throughout
the U.S., Staples analyzes the mechanisms used by blacks to deal with
single life.

A-F 194. VALENTINE, BETTYLOU. Hustling and Other Hard Work: Life Styles
          in the Ghetto. New York: Free Press, 1978. 183 pp.
Strategies for survival in a black ghetto of a Northeastern city are the
focus of this ethnography. The primary subsistence strategies, used in
a variety of combinations by ghetto residents, are work, welfare, and
hustling. The author argues, drawing on five years of participant observation, that "black and poor people in ghettoes have created and follow
life styles that are more the result of poverty than its cause." In the
last two chapters previous ethnography in black ghettoes is reviewed and
the author's fieldwork experiences are described.

A-F 195. VALENTINE, CHARLES A. Black Studies and Anthropology: Scholarly
          and Political Interests in Afro-American Culture. Reading,
          Mass.: Addison-Wesley, 1972. 53 pp.
In a critique of anthropological and sociological studies for their characterization of Afro-American culture as a deviant form of mainstream
culture, Valentine suggests directing research into the area of power
relations between Afro-Americans and whites, and into the social structure
of U.S. society, which he believes depends on oppression of Afro-American
people. He suggests that anthropological participant-observation fieldwork
in Afro-American communities which focused on the distinctiveness and
vitality of Afro-American culture and the relationship of that culture
to the larger society would provide better data for the determination
of courses of action to restructure American society. Valentine advocates
anthropological participation in political issues.

A-F 196. WALLACE, PHYLLIS A. Black Women in the Labor Force. Cambridge,
          Mass.: MIT Press, 1980. 162 pp.
In this book, Wallace surveys and analyzes the segment of the labor market
that is comprised of black American women. She examines the unique labor
market experiences of black women and focuses on the changes in the employment status of these women since 1960. Wallace attributes the general
improvement of the economic status of black women between 1960 and 1970
to fundamental changes in their position in the labor force.

A-F 197. WHITTEN, NORMAN E. and JOHN F. SZWED, eds. Afro-American Anthro-
          pology: Contemporary Perspectives. New York: Free Press,
          1970. 468 pp.
Twenty-two studies of Afro-American cultures from North, Central, and
South America are included in this volume. These articles place Afro-
American culture in the U.S. into the context of the entire Afro-American
experience in the New World, providing data for comparative analysis.
Articles include studies by Carol Stack on the personal kindred of a

black woman, and by Charles and Betty Lou Valentine about anthropological fieldwork in a black ghetto. Issues explored in this wide-ranging collection include Afro-American folklore, religion, music, linguistics, social organization, cultural patterning, and socioeconomic adaptations.

A-F 198. WILLIAMS, MELVIN D. Community in a Black Pentecostal Church: An Anthropological Study. Pittsburgh, Pa.: University of Pittsburgh Press, 1974. 202 pp.
Williams offers an analysis of a black Pentecostal church in Pittsburgh, Pennsylvania. He concentrates on the social relations, community ideology, and social behavior within the congregation rather than on the religious beliefs of the group. His aim is to show how this congregation functions as a community without geographically demarcated patterns of interaction. Emphasizing the symbolic expressions of community which produce cohesion in the group, he shows how behavior patterns from the rural South have been transplanted to Northern cities. Williams demonstrates both the vitality of the urban black community and the desperation caused by conditions of severe poverty.

A-F 199. WILLIE, CHARLES VERT. A New Look at Black Families. 1976; Rev. ed. New York: General Hall, 1981. 250 pp.
Willie's book provides a collection of case studies of black American families with different socioeconomic backgrounds. A New Look at Black Families is a second edition adding six cases to the collection presented in the first edition. Willie compares black and white American families in terms of their social status. He concludes that blacks share a common set of values with white Americans, but that they adapt to these values in a different way.

V.   NATIVE AMERICANS

A-F 200. ABERLE, DAVID F. The Peyote Religion Among the Navajo. New York: Wenner-Gren Foundation for Anthropological Research, 1966. 454 pp.
Aberle studies the factors involved in the development and persistence of the peyote religion in a segment of Navajo society. The author summarizes the positions of the groups in favor of and those in opposition to the use of peyote, and also summarizes pharmacological and physiological data on the use of peyote. A major part of the book is devoted to the history of the Navajo. The author argues that the massive forced stock reductions in the 1930s caused disruptions in Navajo culture which led to the growth of the peyote religion. He classifies the cult as a "redemptive movement" which results when "groups are pushed into new, ambivalently regarded niches, where their engagement with a larger economico-political system is increased."

A-F 201. AXTELL, JAMES. The European and the Indian: Essays in the Ethnohistory of Colonial North America. New York: Oxford University Press, 1982. 402 pp.
This book is a collection of essays on European-Indian contact. Emphasizing the need for theoretical and methodological rapprochement between historical and ethnographic disciplines, Axtell recommends the use of the in-depth knowledge of European history and jargon-free approach of the former, mixed with the analytic sensitivity to structural transformation and to the interrelatedness of belief and behavior of the latter. In particular he is interested in the processes of missionizing and militarizing, seen from both native and European perspectives, and the effects of that interaction.

A-F 202. BAHR, HOWARD M., BRUCE A. CHADWICK, and ROBERT C. DAY, eds.
            Native Americans Today: Sociological Perspectives. New York:
            Harper & Row, 1971. 547 pp.
Although this book was produced for sociologists, the majority of its
forty-two articles are anthropological. The book is divided into seven
sections, each with an introduction by the editors. Several of these
sections reflect the sociological perspectives of the editors, with titles
such as "Patterns of Prejudice and Discrimination" and "Crime and Deviant
Behavior." The articles cover a wide range of subjects representing many
tribes and areas.

A-F 203. BASSO, KEITH H. Portraits of the Whitemen: Linguistic Play
            and Cultural Symbols Among the Western Apache. New York:
            Cambridge University Press, 1979. 120 pp.
The Western Apache's process of inventive caricature of Anglos is here
analyzed linguistically for its symbolic content and social function.
The joking activity operates on two levels: that of an ongoing imaginative
reinterpretation of who "whitemen" are vis-a-vis Apaches, and that of
a framed communicative incident through which social interactions are
negotiated. Basso's claim is that by comprehending the Apache's vision
of whites as a "problem," whites may be brought to a better understanding
of their own culture.

A-F 204. BLANCHARD, KENDALL. The Mississippi Choctaws at Play: The Seri-
            ous Side of Leisure. Urbana: University of Illinois Press,
            1981. 196 pp.
Blanchard is interested in the power of sports to organize ethnic identity
along psychological, social, economic, and ritualistic lines. Choctaw
have a long history of team sports which the author outlines. He then
describes its most recent developments. He also has an applied concern
that this investigation of the integrative functionalism of sports will
be useful for Western work-ethic societies. With leisure time expanding
and the national sense of purpose being diminished, the author asserts
that Americans will need to learn to value less product-oriented activities.

A-F 205. BLU, KAREN I. The Lumbee Problem: The Making of an American
            Indian People. New York: Cambridge University Press, 1980.
            276 pp.
Eschewing "community" and "sub-culture studies," Blu contextualizes the
Lumbee, who identify as Indian, but look black and have no reservation
or "traditional customs." Through an interpretive ethnography of their
attempts to create a corporate identity which rejects but also integrates
the prevailing Southern culture, Blu hopes to promote understanding of
that interaction, especially in the years following the Civil Rights movement. She analyzes the concept of "ethnicity" as a very American product.

A-F 206. BRAROE, NIELS WINTHER. Indian and White: Self-Image and Inter-
            action in a Canadian Plains Community. Stanford, Calif.: Stan-
            ford University Press, 1975. 205 pp.
Braroe applies Erving Goffman's symbolic interactionist approach to the
study of the ways in which a small group of Cree Indians maintain their
cultural distinctiveness in a Southern Canadian ranching community. He
is interested in the ability of the Cree to maintain a positive self-
identity while being held in low esteem by the surrounding dominant society,
and in the ways they present a mutually reinforced identity to the white
world while maintaining their private cultural system. Although this
study was conducted in Canada, its findings have wide applicability to
similar circumstances on reservations in the U.S. Braroe shows how attitudes and behaviors on the part of both whites and Indians are applied
in different, definable social contexts.

A-F 207. **CAHN, EDGAR S.**, ed. Our Brother's Keeper: The Indian in White
America. Washington, D.C.: New Communities, 1969. 206 pp.
This book is a presentation by the staff of the Citizens' Advocate Center
of the American Indians' position in U.S. government policy. It outlines
the ways in which the self-realization of individuals and self-determination of tribes have been hindered by policies of the U.S. Bureau of Indian
Affairs. Three lessons that Indians have learned from dealing with the
Bureau are that self-realization is frustrated, dependency is a virtue,
and cultural alienation is rewarded. The structure of the Bureau is discussed, and the authors attempt to show how change and innovation are
prevented by the position of the Bureau in the U.S. government.

A-F 208. **CAMPBELL, LYLE and MARIANNE MITHUN**, eds. The Language of Native
America: Historical and Comparative Assessment. Austin: University of Texas Press, 1979. 1034 pp.
This selection of essays is meant to present a contemporary analysis of
the classification of Native American languages. An introductory essay
by the editors gives a history of linguistic thought during the past century. Eighteen essays then follow, ranging from Ives Goddard's "Comparative Algonquin" to Susan Steele's "Uto-Aztecan: An Assessment for Historical and Comparative Linguistics" to Eric P. Hamp's concluding work, "A
Glance from Here On." The disciplinary trend at this point is fairly
conservative in its tendency to avoid grouping languages into families
without sufficient evidence, and linguistic borrowing has been given more
credence as the primary influence in creating similarities.

A-F 209. **CLIFTON, JAMES A.** The Prairie People: Continuity and Change
in Potawatomi Indian Culture, 1665-1963. Lawrence: Regents
Press of Kansas, 1977. 529 pp.
Clifton documents the history of the Prairie Potawatomi community over
three centuries, concentrating on changes and continuity in language,
culture, and social organization. This is a chronicle of the significant
events in Potawatomi relations with Europeans and the U.S. government.
The author presents his material by describing the culture of the tribe
at three stages in their history: before European contact, during the
treaty period in the early 19th century, and under present conditions
on the reservation.

A-F 210. **DRIVER, HAROLD E.** Indians of North America. 1961; Rev. ed.
Chicago: University of Chicago Press, 1969. 632 pp.
Dealing with the entire North American continent, from Greenland to the
isthmus of Panama, Driver discusses Indian culture in terms of "universal"
categories of culture such as subsistence, material culture, economics,
marriage and the family, and life cycle. For each category he summarizes
the data in terms of the Culture Areas that he has defined. Thirty-seven
maps at the back of the book depict the distribution of culture traits.

A-F 211. **EGGAN, FRED**, ed. Social Anthropology of the North American Tribes.
1939; Rev. ed. Chicago: University of Chicago Press, 1955.
574 pp.
Reflecting the influence of A. R. Radcliffe-Brown at the University of
Chicago, this volume of essays applies social anthropological principles
to the ethnography of historical and contemporary Indians of the U.S.
It deals with a small number of tribes in detail: Cheyenne and Arapaho,
Kiowa Apache, Chiricahua Apache, Fox, Eastern Cherokee, Klamath-Modoc,
Paviotso, and Plains tribes. Most of the articles deal specifically with
the social organization of the tribes and each follows the same basic
format, discussing kin terms and reciprocal kinship behavior, the social
structure units, and the individual life cycle. The earlier edition has
been expanded by inclusion of a paper on the development of social anthropology, and a chapter which summarizes the usefulness of the method and
theory of social anthropology.

A-F 212. **FRISBIE, CHARLOTTE J.**, ed. Southwestern Indian Ritual Drama.
Albuquerque: University of New Mexico Press, 1980. 372 pp.
In this volume the contributors, with backgrounds in dance, ethnomusicology,
ethnology and ethnolinguistics, have addressed Zuni Kachina Society Songs,
Hopi Ogres Drama, the Picuris Deer dance, the Mescalero Apache Girls'
Puberty Ceremony, Navajo House Blessing Ceremony, Navajo Shootingway,
Papago Skipping Dance, and Havasupai. "Drama" is examined in both its
sociocultural and aesthetic dimensions.

A-F 213. **FUCHS, ESTELLE** and **ROBERT J. HAVIGHURST**. To Live on This Earth:
American Indian Education. Garden City, N.Y.: Doubleday, 1972.
390 pp.
This work is a summary of the findings of a nationwide study which evaluated American Indian education from the perspectives of the students,
teachers, parents, and community leaders. The study was made by the
National Study of Indian Education and sponsored by the U.S. Office of
Education. After tracing the history of the U.S. Government's American
Indian policy to show how it has stressed, with varying force, exclusive
use of the English language and assimilation to mainstream American culture
in its instruction of Indian students, the authors found support at all
levels for bilingual and bicultural education programs which include native
language and cultural materials in the curriculum.

A-F 214. **GEARING, FREDERICK O.** The Face of the Fox. Chicago: Aldine,
1970. 159 pp.
In this ethnography Gearing relates his encounters with and endeavors
to understand Fox Indian culture, and considers what it means to try to
understand another culture. His work with the Fox began in the 1950s
as part of an "action anthropology" project in which anthropological understanding was coupled with an attempt to provide help and to act as an
advocate for the Fox. The author conducted a year of fieldwork in a Fox
community in Iowa in 1952 and 1953, and describes in detail the "structural
paralysis" of the community caused by the Federal government's usurpation
of the traditional patterns of community organization and control. This
paralysis was exemplified most strikingly by the W.W. II veterans who
were attempting, without much success, to establish a satisfying social
position for themselves. The ways in which the Fox community and the
Fox people were seen by the non-Indians in the surrounding farming communities, and by the author himself, are also discussed.

A-F 215. **GUILLEMIN, JEANNE.** Urban Renegades: The Cultural Strategy of
Urban Indians. New York: Columbia University Press, 1975.
336 pp.
Guillemin presents an account of the Micmac in American history and
describes the organization and function of reservation life, and the urban
lifestyle led by many Micmacs who operate in both the reservation and
the urban spheres, or who have made the city their permanent place of
residence. The author focuses on the reservation community and the networks of social ties activated by people in their alternation between
the reservation and the city. Attention is directed to the strategies
by which American Indians have adapted to urban environments of Micmac
culture in isolation from the surrounding dominant culture.

A-F 216. **HAVIGHURST, ROBERT J.** and **BERNICE L. NEUGARTEN**. American Indian
and White Children: A Sociopsychological Investigation. Chicago:
University of Chicago Press, 1955. 335 pp.
Using Piaget's views on human development, measures of emotional and moral
development were designed to test children of six tribes (Hopi, Zuni,
Zia, Papago, Navajo, and Sioux). The tests measured emotional responses,
moral ideology, moral judgment, animism, and acculturation. The results
of the tests were compared with each other and with data from "Jonesville,"
a Euro-American community in the Midwest.

A-F 217. HODGE, WILLIAM H. The Albuquerque Navajos. Tucson: University
of Arizona Press, 1969. 76 pp.
The study seeks to "demonstrate why some Navajos intend to remain permanently in Albuquerque and why others wanted to return or, in fact, did
return to the reservation." Three categories of individuals are identified:
permanent residents, Anglo-modified Indians, and traditional Indians.
The author shows that most of the Navajos studied would prefer to live
on the reservation but are dissatisfied with the economic opportunities
there. The urban and reservation systems thus serve as complementary
parts of one system, although most Navajos eventually return to the reservation to live. Life histories of representative members of each of the
three groups are presented.

A-F 218. HULTKRANTZ, AKE. Belief and Worship in Native North America.
Syracuse, N.Y.: Syracuse University Press, 1981. 330 pp.
This selection of essays from the thirty-year career of a Swedish phenomen-
ologist represents at once a classificatory schema of Native American
belief systems and a theoretical approach to the study of religion in
general. The work is divided into four sections: Belief and Myth, Worship and Ritual, Ecology and Religion, and Persistence and Change;
Hultkrantz's work elaborates a "religio-ecological methodology." A people's
ideology is not treated as a creative corpus apart from their environment,
technology and social structure, but is shown to be directly interactive
with it, transforming through time and circumstance in a series of "alternating configurations."

A-F 219. HYMES, DELL. "In Vain I Tried to Tell You": Essays in Native
American Ethnopoetics. Philadelphia: University of Pennsylvania
Press, 1981. 402 pp.
This work joins literary criticism with ethnolinguistics. Hymes's objective is to analyze Native American oral narratives on the same aesthetic
plane as written literatures, but to use ethno-linguistic tools in order
to make both structure and content accessible--that is, enjoyable and
understandable--to those outside the culture. The texts under consideration are taken from the Northwest Coast. The book is divided into three
parts following Cassirer's semiotic framework: the physical (words),
the presentational (symbolic content), and the personal (the author-
singer's imprint).

A-F 220. JACOBS, WILBUR R. Dispossessing the American Indian: Indians
and Whites on the Colonial Frontier. New York: Scribner, 1972.
240 pp.
Jacobs presents the history of Indian and white relations both from the
Indian viewpoint and from an ecological perspective; he feels that actions
should be evaluated in terms of their effect on the natural environment.
He is critical of historians who portray trappers, mountain men, pioneers,
and Indian fighters as heroes because, he argues, these people had a lack
of concern for future generations. From this perspective he evaluates
Indian and British relations in the Northeastern woodlands area which
led to the Proclamation of 1763 limiting British colonists' access to
land in the area. He then compares the policies of the British toward
colonized people in North America, New Guinea, and Australia.

A-F 221. JILEK, WOLFGANG G. Indian Healing: Shamanic Ceremonialism in
the Pacific Northwest Today. Blaine, Wash.: Hancock House,
1982. 181 pp.
This is an analysis of the revitalization of Northwest Coast Salish spirit
dancing since its official prohibition in 1871. Its history, ethnographic
context, and position vis-a-vis other Native American ritual movements
(for example, the Sun Dance) are explored. Jilek is particularly concerned
with the ritual's psychosocial efficacy as a healing instrument for the

psychophysiological disorders of present-day Salish suffering from persecution and depression.

A-F 222. JORGENSEN, JOSEPH G. The Sun Dance Religion: Power for the
          Powerless. Chicago: University of Chicago Press, 1972.
          360 pp.
Jorgensen analyzes the contemporary and historical Sun Dance Religion
of the Shoshone and Ute tribes of Wyoming, Colorado, and Utah. He
describes the Sun Dance, which in its present form was adopted by the
Shoshone and Ute in the early 20th century as a "redemptive social movement," defined as an attempt by individuals to achieve a more satisfying
cultural orientation. Jorgensen combines ethnographic description of
pre-reservation and reservation life with a detailed analysis of the contemporary Sun Dance. He places his analysis into the context of the larger
white and reservation systems to show how factors external to the Shoshone
and Ute tribal systems have led to the marginal position of these tribes
in general and, especially, of those individuals who take part in the
Sun Dance observances.

A-F 223. KLUCKHOHN, CLYDE and DOROTHEA LEIGHTON. The Navajo. 1947; Rev.
          ed. Cambridge, Mass.: Harvard University Press, 1972. 258 pp.
This book, with its companion volume, Children of the People (see A-F
227), provides the ethnographic background for the Navajo portion of the
Indian Education Research Project (summarized in A-F 216). This is a
basic ethnographic description covering the history, ecology, economy,
material culture, kinship, politics, religion, language, and world view
of the Navajo.

A-F 224. KROEBER, A. L. Cultural and Natural Areas of Native North America.
          Berkeley: University of California Press, 1939. 242 pp.
In this detailed presentation of the culture area concept, Kroeber investigates the relationships between culture areas historically and environ-
mentally. Cultures are seen as a combination of traits which can be isolated and compared among areas. Historical relationships between cultures
and developmental sequences within a culture may be perceived by the
examination of culture traits. At the same time, the author sees cultures
as unified wholes in which traits are combined in unique ways. Bringing
together these two approaches to culture, Kroeber developed the concept
of the culture climax—the culture in which traits were united in such
a way as to epitomize a culture area as a whole. The book also includes
an estimate and discussion of the aboriginal population of North America.

A-F 225. LA BARRE, WESTON. The Peyote Cult. 1938; Rev. ed. New York:
          Schocken Books, 1975. 296 pp.
The Peyote Cult is La Barre's study of a modern pan-Indian religious movement in which participants eat the hallucinogenic plant peyote. This
edition contains La Barre's original study (1938) which documents the
history and diffusion of peyote use among North American Indians, describes
the peyote ceremonies, and discusses the peyote cult and peyote use psychologically and physiologically. It also includes three article-length
reviews of the literature which have been added with each new edition
(1964, 1969, and 1975) and information from recent scientific research
on peyote and other hallucinogens.

A-F 226. LEACOCK, ELEANOR BURKE and NANCY OESTREICH LURIE, eds. North
          American Indians in Historical Perspective. New York: Random
          House, 1971. 498 pp.
This anthology focuses on recent American Indian history and on the ways
in which American Indians have dealt with changing circumstances. The
authors describe the history of American and white relations from an Indian
point of view. America north of Mexico is covered in fourteen chapters

which are organized by culture area. The different areas are discussed either in general terms (Plains, Southwest, California, Subarctic, and Eskimo) or by the selection of a particular tribe which represents the area as a whole. An introductory chapter by Leacock suggests trends in the history of Indian and white relations. A concluding chapter by Lurie describes contemporary Indian issues.

A-F 227. **LEIGHTON, DOROTHEA** and **CLYDE KLUCKHOHN**. Children of the People: The Navajo Individual and His Development. Cambridge, Mass.: Harvard University Press, 1947. 277 pp.

This book and its companion volume (A-F 223) provide the ethnographic background for the Navajo portion of the Indian Education Research Project (see A-F 216 for a summary of the project). In this book the personality development of the Navajo individual is described from childhood through maturity. The authors also describe the administration and results of psychological tests given to Navajo children.

A-F 228. **LELAND, JOY**. Firewater Myths: North American Indian Drinking and Alcohol Addiction. New Brunswick, N.J.: Rutgers Center for Alcohol Studies, 1976. 158 pp.

In an effort to examine the "Firewater Myth" (that American Indians are especially susceptible to alcohol intoxication and addiction), Leland reviews the literature on North American Indian alcohol use and analyzes the data in terms of World Health Organization symptoms of alcohol addiction. She finds that the results of the analysis are inconclusive because of the lack of a clear concept on the part of reporters of the nature of alcohol addiction. She also finds in some of the literature a reverse-firewater hypothesis; several observers express the opinion that American Indian alcohol addiction is rare. She finds the data for this hypothesis inconclusive also. It is suggested that the procedures of ethnoscience might be helpful to sort out problems of the definition of alcohol addiction. By systematically examining each of the World Health Organization symptoms, the author is able to show the inadequacy of the definition of alcohol addiction.

A-F 229. **LEVINE, STUART** and **NANCY OSTREICH LURIE**, eds. The American Indian Today. 1968; Rev. ed. Deland, Fla.: Everett/Edwards, 1971. 229 pp.

This collection presents contemporary American Indian cultures from an Indian point of view. The topics of the papers include Indian history, pan-Indianism, and ethnographic case studies. The book provides a guide to the directions that research on contemporary Indian groups has taken, and addresses the question of cultural renaissance among American Indian tribes as a result of the Civil Rights movements of the 1960s. Most of the authors feel that the American Indians have disassociated themselves from the general Civil Rights movement because Indians regard their case as special.

A-F 230. **LEVY, JERROLD E.** and **STEPHEN J. KUNITZ**. Indian Drinking: Navajo Practices and Anglo-American Theories. New York: Wiley, 1974. 257 pp.

The central research question in this book is whether "Indian drinking is best explained by considering it as a retreatist or escapist response to social disintegration or by viewing it as serving ends that are compatible with pre-existing tribal institutions and values." The authors are also interested in the actual extent of medically-defined alcoholism among the Navajo. Based on quantifiable data about alcohol use and drinking behavior among the Navajo and, for comparison, among the Hopi and the Western Apache, Levy and Kunitz conclude that: (1) the loose structuring of Navajo society promotes the acceptability of visible group drinking; (2) Navajo drinking practices promote behaviors which would be inter-

preted as alcoholic in Anglo-American society, but which are not connected
to alcohol addiction among the Navajo; and (3) the least acculturated
Navajos exhibit drinking behaviors which are most different from Anglo-
American behavior.

A-F 231. LINTON, RALPH, ed. Acculturation in Seven American Indian Tribes.
New York: Appleton-Century, 1940. 526 pp.
In an attempt to understand the process of acculturation, detailed ethnographic accounts of seven American Indian tribes are presented and combined
with a discussion of the implications of acculturation. Acculturation
is defined as "those phenomena which result when groups of individuals
having different cultures come into continuous first hand contact with
subsequent changes in the original culture patterns of either or both
groups." The seven tribes discussed are the Puyallup, White Knife Shoshone,
Southern Ute, Northern Arapaho, Fox, Alkatcho Carrier, and San Ildefonso
Tewa. Data on each tribe were organized according to an outline proposed
by the author, who provides a summary of each tribe's acculturation at
the end of each chapter. In the final three chapters he discusses the
theoretical issues involved with acculturation: the processes of culture
change, the process of culture transfer, and distinctive aspects of acculturation.

A-F 232. LOWIE, ROBERT H. The Crow Indians. New York: Farrar & Rinehart,
1935. 350 pp.
Lowie's description of the Crow Indians is an example of "salvage ethnography." Working with the Crow in 1907 and 1931, Lowie reconstructs their
aboriginal culture by interviewing elderly members of the tribe and collecting their reminiscences. In addition to describing the Crow when
they were a nomadic, warlike, buffalo-hunting tribe on the Northern plains,
he also describes their tribal organization, kinship, life cycle, material
culture, subsistence, mythology, religion, ceremonies, and world view.

A-F 233. MEAD, MARGARET. The Changing Culture of an Indian Tribe. New
York: Columbia University Press, 1932. 313 pp.
Mead describes the conditions on a Plains Indian reservation in Nebraska
with special attention to the position of women in the reservation system.
The cultural disorganization and maladjustment of the Indians on the reservation are stressed. This work is one of the first ethnographic descriptions of an American Indian group which focuses on the contemporary culture
rather than on the traditional pre-reservation culture.

A-F 234. MORGAN, LEWIS HENRY. League of the Ho-de-no-sau-nee or Iroquois.
1851; Reissued. New York: Corinth Books, 1962. 477 pp.
Generally regarded as the first ethnography, Morgan's work includes a
multitude of ethnographic details and is organized around the social,
political, and religious systems of the Iroquois Indian confederacy.
He describes both the traditional religion and the revitalization movement
based on the preachings of Handsome Lake (see A-F 252).

A-F 235. NABOKOV, PETER. Indian Running. Santa Barbara, Calif.: Capra
Press, 1981. 208 pp.
This is a narrative account of the 1980 Tricentennial Run between Taos
and Hopi in memory of the Pueblo Revolt of 1680. Nabokov includes a good
deal of cultural information about the importance of running to Native
Americans, using details from Fox, Mohave, Iroquois and Inca. Taking
a cultural and personality approach, he explores social relations among
the Pueblos in a way that makes their cultural history accessible to non-
anthropologists.

A-F 236. PAREDES, J. ANTHONY, ed. Anishinabe: 6 Studies of Modern Chippewa. Tallahassee: University Presses of Florida, 1980. 436 pp.

These studies done in the 1960s address the ways in which Chippewa people in Northern Minnesota have found to live and operate within American society. The methodology uses both ethnographic/ethnohistorical as well as quantitative sampling techniques to fully uncover the articulation between intrusive behaviors and persistent indigenous "psychological and psychocultural dynamics." Subjects include: powwows, the transformation of wild rice subsistence patterns, a peyote community, a social structural analysis of a Chippewa village, politics in a mixed white and Indian reservation town, and the adaptations of Chippewa to urban North City.

A-F 237. SASAKI, TOM T. Fruitland, New Mexico: A Navajo Community in Transition. Ithaca, N.Y.: Cornell University Press, 1960. 217 pp.

Sasaki describes a series of changes in the community of Fruitland over a period of twenty-five years, including the forced reduction of Navajo sheep herds in the Southwest during the 1930s, and the subsequent relocation of herding families to the Fruitland area where irrigation farming is possible. These changes led to social and cultural disruption as cleavages developed between the longtime residents of Fruitland and the newcomers. W.W. II caused further disruption as many people left for military service or for work in the war industry; their return lessened the isolation of Fruitland. Finally, in 1951, a large construction project opened many wage jobs in the area which led to an economic reorganization of the community. The author describes the social organization of the community as it was affected by these events and proposes some general principles to be applied in future administration of the community.

A-F 238. SCHUSKY, ERNEST LESTER. The Right to Be Indian. San Francisco: Indian Historian, 1970. 67 pp.

Schusky discusses the issue of civil rights for American Indians in light of the Civil Rights Act of 1964. The complexities arising out of various special treaty rights of American Indian tribes in relation to the general Civil Rights Act are considered. The historical circumstances leading to the treaty rights in which tribes have been treated as if they were separate sovereign nations are summarized, and the contemporary civil rights objectives of various Indian political groups are discussed. The author points out that government policies such as the Civil Rights Act concentrate on problems associated with poverty, while many Indian people see the lack of self-government as the central civil rights problem. He argues for self-government as the most effective way to solve "the Indian problem."

A-F 239. SCHUSKY, ERNEST LESTER, ed. Political Organization of Native North Americans. Washington, D.C.: University Press of America, 1980. 297 pp.

These essays devoted to the restructuring of political organization among Native Americans in Canada and the U.S. are divided into two sections. The first investigates Native American reaction to Westerners' intrusion (for example, the rise, decline and resurgence of the Northeast Wabanaki Confederacy; forced education and acculturation of the Eastern Cherokee; John Collier's "Indian New Deal"; and Custer's defeat). The second includes modern case studies of Florida Seminoles, Montana Crow, Quebec Inuit and Cree, and Canadian Arctic Inuit alliance movements.

A-F 240. SCOLLON, RONALD and SUZANNE B. K. SCOLLON. Linguistic Convergence
          An Ethnography of Speaking at Fort Chipewyan, Alberta. New
          York: Academic Press, 1979. 275 pp.
This ethnolinguistic study of a sub-arctic speech community examines the
historical convergence of Chipewyan, Cree, French, and English, and its
relationship to the creation of a "reality set" which the authors term
"bush consciousness." Using a single oral narrative piece to frame the
book, they have analyzed the narrator's use of Chipewyan and English as
well as the storytelling technique. Paralleling the ethnohistoric dimension of the study is an examination of the transformations in ethnographic
and linguistic orientation and methodology over five decades.

A-F 241. SPENCER, ROBERT F., JESSE D. JENNINGS, et al. The Native Ameri-
          cans: Ethnology and Backgrounds of the North American Indians.
          New York: Harper & Row, 1977. 584 pp.
This work presents a brief summary of historic and prehistoric American
Indian cultures organized regionally, with ethnographic sketches of three
or four groups from each culture area which emphasize the material and
economic aspects of traditional life. The work of nine scholars, this
book was written with an essentially uniform goal in mind: "to describe
some important phases in the history and development of the various groups
of American Indians and to convey as well some sense of the nature of
their cultural systems."

A-F 242. SPICER, EDWARD H. Cycles of Conquest: The Impact of Spain,
          Mexico, and the United States on the Indians of the Southwest,
          1533-1960. Tucson: University of Arizona Press, 1962.
          609 pp.
Spicer synthesizes ethnographic and historic data to document the culture
change that has occurred in the Southwestern U.S. and in Northwestern
Mexico since the Spanish Conquest in the mid-1500s. He organizes his
work into four parts. In Part One he describes the relations of individuals and tribal groups with the Spanish invaders and Colonial administrators. Part Two is an analysis of the governmental policies of Spain,
Mexico, and the U.S. toward the Indians of the region. Part Three
describes the ways the political, religious, social, economic, and linguistic systems of the tribal groups have changed. Part Four is a general
discussion of the processes of cultural change evident from the research.

A-F 243. SPICER, EDWARD H., ed. Perspectives in American Culture Change.
          Chicago: University of Chicago Press, 1961. 549 pp.
This work, the result of a seminar on the similarities in culture change
in different cultural groups, presents detailed analyses of culture change
in six groups by different authors. A final summary chapter by Spicer
offers a model to explain various types of contact and processes of change.
The authors use the concept of "contact community" to characterize the
social unit of cultural change and describe the process in terms of networks and social interaction.

A-F 244. SPINDLER, GEORGE and LOUISE SPINDLER. Dreamers Without Power:
          The Menomini Indians. New York: Holt, Rinehart & Winston,
          1971. 208 pp.
The authors present an account of the acculturation of the Menomini of
Wisconsin. They describe four strategies used by the Menomini for dealing
with the incongruities between traditional Menominin and European cultures:
traditional, peyote, transitional, and acculturated. The Menomini reservation was one of the few to which Federal support was terminated. The
authors describe the outcome of the termination policy for this group,
which resulted in the reservation being administered as a county of the
state of Wisconsin. (Since the book was completed the Menomini reservation has been restored to Federal jurisdiction; it was found that termination was not in the best interests of the Indian people.)

64

A-F 245. STEARNS, MARY LEE. Haida Culture in Custody: The Masset Band.
Seattle: University of Washington Press, 1981. 322 pp.
Stearns examines a community of Northwest coast Indians historically,
demographically, sociologically, and ethnographically, using a theoretical
model that interprets structural transformation by tracing individual
roles over time and in reaction to specific events. She is particularly
interested in how the Haida are regulated by a "compulsory system of relations" (imposed by the Canadian government) in social and political matters,
while they also engage in unregulated economic activity with the surrounding service area. The latter is patterned in terms of "a utilitarian
system of relations," within which the Haida are able to retain an obvious
cultural identity within the village-band sphere.

A-F 246. TRIGGER, BRUCE G. The Children of Aataentsic: A History of
the Huron People to 1660. 2 vols. Montreal: McGill-Queen's
University Press, 1976. 913 pp.
Trigger offers an ethnohistorical account of the Huron Indians, emphasizing
the details of Huron culture and the circumstances leading to the dispersal
and incorporation of the Huron people into surrounding Indian groups.
He describes historical events in terms of the motives, values, and assumptions of both the Indians and the Europeans. His critical assessment
of his sources and his use of comparative data from other Indian groups
provide the reader with an understanding of Huron culture and of the
events leading to its final dispersal in 1660.

A-F 247. UNDERHILL, RUTH M. Red Man's Religion: Beliefs and Practices
of the Indians North of Mexico. Chicago: University of Chicago
Press, 1965. 301 pp.
This book offers a general treatment of the belief and ritual systems
of the North American Indians. Underhill combines descriptions of specific
religious practices of different tribes with a discussion of general features of American Indian religions such as impersonal power, visions,
and hunting and agricultural ceremonies. She does not attempt symbolic
analyses of the beliefs and ceremonies but describes the similarities
and differences of the formal aspects of these systems.

A-F 248. WADDELL, JACK O. and MICHAEL W. EVERETT, eds. Drinking Behavior
Among Southwestern Indians: An Anthropological Perspective.
Tucson: University of Arizona Press, 1980. 248 pp.
The editors have gathered papers on Papago, Taos, Navajo, and White Mountain Apache to make a "controlled comparison" of the causes and effects
of drinking among Native Americans. Rejecting the analysis that alcohol
has served a necessary bridging function since the collapse of native
cultures by refocusing status and leadership behavior in newly integrative
ways, the book attempts to contribute to the resolution of the "Indian
drinking problem" by investigating the issue ethnographically at the community level, as well as from the perspective of Native American Public
Health Workers.

A-F 249. WADDELL, JACK O. and O. MICHAEL WATSON, eds. The American Indian
in Urban Society. Boston: Little, Brown, 1971. 414 pp.
This collection of ten original articles concentrates on the experiences
of Indians in urban conditions. A short summary and history of Federal
Indian policy by James Officer provides an introduction. Two articles
deal with the position of Indians on reservations and in the society as
a whole. The remaining articles are case studies of Indians in cities.
The research methods of the various authors differ sharply; some rely
on informal observations while others apply more formal methods of sampling
and quantification. A theme developed by these authors is that Indian
adjustment to urban life closely resembles that of other ethnic groups.
The Navajos and Indians in Chicago receive the greatest attention.

A-F 250. WALKER, DEWARD E., Jr., ed. The Emergent Native Americans:
          A Reader in Culture Contact. Boston: Little, Brown, 1972.
          818 pp.
This collection of readings brings together fifty-two previously published
papers which deal with the patterns and consequences of North American
Indian acculturation. Theoretical, historical, and ethnographic papers
are included, and most areas of the continent are treated. Historical
and contemporary perspectives are represented. The papers selected tend
to accentuate the processes of change rather than patterns of cultural
continuity.

A-F 251. WALKER, DEWARD E., Jr., ed. Systems of North American Witchcraft
          and Sorcery. Moscow, Idaho: Department of Sociology/
          Anthropology, University of Idaho, 1970. 295 pp.
Ten papers in this volume describe the witchcraft and sorcery beliefs
and practices of eleven contemporary American Indian and Latin American
cultures. The papers deal with the functional relationships of witchcraft
and sorcery to other cultural subsystems, and place the beliefs in a historical context of culture contact and intergroup tensions. The groups
from the U.S. include the Western Apache, Pueblo, Skokomish, Iroquois,
Menomini, and Nez Perce. Most of the papers include an appendix in which
personal accounts of witchcraft and sorcery are presented by informants.

A-F 252. WALLACE, ANTHONY F. C. The Death and Rebirth of the Seneca.
          New York: Knopf, 1970. 384 pp.
Wallace documents the early 19th-century cultural revival of the Seneca
Indians, the largest of the tribes in the Iroquois confederacy. This
cultural revival is an example of what Wallace has characterized as a
revitalization movement. The author records the events which preceded
the revitalization movement led by the visionary prophet Handsome Lake,
and the transformations which took place in Iroquois culture as a result
of this movement. The book is divided into three parts: an ethnographic
description of Seneca culture as it existed until the middle of the 18th
century; an historical account of the factors leading to the decline and
disorganization of the Seneca tribe; and a discussion of the process of
renascence during the early reservation period brought about by the acceptance of Handsome Lake's preachings. In addition to documenting a process
of cultural change, the book also tells the story of Indian and white
relations from the Iroquois point of view.

A-F 253. WHITE, RICHARD. The Roots of Dependency: Subsistence, Environ-
          ment, and Social Change Among the Choctaws, Pawnees, and Navajos.
          Lincoln: University of Nebraska Press, 1983. 433 pp.
This study compares the transformation of three Native American groups
from self-sufficient horticultural, hunter-gathering, pastoral groups
to a state of economic and political dependency on the world economic
system. Although material determinants are highlighted, the historical
flux of military, political, social and ideological variables in reciprocal
interchanges of influence and force are given consideration.

A-F 254. WISSLER, CLARK. Indians of the United States. 1940; Rev. ed.
          by Lucy Wales Kluckhohn. Garden City, N.Y.: Doubleday, 1966.
          336 pp.
This is a general survey of American Indian tribes organized by linguistic
groups into six large families: Algonkian-Wakashan, Hokan-Siouan, Penutian,
Nadene, Aztec-Tanoan, and Eskimo-Aleut. Within these families, individual
tribes representing different cultural adaptations are discussed. Descriptions refer to traditional ways of life before the beginning of the reservation system, but the migrations of the various tribes during historical
times are traced. A final section summarizes the general features of
Indian life.

A-F 255. WISSLER, CLARK. The Relation of Nature to Man in Aboriginal
          America. New York: Oxford University Press, 1926. 248 pp.
This book provides an example of the degree to which American anthropologists in the early 20th century used the distribution of culture traits
as a key to the culture history of an area. Looking at cultures as collections of discrete culture traits, and concentrating on material culture,
social organization, and somatology, Wissler discusses the similarities
and differences of these traits as they are distributed geographically
through the North American continent. The purpose of this investigation
is to explain the similarities and differences between cultures in terms
of the diffusion and independent invention of traits. The author argues
that the ecological context of a culture is the major factor which leads
to invention, elaboration, or acceptance of a trait.

A-F 256. WOOD, W. RAYMOND and MARGOT LIBERTY, eds. Anthropology on the
          Great Plains. Lincoln: University of Nebraska Press, 1980.
          306 pp.
All subfields of anthropology are represented in this book of twenty-one
papers--from archeology and physical anthropology to teaching and medical
anthropology. The papers discuss kinship and linguistic analysis, studies
of music and art (especially as symbolic loci for cultural resistance),
and economic and political organization from the position of women and
the question of indigenous control over developmental resources. Included
is a survey of past ethnography in the Great Plains, showing it to have
been a prime source for intra-disciplinary anthropological research.

VI.   SPANISH AMERICANS

A-F 257. ACHOR, SHIRLEY. Mexican Americans in a Dallas Barrio. Tucson:
          University of Arizona Press, 1978. 202 pp.
Achor's study of a Mexican-American neighborhood adds to the ethnographic
literature by concentrating on the adaptations of Mexican-Americans to
urban life. Based on six months of residence and several years of involvement with the barrio of La Bujura, the study emphasizes the position of
the barrio in the larger urban "ecosystem." Within the barrio, Achor
concentrates on the value system of the community.

A-F 258. BERLE, BEATRICE BISHOP. 80 Puerto Rican Families in New York
          City: Health and Disease Studied in Context. New York: Colum-
          bia University Press, 1958. 331 pp.
This is the medical portion of a joint anthropological and medical study
of a Puerto Rican slum in Manhattan (see A-F 285 for the anthropological
portion). The purpose of the book is to study the etiology of disease
in its social context. By focusing attention on the relationship between
social and environmental factors, susceptibility to illness, and the management of such illness, Berle presents data on the health conditions of
Puerto Ricans in New York and speculates on the relation between disease
and changes in social structure.

A-F 259. BROWN, LORIN W., with CHARLES L. BRIGGS and MARTHA WEIGLE.
          Hispano Folklife of New Mexico. Albuquerque: University of
          New Mexico Press, 1978. 279 pp.
The volume consists mostly of Brown's original and unedited folklife materials. These are offered not as accurate history, but as timely portraits
of residents' visions of a traditional way of life now drastically transformed. Weigle and Briggs have arranged the manuscripts, often shifting
genre and point of view, moving from stories of frontier life through

tales about trade and the growth of local fortunes to the aesthetic expressions of social life. Because Brown found these rituals already eroding, the focus then turns to legacies of traditional culture and to Hispano-Catholic institutions such as compadrazgo and church-related ceremonies.

A-F 260. BUITRAGO ORTIZ, CARLOS. Esperanza: An Ethnographic Study of a Peasant Community in Puerto Rico. Tucson: University of Arizona Press, 1973. 217 pp.
Buitrago Ortiz presents a social anthropological study of a rural Puerto Rican barrio. Concentrating on the household, kinship, and the family, the author shows this peasant community to be highly dependent on outside economic influences, especially the fluctuations in the tobacco market. He bases his conclusions on nearly ten years of familiarity with the barrio.

A-F 261. CAMARILLO, ALBERT. Chicanos in a Changing Society: From Mexican Pueblos to American Barrios in Santa Barbara and Southern California. Cambridge, Mass.: Harvard University Press, 1979. 325 pp.
This volume is a social history of the Mexican-American people who have settled in the towns and cities of Southern California. In tracing the history of this group, special attention is placed on the development of Chicano neighborhoods and barrios. The external and internal factors--social, economic, political, racial, cultural and demographic--that have shaped the life experiences of three generations of Mexican-Americans in the U.S. are examined. Another feature of this study is its examination of the origins and evolution of the Chicano working class and the incorporation of these workers into the capitalist labor market.

A-F 262. CLARK, MARGARET. Health in the Mexican-American Culture: A Community Study. 1959; Rev. ed. Berkeley: University of California Press, 1970. 253 pp.
This study, carried out in San Jose, California in 1955, is designed to provide sociocultural information about the medical beliefs of Mexican-Americans. The major part of the book consists of a summary of Mexican-American culture in which economic, religious, and social organization patterns are discussed. The final two chapters are a discussion of theories of disease in the Mexican-American community, including recommendations by Clark as to how medical personnel could respond to their patients in more productive ways.

A-F 263. DAVIDSON, R. THEODORE. Chicano Prisoners: The Key to San Quentin. New York: Holt, Rinehart & Winston, 1974. 196 pp.
Davidson describes the culture of Chicano (Mexican-American) male prisoners in a maximum security Federal prison in California. He describes the social categories of the prisoners, stressing the distinction made between "convicts," who are unified in their opposition to the prison staff, and "inmates," who will inform the staff of illegal behavior in order to improve their own position. The illegal activities of the "Family" (the secret group of Chicano convicts which directs covert activities among the prisoners) are described.

A-F 264. DURAN, LIVIE ISAURO and H. RUSSELL BERNARD, eds. Introduction to Chicano Studies: A Reader. New York: Macmillan, 1973. 585 pp.
This introductory anthology brings together selections from literature, journalism, politics, history, psychology, sociology, and anthropology to portray the culture and society of Mexican-Americans. The book provides a broad context for investigation of issues in contemporary Chicano communities.

A-F 265. DURAN, RICHARD P., ed. Latino Language and Communicative Behavior
Norwood, N.J.: Ablex, 1981. 363 pp.
These essays explore the psycholinguistic and sociolinguistic aspects
of Spanish and English usage in the U.S. The first half addresses the
heterogeneity of Spanish forms and the dependence of code-switching (the
mixing of English and Spanish in discourse) on social background, socialization process, and specific discourse context. The second half studies
the deleterious effects on communication and cognitive skills of negative
attitudes toward bilingualism at school and in the community. Another
study examines how the skills and teaching strategy of the mother are
reflected by the child. Two studies show that bilingualism can be highly
constructive and improve cognitive performance.

A-F 266. GEILHUFFE, NANCY L. Chicanos and the Police: A Study of the
Politics of Ethnicity in San Jose, California. Washington,
D.C.: Society for Applied Anthropology, 1979. 133 pp.
This is a study of minority mobilization and the struggle of Chicanos
to gain more political power. Set in San Jose, the book describes the
internal conflicts of a city with deep cultural and structural divisions.
Geilhuffe researches and interviews both of the mutually hostile camps,
the Chicano militant groups and the police. The study provides an insight
into the militant Chicanos' complaints and the inability of the police
to grasp the meaning of the Chicano struggle.

A-F 267. GONZALEZ, NANCIE L. The Spanish-Americans of New Mexico: A
Heritage of Pride. 1967; Rev. ed. Albuquerque: University
of New Mexico Press, 1969. 246 pp.
In this analysis of the contemporary New Mexico Spanish-American socio-
cultural system, attention is given to historical factors which have influenced cultural persistence and change, but the emphasis is placed on contemporary factors such as juvenile delinquency, availability of higher
education, intermarriage with Anglo-Americans, changes in religious behavior, and the effects of urbanization. Social organization, including
the Spanish-Americans' concepts of community, pride, and social class,
is analyzed. The second edition includes a chapter on contemporary political and social activism.

A-F 268. GRIMES, RONALD L. Symbol and Conquest: Public Ritual and Drama
in Santa Fe, New Mexico. Ithaca, N.Y.: Cornell University
Press, 1976. 281 pp.
Grimes interprets the rituals and symbols of the two major annual celebrations in Santa Fe, New Mexico, showing the significance of the rituals
for each of the traditionally conflicting cultures of the city: Hispanics,
Anglos, and Indians. He also considers their significance for tourists,
the Chamber of Commerce, the merchants, and the art community. He analyzes
the apparently contradictory interpretations of symbols by the different
groups by distinguishing three modes of organizing and acting on deep
cultural concerns: civitas (city-mindedness), ecclesia (institutionalized
religious procedures), and ethnos (organizational styles typical of each
of the three Santa Fe cultures). Through the overlapping and interpenetration of these modes of organization, many of the inconsistencies in
the symbolic system are resolved.

A-F 269. HANSEN, NILES. The Border Economy: Regional Development in
the Southwest. Austin: University of Texas Press, 1981. 225 pp.
This book explores the structure of and changes in employment and earnings
of Mexican labor, the problem of undocumented Mexican immigration, and
related issues. Hansen shows that location theory may not be very helpful
in understanding borderland issues. Instead, he elaborates a regional
model which demonstrates the symbiotic relationship between the urban
areas on both sides of the border. The advantages and limitations of

69

the data sources are noted and explained in detail in the appendices.
The author notes the limitations of the official view of borderland issues
and points to the human element, so often eliminated from quantitative
studies.

A-F 270. **HARWOOD, ALAN.** Rx: Spiritist as Needed: A Study of a Puerto
Rican Community Mental Health Resource. New York: Wiley, 1977.
251 pp.
Harwood presents data on the etiological and nosological system underlying
the approach of traditional Puerto Rican spiritists, who call on various
classes of supernatural spirits to treat a series of specified maladies.
He attempts to show how this system can operate in the modern U.S. health
care system. The author worked in a neighborhood health center in New
York City in 1967 and 1968, participating in spiritists' ceremonies and
surveying a sample of households in the neighborhood. He describes the
setting, the subculture of spiritism, the social structure and rituals
of spiritist groups, diagnosis and treatment in spiritist therapy, spiritism in the context of family relations, and the practical and theoretical
implications of spiritist beliefs and practices.

A-F 271. **HELM, JUNE,** ed. Spanish-Speaking People in the United States.
Seattle: University of Washington Press, 1968. 215 pp.
This volume presents twelve papers by anthropologists and sociologists
which discuss the position of Spanish-speaking people in U.S. society.
The subjects range from Joan W. Moore's study of social class assimilation
and acculturation of a large random sample of Spanish-speaking individuals
in Los Angeles, California, and San Antonio, Texas, to Americo Paredes's
analysis of six Mexican-American intercultural jests. Most of the papers
reflect a concern with acculturation and the maintenance of the cultural
integrity of the Spanish-speaking population of the U.S.

A-F 272. **HENDRICKS, GLENN.** The Dominican Diaspora: From the Dominican
Republic to New York City--Villagers in Transition. New York:
Teachers College Press, 1974. 171 pp.
Hendricks contends that a Dominican Republic village and a New York City
neighborhood are parts of a single social field. He includes ethnographic
descriptions both of life in the Dominican Republic village from which
many of his New York City informants have come, and of the Dominicans'
life in New York. After documenting the various strategies used by the
immigrants to get to the U.S., he examines the role that U.S. schools
play in acculturation, and the conceptions of acculturation held by educational and immigration officials in the U.S.

A-F 273. **HERRERA-SOBEK, MARIA.** The Bracero Experience. Los Angeles,
Calif.: UCLA Latin American Center, 1979. 142 pp.
The author contends that folklore and the "lore" of novels and literature
present very different images of the bracero (Hispanic agricultural day-
laborer): in the former, the depiction is that of a resilient person,
happy and eager to move upward on the social scale; in the latter, the
bracero is seen as a bitter and exploited man. The Bracero Experience
contains numerous first-hand accounts of the lives of braceros to support
Herrera-Sobek's thesis that folklore best reflects the bracero experience
in the U.S.

A-F 274. **HOROWITZ, RUTH.** Honor and the American Dream: Culture and Identity in a Chicano Community. New Brunswick, N.J.: Rutgers
University Press, 1983. 278 pp.
This study of an inner-city Chicano community in Chicago focuses on the
community's youth and the process of growing up. The author is particularly interested in discerning and describing the process by which the
community and its youthful members negotiate the meanings of particular

kinds of conduct and relationships. Because this community exists within, is affected by, and to some extent adopts the larger Anglo culture, community members are provided with alternative meanings or interpretations of situations and behaviors. Tension usually arises between values and norms of the local community, which stress honor and close social ties, and the norms of the wider society, which enforce individual enterprise as a means to achieve the American Dream. The study examines the complex interweaving of structural, ecological, situational, and cultural elements in the local urban community.

A-F 275. **KIEV, ARI.** Curanderismo: Mexican-American Folk Psychiatry. New York: Free Press, 1968. 207 pp.
This work describes the psychological theories and treatment methods of a Mexican-American psychotherapeutic system: curanderismo. Kiev is a psychiatrist whose data come from interviews with curanderos (practitioners of curanderismo). The social and cultural context of Mexican-American mental illness is examined in detail, and the author attempts to show the contribution of culture to personality development and psychic conflict. He compares curanderismo with Euro-American approaches to the treatment of mental illness and shows why Euro-American psychiatrists often do not provide satisfactory treatment for mentally ill Mexican-Americans.

A-F 276. **LA RUFFA, ANTHONY L.** San Cipriano: Life in a Puerto Rican Community. New York: Gordon & Breach, 1971. 149 pp.
La Ruffa examines a predominantly black Puerto Rican community and argues that the black population of Puerto Rico does not represent a distinct subculture. He describes the historical and spatial setting of San Cipriano and presents ethnographic data on economics, social organization, life cycle, and religion—particularly, the Protestant Pentacostalism in the community. He delineates influences on Puerto Rican culture, arguing that through the impact of media such as television, Puerto Rico is becoming more Americanized.

A-F 277. **LLANES, JOSE.** Cuban Americans: Masters of Survival. Cambridge, Mass.: Abt Books, 1982. 229 pp.
Through interviewing 187 Cuban-Americans from diverse communities and classes, Llanes has attempted to sift their stories of escape and survival for symbolic elements. These elements help define and integrate Cuban ethnic identity as it has developed through three waves of migration spread over twenty-one years.

A-F 278. **MADSEN, WILLIAM.** Mexican-Americans of South Texas. 1964; Rev. ed. New York: Holt, Rinehart & Winston, 1973. 124 pp.
This is a general ethnography of the Mexican-American population of Hidalgo County in Southern Texas. The book deals with the conflicts and differential advantages which result when cultural pluralism conflicts with the values of the dominant society. The author provides a general description of the Mexican-American culture of the county, concentrating more on ideals of behavior than on everyday life. He draws on case studies to show how aspects of Mexican-American culture lead to conflicts with the mainstream culture, especially in education and health care delivery. The most detailed analysis is concerned with the ways in which Mexican-American people use two systems of health care: traditional curers and Anglo physicians. This second edition includes an epilogue dealing with developments in Mexican-American political activism.

A-F 279. **MALDONADO-DENIS, MANUEL.** The Emigration Dialectic: Puerto Rico and the USA. New York: International, 1980. 156 pp.
The author analyzes the complex network of social relations that define the Puerto Rican experience in the U.S. Focusing on the Puerto Rican reality from a sociohistoric perspective and using a historical material-

ist framework, Maldonado-Denis sees emigration as an integral part of
what he calls the "anti-development" of Puerto Rico during the last thirty
years; the emigrant is seen as an involuntary exile forced to the metropolis by the exigencies of the Capitalist-Colonial mode of production.
Racial discrimination and cultural assimilation are also analyzed vis-
a-vis U.S. social structure. The return of 150,000 Puerto Ricans in the
last five years is viewed as a result of increased narrowing of the base
of productive labor in monopoly Capitalism; the effects of this return
migration on the Puerto Rican political process are also explored.

A-F 280. MELVILLE, MARGARITA B., ed. Twice a Minority: Mexican American
Women. St. Louis: Mosby, 1980. 270 pp.
This volume gathers in one text a variety of empirical data on Mexican-
American women collected by both Mexican-American and Anglo-American social
scientists. The picture that emerges is one of a population of women
who attempt, with varying degrees of success, to fit into the mainstream
of American life without losing their identity as Mexicans. The book
is divided into three parts. The first deals with the status of women
and several aspects of what constitutes womanhood among Mexican-Americans.
The second part explores gender roles and the changes that seem to be
occurring in their conceptualization. The final section explains cross-
cultural dynamics. The author argues for a redefinition of ethnicity
in which economic considerations and minority status are crucial in understanding the process of selective acculturation.

A-F 281. MINTZ, SIDNEY W. Worker in the Cane: A Puerto Rican Life History.
New Haven, Conn.: Yale University Press, 1960. 288 pp.
This book consists of the autobiographical narrative of Anastacio Zayas
Alvarado ("Don Taso"), with commentary by Mintz. The work is an application of the "life history" technique of anthropological data collection
and presentation. Puerto Rican history, culture and society, and the
experience of "Westernization," are illuminated by Mintz's choice of a
politically active cane worker who had been intimately involved in the
local events which reflected the nature of U.S. Colonial penetration in
the lives of the rural proletariat. After a brief chapter of orientation,
the book proceeds chronologically, mostly in Don Taso's own words, from
childhood and adolescence through early and late manhood. The final section, relating to Don Taso's conversion to the Pentecostal religion, offers
reflections on the substantial changes that have occurred in Puerto Rican
lifeways in the 20th century.

A-F 282. MIRANDE, ALFREDO and ENRIQUEZ EVANGELINA. La Chicana: The Mexican American Woman. Chicago: University of Chicago Press,
1979. 283 pp.
In this critique of erroneous stereotypes, the authors use historical
documents to show the political and economic role of the Chicana woman. The
basic theme that gives organization to the book is the contemporary Chicana
situation. According to the authors, she is triply oppressed: discriminated against as a member of an ethnic minority, as a woman, and as a
victim of acute oppression by males of her own society.

A-F 283. MORA, MAGDALENA and ADELAIDA R. DEL CASTILLO. Struggles Past
and Present. Los Angeles: Chicano Studies Research Center,
University of California at Los Angeles, 1980. 204 pp.
The primary objective of this volume is the documentation and appraisal
of Mexican-American women's participation in the struggle against national
oppression, class exploitation, and sexism. The essays present the complexity and depth of the participation of these women and attest to their
leadership and creativity. This work is divided into five parts. In
Part One, the status of Mexican women is analyzed within the context of
national oppression and class conflict. Part Two addresses sterilization

and the rationale underlying the advocacy of sterilization of minority
women. In Part Three, the authors document the hardships encountered
by women as wage earners and union organizers. The fourth part deals
with working-class movements where women figure as important participants.
Finally, Part Five is a collection of essays on the lives of individual
Mexican-American and Mexican women.

A-F 284. MURGIA, EDWARD. Chicano Intermarriage: A Theoretical and Empiri-
          cal Study. San Antonio, Tex.: Trinity University Press, 1982.
          134 pp.
Murgia examines the condition of Mexican-American people by using inter-
ethnic marriage as an indicator of the amount of assimilation that this
minority group has undergone. Discussed in detail are what the author
sees as the positive and the negative consequences of intermarriage.
The major positive consequence is that intermarriage may result in the
minority's more rapid upward mobility in American society. The negative
consequence analyzed is that intermarriage is a source of assimilation
that threatens ethnic cultural identity and social cohesion. The book
combines empirical research and statistical analysis to illuminate the
dynamics of Anglo-American and Mexican-American interpersonal relationships.

A-F 285. PADILLA, ELENA. Up from Puerto Rico. New York: Columbia Uni-
          versity Press, 1958. 317 pp.
This work presents a social anthropological study of Puerto Ricans in
a New York City neighborhood. The research was conducted in the early
1950s in conjunction with a medical study of the neighborhood (see A-F
258). Padilla concentrates on the social organization of the Puerto Ricans,
describing in detail kinship, family organization, and the ways in which
the people in the neighborhood both define themselves as a group and deal
with other ethnic groups in the society. Socialization, cliques, the
social grapevine, and health are analyzed from a structural-functional
perspective.

A-F 286. ROMO, RICARDO and RAYMOND PAREDES, eds. New Directions in Chicano
          Scholarship. La Jolla: Chicano Studies Program, University
          of California, San Diego, 1978. 268 pp.
Romo and Paredes have put together a series of essays dealing with numerous
aspects of the Mexican-American's life in the U.S. The topics discussed
are from the fields of anthropology, sociology, language, and literature.
The articles criticize anthropological, sociological and educational
studies of Chicano groups that have presented distorted biases and stereotypic views of such groups.

A-F 287. RUBEL, ARTHUR J. Across the Tracks: Mexican-Americans in a
          Texas City. Austin: University of Texas Press, 1966.
          266 pp.
Rubel concentrates on social relations, acculturation, and problems in
professional health delivery in his ethnography of Mexican-Americans in
Texas. He describes the major social institutions of the Mexican-American
community, including the family, men's informal cliques, formal mutual
aid societies, and political structures. The Mexican-Americans are portrayed as perceiving social relationships with anxiety and disaffection.
The author ascribes this phenomenon to the "incongruity which exists
between the family oriented social system for which Chicanos are socialized
and the larger and more complex society with which they must contend."
He suggests avenues by which Mexican-Americans' acculturation can be most
easily achieved.

A-F 288. SAFA, HELEN ICKEN. The Urban Poor of Puerto Rico: A Study in
          Development and Inequality. New York: Holt, Rinehart & Winston,
          1974. 116 pp.
Safa describes the way in which the "economic, family, and community patterns developed in the shantytown . . . promote or hinder the development
of class consciousness and class solidarity among the urban poor." Her
research was conducted over a ten-year period during which time the Puerto
Rican shantytown in which she worked was demolished and the residents
moved to urban housing projects. She describes the pattern of life in
the shantytown and the ways that relocation affected the former residents,
noting that it is difficult for the poor of Puerto Rico to organize politically and to understand the structural roots of poverty because of the
strength of traditional values and patterns of social relations.

A-F 289. SIMMONS, MARC. Witchcraft in the Southwest: Spanish and Indian
          Supernaturalism on the Rio Grande. Flagstaff, Ariz.: Northland
          Press, 1974. 184 pp.
This book surveys, from an historical and cultural rather than a strictly
analytical point of view, the nature of witchcraft belief in the far Southwestern part of the U.S. The author tries to delve below the surface
of supernaturalism to give the reader a basic understanding of the subject,
which continues to be a distinct historical and social phenomenon among
the Hispanic and Indian peoples inhabiting the Southwest. Attention is
also given to folk medicine practices used in the curing of both witch-
caused ailments and biological diseases.

A-F 290. STEWARD, JULIAN H., ROBERT A. MANNERS, ERIC R. WOLF, ELENA
          PADILLA SEDA, SIDNEY W. MINTZ, and RAYMOND L. SCHEELE. The People
          of Puerto Rico: A Study in Social Anthropology. Urbana: Univer-
          sity of Illinois Press, 1956. 540 pp.
This volume is a collaborative effort by a number of anthropologists to
characterize the culture of Puerto Rico. Five individual community studies
are combined with a historical overview and a hypothesis about recurrent
processes in culture change in Puerto Rico. Municipalities, plantations,
and rural areas are discussed as representative settings of different
Puerto Rican subcultures. The focus is on systematic differences in these
regional subcultures, and the institutional frameworks within which they
develop.

A-F 291. TREJO, ARNULFO D., ed. The Chicanos: As We See Ourselves.
          Tucson: University of Arizona Press, 1979. 221 pp.
The essays presented here deal with anthropology, education, history,
literature, political science, and sociology as they relate to Mexican-
Americans. The collection has been compiled for the purpose of giving
both the Mexican-American reader and the non-Mexican-American reader an
inside view of Chicano culture, self-image, socioeconomic status, and
political perspective. Bilingualism and biculturalism are focused on throughout. In addition, there are two essays on women: one on the traditional
women of New Mexico and the other on Chicana women.

A-F 292. VIGIL, JAMES D. From Indians to Chicanos: A Sociocultural His-
          tory. St. Louis, Mo.: Mosby, 1980. 245 pp.
This book offers a historical view of the development of Chicanos by tracing their origins through the multi-faceted cultural heritage of Mexicans
in the U.S. From all these diverse cultural orientations, and after centuries of acculturation, the Chicano emerges as culturally and socially
distinct from the Anglo-American, yet adapted to modern life in Southwest
cities. At the end of each chapter Vigil includes a bibliography related
to the chapter topic.

A-F 293. **WEIGLE, MARTA.** Brothers of Light, Brothers of Blood: The Penitentes of the Southwest. Albuquerque: University of New Mexico
Press, 1976. 300 pp.
Weigle describes the history and organization of the Penitente sect of
Roman Catholicism whose members live in New Mexico and Southern Colorado.
The Penitentes are a secret society best known for the physical penances
the members undergo during the Catholic Holy Week observances. The author
traces Penitente origins to the early Spanish Colonial period. She
stresses the secular aspects of Penitente organization, including mutual
aid and judicial functions, rather than the more sensational activities
for which the Penitentes are known.

A-F 294. **WEST, STANLEY A.** and **JUNE MACKLING**, eds. The Chicano Experience.
Boulder, Colo.: Westview Press, 1979. 318 pp.
This volume collects thirteen articles which exhibit a wide variety of
theoretical viewpoints and scholarly disciplines. The essays emphasize
migrant lifeways, ethnic boundary maintenance, religious beliefs, and
voluntary associations and leadership among Mexican-Americans. The purpose
of the volume is fourfold: (1) to add to the knowledge of Chicano communities; (2) to add to the knowledge and understanding of how Mexican-
Americans have adapted in various urban areas; (3) to present descriptions
and analyses of communities in the Midwest; and (4) to bring an anthropological approach to the understanding of this second-largest minority
group in the U.S.

VII.   URBAN AND APPLIED

A-F 295. **BUELL, EMMETT.** School Desegregation and Defended Neighborhoods.
Lexington, Mass.: Lexington Books, 1982. 202 pp.
In this book Buell analyzes the fierce opposition to forced busing that
erupted in South Boston during the mid-1970s. After contextualizing the
situation with a history of South Boston and the national desegregation
events of the time, he introduces the concept of the "defended neighborhood" and applies it to the South Boston case. By documenting the judicial,
ideological, political, and administrative details of the situation,
Buell offers a view of the functioning and mobilization of the defended
neighborhood, examines four major criticisms of busing for desegregation
in South Boston, and offers policy recommendations for desegregating other
such neighborhoods.

A-F 296. **BURKHART**, LYNNE C. Old Values in a New Town: The Politics of
Race and Class in Columbia, Maryland. New York: Praeger, 1981.
165 pp.
Burkhart lived within and studied the planned pluralism (middle and lower
class, black and white) of a community built in 1967 as an idealistic
alternative to both urban blight and the sterile homogeneity of the suburbs.
To overcome the simplifying techniques of sociology that break down social
reality into statistical variables such as sex, age, race, and income,
the author attempted to enter into and reconstruct the fabric of social
relationships in order to come to a fuller and more constructive analysis
of the outcome of plans for--as well as fears of--community integration.
Burkhart finds a heterogeneous community moving toward functional pluralism,
successfully walking the line between fragmentation and assimilation.

A-F 297. CLIFTON, JAMES A., ed. Applied Anthropology: Readings in the
          Uses of the Science of Man. Boston: Houghton Mifflin, 1970.
          286 pp.
Twenty-one papers published between 1928 and 1966 are selected to present
the general features and research emphases of applied anthropology. Four
chapters are devoted to the development of "action anthropology" in the
University of Chicago Fox Project (see A-F 214). Several articles summarize the role of anthropology in education, in technical assistance,
in medicine, and in Indian Land Claims litigation. Intended as an introduction to the history and diversity of applied anthropology, the collection also includes essays on ethical issues raised by the discipline.

A-F 298. COCHRANE, GLYNN. Development Anthropology. New York: Oxford
          University Press, 1971. 125 pp.
Cochrane, an anthropologist with administrative experience in the Southwest
Pacific, argues that applied anthropology has failed to be of value to
policymakers for five major reasons: (1) the low opinion that applied
anthropologists have shown for administrators; (2) a lack of understanding
of the process by which administrators formulate policy; (3) the inability
of anthropologists to address their academic interests to the problems
faced by administrators; (4) the anthropological specialization in small-
scale problems which have limited utility for administrators who make
policy decisions on a national scale; and (5) the lack of understanding
of the contributions of other social scientists.

A-F 299. DAVIS, W. ALLISON and ROBERT J. HAVIGHURST. Father of the Man:
          How Your Child Gets His Personality. Boston: Houghton Mifflin,
          1945. 245 pp.
Davis and Havighurst here offer a guide—written from the perspective
of psychological anthropology—for parents raising children in American
culture. Individual chapters are devoted to such matters as "The Psychology of the Young Child," "The Battle of Cleanliness," and "Amoral Child
in Moral Society." A chapter on "Like Mother, Like Daughter?" is contributed by Helen Ross, a psychoanalyst.

A-F 300. DEAL, TERRENCE E. and ALLAN A. KENNEDY. Corporate Cultures:
          The Rites and Rituals of Corporate Life. Reading, Mass.:
          Addison-Wesley, 1982. 232 pp.
The premise of this book is that a strong corporate culture will improve
company performance. The values, rituals, and "heroes" of various successful corporations are discussed to demonstrate to business leaders how
companies can manage their cultures.

A-F 301. DOWNS, JAMES F. Cultures in Crisis. 1971; Rev. ed. Beverly
          Hills, Calif.: Glencoe Press, 1975. 237 pp.
In the first part of the book general anthropological concepts are presented to challenge assumptions about the uniformity of U.S. culture.
Downs argues the importance of looking at U.S. society as made up of many
cultures. The second part of the book argues that technological change
has proceeded faster than the society's ability to deal with that change.
Six "crisis areas" are discussed, including drugs, police brutality,
environmental pollution, violence, and changing sexual practices. The
author's position is that Americans should be more willing to accept cultural variety; the crisis is not that there is cultural change, but that
it is occurring so rapidly that individuals have a hard time adjusting
to it.

A-F 302. EAMES, EDWIN and JUDITH GRANICH GOODE. Urban Poverty in a Cross-
          Cultural Perspective. New York: Free Press, 1973. 299 pp.
This study uses data from historical and anthropological sources to explore
the nature of contemporary urban poverty. Special attention is given
to the insights a cross-cultural survey of poverty can provide for understanding poverty in the U.S. Eames and Goode point out that in the U.S.
the term "poverty" confuses three forms of deprivation associated with
low social position: powerlessness, social worthlessness or prestige
deprivation, and natural deprivation. They show how these types of deprivation have occurred separately or in combination in different historical
and cultural circumstances. The final chapter deals specifically with
the U.S.

A-F 303. EDDY, ELIZABETH M. Walk the White Line: A Profile of Urban
          Education. Garden City, N.Y.: Doubleday, 1967. 187 pp.
This is a general discussion of the problems in urban slum schools that
arise from the organizational structure of the school system. The organizing focus of this profile is the relationship between the formal educational system and the urban poor as it is manifested within the schools
that the children of the poor attend. Data collected during observations
in nine public schools were combined with previously published studies
to present this overview.

A-F 304. EDDY, ELIZABETH M. and WILLIAM L. PARTRIDGE, eds. Applied Anthro-
          pology in America. New York: Columbia University Press, 1978.
          484 pp.
Twenty-two original articles concerning past, present, and future trends
in American applied anthropology are brought together here. Many figures
in the field have contributed, among them Margaret Mead, Conrad Arensberg,
Solon T. Kimball, William Foote Whyte, and Ward H. Goodenough. After
an introductory summary of the development of applied anthropology, the
articles are organized into four sections: the dialogue between theory
and application, the place of applied anthropology in institutional settings, the role of anthropology in public policy, and educational and
ethical considerations.

A-F 305. FELDMAN, HARVEY W., MICHAEL H. AGAR, and GEORGE M. BESCHNER,
          eds. Angel Dust: An Ethnographic Study of PCP Users. Lexington,
          Mass.: Lexington Books, 1979. 227 pp.
This volume of essays attempts to fill the gap in knowledge about the
social setting and everyday context for PCP use and abuse. Assumptions
of the extreme pathology of users based on studies of those brought in
for emergency treatment seem to be overturned by this applied ethnography,
which was intended to provide data and impetus for more effectively
designed legislation aimed at controlling the escalating PCP problem.

A-F 306. FITCHEN, JANET M. Poverty in Rural America: A Case Study.
          Boulder, Colorado: Westview Press, 1981. 257 pp.
Fitchen takes a cross-disciplinary tack to exploring the historical causes,
structural realities, and psychological factors of the nonfarming, rural
poor in America, and in so doing hopes to affect policy and projects dealing with these problems. Based on a decade of participant-observation
in a small upstate New York town, her study concentrates on the patterns
of interactions of selected families which are locked into intergenera-
tional poverty.

A-F 307. FUCHS, ESTELLE. Pickets at the Gates. New York: Free Press,
          1966. 205 pp.
This book presents two case studies of black communities confronting educational injustice in their local de facto segregated schools. Fuchs
describes the setting and gives background information relevant to both

events, focusing mainly on socioeconomic data and achievement levels, with a lesser focus (especially in the second study) on the dynamics of community mobilization.

A-F 308. GARDNER, BURLEIGH B. and DAVID G. MOORE. Human Relations in Industry. 1945; Rev. ed. Homewood, Ill.: Richard D. Irwin, 1968. 479 pp.
Gardner and Moore apply anthropological concepts to the study of industrial organization. The purpose of the research is to improve the operation of industrial processes by emphasizing the effect on productivity of inter-personal relations. Case studies of industrial operations are used as examples, though the authors do not stress description. The book is written to be used by business managers and executives, so familiarity with many aspects of industrial management is assumed.

A-F 309. GILBERT, GLENN G. and JACOB ORNSTEIN, eds. Problems in Applied Educational Sociolinguistics. The Hague: Mouton, 1978. 144 pp.
The papers in this volume include general descriptions, research and prog-ress reports, linguistic analyses, and attitudinal and sociolinguistic studies. The majority of the essays are based on research done on Spanish speakers in the Southwestern U.S. The remaining essays are concerned with linguistic problems of other ethnic groups in the U.S., both inside and outside the Southwest.

A-F 310. GLADWIN, THOMAS. Poverty U.S.A. Boston: Little, Brown, 1967. 183 pp.
Gladwin discusses the general nature of the phenomenon of poverty. He compares New Deal policies with the War on Poverty to show how the social and cultural circumstances differed. The New Deal was directed toward a middle-class population which had been economically devastated at a time when there was a general feeling of national crisis. The War on Poverty was instituted in a time of general affluence and was directed toward a group of people who had been living in poverty for generations. Gladwin argues that poverty is the result of the overall structure of society, so that programs designed to alleviate poverty must reallocate money and, most importantly, reallocate the power which is associated with money.

A-F 311. GLASSER, MORTON and GRETEL PELTO. The Medical Merry-Go-Round. Pleasantville, N.Y.: Redgrave, 1980. 167 pp.
This book begins as a study in medical anthropology, the focus of which is the Navajo Shaman's treatment of heart disease. Most of the book, however, is a more general discussion of potentially unnecessary medical practices. Glasser is a practicing physician; Pelto is an anthropologist.

A-F 312. HENRY, JULES. Jules Henry on Education. 1966; Rev. ed. New York: Random House, 1972. 183 pp.
Five of Henry's essays are collected here in one volume. "Vulnerability in Education" deals with the repression of innovation in the socialization process in order to maintain the social and educational structure. "Mental Health Problems in Elementary School" offers suggestions for dealing with disadvantaged and deprived students. "Hope, Delusion and Organization" considers the educational response to student aspirations. "Education of the Negro Child" discusses the need for study of the socializing environ-ment beyond the schools. "A Cross-Cultural Outline of Education" is a statement about the topics that should be covered in a thorough study of education.

A-F 313. HOLTZMAN, WAYNE H., ROGELIO DIAZ-GUERRERO, and JON D. SWARTZ.
Personality Development in Two Cultures: A Cross Cultural Longi-
tudinal Study of School Children in Mexico and the United States.
Austin: University of Texas Press, 1975. 427 pp.
In this study, differences in cognition and personality development in
children in Austin, Texas, and Mexico City are examined over a six-year
period. A battery of primary projective tests were employed. Six hypotheses resulted from the statistical correlation of twenty-one variables.
According to the hypotheses, compared to Mexican children, American children tend to: (1) cope with problems in a more active way; (2) be more
dynamic, technological, and external in terms of subjective culture; (3)
be more complex and differentiated in cognitive structures; (4) be more
individual-centered; (5) be more competitive; and (6) be less fatalistic
and pessimistic.

A-F 314. IANNI, FRANCIS A. J. and EDWARD STOREY, eds. Cultural Relevance
and Educational Issues: Readings in Anthropology and Education.
Boston: Little, Brown, 1973. 533 pp.
The editors have selected thirty-five papers which illustrate five areas:
(1) the general relationships between anthropology and education; (2)
the anthropological impact on educational policy; (3) anthropological
studies of the educational process; (4) cross-cultural approaches to education; and (5) the anthropology of social problems outside of educational
settings.

A-F 315. KIMBALL, SOLON T. and JAMES E. McCLELLAN, Jr. Education and
the New America. New York: Random House, 1962. 402 pp.
The authors see the school as "a transitional institution in which the
process of education gradually separates the young from family and locality
and prepares them to join the great corporate systems and to establish
their own independent nuclear families." The first part of the book is
a description of American society which stresses those aspects of American
culture which are especially important to educators. In the second part
the authors suggest ways that the educational system can instill self-
assurance and commitment to the American system in students.

A-F 316. KURTZ, DONALD V. The Politics of a Poverty Habitat. Cambridge,
Mass.: Ballinger, 1973. 243 pp.
This is an attempt to devise an anthropological approach to the study
and understanding of poverty which is an alternative to the "culture of
poverty" viewpoint. Kurtz's alternative is the idea of a "poverty habitat," which emphasizes the relationship between an impoverished population
and the larger national system of which it is a part, and seeks the causes
of poverty in the larger national system rather than in the culture of
poverty. Data used in the study, conducted near San Diego from 1968 to
1970, derive from a War on Poverty institution, the Border Area Community
Action Council of San Diego County. The study focuses on political conflict, emphasizing the issues, the personnel, and the ways in which the
allocation of resources was manipulated in the final outcome. Kurtz's
conclusions deal with the integration of the poor into the mainstream
of American society, concentrating on the role of local organizations
in the implementation of integration.

A-F 317. LANDES, RUTH. Culture in American Education: Anthropological
Approaches to Minority and Dominant Groups in the Schools.
New York: Wiley, 1965. 330 pp.
Landes describes a training experiment designed to make teachers and social
workers more sensitive to cultural differences when working with pupils
and clients. Conducted in the early 1960s, the experiment had teachers
and social workers engage in short periods of participant-observation
fieldwork to give them an awareness of the influences of families and

communities on school performance and social behavior. Much of the book consists of reports of the experiences and responses of the participants in the program. The study also includes detailed descriptions of various incidents from the experiment which provide insights into both dominant and minority American culture.

A-F 318. LEACOCK, ELEANOR BURKE. Teaching and Learning in City Schools: A Comparative Study. New York: Basic Books, 1969. 263 pp.
Two predominantly black and two predominantly white schools were selected for this study of urban schools. One of the black schools and one of the white schools served low-income neighborhoods while the other two were located in middle-income neighborhoods. The schools were examined in terms of their function in the socialization of American children. Custodial and economic functions are shown to be significant factors in the structure and maintenance of school systems. Leacock also shows how assumptions about the capabilities of students are held by teachers and learned by children. She makes a series of recommendations designed to increase the opportunities for children in the educational system.

A-F 319. LEEMON, THOMAS A. The Rites of Passage in a Student Culture: A Study of the Dynamics of Transition. New York: Teachers College Press, 1972. 215 pp.
Leemon's study of the recruitment, training, and initiation rites of a college social fraternity focuses on the order and context of interactions as the key to understanding the social transitions represented in these specialized rituals and ceremonies. The author uses the tripartite pattern of rites of passage (separation, transition, and incorporation) to structure his description and analysis of fraternity interactions and events.

A-F 320. LEIGHTON, ALEXANDER H. The Governing of Man: General Principles and Recommendations Based on Experiences at a Japanese Relocation Camp. Princeton, N.J.: Princeton University Press, 1945. 404 pp.
Leighton presents a description of the development of a social and political system among evacuees in a Japanese relocation camp in W.W. II and a series of recommendations to administrators who attempt to effect social change. Leighton was in charge of the research team at the Poston Relocation Camp in Arizona. The circumstances that led to a confrontation between the Japanese and the administrators are documented. This case study is then used to provide examples for a series of principles applicable to the administration of people in a time of cultural, social, and psychological stress.

A-F 321. MEAD, MARGARET. Coming of Age in Samoa: A Psychological Study of Primitive Youth for Western Civilization. New York: Morrow, 1928. 176 pp.
Mead, through an ethnographic description of childhood and adolescence in a Polynesian society, attempts to make American readers aware of the ways that American culture influences their own ideas about the processes of maturation. Most of the book is an anthropological description of Samoan socialization. In the final two chapters, "Our Educational Problems in the Light of Samoan Contrasts" and "Education for Choice," Mead compares Samoan and American cultures, points out many values and assumptions held in American society, and advocates an awareness of educational alternatives in America.

A-F 322. MEAD, MARGARET and MARTHA WOLFENSTEIN, eds. Childhood in Contemporary Cultures. Chicago: University of Chicago Press, 1955. 471 pp.
Twenty-six papers by fourteen authors discuss child-rearing from anthropological and psychological perspectives. Data are presented from a variety of cultures but primarily from European and American industrial societies. A recurrent theme of the articles is that U.S. culture can be illuminated by comparisons with other societies. Articles on mainstream and minority American groups are presented in nine chapters which deal specifically with U.S. cultural contexts. The book is organized around particular sources of data about children: observation, child-rearing literature, fantasies of children, interviews, and clinical studies.

A-F 323. MEHAN, HUGH. Learning Lessons. Cambridge, Mass.: Harvard University Press, 1979. 227 pp.
In this study the social organization of interaction in an elementary classroom is examined. Mehan focuses upon one kind of speech event—teacher-led lessons—in an attempt to specify the cultural knowledge that the teacher and students used, but may not have been able to articulate, in order to negotiate their interaction.

A-F 324. MOEN, ELIZABETH, ELISE BOULDING, JANE LILLYDAHL, and RISA PALM. Women and the Social Costs of Economic Development: Two Colorado Case Studies. Boulder, Colo.: Westview Press, 1981. 215 pp.
Using a rural-urban continuum framework, the authors have studied an energy "boom town" and a mining town with potential for rapid economic growth, focusing on the issue of women's status and roles in this transition from a face-to-face social support system to a society based on contractual relationships. Women, the authors claim, tend to bear the brunt of social disalignment, either as newcomer housewives lacking their itinerant husbands' automatic job network, or as longtime residents whose community changes around them, cutting off their economic opportunities. The authors also consider the deleterious impact of economic development on women's position in developing nations.

A-F 325. MOORE, LORNA G., PETER W. VAN ARSDALE, JO ANN E. GLITTENBERG, and ROBERT A. ALDRICH. Biocultural Basis of Health. St. Louis, Mo.: Mosby, 1980. 278 pp.
This volume introduces the reader to the several facets of medical anthropology. Health and disease are seen as intrinsically variable phenomena, depending on biological and cultural variables ranging from ecology to ideology. Three case studies are presented, cross-cultural comparisons are made, and recommendations for changes in the present system of health care in the West are offered.

A-F 326. OGBU, JOHN U. Minority Education and Caste: The American System in Cross-Cultural Perspective. New York: Academic Press, 1978. 410 pp.
Ogbu argues that "the exclusion of blacks from the more desirable social and occupational positions because of their caste-like status is the major source of their academic retardation." He shows that expected social positions of adults in a social status hierarchy are communicated to children who make corresponding adjustments in their academic aspirations and performance. Ogbu constructs an argument in support of his position by drawing on comparisons from West Indians in Britain, Maoris in New Zealand, castes in India, Buraku outcasts in Japan, and Oriental Jews in Israel.

A-F 327. OGBU, JOHN U. The Next Generation: An Ethnography of an Urban Neighborhood. New York: Academic Press, 1974. 275 pp.
Ogbu attempts to understand why minority children living in cities characteristically do poorly in school. His primary interest is in the ways Spanish-speaking and black parents view the city schools, the parents' goals for their children, and how their goals differ from those of their children and those of educators. Particular attention is given to the factors operating outside of the schools which affect the performance of minority-group children.

A-F 328. RICHARDSON, F. L. W., Jr. and CHARLES R. WALKER. Human Relations in an Expanding Company: A Study of the Manufacturing Departments in the Endicott Plant of the International Business Machine Company. New Haven, Conn.: Labor and Management Center, Yale University, 1948. 95 pp.
Using social networks, attitudes, and interactions as their units of analysis, the investigators looked at the relationship in a company between increased mechanization and the quality of human interaction. They show that the efforts by the plant management to streamline the hierarchical and communicational structures of the plant while they were increasing mechanization produced an overall improvement in human relations at the plant.

A-F 329. RIST, RAY. The Urban School: A Factory for Failure. Cambridge, Mass.: MIT Press, 1973. 265 pp.
This study, based on more than two years of participant-observation fieldwork in a black elementary school in St. Louis, Missouri, concentrates on the unequal treatment of children in the school. Rist follows a group of children from their first day in kindergarten to the Christmas holiday in second grade. An important result of this work is the documentation of the way in which students are categorized by the teacher in terms of perceived or assumed ability or potential. Rist shows how the teacher's perceptions of a child's ability influence the quality of the instruction that the child receives. These perceptions are based not only on the academic performance of the child, but also on ideas about the influence of home life on the child's ability. The author includes interviews with the teachers and background information on the organization of the school and the training of the teachers.

A-F 330. ROBERTS, JOAN I. and SHERRIE K. AKINSANYA, eds. Educational Patterns and Cultural Configurations: The Anthropology of Education. New York: MacKay, 1976. 412 pp.
This collection of twenty-nine papers and two bibliographies is a summary of the theoretical and methodological background of anthropological studies of education. The articles included here span the history of anthropology, and are examples of the work of the contributors to the anthropology of education. Two extensive bibliographies--covering anthropology and education, and anthropological studies of enculturation--are included.

A-F 331. ROBERTS, JOAN I. and SHERRIE K. AKINSANYA, eds. Schooling in the Cultural Context: Anthropological Studies of Education. New York: McKay, 1976. 479 pp.
This volume consists of thirty previously published ethnographic studies of conventional formal education. It was produced in conjunction with A-F 330, and the two books together provide an anthropological overview of education.

A-F 332. ROSE, DAN. Energy Transition and the Local Community. Phila-
        delphia: University of Pennsylvania Press, 1981. 189 pp.
Using historical and ethnographic materials, Rose describes how a group
of business people in a coal mining region in Pennsylvania have transformed
their economically depressed city into one in which there is full employment. By relating trends in the world economy to local-level adaptations,
Rose attempts to formulate a general energy-based theory of socioeconomic
development.

A-F 333. SANDAY, PEGGY REEVES, ed. Anthropology and the Public Interest:
        Fieldwork and Theory. New York: Academic Press, 1976. 363 pp.
The nineteen articles in this book evaluate anthropological contributions
to public policy-making and offer substantive studies of variation among
American groups as it affects the ability of individuals in these groups
to succeed in the opportunity structure of U.S. society. Structures of
mainstream society are examined to identify areas where opportunity is
inhibited or enhanced. Minority group behavior patterns and strategies
for operating in the mainstream opportunity structure are also examined.
Specific topics include educational achievement, occupational mobility,
adaptations to poverty, voting behavior, and language.

A-F 334. SPICER, EDWARD H., ASAEL T. HANSEN, MARVIN K. OPLER, and
        KATHERINE LUOMALA. Impounded People: Japanese-Americans in
        Relocation Centers. Washington, D.C.: U.S. Government Printing
        Office, 1946. 342 pp.
This book, written during the last six months of the War Relocation Authority (WRA) by four members of the Community Analysis Division, provides
a chronological narrative of Japanese-American relocation as it was experienced by the administrators and the detainees, and covers all four years
of the program. Five periods are isolated and discussed: (1) the pre-
War conditioning which led to the singling out of the Japanese-Americans
for detention; (2) moving in—the time when people adapted to living in
artificial communities under government supervision; (3) being sorted—
the period when new tensions arose from government attempts to separate
the loyal from the disloyal; (4) settling down—when people made their
adjustment to artificial communities and many saw their situation as an
opportunity to create a model community; and (5) getting out—when the
communities broke up, causing further disruption and tension.

A-F 335. SPINDLER, GEORGE D. The Transmission of American Culture. Cam-
        bridge, Mass.: Harvard University Press, 1959. 51 pp.
In this book, Spindler discusses how American culture is transmitted in
elementary education. He emphasizes the transmission of conflicts in
American values and illustrates with case studies some of the ways that
unintentional transmission of these conflicts takes place. He also points
out ways that teachers' education trains them to reinforce, intentionally
and unintentionally, conflicting American values.

A-F 336. SPINDLER, GEORGE D., ed. Doing the Ethnography of Schooling.
        New York: Holt, Rinehart & Winston, 1982. 504 pp.
The purpose of this volume is twofold: (1) to define and describe educational ethnography; and (2) to clarify the potential of this field for
contributing solutions to educational problems and to the development
of anthropological theory and methods relating to education. The articles,
all of which deal with schooling in the U.S., focus on such topics as
the resistance to change shown by educational institutions; problems in
the diffusion of the information derived from ethnographic studies; and
the nature of the role of ethnography in the school and education.

A-F 337. SPINDLER, GEORGE D., ed. Education and Culture: Anthropological Approaches. New York: Holt, Rinehart & Winston, 1963. 571 pp. The twenty-five articles collected here are organized around three topics: general problems in anthropological studies of education, education in American culture, and education cross-culturally. The essays included were either written especially for the volume or selected on the basis of the following criteria: "each one must represent some dimension of a process particularly significant within the scope of emergent anthropological applications to analysis of the education process in our own society or in other societies; the chapters selected must interrelate to provide a manageable consistency of focus within a very large scope of possibilities; with a very few exceptions where the role of the chapter as a 'think-piece' is especially significant, the chapters must be based upon analysis of empirical data."

A-F 338. SUE, STANLEY and JAMES K. MORISHIMA. The Mental Health of Asian-Americans. San Francisco: Jossey-Bass, 1982. 222 pp. The purpose of this book is to update, examine, and interpret the literature and issues relevant to Asian and Pacific-American mental health. The authors focus on mental health needs and problems, delivery of services, and research and theory. For practitioners, the book provides "an understanding of the clinical symptoms in psychological disturbance, the cultural and social context of such disturbance, and the means to develop effective clinical and community interventions to enhance Asian-American mental health." For researchers, the authors have evaluated the existing research and theories, an evaluation which implicitly suggests ways to improve methodological and conceptual approaches in Asian-American research.

A-F 339. THOMAS, DOROTHY SWAINE. The Salvage: Japanese Evacuation and Resettlement. 1942; Rev. ed. Berkeley: University of California Press, 1975. 637 pp. This study is the first part of a project begun in 1942 by an interdisciplinary team of social scientists from the University of California with the purpose of studying the evacuation, detention and resettlement of Japanese-Americans during W.W. II. Based on participant-observation data, the book analyzes the experiences of detainees stigmatized as "disloyal" who returned to Japan after the war, or who relinquished their American citizenship.

A-F 340. THOMAS, DOROTHY SWAINE and RICHARD S. NISHIMOTO. The Spoilage: Japanese American Evacuation and Resettlement During World War Two. 1946; Rev. ed. Berkeley: University of California Press, 1974. 388 pp. This second volume dealing with the effects of war-time detention on Japanese-Americans (see A-F 339) begins with a sociological history and social demography of Japanese migration to and within the U.S. from 1880 to W.W. II. The focus of the work is the experiences of Japanese-Americans who set up new lives in new areas after detention. Generalized patterns are constructed from sixty-five recorded case histories, fifteen of which are presented in detail here.

A-F 341. VALENTINE, CHARLES A. Culture and Poverty: Critique and Counter-Proposals. Chicago: University of Chicago Press, 1968. 216 pp. In this essay, Valentine outlines and criticizes the culture of poverty concept in anthropology, and offers alternatives. Prompted by the belief that the continued existence of poverty will have serious consequences for the immediate future of society, and that social science can contribute to the resolution of such problems, Valentine traces the relationship between the poverty-culture concept and recent public policy, highlighting the theoretical and methodological underpinnings of three culture-of-poverty formulations. He concludes with proposals for both appropriate public policy and ethnographic research design.

A-F 342. WHITING, BEATRICE B., ed. Six Cultures: Studies of Child Rearing
New York: Wiley, 1963. 1017 pp.
This volume represents the results of a project undertaken through the
Laboratory of Human Development at Harvard University in the 1950s. The
project sought to make available uniform world-wide data on child-rearing.
The volume consists of six separate ethnographies in which there was uni-
form collection and organization of the data. Each ethnography has a
section on adult culture and a section on child training. The cultures
included in the study were a Gusii community in Kenya; the Rajputs of
Khalapur, India; an Okinawan village; the Mixtecans of Juxtlahuaca, Mexico;
an Ilocos barrio in the Philippines; and the New Englanders of Orchard
Town, U.S.A.

A-F 343. WHYTE, WILLIAM FOOTE. Human Relations in the Restaurant Industry.
New York: McGraw-Hill, 1948. 378 pp.
This is one of the early applications of anthropology in industry. The
study was carried out during W.W. II, and is thus a study of individual
and organizational behavior under stressful conditions. Whyte describes
the social system of several restaurants through field observation, interviews, and the presentation of case studies. The topics discussed in
detail include the status and role system of the staffs of the restaurants,
the process of preparing food in terms of social relations, friendship,
and cliques among restaurant employees, and race relations within the
organizations. There is a long section of recommendations for more efficient management of restaurants.

A-F 344. WHYTE, WILLIAM FOOTE. Men at Work. Homewood, Ill.: Dorsey
Press and Richard D. Irwin, 1961. 593 pp.
Whyte divides this volume into seven sections: "Historical and Theoretical
Background"; "The Social and Economic Environment"; "The Technological
and Physical Environment"; "Union-Management Relations"; "The Managerial
Process"; "Service, Staff, and Control Activities"; "A Theoretical Restate-
ment." He stresses interaction, sentiments, and activities in his study
of the problems of organizational relations in business and industry.
Case study material is presented to illustrate problems within an organization to which this approach may be applied.

A-F 345. WOLCOTT, HARRY F. The Man in the Principal's Office: An Ethnography. New York: Holt, Rinehart & Winston, 1973. 334 pp.
The social position of a school principal in the educational system is
examined in this detailed descriptive study, which combines small-scale
analysis of encounters with a larger picture of the principal in the social
and educational systems. The author spent over a year observing one principal in a middle-class suburban school, and he describes the way this
individual operated in his social position of school principal, how the
position is maintained in the educational system, and how he must play
the role of mediator more often than he plays the role of educator.

A-F 346. WOLCOTT, HARRY F. Teachers Versus Technocrats: An Educational
Innovation in Anthropological Perspective. Eugene: University
of Oregon Press, 1977. 255 pp.
Wolcott describes an innovative educational program and devises an explanatory model of the "educational subculture." This history of a school
district's attempt to make education more accountable to the community,
through the implementation of the National Institute of Education's program
SPECS (School Planning, Evaluation, and Communication System), brings
together the views of many of the program participants. In his explanatory
model, Wolcott applies the concept of dual social organization to explain
the conflicting ideologies he finds in the educational system.

VIII. LINGUISTICS

A-F 347. ADAMS, CHARLES C. Boontling: An American Lingo. Austin: University of Texas Press, 1971. 272 pp.
Adams writes that every region of America has unique dialect terms that flavor its speech, but the inhabitants of the region surrounding Boonville in Northern California deliberately invented a dialect (perhaps more accurately a language) that was completely unintelligible to an outsider. Not only were new nouns, verbs, and modifiers invented, often through clipping or abbreviating, but new tense markers, intensifiers, and other grammatical features were developed as well. Boontling—a blend of Boonville and lingo—flourished from 1880 to 1920, but recent linguistic and social investigation has sparked a revival, especially among younger people. This book traces the historical and sociological factors and gives examples of the use of the lingo.

A-F 348. BURLING, ROBBINS. English in Black and White. New York: Holt, Rinehart & Winston, 1973. 178 pp.
This non-technical book is written for educators and other non-linguists who deal with non-standard dialects of English. Drawing on secondary sources, Burling describes the phonology, grammar, and use of the black dialect of English. Various methods for presenting standard English to speakers of non-standard dialects in schools are offered. Burling argues in favor of teaching standard English as a dialect of English which is to be used in socially appropriate circumstances.

A-F 349. CONKLIN, NANCY FAIRES and MARGARET A. LOURIE. A Host of Tongues: Language Communities in the United States. New York: Free Press, 1983. 314 pp.
This sociolinguistic study of the historical and sociological settings for the variety of languages in the U.S. examines the maintenance of some as functioning languages within ethnic groups and the influence of otherwise dead languages on "standard English." The authors' hope is to instigate informed discussion about the future of such matters as bilingual education and multi-cultural community organization, among community leaders and teachers, policy-makers, and public planners.

A-F 350. DILLARD, J. L., ed. Perspectives on American English. The Hague: Mouton, 1980. 467 pp.
These essays on the development of American English have been organized historically, beginning with the first English-speaking colonists, continuing with occupational influences stemming from frontier and maritime life, going on to consider immigrant input, Black English, and the pidgins that have formed. Largely eschewing the position that American dialects grew out of the regional differentiations of the original English settlers, Dillard has selected four positions that explore the effects of multilingual contact situations on variation in English.

A-F 351. FERGUSON, CHARLES A. and SHIRLEY BRICE HEATH, ed. Language in the USA. New York: Cambridge University Press, 1981. 592 pp.
This treatment of American English organizes twenty-three essays into four groups: (1) the forms of American English contrasted to English elsewhere, as well as variations within America; (2) languages preceding English on the continent; (3) immigrant languages; and (4) occupational languages and policy concerning language use. The focus is not on identifiably bounded languages and the reconstruction of their pure roots; rather, the authors concentrate on the ideal types of myths Americans have concerning their language (contrasted with the practical use of that language in everyday speech events), and on the ongoing transformation

of multi-lingual America, which is seen as a locus wherein English operates as a living, changing _lingua franca_.

A-F 352. **FISHMAN, JOSHUA A.** Language Loyalty in the United States: The Maintenance and Perpetuation of Non-English Mother Tongues by American Ethnic and Religious Groups. The Hague: Mouton, 1966. 478 pp.
Fishman presents studies which deal with "the self-maintenance efforts, rationales, and accomplishments of non-English speaking immigrants on American shores." German, Ukrainian, Spanish, and French-speaking communities are examined in detail. The history of immigration is summarized and demographic features of non-English speaking groups are presented. Various means of maintaining languages are discussed, such as periodical publications, radio broadcasts, schools, and religious parishes. Social contexts--for example, family, community, and cultural leadership--are examined to show how they influence language maintenance. The author argues that the existence and perpetuation of many languages is a social resource which should be utilized.

A-F 353. **GEIS, MICHAEL L.** The Language of Television Advertising. New York: Academic Press, 1982. 257 pp.
Using speech act theory to analyze videotapes of 800 commercials, Geis offers an argument that TV advertisers must be held responsible not only for the literal, logical content of the script, but also for the underlying, implied messages which are effective due to the belief systems of the viewers.

A-F 354. **GUMPERZ, JOHN J.** and **DELL HYMES**, eds. Directions in Sociolinguistics: The Ethnography of Speaking. New York: Holt, Rinehart & Winston, 1972. 598 pp.
Nineteen articles provide an introduction to the range of interests of sociolinguists who emphasize the interactional approach to language behavior. The book is divided into three parts: "Ethnographic Description and Explanation," "Discovering Structure in Speech," and "Genesis, Maintenance, and Change of Linguistic Codes."

A-F 355. **HAUGEN, EINAR.** The Norwegian Language in America: A Study of Bilingual Behavior. 2 vols. Bloomington: Indiana University Press, 1969. 699 pp.
Haugen's study of the Norwegian language in America is intended as an analysis of a bilingual community in transition. Volume One discusses the problems of bilingualism, the Norwegian migration to America, the learning of English by the immigrant Norwegians and its subsequent effects on literary and spoken Norwegian. Volume Two presents problems associated with the study of linguistics, the phenomenon of dispersion and borrowing in the Norwegian language, and examples of American Norwegian and English words borrowed from Norwegian. The appendices contain data on Norwegian communities and informants in the U.S., sample questionnaires, maps and statistical tables on Norwegians in America.

A-F 356. **HUBBELL, ALLAN FORBES.** The Pronunciation of English in New York City: Consonants and Vowels. New York: King's Crown Press, 1950. 169 pp.
This work presents a descriptive phonological study of the phonemes in spoken English within the political boundaries of New York City. Phonemes are described and their variation in particular linguistic environments is noted. Stress, intonation, and juncture are not discussed. The informants for the study are described in appendices.

A-F 357. HYMES, DELL, ed. Language in Culture and Society: A Reader
          in Linguistics and Anthropology. New York: Harper & Row, 1964.
          764 pp.
This collection of sixty-nine articles provides a representation of the
interests of anthropological linguists. The selections offer the work
of anthropologists and linguists in many cultures and on many topics.
Hymes provides an introduction which gives background to the study of
the relationship between language and culture. He also provides introductions to each of the sections, and he supplements each author's bibliography in a reference note after each article. The ten sections of the
book are entitled: "The Scope of Linguistic Anthropology," "Equality,
Diversity, Relativity," "World View and Grammatical Categories," "Cultural
Focus and Semantic Field," "Role, Socialization, and Expressive Speech,"
"Speech Play and Verbal Art," "Social Structure and Speech Community,"
"Processes and Problems of Change," "Relationships in Time and Space,"
and "Toward Historical Perspective."

A-F 358. HYMES, DELL and JOHN FOUGHT. American Structuralism. The Hague:
          Mouton, 1981. 296 pp.
This historiography examines Bloomfieldian structuralism as antithetical
to Sapir's "traditional grammar" and as a precursor to Chomsky's synthetic
"transformational grammar." In part, the authors wish to renegotiate
the treatment that structuralism received at the hands of Chomsky, who
referred to it as a meaningless, contentless absorption with pure surface
structure. At the same time, they are interested in sketching both the
personalities responsible for this flux of ideas and the social context--
the community building (at university, foundation, and international
levels) and the boundary-maintenance aspects of ideational trends.

A-F 359. KOCHMAN, THOMAS, ed. Rappin' and Stylin' Out: Communication
          in Urban Black America. Urbana: University of Illinois Press,
          1972. 424 pp.
Twenty-seven articles were selected to describe "the communicative habits
and expressive life style of urban black Americans" in the context of
the community in which such behavior occurs. Although most of the articles
are scholarly, Kochman has also included examples of short stories and
commentaries by political activists which illuminate various aspects of
communication. The articles are divided into four sections: nonverbal
communication, vocabulary and culture, expressive uses of language, and
expressive role behavior.

A-F 360. KURATH, HANS. A Word Geography of the Eastern United States.
          Ann Arbor: University of Michigan Press, 1949. 88 pp.
Kurath presents the results of investigations into regional and local
variations in vocabulary in the Atlantic states from Maine to South Carolina. From nearly every county on the East Coast, Kurath selected at
least two speakers: one having little formal education, and another with
primary or high school education. Using a sample of regionally varying
vocabulary items, he characterizes eighteen speech areas. The distributions of key words and phrases are given in the maps at the end of the
book.

A-F 361. LABOV, WILLIAM. Language in the Inner City: Studies in the
          Black English Vernacular. Philadelphia: University of Penn-
          sylvania Press, 1972. 405 pp.
The reading failure of black students was the incentive for this study
of the language of black children and adolescents in Harlem from 1964
to 1965. The research dealt with vernacular speech used outside of the
classroom. Labov and his co-workers found no correlation between reading
ability and linguistic competence. It is concluded that dialect differences are symbols of political and cultural conflicts in the classroom

arising from poverty and discrimination and that reading failure can be attributed to these conflicts. The book, written to be understood by the general reader, contains both technical and non-technical analyses of the grammatical and phonetic systems of Black English Vernacular which concentrate on the social contexts in which speech takes place.

A-F 362. LABOV, WILLIAM. The Social Stratification of English in New York City. Washington, D.C.: Center for Applied Linguistics, 1966. 655 pp.
This book is a technical study of linguistic variation in a Lower East Side neighborhood of Manhattan. Using quantitative and qualitative analysis of formal and informal interviews, Labov demonstrates that variation in speech sounds which are often attributed to "free" or purely phonetic variation can be explained in terms of sociological indices such as class, sex, age, and ethnic background. A methodological innovation in this work involved using subjective evaluations of examples of speech by the informants. This method provided evidence for linguistic insecurity on the part of the speakers in his sample. Informants often evaluated examples of their own dialect as "poor" or "sloppy" English.

A-F 363. LABOV, WILLIAM. Sociolinguistic Patterns. Philadelphia: University of Pennsylvania Press, 1972. 344 pp.
Nine previously published essays, revised for their inclusion in this book, are presented. Many of the methods and findings of Labov's work in the Lower East Side of Manhattan (A-F 362) are reviewed and evaluated in the first part of the book. The second part synthesizes the Lower East Side data with later work in Martha's Vineyard, Massachusetts, and in Harlem, and consists of theoretical essays on language structure and language change.

A-F 364. MAURER, DAVID W. Language of the Underworld. Lexington: University Press of Kentucky, 1981. 417 pp.
The essays in this volume represent fifty years of Maurer's sociolinguistic investigations of subcultures, focusing largely on four criminal subcultures of varying degrees of parasitic articulation with the dominant society and distinguished from it by varying amounts of behavioral characteristics and patterns. Each essay is prefaced by the author's reasons for the original research and current publication; a short description of the social context, a glossary of the argot, and some linguistic analysis are included.

A-F 365. NEWMEYER, FREDERICK J. Linguistic Theory in America: The First Quarter-Century of Transformational Generative Grammar. New York: Academic Press, 1980. 290 pp.
Newmeyer plots the developmental history of linguistic theory and its philosophical foundations from the empiricist structuralist school of the 1930s through its major crisis in the 1950s. The ensuing Chomsky revolution of transformational-generative grammar is traced through the 1960s and 1970s. The book is written for readers with a basic comprehension of modern linguistic theory.

A-F 366. SCHACH, PAUL, ed. Languages in Conflict: Linguistic Acculturation on the Great Plains. Lincoln: University of Nebraska Press, 1980.
These essays explore aspects of the multilingual situation from Manitoba to Texas over the last century, emphasizing in particular the ways in which linguistic acculturation can be seen as a marker for social assimilation. The languages considered are Lakota (Sioux), Czech, Spanish, three Scandinavian languages, and four German dialects. Political and social pressures that have increased tension over bilingualism are highlighted and ways in which immigrant languages have had a substratum influence on English are discussed.

A-F 367. TURNER, PAUL R., ed. Bilingualism in the Southwest. Tucson:
          University of Arizona Press, 1973. 352 pp.
In this book the interaction among English, Spanish, and various Indian
languages in the Southwest is considered. The papers deal with cultural
as well as linguistic diversity, but with primary emphasis on education
and linguistic acculturation. The topics covered include the teaching
of English to Spanish and Indian language speakers, semantic categories
in the various languages, and the accommodation that speakers of Navajo
or Tiwa make when learning English.

A-F 368. WOLFRAM, WALT and RALPH W. FASOLD. The Study of Social Dialects
          in American English. Englewood Cliffs, N.J.: Prentice-Hall,
          1974. 239 pp.
This is an introductory book dealing with general problems such as field
methodology, social and linguistic variables, and phonological and grammatical indicators of social dialects. Wolfram and Fasold discuss the
characteristics and the sources of linguistic variation in contemporary
American society, the need for an awareness of social dialects in educational institutions, and the bias toward standard written English in standardized educational tests. The book is written for non-linguists and
has a minimum of specialized description and analysis. The authors' concentration on the concept of dialect offers a different perspective on
sociolinguistics from those which examine speech events in detail or which
look at linguistic variation in relation to social problems.

IX.   FOLKLORE AND FOLKLIFE

A-F 369. ABERNETHY, FRANCIS EDWARD, ed. Built in Texas. Waco, Tex.:
          E-Heart Press, 1979. 276 pp.
This is a collection of twenty-four essays covering a variety of folk
building in Texas. Barns and out-buildings, gates and fences, water tanks,
and houses all are illustrated. There are also essays covering methods
and materials (such as corner-notching and adobe), as well as style and
form (such as the shotgun house). The book concludes with a chapter on
outdoor museums in Texas, where folk buildings have been relocated and
restored for preservation.

A-F 370. ABRAHAMS, ROGER D. Deep Down in the Jungle . . . : Negro Nar-
          rative Folklore from the Streets of Philadelphia. 1964; Rev.
          ed. Chicago: Aldine, 1970. 278 pp.
Abrahams describes and discusses the major forms of urban black folklore,
concentrating on the contexts in which it occurs and the factors which
influence its form and style. Verbal forms such as "signifying" and "playing the dozens" are described; folk heroes and their characteristics are
discussed; style and performance of verbal acts are analyzed; and two
major types of narrative--the toast and the joke--are presented.

A-F 371. ABRAHAMS, ROGER D. Positively Black. Englewood Cliffs, N.J.:
          Prentice-Hall, 1970. 177 pp.
This book addresses itself to the question of cultural understanding
between the races. Arguing that black culture is basically different from
that of mainstream white America, Abrahams feels the problem is to teach
whites how to understand and accept this difference. The author uses
examples of black narratives and performances, combined with his own commentary, to show how black culture is organized from the inside and how
liberal whites stereotype blacks.

A-F 372. AMES, KENNETH L. Beyond Necessity: Art in the Folk Tradition.
          New York: Norton, 1977. 131 pp.
The latter part of this book consists of a catalog for an exhibition of
folk art objects from the Winterthur Museum. The major part, however,
is an interpretive essay by Ames that explores the concept of folk art,
looking at its definitions, its history, and its meaning for people today.
Ames asks: is folk art really folk art? He analyzes not only the folk
art objects in the exhibition, but also their cultural context.

A-F 373. BAKER, RONALD L. Folklore in the Writing of Rowland E. Robinson.
          Bowling Green, Ohio: Bowling Green University Popular Press,
          1973. 240 pp.
Although Rowland Robinson (1833-1900) was a creative writer and not a
folklorist, his writings offer a kind of encyclopedia of 19th-century
folkore and folklife in Vermont. In this study, Baker not only enumerates
the occurrences of specific folk genres in various works by Robinson;
he also discusses their cultural contexts and Robinson's methods for incorporating them into his fiction.

A-F 374. BAUMAN, RICHARD and ROGER D. ABRAHAMS, eds. "And Other Neighborly
          Names": Social Process and Cultural Image in Texas Folklore.
          Austin: University of Texas Press, 1981. 321 pp.
This collection of essays by twelve Texas folklorists is divided into
three broad categories: the structure and content of expressive forms:
social types and stereotypes; and expressive dimensions of heterogeneity
and change. The essays adhere to the perspective--formulated by previous
Texas folklorists like John Alan, and Bess Lomax, Mody Boatright, J.
Frank Dobie, J. Mason Brewer, and Americo Paredes--that folklore must
be observed not only in its living place, but also in terms of its social
and political ramifications.

A-F 375. BIANCO, CARLA. The Two Rosetos. Bloomington: Indiana University
          Press, 1974. 234 pp.
Looking at the folklore of two related communities--Roseto, Italy, and
Roseto, Pennsylvania--Bianco shows first how the two communities have
moved apart from each other during the past seventy years. She finds,
nevertheless, that a whole world of traditional values, folk beliefs,
and fantasies still binds the two Rosetos together. In both the Old World
and the New, community members are trying to preserve certain traditions
from the past.

A-F 376   BOATRIGHT, MODY C. Folklore of the Oil Industry. Dallas, Tex.:
          Southern Methodist University Press, 1963. 220 pp.
Based on fieldwork principally in Texas, but also in Pennsylvania, West
Virginia, Oklahoma, and Kansas, Boatright describes and interprets the
folklore of the oil industry up to 1940, when a new generation of oil
workers took over. He shows how those who are involved in the discovery
and production of petroleum have structured their experiences into folkloric patterns, not unlike those that can be found in non-industrial societies.

A-F 377. BOATRIGHT, MODY C. Mody Boatright, Folklorist: A Collection
          of Essays. Austin: University of Texas Press, 1973. 198 pp.
This anthology brings together a number of representative pieces by
Boatright (1896-1970), a folklorist and professor of English who worked
principally on four topics: the cowboy, the American frontier, the oil
industry, and the folklore of contemporary society. Among the essays
collected here are ones on frontier humor, family sagas, and the oil promoter as trickster.

A-F 378. BRIGGS, CHARLES L. The Wood-Carvers of Cordova, New Mexico:
          Social Dimensions of an Artistic "Revival." Knoxville: Uni-
          versity of Tennessee Press, 1980. 253 pp.
Briggs interprets the wood-carvings of Cordova in a broad sociocultural
context--describing not only the craftsmen and their workmanship, but
also their community and ethnic group, the concerns of their patrons,
and the precedents for and subsequent developments of certain artistic
innovations. Particular attention is paid to the emergence of Jose Dolores
Lopez as a major artist.

A-F 379. BRUNVAND, JAN HAROLD. The Study of American Folklore: An Intro-
          duction. 1968; Rev. ed. New York: Norton, 1978. 460 pp.
This is a general topical survey of American folklore which can also serve
as an introductory reference book. Brunvand breaks the study of folklore
into three general areas: oral folklore, customary folklore, and material
folk traditions. Customary folklore includes topics such as beliefs,
rituals, dance, drama, gestures, and games. Material traditions include
architecture, crafts, art, costumes, and foods.

A-F 380. BRUNVAND, JAN HAROLD. The Vanishing Hitchhiker: American Urban
          Legends. New York: Norton, 1981. 208 pp.
Brunvand's primary purpose is to legitimize the study of modern American
urban legends and their meanings. He examines classic automobile legends,
teenage horror stories, food-contamination rumors, fear-of-the-dead anecdotes, and business ripoffs. He also looks at several urban legends in
the making, such as "the economical car," and demonstrates the European
antecedents to American legends, when applicable.

A-F 381. BURRISON, JOHN A. Brothers in Clay: The Story of Georgia Folk
          Pottery. Athens: University of Georgia Press, 1983. 326 pp.
Burrison traces the continuity of Georgia's pottery tradition from the
18th century to the present, revealing in the process a great deal about
the role of the folk craftsman in the South. His material is based on
an examination of census materials, deeds, and land grant records; tax
digests; and oral testimony gathered from visits to pottery operations
(both traditional and non-traditional) that have survived.

A-F 382. COFFIN, MARGARET M. Death in Early America: The History and
          Folklore of Customs and Superstitions of Early Medicine, Funerals,
          Burials, and Mourning. Nashville, Tenn.: Thomas Nelson, 1976.
          252 pp.
Coffin describes traditions from the 18th and 19th centuries that deal
with sickness and death, funerals, coffins, hearses, places of burial,
gravestones, epitaphs, body snatching, mourning, and memorials. In addition, she enumerates some of the causes of premature death in the U.S.,
and identifies some of the early cures and folk remedies that were used
for an assortment of ailments.

A-F 383. COFFIN, TRISTRAM POTTER. Uncertain Glory: Folklore and the
          American Revolution. Detroit, Mich.: Folklore Associates,
          1971. 270 pp.
In the first half of this book, Coffin examines stories and songs (including pieces like "Yankee Doodle Dandy") that were current at the time of
the Revolutionary War and that, in certain cases, have become part of
our oral tradition. The second half of the book deals with some of the
"fakelore" that has survived from the Revolutionary War to our own time,
such as legends that surround figures like Nathan Hale, Ethan Allen, and
Paul Revere.

A-F 384. COFFIN, TRISTRAM POTTER, ed. Our Living Traditions: An Introduction to American Folklore. New York: Basic Books, 1968.
301 pp.
This collection of twenty-three essays describes folklore as a field of
study; identifies the major areas of focus in American folklore (such
as folk music, tales, folk speech); and discusses the place of folklore
in the study of modern life (e.g., the use of folklore by occupational
groups, city lore, and the commercialization of folklore).

A-F 385. COFFIN, TRISTRAM POTTER and HENNIG COHEN, eds. Folklore: From
the Working Folk of America. Garden City, N.Y.: Anchor Press,
1973. 464 pp.
The editors look at examples of folklore collected from members of various
occupational groups (i.e., people who find their identity in the way they
earn their living, rather than in where they live or their racial background). Included are such genres as tales, songs, verses, riddles, jokes,
superstitions, practices, customs, games, rituals, dramas, festivals,
and legendary figures.

A-F 386. COFFIN, TRISTRAM POTTER and HENNIG COHEN, eds. The Parade of
Heroes: Legendary Figures in American Lore. Garden City, N.Y.:
Anchor Press, 1978. 630 pp.
Coffin and Cohen have selected a large sample of stories about remarkable
individuals in America, ranging from Hiawatha to Jimmy Carter, and from
authentic folk heroes to those "fakelore" heroes who have been consciously
popularized in literature. Included among the traditions examined are
those surrounding Paul Bunyan, badmen, frontiersmen, and worker heroes.

A-F 387. COFFIN, TRISTRAM POTTER and ROGER deV. RENWICK. The British
Traditional Ballad in North America. 1950; Rev. ed. Austin:
University of Texas Press, 1977. 297 pp.
This book asks: how does folk poetry originate and what is the history
of the arrival and subsequent spread of British songs in America? The
work is divided into four principal parts: (1) a descriptive essay on
ballad variation in general; (2) a bibliographical guide to story variation; (3) a treatment of how the traditional ballad developed into an
art form; and (4) a general bibliography of titles. Renwick's supplement
updates the original study by Coffin.

A-F 388. COHEN, ANNE B. Poor Pearl, Poor Girl: The Murdered-Girl Stereotype in Ballad and Newspaper. Austin: University of Texas
Press, 1973. 131 pp.
Cohen argues that the ballads based on the Pearl Bryan murder case (1896)
are examples of formulaic composition (i.e., with set sequences of words;
set scenes; set sequences of action; and set characters). By comparing
newspaper and ballad accounts of the crime, she shows that both media
tell the story from the same moral stance, express the same interpretation
of character, and are interested in the same details.

A-F 389. COHEN, DAVID STEVEN. The Folklore and Folklife of New Jersey.
New Brunswick, N.J.: Rutgers University Press, 1983. 253 pp.
The author describes and analyzes the various forms of folklore and folklife in New Jersey, including jokes, names, legends, architecture, furniture, foodways, festivals, and games. Noting the richness and diversity
of New Jersey's folk heritage, Cohen concludes that the character of the
state--like that of the nation as a whole--cannot be reduced to a single
image; rather he feels it is a unique place with its own special identity.

A-F 390. DANCE, DARYL CUMBER. Shuckin' and Jivin': Folklore from Con-
          temporary Black Americans. Bloomington: Indiana University
          Press, 1978. 390 pp.
Dance has compiled 565 stories, jokes, and tales collected over a period
of ten years in a variety of contexts and from individuals with a variety
of backgrounds and ages. The tales are grouped in sections by their themes,
which include etiology, ghosts, conjuring, religion, self-degradation,
sexuality, ethnicity, cruelty of whites, outsmarting whites, and animal
tales.

A-F 391. DORSON, RICHARD M. America in Legend: Folklore from the Colonial
          Period to the Present. New York: Pantheon Books, 1973. 336 pp.
This volume surveys the folklore of selected segments of American society
from the 17th century to the present. From the Colonial period, Dorson
has selected folktales which emphasize religion. From the National period
(1760-1900), he has identified a democratic impulse in the early part
of the period, and an economic impulse in the latter part. In the 20th
century, the folklore of the youth counter-culture is emphasized.

A-F 392. DORSON, RICHARD M. American Folklore. Chicago: University
          of Chicago Press, 1959. 328 pp.
In this survey of American folklore, Dorson describes the major oral traditions in the U.S. from the Colonial period to the Modern era. He covers
native folk humor, regional folk culture, immigrant folklore, folk heroes,
and black folklore. Dorson believes that the only meaningful approach
to U.S. folk traditions is through history.

A-F 393. DORSON, RICHARD M. American Folklore and the Historian. Chicago:
          University of Chicago Press, 1971. 239 pp.
Dorson argues that the study of American folklore should be pursued in
light of the special factors shaping American history (such as the Westward
movement, slavery, regionalism, immigration, democracy, and mass culture).
Among the twelve essays in this volume are ones on folklore in relation
to American Studies, folklore and local history, and folklore in American
literature.

A-F 394. DORSON, RICHARD M. American Negro Folktales. 1956; Rev. ed.
          Greenwich, Conn.: Fawcett, 1967. 384 pp.
In the first section of this book, Dorson explains the origins of black
tales, describes the black communities from which the tales were collected,
and looks briefly at the art of black storytelling. The remaining portion
of the book is devoted to the tales themselves, and subdivided into fifteen
categories, including animal stories, spirits, protest tales, and fool
tales.

A-F 395. DORSON, RICHARD M. Bloodstoppers and Bearwalkers: Folk Tradi-
          tions of the Upper Peninsula. Cambridge, Mass.: Harvard Uni-
          versity Press, 1952. 305 pp.
A variety of folk traditions from Michigan's Upper Peninsula are discussed:
those of European origin (such as French Canadians, Cornish, and Finns);
American Indians (including Ojibway, Potawatomi, and Sioux); and the American pioneers (particularly lumberjacks, miners, and townspeople). Among
the genres included are creation myths, fairy tales, tall tales, occult
tales, romances, exploits, jests, and dialect stories.

A-F 396. DORSON, RICHARD M. Buying the Wind: Regional Folklore in the
          United States. Chicago: University of Chicago Press, 1964.
          574 pp.
Texts from seven regional folk groups are examined: Maine Down-Easters,
Pennsylvania Dutchmen, Southern Appalachian Mountaineers, Louisiana Cajuns,
Illinois Egyptians, Southwest Mexicans, and Utah Mormons. The texts within

each section are divided according to genres of folk material, such as narrative, proverbs, riddles, beliefs, drama, and song. Dorson provides an introduction to each of the sections, and he describes the history of folklore collecting in each area.

A-F 397. DORSON, RICHARD M. Jonathan Draws the Long Bow: New England Popular Tales and Legends. Cambridge, Mass.: Harvard University Press, 1946. 274 pp.
After an introductory chapter on New England storytelling and folktale diffusion, Dorson presents an in-depth treatment of supernatural stories, Yankee yarns, tall tales, local legends, and literary folktales. In this study, direct oral sources of folklore have been bypassed in favor of published material taken from New England newspapers, magazines, and town histories.

A-F 398. DORSON, RICHARD M. Land of the Millrats. Cambridge, Mass.: Harvard University Press, 1981. 251 pp.
In this volume, Dorson has collected folklore from the Calumet region of Northwest Indiana, one of the most heavily industrialized sectors of the U.S. His analysis is centered along five lines of inquiry: the mystique of the region itself; the distinctive folklore of steelworkers; the ethnicity of the region (e.g., Serbs, Greeks, Mexicans, and Puerto Ricans); the folklore of middle-class blacks in Gary; and crimelore in high-crime areas like Gary and East Chicago.

A-F 399. DORSON, RICHARD M. Man and Beast in American Comic Legend. Bloomington: Indiana University Press, 1982. 184 pp.
The first section of this book looks at legendary creatures and "fearsome critters," such as the sidehill dodger, jackalope, hoopsnake, sea serpent, and bigfoot. The second section discusses eight American Munchausens (i.e., folk heroes who have acquired local renown for spinning tall tales about their own feats, in effect creating their own legends, which are then perpetuated by other storytellers).

A-F 400. DORSON, RICHARD M., ed. Folklore and Folklife: An Introduction. Chicago: University of Chicago Press, 1972. 561 pp.
This volume is intended to answer the questions, "what is folklore?" and "what does a folklorist do?" Eighteen authors have contributed chapters on various aspects of folklore and folklife, including oral folklore, social folk custom, material culture, folk arts, and fieldwork methods. The geographic coverage is worldwide, though most of the examples have been taken from the U.S.

A-F 401. DORSON, RICHARD M., ed. Handbook of American Folklore. Bloomington: Indiana University Press, 1983. 584 pp.
Articles by a wide variety of scholars illustrate how American folklore has been studied to date in America, and also how the discipline of folklore is shaping itself in the 1980s. The eight major sections of the book are: American experiences, American cultural myths, American settings, American entertainment, American forms and performers, interpretation of research, methods of research, and presentation of research.

A-F 402. DUNDES, ALAN. Interpreting Folklore. Bloomington: Indiana University Press, 1980. 304 pp.
Claiming that many books on folklore are merely collections of legends, jokes, and proverbs, Dundes seeks ways to interpret these materials. He believes that by analyzing the folklore of a group, the folklorist may well succeed in making the unconscious conscious. In the essays collected here, Dundes interprets, from the point of view of the folklorist, such topics as the number three in American culture, American football, and American male chauvinism.

A-F 403. DUNDES, ALAN, ed. Mother Wit from the Laughing Barrel: Readings
          in the Interpretation of Afro-American Folklore. Englewood
          Cliffs, N.J.: Prentice-Hall, 1973. 673 pp.
Dundes has organized sixty-four examples of interpretive writings on Afro-
American folklore into eight sections, including attitudes toward Afro-
American folklore, discussions and descriptions of folk speech, verbal
art, folk beliefs, folk music, folk narrative, and folk humor. Dundes
provides introductions to each section and to each selection. The authors
of the selections include journalists and social activists, as well as
scholars.

A-F 404. DUNDES, ALAN and CARL R. PAGTER. Urban Folklore from the Paper-
          work Empire. Austin: University of Texas Press, 1975. 223 pp.
Dundes and Pagter have compiled many examples of texts which have been
circulated in the white-collar workers' world, usually on paper, and often
by means of sophisticated duplication techniques. The volume consists
mainly of these texts, with short comments by the authors which place
the documents into the context of American culture. By presenting this
material, Dundes and Pagter hope to expand the conventional definition
of folklore to include mainstream American culture.

A-F 405. EATON, ALLEN H. Handicrafts of New England. New York: Harper,
          1949. 374 pp.
The heart of Eaton's study is a survey of the contemporary scene of New
England handicrafts. Examined are wood crafts, basketry, spinning and
weaving, knitting, crocheting, rugs and carpets, pottery, puppet-making,
metalworking, and gem-cutting. Eaton also describes the cultural and
historical background of the New England handicrafts tradition, as well
as some of the more significant influences on the handicrafts movement.

A-F 406. EATON, ALLEN H. Handicrafts of the Southern Highlands. New
          York: Russell Sage, 1937. 370 pp.
The three-fold purpose of this book, according to the author, is (1) to
help the people of the Southern Highlands better understand their own
handicrafts tradition; (2) to acquaint those outside the region with these
materials and to encourage their wider use; and (3) to contribute to the
development of the handicrafts movement itself.

A-F 407. FERRIS, WILLIAM. Local Color: A Sense of Place in Folk Art.
          New York: McGraw-Hill, 1982. 241 pp.
Looking closely at the work of nine folk artists from Mississippi--
including a cane-maker, basket-maker, painter, needleworker, sculptor, and
quilter--Ferris explains how their work must be considered together with
their lives. He shows how an understanding of their dreams and visions,
their sense of family and tradition, and their religious views can deepen
an understanding of their artistic work.

A-F 408. FERRIS, WILLIAM, ed. Afro-American Folk Art and Crafts. Boston:
          G. K. Hall, 1983. 436 pp.
Ferris maintains that scholars have not given Afro-American material culture the attention it deserves. This book is a collection of some twenty
essays by various authors intended to remedy that deficiency. Following
an introductory chapter discussing the African influence on the art of
the U.S., there are individual sections covering quilters, sculptors,
instrument makers, basket makers, builders, blacksmiths, and potters.

96

A-F 409. **FIFE, AUSTIN and ALTA FIFE.** Saints of Sage and Saddle: Folklore
Among the Mormons. Bloomington: Indiana University Press,
1956. 367 pp.
Drawing upon oral sources, manuscript sources, and published items, the
Fifes present a chronological narrative of Mormon folk history. The
legends and songs that developed around the Mountain Meadows Massacre,
the Three Nephites, Joseph Smith, Brigham Young, and other events and
individuals are emphasized.

A-F 410. **FIFE, AUSTIN, ALTA FIFE, and HENRY GLASSIE, eds.** Forms upon
the Frontier: Folklore and Folk Arts in the U.S. Logan: Utah
State University Press, 1969. 189 pp.
This is a collection of articles emphasizing the material culture and
customs found on the American frontier, a line that shifts with various
stages of American history. The articles are divided into four general
topics: architecture; arts and crafts; medicine and recipes; and folk
life, customs, and ethnic groups.

A-F 411. **FRY, GLADYS-MARIE.** Night Riders in Black Folk History. Knoxville:
University of Tennessee Press, 1975. 251 pp.
Fry describes how fear of the supernatural was a psychological device
employed by whites to control blacks around the time of the Civil War.
By making blacks afraid of encountering supernatural beings, whites were
able to discourage blacks from moving about at night. The author finds
evidence for these practices in the reminiscences, genealogical data,
and legends of Afro-American oral tradition.

A-F 412. **GARDNER, EMELYN ELIZABETH.** Folklore from the Schoharie Hills,
New York. Ann Arbor: University of Michigan Press, 1937.
351 pp.
This is a multi-dimensional study looking at: (1) the folklore (legends,
tales, songs, games, riddles, and superstitions) from the Schoharie Hills;
(2) the history (economic changes, local personalities, and external
events) of the region; (3) the folklore collected in the U.S. among groups
(such as Pennsylvania Germans, Scotch-Irish, and New Englanders) closely
related to the folk of the Schoharie Hills; and (4) the folklore in
European countries from which the Schoharie residents emigrated.

A-F 413. **GEORGES, ROBERT A.** Greek-American Folk Beliefs and Narratives:
Survivals and Living Tradition. New York: Arno Press, 1980.
230 pp.
The author surveys the history of Greek immigration to the U.S.; examines
the basic organizational patterns of the typical Greek-American community;
and then discusses magico-religious beliefs, saints legends, ethnic superstitions, belief tales, and folk tales, to analyze the role played by
these traditions in the lives of Greek-Americans.

A-F 414. **GIZELIS, GREGORY.** Narrative Rhetorical Devices of Persuasion:
Folklore Communication in a Greek-American Community. Athens,
Greece: National Centre of Social Research, 1974. 155 pp.
Gizelis shows how folklore is used in the daily life of a Greek-American
community in Philadelphia for a variety of purposes. He demonstrates
how personal experience stories, anecdotes, jokes, and puns all serve
to express and enhance ethnic identity, as well as to reveal and reinforce
the relative social status of the participants.

A-F 415. GLASSIE, HENRY. Pattern in the Material Folk Culture of the
          Eastern United States. Philadelphia: University of Pennsylvania
          Press, 1968. 316 pp.
Using concepts derived from both folklore and cultural geography, Glassie
offers a wide variety of data to show how regionalism is expressed in
material folk culture. He first discusses the distinctive qualities of
material folk culture, distinguishing it from popular material culture;
he then surveys different types of material folk culture in the region,
paying particular attention to architecture.

A-F 416. GREENWAY, JOHN, ed. Folklore of the Great West: Selections
          from Eighty-three Years of the "Journal of American Folklore."
          Palo Alto, Calif.: American West, 1969. 453 pp.
Fifty-seven selections representing American Indian and immigrant folk
stories and songs are presented with commentary by the editor. The selections are arranged topically into ten chapters, including traditional
Indian life, Indian and white relations, cowboy songs, folk heroes, supernatural beliefs, and recreation. The geographic area covered is the rural
Midwest and the Far West.

A-F 417. HAND, WAYLAND D. Magical Medicine: The Folkloric Component
          of Medicine in the Folk Belief, Custom, and Ritual of the Peoples
          of Europe and America. Berkeley: University of California
          Press, 1980. 345 pp.
This is a collection of Hand's essays on sacred and secular magic, looking
at the folklore of the Western world wherever it deals with injury, disease,
and healing. Topics range from the magical and demonic causes of disease
(including the evil eye and animals in the body) to disease viewed as
divine retribution for sin and a misspent life.

A-F 418. HAND, WAYLAND D., ed. American Folk Legend: A Symposium.
          Berkeley: University of California Press, 1971. 237 pp.
Fourteen papers on various aspects of folk legend are presented to show
that the study of American legends is in its infancy. Topics of the papers
range from theoretical concerns with the definition of legend to specific
investigations of particular legends in particular contexts. Distinctions
between American legends and their Old World counterparts are noted.

A-F 419. HAND, WAYLAND D., ed. American Folk Medicine: A Symposium.
          Berkeley: University of California Press, 1976. 347 pp.
The twenty-five papers in this symposium cover a wide variety of topics
ranging from clinical analyses of folk accounts of miraculous restoration
of limbs to a study of plant hypnotics among the North American Indians.
Historical and contemporary sources are used, with emphasis on the historical. The folk beliefs discussed tend to be those of distinct subgroups
such as Spanish-Americans, Amish, and American Indians, rather than those
of the mainstream culture.

A-F 420. HUFFORD, DAVID J. The Terror That Comes in the Night: An
          Experience-Centered Study of Supernatural Assault Traditions.
          Philadelphia: University of Pennsylvania Press, 1982.
          278 pp.
Hufford concentrates on the Newfoundland tradition of the Old Hag (involving a night-time assault by a supernatural being) and examines the role
of personal experience within that tradition. He also interprets the
tradition of the Old Hag from a psychological perspective and places the
tradition in a broader cultural context.

A-F 421. HURSTON, ZORA NEALE. Mules and Men. Philadelphia: Lippincott,
          1935. 342 pp.
The first half of this book is a collection of black folktales gathered
by Hurston in her home town of Eatonville, Florida. The second half is
a description of the author's investigations into the practice of Hoodoo.
A student of Franz Boas, Hurston apprenticed herself to a series of Hoodoo
doctors in New Orleans and recounts in a narrative style her experiences
of learning and collecting the Hoodoo rituals.

A-F 422. IVES, EDWARD D. Joe Scott, The Woodsman-Songmaker. Urbana:
          University of Illinois Press, 1978. 473 pp.
The first part of this book recreates the life of Joseph William Scott
(1867-1918) in order to examine the matrix out of which his songs grew.
The second part analyzes each of his songs, tracing what happened to them
during some sixty years of oral tradition. The final part of the book
describes the nature of the tradition in which Scott and his songs
developed (i.e., the singing tradition of lumbercamps).

A-F 423. JACKSON, BRUCE. "Get Your Ass in the Water and Swim Like Me":
          Narrative Poetry from Black Oral Tradition. Cambridge, Mass.:
          Harvard University Press, 1974. 244 pp.
Jackson's collection of some 100 toasts, most of them collected from prison
inmates, demonstrates the scope and variety of this particular folk genre.
Included among the topics are: badmen, crime, and jail; pimps, whores,
and other lovers; drinking; and the voyage of the Titanic.

A-F 424. JACKSON, BRUCE. Wake Up Dead Man: Afro-American Worksongs from
          Texas Prisons. Cambridge, Mass.: Harvard University Press,
          1972. 326 pp.
What distinguishes worksongs from other songs, according to Jackson, is
that their aesthetic is one of participation rather than performance;
the ability to keep the music going at a steady beat is more important
than a beautiful voice. In this volume, Jackson analyzes the form and
function of prison worksongs, and provides both photographs and taped
discussions with prison inmates to illustrate the songs' cultural context.

A-F 425. JACKSON, BRUCE, ed. The Negro and His Folklore in Nineteenth-
          Century Periodicals. Austin: University of Texas Press, 1967.
          374 pp.
This is an anthology of some thirty-five articles, letters, and reviews
on black folklore published in such 19th-century periodicals as Atlantic,
Century, Harper's, Lippincott's, Popular Science, and Southern Workman.
The authors range from militant abolitionists to dedicated slaveholders,
with consequently widely-varying attitudes toward blacks and their folklore.
Folksong, speech, belief, and custom are among the topics covered.

A-F 426. JONES, LOUIS C. Things That Go Bump in the Night. New York:
          Hill & Wang, 1959. 208 pp.
Ghostlore, collected by the author in New York during the 1940s, is
described and analyzed. Jones has subdivided the lore into several categories: the dead who return; haunted houses; violence and sudden death;
historical tales from the French and Indian War and the American Revolution; and the ghostly hitchhiker.

A-F 427. JONES, LOUIS C. Three Eyes on the Past: Exploring New York
          Folk Life. Syracuse, N.Y.: Syracuse University Press, 1982.
          194 pp.
This is a collection of articles written over the past thirty-five years
by Jones, a co-founder of the New York Folklore Society and director emeri-
tus of the New York State Historical Association. The essays treat such
topics as folk medicine, Italian werewolves, ghosts, the devil, murder

lore, and folk art. There is also an introductory essay tracing the history of folklore scholarship in New York.

A-F 428. JORDAN, TERRY G. Texas Graveyards: A Cultural Legacy. Austin:
        University of Texas Press, 1982. 147 pp.
Examining three distinct "geographies of death" in Texas--Southern (which includes both blacks and whites), Hispanic, and German--Jordan concludes that the traditional cemeteries of Texas provide one of the best indices to the cultural diversity of the state. He finds that nowhere else is Texas's regional and ethnic variation so well illustrated as in the places that are set aside for the dead.

A-F 429. KLEIN, BARBRO SKLUTE. Legends and Folk Beliefs in a Swedish
        American Community: A Study in Folklore and Acculturation.
        2 vols. New York: Arno Press, 1980. 824 pp.
Examining the legends of several generations of Swedish-Americans in New Sweden, Maine, Klein asks: what legends and beliefs are retained among immigrants and transmitted to the American-born? what adjustments occur in the lore? what accommodations are made between old country beliefs and the American physical scene? and what beliefs and legends have Swedish immigrants and their descendants learned from the native Americans surrounding them?

A-F 430. KNAPP, MARY and HERBERT KNAPP. One Potato, Two Potato . . . :
        The Secret Education of American Children. New York: Norton,
        1976. 274 pp.
The authors have collected a large quantity of folklore from children in all areas of the U.S. to show how children become members of society and learn to deal with stress by using informal and traditional means. The book is divided into sections on: games as legislatures and courts of law; games as stages and laboratories; jeers; jokes; performances; coping with the here and now; and coping with the unknown.

A-F 431. KOCHMAN, THOMAS, ed. Rappin' and Stylin' Out: Communication
        in Urban Black America. Urbana: University of Illinois Press,
        1972. 424 pp.
The twenty-seven articles collected in this volume describe the communicative habits and expressive life style of urban black Americans in the context of the community in which such behavior occurs. The material is divided into four sections: nonverbal communication, vocabulary and culture, expressive uses of language, and expressive role behavior.

A-F 432. KONGAS-MARANDA, ELLI K. Finnish-American Folklore: Quantitative
        and Qualitative Analysis. New York: Arno Press, 1980.
        536 pp.
The quantitative approach considers the corpus of folklore as a whole, analyzing it in terms of specific genres, and yielding statistical data. The qualitative approach describes the process of transmission and considers the single items which make up the total corpus. The author applies these methods to two case studies: a Finnish-American family spanning three generations; and a Finnish-American leader living in Massachusetts.

A-F 433. KORSON, GEORGE. Black Rock: Mining Folklore of the Pennsylvania
        Dutch. Baltimore, Md.: Johns Hopkins University Press, 1960.
        453 pp.
Korson examines the role played by the Pennsylvania Dutch--ordinarily considered an agricultural people--in the development of the anthracite coal-mining industry. Focusing on the miners in Schuylkill County, Pennsylvania, the author describes their folk speech, marriage customs, folk

medicine, religious lore, legends and traditions, and folk songs and ballads.

A-F 434. KORSON, GEORGE. Coal Dust on the Fiddle: Songs and Stories of the Bituminous Industry. Philadelphia: University of Pennsylvania Press, 1943. 460 pp.
Korson uses oral sources, broadsides, pocket songsters, and newspaper files to construct a composite picture of the life and lore of bituminous coal miners from twenty-two states, with emphasis on those in the Appalachian region. Particular attention is paid to the folklore surrounding coal camps (including the camp schools and company store), coal mines (including disaster stories and superstitions), and miners' unions.

A-F 435. KORSON, GEORGE. Minstrels of the Mine Patch. Philadelphia: University of Pennsylvania Press, 1938. 332 pp.
The folklore of anthracite miners in Pennsylvania is documented and analyzed by Korson as part of the heritage of industrial folklore in this country. Korson finds that stories of mine disasters, injury and death, strikes, the Molly Maguires, and many other events inspired a wide array of songs, ballads, stories, superstitions, and legends created by and for the miners.

A-F 436. LAWS, G. MALCOLM, Jr. American Balladry from British Broadsides: A Guide for Students and Collectors of Traditional Song. Philadelphia: American Folklore Society, 1957. 315 pp.
This volume deals with those ballads, originally printed on broadsides in the British Isles, that have crept into folksong tradition and have made their way to America. The author includes descriptions of the ballads by types, an account of their origin in Britain and their distribution in America, an analysis of their relation to the ballads collected by Francis J. Child, and a discussion of their forms and variants.

A-F 437. LAWS, G. MALCOLM, Jr. Native American Balladry: A Descriptive Study and Bibliographical Syllabus. 1950; Rev. ed. Philadelphia: American Folklore Society, 1964. 298 pp.
Some 250 ballads, originating in the New World and distinct from the traditional or broadside ballads imported from the British Isles, are covered in this volume. Laws provides chapters on the origin and distribution of American ballads, the American ballad as a record of fact, American ballad forms and variants, and the British ballad tradition in America.

A-F 438. LEE, HECTOR. The Three Nephites: The Substance and Significance of the Legend in Folklore. Albuquerque: University of New Mexico Press, 1949. 162 pp.
Lee's objective is to assemble, analyze, collate, and interpret all the lore involving the Three Nephites, the white-robed strangers who figure prominently in Mormon belief. The author discusses the legend's frequency, distribution, dominant motifs, supporting elements, comparative motifs, literary aspects, and historical, sociological, and psychological implications.

A-F 439. LEGMAN, GERSHON. Rationale of the Dirty Joke: An Analysis of Sexual Humor. 1st Series, New York: Grove Press, 1968. 811 pp. 2nd Series, New York: Breaking Point, 1975. 992 pp.
The first volume covers the relatively "clean" dirty jokes, including those on children, fools, animals, marriage, and adultery. The second volume deals with the "dirty" dirty jokes, including those on homosexuality, prostitution, disease, and castration. The jokes are analyzed chronologically, geographically, psychologically, and socio-analytically.

A-F 440. McDANIEL, GEORGE W. Hearth and Home: Preserving a People's
         Culture. Philadelphia: Temple University Press, 1982.
         297 pp.
Focusing on five rural counties in Southern Maryland, McDaniel studies
the historical houses and lifestyles of black families from the time of
slavery to the time of tenancy and landownership in the decades following
the Civil War. Two layers of evidence are examined: the material culture
contained in the houses; and the stories and social histories of the people
who lived in the houses.

A-F 441. McDOWELL, JOHN HOLMES. Children's Riddling. Bloomington: Indi-
         ana University Press, 1979. 272 pp.
This study is based on two groups of texts: (1) from working-class Chicano
children, collected in the barrio of Austin, Texas; and (2) from middle-
class Anglo children in the same city. McDowell discusses the cultural
differences between the two groups, the manners in which the children
acquire their riddling skills, the etiquette of riddling, and the ways
in which the riddlers learn from and through the riddling sessions.

A-F 442. MENEZ, HERMINIA Q. Folklore Communication Among Filipinos in
         California. New York: Arno Press, 1980. 257 pp.
Focusing on several Filipino communities in California, the author suggests
that a change in a group's social situation will generate corresponding
changes in the relationships between an act, event, and situation, as
well as in the components of folkloric performance. Storytelling, singing,
joking, proverbs, and folk beliefs are analyzed.

A-F 443. MINTZ, JEROME R. Legends of the Hasidim: An Introduction to
         Hasidic Culture and Oral Tradition in the New World. Chicago:
         University of Chicago Press, 1968. 462 pp.
Following some background material on the Hasidim in Eastern and Central
Europe, the first part of this book examines the Hasidic community in
New York City, looking at customs of youth and marriage, the role of the
rebbe, and the role of the law in Hasidic life and tradition. The second
part presents the tales—mostly legends—that were collected by the author
in the New York Hasidic community.

A-F 444. MONTELL, WILLIAM LYNWOOD. Don't Go Up Kettle Creek: Verbal
         Legacy of the Upper Cumberland. Knoxville: University of Ten-
         nessee Press, 1983. 247 pp.
Relying on personal reminiscences, oral traditions, balladry, song, and
printed materials (which were themselves derived form oral history data),
this book attempts to reconstruct the history of the upper Cumberland
River region in Kentucky and Tennessee. Montell covers the effects of
the Civil War, the importance of the steamboat trade, and the changes
in lifestyle brought on by modern technology.

A-F 445. MONTELL, WILLIAM LYNWOOD. The Saga of Coe Ridge. Knoxville:
         University of Tennessee Press, 1970. 231 pp.
Proposing that folk history can complement standard historical literature,
Montell uses the oral testimony of former residents to reconstruct the
saga of Coe Ridge, a black community in Southern Kentucky from the 1860s
to the 1950s. By analyzing tale types and motifs, the author is able
to separate the more factual from the more folkloric elements.

A-F 446. MULLEN, PATRICK B. I Heard the Old Fisherman Say: Folklore
         of the Texas Gulf Coast. Austin: University of Texas Press,
         1978. 183 pp.
The author's concerns are both functional and contextual: to ascertain
what purposes folklore serves in the lives of the people he interviews;
and to determine how that folklore is used by them. The first part of

102

the book describes the occupational lore of the Gulf Coast fishermen (emphasizing their magic beliefs and legends). The second part looks at the folklore of the region as a whole, discussing the buried treasure legends, local character anecdotes, and tall tales.

A-F 447. PAREDES, AMERICO. "With His Pistol in His Hand": A Border Ballad
          and Its Hero. Austin: University of Texas Press, 1958. 262 pp.
This book is an account both of the life of Gregorio Cortez (1875-1916),
an outlaw on the Texas-Mexico border, and of the ballad about him, El
Corrido de Gregorio Cortez, which developed out of actual events. Paredes
investigates the border country and the people (both Anglo and Hispanic),
as well as the folk traditions that produced the songs, the legends, and
the man himself.

A-F 448. PAREDES, AMERICO and ELLEN J. STEKERT, eds. The Urban Experience
          and Folk Tradition. Austin: University of Texas Press, 1971.
          207 pp.
Based on the proceedings of a conference on urban folklore held in 1968,
this volume includes five papers, as well as the comments and discussion
which followed each. The papers themselves, which are primarily concerned
with the transplantation of rural and traditional folk practices into
an urban setting, discuss Southern mountain beliefs in Detroit, urban
hillbillies, rural migrants in the city, and other topics.

A-F 449. POUND, LOUISE. Nebraska Folklore. Lincoln: University of
          Nebraska Press, 1959. 243 pp.
This collection of Pound's essays covers a wide variety of topics, including: Nebraska cave lore, Nebraska snake lore, Nebraska rain lore, legends
of lovers' leaps, Nebraska strong men, cowboy songs, and the Nebraska
folk customs for deaths, funerals, weddings, and other social events.
In several instances, the author answers questions about the sources of
this folklore and the manner in which it was spread.

A-F 450. PUCKETT, NEWBELL NILES. Folk Beliefs of the Southern Negro.
          Chapel Hill: University of North Carolina Press, 1926.
          644 pp.
Having gathered some 10,000 folk beliefs from blacks in the South, primarily from Mississippi, Georgia, and Alabama, Puckett is interested in
tracing the origins of those beliefs and in understanding some of the
overall principles governing the transmission and content of folklore
in general. The beliefs discussed include those for burial customs, ghosts,
voodooism, minor charms and cures, taboos, and prophetic signs and omens.

A-F 451. QUIMBY, IAN M. G. and SCOTT T. SWANK, eds. Perspectives on American Folk Art. New York: Norton, 1980. 376 pp.
Eleven contributors provide a variety of answers to the question of what
folk art is. The judgments range from ones based on an art aesthetic
to others emphasizing ethnic and regional identity. Representative essays
include those on the material culture and folk art of Norwegian-Americans,
a historical review of trends in the collecting and exhibiting of American
folk art, and the Afro-American tradition in folk art and craft.

A-F 452. ROSENBERG, BRUCE A. The Art of the American Folk Preacher.
          New York: Oxford University Press, 1970. 265 pp.
Based on an analysis of many spontaneous sermons chanted by preachers
both black and white, Rosenberg shows that the art of oral formulaic composition is not limited to ancient or Anglo-Saxon poets. The book's chapters cover the church; sermon content and structure; the formulaic quality
of the chanted sermon; the theme; and the making of a chanted sermon.
The transcripts of some twenty sermons are also provided.

A-F 453. ROSENBERG, BRUCE A. Custer and the Epic of Defeat. University
          Park: Pennsylvania State University Press, 1974. 313 pp.
To reveal the traditional nature of the legend of the defeated hero,
Rosenberg explores ancient and Biblical literature, as well as modern history, to find analogs to the legends surrounding Custer's "Last Stand"
at the Little Big Horn River. Examining the stories of the Spartans at
Thermopylae, the Song of Roland, King Saul at Mt. Gilboa, and many others,
the author shows how historical events can be easily re-arranged to correspond with traditional elements.

A-F 454. STERN, STEPHEN. The Sephardic Jewish Community of Los Angeles:
          A Study in Folklore and Ethnic Identity. New York: Arno Press,
          1980. 417 pp.
Stern's objective is to provide a comprehensive analysis of ethnic identity
as it is manifested in the folklore of the Sephardic Jewish community
of Los Angeles. By examining not only the forms of ethnic expression
(which include such things as prayer, song, proverb, and belief), but
also the mechanisms and processes by which these forms are generated and
transmitted, Stern is able to interpret the motivations, desires, and
goals of the community and its members.

A-F 455. TESKE, ROBERT THOMAS. Votive Offerings Among Greek Philadelphians:
          A Ritual Perspective. New York: Arno Press, 1980. 326 pp.
Teske maintains that votive offerings qualify as folk religious practices
due to their survivalistic character from classical antiquity, their magical aspect, and their character as a self-initiated approach to the supernatural in a time of uncertainty or need. The author applies the model
of ritual-as-communication to the votive offerings, pointing out the similarities of patterning in this and other folk religious practices.

A-F 456. THIGPEN, KENNETH A. Folklore and the Ethnicity Factor in the
          Lives of Romanian-Americans. New York: Arno Press, 1980.
          589 pp.
This is an attempt to explain the ethnicity of Romanian-Americans by way
of their folklore. Thigpen provides chapters on: the historical traditions of the Romanian immigrant; folktales (both dormant and living);
the supernatural world of Romania in America; the American experience;
and the New Ethnicity. Instead of a homogeneous ethnic folk, the author
finds a group of quite diverse people. He concludes that the synthesis
of ethnic traditions in the New World occurs primarily on an individual
basis.

A-F 457. THOMPSON, HAROLD W. Body, Boots and Britches: Folktales, Ballads
          and Speech from Country New York. Philadelphia: Lippincott,
          1939. 530 pp.
Thompson describes and interprets the stories, ballads, legends, and
proverbs from fifty-eight of New York's sixty-two counties. The book is
divided into chapters on pirates, Indian fighters, outlaws, tall-tale
heroes, tricksters, whales, canal lore, lumbermen, mountaineers, soldiers,
place names, and more.

A-F 458. THOMPSON, STITH. The Folktale. New York: Dryden Press, 1946.
          510 pp.
The author identifies the various forms of the folktale, traces their
origins and distribution around the world (according to the historical-
geographical method), and reviews the history of folktale scholarship.
A separate section of the book deals with the folktales of North American
Indians.

A-F 459. TRENT, ROBERT F. Hearts and Crowns: Folk Chairs of the Connecticut Coast, 1720-1840, as Viewed in the Light of Henri Focillon's Introduction to "Art Populaire." New Haven, Conn.: New Haven Colony Historical Society, 1977. 101 pp.
The author uses the "hearts and crowns" chairmaking tradition to attack the "masterpiece approach" to the decorative arts, which tends to consider folk and provincial traditions of design inappropriate for serious consideration as art forms. Trent's approach is to evaluate the objects in terms of the culture which produced them, rather than in terms of conventional high-art analysis.

A-F 460. TULLOS, ALLEN, ed. Long Journey Home: Folklife in the South. Chapel Hill, N.C.: Southern Exposure, 1977. 224 pp.
This collection of articles, originally published as a special issue of Southern Exposure, covers such subjects as music, fishing lore, Afro-American graveyard decoration, North Carolina pottery, Southern barbecue, and clog dancing. In addition, there is an extensive section on folklore resources and bibliography.

A-F 461. VLACH, JOHN MICHAEL. Charleston Blacksmith: The Work of Philip Simmons. Athens: University of Georgia Press, 1981. 154 pp.
Vlach examines the wrought-iron work of Philip Simmons, a blacksmith still working in Charleston, S.C. The author describes Simmons's childhood, apprenticeship, and career--as well as the blacksmith's attitudes toward his work--using oral testimony and observations gathered from 1972 to 1978. Also discussed are the impact of changing markets and technology, the distinctive Charleston tradition in wrought iron, the role of the client in shaping the final product, and the black ethnic heritage of the region.

A-F 462. WATERS, DONALD J., ed. Strange Ways and Sweet Dreams: Afro-American Folklore from the Hampton Institute. Boston: G. K. Hall, 1983. 439 pp.
This volume gathers in one place all the data--on such topics as folktales, rhymes, magic, and music--that the Hampton Folklore Society collected and published in the Southern Workman between 1893 and 1900, as well as other folklore recorded in the Society's notebooks but never published. Waters reviews the history of the Folklore Society and evaluates its overall significance.

A-F 463. WELSCH, ROGER L. Shingling the Fog and Other Plains Lies. Chicago: Swallow Press, 1972. 160 pp.
Welsch describes some 300 tall tales (or traditional lies) collected in the state of Nebraska, covering the time period from early pioneer settlements to the present. Topics of the tales include rough weather, fabulous lands, big men, strange animals, and hard times. The influence of the tall tale on both popular and folk traditions is noted.

A-F 464. WELSCH, ROGER L., ed. Mister, You Got Yourself a Horse: Tales of Old-Time Horse Trading. Lincoln: University of Nebraska Press, 1981. 207 pp.
The classic encounters between the suspicious-and-sometimes-even-hostile farmer in his dooryard and the voluble-and-worldly-wise horse trader are captured in this volume of tales collected by the Federal Writers Project in Nebraska. Welsch interprets these tales as examples both of ancient ritual and of formal, subtle, and complicated games.

A-F 465. WEPMAN, DENNIS, RONALD B. NEWMAN, and MURRAY B. BINDERMAN. The
    Life: The Lore and Folk Poetry of the Black Hustler. Phila-
    delphia: University of Pennsylvania Press, 1976. 205 pp.
Having collected from black inmates in four New York State prisons some
thirty-four texts of toasts, the authors discuss the cultural values and
performance styles associated with this form of narrative. Because one
of the authors was a prison inmate at the time he collected the toasts,
he was able to observe spontaneous performances with audience interaction.

A-F 466. WILGUS, D. K. Anglo-American Folksong Scholarship Since 1898.
    New Brunswick, N.J.: Rutgers University Press, 1959. 466 pp.
This is a history of the British and American scholarship that has been
devoted to ballads and folksongs in English. It covers both the armchair
scholars (who examine literary remains) and the active field collectors
(academic as well as amateur). There are chapters on the controversy
over the communal nature of the ballad and on the collection and publication of folksongs.

A-F 467. WILLIAMS, PHYLLIS H. South Italian Folkways in Europe and America.
    New Haven, Conn.: Yale University Press, 1938. 216 pp.
Intended originally as a handbook for social workers, teachers, and physicians dealing with Southern Italian immigrants in New Haven and New
York, this work describes not only the Old Country beliefs, but also the
retentions and adjustments of the immigrants in the New World. Williams
discusses such topics as employment, housing, diet and household economy,
dress, marriage and the family, recreation, education, and religion.

A-F 468. YODER, DON, ed. American Folklife. Austin: University of Texas
    Press, 1976. 304 pp.
The twelve papers in this volume emphasize the historical, geographical,
and traditional aspects of American folklife. The topics covered include
cultural geography, the use of film in folklore studies, the folk boats
of Louisiana, log houses in Indiana, Afro-American coiled basketry in
South Carolina, and ethnic tensions in the Lower Rio Grande Valley before
1860.

A-F 469. ZEITLIN, STEVEN J., AMY J. KOTKIN, and HOLLY CUTTING BAKER.
    A Celebration of American Family Folklore: Tales and Traditions
    from the Smithsonian Collection. New York: Pantheon Books,
    1982. 291 pp.
This is a selection of family folklore collected at the Smithsonian Institution's Festival of American Folklife during the years 1974 to 1977.
The material includes stories about migration, lost fortunes, family feuds,
courtship, and supernatural happenings, as well as verbal expressions,
customs, and photographs. There are also essays by five folklorists that
comment on the folklore in their own families.

ART AND ARCHITECTURE

The divisions of the Art and Architecture section are, for the most part, self-evident. Nevertheless, a few words of explanation are in order. In the first division, Native American art is understood to be that which was produced by the indigenous populations of what is now the United States of America. Indian art in Canada is treated only peripherally and the art of Central and South America not at all. The division entitled SURVEYS AND MULTIMEDIA STUDIES includes general books that give a comprehensive treatment of the arts in America as well as studies of a more specialized nature that do not fall neatly into the other divisions. Thus, a book dealing with both painting and sculpture during the 1950s would be found in SURVEYS. The WORKS ON PAPER division includes studies of watercolors, drawings, pastels, prints, and illustration. The material covered in the NON-ACADEMIC PAINTING AND SCULPTURE division might also be termed Folk Art. As the title implies, however, this division is restricted to the media of painting and sculpture. Studies of crafts and more utilitarian objects are found in the ANTHROPOLOGY AND FOLKLORE section. Some of the books in the DECORATIVE ARTS and ARCHITECTURE divisions of this section are also related. In accordance with the general policy of this bibliography, studies of single artists or monuments have not been included. Likewise, catalogues of museum collections, unless they feature significant interpretive essays, do not appear. Finally, there are no entries for source books, bibliographies, and other reference aids. The following remarks are designed to fill this gap.

The basic and most comprehensive archival deposit in the field of American art is the Archives of American Art, a branch of the Smithsonian Institution. Manuscript materials are kept in Washington, D.C., but offices in Boston, Detroit, Los Angeles, New York City, and San Francisco contain virtually complete microfilm records of the holdings. Rolls of microfilm can also be secured through interlibrary loan. A guide to this unparalleled collection of documentary material is provided by Garnett McCoy, Archives of American Art: A Directory of Resources (New York: Bowker, 1972), and its 1977 supplement, A Checklist of the Collection. Another valuable service of the Smithsonian Institution is the Inventory of American Paintings Executed Before 1914, a national census of works in oil, watercolor, fresco, pastel, and tempera. Housed in Washington, D.C., the Inventory maintains a collection of thousands of reproductions and an even larger verbal index of paintings. Computerized print-outs are available by artist or by subject classification.

The major bibliographic source is the four-volume Arts in America: A Bibliography, edited by Bernard Karpel (Washington, D.C.: Smithsonian Institution Press, 1979), which has annotations for books published before 1976. Besides the standard visual arts media, this bibliography covers film, dance, theater, and music. Also included is an index of dissertations and theses. At the beginning of each section is a guide to more special-ized, topical bibliographies.

There are numerous biographical collections and dictionaries of Ameri-can artists. The 19th-century classics are William A. Dunlap, A History of the Rise and Progress of the Arts of Design in the United States (1834; rpt. New York: Dover, 1969); Henry T. Tuckerman, Book of the Artists (New York: Putnam, 1867); and Clara Erskine Clement and Laurence Hutton, Artists of the Nineteenth Century and Their Works (Boston: Houghton, Osgood, 1879). More recent publications include the comprehensive George C. Groce and David H. Wallace, The New-York Historical Society's Dictionary of Artists in America: 1564-1860 (New Haven, Conn.: Yale University Press, 1957), and Mantle Fielding, Dictionary of American Painters, Sculp-tors & Engravers, Rev. ed. (New York: Apollo, 1983).

In addition to these general dictionaries, there are a number of specialized publications: Theresa Dickason Cederholm, Afro-American Artists: A Bio-bibliographic Directory (Boston: Boston Public Library, 1973); James L. Collins, Women Artists in America: Eighteenth Century

110

to the Present, 2 vols. (Chattanooga, Tenn.: privately printed, 1973
and 1975); Paul Cummings, Dictionary of Contemporary American Artists
(New York: St. Martin's Press, 1977); Doris Ostrander Dawdy, Artists
of the American West: A Biographical Dictionary, 2 vols. (Chicago:
Swallow Press, 1974 and 1981); Esther Aileen Park, Mural Painters in America
A Biographical Index (Pittsburg, Kans.: Kansas State Teachers College,
1949); Peggy Samuels and Harold Samuels, The Illustrated Biographical
Encyclopedia of Artists of the American West (Garden City, N.Y.: Doubleday,
1976); Jeanne O. Snodgrass, American Indian Painters: A Biographical Dic-
tionary (New York: Museum of the American Indian, 1968); Regina Soria,
Dictionary of Nineteenth-Century American Artists in Italy, 1760-1915
(London: Associated University Press, 1982); and David McNeely Stauffer,
American Engravers upon Copper and Steel (New York: Grolier Club, 1907;
1917 supplement by Mantle Fielding).

Yearly exhibition records of most 19th-century art "academies" are
published as a reference source. Usually, they give lists of artists,
their addresses, the works exhibited, the purchasers, and the prices.
See Mary Bartlett Cowdrey, American Academy of Fine Arts and American
Art-Union (New York: New-York Historical Society, 1953); Mary Bartlett
Cowdrey, The National Academy of Design Exhibition Record, 1826-1860 (New
York: New-York Historical Society, 1943); Maria Naylor, The National
Academy of Design Exhibition Record, 1861-1900 (New York: Kennedy Gal-
leries, 1973); Robert F. Perkins, Jr. and William J. Gavin III, The Boston
Athenaeum Art Exhibition Index, 1827-1874 (Cambridge, Mass.: MIT Press,
1980); and Anna Rutledge Wells, Cumulative Record of Exhibition Catalogues:
The Pennsylvania Academy of Fine Arts, the Society of Artists, and the
Artist's Fund Society (Philadelphia: American Philosophic Society, 1955).

Two collections of writings of American artists and critics provide
a documentary history of art from 1700 to the present. They are John
W. McCoubrey, American Art, 1700-1960: Sources and Documents (Englewood
Cliffs, N.J.: Prentice-Hall, 1965) and Barbara Rose, Readings in American

Art Since 1900 (New York: Praeger, 1968). There are also a number of
collections of interviews with and essays by contemporary artists. These
include: Paul Cummings, Artists in Their Own Words: Interviews (New
York: St. Martin's Press, 1979); Barbaralee Diamonstein, Visions and
Images: American Photographers on Photography (New York: Rizzoli, 1981);
Ellen H. Johnson, ed., American Artists on Art from 1940-1980 (New York:
Harper & Row, 1982); Katherine Kuh, The Artist's Voice (New York: Harper
& Row, 1963); and Lynn F. Miller and Sally S. Swensen, Lives and Works:
Talks with Women Artists (Metuchen, N.J.: Scarecrow Press, 1981).

For an index to reproductions other than that provided by the Inven-
tory of American Paintings Executed Before 1914, see Lyn Wall Smith and
Nancy Dustin Wall Moure, Index to Reproductions of American Paintings
Appearing in more than Four Hundred Books, mostly Published since 1960
(Metuchen, N.J.: Scarecrow Press, 1977).

*   *   *   *   *

Scholars in search of library and archival materials in American
architectural history have been aided greatly by the photographic reproduction in book form of the catalogue cards from several of the most important architectural libraries.

Perhaps the most useful of these is the Catalog of the Avery Memorial
Architectural Library of Columbia University, 2nd ed. enlarged, 19 vols.
(Boston: G. K. Hall, 1968), with the most recent supplemental volumes
published in 1982. This union catalogue includes not only the more than
150,000 volumes on architecture in the Avery Library itself, but also
all architectural and art books on the Columbia University campus.

Two other catalogues that should not be overlooked are the New York
Public Library Dictionary Catalog of the Art and Architecture Division,
30 vols. (Boston: G. K. Hall, 1975) and the Catalogue of the Frances
Loeb Library of the Graduate School of Design, Harvard University, 44 vols.
(Boston: G. K. Hall, 1968).

Other important architectural collections, whose complete catalogues have not been published in book form, include: the Environmental Design Library at the University of California, Berkeley; the Library of Congress, particularly the records on file from the Historic American Buildings Survey and the Historic American Engineering Record, as well as the visual materials located in the Prints and Photographs Division; and the Library and Archives of the American Institute of Architects, also in Washington, D.C.

Scholars in search of additional archival materials on architecture should begin by contacting COPAR (the Cooperative Preservation of Architectural Records), c/o Prints and Photographs Division, Library of Congress, Washington, D.C. 20540. COPAR serves as a national and international clearinghouse of information on the location, preservation, and cataloguing of architectural records. Moreover, several of the local and state units of COPAR have published guides to the architectural resources in their particular geographic regions.

For an especially good overview of the bibliographic resources in American architectural history, see Carl W. Condit, "Architectural History in the United States: A Bibliographical Essay," American Studies International, 16 (Autumn 1977), 5-22. Comparable treatments of the scholarship in American vernacular architecture may be found in Dell Upton, "Ordinary Buildings: A Bibliographical Essay in American Vernacular Architecture," American Studies International, 19 (Winter 1981), 57-75; and Dell Upton, "The Power of Things: Recent Studies in American Vernacular Architecture," American Quarterly, 35 (Bibliography Issue 1983), 262-79.

Bibliographies of American architecture are numerous, but several stand out as particularly useful. Henry-Russell Hitchcock's American Architectural Books: A List of Books, Portfolios, and Pamphlets on Architecture and Related Subjects Published in America Before 1895 (Minneapolis: University of Minnesota Press, 1962) covers the years 1775 to 1894. Hitchcock's bibliography is arranged alphabetically by author and provides

113

known locations for the materials included. This volume was reprinted in 1976 (Da Capo Press) with two new features: a list of architectural periodicals whose starting date precedes 1895; and a chronological short-title list of the books identified by Hitchcock.

Still more comprehensive for this early period is Frank J. Roos, Jr., Bibliography of Early American Architecture: Writings on Architecture Constructed Before 1860 in Eastern and Central United States, Rev. ed. (Urbana: University of Illinois Press, 1968) which lists some 4,400 books and articles. Picking up where Roos leaves off, Lawrence Wodehouse has compiled two annotated bibliographies: American Architects from the Civil War to the First World War (Detroit: Gale Research, 1976); and American Architects from the First World War to the Present (Detroit: Gale Research, 1977). It should be noted, however, that Wodehouse's two volumes—unlike those of Hitchcock and Roos—are limited to books and articles containing biographical information on some 400 architects and architectural firms active in the periods covered. The annotated entries are arranged alphabetically by architect and include references to known repositories of the architects' drawings.

Other sources on American architects include: the Macmillan Encyclopedia of Architects, 4 vols. (New York: Free Press, 1982), covering some 2,400 architects from around the world; Dennis Sharp, Sources of Modern Architecture: A Critical Bibliography, Rev. ed. (London: Granada Publishing, 1981), emphasizing modern architects, perhaps one-third of whom were either born in the U.S. or came here to practice; the Avery Obituary Index of Architects, 2nd ed. (Boston: G. K. Hall, 1980), which lists the obituary notices found in some 500 periodicals indexed by the Avery Library from 1934 to 1979, as well as for a selected few periodicals indexed back to the mid-19th century; and Henry F. Withey and Elsie Rathbone Withey, Biographical Dictionary of American Architects (Deceased) (Los Angeles: New Age Publishing, 1956), describing approximately 2,000 architects and other designers who died in the years between 1740 and

114

1952. While extremely useful, the latter source should be consulted with caution, as its contents have been known to be inaccurate.

Another general bibliography of American architecture worth checking is Arts in America: A Bibliography, 4 vols. (Washington, D.C.: Smithsonian Institution Press, 1979). The section on architecture by Charles B. Wood III provides annotations for some 1,400 books and articles published before 1976. A similar, though less comprehensive, annotated bibliography is David M. Sokol, American Architecture and Art: A Guide to Information Sources (Detroit: Gale Research, 1976), which includes roughly 350 books and articles on American architecture.

Turning to architectural bibliographies that cover more specialized topics, the following should not be overlooked. For vernacular architecture, an essential source is Howard Wight Marshall's American Folk Architecture: A Selected Bibliography (Washington, D.C.: Library of Congress, 1981). On a wide variety of specific topics (including architectural styles, architectural types and individual architects), see the series of Exchange Bibliographies, published by the Council of Planning Librarians from 1958 to 1978, and its two successors: Vance Bibliographies and CPL Bibliographies, both published from 1978 to the present. Indexes to the series come in several sets. See the numbers entitled Index to CPL Exchange Bibliographies and Geographic Index to Exchange Bibliographies, published periodically by the Council of Planning Librarians (Monticello, Ill.), and the three separate indexes--by author, title, and subject-- covering bibliographies Al to Al000 (June 1978 to July 1983) published by Vance Bibliographies (Monticello, Ill.) in July 1983.

Several bibliographies of the literature in American architectural history currently are being compiled on a regular basis. These include: Bibliographic Guide to Art and Architecture, with coverage beginning in 1974 (when it was entitled Art and Architecture Book Guide) for materials, but not including periodical articles, catalogued by the New York Public Library and the Library of Congress; the bibliographical listings of books,

115

articles, and catalogues that may be found in the newsletters of the Society of Architectural Historians and the Vernacular Architecture Forum; and, though its emphasis is not on architecture alone, RILA (Repertoire International de la Litterature de l'Art), published since 1975, covering books, dissertations, museum publications, articles in periodicals, festschriften, and conference proceedings.

Finally, for locating articles published in architectural periodicals, several indexes are available: The Avery Index to Architectural Periodicals, 2nd ed. rev. and enlarged, 15 volumes (Boston: G. K. Hall, 1973), is an author and subject index going back to 1934, covering some 375 American and European architectural periodicals, with three biennial supplements (the last published in 1979). Since 1979, the Avery Index—with coverage expanded to roughly 700 journals—has been made available to researchers as a special on-line data base through the Research Libraries Information Network (RLIN). The Architectural Index, published annually since 1950, covers only ten American architectural and design journals. The Architectural Periodicals Index (a continuation and expansion of the Library Review of Periodical Articles, published by the Royal Institute of British Architects since 1933) indexes some 450 of the world's architectural periodicals, but with emphasis on Great Britain. The Art Index, published annually since 1929, currently indexes some 200 American and European periodicals, including about twenty titles that deal specifically with architecture.

John Davis
Columbia University

James Deutsch
George Washington University

I.   NATIVE AMERICAN

A-A 1. <u>American Indian Art</u>: <u>Form and Tradition</u>. New York: Dutton,
        1972. 154 pp.
This diverse exhibition catalogue is not a comprehensive geographical
and topical survey of Native American art; rather, it is a collection
of essays by noted experts on various specialized topics of particular
interest to them. Instead of surveying the art, the book surveys current
attitudes toward the art and the cultures which produced it. Among other
topics, the essays cover aesthetics, rock art, Pueblo architecture, Iroquois masks, Asiatic sources in Northwest Coast art, and Eskimo sculpture.

A-A 2. BRODER, PATRICIA JANIS. <u>American Indian Painting and Sculpture</u>.
        New York: Abbeville Press, 1981. 165 pp.
Broder's book examines the non-ceremonial art of over seventy contemporary
Native Americans. Beginning about 1885, she traces the gradual acceptance
by Native peoples of the idea of artistic creation as an independent activity rather than a religious or utilitarian one. Broder stresses that
this Indian art must be judged by the same criteria as non-Indian art.
She reacts against the view that because these artists use western materials (commercial paints, paper), they are no longer truly "Indian."
All of the large-scale plates are in color.

A-A 3. BRODY, J. J. <u>Indian Painters and White Patrons</u>. Albuquerque:
        University of New Mexico Press, 1971. 238 pp.
Brody's study weighs the merits of two conflicting interpretations of
modern American Indian painting: first, that it is an extension of traditional forms of expression which has been little diluted by white contact; second, that it has been largely shaped by white patrons who demanded
it evolve into a commercial, subjugated art. Two introductory chapters
outline (1) Native American painting prior to the 20th century and (2)
the relations between Indians and whites. The remainder of the book examines the development and evolution of modern Indian painting.

A-A 4. COE, RALPH T. <u>Sacred Circles</u>: <u>Two Thousand Years of North American</u>
        <u>Indian Art</u>. Seattle: University of Washington Press, 1977.
        252 pp.
The catalogue of an exhibition sent to the Hayward Gallery in London,
this book contains a wide range of information about Native American art.
After an introduction on the "Indianness" of Native North American art,
Coe divides the catalogue into geographical sections. The text, however,
is not a survey; Coe stresses aspects of the art which were previously
given little attention. The book also includes a glossary, time chart,
maps, and an appended discussion of the photographs of Edward Curtis.

A-A 5. CONN, RICHARD. <u>Native American Art in the Denver Museum</u>. Seattle:
        University of Washington Press, 1979. 501 pp.
Five hundred Native American objects selected from the 15,000 in the Denver
Art Museum are illustrated in this large catalogue. The works are selected
first for aesthetic quality, then for breadth of chronological and geographical distribution. An introduction gives historical and societal
perspectives on the appreciation and interpretation of the art. The catalogue entries are divided into ten regional groups.

A-A 6. DOCKSTADER, FREDERICK J. <u>Indian Art in America</u>. Greenwich, Conn.:
        New York Graphic Society, 1962. 224 pp.
Unlike most Native American surveys, this volume does not approach the
art by regions. Five thematic chapters dealing with such topics as the
Indian view of artistic creation, the dating of Indian art, and white

contact precede over 200 plates intended to give a broad survey of media
and tribes. Each plate receives a short commentary indicating function,
iconography, and materials.

A-A 7. DOUGLAS, FREDERIC and RENE d'HARNONCOURT. Indian Art of the United
       States. New York: Museum of Modern Art, 1941. 204 pp.
This early exhibition did much to establish the legitimacy of Native American art history. The authors see North American Indian art as provincial
art, on a smaller scale than the art south of the Rio Grande. They eschew
the label "primitive," and suggest instead the terms "folk" or "regional,"
for Native American art is always an inextricable part of local society.
White ethnologists, they assert, have tended to "oversymbolize" Indian
art. The chapters consist of a number of plates, each of which receives
a short explanatory text.

A-A 8. FEDER, NORMAN. American Indian Art. New York: Abrams, 1965.
       455 pp.
This volume presents over 300 photographs displaying something of the
range of objects produced by the many different cultures identified as
American Indian. Feder provides an introductory discussion of the origins
of the various arts represented and comments on tribal styles, materials,
techniques, change, stability, and other factors. The major emphasis
of the book is on the pictorial chapters devoted to the creation of Indian
art from seven different areas.

A-A 9. FEDER, NORMAN. Two Hundred Years of North American Indian Art.
       New York: Praeger, 1971. 128 pp.
John I. H. Baur writes the preface to this Whitney Museum exhibition catalogue in which he stresses the aesthetic importance of Native American
art. For logistical reasons, Feder excludes pre-historic and contemporary
art. He includes art of the approximate period, 1700-1900, and insists
on the continuing quality of work after white contact. Emphasis is placed
on works from the Plains and Woodlands regions, and the "art" is stressed
more than the "craft." Over 300 objects were in the exhibition, almost
half of which are illustrated here.

A-A 10. FEEST, CHRISTIAN. Native Arts of North America. New York: Oxford
        University Press, 1980. 216 pp.
Feest's approach differs from those of the majority of Native American
surveys. He does not present the art by region but treats it as a cultural
whole, diverse yet linked. He discusses four general types of art: tribal,
ethnic, Pan-Indian, and Indian mainstream. Three introductory chapters
consider approaches to Indian art history, the history of the native peoples of North America, and the specific artistic modifications which
resulted from white contact. Part II examines the art by medium: painting
and engraving, textiles, and sculpture.

A-A 11. FURST, PETER T. and JILL L. FURST. North American Indian Art.
        New York: Rizzoli, 1982. 236 pp.
This survey considers the Native American arts of six regions: the Southwest, California, the Northwest Coast, Alaska, the Plains, and the Eastern
Woodlands. An introductory chapter explains the need to consider the
art as part of an interplay of environment, history, social organizations,
diffusion, and contact with whites. The authors isolate two underlying
religious views which directly affect the art and which are common to
most tribes: a shamanic world view which emphasizes a direct path from
the individual to the spiritual realm and the view that there is no significant difference between humans and other life forms.

A-A 12. HABERLAND, WOLFGANG. The Art of North America. New York: Crown, 1964. 251 pp.
Haberland's text, first published in German, broke new ground in European ethnological circles where the art of Central and South America had formerly been stressed. Haberland does not make a chronological division at the appearance of the white man; he finds relative continuity between the pre- and post-European periods. After two initial chapters which discuss the Palaeo-Indian stage and the early petroglyphs, the remaining portion of the book is devoted to specific regions. Two appendices follow, one examining the art of the West Indies and one providing maps, charts, a bibliography, and an index.

A-A 13. HIGHWATER, JAMAKE. Song From the Earth: American Indian Painting. Boston: New York Graphic Society, 1976. 212 pp.
In this book, Native American painting from before the historic period to the present is examined in light of the particular nature of Indian art. Such concepts as universal harmony, goodness versus beauty, and intentional ambiguity are discussed. Highwater cautions Caucasians that they must suspend the western view of art and the world in order to understand the transcendental character of Native American painting. The last chapter includes sketches of ten contemporary artists.

A-A 14. MATHEWS, ZENA and ALDONA JONAITIS, eds. Native North American Art History. Palo Alto, Calif.: Peek, 1982. 502 pp.
The editors have collected thirty readings (largely previously published articles) which together form an interpretive, scholarly history of Native American art. The articles are grouped by geographical region and are generally specific in theme. Topics include Shamanism, Eskimo houses, Tsimshian prehistoric art, California basketry, Seneca figurines, and Great Lakes pouches.

A-A 15. SLOAN, JOHN and OLIVER LaFARGE. Introduction to American Indian Art, The Exposition of Indian Tribal Arts. 1931; Reissued, Glorieta, N.M.: Rio Grande Press, 1971. 219 pp.
The original publication of this work was a landmark in the study of Native American art. The book is a reprint of the pamphlets issued in conjunction with "the First Exhibition of American Indian Art Selected Entirely with Consideration of Aesthetic Value." The introduction is written by Sloan and LaFarge, but various authors contributed to twelve other chapters. The volume includes an exhaustive list of books on Indian art compiled by Ruth Gaines.

A-A 16. VAILLANT, GEORGE C. Indian Art in North America. New York: Harper & Row, 1939. 63 pp.
This early book features a short but dense text which indicates the state of scholarship in the then budding field of Native American art history. Vaillant discusses the social significance of the art at the time he writes, the social background of the art, and the origins of Indian culture. He distinguishes between pre- and post-contact art and ends with an "appraisal" of the art and architecture. Almost 100 plates are included.

A-A 17. WARNER, JOHN ANSON. The Life and Art of the North American Indian. New York: Hamlyn, 1975. 168 pp.
Warner, a sociologist, is interested in the interplay of Native American art and culture. The full-color illustrations of objects of art are interspersed with photographs by Edward Curtis, which illustrate the life, dress, and ceremonies of early 20th-century Indians. In his introduction, Warner discusses the complex history and historiography of Native American art.

II. SURVEYS AND MULTIMEDIA STUDIES

A-A 18. ALLOWAY, LAWRENCE. Topics in American Art Since 1945. New York: Norton, 1975. 283 pp.
This collection of Alloway's criticism covers American art from Abstract Expressionism to the 1970s. Most of the selections are reprints of previously published articles, but three catalogue essays written for the Guggenheim Museum are also included. Among the artists discussed are Adolf Gottlieb, Jackson Pollock, Sol Lewitt, Jim Dine, Jasper Johns, George Segal, Allan Kaprow, and Robert Smithson.

A-A 19. ASHTON, DORE. American Art Since 1945. New York: Oxford University Press, 1982. 224 pp.
Nine titleless chapters compose this narrative of thirty-five years of American art. Artists and movements are not confined to constricting chapters. Rather, they appear and reappear as their importance in the chronological survey demands. Beginning with Abstract Expressionism, Ashton examines painting, sculpture, conceptual art, and performance. The last chapter considers the work of Miriam Schapiro, William T. Williams, and Bernard Tschumi among others.

A-A 20. ASHTON, DORE. The Unknown Shore: A View of Contemporary Art. Boston: Little, Brown, 1962. 265 pp.
In this book, Ashton deals with post-W.W. II avant-garde painting in Europe and the U.S. She examines the effect of the war on the art which followed it, and notes the influence of 19th-century romantic painting. Ashton rejects the notion of progress in the arts and stresses the need to consider contemporary artists as individuals and not as part of a national or racial style. Among her topics are Existentialism, the Oriental influence, Expressionism, music and painting, and science and art.

A-A 21. BATTCOCK, GREGORY, ed. Minimal Art: A Critical Anthology. New York: Dutton, 1968. 448 pp.
Minimal art, Battcock argues, should not be equated with monumentality. It is neither nihilistic nor anti-past. Problems of scale, viewer-object relationships, and the appraisal of past and present occupy minimal artists. Essays by twenty-nine critics and artists follow Battcock's introduction. The focus is on problems in minimal art rather than on individual artists. There are numerous illustrations throughout.

A-A 22. BATTCOCK, GREGORY, ed. The New Art: A Critical Anthology. New York: Dutton, 1966. 254 pp.
Battcock's anthology is more about criticism than it is about art. The articles and catalogue essays, most from after 1960, were selected to demonstrate the indissoluble bond of contemporary art and criticism. Battcock characterizes contemporary critics as being less concerned with relations between art and other fields (such as literature and philosophy) because they recognize that new definitions must be found for the recent art which transcends the traditional distinctions. Twenty-two critics are featured.

A-A 23. BATTCOCK, GREGORY, ed. Super Realism. New York: Dutton, 1975. 322 pp.
In addition to an introduction by Battcock, this critical anthology on Super Realism, also known as Photo Realism and New Realism, contains seventeen essays dealing with a broad range of responses to the Super Realist paintings and sculpture produced in the 1970s by such artists as Duane Hanson, Richard Estes, Janet Fish, Joseph Raffael, John de Andrea, Robert Bechtle, Ralph Goings, Chuck Close, and Malcolm Morley. The essays are

by Gerrit Henry, Ivan Karp, J. Patrice Marandel, Cindy Nemser, Linda Nochlin, Linda Chase, Kim Levin, H. D. Raymond, Harold Rosenberg, William Dyckes, Joseph Masheck, Gene R. Swenson, Honey Truewoman, and Judith Van Baron. There is also a section of photographs of Super Realist art.

A-A 24. BATTCOCK, GREGORY. Why Art: Casual Notes on the Aesthetics of the Immediate Past. New York: Dutton, 1977. 134 pp.
In this collection of essays, Battcock is interested in contemporary art in its social context. He raises questions about the role of art in society, the exhibition of art in museums and galleries, the relationship between art and its audience, and the importance of aesthetics for the art work. Battcock emphasizes the shift in art away from the art-for-art's-sake rationale toward a concept of art as transportation, and argues for the creation of new criteria, for the evaluation of art as connoisseurship is no longer valid.

A-A 25. BECKER, HOWARD SAUL. Art Worlds. Berkeley: University of California Press, 1982. 392 pp.
Becker presents an extensive discussion of today's art world from a sociological perspective. He focuses on forms of social organization, not aesthetics. In his analysis of art as a social phenomenon, Becker argues for a study of the network of co-operation. Among the issues discussed are the distributing of the art work, aesthetics and critics, arts and crafts, editing, professionals and folk artists, and art and the State.

A-A 26. BENJAMIN, SAMUEL G. W. Art in America: A Critical and Historical Sketch. New York: Harper, 1880. 214 pp.
Benjamin's text provides us with a look at attitudes about American art during the Victorian Age. In 1880, he wrote that it was too soon to expect a "great school of art" in America. In the art which precedes the work of his contemporaries, he finds little that is original and much that depends on the art of Europe. He briefly discusses many major and minor figures in painting and sculpture and ends with a chapter called "Present Tendencies of American Art."

A-A 27. BISHOP, ROBERT and PATRICIA COBLENTZ. The World of Antiques, Art, and Architecture in Victorian America. New York: Dutton, 1979. 495 pp.
This book is primarily devoted to the decorative arts; however, chapters on architecture, painting, and sculpture are included. An introductory chapter examines the influence of Queen Victoria on American taste. Each of the sixteen chapters which follows deals with a specific topic, such as "Clocks" or "Children's World." Emphasis in this extremely broad survey is on the place of art in the lives of Americans of the period. Illustrations are numerous; after a short essay, each chapter is given over to hundreds of illustrations which are treated in the manner of catalogue entries.

A-A 28. BROWN, MILTON WOLF. American Art to 1900. New York: Abrams, 1977. 631 pp.
This college-level text discusses painting and sculpture with special emphasis on American architecture. Also included is a brief chapter on American museums and art associations. The text refers constantly to the historical events which parallel the creation of the objects and buildings. A bibliography organized by medium and individual artists is included.

A-A 29. BROWN, MILTON WOLF., SAM HUNTER, JOHN JACOBUS, NAOMI ROSENBLUM, and DAVID M. SOKOL. American Art: Painting, Sculpture, Architecture, Decorative Arts, Photography. New York: Abrams, 1979. 616 pp.
Five authors have contributed to this survey of American art. Milton Brown discusses painting, sculpture, and architecture to about 1900, Sam Hunter writes on 20th-century painting and sculpture, and John Jacobus deals with the architecture of the same period. Naomi Rosenblum provides four sections on photography, and David Sokol is responsible for the capsule discussions of decorative arts that are scattered throughout the book.

A-A 30. BUETTNER, STEWART. American Art Theory: 1945-1970. Ann Arbor, Mich.: UMI Research Press, 1981. 213 pp.
Buettner surveys much more than the twenty-five years of art theory ("the body of ideas formulated by artists") indicated in the title. He begins in Europe in 1900 and traces both the European and later American developments which led to Abstract Expressionism--his main topic. At the end, he considers the art theory that emerged from the Abstract Expressionists. Throughout, his source material is derived from the statements of the artists in letters, interviews, and manifestoes.

A-A 31. CALAS, NICOLAS. Art in the Age of Risk and Other Essays. New York: Dutton, 1968. 238 pp.
Calas has written on Surrealism, mythology, psychoanalysis, and anthropology. In these essays, he brings a broad humanist background to the art of the present. In the first two essays he discusses Surrealism and Pop art. Other chapters are on poetry and the painted image, art critics, and such artists as Robert Rauschenberg, Jim Dine, Barnett Newman, Alex Katz, and Al Held.

A-A 32. CALAS, NICOLAS and ELENA CALAS. Icons and Images of the 60s. New York: Dutton, 1971. 347 pp.
This collection of essays (some previously published) focuses on the chief artistic figures and movements of the 1960s. The essays are historical, theoretical, and biographical, with the emphasis on painting. The tone of much of the writing is polemical. Nicolas Calas argues that "traceable back to Hegel are the aesthetic theories of the two principal apologists of the New York School, Clement Greenberg and Harold Rosenberg," and that the artists of the 1960s reacted against these Hegelian interpreters. Marcel Duchamp becomes the key figure of the period for them. Illustrations are numerous.

A-A 33. CARMEAN, E. A. The Great Decade of American Abstraction. Houston, Tex.: Houston Museum of Fine Arts, 1974. 138 pp.
This dense catalogue presents a compendium of critical writings on modernism by such authors as Clement Greenberg, Michael Fried, Rosalind Krauss, and Barbara Rose. The painters and sculptors whose work appears in this exhibition are seen as purists, preserving the classical traditions of the media without resorting to gimmickry. Among the artists included are Jack Bush, Friedel Dzubas, Adolf Gottlieb, Hans Hoffman, Barnett Newman, David Smith, and Clyfford Still. In an unusual final section, two conservators discuss the conservation problems particular to recent, large-scale paintings.

A-A 34. CARMEAN, E. A. and ELIZA E. RATHBONE, with THOMAS B. HESS. American Art at Mid-century: The Subjects of the Artist. Washington, D.C.: National Gallery of Art, 1978. 268 pp.
The essays in this exhibition catalogue are based on the repeated affirmation of the Abstract Expressionists that they rejected representational manners, but that their work contains subject matter. The essays focus

on the subjects of the works and how they came into being. Individual
chapters are devoted to: "Gorky: The Plow and the Song"; "Motherwell:
Elegies to the Spanish Republic"; "Pollock: Classic Paintings of 1950";
"De Kooning: The Women"; "Newman: The Stations of the Cross—Lema
Sabachthani"; "Smith: The Voltri Sculpture"; and "Rothko: The Brown and
the Gray Paintings."

A-A 35. CHASE, JUDITH WRAGG. Afro-American Art and Craft. New York:
     Van Nostrand Reinhold, 1971. 142 pp.
Chase's book traces the complete artistic experience of the Afro-American,
beginning with the pre-historic African background and following through
the North American transportation up to the present. She sees these thousands of years of history as one continuous stream of cultural heritage.
Specific chapters examine the years of transition in ante-bellum America,
the urban craftsman, the plantation craftsman, the Depression years, and
contemporary art and craft.

A-A 36. CHENEY, MARTHA CANDLER. Modern Art in America. New York: Whittle-
     sey House, 1939. 190 pp.
Cheney argues for the indigenous character of American art, which she
sees as emerging to produce a new art of universal significance. To support her claim she discusses a broad range of contemporary American art.
Included are chapters on the European authority for American artists and
the pioneer American life and taste. Also studied are artistic and social
developments in the 1930s, the AAA (American Abstract Artists), the museums,
Regionalism, the WPA (Works Progress Administration), and the then modern
mural paintings.

A-A 37. Classical Spirit in American Portraiture. Providence, R.I.:
     Department of Art, Brown University, 1976. 120 pp.
Organized by seven graduate students at Brown University, this exhibition
examined the artistic exploration of classical motifs in 18th- and 19th-
century America. Eight short essays with such subjects as "Jefferson
and Architecture," "Classical Motifs in American Portrait Engravings,"
and "The American Imagination and Italy" accompany the fifty catalogue
entries. The works encompass the media of painting, sculpture, prints,
drawings, photography, architecture, and numismatics.

A-A 38. COHEN, GEORGE M. A History of American Art. New York: Dell,
     1971. 364 pp.
This survey places equal emphasis on painting, sculpture, and architecture
with a shorter discussion of the graphic arts. Cohen sees a heritage
of self-esteem rather than self-consciousness in the art from the Colonial
period to the 20th century. His approach is openly nationalistic. He
seeks to prove that American art can "stand alone" in relation to European art. The American melting pot forms an art which Cohen describes
as "universal," drawing artists from every level of society and all parts
of the world.

A-A 39. CONTRERAS, BELISARIO R. Tradition and Innovation in New Deal Art.
     Lewisburg, Pa.: Bucknell University Press, 1983. 253 pp.
Contreras assigns the roles of the traditionalist and the innovator to
Edward Bruce and Holger Cahill, respectively, the architects of the New
Deal art programs. Bruce's traditionalism is seen as reflecting his European training, while Cahill's less conservative approach is tied to the
American experience. Contreras identifies the three cultural sources
of New Deal art as the Depression era, the contemporary American scene,
and the Mexican mural movement. He examines all three in light of the
opinions expressed by Bruce and Cahill, as well as other prominent artists,
writers, and politicians.

A-A 40. COOKE, HEREWARD LESTER. Eyewitness to Space: Paintings and Drawings Related to the Apollo Mission to the Moon. New York: Abrams,
1971. 227 pp.
This volume, a joint project of the National Gallery of Art and NASA,
reproduces over 250 works of art (most in color) which relate to the Apollo
missions, 1963-1969. Forty-seven artists from Norman Rockwell to Robert
Rauschenberg were present at Cape Kennedy, Mission Control in Houston,
and the Pacific splashdown site. Cooke's essay describes the conception
of this government project as well as the various stages of the mission
which the artists sketched and painted.

A-A 41. CORN, WANDA. The Color of Mood: American Tonalism. San Francisco
DeYoung Memorial Museum, 1972. 46 pp.
Corn's essay essentially defines a new term in the history of American
painting. Tonalism describes the turn-of-the-century predilection for
soft, ethereal, atmospheric effects. Corn traces the origin of the work
in the theory and criticism of the day, and extends the use of the term
to photography as well. Only fourteen works from the original exhibition
are included in this catalogue.

A-A 42. CRAVEN, THOMAS. Modern Art: The Men, the Movements, the Meaning.
1934; Rev. ed. New York: Simon & Schuster, 1940. 378 pp.
The first half of this work is concerned with the European art world from
Van Gogh to the Surrealists. In the second half, Craven interrelates
his own biography, as a native Westerner, with a discussion of America's
culture. Included are chapters on Frank Lloyd Wright, George Grey Barnard,
Alfred Stieglitz, Thomas Hart Benton and the Mexicans, Jose Clemente Orozco
and Diego Rivera. He argues for an art that will open itself to the needs
of a greater number of people, reserving praise for the German artist,
George Grosz, as well as Benton and the two Mexicans, Orozco and Rivera.

A-A 43. CUNNINGHAM, NOBLE E., Jr. The Image of Thomas Jefferson in the
Public Eye: Portraits for the People 1800-1809. Charlottesville:
University Press of Virginia, 1981. 185 pp.
The author seeks to recreate the image of Jefferson as he was known to
the public who elected him president. While familiar today, the painted
portraits and sculpted busts were not seen by the majority of his contemporaries. Rather, Jefferson was known through engraved prints and common
household items which featured his likeness. Cunningham considers the
circumstances of the production and dissemination of these prints. Also
discussed are the media of medals and silhouettes.

A-A 44. DANTO, ARTHUR C. The Transfiguration of the Commonplace: A Philosophy of Art. Cambridge, Mass.: Harvard University Press,
1981. 212 pp.
This is a philosophical treatment of art in which Danto discusses the
nature of art theory. He uses ideas ranging from Plato to Wittgenstein,
and artworks from Bruegel to Roy Lichtenstein. His focus is on the visual
arts (painting and sculpture), but his ideas are intended to stand as
an analytical philosophy of all art. Danto sees theory as that which
detaches the object from the real world and places it in the art world,
a world of interpreted things. He proposes a definition of art in which
the three concepts of rhetoric, style, and expression are connected in
metaphor.

A-A 45. DAVIS, DOUGLAS. Art and the Future. A History/Prophecy of the
Collaboration Between Science, Technology and Art. New York:
Praeger, 1973. 208 pp.
The theme of the book, as stated by Davis, is art's expansion into a sym-
biotic collaboration with "non-art" forces, with the engineer, the scien-
tist, and the computer. Davis begins his extensive survey with the merg-

ings of art and technology in early 20th-century art. The second section covers the period from 1937 to 1965. The blossoming of the collaboration occurs in the late 1960s, with the Art and Technology exhibition in Los Angeles, and with developments in video, computers, holography, and laser light. Included is a section on the process of art with conversations, manifestoes, and statements.

A-A 46. DICKASON, DAVID HOWARD. The Daring Young Men: The Story of the American Pre-Raphaelites. Bloomington: Indiana University Press, 1953. 304 pp.
Making frequent reference to the Pre-Raphaelite Brotherhood of England, Dickason studies the American offshoot, the "Society for the Advancement of Truth in Art," which was based in New York City. He considers the Pre-Raphaelite publications, the doctrine of Art for Art's Sake, the Arts and Crafts movement, Ruskin and other literary influences, and such artists as John La Farge and Peter B. Wight who were sensitive to the principles of the Pre-Raphaelite Brotherhood.

A-A 47. DICKSON, HAROLD E. Arts of the Young Republic: The Age of William Dunlap. Chapel Hill: University of North Carolina Press, 1968. 234 pp.
The exhibition, which took place at the Ackland Art Center at Chapel Hill, examined American architecture, painting, sculpture, and graphic arts during the maturity of William Dunlap (1766-1839), the first chronicler of the arts in America. Dickson's essay, laced with quotes from Dunlap, traces the achievements of a variety of Colonial artists from the Revolutionary War to the Jacksonian Era. There are no catalogue entries; however, almost 200 black and white illustrations are included.

A-A 48. DILLENBERGER, JANE and JOHN DILLENBERGER. Perceptions of the Spirit in Twentieth-Century Art. Indianapolis, Ind.: Indianapolis Museum of Art, 1977. 177 pp.
This catalogue examines relations between theology and the visual arts in 20th-century America. Most of the artists are well known, yet the context in which the authors place them is unfamiliar in American art history. The early 20th century is characterized as dualistic: the more meaningful spiritual realm completely distinct from the material realm. After the 1940s, the authors see a breaking down of barriers, with the perceptions of spirit being anchored in pluralistic humanity rather than the pure concepts of science and morality. The artists range from Arthur B. Davies to Louise Nevelson.

A-A 49. DILLENBERGER, JANE and JOSHUA C. TAYLOR. The Hand and The Spirit: Religious Art in America, 1700-1900. Berkeley, Calif.: University Art Museum, 1972. 192 pp.
The authors contend that in spite of the lack of attention given to it by American art historians, religious painting and sculpture play a major role in the American experience. Artists and churchmen were once intimately associated, and together they dealt with such concepts as nature and science. Art more directly rooted in religion—such as Pennsylvania fracturs and New Mexico santos—is also discussed. The catalogue entries are divided into chronological and thematic (e.g., Biblical, academic, folk) groups.

A-A 50. DOEZEMA, MARIANNE. American Realism and the Industrial Age. Bloomington: Indiana University Press, 1980. 143 pp.
The catalogue of this small exhibition at the Cleveland Museum of Art examines the manner in which 19th- and 20th-century artists responded to the technological aspects of their world. Doezema isolates the concern for the factual as the salient quality of the realistic approach to the industrial environment. She notes, however, that this interest is not

uniquely American, and she stresses a dependence on European models. Among other themes, she discusses illustration, urban iconography, Precisionism, and the art of the Depression.

A-A 51. DOVER, CEDRIC. American Negro Art. Greenwich, Conn.: New York Graphic Society, 1960. 186 pp.
This "picture book," as it is described in the introduction, is a seminal history of Afro-American art and the economic and political situation that shaped its development. It includes "The Manual Arts," on the black craftsmen and artisans under slavery, and "Towards Freedom and Art" on northern black artists in the late 18th and 19th centuries. "Mulattoes and Atelier Art" discusses the role of the black bourgeoisie who, Dover argues, nourished the evolution of an "atelier" art using the received values and techniques of the day but contributed little to the progress of Afro-Americans or American art. "The New Negro" deals with the Black Renaissance of the twenties and the rediscovery of African culture and ancestral arts. "Progress and Problems" discusses the impact of the WPA on Afro-American Art, and "The Continuity of Negro Art" is a survey of more recent 20th-century painters and sculptors.

A-A 52. DRISKELL, DAVID C. Two Centuries of Black American Art. Los Angeles, Calif.: Los Angeles County Museum of Art, 1976. 221 pp.
This is the catalogue to the exhibition which in 1976 was the largest and most comprehensive of its kind. Driskell's text is divided into two chronological segments: "Artists and Craftsmen in the Formative Years, 1750-1920" and "The Evolution of a Black Aesthetic, 1920-1950." The work of black artists is considered not as a separate form of expression but as part of the American art world as a whole. Driskell examines the reasons for the historical obscuration of the accomplishments of black artists and shatters the myth that the subject matter of black artists always reflects "the black experience." Biographies are provided for the artists of the modern period.

A-A 53. EGBERT, DONALD DREW. Socialism and American Art in the Light of European Utopianism, Marxism, and Anarchism. Princeton, N.J.: Princeton University Press, 1967. 159 pp.
Egbert divides the art and architecture he considers into three categories which correspond to the important types of American Socialism: Religious Utopian Socialism, Secular Utopian Socialism, and Marxism. Characteristics of Socialist art which he isolates are usefulness to the group as a whole, subordination of self-expression, and artistic collaboration. Egbert examines the problems of the individual versus society and the relationship of art to propaganda. Throughout the book, the works of art are treated as historical and social documents without qualitative evaluation.

A-A 54. FAIRBANKS, JONATHAN L., et al. Frontier America: The Far West. Boston: Museum of Fine Arts, 1975. 233 pp.
In his introduction Fairbanks outlines the major emphases of the exhibition. The following sections, composed of short essays and selections of appropriate objects, develop several themes: Indians before contact with Europeans, conflicts in the West, Spanish settlements, frontier furniture, and others. Important aspects of the exhibition are its attempts to deal with commonplace objects of the sort not usually included in art exhibitions and to include a balanced treatment of American Indians, acknowledging the primacy of their settlement, the richness of their culture, and the negative aspects of much Indian-white interaction on the frontier.

A-A 55. FINE, ELSA HONIG. The Afro-American Artist. New York: Holt,
         Rinehart & Winston, 1973. 310 pp.
This text is a "history of cultural experience . . . perceived from the
point of view of a Black citizen whose expressive means have been those
of the visual arts." Admittedly hampered by the inadequacies of available
scholarship, Fine traces the development in which artisans and itinerant
limners of the Colonial period became the black painters and sculptors
"producing some of the strongest and most original art to be seen in contemporary America." Fine recognizes militant separatist arguments but
concludes that the success of the modern black artist is simultaneously
a part of and independent of American culture in general.

A-A 56. FINK, LOIS MARIE. Academy: The Academic Tradition in American
         Art. Washington, D.C.: Smithsonian Institution Press, 1975.
         271 pp.
Published for the 150th anniversary of the National Academy of Design,
this exhibition catalogue traces the academic tradition through the 19th
century and into the first half of the 20th. Joshua C. Taylor's introduction explores the word "academic." Fink then traces the early years
of the National Academy when its classes and system of exhibitions were
established as well as the later years of the American Renaissance when
divisive policies and fledgling splinter groups undermined the Academy's
influence. Taylor ends with a chapter examining the vestiges of the academic tradition in the 20th century.

A-A 57. FOSTER, HAL, ed. The Anti-Aesthetic: Essays on Postmodern Culture.
         Port Townsend, Wash.: Bay Press, 1983. 159 pp.
In these collected essays, Postmodernism is explored as a general cultural
phenomenon beginning in the late 1950s. Essays are by: Jean Baudrillard,
Douglas Crimp, Hal Foster, Kenneth Frampton, Jurgen Habermas, Fredric
Jameson, Rosalind Krauss, Craig Owens, Edward W. Said, and Gregory L.
Ulmer. The writers discuss a wide range of subjects, including architecture, sculpture, painting, photography, music, film, and methods of criticism and theory (such as Structuralism and Poststructuralism, Lacanian
psychoanalysis, feminist criticism, and Marxism). Postmodernist theory
sees these methods not as parallel possibilities, but as models in conflict.
The notion of aesthetics, Foster posits, is no longer subversive or critical, and thus a new strategy of criticism is needed.

A-A 58. FUNDABURK, EMMA LILA and THOMAS G. DAVENPORT, eds. Art in Public
         Places in the United States. Bowling Green, Ohio: Bowling Green
         University Popular Press, 1975. 384 pp.
This book provides information about existing public art and indicates
the efforts being made to create and support art in public places.
Included are forty-five short essays on various aspects of public art with
such themes as legislation, the relationship between art and architecture,
organizations and workshops for the urban environment, monuments, the
role of the artist in society, and art as industry. There is also a section of photographs of art in museums, schools, other city buildings,
and outdoor areas.

A-A 59. GARRETT, WENDELL D., PAUL F. NORTON, ALAN GOWANS, and JOSEPH
         T. BUTLER. The Arts in America: The Nineteenth Century. New
         York: Scribner, 1969. 412 pp.
This survey anthology follows Louis Wright's book, The Arts in America:
The Colonial Period (see A-A 145), published three years earlier. Garrett
contributes an introductory chapter examining the historical events which
affected the fine arts. Chapters on architecture, painting and sculpture,
and the decorative arts by Norton, Gowans, and Butler respectively follow.
Each author provides a separate bibliography for his particular area.

A-A 60. GELDZAHLER, HENRY. New York Painting and Sculpture: 1940-1970.
         New York: Dutton, 1969. 494 pp.
At some indefinable point in the 20th century, New York became the dominant
center of world art, or at least of the modern movement. Geldzahler points
to three major causes: the Museum of Modern Art, which put key monuments
of international Modernism on public view; the Works Progrss Administration
(WPA), which gave artists a sense of community; and W.W. II, which drove
leading European artists to this country. Five additional essays by such
critics as Clement Greenberg and Harold Rosenberg indicate the range of
writing about the accomplishments of the New York School.

A-A 61. GERDTS, WILLIAM H. The Art of Healing: Medicine and Science
         in American Art. Birmingham, Ala.: Birmingham Museum of Art,
         1981. 119 pp.
The catalogue of this exhibition is not a catalogue in the usual sense,
for there is no real list of the objects in the exhibition. Instead,
Gerdts offers an extended essay on the theme of medicine in the fine arts.
He begins with early Colonial portraits of doctors and ends with contemporary scenes of racing ambulances and operation rooms. Of primary importance is the Gross Clinic by Thomas Eakins. Along with painting, the
media of sculpture and printmaking are considered.

A-A 62. GERDTS, WILLIAM H. The Great American Nude. New York: Praeger,
         1974. 224 pp.
Perhaps because of the importance of landscape painting in American art,
the nude has never attracted the same artistic attention in the U.S.
as it has in Europe. Nevertheless, Gerdts shows that the nude does have
its history in America. He deals with the societal taboos which prevented
frequent study and depiction of the nude. Public and critical response
is considered. Gerdts's approach is chronological with an emphasis on
painting and sculpture. Partially-clothed figures and works done by artists abroad are also included. The last chapters, which discuss the 20th
century, bring his study up to the present.

A-A 63. GOODRICH, LLOYD. Pioneers of Modern Art in America: The Decade
         of the Armory Show, 1910-1920. New York: Whitney Museum, 1946.
         29 pp.
This exhibition catalogue covers the period between 1908-1922 and includes
thirty-four painters and sculptors. In his essay, Goodrich analyzes the
preceding years, 1900-1908, the Parisian experience for the American artist,
and the artistic world in New York about 1908. He discusses the exhibition
of the Eight, Stieglitz's 291, the critical reaction to these two groups,
the Armory Show of 1913, and the opening of other galleries, societies,
and magazines devoted to the arts.

A-A 64. GOODRICH, LLOYD and JOHN I. H. BAUR. American Art of Our Century.
         New York: Praeger, 1961. 309 pp.
Through the vehicle of the collection of the Whitney Museum, the authors
trace the major currents of 20th-century painting and sculpture. Goodrich
takes the narrative to 1939, and Baur covers the decades of the 1940s
and 1950s. The twenty-five chapters are arranged for the most part by
such descriptive terms as Romantic Realism, semi-abstraction, free-form
abstraction, and formal abstraction, but the text usually deals with more
than purely stylistic concerns. The book ends with a complete catalogue
of the Whitney's 20th-century collection, an index of media, and a list
of Whitney exhibitions.

A-A 65. GOODYEAR, FRANK H., Jr. Contemporary American Realism Since 1960.
Boston: New York Graphic Society, 1981. 255 pp.
This work, published concurrently with the exhibition at the Pennsylvania
Academy of Fine Arts, is both an exhibition catalogue and a survey of
the realist art with the emphasis on painting and the figure. While the
realist painting is ideologically and stylistically diverse, Goodyear
believes it shares with 19th-century American art the same basic concern
with the problems of visual perception and their solution. His discussion
of more recent figure painting includes its history in 20th-century American art and a survey of attitudes toward realist painting, with chapters
on landscape, still life, narrative painting, and sculpture. Goodyear's
treatment is historical and cultural and includes the formal analysis
of specific works.

A-A 66. GREEN, SAMUEL M. American Art, a Historical Survey. New York:
Ronald Press, 1966. 706 pp.
Green designed his history as a college-level textbook. He discusses
painting, sculpture, architecture, graphic arts, photography, and folk
art, excluding the decorative arts and Native American arts as not belonging to the "mainstream" of American (Western) art. The volume contains
numerous plates and a glossary of artistic terms for beginning students.
For instructors, Green makes reference to the College Art Association
Corp. slide set.

A-A 67. GREENBERG, CLEMENT. Art and Culture: Critical Essays. Boston:
Beacon Press, 1961. 278 pp.
While much of this collection of the criticism of Greenberg is devoted
to European art and literature, there is an important section of eight
essays dealing specifically with art in the U.S. These include articles
on Thomas Eakins, John Marin, Winslow Homer, Hans Hoffmann, Milton Avery,
and David Smith as well as two other essays, "'American-Type' Painting"
and "The Late Thirties in New York." As the title indicates, Greenberg
discusses much more than painting. He uses his knowledge of international
art and literature to define and appraise the role of Modernism in contemporary "culture."

A-A 68. GRIFFIN, RACHEL and MARTHA KINGSBURY. Art of the Pacific Northwest:
From the 1930's to the Present. Washington, D.C.: National
Collection of Fine Arts, Smithsonian Institution, 1974. 160 pp.
This exhibition catalogue examines approximately thirty-five years of
artistic production in the Pacific Northwest. Though working in diverse
modes, the artists of the Pacific Northwest nevertheless form a cohesive
"regional" school. With such artists as Morris Graves, Mark Tobey, and
the Kandinsky-inspired Maude Kerns, the school has often been described
as mystical. The two essays discuss Portland and its environs (Griffin)
and Seattle and the Puget Sound (Kingsbury).

A-A 69. HARRIS, NEIL. The Artist in American Society: The Formative
Years, 1790-1860. New York: Braziller, 1966. 432 pp.
Harris is concerned with the period of legitimization of the artistic
profession in the United States. He considers the larger problems of
this process through the personal decisions of individual artists. Discussion of a wide range of issues enhanced by liberal quotations that
capture protagonists' views characterize this book which is not about
art in any narrow sense but is rather a study of artists, their place
in society, and American culture and values between 1790 and 1860.

A-A 70. HARTMANN, SADAKICHI. A History of American Art. 1901; Rev.
ed. New York: Tudor, 1934. 615 pp.
Hartmann's two-volume study was an early work in the field of American
art history. The pronounced tastes of this turn-of-the-century critic
strongly color his personal narrative. Writing before the creation of
the various scholarly "isms," Hartmann treats the art by medium, limiting
his classifications to "old school" and "new school." Much of the study
is devoted to the art of his own period, the late Victorian era. His
appraisals of the tonal, aesthetic school serve as documents of Victorian
taste and criticism. The 1934 version adds a chapter, "An Art-wrangler's
Aftermath," which briefly discusses advances like Cubism, all the time
harking back nostalgically to the decade of the 1890s.

A-A 71. HESS, THOMAS B. and ELIZABETH C. BAKER, eds. Art and Sexual Politics: Women's Liberation, Women Artists, and Art History. New
York: Macmillan, 1973. 150 pp.
In the first essay, "Why Have There Been No Great Women Artists?," Linda
Nochlin offers answers to her question, first by exploring the evidence
behind it, and second by discussing the necessary conditions for producing
art. Thomas Hess argues in his essay that although there may not have
been any great women artists, women have produced great works of art.
This is followed by ten short responses to this issue by women artists.
Elizabeth Baker contributes an essay, "Art and Sexual Politics," in which
she discusses the discrimination within the contemporary museum world.
The final essay by Lee Hall, "In the University," describes the situation
facing the woman artist in the academic world.

A-A 72. HILLS, PATRICIA. The American Frontier: Images and Myths. New
York: Whitney Museum of American Art, 1973. 63 pp.
A rich selection of images is presented in this short exhibition catalogue.
In her brief essay, Hills touches upon the many questions raised by a
consideration of frontier art. The cultural and literary background,
the political tracts, and the historical events themselves all receive
mention. She shows how the art was colored by the doctrine of "Manifest
Destiny," the attitude toward the Indians, and the California gold rush.

A-A 73. HILLS, PATRICIA. Turn-of-the-Century America. New York: Whitney
Museum of American Art, 1977. 194 pp.
Hills's catalogue is a focused look at two decades of American art (1890-
1910) and the way in which it was affected by social, political, and economic activities. She characterizes the period as a time of expansion,
with all eyes turning not to the nation's interior but toward the shores
of Europe. Twelve short essays consider such topics as the mural movement,
art posters, Impressionism, cartoons, portrait and social photography,
and urban life.

A-A 74. HOMER, WILLIAM INNES. Avant-garde Painting and Sculpture in
America: 1910-1925. Wilmington: Delaware Art Museum, 1975.
176 pp.
The purpose of this catalogue is to present a detailed visual study of
the advanced American art of the period 1910-1925 in relation to its modernist sources. The text contains eleven essays that attempt to show the
extent to which the various artists were immersed in the European avant-
garde and point out the distinctive contributions that American artists
made. The essays include: "The Rise of the Avant-Garde in America" by
Paul Schweizer, Priscilla Siegel, and William Rasmussen; "Progressives
versus The Academy at the Turn of the Century"; "Alfred Stieglitz and
'291'"; "The Armory Show and Its Aftermath" by William Innes Homer, and
"The Society of Independent Artists" by Roberta K. Tarbell.

A-A 75. HOWAT, JOHN K. and JOHN WILMERDING. Nineteenth Century America:
      Paintings and Sculpture. New York: New York Graphic Society,
      1970. n.p.
The Metropolitan Museum of Art celebrated its 100th anniversary with a
comprehensive but selective exhibition. In this short introduction, Howat
and Wilmerding broadly trace the themes and development of 19th-century
painting and sculpture in America. Catalogue entries for the 201 works
which are illustrated (some in color) give varied biographical and historical information.

A-A 76. HUNTER, SAM. American Art of the 20th Century; Painting, Sculpture
      Architecture. New York: Abrams, 1972. 487 pp.
Hunter surveys 20th-century painting and sculpture, with particular emphasis on the painting. He begins his discussion with the triumvirate of
Winslow Homer, Thomas Eakins, and Albert P. Ryder whom he sees as a bridge
to the 20th century. The rest of his text emphasizes the art after 1945,
ending with environmental art, videos, and happenings. The expanded version contains additional chapters on architecture by John Jacobus.

A-A 77. KIRBY, MICHAEL, ed. Happenings: An Illustrated Anthology. New
      York: Dutton, 1966. 287 pp.
This book is divided into chapters on five artists who produced happenings
between 1959 and 1963. The artists are: Allan Kaprow, Red Grooms, Robert
Whitman, Jim Dine, and Claes Oldenburg. Each chapter contains a statement
by the artist, one or more scripts of their happenings, and illustrated
descriptions by the artist of the productions. In his introduction, Kirby
discusses characteristics of the happening as an art form and its historical sources in action painting, Surrealism, Dada, the Bauhaus, modern
dance and music, and Artaud's Theater of Cruelty.

A-A 78. KOSTELANETZ, RICHARD. Metamorphosis in the Arts: A Critical
      History of the 1960's. Brooklyn, N.Y.: Assembling Press, 1980.
      316 pp.
Although this book was written in 1968-1969, Kostelanetz has not revised
it for its 1980 publication. Calling this treatment of nonliterary arts--
painting, sculpture, modern dance, music, and film--more historical than
critical, Kostelanetz takes issue with those conservative critics who
lament that there was nothing new about the art produced in the 1960s.
Though art may not always evolve into something more complex, he argues,
it always changes and sometimes (as in the 1960s) the changes become noticeable. He examines fine art, not mass art, and although nonliterary art
is international, he focuses on American--specifically New York--art (New
York having replaced Paris as art capital of the world). He discusses
the two avant-gardes (those who would purify their medium and those who
would "miscegenate" with other media) in each of the five arts mentioned
as well as the relationship between art and the machine (which, he claims,
are not necessarily in opposition). Kostelanetz urges critics to remember
that arts exist in a common environment and influence one another, and
he concludes by speculating that increasing cultural pluralism will allow
several styles to exist simultaneously.

A-A 79. KOZLOFF, MAX. Renderings: Critical Essays on a Century of Modern
      Art. New York: Simon & Schuster, 1969. 352 pp.
Kozloff records his attitudes and observations when he worked as an art
critic during the 1960s. Individual sections are devoted to the European
modern tradition from Courbet to Duchamp; American art and the generation
of W.W. II; modern sculpture; current art (Assemblage, Happenings, and
individual artists); contemporary American photography; and criticism.
The essays were originally published in periodicals between 1961-1968.

A-A 80. KRAMER, HILTON. The Age of the Avant-Garde: An Art Chronicle of 1956-1972. New York: Farrar, Straus & Giroux, 1973. 565 pp.

Kramer was an art critic for the New York Times, and most of the essays in this volume first appeared there. Several of the essays deal with European artists, but more than half the book is devoted to contemporary American artists. Kramer's stated purpose is to reveal how "avant-gardism" has been taken over and exploited by the art establishment in America. He also establishes a case for artists he believes have been neglected or misunderstood, such as Turku Trajan, Ann Arnold, and Arnold Friedman. Highly suspicious of what he takes to be passing fashions in American art like Pop and Op, Kramer argues that it is not necessarily "philistine resistance" to point out how much of the avant-garde is embroiled in ideological clap-trap. He calls for a new criticism which will take into account not only the motives and intentions of artists and their abilities to express and market them, but also the values, the "actuality," of the work of art itself.

A-A 81. LANE, JOHN R. and SUSAN C. LARSEN, eds. Abstract Painting and Sculpture in America, 1927-1944. New York: Abrams, 1983. 256 pp.

Two essays written by the editors introduce this book published in conjunction with an exhibition organized by the Museum of Art, Carnegie Institute. The book seeks to examine the cubist and geometric abstractionist art of the period which is often neglected in favor of "American Scene" painting and Social Realism. The influence of Picasso, Leger, Miro, and Arp as well as movements such as De Stijl and the Bauhaus are considered. Each of the forty-three artists represented receives a separate essay written by one of the twenty-one contributors to the volume.

A-A 82. LARKIN, OLIVER W. Art and Life in America. 1949; Rev. ed. New York: Holt, Rinehart & Winston, 1960. 559 pp.

Art and Life in America was the first major textbook survey of American art from the earliest European settlements to modern times. For each era of American history Larkin sketches a summary of the social and political development that affected the arts, and then proceeds to discuss the architecture, painting, sculpture, and graphics of the period. His major emphasis is on the Anglo-Saxon traditions, with little attention to the Spanish, French, and German architecture that flourished in America, and none at all to American Indian art.

A-A 83. LINDEY, CHRISTINE. Superrealist Painting and Sculpture. New York: Morrow, 1980. 160 pp.

In her introduction, Lindey characterizes the superrealist movement ("verist" in sculpture) as a pan-U.S. phenomenon having no real geographical center or concentration of artists. She examines attitudes toward the "reality" of the photograph and differentiates between pictorially subjective realists and purely photographic realists. Lindey sees all realists as interested in surface quality as opposed to underlying volume and content. She begins by tracing the roots of Superrealism in the art of the 1940s, 1950s, and 1960s and continues with analyses of the work of individual artists.

A-A 84. LIPPARD, LUCY. Changing. Essays in Art Criticism. New York: Dutton, 1971. 320 pp.

In this collection of twenty-one essays written between 1965-70, Lippard discusses individual artists, major exhibitions of the period, and various movements of the late 1960s art world. The focus of these essays is on the New York School during the later half of the 1960s, including such artists as Sol Lewitt, Robert Mangold, Larry Poons, James Rosenquist, and Robert Smithson. In "Rejective Art" she discusses the then recently

coined term of Minimalism, and in "The Dematerialization of Art" she
reviews the developments in conceptual art.

A-A 85. LIPPARD, LUCY. From the Center. Feminist Essays on Women's Art.
New York: Dutton, 1976. 314 pp.
The essays in this collection, some general and some monographic, were
written since the publication of Changing in 1971. In the introduction
Lippard analyzes her own changing Feminism. She presents the essays which
follow as material that can be used to create a separate feminist aesthetic
consciousness, and she envisions the creation of new criteria by which
to evaluate feminist art in an art world still dominated by men.

A-A 86. LIPPARD, LUCY, ed. Pop Art. New York: Praeger, 1966. 216 pp.
Though its repercussions were international, Pop art is seen by Lippard
almost wholly as a phenomenon of America, particularly of New York and
Los Angeles, in the 1960s. She traces Pop art out of an abstract American tradition rather than a figurative one. In this context, Lippard
examines New York Pop while Nancy Marmer discusses California Pop and
Nicolas Calas considers Pop icons. Lawrence Alloway contributes a chapter
on British Pop art which actually preceded the American version. There
is also a chapter on Europe and Canada.

A-A 87. LUCIE-SMITH, EDWARD. Late Modern: The Visual Arts Since 1945.
New York: Praeger, 1969. 288 pp.
This is a pictorial survey with chapters on Abstract Expressionism, the
European scene, post-painterly abstraction, pop, op and kinetic, sculpture,
and environments. Lucie-Smith maintains that all post-war movements,
or "isms," represent a re-evaluation of ideas developed before the war.
The later movements exaggerate the borrowed form while de-emphasizing
the content. Post-war art is characterized by a tendency to redefine
the nature of art itself, and a decreasing concern with the object.

A-A 88. LYNES, RUSSELL. The Art-Makers of Nineteenth-Century America.
New York: Atheneum, 1970. 514 pp.
Lynes is not an art historian, and he approaches his book as an amateur
admirer writing for amateur admirers. The text covers most media but
is limited to only the most prominent figures. Lynes sees the goal of
many 19th-century artists as becoming socially acceptable. He seeks to
show how the artists (art-makers) tried to change the state of the arts
in America by turning a craft into a profession.

A-A 89. McCABE, CYNTHIA JAFFEE. The Golden Door: Artist-Immigrants of
America, 1876-1976. Washington, D.C.: Smithsonian Institution
Press, 1976. 432 pp.
The considerable contribution of foreign-born artists to American modern
art is examined in this bicentennial exhibition catalogue. Over sixty
major figures who became U.S. citizens or settled permanently in America
are considered. The 100-year era is divided into three periods: the
initial massive influx of immigrants (1876-1929), the exodus from central
Europe and the Nazi-controlled states (1930-1945), and the coming of artists who were attracted by America's post-war prominence in the world
of art (1946-1976). In addition to numerous illustrations, the catalogue
includes colorful chronological charts of artists and historical events.

A-A 90. McKINZIE, RICHARD D. The New Deal for Artists. Princeton, N.J.:
Princeton University Press, 1973. 203 pp.
The emphasis here is on the social and political forces behind the Federal
Art Project and the Treasury Department's Section of Fine Arts rather
than on a formal and critical evaluation of the art itself. The FAP under
Holger Cahill is seen as an anti-elitist organization encouraging mass
participation and leveling no critical judgment. Artists in the Treasury

Department under Edward Bruce, however, had stricter aesthetic guidelines.
The demise of both organizations is examined in light of the changing
American political scene in the late 1930s.

A-A 91. McLANATHAN, RICHARD B. K. The American Tradition in the Arts.
New York: Harcourt, Brace & World, 1968. 492 pp.
Covering all media--including architecture--this survey finds American
art reflecting a different set of emphases than its European forerunner.
British influence is nevertheless seen as an important regulating factor
in considering the individuality of the New World. Although social forces
are discussed as well, the text is necessarily selective. With the exception of men like Thomas Cole and the late-century greats, Winslow Homer,
Thomas Eakins, and Albert P. Ryder, general themes are stressed rather
than individuals. Still, "minor" figures do receive treatment.

A-A 92. McLANATHAN, RICHARD B. K. Art in America: A Brief History.
New York: Harcourt, Brace & Jovanovich, 1973. 216 pp.
A survey in the broadest sense, McLanathan's book touches upon architecture,
painting, sculpture, and some non-academic arts from the earliest days
of colonization to the 1960s. The chapters are not divided by media.
Instead, they are organized chronologically, treating all the arts of
a specific period. Illustrations are frequent and are often in color.

A-A 93. MELLQUIST, JEROME. The Emergence of an American Art. New York:
Scribner, 1942. 421 pp.
This book is a partisan account of pre-abstract modern art in America.
It offers a look at attitudes toward American art at a very particular
point in time. The text begins with Sargent and Whistler, who are seen
as forerunners of the modern movement. The Eight are considered the real
heroes of the story, as is Alfred Stieglitz and his "291" coterie. American Scene painting and Social Realism, which Mellquist considers propagandistic and self-limiting, are not discussed.

A-A 94. MENDELOWITZ, DANIEL MARCUS. A History of American Art. 1960;
Rev. ed. New York: Holt, Rinehart & Winston, 1970. 522 pp.
This broad introduction discusses the standard media of painting, sculpture,
and architecture--and more. Recognizing the intrinsic merit of Native
American art as well as its influence on 20th-century expression,
Mendelowitz includes the art of the Indians. Similarly, the decorative arts
are not neglected. By concentrating on "significant personalities,"
Mendelowitz sketches the trends for the novice reader, with an emphasis
on 20th-century art.

A-A 95. MILLER, LILLIAN. Patrons and Patriotism: The Encouragement of
the Fine Arts in the United States, 1790-1860. Chicago: University of Chicago Press, 1966. 355 pp.
In this ambitious book, Miller examines the effect of Nationalism and
patronage on the development of painting and sculpture in the U.S. before
the Civil War. Her work provides perspectives on American art history,
treating the aesthetic premises of the period, the debate over governmental
support of the arts, the establishment of local art academies, and art
in the West. Miller emphasizes the sense of national urgency and self-
consciousness which generated a diverse native vision; focusing on dominant
taste, she outlines the decline of classical values and the paradoxical
attitudes—including paranoia and dependence--toward the European heritage.

A-A 96. MUNRO, ELEANOR. Originals: American Women Artists. New York:
Simon & Schuster, 1979. 528 pp.
Munro emphasizes that her approach to this study of 20th-century women
artists is historical rather than iconographical. The first chapter is
a general history of women's art in the light of 20th-century social and

cultural events. The successive chapters are divided into four "waves" of painters and contain elements of biography and autobiography. Each of the chapters begins with a short summary of that particular generation of women and is followed by essays on individual artists.

A-A 97. New England Begins: The Seventeenth Century. Boston: Museum of Fine Arts, Boston, 1982. 575 pp.
In this three-volume catalogue—divided into "Migration and Settlement," "Mentality and Environment," and "Style"—all 504 objects of the exhibition are reproduced. They represent the media of architecture, furniture, silver and gold, painting, base metals, textiles, ceramics and glass, woodenwares, prints, maps, books, arms and armor, tools, and gravestones. Fifteen scholars are responsible for the essays and catalogue entries. All aspects of 17th-century New England life are examined, including Native American culture. The authors adopt the thesis that while formal values can later be dissociated from an object's use, the members of the culture which produced the object were not able to separate beauty from function.

A-A 98. O'CONNOR, FRANCIS V. Federal Art Patronage 1933-1943. College Park: University of Maryland Art Gallery, 1966. 60 pp.
In the essay in this exhibition catalogue, O'Connor outlines in detail the federal projects undertaken to fund the arts beginning in 1933 when Franklin D. Roosevelt became President. He discusses such projects as the PWAP (Public Works of Art Project), begun in 1933 and run by Edward Bruce, the murals funded by the Section of Painting and Sculpture in the Treasury Department, and the WPA (Works Progress Administration), which had, of all the federal projects in the 1930s, the most extensive impact on the American culture. O'Connor details the working stipulations, the amount and type of art produced, the costs, and the artists employed.

A-A 99. O'CONNOR, FRANCIS V., ed. Art for the Millions; Essays from the 1930s by Artists and Administrators of the WPA Federal Art Project. Boston: New York Graphic Society, 1973. 317 pp.
With minor changes, this volume is a copy of a dummy manuscript produced by the Works Progress Administration in 1939. It comprises sixty-six essays by artists and administrators who worked on the Federal Art Project of the WPA. Murals, graphic arts, photography, posters, art teaching, artists' organizations, and the Index of American Design are all discussed. The original illustrations and plates selected in the 1930s are used throughout. Appendices and a selected bibliography follow.

A-A 100. O'CONNOR, FRANCIS V., ed. The New Deal Art Projects: An Anthology of Memoirs. Washington, D.C.: Smithsonian Institution Press, 1972. 339 pp.
Ten persons connected with the four major New Deal Projects contribute essays to this anthology. Most of their discussion pertains to work done in New York City and State. The various divisions of the projects (mural, easel, sculpture, graphic arts, Index of American Design) are separately considered. Other related subjects—such as the American Abstract Artists and the New York City Municipal Art Galleries—are also examined.

A-A 101. O'DOHERTY, BRIAN. American Masters: The Voice and the Myth. New York: Random House, 1973. 288 pp.
Although O'Doherty focuses on eight American artists, his book can be seen as a selective view of the history of modern American art through the 1960s. He discusses such issues as the relationship between European and American art, the artist and his work, and the work and its audience. Individual chapters are devoted to Edward Hopper, Stuart Davis, Jackson Pollock, Willem de Kooning, Mark Rothko, Robert Rauschenberg, Andrew Wyeth, and Joseph Cornell. The book is illustrated with photographs by Hans Namuth.

A-A 102. O'HARA, FRANK. Art Chronicles, 1954-1966. New York: Braziller, 1975. 165 pp.
Published almost ten years after O'Hara's death, this volume collects fourteen of his essays on such artists as Jackson Pollock, Robert Motherwell, Reuben Nakien, Helen Frankenthaler, and Alex Katz. O'Hara was a poet and sometime composer, and his essays reflect this broad approach as they do his intimacy with most of the artists he considers. A chronology and bibliography indicate the wide range of O'Hara's activities and publications.

A-A 103. PARRY, ELLWOOD. The Image of the Indian and the Black Man in America: 1590-1900. New York: Braziller, 1974. 191 pp.
Parry examines the images of Indians and blacks to determine white Americans' changing perceptions and preconceptions of them. He traces the image of Indians from that of the noble savages of the era of exploration to the fiendish warriors of the era of settlement and finally to a pathetic, dying people in a settled America. Similarly he traces the image of the black from a shadowy servant attending his Colonial master, to the comic butt of genre scenes of the early 19th century and through a sudden rise to heroic stature in the mid-1850s.

A-A 104. Philadelphia: Three Centuries of Art. Philadelphia: Philadelphia Museum of Art, 1976. 665 pp.
This exhibition was the Philadelphia Museum of Art's contribution to the bicentennial celebration. Thirty-seven scholars contributed to the catalogue of over 500 objects of painting, sculpture, architecture, prints, books, photographs, textiles, costumes, and the decorative arts. Lengthy catalogue entries and biographies are arranged chronologically with the emphasis on stylistic interrelations of the media and the ties to the art education, patronage, and cultural life of the city of Philadelphia.

A-A 105. PINCUS-WITTEN, ROBERT. Postminimalism. New York: Out of London Press, 1977. 198 pp.
Postminimalism is Pincus-Witten's term for the art of the ten-year period from 1966-1976 which reacted against the cold, formalist logic of Minimalism. A new feeling for the painterly and frequent autobiographical references are characteristics of this new art. Postminimalism is tied directly to the emerging women's movement and the disillusionment resulting from Watergate and Vietnam. Among the artists discussed are Richard Serra, Eva Hesse, Bruce Nauman, Sol Lewitt, Jackie Ferrara, and James Collins.

A-A 106. PITZ, HENRY C. The Brandywine Tradition. Boston: Houghton Mifflin, 1969. 252 pp.
The region which is the object of this study is the Brandywine River valley in Pennsylvania and Delaware. The Brandywine tradition is mainly one of illustration, beginning with the artists Howard Pyle and N. C. Wyeth. Wyeth's son, Andrew, is perhaps the best-known "Brandywine" artist. Other figures discussed include Frank E. Schoonover, Stanley Arthurs, Harvey Dunn, Elizabeth Shippen Green, Peter Hurd, and John McCoy.

A-A 107. PLAGENS, PETER. Sunshine Muse. Contemporary Art on the West Coast. New York: Praeger, 1974. 200 pp.
Plagens defines the art of the West Coast (California, Oregon, and Washington) as regionalist and does not attempt to transplant a New York construct onto the West Coast art world. He discusses the Los Angeles art scene in the 1960s and the artists associated with the California School of Fine Arts in San Francisco. Included is a review of individual artists and movements, such as the art of assemblage, funk, process, performance, Pop in Los Angeles, and the Los Angeles look.

A-A 108. POESCH, JESSIE. The Art of the Old South: Painting, Sculpture, Architecture and the Products of Craftsmen, 1560-1860. New York: Knopf, 1983. 384 pp.
Poesch's comprehensive survey of a hitherto neglected area of American art history discusses painting, sculpture, architecture, and the decorative arts in an integral manner. She describes a particular southern conscious- ness somewhat different from the rest of ante-bellum America. Anglican- colonial churches, mourning portraits, and sporting paintings of horse racing and breeding are examples of specific southern forms. In addition, a complex blend of English, Spanish, and French influence colors the cul- ture of the Deep South. Illustrations are numerous and are often in color.

A-A 109. PORTER, JAMES A. Modern Negro Art. New York: Dryden Press, 1943. 272 pp.
This book was an early attempt to restore the previously obscured and separate history of black art and artists to the history of American art as a whole. Porter begins with a chapter on ante-bellum artists and crafts- men and traces the development of black artists after emancipation and into the 20th century. Among other topics, the "New Negro Movement" follow- ing W.W. I and naive and popular art are considered.

A-A 110. QUIRARTE, JACINTO. Mexican American Artists. Austin: University of Texas Press, 1973. 149 pp.
The work of Mexican American artists has received little attention. This illustrated text attempts to fill the gap using cultural and artistic rather than political boundaries for the spatial parameters of the study. The introduction is a discussion of European (Anglo) and pre-Columbian frames of reference and pictorial language. Part One contains a history of the exploration and settlement of New Spain, a survey of art and archi- tecture from the 17th through the 19th centuries, and a chapter on the 20th-century Mexican muralists who heavily influenced Chicano artists.

A-A 111. RANDEL, WILLIAM PIERCE. The Evolution of American Taste. New York: Crown, 1978. 212 pp.
Embracing all the arts, but concentrating on architecture and furniture, this book traces the genesis and evolution of the American people's atti- tude toward the visual environment which they create for themselves. The broad text begins in 1607 and ends with the present. Randel singles out personalities (from Joseph Blackburn to Jackson Pollock) and specific works of art which he feels evoke a significant facet of American taste. His narrative is largely historical, relating individuals to the contem- porary national events.

A-A 112. RATHBONE, PERRY T., ed. Westward the Way. St. Louis, Mo.: City Museum of St. Louis, 1954. 280 pp.
Published in conjunction with an exhibition marking the 150th anniversary of the purchase of the Louisiana Territory, Westward the Way combines seven essays and over 200 plates. Word and image are considered together, for each plate is accompanied by an appropriate excerpt from 19th-century travel logs, autobiographies, and textbooks (history, geography, and orni- thology, among others). Rathbone contributes most of the essays, with Frederick E. Voelker providing a "History and Character of the Louisi- ana Territory."

A-A 113. RITCHIE, ANDREW C. Abstract Painting and Sculpture in America. New York: Museum of Modern Art, 1951. 159 pp.
Ritchie's catalogue reviews almost forty years of abstract art in America. At a time when the impact of the Abstract Expressionists was still being felt, this exhibition tried to answer the question: "What is abstract art?" and "Why abstract art?" Ritchie discusses Cubism, Futurism, and the impact of the Armory Show in order to demonstrate the European origins

of abstraction. Most of the book, however, is reserved for the American art which is categorized by such descriptive terms as "naturalistic geometric" and "expressionist biomorphic."

A-A 114. ROSE, BARBARA. American Art Since 1900. 1967; Rev. ed. New York: Praeger, 1975. 320 pp.
This survey of American art begins in the 1880s with Thomas Eakins and ends in the 1970s with the sculpture and painting of Robert Morris and Larry Poons. The emphasis is on theory and criticism rather than cultural history, though artistic developments are tied into broader events in America and Europe. The chapters are arranged to correspond with Rose's primary sourcebook, Readings in American Art Since 1900 (1968).

A-A 115. ROSENBERG, HAROLD. The Anxious Object: Art Today and Its Audience. 1964; Rev. ed. New York: Horizon Press, 1966. 272 pp.
Rosenberg begins with the observation that controversial issues in contemporary art are no longer present. The public unquestioningly accepts all that is offered to it, and the "anxiety" of the art object disappears. By anxiety, Rosenberg means the pathos accompanying the realization that art and gesture do not exist in a personal artistic vacuum but are subject to change via the psychological and social vicissitudes of modern culture. The twenty-three essays examine the relation of the artist and his public, with particular attention given to the ideas and the intellectual tasks each artist sets before him- or herself.

A-A 116. ROSENBERG, HAROLD. Art on the Edge: Creators and Situations. New York: Macmillan, 1971. 303 pp.
In this book, which consists largely of essays previously published in The New Yorker, Rosenberg assesses the possible roles of contemporary art in a culture highly supportive of the arts yet increasingly uncommitted to Modernism. There are essays on thirteen individuals (European and American) whose work exhibits contact with the "actuality" of the 20th century. Seventeen other essays examine such topics as Futurism, WPA art, Photorealism, the art market, and folk art.

A-A 117. ROSENBERG, HAROLD. The De-Definition of Art: Action Art to Pop to Earthworks. New York: Horizon Press, 1972. 256 pp.
Rosenberg maintains that in this "post-art" era, when painting and sculpture have been forsaken for "environment," the artist has become elevated to a godlike status: he or she is the actual personification of art. At the same time, Rosenberg hints that it may be the artists who inevitably lose out by becoming "too big for art." Chapters are devoted to such individual artists as Claes Oldenburg, Frank Stella, and Philip Guston and to such larger issues as earthworks, the dialogue with Europe, and the contemporary museum.

A-A 118. ROSENBERG, HAROLD. The Tradition of the New. New York: Horizon Press, 1959. 285 pp.
This volume brings together previously published criticism of painting, poetry, politics, and general Intellectualism. It reflects Rosenberg's view of Modernism (the "New") as an all-encompassing cultural revolution. As the title implies, however, by 1959 the revolution had already evolved into a tradition tinged with nostalgia. Among other subjects, the essays on painting deal with action painting, Colonial art, and the contemporary public.

A-A 119. RUBINSTEIN, CHARLOTTE STREIFER. American Women Artists: Early
Indian Times to the Present. Boston: G. K. Hall, 1982.
560 pp.
Rubinstein's book is an historical survey of the contribution of American
women to the fine arts. An integrated text rather than a biographical
dictionary, the book proceeds chronologically, with two topical chapters
on Native American artists and folk artists being the only exceptions.
Because of spatial constraints, the discussion is limited to painting
and sculpture. The appendices list the women elected to the National
Academy and the American Academy of Fine Arts and Letters as well as those
who exhibited at the World's Fairs of 1933 and 1939.

A-A 120. RUBLOWSKY, JOHN. Pop Art. New York: Basic Books, 1965.
174 pp.
Rublowsky argues that Pop art is a natural extension of Abstract Expressionism. The great difference between the two movements, however, lies
in the latter's elitist preoccupation with "the unique" and the former's
democratic, commonplace aesthetic. Rublowsky devotes individual chapters
to Roy Lichtenstein, Claes Oldenburg, James Rosenquist, Andy Warhol, and
Tom Wesselmann, and relates them thematically through what he describes
as a common aesthetic concern for everyday images of industrial, urban,
and commercial society.

A-A 121. RUSSELL, JOHN and SUZI GABLIK, eds. Pop Art Redefined. New
York: Praeger, 1969. 240 pp.
Both Russell and Gablik contribute introductions to this anthology, which
emanated from their 1969 Hayward Gallery exhibition in London. They emphasize the formal ideas of Pop rather than the view of the movement as one
extended "joke." There are critical statements by Lawrence Alloway, John
McHale, and Robert Rosenblum as well as statements by twenty-five pop
artists. An index of works reproduced in the volume with short biographies
of the artists follows the statements.

A-A 122. SAINT-GAUDENS, HOMER. The American Artist and His Times. New
York: Dodd, Mead, 1941. 332 pp.
Saint-Gaudens relates numerous remembrances and anecdotes from his childhood years in the Paris and New York studios of his father, sculptor
Augustus Saint-Gaudens. The author knew and visited all the great American
artists of the late 19th and early 20th centuries, and his chatty criticism
and interpretation of their work is based on firsthand discussions with
the artists. After several summary chapters on early American art, Saint-
Gaudens concentrates on the artists of his lifetime, ending in 1941.

A-A 123. SANDLER, IRVING. The New York School: The Painters and Sculptors
of the Fifties. New York: Harper & Row, 1978. 366 pp.
Sandler maintains that the second-generation Abstract Expressionists at
work in the latter half of the 1950s have received insufficient attention
as compared to the pioneers (Jackson Pollock, Willem de Kooning, Mark
Rothko) who preceded them and the pop artists who followed them. He
focuses on such gesture painters as Helen Frankenthaler, Sam Francis, Larry
Rivers, and Alex Katz; assemblage artists such as Richard Stankiewicz,
John Chamberlain, and Robert Rauschenberg; hard-edged and color-field
abstractionists like Ellsworth Kelly, Kenneth Noland, and Al Held; and
the creators of environments and happenings, such as Red Grooms and Claes
Oldenburg.

A-A 124. SCHWARTZ, SANFORD. The Art Presence. New York: Horizon Press,
1982. 246 pp.
This collection of twenty-one short essays on American art is divided
into three sections: Painters and Sculptors, Photographers, and Writers
about Art. The first section reaches from late 19th-century painters

to contemporary artists. The section on photographers includes both European and American 20th-century photographers. In the final section, Schwartz discusses such works as Leo Steinberg's Other Criteria and Susan Sontag's On Photography.

A-A 125. The Shaping of Art and Architecture in Nineteenth-Century America. New York: Metropolitan Museum of Art, 1972. 187 pp.
Eleven papers given at the four-day Metropolitan Museum of Art symposium on "Nineteenth-Century America" in 1972 are collected here. A frequent theme in the papers is the interplay of European and American art and architecture. Among others, James Thomas Flexner discusses methodology in the study of American painting, Barbara Novak considers the influences and affinities of American and European landscape painting before 1860, and Benjamin Rowland, Jr. examines similarities between American and Japanese art.

A-A 126. SONDHEIM, ALAN, ed. Individuals: Post Movement Art in America. New York: Dutton, 1977. 316 pp.
In this volume, artist/critic Sondheim records that which he believes is the newest direction in American art. According to Sondheim, the fifteen artists represented in text and photographs are attempting to clear space for "the world of the self." The "mediated appearance of the self" occurs in their work through the use of new materials (masks, doll clothes) and concepts (personae, obsession). Vito Acconci, Laurie Anderson, Alice Aycock, and Robert Horvitz are among the artists considered.

A-A 127. SPIES, WERNER. Focus on Art. Translated by Luna Carne-Ross and John William Gabriel. New York: Rizzoli, 1982. 279 pp.
This was originally published in Germany in 1979 as Das Auge am Tatort. Spies, a German author and critic, presents a collection of his articles written between 1967 and 1981. They cover a broad range of European and American art, focusing on the art of the 20th century. Included are several articles on the contemporary American scene with such themes as California art, Beuys at the Guggenheim, Pop, Realism, and HyperRealism.

A-A 128. STEIN, ROGER B. Seascape and the American Imagination. New York: Potter, 1975. 144 pp.
This book records an exhibition held at the Whitney Museum of American Art in 1975. Guest Curator Stein departed from typical catalogue format to provide an essay about American visions of the sea. He begins with a discussion of the origins of the American seascape, then goes on to examine its changing modes and functions, giving special emphasis to images from the 19th century. Individual chapters include discussions of the role of the seascape in forging a national identity, the fascination with the sublime, the celebration of commerce, the domestication of the seascape, and tragic and apocalyptic visions in the late 19th century.

A-A 129. STEINBERG, LEO. Other Criteria: Confrontations with Twentieth-Century Art. New York: Oxford University Press, 1972. 436 pp.
In this collection of essays, Steinberg is concerned with various aspects of 20th-century art. He discusses, for example, his own reaction to American art of the last fifteen years, with an analysis of the nature of the relationship between the avant-garde and its audience. In the title essay, he questions the validity and the meaning of the predominantly formalist contemporary criticism. Also included is an essay on the early work of Jasper Johns and several brief reviews of contemporary art written in the 1950s.

A-A 130. STOUDT, JOHN JOSEPH. <u>Early</u> <u>Pennsylvania</u> <u>Arts</u> <u>and</u> <u>Crafts</u>. New
York: Barnes, 1964. 364 pp.
While 17th-century American art was concentrated in New England, the 18th
century saw a shift to Pennsylvania and, specifically, Philadelphia as
the center for the arts. There were English, Scottish, and Swedish settlers, but it was the German culture which set the tone. Stoudt examines
this culture from the founding of the colony in the 1680s to the advent
of the industrial revolution. He gives equal weight to the study of architecture, furniture, crafts, the "fine arts," and illumination.

A-A 131. SWANK, SCOTT, ed. <u>Arts</u> <u>of</u> <u>the</u> <u>Pennsylvania</u> <u>Germans</u>. New York:
Norton, 1983. 309 pp.
This book provides an in-depth survey of Pennsylvania German culture.
Scott Swank traces German immigration, settlement patterns, architecture,
retention, acculturation, and assimilation. Benno Forman discusses German
construction methods, shedding new light on Philadelphia high-style furniture. Arlene Palmer Schwind surveys ceramics and glass; Frederick Weiser,
<u>Fraktur</u>; Don Fenimore, metals; Susan Swan, textiles; and Frank Sommer,
almanacs, manuscripts, and printing. One chapter traces Henry Francis
duPont's interest in collecting Pennsylvania German materials and their
installation at Winterthur. All artifacts are from the Winterthur collection.

A-A 132. TAFT, ROBERT. <u>Artists</u> <u>and</u> <u>Illustrators</u> <u>of</u> <u>the</u> <u>Old</u> <u>West</u>, <u>1850-</u>
<u>1900</u>. New York: Scribner, 1953. 400 pp.
Taft discusses the lives and experiences of many little-known artists
who worked in the Great Plains and the Rockies during the latter half
of the 19th century. More "famous" men like Remington and Russell are
treated only briefly. Taft traces the Pacific Railroad surveys and the
Leslie Excursion of 1877 among others. Some artists, like Heinrich Balduin
Moellhausen and Alfred E. Matthews, are given individual chapters, while
others are grouped in such thematic sections as "The Joining of the Rails"
and "Custer's Last Stand."

A-A 133. TASHJIAN, DICKRAN. <u>Skyscraper</u> <u>Primitives</u>: <u>Dada</u> <u>and</u> <u>the</u> <u>American</u>
<u>Avant-Grade</u>: <u>1910-1925</u>. Middletown, Conn.: Wesleyan University
Press, 1975. 283 pp.
Tashjian presents a cultural history of the influence of Dada, initially
a European phenomenon, on the New York avant-garde. He defines the Skyscraper Primitives as those American artists who were affected by Dada's
interest in the machine and who celebrated modern, technological America.
Specifically, he studies the impact of the two European dadaists living
in New York, Marcel Duchamp and Francis Picabia, on such New York artists
as Alfred Stieglitz, Man Ray, William Carlos Williams, Hart Crane, and
E. E. Cummings. Tashjian describes the conflicting ideas that arose from
this cultural mixture.

A-A 134. TAYLOR, JOSHUA CHARLES. <u>America</u> <u>as</u> <u>Art</u>. New York: Harper &
Row, 1976. 323 pp.
In this volume Taylor traces the evolution of the symbolic representations
of America and Americans that have pervaded their art, literature, and
culture. His discussion moves from the earliest personifications of the
American continent as an Indian princess, to the classical goddesses that
embodied the emergent nation's aspirations to freedom and wisdom, and
on to the early 20th-century caricatures of the American as a rough but
honest rustic. Taylor demonstrates how as the 19th century progressed,
American writers and artists created new mythologies around figures like
Daniel Boone and Rip Van Winkle and thereby added depth to a young culture.

A-A 135. TAYLOR, JOSHUA CHARLES. The Fine Arts in America. Chicago:
University of Chicago Press, 1979. 264 pp.
Taylor's book is offered as a "sketch" of the increasingly complex history
of American painting, sculpture, and graphic arts. He rejects a history
by styles and refuses to speculate on the "Americanness" of American art.
His text seeks to encourage the reader to further investigate the patterns
it outlines. The context of cultural events is an integral part of the
discussion.

A-A 136. TOMKINS, CALVIN. The Bride and the Bachelors: Five Masters
of the Avant-Garde. 1965; Rev. ed. New York: Penguin Books,
1976. 306 pp.
The title of this work is taken from Marcel Duchamp's The Bride Stripped
Bare by Her Bachelors, Even. The five artists discussed are Duchamp,
Jean Tinguely, the maker of sculptural machines; Robert Rauschenberg,
the Pop artist; John Cage, the composer; and Merce Cunningham, the chore-
ographer and dancer. Tomkins is primarily concerned with the influence
of Duchamp on the four other artists. As a friend of the artists, he
offers a unique record of their conversations, their exhibitions, the
reception of their work, and their reactions to their reception.

A-A 137. TRACY, BERRY B. and WILLIAM H. GERDTS. Classical America, 1815-
1845. Newark, N.J.: Newark Museum, 1963. 212 pp.
This exhibition catalogue provides an introduction to the "Empire Style"
in American arts. The first section, written by Tracy, covers classicism
in expensive furniture, silver, ceramics, glass, wallpaper, textiles,
lamps, stoves, and clocks. In the second segment Gerdts discusses painting
and sculpture of the period. The introductory essays for both sections
trace the historical interest in classicism, discuss specific classical
forms and motifs used in American art, explain their derivation from
English and French designs of the 18th and 19th centuries, and comment
on American preferences.

A-A 138. TRENTON, PATRICIA and PETER H. HASSRICK. The Rocky Mountains:
A Vision for Artists in the Nineteenth Century. Norman: University of Oklahoma Press, 1983. 418 pp.
The authors define their territory of study as present-day Washington,
Montana, Idaho, Wyoming, Utah, Colorado, and New Mexico. Eschewing the
over-simplified classification of "The Rocky Mountain School," they demonstrate the variety of reactions to America's greatest natural monument.
Extensive discussion of the various scientific, military, and railroad
survey expeditions which employed artists is augmented by separate chapters
on Albert Bierstadt and Thomas Moran as well as a detailed account of
the activities of the many other painters who journeyed west.

A-A 139. TRUETTNER, WILLIAM H. and ROBIN BOLTON-SMITH. National Parks
and the American Landscape. Washington, D.C.: National Collection of Fine Arts, 1972. 141 pp.
Organized for the 100th anniversary of the founding of Yellowstone National
Park, this exhibition considered both personal and official American attitudes toward the wilderness of the West. Landscape art (painting and
photography) is tied to the creation of vast parklands as the "first massively endowed national works of art." The catalogue essay discusses
concepts of "virgin" land from the time of Ralph Waldo Emerson and Thomas
Cole to the turn of the century. The plates are arranged by the national
park they depict. Parks from twelve different states including Alaska
and Hawaii are treated.

A-A 140. Video Art. Philadelphia: University of Pennsylvania, Institute of Contemporary Art, 1975. 116 pp.
This exhibition catalogue contains four essays: D. Antin's "Video: The Distinctive Features of the Medium"; L. Borden's "Directions in Video Art"; J. Burnham's "Sacrament and Television"; and J. McHale's "The Future of Television: Some Theoretical Considerations." The essays include a discussion of individual tapes as well as broader issues concerning video—for example, its relationship to television, as parody or alternative, the economic limitations on video artists, and formal features peculiar to video.

A-A 141. WILMERDING, JOHN. American Art. New York: Penguin Books, 1976. 322 pp.
Wilmerding's survey begins with the first extant drawing by a European on American soil (1564) and ends over 400 years later with the U.S. bicentennial. There are six chronological sections with such thematic chapters as "The Grand Tour," "The Luminist Vision," and "Cubism in America." Discussion of each artist is necessarily brief, and the text is followed by 300 black and white plates.

A-A 142. WILMERDING, JOHN, ed. American Light: The Luminist Movement, 1850-1875. Paintings, Drawings, Photographs. Washington, D.C.: National Gallery of Art, 1980. 330 pp.
With an introduction by John Wilmerding and essays by most of the leading scholars in the field, this exhibition catalogue offers a detailed, if diverse, consideration of the luminist "movement" in American art. Chapters on luminist drawing and photography round out the discussion of painting. There are numerous color plates and a bibliography tracing the scholarship on the subject.

A-A 143. WILMERDING, JOHN, ed., with LINDA AYERS and EARL A. POWELL. An American Perspective: Nineteenth Century Art from the Collection of JoAnn and Julian Ganz, Jr. Hanover, N.H.: University Press of New England, 1981. 180 pp.
Wilmerding describes the Ganzes' collection as "the finest private collection in the country of nineteenth-century American art." The works are concentrated in the 1860s and 1870s; however, works by Thomas Cole and John Singleton Copley are also present. Three essays consider the particular strengths of the collection. Powell discusses landscape paintings and drawings, Ayers treats genre painting and sculpture, and Wilmerding examines still-life painting.

A-A 144. WILSON, RICHARD GUY, DIANNE H. PILGRIM, and RICHARD N. MURRAY. The American Renaissance, 1876-1917. New York: Pantheon Books, 1979. 232 pp.
Variously referred to as The Gilded Age or The Brown Decades, the American Renaissance remains a little-studied area of American art history. This volume, the catalogue of a travelling exhibition, is the work of the show's organizers. Wilson discusses the cultural backdrop against which the artists worked and contributes a chapter on architecture, landscape, and city planning. Pilgrim examines the decorative arts, and Murray studies the painting and sculpture. A selected bibliography and a short illustrated checklist of the exhibition conclude the volume.

A-A 145. WRIGHT, LOUIS, GEORGE TATUM, JOHN McCOUBREY, and ROBERT SMITH. The Arts in America: The Colonial Period. New York: Scribner, 1966. 368 pp.
The contributions of the four authors begin with Wright's social and political survey of the colonies. Tatum's following essay on architecture concentrates on buildings of English derivation but also touches on French, Spanish, German, Swedish, Dutch, and Flemish influences. McCoubrey's

essay on painting and sculpture covers the important stylistic trends
and artists of the period and traces the development of individualism
in American art. The decorative arts section by Smith is divided both
by style and region, attempting to give a basic sense of regional variation
and influence as well as stylistic progression.

III. A. PAINTING: SURVEYS

A-A 146. ANDERSON, DENNIS R. American Flower Painting. New York: Watson-
         Guptill, 1980. 84 pp.
Anderson supplies a short text to this book primarily devoted to thirty-
two color plates which indicate the evolution of flower paintings from
Colonial times to the present. His text seeks to outline only the broad
currents of this genre of American painting. Each plate is given a
detailed discussion, and a selected bibliography follows.

A-A 147. BAIGELL, MATTHEW. A History of American Painting. New York:
         Praeger, 1971. 288 pp.
Baigell's survey begins about 1660 and ends in the 1970s. He eschews
American art history rooted in the celebration of European art as well
as its opposite, art history which focuses only on the indigenous qualities
of the painting. His book is not a compendium of names; indeed he concentrates on only a few artists of a given period. Movements rather than
influences interest him. The book is illustrated with both black and
white and color plates.

A-A 148. BARKER, VIRGIL. American Painting: History and Interpretation.
         New York: Macmillan, 1950. 717 pp.
This book begins with the first Spanish Colonial painting and ends with
the work of Thomas Eakins. Barker chooses the year 1790 to divide his
two comprehensive periods, the Colonial and the Provincial. As indicated
by the subtitle, the lengthy text combines documentation and criticism.
Throughout this work, Barker discusses the familiar names as well as numerous lesser-known painters. His treatment of the artists and paintings
of the early Colonial years is particularly extensive.

A-A 149. BURROUGHS, ALAN. Limners and Likenesses: Three Centuries of
         American Painting. Cambridge, Mass.: Harvard University Press,
         1936. 246 pp.
This survey is unique in that the text continues up to the publication
date, giving an early "historical" consideration of such modern artists
as John Marin, Georgia O'Keeffe, Edward Hopper, and Grant Wood. Burroughs
devotes much attention to the Colonial and Victorian eras, but 19th-century
landscape painting receives only eleven pages. His biographical text
emphasizes the "fact" (likeness) in American painting, a characteristic
he traces throughout the three centuries he considers.

A-A 150. CAFFIN, CHARLES HENRY. The Story of American Painting: The
         Evolution of Painting in America from Colonial Times to the
         Present. New York: Stokes, 1907. 396 pp.
Primarily a document of turn-of-the-century taste, Caffin's early work
practically dismisses the "scanty beginnings" of painting during the
Colonial era as well as the subsequent "native growth of landscape painting." He concentrates on the painters of his own time, the so-called
American Renaissance or Gilded Age. The artists of this period are discussed in some detail with the extent of each painter's treatment based
largely on Caffin's personal preferences.

A-A 151. DAVIDSON, ABRAHAM. The Eccentrics and Other American Visionary
          Painters. New York: Dutton, 1978. 202 pp.
Somewhere between the much discussed American dichotomy of the real and
the ideal lies the little explored stream of visionary painting. Davidson
considers painters from 1800 to 1950 whose works seem dreamlike, fantastic,
and perhaps anguished. His roster is a varied one, encompassing such
artists as Thomas Cole, Edward Hicks, William Rimmer, Thomas Dewing and
Arshile Gorky. Davidson's approach is chronological, but artists of different eras are frequently related. The bibliography is useful particularly for the lesser known artists discussed.

A-A 152. ELDREDGE, CHARLES C. American Imagination and Symbolist Painting.
          New York: Grey Art Gallery and Study Center, 1979. 176 pp.
This exhibition defined a new type of American painting roughly equivalent
to the French symbolist movement. Designated "Introspective" painting,
these works span the period from 1855 to 1917. Part I of this catalogue
examines the cultural background in literature and international Symbolism.
Part II focuses on the art, discussing themes of seduction, virgins, dreams,
life and death, and Neo-paganism. Although several of the artists—Albert
P. Ryder and Arthur B. Davies, for example—are well known, the majority
of painters were previously undiscussed in the literature.

A-A 153. GERDTS, WILLIAM H. Painters of the Humble Truth: Masterpieces
          of American Still Life 1801-1939. Columbia: University of
          Missouri Press; Tulsa, Okla.: Philbrook Art Center, 1981.
          293 pp.
The catalogue of this exhibition curated by Gerdts appeared ten years
after his initial American Still-life Painting (see A-A 154). In his
catalogue essay, Gerdts concentrates on fewer artists in greater detail.
His eleven chapters are arranged thematically, covering 300 years of American still-life painting. Both the cultural context and the contemporary
criticism are considered in some detail.

A-A 154. GERDTS, WILLIAM H., and RUSSEL BURKE. American Still-Life Paint-
          ing. New York: Praeger, 1971. 264 pp.
In this book Gerdts and Burke reappraise the still life, which they feel
merits greater esteem. They have drawn together the work of dozens of
artists who specialized in this genre. Aside from the first chapter on
antecedents and the final one on the 20th century, the book is an exploration of the work of the 19th century, when the still-life enjoyed its
greatest popularity. American Still-Life Painting is an introductory
work; the authors neither seek nor offer answers to broad cultural questions.

A-A 155. ISHAM, SAMUEL. The History of American Painting. New York:
          Macmillan, 1905. 608 pp.
Isham's pioneering study was the first serious attempt at chronicling
American painting from "The Primitives" to the beginning of the 20th century. In 1927, Royal Cortissoz added five chapters dealing with later
developments in Impressionism and The Eight. A painter himself, Isham
approached his material by movements and subject matter rather than biography.

A-A 156. KOKE, RICHARD J. American Landscape and Genre Paintings in the
          New-York Historical Society. 3 vols. New York: G. K. Hall,
          1982. 1243 pp.
The result of ten years' labor, these three volumes contain entries for
over 3000 oil paintings and works on paper (excluding prints) which fall
into the categories of landscape, genre, anecdotal, historical, naive,
and marine painting. Most works are illustrated. Each entry contains
a physical description, provenance, reference, and short comment. Works

are grouped alphabetically by artist (the best-represented painter is
Asher B. Durand with 375 landscapes). This is a major resource for scholars of American art in general and of American landscape painting in particular.

A-A 157. LITTLE, NINA FLETCHER. American Decorative Wall Painting 1700-
1850. 1959; Rev. ed. New York: Dutton, 1972. 169 pp.
This is essentially a reprint of the 1952 first edition, with an additional
chapter recording information discovered since initial publication. Little
discusses "The influence of the traveling decorator on the early homes
of rural America. . . ." She explores in detail the stylistic, technical,
social, and economic aspects of decorative wall painting. The book is
divided into two parts. The first part covers painted woodwork and concentrates on New England. The second part is concerned with painted plaster walls and, although also concentrating on New England, it is organized
by decorative motifs. Appendices provide biographical entries on painters
and lists of pictorial panels.

A-A 158. McCOUBREY, JOHN W. American Tradition in Painting. New York:
Braziller, 1963. 128 pp.
McCoubrey's short essay has been called an exercise in geographic determinism. He attributes what he sees as characteristic traits in American
painting to the continuing impact of the American landscape on generations
of painters. McCoubrey argues that this country's vast scale, its unfinished and uncontrolled quality, and its people's relative powerlessness
over the environment have all helped shape a continuity in the American
vision that has persisted for nearly three centuries.

A-A 159. McSHINE, KYNASTON, ed. The Natural Paradise: Painting in America.
1800-1950. New York: Museum of Modern Art, 1976. 178 pp.
This bicentennial exhibition examines the romantic tradition in 19th-
and 20th-century painting. The catalogue presents works of startling
diversity, which essays by Robert Rosenblum and John Wilmerding attempt
to relate. Particular stress is given to the affinities between 19th-
century landscape painting and 20th-century Abstract Expressionism. A
lengthy chronology and a bibliography are appended.

A-A 160. NORELLI, MARTINA R. American Wildlife Painting, 1720-1920.
New York: Watson-Guptill, 1975. 224 pp.
In her introduction, Norelli traces the scientific interest in nature
which has characterized American explorers since the 16th-century. The
catalogue, however, concentrates on six specific artist-naturalists:
Mark Catesby, Alexander Wilson, John James Audubon, Martin Johnson Heade,
Abbott Handerson Thayer, and Louis Agassiz Fuertes. Numerous descriptive
and analytic paintings and drawings of these six men are reproduced, many
in color. Each artist receives an in-depth discussion of his work and
naturalist theories.

A-A 161. NOVAK, BARBARA and ANNETTE BLAUGRUND, eds. Next to Nature:
Landscape Paintings from the National Academy of Design. New
York: Harper & Row, 1980. 213 pp.
The work of a group of Columbia University graduate students, this exhibition drew from the unique collection of the National Academy of Design.
Novak and her students sifted the collection for the outstanding landscape
paintings of over fifty artists, some of whom were still living. The
catalogue entries were written by the students; an introduction is provided
by Novak.

A-A 162. PROWN, JULES DAVID. American Painting from Its Beginnings to
the Armory Show. Geneva: Skira, 1969. 144 pp.
Prown has written a survey which touches on all the major figures with
particular emphasis on John S. Copley, Winslow Homer, Thomas Eakins, and
James A. M. Whistler. His five chapters are both chronological and thematic, positing general trends for particular time periods such as "The
Search for Identity" during the early 19th century. All of the reproductions are in color.

A-A 163. PROWN, JULES DAVID and BARBARA ROSE. American Painting: From
the Colonial Period to the Present. New York: Rizzoli, 1977.
276 pp.
This is a combined reprint of two volumes published separately in 1969.
See Jules David Prown's American Painting: From Its Beginnings to the
Armory Show (A-A 162) and Barbara Rose's American Painting: The Twentieth
Century (A-A 226).

A-A 164. QUICK, MICHAEL, et al. American Portraiture in the Grand Manner,
1720-1920. Los Angeles, Calif.: Los Angeles County Museum
of Art, 1981. 228 pp.
This catalogue examines large-scale, full-length American portraits in
the English tradition. Such ambitious portraits are necessarily rooted
in art historical traditions. They represent "Aesthetic objectives of
each historical period." The 200 years covered by this exhibition are
treated in four chronological essays by Quick, Marvin Sadik, and William
H. Gerdts. The seventy-four catalogue entries are all reproduced in color
plates.

A-A 165. RICHARDSON, EDGAR PRESTON. American Romantic Painting. New
York: Weyhe, 1944. 50 pp.
Richardson provides a short introduction to this volume of black and white
reproductions. He contrasts American romantic painting with its more
literary European equivalent. American romantic painting, he states,
comes more naturally from within the artist. Brief biographical sketches
are provided for over eighty artists.

A-A 166. RICHARDSON, EDGAR PRESTON. Painting in America: The Story of
Four Hundred and Fifty Years. New York: Crowell, 1956.
447 pp.
When it appeared, Richardson's initial effort provided information about
dozens of artists never before discussed. He subscribes to neither the
"frontier fallacy" that only native-born, self-taught artists can be considered truly American nor to the view that all artistic progress in
America must be related to European developments. Instead, his survey
considers both the art and the craft of painting—both the lofty European-
derived associations and the localized social aspects of the works.

A-A 167. WILLIAMS, HERMANN WARNER, Jr. Mirror to the American Past.
A Survey of American Genre Painting: 1750-1900. Greenwich,
Conn.: New York Graphic Society, 1973. 248 pp.
Williams's book is not meant to be a general history of American genre
painting; rather, it is a selective survey of aspects of the field.
Williams excludes, for example, literary genre, primitive painting, and
paintings with Native American subject matter. He concentrates instead
on scenes of American daily life, discussing almost 150 painters from
the well-known greats to the most obscure. Illustrations are plentiful,
and the policy has been to reproduce less familiar works rather than the
"old favorites."

A-A 168. **WILMERDING, JOHN.** A History of American Marine Painting. Salem,
          Mass.: Peabody Museum of Salem, 1968. 279 pp.
Wilmerding's study of "salt-water" painting is the first of its kind.
The text begins with the Colonial era and continues to the present,
although the emphasis is on the 19th century. Marine painting is characterized as being freer from idealization and literary themes and more
prone to experimentation than landscape painting. The fourteen chapters
consider the relationship of marine painting to Colonial portraiture,
folk art, and the Dutch tradition. Such themes as the contribution of
French romantic painting and the introduction of steam-driven vessels
are also examined. An extensive bibliography is included.

A-A 169. **WILMERDING, JOHN,** ed. The Genius of American Painting. New
          York: Morrow, 1973. 352 pp.
In this richly illustrated book, Wilmerding discusses American painting
during the first half of the 19th century and introduces essays by R.
Peter Mooz on Colonial Art, Richard J. Boyle on the second half of the
19th century, Irma B. Jaffe on the years 1900-1930, Harry Rand on the
1930s and Abstract Expressionism, and Dore Ashton on contemporary art.
The book is intended primarily for the general reader.

III. B. PAINTING: COLONIAL

A-A 170. **ALLEN, EDWARD B.** Early American Wall Paintings: 1710-1850.
          New Haven, Conn.: Yale University Press, 1926. 110 pp.
This book deals with the panel paintings and frescoes in 18th- and early
19th-century residences largely from the New England region where this
art form seems to have been concentrated. Allen's approach is that of
an antiquarian. His text is descriptive, discussing each house separately
and taking pains to situate each painting within the fabric of its building.

A-A 171. **BELKNAP, WALDRON PHOENIX,** Jr. American Colonial Painting: Mate-
          rials for a History. Cambridge, Mass.: Harvard University
          Press, 1959. 377 pp.
Charles Coleman Sellers edited this posthumous publication of the research
of Belknap. The diverse chapters illustrate the painstaking historical/
genealogical method which Belknap championed. Included are his contribution to the identity of Robert Feke, his "discovery" of the English mezzotint as a source for Colonial portraiture, and his exhaustive treatment
of early New York portraits and painters.

A-A 172. **EVANS, DORINDA.** Benjamin West and His American Students. Washing-
          ton, D.C.: Smithsonian Institution Press, 1980. 203 pp.
Benjamin West has been called "the father of American painting" less for
his frequently undistinguished paintings than for the profound influence
he exerted on American painters studying in London and on American shores.
This catalogue of the National Portrait Gallery exhibition focuses on
twenty-four pupils of West's during the sixty-year period, 1760-1820.
After a ten-page introduction to the career of West, Evans devotes the
rest of the volume to the students who are grouped in three "generations."
A bibliography of manuscript material listed by artist is included.

A-A 173. **FLEXNER, JAMES THOMAS.** America's Old Masters. 1939; Rev. ed.
          Garden City, N.Y.: Doubleday, 1980. 369 pp.
Ten years before the first scholarly survey of American painting, Flexner
published this volume dealing with four Colonial artists: Benjamin West,
John S. Copley, Charles W. Peale, and Gilbert Stuart. He puts forward

the view that the methodology of American art history differs from its
European counterpart, an opinion which parallels his thesis that while
American painting is linked to a European tradition, it nevertheless is
highly colored by the exigencies of Colonial life.

A-A 174. FLEXNER, JAMES THOMAS. First Flowers of Our Wilderness: American
Painting, the Colonial Period. Boston: Houghton Mifflin, 1947.
367 pp.
This first book of Flexner's three-volume history of American painting
deals with the pre-revolutionary era. Flexner writes what he terms a
"social history of American painting" in which he considers the artist
as a reflection of his place and time. Thus, Colonial painting is
explained in terms of Colonial life. Flexner treats the works (mainly portraits) as historical documents, rejecting the view that a work must be
painted in a non-European manner in order to be considered truly "American." Separate chapters are devoted to John Smibert, Robert Feke, Benjamin
West, and John S. Copley.

A-A 175. FLEXNER, JAMES THOMAS. The Light of Distant Skies: American
Painting, 1760-1835. New York: Harcourt Brace, 1954.
307 pp.
The second of Flexner's three-volume history of American painting, this
book concerns itself with history painting, portraiture, and the genesis
of an American approach to both. Flexner considers the state of art
instruction in the colonies and the somewhat ambivalent American relationship to English art. General political and cultural information is integrated into the anecdotal text. Flexner includes a bibliography for more
than sixty artists, many of whom are still relatively unknown.

A-A 176. PRESSLY, NANCY L. Revealed Religion: Benjamin West's Commissions
for Windsor Castle and Fonthill Abbey. San Antonio, Tex.:
San Antonio Museum of Art, 1983. 76 pp.
George III commissioned Benjamin West to decorate his private chapel at
Windsor, but the project was cancelled before completion. This catalogue,
like the exhibition, comprises forty-one paintings, oil sketches, and
drawings that West prepared for the cycle, which was to be on revealed
religion. Also included are a set of stained glass designs for St.
George's chapel in Windsor Castle and seventeen paintings and stained glass
designs commissioned by William Beckford for his neo-Gothic mansion,
Fonthill Abbey, also cancelled before completion. Prevailing scholarly
opinion on some points is challenged in the text. Entries offer comments
and give biblical excerpts to illuminate West's symbolism.

A-A 177. QUIMBY, IAN M. G., ed. American Painting to 1776: A Reappraisal.
Charlottesville: University Press of Virginia, 1971. 384 pp.
This is a collection of papers presented by art historians and conservators
at the 1971 Winterthur Conference. Included are individual essays on
Gustavus Hesselius, John Smibert, Robert Feke, and Pieter Vanderlyn, as
well as on the more general subjects of decorative painting and New York
metropolitan painting. The conservators discuss X-radiography, pigment
analysis, and the methodology of technical examination.

A-A 178. SHERMAN, FREDERIC FAIRCHILD. Early American Painting. New York:
Century, 1932. 289 pp.
Sherman's early book is essentially a compilation of individual biographic
entries for the artists of the 17th, 18th, and early 19th centuries.
The stress is on portrait painters, with additional chapters on miniature
painters, landscape painters, historical painters, religious painters,
and genre painters.

III.   C. PAINTING: 19TH CENTURY

A-A 179.   BAUR, JOHN I. H.   M. & M. Karolik Collection of American Paintings
           1815-1865. Museum of Fine Arts, Boston. Cambridge, Mass.:
           Harvard University Press, 1949. 544 pp.
At a time when John S. Copley was thought to be the only significant American painter before Winslow Homer, Maxim Karolik filled his collection
with works by luminists and "primitive" painters whose importance to American art history is no longer disputed. Baur's catalogue essay, "Trends
in American Painting, 1815-1865," has become a classic of American art
history. Among other topics, it presents an early discussion of Luminism
and a consideration of the American relationship to the real and the ideal.
The catalogue entries frequently provide information about some of the
artists which cannot be found elsewhere.

A-A 180.   BERMINGHAM, PETER. American Art in the Barbizon Mood. Washington,
           D.C.: Smithsonian Institution, 1975. 191 pp.
The Barbizon style of landscape painting, which flourished in France from
the 1830s through the 1880s, was evidence of an opposition to growing
industrialization and an attempt to find release in nature and the rural
past. French painters' sombre images of peasants at work had no counterpart in America, but American artists welcomed the freedom to paint unspec-
ified, idyllic scenes from nature and imbued them with their own sense
of optimism and promise. Bermingham records the development of American
painters who worked in the Barbizon mode and contrasts the style's development in America and France.

A-A 181.   BOYLE, RICHARD J. American Impressionism. Boston: New York
           Graphic Society, 1974. 236 pp.
Boyle's purpose is threefold: to offer a general survey of the American
impressionists of the late 19th century, to trace the development of the
style in America, and to determine the purely "American" characteristics
of the paintings. He argues that too many artists have been mislabeled
as impressionists, and he excludes such painters as Frank Duveneck, J.
Francis Murphy, and Robert Henri. Boyle begins by discussing both the
European and American backgrounds to Impressionism. He then devotes two
chapters to the "pre-impressionists" (James A. M. Whistler, John La Farge,
John Singer Sargent), while the "true" impressionists of the years 1875-
1915 are examined in the last six chapters.

A-A 182.   BURKE, DOREEN BOLGER. American Paintings in the Metropolitan
           Museum of Art. Volume III: A Catalogue of Works by Artists
           Born Between 1846 and 1864. Edited by Kathleen Luhrs. Princeton,
           N.J.: Princeton University Press, 1980. 528 pp.
This large catalogue includes paintings from the 1870s to the 1940s in
the collection of the Metropolitan Museum. Every painting is reproduced
and discussed in an individual essay. Artists' biographies, provenance,
exhibition records, and bibliographic references are supplied for each
entry. Related works are frequently discussed and illustrated. A consideration of forgeries and their detection is included.

A-A 183.   CURRY, LARRY. The American West: Painters from Catlin to Russell.
           New York: Viking Press, 1972. 198 pp.
Curry begins his catalogue essay by sketching the history of westward
expansion. He discusses the early artists of the Hudson River School
and the interest in Thomas Cole's "wilder image." Curry maintains that
this search for wilderness scenes led such artists as Karl Bodmer, George
Catlin, George Caleb Bingham, Worthington Whittredge, and Samuel Colman
further and further west. He briefly discusses these figures and their

colleagues, providing a chronological time chart for each of the twenty-four painters he considers.

A-A 184. ELY, CATHERINE BEACH. The Modern Tendency in American Painting.
New York: Frederick Fairchild Sherman, 1925. 93 pp.
In her opening chapter, Ely bemoans the unfertile climate for the fine arts in the early 20th century. She cites the aggrandizement of European reputations and the American passion for scientific developments as two factors causing indifference toward American painters. Ely writes as a partisan critic. Many of her chapters on such artists as Robert Henri, Abbott Thayer, and Arthur B. Davies first appeared as reviews in contemporary periodicals.

A-A 185. FLEXNER, JAMES THOMAS. Nineteenth-Century American Painting.
New York: Putnam, 1970. 256 pp.
In his foreword, Flexner repeats his plea advanced in earlier publications for American painting to be considered in American terms without reference to the French norm which had dominated 19th-century art history. He sees American artists as unique individuals coming from predominantly self-taught roots, and argues that it is therefore difficult to divide them into schools and influences. This book covers a broader area than Flexner's earlier volume, That Wilder Image (see A-A 186) providing more extensive discussions of early 19th-century painters and the American impressionists.

A-A 186. FLEXNER, JAMES THOMAS. That Wilder Image: The Paintings of
America's Native School from Thomas Cole to Winslow Homer.
Boston: Little, Brown, 1962. 407 pp.
Covering the period from 1825-1900, the last volume of Flexner's trilogy (see A-A 174 and 175) makes a case for a "native school" of American painting. Embracing such diverse figures as Asher B. Durand and George Inness, this "school" would nevertheless reflect a common foundation in the universal optimism and popularism of the period and the orientation away from European models. .Flexner cites a "vernacular tradition" which reigns through these years. His emphasis is on landscape, but genre, portraiture, and print-making are also discussed.

A-A 187. FRANKENSTEIN, ALFRED. After the Hunt: William Harnett and Other
American Still Life Painters, 1870-1900. 1953; Rev. ed.
Berkeley: University of California Press, 1969. 200 pp.
While focusing on Harnett, Frankenstein also discusses the painters John F. Peto and John Haberle at some length. There are two additional chapters on the "second circle"—Jefferson D. Chalfant, George W. Platt, Richard L. Goodwin, John F. Francis, George Cope, and Alexander Pope—and the "third circle"—thirty-six little-known still life painters. The book is mainly an account of the archival and critical methodology employed by Frankenstein in his research on Harnett. He includes a critical catalogue of the artist's frequently forged work and a list of owners of "genuine" Harnetts.

A-A 188. GERDTS, WILLIAM H. American Impressionism. Seattle, Wash.:
Henry Art Gallery, 1980. 179 pp.
The text of this book stands alone as an independent scholarly achievement as well as serving as the catalogue of an important exhibition. Gerdts contests the notion that the somewhat conservative American Impressionism was hindered by "the tradition of American Realism." Paying particular attention to impressionist subject matter, he argues that what is "American" about American Impressionism is actually a complex amalgam of the many factors which he touches upon in the seventeen chapters of the book. A detailed bibliography is included.

A-A 189. GERDTS, WILLIAM H. Revealed Masters: Nineteenth-Century American Painting. New York: American Federation of Arts, 1974.
152 pp.
Revealed Masters was an exhibition designed to familiarize the public
with certain 19th-century artists who were out of the mainstream but whose
work demanded greater recognition. Gerdts's essay traces the stream of
19th-century painting, discussing such lesser known subjects as the White
Mountain School, the schools of Buffalo and California, and square format
painting. This essay precedes the catalogue proper, which includes the
work of such artists as John White Alexander, David Johnson, and Harriet
Hosmer.

A-A 190. GOETZMANN, WILLIAM H. and JOSEPH C. PORTER, with artists' biographies by David C. Hunt. The West as Romantic Horizon. Omaha,
Neb.: Joslyn Art Museum; Lincoln: University of Nebraska Press,
1981. 128 pp.
This book is a catalogue of the collection of InterNorth, Inc., a natural
gas company devoted to scholarship on art pertaining to America's western
frontier. Karl Bodmer, the German artist who accompanied Prince
Maximillian on his 1832 North American expedition, and Alfred Jacob Miller,
the artist of the 1837 Stewart expedition to the Northern Plains, are
particularly well represented. Goetzmann sees the works of the West as
an important source of romantic sentiment in art, and Porter examines
the watercolor sketches of Indians and settlers which are valuable to
historians and ethnologists.

A-A 191. HILLS, PATRICIA. The Painters' America: Rural and Urban Life,
1810-1910. New York: Praeger, 1974. 160 pp.
Hills's catalogue is concerned with the broad meaning of genre and, more
specifically, with the American values it reflects in the hundred-year
time span she examines. She traces an early tone of optimism and nationalism which gives way to a "cosmopolitan and aesthetic viewpoint." The
painters whom one would expect to find in such a show--William Sydney
Mount and Eastman Johnson, for example--are presented alongside many lesser-
known figures. Hills's treatment is topical, with such subtitles as "Paintings of Town and Village Life" and "Black People in Pre-Civil War Painting."

A-A 192. MORGAN, H. WAYNE. New Muses: Art in American Culture, 1865-
1920. Norman: University of Oklahoma Press, 1978. 232 pp.
New Muses is one of a number of recent contributions to American cultural
history through reference to American art. Morgan concentrates on painting
and the context of art and artists during the years of transition from
1865-1920. He examines such themes as the response of people to painting,
the relationship of art to materialistic and egalitarian values, and the
place of art in America's role as an emerging, urbanized world power.
He refers constantly to original source material housed in such repositories as the Archives of American Art. A comprehensive bibliography
is included.

A-A 193. NOVAK, BARBARA. American Painting of the Nineteenth Century:
Realism, Idealism, and the American Experience. New York:
Praeger, 1969. 350 pp.
Novak sees her book as occupying a middle ground between the familiar
hurried surveys on the one hand and detailed monographs on individual
painters on the other. She makes no claims to inclusiveness but only
to provide an investigation of some dozen or so painters whose work seems
to reveal and perpetuate certain persisting traditions in American painting.
Novak is fascinated by the continuing tension between the real and the
ideal. While what she calls "the respect for fact" is often dominant,
it is frequently wedded to a poetic vision, as in the case of those mid-
century painters known as luminists, whom she discusses at length.

A-A 194. NOVAK, BARBARA. The Arcadian Landscape: Nineteenth Century
          American Painters in Italy. Lawrence: University of Kansas
          Museum of Art, 1973. n.p.
This exhibition catalogue traces the American fascination with the Italian
landscape which began with Benjamin West's trip to Rome in 1760. Novak's
essay, "Arcady Revisited," examines the deeply felt literary and historical
associations which drew so many artists to the campagna, many of whom
lived there for a number of years as expatriates. Charles Eldredge's catalogue entries briefly discuss each work, giving provenance and exhibition
records.

A-A 195. NOVAK, BARBARA. Nature and Culture: American Landscape Painting,
          1825-1875. New York: Oxford University Press, 1980. 323 pp.
In this study, Novak examines the great era of American landscape painting,
1825-1875. Relying heavily on contemporary manuscripts and texts, she
places the painters and their works within the changing cultural context
of 19th-century life. Novak is concerned with thought and with ideas,
and her ten chapters reflect this emphasis. Each could stand as a separate
essay. In one section, she discusses the relationship of 19th-century
advances in geology, meteorology, and botany to the art, while in others
she studies the western exploratory expeditions, the introduction of the
train into the landscape, and the American concept of the "Sublime."

A-A 196. OWENS, GWENDOLYN and JOHN PETERS-CAMPBELL. Golden Day, Silver
          Night: Perceptions of Nature in American Art, 1850-1910. Ithaca,
          N.Y.: Herbert F. Johnson Museum of Art, 1982. 111 pp.
In her introduction to the exhibition catalogue, Owens distinguishes
between the landscapes of the great mid-century period (Golden Day) and
the later works which responded to and occasionally rebelled against this
tradition (Silver Night). The mid-century predilection for cultivated
bucolic scenes and inaccessible wilderness views gives way to a more personal mode characterized by looser brush strokes and an interest in pal-
pable atmosphere. Over forty artists are represented, their works being
drawn from the collections of six upstate New York museums.

A-A 197. WOLF, BRYAN JAY. Romantic Revision: Culture and Consciousness
          in Nineteenth-Century American Painting and Literature. Chicago:
          University of Chicago Press, 1982. 272 pp.
Wolf is concerned with the "modernity" of the American romantic vision
in painting. He looks at three artists--Washington Allston, John Quidor,
and Thomas Cole. The fact that he comes from the broader field of American
cultural studies is reflected by his integrated discussion of such literary
figures as John Milton and Washington Irving. Wolf sees romantic art
less as a simple celebration of nature than as a vehicle for the mind
of the painter to achieve "consciousness" with itself and the world around
it. In a concluding chapter Wolf relates Romanticism to Luminism.

III.   D. PAINTING: 20TH CENTURY

A-A 198. AGEE, WILLIAM C. Synchromism and Color Principles in American
          Painting, 1910-1930. New York: Knoedler, 1965. 53 pp.
Agee argues that Synchromism and the Synchromists have been unduly slighted
by historians who only consider the presumptuous 1913 statement issued
by Morgan Russell and Stanton Macdonald-Wright and the few "typical" (and
often misdated) canvases which have come to be associated with the movement.
He feels that the principles of Synchromism endured much longer than is
commonly thought, and he cites such artists as Thomas Hart Benton, Andrew

Dasburg, and Morton L. Schamberg as having felt the influence of Synchromism.

A-A 199. **ALLOWAY, LAWRENCE.** American Pop Art. New York: Collier Books, 1974. 144 pp.
In this exhibition catalogue, Alloway contends that Pop art is neither realistic nor abstract but an art about signs and sign systems that shares themes with popular culture. Alloway links Pop art to the 20th-century growth and consumption of popular culture and the tendency to treat our whole culture as if it were art, as an alternative to an aesthetic that isolated visual art from life. The text gives a brief history of popular culture and looks at the study of popular art. It includes a chapter which ties Pop art to the 19th-century trompe l'oeil painting of William Harnett and the 20th-century Precisionist Charles Sheeler.

A-A 200. **ARNASON, H. H.** American Abstract Expressionists and Imagists. New York: Guggenheim Museum, 1961. 131 pp.
This catalogue to the exhibition at the Guggenheim Museum is intended as a survey of painting loosely described as Abstract Expressionist. Arnason recognizes that Abstract Expressionism is a complex of different approaches to painting. He makes a distinction between Abstract Expressionists (Jackson Pollock, Willem de Kooning, Jack Tworkov, Norman Bluhm, Joan Mitchell) who make the act of painting the subject, and the "Imagists" (Mark Rothko, Barnett Newman, Ad Reinhardt, Robert Motherwell) who attempt "to present in abstract terms a conflict or relationship" through dramatically isolated shapes and simplified color areas.

A-A 201. **ASHTON, DORE.** The New York School: A Cultural Reckoning. New York: Viking Press, 1972. 246 pp.
Harold Rosenberg has described the New York School as a group of "individuals bewildered, uncertain, and straining after direction and an intuition of themselves." Ashton's study of the period leading up to 1940 and the following decade supports this view, as she examines the personalities and conflicting interests which prevented the emergence of a common ideology. Her work is a cultural history of artists in American society. It is not about works of art or artists as individuals, but an examination of the ingredients that went into making painting an important force in American culture.

A-A 202. **ASHTON, DORE.** A Reading of Modern Art. Cleveland, Ohio: Press of Case Western Reserve University, 1969. 208 pp.
Ashton sees her consideration of 20th-century European and American art (mostly painting) as a critical essay, not a general survey. She examines selected artists and topics in a way which emphasizes connections and ideas by going beyond traditional appraisals of the well-known modern works reproduced in the book. Her unhistorical approach allows her to draw ties between disparate artists and movements in the U.S. and Europe. The Americans discussed include Mark Rothko, Philip Guston, Robert Motherwell, Willem de Kooning, Helen Frankenthaler, Jasper Johns, and Morris Louis.

A-A 203. **BAIGELL, MATTHEW.** The American Scene: American Painting of the 1930s. New York: Praeger, 1974. 214 pp.
This heavily illustrated text examines the genesis of American Scene Painting together with the government-sponsored work projects that developed with it. The book includes monographic studies of Thomas Hart Benton, Grant Wood, John Steuart Curry, Reginald Marsh, Stuart Davis, and Ben Shahn. Baigell also discusses Social Realists, asserting that while they did not develop one characteristic style or point of view, they shared assumptions about the function of art and its relationship to society.

A-A 204. BARKER, VIRGIL. From Realism to Reality in Recent American Paint-
ing. Lincoln: University of Nebraska Press, 1959. 93 pp.
The author defines Realism as a growing awareness of pigmental reality—
the expressive character of the medium of paint. Beginning with Maurice
Prendergast, he discusses works by Stuart Davis, Max Weber, John Marin,
Charles Sheeler, Georgia O'Keeffe, Marsden Hartley, Yasuo Kuniyoshi,
Reginald Marsh, Edward Hopper, Morris Graves, Andrew Wyeth, Hans Hofmann,
Theodoros Stamos, and Mark Rothko. In his chapter on action painting,
he describes his reaction to the then new paintings by Jackson Pollock,
Hofmann, and Stamos. Illustrations are primarily of works in the Univer-
sity of Nebraska Art Gallery.

A-A 205. BAUR, JOHN I. H. Revolution and Tradition in American Painting.
Cambridge, Mass.: Harvard University Press, 1951. 170 pp.
Baur's study traces the development of American painting and sculpture
in the first half of the 20th century. The picture is a complex maze
of "isms" (Cubism, Futurism, Precisionism, etc.) and a confrontation of
opposites (conservative and liberal, realistic and abstract, objective
and subjective, classic and romantic, etc.). Baur imposes a formal scheme
upon the whole, outlining first the revolutionary and then the traditional
aspects of the art of the period. While he is concerned with biography,
chronology, and the critical climate, he concentrates on larger trends
and motivations, especially the impact of European Modernism.

A-A 206. BROWN, MILTON. American Painting from the Armory Show to the
Depression. Princeton, N.J.: Princeton University Press, 1955.
243 pp.
According to Brown, the dates 1913 for the Armory Show and 1929 for the
Depression delimit an important period in American art. Those years saw
an older tradition of "Realism" being displaced by more modern European
concepts of art and the cataclysmic economic event of 1929. Brown sets
the development of modern art movements against the established "Realism"
of the academy. He is concerned not only with this stylistic battle but
also with the relationship of "these artistic developments to the changing
social conditions which determined them."

A-A 207. COX, ANNETTE. Art-as-Politics: The Abstract Expressionist Avant-
Garde and Society. Ann Arbor, Mich.: UMI Research Press, 1982.
206 pp.
Cox explores the relationship of the Abstract Expressionists to Stalinism
and Surrealism and their initial attraction to these movements. She proposes that the radical nature of Abstract Expressionism lies in its desire
to be free of any political or aesthetic dogma, while retaining the expressive qualities produced by these dogmas. Cox analyzes the political dimensions of the work and writings of Barnett Newman, Jackson Pollock, and
Ad Reinhardt, as well as the writings of the two major critics of the
period, Harold Rosenberg and Clement Greenberg.

A-A 208. DAVIDSON, ABRAHAM A. Early American Modernist Painting, 1910-
1935. New York: Harper & Row, 1981. 324 pp.
Davidson sets the beginning of American modernist painting at about 1910—
the year of Arthur G. Dove's first non-objective paintings, Max Weber's
nudes based on Picasso's figures, and Morgan Russell's still lifes in
the manner of Cezanne. The author finds that an important aspect in the
development of early Modernism in America is that it appeared suddenly,
and he argues that this factor accounts for many features of American
painting. The book is divided into six major chapters with smaller sub-
sections: The Stieglitz Group; The Arensberg Circle; Color Painters;
Early Exhibitions, Collectors, and Galleries; Precisionism; and The Independents.

A-A 209. FRIEDMAN, MARTIN. The Precisionist View in American Art. Minneapolis, Minn.: Walker Art Center, 1960. 62 pp.
This exhibition catalogue includes the work of sixteen artists, focusing
on Georgia O'Keeffe, Charles Sheeler, and, to a lesser degree, Charles
Demuth, Preston Dickinson, and Niles Spencer. In his introduction,
Friedman defines the Precisionist view as an essentially realistic view
that reflects an idealized state of absolute order. He describes the
characteristics of Precisionist painting, its process, its approach, and
its aesthetic. The essay also offers a consideration of the relationship
of Precisionism to native American style, modern European art, and its
attraction to industry and the modern city.

A-A 210. GELDZAHLER, HENRY. American Painting in the 20th Century. Greenwich, Conn.: New York Graphic Society, 1965. 236 pp.
This catalogue traces the development of American painting from 1900,
beginning with the Eight, to the 1960s and the second generation of
Abstract Expressionists. Geldzahler bases his survey on works selected
from the collection of the Metropolitan Museum. The book is divided by
chapters into the major 20th-century trends. Each chapter begins with
general remarks on the period, followed by small sections on individual
artists. The approach is historical and biographical, and individual
works are discussed. Short biographies of each artist are included.

A-A 211. GUILBAUT, SERGE. How New York Stole the Idea of Modern Art:
Abstract Expressionism, Freedom, and the Cold War. Translated
by Arthur Goldhammer. Chicago: University of Chicago Press,
1983. 277 pp.
Guilbaut argues for a reinterpretation of the development and acceptance
of abstraction in post-W.W. II American Art. Noting that most studies
of the art of the period have dealt with either the aesthetics of action
or the formal qualities of the work, Guilbaut offers a social study of
Abstract Expression which attempts to grasp the reasons American avant-
garde art took the abstract form that it did. His central thesis is that
the success of an American avant-garde was due "not solely to aesthetic
and stylistic considerations," but "to the movement's ideological resonance."

A-A 212. HELLER, NANCY and JULIA WILLIAMS. The Regionalists. New York:
Watson-Guptill, 1976. 208 pp.
This volume is essentially a picture book of the "Regionalist" (sometimes
called "American Scene") art of the 1930s. It includes a short chapter
on the "Concept of Realism." Successive chapters group the paintings
by subject matter—rural, urban, mythic, or socio-political. The last
chapter concerns itself with "the fate of Regionalist painting" and "the
ultimate significance of the Regionalist movement in the context of American Art history."

A-A 213. HESS, THOMAS B. Abstract Painting: Background and American
Phase. New York: Viking Press, 1951. 164 pp.
Hess traces the aesthetic characteristics of Western art to establish
a link between the art of the Abstract Expressionists and the art of the
past. His discussion is divided into three parts. The first describes
the nature of abstract art in general, focusing on art up to the 20th
century. The second part surveys the period from Post-Impressionism to
W.W. II in Europe and America, and the third discusses the art of the
New York School, positing that New York has replaced Paris as the center
of world art.

A-A 214. HOBBS, ROBERT CARLETON and GAIL LEVIN. Abstract Expressionism:
The Formative Years. Ithaca, N.Y.: Cornell University Press,
1978. 140 pp.
In the first essay in this exhibition catalogue, "Early Abstract Expressionism: A Concern with the Unknown Within," Hobbs examines the
Surrealist/Cubist context from which Abstract Expressionism developed in the
1930s and 1940s. Focusing on the Surrealist content, he traces the works
from an earlier, more complex state to their later, condensed form. In
particular, he discusses the concepts of peripheral viewing and peripheral
imagery. Levin, in her essay, "Miro, Kandinsky and the Genesis of Abstract
Expressionism," outlines and documents the influence of Miro and Kandinsky
on the Abstract Expressionists. Individual essays on the fifteen artists
exhibited also are included.

A-A 215. HUNTER, SAM, ROSALIND KRAUSS, and MARCIA TUCKER. Critical Perspectives in American Art. Amherst, Mass.: Fine Arts Center
Gallery, University of Massachusetts, 1976. 66pp.
In the introduction to this catalogue, Hugh M. David writes that "the
art movements of the sixties which succeeded Abstract Expressionism may
be seen as a reaction to the heroic individualism" of the earlier movement.
The text for the catalogue takes five issues which might be described
as central preoccupations of recent art: "Field Painting," "Perceptual
Fields," "Objecthood," "Cultural Irony," and "Narrative Art." For each
topic, three artists are discussed who represent chronologically successive
contributions to the aesthetic focus they share.

A-A 216. JANIS, SIDNEY. Abstract and Surrealist Art in America. New
York: Reynal & Hitchcock, 1944. 144 pp.
This work, written thirty years after the Armory Show, is an early attempt
to present American Modernist painting against the background of the European avant-garde. Many of the Abstract Expressionists included were virtually unknown in 1944, and they awaited the publication of the book to
discover whether they had been categorized as Abstractionists or as the
more fashionable Surrealists. Janis considers Robert Motherwell, John
Ferren, Hans Hofmann, and Willem de Kooning as Abstractionists, while
Jackson Pollock, Mark Rothko, Adolph Gottlieb, and Mark Tobey emerge as
Surrealists.

A-A 217. KOOTZ, SAMUEL. Modern American Painters. Norwood, Mass.:
Plimpton Press, 1930. 64 pp.
This early work reads as a manifesto calling for a New American painting.
Kootz finds in most contemporary painting "nothing more substantial than
office-memoranda." Early American masters fare no better: Homer at best
"was a super-illustrator" and Ryder's "so-called poetry was a mixture
of dense muddy pigmentation." Among "Some Important American Painters
of Today," who display a much-needed new consciousness, Kootz includes
Charles Demuth, Arthur G. Dove, Max Weber, and Walt Kuhn.

A-A 218. LEVIN, GAIL. Synchromism and American Color Abstraction: 1910-
1925. New York: Braziller, 1978. 144 pp.
Launched in Munich in 1913 by Morgan Russell and Stanton Macdonald-Wright,
Synchromism intended nothing less than to change the course of western
painting. This catalogue, published with the exhibition of the same name
at the Whitney Museum of American Art, continues the work begun by William
C. Agee in his pioneering study Synchromism and Color Principles in American Painting: 1910-1930 (see A-A 198). Levin presents the work of the
two founders with paintings by other American artists who explicitly relied
on the impact of color for expression.

A-A 219. MARLING, KARAL ANN. <u>Wall-to-Wall</u> America: <u>A Cultural History of Post Office Murals in the Great Depression</u>. Minneapolis: University of Minnesota Press, 1982. 348 pp.
Marling presents a cultural history of the murals painted in post offices by Treasury Section artists during the 1930s. Her prime concern is with the ways in which the murals were perceived by the local population for which they were painted. The chapters are organized topically and geographically: Marling focuses on one or two murals in order to develop a particular theme and to elucidate the regional character of the popular appraisal. Her "Note on Sources" is a practical guide to the use of the pertinent documents and archives.

A-A 220. McROBERTS, JERRY WILLIAM. <u>The Conservative Realists' Image of America in the 1920's: Modernism, Traditionalism, and Nationalism</u>. Ann Arbor, Mich.: University Microfilms International, 1983. 274 pp.
This study is devoted to the visual arts in America during the 1920s. McRoberts has chosen artists who he believes are united in their commitment to the native tradition of realistic representation and American subject matter. In the first two chapters he delineates the trends—Modernism, Traditionalism, and nationalism—which led to the art boom and the crisis in national values. He follows this with individual chapters on Edward Hopper, Charles Burchfield, Ben Shahn, Thomas Hart Benton, Grant Wood, John Steuart Curry, Paul Manship, and Solon Borglum.

A-A 221. MEISEL, LOUIS K. with HELENE ZUCKER SEEMAN. <u>Photo-Realism</u>. New York: Abrams, 1980. 528 pp.
Meisel presents this book as a complete reference work on the art of the Photo-Realists up to 1979. He illustrates almost every painting by a major Photo-Realist from 1967-1979. In his introduction, Meisel outlines the definition of the term Photo-Realism, which he coined in 1968, and a brief history of the style. Introductions to thirteen major Photo-Realists are followed by biographical and extensive bibliographical material. A final section includes a discussion of fifteen painters related to Photo-Realism.

A-A 222. MILLER, DOROTHY C. and ALFRED H. BARR, Jr. <u>American Realists and Magic Realists</u>. New York: Museum of Modern Art, 1943. 67 pp.
In the short essay to this exhibition catalogue, Miller identifies Realism as a widespread but unrecognized trend in American art. The exhibition is limited, in particular, to realist pictures characterized by their sharp focus and precise representation. It is primarily devoted to young American contemporaries (twenty-six artists), with an introductory section on 19th-century American painting and the work of Charles Sheeler and Edward Hopper. Statements by the artists are included.

A-A 223. <u>The New American Painting</u>. New York: Museum of Modern Art, 1959. 96 pp.
Organized by the International Program of the Museum of Modern Art and shown in eight European countries in 1958-1959, this exhibition was the first large-scale collection of Abstract Expressionist paintings to travel to Europe. The catalogue includes excerpts from foreign reviews, and an essay by Alfred Barr, in which he posits that the seventeen artists in the exhibition are uncompromising in their individualism. Statements by the artists are published together with illustrations of the works exhibited.

A-A 224. PERLMAN, BENNARD B. The Immortal Eight: American Painting from Eakins to the Armory Show (1870-1913). New York: Exposition Press, 1962. 226 pp.

Perlman offers an account of American art from Thomas Eakins in 1870 to the Armory Show in 1913. In the opening statement, turn-of-the-century art is described as "at its lowest ebb." Out of this academic stagnancy, the author sees the emergence of the art of The Eight. The "biting realism" and "love of truth" of these painters is celebrated throughout the work. The text is largely biographical, relying on letters, diaries, and reports of conversations. An introduction is provided by Mrs. John Sloan.

A-A 225. ROSE, BARBARA. American Painting: The Eighties. New York: Vista Press, 1979. 110 pp.

Ten years before the publication of this exhibition catalogue the question "Is painting dead?" was being seriously entertained. The tradition-smashing aesthetic of innovation had led to ephemeral art (conceptual and performance art) and works made of materials destined to disintegrate. The painters included in this catalogue are intended to represent a new direction in American Art—a return to easel painting and tradition without ignoring the fundamental assumptions of Modernism. Many of the artists in this catalogue and exhibition—Elizabeth Murray, Susan Rothenberg, Lois Lane, Howard Buchwald, Thornton Willis, Robert Moskowitz, and Bill Jenson—are now well established.

A-A 226. ROSE, BARBARA. American Painting: The Twentieth Century. Geneva: Skira/World, 1970. 126 pp.

Rose sees a somewhat delayed American reaction to the 1913 Armory Show, which kept artists grappling with technical and formal advances through the difficult 1930s. The New York School emerges in the 1940s to resolve many of the problems and set the generally positive tone with which Rose characterizes the ensuing art. Her text is illustrated with numerous plates, all reproduced in color.

A-A 227. ROSENBLUM, ROBERT. Modern Painting and the Northern Romantic Tradition: Friedrich to Rothko. New York: Harper & Row, 1975. 240 pp.

The chapters of this book, originally presented in 1972 at Oxford University as The Slade Lectures, offer a broad and speculative interpretation of the modern period. Rosenblum presents an alternative to the French tradition of Modernism which he calls the northern romantic tradition. He includes a discussion of work by Caspar David Friedrich, Vincent Van Gogh, Edvard Munch, Wassily Kandinsky, Paul Klee, Piet Mondrian, and the Abstract Expressionists (in particular, Barnett Newman and Mark Rothko). The roots of Abstract Expressionism are traced to both the European romantic tradition and the local American tradition.

A-A 228. SANDLER, IRVING. The Triumph of American Painting. A History of Abstract Expressionism. New York: Praeger, 1970. 301 pp.

Sandler surveys the development of Abstract Expressionism, providing extensive information on the period. He attempts to broaden the interpretation of the art beyond formalism to include an analysis of the content. Sandler discusses the artists' intentions as their styles developed, focusing on the years 1942 to 1952 and the work of fifteen artists. They are separated into two mainstreams—gesture and color-field painting—and individual chapters are devoted to each of the fifteen artists.

A-A 229. SCHAPIRO, MEYER. Modern Art: Nineteenth and Twentieth Centuries.
          New York: Braziller, 1978. 277 pp.
This is Volume 2 of Schapiro's selected papers. The essays in this volume
originally were published between 1941 and 1978. Two of the pieces are
concerned specifically with American art: "Introduction of American Art
in America: The Armory Show" (pp. 135-178) and "Abstract Art" (pp. 185-
232). These essays discuss the advent of a new art, its critical reception,
and the cultural and historical reasons behind the critical reception.

A-A 230. SEITZ, WILLIAM CHAPIN. Abstract Expressionist Painting in America.
          Cambridge, Mass.: Harvard University Press, 1983. 490 pp.
Originally written as a doctoral dissertation in 1955, Seitz's early study
of Abstract Expressionism was published without change almost thirty years
later. Six artists have been chosen to represent the movement: Willem
de Kooning, Arshile Gorky, Hans Hofmann, Robert Motherwell, Mark Rothko,
and Mark Tobey. After an initial chapter on the spread of the movement,
Seitz examines the pictorial and metaphysical core of the paintings.
Later chapters consider the societal and historical ramifications. Almost
300 illustrations accompany the text, many of which are in color.

A-A 231. SHAPIRO, DAVID, ed. Social Realism: Art as a Weapon. New York:
          Ungar, 1973. 340 pp.
This anthology is a collection of critical responses to Social Realism.
The first section, written by David Shapiro as an introduction, gives
a brief history of artists' organizations under the WPA Arts Project,
focusing on the Artists Union, the American Artists Congress, and the
John Reed Clubs, which published the ideas and aesthetics of Social Realism.
The second section provides the social and aesthetic background, with
articles, essays, and manifestos by Diego Rivera, Thomas Benton, Meyer
Schapiro, and others. The third section consists of essays about five
Social Realists--Philip Evergood, William Gropper, Jacob Lawrence, Jack
Levine, and Ben Shahn--and of writing by the artists themselves.

A-A 232. STRAND, MARK, ed. Art of the Real: Nine American Figurative
          Painters. New York: Potter, 1983. 240 pp.
This book argues against the contention that little realistic painting
existed in the 1950s and that realism was only "reborn" in the 1980s.
The nine artists included--William Bailey, Jack Beal, Jane Freillicher,
Philip Pearlstein, Alex Katz, Lennart Anderson, Louisa Mattiasdottir,
Wayne Thiebaud, and Neil Ashton--all began their careers at the time of
Abstract Expressionism. They have nothing to do with the later super
realists and their "photographic" painting. Each of the nine is presented
by means of an edited transcription of a taped interview.

A-A 233. TUCHMAN, MAURICE, ed. New York School, The First Generation:
          Paintings of the 1940's and 1950's. Los Angeles, Calif.: Los
          Angeles County Museum of Art, 1965. 253 pp.
This heavily illustrated book is a catalogue of an exhibition of the work
of fifteen artists usually referred to as "Abstract Expressionists" who
helped create the "New American Painting" in the 1940s and 1950s. It
contains statements by the artists--including Mark Rothko, Ad Reinhardt
Philip Guston, and Arshile Gorky--statements by the critics--Lawrence
Alloway, Robert Goldwater, Clement Greenberg, Harold Rosenberg, William
Rubin, and Meyer Schapiro--and an extensive bibliography of artists,
critics, and related contemporary writing.

A-A 234. WECHSLER, JEFFREY. Surrealism and American Art, 1931-1947.
New Brunswick, N.J.: Rutgers University Art Gallery, 1978.
116 pp.
Jack J. Spector contributes an introductory essay on European Surrealism
to this catalogue, which explores the introduction, transformation, and
demise of Surrealism in the United States. The main essay by Wechsler
considers the three European-derived styles--Naturalistic Surrealism,
automation, and Magic Realism--and the two indigenous strains--Social
Surrealism and Post-surrealism. Wechsler discusses many individual artists
and concludes that there is one underlying factor which places a cultural
stamp on American Surrealism: the emphasis on the fact and its corresponding tie to reality.

IV.   A. SCULPTURE: SURVEYS

A-A 235. **ADAMS, ADELINE VALENTINE POND.** The Spirit of American Sculpture.
New York: National Sculpture Society, 1923. 234 pp.
This early work on American sculpture was written in conjunction with
an exhibition sponsored by the National Sculpture Society in 1923. Adams
seeks to contrast the qualities of sculpture created during times of peace
with those of sculpture done under the stress of war. Thus in the former
she sees characteristics of repose and symmetry while in the latter she
observes agitation and disjunction. Her object is to uncover formal and
expressive features in the examples she discusses rather than to deal
with the patriotic, historical, biographical, and civic themes most of
the works present.

A-A 236. **BRODER, PATRICIA JANIS.** Bronzes of the American West. New York:
Abrams, 1974. 431 pp.
As Harold McCracken notes in the introduction to this book, there was
no comprehensive book on sculpture of the American West before this one.
And, as Broder makes eminently clear, the now legendary world of the cowboys and Indians, popularized and mythologized in novels and the cinema,
fascinated a considerable number of American sculptors, particularly in
the early 20th century. Gutzon and Solon Borglum, Frederick Remington,
Charles M. Russell, and James Earle Fraser are generally well known, but
Broder has also written about many others less familiar who produced notable work. She shows that this subject matter is not extinct; it still
appeals to some sculptors today.

A-A 237. **CRAVEN, WAYNE.** Sculpture in America. New York: Crowell, 1968.
722 pp.
Craven's book of about 600 pages of text recounts the work of scores of
sculptors who contributed to the development of fine art sculpture in
this country. Although he includes a discussion of 20th-century accomplishments, Craven's real interest and affection are for the 19th century.
The book consists of a vast number of carefully detailed sketches of individual sculptors, grouped in approximate chronological sequence and accompanied by brief introductions which provide a fuller context for the artists and their work.

A-A 238. **FRIEDLANDER, LEE.** The American Monument. New York: Eakins
Press, 1976. n.p.
The book is essentially a collection of Lee Friedlander's photographs
of American public sculpture. Friedlander believes that the significance
of civil statuary and sculptural monuments has been overlooked in the
history of American art, and his purpose here is to provide a visual record
of some of them. An essay by Leslie Katz provides descriptive and tech-

nical information for each of the sculptures illustrated. Katz suggests
that an analysis of the works would reveal much of interest regarding
changing attitudes toward war, immigration, and other aspects of American
culture.

A-A 239. TAFT, LORADO. The History of American Sculpture. 1903; Rev.
ed. New York: Macmillan, 1930. 622 pp.
In this early synthesis, Taft divides the history of American sculpture
into three periods: beginnings, 1750-1850; middle, 1850-1876; and contemporary, 1876-1903. A supplementary chapter by Adeline Adams was added
in 1923 to bring the work up to that date. Taft suggests that the early
American colonists did not arrive from England with a vital sculptural
tradition, because British sculpture of the period was inferior. Therefore,
Taft argues, American sculpture did not have a basis from which it could
develop, and so it took until 1850 for America to begin to produce significant works. The middle period saw the appearance of several American Neoclassical masters, some of whom Taft believes compare with the
great sculptors of Europe. Taft sees America finding its own distinctive
and pluralistic way in the contemporary period.

A-A 240. 200 Years of American Sculpture. New York: Whitney Museum
of American Art, 1976. 350 pp.
This heavily illustrated publication, recording a bicentennial exhibition
at the Whitney, is an introductory treatment of American sculpture. While
the 20th century is emphasized, the volume attempts to be inclusive; most
varieties of American sculpture, if not discussed at length, are at least
mentioned. Seven scholars contributed to the volume: Norman Feder discusses American Indian objects; Wayne Craven deals with the 19th century;
Tom Armstrong with folk sculpture; Daniel Robbins with sculpture created
between 1890 and 1930; Rosalind Krauss, 1930 to 1950; and Barbara Haskell
and Marcia Tucker each write about more recent work.

IV. B. SCULPTURE: COLONIAL

A-A 241. BENES, PETER. The Masks of Orthodoxy: Folk Gravestone Carving
in Plymouth County, Massachusetts, 1689-1805. Amherst: University of Massachusetts Press, 1977. 273 pp.
Benes identifies three schools of county gravestone cutters, and he forms
three hypotheses about the artistic intentions of those carvers. First,
the skull images probably symbolized ghosts and spirits rather than Death;
second, the animated facial caricatures resulted from a deliberate refine-
ment and a playful manipulation of traditional design motifs to illustrate
complex religious concepts of grace, resurrection, and salvation; third,
the visual language of the grave markers derived from a Puritan folk
heraldry that was itself representative of the spiritual attitudes of a
local community.

A-A 242. BREWINGTON, MARION VERNON. Shipcarvers of North America. Barre,
Mass.: Barre, 1962. 173 pp.
With the advent of "ironclad" vessels, the American shipcarver was gradually put out of business. Today, his work is relegated to a few public
museums and to various private collections where the objects are frequently
used as architectural ornament or garden sculpture. Because of the scattered nature of this material, the author makes no claim of completeness
in this small book. The text is chronological with numerous illustrations.
A list of American shipcarvers and a detailed study of the figureheads
of the frigate Constitution are appended.

A-A 243. FORBES, HARRIETTE M. Gravestones of Early New England and the
          Men Who Made Them, 1653-1800. Boston: Houghton Mifflin, 1927.
          141 pp.
In this early study, Forbes considers several prominent stonecutters whose
gravestones are representative of the type of work done in the Boston
area. She discusses the nature of gravestone art as well as its symbolism.
The carvers are primarily from Massachusetts, but there are two chapters
on the gravestones of Rhode Island and Connecticut. An appendix of early
New England stonecutters follows the text.

A-A 244. LUDWIG, ALLAN I. Graven Images: New England Stonecarving and
          Its Symbols, 1650-1815. Middletown, Conn.: Wesleyan University
          Press, 1966. 482 pp.
The first chapter of this book is both a general discussion of the complex
relationship of image, religion, and symbol and a specific treatment of
the historical context of Puritan art, theology, and ritual. Succeeding
chapters analyze New England gravestones in terms of visual vocabulary,
design sources, stylistic evolution, and individuation among the identifiable craftsmen. Ludwig utilizes the iconographic method of linking
pictorial emblems with contemporary literary sources to arrive at an important conclusion: the "iconophobic" Puritans not only produced religious
art, but imbued their visual imagery with profound symbolic meaning.

A-A 245. PINCKNEY, PAULINE. American Figureheads and Their Carvers.
          New York: Norton, 1940. 223 pp.
Pinckney's book was the first to examine American ship carving in detail.
Although there were many more merchant ships than naval vessels, she concentrates on the latter because of their greater documentation. Pinckney
attempts to define the hands of many carvers, and her appendixes include
a list of carvers, a list of extant figureheads, contemporary descriptions
of figureheads, and a chapter-by-chapter bibliography.

A-A 246. TASHJIAN, DICKRAN and ANN TASHJIAN. Memorials for Children of
          Change: The Art of Early New England Stonecarving. Middletown,
          Conn.: Wesleyan University Press, 1974. 309 pp.
The Tashjians' book picks up where Forbes and Ludwig left off (see A-A
243 and 244). In this well-documented study of New England gravestones,
they consider the object first and foremost as a cultural artifact, a
reflection of a group of ideas and values. Puritan attitudes toward art
are considered alongside iconographic problems and discussions of specific
regions and shops. An appendix gives over 160 epitaphs which illustrate
the text and are, for the most part, rubbings taken from the actual stones.

A-A 247. WATTERS, DAVID H. "With Bodilie Eyes": Eschatological Themes
          in Puritan Literature and Gravestone Art. Ann Arbor, Mich.:
          UMI Research Press, 1981. 225 pp.
"Bodilie eyes," a term coined by Increase Mather in the 17th century,
describes the moment at the Resurrection when the elect see the beauty
of Christ and the Millennium through "human but glorified eyes." Watters
sees this as the underlying concept of Puritan eschatological literature
(particularly Edward Taylor's poetry) and gravestone art. He asserts
that this singular concept pervaded all levels of New England culture
in the 17th century. His is an iconographic study, emphasizing the continuities between literature and art.

163

IV.   C. SCULPTURE: 19TH CENTURY

A-A 248. CAFFIN, CHARLES HENRY. American Masters of Sculpture. New York:
            Doubleday, Page, 1913. 195 pp.
Caffin reacts against the expatriate movement which demanded that American
sculptors work in Florence and Rome. He applauds his contemporaries,
the "new" generation, who chose Parisian academies for their training
and who subsequently returned home to do "American" subjects. He rejects
the overly sentimental Italian sculpture in favor of the French sensitivity
to modelling and surface texture. Eleven American sculptors receive individual chapters. The text concludes with an examination of "The Decorative
Motive" and "The Ideal Motive."

A-A 249. CLARK, WILLIAM J. Great American Sculptures. Philadelphia:
            Gebbie & Barrie, 1878. 144 pp.
In this early attempt to analyze the 19th-century American Neoclassic
style in sculpture, Clark contrasts the American works with Classical
sculpture from Greece and Rome. He suggests that the American sculptures
adapted similar norms of beauty to modern times where the gods and rulers
of the Classical World have been replaced by human heroes from literature
and history. Clark includes brief biographical sketches of the most prominent sculptors, but he devotes most of the text to a description and analysis of individual works. He suggests that with the work of its Neoclassical sculptors, American sculpture had at last reached a maturity of expression with its own distinctive values.

A-A 250. GARDNER, ALBERT TEN EYCK. Yankee Stonecutters: The First Ameri-
            can School of Sculpture, 1800-1850. New York: Columbia Uni-
            versity Press, 1947. 84 pp.
Gardner argues that the American expatriate sculptors who worked in Rome
and Florence during the middle of the 19th century created the "first
school" of American sculpture. However, he believes that the works they
produced cannot compare with European work in the Neoclassical style.
The American work should be considered as an expression of prevailing
American social and cultural attitudes, Gardner suggests. The sculptures
reflect the tastes of American patrons of the period for the sentimental
and the pretentious. Gardner concludes that the American Neoclassical
style in sculpture was ultimately inferior because it was only a superficial imitation of an important European movement.

A-A 251. GERDTS, WILLIAM H. American Neo-Classic Sculpture: The Marble
            Resurrection. New York: Viking Press, 1973. 160 pp.
This work discusses Neoclassicism as the favorite mode of American high
culture sculptors in the middle years of the 19th century. Gerdts has
organized his material in two ways: first, he provides a chronological
discussion of the sculptors--Horatio Greenough, Thomas Crawford, Hiram
Powers, William Henry Rinehart, and many others; then he offers an illustrated treatment of major sculptural themes: female nude, male nude,
group compositions, funerary monuments, fountain sculpture, biblical themes,
the American Indian, and hand and foot sculpture.

A-A 252. THORP, MARGARET. The Literary Sculptors. Durham, N.C.: Duke
            University Press, 1965. 206 pp.
According to Thorp, what is usually called Neoclassical sculpture may
be defined as sculpture presenting or alluding to a literary or narrative
theme. She believes that American sculptors of the 19th century were
primarily concerned with expressing themes of patriotism. Even those
expatriates who chose to live and work in Florence and Rome produced allegorical works dealing with ideas of freedom and the value of the individual

traditionally associated with life and politics in America. Thorp argues
that their interest in such themes gained in intensity in proportion to
the perspective and appreciation they acquired by their exodus from an
America they believed was ignoring its traditional values and turning
toward materialism. She suggests that patriotic themes in American sculpture were as much a revitalization of patriotism from abroad as they were
expressions of contemporary sentiment back home.

IV.   D. SCULPTURE: 20TH CENTURY

A-A 253. ANDERSEN, WAYNE V. American Sculpture in Process, 1930-1970.
          Boston: New York Graphic Society, 1975. 278 pp.
The book attempts to uncover the origins of such movements as minimalist,
Pop, and earth art. Andersen believes most of them can be traced to the
social and artistic discontents of the 1930s when traditional and formalist
art became closely associated with an oppressive elite and political conservatism. By searching out new materials and techniques, Andersen suggests that American sculptors attempted to find alternatives to "collectors' art" and to create works for environments other than the museum.
Andersen concludes that the process of creation may hold more significance
as a social expression for some American sculptors than the finished work
itself.

A-A 254. ASHTON, DORE. Modern American Sculpture. New York: Abrams,
          1968. 54 pp.
The sculptures considered in this work are mostly from the New York School
and include works by George Rickey, Alexander Calder, Gary Segal, David
Smith, and Leonard Baskin. Ashton tries to find a common stylistic link
between them. Ultimately she traces all the major "Progressive" 20th-
century American trends back to sculpture inspired by European work.
Thus Cubism, Surrealism, Dada, and other European movements emerge as
forerunners of modern American sculpture in Ashton's view.

A-A 255. BATTOCK, GREGORY, ed. Idea Art: A Critical Anthology. New
          York: Dutton, 1973. 203 pp.
The fifteen essays by Ursula Meyer, Jack Burnham, and others in this volume
define idea art very broadly; they include body art and earth art under
the rubric. Idea art emerges from the essays as being any art more concerned with theory than with the objects or events presented by the work.
The essays deal with artistic ideologies behind such issues as art and
politics, art and the environment, anti-art, art criticism, and other
topics of a similar conceptual nature. The purpose of the book as stated
by Battock is to provide a basis for understanding the meanings behind
a variegated array of conceptual forms and techniques.

A-A 256. BURNHAM, JACK. Beyond Modern Sculpture: The Effects of Science
          and Technology on the Sculpture of This Century. New York:
          Braziller, 1968. 402 pp.
Burnham attempts an overview of the origins and developments of contemporary sculpture beginning with the post-W.W. II period and continuing
into the 1960s. He emphasizes the disillusionment of modern sculptors
with the purpose and aesthetic of traditional sculpture. Burnham suggests
that the sculptors first rejected the inherited aesthetic basis of sculpture and then began to formulate a variety of new aesthetics. He argues
that scientific principles and technological advances played a vital role
in the definition of the new sculpture. Burnham sees such forms and styles
as Constructivism, automata, kinetic sculpture, and light sculpture as

being expressive of the hope that science may hold the key to aesthetic and creative discovery.

A-A 257. Fourteen Sculptors: The Industrial Edge. Minneapolis, Minn.: Walker Art Center, 1969. 53 pp.
Christopher Finch, Morton Friedman, and Barbara Rose contributed essays to this catalogue. They suggest that there is a coherent school in contemporary American sculpture characterized by the use of such common industrial materials as aluminum, structural steel, glass, and plastic. Friedman stresses that by using commercially available materials, the sculptors are attempting to provide a synthesis between art and industry. Rose believes that artists today are as accomplished in the manipulation of common materials as are industrialists, but sculptors apply their proficiency to different ends. Finch finds a commentary on materialism in the works by these sculptors because he believes they are attempting to re-direct the meanings in industrial techniques by adapting them to an artistic idealism.

A-A 258. HARTMANN, SADAKICHI, ed. Modern American Sculpture: A Representative Collection of the Principal Statues, Reliefs, Busts, Statuettes and Specimens of Decorative and Municipal Work, Executed by the Foremost Sculptors in America Within the Last Twenty Years. New York: Paul Wenzel, 1918. 62 pp.
Every sculptor of importance at the time is represented here by at least one work. The volume serves as a record of taste in a period for which there is little available visual documentation. The sculpture is primarily in the beaux-arts tradition, and it is representative of public and architectural sculpture at the turn of the century. War memorials, American heroes, Indians, and themes from ancient Greece and Rome predominate. Many now famous works by Frederic Remington and Augustus St. Gaudens are illustrated in the context of their contemporaries. Hartmann suggests that he has illustrated all the sculptures which most influenced the design of public monuments throughout the U.S.

A-A 259. KAPROW, ALLAN. Assemblage, Environments & Happenings. New York: Abrams, 1966. 341 pp.
Conceived as a document of the period (late 1950s and early 1960s) which saw the rejection of traditional artistic media and traditional artists' identities, Assemblage sandwiches Kaprow's text between two extensive photographic sections. As an artist, Kaprow discusses artists' concerns: materials, attitudes toward art, and the creators themselves. He differentiates between assemblage, environments, and happenings, suggesting that the latter grew out of the freedom and spontaneity of the first two. Among the artists whose happenings are photographically reproduced are Wolf Vostell, Kenneth Dewey, and Kaprow himself.

A-A 260. LICHT, JENNIFER. Spaces. New York: Museum of Modern Art, 1969. n.p.
This is an exhibition catalogue of environmental installations and light art projects by Michael Asher, Larry Bell, Dan Flavin, Robert Morris, Pulsa (Group), and Franz Walther. Licht describes their work as examples of "contemporary investigations of actual, real space as a nonplastic, yet malleable, agent in art." The sculptures, she believes, create new spaces or imply space where none previously existed by delimiting or contradicting existing space with light.

A-A 261. MARSHALL, RICHARD and SUZANNE FOLEY. Ceramic Sculpture: Six
          Artists. Seattle: University of Washington Press, 1981.
          144 pp.
This exhibition catalogue traces the development of ceramic sculpture
in California from its beginnings in the mid-1950s. The authors point
out that since the 1950s ceramic sculpture has become an important part
of the curriculum in many university art departments, a fact which they
suggest indicates its importance as a major art form. The six artists
discussed in this catalogue are Peter Voulkes, John Mason, Kenneth Price,
Robert Arneson, David Gilhooly, and Robert Shaw. The authors contend
that these six sculptors have established the medium of ceramic sculpture
on an equal basis with contemporary painting and sculpture in other media.

A-A 262. MEYER, URSULA. Conceptual Art. New York: Dutton, 1972.
          227 pp.
Meyer defines conceptual sculpture as work in which the idea behind the
material presence of the object is not important. According to her, conceptual sculptors wish to restore artistic values to sculpture in the
midst of what they perceive to be a growing tendency toward materialism
and a commodity art market. Because of an emphasis on ideas rather than
the object itself, Meyer suggests that conceptual sculpture can at times
appear to be "anti-sculptural." But she maintains that conceptual sculptors do not disdain the finished work. Rather they exhibit a deep concern
for the meanings of the materials they use, and they seek to re-establish
those meanings in the commercial market place.

A-A 263. SCHNIER, JACQUES PRESTON. Sculpture in Modern America. Berkeley:
          University of California Press, 1948. 224 pp.
Schnier's study surveys general movements in American sculpture under
three main divisions: Realism, Surrealism, and Expressionism. The purpose
is to present in broad strokes the main features of work done shortly
before, during, and after W.W. II. Illustrations are grouped by topics:
heads, figures, animals, and reliefs. By analyzing developments and permutations in each of these categories, Schnier traces the evolution of
modern American sculpture out of the beaux-arts and Neoclassical styles.

A-A 264. SEITZ, WILLIAM C. The Art of Assemblage. New York: Museum
          of Modern Art, 1961. 176 pp.
The catalogue of a major exhibition, this work surveys "found-object"
sculpture and collage as specific and distinct media. It also relates
assemblage to equivalent forms in literature and music. In a section
on "Attitudes and Issues," Seitz attempts to define the art of assemblage
in terms of the ideas behind the techniques. He establishes the art of
assemblage as a conceptual sculpture. Found objects, on the other hand,
he suggests, have associations with the randomness of the real world.
Collages, according to Seitz, deal more with a traditional artistic formalism. While the book treats some European artists, it also includes discussions of such leading Americans as Joseph Cornell and Louise Nevelson.

A-A 265. SHARP, WILLOUGHBY and WILLIAM C. LIPKE. Earth Art. Ithaca,
          N.Y.: Cornell University Press, 1970. n.p.
This catalogue is a cooperative attempt by artists and critics to establish
the meaning and limits of earth art. Nine artists took part in the effort,
and they produced works for an exhibition at Cornell University immediately
before it opened. Sharp offers an overview of the history of earth art,
tracing its development out of ancient earth mounds and pyramids. Lipke
tries to establish a critical rationale for the form. He sees a meaning
in the works exhibited expressed by their relation to the real topography
of the actual global environment. Lipke believes that earth art strives
to break away from the confines of the museum and establish art as a function of the real world.

A-A 266. TUCHMAN, MAURICE, ed. American Sculpture of the Sixties. Los
Angeles: Los Angeles County Museum of Art, 1967. 258 pp.
Almost every major sculptor of the 1960s offers comments in this anthology.
Although no single theme is developed, the artists' statements provide
insight into the sculpture of the period. The book illustrates many of
their works, and it includes a section listing exhibitions, biographical
data, and bibliographical references for such sculptors as Dan Flavin,
Alexander Calder, Anthony Caro, John Chamberlain, Donald Judd, Robert
Rauschenberg, Claes Oldenburg, George Segal, David Smith, George Rickey,
and Lucas Samaras. Ten critical essays on various subjects are also
included in the catalogue.

A-A 267. Vanguard American Sculpture, 1913-1939. New Brunswick, N.J.:
Rutgers University Art Gallery, 1979. 161 pp.
This exhibition catalogue undertakes to identify and define the avant-
garde characteristics in early 20th-century American sculpture. The analysis does not indicate that there was a particular style or school to which
the sculpture adhered, but it suggests that there were features in the
American work which can be related to modernist movements in Europe.
The term "vanguard" is chosen to embrace all these aspects of Modernism
as they appeared in American sculpture. "Vanguard" also includes the
streamlined and the machine aesthetic as they developed in America. Essays
on Dada, Surrealism, art deco, and early nonobjective sculpture deal with
their transformations in American sculpture. The essays also associate
some of the American manifestations of the vanguard with progressive social
innovations of the 1930s.

A-A 268. VARIAN, ELAYNE H. Art in Process: The Visual Development of
a Collage. New York: Finch College Museum of Art, 1966.
32 pp.
This exhibition catalogue attempts to present collage as a process rather
than as a finished work of art. The works-in-process range from the traditional collage to what is now called an assemblage. Projects by Claes
Oldenburg, Robert Rauschenberg, Larry Rivers, and Theodoros Stamos are
illustrated in various stages of completion. The illustrations also show
preliminary sketches and tests of materials and techniques relevant to
the works. Photographs, literary and biographical associations, and whatever else contributed to the sculptor's creative approach are included.
The stated object of the catalogue is to reveal as much as possible about
the motivations and presumptions behind each piece.

V.   A. WORKS ON PAPER: SURVEYS

A-A 269. GARDNER, ALBERT TEN EYCK. History of Water Color Painting in
America. New York: Van Nostrand Reinhold, 1966. 160 pp.
Gardner discusses general technical aspects of watercolor painting and
cites the 18th-century and 19th-century English influence as seminal for
the development of the medium in America. His book was one of the first
considerations of the specific medium of watercolor painting in American
art. In his short text, Gardner refrains from developing his points in
great detail.

A-A 270. GOLDMAN, JUDITH. American Prints: Process & Proof. New York:
Whitney Museum of American Art, 1981. 176 pp.
This exhibition catalogue fulfills two functions: It provides a general
survey of 300 years of American printmaking, and it highlights the work
of fourteen contemporary painter/printmakers. As the title indicates,

the emphasis is on the creative process of making a print. Working and trial proofs constitute a major portion of the exhibition. Part I gives a general survey of the development of the American print from 1670 to 1960. Building on this background, Part II examines in detail several works by Chuck Close, Jim Dine, Vincent Longo, Philip Pearlstein, Frank Stella, and others.

A-A 271. HORNUNG, CLARENCE P. and FRIDOLF JOHNSON. 200 Years of American Graphic Art: A Retrospective Survey of the Printing Arts and Advertising Since the Colonial Period. New York: Braziller, 1976. 211 pp.
The authors have divided what is actually over 300 years of the development of the graphic arts in America into nine chronological sections. Each section begins with a concise (five-page) summary of the political, social, economic, and technological influences on the art of printing during that period, followed by numerous illustrations of the graphic styles discussed. The book is most useful to anyone already familiar with printing terminology and techniques, since the authors frequently employ terms of the trade without benefit of definition or explanation. The book is well indexed and includes a secondary bibliography arranged by subject.

A-A 272. MEYER, SUSAN E. America's Great Illustrators. New York: Abrams, 1978. 311 pp.
In America's Great Illustrators Meyer offers evidence of the craft and imagination of ten illustrators prominent in the late 19th and early 20th century: Howard Pyle, N. C. Wyeth, Frederic Remington, Maxfield Parrish, J. C. Leyendecker, Norman Rockwell, Charles Dana Gibson, Howard Chandler Christy, James Montgomery Flagg, and John Held, Jr. Meyer starts with a brief historical survey of publishing and the periodicals that employed these artists, and then comments on the artists' life styles and their attitudes toward their work. Each artist is then discussed individually.

A-A 273. MORSE, JOHN D., ed. Prints in and of America to 1850: Winterthur Conference Report 1970. Charlottesville: University Press of Virginia, 1970. 355 pp.
The papers delivered at the 1970 Winterthur Conference deal with printmaking in America from first attempts in 16th-century Mexico and 17th-century New England to the growing market and competence evident in the 18th century. Additional presentations on the influence of the English Whig tradition of dissent on pre-Revolutionary America, scientific illustration, counterfeit printing, lithographic technology, and the popularity of sheet music covers extend the range of topics and the volume's temporal scope.

A-A 274. SHADWELL, WENDY J., et al. American Printmaking: The First 150 Years. New York: Museum of Graphic Art, 1969. 180 pp.
This volume is a catalogue of an exhibition organized by the Museum of Graphic Art and circulated to several other institutions. It illustrates and discusses 115 prints produced between 1670 and 1821. Although a few prints produced in England are included, the majority were made in the U.S. The volume has virtually no text in the normal sense, but Shadwell has written paragraph captions to accompany each catalogue entry. Read in sequence, these become a text of sorts and provide a good deal of information about the prints and their context.

A-A 275. STEBBINS, THEODORE E., Jr., with the assistance of JOHN CALDWELL
and CAROL TROYEN. American Master Drawings and Watercolors:
A History of Works on Paper from Colonial Times to the Present.
New York: Harper & Row, 1976. 464 pp.
Stebbins's survey of American drawings and watercolors from the 17th century to the present treats major and little-known artists, including Native
Americans and expatriates, as well as foreign-born draftsmen who produced
important work in America. The study discusses stylistic trends, cultural
contexts, and the uses, collecting, and exhibition of drawings. The text
is keyed to the illustrations of 360 drawings, watercolors, gouaches,
and pastels (but not architectural drawings or cartoons). A complete
bibliography is included.

A-A 276. WEITENKAMPF, FRANK. American Graphic Art. 1912; Rev. ed. New
York: Macmillan, 1924. 328 pp.
Originally published more than seventy years ago, this remains the most
complete study of American printmaking. Weitenkampf's approach is topical
rather than chronological, with each chapter devoted to a specific medium.
Weitenkampf considers etching, engraving, mezzotint, aquatint, wood-
engraving, lithography, comics, bookplates, and posters, and he includes
a lengthy bibliography and index.

V.   B. WORKS ON PAPER: COLONIAL

A-A 277. Boston Prints and Printmakers, 1670-1775. Charlottesville:
University Press of Virginia, 1973. 294 pp.
This is a collection of eight papers given at a conference sponsored by
the Colonial Society of Massachusetts. The foreword by Walter Muir
Whitehill and Sinclair H. Hitchings outlines some of the conclusions reached
by the participants during their discussions. The papers themselves touch
on Boston topography, heraldic and emblematic engraving, scientific illustration, prints of the American Indian, and several individual printmakers.

A-A 278. DREPPERD, CARL WILLIAM. Early American Prints. New York: Century, 1930. 232 pp.
Drepperd's text is written for the amateur collector. He gives general
printmaking information regarding processes and states and summarily treats
Colonial prints, revolutionary prints, engravings, lithography, book and
magazine illustration, and caricature. Currier and Ives receive special
attention. Most of the book is devoted to lists of artists and selected
examples of their work.

A-A 279. WICK, WENDY C. George Washington: An American Icon. The Eighteenth-Century Graphic Portraits. Washington, D.C.: Smithsonian Institution Travelling Exhibition Service and the National
Portrait Gallery, 1982. 186 pp.
This book and the exhibition it documents celebrate the 250th anniversary
of George Washington's birth. While thousands of portrait prints of Washington have been published, the focus here is on those made during his
lifetime. In order to gain the broadest insight into his contemporary
culture, book and magazine illustrations, broadsides, almanacs, music
sheets, and primers with Washington's likeness are included. He is considered as a military commander, a president, and a national symbol.
Catalogue entries, notes, references, a checklist, and an index follow
the essays.

V. C. WORKS ON PAPER: 19TH CENTURY

A-A 280. Art & Commerce: American Prints of the Nineteenth Century. Charlottesville: University Press of Virginia, 1978. 179 pp. Eight papers given at the American Prints Conference in Boston (1975) are collected in this volume. An effort was made to give equal treatment to "prints made for the masses" and "artistic," limited-edition prints. A recurrent theme is the mechanization of the printmaking process in the 19th century. The essays deal with whaling panoramas, chromolithography, painter-lithographers, and monotypes. Appended is a checklist of a concurrent exhibition held at the Museum of Fine Arts, Boston.

A-A 281. GLANZ, DAWN. How the West Was Drawn: American Art and the Settling of the Frontier. Ann Arbor, Mich.: UMI Research Press, 1982. 205 pp. A revision of her doctoral dissertation, Glanz's book is an iconographic study of westward expansion in 19th-century America. She considers not only how the West was drawn, but also how it was painted and sculpted. Images of the West, she feels, can be related to the broader issues of American culture studies. The four chapters examine 19th-century representations of Daniel Boone, fur trappers and traders, pioneers and homesteaders, and wild animals.

A-A 282. HOOPES, DONELSON F., GUDMUND VIGTEL, and WEND VON KALNEIN. The Dusseldorf Academy and the Americans. Atlanta, Ga.: High Museum of Art, 1973. 135 pp. Watercolors and drawings make up this comparative exhibition of the German masters of the Dusseldorf Academy and the American students who came there during the middle decades of the 19th century. The Dusseldorf tradition, one of "gloss and sentiment," can be seen in the works of such Americans as George Caleb Bingham and Eastman Johnson, as well as in the landscapes of William Trost Richards and William Stanley Haseltine. Hoopes discusses the American importation of the Academy style, and Von Kalnein, the director of the Dusseldorf art museum, concentrates on the German teachers themselves.

A-A 283. LOONEY, ROBERT F., ed. Philadelphia Printmaking: American Prints before 1860. West Chester, Pa.: Tinicum Press, 1977. 175 pp. This volume commemorates the fourth American Prints Conference held in 1973. Eight papers by such scholars as Sinclair H. Hitchings, Peter C. Marzio, E. P. Richardson, and Alan Fern are here published for the first time. The subjects include print sellers, American drawing books, political caricature, and several monographic studies of artists (i.e., Mathew Clark, William Charles, Thomas Doughty, and John Plumbe).

A-A 284. M. and M. Karolik Collection of American Watercolors and Drawings, 1800-1875. 2 vols. Boston: Museum of Fine Arts, Boston, 1962. 682 pp. These two volumes catalogue almost half of the vast collection of works on paper given to the Museum of Fine Arts, Boston, by the Karoliks. There are well-researched entries for 1465 works. Volume 1 deals with some 200 "academic" artists, while Volume 2 covers visiting foreign artists, Civil War artists, and folk artists. Illustrations are numerous, and a series of appendices lists artists, portrait sitters, places represented, and subjects.

A-A 285. MARZIO, PETER C. The Democratic Art: Pictures for a 19th-Century
          America. Boston: Godine, 1979. 357 pp.
Marzio's large book is a study of chromolithography in America from 1840
to 1900. Although he focuses on the colored lithograph as a means of
reproducing paintings for the mass public, the role of chromolithography
in advertising is also discussed. Marzio considers materials, machines,
distribution, artists, and buyers. Particular emphasis is given to the
place of chromolithography in American life. The notes and the bibliography are extensive. Two appendices list chromolithographic color formulas
used from 1860 to 1890 and a list of chromos advertised for sale by New
York dealer George Munro in 1880.

A-A 286. MORITZ, ALBERT F. America the Picturesque in Nineteenth Century
          Engraving. New York: New Trend, 1983. 167 pp.
Moritz examines the period when American engraved illustration was at
its height. Both the traveling engravers who interpreted the landscape
and events around them and the engravers (sometimes the same men) who
did copies of landscape paintings are considered. Considerable attention
is given to European (English) developments which shaped American engraving
and helped mold the hybrid American idiom of the picturesque. Two important books are considered in detail: American Scenery (1840) and Picturesque America (1872).

V.   D. WORKS ON PAPER: 20TH CENTURY

A-A 287. ADAMS, CLINTON. American Lithographers 1900-1960: The Artists
          and Their Printers. Albuquerque: University of New Mexico
          Press, 1983. 228 pp.
Unlike the established media of etching and engraving, the technique of
lithography has had a checkered history in America. An artist himself,
Adams traces the vain attempts of early 20th-century artists to exhibit
and sell their lithographs. He describes the wide use of lithography
by Social Realists and Regionalists and its subsequent rejection by
Abstract Expressionists. His focus is on individual artists and their
printers. A technical appendix explains the various lithographic processes.

A-A 288. CUMMINGS, PAUL. American Drawings: The 20th Century. New York:
          Viking Press, 1976. 207 pp.
One to three drawings by 118 artists from Thomas Dewing to Christo are
reproduced in this survey. In his short introduction, Cummings sketches
the broadest possible overview of American art of the 20th century, giving
less attention to drawing than to the general currents of the national
art scene. Each artistic stylistic evolution in works on paper is then
characterized in a series of brief statements.

A-A 289. JOHNSON, UNA E. American Prints and Printmakers: A Chronicle
          of Over 400 Artists and Their Prints from 1900 to the Present.
          Garden City, N.Y.: Doubleday, 1980. 266 pp.
Johnson's book is the first general survey of American printmaking of
the 20th century. Her approach is loosely chronological, but because
of the variety of techniques and means of expression, different subjects
are frequently interwoven. Topics discussed include the Mexican influence,
Regionalism, prints by sculptors, monotypes, embossed prints, graphic
workshops, and the relationship of prints to the painting movements of
the 1960s and 1970s.

A-A 290. ROSE, BERNICE. Drawing Now. New York: Museum of Modern Art,
          1976. 96 pp.
In a substantial catalogue essay, Rose examines contemporary drawing beginning about 1960. She emphasizes the historical traditions of the medium
and the manner in which 20th-century practice differs from and at the
same time perpetuates drawings of the past. Each artist receives a short
biography and list of references. While there are some Europeans included,
the emphasis is on American artists. Particularly well represented are
Jim Dine, Jasper Johns, Roy Lichtenstein, Robert Rauschenberg, and Cy
Twombly.

VI. NON-ACADEMIC PAINTING AND SCULPTURE

A-A 291. American Folk Art: The Art of the Common Man in America, 1750-
          1900. New York: Museum of Modern Art, 1932. 152 pp.
An introductory essay written by Holger Cahill defines folk art as the
work of people with little book learning in art techniques and with no
formal academic training. According to Cahill, the great period of American folk art was from 1650 to 1875, with New England and Pennsylvania
as the most productive areas. Originally published as a catalogue for
an exhibition of American folk art at the Museum of Modern Art, the book
also contains detailed notes on the artists and objects presented.

A-A 292. American Folk Art: The Herbert Waide Hemphill Jr. Collection.
          Milwaukee, Wis.: Milwaukee Art Museum, 1981. 112 pp.
This catalogue for a travelling exhibition features three extended essays:
(1) Herbert W. Hemphill discusses his collection and how it was built;
(2) Russell Bowman analyzes some of the contradictory attitudes toward
what constitutes American folk art; and (3) Donald B. Kuspit examines
the attitudes of and toward makers of folk objects in the 20th century.
The Hemphill collection is said here to represent and to include almost
every type of object that might fit any of the various definitions of
American folk art.

A-A 293. American Folk Sculpture: The Work of Eighteenth and Nineteenth
          Century Craftsmen. Newark, N.J.: Newark Museum, 1931.
          108 pp.
Among the objects represented are ships' figureheads, cigar-store figures,
weathervanes, toys, firemarks, and bird and animal carvings, most of them
dating from the 19th century and primarily from New England and Pennsylvania. In an introductory essay, Holger Cahill notes that the work on
display "is folk art in its truest sense—it is an expression of the common
people and not an expression of a small cultured class." This exhibition
of sculpture complemented an earlier one of painting (called "American
Primitives") at the Newark Museum (see A-A 294).

A-A 294. American Primitives: An Exhibit of the Paintings of Nineteenth
          Century Folk Artists. Newark, N.J.: Newark Museum, 1930.
          76 pp.
This is generally regarded as the first exhibition of what has come to
be known as "folk art" that was held in a major art museum. According
to Holger Cahill's introductory essay, the word "primitive" is used to
describe "the work of simple people with no academic training and little
book learning in art." The paintings are divided into several broad categories, including portraits, landscapes and other scenes, and decorative
pictures.

A-A 295. BISHOP, ROBERT. American Folk Sculpture. New York: Dutton,
         1974. 392 pp.
The author surveys the field of sculpture by self-taught artists who generally were working in rural areas and small towns, from Colonial times
to the present. Their output covers a wide variety of subjects, used
for a wide variety of purposes, and made from a wide variety of materials.
Among the objects described are gravestones, weathervanes, scrimshaw,
decoys, religious objects, whirligigs, trade signs, cigar-store Indians,
and carousel sculpture.

A-A 296. BISHOP, ROBERT. Folk Painters of America. New York: Dutton,
         1979. 255 pp.
In this survey of American folk painting, broadly defined and organized
by geographic region, Bishop identifies two major categories: (1) pictures
that recorded people, places, and time; and (2) paintings that decorated
essentially utilitarian objects (such as signs, fireboards, mantels, carpets, window shades, walls, ceilings, and furniture). The author maintains
that folk painting includes not only "the supreme masterpiece," but also
"the simple genre picture and the crudely painted portrait."

A-A 297. BLACK, MARY and JEAN LIPMAN. American Folk Painting. New York:
         Potter, 1966. 244 pp.
The authors provide a chronological survey of painting from the Colonial
period to the present, with emphasis on the period between the American
Revolution and the Civil War, which they call "the heyday of the American
folk artist." During that time, the work of several types of artists
is examined, including professional portrait painters (both itinerant
and residential); painters of landscapes, townscapes, seascapes, and genre
scenes; painters of colloquial history; art instructors; and fraktur makers.

A-A 298. CHRISTENSEN, EDWIN. Early American Wood Carving. Cleveland,
         Ohio: World, 1952. 149 pp.
This work was the first broad survey of wood carving from the Colonial
era to the end of the 19th century. Because of the variety of objects,
Christensen finds no seizable "American" style of carving. He discusses
academic figures, tavern signs, circus art, portrait busts, architectural
ornament, cake molds, decoys, and New Mexico religious bultos. Academic
art is characterized as being more European in flavor, "folk" art as more
dependent on native talent.

A-A 299. DEWHURST, C. KURT, BETTY MacDOWELL, and MARSHA MacDOWELL. Artists
         in Aprons: Folk Art by American Women. New York: Dutton,
         1979. 202 pp.
This volume focuses on those women who, without formal training or professional stature, produced works of art in their homes that the authors
judge to be of "superior aesthetic quality." The art of roughly seventy-
five women, from Colonial times to the present, including embroideries,
drawings, watercolors, and oil paintings, is described.

A-A 300. DEWHURST, C. KURT, BETTY MacDOWELL, and MARSHA MacDOWELL. Religi-
         ous Folk Art in America: Reflections of Faith. New York:
         Dutton, 1983. 163 pp.
Although many of the objects described in this survey of American religious
art are not the products of traditional folk culture, the authors try
to focus on those objects that are. As a result, their coverage extends
not only to the religious paintings and carvings of independent artists
working outside of any folk tradition, but also to the material culture
and folkways that serve as religious expressions for a number of traditional groups.

A-A 301. EBERT, JOHN and KATHERINE EBERT. American Folk Painters. New
York: Scribner, 1975. 225 pp.
The authors survey the development of non-academic painting in the U.S.
from roughly 1700 to 1900. A wide range of painting types is discussed,
including portraits, ship and marine pictures, still-lifes, landscapes,
patriotic and religious paintings, frakturs, and calligraphy. Considerable
attention is placed on the artists themselves, with an attempt made throughout to distinguish the professional from the amateur.

A-A 302. ERICSON, JACK T., ed. Folk Art in America: Painting and Sculpture. New York: Mayflower Books, 1979. 175 pp.
This is an anthology of articles on non-academic painting and sculpture
that were published in the magazine Antiques from 1935 to 1977. Ericson
has organized the material into three sections: (1) attempts at defining
"folk art," including the 1950 symposium on "What Is American Folk Art";
(2) paintings, especially portraiture; and (3) sculpture, especially gravestones, weathervanes, and wood carvings.

A-A 303. ESPINOSA, JOSE E. Saints in the Valleys: Christian Sacred Images
in the History, Life and Folk Art of Spanish New Mexico. Albuquerque: University of New Mexico Press, 1960. 122 pp.
Examining the religious folk art of Spanish New Mexico during the years
from 1775 to 1900, Espinosa provides some historical background before
discussing the classification and technology of the santos—both retablos
(painted boards) and bultos (statues)—as well as their images in New
Mexican life. He notes that the motivation of New Mexican folk artists
is analogous to that of the carvers and painters of medieval Europe in
that they did not always establish convincing likenesses as their goal.

A-A 304. FORD, ALICE. Pictorial Folk Art: New England to California.
New York: Studio, 1949. 172 pp.
In this broad survey of non-academic painting from Colonial times to the
present, Ford examines a wide variety of types, including: portraiture;
landscape painting; religious and allegorical painting; historical and
patriotic painting; genre and still-life painting; female seminary art;
scrimshaw drawing; and regional painting and drawing. There is also a
concluding chapter on "the rediscovery of American folk art" in our own
time.

A-A 305. FRIED, FREDERICK. Artists in Wood: American Carvers of Cigar-
Store Indians, Show Figures, and Circus Wagons. New York:
Potter, 1970. 320 pp.
Fried's book is as much a detective story as it is a history of the work
of American woodcarvers. Because this area of folk sculpture lay largely
unexplored, the research tasks were formidable. Nevertheless, Fried offers
thirty-eight biographies of the artists who carved shop figures, cigar-
store Indians, and circus wagons in the 18th and 19th centuries. A number
of appendices follow the text, listing artists, auctions, and collections
of show figures.

A-A 306. HEMPHILL, HERBERT WAIDE, Jr., ed. Folk Sculpture USA. Brooklyn,
N.Y.: Brooklyn Museum, 1976. 96 pp.
This catalogue for an exhibition of American sculpture spans three centuries (the 18th through the 20th) and several ethnic groups (Anglo-
American, Spanish-American). The objects in the exhibition were selected
on the basis of their aesthetic merit and for their evocation of the individualistic visions of artists working outside the mainstream of American
culture.

A-A 307. HEMPHILL, HERBERT WAIDE, Jr. and JULIA WEISSMAN. Twentieth-
Century American Folk Art and Artists. New York: Dutton, 1974.
237 pp.
Some 130 artists, working in many different media, are represented in
this survey of art and artists in the 20th century. The authors maintain
that the vision of the folk artist is a private one: a personal universe,
a world of his or her own making. Among the types of objects covered
are needlepoint, wood sculpture, and works in crayon, watercolor, oil,
and acrylic.

A-A 308. KAUFFMAN, HENRY. Pennsylvania Dutch: American Folk Art. 1946;
Rev. ed. New York: Dover, 1964. 146 pp.
Kauffman notes that the spirit of Pennsylvania Dutch craftsmanship flourished during the years from 1750 to 1850, reaching a peak in the first
half of the 19th century. After providing some historical background
on the Pennsylvania Dutch, the author surveys a variety of their art forms,
including architecture, furniture, pottery, glasswork, metalwork, textiles
and needlework, and certificates and manuscripts.

A-A 309. KLAMKIN, MARIAN and CHARLES KLAMKIN. Wood Carvings: North American Folk Sculptures. New York: Hawthorn Books, 1974. 213 pp.
The Klamkins survey wood carving in America from Colonial times to the
present, but with emphasis on the 19th century. Among the objects
described are: figureheads, ship carvings, and sailors' carvings; patriotic symbols and parade carvings; trade signs and shop figures; Indian
carvings; weathervanes and whirligigs; circus, carnival, and carousel
carvings; toys, dolls, and small animal figures; bird and fish decoys;
and butter molds and other carved household objects.

A-A 310. LICHTEN, FRANCES. Folk Art of Rural Pennsylvania. New York:
Scribner, 1946. 276 pp.
Focusing on the applied decorative arts of the Pennsylvania Dutch, Lichten
identifies the era of highest craftsmanship as that between the middle
of the 18th century and the middle of the 19th century. Among the types
of objects discussed are plates, linen, coverlets, needlework, baskets,
wood carvings, gravestones, iron ware (such as stove plates and trivets),
tinware (such as coffee pots and lanterns), quilts, and rugs.

A-A 311. LIPMAN, JEAN. American Folk Art in Wood, Metal and Stone. New
York: Pantheon Books, 1948. 193 pp.
The author examines the art done in wood, metal, and stone, paying particular attention to the following categories: ship figureheads and orna-
ments; weathervanes, cigar-store figures and other trade signs; circus
and carousel carvings; toys; decoys; sculpture for house and garden; and
portraits. Lipman subscribes to the definition of folk art established
by Holger Cahill in American Folk Art (see A-A 291) and American Folk
Sculpture (see A-A 293).

A-A 312. LIPMAN, JEAN. American Primitive Painting. New York: Oxford
University Press, 1942. 158 pp.
Lipman defines primitive paintings as those that are directly opposed
to academic. Typically, they are non-derivative, individual, unpretentious,
and anonymous; generally, they flourished in the first three quarters
of the 19th century. Among the paintings represented in this volume are
portraits, landscapes, genre scenes, ship pictures, memorials, and still
lifes.

A-A 313. LIPMAN, JEAN and ALICE WINCHESTER. The Flowering of American
Folk Art, 1776-1876. New York: Viking Press, 1974. 288 pp.
The authors have collected an array of what they call American folk art
from the period 1776 to 1876, which they view as the century of the greatest development of folk art in this country. The objects were selected
for inclusion on the basis of artistic merit; that is, the authors sought
objects that displayed "originality of concept, creativity of design,
craftsmanly use of the medium and flashes of inspiration." They have
included large and numerous illustrations of American folk art including
paintings, needlework, sculpture, the decorative arts, and furniture,
with a brief introduction as background to each section.

A-A 314. LIPMAN, JEAN and TOM ARMSTRONG, eds. American Folk Painters
of Three Centuries. New York: Hudson Hills Press, 1980.
233 pp.
The thirty-seven artists included here represent the editors' choices
of the best American painters they call folk, grouped by century and then
arranged alphabetically. For each artist—most of whom painted during
the 19th century—there is an individual essay that includes biographical,
art historical, and bibliographical information. This volume was published
in conjunction with an exhibition of painting organized by the Whitney
Museum of American Art.

A-A 315. LIVINGSTON, JANE and JOHN BEARDSLEY. Black Folk Art in America,
1930-1980. Jackson: University Press of Mississippi, 1982.
186 pp.
According to Livingston, black folk art is paradoxically based in a deeply
communal culture, while springing at the same time from the hands of a
relatively few, physically isolated individuals. This volume—which served
as the catalogue for an exhibition organized by the Corcoran Gallery of
Art—examines the work of twenty self-taught artists, primarily painters
and sculptors, during the fifty years from 1930 to 1980. Two introductory
essays are also included: one that traces the forms of black art to their
African origins, and another that analyzes the voyage and vision of the
black artist.

A-A 316. LORD, PRISCILLA SAWYER and DANIEL J. FOLEY. The Folk Arts and
Crafts of New England. Philadelphia: Chilton Books, 1965.
282 pp.
The authors are interested in objects made by hand in New England that
display the inventiveness and creative skill of the maker. Covering
several hundred years, up to the end of the 19th century, the book includes
sections on spinning, weaving, needlework, quilting, rugmaking, itinerant
painting, silversmithing, basketmaking, wood carving, making of jewelry,
and gravestone carving.

A-A 317. RHODES, LYNETTE I. American Folk Art: From the Traditional
to the Naive. Cleveland, Ohio: Cleveland Museum of Art, 1978.
117 pp.
The first part of this volume consists of an extended essay on folk art,
which Rhodes defines as the "art of the general people, by the people,
and for the people." Noting the contemporary interest in American folk
art, the author examines its wide diversity and traces its historical
development. In the book's second part, Rhodes explores several different
types of objects, from the utilitarian (including frakturs, cookie molds,
and fish decoys) to the visionary (including the paintings of Edward Hicks,
the sculpture of Edgar Tolson, and the religious art of the Shakers, Zoars,
and Hispanic New Mexicans).

A-A 318. SHELLEY, DONALD A. The Fraktur-Writings or Illuminated Manuscripts of the Pennsylvania Germans. Allentown: Pennsylvania
German Folklore Society, 1961. 375 pp.
This detailed study of fraktur-writing traces the transplantation of forms
and techniques from Europe to the New World, and then examines its development and popularity in the 19th century, especially during the years 1800
to 1835, which Shelley calls its "high point." In addition, the various
schools of fraktur-writing--each with its own individual artists, forms,
and characteristic motifs--are identified.

A-A 319. STOUDT, JOHN JOSEPH. Pennsylvania Folk-Art: An Interpretation.
Allentown, Pa.: Schlechter, 1948. 402 pp.
Stoudt interprets the art of the Pennsylvania Dutch as an expression of
their cultural perspective, deriving from and manifesting a common fund
of ideas, images, and iconography. Among the materials he examines are
frakturs, portraits, decorated household objects, ceramics, textiles,
architectural decoration, and tombstones. This is a revised version of
the author's Consider the Lilies, How They Grow: An Interpretation of
the Symbolism of Pennsylvania German Art (1937).

A-A 320. WILDER, MITCHELL A. and EDGAR BREITENBACH. Santos: The Religious
Folk Art of New Mexico. Colorado Springs, Colo.: Taylor Museum,
1943. 49 pp.
This is a general introduction to the subject, in which the authors provide
some historical background to the art of the santos; categorize it by
type (bultos and retablos); discuss the techniques of artistic construction;
explain the acts of devotion and offerings that are associated with the
santos; and survey the various artistic styles that have been identified.

VII.   A. PHOTOGRAPHY: SURVEYS

A-A 321. CAHN, ROBERT and ROBERT GLENN KETCHUM. American Photographers
and the National Parks. New York: Viking Press, 1981.
180 pp.
This book documents the direct relationship between landscape photography
and the national park ethic in the U.S. It is Cahn's contention that
the idea of setting aside large pieces of wild land for careful public
use is a uniquely American one. And, while it was not invented by photographers, it was consciously promoted by certain photographers, ranging
from Carlton E. Watkins and William Henry Jackson through Ansel Adams
and Edward Weston (as well as such modernists as David Mussina and Richard
Misrach).

A-A 322. COLEMAN, A. D. The Grotesque in Photography. New York: Summit
Books, 1977. 208 pp.
A short essay introduces this lengthy book. Coleman points out that an
element of the grotesque has always been a part of photography--either
intentionally or unintentionally. Beginning in the 1960s, however, there
was a new and greater tendency to use the grotesque among this country's
best and most serious art photographers. Coleman contends that this
development suited the time and must be confronted by those who wish to
understand the era and the photography that mirrored it.

178

A-A 323. DOHERTY, ROBERT J. Social Documentary Photography in the USA.
      Garden City, N.Y.: Amphoto, 1976. 92 pp.
Doherty traces the development of a documentary photographic tradition
in the U.S. through the work of three men: Jacob Riis, who used the camera
to expose slum conditions in New York in the 1890s; Lewis Hine, whose
work for the Child Labor Commission in the early 20th century helped to
eliminate child labor; and Roy Stryker, who directed the Farm Security
Administration photographic project during the Depression. Doherty contends that the documentary tradition has always been associated with social
reform.

A-A 324. DOTY, ROBERT, ed. Photography in America. New York: Random
      House, 1974. 255 pp.
An introduction by Minor White and an essay by Doty define the outlines
of this survey. Each major style is treated, including the earliest primitive portraits, the great western landscapes, the Photo-secession, and
contemporary developments in the work of such photographers as Less Krims
and Todd Walker.

A-A 325. MELTZER, MILTON and BERNARD COLE. The Eye of Conscience: Photog-
      raphers and Social Change; With One Hundred Photographs by Noted
      Photographers, Past and Present. Chicago: Follett, 1974.
      192 pp.
Meltzer and Cole are interested in American photographers who have used
their cameras to try to change social conditions. Their method of investigation is idiosyncratic. They pick four very well known photographers
from the past (Timothy O'Sullivan, Jacob Riis, Lewis Hine, and Dorothea
Lange) and present their work alongside that of six virtually unknown
modern photographers. Their purpose is to show the reader that he or
she can also use a camera to engender social change.

VII. B. PHOTOGRAPHY: 19TH CENTURY

A-A 326. CAFFIN, CHARLES HENRY. Photography as a Fine Art: The Achieve-
      ments and Possibilities of Photographic Art in America. New
      York: Doubleday, Page, 1901. 191 pp.
Caffin was a great defender of Alfred Stieglitz and "straight" photography.
He believed that art and science met in photography and the medium should
never be violated by "faked effects." Like most writers on photography
at the turn of the century, however, Caffin was ambivalent about photography as art and often celebrated those photographs which looked most
like the academic art with which he was most familiar.

A-A 327. EARLE, EDWARD W., ed. Points of View: The Stereograph in America.
      A Cultural History. Rochester, N.Y.: Visual Studies Workshop
      Press, 1979. 119 pp.
The history of the stereograph--with photographic images which can be
viewed as three-dimensional with the proper apparatus--is traced in detail
from 1850 to 1914. Earle's essay relates the growth of this popular form
of material culture to major aesthetic movements in both Britain and the
U.S. Particular emphasis is placed on the writings of Oliver Wendell
Holmes who did a great deal to popularize the medium in America. Earle's
essay is followed by an interpretive chronology. The book includes essays
by Howard S. Becker, Thomas Southall, and Harvey Green.

A-A 328. NAEF, WESTON J., JAMES N. WOOD, and THERESE THAU HEYMAN. Era of Exploration: The Rise of Landscape Photography in the American West, 1860-1885. Boston: New York Graphic Society, 1975. 260 pp.

The 19th-century landscape genre is treated in detail. Naef traces the rise of landscape photography in Europe in the 1850s and in the U.S. in the 1860s. Special attention is paid to the work of Carlton E. Watkins, Timothy H. O'Sullivan, Eadweard J. Muybridge, A. J. Russell and William Henry Jackson. A chronology and selected bibliography are provided.

A-A 329. NEWHALL, BEAUMONT. The Daguerreotype in America. New York: Duell, Sloan & Pearce, 1961. 176 pp.

This pioneering work discusses the evolution of daguerrean technology from the first very slow exposures through efforts to cut exposure time, as well as early attempts to produce color daguerreotypes. Major daguerreotypists discussed include Samuel F. B. Morse, Albert Sands Southworth, and Frederick Langenheim. Studio design and business aspects of operating a successful daguerreotype salon are treated in some detail. A short discussion treats the impact of the daguerreotype on American art. Finally, Newhall suggests reasons why the daguerreotype was superseded by the glass-plate process.

A-A 330. OSTROFF, EUGENE. Western Views and Eastern Visions. Washington, D.C.: Smithsonian Institution and the U.S. Geological Survey, 1981. 118 pp.

In this book Ostroff attempts to relate mid-19th-century Eastern art conventions to Western landscape photographs. A large selection of photographs is presented along with a group of lithographs, sketches, and paintings. In his introductory essay, Ostroff suggests that hand-made "art" was less trusted in the 19th century than machine-made photographs and, therefore, only the camera could really show Americans the grandeur of the West.

A-A 331. RINHART, FLOYD and MARION RINHART. The American Daguerreotype. Athens: University of Georgia Press, 1981. 446 pp.

This large book treats both the technical and business aspects of early daguerrean studios. The Rinharts advance the theory that daguerrean art reached a higher level of development in the U.S. than in Europe because American photographers were generally professionals and operated under a competitive impetus that their amateur counterparts in Europe did not face. Color daguerreotypes are discussed. Technical chapters include information on apparatus and processes, art influences, and the identification of cases.

A-A 332. RINHART, FLOYD and MARION RINHART. American Miniature Case Art. New York: Barnes, 1969. 205 pp.

The authors trace the history of the miniature case, a popular 19th-century object used to hold silvered-copper daguerreotypes (as of 1839) and later glass, tin, and paper prints. Both leather- or cloth-covered wood-frame cases and molded plastic cases are discussed. The various scenes and designs which appear in relief on the covers are seen as broadly reflective of 19th-century American culture. The Rinharts examine the many types, shapes, and relief designs of miniature cases and provide a technical chapter on their manufacture. Following are over 200 plates, a list of case designs, and biographies of case manufacturers.

A-A 333. TAFT, ROBERT. Photography and the American Scene: A Social History, 1839-1889. New York: Macmillan, 1938. 546 pp.

This work, done in the early 20th century, remains a useful source of information on photography within the dates stated in the title. No single thesis informs the work, but there are chapters on daguerreotypes, tintypes, ambrotypes, the family album, the Civil War, and photographing the frontier. The author knew personally many early photographers and often inserts long quotes from their letters to him.

A-A 334. TALBOT, GEORGE. At Home: Domestic Life in the Post-Centennial Era, 1876-1920. Madison: State Historical Society of Wisconsin, 1976. 88 pp.
This exhibition catalogue addresses a particular question about photographic data: How can photographs help us understand the social role played by taste--by the things with which people choose to surround themselves? Talbot suggests that photographs can amplify what we already know about an era and show us things that we might easily miss without photographic data. Popular photographs (snapshots) can elucidate the functional myths that form the bases for much of life if we know how to look carefully.

A-A 335. WELLING, WILLIAM B. Photography in America: The Formative Years, 1839-1900. New York: Crowell, 1978. 431 pp.
In the preface to this year-by-year encyclopedia of 19th-century photography, Welling notes the early predominance of portrait photography in the U.S. Landscape photography, he asserts, only came into its own after the flourishing of the Hudson River school of painters. Following a prologue briefly treating the early developments, 1800-1839, Welling discusses in detail the progress made in the field of American photography during the rest of the century. Each year constitutes a separate chapter of this book. The narrative is embellished by catalogue-style mini-features which rely on contemporary documents and photographs to tell the stories of specific events, such as the introduction of the albumen process and the founding of the American Photographic Society.

A-A 336. WOLF, DANIEL, ed. The American Space: Meaning in Nineteenth-Century Landscape Photography. Middletown, Conn.: Wesleyan University Press, 1983. 122 pp.
This volume is a collection of 108 19th-century photographs of the American West taken between 1842 and 1906. It includes the efforts of amateur photographers as well as the pioneering work of such important landscape photographers as Carleton E. Watkins and Timothy O'Sullivan. An introductory essay by Daniel Wolf attempts to indicate how all the photographs illustrate themes and meanings peculiar to American space. Wolf discusses how the works deal with the silence of space, the timeless and motionless qualities of space, the role of light, the absence of human intrusion, and ideas of freedom implied by limitless space. He also suggests that 19th-century photographs of the West are more successful than Western landscape painting because the photographers did not dramatize, exaggerate, or fill up space with imaginary detail.

VII. C. PHOTOGRAPHY: 20TH CENTURY

A-A 337. DESMARAIS, CHARLES. The Portrait Extended. Chicago: Museum of Contemporary Art, 1980. 48 pp.
According to Desmarais, the eight young contemporary photographers whose work is presented in this exhibition catalogue have felt the need to reintroduce or re-emphasize the narrative context of the portrait. They believe that a single isolated picture cannot convey the nature of their subjects, so they have developed a form of serial portraiture in which a whole range of documents are combined with several portraits in order to present many aspects of the subject's personality and character.

Desmarais sees a tradition for this in the work of Alfred Stieglitz who assembled what was perhaps the first extended portrait in a series of photographs of Georgia O'Keeffe. He believes that the extended portrait is a logical artistic extension of the amateur's tendency to take many snapshots of friends and relatives.

A-A 338. EAUCLAIRE, SALLY. The New Color Photography. New York: Abbe-
ville Press, 1981. 287 pp.
Eauclaire argues that the use of color by photographers in a way that is both restrained and integral to composition is a relatively new develop-ment (since the 1960s). She defends the new colorists as fundamentally different from those painters who are called photo-realists; they are more restrained and less emotional than the painters. Eauclaire also suggests that the new colorists represent a rejection of the "new journal-ism" photographers of the 1960s and 1970s (such as Diane Arbus and Gary Winogrand). The work of a large number of color photographers is showcased, and the biographies of forty-six contemporary photographers are included.

A-A 339. GEE, HELEN. Photography of the Fifties: An American Perspective.
Tucson, Ariz.: Center for Creative Photography, 1980. 161 pp.
Gee, who operated a gallery for photographers in New York during the 1950s, brings a personal perspective to this book. The disjointed nature of the period is reflected in the broad stylistic variety presented. Richard Avedon, W. Eugene Smith, Lotte Jacobi, and Robert Frank are among the photographers whose work is presented and commented upon.

A-A 340. GREEN, JONATHAN, ed. The Snapshot. Millerton, N.Y.: Aperture,
1974. 126 pp.
This work presents informal photographs by several of the country's leading photographers. In general, photographs involve family and friends in unguarded moments or street scenes. Among those whose work is presented are Emmet Gowan, Joel Meyerowitz, Nancy Rexroth, and Gary Winogrand. The title refers to the unplanned nature of the pictures and not to the usual naive images taken by people with untrained eyes.

A-A 341. HARTMANN, SADAKICHI. The Valiant Knights of Daguerre: Selected
Critical Essays on Photography and Profiles of Photographic
Pioneers. Edited by Harry W. Lawton and George Knox. Berkeley:
University of California Press, 1978. 364 pp.
This book collects forty-six of Hartmann's essays published between 1898 and 1913. During those years, Hartmann inhabited the world of Alfred Stieglitz's photo-secession. As a critic, he was never attracted to the "artistic excesses" of some of Stieglitz's followers and always advocated the creative possibilities of "straight" photography. His various essays are here evenly divided between general critical articles and specific profiles of the "pioneers" of photography.

A-A 342. HOMER, WILLIAM INNES. Alfred Stieglitz and the Photo-Secession.
Boston: New York Graphic Society, 1977.
Homer treats Stieglitz's personal background, the evolution of his ideas, and his relations with other people in the movement. A clear distinction is drawn between the early phase of the photo-secession, which was influ-enced by people like F. Holland Day, Gertrude Kasebier, Joseph T. Keiley, and Edward Steichen, and the later phase of the movement which was influ-enced by such people as Frank Eugene and Alvin Langdon Coburn. The move-ment from the manipulated print back toward straight photography is docu-mented. The book ends with a strong defense of Stieglitz as the pivotal figure in American art and photography in the early 20th century.

A-A 343. HURLEY, F. JACK. Portrait of a Decade: Roy Stryker and the Development of Documentary Photography in the Thirties. Baton Rouge: Louisiana State University Press, 1972. 196 pp.
Hurley's book describes in some detail "the birth, productive years, and the death of the 'historical section' of the Farm Security Administration." The focus of the study is on Roy Stryker, chief of the historical section, but attention is also paid to those photographers--Walker Evans, Dorothea Lange, Arthur Rothstein, and Russell Lee among others--who contributed to the total documentary effect. Hurley's concern throughout the book is with "the development of the documentary style by the historical section photographers, the uses made of the pictures, and the long-term influence of the project."

A-A 344. HURLEY, F. JACK, ed. Industry and the Photographic Image: 153 Great Prints from 1850 to the Present. New York: Dover, 1980. 150 pp.
In his complementing text to the images by such photographers as Lewis Hine, Alvin Langdon Coburn, Paul Strand, and Margaret Bourke-White, Hurley explores the interrelationship of industry and photography. Among other topics, he discusses the birth and growth of industrial photography, the impact of technical improvements in cameras and film; how photography reflected changing attitudes toward industrialization; the role of Fortune magazine as a disseminator of industrial photography; and the transformation of the medium from straightforward socio-documentary record to its broader role as an instrument of art, criticism, and social commentary.

A-A 345. JENKINS, WILLIAM. New Topographics: Photographs of a Man-Altered Landscape. Rochester, N.Y.: International Museum of Photography at George Eastman House, 1975. 48 pp.
Jenkins's introduction creates a context for understanding new formalism in photography in the mid-1970s. Nicholas Nixon, Lewis Baltz, Joe Deal, and Robert Adams are quoted concerning their own work. This catalogue of an exhibition at the George Eastman House includes photographs by Adams, Baltz, Bernd and Hilla Becher, Joe Deal, Frank Gohlke, Nixon, John Scott, Stephen Shore, and Henry Wessel, Jr.

A-A 346. Landscape: Theory. New York: Lustrum Press, 1980. 175 pp.
This work contains photographs and essays by ten contemporary photographers. Their photography and commentary provide a broad sampling of contemporary approaches to landscape photography. Most of them, led by Robert Adams and Lewis Baltz, photograph "the new American frontier" in which land and human settlement come together, sometimes reversing the qualities usually associated with the landscape and with buildings. The dominant theme is the process of change and the interplay between the American myth of the unspoiled landscape and the reality of urban development. William Garnett and Eliot Porter, on the other hand, are prominent among the photographers who seek a return to images of pure nature. They often rely upon the close-up to exclude any surrounding encroachment of the "man-altered landscape." Their aim is to re-awaken the awe and respect for nature they believe was characteristic of 19th-century American photography.

A-A 347. LYONS, NATHAN, ed. Contemporary Photographers: Toward a Social Landscape. New York: Horizon Press, 1966. 67 pp.
In his short introduction to this catalogue of the work of five photographers, Lyons discusses the "natural" landscape, the "man-made" landscape, and the "human" landscape. With the ever expanding reference point of contemporary environment and landscape, Lyons argues that a new category-- the social landscape--established itself in the 1960s. Moving beyond the identity of form, this work looks very little like the social-documentary style of the 1930s. Artists represented are Bruce Davidson, Lee Friedlander, Garry Winograd, Danny Lyon, and Duane Michals.

A-A 348. MORGAN, HAL and ANDREAS BROWN. Prairie Fires and Paper Moons:
The American Photographic Postcard, 1900-1920. Boston: Godine,
1981. 191 pp.
According to Morgan and Brown, there was a booming international postcard
fad in the early 20th century, and this book is essentially a collection
of American photographic postcards indicating the wide variety of examples
available in the U.S. during the height of their popularity. The authors'
introduction attributes the great demand for postcards in America to newly
established free delivery routes and reduced rates for privately printed
postcards. They also note that the Eastman Kodak Company manufactured
postcard-size photographic paper upon which photographs could be printed
immediately from negatives. Many studios were opened specializing in
photographic postcards, and the postcard continued to flourish into the
1930s. For these reasons, the authors believe, there is an unusually
complete record of American life during the period on photographic postcards.

A-A 349. STOTT, WILLIAM. Documentary Expression and Thirties America.
New York: Oxford University Press, 1973. 361 pp.
Stott is interested in photography, but also a good deal more. Art, literature, music, and dance figure at least peripherally in this study. Stott
defines the documentary tradition as people-oriented and aimed toward
program implementation, ". . . and its people tend, like the innocent
victims in most propaganda, to be simplified and ennobled--sentimentalized,
in a word." Stott attempts to define the Depression era's Zeitgeist in
such a way as to account for the upsurge of interest in documentary expression.

A-A 350. STRYKER, ROY and NANCY WOOD. In This Proud Land: America 1935-
1943 as Seen in the FSA Photographs. Greenwich, Conn.: New
York Graphic Society, 1973. 191 pp.
In his eightieth year, Roy Stryker was encouraged to select a group of
his favorite images from the Farm Security Administration project that
he directed for the federal government during the 1930s. A short essay
concerning the FSA project and the documentary tradition was taken from
his files and Woods provided a somewhat longer essay placing the photographs and Stryker in context.

A-A 351. SZARKOWSKI, JOHN. American Landscapes. New York: Museum of
Modern Art, 1981. 80 pp.
The book reviews the classic American landscape photographers of the 19th
century and then brings the survey well into the recent past, exploring
the work of Ansel Adams and the Westons (Edward and Brett). Even more
recent, very stylized work by such photographers as Roger Merton, Robert
Adams and Frank Gohlke complete the collection.

A-A 352. SZARKOWSKI, JOHN. Mirrors and Windows: American Photography
Since 1960. New York: Museum of Modern Art, 1978. 152 pp.
Is serious photography a mirror (reflecting the inner life of the photographer) or a window (looking out and recording the objective world)?
Szarkowski's answer is that it can be either or even both. This book,
designed as a catalogue for the Museum of Modern Art exhibit by the same
name, explores the dual functions of photography in the recent past.

A-A 353. TRAVIS, DAVID. Photography Rediscovered: American Photographs,
1900-1930. New York: Whitney Museum of American Art, 1979.
190 pp.
This catalogue features the work of thirty-four major early 20th-century
photographers. The theme of the book is the movement from straight documentation by people like Adam Clark Vroman to the extreme emphasis on
self-realization by photographers such as Paul Outerbridge and, finally,

184

back to the use of the camera to both record and make sense out of the world around us (as exemplified by the work of Walker Evans and Edward Weston). Travis suggests that the movement from one style to another has constituted a constant process of "rediscovery" of photography. Early critical debates concerning style and approach are discussed.

A-A 354. Twelve Photographers of the American Social Landscape: Bruce
          Davidson and Others. Waltham, Mass.: Poses Institute of Fine
          Arts, Brandeis University, 1967. n.p.
The exhibition takes its title from a statement by Lee Friedlander in the journal Contemporary Photographer (Fall 1963), where he described his work as preoccupied with "the American social landscape and its conditions. . . ." In an introduction to the catalogue, Thomas H. Garver finds a tradition for Friedlander's social landscape in "straight" or "things as they are" photography beginning with Roy Stryker and the Farm Security Administration photographic project. Garver believes that Walker Evans's American Photographs (1938) and Robert Frank's The Americans (1959) were other important landmarks in the tradition. According to Garver, the twelve photographers who contributed to the exhibition dealt with the American urban landscape in much the same way in which Evans and Frank strove to find "implicit commentary" rather than "explicit messages" in the rural American scene.

VIII. DECORATIVE ARTS

A-A 355. ANDREWS, EDWARD DEMING and FAITH ANDREWS. Shaker Furniture:
          The Craftsmanship of an American Communal Sect. New York:
          Dover, 1937. 133 pp.
This book contends that the Shakers, unlike other separatist societies, were able to fuse their religious principles into their craftsmanship and create an original style of functional furniture. The authors, who concentrate on the Eastern sects and specifically on the New Lebanon community, consider the period between 1800 and 1860 to provide the purest samples of Shaker production. After this period the barriers with the outside world started to break down and the sect became liberalized, diluting the creative communal energy that produced the furniture. Short chapters provide background on Shaker cultural traditions, stylistic development, the nature of craft, and Shaker interiors.

A-A 356. AYRES, WILLIAM, ed. A Poor Sort of Heaven A Good Sort of Earth:
          The Rose Valley Arts and Crafts Experiment. Chadds Ford, Pa.:
          Brandywine River Museum, 1983. 134 pp.
This volume is the catalogue of an exhibition which documents the history and production of Rose Valley, a utopian craft community modeled on the tenets of John Ruskin and William Morris. Rose Valley was founded by architect William Price near Media, Pennsylvania, and operated from 1901 to 1916. Craftsmen stressed the beauty of the well-made object, handcraft over the machine, and ornamented surfaces. Essays trace the development of the community and its cultural life, as well as Rose Valley architecture, furniture, and pottery. The life of William Price is examined as is the house publication, The Artsman.

A-A 357. BARBER, EDWIN ATLEE. The Pottery and Porcelain of the United
    States and Marks of American Potters. 1904; Rev. ed. New York:
    Feingold & Lewis, 1909. 795 pp.
This volume was Barber's attempt to raise the consciousness of American
collectors concerning the value of their nation's pottery and porcelain.
Since imported ware was preferred by consumers during the 18th and 19th
centuries, most American manufacturers hid their identification marks
and imitated foreign styles. Consequently, Barber is concerned with accumulating data and providing information to help collectors and scholars
identify American ceramics. He covers techniques, products, chronology,
and specific manufacturers.

A-A 358. BING, SAMUEL. Artistic America, Tiffany Glass, and Art Nouveau.
    Cambridge, Mass.: MIT Press, 1970. 260 pp.
Bing, a Parisian art dealer and creator of the term Art Nouveau, visited
America in the 1890s to observe the art scene. This book offers four
of the articles he wrote about America. His report to the French government, "Artistic America," discusses painting, sculpture, architecture,
and the industrial arts. An article on Tiffany and two on the Art Nouveau
are also included. Bing found much to admire in the U.S., especially
in the industrial arts with their use of up-to-date machinery. He saw
the best of American design as judiciously taking ideas from every culture,
altering them, and adding something new based on the study of nature to
produce an aesthetic that was "attuned to local conditions" and "imbued
with the spirit of the people."

A-A 359. BISHOP, ROBERT CHARLES. Centuries and Styles of the American
    Chair 1640-1970. New York: Dutton, 1972. 516 pp.
Bishop uses over 900 illustrations to present the history of the American
chair through 1970. Chairs of every style, quality, and region are shown.
Period illustrations are included to indicate how the chair was used,
and advertisements, patent drawings, and other contemporary sources complete the picture. The text discusses the history of the chair and the
captioned illustrations contain detailed analyses.

A-A 360. BISHOP, ROBERT CHARLES and PATRICIA COBLENTZ. American Decorative
    Arts: 360 Years of Creative Design. New York: Abrams, 1982.
    405 pp.
This volume presents a comprehensive history of American decorative arts
through 1980. The authors use period representations and modern photographs of interiors and exteriors to illustrate the book. Individual
artifacts are presented with captions that include stylistic observations
and anecdotal information. Social, economic, and historical trends are
noted and contemporary sources of design philosophy are mentioned and
quoted. Parallel developments in other art media are also discussed.
The authors concentrate on the formal analysis of artifacts and the history
of style.

A-A 361. BIVINS, JOHN, Jr. The Moravian Potters in North Carolina. Chapel
    Hill: University of North Carolina Press, 1972. 300 pp.
Due to their "practical religion" and well-organized social system, the
Moravians were able to develop a culture in which high levels of accomplishment were often achieved. This level of achievement can be seen
in the pottery excavated at the Wachovia tract in North Carolina from
the 18th through the middle of the 19th centuries. The Moravian habit
of keeping copious records provided Bivins with the opportunity to "attempt
to correlate archaeological finds in Wachovia" with the documentation
still in existence. Chapters are devoted to materials, tools, techniques,
and to the master potters and their apprentices. Stylistic analysis of
the pottery and glossaries of ceramic and Moravian terms are included.

A-A 362. BJERKOE, ETHEL HALL. The Cabinetmakers of America. Garden City, N.Y.: Doubleday, 1957. 252 pp.
This book is a collection of biographical sketches of furniture makers active through the middle of the 19th century. An introductory chapter surveys the development of cabinetmaking in America through the Classical Revival with brief mention of later styles. Families of cabinetmakers are grouped together for convenience and to show stylistic influences. Captioned photographs, attributed to a specific craftsman where possible, are also provided. A glossary of furniture terminology is included.

A-A 363. BOHAN, PETER and PHILIP HAMMERSLOUGH. Early Connecticut Silver 1700-1840. Middletown, Conn.: Wesleyan University Press, 1970. 288 pp.
The authors here offer most of the known examples of Connecticut hollow ware, nearly 200 items, and representative examples of flatware. An introductory chapter discusses the economic and social character of silversmithing. The authors emphasize that many silversmiths worked at their trade part-time and held down other jobs, either in related fields such as engraving or in quite different fields such as law. Another chapter explains the stylistic development of Connecticut silver by breaking it down into three phases terminating in mass production. An index of biographical notes on silversmiths is included as well as an index of marks.

A-A 364. BRIDENBAUGH, CARL. The Colonial Craftsman. New York: New York University Press, 1950. 214 pp.
A collection of lectures on the place of the craftsman in Colonial society is presented in this volume. The author, however, is not interested in the antiquarian aspects of Colonial craftsmanship, but concentrates on social history. Bridenbaugh devotes his discussion to the 18th century when the standard of living had risen high enough to support a distinct class of artisans. Chapters explore the role of the craftsman in the rural South, the rural North, and the city. One chapter emphasizes the "small business" nature of most Colonial crafts, and the final chapter deals with the social status of craftsmen.

A-A 365. BURTON, E. MILBY. Charleston Furniture, 1700-1825. Charleston, S.C.: Charleston Museum, 1955. 150 pp.
This study is limited to cabinet makers who produced furniture in Charleston from the end of the 17th century through the first quarter of the 19th. It opens with an introduction which details the social and cultural background of this period and discusses problems of locating and identifying representative pieces. A second chapter decribes woods used for the furniture. Following these essays are photographs of objects accompanied by biographical information about the cabinet makers who produced them. Also included are photographs of wills, newspaper ads, obituaries, deeds, and inventories, primary texts which yield information about trends in design and changes of fashion.

A-A 366. BUTLER, JOSEPH T. Sleepy Hollow Restorations: A Cross-Section of the Collections. Tarrytown, N.Y.: Sleepy Hollow Press, 1983. 308 pp.
This survey documents 425 objects from the Phillipsburg and Van Cortlandt Manors and Sunnyside, Washington Irving's home. The three properties are located in the lower Hudson River Valley and are managed by Sleepy Hollow Restorations. A chronological study, black-and-white photographs, and catalogue notes cover furniture, paintings, drawings, prints, woodenware, ivory, ceramics, glass, metals, and textiles. Formed from family pieces and household inventories, the collections span the 17th through the 19th centuries and are particularly strong in New York, Dutch and English pieces. Included are extensive bibliographical and genealogical indices on the Phillipse, Van Cortlandt and Irving families.

A-A 367. CARPENTER, CHARLES H., Jr. Gorham Silver: 1831-1981. New York:
Dodd, Mead, 1982. 332 pp.
Amply illustrated, this survey of the Gorham Company melds company history,
stylistic trends, social history, and manufacturing processes in one volume.
Based on secondary sources as well as company files and photographs,
Carpenter's text covers everything from Gorham's silver matchboxes, flatware
loving cups, and souvenir spoons, to Mrs. Lincoln's "chicken-leg" tete-
a-tete. An authority in the field, Carpenter also deals with Gorham
bronzes, artwares, hammered wares, and Martele. A biographical study of
the company's leaders and designers is included as well as a survey of
the major design influences (High Victorian, Art Nouveau, Art Deco, etc.)
during the firm's 150-year career.

A-A 368. CATHERS, DAVID M. Furniture of the American Arts and Crafts
Movement: Stickley and Roycroft Mission Oak. New York: New
American Library, 1981. 275 pp.
Cathers has provided a book for connoisseurs, collectors, and art historians. Information on style, attribution, and cultural influences is presented. Although Cathers concentrates on the work of Gustav Stickley,
he also examines the furniture of Roycroft and of Stickley's brothers.
The background of the Arts and Crafts movement, and the story of Stickley
and his competitors are discussed, but the majority of the book is given
to stylistic comparisons. Individual sections of the book are devoted
to various categories of furniture.

A-A 369. CHRISTENSEN, ERWIN O. The Index of American Design. New York:
Macmillan, 1950. 229 pp.
Christensen presents nearly 400 photographs and watercolors from the WPA-
sponsored Index of American Design. The text is arranged thematically.
All forms of American design are included, from fire helmets and dolls
to furniture. Each section features a short introduction by Christensen,
and every illustration is also discussed by the author. A general introduction to the text by Holger Cahill traces the growth of interest in
American design and the purpose and development of the Index of American
Design. An index of the artists and the locations of the original photographs and watercolors are included, as is a comprehensive list of all
subjects covered by the Index.

A-A 370. CLARK, GARTH and MARGIE HUGHTO. A Century of Ceramics in the
United States, 1878-1978: A Study of Its Development. New
York: Dutton, 1979. 371 pp.
This exhibition catalogue traces the growth of art ceramics during the
period 1878-1978 from a hobby to a well-respected art form. The preface
discusses the ceramics collection of the Everson Museum (Syracuse, N.Y.),
the process of organizing the exhibit, and some aspects of ceramic art.
The chapters are divided by decade, and style, aesthetics, and technique
are considered. A chronology of major events in American ceramics and
biographies of many ceramists are included.

A-A 371. CLARK, ROBERT JUDSON. The Arts and Crafts Movement in America
1876-1916. Princeton, N.J.: Princeton University Press, 1972.
190 pp.
This is the catalogue to the first comprehensive exhibit of American Arts
and Crafts design. After an introduction by Clark, the book is divided
into geographical sections: the Eastern Seaboard, Chicago and the Midwest,
and the Pacific Coast. Chapters on the Arts and Crafts book and on Art
Pottery are also included. Each chapter is written by a different scholar
or in collaboration with Clark. The sections contain a brief introduction
to activity in the area, and a synopsis of each artist is presented before
examples of the artist's work are shown.

188

A-A 372. COMSTOCK, HELEN. American Furniture: Seventeenth, Eighteenth
and Nineteenth Century Styles. 1962; Rev. ed. New York: Viking
Press, 1966. 336 pp.
Comstock establishes the European background of American furniture design.
The book ranges from the Jacobean period to the Early Victorian; she contends that furniture designed after 1870 is better treated in a work on
20th-century styles. Primarily a history of style, the book also stresses
American regional traits but is not solely devoted to this subtopic.
A short introduction to each period is followed by a chart summarizing
design, material, technique, and European developments. Each chapter
illustrates individual pieces and interior arrangements.

A-A 373. COOKE, EDWARD S., Jr. Fiddle-backs and Crooked-backs: Elijah
Booth and Other Joiners in Newtown and Woodbury 1750-1820.
Waterbury, Conn.: Mattatuck Historical Society, 1982.
120 pp.
Using tax lists, account books, and inventories, and studying the social,
cultural, and economic make-up of two Connecticut towns, Cooke shows that
each town had distinctive furniture forms and designs. Cooke documents
the existence of previously unknown cabinetmakers, and, through documentary
sources and an examination of construction details and design, he sheds
new light on furniture previously attributed to the shop of Elijah Booth.
The thirty-five photographs of chairs, tables, and case pieces are accompanied by extensive catalogue notes which compare and contrast design
and construction elements of different makers and communities. Appendices
list Newtown and Woodbury joiners and cite furniture inventories of each
town.

A-A 374. COOPER, WENDY A. In Praise of America: American Decorative
Arts, 1650-1830/Fifty Years of Discovery Since the 1929 Girl
Scouts Loan Exhibition. New York: Knopf, 1980. 280 pp.
Like the 1929 Girl Scout Loan Exhibition, which this catalogue commemorates,
the 1980 show took a dualistic approach to decorative arts by presenting
the material in the light of both cultural and aesthetic interpretations.
Reflecting recent scholarship, the material is arranged by topic, as
opposed to the chronological format of the 1929 show. Consequently, some
chapters, like "Search and Research," which concentrates on documented
objects, cut across art forms and time periods; "Form and Fabric," however,
treats a specific art form. Other chapters discuss patronage, regionalism,
ornamentation, and objects made in secondary design centers. The final
chapter examines the Classical style in a chronological fashion.

A-A 375. CUTTEN, GEORGE BARTON. The Silversmiths of Virginia Together
with Watchmakers and Jewelers, from 1694-1850. Richmond, Va.:
Dietz Press, 1952. 259 pp.
Cutten has assembled a collection of short biographies of silversmiths,
watchmakers, and jewelers from Virginia and West Virginia who were active
during the period from 1694, when the first reliable information is available, to the end of hand-made silver around 1850. An introduction gives
a history of silver in Virginia and some reasons why very little silver
has survived. The book is arranged alphabetically by town with silversmiths arranged chronologically. Marks have been included as well as
examples of silver and portraits of the craftsmen.

A-A 376. DAVIDSON, MARSHALL B., ed. Three Centuries of American Antiques.
New York: Bonanza Books, 1979. 1215 pp.
This is a comprehensive history of American antiques written for a wide
audience. Particular attention is given to the cultural context of the
artifacts, but style and technique are also discussed. Decorative arts
are emphasized, but all other visual artifacts are depicted and mentioned
in the text. The larger divisions of the book, such as "The Puritan Cen-

tury," are broken up into feature articles such as "The Children's Corner." The first volume of the book covers the Colonial period, the second discusses the antebellum period, and the final volume treats the period up to W.W. I. Each volume contains style charts and a glossary of terms.

A-A 377. Design in America: The Cranbrook Vision 1925-1950. New York: Abrams, 1983. 352 pp.
This text accompanied an exhibit mounted by the Metropolitan Museum and the Detroit Institute of the Arts. It centers on one of America's first institutions devoted to the study of design, the Cranbrook Academy. Located in Bloomfield Hills, Michigan, the Academy's impact on the arts from 1925-1950 made it comparable to the Bauhaus. Photographs of 265 pieces document the work of such students and teachers as Eero and Eliel Saarinen, Charles Eames, and Florence Kroll. This is both a history of the Academy and an evolutionary study of furniture, architecture, metalwork, textile, ceramic, sculpture, and interior design.

A-A 378. DONHAUSER, PAUL S. History of American Ceramics: The Studio Potter. Dubuque, Iowa: Kendall/Hunt, 1978. 260 pp.
Donhauser explores the reasons for the birth of studio pottery and its growth into a significant art form. As such, this is not a definitive history of American ceramics, but an interpretive overview. Important artists and companies are discussed as is the impact of historical events such as the Depression. Foreign ceramics are mentioned, and the influence of post-W.W. II modernisms (up to the 1970s) are detailed. A glossary is included, and a series of appendices lists individuals, societies, and institutions that have been active in studio pottery.

A-A 379. ELDER, WILLIAM VOSS, III. Baltimore Painted Furniture. 1800-1840. Baltimore, Md.: Baltimore Museum of Art, 1972. 132 pp.
Elder's emphasis is on the unique characteristics which distinguish Baltimore painted furniture from that of other regions, where the painted tradition did not attain the same importance. He includes a bibliography for broader studies on the Classical taste in America and an exhaustive list of Baltimore cabinetmakers of the period. A section on conservation and restoration sheds light on this often ignored aspect of the decorative arts.

A-A 380. ELDER, WILLIAM VOSS, III. Maryland Queen Anne and Chippendale Furniture of the Eighteenth Century. New York: October House, 1968. 128 pp.
This catalogue records the first exhibit of Queen Anne and Chippendale furniture manufactured in Maryland. It is intended to serve as a base for more detailed research and to help re-identify furniture that had been sold out of the state and later given the wrong provenance. Not enough furniture remains for a comprehensive selection of the varieties of furniture, and many attributions are tentative. Stylistic characteristics and the choice of secondary woods are emphasized. The book consists of seventy-five captioned photographs, examples of cabinetmakers' labels, and a list of cabinetmakers and clockmakers.

A-A 381. FAILEY, DEAN F., with ROBERT J. HEFNER and SUSAN E. KLAFFKY. Long Island Is My Nation: The Decorative Arts and Craftsmen, 1640-1830. Setauket, N.Y.: Society for the Preservation of Long Island Antiquities, 1976. 304 pp.
This exhibition catalogue draws together a large collection of household furnishings, especially furniture and silver, known to have been owned on Long Island prior to 1830. The range of objects, many expensive and associated with prominent families but a few of a commonplace sort, reveals patterns of contact with other areas, New York and New England in particular, as well as distinctive regional traits.

A-A 382. FAIRBANKS, JONATHAN L. and ELIZABETH BIDWELL BATES. American
Furniture, 1620 to the Present. New York: Marek, 1981.
561 pp.
The authors argue that since so much data are available on American furniture, it is as easy to create as it is to disprove theories concerning
its development through selective sampling. Bates and Fairbanks claim
that the most important function of their revisionist study is to be a
source of factual information. Both grand and modest pieces of furniture
are examined, since the authors believe that such comparisons best train
the reader's eye. The book concentrates on stylistic analysis, but cultural interpretations are not neglected. A primary thesis is that furniture of high and low quality was produced in all periods.

A-A 383. FALES, DEAN A. American Painted Furniture, 1660-1880. New York:
Dutton, 1972. 299 pp.
Fales's purpose in writing this book is to indicate for the first time
the immense variety of painted decoration in American furniture. His
text briefly describes the characteristics of each category of painted
furniture, then highlights several outstanding examples of the art. Perhaps of greater importance, however, are the photographs which not only
illustrate the text, but also are by themselves a major resource, forming
the largest published body of information on American painted furniture.

A-A 384. FITZGERALD, OSCAR P. Three Centuries of American Furniture.
Englewood Cliffs, N.J.: Prentice-Hall, 1982. 323 pp.
Fitzgerald covers American furniture from the late 17th century through
the birth of Modernism in the early 20th century. Both cultural and aesthetic factors are discussed, and the evolution of shop practices, from
the 17th-century joiner to the 19th-century factors is also evaluated.
Acknowledged masterpieces are presented but many of the artifacts illustrated are offered for the first time and are considered of representative,
not exceptional, quality. The book is organized around stylistic terms.
Furniture catalogues from 1786 and 1850 are included to show changing
attitudes toward furniture.

A-A 385. GARVAN, BEATRICE B. and CHARLES F. HUMMEL. The Pennsylvania
Germans: A Celebration of Their Arts 1683-1850. Philadelphia:
Philadelphia Museum of Art, 1982. 196 pp.
This volume is the catalogue of an exhibition mounted by the Philadelphia
Museum of Art and Winterthur. Over 300 objects made or used by Pennsylvania Germans from 1683 to 1850 are pictured, described, and discussed
within their socio-cultural framework. This daily-life approach explores
the objects in chapters entitled: "From Diversity," "Pockets of Settlement," "The Marketplace," "Good Neighbors," "Liberty and Freedom," "For
the Home," and "Religion and Education." Three years in the making, the
catalogue draws on the expertise of nine curators as well as recent
research done in Europe. The authors assert that the largest quantity of
extant Pennsylvania German artifacts underscores the viability of their
cultural impact as well as their good craftsmanship.

A-A 386. GORDON, BEVERLY. Shaker Textile Arts. Hanover, N.H.: University
Press of New England, 1980. 329 pp.
Gordon's "comprehensive study" is an attempt to rectify the shortage of
scholarly commentary on Shaker textile art while remaining accessible
to the general reader. A brief introductory chapter discusses the nature
of the Shaker community. The next chapter provides basic information
on the design, manufacture, and use of textiles by the Shakers. Further
chapters detail the materials and techniques employed and the variety
of the textiles produced. A number of appendices present information
on, among other things, Shaker community organization, weaving patterns,
and textile recipes.

A-A 387. HENZKE, LUCILE. <u>American</u> <u>Art</u> <u>Pottery</u>. Camden, N.J.: Nelson,
    1970. 336 pp.
Short histories of late 19th-century art potteries are presented in this
book. The thirty-seven entries are arranged chronologically by date of
establishment. Most sections are only a few pages long, but the Weller
pottery is given ninety pages. The sections provide information on the
history of the firm and the types of pottery produced, and the marks of
individual craftsmen and companies are included. Technical processes
are explained, and innovations are detailed. A separate section, with
a glossary of terminology, is devoted to pottery tiles.

A-A 388. HILLIER, BEVIS. <u>The</u> <u>Decorative</u> <u>Arts</u> <u>of</u> <u>the</u> <u>Forties</u> <u>and</u> <u>Fifties</u>:
    <u>Austerity/Binge</u>. New York: Potter, 1975. 200 pp.
A history of decorative arts in Britain and the U.S. from 1940-1960, with
a foreword by Sir John Betjeman, this book is written from a British perspective, although approximately 50% of the content is devoted to American
items or to their influence on British material culture. The two decades
are seen from an art historical and social historical perspective as
sharply divided in tastes and products. The section titled "The Arts of
War" reproduces W.W. II items (including all forms of propaganda) and
comments on the influence of camouflage on shapes in art, comics, book
jackets, advertising, and toys. "The Post-War Temper" covers the boom
in consumer goods, the New Look, escapist art, automobiles, hair styles,
and motifs in decoration. "The Fifties" studies eccentricity in buildings,
dress and photography, rock 'n' roll and rock culture, fashions, television
and science fiction. "The Best of Austerity/Binge" features the best
design in all modes during the period, and the book concludes with a discussion of the contemporary revival of this period, with its characteristic
motifs and styles. This is an illustrated survey of the period, including
many types of art not considered in standard texts.

A-A 389. HOLSTEIN, JONATHAN. <u>The</u> <u>Pieced</u> <u>Quilt</u>: <u>An</u> <u>American</u> <u>Design</u> <u>Tra-</u>
    <u>dition</u>. Greenwich, Conn.: New York Graphic Society, 1973.
    191 pp.
Holstein concentrates on the stylistic elements of the pieced quilt.
He is not concerned with the varieties of stitching; rather, his interest
is in the visual designs of different types of quilting. He acknowledges
the functional nature of quilts, but states that they were also intended
as objects of beauty. Holstein traces the history of quilting by exploring
stylistic developments, and he states that the most efficient techniques
produced geometric designs. He also discusses the resemblance between
quilts and abstract painting, and argues that a general appreciation for
geometric forms was growing and that the appreciation could be reflected
in decorative art before it was allowed in fine art.

A-A 390. HOOD, GRAHAM. <u>American</u> <u>Silver</u>: <u>A</u> <u>History</u> <u>of</u> <u>Style</u> <u>1650-1900</u>.
    New York: Praeger, 1971. 255 pp.
As the title indicates, this book is primarily intended as a study of
the formal evolution of American silver. The author is concerned with
helping the reader develop an aesthetic appreciation for silver through
examples of stylistic analysis. The social importance of silver and of
the silversmith are also mentioned. The first chapter explains the nature
of the profession, and the rest of the book traces the stylistic development of silver.

A-A 391. KAUFFMAN, HENRY J. <u>The</u> <u>Colonial</u> <u>Silversmith</u>: <u>His</u> <u>Techniques</u>
    <u>and</u> <u>His</u> <u>Products</u>. Camden, N.J.: Nelson, 1969. 176 pp.
This history of Colonial silver concentrates on the materials, tools,
and techniques of the profession. Kauffman argues that a knowledge of
the technology of the craft can aid scholars in determining an artifact's
date, place of origin, and purpose, as well as providing insights about

the society in which it was produced. After a short discussion of the characteristics of silver and the nature of the workshop, chapters are presented on the techniques of creating various objects. Technical drawings, by Dorothy Briggs, are used to illustrate procedures, and photographs depict the finished product. Technical terminology is used and is explained in the text.

A-A 392. KAUFFMAN, HENRY J. Early American Ironware, Cast and Wrought. Rutland, Vt.: Tuttle, 1966. 166 pp.
This work is a history of American cast and wrought ironware through the middle of the 19th century. Kauffman discusses the history of the professions, and the development of the technologies beginning with the blast furnace. He establishes the social status of the craftsmen and explores the products that they made. After the first three chapters, which explain the early technical developments of iron-making, the book is divided by profession, i.e., blacksmith, farrier, cutler.

A-A 393. KETCHUM, WILLIAM C., Jr. Early Potters and Potteries of New York State. New York: Funk & Wagnalls, 1970. 278 pp.
Ketchum considers this study as the groundwork for more intensive research. The book concentrates on the history of utilitarian kitchen wares through the 19th century. The first chapter introduces the variety of wares produced and explains the techniques and materials employed. Few illustrations are included due to the consistency of shape in utilitarian pottery, but a chart shows the basic forms. An appendix lists potters, their period, identification mark, and products.

A-A 394. KIRK, JOHN T. American Chairs: Queen Anne and Chippendale. New York: Knopf, 1972. 208 pp.
Kirk's examination of chairs, produced in that continuum of English-derived styles generally identified in America as Queen Anne and Chippendale, has three major components. First, after a brief introduction and discussion of the concept of regional characteristics, Kirk analyzes in detail distinctive construction and design traits of chairs produced in six regions of the eastern U.S. Next he provides a collection of photographs of nearly 200 different Queen Anne and Chippendale chairs, accompanied by comments on salient construction and design features. Finally, he offers conclusions about regional aesthetics.

A-A 395. KIRK, JOHN T. American Furniture and the British Tradition to 1830. New York: Knopf, 1982. 397 pp.
Kirk seeks to remedy a problem he sees in recent decorative arts scholarship. Although artifact analysis grows increasingly sophisticated, too little attention is paid to international relationships. Through scholarly essays and comparative illustrations this book examines the relationship between American and British furniture. The nine essays discuss such topics as the distribution of motifs, the role of wood identification, the problem of style lag, and the tradition of painted furniture. The visual survey is arranged by form and by period style within each form. Basic information on provenance is included. Little emphasis is given to stylistic analysis since Kirk believes the visual juxtaposition of the American and British pieces is sufficient. Over 1500 illustrations are included.

A-A 396. KLAMKIN, MARIAN. American Patriotic and Political China. New York: Scribner, 1973. 215 pp.
Klamkin details the history of patriotic and political china, discussing both import and export varieties. She explains the techniques involved and shows the impact of mechanization on price and quality. Individual chapters are concerned with specific manufacturers such as Wedgwood, or a specific type such as blue and white china. Special attention is given

193

to presidential imagery, but topics such as anti-slavery and women's suffrage are also discussed. A glossary of pottery and porcelain terms is
included.

A-A 397. KOVEL, RALPH M. and TERRY H. KOVEL. A Directory of American
          Silver, Pewter and Silverplate. New York: Crown, 1961.
          352 pp.
This book is a collection of basic data assembled by the Kovels for the
identification of silver, pewter, and silverplate. Each chapter has a
short section that discusses the history of the medium and presents typical
"shapes" in which the mark of a craftsman would have been contained.
Following this is a large section containing the names of known craftsmen,
birth, death, and/or working dates, their city, and references by number
to the Kovels' extensive bibliography. When available, an example of
the craftsman's mark is included

A-A 398. LASANSKY, JEANETTE. To Cut, Piece and Solder: The Work of the
          Rural Pennsylvania Tinsmith 1778-1908. University Park: Penn-
          sylvania State University Press, 1982. 80 pp.
Relying on period newspapers, trade catalogues, business directories,
personal interviews, and secondary sources, Lasansky documents the life
and work of the Pennsylvania tinsmith. Numerous black-and-white photographs show shop interiors, advertisements, and artifacts from museums
and private collections. Lasansky traces the craft from its first documentation in 1757 to the early 20th century. Interweaving social and
design history, Lasansky describes the tinsmithing process, innovations
which brought uniformity of design, and the change in emphasis from household wares to roofing and furnace work. Cheese biggins, ale tasters,
coffee pots, quilt patterns, and cookie cutters are but a few of the
objects identified and discussed.

A-A 399. LAUGHLIN, LEDLIE IRWIN. Pewter in America: Its Makers and Their
          Marks. 3 vols. Vols. 1 & 2, Boston: Houghton Mifflin, 1940;
          Vol. 3, Barre, Mass.: Barre, 1971. 655pp.
Updated by the addition of a third volume, this 1940 history of American
pewter attempts to be a comprehensive source of information for collectors
within the limits of surviving documentation. Early manufacturers are
grouped geographically since styles within an area were often very similar.
With improved communication, styles became national and, consequently,
Laughlin organizes britannia period pewterers alphabetically. Since most
britannia was plated after 1850, Laughlin essentially ceases his history
at that date. The third volume follows the plan of the first two but
presents new information on previously mentioned pewterers and on those
newly discovered.

A-A 400. LEA, ZILLA RIDER, ed. The Ornamented Chair: Its Development
          in America 1700-1890. Rutland, Vt.: Tuttle, 1960. 173 pp.
This collection of seven essays is devoted to the history of this highly
regional furniture style which features painted decoration. The development of ornamentation is traced from hand-painted motifs through stenciling
to the end of the technique in mass-production. The authors point out
that although the chair manufacturers are often known, the decorators
are usually anonymous.

A-A 401. LITTLE, NINA FLETCHER. Neat and Tidy: Boxes and Their Contents
          Used in Early American Households. New York: Dutton, 1980.
          205 pp.
This book is concerned with the social and decorative importance of boxes.
Using wills, inventories, and other primary sources, Little analyzes the
role these storage containers played in American life through the middle
of the 19th century. Chapters are devoted to boxes for general convenience,

personal use, domestic purposes, and boxes of unique design. Both hand-crafted and factory-made boxes are considered, as are imported boxes. The styles and techniques of box decoration are also discussed. Chapters are subdivided into sections concentrating on the form of the box and the purpose and contents of the box.

A-A 402. LYNN, CATHERINE. Wallpaper in America: From the Seventeenth Century to World War I. New York: Norton, 1980. 533 pp.
Wallpaper was often considered the most important aspect of a room's decor and was given symbolic and moral implications by 19th-century writers. This book attempts to provide a comprehensive introduction to wallpaper usage in America. Lynn presents a history of style, tracing not only the historical evolution of patterns but also their geographical dissemination across the country. The social importance of wallpaper is explored, and the theories of wallpaper design are also detailed.

A-A 403. MADIGAN, MARY JEAN and SUSAN COLGAN, eds. Early American Furniture, From Settlement to City: Aspects of Form, Style, and Regional Design from 1620 to 1830. New York: Billboard, 1983. 160 pp.
This is a collection of articles which originally appeared in Arts and Antiques magazine. Essentially revisionist, many of these studies not only discuss style but present scientific data on construction and wood analysis. Period documents are examined, and the interrelationship between American and European furniture design is emphasized by most of the writers. The topics covered include: Country Chippendale, Georgia Piedmont Furniture, The Fiddleback Chair, and Painted Furniture.

A-A 404. MAYHEW, EDGAR de N. and MINOR MYERS, Jr. A Documentary History of American Interiors from the Colonial Era to 1915. New York: Scribner, 1980. 399 pp.
This study concentrates on the economic and social factors that influence interior design. The authors compiled their information on the contents of interiors from such primary sources as pattern books, inventories, and diaries. For evidence concerning the arrangement of furniture they used contemporary illustrations. The book is intended to be helpful to restorationists by providing accurate information concerning all aspects of a room's interior design. Consequently, each chapter contains sections on floors, walls, furniture, lighting, etc.

A-A 405. McKEARIN, GEORGE S. and HELEN McKEARIN. American Glass. New York: Crown, 1941. 622 pp.
The McKearins offer an extensive history of American glass from its begin-nings through the end of the 19th century. The book is aimed at collectors and scholars. Detailed information is presented on style, technique, and attributions. Two chapters present the history of glass and the basic techniques for its production and ornamentation. The story of American glass is told by city, region, or manufacturer. Specific techniques such as Blown Three Mold or pressed glass and types such as historical flasks are extensively discussed. Various charts on particular types of glass—using the McKearin coding system—are provided, as are a glossary and a chronological list of American glass houses.

A-A 406. McKEARIN, HELEN and GEORGE S. McKEARIN. Two Hundred Years of American Blown Glass. 1950; Rev. ed. New York: Crown, 1966. 382 pp.
Considering glass crucial to the development of American civilization, the McKearins have produced a comprehensive history of American blown glass through the 19th century and with some mention of 20th-century developments. The political and economic factors influencing glassmaking are closely examined and the rise and fall of numerous glasshouses is

explained in the light of these undercurrents. For example, the effects
of the revolution, the growth of the infrastructure, and the introduction
of protective tariffs are considered. The book is organized both chronologically and topically.

A-A 407. MELCHOR, JAMES R., N. GORDON LOHR, and MARILYN S. MELCHOR.
Eastern Shore, Virginia Raised-Panel Furniture 1730-1830. Norfolk
Va.: Chrysler Museum, 1982. 135 pp.
By the time proper attention was paid to southern furniture, many of the
objects had been sold north and had lost their southern pedigree. One
group that survived due to its large size, durable construction, and utilitarian nature is the raised-panel furniture, usually cupboards, of Eastern
Virginia. The stated intention of the authors "is to provide a comprehensive documentation and comparative study" of this furniture. Emphasis
is given to aspects of technique, and the book contains many photographs
and drawings of construction details. The first chapter provides the
socioeconomic background, and the remaining six chapters concentrate on
the six types of raised-panel furniture.

A-A 408. MONTGOMERY, CHARLES F. A History of American Pewter. New York:
Praeger, 1973. 246 pp.
Montgomery explores the everyday use of pewter and the techniques of pewter
manufacture. One chapter discusses aspects of the connoisseurship of
pewter, but the majority of the book details the variety of objects made
from pewter with stylistic, technical, and cultural factors considered.
An appendix presents the marks of the pewter and britannia manufacturers
that are represented in the text. Other appendices present lists of significant public collections of pewter, plates, and dishes in the Winterthur
collection with a chart of their metal composition, and a section on how
to clean old pewter.

A-A 409. MONTGOMERY, CHARLES F. and PATRICIA E. KANE, eds. American Art:
1750-1800, Towards Independence. Boston: New York Graphic
Society, 1976. 320 pp.
This volume was published as a catalogue for the landmark bicentennial
exhibition of American arts that opened at Yale University and traveled
to the Victoria and Albert Museum in London. Divided into three parts,
it comprises a series of essays on American style and culture, an extensively annotated and illustrated discussion of each of the approximately
250 objects in the exhibition, and a brief descriptive catalogue of the
objects.

A-A 410. ORMSBEE, THOMAS H. The Windsor Chair. New York: Deerfield
Books, 1962. 304 pp.
Ormsbee traces the history of the Windsor chair from its Gothic birth
in England through the 19th century. Although a short chapter is devoted
to the English Windsor chair, Ormsbee concentrates on the American varieties. He considers the American chair "outstanding" because it is of
solid construction but does not sacrifice graceful proportion. The author
discusses material, technique, and design, and he points out regional
variations in Windsor construction. A large section of captioned illustrations is presented and a chapter discusses historically important Windsor chairs. A checklist of Windsor chairmakers is also included.

A-A 411. OTTO, CELIA JACKSON. American Furniture of the Nineteenth Century.
New York: Viking Press, 1965. 229 pp.
Concentrating on the influence of French design, Otto distinguishes between
the furniture styles of such French immigrants as Charles Lannuier, Michel
Bouvier, and those of such indigenous craftsmen as Duncan Phyfe, and John
and Thomas Seymour. She also traces regionalist differences in material,
technique, and form. Examples of French prototypes are included, and

the continuing importance of French design through the 1870s is detailed.
The analysis of all examples emphasizes the distinguishing characteristics
of each period and craftsman. The influence of social and historical
developments is also mentioned.

A-A 412. PEPPER, ADELINE. The Glass Gaffers of New Jersey and Their Creations from 1739 to the Present. New York: Scribner, 1971.
330 pp.
In this study Pepper focuses on the history of handblown glass in New
Jersey. The book is arranged around individual glassworks, towns, or
specific craftsmen and their descendants. This method maintains the "continuum of events" by showing how the "intermarriage of glassmaking families" and the effects of "historical and natural calamities" have influenced glassmaking. Pepper has endeavored to correct factual errors in
earlier histories and to contribute new data. Furthermore, the author
has interviewed old gaffers and has researched a variety of primary sources
that had never been examined before. She also discusses relevant events
in New Jersey history and presents some of the social implications of
glass manufacturing.

A-A 413. QUIMBY, IAN M. G., ed. Ceramics in America. Charlottesville:
University Press of Virginia, 1973. 374 pp.
This volume gathers together fourteen papers presented at a conference
at the Winterthur Museum in 1972. Chairperson Dwight Lanmon invited anthropologists, archaeologists, historians, and curators to address a variety
of questions about ceramics made or used in America in the 17th, 18th,
and early 19th centuries. The papers by Bernard Fontana and James Deetz
are concerned with methodological issues. The remaining papers seek to
interpret the range and popularity of certain forms, examine the roles
of technology and taste, or document design, manufacture, ownership, or
trade patterns with greater precision.

A-A 414. REVI, ALBERT CHRISTIAN. American Art Nouveau Glass. Camden,
N.J.: Nelson, 1968. 476 pp.
A detailed history of American Art Nouveau glass is presented in this
volume. The introduction contains a general history of the Art Nouveau
movement as well as an exploration of its stylistic sources. The text
concentrates on eighteen manufacturers. The history of each studio is
recounted, and analyses of specific types of glass from the studio are
presented. Techniques are explained and style is considered; some trademarks are shown.

A-A 415. REVI, ALBERT CHRISTIAN. American Cut and Engraved Glass. New
York: Nelson, 1965. 497 pp.
In this work, Revi covers the history and manufacturers of American cut
and engraved glass from its beginnings in the late 18th century well into
the 20th century. He concentrates on the middle Atlantic and northeastern
states but includes companies from a few midwestern states as well. The
opening chapter presents a brief overview of the development of the industry and includes information on procedures and technological improvements.
The rest of the book details the history and styles of the various companies operating in each of the states covered. An appendix presents
the trademarks and labels for forty-seven companies. There is both a
general index and a pattern index.

A-A 416. REVI, ALBERT CHRISTIAN. American Pressed Glass and Figure Bottles.
New York: Nelson, 1964. 446 pp.
Revi traces the history of pressed glass and figure bottles into the 20th
century. The glass companies discussed in the book are arranged alphabetically; the history of a firm and the styles that it produced are
explained. Photographs, drawings, diagrams, and illustrations are used

to present the glass styles. A chapter depicts patent designs that could not be associated with any company, and a final chapter discusses the varieties of American figure bottles.

A-A 417. ROGERS, MEYRIC R. American Interior Design: The Traditions and Development of Domestic Design from Colonial Times to the Present. New York: Norton, 1947. 309 pp.
Rogers, writing in 1947, presents a history of the American interior through the 1940s. He emphasizes the historical and social influences on design, but style and technique are also considered. The book is divided into five chapters which feature different periods in design history The individual chapters are broken down into discussions of different decorative art forms, as well as cultural and historical trends. A collection of plates features photographs of miniature model rooms designed by Mrs. James Ward Thorne for the Chicago Art Institute. All illustrations are captioned and the plates present an extensive discussion of the interiors. A glossary and biographical notes on craftsmen are included.

A-A 418. SAFFORD, CARLETON L. and ROBERT BISHOP. America's Quilts and Coverlets. New York: Dutton, 1972. 313 pp.
The authors present a lavishly illustrated introduction to American bed-coverings. Although of use to the scholar—many of the illustrations were never published before—the book is designed for the lay person. The history of style, materials, and technique is explained in non-technical terminology. The chapters are organized according to type of bed-covering: Linsey-Woolsey, Overshot coverlet, etc. The text of each chapter features basic information on the bedcovering, while the captioned illustrations discuss specific aspects of the artifact.

A-A 419. SCHIFFER, MARGARET BERWIND. Furniture and Its Makers of Chester County Pennsylvania. Philadelphia: University of Pennsylvania Press, 1966. 280 pp.
This is a history of non-Germanic country furniture manufactured in the area immediately west of Philadelphia from 1682 to 1850. An alphabetical list of craftsmen that includes relevant contemporary documentation is presented. A section discusses specific characteristics of Chester County furniture, and a collection of miscellaneous information is included. The illustrations provide basic information, dimensions, and provenance concerning the artifacts.

A-A 420. SCHWARTZ, MARVIN D. and RICHARD WOLFE. A History of American Art Porcelain. New York: Rennaissance Editions, 1967. 93 pp.
This short survey was the first book devoted solely to the study of American art porcelain. Schwartz and Wolfe provide a stylistic and cultural history of American porcelain from its beginnings in the 18th century through the 20th century. After an introductory chapter on the world history of porcelain and a discussion of early American efforts at the craft, the authors explore the Empire style, the Rococo revival, and varieties of eclecticism before concluding with a chapter on the 20th century. A short annotated bibliography of American ceramics is included.

A-A 421. SEALE, WILLIAM. The Tasteful Interlude: American Interiors Through the Camera's Eye, 1860-1917. New York: Praeger, 1975. 256 pp.
Seale introduces this pictorial study of Victorian taste with an unconventional explication of the major trends in interior decoration between 1860 and 1917. He recognizes that style and taste appear in the selection and arrangement of objects in a room setting as well as in the design of the objects themselves. Gleaned from sources across the country, these high quality reproductions constitute an important published pictorial archive of Victorian culture in America.

A-A 422. <u>Shaker</u> Furniture <u>and</u> Objects <u>from</u> the <u>Faith and</u> Edward <u>Deming</u>
<u>Andrews</u> Collections <u>Commemorating</u> the <u>Bicentenary of</u> the <u>American</u>
<u>Shakers.</u> Washington, D.C.: Smithsonian Institution, 1973.
88 pp.
This volume contains a summary of the history of the Shakers in New England
by Edward Deming Andrews, comments on Shaker design by Jane Malcolm, and
a small collection of photographs of Shaker artifacts. It also includes
an interview with Faith Andrews, who, with her husband Edward, was instrumental in bringing Shaker culture to its current level of appreciation.

A-A 423. SHEA, JOHN G. <u>Antique</u> Country <u>Furniture</u> of <u>North</u> America. New
York: Van Nostrand Reinhold, 1975. 228 pp.
Shea presents a cultural and stylistic guide to country furniture through
the 19th century, including detailed structural information. The first
section of the book discusses the historical background of regional styles
and includes information on European sources. Emphasis is given to regions
with the highest quality or most significant furniture. The second section
presents photographic comparisons of the regional variations in different
categories of furniture. The third section provides an illustrated study
of country construction techniques, and the fourth section contains measured drawings of a large number of pieces of country furniture.

A-A 424. STILLINGER, ELIZABETH. <u>The</u> Antiques <u>Guide</u> to <u>Decorative</u> Arts
<u>in</u> America, <u>1600-1875.</u> New York: Dutton, 1972. 463 pp.
Stillinger treats almost three centuries of craftsmanship in increments
of twenty-five years. Each of her divisions constitutes a particular
style (e.g., William and Mary [1700-1725], Chippendale [1750-1775], and
Victorian [1850-1875]), and every section begins with a short discussion
of historical background and stylistic development. The different media
of furniture, silver, ceramics, and glass are considered separately in
each division.

A-A 425. STOREY, WALTER RENDELL. <u>Period</u> Influences <u>in</u> Interior <u>Decoration.</u>
New York: Harper, 1937. 211 pp.
Storey examines "period style" from the early Colonial dwellings to the
modern New York penthouse. Rooms which are wholly of a specific period,
the author maintains, can offer unique insights into the general temperament of the society of that period. American furnishings are the subject
of the book; however, European movements and influences receive extensive
treatment insofar as they shaped the evolution of the decorative arts
of the U.S.

A-A 426. TRACY, BERRY B., MARILYNN JOHNSON, MARVIN D. SCHWARTZ, and
SUZANNE BOORSCH. <u>19th-Century</u> America: <u>Furniture and</u> Other
<u>Decorative</u> Arts. New York: Metropolitan Museum of Art, 1970.
n.p.
The catalogue of an exhibition held at the Metropolitan Museum of Art
in 1970 to celebrate its founding a century before, this is an important
treatment of high culture decorative arts of the 19th century. Tracy's
concise introductory essay provides a discussion of the evolution of styles
in 19th-century America, and establishes a conceptual context for the
catalogue of nearly 300 entries that follows. All objects are illustrated
and accompanied by descriptive and interpretive paragraphs.

A-A 427. VERMEULE, CORNELIUS. <u>Numismatic</u> Art <u>in</u> America: <u>Aesthetics</u>
<u>and</u> the <u>United</u> States <u>Coinage.</u> Cambridge, Mass.: Harvard Uni-
versity Press, 1971. 266 pp.
Vermeule's view is that American coins have been unfairly disparaged or
ignored by art historians and that, in fact, they constitute an important
form of official historical art. Vermeule organizes his discussion chronologically. At the beginning he examines the background for Federal coinage;

at the end he offers a prognosis for the future of the medallic art in
America. Between these two boundaries he illustrates and discusses in
detail not only such familiar coins as the Indian Head and Lincoln pennies,
but also an immense range of commemorative medals known largely only to
coin collectors.

A-A 428. VLACH, JOHN. The Afro-American Tradition in Decorative Arts.
Cleveland, Ohio: Cleveland Museum of Art, 1978. 175 pp.
This book is a cultural history account of nine media in which black artisans have made a distinctive imprint on American arts and crafts: basketry,
musical instruments, wood carving, quilting, pottery, boatbuilding, black-
smithing, architecture, and graveyard decoration. The objects described
are of two kinds: some are directly related to antecedents in Africa;
others are indirectly related to African examples in their iconography,
technology, spatial organization, or conceptual inspiration. Vlach asserts
that an improvisational mind set is the most significant and continuous
contribution of Afro-American craftsmen.

A-A 429. WARING, JANET. Early American Stencils on Walls and Furniture.
New York: W. R. Scott, 1937. 149 pp.
Waring, hoping to rekindle an interest in the disappearing craft of stencilling, here offers an overview of the techniques and styles of wall
and furniture stencilling. The book is divided into two parts. The first
part discusses the stencilled walls of New England, New York, and Ohio.
The styles and techniques of individual walls are analyzed and information
on the craftsmen is provided. The second part of the book consists of
a selective chronological history of stencilled furniture. Style and
technique are detailed, and the rise and fall of stencilled furniture
in the popular taste is explored. A short section mentions the use of
stencils on tin and velvet.

A-A 430. WATKINS, LURA WOODSIDE. Early New England Potters and Their
Wares. Cambridge, Mass.: Harvard University Press, 1950.
291 pp.
This book is concerned with two categories of New England pottery: common
red earthenware made from local clay and stoneware fashioned from imported
materials. Two other categories, mass-produced buffware and art pottery,
are discussed briefly. A chapter is devoted to the technical procedures
used in the manufacture of redware and stoneware. The remainder of the
book details the history and products of pottery manufacturers in various
parts of New England. A separate chapter is specifically concerned with
the styles of redware. Some 18th-century documents are included in an
appendix, and a checklist of New England potters is also provided.

A-A 431. WHITEHILL, WALTER MUIR, ed. Boston Furniture of the Eighteenth
Century. Boston: Colonial Society of Massachusetts, 1974.
316 pp.
The eight papers printed in this volume were presented at a 1972 symposium,
the purpose of which was to publicize recent scholarship about furniture
and furniture makers in early America. Although the various authors
limited their inquiries to the Boston area, their findings and research
designs constitute a survey of current directions and techniques utilized
by decorative arts researchers. Articles on japanned, blockfront, bombe,
and carved furniture draw upon the written as well as the artifactual
record to demonstrate regional cabinetmaking characteristics. Construction
and materials, along with style, proportion, and decoration, are visual
criteria for distinguishing among woodworking shops.

A-A 432. WILSON, KENNETH M. New England Glass and Glassmaking. New York: Crowell, 1972. 401 pp.
The minutia of glassmaking in New England through the 19th century and into the 20th is presented in this volume. Excerpts from letters, diaries, advertisements, and other primary sources are used to detail the histories of various firms. The styles produced by each firm are specified, utilizing (when appropriate) the flask coding system formulated by Helen and George McKearin. A chapter explaining the influence of imported glass precedes several chapters, each of which details the activities of numerous individual companies in the window, bottle, and flint glass industries. The economic importance of the glass industry is covered, as is the sociology of glass usage, e.g., the rise of the bitters industry is connected to the temperance movement.

IX.   A. ARCHITECTURE: SURVEYS

A-A 433. ANDREWS, WAYNE. American Gothic: Its Origins, Its Trials, Its Triumphs. New York: Random House, 1975. 154 pp.
Although photographs predominate in this volume, there is also an interpretive essay by Andrews that connects the Gothic Revival in America both to its European antecedents and to the modern movement that succeeded it. The author analyzes the products and the philosophies of the architects and writers associated with the Gothic style.

A-A 434. ANDREWS, WAYNE. Architecture, Ambition, and Americans: A Social History of American Architecture. 1955; Rev. ed. New York: Free Press, 1978. 332 pp.
Surveying American architectural styles from the 17th century to the present, Andrews deals not with the average or the typical, but with the architectural monuments that were embraced by the rich and powerful. His point is that ambition and money are the catalysts that produce artistic and hence architectural taste, or at least the desire for such taste.

A-A 435. ARTHUR, ERIC and DUDLEY WITNEY. The Barn: A Vanishing Landmark in North America. Greenwich, Conn.: New York Graphic Society, 1972. 256 pp.
The authors have high regard for the barns in Canada and the U.S. that were hand-built by master carpenters and their crews in the days before prefabrication and modern technology brought us the factory-built version. They discuss the Dutch Barn, the English Barn, the Pennsylvania Barn, the Connected Barn, and Circular and Polygonal Barns.

A-A 436. BENES, PETER and PHILIP D. ZIMMERMAN. New England Meeting House and Church, 1630-1850. Boston: Boston University Scholarly Publications, 1979. 177 pp.
Benes and Zimmerman describe New England meeting houses and churches not only in terms of their architectural features, but also in terms of their interior furnishings, construction techniques, seating arrangements, and more. The authors' purpose is to recreate in its entirety the "world" of the New England meeting house and church, including its social, political, religious, and artistic functions.

A-A 437. BUNTING, BAINBRIDGE. Early Architecture in New Mexico. Albuquerque: University of New Mexico Press, 1976. 122 pp.
The author explores the cultural differences among the Indian, Spanish, and Anglo-American inhabitants of New Mexico, as reflected in their architecture. According to Bunting, a basic unity prevailed in the architecture

of New Mexico from roughly 1700 to 1880; the only major differences found in the communities of the three cultures were the ways in which their modular units were composed.

A-A 438. BURCHARD, JOHN ELY and ALBERT BUSH-BROWN. The Architecture of America: A Social and Cultural History. Boston: Little, Brown, 1961. 595 pp.
This is a survey of architects, buildings, and architectural styles in America from the early 17th century to 1960. An introductory chapter on "The Nature of Architecture" explains the interrelationship between architecture and society--a theme the authors address throughout by noting achievements not only in architecture, but also in painting, literature, technology, business, and more.

A-A 439. CIUCCI, GIORGIO, FRANCESCO DAL CO, MARIO MANIERI-ELLA, and **MANFREDO TAFURI,** Translated by Barbara Luigia La Penta. The American City: From the Civil War to the New Deal. 1973; Transl. Cambridge, Mass.: MIT Press, 1979. 563 pp.
While the title of the book might suggest a survey of urban history from the 1860s to the 1930s, this is instead a collection of four separate essays on the American city. The topics are: Daniel H. Burnham and the City Beautiful movement; Progressive ideology and reform of the city; Frank Lloyd Wright and agrarian ideology; and the skyscraper and the city.

A-A 440. COHN, JAN. The Palace or the Poorhouse: The American House as a Cultural Symbol. East Lansing: Michigan State University Press, 1979. 267 pp.
Operating on the premise that the house has been, and continues to be, the dominant symbol for American culture, Cohn examines the writings of architects, politicians, novelists, reformers, and others to explain the complexities and contradictions inherent in that symbol. The author emphasizes how American attitudes toward houses of the rich contrast greatly with attitudes toward houses of the poor; she also discusses in some detail the mythology and nostalgia surrounding the home in the U.S.

A-A 441. CONDIT, CARL W. American Building: Materials and Techniques from the First Colonial Settlements to the Present. Chicago: University of Chicago Press, 1968. 329 pp.
This is a revised and corrected, though also condensed, version of Condit's more technical two-volume work, American Building Art (1960, 1961). Included here is a discussion of both the materials (e.g., wood, stone, iron, steel, concrete) and the techniques (e.g., timber-framing, masonry, steel-frame, reinforced concrete) that have played a major role in American building development. Condit is interested in the relationship between these materials and techniques and the course of American history.

A-A 442. CRAIG, LOIS A. and the staff of the Federal Architecture Project. The Federal Presence: Architecture, Politics, and Symbols in United States Government Building. Cambridge, Mass.: MIT Press, 1978. 580 pp.
This study, essentially a collection of thematic essays and photographs arranged in rough chronological order, tells of the growing architectural and environmental presence of the U.S. government from the end of the 18th century to the present. The authors treat not only the actual buildings erected by the government, but also how those buildings are perceived by society and how those perceptions relate to changing political and economic developments in the nation.

A-A 443. CRANZ, GALEN. The Politics of Park Design: A History of Urban
         Parks in America. Cambridge, Mass.: MIT Press, 1982. 347 pp.
The author's overall objective is to examine the significance of urban
parks within the intellectual and moral life of American society and culture. Using the park systems of three cities--New York, Chicago, and
San Francisco--as case studies, Cranz analyzes the roles played by philanthropists, professionals, bureaucrats, idealists, and all kinds of park
users in trying to understand the major forces that have shaped the movement for urban parks in the U.S.

A-A 444. DAVIDSON, MARSHALL B., ed. The American Heritage History of
         Notable American Houses. New York: American Heritage, 1971.
         383 pp.
Aimed primarily at a popular audience, this volume tells the story of
American life in terms of the houses that Americans have planned, built,
and lived in. With a selection of houses that the editor terms "the best
and, for the most part, the most typical" of all that have been built
from the 17th century to the present, an attempt is made to identify the
needs, tastes, and dreams of the people who lived in them.

A-A 445. DOWNING, ANTOINETTE F. and VINCENT J. SCULLY, Jr. The Architec-
         tural Heritage of Newport, Rhode Island, 1640-1915. 1952; Rev.
         ed. New York: Potter, 1967. 526 pp.
Although this is primarily a chronological history of Newport's architectural growth from its founding in 1639 to the first years of the 20th
century, larger developments in American social and economic history are
also considered. The sections written by Scully argue that Newport's
19th-century domestic buildings (especially the cottages and the country
houses done in the Stick and Shingle styles) can represent, in a microcosm,
American domestic architecture of that period.

A-A 446. FISHWICK, MARSHALL and J. MEREDITH NEIL, eds. Popular Architec-
         ture. Bowling Green, Ohio: Bowling Green Popular Press, 1974.
         120 pp.
Published originally as a special section in the Fall 1973 issue of the
Journal of Popular Culture, this is a collection of twelve essays--written
by architects, art historians, and architectural historians--that deals
with architecture as symbol and archetype. Among the topics considered
are: the skyscraper as popular icon; the American courtship of house
and car; squatter settlements as vernacular environments; and the aesthetics of bigness in late 19th-century American architecture.

A-A 447. FITCH, JAMES MARSTON. American Building, I: The Historical
         Forces That Shaped It. 1948; Rev. ed. Boston: Houghton Mifflin,
         1966. 350 pp.
Dividing American architectural history into nine chronological periods,
Fitch examines the forces within each that have shaped both the stylistic
and functional character of American building. Among the forces identified
by the author are industrialization, technological innovation, urbanization,
war, prosperity, and abundance. Volumes I (1966) and II (1972) of American
Building (see A-A 448) represent an updated and greatly enlarged version
of Fitch's single-volume study, American Building: The Forces That Shape
It (1948).

A-A 448. FITCH, JAMES MARSTON. American Building, II: The Environmental
         Forces That Shape It. 1948; Rev. ed. Boston: Houghton Mifflin,
         1972. 349 pp.
In this volume, Fitch seeks a holistic concept for explaining the relationship between human beings and the environmental forces that shape the
form and function of their buildings. These forces include: the thermal
environment; the atmospheric environment; the luminous environment; the

sonic environment; and space, time, and gravity. Fitch's synthesis is
based on more specialized studies by anthropologists, ecologists, physiolo-
gists, and psychologists.

A-A 449. FOLEY, MARY MIX. The American House. New York: Harper & Row,
1980. 299 pp.
In this survey of American domestic architecture, Foley provides a guide
to the various styles, identifying what it is that makes a house Georgian,
Greek Revival, Victorian, etc. Her chronology is in five parts: the
earliest years (when houses were transplanted from European traditions);
the Classical period (including Georgian, Federal, and Greek Revival);
the Victorian age (including the Romantic revivals); the American Renaissance (with its Beaux-Arts style); and the era of the modern house.

A-A 450. FORMAN, HENRY CHANDLEE. The Architecture of the Old South:
The Medieval Style, 1585-1850. Cambridge, Mass.: Harvard University Press, 1948. 203 pp.
Forman maintains that the American colonists in the South tended to cling
to the medieval building practices and architectural style they had left
behind in England. And since American architecture tended to lag about
fifty years behind the style in England across the ocean, Forman claims
that by the end of the 17th century, American architecture was even more
medieval than the coeval English version.

A-A 451. GEBHARD, DAVID and DEBORAH NEVINS. 200 Years of American Architectural Drawing. New York: Watson-Guptill, 1977. 301 pp.
The drawings of some eighty architects and architectural firms are represented in this survey, covering the years 1776 to 1976. Gebhard outlines
the history of architectural drawing in America, relating it to the evolution of the architectural profession and emphasizing the connection
between drawings and the built work. Nevins summarizes the careers of
the individual architects, placing their drawings in the context of their
professional development.

A-A 452. GLASSIE, HENRY. Folk Housing in Middle Virginia: A Structural
Analysis of Historic Artifacts. Knoxville: University of
Tennessee Press, 1975. 231 pp.
Examining vernacular houses in a rural area of Virginia, the author's
objective is to understand not so much how these houses were built, but
rather how they were conceived. Influenced by French structuralist theory,
Glassie translates these buildings into formulas that demonstrate how
these seemingly simple houses are actually the product of an intricate
architectural competence.

A-A 453. GOODE, JAMES M. Capital Losses: A Cultural History of Washington's Destroyed Buildings. Washington, D.C.: Smithsonian Institution Press, 1979. 517 pp.
This work is divided into two major categories of building types--
residential and non-residential--and is further subdivided according to building function (e.g., commercial, government, rowhouse, apartment house,
etc.) and date of design. Although on one level it is simply a guide
to buildings that have been destroyed, the book's chronological and functional format allows also for a broad cultural history of Washington architecture to emerge.

A-A 454. GOWANS, ALAN. Architecture in New Jersey: A Record of American
Civilization. Princeton. N.J.: Van Nostrand, 1964. 161 pp.
The author argues that because New Jersey has always been more a corridor
for the transmission of people and ideas than an originating center of
culture, its architecture can be regarded as a revealing record of the
development of American civilization. In the state's architecture, Gowans

traces the diverse influences, the great ideas, the changing tastes, and the permanent values of American character and culture from the 17th century to the present.

A-A 455. GOWANS, ALAN. Images of American Living: Four Centuries of Architecture and Furniture as Cultural Expression. Philadelphia: Lippincott, 1964. 498 pp.

This volume is based on the idea that there have been certain trends of historical development (such as the conquest of nature and the evolution of democracy) that reflect the fundamental character, aspirations, and moods of American civilization. The basic design concepts used in architecture and furniture are very much influenced by these trends, according to Gowans, and therefore may be seen as history in its most tangible form.

A-A 456. GRANT, H. ROGER and CHARLES W. BOHI. The Country Railroad Station in America. Boulder, Colo.: Pruett, 1978. 183 pp.

This study of the small-town or country railroad depot is divided into two parts: (a) an assessment of the depot as a community hub; and (b) an architectural overview of the combination freight and passenger depot, tracing its evolution and surveying its regional variations. The authors note that, for existing country depots, the future appears to be bleak.

A-A 457. GROW, LAWRENCE. Waiting for the 5:05: Terminal, Station and Depot in America. New York: Main Street/Universe Books, 1977. 128 pp.

Through a number of brief sketches, the author traces the history of railroad stations and describes the evolution of their architectural styles (including Country Gothic, Spanish Mission, Beaux Arts, and what came to be known simply as Railroad Style). Special attention is paid to the stations designed by H. H. Richardson and Frank Furness.

A-A 458. GUTMAN, RICHARD J. S. and ELLIOTT KAUFMAN. American Diner. New York: Harper & Row, 1979. 154 pp.

Maintaining that the diner has always been a faithful reflection of public taste and public need, Gutman traces its history from the first mobile lunch cart in 1872 to the present. Especially noted is how various architectural styles (such as the modernism of the 1920s, the streamlined look of the 1930s, and the futuristic manner of the 1960s) have influenced diner design over the years.

A-A 459. HAMLIN, TALBOT FAULKNER. The American Spirit in Architecture. New Haven, Conn.: Yale University Press, 1926. 353 pp.

This general survey of American architectural history is part of The Pageant of America series edited by Ralph Henry Gabriel. In this volume, Hamlin covers the succession of architectural styles; looks at specific types of buildings (e.g., banks, factories, theaters, and churches); and tries to integrate this material into larger themes of American cultural history, including contact with England, westward expansion, and urbanization.

A-A 460. HAMMETT, RALPH W. Architecture in the United States: A Survey of Architectural Styles Since 1776. New York: Wiley, 1976. 409 pp.

The history of American architecture, according to Hammett, is divided into cycles of approximately twenty years, during which each generation develops its own identity and characteristic style. In this volume, the style of each of nine periods is described in relation to its contemporary culture and as a reflection of the social, economic, and technical changes that influence architectural development.

A-A 461. HAYDEN, DOLORES. The Grand Domestic Revolution: A History of
          Feminist Designs for American Homes, Neighborhoods, and Cities.
          Cambridge, Mass.: MIT Press, 1981. 367 pp.
Hayden brings to light the work of American "material feminists," who,
in the years between the Civil War and the 1930s, called for a "grand
domestic revolution" in the material conditions of women. By redefining
housework and the housing needs of women, these feminists, according to
the author, impelled architects and urban planners to reconsider the
effects of design on family life.

A-A 462. HAYDEN, DOLORES. Seven American Utopias: The Architecture of
          Communitarian Socialism, 1790-1975. Cambridge, Mass.: MIT
          Press, 1976. 401 pp.
This study explores the relationship between social organization and building in communities built by Shakers, Mormons, Fourierists, Perfectionists,
Inspirationists, Union Colonists, and Llano Colonists at seven different
sites in the U.S. Hayden is particularly interested in the ways the com-
munards resolved conflicts between their needs for authority and participation, community and privacy, and uniqueness and replicability.

A-A 463. Historic America: Buildings, Structures, and Sites. Washington,
          D.C.: Library of Congress, 1983. 708 pp.
Published to commemorate the first fifty years of the Historic American
Buildings Survey (HABS), this is in part a checklist of the sites and
structures that have been documented by HABS and/or HAER (Historic American
Engineering Record). In addition, there are sixteen essays written by
architectural historians, librarians, architects, archivists, and curators
on a wide variety of topics dealing with HABS, historic preservation,
construction, engineering design, and future directions.

A-A 464. HITCHCOCK, HENRY-RUSSELL and WILLIAM SEALE. Temples of Democracy:
          The State Capitols of the USA. New York: Harcourt Brace
          Jovanovich, 1976. 333 pp.
The authors survey the histories of the state capitol buildings in each
of the fifty states, paying particular attention to the structures as
symbols of democracy, as well as to the overall evolution of architectural
styles and building features. They maintain that the state capitol is
one of America's two unique contributions to monumental architecture;
the other, they say, is the skyscraper.

A-A 465. HITCHCOCK, HENRY-RUSSELL and ARTHUR DREXLER, eds. Built in USA:
          Post-war Architecture. New York: Museum of Modern Art, 1952.
          128 pp.
Hitchcock contributes an essay on the state of contemporary architecture
in the U.S.; and Drexler discusses some forty-five buildings selected—
on the basis of "quality and significance of the moment"—for an exhibition
at the Museum of Modern Art on post-war architecture. Among the architects
represented are Marcel Breuer, Philip Johnson, Mies van der Rohe, and
Frank Lloyd Wright.

A-A 466. JACKSON, JOHN BRINCKERHOFF. The Necessity for Ruins and Other
          Topics. Amherst: University of Massachusetts Press, 1980.
          129 pp.
This collection of essays addresses Jackson's foremost concern: the history of the American cultural landscape. His objective is to think of
landscapes not merely in terms of how they look (i.e., how they conform
to an aesthetic ideal), but how they satisfy our elementary needs. Among
the topics covered by Jackson are the sacred grove in American cultural
history; the incentive provided by ruins for restoration, renewal, and
reform; and the significance of the garage in American vernacular architecture.

A-A 467. JACOBS, STEPHEN W. Wayne County: The Aesthetic Heritage of a Rural Area: A Catalogue for the Environment. Lyons, N.Y.: Wayne County Historical Society, 1979. 288 pp.
Although the focus of this work may seem somewhat restricted—limited as it is to the study of one rural county in upstate New York—its objective is broad: to serve as a model for inventorying, cataloguing, and classifying the design resources (particularly the architectural elements) that can be found in any rural area in the U.S. According to the author, the conventional wisdom regarding rural America (i.e., that it is relatively immutable and slow to change) is wrong.

A-A 468. JOHNSTON, NORMAN. The Human Cage: A Brief History of Prison Architecture. New York: Walker, 1973. 68 pp.
Johnston traces the history of prison architecture from its antecedents in castle, dungeon, and fortress, through the large, high-security institutions of the 19th century, and down to the new breed of open, dispersed minimum-security facilities in the 20th century. He concludes that the "history of prison architecture stands as a discouraging testament of our sometimes intentional, sometimes accidental degradation of our fellow man."

A-A 469. JORDAN, TERRY G. Texas Log Buildings: A Folk Architecture. Austin: University of Texas Press, 1978. 230 pp.
According to Jordan, the products of folk architecture come not only from professional architects, but from the collective memory of the people, whose mental images change little from one generation to the next. In this volume, the author examines a specific product of folk architecture— log building in Texas—by tracing its origins and diffusion, from Europe to North America and westward to Texas; its construction techniques and methods; and its various types and plans as found in the different cultural regions of Texas.

A-A 470. KAISER, HARVEY H. Great Camps of the Adirondacks. Boston: Godine, 1982. 240 pp.
From the end of the Civil War to the beginning of the Depression, a group of industrialists, financiers, and railroad builders came to the Adirondack mountain region in northern New York to build family vacation retreats and camps. Kaiser provides a history of this development. He notes the social life of the camps, considers some of the major builders and buildings, and describes the rustic use of native timber and stone that came to be known as the Adirondack Style.

A-A 471. KAUFFMAN, HENRY J. The American Farmhouse. New York: Hawthorn Books, 1975. 265 pp.
Kauffman's survey of American farmhouses is limited only to three regions— New England, the Middle States (from New York to Ohio), and the Southeast— and only to those structures that were built during the 17th, 18th, and 19th centuries. Within this sample, the author observes patterns in the variable sizes of the structures, in the mobility of the farm population, and in the influence of regional and ethnic traditions on farmhouse construction and design.

A-A 472. KENNEDY, ROGER G. American Churches. New York: Stewart, Tabori & Chang, 1982. 295 pp.
Kennedy's central notion is that what makes a building religious is not so much its container (i.e., its physical style and structure), as its content (i.e., the degree to which it functions as a religious edifice and reinforces religious feelings and actions). To illustrate this point, the author interweaves some general reflections on American religious life together with material on the architects, architecture, and worshippers of specific religious buildings.

A-A 473. KIDNEY, WALTER C. The Architecture of Choice: Eclecticism in
America, 1880-1930. New York: Braziller, 1974. 178 pp.
The author's history of eclecticism in America covers its European backgrounds, its numerous examples in this country, and some of the psychological and aesthetic reasons for its great popularity here. Kidney maintains that eclecticism—just like the modernism espoused by members of
the Chicago and Prairie Schools—was a rejection of the values and culture
of the mid-19th century.

A-A 474. KIMBALL, FISKE. American Architecture. Indianapolis, Ind.:
Bobbs-Merrill, 1928. 262 pp.
This history of architecture in America traces its development from Colonial beginnings, through the various Georgian styles, Greek Revival, Romanticism, Gothic Revival, classical form, and finally Modernism. Kimball
observes that it is in architecture, of all the arts, that America best
expresses its newness, its vitality, and its greatness.

A-A 475. KOUWENHOVEN, JOHN A. Made in America: The Arts in Modern Civilization. Garden City, N.Y.: Doubleday, 1948. 303 pp.
Kouwenhoven looks at a variety of art forms—including painting, literature,
and music—but he pays particular attention to architecture in distinguishing between the cultivated tradition (with modes borrowed from Europe
and characterized by ornateness, embellishment, and decoration) and the
vernacular tradition (arising out of the everyday life of the American
environment and characterized by lightness, constraint, and simplicity).

A-A 476. KUBLER, GEORGE. The Religious Architecture of New Mexico in
the Colonial Period and Since the American Occupation. Colorado
Springs, Colo.: Taylor Museum, 1940. 232 pp.
Following a discussion of the missionary enterprise in the New Mexico
region (noting both the methods and the historical causes of evangeliza-
tion), Kubler analyzes the religious buildings in Indian pueblos and in
Spanish towns and villages. Attention is paid to each building's location, orientation, distribution, utilization of materials, plan, structure,
mass, and use of visual effects.

A-A 477. LANCASTER, CLAY. Architectural Follies in America; or, Hammer,
Sawtooth, and Nail. Rutland, Vt.: Tuttle, 1960. 243 pp.
Lancaster defines architectural follies as those buildings that are offensive to the sense of good taste and restraint; that are out of key with
their neighbors in size, style, or planning; or that were financial disasters for their builders or investors. Among the follies he describes
are: oriental exoticisms, such as Iranistan and Trollope's Bazaar; octa-
gons, hexagons, and other geometric forms; corn palaces; elephant hotels;
and wedding-cake houses.

A-A 478. LANCASTER, CLAY. The Japanese Influence in America. New York:
Walton H. Rawls, 1963. 292 pp.
Lancaster covers a number of topics in this volume, including the Japanese
influence upon the Chicago School of architecture; the Japanese contribution to the development of the American bungalow; the influence of Japan
on modern architecture; the effect of Japanese gardens on landscaping
in America; and the impact of Japanese exhibitions at expositions and
world's fairs in the late 19th and early 20th centuries.

A-A 479. LOCKWOOD, CHARLES. Bricks and Brownstone: The New York Row
House, 1783-1929, An Architectural and Social History. New
York: McGraw-Hill, 1972. 262 pp.
Lockwood looks not only at the architectural styles (including Federal,
Greek Revival, Gothic Revival, Italianate, and Second Empire) of the New
York row house from the late 18th to the early 19th centuries, but also

at the aesthetic, social, and technological forces that helped to shape those styles. In addition, Lockwood discusses the lives of the families who inhabited the row houses.

A-A 480. LOTH, CALDER and JULIUS TROUSDALE SADLER, Jr. The Only Proper Style: Gothic Architecture in America. Boston: New York Graphic Society, 1975. 184 pp.
This volume traces the wide range of architectural interpretations of the Gothic style in the U.S. and examines our changing attitudes toward it. Among the building types covered are churches, colleges, mortuary chapels, cottage residences, pavilions, and outbuildings. The coverage extends from the Gothic Survival of the 17th century to the Skyscraper Gothic of the early 20th century.

A-A 481. LYNES, RUSSELL. The Tastemakers. New York: Harper, 1954. 362 pp.
The author's survey of taste in America identifies three distinct eras: (1) the Age of Public Taste, beginning with the election of Andrew Jackson in 1828, when taste became everybody's business; (2) the Age of Private Taste, when the tastemakers directed their messages at individuals, such as the rich who were looked up to as models of behavior; and (3) the Age of Corporate Taste, when the tastemakers took to working through the mass media to reach the millions. For each era, Lynes cites a number of examples from the built environment, including landscaping, building design, and the idea of a home.

A-A 482. MARSHALL, HOWARD WIGHT. Folk Architecture in Little Dixie: A Regional Culture in Missouri. Columbia: University of Missouri Press, 1981. 146 pp.
Using Henry Glassie's Folk Housing in Middle Virginia (see A-A 452) as a basis for understanding the ways of folk builders, Marshall examines the vernacular architecture of the Little Dixie region of eight counties in northeastern Missouri. The author's aim is to suggest how folk architecture can help both to define a particular region and to illustrate its settlement history. The topics addressed include construction methods; materials; building types and their variations; and the relationship of architecture to one's sense of place.

A-A 483. MOORE, CHARLES W., GERALD ALLEN, and DONLYN LYNDON. The Place of Houses. 1974; Rev. ed. New York: Holt, Rinehart & Winston, 1979. 278 pp.
Moore, Allen, and Lyndon begin by describing three towns they admire greatly: Edgartown, Mass., a 300-year-old settlement on Martha's Vineyard; Santa Barbara, Calif., with its architectural allusions to its Spanish heritage; and Sea Ranch, a second-home community begun along the northern California coast in 1965. From each of these places, the authors draw lessons that they then use to establish a conceptual framework for understanding the patterns and purposes of the house in society and culture.

A-A 484. MOORE, CHARLES W., KATHRYN SMITH, and PETER BECKER, eds. Home Sweet Home: American Domestic Vernacular Architecture. Los Angeles, Calif.: Craft and Folk Art Museum; New York: Rizzoli, 1983. 150 pp.
American domestic vernacular architecture, according to the editors, is defined by a vast conglomeration of building types (including New England saltboxes, California ranch houses, Great Plains sodhouses, and Southern shotgun houses). This collection of essays, written by some twenty-five contributors, observes that all vernacular dwellings are built in response to the particular needs of people within the limitations of a given time and the demands (or resources) of a given region.

A-A 485. MORGAN, WILLIAM N. Prehistoric Architecture in the Eastern United States. Cambridge, Mass.: MIT Press, 1980. 197 pp.
Writing as an architect, Morgan provides an overview of the architecture--primarily earth mounds--built by Native Americans in the Eastern U.S. from about 2200 B.C. until the time of the first contact with Europeans. His introductory chapter examines the mounds' general architectural elements (such as planning, structure, and design); then he describes some eighty specific sites whose plans he has reconstructed on the basis of archaeological data.

A-A 486. MORRISON, HUGH. Early American Architecture: From the First Colonial Settlements to the National Period. New York: Oxford University Press, 1952. 619 pp.
All types of structures--domestic, ecclesiastical, commercial, public, and private--are discussed in this treatment of American building from the earliest colonies (including those of the Spanish, French, Swedish, Dutch, and English) to San Francisco in 1848. Although Morrison occasionally alludes to technical matters like heating, lighting, and structural underpinnings, his primary concern is stylistic evolution.

A-A 487. MUMFORD, LEWIS. The South in Architecture. New York: Harcourt, Brace, 1941. 147 pp.
The four lectures contained in this volume examine the contribution of the South to American culture in terms of its architects and architecture. The lectures cover: (1) the basis for American form (i.e., what the colonists brought to the New World); (2) the universalism and rationality of Thomas Jefferson; (3) the Romanticism and Regionalism of H. H. Richardson; and (4) the social task of architecture (i.e., to interpret and embody the needs of our democracy).

A-A 488. MUMFORD, LEWIS. Sticks and Stones: A Study of American Architecture and Civilization. 1924; Rev. ed. New York: Dover, 1955. 238 pp.
Mumford discusses the evolution of major architectural styles in America from the medieval traditions of 17th-century New England towns and the heritage of the Renaissance in the 18th century to the machine age of the early 20th century. He makes an effort to treat buildings not as self-sufficient entities and aesthetic abstractions, but as structures that are closely related culturally to their sites and settings.

A-A 489. NATIONAL TRUST FOR HISTORIC PRESERVATION, TONY P. WRENN, and ELIZABETH D. MULLOY. America's Forgotten Architecture. New York: Pantheon Books, 1976. 311 pp.
Using examples taken from homes, farms, civic and community buildings, commercial and industrial buildings, as well as sites and memorials, the authors suggest ways in which these background buildings can be not only identified, but also recognized as valuable resources. One way is to see how the personality of a community (urban or rural) can be reflected in its often-overlooked vernacular architecture.

A-A 490. NEWCOMB, REXFORD. Architecture in Old Kentucky. Urbana: University of Illinois Press, 1953. 185 pp.
Asking to what extent Kentucky architecture up to the late 19th century exemplifies a distinctive regional culture, Newcomb examines a number of topics, including the environmental setting, the manner of life of the people, the traditions of Kentucky crafts and craftsmen, and the work of Kentucky painters, sculptors, and decorators. In addition, he considers the architectural styles--including Georgian, Greek Revival, Romanticism, and Eclecticism--found in the state.

A-A 491. NEWCOMB, REXFORD. Architecture of the Old Northwest Territory: A Study of Early Architecture in Ohio, Indiana, Illinois, Michigan, Wisconsin, and Part of Minnesota. Chicago: University of Chicago Press, 1950. 175 pp.
In this history of architecture in the Northwest Territory up to the time of the Civil War, Newcomb notes not only the various architectural styles, but also the social and economic status of the builders, the material resources of the region, the history of the westward movement, the architecture of communitarian groups in the area, and the influence of both Southern and Yankee traditions.

A-A 492. NEWTON, NORMAN T. Design on the Land: The Development of Landscape Architecture. Cambridge, Mass.: Harvard University Press, 1971. 714 pp.
Although the first section of this volume deals with developments outside the U.S., going back to ancient times, the bulk of the book concentrates on the history of landscape architecture in this country. Newton covers metropolitan park systems, town planning, the national park system, the City Beautiful movement, open-space systems in urban environments, and more.

A-A 493. NOFFSINGER, JAMES PHILIP. The Influence of the Ecole des Beaux-Arts on the Architects of the United States. Washington, D.C.: Catholic University of America Press, 1955. 123 pp.
The author examines the accomplishments of the comparatively small group of American architects who received their training at the Ecole des Beaux-Arts in Paris. Noffsinger's coverage extends from 1846, when Richard Morris Hunt became the first American to enter the French school, to 1955. Among the architects who attended in the years between are H. H. Richardson, Charles Follen McKim, Louis Sullivan, Paul Cret, John Russell Pope, and John Wellborn Root.

A-A 494. OLIVER, RICHARD, ed. The Making of an Architect, 1881-1981: Columbia University in the City of New York. New York: Rizzoli, 1981. 263 pp.
In this volume, the administrative history of the Graduate School of Architecture and Planning at Columbia University is placed in a larger context through the use of historical essays on related topics, including the rise of the metropolitan ideal, the Beaux-Arts system of education, the development of new ideas in city planning, the concern for historic preservation, and the student protest movement.

A-A 495. PARE, RICHARD, ed. Court House: A Photographic Document. New York: Horizon Press, 1978. 255 pp.
Essays by Calvin Trillin (on "county thoughts"), by Henry-Russell Hitchcock and William Seale (on courthouse architecture), and by the Hon. Paul C. Reardon (on the origins and impact of the county court system) accompany a collection of photographs of some 300 county courthouses in the U.S. While county courthouses are sometimes overshadowed by larger structures in major urban areas, they dominate the skylines of smaller cities.

A-A 496. PETERSON, CHARLES E., ed. Building Early America: Contributions Toward the History of a Great Industry. Radnor, Penn.: Chilton Book, 1976. 407 pp.
This is a collection of twenty essays on building history and building preservation, addressing such topics as frame houses, central heating, brick and stone, 19th-century lighting, and the use of window glass. The discipline of building history is seen not only as an important element within the larger context of the histories of science, technology, economics, and architecture, but also as a distinct field of study with its own values and questions.

A-A 497. PICKERING, ERNEST. The Homes of America: As They Have Expressed
          the Lives of Our People for Three Centuries. New York: Crowell,
          1951. 284 pp.
Arguing that the history of American homes is necessarily a history of
American life, Pickering studies our country's domestic architecture in
chronological sequence, looking not only at the evolution of architectural
styles and treatments, but additionally at the people who produced the
homes. The influences of geography and climate are also surveyed.

A-A 498. PIERSON, WILLIAM H., Jr. American Buildings and Their Architects,
          I: The Colonial and Neo-Classical Styles. Garden City, N.Y.:
          Doubleday, 1970. 503 pp.
Pierson begins with the medieval origins of American Colonial architecture
and continues through all of its neo-Palladian and neo-Classical stages
up to the second quarter of the 19th century. Throughout, the author
refers to the English and continental influences that have shaped American
architecture, both secular and religious. Also included is a brief section
on the Southwest in the Colonial period. (See A-A 583 for Vol. II of
this work.)

A-A 499. REED, HENRY HOPE, Jr. The Golden City. Garden City, N.Y.:
          Doubleday, 1959. 160 pp.
In this book, Reed celebrates the exuberance of the Classical tradition
(as exemplified in the United States by New York's Grand Central Terminal,
San Francisco's City Hall complex, and Washington's Federal Triangle).
He asks why, in a land of plenty, our modern architecture--typified by
Reed as one functional glass box after another--should be so unornamented
and desolate.

A-A 500. RHOADS, WILLIAM B. The Colonial Revival. 2 vols. New York:
          Garland, 977. 1134 pp.
The author looks at manifestations of the Colonial Revival from about
1870 to 1924 in houses, exhibition pavilions, colleges, churches, civic
buildings, arts and crafts, and furniture. In trying to explain why the
Colonial Revival came into being in the late 19th century and why it
thrived well into the 20th century, Rhoads examines the attitudes of architects, clients, preservationists, and others.

A-A 501. RIFKIND, CAROLE. A Field Guide to American Architecture. New
          York: New American Library, 1980. 322 pp.
Intended as a guidebook to three centuries of American architecture up
to 1940, this volume uses line drawings and photographs to identify construction and design elements in residential, ecclesiastical, civic, commercial, and utilitarian buildings. For each building type, Rifkind's
approach is primarily chronological, showing sequential development and
successive stylistic phases.

A-A 502. RIFKIND, CAROLE. Main Street: The Face of Urban America. New
          York: Harper & Row, 1977. 267 pp.
Rifkind tells the story of the birth, growth, and decline of America's
main streets (which she calls the heart and soul of our villages, towns,
and cities). Among the topics addressed are: the origins of main streets
in a variety of settings (New England villages, cattle towns, mining towns,
railroad towns); the main street as an expression of a town's identity;
the daily life of years ago on the nation's main streets; and the prospects
for our main streets today.

A-A 503. ROBINSON, WILLARD B. American Forts: Architectural Form and Function. Urbana: University of Illinois Press, 1977. 229 pp.
Examining American military forts—but not fur trader posts or civilian forts—from Colonial times to the second half of the 19th century—Robinson finds a beauty of form that he feels is the result of the forts' clarity of function. Among the specific topics covered by Robinson are the transition from a system of impermanent to permanent works, the influence of the Civil War on fortification theory, and the historical and regional development of the Army forts that were built for defense on the American frontier.

A-A 504. ROBINSON, WILLARD B. Gone from Texas: Our Lost Architectural Heritage. College Station: Texas A & M University Press, 1981. 296 pp.
Robinson's objectives are: to provide a history of Texas buildings that have been destroyed; to explain the conditions (in terms of the environment, society, art, and technology) under which this architecture was produced; and to understand the values that were current at that time. In the process, it is the author's hope that an accurate cross-section of the state's architectural history will be revealed.

A-A 505. ROBINSON, WILLARD B. The People's Architecture: Texas Courthouses, Jails, and Municipal Buildings. Austin: Texas State Historical Association, 1983. 365 pp.
The purpose of this study is to survey the poetic and rational determinants that gave form and character to local governmental buildings in Texas, and then to survey the material and human conditions reflected in their design and construction. Robinson examines the buildings as a whole, as well as specific architectural features (including domes, clocktowers, colonnades, and roof forms), relating them to historical events and trends, political circumstances, and building codes and laws.

A-A 506. ROTH, LELAND M. A Concise History of American Architecture. New York: Harper & Row, 1979. 400 pp.
This survey of American architecture is concerned with the dilemma faced by American builders and architects—i.e., whether to build pragmatically and efficiently or to build according to a conceptual ideal. Roth notes that many settlers came to the New World in order to find a measure of perfection, only to learn that they first had to shelter themselves in the most rudimentary of ways.

A-A 507. SANFORD, TRENT ELWOOD. The Architecture of the Southwest: Indian, Spanish, American. New York: Norton, 1950. 312 pp.
The Southwest, according to the author, represents a blending of three cultures—Indian, Spanish, and Anglo-American—whose imprints are most visible in their architecture. The book's purpose, therefore, is to tell not only what was built by members of these three cultures, but to describe how it was built and to ascertain what inspired them to build it.

A-A 508. SCULLY, VINCENT J., Jr. American Architecture and Urbanism. New York: Praeger, 1969. 275 pp.
Scully's aim is to give a total picture of the interrelated forces of society, environment, and architecture, and to demonstrate how these forces have interacted to produce the characteristic urban landscape in the U.S. He deals with the architecture chronologically and stylistically, bringing in European precedents and influences, but also asserting the dynamic nature of architectural development.

A-A 509. SCULLY, VINCENT J., Jr. Pueblo: Mountain, Village, Dance.
          New York: Viking Press, 1975. 398 pp.
Intended neither as a complete history of Pueblo buildings nor as an anthropological study of Pueblo mythology and ceremonials, this volume seeks
to explore several broad ideas relating to the meaning of human action
within both the natural and the built environment. Scully examines the
architecture and the dances found in pueblos along the Rio Grande and
in other parts of New Mexico, as well as the Navajo hogans and Hopi towns
in Arizona.

A-A 510. SEARING, HELEN. New American Art Museums. New York: Whitney
          Museum of American Arts; Berkeley: University of California
          Press, 1982. 142 pp.
According to the author, the art museum is significant both as an embodiment and as a repository of a given society's aesthetic values. In this
volume, designed as a catalogue to an exhibition on new American art
museums, Searing provides an historical overview of the art museum as a
specific building type during the past 200 years; she then focuses on
seven new museums for the 1980s, including buildings in New York, Atlanta,
Dallas, and Richmond.

A-A 511. SEVERENS, KENNETH. Southern Architecture: 350 Years of Distinc-
          tive American Buildings. New York: Dutton, 1981. 208 pp.
Severens identifies a distinctive Southern architecture, which he attributes to the ideology, ambience, economy, religion, and cultural life of
the region. The author examines a number of building types (including
plantations, churches, and colleges), looks at the connections between
architects and their clients, notes the architecture of antebellum cities
like Charleston and New Orleans, and concludes with a description of what
he calls the "progressive resurgency" of the new South.

A-A 512. SKY, ALISON and MICHELLE STONE. Unbuilt America: Forgotten
          Architecture in the United States from Thomas Jefferson to the
          Space Age. New York: McGraw-Hill, 1976. 308 pp.
The authors have collected some 200 architectural proposals which, in
most cases, were intended to be realized and were technically possible
when conceived, yet for a variety of reasons remained unbuilt. The proposals range in time from Thomas Jefferson's plans for observatory towers
at Monticello in the late 18th century to the designs of Gerard O'Neill
and Brian O'Leary in the 1970s for a space habitat to house 10,000 workers.

A-A 513. STERN, ROBERT A. M. and JOHN MONTAGUE MASSENGALE, eds. The Anglo
          American Suburb. New York: St. Martin's Press, 1981. 96 pp.
This book looks at the tradition of the planned suburb and suburban enclave
that flourished between 1790 and 1930 in both England and the U.S., but
primarily in the latter. The fifty-or-so suburbs analyzed are those considered the best and most comprehensively designed of their types, including: railroad suburbs, streetcar and subway suburbs, industrial villages,
resort suburbs, and automobile suburbs.

A-A 514. STILGOE, JOHN R. Common Landscape of America, 1580 to 1845.
          New Haven, Conn.: Yale University Press, 1982. 429 pp.
Stilgoe analyzes the landscape made by Americans between 1580, when the
Spanish colonists crossed the Rio Grande, and 1845, when pioneers moving
west from Indiana and Illinois encountered the great prairie. His study
looks for common patterns (i.e., patterns that are understood and agreed
upon by all) in the landscape: in our cities, turnpikes, farmsteads,
fences, crop plantings, graveyards, rural churches, mills, factories,
and elsewhere.

A-A 515. SWAIM, DOUG, ed. Carolina Dwelling: Towards Preservation of
Place: In Celebration of the North Carolina Vernacular Landscape.
Raleigh: North Carolina State University School of Design,
1978. 257 pp.
This collection of essays seeks to describe, analyze, and suggest possible
meanings for various features of the North Carolina landscape. Aspects
of traditional design are highlighted. Included are essays on: folk
housing; the "L" house as a carrier of style; the North Carolina porch
as a climatic and cultural buffer; country churches; Carolina tobacco
barns; and the North Carolina courthouse square.

A-A 516. TALLMADGE, THOMAS E. The Story of Architecture in America.
1927; Rev. ed. New York: Norton, 1936. 332 pp.
Written by a practicing architect, this is a general survey of American
architecture from the earliest settlements to the 1920s. The history
is divided into a number of stylistic periods: Colonial, Post-Colonial,
Greek Revival, Parvenu Period (i.e., the age of innocence), Romanesque
Revival, and the 1893 World's Columbian Exposition and eclecticism.
Tallmadge also includes a chapter on Louis Sullivan as "parent and prophet."

A-A 517. TATUM, GEORGE B. Penn's Great Town: 250 Years of Philadelphia
Architecture Illustrated in Prints and Drawings. Philadelphia:
University of Pennsylvania Press, 1961. 352 pp.
Tatum tells the story of Philadelphia architecture from the town's inception in 1682 to 1960, maintaining that the history of Philadelphia's buildings and the people who built them is highly representative of all of
American architectural history. From the early 18th to the early 20th
centuries, the architects and architecture of Philadelphia, according
to Tatum, either helped to create new styles for the country or helped
to lead the way for the acceptance of those styles.

A-A 518. TORRE, SUSANA, ed. Women in American Architecture: A Historic
and Contemporary Perspective. New York: Watson-Guptill, 1977.
224 pp.
Some twenty articles by a variety of designers, architects, critics, and
architectural historians outline the participation of women in architecture
and related design disciplines in the U.S., from both a historical and
a contemporary perspective. Sections of the book focus on the design
of domestic space, women in the architectural profession, women as critics,
and the spatial symbolism of women.

A-A 519. TUCCI, DOUGLASS SHAND. Built in Boston: City and Suburb, 1800-
1950. Boston: New York Graphic Society, 1978. 269 pp.
Tucci places the architectural history of the Boston area--including its
major buildings, architectural styles, downtown development, and processes
of suburbanization--in the larger context of cultural history. He also
emphasizes the work in Boston of six prominent architects: Charles
Bulfinch, H. H. Richardson, Charles Follen McKim, Ralph Adams Cram, Louis
Sullivan, and Walter Gropius.

A-A 520. TUNNARD, CHRISTOPHER and HENRY HOPE REED. American Skyline:
The Growth and Form of Our Cities and Towns. Boston: Houghton
Mifflin, 1955. 302 pp.
Maintaining that the development of our cities and towns closely reflects
our people and history, the authors describe various aspects of the American built environment from Colonial times to the present. Considered
are homes, skyscrapers, civic buildings, hotels, highways, parking lots,
industrial plants, and more. Tunnard and Reed explain how these forms
were shaped and how they may affect the lives we lead.

A-A 521. VAUGHAN, THOMAS, ed. Space, Style and Structure: Building in
Northwest America. 2 vols. Portland: Oregon Historical Society,
1974. 750 pp.
This is a collection of forty-four articles covering a wide array of building types, design, and history in the Pacific Northwest region (Oregon,
Washington, and Idaho) from the time of the Indians to the present. Among
the topics covered are fur trading posts, early missions, inns and hotels,
churches, industrial buildings, farmhouses and barns, spas and resorts,
parks and gardens, and cities and towns.

A-A 522. WALKER, LESTER. American Shelter: An Illustrated Encyclopedia
of the American Home. Woodstock, N.Y.: Overlook Press, 1981.
320 pp.
Walker delineates some 100 styles of American homes from the conventional
(e.g., bungalow, Italianate, Queen Anne) to the nontraditional (e.g.,
converted railroad cars, floating houses, and quonset huts). Each of
the styles is illustrated by line drawings with detailed annotations.
The styles are arranged in chronological order, beginning with the Indians
and early settlers and extending up to the present.

A-A 523. WELLS, CAMILLE, ed. Perspectives in Vernacular Architecture.
Annapolis, Md.: Vernacular Architecture Forum, 1982. 237 pp.
The twenty-two essays in this volume are derived from papers presented
at meetings of the Vernacular Architecture Forum in 1980 and 1981. According to the editor, vernacular architecture recognizes buildings as cultural
artifacts, durable and stationary, that can complement more traditional
historic sources. Among the topics covered here are: 18th-century grist
mills in Pennsylvania; impermanent camp architecture of the Civil War;
one-room school houses in Montana; and primitive Baptist church houses
in Appalachia.

A-A 524. WESLAGER, C. A. The Log Cabin in America: From Pioneer Days
to the Present. New Brunswick, N.J.: Rutgers University Press,
1969. 382 pp.
Weslager's primary objective is neither to analyze architectural forms
and patterns nor to describe log construction techniques, but rather to
understand the part played by the log cabin in early American family life,
in the political arena, and in the process of Americanization on the frontier. To this end, he tries to associate the log cabins in various parts
of the country with the people who built them. Weslager includes a section
on the log cabin in American politics, paying special attention to the
Log Cabin campaign of 1840.

A-A 525. WHIFFEN, MARCUS. American Architecture Since 1780: A Guide
to the Styles. Cambridge, Mass.: MIT Press, 1969. 313 pp.
Although he admits that architectural taxonomy is not as well-developed
as bird-watching may be, Whiffen's aim in this volume is to help "building
watchers" increase their knowledge of the architecture around them. Consequently, he describes in detail the styles that have developed in this
country from the end of the 18th century to the present, including: the
wide array of architectural revivals, the Victorian styles, the Beaux-
Arts forms, and the varieties of Modernism.

A-A 526. WHIFFEN, MARCUS and FREDERICK KOEPER. American Architecture,
1607-1976. Cambridge, Mass.: MIT Press, 1981. 495 pp.
This survey asks if there are any elements in our architectural history
that are specifically American (i.e., distinct from other architectures
of the western world). Whiffen (who covers the period from 1607 to 1860)
and Koeper (who takes 1860 to 1976) suggest several such elements, both
in terms of external house and the temple-form of Greek Revival buildings,
and in terms of attitudes of mind (such as empiricism and pragmatism).

A-A 527. WILLIAMS, HENRY LIONEL and OTTALIE K. WILLIAMS. A Guide to Old
American Houses, 1700-1900. New York: A. S. Barnes, 1962.
168 pp.
The authors describe the different domestic architectural styles (as well
as the more common variations in style) that became popular during the
years 1700 to 1900. Each of the styles is examined in turn, including:
late Colonial, Georgian, Federal, Greek Revival, Gothic Revival, and Victorian Eclecticism. The authors emphasize that the style of the houses
may vary not only geographically and chronologically, but also according
to the national or cultural origins of the builders and owners.

A-A 528. WISCHNITZER, RACHEL. Synagogue Architecture in the United States:
History and Interpretation. Philadelphia: Jewish Publication
Society of America, 1955. 204 pp.
The author's aim is to explain American synagogue architecture, from the
Colonial period to the present, in the context of the history of ideas
in this country. She notes the battle of architectural styles and the
Classical countercurrents in the 19th century, the beginnings of the Orien-
tal trend after the Civil War, the new Classicism in the early 20th century,
and the impact on the synagogue and its architecture of the increased
suburbanization after W.W. II.

A-A 529. WRIGHT, GWENDOLYN. Building the Dream: A Social History of
Housing in America. New York: Pantheon Books, 1981. 329 pp.
The author examines thirteen different kinds of domestic dwellings--
including the Puritan home, urban rowhouse, slave quarters and the master's
house, rural cottage, Victorian suburb, urban tenement, and company town--
in an effort to explain the symbolism and imagery attached to the ordinary
home in America. Among the questions posed by Wright are: What kinds
of people lived in these houses? What kinds of places did they fashion
for themselves? How did they live in their homes? How were they told
they should live?

A-A 530. ZELINSKY, WILBUR. The Cultural Geography of the United States.
Englewood Cliffs, N.J.: Prentice-Hall, 1973. 164 pp.
Zelinsky is interested in examining two sides of American cultural geography: how our cultural system has shaped spatial processes, features,
and structures; and how those geographic facts have in turn modified and
channeled the development of our cultural system. After looking at a
number of such cultural manifestations as house forms, settlement features,
and place names, Zelinsky establishes an overview of five major cultural
regions in the U.S., each with a number of distinct subregions.

A-A 531. ZIMILES, MARTHA and MURRAY ZIMILES. Early American Mills. New
York: Potter, 1973. 290 pp.
Although concerned primarily with aesthetic considerations, this survey
of early American mills in New England and New York also attempts to highlight some of the social, economic, and historical factors affecting mill
development through the 19th century. The authors are interested not
only in how the mills look and how they were built, but also how they
work. Textile mills receive the most attention, but mills for other industries (e.g., clocks, paper, furniture) are briefly noted.

A-A 532. ZUBE, ERVIN H., ed. Landscapes: Selected Writings of J. B.
Jackson. Amherst: University of Massachusetts Press, 1970.
160 pp.
This is a collection of essays by J. B. Jackson on the social values and
cultural patterns reflected in the American landscape. Most of the essays
were written by Jackson during the years 1951 to 1968 for Landscape, a
magazine that he founded and edited. Among the topics covered are: images
of the city; street scenes; other-directed houses; and the westward-moving
house (a study of three American houses and the people who lived in them).

A-A 533. ZUBE, ERVIN H. and MARGARET J. ZUBE, eds. Changing Rural Land-
          scapes. Amherst: University of Massachusetts Press, 1977.
          151 pp.
Change--as it occurs in the rural landscape--is the focus for this collection of articles published in Landscape magazine during the years 1951
to 1969. Most of the essays are by J. B. Jackson, though there are also
contributions by other writers (including Carl Sauer and Wilbur Zelinsky).
Among the subjects addressed are: the spatial organization among different
elements of the landscape (such as front yards, walls, and fences); the
role of rural towns and cities; and the values that individuals associate
with the landscape.

A-A 534. ZURIER, REBECCA. The American Firehouse: An Architectural and
          Social History. New York: Abbeville Press, 1982. 286 pp.
According to Zurier, fire stations are usually modest buildings, reflecting
existing architectural trends and rarely displaying radical innovations.
In this history, the author surveys the various styles that have characterized stations over the years (including castles and palaces, streamlined
stations, and recent alternatives to the box). Some attention is also
given to the history of the modern fire department and its administration.

IX.   B. ARCHITECTURE: COLONIAL

A-A 535. BRIGGS, MARTIN S. The Homes of the Pilgrim Fathers in England
          and America, 1620-1685. New York: Oxford University Press,
          1932. 211 pp.
The author's objective is to examine the links between the timber-framed
houses of New England and their counterparts in the districts of England
from which the Pilgrims came. House types in 17th-century Holland likewise
are investigated to determine whether they may have helped dictate architectural forms in the New World. The origins of the Pilgrim movement
and its cultural context in the region are also discussed by Briggs.

A-A 536. CHANDLER, JOSEPH EVERETT. The Colonial House. 1916; Rev. ed.
          New York: McBride, 1924. 222 pp.
Chandler divides Colonial architecture into three distinct periods, noting
differences in plans, materials, and construction details. Although the
detailed treatment of construction details and architectural features
(such as roof profiles, dormer windows, and interior plans) is intended
in part for architects and builders who wish to be accurate in creating
homes in the Colonial Revival style, this volume is useful also for its
chronological history of the Colonial house in the New World.

A-A 537. CUMMINGS, ABBOTT LOWELL. The Framed Houses of Massachusetts
          Bay, 1625-1725. Cambridge, Mass.: Harvard University Press,
          1979. 261 pp.
In this detailed treatment of house plans and building techniques in early
New England, Cummings is interested in the ways that the English settlers
both perpetuated and modified a long-standing tradition of timber building.
Using historic documents as well as surviving buildings, Cummings is able
to reconstruct the architectural scene not only in Massachusetts Bay,
but also in the English districts from which the colonists came.

A-A 538. DONNELLY, MARIAN CARD. The New England Meeting Houses of the
Seventeenth Century. Middletown, Conn.: Wesleyan University
Press, 1968. 165 pp.
In comparing New England meeting houses of the 17th century to their
English and Continental contemporaries, the author concludes that the meet-
ing houses apparently were not linked to fashionable developments in the
English Renaissance, nor to experimental Protestant architecture in north-
ern Europe, but rather were derived naturally from late medieval English
village traditions.

A-A 539. EBERLEIN, HAROLD DONALDSON. The Architecture of Colonial America.
Boston: Little, Brown, 1915. 289 pp.
Eberlein's purpose is to survey and analyze the architectural history
of Colonial America, noting a close connection between architecture and
the social and economic circumstances of the period. The various geographical regions are covered, as well as such specific topics as public buildings, churches, materials and textures, and American architects.

A-A 540. EBERLEIN, HAROLD DONALDSON and CORTLANDT VAN DYKE HUBBARD. American Georgian Architecture. Bloomington: Indiana University
Press, 1952. 55 pp.
This is an examination of the Georgian style in America, from its medieval
beginnings to its evolution into the Federal manner. The authors identify
three distinct periods of Georgian building, and survey the scene in each
of three geographical regions (the South, the Middle Colonies, and New
England). There is also a chapter devoted to the architects, the builders,
and the books of American Georgian architecture.

A-A 541. FORMAN, HENRY CHANDLEE. Early Nantucket and Its Whale Houses.
New York: Hastings House, 1966. 291 pp.
The author is interested not so much in the rich sea captains and affluent
merchants of Nantucket in the 17th and early 18th centuries, as he is
in what he calls the plain islanders--in their economy, society, history,
and buildings. While noting Nantucket's medieval heritage--particularly
in terms of its town plan and construction methods--Forman also points
out how building on the island was never static, but always changing and
growing.

A-A 542. GARRETT, WENDELL D. Apthorp House, 1760-1960. Cambridge, Mass.:
Harvard University Press, 1960. 100 pp.
This investigation of a single house in Cambridge, Massachusetts, is partly
architectural history, partly social history, and partly local history.
Garrett sees the Apthorp house as representative of the American effort
to carry out the Palladian ideals of the 18th century. Attention is paid
to details of construction, the lives of the house's residents, and its
setting on the Harvard campus.

A-A 543. GARVAN, ANTHONY N. B. Architecture and Town Planning in Colonial
Connecticut. New Haven, Conn.: Yale University Press, 1951.
166 pp.
Using a variety of sources (including serial photographs, demographic
data, and land surveys), Garvan explains how the architecture and plans
of Connecticut towns developed visually. He maintains that although the
Colonial town was never an exact imitation of the town in Europe, it was
much closer in appearance to its Old World origins than to any kind of
amalgam or merger of European and American characteristics.

A-A 544. GOULD, MARY EARLE. The Early American House. New York: McBride,
        1949. 143 pp.
Gould is concerned not only with early American houses and their furnishings, but also with how they were built, how they were used, and what
they meant to their inhabitants. Among the topics addressed are: early
one-room houses and how they grew; chimneys and fireplaces; kitchenware
and miscellaneous household utensils; food and drink; and everyday Colonial
life throughout the year.

A-A 545. ISHAM, NORMAN MORRISON. Early American Houses. Boston: Walpole
        Society, 1928. 61 pp.
The author describes the plans and construction techniques—including
framing details and interior treatments—of the houses built along the
Atlantic seaboard during the 17th century. Isham notes how the building
traditions brought by English and Dutch craftsmen to the New World grew
in their own way here, producing for the American home something that
was new and distinctive.

A-A 546. JACKSON, JOSEPH. American Colonial Architecture: Its Origin
        and Development. Philadelphia: McKay, 1924. 228 pp.
The author traces the origin of the Colonial style in America, noting
that it was developed not by professionally trained architects but rather
by hard-working carpenters and builders. The evolution of this style
is followed in a number of geographical regions until the late 18th century,
with some attention paid to the attitudes and customs of the settlers
themselves.

A-A 547. KELLY, J. FREDERICK. The Early Domestic Architecture of Connecti-
        cut. New Haven, Conn.: Yale University Press, 1924. 210 pp.
According to Kelly, the early houses in Connecticut shared with contemporaneous houses in the other New England colonies two fundamental characteristics: (1) they were true to their milieu, reflecting with simplicity
and directness the conditions that produced them; and (2) they were true
to their purpose, reflecting the intimacy of the domestic environment.
The author covers house design, construction, and decoration, noting the
Colonial inheritances from England, as well as the changes that occurred
over time in the New World.

A-A 548. KIMBALL, SIDNEY FISKE. Domestic Architecture of the American
        Colonies and of the Early Republic. New York: Scribner, 1922.
        314 pp.
The author examines the evolution of the early American home from the
primitive shelters and frame houses of the 17th century to the application
of academic architectural forms in the 18th century, and finally to the
new ideals (especially classical details) that came after the American
Revolution in the houses of the early republic. Kimball employs a wide
variety of sources (including building contracts, inventories, and deeds)
to reconstruct the histories of some 200 houses.

A-A 549. McNAMARA, BROOKS. The American Playhouse in the Eighteenth Cen-
        tury. Cambridge, Mass.: Harvard University Press, 1969.
        174 pp.
McNamara traces the patterns of expansion and change that characterized
the work of theater builders in 18th-century America. He notes how trained
architects gradually assumed a larger role in playhouse design, taking
over this responsibility from the theater managers who had held it earlier.
The designs of a number of major theaters (including the Chestnut Street,
Haymarket, and Park) are examined in detail.

A-A 550. MIXER, KNOWLTON. Old Houses of New England. New York: Macmillar
1927. 346 pp.
The author's aim is to present the houses of Colonial New England as an
expression of that region's unique history, with particular emphasis on
the Puritan heritage and the trading and seafaring economy. The New
England homestead, according to Mixer, has its roots in medieval England
but, having adapted to conditions and to materials in the New World, differs characteristically from its prototypes.

A-A 551. MURTAGH, WILLIAM J. Moravian Architecture and Town Planning:
Bethlehem, Pennsylvania, and Other Eighteenth-Century American
Settlements. Chapel Hill: University of North Carolina Press,
1967. 145 pp.
Murtagh examines the 18th-century architecture of the Moravians in America,
noting how their concern for a closely knit society is reflected in the
sense of unity and completeness found in their buildings and towns.
Although the author focuses on the Moravian architecture in Bethlehem,
Pa. (the Moravians' first permanent settlement in America), he looks
briefly at other Moravian communities in Pennsylvania, New Jersey, and
North Carolina.

A-A 552. NORTON, PAUL F. Latrobe, Jefferson and the National Capitol.
New York: Garland, 1977. 362 pp.
Norton addresses several questions: how the new design for the Capitol
Building was used to meet the needs of a unique legislative system; how
the Capitol influenced later architecture in the U.S.; and how the details
of its design and construction were handled during the time that Thomas
Jefferson was the president and Benjamin Henry Latrobe was the architect.

A-A 553. ROSE, HAROLD WICKLIFFE. The Colonial Houses of Worship in America:
Built in the English Colonies Before the Republic, 1607-1789,
and Still Standing. New York: Hastings House, 1963. 574 pp.
The author is interested not only in describing the architecture of the
houses of worship built during the years 1607 to 1789, but also in understanding the spirit those buildings represent in American civilization.
Rose surveys the houses of worship used by members of the various religious
denominations (including the Church of England, Catholicism, Judaism,
Methodism, Presbyterianism, and others).

A-A 554. SHURTLEFF, HAROLD R. The Log Cabin Myth: A Study of the Early
Dwellings of the English Colonists in North America. Edited
by Samuel Eliot Morison. Cambridge, Mass.: Harvard University
Press, 1939. 243 pp.
Published posthumously, this volume seeks to overturn the common public
belief that the log cabin was the earliest form of dwelling of the first
English settlers in North America. In addition to proving that there
were no log cabins until at least the end of the 17th century, Shurtleff
is interested also in discovering how and why the myth of the log cabin
originated and flourished in the U.S.

A-A 555. TATUM, GEORGE B. Philadelphia Georgian: The City House of Samuel
Powel and Some of Its Eighteenth-Century Neighbors. Middletown,
Conn.: Wesleyan University Press, 1976. 187 pp.
This history of the owners, architectural features, and furnishings associated with the Powel House covers more than just this one Colonial mansion
in Philadelphia. Tatum asks: how did the Powel House compare to others
of its time and place? what were the origins of the architectural forms
selected and who were the craftsmen employed to execute them? how authentic is the structure we see today? and what insight into the values and
living patterns of the period does the house provide?

A-A 556. WATERMAN, THOMAS TILESTON. The Dwellings of Colonial America.
          Chapel Hill: University of North Carolina Press, 1950.
          312 pp.
Waterman finds a wide variety of influences evident in American architectural development between the time of the first English settlements and
the close of the American Revolution. Members of the different cultural
groups in the New World each contributed their own traditional methods
of building, which were then modified to meet the varying demands of the
American climate and the living conditions encountered on the expanding
American frontier.

A-A 557. WERTENBAKER, THOMAS JEFFERSON. The Founding of American Civili-
          zation: The Middle Colonies. New York: Scribner, 1938.
          367 pp.
In the middle colonies of America--with their heterogeneous population,
diversity of economic conditions, and distinct isolation from the Old
World--Wertenbaker finds a "perfect laboratory for observing a new civilization in the process of formation." Most of the evidence the author
presents is architectural: comparing the houses, cottages, churches,
city plans, etc., in the middle colonies to those in western Europe.

A-A 558. WERTENBAKER, THOMAS JEFFERSON. The Old South: The Founding
          of American Civilization. New York: Scribner, 1942. 364 pp.
In this study of the South, as in Wertenbaker's earlier volume on the
middle colonies, architectural evidence is emphasized because, as the
author writes, "it serves so admirably to illustrate the forces which
created our civilization." Wertenbaker describes a variety of buildings
in Maryland, Virginia, and the Carolinas during the Colonial and early
national periods in order to point out the differences in nationality,
religion, and social and economic class found in the region.

A-A 559. WHIFFEN, MARCUS. The Eighteenth-Century Houses of Williamsburg:
          A Study of Architecture and Building in the Colonial Capital
          of Virginia. Williamsburg, Va.: Colonial Williamsburg, 1960.
          223 pp.
Although the second part of this volume is simply a guide to extant houses
in Williamsburg, the first part is much broader in scope, placing Williamsburg in the context of its times and using its domestic architecture as
representative of development throughout the colonies in the 18th century.
Whiffen includes chapters on: materials; master builders and craftsmen;
professional equipment (such as books and tools); and the cultural, economic, climatic, and legal factors that affected the design of the Williamsburg house.

A-A 560. WHIFFEN, MARCUS. The Public Buildings of Williamsburg, Colonial
          Capital of Virginia: An Architectural History. Williamsburg,
          Va.: Colonial Williamsburg, 1958. 269 pp.
Examining the public buildings of Colonial Williamsburg, from the early
17th century to 1780 when the capital was moved to Richmond, Whiffen
describes how, why, and through whom these buildings came to be erected.
The author relates these structures (built primarily for the government,
the college, and the church) to contemporary ones in England, and he shows
how the architecture of Williamsburg influenced that of the rest of Virginia.

IX.   C. ARCHITECTURE: 19TH CENTURY

A-A 561. ANDREW, LAUREL B. The Early Temples of the Mormons: The Archi-
          tecture of the Millennial Kingdom in the American West. Albany:
          State University of New York Press, 1978. 218 pp.
Andrew analyzes the six Mormon temples that were completed in the 19th
century (in Ohio, Illinois, and Utah) not only in terms of their architectural design, but also in terms of what they meant to the people who
built them. She concludes that the architecture of the 19th-century temples was that of a true religious utopia, providing a visual analogue
for the new and unique theology of the Mormons.

A-A 562. BUNTING, BAINBRIDGE. Houses of Boston's Back Bay: An Architec-
          tural History, 1840-1917. Cambridge, Mass.: Harvard University
          Press, 1967. 494 pp.
The example of Boston's Back Bay is used by Bunting to represent American
architectural development in several ways: to follow changes in architectural style and building technology during the latter half of the nineteenth century; to understand the development of city planning in the
U.S.; and to study the sociology of the Boston scene and some of the forces
that have shaped it.

A-A 563. CARROTT, RICHARD G. The Egyptian Revival: Its Sources, Monuments,
          and Meaning, 1808-1858. Berkeley: University of California
          Press, 1978. 221 pp.
In this history of the Egyptian Revival, Carrott investigates the sources
that stimulated the movement, the differences between the original structures and those of the revival, and the meaning and iconography of the
American versions. In addition, he discusses the significance of the
Egyptian Revival within the overall history of 19th-century architecture
and within the history of revival architecture specifically.

A-A 564. CONDIT, CARL W. The Chicago School of Architecture: A History
          of Commercial and Public Building in the Chicago Area, 1875-
          1925. Chicago: University of Chicago Press, 1964. 238 pp.
This is an outgrowth of the author's earlier work, The Rise of the Skyscraper (1952), with new material on the social, economic, and intellectual
history of Chicago. Condit describes how the city's growing population
and soaring land prices combined with changes in science, technology,
and aesthetics to produce the skyscraper. Much attention is focused on
the work of the city's most prominent architects, including William LeBaron
Jenney, Daniel Burnham, John Wellborn Root, Dankmar Adler, and Louis
Sullivan.

A-A 565. COOLIDGE, JOHN. Mill and Mansion: A Study of Architecture and
          Society in Lowell, Massachusetts, 1820-1865. New York: Columbia
          University Press, 1942. 261 pp.
As the largest and wealthiest of Massachusetts mill towns, Lowell also
developed the most splendid architecture. Coolidge is interested in the
relationships between architecture and society in the 19th century, asking
to what extent the architecture (in terms of both form and function) of
Lowell's private houses, public buildings, and commercial mills was consistent with the patterns of its social, industrial, and cultural history.

A-A 566. DUNCAN, HUGH DALZIEL. Culture and Democracy: The Struggle for Form in Society and Architecture in Chicago and the Middle West During the Life and Times of Louis H. Sullivan. Totowa, N.J.: Bedminster Press, 1965. 616 pp.

Duncan maintains that the architectural legacy of Louis Sullivan can be found in the work of Frank Lloyd Wright and Mies van der Rohe in Chicago; and that Sullivan's spirit, moreover, passed beyond architecture to a more philosophical and sociological realm represented in the work of Thorstein Veblen, John Dewey, George H. Mead, Charles H. Cooley, Robert Park, and others.

A-A 567. EARLY, JAMES. Romanticism and American Architecture. New York: A. S. Barnes, 1965. 171 pp.

This is a study not so much of specific buildings as of what the author calls "the patterns of thought and feeling" that fostered them. Early's emphasis is on the history of ideas that shaped American architecture in the 19th century, particularly as expressed by the architects, philosophers, and writers associated with the romantic era in the U.S.

A-A 568. FITCH, JAMES MARSTON. Architecture and the Esthetics of Plenty. New York: Columbia University Press, 1961. 304 pp.

Fitch argues that the technological revolutions of the last half of the 19th century—including the introduction of electricity, plumbing, refrigeration services, and new methods of construction—have demanded a totally new approach to architectural form and function. He maintains that what is most American about our aesthetic and technological innovations is that they quickly pervade all classes of the population and all regions of the country.

A-A 569. FRANCAVIGLIA, RICHARD V. The Mormon Landscape: Existence, Creation, and Perception of a Unique Image in the American West. New York: AMS Press, 1978. 177 pp.

In order to identify the type of landscape (i.e., the visual image of a place or area based upon some abstraction of reality) that is created by Mormon residents of rural villages and settlements in the West, the author examines such distinctive features as roads, ditches, spacing of houses on the block, house plans, house styles, barns and outbuildings, fences, gardens, schools, and churches.

A-A 570. HAMLIN, TALBOT. Greek Revival Architecture in America: Being an Account of Important Trends in American Architecture and American Life Prior to the War Between the States. New York: Oxford University Press, 1944. 439 pp.

Regarding the Greek Revival as the first truly American architecture, Hamlin traces its development from its late 18th-century roots to its manifestation in both urban and rural areas during the years 1820 to 1860. He notes that the Greek Revival was able to flourish in an American culture that had high regard for Classical literature, Classical art, and Classical ideals, before it succumbed to the changed climate following the Civil War.

A-A 571. HANDLIN, DAVID P. The American Home: Architecture and Society, 1815-1915. Boston: Little, Brown, 1979. 545 pp.

According to Handlin, it was not until the first decades of the 19th century that Americans began to challenge the assumptions inherited from European precedent regarding the homes in which they lived. At that time, Americans started to formulate new ideas for their domestic architecture—ideas that Handlin traces through an examination of people (including architects, planners, designers, and reformers), places, and events.

A-A 572. HENRY, ANNE W. D. The Building of a Club: Social Institution and Architectural Type, 1870-1905: A Study of the Precedents and Building of the University Cottage Club, Princeton. Princeton, N.J.: Princeton University School of Architecture and Urban Planning, 1976. 116 pp.
Henry uses the building of the University Cottage Club House at Princeton University in the first decade of the 20th century as a way of analyzing both the institution of the club in the U.S. and the architectural development of a club type. She finds that new developments in club architecture during the last quarter of the 19th century coincided with changes in architectural theory, as the picturesque aesthetic was being displaced by a more abstract formality.

A-A 573. JACKSON, JOHN BRINCKERHOFF. American Space: The Centennial Years, 1865-1876. New York: Norton, 1972. 254 pp.
Jackson maintains that many of the distinctive regional characteristics of our major cities and rural districts evolved under the pressure of rapidly changing technological, social, and aesthetic forces in the decade following the Civil War. Jackson examines conditions in both urban and rural areas in several regions of the country, paying particular attention to the American attitudes toward space, planning, nature, and industrialization.

A-A 574. JACKSON, JOSEPH. Development of American Architecture, 1783-1830. Philadelphia: McKay, 1926. 230 pp.
This volume continues the history of American architecture for another fifty years from the point where the author's previous work, American Colonial Architecture (see A-A 546), concluded. Jackson surveys the scene in a number of major cities, noting the close connection between what he terms "the advent of civilizing domestic conveniences" and "the improvement of national taste."

A-A 575. KAUFMANN, EDGAR, Jr., ed. The Rise of an American Architecture. New York: Praeger, 1970. 241 pp.
This is a collection of four essays on the contribution of 19th-century America to the history of architecture and city planning. The essay topics (and their authors) are: the American influence on architecture in Europe (Henry-Russell Hitchcock); the American city, real and ideal, with emphasis on the work of Frederick Law Olmsted (Albert Fein); a history of skyscraper development (Winston Weisman); and a discussion of American houses from Thomas Jefferson to Frank Lloyd Wright (Vincent Scully).

A-A 576. KIRKER, HAROLD. California's Architectural Frontier: Style and Tradition in the Nineteenth Century. San Marino, Calif.: Huntington Library, 1960. 224 pp.
Kirker's primary objective is to demonstrate how the Colonial nature of California's frontier society in the 19th century is reflected in its architecture. To this end, he shows that each group on the California frontier (including Yurok Indians, Russians, Spaniards, Mexicans, and Americans) built from the memory of their old homes and in the manner of their old habits to reproduce—in a manner consistent with their Colonial status—the houses they had left behind.

A-A 577. LONGSTRETH, RICHARD. On the Edge of the World: Four Architects in San Francisco at the Turn of the Century. Cambridge, Mass.: MIT Press, 1983. 455 pp.
Examining the work of Ernest Coxhead, Willis Polk, A. C. Schweinfurth, and Bernard Maybeck at the end of the 19th century, Longstreth finds that in its distinctiveness and innovation, their work was very much a product of its environment. At the turn of the century, San Francisco was seen as a land of infinite potential, thereby engendering an independence of

spirit and action that, according to the author, was reflected in the architecture of the age.

A-A 578. MAASS, JOHN. The Gingerbread Age: A View of Victorian America. New York: Rinehart, 1957. 212 pp.
Covering the period from 1837 to 1876, Maass strives to overturn the notion that Victorian architecture represents an "age of horror" or a "disintegration of taste." According to the author, Victorian architecture--with its boldness and vitality--has important lessons to offer the Modernist designers and builders of the 20th century whose output, Maass believes, is too conformist in appearance.

A-A 579. MAASS, JOHN. The Victorian Home in America. New York: Hawthorn Books, 1972. 235 pp.
Maass follows the development of American domestic architecture during the years 1840 to 1900, noting the various historical styles from Gothic Revival to Colonial Revival. His survey embraces all types of houses in the period--whether products of the professional designer, the amateur, or the rural carpenter. Attention is also paid to the question of social and cultural context, particularly in terms of the influences of technology and Romanticism.

A-A 580. MEEKS, CARROLL L. V. The Railroad Station: An Architectural History. New Haven, Conn.: Yale University Press, 1956. 203 pp.
Meeks traces the evolution of the passenger railroad station around the world, though he emphasizes developments in North America. According to the author, 19th-century architecture is unified by a style he calls Picturesque Eclecticism, which reached its fullest expression in the years between 1860 and 1890. For railroad stations, Picturesque Eclecticism meant soaring towers, agitated and unbalanced contours, and bold contrasts of shapes and colors.

A-A 581. MUMFORD, LEWIS. The Brown Decades: A Study of the Arts in America, 1865-1895. 1931; Rev. ed. New York: Dover, 1955. 266 pp.
The term "the brown decades" refers to the years following the Civil War when the mood of the United States, according to the author, was darker, sadder, and soberer. Mumford maintains that in terms of creative achievements in architecture, literature, and philosophy, the brown decades deserve greater recognition. In architecture, Mumford calls attention to such "genuine successes" as the skyscraper, the Brooklyn Bridge, and the homes designed by H. H. Richardson.

A-A 582. PERRIN, RICHARD W. E. Historic Wisconsin Buildings: A Survey in Pioneer Architecture, 1835-1870. 1962; Rev. ed. Milwaukee, Wis.: Milwaukee Public Museum, 1981. 123 pp.
Although Perrin's focus is on Wisconsin, his inquiries into the nature of materials, craftsmanship, and design elements in the buildings he describes have broad applications to pioneer architecture in the U.S. during the 19th century. Among the specific topics covered are: open-timber framing, palisaded walls, balloon-frame construction, brick veneer, fieldstone masonry, and gravel-wall construction.

A-A 583. PIERSON, WILLIAM H., Jr. American Buildings and Their Architects, II: Technology and the Picturesque, the Corporate and the Early Gothic Styles. Garden City, N.Y.: Doubleday, 1978. 500 pp.
Tracing the European roots of the Gothic Revival in America back to the Middle Ages, Pierson's aim is to identify the larger forces and the important people associated with the romantic styles in the United States during the 19th century. The effects of technology on American architecture,

as well as the influences of the nation's changing social system, are also noted. (See A-A 498 for Vol. I of this work.)

A-A 584. SCULLY, VINCENT J., Jr. The Shingle Style and the Stick Style: Architectural Theory and Design from Richardson to the Origins of Wright. 1955; Rev. ed. New Haven, Conn.: Yale University Press, 1971. 184 pp.
Scully is concerned primarily with a single phase in the development of American domestic architecture: the country and suburban residences made of wood during the years 1872 to 1889 which were characterized by surface continuity and flowing interior spaces. This phase, according to the author, embodies some of the most lively and original achievements of the last century.

A-A 585. STANTON, PHOEBE B. The Gothic Revival and American Church Architecture: An Episode in Taste, 1840-1856. Baltimore, Md.: Johns Hopkins University Press, 1968. 350 pp.
The author focuses on one aspect of church building in 19th-century America: the movement within the Episcopal Church to erect structures in an English Gothic style deemed suitable to the Church's changed attitudes toward history, ceremony, and moral purpose. Stanton explores the close links between the British generators of these changes and their American counterparts. She also studies several of the church buildings and the architects associated with this movement.

A-A 586. TURNER, PAUL V., MARCIA E. VETROCQ, and KAREN WEITZE. The Founders and the Architects: The Design of Stanford University. Stanford, Calif.: Stanford University Department of Art, 1976. 96 pp.
Although this study focuses on the design plan for Stanford University in the late 19th century, it also assesses the significance and influence of that plan on university architecture in the U.S. and comments upon the relationships between architects, planners, and patrons at the turn of the century. Moreover, in explaining the popularity of the Spanish-Mission style of architecture at Stanford, the book describes some of the related literary and artistic trends.

A-A 587. VAN RAVENSWAAY, CHARLES. The Art and Architecture of German Settlements in Missouri: A Survey of a Vanishing Culture. Columbia: University of Missouri Press, 1977. 533 pp.
Settling in Missouri from the early 1830s to the late 19th century, German immigrants became the dominant cultural group in several sections of the state. This volume studies those immigrants, discussing not only why they travelled and how they adjusted to the New World, but especially how their German-American culture developed and how it is expressed in the design and craftsmanship of their buildings and household furnishings.

A-A 588. WACKER, PETER O. Land and People: A Cultural Geography of Pre-industrial New Jersey: Origins and Settlement Patterns. New Brunswick, N.J.: Rutgers University Press, 1975. 499 pp.
The author's major objective is to describe the varied cultural landscapes, particularly forms of settlement and land division, in New Jersey up to the early 19th century—and then to place those landscapes in the context of the historical cultural geography of both the Atlantic seaboard and the trans-Atlantic diffusion of Old World culture traits. According to Wacker, the example of New Jersey is a significant one, due not only to its culturally diverse population but also to its location between the cultural hearths of Pennsylvania and New England.

A-A 589. WELSCH, ROGER L. Sod Walls: The Story of the Nebraska Sod House.
          Broken Bow, Neb.: Purcells, 1968. 208 pp.
Indigenous to the Great Plains, the sod house, according to Welsch, is
an American form through and through, clearly displaying the pioneers'
ingenuity as well as the folk processes by which sod construction techniques were developed and disseminated. Using letters, photographs,
stories, songs, and oral interviews, the author combines a detailed study
of sod house construction with a discussion of pioneer culture in Nebraska.

A-A 590. WILHELM, HUBERT G. H. Organized German Settlement and Its Effects
          on the Frontier of South-Central Texas. New York: Arno Press,
          1980. 237 pp.
Focusing on the hill country of Texas, Wilhelm is interested in learning
how German immigrants reacted to new conditions on the American frontier
and also how the landscape was affected by the imprint of German culture.
To answer these questions, he looks at architectural features, including
houses, barns, and fences. Wilhelm finds that during the initial settlement phase, German immigrants adopted American building types, but that
in later years they returned to traditional German materials and methods
of construction.

A-A 591. WILSON, RICHARD GUY, ed. Victorian Resorts and Hotels. Phila-
          delphia: Victorian Society in America, 1982. 127 pp.
During the period from 1820 to 1914, Wilson contends, the resort as a
specialized activity and the hotel as a building type reached the apogee
of development. This collection of essays addresses a number of the
aspects associated with Victorian resorts, both as buildings and as activities. Among the topics covered are: hotel design, amusement parks, resort
casinos, national park hostelries, health-restoring resorts, wicker furniture, and the foreign traveller in the American hotel.

A-A 592. WRIGHT, GWENDOLYN. Moralism and the Model Home: Domestic Archi-
          tecture and Cultural Conflict in Chicago, 1873-1913. Chicago:
          University of Chicago Press, 1980. 382 pp.
Using Chicago as a case study, Wright discovers that in the years between
1873 and 1913 the form of the ideal middle-class domestic dwelling underwent a major transformation: from an exuberant highly personalized display
of irregular shapes, picturesque contrasts, and varieties of ornament
(supposedly symbolizing the uniqueness of the family) to a restrained
and simple dwelling with the focus on its scientifically arranged kitchen.

IX.   D. ARCHITECTURE: 20TH CENTURY

A-A 593. BANHAM, REYNER. Los Angeles: The Architecture of Four Ecologies.
          New York: Harper & Row, 1971. 256 pp.
According to Banham, the special mixture in Los Angeles of geography,
climate, economics, demography, mechanics, and culture has created a very
unusual American city. He divides this sprawling metropolis into four
"ecologies": (1) "surfurbia" (the beach communities); (2) the foothills
(Beverly Hills, Bel Air, Hollywood); (3) the plains area (Burbank, Watts,
Torrance);.and (4) "autopia" (the freeways).

A-A 594. BLOCK, JEAN F. The Uses of Gothic: Planning and Building the
Campus of the University of Chicago, 1892-1932. Chicago: University of Chicago Library, 1983. 262 pp.
This volume explores how the use of the Gothic style and quadrangular
plan at the University of Chicago was a reflection of the University's
intellectual, social, and aesthetic needs and aspirations during the years
1892 to 1932. The Gothic architecture served in part as a symbol of reassurance, providing the University with a connection to the outside world
at the same time that it imposed order upon the school itself.

A-A 595. BROOKS, H. ALLEN. The Prairie School: Frank Lloyd Wright and
His Midwest Contemporaries. Toronto: University of Toronto
Press, 1972. 373 pp.
Brooks covers the history of the Prairie School, describing the architects,
the buildings, and the guiding philosophy that sustained the movement.
According to the author, the school flourished from 1900 to W.W. I--though
it continued into the 1920s and 1930s--and was characterized by horizontal
lines; clear, precise and angular features; a rejection of historical
styles and ornament; and the use of brick, wood, and plaster.

A-A 596. CLARK, ROBERT JUDSON and THOMAS S. HINES. Los Angeles Transfer:
Architecture in Southern California, 1880-1980. Los Angeles,
Calif.: William Andrews Clark Memorial Library, 1983. 122 pp.
Each of the authors treats a different period of architectural history
in Southern California, tracing the evolution and transfer of architectural
ideas and ideals. Clark covers the years from 1880 to 1930, describing
the rapid growth of the region; Hines examines the years 1920 to 1980,
noting the region's encounter with the forces of Modernism, with particular
emphasis on the work of Frank Lloyd Wright, Richard Neutra, and Charles
Moore.

A-A 597. EATON, LEONARD K. American Architecture Comes of Age: European
Reaction to H. H. Richardson and Louis Sullivan. Cambridge,
Mass.: MIT Press, 1972. 256 pp.
Although Frank Lloyd Wright has often been regarded as the first American
architect to exert any real international influence, Eaton maintains that,
based on the reactions of European architects in the 1890s and early 20th
century to the work of H. H. Richardson and Louis Sullivan, American architecture had come of age before Wright established his reputation abroad.

A-A 598. EATON, LEONARD K. Two Chicago Architects and Their Clients:
Frank Lloyd Wright and Howard Van Doren Shaw. Cambridge, Mass.:
MIT Press, 1969. 259 pp.
Wondering what kinds of clients sponsored Frank Lloyd Wright's innovative
early houses from about 1890 to 1920, Eaton compares Wright's patrons
to those of Howard Van Doren Shaw, a more conservative architect of the
same period. Eaton notes many similarities between the two groups but
points out that Shaw's clients tended to be better educated, more successful economically, more socially active, and more conventional in their
leisure-time activities.

A-A 599. EDGELL, G. H. The American Architecture of To-day. New York:
Scribner, 1928. 401 pp.
Edgell reviews the architecture of his day, subdividing it into three
categories: domestic and academic architecture, ecclesiastical and monumental architecture, and commercial architecture. Although he generally
praises the work of the modernists, he cautions them not to fear the precedent of the past, but rather to look for ways in which it can assist in
the solution of contemporary architectural problems.

A-A 600. GEBHARD, DAVID and HARRIETTE VON BRETON. L.A. in the Thirties, 1931-1941. Layton, Utah: Peregrine Smith, 1975. 165 pp.
Los Angeles architecture in the 1930s, according to the authors, represents the convergence of two trends in American cultural history: (1) the migration to the Los Angeles area of some of the most innovative designers in the world, and (2) the flourishing during that time of a new American style based on streamlined design, the use of new materials (especially glass, but also aluminum and chrome-plated steel), and new techniques in mass production.

A-A 601. GIEDION, SIGFRIED. Space, Time, and Architecture: The Growth of a New Tradition. 1941; Rev. ed. Cambridge, Mass.: Harvard University Press, 1967. 897 pp.
Although much of this book's focus is on architectural development in Europe, it does give considerable attention to the antecedents of modern architecture in the U.S. Giedion emphasizes the significance of the invention of the balloon frame in this country and highlights the contributions of Frank Lloyd Wright and members of the Chicago School of architecture.

A-A 602. GOLDBERGER, PAUL. On the Rise: Architecture and Design in a Postmodern Age. New York: Times Books, 1983. 340 pp.
This is a collection of some eighty pieces of architectural criticism written by Goldberger for the New York Times over the past ten years. A wide variety of topics is addressed: the architecture of American cities (including Los Angeles, Houston, Denver, Detroit, and Seattle), new buildings and monuments erected around the country, battles for historic preservation, and the work of contemporary architects.

A-A 603. GOLDBERGER, PAUL. The Skyscraper. New York: Knopf, 1981. 180 pp.
This is a history of the skyscraper, from the late 19th century to the present. Goldberger maintains that the skyscraper, more than any other type of building, is both quintessentially American and quintessentially of the 20th century. Yet, he cautions, while the skyscraper is often regarded as the city's triumphant symbol, it can also be regarded as an unwelcome intruder.

A-A 604. HALL, BEN M. The Best Remaining Seats: The Story of the Golden Age of the Movie Palace. New York: Potter, 1961. 266 pp.
In this history and description of movie theaters in the U.S.--particularly the luxury theaters built during the 1920s--the theater building and its decoration are considered for their effect on the total movie experience. Hall concludes that, like the films of the period, the ornate theaters satisfied a public taste for illusion and fantasy; they declined as tastes changed in the 1930s and afterwards.

A-A 605. HAMLIN, TALBOT, ed. Forms and Functions of Twentieth-Century Architecture. 4 vols. New York: Columbia University Press, 1952. 3265 pp.
Written primarily for professional architects and designers, this work is in large part technical and theoretical, containing descriptions of structural methods and design principles. Yet, in the final two volumes, all types of buildings are surveyed in detail (including residences, schools, churches, courthouses, theaters, banks, factories, settlement houses, asylums, and much more), with some historical background provided as context for each building type.

A-A 606. HIRSHORN, PAUL and STEVEN IZENOUR. White Towers. Cambridge,
Mass.: MIT Press, 1979. 190 pp.
The authors maintain that in more than fifty years of development, the
architecture of White Tower restaurants has "formed a particularly complete
and sophisticated set of stylistic variations on one strict symbolic
theme—a white building with a tower over its entrance—for one strict
functional purpose: selling hamburgers." Hirshorn and Izenour try to
shed some light on the nature of commercial architectural design, its
conscious use of both signs and symbols, and how it incorporates contemporary styles.

A-A 607. HUXTABLE, ADA LOUISE. Kicked a Building Lately? New York:
Quadrangle/New York Times Book, 1976. 304 pp.
This is the author's second collection of material written for the New
York Times on architecture and the urban scene. Covering the years from
1970 to 1976, Huxtable not only reviews specific buildings, but also comments upon such topics as: the work of architects like Marcel Breuer
and Louis Kahn, historic landmarks, Victorian architecture, and the urban
landscape (from New York and New Orleans to Salem, Massachusetts).

A-A 608. HUXTABLE, ADA LOUISE. Will They Ever Finish Bruckner Boulevard?
New York: Macmillan, 1970. 268 pp.
This is a selection of Huxtable's criticism, written for the New York
Times during the years 1963 to 1969, divided into two sections: (1) the
urban scene (focused mostly on New York, but also addressing problems
in other American cities), including an evaluation of particular buildings;
and (2) architecture (with sections on the art of expediency, the state
of the art, preservation, and the past).

A-A 609. JAKLE, JOHN A. The American Small Town: Twentieth-Century Place
Images. Hamden, Conn.: Archon Press, 1982. 195 pp.
Jakle's objective is to describe the American small town in the 20th century not in terms of its history, but rather in terms of its idea—i.e.,
to identify and interpret the elements of the landscape which traditionally
serve to symbolize the small town in America. These elements include
many features of the built environment, such as railroad depots, main
streets, courthouse squares, mills and mines, residential streets, churches,
and highways.

A-A 610. JENCKS, CHARLES. Architecture Today. New York: Abrams, 1982.
359 pp.
Analyzing recent developments in architecture, Jencks identifies three
major directions: (1) Late-Modernism (which retains the ideas, forms,
and language of the modern movement, often to an extreme); (2) Post-
Modernism (which, in reaction to what it sees as the visual dullness of
Modernism, tries to combine it with something else, often traditional
building); and (3) Alternatives (including alternative technologies and
nomadic designs). Much of the material here is derived from two of
Jencks's earlier books which are more international in scope, The Language
of Post-Modern Architecture (1977) and Late-Modern Architecture and Other
Essays (1980).

A-A 611. JORDY, WILLIAM H. American Buildings and Their Architects, III:
Progressive and Academic Ideals at the Turn of the Twentieth
Century. Garden City, N.Y.: Doubleday, 1972. 420 pp.
Beginning with a study of the Chicago School and the growth of the sky-
scraper, Jordy goes on to discuss what he sees as the major works of the
most important progressive and academic architects from 1880 to W.W. I.
Emphasizing the contributions of Louis Sullivan, Frank Lloyd Wright,
Charles and Henry Greene, Irving Gill, Bernard Maybeck, and Charles Follen
McKim, the author provides a general critical framework for the study
of architecture in this period.

A-A 612. JORDY, WILLIAM H. American Buildings and Their Architects, IV: The Impact of European Modernism in the Mid-Twentieth Century. Garden City, N.Y.: Doubleday, 1972. 469 pp.
Instead of trying to survey all of modern architecture, Jordy focuses on six different buildings as a way of gaining insight into the larger social, economic, technological, aesthetic, and ideological context of the period. The projects he considers are: Rockefeller Center in New York, the PSFS Building in Philadelphia, a dormitory at Vassar College by Marcel Breuer, two buildings by Mies van der Rohe, the Guggenheim Museum by Frank Lloyd Wright, and a medical research building by Louis Kahn.

A-A 613. KRINSKY, CAROL HERSELLE. Rockefeller Center. New York: Oxford University Press, 1978. 223 pp.
According to Krinsky, Rockefeller Center--a coordinated group of commercial buildings in midtown Manhattan--holds a place in our contemporary capitalist democracy comparable to that of cathedrals and other major monuments in earlier times. Her study examines the Center's sponsors and financial backing; the arrangement and order of the buildings; and other aspects of planning, design, commerce, promotion, technology, and urban renewal.

A-A 614. KURTZ, STEPHAN A. Wasteland: Building the American Dream. New York: Praeger, 1973. 125 pp.
Kurtz emphasizes the dependency of the architect upon the social order: The architect relies upon the world first to present a problematic situation and then to provide the means for its resolution. Filled with black-and-white photos, the book is divided into four sections: the road, exurban communities, the city, and the profession. The first section points out that the American road provides illusions of home, security, refuge. Howard Johnson restaurants, which dot highways throughout America, are especially responsible for this "home away from home" tradition. Section two looks at Levittown and the problems of a Utopian community; Kurtz concludes that the horror of suburban life cannot be planned out of existence by designers since the problems reside within the social structure and family relations. The next section emphasizes the architect's primary responsibility to fulfill the city dwellers' basic needs. In his concluding section, Kurtz notes that architecture must be given back to the people.

A-A 615. MAHER, JAMES T. The Twilight of Splendor: Chronicles of the Age of American Palaces. Boston: Little, Brown, 1975. 453 pp.
In this study of five American palaces completed between W.W. I and the 1930s, the aim is not so much to describe the buildings' architecture and decoration as it is to study the individuals who commissioned, designed, and decorated the palaces. The five palaces (and their owners) are: Whitemarch Hall (Edward Townsend Stotesbury), Ca' d'Zan (John Ringling), Vizcaya (James E. Deering), San Marino (Henry E. Huntington), and Shadow Lawn (Hubert Templeton Parson).

A-A 616. McCALLUM, IAN. Architecture USA. New York: Reinhold, 1959. 216 pp.
McCallum's purpose is to present a cross-section of what he considers the best of American architecture, by way of examining the work of thirty-three architects. According to McCallum, the biographical approach is necessary "because, in architecture today, quality is in direct ratio to the calibre of the individual architect." The architects are arranged chronologically according to the year of their birth.

A-A 617. **MOCK, ELIZABETH**, ed. Built in USA: Since 1932. New York:
Museum of Modern Art, 1945. 127 pp.
This catalogue of an exhibition at the Museum of Modern Art covers forty-
five examples of "good building in the United States" erected since the
Museum's 1932 exhibition of International-Style modern architecture.
An introductory essay by Mock surveys new developments in design, the
adaptation of building form and structure to climate and topography, and
the use of new materials (such as reinforced concrete and laminated wood).

A-A 618. **MUMFORD, LEWIS.** From the Ground Up: Observations on Contemporary
Architecture, Housing, Highway Building, and Civic Design.
New York: Harcourt, Brace, 1956. 243 pp.
This is a collection of essays by Mumford that appeared in the Sky Line
department of the New Yorker magazine between 1947 and 1955. Various
topics are covered, including: housing projects (both urban and suburban),
the United Nations complex of buildings, the architecture of Frank Lloyd
Wright, school buildings, modern skyscrapers, New York traffic, and highway
design.

A-A 619. **MUMFORD, LEWIS.** The Highway and the City. New York: Harcourt,
Brace & World, 1963. 246 pp.
In this collection of twenty-two essays on the problems of the contemporary
city, Mumford deals first with European examples but concentrates in the
second half of the book on developments in the U.S. Among the topics
addressed are the impact of Frank Lloyd Wright, the desecration of New
York's Pennsylvania Station, historic architecture in Philadelphia, and
the relationship of landscape to townscape.

A-A 620. **NAYLOR, DAVID.** American Picture Palaces: The Architecture of
Fantasy. New York: Van Nostrand Reinhold, 1981. 224 pp.
According to the author, no buildings have been so loudly hyped by their
owners, so totally reviled by architectural critics, and yet so well
received by local citizens, as the motion picture palaces, built in a wide
variety of styles generally in the years between W.W. I and the 1930s
Depression. After some discussion of what preceded these luxury theaters,
Naylor focuses on the architects and architecture of the grand picture
palaces.

A-A 621. **PEISCH, MARK L.** The Chicago School of Architecture: Early Followers of Sullivan and Wright. New York: Random House, 1964.
177 pp.
According to Peisch, a number of Chicago architects, though not all as
well known as Louis Sullivan and Frank Lloyd Wright, made important contributions to the development of modern architecture during the years
1893 to 1914. These architects include Barry Byrne, William E. Drummond,
George Grant Elmslie, Hugh M. Garden, Walter Burley Griffin, George W.
Maher, and William G. Purcell.

A-A 622. **POLYZOIDES, STEPHANOS, ROGER SHERWOOD, JAMES TICE,** and **JULIUS
SHULMAN.** Courtyard Housing in Los Angeles: A Typological Analysis. Berkeley: University of California Press, 1982. 219 pp.
Although focusing on courtyard housing in the Los Angeles area, the authors
relate this particular style of housing to larger developments in urban,
social, and cultural history. Their typological analysis looks at some
of the conscious and unconscious factors that generated the courtyard
houses, at some of the architectural and historic precedents, and at more
general ideas of spatial organization.

A-A 623. ROBINSON, CERVIN and ROSEMARIE HAAG BLETTER. Skyscraper Style:
          Art Deco New York. New York: Oxford University Press, 1975.
          88 pp.
In this study of art deco skyscrapers in New York, the question of architectural style is placed within the framework of developments in science,
industry, and business. Robinson contributes an essay on the architects
(including their backgrounds and education) and their buildings, while
Bletter describes the origins and cultural significance of the art deco
style.

A-A 624. ROBINSON, SIDNEY K. Life Imitates Architecture: Taliesin and
          Alden Dow's Studio. Ann Arbor: University of Michigan Archi-
          tectural Research Library, 1980. 74 pp.
The author examines what he calls "the composed places" created by two
architects in the 20th century: Frank Lloyd Wright's Taliesin in Wisconsin
and Alden Dow's studio in Michigan. According to Robinson, each of these
architects wanted to compose in their places an enduring relationship
between architecture and life, and to have the beauty of their places
intimately related to the harmony of nature.

A-A 625. SCHAFFER, DANIEL. Garden Cities for America: The Radburn Experi-
          ence. Philadelphia: Temple University Press, 1982. 276 pp.
This analysis of the garden city movement in the U.S. emphasizes the history of Radburn, New Jersey, a garden city community that was planned
in 1929 as an alternative to conventional suburban development. In addition, Schaffer describes some of the movement's earlier history (such
as the Sunnyside Gardens experiment in Queens and the Regional Planning
Association of America), and takes a brief look at the legacy left by
the Radburn experience.

A-A 626. SCULLY, VINCENT J., Jr. The Shingle Style Today; or, the His-
          torian's Revenge. New York: Braziller, 1974. 118 pp.
Looking at some of the single-family houses designed by a number of contemporary architects—including Charles Gwathmey, John Hagmann, Charles
Moore, Jaquelin Robertson, Robert Stern, and Robert Venturi—Scully maintains that there are important stylistic connections between their body
of work and that of the Shingle-Style architects of the 1880s.

A-A 627. SMITH, C. RAY. Supermannerism: New Attitudes in Post-Modern
          Architecture. New York: Dutton, 1977. 354 pp.
According to the author, Supermannerism is a new design movement in the
U.S. that is radically changing our vision, altering our cultural consciousness, and reshaping our country. The movement is characterized by the
systematic manipulation of established principles, alteration of scale,
and reordering of surface details. Among its most prominent exponents
are Romaldo Giurgola, Hugh Hardy, Charles Moore, and Robert Venturi.

A-A 628. STERN, ROBERT A. M. New Directions in American Architecture.
          1969; Rev. ed. New York: Braziller, 1977. 152 pp.
In the first part of this study, Stern discusses and illustrates the work
of seven prominent architects: Louis Kahn, Kevin Roche, Paul Rudolph,
Philip Johnson, Robert Venturi, Romaldo Giurgola, and Charles Moore.
The book's second section offers an essay on architecture and today's
cities, with comments on how architects might involve themselves in the
remaking of our urban environments.

A-A 629. STERN, ROBERT A. M., GREGORY GILMARTIN, and JOHN MONTAGUE
MASSENGALE. New York 1900: Metropolitan Architecture and Urbanism
1890-1915. New York: Rizzoli International, 1983. 502 pp.
The authors regard New York City at the turn of the century as the nation's
ultimate example of metropolitanism and urban grandeur. Their study
addresses in part the larger question of urbanism in 1900 while focusing
on the architecture of New York, including its palaces of production
Ooffice buildings, banks, stores), its palaces of pleasure (theaters, clubs,
Coney Island), and its palaces for the people (hotels, apartments).

A-A 630. VENTURI, ROBERT, DENISE SCOTT BROWN, and STEVEN IZENOUR. Learning
from Las Vegas: The Forgotten Symbolism of Architectural Form.
1972; Rev. ed. Cambridge, Mass.: MIT Press, 1977. 192 pp.
After describing the architecture of the commercial strip in Las Vegas,
the authors offer some generalizations on the iconography of urban sprawl.
They note that on the Strip—as was the case also with Roman triumphal
arches and medieval European cathedrals—form is overshadowed by symbolism,
allusion, and emotional association. Venturi, Brown, and Izenour do not
necessarily champion the values of Las Vegas, but they do admire a number
of its elements as apt means of architectural communication in the age
of the automobile.

A-A 631. VIEYRA, DANIEL I. "Fill 'Er Up": An Architectural History of
America's Gas Stations. New York: Macmillan, 1979. 111 pp.
According to the author, the gas station is paradoxically both the most
widespread type of commercial building in the U.S. and the most ignored.
Vieyra's architectural history of America's gas stations does not emphasize
chronological or stylistic developments; rather it is interested primarily
in the imagery and symbolism that the stations have represented and projected in our 20th-century, drive-in civilization.

A-A 632. WEKERLE, GERDA, REBECCA PETERSON, and DAVID MORLEY, eds. New
Space for Women. Boulder, Colo.: Westview Press, 1980.
332 pp.
This is a collection of twenty essays—written by architects, designers,
sociologists, geographers, psychologists, and historians—on some of the
problems encountered by women in homes, office buildings, suburban areas,
neighborhoods, and elsewhere. Specific topics include: the institutional
constraints affecting women in the decision-making process, women as
environmental activists, women and urban design, and the design of the
domestic workplace.

A-A 633. WINTER, ROBERT. The California Bungalow. Los Angeles, Calif.:
Hennessey & Ingalls, 1980. 95 pp.
Seeking to establish an overall concept and definition for the bungalow,
the author finds his answer in California—where the style of life, the
mild climate, and the closeness to nature all suggest to him the bungalow
concept and bungalow mystique. Consequently, Winter focuses on developments in California, though he also traces the origins of the bungalow
back to 17th-century India, where he finds it was invented by the British.

A-A 634. WOLFE, TOM. From Bauhaus to Our House. New York: Farrar, Straus
& Giroux, 1981. 143 pp.
According to Wolfe, modern architecture in the 20th century was created
in Europe and transported by "white gods" (primarily members of the Bauhaus
movement) to the New World. Maintaining that this architecture is both
completely alien to and inexpressive of American culture—and that clients
for the most part either are puzzled by it or hate it—the author is
bemused by the fact that the Modernist style, particularly in the form
of the glass-box, nevertheless became widespread in this country.

HISTORY

History, of course, is by nature an ambitious discipline; its boundaries expand with each passing day. Its components—people, events, processes—are innumerable, capable of being viewed in an endless variety of combinations and from any number of perspectives. In the last few decades, moreover, the discipline has willfully expanded its purview, increasingly interesting itself in lives and developments less attended to by contemporaries, in subject matter traditionally treated by other disciplines, and in analytical techniques pioneered by those "rival" disciplines. Indeed, some might accuse American historians of a kind of methodological imperialism as they exploit the resources of alien fields and relentlessly impinge upon their territory. History's inherent ambitiousness and recent expansionism has bred a multiplicity of sub-fields and each, in fact, possesses its own body of reference works. One cannot begin to approach these many tools, however, without some familiarity with the more general and most basic reference sources for American history.

There exist a number of works whose purpose is to describe the reference material available to the scholar. Both Eugene P. Sheehy's <u>Guide to Reference Books</u> (Chicago: American Library Association, 1976) and Carl White and associates' <u>Sources of Information in the Social Sciences</u> (Chicago: American Library Association, 1973) include sections on history, noting the bibliographies, biographical sources, dictionaries, and encyclopedias that might be of particular use to the researcher. Helen J. Poulton's <u>The Historian's Handbook: A Descriptive Guide to Reference Works</u> (Norman: University of Oklahoma Press, 1972) is, as the title would indicate, a more extensive and detailed inventory of research aids in history, including national bibliographies, dissertation indexes, and guides to government publications and legal sources. In terms of American history, the most ambitious guide to bibliographies has been the Henry P. Beers volumes, <u>Bibliographies in American History</u>, originally published in 1942

239

and now updated through 1978 (Woodbridge, Conn.: Research Publications, 1982). Beers lists both catalogues of publications and "archival and manuscript research aids"; bibliographies, in other words, both of source material and of secondary work. For the post-1789 material he groups bibliographies by topic (e.g., diplomatic, economic, political, and ethnic history) or by region addressed in the work.

As for bibliographies themselves, of the general treatments of American history probably the two-volume Harvard Guide to American History, edited by Frank Freidel (Cambridge, Mass.: Harvard University Press, 1974), is most basic. The Harvard Guide presents the "most immediately useful" historical work published through mid-1970 under topical and chronological headings. Also in the guide are references to more specialized bibliographies in various subfields, to biographies and personal records, and to other research aids as well as a discussion of the methods and materials of historical research. The listings in The American Historical Association's Guide to Historical Literature, edited by George Frederick Howe, et al. (New York: Macmillan, 1961), are necessarily much less comprehensive as the volume attempts a "bibliographic panorama" of all eras and parts of the globe. They do, however, have the virtue of being briefly annotated while the Harvard Guide's listings are simply listings. An earlier edition of the AHA guide, edited by George Mathew Dutcher, et al. (New York: Macmillan, 1931), has not been entirely superseded—it merits consultation for work published before 1930 as well as for its often somewhat fuller annotation and its references to contemporary reviews of works cited. Other volumes which, similarly, list fewer titles but consider them more fully than the Harvard Guide include the Library of Congress General Reference and Bibliography Division's A Guide to the Study of the United States of America: Representative Books Reflecting the Development of American Life and Thought (Washington, D.C.: Library of Congress, 1960; supplement, 1976), and Josephus N. Larned, ed., The Literature of American History: A Bibliographic Guide (Boston: Houghton

Mifflin, 1902). The Library of Congress guide boasts comparatively extensive treatment of the selected work. It contains a general history section
as well as sections for such sub-disciplines as military, intellectual,
and local history. Historical works are also included within other sections, such as "Population, Immigration, and Minorities." The Larned
guide, of course, only addresses books published through the end of the
19th century. Its annotations, however, often prove useful, being of
a particularly scholarly, critical bent.

The researcher needs also to consult more specialized bibliographies.
These include listings devoted to a certain subject (e.g., Samuel F. Bemis
and Grace G. Griffin, Guide to the Diplomatic History of the United States,
1775-1921 [Washington, D.C.: U.S. Government Printing Office, 1935]),
those attending to resources available in a particular region (e.g., Harry
J. Carman and Arthur W. Thompson, A Guide to the Principal Sources for
American Civilization, 1800-1900, in the City of New York: Printed Materials [New York: Columbia University Press, 1962]), and those addressing
a certain period (e.g., William J. Stewart, Era of Franklin D. Roosevelt:
A Selected Bibliography of Periodical, Essay, and Dissertation Literature
[Hyde Park, N.Y.: National Archives & Record Service, 1974]). The Golden-
tree Bibliographies in American History series, under the general editorship of Arthur Link, is of particular note, having already issued a number
of volumes on various eras and topics. One ought not neglect catalogues
of special collections and notable library holdings increasingly available
in bound volumes. A student of American radicalism, for instance, would
not want to miss the catalogue of the Tamiment Institute Library at New
York University (Boston: G. K. Hall, 1980).

A great deal of historical literature is published initially, or
appears solely, in periodical or dissertation form. America: History
and Life, issued three times a year, represents a most valuable guide
to periodical literature. An offspring of the more broadly focused Historical Abstracts, 1775-1945, America: History and Life has, since 1964,

abstracted current articles in U.S. and Canadian history and culture and
has provided bibliographic citations and references to book reviews.
Well-indexed, its entries are subdivided by period and by subject or
grouped by regional focus. For the greater part of this century the American Historical Association's Writings on American History volumes have
indexed available periodical literature. Typically, these describe the
output of a single year. More recent editions have simply listed articles,
arranging them by subject. Supplementing Writings on American History
since 1976 has been the AHA's Recently Published Articles which, again,
simply lists (under chronological or regional headings) and does not anno-
tate. The Association also periodically reports on recently completed
dissertations and work in progress in Doctoral Dissertations in History.
In addition to this and more general references, such as the Comprehensive
Dissertation Index (Ann Arbor, Mich.: University Microfilms, 1973-),
such work is addressed in Warren F. Kuehl's Dissertations in History:
An Index to Dissertations Compiled in History in United States and Canadian
Universities, 2 vols. (Lexington: University of Kentucky Press, 1965-
72).

As the range of historical study broadens—both in terms of subject
matter and method—so too does the nature of the evidence the historian
seeks. Manuscripts and documents, though, remain central to the work
of the profession. The indispensable references to this sort of material
are A Guide to Archives and Manuscripts in the United States, edited by
Philip Hamer (New Haven, Conn.: Yale University Press, 1961), Directory
of Archives and Manuscript Repositories in the United States (Washington,
D.C.: National Historical Publications and Records Commission, 1978),
and the Library of Congress National Union Catalog of Manuscript Collections (Washington, D.C.: Library of Congress, 1959/61-). The first two,
published under the auspices of the National Historical Publications and
Records Commission, list collections of papers and records of business,
political, and social organizations, as well as of thousands of individuals

by location. They are indexed by name or organization. The Library of
Congress volumes, issued annually, describe collections as they are catalogued. These descriptions are usually more extensive than those of the
other guides, though consulting the volumes may require going through
any number of indexes. For Federal documents and records the National
Archives and Records Service has published a Guide to the National Archives
of the United States (Washington, D.C.: United States Government Printing
Office, 1974). It covers the Archives's central and regional holdings
of material from the legislative and judicial branches and from executive
departments and agencies, as well as documents from the pre-Constitutional
period and from foreign governments. The Carnegie Institution of Washington's guides to manuscript material for the history of the U.S., produced
between 1906 and 1943, though necessarily dated, remain important for
their description of America-related collections in foreign nations.
Finally, as with bibliographies, there are any number of manuscript guides
of a more specialized nature, such as those to holdings of American Revolution and Civil War material, or to resources available in a particular
area.

Similarly, there are almost certainly more encyclopedias and dictionaries that deal with distinct periods, groups, regions, or subfields
than with American history in general. Stephan Thernstrom, ed., Harvard
Encyclopedia of Ethnic Groups (Cambridge, Mass.: Harvard University Press,
1980) is but one of many examples of more specialized basic reference.
The eight volume Dictionary of American History, Rev. ed. (New York:
Scribner, 1976), however, aspires to answer the need, in the words of
its first editor, James Truslow Adams, "for one source to which an inquirer
might go to find, and quickly, what he wishes to know as to specific facts,
events, trends, or policies in our American past." Alphabetically arranged,
but in one volume (and including significant personalities) is the Oxford
Companion to American History (New York: Oxford University Press, 1966),
edited by Thomas Johnson. One volume references ordered chronologically

243

include Richard Morris, ed., Encyclopedia of American History (New York: Harper & Row, 1982), Webster's Guide to American History (New York: G. & C. Merriam, 1971), and Arthur Schlesinger, Jr., ed., The Almanac of American History (New York: Putnam, 1983). The Morris Encyclopedia is divided into a basic chronology of national events, especially political and military ones, and a topical chronology of events in the social, cultural, economic, and scientific realms. It and the Webster Guide contain separate biographical sections. For more comprehensive biographical information one would probably want first to consult The Dictionary of American Biography (New York: Scribner, 1928-). Since the publication of the first volume in 1928, the Dictionary has sought to detail the lives of notable deceased Americans. The work, with supplemental volumes, now covers those whose lives extended into the mid-1960s. Who Was Who in America (Chicago: Marquis-Who's Who, 1942-73) and the National Cyclopedia of American Biography (New York: James T. White, 1892-) are among other multi-volume biographical references. There also exist more focused biographical encyclopedias--e.g., the four volume Notable American Women, edited by Edward T. James, et al. (Cambridge, Mass.: Harvard University Press, 1971-80)--and various single volume arrangements. One of the most interesting of the latter is John A. Garraty, ed., Encyclopedia of American Biography (New York: Harper & Row, 1974). Each of the more than 1,000 entries include two sections--a straightforward summary of the subject's life and a more reflective essay, typically by a prominent historian or biographer, considering the individual and his or her significance.

Patrick Williams
Columbia University

I. OVERVIEWS AND SPECIAL STUDIES

H 1. AYDELOTTE, WILLIAM O. Quantification in History. Reading, Mass.:
Addison-Wesley, 1971. 181 pp.
This volume contains five essays and a collection of letters between the
author and J. H. Hexter, an historian also concerned with the problems
of quantitative historical data. To clarify the value of a quantitative
approach to history, Aydelotte points to specific areas in which such
a methodology proves useful. His essays weigh the advantages and disadvantages of quantitative techniques, examine their uses, and discuss in detail
the practical limitation of the methodology.

H 2. AYDELOTTE, WILLIAM O., ALLAN G. BOGUE, and ROBERT WILLIAM FOGEL.
The Dimensions of Quantitative Research in History. Princeton,
N.J.: Princeton University Press, 1972. 435 pp.
This collection of essays explains the uses and limitations of quantification in historical research. The essays emphasize historical substance
rather than methodology and deal with both American and non-American topics.
Problems in American history are addressed in essays on the following:
social mobility; the effects of incumbency, the party in power, economic
conditions, and other factors in congressional election results; an analysis of roll call votes establishing how power was used in the Thirty-
Seventh Senate; variable expenditures by some American cities at the beginning of the 20th century; and the extent to which Federal land policy
contributed to inefficiency in agriculture.

H 3. BAILYN, BERNARD, et al. The Great Republic: A History of the American People. Boston: Little, Brown, 1977. 1316 pp.
The authors of this work--Bailyn, David Brion Davis, David Herbert Donald,
John L. Thomas, Robert H. Wiebe, and Gordon S. Wood--have assembled a
survey of American history from the earliest settlers in Virginia to the
present. Though each of the six sections of the work is written by a
different historian, two major themes dominate the work: the development
of free political institutions in America; and the mediation between majority rule and minority rights.

H 4. BEARD, CHARLES A. and MARY R. BEARD. The Rise of American Civilization. 1927; Rev. ed. New York: Macmillan, 1933. 865 pp.
This survey examines American civilization from its beginnings through
the machine age of the 1920s. The Beards isolate the conflicts of diametrically opposed economic interests--merchants and planters, capitalists
and laborers, businessmen and farmers--as the determinative factors shaping
American society and culture. They trace the cyclical rise of various
business interests and the ultimately successful efforts to harness these
interests through liberal reform. Their work is not economic or business
history per se, but rather an economic interpretation of all of American
history.

H 5. BERNSTEIN, BARTON J., ed. Toward a New Past: Dissenting Essays
in American History. New York: Random House, 1968. 364 pp.
The twelve articles in this work represent a broad range of historical
analyses by liberal scholars, including: Eugene Genovese's critique of
traditional "Marxist" interpretations of the economic function of slavery,
Christopher Lasch's discussion of the Cold War and its impact on American
intellectuals, Staughton Lynd's review of interpretations of the constitution, and Jesse Lemisch's essay on "History from the Bottom Up." This
diverse collection offers the opinions and writing of American historians
outside the mainstream of their discipline.

H 6. **BERTHOFF, ROWLAND T.** Unsettled People. New York: Harper & Row, 1971. 528 pp.
Berthoff maintains that economic development often undermines social order. The class structure, the family, church influences, and community values maintained stability during the Colonial period. Industrial and economic growth during the 19th century, resulting in an increased emphasis on individual success and status, caused the institutions that had stabilized society to erode under the new economic system. Berthoff concludes that a new era may be approaching in which economic sources of disorder, competition, and individualism in particular, may be resolved and the traditional conservative values of community and social responsibility restored.

H 7. **BOORSTIN, DANIEL J.** The Americans: The Democratic Experience. New York: Random House, 1973. 717 pp.
Boorstin chronicles the development of a democratic culture in America. From cowboys and explorers to 20th-century advertising and consumer consumption, he offers a patchwork sampling of American culture. Concluding with an analysis of the repercussions of technology, Boorstin warns of the "unfreedom of omnipotence" wrought by scientific advances. The bibliographical section provides a comprehensive listing of sources.

H 8. **BOORSTIN, DANIEL J.** The Americans: The National Experience. New York: Random House, 1965. 517 pp.
In this second volume of a three-part series on American culture (see H 7 and H 60), Boorstin explores various social and political factors that fueled expansion in America and helped Americans adjust to and exploit their surrounding environments. Focusing on the period from the Revolutionary era to the Civil War, the author explains how early Americans responded to the uncertainties of life on the developing continent and created new concepts of community and nationhood. Boorstin also discusses the uniquely American symbols, language, and institutions that developed in response to the American experience.

H 9. **BREMNER, ROBERT H.** American Philanthropy. Chicago: University of Chicago Press, 1960. 230 pp.
Bremner relates the history of American philanthropy, good deeds, and social reforms from the Native Americans who welcomed Columbus and taught the starving Pilgrims to plant corn through John D. Rockefeller and the Ford Foundation. Bremner describes the book as "a survey of voluntary activity in the fields of charity, religion, education, humanitarian reform, social service, war relief, and foreign aid." He deals with representative donors, whether of money or service, with promoters of moral and social reform, and with the various institutions and associations Americans have founded to implement philanthropy. Covering such specific agents as Cotton Mather, Benjamin Franklin, Dorothea Dix, CARE, and the March of Dimes, the work serves as an introduction to the philanthropic elements of American life.

H 10. **BREMNER, ROBERT H.** From the Depths: The Discovery of Poverty in the United States. New York: New York University Press, 1956. 364 pp.
Bremner provides a study of the "discovery of poverty" in the U.S. by reformers and humanitarians and an examination of how and why attitudes and actions toward poverty have changed. While explaining the factors that made Americans aware of poverty and sympathetic to the misfortunes of fellow citizens, the author traces the shift from a view of poverty as the result of character defects and unequal endowments to the newer view which sees poverty as essentially a result of social and economic conditions which can be corrected by social action. Bremner also examines the relationship between these changing attitudes and the growing emphasis

on factual statistics in social surveys. He is one of the first historians
to make use of such sources of information as popular magazines, popular
novels, and graphic arts.

H 11. CARSTENSEN, VERNON, ed. The Public Lands: Studies in the History
        of the Public Domain. Madison: University of Wisconsin Press,
        1962. 522 pp.
This collection of articles by various authors examines the ways in which
the public lands were conceptualized, utilized, and given away. The articles are grouped according to "Origins of the Public Land System," "Distribution of the Public Lands," "Comment, Criticism and Concern with Consequences," and "Problems of Protection and Management of Public Domain."
In his introduction, Carstensen argues that although historians generally
have taken a hostile view of land disposal operations, calling attention
to political favoritism and fraud, quite often what was termed fraud was
simply "local accommodation to the rigidities and irrelevance of the laws."

H 12. CARTWRIGHT, WILLIAM H. and RICHARD L. WATSON, eds. Reinterpretation
        of American History and Culture. Washington, D.C.: National Coun-
        cil for the Social Studies, 1973. 554 pp.
Cartwright and Watson contend that historians constantly reinterpret history according to the interaction between the past and the present, either
consciously or subconsciously answering the questions raised by the current
milieu. Having established this understanding of the complexity and relevance of historical scholarship, the editors present twenty-five essays
as examples of contemporary interpretations of U.S. history. Race and
nationality, women's history, and historiographical questions are addressed
in the first half of the volume where new areas of historical investigation
are highlighted. The second half offers a series of fifteen essays rein-
terpreting American history from the Colonial period through post-W.W.
II foreign relations.

H 13. CUMMINGS, RICHARD. The American and His Food: A History of Food
        Habits in the United States. 1940; Rev. ed. New York: Arno Press,
        1944. 291 pp.
In this chronological survey from 1789 to 1940, Cummings documents sociological, technological, cultural, and environmental influences on American
eating habits. The author draws on contemporary travel accounts, cookbooks,
periodicals, and government documents. He treats foodways on the family
farm and within the growing cities and incorporates the effects of refrigeration and rapid transportation as well as improvements in food processing
and packaging. Food faddists are covered, as is the rise of such industry
titans as Campbell's Soups and Quaker Oats. Other topics include the
growth of government control over sanitation, purity, and packaging, and
the development of nutritional science.

H 14. CURTI, MERLE. American Philanthropy Abroad: A History. New Bruns-
        wick, N.J.: Rutgers University Press, 1963. 651 pp.
Curti provides an extensive study of the many forms of American foreign
philanthropy. Although he concentrates on private, nongovernmental philanthropic efforts, attention is given to the increasing correlation of private and governmental measures, especially since the beginning of W.W. II
Curti suggests that American philanthropic projects are motivated by the
humanitarian concerns of the Judeo-Christian tradition which stress an
obligation to try to relieve human need. Other less altruistic reasons
for philanthropy include the promotion of business, the creation of a
favorable foreign image of the U.S., and ethnic loyalties of the type
exhibited in the aid to Ireland during the 19th-century famines.

H 15. DANIEL, ROBERT L. American Philanthropy in the Near East, 1820-1960.
       Athens: Ohio University Press, 1970. 322 pp.
Daniel considers America's early philanthropic efforts and their subsequent
developments. Included are detailed accounts of private charities spanning
the time from Samuel Gridley Howe's relief work in Greece in the 1820s
to the work of the Near East Foundation in the 1950s. Because philanthropy
in the Near East grew out of American religious efforts, much of the book
is given over to missions and the people who proselytized in the region.
Among the philanthropic enterprises that developed from the missionary
attempt were hospitals and schools, notably the American University of
Beirut.

H 16. DEGLER, CARL N. Out of Our Past. New York: Harper & Row, 1959.
       484 pp.
Viewing the past through the "lens of the present," Degler endeavors to
trace the development of America's unique national character in the middle
of the 20th century. Degler's analysis highlights the ideas, beliefs,
and values of the American people that have shaped contemporary American
culture. The history of black people in America and the rise and influence
of the city are emphasized as key facets of the American experience.

H 17. FISCHER, DAVID HACKETT. Growing Old in America: The Bland-Lee
       Lectures Delivered at Clark University. New York: Oxford Uni-
       versity Press, 1977. 242 pp.
This is the first major study to place the process of aging in America
into an historical perspective. Fischer begins with the Puritans and
their veneration of the aged. He argues that between 1770 and 1820 the
focus of age group bias began to change as respect for the old declined
and the young began to acquire new advantages. In the 19th and 20th centuries this process reached its climax; old age came to be regarded with
contempt and a cult of youth took shape. Nineteenth- and 20th-century
Americans have repudiated their elders instead of respecting them as they
did in earlier centuries, thus removing them from the society as much
as possible. Due to the increasing number of elderly in the society,
old age has emerged as a social problem. Attempts to deal with the problem
through such devices as social welfare and pensions, Fischer notes, have
created many other problems.

H 18. FORSTER, COLIN and G. S. L. TUCKER. Economic Opportunity and White
       American Fertility Ratios, 1800-1860. New Haven, Conn.: Yale
       University Press, 1972. 121 pp.
At the beginning of the 19th century, the American birth rate was much
higher than that which prevailed throughout most of Europe. Moreover,
it began to decline much earlier in the century than European rates.
The authors reexamine the hypotheses of Yasukichi Yasuba (see H 47), who
concluded that the exceptional behavior of the birth rate in 19th-century
America was due to the declining availability of new land and the consequent growth in concentration of the rural population. Using more sophisticated statistical techniques, Forster and Tucker substantially confirm
Yasuba's conclusions. They determine that a meaningful socio-economic
relationship did indeed exist between the white birth ratio and the opportunities for the establishment of new farms. Urbanization, they conclude,
does not become a major variable until well into the second half of the
century. Whatever the case in Europe, urbanization was not a necessary
condition for the reduction of fertility in America in the first half
of the 19th century.

H 19. GOLDMAN, RALPH M. Search for Consensus: The Story of the Democratic Party. Philadelphia: Temple University Press, 1979.
417 pp.
Goldman chronicles the Democratic party's attempt to give "practical effect
to the idea of representativeness." From the earliest emergence of popular
sovereignty to the Democratic party's current state, this work investigates
the party's attempts throughout its history to coalesce many different
interests in order to reflect a national civic consensus. Goldman highlights the Democratic party's enhancement of the representative nature
of the American system, and its struggle to remain a dominant force in
American politics.

H 20. HASSLER, WARREN W. With Shield and Sword. Ames: Iowa State University Press, 1982. 462 pp.
Hassler chronicles American military activity from the French and Indian
War through present military commitments and policy. Hassler employs
an integrated approach to the military history of the U.S., which "discusses the participation of significant individuals interacting with American military operation on land, sea and in the air and their search throughout history for a viable military policy in times of peace and war."

H 21. HOFSTADTER, RICHARD. The American Political Tradition. New York:
Knopf, 1948. 381 pp.
In twelve essays, Hofstadter characterizes key figures from the Revolutionary era to Franklin Roosevelt, all of whom typified the sentiments
of their period and contributed to major currents in American political
thought. Hofstadter argues that "above and beyond local conflicts there
has been a common ground, a unity of cultural and political tradition,
upon which American civilization has stood," and that concurrence about
the rights of property, economic individualism, and the value of opportunity served as "staple tenets of the central faith in American political
ideologies" since the founding of the nation.

H 22. HOOKER, RICHARD J. Food and Drink in America: A History. Indianapolis, Ind.: Bobbs-Merrill, 1981. 436 pp.
Drawing on social histories and unpublished travel accounts, Hooker covers
American eating and drinking habits from Colonial times to the present.
He provides anecdotal surveys of regional foodways; the introduction of
new exotica such as the tomato; the rise of the fast-food industry with
its fashionable precedents such as Delmonico's; urban lunch counters;
and the convenience food industry with its innovations in packaging and
freezing. Foods of different regions are covered, as are foodways of
various ethnic groups. Hooker blends social and cultural history to show
the rationale behind certain habits such as drinking ice water with meals
(a temperance movement ploy). Native abundance is stressed throughout
this survey. A final chapter treats contemporary reliance on highly pro-
cessed and chemically treated foodstuffs.

H 23. HUBER, RICHARD M. The American Idea of Success. New York: McGraw-
Hill, 1971. 563 pp.
The maxims of Benjamin Franklin, the "old boy network," the "school of
hard knocks," and "how-to" books are explored in this examination of the
American preoccupation with the notion of success. Huber sees success
in dualistic terms, noting both its materialistic dimension (money, position, status) and its spiritual side (the inner peace that comes from
hard-sought accomplishment). Paradoxically, Huber argues, the "struggle"
for success is often more rewarding than the final pay-off. The dimensions
of the "success ethic," its origins, and its implications for American
society are examined through the lives of Horatio Alger, Dale Carnegie,
Norman Vincent Peale, Ralph Waldo Emerson, and others. The idea of success
is seen as an integral component of American religion, schooling, and

character. Huber shows that while society values the successful individual, it does so only when such success has been achieved honestly and when some return in the form of "good works" or community service is offered.

H 24. **KATZ, JONATHAN.** Gay American History: Lesbians and Gay Men in America. New York: Crowell, 1976. 690 pp.
This work uncovers a 400-year history of homosexuality in America. Investigation of gay and lesbian history, Katz suggests, reveals a largely uncharted area of American history and the "influence of a particular national setting on the historical forms of homosexuality found within it." Six chronological, topical sections explore gay Americans' experience with homosexual oppression, resistance, and love. Each section presents the influences and social conditions that affected homosexuality in a given period.

H 25. **LECKIE, ROBERT.** The Wars of America. 1968; Rev. ed. New York: Harper & Row, 1981. 1160 pp.
Leckie chronicles America's extensive involvement in warfare from the Colonial period through the Vietnam era. He illustrates how and why this nation fought various wars, and what the resort to arms yielded the country. Besides giving a description of changes in the scope and tactics of war through history, Leckie describes "the men who made and fought in these wars." In his consideration of the course and personalities of American warfare, Leckie acknowledges the reality of "men as fighting creatures" and the U.S. as "the fightingest nation since the advent of modern warfare."

H 26. **LEE, RONALD DEMOS,** ed. Population Patterns in the Past. New York: Academic Press, 1977. 376 pp.
Although only one of the twelve essays in this collection specifically focuses on the U.S., they all explore methodological issues and various hypotheses of general interest to demographers. In addition, the essays share common, cross-cultural themes of "preindustrial institutions and population control," "socioeconomic determinants of modern demographic behavior," or "new methods for analyzing aggregate demographic data" which serve as the organizational framework of the book.

H 27. **LIFTON, ROBERT JAY** and **ERIC OLSON.** Explorations in Psychohistory. New York: Simon & Schuster, 1974. 372 pp.
This collection of essays considers the interrelationship of psychology and history. Four psychological approaches to history—prehistorical confrontation, the leader's individual psychopathology, the great man in history, and shared psycho-historical themes—are represented. The effort to combine the two disciplines, Lifton explains, stems from the conviction that a synthesis of history and psychology can address "the extraordinary confusions of our times" and generate "a new conceptual . . . and therapeutic vitality within the psychological professions."

H 28. **MANN, ARTHUR.** The One and the Many: Reflections on the American Identity. Chicago: University of Chicago Press, 1979. 209 pp.
Mann presents an essay, not a history, on the characteristics of the American nationality and its relationship to ethnic affiliation in the U.S. He discusses the white ethnic revival, the histories of the melting pot, Anglo-Saxon supremacy, and cultural pluralism theories, which, in the author's opinion, "still define the boundaries of present thinking on the One and the Many." Finally, Mann compares, when applicable, the U.S. experience with that of other countries' national experiences.

H 29. McCLELLAND, PETER D. and RICHARD J. ZECKHAUSER. Demographic Dimensions of the New Republic: American Interregional Migration, Vital Statistics, and Manumissions, 1800-1860. New York: Cambridge University Press, 1982. 222 pp.
This quantitative analysis of statistical data defines the demographic patterns in the U.S. between the Revolution and the Civil War. After discussing the significance of a regional approach, the authors offer observations on trends in migration, manumissions, death rate, birth rate, and the rate of natural increase for both the white and black populations.

H 30. MERK, FREDERICK. Manifest Destiny and Mission in American History: A Reinterpretation. New York: Knopf, 1963. 265 pp.
This study, based on periodical research, separates base from noble motives behind American expansionism. Merk argues that the term "Manifest Destiny" properly applies only to the notion that the U.S. must expand to the continental limits of North America. This theory, the author maintains, became important to American expansion starting in 1845, after which it flourished only for three or four years. Merk characterizes the expansion of the Polk years as primarily ideological. He then traces the decline of the "Manifest Destiny" theory and reveals that Colonialism characterized later American expansion. While the ideas of Manifest Destiny persist no longer, Merk contends that America still sees itself as a guiding light to political and individual freedom.

H 31. MORISON, SAMUEL ELIOT. The Oxford History of the American People. New York: Oxford University Press, 1965. 1150 pp.
Morison offers not a textbook "but a history written especially for my fellow citizens to read and enjoy." The work covers the period from "America Under Her Native Sons" to "The Kennedy Administration, 1961-1963." Concentrating on social and economic developments, Morison pays particular attention to sea power, American Indians, and the Colonial period, during which time, he maintains, America's most basic cultural principles were established.

H 32. POTTER, DAVID M. History and American Society. New York: Oxford University Press, 1973. 422 pp.
Potter divides sixteen essays on diverse subjects into two categories, "History" and "American Society." Broad issues such as historical methodology, the use of nationalism as a concept, and the relation of history to the social sciences are discussed in the first section. The essays of the second section, which focus specifically on the U.S., address American individualism, the influence of women on the American character, and the sources of social alienation. The role and nature of historical discourse are also discussed.

H 33. POTTER, DAVID M. People of Plenty: Economic Abundance and the American Character. Chicago: University of Chicago Press, 1954. 219 pp.
Potter's brief volume has two related but distinct purposes. First, he examines the tools historians have used to construct general interpretive statements about human behavior; he points out that they have largely produced loose impressionistic statements more notable for their breadth than their rigor. Second, Potter suggests that historians should employ methods and theories drawn from the behavioral sciences in order to lend their generalizations a greater degree of rigor. Potter offers as a particular example of this approach an analysis of the American national character. Accepting the behaviorist conclusion that the most important trait of Americans is their competitiveness, Potter explains this trait by reference to America's superior endowment of resources. An economy of abundance has shaped American culture, he says, and has had a dramatic influence upon our social and political behavior at home and abroad.

H 34. ROBBINS, ROY M. Our Landed Heritage: The Public Domain, 1776-1936.
       1942; Rev ed. Princeton, N.J.: Princeton University Press, 1976.
       503 pp.
Robbins surveys the public domain and the laws governing it. He considers
the period from the formation of the public domain in 1776 to the year
1935 when President Roosevelt withdrew all lands from public entry. The
work is broken into four sections: Part I covers 1776 to 1850 and depicts
individual settlers as the greatest influence in the occupation of the
lands; Part II covers 1850 to 1862 and deals with attempts by corporations
to challenge the settler's claims and influence; Part III shows the triumph
of capital and corporations over the pioneering forces of the settlers
between 1862 and 1901; and Part IV, which covers 1901 to 1936, includes
the conservation effort and the setting aside of remaining public land
in a permanent national domain.

H 35. ROOT, WAVERLY and RICHARD DeROCHEMONT. Eating in America: A History.
       New York: Morrow, 1976. 482 pp.
The authors contend that despite ethnic assimilation, American foodways
retain vestigal ties to English culture. This chronological overview
begins with the findings of early explorers and ends with an assessment
of foodways in the 20th century. They examine Native American culture
as well as regional influences of ethnic groups. The development of the
cooking process is examined through a study of culinary artifacts. Chapters devoted to the transformation of agri-"culture" into agri-"business"
are also included. These discussions treat the evolution of the American
restaurant, the cookbook industry, meat packing, the sociology of drinking
habits, and the American penchant for sweets. Anecdotes about such well-
known gourmands as Thomas Jefferson and Benjamin Franklin and comments
on American foodways by chroniclers such as Anthony Trollope and Charles
Dickens are also included.

H 36. RUTLAND, ROBERT A. The Democrats: From Jefferson to Carter. Baton
       Rouge: Louisiana State University Press, 1979. 254 pp.
In a history of the Democratic party designed for a general audience,
Rutland traces the development of America's oldest political party from
its birth almost 200 years ago to its present-day standing. The author
traces the ideas of Jefferson, the father of the party, who set the primary
direction for its development, through the "Era of Good Feelings," and
describes the transformation of the party at the hands of Jackson. The
author then examines the Democratic party's response to the slavery issue
and the Civil War, and the resulting impotence of the party until Franklin
D. Roosevelt's administration. After an examination of Roosevelt's impact
upon the party, Rutland traces the history of the Democrats down to the
presidency of Jimmy Carter. He emphasizes throughout the outstanding
men of the party, its philosophical goals, and major issues.

H 37. SHOVER, JOHN L. First Majority-Last Majority: The Transformation
       of Rural Life in America. DeKalb: Northern Illinois University
       Press, 1976. 338 pp.
Shover traces the evolution of agriculture from family farms to large-
scale agribusiness, looking at the technological innovations that triggered
this process. Using several case studies, the first half of Shover's
book examines the conditions of agriculture before 1945. The second half
is devoted to the emergence of agriculture after W.W. II as big business
that became dominated by a few corporations. Technological changes following W.W. II signified a tremendous historical transformation, according
to Shover, as small farmers were forced out of busines by oligopolistic
corporations.

H 38. STANNARD, DAVID, ed. Death in America. Philadelphia: University
of Pennsylvania Press, 1975. 158 pp.
In this work, scholars from the fields of history, anthropology, literature,
and art history view approaches to death in America from Puritan times
to the present. Changing attitudes toward death are considered in essays
on childhood death in New England; 19th-century sentimentality as evoked
through consolation literature; the rise of the garden cemetary; and cultural attitudes among Mexican-Americans and Mormons. In these essays,
death is alternatively viewed as terrifying, as an avenue to a better
world, and as a catalyst of community and familial change. In a final
essay by Philip Aries, 20th-century attitudes are seen as a reversal of
the nascent individualism of the Middle Ages. The current anonymity of
the individual and his passing is now being countered by forthright dialogue through hospital seminars, new literature on death, and the "openness" of present secular society.

H 39. VINOVSKIS, MARIS A., ed. Studies in American Historical Demography.
New York: Academic Press, 1979. 282 pp.
Vinovskis has assembled a collection of twenty-five articles which origi-
nally appeared in thirteen different journals. John Demos, Philip J.
Greven, Jr., Robert Wells, and Tamara Haraven are among the contributors.
The articles discuss a variety of periods and aspects of "historical demog-
raphy" in the U.S. Family, fertility, and ethnicity are recurrent themes.
In terms of geographic representations, the Northeast receives most of
the attention.

H 40. WEIGLEY, RUSSELL. History of the United States Army. New York:
Macmillan, 1967. 688 pp.
Weigley documents the lengthy history of both the professional army in
America and the citizen militia from their origins in the Colonial period
to contemporary times. The development of the military institution, its
organization, and the ideas behind its administration are outlined. In
conclusion, the author assesses the future of the military in America
and the patterns that war will follow, asserting that a new military pattern has been established since W.W. II. The wars in Korea and Vietnam,
unsupported by strong national pro-military commitment, represent a new
form of conflict. Weigley's history reflects a pro-military slant and
supports the view that the army will remain strong and able to defend
the U.S. in the future.

H 41. WELLS, ROBERT V. Revolutions in Americans' Lives: A Demographic
Perspective on the History of Americans, Their Families, and Their
Society. Westport, Conn.: Greenwood Press, 1982. 311 pp.
This demographic "synthesis" examines broad changes in living patterns
over the entire span of U.S. history rather than narrowly focusing on
small shifts over relatively brief periods. The author concludes that
"as individual and legislative whim have replaced biological and sociological regularities as determining influences" on matters ranging from
fertility to living conditions, Americans have come to have less control
over the patterns of their lives.

H 42. WIEBE, ROBERT H. The Segmented Society: An Introduction to the
Meaning of America. New York: Oxford University Press, 1975.
209 pp.
Wiebe argues that America can be understood only in terms of its "unique
pattern of relationships" rather than as a traditional, unified culture.
In his emphasis on social structure rather than culture, Wiebe presents
America as a stable system of boundaries and as a country that holds
together in spite of its lack of a unifying, national tradition. He views
America from the 18th to the 20th centuries as a changing collection of
segments: in the 18th and 19th centuries it consisted of family-centered,

geographically-segregated communities; but in the 20th century it has become an interlocking structure of occupations. Wiebe uses this thesis to examine beliefs and institutions he thinks are basic to America, such as a weakness of class consciousness.

H 43. WILLIAMS, T. HARRY. The History of American Wars: From 1745 to 1978. New York: Knopf, 1981. 435 pp.
This account of American military history traces the changes in style and scope of warfare as reflected in this country's involvement in various conflicts. Williams's view of warfare as a "continuation of (political) policy carried out by other means," provides an investigative framework for the book. Within this framework, Williams describes the various policies, objectives, and strategies that governed American warfare from the Colonial period to Vietnam, in conflicts ranging from wars of limited objectives to total war.

H 44. WILLIAMS, WILLIAM APPLEMAN. America Confronts a Revolutionary World: 1776-1976. New York: Morrow, 1976. 224 pp.
This work describes the challenge facing the U.S. to live up to its own image and the world's expectations. Williams maintains that this country has denied its commitment to the "revolutionary right of self-determination." Imperialism and a fierce desire to "preserve the present" have blinded the country to a changing world. Williams insists that in order to thrive the U.S. must broaden its perspective to learn from the past and proceed into the future committed to the ideals of humanistic equality and self-determination.

H 45. WILLIAMS, WILLIAM APPLEMAN. The Contours of American History. Cleveland, Ohio: World, 1961. 513 pp.
Williams, a Marxist historian, surveys broad phases of American culture with particular reference to the economic dimensions of cultural ideals and values. The author argues that elements such as the fragmentation of American society along economic and technological lines, the frontier expansion outlook, commitment to private property, and loyalty to an ideal of human standards persisted as features of American society throughout history. Williams asserts that the potential for a democratic socialist state exists in the U.S., if Americans seize the opportunity to foster new moral values.

H 46. WILLIAMS, WILLIAM APPLEMAN. Empire as a Way of Life: An Essay on the Causes and Character of America's Present Predicament Along with a Few Thoughts About an Alternative. New York: Oxford University Press, 1980. 226 pp.
Williams sees Americans as having always been expansionists, even though their leaders have sometimes obscured this tendency behind rhetoric. The concept of empire, resulting in efforts to impose American will and values on North America and elsewhere, has had both material and psychological benefits. But its costs have outweighed these assets in Williams's analysis, which considers various aspects of American history from colonization to 20th-century foreign policy. Although most American leaders have identified themselves with the expansionist, imperialist spirit, Williams includes discussion of some, such as Herbert Hoover, who in his view have dissented from the mainstream.

H 47. YASUBA, YASUKICHI. Birth Rates of the White Population in the United States, 1800-1860. Baltimore, Md.: Johns Hopkins University Press, 1962. 198 pp.
Historians have generally agreed that in the early decades of the 19th century the white American birth rate was far above the rates of comparable European countries while by mid-century the rate was declining considerably in advance of the same trend in Europe. Yasuba's study confirms these

phenomena through the use of "crude" and "refined" age ratios. Much of the difference between American and European ratios, Yasuba finds, is explained by differences in the age and incidence of marriage. Yasuba also points out that regional differences in particular, and the 19th-century trend as a whole, are associated with regional and national levels of economic development. Industrialization-urbanization, population density, and per capita income, he finds, are all negatively and significantly correlated with the refined white birth ratio. Yasuba further concludes that in the first decades of the century, fertility was positively associated with the availability of land and that, later, industrialization-urbanization became the major determinant of American fertility patterns.

II. AGE OF DISCOVERY/COLONIAL

H 48. ADAMS, JAMES TRUSLOW. The Founding of New England. Boston: Atlantic Monthly Press, 1921. 482 pp.
Adams's study is a general history of the early settlement of New England, with a special focus on the economic reasons why Englishmen chose to leave their homeland and how the Colonies fit into the larger sphere of British imperialism. Adams points out that of the 65,000 Englishmen who settled in the region during the period, only 4,000 joined the churches. He concludes that the internal struggle within the theocracy was a more important quest for freedom than the ensuing Revolution.

H 49. ALLEN, DAVID GRAYSON. In English Ways: The Movement of Societies and the Transferral of English Local Law and Custom to Massachusetts Bay in the Seventeenth Century. Chapel Hill: University of North Carolina Press, 1981. 312 pp.
Allen argues that historians have overstated the differences between life in 'Old' and 'New' England. Based on a study of five Massachusetts towns, he contends that early New England settlers reproduced traditional British institutions and agricultural practices in their new location. Allen also contends that early Massachusetts towns were strikingly diversified, reminiscent of the regional differences of Old England. He suggests that economic and demographic expansion, as well as increased social stratification, effected increased centralization and uniformity in Massachusetts life later in the century. Even at this later date the settlers turned to English models of provincial government.

H 50. ANDREWS, CHARLES M. The Colonial Period of American History. 4 vols. New Haven, Conn.: Yale University Press, 1934-1938. 1789 pp.
Approaching the Colonial Era from a British perspective, Andrews examines the Colonies' status as integral parts of the British empire and as subordinate, dependent communities. From this vantage point, he suggests that England's role as a dominant influence on later American achievement has been underestimated. The first three volumes of the study cover all Colonial settlements in British America founded in the 17th century, including those in Canada and the West Indies. The fourth volume looks at the evolution of England's commercial and Colonial policies to 1763. Andrews surveys the transition of the Colonies from a 17th-century "English world in America" to the duality of interest in 18th-century Anglo-American society.

H 51. ANDREWS, K. R., N. P. CANNY, and P. E. H. HAIR, eds. The Westward
Enterprise: English Activities in Ireland, the Atlantic, and
America 1480-1650. Detroit, Mich.: Wayne State University Press,
1979. 326 pp.
These essays explore early British efforts to colonize the New World,
discussing social control in English settlements in Ireland and Virginia.
Topics covered include "native" reaction to English colonization; the
English in the Caribbean; the contraband tobacco trade from Trinidad and
Guiana; English commercialization and American colonization; the place
of the Amerindian in literature promoting colonization; English law in
Virginia; religion in Virginia; differences between settlement in Massachu-
setts and the Caribbean; and the problem of "perspective" in early American
history (especially in regard to the historiographical predominance of
New England).

H 52. ANDREWS, MATTHEW PAGE. The Founding of Maryland. Baltimore, Md.:
Williams & Wilkins, 1933. 367 pp.
Andrews presents a history of Maryland from its founding to the Revolution
and argues that religious liberty in America was first established in
Maryland, a refuge for Catholic Englishmen. In contrast to the theocracy
of New England, Maryland established a "pure democracy"; the people had
the power to convene their own assemblies, to initiate their own laws,
and to reject any law imposed on them. Andrews maintains that the Calverts,
under the influence of Thomas More's Utopia, were the first to promote
religious toleration in the colonies. Moreover, he celebrates "The Toleration Act" of 1649 as an attempt to protect the Catholic minority in Maryland from religious persecution by the rising Puritan element.

H 53. AXTELL, JAMES L. The School upon a Hill: Education and Society
in Colonial New England. New Haven, Conn.: Yale University Press,
1974. 298 pp.
Axtell believes that education, a process whereby children are socialized,
includes but is not limited to formal schooling. Working from the perspectives of anthropology, sociology, and psychology, he considers the
cultural forces that shaped the identities of Colonial children and that
bound them to their society until they were twenty-one years old. Instruction in the catechism, the doctrines of public and private calling, and
a system of apprenticeship are only a few of the mechanisms which Axtell
considers in his discussion of the way in which the Puritan church, family,
and school controlled the development of children. He also analyzes the
impact of the frontier experience on children, the interaction between
New Englanders and Native Americans, and the experience of attending
Harvard College.

H 54. BAILYN, BERNARD. The New England Merchants in the Seventeenth Century. Cambridge, Mass.: Harvard University Press, 1955. 249 pp.
Although New England merchants were an influential group during the 17th
century, Bailyn states that they did not constitute a homogeneous segment
of society. Rather, their interests became increasingly diversified as
the New England settlements began to develop a unique character that consisted of a mixture of Old and New World forces. Bailyn's study focuses
on early 17th-century trade, detailing how it became increasingly alienated
from religious foundations and ultimately developed into a merchant business and culture which remained stable until the eve of the Revolution.

H 55. BAILYN, BERNARD. The Origins of American Politics. New York:
Knopf, 1968. 161 pp.
Comparing the political culture and institutions of Augustan England and
Colonial America, Bailyn concludes that Colonial leaders adopted an English
opposition ideology predicated on a dominant executive influence which

could control political life. Although American Colonial executives had great legal powers, in practice they lacked extra-institutional sources of influence. The result was a highly unstable, factious political situation in which rhetoric led American politicians to view their opponents either as seditious or as representatives of a corrupt government.

H 56. BATTIS, EMORY. Saints and Secretaries: Anne Hutchinson and the Antinomian Controversy over Massachusetts Bay. Chapel Hill: University of North Carolina Press, 1962. 379 pp.
Battis's account of Anne Hutchinson's defiance of the Massachusetts clergy explores the motives and the personalities of Hutchinson and her followers. Suggesting that her activist religious views were part of a "psychological response to a complex set of emotional pressures," Battis examines the circumstances which he feels compelled her to rebel. He finds the cause for her assertiveness in an unsatisfied search for masculine authority which she sought in her father, in her husband, in John Cotton, and finally in God. Battis also looks into the backgrounds of those who took up the antinomian cause, suggesting needs and attitudes which could have led to such a commitment.

H 57. BILLIAS, GEORGE A., ed. Law and Authority in Colonial America. Barre, Mass.: Barre, 1965. 208 pp.
The essays included in Part I of this collection consider the influence of English Law on the formation of a legal code in the Colonies. They identify those portions of English law which the Colonists either adopted unchanged or rejected. Moreover, they determine the extent to which English custom defined particular laws and the way in which the Colonists both modified English statutes and invented new ones in order to meet the challenges posed by settlement. In Part II, the contributors address issues of authority. They analyze the consequences of importing an English political structure to the Colonies; the gradual refusal of settlers to defer to England as well as to the Colonial elite; the disintegration of family ties; and the diminution of clerical influence in political affairs.

H 58. BILLINGTON, RAY ALLEN, ed. The Reinterpretation of American History: Essays by Ten Leading Historians of Colonial America. Los Angeles, Calif.: Henry E. Huntington Library, 1966. 268 pp.
These essays in honor of John Edwin Pomfret cover a variety of subjects in early American history, evaluating scholarly criticism in the field as well as recent methodological approaches to the material. The first section contains three essays on John Pomfret and the Huntington Library. The second section is composed of five essays dealing with scholarship concerning early New England, the Middle Colonies, the Southern Colonies, and the American Revolution. The final five essays treat such approaches to the study of American history as the imperial (addressing English Colonialism), the international (addressing early America's relations with Europe and America's own adjoining neighbors), the archaeological (studying the physical artifacts of historic sites in North America in order to complement and corroborate written records), and the archival (dealing with the proliferation of journal publications in the field).

H 59. BONOMI, PATRICIA. A Factious People: Politics and Society in Colonial New York. New York: Columbia University Press, 1971. 342 pp.
Suggesting that understanding special interest groups is essential to comprehending the politics of Colonial New York, Bonomi explores the relationship between political and social life in that colony from Leisler's Rebellion until 1770. She also examines the cultural and socio-economic atmosphere from which New York political activity—with all its factionalism and competing interests—evolved. Bonomi provides background on the historiography, early settlement patterns, and geographic expansion of

Colonial New York, and discusses a series of political conflicts over imperial authority and gubernatorial power, economic interests, and the land system.

H 60. BOORSTIN, DANIEL J. The Americans: The Colonial Experience. New York: Random House, 1958. 434 pp.
Tracing the beginnings of what Boorstin interprets as national character, The Americans opens with a section on the transformation of Utopian dreams into actual Colonies faced with the "reality of America." Boorstin looks at the Colonists' development of new perspectives in a New World unencumbered by the past, suggesting that these Americans' ways of thinking were common to all. He explores American thought patterns in the realms of education, knowledge, medicine, science, occupation, language and printing, and warfare and diplomacy. Boorstin concludes that a national trait of practicality, originating in the earliest Colonial experiences, shaped the ideals and principles that united the Colonists into one people. This volume is the first in a three-part series on American culture (see H 7 and H 8).

H 61. BOWES, FREDERICK P. The Culture of Early Charleston. Chapel Hill: University of North Carolina Press, 1942. 156 pp.
Bowes looks at various aspects of life in Colonial Charleston: religion, education, books and publishing, science, literature and the arts, and "the Charleston Aristocracy." Charleston was a thriving city, rich in luxuries, and though not exceptionally large, it was very important as a seaboard center for the importation of slaves and for trade. Concentrating on the white society of Charleston, Bowes documents its rapid cultural and intellectual growth during the Colonial era.

H 62. BREEN, TIMOTHY H. The Character of the Good Ruler: A Study of Puritan Political Ideas in New England 1630-1730. New Haven, Conn.: Yale University Press, 1970. 301 pp.
Breen contends that the distinction between "discretion" and "delegation" constituted a fundamental debate in the Puritan sphere. Those who favored discretion assumed that magistrates should have substantial freedom in their decision-making power, while those who favored delegation suggested that magistrates possessed only those powers explicitly granted by the community. With the Glorious Revolution, however, the distinction between "court" and "country" replaced the debate concerning discretion and delegation as the primary political conflict. In addition, whereas 17th-century magistrates concentrated on the preservation of godliness, during the 18th century, magistrates derived their mandate from the preservation of liberty and property.

H 63. BREEN, TIMOTHY H. Puritans and Adventurers: Change and Persistence in Early America. New York: Oxford University Press, 1980. 270 pp.
In his examination of the relationship between values and social institutions in Colonial Massachusetts and Virginia, Breen argues that historians have overestimated the degree of change and underestimated the degree of local diversity in Colonial America. He proposes an approach grounded in cultural anthropology which emphasizes the cultural continuities underlying institutional changes. Breen applies this approach to such topics as the Colonial militia, taxation, migration, the labor force, and the gambling habits of Virginian gentry.

H 64. BREMER, FRANCIS J. The Puritan Experiment: New England Society
from Bradford to Edwards. New York: St. Martin's Press, 1976.
255 pp.
This book offers an overview of Puritan New England from its origins to
the Great Awakening of the 18th century. Bremer addresses the British
roots of Puritanism in the 16th century, the movement's theology, the
establishment of settlements in Massachusetts Bay, Connecticut, and Rhode
Island, and the role of church and state in these communities. The effects
on New England of growing secularization and religious pluralism, political
developments in Britain, and Native American discontent are detailed.
Included are sketches of New England family and community life, arts and
sciences, and race relations.

H 65. BRIDENBAUGH, CARL. Cities in Revolt: Urban Life in America, 1743-
76. 1955; Rev. ed. New York: Oxford University Press, 1971.
547 pp.
This book is a continuation of Bridenbaugh's earlier Cities in the Wilderness (H 66). From 1743-1760, the five major Colonial cities prospered
from the "war economy" established by the British in their efforts to
wrest control of North America from the French. Combined with the increasing commercial trade between the Colonial cities, the urban economies
were increasingly interconnected, forever removing their previous isolation.
This prosperity was short-lived, and with the removal of the French from
North America, a period of depression, tension, and ultimately revolt
set in from 1760-1776. Bridenbaugh also examines the social practices
and urban problems found in Colonial cities during the three decades prior
to the Revolution.

H 66. BRIDENBAUGH, CARL. Cities in the Wilderness: The First Century
of Urban Life in America, 1625-1742. New York: Capricorn, 1938.
500 pp.
Looking at Boston, Charlestown, New York (New Amsterdam), Newport, and
Philadelphia, Bridenbaugh argues that the Colonial cities were commercial
communities comparable to their English counterparts. These cities were
large enough to be similar to one another, yet distinct from other Colonial
towns. From their village origins, Colonial cities developed a new civic
consciousness at the turn of the 18th century before entering into urban
maturity from 1720-1742. Bridenbaugh gives an overview of the social
and economic life in these cities, and pays special attention to the new
urban problems of disease, crime, fire, and poverty, and the means adopted
to solve them. The mercantile foundations of these cities created a society that attached great importance to wealth and commercial success.

H 67. BRIDENBAUGH, CARL. Early Americans. New York: Oxford University
Press, 1981. 281 pp.
This collection of essays stresses "underemphasized or unknown features"
in the growth of early American society. Bridenbaugh deals with various
aspects of the theme of movement. Special attention is devoted to the
migration of individuals throughout the Colonies, the settlement patterns
of early European immigrants, and their interaction with Native Americans
and the environment. The introduction and adaptation of European ideals
and habits into the American social structure are also considered.

H 68. BRIDENBAUGH, CARL. Fat Mutton and Liberty of Conscience: Society
in Rhode Island, 1636-1690. Providence, R.I.: Brown University
Press, 1974. 157 pp.
This study of Rhode Island and Providence Plantations in the 17th century
describes the successful initiation and development of commercial agriculture in an economy characterized by large-scale gentry investment in
landed estates devoted to stock-rearing and grazing. The author also
describes how the Colonists established important trading networks, at

first with neighboring Colonies and later with the whole North Atlantic commercial system. The initial gentry investment, according to Bridenbaugh, was a conscious attempt to construct an economy which would fit the North Atlantic commercial-agricultural trading system. The success of the experiment was greatly facilitated by the plantations' religious tolerance, which also spurred the later influx of Quakers, who brought with them the contacts necessary to ensure commercial prosperity. Thus by the early 18th century, the Narragansett region was a thriving mercantile and maritime community.

H 69. BRIDENBAUGH, CARL. Jamestown, 1544-1699. New York: Oxford University Press, 1980. 199 pp.
Bridenbaugh offers a general history and interpretation of Jamestown's significance as an American symbol. He suggests that due to a lack of accurate records, much of our understanding of this colony has been distorted. The following topics are emphasized: the settlers' backgrounds; religion and government in the colony; the Jamestown site and its role as a port; and Bacon's Uprising and Lawrence's Rebellion. Also examined is the colony's ultimate failure as a community. The viewpoints of both English settlers and Native Americans are considered.

H 70. BRIDENBAUGH, CARL. Myths and Realities: Societies of the Colonial South. Baton Rouge: Louisiana State University Press, 1952. 208 pp.
Bridenbaugh asserts that before the Revolution there was no conception of a "South." The land and its mixture of inhabitants were the least homogeneous of the Colonies. In his research on the origins of Southern society, Bridenbaugh discovered various myths which he considers to have been misinterpretations; he contends that only through a comprehension of the Colonial South's rural character and its dependence upon slavery can the region be properly understood. Various geographical areas are treated separately: the Chesapeake and its tobacco culture; the Carolinas which specialized in the cultivation of rice and indigo; and the informal "Back Country" which constituted a hodgepodge of farming and hunting.

H 71. BROWN, ROBERT ELDON and B. KATHARINE BROWN. Virginia, 1705-1786: Democracy or Aristocracy? East Lansing: Michigan State University Press, 1969. 333 pp.
The authors consider class conflict as a factor precipitating Virginia's involvement in the Revolution. They begin with the assumption that democracy and aristocracy "may be involved not only in the voting franchise and political representation but also in such fundamental aspects of society as economic and educational opportunity, religious freedom, and class attitudes." They address such topics as the impact of slavery on white society, methods of property exchange, education, and electoral practices. While they identify slavery as the single most important feature of aristocratic Virginia, they argue that democratic elements prevailed in the colony. "Middle-class, representative democracy was well-entrenched in the Old Dominion long before the American Revolution."

H 72. BRUCE, PHILIP ALEXANDER. Economic History of Virginia in the Seventeenth Century. 2 vols. New York: Macmillan, 1895. 1285 pp.
Bruce traces the economic development of Virginia from 1606 to 1700. His account of the first quarter of the century relies on the writings of John Smith, and is consequently critical of the Virginia Company of London. While discussing the factors that led to the colonization of the Chesapeake Bay, he considers the topography of Virginia as well as the Native Americans who resided there. Moreover, he considers Virginia's agricultural development in four stages: 1607-1624; 1624-1650; 1650-1685; 1685-1700. Throughout he discusses Virginia's labor system, which included indentured servants and slaves, transportation, the domestic economy of

planters, and Virginia's role in the mercantilistic British Empire. Bruce argues that the revocation of Virginia's charter liberated economic forces in Virginia in ways which allowed it to prosper economically.

H 73. BRUCE, PHILIP ALEXANDER. Institutional History of Virginia in the Seventeenth Century: An Inquiry into the Religious, Moral, Educational, Legal, Military and Political Condition of the People Based on Original and Contemporary Records. 2 vols. New York: Putnam, 1910. 1404 pp.
In the first volume of this work Bruce examines the religious, moral, educational, and legal institutions which existed in 17th-century Virginia; in the second volume he considers the military and political features of the colony. Bruce argues that the colonists in Virginia did not present problems for England. They were not averse to hard work and they shared the cultural values and beliefs of New England's Puritans. While Virginia's scattered plantations did not allow for the establishment of a system of public education similar to that of New England, Virginians compensated by either sending their children to be educated in England or by hiring tutors and establishing private schools for those children who remained in the Colonies. In conclusion, Bruce draws attention to the democratic elements in Virginia's political and economic institutions.

H 74. BRUCE, PHILIP ALEXANDER. Social Life of Virginia in the Seventeenth Century. Richmond, Va.: Whitter & Shepperson, 1907. 268 pp.
Bruce studies the social life of Virginia's gentry. He argues that the colony's gentry was composed of the younger sons of English aristocrats who, because laws of primogeniture prohibited their inheriting their fathers' estates, transported the possessions and values of their class to the New World where they could establish a new aristocracy. Throughout, the book discusses the promotion of emigration in England; the evolution of social distinctions and a higher class of planters in Virginia; and the social codes which governed all aspects of life in the colony.

H 75. CASSEDY, JAMES H. Demography in Early America: Beginnings of the Statistical Mind, 1600-1800. Cambridge, Mass.: Harvard University Press, 1969. 357 pp.
Cassedy examines what he views as the tendency of early Americans to think about people and things "in the aggregate." He outlines the political, economic, and social factors--including the necessities of Colonial governance and taxation and the age's empiricism and scientific curiosity--that helped create the demand, and means, for a more thorough collecting of demographic data. He considers statistical thinking during the Revolutionary Era and the quantitative efforts of the Colonial Period--the census, parish records, collections of fertility, mortality, life expectancy, and medical data. Cassedy uses 17th- and 18th-century scientific tracts and periodicals, as well as other primary and secondary sources as the basis for his thesis.

H 76. CLARK, CHARLES E. The Eastern Frontier: The Settlement of Northern New England, 1610-1763. 1970; Rev. ed. Hanover, N.H.: University Press of New England, 1983. 436 pp.
Clark examines the settlement and growth of the area which eventually became New Hampshire and Maine from its original "conquering" by the settlers to the end of the Colonial era. He argues that northern New England constituted a separate region, as distinct from southern New England as the latter was from the Middle Atlantic region. Clark focuses on the social history of the people--their way of life, their problems, their cultural achievements, and their distinctive characteristics and thought-- yet includes brief narratives on political, economic, and institutional developments. He concludes that although northern New England eventually

came under the political domination of Massachusetts, the region retained many of its original, distinctive qualities and characteristics.

H 77. CONDON, THOMAS J. New York Beginnings: The Commercial Origins of New Netherland. New York: New York University Press, 1968. 204 pp.
In his study of the commercial influences on New York, Condon finds that early immigrants came to the colony with the intention of securing quick profits and a speedy return to Europe, rather than of establishing a permanent Dutch society. He explores the colony's relationship with both the Netherlands and the West India Company through the 1660s. The significance of the Dutch Period of New York history, as Condon sees it, is the similarity of reaction in both New Netherland (despite its commercial origins) and New England to the challenge of building a new society.

H 78. COOK, EDWARD M., Jr. The Fathers of the Towns: Leadership and Community Structure in Eighteenth-Century New England. Baltimore, Md.: Johns Hopkins University Press, 1976. 273 pp.
Cook examines the nature of political and social structures in 18th-century New England communities in order to uncover the similarities between local leaders of the various towns. He considers a variety of social influences on political behavior, thus illuminating similarities of motivation in the management of seventy-four towns. He also discovers five major types of towns which share distinct political patterns: the urban center, the major county town, the proto-suburbs, the small farming village, and the frontier town.

H 79. COOK, WARREN. Flood Tide of Empire: Spain and the Pacific Northwest, 1543-1819. New Haven, Conn.: Yale University Press, 1973. 620 pp.
Cook's account of Spanish ventures in the Pacific Northwest suggests that the Spanish influence on America's northern coastline has not been fully recognized. Examining historical fact, myth, and legend about the Northwest, he treats settlement of California, voyages to the Northwest by explorers of various nationalities, and Spanish cultural and diplomatic interaction with Russians, British, European settlers, and native Americans. Cook discusses the Nootka Sound confrontation with Britain where Spain lost her Northwest Coast empire, and concludes with a chapter on Spain and manifest destiny.

H 80. COVEY, CYCLONE. The American Pilgrimage: The Roots of American History, Religion and Culture. New York: Collier Books, 1961. 122 pp.
Covey characterizes the period between 1600 to 1750 as an era of pilgrimage. He considers more than merely physical pilgrimages; an intellectual outlook prevailed during this period wherein an individual undertook a symbolic journey through this life to the afterlife. Also discussed is the influence of the Great Awakening, and the disparate philosophical and cultural notions of Jonathan Edwards and Benjamin Franklin.

H 81. CRANE, VERNER W. Benjamin Franklin and a Rising People. Boston: Little, Brown, 1954. 219 pp.
Crane emphasizes Franklin's contribution to the definition of America's national identity. At the same time, he brings to light other facets of Franklin's career as scientist, businessman, and newspaper editor. The study examines the influential roles Franklin played in the Revolution, the conceptualization of America's democratic creed, the formulation of the Albany plan, and the development of American foreign relations. Crane also argues that even though Franklin advocated laissez faire, he promoted a social morality which depended on the cultivation of religious sentiment.

262

H 82. CRAVEN, WESLEY FRANK. The Colonies in Transition: 1660-1713.
       New York: Harper & Row, 1968. 363 pp.
Suggesting that a dual process of "Americanization" and "Anglicanization"
marked the Colonial Period from 1660 to the conclusion of Queen Anne's
War, Craven contends that although the Colonists developed stronger indigenous political and social structures, they nevertheless became further
integrated into the imperial world. With this thesis in mind, Craven
examines the following topics: the Navigation Acts and the changing imperial system; the conquest of New York and establishment of proprietary
Colonies; the Glorious Revolution and Revolutionary settlement; relations
with Native Americans; early slave history; and the rise of Colonial assemblies.

H 83. CRAVEN, WESLEY FRANK. The Southern Colonies in the Seventeenth Cen-
       tury, 1607-1689. Baton Rouge: Louisiana State University Press,
       1949. 451 pp.
Craven argues that small farms and indentured servitude prevailed in the
Southern Colonies of the 17th century. Political rather than institutional
in focus, Craven's history concentrates mainly on Virginia and discusses
the Spanish efforts at colonization; the history of Roanoke, the lost
colony; the settlement of Jamestown; the efforts of the Virginia Company
of London and its dissolution by the King; the emergence of the tobacco
economy; the influence of the Puritan Revolution in England; the settlement
of Maryland and Carolina; Bacon's Rebellion; and the emergence at the
end of the century of an effective, British imperial system.

H 84. CRONON, WILLIAM. Changes in the Land: Indians, Colonists, and
       the Ecology of New England. New York: Hill & Wang, 1983.
       241 pp.
Cronon analyzes the radical change in the landscape of New England as
large areas were deforested, land was fenced in, dams were built, and
Europeans introduced new types of wildlife and forestation. The human
ecology was transformed as well, as Native Americans were killed by disease
and war, and their lands were circumscribed. Although Cronon discusses
a variety of causes and factors underlying this transformation, he believes
that ultimately European notions of property and the workings of the market
were most important. As nature became a commodity, the "transition to
capitalism alienated the products of the land as much as the products
of human labor."

H 85. CROWLEY, J. E. This Sheba, Self: The Conceptualization of Eco-
       nomic Life in Eighteenth-Century America. Baltimore, Md.: Johns
       Hopkins University Press, 1974. 161 pp.
Crowley argues that, until the American Revolution, the Colonists never
legitimized the individual's pursuit of economic self-interest. Instead,
they strove economically to retain "social wholeness" in an increasingly
depersonalized environment. Claiming that human values are defined by
human behavior, Crowley looks at the terms used in association with labor--
industry and frugality--and rather than ascribing them to religious motives,
he sees them as responses to fears of the curtailment of luxury and the
destruction of autonomy, in addition to the danger of anarchy arising
from idleness.

H 86. CUMMINGS, W. P., S. HILLIER, D. B. QUINN, and G. WILLIAMS. The
       Exploration of North America, 1630-1776. New York: Putnam, 1974.
       272 pp.
This highly illustrated treatment of the exploration of North America
is divided geographically, with sections comprised of general historical
summaries of various area, and accompanying texts, maps, and illustrations
dating from the time of exploration. Suggesting that the uneven 17th-
and 18th-century phase of exploration and "re-exploration" of North Ameri-

can territories ended with a "breathing space" during which "the realities
of power politics were to prepare for a decisive period in American exploration," the book examines discovery in New France, the Great Lakes and
the Mississippi; Westward movements originating in the Southern Colonies
and on the Northeastern seaboard; penetration of the Southeastern mountains;
Spanish and French exploration of Louisiana and the Southwest; surveys
of the Arctic, the Rocky Mountains, and the Pacific Coast.

H 87. DANIELS, BRUCE C. The Connecticut Town: Growth and Development,
1635-1790. Middletown, Conn.: Wesleyan University Press, 1979.
249 pp.
Daniels contends that Connecticut was in the process of urbanization as
"concentration points" of population and complex organization appeared
during the Colonial and Revolutionary periods. Examining ideological
development within the towns in the context of continually changing political and economic structures, Daniels uses local histories for his study,
as well as quantitative material which he includes in an index.

H 88. DEMOS, JOHN. A Little Commonwealth: Family Life in Plymouth Colony.
New York: Oxford University Press, 1970. 201 pp.
Integrating anthropological and historical methods, Demos examines physical
artifacts, wills, inventories, and official records in this case study
of the Pilgrim family and community life. He describes the physical setting of Plymouth and its early community problems regarding housing, heating, and the physical environment. Social organization was based upon
the family unit and kinship networks, and eventually they served as the
primary means for owning, using, and distributing property. Demos concludes that families served social welfare functions as well, acting
as schools, hospitals, and welfare agencies. Women and children had formidable responsibilities in the Plymouth community, with sharply defined
roles. Consequently, the process of growing up was much different for
children, to the point that no concept of adolescence existed.

H 89. DeVOTO, BERNARD AUGUSTUS. The Course of Empire. Boston: Houghton
Mifflin, 1952. 647 pp.
This account tells the story of European exploration of the North American
continent from its discovery to the Lewis and Clark expedition. Principal
themes are "the geography of North America insofar as it was important
in the actions dealt with; the ideas which the men involved in these
actions had about this geography . . .; the exploration of the United States
and Canada; the contention of four empires for the area that is now the
United States . . .; the relationship to all these things of various Indian
tribes." DeVoto also places heavy emphasis on the personalities of the
explorers, providing short vignettes about major figures.

H 90. DINKIN, ROBERT J. Voting in Provincial America: A Study of Elections in the Thirteen Colonies, 1689-1776. Westport, Conn.: Greenwood Press, 1977. 284 pp.
Dinkin uses secondary sources as well as voting records to provide a comprehensive study of early American voting patterns. Voting in colony-
wide elections between 1689 and 1776 is most closely examined. The type
of candidates, campaigning activities, nominations, eligible voters, and
the various methods of voting itself are discussed, accompanied by several
statistical tables. Dinkin concludes that while no overall statement
can be made concerning provincial voting behavior, ethno-cultural origins
as well as specific issues and political awareness were important factors
in determining the vote of the Colonial citizen.

H 91. **DOW, GEORGE FRANCIS.** Domestic Life in New England in the Seventeenth Century. Topsfield, Mass.: Perkins Press, 1925. 48 pp.
First delivered as a lecture in conjunction with ceremonies at the opening
of the American Wing of the Metropolitan Museum of Art in New York City,
Dow's essay is an extensively illustrated recreation of various aspects
of daily life in 17th-century New England, including housing, food, fashion,
and relations with family and friends. Dow gleans information from records
and letters to reconstruct domestic life and describes the average as
well as the outstanding characteristics of living conditions and daily
affairs.

H 92. **DUNN, RICHARD S.** Puritans and Yankees: The Winthrop Dynasty of
New England, 1630-1717. Princeton, N.J.: Princeton University
Press, 1962. 379 pp.
Dunn suggests that the history of the three generations of Winthrops represents not only the weakening of the Winthrops's political and social position but also the transformation of New England from Puritan to Yankee,
or the secularization of the society. Autonomy from England decreased
through the years, and the various ways in which the Winthrops related
to the mother country illustrate the increasing pressures that would eventually precipitate the American Revolution.

H 93. **EARLE, ALICE MORSE.** Home Life in Colonial Days. 1898; Rev. ed.
New York: Macmillan, 1935. 451 pp.
Earle's survey covers all aspects of home life from the 17th through 18th
centuries. Period documents and travel accounts are used with household
artifacts to recreate a highly visual account of everyday life, primarily
in New England, but also in the Middle Colonies and in the South. The
regional and historical topics covered include housing forms, lighting
methods, Indian culture, foodways, manners, home textile manufacture,
travel, taverns, women's work, jack-knifing, dress, religion, community
life, and flower gardening. The "waste not, want not" ethos, the enforced
self-sufficiency, and the labor-intensiveness of everyday life become
evident in this socio-cultural study. Artifacts are viewed from a utilitarian standpoint and as cultural barometers of rising affluence. Processes such as spinning, dyeing, and weaving are viewed in depth.

H 94. **EARLE, ALICE MORSE.** The Sabbath in Puritan New England. New York:
Scribner, 1891. 335 pp.
Earle provides a study of the physical and social structure of Puritan
meetinghouses. She describes the interiors of the churches, the fashion
of Sabbath dress, the church leaders, ecclesiastical finances, and the
nature of the services themselves. She also recounts a variety of anecdotes including the fact that in some Puritan communities it was customary
to bring the family dog to church so that the animal might provide warmth
by laying on its owner's feet.

H 95. **ECCLES, WILLIAM J.** France in America. New York: Harper & Row,
1972. 249 pp.
Eccles's revisionist history deals primarily with the French colonization
and administration of Canada, with minimal reference to the other French
holdings in the New World--Louisiana, and the West Indies. Particularly
stressed are the political and military relations with the Indians and
the British Colonies, and the economic growth of the French colony. Eccles
refutes the concept of great Catholic power in Colonial Canada, insisting
that after 1663 the Crown had established dominance over the clergy.
In addition, he asserts that Canadian habitants were economically and
politically more powerful than their rural European counterparts, overturning previous historical thought. However, the book's significance
lies in its account of the British conquest and its rebuttal of the belief
that French Canada's fall was inevitable.

H 96. EKIRCH, A. ROGER. "Poor Carolina": Politics and Society in
Colonial North Carolina, 1729-1776. Chapel Hill: University of
North Carolina Press, 1981. 305 pp.
In his study of the social, economic, and cultural context of politics,
Ekirch addresses the problem of mid-18th-century North Carolina's failure
to develop secure governing elites and a stable polity. He provides a
description and analysis of North Carolina's economy, demography, and
social structure, and discusses conflicts over land, regional disagreements,
and struggles between the Governor and the State Assembly. Ekirch suggests
that poverty and slow economic growth were the most important factors
in Colonial North Carolina's political life.

H 97. FLAHERTY, DAVID H. Privacy in Colonial New England. Charlottesville: University Press of Virginia, 1972. 287 pp.
Flaherty views the Puritan era as a transitional phase between medieval
communalism--keeping an eye on your neighbor--and modern individualism
as manifested in the Puritan emphasis on introspection. In the first
half of his book, Flaherty examines a variety of issues concerning family
life, including the structure of physical space within the home and in
the town, and the relations of the members of the household to guests,
neighbors, and the surrounding community. The second half focuses on
the individual's relationship to Colonial institutions such as the church,
the law, and the court. Flaherty asserts that by the 17th century, privacy
had become an important and accepted value throughout the Western world.
Despite their subjection to the scrutiny of village life (due primarily
to surveillance by the church), the Puritans nevertheless had ample opportunity to attain the privacy they sought in the sparsely populated countryside and through various solutions within the home.

H 98. FLAHERTY, DAVID H., ed. Essays in the History of Early American
Law. Chapel Hill: University of North Carolina Press, 1969.
534 pp.
Flaherty introduces this collection with an outline of the positions taken
by the various historians of Colonial law and a survey of primary sources.
The contributors then address a series of different issues: George Haskins
considers law in Colonial New England; Julius Goebbel, Jr. provides three
selections on the legal systems and values of Plymouth and New York; and
Richard Morris analyzes Massachusetts's Declaration of 1646 and the arrival
of trained lawyers. Also included are a number of essays which evaluate
the influence of English law on the formation of Colonial law.

H 99. FLEMING, SANDFORD. Children and Puritanism: The Place of Children
in the Life and Thought of the New England Churches, 1620-1847.
New Haven, Conn.: Yale University Press, 1933. 236 pp.
Fleming discusses the religious education of New England Puritan children
from the establishment of Plymouth Plantation to Horace Bushnell's 19th-
century essays on "Christian Nurture." In the first section of the book,
Fleming documents the history and distinguishing features of the New
England churches. In parts two and three he analyzes the importance of
children to orthodox Puritans, the forms of religious appeal made to them,
and the children's responses to their religious experiences. According
to Fleming, children were considered by early Puritans primarily as
depraved sinners requiring conversion. Throughout the Great Awakening of
the 18th century, children experienced conversion in large numbers because
they were made to feel God's wrath so severely. Fleming stresses that
children's conversions were regarded as identical to adults' conversions,
and suggests that the demand for religious conviction from such young
people must have resulted at times in psychological damage. In the final
section of "Christian Nurture," Fleming recounts the emergence of the
view that children are different from adults. He concludes with a lengthy
discussion of the life and work of Horace Bushnell, who promoted the doc-

trine that Christian education consisted not of conversion but of the
forging of Christian character.

H 100. **FOSTER, STEPHEN**. Their Solitary Way: The Puritan Social Ethic
   in the First Century of Settlement in New England. New Haven,
   Conn.: Yale University Press, 1971. 214 pp.
Their Solitary Way is a study of normative literature and beliefs in early
New England. Foster describes and analyzes the 17th-century New England
vision of proper individual behavior within civil society. He discusses
the two foundations of Puritan society, order and love, and shows how
Puritan ideas of Godly order and love led to a vision of a naturally hierarchical society bound together by mutual responsibilities. He also
describes how the Puritan social ethic deals with the more specific problems
of government, wealth, and poverty, and examines the ambiguous relationship
between Puritanism and democracy.

H 101. **FOX, SANFORD J.** Science and Justice: The Massachusetts Witchcraft
   Trials. Baltimore, Md.: Johns Hopkins University Press, 1968.
   121 pp.
Adopting an interdisciplinary approach which involves law, science, and
history, Fox argues that science and religion were intertwined in Colonial
New England; when a witchcraft episode occurred science could not provide
a check on religion. Massachusetts law finally established that those
accused of witchcraft could be prosecuted only if there was proof of
maleficium--any illness that lay beyond the diagnostic skills and medical
treatment available in the Colony. Given this provision, doctors and
midwives who suspected witchcraft "found" anatomical evidence which today
would be dismissed as normal physiological or psychological variations.
Moreover, Fox concludes, scientists would not challenge this often spectral
evidence and consequently it frequently established the guilt of a
suspected witch.

H 102. **FRIES, SYLVIA DOUGHTY.** The Urban Idea in Colonial America. Philadelphia: Temple University Press, 1977. 218 pp.
Fries attempts to employ graphic sources to interpret perceptions of the
city instead of relying upon personal expressions. She argues
that the American city was a reactionary attempt by Englishmen to recreate
ideal parts of their society in North America. Looking at the four most
important planned Colonial cities--Boston, Philadelphia, Williamsburg,
and Savannah--she shows how they were conceived by men who saw the city
as capable of imposing order over chaos, and cohesion over disintegration.
The most successful of these plans was Savannah's, which integrated rural
and urban ecologies by granting land in urban-rural, geometric units.
The ideas of John Winthrop, William Penn, and James Oglethorpe continued
into the 20th century with the garden city and "city beautiful" movements
which attempted to impose upon the city an aesthetic at odds with the
city itself. Rather than accepting the diversity characteristic of city
life, these men and later reformers sought to impose a specific order
on urban life that never successfully took hold.

H 103. **GEDDES, GORDON E.** Welcome Joy: Death in Puritan New England.
   Ann Arbor, Mich.: UMI Research Press, 1976. 262 pp.
Geddes examines Puritan ideas concerning death, signs of imminent death,
the dying of the saved and unsaved, funeral rites, and mourning, arguing
that, while the Puritans had some sense of comfort that God would preserve
the saints from damnation, they could not finally shake off the horror
of death and damnation common to the medieval religion they sought to
reform. Conversion became more important as a preparation for death than
as a central event in the religious progress of the saint while on earth.
Geddes examines Puritan ideas concerning death, signs of imminent death,
the dying of the saved and unsaved, funeral rites, and mourning.

H 104. **GIBSON, CHARLES.** Spain in America. New York: Harper & Row, 1966.
216 pp.
Spain in America is a general summary of Spanish-American civilization
in the New World through the Spanish Colonies' move toward independence
in the early 19th century up to the Mexican revolution. Gibson traces
the development of Spanish Colonial society stressing the decline of popular participation in government and the efforts of the ruling class to
increase economic exploitation. The author frequently compares the Spanish
Colonies with those of the British, insisting that the Spanish-American
colonists did not wipe out the indigenous culture, but fused it with their
own. Of special interest to the author are the economic and political
relationships of the two New World continents.

H 105. **GILDRIE, RICHARD P.** Salem, Massachusetts 1626-1683: A Covenant
Community. Charlottesville: University Press of Virginia, 1975.
187 pp.
Gildrie contends that covenants were not only religious creeds but "social
compacts" as well. He develops this notion by outlining the importance
of several covenants in Salem, Massachusetts, and illuminates the process
by which Salem developed into a commercial town. He examines the changing nature of covenants, claiming they reflect internal social and political changes and the effort to conciliate secular developments to Puritanism.
Gildrie examines implicit and explicit covenants, communal society and
dissent, Colonial politics, and the emergence of commercial Salem.

H 106. **GIPSON, LAWRENCE H.** The British Empire Before the American Revolution. 15 vols. New York: Knopf, 1958-1974. 5625 pp.
Gipson examines the decades immediately prior to the American Revolution
and argues that the colonists were able to break with the mother country
only after England removed the French threat from North America. After
1763 the colonists no longer needed British protection and did not want
to shoulder the financial burden of maintaining the British Empire.
Volumes I through III discuss the British Empire from 1748 to 1754.
Volumes IV and V consider the friction between England and France which
arose not only in North America but throughout the world. Volumes VI,
VII, and VIII focus on the causes and effects of the French and Indian
War; Volumes IX through XII expose the consequences of English victory.
Volume XIII summarizes the series and provides historical sketches of
the British Empire from 1748 to 1776. Volume XIV is a bibliographic guide
to the topic, and Volume XV is a guide to manuscripts.

H 107. **GREENE, JACK P.** The Quest for Power: The Lower Houses of Assembly
in the Southern Royal Colonies 1689-1776. Chapel Hill: University of North Carolina Press, 1963. 522 pp.
Greene traces the rise of the Assemblies in Georgia, the Carolinas, and
Virginia. He argues that the Assemblies' "Quest for Power" was a battle
for political identity on the part of emerging elites in the Colonies.
According to Greene, a "marked correlation" existed between the growth
of socio-economic elites in the Colonies and the Assemblies' demands for
authority. Greene supports his arguments with references to the struggles
over finance, the civil lists, legislative proceedings and identity, and
executive power. He concludes with a discussion of the imperial attempts
in the 1760s and 1770s to control the Assemblies' authority, attempts
which helped trigger the American Revolution.

H 108. GREVEN, PHILIP J. <u>Four Generations</u>: <u>Population</u>, <u>Land</u>, <u>and Family</u>
in <u>Colonial Andover</u>, <u>Massachusetts</u>. Ithaca, N.Y.: Cornell University Press, 1970. 329 pp.
Examined within the broader context of Western European family history,
this case study draws on general demographic data to trace the histories
of the original families of Andover. Greven relates population pressures
to land transmission patterns and to family structure, showing how interpersonal (particularly father-son) relationships and inheritance patterns
changed over time. He argues that as Andover's population grew, increasing pressure over land availability eroded patriarchal control and encouraged migration in search of greater opportunity.

H 109. HALL, DAVID, ed. <u>Puritanism in Seventeenth-Century Massachusetts</u>.
New York: Holt, Rinehart & Winston, 1968. 122 pp.
This collection of essays is divided into four sections: "Puritanism
as a Religious and Intellectual Movement"; "Puritanism as a Political
System"; "Church and State: Was Massachusetts a Theocracy?"; and "Declension." Authors include Edmund S. Morgan, Perry Miller, Bernard Bailyn,
Vernon L. Parrington, Samuel Eliot Morison, James Truslow Adams,
B. Katherine Brown, Alan Simpson, Aaron B. Seidman, Herbert W. Schnieder,
Brooks Adams, and Darrett B. Rutman. Many of the essays consider whether
the Puritans are responsible for what is repressive in our culture, and
to what extent they can be considered the founders of democracy. The
role of increasing commercial interests, internal social conflict, and
the intellectual problems of the Puritans are discussed.

H 110. HALL, MICHAEL GARIBALDI. <u>Edward Randolph and the American Colonies</u>,
<u>1676-1703</u>. Chapel Hill: University of North Carolina Press,
1960. 241 pp.
Americans tend to think of their Colonial past in terms of either Jamestown
and the Mayflower (1607-1620) or the developments of the 18th century
which led to the Revolution. According to Hall, much of the progress
in between has been ignored. He presents a history of that transition
and one of its prime movers—Edward Randolph. The crucial period between
1660 and 1700 witnessed the economic, political, and social growth of
many of the Colonies, and Hall argues that Randolph wielded significant
influence in America and in England as Britain's authority on the Colonies
during these years.

H 111. HENRETTA, JAMES A. <u>Salutary Neglect</u>: <u>Colonial Administration</u>
<u>Under the Duke of Newcastle</u>. Princeton, N.J.: Princeton Uni-
versity Press, 1972. 381 pp.
Henretta's book is a study of the role of the Duke of Newcastle as Colonial
administration changed over the years from 1721 to 1754. During this
period of "salutary neglect," Colonial policy was formed as the result
of shifts in power and interest among Colonial administrators. Henretta
argues that, as political power in England shifted to the hegemony of
parliament, patronage powers became more concentrated among British officials, and the authority of the Colonial governors declined; the result
was a Colonial administration determined largely by private interests.
This "inevitable development," Henretta argues, "was accelerated by the
neglect of colonial problems by those in London and by the shortsighted
and selfish patronage policies pursued by politicians such as Newcastle."

H 112. HULL, N. E. H. and PETER C. HOFFER. <u>Murdering Mothers</u>: <u>Infanticide</u>
<u>in England and New England</u>, <u>1558-1803</u>. New York: New York Uni-
versity Press, 1981. 211 pp.
Hull and Hoffer analyze court records of infanticide in England and New
England. According to them, the prosecution of and conviction for infanticide increased in Britain after the 1580s and then slowed down markedly
during the 18th century. In New England, the Puritan effort to root out

concealed sin and a fear of social and religious decline led to sharp
legal sanctions against infanticide. In the 18th century Colonial legal
authorities, influenced by new social values and an improved quality of
life, tempered the harsh punishment of the previous century. The authors
also discuss the environmental factors (economic conditions, levels of
violence, and social stress) which encouraged infanticide in both England
and New England.

H 113. **INNES, STEPHEN.** Labor in a New Land: Economy and Society in
Seventeenth-Century Springfield. Princeton, N.J.: Princeton University Press, 1983. 463 pp.
Innes challenges the view that 17th-century New England communities were
egalitarian and harmonious. Based on the account books of Springfield,
Massachusetts' major leaders, he claims that economic dependence, inequality, and contention marked Springfield's social and economic life. He
argues that our traditional model of the New England town must be modified
to include the larger seaports and smaller commercial towns. Innes suggests that, given the population and influence of the commercial towns,
the communalistic, egalitarian, provincial New England towns like Dedham
and Andover may be the exception rather than the rule.

H 114. **JEDRY, CHRISTOPHER M.** The World of John Cleaveland: Family and
Community in Eighteenth-Century New England. New York: Norton,
1979. 234 pp.
Jedry's social history of the people of a small Massachusetts town focuses
on domestic affairs as well as on intellectual development. The minister
was the most important figure in the life of the mind for small Colonial
towns. Examining the personal papers of John Cleaveland, Jedry traces
the minister of Ipswich through the turmoils of the Great Awakening and
the Revolutionary War. An extensive examination of records left concerning
the townspeople of Ipswich reveals patterns of property inheritance, marriages, births, migrations, and personal property rights, which, in combination with the record of their intellectual leader, sketch a detailed
portrait of 18th-century life.

H 115. **JOHNSON, JAMES TURNER.** A Society Ordained by God: English Puritan
Marriage Doctrine in the First Half of the Seventeenth Century.
Nashville, Tenn.: Abingdon Press, 1970. 219 pp.
This is an intellectual history of Puritan marriage ethics in the first
half of the 17th century, based on the writings of Alexander Niccholes,
John Milton, and others who fueled theological debate over marriage by
producing scholarly treatises on the subject. Although the text focuses
on the evolution of certain ideas about what form the relationships of
husbands and wives should ideally take, it also deals with social dimensions (friendship, government, church, and business partnership) which
reinforced the Biblically inspired covenantal model of marriage.

H 116. **JOHNSON, RICHARD R.** Adjustment to Empire: The New England Colonies,
1675-1715. New Brunswick, N.J.: Rutgers University Press, 1981.
470 pp.
Treating the New England Colonists' relationship with England and their
"accommodation to royal supervision," Johnson examines the forces which
shaped that relationship: common heritage; trade; the Colonists' needs
and ambitions; English attempts to increase American dependence; and the
pressures of the French and Indian War. He analyzes political and institutional New England history, emphasizing the Colonies' dealings with
each other and with the outside world. In examining this period of trans-
Atlantic interaction, Johnson compares the Colonies of Massachusetts,
Plymouth, Connecticut, Rhode Island, and New Hampshire, contrasting their
problems and solutions in light of British aims and policies.

H 117. JONES, DOUGLAS L. Village and Seaport: Migration and Society in Eighteenth Century Massachusetts. Hanover, N.H.: University Press of New England, 1981. 167 pp.

Jones, in the tradition of Kenneth A. Lockridge and Wesley Frank Craven, argues that 18th-century Massachusetts underwent economic changes that altered the character of Colonial New England. As the land-to-man ratio decreased, the younger generation was forced either to migrate West where land was more abundant or to move and seek employment in the emerging commercial centers along the coast. The author compares two neighboring towns--Beverly, an expanding seaport near Salem, and Wenham, a farming community. The first offered opportunities typical of those found in the emerging commercial cities that adapted to population growth and migration. On the other hand, Wenham represented the limitations of an agricultural economy and the problems facing a community that relied on outward migration to balance population growth and to compensate for diminishing resources. In conclusion, Jones sees the 18th century as a transitional period between the low level of mobility in the 17th century and the higher levels which followed in the next two centuries.

H 118. JONES, JAMES W. The Shattered Synthesis: New England Puritanism Before the Great Awakening. New Haven, Conn.: Yale University Press, 1973. 207 pp.

Jones argues that the Puritans who settled New England brought with them a religion which synthesized, but did not reconcile two conflicting forces: a belief in diverse predestination and the impotence of man; and a commitment to human industry in worldly affairs that allowed them to establish colleges, prosperous businesses, and communities. The Antinomian crisis of the 1630s revealed the tension beneath this synthesis, a tension which finally divided New Englanders during the Great Awakening. Examining the work of nine preachers of the 17th and 18th centuries, Jones shows that the Great Awakening did not create the schism, but that the division had been present for almost a century prior to that event.

H 119. JONES, RUFUS M. The Quakers in the American Colonies. London: MacMillan, 1911. 603 pp.

Jones examines the spreading influence of Quakerism between 1656 and 1780, when it seemed likely to become one of the most prominent religious and cultural forces in America. The Quakers in America for the most part did not encounter the exclusion from political office that they suffered in Britain. In many areas even outside Pennsylvania, Quakers formed a large percentage of the population. Jones believes that the power of Quakerism resided in its emphasis on lay religion which provided ordinary men and women with a feeling of community and equality through spiritualism, in that each person was equal in his or her ability to feel God.

H 120. JUDD, JACOB and IRWIN H. POLISHOOK, eds. Aspects of Early New York Society and Politics. Tarrytown, N.Y.: Sleepy Hollow Restorations, 1974. 150 pp.

The editors collected these essays from those given at a 1971 conference in Tarrytown, N.Y. on New York Colonial and Revolutionary history. The thrust of many of the essays is historiographical: Patricia U. Bonomi argues that the dearth of New York local history is in itself a subject for study; Irwin Polishook calls for the application of quantification to New York history; and Lawrence Leder suggests that New York studies provide a prototype for American studies. Among the other essays included are Richard B. Morris's "The American Revolution Comes to John Jay," Edwin G. Burrows's "Military Experience and the Origins of Federalism and Anti-federalism," and Thomas J. Archdeacon's "The Age of Leisler--New York City, 1689-1710: A Social and Demographic Interpretation."

H 121. KATZ, STANLEY N. Newcastle's New York: Anglo-American Politics, 1732-1753. Cambridge, Mass.: Harvard University Press, 1968. 285 pp.

Katz bases his study of Anglo-American politics in pre-Revolutionary New York on the Newcastle Papers in the British Museum. He contends that the permissiveness of imperial officials, anxious for the most part to run the Colonies economically, made possible a relatively open and non-provincial political system in New York. As the requirements of the revolution demanded more accountability on the part of officials, however, "a more impersonal, rigid situation" came to prevail in Colonial government. Katz studies the roles of Governors William Cosby, George Clinton, and Lieutenant Governor Clarke.

H 122. KELLAWAY, WILLIAM. The New England Company, 1649-1776: Missionary Society to the American Indians. New York: Barnes & Noble Books, 1961. 303 pp.

The New England Company was established in 1649 in England with the sole purpose of converting the New England Indian to Christianity. The Company collected funds, invested them, and returned the interest to the commissioners who paid the ministers. Kellaway examines the Company in England as well as in the Colonies. The English wanted to be certain to convert the American Indians to true Protestantism not only for religious reasons but also for political reasons--to goad the Spanish and Portuguese. The barriers of language and culture had to be overcome before conversion could take place, and much of the work of the Company was spent in trying to Anglicize the Indians. Converts were few, but Kellaway reminds the reader that so, too, were the evangelizing ministers.

H 123. KINNEY, CHARLES B., Jr. Church and State: The Struggle for Separation in New Hampshire, 1630-1900. New York: Teachers College, Columbia University, Bureau of Publications, 1955. 198 pp.

Prompted by contemporary efforts to abolish religious education in public schools, Kinney reviews almost three centuries of debate over separation of church and state in New Hampshire. He recounts the initial establishment of Puritan religion in the colony and the gradual disintegration of official Puritan unity with the growing political and economic power of dissenting sects. Then he discusses the close relation of church, state, and public education throughout New Hampshire's history. Kinney emphasizes the "religious overtones and undertones" in the legislative language of the two opposing traditions. He concludes by calling for the establishment of principles which are common to all religions, and which can be taught in public schools and studied by all children.

H 124. LABAREE, BENJAMIN W. Colonial Massachusetts: A History. Millwood, N.Y.: K.T.O. Press, 1979. 399 pp.

Labaree synthesizes older traditions of historiography that emphasize individuals and newer monographic literature emphasizing communities. After initial chapters on the land, Native American societies, and the English roots of the colonists, he examines early attempts to establish communities, the religious mission of the 17th century, economic expansion, and the end of the Puritan era. Describing provincial politics, life and culture, and the process whereby Massachusetts became part of the British Empire, Labaree concludes with a discussion of the breakdown of the imperial relationship and the coming of independence and statehood.

H 125. LABAREE, LEONARD WOODS. Royal Government in America: A Study of the British Colonial System Before 1783. New Haven, Conn.: Yale University Press, 1930. 491 pp.

Labaree examines the political structure of the royal provinces, with attention to the ways in which royal authority was invoked and enforced, how Colonial administration functioned, and the responses of the colonists to royal policy. The central theme of this age, Labaree argues, was "the great contest between the assemblies and the crown over the royal prerogative." He explores the role of the Captain General, the Governor, the Provincial Assembly, and the Board of Trade; he also discusses the workings of legislation, provincial finance, and the administration of justice.

H 126. LAND, AUDREY C., LOIS GREEN CARR, and EDWARD C. PAPENFUSE, eds.
        Law, Society, and Politics in Early Maryland. Baltimore, Md.:
        Johns Hopkins University Press, 1974. 350 pp.
These essays, first presented at The Conference on Maryland History, trace the development of social and economic stratification and analyze the careers of slaves, servants, and farmers in Maryland. They connect voting behavior and distribution of political power to social and economic groups in the community. The collection includes essays on the evolution of Maryland's legal system; immigration; servitude and opportunity in Colonial Maryland; the black family; and the growth of Baltimore and its impact on the countryside.

H 127. LANGDON, GEORGE D. Pilgrim Colony: A History of New Plymouth,
        1620-1691. New Haven, Conn.: Yale University Press, 1966.
        257 pp.
Langdon presents a history of the Plymouth Colony until its incorporation in Massachusetts Bay in 1691. Included are discussions of the European background and experience of the Pilgrims, the initial attempts at settlement, early conflict and factionalism, the development of religious and political institutions, and land policy. Langdon explains Plymouth's failure to get a royal charter, first in the 1660s and later in the 1690s, suggesting that this failure resulted from a lack of commitment to the historical identity of the colony and the unwillingness of its members to embroil themselves in British politics.

H 128. LEACH, DOUGLAS EDWARD. Flintlock and Tomahawk: New England in
        King Philip's War. New York: Norton, 1958. 304 pp.
King Philip's War of 1675-6 was the most serious of the wars between the colonists and the Native American population. One thousand English colonists were killed in the war, and their line of settlement was pushed back southward and eastward into the Connecticut Valley, resulting in a severe economic setback. Leach contends that King Philip's War was a decisive defeat for Native Americans which finally forced them to recognize that they had lost control of New England. Afterwards, Indian activities were supervised by the colonists and the Indian people were kept under observation. Eventually, they were forced by English expansion into the position of tenant farmers. For the colonists, the wartime destruction of towns and the breakup of families exposed the internal tensions of Puritan society which would blatantly manifest themselves later in the American Revolution.

H 129. LEACH, DOUGLAS EDWARD. The Northern Colonial Frontier, 1607-1763.
        New York: Holt, Rinehart & Winston, 1966. 266 pp.
Leach covers what he considers to be a neglected aspect of Colonial history—the history of the northern half of the earliest American frontier. Alternating between chronological and topical sections, he begins with the English settlement at Plymouth, moves to the Dutch at New Netherland, and then turns to other English settlements in New England. He discusses Indian wars prior to the French and Indian War, the pioneer's life, the fur trade, land speculation, and missionary efforts. The work includes an extensive annotated bibliography.

H 130. **LEDER, LAWRENCE H.** Liberty and Authority: American Political
Ideology, 1689-1763. Chicago: Quadrangle Books, 1968. 167 pp.
Leder outlines the political theory in Colonial America that emerged in
response to the necessity of justifying demands for rights and privileges
from England. Using popular accounts of political thought in newspapers,
sermons, magazines, and pamphlets, as well as material from the Colonial
press, Leder provides contemporary opinions of the relationship between
England and the Colonies before "the conscious effort of the British to
reshape the empire." He finds that the years before 1763 were not characterized by a smooth flow of ideas leading to rebellion. Rather, the
political views of this period tended to reject the idea of independence
from England.

H 131. **LEDER, LAWRENCE H.** Robert J. Livingston, 1654-1728, and the Politics of Colonial New York. Chapel Hill: University of North
Carolina Press, 1961. 306 pp.
Leder studies Robert Livingston's career from the perspective of how it
illuminates the formative years of American politics; he argues that a
biographical approach can reveal at least as much as the study of institutions. As New York changed from a trading outpost to a royal province,
Livingston became "one of the colony's wealthiest and most influential
leaders." He discusses Livingston's relations with such figures as
Ingoldesby, Bellomont, and Dongan; his role in the Leisler Rebellion; his
career as an assemblyman; and his services in Indian affairs.

H 132. **LEVY, BABETTE MAY.** Preaching in the First Century of New England
History. Hartford, Conn.: American Society of Church History,
1945. 215 pp.
Levy examines a period of history when ministers born and trained in
England were the leaders of New England churches. She devotes particular
attention to the following topics: the preparation of sermons; church
doctrine as delivered from the pulpit; the apprehensiveness of the Puritan
ministers toward their own success; preaching on politics and war; and
style of sermons. Also discussed is the growing disaffection of the congregation from the message they were receiving from their church leaders.

H 133. **LOCKRIDGE, KENNETH A.** Literacy in Colonial New England: An Inquiry
into the Social Context of Literacy in the Early Modern West.
New York: Norton, 1974. 164 pp.
In a controversial study of signatures on Colonial New England wills,
Lockridge argues that the literacy level of the first settlers was lower
than that of their children. Almost universal male literacy was achieved
in the 18th century when towns became large enough to support schools.
Lockridge compares New England's literacy rates with those of Virginia,
England, Scotland, and Sweden. He attributes the higher literacy rates
of New England, Scotland, and Sweden to the predominance of Protestantism
and sees literacy as Protestantism's contribution to modernization.

H 134. **LOCKRIDGE, KENNETH A.** A New England Town, the First Hundred Years:
Dedham, Massachusetts, 1636-1736. New York: Norton, 1970.
208 pp.
Lockridge focuses on the interactions of ideology, polity, and economic
setting in Colonial Dedham. Describing the town at its foundation as
a "Christian Utopian Closed Corporate Community," he shows how Dedham's
early economic structure, particularly its pattern of land distribution,
was related to the settlers' commitment to Puritan values of order and
communitarianism, and to the corporate ideals of European peasant society.
Dedham's residents remained primarily subsistence farmers for most of
this period. Although Lockridge finds no evidence of dramatic social
and economic changes, by the early 18th century the people of Dedham witnessed a reduction in the size of land holdings due to disparity of wealth,

the practice of partible inheritance, and outward migration in search
of economic opportunities. Lockridge claims that these changes combined
to alter the original communal order and its associated values.

H 135. LOCKRIDGE, KENNETH A. Settlement and Unsettlement in Early America:
The Crisis of Political Legitimacy Before the Revolution. New
York: Cambridge University Press, 1981. 134 pp.
Lockridge's short work, originally presented as the 1980 Goodman Lectures
at the University of Western Ontario, compares and contrasts the development of society in New England and Virginia before the Revolution. Particular emphasis is given to penetrating the "mental world" of the Colonies.
Lockridge finds that "the colonial era was marked by a fruitless struggle
to achieve a legitimate political order." Clashes between the attitudes
of landed aristocracies and evangelical localism characterized the struggle
in both Colonial settings.

H 136. McGIFFERT, MICHAEL, ed. Puritanism and the American Experience.
Reading, Mass.: Addison-Wesley, 1969. 280 pp.
Beginning with a historiographical preface by Richard Schlatter, this
volume of twenty-nine essays by historians as well as Puritans is divided
into three sections. The first focuses on the Puritan utopia of "a city
upon a hill" as envisioned by John Winthrop and the first generation to
settle in the New World. The second section examines the transition of
this Puritan ideal as it confronted the American environment and developed
traits far too secular for the minds of the earliest settlers. In the
last section, the essays discuss the legacy left by the Puritans and the
impact of their ideas on succeeding generations with reference to the
three specific areas: "The Protestant Ethic"; "Puritanism and Democracy";
and "Puritanism and the American Character."

H 137. McINTYRE, RUTH A. Debts Hopeful and Desperate: Financing the
Plymouth Colony. Plymouth, Mass.: Plimoth Plantation, 1963.
86 pp.
From the decision to emigrate to the discharge of Plymouth's debts in
1645, McIntyre traces the financial difficulties and developments of the
Pilgrims. She contends that the commercial life of the colony stands
on its own as an early example of business success. The formation of
a joint stock company between the Pilgrims and merchants, differences
of opinion and the breakup of the company, the Pilgrims' involvement in
the fur trade, trading rights, conflict over accounts with London, and
final settlement are documented.

H 138. MERRENS, HARRY ROY. Colonial North Carolina in the Eighteenth
Century: A Study in Historical Geography. Chapel Hill: University of North Carolina Press, 1964. 293 pp.
Merrens provides an introduction to the geography and economy of Colonial
North Carolina. Concentrating primarily on the period of rapid population
increase in the middle of the 18th century, he describes the extent and
topography of the colony, its natural resources, and the demographic and
settlement patterns of its inhabitants. Merrens analyzes regional variations in economic activity within the colony, describing in particular
the forest and naval store industries, the expansion of commercial agriculture, and the role of urban settlements in the economic development
of their hinterlands. He finds that cultural factors influenced patterns
of economic growth and rejects the idea that a series of well-defined
frontier stages or zones of development existed in Colonial North Carolina.

H 139. MERRITT, RICHARD L. Symbols of American Community, 1735-1775.
        New Haven, Conn.: Yale University Press, 1966. 279 pp.
Merritt provides a quantitative analysis of symbols of communication taken
from Colonial newspapers published prior to the American Revolution in
an effort to find patterns which may reflect changes in Colonial thought.
The focus is on "political disintegration and integration," and the development of community awareness both within separate colonies and in America
as a whole. Merritt offers a number of hypotheses which, while based
on American data, address broad questions concerning political community
awareness in general.

H 140. MIDDLEKAUFF, ROBERT. Ancients and Axioms: Secondary Education
        in Eighteenth Century New England. New Haven, Conn.: Yale Uni-
        versity Press, 1963. 218 pp.
Colonial New Englanders were committed to establishing and maintaining
a school system, despite wars and economic hardships. Middlekauff argues
that "liberal" education, which emphasized the classics, was brought to
New England from England and prevailed throughout the century; new educational ideas, religious and social decline, and the emergence of a large
commercial class did not affect secondary education. Middlekauff also
studies the economics of education and points out that the Puritans
believed in education supervised by the state and financed by the public.
In fact, schools absorbed the largest share of town revenues in 18th-
century New England.

H 141. MIDDLEKAUFF, ROBERT. The Mathers: Three Generations of Puritan
        Intellectuals, 1596-1728. New York: Oxford University Press,
        1976. 440 pp.
Intended not as a biographical study, but as an examination of the Mathers
as representative of many Puritan ministers who were also intellectuals,
Middlekauff's book discusses the Puritan Millenialism brought from England
by Richard Mather, which was refined and intensified by his son Increase
and grandson Cotton Mather. Middlekauff finds, contrary to earlier scholarship, that Puritan intellectuals made use of science and reason in developing theories of religious belief without "accommodating or rationalizing
existing belief." He describes the Mathers as men of moral and intellectual creativity and courage.

H 142. MILLER, PERRY. Orthodoxy in Massachusetts 1630-1650. Cambridge,
        Mass.: Harvard University Press, 1933. 353 pp.
This study of the institution of Congregationalism in Massachusetts Bay
examines conflicts within England over the proper forms of civil and ecclesiastical organization, and traces the history of English Puritanism and
its attempts to further the reformation of the Church of England. Miller
distinguishes between separatist and non-separatist Congregationalism,
demonstrating how the logic of the non-separatists led to the suppression
of dissent with the establishment of orthodoxy in Massachusetts. He concludes with a discussion of the Cambridge Platform.

H 143. MORGAN, EDMUND S. American Slavery, American Freedom: The Ordeal
        of Colonial Virginia. New York: Norton, 1975. 454 pp.
Morgan offers a general history of 17th-century Virginia. He argues that
the replacement of white servants with black slaves after Bacon's rebellion
made possible an inter-class alliance among white Virginians. By creating
a laboring class that was literally a race apart, Virginia's gentry could
be ardent republicans, at least as far as whites were concerned. Virginia's Republicanism was predicated on slavery and not contradictory
to it.

H 144. MORGAN, EDMUND S. The Puritan Dilemma: The Story of John Winthrop.
Boston: Little, Brown, 1958. 224 pp.
Combining a biography of John Winthrop with a social and political history
of early Massachusetts, Morgan probes the interplay between the individual
and society, and highlights the Puritan dilemma of "doing right in a world
that does wrong." He describes Winthrop's early life, education, and
religious beliefs. The Atlantic crossing and the formation of Massachusetts's government are discussed in the context of the problem of dissent
and the struggles between magistrates and freemen.

H 145. MORGAN, EDMUND S. The Puritan Family: Essays on Religion and
Domestic Relations in Seventeenth-Century New England. 1944;
Rev. ed. New York: Harper & Row, 1966. 196 pp.
Morgan discusses love, child-rearing, education, the relationship between
servants and masters, and the position of the family in Puritan society.
In the last chapter, he contends that the tremendous concern Puritan parents had with the salvation of their own children caused them to turn
away from the outside world. By segregating themselves from the non-
Puritan world, rather than attempting to draw outsiders into the faith,
they became "tribal" and "clannish." If the Puritans had shown more concern with the outside world rather than concentrating almost exclusively
on their own children, Morgan believes that the Puritan "Kingdom of God
on earth" might have proved far more successful and long-lived.

H 146. MORISON, SAMUEL ELIOT. Builders of the Bay Colony. 1930; Rev.
ed. Boston: Houghton Mifflin, 1958. 405 pp.
Morison offers a collection of biographical essays, each devoted to a
person of the first generation Bay colony who was chosen not by public
prominence but as representative of the spectrum of early Colonial life
in the Puritan community. Among those included are Captain John Smith,
John Winthrop, Henry Dunster (president of Harvard), John Eliot (missionary
to the Indians), and the frontier leader and fur trader William Pynchon.

H 147. MORISON, SAMUEL ELIOT. The European Discovery of America. Volume
I, The Northern Voyages A.D. 500-1600. New York: Oxford University
Press, 1971. 712 pp; Volume II, The Southern Voyages 1492-1616.
New York: Oxford University Press, 1974. 758 pp.
The first volume of Morison's account of European voyages of discovery
to North America discusses pre-Columbian travels, alleged and actual,
analyzes English ship-building and navigation from 1490 to 1600, and reconstructs the voyages of Cabot and his successors. Morison examines French
maritime experience, the search for a Northwest passage and the first
two attempts to establish colonies in Virginia. Volume II deals primarily
with the voyages of Columbus, Magellan, and Drake to posts further south;
Morison claims to have "retraced their courses at sea," treating explorations of the North American coastline from Florida to California and ports
south of the Caribbean. Both volumes are heavily illustrated with maps,
photographs, and sketches.

H 148. MORISON, SAMUEL ELIOT. The Founding of Harvard College. Cambridge,
Mass.: Harvard University Press, 1935. 472 pp.
Morison presents a history of Harvard College from its founding to 1650.
He argues that while the example of English universities, especially that
of Cambridge, guided the founders of Harvard College, no other European
institution had a direct impact. Emmanuel College, established in 1504,
influenced Harvard because a number of its graduates, particularly its
ministers, came to New England. The town of Cambridge, chosen as the
college's site, appealed to the founders primarily because it was never
contaminated by Antinomian ideas. Morison emphasizes the role of the
General Court and the college's first president in its development. In
1646, the laws of the college were codified and Harvard laid the founda-

tions for American education by not requiring members of the college community to take a religious oath, and by advocating broad educational goals.

H 149. MORRIS, RICHARD B. Government and Labor in Early America. New York: Columbia University Press, 1946. 557 pp.
Morris makes extensive use of local court records to examine governmental regulations of labor relations during the Revolutionary era. He begins with a description of the mercantilist background of the American economy. A discussion of free labor investigates the control of wages, collective actions by workers and their legal standing, contracts and the condition of labor, maritime labor relations, and the relationship between labor and the military. Finally, a section on "unfree" labor evaluates the nature and sources of bound labor, and the legal status of servants.

H 150. MUNROE, JOHN A. Colonial Delaware: A History. Millwood, N.Y.: K.T.O. Press, 1979. 292 pp.
Munroe traces the history of Colonial Delaware from its Swedish origins to the Revolutionary Era. Included are examinations of New Sweden, the Dutch occupation, Delaware under the Duke of York and under William Penn, the founding of Wilmington and the demographic expansion of the countryside, religion and education, economics, and the Revolutionary order. Munroe demonstrates how the "vagaries of political organization in the Old British Empire permitted the accidental development of a remarkably independent commonwealth." A bibliographic essay follows the text.

H 151. NASH, GARY B. Quakers and Politics: Pennsylvania, 1681-1726. Princeton, N.J.: Princeton University Press, 1968. 362 pp.
Nash's book is an exploration in "the sociology of politics" among the Pennsylvania Quakers, a concept that includes such topics as their social structure, connections between their behavior and their social views, the role of William Penn in their society, and their society's class structure. Nash argues that the "Holy Experiment" of the Friends was typical of the American Colonial experience, and that the Quaker experience of social and political disequilibrium in the face of a strong belief system had analogues in such early societies as Puritan New England and Anglican Virginia.

H 152. NASH, GARY. Red, White, and Black: The Peoples of Early America. 1974; Rev. ed. Englewood Cliffs, N.J.: Prentice-Hall, 1982. 350 pp.
Nash examines the interrelationships between Indian, white, and black cultures in America during the Colonial Period. The predominantly negative consequences for both Indian and black peoples of European incursions in America and Africa are discussed. Nash's principal themes include the advanced nature of the societies of native peoples that Europeans encountered, and the changes that evolved in European societies which were transplanted to America. Included is a comparative study of slavery as practiced in North and Latin America.

H 153. OBERHOLZER, EMIL, Jr. Delinquent Saints: Disciplinary Action in the Early Congregational Churches of Massachusetts. New York: Columbia University Press, 1956. 379 pp.
Oberholzer looks at various offenses committed by Puritans, among them heresy, marital quarreling, extra-marital relations, drunkenness, acts of cruelty, lying, and unethical business transactions. The Puritan church as a court of law is examined, as well as the relationship between church and state. A code enacted in 1641 dictated that the church had the power to punish by excommunication, but could not overstep the boundaries of the civil courts, which could punish secular or religious transgressions. By the beginning of the Revolution, it had become clear that the Puritan utopia so hoped for by Massachusetts Puritans had failed and the covenant had been broken.

H 154. OLSON, ALISON G. Anglo-American Politics, 1660-1775. New York: Oxford University Press, 1973. 192 pp.
The interaction between political factions and imperial politics from the Restoration to the American Revolution provides the primary focus of Olson's work. She argues that the imperial context made possible a "diversity of authorities, associations, interests and issues" which fragmented the political community, leading to the growth and legitimization of parties. These parties, she suggests, were crucial to the everyday functioning of the empire prior to the Stamp Act crisis. The changed context of English and Colonial politics in the 1760s meant, however, that instead of helping to hold the empire together, factions now helped to tear it apart.

H 155. OSGOOD, HERBERT LEVI. The American Colonies in the Eighteenth Century. 4 vols. New York: Columbia University Press, 1924. 2268 pp.
Osgood describes a process in which thirteen separate colonies gradually coalesced into one system under the control of the British government. He argues that a national impulse matured during the 18th century and that the break with the mother country was the natural end of that process. Part I includes detailed discussions of the Colonies during the first two inter-Colonial wars, which occurred between 1690-1714. In part II Osgood discusses the years of peace (1714-1740), which intervened before the third inter-Colonial war. Part III decribes the growth of the nationalistic impulse in America during the third and fourth inter-Colonial wars, 1740-1763.

H 156. OSGOOD, HERBERT LEVI. The American Colonies in the Seventeenth Century. 3 vols. New York: Macmillan, 1904-1907. 1619 pp.
In this institutional history of the British Colonies in North America, Osgood is concerned with forms of government and types of administration. Volume I looks at the birth of the first Colonies (Virginia, Maryland, Massachusetts, Connecticut, and Pennsylvania), early forms of government, ideologies, internal histories, economic structures, and relations with Native Americans. Volume II concentrates on colonies established after the 1660s, and discusses their government, economy, history, and religion; Osgood argues that by the 1690s, the residents of the British Colonies began to develop a national impulse, separate from their English identity. Volume III is concerned with the British imperial system and its impact on Colonial life. Osgood concludes that in the 17th century events in England such as the Puritan Revolution, the English Civil War, and the Restoration had a major impact on Colonial life and institutions.

H 157. PARRY, J. H. The Age of Reconnaissance. Cleveland, Ohio: World, 1963. 327 pp.
This book summarizes the exploration, trade, and settlement of Europeans in non-European lands in the 15th, 16th, and 17th centuries. Parry stresses the primary importance of technological supremacy for the success of European conquest, and details the scientific and technological innovations of the 15th and 16th century which made geographical exploration possible. In describing the founding of the early colonies, Parry accentuates the economic, religious, and political factors in the European drive for territory. The book describes the European preconditions for colonization.

H 158. PENCAK, WILLIAM. War, Politics, and Revolution in Provincial Massachusetts. Boston: Northeastern University Press, 1981. 314 pp.
Pencak's study is based on the proposition that military conflict defines the 18th century as Puritanism does the 17th. He studies the economic, social, and political unrest which conflict brought to 18th-century Massachusetts, and the attitude of the general populace to those who guided

the war. Pencak argues that the Massachusetts Revolution was a true "people's revolt . . . the product neither of personal elite squabbling, paranoid fear of British tyranny, nor class conflict." Pencak addresses the behavior of the General Court, including its disputes with Governors Bernard and Hutchinson, and then moves on to discuss the "membership, tactics, and ideology" of the Revolutionary movement.

H 159. PERKINS, EDWIN J. The Economy of Colonial America. New York: Columbia University Press, 1980. 177 pp.
Contrasting Colonial American economy with modern economic trends in a comparative global context, Perkins discusses demography, growth rates, living standards, and wealth distribution, converting all monetary figures into 1980 equivalents. He focuses on rural agricultural economy and the economic behavior of farmers, planters, artisans, and merchants. Although primarily describing free white lifestyles, Perkins devotes a chapter to the role of slaves and indentured servants in the Colonial economy.

H 160. POCOCK, J. G. A. The Machiavellian Moment: Florentine Political Thought and the Atlantic Republican Tradition. Princeton, N.J.: Princeton University Press, 1975. 602 pp.
Tracing the roots of the republican ideals of Revolutionary America from Classical and Christian thought through republican Florence and civil-war England, Pocock suggests that early American thinkers sought to overcome the tendency toward instability displayed in republican countries which relied on a combination of popular virtue and governmental mechanism. He examines the debates over the state and a standing army, fears of corruption, and responses to a growing commercial society.

H 161. POLE, J. R. The Gift of Government: Political Responsibility from the English Restoration to American Independence. Athens: University of Georgia Press, 1983. 185 pp.
Pole argues that during the 17th and 18th centuries, a utilitarian justification of government as the means to secure the happiness of the people replaced an earlier notion of government as a "gift" graciously bestowed by the ruler. This transition is discussed in relation to the rise of Parliament, the role of the Crown in the Colonies, and the emergence of Colonial assemblies. Pole suggests that as the newer utilitarian conception of government took hold, it was accompanied by the modern notion that constituents should have general access to information regarding their political institutions and leaders.

H 162. POWELL, SUMNER CHILTON. Puritan Village: The Formation of a New England Town. Middletown, Conn.: Wesleyan University Press, 1963. 215 pp.
Powell relates the founding and early history of a representative New England village. He traces the prominent citizens of 17th-century Sudbury, Massachusetts back to their origins in English manorial villages, incorporated boroughs, and East Anglian enclosed-farm villages, analyzing how their respective regional heritages influenced the emerging social order of the settlement in New England. Sudbury's founders, Powell argues, had abandoned almost every form of traditional hierarchy--political, ecclesiastical, and legal--in order to forge a society of free townsmen governing themselves according to common consent and law, rather than powerful central authorities. He looks at how the town managed land, government, taxation, church government, quarrels among townspeople, and relations with neighboring communities.

H 163. POWERS, EDWIN. Crime and Punishment in Colonial Massachusetts 1620-1692: A Documentary History. Boston: Beacon Press, 1966. 647 pp.
Powers interprets the history and significance of cases involving the social offender as documented in court records and other primary sources, many of which are excerpted in the text. The book is arranged topically and includes material on civil rights and liberties; penalties; types of offenses (Quaker heresies, witchcraft, drunkenness); general background on lawmaking; and the respective roles of church and state in 17th-century Massachusetts. An appendix compares the civil rights and liberties of the Massachusetts Bay Colony with those of the Commonwealth of Massachusetts today.

H 164. QUINN, DAVID B. North America from Earliest Discovery in First Settlements: The Norse Voyages to 1612. New York: Harper & Row, 1977. 621 pp.
Quinn's detailed narrative describes the discovery of the New World and explores the different ways the early European colonizers attacked the problem of settlement. Though including chapters on Amerindian culture, European ideology and institutions, and economic exploitation of the new continents, Quinn deals most thoroughly with the founding of the major early settlements by the French, Spanish, and English. The discovery and the early colonization of the Americas is presented not only as the basis for later American civilization, but also as a relatively minor expression of the great European Age of Discovery of the 16th century.

H 165. REPS, JOHN. Tidewater Towns: City Planning in Colonial Virginia and Maryland. Williamsburg, Va.: Colonial Williamsburg Foundation, 1972. 345 pp.
This heavily illustrated study is chiefly concerned with the physical layouts of towns, although it also considers the process of founding a town in the 17th and 18th centuries. Reps argues that 17th-century governmental policies of producing towns wholesale as a precondition for settlement shifted in the 18th century to concentration on a few towns whenever population expansion produced a need. In his discussion of town-planning, Reps stresses the influence of tradition and the grid pattern of laying out a town.

H 166. ROWSE, A. L. The Elizabethans and America. New York: Harper, 1959. 221 pp.
Rowse proposes to push back the story of the foundation of America to the 1580s--the high point of the Elizabethan Age. He points out the activities and avid interest of Queen Elizabeth and her contemporaries in the colonization of North America. Beginning with a history of the struggle for Colonial territories between Spain, France, England, and Portugal, Rowse devotes subsequent chapters to the following topics: life in Virginia; the Elizabethan qualities of the Pilgrims and Puritans; the areas north of New England (Nova Scotia and Newfoundland); and the image of North America in Elizabethan culture.

H 167. RUTMAN, DARRETT B. Husbandmen of Plymouth: Farms and Villages in the Old Colony, 1620-1692. Boston: Beacon Press, 1967. 100 pp.
Rutman describes the development of the grain-producing, agricultural economy of Plymouth colony. He attributes the settlers' early concentration on agriculture to two factors: first, their inability to establish the anticipated trade in fish and furs; second, the influx in the 1630s of immigrants into the Massachusetts Bay region. By creating a strong demand for food, the migration encouraged the Plymouth farmers to expand their agricultural activities. Rutman shows how Native American practices influenced the colonists and explains why they turned to extensive methods

of farming. Agriculture, he says, continued to dominate all aspects of
life in Plymouth through the end of the 17th century.

H 168. RUTMAN, DARRETT B. Winthrop's Boston: A Portrait of a Puritan
        Town, 1630-49. New York: Norton, 1965. 324 pp.
According to Rutman, the "City upon a Hill" founded by John Winthrop and
his Puritan followers never achieved its founders' original goals. From
the start, Boston was so fragmented that the adjective "Puritan" seems
inapplicable. The religious ideals of the Puritans were soon discarded
for those of individualism, materialism, and the separation of church
and state. As the city grew, homogeneity was replaced with heterogeneity,
commerce was substituted for agriculture, and religious toleration overwhelmed orthodoxy. In less than twenty years, Rutman argues, Boston transformed itself from a small, medieval, religion-based community to a modern,
secular, commercial-based society.

H 169. SLATER, PETER GREGG. Children in the New England Mind in Death
        and Life. Hamden, Conn.: Shoe String Press, 1977. 248 pp.
Slater discusses children from the 17th century to the middle of the 19th
century from the perspective of an intellectual historian. He divides
his book into two sections. The first part examines ideas about the dead
child, an important aspect to be considered in an era of high infant mortality and a belief in infant damnation. The second section looks at
child-rearing practices during the Colonial and early national periods.

H 170. SMITH, ABBOT EMERSON. Colonists in Bondage: White Servitude and
        Convict Labor in America, 1607-1776. New York: Norton, 1971.
        435 pp.
More than half of the English who settled in the New World during the
17th century arrived as indentured servants, or especially in the Chesapeake colonies, as redemptioners. Given the scarcity of labor, economic
development in the 17th century depended on the importation of workers.
Most planters used indentured servants who were drawn from the surplus
population of England's poor. The economic factors that determined the
number of imported servants were the lack of employment in England and
the financial promise of the Colonies, especially in the Chesapeake area.
In the 1670s, a rise in employment opportunities in England combined with
a decline in opportunities to make money in the Colonies to bring about
the decline in the importation of indentured servants. Smith also shows
that many indentured servants were forced out of England and he describes
the conditions in which these workers traveled to and lived in the Colonies.

H 171. SMITH, JAMES MORTON, ed. Seventeenth Century in America: Essays
        in Colonial History. Chapel Hill: University of North Carolina
        Press, 1959. 238 pp.
These essays, first presented at a symposium celebrating the 350th anniversary of the settlement of Jamestown, consider the ways in which the
colonists adjusted to the conditions of 17th-century North America. They
address a variety of issues: the colonists' justifications for dispossessing Native Americans of land and resources; the cultural adjustment of
Native Americans to European civilization; the social origins of the colonists; the evolution of Virginia's government; the development of European
religious practices in America; and the definition of a perception of
history distinct from the English one.

H 172. SOSIN, JACK M. English America and the Restoration Monarchy of
        Charles II: Transatlantic Politics, Commerce, and Kinship. Lin-
        coln: University of Nebraska Press, 1980. 389 pp.
Sosin's account of the Stuarts's attempts to govern the North American
Colonies during the Restoration begins with a discussion of kinship and
trade connections before 1660. He goes on to describe attempts to bring

the Colonies under a unified administration and the eventual collapse of these centralizing efforts. Maintaining that there was no continuous unified plan of imperial action, Sosin contends that Charles II and James II made their Colonial policy in response to an unstable constellation of interests and pressures. The end result was not unified Colonial administration, but the proliferation of disparate Colonial governmental forms.

H 173. SOSIN, JACK M. English America and the Revolution of 1688: Royal Administration and the Structure of Provincial Government. Lincoln: University of Nebraska Press, 1982. 321 pp.
The second part of Sosin's proposed trilogy on the "English Atlantic Community" from the Restoration of Charles II until the Hanoverian ascension to the throne in 1714, this volume examines the roots, events, and outcome of the series of rebellions which shook the Colonies in the aftermath of the Glorious Revolution. Sosin argues that social and political instability, combined with conflicts between ambitious local leaders, led to the uprisings. He suggests that the conflicts were less about ideology than about who would rule under English authority.

H 174. STANNARD, DAVID. The Puritan Way of Death: A Study in Religion, Culture, and Social Change. New York: Oxford University Press, 1977. 236 pp.
Considering anthropology and sociology as well as history, Stannard's interdisciplinary study describes death and dying as a paradigm of the Puritan way of life. While the Puritans saw themselves as God's chosen people and viewed death as a gate to eternal life, they nevertheless lived in terror of death due to the doctrines of predestination and assurance. Stannard claims that this view of death changed with the decline of Puritanism; in the 19th century a more optimistic outlook emerged.

H 175. TATE, THAD W. and DAVID L. AMMERMAN, eds. The Chesapeake in the Seventeenth Century: Essays on Anglo-American Society. Chapel Hill: University of North Carolina Press, 1979. 310 pp.
Eleven scholars contributed to this volume of 17th-century Chesapeake socio-political history. Their essays consider the following topics: settlement patterns; marriage and family; disease and mortality in early Virginia; immigrant opportunities in Maryland; the social origins of servants; and the emergence of native-born elites. Each essay shows the transformation of Chesapeake society from a world marked by strife, instability, disease, and death to one noted for its socio-political stability and secure elites.

H 176. TAYLOR, ROBERT J. Colonial Connecticut: A History. Millwood, N.Y.: K.T.O. Press, 1979. 285 pp.
Discussing the importance of Connecticut's political institutions in helping to maintain political stability during the Colonial period, Taylor suggests that Connecticut's relative independence from the intervention of the Crown kept imperial politics from disrupting political life. According to Taylor, the desire to remain free from British control led Connecticut elites to compromise their differences. The following topics are highlighted: demographic expansion; sectarian conflicts and the growth of religious liberty; increased social stratification; developments in science and culture; and Connecticut's move toward independence.

H 177. TULLY, ALAN. William Penn's Legacy: Politics and Social Structure in Provincial Pennsylvania, 1726-1755. Baltimore, Md.: Johns Hopkins University Press, 1977. 255 pp.
Tully's book is a study of political Pennsylvania in the years following the crises of the 1720s and ending with the Quakers' withdrawal from politics in the mid-1750s. Tully argues that these years were not marked

by the factionalism and internal conflict that many historians cite as
distinguishing features of Colonial societies; rather, a fully formed
political and decision-making system evolved to settle possible conflicts.
Uncertainties and factionalism did exist, but only periodically and in
response to changes in British policy; mid-18th century Pennsylvania was
marked by political stability.

H 178. VAUGHAN, ALDEN T. American Genesis: Captain John Smith and the
       Founding of Virginia. Boston: Little, Brown, 1975. 207 pp.
A consideration of John Smith's involvement in the first years of Virginia's settlement, Vaughan's study traces the transformation of the errant
dream of a soldier of fortune into an early American social order. Smith
spent only two and a half years in Virginia, yet he saved Jamestown in
its darkest hours. After leaving Jamestown, Smith explored and mapped
New England and promoted colonization efforts in England. For Vaughan,
John Smith symbolizes young America--bold, energetic, and optimistic,
yet intolerant, proud, and seeking approval.

H 179. VAUGHAN, ALDEN T. and FRANCIS J. BREMER, eds. Puritan New England:
       Essays on Religion, Society, and Culture. New York: St. Martin's
       Press, 1977. 395 pp.
The editors present twenty-one articles which, with a single exception,
have appeared in scholarly journals between 1961 and 1976. Intended to
serve as an introduction to American Puritanism, the essays are divided
into eight sections which discuss the following subjects: English origins;
the practice of religion in New England; social order; religious dissent;
women, children, and witchcraft; Puritan literature; developments in Puritan intellectual life; and a final essay by Edmund S. Morgan concerning
the legacy of American Puritanism. Each article is preceded by a brief
historiographical introduction by the editors, and a chronology of American
and English Puritanism is provided.

H 180. WARCH, RICHARD. School of the Prophets: Yale College 1701-1740.
       New Haven, Conn.: Yale University Press, 1973. 184 pp.
Warch describes the tumultuous birth and early development of Yale College.
He argues that the story of the college illuminates the goals and authority
of the Congregationalist leaders of Connecticut. He analyzes the crisis
that followed the death of the first rector, Abraham Pierson; the battle
between Hartford and New Haven over the location of the institution; and
the sensational conversion to Anglicanism in 1722 of the College rector,
Timothy Cutler, as well as some members of the faculty. The book also
includes discussions of curriculum, finance, and student life. Finally,
Warch considers how the ideas of Newton and Locke took hold at the college
during the 1730s.

H 181. WEBB, STEPHEN SAUNDERS. The Governors-General: The English Army
       and the Definition of the Empire, 1569-1681. Chapel Hill: Uni-
       versity of North Carolina Press, 1979. 549 pp.
Suggesting that historians have overemphasized the commercial nature of
the first British Empire, Webb contends that military and imperial considerations dominated Anglo-American attitudes toward the empire. He
develops this argument through an examination of the military administration
in the British Isles and the "garrison government" of the Governors-General
in the Colonies. Webb concentrates on the Crown Colonies of Jamaica and
Virginia, but also treats attempts to impose royal authority on other
Colonies. He concludes with a general overview of the role of garrison
government and the military in the history of early America.

H 182. WELLS, ROBERT V. The Population of the British Colonies in America Before 1776: A Survey of Census Data. Princeton, N.J.: Princeton University Press, 1975. 342 pp.
Wells analyzes 124 censuses taken between 1623 and 1775 in twenty-one British colonies from Canada to the West Indies. The bulk of the book describes population patterns in each colony for which a census survived. Through a comparison of demographic data, Wells discusses the different patterns of development which emerged in colonies on both the mainland and the islands, emphasizing the differences in household composition and family experiences. The author discusses the geographical distribution of each colony's population, racial composition, the extent of slavery and indentured servitude, and differences in marital customs, household size, and family structure.

H 183. WINSLOW, OLA E. A Destroying Angel: The Conquest of Smallpox in Colonial Boston. Boston: Houghton Mifflin, 1974. 137 pp.
Winslow describes the struggle against smallpox in 18th-century New England. She argues that the initiative of individual physicians, rather than the role played by governmental authorities, was largely responsible for controlling the disease. She devotes a chapter of her study to Edward Jenner, the English discoverer of the smallpox innoculation. A consideration of Benjamin Waterhouse, who first used the innoculation in Boston, gives way to a study of the way in which Cotton Mather and Zabdiel Boylston of Boston promoted the use of innoculation in 1721.

H 184. WORRALL, ARTHUR J. Quakers in the Colonial Northeast. Hanover, N.H.: University Press of New England, 1980. 238 pp.
Worrall discusses Quakers in the Northeast from the time of the "Quaker Invasion," beginning in 1656, to the year 1790. He concludes that the sudden increase in the expulsion of Quakers from membership in the church was not due to the Revolutionary War but rather to a wave of internal reform. The emphasis on traditional Quakerism both interrupted Quaker accommodation to the outside world and caused tensions within the church to rise to the surface.

H 185. WRIGHT, LOUIS B. The Cultural Life of the American Colonies, 1607-1763. New York: Harper, 1957. 292 pp.
Wright provides an overview of American culture from Jamestown to the conclusion of the French and Indian War. In order to demonstrate the cultural diversity of the Colonial period, he discusses a wide variety of topics, including: agrarian societies and elites in the South and in New York; the work ethic and the emergence of a mercantile elite in the Northern Colonies; ethnic and national diversity; religion, education, libraries, literature, drama, music, architecture, science, and the press. Wright suggests that the spread of commerce and communication systems helped to create a more unified and less parochial American culture.

H 186. WRIGHT, LOUIS B. The Dream of Prosperity in Colonial America. New York: New York University Press, 1965. 96 pp.
Four of Wright's lectures are collected in this volume: "American Cornucopia for All the World," "The Lure of Fish, Furs, Wine, and Silk," "Cures for All the Ills of Mankind," and "The Continuing Dream of an Economic Utopia." Wright points to the universal faith in the wealth of the New World as a continuous theme beginning with Columbus, and discusses its profound effect on historical development. He concentrates his discussion of "the dream of prosperity" in America on the period before the Revolution.

H 187. WRIGHT, LOUIS B. Everyday Life in Colonial America. New York:
        Putnam, 1965. 255 pp.
Wright contends that Colonial life was colored by a pervasive concern
with religion and with the personal attributes of courage, hard work,
and ingenuity. His survey begins with an overview of the mystique of
the new land--its physical bounty, and the folklore of indigenous plants
(e.g., sassafras and tobacco). Realities of the crossing, land clearing,
and adaptations in housing and eating habits are covered. Rural life
is treated regionally, with attention given to foodways and harvesting,
animal care, and to such leisure activities as cockfighting and turtle
gigging. The "how-to" of whaling and ship building, and the rice, tobacco,
and indigo industries are surveyed, as are the dynamics of being an apprentice in printing, silver-smithing, and other trades. "Hickory stick"
education; the establishment of the nation's first universities; sports
and pastimes; musket-loading and volleying; and the social and cultural
dimensions of the Puritan, Anglican, and other faiths are also covered.

H 188. ZUCKERMAN, MICHAEL. Peaceable Kingdom: New England Towns in the
        Eighteenth Century. New York: Knopf, 1970. 329 pp.
Zuckerman refutes the idea that the first American settlers lost their
sense of community under the influence of frontier individualism. Using
New England town records, especially those concerning elective offices,
Zuckerman proposes the alternative thesis that concern for the community
over and above the self continued up to the time of the American Revolution.
He traces a continuum of values and behavior in Massachusetts throughout
the 18th century, with special reference to the common citizen.

III.   REVOLUTIONARY AND NEW REPUBLIC

H 189. ADAIR, DOUGLASS. Fame and the Founding Fathers. Edited by Trevor
        Colbourn. New York: Norton, 1974. 315 pp.
This posthumously issued collection of Adair's essays, articles, reviews,
notes, and documents are concerned with the intellectual world of the
Founding Fathers and with their place in American history. Adair demonstrates the intellectual sophistication of their political theory, while
discussing the "Tenth Federalist," the influence of David Hume on James
Madison, the "authorship of the disputed Federalist Papers," the papers
of Thomas Jefferson, and the Constitution.

H 190. ALDEN, JOHN RICHARD. The First South. Baton Rouge: Louisiana
        State University Press, 1961. 144 pp.
Alden treats the origins of Southern sectionalism in terms of the national
politics of the period 1776-1789. He argues that Southern sectionalism
had its origins in the 18th rather than in the 19th century, and that
a considerable number of cultural patterns typical of the South were operative by the time of the Constitutional Convention. The emergence of a
distinctly Southern interest in the Continental Congress is discussed,
and the role of Southern politicians in the Confederation period is shown
to be consistent and mutually supportive. Finally, the impact of the
Southern bloc on the Constitutional Convention and the battle for ratification is assessed.

H 191. **ALEXANDER, JOHN K.** Render Them Submissive: Responses to Poverty in Philadelphia, 1760-1800. Amherst: University of Massachusetts Press, 1980. 234 pp.
Alexander analyzes the ways Philadelphians responded to poverty in the late 18th century. He argues that although the actual condition of the poor remained largely unaltered, the Revolution dramatically changed the nature and aims of poor relief. Increasingly, relief within institutions became more common and separation of the "deserving" from the "vicious" poor received greater emphasis. Poor relief, whether public or private, was employed both to control and uplift the poor. Alexander believes that although these trends began in pre-Revolutionary Philadelphia, a heightened concern about social disorder and insubordination accelerated their development during the Revolutionary era.

H 192. **AMMON, HARRY.** The Genet Mission. New York: Norton, 1973. 194 pp.
Ammon describes the diplomatic mission of Edmund Genet, the first ambassador to America from post-Revolutionary France. Between April and December of 1793, Genet caused a series of political scandals which resulted in his recall at the insistence of the Washington Administration. Ammon recounts Genet's numerous political intrigues, and discusses the impact of his mission on the first American party system, the Democratic-Republican societies, the ideological factions of the Washington Administration, and American reaction to the French Revolution. Although this book focuses largely on Genet himself, it also touches upon the theory and practice of politics in the Federalist era.

H 193. **APTHEKER, HERBERT.** The American Revolution. New York: International, 1960. 304 pp.
In this Marxist analysis of the Revolutionary era in American history from 1763 to 1783, Aptheker rejects the notion that the Revolution was the triumph of a new aristocracy. The philosophy of the Revolution is explored in view of sectional conflicts and such institutions as chattel slavery. Also considered is the significance of class and class conflict in assessing the extent of popular support for the Revolution. Finally, Aptheker examines the social and economic effects of the American Revolution in terms of America's increasingly stratified social structure and the development of commercial capitalism.

H 194. **BAILYN, BERNARD.** The Ideological Origins of the American Revolution. Cambridge, Mass.: Harvard University Press, 1967. 335 pp.
Bailyn suggests that the English Commonwealth tradition of political opposition shaped American political ideas even more than did Locke. This tradition led Revolutionary leaders to interpret politics as a continuing struggle between power and liberty. Within this mind-set, Colonial leaders saw English attempts to restructure imperial relationships as part of the broader conspiracy to undermine liberty and impose tyranny. The colonists' "real fears and anxieties" over this conspiracy led first to the resistance movement and then to the elaboration of a new theory of political authority.

H 195. **BAILYN, BERNARD** and **JOHN B. HENCH**, eds. The Press and the American Revolution. Worcester, Mass.: American Antiquarian Society, 1980. 383 pp.
The belief that "those who controlled the printed word were the persons crucial to the formation of a revolution within the minds of Americans, as well as to the act of overt revolt" represents the unifying theme of this collection of essays. Stephen Botein's "Printers and the American Revolution" chronicles the impact of the Revolution on the "occupational identity" of his subjects. Richard Buel's contribution, "Freedom of the

Press in Revolutionary America: The Evolution of Libertarianism, 1760-1820," demonstrates that freedom of the press as we understand it today did not truly exist in America until Jefferson's presidency. The other contributions to this volume are: Robert M. Weir, "The Role of the Newspaper Press in the Southern Colonies on the Eve of the Revolution: An Interpretation"; Willi Paul Adams, "The Colonial German-Language Press and the American Revolution"; Janice Potter and Robert M. Calhoon, "The Character and Coherence of the Loyalist Press"; Paul Langford, "British Correspondence in the Colonial Press, 1763-1775: A Study in Anglo-American Misunderstanding before the Revolution"; and G. Thomas Tanselle, "Some Statistics on American Printing, 1764-1783."

H 196. BONWICK, COLIN. English Radicals and the American Revolution. Chapel Hill: University of North Carolina Press, 1977. 362 pp. Bonwick examines the reactions of English radicals to the rebellion of their Colonies in America. He distinguishes between "Old" (Commonwealth) and "New" (Artisanal) radicals. The former saw America as a model of liberty; the latter as an example of equality. Bonwick finds that although they were admirers of the new American Republic and critics of George III, the English radicals "displayed a strong sense of loyalty to the state" and believed that the principles of constitutional monarchy were still sound.

H 197. BORDEN, MORTON. Parties and Politics in the Early Republic, 1789-1815. New York: Crowell, 1967. 119 pp. Borden surveys the first twenty-five years of national politics under the Federal Constitution. He traces the debates surrounding philosophical, economic, and foreign policy issues in the 1790s and links these to the development of political parties. Despite the intense partisanship, even extremism, of the Adams years and the stresses generated by international events during Thomas Jefferson's second term and James Madison's presidency, Borden finds that politicians of both parties contributed to the development of an effective Federal government and established precedents for legitimate opposition and the orderly transfer of power. In treating major figures, such as George Washington, Alexander Hamilton, and James Madison, the author seeks to provide both objective assessment and a feeling for how contemporaries perceived these leaders.

H 198. BRUNHOUSE, ROBERT L. The Counter-Revolution in Pennsylvania 1776-1790. Harrisburg: Commonwealth of Pennsylvania, Department of Public Instruction, Pennsylvania Historical Commission, 1942. 368 pp. Brunhouse examines the replacement of Pennsylvania's radically majoritarian Constitution of 1776 with the more "balanced" Constitution of 1790. He traces the rise of a radical party in Pennsylvania during the early 1770s and 1780s, and the eventual triumph of more conservative elements. The conservatives' objections to provisions in the Constitution of 1776 for a unicameral legislature, split executive, and democratically controlled courts fueled conflict. Brunhouse views the Constitution of 1790 as a counter-revolution undertaken by conservative elites who sought to curtail or at least control the democratization of politics fostered during the Revolutionary period.

H 199. BUEL, RICHARD. Securing the Revolution: Ideology in American Politics, 1789-1815. Ithaca, N.Y.: Cornell University Press, 1972. 391 pp. Buel examines the relationship between political theory and practice in the era of the first American party system, and emphasizes the function of ideology in forming the organizational structure of the Federalist and Jeffersonian Parties. He argues that the first American party system arose not because opposing groups competed for office, but because the

leaders of the Revolution disagreed on the means of implementing the promises of the Revolution. Also discussed are fiscal policy, sectionalism,
and foreign policy. Buel concludes that ideological issues raised during
the 1790s were not resolved until the demise of the Federalist Party after
the War of 1812.

H 200. **CHAMBERS, WILLIAM N.** Political Parties in a New Nation: The American Experience, 1766-1809. New York: Oxford University Press,
1963. 231 pp.
Chambers describes the unique characteristics of party development in
America, paying particular attention to the nature of political parties
and their role in the molding of a nation. Included is a comparison
between the new American nation and nations that were emerging in the early
1960s. According to Chambers, the 1790s showed the greatest manifestation
of American political genius. He traces the political development from
the chaotic factionalism of the early years through the stable order of
the Federalist period. Chambers concludes with an examination of the
emergence of the Republican Party during the two terms of Jefferson's
presidency.

H 201. **COHEN, LESTER H.** The Revolutionary Histories: Contemporary Narratives of the American Revolution. Ithaca, N.Y.: Cornell University Press, 1980. 286 pp.
Cohen explores the philosophical, ideological, and formal characteristics
of the patriot histories which were produced to explain the Revolution.
He argues that the "Revolutionary histories" rejected the traditional
Providential philosophy of history which relied on faith in a divine plan
or guidance. Instead, the historians of the Revolution saw their story
as essentially human. Their narratives, romantic in character, chronicled
the story of a heroic people overthrowing British corruption and tyranny.
Consequently, their histories also served as ethical and political manuals
of Republicanism.

H 202. **COMMAGER, HENRY S.** The Empire of Reason: How Europe Imagined
and America Realized the Enlightenment. New York: Anchor Press,
1977. 342 pp.
Commager argues that although Europeans conceived the Enlightenment, it
was most completely realized in America. He broadly defines the Enlightenment as belief in the lawfulness of nature and God, faith in reason's
ability to understand these laws and to bring society into conformity
with them, and commitment to intellectual freedom, progress, and reform.
Commager discusses some of the major figures of the Enlightenment in Europe
and America, different visions of America and Americans, and the early
attempts to forge a nation and an enlightened political system.

H 203. **COUNTRYMAN, EDWARD.** A People in Revolution: The American Revolution and Political Society in New York, 1760-1790. Baltimore,
Md.: Johns Hopkins University Press, 1981. 388 pp.
Countryman begins with an examination of the "old order" in New York State,
highlighting the contradictions of the Colonial political system, and
the formation of a popular coalition which sought to break down that order.
Next, the author considers what he calls the "crisis" of 1774-7 in which
the new coalition and the old order fought for control. Finally, he portrays the aftermath of this political uprising, which pitted radicals
and conservatives in a struggle to gain control of the new political order.
Countryman pays particular attention to the activities of crowds and mobs
which he believes were the social manifestations of the political upheaval.

H 204. DICKERSON, OLIVER M. The Navigation Acts and the American Revo-
        lution. Philadelphia: University of Pennsylvania Press, 1951.
        344 pp.
Dickerson argues that the British Navigation Acts and traditional regulation of trade were not causes of the American Revolution. Instead,
legal and administrative innovations after 1763 sparked Colonial unrest.
Dickerson divides his book into two parts. The first, "The Cement of
Empire," examines the functioning of the British mercantile system until
1763, debates the oppressiveness of the Navigation Acts, investigates
evasions of the system, and treats the attitudes of leading Americans
toward the Acts. Part Two, "Dissolving the Cement of Empire," treats
the new system of taxation in the 1760s, the enlarged customs administration, and English opinions toward the crisis.

H 205. FAY, BERNARD. The Revolutionary Spirit in France and America:
        A Study of Moral and Intellectual Relations Between France and
        the United States at the End of the Eighteenth Century. Translated
        by Ramon Guthrie. New York: Harcourt, Brace, 1927. 613 pp.
Disillusioned by the mediocrity of their own monarchy and inspired by
the writing of Abbe Raynal, Frenchmen of the 1770s looked to America as
a "sort of moral and social ideal." Thus between 1775 and 1800, "there
reigned an impassioned intellectual union between the two countries,"
perhaps best embodied in the adulation given Franklin in France and
LaFayette in America. Fay supplies the reasons for and manifestations of
this union, and he charts the dissolution of this friendship at the end
of the century.

H 206. FONER, ERIC. Tom Paine and Revolutionary America. New York:
        Oxford University Press, 1976. 326 pp.
Foner examines the impact Tom Paine and his writings had on Revolutionary
America. The experiences and attitudes which shaped this radical political
theoretician are considered in view of the social and cultural milieu
of Philadelphia. Foner discusses the political ideology that Paine
espoused in Common Sense and other tracts, and analyzes the theoretical
contours of his Republicanism. He then examines Paine's position in the
debate over price controls and laissez-faire. Foner concludes that Paine
helped build the foundations of a republican empire in America.

H 207. GILBERT, FELIX. To the Farewell Address: Ideas of Early American
        Foreign Policy. Princeton, N.J.: Princeton University Press,
        1961. 173 pp.
Gilbert examines American foreign policy from the founding of the Republic
to George Washington's famed Farewell Address in 1797, in which he advocated isolationism from European entanglements. Gilbert focuses on both
the intellectual and political influences on American foreign policy,
and he argues that U.S. diplomacy evolved from many disparate elements
and was truly eclectic in nature. One of the main ideas behind American
isolationism was the notion—extant from the Revolution—that America
was a virtuous, regenerated society distinct from Old World "corruption"
and declension. Also at work, however, was an antipathy toward political
power: ambivalence over the development of industrial and commercial
interests; and troubling questions on the role of the military in American
society and government.

H 208. GROSS, ROBERT. The Minutemen and Their World. New York: Hill
        & Wang, 1976. 242 pp.
Gross attempts to recreate the social world of Revolutionary Concord.
Combining a detailed narrative of the Revolutionary crisis with a quantitatively based "new social history," he argues that factional, religious,
and generational conflicts racked mid-18th-century Concord due to the
growing scarcity of land. The growing hostility between the Colonies

and Great Britain intensified the strain on the inhabitants of Concord. Gross suggests that the Revolution in Concord was of a paradoxical nature; the Minutemen fought to protect an older world order from imperial and commercial encroachments, creating a new forward-looking community in the process. He concludes by tracing the transformation of Concord from the home of the Minutemen to the home of Henry David Thoreau.

H 209. HANDLIN, OSCAR and LILIAN HANDLIN. A Restless People: Americans in Rebellion, 1770-1787. New York: Doubleday, 1982. 274 pp.
The Handlins argue that America's unique "style of life . . . developed habits of risk-taking that made possible the plunge into war and independence." The loneliness of the rural frontier, the stress which characterized life in the American cities, and other distinctive features of the New World produced a desire among Americans to create a "new society." The authors conclude that the success of the Revolution could not satisfy America's habitually restless inhabitants, and that Americans' restless tendency to abandon one way of life for another is a trait which has been inherited from the Revolution.

H 210. HIGGINBOTHAM, DON. The War of American Independence: Military Attitudes, Policies, and Practice, 1763-1789. New York: Macmillan, 1971. 509 pp.
Although this work contains accounts of the major battles of the Revolutionary War, Higginbotham concentrates primarily on an analysis of American military policy and the attitudes of the revolutionaries toward the war. He also examines how 18th-century military attitudes helped precipitate the Revolutionary War, and how these same attitudes affected the war's outcome. Higginbotham believes that many of the American participants in the Revolution, especially those from Massachusetts, viewed the war as a test of the superiority of the Colonial militia over the regular, professional army of the British.

H 211. HIGGINS, W. ROBERT, ed. The Revolutionary War in the South: Power, Conflict, and Leadership. Durham, N.C.: Duke University Press, 1979. 291 pp.
Higgins divides his collection of essays into three parts. The first group of essays focuses on the context of the Revolution in the South, covering such issues as styles of leadership, race relations, and the role of Native Americans in North Carolina. The second group of articles deals with important individuals, focusing on Benjamin Lincoln, Horatio Gates, Arthur Lee, and John Laurens. The final three essays consider military aspects of the Revolution in the South, with special emphasis on British military strategy and withdrawal.

H 212. HOERDER, DIRK. Crowd Action in Revolutionary Massachusetts, 1765-1780. New York: Academic Press, 1977. 394 pp.
Hoerder argues that through the Colonial period crowd action served as a legitimate means of enforcing communal norms. The crowd action incorporated an ideology of the common good, which was subjected to increasing attack as class distinctions in the colony became more defined. As the conflict between England and the Colonies intensified, the antagonistic relationship between the elite and the lower classes changed as well. Hoerder contends that the people began to articulate a more egalitarian and democratic ideology than the established orders wished to accept.

H 213. HOFFMAN, RONALD and PETER J. ALBERT, eds. Sovereign States in an Age of Uncertainty. Charlottesville: University Press of Virginia, 1981. 261 pp.
In this volume, eight contributors offer essays on the politics of the Confederation period. An introductory essay by Jackson T. Main looks at the Confederation era in terms of state problems and accomplishments.

Stephen Patterson, Jerome Nadelhaft, and Richard Ryerson examine the development of state politics and parties in Massachusetts, South Carolina, and Pennsylvania, respectively. Edward Papenfuse analyzes the relationship between factionalism and fiscal policy in Maryland, and Edward Countryman treats the development of factions in the New York State legislature. Emory Evans depicts executive leadership in Virginia, and Merrill Jensen concludes with a discussion of the antagonisms which arose between the states.

H 214. HUMPHREY, DAVID C. From King's College to Columbia, 1746-1800. New York: Columbia University Press, 1976. 413 pp.
Humphrey shows how religious diversity and urban surroundings defined the character of Columbia College. King's College was chartered as an Anglican school, yet from the start some non-Anglican clergymen served on the governing board. After the American Revolution, the college distinguished itself from its American counterparts when the complexities of its urban setting became more defined and began to infiltrate life on campus, and when the administration allowed students to live off campus. Humphrey argues that the school and its curriculum were essentially designed to serve the economic and social elite. Consequently, his study includes chapters on educating the elite and an evaluation of education from an elitist perspective.

H 215. JENSEN, MERRILL. The New Nation: A History of the United States During the Confederation, 1781-1789. New York: Knopf, 1950. 433 pp.
This work presents the economic, financial, cultural, and political history of the era of Confederation. Jensen explores problems posed by the termination of the War for Independence: the demobilization of soldiers; the public debts; and economic dislocations. He also examines interest groups in the new nation, struggles for power within the states, and debates between Federalists and Nationalists over the proper relation of central to local authority.

H 216. KAMMEN, MICHAEL G. Season of Youth: The American Revolution and the Historical Imagination. New York: Knopf, 1978. 384 pp.
Kammen examines the role of the American Revolution as a national tradition. Included is an explanation of how personal memory changes into tradition, which is based on a study of popular historiography of the Revolution after the death of those who took part in it. Kammen traces American sentiments toward the Revolution as displayed in art, poetry, drama, and the historical novel. He argues that these sources indicate that historically Americans have viewed the Revolution as a "coming of age" which has advanced their quest for a national character.

H 217. KETCHAM, RALPH. From Colony to Country: The Revolution in American Thought, 1750-1820. New York: Macmillan, 1974. 318 pp.
This work concentrates on a multitude of influential agents to illustrate the transformation of political ideas during the Revolutionary era. Ketcham discusses Benjamin Franklin, the early state constitutions, the U.S. Constitution and the ratification debates, attempts to create a republican character, the Hamilton-Jefferson debates, race and slavery, science and religion, and the search for an American art and literature. Ketcham argues that though originally an effort was made to gain representation in England, Colonial protest spawned theories of government founded on the sovereignty of the people, and culminated in the Declaration of Independence, which united concepts of individual rights and majority rule. He examines both the problems that arose from this tenuous union and the ultimate solution—the Constitution's provisions for a strong but representative central government.

H 218. KOCH, ADRIENNE. Jefferson and Madison: The Great Collaboration. New York: Oxford University Press, 1950. 294 pp.
Koch uses the friendship of Thomas Jefferson and James Madison as the focus for this study of the two men's political philosophies. She discusses their views on religious freedom, civil liberties, education, federal authority, the nascent party system, the Alien and Sedition Acts, the French Revolution, American expansion, the national debt, the role of the Supreme Court, and the construction of Washington, D.C. The study refutes the common misconception that Jefferson and Madison were uncompromising idealists, and shows how they adapted their principles to the realities of governing their growing nation. Her reappraisal of their views also sheds new light on the American traditions of democratic theory.

H 219. KURTZ, STEPHEN G. and JAMES H. HUTSON, eds. Essays on the American Revolution. Chapel Hill: University of North Carolina Press, 1973. 320 pp.
This collection of essays on topics important to the history of the American Revolution includes entries by such scholars as Bernard Bailyn, Jack P. Greene, John Shy, and Edmund S. Morgan. The first and final essays, by Bailyn and Morgan respectively, provide general interpretations of the meaning of the American Revolution. The remaining essays discuss the underlying causes of the Revolution, the nature of its military strategy and violence, the politics of the Continental Congress, the role of religion in the ideology of the movement, and the ramifications of the war in relation to the preservation of social order.

H 220. MAIER, PAULINE. From Resistance to Revolution; Colonial Radicals and the Development of American Opposition to Britain, 1765-1776. New York: Knopf, 1972. 318 pp.
Maier traces the escalation of opposition to British authority beginning with the Stamp Act crisis. She argues that initially the "radicals" remained loyal citizens and attempted to organize "ordered" resistance. Gradually, however, the perceptions of radical leaders changed. They came to oppose not merely certain aspects of British legislation, but British authority itself. Maier concentrates on the resistance leaders and the organizations they created (e.g., Sons of Liberty and Committees of Correspondence). An examination of the relationship between these radical leaders and their popular following is included. Maier insists that the "Real Whig" tradition was crucial in forming the radicals' perceptions of British actions.

H 221. MAIN, JACKSON T. The Antifederalists: Critics of the Constitution, 1787-1788. Chapel Hill: University of North Carolina Press, 1961. 308 pp.
Main's study of the opposition to the proposed Federal Constitution during the 1780s describes the vitality of Antifederalism and suggests several causes for the coalition's defeat. The author finds the Antifederalists' strength in areas such as opposition to taxation and regulation of commerce, and in other domains where "traditional fear of centralized authority" abounded. Main concludes that lack of party organization, ineffective leadership, and failure to establish a clear program to improve the central government weakened the Antifederalist cause. Also contributing to the group's ultimate failure were isolation and sectionalism, class divisions, competition between commercial and noncommercial elements, and antagonism between debtors and creditors.

H 222. MAIN, JACKSON T. Political Parties Before the Constitution. Chapel Hill: University of North Carolina Press, 1973. 481 pp.
This study traces the development of political parties during the period between the Revolution and the creation of the Constitution. Main utilizes computer technology to detail the voting patterns in the lower houses

293

of seven state legislatures. He argues that groups of legislators who
voted together existed in all of these states and represented various
sectional, economic, and cultural interests which corresponded to voting
blocks in other states. These legislators tended to fall into one of
two polarized groups, Localists or Cosmopolitans, who differed in their
attitude toward the Constitution and other issues. Thus, their existence
underscored the cultural, economic, and political divisions in the new
nation.

H 223. MAIN, JACKSON T. The Social Structure of Revolutionary America.
Princeton, N.J.: Princeton University Press, 1965. 330 pp.
Main discusses the existence of recognizable class distinctions in Revolutionary American society. He is especially concerned with class mobility,
endeavoring to determine both the extent to which propertyless Americans
were able to obtain property in their lifetimes, and the social origins
of the existing "wealthy 'upper class.'" He concludes that although Revolutionary America lacked the class consciousness of Europe, a social ranking based on "a prestige order" did exist. Yet he also believes that
traditional factors which had historically determined social standing,
such as wealth, heredity, and property, possessed far less significance
during the Revolution.

H 224. MARTIN, JAMES K. In the Course of Human Events: An Interpretive
Exploration of the American Revolution. Arlington Heights, Ill.:
AHM, 1979. 271 pp.
Martin describes two distinguishable phases of the Revolution. First,
discussing the period from 1765 to 1775, he examines the "Conspiracy from
Above" whereby the most respected American leaders inspired the people
to revolt. He characterizes the second part of the Revolution as a "con-
vulsion from below, dating from 1775 to 1787. He discusses the colonists'
mobilization in preparation for war and tells how, with this accomplished,
the newly active American populace maintained political power until the
ratification of the Constitution.

H 225. McCOY, DREW R. The Elusive Republic: Political Economy in Jeffersonian America. Chapel Hill: University of North Carolina
Press, 1980. 268 pp.
McCoy suggests that Republican thinkers sought to fashion a system of
government which preserved classical political ideals within a commercial
economy. He develops this argument by examining the philosophies of
Franklin, Jefferson, and Madison, and by considering the debates over the
Constitution, Hamilton's policies, the Louisiana Purchase, and the War
of 1812. McCoy believes that Jeffersonian thinkers were specifically
concerned with social decay in America and aimed to prevent or postpone
this decay by means of westward expansion. They hoped that expansion
over space would prevent the development of the extreme stratification,
luxury, and dependence which they believed was destroying Europe.

H 226. MIDDLEKAUFF, ROBERT. The Glorious Cause: The American Revolution
1763-1789. New York: Oxford University Press, 1982. 697 pp.
Middlekauff offers a narrative history of the American War of Independence
and the founding of the new nation. He attends to the ways in which popular life and culture shaped, and were shaped by, events, maintaining that
the American people evidenced an intense engagement in the public issues
of the period. Middlekauff shows how traditional Protestantism defined
their concepts of freedom, equality, and the nation, and how these years
recast such notions.

H 227. MILLER, JOHN C. Crisis in Freedom: The Alien and Sedition Acts. Boston: Little, Brown, 1951. 253 pp.
This volume deals with four acts of Congress passed in 1798: the Naturalization Act; the Act Concerning Aliens; the Act Respecting Alien Enemies; and the Act for the Punishment of Certain Crimes. Miller analyzes the political, ideological, and philosophical elements which underlay these acts and the degree to which these statutes constricted freedom of speech. Also considered are the conflicts between Federalists and Jeffersonians which prompted these laws. Miller investigates the influence of John Adams, Thomas Jefferson, Alexander Hamilton, and other major figures of this period. The legal, constitutional, and political implications of restraining freedom of the press are discussed in the context of Federalist ideology.

H 228. MILLER, JOHN C. The Federalist Era, 1789-1801. New York: Harper, 1960. 304 pp.
In this study of politics and public policy during the Washington and Adams administrations, Miller describes the following topics: the Hamiltonian economic program; the conflict between Hamilton and Jefferson within Washington's cabinet; the rise of the first party system; foreign affairs; the Whiskey Rebellion and domestic unrest; the Genet Affair; and the Alien and Sedition Acts. Throughout the book the author focuses on the twin themes of "Union" and "Liberty"; he examines how early leaders sought to promote the prosperity and cohesion of the new nation, and how they sought to protect (or attack) individual civil rights.

H 229. MORGAN, EDMUND M. and HELEN M. MORGAN. The Stamp Act Crisis: Prologue to Revolution. Chapel Hill: University of North Carolina Press, 1953. 310 pp.
This work describes England's attempt to implement the Stamp Act. The authors include biographical studies and discuss general trends and issues. They suggest that the Colonies would have gone to war if the English Parliament had not repealed the act. They contend, however, that the great importance of the Stamp Act lies not in its incitement of Revolutionary organizations and leaders, but in its crystallization of political and constitutional differences between England and the Colonies, differences which in ten years led to the Revolution.

H 230. MORRIS, RICHARD B. The Peace Makers: The Great Powers and American Independence. New York: Harper & Row, 1965. 572 pp.
This history details the diplomacy which concluded the War of Independence. Morris reconstructs the negotiations between the great powers of the world and the U.S., the domestic political and economic developments of England, France, Spain, and the U.S., and the relationships between the countries and their envoys. Although concerned primarily with the experiences and accomplishments of John Adams, Benjamin Franklin, John Jay, and Henry Laurens, Morris looks at European leadership as well. He concludes with a discussion of the subsequent careers of these diplomats and their reputations after the war.

H 231. NASH, GARY B. The Urban Crucible: Social Change, Political Consciousness, and the Origins of the American Revolution. Cambridge, Mass.: Harvard University Press, 1979. 548 pp.
In a comparative study of Boston, New York, and Philadelphia during the 18th century, this work investigates the role of the city as a center of social upheaval. Nash argues that the American Revolution found a catalyst in popular collective action and the lower class' challenge to the elite's claim to power. The author focuses primarily on the urban lower class and the development of a class consciousness based on economic and social position. Nash stresses the importance of ideology for the coming Revolution, and traces the rise of poverty and the narrowing of opportunities in the Colonial city.

H 232. NYE, RUSSEL BLAINE. The Cultural Life of the New Nation, 1776-
1830. New York: Harper, 1960. 324 pp.
The exuberant nationalism of a unique country not tied to tradition by
aristocracy or established churches, and its maturing culture and thought,
are the subjects of Nye's book. He traces how scientific advances and
Enlightenment thought in America set the pattern for education, religion,
literature, and art. The book is split into two parts: the first considers "The Fame of the American Enlightenment"; the second discusses
"The Growth of the American Point of View."

H 233. PALMER, ROBERT R. The Age of the Democratic Revolution: A Political History of Europe and America, 1760-1800. 2 vols. Princeton,
N.J.: Princeton University Press, 1959. 1118 pp.
Palmer divides this survey of the revolutionary character of the 18th
century into two volumes. The first, entitled The Challenge, examines
the period from 1760-90 from an international perspective, concentrating
on the American and French Revolutions. He views these two events as
part of a larger democratic movement that altered the course of Western
civilization in the 18th century. The second volume, The Struggle, offers
an analysis of European and American political development after the democratic "challenges" of the period prior to 1790. Palmer documents the
conflict between democratic ideals and older aristocratic structures.

H 234. RAKOVE, JACK N. The Beginnings of National Politics: An Interpretive History of the Continental Congress. New York: Knopf,
1979. 484 pp.
Rakove focuses on the relationship between Congressional and local authority and the development of Federal and national viewpoints. He argues
that historians have overestimated the influence of clearly defined class
or ideologically-based political groupings. Instead, he suggests, political decisions were shaped most by immediate wartime realities. The book
has four sections: the first examines the shaping of the strategy of
opposition to Great Britain in the early 1770s; the second considers the
framing of the Articles of Confederation and the administration of the
war until 1781; the third describes the crisis years of the early 1780s;
and the fourth outlines the deterioration of Congress's authority and
the reform movement leading to the Constitutional Convention.

H 235. REZNECK, SAMUEL. Unrecognized Patriots: The Jews in the American
Revolution. Westport, Conn.: Greenwood Press, 1975. 299 pp.
As described by Rezneck, the American Revolution was a pivotal event in
American Jewish life. The author finds that the small Jewish community
concentrated in seaboard cities identified, for the most part, with the
patriots' cause, seeing in the philosophy of natural rights a promise
of emancipation and opportunity. Jews contributed to the war effort both
militarily and economically, and, by doing so, involved themselves in
political life to a much greater degree than had previously been the case.
America accepted their service, allowing them to participate in public
affairs to an extent hardly typical in the Western world. Jews continued
in this new-found public role in the post-Revolutionary years, and thus
raised the perennial issue of Jewish identity versus assimilation.

H 236. RISJORD, NORMAN K. Chesapeake Politics, 1781-1800. New York:
Columbia University Press, 1978. 715 pp.
Risjord discusses the political development of Maryland, Virginia, and
North Carolina during the Confederation and early national periods. He
investigates the conflict between Federalists and Anti-federalists, as
well as the emergence of the first party systems and the ultimate victory
of Republicans over Federalists. Risjord treats such specific variables
as geography, ethnicity, race, and ideology in a qualitative manner, and
also brings quantitative data to bear on the question of party formation.

On the basis of legislative voting patterns and election returns, Risjord concludes that a mature political party system existed between 1793 and 1800 in the Chesapeake Bay area, and that the Federalists became a noninfluential minority thereafter.

H 237. ROBINSON, DONALD L. Slavery in the Structure of American Politics, 1765-1820. New York: Harcourt Brace Jovanovich, 1971. 564 pp.
Robinson records and evaluates the founding fathers' treatment of the institution of slavery, and discusses its impact on the political foundation of the U.S. Included is a history of the development of slavery from its first establishment in British America through the early Presidential administrations. Robinson examines attempts to end the importation of slaves, and the effect of slavery on the Northwest Ordinance, the Missouri Compromise, and Jay's Treaty.

H 238. ROSSITER, CLINTON. Seedtime of the Republic: The Origin of the American Tradition of Political Liberty. New York: Harcourt, Brace, 1953. 558 pp.
Three major themes--circumstance, men, and heritage--underlie this study of American thought during the 18th century. Rossiter examines six representative Colonial men: Thomas Hooker, Roger Williams, John Wise, Jonathan Mayhew, Richard Bland, and Benjamin Franklin. Analyzing the political theory of the Revolution, Rossiter contends that though this Revolutionary creed failed to produce a universal thinker or a definitive book, it nevertheless formed the basis of action for thousands of Americans. This creed stated that the finest form of government incorporated popular, limited, separated, balanced, republican, constitutional, representative, and virtuous elements.

H 239. ROYSTER, CHARLES. A Revolutionary People at War: The Continental Army and American Character, 1775-1783. Chapel Hill: University of North Carolina Press, 1979. 452 pp.
Royster examines the character of those who fought for American independence. Such a study is significant, he says, because "the national character of the revolutionaries formed one of the principal bases of their wartime allegiance." Royster pays particular attention to the strong religious sentiment which the Continental Army used to justify its resistance to England, and to the way in which morale was maintained during this eight-year struggle. The importance of the Valley Forge winter, and the creation of a "self-conscious professionalism" under Steuben, are also emphasized.

H 240. RYERSON, RICHARD. The Revolution Is Now Begun: The Radical Committees of Philadelphia, 1765-1776. Philadelphia: University of Pennsylvania Press, 1978. 305 pp.
Ryerson investigates Philadelphia's Revolutionary institutions, specifically their mode of operation, their personnel, and their method of mobilizing the population. He suggests that these Revolutionary committees, along with increased participation and democratization, prepared Pennsylvania for dramatic social and political transformation after 1776. Ryerson suggests that the Revolution created a modern democratic political life in Philadelphia, based on parties and widespread mobilization. The Revolution served to alter the social roots of political power and effectively institutionalized the people as a locus of political authority.

H 241. SCHLESINGER, ARTHUR MEIER. The Colonial Merchants and American Revolution, 1763-1776. New York: Columbia University Press, 1917. 647 pp.
Schlesinger attributes the political behavior of Colonial merchants during the Revolutionary era directly to their economic interests. The increased Parliamentary restrictions on trade during the 1760s alarmed the merchants.

Seeking to restore the pre-1764 commercial order, Colonial merchants concluded non-intercourse agreements and relied on the radicals of the Revolution to enforce these compacts on all commercial interests. Finally, the radicals, in pursuit of wider goals, overwhelmed the merchants. Although the merchants again sought to use popular sentiment in 1773-4 to defeat the threat of the East India Company monopoly, their waning influence rendered the attempt ineffectual.

H 242. SHAW, PETER. American Patriots and the Rituals of Revolution.
Cambridge, Mass.: Harvard University Press, 1981. 279 pp.
Shaw combines psychological and anthropological analyses in this interpretation of the "ritual language" of the American Revolution. His book is divided into three sections. The first discusses the Patriot crowds of the 1760s, Thomas Hutchinson, and popular politics and symbolism in London. The second section analyzes James Otis, John Adams, Joseph Hawley, and Josiah Quincy, especially in terms of their relationships with Hutchinson. The last section offers a reading of the festival and ritual traditions which American patriots drew upon during the Revolution and suggests ways in which they altered the rituals by politicizing them.

H 243. SMITH, PAGE. A New Age Now Begins; A People's History of the American Revolution. 2 vols. New York: McGraw-Hill, 1976. 1899 pp.
These two volumes provide an account of the Revolutionary era from its origins in Colonial thought to its aftermath. Smith emphasizes the creation of a uniquely American character that gave rise to the Revolutionary spirit. Smith emphasizes the British interests in the conflict as well as those of the Colonies. He weaves together military and political events to show how this period of history influenced and united the American people.

H 244. SYDNOR, CHARLES S. Gentlemen Freeholders: Political Practices in Washington's Virginia. Chapel Hill: University of North Carolina Press, 1952. 160 pp.
Sydnor presents a study of political practices in 18th-century Virginia. He discusses the institutions of government, techniques of electioneering, the electorate, and the relationship of voters to candidates. He also studies the gentry of Virginia which produced Washington, Jefferson, Madison, and Monroe. Sydnor argues that the political system of 18th-century Virginia combined aristocratic and democratic elements and suggests that this system proved successful in choosing its leaders.

H 245. SZATMARY, DAVID P. Shays' Rebellion: The Making of an American Insurrection. Amherst: University of Massachusetts Press, 1980. 184 pp.
Szatmary examines Shays' Rebellion in the context of the capitalist transformation of Massachusetts society. He argues that the insurrection grew out of conflict between an expanding commercial sector (and burgeoning commercial elites) and a more traditional subsistence culture. He documents the ways in which the economic crisis of the 1780s led to increased indebtedness, which helped to instigate the uprising. The stages of the uprising and the ideology that informed its suppression are considered. Finally, Szatmary discusses how the social turmoil of the 1780s strengthened the movement for a new constitution.

H 246. THACH, CHARLES C. The Creation of the Presidency, 1775-1789.
Baltimore, Md.: Johns Hopkins University Press, 1923. 182 pp.
Thach discusses the shift of public opinion from a widespread fear of strong government to an overwhelming support for a powerful executive. In tracing this development in the years 1775-1789, the author provides a synthesis of the thought of America's earliest leaders on the proper role of the executive. He analyzes the chief political events of the

period, the Revolution itself, and considers the influence of the state constitutions and the British system on plans for the Federal government. Thach concludes with a discussion of the Constitutional Convention and the subsequent Removal Debate.

H 247. TUCKER, ROBERT W. and DAVID C. HENDRICKSON. The Fall of the First British Empire: Origins of the War of American Independence. Baltimore, Md.: Johns Hopkins University Press, 1982. 450 pp.
The authors of this work offer a reconsideration of the origins of the American Revolution, arguing that the Revolution emerged not out of a change in perspective in London, but out of new attitudes and capacities in the Colonies. The authors combine analysis of imperial problems such as imperial defense, the Trade and Navigation acts, and Colonial autonomy, with a history of the development of imperial politics in the 1760s and 1770s. They stress constitutional conflicts and the growth of irreconcilable differences between various partisan views.

H 248. VAN ALSTYNE, RICHARD W. Empire and Independence: The International History of the American Revolution. New York: Wiley, 1965. 255 pp.
Van Alstyne discusses the diplomatic, military, and political history of England, France, and the American Colonies in an attempt to write an international history of the era of the American Revolution. Beginning with a discussion of pre-Revolutionary conflicts of interests, Van Alstyne suggests that the debates of the 1780s, at least on the Colonial side, focused less on Constitutional issues and more on Americans' perception that they no longer needed British protection. He traces the growing conflict and eventual war, the failed attempts at reconciliation, and the European political context.

H 249. WALSH, RICHARD. Charleston's Sons of Liberty: A Study of the Artisans, 1763-1789. Columbia: University of South Carolina Press, 1959. 166 pp.
Walsh describes the artisans' central importance to the Revolution in South Carolina, disagreeing with historians who see Charleston's artisans as a politically dependent and economically insignificant group. He discusses the socio-economic importance of the artisans and argues that they constituted a radical element during the Revolutionary era. Walsh maintains that the Revolutionary period marked the high point of the artisans' achievement and power. Chapters cover the 1760s, 1770s, the British occupation, and the conclusion of the Revolution in the 1780s.

H 250. WHITE, LEONARD D. The Federalists: A Study in Administrative History. New York: Macmillan, 1948. 538 pp.
This history of bureaucracy in the Federal government covers the presidencies of Washington and Adams. White presents the problems of central management in the President's office and on the departmental and bureaucratic levels. Among other subjects, this work investigates the acquisition and expenditure of money, procurement of supplies, personnel recruitment, departmental organization, interdepartmental relations and conflicts, the relations of the various departments and the Executive branch to Congress, and the development of administrative law.

H 251. WHITE, MORTON. The Philosophy of the American Revolution. New York: Oxford University Press, 1978. 299 pp.
In his philosophical and historical analysis of some of the leading ideas of the Revolutionary generation, White discusses Revolutionary epistemology, metaphysics, theology, and ethics. He analyzes their notions of self-evident truths, the essence of man, and divinely ordained ends, rights, and duties, carefully delineating the ambiguities and contradictions in the philosophy of the American Revolution. In addition, White provides

a historical context for these ideas by examining those thinkers who most influenced the revolutionaries, and by describing the manner in which political practices embodied their philosophical notions.

H 252. WILLS, GARRY. Explaining America: The Federalist. New York: Doubleday, 1981. 270 pp.
In this work, the second in a series entitled America's Political Enlightenment, Wills attempts to explain the genesis and the text of The Federalist Papers which are, he notes, a sort of explanation of America. He describes these documents, without which the Constitution might not have been ratified, as a "spectacle of rhetorical and analytic overkill." In the first two parts of his book, Wills examines first Madison's, then Hamilton's involvement in the drafting of the Constitution and The Federalist Papers. Both men, he notes, were greatly influenced by Hume and were convinced of the "need for a stronger central government." The third author, Jay, is mentioned only briefly. The last two sections deal with Papers No. 51 (checks and balances) and No. 10 (representation)—papers which, as Wills notes, contradict one another; if tyrannical majorities are impossible, as argued in No. 10, why is the separation of powers urged in No. 51 necessary?

H 253. WILLS, GARRY. Inventing America: Jefferson's Declaration of Independence. New York: Doubleday, 1978. 398 pp.
The first volume of a series entitled America's Political Enlightenment, Wills's interpretation elucidates three distinct 'Declarations.' The first is Jefferson's Declaration which Wills describes as an 18th-century philosophical document rooted in the Scottish Enlightenment. The second is the Congressional Declaration, a political document designed for the audience of the contemporary 18th-century world. The third view characterizes the Declaration as a "National Symbol," a retroactive and romantic notion of the Declaration as a founding act. Wills argues that the confusion over the Declaration's historical context has led Americans to romanticize their place in the world and idealize the purity of their purposes.

H 254. WOOD, GORDON S. The Creation of the American Republic 1776-1787. Chapel Hill: University of North Carolina Press, 1969. 653 pp.
In his examination of American political thought during the years 1776-87, Wood argues that Americans borrowed the most radical components of British Whig political theory to create a uniquely American conception of the role of government in society. These ideas, based on a set of common assumptions about society, history, and politics, moved political discussion from an essentially classical world into one that was recognizably modern. This new political theory laid the foundations for the American Constitution. Wood asserts that the Revolutionary period greatly influenced the formation of subsequent American political ideas.

H 255. YOUNG, ALFRED F. The Democratic-Republicans of New York: The Origins, 1763-1797. Chapel Hill: University of North Carolina Press, 1967. 636 pp.
Young addresses four questions about the Democratic-Republicans: who they were; what issues caused their mobilization; how they were organized; and what their philosophy entailed. He suggests that though Antifederalists and Republicans shared certain similarities, the Republicans emerged in response to the issues of the 1790s: the Hamiltonian programs, foreign affairs, and the Federalist response to the increasingly democratized character of politics. While concentrating on the Washington administration, Young provides background on the politics of Revolutionary New York as well.

H 256. YOUNG, ALFRED F., ed. The American Revolution: Explorations in the History of American Radicalism. DeKalb: Northern Illinois University Press, 1976. 481 pp.

Each essay in this volume explores themes of radicalism during the Revolutionary era. The authors look at the relation between classes, arguing that a complete understanding of society requires an examination of the beliefs and behavior of the classes at the bottom of the Colonial social structure. The formation of the consciousness of radicals and artisans, the relation between tenants and landlords, the role of religion in the development of revolutionary consciousness, and the consequences of the Revolution for blacks and women constitute major themes in this work. The authors maintain that a social revolution, characterized by a move toward a more egalitarian and democratic ideology, accompanied the political revolution of the 1770s.

IV. NINETEENTH CENTURY

H 257. ABERNETHY, THOMAS PERKINS. The Burr Conspiracy. New York: Oxford University Press, 1954. 301 pp.

Using a considerable body of unexploited primary sources, Abernethy traces Aaron Burr's legendary conspiracy of 1804-1806 to separate the Western territories of the U.S. from its Eastern half and create an independent nation. Abernethy sifts through the many myths surrounding the conspiracy to distinguish fact from hearsay. He maintains that three main factors made the conspiracy possible. First, he cites the lack of a strong nationalist sentiment in the early days of the Republic, especially in the West. Burr's plan, in this sense, was but the most significant of several such plots. Second, the explosive atmosphere of the Western region--the status of which was still ambiguous--was ripe for separatist callings. Westerners were highly resentful of the preferred status of Eastern commercial interests in the national economy. Finally, and most significantly, was Burr's own strong personal ambition for power--which remained unsatisfied within the confines of the American political system.

H 258. ATHERTON, LEWIS. Main Street on the Middle Border. Bloomington: Indiana University Press, 1954. 423 pp.

In looking at small town life in Ohio, Indiana, Illinois, Missouri, Michigan, Minnesota, Wisconsin, Iowa, and the eastern farming fringe of Kansas, Nebraska, and the Dakotas since the Civil War, Atherton studies the effect of industrialization on hundreds of communities, and discusses changing value systems and lifestyles and other problems faced by small towns. Maintaining that the prospects are not entirely gloomy for the survival of small villages, he examines the bonds of community they offer their inhabitants. He notes, for example, that the population of "country towns" has increased since 1900, and that "farm loyalty" is as strong as ever in smaller villages.

H 259. BAKER, JEAN H. Affairs of Party: The Political Culture of Northern Democrats in the Mid-Nineteenth Century. Ithaca, N.Y.: Cornell University Press, 1983. 368 pp.

Baker presents a study of the Democratic Party between 1850 and 1870. She analyzes the party in terms of political culture and surmises that the Democrats of the mid-19th century were influenced strongly by traditions of American Republicanism, economic liberalism, and the democratic ideas of 18th-century English opposition. Baker pays particular attention to the racism of Northern Democrats, describing it as a major tenet of their ideology, yet concludes that they nevertheless generally supported the Union's Civil War effort, even after emancipation became a war objective.

H 260. **BANNER, JAMES M.** To the Hartford Convention: The Federalists and the Origins of Party Politics in Massachusetts, 1789-1815. New York: Knopf, 1969. 378 pp.

This work examines the Federalist Party in Massachusetts in terms of ideology, organization, and international developments, from its origins to the Hartford Convention. Banner suggests that much of the Federalists' ideology was carried over from the neo-Whig agitators of the Revolutionary era; and he denies that the Federalism of Massachusetts was an elitist, archaic form of regionalism. The influences of Jeffersonian thought, the Embargo Acts, the War of 1812, and the development of sectionalism within the Federalist Party are treated.

H 261. **BANNING, LANCE.** The Jeffersonian Persuasion: Evolution of a Party Ideology. Ithaca, N.Y.: Cornell University Press, 1978. 307 pp.

Arguing that it has been a topic slighted by historians, Banning presents a survey of the ideology of the Jeffersonian Republicans, from its origins as a reaction to the perceived threat of Federalist "monarchism," to the "Revolution of 1800," when Jefferson came to power. Banning claims that it is valid to speak of a more or less coherent party ideology, even at a time when parties themselves were eschewed as dangerous manifestations of "factionalism." He further argues that central to Jeffersonian ideology was the genuine fear that the Federalists posed a very real danger to the existence of the young Republic. Banning maintains that the Jeffersonian Republicans were influenced to a large degree by the British heritage, and that there was a greater transatlantic exchange of ideas than has hitherto been recognized.

H 262. **BEISNER, ROBERT L.** Twelve Against Empire: The Anti-Imperialists, 1898-1900. New York: McGraw-Hill, 1968. 310 pp.

Beisner presents a collective biography of twelve spokesmen, inside and outside the government, who opposed the Spanish-American War and the "empire" acquired by the U.S. as a result of the War. Six of the spokesmen are Republicans and six are Mugwumps; among them, William James, E. L. Godkin, Charles Eliot Norton, Andrew Carnegie, and Benjamin Harrison. Beisner's purpose is to discern the emotional and intellectual basis of the anti-imperialist movement. He argues that these men were traditionalists. They believed that the acquisition by the U.S. of Colonial possessions, and its imposition of imperial rule upon unwilling subjects, was a betrayal of its most cherished principles. This both endangered democracy at home and exposed the U.S. to dangerous complications abroad.

H 263. **BENSON, LEE.** The Concept of Jacksonian Democracy: New York as a Test Case. Princeton, N.J.: Princeton University Press, 1961. 351 pp.

Benson's study of the differing characteristics of the Democratic and Whig Parties in New York is based on statistical analysis of voting behavior during the 1830s and 1840s. Benson examines the social characteristics of party leadership; the parties' differing concepts of political economy; the images they projected in their platforms; and religions, class, and ethnic characteristics of their supporters. He argues that ethnicity and religion, rather than economic and class factors, governed voting behavior, and he contends that the egalitarian impulse associated with the Democratic Party of Jackson actually developed among anti-Jackson groups in New York.

H 264. BENSON, LEE. Merchants, Farmers, & Railroads: Railroad Regulation and New York Politics, 1850-1887. Cambridge, Mass.: Harvard University Press, 1955. 310 pp.
The rift between the urban-industrial East and the rural-agrarian West between 1850 and 1890 is the subject of Benson's study. The traditional explanation for this feud was the movement, apparently inspired by Western agrarian interests, to bring the railroads under state and Federal control. Benson contends, however, that agrarian protests were less important than the commercial interests, centered in New York City, in forcing the adoption of the Interstate Commerce Act of 1887. The commercial policies of New York and other states led to the proliferation of railroad development beyond competitively feasible limits. These policies resulted in rate wars which both lowered transport costs in the West, and averted destructive wars for markets in the East. This led, according to Benson, to the Eastern fight against the railroads which was to result, by 1887, in Federal regulation.

H 265. BENTLEY, GEORGE R. A History of the Freedmen's Bureau. Philadelphia: University of Pennsylvania Press, 1955. 298 pp.
Bentley presents a survey of the famed Bureau of Refugees, Freedmen, and Abandoned Lands—or the Freedman's Bureau—of the Reconstruction period, from its inception to its final dissolution in 1872. He details the functioning of the Bureau at the state and local levels, discussing in particular the courts and legal aspects, education, and political organization. He describes the debates—especially between Andrew Johnson and Congress— and interacting forces in Washington which affected the Bureau, devoting special attention throughout to Oliver O. Howard, who headed the Bureau. Bentley argues that while the Bureau provided essential services, relief, and protection for the erstwhile slave population in the immediate aftermath of the war, its ultimate effect was detrimental, for it intensified the racial prejudice of the Southern people, and left Southern blacks in a particularly compromising position once Federal protection was removed and "Redemption" had taken place.

H 266. BERWANGER, EUGENE. The Frontier Against Slavery: Western Anti-Negro Prejudice and the Slavery Extension Controversy. Urbana: University of Illinois Press, 1967. 176 pp.
In examining state constitutional debates, legislative laws and reports, newspaper correspondence and editorials, and manuscript collections, Berwanger asserts that prejudice against the Negro was a prime factor in the development of anti-slavery feeling in the Western U.S. before the Civil War. By looking at various sections of the American West, Berwanger traces the spread of anti-Negro sentiments from the old Northwest to the frontier regions. Negro prejudice was predicated upon the fear of being inundated by freed slaves from the South. Hence, Berwanger insists, most Westerners did not support the abolition of slavery, though they were opposed to its expansion into the territories.

H 267. BILLINGTON, RAY. The Protestant Crusade, 1800-1860: A Study of the Origins of American Nativism. New York: Macmillan, 1938. 514 pp.
Billington examines the development of anti-Catholic and anti-foreign attitudes as they rose to national prominence during the first half of the 19th century, leading eventually to the nativist outbursts of the 1850s and the rise of the Know-Nothing Party. Billington focuses on the activities of the nativists, rather than on the Catholic reaction—which, he contends, only further intensified the nativists' anti-Catholicism. Billington maintains that Nativism had become so pervasive that only the sectional divisions over slavery during the 1850s and the Civil War in the 1860s were large enough to overshadow Nativism in general and the Know-Nothings in particular.

H 268. BOGUE, ALLAN G. The Earnest Men: Republicans of the Civil War Senate. Ithaca, N.Y.: Cornell University Press, 1981. 369 pp. Arguing that previous writers on Civil War politics have used the terms "Radical" and "Conservative" with a great deal of imprecision, Bogue employs legislative roll-call analysis in order to examine the nature of radicalism in the U.S. Senate during the Civil War. He describes the extent to which Federal lawmakers adapted to the changing issues and patterns of alignment throughout the conflict. After discussing individual Senators, Bogue seeks to measure the effect of their particular characteristics on their voting behavior. Bogue argues that there was no distinct cleavage in Republican ranks, but rather there was a continuum of views. Nevertheless, he maintains that there was a great deal of conflict among Republican Senators over the issues surrounding the war. Hence, the goal of winning the war was often not enough to create legislative consensus. Bogue suggests that the party's commanding majority was a major factor in the development of political factions in the Republican Party.

H 269. BROUSSARD, JAMES H. The Southern Federalists, 1800-1816. Baton Rouge: Louisiana State University Press, 1978. 438 pp. Broussard combines chronological treatment of the Federalists' changing political fortunes in the Carolinas, Georgia, and Virginia, with topical treatment of their political positions, party organizations, and the social, economic, and demographic situation of Federalist voters. He suggests that the Federalists' fortunes can be tied to fear of France and the French Revolution. When fear of France was widespread, the Federalist Party gained support; when the threat seemed less important, support declined. The collapse of the Federalists in the South, Broussard speculates, was due more to the fall of Napoleon than to the end of the war with England. Broussard combines research in literary sources with quantitative data.

H 270. BROWN, ROGER. The Republic in Peril: 1812. New York: Columbia University Press, 1964. 238 pp. Brown suggests that concern over the success of the Republican Experiment was the primary motivation for the U.S.'s 1812 declaration of war against Britain. The author, although recognizing that impressment had been a long-standing irritation, does not cite it as a primary factor in the decision to go to war. Most Americans, according to Brown, regretted the drift to war, but saw it as inevitable. The author dismantles the legend of the War Hawks, maintaining that even such territorial ambitions as the annexation of Canada, often cited as a motivating factor, were in reality matters of war strategy, not war aims. Furthermore, through the examination of Congressional correspondence, Brown found little evidence of an economic rationale for the war; rather, the author concludes, national honor played the crucial role.

H 271. CAMPBELL, CHARLES S. The Transformation of American Foreign Relations, 1865-1900. New York: Harper & Row, 1976. 393 pp. Campbell offers a broad survey of the diplomacy and foreign policy of the U.S. from the Civil War to 1900, a period which witnessed the fruition of the nation as an international power. The two dominant themes are the steady melioration of Anglo-American relations, and the American quest for overseas territory. Campbell also examines such topics as America's strained relations with Latin America, the causes of the Spanish-American War, and the steady expansion of the U.S. as both a commercial and political-military power.

H 272. CATTON, BRUCE. This Hallowed Ground: The Story of the Union
        Side of the Civil War. Garden City, N.Y.: Doubleday, 1956.
        437 pp.
Catton offers a narrative account of the military aspects of the Civil
War, concentrating on the Union side. He describes the major battles,
the personalities involved, and the strategies employed, from the Fort
Sumter crisis to Lee's surrender at Appomattox. He analyzes the Union's
initial failures and its inability to create an efficient and bold group
of commanders. Catton details the rise of Ulysses S. Grant to Commander
of the Union Army and his eventual successes. Yet Catton emphasizes
throughout that it was the "rank and file" who endured the hardships of
war, and who were most responsible for the successful conclusion of the
war by the North, and hence for the preservation of the Union.

H 273. CHANNING, STEVEN. Crisis of Fear: Secession in South Carolina.
        New York: Simon & Schuster, 1970. 315 pp.
By studying contemporary opinion as expressed in primary sources, Channing
evokes the mood of South Carolina during the year preceding its secession
from the Union in December 1860. He also presents the political history
of events in this crucial Southern state which led to secession. From
John Brown's raid on Harper's Ferry onward, the psychic fears of white
South Carolinians, especially of their leadership class, became increasingly intense. Channing argues that after Lincoln's election in 1860,
the fears of a major abolition movement and of a general emancipation,
became manifest in the movement to secede from the Union.

H 274. COLES, HARRY L. The War of 1812. Chicago: University of Chicago
        Press, 1965. 298 pp.
Coles concentrates on military action in the War of 1812, on both land
and sea. The study encompasses American, British, and Canadian war perspectives, and places the war within the context of the general war in
Europe, which affected the North American war's appearance and sudden
demise. To Coles, the War of 1812 is perhaps the most enigmatic war
America has fought: it is difficult to say why it was fought and by whom
it was won. He contends that it was also a "sobering" war, because not
only did the defeats and mistakes have a sobering effect on its generation,
but they led to administrative reorganization of the Federal war effort.
Its relevance to 20th-century history is also discussed: the small scale
of the war and the uncertainties of the conclusions reveal the ambiguities of international conflict more sharply than later battles of the
U.S. would do, and hence is of value to present day political studies.

H 275. COX, LaWANDA and JOHN H. COX. Politics, Principle, and Prejudice,
        1865-1866: Dilemma of Reconstruction America. Glencoe, Ill.:
        Free Press, 1963. 294 pp.
This work analyzes the politics of early Reconstruction, building up to
and culminating in the break between Congress and President Andrew Johnson
in 1866. The Coxes argue that the radical Republicans did not represent
a unity of economic interests, but were rather a political coalition,
sincere in its espousal of justice to the freedmen, which found itself
in danger of being eliminated as an effective political force during the
first year of Reconstruction. According to the Coxes, two factors contributed to the break between Johnson and the Republican Party in 1866.
The first factor was Johnson's lack of commitment to the freedmen's civil
rights. The second and more important factor was Johnson's attempt to
jettison the old Republican coalition and build a new conservative Union
Party of conservative Republicans, Southern yeomen, Northern Democrats,
and Western farmers.

H 276. CRAVEN, AVERY O. The Coming of the Civil War. New York:
        Scribner, 1942. 491 pp.
Craven argues that the American Civil War was not an irrepressible or
inevitable conflict, but rather resulted from the work of politicians
and others, mostly from the North, who agitated public opinion over the
evils of Southern society. He focuses primarily on the Southern perspective, arguing that the causes of the war were Northern attacks on the
South's institution of slavery, the raising of the moral argument by abolitionists and other extremists, and the gratuitous and unnecessary injection
of slavery into the political sphere. In the face of such attacks the
South rose to defend its way of life. Craven maintains that while there
were obvious differences between the Northern and Southern ways of life,
these differences were not great enough to cause civil war between them.
Hence, the real tragedy of the war, according to Craven, was that it could
have been avoided.

H 277. CRAVEN, AVERY O. The Growth of Southern Nationalism, 1848-1861.
        Baton Rouge: Louisiana State University Press, 1953. 433 pp.
In this volume of A History of the South, Craven considers the South's
role in the events which culminated in the Civil War. The author does
not discuss precise causes of the Civil War, but rather attempts to state
his general impression of how events escalated to the point where they
could no longer be handled by the democratic process. Craven argues that
slavery came to symbolize values in both the Northern and Southern social-
economic structures which neither would compromise. Furthermore, Craven
asserts that with the election of Lincoln, the South was reduced to the
status of a permanent minority—subject to the will of a numerically
stronger North, whose purpose was the alteration of their social structure.
Consequently, Southerners accepted the Civil War as necessary to preserve
their property, self-respect, and rights. Craven includes an extensive
bibliographic essay at the conclusion of this work.

H 278. CUNLIFFE, MARCUS. The Nation Takes Shape, 1789-1837. Chicago:
        University of Chicago Press, 1959. 222 pp.
Cunliffe presents a general survey of the U.S. from the founding of the
Republic to the end of Andrew Jackson's presidency. He argues that there
were many conflicting tendencies during the early days of the nation over
what America was to be. He examines the conflicts between city and countryside, nationalism and regionalism, and conservatism and experimentalism.
Hence, Cunliffe maintains that the dominant themes and characteristics
of American society and politics were not static and permanent, but
developed out of these contending forces and were ever evolving throughout
this period. Cunliffe also argues that a truly national character
developed out of the conflicts and struggles of these early years.

H 279. CUNNINGHAM, NOBLE E. The Jeffersonian Republicans in Power:
        Party Operations, 1801-1809. Chapel Hill: University of North
        Carolina Press, 1963. 318 pp.
Cunningham examines the practical operations of the Jeffersonian-Republican
Party under the administration of Thomas Jefferson. He deals with
Jefferson both as president and as the leader of an inchoate political
apparatus. Cunningham examines the role and structure of political parties,
party machinery, campaign methods, patronage, relations with the press,
and the variety of Jeffersonian parties throughout the states. Cunningham
argues that while during this period the American political system was
still in its formative stage of development, it was here that the main
characteristics of the modern political system originated. He cites the
implementation of coherent programs of public policy, and the organization
and discipline necessary to insure party succession and power in particular.

H 280. CUNNINGHAM, NOBLE E. The Process of Government Under Jefferson.
     Princeton, N.J.: Princeton University Press, 1978. 357 pp.
Cunningham examines the functioning of government under Thomas Jefferson.
He focuses on the processes by which decisions were made and implemented,
rather than on their content. Cunningham describes the workings of the
Executive branch as well as that of Congress, yet eschews pure administrative history by examining the influences and pressures which affected
how policy was made. He argues that contrary to traditional notions
Jefferson was not uninvolved in the government's day-to-day operations,
but rather was a skilled and effective manipulator of the Federal bureaucracy. Special attention is devoted to Jefferson's efforts to influence
Congress, especially in its important committees.

H 281. DANGERFIELD, GEORGE. The Awakening of American Nationalism, 1815-
     1828. New York: Harper & Row, 1965. 331 pp.
Dangerfield examines the origins and development of American nationalism
during the early 19th century. He argues that the central controversies
of this period can be classified under two broad categories: economic
nationalism and democratic nationalism. He further claims that there
were three factors of primary importance in the growth of nationalist
sentiment. First was the power of Jeffersonian ideals in spite of the
disintegration of the Jeffersonian system. Second was the increased activity on the part of the Federal government, as evidenced by the War of
1812. And third was the expansion of the economy and the increase of
economic opportunities.

H 282. DANGERFIELD, GEORGE. The Era of Good Feelings. New York:
     Harcourt, Brace, 1952. 525 pp.
Dangerfield examines the last years of the Monroe Administration and that
of John Quincy Adams as a critical transition period from Jeffersonian
to Jacksonian Democracy. He argues that deep political and social divisions were extant during this "era of good feelings." Dangerfield also
discusses the sectional divisions which underlay the boisterous nationalism
of the period, including the first outbreak of the slavery issue and the
conflict between agrarian debtors and Eastern bankers. These conflicts
were latent during the administrations of Monroe and Adams, but exploded
on to the national scene with the ascendency of Andrew Jackson and the
policies which his administration implemented.

H 283. DANHOF, CLARENCE H. Change in Agriculture: The Northern United
     States, 1820-1870. Cambridge, Mass.: Harvard University Press,
     1969. 322 pp.
Danhof analyzes the rapid growth that took place in the productivity of
Northern agriculture after 1820. The author concentrates on the entrepreneurial role of a small group of farmers, and shows how economic developments outside the agricultural sector--urban-demographic change, expansion
of transportation, growth of external markets--stimulated these leading
groups to seek means of expanding production. Although the great majority
of the nation's farmers remained cautious and noncommercial, they gradually were converted to the new techniques of farming. Western migration
and European immigration helped weaken the inhibitions of the conservative
majority. Pursuit of personal advancement translated into a commercial
approach to farming. The Civil War accelerated the mechanization of farming, and by 1870 a new commercial agriculture system was in place.

H 284. DEARING, MARY R. Veterans in Politics: The Story of the G.A.R.
     Baton Rouge: Louisiana State University Press, 1952. 523 pp.
Dearing presents a narrative account of the efforts of the Grand Army
of the Republic--the Northern Civil War Veteran's association--to influence
national politics in the years following the war. The author details
their efforts to gain favors, especially pensions, from the Federal govern-

ment. Her study also describes the techniques used by the Republican
Party to appeal to this interest group. Manuscripts, newspapers, and
extensive G.A.R. records were utilized in the author's research.

H 285. DEGLER, CARL N. The Other South: Southern Dissenters in the
Nineteenth Century. New York: Harper & Row, 1974. 392 pp.
This work examines white Southerners who contested the values and ethos
of the 19th-century South. Degler traces the threads of a Southern liber-
tarian, rationalist, patriotic, and Christian tradition through the social
struggles of the 19th century. The book is divided into three general
sections, each detailing an aspect of Southern dissent. The first deals
with Southerners who opposed slavery on behalf of both blacks and whites.
The second focuses on those Southerners who opposed secession and remained
loyal, at least in sentiment, to the Union. In the final section, Degler
examines those Southerners who became Republicans during Reconstruction,
rejected the Democratic party in the 1880s, and participated in the Populist revolt of the 1890s.

H 286. DEW, CHARLES. Ironmaker to the Confederacy: Joseph R. Anderson
and the Tredegar Iron Works. New Haven, Conn.: Yale University
Press, 1966. 345 pp.
Dew examines one aspect of the industrial history of the Confederate South
in his study of the Tredegar Iron Company of Virginia, under the proprie-
torship of Joseph Anderson, from 1859 to 1867. Dew utilizes the hitherto
unexploited company records for the basis of the work, and examines the
attitudes of Southern businessmen and the problems facing Southern industry
before, during, and after the war. While it has long been axiomatic that
the lack of industry was a major cause for the Confederate defeat, Dew
argues that the inadequate supply of raw materials, rather than the lack
of industrial equipment, was the crucial difficulty faced by Confederate
war planners.

H 287. DILLON, MERTON. The Abolitionists: The Growth of a Dissenting
Minority. DeKalb: Northern Illinois University Press, 1974.
298 pp.
This work examines the development of Abolitionism in antebellum America
and places Abolitionism in the context of other reform movements such
as temperance and prison reform. The roles of such leading Abolitionist
figures as Wendell Phillips and William Lloyd Garrison are assessed. The
transformation of Abolitionism from a small, apolitical, religiously oriented movement to an antislavery movement of great political importance
is placed within the framework of antebellum politics as a whole. The
role of Abolitionism in increasing the political tensions of the 1850s
through the agitation surrounding the Fugitive Slave Law is also treated.

H 288. DOENECKE, JUSTUS D. The Presidencies of James A. Garfield and
Chester A. Arthur. Lawrence: Regents Press of Kansas, 1981.
229 pp.
Doenecke presents a general survey of the administrations of James A.
Garfield and Chester A. Arthur. He attempts to revise the traditional
view of these two presidents as inept and thoroughly corrupt by looking
at their achievements: the development of the navy, civil service reform,
and the attempt to implement a scientific, rational tariff system.
Doenecke also contests the traditional view of America as isolationist at
this time, and argues that the Garfield and Arthur administrations deployed
an aggressive foreign policy, intervening throughout the world. Yet
Doenecke maintains that this period was one of transition for the American
presidency from the weak or questionable leadership of Andrew Johnson
and Ulysses S. Grant to the forceful direction of Theodore Roosevelt.
He also examines the tensions within the Republican Party, such as that
between the Half-Breed and Stalwart factions, and offers a general overview
of ˉmerican politics, economics, and society during the Gilded Age.

H 289. DONALD, DAVID. The Politics of Reconstruction, 1863-1867. Baton
Rouge: Louisiana State University Press, 1965. 105 pp.
In his examination of postbellum politics, Donald applies quantitative
roll-call analysis to the major pieces of legislation in order to determine
what distinguished "Radicals" from "Conservatives," and to discern the
nature of Republican factionalism during Reconstruction. He argues that
too much attention has previously been devoted to the major personalities
of the period, and that the actual voting behavior of all representatives,
rather than their speeches, is a more exact method of categorization,
as speeches were often directed toward constituencies and did not address
the issues at hand. Donald finds that the greater electoral support given
a Republican representative, the more radical the measure he supported
in Congress. Yet most of the significant legislation, Donald argues,
was not formulated solely by Radicals, but was arrived at through compromise by the various Republican factions.

H 290. DONALD, DAVID, ed. Why the North Won the Civil War. Baton Rouge:
Louisiana State University Press, 1960. 128 pp.
This collection of essays deals with various aspects of the Civil War
in trying to explain why the North was ultimately victorious. Each section
examines a particular disadvantage under which the Confederacy labored.
Among the factors discussed are deficiencies in the political system of
the one-party South; shortcomings in the leadership of Jefferson Davis;
and the deficiencies in Confederate supplies, ammunition, and manpower.
Northern advantages included industrial superiority, more capable political
leadership, and diplomatic success in Europe, all of which were crucial
elements in the North's victory. The collection includes essays by the
historians Richard Current, T. Harry Williams, Norman Graebner, David
Donald, and David M. Potter.

H 291. EATON, CLEMENT. A History of the Southern Confederacy. New York:
Macmillan, 1954. 351 pp.
Eaton's analysis of the Confederacy's struggle is based upon an integration
of its political, social, and military history. He traces the continuity
of Southern political traditions throughout the Confederacy to support
his argument that secession was actually a conservative revolt and also
finds significant continuities between the social histories of the antebellum and Confederate South. The book examines the roles of women, the
common soldier, and the personalities of Confederate leaders. It attempts
to explain the military history of the Confederacy and why it lost the
war, with particular emphasis on the impact of logistics, strategy, and
the Western campaigns.

H 292. ELLIS, RICHARD E. The Jefferson Crisis: Courts and Politics
in the Young Republic. New York: Oxford University Press, 1974.
377 pp.
Ellis examines the changing role of the judiciary during the Jefferson
administration. Based on a wide range of primary materials, his study
traces the transformation of the judicial system from its status as an
inferior partner of the other two branches of government into an equal
partner in the American political system. The repeal of the Judiciary
Act of 1801, the details of the landmark Marbury v. Madison decision,
the impeachment trials of Judges John Pickering and Samuel Chase, and
the disputes over state-level judicial reform between 1796 and 1808 are
all discussed in detail.

H 293. **ESCOTT, PAUL D.** After Seccession: Jefferson Davis and the Failure
of Confederate Nationalism. Baton Rouge: Louisiana State University Press, 1978. 295 pp.
Escott recounts the failed efforts of President Jefferson Davis to create
the Southern nationalist sentiment that might have enabled the fledgling
nation to survive. The strong Southern tradition of localism provided
Davis with many problems; but according to Escott, Davis's own shortcomings were also part of the difficulties. Davis failed to adequately comprehend the suffering of poor Southerners, and this short-sightedness
inhibited Southerners' willingness to sacrifice everything for the war
effort. The author makes extensive use of personal correspondence found
in the Confederate Record.

H 294. **EVANS, W. McKEE.** Ballots and Fence Rails: Reconstruction on
the Lower Cape Fear. Chapel Hill: University of North Carolina
Press, 1967. 314 pp.
Evans's case study of the impact of the Civil War and its aftermath on
a region of North Carolina chronicles the military campaign which touched
the area in 1865, its occupation, reconstruction, and eventual redemption
by the local whites. The book unfolds through the presentation of biographical portraits of important local figures. The author concludes
that voting rights alone were woefully insufficient to bring about a true,
long-lasting shift in political power in the area, and that the result
of the overthrow of Reconstruction was the restoration of the antebellum
values concerning race and social position.

H 295. **FEHRENBACHER, DON E.** Prelude to Greatness: Lincoln in the 1850's.
Stanford, Calif.: Stanford University Press, 1962. 205 pp.
Fehrenbacher offers a collection of seven essays covering various aspects
of Lincoln's political career in the decade prior to his election as President. His participation in the formation of the Republican Party in Illinois, his formulation of the Freeport Doctrine, and his other activities
of the 1850s are discussed. Fehrenbacher also examines the conditions
which produced the anomalous senatorial contest of 1858 between Lincoln
and Douglas, as well as the consequences of the campaign for the participants and their respective parties. Finally, Fehrenbacher examines the
circumstances by which Lincoln, with a previously unspectacular political
record, managed to gain the Republican nomination in 1860.

H 296. **FELDBERG, MICHAEL.** The Turbulent Era: Riot and Disorder in Jacksonian America. New York: Oxford University Press, 1980.
136 pp.
The Philadelphia experience with mob violence in the Jacksonian era is
used as a model for a general interpretation of rioting in America during
the Jacksonian years. Feldberg distinguishes two categories of riots:
those meant to reinforce existing ethnic stratification and to discourage
marginal groups from asserting their rights, and those meant to reinforce
group solidarity. The author sees a relationship between the rioting
and the perceived behavior of Andrew Jackson, the quintessential example
of the common man.

H 297. **FISCHER, DAVID HACKETT.** The Revolution of American Conservatism:
The Federalist Party in the Era of Jeffersonian Democracy. New
York: Harper & Row, 1965. 455 pp.
Fischer describes the efforts of a new, younger generation of Federalist
leaders to respond energetically to the rise of Jeffersonian Democracy
during the early years of the 19th century. Their response was to create
vote-seeking political organizations of their own. This practice, Fischer
claims, was in violation of their traditional ways of thinking about politics, which viewed formal political organizations as dangerous to a republic. The Federalists did not pass from the political scene after the

"Revolution of 1800" because younger Federalists had considerable success in their adaptation of Jeffersonian political techniques. Finally, Fischer argues, this resulted in a generation gap between old and new Federalists. The work includes an appendix with brief biographies of important Federalist leaders.

H 298. FISH, CARL RUSSELL. A History of American Life: The Rise of the Common Man, 1830-1850. New York: Macmillan, 1950. 391 pp.
Fish traces the evolution of American culture and civilization between 1830 and 1850. During this period, he maintains, the aristocratic European heritage disappeared, to be replaced by a more egalitarian and indigenous culture. Fish contrasts the lifestyle and attitudes predominant in 1830 with those of 1850, and decribes the distinctly regional ways of life, and the trends toward national diversity. Fish gauges the impact of technological innovation on American institutions and values and examines the development and growth of American art, literature, and architecture. He further analyzes the rise and impact of religious and communal groups, immigration, and education.

H 299. FONER, ERIC. Free Soil, Free Labor, Free Men: The Ideology of the Republican Party Before the Civil War. New York: Oxford University Press, 1970. 353 pp.
Foner analyzes the ideology of the Republican Party in the years leading up to the Civil War. The Republican Party was a classically American political coalition of many disparate groups and ideas: ex-Whigs, ex-Democrats, Abolitionists, and nativists. The one idea which they held in common, however, was opposition to the expansion of slavery into the territories. Republicans believed in the idea of "free labor"--that all men were free of constraints to succeed or fail in life on the basis of their own merits. They increasingly perceived the South, with its basis in slave labor, as an expanding "slavocracy" which threatened the very existence of Northern society and its free institutions. Foner claims that the ideology of the Republican Party reflected views and beliefs common, indeed fundamental, to Northern society, and was a major factor in mobilizing the North for total, civil war. In separate chapters he discusses the Republican critique of the South, the various groups which made up the Republican Party and their contributions to its ideology, and the Republicans on the race question and their views on ethnicity.

H 300. FONER, ERIC. Politics and Ideology in the Age of the Civil War. New York: Oxford University Press, 1980. 250 pp.
Foner attempts to integrate the social, political, economic, and ideological aspects of the history of the Civil War period. The eight essays in the work revolve around the apparent contradiction between the Republican ideology of independent, free labor, and the expansion of capitalism and capitalist relations in which labor was becoming increasingly dependent upon an impersonal market. The first part of the book discusses the origins of the Civil War, including a historiographical essay on the causes of the war. In the second section the racial attitudes of Northern Republicans, and the tensions between the Abolitionist and labor movements, are examined. The final section is concerned with land and labor after the Civil War, outlining the development of an American radicalism which considered economic independence essential to personal liberty.

H 301.   **FOOTE, SHELBY.** The Civil War: A Narrative History. Vol. 1.
Fort Sumter to Perryville. New York: Random House, 1958; Vol.
2. Fredericksburg to Meridian. New York: Random House, 1963;
Vol. 3. Red River to Appomattox. New York: Random House, 1974.
2934 pp.
In this multi-volume history of the Civil War, military events and strategies are emphasized, and Foote attempts to balance the attention normally
devoted to the Eastern theater with coverage of the often-neglected Western
theater. Although primarily a military history, Foote also considers
the effects of political and social issues, as well as the personalities
of those involved in the conflict. Foote's primary sources consist chiefly
of official records of the Confederate and Union forces as well as reminiscences of the participants. He employs the historian's standards with
the style of the novelist, and while references have been excluded from
the text, the volumes do contain bibliographic essays and extensive indices.

H 302.   **FORGIE, GEORGE B.** Patricide and the House Divided: A Psychological Interpretation of Lincoln and His Age. New York: Norton,
1979. 308 pp.
American political leaders in the mid-19th century belonged to a generation
born and socialized in the early Republic, when the memory of the Revolution was still fresh and founding heroes still held political power.
This fact, Forgie asserts, provides a key to understanding more clearly
not only the mentality of mid-19th century leadership, but also the structure and style of the long struggle to preserve the Union and hence the
origins of the American Civil War. The author discusses the peculiarly
deferential mentality that was characteristic of most American political
leaders which led them to refer almost all important political and policy
matters to the standards of the founding period. This encouraged a solidarity that prevented disunion during the 1850s, but in the long run frustrated efforts at sustained compromises.

H 303.   **FORMISANO, RONALD P.** The Transformation of Political Culture:
Massachusetts Parties, 1790's-1840's. New York: Oxford University Press, 1983. 496 pp.
Formisano traces the development of the party system in Massachusetts
during the half century between 1790, when political associations were
believed to be dangerous, and 1840, when the second party system was fully
developed. This transformation in political culture was a gradual one,
Formisano argues, and thus enabled the traditional elite to retain much
of their power. Formisano focuses on the 1820s and 1830s—when the generation of the Founding Fathers had passed and was replaced by a generation
which had grown up with the idea of political parties. Furthermore,
improvements in communication and transportation, increased economic opportunity, and greater political organization all stimulated popular political
participation. The two-party system became entrenched, Formisano claims,
as national political issues began to appear in response to Andrew
Jackson's Presidency.

H 304.   **FRANKLIN, JOHN HOPE.** Reconstruction: After the Civil War.
Chicago: University of Chicago Press, 1961. 258 pp.
Writing within the revisionist school of Reconstruction historiography,
Franklin challenges the traditional view that Reconstruction was a period
of unprecedented sordidness, corruption, and injustice in American life.
Instead, he argues that the failure of Reconstruction was the inability
of political leaders, in the face of intense Southern resistance, to
achieve justice for both blacks and whites in postbellum Southern society.
Franklin focuses on the primary role which blacks themselves played in
the process of Reconstruction, arguing that Afro-Americans were not merely
"passive" participants, but rather were shapers of their own destiny.
Finally, he maintains that Reconstruction was not a total failure, for

in spite of incredible hardships and obstacles, blacks made great achievements in education and in their initial experiences in the American political system.

H 305. FREEHLING, WILLIAM M. Prelude to Civil War: The Nullification
Crisis in South Carolina, 1816-1836. New York: Harper & Row,
1965. 395 pp.
Freehling examines the Nullification Crisis in South Carolina during the
1830s. He argues that the strident defense of the doctrine of States'
Rights by South Carolina's political leaders was but a veneer to mask
popular anxiety over the agitation of the issue of slavery by Northern
Abolitionists. Freehling cites as prime examples the efforts of Southern
Congressmen to impose the "Gag Rule"--a resolution automatically tabling
and thus stifling Congressional debate over the Abolitionist petitions
which were inundating Congress at the time--and the refusal of Southern
postmasters to deliver inflammatory Abolitionist tracts in the South.
Freehling also denies an economic cause for the crisis by arguing that
a disproportionate number of nullification advocates were from the coastal,
rice-producing districts--an area which unlike the cotton region was not
beset by falling prices. Finally, Freehling argues that a major secession
movement failed to materialize because of President Andrew Jackson's
threats to put down with military force any such movement.

H 306. FULLER, EDMUND. Prudence Crandall: An Incident of Racism in
Nineteenth Century Connecticut. Middletown, Conn.: Wesleyan
University PRess, 1971. 113 pp.
Fuller's book documents the arrest in 1833 of Prudence Crandall and the
debate which ensued between Abolitionist and pro-slavery forces. For
Fuller, the arrest of the young Quaker schoolmistress who opened a school
for black girls in the heart of Canterbury, Connecticut, is important
for several reasons: it reveals the deeply ingrained racism in U.S. history;
it delineates the many facets of the New England reform spirit and the
diverse persons touched by it; and it "shows the problems of free blacks
in the heart of a state that even then believed itself to be the paragon
of the enlightened liberal North."

H 307. FURNISS, NORMAN. The Mormon Conflict 1850-1859. New Haven, Conn.:
Yale University Press, 1960. 311 pp.
Furniss chronicles the mounting tension in Utah in the 1850s between Mormons, "Gentile" settlers, and the U.S. government, culminating, in 1857,
in the "Mormon War," an essentially bloodless show of Federal force.
The Mormons' desire to dominate the territory they had settled clashed
with popular animosity toward them. President Buchanan ultimately dis-
patched troops to assert the government's authority. Furniss finds fault
on both sides, citing, for instance, the ill effects of Mormon theocracy
and the incompetence of a number of Federal representatives in Utah.
He works from manuscripts, public documents, newspapers, memoirs, and
secondary sources, and provides a detailed bibliographic essay.

H 308. GAMBILL, EDWARD L. Conservative Ordeal: Northern Democrats and
Reconstruction, 1865-1868. Ames: Iowa State University Press,
1981. 188 pp.
Gambill examines the Northern wing of the Democratic Party during the
early years of Reconstruction, delineating the nuances and variety in
their ideology. Their overall strategy, he argues, can be described as
more of an ad hoc response to the volatile course of Reconstruction politics than as a carefully formulated program. The Democrats' strategy
in appealing for votes from the Northern electorate was founded on white
antipathy toward blacks and their aspirations for equal rights, as well
as on the constitutional defense of States' Rights and the fear of Radical
Republican tyranny. Northern Democrats supported the calls for the resto-

ration of "home rule" in the South. And in Congress Democrats attempted unsuccessfully to exploit the divisions within Republican ranks. Gambill argues that Democrats were often as disenchanted with the Administration of Andrew Johnson as were Republicans, and many desired to disavow him completely as a liability to the party, though they ultimately defended him at his impeachment trial. Indeed, a main point of intra-party tension was between Democrats who desired to participate in Johnson's National Union movement along with conservative Republicans and those who wanted to maintain the independent course of the party. Democrats also failed to develop leadership at the national level, around which all factions could unite. It was these problems, combined with the stigma of treason attached to the party because of the Civil War, that destined the Democrats to fail in early Reconstruction and enabled the Republican Party to maintain hegemony in the North.

H 309. GARRATY, JOHN A. The New Commonwealth, 1877-1890. New York: Harper & Row, 1968. 364 pp.
Garraty presents a synthesis of political, social, and economic trends in American life during the latter years of the 19th century. He argues that during these years American civilization underwent a gradual transformation in its beliefs about the relationship between the individual and society. The earlier belief was that the individual was completely independent and free from intrusion by other individuals or institutions. This traditional assumption was transformed, Garraty argues, with the development of the idea of the "commonwealth," or the necessity of collective action to deal with modern problems.

H 310. GATES, PAUL W. Agriculture and the Civil War. New York: Knopf, 1965. 383 pp.
This book looks at the impact of the Civil War on agriculture in the 1860s. Gates discusses the South during the War, the shift from cotton to corn production, and the growing distress of Southern planters when deprived of both supplies and markets. He also analyzes Northern farming, focusing on livestock, farming, dairy farming, farm labor, and machinery. Finally, he examines general farming issues such as the Homestead Act and the beginnings of agricultural education.

H 311. GATES, PAUL W. The Farmer's Age: Agriculture, 1815-1860. New York: Holt, Rinehart & Winston, 1960. 460 pp.
Gates provides a general overview of farming in the U.S. from 1815 to the eve of the Civil War. He opens with chapters on the status of Southern and Northern agriculture in 1815. He examines the development of commercial, market-oriented agriculture in the West and the North by analyzing grain, prairie, and dairy farming. Gates then examines the explosion of cotton production in the South, and the eventual emergence of "King Cotton" as the region's main staple. He also examines the controversial issue of the degree to which the South produced its own food supply, as well as public land policy, agricultural journalism, and the relationship between labor and farm machinery.

H 312. GILLETTE, WILLIAM. Retreat from Reconstruction, 1869-1879. Baton Rouge: Lousiana State University Press, 1979. 463 pp.
This account of the decline of Reconstruction centers on the Southern policy of the Grant Administration. Among the most important factors in Reconstruction's demise were increasing Southern resistance, the inefficiency of Federal officials, severe factionalism among Southern Republicans and their allies, and a general tiring of the effort in the North. When Republican support of civil rights legislation in 1874 led to repudiation in that year's Congressional elections, pressure to give up on the cause in order to save the Republican party was greatly enhanced. Finally, the failure of the Grant Administration to support with any consistency

the Southern Republican state governments, which were repeatedly placed under severe pressure, was crucial to their ultimate demise.

H 313. GINGER, RAY. Altgeld's America: The Lincoln Ideal Versus Changing Realities. Chicago: Quadrangle Books, 1958. 376 pp.
Ginger examines the efforts of Gilded Age reformers in Chicago, led by John Altgeld, who became Mayor in 1893. In the years following the Civil War, Ginger argues, the memory of Abraham Lincoln dominated Americans' notions of what was good about America. Yet the harsh realities of life resulting from rapid industrialization simultaneously belied that idyllic vision. By the time Altgeld ascended the Chicago mayoralty, the ideal had been eradicated, and in its place stood the notion of "Success." Altgeld and his supporters attempted to turn away from this emphasis on pecuniary, material achievements and to reestablish a more humanistic orientation in Chicago life. Ginger describes the efforts, occasional successes, and ultimate failures of these reformers.

H 314. GLAD, PAUL W. McKinley, Bryan, and the People. New York: Lippincott, 1964. 222 pp.
Glad focuses on the personalities, issues, and events surrounding the election of 1896, which he considers one of the most important in American history. He devotes equal attention to the familiar economic issues, such as the conflict over the gold and silver standards, as well as the two key individuals involved. Indeed, McKinley and Bryan personified the dominant and often conflicting values, assumptions, and beliefs of their time. The former was the self-made millionaire who represented corporate wealth and power, while the latter reflected the ideals of the agrarian hero, who championed the cause of the yeoman farmer. The outcome of the election reflected the increasing influence of the corporation and wealth in American society and politics.

H 315. GOETZMANN, WILLIAM H. When the Eagle Screamed: The Romantic Horizon in American Diplomacy, 1800-1860. New York: Wiley, 1966. 138 pp.
Goetzmann presents a brief survey of American diplomacy and foreign policy from 1800 to 1860, tracing U.S. activities in Latin America, the Far East, and the American West, as well as describing American military engagements and wars with England and Mexico. He describes American expansionism during this period as a manifestation of the romantic visions of "Manifest Destiny," and argues that these visions were the prime motivation for expansion. Hence, Goetzmann views American imperialism as a social and cultural phenomenon as much as a political one. He further maintains that the American impulse to explore, conquer, and settle was but a continuance of the European imperialist tradition, as exemplified by English and French Colonialism, and thus 20th-century American intervention is but an extension of this tradition.

H 316. GOODWYN, LAWRENCE. Democratic Promise: The Populist Moment in America. New York: Oxford University Press, 1976. 718 pp.
This survey of Populism discusses the rise of the Populist movement, its regional and national manifestations, and its eventual decline. Emphasis is placed on the economic orientation of the movement, and its Southern roots as manifested in the Farmers Alliance and Texas Populism. Populism is interpreted favorably as "the largest democratic mass movement in American history," realizing itself in the alternative institutions and culture generated by its cooperative and educational efforts. The free silver issue that has preoccupied historians, and increasingly preoccupied many Populists, stimulated, according to Goodwyn, a "shadow movement," a caricature which neglected Populism's original devotion to building an independent, democratic existence for the nation's farming and laboring populations. With Populism's failure, a direct result of the choice of fusion with the Democrats in 1896, an emerging corporate culture triumphed.

315

H 317. **HALTTUNEN, KAREN.** Confidence Men and Painted Women: A Study of
Middle Class Culture in America, 1830-1870. New Haven, Conn.:
Yale University Press, 1982. 262 pp.
Halttunen explores the culture of middle-class America through an examination of literature for young men and women, such as etiquette books and
popular periodicals. The "confidence man" was a symbol of hypocrisy in
Jacksonian America and beyond; ambition increasingly substituted for virtue
in the scramble for success in a mobile, socially fluid, and increasingly
urban society. The advice literature suggested as an antidote the cultivation of a transparent sincerity. Thus, a social code of "respectability" developed, behind which the ever-present ambitions could move.

H 318. **HAMILTON, HOLMAN.** Prologue to Conflict: The Crisis and Compromise
of 1850. Lexington: University of Kentucky Press, 1964. 236 pp.
In examining the crisis and Compromise of 1850, Hamilton has two objectives.
First, he contends that the national peace-time crisis and the resultant
compromise bring to the forefront issues equal to, though different from,
the secession crisis of 1860 and the Civil War itself. Second, Hamilton
examines the words and actions of political leaders such as Stephen Douglas,
Zachary Taylor, and William Corcoran in order to reassess the role which
they played in the crisis. Hamilton also includes an appendix of Congressional voting patterns concerning various aspects of the Compromise of
1850.

H 319. **HARRIS, WILLIAM C.** The Day of the Carpetbaggers: Republican Reconstruction in Mississippi, 1867-1877. Baton Rouge: Louisiana
State University Press, 1979. 760 pp.
Harris offers a comprehensive account of Reconstruction politics in Mississippi from 1867 to 1877. He measures the impact of military reconstruction
and Republican civilian rule in the state as a case study of Radical Reconstruction. Though primarily a political history, Harris's work also
describes the common perceptions of contemporaries who were not involved,
or even highly interested, in the course of political events. He contends
that while there was relatively little corruption or abuse of power by
Mississippi Republicans, they failed to take full advantage of the Federal
aid which was potentially available to them, both for economic development
and the protection of freedmen's rights. Harris maintains that although
many Mississippi Republicans were committed to equal rights for blacks
even after passage of the Fifteenth Amendment, they were unable to prevent
the state's eventual "Redemption" by the Democrats. Republicanism ultimately
became virtually nonexistent in Mississippi after Reconstruction despite
the state's significant black population.

H 320. **HATTAWAY, HERMAN** and **ARCHER JONES.** How the North Won: A Military
History of the Civil War. Urbana: University of Illinois Press,
1983. 762 pp.
Hattaway and Jones consider the factors which shaped the various battles
and led to the outcome of the Civil War. They focus on the high
command, emphasizing the importance of strategy and logistics over tactics.
While stressing the purely military factors in the eventual Northern victory, they also analyze the management of resources as well as economic
and political planning. Hattaway and Jones credit Grant with developing
the "strategy of exhaustion," which produced ultimate success. Lee is
portrayed as a master of defensive strategy, even when, during his two
invasions of the North, he was ostensibly conducting offensive campaigns.
The work includes over 200 map diagrams and an appendix on the study of
military operations.

H 321. HICKS, JOHN D. The Populist Revolt: A History of the Farmers'
         Alliance and the People's Party. Minneapolis: University of
         Minnesota Press, 1931. 473 pp.
Hicks views the post-Civil War conflict between the indebted agrarian
South and West and the financial interests of the East as central in his
survey of the Populist movement. He examines both the Northern and Southern
Alliances, which were the immediate precursors of the Populists. Of the
two Alliances, the Southern became the larger, more visible, and ultimately
more radical. And the Southern Alliance eventually came to favor direct
political action, which manifested itself in the People's Party in 1892.
Despite their ultimate failure, Hicks argues that the Populists fulfilled
their main objectives by forcing the two major parties to recognize and
accommodate the third party threat. Indeed, over the next fifteen years,
much of the Populist program became public policy, an outcome which Hicks
considers favorable to both the farmers and the nation at large.

H 322. HIRSHSON, STANLEY P. Farewell to the Bloody Shirt: Northern Repub-
         licans and the Southern Negro, 1877-1893. Bloomington: Indiana
         University Press, 1962. 334 pp.
Hirshson examines the attitudes of Northern Republicans toward blacks
in the South after Reconstruction and argues that those attitudes were
shaped more by selfish political considerations than by humanitarian concern. Some Republicans looked to Southern blacks to form the basis of
a Southern wing of the party and render it a truly national one. Others
believed blacks to be undependable or inferior and tried to build a white
Republican Party through racist appeals and demagoguery. Hirshson
describes the conflict between these two factions, but argues that all
Republican leaders ultimately tended to "wave the bloody shirt" or did
not, depending upon the political exigencies of the moment.

H 323. HOLT, MICHAEL F. The Political Crisis of the 1850's. New York:
         Wiley, 1978. 330 pp.
Holt argues that the Civil War resulted not from the debate over slavery,
but from a crisis in the American political structure during the 1850s.
Slavery and sectional tensions had been extant, he maintains, since the
founding of the Republic without resulting in war. During the 1850s,
however, the electorate lost faith in the Second Party System because
conflict no longer continued to be resolved in the existing political
apparatus. Republicans rose to dominance in the North, not in opposition
to slavery per se, but because they reflected the traditional republican
ideals of free labor and free men. Concomitantly, secessionists were
victorious in the South because there was no effective political opposition
to the Democratic Party. Consensus disintegrated over differing interpretations of what actually constituted a "republican" form of government.
Hence, preservation of republican government, rather than slavery, was
the decisive motivation for both sides in choosing to go to war.

H 324. HOWE, DAVID WALKER. The Political Culture of American Whigs.
         Chicago: University of Chicago Press, 1979. 404 pp.
In attempting to correct a perceived overemphasis on the Jacksonian Democrats during the Second Party System, Howe examines their opponents, the
Whigs. He concentrates on their political culture, rather than on the
party itself, to show that the social basis of Whiggism was as broad as
that of the Jacksonians, who are traditionally perceived as representing
the interests of the common man. Thus, the Whig Party also transcended
social, economic, and even ethnic divisions. Indeed, although the Jacksonians won more presidential elections, Whiggism more profoundly influenced the emerging industrial society and had a greater impact in developing the values and beliefs of 19th-century America. American Whiggism
was not merely a political creed, but reflected an entire way of life
for a generation of Americans.

H 325. JAFFA, HARRY V. Crisis of the House Divided: An Interpretation
of the Issues in the Lincoln-Douglas Debates. Chicago: University
of Chicago Press, 1959. 451 pp.
Jaffa presents an analysis of the famous debates between Lincoln and
Douglas during the 1850s. He maintains that the two were not engaging
in mere rhetoric or polemics, but were indeed debating the fundamental
moral issues confronting the American political system. Douglas's contention that the extension of slavery ought to be contingent upon the
will of the majority was devoid of moral content, according to Jaffa.
Lincoln, on the other hand, recognized the incompatibility of chattel
slavery with a republican form of government, and felt the extension of
such a morally repugnant institution could not be left to majority rule.
Hence, Lincoln's position possessed the ethical element missing from the
position of Douglas. Jaffa maintains that the debates have implications
for the development of modern political philosophy and theory.

H 326. JENSEN, RICHARD. The Winning of the Midwest: Social and Political
Conflict, 1888-1896. Chicago: University of Chicago Press, 1971.
357 pp.
Jensen examines the American Midwest during the turbulent decade of the
1890s, and concentrates on campaigns and voting behavior to discern the
beliefs, values, and wants of Midwesterners at the time. He argues that
religion and ethnicity, rather than social or economic class, were the
prime determinants of political affiliation. Hence, politics tended to
be extremely volatile and, at times, violent. Yet politicians displayed
remarkable flexibility in changing with the whims of their unpredictable
constituencies. Jensen concludes that the political system proved stable
and equal to the challenge of intense, often irrational, conflict-ridden
times.

H 327. KELLER, MORTON. Affairs of State: Public Life in Late 19th Century
America. Cambridge, Mass.: Harvard University Press, 1977.
631 pp.
Keller's subject is the character of America's public experience from
the Civil War to the end of the 19th century. He finds that the impetus
generated by the Civil War toward strong centralized government was dis-
sipated in the 1870s by Reconstruction and by the resurgence of racism,
localism, and cultural diversity. The state was effectively prevented
from implementing new policies encouraging economic development by the
reemergence of older American localist and laissez-faire values. The 1880s,
according to Keller, saw the first hesitant break in this trend as industrialization finally dislodged the Civil War and its aftermath from the
center of public attention. The values of the 1870s, however, remained
strong. It was not until the crisis of the 1890s precipitated a political
realignment and the emergence of the Republican party as the identifiable
voice of industrial and middle-class America, that the way was cleared
for a significant degree of institutional and political innovation. Even
then, 19th-century values persisted, qualifying the transition to a modern,
highly organized society.

H 328. KLEPPNER, PAUL. The Third Electoral System, 1853-1892: Parties,
Voters, and Political Cultures. Chapel Hill: University of North
Carolina Press, 1979. 424 pp.
This synthesis of recent studies of American political behavior in the
first era of Republican-Democrat rivalry downplays the influence of socio-
economic factors on voting patterns. Through a discussion of many case
studies—for example, the prohibition movement in Iowa and the suffrage
fight in Rhode Island—and the use of quantitative evidence, Kleppner
stresses the influence of ethnic and especially religious factors in influencing how people voted. He also claims ideology played a strong role
in determining political identification.

H 329. KRADITOR, AILEEN S. Means and Ends in American Abolitionism:
        Garrison and His Critics on Strategy and Tactics, 1834-1850.
        New York: Random House, 1967. 296 pp.
Kraditor argues that the tactics developed by William Lloyd Garrison and
his American Anti-Slavery Society between its founding in 1834 and 1850
were developed to promote the goal of eradicating racist attitudes in
the minds of white Americans, and not simply to abolish the institution
of slavery. The first two chapters deal with the role of Abolitionists
as agitators and the significance of women Abolitionists in light of the
development of Feminism. The next three chapters deal with the differences
that arose within the Abolition movement over the issues of means and
ends, constituency, and image. The last three chapters explain how theories of means and ends were adjusted to cope with the problems of agitation and conversion that the movement encountered in American society.

H 330. LACOUR-GAYET, ROBERT. Everyday Life in the United States Before
        the Civil War: 1830-1860. Translated by Mary Ilford. New York:
        Ungar, 1969. 300 pp.
Lacour-Gayet offers a survey of the everyday life of Americans in the
thirty years before the Civil War. He first examines material culture:
the growth of cities, housing patterns, food, clothing, and the development
of a complex postal and telegraph system. Next he analyzes "private"
routines of leisure, sports, and etiquette, as well as "public" routine
revolving around commerce, the market, and the realities of slave and
plantation life. Lacour-Gayet further examines religious and intellectual
developments, the rise of free, public education, the growth of indigenous
art and literature, and the ubiquity of newspapers and journals. Finally,
he focuses on the various antebellum reform movements and American political culture. He concludes that the five components of the American character at this time were bustle, inquiry, optimism, the work ethic, and
the drive for success.

H 331. LaFEBER, WALTER. The New Empire: An Interpretation of American
        Expansion, 1860-1898. Ithaca, N.Y.: Cornell University Press,
        1963. 444 pp.
LaFeber examines U.S. foreign policy during the late 19th century by concentrating on the economic forces behind American expansion. This period
witnessed the full manifestation of the Industrial Revolution in America,
as well as the rise of the U.S. as a legitimate world power. LaFeber
draws the connection between, on the one hand, the perceived need for
foreign markets in order to accommodate the rapidly expanding U.S. economy,
and on the other hand, political and military expansion. He argues that
overseas expansion did not constitute a sharp break in American history,
but represented a culmination of previous trends, and that there was no
passivity on the part of the shapers of American foreign policy. Rather,
expansion was a conscious decision of the political and business leaders
to resolve the problems of American society.

H 332. LATNER, RICHARD B. The Presidency of Andrew Jackson: White House
        Politics, 1829-1837. Athens: University of Georgia Press, 1979.
        291 pp.
Latner's account of Jackson's presidency emphasizes his personal leadership
and the Western orientation of both the President and his principal
advisors. Jackson's interpretation of Jeffersonian ideology guided his
policy decisions; he and his "Kitchen Cabinet" of informal advisors
employed a general opposition to "special privilege" as their guiding principle. Especially important in the formation of policy were Westerners
Amos Kendall and Francis P. Blair, both veterans of antibank agitation
in Kentucky that profoundly influenced the formation of their influential
political philosophy.

H 333. **LEVY, LEONARD.** Jefferson and Civil Liberties: The Darker Side.
Cambridge, Mass.: Harvard University Press, 1963. 225 pp.
Levy provides a historical corrective to the traditional view of Thomas
Jefferson as the principled defender of civil liberties and the rights
of the individual, and as the personification of Enlightenment thought.
To the contrary, Levy documents Jefferson's support and use of loyalty
oaths, deployment of the army to enforce the law, censorship of the press,
and other violations of civil liberties. Levy consciously eschews historical "objectivity" in his account. And while he simultaneously attempts
to avoid "presentism," he argues that even when judged by the standards
of his own time, Jefferson displayed an authoritarian impulse contrary
to the Enlightenment values which he is traditionally credited with defending.

H 334. **LIVERMORE, SHAWN.** The Twilight of Federalism: The Disintegration
of the Federalist Party, 1815-1830. Princeton, N.J.: Princeton
University Press, 1962. 292 pp.
Livermore argues, contrary to traditional interpretation, that the Federalist Party lasted--at least at the local level--up until 1830. He contends
that although the Federalists were profoundly damaged by the Hartford
Convention and by the Jeffersonian Republicans' successful conclusion
of the war with England, they continued as an important force in state
and local politics until the ascendency of Andrew Jackson. The Federalists
were especially influential in the Northeast, and Livermore documents
the region's political battles to support his view. He also includes
an appendix with a reference list of the important Federalist personalities
during these years.

H 335. **LONN, ELLA.** Foreigners in the Confederacy. Chapel Hill: University of North Carolina Press, 1940. 566 pp.
Lonn corrects the misconception of a Cavalier South by identifying and
describing the numbers of immigrants and foreigners who lived in the South
and served or resisted the Confederacy. Foreigners volunteered for Southern commands and participated in blockade-running, and immigrants enlisted
or were drafted into Confederate service. Anti-foreign feelings occasionally erupted during the war, as native-born Southerners blamed European
powers for failing to recognize the Confederacy, and charged Jews with
hoarding goods. Overall, however, foreigners in the Confederacy shared
the values and interests of their Southern neighbors.

H 336. **LURAGHI, RAIMONDO.** The Rise and Fall of the Plantation South.
New York: New Viewpoints, 1978. 191 pp.
Luraghi offers a comprehensive interpretation of the culture and society
of the Old Plantation South, from its origins and early growth to its
full development during the antebellum era, and finally up to the Civil
War. He places the American South within a broad comparative framework,
contrasting it to other seigneurial societies of New France, the Caribbean,
and South America. Luraghi argues that the Italian Renaissance was central
to the development of the New World and the slave society to which it
gave rise. He finds that the American South developed a seigneurial culture entirely distinct from that of the North, which contrasted with the
latter's basis in Capitalism and the notion of free labor. Luraghi further
argues that the experience of the Confederacy, with its forced industrialization and centralization, constituted a distinct historical break from
the antebellum South.

H 337. **MAY, ERNEST R.** The Making of the Monroe Doctrine. Cambridge,
Mass.: Harvard University Press, 1975. 306 pp.
In his examination of the formulation of the Monroe Doctrine, May portrays
the policy as a product of concern over the coming 1824 election, rather
than as a foreign policy concern. Neither U.S. political leaders nor

the population as a whole felt any danger in 1823 from foreign imperialist
powers. Secretary of State John Quincy Adams felt, however, the need
to counter political pressure from such ardent nationalists as Henry Clay,
whose bellicosity toward Latin America and Europe engendered much popular
support. Adams's response was the statement which became known as the
Monroe Doctrine. May minimizes intellectual or ideological convictions
on the part of Adams as a significant factor in the formulation of the
Monroe Doctrine, and further maintains that American foreign policy during
this period was largely determined by domestic political struggles.

H 338. MAY, ROBERT E. The Southern Dream of a Caribbean Empire, 1854-
        1861. Baton Rouge: Louisiana State University Press, 1973.
        286 pp.
This work examines the attempts of Southerners to extend slavery southward
into the Caribbean and Latin America after the Kansas-Nebraska Act. The
newly formed Republican Party opposed the Southern expansionists, and
the ensuing conflict became an important factor in the tensions building
up to the Civil War. May suggests that the expansion of slavery was as
important in terms of symbolism and ideology as it was in terms of pure
economics. Expansion represented, for Southerners, the vitality of slavery,
and reaffirmed their commitment to a way of life which was increasingly
perceived as being threatened by the North.

H 339. MAYFIELD, JOHN. Rehearsal for Republicanism: Free Soil and the
        Politics of Antislavery. Port Washington, N.Y.: Kennikat Press,
        1980. 220 pp.
Mayfield offers a survey of the Free Soil Party of the 1840s, which was
the first major political manifestation of antislavery sentiment in the
U.S. Mayfield examines the formation and political strategies of the
party, but concentrates on its ideology, arguing that the Free Soilers
were primarily motivated by an ideological antagonism toward slavery.
The party's roots were to be found in three groups: the Liberty Party,
the Conscience Whigs, and the "Barnburner" faction of the New York Democratic Party. Mayfield argues that while Free Soilism failed as a political movement, it was ultimately successful in establishing slavery as
a national political concern, and also was integral to the later development of the Republican Party in the 1850s.

H 340. McCORMICK, RICHARD. The Second American Party System: Party Forma-
        tion in the Jacksonian Era. Chapel Hill: University of North
        Carolina Press, 1966. 389 pp.
McCormick presents a state-by-state analysis of the formation of political
parties during the Jacksonian era, or what is known as the "Second Party
System." He argues that the Second Party system developed in different
regions essentially over identification with presidential candidates.
McCormick views parties as political machines, and argues that ideology,
issues, and constituencies were of only secondary importance. He argues
that this party system developed gradually, commencing in earnest in 1824
with the renewed interest in the presidency, and proceeded at varying
paces in the different regions. But between 1824 and 1854 the two-party
system existed in all regions of the nation, which was not the case either
before or after these dates. McCormick also examines the significant
changes in political styles, leadership, and campaigns during this crucial
period in the development of American politics.

H 341. McDONALD, FORREST. The Presidency of Thomas Jefferson. Lawrence:
        University Press of Kansas, 1976. 201 pp.
McDonald presents a critique of Jefferson's administration from a viewpoint
sympathetic to Jefferson's adversary, Alexander Hamilton. Although politically skilled in dealing with Congress and his countrymen, Jefferson is
nonetheless portrayed as temperamentally and idealistically more appro-

priately suited to an oppositional rather than a governing position and, furthermore, as evasive in regard to civil liberties. McDonald is critical of the poor preparations made for the military defense of the country even as the British-French struggle continued. He maintains that Jefferson's agrarianism and antipathy toward commerce and industrial development rendered him an essentially retrogressive American President.

H 342. McKITRICK, ERIC L. Andrew Johnson and Reconstruction. Chicago: University of Chicago Press, 1960. 533 pp.
McKitrick offers a major revision of Andrew Johnson's role during the first years of Reconstruction, 1865-1866. Traditional views consider Johnson a principled defender of the Constitution against attacks by the Radical Republicans. McKitrick, however, argues that Johnson was an "out-sider," foreign to the ways of the Washington inner political circles, and that it was his intransigence and unpredictability which alienated Radicals, Conservative Republicans, and even Southerners. Indeed, opposition to Johnson was the primary reason for the rise of Radicalism. Yet compromise did not become distinctly impossible until well into 1866. McKitrick is also critical of the Radical Republicans, and argues that moderates such as William Fessenden of Maine could have created an amicable restoration of the rebellious states. McKitrick argues that despite the complexity and magnitude of the problems of Reconstruction, these problems could have been resolved within the political-institutional context, and that the failure to achieve that end was primarily Johnson's responsibility.

H 343. McPHERSON, JAMES M. Ordeal by Fire: The Civil War and Reconstruc-tion. New York: Knopf, 1982. 694 pp.
McPherson presents a broad survey of the Civil War and Reconstruction period, concentrating heavily on the military aspects of the war, as opposed to social and political developments. As the work is a synthesis, McPherson devotes attention to the many historiographical debates, and presents arguments from all sides. He describes the strategies and objec-tives of the opposing militaries during the war. And he argues that Recon-struction was ultimately a failure, despite many important reforms, because it did not succeed in restructuring Southern society along more egalitarian lines. The text includes many maps showing military strategy, as well as an extended bibliographical note and a glossary of military terms.

H 344. McWHINEY, GRADY and PERRY D. JAMIESON. Attack and Die: Civil War Military Tactics and the Southern Heritage. University: University of Alabama Press, 1982. 209 pp.
This work investigates the question of why the South suffered so many casualities during the Civil War. An equivalent loss of men for the U.S. during W.W. II would have constituted a loss of 6,000,000 men instead of 300,000. McWhiney and Jamieson find the reason in the rapid development of firepower coupled with a reliance on increasingly outmoded strategies and tactics. They find the reason for this damaging reliance on old ways not to be the legacy of Napoleon nor his historical interpreter Jomini, as has been argued; neither was it the influence of West Point instructor Dennis Hart Mahan. The source of the ideas behind Civil War strategy and tactics was the experience gained by officers who took part in the Mexican War. This historical explanation is buttressed by an ethno-cultural one. The authors maintain that Southerners were primarily of Scot-tish, Welsh, and Scots-Irish stock, as opposed to the more purely English Yankees. The Confederates chose to fight in traditional Celtic fashion, constantly on the offensive, preferring to attack and favoring frontal assaults which proved suicidal.

H 345. MERK, FREDERICK and L. B. MERK. The Monroe Doctrine and American
Expansionism, 1843-1849. New York: Knopf, 1966. 289 pp.
The work examines the rationale behind American imperialism under the
administration of James K. Polk. The authors maintain that the Democratic
expansionists justified territorial conquest by applying the Monroe Doctrine to the territory just beyond American boundaries, and by exaggerating
and misconstruing European interest in the Western Hemisphere. According
to this view, Polk deliberately deceived the public in his assertion of
the threat to American security posed by Europe, and the ultimate manifestation of this policy was an unnecessary war with Mexico. The Whigs,
by contrast, emerge as the more honest and forthright, as well as the
more politically astute of the two parties.

H 346. MEYERS, MARVIN. The Jacksonian Persuasion: Politics and Belief.
Stanford, Calif.: Stanford University Press, 1957. 231 pp.
In this analysis of both Andrew Jackson and the age in which he lived,
Meyers puts to rest the mystique surrounding the seventh President and
argues that it was his dramatic personal talents, rather than his philosophy of reform or his policies, which lent Jackson his political success.
Nonetheless, using a wide range of materials and inter-disciplinary
approaches, Meyers scrutinizes the psychological and philosophical dimensions
of the era. He devotes particular attention to Jackson's banking policy,
which both concretely and symbolically was central to his creed, and
analyzes it within the broader ideological context of the Jacksonian Era.

H 347. MILLER, DOUGLAS T. Jacksonian Aristocracy: Class and Democracy
in New York, 1830-1860. New York: Oxford University Press, 1967.
228 pp.
In examining social and economic class relationships in antebellum New
York, Miller challenges the traditional view that political egalitarianism
was the dominant theme of the Jacksonian era. Miller argues that the
period was not one of optimism and upward social mobility, nor was society
free from class divisions. Rather, between 1830 and 1860 New York experienced an industrial revolution which, complicated by an influx of cheap
immigrant labor and an improved transportation system, lowered the status
of skilled craftsmen and created a new privileged class. The result was
a society increasingly characterized by social stratification, low social
mobility, and class animosity.

H 348. MILLER, JOHN CHESTER. The Wolf by the Ears: Thomas Jefferson
and Slavery. New York: Free Press, 1977. 319 pp.
Through an examination of Thomas Jefferson's views on race, Miller attempts
to explain why Jefferson continued to hold slaves in spite of his avowed
opposition to slavery. He analyzes the importance of his conception of
race to the Declaration of Independence, his advocacy of returning the
slaves to Africa, and his role in the Missouri controversy of 1819-21.
Jefferson's ideas on racial issues are placed within the larger framework
of his thought as a whole. Although he was one of the most progressive
and enlightened thinkers of his day, Miller suggests that Jefferson's
ideas on race were marred by the values and assumptions of the society
in which he lived, and that he was ultimately unable to transcend those
values.

H 349. MORGAN, HOWARD WAYNE. From Hayes to McKinley: National Party
Politics, 1877-1896. Syracuse, N.Y.: Syracuse University Press,
1969. 618 pp.
Morgan presents a synthesis of American political history in the Gilded
Age. He argues that this period saw the development of a national party
system in which the Republicans triumphed by emphasizing national concerns
over local interests. Morgan stresses the Republican programs of the
tariff, internal improvements, and Federal spending. He contends that

the "constructive nationalism" of the Republicans provided a foundation
for the modern political party system. Major politicians of the period
are reevaluated in an effort to assess the Republican Party and its leading
organizers in a more favorable light.

H 350. MORGAN, HOWARD WAYNE, ed. The Gilded Age. 1963; Rev. ed. Syracuse, N.Y.: Syracuse University Press, 1970. 329 pp.
The essays in this collection attempt to show how the postbellum Civil
War generation sought to create national unity and to develop a meaningful
body of policy, ideals, and taste. The authors discuss the many different
aspects of American society, culture, and politics during the Gilded Age.
They examine such topics as the development of corporations, labor, civil
service reform, literature, popular culture, science and technology, political culture, Populism, and foreign policy. The contributors include Howard
Wayne Morgan, Herbert Gutman, John Ripple, Lewis Gould, and Ari Hoogenboom.

H 351. MORRIS, ROBERT C. Reading, 'Riting, and Reconstruction: The Education of Freedmen in the South, 1861-1870. Chicago: University
of Chicago Press, 1981. 341 pp.
Morris describes the education of Southern freedmen, under the auspices
of the Freedmen's Bureau, during Reconstruction. He argues that the lofty
idealism of educators was modified by pragmatism and an awareness of the
need for sectional accommodation. Furthermore, the basic philosophy of
black education was moderate in tone, stressing order and gradualism--
the notion that racial prejudice and discrimination would disappear as
blacks made socio-economic gains. Morris also devotes considerable attention to the individual instructors who played the crucial role of implementing the policies of the Bureau at the local level. He examines their
backgrounds, social and racial attitudes, and politics, as well as their
motivations, goals, and objectives. Morris bases his study on the educators' statements and letters, class lessons, and textbooks written specifically for the freedmen.

H 352. MORRISON, CHAPLAIN W. Democratic Politics and Sectionalism: The
Wilmot Proviso Controversy. Chapel Hill: University of North
Carolina Press, 1967. 244 pp.
Morrison argues that the 1846 Wilmot Proviso, which sought to prevent
the extension of slavery into those territories which might be acquired
from Mexico as a result of the Mexican-American War, polarized sectional
loyalties in the subsequent two years, especially within the Democratic
Party. The short-term result was the creation of the Free Soil Alliance
and the Democratic defeat in the 1848 presidential election. The long-
term consequence was disunion and war. Thus, Morrison treats the Wilmot
Proviso as an episode of crucial significance in the development of the
sectionalization of politics during the Second Party System.

H 353. NELSON, WILLIAM E. The Roots of American Bureaucracy, 1830-1900.
Cambridge, Mass.: Harvard University Press, 1982. 208 pp.
Nelson argues that post-Civil War reformers intended to institutionalize
pluralism. The author sees the rise of bureaucratic institutions as a
conscious attempt to initiate minority rule. Party government, he argues,
evolved after the war into minority rule with a greater concern for the
welfare of individuals and minority groups. Nelson locates the greatest
change at the national level, as all areas of the Federal government became
more specialized and more dependent upon professional advice. The author
contends that bureaucratic institutions have contributed to the maintenance
of civil liberties.

H 354. NEVINS, ALLAN. The Emergence of Lincoln. 2 vols. New York:
    Scribner, 1950. 996 pp.
The first volume, "Douglas, Buchanan and Party Chaos: 1857-1859," focuses
on the factionalism within the Democratic Party, and specifically on the
rivalry between Stephen Douglas and James Buchanan. Nevins sees this
struggle as a precursor to the war itself. Douglas's pyrrhic victory
over Lincoln in the Illinois senatorial contest of 1858 is analyzed.
Volume II, "Prologue to Civil War: 1859-1861," discusses the train of
events which led to Lincoln's nomination, the election of 1860, and the
secession crisis during the winter of 1860-1861.

H 355. NEVINS, ALLAN. Ordeal of the Union. 2 vols. New York: Scribner,
    1947. 1183 pp.
This is a historical narrative of political, social, and military events
between 1847 and 1865. In Volume I, subtitled "Fruits of Manifest Destiny:
1847-1852," Nevins discusses the consequences of the Mexican War and its
effects on the respective regions and political parties. He discusses
Abolitionism and its relations to the general reform movements. Nevins
also examines slavery and its centrality to the South. The second volume,
subtitled "House Dividing: 1852-1857," covers both the elections of
Franklin Pierce and James Buchanan. Nevins discusses the problems of
immigration, the rise of Nativism, the Kansas-Nebraska Act, and the birth
of the Republican Party.

H 356. NEVINS, ALLAN. The War for the Union. 4 vols. New York: Scribner,
    1959. 1959 pp.
The first volume, "The Improvised War: 1861-1862," chronicles the growing
realization by the Lincoln Administration and the Northern and Southern
populations that the war would not be short and would have to be waged
more efficiently. The unanimity following the Fort Sumter crisis gave
way to a more realistic reappraisal of the necessities of war as a consequence of the first battle of Bull Run. Volume II, "War Becomes Revolution: 1862-1863," focuses on the nature of the Emancipation Proclamation
and its effects on war aims, conscription, war-time diplomacy, and the
importance of the battle of Antietam as a prerequisite for the Proclamation.
The third volume, "The Organized War: 1863-1864," examines the victory
at Gettysburg, the New York City draft riots, and the rise of U. S. Grant
to supreme commander. The final volume, "The Organized War to Victory:
1864-1865," covers Lincoln's reelection, Grant's pursuit of Lee, the surrender at Appomattox, and the assassination of Lincoln.

H 357. NICHOLS, ROY F. The Disruption of American Democracy. New York:
    Macmillan, 1948. 612 pp.
Nichols, in analyzing the Democratic Party in the five years preceding
the Civil War, contends that conflicts among the Democrats lay at the
root of secession. He examines the chaotic state of the Democratic Party
during the Buchanan administration, and places the confused party politics
of the period within the context of national violence and emotionalism.
Nichols argues that disorganization among state Democrats, the lack of
a strong national party leadership, and obstinate Southern Democrats created a climate in which political disruption led to secession and war.

H 358. NIVEN, JOHN. Martin Van Buren: The Romantic Age of American Poli-
    tics. New York: Oxford University Press, 1983. 715 pp.
Martin Van Buren is the focal point of this study of the emergence of
the second party system. As creator of the Albany Regency political
machine in New York State and chief promoter of Andrew Jackson to the presidency, Van Buren represented, and indeed led, a new style in American
politics. The major part of Niven's work discusses Van Buren's relationship with Jackson during the latter's presidency, with less attention
devoted to Van Buren's own troubled administration. Niven does, however,

325

pay close attention to the machinations of partisan politics during these years.

H 359. NOBLE, DAVID F. America by Design: Science, Technology, and the Rise of Corporate Capitalism. New York: Knopf, 1977. 384 pp.
Noble's study describes the role of business and business leaders in directing scientific research in the late 19th and early 20th centuries toward the creation of modern corporate Capitalism. Noble argues against the alleged "inevitability" of society's adjusting to the modernizing effects of technological innovation. Instead, he describes the connections between business and education leaders during these critical years which produced the particular, hierarchical set of social and economic arrangements which continue to dominate the U.S.

H 360. NYE, RUSSEL BLAINE. Society and Culture in America, 1830-1860. New York: Harper & Row, 1974. 432 pp.
Nye examines the transformation of American life from the age of Jackson to the Civil War. This was a period of tremendous growth in population, area of settlement, industry, and in the economy in general. Nye argues that the U.S. concomitantly began to develop its own indigenous institutions, philosophy, art, and literature, rather than merely adapting European models. Nye examines beliefs and ideology, antebellum reform movements, the growth of education, literature, philosophy, and the arts and, finally, the status of blacks in the thirty-year span leading up to the Civil War, showing how each was a distinct result of the American environment.

H 361. O'CONNOR, THOMAS H. Lords of the Loom: The Cotton Whigs and the Coming of the Civil War. New York: Scribner, 1968. 214 pp.
O'Connor examines the reactions of American businessmen toward the coming of the Civil War. He concentrates on one group of businessmen, the textile manufacturers of Massachusetts, to analyze their material productivity and influence on society as well as society's demands on them. O'Connor describes the clash between the "Yankee zeal" for profit and the "Puritan conscience," and argues that while the latter concerned itself with uprooting the evils of slavery, the former focused on the economic demand for more slave-produced cotton. A decisive answer either way, according to O'Connor, seemed bound to endanger the Union.

H 362. OLSEN, OTTO H., ed. Reconstruction and Redemption in the South. Baton Rouge: Louisiana State University Press, 1980. 250 pp.
Olsen presents a collection of state studies concerning various aspects of Southern Reconstruction and redemption. States included are Alabama, Louisiana, Mississippi, North Carolina, and Virginia. According to Olsen, Reconstruction failed because the Republicans in each state were never able to establish a foothold firm enough to effectively withstand the later pressure from their political opponents, especially when assistance from Washington was no longer forthcoming. Bibliographies for each article are included.

H 363. OWSLEY, FRANK L. King Cotton Diplomacy; Foreign Relations of the Confederate States of America. Chicago: University of Chicago Press, 1931. 617 pp.
Owsley argues that the Southern economic dependence on cotton dominated the Confederacy's foreign affairs, and he discusses the political ramifications of the region's reliance on one staple. The author details the Confederacy's diplomatic efforts at obtaining European intervention in the war. In Confederate eyes, Owsley asserts, any form of diplomatic recognition would have resulted in independence for the South. The book also contains an analysis of England's decision not to intervene in the Civil War. Owsley contends that many British industrialists actually benefited from the war, which offset the economic disadvantage of curtailed trade with the Confederacy.

H 364. **PERKINS, BRADFORD.** Castlereagh and Adams: England and the United
States, 1812-1823. Berkeley: University of California Press,
1964. 304 pp.
Perkins describes Anglo-American relations from the outbreak of the War
of 1812 to the promulgation of the Monroe Doctrine, concentrating on the
two respective foreign policy shapers, Viscount Robert Castlereagh and
John Quincy Adams. He argues that this period witnessed America's search
for true independence and its assertion of national sovereignty. Indeed,
the War of 1812 resulted from Republican assertions of the U.S. as an
international power, and the war for the U.S. was mainly a struggle to
maintain the position it had hitherto achieved. The Monroe Doctrine,
Perkins argues, combined the "realism" of the Federalist's foreign policy
with the Republican aspirations; it proclaimed American isolation from
Europe while simultaneously asserting the U.S.'s independent course of
action in dealing with Latin America. Perkins maintains that too much
attention has hitherto been devoted to the development of American foreign
policy at this time, and he corrects this view by investigating the development of British foreign policy.

H 365. **PERKINS, BRADFORD.** Prologue to War: England and the United States,
1805-1812. Berkeley: University of California Press, 1961.
457 pp.
Perkins examines the factors which led to the War of 1812. He describes
the course of events in the decade before the war: the treaty negotiations
of 1806, the Embargo, the Chesapeake affair, non-intercourse, the rise
of the War Hawks, and finally, the forces which led James Madison and
Congress to declare war against Britain. Perkins stresses as a key factor
the perceptions which Americans had of these developments, as well as
other notions that the British were attempting to foment domestic strife,
especially among Indians on the frontier. Ultimately, Perkins argues
that the main cause for war was impressment by the Royal Navy and the
response of outrage on the part of the American public.

H 366. **PERMAN, MICHAEL.** Reunion Without Compromise: The South and Reconstruction, 1865-1868. New York: Cambridge University Press,
1973. 376 pp.
By investigating the political leadership of the Southern states in the
first three years of Reconstruction, Perman argues that much of the leadership of the Confederacy remained intact after the war, and the Reconstruction measures were not nearly as stringent or enforced as scrupulously
as they might have been. The various strategies employed by the Southerners to gain readmission are viewed by Perman as evidence of the vitality
of ex-Confederate leadership. This added momentum to the Radical Republican program. Finally, Perman concludes that Reconstruction was almost
over by 1868, and completely eroded shortly thereafter.

H 367. **PESSEN, EDWARD.** Jacksonian America: Society, Personality and
Politics. Homewood, Ill.: Dorsey Press, 1969. 408 pp.
Pessen offers a comprehensive overview of the Jacksonian period (roughly
1825-1845), discussing values and ideologies; economic development (agriculture, industry, labor, banking, commerce, transportation); and politicians and the political system (especially the Whig and Democratic
parties). Pessen contends that this period was not one in which democracy
and social equality flourished; instead it was an age in which the shrewd
and the wealthy—not the common man—gained political power, and it was
a time in which society remained class-stratified. Jackson had little
effect on the economic, social, and intellectual trends of the time.
Consequently, Pessen believes the time period has been misnamed. "There
is something to be said," he concludes, "for calling it an age of materialism and opportunism, reckless speculation and erratic growth, unabashed
vulgarity, and a politic, seeming deference to the common man by the uncom-

mon man who actually ran things." An extensive bibliographic essay is
included.

H 368. POTTER, DAVID M. The Impending Crisis, 1848-1861. Edited by Don
        Fehrenbacher. New York: Harper & Row, 1976. 638 pp.
Potter examines how, in the 1850s, the final efforts to maintain national
unity collapsed. The Compromise of 1850, thought to be the final settlement, was an armistice rather than a settlement, according to Potter.
The Kansas-Nebraska Act of 1854 tore at the nation and its political parties, showing how fragile the "unity" gained in 1850 was. Potter defends
the elaborate discussion of the slavery question in the Supreme Court's
Dred Scott case, but disagrees with its conclusion that Congressional
power over slavery in the territories was limited. Lincoln is discussed
as well, and is portrayed as a moderate, both during the 1850s and as
President-elect.

H 369. POTTER, DAVID M. Lincoln and His Party in the Secession Crisis.
        New Haven, Conn.: Yale University Press, 1942. 408 pp.
Potter examines Lincoln's actions from his presidential election to the
Civil War. He argues that the victorious Republicans of 1860 were a minority party. They were composed of mutually suspicious factions which lacked
a true policy regarding the sectional controversy, and which believed
that secession was a bluff. Lincoln rejected compromise and was determined
to preserve the status quo until the pro-Union Southerners would bring
the states back into the Union. Failure eventually came, Potter claims,
because Lincoln and his party misunderstood both the nature of Southern
Unionism and the resolve of Southern secessionists.

H 370. POTTER, DAVID M. The South and the Sectional Conflict. Baton
        Rouge: Louisiana State University Press, 1968. 321 pp.
In this collection of eleven essays, Potter examines different aspects
of the Civil War. The work is divided into three sections. The first
contains essays dealing with the essence of the South as a distinct
regional entity. The second section deals with the evolution of the historical literature which, Potter suggests, is helpful in examining the
changing views of the South and its past. The third section contains
five essays dealing with various aspects of the Civil War, including Horace
Greeley's views on secession, John Brown and the American Negro, Republicans and the Secession Crisis, and an assessment of Jefferson Davis as
a political leader.

H 371. POWELL, LAWRENCE. New Masters: Northern Planters During the Civil
        War and Reconstruction. New Haven, Conn.: Yale University Press,
        1980. 253 pp.
Powell recounts the experiences of Northerners who relocated to the South
and acquired plantations during the Civil War and Reconstruction. These
Northern planters tried to resolve the fundamental problem of the transition from a slave labor to a free labor economy. Powell finds that
these "Yankee" planters were more numerous than has generally been thought,
estimating that there were between twenty and fifty thousand in the South
during the period. Powell also describes the freedmen's efforts to assert
their independence from their new employers, in both the plantation fields
and the rural country stores, and maintains that this struggle was central
in the transition from the Old to the New South. This process, Powell
maintains, is an example of the limits of liberal reform during a period
when America was evolving into a modern, industrial society.

H 372. **RISJORD, NORMAN.** The Old Republicans: Southern Conservatism in
the Age of Jefferson. New York: Columbia University Press, 1965.
340 pp.
The conservative wing of the Jeffersonian Party shows both the development
of Southern conservative thought and the Southern sectional self-image,
according to Risjord. This group, the "Old Republicans," is seen as the
intermediaries between the anti-Federalists of the 1780s and the States'
Rights Southerners of the Jacksonian era. The interpretation of the Constitution, specifying what it permitted the Federal Government to do,
was the most important factor in the development of political factions
and alliances. And the Old Republicans, Risjord argues, opposed all
efforts to grant the central government more authority.

H 373. **ROARK, JAMES L.** Masters Without Slaves: Southern Planters in
the Civil War and Reconstruction. New York: Norton, 1977.
273 pp.
In his study of plantation life after slavery, Roark argues that the
planter class continued to dominate Southern society and politics during
Reconstruction, to the detriment of the freedmen and white yeomanry.
Planters by and large retained their ownership of land, which in turn
enabled them to control the political and legal apparatus. True, slavery
was dead, but the planter class instituted the sharecropping system, which
kept the black population as a whole in a state of peonage. Roark traces
the various legal and, when necessary, extra-legal strategies and practices
which were used to oppress the freedmen. Roark concludes that "revolutions
may go backwards"--that is, that the possibilities for racial equality
opened up during the Civil War were quickly extinguished, and that there
was actually little change in the social and economic class relations
in the South as a result of the Civil War.

H 374. **RORABAUGH, W. J.** The Alcoholic Republic: An American Tradition.
New York: Oxford University Press, 1979. 302 pp.
In the first decades of the 19th century Americans consumed alcohol in
greater quantity than ever before or since. This account of the "alcoholic" era in American history documents the extensive use of whiskey and
examines the sources of the nation's dependence on drinking. Rorabaugh
ties this use of alcohol to economic conditions, to the country's unappe-
tizingly bland diet, and to psychological frustrations stemming from unfulfilled ambitions. The author then places the rise of the temperance movement within the context of these conditions.

H 375. **ROSE, WILLIE LEE.** Rehearsal for Reconstruction: The Port Royal
Experiment. Indianapolis, Ind.: Bobbs-Merrill, 1964. 442 pp.
Rose provides an account of how Northern philanthropists attempted to reconstruct Port Royal society after the U.S. Army captured South Carolina's
Sea Islands in 1861. As the local inhabitants fled from the occupying
forces, they abandoned large plantations and a labor force of approximately
10,000 slaves. This effort to rebuild Port Royal entailed participation
from the Army and the Federal government, business and educational organizations, religious institutions, and abolitionist and philanthropic societies. The aim of these groups was to render the freedman an economically
self-sufficient citizen who could contribute to the new society which
was to arise after the war. Their main concern was to educate the freedmen,
though they also provided economic support and even helped organize a
regiment of black troops. Rose shows how many of the freedmen's initial
gains were lost because of in-fighting among the various groups and individuals, racism, planter redemption, and the lack of resolve on the part
of the Federal government to protect the freedmen's civil rights. Nevertheless, she argues that many long-lasting, indeed fundamental, changes
occurred in Port Royal society, and that the Port Royal experiment provides
an example of the possibilities Reconstruction held if the North and the

Federal government had been fully committed to rebuilding Southern society
on the principle of racial egalitarianism.

H 376. **ROTHMAN, DAVID J.** The Discovery of the Asylum: Social Order and
        Disorder in the New Republic. Boston: Little, Brown, 1971.
        376 pp.
The Jacksonian period was marked by a revolution in social practice.
Increasingly, the family was replaced by institutions and asylums to solve
poverty, crime, delinquency, and insanity. At the time, this was seen
as a progressive, far-sighted development and thus a reform. The asylum
served two basic purposes: rehabilitation and the establishment of an
example for correct and moral behavior. As different asylums began
appearing--the alms house, the penitentiary, the orphanage, the insane asylum
the reformatory--they assumed increasing and unexpected responsibilities
and burdens. By the 1850s asylums were increasingly forced to abandon
their original goals of reform and to replace them with simple incarcera-
tion and custodianship.

H 377. **ROTHMAN, DAVID J.** Politics and Power: The United States Senate,
        1869-1901. Cambridge, Mass.: Harvard University Press, 1966.
        348 pp.
Rothman examines the process of professionalization in the U.S. Senate
between 1869 and 1901. He describes the manner in which bureaucratic
forms were developed to administer the Senate's business. The committee
system replaced decision-making on the floor while the party caucus served
to discipline the committees. Political competence, rather than social
prominence, became a decisive determinant of who would be elected. As
parties became more organized, economic interest groups sought to transfer
their attention to the parties themselves. The degree of their success,
Rothman argues, was not determined by the particular ideological predilec-
tions of the parties, but by the capability and extent of their own organizations. In these regards, the Senate shared the general patterns of
organizational change which characterized American society at the turn
of the century.

H 378. **SCHLESINGER, ARTHUR M., Jr.** The Age of Jackson. Boston: Little,
        Brown, 1945. 545 pp.
In his classic study of the Jacksonian era, Schlesinger examines the conflicting ideologies and political associations which were emerging during
this crucial period of American history. Schlesinger argues that politics
did not revolve purely around personalities--such as Jackson--to the complete neglect of ideology, but rather that Jacksonian Democracy was shaped
much more by reasoned and systematic notions about society than has
hitherto been recognized. He also questions the traditional notion of
Jackson's ascendency as representing the triumph of the West in American
politics, and contends that many dominant ideas and motives of Jacksonian
democracy originated in the East or South of American democracy, and he
maintains that the ambiguities and questions surrounding American democracy
have their roots in the Jacksonian period, when the critical issues involving the type of society America was to be were debated.

H 379. **SEIP, TERRY L.** The South Returns to Congress: Men, Economic Mea-
        sures, and Intersectional Relationships, 1868-1879. Baton Rouge:
        Louisiana State University Press, 1983. 322 pp.
Seip uses quantitative techniques to analyze the voting behavior of 251
Southern members of Congress on issues concerning economic development
during the later Reconstruction. Northern and Southern Democrats, Seip
finds, tended to display greater unity on three types of issues than did
the two wings of the Republican Party. Indeed, Seip is highly critical
of Northern Republicans for concerning themselves too much with sectional
interests at the expense of national interests. Furthermore, intraparty
disputes among Southern Republicans was the main reason for the party's
demise in that section and for the subsequent Democratic redemption.

H 380. SEWELL, RICHARD H. Ballots for Freedom: Antislavery Politics in the United States, 1837-1860. New York: Oxford University Press, 1976. 379 pp.
Sewell's primary concern in this study is political antislavery, especially as manifested in the Liberty Party, the Free Soil movement and Party, and finally the Republican Party. Sewell argues that the leaders of these organizations were committed both to the elimination of slavery and to basic civil rights for blacks. He denies that they were unduly bigoted when judged by the standards, values, and beliefs of their own time. The work contains much information concerning hitherto obscure figures in the Liberty party, the first significant political antislavery organization.

H 381. SHANNON, FRED A. The Farmer's Last Frontier: Agriculture, 1860-1897. New York: Holt, Rinehart & Winston, 1945. 434 pp.
Shannon discusses the Westward expansion of agriculture to the limits of the "last frontier," the area lying between the Mississippi River and the Rocky Mountains. Shannon describes migration and settlement, public land policies, mechanization, the spread of prairie and of livestock farming, and the agrarian problems associated with transportation, marketing, and farm financing. He stresses the rapacity of Southern landowners and merchants and their responsibility for the high interest rates and other exploitative policies which inhibited capital formation and the improvement of Southern farms. Shannon concludes with a discussion of the agrarian protest movements of these decades.

H 382. SILBEY, JOEL H. The Shrine of Party: Congressional Voting Behavior, 1841-1852. Pittsburgh, Pa.: University of Pittsburgh Press, 1967. 292 pp.
Silbey presents a quantitative roll-call analysis of Congressional voting from 1841 to 1852, the later years of the Second Party System. He finds, contrary to traditional interpretation, that although political parties were weakened by the issues of slavery and territorial expansion, they continued to maintain a high degree of cohesion throughout the 1840s. Nevertheless, while it was of secondary importance, sectionalism continued to grow steadily; indeed, the origins of party disintegration, Silby argues, are to be found during the 1840s.

H 383. SINGLETARY, O. The Mexican War. Chicago: University of Chicago Press, 1960. 181 pp.
Singletary examines the military conflict between the U.S. and Mexico between 1846 and 1848, detailing the war's background and the events which precipitated it. He views the war as limited and obscure, both to contemporaries and in American historiography, one largely overshadowed by the issues and domestic conflicts which eventually led to the Civil War. Singletary argues that behind the military conflict was a political struggle within the U.S. between the predominantly Whig Army Generals and a Democratic President. And although the ultimate outcome was propitious to the interests of the U.S., this political struggle noticeably hampered the U.S. war effort.

H 384. SMELSER, MARSHALL. The Democratic Republic, 1801-1815. New York: Harper & Row, 1968. 369 pp.
Smelser presents a general history of the years between the inauguration of Thomas Jefferson and the conclusion of the War of 1812, focusing on the policies and practices of the Federal government. He portrays Jefferson sympathetically, attributing his failures to external events and circumstances beyond his control. And while not going so far as to call James Madison an incapable president, Smelser argues that his literal interpretation of the divisions of powers under the Constitution prevented him from lobbying Congress effectively or from establishing any significant

influence over it. Smelser describes the U.S. as being bitterly divided over the War of 1812.

H 385. SMITH, HENRY NASH. Popular Culture and Industrialism, 1865-1900. Garden City, N.Y.: Doubleday, 1967. 522 pp.
Smith examines the beliefs, attitudes, and behavior of the American people during the later half of the 19th century. He focuses attention on the questions of nationalism, labor protest, the rise of the city, and the religious revival of the period. The development of the forms and importance of mass communication, Smith argues, enabled popular culture to become a national culture. He bases his argument not only on contemporary writings and speeches, but also on an examination of popular physical culture: paintings, drawings, sculptures, and the like; and he argues that this culture was reflective of the emergent industrial order and the values it espoused.

H 386. SORIN, GERALD. Abolitionism: A New Perspective. New York: Praeger, 1972. 179 pp.
Sorin differentiates between Abolitionists and anti-slavery advocates in arguing that the former not only sought to eradicate slavery but also envisioned full equality for blacks. He perceives the Abolitionists as sincere, visionary idealists whose origins lay in both religious revivalism and the thought of the Enlightenment. He details the transition from gradualism to immediatism and from moral suasion to organized, political action, and shows that violence occasionally erupted within Abolitionist ranks. Sorin also examines the differences in timing and strategy among the various Abolitionist groups, black and white. After discussing the role of the Abolitionists during the Civil War and Reconstruction, Sorin concludes that they succeeded in achieving only one of their two major goals: emancipation of the slave.

H 387. SPROAT, JOHN G. The Best Men: Liberal Reformers in the Gilded Age. Chicago: University of Chicago Press, 1968. 356 pp.
In a detailed, revisionist examination of the Liberal Reform movement from Reconstruction to the 1890s, Sproat argues that liberal reformers were primarily economic or intellectual elites. As such, these men perceived corruption, political and otherwise, as sinful and indecent. It was this perception which made the liberal reformers disheartened with Reconstruction, and which further motivated their efforts for civil service reform. Sproat examines liberal reformers as both a political and social group. He argues that they had great difficulties in upholding traditional standards of moral conduct in a society mesmerized by progress and material wealth.

H 388. STAMPP, KENNETH M. And the War Came: The North and the Secession Crisis, 1860-61. Baton Rouge: Louisiana State University Press, 1950. 331 pp.
Stampp is concerned with determining why the Civil War occurred. He asserts that the war was the product of deep and fundamental differences between the North and the South, rendering ineffectual most attempts at compromise. Stampp contends that there was no basis for sectional harmony as long as blacks remained slaves, and so long as Northerners used their overwhelming political power in Congress to advance their special interests at the expense of the South. The dominant groups on each side would not yield on these points, so secession became the last hope for a peaceful settlement. Why the South attempted to secede and why it did not produce the desired peace is the central theme of the book.

H 389. STAMPP, KENNETH M. The Era of Reconstruction: 1865-1877. New York: Knopf, 1965. 228 pp.
In this revisionist survey of Reconstruction, Stampp reevaluates every traditional interpretation of the period. He sees the Radical Republicans not as cruel, vindictive, and greedy individuals determined to punish the South, but rather as an eclectic political coalition resulting primarily from the intransigence of Andrew Johnson and Southern whites. The Radicals, furthermore, did have a genuine concern for the basic civil rights of the emancipated black population. On the other hand, Johnson is viewed not as the idealistic defender of constitutional liberties, but as an intransigent, and sometimes incompetent President who really had little concern for the freedmen. Stampp also attempts to incorporate the central role played by blacks in the Reconstruction process. He argues that the era of Reconstruction was tragic not because of injustices done to a "Prostrate South," but because "Radical" Reconstruction failed to go far enough in re-casting Southern society along more egalitarian principles and in guaranteeing the basic rights of the freedmen.

H 390. STAMPP, KENNETH M. The Imperiled Union: Essays on the Background of the Civil War. New York: Oxford University Press, 1980. 320 pp.
This collection of essays written over several years deals with the sectional crisis of the 1850s and the causes of the Civil War. Stampp examines the major issues of the period: the idea of the perpetuity of the Union, and slavery and slave personalities, including critiques of Fogel and Engerman's Time of the Cross and the Elkins thesis, as well as modification of Stampp's own views expressed earlier in the Peculiar Institution. Finally, he discusses the causes and consequences of the Civil War itself. Stampp argues that the war was not an inevitable or irrepressible conflict, and that it might have been avoided were it not for the intransigence of Southern ideologues.

H 391. STERN, MADELEINE B. Heads and Headlines: The Phrenological Fowlers. Norman: University of Oklahoma Press, 1971. 348 pp.
Stern examines the discipline of phrenology during the 19th century by focusing on the lives and work of Orson Squire Fowler, his brother Lorenzo, and other kin. The Fowlers were prime movers in the development of the discipline, and they wrote and lectured on the subject for almost a century. Indeed, phrenology developed a certain mass appeal, and Stern views it within the context of other 19th-century reform movements such as women's rights, temperance, spiritualism, revivalism, and education. Stern also describes the Fowlers's association with such well-known literati of the period as Mark Twain, Edgar Allan Poe, and Walt Whitman.

H 392. THISTLETHWAITE, FRANK. The Anglo-American Connection in the Early Nineteenth Century. Philadelphia: University of Pennsylvania Press, 1959. 222 pp.
Thistlethwaite examines American-British economic relations during the 19th century. These two economies were so closely related, he argues, that one can speak of an "Atlantic Economy." After the War of 1812 and up to the American Civil War was the period of greatest economic activity. And this activity provided the resources for America's Westward expansion. Thistlethwaite discusses reformist ideologies and movements that occurred simultaneously in the two countries: the utopian experiments at the Owenite and Transcendental communities, humanitarian efforts, and the political movements for women's rights and the abolition of slavery. He also assesses the effects each had upon its transatlantic counterpart. Thistlethwaite concludes, however, that America turned increasingly toward domestic markets and resources after its Civil War, bringing the Atlantic economy to an end.

H 393. THOMAS, EMORY M. The Confederate Nation, 1861-1865. New York:
Harper & Row, 1979. 384 pp.
Thomas offers a general survey of the Confederate States of America during
the Civil War. He argues that Southern moderates, rather than "fire-
eaters," led the secessionist movement, and filled most of the offices
of Confederate state and national government. Thomas's thesis is that
the Southern tradition of local autonomy, which was central to the pre-
war political culture of the region, conflicted with the emergent Confederate nationalism produced by the war. Thus, except for several outstanding
examples of centralized, state-controlled industry, attempts by Jefferson
Davis to centralize authority were bitterly and often effectively opposed,
to the ultimate detriment of the Southern war effort.

H 394. THORNTON, J. MILLS. Politics and Power in a Slave Society: Alabama,
1800-1860. Baton Rouge: Louisiana State University Press, 1978.
492 pp.
Thornton examines the relationship between slavery and Jacksonian ideology
in the politics of antebellum Alabama. The first part of the book covers
Alabama's politics in the first fifty years of the 19th century. Using
both traditional and quantitative sources, the author examines the various
parties, their social foundations, and the institutions through which
they interacted in this period of Alabama's political history. The second
part of the book looks at the impact of the sectional crisis of the 1850s
on Alabama politics and the role of "fire eaters" in the secession movement.
Mills argues that Alabama's yeomen, valuing personal freedom and political
democracy, perceived their independence as predicated upon the preservation
of black slavery.

H 395. TOMSICH, JOHN. A Genteel Endeavor: American Culture and Politics
in the Gilded Age. Stanford, Calif.: Stanford University Press,
1971. 236 pp.
Tomsich examines eight writers and critics of the Gilded Age, such as
Charles Eliot Norton and George W. Curtis. These men, known as "mugwumps,"
or genteel political reformers, propagated a cultural ideal in important
periodicals of the time. Tomsich argues that the genteel type was split
between his public and private self; the private man was frank and open,
but the public man rejected realism. These men believed the function
of culture was to promote social stability, to elevate the middle class,
and to humanize the nouveau riche. Tomsich argues that this split trapped
reformers in their attempt to create a self-justifying aristocracy of
their own.

H 396. TRACHTENBERG, ALAN. The Incorporation of America: Culture and
Society in the Gilded Age. New York: Hill & Wang, 1982.
261 pp.
Trachtenberg traces the ascent of the corporation in American economic
life during the late 19th century, and the effects of the corporate system
on culture, on values and outlook, and on the "way of life." He argues
that the change in perceptions of the corporation was as significant as
the changes in the enterprises and institutions themselves. In pre-Civil
War America, the corporation was still perceived as a public or semi-public
institution contributing to national development. The large, amorphous
corporation developed out of economic and geographic expansion after the
Civil War, which increasingly required the concentration of capital and
resources. This process of incorporation, however, was not without conflict. And it engendered opposing views about the very meaning of the
word "America," as opponents believed that the new corporate America
betrayed the original values of the nation. The conflict culminated in
the bloody labor conflicts of the 1890s, which resulted in the victory
of the corporation in American political, economic, and cultural life.
Trachtenberg's method is topical and thematic rather than chronological,

and includes chapters on the Old American West, machines, capital and labor, the growth of cities, the relationship between culture and politics, and the final triumph of the corporation in America.

H 397. **TRASK, DAVID F.** The War with Spain, 1898. New York: Macmillan, 1981. 546 pp.
Trask offers a detailed narrative of the Spanish-American War, which confirmed America as a Colonial power in the Caribbean and the Pacific. He argues that the war resulted not from strategic, economic, or ideological motives, but rather from the extreme and irrational feelings of the American public which no politician could ignore. Trask maintains that the U.S. government did not want war, and President McKinley desired it even less. Indeed, McKinley is portrayed as a most reluctant imperialist. Frank faults Philippine leader Emilio Aguinaldo, rather than U.S. policymakers, for the violent course of Philippine resistance to American rule.

H 398. **TREFOUSSE, HANS L.** The Radical Republicans: Lincoln's Vanguard for Racial Justice. New York: Knopf, 1969. 492 pp.
Trefousse examines the ideology and practice of the leaders of the radical wing of the Republican Party during the 1860s, focusing on Benjamin Wade, Charles Sumner, Thaddeus Stevens, and Zachariah Chandler. These men were racial egalitarians, Trefousse maintains, but being impatient with the slow process of change, they often favored bold and aggressive steps without always considering the unintended consequences which would invariably result. Trefousse examines their role in the founding of the Republican Party, their often troubled relations with the rest of the party, especially Lincoln, their efforts to develop a policy for the abolition of slavery, and their desire to make the Republican Party the party of racial justice in America.

H 399. **TYLER, ALICE FELT.** Freedom's Ferment: Phases of American Social History from the Colonial Period to the Outbreak of the Civil War. New York: Harper & Row, 1944. 608 pp.
This work examines the major humanitarian crusades for reform in the U.S. from the end of the War of 1812 to the beginning of the Civil War. Topics covered include Feminism, temperance, pacifism, and Abolitionism. Besides a discussion of utopian Socialism, there is an extended look at the various groups involved in the religious revival known as the Second Great Awakening. The Shakers, Mormons, and other millenialists, such as the Millerites, are examined. Tyler contends that America was seen as both a great experiment and a land of experimentation. It was this openness to experimentation, coupled with the perfectionist spirit of the Second Great Awakening, which called for the myriad of movements for social reform in the middle of the 19th century.

H 400. **VAN ALSTYNE, R. W.** The Rising American Empire. New York: Oxford University Press, 1960. 215 pp.
Van Alstyne surveys the American "empire," from the founding of the Republic through the end of the 19th century. He argues that expansionism has been an inherent characteristic of America, as both a colony and an independent nation. Furthermore, the development of the U.S. coincides with the rise of modern nationalism and the idea of the sovereign nation-state, and Van Alstyne believes that it ought to be examined within that context. This process continued unencumbered throughout the 19th century and culminated with the Spanish American War: an unabashed exercise in political and military imperialism. Since then, Van Alstyne argues, American leaders have been concerned with consolidation and defense of the American "empire," rather than with its further expansion.

H 401. VAN DEUSEN, GLYNDON. The Jacksonian Era, 1828-1848. New York: Harper & Row, 1959. 290 pp.
Van Deusen presents a general survey of the Jacksonian era, commencing with Jackson's ascendency to the presidency in 1828. He sees the years that followed as a period of American expansion—physical, economic, and even psychological—fostered by laissez-faire economics and fervent nationalism. Van Deusen treats the Whigs and Jacksonian Democrats even-handedly, minimizing the differences between them and stressing their common characteristics. He concludes that with the spoils of the Mexican War rekindling the debate over slavery, an issue which had been deliberately avoided, the Second Party System was beginning to show signs of disintegration.

H 402. WALKER, ROBERT H. Everyday Life in the Age of Enterprise, 1865-1900. New York: Putnam, 1967. 255 pp.
Walker traces the changes in American daily life during the last third of the 19th century: from its insularity and self-sufficiency to its reliance upon technological innovation and its metamorphosis into a more democratic and egalitarian culture. He describes how electrification, the rise of the steel and railroad industries, the expansion of opportunities for women, and changes in fashion and leisure affected the American home. Walker examines the changing roles of family members as well as the distinct customs and attitudes of various regions, and argues that the tendency was toward individual independence and greater national homogeneity.

H 403. WALTERS, RONALD G. American Reformers, 1812-1860. New York: Hill & Wang, 1978. 235 pp.
Walters examines the antebellum reform movements in America, commencing in 1815, by concentrating on the various political ideologies and religious beliefs behind the movements. He places antebellum reform within its political and cultural context: from the end of the Jeffersonian period, to the Jacksonian era, the collapse of the Second Party system, and finally the tumultuous decade of the 1850s. Walters demonstrates how reform movements reflected the perplexities, anxieties, and aspirations of ordinary Americans during this period. He concludes that reform did not survive the Civil War period because of its inability to build institutions and traditions capable of surviving across generations.

H 404. WAYNE, MICHAEL. The Reshaping of Plantation Society: The Natchez District, 1860-1880. Baton Rouge: Louisiana State University Press, 1983. 226 pp.
Wayne examines the new social and economic class relations in the Natchez District of Mississippi and Louisiana in the two decades following the Civil War. He argues that a "New South Plantation" had emerged by the 1880s, and that these new plantations were generally owned by the former slaveowners. Wayne claims that the old planter class maintained their hegemony over the local social and economic hierarchy, but that there was a transformation in their ideology. While blacks continued to perform the labor on the plantations and had little opportunity for land ownership, he finds that there was a high turnover of blacks on the plantations, and that the freedmen had a high degree of geographic mobility. Consequently, Wayne argues, the planters eschewed their old paternalistic attitudes toward the blacks and adopted a more "bourgeois" ideology, basing these new relations with the freedmen on a cash nexus, and espousing the values of profit and the supremacy of the marketplace.

H 405. **WHITE, LEONARD D.** The Republican Era, 1869-1901: A Study in
        Administrative History. New York: Macmillan, 1958. 406 pp.
White examines the Federal bureaucracy during the Gilded Age by analyzing
the presidential administrations of Ulysses S. Grant, and those that followed, until the assassination of McKinley in 1901--a period when Republicans dominated the office of President. A dominant theme is the perennial struggle between the President and Congress for control of the bureaucratic apparatus. White argues that the Congress wanted to reduce the
Presidents' administration of law to purely ministerial functions, but
that this desire was frustrated by the strength of Presidents Hayes,
Cleveland, and Garfield. White devotes chapters to each administration,
and details as a central theme the struggle for civil service reform and
a new personnel system.

H 406. **WIENER, JONATHAN M.** Social Origins of the New South: Alabama,
        1860-1885. Baton Rouge: Louisiana State University Press, 1978.
        247 pp.
Wiener examines a six-county area of Alabama's western black-belt as a
case study of social and economic class relations in the South during
Reconstruction. He argues that after the war there was a high degree
of continuity in the land-owning patterns from the antebellum period.
Wiener claims that while the mode of production and resultant social relations had undergone transformation, as nominally "free" labor had replaced
slavery, the same individuals or families tended to maintain their hegemony
over the new system. Indeed, there was greater social stability among
the largest landowning class after the war than in the decade before it.
The planter class, Wiener argues, withstood challenges from the freedmen,
the white yeomanry, and the merchant and industrial classes, maintaining
their dominance over the land. And although his study was of a small,
well-defined area, Wiener extrapolates upon his findings and suggests
that the same process may have occurred throughout the South after the
Civil War.

H 407. **WILEY, BELL I.** The Plain People of the Confederacy. Baton Rouge:
        Louisiana State University Press, 1943. 104 pp.
Primarily through the use of letters and diaries, Wiley examines the lives
of soldiers, blacks, and poor-to-middling farmers during the Confederacy's
struggle for existence. Their lives were harsh: having been disrupted
by war, social conflict, and especially inflation, which had grown out
of control toward the end of the War. After Gettysburg and Vicksburg,
according to Wiley, the patriotism of these plain folks dwindled, more
as a result of their conviction that they were being discriminated against
by the privileged classes than because of defeat and the deprivations
of war. The Confederate government, besieged by Northern armies and recal-
citrant local officials, proved completely unable to alleviate the suf-
ferings of the common folk, both in and out of the army.

H 408. **WILLIAMS, T. HARRY.** Lincoln and His Generals. New York: Grosset
        & Dunlap, 1952. 363 pp.
Williams's study details the military leadership of the Union Army during
the Civil War. It is his contention that in the early phases of the war,
generals were often appointed for political reasons. Not surprisingly,
many were incompetent. Thus, a frustrated Lincoln searched continually
for men with military competence, finally deciding on General McClellan
in late 1862. A modern command system was instituted in the winter of
1863-64, with Ulysses S. Grant assuming greater influence. Grant, according to Williams, understood the reality of modern, total war, and correctly
viewed the war as a conflict between two entire societies rather than
between small, professional armies. Lincoln, however, is credited more
than any of his generals with possessing the better grasp of war strategy.

H 409. **WILLIAMS, T. HARRY.** <u>Lincoln and the Radicals</u>. Madison: University of Wisconsin Press, 1941. 413 pp.
Williams examines the relations between Lincoln and the Radical Republicans of the Civil War Congresses. He describes their conflicting views over the conduct, policy, and objectives of the war, beginning with the disputes over Lincoln's choices of generals, and continuing through the end of the war and into the era of Lincoln's successor, Andrew Johnson. Williams portrays the Radicals as vindictive, ruthless extremists who welcomed the outbreak of the war in order to destroy slavery and the civilization to which it gave rise; and he claims that the Radicals had little sincere concern for the slaves of the South, referring to them disparagingly as the "Jacobins." Lincoln, on the other hand, is seen as a steady, moderate influence on the party, more in touch with political realities, yet more genuinely concerned with a just and equitable restoration of the Union.

H 410. **WILLIAMS, T. HARRY.** <u>Romance and Realism in Southern Politics</u>. Athens: University of Georgia Press, 1961. 84 pp.
In four separate essays Williams discusses Southern distinctiveness, Reconstruction, Populism and Progressivism in the South, and the development of Huey Long's political dynasty in Louisiana. The history of the post-Civil War South, Williams argues, has run in two directions: the romantic, which stresses the glories of the past, and the "realist," which tries to recognize the South's economic backwardness, and emphasizes the necessity of struggling to overcome the region's economic problems. The chapter on Long illustrates the potential role of the "realist" within the realm of Southern politics.

H 411. **WILTSE, CHARLES M.** <u>The New Nation, 1800-1845</u>. New York: Hill & Wang, 1961. 237 pp.
Wiltse surveys the first half of the 19th century in America, examining both the major social, political, and economic developments as well as the individuals who shaped them. He sees the achievement of a unified nationalist sentiment primarily as a result of the War of 1812 and its successful conclusion for the U.S. Yet this unified sentiment proved ephemeral. Consensus quickly broke down after the war, as the Missouri Crisis of 1820 clearly demonstrated. Wiltse examines how sectional antagonisms developed during the 1830s, and how the debate over slavery began to dominate national politics.

H 412. **WOOD, FORREST G.** <u>Black Scare: The Racist Response to Emancipation and Reconstruction</u>. Berkeley: University of California Press, 1968. 219 pp.
Wood examines the growth and development of the racism endemic not only to the South but to the entire nation after the demise of slavery. He argues that modern racism did not begin during the Civil War, but that the war and Reconstruction polarized racism for the first time into a psychological force of massive national proportions. The racist demagoguery of the Civil War and Reconstruction era was the first instance of "white backlash" against black freedom and the attempts by humanitarians to help meliorate the negro's status. Wood recounts the major events of the era, but more importantly he examines the popular racial attitudes from which such events rose, as well as the perceptions of and reactions to them.

H 413. **WOODWARD, C. VANN.** <u>Reunion and Reaction: The Compromise of 1877 and the End of Reconstruction</u>. Boston: Little, Brown, 1951. 297 pp.
Woodward examines the political and economic agreement among Republicans, Southerners, and railroad interests which ended the era of Reconstruction in 1877. He details the intricate political maneuverings and alignments which eventually left the South firmly Democratic and its economy dependent on Eastern financial and industrial interests. Woodward's analysis challenges the traditional interpretation of the Compromise of 1877 as an outcome of the Wormley Conference, and instead views the compromise as fundamentally affected by a deal over a Southern transcontinental railroad.

V. TWENTIETH CENTURY

H 414. AARON, DANIEL. Men of Good Hope: A Story of American Progressives.
New York: Oxford University Press, 1951. 329 pp.
In an effort to "rehabilitate the progressive tradition," Aaron places
the movement in a philosophical tradition of Jeffersonian ideals and Protestant evangelicalism. The bulk of this analysis deals with five Progressive
theorists--Henry George, Edward Bellamy, Henry Demerest Lloyd, William
Dean Howells, and Thorstein Veblen. A final section on Theodore Roosevelt
and Brooks Adams considers the pragmatic side of progressivism.

H 415. ABRAHAMSON, JAMES L. America Arms for a New Century: The Making
of a Great Military Power. New York: Free Press, 1981. 253 pp.
Abrahamson's book is a study of the role played by professional military
officers in the development of American defense capabilities between 1880
and 1920. These officers from both the Army and the Navy, believed the
U.S. military establishment had to keep pace with a changing world. With
the advent of W.W. I, the officer corps pushed for a greatly increased
standing military force. Their effort foundered on the traditional American disdain, still strong in that period, for a permanent defense force
of any proportions. Abrahamson's sources include contemporary periodicals
and articles by the military officers themselves.

H 416. ALEXANDER, CHARLES C. Holding the Line: The Eisenhower Era, 1952-
1961. Bloomington: Indiana University Press, 1975. 326 pp.
Alexander's survey of the Eisenhower years is favorable to the President,
who is credited with keeping the U.S. out of war, fighting his party's
extremist right wing, and seeking to contain the expansion of the American
Cold War state. Eisenhower is criticized, however, for excessive timidity
in the area of civil rights, for agreeing to CIA adventurism, and for
rigid anti-Communism in general. The emphasis in this book is on
politics, but a long chapter deals with economic, social, and intellectual
trends of the 1950s.

H 417. ALLEN, FREDERICK LEWIS. The Big Change: America Transforms Itself
1900-1950. New York: Harper & Row, 1952. 308 pp.
Dividing his study into three sections, "The Old Order" (1900), "Momentum
of Change," and "The New America," Allen contends that marked social
stratification was erased in the first half of the century, and that social
reform, expanding industrialism, and democratic government combined to
produce a "Big Change." That change was the emergence of a newly viable,
politically recognized middle-class. This chronological survey discusses
the cultural dimensions of the loosened morals of the 1920s, the Muckrakers,
the economic and social ramifications of the Depression and the New Deal,
the two World Wars, increased productivity and the gradual emergence of
America as a world power.

H 418. ALTBACH, PHILIP G. Student Politics in America: A Historical
Analysis. New York: McGraw-Hill, 1974. 249 pp.
This study examines the political activity of American college students
from 1900 to 1960, with brief consideration of activism in earlier and
later periods. Altbach concentrates on organizations which were liberal
or radical in orientation and national, or at least regional, in scope.
He sees both continuity and change within student politics: the roots
of the 1960s New Left, for example, can be traced to student movements
of the 1920s and 1930s. Further, activity in foreign affairs, world peace,
and civil liberties has been fairly constant. On the other hand, efforts
aimed at university reform have waxed and waned. Altbach identifies
several factors which rendered American students less effective than their

counterparts in other countries: the American political structure is
complex and highly developed; American universities are large, geographically diverse, and administratively diffuse; and students have neither
a sense of community nor a long tradition of political activism. While
students have had limited successes, Altbach concludes, they have not
effected deep or lasting changes in the American socio-political system.

H 419. BEALE, HOWARD. Theodore Roosevelt and the Rise of America to World
        Power. Baltimore, Md.: Johns Hopkins University Press, 1956.
        600 pp.
Beale focuses on the role of Theodore Roosevelt in the formation of American
foreign policy, specifically, his knowledge, his attitudes toward different nations, and his dealings with foreign representatives. Roosevelt
is portrayed as a cultural parochial and a believer in the sufficiency
of military power as the chief instrument of international relations.
Beale also examines the Anglo-American rapprochement of these years, a
movement strongly encouraged and aided by Roosevelt.

H 420. BELL, DANIEL. Marxian Socialism in the United States. Princeton,
        N.J.: Princeton University Press, 1952. 212 pp.
Bell's history of major radical movements in the U.S. focuses on the Socialist and Communist parties. The failure of American radicals to develop
a strong base of support is due, in large part, to their inability to
resolve the basic conflict between politics and ethics. In their rejection
of Capitalism, radicals could not relate to specific problems of the immediate world. A religious movement can do this, but a political one cannot.
Employing Martin Luther's metaphor, Bell describes the Socialist Party
as being "in the world, but not of it." It had a set of goals, but was
not an integrated part of society. The Communist Party went beyond this
point, refusing to live in as well as be part of the world and creating
instead a new world of its own.

H 421. BELLUSH, BERNARD. The Failure of the NRA. New York: Norton,
        1975. 197 pp.
Drawing on primary sources, Bellush traces the rise and fall of the
National Recovery Administration, the agency FDR intended to be the centerpiece of his New Deal economic program. The NRA, the administrative arm
of the National Industrial Recovery Act, was to police business activity
and, as a result, to revive the economy and put millions of people back
to work. Bellush attributes NRA's failure to internal weakness due to
the alcoholism of its leader, Hugh Johnson, and to self-regulating businesses' insensitive policy toward labor and resulting labor disputes.
The author discusses details of the Supreme Court decision declaring the
NRA unconstitutional, and its effect on the overall economic policy of
the New Deal.

H 422. BENNETT, DAVID H. Demagogues in the Depression: American Radicals
        and the Union Party, 1932-36. New Brunswick, N.J.: Rutgers Uni-
        versity Press, 1969. 341 pp.
Bennett examines the forces that contributed to the formation of the Union
Party in 1936. A coalition of several different movements led by Charles
Coughlin, Francis Townsend, Gerald L. K. Smith, and William Lemke, the
party sought to end the Great Depression through the manipulation of the
money supply. All members of the coalition were former supporters of
Franklin Roosevelt and the New Deal, but became convinced that neither
went far enough. In focusing upon the money supply as a panacea, they
continued a tradition that stretched back to the Greenback and Populist
movements. Their desire to re-create the past, their appeal to the powerless in an industrial and urban society, their emphasis on money, and
their occasional anti-Semitism reveal that they were closer to the right
than the left, more of a precursor to McCarthy than the New Left.

340

H 423. **BLUM, JOHN MORTON.** The Progressive Presidents: Theodore Roosevelt, Woodrow Wilson, Franklin D. Roosevelt, Lyndon B. Johnson. New York: Norton, 1980. 221 pp.
As the title suggests, Blum finds significant similarities among these four presidents. All, he argues, were strong chief executives who were talented in political maneuvering, committed to promoting gradual social reform, and accomplished in directing foreign policy. The author believes that each of these presidents made mistakes in policy judgments, but his assessment is essentially favorable.

H 424. **BLUM, JOHN MORTON.** V Was for Victory: Politics and American Culture During World War II. New York: Harcourt Brace Jovanovich, 1976. 372 pp.
Blum surveys American society during W.W. II, and considers how the wartime experience at home shaped expectations about the post-war world. Among the subjects covered in this book are wartime propaganda, congressional actions, civil rights, and the experiences of ethnic and religious minorities. Blum concludes that the experience of the war resulted in a heavily consumer-oriented post-war society.

H 425. **BONNIFIELD, PAUL.** The Dust Bowl: Men, Dirt and Depression. Albuquerque: University of New Mexico Press, 1979. 232 pp.
Bonnifield's study, based on local sources, describes the effects of drought and wind erosion on the "Dust Bowl" region of the Southwestern U.S. in the years 1932-1938. The author suggests that the supposedly remedial policies of the Federal government were actually intended to drive people off the land, and thereby to restore a grazing economy. Hard times and the relative failure of government policy to relieve the distress inspired the great "Okie" migration to California.

H 426. **BOWERS, WILLIAM L.** The Country Life Movement in America, 1900-1920. Port Washington, N.Y.: Kennikat Press, 1974. 189 pp.
Bowers examines the early 20th century's country life movement, which sought to preserve the imagined virtues of agrarian life within an increasingly urbanized society. The movement, which Bowers portrays as a current of Progressivism, hoped the much-noted migration out of rural areas might be stemmed if country living could be made more economically, socially, and intellectually attractive. The movement worked at cross purposes-- it attempted to make farm life more businesslike, scientific and cosmopolitan and to preserve vaunted rural tradition. Bowers concludes that industrialization proved too formidable a force for such efforts to succeed.

H 427. **BREINES, WINI.** Community and Organization in the New Left, 1962-1968; The Great Refusal. New York: Praeger, 1982. 187 pp.
Breines represents the emergence of the New Left as a serious reform effort with imaginative programs and a sophisticated conceptual basis. In this history, Students for a Democratic Society (SDS) is described as the quintessential New Left organization, one capable of practical action. A major theme of the work is the constant tension between the New Left's desire for open participation and democratic decision-making and its need for strong decisive leadership.

H 428. **BRINKLEY, ALAN.** Voices of Protest: Huey Long, Father Coughlin, and the Great Depression. New York: Knopf, 1982. 348 pp.
Brinkley examines the rhetoric and composition of the "Share Our Wealth" and "Social Justice" movements of the 1930s. He finds that the language and ideology of Long and Coughlin were more reminiscent of American Populism than of, as is often asserted, Fascism. Their evocation of individual autonomy, decentralization, and community independence and their railing against distant, powerful malefactors appealed especially to a middle class whose status and community position were imperiled not only by eco-

nomic crisis but also by an emerging mass society. Brinkley considers
the limits of the discontent in this period, especially the ultimate reluctance of many of Long and Coughlin's followers to decisively renounce
the popular FDR.

H 429. BUCHANAN, A. RUSSELL. The United States and World War II. 2 vols.
New York: Harper & Row, 1964. 635 pp.
Buchanan studies the American role in W.W. II--a total war conducted in
the military, diplomatic, scientific, and economic arenas. Buchanan details
the campaigns in the Pacific, Africa, and Southern and Western Europe,
attending less to social and cultural developments. He also discusses
Allied statesmanship and varied elements of the home front experience.

H 430. BURNER, DAVID. The Politics of Provincialism: The Democratic
Party in Transition, 1918-1932. New York: Knopf, 1968.
293 pp.
Burner examines the emergence of the Democratic party from its rural base
to form a coalition with the urban political powers. From 1900 to 1932,
a period of Republican dominance, the Democratic party lost its largely
rural orientation and leadership, and came to represent the ideals of
urban Americans, especially of more recent immigrants. The transition
was bitter: rural Democrats struggled to retain strength through the
issues of nativism, prohibition, and Protestantism; losing presidential
candidates of the era had strong associations with city political machines.
The two factions were finally united in a coalition forged by the Great
Depression and the personality of Franklin Roosevelt.

H 431. CARTER, PAUL A. Another Part of the Fifties. New York: Columbia
University Press, 1983. 328 pp.
Carter portrays the 1950s as a decade that was politically and culturally
richer than is usually imagined. Beginning with the election of Eisenhower
in 1952, he chronicles various aspects of the social and political history
of the Eisenhower years. Among these are religion, changes in higher
education, the advent of the atomic age, and mass entertainment, especially
the emergence and development of television.

H 432. CARTER, PAUL A. Another Part of the Twenties. New York: Columbia
University Press, 1977. 229 pp.
Carter argues that the popular recollections of the "Roaring Twenties"
fail to take into account the broader spectrum of social and political
behavior. The more commonplace aspects of daily life, he argues, show
the decade to have had a calm, progressive side. This collection of essays
explores such topics as prohibition, the peace movement, scientific progress, advertising, church responses to the modern world, and the persistence of traditional, rural values even in those movements perceived to
be rebelling against them.

H 433. CASHMAN, SEAN DENNIS. Prohibition: The Lie of the Land. New
York: Free Press, 1981. 290 pp.
Cashman offers a general survey of the era of national Prohibition (1920-
33). He discusses the social and political reasons for which Prohibition
was adopted; its impact on American society and political life; its relationship to criminal activity; its repeal during the early days of the
Roosevelt Administration; and its lingering image, especially in popular
culture.

H 434. CHAMBERLAIN, JOHN. Farewell to Reform: The Rise, Life and Decay of the Progressive Mind in America. New York: John Day, 1932. 333 pp.
Chamberlain's book is one of the earliest studies of Progressivism, and emphasizes its intellectual and social rather than its political aspects. Attention is given to muckrakers, novelists, and some progressive politicians such as Theodore Roosevelt, Robert La Follette, and Woodrow Wilson. The author argues that progressive reformers were often ineffectual and backward-looking, seeking a return to the "virtuous" America of the past. Progressivism proved too weak to oppose the emotionalism of W.W. I, and collapsed with Wilson's Presidency.

H 435. CLARK, NORMAN H. Deliver Us from Evil: An Interpretation of American Prohibition. New York: Norton, 1976. 246 pp.
The Temperance and Prohibition movements became significant social and political forces during a time when different groups in America were developing a bourgeois culture. As the slow articulation of deep anxieties, both movements intended to protect the values sheltered by the nuclear family. This theme, Clark argues, connected the arguments of Lyman Beecher in the 1820s, Elizabeth Cady Stanton in the 1850s, and Herbert Hoover in the 1920s. Since no church, state, or private organization existed to protect public virtue, these movements were formed to defend the sanctity of the bourgeois family. The repeal of Prohibition in the 1930s marked the decline of pietistic Capitalism and the appearance of a new society and order, but one still rooted in bourgeois values.

H 436. CLECAK, PETER. America's Quest for the Ideal Self: Dissent and Fulfillment in the 60's and 70's. New York: Oxford University Press, 1983. 395 pp.
Clecak interprets recent trends in American society favorably, arguing that what others refer to as the "me decade" phenomenon—an exploration of self-indulgent narcissism—is, rather, the "democratization of personhood." Under this rubric Clecak includes the drive for greater cultural recognition on the part of born-again Christians, feminists, homosexuals, and various ethnic groups. The quest for fulfillment during these years, Clecak agrees, has been a largely personal one.

H 437. COLE, WAYNE S. Roosevelt and the Isolationists, 1932-1945. Lincoln: University of Nebraska Press, 1983. 698 pp.
This study of the isolationist movement in the FDR years is based on research in both the U.S. and Britain. Cole's sources include FBI files, over 100 archive and manuscript collections, and personal interviews. Cole maintains that there were three distinct phases in Roosevelt's relationship with the isolationists: first, an uneasy accommodation; second, a widening split after 1937, occasioned by the President's increasing attention to foreign affairs (as his domestic program faltered); and, finally, the defeat and, in some cases, persecution of isolationists as FDR's interventionist policy triumphed. The case for interventionism could be argued on its own merits, yet FDR fought his isolationist opponents with less elevated political methods. Cole's attention is often drawn to the U.S. Senate, a primary seat of the isolationist cause.

H 438. CONKIN, PAUL K. The New Deal. New York: Crowell, 1967. 118 pp.
This book provides an overview of the politics, legislation, and personalities of the New Deal era (1932 to 1939). Conkin argues that the New Deal consisted of a series of pragmatic, non-ideological reforms, unified primarily by the charismatic personality of Franklin Delano Roosevelt. The specific reforms enacted in the first "hundred days" are discussed at length, and Conkin concludes that the emphasis of the New Deal as a whole moved from economic recovery to economic reform. Conkin sees the origins of the contemporary welfare state in the politics of the New Deal.

H 439. CONKIN, PAUL K. Tomorrow a New World: The New Deal Community Program. Ithaca, N.Y.: Cornell University Press, 1959. 350 pp.

The New Deal's community program, with its construction of approximately 100 communities, departed sharply from the American individualist tradition. Initially planned by the Division of Subsistence Homesteads in the Department of the Interior and the Federal Emergency Relief Administration, by 1935 most of the projects became the responsibility of the Resettlement Administration headed by Rexford Tugwell. Influenced by planned land settlement, the city planning movement, and national economic planning, the community idea was appealing in the abstract, but difficult to realize. Examining Arthurdale, Jersey Homesteads, Penderlea Homesteads (North Carolina), and the Greenbelt towns, Conkin finds that settlers were not anxious to participate in an experiment they could not understand or appreciate. They simply wanted economic security.

H 440. CROSBY, DONALD F. God, Church, and Flag: Senator Joseph R. McCarthy and the Catholic Church, 1950-1957. Chapel Hill: University of North Carolina Press, 1978. 307 pp.

Crosby considers the Catholic response to Senator Joseph McCarthy's anti-Communist crusade, and concludes it was not fundamentally different from the response of other Americans. Support or opposition was a function of the political preferences and beliefs of the individuals; there was no uniform response by either the church hierarchy or the laity. The Vatican order that the Jesuit weekly America cease its severe criticism of McCarthy and adopt a more aloof posture is interpreted primarily as a pragmatic rather than a partisan move.

H 441. CRUNDEN, ROBERT. Ministers of Reform: The Progressives' Achievement in American Civilization, 1889-1920. New York: Basic Books, 1982. 307 pp.

Crunden argues that a common background of Republicanism and devout Protestantism shaped a whole generation's agenda. The Progressive's manifold efforts to provide for the spiritual reformation of the nation and to fulfill a divine plan for American democracy emerged from a shared set of moral values. Crunden has examined 100 members of the Progressive generation, and emphasizes the lives and work of twenty-one individuals, including John Dewey, Woodrow Wilson, Frank Lloyd Wright, Charles Ives, Frederick Jackson Turner, George Herbert Mead, and Richard Ely. He believes Progressivism to have made its most lasting impact in the arts, philosophy, and diplomacy, and describes the "innovative nostalgia" of many of its efforts—the simultaneous gaze into past and future.

H 442. CUFF, ROBERT D. The War Industries Board: Business-Government Relations During World War I. Baltimore, Md.: Johns Hopkins University Press, 1973. 304 pp.

Cuff examines the origins of the War Industries Board (WIB) which presided over America's industries during W.W. I. Numerous forces and ideas competed for power before and immediately after the U.S. entered the war in April 1917. The organization that finally emerged was the WIB, under the leadership of businessman and political patron Bernard M. Baruch. The WIB brought industry under regulation by working with and frequently accommodating the nation's business leaders. The system operated on the basis of compromise more than of centralized control. Furthermore, the authority that did exist was often left in the hands of administrators with strong professional ties to the business community.

H 443. DEBENEDETTI, CHARLES. Origins of the Modern American Peace Movement 1915-1929. Millwood, N.Y.: K.T.O. Press, 1978. 281 pp.
This book studies the peace movement in the U.S. from the founding of the League to Enforce Peace to the Kellogg-Briand Pact, which sought to outlaw war as an instrument of national policy. Within the movement, conservatives stressing the need for international law conflicted with liberals pursuing a world political organization. The movement of this period was an important predecessor of later peace movements.

H 444. DeWEERD, HARVEY A. President Wilson Fights His War: World War I and the American Intervention. New York: Macmillan, 1968. 457 pp.
DeWeerd's account primarily discusses the role of the U.S. in the European military theater during W.W. I. The roles played by Secretary of War Newton Baker and General John J. Pershing are stressed, especially the mobilization of nearly 5 million men by the U.S. in less than two years. Strategy, tactics, and the deployments of military units are also covered.

H 445. DOBSON, JOHN M. America's Ascent: The United States Becomes a Great Power. DeKalb: Northern Illinois University Press, 1978. 251 pp.
The author describes how the great influence of a small circle of leaders produced the American expansion in the late 19th and early 20th centuries. Among the motivations stressed by Dobson for this development are a belief in the American way of life as inherently superior; the desire for status and world power; and the economic drive for markets as a solution to the recurring problem of depression. Of less importance, in Dobson's view, was strategic thinking, such as is often cited as the cause of U.S. actions regarding Panama. Dobson paints a favorable portrait of President Theodore Roosevelt and Secretary of State Elihu Root.

H 446. DODDS, JOHN W. Everyday Life in Twentieth Century America. New York: Putnam, 1965. 254 pp.
Dodds explores the evolution of various elements of daily life in the 20th century. The history of transportation is traced from horse and buggy to the assembly line to Kitty Hawk. Daily living patterns in the small town and the growing city are contrasted. Changing attitudes toward living space are revealed in such phenomena as the demise of the palatial mansion and the rise of interest in "organic architecture." Dodds discusses reading matter--from the sentimental novel to the realistic fiction of Hemingway--and the institution of the paperback. He treats changes in music and humor as well as the move from "home centered" entertainment to the cult of movie theaters and spectator sport. The changes technology has occasioned are considered in discussions of frozen foods, electricity, synthetics, plastics, and "wonder drugs."

H 447. DRAPER, THEODORE. American Communism and Soviet Russia: The Formative Period. New York: Viking Press, 1960. 558 pp.
This study of American Communism covers the years 1923 to 1929, and focuses on how the relationship of the American Communists to Moscow completely dominated the party in the U.S. Draper shows how shifts within the American organization followed the power struggles in the Soviet Union, linking the fortunes of American Communist leaders such as William Z. Foster and Jay Lovestone to the infighting among Trotsky, Kamenev, Zinoviev, Bukharin, and Stalin. He also argues that the party had to choose between ideology and influence, and thus, alternated between doctrinaire sectarianism and a cultivation of more influential non-Communists in the Farmer-Labor and Progressive movements, the AFL, and similar organizations.

H 448. DRAPER, THEODORE. The Roots of American Communism. New York:
Viking Press, 1957. 498 pp.
Draper traces the political origins of the Communist movement in America
prior to 1922. Examined in detail are the movement's emergence within
the Socialist Party's left wing, its relationship to the Bolshevik Revolution, and the sectarianism that marked its early years. In addition,
Draper addresses American Communism's constituency, particularly its ethnic
composition. He demonstrates that the Communists' support came primarily
from those outside the mainstream of American society, particularly recent
immigrants.

H 449. DYSON, LOWELL K. Red Harvest: The Communist Party and American
Farmers. Lincoln: University of Nebraska Press, 1982. 259 pp.
The study focuses on several Communist dominated farmers' organizations.
Despite the commitment of local Communist organizers and several successes
in the interwar period, the Communist Party U.S.A. failed to win wide
farm support. The reasons for this failure include the lack of attention
by the party's Central Committee, the failure to capitalize on the rich
populist tradition, and the individualism of American farmers which forced
the party to "mute the goal of collectivization."

H 450. EKRICH, ARTHUR A. Progressivism in America: A Study of the Era
from Theodore Roosevelt to Woodrow Wilson. New York: Franklin
Watts, 1974. 308 pp.
Ekrich treats many aspects of American Progressivism, including the
reformers—socialists, urban liberals, muckrakers, proponents of the social
gospel; the efforts to build a national Progressive program; and the
dynamic relationship between foreign policy and American life. But his
particular concern is to highlight the interrelatedness of Western Europe
and the U.S., not only in the shared experience of industrialism and nationalism but also in the borrowings of American Progressives from European
social and political thought. Governmental activism and social welfare
measures were, in some form, sought by Progressives as well as by the
social democrats and socialists of Western Europe and Britain.

H 451. FEIS, HERBERT. The Diplomacy of the Dollar, 1919-1932. Baltimore,
Md.: Johns Hopkins University Press, 1950. 81 pp.
Feis details the close relationship between the State Department and private business between the end of W.W. I to the beginning of the New Deal.
The State Department directed private funds toward investments which it
hoped would advance the national interest. Feis recounts how large firms,
anxious for profits, made considerable investments in Europe, Latin America
and Japan at the behest of the Coolidge and Hoover administrations, and
how this process was abruptly halted after the Stock Market Crash of 1929.
According to Feis the end of "dollar diplomacy" resulted in the new internationalism of FDR.

H 452. FELIX, DAVID. Protest: Sacco-Vanzetti and the Intellectuals.
Bloomington: Indiana University Press, 1965. 274 pp.
In this study, Felix shifts the reader's attention from Sacco and Vanzetti
as men or as Italian-Americans to Sacco and Vanzetti as radicals, and
suggests that their trial was far more than a simple legal procedure—
that it was "a legend called into life to fill a need." According to
Felix, the Sacco-Vanzetti case was a vehicle for protest and an inspiration
to the American intellectuals, a group that he asserts lived on the outer
fringes of American society, "ignored or despised in a country impatient
of thought and busy organizing its physical resources." It was in this
context that the intellectuals discovered the Sacco-Vanzetti case—a case
that provided the hard, definable issue they had been waiting for, around
which they could crystallize their more general protest. He suggests
that this protest became, in fact, an important stage in the reintegration
of intellectuals into American society.

H 453. FOGARTY, ROBERT S. The Righteous Remnant: The House of David.
Kent, Ohio: Kent State University Press, 1981. 195 pp.
Fogarty begins his account of The House of David with an overview of its
origins in 18th- and 19th-century theology. He cites the prophetic careers
of such figures as Joanna Southcott, John Wroe, and James Jershem Jezreel;
he then discusses the lives and careers of the founders of The House of
David, Benjamin and Mary Purnell. Succeeding chapters document the theology and religious practices which characterize the sect's history.
Fogarty also treats the relationship between the sect and society. The
volume concludes with several appendices which provide the "Sixty Propositions" of The House of David, a Colony membership list, and biographical
information concerning major sect members and their families.

H 454. FREIDEL, FRANK. F.D.R. and the South. Baton Rouge: Louisiana
State University Press, 1965. 102 pp.
Freidel argues that the South was initially supportive of New Deal legislation, especially agricultural relief measures, but that this support
eroded as blacks entered the New Deal coalition and FDR began to advocate
steps toward racial justice. Freidel also treats the conflict that emerged
between FDR and the Bourbon governments of several states, and the waning
of support for the New Deal on the part of powerful Southern senators
such as Virginia's Carter Glass.

H 455. GIESKE, MILLARD L. Minnesota Farmer-Laborism: The Third Party
Alternative. Minneapolis: University of Minnesota Press, 1979.
389 pp.
Growing out of the Populist and Progressive traditions, the Farmer-Labor
Party of Minnesota offered a regional alternative to the major political
parties in the period 1918-1944. Originally founded by a group of dissatisfied socialists, the party held that "the political and economic
systems were unresponsive and malfunctioning." It grew with support from
farmer's cooperatives, labor union activists, and the Non-Partisan league.
The party elected a Senator in 1922 and two governors in the 1930s, but
declined, Gieske argues, as a result of intra-party disputes and factionalism.

H 456. GLAZER, NATHAN. The Social Basis of American Communism. New York:
Harcourt, Brace & World, 1961. 244 pp.
Between 1920 and 1950 the American Communist Party chiefly sought to
enlarge and take care of its membership. While throughout the 1920s the
Party was composed almost exclusively of recent immigrants, after 1930
it was transformed from a largely working-class organization into one
that was half middle-class. Between 1935 and 1950, the Party became the
"vanguard of the intellectual and professional worker." The white-collar,
middle-class cast differentiated the American Communist Party from almost
every other Communist Party in the world. During both periods, Glazer
finds a large number of Jewish members. Joining the party out of a faith
and a desire for community, not economic interest, Jews and other ethnic
members perceived party membership as shedding the limitations of one's
social reality and joining a fraternity that transcended the divisions
of the world.

H 457. GOLDMAN, ERIC F. The Crucial Decade and After: America 1945-1955.
New York: Knopf, 1956. 298 pp.
Goldman argues that the decade following W.W. II was one of rapid political
change and innovative foreign and domestic policy which began to stabilize
and slow down under the Eisenhower administration. The era's political
figures receive most of the book's attention: Goldman describes the activities and ideas of Truman, Robert Taft, Alger Hiss, Joseph McCarthy, and
Eisenhower. He also discusses the challenge to reformist philosophy and
the growing acceptance of a foreign policy which stressed co-existence
rather than confrontation.

H 458. GOLDMAN, ERIC F. Rendezvous with Destiny. New York: Knopf, 1952.
503 pp.
Goldman's narrative, spanning the years from Grant to Truman, traces
liberal reform efforts in an increasingly urban and industrial society.
Distinguishing these reformers from the socialists to their left, Goldman
examines patrician reform in the years immediately following the Civil
War, Populism, the influence of Henry George, Progressivism—both as
Herbert Croly's New Nationalism and Woodrow Wilson's New Freedom—and liberalism during W.W. I, the 1920s, and the New Deal years. In examining
these movements, Goldman is particularly attentive to the doctrine he
terms "Reform Darwinism," which stressed the environmental and economic
motivations of behavior.

H 459. GOLDMAN, ERIC F. The Tragedy of Lyndon Johnson: A Historian's
Personal Interpretation. New York: Knopf, 1969. 531 pp.
This account of the Johnson Administration offers a portrait of the Presi-
dent and his political struggles in such crises as the Vietnam war, a
massive railway strike, and the Santo Domingo conflict. Written by a
former consultant to Johnson, this book focuses on the personality of
Johnson and on the author's attempt to open communication between the
President and the worlds of academia and the arts.

H 460. GRAHAM, OTIS L., Jr. An Encore for Freedom: The Old Progressives
and the New Deal. New York: Oxford University Press, 1967.
256 pp.
This study takes issue with the traditional view that the New Deal was
merely the logical extension of the Progressive reform movement. In a
survey of more than 100 Progressive-era reformers, Graham finds that half
were adamantly opposed to the New Deal. Graham contends that the two
movements were fundamentally different. The Progressive movement, Graham
concludes, was based on the ideals of reform through politics and muckraking journalism, within the bounds of white, Protestant, provincial
society, while the New Deal concentrated on economic security, urban problems, and the use of concentrated Federal power.

H 461. GRAHAM, OTIS L., Jr. Toward a Planned Society: From Roosevelt
to Nixon. New York: Oxford University Press, 1976. 357 pp.
Otis discusses "planning"—coordinated "public intervention" in the pursuit
of national goals—as advocated or carried out in America since the 1930s.
He examines the attractions planning held for a number of New Dealers
and how a "broker state"—a government given to ad hoc intervention—
emerged from those years. The 1960s witnessed a reawakening of interest
in broader notions of planning, in structural reform and the expansion
of public control. By the time of the Nixon Presidency, a consensus embracing Right and Left had been created favoring an articulation of long-range
economic and social goals and public involvement in the achievement of
them.

H 462. GREEN, JAMES R. Grass-Roots Socialism: Radical Movements in the
Southwest, 1895-1943. Baton Rouge: Louisiana State University
Press, 1978. 450 pp.
Before W.W. I, Oklahoma, Texas, Louisiana, and Arkansas gave the Socialist
Party its strongest national support. The socialist movement in the Southwest was built by former Populists, militant miners, blacklisted railroad
workers, women's suffragettes, renegade preachers of Christian socialism,
and amateur agitators and writers. The Party organized itself around
local issues and a wide range of class struggles: debtor-creditor, tenant-
landlord, worker-industrialist. Green finds that support for Eugene Debs
was a class phenomenon, not a religious or ethnic one. In politicizing
the class struggle for poor white workers and farmers, the Party countered
the narrow, racist appeal used by the status quo in the Democratic Party.

348

H 463. GREENSTEIN, FRED I. The Hidden-Hand Presidency: Eisenhower as
    Leader. New York: Basic Books, 1982. 286 pp.
Greenstein's revisionist account of the Eisenhower Presidency characterizes
Ike as a shrewd, subtle political leader. His leadership strategies
stressed behind the scenes, or "hidden-hand," influence; a simultaneous
refraining from personal criticism and manipulation of personality traits;
and a careful delegation of power. Greenstein presents as a case study
the McCarthy episode, in which Eisenhower and his administration worked
steadily--but not publicly--to undermine the Senator from Wisconsin.

H 464. GREGORY, ROSS. The Origins of American Intervention in the First
    World War. New York: Norton, 1971. 62 pp.
This book is a short account of the background to American entry into
W.W. I between 1914 and 1917. Gregory examines Wilson's policy of neutrality, and the complex events which ultimately undermined that policy.
He argues that America's place in the world economy made involvement inevitable. Wilson is depicted as an idealistic man surrounded by advisors
who were inept and outright insubordinate. These problems were compounded
by the divided opinions of Americans of different national origins.
Gregory argues that right up to the moment war was declared, Wilson was
unable to accept the drift toward intervention, and stretched his political
credibility, domestically and internationally, with his efforts to remain
non-belligerent.

H 465. GRUBER, CAROL S. Mars and Minerva: World War I and the Uses of
    the Higher Learning in America. Baton Rouge: Louisiana State
    University Press, 1975. 293 pp.
Gruber criticizes members of highly respected professions, especially
historians such as Carl Becker and Frederick Jackson Turner, who committed
their academic knowledge and prestige to portraying W.W. I as a clear
and simple struggle between democracy and autocracy. The militarization
of college campuses, the sacrifice of academic freedom and independence,
and the production of cheap propaganda, argues Gruber, served the interests
of established power rather than the standards of truth and of intellectual
integrity.

H 466. GUTTMANN, ALLEN. The Wound in the Heart: America and the Spanish
    Civil War. New York: Free Press of Glencoe, 1962. 292 pp.
Guttmann examines the impact of the Spanish Civil War (1936-1939) on Americans and why it moved them to such intense partisanship. He discusses
the many responses to the conflict thematically, according to whether
they operated from conservative, liberal, anti-democratic, Catholic, radical, or irrationalist assumptions or perspectives. Guttmann finds, however,
that the majority of concerned Americans defined their opinions in terms
of the liberal democratic tradition--backers of the Republic spoke of
preserving a democratic, rather than a radical, government; supporters
of Franco pictured him as a defender of religious or individual liberty.
Guttman treats as well the "post-liberal" irrationalist response, especially on the part of a number of artists, that viewed the conflict as
one of man versus machine or primitivism versus progress.

H 467. HARPER, ALAN. The Politics of Loyalty: The White House and the
    Communist Issue, 1946-1952. Westport, Conn.: Greenwood Press,
    1969. 318 pp.
Harry Truman, the central figure in this study, is portrayed quite favorably as a president committed to civil liberties, but forced by political
pressure to institute internal security measures. Truman gave Justice
Department officials wide latitude in their enforcement of these measures,
and also supported loyalty tests for civil servants. Harper examines
Truman's attempts to balance civil liberties against these security measures, to pursue a coherent foreign policy in spite of political attacks

on the State Department, and to contend with the maneuvering of powerful administrators within the Federal bureaucracy.

H 468. HAWLEY, ELLIS W. The Great War and the Search for a Modern Order: A History of the American People and Their Institutions, 1917-1933. New York: St. Martin's Press, 1979. 264 pp.
Hawley's portrait of American society from the U.S. entry into W.W. I through the Hoover administration attends, in particular, to wartime mobilization, the rise of "mass consumption society" in the 1920s and its collapse during Hoover's term. An overriding theme of American development in these years, Hawley suggests, was the search for a "modern managerial order" which might provide for coordination and rationalization in an industrial society, without infringing upon America's traditional liberal individualism and anti-statism. Hawley sees in this era a laying of ideological and institutional foundations for the "new liberalism" of the post-W.W. II years, and not simply the decline of Progressivism or the beginnings of the New Deal.

H 469. HAYS, SAMUEL P. Conservation and the Gospel of Efficiency: The Progressive Conservation Movement, 1890-1920. Cambridge, Mass.: Harvard University Press, 1959. 297 pp.
Hays reexamines the progressive conservation measures involving the nation's forests, public lands, rivers, and range lands. He finds in the drive for conservation a curious combination of forces. Corporate interest frequently turned up on the side of conservation; the long-term interests of the large corporation actually made it an ally more often than an opponent. Smaller, speculative businesses, on the other hand, were among the fiercest opponents of conservation measures, which threatened their short-run economic gains.

H 470. HAYS, SAMUEL P. The Response to Industrialism, 1885-1914. Chicago: University of Chicago Press, 1957. 210 pp.
Hays examines how the growth of an industrialized, interdependent, complex society affected various groups of Americans. The vast expansion of business and industry in the decades preceding W.W. I provided for increased material prosperity; at the same time it brought drastic changes to which individuals and the nation as a whole were forced to respond. Hays proceeds topically, exploring economic, political, urban, and international developments, as well as such subjects as the impact of industrialism on religion. He argues that the era was not characterized simply by divisions between the haves and have-nots, but that industrialism generated more complex conflicts and responses. He discusses, for example, how the impetus for reform often came from prosperous classes seeking in bureaucracy and government a counterweight to big business; that city and country were often at odds; and that some worked to reap the maximum benefit from, and some simply rejected, the new order.

H 471. HEATH, JIM F. Decade of Disillusionment: The Kennedy-Johnson Years. Bloomington: Indiana University Press, 1975. 332 pp.
Heath traces the shifts in national mood from the optimistic, expectant inauguration of the Kennedy presidency through the unraveling of the Johnson Administration. The Kennedy Administration is portrayed as having been highly cautious domestically but aggressive internationally, both in the military buildup in Vietnam and in the expansion of the U.S. military establishment. Johnson's record of domestic legislative reforms was substantial, according to Heath, but was soon overshadowed by the social and political effects of urban rioting and of the deep divisions in public opinion over the war in Southeast Asia.

H 472. **HICKS, JOHN.** Republican Ascendancy, 1921-1933. New York: Harper
& Row, 1960. 317 pp.
Hicks portrays the 1920s as a decade of withdrawal from reform movements
at home and from international responsibility abroad. Though much attention is paid to the dissenters (especially the Progressives) of the "prosperity decade," Hicks also chronicles the rise of the automobile, the
motion picture, and the radio. Hicks concludes by discussing the futile
attempts of the old order to deal with the crisis of the Great Depression,
and the rejection of that order by the voters in the election of 1932.

H 473. **HIGBEE, EDWARD C.** Farms and Farmers in an Urban Age. New York:
Twentieth Century Fund, 1963. 183 pp.
This account of American agriculture in the post-W.W. II years stresses
the impact of technological and organizational change on the industry.
Russell argues that most of the basic commodities in the U.S. are produced on a relatively small number of large, very productive farms, while
the rest of the nation's farmers are marginal in producing needed agricultural products. The author also outlines American attitudes toward
farm life and how they affect government policy and urban life. The author
believes that the future of the industry lies with the agribusinesses
which are heavily capitalized and dependent on technological advancements.

H 474. **HIMMELBERG, ROBERT F.** The Origins of the National Recovery Administration: Business, Government, and the Trade Association Issue,
1921-33. New York: Fordham University Press, 1976. 232 pp.
Studying the business community's efforts during the 1920s and 1930s to
emasculate Federal antitrust legislation, Himmelberg argues that the NRA
represented the culmination of a secular movement for antitrust revision
that began after W.W. I. In their attempts to redefine the limits upon
industrial cooperation, the goal of business was not to promote, but limit
competition. During the 1920s, Republican administrations systematically
relaxed controls over competition and promoted the activities of various
trade associations. With the passage of the National Industrial Recovery
Act of 1933, business achieved most of its goals. The act, however, did
little for economic recovery and illustrated the tendency of businessmen
to seize state power, use it to defend their position, and enhance their
wealth.

H 475. **HODGSON, GODFREY.** America in Our Time. New York: Random House,
1976. 564 pp.
Hodgson's account of American society since W.W. II focuses on an examination of the "liberal consensus" which prevailed in the late 1940s and
the 1950s, and declined under the pressures of Vietnam, the counterculture,
and the New Left in the 1960s. He argues that the "discovery of Middle
America" by Nixon in 1968, and the advent of a more conservative political
majority, brought about the very different climate of the 1970s. Hodgson
pays particular attention to the important role of the news media, notably
television, in determining both the subjects of public discussion and
their popular perception.

H 476. **HOFSTADTER, RICHARD.** The Age of Reform: From Bryan to F.D.R.
New York: Knopf, 1955. 350 pp.
Hofstadter analyzes the major movements for reform from 1890-1940. He
examines the phenomena of Populism, Progressivism, and Liberalism.
Hofstadter views Populism as based upon a nostalgic desire for a return
to an arcadia. He also says that this movement was anti-urban and anti-
Semitic. Progressivism is seen as representing the anxieties of the urban
middle classes, most of whom had suffered loss of power and prestige during
industrialization in the late 19th century. This "status revolution"
explains the inordinate presence of ministers, professors, businessmen,
and lawyers in the Progressive movement. From W.W. I until the New Deal,

351

Progressivism shed its intellectualism and moralism. According to
Hofstadter, FDR's New Deal liberalism was different because it was pragmatic, relativistic, and opportunistic. FDR's liberalism was amoral not
moralistic, asking not whether it was right but whether it worked.

H 477. HOWE, IRVING and LEWIS COSER. The American Communist Party: A
    Critical History (1919-1957). Boston: Beacon Press, 1957.
    593 pp.
Howe and Coser examine the inner workings of the Communist Party from
its founding in 1919 to its decline in the 1950s. In its first fifteen
years, the Party isolated itself from Progressive unions, other Leftist
movements such as the Farmer-Labor movement in Minnesota, Progressive
political campaigns such as that of Robert LaFollette in 1924, and even
the Socialist Party (which they derided as "social fascists"). During
the Popular Front and W.W. II, a ten-year period of cooperation emerged.
After 1945, however, this was abandoned with the ouster of Earl Browder
as leader of the American Party and a rising tide of anti-Communism.
By 1957, the Communist Party, for all intents and purposes, was dead.
The authors argue, finally, that the failure and great defeats suffered
by European and American radical movements after 1920 provided an essential
condition for the growth of Stalinism during the Depression and War years.

H 478. HURT, R. DOUGLAS. The Dust Bowl: An Agricultural and Social His-
    tory. Chicago: Nelson-Hall, 1981. 214 pp.
The author describes the region known as the Dust Bowl and discusses its
environmental history, focusing on the great dust storms of the 1930s.
The storms that gave the region its name appeared on a relatively predictable schedule, but few long-term measures have been adopted to deal with
them; Hurt asserts that nature has been as responsible for their decline
as the efforts of man have. He concludes that while future storms and
a return to the worst years of the Dust Bowl are not inevitable, they
are possible.

H 479. ISRAEL, JERRY, ed. Building the Organizational Society: Essays
    on Associational Activities in Modern America. New York: Free
    Press, 1972. 341 pp.
This collection of essays examines the new type of social organization
that arose in an increasingly cosmopolitan, technical America between
1890 and 1929. "The new organizational society" saw the emergence of
specialized groups based on function, which sought, through self-conscious
collective action, to shape the environment around them. The contributors
discuss professional associations in fields such as law and medicine;
social institutions such as schools, labor unions, and churches; policy-
making groups; and governmental organizations. Many of the authors critique as well as describe the activities of these groups.

H 480. ISSERMAN, MAURICE. Which Side Were You On?: The American Commun-
    ist Party During the Second World War. Middletown, Conn.: Wes-
    leyan University Press, 1982. 305 pp.
During the 1940s and 1950s the Communist Party adopted policies of "suicidal delusions." During the war, they accepted a no-strike pledge, arbi-
tration, and incentive pay plans in a unified effort to defeat the Nazis.
This alienated them from other groups within organized labor, and won
them few allies in the Democratic Party. After 1945, the Party operated
with a "last-ditch-stand mentality" and failed to take advantage of the
political space available to them. They squandered resources on the Henry
Wallace campaign, forced sympathetic unions to choose between the party
and their members' interests, and assumed from 1946-56 that war, fascism,
and economic collapse were close at hand. For all intents and purposes,
Isserman contends, the Party was dead by 1960 and had little influence
on the then-emerging New Left.

H 481. KENNEDY, DAVID M. Over Here: The First World War and American
        Society. New York: Oxford University Press, 1980. 404 pp.
Kennedy examines W.W. I on the home front, considering economic and industrial mobilization, finance, diplomacy, civil liberties, and the experience
of blacks, labor, women, and intellectuals. He discusses, as well, interpretations of the war's meaning as they emerged in the 1920s. Kennedy
sees American behavior during the war as manifesting national characteristics, such as the suspicion of concentrated power and the tradition
of voluntarism. His work draws on recent scholarship, literary evidence,
and archival research in the U.S. and Britain.

H 482. KOLKO, GABRIEL. The Triumph of Conservatism: A Reinterpretation
        of American History, 1900-1916. New York: Free Press of Glencoe,
        1963. 344 pp.
Kolko asserts that at the heart of Progressivism, at least at the national
level, was not reform but a regulation of the economy that was to the
ultimate advantage of big business. The largest industries, unable to
bring "cutthroat competition" under control, sought a rationalized, stabilized environment and worked with the nation's political leaders to create
the system Kolko calls "Political Capitalism." Through informal detente
with the Roosevelt administration, through pure food and drug regulation,
anti-trust activity, and the development of the Federal Reserve System
and the Federal Trade Commission, big business and finance was able to
consolidate its position within a more secure and predictable economy.
Kolko's sources include personal and state papers and, most notably, trade
journals from the period.

H 483. KUTLER, STANLEY. The American Inquisition: Justice and Injustice
        in the Cold War. New York: Hill & Wang, 1982. 285 pp.
Kutler's study looks at the demands for national security and loyalty
in the post-W.W. II era, and the specific measures instituted to meet those
demands. He presents case studies of political harassment, such as that
of Owen Lattimore, and argues that legal recompense for victims was often
belated and inadequate. Kutler also discusses the power wielded by agencies and individuals of the Federal bureaucracy, notably the FBI, the
Departments of State, Defense, and Justice, and the Passport Office; he
sees personal and parochial ambitions as often motivating anti-communist
activity.

H 484. LADER, LAWRENCE. Power on the Left: American Radical Movements
        Since 1946. New York: Norton, 1979. 410 pp.
Chronicling the activities of leftist groups since W.W. II, Lader finds
that American radicalism has diverse ideological sources, is essentially
pragmatic, and has lacked a single, united leadership, body of doctrine,
or organizational structure. Relying on oral histories and archival
sources, the author discusses the labor movement, the Communist Party,
and the dark years of McCarthyism. The bulk of his analysis, however,
concerns the civil rights movement, student radicalism, and the anti-war
and women's movement of the 1960s. Lader examines these currents of radicalism and assesses the sources of the Left's failures in the period.

H 485. LAWSON, STEVEN F. Black Ballots: Voting Rights in the South,
        1944-1969. New York: Columbia University Press, 1976. 474 pp.
Lawson's book is an account of the struggle in the South to secure voting
rights for blacks. Case studies from Alabama and Mississippi show the
obstacles and fierce resistance, including physical violence, which the
effort encountered. The roles of private groups, such as SNCC and the
NAACP, and the activities of various presidential administrations are
described. The climax of the effort was the enactment of the Voting Rights
Act in 1965, which at last succeeded in securing the right to vote throughout the South.

H 486. LEUCHTENBERG, WILLIAM E. Franklin D. Roosevelt and the New Deal,
        1932-1940. New York: Harper & Row, 1963. 393 pp.
Leuchtenberg concentrates on New Deal policy, administration, and political
impact rather than on the personality of Roosevelt himself. He is
impressed by FDR's economic flexibility, administrative abilities, and the
experimentalism of many of his programs. Unlike many other historians,
who have stressed continuities in the New Deal and the administrations
and reform programs that preceded it, Leuchtenberg emphasizes its revolutionary impact--in bringing new groups into the political arena, in
recasting the functions of the president and of the Federal government,
in focusing new attention on social security and collective action, and
in the setting of a new agenda for the national state.

H 487. LEUCHTENBERG, WILLIAM E. In the Shadow of FDR: From Harry Truman
        to Ronald Reagan. Ithaca, N.Y.: Cornell University Press, 1983.
        346 pp.
This book is an account of the enduring impact of Franklin D. Roosevelt
on American politics, as seen in the history of the Presidency from 1945
into the 1980s. FDR influenced domestic and foreign policies, campaign
styles, and the very conception of the presidential office. The author
focuses on Democratic presidents and the post-New Deal platforms of the
Fair Deal, the New Frontier, and the Great Society. Johnson was probably
most affected, according to Leuchtenberg, while Kennedy and Carter seem
to have been influenced more politically than personally by FDR. Even
Reagan, despite obvious differences, is depicted as having been influenced
by, and seeking to associate himself with, FDR.

H 488. LEUCHTENBERG, WILLIAM E. The Perils of Prosperity, 1914-1932.
        Chicago: University of Chicago Press, 1958. 313 pp.
Leuchtenberg examines American society as it was transformed in the years
between W.W. I and the end of the Hoover Administration. He attends, in
particular, to the rise of the city and the challenges this presented
to traditional economic, social, and moral arrangements. Discussed specifically are the nation's experience of the war, the Red Scare, domestic
politics and foreign affairs in the 1920s, culture, economy and industry,
reaction to the moral revolution, and the Crash. According to Leuchtenberg,
the perils of the prosperity and technological innovation of the 1920s
included the concentration of power and profit in the hands of a class
ill-prepared for social leadership. At the same time, he believes America
to have emerged from the 1920s a more cosmopolitan, tolerant, and inter-
nationalist nation.

H 489. LINGEMAN, RICHARD. Don't You Know There's a War On? The American
        Home Front 1941-1945. New York: Putnam, 1970. 400 pp.
Lingeman describes the domestic life of the nation during W.W. II. He
discusses civil defense measures, wartime migration, propaganda and popular
culture, shortages and rationing, race relations, and domestic politics.
He also considers war production and labor, particularly issues of morale,
of women and blacks in the industrial workforce, and of trade unionism.

H 490. LINK, ARTHUR S. Wilson the Diplomatist: A Look at His Major For-
        eign Policies. Baltimore, Md.: Johns Hopkins University Press,
        1957. 165 pp.
This book analyzes the foreign policy of Woodrow Wilson, with special
reference to the origins of W.W. I. Link details the intellectual preconceptions which guided Wilson's choices in foreign affairs, and lays
considerable emphasis on Wilson's highly moral conception of international
relations. This work analyzes the problem of German submarine warfare
and its implications for American neutrality, as well as Wilson's reasons
for entering the war. Wilson's conception of a new era of international
relations based on the League of Nations was never realized in practical

354

politics, and Link analyzes the reasons for the rejection of the League
of Nations, as well as the demise of Wilsonian idealism in foreign policy
in the 1920s.

H 491. LINK, ARTHUR S. Woodrow Wilson and the Progressive Era, 1910-1917.
          New York: Harper & Row, 1954. 96 pp.
Two themes are explored in this book: Wilson's diplomatic efforts during
W.W. I, and the role of progressives in national politics. Link analyzes
party conflicts and factionalism over progressive reforms, but his emphasis
remains on Wilson, his motivations, and his role both in furthering the
progressive movement and in bringing the U.S. into W.W. I.

H 492. LUBOVE, ROY. The Struggle for Social Security, 1900-1935. Cam-
          bridge, Mass.: Harvard University Press, 1968. 276 pp.
Lubove traces the years of effort on the part of reformers which culminated
in the final passage of the 1935 Social Security Act. The author focuses
on individual policies that addressed the needs of America's economically
disadvantaged; unemployment benefits, health insurance, retirement pensions,
and workmen's compensation are discussed in separate chapters. Lubove
maintains that the traditional American work ethic has relegated the poor
and those who are not able to work to a demeaning welfare system, rather
than providing them with some more meaningful source of income.

H 493. LYONS, EUGENE. The Red Decade: The Stalinist Penetration of
          America. New York: Bobbs-Merrill, 1941. 423 pp.
In this examination of the rise of the Communist Party in the U.S. during
the 1930s, Lyons insists that Stalinism is the most serious threat to
American security at the time of his writing. He considers the Party
to be more of a conspiracy than a social movement, "more a hoax than a
social upsurge." Displaying little sympathy for its leaders, he defends
red-baiting and describes American Communists as "a horde of part-time
pseudo-rebels who have neither courage nor convictions." The cult of
Russia-worship, according to Lyons, has penetrated numerous American institutions and movements, including organized labor, churches, education,
theater, movies, and the arts. This development has been fostered by
liberal sympathizers and fellow travellers who failed to understand the
true nature of the Party.

H 494. MANGIONE, JERRE. The Dream and the Deal: The Federal Writers'
          Project, 1935-1943. Boston: Little, Brown, 1972. 416 pp.
This account of the New Deal programs for writers is by one of the participants. The writers' project put jobless authors (some later prominent)
to work producing guidebooks and, later, the "Life in America" series,
a collection of life stories, slave narratives, ethnic material, and other
documents. Mangione concludes that the history of Federal Writers' Project
offers no clear lesson to those championing the cause of governmental
subsidy of the arts.

H 495. MANGIONE, JERRE. An Ethnic at Large: A Memoir of America in the
          Thirties and Forties. New York: Putnam, 1978. 378 pp.
Mangione's memoir begins with a description of life in a Sicilian immigrant
family in Rochester, New York. After attending Syracuse University,
Mangione moved to New York and became part of the group of intellectuals
gathering in Greenwich Village. He describes the life styles of these
intellectuals as well as their attraction to communism during the Depression years. Mangione goes on to discuss the life of an intellectual during
the war years, and describes a part of the American war experience often
ignored: the internment of 10,000 Germans, Italians, and Japanese by
the Department of Justice. Mangione directed the public relations program
of the Immigration and Naturalization Service during W.W. II.

H 496. McAULIFFE, MARY. Crisis on the Left: Cold War Politics and American Liberals, 1947-1954. Amherst: University of Massachusetts Press, 1978. 204 pp.
McAuliffe describes the liberal community's response to the Cold War and to the domestic anti-communism of that period. She finds that the more or less united Left of the 1930s was replaced by a "liberal center"--more cautious, conservative, elitist--which prevailed until the Vietnam era. She documents the failure of the American Civil Liberties Union, democratic socialists like Norman Thomas, and mainstream Liberals such as Hubert Humphrey, to effectively challenge anti-communist hysteria.

H 497. McCOY, DONALD R. Angry Voices: Left-of-Center Politics in the New Deal Era. Lawrence: University of Kansas Press, 1958. 224 pp.
McCoy studies four leftist political organizations that emerged during the 1930s due to dissatisfaction with the two-party system. The League for Independent Political Action was formed in 1929 expressly to work for a new political party. Led by John Dewey, its early membership included James Mauer, Paul Douglas, Oswald Garrison Villard, Reinhold Niebuhr, and W. E. B. DuBois. Frustrated by its inability to sell its theories and by the popularity of Roosevelt, the LIPA gave rise to the Farmer-Labor Political Federation in 1934 and later the American Commonwealth Political Federation. Like their parent organization, each of these failed to develop a large following. Along with the Union Party of 1936, these efforts were unsuccessful because of internal weaknesses, organizational problems, the strategy of the Democratic Party, and the social-psychological attitudes of their potential followers.

H 498. McDONALD, WILLIAM F. Federal Relief Administration and the Arts. Columbus: Ohio State University Press, 1969. 869 pp.
This study examines five professional programs of the Works Progress Administration: the Federal Art, Music, Theater, and Writers' projects, and the Historical Records Survey. The author first presents the origins and administrative history of the entire effort, then the origins and organization of each individual project. McDonald offers evidence that Federal relief for artists came only after all traditional and private means of support had been exhausted. Other themes discussed are the concern of social workers to democratize and socialize the arts, and the frustration of these aims by the Federal directors of the projects.

H 499. McELVAINE, ROBERT S., ed. Down and Out in the Great Depression: Letters from the Forgotten Man. Chapel Hill: University of North Carolina Press, 1983. 222 pp.
McElvaine blends political history, period photographs and words of the people to reveal the daily life of Americans during the Depression. This work begins with a political, economic, and social overview of the Depression years. The study then draws on almost 200 randomly selected letters addressed to Franklin and Eleanor Roosevelt. Letters are arranged in topical chapters which focus on the causes and cures for the Depression, problems endemic to particular groups (e.g., homeowners, rural poor, blacks, the aged, and children), reactions to relief and the New Deal, and personal feelings toward the Roosevelts--virtually parent figures for the struggling populace. McElvaine asserts that the Depression populace "may have been down, but not out"; individuals were not inert, but were struggling to find answers to their personal difficulties.

H 500. MERTZ, PAUL E. New Deal Policy and Southern Rural Poverty. Baton Rouge: Louisiana State University Press, 1978. 279 pp.
This survey of New Deal efforts to alleviate pervasive Southern rural poverty describes the origins of agrarian relief policies in the Federal Emergency Relief Administration and their implementation throughout the

356

1930s. While praising the aims and efforts of the New Dealers, Mertz concludes that these efforts were inadequate, given the extent of the problems (financing, labor, poor soil conditions, etc.), and that the preoccupation of the Roosevelt Administration with broader political problems prevented it from sufficiently addressing the problem of Southern rural poverty.

H 501. MORSE, ARTHUR D. While Six Million Died: A Chronicle of American
     Apathy. New York: Random House, 1968. 420 pp.
Morse records the seeming indifference of a great many Americans to the fate of European Jews in the period from the beginning of the Hitler regime through the establishment of the War Refugee Board in early 1944. Considering the question of what was known, Morse concludes that American policy-makers could hardly have remained unaware of Nazi intentions toward European Jewry nor, after 1942, of the policy of systematic extermination carried out. Yet the U.S. government refused to liberalize immigration policy to provide for refugees in the years before the holocaust or to divert resources from the war effort to rescue attempts during the conflict. Morse's indictment of official inaction is based both on official, especially State Department, documents and on a variety of material published for public consumption in the years 1933 to 1945.

H 502. MOWRY, GEORGE E. The California Progressives. Berkeley: Univer-
     sity of California Press, 1951. 349 pp.
California Progressivism was an expression of an older America objecting to the ideological and social drift of the early 20th century. Three political struggles dominated California from 1900-20: North versus South, labor versus capital, and general opposition to corporate rule, especially by the Southern Pacific Railroad. Progressivism was a militant, middle-class individualism that sought a classless society, but felt threatened by corporate power on one hand and labor unions on the other. Coming to power with the election of Governor Hiram Johnson in 1910, California Progressives adopted civil service, child labor laws, prison and court reform, utility regulation, a business-like state budgetary system, and electoral reforms such as initiative, referendum and recall. Although Progressives failed to end corporation-dominated state government, they supplied a "middle way" between the perceived corruption of a labor party and big business.

H 503. MOWRY, GEORGE E. The Era of Theodore Roosevelt, 1900-1912. New
     York: Harper & Row, 1958. 330 pp.
Mowry's study consists of three parts: the first concerns the economic, political, and intellectual currents which produced "the progressive" in American life; the second, the presidency of Theodore Roosevelt; the third, the administration of William Howard Taft, which ultimately led to a split in the Republican ranks and the restoration of Democratic rule. Roosevelt is presented as the dominant and most representative figure of a period in which America's government, economy, and international role were transformed and began to take their modern forms.

H 504. MOWRY, GEORGE E. Theodore Roosevelt and the Progressive Movement.
     Madison: University of Wisconsin Press, 1947. 405 pp.
Mowry's treatment of Roosevelt and Progressivism examines the reciprocal influences of man and political movement. Concentrating on the years following the Roosevelt presidency, Mowry studies the growing rift between Roosevelt and Taft and, more generally, between conservative and progressive Republicans. He describes the factors, including the personal ones, which led Roosevelt to stake out an increasingly "radical" position and, eventually, to sanction the splitting of the GOP with the Bull Moose challenge of 1912. Roosevelt, Mowry says, entertained third-term hopes until the time of his death. The author ends by noting that while progressive

Republicanism had been vanquished by the 1920s, elements of its "New Nationalism" appeared in New Deal policies.

H 505. MOWRY, GEORGE E. The Urban Nation, 1920-1960. New York: Hill & Wang, 1965. 278 pp.
Mowry's thesis is that the two World Wars and the Great Depression greatly stimulated the trends toward urbanization and toward a mass production, consumer-oriented American society. These trends weakened county and state governments, reconcentrating power at the city and especially the Federal levels of government. Mowry also examines the turn of U.S. foreign policy from relative isolationism to internationalism and interventionism.

H 506. MULDER, RONALD A. The Insurgent Progressives in the United States Senate and the New Deal, 1933-1939. New York: Garland, 1979. 334 pp.
This is a study of a group of "old" Progressives in the U.S. Senate during the New Deal, including William Borah, Robert LaFollette, Burton K. Wheeler, Hiram Johnson, George Norris, and Gerald P. Nye. The author focuses on the ideological relationship between the traditional Progressive views of these senators and the developing welfare state of the New Deal. Uneasy with the business-government "partnership" of the early New Deal, they were happier with the renewed anti-trust activity of the later 1930s. They continued to fear centralized power, private or public; of the group, Norris and LaFollette were friendliest to the New Deal.

H 507. MURRAY, ROBERT K. The Harding Era: Warren G. Harding and His Administration. Minneapolis: University of Minnesota Press, 1969. 626 pp.
Murray challenges the traditional derogatory portrayals of the Harding presidency (1921-23). Having had access to the Harding papers, Murray is persuaded that the President had a developed program of his own and that this administration engineered the transition from postwar socioeconomic dislocation to relative prosperity. Harding, he asserts, is best understood as a centrist whose administration established the Republican policies sustained for the rest of the decade.

H 508. MURRAY, ROBERT K. Red Scare: A Study in National Hysteria, 1919-1920. Minneapolis: University of Minnesota Press, 1955. 337 pp.
Murray analyzes the nation's collective "state of mind" during the post-W.W. I "Red Scare"; he looks particularly at a series of major public events, including the Seattle general strike, the Boston police strike, the Palmer raids, and government deportation activities. Murray's sources include periodicals, newspapers, pamphlets, memoirs, and government publications of the period. He concludes that the restrictive legislation and mob violence which characterized the public reaction to "Red Scare" may well have been more damaging than the original perceived threat of subversion.

H 509. NAISON, MARK. Communists in Harlem During the Depression. Urbana: University of Illinois Press, 1983. 355 pp.
During the 1930s, the Communist Party had more influence on Afro-American life than any other socialist organization in U.S. history. By organizing unemployment councils, attacking lynchings, and supporting the Scottsboro defendants, the Party was brought into the mainstream of black community life in Harlem. Although black membership in the party remained small, its influence was seen in the support it received from such black intellectuals as Langston Hughes, Ralph Ellison, and Richard Wright. With the adoption of a "united front" in 1934 (a precursor to the Popular Front after 1935), the Party worked with diverse black organizations and leaders, including Adam Clayton Powell, Jr., Father Divine, and the NAACP. In Harlem, Naison argues, the Party did not simply act upon direct orders

from Moscow, but on numerous occasions developed their own independent strategy based upon local conditions and circumstances.

H 510. **NOGGLE, BURL.** Teapot Dome: Oil and Politics in the 1920s. Baton Rouge: Louisiana State University Press, 1962. 234 pp.
Noggle examines the meaning and the ramifications of the oil-leasing scandals of the Harding Administration. The scandals, Noggle demonstrates, were a phase in the struggle between government and the private sector for control of the public domain. A bibliographic essay is appended.

H 511. **NYE, RUSSEL B.** Midwestern Progressive Politics: A Historical Study of Its Origins and Developments, 1870-1950. East Lansing: Michigan State College Press, 1951. 398 pp.
Nye examines the various phases of Midwestern protest in chronological sequence and contends that the region's radicalism was distinctive. He considers Midwestern dissent from its beginnings to the 1950s and finds an essential continuity in radical movements such as the Grangers, the Greenbackers, the Populists, and the LaFollette Progressives. Nye contends that these movements usually started with the people, and either acquired leaders after their inception or remained leaderless. The author interprets Midwestern radicalism as a series of logical attempts to protect the economic interests of its proponents.

H 512. **O'NEILL, WILLIAM L.** Coming Apart: An Informal History of America in the 1960s. Chicago: Quadrangle Books, 1971. 442 pp.
In this survey of the tumultuous 1960s, O'Neill considers the foreign and domestic policies of the era's presidential administrations, the student and civil rights movements, ghetto riots, and political campaigns. O'Neill defends the liberal positions of Presidential candidates and Senator Eugene McCarthy, denounces the war and American exploitation of the Third World, and pins his hopes for change on activists such as Ralph Nader.

H 513. **O'NEILL, WILLIAM L.** Divorce in the Progressive Era. New Haven, Conn.: Yale University Press, 1967. 295 pp.
O'Neill sees the study of divorce as a way of shedding light on larger issues and developments of the early 20th century, such as the "moral revolution"--which he sees more as reform than revolution. In his view, it also offers a means of exploring the ideological debate over the Victorian family, and how this debate led to a new concept of family in the 20th century. More generally, "since divorce was the cause of much anxious soul-searching by the Progressive generation, it reveals a good deal about the assumptions on which the Progressives' view of themselves and their world was based."

H 514. **PARMET, HERBERT S.** The Democrats: The Years After F.D.R. New York: Macmillan, 1976. 371 pp.
This book discusses the Democratic Party and its ideology, from Harry Truman to Lyndon Johnson. The author delineates the strengths and weaknesses of the Democratic party during these years, arguing that the Democrats were too conventional to justify the faith humanitarians often placed in them. Included are discussions of John F. Kennedy's administration and the fight over the civil rights plank of the 1948 platform.

H 515. **PATTERSON, JAMES T.** America's Strategy Against Poverty, 1900-1980. Cambridge, Mass.: Harvard University Press, 1981. 268 pp.
Patterson analyzes efforts to ameliorate poverty in the U.S., particularly in the years since 1930. Patterson argues that even the poorest in the U.S. lead more comfortable lives than many people elsewhere in the world, but that economic expectations are higher in America, influenced by television images of affluence. Patterson's position is that protest against poverty in the 1960s resulted in landmark social welfare programming; however, social welfare spending remains significantly lower than in most

industrialized countries. He suggests that this may be the result of continuing middle-class fears of fostering a permanently dependent "culture of poverty."

H 516. **PELLS, RICHARD H.** Radical Visions and American Dreams: Culture and Social Thought in the Depression Years. New York: Harper & Row, 1973. 424 pp.
Pells explores the impact of the Great Depression on American culture and social thought. In focusing on intellectuals seeking alternatives to the political beliefs, economic institutions, social values and artistic preoccupations that existed before 1929, the author shows the intellectual diversity of the 1930s. Since intellectuals were on the fringe or "outside" of American society, they felt great empathy for the plight of the unemployed. Becoming increasingly collectivist while much of the U.S. grew more conservative, American social and literary thinkers rejected liberalism for radical existentialism. Pells is wide-ranging in his coverage, including novelists like John Steinbeck and John Dos Passos, movie directors John Ford and Orson Welles, social critics John Dewey and Lewis Mumford, and photographer Walker Evans.

H 517. **POLENBERG, RICHARD.** One Nation Divisible: Class, Race, and Ethnicity in the United States Since 1938. New York: Viking Press, 1980. 363 pp.
Polenberg examines class, racial, and ethnic divisions in America over the course of forty years, detailing the impact of W.W. II, Cold War anti-communism, suburbanization, the reform efforts of the 1960s, and Vietnam on social stratification. He shows these effects to have been somewhat contradictory--some have diminished social distinctions, some have exacerbated them. Though patterns of class, race, and ethnicity have been greatly changed, Polenberg believes the U.S. continues as a "segmented society."

H 518. **POLENBERG, RICHARD.** War and Society: The United States, 1941-45. Philadelphia: Lippincott, 1972. 298 pp.
According to Polenberg, W.W. II radically altered the character of American society and challenged its most durable values. The war linked economic regulation with politics and social policy for the first time through a combined approach of compulsion and volunteerism. Business gained new prestige during the war, while liberalism went into a period of decline, a development exemplified by the birth and nurturing of the military-industrial complex. Numerous political developments that began in the 1930s crystallized during the war: the Republican and Southern Democratic alliance in Congress, the expanded power of the Federal government, the acceptance of the welfare state by the GOP, the consolidation of Democratic power in large cities, and the more active role of organized labor in national elections.

H 519. **RIMLINGER, GASTON V.** Welfare Policy and Industrialization in Europe, America, and Russia. New York: Wiley, 1971. 362 pp.
Rimlinger compares the approaches of several industrial nations to modern social insurance: Germany's paternalism, Russia's collectivism, and America's liberalism. In the U.S., social insurance came very late--in the 1930s--because of the widespread belief that it meant curtailment of individual freedom. The Great Depression, by destroying private security plans and exposing the weaknesses of programs at the state level, finally broke down this resistance; even then, the plan that emerged reflected certain reservations. (For example, farmers were not believed to need such insurance, and each state was authorized to decide who needed assistance and what the rate of taxation for unemployment insurance would be.)

H 520. **ROMASCO, ALBERT U.** The Politics of Recovery: Roosevelt's New
Deal. New York: Oxford University Press, 1983. 276 pp.
Romasco focuses on the first two years of Franklin D. Roosevelt's term,
when both the economic crisis and the opportunities for reform were greatest. According to Romasco, political considerations dominated decision-
making, and New Deal economic policies of 1933-34 had no perceivable unity.
The author also examines briefly the political leadership of FDR himself.

H 521. **ROMASCO, ALBERT U.** The Poverty of Abundance: Hoover, the Nation,
and the Great Depression. New York: Oxford University Press,
1965. 282 pp.
Romasco examines the Hoover years of the Great Depression, considering,
especially, how existing institutions were used or adapted to cope with
the paradox of increased scarcity in a land of abundance. Contrary to
popular imagining, Hoover did act in this crisis--more so, in fact, than
had any of his predecessors when faced with economic distress. He established a precedent for increased governmental activism, Romasco believes,
yet his guiding ideology prevented the full use of Federal power required
to cope with this Depression.

H 522. **ROSENBERG, EMILY S.** Spreading the American Dream: American Economic and Cultural Expansion, 1890-1945. New York: Hill & Wang,
1982. 258 pp.
Rosenberg focuses on the spread of America's economic and cultural influence throughout the world during the first half of the 20th century.
Business people, religious figures, writers, and movie-makers participated
in this development, and the Federal government supported these private
initiatives. Rosenberg describes how, by the end of W.W. II, powerful
members of American society, within and outside of government, had assumed
world leadership roles in this expansion.

H 523. **SALE, KIRKPATRICK.** SDS. New York: Random House, 1973. 752 pp.
Sale traces the history of the Students for a Democratic Society (SDS)
through the "decade of defiance," the 1960s. He divides the decade into
four periods: reorganization of forerunner groups and foundation-setting;
reform efforts; resistance (or militant confrontation); and revolution.
Sale considers the projects of SDS (e.g., Economic Research and Action
Projects, civil rights demonstrations) as well as the factional battles
within the organization. His study concludes with the split of SDS into
the Weather Underground and the Progressive Labor-SDS, and the demise
of SDS shortly thereafter. Sale's assessment of SDS is favorable, seeing
in the organization's history both the possibility for a permanent American
left, and evidence of concrete progress in university governance, civil
rights, and peace.

H 524. **SALOUTOS, THEODORE.** The American Farmer and the New Deal. Ames:
Iowa State University Press, 1982. 327 pp.
Almost a fifth of American Farmer and the New Deal is devoted to the proposals generated by farmers and legislators during W.W. I and the succeeding decade which were subsequently instituted in the 1930s. Later chapters
focus on attempts to stabilize incomes and eliminate surplus under the
Agricultural Adjustment Act in 1933, the invalidation of the first AAA
by the Supreme Court in 1935, the creation of the Farm Security Administration in 1937, and the battle for rural electrification. While recognizing that many of the New Deal farm programs were inadequate to the
needs of farmers during the Depression, Saloutos shifts the emphasis away
from leadership to the problems of sharecroppers, tenants, and black
farmers.

H 525. SCHLESINGER, ARTHUR M., Jr. The Age of Roosevelt, Volume I: The
        Crisis of the Old Order, 1919-1933. Boston: Houghton Mifflin,
        1957. 557 pp.
In the first volume of his study of the era of Franklin Roosevelt's presidency, Schlesinger examines the intellectual, social, and political origins
of the New Deal. Schlesinger opens with a prologue devoted to Roosevelt's
inauguration on March 4, 1933, then moves back in history to deal with
Populism, Progressivism, W.W. I, the 1920s, the first years of the Great
Depression, and finally the arrival of Roosevelt on the national scene.
Schlesinger finds the origins of the New Deal in earlier American reform
programs such as the New Freedom and the New Nationalism.

H 526. SCHLESINGER, ARTHUR M., Jr. The Age of Roosevelt, Volume II:
        The Coming of the New Deal. Boston: Houghton Mifflin, 1958.
        669 pp.
This book deals chiefly with the domestic aspects of the New Deal in 1933
and 1934. Schlesinger focuses on the President but, after an introductory
chapter, develops other topics, such as agriculture, industry, money,
the tariff, relief efforts, public works, social security, conservation
and resource development, labor, business regulation, the air mail crisis,
the rise of conservative opposition, and 1934 electoral victories for the
administration. In the last four chapters Schlesinger examines Roosevelt
as both President and private person.

H 527. SCHLESINGER, ARTHUR M., Jr. The Age of Roosevelt, Volume III:
        The Politics of Upheaval. Boston: Houghton Mifflin, 1960.
        749 pp.
This volume of Schlesinger's FDR series examines the personalities and
crises of 1935 and 1936 and the development of the "Second New Deal."
The first part of the volume discusses the social and political ferment
of these years, considering the impact of Father Charles Coughlin, Senator
Huey P. Long, American fascist intellectuals, socialists, and the Communist
Party. The remainder of the book deals with the reform and relief efforts
of the Second New Deal, Roosevelt's problems with the Supreme Court, and
the 1936 campaign.

H 528. SCHLESINGER, ARTHUR M., Jr. A Thousand Days: John F. Kennedy
        in the White House. Boston: Houghton Mifflin, 1965. 1087 pp.
Schlesinger's account of the Kennedy presidency is intended not as an
exhaustive history, but as a personal memoir; its focus is primarily on
Kennedy's handling of foreign affairs. Schlesinger begins with the presidential campaign and considers critical episodes such as the invasion
of the Bay of Pigs, the Cuban missile crisis, and the revolt in the Congo,
as well as JFK's policies in Vietnam. He also looks at reform efforts
such as the Alliance for Progress. Schlesinger concludes by praising
Kennedy's achievements in his relatively brief tenure in the White House;
chief among these achievements were the nuclear test ban treaty, national
economic policy reform, expanded civil rights efforts, and progress in
America's relationship with Latin America and the Third World.

H 529. SKOWRONEK, STEPHEN. Building a New American State: The Expansion
        of National Administrative Capacities, 1877-1920. New York:
        Cambridge University Press, 1982. 389 pp.
Institutional innovation and reform efforts in government agencies are
explored through three case studies: civil service reform, the revamping
of the army, and the regulation of railroads. Skowronek's book is a study
of the interaction between government structure and politics. He concludes
that after 1900, the bureaucratic mode of government prevailed, supported
by institutional innovators, as well as political progressives such as
Theodore Roosevelt.

H 530. SMITH, DANIEL. The Great Departure: The United States and World
        War I, 1914-1920. New York: Wiley, 1965. 221 pp.
This is a political and diplomatic history of the decision by President
Woodrow Wilson and his administration to commit the U.S. to the Allied
side of the European conflict. Smith describes the thinking which led
to the decision, U.S. diplomatic efforts during the war, and American
conduct at the Paris peace conference. Smith does not give an account
of the military side of U.S. involvement.

H 531. STEIN, HERBERT. The Fiscal Revolution in America. Chicago: Uni-
        versity of Chicago Press, 1969. 526 pp.
Stein studies the transition in American ideology and public policy between
1932 and the 1960s. During those years, fiscal policy came to be understood in Keynesian terms, with deficits and surpluses a means of achieving
certain national economic objectives. This sort of compensatory fiscal
policy was unacceptable to Herbert Hoover and unpalatable to FDR, but
the economy's response to the wartime situation convinced many skeptics
of its legitimacy. Stein traces this conversion, showing how even conservative business leaders came to support the new approach to Federal
finances.

H 532. STOFF, MICHAEL B. Oil, War, and American Security: The Search
        for a National Policy in Foreign Oil, 1941-1947. New Haven, Conn.:
        Yale University Press, 1980. 249 pp.
Realizing that its oil reserves were shrinking, the U.S. government during
W.W. II sought to develop a national policy on foreign oil, focusing on
the Persian Gulf area. Bureaucratic infighting, especially between Secretary of State Cordell Hull and Secretary of the Interior Harold Ickes,
oil company resistance, and British objections were instrumental in the
failure of this effort, and control of the flow of oil remained in the
private sector.

H 533. STONE, RALPH. The Irreconcilables: The Fight Against the League
        of Nations. Lexington: University Press of Kentucky, 1970.
        208 pp.
This book examines the group of Senators who formed the core of opposition
to the Treaty of Versailles in 1919. This group was led by Robert
LaFollette, Henry Cabot Lodge, William Borah, and George Norris. The
"irreconcilables'" opposition to the Treaty centered on the League of
Nations, though they never agreed on specific objections to the League.
This heterogeneous group, according to Stone, was united more in its opposition to Wilsonian foreign policy than in any positive program. Stone
concludes that the "irreconcilables" were the vanguard of 1920s isolationism.

H 534. TERKEL, STUDS (LOUIS). Hard Times: An Oral History of the Great
        Depression. New York: Pantheon Books, 1970. 462 pp.
Terkel collects reflections of people of all ages and occupations regarding
the Great Depression. The book describes the meaning of 1930s "hard times"
to those who lived through them and to the subsequent generations that
grew up in relative affluence. Terkel's interviews address a range of
subjects, including labor unions, the New Deal, farming, popular political
movements, the arts, public service, and the everyday experience of different social classes.

H 535. UNGER, IRWIN. The Movement: A History of the American Left,
        1959-1972. New York: Dodd, Mead, 1974. 217 pp.
This work discusses the origins and impact of the New Left in America
and provides a chronology of events and a summary of movement philosophy.
A central theme is the increasing radicalization of the New Left in the
1960s, leading up to the 1968 Chicago SDS convention, where an eventually

fatal rift developed in the movement. Unger defines the New Left as a
political and cultural movement of white, middle-class youth who sought
self-realization in political activism, and attempts to explicate the
tangled interrelationships of political and cultural dissent during the
period.

H 536. VIORST, MILTON. Fire in the Streets: America in the 1960s. New
         York: Simon & Schuster, 1979. 591 pp.
The 1960s, according to Viorst, were marked by major popular challenges
to public order, to established institutions and social values, and to
traditional processes of government. These challenges included campus
activism, peace demonstrations, civil rights actions, and the black power
movement. The scenes for their most dramatic manifestations were the
1968 Democratic Convention in Chicago, the March on Washington, the
Berkeley campus, the Watts ghetto in Los Angeles, and Kent State. Viorst's
study is not a formal history or a theoretical work; rather, it attempts
to give a coherent descriptive account of the events, ideas, and personalities of the turbulent decade. Viorst organizes his account around interviews with a dozen key figures of the period. He concludes that the 1960s
yielded some expansion of rights for disadvantaged and minority groups
in American society, and resulted in greater popular participation in
government decision-making. On the other side, Viorst sees the reformist
energies of the 1960s turning away from social issues and toward personal
self-indulgence in the 1970s.

H 537. WEGLYN, MICHI. Years of Infamy: The Untold Story of America's
         Concentration Camps. New York: Morrow, 1976. 351 pp.
Weglyn, an inmate in a Japanese-American internment camp in Arizona during
W.W. II, interviewed other former inmates to write this account of American
policy toward Japanese-Americans during the war. The book covers the
background of the detainment decision, its implementation and the eventual
return home of the detainees. The concern of officials across the nation
regarding the loyalty of Japanese-Americans is documented. Weglyn shows
that, at the time of his executive order, FDR had in hand a secret study
(the Munson Report) which denied the existence of any "Japanese problem."

H 538. WEINSTEIN, ALLEN. Perjury: The Hiss-Chambers Case. New York:
         Knopf, 1978. 674 pp.
Using previously unavailable FBI files, Weinstein studies one of the most
celebrated cases of the 20th century. The book describes the activities
of both Alger Hiss and Whittaker Chambers in the 1930s, Chambers's post-
Communist Party career, his accusation in August 1948 that Hiss had been
active in espionage for the Soviet Union, and the culmination of the subsequent legal maneuvering: Hiss's conviction for perjury in 1950 (the
statute of limitations for espionage having run out). The subsequent
careers of the two men, and the lasting symbolism and impact of the case,
are described. Weinstein concludes that the evidence supports the jury's
conviction of Hiss.

H 539. WEINSTEIN, JAMES. Ambiguous Legacy: The Left in American Politics.
         New York: Franklin Watts, 1975. 179 pp.
Weinstein argues that the American Left has failed three times since 1900.
The Socialist Party from 1901-19, the Communist Party from 1919-56, and
the New Left during the 1960s evidence the existence of a radical past
in America, one that failed primarily because of political and internal
weaknesses. Each movement accepted the syndicalist belief that in fighting
for immediate goals, they would promote larger revolutionary aims. Both
the Communist Party and the New Left failed to base their politics on
the changing nature of corporate Capitalism and instead tried to use foreign models. During the course of the 20th century, American radicalism
moved from a trade union, working-class, and immigrant base to one repre-

sented by universities and the white middle-class. Weinstein concludes
that trade unions and Left organizations unchallenged from the outside
by a party raising questions of socialist values has to accept Capitalism
and cannot develop alternatives to oppose their subordinate position.

H 540. WEINSTEIN, JAMES. The Corporate Ideal in the Liberal State, 1900-
1918. Boston: Beacon Press, 1968. 263 pp.
Weinstein argues that the reform measures of the Progressive era were
shaped by the nation's business and financial elite, who saw in them a
means of securing the existing order and containing challenges from the
left and of increasing the efficiency of the economic system. Dispensing
with ideological laissez faire and social Darwinism, the most sophisticated
business leaders advocated Federal intervention and a system by which
various social groups would be granted representation in decision-making
processes on the condition they support existing social arrangements.
From this perspective, Weinstein examines the National Civil Federation
as an important source of corporate liberalism, and discusses specific
measures and movements including workmen's compensation. The Federal
Trade Commission Act, the city commission and city manager programs, and
the efforts to organize American industry in W.W. I.

H 541. WEINSTEIN, JAMES. The Decline of Socialism in America, 1912-25.
New York: Vintage Books, 1967. 367 pp.
Before 1920, the Socialist Party had mass support at the polls, a widespread and vital press, a large union following, and influence on reformers.
As a social force, the Party was the leading radical organization in the
U.S. before 1920. Socialism did not decline after the 1912 election as
others have assumed. The Party grew in membership during W.W. I, and
by 1919 its membership of 109,000 nearly matched that of 1912. The different nature of the membership (East coast based, largely immigrants,
and more radical after the Russian Revolution), however, created new splits
and factions. The formation of competing socialist parties (Communist
Party and Communist Labor Party), the failure of the 1919 steel strike,
and the internal splits between native-born and immigrant members tore
the Party apart. The legacy of 1919, then, was the alienation of American
Socialism.

H 542. WELCH, RICHARD E. Response to Imperialism: The United States
and the Philippine-American War, 1899-1902. Chapel Hill: University of North Carolina Press, 1979. 215 pp.
Welch describes the effects of the U.S. suppression of the Philippine
Insurrection on American politics, economic life, religion, racial attitudes, intellectuals, and the presidency. He finds that support for the
war arose from the romantic nationalism prevalent at the turn of the century (which saw the U.S. as a force for good), and the optimistic belief
in the possibilities of progress. His conclusion is that long-term impact
on the American political scene was slight.

H 543. WHITE, THEODORE. America in Search of Itself; The Making of the
President 1956-1980. New York: Harper & Row, 1982. 465 pp.
This book describes changes in the presidential election process in the
years from Eisenhower to Reagan. White discusses, as well, how the elections themselves reflect larger changes in American society. He treats
the pervasive influence of television, and its role in the decline of old-
fashioned political machines. The failure of liberalism is frequently
addressed, especially as evidenced in the difficulties encountered in
implementing Lyndon Johnson's Great Society reform programs. White
believes that the 1980 election marked the final break-up of the New Deal
coalition.

H 544. WIEBE, ROBERT H. Businessmen and Reform: A Study of the Progressive Movement. Cambridge, Mass.: Harvard University Press, 1962.
283 pp.
The author examines the political activities of a wide range of businessmen
and business organizations. He concludes that businessmen can be found
on both sides of most reform issues and that on those questions of greatest
interest to business--e.g., legislation creating the Federal Trade
Commission--business spokesmen played dominant roles in shaping the laws
and their administration. On other issues, however, they were less concerned about the particular form that legislation took and thus less
involved. Wiebe's book portrays the businessman as an active and frequently
positive force in liberal reform.

H 545. WIEBE, ROBERT H. The Search for Order, 1877-1920. New York:
Hill & Wang, 1967. 333 pp.
Wiebe describes the evolution of America from a country of "island
communities"--autonomous and isolated--to one that was both more coherent
and more impersonal. Wiebe sees Progressivism as emerging from the efforts
of a "new middle class," chiefly urban professionals, to construct a new
bureaucratic order capable of coping with an increasingly urbanized, industrialized nation. Favoring centralized administration, professional management, and specialization, this class aided in the creation of the more
integrated, national society of 1920. Wiebe appends a detailed bibliographic essay.

H 546. WILSON, JOAN HOFF. American Business and Foreign Policy 1920-1933.
Boston: Beacon Press, 1971. 339 pp.
In this reinterpretation of American foreign policy, Wilson argues that
between the end of W.W. I and the inauguration of the New Deal, business
and government were in substantial cooperation about the conduct of foreign
policy. The peace and disarmament movements, allied war debts, and the
German reparations are discussed in terms of business and finance in the
U.S. This book also contains an extensive treatment of American commercial
policy in the Far East, Europe, and the Middle East, as well as chapters
on protectionism and the Open Door Policy. Wilson concludes with an examination of the foreign policy of the Hoover administration and its relationships with multinational corporations.

H 547. WOLFSKILL, GEORGE and JOHN A. HUDSON. All but the People: Franklin
D. Roosevelt and His Critics, 1933-1939. New York: Macmillan,
1969. 386 pp.
The authors examine a cross-section of contemporary criticism of FDR and
the New Deal. Personal, Fascist, Communist/radical, and business community
criticism are discussed, as well as that emerging from the major political
parties and the press. The authors believe that the New Deal was a search
for a "middle way" between laissez faire Capitalism and Socialism, and
that Roosevelt was unable to communicate his social plans to the public
successfully. They argue that critics, in their impatience with or lack
of belief in FDR's policies, damaged the efforts of the New Deal. This
study is based on holdings in the Roosevelt presidential library in Hyde
Park, New York.

H 548. WORSTER, DONALD. Dust Bowl: The Southern Plains in the 1930s.
New York: Oxford University Press, 1979. 277 pp.
One of the three worst ecological disasters in human history, the Dust
Bowl in the Southern Plains states, combined with the Great Depression
to reveal fundamental weaknesses in traditional American culture. Capitalism, according to Worster, was the major cause of the Dust Bowl. Plainsmen
sought land not simply to make a living, but to treat it as capital and
make money. Believing man has a right and an obligation to use such capital for self-advancement, the social order rejected any restraint, natur-

ally or man-imposed. Shock was the reaction when the Dust Bowl, like
the Depression, harshly illustrated the expansionary limits to Americans
for the first time. Land no longer was seen as a means of opportunity,
thereby destroying Jefferson's agrarian ideal of man's harmony with nature.

VI.   INTELLECTUAL HISTORY

H 549. AMES, VAN METER. Zen and American Thought. Honolulu: University
         of Hawaii Press, 1962. 293 pp.
Zen, according to Ames, may be more American than most consider it to
be. Zen, which denies the dualism associated with religion in the West,
finds a mirror in the American philosopher George Mead's notion of accounting for the human self and mind without any transcendent principle. The
principles of Zen are particularly applicable to North America, according to Ames, because of its ability to meet a cultural need for reassurance
without being anachronistic. Chapters of this book deal with various
American philosophers, such as Thoreau, Santayana, and Mead, demonstrating
how much Zen, in principle if not in name, has penetrated American thought.

H 550. ARIELI, YEHOSHVA. Individualism and Nationalism in American Ideo-
         logy. Cambridge, Mass.: Harvard University Press, 1964.
         442 pp.
This book is an investigation into how a heterogeneous society, recent
in origin, mobile and diverse in population, comes to consider itself
a national entity. Arieli focuses primarily upon the "concepts which
have played a major role in American public opinion and have served to
crystallize a sense of collective identification." By examining their
meaning and historical significance, the author hopes to understand better
the nature of American national consciousness. It is Arieli's opinion
that only a concept that interpreted Americanism in terms of a social
order based on "universally valid ideals of humanity" could serve as a
basis of national identification.

H 551. BAILYN, BERNARD. Education in the Forming of American Society:
         Needs and Opportunities for Study. Chapel Hill: University of
         North Carolina Press, 1960. 147 pp.
This work broadens the concept of education to include the home, the work
place, the church, and the community as well as schools and colleges,
bringing together essays that are, first, revisionist interpretations of
Colonial educational history, and second, lengthy critical commentaries
on sources. In his broadening definition of education as more than formal
pedagogy, Bailyn enunciates several theses. He argues, for example, that
the effort to convert Native Americans to Christianity forced a new social
role on the schools that endured with the continued diversity of the population, and that public support for education resulted from a chronic
lack of private wealth rather than from ideological principles.

H 552. BALTZELL, E. DIGBY. Puritan Boston and Quaker Philadelphia.
         Boston: Beacon Press, 1982. 585 pp.
Baltzell seeks to explain why Philadelphia's contribution to American
intellectual and public life has been so far below the level of Boston's.
The key is to be found in each city's prevailing religious conviction.
Puritans saw life as a calling and stressed class leadership, class authority, and class responsibility; the Quaker religious ethos, however, was
one of egalitarian individualism with a dose of anti-intellectualism.
Thus the Quaker City produced merchants rather than magistrates and ministers, and its upper class failed to assert class authority while that

of Boston stressed community goals over the pleasures of private life.
Baltzell discusses the effect of the cultures of the two cities on their
art, professions, political and public life, religion, and institutions
of education, especially Harvard University and the University of Pennsylvania.

H 553. BARRET, DONALD N., ed. Values in America. Notre Dame, Ind.:
        University of Notre Dame Press, 1961. 182 pp.
A symposium held at the University of Notre Dame to explore, develop,
and criticize the "reality" of values in America, provides the basis for
this volume of essays by American social scientists. Each of the symposium
sessions has become a section of the book: Analysis of Values in Behavioral Sciences; Values and Education in America; Values and American Economic Life; Values and Religion in America; and Values and Mass Communication in America. An introductory essay, "Value Problems and Present Contributions," provides a focus for the book.

H 554. BARRETT, WILLIAM. The Truants: Adventures Among the Intellectuals.
        Garden City, N.Y.: Anchor Press, 1982. 270 pp.
As the book's title makes clear, the thesis underlying Barrett's memoir
of the personalities clustered around the influential journal Partisan
Review from the late 1930s to the early 1960s is that these New York intellectuals often deluded themselves about the nature of the world around
them and avoided political and economic realities by fleeing into their
own world of warring abstractions. Barrett gives in his book portraits
of the Partisan Review crowd, their ideas and influences, conflicts and
crises, as well as reminiscences of "outside" figures such as Albert Camus,
Hannah Arendt, and Lionel Trilling. There is even a chapter recalling
the Abstract Expressionist painters Barrett met in the 1950s. The result
is a highly personal account of an important place and time in American
literary and intellectual life.

H 555. BECKER, CARL L. The Declaration of Independence: A Study in the
        History of Political Ideas. New York: Harcourt, Brace, 1922.
        286 pp.
Becker separates his discussion of the creation and the influence of the
Declaration of Independence into five chapters. He examines the "Historical Antecedents of the Declaration," the philosophy of natural rights
and the British empire, the drafting of the document, its "literary qualities," and its philosophical interpretations in the 19th century. The
purpose of the Declaration was to justify American rebellion to the world,
to set forth an argument against monarchies, and to create a theory of
government that would accept the idea of a just revolution. It was Locke
who allowed the 18th-century man to believe that institutions might be
brought "into perfect harmony with the Universal Natural Order." Becker
provides the text of the document, showing the stages of editing and
development, and an insight into Jefferson's literary considerations.
He concludes that the optimistic and naive faith of the founding fathers
suffered under the forces of a modernizing society during the 19th century
when "humanity" was abandoned.

H 556. BECKER, CARL L. Freedom and Responsibility in the American Way
        of Life. New York: Knopf, 1945. 122 pp.
Freedom and Responsibility is a collection of lectures delivered by Becker
at the University of Michigan in December of 1944, a few months before
his death. Becker addresses "The American Political Tradition," "Freedom
of Speech and Press," "Freedom of Learning and Teaching," "Constitutional
Government," and "Private Free Enterprise." He sees the conflict between
freedom and responsibility as "central to all political philosophy and
practice." The conflict concerns the need to balance justly individual
liberty with necessary government as well as possible "to the desires
and interests of all individuals and classes in society."

H 557. BECKER, CARL L. New Liberties for Old. New Haven, Conn.: Yale
        University Press, 1941. 181 pp.
The issue of democracy is the focus of this collection of six essays,
written in as many years during the prewar tensions of the 1930s. In
his opening essay, "New Liberties for Old," Becker traces the change in
the meaning of liberty from "the liberal-democratic social philosophy
of the eighteenth century" to its later conception under the influence of
Marx. The second essay, "Loving Peace and Waging War," discusses justifications offered for war. The following essays, "Afterthoughts on Constitutions," "When Democratic Virtues Disintegrate," "Some Generalities
That Still Glitter," and "The Old Disorder in Europe" look at totalitarian-
ism and liberties. The question "What is the value of the new liberties
that are now offered in place of the old?" is the central theme.

H 558. BERMAN, RONALD. America in the Sixties: An Intellectual History.
        New York: Free Press, 1968. 291 pp.
Berman believes most intellectuals felt that the 1960s would usher in
a new age, although they were not sure what that would bring. They did
agree that the intellectual should assume an active public life to give
the society "morals" not provided by politicians--a "class antagonistic
to intellect." The intellectuals found themselves in positions of power
within the revitalized university and in the government, but quickly discovered the snare of bureaucracy. Berman believes the "new left" failed:
"it could not justify the political supremacy of an intellectual minority
and it could not shape the academic institution to its own demands."
Besides three chapters discussing the "new left," other chapters focus
on religion, blacks, authors, and "culture heroes"--including such personages as Castro, Norman Mailer, and C. Wright Mills.

H 559. BILLINGTON, RAY ALLEN. Land of Savagery, Land of Promise: The
        European Image of the American Frontier in the Nineteenth Century.
        New York: Norton, 1981. 364 pp.
This is a study of the views of America held and expressed by a variety
of Europeans--writers, adventurers, immigrants--in novels, letters, and
promotional literature. A dual vision of the U.S. as both a savage wilderness, forbidding yet intriguing, and a land of opportunity was conveyed.
Billington contends that the image of the U.S. was as significant as its
reality. Many immigrants wrote to European friends and relatives of the
opportunity and equality they found in the New World, especially in the
American West. In the end, the U.S. took on elements of myth that were
important to its image abroad as well as to its self-perception.

H 560. BLEDSTEIN, BURTON. The Culture of Professionalism: The Middle
        Class and the Development of Higher Education in America. New
        York: Norton, 1976. 354 pp.
Bledstein argues that a stress on values rather than material wealth characterized the ascendant professional class in America. The vision of
a society grounded on the foundation of a career permeated middle-class
values; these values served increasingly to satisfy the emotional and
intellectual needs of this sector of society. The author traces the historical continuities found in cultural responses of the middle class in
the 19th and 20th centuries and outlines the American university's role
in cementing middle class acceptance of merit, competence, discipline
and control as fundamental components of achievement and success.

H 561. BOLLER, PAUL F., Jr. American Thought in Transition: The Impact
        of Evolutionary Naturalism, 1865-1900. Skokie, Ill.: Rand McNally,
        1969. 271 pp.
Beginning with the revolutionary impact of Darwinism in America, this
intellectual history traces the subsequent development of theories in
the social sciences, religion, and philosophy through the 19th century.

Attention is focused on the thought of William James, Oliver Wendell Holmes, Jr., and Thorstein Veblen as representative of evolutionary Naturalism.

H 562. BOLLER, PAUL F., Jr. American Transcendentalism, 1830-1860: An Intellectual Inquiry. New York: Putnam, 1974. 227 pp.
An introduction to the Transcendentalists, this book concisely discusses the intellectual origins of the movement and its vast impact on American life. From the Puritan roots of Transcendentalism to the influence of Darwin and Freud, Boller places intellectual activity within its historical context. His final chapter provides an analysis of the significance of Transcendentalism, and particularly Emerson, in the 19th and 20th centuries.

H 563. BOLLER, PAUL F., Jr. Freedom and Fate in American Thought: From Edwards to Dewey. Dallas, Tex.: Southern Methodist University Press, 1978. 300 pp.
This volume is a collection of interpretive essays by Boller that follow the thoughts of nine well-known Americans from Jonathan Edwards to John Dewey, offering "the richness and variety contained in American definitions of freedom and causality. . . ." Boller believes that the mood of the U.S. was becoming increasingly fatalistic in the 1960s. This gloom was accompanied by social unrest, the Vietnam War, and political corruption in high office during the 1960s and 1970s, which produced "a serious crisis in self-confidence." During these same two decades, he also sees professional philosophers challenging the doctrine of universal determinism and accentuating the role of free will.

H 564. BOORSTIN, DANIEL J. America and the Image of Europe: Reflections on American Thought. New York: Meridian Books, 1960. 192 pp.
Boorstin's eight essays on various topics, ranging from intellectual history, style of historical monuments, public relations and political figures, to a "dialogue" between Jewish and American history, constitute an effort to discover what is unique in American history. These essays "are concerned with how the image of Europe has given us our bearings, and yet how un-European is the framework of our life and the pattern of our history." Boorstin stresses the importance of the American people accepting non-Europeans as equals, and of the U.S. perceiving itself within "a new map of the whole world," lest America remain only an afterword to European civilization.

H 565. BOORSTIN, DANIEL J. The Lost World of Thomas Jefferson. New York: Holt, 1948. 306 pp.
This book explores the intellectual environment, the spirit and the ideas of Jefferson's world. Boorstin's discussion of Jefferson and the elite group of thinkers who influenced him examines the philosophies of seven men: Benjamin Franklin, David Rittenhouse, Dr. Benjamin Rush, Joseph Priestly, Benjamin Smith Barton, Tom Paine, and Charles Willson Peale. In Boorstin's interpretation, the group revolved around Jefferson and exchanged their political and social philosophies with the statesman.

H 566. CALHOUN, DANIEL. The Intelligence of a People. Princeton, N.J.: Princeton University Press, 1973. 408 pp.
This study attempts to assess the peculiar nature of American talents and intellectual strengths and weaknesses between the Revolution and the Civil War. Calhoun builds his arguments on such sources as the exhortations of educational critics and reformers, the published remains of professional groups (bridge-builders, shipbuilders, and clergymen), and popular handbooks on child-rearing. Calhoun argues that the period saw a narrowing of the American mind; the national intelligence was degraded by citizens who either could not live up to or did not value the achievements of their ancestors or of their contemporaries in England.

H 567. CASH, WILBUR J. The Mind of the South. New York: Knopf, 1941.
      444 pp.
In this work, Cash penetrates the dense psychological makeup of the South
from the antebellum emphasis on individualism, Romanticism, and Puritanism
to the class identities of the New South. Relations between the races,
sexes, and classes are interpreted in light of the region's violence and
its guilty conscience over slavery.

H 568. CHESTER, RONALD. Inheritance, Wealth, and Society. Bloomington:
      Indiana University Press, 1982. 235 pp.
Chester offers an intellectual history of the institution of inheritance
and examines issues raised by its concentration of wealth and power within
a society committed to some sort of egalitarianism. The book details
developing attitudes toward inheritance in Western Europe and America
in the 17th, 18th, and 19th centuries, modern debates over the fairness
of the institution, and its effects on other institutions, particularly
in respect to charity, creditors' rights, and criminality. Chester has
directed his work toward those involved in policy making, and he ends by
considering reform of the institution. He works from a wide range of
legal, economic, sociological, philosophical, and historical texts.

H 569. CHURCH, ROBERT L. and MICHAEL W. SEDLAK. Education in the United
      States: An Interpretive History. New York: Free Press, 1976.
      489 pp.
This survey provides a broad social and political context for the history
of American education. The work's theme is "the varying commitment among
Americans to 'mass schooling' and equality of education." This has
involved both the expansion of opportunities to go to school and the limiting
of these opportunities on the basis of race and social class, with a simultaneous broadening of responsibility for the schools. Among the topics
covered are antebellum district schools, the common school movement, colleges and universities, vocational education, educational reform in the
South, progressivism in education, and equality of educational opportunity.

H 570. COMMAGER, HENRY STEELE. The American Mind: An Interpretation
      of American Thought and Character Since the 1880s. New Haven,
      Conn.: Yale University Press, 1950. 476 pp.
Commager begins with the premise "that there is a distinctively American
way of thought, character and conduct." Consideration of the cultural
and intellectual developments widely shared throughout the Western world
has not been overlooked, and Commager uses his awareness of European influences to shed light on the aspects of the American mind he finds unique.
Through twenty chapters he discusses literature, journalism, philosophy,
religion, economics, historiography, politics, law, art, and architecture.
While the material changes since the 1880s have been astounding, Commager
concludes that the most significant changes have been philosophical.
Like Henry Adams, he sees the shift from a religious to a scientific society causing certainty to become uncertainty, order to become disorder.
Optimism, idealism, and a belief in industry and honor had been retained.
Yet he saw fundamental changes underlying these persistent attitudes.
Intolerance was gaining ground, and as approval of conformity arose, individualism naturally declined. Advertising emphasized a growing class
consciousness. Humor, which had been amiable in the 19th century, became
malicious in the 20th. Moral standards and religious practice became
lax. As America emerged as a world power, these changes in the American
character have held frightening implications.

H 571. CONKIN, PAUL K. Puritans and Pragmatists: Eight Eminent American
        Thinkers. New York: Dodd, Mead, 1968. 495 pp.
Eight quite different thinkers--Jonathan Edwards, Benjamin Franklin, John
Adams, Ralph Waldo Emerson, Charles Pierce, William James, John Dewey,
and George Santayana--are the subjects of this analysis of American intellectual history. Aware of the differences among these men's views, Conkin
nevertheless finds each shares a pragmatic world view, an instrumental
conception of knowledge and art. Similarly, the author argues that,
although not Puritan in any strictly technical sense, these important
American intellectuals held in common a tendency to think within a
Calvinist framework.

H 572. COTTON, JAMES HARRY. Royce on the Human Self. Cambridge, Mass.:
        Harvard University Press, 1954. 347 pp.
To fulfill the need for a systematic study of Royce in English, the author
has concentrated in this book on Josiah Royce's writings on the self.
The book is broken into three sections: the first culminates in 1885,
with The Religious Aspects of Philosophy; the second section concludes
with Royce's most comprehensive work, The World and the Individual; finally,
the third part examines Royce's published work after 1901. Comparisons
of Royce with other modern and classical philosophers is avoided with
the exception of William James and Charles Peirce. These two, along with
Royce, formed the nucleus of the "Classical" period in American philosophy.
The author includes his own critical comments. Many unpublished sources
are used in this study. A selected bibliography as well as a brief appendix of Royce-James correspondence is included.

H 573. CREMIN, LAWRENCE A. American Education: The National Experience,
        1783-1876. New York: Harper & Row, 1980. 607 pp.
In the second volume of a history of American education, Cremin traces
the development of an authentic American vernacular education from the
early Republican period through Reconstruction. He argues that this vernacular education is rooted in a popular paideia which incorportes religious pieties, Republican ideals and utilitarian values. This paideia was
critical to the development of a unified society, yet it provided justification for both abolitionists and pro-slavery defenders. The concept
of education is broadly defined to include religion, newspapers, museums,
libraries and intellectual currents as well as the institutional history
of public and private schools. The author's cultural concerns allow the
discussion of both Horace Mann and Harriet Beecher Stowe as American educators. Cremin also discusses the efforts of those outside the mainstream--
Catholics, blacks, and Indians--to educate themselves.

H 574. CREMIN, LAWRENCE A. The Transformation of the School: Progressiv-
        ism in American Education, 1876-1957. New York: Knopf, 1961.
        387 pp.
Cremin locates the origins of educational reform in the Progressive era
and views Progressive education as part of the liberal response to the
forces of industrialization, immigration, urbanization, and science that
were transforming America. The author's primary theme is the degeneration
of what was an exciting revolt against formalism at the turn of the century
into a mockery of itself after 1920. Cremin describes the debased state
of education at the turn of the century which the reformers wished to
correct by broadening the functions of the school and making learning
relevant to the students, but he points out that once reform started,
its momentum became self-generated, reaching a peak in the 1920s and 1930s,
declining in the 1940s, and dying in the 1950s. Although Cremin points
out the eventual absurdities of some Progressive educational reform, he
refuses to hold pioneers like John Dewey responsible for the excesses
of their disciples.

H 575. CRUNDEN, ROBERT M. From Self to Society, 1919-1941. Englewood
Cliffs, N.J.: Prentice-Hall, 1972. 212 pp.
This book offers an interdisciplinary look at the era between 1919 and
1941. As an "intellectual history of culture," the book focuses on several
prominent or significant personalities of the period and examines their
contributions to American intellectual currents. Crunden suggests that
the era was marked by three ideological shifts: the Progressive era,
which left an intellectual legacy that valued the individual as an active
participant in society; the post-W.W. I years, in which individualism
was idealized; and, finally, the Depression era, which valued community
and the submergence of the individual within society. Within this broad
framework, the book discusses the intellectual themes and cultural achievements characterizing the era.

H 576. CURTI, MERLE. The Growth of American Thought. 1943; Rev. ed.
New York: Harper, 1964. 939 pp.
Curti defines his synthesizing study as "a social history of American
thought," stressing the dissemination of knowledge and the growth of education in the U.S. He examines European influences upon the development
of intellectual life and institutions in America. His effort is to
"describe in broad outline the nature of dominant ideas and to indicate
the major contributions made by Americans to exact knowledge." Although
Curti is primarily interested in placing the development of American
thought within its social context, the revised edition incorporates recent
literature on the topic, which concentrates more on the internal structure
and philosophical foundations of ideas than on their social milieu.

H 577. CURTI, MERLE. Human Nature in American Thought: A History. Madison: University of Wisconsin Press, 1980. 424 pp.
Curti examines American conceptions of human nature from the arrival of
Europeans on this continent to the present. He notes that the phrase
"human nature" has often formed the basis for important philosophies or
political doctrines, cropping up particularly often during periods of
upheaval (the American Revolution and the Civil War, for instance), but
also claims that those who use it seldom define it. He therefore examines
a wide range of not only literary but also philosophical, theological,
political, and scientific writings for their implied notions of human
nature. American intellectuals have drawn upon classical Greek, ancient
Oriental, medieval Christian, and modern Western notions about human nature.
Since the mid-19th century, sciences—natural and social—have contributed
significantly to the definition of human nature. Old World notions of
human nature, when transplanted, generally are modified to fit circumstances in the New World.

H 578. CURTI, MERLE. The Social Ideas of American Educators. 1935; Rev.
ed. Totowa, N.J.: Littlefield, Adams, 1968. 613 pp.
Curti looks at the intellectual and spiritual leaders of American elementary and secondary schools in order to define their relation to social
movements, especially those associated with business and industry. At
once chronological, topical, and biographical, his history traces the
relations between social concerns and educational leadership in various
time periods, which range in this revised edition from Colonial times
through the 1960s.

H 579. DAVIS, RICHARD BEALE. Intellectual Life in the Colonial South,
1585-1763. 3 vols. Knoxville: University of Tennessee Press,
1978. 1810 pp.
This work is a broad survey of the Southern mind and Southern culture
as expressed in architecture, political discourse, religion, literature,
art, music, and education. A distinct "Southern" mind is seen as emerging
before the American Revolution. Among the many topics considered are

the promotion and discovery of the South, scientific efforts there, and Southern responses to Indians. The mind of the Colonial South is portrayed as fragmented rather than systematic.

H 580. DIEHL, CARL. Americans and German Scholarship, 1770-1870. New Haven, Conn.: Yale University Press, 1978. 194 pp.
Diehl presents a study of Americans at German universities before 1870 who lived through the transformation of German scholarship. He argues that at the end of the 18th century German scholars began losing a humanistic vision and historical imagination as they became more concerned with the techniques of historical and philological research. Although this was a major crisis in Western scholarship, the Americans in Germany, Diehl contends, were not aware of its significance. They acquired the research techniques and rejected the humanistic vision, committing themselves to specialization, research, and the professionalization of the academic community at the expense of humanism.

H 581. DIGGINS, JOHN P. Up from Communism: Conservative Odysseys in American Intellectual History. New York: Harper & Row, 1975. 522 pp.
The migration of former Communists into the camp of conservatism during the 1940s, 1950s, and 1960s is viewed through the lives of four men: Max Eastman, John Dos Passos, Will Herberg, and James Burnham. These four journeyed from the Old Left of the 1930s to the ranks of arch-conservatives in the 1960s; however, Diggins sees a continuity of intellectual position in both the Communist and the conservative attitudes toward liberalism.

H 582. DUGGER, RONNIE. The Invaded Universities: Form, Reform, and New Starts. New York: Norton, 1974. 457 pp.
Through a case-study of the University of Texas, Dugger critiques higher education in America and argues that it has suppressed independent thought. According to Dugger, the nation's universities have been used by business to legitimate its economic and political values. Within this work, Dugger raises critical questions concerning the structure and function of the university.

H 583. EAMES, S. MORRIS. Pragmatic Naturalism. Carbondale: Southern Illinois University Press, 1977. 242 pp.
Eames intends his book to be a guide to the leading ideas of the philo-sphical movement he calls "pragmatic naturalism." This study is limited to four representatives of this movement: Charles Sanders Pierce, William James, George Herbert Mead, and John Dewey. These four men are generally considered the intellectual founders and chief exponents of the Pragmatic movement in America—through which it is often said America came of age intellectually. At the end of each section, the author provides a list of further readings.

H 584. EASTON, LOYD D. Hegel's First American Followers. Athens: Ohio University Press, 1963. 353 pp.
In this book, Easton presents and interprets the Hegelian views of J. B. Stallo, Peter Kaufmann, Moncure Conway, and August Willich within their historical settings. These four men "championed and applied" Hegel's philosophy in America a decade before the St. Louis Hegelian Society was organized. One wrote a book in 1848 that was studied in St. Louis sixteen years later; two became auxiliaries of the St. Louis Society. Easton also includes an appendix of inaccessible and rare key writings of these men, some translated from German, in which they write on the meaning and application of Hegel's thought.

H 585. EATON, CLEMENT. The Mind of the Old South. Baton Rouge: Louisiana
State University Press, 1964. 271 pp.
This book examines the complex patterns of thought and social values that
Southerners developed between 1820-1860, the period when the civilization
of the South was most distinct from the culture of the North. Eaton claims
that the foundations of long-enduring sectional attitudes, particularly
in regard to blacks and the Federal government, were laid in this antebellum period. Eaton studies the Southern mind through a study of representative individuals. The book illuminates the process of historical
change in the South and the reasons that Southerners made the decisions
they did by focusing on the lives and the often contradictory experiences
of representative Southerners.

H 586. EKIRCH, ARTHUR A., Jr. Ideologies and Utopias: The Impact of
the New Deal on American Thought. Chicago: Quadrangle Books,
1969. 307 pp.
Ekirch discusses the intellectual response to the economic collapse of
the 1930s, the fitful development of the New Deal's policies and programs,
the successes and failures of the New Deal's attempts to bolster the arts
by providing government support, the views of FDR's detractors and supporters, and, finally, the terms of the foreign policy debate that dominated the period before Pearl Harbor. He concludes that the political
and intellectual changes the Depression and New Deal brought about have
cast a long shadow over the 20th century and remain crucial to understanding subsequent American history.

H 587. FAUST, DREW. A Sacred Circle: The Dilemma of the Intellectual
in the Old South, 1840-1860. Baltimore, Md.: Johns Hopkins University Press, 1977. 189 pp.
The "sacred circle" to which the title of this book refers was a group
of five intellectuals in the South who collectively sought a mission and
an identity within a society from which they felt estranged. Virginians
George Frederick Holmes, Nathaniel Beverley Tucker, and Edmund Ruffin
kept in close contact with William Gilmore Simms and James Henry Hammond
in South Carolina, responding to each other's work and developing among
themselves a religious sense of their reformist mission. Their "dilemma"
centered on their defense of the slave system. Faust suggests that these
five men envisioned a society in which slavery could be legitimated.

H 588. FERMI, LAURA. Illustrious Immigrants: The Intellectual Migration
from Europe, 1930-1941. 1968; Rev. ed. Chicago: University
of Chicago Press, 1972. 431 pp.
This book deals with the wave of intellectuals who emigrated to America
from Fascist-controlled Europe in the 1930s and early 1940s. Fermi's
study of this movement draws on the experiences of some 1900 "illustrious
immigrants," as well as her own participant's perspective. (She was married to emigre physicist Enrico Fermi.) After describing the encroachment
of politics on European university life during the early 1930s, Fermi
gives an account of the agencies established to aid displaced scholars.
She then analyzes the pattern of migration of European scholars to the
U.S. from 1930 to 1941, discussing trends in the number and nationality
of immigrants and their geographical distribution in the U.S. The second
part surveys the achievements of European-born intellectuals in various
spheres of American culture, including art, psychoanalysis, science, and
mathematics.

H 589. FLEMING, DONALD and BERNARD BAILYN, eds. The Intellectual Migration Europe and America, 1930-1960. Cambridge, Mass.: Harvard University Press, 1969. 748 pp.
This collection of essays focuses on the contributions to American culture made by the European intellectuals and artists who fled Hitler's regime. Three broad sections discuss the roles played by emigres in the sciences, in the social sciences, and in the humanities, gathering together such a diverse group of Europeans as the Frankfurt School theorists. The intellectual exchange between the U.S. and Europe during this critical era was a timely, productive one, as disciplines that were in the process of developing in America were given new direction by the European emigres. This volume provides an overview of the effect of the Europeans' ideas and achievements on American intellectual life and culture.

H 590. FLIEGELMAN, JAY. Prodigals and Pilgrims: The American Revolution Against Patriarchal Authority, 1750-1800. New York: Cambridge University Press, 1982. 328 pp.
Fliegelman's subject is the cultural revolution in 18th-century England and America, only one of whose manifestations was the American Revolution. The distinguishing feature of this cultural revolution was "a revolution in the understanding of the nature of authority that affected all aspects of eighteenth-century culture": the revolt against patriarchal authority. After discussing the ideological shift from traditional parental (patriarchal) authority to Lockean non-coercive familial relations--a shift that displaced the burden of responsibility from the parent and onto the child, and that resonated with political implication--Fliegelman examines in a comparative and interdisciplinary manner the thematic connections between key historical events and the important literary, pedagogical, theological, and political texts of the period. The outcome of such an ideological shift is seen to have resulted in filial anxiety over the ability of children to govern themselves in the world, as well as increased Federalist anxiety over the ability of America's "children" democratically to govern themselves: the price of establishing a new egalitarian model for the family and for the country.

H 591. FLOWER, ELIZABETH and MURRAY G. MURPHEY. A History of Philosophy in America. 2 vols. New York: Putnam, 1977. 972 pp.
In two comprehensive volumes, the authors survey American philosophy from the Puritans to the Pragmatists. Volume I begins with the religious thought of Colonial days and concludes with a brief essay on Transcendentalism; the second volume is primarily devoted to the Pragmatists, with essays on Peirce, James, Royce, Santayana, Dewey and Lewis. The volumes synthesize a large amount of material and provide summaries of the thought of major American philosophers.

H 592. FREDERICKSON, GEORGE M. The Inner Civil War: Northern Intellectuals and the Crisis of the Union. New York: Harper & Row, 1965. 277 pp.
This study traces the reactions of Northern intellectuals to the Civil War. Examining a diverse group of individuals from Whitman and Emerson, to William Lloyd Garrison, to Horace Bushnell, Fredericksen argues that a lost generation found itself. Pacifists became militarists, moral reformers turned from the issue of slavery to the issue of civil service reform, and dissenters became powerful. The post-1865 effects of the Civil War on the intellectual community are examined in the book's final segment.

H 593. FUSS, PETER. The Moral Philosophy of Josiah Royce. Cambridge,
Mass.: Harvard University Press, 1965. 268 pp.
Historians of American philosophy generally include Josiah Royce as one
of the classic American philosophers, but to many, according to Fuss,
Royce's philosophical doctrines dealing with absolute idealism are no
longer valid. It is the author's contention that any revival of Royce's
work should be in the area of his moral philosophy. In this book, Fuss
asserts that Royce did "develop an integrated, intelligible and not implaus-
ible ethical theory." Fuss presents his theory in a combination of chronological presentation and systematic exposition. He does not offer a definitive evaluation, but merely criticism from within Royce's philosophical
framework. Use is made of Royce's unpublished writings.

H 594. GABRIEL, RALPH HENRY. American Values: Continuity and Change.
Westport, Conn.: Greenwood Press, 1974. 230 pp.
Eleven essays by Gabriel are collected in this volume, which originally
appeared between 1938 and 1964 as pamphlets, articles, and addresses.
Gabriel's theme is the current of "democratic faith" underlying the historical development of American values, including "the doctrine of moral
law, the belief in progress, and the gospel of liberty." Ranging chronologically from the age of Jefferson to the Cold War, he discusses the
influence of religion, the Enlightenment, rationalism, the atomic bomb,
nationalism, and the Cold War. Gabriel states that "values are beliefs,"
forming the national ideal for society's behavior and thus becoming society's standards. In his last chapter, Gabriel sums up American values
regarding politics, religion, education, law, social relations, science,
economy, the arts, and international relations.

H 595. GABRIEL, RALPH HENRY. The Course of American Democratic Thought.
1940; Rev. ed. New York: Ronald Press, 1956. 508 pp.
In this survey, Gabriel traces the development of democratic ideals through
six periods of American history. Beginning with "Middle Period" thinkers
such as Emerson, Thoreau, and Beecher, he next analyzes the Civil War's
significance in intellectual life, focusing on Whitman, and then examines
the effects of Darwinism and industrialization after the war. Part IV
studies the rise of American scholarship from philosophers Royce and James
to Sumner and Adams. His analysis of the Progressive era is followed
by a discussion of the years after W.W. I and the intellectual ramifications of wartime. Three themes emerge through all six periods: individualism, natural law, and the world mission of America have consistently
shaped the country's intellectual life.

H 596. GAY, PETER. A Loss of Mastery: Puritan Historians in Colonial
America. Los Angeles: University of California Press, 1966.
164 pp.
Gay, primarily a European historian, looks at the hopeful beginnings of
historical writing amidst the religious climate of the Colonial age.
He contends that the Puritan experiment and the recording of that history
failed to live up to expectations; Puritan history died of atrophy as
the Americans' European colleagues moved on and adapted new ideas. Gay
examines William Bradford, Cotton Mather, and Jonathan Edwards in separate
sections of the book, arguing that they all placed piety first in the
writing of history, and that they relied on older historiographical methods
in approaching their subjects.

H 597. GILBERT, JAMES B. Work Without Salvation: America's Intellectuals
and Industrial Alienation, 1880-1910. Baltimore, Md.: Johns
Hopkins University Press, 1977. 240 pp.
Gilbert discusses the shock of the new order of industrialism and forces
of urbanization upon the "relationship of individuals and labor," primarily
concentrating on the New England region. The book is divided into three

sections: a look at the first awareness of the problem, individuals and movements that tried to regain "the hegemony of the work ethic," and a discussion of "the movements in psychology and philosophy that attempted to restate the relationship of mankind to work in the new behaviorist form." He concludes that contemporary America lies somewhere between the traditional work ethic and "the new compulsions of alienated labor." Hence, "in the unresolved crisis of modern industrialism, critics such as Dewey, Veblen and James, with one foot in tradition and the other advanced toward industrial behaviorism, strike us as fresher and more up-to-date than the apostles of a managerial society."

H 598. GOETZMANN, WILLIAM H., ed. The American Hegelians: An Intellectual Episode in the History of Western America. New York: Knopf, 1973. 397 pp.
This collection of essays examines the impact of German philosophy on a circle of intellectuals in St. Louis, in other parts of the Midwest, and in Concord, Massachusetts, in the mid-19th century. These "American Hegelians" raised ideas and themes central to the American character, upholding the values of urbanization and progress. Their application of Hegel's thought to American social processes perpetuated idealism in the nation's intellectual life. This anthology gathers together many essays on the important, though neglected, St. Louis thinkers (and their impact on public education), on the Concord School of philosophy, and on Pragmatism and Marxist movements.

H 599. GOSSETT, THOMAS F. Race: The History of an Idea in America. Dallas, Tex.: Southern Methodist University Press, 1963. 510 pp.
This wide-ranging book presents a social and intellectual history of American racism. Gossett not only deals with racism directed at blacks in America, but also examines the concept in relation to Orientals, Indians, and Southern and Eastern Europeans. Among the multitude of topics Gossett treats are the attitudes of scholars, writers, and ministers; the status of Indians and blacks; immigration restrictions; nativism; scientific theories about race; the Teutonic and Anglo-Saxon theories of historians and literary critics; and what Gossett sees as the distaste for racism in the 20th century.

H 600. GUTTMAN, ALLEN. The Conservative Tradition in America. New York: Oxford University Press, 1967. 214 pp.
Guttman's volume is a collection of six of his own essays, "The Decline of Conservatism in America," "Images of Value and a Sense of the Past," "The Establishment of Religion," "Conservatism and the Military Establishment," "The Revival of Conservative Ideas," and "The Present and the Future." In his introductory essay, "Liberalism and the Political Theory of Edmund Burke," he argues that because liberalism in America has been the dominant force the conservative opposition has often been misunderstood. Many historical interpretations have been marred, Guttman believes, by inaccurate interpretation of certain views that have become part of the defended status quo as conservative, when in fact in their own time they were part of an effort to reform. He traces the decline of conservatism politically, its survival in literature, and the attempts made to revive conservatism in this century.

H 601. HALL, PETER DOBKIN. The Organization of American Culture, 1700-1900: Private Institutions, Elites, and the Origins of American Nationality. New York: New York University Press, 1982. 325 pp.
American nationality, "the ability of Americans to conduct their economic, political, and cultural activities on a national scale as opposed to a local or regional one, evolved as the result of private corporate insti-

tutions and a corresponding elite. Hall traces the evolution of American nationality from the New England Puritans, through the ideology of Federalism, the post-Civil War educational reformers and businessmen, to the Progressives. After exploring the diversity of social and economic systems in early 18th-century America, Hall describes the development of corporate models of authority and collective action among the New England merchants. He then examines the transformation of American culture in light of specific institutional developments from 1780-1860: the legal foundations of the corporation; the medical profession; and higher education, particularly the comparative impact of Yale and Harvard. The Civil War is discussed as being a major impetus in the development of American nationalism. Hall closes with a challenge as America is forced to move beyond its nationalistic awareness to a new international stance.

H 602. HARTZ, LOUIS. Economic Policy and Democratic Thought: Pennsylvania, 1776-1860. Cambridge, Mass.: Harvard University Press, 1948. 366 pp.
Government policy played an important role in the economic development of Pennsylvania in the period between the Revolution and the Civil War. Hartz disputes the traditional contention that this period was characterized by laissez-faire policy. While the Federal government maintained a low profile, the state government in Pennsylvania was extremely active in the development of the state's resources and enterprises—acting as promotor, entrepreneur, and owner, as well as regulator. The author discusses the opposition to this state activity. He shows how the state's problems in administering its programs fed this opposition, particularly after the depression of the late 1830s. By mid-century, the author says, opposition to state involvement in economic life had become widespread—even among privileged corporations themselves. By this time, private interests were in a strong enough position to forego state support and to end state limitations on their activities (just when the controls were most needed).

H 603. HASKELL, THOMAS L. The Emergence of Professional Social Science: The American Social Science Association and the Nineteenth-Century Crisis of Authority. Urbana: University of Illinois Press, 1977. 276 pp.
The formation of an institutionalized "modern perspective" on mankind is attributed to the social sciences, but Haskell argues that this way of looking at man has pervaded other areas of thought. Indeed, Haskell believes that the broad acceptance of this perspective paved the way for the professionalization of the social sciences. Here, he looks to the generation before professionalization, at their replacement by "professionals." He focuses on the American Social Science Association, founded in 1865, from which other associations were born: the American Historical Association, the American Economic Association, and civil service reform among them. The history of the ASSA encompasses three larger issues: professional authority, the rise of the social scientist, and the realignment of social thought in the pivotal decade of the 1890s. Haskell addresses this study to historians as well as social scientists, hoping to "bridge the gap" between the two disciplines.

H 604. HERRESHOFF, DAVID. American Disciples of Marx from the Age of Jackson to the Progressive Era. Detroit, Mich.: Wayne State University Press, 1967. 215 pp.
This is a brief series of biographical studies of American intellectuals and activists on the Left, ranging from Emerson to Eugene Debs. Herreshoff's overview provides an account of the conflicts faced by 19th-century radicals as they attempted to discern which elements of Marx's thought could profitably be applied to American society. He explores the range of options of radical schools of thought and movements available to American intellectuals.

H 605. HERSCHER, URI D. Jewish Agricultural Utopias in America, 1880-1910. Detroit, Mich.: Wayne State University Press, 1981. 197 pp.

The constant failure of the farming cooperatives established by Russian Jewish immigrants is detailed by Herscher in his case studies of these enterprises. In addition to describing the relationship between the settlers and their Jewish-American sponsors, the author traces the ideological influence of Russian Socialism and of the American agrarian utopianist Henry George. Herscher describes in great detail the one success of the movement, which was at Woodbine, New Jersey; though it relied heavily on foreign philanthropy and compromised its agrarian ideals by establishing industries, it survived to become a municipality and what one contemporary observer called the "First Self-Governed Jewish Community Since the Fall of Jerusalem." Herscher finds in the utopianists a messianic urgency to escape industrialized society, which they identified with the persecution of their homeland.

H 606. HIGHAM, JOHN and PAUL K. CONKIN, eds. New Directions in American Intellectual History. Baltimore, Md.: Johns Hopkins University Press, 1979. 245 pp.

This collection of essays culled from those submitted by the participants in the Wingspread Conference on New Directions in American Intellectual History of 1977 includes pieces by a number of the nation's intellectual historians, including Gordon S. Wood, Sacvan Bercovitch, Henry F. May, David D. Hall, and Warren I. Sussman. Each essay comes to terms in one way or another with the decline in popularity of intellectual history in the late 1960s and 1970s and suggests explicitly or by example new alternatives for writing the history of ideas. The subjects considered in this collection are wide-ranging, from Wood's essay on "Intellectual History and the Social Sciences" to Hall's remarks on the history of culture in "The World of Print and the Collective Mentality in Seventeenth-Century New England."

H 607. HOFSTADTER, RICHARD. Anti-Intellectualism in American Life. New York: Knopf, 1963. 434 pp.

This book considers religion, politics, business, and educational institutions in interpreting the phenomenon of anti-intellectualism in the U.S. Responding to the McCarthyism of the 1950s, Hofstadter seeks the source of the denigration of intellectualism deep in the American past, discussing the Puritans, religious fundamentalism, and 20th-century business attitudes. Hofstadter offers an interpretation of the American traditions of practicality and emotionalism, which created a climate unsympathetic to intellectual life.

H 608. HOFSTADTER, RICHARD. The Idea of a Party System: The Rise of Legitimate Opposition in the United States, 1780-1840. Berkeley: University of California Press, 1969. 280 pp.

In this work Hofstadter addresses the intellectual origins of the two-party system through the Jeffersonian and Jacksonian eras. He argues that the development of legitimate party opposition and a theory of politics that accepted it was quite new in world history and that its emergence required a bold act of understanding on the part of its contemporaries. Hofstadter contends that the crisis of 1797-1801, in which power passed to a legitimate opposition, was as important to the young nation as the constitutional crisis of 1787-1788. He examines the anti-party views that dominated the Anglo-American political tradition before the Revolution, the anti-party bias in the drafting of the Federal constitution, and the position of Jefferson and Madison as anti-party theorists who discovered themselves organizing an opposition party in the 1790s.

H 609. HOFSTADTER, RICHARD. The Paranoid Style in American Politics and
        Other Essays. New York: Knopf, 1965. 314 pp.
Assembled in this volume is a collection of Hofstadter's essays written
over a span of fourteen years. The essays are divided into two groups:
the first concerns the contradictions that produced the extreme right
of the 1950s and 1960s; the theme of the second section is the reaction
to the industrialism and world power of the earlier modern era. "All
deal with public responses to a critical situation or an enduring dilemma,"
such as the rise of big business, the Cold War, and imperialism. Hofstadter is more concerned with "the milieu of politics rather than its structure,"
looking at the public response to political issues rather than institutions
and distribution of power. Hofstadter was interested in "the conspira-
torial mind," the belief that all problems stem from a single source,
and therefore, "can be eliminated by some kind of final act of victory
over the evil source." Contemporary conservatism can still be traced
to "ascetic Protestantism," a religious world view and the work ethic,
and a fear that "an adherence to the decline of entrepreneurial competition
will destroy our national character."

H 610. HOLLANDER, PAUL. Political Pilgrims; Travels of Western Intellec-
        tuals to the Soviet Union, China, and Cuba, 1928-1978. New York:
        Harper & Row, 1983. 544 pp.
Hollander's book is a description of what he sees as high gullibility.
He tells the story of certain Western intellectuals, highly alienated from
their own societies, whose need to believe manifested itself in a pervasive
blindness to possible flaws in various totalitarian utopias of the 20th
century. He critically surveys the literature produced by the "pilgrims"
in their travels in 20th-century totalitarian states, stressing with some
sympathy and much criticism the travelers' motivations.

H 611. HORSMAN, REGINALD. Race and Manifest Destiny: The Origins of
        American Racial Anglo-Saxonism. Cambridge, Mass.: Harvard Uni-
        versity Press, 1981. 367 pp.
Focusing on the years 1800-1850, this study discusses the origins of the
belief in racialism and white supremacy in the U.S., showing that such
ideas were well-established in America by 1850. The American expansionism
of the 19th century was understood by its proponents as the manifest destiny of superior whites; this concept helped to justify the fates of the
non-whites who were in the way. European theorizing about the Anglo-Saxon,
Teutonic races and their presumed characteristics merged with the epic
story of America's conquest of the continent. From the years of the Revolution to the Civil War, the increase in harshness of general attitudes
toward blacks, Indians, and Mexicans was notable. Greater attention is
paid here to the racial ideas themselves than to why such beliefs arose
during these years. The Anglo-Saxonism often associated with the late
19th century, it is shown, actually dates further back.

H 612. HUTH, HANS. Nature and the American: Three Centuries of Changing
        Attitudes. Berkeley: University of California Press, 1957.
        250 pp.
Using literary, pictorial, and historical references, this study addresses
the relationship of Americans to their natural environment. Huth covers
such diverse topics as 19th-century Naturalists, Puritan ideas toward nature,
and the rise of 20th-century public policy regarding conservation.

H 613. JONES, HOWARD MUMFORD. The Age of Energy: Varieties of American
        Experience, 1865-1915. New York: Viking Press, 1971. 545 pp.
This is the final volume of Jones's three-part intellectual history, includ-
ing O Strange New World (H 615) and Revolution and Romanticism (H 617).
Jones sees the era (1865-1915) as represented by "the discovery, use,

exploitation, and expression of energy, whether it be that of personality
or of prime mover or of words." The level of energy reached during the
Civil War, Jones believes, caused "gigantic verbal clashes" over reconstruction policies, industrialism, politics and religion. Jones sees
his work as a study of American culture from the end of the Civil War,
through national and regional tensions, and the spirit of unity fostered
by the Spanish-American War, to the "new nationalism" of Theodore Roosevelt
and the eve of W.W. I.

H 614. JONES, HOWARD MUMFORD. Ideas in America. Cambridge, Mass.:
        Harvard University Press, 1944. 304 pp.
This collection of thirteen addresses and essays, which Jones wrote between
1934 and 1942, represents contributions to the history of ideas, morals,
and taste in the U.S. Jones groups the essays according to subject.
The first group admonishes American scholars to recognize their responsibility to study American culture, delineates the most neglected and
misunderstood areas of the culture, and argues for the use of American
literature as an instrument for cultural analysis. The second group discusses the history of ideas and their influence. The final group deals
with the responsibilities that American scholars, writers, and publishers
have toward their contemporary audiences; most of these concern the rise
of Fascism in Europe and its corollaries in America.

H 615. JONES, HOWARD MUMFORD. O Strange New World, American Culture:
        The Formative Years. New York: Viking Press, 1964. 464 pp.
Jones analyzes American culture from the discovery of the New World to
the early years of the Republic by examining European and American reactions to America. American culture, Jones claims, arose from the interplay of the Old World and the New. Initially, Europe projected certain
values into America which the colonists accepted, modified, or rejected.
Jones traces the vague Renaissance image of America, at first golden but
later tarnished by Europe's unscrupulous search for wealth, and then considers the Renaissance man in America, the European view of Colonialism,
and literature written to promote emigration. Later, he considers the
transfer of the Protestant ethic from Europe to America and the American
Enlightenment's rediscovery of the classical past. After independence,
America tried to create a culture free from the Old World's corruption;
hence the rise of nationalism in the arts and sciences.

H 616. JONES, HOWARD MUMFORD. The Pursuit of Happiness. Cambridge, Mass.:
        Harvard University Press, 1953. 168 pp.
Jones takes the phrase "the pursuit of happiness" and traces the ways
in which it has been interpreted from before its appearance in the Declaration of Independence to contemporary America. Religion, government,
business, psychology, and especially 20th-century popular culture and
advertising reflect the underlying belief that the pursuit of happiness
is a national right. Today's interpretation of the meaning of happiness
has changed following revolutions in philosophical and psychological
thought. Happiness is a reflection of one's inner life, a harmonious
adjustment to a hostile world. Jones speculates that perhaps the 18th-
century author of the Declaration of Independence was "wiser than are
we." To Jefferson and his contemporaries, happiness was "contentment"
with the limited "opportunities and powers" we are able to "achieve in
an indifferent universe."

H 617. JONES, HOWARD MUMFORD. Revolution and Romanticism. Cambridge,
        Mass.: Harvard University Press, 1974. 487 pp.
Following O Strange New World (H 615), and before The Age of Energy (H
613), Revolution and Romanticism completes Jones's trilogy concerning
the "relationships of art and thought" between the U.S. and Europe. Jones
principally looks at the American and French Revolutions to consider the

origins and the cultural and social results of the two "convulsions" of Romanticism and Revolution, using examples from Great Britain and Germany as well. Romantic individualism, romantic genius, classicism, and the "Faustian Man" are among the topics Jones addresses. Jones concludes that the major contribution of Revolution and Romanticism is the right of individualism, which became the foundation for the "Rights of Man."

H 618. KAESTLE, CARL F. Pillars of the Republic: Common Schools and American Society, 1780-1860. Edited by Eric Foner. New York: Hill & Wang, 1983. 266 pp.
In this reinterpretation of the movement to establish state systems of elementary schools, Kaestle argues that few Americans opposed popular education in either ideology or behavior; many, however, strongly resisted the intrusion of the state into local institutional life. Reformers advocating centralized support and control prevailed; localists, who were divided along racial, ethnic, religious, class, and regional lines, forced some adjustments in the system. Kaestle describes extensive local arrangements for schooling in existence prior to reform; the context of social change; and an ideology based on Republicanism, Protestantism, and Capitalism, which was forged by reformers but shared by many of the localists who opposed them. He assesses regional differences, as well as limits justified on the basis of sex and race.

H 619. KALLEN, HORACE M. Cultural Pluralism and the American Idea: An Essay in Social Philosophy. Philadelphia: University of Pennsylvania Press, 1956. 208 pp.
This volume begins with Kallen's essay "Cultural Pluralism and the American Idea," is followed by a critical commentary from several specialists, and closes with a response from Kallen to his critics. "Cultural Pluralism and the American Idea" looks at the need for social responsibility and national unity as well as the need for freedom of the individual. Kallen discusses the negative impact of the widening gap between work and leisure upon the individual, and "lays the iniquities of social, political, economic and religious authoritarianism." In his reprise, Kallen asserts, "I do not see how the individualizing trait of the authentic American can be anything else than his commitment to this common undertaking in American society." It is the cultural pluralist who can peacefully communicate through the "American idea" of the "morality of freedom" and open-minded tolerance.

H 620. KAMMEN, MICHAEL. People of Paradox. New York: Knopf, 1972. 316 pp.
This interpretation of the dominant traits of American culture searches out the large tendencies and contradictions that have shaped the national character. Kammen's discussion of "biformity" in the American experience asserts that the tensions and ambiguities first faced by the country during its Colonial years have become the basis of American society. Conflicting ideas about work, individuality, nature, community, and the search for identity have continued through the centuries to produce a unique society. Kammen emphasizes the 16th and 17th centuries in this analysis of the cultural paradoxes that have shaped the American nation.

H 621. KARL, BARRY D. Charles E. Merriam and the Study of Politics. Chicago: University of Chicago Press, 1974. 337 pp.
The work is a "biography" of a whole generation of professional academics, of which Merriam is but a leading example, who came to maturity during the Progressive Era and whose power lasted until the 1950s. Impressed by the idea that there ought to be one national American civilization, Merriam and his generation first attempted to reconcile expertise, the new behaviorism, and appeals to the electorate during the Progressive era. When the apparent collapse of the alliance between the "experts" and the rest of the population occurred in the late 1910s, as symbolized

by Merriam's disastrous campaign for mayor of Chicago, the experts worked out a new strategy of implementing professionalism and cultural nationalism: they became appointed advisers to government officials. By the 1950s, however, with Merriam's death, a new group of American natural culturalists was emerging, eventually to replace Merriam's.

H 622. KAUFMAN, ALLEN. Capitalism, Slavery, and Republican Values: Ante-bellum Political Economists, 1819-1848. Austin: University of Texas Press, 1982. 189 pp.
Kaufman examines the ideological roots of the terms of political discourse in antebellum America, using the logical and ideological structure of the works of three writers on political economy: Daniel Raymond, a Northern protectionist; Thomas Dew, a Southern free-trader; and Jacob Cardozo, a South Carolina journalist. The book analyzes the views of these men on such issues as slavery, trade, and industrialization. Kaufman attempts to use "political economy" as an "interpretive tool for reevaluating the political equilibrium and disequilibrium of the antebellum period." An introduction by Elizabeth Fox-Genovese and Eugene Genovese places Kaufman's work in the context of Marxist historiography.

H 623. KERBER, LINDA K. Federalists in Dissent: Imagery and Ideology in Jeffersonian America. Ithaca, N.Y.: Cornell University Press, 1970. 233 pp.
In this account of Federalist objections to Jeffersonianism, Kerber examines the set of beliefs Federalists held and how they differed with the Republicans on grounds other than partisanship. Kerber concentrates on the writings of mainly New England "articulated Federalists." She focuses on their attitudes toward science, the arts, law, and education, and concludes that they perceived their world in disarray. She argues that the Federalists, looking at the new nation through a different world view than the Republicans, thought the cultural fabric of the Republic was under attack.

H 624. KING, RICHARD H. The Party of Eros: Radical Social Thought and the Realm of Freedom. Chapel Hill: University of North Carolina Press, 1972. 227 pp.
This book examines the influence of Freud on three radical American theorists. The ideas of Paul Goodman, Herbert Marcuse, and Norman O. Brown are analyzed with an emphasis on their understanding of human consciousness and cultural processes. King discusses the sexual radicalism of the three theorists, asserting their contribution to a broader post-war "cultural radicalism."

H 625. KIRKLAND, EDWARD C. Dream and Thought in the Business Community, 1860-1900. Ithaca, N.Y.: Cornell University Press, 1956. 175 pp.
These six essays, the published version of a series of lectures delivered at Cornell in 1956, explore the ideology of American business leaders in the second half of the 19th century. Kirkland's conclusions are based principally on businessmen's attitudes, as reflected in their homes and their domestic habits, and as expressed in their statements regarding public school education, college education, the role of government, and philanthropy. According to Kirkland, business leaders did not as a whole subscribe to a consistent ideology. Indeed, he finds that contemporary intellectual systems such as Social Darwinism influenced business attitudes only to the extent that they provided a new vocabulary for expressing prevailing opinions. Nevertheless, businessmen shared a generalized commitment to values of order and to attempts to rationalize business affairs. They thus preferred education over ignorance but insisted that education itself be ordered and hierarchical: to each as much as was necessary to perform his function and no more. Similarly, business opposed govern-

ment interference less out of fear of democracy's revenge than out of suspicion that government meddling would disrupt the orderly operation of natural economic laws.

H 626. KOSTER, DONALD N. Transcendentalism in America. Boston: Twayne, 1975. 126 pp.
Koster's volume provides a study of the historical and philosophical background to the appearance of the Transcendentalist movement, its development and literary landmarks, and an assessment of the movement's implications for American thought to the present day. Koster traces Transcendental influences on succeeding writers, such as Emily Dickinson, Robert Frost, Wallace Stevens, and Eugene O'Neill, as well as on the Beat Generation and the 1960s generation, including Abbie Hoffman, S.D.S., and the Beatles. In conclusion, while Koster agrees with the view that the Transcendentalists' effort to gain a deeper spiritual meaning of life seems at odds with 20th-century society, the "contemporary underground," in fact embraced the values set forth by Emerson, Thoreau, and Whitman.

H 627. KRADITOR, AILEEN S. The Radical Persuasion, 1890-1917: Aspects of the Intellectual History and Historiography of Three American Radical Organizations. Baton Rouge: Louisiana State University Press, 1981. 381 pp.
In this study of the American radical Left at the turn of the century, Kraditor sees a disjunction between radical rhetoric and ideology as pronounced by leaders of the Socialist Labor Party, the Socialist Party of America, the International Workers of the World, and the real sentiments of the working class and a number of ethnic groups. Works were viewed inaccurately, the American social order misperceived, and the ability of a democratic political culture to address the ills of Capitalism was underestimated by radical leaders. Kraditor argues that the radicals' preconceptions of the groups with whom they attempted to work hurt their efforts to mobilize the working class in a unified class struggle.

H 628. KUKLICK, BRUCE. The Rise of American Philosophy, Cambridge, Massachusetts, 1860-1930. New Haven, Conn.: Yale University Press, 1977. 674 pp.
This work traces the development of philosophical thought at Harvard University and provides an account of the impact of Darwinism and the subsequent rise of Pragmatism. Kuklick offers an analysis of the Cambridge circle of philosophers from Francis Bowen and Unitarianism through the Pragmatic response to Darwinism in the ideas of Wright, Peirce, James, Royce, and others. The book then discusses the specialization of philosophical thought into academic disciplines as the university became increasingly systematized in the 20th century. Kuklick analyzes American philosophical trends within the framework of a changing educational system.

H 629. LASCH, CHRISTOPHER. The Agony of the American Left. New York: Knopf, 1969. 212 pp.
This collection of essays on the Left and American life includes examinations of the decline of populism and Socialism, black power, the New Left of the 1960s, and the Congress for Cultural Freedom (a liberal and anti-Communist group of the 1950s). The author describes the Left's failure to become more than a marginal force in American politics, and is particularly critical of intellectuals' abdication of their independent, critical role. Lasch believes that liberalism cannot overcome certain contradictions inherent in Capitalism, and that a coherent programmatic radicalism is needed for true restructuring of American society.

H 630. LASCH, CHRISTOPHER. The Culture of Narcissism: American Life
        in an Age of Diminishing Expectations. New York: Norton, 1979.
        268 pp.
Lasch offers an extensive critique of contemporary American society, focusing on the loss of confidence in America and on increasing social pessimism.
He examines the crisis of Western culture and the bankruptcy of liberalism
and the intellectual disciplines. Lasch criticizes the unwillingness
of citizens to take part in the political system as well as bureaucratic
behavior which undermines earlier political traditions. He further
describes the culture of competitive individualism which, he maintains,
has created the pervasive hedonism and self-indulgence in American society.
Lasch argues that the "cultural revolution" of the present only tends
to reproduce the fears of narcissistic survival and further engenders
the collapse of civilization.

H 631. LASCH, CHRISTOPHER. The New Radicalism in America, 1889-1963;
        The Intellectual as Social Type. New York: Knopf, 1965.
        349 pp.
Lasch treats the emergence of a "new" radicalism at the turn of the century
as "a phase of the social history of intellectuals." The growth of a
secular radicalism that treated political and cultural issues as intimately
related was associated with the rise of a sort of intellectuals' subcul-
ture--self-consciously distinct and identifying with the nation's outcasts
and down-trodden rather than with its dominant classes. Lasch proceeds
primarily by means of biographical treatment--he considers Jane Addams,
Randolph Bourne, Lincoln Steffens, Mabel Dodge Luhan, Lincoln Colcord,
and the New Republic circle, concluding with a study of Norman Mailer.

H 632. LATOURETTE, KENNETH SCOTT. Missions and the American Mind.
        Indianapolis, Ind.: National Foundation, 1949. 40 pp.
Latourette surveys the many missionary endeavors carried on in the U.S.
and by Americans outside the national boundaries. Christian missions
have had an important influence on the American mind since Colonial days,
when America was a field for European missionary agencies concerned with
both unregenerate whites and the Indians. The Western movement subsequently provided a fertile area for missionaries within the nation, as did
the slave population of the South. Latourette also examines American
efforts to christianize the World and the effects of this on American
culture.

H 633. LEARS, T. J. JACKSON. No Place of Grace: Antimodernism and the
        Transformation of American Culture 1880-1920. New York: Pantheon
        Books, 1981. 364 pp.
Antimodernism, as Lears defines it, was a revolt against positivism by
the middle- and upper-class intellectuals who sought "authentic" experience.
Characterized by ambivalence toward--not outright repudiation of--material
progress, antimodernism was not mere "escapism." As Lears points out,
it has much in common with 20th-century literary modernism--both rejected
"stodgy moralism." He has two aims: (1) to correct the notion that antimodernism was the "death rattle" of the old-stock Northern elite; and
(2) to suggest a new way of understanding the shift from the 19th-century
(i.e., Protestant, entrepreneurial) to the 20th-century (i.e., therapeutic,
consumer) world view. In his methodology, Lears has drawn upon the theories of Weber, Freud, and Gramsci. Among those he discusses are Henry
and Brooks Adams, V. W. Brooks, J. B. Cabell, Samuel Clemens, Henry and
William James, Frank Norris, C. E. Norton, Horace Traubel, and Edith
Wharton.

H 634. LYND, STAUGHTON. Intellectual Origins of American Radicalism.
New York: Pantheon Books, 1968. 184 pp.
Lynd discovers the roots of American radicalism in 18th- and 19th-century
writings of Joseph Priestly, John Wilkes, Granville Sharp, Thomas Paine,
William Lloyd Garrison, Theodore Parker, and Henry David Thoreau. His
contention is that a strong tradition of dissent in American thought characterized pre-Civil War American culture. He shows that, from the start,
these thinkers raised basic questions challenging private property and
state authority. Each of the thinkers held in common views that the correct foundation for government is a universal law of right and wrong that
was based on the intuitive common sense of every person, that freedom
cannot be delegated, and that the purpose of society is the fulfillment
of the self.

H 635. MARCELL, DAVID W. Progress and Pragmatism: James, Dewey, Beard,
and the American Idea of Progress. Westport, Conn.: Greenwood
Press, 1974. 402 pp.
Marcell places Pragmatism within the American idea of progress to illustrate its unique characteristics, its popularity, and its diversity.
Choosing the three Pragmatists he considers the most influential--James,
Dewey, and Beard--Marcell argues that they held responses common to the
"intellectual crisis of their times," molding Pragmatism into a philosophy
of progress. This, he believes, will illuminate Pragmatic liberalism
throughout the development of American thought. Marcell wishes to show
how the ideas of these three Pragmatists connected "the traditional faith
in progress" with "the more scientific, critical approach to history,
morality, and experience" that characterizes the 20th century.

H 636. MAY, HENRY F. The End of American Innocence: A Study of the First
Years of Our Own Time, 1912-1917. New York: Knopf, 1959. 413 pp.
While most Americans feel that it was W.W. I that projected America into
the modern age, May argues that beneath a placid exterior many new ideas
that would not emerge in full bloom until after the war were already present. The exterior stability of prewar America was characterized by traditional values, and it was these values that began to shift, first among
small groups and then in the rest of society. May considers Victorian
ideas of art and those of newer poets; and in addition he examines the
thought of conservatives and radicals. He believes that the dislocation
felt by many intellectuals after W.W. I can be traced to the blind optimism
which he identifies as the primary flaw of the 19th century.

H 637. MAY, HENRY F. The Enlightenment in America. New York: Oxford
University Press, 1976. 419 pp.
May's account of the influence of the European Enlightenment on America
broadly defines the Enlightenment to include "all those who believe two
propositions: first, that the present age is more enlightened than the
past; and second, that we understand nature and man best through the use
of our natural faculties." Explaining the American versions of the Enlightenment in terms of conflict and compromise with American Protestantism--
the central fact of 18th-century American experience--May discusses the
successive influence of four stages of European Enlightenment thought
in America: what he calls the Moderate, Skeptical, Revolutionary, and
Didactic Enlightenment. These categories allow him to draw distinctions
where traditional interpretations have often been confused, as, for example,
in the differences between the beliefs of Jefferson and Adams.

H 638. McDERMOTT, JOHN J. The Culture of Experience: Philosophical Essays
        in the American Grain. New York: New York University Press, 1976.
        237 pp.
In this collection of essays, McDermott's primary concern is that of experience, which he believes is the common thread linking American philosophers
from John Winthrop to George Herbert Mead. The topics he addresses are
of contemporary interest, and his emphasis on Dewey's "aesthetic sensibility" is used to define 20th-century repression, nature nostalgia, nature
space, nature time, urban space, urban time, and technological artifact."
How we "feel" about our experiences should be the guiding force behind
our decisions at the personal, social, and political levels. McDermott
looks at the commonplace and seemingly obvious aspects of American life
through the ideas of the American philosophical tradition, which gains
power and meaning from its application to the entire scope of American
culture. McDermott hopes that through his essays the creative forces
unique to America and essential to the preservation of its ideals will
be illuminated.

H 639. McWILLIAMS, WILSON C. The Idea of Fraternity in America. Los
        Angeles: University of California Press, 1973. 695 pp.
McWilliams argues that the 18th-century doctrine of fraternity was inaccurate and might have done as much to damage the idea as to strengthen it.
For all their enthusiasm, the founding fathers shed little light on fraternal relations. McWilliams "presumes there is a nature of man, and consequently a nature of fraternity." He agrees with the earliest philosophers who saw fraternity as a way to achieve freedom and equality. The
reversal of this idea in modern times he sees as a serious fault.
McWilliams defines fraternity as a bond of shared values or goals, shared
affection, recognizing failure but providing emotional support, and a
sense of identity. His definition "implies a necessary tension with
loyalty to a society at large." We are all kinsmen more than we may expect,
and fraternity is essential to modern human relations.

H 640. MERRILL, KENNETH R. and ROBERT W. SHAHAN, eds. American Philosophy:
        From Edwards to Quine. Norman: University of Oklahoma Press,
        1977. 200 pp.
This book is a collection of essays read at the sixth Annual Oklahoma
Conference in Philosophy in 1976. Roland A. DeLattre discusses Jonathan
Edwards's reconciliation of his idea of beauty with its implications for
politics. Robert Caponigri explores notions of the individual and the
state in Transcendentalist thought. Max H. Frisch discusses American pragmatism, Peter Fuss writes on Josiah Royce and the concept of the self,
and Frederick A. Olaffson discusses Santayana. A final essay by W. V.
Quine "argues for an undogmatic, nonreductionist physicalism, justifying
its ontology in (roughly) pragmatic grounds."

H 641. MILLER, DAVID L. George Herbert Mead: Self, Language, and the
        World. Austin: University of Texas Press, 1973. 280 pp.
Miller locates Mead in the tradition of Pragmatism, tracing his intellectual changes from the early influence of Darwin to the later influence
of Whitehead, when Mead grew more concerned with perception and relativity.
He explores Mead's primary concerns: his theory of the self and its relation to material reality; objectivity and creativity; and the aesthetic
experience. Miller contends that "Mead was a pragmatist who placed special
emphasis on social behavior and finally on the principle of sociality."

H 642. MILLER, PERRY. Errand into the Wilderness. Cambridge, Mass.:
        Harvard University Press, 1956. 244 pp.
As Miller says, his essays "add up to a rank of spotlights on the massive
narrative of the movements of European culture into the vacant wilderness
of America." Once the early colonists realized they could not redeem

Europe, their "errand" took second place in adapting to the "wilderness." Miller considers this thesis from the viewpoints of theology, literature, and intellectual history. He believes the Great Awakening in the 18th century was the point where the wilderness began to define the objectives of the Puritan errand; and that the prophet of the Great Awakening in America, Jonathan Edwards, broke with the Puritan past in methodology, though not in content. This work traces continuities from Edwards to Emerson and shows that the theme of Nature and Civilization pervaded 19th-century American literature. Finally, Miller considers whether this theme can run indefinitely in America.

H 643. MILLER, PERRY. The Life of the Mind in America: From the Revolution to the Civil War. New York: Harcourt, Brace & World, 1965. 327 pp.
In this work, which was unfinished at his death in 1963, Miller examines revivalism and legalism in America from roughly 1800 to 1860; in the partially finished third section, he discusses the science and technology of that same era. Religious revivalism was, according to Miller, a reaction against 18th-century rationalism and an attempt to assert national unity through religion. Legalism sought, on the other hand, to unify the nation by accommodating the "ubiquitous [English] Common Law" to the American legal system. Americans of the era, Miller claims, also fostered the hope of achieving national eminence in science and technology. Realization of this hope, he notes, was furthered by the democratic urge to disseminate knowledge and to put it to practical use.

H 644. MILLER, PERRY. Nature's Nation. Cambridge, Mass.: Harvard University Press, 1967. 298 pp.
This collection of fifteen essays attempts to define the essence of American Romanticism, covering a broad range of material. While the main focus concerns Puritan thought, predominant 19th-century ideas about nature and religion are also analyzed, and essays on Emerson, Thoreau, Melville, and Theodore Parker are included. Miller's concern is "the problem of American self-recognition," how immigrants settled in the new American wilderness.

H 645. MILLER, PERRY. The New England Mind: From Colony to Province. Cambridge, Mass.: Harvard University Press, 1953. 513 pp.
This book and Miller's earlier The New England Mind: The Seventeenth Century (H 646) are complementary: the first takes a microscopic view of 17th-century New England, while the second takes a macroscopic view. From Colony to Province documents and explores those local events that shook the provincial scene: for example the "Half-Way Covenant," Revivalism, the Salem witch trials, and the controversy over smallpox vaccination. Miller analyzes these events to show the public "mind" of New England. He also shows how, by the start of the 18th century, the society had evolved into heterogeneous elements that spelled the end of the Puritan system. This movement from what one scholar has called "piety" (religious conscience) to "moralism" (social conscience) is also interpreted through such key figures as Cotton and Increase Mather, Charles Chauncy, Thomas Hooker, Anne Hutchinson, and Benjamin Franklin.

H 646. MILLER, PERRY. The New England Mind: The Seventeenth Century. New York: Macmillan, 1939. 528 pp.
Miller's topical analysis of various Puritan documents demonstrates that the first three generations of New England Puritans subscribed to a coherent body of thought. Largely derivative in their thinking, these Puritans believed that human nature was depraved and that only God's Grace could convert men. Such beliefs shaped their contractual view of man's relation to man and to God. Theological beliefs underlay church and civil government. Both the universe and man's activities--his thinking, his daily

actions, and his art--were designed to glorify God and to prepare man for possible salvation.

H 647. MILLER, PERRY. The Responsibility of the Mind in a Civilization of Machines. Amherst: University of Massachusetts Press, 1979. 213 pp.
This third volume of Miller's assorted lectures and essays--after Errand into the Wilderness (H 642) and Nature's Nation (H 644)--ranges in subject from the Bay Psalm Book and the Cambridge platform of the 17th century to conditions of American culture in the mid-20th century. Included are such essays as "The Social Context of the Covenant," "Equality in the American Setting," "The New England Conscience," and "Liberty and Conformity." "The Plight of the Lone Wolf" and the title essay address the business of scholarship, which Miller describes as a "perverse dedication to failure."

H 648. MOORE, ARTHUR. The Frontier Mind. Lexington: University Press of Kentucky, 1957. 246 pp.
Focusing on early Kentucky, where the author believes the major American attitudes toward the frontier were formed, Moore's interpretations are aimed at the whole of the American frontier. He criticizes the frontiersman as drawn by such romantic writers as Cooper and Simms, and rejects the Turner thesis that frontier conditions produced more democratic institutions and freer individuals, attributing the general acceptance of this thesis by earlier historians to blatant nationalism.

H 649. MORISON, ELTING E., ed. The American Style: Essays in Value and Performance. New York: Harper, 1958. 426 pp.
This book is a record of a 1957 conference dedicated to the examination of new approaches to the analysis of American culture. The idea of the participants was that a constructive international stance by the U.S. was inhibited not only by outside forces but by American values, government, national self-image, and national lifestyle. Themes of the papers center on: theory versus practice in American life; the meaning and content of individuality in an increasingly bureaucratic and specialized society; the manner in which good and evil is handled in American society; and evolution of values in American society. The book also offers comment on the debate generated by the formal paper presentations.

H 650. MORRIS, CHARLES. The Pragmatic Movement in American Philosophy. New York: Braziller, 1970. 210 pp.
Basing his book directly upon the writings of Peirce, James, Dewey, and Mead, Morris critically presents the Pragmatists' basic ideas and the interrelationships of those ideas. His primary intention is not to deliver an overall history of Pragmatic philosophy or to relate the movement to American culture. He wishes the book to be "a work within American pragmatic philosophy and not simply a book about it." The book begins with a general view of Pragmatic philosophy, and by chapter looks at Pragmatic semiology, methodology, axiology, cosmology, and contemporary Pragmatic thought.

H 651. NAGEL, PAUL C. This Sacred Trust: American Nationality, 1798-1898. New York: Oxford University Press, 1971. 376 pp.
This book deals with an area of intellectual history termed the history of public sentiment. Nagel represents the process of American self-definition and the development of a national ideology as a dialectic between Republican order and human nature--or, in his terms, between the responsibility of an American "trust" or "vineyard," and the obligation of "stewardship," with the President as the chief steward. He traces this dialectic from 1798 to 1898 by breaking the century into five time periods. Each chapter opens with a survey of the ideas of the period

and then presents the period's characteristic hopes and fears. Nagel
discusses the presidents of each period as spokesmen and, finally, details
the type of nationality expressed by leading religious, philosophical,
and literary figures of the period.

H 652. NASAW, DAVID. Schooled to Order: A Social History of Public School
     ing in the United States. New York: Oxford University Press,
     1979. 303 pp.
This volume examines the history of public schooling between 1835 and
1970, and essentially argues that the public school system served the
function of socializing and exerting social control over the industrial
work force. Nasaw argues that the rise of the common schools was the
most important development between 1835 and 1855, that the increase in
the importance of and attendance at high schools occurred in the period
1895 to 1915, and that higher education became most important in the post-
W.W. II period. This book also touches upon the impact of ethnic, class,
and religious factors in the development of educational institutions.

H 653. NASH, GEORGE H. The Conservative Intellectual Movement in America:
     Since 1945. New York: Basic Books, 1976. 463 pp.
Nash comprehensively describes the various strands of American conservatism
since W.W. II--libertarian, Burkean-organic, and "fusionist," the latter
of which seeks to reconcile the first two. He tells the story of the
development of a movement acutely aware of its own marginality to one
that by the 1970s was beginning to believe that it owned the future.
Nash stresses ideas themselves and the intellectuals who produced and
argued about them rather than on actual political battles. Nash's book
is a history of the "respectable," rather than "radical," Right.

H 654. NASH, RODERICK. Wilderness and the American Mind. 1967; Rev.
     ed. New Haven, Conn.: Yale University Press, 1973. 300 pp.
Nash traces the history of American attitudes toward nature from their
European origins and Puritanism to the ecological movement of the 1960s
and 1970s. Chapters on John Muir and the development of environmental
concern, the creation of national parks, and the philosophical underpinnings of preservationism offer an account of American views of wilderness
from the Puritans (who feared it) to the conservationists (who have sought
to preserve it).

H 655. NOBLE, DAVID W. The Paradox of Progressive Thought. Minneapolis:
     University of Minnesota Press, 1958. 272 pp.
Noble discusses the themes that run through the thought of several prominent Progressive theorists, including Charles Cooley, Thorstein Veblen,
Herbert Croly, and Walter Rauschenbusch. The book emphasizes the "paradox"
of expecting industrialization to offer a return to humanity's primordial
state of goodness, an idea that Noble consistently finds among Progressive
thinkers. Belief in an evolutionary movement toward an ideal social structure is another theme unifying the men studied by Noble.

H 656. NOVAK, MICHAEL, ed. American Philosophy and the Future: Essays
     for a New Generation. New York: Scribner, 1968. 367 pp.
These eleven essays are introduced as an attempt to move toward a new
"revolution in philosophy" that can answer the needs of an increasingly
technical, dehumanized society. The essays are unified by reaching back
to "the 'Golden Age' of American philosophy--the age of Royce and Peirce,
of Mead, Dewey, James, Santayana and Whitehead" for useful ways of perceiving current problems. Novak's secondary purpose in the volume is to free
American theology from its dependence upon "European traditions." Almost
all the essays look at "fundamental beliefs" regarding human values in
contemporary America. Novak hopes that American theology can open itself
to new creative possibilities offered by the perspective of American philosophy.

H 657. NYE, RUSSEL B. This Almost Chosen People: Essays in the History
        of American Ideas. East Lansing: Michigan State University Press,
        1966. 374 pp.
Nye's intention in this collection of his own essays is to show how a
few ideological concepts in America were shaped by the American experience.
Starting from Gunnar Myrdal's view that in America national ideology is
more explicitly stated and popularly known than that of any other Western
country, Nye discusses progress, nationalism, free enterprise, missionary
tendencies, individualism, nature, and equality "to show how they have
given an ideological backbone" to American leaders and the American people.

H 658. O'BRIEN, MICHAEL. The Idea of the American South: 1920-1941.
        Baltimore, Md.: Johns Hopkins University Press, 1979. 273 pp.
Varied concepts of "the South" held and articulated by such Southern intel-
lectuals as Allen Tate, Howard Odum, John Crowe Ransom, Frank Owsley,
John Donald Wade, and Donald Davidson are explored in this study. The
assertion of a Southern identity is seen as a response to modernist ideas.
In the debate over the meaning of Southern regionalism in the years between
W.W. I and W.W. II, the participants saw their alienation from the emerging
"New South" as an unavoidable response to its industrialism.

H 659. O'NEILL, WILLIAM L. A Better World--The Great Schism: Stalinism
        and the American Intellectuals. New York: Simon & Schuster,
        1982. 447 pp.
O'Neill tells the story of the struggle within the American Left over
relations with the U.S.S.R. from 1939 through the 1950s, attacking those
who refused to disassociate themselves from or denounce Stalinist Russia
once its crimes had become known. A story of the politics of intellectuals,
the book is an attack on the Left, using Left-liberal publications of
the period as its principal source. Stalinism is seen as McCarthyism's
root cause, and it is argued that the Left's failure to distinguish itself
utterly, in the public mind, from Stalinist Russia hurt its own cause.
O'Neill concludes, however, that some intellectuals on the Left--George
Orwell, James Baldwin, Dwight MacDonald, Lionel Trilling, Mary McCarthy,
and Edmund Wilson--were able to change their political positions accordingly.

H 660. OSTRANDER, GILMAN. The Rights of Man in America 1606-1861. Colum-
        bia: University of Missouri Press, 1960. 356 pp.
Ostrander states that his purpose in this volume is to trace American democracy from its earliest Colonial beginnings, when "democracy" was a pejora-
tive term synonymous with "mob rule," to the mid-19th century usage of
the term to describe American representational government and a relatively
classless society (among the white population). Ostrander examines the
internal problems of the American definition of democracy: individualism
versus majority rule, the meaning of equality, the idea of fraternity,
and the changes in meaning brought about by the progress of time. He
concludes, however, that Americans have held onto ideas from the Old World
since the Colonial period.

H 661. PELLS, RICHARD H. Radical Visions and American Dreams: Culture
        and Social Thought in the Depression Years. New York: Harper
        & Row, 1973. 424 pp.
This history of the 1930s emphasizes the political ideals of the writers
and intellectuals of the period, arguing that the radicals of the 1930s
emerged as an elite group of experts in the post-W.W. II era after they
had surrendered their leftist goals to rally around the wartime call for
patriotic antifascism. The critical intellectual community of the 1930s
thus became incorporated into the modern corporate state as a privileged
professional group. Pells analyzes both the social history and mass culture of the 1930s and the development of the American intellectual's role
in society.

H 662. PERSONS, STOW. American Minds: A History of Ideas. New York: Holt, 1958. 467 pp.
Person's book is an introduction to American intellectual history, focusing on the five "social minds" he defines as the major distinctive intellectual trends. He begins in the 17th century with "The Colonial Religious Mind, 1620-1660," and moves through the Enlightenment, 19th-century democratic thought, Naturalism, and "The Contemporary Neodramatic Mind." Within each large section Persons traces the development of ideas, stating that his primary purpose in this volume is to describe the movements and the intellectuals who shaped them.

H 663. PERSONS, STOW, ed. Evolutionary Thought in America. New Haven, Conn.: Yale University Press, 1950. 462 pp.
One of the earliest products of the interdisciplinary approach to American culture represented by the concept of American Studies, this collection of essays on the topic of Evolution cuts across areas of scholarship as well as areas of culture. The work discusses the theory of Evolution, and contains essays on the rise and impact of Evolutionary concepts, the relation of Evolution to sociology, political and constitutional traditions, economics, literature, architecture, psychology, ethics, and theology.

H 664. PETERSON, MERRILL D. The Jefferson Image in the American Mind. New York: Oxford University Press, 1960. 548 pp.
Peterson's intention in this volume is not to write a book about Thomas Jefferson's life, but rather how Jefferson's "ideas and ideals, policies and sentiments" influenced American thought. He traces the "shadow" of Jefferson upon the changing intellectual and cultural life of the U.S. from Jefferson's death in 1826 through post-W.W. II society, "how the accidents of time have turned Jefferson's political doctrines all around without, however, disturbing the axis of his faith." Peterson documents the peaks and valleys of Jefferson's popularity, and concludes that although many of his values have slipped away, "he may yet go on vindicating his power in the national life as the heroic voice of imperishable freedoms."

H 665. POCHMAN, H. A. German Culture in America. Madison: University of Wisconsin Press, 1957. 865 pp.
Pochman's study chronicles the influence of German scholarship and literature on American life, from the Colonial era through the 20th century. The first section of this book explores the impact of German philosophy on America, pointing to the correspondence between Colonial men of letters and German intellectuals, and the later familiarity of American scholars with German philosophical trends. Transcendentalism is analyzed in relation to the influence on it from German thought. The second part of the book examines German literature in American culture, covering German drama, poetry, fiction, and Germanic themes running through the works of American short story writers.

H 666. POLE, J. R. Paths to the American Past. New York: Oxford University Press, 1979. 348 pp.
The essays in this collection, written between 1958 and 1978, have been chosen and arranged to illustrate Pole's interest in the relation between American history and U.S. historiography. Sections one and two treat the Revolutionary era and the early Republic, and slavery and race, respectively. Pole's perspective is grounded in comparativism but wary of unfettered relativism. An early essay on Lincoln and the British working class, for example, illustrates how emancipation, implemented by Lincoln only after less radical strategies for preserving the Union had failed, symbolized for British workers his dedication to the rights and dignity of the common man. The writings in section three, primarily historiographical, focus mostly on the complex influences on and developments in Progressive and consensus history.

H 667. POLE, J. R. The Pursuit of Equality in American History. Berkeley:
University of California Press, 1978. 380 pp.
Equality as a central issue in American public policy is the focus of
this work. Throughout American history there has been a discrepancy
between public commitment to the ideology of equality and egalitarian
policy and action. Pole explores the historical sources and characteristics of this discrepancy. After establishing the philosophical origins
of the idea of equality, he examines the operative effects of egalitarian
ideas in American history from the rhetoric of the Revolutionary War to
the 1970s. Pole focuses on three types of equality: religious, racial,
and gender. Using extensive references to legal and legislative materials,
he urges that America has evolved on egalitarian principles without the
corresponding society of equals. While the U.S. has slowly developed
a "nationalism of consciousness" based on egalitarian concerns, it remains
in a struggle with an "incomplete revolution."

H 668. POWELL, ARTHUR G. The Uncertain Profession: Harvard and the Search
for Educational Authority. Cambridge, Mass.: Harvard University
Press, 1980. 341 pp.
This history of the Graduate School of Education at Harvard University
from the first appointment of faculty in education in 1890 through its
founding as a school in 1920 and on to the end of the 1960s stresses the
numerous shifts in the school's sense of its purpose as it tried to respond
to the demands of university officials, outside forces, and society at
large. Special attention is paid to the school's difficulties in coping
with the strong anti-elitist, even anti-intellectual, proclivities of
its presumed constituency, professional "educationists." The author,
who served as the school's associate dean from 1968 to 1976, gives an
insider's account, emphasizes the internal story, sees the school as a
mirror for conflicting views of education within the U.S., and questions
the very need for such an institution to exist.

H 669. RUCKER, EGBERT DARNELL. The Chicago Pragmatists. Minneapolis:
University of Minnesota Press, 1969. 200 pp.
It is Rucker's contention that only at the University of Chicago did
a school of Pragmatic philosophy emerge. While influenced by James and
Peirce, the intellectual development of the Chicago school was largely
indigenous. They saw "both science and values arising from human action,"
and the analysis of action was central to their philosophy, a different
approach from that of either James or Peirce. The Chicago school included
scholars from various disciplines, among them Dewey, Mead, Ames, and Veblen.
Through a philosophical consideration of the influences of scientific
advances and progress in the social sciences, plus the untraditional attitude of the then-new test university (est. 1892), meant that Chicago could
take advantage of a unique "experimental spirit."

H 670. RUDOLPH, FREDERICK. The American College and University: A History.
New York: Knopf, 1962. 516 pp.
This study follows as a central theme the development of the British-
inspired, classically oriented college of pre-Civil War America into the
modern, partly German-inspired university that dominates 20th-century
higher education. Among the many aspects of the university that Rudolph
examines are the curriculum, the extracurriculum, the education of women,
the role of religion, finance, the role and status of the professor, the
land grant college and state university, football, and the great importance
of students in shaping and changing the development of American higher
education.

H 671. SANFORD, CHARLES L. The Quest for Paradise: Europe and the American Moral Imagination. Urbana: University of Illinois Press, 1961. 282 pp.
Sanford defines "the dominant American mode of apprehending reality" as the never-ending search for an earthly paradise. He traces this search from the American beginnings through the 19th century in various imaginative and religious forms, paying particular attention to Thomas Jefferson and Henry James. He concludes with chapters on 20th-century diplomacy (seen in the light of this quest) and literature the main theme of which "has been the dispossession from paradise." Nevertheless, "the myth of Eden continues to dominate the American imagination."

H 672. SAVELLE, MAX. Is Liberalism Dead? And Other Essays. Seattle: University of Washington Press, 1967. 214 pp.
This volume is a collection of Savelle's essays, which originally appeared between 1945 and 1964. They fall under three headings: "Liberalism," "The Colonies in America," and the "Philosophy of History," and while most rest on Savelle's area of expertise--Colonial history--they cast a wide net, discussing 20th-century minds as well as the minds of Jonathan Edwards and Benjamin Franklin.

H 673. SAVELLE, MAX. Seeds of Liberty: The Genesis of the American Mind. Seattle: University of Washington Press, 1965. 618 pp.
Savelle has written this book for the general reader, as a broad description of the origin of the "American Way of Life." He consciously makes extensive use of quotations by Americans of the time in conjunction with illustrations to give the reader a sense of the era, to "let the mind of the eighteenth-century Americans speak for itself." Savelle's book attempts to impart cultural life as a whole, so as not to distort any part, and discusses religion, science, philosophy, economics, society, politics, literature, art and architecture, music, and nationalism in separate chapters. The years between 1740 and 1760 are looked at most carefully, as those decades saw the growth of a national self-consciousness and influenced the Revolutionary generation.

H 674. SCHLESINGER, ARTHUR M., Jr. The Crisis of Confidence: Ideas, Power and Violence in America. Boston: Houghton Mifflin, 1969. 313 pp.
Writing at the end of a turbulent decade, Schlesinger sees the U.S. suffering from "a double crisis--the crisis of our own internal character as a nation and the crisis of the relationship between America and the world." Americans had always felt the U.S. was equal to any challenge, but the rise of internal turmoil, the loss of respect and trust from abroad, and the rise of the Cold War led to the "illusions [that] have created the crisis" that climaxed in Vietnam. "The time has surely come for a reassessment of our institutions and values." Through essays organized into six chapters, Schlesinger looks at the rise of violence in the U.S., the role of the intellectual, the Cold War, Vietnam, student unrest ("Joe College, R.I.P."), and the future of American politics.

H 675. SCHLESINGER, ARTHUR M., Jr. and MORTON WHITE, eds. Paths of American Thought. Boston: Houghton Mifflin, 1963. 614 pp.
In this collection of twenty-seven essays ranging from the intellectual history of the American Revolution to a consideration of 20th-century science, the editors have consciously arranged a "display" of "the achievements" in the field of American intellectual history. Aspects of American social, cultural, political, and economic developments are included. Among the contributors are Richard Hofstadter, Irving Howe, Edmund S. Morgan, and Paul A. Samuelson. This volume was assembled to show the abundant resources provided by the American intellectual past, with the hope that these essays can convey its diversity and significance.

H 676. SCHNEIDER, HERBERT W. A History of American Philosophy. 1946;
       Rev. ed. New York: Columbia University Press, 1963. 590 pp.
Addressing what he interprets as unpatterned trends of thought in the
U.S., Schneider examines the impact of European philosophers on America,
particularly Hegel, Locke, and Kant. He concludes his volume with an
in-depth analysis of the Pragmatists, presenting the thought of James,
Peirce, Dewey, and others. Schneider finds no dominant theme for the
eclectic philosophy of America.

H 677. SHAPIRO, HENRY D. Appalachia on Our Mind: The Southern Mountains
       and Mountaineers in the American Consciousness, 1870-1920. Chapel
       Hill: University of North Carolina Press, 1978. 376 pp.
Shapiro examines the processes by which Americans in the late 19th and
early 20th centuries, perceiving their nation as a homogeneous entity,
reconciled their image of the nation with the "otherness" they saw in
Appalachia. The "discovery" of the region by local-color writers and
the work of religious missions are examples of the ways Americans attempted
to deal with the "problem" posed by the distinctiveness of the region
and its people. This book is, as the author states, not a history of
Appalachia but rather a history of the idea of Appalachia and its significance.

H 678. SLOAN, DOUGLAS. The Scottish Enlightenment and the American College
       Ideal. New York: Teachers College Press, 1971. 298 pp.
This book recognizes the significance of the Scottish Enlightenment for
American thought and provides a perspective for the study of early American
education. The work is a collection of seven essays on "the thoughts
and careers of representative individual educators who were related to
the Presbyterian Academy and early Princeton traditions." Sloan documents
the use his subjects made of the Scottish Enlightenment to place their
predominantly church-related institutions and educational concerns in
contact with the advanced intellectual currents of the time.

H 679. STARR, KEVIN. Americans and the California Dream, 1850-1919.
       New York: Oxford University Press, 1973. 494 pp.
The emergence of California as a unique symbol of expansion and success
is analyzed in this book. Beginning with California's admission into
statehood in 1850 and closing with the San Francisco Panama-Pacific International Exposition in 1915, Starr documents the rich history of California
settlement and its significance in the American mind. The reality of
violence and struggle is juxtaposed against the myth spawned by the West
as Starr examines the lives of several important Californians of the era.

H 680. STEIN, ROGER B. John Ruskin and Aesthetic Thought in America,
       1840-1900. Cambridge, Mass.: Harvard University Press, 1967.
       321 pp.
Stein synthesizes a broad array of subjects that go far beyond the influence of Ruskin on aesthetics. The responses of writers, scientists, the
clergy, and philosophers to Ruskin's thought are analyzed as the critic's
popularity rose and fell during the sixty-year period in question. Stein
argues that Ruskin's original popularity derived from his moral view of
aesthetics; as economic and social changes were wrought by the industrial
revolution, however, his theological aesthetic concepts lost their appeal.

H 681. STROUT, CUSHING. The American Image of the Old World. New York:
       Harper & Row, 1963. 288 pp.
It has almost always been the case, Strout believes, that Americans have
defined themselves in relation to Europe, which is often defined by Americans as including Russia. In his effort to trace the image, he examines
biography, literature, and politics to form a work of intellectual history
also containing literary and diplomatic strains. Beginning with the first

settlers from England and the formation of an "Old World," he continues through the end of W.W. II and the formation of NATO, stating that Americans "come of age when they perceive the tension between myth and history—and so learn to revise their outlook."

H 682. STROUT, CUSHING. The Pragmatic Revolt in American History: Carl Becker and Charles Beard. New Haven, Conn.: Yale University Press, 1958. 182 pp.
Strout chooses Becker and Beard because of their closeness to a modern philosophical crisis of history: "When all points of view are understood as passing phases of a historical process, neither the historian as knower nor the liberal as philosopher, can claim to a place to stand outside the stream of history." The two historians attempted to find a new philosophy for history, and were part of the movement away from the almost exclusive study of institutional forms to social, cultural, intellectual, and economic history. Strout divides his study into three parts: "The Revolt of Relativism," "The Revolt against Formalism," and "Liberals in Crisis." Strout concludes that Becker and Beard jolted historians into a new, but destructive, skepticism, and sought hope in a theory of history progressing toward a "vague goal," though "at odds with both the historical spirit and the liberal mind."

H 683. STROUT, CUSHING, ed. Intellectual History in America. 2 vols. New York: Harper & Row, 1968. 453 pp.
Twenty-nine essays in all, these two volumes form an anthology of American intellectual history from Puritanism to the Cold War. (Vol. I is devoted to "Contemporary Essays on Puritanism, the enlightenment, and Romaniticism"; Vol. II covers the period "From Darwin to Niebuhr.") Strout does not attempt to define "intellectual history"; the topics include theology, historiography, political ideology, literature, and science. Strout does, however, identify the intellectual historian as one who looks more closely at social setting than the philosopher and also examines man's theories more than the political or social historian, "putting ideas into contexts and finding ideas in the complex currents of historical change." Edmund S. Morgan, Perry Miller, and Stow Persons are a few of the contributors to Volume I, and John Higham, David Noble, Warren I. Susman and Arthur Schlesinger, Jr. are contributors to the second volume.

H 684. STUART, REGINALD C. War and American Thought: From the Revolution to the Monroe Doctrine. Kent, Ohio: Kent State University Press, 1982. 245 pp.
Stuart presents a reassessment of American attitudes toward war, contradicting the assumption that Americans historically rejected war as an instrument of national policy. Instead, he argues that a limited-war mentality (a restrained approach to conflict) is the legacy left by the Revolutionary generation. The origin, development, and application of this limited-war mentality are the themes of this work. Stuart reconstructs the matrix of ideas the Revolutionary Americans held toward war, comparing European and American attitudes. After exploring the role that a limited-war mentality played in the American Revolution, Stuart examines the chronological development of the American war myth. He suggests that the combination of a limited-war mentality and a growing nationalism helped forge this myth—the belief that war is inevitable; that Americans fight only for defense and retaliation; that force is needed as an instrument of policy. Stuart argues that it is only by acknowledging the significance of a limited-war mentality—the true historical American attitude toward war—that we can comprehend the "anomalies of armed forces, civilization, and national ambitions" in U.S. history.

H 685. THAYER, H. S. Meaning and Action: A Critical History of Pragmatism
        Indianapolis, Ind.: Bobbs-Merrill, 1968. 572 pp.
This philosophically oriented historical study is a summation and evaluation of the Pragmatic tradition in European and American philosophy as
well as a history. Thayer defends the Pragmatists as important, effective,
and correct. He begins with the mid-17th century when the Cartesian revolution first raised the fundamental problem of Pragmatism: how to find
an "integral relation between the nature of scientific knowledge and the
status of moral values." He then moves quickly to the major American Pragmatists, Peirce, James, and Dewey, and also examines lesser figures and
followers of the tradition in England. Thayer contends that these people
developed an epistemology which they found consistent with science and
productive of a successful ethic; he also suggests that Pragmatism, while
a response to late 19th-century American conditions, has had a major effect
on the thought and behavior of Americans and others.

H 686. VEYSEY, LAURENCE R. Emergence of the American University. Chicago:
        University of Chicago Press, 1963. 505 pp.
Veysey describes how and why the American university has developed its
characteristic atmosphere, purposes, and goals. The first section of
the work which is intellectual history, examines the academic philosophies
competing for control of the universities between 1865 and 1910—utility,
research, and liberal culture. The second section, which covers the years
from 1890 to the present, describes the academic structure that developed,
"the younger men who took command of it, and its effect on a variety of
professional temperaments." Veysey concludes that social ambition rather
than a search for academic excellence eventually has overtaken the university.

H 687. WELTER, RUSH. The Mind of America, 1820-1860. New York: Columbia
        University Press, 1975. 603 pp.
Welter believes that the generation that came of age between 1820 and 1850
was the most significant for the formation of American national character
and political direction. His book is a study of the "national attitudes"
not of the elite but of the common men and women of the period. Welter
finds these attitudes to include the women of the period. Welter finds
these attitudes to include the belief that history "culminated" in America,
a belief in the power of the individual, and a tendency toward a limited,
democratic government which would preserve social order and promote liberty.
Within this intellectual framework a number of problems arose: they became
"expansionists at home and isolationists abroad," they curtailed government
authority and encouraged economic exploitation. Their "doctrine . . .
had overridden common sense." Welter believes the Civil War was at least
in part a result of these earlier attitudes, and that "the democratic
heritage had reached its highest expression in the war," as "the ultimate
test of the American experiment."

H 688. WELTER, RUSH. Popular Education and Democratic Thought in America.
        New York: Columbia University Press, 1962. 473 pp.
Welter's intention in this work is to discuss the political ramifications
of the American idea of education. He believes that American democratic
theory is often so close to American educational theory that both have
been blended in American society. Welter looks at groups of intellectuals
and politicians and their public documents to trace the dialogue between
"popular rule and public education" from Colonial times to the mid-20th
century. Faith that education would answer the needs of Americans when
facing social dilemmas was established between the Jacksonian era and
W.W. II. Since the war our faith in political education has been ebbing,
which weakens the structure of our theory of democracy. Welter asserts,
however, that "both conclusions indicate . . . that our faith in education
has been and remains our most characteristic belief."

H 689. **WHITE, MORTON.** Pragmatism and the American Mind: Essays and Reviews in Philosophy and Intellectual History. New York: Oxford University Press, 1973. 265 pp.
As an analytic philosopher who wishes to connect philosophy to other disciplines, White collected these essays reflecting the variety of interests he had pursued over the course of more than thirty years. The essays are divided into three categories. The first, "The Mind of America," concerns the intellectual and the city, William James, the "Revolt against Formalism" and anti-intellectualism. The second set, "Pragmatism and Analytic Philosophy," is more technically philosopical, addressing the differences or lack of differences between the methods of science and of philosophy. The last section, "Philosophy and Civilization," looks at the relationship between philosophical thought and science, history, education, and religion. It is White's "hope that these essays will strike a blow for rationality at a time when rationality is once again under attack."

H 690. **WHITE, MORTON.** Social Thought in America: The Revolt Against Formalism. New York: Viking Press, 1947. 301 pp.
This book is an intellectual history of the early 20th century that analyzes the work of Charles A. Beard, John Dewey, Oliver Wendell Holmes, Jr., James Howey Robinson and Thorstein Veblen. White argues that, taken together, these "progressive" thinkers constitute a coherent intellectual movement that may be characterized as a "revolt" against formalism. The group of thinkers whose work White analyzes rejected the sentimental idealism of 19th-century American thought in favor of a pragmatic, scientific approach to knowledge, which eventually generated a new intellectual ethos. The emergence of this new intellectual ethos is discussed in relation to history, law, sociology, politics, and philosophy.

H 691. **WHITE, MORTON and LUCIA WHITE.** The Intellectual Versus the City: From Thomas Jefferson to Frank Lloyd Wright. Cambridge, Mass.: Harvard University Press and M.I.T. Press, 1962. 270 pp.
In this work, the Whites investigate the persistently negative attitudes toward the city, which have been "voiced in unison" by members of every important intellectual group throughout American history. These criticisms, however distant, supply the central views that are still held today. Analyzing and classifying reactions to the city, the Whites "examine the intellectual roots of anti-urbanism and ambivalence toward urban life in America." They conclude that the "moral message" from Jefferson's era remains the same. The city must answer its critics and solve three problems: the education and employment of minorities, the fostering of individuality, and the communication breakdown that arises from the city's diverse population.

H 692. **WIENER, PHILLIP P.** Evolution and the Founders of Pragmatism. Cambridge, Mass.: Harvard University Press, 1949. 288 pp.
Wiener's book examines the relationship between ideas of Evolution and the development of Pragmatism. The book provides an introduction to the ideas developed by such early Pragmatists as Chauncey Wright, C. S. Peirce, and William James. Evolution was an important catalyst for these thinkers as they reexamined a world in which older certainties were being questioned and discarded, and alternate answers were being sought.

H 693. **WILD, JAMES.** The Radical Empiricism of William James. Garden City, N.Y.: Doubleday, 1969. 430 pp.
William James's philosophical and psychological work has, in this study, been viewed in relation to European phenomenology, particularly that of Husserl. Viewing phenomenology as the search for the "brute structure of experience," Wild examines the phenomenological aspects of James's empirical inquiries in four parts. The first section discusses The Principles of Psychoanalysis as a phenomenological psychology using Husserlian terminology. The next section discusses the second volume of the Prin-

ciples, describing the "three departments of the mind"--"perceptual facts,"
"conceptual meanings" and "human choices and emotions." The third section
is devoted to the ethical and religious base of the active life and the
"pragmatic theory of truth to which [this] lead[s]." In the fourth section,
Wild addresses the Essays in Radical Empiricism and outlines the progress
of James's whole system while indicating the importance of James's work
to phenomenological thought.

H 694. WILLIAMSON, CHILTON. American Suffrage from Property to Democracy,
       1760-1860. Princeton, N.J.: Princeton University Press, 1960.
       306 pp.
Williamson offers a survey of American suffrage and the gradual removal
of property qualifications between the American Revolution and the Civil
War. He describes the process and circumstances by which universal white
male suffrage became the prime characteristic of the American political
system, and argues that this distinguished America from all other nations.
Universal white male suffrage was a "reform" which caused remarkably little
social conflict, unlike the movements to secure the vote for blacks and
women. Williamson argues that property qualifications regulating suffrage
had been substantially removed even before the coming of Jacksonian Democracy. He cites the widespread availability of land, natural rights philosophy, and both war and rumors of war as contributing to this phenomenon.

H 695. WOLFE, DON M. The Image of Man in America. 1957; Rev. ed. New
       York: Crowell, 1970. 507 pp.
Wolfe writes an intellectual history of the U.S. which extends from the
thoughts of Thomas Jefferson to the ideas prevalent in the 1960s and which
is unified by an underlying concern: how have the greatest thinkers in
American history dealt with the opposition between nature and nurture?
In other words, he considers whether human behavior and capability are
formed by genetic inheritance or by environment. The "concept of plastic-
ity," according to him, pervades the American conception of human nature;
consequently, Americans base their faith in education and equality on
the belief that any person's position can be improved. Wolfe concludes
his discussion with the assertion that a "true science of man" is needed
in order to test American conceptions of the capability for change and
to understand why great thinkers have emerged at particular times in American history.

H 696. WYLLIE, IRVIN G. The Self-Made Man in America: The Myth of Rags
       to Riches. New Brunswick, N.J.: Rutgers University Press, 1954.
       210 pp.
This treatise, which focuses on the literature of self-help, chronicles
the rise and fall of the gospel of success. Tracing the development of
the idea of material success from Colonial days to the crash of 1929,
Wyllie finds that it was a means for creating faith and hope in the American economic system, but also that it was more of a myth than a reality.
The self-made man of American faith rose from a low origin to become a
person of wealth and substance through the cultivation of such virtues
as diligence, thrift, and sobriety. The "hero" began to lose credibility,
however, as turn-of-the century muckrakers revealed that the great American
financial successes resulted from sharp and less than honest practices
rather than from diligence and sobriety. Then, with the Great Depression,
a group of cynics began to question the very notion of material success.
Still, the dream continues to hold appeal for many contemporary Americans.

H 697. ZOLL, DONALD ATWELL. The Twentiety-Century Mind: Essays on Contemporary Thought. Baton Rouge: Louisiana State University Press, 1967. 152 pp.
Zoll's collection of seven of his own essays are his response to the popular forms of protest which were surfacing during the 1960s. He conveys in this volume a "widened conception of protest" tempered by "philosophical detachment." Included are his comments upon "The Coming Collapse of the American Democracy," "Conscience, Law and Civil Disobedience," and "The Artist as Academician." Zoff analyzes contemporary developments in Western society from a self-consciously American viewpoint. In the closing essay, "The Twentieth-Century Mind," Zoll discusses the "modern man"; while enjoying material abundance and leisure feels he has lost control over his destiny. He suggests that as members of late 20th-century society Americans should understand their "primordial connections" and "know and accept what it is to be a social creature in the most fundamental sense of the term."

VII. WOMEN

H 698. ALTBACK, EDITH HOSHINO. Women in America. Lexington, Mass.: Heath, 1974. 205 pp.
Women in America was written as a "restitution to ordinary American women." Since much of women's history is devoted exclusively to "exceptional" women, Altback has focused on the housewife--middle class and working class--and the average paid working woman. Although she does not exclude the Feminist movement from her study, she does emphasize the "underlying grass roots sources" rather than the elite leaders of both the 19th century movement and the modern day movement. The book includes statistical information on marriage, birthrates, employment rates, and occupational status. There is a chapter on child care, as well as a data chart noting such things as employment, inventions, fashions, events, and achievements.

H 699. ANDERSON, KAREN. Wartime Women: Sex Roles, Family Relations, and the Status of Women During World War II. Westport, Conn.: Greenwood Press, 1981. 198 pp.
Analyzing newspapers and government reports, Anderson concludes that women's employment during W.W. II did not challenge women's traditional domestic role or the division of family responsibilities. The war created opportunities for women to expand their experiences, but it also reaffirmed male hegemony. Anxiety and apprehension shrouded wartime changes in family life, child care, and the workplace. In the post-war period, many women returned to the home; the war had little lasting effect on the overall position of women.

H 700. APTHEKER, BETTINA. Woman's Legacy: Essays on Race, Sex and Class in American History. Amherst: University of Massachusetts Press, 1982. 177 pp.
Woman's Legacy is written from a Marxist-Feminist perspective and "insists that the source of woman's oppression must be rooted in the social conditions of each particular historical period." It focuses on black women because "the black female experience, by the very nature of its extremity, illuminates the subjugation of all women." With these assumptions in mind, Aptheker has written a series of seven essays dealing with such topics as women and the Fifteenth amendment, women and the fight against lynching, domestic labor, and the Moynihan Report.

H 701. BAKER, ELIZABETH FAULKNER. Technology and Women's Work. New York: Columbia University Press, 1964. 460 pp.

Baker devotes most of her study to descriptions and analyses of women's place in a large number of occupations--mainly industrial and professional-- in the 19th and 20th centuries. Her discussion focuses on technology, but she also includes information on such other factors affecting the workplace as education and unionization. Protective labor legislation and women's role in labor organizations are also discussed.

H 702. BANNER, LOIS W. American Beauty: A Social History Through Two Centuries of the American Idea, Ideal, and Image of the Beautiful Woman. New York: Knopf, 1983. 369 pp.

Drawing on period advice literature, fashion magazines, travel accounts, and theatrical memorabilia, Banner examines the mystique behind the "ideal beauty." Changes in the cosmetics industry and the evolution of attitudes, fashions, and behavior which accompanied or precipitated changes in this ideal are examined. Whereas role models in the past were typically from the upper class, recent "ideals of beauty" have emerged from all strata of society. Banner argues that she stresses the role of popular culture, film, and the media in affecting changing stereotypes. Four ideal types are identified: the pale and passive "steel engraving" lady of the ante- bellum period; the big-busted beauty personified by Lillian Russell after the Civil War; the athletic Gibson Girl and the boyish, short haired Flapper typified by the film stars Mary Pickford and Clara Bow. Reasons behind the popularity of the stereotypes are explored, as are the cultural ramifications of dieting and tobacco usage. Banner draws parallels to male counterparts during the same time period. Calling the female quest for beauty the "Cinderella Myth," Banner equates it with the "Horatio Alger" myth, its male counterpart.

H 703. BANNER, LOIS W. Women in Modern America: A Brief History. New York: Harcourt Brace Jovanovich, 1974. 276 pp.

In writing a history of American women from 1890 through the 1970s, Banner has divided the experience of these years into three periods. The period 1890 to 1920, she says, was a time when many "traditional discriminations came to an end"; Feminist and reform groups were organized. The period 1920 to 1960 marked the decline of Feminist groups; there was general apathy regarding women's issues as the country concentrated on the Depres- sion and war. The period from 1960-1974 saw a re-emergence of a Feminist movement even more radical than its predecessor. Banner's aim is to explore the reasons behind this pattern of rise and fall and rise again, and to concentrate on the differing responses of various groups of women-- working class, middle class, blacks, immigrants, farm women--to the times in which they lived.

H 704. BARKER-BENFIELD, G. J. The Horrors of the Half-Known Life: Male Attitudes Toward Women & Sexuality in 19th Century America. New York: Harper & Row, 1976. 894 pp.

Sexual beliefs and the sex roles they created are the subjects of this interpretation of 19th-century sexuality. Beginning with an analysis of Tocqueville's account of American sexual segregation, Barker-Benfield proceeds to discuss childbirth practices, male psychology, and the com- petitive nature of society which led to male fear and repression of women.

H 705. BAUM, CHARLOTTE, PAULA HYMAN, and SONYA MICHAEL. The Jewish Woman in America. New York: Dial Press, 1976. 290 pp.

The authors trace the experience of Jewish immigrant women in this country from its roots in the traditional religious cultures of Germany and Eastern Europe through the contemporary suburban family. Women are discussed as breadwinners, participants in trade union movements, prostitutes, social workers and philanthropists, and as "Jewish Mothers" and "Jewish-American

Princesses"--negative stereotypes which, the authors argue, represent
ambivalence on the part of assimilated male writers toward their Jewish
heritage and the strong women who created and preserved it. The authors
"have tried to destroy some of the myths about Jewish women that have
severely affected their self-images, and to replace the myths with the
truth about an admirable heritage that conventional histories have ignored.'

H 706. BAXTER, ANNETTE K., with CONSTANCE JACOBS. To Be a Woman in America
        1850-1930. New York: Times Books, 1978. 240 pp.
This is primarily a collection of photographs, in which Baxter argues
that during the period between 1850 and 1930, as in most of American history, women were subjects of exploitation. In the 19th century, "with
the advent of a full-scale philosophy of domesticity," most women were
relegated to the home. Those who worked in the mills or other factories
experienced long hours and low wages. The same was true for 20th-century
women who worked as typists and switchboard operators. "Yet," says Baxter,
"all along there were women who declined to be discouraged by setbacks
or stereotypes." Thus Baxter's photographic essay portrays active,
involved women who, according to the author, exude "charm, stamina and versa-
tility." The photographs are arranged thematically rather than chronologically; Baxter suggests that this arrangement more accurately portrays
the "complex truth" of women's history, a history characterized by "shifting goals and reversals of status."

H 707. BECKER, SUSAN D. The Origins of the Equal Rights Amendment: Ameri-
        can Feminism Between the Wars. Westport, Conn.: Greenwood Press,
        1981. 300 pp.
This study focuses on equalitarian Feminists and especially on the National
Women's Party and its allies and opponents during the 1920s and 1930s.
Becker inquires into the nature of American Feminism between the wars;
the origins of the ERA and the bases on which it was supported or opposed;
and the achievement of the women's movement by the time of W.W. II? Becker
notes that the equality of the National Women's Party sought was an equality defined by men. She agrees with the Party's demand for equality,
but also concludes that in its failure to develop a feminine ideology
and to consider the social and psychological aspects of equality, the
National Women's Party arguments were weak, their effect ultimately limited.

H 708. BERG, BARBARA J. The Remembered Gate: Origins of American Femin-
        ism: The Woman and the City, 1800-1860. New York: Oxford Uni-
        versity Press, 1978. 270 pp.
The Remembered Gate explores the origins of Feminism. Berg argues against
the often-held theory that Feminism originated with Abolitionism. Feminism,
she claims, was a reaction to the woman-belle ideal; both of these concepts
were results of the urbanization process which took place between 1800
and 1860. With the mass movement to cities, the self-perceptions of
females changed. They were able to observe women of all backgrounds, and
could thus see the plight of their sex as a whole. Subsequent to these
observations, benevolent societies were formed. It is within these early
societies (not within the Abolition societies that were to follow) that
the roots of Feminism were formed.

H 709. BERKIN, CAROL RUTH and MARY BETH NORTON, eds. Women of America:
        A History. Boston: Houghton Mifflin, 1979. 442 pp.
This is an anthology of articles--all written specifically for Women of
America--on American women from the Puritans to the present. Original
documents as well as secondary articles are included, organized by three
time frames: Colonial, 19th century and 20th century. The editors dispute
the prevailing view of Colonial women as equal partners with men, and
the 19th-century view of "ladies of leisure," or prisoners of domesticity.
They view this "myth of the golden age," followed by a period of status

loss and finally recovery through Feminism, as appealing but inaccurate. Instead, they see the history of women as one of steady improvement.

H 710. BLAIR, KAREN J. The Clubwoman as Feminist: True Womanhood Redefined, 1868-1914. New York: Holmes & Meier, 1980. 199 pp.
Blair studies the several strands that were woven together in 1890 to form the General Federation of Women's Clubs, and surveys the impact of that organization on its members and society. The career and reform-oriented Sorosis and New England Women's club, the literary clubs of the late 19th century, and the Women's Educational and Industrial Unions, all prefigured and contributed to the General Federation. Blair argues that the club movement was Feminist in nature, though it was more moderate than the suffrage movement. Through the women's clubs, women developed gender solidarity and eventually extended their influence to the public sphere.

H 711. BLAXALL, MARTHA and BARBARA REAGAN, eds. Women and the Workplace: The Implications of Occupational Segregation. Chicago: University of Chicago Press, 1976. 326 pp.
In these expanded proceedings of a conference held during International Women's Year, occupational segregation is considered by various scholars concerned with "combating" this kind of segregation. The historical articles are not focused especially on the U.S.; but the papers in sociology and economics generally are, and they provide perspectives on, and insights into, topics as diverse as the law, poverty among female-headed families, and selection of specialized fields by economists. The volume originally appeared as a supplement to the Spring 1976 issue of Signs: A Journal of Women and Culture.

H 712. BORDIN, RUTH. Woman and Temperance: The Quest for Power and Liberty, 1873-1900. Philadelphia: Temple University Press, 1981. 211 pp.
Bordin describes the Women's Christian Temperance Union during its formative and most powerful years. She discusses the organizational contributions and personal style of Frances Willard, who was president of the Union from 1879-1898. Although the WCTU had its limits, says Bordin, it nevertheless served to raise the consciousness of its members and thus helped in the movement toward suffrage and political involvement.

H 713. BUHLE, MARI JO. Women and American Socialism, 1870-1920. Urbana: University of Illinois Press, 1981. 344 pp.
This history of women involved in Socialism in America from 1870 to 1920 documents the development of their ideology and discusses the organizational structure of their politics. Buhle notes that these women tried to mold American socialism to meet their priorities with regard to diverse social issues. The successes and failures of their efforts are considered in the context of the personalities of various important figures of the era. Buhle's central theme is the "interplay of two parallel traditions, immigrant and native-born," with special reference to the class versus gender argument which characterized the Socialist movement.

H 714. CAMPBELL, BARBARA KUHN. The "Liberated" Woman of 1914: Prominent Women in the Progressive Era. Ann Arbor, Mich.: UMI Research Press, 1979. 220 pp.
Drawing on statistical information and on sources such as Who's Who in America, 1914-1915; Notable American Women; and Women of the Century, Campbell considers related factors such as education, urban and rural life, professions, women's organizations, marriage, divorce, birth control, as well as various attitudes toward, and forms of, participation in reform movements. She finds that career type, or choice of profession, was the most significant factor in shaping prominent women's adult lives during

the Progressive Era. Although the women she studies did not greatly challenge the institutions of marriage and the family, Campbell claims that
they did gain greater equality. The book concludes that a "determination
to control their own lives and develop their own capabilities—whether
inside or outside of marriage—was a hallmark of the notable women in
the early twentieth century."

H 715. CANTOR, MILTON and BRUCE LAURIE, eds. Class, Sex, and the Woman
        Worker. Westport, Conn.: Greenwood Press, 1977. 253 pp.
An introduction by Caroline F. Ware ties together the ten essays in this
volume, especially in their use of class and sex as analytical tools.
Monographs are included on the Lowell Mill workers, immigrant women workers
(Irish, Italian and Jewish), trade union women, and the Women's Trade
Union League. Included are Susan J. Kleinberg's article on methods for
studying urban women; Alice Kessler-Harris's on Pauline Newman, Fannia
Cohn, and Rose Pesotta; Elizabeth Jameson's on women in Western mining
towns; and Robin Miller Jacoby's on the WTUL and Feminism in the U.S.

H 716. CARROLL, BERENICE, ed. Liberating Women's History: Theoretical
        and Critical Essays. Urbana: University of Illinois Press, 1976.
        434 pp.
The first part of Carroll's volume addresses issues concerning the historiography of women. Contributors focus on a variety of traditional
approaches to history which exclude or diminish the role of women. Essays
in this section include "Women in Society: A Critique of Frederick Engels"
and "Historical Phallicies: Sexism in American Historical Writing."
Parts Two and Three are devoted to particular case histories which, respectively, address the relationship between ideology, sex, and history and
class, sex, and social change. Topics discussed include education and
ideology in 19th-century America; Feminism and class consciousness in
the British and American labor movements; sex and class in America from
the Colonial era through the 19th century; and women, their work, and
the social order. The volume concludes with a selection of essays concerned with the future of women's history. This section incorporates
essays on "New Approaches to the Study of Women in American History,"
"Feminism and the Methodology of Women's History," and on the possibilities
of "Herstory" as a scholarly discipline.

H 717. CHAFE, WILLIAM H. The American Woman: Her Changing Social, Eco-
        nomic, and Political Roles, 1920-1970. New York: Oxford Uni-
        versity Press, 1972. 351 pp.
Chafe analyzes the roles of women in politics and the economy since the
passage of the Nineteenth Amendment. He finds that gains by women were
inhibited by the attitude that a woman's place was in the home. World
War II, a period when women were actively solicited for the labor force,
was a turning point; women entered the job market during the war and
remained there afterward. Chafe argues that it was this increase in participation in the labor force in the post-War era that set the stage for
the drive for equality in the 1960s.

H 718. CHAFE, WILLIAM H. Women and Equality: Changing Patterns in Ameri-
        can Culture. New York: Oxford University Press, 1977. 207 pp.
Writing from the assumption that one can best understand a society by
studying those who are "ordinarily left out," Chafe gives both a basic
overview of women's history and a theoretical discussion of the inherent
problems in defining women's history and the inherent obstacles in achieving equality in America. Although he concentrates on the role of sex
in society, Chafe believes that race and class are also important social
influences. In fact, he dedicates a good portion of this book to a comparison of the histories of sex and race in America; the purpose of the
comparison is not to point out the differences between race and sex as

social indicators but to illustrate the influence of social control in general.

H 719. CLINTON, CATHERINE. The Plantation Mistress: Woman's World in the Old South. New York: Pantheon Books, 1982. 331 pp.
Clinton examines the white woman's role as mistress on the Southern plantation between the Revolution and 1835. She argues that sex is as important a factor as race in analyzing Southern society. Through examination of white mistresses' work, marital situations, kin relations, education, health, and their relations with black slaves, Clinton concludes that women sustained wearisome responsibilities in terms of domestic production and plantation management.

H 720. CONRAD, SUSAN PHINNEY. Perish the Thought: Intellectual Women in Romantic America, 1830-1860. New York: Oxford University Press, 1976. 292 pp.
Conrad's introduction extends the definition of "intellectual woman" beyond the traditional stereotypes. Margaret Fuller is the subject of chapter two, while chapter three deals with the influence of American Romanticism on women's history and Feminist thought. Chapter four covers intellectual women and the institutions of American Feminism, and the final chapter discusses the female intellectual in transition. Some of the women intellectuals discussed are Elizabeth Oaks Smith, Elizabeth Cady Stanton, Sarah Helen Whitman, Lydia Maria Child, Elizabeth Palmer Peabody, and the Grimke sisters.

H 721. COTT, NANCY F. The Bonds of Womanhood: 'Woman's Sphere' in New England, 1780-1835. New Haven, Conn.: Yale University Press, 1978. 225 pp.
Cott discusses the work, education, religion, and self-perceptions of New England women, concentrating on the white middle class sector. According to Cott, the 1830s witnessed the development of the social status of women in the following areas: an overwhelming recruitment of women into the textile factories and into the teaching field occurred; literacy rates increased; and women became increasingly organized in Christian benevolent societies and in the anti-slavery movement. In fact, Cott dates the beginning of organized Feminism in the 1830s while at the same time stressing the importance of the concept of domesticity during the era. Cott explains this paradox by pointing out that although Feminism and domesticity might seem mutually exclusive, Feminism actually grew out of domesticity. The separate sphere of domesticity "bound women together even as it bound them down." A group-consciousness among women developed, thus providing a key ingredient for an organized women's movement.

H 722. COTT, NANCY F. and ELIZABETH H. PLECK. A Heritage of Her Own: Toward a New Social History of American Women. New York: Simon & Schuster, 1979. 608 pp.
The twenty-four essays in this volume focus on three major themes: women and the family, women and work, women and Feminism. (Feminism, as defined by the editors, is a "shorthand to denote the complicated subject of how women thought about themselves.") Because they deal with the lives of "ordinary" women, these essays fit the category of social history, but "the majority," explain the editors, "because of their concern with women's consciousness . . . tackle essentially political questions." The essays range from the 17th century through the 20th century. Contributing authors include: Ruth Milkman, Alice Kessler-Harris, Gerda Lerner, Herbert Gutman, Linda Gordon, Eugene Genovese, and Carroll Smith-Rosenberg.

H 723. DAVIES, MARGERY W. Woman's Place Is at the Typewriter: Office
        Work and Office Workers, 1870-1930. Philadelphia: Temple Uni-
        versity Press, 1982. 217 pp.
Davies analyzes the historical circumstances that led to women's predominance in the field of secretarial work. She finds that prior to the Civil
War clerical work was typically performed by men. However, as businesses
expanded office work was "rationalized" and broken up into discrete tasks
such as billing, filing, and typing. The result was the "proletariani-
zation" of clerical work into routinized jobs and declining opportunities.
At this point, women began to dominate the clerical field. The author
examines the social and economic backgrounds of these women, their efforts
to organize, and their attempts to adapt to new technologies.

H 724. DAVIS, ANGELA Y. Women, Race and Class. New York: Random House,
        1981. 271 pp.
In this history of black women in the U.S., Davis provides a Marxist-
Feminist interpretation of such topics as women's rights and Abolition,
black women and education after the Civil War, and black women and the
women's club movement. Five Communist women are profiled: Lucy Parsons,
Ella Reeve Bloor, Anita Whitney, Elizabeth Gurley Flynn, and Claudia Jones.
Davis concludes with three chapters that analyze and trace the roots of
contemporary issues: the myth of the black rapist, birth control and
sterilization, and black women and housework.

H 725. DEGLER, CARL N. At Odds: Women and the Family in America from
        the Revolution to the Present. New York: Oxford University Press,
        1980. 527 pp.
Degler synthesizes recent scholarship from the fields of family history
and women's history, arguing that the fusion of these two fields is necessary for a full understanding of either field. A primary assumption of
this book is that the development of concern for women's equality runs
counter to the preservation of the family, since the existence of the
family as it developed in the early 19th century depends, in part, on
the subordination of women. Organized topically to discuss such issues
as family relationships, limitations on family size, growth of women's
organizations, and women in the work force, this book argues that, despite
gains in broadening the scope of women's activities, the family continues
to provide the basic pattern for women's work and associations.

H 726. DELANY, JANICE, MARY JANE LUPTON, and EMILY TOTH. The Curse:
        A Cultural History of Menstruation. New York: Dutton, 1978.
        276 pp.
In this work, menstruation is examined in folklore, humor, advertising,
arts, and literature, and in its anthropological, cultural, medical, and
social contexts. As a "curse," menstruation has been avoided, feared,
despised, seen as a talisman, linked to the defeat of the ERA, and seen
as the cause of monthly variations in emotional health. The authors
explore the history of sanitary products and their changing treatment in
the media; cultural rituals and meanings of the menarche; the physiological
and emotional impact of the "change of life"; Biblical references to the
"unclean woman"; the dynamics of menstruation as viewed by Aristotle and
Freud; and advice books and current medical thought. Through this work,
the authors hope to lift the curse and view it as "Eve's blessing."

H 727. DEXTER, ELISABETH ANTHONY. Career Women of America, 1776-1840.
        Francestown, N.H.: Marshall Jones, 1950. 262 pp.
Dexter here provides a historical and sociological discussion of ways
in which women could earn a living or pursue a career in the years after
the American Revolution. She describes teachers, doctors and midwives,
actresses and entertainers, writers, domestic shopkeepers, seamstresses,
outdoor workers, and millworkers, and considers such topics as marriage,

urbanization, and industrialization. According to Dexter, a larger proportion of women worked outside the home after 1776 and as a result the
patriarchal household of Colonial days became less and less typical.
But she also notes that while women had new opportunities for careers,
new handicaps accompanied these opportunities.

H 728. DEXTER, ELISABETH ANTHONY. Colonial Women of Affairs: A Study
of Women in Business and the Professions in America Before 1776.
Boston: Houghton Mifflin, 1924. 204 pp.
Dexter documents the participation of women in many areas of life before
the Revolution. Women were tavernkeepers; producers and merchants of
a wide variety of goods and services; midwives, nurses, and doctors;
teachers; land proprietors and managers of farms and businesses; authors
of poetry, captivity narratives, diaries, and tracts; religious leaders;
actresses; printers and editors. Dexter also notes the activity of women
in political life and as parties to litigation. Her conclusion suggests
that women in this period participated with more ease and less social
stigma than they would in the 19th century.

H 729. DICKINSON, JOAN YOUNGER. The Role of Immigrant Women in the
U.S. Labor Force, 1890-1910. New York: Arno Press, 1980.
218 pp.
Working from census data and from Department of Labor and Department of
Immigration reports, the author analyzes labor force participation of
immigrant women as compared to other women and men. She breaks these
categories down further by ethnicity, age, job category, and period of
immigration. Dickinson concludes that immigrant women were more likely
to work than native-born white women, more likely to continue work after
marriage, and more likely to work in low-status jobs such as domestic
service, cotton mills, and the garment industry. Dickinson explains these
trends through theories of "substitution" and "schin migration": the
entry of each new group into the labor force permits the earlier group
to move up in status and pay.

H 730. DUBLIN, THOMAS. Women at Work: The Transformation of Work and
Community in Lowell, Massachusetts, 1826-1860. New York: Columbia University Press, 1979. 312 pp.
Dublin traces the employment of women in the early textile mills of Lowell
from the arrival of the rural northern New England Yankees in the 1820s
to their replacement by Irish immigrants by the 1850s. He examines such
issues as employment, pay, the work itself, housing, and collective protest,
and he emphasizes the brevity of the mill girls' moment on the industrial
stage. Many tables and five appendices are included.

H 731. DUBLIN, THOMAS, ed. Farm to Factory: Women's Letters, 1830-1860.
New York: Columbia University Press, 1981. 191 pp.
Dublin reproduces four groups of letters sent or received by women working
in the New England mills before the Civil War. In most respects, the
correspondents are typical of the many thousands of young women who left
the region's farms in these years to find employment, and a measure of
economic and social independence, in the mill towns. Most did not become
lifelong industrial workers, but either returned to farms or pursued other
activities in the cities. These correspondents illuminate the everyday
life and experience of working women of the period. Dublin's introductory
essay, afterword, and chapter notes place the letters in broader contexts
of the economic and social life of the region and the typical life cycle
of 19th-century American women.

H 732. DuBOIS, ELLEN CAROL. Feminism and Suffrage: The Emergence of
an Independent Women's Movement in America, 1848-1869. Ithaca,
N.Y.: Cornell University Press, 1978. 220 pp.
DuBois argues that the first American Feminist movement was a response
to the upsurge in popular politics in the 1820s and 1830s. At this time,
women were relegated to a domestic sphere that insured their inequality.
Women were drawn to organize, Dubois argues, "by the promise that political
activity held for the creation of a truly democratic society." The book
traces the formation of a conscious women's movement, its alliance with
Abolitionism, and its maturation into a movement dedicated to obtaining
suffrage.

H 733. DYE, NANCY SCHROM. As Equals and as Sisters: Feminism, the Labor
Movement, and the Women's Trade Union League of New York. Columbia: University of Missouri Press, 1980. 220 pp.
Dye describes the Women's Trade Union League as a "unique coalition of
women workers and wealthy women." Its goal was to integrate all women
into the labor movement, and it consequently crossed over class lines.
Dye focuses on the New York branch of the WTUL in the years from its founding in 1903 to W.W. I, and includes additional information about the garment trades and women's employment and politics during these years. The
shift of the WTUL from union organizer to a women's reform organization
is seen by Dye as a retreat, not a Feminist victory.

H 734. EHRENREICH, BARBARA and DEIRDRE ENGLISH. Complaints and Disorders:
The Sexual Politics of Sickness. Old Westbury, N.Y.: Feminist
Press, 1973. 94 pp.
Complaints and Disorders is a Feminist analysis of the social role of
medicine. Ehrenreich and English examine the 19th and early 20th century
stereotypes of the "sick" woman of the upper and middle classes and the
"sickening" woman of the lower class. They conclude with reflections
on the persistence of aspects of these stereotypes in today's health care
system.

H 735. EHRENREICH, BARBARA and DEIRDRE ENGLISH. Witches, Midwives, and
Nurses: A History of Women Healers. Old Westbury, N.Y.: Feminist Press, 1973. 43 pp.
Although in 1973, 93% of American doctors were male (according to the
authors' figures), this certainly had not always been the case; until
relatively recently, the medical sphere had been dominated by women.
Witches, Midwives, and Nurses deals with the problem of why and how women
became subservient where they had once dominated. Toward this end,
Ehrenreich and English look at two historical episodes in the "male takeover
of healthcare": the suppression of witches in medieval Europe, and the
rise of the male-dominated medical profession in 19th-century America.
These two episodes exemplify the political clash between women healers
and the male medical profession which, according to the authors, is part
of the larger, more general political struggle for women's rights. The
aim of this pamphlet is thus twofold: to recapture history, and to further
the rights of women.

H 736. ENGLE, PAUL. Women in the American Revolution. Chicago: Follet,
1976. 299 pp.
Colonial American women were unlike their British counterparts, Engle
claims, because American women worked alongside men. They "had to share
the total new experience," and this held true during the Revolution as
well. American women contributed to the war in several ways. Women in
the American Revolution describes eighteen of these women, whose contributions varied from printing and publishing newspapers, to influencing important men of the Revolution, to actually fighting in the battles.

409

H 737. EPSTEIN, BARBARA LESLIE. The Politics of Domesticity: Women, Evangelism, and Temperance in Nineteenth-Century America. Middle-town, Conn.: Wesleyan University Press, 1981. 188 pp.
This work looks at the development of conflict between men and women in women's consciousness by the end of the 19th century. Utilizing a sample of 18th-century conversion narratives and the 19th-century religious press, Epstein contrasts the shared male-female experience of the First Great Awakening with the militancy of women against impious men in the Second Great Awakening. A comparison of the Women's Crusade and the Women's Christian Temperance Union serves as Epstein's second example of a growing sense of conflict. Epstein sees the popular women's culture of the 19th century as reflecting the angry feminine response to the subordination and confinement of their domestic positions.

H 738. EVANS, ELIZABETH. Weathering the Storm: Women of the American Revolution. New York: Scribner, 1975. 372 pp.
Weathering the Storm is a collection of diary and journal entries written by eleven women who lived during the time of the Revolution. Evans prefaces each chapter with biographical information on the particular diary or journal author. In addition, the book contains a general introduction which gives an overview of women's position during the Revolution. It includes discussions of women's legal and economic status, their role in particular religious sects, their performance as soldiers in the Revo-lution, their stance regarding independence (were they patriots, loyalists, or neutral?), and even the state of medicine and childbirth at this point in America's history.

H 739. EVANS, RICHARD J. The Feminists: Women's Emancipation Movements in Europe, America, and Australasia, 1840-1920. New York: Barnes & Noble, 1977. 266 pp.
Evans's book is a comparative history. Its intention, as the author notes, is "to establish a general framework of interpretation tracing the origins, development and eventual collapse of women's movements in relation to the changing social formations and political structures of Europe, America, Australia, and New Zealand in the era of bourgeois liberalism." In the first section of the book, Evans examines the origins of organized Feminism and the main features of its development. In the second part, he uses case studies of individual Feminist movements to illustrate the main varie-ties of organized Feminism. Socialist women's movements as alternatives to women's emancipation movements are discussed in the following section, and, in the last, Evans offers reasons for the collapse of bourgeois Femin-ist movements after W.W. I.

H 740. FADERMAN, LILLIAN. Surpassing the Love of Men: Romantic Friend-ship and Love Between Women from the Renaissance to the Present. New York: Morrow, 1981. 496 pp.
A book which arose out of Faderman's study of Emily Dickinson's love poems and letters to Sue Gilbert, this volume surveys romantic friendship and sexual love among women from the 16th through the 20th centuries in Europe and America. Faderman places women's intimacies in a historical and cul-tural framework, examining both the expressions of and changes in women's friendship through time, and social perceptions of attitudes toward such intimacies. The book includes biographical information and primary source material (letters, diaries, etc.).

H 741. FEINSTEIN, KAREN WOLK, ed. Working Women and Families. Beverly Hills, Calif.: Sage, 1979. 295 pp.
These essays deal with themes relating to the increase of women in the labor force and the new pressures on women workers and their families as a result of this trend. Broadly, the editor summarizes the issues: "the class of traditional mores and attitudes, which assign homemaking

and childrearing responsibilities to wives, with increased labor force
participation by women has placed an enormous physical and emotional burden
on women workers with families. The absence of wives and mothers from
the home during all or part of the day has also created new demands on
husbands, new needs related to the care of children, and new attitudes
toward work on the part of both husbands and wives." Feinstein notes
that the intent of the book is both to study these related issues and
to provide pragmatic answers which will contribute to constructive social
change.

H 742. FLEXNER, ELEANOR. Century of Struggle: The Woman's Rights Move-
        ment in the United States. Cambridge, Mass.: Harvard University
        Press, 1959. 384 pp.
Century of Struggle is divided into three sections. Part I focuses on
the position of women in society and the origins of suffragism prior to
the Civil War. Part II looks at the emergence of a solid organization
of suffragists in the last decades of the 19th century. Part III analyzes
the 20th-century suffrage movement, its strategies, and eventual success.
Flexner views the suffrage movement within the context of women's position
in the labor force and within the context of the educational system.
She also discusses the political strategies of anti-suffragism.

H 743. FONER, PHILIP S. Women and the American Labor Movement. New
        York: Free Press, 1979. 621 pp.
This study documents the role of women in labor struggles from the Colonial
era through the Progressive movement. Foner examines the status of working
women and discusses the persistent efforts of such labor organizers as
Mother Jones, Harriet Tubman, Elizabeth Chambers Morgan, and Florence
Kelley. The book tells the story of women within the Knights of Labor,
the AFL, the IWW, the National Women's Trade Union League, among others,
and details the strikes and demonstrations that shaped labor history.

H 744. FRANKFORT, ROBERTA. Collegiate Women: Domesticity and Career
        in Turn of the Century America. New York: New York University
        Press, 1977. 121 pp.
Frankfort's book is an analysis of women's collegiate education in the
19th and early 20th centuries based on a detailed study of the graduates
of Bryn Mawr and Wellesley Colleges. Utilizing data from alumnae career
patterns, the book explores the long-term significance and interdisciplinary approach of these institutions as well as the changing image of the
celibate woman scholar in higher education.

H 745. FREEDMAN, ESTELLE B. Their Sisters' Keepers: Women's Prison
        Reform in America, 1830-1930. Ann Arbor: University of Michigan
        Press, 1981. 248 pp.
Freedman provides full portraits of Progressives Frances Kellor and
Katherine Bement Davis, as well as tables describing the personal backgrounds of fifty other selected reformers. Changing attitudes toward
women prisoners are described and related to larger social trends. Also
reviewed are the prisoners' experiences and the institutions' focus, staff,
and routine. Freedman concludes with an evaluation of the gender-separate
prison system.

H 746. FREEMAN, JO. The Politics of Women's Liberation: A Case Study
        of an Emerging Social Movement and Its Relation to the Policy
        Process. New York: McKay, 1975. 268 pp.
The author examines the relation of social movement to public policy,
noting that while the women's liberation movement is strong, it is only
beginning to have an impact on economic conditions. Freeman is interested
in the question of what precipitated the movement and when it occurred.
She describes "the grand press blitz of 1969-70," major figures in the

government at this time, and the numerous organizations resulting. She also reviews major policy arising from the women's movement and the way in which sex discrimination and race discrimination are related.

H 747.   FREEMAN, JO, ed. Women: A Feminist Perspective. Palo Alto, Calif.: Mayfield, 1975. 487 pp.
Freeman's anthology contains nearly thirty articles by almost as many authors on a diverse range of subjects pertaining to women in America. The issues covered include: the female body, sexuality, and rape; women in and out of the family; growing up female; the working woman; images of women in art and popular culture; and Feminism. The essays in the volume, all written from a Feminist point of view, examine why social and political institutions and socialization processes create different choices and role expectations for men and women, how and why women have been and are discriminated against, and how the Feminists have challenged women's status in America.

H 748.   FRIEDMAN, JEAN E. and WILLIAM G. SHADE, eds. Our American Sisters: Women in American Life and Thought. Boston: Allyn & Bacon, 1973. 354 pp.
This collection of essays covers the history of women in America from Colonial times through the Victorian era, Progressivism, and 20th-century Feminism. In chronological sections on each period the articles discuss ideas concerning sex roles, the realities of women's everyday lives, and the rise of Feminist movements in the U.S. Introductions to each section synthesize the divergent material and draw out the dominant historical themes.

H 749.   GEORGE, CAROL, V. R., ed. "Remember the Ladies": New Perspectives on Women in American History. Syracuse, N.Y.: Syracuse University Press, 1975. 201 pp.
Focusing on social history, the book is composed of three sections: "The Growth of American Feminist Thought" (1600-1800); "The 'Cult of True Womanhood'" (1800-1920); and "The 'New Woman' and Social Change" (1920-1970s). Attempting to suggest ways into which scholars might reconstitute the past in order to incorporate women, the authors consider a wide range of subjects: women and religion, women in politics, women as patients of male gynecologists, women and divorce. They also discuss "flappers," philosophers, slave-conductors, and nativists, and talk specifically about women such as Anne Hutchinson, Abigail Adams, and Harriet Tubman.

H 750.   GLUCK, SHERNA, ed. From Parlor to Prison: Five American Suffragists Talk About Their Lives. New York: Vintage Books, 1976. 285 pp.
Five women who were active in the suffrage movement between the late 19th century and 1920 tell their own stories in this oral history. Reprints of newspaper and magazine articles of the era are juxtaposed with the reminiscences of Sylvie Thygeson, Jesse Haver Butler, Miriam Allen Deford, Laura Ellsworth Seiler, and Ernestine Hara Kettler. The book begins with an interpretive history of the women's suffrage movement and concludes with a chronology from 1776-1920.

H 751.   GORDON, LINDA. Woman's Body, Woman's Right: A Social History of Birth Control in America. New York: Grossman, 1976. 479 pp.
This Feminist history of birth control is based on a class analysis of sexual politics. According to Gordon, the fight for birth control and the regulation of contraceptives were tied inextricably to economic inequities stemming from Capitalism and a male-dominated political system. The book discusses the move in the 1870s toward advocating women's right to choose motherhood; the movement's radical stage in the first two decades

412

of the 20th century, when Margaret Sanger led the battle; and the 1920s
and 1930s, when a professional class began a more conservative appeal
for birth control.

H 752.   GRAY, DOROTHY. Women of the West. Millbrae, Calif.: Les Femmes,
         1976. 179 pp.
Gray contends that while the Victorian Age and the Industrial Revolution
debased women, women of the West in the 19th century had greater opportunity for independence and equality. She presents portraits of representative and outstanding women of the West including: Sacajawea, Lewis
and Clark's guide; Narcissa Whitman, a missionary; Juliet Brier, a forty-
niner pioneer; Dame Shirley, a mining town woman; Esther Morris and Carrie
Chapman Catt, who fought for women's suffrage; Ann Eliza Young, a rebellious wife (the nineteenth) of Brigham Young, the Mormon leader; Bright
Eyes La Flesche, a well-educated Omaha Indian woman who fought white injustice through the legal and political system; and Willa Cather, the author
who portrayed real Western women. Gray also includes chapters on minority
women, professional women, women on the cattle frontier, and women on
the farm. She notes that despite the heroism and achievements of these
women, stereotypical views of Western women have prevailed and that women
of the West have not become role models for women in general.

H 753.   GREEN, HARVEY with MARY-ELLEN PERRY. The Light of the Home:
         An Intimate View of the Lives of Women in Victorian America.
         New York: Pantheon Books, 1983. 205 pp.
Concentrating on the Northeastern region of the U.S., Green discusses
middle-class Victorian women (1870-1910) through an illustrated examination
of aspects of domestic culture as represented by household objects, diaries,
letters, fiction, etiquette books, and advice literature of the period.
According to Green, the material and technological advances of the late
19th century, coupled with the rise of corporate Capitalism, intensified
the conception of woman as the guardian of the "domestic altar"; women
were to provide a civilizing influence to counteract the competitive,
unchristian realities of the economic sector. Despite being designated
as the source of the nation's moral integrity, women were represented
as fragile beings who could not measure up to the physical and mental
strength of their noble ancestors. Thus, "the cult of motherhood became
an institutionalized, but powerless, conscience for capitalism."

H 754.   GREENWALD, MAUREEN WEINER. Women, War and Work: The Impact of
         World War I on Women Workers in the United States. Westport,
         Conn.: Greenwood Press, 1980. 309 pp.
Greenwald discusses four case studies of women's employment during W.W. I.
The first study deals with Federal labor policy. The other three studies
concentrate on women railroad workers, streetcar conductors, and telephone
operators. Greenwald considers management strategies and goals, women's
own perceptions of their employment and their rights, the relationships
between men and women in the workplace, and the role of the Federal government in reform. She also looks at the perpetuation of such trends as
the exclusion of women from labor unions in the post-war years.

H 755.   GRIMES, ALAN P. The Puritan Ethic and Woman Suffrage. New York:
         Oxford University Press, 1967. 159 pp.
Grimes examines the origins of the success of the women's suffrage movement
in Utah and Wyoming in an attempt to understand why these states were
the first to allow women the vote. He finds that male support for prohibition and for the restriction of immigration were major factors, while
radical activism played a lesser role. Grimes argues that suffrage was
achieved because of the traditional values of Protestantism and the Puritan
ethic.

H 756.   **HALL, JACQUELYN DOWD.** Revolt Against Chivalry: Jessie Daniel
         Ames and the Women's Campaign Against Lynching. New York: Colum-
         bia University Press, 1974. 373 pp.
Hall's book serves both as a history of women's campaign against lynching
in the 20th century and as a biography of Jessie Daniel Ames, a major
leader within this campaign. Hall's emphasis is on the participants within
the movement and she is, thus, primarily concerned with white, middle-
class women and "their place within the intertwining of racial tensions,
sexual stereotypes, and class assumptions." In addition to background
information on Jesse Daniel Ames's childhood in Texas and the suffrage
movement in this state, Hall includes chapters on the Commission on Interracial Cooperation in the 1920s, the relationship between lynching and
sexual attitudes, and the strategy of the Association of Southern Women
for the Prevention of Lynching.

H 757.   **HARLEY, SHARON** and **ROSALYN TERBORG-PENN**, eds. The Afro-American
         Woman: Struggles and Images. Port Washington, N.Y.: Kennikat
         Press, 1978. 137 pp.
This volume is an anthology of essays documenting black women's struggles
against sexism and racism in 19th- and 20th-century America. Essay topics
include Northern black female workers in the Jacksonian Era; discrimination
against black women in the women's movement, 1830-1920; black male perspectives on the 19th-century woman; the black woman's struggle for equality in the South, 1895-1925; black women in the blues tradition; images
of black women in Afro-American poetry; and a focus on the contributions
of three activists, educators Anna J. Cooper and Nannie Burroughs, and
politician Charlotta A. Bass.

H 758.   **HARRIS, BARBARA J.** Beyond Her Sphere: Women and the Professions
         in American History. Westport, Conn.: Greenwood Press, 1978.
         212 pp.
Based on a series of lectures delivered by the author at a career management program for women, Beyond Her Sphere provides a history of women
in Western society, "focusing particularly on those aspects of women's
history that bear directly on the experience of females with professional
and intellectual aspirations." Harris's study begins with the ideology
surrounding women which grew out of the Middle Ages and which influenced
Western European civilization, then discusses the rise of the "cult of
domesticity" in 19th-century society. She pays particular attention to
the history of women in the U.S., from the First Woman's Rights Convention
held in New York in 1848 to the "New Feminism" of the 1960s and 1970s.
The study focuses on white, middle-class women.

H 759.   **HARTMAN, MARY S.** and **LOIS BANNER**, eds. Clio's Consciousness Raised:
         New Perspectives on the History of Women. New York: Harper
         & Row, 1974. 253 pp.
Among the articles in this collection are six which deal with women in
Europe, thus providing a cross-cultural perspective. Four of the
articles--written by Ann Douglas Wood, Carroll Smith-Rosenberg, Regina Morant
and Linda Gordon--deal with Victorian sexuality. There are also articles
on the feminization of religion, libraries, and the home--written by
Barbara Welter, Dee Garrison and Ruth Schwartz, respectively.

H 760.   **HARTMANN, SUSAN M.** The Home Front and Beyond: American Women
         in the 1940s. Boston: Twayne, 1982. 235 pp.
This book provides a general study of women's lives during the 1940s,
primarily in the public domain. Hartmann notes that women's service in
the military establishment shows a dramatic break from the past. She
also discusses women in the labor force, the education of women, their
relation to the legal system and to government. She analyzes changing
marriage, divorce, childbearing, childrearing, and domestic patterns.

Finally, she surveys the range of models available to women in popular culture and concludes with the view that the appearance of the women's movement in the public domain represents the most substantial change of the 1940s.

H 761. HERSH, BLANCHE GLASSMAN. The Slavery of Sex: Feminist-Abolitionists in America. Urbana: University of Illinois Press, 1978. 280 pp.
Hersh profiles fifty-one Feminist Abolitionists, establishing their Puritan-Yankee heritage and comfortable class position as well as their life-long interest in universal perfectionist movements. She finds that the key to their ideology is their generally liberal, non-Calvinist approach to religion; they were heirs of the Transcendentalists and of 18th-century democratic humanitarianism. Hersh devotes a chapter to the role of their husbands as well. Each woman is at least briefly discussed, and major leaders receive careful consideration.

H 762. HUMMER, PATRICIA M. The Decade of Elusive Promise: Professional Women in the United States, 1920-1930. Ann Arbor, Mich.: UMI Research Press, 1979. 182 pp.
Hummer examines the growing opportunities for women in professional life during the 1920s, particularly in the fields of law, medicine, and higher education. She argues that, while expectations for professional careers and equality were high, they were largely unrealized. Factors such as class and regional distribution, the expectations of society, sexual prejudice, and the employment situation of the period weighed heavily against women's entry or success in the learned professions. Hummer notes that while institutional barriers were often lowered, these problems were not eliminated.

H 763. HYMOWITZ, CAROLE and MICHAELE WEISSMAN. A History of Women in America. New York: Bantam Books, 1978. 400 pp.
This general survey divides its attention between the lives of ordinary women and those of notable personages. The authors outline the role of women in American development--in the Colonial period, the American Revolution, the Westward movement, industrialization, the Civil War, the massive immigration of the latter half of the 19th century, Progressive era reform, and labor organizing early in the 20th century. They also address the histories of discrete groups of females, such as slave women, 19th-century women's rights activists, and the birth control advocates of the 20th century. The book concludes with a discussion of the role of the housewife, birth control, women in the workplace, and the "New Feminism."

H 764. JAMES, JANET WILSON. Changing Ideas About Women in the United States, 1776-1825. New York: Garland, 1981. 337 pp.
Wilson explores upper- and middle-class Americans' varying conceptions of women's roles in the Colonial and the early National period. Despite the title, the book devotes considerable attention to the years before the Revolution. She demonstrates that such ideas developed in a complex fashion, instead of linearly progressing toward greater freedom and opportunity for women. The 18th century, for instance, saw a diminishing of the economic role of women but greater attention to their intellectual elevation. The American Revolution's perhaps unintended stimulation of an urge for a more meaningful public life for women was met, after 1800, both by religious revivalism's emphasis on domesticity and feminine duty and industrialization's removal of economic life from the household. Evangelicism and the Industrial Revolution, however, also allowed for women's involvement in such public activity as charity work and education. Wilson bases her work on didactic literature and fiction of the day, diaries, letters, memoirs, and travellers' accounts, as well as general histories, biographies, and literary criticism.

415

H 765. JEFFREY, JULIE ROY. Frontier Women: The Trans-Mississippi West:
        1840-1880. New York: Hill & Wang, 1979. 240 pp.
Drawing from women's journals, reminiscences, collections of letters,
and a number of interviews, Jeffrey has written a history of pioneer women
spanning the era of the American frontier from 1840-1880. Her intention
is to remedy the scant attention paid by previous historians to the role
women played in the movement Westward. She considers both the personal
and public experiences of the frontier woman as wife, mother, daughter,
cultural mediator, and emancipated citizen. Jeffrey is especially interested in how the new standards for women created in the 19th century
affected women's attitudes toward themselves. She concludes that the pioneer woman used these new standards to establish and maintain her identity,
rather than to liberate herself from the established, gender-specific,
female role.

H 766. JOSEPHSON, HANNAH. The Golden Threads: New England's Mill Girls
        and Magnates. New York: Duell, Sloan & Pearce, 1949. 325 pp.
Josephson's account focuses on two groups in 19th-century Lowell, Massachusetts: the textile business pioneers and the women factory workers.
The study begins with the early exploration of Francis Cabot Lowell and
ends with the collapse of the Pemberton Mill in Lawrence in 1860.
Josephson discusses the labor unrest which she says was evident from the
very beginning of the mills' operations, as well as the New England mill
girls, whom she describes as being extremely independent.

H 767. KATZMAN, DAVID M. Seven Days a Week: Women and Domestic Service
        in Industralizing America. New York: Oxford University Press,
        1978. 374 pp.
This is a study of domestic service in America between 1870 and 1920.
Katzman argues that, as a result of rapid industrialization, several
changes occurred in the field of domestic service. Native-born Americans
began to leave the field to enter shop work. The number of immigrant
servants dwindled. The field became dominated by blacks, many of whom
migrated North. Utilizing quotations of domestic servants, Katzman discusses working conditions, the special relationships that were formed
between women employers and employees, the sexual tensions that existed
between men and their servants, and the South's unique inability to distinguish race from domestic service.

H 768. KENNEDY, SUSAN ESTABROOK. If All We Did Was to Weep at Home:
        A History of White Working-Class Women in America. Bloomington:
        Indiana University Press, 1979. 331 pp.
Kennedy has written a history of white, working-class women between 1600
and 1977. In the early stages of the factory system, she says, women
saw their tenure in the workplace as temporary. They saw no reason to
identify with other working women; in fact, it would have been demeaning
to do so. Slowly, however, this is beginning to change. Kennedy is primarily interested in tracing the roots of a collective consciousness among
working women. She claims that these "contemporary beginnings of awareness" did not come into being until the mid-1970s. The author looks at
such influences as immigration, industrialization, and war on the position
of working-class women.

H 769. KERBER, LINDA K. Women of the Republic: Intellect and Ideology
        in Revolutionary America. Chapel Hill: University of North Caro-
        lina Press, 1980. 304 pp.
Kerber analyzes the roles of women in Revolutionary America. She argues
that the day-to-day necessities of supporting the war effort conflicted
with the traditional exclusion of women from civic life. Nonetheless,
the Revolution did not empower women nor did it fundamentally alter their
status. Instead, a concept of "Republican Motherhood" emerged, which called

upon women to exercise their virtue within the home by educating and nurturing virtuous (male) citizens. "Republican Motherhood" linked women's virtue to the polity while successfully excluding them from active participation in the political world. Kerber discusses this development in relation to patriotism, education and divorce.

H 770. **KERBER, LINDA K.** and **JANE DE HART MATTHEWS**, eds. Women's America: Refocusing the Past. New York: Oxford University Press, 1982. 478 pp.
Women's America combines analytical essays with primary documents. The book is divided into four sections: Traditional America (1600-1820), Industrializing America (1820-1880), Industrializing America (1880-1920), and Modern America (1920-1980). Within each section there are essays devoted to the economics, politics, biology, and ideology of women. The book includes works by Julia Cherry Spruill, Anne Firor Scott, Kathryn Kish Sklar, Carroll Smith-Rosenberg, Alice Kessler-Harris, William Chafe, and Betty Friedan. A section of "essential documents" is also included.

H 771. **KESSLER-HARRIS, ALICE.** Out to Work: A History of Wage-Earning Women in the United States. New York: Oxford University Press, 1982. 400 pp.
Kessler-Harris has written a history of women as wage laborers. Her discussion begins with the Colonial period and continues through the industrialization process to the present. Kessler-Harris is particularly interested in the relationship between women's position in the labor force and their position in the home; wage work, she says, "simultaneously sustained the patriarchal family and set in motion the tensions that seem to be breaking it down." Beginning in the 1920s, it became increasingly expected that women would work outside the home. Here, too, says Kessler-Harris, there was an ironic relationship between work and family: women had to work outside the home to fulfill their obligations within the home.

H 772. **KESSLER-HARRIS, ALICE.** Women Have Always Worked: A Historical Overview. Old Westbury, N.Y.: Feminist Press, 1981. 193 pp.
The various forms of women's labor from Colonial times through the present are covered in this book. Kessler-Harris discusses the shift from Colonial times when all people--men and women--were involved in domestic non-paid labor, to industrial times when women began to be defined as non-wage earners and, consequently, as inferior to men. In the 19th century, women's involvement in the "helping professions" stemmed from an ideology which saw women as pure, pious, and unselfish. In the 20th century, the effects of the Depression and War on the positions of women were negligible; despite huge increases in the number of women in the paid labor force, "the jobs open to women continued to be obstinately sex-segregated." Kessler-Harris ends with a discussion of such contemporary issues as: the pros and cons of day care, the concept of government subsidized housework, and the possibility of a tax on male wages to entice men to remain at home and care for children.

H 773. **KOEHLER, LYLE.** A Search for Power: The "Weaker Sex" in Seventeenth-Century New England. Urbana: University of Illinois Press, 1980. 561 pp.
Koehler traces the institutionalization of attitudes toward women in the New World back to England and the early Puritan Colonies. He explains that forms of rebellion, religious heresies, witchcraft, or other behavioral aberrations were women's ways of coping with the prevailing Puritan value system. Koehler concludes by looking at all women in the New World-- Puritan and non-Puritan--and suggests that this wider view contradicts the notion that the Puritan age was one of relative liberation for women.

H 774. **KRADITOR, AILEEN.** The Ideas of the Woman Suffrage Movement, 1890-
1920. New York: Columbia University Press, 1965. 313 pp.
Kraditor sees the 1890s as a crucial point in the woman's suffrage movement.
She explains that it was during this time that most of the original radical
Feminists died or retired. The new leaders were more conservative and
more willing to compromise. They maintained that women were different
from, not equal to, men, and that they should be given the vote not just
for their own benefit but for the benefit of society; women voters would
expedite the passage of social reform legislation. These Feminists were
anti-immigrant and anti-black, and they believed their votes would counter-
balance the votes of "undesirables." Moreover, it was in the 1890s that
Southern white women joined the suffrage movement and this marked the
movement's permanent split from the Abolitionist movement.

H 775. **LAGEMANN, ELLEN CONDLIFFE.** A Generation of Women: Education
in the Lives of Progressive Reformers. Cambridge, Mass.: Harvard
University Press, 1979. 207 pp.
Lagemann examines the educational backgrounds of five prominent progressive reformers: Grace Hoadley Dodge (1856-1914), who was involved in
the founding of the YMCA; Maud Nathan (1862-1946), the president of the
New York Consumers' League; Lillian Wald, the founder of the Visiting
Nurse Association and the Henry Street Settlement; Leonora O'Reilly (1872-
1927) and Rose Schneiderman (1882-1972), both of whom started as working
girls and climbed the trade union ladder to become important organizers
for the Women's Trade Union League. Lagemann argues that even though
the five women were not from the same class they all developed an early
sense of self-esteem. She also examines the close bonds between women
and concludes that shared gender experiences transcend class divisions.

H 776. **LAGEMANN, ELLEN CONDLIFFE,** ed. Nursing History: New Perspectives,
New Possibilities. New York: Teachers College Press, 1983.
219 pp.
Nursing History is a collection of nine papers from a conference sponsored
in May 1981 by the Rockefeller Archive Center. The authors situate nursing
history within the developing fields of women's history and professional
history and explore such issues as the relation of nursing to philanthropy
and "social feminism"; the professionalization of nursing through development of training schools, registration, and regulation; the disappearance
of some kinds of nurses (midwives and visiting nurses), and changes in
the role of others (public health nurses and private duty nurses); and
the image of nurses presented by popular culture. An annotated bibliography is included.

H 777. **LEACH, WILLIAM.** True Love and Perfect Union: The Feminist Reform
of Sex and Society. New York: Basic Books, 1980. 449 pp.
Focusing on the period from 1850-1880, Leach argues that Feminists at
this time—male and female—developed a "new ideology" geared toward reforming the lives of the bourgeoisie and toward creating gender equality.
Rooted in earlier humanitarian reform, these Feminists were urban-based,
secular, and intent on incorporating science and organization into their
world view. Some, particularly Elizabeth Cady Stanton, reworked the positivism of Auguste Comte so as to emphasize the feminine role in a rationalized social order. Leach addresses topics as diverse as sexual passion,
the new department stores, and the American Social Science Association.
A long biographical chapter is included, as well as shorter sketches of
other Feminists.

H 778. LEMONS, J. STANLEY. The Woman Citizen: Social Feminism in the
     1920s. Urbana: University of Illinois Press, 1973. 266 pp.
Lemons analyzes the work and achievements of Feminist organizations during
the 1920s. He disputes the stereotypical characterization of the 1920s
as the decade of the frivolous flapper and, instead, emphasizes the serious
efforts of women's organizations to generate social reforms. He looks
at the factional rivalry among the Feminist groups as well as the treatment
these groups received from the larger society. Lemons suggests that the
reformist activities of women during the 1920s can be seen as a bridge
between Progressivism and New Deal reformism.

H 779. LEONARD, EUGENIE ANDRUSS. The Dear Bought Heritage. Philadelphia:
     University of Pennsylvania Press, 1965. 658 pp.
Leonard claims that "it was not the meek and the mild who braved the ocean
and came to our shores but the daredevils, the staunch and the courageous.
This was equally true for men and women." Despite a lack of economic
and legal power, says Leonard, these "daredevil" women accomplished a
great deal in Colonial America. Leonard maintains that a prime concern
of women has always been to improve the environment in which their children
lived. In attempting to do this, Colonial women helped their husbands
to build up homes, food supplies, clothing, and protection against Indians.

H 780. LERNER, GERDA. The Majority Finds Its Past. New York: Oxford
     University Press, 1979. 217 pp.
This collection of twelve essays, written by the author over a period
of ten years, raises crucial questions concerning the history of women.
Lerner touches on broad issues dealing with the methodology of studying
women's history, the definition of women as a class or group in society,
and the historical origins of women's repressive roles. The essays also
focus on specific issues concerning the different experiences of black
and white women in America, Abolitionism and the women's movement, and
the relationship between working women and upper-class women in the Jacksonian Era.

H 781. LERNER, GERDA. The Woman in American History. Menlo Park, Calif.:
     Addison-Wesley, 1971. 207 pp.
Lerner surveys the role of women in America beginning in Colonial times
through the 20th century. She discusses their positions in the home,
in the paid work force, and as politically active citizens. The book
notes the contributions of "outstanding women," but it is also "concerned
with tracing the ways in which ordinary women have contributed to the
American quest for freedom, security, and abundance."

H 782. LUTZ, ALMA. Crusade for Freedom: Women of the Antislavery Move-
     ment. Boston: Beacon Press, 1968. 398 pp.
This is a chronicle of thirty years of women's participation in the Abolitionist movement prior to the Civil War. Lutz argues that the Abolitionist movement was the first reform movement through which women organized. She offers an anecdotal account of the leaders of the movement:
Maria Weston Chapman, Lydia Maria Child, Harriet Beecher Stowe and the
Grimke sisters, among others. Lutz locates the genesis of women's rights
movements within the Abolitionist movement, and discusses the roles which
Lucretia Mott, Elizabeth Cady Stanton, and Susan B. Anthony played in
both efforts.

H 783. MARSH, MARGARET S. Anarchist Women, 1870-1920. Philadelphia:
     Temple University Press, 1981. 214 pp.
Marsh analyzes the theories of anarchist women, and contrasts these to
the theories of male Anarchists, Socialists, and mainstream Feminists.
The anarchist Feminists challenged the patriarchal family and advocated
sexual non-conformity. Marsh considers activists such as Emma Goldman,

and includes a portrait of Voltairine de Dleyre, whom she sees as a primary theorist of the movement. In addition, the lives of six representative women, Florence Finch Kelly, Helena Born, Mollie Steimer, Marie Ganz, Margaret Anderson, and Marie L. are discussed in brief biographies.

H 784. MASSEY, MARY ELIZABETH. Bonnet Brigades. New York: Knopf, 1966. 371 pp.
This text examines the impact of the Civil War on the lives of women in both the Confederacy and the Union. Through the study of letters and diaries, the author concludes that the war experience had similar effects on the women of both sides. She argues that the war compelled Southern and Northern women to become self-reliant activists and that this, in turn, allowed for their intellectual and physical achievements.

H 785. MATTHAEI, JULIE A. An Economic History of Women in America: Women's Work, the Sexual Division of Labor, and the Development of Capitalism. New York: Schocken Books, 1982. 381 pp.
Matthaei's economic history is divided into three sections. Part One is a study of women in the Colonial period, a time when family life and economic life were connected and there was little distinction between the economic roles of men and women. Part Two deals with women's work in the 19th century, the point at which family life and economic life-- men's spheres and women's spheres--separated. At the same time, however, women began to be drawn into the labor force and into "men's jobs." "In this way," says Matthaei, "the sexual division of labor has begun to under- mine itself." In Part Three, she discusses the disintegration of separate spheres which is taking place in the 20th century. She also speculates about the future of women's place in the economy.

H 786. MAY, ELAINE TYLER. Great Expectations: Marriage and Divorce in Post-Victorian America. Chicago: University of Chicago Press, 1980. 200 pp.
This study compares divorce cases in Los Angeles in 1880 and 1920, to determine a rationale for the escalating divorce rate noted in post- Victorian times. May asserts that pre-20th-century divorce was predicated on "breach of contract," or a negating of marital duties. Post-Victorian divorce reflected a concern with personal happiness--the achieving of certain implied "expectations" regarding personal liberty, affluence, and mobility. She refutes earlier scholars who attribute rising divorce in the Progressive era to women's rights or relaxed divorce laws, arguing that women's autonomy was more myth than reality. Actual divorce court testimonies shed new light on changing attitudes regarding sexuality, material goods, working wives, and the changing role of men in post- Victorian society.

H 787. MAZEY, MARY ELLEN and DAVID R. LEE. Her Space, Her Place: A Geography of Women. Washington, D.C.: Association of American Geographers, 1983. 83 pp.
Her Space, Her Place is a Feminist application of traditional geographical methodologies, such as spatial distribution, spatial analysis, and dif- fusion. Beginning with a consideration of the ratio of men to women in various localities, and the geographical patterns by which such reforms as suffrage and reproductive rights have been diffused, Mazey and Lee take up such diverse topics as daily spatial activity patterns, anxiety away from home, and women's relation to the environment. They demonstrate the fruitfulness of adding special consideration of women to the study of geography and vice versa.

H 788. MELDER, KEITH E. Beginnings of Sisterhood: The American Woman's Rights Movement, 1800-1850. New York: Schocken Books, 1977. 199 pp.

Melder chronicles the origins of American Feminism in the half-century before the 1848 Seneca Falls Convention. He begins by describing the changing circumstances of the 19th century as regards women's work, legal status, educational opportunities, and what was regarded by the upper and middle classes as their proper "sphere." Shared experience in schools, the new industrial workplace, the Evangelical movement, and moral reform organizations stimulated new sorts of relationships among women and a new activism. Evangelicism, anti-slavery, and temperance assigned a role to women in the perfecting of the world. By the 1840s, a self-conscious, autonomous movement challenging legal discrimination against women and the concept of separate spheres had arisen out of the anti-slavery crusade. Melder works from manuscripts of women's rights and anti-slavery activists; proceedings, reports, and publications of reform organizations, as well as other contemporary sources; and biography and similar secondary work.

H 789. MOHR, JAMES C. Abortion in America: The Origins and Evolution of National Policy, 1800-1900. New York: Oxford University Press, 1978. 331 pp.

Mohr traces the legal, social, and medical issues involved in the medical practice during the 19th century, noting the complications and ambiguities in state and Federal legislative policies. He observes that, although in 1800 there was virtually no abortion legislation in the U.S., by 1900 abortion in most jurisdictions was a criminal offense. The author attempts to account for the "dramatic and still intensely debated shift in social policy," asking such questions as: When did anti-abortion laws begin to appear in the criminal codes? How rapidly did early abortion policies change? What were law makers responding to? What groups fought to make abortion a criminal offense in the U.S. and why? Mohr suggests that the answers to these questions are important for understanding the present debates on the legality of abortion.

H 790. MORGAN, DAVID. Suffragists and Democrats. East Lansing: Michigan State University Press, 1972. 225 pp.

Morgan focuses on the period from 1916-1920 in his analysis of the ratification of the Nineteenth Amendment to the U.S. Constitution. He examines the role of Democratic President Woodrow Wilson in the political battle over votes for women and finds that the suffrage movement became enmeshed in party politics. The author analyzes opposition to the Amendment by Southern politicians, and by the liquor and textile industries.

H 791. NEIDLE, CECYLE S. America's Immigrant Women: Their Contribution to the Development of a Nation from 1609 to the Present. Boston: Twayne, 1975. 312 pp.

Neidle seeks first to redefine the image of American immigrant women to include not only those women who arrived in America during the 19th and 20th centuries, but also those who arrived as the first wave of European settlers during the 17th century. Her contention is that these women, in leaving their homes behind, brought with them certain skills and values which were as important in shaping our present culture as those of later immigrant women. Neidle treats both individuals and groups, and proceeds chronologically, treating first the Puritans and Quakers, then women's trade unions and other, mostly urban, women's organizations. She concludes with an examination of women's contributions in the 20th century in the fields of science, medicine, music, literature and business.

H 792. NIELSEN, GEORGIA PANTER. From Sky Girl to Flight Attendant: Women
        and the Making of a Union. Ithaca, N.Y.: I.L.R. Press, 1982.
        160 pp.
Nielsen examines the situation of women in the American trade union movement through a case study of the Air Line Stewardess Association. After
a brief history of the aviation industry, and of the birth and growth
of the profession of stewardess within that industry, she traces the
attempts of stewardesses to bargain collectively for better wages and working conditions and, eventually, for an end to such discriminatory practices
as weight requirements and no-marriage rules. The history of this particular union presents interesting conflicts with all-male unions within
the same industry, such as the Air Line Pilots Association, which was
reluctant to recognize the right of the women to bargain separately or
to have equal privileges within a joint union.

H 793. NIES, JUDITH. Seven Women: Portraits from the American Radical
        Tradition. New York: Viking Press, 1977. 235 pp.
Nies draws portraits of seven politically active, influential American
women: Sarah Grimke, Harriet Tubman, Elizabeth Cady Stanton, Mother Jones,
Charlotte Perkins Gilman, Anna Louise Strong, and Dorothy Day. Suggesting
a tradition of radical women in American history, Nies maintains that
there has existed a coherent network of female activists from the earliest
Suffragists and Abolitionists to 20th-century radical organizers.

H 794. NOBLE, JEANNE. Beautiful, Also, Are the Souls of My Black Sisters:
        A History of Black Women in America. Englewood Cliffs, N.J.:
        Prentice-Hall, 1978. 353 pp.
This book examines the social and cultural history of American black women.
Beginning with the place of women in African legend, Noble proceeds to
trace the feminine experience of slavery, emancipation, and the continued
servitude to whites. Subjects examined include domestic labor, black
family life, black women in the arts, entertainment, and the professions,
and the relations of black women to black men and white women. Such leading personalities as Harriet Tubman, Sojourner Truth, Ida B. Wells Barnett,
Mary McLeod Bethune, Zora Neale Hurston, and Bessie Smith are discussed
as well.

H 795. NORTON, MARY BETH. Liberty's Daughters: The Revolutionary Experi-
        ence of American Women 1750-1800. Boston: Little, Brown, 1980.
        384 pp.
Norton suggests that images of a Colonial "Golden Age" of women have been
overdrawn. In fact, the traditional role and place of women was highly
circumscribed and clearly inferior to that of men. Norton argues that
the Revolutionary War altered this traditional organization as the disruption of society created new opportunities for women and Republican
ideology led to a reconsideration of women's roles. Women's educational
opportunities increased and the domestic sphere was seen as a crucial
arena for creating Republican citizens. However, this "domestic sphere"
also limited women's influence as it prevented them from entering other
arenas such as politics and professional careers.

H 796. O'NEILL, WILLIAM L. Everyone Was Brave: The Rise and Fall of
        Feminism in America. Chicago: Quadrangle Books, 1969. 369 pp.
O'Neill's study of Feminism from the 1840s to the 1960s rests on the underlying assumption that American Feminism failed because its leaders refused
to take into account that women's problems were social and economic as
well as political. Feminists did not focus enough of their attention
on altering the prevailing belief that women's place was in the home.
According to this analysis, the source of sexist restrictions on women
lies in the family and marriage structure, to which radical Socialism
provides an egalitarian alternative.

H 797. O'NEILL, WILLIAM L. The Woman Movement: Feminism in the United States and England. New York: Barnes & Noble Books, 1969. 208 pp.

O'Neill traces the development of the women's rights movement in America and, to a lesser extent, in England. Beginning with Mary Wollstonecraft's attack on British institutions in 1790, he relates in narrative (and illustrates with twenty-two documents) the continuing efforts of Feminists. The story covers several facets of the movement: the struggle for the vote, for property rights, for education, for entry into industry, as well as for temperance and general social reform.

H 798. OPPENHEIMER, VALERIE KINCADE. The Female Labor Force in the United States: Demographic and Economic Factors Governing Its Growth and Changing Its Composition. Berkeley: Institute of International Studies, University of California, 1970. 203 pp.

Oppenheimer uses methods of economics, demographics, and (to some extent) sociology to investigate the increasing participation of women, particularly married women, in the labor force, from 1900 to 1940 and very dramatically from 1940 to 1960. She first examines supply factors (economic and social incentives for women to work), finding these an insufficient explanation. She then argues that the labeling of certain jobs as "women's work" made it possible to speak of a separate female labor market. Oppenheimer concludes that an increase in demand in this market interacted with supply factors to produce the trend toward increased female participation.

H 799. O'SULLIVAN, JUDITH and ROSEMARY GALLICK. Workers and Allies: Female Participation in the American Trade Union Movement, 1824-1976. Washington, D.C.: Smithsonian Institution Press, 1975. 96 pp.

This book was originally issued as a catalog for a Bicentennial exhibit on women's role in the labor movement. In addition to photographs, it includes a chronology of the history of women's labor, a bibliography, and a section of short biographical paragraphs on important women organizers and allies from Victoria Woodhull to Elizabeth Gurley Flynn to Bella Abzug. An introductory essay offers an overview of the history of American women working from the earliest days of the Industrial Revolution in New England through the Civil War, W.W. I and W.W. II to more recent struggles to organize and to challenge sexual discrimination.

H 800. PIVAR, DAVID J. Purity Crusade: Sexual Morality and Social Control, 1868-1900. Westport, Conn.: Greenwood Press, 1973. 308 pp.

Pivar contends that neither of the two prevailing historical interpretations of Victorian morality—that it was excessively repressive, or that "there was a persistence of illicit and subterranean sex"—is to the point. Instead, what should be emphasized is that it was moderate social reformers, like the social purists, who dealt with the problems resulting from a changing sexual morality. In addition to describing the movement (which he credits to urban Progressives), Pivar discusses the context and background of the social purity movement: Suffragists and Abolitionists were often members. And he discusses the consequences of the movement: it was the forerunner of the social hygiene movement, and one of the bases of an increasing emphasis on better childrearing practices.

H 801. RICHEY, ELINOR. Eminent Women of the West. Berkeley, Calif.: Howell-North Books, 1975. 276 pp.

Richey maintains that "there was something about the West that activated . . . creativity, that stimulated women to transcend their customary roles." She writes about nine women, most of whom grew up in the late 19th century: Imogen Cunningham (photographer), Florence Sabin (medical researcher), Abigail Scott Dunway (teacher and activist), Gertrude Atherton (novelist), Sarah Winnemucca (Indian Chief), Gertrude Stein (writer), Jeanette Rankin (social worker and suffragist), Isadora Duncan (dancer), and Julia Morgan (architect). These women were able to accomplish what they did, says Richey, because women were more highly valued in the West, due to their relative scarcity; young women were rarely influenced by older, more conservative women (who remained in the East); and women of the West could take advantage of higher education. Moreover, freedom, individuality, and developing one's potential were highly valued in the West.

H 802. ROSEN, RUTH. The Lost Sisterhood: Prostitution in America, 1900-1918. Baltimore, Md.: Johns Hopkins University Press, 1981. 245 pp.
Rosen examines the growth of urban prostitution and the reaction of reformers who attempted to eradicate it during the Progressive era. She argues that reformers not only failed in their attempts to end prostitution; they also intensified problems experienced by prostitutes. Rosen looks at prostitution in the larger context of women's place in a sexually divided job market and concludes that women chose prostitution voluntarily as a way of earning better wages. The book focuses on the interaction among the prostitutes and the class divisions that divided women in this occupation.

H 803. ROSENBERG, ROSALIND. Beyond Separate Spheres: Intellectual Roots of Modern Feminism. New Haven, Conn.: Yale University Press, 1982. 288 pp.
Prior to the 1920s, in accordance with the Victorian ideal, women were perceived, by themselves and by others, as separate and distinct from males. In the 1920s, however, women began viewing themselves as equal to males. It is with this change in female self-perception, argues Rosenberg, that the women's movement fades, giving way to a new type of Feminism. The process was buttressed by the expanding opportunities for females in higher education during the 1920s, and the resulting group of female intellectuals. Beyond Separate Spheres concerns itself with those researchers--women such as Marion Talbot, Helen Thompson, Leta Hollingworth, Margaret Mead (to name just a few)--who initiated the study of sex differences. They contended that the biological differences between men and women had no bearing on intellectual capabilities and that the observable differences between the sexes were due mainly to social upbringing. In so claiming, they forged a new path for modern Feminism.

H 804. ROTELLA, ELYCE J. From Home to Office: U.S. Women at Work, 1870-1930. Ann Arbor, Mich.: UMI Research Press, 1981. 233 pp.
Rotella attempts a "new economic history" of women in the non-agricultural labor force from 1870 to 1930. Using econometric techniques, she explores the increasing participation of women in the work force, especially the young and single, and particularly in clerical positions. Behind this development was an expansion of supply--the decline of the household-centered economy and the rise of labor-saving technology, for instance, made more educated young women available for work outside the home--and of demand--industry evolved in such a way as to require large numbers of clerical workers. Rotella bases her work on official statistics, governmental reports, and secondary material.

H 805. ROTHMAN, SHEILA. Woman's Proper Place: A History of Changing
Ideals and Practices, 1870 to the Present. New York: Basic Books,
1978. 322 pp.
Rothman discusses the interplay between changing ideas of women's proper
roles and changing principles of American social policy toward women.
She provides an account of the experiences of women within the family,
the workplace, and public life, paying special attention to the role of
technology, education, and the professions. She explores the role of
the settlement houses and suffrage groups, the work of the National Organization of Women, as well as the ideology of educated motherhood and liberation politics in America. A special focus of the book is on the role
of the medical profession.

H 806. RYAN, MARY P. Cradle of the Middle Class: The Family in Oneida
County, New York, 1790-1865. New York: Cambridge University
Press, 1981. 321 pp.
Analyzing census data, wills, letters, and other primary sources, Ryan
seeks to show that "early in the nineteenth century the American middle
class molded . . . its distinctive identity around domestic values and
family practices." She argues that mothers increasingly shaped the character and mores of middle class children, and that there was a complex
interaction between the middle class family and various historical developments from the "frontier generation" of the 18th century, to "women's
larger place in the city" in the mid-19th century.

H 807. RYAN, MARY P. The Empire of the Mother: American Writing About
Domesticity 1830-1860. New York: Institute for Research in History and the Haworth Press, 1982. 170 pp.
Ryan examines "the development of domestic ideology" from its roots in
the rather restrained advice literature (written mostly by the clergy)
of the 1830s to its flourishing in the "feminine" novels of the 1860s.
She describes the process by which mothers simultaneously gained new ideological power and yet became more isolated within the home. Ryan explores
the contradictions in this ideology and summarizes historiographical
debates about domesticity.

H 808. RYAN, MARY P. Womanhood in America: From Colonial Times to the
Present. New York: New Viewpoints, 1975. 496 pp.
The history of American women is surveyed in this analysis of family structure, the work force, and Feminist activity. Chronological sections examine these three topics in various periods of U.S. history from the agrarian
lives of Colonial women through 19th-century industrialization and finally
to the 20th century with its consumption ethic. The text takes into
account diverse factors of race, class, and religion. Ryan maintains that
a gender-segregated society has continued to exist throughout America's
history.

H 809. SCHARF, LOIS. To Work and To Wed: Female Employment, Feminism,
and the Great Depression. Westport, Conn.: Greenwood Press,
1980. 240 pp.
Scharf focuses on the employment of married, middle-class women. She
finds that during the Depression, family necessity replaced Feminist arguments as the rationale for working wives. Moreover, during this time,
women in the work force experienced a decline in status and in salary.
Specific chapters look at government; professional, clerical, and teaching
employment patterns; and New Deal attitudes and programs.

H 810. SCHARF, LOIS and JOAN M. JENSEN, eds. Decades of Discontent:
        The Women's Movement, 1920-1940. Westport, Conn.: Greenwood
        Press, 1983. 313 pp.
Scharf and Jensen see the period from 1920 to 1940 as decades of discontent
which were marked by paradoxes that touched every aspect of the female
experience. They argue that although the economic structure, political
institutions, and social ideology of the time made it possible for individual women to achieve, "the same conditions made it difficult for the
women's movement to either maintain its strength or expand as an organized
group committed to social change in opposition to the established order."
The essays in this collection--which range from Estelle B. Freedman's
consideration of "The New Woman: Changing Views of Women in the 1920s"
to Sherna Gluck's "Socialist Feminism Between the Two World Wars: Insights
from Oral History"--attempt to explain the decline of the women's movement
after 1920.

H 811. SCHILPP, MADELON GOLDEN and SHARON M. MURPHY. Great Women of the
        Press. Carbondale: Southern Illinois University Press, 1983.
        248 pp.
This collection of eighteen biographical profiles of women journalists
spans three centuries. Though such familiar figures as Margaret Fuller
and Mary Katherine Goddard are represented, the authors also recover such
uncanonized names as Elizabeth Timothy, the first woman publisher in
America; Anne Newport Royall, a Washington correspondent during John Quincy
Adams's administration; and Rheta Childe Dorr, an activist in the late
19th- and early 20th-century women's movement, an editor for the New York
Evening Post, and the first editor of Suffragist, the official organ of
the Congressional Union for Women Suffrage. The book contains extensive
bibliographies for each woman profiled.

H 812. SCHLISSEL, LILLIAN. Women's Diaries of the Westward Journey.
        New York: Schocken Books, 1982. 262 pp.
Schlissel seeks new perspectives on the overland migration of 1840 to
1870 by examining the diaries of the women who made the journey. She
finds the women more attentive to the rhythms of everyday life and death
along the trail, and less taken by the adventurous aspects of their trek
than were the men with whom they traveled. They often, in fact, attempted
to re-establish traditional roles and domestic routines as best they could.
In the first section of the work Schlissel describes the changing nature
of the Westward journey in the 1840s, 1850s, and 1860s. In the second,
four diaries are reproduced. Schlissel includes many photographs and
a table of individual characteristics of ninety-six diarists.

H 813. SCHRAMM, SARAH SLAVIN. Plow Women Rather than Reapers: An Intel-
        lectual History of Feminism in the United States. Metuchen, N.J.:
        Scarecrow Press, 1979. 441 pp.
Schramm's intention is to trace the ideological roots and intellectual
developments of Feminism, as well as to provide definitions of Feminism.
The book includes discussions of Feminist views of the family, education,
and women's and men's roles in society. In conclusion, Schramm suggests
that while women never fully reap the benefits of Feminism, the very activity of Feminist thinking is a vital and necessary step toward progress.

H 814. SCOTT, ANNE F. The Southern Lady: From Pedestal to Politics,
        1830-1930. Chicago: University of Chicago Press, 1970.
        247 pp.
Covering a span of 100 years, Scott examines women's domestic roles and
their activities in reform and suffrage movements. Contrasting the dominant, traditional image of Southern women with the realities of their
daily lives in the 19th century, she concludes that an awareness of this
contradiction led Southern women into the political arena, particularly

after the Civil War, when women were thrust into positions of responsibility. Scott describes the long struggle of these Southern suffragists who were able to maintain their staunch moralism and genteel image.

H 815. SCOTT, ANNE FIROR and ANDREW MacKAY SCOTT. One Half the People: The Fight for Woman Suffrage. Philadelphia: Lippincott, 1975. 174 pp.
This collection of primary documents related to American women's struggle for the vote is introduced at length by the authors. They seek to answer the questions of who participated in the suffrage movement; how its strategy and tactics developed and changed, and which were successful; why the movement split twice, and with what consequences; why men were opposed to it; and how it was related to other social movements such as Progressivism, and voluntary associations like the Women's Christian Temperance Union.

H 816. SIMKINS, FRANCIS BUTLER and JAMES WELCH PATTON. The Women of the Confederacy. New York: Garrett & Massie, 1936. 306 pp.
The authors provide a study of women's participation in the secessionist cause and the conditions for existence in the occupied South. Relying heavily upon diaries and reminiscences, Simkins and Patton show "feminine champions of the Southern cause" enthusiastically encouraging their male relatives to battle, helping to equip them and later nurse them, supporting them as spies and smugglers. Moreover, says Simkins, these women deserved praise simply for managing to survive in conditions of scarcity and danger.

H 817. SINCLAIR, ANDREW. The Better Half: The Emancipation of the American Woman. New York: Harper & Row, 1965. 401 pp.
Sinclair offers a general social history of women in the U.S. from the 19th century into the 20th century. He notes that 19th-century Feminists were restricted because they had to project a "lady-like" image, and he maintains that it was only after working-class and middle-class suffragists joined hands that the movement gained force. Sinclair traces the flux of the suffragists' movement from city to country and back to city, and notes the effect of Western expansion on the women's movement.

H 818. SMITH, PAGE. Daughters of the Promised Land: Women in American History. Boston: Little, Brown, 1970. 392 pp.
Smith provides background for his study of the role and importance of women in American history with a short analysis of the status of women in ancient cultures (Greek, Egyptian, etc.), and the subsequent modifications of their status through the influence of Christian dogma. In Colonial America, as in the Israel of Old Testament Jews, women enjoyed substantial social equality with men, despite growing anxiety over female sexuality. The relative power and independence of American women suffered as the emerging middle class of the 18th and 19th centuries capitalized on the restrictive aspects of Christian morality: the home was the proper sphere for women, whose main function was to nurture children.

H 819. SMUTS, ROBERT W. Women and Work in America. New York: Schocken Books, 1971. 176 pp.
Smuts finds that "the picture of women's occupations outside the home has changed since 1890 in only a few essentials: a sharp decline in the relative importance of manual work on farm, in factory, and in household service occupations; and sharp increases in the importance of clerical and sales work, teaching and nursing, and non-household service jobs." He notes that despite increasing opportunities in the paid work force, women believe their primary responsibilities to be within the home. Smuts stresses the causes rather than the consequences or change in women's roles through the 1950s.

H 820. SOCHEN, JUNE. Movers and Shakers: American Women Thinkers and
    Activists, 1900-1970. New York: Quadrangle Books, 1973. 320 pp.
Sochen's book focuses on women intellectuals and activists of the 20th
century. Although there are women who fought for equal rights in their
personal lives, Sochen has written about those who made this fight a public
effort. She is interested in women "who agonized externally, who shared
their concerns with others, who organized similarly disposed women. . . ."
Movers and Shakers is also a study of the interaction between these women
and their environments and times. Women activists, says Sochen, react
to the times in which they live; thus, the actions of Feminists in one
decade will be different from those of Feminists in another decade.

H 821. SOCHEN, JUNE. The New Woman in Greenwich Village, 1910-1920.
    New York: Quadrangle Books, 1972. 175 pp.
Sochen traces the bohemian, radical, Socialist, and Feminist perspectives
in New York City's Greenwich Village during the second decade of the 20th
century by focusing on five Feminists. She details the lives and works
of Henrietta Rodman and Crystal Eastman (writers and activists in the
peace movement reform of New York City's school system), Neith Boyce and
Susan Glaspell (professional Feminist writers), and Ida Rauh (an actress
with the Provincetown Players who performed a number of Feminist plays
written by Glaspell). Sochen also makes note of the roles which men played
in the emergence of the "new women" of Greenwich village.

H 822. SPRUILL, JULIA CHERRY. Women's Life and Work in the Southern Colo-
    nies. Chapel Hill: University of North Carolina Press, 1938.
    426 pp.
Four chapters of this book deal with women as workers: eight chapters
deal with women's primary focus, domestic life, and two are devoted to
women's intellectual pursuit, and women and the law. In each case, Spruill
begins her analysis in the early 17th century, and generally continues
through the 1780s. She focuses on "the elite," but speculates on the
life of other classes as well. Spruill often compares the life in the
Southern Colonies to life in England.

H 823. STEINSON, BARBARA J. American Women's Activism in World War I.
    New York: Garland, 1982. 440 pp.
During W.W. I, says Steinson, an unprecedented number of women joined
the public sector. Three types of women's groups are explored: peace
movements, such as the Woman's Peace Party; military preparedness groups,
such as the Woman's Section of the Navy League; and women's relief groups.
The members of these groups differed not only in their goals, but in their
age, wealth, employment, and attitudes toward suffrage. Steinson discusses
the competition that existed between different groups and individuals.
But she is most interested in looking at the ways in which these women
"with very different purposes used the traditional ideology regarding
woman's role to support their cause."

H 824. STELLMAN, JEANNE MAGER. Women's Work, Women's Health: Myths and
    Realities. New York: Pantheon Books, 1977. 262 pp.
Stellman examines both the social and legal issues raised by women working
and the impact on women's health of their work in office, factory, and
home. The author regrets that discussions of women's health on the job
are usually limited to the effect of work on reproductive capacity, so
she devotes attentions to other considerations, such as work-related stress
and the range of occupational hazards specific to fields in which women
are concentrated--the health services, office and clerical work, domestic
work and service industries. The dilemma of trying both to protect women
from such hazards and to prevent job discrimination based on the presence
of such hazards is treated, and Stellman proposes a number of measures
that might make for a fuller and healthier working life for women.

H 825. STIMPSON, CATHARINE R., ELSA DIXLER, MARTHA J. NELSON, AND KATHRYN B. YATRAKIS, eds. Women and the American City. Chicago: University of Chicago Press, 1981. 277 pp.
Operating on the premise that women's needs in urban environments often differ from those of men, the editors point out the importance of establishing non-sexist cities. In the twenty-one articles which constitute the book, the position of women in cities is analyzed, using history to clarify contemporary concerns. Issues of particular importance which are discussed include: the role of women in political and community organizations; the urban experiences of minority and immigrant women; the influence of society's conception of gender on the design of urban space; and the problems confronting old people in cities. Suggestions for positive change in urban policy are proposed.

H 826. STRASSER, SUSAN. Never Done: A History of American Housework. New York: Pantheon Books, 1982. 365 pp.
Strasser contends that historians have overlooked the subject of housework since American society construes all "work" as "paycheck-related." Her study examines the evolution of household tasks from Colonial times to the present and includes discussions of the impact of technological and industrial growth on household work. Strasser notes that the intrafamily dependence network which was endemic to Colonial life was eliminated by innovations such as running water, gas stoves, washing machines, and convenience foods. Concomitantly, the family foodways industry evolved from home-grown, to preserved and prepared, to modern-day "drive-thru" restaurants. A final chapter, "Life on the Market," treats "two income" families, the rise of single family living, and men as household consumers.

H 827. TAX, MEREDITH. The Rising of the Women: Feminist Solidarity and Class Conflict, 1880-1917. New York: Monthly Review Press, 1980. 322 pp.
Tax examines the connections between Feminism, trade unionism, and the Socialist movement. She focuses upon the organizations women formed, their activities in industrial disputes, and their struggle for women's suffrage. Tax describes the ephemeral relationship between working-class organizations and the women's movement. She also explores the theoretical and practical questions facing historians of working-class women.

H 828. TENTLER, LESLIE WOODCOCK. Wage-Earning Women: Industrial Work and Family Life in the United States, 1900-1930. New York: Oxford University Press, 1979. 266 pp.
Tentler investigates the economic and social experiences of working class women in factory, sales, and non-domestic service work in the urban centers of the Northeast and Midwest. She concludes that the work experience of these women, primarily concentrated in a brief period before marriage, was part of a conservative sex-role socialization which tended to confirm rather than contradict women's psychological dependence on the family, her sense of inferiority, and her role as mother and housekeeper. Tentler maintains that women experienced rigid sex-segregation in terms of job opportunities, and consistent below-subsistence pay.

H 829. THOMPSON, ROGER. Women in Stuart England and America: A Comparative Study. Boston: Routledge & Kegan Paul, 1974. 276 pp.
While for three or four generations after the founding of the Colonies American women enjoyed better economic opportunities than they would have in Stuart England, the gap between English and American opportunities began to close as distinct upper and lower classes emerged in America. As communities grew into cities, the previously open interpretation of legal rights for women in America began to follow the English model more closely. Liberating gains made by American women in the 17th century were not maintained; but on the whole, Thompson concludes, women enjoyed

a more attractive position in American society in the 17th century and beyond than English society would have allowed.

H 830. ULRICH, LAUREL. Good Wives: Image and Reality in the Lives of Women in Northern New England 1650-1759. New York: Knopf, 1982. 296 pp.
Ulrich examines the roles which helped shape women's experiences in Colonial New England. She analyzes both the prescriptive images of the "woman's place" and the actual practices of women's economic, family, and religious lives. Challenging the view that a Colonial woman's life as static, Ulrich suggests that many of the transformations which have been attributed to antebellum and Victorian America took place before 1750.

H 831. WANDERSEE, WINIFRED. Women's Work and Family Values, 1920-1940. Cambridge, Mass.: Harvard University Press, 1981. 165 pp.
Wandersee claims that a higher standard of living in the 1930s, relative to previous decades, made it acceptable for middle-class women to be employed outside the home in order to increase family income. She looks at the 20th-century changes in women's employment, from agriculture and manual labor to business and sales. She also looks at the impact of the Depression and widespread unemployment on women in the workforce. Though women were working outside the home in greater numbers, women's ideal place was still believed to be in the home. Wandersee concludes by suggesting that this paradox has continued in subsequent decades.

H 832. WARE, SUSAN. Beyond Suffrage: Women in the New Deal. Cambridge, Mass.: Harvard University Press, 1981. 204 pp.
Attempting to dispel the idea that the 1930s was a decade of decline in women's position in society, Ware studies twenty-eight females who held government positions during the New Deal. She discusses the influence of these women on New Deal policies (especially regarding social welfare) and on New Deal politics (especially regarding appointments). These women, Ware contends, created a network of female influence in the government during the Depression which has been unequaled since. Brief, individual biographies and a table of biographical data are provided.

H 833. WARE, SUSAN. Holding Their Own: American Women in the 1930s. Boston: Twayne, 1982. 223 pp.
Ware believes that the Depression reinforced traditional ideas about women's role in the family; she sees the roots of the "feminine mystique" of the 1940s and 1950s in the 1930s. Yet women did make some strides during this decade. Working women were less affected by the Depression than working men, basically because clerical and sales jobs were affected less than industrial work. Moreover, the percentage of women in the labor force increased during the 1930s; and the decade saw the shift from younger, unmarried women to older, married women making up the majority of female workers. (Ware disagrees with the prevailing interpretation that this shift took place as a result of W.W. II.) In addition to discussing women's position in the labor force, Ware looks at women's position in education, social reform, the Left, literature, fine arts, and popular culture.

H 834. WELTER, BARBARA. Dimity Convictions: The American Woman in the Nineteenth Century. Athens: Ohio University Press, 1976. 230 pp.
Welter has examined 19th-century literature by, for, or about women, as well as manuscript and secondary sources, in order to assess feminine roles and female experience in that period. Her essays address such subjects as adolescence, the Cult of True Womanhood, medical views of women and sexuality, women's fiction, prevailing views of women's intellectual

capabilities, and the increasing feminine influence in American religion.
The collection concludes with a long piece on Margaret Fuller.

H 835. WELTER, BARBARA, ed. The Woman Question in American History.
Hinsdale, Ill.: Dryden, 1973. 177 pp.
This volume offers a collection of fifteen essays surveying numerous
aspects of women's history. Three sections deal with women's "Life," their
"Liberty," and their "Pursuit of Happiness," ranging from Colonial women
to the Suffragists and contemporary Feminists. Individual articles in
this collection touch on Indian and black women, women of the frontier
and of the South, changing sex roles, and the origins of women's movements
for liberation.

H 836. WERTHEIMER, BARBARA MAYER. We Were There: The Story of Working
Women in America. New York: Pantheon Books, 1977. 427 pp.
Wertheimer has written a history of the American working woman from
Colonial times through the 20th century. She omits women who worked in
the arts, in the professions, and in reform work, and concentrates instead
on such women as black workers (including slaves), garment workers, mill
workers, and mine workers. Much of the book is devoted to women's struggles with labor unions. Annotated bibliographies are included for each
chapter.

H 837. WERTZ, RICHARD W. and DOROTHY G. WERTZ. Lying-In: A History of
Childbirth in America. New York: Free Press, 1977. 260 pp.
This critique of childbirth in the U.S. analyzes the attitudes and practices surrounding labor and birth from Colonial times to the present.
The decline of midwifery and the rise of an expensive, inequitable obstet-
rical system are examined by the authors in their attempt to understand
the inadequacies of present childbirth practices.

H 838. WILSON, MARGARET GIBBONS. The American Woman in Transition: The
Urban Influence, 1870-1920. Westport, Conn.: Greenwood Press,
1979. 252 pp.
Noting the emergence of a "New Woman" in the late 19th century and an
increasing sphere of activity open to women, Wilson writes, "it is to
the phenomenal upsurge in urbanization and industrialization occurring
between 1870 and 1920 that we must turn to account for the permanent enlarg-
ing of the accepted sphere of activity for women and the change in the
image of feminine propriety." Wilson undertakes a systematic study of
white middle-class women in an attempt to distinguish patterns of behavior
specific to urban areas.

H 839. WRIGHT, CARROLL D. The Working Girls of Boston. Boston: Wright
& Potter, 1889. 133 pp.
This study was originally published in 1884 as part of the annual report
of the Massachusetts Bureau of Statistics of Labor. The Bureau interviewed
1,032 of the 20,000 non-domestic women workers in Boston for personal
histories. Statistical information is presented, mostly in tabular form,
about occupation, place of work, ethnic origin, age, duration and perman-
ency of employment, hours worked, health, working conditions, living conditions (in the family home and in boarding houses and institutions),
earnings, economic condition, and "moral condition." A final section
is devoted to refuting the widely believed contention that factory and
shop workers are prone to prostitution.

H 840. ZELMAN, PATRICIA G. Women, Work, and National Policy: The Kennedy-Johnson Years. Ann Arbor, Mich.: UMI Research Press, 1982. 160 pp.

In focusing narrowly on Washington politics, Zelman gains a clear perspective on how political developments, especially in the executive branch, facilitated and aroused a developing Feminist consciousness. Zelman details the roles of such women as Esther Peterson, Martha Griffiths, and Edith Green in obtaining the President's Commission on the Status of Women, the inclusion of "sex" in Title VII, and the Women's Job Corps. Zelman notes that the victories of the Feminist movement in the 1960s were won despite the fact that broad, popular support had still not been achieved.

VIII. ETHNICITY

H 841. ADLER, SELIG and THOMAS E. CONNOLLY. From Ararat to Suburbia: The History of the Jewish Community of Buffalo. Philadelphia: Jewish Publication Society of America, 1960. 498 pp.

This work traces the rise of the Jewish community in Buffalo from its beginnings, when Buffalo was an outpost during the War of 1812, until the date of publication. The relatively quiet period of German-Jewish activity during the middle of the 19th century is contrasted with the rapid expansion caused by the arrival of East European Jews at the end of the century. The arrivals from the Russian Pale brought with them both religious and secular customs which alienated them from the established German-Jewish community. The authors show that factionalism brought on by differing views toward Zionism fractured the solidarity of the Buffalo Jews even further; they conclude, however, that the Holocaust of W.W. II and antagonism toward the treatment of Jews in the Soviet Union will help bring the Jews of Buffalo closer together in the years to come.

H 842. ALLSWANG, JOHN M. A House for All People: Ethnic Politics in Chicago, 1890-1936. Lexington: University Press of Kentucky, 1971. 253 pp.

Allswang investigates the relationship between ethnic pluralism and American politics in an era of political and social change in the U.S. The study centers on the role of ethnic groups in the unprecedented rise to power of the Democratic Party in Chicago. Emphasis is on the period from the end of W.W. I to the first Roosevelt election. A secondary theme is the exploration of how ethnic groups make their way into the American political system. Quantitative analytical techniques are employed in the analysis of political behavior.

H 843. ANDERSON, ARLOW W. The Norwegian-Americans. Boston: Twayne, 1975. 274 pp.

Anderson details the background and adaptation of Norwegians in America, emphasizing initial assimilation. Because Norwegians were compelled to emigrate for economic reasons rather than persecution or discrimination, they were grateful for the opportunity America offered while maintaining an attachment to their homeland. Also examined is the Norwegian penchant for reforming America through social criticism, and their support for the Populist and Farmer-Labor Movements. A bibliographic essay is included.

H 844. **BARTH, GUNTHER.** Bitter Strength: A History of the Chinese in
the United States, 1850-1870. Cambridge, Mass.: Harvard University Press, 1964. 305 pp.
The transition of Chinese immigrants from transient laborers to permanent
American residents is the subject of Barth's study. Beginning in the
1850s, large numbers of Chinese men left the economically and politically
unstable Pearl River Delta for California, where they worked as indentured
servants in hope of supporting their families and eventually returning
to their homeland. Work camps and San Francisco's Chinatown isolated
them from American society and perpetuated Chinese social structures.
Not until the Chinese looked beyond the work camp for opportunity did
the process of acculturation to American life begin. By 1870, an increasing number of Chinese elected to settle in the U.S.

H 845. **BARTON, JOSEF J.** Peasants and Strangers: Italians, Rumanians,
and Slovaks in an American City, 1890-1950. Cambridge, Mass.:
Harvard University Press, 1975. 217 pp.
This book is a social history of three Southern and Eastern European immigrant groups who left their economically declining rural villages for
industrial Cleveland. Although most newcomers returned to their homes,
those who stayed encouraged other villagers or relatives to join them.
The communities these immigrants established were thus both "a reconsti-
tution of a village and partly an accommodation to the fragmented social
order of the metropolis." Each group brought with it distinct values
which affected economic mobility: Italians and Slovaks remained laborers,
while Rumanians moved rapidly into middle-class occupations. Assimilation
occurred in the 1930s and 1940s after the restriction of immigration.
Ethnic communities declined but group loyalties reasserted themselves in
the broader context of religious organizations.

H 846. **BAYOR, RONALD H.** Neighbors in Conflict: The Irish, Germans, Jews,
and Italians of New York City, 1929-1941. Baltimore, Md.: Johns
Hopkins University Press, 1978. 232 pp.
Bayor argues that long-term economic competition and ethnic group reaction
to politics of the 1930s resulted in intense intergroup conflict in
Depression-era New York. The Great Depression exacerbated economic tensions
between groups as competition for jobs stiffened. Simultaneously, conflict
over local, domestic, and international politics pitted group against
group. The Irish feared the loss of their control over the New York City
government to Jews and Italians; events in Nazi Germany and growing anti-
German sentiment fueled Jewish-German conflict. Irish-Jewish antagonism
resulted from the association of Jews and Communists and the anti-Semitism
of the Coughlin movement. Bayor examines the impact of these divisions
on intergroup relations in two neighborhoods.

H 847. **BENSON, ADOLPH B.** and **NABOTH HEDIN**, eds. Swedes in America 1638-
1938. New York: Haskell House, 1938. 614 pp.
Published as a part of the New Sweden Tercentenary Celebration, this volume
is an attempt to recall by summaries and examples the role played by Swedes
as American pioneers and citizens. It reviews activities and influences
of the Swedes in various fields of endeavor from 1638 to the 20th century.
Commentary is made on Swedish Americans as farmers, writers, athletes,
professionals, musicians, artists, military personnel, and businessmen
and women. Illustrations are contained and an index of prominent Swedish
Americans concludes the volume.

H 848. **BERGER, DAVID,** ed. The Legacy of Jewish Migration: 1881 and Its
Impact. New York: Columbia University Press, 1983. 187 pp.
Eighteen eighty-one marked the outbreak of a wave of pogroms against the
Jews of Russia and the beginning of the massive cultural, ideological
and demographic changes, which, according to Berger, "transformed modern

Jewry profoundly and irrevocably." This book is the outcome of a 1981 conference in New York that marked the 100th anniversary of that event, and re-examined its impact on Jewry and its implications for 20th-century Jewish life. Included are sections on the Old World Context, Ideology and Culture, and New Modes of Jewish Community.

H 849. BERGER, MAX. The British Traveller in America, 1836-1860. New York: Columbia University Press, 1943. 239 pp.
Berger recounts the experiences of British travellers in America between 1836-1860 and discusses their viewpoints of America. Matters discussed unique to the pre-Civil War era include democratic government, slavery, the national character, and manners and customs. Berger also has devoted a chapter to religion which outlines the British view toward American tolerance toward other religions. Public education was an issue which also surprised the British traveller. The final chapter is devoted to emigration. Discussed are the reasons for emigration as well as which groups of people from England came to the U.S. Berger successfully portrays the British surprise and skepticism toward the American democratic lifestyle.

H 850. BERMAN, MYRON. Richmond's Jewry, 1769-1976: Shabbat in Shockoe. Charlottesville: University Press of Virginia, 1979. 438 pp.
In tracing over two centuries of Jewish history in Richmond, Berman focuses primarily on the forty to fifty Jewish families in antebellum Richmond and the 5,000 to 10,000 Jews living in Richmond in the first half of the 20th century. He devotes his narrative to the great Jewish families of the city and to the spiritual and intellectual leaders, such as Dr. Edward N. Calisch, who preached and practiced Jewish accommodation with the host Southern culture. The Jews of Richmond, Berman suggests, abandoned much of their distinctly ethnic ritual and social cohesion, conformed to Southern social values, and became as much Southern as Jewish in identity.

H 851. BERNARD, RICHARD M. The Melting Pot and the Altar: Marital Assimilation in Wisconsin, 1850-1920. Minneapolis: University of Minnesota Press, 1980. 162 pp.
Assuming that ethnic groups which intermarried accepted each other, Barnard examines marriage patterns in Wisconsin to gauge ethnic group assimilation. Because intermarriage guaranteed other forms of social interaction, Bernard contends new light can be shed on immigrant assimilation by centering attention on the extent, patterns, and causes of such marriages. Barnard does not attempt to explain why particular couples married, but he does show the rates at which members of different ethnic groups married and to analyze the influences in their decision-making. He draws his data primarily from the manuscripts of Wisconsin's state marriage registrations for the decennial years 1890-1920.

H 852. BERTHOFF, ROWLAND T. British Immigrants in Industrial America, 1790-1950. Cambridge, Mass.: Harvard University Press, 1953. 296 pp.
Berthoff includes in his study of British immigrants the English, Scottish, Welsh, Protestant Irish, and English-speaking Canadian immigrants. An introductory chapter deals with immigration statistics and surveys the topic in broad terms. The remainder of the work consists of two main sections treating economic and cultural adjustment. Berthoff shows that in contrast to most immigrant groups, the British generally had prior experience in industrial trades and were more skilled. The British therefore tended to secure better paying employment than many immigrant groups. Furthermore, the cultural background of British immigrants made assimilation into American society relatively easy.

H 853. BIRMINGHAM, STEPHEN. The Grandees: America's Sephardic Elite.
New York: Harper & Row, 1971. 368 pp.
Birmingham's work takes a biographical look at the Jews who arrived in
America before 1840. The lives of affluent Jewish merchants such as Newport's Aaron Lopez and New York's Moses Levy are depicted, and the respect
they commanded in American society is stressed. The life of the first
Jewish Naval Officer of the U.S., Uriah Levy, is portrayed in great detail
as well. The Cardozo family, which excelled in the legal circles of New
York City, is traced through several generations, as was the Nathan family,
which became famous because of the murder of one of the family. By telling
the stories of these families, Birmingham portrays the creation of a social
elite which he demonstrates still exists in American Judaism today.

H 854. BIRMINGHAM, STEPHEN. Our Crowd: The Great Jewish Families of
New York. New York: Harper & Row, 1967. 404 pp.
Birmingham admits that his work is not a scholarly examination of New
York's most famous and influential German Jewish banking families. Rather,
he seeks to look "behind the marble facades" and see whether these families
possessed the same "capacity for folly and grandeur" as most people.
Among the families whose histories are chronicled are those of the Selig-
mans, the Guggenheims, the Lehmans, the Belmonts, the Kuhns, the Lewisohns,
and the three Loebs. Birmingham concludes that these Jewish families
formed the only real aristocracy in the city, if not the country.

H 855. BLEGEN, THEODORE C. Norwegian Migration to America: 1825-1860.
Northfield, Minn.: Norwegian-American History Association, 1931.
413 pp.
This study examines both the Norwegian immigrants' adaptation to America
and the migration's affect on the Europe that they left. Blegen emphasizes
that the immigrant experience is quintessentially "modern," and asserts
that America's attraction for Norwegians was a total one, not attributable
to economic motives alone. Support for this claim is based, in part,
on a study of immigrant songs and ballads.

H 856. BODNAR, JOHN. Immigration and Industrialization: Ethnicity in
an American Mill Town, 1870-1940. Pittsburgh, Pa.: University
of Pittsburgh Press, 1977. 213 pp.
In this study of Steelton, Pennsylvania in the late 19th and early 20th
centuries, Bodnar concludes that the town's social relations were characterized not by destruction and subsequent integration of ethnic and
socio-economic groups but by a reorganization of ethnic and class alignments.
Steelton offers an example of internal community reactions to industrial
life as well as a view of the experience of Slavic immigrants in American
mill towns. Bodnar suggests a model for explaining the evolution of social
relationships in various industrial towns since the 19th century.

H 857. BRANDES, JOSEPH. Immigrants to Freedom: Jewish Communities in
Rural New Jersey Since 1882. Philadelphia: University of Pennsylvania Press, 1971. 424 pp.
Immigrants to Freedom documents the rarely acknowledged story of the Eastern European Jews who chose to continue their rural lifestyles when they
arrived in the U.S. According to Brandes, many of these settlers believed
that a rural lifestyle would help discredit the Jewish stereotypes which
bred anti-Semitism, and that this helped them gain financial support from
wealthy, urban Jews. Brandes also argues that a growing fear among Jews
that emigration would be curtailed because of the pernicious conditions
in city slums convinced many Jews that agricultural communities would
insure that Jewish immigration would be allowed to continue. He finds
that in contrast to the experience of urban Jews, very few of the rural
settlers embraced either Socialism or Zionism.

H 858. BRIGGS, JOHN W. An Italian Passage: Immigrants to Three American
        Cities, 1890-1930. New Haven, Conn.: Yale University Press,
        1978. 348 pp.
In this account of the Italian experience in Rochester and Utica, New
York, and in Kansas City, Missouri, Briggs eschews the "well-studied theory
of exploitation, discrimination, and rejection." He places his main emphasis on the continuity of life the immigrants experienced. According to
Briggs, the melting pot theory is not useful because it masks areas of
fundamental agreement between different ethnic groups. He devotes the
first four chapters of this book to the experience of these Italian immigrant populations in Italy before turning to their American experience.
He portrays the immigrants as active agents, "capable of initiative as
well as of accommodation." He examines their transformation from Italian
to Italian-American and closely studies the growth of organizations in
their communities, their education, their businesses, and their political
involvement.

H 859. BROEHL, WAYNE G., Jr. The Molly Maguires. Cambridge, Mass.:
        Harvard University Press, 1964. 409 pp.
The struggle between the railroad-coal combination led by Franklin B.
Gowan and Irish miners in the anthracite fields of eastern Pennsylvania
was one of the most violent and controversial in American history. The
failure of Irish miners to form a union as a result of the laissez-faire
environment and economic individualism imposed by the operators produced
resentment by the miners. Social tensions were exacerbated because the
mine bosses and owners were English and Welsh Protestants, while their
poor employees were Irish Catholics. When the miners, building upon Irish
tradition, formed a secret society called the Molly Maguires and murdered
several opponents, Gowan hired a Pinkerton agent, James McParlan, who
infiltrated the organization and then testified against the Mollies.
Eventually twenty-one miners were executed for their alleged participation
in the murders. Broehl treats the subject as ethnic, labor, business
and social history, examining the cultural, as well as economic, dimensions
of the story.

H 860. BROWN, THOMAS N. Irish-American Nationalism, 1870-1890. Phila-
        delphia: Lippincott, 1966. 206 pp.
The depression of the 1870s unleashed two forces within the Irish-American
community: nationalism and the search for social justice. Of the two,
the former was more powerful. The Irish-American press proved to be the
main instrument in the spread of Irish-American nationalism. Four ingredients made up Irish-American nationalism: (1) loneliness derived from
the immigrant experience, (2) alienation in the new American environment,
(3) prejudice by the Protestant majority, and (4) poverty. This combination produced a contradiction. Confronting the radical rhetoric of leaders
like Patrick Ford, O'Donovan Rossa and John Mitchell were intensely conservative demands. In the effort to overcome a pervasive sense of inferiority, there was an intense longing for acceptance which exhibited itself
in middle-class respectability.

H 861. BURCHELL, R. A. The San Francisco Irish, 1848-1880. Berkeley:
        University of California Press, 1980. 227 pp.
The experience of the Irish in San Francisco differed from those Irish
who settled in Eastern cities. California was a much more fluid society
in the 19th century, making Catholic-Protestant relations less volatile
than elsewhere in the U.S. The Chinese presence also eliminated scapegoating prejudice found in other parts of the country. The Irish were
successful from the start. By 1870, three Irishmen had been elected to
the Senate and another mayor of San Francisco. Others held prominent
positions in banking and business. Because of their widespread diffusion
in many occupations, the large numbers of fraternal associations, and

upward mobility between the first and second generations, the Irish were not exclusively supporters of the Democratic Party and the large, boss-run machine failed to appear in San Francisco.

H 862. CADA, JOSEPH. Czech-American Catholics, 1850-1920. Lisle, Ill.: Center for Slavic Cultures, St. Procopius College, 1964. 124 pp.
Essentially a short sketch of early Czech Catholics in America, Cada's work parallels similar accounts of national and spiritual enterprises in the late 19th and early 20th centuries. The first part of the book covers pioneer Czechs and those arriving after 1850 to settle both rural and urban parishes. Part two encompasses Czechs who arrived after 1890. Their institutions included high schools, religious communities and cultural organizations to transfer their cultural heritage to American-born Czechs. Efforts of Czech Americans at freeing their homeland are also examined. Cada relies primarily on bulletins, almanacs, Catholic periodicals and papers, and parish reports as his sources. Cada hopes to provide thematic materials for future scholarly studies on American immigration. A bibliography of general works, periodicals, and newspapers is included.

H 863. CHIU, PING. Chinese Labor in California, 1850-1880: An Economic Study. Madison: State Historical Society of Wisconsin, 1967. 180 pp.
Chiu attempts to analyze and describe the role of the Chinese immigrants within the general framework of the economic development of California. Emphasis is placed upon the entry and exit of the Chinese in the economy during the years of regional and national economic change from 1848 to 1880. Contributions of Chinese labor are discussed in a general description of their economic activities; discrimination against Chinese labor is discussed in conjunction with economic development. Chiu's aim is to incorporate only factual data, leaving out social, political, religious and moral arguments.

H 864. CLARK, DENNIS. The Irish in Philadelphia: Ten Generations of Urban Experience. Philadelphia: Temple University Press, 1973. 246 pp.
Although this book covers the influence of the Irish in Philadelphia from its founding to the present, the primary focus of the work is on the 19th century. The experience of the Irish in Philadelphia differed significantly from other immigrant experiences in Eastern cities. This difference is attributed to the greater land area of Philadelphia relative to Boston or New York City which allowed for cheaper land prices and a dispersed population. The easy availability of land enabled many working-class Irish to own their own two-story brick row houses. By 1883, half the Philadelphia work force owned their houses and worked a ten-hour day. A short time after arriving, the Irish entered the business world as real estate brokers, saloon keepers, grocers, and building contractors. Through these professions, the Irish became supporters and defenders of the free enterprise systems. The construction industry became a special Irish concern and was a link to the political machine through the awarding of public works projects to Irish-controlled enterprises. The "Victorian compromise" which permitted the Irish to build their own institutions, provided they leave the dominant Protestant structure and order alone, enabled the Irish to develop their own subculture. As in other cities, Irish life centered around the church, the parish school, the saloon, and the fire company.

H 865. CLARK, DENNIS. The Irish Relations: Trials of an Immigrant Tradition. Rutherford, N.J.: Fairleigh Dickinson University Press,
1982. 255 pp.
In this wide-ranging collection of topically arranged essays, Clark offers
an overview of the history of Irish-Americans from the 1830s to the present.
Three chapters on labor include discussion of indentured servants, women
workers in the 1880s, and the exploitation of Irish industrial workers.
Three chapters deal with Irish-American urban businesses--saloons, travel
agencies, and building contractors. Another section of three chapters
focuses on Irish nationalist movements and their leaders. Clark also
discusses Irish relations with other ethnic groups, concentrating on blacks,
the Anglo upper class, and Jews. In the final section he analyzes recent
Irish-American attempts to preserve ethnic distinctiveness in the U.S.

H 866. COHEN, BERNARD. Sociocultural Changes in American Jewish Life
as Reflected in Selected Jewish Literature. Cranbury, N.J.:
Associated University Presses, 1972. 282 pp.
Cohen traces development within the American Jewish community during the
nine decades since the mass emigration of Eastern European Jews which
began in the 1880s. During this period America became a new center of
Jewish life; at the same time, social factors in American life transformed
the Jewish community, especially over the course of the last three generations. Cohen's primary objectives in this study are first, to analyze
socio-cultural change in American Jewish life and, second, to determine
how these changes are mirrored in contemporary, selected literature of
American Jewish writers. He is concerned primarily with the issue of
creative survival versus assimilation of American Jews.

H 867. COHEN, NAOMI W. Not Free to Desist: The American Jewish Committee,
1906-1966. Philadelphia: Jewish Publication Society of America,
1972. 652 pp.
This work studies the origins and achievements of the first American Jewish
"defense" organization. Cohen points out that at the organization's inception, its function was primarily to "prevent infringements upon the civil
and religious rights of Jews." But within a few years, the Committee
became an influential lobbying power in Washington. More recently, Cohen
finds that the Committee has turned its attention "inward," concerning
itself more with young Jews searching for their "Jewish identity."

H 868. COLE, DONALD B. Immigrant City: Lawrence, Massachusetts, 1845-
1921. Chapel Hill: University of North Carolina Press, 1963.
248 pp.
Cole proposes in this work to "find the truth about Lawrence" and, at
the same time, to illuminate the condition of the immigrant in all of
urban America. He questions the assumption that all immigrants were poverty-
stricken and un-American. He begins with an account of Lawrence during
the strike of 1912 through the eyes of the native Americans and then turns
to a narrative of the city's history from 1845 to 1912, a narrative that
he argues puts the strike in its proper perspective. Most important,
however, is the section he devotes to the immigrants' search for security
in the new world and his conclusion that these immigrants may have been
poverty-stricken to a great extent, but that they were nevertheless successful in their search. They found security in their families, in the mills,
in groups, and in their Americanism. The strike was less an expression
of violent radicalism than an attempt by patriotic Americans to improve
their working and living conditions.

H 869. COMMAGER, HENRY STEELE, ed. Immigration and American History. Minneapolis: University of Minnesota Press, 1961. 166 pp. The main themes running through this collection of essays dedicated to Theodore C. Blegen are that the emigrant and immigrant are one and that there are great potentialities for pluralism in our loyalties. Topics include the image of America in Europe, the place of the immigrant in Western fiction, the migration of ideas, and the prospects for the study of immigration. Also included are an essay entitled "The Saga of the Immigrant" by Blegen and a bibliography of his written works.

H 870. CONROY, HILARY and T. SCOTT MIYAKAWA. East Across the Pacific: Historical and Sociological Studies of Japanese Immigration and Assimilation. Santa Barbara, Calif.: Clio Press, 1972. 322 pp. The authors of this book attempt to assemble recent research on Japanese immigration and settlement in North America, Hawaii, and the Pacific Islands through this collection of historical and sociological essays. As a whole, the collection refutes the anti-Oriental organizations' claims that Asians would not be assimilated into America by citing the significant contributions of Asian Americans to the U.S. economy and culture. The volume also is a source of comparative data for testing explanatory general- izations regarding American ethnic and race relations and the experience of Asian and European immigration.

H 871. CONZEN, KATHLEEN NEILS. Immigrant Milwaukee, 1836-1860: Accom- modation and Community in a Frontier City. Cambridge, Mass.: Harvard University Press, 1976. 300 pp. Conzen uses manuscript census data, city directories, and local newspapers to identify and analyze the demographic, residential, economic, social, and political configurations of the German community in Milwaukee. She argues that German immigrants tended to cluster together because they entered Milwaukee in large numbers when the city had ample space and employ- ment opportunities. The coincidence of rapid urban growth and the arrival of a skilled immigrant group allowed the Germans to prosper, to enjoy good living conditions, and to adjust painlessly to American urban life, all the while postponing assimilation.

H 872. COOK, ADRIAN. The Armies of the Streets: The New York City Draft Riots of 1863. Lexington: University Press of Kentucky, 1974. 323 pp. Cook provides an in-depth analysis of the worst riot in American history. From July 11-14, 1863 opponents of the Federal government's draft violently attacked draft offices, Republican sympathizers of the Civil War, and innocent blacks. Most of the rioters were Irish and at times the violence evolved into a type of class warfare. At least 105 people were killed in the disturbance, although Cook believes that the reports of over a thousand dead were exaggerations. The widespread poverty and poor employ- ment conditions among the immigrant and working population of New York were the ultimate contributors to America's worst episode of urban violence.

H 873. CORDASCO, FRANCESCO, ed. Studies in Italian American Social History. Totowa, N.J.: Rowman & Littlefield, 1975. 264 pp. This volume is a collection of various essays concerned with Italian- American experience, compiled in honor of Leonard Covello. Included are papers on conflict, acculturation and assimilation; the Italian language press, anti-Fascist reactions in the U.S.; Italian political refugees, and the contemporary patterns of Italian emigration. The contributors include Jerre Mangione, Humbert Nelli, and Andrew Rolle. In the opening essay, Cordasco provides an overview of Leonard Covello's early efforts at systematic study of the Italian-American experience. Also included are three appendices, the first two pieces written by Covello and the third a handlist of selected writings by Covello.

H 874. COWAN, HELEN I. British Emigration to British North America: 1783-1837. Toronto: University of Toronto Library, 1928. 273 pp.

Cowan examines a variety of ethnic groups that emigrated from the U.K. to North America, including the Scotch and Irish. She demonstrates that settlements established before 1783 influenced the experiences of later groups of immigrants. Other topics discussed include the transatlantic trade in indentured servants, and British plans to alleviate domestic poverty by facilitating "pauper emigration."

H 875. CUNZ, DIETER. The Maryland Germans: A History. Princeton, N.J.: Princeton University Press, 1948. 476 pp.

With the exception of Pennsylvania, Germans played a greater role in Maryland than in any other state. Cunz examines why immigrants from German-speaking regions of Europe chose to settle in Maryland, and narrates the history of the Calvert Colony on the Chesapeake Bay. He discusses its settlement; the role of some of its prominent figures; its Americanization; and the characteristics of second and third generation German Americans. Finally, Cunz considers the experience of Maryland Germans a case history of American immigration that generates conclusions applicable to immigration history in general.

H 876. CURRAN, THOMAS J. Xenophobia and Immigration: 1820-1930. Boston: Twayne, 1975. 214 pp.

Curran attempts a sweeping survey of persistent anti-foreign attitudes in the U.S. He finds two types of xenophobic movements: one which sought to control the power and influence of immigrants, another which strove to restrict immigration. Curran then describes the various manifestations of xenophobia: the nativist movements of antebellum years; the anti-foreign politics of the American Republicans and Know Nothings; the late 19th-century reaction to Asian, Southern, and Eastern European immigration; the exclusionary policies of trade unions; the early 20th-century drive toward restriction; and the renascence of the Ku Klux Klan in the 1920s.

H 877. DANIELS, ROGER. The Politics of Prejudice: The Anti-Japanese Movement in California and the Struggle for Japanese Exclusion. Berkeley: University of California Press, 1962. 165 pp.

Daniels sketches a brief history of Japanese immigration to California and then traces anti-Japanese prejudice from its origins to the Immigration Act of 1924. He argues that though anti-Oriental attitudes were deeply rooted in the popular culture of the American West, the politics of trade unionists and progressive politicians rather than public sentiment spurred the crusade against Japanese immigration. In 1901 and again in 1913, the California legislature passed anti-Japanese legislation. In the W.W. I years, anti-Japanese sentiment spread throughout the U.S., encouraged by "yellow peril" propaganda. By the early 1920s, California's anti-Japanese politics were emblematic of American xenophobia, and in 1924 immigration legislation excluded Japanese from the U.S.

H 878. DAVIS, ALLEN F. and MARK H. HALLER, eds. The Peoples of Philadelphia: A History of Ethnic Groups and Lower Class Life, 1790-1940. Philadelphia: Temple University Press, 1973. 301 pp.

Davis and Haller have collected twelve essays on the urban history of Philadelphia, focusing on the experience of immigrants, laborers, and the poor. Recurring themes include the adjustment of immigrants to life and work in the city, and urban social problems. The essays treat topics such as economic mobility, housing conditions, community organization and social order in immigrant ghettos, riots, crime, and violence.

H 879. DAVIS, LAWRENCE B. Immigrants, Baptists, and the Protestant Mind
in America. Urbana: University of Illinois Press, 1973.
230 pp.
Davis focuses on the attitudes of Northern Baptists toward immigrants
during the period between 1880 and 1925. Such issues as the Chinese immigration of the 1880s and the debate over limiting immigration after W.W.
I are discussed in relation to the Baptist stance on newcomers. Davis
argues that, in the final analysis, Northern Baptists supported the new
ethnic groups and actively conducted missionary work among them. The
conversion of German immigrants to the Baptist faith before the turn of
the century accounted, in part, for the church's sympathy for the foreigner
in America.

H 880. DAVIS, MOSHE. The Emergence of Conservative Judaism: The Historical School in the Nineteenth Century. Philadelphia: Jewish Publication Society of America, 1983. 527 pp.
Davis describes the emergence of Conservative Judaism by tracing its roots
to what 19th-century contemporaries called the Historical School. These
Jews, who Davis points out possessed a wide variety of views on many subjects, were able to unite because they agreed on the following: (1) secular enlightenment must be accepted and encouraged; (2) Jews should take
advantage of American religious freedom; (3) the search for a home in
Israel must continue until it is achieved. According to Davis, the Historical School sought a new approach to Judaism that would maintain Jewish
tradition but would be consonant with American democratic tradition.

H 881. DeJONG, GERALD F. The Dutch in America, 1609-1974. Boston: Twayne,
1975. 326 pp.
In comparison to other European groups, Dutch migration to the U.S. was
not extensive. The important periods of migration were: (1) the settlement of New Netherlands from 1609-64, (2) the antebellum period from 1840-
61, and (3) the 1880s. Upon arrival in the U.S., most Dutch tended to
be conservative, sought to become Americans, and were heavily influenced
by religion. Ironically, Dutch influence spread after 1664 because of
the growth of the Dutch Reformed Church, which used the Dutch language
as late as the 19th century. The earliest immigrants settled primarily
in New York and New Jersey, while the 19th-century voortrekkers were
attracted to cheap land in the Midwestern states of Wisconsin, Michigan,
Iowa and Minnesota.

H 882. DIGGINS, JOHN P. Mussolini and Fascism: The View from America.
Princeton, N.J.: Princeton University Press, 1972. 524 pp.
Diggins traces the rise of Fascism in Italy and studies the response of
Americans of both native and Italian origin to this rise. He delineates
their early reactions, paying close attention to the dominant symbols
and images of Mussolini. He then examines the particular responses of
various social groups and institutions in American society and describes
the shift in American opinion that came after the U.S. entered the war.
He suggests that while 90% of the Italian-American press was pro-Mussolini
in 1941, it was more out of a sense of nostalgic patriotism than out of
a strict adherence to ideology, and that this support quickly diminished
after 1941.

H 883. DIMONT, MAX I. The Jews in America: The Roots, History, and
Destiny of American Jews. New York: Simon & Schuster, 1978.
286 pp.
The Jews in America attempts to revise what Dimont calls the standard
history of the Jews as sufferers and instead proposes that the "real"
Jewish history is "rich, rebellious, and full of intellectual adventure."
He believes that American Judaism is "a unique outgrowth of the American

soil, shaped as much by the American spirit as by the Jewish ethic," and
that this experience gave American Jews a "resilience" unique to this
country. Dimont also argues that past scholars have erred in attributing
to religious incentives the arrival of the first Jews in America. Rather,
Dimont believes that economic incentives enticed the "pioneer" Jews to
come to America. Finally, Dimont's survey discredits those who have stated
that the tendency toward assimilation endangers the survival of Judaism;
it posits instead that the American experience will not only preserve
the religious and cultural traditions of the Jewish faith, but enrich
them.

H 884. DINER, HASIA R. Erin's Daughters in America: Irish Immigrant
      Women in the Nineteenth Century. Baltimore, Md.: Johns Hopkins
      University Press, 1983. 192 pp.
The Irish were the only major immigrant group to the U.S. predominately
composed of females. Unlike other immigrants, Irish women did not seek
factory or day labor work; most were servants and mill girls, and the
former profession changed little from 1840 to 1900. Seeing themselves
as self-sufficient women, the Irish did not accept the "cult of domesticity" and worked for long periods of adulthood, postponed or forsook marriage, and saved money. Irish women suffered less job discrimination
than their male compatriots, allowing greater mobility into semi-profes-
sional positions like nursing, teaching, stenography, sales and clerical
work. Despite their aggressive, independent efforts to achieve economic
security, most Irish women rejected the women's movement and tended to
identify with their fellow immigrants. The sexual segregation characteristic of the Irish produced low rates of illegitimacy, premarital sex,
and prostitution among Irish-American women. The economic independence
of Irish women allowed for a rise in status while Irish men suffered the
reverse. This produced unresolved and sometimes violent tensions within
many families. Consequently, high rates of female-headed households resulting from discord, desertion and death of the male breadwinner were not
uncommon.

H 885. DINNERSTEIN, LEONARD. The Leo Frank Case. New York: Columbia
      University Press, 1968. 248 pp.
Dinnerstein's work recounts the trial of Leo Frank, a Jew living in Georgia
who in a wave of anti-semitism was convicted of murdering thirteen-year-
old Mary Phagan. Although Governor John M. Slaton commuted Frank's death
sentence, an angry mob kidnapped and lynched him. Dinnerstein points
out that the Ku Klux Klan developed out of a group called the Knights
of Mary Phagan, which had been instrumental in Frank's murder. Conversely,
he notes that Jewish reaction to this incident was strong, for only days
after Frank's death the B'nai Brith Anti-Defamation League was formed.
The case's implications for national politics and historians' conceptions
of the Progressive Era are also considered.

H 886. DINNERSTEIN, LEONARD and MARY DALE PALSSON, eds. Jews in the South.
      Baton Rouge: Louisiana State University Press, 1973. 392 pp.
An anthology of twenty-one previously-published essays, this book examines
life in the antebellum, Confederate, New South, and 20th-century eras,
as well as Southern views of and responses to Jews and Jewish reactions
to desegregation. The editors' choice and arrangement of essays reinforce
their argument that, although few in number, Jews in the South contributed
significantly to Southern economic expansion because Jewish enterprise
and prosperity supported growing communities. The editors and various
authors also agree that Jews in the South adopted life-styles and values
similar to other Southerners, although Jews evinced, even if only privately,
greater intolerance on matters of race and social reform than did non-
Jews in the South.

H 887. DINNERSTEIN, LEONARD, ROGER L. NICHOLS, and DAVID M. REIMERS.
Natives and Strangers: Ethnic Groups and the Building of America.
New York: Oxford University Press, 1979. 333 pp.
The authors offer a synthesis of ethnic American history. The book is
arranged chronologically and emphasizes the role of ethnic minorities
in "the emergence of modern America." Immigrants, argue the authors,
made significant contributions to the economic growth and cultural development of the U.S., but despite their contributions suffered oppression
and discrimination. The authors recount in detail the conflict and struggle which has consistently shaped the experience of newcomers to America.

H 888. DINNERSTEIN, LEONARD and FREDERIC COPLE JAHER, eds. The Aliens:
A History of Ethnic Minorities in America. New York: Appleton-
Century-Crofts, 1970. 347 pp.
This collection of essays emphasizes "the harsher aspects" of minority
group experiences in the U.S. and treats all groups of non-English origin.
The book is divided chronologically, starting in the Colonial period,
with essays on the various groups present in American society. The authors
trace waves of immigrants and the reception of immigrants, paying particular attention to nativism in the young republic. Emphasis is placed on
the struggle and ordeal of the immigrant experience in America.

H 889. DIVINE, ROBERT A. American Immigration Policy, 1942-1952. New
Haven, Conn.: Yale University Press, 1957. 220 pp.
Divine traces the course of restrictive immigration policy from 1924 to
1952, after a thorough discussion of its origins in earlier policy. Until
the 1880s a policy of laissez-faire was followed. Selectivity was first
employed in 1882 when convicts, lunatics, idiots, and paupers were barred
from entry, but found its fullest expression in the 1921 temporary quota
measure (a measure made permanent three years later). Divine enumerates
four principles that are incorporated in the formation of immigration
policy--economic, social (racial), nationalistic, and foreign policy con-
siderations--and suggests that these principles can be put together in
many different ways. He ends his study with a chapter on the McCarran
Act, a piece of legislation that codified all the previous acts and established the U.S. as a bastion against Communism.

H 890. DOLAN, JAY P. The Immigrant Church: New York's Irish and German
Catholics, 1815-1865. Baltimore, Md.: Johns Hopkins University
Press, 1975. 221 pp.
Dolan examines the evolution of American Catholicism in the context of
immigrant interaction and responses to urban life. He observes that the
Irish and Germans shared conceptions of Tridentine piety, but that they
clashed over ethnic permutations regarding devotions and control over
the church. Dolan concludes that the basic structure of the American
Catholic church, and its culture, grew out of the interplay between ethnic
groups in the urban environment. What existed only in inchoate terms
in 1815 had become clearly defined by 1865--namely, an American Catholic
church marked by ethnic pluralism, the national parish, and the parochial
school all under Irish hegemony, and a church withdrawn into its own community and maintained by discipline and loyalty to church institutions.

H 891. DOWIE, JAMES IVERNE. Prairie Grass Dividing. Rock Island, Ill.:
Augustana Historical Society, 1959. 262 pp.
Dowie portrays the lives of a small group of immigrants who settled in
the Platte Valley of Nebraska after the Civil War, detailing the difficulties of pioneer life. The account is centered around this limited
group not because of their accomplishments but because of the faith which
they held in America, and for that faith Dowie sees these people as a
chapter in both American history and the history of Nebraska. That this
group of pioneers was Swedish remains incidental except insofar as the

fact relates to the contributions of immigrant groups to U.S. history.
Dowie also details the establishment of the Nebraska Conference of the
Augustana Lutheran Church and the first twenty years of Luther College
in Wahoo, Nebraska, as part of the Swedish effort to transfer their heritage to Nebraska.

H 892. DOWIE, JAMES IVERNE and ERNEST M. ESPELIE, eds. The Swedish Immi-
        grant Community in Transition. Rock Island, Ill.: Augustana
        Historical Society, 1963. 246 pp.
Although not intended as a continuous account of Swedish migration to
the U.S., the essays contained in this volume are presented in chronological order, centered around specific epochs in Swedish life in America.
The volume begins with the arrival of Swedes, the establishment of religious and educational institutions, and the settling into American life.
The essays then turn to the language, politics, and press of Swedish Americans in transition in American society, closing with an essay by Conrad
Bergendoff on the changing world of the immigrant. A bibliographic essay
on the writings of Conrad Bergendoff is included.

H 893. EHRLICH, RICHARD L., ed. Immigrants in Industrial America: 1850-
        1920. Charlottesville: University of Virginia Press, 1977.
        218 pp.
The common objective of these ten essays is to dispel the notion that
the encounter with America destroyed the traditional lifestyles of immi-
grants, and to demonstrate instead how transplanted European cultures
survived in, adapted to, and influenced their American environs. Caroline
Golab writes on "The Impact of the Industrial Experience on the Immigrant
Family"; Carol Groneman on "Women Workers in Mid-Nineteenth-Century New
York City"; Tamara K. Hareven on "Family and Work Patterns of Immigrant
Laborers in a Planned Industrial Town, 1900-1930"; Virginia Yans-McLaughlin
on the work experience of Southern Italian immigrants in Buffalo, New
York, at the turn of the 20th century; Douglas V. Shaw on the development
of political leadership among the Irish in Jersey City; David Montgomery
on "Immigrant Workers and Managerial Reform"; Michael Gordon on "Irish
Immigrant Culture and the Labor Boycott in New York City, 1880-1886";
Bruce Laurie on "Immigrants and Industry: The Philadelphia Experience,
1850-1880"; Laurence Glasco on "Ethnicity and Occupation in the Mid-
Nineteenth-Century: Irish, German, and Native-born Whites in Buffalo, New
York"; and Clyde Griffen on "The 'Old' Immigration and Industrialization:
A Case Study."

H 894. ELOVITZ, MARK H. A Century of Jewish Life in Dixie: The Birmingham
        Experience. University: University of Alabama Press, 1974.
        258 pp.
Elovitz describes the settlement, occupations, and social adjustments
of Jews in Birmingham from 1871 through the 1960s. He argues that the
German Jews who arrived in the city in the 1870s and 1880s earned the
respect of their Christian neighbors by their business skills, integrity,
generosity, and accommodation to local ways. German Jews prospered and
even won election to public office, and they escaped Ku Klux Klan harassment.
By contrast, the Eastern European Jews who arrived in Birmingham after
1890 found little favor among German Jews and Christians. Their clannish-
ness and religious orthodoxy set them apart from the German Jews, Elovitz
argues, and the two Jewish communities did not converge until the 1930s,
when new immigration had ended and Eastern European and German Jews found
it more advantageous to cooperate with one another.

H 895. EPSTEIN, MELECH. Jewish Labor in the United States: An Industrial,
        Political, and Cultural History of the Jewish Labor Movement,
        1882-1914. New York: Trade Union Sponsoring Committee, 1950.
        922 pp.
Epstein attempts to determine the extent to which both American economic
development and the "peculiar" background of East European Jews shaped
the Jewish labor movement. He asserts that the distinctive features of
Jewish labor included (1) their militant adherence to radical beliefs;
(2) their ideological and political unity held before industrial organization;
and (3) young intellectuals playing a decisive role in its formative stages.
He concludes that social romanticism and activist fervor accounted for
the activism of Jews in the labor movement.

H 896. ERICKSON, CHARLOTTE. Invisible Immigrants: The Adaptation of
        English and Scottish Immigrants in Nineteenth Century America.
        Coral Gables, Fla.: University of Miami Press, 1972. 531 pp.
This work is based on the correspondence of twenty-five families of Scottish and English immigrants, for which Erickson has provided interpretive
introductions. She has also written biographical sketches for each family
based on census schedules, passenger lists, and county histories. Erickson
questions the conclusions of earlier immigrant historians and argues that
assimilation in America was not a painless process for British immigrants;
she also attacks the conventional view of eager Europeans emigrating after
reading guidebooks or letters from America.

H 897. ERNST, ROBERT. Immigrant Life in New York City, 1825-1863. New
        York: King's Crown Press, 1949. 331 pp.
When the Erie Canal opened in 1825, immigrants made up only 7% of the
population of New York City; by 1860, almost half of the city's population
was foreign-born. In this book, Robert Ernst describes the experience
of immigrant New Yorkers, especially the Irish and Germans. He examines
in depth immigrant employment, working conditions, the integration of
the foreign-born into the city's unions, and the emergence of a powerful
German labor movement. Ethnic consciousness was "of a kind," fostered
by ethnic churches and fraternal organizations, but newspapers, politics,
and labor as well as factionalism within ethnic communities contributed
to assimilation.

H 898. Essays in American Jewish History. Cincinnati, Ohio: American
        Jewish Archives, 1958. 534 pp.
This volume commemorates the tenth anniversary of the founding of the
American Jewish Archives under the direction of Jacob Rader Marcus. An
article by Ellis Rivkin examines Jews' relations to American Capitalism
and patterns of anti-Semitism in U.S. history, noting its regular appearance at times of social and economic stress. The twenty other essays
reflect more specialized and narrowly focused concerns on the part of
the assembled scholars. Topics addressed include genealogy, slaveholding
among Jews in 17th-century New York, the economic life of Jews in the
mid-19th century, and the work of several American scholars of Judaism.
Assorted archival material is also reproduced.

H 899. ESSLINGER, DEAN R. Immigrants and the City: Ethnicity and Mobility
        in a Nineteenth-Century Midwestern Community. Port Washington,
        N.Y.: Kennikat Press, 1975. 156 pp.
Using both traditional methods of historical research and the newer techniques of quantitative analysis, Esslinger examines urbanization as it
affects and was affected by the lives of thousands of immigrants. The
urban community under study is that of South Bend, Indiana; a community
that experienced rapid growth, thereby making the impact of immigration
highly visible. Over 10,000 cases were reviewed in an attempt to determine
geographical, residential, and occupational mobility as well as patterns

of immigrant leadership. Esslinger finds a high rate of geographical mobility and a low level of ethnic segregation, but acknowledges that these factors and variables, and assimilation became more difficult with the increase of urban growth in the 1880s and the rising level of prejudice that accompanied this growth.

H 900. FEIN, ISAAC M. The Making of an American Jewish Community: The History of Baltimore Jewry from 1773 to 1920. Philadelphia: Jewish Publication Society of America, 1971. 348 pp.
Fein characterizes the first century of Baltimore Jewry as a "pioneering" age, in which Jewish immigrants were as much adventurers as freedom seekers. The years from 1830 to 1855 saw the formation of a true Jewish "community," with synagogues built and Jewish educational apparatus developed. The next twenty-five years are seen by Fein as years of dissension, in which men like David Einhorn and Benjamin Szold divided the Baltimore Jews. The arrival of the East European Jews caused further discord, but the rising popularity of the Zionist movement is portrayed as the unifying force of the early 20th century.

H 901. FEINGOLD, HENRY L. The Politics of Rescue: The Roosevelt Adminis-tration and the Holocaust, 1938-1945. New Brunswick, N.J.: Rutgers University Press, 1970. 394 pp.
Feingold describes the competing forces which produced the Roosevelt administration's lack of effort to help the victims of the Holocaust. His study of State Department documents suggests to him that its fear that German spies could infiltrate the U.S. if refugees were admitted into the country prevented more action by the government. In the period before Pearl Harbor, the zealous manner in which Congress and the State Department sought to maintain neutrality is portrayed as thwarting Roosevelt's desire to satisfy American Jewish groups with an organized program of relief. By the time American Jews were able to convince the Administration that relief efforts should be separated from the State Department, resulting in the formation of the War Refugee Board, the war was nearly over.

H 902. FEINSTEIN, MARNIN. American Zionism: 1884-1904. New York: Herzl Press, 1965. 320 pp.
Feinstein sees three significantly distinct phases in the pre-W.W. I Ameri-can Zionist movement. The first stage involved the formation of Hoveve Zion societies. These were formed, according to Feinstein, primarily by Russian "sentimentalists" who hoped only that small settlements could be formed in Palestine where persecuted Russian Jews might settle. The second stage described by Feinstein commenced in 1897 with Theodor Herzl's call for the convocation of a World Zionist Congress, and is portrayed as one of unity both in vision and action. Feinstein argues that by 1905, the different factions could no longer cooperate effectively, and that in the third stage "religious," "labor," and "general" Zionists each formed their own organizations which remained autonomous until the creation of Israel.

H 903. FELDBERG, MICHAEL. The Philadelphia Riots of 1844: A Study in Ethnic Conflict. Westport, Conn.: Greenwood Press, 1975. 209 pp.
Feldberg examines two major anti-immigrant riots in mid-century Philadel-phia. In 1844, the Kensington riot erupted because of a dispute over the reading of the Protestant version of the Bible in the public schools, which was protested by the Irish Catholic minority. Conflict was provoked by nativists who went so far as to organize anti-Catholic rallies in Irish neighborhoods. Later that same year, in the Southwark riot, the Irish and the police clashed and for the first time American public authorities took human lives to control the disturbance. These riots marked a tran-

sition in collective violence from a struggle between two religious groups
to strife between a group and the state. Most of the riots that occurred
in the late 19th and 20th centuries tended to be the latter, pitting different ethnic, racial, or labor groups in violent confrontations with
the state. This marked a departure from the Colonial and antebellum mobs
who attacked each other or representative institutions they deplored.

H 904. FELDSTEIN, STANLEY. The Land That I Show You: Three Centuries
of Jewish Life in America. Garden City, N.Y.: Anchor Press,
1978. 512 pp.
Feldstein's survey concentrates primarily on the post-bellum period.
Feldstein points out that during the Civil War there was great disagreement
on the question of slavery among Jewish Americans. He also juxtaposes
the experiences of urban and rural Jews in the U.S. The sweatshop culture
is examined, especially the manner in which this experience led to the
formation of Jewish unions. Jewish radicalism and criminality are treated,
and anti-semitism is compared in the various periods of American history.
The final chapters consider the creation of Israel, suburbanization, and
the problems of maintaining Judaism in modern America.

H 905. FELL, MARIE LEONORE. The Foundation of Nativism in American Textbooks, 1783-1860. Washington, D.C.: Catholic University of
America Press, 1941. 259 pp.
The author attempts to determine the extent to which textbooks used in
the period between 1783 and 1860 laid the foundations of the anti-foreign
and anti-Catholic attitudes which bore full expression in the nativist
movements of the 1830s and 1840s and in the Know Nothing party of the
1850s. In the course of her research Fell examined more than 1,000 texts
(500 readers, 250 histories, and 250 geographies) and offers many excerpts
from these texts. She suggests that their bias was more anti-Catholic
than anti-foreign and thus most significantly affected immigrants from
Roman Catholic countries.

H 906. FERMI, LAURA. Illustrious Immigrants: The Intellectual Migration
from Europe, 1930-41. Chicago: University of Chicago Press,
1968. 440 pp.
According to Fermi, "The wave of intellectuals from continental Europe
arriving in the thirties and early forties, driven here by the forces
of intolerance and oppression, was so large and of such high quality that
it constituted a new phenomenon in the history of immigration." In this
book Fermi examines this wave; the circumstances behind the migration,
the reception of this new immigrant population, and the performance of
these new immigrants in the U.S. in such varied fields as psychoanalysis,
atomic science, art, literture, and the social sciences. The data were
collected from the reminiscences of those who migrated.

H 907. FEUERLICHT, ROBERTA STRAUSS. Justice Crucified: The Story of
Sacco and Vanzetti. New York: McGraw-Hill, 1977. 480 pp.
Feuerlicht looks at the famous case of Sacco and Vanzetti through the lens
of the immigrant experience in America. She suggests that the story of
Sacco and Vanzetti begins not in 1920 with their arrests, but in 1620
with the Puritan Commonwealth—that the story of Sacco and Vanzetti is
representative of the experience of unwanted immigrants and dissenters
throughout American history. In the first part of the book she takes
what she calls a "detour through a three-hundred-year history of hate
in white America." The remainder of the book analyzes the case itself
in light of this heritage. Her emphasis is on the personalities of the
two men and on their experiences as immigrants in an increasingly hostile
nation.

H 908. **FRIEDMAN, SAUL S.** No Haven for the Oppressed: United States Policy Toward Jewish Refugees, 1938-1945. Detroit, Mich.: Wayne State University Press, 1973. 315 pp.

Like other works on the subject, Friedman blames State Department officials and Congressional conservatives for much of America's inaction toward Jewish refugees during W.W. II. Friedman also believes that too little attention has been focused on the opposition of organized labor to liberalizing immigration laws; a position they took, he says, because they feared the competition for jobs which immigrants would pose. Another aspect of the subject which Friedman analyzes more closely than past authors is the aborted plan to relocate European Jews in North Africa.

H 909. **FUCHS, LAWRENCE H.** The Political Behavior of American Jews. Glencoe, Ill.: Free Press, 1956. 220 pp.

Although Jewish political behavior in the 18th and 19th century is covered in brief, a majority of Fuchs's work analyzes Jewish political opinions since the administration of Franklin Roosevelt. He asserts that the organizing experience of American Jews' has helped them wield more political power than their numbers should allow, and adds that anti-semitism has consistently mended rifts within the Jewish political community.

H 910. **GAMBINO, RICHARD.** Blood of My Blood: The Dilemma of the Italian-Americans. Garden City, N.Y.: Doubleday, 1974. 350 pp.

Gambino combines scholarly research with his own personal experiences-- experiences that he suggests are typical and illustrative of the Italian-American saga--in this book. He examines the Italian family system, a system that includes all of one's blood relatives, and chronicles the strain second generation Italian-Americans experienced as a result of the differing conceptions of family. Gambino outlines the reasons the immigrants came to America as well as the way American society received them. Attention is paid to the transplantation of the prejudice of the Northerners toward the Southerners as well as to the anti-Italian "fever" that raged among native Americans. Chapters are devoted to the images of the Italian-American male and female, the Italian-American conception of sexuality, the role of religion, and the role of education. Gambino also studies the problem of the Mafia image and ends with an examination of what it means to be an Italian-American in today's U.S.

H 911. **GAMBINO, RICHARD.** Vendetta: A True Story of the Worst Lynching in America, the Mass Murder of Italian-Americans in New Orleans in 1891, the Vicious Motivations Behind It, and the Tragic Repercussions That Linger to This Day. Garden City, N.Y.: Doubleday, 1977. 198 pp.

Gambino argues that the lynching of eleven Sicilians accused of murdering the New Orleans police chief was part of a conspiracy by the city's elite to intimidate upwardly mobile Italians and other minorities who challenged the city's political machine and conservative rule. Anti-Italian prejudices in the city, which Gambino insists still linger, contributed to the lynching.

H 912. **GARCIA, JUAN RAMON.** Operation Wetback: The Mass Deportation of Mexican Undocumented Workers in 1954. Westport, Conn.: Greenwood Press, 1980. 268 pp.

Undocumented Mexican workers seeking jobs after W.W. II created social and economic pressures that politicians sought to relieve through government action. By 1954 the Federal government had launched a program to address the issue through deportation, repatriation, or "voluntary" departure. In the final analysis, however, Operation Wetback, as it was called, failed because it was a stopgap measure serving only to irritate relations between Mexico, the U.S., and Hispanic-Americans.

H 913. GARTNER, LLOYD P. History of the Jews of Cleveland. Cleveland,
    Ohio: Western Reserve Historical Society, 1978. 385 pp.
Although Gartner's work focuses upon Jewish life in Cleveland, it consciously attempts to relate events in Cleveland to Judaism throughout
America. He examines Jewish economic and cultural life most closely, providing copious statistics to support his contentions. Immigration and
its ramifications for the Cleveland Jewish community are given close scrutiny, for Gartner feels that the continual arrival of European Jews throughout the 19th and 20th centuries has been the characteristic which has
most shaped American Judaism.

H 914. GERLACH, RUSSEL L. Immigrants in the Ozarks: A Study in Ethnic
    Geography. Columbia: University of Missouri Press, 1976.
    206 pp.
Gerlach provides a detailed mapping of the various ethnic groups in the
rural Ozark highlands of Missouri. By concentrating on the German groups
who comprised about 80% of the European-based ethnic groups in the region
and comparing their patterns of land usage, population growth, settlement,
and occupation with the other rural Ozark ethnic groups, Gerlach discovers
that different ethnic groups created different landscapes. He further
concludes that the German groups proved more resilient than the smaller
ethnic groups in resisting assimilation and, consequently, affected rural
Ozark geography more profoundly than did other immigrants.

H 915. GIBSON, FLORENCE E. The Attitudes of the New York Irish Toward
    State and National Affairs, 1848-92. New York: Columbia Univer-
    sity Press, 1951. 480 pp.
Three major themes dominated Irish-American attitudes in the last half
of the 19th century. First, Irish immigrants brought strong anti-British
feelings with them, a trait compatible with the poor Anglo-American relations of the 19th century. Second, most Irish tended to join the Democratic Party and made it their vehicle to involvement in local and national
politics. Third, their loyalty to the Roman Catholic Church transformed
that institution into an Irish-dominated one. For most of the period
Gibson studies, the American-Irish were militant and radical regarding
Irish independence, yet conservative on most American domestic issues.

H 916. GLANZ, RUDOLF. Jew and Irish: Historic Group Relations and Immi-
    gration. New York: Waldon Press, 1966. 159 pp.
Glanz's study compares and contrasts the circumstances surrounding the
immigration of both groups, and how these circumstances affected their
behavior upon arrival. Most of the conflicts between the two groups in
the mid-19th century are ascribed primarily to competition between Irish
and Germans, not Irish and Jews. Later on, the East European Jews and
the Irish are portrayed forming close political bonds. The place of the
Jew and Irish in native American folklore and humor is contrasted, as
is the depiction of the Jews in the Irish press.

H 917. GLANZ, RUDOLF. The Jewish Woman in America: Two Female Immigrant
    Generations, 1820-1929. New York: KTAV, 1976. 213 pp.
Glanz begins his study with a look at the women of the German Jewish immigration. Social life and communication are covered in the next chapter,
while social mores, style, fashion, and etiquette are also examined.
Family problems, including marriage and divorce patterns, are treated,
as are the educational opportunities for German Jewish women. While German
Jewish women advanced through education, Glanz argues that Russian women
relied on the industrial opportunities of America to advance their status
within the Jewish community. Finally, Jewish women's involvement in the
Women's Rights Movement is discussed.

449

H 918. GLANZ, RUDOLF. The Jews of California: From the Discovery of
         Gold until 1880. New York: Waldon Press, 1960. 188 pp.
Glanz portrays the special conditions which Jews faced when migrating
to California with the other Forty-Niners. Glanz is primarily concerned
with providing documentation of Jewish life in early California, and he
admits that little interpretation is provided. The founding of the first
synagogues in California is documented. The rise of the Jewish communities in San Francisco and Sacramento is described, as is the role of Jewish
merchants and traders in the mining camps. Life in the Northern California
mining country is compared with that of the Jews who settled in Southern
California.

H 919. GLANZ, RUDOLF. Studies in Judaica Americana. New York: KTAV,
         1970. 407 pp.
Among the topics covered in this collection of essays are early Jewish
peddling in America, German Jewish life in 19th-century New York City
and the rise of the Jewish club in the U.S. Also treated is the Jewish
social condition as seen by the "muckrakers," the Rothschild legend, and
the place of Jews in 19th-century American humor. Another chapter examines
Jews in the literature of German Americans, while another compares Jewish
and Chinese immigration. Finally, source material on Jewish immigration
to America from 1800 to 1880 is discussed.

H 920. GOLAB, CAROLINE. Immigrant Destinations. Philadelphia: Temple
         University Press, 1977. 246 pp.
Golab's book is divided into two parts. In the first section, the author
discusses the Atlantic economy and the movement of rural peoples to industrializing cities in Europe and the U.S. Golab argues that the migratory
experience influenced the destinations and behavior of newcomers and
stresses the impact of the cultural heritage of immigrant groups (especially
the Polish immigrants she has studied) on patterns of settlement and adjustment. In the second section, she focuses on the experience of Polish-
Americans. Concentrating on community institutions, she maintains that
Poles substituted the urban neighborhood for the urban village.

H 921. GOODMAN, ABRAM V. American Overture: Jewish Rights in Colonial
         Times. Philadelphia: Jewish Publication Society of America,
         1947. 285 pp.
Goodman points out that although the House of Commons granted Jews few
rights in England, they were more willing to grant them rights in the
Colonies, probably in the hope of promoting settlement there. Special
attention is given to Rhode Island, and the manner in which Roger
Williams's liberal influence helped the Jews while his influence persisted.
This situation is compared with that of New York, in which Jews initially
gained their rights with great difficulty from Peter Stuyvesant. The
other colonies are also examined, though in less detail.

H 922. GOREN, ARTHUR A. New York Jews and the Quest for Community: The
         Kehillah Experiment, 1906-1922. New York: Columbia University
         Press, 1970. 361 pp.
Goren is concerned with the struggle of New York Jews to preserve their
ethnic identity and provide a measure of personal security through the
establishment of group institutions. The main focus is on the efforts
of New York Jews to establish a comprehensive communal structure in the
second decade of the 20th century. These Jews envisioned a democratically
governed polity which would unite the city's Jewish population, utilize
its intellectual and material resources, and build a model ethnic community.
This in turn was to ease the adjustment of the Jewish immigrant and direct
their Americanization. After ten years, however, this organization, known
as the Kehillah Experiment, began to decline. The story of its brief
existence is the content of Goren's book.

H 923. **GREELEY, ANDREW M.** That Most Distressful Nation: The Taming of the American Irish. Chicago: Quadrangle Books, 1972. 281 pp.
That Most Distressful Nation discusses the assimilation of the American Irish. Greeley recounts the historical background of Irish Americans, their transferred family, community, and religious institutions, their structural assimilation into American institutions, their achievements and their failures. According to the author, the current status of the American Irish is largely attributable to their economically stimulated migration (the result of the Potato Famine in the mid-19th century) and the state of American society at the time. "The legitimation of ethnicity came too late for the American Irish," Greeley concludes. "They are the only European immigrant group to have overacculturated. . . . The WASPS won the battle to convert the Irish into WASPs just before the announcement came that permanent peace had been made with ethnic diversity."

H 924. **GREENE, VICTOR.** For God and Country: The Rise of Polish and Lithuanian Ethnic Consciousness in America, 1860-1910. Madison: State Historical Society of Wisconsin, 1975. 202 pp.
Greene contends that among the various immigrant groups whose ethnic consciousness evolved into a new understanding of their native lands once they had arrived in America, the Poles and Lithuanians are outstanding examples. These two groups first entered the U.S. in the mid-19th century without strong ethnic feelings or political interests. After several decades, Greene notes a decisive shift. By W.W. I both groups supported an independent Poland and Lithuania. Greene concludes that the process of ethnicization took place after arrival in the U.S. Finally he offers a hypothesis about the compatability of ethnic awareness and American identity not only for Poles and Lithuanians but for all immigrant groups which experienced a similar transformation.

H 925. **GRINSTEIN, HYMAN B.** The Rise of the Jewish Community of New York, 1654-1860. Philadelphia: Jewish Publication Society of America, 1945. 645 pp.
In studying American Jewish life before the Civil War, Grinstein draws several conclusions. First, he believes that American democratic spirit had a profound affect on the character of American Judaism, because that spirit broke down the barriers which had separated the social classes within the Jewish community. Grinstein also holds that the belief in "liberty" so prevalent in America helped justify dissent within the Jewish community. This allowed the frequent "secessions" from established synagogues to take place, which Grinstein believes led to the anarchy he finds within the New York Jewish community of the 1820s and 1830s. The disappearance of "excommunication" from Jewish religious practice in America is said to have hastened the "chaos" which Grinstein chronicles.

H 926. **GRISWOLD del CASTILLO, RICHARD.** The Los Angeles Barrio, 1850-1890: A Social History. Berkeley: University of California Press, 1979. 217 pp.
"Between 1848 and 1900 . . . the Spanish-speaking peoples of the Southwestern United States changed from a Mexican frontier society into an ethnic group marginal to both Mexican and Anglo-American cultures," according to the author. Using the methodology of the New Urban History, he studies 19th-century Los Angeles, when the city changed from being Mexican to American, with Mexicans subsequently living in Sonora Town, a Los Angeles barrio. The main theme of this work is the economic, familial, societal, and geo-political metamorphosis of Mexican-American culture.

H 927. GUMINA, DEANNA PAOLI. The Italians of San Francisco, 1850-1930.
New York: Center for Migration Studies of New York, 1978.
224 pp.
In this bilingual edition, Gumina focuses on the Italian-American community
in San Francisco from 1850 when California was admitted to the Union,
until 1930 when the community began to lose its cohesiveness as a result
of the rise of Fascism and the growing independence of the younger generation. She looks at the community from the point of view of the first
generation of Italian migrants and asserts that while these migrants were
devoted to the progress of the state and were highly successful in the
fishing industry and agriculture, their main goal was to remain Italian.
They were slow to become Americanized, celebrating their own holidays,
reading their own newspapers and periodicals, and attending their own
variety theater.

H 928. GUROCK, JEFFREY S. When Harlem Was Jewish: 1870-1930. New York:
Columbia University Press, 1979. 216 pp.
Harlem was the second largest Jewish community in the U.S. by 1910. Unlike
the Lower East Side, Harlem was populated with the exceptional immigranta--
the skilled worker, the shopkeeper, the professional businessman, and
the building trades worker. This contradicts the "Chicago School" theory
that immigrant migration from one area to another reflects economic advancement and abandonment of the ghetto culture. Harlem, in fact, was at once
a primary and secondary area of settlement. This distinctive difference
from the Lower East Side made Socialism less influential and successful,
and produced an elite that tried to assimilate and still retain Judaic
culture, usually through the Talmud Torah movement. For the second generation Jews, however, it was the synagogue that emerged as the institution
to reach out and retain their Jewish identity. Gurock minimizes the differences between orthodox and conservative Jews, arguing that cooperation
between the groups was typical prior to 1930. Divisions thereafter were
not the culmination of years of conflict, but an end to cooperation.
After 1920 Jews began leaving Harlem for Washington Heights and the West
Side, not because of the rising black population but because better housing
was available in other communities.

H 929. HALPERIN, SAMUEL. The Political World of American Zionism.
Detroit, Mich.: Wayne State University Press, 1961. 431 pp.
Halperin's work traces the growth of pro-Zionist opinion among Americans
in the first half of the 20th century. He describes the ideological barriers which separated the various factions of organized Judaism at the
beginning of the century, but then argues that the political issues of
the 1920s and 1930s, even those which had little to do with religion,
were able to unite Conservative, Reconstructionist, Reform, and Orthodox
Jews. He points out that the only organized groups that put up any opposition to American Zionism were the Jewish labor unions, and compares
the manner in which pro- and anti-Zionist groups fought for hegemony within
the Jewish community.

H 930. HANDLIN, OSCAR. Adventure in Freedom: Three Hundred Years of
Jewish Life in America. New York: McGraw-Hill, 1954. 282 pp.
Handlin cites a number of factors which he believes most influenced Judaism
in America. The diversity of America, according to Handlin, made seeking
diverse positions within the Jewish community more acceptable, and thus
made American Jews seem greatly divided when compared to their European
ancestors. Although this situation led to "anarchy" in the 18th and 19th
centuries, by the 20th this experience set a precedent for freedom of
action which was unthinkable in European Jewish communities. Handlin
sees the period from 1890 to 1941 characterized primarily by Jewish reaction to anti-semitism, and he sees the improving reception of the Zionist
movement over this period as the result.

452

H 931. HANDLIN, OSCAR. Boston's Immigrants, 1790-1880. 1941; Rev. ed.
New York: Atheneum, 1968. 382 pp.
Handlin's book was originally published in 1941 as Volume 50 of the Harvard
Historical Studies series, and covered Boston's immigration through 1865;
the revised edition continues the coverage to 1880. Handlin is primarily
concerned with the Irish, Boston's largest immigrant group, and he attempts
to answer such questions as: how the Irish happened to come to Boston,
why they stayed, what hardships they endured, what problems they created,
and the place the Irish eventually came to claim in the city. Handlin
shows that the Irish did not fit the occupational pattern of Boston and
instead provided a large pool of cheap labor which in turn intensified
such problems as vice, crime, disease, and poor housing conditions. The
Irish created conflict in the intellectual realm because they were Roman
Catholic and Boston, on their initial arrival, was a Protestant city.
The Boston Irish opposed social reform and President Lincoln, and were
allied to slavery, the Democratic Party, and the South.

H 932. HANDLIN, OSCAR. The Newcomers: Negroes and Puerto Ricans in
a Changing Metropolis. Cambridge, Mass.: Harvard University
Press, 1959. 171 pp.
In looking at New York City and a seventeen-county area surrounding the
city, termed the New York Metropolitan Region, Handlin attempts to dispel
the notion that there is no historical context in which to view the problems of urban life facing blacks and Puerto Ricans. Rather, these
ethnic groups constitute the most recent of a long series of newcomers.
New York had historically benefitted from European immigration--which
provided the large, unskilled labor force needed for urban growth. Social
disorders followed this growth, but earlier immigrants had overcome these
disorders through the capacity to expand and the opportunities resulting
from such expansion. However, the progress of blacks and Puerto Ricans,
as the most recent newcomers, has been impeded by color prejudice. Handlin
predicts, nevertheless, that they can overcome this obstacle through the
development of communal institutions and ethnic neighborhoods at various
income levels, by amelioration of prejudice, by a continued need for cheap
labor, and through a greater reliance upon governmental agencies than
their predecessors had known.

H 933. HANDLIN, OSCAR. The Uprooted: The Epic Story of the Great Migrations that Made the American People. 1951; Rev. ed. Boston:
Little, Brown, 1972. 333 pp.
The Uprooted is an impressionistic account of the impact of immigration
on the 35 million European men and women who settled in the U.S. Handlin
argues that the process of relocation was tragic: immigrants were forcibly
removed from their stable, cohesive peasant communities, suffered the
indignities and hardships of the transatlantic crossing, and found the
cities of the U.S. where they landed to be harsh and unaccommodating.
Widespread alienation resulted as the social bonds of the Old World were
torn asunder in the New. The revised second edition includes a discussion
of recent immigration history and an updated bibliography.

H 934. HANSEN, MARCUS LEE. The Atlantic Migration, 1607-1860. Cambridge,
Mass.: Harvard University Press, 1940. 391 pp.
This study traces the transatlantic migration of white Europeans from
the time of the first Colonies through the beginning of the American Civil
War. Special emphasis is given to the period after the Revolutionary
War. The author concentrates on the European origins of the migrants,
offers explanations for the movement Westward, and analyzes the effects
on the rate of migration from improved intra-European and transatlantic
communications and transportation. Although he includes some numerical
estimates, Hansen's book is primarily descriptive.

H 935. HERTZBERG, STEVEN. Strangers Within the Gate City: The Jews
of Atlanta, 1845-1915. Philadelphia: Jewish Publication Society
of America, 1978. 325 pp.
Hertzberg studies the adaptation and assimilation of Jewish immigrants
to Atlanta, noting the rapid upward mobility and acculturation of German
Jews arriving in the mid-19th century and the less successful and more
culturally resilient Eastern European Jews coming in the late 19th century.
Ethnic and class differences divided the Jews of Atlanta, but Jews increasingly came together in the 20th century. The self-selection of Jews entering Atlanta favored the ambitious, and competition from less well-educated
black and white Southern migrants also contributed to Jewish success.
The Jews enjoyed public acceptance in Atlanta from the city's elite because
their presence and activities heralded prosperity.

H 936. HIGHAM, JOHN. Send These to Me: Jews and Other Immigrants in
Urban America. New York: Atheneum, 1975. 259 pp.
Among the essays collected in this book is an evaluation of the career
of Abraham Cahan, whom Higham characterizes as a "novelist between three
cultures." Higham also analyzes "ideological" anti-semitism in the Gilded
Age and in the life and works of such later figures as Henry Ford and
Father Coughlin. Another selection treats social discrimination against
Jews from 1830-1930, and another puts American anti-semitism in the context
of the American cultural tradition. The historical tradition of ethnic
pluralism in American thought is also considered.

H 937. HOFFMAN, ABRAHAM. Unwanted Mexican Americans in the Depression:
Repatriation Pressures, 1929-1939. Tucson: University of Arizona
Press, 1974. 207 pp.
Hoffman prefaces his study of repatriation with a chapter-long overview
of their earlier migrations into the U.S. He proceeds to examine the
California experience in detail, paying close attention to the Federal
and local bureaucratic procedures that were employed. The most ambitious
of the organized repatriation plans, according to Hoffman, was pursued
by Los Angeles County. He therefore devotes several chapters outlining
it, as well as the variety of assumptions county officials relied on to
justify repatriation: that treatment of Canadians and Mexicans was comparable; that Mexicans were unassimilable; that they constituted a disproportionate share of relief cases; and that, because nationality was
determined by culture and not by birthplace, American-born children should
be deported along with their Mexican parents.

H 938. HOLLI, MELVIN G. and PETER D'ALROY JONES, eds. The Ethnic Frontier:
Essays in the History of Group Survival in Chicago and the Midwest.
Grand Rapids, Mich.: Eerdmans, 1977. 422 pp.
This collection of nine essays addresses the continuing role of ethnicity
in the culture and politics of the American Midwest. Three essays treat
the problem of ethnic conflict in the Old Northwest: Jacqueline Peterson
traces the clash of the values of Yankee settlers in Chicago with those
of the older multi-racial settlement there; Melvin Holti examines the
triumph of Yankee democracy over French feudalism in early Detroit, and
Hugo Leaming examines the history of the nomadic Indian/poor-white/black
Ben Ishmael tribe. Four essays examine the formation of ethnic communities
in Chicago, and a final essay by Arnold Hirsch is an analysis of the black
protest over housing discrimination in Chicago after W.W. II.

H 939. HOWE, IRVING. World of Our Fathers. New York: Simon & Schuster,
1976. 714 pp.
This work, which became a national best-seller in 1976, is a social history of the East European Jews' journey to America and "the life they
found and made" there. Howe traces the vast migration of East European
Jewry in the late 19th century and discusses the settlement patterns and

development of the Jewish community in the U.S. He offers a detailed picture of life in the ghetto, of early Jewish enterprise, and of occupational and economic adjustment. He describes the lives of the early immigrants, their education and acculturation, their involvement in American radical politics, and the responses of Americans to these new immigrants. Howe also examines the dynamics of Yiddish culture in America through Yiddish literature, theater, press, and academe. Finally, he analyzes the dispersion and assimilation of the Jewish people into all facets of the mainstream of American life.

H 940. HUNDLEY, NORRIS, Jr., ed. The Chicano. Santa Barbara, Calif.: Clio Books, 1975. 168 pp.
The work is a collection of essays on selected aspects of Mexican-American history, with an emphasis on the 20th century. Hundley, while stressing the need for ethnic minority groups to discover their own history rather than having the dominant culture write it for them, attempts a rapprochement between the "insider's" view and the "outsider's" view of Mexican-American history. Essays discuss such topics as the formative years of Carlos Eduardo Castaneda; a general assessment of Mexican-American history; southern Colorado in the late 19th century; the Pacific Electric strike of 1903; the 1931 Federal Deportation drive; and Mexican life in Gary, Indiana during the Depression.

H 941. HVIDT, KRISTIAN. Flight to America: The Social Background of 300,000 Danish Emigrants. New York: Academic Press, 1975. 214 pp.
Flight to America focuses on the demographic and economic background of Danish immigrants to the U.S. before 1914. Hvidt argues that immigration to America was an outgrowth of the internal migration from rural to urban areas in Denmark. A large number of rural migrants found little opportunity in older Danish urban centers and hence left their homeland for the U.S. Most immigrants were between ages sixteen and twenty-four, or over forty; a majority were men; and an increasing number by 1900 migrated individually. Over two thirds of Danish immigrants came from working class occupations. Hvidt broadens the scope of his conclusions by comparing Danish immigration statistics with those of other countries.

H 942. ICHIHASHI, YAMATO. Japanese in the United States: A Critical Study of the Problems of Japanese Immigrants and Their Children. Stanford, Calif.: Stanford University Press, 1932. 426 pp.
Ichihashi's aim is to provide an accurate, objective story of the Japanese immigrants in the U.S. and their children. The Japanese, by virtue of their race, cultural background, and economic status have given the U.S. numerous problems, some assuming diplomatic importance, which have generally been presented to the U.S. public in a biased tone. This book is an attempt to clarify these difficulties. A brief introductory chapter details Japanese migration in general. The main body of the book consists of four parts: Japanese arrival in America; analysis of the facts relating to alien Japanese residents; a historical examination of anti-Japanese agitation; and the so-called "second generation" problems.

H 943. IORIZZO, LUCIANO J. and SALVATORE MONDELLO. The Italian-Americans. New York: Twayne, 1971. 273 pp.
In this study, Iorizzo and Mondello have chronicled the Italian-American experience as an integral part of American history rather than an isolated social phenomenon, showing how it integrated with such major themes as nativism, urbanization, and industrialization. They stress, however, that it is a mistake to view Italian immigration only in terms of the urban experience as this ignores the role of the Italian-American in the settlement of small towns, and on the land. They trace the developments in Italy that led to mass emigration and show how the animosities between

Northern and Southern Italians were transplanted to American soil. Chapters are also devoted to the relationship between crime and the Italian-American, Italian-American religion, and Italian-American fascism. They turn their attention in their epilogue to the outstanding figures of Italian ancestry--including such notables as Fiorello LaGuardia, Enrico Fermi, and Frank Sinatra.

H 944. JENKINS, BRIAN. Fenians and Anglo-American Relations During Reconstruction. Ithaca, N.Y.: Cornell University Press, 1969. 346 pp.
The Fenian Brotherhood, founded in 1858 by Irish revolutionaries attached to the Young Ireland movement of 1848, was an effort by Irish-Americans to instigate a nationalist republican revolution in Ireland. Based primarily in New York, the Fenians set up a government-in-exile, recruited followers, and raised money for a planned invasion to liberate Ireland from the British. The large number of naturalized Irish-Americans and their high rate of political participation made their support for a free Ireland a domestic political concern. After the Fenians failed in an attempted invasion of Canada, British treatment of the prisoners became an election issue in 1866. Secretary of State Seward did not want the Fenians to widen the already existing diplomatic division between the U.S. and British stemming from the Alabama controversy. At the same time, he wanted Irish-American support and believed he had to defend the constitutional rights of naturalized citizens, however bogus the process may have been. Throughout the Reconstruction period, therefore, Anglo-American diplomatic policy was based upon the ultimate desire to avoid war with each other. After 1867, the Fenians' significance declined in North America, but not before succeeding in changing British attitudes toward remedial measures in Ireland.

H 945. JONES, MALDWYN ALLEN. American Immigration. Chicago: University of Chicago Press, 1960. 359 pp.
Jones presents a standard chronological survey of immigration to the U.S. from 1607 to 1960. The author treats in detail the background of European immigrants, the process of immigration, and the transition of ethnic groups to American culture. Jones is especially concerned with the role immigration played in shaping American society and institutions and he examines at length the relationship of immigrants to political movements, westward expansion, and economic growth.

H 946. JORDAN, TERRY G. German Seed in Texas Soil: Immigrant Farmers in Nineteenth-Century Texas. Austin: University of Texas Press, 1966. 237 pp.
Jordan contrasts the agricultural heritage and practices of Texas Germans with those of their Southern-born neighbors and then compares the experiences of Texas Germans and their neighbors in western and eastern Texas environments. Relying on manuscript census data between 1850 and 1880, German-language sources, and travel accounts, Jordan tests the conventional argument that German immigrant farmers were superior to American (Southern) ones. He concludes that the Germans' reputation for superiority derived principally from their own writings and the favorable depictions left by travelers, such as Frederick Law Olmsted, who used the Germans as a foil to criticize slave-based agriculture. In fact, says Jordan, the Germans were no better than their Southern-born neighbors in such activities as gardening, fruit-growing, and milk and butter production, and, indeed, the Germans tried, selected, and adapted readily to Southern or Western crops and customs. Jordan adds that the Texas Germans evinced few, if any, antislavery convictions and that they became Southern in sentiment and culture, as they did in agricultural practices.

H 947.   JOSELIT, JENNA WEISSMAN. Our Gang: Jewish Crime and the New
         York Jewish Community, 1900-1940. Bloomington: Indiana Univer-
         sity Press, 1983. 209 pp.
Crime and the perceptions of crime in New York's Jewish community are
the subjects of Joselit's study. Jewish crime--extortion, pickpocketing,
arson, and prostitution--resulted from the economic pressures of ghetto
life. In the early years of the 20th century, New York Jews denied the
existence of crime, fearful of threatening their place in American society.
By 1912, however, Jews recognized the gravity of the crime problem and
worked to no avail to mitigate it. By the 1920s and 1930s, Jewish crime
began to lose its ethnic particularity as Jews became increasingly acculturated to American society. When Jews moved out of the downtown and
Harlem ghettos, Jewish crime decreased in importance and the community's
concern about criminality likewise diminished.

H 948.   KANTOWICZ, EDWARD R. Polish-American Politics in Chicago, 1888-
         1940. Chicago: University of Chicago Press, 1975. 260 pp.
Kantowicz chronicles the involvement of first- and second-generation Polish
immigrants in Chicago's politics. Throughout their first thirty years
in Chicago, Polish voters found Democrats generally responsive to their
ethnic and working class interests; Poles had little affinity with turn-
of-the-century reform politics. The 1920s marked a transition in Polish-
American politics: assimilated Poles entered the middle class and placed
less emphasis on working-class issues, but simultaneously sought recognition as an ethnic force in city politics. Recognition was, however,
only partially attained because Polish-American politicians did not achieve
the balance between reform and boss politics necessary for success at
Chicago's polls.

H 949.   KELLY, GAIL P. From Vietnam to America: A Chronicle of the Viet-
         namese Immigration to the United States. Boulder, Colo.: West-
         view Press, 1977. 254 pp.
Kelly details the emigration of 130,000 Vietnamese refugees from their
departure from Vietnam in 1975 to their resettlement in the U.S. The focus
is on the process by which the Vietnamese went from being political refugees, many fully intending to return to their homeland, to immigrants,
adjusting to a modern industrial American society. The book is organized
by the chronology of the Vietnamese transition. Part one describes the
refugees, who they were and how they departed Vietnam. Part two is concerned with the refugee camps where the Vietnamese awaited resettlement.
Part three addresses initial Vietnamese integration into the U.S. economy
and the development of a Vietnamese community within the U.S. Kelly concentrates on the "interplay of American policies and Vietnamese responses
to them" and the American management of Vietnamese immigration.

H 950.   KESSNER, THOMAS. The Golden Door: Italian and Jewish Immigrant
         Mobility in New York City, 1880-1915. New York: Oxford Univer-
         sity Press, 1977. 224 pp.
Kessner compares the Italian and Jewish immigrant experience in New York
during the peak period of immigration to determine how each group fared
in adapting to American life and in achieving economic mobility. By studying each group's rates of literacy and pre-emigration work experiences,
aspirations, occupational structure, education, contributions of spouses
and children to the household, individual and inter-generational career
mobility, length of residence in the U.S., residential patterns in the
city, and ghetto economy and society, Kessner learns that both Italians
and Jews experienced significant upward mobility and had higher rates
of mobility than immigrants in other urban settings.

H 951. KORN, BERTRAM W. American Jewry and the Civil War. Philadelphia:
        Jewish Publication Society of America, 1951. 331 pp.
Korn's subject is the experiences of the American Jewish community during
the Civil War. It is an effort at "group biography," the primary interest
of the author being the efforts, during this war, to extend freedom and
to lift restrictions based on race or religion, thereby granting all minority Americans their due respect and liberty. The Jews in both the Confederate and Union war efforts; the attitudes of Jewish leaders on secession, war, and peace; and opinions on slavery are all explored. In addition, Korn examines the reality of equal treatment before the law, prejudices against the Jews during the war, Abraham Lincoln's attitude toward
American Jews, and the effect of the war on the development of the American
Jewish community. Finally, Korn considers whether the Jewish community
has changed significantly since the Civil War years.

H 952. LaGUMINA, SALVATORE J. and FRANK J. CAVAIOLI. The Ethnic Dimension
        in American Society. Boston: Holbrook Press, 1974. 364 pp.
LaGumina and Cavaioli contend that the American experience can be understood through the study of American immigrant and ethnic minorities.
Toward this end, they have compiled this reader, the purpose of which
is to "fathom the American social fabric through the perspectives and
experiences of American ethnic groups." The primary emphasis is on the
era of New Immigration, dating from the last quarter of the 19th century,
but earlier periods are covered to lend continuity to the idea of ethnic
presence and influence in American history. Official U.S. immigration
policy, as it has reacted to and reflected ethnic biases, is also treated.
Selections are based both on primary and secondary sources.

H 953. LEVINE, EDWARD M. The Irish and Irish Politicians: A Study of
        Cultural and Social Alienation. Notre Dame, Ind.: University
        of Notre Dame Press, 1966. 241 pp.
Levine analyzes and explains the American phenomenon of the "Irish politician." As a result of their oppression by the English, the Irish lived
in an alienating environment. These conditions were replicated upon
arrival in the U.S., where they were an intensely disliked and distrusted
alien, lower-class Catholic minority in a middle-class Protestant society.
The Catholic-Protestant cleavage made them pariahs. The parish and parochial school became the institutionalized symbols of Irish separatism,
both nurtured by Irish Catholicism. The Democratic Party, the one institution that did not spurn them, became the secular extension of their
religious identity. Since the Irish social environment thoroughly blended
politics and religion with daily life, the Irish developed a personalized,
informal style. Identification with "the people" and being popular was
a sharp contrast to the Protestant middle-class norm. The new generation
of Irish politicians, however, is moving away from this alienated working-
class style as more of them are college-educated, married to non-Irish
women, live in middle-class neighborhoods, and retain no meaningful relationship to the Democratic Party.

H 954. LEYBURN, JAMES G. The Scotch-Irish: A Social History. Chapel
        Hill: University of North Carolina Press, 1962. 377 pp.
Three major epochs divide Scotch-Irish history: Scotland before 1610;
the settlement of Ireland after 1610; and migration to America in the
18th century. The Scotch-Irish were part of two major migrations; the
migration to Ulster in Northern Ireland and the migration to the backcoun-
try of Pennsylvania, Virginia, and the Carolinas. At the time of the
Ulster migration, Scotland was experiencing a religious revival. This
was still alive when the Scotch-Irish moved to America and gave them a
unique character which lasts to this day. The Presbyterianism of the
Scotch-Irish was Calvinist in its emphasis on the Old Testament, the denunciation of sin, the disdain for beauty and their belief that they were

the chosen people. Although they were initially called "Irish," the massive migration from the poor Catholic South after 1840 led many to distinguish themselves by employing the term "Scotch-Irish."

H 955. LOEWEN, JAMES W. The Mississippi Chinese: Between Black and White. Cambridge, Mass.: Harvard University Press, 1971. 237 pp.

Loewen reconstructs the history of the Chinese contract laborers brought to Mississippi after Reconstruction to work on cotton plantations and, more especially, the descendants of those laborers who, by 1970, comprised the largest concentration of Chinese in the South. He argues that the almost wholly male immigrant population viewed themselves as sojourners, but many married or entered common-law relationships with blacks and settled in Mississippi. The Chinese abandoned agriculture to set up small businesses in towns that catered to a black clientele. The dual associations with blacks by marriage and business made the Chinese "black" in white Southern eyes. As the Chinese prospered, they tried to gain acceptance by moving away from their black associations. By the 1940s Chinese children were admitted to white schools.

H 956. LUCAS, HENRY S. Netherlanders in America: Dutch Immigration to the United States and Canada, 1789-1950. Ann Arbor: University of Michigan Press, 1955. 744 pp.

This is a comprehensive study of Dutch immigration from the earliest settlements in New Netherlands to the mid-20th century. During the early national period, Dutch immigration was slow and small in number. After 1846, immigration increased as religious disputes between King William I and the Dutch church produced dissenters who migrated to the U.S. in search of religious freedom. Most immigrants went to the Midwest in search of cheap land. Whether Protestant or Catholic, religion determined the pattern of settlement and by 1875 there were substantial Dutch communities in Michigan, Iowa, Wisconsin and Minnesota. Settling as compact but rural groups, the Dutch were slow to assimilate. Yet, by the 20th century, the Dutch influence was less substantial than other immigrant groups as a result of their dispersal across the U.S.

H 957. LUEBKE, FREDERICK C. Bonds of Loyalty: German-Americans and World War I. DeKalb: Northern Illinois University Press, 1974. 366 pp.

Luebke challenges conventional histories of German America which ignore the different types of ethnic identity within the German-American community. He argues that "Teutonic unity" was largely a product of the German language press and German fraternal associations but represented only one segment of German-American thought and culture. "Club" Germans, continues Luebke, purveyed the idea of a Teutonic unity and sought to implant high German culture in America. "Church" Germans, who placed religion over culture, did not share the club Germans' goals, rather using the German language and customs to prevent heresy and declension within their churches. Americans, concludes Luebke, failed to appreciate the distinctions among German Americans and regarded the more visible and vocal club Germans' dual loyalty to Germany and the U.S. as the norm in German America. In the angry atmosphere of W.W. I, anti-German feelings in the U.S. lashed out at German Americans regardless of their ties to German culture and hastened the demise of any common, national German America.

H 958. LYMAN, STANFORD, ed. The Asian in the West. Reno: University of Nevada Press, 1970. 168 pp.

Lyman has assembled nine essays by the behavioral and historical faculty of the University of Nevada System. Individually they are historical or sociological in emphasis. Collectively they seek to contribute to Asian-American studies and to the broader topic of ethnic relations in the American West. Topics discussed include marriage and the family, Chinese secret societies and community and youth organizations, Asians in America, and the contribution of Asians to American society.

H 959. MANGIONE, JERRE. Mount Allegro: A Memoir of Italian-American
        Life. Boston: Houghton Mifflin, 1943. 285 pp.
In telling the story of his family life (the names are changed), Mangione presents the reader with a description of immigrant Sicilian life in Rochester, New York and, more generally speaking, a portrait of the Italian-American experience in America. He gives an account of successful and failed ventures in upward mobility as well as the concurrent beginnings of acculturation and, in some cases, assimilation. The emphasis is on process and not on the end result. This book represents the committing of the oral tradition to paper.

H 960. MARCUS, JACOB RADER. Early American Jewry. 2 vols. Philadelphia:
        Jewish Publication Society of America, 1951, 1953. 895 pp.
Marcus bases this study of American Jews in the Colonial and early national periods chiefly on personal letters from the time, thus seeking to capture everyday Jewish life and "the spirit of the age." He explores the impact of environment and events, especially the American Revolution, on individual Jews, their religious outlook, and their political goals. The two volumes study Jewish life settlement by settlement, ones in New York, New England, and Canada in the first volume; and those in Pennsylvania and Georgia in the second. The work closes, however, with an overview of the small, predominantly urban and commercial American Jewish community. The survey considers the nature of immigration and acculturation, religious and community organization, as well as cultural, political and economic activity. Marcus refers to these years as the Sephardic period of American Jewry, asserting that, though those of Spanish-Portuguese origin represented the majority of American Jews only through the early 18th century, their religious culture dominated the community well into the 19th.

H 961. MARCUS, JACOB RADER, ed. Critical Studies in American Jewish
        History. 3 vols. New York: KTAV, 1971. 929 pp.
This work consists of scholarly articles reprinted from the journal of the American Jewish Archives. The essays in the first two volumes deal with aspects of Jewish life and with prominent Jewish citizens from Colonial times through the beginnings of the 20th century. Topics discussed include the antebellum immigrants, the Jewish arts, and Jews in America's Westward migration. The third volume covers the decades since the beginning of the mass immigration of Eastern European Jews at the end of the 19th century. Subjects and personalities addressed include Jewish radical and reform efforts, Zionism in America, Justice Louis Brandeis, and the Leo Frank case. The collection closes with Marcus's 1964 essay "Major Trends in American Jewish Historical Research."

H 962. McCAFFREY, LAWRENCE J. The Irish Diaspora in America. Bloomington:
        Indiana University Press, 1976. 214 pp.
McCaffrey argues that Irish-American identity and culture derive from the interaction of Irish, British, and American forces on both sides of the Atlantic. He identifies Anglicization and Romanization as the principal influences on Irish character and history, relating the loss of Gaelic culture to Irish political nationalism after the English conquest, the Great Famine, the Catholic Church, and 19th-century Irish emigration, on the one hand, and to American nativism, Irish-American politics, the American Catholic church, and Irish nationalism in America, on the other hand. McCaffrey links Irish nationalism in both Ireland and America to historical European liberalism and contemporary struggles for national liberation and rejects the stereotype of Irish-Americans as political conservatives. In essaying contemporary Irish-American culture, however,

he concludes that the Catholic parochial school system and social mobility among Irish-Americans have significantly eroded Irish identity.

H 963. McWILLIAMS, CAREY. The Mexicans in America: A Students' Guide to Localized History. Edited by Clifford L. Lord. New York: Teachers College Press, 1968. 32 pp.
McWilliams offers a brief survey of the history of Mexican-Americans (Hispanos) in the American Southwest, from the settling of the area by the Spanish in the 16th century down to the present day. Geographic similarity between, and the history of Spanish domination of, Mexico and the American Southwest renders Mexican immigrants unique from European immigrants. The mass immigration of the early 20th century resulted largely from "pull" factors in the U.S., in which the expanding economy created many opportunities in the railroad, mining, sheep, and cattle industries, and later in cotton and agriculture. However, the recent Mexican "problem" and the disadvantaged status of Hispanos, are due to specific historical circumstances, not to alleged Hispanic inferiority. Finally, McWilliams says Hispanos have made great advances in social and economic status, and have gained national recognition in their fight for equality in America.

H 964. McWILLIAMS, CAREY. North from Mexico: The Spanish-Speaking People of the United States. Philadelphia: Lippincott, 1949. 324 pp.
This narrative spans four centuries, from the implantation of Spanish culture into Mexico and the Southwestern U.S. during the 16th century, to the establishment of nuclear research laboratories in New Mexico during the 1940s. Though essentially chronological, the socio-economic character of 20th-century Mexican Americans is addressed throughout, and thus portrayed against the historical backdrop of (1) the Spanish "fantasy heritage" that disparaged Mexican and Indian ancestry; and (2) the two "defeats" that dominate Mexican-American consciousness: the 19th-century conquest of the Southwest by the U.S., and the social subordination of Mexican immigrants during the early decades of the 20th century. McWilliams's primary concerns are to document the limited opportunities Mexican Americans have had for acculturation, and to establish their unique problems as an ethnic minority, which, unlike others within the U.S., shares a common culture with a geographically adjacent population.

H 965. MEIER, MATT S. and FELICIANO RIVERA. The Chicanos: A History of Mexican Americans. New York: Hill & Wang, 1972. 302 pp.
The bulk of this history covers the period following the 1848 Treaty of Guadalupe Hidalgo; however, its three initial chapters discuss the earlier "Indo-Hispanic" and "Mexican" periods, examining the roots of the cultural conflict between Anglos and Mexican Americans. Subsequent chapters detail the loss of land by tejanos to Anglos, spurred by the Texas cattle boom of the 1870s and 1880s; the effects of the 1910 Mexican Revolution; the socio-economic segregation of Mexican immigrants between 1900 and 1930; repatriation during the Depression; union militancy during the 1920s and 1930s; the bracero programs, both during W.W. II and the more extensive one between 1948 and 1964; the development of Mexican-American organizations; and the 1960s Chicano movement. A bibliographic essay is included.

H 966. MEIER, MATT S. and FELICIANO RIVERA, eds. Readings on La Raza: The Twentieth Century. New York: Hill & Wang, 1974. 277 pp.
The editors, drawing on contemporary and secondary readings, attempt to briefly trace the history of Mexican-Americans since 1900. Not intending to present a comprehensive survey, Meier and Rivera touch upon the important and significant events of the period. Their method is chronological as well as topical. They maintain that Mexican-Americans have, collectively, an experience distinct from other immigrant groups in the U.S. Separate sections examine the initial mass immigration (1900-1920); dispersion (1920-1930); repatriation—as Mexican-Americans were forced out

of the U.S. during the Depression; their W.W. II experience; the postwar
period, characterized by increasing Mexican-American labor militancy;
and the contemporary activity and ideology of Mexican-Americans.

H 967. MELENDY, H. BRETT. Asians in America: Filipinos, Koreans, and
East Indians. Boston: Twayne, 1977. 340 pp.
In the wave of 20th-century immigration, the Filipinos, Koreans, and East
Indians (of Bangladesh, Pakistan and India) hold a significant place.
Through a study of these three ethnic groups, Melendy traces motivations
for their emigration and subsequent encounters with white America. Most
Asians, according to Melendy, planned to stay only a short time in the
U.S.; many remained permanently. The alteration of the original plans
of these immigrants is analyzed as is the economic adjustment of these
Asians in America. Contrary to ethnic Europeans in America, the Asians,
in Melendy's opinion, do not see themselves as becoming readily absorbed
into American society. Immigration tables and statistics on Asians in
America are included.

H 968. MELENDY, H. BRETT. The Oriental Americans. New York: Hippocrene
Books, 1972. 235 pp.
This is a survey of Chinese and Japanese immigration. Melendy summarizes
the history and culture of China and Japan before narrating the immigrant
experience. He then describes how the Chinese and Japanese managed to
finance their trips to America; the adoption of anti-Oriental legislation
in the U.S.; the problems these immigrants encountered in American society;
and the economic gains they were able to make despite adverse conditions.

H 969. MILLER, RANDALL and THOMAS D. MARZIK, eds. Immigrants and Religion
in Urban America. Philadelphia: Temple University Press, 1977.
170 pp.
A collection of eight essays, each of which is based on the relationship
between religious beliefs and the ethnic experience in post-Civil War
urban America, comprise this study on immigrants in urban America. Separate ethnic groups in various geographic settings are examined in order
to detail the unique experience of each immigrant group. All the essays
deal with the New Immigration of the late 19th and 20th centuries. Aspects
of the Czech, East European Jewish, Polish, Armenian, and Slovak experiences are presented, as well as those of the Italian, Irish, and German
immigrants.

H 970. MILLER, STUART CREIGHTON. The Unwelcome Immigrant: The American
Image of the Chinese, 1785-1882. Berkeley: University of California Press, 1969. 259 pp.
Miller challenges the views that anti-Chinese attitudes in the U.S.
developed in the late 19th century as a response to the importation of
"coolie" labor and that the prejudice was limited to California and the
American West. Most American traders, diplomats, and missionaries brought
to the U.S. a negative image of China, which reached the American public
through magazines, newspapers, geography textbooks, and travel accounts.
Widely held negative perceptions of the Chinese and fears of a revival
of slavery galvanized American opinion in favor of the 1882 legislation
restricting Chinese immigration.

H 971. NELLI, HUMBERT S. The Business of Crime: Italians and Syndicate
Crime in the United States. New York: Oxford University Press,
1976. 314 pp.
Nelli uses newspapers, local police and court records, and Federal records
to trace the development of Italian-American criminal organizations from
the late 19th century through W.W. II. Nelli argues that Italian-Americans
developed their criminal organizations in response to local American social,
economic, and political conditions because Old World patterns of intimi-

dation and extortion did not transplant well. He further maintains that organized crime served as a ladder of social mobility for Italians and other ethnic groups. As Italians moved into the middle class, other ethnic groups began to gain power in the syndicates.

H 972. NELLI, HUMBERT S. From Immigrants to Ethnics: The Italian Americans. New York: Oxford University Press, 1983. 225 pp.
This book is a socio-historical analysis of Italian Americans. Part I examines the nature of traditional Italian society and culture and the characteristics of Italian immigration prior to 1880. The largest section, Part II, focuses on the period of peak migration during the late 19th and early 20th centuries when the vast majority of Italians entered the U.S. Nelli examines the problems Italians encountered in adapting not only to a new society, but to urban life. Part III is concerned with the emergence of Italian-American consciousness and the post-W.W. II migration from Italy to the U.S. Nelli contends that Italian-Americans are among the most prominent of the American ethnic groups to have participated in an ethnic revival during the 1970s.

H 973. NELLI, HUMBERT S. Italians in Chicago, 1880-1930: A Study in Ethnic Mobility. New York: Oxford University Press, 1970. 300 pp.
Nelli examines the transition of Southern Italian immigrants to life in Chicago. Central to the experience of Chicago's Italians was high residential mobility--few immigrants remained long in areas of first settlement and most moved frequently in search of better housing, neighborhoods, and jobs. Though initially immigrants found limited occupational mobility, Nelli argues that by the 1920s Italians began to advance economically because they recognized the importance of education and participated in commerce, politics, and organized crime. Simultaneously, Italians grew increasingly acculturated to American society. Community institutions, most importantly churches, mutual benefit societies, and the Italian press, facilitated adjustment to life in Chicago.

H 974. NIEHAUS, EARL F. The Irish in New Orleans, 1800-1860. Baton Rouge: Louisiana State University Press, 1965. 194 pp.
Niehaus treats the differences between, and eventual convergence of, the old immigrants and the famine immigrants in New Orleans, but he centers his discussion on the years between 1830 and the Civil War. Niehaus maintains that the Irish were dispersed throughout the city rather than confined to any single area, as often supposed. He shows that Irish Catholics exerted sufficient strength in different areas of the city to gain control over parochial education, to get sermons delivered in English rather than French, and to Americanize the Catholic church. Niehaus concludes that the vast majority of Irish adapted easily to American ways and sought entrance into the host Southern society.

H 975. NOVOTNY, ANN. Strangers at the Door: Ellis Island, Castle Garden, and the Great Migration to America. Riverside, Conn.: Chatham Press, 1971. 250 pp.
Novotny's book is an illustrated work on the ports of entry for immigrants to the U.S. The narrative begins with a portrait of Ellis Island in 1907, covers the history of immigration from 1855 through 1890 at Castle Garden, and proceeds to the early years of Ellis Island. The final chapters are devoted to the "closing door" period from 1914 to 1932, and to the reception of deportees and displaced persons since 1932. Novotny also decribes the living and working conditions immigrants faced in the U.S.

H 976. O'BROIN, LEON. Fenian Fever: An Anglo-American Dilemma. New
York: New York University Press, 1971. 264 pp.
The Fenian Brotherhood, founded by John O'Mahoney in New York in 1858,
and its Irish counterpart, the Irish Revolutionary Brotherhood (later
Irish Republican Brotherhood), were the leading national revolutionary
movements for the mid-19th-century Irish people. The Fenians were the
first such movement in Ireland to be supported by foreign money. Many
Irish peasants believed poverty and emigration were the twin products
of British policy, and that a revolution would resolve these problems.
Fenian leaders James Stephens and O'Mahoney tried to attract support for
their cause in Europe and the U.S. These efforts culminated in two unsuccessful assaults on Canada in 1866 and then several more in Ireland in
1867. Because of well-placed spies in the Fenian organizational structure,
splits within its leadership, and lack of financial and mass support,
the British were able to successfully thwart the Fenian-led revolution.
After the fall of the Fenians in 1867, land reform became the galvanizing
issue for the landless peasantry in Ireland, a movement with greater support from the clergy and consequently more successful.

H 977. O'GRADY, JOSEPH P., ed. The Immigrants' Influence on Wilson's
Peace Policies. Lexington: University of Kentucky Press,
1967. 329 pp.
O'Grady has assembled a cooperative and comparative study of immigrant
groups and their efforts to influence the peace-making policies of Woodrow
Wilson at the end of W.W. I. By studying several ethnic groups, O'Grady
hoped to note both successes and failures of each group to better determine
the actual level of influence such groups had on the peace-making policies.
Ethnic groups examined include the Germans, Irish, British, Italians,
Magyars, South Slavs, Czechs, Slovaks, Carpatho-Ruthenians, Poles and
Jews. The Mid-European Union is also discussed.

H 978. PITT, LEONARD. The Decline of the Californios: A Social History
of the Spanish-Speaking Californians, 1846-1870. Berkeley: University of California Press, 1966. 324 pp.
The story of the winning of the Old American West has been told, almost
by definition, from the viewpoint of the conquerors. Pitt provides a historical corrective by studying the vanquished: the Spanish-speaking population of California after the Mexican War. He maintains that the significance of the process was that the aftermath of the Mexican War was
the first instance, except for the Italians, in which the U.S. defeated
and absorbed an entire culture. He thus tied his case study to the larger
themes of Manifest Destiny and imperialism, nativism, racism, as well
as the worldwide defeat of static, traditional societies by those oriented
toward ideas of technology and progress. It is demonstrated that Californios vacillated in declaring independence from Mexico, and were then
ripe for conquest by the Yankees. Succeeding chapters describe the political, social, economic, and cultural implications of such a thoroughgoing
and systematic defeat. In a minor theme, Pitt relates the historical
experience of California's Spanish-speaking population to its contemporary
situation.

H 979. PRPIC, GEORGE. The Croatian Immigrant in America. New York:
Philosophical Library, 1971. 519 pp.
Prpic presents a history of Croatians in America, beginning with historical
background of the earliest Croatian immigration. The bulk of his study,
however, is concerned with the largest influx of Croatian immigrants
from 1880 onward. Religions, organizations, and the press of Croatian
immigrants are examined as well as the reaction in Croatia to the emigration to America. One section is devoted to Croatian American literature
and scholarly work, while others detail Croatian contributions to American
society in the U.S. military, the arts, education, sports, and other fields.

The book concludes with a section on recent Croatian-American history and future prospects for Croatian Americans. Illustrations, appendices, and a bibliography are included.

H 980. RAPHAEL, MARC LEE. Jews and Judaism in a Midwestern Community: Columbus, Ohio, 1840-1975. Columbus: Ohio Historical Society, 1979. 483 pp.
Raphael tells the story of a community of American Jews which existed outside the great metropolises. Examined are the economic, social, and organizational lives of upwardly mobile German Jews in the mid-19th century; of the more distinct Eastern Europeans in later decades; and of the assimilated second and third generations in this century. Raphael seeks to explore the experience of the more prominent and articulate as well as that of the more anonymous. He thus makes use of traditional sources, such as newspapers, biographies, and institutional records, and of the methods and resources of the new social history, such as statistical description based on census reports, election results, legal records, city directories, and birth and death data. Bespeaking Raphael's attention to detail are the many photos and tables, including, for instance, one of the 1947 batting averages of local ballplayers.

H 981. REISLER, MARK. By the Sweat of Their Brow: Mexican Immigrant Labor in the United States, 1900-1940. Westport, Conn.: Greenwood Press, 1976. 298 pp.
The story of the Mexican worker in the U.S. between 1900 and 1940 was one of incessant racial discrimination and class oppression, argues Reisler. Mexican immigration had been inextricably linked to economic development in the Southwestern U.S. The mass immigration after 1900 was a response to the need for unskilled labor, and Mexicans had little problem crossing the border before 1917. The first restrictive law was passed in 1917, but it went unenforced because of the W.W. I labor shortage, and the policy of "temporary admission" was employed. The 1920s was a period of ebb and flow for Mexican immigration: when the economic outlook was bright, Mexicans were recruited; but when the economy stalled, they were ostracized. Mexican labor continued to predominate in agriculture, but was involved only in the most arduous and lowest-paying of industrial positions. Popular nativist and racist sentiment forced Congress in the 1920s to further restrict immigration, in spite of employers' claims of a shortage of labor. And when the Depression came, Mexican immigrants fared the worst of all in the Southwest: their union movement was weak at best, and the gains made were modest and temporary.

H 982. RIPPLEY, LA VERN J. The German-Americans. Boston: Twayne, 1976. 271 pp.
Rippley surveys the German experience in America from the 17th century through the 20th century, with particular attention to immigration patterns, cultural adaptations, religion, politics, and German reactions to the American Civil War, W.W. I, and Nazism. He includes Russian-Germans in his survey but excludes German Jews. He views the erosion of German-American national identity as a natural concomitant of long residence in the U.S., diverse religious and social traditions among Germans, and responses to international developments.

H 983. ROLLE, ANDREW F. The Immigrant Upraised: Italian Adventurers and Colonists in an Expanding America. Norman: University of Oklahoma Press, 1968. 391 pp.
Rolle breaks with the common historiography of the immigrant experience in his rejection of the view that while immigrants contributed much to the improvement of the nation they were themselves degraded. He turns his attention instead to the immigrant who escaped the Eastern cities, to the immigrant who traveled to and settled in one of the twenty-two

states west of the Mississippi. He shows that the portion of Italian-Americans who did migrate West (approximately 15 to 20%) suffered little discrimination, were readily assimilated, and rivaled the native-born in their social mobility—that these immigrants were upraised, not uprooted. He emphasizes the upgrading function of the American West, the opportunity the frontier provided the individual (whether native or immigrant) for self-betterment.

H 984. ROWE, JOHN. The Hard-Rock Men: Cornish Immigrants and the North American Mining Frontier. Liverpool: Liverpool University Press, 1974. 322 pp.
By the early 19th century, copper mines in Cornwall were the most modern in the world; however, both a deterioration in economic conditions and non-conformist religious ferment within Cornish Methodism helped spur Cornish immigration to the U.S., according to Rowe. His account of Cornish immigrant life revolves around their experiences as lead miners in Wisconsin and copper miners in Michigan between 1830 and 1850, as well as the acceleration in immigration that followed the 1848 discovery of gold in California. The emphasis in this volume is on the vicissitudes of the 19th-century mining industry in the U.S., rather than on the social life of Cornish immigrants.

H 985. ROWSE, ALFRED L. The Cousin Jacks: The Cornish in America. New York: Scribner, 1969. 451 pp.
Rowse's study of Cornish Americans is organized by region rather than by period. He devotes separate chapters to areas where the Cornish settled, and details the history of that settlement, usually through the experiences of prominent Cornish families. Included are discussions of 17th-century settlements in Virginia and New England, with special emphasis on Pennsylvania; the few Cornish families which located in the Southern Colonies; the waves of immigration by Cornish miners to the Great Lakes region, the Northwest, and the Southwest; and the Cornish Mormons in Utah. Rowse concludes with an overview of 20th-century Cornish immigration.

H 986. RUDOLPH, B. G. From a Minyan to a Community: A History of the Jews of Syracuse. Syracuse, N.Y.: Syracuse University Press, 1970. 314 pp.
Rudolph recounts the history of the Syracuse Jewish community from its beginnings in the 1830s through the 1960s. His chronicle encompasses the experience of the first generation, the increasing presence of Russian and Polish immigrants in the late 19th century, and the development of charitable organizations, schools, and religious institutions. Syracuse Jews' role in the larger local community and their reactions to national and international events are touched upon as well. Rudolph bases his study on archival material, literary, and oral sources. His book includes numerous excerpts from manuscripts and newspaper accounts and many photographs.

H 987. SAMORA, JULIEN. Los Majados: The Wetback Story. Notre Dame, Ind.: University of Notre Dame Press, 1971. 205 pp.
According to Samora, the illegal immigration of hundreds of thousands of Mexicans a year to the U.S. poses severe problems for many: the "wetbacks" themselves, their American employers, and the American unemployed who lose jobs to them. A critical chapter in the book, "Through the Eyes of a Wetback—A Personal Experience" traces the entire journey from the swim across the Rio Grande, capture, detention, to the return to Mexico. The author looks at both sides of the problem. He juxtaposes the devastating poverty in Mexico from which these people are fleeing with the threat that they pose to American labor. On the one hand, Samora is sympathetic with the Mexican's plight but on the other, he considers how they effect American communities, public health, welfare, delinquency, and crime.

H 988. SANDERS, RONALD. The Downtown Jews: Portraits of an Imigrant
Generation. New York: Harper & Row, 1969. 477 pp.
Sanders tells the story of first generation American Jews in New York's
Lower East Side by focusing on the life of Abraham Cahan, a Russian immigrant who, as editor of the Jewish Daily Forward, became one of the pillars
of the community. Jewish radicalism, literary life, and labor organizing,
all of which Cahan was in some way involved with, are detailed. The vivid
depictions of elements of American Jewish life from the 1880s through
W.W. I are based on contemporary writings, secondary sources, and Sanders's
conversations with veterans of the era.

H 989. SAVETH, EDWARD N. American Historians and European Immigrants,
1875-1925. New York: Columbia University Press, 1948. 244 pp.
Saveth presents a study of the views of various American historians, most
of whom came from Anglo-Saxon Protestant backgrounds, toward the immigrant
in America between 1875 and 1925. The book is concerned primarily with
immigrants of non-English derivation, and begins with background on historians' attitudes toward immigrants and on the influence of the Teutonic
germ theory of institutional development on late 19th-century American
historians. This theory is in turn compared to aspects of Social Darwinism.
The frontier theme in American historiography and its influence on the
treatment of immigrants by historians is examined, as is the role of the
European immigrant in U.S. political history and the immigrants' part
in American social history.

H 990. SCHOENER, ALLON, ed. Portal to America: The Lower East Side
1870-1925. New York: Holt, Rinehart, & Winston, 1967.
256 pp.
The book offers a portrait of New York's Lower East Side, which was the
first American stopping place so many Jewish immigrants. Schoener has
compiled both period photographs, such as those of Jacob Riis and Lewis
Hines, and descriptions of the community's life gleaned from the New York
daily and Yiddish presses. Photos and text depict the process of immigration, Jewish home and street life, local culture, and the immigrants'
work experience.

H 991. SEMMINGSEN, INGRID. Norway to America: A History of the Migration.
Minneapolis: University of Minnesota Press, 1978. 213 pp.
Semmingsen examines 100 years of the Norwegian-American experience, noting
the social and economic dynamics in Norway which fueled immigration, tracing the immigrants' journey from the fjords of their homeland to the farms
of the American Midwest, and chronicling their adjustment to the U.S.
She notes two periods of immigration: before 1865, when small numbers
of families headed to the U.S. for a variety of idiosyncratic reasons,
and after 1865, when those who left Norway were generally young men seeking
the economic opportunity which was increasingly limited in Norway. Throughout the period of mass migration, Norwegians established strong communities
and maintained their ethnic distinctiveness, but by the 1920s U.S. immigration restrictions and the Americanization of the second generation
weakened ethnic solidarity.

H 992. SHANNON, WILLIAM V. The American Irish: A Political and Social
Portrait. New York: Macmillan, 1966. 484 pp.
Beginning with an overview of Irish history and continuing through the
years of immigration and settlement in the U.S. to the presidency of John
F. Kennedy, Shannon describes the role and impact of the Irish in the
U.S. The underlying theme of the work is the varied and pluralistic experi-
ences of the American-Irish. In politics, Tammany Hall's Al Smith, the
confrontational James Michael Curley, red-baiting Joseph McCarthy, and
Harvard-educated John F. Kennedy represented diverse, yet important parts
of Irish-American culture and ideas during the 20th century. In religion,

this contrast was evident in the careers of liberal clerics like James Cardinal Gibbons, John Cardinal Ireland, and Monsigneur John A. Ryan and their more conservative opponents like Archbishop Michael Corrigan, William Cardinal O'Connell, and Father Charles Coughlin. Even the literature produced by Finley Peter Dunne, James T. Farrell, and Eugene O'Neill evoked controversy from important elements within the Irish community who resented the less-than-ideal manner these writers treated their fellow ethnics in their writing. Shannon tries to explain these contradictions by showing the different ways the Irish adapted to life in America, what aspects of it they rejected, and most importantly what parts they finally accepted.

H 993. SHAPIRO, JUDAH. The Friendly Society: A History of the Workmen's Circle. New York: Media Judaica, 1970. 251 pp.
Shapiro presents a narrative account of the organization which grew out of the Workmen's Circle, a self-help benevolent association established in New York City in 1892. This group introduced large numbers of Eastern European Jewish immigrants into the labor movement. Although the links between the Circle and other labor organizations are not explored in depth, the study does emphasize the significance of this and similar Jewish self-help groups in providing a forum for political dissent. Shapiro stresses the American political system. She explains that the Circle, a national organization by 1900, helped redefine Jewishness in a way which made it relevant to the lives of its members and reconnected with Jewish life many who could not act on traditional Jewish patterns in modern circumstances. Material on the organization's recent support of hospitals, such as New York's Montefiore, and homes for the aged suggests other ways in which the Circle has helped transform traditional Jewish values into forces for social change within society.

H 994. SHAPIRO, YONATHAN. Leadership of the American Zionist Organization, 1897-1930. Urbana: University of Illinois Press, 1971. 295 pp.
Shapiro traces the course of Zionism in America in the first thirty years of the century. Zionism in Europe had emphasized a cultural nationalism and a separate Jewish identity, but in America it was transformed into what Shapiro terms "Palestinianism," which focused on building a Jewish homeland in distant Palestine. Shapiro locates the source of this transformation in groups like the Federation of American Zionists and the Zionist Organization of America, and leaders like Louis Brandeis. "Palestinianism" represented a strategy by which assimilated, socially prominent Jews of German background could assert identity and self-respect in the face of anti-Semitism while not committing themselves to any withdrawal from American society. Shapiro works from documents of Zionist organizations, Yiddish and Hebrew periodicals, the papers of men like Brandeis, and personal interviews.

H 995. SHARFMAN, I. HAROLD. Jews on the Frontier. Chicago: Regnery, 1977. 337 pp.
The American frontier had an erosive effect on all ethnic and religious groups which ventured into it, and it is Sharfman's thesis that the Jews on the Western fringes of America were no exception to this process. No links with past traditions or heritage were available to Jews on the frontier; thus the Jews' role in Western expansion was largely obscured by the Jews' own lack of identity. According to Sharfman, the frontier accelerated this disintegration of Jewish identity in two major ways. First, Jews tended to move West as individuals and were subject to alien pressures without the benefit of group support which would serve to preserve traditional beliefs. Second, men, Jewish and otherwise, outnumbered women on the frontier by a considerable percentage, making marriges outside the Jewish faith common, merging the Jews into the mainstream in the process.

H 996. SHOCKLEY, JOHN STAPLES. Chicano Revolt in a Texas Town. Notre
    Dame: University of Indiana Press, 1974. 302 pp.
In 1963 and in 1969, in Crystal Cty, Texas, Mexican-Americans revolted
against the local government and ousted the Anglos in power. In an effort
to better understand the Chicano movement, race relations and conflicts,
and political change in general in the U.S., Shockley makes a close study
of these revolts, dealing with such questions as: Why did the revolts
occur? How were they carried out? Why did the first fail? And, does
the second seem more permanent?

H 997. SILVERBERG, ROBERT. If I Forget Thee O Jerusalem: American
    Jews and the State of Israel. New York: Morrow, 1970. 620 pp.
This is a study of the role of the U.S. and of American Jewry in the creation of the State of Israel, with emphasis on the 20th-century Zionist
movement. The author synthesizes a wide range of material on the growth
of American Jewry, its various factions, and policies toward the New
Jerusalem as expressed by government policy advisors such as Bernard Baruch
during and after W.W. I as well as the many private and philanthropic
organizations that have supplied political support and funds for building
the modern Jewish state. Although the book is primarily a work in international relations, it reflects a keen grasp of the role of private and
domestic interest groups in shaping U.S. foreign policy.

H 998. SOWELL, THOMAS. Ethnic America: A History. New York: Basic
    Books, 1981. 353 pp.
Economist Thomas Sowell seeks to explain the differences--in income, occupation, unemployment, crime, alcoholism, fertility, business ownership,
and education--among the ethnic groups that make up the "American mosaic."
He devotes separate chapters to the historical experiences of the Irish,
Germans, Jews, Italians, Chinese, Japanese, Blacks, Puerto Ricans, and
Mexicans. He dismisses discrimination as an explanation for the myriad
differences he finds, since "all have been discriminated to one degree
or another," and today the intensity of discrimination "has lessened and
in some respects disappeared." His explanation for the "wide variations
in the rates of progress among American ethnic groups" is cultural; the
distinctive values and attitudes, especially attitudes toward learning,
self-improvement, and work, that each group brought with them have determined their adaptation to this country.

H 999. STACK, JOHN F., Jr. International Conflict in an American City:
    Boston's Irish, Italians, and Jews, 1935-1944. Westport, Conn.:
    Greenwood Press, 1979. 181 pp.
Stack explores the tense inter-ethnic relations in Boston during the Great
Depression and W.W. II. He finds that cultural differences--Jewish economic mobility, Italian economic and political isolation, and Irish political activism--divided ethnic groups throughout Boston's history. The
fiscal upheaval of the Depression increased intergroup rivalry, and most
importantly, each group's differing reactions to the international crises
of the 1930s and 1940s precipitated ethnic conflict. Irish anti-Communism,
isolationism, and association with the Coughlin movement, Italian support
of Mussolini, and Jewish fear of the German threat coupled with a rise
in domestic anti-semitism, aggravated long-standing ethnic tension.

H 1000. SZAJKOWSKI, ZOSA. Jews, Wars, and Communism. 2 vols. New York:
    KTAV, 1974. 1111 pp.
In the first of these two volumes Szajkowski discusses the years during
and after W.W. I and their impact on American Jewish life. Until the
war, American Jews represented "a carryover from European ideologies."
Afterwards, American Jewry came to maturity, taking over the leadership
in world Jewry from a nationally divided European Jewry. With this development, American Jews were beset by accusations, being held responsible

especially for the Russian, German, and Hungarian revolutions. In volume
two, the author examines the Red Scare of 1919-1920 and the raids, arrests,
internments, and deportations which accompanied those years as well as
attacks on pro-Germans, pacifists, and radicals.

H 1001. TAYLOR, PHILIP. The Distant Magnet: European Emigration to the
        U.S.A. New York: Harper & Row, 1971. 326 pp.
Taylor offers a synthesis of histories of the immigration from Europe
to the U.S. from 1830 to 1930. Unlike most surveys, about half of Taylor's
book is devoted to the European background to immigration. He chronicles
the sweeping economic and demographic changes which simultaneously spurred
immigration; the local factors which led to the exodus abroad; and the
perceptions of America which attracted Europeans. Taylor also focuses
on the passage to the U.S. by sail and steam. The remainder of the book
treats the adaption of immigrants to their American environment, including
discussions of immigrant laborers, ethnic communities, and the relations
of newcomers and established Americans.

H 1002. TOLL, WILLIAM. The Making of an Ethnic Middle Class: Portland
        Jewry over Four Generations. Albany: State University of New
        York Press, 1982. 242 pp.
Toll traces the history of Jewish-Americans in Portland, Oregon between
1855 and 1945. Analyzing census data, city directories, death certificates,
school records, and other manuscript material, Toll presents a profile
of the Jewish community and highlights economic opportunity and social
structure. The author also focuses on Jewish social organizations, benevolent societies, and religious associations. Toll's chronological narrative
emphasizes the cultural continuity of Portland's Jews.

H 1003. TOMASI, SILVANO M. Piety and Power: The Role of the Italian
        Parishes in the New York Metropolitan Area, 1880-1930. New York:
        Center for Migration Studies of New York, 1975. 201 pp.
Tomasi details the experience of Italian immigrants with American Catholicism in order to understand the process of adaptation of immigrants in
a new society and the use they made of religious institutions. The Italian
Catholic experience, according to Tomasi, provides evidence of the need
to re-write American church history through the expectations and values
of the people rather than through the biographies of the Church hierarchy.
This study outlines a concept of assimilation which rejects the traditional
theory of total conformity to Anglo-Protestant society and the melting
of cultures into one American culture.

H 1004. UROFSKY, MELVIN I. American Zionism from Herzl to the Holocaust.
        Garden City, N.Y.: Anchor Press, 1976. 506 pp.
Stressing the unique relationship between Israel, the U.S., and American
Jews, Urofsky attempts to explore the roots of this relationship and the
growth and development of the Zionist movement in America. While modern
Zionism was largely discounted in the U.S. prior to 1914, the outbreak
of W.W. I saw a new group of American Jews assume the leadership of the
Zionist Movement. Urofsky contends that this new leadership resulted
in an American Zionism which was "part of and reflective of larger trends"
in American society. The history of this movement--its leaders, successes,
failures and philosophy--within the context of American history, is the
subject of this work.

H 1005. VORSPAN, MAX and LLOYD P. GARTNER. History of the Jews of Los
        Angeles. San Marino, Calif.: Huntington Library, 1970.
        362 pp.
A part of the Regional History Series of the Jewish History Center of
the Jewish Theological Seminary, Vorspan and Gartner's work is concerned
primarily with American Jewry's role in urban communities. This volume

traces the transplantation of European and Eastern American Jewish life to Southern California. Specifically concerned with Los Angeles, the authors document the important cultural, religious, social service, and educational institutions which have developed in the Jewish community since W.W. I, and the maintenance in Los Angeles, as in other urban American centers, of a distinctive Jewish life.

H 1006. WARD, DAVID. Cities and Immigrants: A Geography of Change in Nineteenth Century America. New York: Oxford University Press, 1971. 164 pp.
In this historical geography, Ward examines the changing urban landscape in the 19th century. Between 1820 and 1920 most immigrants in America settled in urban centers, fueling the rapid growth of these areas and the expansion and redistribution of urban populations. Early chapters in the book detail the effects of regional economic growth and migration on American cities. The latter part examines the internal differentiation of urban centers. Ward bases his conclusions primarily upon quantitative and statistical analysis.

H 1007. WITTKE, CARL. The Irish in America. Baton Rouge: Louisiana State University Press, 1956. 319 pp.
Wittke's study is an examination of Irish life in the U.S. from the potato famine of the 1840s to the end of W.W. I. Starting at the lowest rungs of the social and economic ladders in the U.S., the Irish by the end of the 19th century achieved success in a variety of fields. Although politics and the Roman Catholic Church are frequently cited as the obvious examples of this rise to middle-class respectability, Wittke shows the impact of the Irish in business, organized labor, journalism, entertainment, and the popular arts. Wittke emphasizes the continual cultural exchange between Irish immigrants in the U.S. and their countrymen across the Atlantic. This communication was fostered by Irish radicals who were frequently forced to emigrate because of their anti-British activities. Conflict within the Irish community between the radical and more conservative elements, especially the Church, was a continual theme prior to the achievement of Irish independence in 1922.

H 1008. WITTKE, CARL. We Who Built America: The Saga of the Immigrant. 1939; Rev. ed. Cleveland, Ohio: Press of Western Reserve University, 1984. 550 pp.
Wittke presents a broad historical survey of European immigration to the U.S. in three time periods: the Colonial era; the period of Old Immigration; and the New Immigration of the post-1880 years. While most immigrants sought refuge for economic reasons, Wittke emphasizes the belief of many native-born Americans that their nation was "divinely created . . . to give freedom to the downtrodden of the earth." Consequently, Wittke sees the impact of successive waves of immigration upon the American scene and the subsequent interaction of immigrant and American culture as a primary force in American history.

H 1009. WYTRWAL, JOSEPH A. America's Polish Heritage: A Social History of Poles in America. Detroit, Mich.: Endurance Press, 1961. 350 pp.
While presenting a social history of one of American society's more prominent ethnic components, Wytrwal also examines the process of acculturation and presents an analysis of pluralism in American society. After providing a brief history of Poland, the author delves into the life of the Polish family, parish, and organizations, all documented by a detailed historical and sociological study of Poles in America. Case studies on the two largest American Policy organizations, the Polish National Alliance and the Polish Roman Catholic Union, are included.

H 1010. WYTRWAL, JOSEPH A. Poles in American History and Tradition.
Detroit, Mich.: Endurance Press, 1969. 485 pp.
Poles have been present in American history from its earliest origins
and it is Wytrwal's aim in this book to provide a history of this presence.
Included are sections on Poles in the War for American Independence; the
Union and Confederate armies; the Spanish American War; and the World
Wars of the 20th century. Poles as pioneers, as immigrants and as political refugees and exiles of the post-W.W. II era are also examined. The
history concludes with a report on prominent Polish Americans and organizations, from the Polish press, to Poles in athletics and politics. An
extensive bibliography is included.

H 1011. YANS-McLAUGHLIN, VIRGINIA. Family and Community: Italian Immigrants in Buffalo, 1880-1930. Ithaca, N.Y.: Cornell University
Press, 1977. 286 pp.
Using church records, newspapers, government documents, Federal censuses,
foreign-language materials, and oral interviews, Yans-McLaughlin examines
the daily lives of Italian men and women who made the adjustment from
a pre-industrial culture to an urban one. She suggests that immigrant
families served as the principal control factor in immigrant communities
and that the families' retention or modification of traditional culture
guided immigrant responses to new socio-economic conditions. Italian immigrant men suffered underemployment and the women tended to remain at home,
but the families proved flexible and, so, durable in the industrial city.

IX.   BLACK HISTORY

H 1012. ANDERSON, ERIC. Race and Politics in North Carolina, 1872-1901:
The Black Second. Baton Rouge: Lousiana State University Press,
1981. 372 pp.
Anderson attempts to explore the black experience in the postbellum South
by focusing on the Second Congressional District in North Carolina from
the end of Reconstruction until the disenfranchisement of blacks in the
1890s. During the late 19th century, the "Black Second" elected numerous
blacks to local offices and four black representatives to the U.S. Congress.
Anderson analyzes demographic, political, and economic conditions in the
district and traces the decline of black electoral strength which ended
in disenfranchisement.

H 1013. APTHEKER, HERBERT. American Negro Slave Revolts. New York:
Columbia University Press, 1943. 409 pp.
This account was the first fully documented study of slave revolts and
resistance to slavery in the Old South. Focusing on the revolts of Nat
Turner, Denmark Vesey, and Gabriel Prosser, Aptheker contrasts the historical record of slave revolts with the popular belief that blacks did
not resist their servile status. The author argues that uprisings and
plots came in waves. He finds that before 1850 the uprisings were made
up almost exclusively of slaves, with rarely any free black or white participation. It was not until after 1850, the period of greatest unrest,
that Aptheker finds evidence of Southern white participation in the slave
revolts.

H 1014. BERLIN, IRA. Slaves Without Masters: The Free Negro in the Antebellum South. New York: Pantheon Books, 1975. 423 pp.
This discussion of race relations and the plight of free blacks in the
South offers a comparison between the status of free blacks in the upper
and lower Southern states. Examining differences in income, education,

and job skills, Berlin concludes that the free blacks in the Deep South
were allowed fuller lives than those of the states further North. The
book argues that this difference can be attributed to the smaller number
of free blacks in the lower states, and to the tendency of this group
to be lighter-skinned.

H 1015. BERRY, MARY FRANCES and JOHN W. BLASSINGAME. Long Memory: The
        Black Experience in America. New York: Oxford University Press,
        1982. 486 pp.
Each chapter of Long Memory treats a specific theme in black history in
relation to the whole of the Afro-American experience. The book is a
discussion of the obstacles to black participation in American life, and
an analysis of the black reaction to this exclusion. Issues such as segregation and discrimination in politics, education, criminal justice, and
the job market are all analyzed. Protest movements and black nationalism
are seen as part of the ongoing black struggle against oppression. The
authors also devote attention to the role of black churches and the black
family in American life.

H 1016. BLASSINGAME, JOHN W. Black New Orleans, 1860-1880. Chicago:
        University of Chicago Press, 1973. 301 pp.
Blassingame's study focuses on the economic and social life of the blacks
of New Orleans during the Civil War and Reconstruction years. Emancipation,
the author argues, brought significant changes to the black community:
family bonds were strengthened as the patriarchal family replaced the
unstable slave family, blacks agitated successfully for increased educational opportunities for their children, and strong communal institutions
were established. Race relations in New Orleans, while more amicable
than those in other Southern cities, were still overwhelmingly segregationist. Despite discrimination, blacks adjusted successfully to the
city's economy.

H 1017. BLASSINGAME, JOHN W. The Slave Community: Plantation Life in
        the Antebellum South. New York: Oxford University Press, 1972.
        262 pp.
Blassingame combines evidence from slave narratives with psychological
theory to present a revisionist view of slave culture and personality.
He contends that fellow slaves, the black church, and the family were
more important in shaping black behavior than masters and overseers.
Blassingame presents a direct challenge to Elkins's thesis and argues
that most slaves were able to maintain some autonomy under chattel slavery
and resisted white domination. Applying psychologist H. S. Sullivan's
interpersonal theory to slavery, Blassingame finds there were seven possible slave personality types.

H 1018. BOLES, JOHN B. Black Southerners, 1619-1869. Lexington: Uni-
        versity Press of Kentucky, 1983. 244 pp.
Boles offers a broad survey of the experience of blacks in the American
South from the origins of slavery in the 17th century up until 1869.
He argues that blacks have played an integral role in Southern society
almost from the beginning, and that one cannot understand the history
of the region without understanding the history of its Afro-American population. In the first half of the work, Boles traces the historical development of the plantation and of slavery as a system of labor. In the second
half he examines the richness and diversity of black culture during slavery,
and the complex master-slave relationship. Boles concludes with a chapter
on the early Reconstruction, and discusses the difficult transition both
blacks and whites went through in adapting to a new set of social relations.

H 1019. BREEN, T. H. and STEPHEN INNES. "Myne Owne Ground": Race and
         Freedom on Virginia's Eastern Shore 1640-1676. New York: Oxford
         University Press, 1980. 142 pp.
This book focuses on a small group of free black men and women in North-
hampton County, Virginia. Between 1640 and 1676, Anthony Johnson, his
family and other blacks schooled themselves in the laws of the county,
cultivated white patrons, and worked the land. They acquired their freedom,
and owned property. The authors trace this history and argue that it
was not until the slave codes of 1705 that the possibility of a racially
integrated society in Virginia became doubtful.

H 1020. BROWN, LETITIA WOODS. Free Negroes in the District of Columbia,
         1790-1846. New York: Oxford University Press, 1972. 226 pp.
Although 18th-century Washington was characterized by a slaveholding economy, by the mid-19th century Washington, D.C. had a sizeable population
of free blacks. Brown traces the decline of slavery in the District,
focusing upon means of manumission. The nation's capital, because of
its urban setting, offered blacks a degree of freedom unattainable elsewhere in the South. Although racial barriers in the District of Columbia
were as rigid by the 1840s as they were in other Southern cities, the city's
legacy of relative freedom was to continue to offer greater opportunities
to its black population.

H 1021. CARSON, CLAYBORNE. In Struggle: SNCC and the Black Awakening
         of the 1960s. Cambridge, Mass.: Harvard University Press, 1981.
         359 pp.
Carson presents an account of the Student Non-Violent Coordinating Committee (SNCC) from its founding in 1960 to its disintegration in the early
1970s. Central to his study is the intellectual development of SNCC.
The organization's history, he argues, can be divided into three stages.
From 1960 until the 1964 Democratic Convention SNCC emerged as a major
force in the movement for black equality, resulting in a vision of non-
violent change. From 1964 to 1966 there was a period of internal debate
about the organization's future. With the election of Stokely Carmichael
as its head in 1966, SNCC changed its focus to a program advocating racial
separatism. Athough it remained an influential political voice in the
black community through the second half of the 1960s, SNCC dissolved by
1971, torn by internal dissension.

H 1022. CHAFE, WILLIAM H. Civilities and Civil Rights: Greensboro, North
         Carolina and the Black Struggle for Freedom. New York: Oxford
         University Press, 1980. 436 pp.
Chafe places Greensboro's sit-in movement and black activism of the 1960s
in the context of the city's social and political history from 1940 to
1970. Whites in Greensboro, he argues, held an ambiguous "progressive
mystique" that emphasized "civility" in politics and race relations.
This progressivism served as a means of social control and created an
atmosphere of openness that encouraged vocal protest. Throughout the
thirty years discussed, protest had been central to the black community.
The author concludes that the 1960s' protests were not a departure from
tradition for the black community of Greensboro.

H 1023. COUGHTRY, JAY. The Notorious Triangle: Rhode Island and the
         African Slave Trade, 1700-1807. Philadelphia: Temple University
         Press, 1981. 361 pp.
Coughtry has constructed a census of the American slave trade which documents the evolution of slave importation as a speculative commercial experiment begun by a handful of Newport's commercial elite who were actively
involved in foreign trade. Throughout the 1700s, Rhode Island controlled
60 to 90% of American trade in foreign slaves. Although the number transported on Rhode Island ships was only a small part of the total number

of slaves brought to the New World, the study argues that in no other colony did the slave trade play such a significant role in the economy.

H 1024. CURRY, LEONARD P. The Free Black in Urban America 1800-1850: The Shadow of the Dream. Chicago: University of Chicago Press, 1981. 346 pp.

Curry employs a comparative approach to examine the free black experience in the fifteen largest American cities. Free blacks, he argues, found the American dream of equality and prosperity unattainable. Although there was little segregation on a 20th-century scale, black residences were generally substandard and located in poorer neighborhoods. Prejudice was widespread, often manifesting itself in interracial violence. Despite these obstacles, urban free blacks developed a strong sense of community through churches, mutual and fraternal organizations and schools, and gained the cohesiveness necessary to protest discrimination.

H 1025. CURTIN, PHILIP D. The Atlantic Slave Trade: A Census. Madison: University of Wisconsin Press, 1969. 338 pp.

Curtin writes a revisionist account of the North Atlantic slave trade and looks at the countries and "businesses" behind it. Beginning with a review of the literature behind the subject, the author combines modern historiographical research techniques and statistical analysis to better view the situation of slave trading from the 15th through the 19th centuries, and the radical social and political consequences of such an enterprise. Curtin examines slave trading from both sides. Not only was slave-trading devastating to the African population, but it was also dangerous for the traders and buyers as well, for the disease-ridden environment of Africa claimed the lives of half the European merchants, officials, and soldiers sent to man the slave trading posts. Curtin claims that slave trade was central to European economics and not peripheral, as was once believed. Included are extensive statistics regarding the ethnic and geographical origins of slaves, an extensive bibliography, and a linguistic inventory of the native languages spoken by the blacks who were taken into slavery.

H 1026. DAVIS, DAVID BRION. The Problem of Slavery in the Age of Revolution: 1770-1823. Ithaca, N.Y.: Cornell University Press, 1975. 576 pp.

Davis opens his book in 1770 when the French Abbe Reynal called for a "Black Spartacus" to rise up and fight slavery in the New World. This champion for human rights was to be Toussaint L'Ouverture, who led the Haitian Revolution. Davis discusses the American, French, and Haitian Revolutions in this study. Davis also illuminates the role played by the Quakers as leaders and connecting links in a transatlantic Abolitionist network. The study ends in 1823, the year in which British Abolitionists were directing their protest efforts not merely against the slave trade, but against slavery itself in the British West Indies. Within the U.S. the year 1822 witnessed both the Missouri Compromise which extended the physical domain of slavery and the suppression of Denmark Vesey's attempt to lead a slave rebellion.

H 1027. DEGLER, CARL. Neither Black Nor White: Slavery and Race Relations in Brazil and the United States. New York: Macmillan, 1971. 302 pp.

This study compares slavery and racism in America and in Brazil, and finds that perceptions of skin color and of racial type vary between the two countries. Degler contends, for example, that black integration into the mainstream culture and society is more successful in Brazil than in the U.S. Included in this discussion is the status of the mulatto in Brazil, and the acceptance of racially mixed marriages. Also examined is the contrast between the emancipation processes in these two countries.

H 1028. ELKINS, STANLEY. Slavery, a Problem in American Institutional
         and Intellectual Life. 1959; Rev. ed. Chicago: University
         of Chicago Press, 1976. 263 pp.
The four essays collected in this book analyze slavery from an interdisciplinary perspective. First outlining the history of slavery in the
U.S., Elkins moves on to compare American slavery with that of Latin
America. The third essay presents Elkins's well-known argument on the
psychological dimensions of slavery, in which he compares the personality
traits exhibited by slaves with those shown by prisoners held in German
concentration camps in W.W. II. Finally, Elkins argues that it was the
lack of institutional channels in the 19th century that prevented Abolitionists from confronting slavery on a practical rather than merely on
an abstract basis.

H 1029. ENGS, ROBERT FRANCIS. Freedom's First Generation: Black Hampton,
         Virginia, 1861-1890. Philadelphia: University of Pennsylvania
         Press, 1979. 236 pp.
Through an examination of the history of Hampton, Virginia, Engs traces
the black experience in the post-Emancipation era. He begins his account
with several chapters devoted to Hampton during the Civil War, and the
role played by the Union army and the American Missionary Association
during the establishment of the independent black community. The second
section treats the post-bellum Reconstruction, and focuses on the activities
of the Freedmen's Bureau during Andrew Johnson's administration. Engs
then examines the way in which the Bureau's power was undermined by the
Military Reconstruction Acts of 1867. The final section treats the issues
of education for blacks, black property ownership, and social and political
freedom. In particular, Eng focuses on the establishment of the Hampton
Agricultural and Normal Institute by Samuel Chapman Armstrong. Throughout
the study, he documents the conflict between the values of independent
blacks and paternalistic whites.

H 1030. ESSIEN-UDOM, E. U. Black Nationalism: A Search for an Identity
         in America. Chicago: University of Chicago Press, 1962.
         367 pp.
This history of black nationalist movements in America and the ideas associated with them is primarily a sociologial treatise on the Black Muslims,
although it also includes a section on black nationalist movements prior
to W.W. I. The author discusses the Black Muslim movement in the context
of the ambivalence of American blacks toward both race and nation, and
argues that the movement has appealed mainly to alienated, lower-class
urban blacks who are rejected by both whites and middle- and upper-class
blacks. Essien-Udom argues that even though the cult has a vision of
the white man's doom and black supremacy, on a practical level the leaders
of the group are mainly concerned with encouraging both moral reform and
economic accumulation within the black lower classes.

H 1031. FOGEL, ROBERT W. and STANLEY L. ENGERMAN. Time on the Cross:
         The Economics of American Negro Slavery. 2 vols. Boston: Little,
         Brown, 1974. 553 pp.
In this controversial study, Fogel and Engerman maintain that plantation
slavery represented a more rational allocation of factor supplies than
any alternative available at that time, and was a dynamic and efficient
mode of commercial agriculture. Slave plantations were productive and
profitable; the slave plantation system was the most important sector,
they contend, in the rapidly expanding Southern economy in the 1850s.
Slaves themselves showed levels of productivity equal to or exceeding
those achieved by free labor on Western farms or in Eastern factories.
Furthermore, the slaves had as good a standard of living as the free
workers or better. They maintain that the planter-entrepreneurs of the
antebellum South contributed in important measure to the region's economic
expansion in the years immediately prior to the Civil War.

H 1032. FONER, ERIC. Nothing but Freedom: Emancipation and Its Legacy.
Baton Rouge: Louisiana State University Press, 1983. 142 pp.
Foner attempts to re-assert the fundamental radicalism of the abolition
of slavery in the U.S. In an introductory chapter, he applies a comparative approach to the process of emancipation, describing the post-
emancipation experience of blacks in Haiti, in the British Caribbean, and
southern and eastern Africa. In developing this broad framework, Foner
stresses the essential revolutionary nature of emancipation in the U.S.
For a short time at least blacks were able to influence the state apparatus
and use it in their fight with white planters over control of their labor
power. In the third chapter, Foner offers a case study of this interpretation by examining a strike by black rice workers in the rice region
of South Carolina in 1876. Here, black workers utilized their influence
on the state to resist attempts by the planters to assert total control
over their labor. Although blacks were eventually dispossessed of political power, and suffered short-lived gains, Foner maintains that Reconstruction vindicated a revolutionary experiment.

H 1033. FONER, PHILIP S. Essays in Afro-American History. Philadelphia:
Temple University Press, 1978. 244 pp.
In this collection of eleven essays, Philip Foner traces the resistance
by blacks to political inequality and economic injustice from the end of
the American Revolution to the eve of W.W. I. The first essay deals with
aspects of the First or Northern Emancipation, which took place after
the Revolutionary War. The last three essays deal with early 20th-century
black Socialists and the relations between blacks and the Industrial
Workers of the World. Foner's prime contention is that labor is a "house
divided," and that racial unity is the key to both black advancement and
labor progress.

H 1034. FRANKLIN, JOHN HOPE. From Slavery to Freedom: A History of Negro
Americans. 1947; Rev. ed. New York: Knopf, 1974. 548 pp.
Franklin traces black culture to its African origins and examines the
effects of slavery on black life, emphasizing the resistance of slaves
to the plantation system. Franklin continues his broad survey into the
20th century through W.W. II, analyzing the persistence of racism and
the efforts of black leaders to bring about change. He also outlines
the achievements of blacks in literature, in intellectual life, and in
the military.

H 1035. FREDRICKSON, GEORGE. The Black Image in the White Mind: The
Debate on Afro-American Character and Destiny; 1817-1914. New
York: Harper & Row, 1971. 343 pp.
Fredrickson analyzes the development during the 19th century of various
theories used to support racist social policies. He discusses the debate
concerning the colonization or deportation of primarily free blacks to
Liberia as well as the Abolitionist critique toward this antebellum scheme.
The author then delineates the various approaches used to proclaim Negro
inferiority: biblical as well as scientific sources were relied upon.
The idea of full or social racial equality seemed to elude all, says
Fredrickson, although this did not prevent some from advocating political
or even economic equality. The beginning of the 20th century witnessed
the coalescing of Northern and Southern thoughts on race around the concepts of Anglo-Saxon supremacy and the "White Man's Burden."

H 1036. GENOVESE, EUGENE D. The Political Economy of Slavery: Studies
in the Economy and Society of the Slave South. 1965; Rev. ed.
New York: Vintage Books, 1967. 304 pp.
In these essays, Genovese examines the relationships between plantation
slavery and the Southern economic and social structure which that labor
system supported. Genovese maintains that by the mid-19th century, the

South was approaching an economic crisis due to the inefficiency and unprof-
itability of plantation slavery. Slavery prolonged wasteful cotton monoculture, inhibited agricultural reform, and retarded Southern industrial
development. The economic crisis of the South, moreover, caused a social
and political crisis for America as a whole. Plantation slavery supported
in the South a pre-capitalist slave-owning planter aristocracy whose interests were bound up in the slave system. This elite's realization of its
deteriorating economic position, and its refusal to sacrifice its distinctive culture led to efforts to expand slavery into free territory and,
ultimately, to secession and civil war.

H 1037. GENOVESE, EUGENE D. Roll, Jordan, Roll: The World the Slaves
         Made. New York: Knopf, 1972. 823 pp.
Roll, Jordan, Roll is a comprehensive portrait of plantation slavery in
the American South. Genovese focuses on the ambiguities of master-slave
relations, which he defines in terms of "the culture of paternalism."
Plantation slavery was characterized by tension as the slaveholder ruled
as both authoritarian master and benevolent father, to whom slaves often
deferred out of loyalty and/or fear. But the hold of paternalism was
never secure, because slaveholders lived in constant fear of slave uprising,
and slaves continually resisted the power of their masters. Genovese
also offers an analysis of slave religion and its role on the plantation.

H 1038. GILMORE, AL-TONY, ed. Revisiting Blassingame's The Slave Community:
         The Scholars Respond. Westport, Conn.: Greenwood Press, 1978.
         206 pp.
In his 1972 study The Slave Community (H 1017), John Blassingame presented
a reinterpretation of the history of slavery from the perspective of the
slave. In this work, Al-Tony Gilmore has collected critical challenges
to Blassingame's methodology and conclusions. Essays by Eugene Genovese,
Earl Thorpe, and Leslie Howard Owens take issue with the use of psychological theory to explain slave behavior. Other essays treat such issues
as the significance of The Slave Community in public policy debates, the
political aspects of slave culture, and the relation of recent quantitative
research to Blassingame's analysis. A response by Blassingame is included.

H 1039. GOLDIN, CLAUDIA DALE. Urban Slavery in the American South, 1820-
         1860: A Quantitative History. Chicago: University of Chicago
         Press, 1976. 168 pp.
Goldin, who bases her argument on an analysis of Southern urban attitudes
and on a quantitative study of the comparative demand for slaves in urban
and rural areas, concludes that slavery and the antebellum Southern cities
were not inherently incompatible. Urban slavery, she points out, showed
no tendency toward decline in the period before the Civil War. Rather,
it varied directly with the level of slave prices and hiring rates. Goldin
maintains that urban demand for slaves was actually increasing throughout
the period under study, but that it varied. Thus at times of high slave
prices urban demand fell more rapidly than rural demand, a phenomenon
explained by the availability of substitutes for slave labor (in particular
immigrant labor) in the cities. Agricultural slavery was less responsive
to price movements because immigrant labor was not available in rural
areas of the South.

H 1040. GREEN, CONSTANCE McLAUGHLIN. The Secret City: A History of Race
         Relations in the Nation's Capital. Princeton, N.J.: Princeton
         University Press, 1967. 389 pp.
The black population of Washington, D.C., argues Green, remained a "secret
city" from 1790 to the 1950s. This book examines the relations of black
and white in the District of Columbia which preserved the secrecy of the
black community for over 150 years. Black codes which grew increasingly
strict in the antebellum years restricted the activities of the city's
blacks. Even after the relaxation of the anti-black laws during Recon-

struction, blacks continued to suffer discrimination and poverty. Increasing racism and the lack of economic opportunity hastened a decline of the black community before the turn of the century. Green chronicles the oscillations of protest in the 20th century, focusing on black community organizations which attempted to break the race barrier.

H 1041. **GREENE, LORENZO JOHNSTON.** The Negro in Colonial New England, 1620-1776. New York: Columbia University Press, 1942. 404 pp.
Greene's study discusses the Colonial slave trade and status of slaves in all the New England societies and examines how this institution functioned within the Puritan system of beliefs. He looks at the black population, Colonial authority, slave laws and punishments, the slave family, the relationship between master and slave, religious conversion, and freed blacks. Greene contends that for the most part, the status of the black slave in Colonial New England could be compared to the status of the European indentured servant.

H 1042. **GUTMAN, HERBERT G.** The Black Family in Slavery and Freedom, 1750-1925. New York: Pantheon Books, 1976. 664 pp.
Gutman contends that the black family survived slavery and racism with more stability and strength than historians traditionally have believed. His analysis of the black family's adaptations to the pressures of a racist society focuses primarily on the effects of slavery, and he maintains that black families created a domestic realm inaccessible to whites. The book presents data on the family structure of slaves drawn from plantation records and files kept by the Freedmen's Bureau.

H 1043. **GUTMAN, HERBERT G.** Slavery and the Numbers Game: A Critique of Time on the Cross. Urbana: University of Illinois Press, 1975. 183 pp.
In this response to Fogel and Engerman's statistically based analysis of slavery, Gutman challenges the scientific methodology and theoretical underpinnings of Time on the Cross (H 1031). Gutman charges that factual errors, theoretical exaggerations, and quantitative miscalculations were made in the earlier work. According to Gutman's critique, Fogel and Engerman's study suffers because it casts aside historical context in favor of quantitative data.

H 1044. **HARDING, VINCENT.** There Is a River: The Black Struggle for Freedom in America. New York: Harcourt Brace Jovanovich, 1981. 416 pp.
Harding's book is a narrative history of the attempts by Afro-American people to achieve racial equality. This work begins with the trans-Atlantic crossing and ends with the close of the Civil War. Harding views the history of blacks in America as one of struggle against oppression. He concentrates on movements of social change and on those who took part in these protests. For Harding, opposition to racial injustice is symbolized by the "river," which is what he wishes to chart. The various individuals examined are all considered part of the "river." The major focus is on black opposition such as that demonstrated by Frederick Douglass and Martin Delaney.

H 1045. **HARRIS, WILLIAM H.** The Harder We Run: Black Workers Since the Civil War. New York: Oxford University Press, 1982. 259 pp.
Harris traces the struggle of blacks to gain opportunity and equality in the American workplace. He argues that the history of the black worker is the history of discrimination and oppression. Much of his work centers on an examination of racism in a white labor force, the transition of blacks from a rural agricultural to an urban industrial culture, and the organizational efforts of blacks within the labor movement. In addition,

Harris examines the impact of the Great Depression, W.W. II, and the Civil Rights Movement on the black labor force. He concludes that blacks have made only marginal progress, as little has been done to limit the effects of racial discrimination against blacks in employment and income.

H 1046. HERMANN, JANET SHARP. The Pursuit of a Dream. New York: Oxford University Press, 1981. 290 pp.
The dream of which Hermann writes belonged to Joseph Davis, elder brother of Confederate President Jefferson Davis, and to Ben Montgomery, "the most influencial slave" on Davis's plantation. The book traces Joseph Davis's efforts to apply elements of Robert Owen's utopian theory to his own plantation south of Vicksburg, Mississippi. Hermann follows the experiment from its "humane" ante-bellum treatment of slaves through the post-bellum ownership of the plantation by Ben Montgomery and later by his son Isaiah Montgomery.

H 1047. HIGGS, ROBERT. Competition and Coercion: Blacks in the American Economy, 1865-1914. New York: Cambridge University Press, 1977. 208 pp.
According to Robert Higgs, both economic competition and racial coercion determined the material status of blacks in the first fifty years after Emancipation. Competition, he argues, allowed blacks to make economic gains despite the political and legal obstacles to equality they faced. Specifically, a high demand for labor and black mobility prevented white landowners from forming cartels to restrict black contracts. Although the mass of blacks remained poor, their real income per capita rose significantly in their first half-century of freedom, doubling between 1867 and 1900, and tripling by 1915.

H 1048. HOLT, THOMAS. Black Over White: Negro Political Leadership in South Carolina During Reconstruction. Urbana: University of Illinois Press, 1977. 269 pp.
Holt analyzes the social background and voting behavior of black political leaders in South Carolina, the only state to have a black majority-led state legislature during Reconstruction. Holt finds that of the 255 blacks elected to state and Federal offices between 1868 and 1876, about one-fourth had been free before the war. Further, he notes that most black leaders were professionals or artisans, and 65% were literate. Few were sharecroppers or laborers. Holt finds that as a whole black leaders did not make economic and land reforms their highest priority. In fact, the most important leaders frequently failed to act in the interests of share-croppers, tenant-farmers or farm workers, preferring educational reform over agrarian reform.

H 1049. HORTON, JAMES OLIVER and LOIS E. HORTON. Black Bostonians: Family Life and Community Struggle in the Antebellum North. New York: Holmes & Meier, 1979. 175 pp.
The Hortons present a quantitative survey of antebellum Boston's black population. They include data on residence, nativity, occupational status, and literacy as background for their discussion of the family networks and community institutions which shaped the lives of black Bostonians. The family, they contend, was the central unit of the community's social life. Important also were cooperative organizations which responded to the needs of the black population—schools, fraternal societies, benevolent service groups, and black churches. The Hortons argue that these institutions became crucibles for the antislavery movement.

H 1050. HUGGINS, NATHAN I. Black Odyssey: The Afro-American Ordeal in
         Slavery. New York: Pantheon Books, 1977. 250 pp.
Huggins offers an account of the slave experience. He emphasizes the
extent to which the comprehensive world view of the American villager
was disrupted by capture and forced emigration. Further, he recounts
the attempts by blacks to construct new communities and keep alive cultural
traditions in the face of difficulties encountered in America. Slave-
planter relations, life and the struggle for survival in the slave quarters,
and slave accommodation and resistance are also discussed.

H 1051. KATZMAN, DAVID M. Before the Ghetto: Black Detroit in the Nine-
         teenth Century. Urbana: University of Illinois Press, 1973.
         254 pp.
Detroit's black population before the large influx of Southern migrants
to the city in the early 20th century is the subject of Katzman's study.
He argues that caste and segregation defined the status of blacks in the
city, so that by 1900, they were socially, economically, and politically
isolated. The black elite sought to preserve its precarious prosperity
rather than to challenge unjust race relations. Moreover, black
institutions--churches, fraternal organizations, and clubs--divided the
black community by class and prevented group solidarity.

H 1052. KIRBY, JOHN B. Black Americans in the Roosevelt Era: Liberalism
         and Race. Knoxville: University of Tennessee Press, 1980.
         254 pp.
Two themes underlie Kirby's study: the link of white racial liberalism
to the reform policies of the New Deal, and the effect of the New Deal
on black ideas and political activity in the 1930s. Southern interracial
lists had a powerful influence on the Roosevelt administration, and Eleanor
Roosevelt symbolized the merger of the racial liberalism of the 1930s
with economic reform. Blacks generally supported Roosevelt and the New
Deal, but the President's policies also spurred significant debate among
black intellectuals, especially over issues of race and class. Kirby
concludes that the results of Roosevelt's policies toward blacks were
mixed.

H 1053. KLEIN, HERBERT S. The Middle Passage: Comparative Studies in
         the Atlantic Slave Trade. Princeton, N.J.: Princeton University
         Press, 1978. 282 pp.
Klein analyzes both the basic demographic features of the trans-Atlantic
slave trade and the part of that trade dealing with the experiences of
what contemporaries called the "Middle Passage," or the trans-oceanic
crossing. The study examines how and when the slaves were moved trans-
Atlantically and which European merchants controlled this vast migration
enterprise. Klein finds that whatever their nationality, all the individual traders were strongly similar because of certain characteristics
of the business. He also suggests that they seem to have found "an optimal
way of carrying slaves": their ships became more similar, for instance,
and all the European traders used the same African staples (rice and yams)
to feed the slaves during the voyage.

H 1054. KLEIN, HERBERT S. Slavery in the Americas: A Comparative Study
         of Virginia and Cuba. Chicago: University of Chicago Press,
         1967. 270 pp.
In this comparison of legal, social, and economic aspects of slavery in
two slaveholding regions, Klein contends that Virginia's slaves were
entrapped in a rigid caste system which contrasted to the more flexible
"labor system" in Cuba. Virginia adopted a restrictive slave code which
defined blacks as chattel; Cuba's traditional slave codes treated slaves
as legal persons. Whereas Virginia's Anglicans had little interest in
slaves' welfare, the Catholic Church in Cuba reached out to blacks, offer-

ing them equality and opportunity for manumission. Economically, Virginia's slaves were primarily unskilled plantation or farm workers while Cuban slaves found considerable economic opportunity. Attitudes toward slavery also differed considerably: Virginia had few free blacks and strict anti-miscegenation laws, whereas Cuba had racial intermixture and a large population of free blacks.

H 1055. KOLCHIN, PETER. First Freedom. The Responses of Alabama's Blacks to Emancipation and Reconstruction. Westport, Conn.: Greenwood Press, 1972. 215 pp.

Peter Kolchin argues that Emancipation revolutionized the lives of blacks in Alabama. Freedmen demonstrated their independence by breaking their ties to plantations and migrating; those who remained on plantations became more assertive in relations with planters. No longer subject to arbitrary dissolution, the black family was strengthened under freedom. A black educational system emerged with the wide support of the black community, and black churches were organized as former slaves broke ties with white denominations. The black social structure also changed significantly—most importantly in the stratification which resulted from the creation of an independent black upper class. And though black political gains were limited, blacks became involved in the political process.

H 1056. KUSMER, KENNETH L. A Ghetto Takes Shape: Black Cleveland, 1870-1930. Urbana: University of Illinois Press, 1976. 305 pp.

By 1913, Cleveland had a clearly defined black ghetto. Kusmer finds transformations in race relations and the social structure of the black community central to an understanding of this development. Beginning in the 1870s, a pattern of racial tension destroyed the "almost equal" status which blacks enjoyed in mid-19th century Cleveland. As racism and discrimination worsened because of the white response to increased black migration, black economic opportunity declined and a segregated black district emerged. Kusmer examines the effect of "ghettoization" on community institutions and leadership, and effectively compares the black population of Cleveland with other Northern black communities.

H 1057. LANE, ANN J, ed. The Debate over Slavery: Stanley Elkins and His Critics. Urbana: University of Illinois Press, 1971. 378 pp.

The publication of Stanley Elkins's controversial Slavery in 1959 was the catalyst of a widespread reevaluation of black history. Ann Lane has gathered essays critical of Elkins's theses from twelve prominent historians. The major issues of debate include Elkins's acceptance of the Sambo stereotype, his comparison of Northern and Latin American slave systems, his use of the plantation-concentration camp analogy, and his discussion of the anti-institutionalism of Abolitionists. In a lengthy response, Elkins addresses his critics and suggests directions for future research.

H 1058. LEWIS, RONALD L. Coal, Iron, and Slaves: Industrial Slavery in Maryland and Virginia, 1715-1865. Westport, Conn.: Greenwood Press, 1979. 283 pp.

Lewis outlines the business and technological history of the Southern iron industry, focusing on the use of slave labor in the main center of regional production. The chapters emphasize social as well as economic aspects of such topics as discipline and motivation of slave workers, daily life in the mines and mills, and conflicts between planters and industrialists over how the region's human and financial resources should be employed. The author argues that industrialists were far from being the vanguard of a new industrial order; rather, they preferred black labor over a free white work-force and clung just as much to conceptions of a plantation society as did their plantation counterparts.

H 1059. LITTLEFIELD, DANIEL C. Rice and Slaves: Ethnicity and the Slave
         Trade in Colonial South Carolina. Baton Rouge: Louisiana State
         University Press, 1981. 199 pp.
Littlefield argues that historians have not paid sufficient attention
to African contributions to the development of plantation society and
culture in the New World. South Carolina, which had a large black population, provides a locale for viewing the African component in the formation of the plantation system in America. The author finds evidence that
planters were aware of cultural distinctions between the Africans and
slaves from Gambia who were preferred because they were more familiar
with rice production.

H 1060. LITWACK, LEON F. North of Slavery: The Negro in the Free States,
         1790-1860. Chicago: University of Chicago Press, 1961. 318 pp.
Conditions for blacks north of the Mason-Dixon line, Litwack argues, were
little better than those in slave states prior to the Civil War. However,
different avenues of resistance were open to Northern blacks. Being free,
they could resist oppression through education, economic advancement,
and political action, whereas Southern blacks were largely restricted
to open revolt. Litwack chronicles the ultimate failure of the Federal
government to protect Northern blacks, and documents the legal restrictions
placed on their activity.

H 1061. MANDLE, JAY R. The Roots of Black Poverty: The Southern Plan-
         tation Economy After the Civil War. Durham, N.C.: Duke Univer-
         sity Press, 1978. 144 pp.
The enduring problem of black poverty, according to Mandle, can be traced
to the persistence of the plantation mode of production in the post-Civil
War South. Despite Emancipation, land in the South remained in the hands
of planters who found mechanisms of control over black laborers to replace
slavery. Legal restrictions, a limited labor market, and the use of violence to enforce authority trapped blacks in a system of tenant farming
and sharecropping. W.W. II marked the decline of plantation economy,
but the poverty which it engendered remained. Because of their lack of
property and capital, as well as their late entrance into the U.S. industrial economy, blacks found themselves with few economic opportunities.

H 1062. McGOVERN, JAMES R. Anatomy of a Lynching: The Killing of Claude
         Neal. Baton Rouge: Louisiana State University Press, 1982.
         170 pp.
In October 1934, a Jackson County Florida mob brutally tortured and killed
Claude Neal, a young black murder suspect. The events surrounding the
lynching of Neal are the subject of McGovern's book. The author examines
the social background of the country's white residents and posits that
their traditional values, frontier-like experience, racism, and economic
frustration precipitated the lynching. The incident fueled the national
campaign for anti-lynching laws led by the NAACP. The extensive publicity
surrounding the Neal case, argues the author, led to a rapid decline in
racially motivated Southern mob violence. Anatomy of a Lynching sheds
light on the causes and effects of the nearly 3,000 lynchings in the South
between 1880 and 1940.

H 1063. MEIER, AUGUST and ELLIOTT RUDWICK. Along the Color Line: Explora-
         tions in the Black Experience. Urbana: University of Illinois
         Press, 1976. 404 pp.
The authors have gathered in this collection essays dealing with Afro-
American leadership, black nationalism and black power, and the history
of nonviolent direct action as a tactic of black protest. They discuss
the impact of such leaders as Frederick Douglass, W. E. B. Du Bois, Booker
T. Washington, and Martin Luther King, Jr. Several essays examine the
NAACP and its role in the black struggle for equality. The final section,

on nonviolence, examines black protests and boycotts in the century preceding the mass resistance of the civil rights movement.

H 1064. MORRIS, MILTON D. The Politics of Black America. New York: Harper & Row, 1975. 319 pp.
Morris's account of the political experience of black Americans begins with an examination of various approaches to the problem of race and politics. After his comparative analysis of the possible approaches, Morris addresses the struggles for change in both the U.S. and South Africa. The second section addresses the particular issues of subordination in a democratic polity. For this discussion, the author traces the roots of black subordination in American society and politics, examines the issues of citizenship for black Americans, and analyzes the growth and development of black nationalism. Section three is devoted to an analysis of the political attitudes of black Americans, their participation in the electoral process and party politics, and the activities of black political action groups. Morris concludes with a section which addresses the responses and challenges of blacks to the political system. He includes discussions of the judicial, executive, and congressional responses to blacks, the 1964 Civil Rights Act, and the problematic political future of black Americans.

H 1065. MULLIN, GERALD W. Flight and Rebellion: Slave Resistance in Eighteenth Century Virginia. New York: Oxford University Press, 1972. 219 pp.
Mullin uses advertisements for runaway slaves, plantation records, and other sources to analyze forms of slave resistance and the relation of slave acculturation to behavior. He argues that there were three distinct groups of slaves: those who ran off to establish traditional villages shortly after arrival, "new negroes" who had been in the Colonies for a while and did not attempt to escape plantation life totally, and skilled, American-born blacks who ran off alone and attempted to go North or to pass as free blacks in cities. The book concludes with a discussion of Gabriel's Rebellion. Mullin argues that the slave insurrection failed to garner support because of the various cultural experiences of Virginia's black population. Gabriel Prosser and the rebellion's other leaders were highly assimilated, skilled, and well-traveled, and consequently lacked cultural ties with the majority of the slave population.

H 1066. NIELSON, DAVID GORDON. Black Ethos: Northern Urban Negro Life and Thought, 1890-1930. Westport, Conn.: Greenwood Press, 1977. 248 pp.
In this examination of the culture and thought of black "ordinary people," David G. Nielson concludes that the deterioration of race relations after 1890 led blacks to adopt a new view of themselves and of their relationship to white society, thus bringing about the emergence of racial consciousness. Isolated by whites, blacks turned inward, developing their own economic and social institutions. Black-white tensions during and immediately following W.W. I culminated in racial separation and the flourishing black culture of the 1920s. Nielson draws extensively from black literature, newspapers, and magazines.

H 1067. OSOFSKY, GILBERT. Harlem, the Making of a Ghetto: A History of Negro New York, 1890-1920. New York: Harper & Row, 1966. 239 pp.
Osofsky argues that urban blacks are not recent migrants to American cities. Looking at Harlem, the most famous black community in the U.S., the author demonstrates how a previously white ethnic neighborhood evolved into a black ghetto in the early decades of the 20th century. Harlem differed from earlier immigrant and racial ghettos by not beginning as a slum. Unlike other black communities of 19th-century New York--such as Five

Points, the Tenderloin, and San Juan Hill--Harlem was the first residentially and racially segregated neighborhood in New York. This development would eventually typify most 20th-century American cities. By the 1920s, the detrimental effects of this were evidenced in the problem of inadequate housing, racial discrimination, and high rates of mortality, disease, and crime typical of Harlem.

H 1068. OUBRE, CLAUDE F. Forty Acres and a Mule: The Freedmen's Bureau
         and Black Land Ownership. Baton Rouge: Louisiana State University Press, 1978. 212 pp.
Claude Oubre's book traces the failure of efforts to secure land for freedmen during and after the Civil War. Oubre provides several reasons for the ineffectiveness of the Bureau, including the unresponsiveness of Congress to the needs of freed blacks, the disorganization of Bureau offices, and Southern white opposition to black land ownership. The effectiveness of the Bureau was further weakened by the difficulties of blacks' transition from slavery to freedom in the depressed economy of the postbellum South.

H 1069. OWENS, LESLIE HOWARD. This Species of Property: Slave Life and
         Culture in the Old South. New York: Oxford University Press, 1976. 291 pp.
Drawing from extensive research into plantation records and slave narratives, Owens presents an interpretation of slave personality and behavior which challenges recent historical interpretations of slavery. The laziness and docility attributed to slaves were the result of grueling labor, poor health care, and an inadequate diet. But regardless of these oppressive conditions, slaves asserted their humanity. Slave resistance, though it was seldom manifested in open revolt, was widespread and often effective in subverting the masters' dominance. The relations between planters and the "favored" household slaves and black slave drivers were as often antagonistic as amicable. The culture of the slave quarters--religion, folklore, music, and most important, the family--allowed the slaves a means of asserting their autonomy.

H 1070. PAINTER, NELL IRVIN. Exodusters: Black Migration to Kansas after
         Reconstruction. New York: Knopf, 1977. 288 pp.
In 1879 and 1880, thousands of blacks migrated up the Mississippi River and Westward, hoping to find in Kansas the freedom denied them in the deep South. Emancipation and Reconstruction, argues Painter, brought blacks limited freedom: white violence, political oppression, and landlessness plagued most blacks. By the late 1870s, many black leaders advocated migration as a solution to race problems, thus creating a favorable climate for the "Kansas Fever Exodus" of 1879. Approximately 6,000 blacks left Mississippi, Louisiana, Texas, and Tennessee in what Painter concludes was a large-scale repudiation of Southern intolerance.

H 1071. PLECK, ELIZABETH HAFKIN. Black Migration and Poverty: Boston
         1865-1900. New York: Academic Press, 1979. 239 pp.
According to Pleck, the majority of black newcomers to Boston--ex-slaves from the urban South--found initial adjustment to the Northern city difficult. At the start, there were divisions within the black community between the newcomers and those who had been free blacks in the antebellum North. Later, as the migrants became acculturated to the Northern black community, and adopted their economic values, whites systematically denied them economic opportunity; the former slaves were thus unable to attain upward mobility. Pleck contends that discrimination was at the root of black poverty in the North, and notes that poverty had debilitating effects on black social life, resulting most notably in the increase of households headed by unmarried women.

H 1072. QUARLES, BENJAMIN. Black Abolitionists. New York: Oxford University Press, 1969. 310 pp.
Quarles analyzes the efforts of Northern blacks to free their Southern brethren, and emphasizes Abolitionist methods of agitating against slavery. The author discusses the growth of militancy among Northern black activists and their influence on the white anti-slavery movement. Quarles outlines the political conditions that helped shape the strategies of reform and focuses on the roles played by the Church and the press in the growth of the black Abolitionist movement. In later chapters he addresses the question of black suffrage; examines the response to the Fugitive Slave Law on the part of black Abolitionist leaders; and traces the events leading to the Civil War, with a particular emphasis on John Brown's raid on Harper's Ferry in 1859 and its aftermath.

H 1073. RABINOWITZ, HOWARD N. Race Relations in the Urban South, 1865-1890. New York: Oxford University Press, 1978. 441 pp.
In his examination of Atlanta, Montgomery, Nashville, Raleigh, and Richmond, Rabinowitz finds that blacks who settled in Southern cities after the Civil War faced difficulties adjusting to their new environment. Whites attempted to assert control over the threatening mass of urban blacks and restricted black activities harshly. Blacks received little justice in the legal system and had no effective political voice. Black Southerners were at first excluded from public services, and a system of segregation—separate and unequal—took hold. Only by building strong community institutions were blacks able to overcome some of the indignities of race relations in the urban South.

H 1074. RANSOM, ROGER L. and RICHARD SUTCH. One Kind of Freedom: The Economic Consequences of Emancipation. New York: Cambridge University Press, 1977. 409 pp.
This volume explores the reasons for the stagnation of the post-bellum Southern economy. Ransom and Sutch maintain that Emancipation's major effect was to shatter the web of economic institutions that had developed to serve the plantation system. The post-bellum South thus faced a dual challenge: to replace the labor lost with the demise of slavery, and to reorganize the institutions serving agriculture. The new agricultural system discourged capital investment and technical improvement. Sharecropping, for example, provided no incentive to improve the land. Southern farmers lacked the incentives of their Northern counterparts, and the Southern rural economy thus remained undeveloped. Racism exacerbated the distortions inherent in the region's economic institutions, denying blacks the educational opportunities necessary to their own and to overall regional growth.

H 1075. RAWICK, GEORGE P. From Sundown to Sunup: The Making of the Black Community. Westport, Conn.: Greenwood Press, 1972. 209 pp.
Rawick draws from sociological and anthropological research in this interdisciplinary history of slave culture in the American South. Challenging Stanley Elkins's plantation-concentration camp analogy, the author argues that because of the flourishing community institutions which they created in the slave quarters, blacks did not become submissive victims of slavery. Rawick highlights the importance of African cultural traditions in slave life, and argues that religion and family made communal autonomy possible. Rawick is the first historian to rely extensively upon the WPA oral history of slavery compiled in the 1930s.

H 1076. ROSE, WILLIE LEE. Slavery and Freedom. Edited by William W. Freehling. New York: Oxford University Press, 1982. 224 pp.
In this collection of essays, speeches, and book reviews, Rose argues that the nature of the institution of slavery was a changeable one, and not the static institution presented by recent historiography. The author

offers an interpretation of slave life which finds middle ground between
the Elkins "thesis" and the slave autonomy thesis. Other topics addressed
include Reconstruction; the presentation of slavery and freedom in American
historical fiction; contemporary views of slavery and Emancipation; and
documentary sources.

H 1077. RUDWICK, ELLIOTT. Race Riot at East St. Louis, July 2, 1917.
Carbondale: Southern Illinois University Press, 1964. 300 pp.
Rudwick examines what was to be the most serious American race riot to
occur in the first half of the 20th century. He argues that black migration, the perceived threat of black competition in the white job market,
and increasing black political power were the underlying causes of the
conflagration. In his provocative concluding chapter, Rudwick compares
the East St. Louis riot with later race riots in Chicago and Detroit,
and finds preconditions and consequences common to both.

H 1078. SCHEINER, SETH M. Negro Mecca: A History of the Negro in New
York City, 1865-1920. New York: New York University Press,
1965. 246 pp.
Though Scheiner takes into account the white world within which the American black has lived, he is more interested in looking at black society
on its own terms, and in New York City in particular. Beginning with
a history of slave population in New York in 1626, the author examines
the evolving stature of the New York City black up until 1920. In 1795,
the rigid slave laws were relaxed by Abolitionist governor John Jay paving
the way for growth in the black population. After the Civil War, there
was an even greater influx of blacks who were driven North by economic
hardships in the South. The author points out, however, that though
slavery died early in New York, "political, legal, economic, and social
discrimination persisted." Because the black communities were ostracized
from mainstream society, they developed their own--building their own
churches for example, while growing in awareness of their curtailed civil
rights. The years between the Civil War and 1920 are crucial ones.
Scheiner believes that only by taking a careful look at what went on during
that time can one understand the roots of today's de facto segregation
and discrimination in employment.

H 1079. SITKOFF, HARVARD. A New Deal for Blacks: The Emergence of Civil
Rights as a National Issue: The Depression Decade. New York:
Oxford University Press, 1978. 397 pp.
Sitkoff studies the events, institutions, and individuals which combined
to make civil rights a national issue from the New Deal era through the
1970s. In his study, Sitkoff looks at the interplay of local control,
borough politics, the poll tax and the white primary. He also considers
the impact on civil rights of the Left, and of organized labor. Sitkoff
argues that Roosevelt was far from being radically progressive and humanitarian, but that the roots of later civil rights advances can be traced
to the New Deal.

H 1080. SPEAR, ALLAN H. Black Chicago: The Making of a Negro Ghetto,
1890-1920. Chicago: University of Chicago Press, 1967.
254 pp.
In 1920, Chicago's blacks lived in segregated neighborhoods wherein they
created community institutions, businesses, and a political machine.
Spear's book traces the origins of the black ghetto to the sharp demarca-
tion of the color line in the 1890s. Discrimination and racial hostility
had created a physical ghetto, limited black economic mobility, and
restricted black access to public services. Segregation brought internal
changes to Chicago's black community: a new black elite emerged as the
ghetto's leadership group, and strong social organizations drew the community together. The heavy migration of Southern blacks to the city after

1915 reinforced patterns of the ghetto which were to endure throughout
the next fifty years.

H 1081. STAMPP, KENNETH M. The Peculiar Institution: Slavery in the
         Ante-Bellum South. New York: Knopf, 1956. 435 pp.
Stampp maintains that slavery as an economic system was a success. It
was a practical solution to Southern labor needs and continued to attract
the investments of planters (whom Stampp regards as practical businessmen) up to the Civil War. Slavery did not inhibit agricultural reform;
it was not the cause of soil exhaustion; nor did it retard Southern industrialization. Stampp concludes, however, that slavery was an obstacle
to Southern social, cultural, and long-term economic development.

H 1082. STAROBIN, ROBERT S. Industrial Slavery in the Old South. New
         York: Oxford University Press, 1970. 320 pp.
Starobin examines the lives of the Southern slaves hired to perform industrial labor in the first half of the 19th century. He finds that industrial working conditions were abysmal, and that most industrial slaves
lived at the brink of subsistence in housing no better than that of the
plantation quarters. Slave discontent in the workplace was widespread;
protest ranged from subtle resistance such as negligence, to refusal to
work, escape attempts, and outright rebellion. Industrial discipline,
often in the form of brute repression, maintained workforce stability
and productivity. Starobin also addresses the question of the economics
of industrial slavery, arguing that slave labor was more profitable and
efficient than wage labor, and that white Southerners favored the use
of slavery to industrialize the South.

H 1083. STAUDENRAUS, P. J. The African Colonization Movement, 1816-1863.
         New York: Columbia University Press, 1961. 323 pp.
This study of the American Colonization Society examines a popular 19th-
century solution to the "problem" posed by free blacks. Staudenraus discusses the supporters of the colonization movement, their political intentions, and the economic support tendered by the Society. The proponents
of colonization sought to civilize and Christianize Africa with properly
indoctrinated free blacks while ridding the U.S. of its racial dilemma.
Staudenraus concludes with an account of the frustrations encountered
by black colonists attempting to settle in Liberia.

H 1084. TOLL, WILLIAM. The Resurgence of Race: Black Social Theory from
         Reconstruction to the Pan-African Conferences. Philadelphia:
         Temple University Press, 1979. 270 pp.
Central to an understanding of the transformation of black social thought
between 1880 and 1930 is the debate between the supporters of Booker T.
Washington, who argued the necessity of black "social rehabilitation,"
and the supporters of W. E. B. DuBois, who emphasized the need for black
group cohesiveness through "cultural vitalization." Toll traces these
ideas and their effect on black intellectuals. From the 1880s until W.W.
I, most black social observers compared ex-slaves to emancipated peasants,
and posited the need for modernization. But by the turn of the century,
strong voices of opposition argued for an emphasis on black ethnic distinctiveness and the unique black contribution to American culture. By
the 1920s, the latter view dominated and found its expression in black
literary culture and the Pan-African movement.

H 1085. WADE, RICHARD C. Slavery in the Cities: The South 1820-1860.
         New York: Oxford University Press, 1964. 340 pp.
This book examines the nature of slavery in a setting less familiar than
the plantation. Wade finds that just at the time when the institution
of slavery appeared stable in the rural South, it was declining rapidly
in the cities. The urban environment, he says, was inimical to slavery.

Efficient performance in the urban environment required that slaves be
granted a substantial degree of autonomy. Such freedoms were incompatible
with the master-slave relationship, and slaves were regarded less as chat-
tels and more as employees with a signific[c]nt degree of personal liberty.
For example, slaves were hired out to third parties, no longer working
under the immediate supervision of their owners; they were even allowed
to live away from the owner's home. These changes, Wade concludes, undermined the institution from within; they account for the rapid decline
in the urban slave population in the pre-Civil War decade.

H 1086. WEBBER, THOMAS L. Deep Like the River: Education in the Slave
         Quarter Community, 1831-1865. New York: Norton, 1978.
         339 pp.
Webber argues that there was a dramatic contrast between what plantation
slaves learned and what slaveholders intended to teach them. Section
one of this volume examines the secular training and religious instruction
provided by whites. Webber discusses the way in which whites attempted
to control slaves' attitudes and ideas by teaching them fear and submis-
siveness, then demonstrates that the predominant black culture of the
slave quarters challenged the values of the master. Section two focuses
on various "cultural themes" of the quarter community. These themes,
which stood in opposition to the tenets of white instruction, include
communality, antipathy toward whites, the importance of the family, Christianity and the "spirit world," and the immorality of slavery. Section
three examines the educational "instruments" available to the quarter
community. Such means of instruction and socialization included the family,
the peer group, the clandestine congregation, and folklore. This volume
concludes with a comparison of the slave quarter with the Indian reservation.

H 1087. WEISS, NANCY J. Farewell to the Party of Lincoln: Black Politics
         in the Age of FDR. Princeton, N.J.: Princeton University Press,
         1983. 333 pp.
In 1932, blacks voted overwhelmingly Republican; in 1936 blacks supported
Roosevelt's candidacy enthusiastically. This political shift, argues
Weiss, was the result of the appeal of the New Deal's economic policy
to blacks. Despite breakthroughs such as the appointment of an unofficial
"black cabinet" and the openness of Eleanor Roosevelt to black constituents,
the racial policies of the Roosevelt administration were conservative.
Discrimination in Federal programs was common, and the failure of the
NAACP anti-lynching campaign indicated the unwillingness of FDR to make
civil rights a priority. But Federal relief programs did indeed respond
to the needs of poor urban blacks and thus won black voters over to the
Democratic Party.

H 1088. WEISS, NANCY J. The National Urban League, 1910-1940. New York:
         Oxford University Press, 1974. 402 pp.
This book is an institutional history of the National Urban League in
regard to race relations and the urbanization of blacks in the early 20th
century. In its first three decades, the Urban League was committed to
improving the conditions of blacks in American cities. The league provided
welfare services, trained social workers, and organized efforts to integrate black-dominated occupations. Weiss concludes that the League aided
black migrants in their adjustment to urban life and ameliorated different
living conditions. But by clinging to the ideals of Progressivism and
looking to the American system for solutions, it made little headway in
challenging racism.

H 1089. WILLIAMS, LEE E. and LEE E. WILLIAMS II. Anatomy of Four Race
         Riots: Racial Conflict in Knoxville, Elaine (Arkansas), Tulsa
         and Chicago, 1919-1921. Jackson: University and College Press
         of Mississippi, 1972. 128 pp.
This book focuses on racial riots which occurred in three cities and one
small town during the tumultuous post-W.W. I years. Especially concerned
with the motivation and aftermath of each event, the authors contend that
common to each conflict was the attempt by whites to preserve traditional
race relations. The Williamses conclude that white attacks on blacks
were motivated by differing tensions: fear of black economic competition;
reaction to alleged black crimes, especially those with sexual overtones;
or insecurity over increasing black political power and assertion of equality.

H 1090. WILLIAMSON, JOEL. After Slavery: The Negro in South Carolina
         During Reconstruction, 1861-1877. New York: Norton, 1965.
         442 pp.
This book studies the history of blacks during the Reconstruction Era
in South Carolina, a state where blacks played an important political
role because they constituted a majority of the electorate. Williamson
attempts to answer the question of why blacks were unable to sustain their
political freedom and influence beyond 1877. He examines their limited
freedoms in light of new economic patterns, racial conflict, and the tensions between whites and freemen. Williamson also examines the new black
middle class that emerged with the rise of segregation.

H 1091. WILLIAMSON, JOEL. New People: Miscegenation and Mulattoes in
         the United States. New York: Free Press, 1980. 221 pp.
According to Williamson, the history of the "new people" reflects larger
trends in black history. His book focuses upon perceptions of race in
the U.S. In the Colonial period and in the South as late as 1950, mulattoes
were viewed as a group separate from blacks and whites, but by the 20th
century mulattoes were universally identified as blacks. As whites adopted
the notion that any degree of black ancestry made an individual black,
mulattoes simultaneously asserted their blackness. Miscegenation has
been generally disdained by white society and though there has been some
acceptance of the value of black culture by whites, intermarrige, according
to Williamson, is still not widely accepted.

H 1092. WOLTERS, RAYMOND. Negroes and the Great Depression: The Problem
         of Economic Recovery. Westport, Conn.: Greenwood Press, 1970.
         398 pp.
Wolters' monograph analyzes the effects of recovery legislation upon black
life during the Depression and the general economic recovery program and
its value to America's black labor force. The book is divided into three
organizational sections which discuss the AAA, the NRA, and the NAACP.
The first part details the effects of the AAA on black tenant farmers
in the South; the second section, an analysis of the NRA, shows the New
Dealers' tendency to harm the blacks they were trying to help in the areas
of wages and work hours. The book concludes with an examination of the
NAACP and the in-fighting that split the organization between 1933 and
1936.

H 1093. WOOD, PETER H. Black Majority: Negroes in Colonial South Carolina
         from 1670 through the Stono Rebellion. New York: Knopf, 1974.
         346 pp.
Wood discusses the settlement and early economic and social history of
Colonial South Carolina, concentrating on the colony's transition from
diversified production to dependence upon the cultivation of rice as a
commercial staple. The author closely examines the nature and transformation of the colony's labor system. Black slavery was present in South

Carolina from the colony's inception. This was due to the high proportion of West Indian planters among the early inhabitants, the relative proximity of the West Indies as a source of supply, and the sluggishness of European immigration. During the period of economic diversity, the slaves performed a variety of tasks, but with the development of rice production, boring, repetitive work became the norm on the plantation.

H 1094. WOODWARD, C. VANN. The Strange Career of Jim Crow. 1955; Rev. ed. New York: Oxford University Press, 1974. 233 pp.
Woodward tells the history of segregation in America and argues that segregation in Southern public accommodations did not exist until the rise of the "Jim Crow" laws that first restricted blacks around the turn of the century. He examines the motives of the Southern conservatives who feared the Populist alliance of blacks and poor whites and responded with the rigid system of segregation. The relative newness of legal and total segregation in the South, according to Woodward, facilitated the gradual, yet eventual erosion of the system.

X.   NATIVE AMERICAN

H 1095. ANSON, BERT. The Miami Indians. Norman: University of Oklahoma Press, 1970. 329 pp.
Anson examines the tribal history of the Miami Indians in terms of their economic, political, and military struggles to retain their strategically located homeland in Ohio and Indiana. By employing a variety of strategies, the Miami effectively thwarted American settlement north of the Ohio River until their defeat at the Battle of Fallen Timbers at the end of the 18th century. After that battle, despite their persistent efforts to compromise and acculturate themselves to American society, the Miami were steadily dispossessed of their land until their forced removal to Oklahoma in the 1840s. Anson traces the developments of that segment of the tribe which resettled in Oklahoma and that segment which remained in Indiana from 1846-1968, and he discusses their modern ethnic identity in the light of extensive intermarriage with whites.

H 1096. ARMSTRONG, WILLIAM H. Warrior in Two Camps: Ely S. Parker, Union General and Seneca Chief. Syracuse, N.Y.: Syracuse University Press, 1978. 244 pp.
Armstrong's biography of Ely S. Parker is a case study of the difficulties faced by those American Indian intellectuals in the 19th century who attempted to achieve success in American society while retaining their traditional values and beliefs. A legal defender of the Seneca during two decades of court battles against the Ogden Land Company and an assistant to anthropologist Lewis Henry Morgan, who attempted to document Seneca culture, Parker was U. S. Grant's military secretary during the Civil War and was later chosen by Ulysses S. Grant to become Commissioner of Indian Affairs. Armstrong focuses on the conflicts between Parker and the Anglo-American reformers and philanthropists who eventually forced his resignation and describes Parker's ambiguous standing among his native people and his attempts to reconcile his position.

H 1097. BAILEY, JOHN W. Pacifying the Plains: General Alfred Terry and the Sioux, 1860-1890. Westport, Conn.: Greenwood Press, 1979. 236 pp.
Bailey details the implementation of the U.S. Federal government's removal policy among the Sioux Indians during the Reconstruction era. Bailey focuses on the frustrations and difficulties faced by U.S. agents charged

with managing the Sioux, who were the most resistant of all Plains Indians
toward government domination. He examines the administration of General
Terry, who was responsible for relocating the Sioux from their enormous
territory on the Northern Plains to confinement in a small portion of
South Dakota. Although the process of removal was harsh and devastating
for the tribe, Bailey argues that Terry attempted to manage the Sioux
fairly, but was constrained by the values and economic exigencies of
America in the 19th century.

H 1098. BAIRD, W. DAVID. The Quapaw Indians: A History of the Downstream
         People. Norman: University of Oklahoma Press, 1980. 290 pp.
Baird describes the history of the Quapaw, a tribe which successfully
used the Federal allotment policy of the late 19th century to secure a
significant land base. Although the Quapaw population was dramatically
reduced by European diseases and was splintered by removal policies in
the early 1880s, the tribe retained a cultural identity and increased
its number by absorbing members from other tribes. Baird describes their
strategies for cultural survival and their efforts to protect their land
base against the intrigues of Oklahoma politicians and the threat of dissolution in the post-W.W. II era.

H 1099. BARSH, RUSSEL LAWRENCE and JAMES YOUNGBLOOD HENDERSON. The Road:
         Indian Tribes and Political Liberty. Berkeley: University of
         California Press, 1980. 301 pp.
Barsh and Henderson examine the legal history of political sovereignty
insofar as the concept has figured in the relations between American Indian
tribes and the U.S. Federal government. The authors emphasize that the
goal of Federal Indian policy throughout the past 200 years has been to
replace the tribal status of American Indians with individual status as
the basis and framework for litigation. The authors analyze Congressional
Acts and Supreme Court decisions involving Indians between 1700 and 1970,
and they claim that Federal courts have perpetuated historically inaccurate
notions of justice in their use of historical precedent as a basis for
contemporary Court decisions.

H 1100. BEE, ROBERT L. Crosscurrents Along the Colorado: The Impact
         of Government Policy on the Quechan Indians. Tucson: University
         of Arizona Press, 1981. 184 pp.
Bee examines the impact of Federal Indian policy on one Indian community
throughout the 1960s and 1970s. Arguing that the development of Federal
Indian policies and their impact on Indian peoples constitutes a form
of Colonialism, Bee traces the historic development of the Quechan (or
Yuma) reservation in Arizona and California. Focusing on the relationship
between Federal regulation and the tribal administration, Bee describes
how these interest groups clashed over water and resource rights in the
1970s, when the Quechan requested the restoration of thousands of acres
of former reservation land. Basing his study on fifteen years of fieldwork
among the Quechan, Bee details the tribe's struggle to gain political
autonomy and their participation in several Federal programs designed
to improve the tribal economy.

H 1101. BERKHOFER, ROBERT F., Jr. The White Man's Indian: Images of
         the American Indian from Columbus to the Present. New York:
         Knopf, 1978. 660 pp.
Arguing that the images we have of the "other" are never objective but
are always related to how we perceive our own society, Berkhofer traces
the transformations in the symbolic value of Indians for Anglo-Americans
throughout American history. Exploring the origins of persistent images
and themes associated with the Indians and analyzing our changing perception
of them, the author relates these image patterns to events and crises
in Western society. He traces the evolution of Indian images in the dis-

ciplines of anthropology, history, literature, art, philosophy, and political science. A large section is devoted to examining how cultural representations of Indians relate to legal policy, both in theory and in practice. Notions of the Indian as noble savage, environmentalist, and counter-culture hero are evaluated. Throughout the book the author contends that Indians exist only as images to most Americans.

H 1102. BERTHRONG, DONALD J. The Cheyenne and Arapaho Ordeal: Reservation and Agency Life in the Indian Territory, 1875-1907. Norman: University of Oklahoma Press, 1976. 402 pp.
This study of Cheyenne and Arapaho history during the reservation and allotment periods is a sequel to Bethrong's earlier study of Indian-Anglo military conflict in The Southern Cheyennes (H 1103). Here Berthrong examines the implementation of Federal policies designed to acculturate the Cheyenne and Arapaho through Christianization and farming programs. He argues that these attempts failed due to a congressional refusal to allocate enough funds, the fracture of tribal land base under the 1887 Dawes Act, and the determination of the Cheyenne and Arapaho to maintain their traditional culture. He details the hardships suffered by these tribes after their removal from the Plains and confinement on a reservation in Oklahoma.

H 1103. BERTHRONG, DONALD J. The Southern Cheyennes. Norman: University of Oklahoma Press, 1963. 446 pp.
Berthrong presents the history and ethnography of the division of Cheyenne Indians who occupied the Central and Southern Plains from 1650 until 1875. He describes their migration to the Plains from the Great Lakes and their frequent relocations throughout the area due to pressure from competing groups. He focuses on the relations between the Cheyenne and other tribes, including their pivotal role in the trading economy. Using primary historic sources, Berthrong details the decline of their circumstances due to the near extinction of bison and to pressure from colonists, as well as their repeated attempts to uphold peace treaties. The bulk of the text is devoted to the era of military struggles against U.S. forces and to their life in the early reservation period.

H 1104. BLAINE, MARTHA ROYCE. The Ioway Indians. Norman: University of Oklahoma Press, 1979. 364 pp.
Blaine's volume provides a history of the Ioway Indians from the pre-Colonial period through the 19th century. The Ioway tribe, according to Blaine, exerted great influence on neighboring tribes and on the early fur traders because of their central location between the Missouri and Mississippi Rivers. Despite their early influence, the Ioway people were subjected to a gradual loss of independence. As Blaine's history demonstrates, the Ioway tribe became economically dependent, suffered the loss of their land, and were eventually relocated as part of the exploitation of the American frontier. In addition, the Ioway Indians were deprived of many traditions as their cultural heritage was further assailed by Anglo-Americans throughout the late 19th century.

H 1105. BROWN, DEE. Bury My Heart at Wounded Knee: An Indian History ot the American West. New York: Holt, Rinehart & Winston, 1971. 487 pp.
Brown argues the Indian viewpoint in this re-telling of the Western Indian wars between 1860 and 1890, when the Sioux were militarily defeated at Wounded Knee. Although he details the struggles of many different tribes and their leaders, he pays primary attention to the Indians of the Northern and Southern Plains, recounting their tragically persistent attempts to retain their land and their traditional ways of life. Dee emphasizes the economic motives behind the Euro-American expansion and the cruelties inflicted upon the Indians as a result of Federal policies.

H 1106. **CARLSON, LEONARD A.** Indians, Bureaucarts and Land: The Dawes
Act and the Decline of Indian Farming. Westport, Conn.: Greenwood Press, 1981. 219 pp.
Carlson chronicles the evolution of the 1887 Dawes Act as a solution to
the problem of assimilating American Indians into Anglo-American society.
He documents the implementation of the allotment policy and assesses its
effect on Indian farming and property rights. Using the Dawes Act as
an example, the author considers the role of economic interests in the
formation of Federal Indian policy. He argues that the Dawes Act responded
to the demands of the Anglo-American market for land and was not designed
to benefit Native Americans, who lost a considerable amount of their land
base as a result of allotment policies.

H 1107. **CARTER, SAMUEL III.** Cherokee Sunset, a Nation Betrayed: A Narrative of Travail and Triumph, Persecution and Exile. Garden
City, N.Y.: Doubleday, 1976. 318 pp.
Basing his account on primary sources, Carter chronicles the social and
political development of the Cherokee in the Southeast, focusing on their
struggle to maintain their homeland and to resist removal to Oklahoma.
Citing passages from the Phoenix, a Cherokee newspaper extant in the 1930s,
from missionary records, and from legal documents, Carter attempts to
recreate the personalities and events that shaped Cherokee history. He
discusses the influence of tribal factionalism on the Cherokee response
to removal, and the experiences of the tribe during the relocation process.

H 1108. **CHAMBERLAIN, J. E.** The Harrowing of Eden: White Attitudes Toward
Native Americans. New York: Seabury Press, 1975. 248 pp.
Chamberlain presents a historical examination of the official policies
toward native peoples adopted by the governments of Canada and the U.S.
He compares Indian and European cultural values, focusing on the disjunc-
ture in their belief systems and on how this separation both alienated
Indians from white culture and shaped major developments in Federal policy.
He describes the efforts of U.S. policy makers to acculturate the Indian
through policies of land allotment, Christian missions, and education.
Chamberlain compares the Indian policies of the U.S. and Canada and concludes that, although Canadian legislation has often protected Indian
traditions, the differences in governmental approach are more apparent
than real and that both governments have sought to eradicate Indian cultures.

H 1109. **CLARK, JERRY E.** The Shawnee. Lexington: University Press of
Kentucky, 1977. 99 pp.
Clark uses archaeological and ethno-historical data to trace the early
migrations of the Shawnee and to argue that these Algonkian speakers represent the continuation of the prehistoric Fort Ancient culture of the Ohio
River Valley. He also evaluates their claim to the territory of Kentucky
despite their use of the area only as a hunting locale and their permanent
settlement elsewhere. The author attempts to locate the major Shawnee
divisions throughout the Southeast prior to their resettlement in Oklahoma
and analyzes their social and economic relations with Euro-Americans and
other Indian nations. Also included is a short chapter on social organization.

H 1110. **COLLIER, JOHN.** The Indians of the Americas. New York: Norton,
1947. 326 pp.
Collier critiques the materialism and destructiveness of the modern world
by presenting in contrast the history and cultures of the American Indian,
which he sees as representing hope for world salvation. Collier advocated
retaining Indian socio-cultural institutions, and as Commissioner of Indian
Affairs under Franklin Roosevelt he attempted to institute policies that
would encourage Indian self-determination and retard acculturation.

In this work the author re-examines Indian-white relations both north
and south of the Rio Grande, and he documents the failure of past U.S.
policies among many tribes. He provides a first-hand account of the
development of New Deal Indian policies during his administration and comments on events between 1940-1945. Throughout the work Collier emphasizes
that it is the community life of Indians that has preserved their cultural
integrity and that must in turn be preserved.

H 1111. COLSON, ELIZABETH. The Makah Indians: A Study of an Indian Tribe
in Modern American Society. Manchester, England: University
of Manchester Press, 1953. 308 pp.
Based on the author's fieldwork among the Makah Indians of Washington State
from 1941-42, this work provides an ethnographic description of the tribe
with an emphasis on the problem of culture change and assimilation. Colson
argues that favorable economic conditions enabled the Makah to modernize
and make them less dependent upon traditional culture patterns than were
many other Indian groups and points out that their small population rendered them especially vulnerable to the Indian services efforts to assimilate the tribe. She examines the complexity of Makah identity on both
an individual and a group level and also analyzes patterns of interaction,
particularly as they exemplify traditional notions of a Makah class system.
Included is a treatment of the interplay between indigenous and Christian
notions of the supernatural.

H 1112. COOK, SHERBURNE F. The Conflict Between the California Indian
and White Civilization. Berkeley: University of California
Press, 1976. 522 pp.
Cook analyzes the effect of white contact on the California Indian tribes
throughout several eras of their colonized history. He focuses on relations between Indians and Spanish in the California missions; on the
impacts of Spanish, Mexican and American policies on Indian cultures; and
on the tribes' techniques of resistance to acculturation. Emphasizing
the importance of demographic data, dietary shifts and disease patterns,
the author compares the experience of mission Indians to that of non-mission
Indians, and he discusses the physical and social adaptation of Western
Indians to their changed environment.

H 1113. COTTERILL, R. S. The Southern Indians: The Story of the Civilized
Tribes Before Removal. Norman: University of Oklahoma Press,
1954. 255 pp.
Cotterill examines the cultures of the Cherokee, Chickasaw, Creek, and
Chocktaw peoples from the years following the American Revolution to
the 1830s and the beginning of Indian relocation programs. After an introductory description of these societies during their early years of contact
with Europeans, he concentrates on the changes that occurred in Southern
Indian political and social structures in response to increasing pressure
from surrounding Anglo-American populations. The author focuses on the
difficulties that beset intertribal relations, the strategies of various
Indian leaders, and the growing divisions between those Indians who adopted
many elements of Anglo-American culture and those who persisted in their
traditional lifestyles.

H 1114. CRAMPTON, C. GREGORY. The Zunis of Cibola. Salt Lake City:
University of Utah Press, 1977. 201 pp.
In recounting the history of the Zuni of New Mexico from their initial
contact with the Spanish to the present, Crampton argues that the Zuni
were much less xenophobic than their neighbors, the Navajo and the Hopi.
He emphasizes Zuni adoption of Spanish material culture and aspects of
their religion, and he details later relations with American adventurers
and settlers. Crampton also describes Zuni diplomatic efforts at assuaging
conflicts between whites and Indians, the Zuni-U.S. alliance in the Navajo

wars of the mid-19th century, and the increased contact with Western society at the advance of the railroad in the 1880s. The impact of foreign culture on Zuni life is stressed, and Crampton focuses in particular on the influence exerted by those cultural programs instituted by the missionaries and reformers of the late 19th and early 20th centuries.

H 1115. CRANE, VERNER W. The Southern Frontier: 1670-1732. Ann Arbor: University of Michigan Press, 1929. 359 pp.
Crane reviews the early history of Anglo-American settlement in the Southeastern U.S., focusing on the importance of the Indian trade for the expansion of the Carolina colonies, describing the struggle between the European powers to control it—including the events of Queen Anne's War—and arguing that the trading relationship enjoyed by the British with the Creeks and Cherokees provided them with an advantage over the French and Spanish. The author discusses the importance of Charles Town as a trade center and describes the way in which it was regulated. He chronicles the Creek, Choctaw and Cherokee revolt against the trading regime in the Yamasee War, and explains how this event resulted in new British policies toward the Indians. Crane concludes by assessing the relations between the Creek Confederacy and the Spanish, French and British in the early 18th century, and by discussing the founding of the colony of Georgia.

H 1116. CRAVEN, WESLEY F. White, Red, and Black: The Seventeenth-Century Virginian. Charlottesville: University Press of Virginia, 1971. 114 pp.
Craven explores the situation of whites, blacks, and Indians in Colonial Virginia in order to evaluate the nature of their interaction patterns. Treating each group in a separate essay, the author emphasizes the importance of demographic data for the analysis of these societies and their relations with one another. Craven argues that population declines among Eastern Native Americans shortly after contact undermined their efforts to confederate in order to resist Virginia colonists as a group. The author analyzes the reasons why blacks and Indians were treated differently by Colonial society and attempts to evaluate the extent of black slavery in early Virginia.

H 1117. CROSBY, ALFRED W. The Columbian Exchange: Biological and Cultural Consequences of 1492. Westport, Conn.: Greenwood Press, 1972. 268 pp.
Crosby examines the impact of Columbus's discovery of the New World on the American and European ecosystems. He argues that the chief reason for the European conquest of indigenous Americans was that the introduction of Old World diseases decimated the Native American populations. Crosby details the transformation of the American ecosystem by the importation of Spanish plants, animals, and subsistence technologies, focusing on how European imports such as swine damaged the ecology of the Americas by competing with and displacing indigenous biotic forms. The author re-analyzes the debate over the origins of syphilis, and also claims that the introduction of American crops to Europe contributed to population growth there. Crosby concludes the work with a chapter examining the continuing process of biological exchange between Europe and America.

H 1118. DALE, EDWARD EVERETT. The Indians of the Southwest: A Century of Development under the United States. Norman: University of Oklahoma Press, 1949. 283 pp.
Dale chronicles relations between the U.S. government and Indian peoples in the territory acquired by the U.S. after the Mexican War. After providing a summary account of early European penetration of the Southwest, the author examines administrative difficulties on both the Federal and state levels throughout the latter half of the 19th and first half of the 20th centuries. The analysis focuses on the implementation of Federal

policies by various Indian agents and officials. Individual tribes are discussed state by state. The latter half of the book deals with the problems of modernization throughout the Southwest region, with an emphasis on medical and educational developments.

H 1119. DANZIGER, EDMUND JEFFERSON, Jr. The Chippewas of Lake Superior.
        Norman: University of Oklahoma Press, 1978. 263 pp.
Danziger examines the relations between Lake Superior Chippewas and the Euro-American population from their initial contact with the French in 1641 to the late 1970s. The author focuses on the development and implementation of European and American policies toward the Chippewa as a tribal entity, emphasizing their attempts to retain their cultural heritage. In the chapters dealing with 20th-century socio-political affairs, Danziger offers information gained from oral interviews with Chippewa people on their reservation.

H 1120. DEBO, ANGIE. And Still the Waters Run. Princeton, N.J.: Princeton University Press, 1940. 417 pp.
Debo critiques the management of Southeastern Indian tribes removed to Oklahoma in the 1830s. Focusing on the so-called "Five Civilized Tribes," Debo chronicles the methods and motives behind the usurpation of their lands in the East and their exile to Oklahoma on the "Trail of Tears." The work concentrates on their subsequent success and then decline in Oklahoma, where their original land allotments were steadily reduced despite treaties which stipulated that their ownership would extend into perpetuity. The interplay of Federal law with the intrigues of early Oklahoma politics and social factors such as intermarriage are described against a background of economically-based exploitation. The impact of Oklahoma statehood and the process of land litigation cases are detailed, and the author explores the position of Indians in the social system of Oklahoma.

H 1121. DEBO, ANGIE. Geronimo: The Man, His Time, His Place. Norman:
        University of Oklahoma Press, 1976. 480 pp.
Debo explores Geronimo's personal life and his character and portrays the man in the context of his social and political milieu. She bases her study on historical documents and on her interviews with his family members and friends, conducted on the Mescalero Apache Reservation. In the first part of the work, the author presents Geronimo's family background and the historic events that motivated him to lead the Apaches' armed resistance to U.S. military forces in the late 19th century. Much of the second half of the book is devoted to examining Geronimo's life at Fort Sill after his surrender in 1886, and the efforts of his people to adjust to reservation life. More than sixty photographs of Apache life in the late 19th century augment the text.

H 1122. DEBO, ANGIE. A History of the Indians of the United States.
        Norman: University of Oklahoma Press, 1970. 386 pp.
In this broad survey of American Indian history, Debo pays primary attention to Indian-white relations during the Colonial era and the frontier wars, and to the post-removal reconstruction of Indian societies in Oklahoma throughout the 19th and 20th centuries. Focusing on the nature of the U.S. government's relations with the American Indian population, the author decribes the system of land allotment and the effects of the Indian Reorganization Act of 1934 on reservation properties and discusses tribal termination policies. Debo concludes with a review of key Federal Indian policy decisions during the 1960s.

H 1123. DEBO, ANGIE. The Road to Disappearance. Norman: University
of Oklahoma Press, 1941. 399 pp.
This work chronicles the history of the Creek Indians from the era of
the historic Creed Confederacy in Alabama and Georgia to the tribe's
post-removal decline in Oklahoma at the end of the 19th century. Debo
details the diplomatic and militaristic strategies employed by the Creeks
to maintain their homelands, their relations with other Southeastern
Indians, and their removal to Oklahoma in the 1830s. The bulk of the work
treats their long process of adjustment to life in their new home, their
participation in the Civil War, and their socio-political history thereafter
Particular emphasis is given to the role of mixed-blood Creeks as political
leaders, to the factionalism that emerged between full bloods and mixed
bloods, and to the tribe's process of acculturation in Oklahoma, including
their adoption of Christianity.

H 1124. DeROSIER, ARTHUR H. The Removal of the Choctaw Indians. Knoxville
University of Tennessee Press, 1970. 208 pp.
DeRosier presents a summary of Federal Indian policies implemented from
the time of Washington's administration through the term of Andrew Jackson
and discusses their effects on the Choctaw Indians. Emphasizing the importance of the "problem" the Southeastern Indians raised for national policy-
makers early in the 19th century, DeRosier compares the strategies of
early government officials such as John C. Calhoun with the removal tactics
of Andrew Jackson. He documents the erosion of the Choctaw political
structure under pressure from Jackson's administration and the relocation
of the tribe to Oklahoma in the 1830s.

H 1125. DIAL, ADOLF L. and DAVID K. ELIADES. The Only Land I Know: A
History of the Lumbee Indians. San Francisco: Indian Historian
Press, 1975. 188 pp.
Dial and Eliades present an ethno-historic account of the Lumbee Indians
of North Carolina. The authors describe their daily life, folklore, and
ethnic identity throughout two centuries of white domination. A large
portion of the work is devoted to the career of Henry Berry Lowrie, a
Civil War-era Lumbee and leader of a military anti-white band of local
Indians. The authors present primary documents that narrate Lumbee-white
relations during Lowie's career, and describe his evolution into a local
folk hero. Biographical sketches of other important Lumbee figures are
provided, and the authors detail the farming economy of the tribe and
their struggle to maintain legal status as Indians throughout the 20th
century.

H 1126. DIPPIE, BRIAN W. The Vanishing American: White Attitudes and
U.S. Indian Policy. Middletown, Conn.: Wesleyan University
Press, 1982. 423 pp.
Dippie examines the notion of the American Indian as a vanishing race,
and the impact of that perception on government policy-making throughout
U.S. history until the Indian Reorganization Act of 1934. Dippie demonstrates how the concept of the "Vanishing American" changed from the early
frontier days, when it was widely assumed that Indians would literally
die out, to the late-19th-century policy of acculturation which envisioned
that assimilation into Anglo-American society would destroy Indian culture
and identity. Dippie also examines the segregationist policy taken before
the Civil War, the policy of assimilation which occurred from the Civil
War through W.W. II, and the condition of the Indian since W.W. II. Dippie
takes the view of a cultural historian, examining the attitudes and beliefs
that create policy, rather than focusing on the policy itself, and brings
into his discourse discussions of anthropology, artistic notions and popu-
larly-held beliefs.

H 1127. DOWNES, RANDOLPH C. Council Fires on the Upper Ohio: A Narrative of Indian Affairs in the Upper Ohio Valley Until 1795. Pittsburgh, Pa.: University of Pittsburgh Press, 1940. 369 pp.
This work traces the history of Indian-white relations throughout the early years of white encroachment into the Upper Ohio Valley. The author describes the Shawnee conflicts with settlers over the territory of Kentucky and the struggle of the Iroquois to maintain Pennsylvania, as well as the defeat of the Delaware by the English. Downes provides a decade-by-decade chronology of events during the French-English struggle for the region, and of the roles played by the affected Indian tribes in that struggle and in the American Revolution. He traces the advancement of the American frontier into the Midwest and chronicles the careers of Daniel Boone, George Rogers Clark, and other leaders of the Euro-American penetration into Indian country.

H 1128. DRURY, CLIFFORD M. Chief Lawyer of the Nez Perce Indians, 1796-1876. Glendale, Calif.: Clark, 1979. 304 pp.
Drury examines the history of the Nez Perce throughout the 19th century by recounting the life experiences of The Lawyer, a Nez Perce diplomat who signed treaties in 1855 and 1863 that ceded tribal land and mineral rights to the U.S. government. In this study Drury portrays The Lawyer as the antithesis of Chief Joseph, the militant Nez Perce leader who resisted U.S. attempts to confine the tribe to a portion of their former territory. By contrasting the different political positions of the two men, the author describes the cultural change Nez Perce underwent during the 19th century and the factionalism that it generated. He chronicles the early attempts to missionize the Nez Perce, their political negotiations with the Federal government at the Walla Walla Council and the Lapwai Council, and their military engagements with U.S. troops.

H 1129. EASTMAN, ELAINE GOODALE. Pratt, the Red Man's Moses. Norman: University of Oklahoma Press, 1935. 285 pp.
Eastman presents a biography of General Richard Henry Pratt, 19th-century crusader for Indian rights and founder of the Carlisle Indian School in Pennsylvania. Eastman emphasizes Pratt's advocacy of assimilating American Indians through education, a position that was considered liberal in the late 1800s. She evaluates Pratt's influence on Federal Indian affairs; details his opinions on racism, intelligence, missionization, and various government policies related to Indian development; and describes Pratt's struggle to support his educational institutes and the success of his students, such as Dr. Carlos Montezuma and Dr. Charles A. Eastman.

H 1130. EDMUNDS, R. DAVID. The Potawatomis: Keepers of the Fire. Norman: University of Oklahoma Press, 1978. 367 pp.
In this tribal history, Edmunds examines the culture and society of the Potawatomis, focusing on the lifestyle changes introduced by European contact. The author discusses their horticultural heritage and their increasing dependence on European trade goods provided by French, British, and Euro-American colonists. Edmunds describes the political factionalism that emerged in the mid-18th century, when the Potawatomis became increasingly divided between allegiance to the French and to the British. He also examines the impact of the expanding American frontier and the forced removal of the Potawatomis to Kansas.

H 1131. EDMUNDS, R. DAVID, ed. American Indian Leaders: Studies in Diversity. Lincoln: University of Nebraska Press, 1980. 257 pp.
This collection of twelve essays by Edmunds and other historians examines Native American leadership from the 18th through the 20th centuries. The studies explore the various strategies (negotiation, accommodation, violence, etc.) employed by Indian leaders to come to terms with the prob-

lems of Indian-white contact, focusing upon their diplomatic approaches. Among the leaders whose biographies are included are Quannah Parker, Alexander Mcgillivray, Sitting Bull, and Peter MacDonald.

H 1132. EVANS, W. McKEE. To Die Game: The Story of the Lowry Band, Indian
         Guerillas of Reconstruction. Baton Rouge: Louisiana State Uni-
         versity Press, 1971. 282 pp.
Evans focuses on the rise of the Lowry Band, a group of North Carolina Lumbee Indians that organized during the Civil War in order to resist the forced labor imposed on all "colored" peoples during the Confederate war effort. This guerilla band existed until 1872 and fought both local governments and the Ku Klux Klan. Evans also provides a general history of the Lumbee nation, emphasizing their continued allegiance to their heritage and their struggle against racism.

H 1133. EWERS, JOHN C. Indian Life on the Upper Missouri. Norman: Uni-
         versity of Oklahoma Press, 1968. 222 pp.
Ewers examines the cultural and economic milieu of the tribes who occupied the Upper Missouri region prior to European contact and assesses the impact of their meeting on both peoples. Placing primary importance on trade relations between Anglo-Europeans and Indians, he evaluates their cultural exchange, and by examining the artwork of the era, he also explores the symbolic representation of European and Indian contact. Ewers assesses the effect of Anglo-European culture on the art of the Plains Indians and explores the role of the Plains tribes as a symbol among other Indian peoples.

H 1134. FEY, HAROLD E. and D'ARCY, McNICKLE. Indians and Other Americans:
         Two Ways of Life Meet. New York: Harper, 1959. 220 pp.
This work describes Native American/Euroamerican relations from the two groups' initial contact through the post-W.W. II era, with the object of assessing the Indians' situation in the 1950s and evaluating Federal regulation of that situation. The authors use demographic and economic data to support their unfavorable evaluation of the U.S. government's management of Indian affairs, and they also argue that Federal policy has resulted in the increased dependency of American Indians. They critique as short-sighted the history of tribal education and other forms of management, while defending the Indian Reorganization Act and other proposed measures that would encourage tribal self-determination.

H 1135. FORBES, JACK D. Apache, Navajo and Spaniard. Norman: University
         of Oklahoma Press, 1960. 304 pp.
Forbes examines the 17th-century Pueblo and Apache Indians and their con-tact with Spanish immigrants. He presents his material chronologically, beginning with a description of the first meeting of the Apache with the Spaniard and the story of Coronado's explorations. He then discusses Spanish efforts at mining and religious proselytizing, the establishment of a permanent Spanish colony in New Mexico, and the restoration of Spanish authority following the Pueblo Revolt of 1698. The author disputes the widely accepted opinion that the Apache and Pueblo Indians were enemies prior to Euro-American contact; instead, he credits Spanish intrusion with having generated most of Southwestern warfare.

H 1136. FORBES, JACK D. Warriors of the Colorado: The Yumas of the
         Quechan Nation and Their Neighbors. Norman: University of Okla-
         homa Press, 1965. 378 pp.
Forbes presents the ethnography and history of the Yuma Indians. Describ-ing their creation myth and treating the Yuma as a small folk culture, Forbes focuses on the effect upon such a culture of a meeting with a larger mass culture, and he examines the confrontation of the Yuma culture with the first Spanish conquerors, and later with the Mexicans and Anglo-

Americans. The chronology proceeds until the year 1852, when, after a 312-year struggle with the Europeans, the Quechan Nation ceased to exist as an independent tribe of American Indians.

H 1137. FOREMAN, GRANT. Indian Removal: The Emigration of the Five Civilized Tribes of Indians. Norman: University of Oklahoma Press, 1932. 415 pp.
Foreman examines the effects of President Jackson's Federal removal policy on each of the so-called "Five Civilized Tribes." He emphasizes that prior to these Southeastern Indians' relocation in Oklahoma, these tribes made great advances in the areas of education, commerce, and government, and he argues that the Federal government was unprepared to implement the complex goal of removal, the lack of preparation of which resulted in tragic consequences for the Indians. While criticizing the governmental and bureaucratic management of the affair, the author describes the efforts of enlisted men and civilians who attempted to aid the emigrants. The commentary is augmented by first-hand accounts of events, maps, and photographs of historic sites.

H 1138. FOWLER, LORETTA. Arapahoe Politics, 1851-1978: Symbols in Crises of Authority. Lincoln: University of Nebraska Press, 1982. 378 pp.
The product of both fieldwork and ethno-historic research, Arapahoe Politics examines the way in which Arapahoe history serves as a charter for contemporary political organization and social relationships among the reservation Arapahoe of Wind River, Wyoming. The author attempts to account for the Arapahoe government's uniquely successful accommodation to modern political systems, describing how new authority relations were legitimized and how tribal goals were implemented without undermining the structure of traditional leadership. Fowler examines the symbolism of political events among the Arapahoe and the ways in which ideologies have directed social action. She emphasizes the influence of the traditional Arapahoe age-grade system and details the tribal leadership of the past 150 years in order to illustrate the transformation of the tribe's political system.

H 1139. FRITZ, HENRY E. The Movement for Indian Assimilation, 1860-1890. Philadelphia: University of Pennsylvania Press, 1963. 244 pp.
In this study of the Indian policy reform era of the late 19th century, Fritz concentrates on the goals and implementation of Grant's peace policy. He contends that previous historians have judged this peace policy too harshly, pointing out improvements in recruiting agency employees and in bureaucratic administrative procedure. The failures of Grant's policy are blamed on Congress and on the political influence of the Catholic Church, a chief opponent of the Federal program. Fritz also examines the passage of the General Allotment Act of 1887 and the pressure exerted on Senator Dawes by voters seeking to secure Indian reform legislation.

H 1140. GIBSON, ARRELL MORGAN. The American Indian: Prehistory to the Present. Lexington, Mass.: Heath, 1980. 618 pp.
Gibson provides an overview of the Indian's role in American history, summarizing North American prehistory, describing cultural diversity among Indians in the post-contact era, and focusing on the history of Indian-white relations from the Colonial era to the 1970s. Gibson discusses the French, English, Spanish and American political regimes and their differing Indian policies, and describes the Indian wars, the removal of tribes to the West, their confinement on reservations, and their political and economic development throughout the 20th century.

H 1141. **GRAYMONT, BARBARA.** The Iroquois in the American Revolution. Syracuse, N.Y.: Syracuse University Press, 1972. 359 pp. Graymont details the political role of the Six Nations Confederacy in the British-American struggle for the North American continent. She recounts the Iroquois struggle to remain neutral toward both governments and describes the factionalism that destroyed the confederacy after the American Colonies began their bid for independence and both sides struggled to gain an alliance with the Iroquois. The role of leaders on all sides is described, with particular emphasis on the chieftainship of Joseph Brant. An underlying theme throughout the work is the detrimental effect of Iroquois dependency on Euro-Americans on the political viability of the Iroquois themselves.

H 1142. **GREEN, MICHAEL D.** The Politics of Indian Removal: Creek Government and Society in Crisis. Lincoln: University of Nebraska Press, 1982. 237 pp. Green focuses on the social and political history of the Creeks between 1814 and 1836, tracing the political events which culminated in their removal to Oklahoma in the early 1830s. Beginning with an overview of Creek social organization in the pre-Colonial era, Green describes their rapid loss of autonomy vis-a-vis the U.S. government. He examines the interplay of four decision-making bodies in the political process of removal: the Federal government; the state governments of Georgia and Alabama; the local, town governments of the Creeks; and the Creek National Council. Green emphasizes the actions of the latter as the center of opposition to removal. Descriptions of Andrew Jackson, Alexander Mcgillivray and other influential leaders are also included.

H 1143. **GREEN, NORMA KIDD.** Iron Eye's Family: The Children of Joseph La Flesche. Lincoln: Johnsen Publishing for Nebraska State Historical Society, 1969. 225 pp. Green provides a study of the late 19th-century La Flesche family, of mixed Omaha Indian and French descent. Iron Eye was the last hereditary chief of the Omaha and a progressive who advocated adoption of Euro-American customs. His dual allegiance was perpetuated in the careers of his children, who became famous intellectuals of their day. The author offers insight into the problems that faced American Indian people during a time of intense acculturation pressure by examining the lives of Susan, who became an M.D. and served as a tribal physician; Rosalie, who served as financial advisor to the Omaha; Susette, a nationally known reformer for Indian rights; and their brother Francis, who became the first professional American Indian anthropologist.

H 1144. **GRINNELL, GEORGE BIRD.** The Cheyenne Indians: Their History and Ways of Life. 2 vols. New Haven, Conn.: Yale University Press, 1923. 430 pp. Grinnell chronicles the social history and cultural practices of the Cheyenne Indians throughout the 19th century, based on his extensive fieldwork among the tribe. In Volume I, the author focuses on gender roles, marriage and child rearing practices, daily life, and other aspects of Cheyenne social organization. He also describes the subsistence economy, government, and material culture of the tribe. In Volume II, Grinnell presents the cultural beliefs of the Cheyenne: their cosmological notions, their medical philosophy and practices, and their ceremonial practices. He discusses the role of mythological symbolism in Cheyenne social organization and includes three appendices on Cheyenne village sites, songs, and the formation of the women's quilling society.

H 1145. GUNNERSON, DOLORES A. The Jicarilla Apaches: A Study in Survival.
DeKalb: Northern Illinois University Press, 1974. 326 pp.
In the first half of this work, Gunnerson traces the political and social
history of various Apache divisions after their arrival in the Southwest
in the early 16th century. Using linguistic and historic data, she
attempts to identify the many Apachean groups described in the early records
of Spanish explorers in order to reconstruct the Apache's social evolution.
The author re-examines the relations between the Apache and the Pueblo
Indians and describes their reactions to Spanish rule. The latter part
of the book deals specifically with the Jicarillas and the social flexibility which enabled them to retain their identity.

H 1146. GUNTHER, ERNA. Indian Life of the Northwest Coast of North America
As Seen by the Early Explorers and Fur Traders during the Last
Decades of the Eighteenth Century. Chicago: University of Chicago Press, 1972. 277 pp.
Gunther reconstructs the cultures of the Northwest Coast at the time of
white contact by combining information provided by native informants with
the written records of early explorers, traders and travelers to the region.
Employing ethnohistoric methodology, the author analyzes the journals,
diaries, and political documents of European explorers to interpret their
collections of material artifacts and their place in the cultures of the
Northwest Coast. She also examines the artistic representations of Indian
life rendered by members of Spanish, French, and English expeditions to
the area in order to gain ethnographic information about the indigenous
populations of the region.

H 1147. HAGAN, WILLIAM T. American Indians. Chicago: University of
Chicago Press, 1961. 190 pp.
Hagan presents a history of Indian-white relations from Colonial times
to the present, emphasizing the Indian policies of the Federal government.
He describes the importance of Indian alliances to the colonists in fighting with Spanish, and later with British, troops. Once the U.S. became
free from the threat of foreign dominance after 1812, the importance of
an Indian alliance diminished and the government could begin expanding
the country's frontier with less consideration of Indian interests. The
author details the Indian Removal of 1816-1850, and chronicles the resistance of Midwestern and Western Indians to government allotment policies
of the late 19th century. Hagan traces the roots of New Deal Indian policy
to the reform efforts of the turn of the century, stressing the often
unsuccessful attempts at acculturation.

H 1148. HAGAN, WILLIAM T. Indian Police and Judges: Experiments in Acculturation and Control. New Haven, Conn.: Yale University Press,
1966. 194 pp.
Hagan examines the Indian's participation in legal systems and law enforcement on reservations since the second half of the 19th century. The author
emphasizes the special problems of law enforcement in the old West, focusing on problems related to Indian lands and property. He explores the
origin of tribal police and the U.S. Army's subsequent recruitment of
Indians for the purpose of helping to subdue the militant factions within
the tribes. The work examines tribal police on Apache and Sioux reservations and the judgeship of Quannah Parker, former war leader of the
Comanche.

H 1149. HAGAN, WILLIAM T. United States-Comanche Relations: The Reservation Years. New Haven, Conn.: Yale University Press, 1976.
336 pp.
Hagan documents the political and social history of the Comanche from
their signing of the Medicine Lodge Treaty in 1867 until the death of
Quannah Parker in 1911. Using the stated goals of the treaty as a framework

503

for evaluating the implementation of Federal policy among the Comanche, the Kiowa, and the Kiowa-Apache during the last quarter of the 19th century, Hagan chronicles the government's efforts to assimilate the tribes and to reduce their land holdings. The work stresses the difficulties of reservation management and the factionalism that emerged among politicians, army personnel, and the Indians themselves regarding the issues of allotment, land sales, self-sufficiency, and law enforcement. Hagan also addresses the complications produced by cattlemen, businessmen, and missionaries who had an interest in Indian affairs, and discusses the influence of the Ghost Dance and the peyote cult on Comanche culture.

H 1150. HAINES, FRANCIS. The Nez Perces: Tribesmen of the Columbia Plateau. Norman: University of Oklahoma Press, 1935. 329 pp.
Haines chronicles the tribal history of the Nez Perce people of the intermontane Northwest, focusing on their adaptation to Anglo-American migration to the region in the 19th century. The author provides an overview of Nez Perce ethnography, describing their indigenous economy, political organization and cosmology. He treats their historic importance as traders and their relations with the other area Indian groups. Haines shows that the Nez Perce accepted Christianity and education at an early time, despite ensuing tribal factionalism over these issues. The latter half of the work analyzes the events that plunged the Nez Perce into warfare with the U.S. government over territorial rights, and the role of Chief Joseph in the Nez Perce War of 1877.

H 1151. HALLIBURTON, R., Jr. Red Over Black: Black Slavery Among the Cherokee Indians. Westport, Conn.: Greenwood Press, 1977. 218 pp.
Halliburton describes the history of black enslavement within the Cherokee Nation from the introduction of African slaves to America through their emancipation. He finds that the growth in the black slave population among the Cherokee was contemporary with the tribe's adoption of a sedentary agrarian society modeled on Southern plantation culture. The author argues that the Cherokee incorporated blacks into their kinship system and did not exploit them as a labor source as much as the Southern whites did. Halliburton details the adoption of a slave code by the Cherokee Nation, the activities of white missionaries and abolitionists in Cherokee country, and the friction between Southern states and the Indians in regard to the Cherokee's protection of runaway slaves.

H 1152. HASSRICK, ROYAL B. The Sioux: Life and Customs of a Warrior Society. Norman: University of Oklahoma Press, 1964. 379 pp.
Hassrick reconstructs Lakota Sioux society and culture as it existed in the period 1830-1870, when they were the dominant nation on the Northern Plains. The author provides a description of Lakota social organization, political structure, material culture, kinship, hunting and warfare patterns, and recreational activities. Focusing on the personality structure of the Lakota individual, Hassrick examines the conflict between self-interest and social demands in a small-scale, communal society, basing his reconstruction of the Sioux gestalt on information from older Sioux informants who lived during that era. The latter part of the study focuses on the function of self-sacrifice in the religion and status system of the Sioux.

H 1153. HAUPTMAN, LAWRENCE M. The Iroquois and the New Deal. Syracuse, N.Y.: Syracuse University Press, 1981. 256 pp.
Hauptman assesses the impact of the Indian New Deal policies, concentrating on the Iroquois populations in New York, Oklahoma and Wisconsin. He examines the benefits of tribal reorganization and of various legislative programs implemented by Roosevelt, focusing especially on the WPA program. Hauptman criticizes the means used by Commissioner of Indian Affairs John

Collier in his effort to secure tribal acceptance of the Indian Reorganization Act. The author examines the reasons behind the New York Iroquois'
rejection of the I.R.A., and reappraises Collier's leading critic, Alice
Lee Jamison.

H 1154. HERTZBERG, HAZEL W. The Search for an American Indian Identity:
Modern Pan-Indian Movements. Syracuse, N.Y.: Syracuse University
Press, 1971. 362 pp.
Hertzberg examines the emergence of pan-Indian movements throughout the
20th century, as Indian groups began working together for political and
ethnic unity. He analyzes the development of political reform organizations such as the National Congress of American Indians, and the rise
of inter-tribal religious movements such as the Native American Church.
Emphasizing the historical development of reform movements, Hertzberg
chronicles the formation of the first 20th-century national Indian movement,
the Society of American Indians, which was founded in 1911. The study
also extends to recent decades, discussing the rise of the American Indian
movement and other militant Indian rights organizations.

H 1155. HIGHWATER, JAMAKE. The Primal Mind: Vision and Reality in Indian
America. New York: New American Library, 1981. 234 pp.
Defining Indian thought as primal, Highwater examines its epistemological
foundations and explores the boundaries that separate the primal reality
from the world view of Western civilization. According to the author,
both systems of thought are in crisis, and the Western world has become
increasingly attracted to and influenced by the primal philosophic orientation. Highwater argues that these disparate orientations are a valuable
resource for each other and that they should complement and enhance one
another. He examines the behavioral implications of conceptual systems
as revealed through language, art, and other expressive domains of culture,
and suggests how these effect the identity and position of American Indians
in the modern world.

H 1156. HOLDER, PRESTON. The Hoe and the Horse on the Plains: A Study
of Cultural Development Among the American Indians. Lincoln:
University of Nebraska Press, 1970. 176 pp.
Holder compares the adaptations of nomadic bison hunters and village horti-
culturalists in the upper Missouri region of the Northern Plains and evaluates the interaction of the two groups throughout the 19th century. Using
archeological, ethnological and historical materials, he focuses on the
subsistence strategies and social organization of the Caddoan-speaking
village Indians. He provides an overview of the rise of the equestrian
hunting economy on the plains in the 18th century, and describes the evolution of the Dakota Sioux as prototypical of the nomadic patterns.
The author describes the decline of the village cultures under military
pressure from equestrian groups, the demands of Euro-American trades, and
the influence of epidemic diseases.

H 1157. HOOVER, DWIGHT W. The Red and the Black. Chicago: Rand McNally,
1976. 469 pp.
Hoover presents a survey of the racial ideas and images of Indians and
blacks in the New World from Colonial days to the present, concentrating
on the 20th century. The premise upon which the book is based is that
racial views both reflect prevailing social assumptions and political
events and influence them. The structure is Kuhnsian insofar as the author
argues that changing ideas are not the product of gradual progress brought
about by new discoveries, but are the result of paradigm shifts which
occur when old paradigms prove inadequate. Hoover considers both the
ideas and images held by the dominant white majority and those of the
minority groups themselves. His evidence is drawn from popular culture,
literature, plays, movies, and television, as well as from anthropological,
religious, and genetic theory.

H 1158. **HOROWITZ, DAVID.** The First Frontier: The Indian Wars and
America's Origins, 1607-1776. New York: Simon & Schuster, 1978.
251 pp.
Horowitz reconstructs the early history of relations between Eastern Indian
nations and the Colonists. The author shows that many of the Colonial
Indian wars were sparked by the desire for revenge on the part of Indian
groups who had been attacked without provocation. He describes the alliances of the Hurons and Iroquois with French, English, and American military forces and the consequent inter-tribal wars, as well as Pontiac's
War. The work closes with the American Declaration of Independence in
1776.

H 1159. **HORSMAN, REGINALD P.** Expansion and American Policy, 1783-1812.
East Lansing: Michigan State University Press, 1967. 209 pp.
Horsman examines the evolution of American Indian policy during the first
twenty-five years after the establishment of the American Republic. He
concludes that despite the well-organized plans for fair treatment of
Indian peoples made by administrators such as Washington's Secretary of
War Henry Knox, the unwillingness of both whites and Indians to compromise
their claim to frontier lands made conflict inevitable. The author argues
that government policy-makers justified seizure of Indian lands according
to their ethnocentric belief that they were "civilizing" Native Americans.

H 1160. **HUDDLESTON, LEE ELDRIDGE.** Origins of the American Indians:
European Concepts, 1492-1729. Austin: University of Texas Press,
1967. 179 pp.
Huddleston investigates 16th- and 17th-century European literature in
order to reveal the attitudes of European Americans toward the problem
of the origins of New World Indians. Noting that the classification and
origins of Indians was primarily a theological problem, Huddleston documents the attempts of the early writers to argue the affinities between
American Indians and other more well-known peoples, including the Hebrews.
The author evaluates the impact of various prominent writers (predominantly
Spanish) on the question, including Joseph de Acosta and Gregorio Garcia,
each of whom he credits with establishing a major tradition of thinking
in the oral literature. Historical landmarks in the debate, such as the
Grotius-DeLaet controversy, are evaluated.

H 1161. **HUDSON, CHARLES.** The Southeastern Indians. Knoxville: University
of Tennessee Press, 1976. 573 pp.
Hudson provides an overview of Indian culture in the Southeast from prehistory through the 20th century. Using archaeological data, he describes
the major prehistorical traditions in the region from the Paleo-Indian
era to the Mississippian. Through an analysis of regional myths and artifacts of material culture, Hudson discusses the belief system of the
Indians with an emphasis on the Southeastern Ceremonial complex. His
description of the social organization of the Indians focuses on the role
of dual organization and ranking in the regional kinship systems. He
also includes descriptions of subsistence systems, ceremonial organization,
artistic forms, and games, and he analyzes their position in ideological
frameworks. Hudson concludes with a discussion of the impact of European
and American colonization on the Indians, paying attention to the removal
of Southeastern Indians under President Jackson in the 1830s. He briefly
evaluates the impact of Indian culture on contemporary Southern society
and discusses the acculturation of the Indians in the 1960s.

H 1162. **HUMPHREY, SETH K.** The Indian Dispossessed. Boston: Little,
Brown, 1905. 298 pp.
The Indian Dispossessed is an early indictment of 150 years of legislative
policy in America during which Indian peoples were dispossessed of their
lands. Humphrey points out that governmental policies toward Native Ameri-

cans violated the principles of Christianity and the Constitution of the
U.S. At the same time, Humphrey traces the efforts of missionaries and
reformers to help the Indian by encouraging acculturation, an approach
that he attributes to the ethnocentric sentiments of the turn-of-the-
century Indian reform movement. The author provides case studies of the
process of dispossession among the Umatillas, the Nez Perce, the Ponca,
and the Mission Indians of California, and describes U.S. Federal violations of its own policies and treaties throughout the country.

H 1163. HYDE, GEORGE E. Indians of the High Plains: From the Prehistoric
Period to the Coming of the Europeans. Norman: University of
Oklahoma Press, 1959. 231 pp.
Hyde documents the changing balance of power among Plains Indians prior
to the 19th century. He begins by describing the Athapaskan group's
advancement into the Southwest in the 17th century and then chronicles
their evolution into the Navajo nation and the Padoucas, or Plains Apache,
who controlled the Plains from the Dakotas to Texas. He details their
relations with the other regional tribes, paying particular attention
to the Pawnee and the Kiowas. He describes this group's demise and the
ensuing ascendancy of the Shoshonean tribes, including the Shoshone, the
Utes, and the Comanches. Hyde focuses on their intertribal wars with
the Cheyennes, Arapahoes, and the Crows, who abandoned a horticultural
village existence in the 18th century and moved onto the Plains after
the acquisition of horses and European firearms.

H 1164. HYDE, GEORGE E. Indians of the Woodlands: From Prehistoric Times
to 1725. Norman: University of Oklahoma Press, 1962. 295 pp.
Hyde combines archeological analysis with ethno-historic tradition to analyze the prehistoric and early historic cultures of the north-central
woodlands of the Midwest. Emphasizing the early development of the Siouan
language group, Hyde details their origins in the Ohio Valley and the
Iroquoians' introduction of the Hopewell culture to the Siouan groups.
He examines their transformation from hunter-gatherers to village horti-
culturists and traces the persistence of Hopewellian culture themes among
the woodland Siouan groups after their subsequent migrations to the North
and West. The author evaluates various theories concerning the rise of
the Southwestern Mississippian tradition and the Iroquoian migration to
the north. He describes the impact on the Siouan and Algonquian people
of the early French penetrations into the Great Lakes and the central Ohio
Valley, and he evaluates the role of the Iroquois in subsequent inter-
tribal wars. Throughout the work, Hyde critiques the various research
methodologies employed by other anthropologists at the time of this study.

H 1165. HYDE, GEORGE E. Red Cloud's Folk: A History of the Oglala Sioux
Indians. Norman: University of Oklahoma Press, 1937. 331 pp.
Hyde details the tribal history of the Oglala Sioux from the time of their
migration from the Great Lakes Region of Minnesota to the Great Plains
through the early reservation era. He focuses on the historic events
that transformed the Sioux into the dominant Indians on the plains and
on the Sioux individuals and families who influenced the ensuing social
transformation. He also documents relationships between the Oglala and
various traders and U.S. government officials in order to explain the
chain of events that resulted in the Siouxs' confinement on reservations.

H 1166. IVERSON, PETER. Carlos Montezuma and the Changing World of American Indians. Albuquerque: University of New Mexico Press, 1982.
222 pp.
Iverson examines the life of Carlos Montezuma, a Yavapai physician, Indian
rights activist, and controversial opponent of the Bureau of Indian Affairs.
Iverson considers the activities of Montezuma, which includes publishing
an Indian rights newspaper, Wassaja, and lobbying among members of dif-

ferent tribes for the development of a Pan-Indian movement, against the
backdrop of the transformation of Indian life in the late 19th and early
20th centuries. Here Iverson explores the adjustment to reservation confinement, the struggle for a land base and water rights, and the crusade
for greater autonomy within the political framework of the reservation.

H 1167. IVERSON, PETER. The Navajo Nation. Westport, Conn.: Greenwood
Press, 1981. 273 pp.
Focusing on the 20th-century history of the Navajo people, Iverson
describes their evolution into a unified and prosperous nation. The author
presents a decade-by-decade chronology of the economic and cultural crises
faced by the Navajo in the process of their development into one of the
most numerous and successful Indian peoples in America. Their successful
retention of traditional values is highlighted in a discussion of their
educational and medical systems. Iverson includes an in-depth examination
of contemporary Navajo politics under the tribal chairmanship of Peter
MacDonald.

H 1168. JAENEN, CORNELIUS J. Friend and Foe: Aspects of French-Amerindian
Cultural Contact in the Sixteenth and Seventeenth Centuries.
New York: Columbia University Press, 1976. 207 pp.
Jaenen examines the widely accepted notion that French relations with
American Indians were more benevolent than those of the English and Spanish.
Focusing on the ideological context of the French-Indian contact, he
describes the "invention" of America and its inhabitants by early European
writers and explorers, analyzes the concept of the "noble savage" as it
reflects the 16th-century French world view, and discusses the difficulties
the Jesuit missionaries encountered in their attempt to Christianize the
Iroquois and other Indians in New France. Jaenen argues that while all
European nations shared a similar conceptual framework, their relations
with Native Americans varied according to their economic motives in the
New World. He notes that while French-Indian relations were friendly
in the pre-Colonial era, the rise of Canadian nationality in the modern
era generated a new gap between the two cultures.

H 1169. JENNINGS, FRANCIS. The Invasion of America: Indians, Colonialism,
and the Cant of Conquest. Chapel Hill: University of North
Carolina Press, Institute of Early American History and Culture,
1975. 369 pp.
Jennings critiques both the sources and interpretations used by historians
to describe the conquest of Native American peoples by Euro-American society. The author analyzes the ideologies that influence historical documentation and offers alternative assumptions for ethno-historic methodology
and analysis. He presents new aspects of Indian-white relations in the
Northeast and South, concentrating on the Colonial era. He also examines
the influence of early anthropological and liberal theory on our perception
of Native American life.

H 1170. JOHN, ELIZABETH A. H. Storms Brewed in Other Men's Worlds: The
Confrontation of Indians, Spanish and French in the Southwest,
1540-1795. College Station: Texas A&M University Press, 1975.
805 pp.
John provides a comprehensive examination of the interaction between European and Indian peoples in the American Southwest during 250 years of
Spanish rule in that region. Beginning with the first documentation of
each of the regional Indian groups, the author narrates their varying
experiences under the Spanish, the concurrent development of Hispanic
communities throughout the area, and the changing relationships of these
groups. She analyzes the development of Spanish Indian policy and assesses
the cultural and social impact of Spanish government on the indigenous
populations, with particular attention to the Pueblo, Comanche, Apache,
Caddoan, and Navajo groups.

H 1171. JOSEPHY, ALVIN M., Jr. The Indian Heritage of America. New York: Knopf, 1968. 384 pp.

Josephy provides a summary account of the cultural developments of North and South American Indians, describing the major culture areas of the Americas with regard to economy, language, material culture and social organization. The first part of the work focuses on the Precolumbian era in the Western hemisphere, including a description of South and Central American ethnographic areas. In the latter half of the book, Josephy describes the conquest of the Indians in the U.S., Canada, and Latin America, and examines the Indian resistance to assimilation in the 1960s and 1970s.

H 1172. JOSEPHY, ALVIN M., Jr. The Nez Perce Indians and the Opening of the Northwest. New Haven, Conn.: Yale University Press, 1965. 705 pp.

Josephy provides a lengthy, detailed treatment of the political and social history of the Nez Perce from the time of their contact with American traders until the dramatic surrender of Chief Joseph in 1877. The author describes the various strategies employed by leading Nez Perce headmen in dealing with white encroachment, and he analyzes the influence of particular Indian agents, military personnel, missionaries, and educators who participated in tribal affairs. Josephy chronicles the escalation of violence in the interior Northwest following the Whitman massacre, the Indians' attempt to unify in resistance against U.S. pressures, and the long military struggle of the Nez Perce to retain their homeland in the Walla Walla Valley.

H 1173. KELLY, LAWRENCE C. The Assault on Assimilation: John Collier and the Origins of Indian Policy Reform. Albuquerque: University of New Mexico Press, 1983. 445 pp.

Kelly's study is both a biography of John Collier, Commissioner of Indian Affairs under Franklin Roosevelt, and an analysis of Federal Indian policy between 1920 and 1945. The author details Collier's personal development into an idealistic reformer deeply concerned with global social and environmental problems, as well as his early involvement in community development. He characterizes Collier's interest in Indian problems as a natural outcome of his early interests, and details his participation in various legal disputes concerning Indian rights, both as a private citizen and as Indian commissioner. The author describes Collier's political acumen in reforming Indian health services, protecting their religious freedom and fighting policies of Indian assimilation, while noting that Collier's inability to compromise hampered his effectiveness and foiled his goals as Commissioner of Indian Affairs.

H 1174. KELLY, LAWRENCE C. The Navajo Indians and Federal Indian Policy, 1900-1935. Tucson: University of Arizona Press, 1968. 221 pp.

Kelly discusses the political history of the Navajo from the establishment of their reservation to the implementation of the Indian Reorganization Act. He examines the effect of the 1887 Dawes Act on the Navajo land base and on Navajo relations with the Federal government. Focusing on the historical development of Navajo land-rights conflicts, the author describes the foundation of Federal laws that provided for the exploitation of oil and mineral resources on the reservation. In the latter half of the study, Kelly describes tribal efforts to expand reservation holdings and analyzes the effects of New Deal policies on Navajo range management, health and educational services, and political status.

H 1175. KELLY, LAWRENCE C. Navajo Roundup: Selected Correspondence of
         Kit Carson's Expedition Against the Navajo, 1863-1865. Boulder,
         Colo.: Pruett Press, 1970. 192 pp.
Kelly provides almost 100 samples of the correspondence between the military personnel (including General James H. Carleton and Kit Carson) who
carried out the defeat and forced march of the Navajo to the Bosque Redondo
reservation. The author utilizes these data to reinterpret many of the
events of the expedition, such as the Canyon de Chelly campaign, and to
re-evaluate the role of Kit Carson. The hope of the Indian policy makers
to achieve rapid acculturation and the damaging effect of the military
campaign on the Navajo people are underlying themes in Kelly's commentary.

H 1176. KENNEDY, J. H. Jesuit and Savage in New France. New Haven, Conn.:
         Yale University Press, 1950. 206 pp.
Kennedy analyzes the impact of French Jesuit experiences in Canada and
the Northeastern U.S. on European thought in the 17th and 18th centuries,
with particular emphasis on the notion of "savagism." The author examines
the writing of the early Jesuit missionaries to reconstruct their impressions of Indian intelligence, morality, reason, religion, and political
organization. He emphasizes that the Jesuits were impressed by the physical vigor and generosity of the Indians they encountered, and were the
first Europeans to perceive Native Americans as individual human beings.
The author focuses on how these impressions were used in European theological debates of the era, and on the relationship between Catholicism
and politics in France.

H 1177. KENNER, CHARLES L. A History of New Mexican-Plains Indian Rela-
         tions. Norman: University of Oklahoma Press, 1969. 250 pp.
Kenner describes social and political relations on the northern frontier
of the Southwest from the early Spanish settlement of New Mexico through
the end of the 19th century. The author emphasizes the continuity in
informal relations of trade and warfare despite changes in territorial
control from Spain to Mexico to the U.S. Focusing on 19th-century events,
Kenner discusses the relations between Anglo-Americans, Pueblo Indians
and Plains tribes, emphasizing the Comanche resistance to white settlement
and their participation in the cattle trade. The author explores the
role of professional buffalo hunters and traders in the area and the dangers they faced from the Indians. He emphasizes the development of a
regional culture among village Indians, Plains Indians, and Hispanic settlers.

H 1178. KESSELL, JOHN L. Kiva, Cross and Crown: The Pecos Indians and
         New Mexico, 1540-1840. Washington, D.C.: U.S. Park Service,
         1979. 587 pp.
Kessell examines the cultural history of the Pueblo Indians under the
dominion of the Spanish and Mexican governments. Focusing on the history
of Pecos Pueblo, the author describes the imposition of Catholicism and
forced labor on the Pueblos by the Spanish, and the missionization attempts
by several prominent friars who worked in Pecos. The author details the
importance of Pecos as a trading center, the Pecos' relations with Plains
Indians, and their prominent role in the Pueblo Revolt of 1680. Kessell
describes the near-destruction of the Pecos population by Comanche raiders
and by small-pox in the late 18th and early 19th centuries and the abandonment of the Pueblo in 1838. He chronicles the subsequent near-destruction
of the village by Hispanic settlers and treasure-hunters until the Pueblo
was excavated and restored by archeologists throughout the 20th century.
The text is augmented by more than 500 illustrations, photographs, and
maps.

H 1179. KESSELL, JOHN L. Mission of Sorrows: Jesuit Guevavi and the Pinas, 1691-1767. Tucson: University of Arizona Press, 1970. 224 pp.

Kessell focuses on the Jesuit mission of Los Santos Angeles de Guevavi in this study of Spanish-Pima relations in southern Arizona during the late 17th and early 18th centuries. Drawing from the archives of the Roman Catholic Diocese in Tucson, Arizona, Kessel presents the Jesuit padres' point of view on their efforts to convert the Pima to Spanish Christianity, and he notes the ethnocentric manner in which they portray the Pima as resisting the assault on their culture. Kessel maintains that the position of the mission on the advanced northern frontier of Mexico separated it from missions further south in that it was largely exempt from the competition for resources between missionaries and colonists that characterized the southern territories.

H 1180. KICKINGBIRD, KIRKE and KAREN DUCHENEAUX. One Hundred Million Acres. New York: Macmillan, 1973. 240 pp.

The authors, both of whom are Indian, direct the American readers' attention away from historical portrayals of Indian life and toward an examination of contemporary Indian struggles to control the remnants of their land base. Case studies of the legal status and management of Indian land resources focus on Alaskan natives, the Crow, the Sioux, the Menominee, and also on smaller, lesser-known tribes. The authors criticize Federal Indian policies and advocate new reform measures that would provide Indian peoples with the economic foundations and land base necessary for tribal self-determination.

H 1181. KRECH, SHEPARD III, ed. Indians, Animals, and the Fur Trade: A Critique of "Keepers of the Game." Athens: University of Georgia Press, 1981. 207 pp.

In this collection of essays, seven authors discuss the North American Indian participation in the fur trade in terms of Calvin Martin's 1978 publication Keepers of the Game: Indian-Animal Relationships and the Fur Trade (H 1193). Martin attempts to present the Indian point of view, proposing that before the arrival of the Europeans the Indians lived in balance with nature, enforced by taboos against excess hunting. The Europeans brought disease with them which was misunderstood by the Indians who blamed the animals. The original harmonious relationship was destroyed; taboos were ignored, prompting the Indians to overkill the wildlife in their participation in the fur trade. Martin's work addresses many issues, including whether his thesis can be applied to other areas of the continent, and whether there were more materialist reasons for the Indian involvement in the fur trade. This book concludes with a response by Martin to some of these arguments.

H 1182. KUPPERMAN, KAREN ORDAHL. Settling with the Indians: The Meeting of English and Indian Culture in America, 1580-1640. Totowa, N.J.: Rowman & Littlefield, 1980. 224 pp.

Kupperman examines the world view of the English colonists by presenting descriptions of American Indians written by colonists for an English audience. Taking the view that the English colonists had a perspective on their environment that was not much more sophisticated than that of the Indians, the author then describes the confrontation of their cultures, and the similarities and differences inherent in their world views. Kupperman asserts that the English were impressed by the stability of the Indians, often holding it up as a paradigm of strength against the backdrop of their own decaying social order, and concludes by cautioning against exaggerating the modernity of the "rank and file" English colonists.

H 1183. LA FARGE, OLIVER. As Long as the Grass Shall Grow. New York:
         Longmans, Green, 1940. 144 pp.
La Farge's text is supplemented by more than 100 of Helen M. Post's photographs of Native American life. Both the narrative and the illustrations
portray a dual theme: the despondent atmosphere of reservation life on
the one hand, and the hope for improvement through education and modernization on the other. The author describes the struggles of Native peoples
attempting to adapt themselves to the reservation era while trying to
preserve their traditional cultures and world view. Speaking from the
Indian viewpoint, La Farge expresses the despair and confusion they have
experienced as a consequence of losing control over their lives and the
lives of their children.

H 1184. LAWSON, MICHAEL L. Dammed Indians: The Pick-Sloan Plan and the
         Missouri River Sioux, 1944-1980. Norman: University of Oklahoma
         Press, 1982. 261 pp.
Lawson's Dammed Indians provides a case study of contemporary land rights
struggles between the U.S. Federal government and American Indian tribes.
The book examines the impact of the Army Corps of Engineers' construction
of flood control dams along the Missouri River upon the Sioux people,
whose land and water resources were seriously damaged by the project.
Much of the book is devoted to a review of the Sioux people's increasing
ability to press their legal claims against the government for its violation of treaty rights and to sue for compensation for the loss of their
property and economic resources.

H 1185. LEUPP, FRANCIS E. In Red Man's Land: A Study of the American
         Indian. New York: Revell, 1914. 160 pp.
Former Commissioner of Indian Affairs Leupp presents his view of Native
American cultures and individuals. Despite the author's conviction that
Western civilization is superior to that of the Indians, he critiques
government wardship over Indian peoples and the negative effects of Federal
policies on tribal development in the early years of the 20th century.
Leupp describes the beauty of indigenous Indian life and philosophy, and
condemns the government's efforts to ban traditional forms of religious
practice, dress and home life. He advocates greater sensitivity on the
part of Federal policy makers in their design of acculturation programs,
which Leupp feels should capitalize on the strengths of Indian culture
rather than effect whole-scale replacement of their lifestyles.

H 1186. LIBERTY, MARGOT and JOHN STANDS IN TIMBER. Cheyenne Memories.
         New Haven, Conn.: Yale University Press, 1967. 330 pp.
The authors provide an ethno-historic account of the Cheyenne in the 19th
century as related by the tribal historian in the 1950s. The narrative
is augmented by photographs and old ledger drawings. Stands In Timber
recounts Cheyenne mythology, the biographies of famous tribal personalities,
the social organization of the Cheyenne and their historic relations with
other tribes. He describes the structure and function of Cheyenne political and religious institutions and men's societies and recounts the Cheyenne version of the Little Big Horn and other important military engagements with the U.S. army. The work includes an account of life throughout
the reservation era from a Cheyenne perspective.

H 1187. LINDQUIST, G. E. E., ed. The Indian in American Life. New York:
         Friendship Press, 1944. 185 pp.
The chapters of this work, some of which are authored by contributors
other than Lindquist, address the topics of culture areas, Indian-white
relations, acculturation, education, and tribal leadership. Lindquist
includes the life experiences of individual Indian families in order to
assess the roles of American Indians in U.S. society in the W.W. II era.
He advocates Christian leadership in the acculturation of Native Americans

and commends the missionary effort while criticizing the 1934 Indian Reorganization Act.

H 1188. LITTLEFIELD, DANIEL F., Jr. Africans and Creeks: From the
         Colonial Period to the Civil War. Westport, Conn.: Greenwood
         Press, 1979. 286 pp.
Littlefield examines the impact of black slavery on the Creek people as
well as the Seminoles, the subject of a previous study (see H 1189).
As the Creek nation developed a plantation economy, they adopted the white
practice of slavery. Black slaves from both white and Creek planters
escaped, whenever they could, into Seminole country. Littlefield devotes
much of his discussion to a description of how this nearby refuge affected
Creek-Seminole relations, particularly after the Creek's removal to Oklahoma as the close proximity of black slaves among the Creeks and free
blacks among the Seminoles gave rise to conflict. Littlefield also gives
an account of the institution of slavery in the West and of the involvement
of the Creeks and their blacks in the American Civil War, which resulted
in the emancipation of the blacks and their subsequent adoption as members
of the Creek nation. It is Littlefield's hope that this study will lend
new insight into the extent of social discontinuity and the rate of acculturation of the Creeks before the Civil War.

H 1189. LITTLEFIELD, DANIEL F., Jr. Africans and Seminoles: From Removal
         to Emancipation. Westport, Conn.: Greenwood Press, 1977.
         278 pp.
Littlefield examines the relations between blacks and Seminole Indians
from the development of their alliance against slaveholders in the 18th
century to the Civil War era. He chronicles the evolution of the institution of slavery among the Seminoles; describes how the nature of Seminole
slavery differed from that of other Southeastern tribes; documents the
military alliance between blacks and Seminoles during the War of 1812,
the two Seminole wars, and during the implementation of the Removal Act
in the 1830s; emphasizes how the Seminole policy of harboring run away
slaves complicated their relations with the white community both in Florida
and in the West after removal; explores the roles of blacks within Seminole
society as slaves, warriors, and interpreters; and discusses the extent
of cultural exchange between the two groups.

H 1190. LLEWELLYN, K. N. and E. ADAMSON HOEBEL. The Cheyenne Way: Con-
         flict and Case Law in Primitive Jurisprudence. Norman: Univer-
         sity of Oklahoma Press, 1941. 360 pp.
In this study of Cheyenne law, the authors analyze data collected from
the Northern Cheyenne of the Tongue River Reservation in Montana to examine
the interplay between legal institutions, legal ideologies and actual
behavior. Using the case study method of analysis, they explore the patterns that underlay the complexity of legal process in a society that
was flexible and loosely organized in comparison with Euro-American civilization. The authors trace the evolution of the Cheyenne legal system from
1820-1880 by presenting fifty-three case studies of the application of
Cheyenne laws regarding property rights, inheritance, homicide, marriage,
religious infractions and other issues. From this evidence they provide
an examination of Cheyenne culture, social organization, and tribal ethics.

H 1191. MAILS, THOMAS E. The Mystic Warriors of the Plains. Garden City,
         N.Y.: Doubleday, 1972. 618 pp.
Mails offers a comprehensive summary of Plains Indian life in its strongest
era, between 1750-1875. Illustrated throughout by the author, the work
describes the daily life, social organization and government of many Plains
tribes. A Lutheran pastor, Mails concentrates on tribal religious ideology
and ceremonies and on their expressive manifestations in objects, art,
songs, and dance. The underlying focus of the book is a description and

defense of the ethos of Plains cultures as seen by a contemporary theologian. The author draws on the accounts of early observers of Plains life to reconstruct their lifestyle and world view.

H 1192. MARDOCK, ROBERT W. The Reformers and the American Indian. Columbus: University of Missouri Press, 1971. 245 pp.
Mardock chronicles the rise of Indian reform movements during the post-Civil War years and their liberal, political and theological background. The author emphasizes the Christian mission that guided the work of reformist groups, including their belief that frontier society was morally unjust and hampered Indian social development. The author describes the regional factionalism that characterized political debate over the development of Federal Indian policy, and describes the political influence of the largely Eastern reform organizations. The book includes an analysis of the controversial Dawes Act of 1887, which provided for individual land-titles as part of an attempt to acculturate Indians into the national economic system.

H 1193. MARTIN, CALVIN. Keepers of the Game: Indian-Animal Relationships and the Fur Trade. Berkeley: University of California Press, 1978. 226 pp.
Martin characterizes the American Indian as an environmentalist and calls for further study of the role played by Native Americans in the fur trade of the 17th, 18th, and 19th centuries. Focusing on the Micmac and Ojibway peoples of Canada, Martin suggests that the tremendous disruption (principally epidemic diseases) brought to the Indian environment by European contact upset the Indian spiritual view of the balance of nature. Martin contends that with the breakdown of this contract between man and his environment, Indian peoples began a wholesale slaughter of fur-bearing animals as an act of revenge against the ecosystem which they felt had betrayed them.

H 1194. McKEE, JESSE O. and JON SCHLENKER. The Choctaws: Cultural Evolution of a Native American Tribe. Jackson: University Press of Mississippi, 1980. 227 pp.
In this introduction to the history of the Choctaw tribe from prehistory to the present, the authors stress the changing structure of Choctaw culture. They place particular emphasis on the transformation of Choctaw social structure due to political control by the U.S. Federal government. They also discuss the effects of the 1830s removal policy on the Mississippi and the Oklahoma Choctaw, paying particular attention to their socio-economic status, demography, and settlement pattern. The administrations of contemporary tribal leaders are described. Statistical tables of Choctaw land use, labor, political organization, and demography supplement the text.

H 1195. McNICKLE, D'ARCY. They Came Here First: The Epic of the American Indian. Philadelphia: Lippincott, 1949. 325 pp.
McNickle provides a general history of Native Americans from their prehistoric migration across the Bering Strait through the passage of John Collier's Indian Reorganization Act in 1934. The author describes the flavor of Indian cultures by presenting examples of their languages, arts, and myths. He assesses the discovery and colonization of North America from both the Indian and white viewpoint; examines the major tenets of English and American Indian policies; and geographically traces the process of Indian displacement and U.S. governmental land acquisition. The author reviews important court cases in order to illustrate the government's continuing efforts to control the destiny of the Indian people and to acquire their land and resources.

H 1196. McNITT, FRANK. The Indian Traders. Norman: University of Oklahoma Press, 1962. 393 pp.
McNitt discusses the major Southwestern Indian traders in the 19th and
early 20th centuries, emphasizing the trading industry's critical role
in Indian-white relations, and tracing the careers of such prominent
traders as Lorenzo Hubbel, C. M. Cotton, Jacob Hambline, and Solomon Bibo.
The author stresses the fact that although the traders' economic motives
often induced them to take advantage of their Indian clientele, their
intimate association with the tribes also facilitated transmission of
more positive influences on Indian life. McNitt cites as an example the
development of craft industries, which supplemented the income of reservation Indians, and he details the evolution of rug production among the
Navajo and the role of several traders in its development and marketing.
The work also describes the Southwestern trade industry in general, including the primary commodities exchanged, the price scale, and the operation
of particular trading posts.

H 1197. MEYER, ROY W. The Village Indians of the Upper Missouri: The
Mandans, Hidatsas, and Arikaras. Lincoln: University of Nebraska
Press, 1977. 354 pp.
Meyer chronicles the history of the Mandan, Hidatsa and Arikara Indians
from the proto-historic era through the 1970s, focusing on the history
of the Upper Missouri region during the 19th century, when these village
groups played an important role in the regional trading system. The author
details the relation between the three tribes with other area Indians and
with Lewis and Clark and other explorers; chronicles the increased affiliation of the three groups after the 1837 smallpox epidemic that reduced
their population; and details their placement on a common reservation
and their subsequent relocations. The political and social organization
of the tribes throughout the 20th century is described, with an emphasis
on their increasing modernization and acculturation. Meyer discusses the
impact of the construction of the Garrison Dam on the reservation in 1948
and the legal battles over tribal rights that followed. He also examines
tribal political and economic affairs in the 1960s and 1970s.

H 1198. MINER, H. CRAIG. The Corporation and the Indian: Tribal Sovereignty and Industrial Civilization in Indian Territory, 1865-
1907. Columbia: University of Missouri Press, 1976. 236 pp.
Miner examines the relationship between Indian tribes and corporations
in Oklahoma prior to its statehood. The study focuses on how capitalist
expansion in the post-Civil War years influenced Indian policy in such
a way as to facilitate corporate ownership of Indian lands. The author
argues that it was the process of corporate expansion that destroyed the
sovereignty of the Indian tribes and undercut their political rights vis-
a-vis the Federal government. Miner describes the expansionist strategies
of the early coal and oil and cattle industries and how these affected
the Choctaw, the Osage, the Cherokee, and other Oklahoma Indian tribes.

H 1199. MINER, H. CRAIG and WILLIAM UNRAU. The End of Indian Kansas:
A Study of Cultural Revolution, 1854-1871. Lawrence: Regents
Press of Kansas, 1978. 179 pp.
Miner and Unrau document the second era of Indian removal, in which 10,000
Indians already resettled in Kansas were removed to Oklahoma by the Federal
government in order to open the territory for settlement. The authors
examine how the removal process was accomplished by means of negotiation,
fraud and government pressure, and they detail the role of prominent local
and national political figures in the policy's development and implementation. They emphasize the population decimation suffered by the Indians
in the course of their forced removal, the decline of their economic base
in Oklahoma, and the effects of these factors on their cultural vitality.

H 1200. MINGE, WARD ALLEN. Acoma: Pueblo in the Sky. Albuquerque:
University of New Mexico Press, 1976. 180 pp.
Using both ethno-historical and archaeological data, Minge provides a historic summary of the people of Acoma Pueblo from the time of their first
contact with Europeans in 1540 to the 1970s. The study focuses on the
cultural adjustments made by the Acoma in response to the rule and policies
of Spain, Mexico, and finally the U.S. Numerous photographs, maps, and
tables augment the text.

H 1201. MOHR, WALTER H. Federal Indian Relations, 1774-1788. Philadelphia
University of Pennsylvania Press, 1933. 247 pp.
Mohr examines the early attempts of the U.S. government to develop policies
for dealing with Indian populations and the struggle between Federal and
state polities for legal jurisdiction over Native Americans. He chronicles
the collapse of English rule and its effect on the Indians of the Northeast,
many of whom had aligned themselves with the British during the Revolutionary War; describes early treaty negotiations with the Indians of the
Northeast and with the Southeastern tribes throughout the 18th century;
and examines how concern about regulating trade and warfare colored Indian
policy as it was outlined by the Continental Congress in the Articles
of Confederation and other early articles of legislature.

H 1202. MOONEY, JAMES. The Ghost Dance Religion and the Sioux Outbreak
of 1890. Washington, D.C.: Government Printing Office. 14th
Annual Report of the Bureau of American Ethnology, 1896.
1136 pp.
Mooney uses his fieldwork among various tribes during the 1890s to present
a first-hand ethnographic account of the Ghost Dance religion, which he
analyzes within the context of earlier Indian revitalization movements
in the Midwest and Pacific Northwest. Mooney presents the doctrine of
the Ghost Dance religion and describes its practice among tribes east
and west of the Rockies, especially among the Sioux, focusing on the relationship of the Ghost Dance to the Wounded Knee Massacre and other events
among Plains Indians. The author presents a detailed evaluation of parallels to the Ghost Dance among various Western religions, and transcribes
the Ghost Dance songs of the Arapaho, Cheyenne, Paiute, Sioux, Kiowa and
Caddoan Indians. The text is augmented by over 100 photographs taken
by the author of the Ghost Dance in progress and of the religious parapher-
nalia used in its performance.

H 1203. NEITHAMMER, CAROLYN. Daughters of the Earth: The Lives and
Legends of American Indian Women. New York: Macmillan, 1977.
281 pp.
Neithammer examines the role of women in Indian societies prior to their
contact with European civilization. Relying primarily on anthropological
studies, the author attempts to assess both the symbolic and pragmatic
position of women by analyzing data on the role of women in the cosmological, sexual, economic, and social realms of various Indian peoples. She
attempts to recreate the life experience of women in these societies from
birth until death in order to re-examine old stereotypes about the under-
evaluation of this gender.

H 1204. NICHOLS, DAVID A. Lincoln and the Indians: Civil War Policy
and Politics. Columbia: University of Missouri Press, 1978.
223 pp.
In this examination of U.S. Indian policy during Lincoln's administration,
Nichols discusses three problematic issues that the president faced.
The first was the presence of Indian peoples in Confederate territory.
Secondly, Lincoln had to decide how to respond to the 1862 Santee Sioux
uprising in Minnesota. Finally, Lincoln had to deal with reformers who
sought to assimilate Native Americans into white society and to clean

516

up the corrupt Indian Office. Nichols concludes that Lincoln's sympathies, as well as those of his Commissioner of Indian Affairs, William P. Dole, lay with those interested in expanding the frontier and using the military to remove Native Americans from their territories.

H 1205. O'DONNELL, JAMES H., III. Southern Indians in the American Revolution. Knoxville: University of Tennessee Press, 1973. 171 pp.

O'Donnell focuses on Indian-white conflicts during the years of the American Revolution (1775-1783). He provides an overview of the dynamics of struggle during these years on the Western frontier, treating the activities of the great Southern tribes—the Cherokees, Chickasaws, Choctaws, and Creeks—as well as the activities of the Americans and British. O'Donnell documents the efforts of both Americans and British to urge Indian neutrality in the struggle, and he asserts that the Indians fought to preserve their land and autonomy, not simply to gain immediate favor with the side that possessed the most gifts. O'Donnell points out that in fact a large number of Indian peoples chose the losing British side of the conflict since it was clear that the primary threat to Indian land came from the expanding Colonial settlements.

H 1206. OLSON, JAMES C. Red Cloud and the Sioux Problem. Lincoln: University of Nebraska Press, 1965. 375 pp.

Olson presents the 19th-century history of the Sioux by focusing on the life of their prominent leader Red Cloud, who attempted to prevent white penetration of the Powder River country and staged successful military campaigns against Colonel Carrington and other U.S. Army commanders. After arguing that Red Cloud did not fully comprehend the conditions of the Fort Laramie Treaty, which he signed in 1868, Olson details the political controversy that surrounded the creation of the Sioux reservation, with an emphasis on state-Federal land disputes. The author describes Red Cloud's many trips to Washington to argue his people's position with government officials and to win them land ownership and land-use rights. The continued leadership of Red Cloud, Spotted Tail, and other chiefs throughout the difficult early reservation years is discussed. The work includes a text of the 1868 Fort Laramie Treaty.

H 1207. ORTIZ, ROXANNE DUNBAR. The Great Sioux Nation: Sitting in Judgment on America. New York: American Indian Treaty Council Information Center, 1977. 223 pp.

Ortiz chronicles political relations between the Sioux and the U.S. government in the 1970s. She provides transcripts of the Sioux Treaty Hearing held in Nebraska in December of 1974, during which time sixty-five defendants were tried for criminal offenses resulting from their participation in the Wounded Knee siege of 1973. Ortiz presents the testimony of forty-nine "expert witnesses" who argued for the defense, including traditional Sioux leaders, historians, attorneys and anthropologists. The work includes the text of the 1868 Fort Laramie Treaty, upon which the Sioux base their legal claim to national sovereignty, and the second half of the work presents the oral history of Lakota Indians regarding their knowledge of and opinion about the Treaty and its implications for contemporary land rights issues.

H 1208. ORTIZ, ROXANNE DUNBAR. Roots of Resistance: Land Tenure in New Mexico, 1680-1980. Los Angeles: Chicano Studies Research Center Publications and American Indian Studies Center, University of California, 1980. 202 pp.

Ortiz offers a comparative study of Pueblo and Hispanic efforts to control and preserve their land base in New Mexico under Spanish, Mexican, and U.S. rule. Analyzing the historic events in the Southwest as an economically based class struggle, Ortiz focuses on the history of land tenure in the Southwest, arguing that indigenous populations in New Mexico were able to maintain traditional patterns of land ownership until the U.S. gained control of the territory in 1848. The author discusses the recent political struggles between Southwestern Indians and the Federal government, including the Indians' defeat of the Bursum Bill and the reclamation of Blue Lake from the U.S. Forest Service by Taos Pueblo.

H 1209. OURADA, PATRICIA K. The Menominee Indians: A History. Norman:
         University of Oklahoma Press, 1975. 274 pp.
In this work, Ourada offers a historic overview of this Wisconsin tribe from their earliest contact with Europeans until 1975. She discusses the military allegiance of the Menominee to the French, and, later, to the British, and asserts that prolonged trading relationships with Euro-Americans left the Menominee economically vulnerable despite their accept-ance of U.S. government sovereignty. This work describes the treaty era during which the Menominee succeeded in retaining a portion of their ances-tral land; early problems with the management of their timber resources; the tribe's termination from the auspices of the Bureau of Indian Affairs in 1953; the disastrous consequences of that action; and the eventual resto-ration of B.I.A. management, which created factionalism on the reservation.

H 1210. PARMAN, DONALD L. The Navajos and the New Deal. New Haven, Conn.:
         Yale University Press, 1976. 316 pp.
Parman explores the experiences of the Navajo under the New Deal policies of Commissioner of Indian Affairs John Collier from 1935 until 1941. The author examines the responses of various tribal factions to Collier's program as well as the reaction of whites active in Navajo affairs. Focus-ing on Collier's reforms concerning land use, stock management, and edu-cation among the Navajo, and attempting to analyze the reasons behind the tribe's denunciation of the commissioner's efforts, he notes that while Collier hoped to develop tribal unity by encouraging Navajo self-government, political resistance to his proposals on the part of both tribal and govern-ment officials thwarted the implementation of his plans and produced uni-fied opposition instead. Parman assesses the long-term effects of the era and concludes that Collier succeeded in redirecting Navajo development in ways that have benefited the tribe economically and culturally.

H 1211. PARSONS, ELSIE CLEWS. Pueblo Indian Religion. 2 vols. Chicago:
         University of Chicago Press, 1939. 1275 pp.
Parsons presents a detailed account of Pueblo society and culture from the vantage point of their extensive cosmological and ceremonial life. The author provides ethnographic data from the early 20th century in order to evaluate Pueblo acculturation, cultural change, and ethos against the backdrop of traditional institutions. An overview of the ceremonial pat-terns of the Western and Eastern Pueblos is followed by a description of the ritual cycles of individual towns. Variations in ceremonial form and content and their apparent origins among non-Puebloan Indians and Anglo-Americans are assessed. The study focuses throughout on the inter-play between cultural continuity and numerous forms of change.

H 1212. PEARCE, ROY HARVEY. Savagism and Civilization: A Study of the
         Indian and the American Mind. 1953; Rev. ed. Baltimore: Johns
         Hopkins University Press, 1965. 260 pp.
In order to present a history of the notion of "savagism," Pearce examines American attitudes toward the Indian as reflected in political pamphlets, missionary reports, drama, poetry, novels and anthropological accounts. The author focuses on the conflict between the image of the Indian as "noble savage" and the impulse of Americans to Christianize and acculturate Native Americans. He stresses the complex nature of our images of Indians and explores their place in the Western intellectual tradition of primitivism as the antithesis of civilization.

H 1213. PERDUE, THEDA. Slavery and the Evolution of Cherokee Society,
         1540-1866. Knoxville: University of Tennessee Press, 1979.
         207 pp.
Perdue emphasizes the importance of slavery in the development of the Cherokee socio-economic system. Chronicling the history of slavery among the
Cherokee before and after their contact with Euro-Americans, Perdue contends
that the Indians used slaves to maintain their kinship system rather than
as an economic resource. She describes the changing function of slavery
among the Cherokee as they replaced their traditional economy with the
plantation system under the influence of the U.S. government, and documents
the increasing importance of slave labor to Cherokee economic production.
The author describes the effects of Cherokee removal to Oklahoma and the
Civil War on their tradition of keeping slaves.

H 1214. PEROFF, NICHOLAS C. Menominee Drums: Tribal Termination and
         Restoration, 1954-1974. Norman: University of Oklahoma Press,
         1982. 282 pp.
Arguing that the overt motive behind Federal Indian policy is the assimilation of Native Americans, Peroff examines how this explicit goal was
achieved in the Menominee Termination Act of 1954, which dissolved that
tribe's reservation into a county and withdrew Federal protection of their
resource management. The author explains how termination policy evolved,
how its implementation had disastrous effects, and how and why it was
reversed. The author argues that this Federal approach has gained in
momentum, and he stresses the importance of community action in devising
different directions for tribal government. Includes the text of the
Menominee Termination Act and the Menominee Restoration Act.

H 1215. PHILLIPS, GEORGE HARWOOD, Jr. Chiefs and Challengers: Indian
         Resistance and Cooperation in Southern California. Berkeley:
         University of California Press, 1975. 225 pp.
Phillips examines the role of Indians in California history, focusing
on the various strategies they employed when dealing with missionaries,
settlers, and the military. The author details the events of the Garra
uprising and other Indian attempts forcibly to resist the American settlement of California, as well as the efforts of some Indians to bring about
peaceful negotiations between Indians and whites. Phillips describes
the actions of three prominent Indian leaders: Juan Antonio, Antonio
Garra, and Manuelito Cota; analyzes the influence of important American
politicians and Indian agents throughout the 19th century; and examines
the role of the military in law enforcement.

H 1216. PHILLIPS, GEORGE HARWOOD, Jr. The Enduring Struggle: Indians
         in California History. San Francisco: Boyd & Fraser, 1981.
         110 pp.
Phillips provides an overview of Indian history in California, examining
the changes in the Indian culture that have emerged between Spanish colonization and the present. He discusses cultural exchange between Indian
and European populations as well as the implementation of U.S. Federal
policies on California tribes, and he evaluates the reaction of the Indians
to these Federal measures. He also addresses the growth of pan-Indianism,
particularly in the post-W.W. II period when many American Indians migrated
to California from other parts of North America.

H 1217. PHILP, KENNETH R. John Collier's Crusade for Indian Reform:
         1920-1954. Tucson: University of Arizona Press, 1977.
         304 pp.
Philp provides a biography of John Collier from the time of his first visit
to Taos Pueblo in 1920 and throughout his tenure as Commissioner of Indian
Affairs until his death at age eighty-four. An idealist troubled by the
materialism and individualism of modern Western society, Collier felt

that the tribal life of the American Indian should be encouraged and should
serve as a model for the rest of the world. After beginning his investigation of the reservation system as the employee of a welfare organization, Collier continued to crusade against Federal Indian policies
until appointed Indian commissioner in 1933. His subsequent implementation
of "New Deal" reformist policies regarding American Indians generated
controversy among both Indians and non-Indians. The work details his
efforts, in and out of office, to encourage cultural plurality and to
champion the cause of dependent minority groups.

H 1218. PORTER, H. C. The Inconstant Savage: England and the North
       American Indian, 1500-1660. London: Duckworth Press, 1979.
       588 pp.
Porter examines the development of English perceptions of the American
Indian during Tudor and Stuart times by presenting the writings of Thomas
More, Shakespeare and other literary figures of the 16th and 17th centuries,
as well as English records of exploration and colonization. Porter focuses
on published commentaries regarding Indian-white relations in the colony
of Virginia, and discusses the activities there of Alexander Whitaker
and other clergymen and intellectuals. The study includes an English
translation of the writings of Bartholomew de Casas and a list of publications about American Indians that appeared in England during the early
Colonial era.

H 1219. POWELL, PETER J. People of the Sacred Mountain: A History of
       the Northern Cheyenne Chiefs and Warrior Societies, 1830-1879,
       with an Epilogue 1969-1974. 2 vols. New York: Harper & Row,
       1981. 1441 pp.
Powell, an Episcopal priest, has produced an ethno-historic account of
the Cheyenne throughout their years of conflict with the American military
and with other Plains tribes. In Volume I, the author emphasizes two
events that shaped the Cheyenne world during the first half of the 19th
century: the Pawnees' capture of their Sacred Medicine Arrows in 1830,
and a Cheyenne woman's desecration of their Sacred Buffalo Hat in 1872.
Volume II focuses on political and social developments among the Cheyenne
after the 1868 Sand Creek Massacre, which created tribal factionalism
between those who advocated war and those who continued to seek peaceful
relations with whites. Utilizing Cheyenne sources, Powell recreates their
tribal history throughout an era of rapid change. A primary source of
information is a collection of Cheyenne ledger drawings that are interpreted and reproduced in the text, which is also augmented by rare photographs of Cheyenne leaders. The Cheyenne version of major battles and
other events is presented, as well as biographical information on little-
known Indian individuals.

H 1220. POWELL, PETER J. Sweet Medicine: The Continuing Role of the
       Sacred Arrows, the Sun Dance, and the Sacred Buffalo Hat in North-
       ern Cheyenne History. 2 vols. Norman: University of Oklahoma
       Press, 1969. 935 pp.
An Episcopal priest, Powell provides an in-depth look at the tribal history
of the Northern Cheyenne, placing particular emphasis on religious ideology
and ceremonies as they have been practiced for the last 200 years. The
author examines the function and historic movement of the sacred objects
of the Cheyenne and details the factionalism and social life of the tribe
throughout the era of warfare and into the modern reservation period.
Indigenous belief systems are credited with having maintained the cultural
identity of the Cheyenne, and the influence of important Cheyenne religious
figures is discussed. The work includes Cheyenne drawings of important
19th-century events and photographs of tribal religious ceremonies during
the 1960s.

H 1221. POWERS, WILLIAM K. Oglala Religion. Lincoln: University of
Nebraska Press, 1977. 233 pp.
Powers employs structuralist theory to explain the transformations in
and persistence of social organization and world view among the Oglala,
a major division of the Teton Sioux. Religion is considered the primary
framework that guides Oglala conceptions of time, space, ritual, and cultural identity. Powers explains how the conceptual universe of the Oglala
has shaped their social organization within the contemporary reservation
era through the Yuwipi ceremony, the Sun Dance, and other ritual performances.

H 1222. PRIEST, LORING BENSON. Uncle Sam's Stepchildren: The Reformation
of United States Indian Policy, 1865-1887. New Brunswick, N.J.:
Rutgers University Press, 1942. 310 pp.
Priest chronicles the U.S. government's struggle to develop a cohesive
Federal policy toward American Indians from the close of the Civil War
to the final passage of the Dawes Act in 1887, which mandated tribal land
allotments. The author assesses the role played by prominent individuals
and organizations such as the church, the Indian Rights Organization,
and various reform groups; he discusses the bureaucratic entanglements
between Grant's peace policy and sectional rivalries between Eastern and
Western states regarding Indian rights; and he evaluates the roles of
citizenship, land allotment, and educational policies in acculturation.
Priest chronicles the political contests in Congress over policy implementation and their eventual resolution.

H 1223. PRUCHA, FRANCIS P. American Indian Policy in Crisis: Christian
Reformers and the Indian, 1865-1900. Norman: University of
Oklahoma Press, 1976. 456 pp.
Prucha examines the influence of Christian reformers on U.S. Indian policy
formulated in the last third of the 19th century. He argues that the
success of the reformers in changing the Federal practice of dealing with
Indians as tribal entities to an orientation of individualism revolutionized Indian policy and laid the groundwork for 20th-century Indian-white
relations. He details the struggle between governmental factions which
advocated military control of the Indians and those which argued for the
peaceful reform of Indian policy, and he evaluates the influence of events
such as the Modoc War on Grant's peace policy. Prucha details the efforts
of the reformers to assimilate Native Americans into U.S. society through
land allotment policies, Christianization, and education. Their efforts
to assimilate the Five Civilized Tribes as a model for other Indians are
discussed, and Prucha evaluates the long-term success of the reformers'
attempts to change Native American culture.

H 1224. PRUCHA, FRANCIS P. American Indian Policy in the Formative Years:
The Indian Trade and Intercourse Acts, 1790-1834. Cambridge,
Mass.: Harvard University Press, 1962. 303 pp.
Prucha examines the goals and implementation of Federal Indian policy
from the early years of American independence through the Jacksonian era.
He outlines the principles by which the U.S. dealt with the problems of
land titles, white encroachment onto Indian lands, protection of Indian
rights, promotion of acculturation, and regulation of Indian-white economic
relations. The work deals topically with legislative handling of the
fur trade, liquor trafficking, the management of lands and criminal punishment, and removal. Prucha focuses on the reasons for the failure of many
Federal mandates and in particular on the efforts of frontier traders
and settlers to circumvent restrictive laws wherever possible.

H 1225. PRUCHA, FRANCIS P. The Churches and the Indian Schools, 1888-
1912. Lincoln: University of Nebraska Press, 1979. 278 pp.
Prucha chronicles the struggles between Catholics and Protestants to gain
control over Indian education. He focuses on the disputes over Catholic
mission schools on Indian reservations, and on how the bitter rivalry
between the two religious factions reflected opposing notions of how
Indians should be incorporated into American society. The work covers
the many legal and Congressional battles over the issues involved and
details the participation of influential political and religious figures
of the day. It also explores the symbolic import of religious garb and
insignia. Included are the texts of tribal petitions to the government
regarding the management of reservation school systems.

H 1226. RAHILL, PETER J. The Catholic Indian Missions and Grant's Peace
Policy, 1870-1884. Washington, D.C.: Catholic University of
America Press, 1953. 369 pp.
Rahill explores the Catholic Church's reaction to Grant's Peace Policy,
which placed most Indian agencies under the control of Protestant denominations. He describes how the funding and function of Catholic mission
schools and churches on Indian reservations came under attack during an
era of anti-Catholic sentiment in America, focusing primarily on the Bureau
of Catholic Indian Missions' struggle to regain control of a number of
Federal Indian agencies and on the political reorganization of the bureau.
Rahill includes a description of Catholic mission work among the Sioux
in order to illustrate the operation of the B.C.I.A.

H 1227. RANDOLPH, J. RALPH. British Travelers Among the Southern Indians,
1660-1763. Norman: University of Oklahoma Press, 1973. 183 pp.
Randolph's study examines Colonial attitudes toward the American Indian
as they developed among itinerant Englishmen such as diplomats and missionaries who traveled among the Southeastern peoples. Randolph identifies
the ethnocentric viewpoint at the heart of English observations on native
religion and life styles. The author notes that although most of the
travelers were educated and showed interest in native dress and religion,
their interest was purely a case of curiosity; they did not show any
inclination in preserving such customs. Randolph also suggests that English
racism seemed to intensify, according to Randolph, as contact increased
between the two cultures.

H 1228. RAY, ARTHUR J. and DONALD B. FREEMAN. "Give Us Good Measure":
An Economic Analysis of Relations Between the Indians and the
Hudson's Bay Company before 1763. Toronto: University of Toronto
Press, 1978. 288 pp.
Ray and Freeman examine the economic institutions and relationships between
the Hudson's Bay Company and Indians throughout the company's first century
of operation. Based on the transaction records of six trading posts,
the study emphasizes the function of trade as an economically based enterprise rather than as an alliance system. The struggle between the French
and the English for control of the fur trade and the intertribal conflicts
that resulted from trading partnerships are discussed. The authors emphasize that the economic interaction between Native Americans and European
entrepreneurs presents theoretical problems for the analysis of trade
and exchange, and the implications of these data for comparative economic
theory are discussed.

H 1229. REID, JOHN PHILLIP. A Better Kind of Hatchet: Law, Trade, and
Diplomacy in the Cherokee Nation During the Early Years of European Contact. University Park: Pennsylvania State University
Press, 1976. 249 pp.
Reid's study examines Cherokee-white relations in the Carolinas throughout
the 17th and 18th centuries. He emphasizes the differences between Cherokee and Euro-American legal and political structures, and describes how
these differences affected the interaction of the two groups. The author
shows how unilateral trade regulations favoring the British often undermined diplomatic efforts, and discusses the interaction of these factors
with regard to the Yamasee War and other historic events. He also notes
that European misconceptions about Cherokee social organization and inter-
tribal relations undermined the efficiency and success of proposed Indian
policy. Throughout the work Reid focuses on how Indian-white relations
in the new world challenged European legal traditions.

H 1230. ROE, FRANK GILBERT. The Indian and the Horse. Norman: University
of Oklahoma Press, 1955. 434 pp.
Roe evaluates the importance of the horse to Plains Indian culture. He
describes how horses replaced dogs as beasts of burden and concludes that
the acquisition of the horse did not transform Plains Indian society but
rather strengthened an indigenous nomadic pattern among hunter-gatherers.
Roe traces the evolution of the post-horse social organization in different
geographical regions and explores tribal systems of horse breeding, herd
management, and training. He examines the role of the horse in the social,
economic, and psychological life of the Indians and discusses its importance to Indian hunting and warfare strategies.

H 1231. ROGIN, MICHAEL PAUL. Fathers and Children: Andrew Jackson and
the Subjugation of the American Indian. New York: Knopf, 1975.
373 pp.
Rogin presents a psycho-historical study of Andrew Jackson and the age
of American expansion he helped to create. The author explores 19th-
century philosophic notions, such as Manifest Destiny, that supported American
territorial advancement and the subjugation of Indian peoples, and discusses the rise of individuals who seemed to personify the national ethos,
such as Daniel Boone. Arguing that Jackson's antipathy toward American
Indians and the zeal with which he pursued their surrender grew out of
his own deep-seated fears and political ambitions, Rogin contends that
Jackson felt a need to duplicate the achievements of the Revolutionary
War heroes by extending America's territorial claims through warfare.

H 1232. RUBY, ROBERT H. and JOHN A. BROWN. The Cayuse Indians: Imperial
Tribesmen of Old Oregon. Norman: University of Oklahoma Press,
1972. 345 pp.
The authors present the 19th-century history of the Cayuse, a small tribe
of the intermontane Pacific Northwest whose geographic location placed
them in a strategic trade location and thrust them into the forefront
of Indian-white struggles for the territory of Oregon. Detailed treatment
is given to the massacre of missionary Marcus Whitman and his associates
by the Cayuse in 1847 and to the subsequent series of wars. The Cayuse
attempted to incite the Northwest Indians to unify against the incursions
of the whites, and the authors use primary documents to recreate the tense
relations between the tribal members and the agents sent to manage them.
They also describe Cayuse relations with the Nez Perce and detail the
political and personal battles over Indian policy between Federal, state,
and church officials.

H 1233. RUBY, ROBERT H. and JOHN A. BROWN. Indians of the Pacific North-
         west: A History. Norman: University of Oklahoma Press, 1981.
         294 pp.
Ruby and Brown present the history and ethnography of the Indians of the
intermontane Northwest. Beginning with a description of indigenous subsistence techniques, they discuss the importance of the riverline interior
Northwest as a trading center and the early acculturation of the coastal
groups. The book focuses on the warfare between the Indians and the U.S.
government for the territories of Oregon, Washington, and Idaho, including
the Nez Perce War, the Modoc Wars and the Bannock-Paiute Wars of 1878.
The authors discuss the early reservation era and the effects of Grant's
peace policy on the acculturation of Northwestern tribes.

H 1234. RUSSELL, HOWARD S. Indian New England Before the Mayflower.
         Hanover, N.H.: University Press of New England, 1980. 284 pp.
Russell examines the lifestyles of New England Indian peoples prior to
their contact with British settlers. Using primarily archeological data,
he reconstructs the subsistence technology, village construction and material culture of late prehistoric, horticultural populations, emphasizing
the influence of economic production on Indian social organization and
cultural tradition. Russell describes the Indians' use of wild food
resources and their cultivation techniques; their seasonal round of hunting,
fishing, and planting; and trade, war and other interactions between prehistoric Indian groups. The work includes an appendix that lists common
trees, shrubs, and herbaceous plants used by the prehistoric Indian populations of New England.

H 1235. SALISBURY, NEAL. Manitou and Providence: Indians, Europeans,
         and the Making of New England, 1500-1643. New York: Oxford
         University Press, 1982. 316 pp.
Salisbury examines Puritan-Indian relations in New England up to and including the Pequot War. In his investigation of historical process, Salisbury
critiques the models of Indian-white relations that have been presented
by other scholars to account for the destruction of native cultures by
Euro-American settlers. He argues that it was not cultural incompatibility
that guided the conquest of America, but rather that the success of the
English colonization effort was primarily due to the spread of diseases
introduced by the early French and English explorers, and the subsequent
decimation of Indian populations. Salisbury uses anthropological data
to chronicle the cultural history of the Algonquian Indians in New England
and to reconstruct their relations with Europeans both prior to actual
colonization and after the establishment of permanent settlements.

H 1236. SANDOZ, MARI. Crazy Horse: The Strange Man of the Oglalas.
         New York: Knopf, 1942. 428 pp.
In this biography of Crazy Horse, the most renowned leader of the Sioux,
Sandoz details the daily life of the Plains Indians during an era of rapid
social and economic change. The author describes the tactics taken by
various Sioux leaders in their attempts to protect their relatives and
preserve their ancestral homeland. Written from a Native American perspective and rich in ethnographic detail about the Sioux, the book reveals
the personal and social dilemmas faced by Crazy Horse in his rise to fame
as a war leader on the Plains.

H 1237. SATZ, RONALD N. American Indian Policy in the Jacksonian Era.
         Lincoln: University of Nebraska Press, 1975. 343 pp.
Satz offers a systematic analysis of government Indian policy during the
Jacksonian era, during which the Federal government consolidated its legal
jurisdiction over American Indian tribes and effected the Southeastern
tribes' removal to the territory of Oklahoma. The author examines the
factors behind the removal policy, the political response that was forth-

coming, and the Federal government's failure to live up to the conditions of the relocation program. The study focuses on legislative debates and administrative difficulties that characterized this political era, and on the non-governmental influences (such as land speculators) that made the implementation of well-meaning policies impossible.

H 1238. **SAUER, CARL ORTWIN**. Sixteenth-Century North America: The Land and Its People as Seen by Europeans. Berkeley: University of California Press, 1971. 319 pp.
Sauer reconstructs the North American landscape as it appeared to 16th-century explorers by examining their own accounts and official documents. The author describes their geographic knowledge by analyzing maps of the New World as it was perceived by the French, English, Spanish and Portuguese; presents the early explorers' impressions of the Atlantic Coast, Canada, the Far West, and Florida; details the expeditions of De Soto, Coronado, and other important travelers; describes their view of New World flora, fauna, and American Indians; and chronicles their relations with the tribes they encountered on their journeys.

H 1239. **SAUM, LEWIS O.** The Fur Trade and the Indian. Seattle: University of Washington Press, 1965. 324 pp.
Referring often to the accounts of Indians by fur traders, the author examines the European conception of Native Americans as it developed among fur traders, from their earliest contact with Indians through the mid-19th century. The period from 1800 to 1850 is highlighted in view of the traders' observations of Native American culture and personality traits, suggesting both the positive and negative views of the Indian. This study offers a record of the Euro-American response to Indians on the frontier, as well as the reaction of Native Americans to the fur traders. In doing this, Saum contrasts the relationships of the Englishman and the Frenchman with the Indian, arguing that the more flexible French were better able to deal with the Native Americans.

H 1240. **SAVAGE, WILLIAM W., Jr.** The Cherokee Strip Live Stock Association: Federal Regulation and the Cattleman's Last Frontier. Columbia: University of Missouri Press, 1973. 154 pp.
Savage chronicles the relationships between the Oklahoma Cherokee and the ranching community regarding the Cherokee Outlet, a 6-million-acre tract of land originally granted to the tribe in perpetuity by the Federal government. In 1833, the Cherokee began leasing the grazing land to a cattleman's association called the Cherokee Strip Live Stock Association, and Savage focused on this historic event to analyze the interrelationships between four social and economic factions: homesteaders, cattlemen, Indians, and the Federal government. He argues that the government's interest in controlling Western lands for settlement led to the Federal dissolution of the Association and fiscal confiscation of the acreage in 1891 in order to open the area to homesteaders. Throughout the work, the author focuses on the role of the Indians as businessmen and the issue of tribal involvement in the national economy.

H 1241. **SAVAGE, WILLIAM W., Jr., ed.** Indian Life: Transforming an American Myth. Norman: University of Oklahoma Press, 1977. 286 pp.
A collection of essays written by observers of Indian life in the late 19th and early 20th centuries, Indian Life explores stereotypic and symbolic representations of Native Americans at that time. Many of the contributions to this volume reflect the ethnocentric perspective on Indian culture typical of that era, a perspective that contributes to the image-making of Indians by the contemporary writers and film-makers. The selections focus on the life-styles of the Plains Indians during their territorial wars with the U.S. and throughout the early reservation period. The work includes photographs demonstrating the situation of the reservation Indian.

H 1242. SAYRE, ROBERT F. Thoreau and the American Indians. Princeton,
N.J.: Princeton University Press, 1977. 239 pp.
Sayre examines the life and writings of Henry David Thoreau in order to
comment on the 19th-century notion of savagism, which informed Euro-American
ideas about American Indians. The author acknowledges Thoreau's philosophical transcendence of this ethnocentric notion and his tremendous
appreciation of Indian culture. At the same time, Sayre notes that Thoreau
had only an ideal notion of Indians and did not comprehend the diversity
and complexity of Native American socio-cultural forms. The work analyzes
a variety of Thoreau's writings, including his unpublished manuscript
notebooks regarding Indian history and philosophy.

H 1243. SCHULTZ, GEORGE A. An Indian Canaan: Isaac McCoy and the Vision
of an Indian State. Norman: University of Oklahoma Press, 1972.
230 pp.
Isaac McCoy was a missionary-reformer who worked actively for the establishment of an Indian State West of Missouri in the 1820s and 1830s.
Schultz examines McCoy's career and ideals in the context of both philanthropic and governmental attitudes toward Indians. Although Schultz notes
that McCoy shared the philanthropic attitude of his day, which advocated
the removal of Eastern Indians to protect them from white frontier societies and the accompanying social disruptions resulting from the clash
of cultures, he was also more forward-thinking than many of his contemporaries. Among McCoy's goals for the Indian State was higher education
for Indians in law, religion and medicine. Finally, however, Schultz
notes that McCoy was used, without his knowledge, by the Jackson Administration to support and facilitate its own Indian Removal policies.

H 1244. SEYMOUR, FLORA WARREN. The Story of the Red Man. New York:
Longmans, Green, 1929. 421 pp.
Seymour offers an overview of American Indian history from the arrival
of Columbus through the end of the Indian wars and the onset of acculturation policies in the early reservation era. The work focuses on major
historical incidents and on famous Indian personalities, such as Sacajawea,
Joseph Brant, Tecumseh and Red Cloud. In the last three chapters the
author examines the benefits of U.S. education policies for Native Americans, the erosion of their land base, and the influence of Indian sympathizers on their affairs.

H 1245. SHEEHAN, BERNARD W. Seeds of Extinction: Jeffersonian Philanthropy and the American Indian. Chapel Hill: University of
North Carolina Press, 1973. 301 pp.
Sheehan examines the history of the Jeffersonian-era humanitarians who
advocated assimilation of American Indians in opposition to those who
favored extermination of the tribes. Emphasizing the interplay between
ideology and historic events, the author explores 18th-century notions
about Indian origins and moral status and discusses the image of the Indian
as Noble Savage. He describes the influence of Protestant religious groups
on the Federal Indian policy of Washington and Jefferson and their administrative efforts to incorporate Indians into American society. He also
chronicles the evolution of humanitarian reformist groups throughout the
era of removal and credits them with having saved indigenous populations
from complete destruction.

H 1246. SPICER, EDWARD H. Pascua: A Yaqui Village in Arizona. Chicago:
University of Chicago Press, 1940. 319 pp.
In this case study of one Yaqui community, Spicer analyzes the process
of acculturation among Indians who have been removed from their indigenous
homeland and cultural context. After escaping from Mexico in the 1890s,
the Yaqui resettled in Arizona, where they became employed as day laborers
outside their village. Spicer describes the increasing dissociation

between their economic and ceremonial lives, and attempts to determine whether their socio-cultural system can survive without their traditional horticultural subsistence base. He describes the increasing "compartmentalization" of Yaqui life, and the community's attempts to retain ceremonial institutions that no longer function except in a ritual sense.

H 1247. STEDMAN, RAYMOND WILLIAM. Shadows of the Indian: Stereotypes in American Culture. Norman: University of Oklahoma Press, 1982. 281 pp.
Stedman explores the many stereotypes used to represent American Indians in the media over the course of the past century. Arguing that Indians exist only in the imagination of most Americans, Stedman describes how popular images of the Indian evolved from the changing context of Indian-white relations. He examines characterizations of the Indian as enemy, noble savage, alcoholic, sexual object and environmental crusader, paying particular attention to the film industry's inattention to realism in its oversimplified portrayal of the American Indian as either good or bad.

H 1248. STRICKLAND, RENNARD. Fire and the Spirits: Cherokee Law from Clan to Court. Norman: University of Oklahoma Press, 1975. 260 pp.
Strickland describes the Cherokee legal system's development into a combination of tribal tradition and Anglo-American legal institutions. Basing his work on the official records of the Cherokee Nation, Federal Indian records and the writing of early observers, the author focuses on the evolution of the legal system among Western Cherokees since their removal to Oklahoma in 1838, when their tribal courts were abolished. Strickland emphasizes the fact that Cherokee acculturation has been regarded as a model of successful Indian change, and he refutes this view. Arguing that "law" is a more culturally relative concept than has been accepted, he examines both the formal and informal forms of legal process among the Cherokee and analyzes them within the context of their culture.

H 1249. STUART, PAUL. The Indian Office: Growth and Development of an American Institution, 1865-1900. Ann Arbor, Mich.: UMI Research Press, 1979. 243 pp.
Stuart chronicles the development of the U.S. Office of Indian Affairs between the end of the Civil War and the beginning of the 20th century. Focusing on the process of institutionalization within the context of global modernization, the author examines how Federal Indian policy became increasingly internalized within the Bureau of Indian Affairs. He discusses the centralization of organizational control and the hierarchical reorganization of the office in respect to personnel recruitment, the control of official behavior, the inspection of agency conditions, and the evolution of the Board of Indian Commissioners. Throughout the study Stuart emphasizes the growing importance of education as a tool of assimilation policies.

H 1250. SZASZ, MARGARET C. Education and the American Indian: The Road to Self-Determination Since 1928. Albuquerque: University of New Mexico Press, 1974. 251 pp.
Szasz provides a broad historical treatment of Indian education from 1928-1970. Focusing on the administrations of the directors of the Bureau of Indian Affairs Education division, she chronicles the harsh acculturation tactics of the early years and the reformist policies that succeeded them. Throughout the work, the author emphasizes that although the nature of educational problems has changed, Indians still receive poor quality education. Szasz analyzes the major factors that have shaped the educational experiences of Native Americans, both external and internal to the B.I.A. She concludes with an examination of the move toward Indian-controlled schools in the 1960s and 1970s.

H 1251. TAYLOR, GRAHAM D. The New Deal and American Indian Tribalism: The Administration of the Indian Reorganization Act, 1934-45. Lincoln: University of Nebraska Press, 1980. 203 pp.
Taylor examines the reasons why the 1934 passage of the Indian Reorganization Act did not achieve the intended effects of tribal economic development and self-determination. The author critiques the Indian New Deal on the grounds that Collier and other reformers made incorrect assumptions about the nature of Indian societies and tribal organizations, and also failed to come to terms with the lack of support Indians showed toward the implementation of the new policies. The work evaluates both the positive and the negative legacies of the I.R.A., including the form of contemporary tribal leadership.

H 1252. THOMPSON, GERALD. The Army and the Navajo: The Bosque Redondo Reservation Experiment, 1863-1868. Tucson: University of Arizona Press, 1976. 196 pp.
Thompson presents an administrative study of the Bosque Redondo Reservation, created in 1863 as a solution to the problem of managing the Navajo and assimilating them into white society. The author argues that the reservation system developed out of a humanitarian motive—to protect the Indians from the hostility of the military and private sectors, and to provide them with the skills and Christian values necessary for survival in the modern world. This case study reveals the difficulties of implementing this goal through forced culture change. The author analyzes the reasons behind the failure of the Bosque Redondo experiment and concludes it did succeed in preparing the Navajo for their continuing reservation experience.

H 1253. THOMPSON, LAURA. Culture in Crisis: A Study of the Hopi Indians. New York: Harper, 1950. 221 pp.
Thompson's report addresses conditions faced by the Hopi during the 1940s. An early work in applied anthropology, the aim of the study was to evaluate the effects of Federal Indian policy and to make recommendations for improving tribal management and for fostering economic development. The researchers isolate two levels of crisis facing the Hopi: an economic one resulting from the effects of overpopulation, overgrazing of herds, drought, and the reduction of Hopi lands by Navajo annexation; and a high level of psychological distress among Hopi individuals as a result of the social environment of reservation life. The book includes data on reservation economics, crime, enculturation, education, and a chapter on concepts of time, space and language by Benjamin Lee Whorf.

H 1254. TRENNERT, ROBERT A., Jr. Alternative to Extinction: Federal Indian Policy and the Beginnings of the Reservation System, 1846-51. Philadelphia: Temple University Press, 1975. 263 pp.
Trennert examines the effect of frontier expansion into the Far West upon Federal Indian policy in the years 1846-1851. He explains that once Americans came into contact with the powerful nomadic tribes of the Plains and realized that they would present a barrier to Western advancement, the U.S. government abandoned its plan to consign Indians to lands west of the Mississippi. Trennert examines the origins of the modern reservation system in this era of expansion; explores how Federal policies attempted to acculturate Native Americans under controlled conditions; and assesses the role played by William Medil, Thomas Hart Benton, and other prominent politicians in the formulation of Federal Indian policy.

H 1255. TRENNERT, ROBERT A., Jr. Indian Traders on the Middle Border: The House of Ewing, 1827-54. Lincoln: University of Nebraska Press, 1981. 271 pp.

Trennert explores the influence of the House of Ewing, an Indian trading company, on the formulation of Federal Indian policy during the late 1840s and early 1850s. The Ewings conducted their trading business in the Wabash region of Northern Indiana at a time when the regional Indians were receiving payment for lands they had been obliged to cede to the U.S. government. Trennert provides a case study of the relationship between entrepreneurial capitalist interests on the frontier and tribes that were undergoing forced economic and social change. He emphasizes the considerable interdependence among merchants, land speculators, Indian agents, and government in the process of removing Indians from their land in the interests of advancing the frontier and clearing it for the benefit of American economic development.

H 1256. TURNER, GEOFFREY. Indians of North America. Poole, England: Blanford Press, 1979. 261 pp.

Turner presents a broad overview of North American Indian and Eskimo cultures both of which he classifies under eleven geographically based culture areas. Each culture area is described with an emphasis on technologies of subsistence, settlement patterns, material culture, and traditional ceremonial life. Also discussed are the prehistory of Native Americans from the time of their migration to North America and the socio-economic conditions of Indians in the 1960s. The text is supplemented by color illustrations and photographs.

H 1257. UNDERHILL, RUTH M. The Navajos. Norman: University of Oklahoma Press, 1956. 288 pp.

Underhill presents a history of the Navajo throughout the past 500 years with an emphasis on the interplay between tradition and cultural change. She uses archaeological and archival data as well as ethnographic accounts collected during her thirteen years as an employee of the U.S. Indian Service. The Navajo view of their relations with Pueblo people, the Spanish, and American society is presented with reference to their mythological, poetic, and material cultural expressions. The work reviews the military subjugation of the Navajos and their difficult reconstruction in the modern world. Particular attention is paid to the economic and social influence of traders throughout the early reservation period, and to the development of education among the rural Navajo.

H 1258. UNDERHILL, RUTH M. Red Man's America. Chicago: University of Chicago Press, 1953. 395 pp.

In this summary of North American Indian life from prehistory until the 1950s, Underhill sketches the major distinctions between Indian peoples by employing their concept of the "culture area." The author delimits ten culture areas on the basis of subsistence techniques, social organization, and material traits and provides an ethno-historical account of the major tribes in each area. She includes an overview of both prehistoric developments and U.S. Federal Indian policies from the Colonial era to the middle of the 20th century.

H 1259. UPTON, L. F. S. Micmacs and Colonists: Indian-White Relations in the Maritimes, 1713-1867. Vancouver: University of British Columbia Press, 1979. 243 pp.

Upton details the 18th- and 19th-century history of the Micmacs, one of the first North American Indian groups to come into contact with Europeans, and the only Canadian tribe forcefully to resist settlement and displacement. The work focuses on the choices exercised by the Micmac regarding their political relations with European powers: their accommodation to the French, their enmity toward the British, and their passive resistance

throughout the reservation era. The author emphasizes their retention
of traditional values and their development as artists and traders throughout the past 250 years.

H 1260. UTLEY, ROBERT M. Frontier Regulars: The United States Army and
the Indian, 1866-1891. New York: Macmillan, 1973. 462 pp.
Utley examines the structure and character of the Regular Army, which
fought the Indians in the period between the Civil War and the Wounded
Knee Massacre of 1891. He contrasts the negative stereotype of the army
held by humanitarian civilians with their own self image as the advance
guard of civilization, and describes the daily reality of their circumstance. Utley assesses the capabilities of various Army commanders and
analyzes the effect of their personalities on 19th-century military history.
He describes the equipment of the soldiers, the formulation of Army policy,
and the relationship between the Army and Congress. In presenting the
major Indian campaigns, Utley identifies the military motives and capabilities of the Plains tribes, and analyzes the political policies of the
Indian leaders.

H 1261. VAUGHAN, ALDEN T. New England Frontier: Puritans and Indians,
1620-1675. 1965; Rev. ed. New York: Norton, 1979. 430 pp.
Vaughan's study explores contact between Puritans and Native Americans
during the half century between the arrival of the Pilgrims and King
Philip's War. Challenging the scholarly claim that the Puritans were pious
hypocrites insofar as they theologically justified dispossessing Native
Americans of land and resources, Vaughan contends that, by 17th-century
standards, the Puritans pursued a relatively humane policy of peaceful
and voluntary assimilation. The Puritans offered the Indians education,
Christianity, and justice. While Vaughan does not overlook the atrocities
that did occur, he maintains that the clash between such vastly different
cultures was inevitable and not attributable merely to Puritan greed for
lands. Qualifying this assertion in the introductory essay to the revised
edition, he grants that the cultural imperialism and ethnocentrism of the
Puritans indisputably poisoned their relations with the Native Americans.

H 1262. VIOLA, HERMAN J. Diplomats in Buckskins: A History of Indian
Delegations in Washington City. Washington, D.C.: Smithsonian
Institution Press, 1981. 233 pp.
Viola chronicles the history of American Indian delegations to the capital
from the Colonial era through the civil rights period of the 1970s. The
author discusses the nature of their official negotiations with U.S.
Presidents and congressmen and their participation in political functions
such as inaugural parades and dedication ceremonies. He also describes
their accommodations in Washington, their social life there, the execution
of their official portraits for the Washington gallery, and their occasional illness and death while there. The text is augmented by photographs
and drawings of tribal delegations throughout the 19th and 20th centuries.

H 1263. WALLACE, ANTHONY F. C. King of the Delawares: Teedyuscung, 1700-
1763. Philadelphia: University of Pennsylvania Press, 1949.
305 pp.
Wallace chronicles the life of Teedyuscung, an 18th-century Delaware leader
who urged his people to adopt Euro-American practices while championing
his people's rights against the European government. The study describes
the personal struggles of an intellectual who understood the reasons for
his people's decline but was socially powerless to address them. Wallace
describes Teedyuscung's involvement in the political history of 18th-
century New England and details the relations of the Delawares with other
Indians and with the English and French. The work focuses on the joint
efforts of Teedyuscung and Iroquois leaders to preserve the land base
of regional Indian groups, and provides a case study of Indian-white relations throughout 18th-century New England.

H 1264. **WALLACE, ERNEST** and **E. ADAMSON HOEBEL.** The Comanches: Lords of
the South Plains. Norman: University of Oklahoma Press, 1952.
381 pp.
Wallace and Hoebel use both historical records and native informants to
present the history and ethnography of the Comanches from the time of
their migration into the Southwest until their confinement on an Oklahoma
reservation in the 1870s. Focusing on the military prowess of the Comanche,
they describe their successful repudiation of French, Spanish, and American
settlers. The authors also provide an overview of Comanche culture: their
nomadic hunting economy, material culture, religion, political organization
and mythology. They describe the life-cycle of the Comanche individual
and the structure of their kinship system, and include first-hand accounts
by informants about the tenor of life as they experienced it late in the
19th century.

H 1265. **WASHBURN, WILCOMB E.** The Indian in America. New York: Harper
& Row, 1975. 296 pp.
Washburn provides a summary of the beliefs and behavioral patterns of
American Indians from prehistory to the present. Drawing on the work
of various scholarly and historic accounts, Washburn presents Native American ethnography by topic, addressing such subjects as Indian religion,
social structure and what the author terms "Indian personality." He
describes major events in Indian-white relations from the Colonial era
through the establishment of reservations and the implementation of allotment policies in the early 20th century; discusses changes in the political
and economic circumstance of Native Americans in the 1960s and 1970s;
and concludes that acculturation has eclipsed traditional values.

H 1266. **WASHBURN, WILCOMB E.** Red Man's Land, White Man's Law: A Study
of the Past and Present Status of the American Indian. New York:
Scribner, 1971. 280 pp.
Washburn provides a comprehensive treatment of the philosophic and legal
position of the American Indian vis-a-vis the Federal government and analyzes the economic factors behind the development of Federal Indian policy.
Following a historic introduction to the modern situation of Native Americans, the author examines the complexities of land titles, inheritance,
and land management in the major geographic regions of the U.S. and Canada.
He explores the roles of the U.S. constitutional congress, tribal governments, and Federal agencies such as the Bureau of Indian Affairs in the
accelerating legal struggles over land and resource rights. The influence
of education systems, anthropologists, and white social activist groups
on the Indian situation are assessed as the author explores the paradox
of America's symbolic elevation of the Indian while denying them social
and economic viability in the modern world.

H 1267. **WASHBURN, WILCOMB E.** and **ROBERT M. UTLEY.** The American Heritage
History of the Indian Wars. New York: American Heritage, 1977.
352 pp.
The authors present the history of Indian-white relations through an
account of their chief military encounters from the time of Columbus to
the defeat of the Sioux at Wounded Knee in 1890. In the first half of
the volume, Washburn details conflicts in the Eastern U.S. up to 1850,
when the Southeastern tribes had been militarily defeated and relocated
to Oklahoma. He includes accounts of inter-tribal wars and discusses
the role played by Indians in both the French and Indian War and the American Revolution. In the second half of the book, Utley describes the Indian
populations indigenous to the Western U.S. and chronicles their wars
against settlers and Federal troops after the Civil War.

H 1268. WILKINS, THURMAN. Cherokee Tragedy: The Story of the Ridge Family
and the Decimation of a People. New York: Macmillan, 1970.
398 pp.
Wilkins presents the 18th- and 19th-century history of the Cherokee by
examining the Ridge family, prominent mixed-bloods who encouraged their
tribe to become educated so they could deal more effectively with the
Federal government. The author describes traditional Cherokee beliefs
and practices; explores the difficulties faced by the people in an era
of rapid change; and details the political and cultural developments of
the Cherokee prior to removal: their diplomatic skills, their invention
of a Cherokee alphabet, their embrace of education, and their leadership
among the Southeastern tribes. Focusing on the efforts of the Ridge Family,
John Ross and other educated Cherokee to prevent the implementation of
the Indian Removal Act, Wilkins describes their despair when it was mandated and the devastating effects of relocation on the tribe.

H 1269. WILLIAMS, WALTER L., ed. Southeastern Indians Since the Removal
Era. Athens: University of Georgia Press, 1979. 253 pp.
This collection of articles deals with the history of those Southeastern
Indian groups that avoided relocation to Oklahoma in the 1860s. Various
authors present ethnographic and historical studies of the struggles of
small Indian populations to retain an ethnic identity and to gain political
and economic viability in the modern world. A persistent theme is the
marginal legal and ethnic status of Indians in the South, and their various
strategies for development are documented in individual case studies.
The editor concludes with an analysis of political and social factors
that influenced the direction of all the groups, and he describes the
pattern of their response.

H 1270. WISE, JENNINGS C. The Red Man in the New World Drama: A Politico-
Legal Study with a Pageantry of American Indian History. Revised,
edited, and introduced by Vine Deloria, Jr. New York: Macmillan,
1971. 418 pp.
Wise describes the history of Indian-white relations within the context
of a world drama of conflicting religions, emphasizing the religious motive
of the early Europeans in America, and discussing the relations between
the Dutch, English and Iroquois in New York, and the role of the Indians
in the Revolutionary War. Wise details early Indian policy in the Independence Era and as the frontier extended to the Midwest in the 19th century; the removal of Indian tribes to the West before the Civil War and
their subjugation and confinement to reservations in the 1870s; the era
of the reform movements under Grant's Peace Policy; and the organization
of the Indian Bureau in the early part of the 20th century. Deloria adds
chapters on the political history of Native Americans from the time of
the New Deal policies through the activism of the American Indian Movement
in the 1970s.

H 1271. WITHERSPOON, GARY. Language and Art in the Navajo Universe. Ann
Arbor: University of Michigan Press, 1977. 214 pp.
Witherspoon explores the cognitive organization underlying Navajo art
and language, analyzing culture as a system of classification and using
structuralist theories to explore the conceptual basis of Navajo grammatical form and function. He isolates key principles of classification in
the Navajo language, such as shape categories, explores how these distinctions relate to other cultural domains, and argues that the metaphysical
premises of Navajo culture are substantively different from those that
support Western thought, and that these differences must be acknowledged
in order systematically to analyze Navajo ideology and behavior. He rein-
terprets the meaning of Navajo art and language according to what he feels
to be their own principles of perception and conceptualization.

H 1272. WRIGHT, J. LEITCH, Jr. The Only Land They Knew: The Tragic Story of American Indians in the Old South. New York: Free Press, 1981. 372 pp.
Wright's study is an ethno-historical account of the American Indians of the Atlantic and Gulf Coast region and its hinterland during the Colonial era. The author examines the process of rapid demographic decline and social disorganization among indigenous populations throughout the 16th, 17th, and 18th centuries. Wright contends that the extent and impact of Indian slavery has been underestimated, and emphasizes the genetic and cultural exchanges between American blacks and Indians captured and forced into slave labor. He argues that President Jackson's policy of enforced removal of Native Americans saved them from enslavement and further population decline in the East.

H 1273. WOODS, PATRICIA DILLION. French-Indian Relations on the Southern Frontier, 1699-1762. Ann Arbor, Mich.: UMI Research Press, 1980. 239 pp.
Woods describes the interaction between the French colony of Louisiana and three Southern tribes: the Natchez (exterminated by the French in 1729), the Chikasaw (whom the French were unable to subdue), and the Choctaw. The latter proved to be important allies to the French, providing a buffer against British Colonies to the East. Woods suggests that the difficulties involved in the colonization of Louisiana were due to the political disorganization of the French, as well as to shifting loyalties within Native American tribes.

XI.   URBAN HISTORY

H 1274. ABBOTT, CARL. Boosters and Businessmen: Popular Economic Thought and Urban Growth in the Antebellum Middle West. Westport, Conn.: Greenwood Press, 1981. 266 pp.
Abbott pursues themes set forth by Richard Wade, The Urban Frontier (see H 1391), and others by examining the role of four Midwestern cities (Cincinnati, Chicago, Indianapolis, and Galena) in stimulating the development of intra- and interregional trade networks during the decades preceding the Civil War. The first three chapters describe the economic structure of each city as it evolved in response to national business cycles and trends, improved transportation facilities, accelerating migration, and the expansion of agricultural production. Subsequent chapters relate the functional specialization of these communities instigated by the diverse ways in which their business leaders responded to the opportunities available to them. The study links a voluminous body of booster literature to census and shipment data to see why some cities were more successful prognosticators of their prospects than others. Chicago and Indianapolis fared better than Cincinnati and Galena because their efforts to build distribution facilities were more closely related to railroading. The account of Chicago's displacement of Cincinnati as the Queen City of Midwestern trade adds to previous studies by emphasizing labor and ethnic tensions which handicapped the Ohio monarch "grown fat" on its early rise in manufacturing and river trade.

H 1275. ABBOTT, CARL. The New Urban America: Growth and Politics in Sunbelt Cities. Chapel Hill: University of North Carolina Press, 1981. 317 pp.
This book defines the sunbelt as a region which includes twenty-five states from Delaware to Washington. Following an introductory chapter describing the emergence of the sunbelt from 1940 to 1970, Abbott considers the growth

of five sunbelt cities: Norfolk, Atlanta, San Antonio, Denver, and Portland. He then analyzes suburbanization; changes wrought by W.W. II; post-
war political changes; urban renewal struggles; the fight for suburban
equality; and the rise of neighborhood politics in these cities. Abbott
concludes that urban growth in the sunbelt has led to increasing friction
between older and newer sections of cities, decreasing municipal unity,
and decay in neo-progressive reform movements.

H 1276. ALLSWANG, JOHN M. Bosses, Machines, and Urban Voters: An American
      Symbiosis. Lexington: University Press of Kentucky, 1977.
      253 pp.
In his discussion of the role of machine politics in the municipal governments of New York and Chicago from the second half of the 19th century
on, Allswang analyzes the careers of five bosses: Boss Tweed, Charles
Francis Murphy, Big Bill Thompson, Tony Cermak, and "The Last of the
Bosses," Richard Daley. The author proposes that machine politics served
the needs of a rapidly growing and alien population, which the old ruling
class was unwilling and unable to serve. Allswang details the patronage
system, "honest and dishonest graft," party politics, and the developing
needs of the urban dweller.

H 1277. ANDERSON, ALAN D. The Origins and Resolution of an Urban Crisis:
      Baltimore, 1890-1930. Baltimore, Md.: Johns Hopkins University
      Press, 1977. 143 pp.
Conceiving the city as a system, Anderson shows how growth in Baltimore
generated disequilibria that theoretically could have been resolved in
a variety of ways. As it turned out, the system restored equilibrium
through progressive administrative reform and through technical innovation
in producing services. The former response was more successful than the
latter, and Anderson demonstrates why this was the case. His book analyzes
the development of municipal services in Baltimore, with particular reference to the means of handling sewage and providing water and transportation.
Anderson also shows how the automobile--a solution outside the control
of the city--finally resolved Baltimore's most serious transportation
problem.

H 1278. ARCHDEACON, THOMAS J. New York City, 1664-1710: Conquest and
      Change. Ithaca, N.Y.: Cornell University Press, 1976. 197 pp.
This work offers an examination of the first serious ethnic conflict in
New York City. Archdeacon describes the heterogeneous population of
17th-century New York, its merchant class, and the social geography that
these different groups occupied. The divisions between older Dutch settlers and the newer English counterparts came to the fore in Leisler's
Rebellion of 1689. Unlike similar uprisings elsewhere in the Colonies,
this rebellion did not attempt to assert the rights of Englishmen and
instead reflected suppressed ethnic tensions. Leisler's followers tended
to be economically declining older Dutch settlers making a last grasp
for power against the demographically increasing and powerful English.
Wealth and class were secondary to nationality in the formation of political affiliations at this time. Politics based on ethnicity thereby undermined traditional patterns of deference in this first encounter with democratically oriented politics in New York City.

H 1279. ARNOLD, JOSEPH L. The New Deal in the Suburbs: A History of the
      Greenbelt Town Program, 1935-54. Columbus: Ohio State University
      Press, 1971. 272 pp.
The greenbelt town program represented a radical change in the pattern
of urban growth and real estate practice in the U.S. Based upon the garden
city idea of Ebenezer Howard, the program's communal ownership of real
estate cut across a very tough American grain and was frequently attacked
by opponents for its "socialist" and collectivist goals. Three towns--

Greenbelt, Maryland, Greenhills, Ohio, and Greendale, Wisconsin—were physically, economically, and socially planned by the Federal government in an effort to reverse the economic and social segregation of metropolitan America. In time, the cooperative enterprise expanded at Greenbelt, declined at Greenhills, and disintegrated at Greendale, eventually forcing the Federal government to abandon the program. Despite its failure, the greenbelt program marked a bold departure in the way community life is planned and organized in the U.S.

H 1280. BARRETT, PAUL. The Automobile and Urban Transit: The Formation of Public Policy in Chicago, 1900-1930. Philadelphia: Temple University Press, 1983. 295 pp.
This study explores Chicago's diverse responses to its transportation needs. Focusing mainly on automobiles and transit lines, Barrett traces current commuter dissatisfactions to their roots in conflicting science definitions that kept planners from integrating these modes into a single coordinated system. The work demonstrates the multifaceted role transit played in urban social and political life.

H 1281. BARTH, GUNTHER. City People: The Rise of Modern City Culture in Nineteenth-Century America. New York: Oxford University Press, 1980. 289 pp.
Barth believes that modern city culture was a product of the 19th century and drastically changed, and in some ways vanished with the adoption of the automobile as the most popular form of transportation. New innovations and technology led to the creation of such new urban forms as the apartment house and streetcar, which fostered a new use and different division of urban space. Four institutions in particular encouraged the development of a mass culture with popular appeal: the metropolitan press, the department store, the ball park, and the vaudeville house. Egalitarian at their core, these institutions inculcated the work ethic and middle-class values. With the aid of modern communications, big city culture was soon transformed into a new national culture.

H 1282. BENDER, THOMAS. Community and Social Change in America. New Brunswick, N.J.: Rutgers University Press, 1978. 159 pp.
Bender examines a familiar theme in American historical writing: the process of community breakdown resulting from the forces of modernization, urbanization, and industrialization. Ever since Ferdinand Tonnies developed his theories of Gemeinschaft and Gesellschaft (community and society), social theorists have argued that the two concepts are polar opposites, with modern urban society moving from the former to the latter. Recent sociological studies, however, have shown that often urban and folk ways exist simultaneously in modern society. Bender develops this theme, arguing that community is not a mere base or line of change, but an enduring form of social interaction. Historians err in depicting the American past in terms based simply upon social change and community collapse. Rather than deteriorating or falling apart, community life in most instances has been transformed into something with characteristics associated with modern and pre-modern urban society.

H 1283. BENDER, THOMAS. Toward an Urban Vision: Ideas and Institutions in Nineteenth-Century America. Lexington: University of Kentucky Press, 1975. 277 pp.
Bender analyzes emergent theories of urban planning in the 19th century, beginning with the challenge that early manufacturing towns posed to Romantic ideas of nature. Reconciling nature with civilization was the central concern of early urban planners, and introducing parks into city development became a popular solution to the conflict between city life and country values. Bender analyzes Lowell, Massachusetts, as a representative of the early urban ideal and examines the efforts of Charles Loring Brace and Frederick Law Olmsted.

535

H 1284. BERNARD, RICHARD M. and BRADLEY R. RICE, eds. Sunbelt Cities: Politics and Growth Since World War II. Austin: University of Texas Press, 1983. 346 pp.

This work is a collection of twelve essays which focuses on individual major cities in the sunbelt. Alaphabetically arranged from Atlanta to San Diego and written by academics who have worked in these cities, a pattern emerges from their varied experiences. Traditional political leaders have faced an increasing number of similar challenges from suburbanites and minorities. The cities can be ranked into three categories according to the degree of success the minorities and suburbs have won in their confrontation with established politicians.

H 1285. BLAKE, NELSON M. Water for the Cities: A History of the Urban Water Supply Problem in the United States. Syracuse, N.Y.: Syracuse University Press, 1956. 341 pp.

Blake tells how American cities came to recognize their need for a central water supply and how they met that need. His major focus is on New York City, Boston, Philadelphia, and Baltimore, with others briefly mentioned. During the period of America's most rapid urban growth, 1790 to 1860, cities replaced such water sources as springs, wells, and cisterns with large-scale, centralized water systems. In the early 19th century, most water needs were filled by private companies with Aaron Burr's Manhattan Company (later to evolve into Chase Manhattan Bank) being the most notorious. The profit motive, however, proved a poor incentive to provide water to all sections and groups in the city and only Philadelphia's municipally run system was considered a success. In the 1840s, New York's Croton System and Boston's Cochituate Aqueduct opened, paving the way for more city-sponsored operations. By 1860, only four of the sixteen largest U.S. cities had private companies providing water for them. After the Civil War, engineers began studying water filtration techniques, although cities with upland water supplies did not seriously consider them. By 1940, Americans took water almost for granted. The ten largest European cities averaged 39 gallons a day per capita, while their ten largest American counterparts consumed 155 gallons.

H 1286. BLOUIN, FRANCIS X. The Boston Region, 1810-1850: A Study of Urbanization. Ann Arbor, Mich.: UMI Research Press, 1980. 220 pp.

This study of the area surrounding Boston in the early industrial period addresses questions concerning the region's boundaries, the spatial distribution of activities, the extent of specialization, and the connections among components and activities within the region. Blouin concludes that with Boston serving as an economic foundation the 219 cities and towns of the region were interdependent at this time, and that decisions relating to the location of businesses were based on obtaining specific resources at competitive costs.

H 1287. BORCHERT, JAMES. Alley Life in Washington: Family, Community, Religion and Folklife in the City, 1850-1970. Urbana: University of Illinois Press, 1980. 326 pp.

In this work, Borchert reveals the impact of urban environment on residents through the reconstruction of the life of black migrants in the alleys of Washington, D.C. Newspaper accounts, photographs, personal interviews, census records and building permits are used to reconstruct and view family and neighborhood groups, and childhood, work, religion and folklife in the city. The survival of black culture, strong patriarchal family units with viable kinship links, cohesiveness, and solidarity lead Borchert to conclude that black life was not harmful to the community or culturally fragmented. Instead, blacks adapted their rural culture and remade the urban environment to fit their needs.

H 1288. BOYER, PAUL S. Urban Masses and Moral Order in America, 1820-1920.
         Cambridge, Mass.: Harvard University Press, 1978. 387 pp.
Boyer studies the 19th-century struggle between the individual's rights
in an egalitarian society and the perceived need to construct an enduring
moral order. He finds that reformers, convinced that urbanization and
industrialization were undermining moral order and stability, attempted
through a variety of measures such as tract societies and organized youth
programs to duplicate the atmosphere of moral order found in the idealized
village. The author traces the development of this concept of social
control and various efforts to achieve it.

H 1289. BROWNE, GARY LAWSON. Baltimore in the Nation, 1789-1861. Chapel
         Hill: University of North Carolina Press, 1980. 349 pp.
Motivated by the question of how Baltimore was transformed from a Colonial
commercial city into a modern American industrial city, the author looks
at the city's social, political, and economic relations through the eyes
of the business community. He finds that with the Revolution as a catalyst,
interactions between society and the economy produced a Republicanism
that took control away from the elite and eventually embraced Jacksonian
ideas about money while encouraging the building of an industrial economy.

H 1290. BROWNELL, BLAINE A. The Urban Ethos in the South: 1920-1930.
         Baton Rouge: Louisiana State University Press, 1975. 237 pp.
In his study of the Southern city in the 1920s, Brownell attempts to define
a distinct urban ethos held by leading commercial and civic groups, and,
in some measure, by the general public. The author primarily examines
the printed media in exploring the "urban imagery, urban boosterism, and
concepts of the urban community," as well as views of local histories,
held by the conscious urban elite. Brownell finds that municipal policy
was based on the concept of an organic metropolis, in which civic voluntarism would unite the populace and form and implement policy. Brownell
concludes that this vision of civic participation, though it left its
mark on the appearance and structure of Southern cities well after the
1920s, was bound to fail because it ignored ethnic and class differences
within the city population.

H 1291. BURG, DAVID F. Chicago's White City of 1893. Lexington: Univer-
         sity Press of Kentucky, 1976. 379 pp.
In this interpretive account of the World's Columbian Exposition of 1893
(based on extensive research of fair records, photographs, and memorabilia),
Burg argues that the wonders of the fair revealed American values, antici-
pations, and aspirations. He emphasizes the combination of technical
genius and cooperative endeavor which provided directions for social planners of the modern age. Chapters include detailed information on such
topics as landscaping and architecture; the participation of writers and
artists; the World's Congress auxiliary; and what the exposition reveals
of late 19th-century professional and academic life.

H 1292. CALLOW, ALEXANDER B., Jr. The Tweed Ring. New York: Oxford Uni-
         versity Press, 1965. 351 pp.
In its five years of power from 1866-1871, the "Tweed Ring," as it was
derogatorily labeled, became and remains the classic symbol of urban political corruption. In the years just prior to and during the Civil War,
William M. Tweed successfully built a powerful political organization
around Tammany Hall, originally a fraternal society. Based strictly on
self-interest, the first modern political machine in America attempted
to serve the needs of poor Irish immigrants in New York, as well as aspir-
ants for political power. As a result, the Irish were assimilated into
the political culture of the U.S. and a new form of urban politics in
the 19th century was created. The conflict between upper-class Protestant
reformers and Tweed and his immigrant allies finally erupted in charges
of corruption and his ouster from office in 1871.

H 1293. CARO, ROBERT A. The Power Broker: Robert Moses and the Fall of
New York. New York: Knopf, 1974. 1278 pp.
In this work, Caro explains the physical development of 20th-century New
York through the life of the man he believes was most responsible for
shaping it, Robert Moses. Holding numerous city and state positions,
Moses dominated the planning and construction of most public works projects
in New York State from 1924-1968, spending over $27 billion on highways,
parks, playgrounds, bridges, houses, stadiums, and entertainment centers
during that time. While Caro considers Moses the greatest builder of
his era, he recognizes that the long-term impact of his work was a colossal
failure. Moses's paternalistic approach, elitist attitudes, and bulldozing
tactics provided little opportunity for input by residents of the city
and created as many new problems as he allegedly solved.

H 1294. CAVALLO, DOMINICK. Muscles and Morals: Organized Playgrounds
and Urban Reform, 1880-1920. Philadelphia: University of Pennsylvania Press, 1981. 188 pp.
From 1880 to 1920, urban social reformers sought to transfer control of
children's play from their families to the state. Playgrounds were built
in American cities in large numbers after 1900 so that city youths could
be supervised and controlled. Influenced by psychologists like James
Mark Baldwin, Edward Thorndike, John Dewey, and especially Stanley Hall
and his theory of recapitulation, play organizers believed supervised
play would alter the behavior of children. Since muscle control was a
primary link between a child's "inner" realm of feeling and his "outer"
world of social interaction, structured and supervised play strengthened
the youth's moral fiber as much as it fortified his or her body. The
playground, then, became an ideal alternative to unsupervised and chaotic
street play. Rather than destroy adolescent peer groups and gangs, play
organizers wished to structure their activity by channeling it into team
games and team experiences. Cavallo focuses on the leaders of the Playground Association of America who promoted these ideas, especially Luther
Gulick, Joseph Lee, and Jane Addams. Although play organizers and child
psychologists differed on points of child development, each emphasized
a mode of child training that could be practiced by rigorous physical
drill and games on organized playgrounds, which explains the popularity
of this popular Progressive reform.

H 1295. CHEAPE, CHARLES W. Moving the Masses: Urban Public Transit in
New York, Boston, and Philadelphia, 1880-1912. Cambridge, Mass.:
Harvard University Press, 1980. 285 pp.
Cheape places urban mass transit in the context of changing strategies
and structures of business management in this study of three East Coast
cities in which private companies built extensive systems before the turn
of the century. The book focuses on the financing of transit companies
and their consolidation into monopolies in much the same pattern that
characterized the nation's railroad industry and other municipal utilities
such as electricity and gas. The study addresses the point made by Gabriel
Kolko and others that utility officials had a vested interest in supporting
greater public regulation.

H 1296. CHUDACOFF, HOWARD P. The Evolution of American Urban Society.
1975; Rev. ed. Englewood Cliffs, N.J.: Prentice-Hall, 1981.
312 pp.
This work provides a synthesis of the most recent literature associated
with the variety of "new" histories: urban, labor, ethnic, women, and
black. Cudacoff describes how American cities evolved from the Colonial
period to the 1970s by examining them from three general perspectives:
spatial and physical; social and demographic; and political. The text
is divided into nine chapters with three general chronological parts.
The first considers the pre-industrial and walking city, emphasizing the
Colonial period, the rise of national urban networks, and the beginnings

of urban sprawl and industrialization. The middle portion emphasizes
the impact of immigration, the social and health problems it caused, and
the rise of the political boss and reform movements to meet those problems.
The final chapters consider the U.S. as an urban nation after 1920 and
the impact of the changing relationship of the Federal government and
American cities during the New Deal and beyond. Finally, the author provides an extensive bibliography at the end of each chapter including the
most recent important works on American urban history.

H 1297. COHEN, RONALD D. and RAYMOND A. MOHL. The Paradox of Progressive
Education: The Gary Plan and Urban Schooling. Port Washington,
N.Y.: Kennikat Press, 1979. 216 pp.
Cohen and Mohl describe the Gary plan, which gained much attention during
the first years of the 20th century. The plan encouraged the use of school
physical facilities during weekends and evenings, and it advocated the
involvement of more adults in education. The authors note that the proposition attracted support from a variety of sources; some conservatives
saw it as a way to obtain cheaper education, while some reformers saw
it as a way to change society.

H 1298. CONDIT, CARL W. The Railroad and the City: A Technological and
Urbanistic History of Cincinnati. Columbus: Ohio State University
Press, 1977. 335 pp.
The interaction between the railroad and Cincinnati, between the completion
of the first line in 1836 and the opening of Union Terminal in 1936, demonstrates how railroads influenced land-use patterns and the overall form
of the city. As the nexus of railroad systems linking the North and the
South, Cincinnati generated a huge traffic in freight and passengers in
the 19th century which was vital to the city. Numerous companies formed,
failed, merged, consolidated, and reorganized, but in the process planned
and built terminals in the city. The location of the terminals reflected
the topography of the area as well as the engineering capacity of the
roads. In turn, railroad depots provided a focus to the material life
and activity of the city while serving a symbolic role to the local populace.

H 1299. DANBOM, DAVID B. The Resisted Revolution: Urban America and the
Industrialization of Agriculture 1900-1930. Ames: Iowa State
University Press, 1979. 195 pp.
Danbom traces the rise of the "Country Life Movement" and the efforts
of its adherents to raise rural America to a 20th-century standard of
social and economic organization and efficiency. This little-studied
facet of Progressive reformist zeal grew out of the Country Life Commission
appointed by President Theodore Roosevelt in 1907 to study the causes
of the perceived economic backwardness and social stagnation of farming
regions. Working through the U.S.D.A. and other government and private
agencies, the Country Lifers sought to model the rural educational system
and promote more rational, scientific farming methods. While not explicitly
linked to a broader interpretation of the Progressive period, the account
raises important questions about the declining status of farmers in an
industrializing society.

H 1300. DAVIS, ALLEN F. Spearheads for Reform: The Social Settlements
and the Progressive Movement, 1890-1914. New York: Oxford University Press, 1967. 322 pp.
Davis claims that the settlement house movement of the early 20th century
was one of the principal instruments in the first war on poverty in the
U.S. Most settlement house workers, he contends, believed in the ideals
of American government, supported the goals of organized labor, and adopted
a less paternalistic stance in their treatment of the poor and immigrants
than other Progressive reformers. The settlement house movement encouraged

young Americans to forsake philanthropy for reform. The variety of important Americans involved--Jane Addams, Lillian Wald, Charles Beard, Harry Hopkins, Henry Morganthau, Herbert Lehman, Gerard Swope, and John Dewey-- attests to the impact of the movement which continued despite its decline after W.W. I.

H 1301. DICKINSON, JOHN N. To Build a Canal: Sault Ste. Marie, 1853-1854 and After. Columbus: Ohio State University Press, 1981. 192 pp. Completed some thirty years after the Erie Canal, the St. Mary's Falls Canal has been no less significant in connecting the Great Lakes interior with the Eastern seaboard. The discovery of vast copper deposits in Michigan provided the impetus for construction, and this study describes the diverse interests, both public and private, involved in the project at the local and national level.

H 1302. DINER, STEPHEN J. A City and Its Universities: Public Policy in Chicago, 1892-1919. Chapel Hill: University of North Carolina Press, 1980. 263 pp. Diner focuses on the professionalization of academia and discusses the impact of the professional academic on public policy. Concentrating particularly on the University of Chicago and its relationship with that city, Diner outlines social scientists' activities in reforming local government, public education, the treatment of deviant behavior, and welfare. Though the profesors did accomplish much, they began to avoid public advocacy after political scientist Charles E. Merriam lost his campaign for mayor in 1919, and they assumed the less active role of advisers to officeholders.

H 1303. DUFFY, JOHN. A History of Public Health in New York City, 1625- 1866. New York: Russell Sage, 1968. 619 pp. Duffy provides a chronological account of the way in which New York City dealt with its sanitary and health problems from its early days as a Dutch settlement to the creation in 1866 of the Metropolitan Board of Health, the forerunner of the current Department of Health. During its first century, the settlement suffered few major health problems. Whenever problems arose, a temporary board of health was created. Epidemics constituted the major problem during the 18th and 19th centuries, and although quarantine laws were frequently strengthened, no permanent agency was created to prevent repetition of the problem. After 1790 sanitation problems were exacerbated by a rapidly rising population, much of it with predominantly rural backgrounds and primitive concepts of hygiene. Political corruption hindered the impressive reform efforts of people like John Griscom and Elisha Harris to solve these problems until the creation of the Metropolitan Board of Health. Duffy discusses the various ways the modern city created new services to alleviate health problems--the Croton water and sewage system, the hospital, the quarantine, and food and market regulations.

H 1304. DUIS, PERRY R. The Saloon: Public Drinking in Chicago and Boston, 1880-1920. Urbana: University of Illinois Press, 1983. 376 pp. This book is a case study of the rise and fall of the saloon in Chicago and Boston during a period of considerable agitation over the problems of drinking. Duis chose the two cities because of their different approaches to saloon regulation; unlike Chicago, Boston exerted a great deal of control over its saloons. His book, however, extends far beyond a consideration of the fate of the saloon; it identifies changes in the social and economic life of American cities of the period which first promoted growth and then contributed to decline. Finally, Duis examines the complex problems of the liquor industry.

H 1305. DYKSTRA, ROBERT. The Cattle Towns: A Social History of the Kansas
Cattle Trading Centers, Abilene, Ellsworth, Wichita, Dodge City
and Caldwell, 1867-1885. New York: Knopf, 1968. 386 pp.
Using social science methodology in his analysis of population characteristics, Dykstra analyzes the economic development of Abilene, Ellsworth,
Caldwell, Wichita, and Dodge City. He argues that the emergence of the
towns was a complicated process marked by competition among the five cattle
centers as well as by rivalry within each town's citizenry. Growth emerged
from conflict rather than consensus in Dykstra's model of urban development.

H 1306. ELAZAR, DANIEL J. Cities of the Prairie: The Metropolitan Frontier and American Politics. New York: Basic Books, 1970.
514 pp.
This book transcends disciplinary boundaries by combining local research
with a large synthesis of American history. The author examines the political systems of seventeen medium-sized (50-250,000 inhabitant) cities of
the prairie region, such as Peoria and Joliet, Illinois, and emphasizes
the historical and cultural context of government and politics. Elazar
concentrates on the years from the end of W.W. II to the Kennedy administration, but he also includes a discussion of the cultural and historical
forces which shaped these cities. The four key forces Elazar isolates
are the frontier, migration, sectionalism, and Federalism.

H 1307. ERENBERG, LEWIS A. Steppin' Out: New York Nightlife and the
Transformation of American Culture, 1890-1930. Westport, Conn.:
Greenwood Press, 1981. 291 pp.
Erenberg examines the cabaret and the nightlife associated with it in
the early part of the 20th century. Before 1910 cabarets were little
known by the middle class and were usually considered "dives," and associated with saloons, red-light districts, and male culture. Their transformation into a respectable institution reflected changing standards
of social and sexual life, especially the gradual decline of Victorian
values. For some, the cabaret eased many of the institutional demands
of the social group, the community, and the family. For professionals,
the wealthy, entertainers, and tourists, the cabaret offered more personal
choices, an informal social life, and a new realm of public privacy.
This development marked a profound reorientation in American culture toward
greater informality, fewer restrictions on the individual, and an emphasis
on self-fulfillment, self-expression, and personality development. Rejecting the Chicago School of Sociology and its thesis that nightlife represented cultural decline, anonymity, and urban pathos, Erenberg sees it
as an outlet for creative desires and urges.

H 1308. FEIN, ALBERT. Frederick Law Olmsted and the American Environmental Tradition. New York: Braziller, 1972. 180 pp.
Frederick Law Olmsted, Sr. was one of the first landscape architects
and comprehensive environmental planners in the U.S. Best known
for his design of New York's Central Park, Olmsted was a pioneer in the
movement for urban parks, parkways, planned suburbs and college campus
communities. He sought to integrate an appreciation of the ecological
facts of nature with the belief that cities were necessary centers of
civilization and culture. The planning and design of cities, Olmsted
believed, cannot ignore the intimate relationship between community needs
and ecological realities. Fein argues that Olmsted's espousal of social
democracy is especially relevant to contemporary urban life with its unresolved conflicts over the use of space and political power.

H 1309. FOGELSON, ROBERT M. Big City Police. Cambridge, Mass.: Harvard
        University Press, 1977. 374 pp.
Fogelson's book is a study of 20th-century policy in large metropolitan
cities. He analyzes what urban police forces do, what they are theoretically supposed to do, how they evolved, and how they relate to the large
social structure of which they are part. Fogelson also examines the inside
of the bureaucracy of a police department and how these processes respond
to external pressure.

H 1310. FOGELSON, ROBERT M. The Fragmented Metropolis: Los Angeles,
        1850-1930. Cambridge, Mass.: Harvard University Press, 1967.
        362 pp.
Fogelson describes Los Angeles before the invention of the automobile
and argues that the dispersal of the city occurred prior to that technological innovation. Two major forces, according to the author, combined
to create a city with no center: the streetcar system and the desire
of Midwestern migrants to have homes with lawns. This conclusion challenges those theories which contend that urban sprawl began only in the
1930s.

H 1311. FOLSOM, BURTON W., Jr. Urban Capitalists: Entrepreneurs and
        City Growth in Pennsylvania's Lackawanna and Lehigh Regions,
        1800-1920. Baltimore, Md.: Johns Hopkins University Press,
        1981. 191 pp.
In his study which describes the transformation of several old rural areas
into coal and iron centers, Folsom places the rapid rise of two Pennsylvania cities (Scranton and Bethlehem) in a regional context. After reviewing various theoretical frameworks of urban development, such as central
place models, initial and locational advantages, and environmental explanations, he argues that the true reasons for the different economic structures in these two locales are found in the biographies of their early
entrepreneurial elites. His sample of forty Scranton business leaders
during the 1880s reveals diverse social and ethnic backgrounds and more
risk-taking behavior than was typical of neighboring communities which
were more socially homogeneous.

H 1312. FOSTER, MARK S. From Streetcar to Superhighway: American City
        Planners and Urban Transportation, 1900-1940. Philadelphia:
        Temple University Press, 1981. 246 pp.
Foster examines the changing perspectives and reactions of city planners
to the rapid evolution of urban transportation and automotive technology.
Focusing mainly on Boston, Detroit, Chicago, and Seattle, he argues that
planners did the best they could, given the public's enthusiasm for automobiles and new suburban developments, to promote public transportation
systems for inner-city and regional areas. His account shows that many
planners viewed suburbs and highway construction as more positive long-
range solutions to urban congestion.

H 1313. FOX, KENNETH. Better City Government: Innovation in American
        Urban Politics, 1850-1937. Philadelphia: Temple University
        Press, 1877. 222 pp.
Fox studies municipal reform during a period of great urban growth and
considers the complexity of the times in an attempt to dispel myths about
boss rule and the goals of reformers. Boss rule, according to Fox, was
never as strong as portrayed by the reformers; instead, local wardheelers
exercised much power. In Chicago, for example, an effective machine did
not appear until the 1930s. Moreover, although usually thought of as
polarized forces, bosses and urban supporters often shared the same goals
for different reasons.

H 1314. FRISCH, MICHAEL H. Town into City: Springfield, Massachusetts, and the Meaning of Community, 1840-1880. Cambridge, Mass.: Harvard University Press, 1972. 301 pp.

Frisch examines the city-building process in a specific medium-sized city in western Massachusetts. The author analyzes the objective dimensions of growth and how people understood and reacted to it. The pre-Civil War town had a strong sense of community typified by a limited government run by and for the interests of taxpayers, a politics of deference and indistinguishable public and private sectors. For the most part, the Springfield of 1840 had much more in common with the Colonial town of a century earlier than with the city that emerged only forty years later. Politics, for example, was a curious blend of aristocracy and egalitarianism; political activity stopped after elections and did not extend to the conduct of government. This narrow view of public life changed after the Civil War. As a result of wartime contracts, an already-diversified economy, and demographic growth, the local government was forced to assume responsibilities previously left to the private sector. This new government role produced political conflict, the politicization of businessmen, and the professional politician. By 1880 a more bureaucratic and administrative interpretation of democracy emerged that heralded the Progressive concept of public interest in the next century. Despite this transformation, Frisch concludes that the idea of local community did not disappear as much as change its form and manifestation.

H 1315. FUNNELL, CHARLES E. By the Beautiful Sea: The Rise and High Times of that Great American Resort, Atlantic City. New Brunswick, N.J.: Rutgers University Press, 1983. 250 pp.

This book attempts to construct a pattern of social history for the greatest popular Victorian American resort, using the themes of the machine and the city, nature, morality, and pleasure--terms which occupied a prominent place in the public mind at the end of the 19th century. Funnell sees Atlantic City as fairly typical of resort parks of the period, and paradigmatic of the social phenomenon of Victorian America: urban vigor and squalor, massed humanity and new popular culture, florid but charming sentimentality, sinister but inventive criminality, ingenuity and bad taste, optimism and eccentricity.

H 1316. GELFAND, MARK I. A Nation of Cities: The Federal Government and Urban America, 1933-65. New York: Oxford University Press, 1975. 476 pp.

In urban areas, the New Deal of Franklin Roosevelt represented a break from other reform movements in American history. In transforming attitudes of business and the private sector, the Federal government's intervention was for the first time seen as a positive and necessary influence in the growth and development of cities. Rising relief expenditures and growing tax delinquencies forced cities to seek Federal help after 1930. Gelfand argues that FDR, however, possessed an anti-urban outlook and was more interested in assisting the city dweller, not the city itself. Unlike the efforts of the TVA, Resettlement Administration, or Rural Electrification Administration, little was done during his administration to change the physical contours of the city. This changed after World War II as Federal programs emphasized massive physical construction projects. Many skyscrapers, convention halls, parking garages, freeways, and pedestrian malls were built with the aid of large Federal subsidies. Along with highway and urban renewal, public housing and home mortgage insurance projects constituted the four major Federal programs having the greatest impact on cities from 1933-1960. Good intentions aside, parts of these programs failed because their planning focused on houses and highways instead of communities.

H 1317. **GLAAB, CHARLES N.** Kansas City and the Railroads: Community Policy
in the Growth of a Regional Metropolis. Madison: State Historical Society of Wisconsin, 1962. 260 pp.
Glaab traces the successful campaign by Kansas City, Missouri residents
for rail connections with the West. Glaab outlines the arguments for
the railroad used by urban boosters and details their frequently dirty
politics. Federal policy is also examined; it was the Pacific Railway
Act of 1862 that allowed the establishment of the Kansas Pacific Railroad,
and it was the Railroad that transformed Kansas City from a small antebellum military freight and Southwest trade center into a regional economic
power.

H 1318. **GLAAB, CHARLES N.** and **THEODORE A. BROWN.** A History of Urban
America. 1967; Rev. ed. New York: Macmillan, 1976. 400 pp.
Glaab and Brown use urban growth as an organizing theme for American history and assign dominant traits to successive periods. They begin with
the Colonial towns, then move to the social and cultural life of the city
in the first half of the 19th century. The years from 1860 to 1910, which
receive similar treatment, are discussed in terms of population changes,
technology, government, the development of city planning, and the rise
of the metropolis. Other subjects covered are Federal urban policy,
suburbs, and super-cities.

H 1319. **GOIST, PARK DIXON.** From Main Street to State Street: Town and
Community in America. Port Washington, N.Y.: Kennikat Press,
1977. 180 pp.
Goist contends that the search for community has been, and remains, a
major concern in American life. Drawing on literature, advertising, sociology, social work, journalism and city planning, Goist examines the changing
concept of community from the perspectives of the city and of the town.
This study covers the period between 1890 and 1940 and is divided into
two sections. The first explores the American literary imagination (Booth
Tarkington, Sherwood Anderson, Sinclair Lewis) and automative industry
advertising, both of which viewed and promoted the town as ideal community.
The second section offers individual perspectives of the city and its
community-making possibilities. The afterword treats contemporary theories
of community such as the work of Richard Sennett.

H 1320. **GOLDFIELD, DAVID R.** Cotton Fields and Skyscrapers: Southern
City and Region, 1607-1980. Baton Rouge: Louisiana State University Press, 1982. 232 pp.
The Southern experience of race, Colonial economy, and a predominantly
rural population produced an economy and a society with no need for large
cities. The numerous small towns scattered across the region filled the
role played by large cities in other areas of the nation. Those Southern
urban areas which could be termed cities held the same values, sheltered
the same society, and supported the same economy as the cotton fields.
As a result, Goldfield concludes, the "worlds of the cotton field and
the skyscraper are essentially the same."

H 1321. **GOLDFIELD, DAVID R.** Urban Growth in the Age of Sectionalism:
Virginia, 1847-1861. Baton Rouge: Louisiana State University
Press, 1977. 336 pp.
In exploring the growth of various Virginian cities in the decade prior
to the Civil War, Goldfield argues that the development of an urban society
in the South decisively influenced that region's attitude toward the North
and Secession. The author points to the paradox of Southern urbanization:
while the city integrated Virginia into the national economy, its economic
weakness in comparison to its Northern counterparts underscored the South's
inferior economic position, thus nurturing resentment of the North.
Goldfield treats the development of an urban economic superstructure in
the South, the rise of a civic elite and urban consciousness, and the

extension of urban and commercial services. Also detailed are the relations between Southern city and country, and the distinct economic orientations of different cities, which determined their attitudes toward the
sectional issue.

H 1322. GOLDFIELD, DAVID R. and BLAINE A. BROWNELL. Urban America: From
Downtown to No Town. Boston: Houghton Mifflin, 1979. 435 pp.
Goldfield and Brownell trace the spatial development of American cities
from their Colonial beginnings to the present. Pointing out that change
has been the most fundamental law of urbanization, they outline four stages
through which American cities have passed. Pushed along by shifts in
social, political, and economic patterns, cities have progressed from
a cluster (settlement-1790) to a market place (1790-1870) to a radical
center (1870-1920) and, finally, to a vital fringe (1920-present). Within
each of these eras, the authors discuss the impact of social arrangements,
transportation and communication patterns, ethnic groups, and economic
growth on a wide variety of cities.

H 1323. GREEN, CONSTANCE M. The Rise of Urban America. New York: Harper
& Row, 1965. 208 pp.
This survey highlights important developments in the rise of urban America
as well as the role of cities in creating a distinctive American culture.
Green's account begins with the Colonial era and progresses to the 1960s.
The first century of American urban life centered on such seaports as
Boston, New York, and Philadelphia; rapid population growth and favorable
climate allowed many towns to develop into cities. Industrialization
quickened this process and created the need for social and political adjustments.

H 1324. GREEN, CONSTANCE M. Washington: Village and Capital, 1800-78.
Princeton, N.J.: Princeton University Press, 1962. 444 pp.
In this, the first of a two-volume urban biography (see H 1325), Green
reviews the evolution of Washington from a small, Southern town into the
national capital of the U.S. Initially, the District was three distinct
and separate towns--Washington (Capitol Hill), Georgetown, and Alexandria--
each engaged in cut-throat economic competition with one another. In
1844, Alexandria was ceded back to Virginia, but the rivalry between the
other two cities continued into the 1860s. Continued dependence on the
Federal government and the lack of a good location inhibited the economic
growth of Washington through most of the 19th century. As late as 1870,
some considered it the ugliest city in the U.S. Green also devotes space
to describing the race relations, characterized by large numbers of freemen
before the Civil War and a rising black population thereafter.

H 1325. GREEN, CONSTANCE M. Washington: Capital City, 1879-1950. Princeton, N.J.: Princeton University Press, 1962. 558 pp.
In this second volume of her biography of the U.S. capital (see H 1324)
Green describes the development of Washington from a small Southern city
to a modern American metropolis. By the mid-20th century, Washington
was an anomaly among American cities. Over half its real estate was tax
exempt, its citizens had no representation in Congress, political power
was in the hands of a small group of businessmen on the Board of Trade,
and it had an important and influential upper-class black community.
A non-industrial and non-commercial city, political power was the business
that distinguished Washington. Washington never experienced the massive
European immigration and its corresponding social problems that other
cities suffered. Instead, it experienced a massive black migration that
created two different cities--a small white community focused around
Federal government institutions and a large, poor, black minority. This
contradiction allowed for the construction of the most impressive physical
development project of the City Beautiful movement, the Washington Mall,

while most of the city's inhabitants suffered from poor and inadequate housing, many living in alley slums sprinkled throughout the city. After 1930 this situation began to change with the advent of the New Deal and the experience of W.W. II.

H 1326. GRIFFEN, CLYDE and SALLY GRIFFEN. Natives and Newcomers: The Ordering of Opportunity in Mid-Nineteenth-Century Poughkeepsie. Cambridge, Mass.: Harvard University Press, 1978. 291 pp.
The Griffens study the occupational mobility of both new and long-term residents of 19th-century Poughkeepsie, New York. Mobility, they discover, went both ways. Using credit ledgers and business records, they conclude that small businesses had a high rate of failure, and that families played a critical role in the success or failure of business ventures. Considerable kinship involvement sustained numerous businesses in a competitive and often hostile environment.

H 1327. HAMMACK, DAVID C. Power and Society: Greater New York at the Turn of the Century. New York: Russell Sage, 1982. 422 pp.
Hammack rejects the elite theory of political power and argues that the pluralist model is more accurate when examining New York City from 1880 to 1920. Political power during this period was distributed among several distinct economic, social, and political elites, not one single power elite, machine, or genteel class. The author examines different theories of how political power is dispersed, and then attempts to test them. He discusses the changing economy from one based on commerce to one reliant on light, small industrial establishments. This transformation divided the city's upper class into five differing elite groups. The resulting fragmentation prevented any one of these groups from controlling mayoral elections and gave organized labor and different ethnic groups a greater role in municipal politics. These divisions are illustrated in several important issues on which Hammack focuses: the consolidation movement, the construction of the New York subway, and the centralization of the city's public school system.

H 1328. HANDLIN, OSCAR and JOHN BURCHARD, eds. The Historian and the City. Cambridge, Mass.: MIT Press, 1963. 299 pp.
Though many of the essays in this collection do not deal with the historical problems presented by the American city, some do make the American city their primary concern, and all put the American city in the perspective of the development of modern urban society. Included are those by Sam B. Warner, Jr. on the interplay between technical innovation and industrialization in early 19th-century Philadelphia, Morton White on the causes of the American intellectual's disaffection for the city, and Frank Freidel on the reactions of four generations of Boston Adamses to urban life. More general essays deal with the philosophy of the city, the economic, technical, and social structure of different types of cities, and the problems facing the urban historian.

H 1329. HARRIS, CARL V. Political Power in Birmingham, 1871-1921. Knoxville: University of Tennessee Press, 1977. 318 pp.
Harris studies those who wielded power in a Southern city during the Progressive Era. He traces the backgrounds of office holders and identifies those groups which benefited most from their decisions. Based on this study, Harris concludes that there was a power elite: the wealthy dominated the leading political positions. The power to make decisions, however, was less clearly distributed and defined, because competition for benefits forced compromises and changes in policy-making.

H 1330. HAWES, JOSEPH M. Children in Urban Society: Juvenile Delinquency
in Nineteenth Century America. New York: Oxford University
Press, 1971. 315 pp.
Hawes examines 19th-century America's concepts of youth, family, social
order, and deviance. He begins by surveying notions about wayward youth
in both American and European literature, science, and popular culture.
He then focuses on the development of American institutions for juvenile
delinquents in the 19th century from "houses of refuge," to reform schools,
to "placing out" systems. He emphasizes the continuity of these institutions, especially in the notions of children as small adults and of
the central importance of environment in personality development. He
argues that it was not until the end of the century--with the emergence
of G. Stanley Hall's psychology and Judge Ben Lindsey's humanitarianism--
that a truly child-sensitive juvenile court began to develop.

H 1331. HERSHBERG, THEODORE, ed. Philadelphia: Work, Space, Family,
and Group Experience in the Nineteenth Century: Essays Toward
an Interdisciplinary History of the City. New York: Oxford
University Press, 1981. 523 pp.
A collection of thirteen empirical essays based on data gathered by the
Philadelphia Social History Project, the authors explore the elements
that molded the lives of late 19th-century Philadelphians. The essays
move toward an interdisciplinary approach to urban history in which urban
is defined as a process rather than simply a collection of events that
happened in a city. It is this process, "the interrelationships among
environment, behavior, and group experience," that the authors address
in these essays.

H 1332. HERSHKOWITZ, LEO. Tweed's New York: Another Look. Garden City,
N.Y.: Anchor Press, 1977. 409 pp.
Leo Hershkowitz insists that Boss Tweed was innocent because New York
City was too large and too complex for a single political organization
to dominate so thoroughly. Tweed's confession, a last minute act of desperation to regain his freedom, provided the only tangible evidence that
a "Tweed ring" existed. Tweed's crimes were never major. He was never
tried for theft or graft, but rather subterfuge. The first trial ended
in a hung jury with a majority in favor of acquittal. The second jury
was chosen in a questionable fashion. The judge and prosecution deliberately misled the jury into believing the maximum sentence would only
be one year, not the thirteen years Tweed finally received. Hershkowitz
concludes that lower echelon officials were the individuals responsible
for making corrupt deals with contractors and the real perpetrators of
municipal graft.

H 1333. HOLLI, MELVIN. Reform in Detroit: Hazen G. Pingree and Urban
Politics. New York: Oxford University Press, 1968. 269 pp.
Holli's book examines reform and machine politics in late 19th-century
American cities, using Detroit as an example. Reformers became alarmed
at political corruption and boss rule and, consequently, campaigned to
clean up cities. Holli describes how the Republican mayor of Detroit,
who entered office as a businessman's advocate of efficient government,
became a social reformer fighting for municipal ownership of electrical
generating facilities. In the process, Holli develops a model that
explains movements for urban reform by dividing them into two categories:
structural reform and social reform.

H 1334. HOLLINGSWORTH, J. ROGERS and ELLEN JANE HOLLINGSWORTH. Dimensions
         in Urban History: Historical and Social Science Perspectives
         on Middle-Size American Cities. Madison: University of Wisconsin
         Press, 1979. 184 pp.
Lamenting the lack of attention given cities ranging from 10,000 to 250,000
inhabitants, the authors offer case studies of three cities in Wisconsin
to fill that void. Their studies of Eau Claire, Janesville, and Green
Bay focus on the changing social, political, and economic dynamics of
the late 19th century. While they suggest that it is too early for generalizations, they conclude that it is possible to construct a typology of
cities of this size.

H 1335. JACKSON, ANTHONY. A Place Called Home: A History of Low-Cost
         Housing in Manhattan. Cambridge, Mass.: MIT Press, 1976.
         359 pp.
Since the Industrial Revolution, every generation in New York has suffered
from a housing crisis and Jackson argues that the problem is endemic,
not just temporary. After 1840 the tenement began replacing the alley,
rookery, and cellar as the living place for the poor. Efforts by philanthropists were inconsequential. Model tenements such as Silas Wood's
Gotham Court quickly degenerated into disease-ridden abodes doing little
to solve the problem of adequate housing for the city's working and immigrant populations. Tenement house laws passed in 1867, 1887, and 1901
proved to be inadequate or ill-enforced. Even government intervention
after 1935 did little to solve the basic housing problems of the poor
and often only benefitted the middle-class. Jackson attributes this to
the "filtering" theory of housing supply which has dominated housing policy
for most of the 19th and 20th centuries. This argument assumes that construction of new housing in any price range will reshuffle the entire
housing stock so that everyone, including the poor, will benefit by either
improved accommodation or lower cost.

H 1336. JACKSON, KENNETH T. The Ku Klux Klan in the City, 1915-1930.
         New York: Oxford University Press, 1967. 326 pp.
Jackson rejects the interpretation that the Ku Klux Klan was a violent,
rural-based, small town, Southern, white supremacy organization in the
early 20th century. Rather, the Klan's largest concentration of members
was located in the big cities of such Midwestern states as Ohio, Indiana,
and Illinois. Race prejudice was less of a reason for joining the Klan
than such issues as immigration restriction, prohibition, and Protestant
fundamentalism. By the 1920s, the Klan was seen as a large fraternal
organization with significant numbers of white-collar workers and businessmen as members. Fear of change and certain elements within American cities
encouraged the growth of the Klan, which successfully integrated itself
into local American political, social, and religious life during this
period.

H 1337. JACOBS, JANE. The Death and Life of Great American Cities. New
         York: Random House, 1961. 458 pp.
Jacobs attacks modern city planning and rebuilding. Since the start of
the 20th century with the City Beautiful movement, planners and architects have erroneously tried to treat the city in an aesthetic way, as
a work of art. Designs conceptualized by Ebenezer Howard, Daniel Burnham,
Patrick Geddes, Lewis Mumford, and Le Corbusier, despite their many differences, share an emphasis on self-containment, organization, and imposed
order. This, Jacobs argues, is anti-city. By sorting out different functions to different parts of the city, they create the illusion of privacy
and suburban isolation. The best city neighborhood is one with lively
streets, functional integration, and parks, squares, and buildings being
used together. The big city is a natural generator of diversity and this
should be encouraged, not suppressed. Four factors are necessary for

diversity: more than one primary function, short blocks, different types
and ages of buildings, and a dense population. This diversity encourages
people to engage in activities in the street, thereby making it safe and
free from crime. High density should not be equated with slums and poverty.

H 1338. **JAHER, FREDERIC COPLE.** The Urban Establishment: Upper Strata
in Boston, New York, Charleston, Chicago, and Los Angeles. Urbana:
University of Illinois Press, 1982. 777 pp.
By describing the rise and fall of the elite classes in five American
cities, Jaher attempts to illuminate the role of the leadership echelons
in society, and, more specifically, in the city (as only the Charleston
patriciate lived in a non-urban environment). Concentrating on the 19th
century, Jaher explores the mentality and composition of each city's upper
class, as well as its economic power. In conclusion, Jaher relates the
five case studies to other urban strata in the U.S., to ruling establishments in Europe, and to the alleged existence of an American oligarchy.

H 1339. **KASSON, JOHN F.** Amusing the Million: Coney Island at the Turn
of the Century. New York: Hill & Wang, 1978. 120 pp.
Kasson argues that the establishment of amusement parks signified a major
transition in American culture. Using Coney Island as a case study, he
explores the connection between urbanization and popular culture, emphasizing the growth of leisure time and spending power within the working
class, and the development of cheap mass transit that allowed excursions
from the city. As a "harbinger of modernity," the sensual and participa-
tory amusements of Coney Island represent to Kasson a cultural revolt
against Victorian standards of taste and conduct by the new urban American.

H 1340. **KIRSCHNER, DON S.** City and Country: Rural Responses to Urbanization in the 1920s. Westport, Conn.: Greenwood Press, 1970.
279 pp.
The first two decades of the 20th century were prosperous times for farmers.
When this changed after 1920, farmers in Illinois and Iowa blamed certain
factors associated with the city. Whereas farmers previously attacked
urban wealth, now urban lifestyles became synonymous with indecency.
The leading objects of this assault were immigrants, Jews, and Catholics,
frequently symbolized in the issue of prohibition. The ensuing city-
country division that emerged saw urban areas united on economic issues
and divided on cultural ones. In rural areas, the opposite occurred.
Kirschner alleges that this development refutes the Hofstadter thesis
that cultural issues take precedence during periods of economic prosperity
and recede in favor of economic concerns during depressions.

H 1341. **KNIGHTS, PETER R.** The Plain People of Boston, 1830-1860: A Study
in City Growth. New York: Oxford University Press, 1971.
204 pp.
Knights's study concentrates on determining the population patterns, demographic mobility, and wealth trends in Boston before the Civil War.
Although the author approaches this subject with certain questions in mind--
Where did the people come from and go to? Where did they live? What
occupations did they pursue and how successfully?--he devotes most of
his research to the difficult task of establishing a thorough statistical
profile of Boston's population. Using census materials and a variety
of other sources, Knights establishes that Boston's population was characterized by very high rates of in- and out-migration, that the poor were
more mobile than the rich, and that the tendency early in the period was
for immigrants to originate in rural New England, but that this changed
after the mid-1840s with a growing influx of foreign-born migrants. As
the century progressed, wealth became more concentrated and opportunities
for upward mobility declined. The book includes an afterword by Eric
E. Lampard, who suggests explanations for some of the trends uncovered

by Knights and outlines the opportunities in this field for further research and analysis.

H 1342. KOUWENHOVEN, JOHN A. The Columbia Historical Portrait of New York: An Essay in Graphic History. 1953; Rev. ed. New York: Harper & Row, 1972. 350 pp.
Using drawings, prints, paintings, advertisements, and photographs, Kouwenhoven provides a visual history of New York City. The book's emphasis is on the 19th century, as over half the illustrations focus upon that period. The author employs a wide variety of images that touch upon a diversity of topics—commerce, architecture, physical development, social life, leisure, and work being the most prominent. The pictures are arranged in rough chronological order representing successive phases of the city's evolution. As historical documents, the pictures serve two roles. First, they are a source of factual information on the city's topography, customs, and manners. Secondly, they reveal attitudes and interests unavailable in written documents. A brief essay runs through the book and ties the sequence of pictures together.

H 1343. LANE, ROGER. Policing the City: Boston, 1822-85. Cambridge, Mass.: Harvard University Press, 1967. 299 pp.
By the early 19th century, the problem of crime and order was a paramount urban dilemma. Boston, in 1837, was among the first American cities to resort to a professional police force. Resistance centered on traditional Republican fears of police power as a threat to freedom and civil liberties. For the first time, city officials were preoccupied with preventing crime, not merely responding to it. Over time, police functions became more narrowly defined as new departments for sewers, streets, buildings, and health were created. Social problems of drunkenness, prostitution, and vagrancy remained high on their agenda for the remainder of the century. The failure to solve these problems, combined with political divisions between native-born and immigrants, convinced state officials to remove the police from local control in 1885 and hand it over to the state government.

H 1344. LANE, ROGER. Violent Death in the City: Suicide, Accident and Murder in Nineteenth-Century Philadelphia. Cambridge, Mass.: Harvard University Press, 1979. 193 pp.
Primarily employing records from Philadelphia's board of health and the county coroner, Lane studied all the victims of violent death in the city from 1839 to 1901. His analysis of these statistics is based on the assumption that the manner of violent death often reflects the life led by the victim. He categorizes the number of deaths and provides per capita statistics to reflect the variance in the incidence of suicide, accident, and murder during the 19th century. In conclusion, Lane finds that in this urban setting there were fewer murders and accidents and more suicides for the white than for the black population.

H 1345. LARSEN, LAWRENCE. The Urban West at the End of the Frontier. Lawrence: Kansas University Press, 1978. 173 pp.
The author argues that the "urban frontier" was not really a frontier by 1880, for Western cities adopted the characteristics of older centers. The Western environment did not produce a new society but rather cities which looked and functioned like those in the East. Larsen uses several sources, especially statistics from the 1880 census, to examine twenty-four Western cities (e.g., Austin, Galveston, Houston, Dallas, Saint-Joseph, Denver, Los Angeles, and San Francisco). After a brief overview of the cities, he discusses urban life in the West at the close of the frontier with special attention to such topics as ethnic composition, religion, architecture, city planning, recreation, city services, and education.

H 1346. LAZERSON, MARVIN. Origins of the Urban School: Public Education in Massachusetts, 1870-1915. Cambridge, Mass.: Harvard University Press, 1971. 278 pp.
Lazerson's book "treats the assumptions, ideologies, and practices of the generation of educators who shaped America's city schools." The study focuses on the kindergarten, manual training, vocational education, evening school, and citizenship education programs of ten Massachusetts cities. It is in these programs that educational policy changed most drastically: between 1870 and 1900, education aimed to ameliorate the social conditions of a newly urban immigrant population by teaching traditional moral values; after 1900, vocational guidance became more pronounced in order to direct the child into his proper role in the economic order.

H 1347. LINDSTROM, DIANE. Economic Development in the Philadelphia Region, 1810-1850. New York: Columbia University Press, 1978. 255 pp.
Lindstrom is essentially concerned with the reasons for industrialization in Philadelphia. Examining this development through a regional approach she finds the early interdependence between Philadelphia and its hinterland resulted in specialization of both. The quicker pace of specialization in the city and greater rewards reversed the old relationship making the hinterland dependent on the core while encouraging the core to grow rapidly and enter new markets. This pattern confirms that market opportunities shaped regional production.

H 1348. LOCKWOOD, CHARLES. Manhattan Moves Uptown: An Illustrated History. Boston: Houghton Mifflin, 1976. 343 pp.
Lockwood provides an account of the rapid, unprecedented physical development of Manhattan in the 19th century. During this period, in both sheer size and population, Manhattan grew faster than at any other time in its history. Numerous physical and health problems such as insufficient water, sewage, garbage removal, heat, plumbing, and building safety had to be solved. Neighborhoods were rapidly transformed as a consequence of the swift growth, usually changing from well-to-do to working-class areas. Lockwood delineates how and when this process occurred in such areas as Bowling Green, Tompkins Square, and St. John's Park. The laissez-faire, unplanned development also left behind a trail of poverty, evident in the ever-present problem of squatters and shantytowns throughout this period.

H 1349. LUBOVE, ROY. Community Planning in the 1920s: The Contribution of the Regional Planning Association of America. Pittsburgh, Pa.: University of Pittsburgh Press, 1963. 155 pp.
The Regional Planning Association of America (RPAA) was born out of Al Smith's Reconstruction Commission of 1919 and influenced by some of the leading architects and planners of the early 20th century, including Clarence Stein, Henry Wright, Raymond Unwin, Frederick Ackerman, and Lewis Mumford. The RPAA rejected planning for its concern with palliatives and ignored fundamental structural problems. Critical of the City Beautiful movement and the early emphasis on physical planning, the RPAA opposed metropolitan centralization and suburban diffusion. At a certain point, the RPAA argued, the size of a city could no longer be productive or achieve an equilibrium. Rather than seeking to impose one plan or ideal on the city (like the garden city or new town plan), the RPAA wanted to coordinate social and physical concerns in the form of community planning. Some of these ideas were tested in the planned communities of Sunnyside Gardens in New York City and Radburn, New Jersey. Aware that the automobile and electricity were going to expand the limits of the city, the RPAA argued for more careful and deliberate planning. Although the RPAA eventually broke up in 1933, it exerted its influential ideas through other planning, housing, and architectural groups in New York.

H 1350. LUBOVE, ROY. The Progressives and the Slums: Tenement House
Reform in New York City, 1890-1917. Pittsburgh: University
of Pittsburgh Press, 1962. 284 pp.
Lubove examines the ideas of housing reformers in New York City. He is
concerned less with national politics and more with the concrete ideas
of local reformers and how they were implemented. Housing reformers sought
to implement a form of social control by placing great faith in changing
the physical environment. There was little concern for the economic,
ethnic, or social dimensions of many of the housing problems associated
with the tenement. Two major individual figures behind the housing reform
movement were Jacob Riis and Lawrence Veiller. Riis believed in restrictive legislation, the model tenement, and the Octavia Hill plan to improve
the housing conditions of the poor. His was a humanitarian approach with
an environmental emphasis. Veiller likewise was an apostle of restrictive
legislation, but also sought a comprehensive housing code based on professional planning and expertise. Lubove concludes that ignoring the need
for larger state subsidies through loans, land purchases, and easy
mortgages—methods eventually adopted by the New Deal—was the greatest
failure of Progressive reformers.

H 1351. MANDELBAUM, SEYMOUR J. Boss Tweed's New York. New York: Wiley,
1965. 196 pp.
Mandelbaum believes that the rise of the urban political machine was the
product of the destruction of traditional family and social structures
resulting from migration to the New World. A communication problem emerged
between new and competing groups in American society, and the machine
emerged as a solution to bridge that gap. The chaos resulting from rapid
physical growth left New York with a poor and inadequate system of streets,
schools, health care, and transportation. The decentralized structure
of urban government provided little opportunity for comprehensive, city-
wide solutions to these problems. The demand for a more centralized,
rationally planned approach to urban problems justified the adoption and
acceptance of the machine by numerous groups in the metropolis.

H 1352. MAYER, HAROLD M. and RICHARD C. WADE. Chicago: Growth of a
Metropolis. Chicago: University of Chicago Press, 1969.
510 pp.
The authors, a geographer and a historian, look at the history of the
growth and development of the city of Chicago. They use photographs as
evidence—not merely as illustration—to reveal the physical conditions
of the city and to document the city as residents and visitors knew it.
The book covers commercial and residential districts, rich and poor,
throughout the metropolitan area from the 1850s to the late 1960s.

H 1353. McCARTHY, KATHLEEN D. Noblesse Oblige: Charity and Cultural
Philanthropy in Chicago, 1849-1929. Chicago: University of
Chicago Press, 1982. 230 pp.
"Noblesse oblige" translates to "civic stewardship" in the American city,
according to McCarthy. She describes four generations of these stewards:
benevolent ladies and Christian gentlemen before the 1871 fire; Gilded
Age institution builders after; Progressives who shifted support to
neighborhood-oriented reformers; and Jazz Age philanthropists who promoted
the activities of the new professional class. Using organizational records,
contemporary published works, biographies, and a wide range of contemporary
sources, McCarthy reveals one of the more subtle aspects of the evolution
of the city: donor responsibility for the development and direction of
non-profit organization.

H 1354. McKELVEY, BLAKE. The Emergence of Metropolitan America, 1915-1966. New Brunswick, N.J.: Rutgers University Press, 1968. 311 pp.
McKelvey continues his narrative account of American urbanization into the 20th century in this second volume on American cities (see H 1355). The author divides the study into six chapters covering each decade from 1915 to the 1960s. Two themes are emphasized: the struggle by city politicians to control and master the problems of urban growth; and the migration of European immigrants in the early part of the century, and Afro-Americans after W.W. I. The Great Depression, more than any other event, transformed the power relationships of urban America. For the first time, the Federal government became a leading influence and actor in shaping urban development. As metropolitan areas grew more diffuse and expansive, the Federal government became a connecting link between different interests. The impact of the Federal government was felt most in the massive urban renewal and redevelopment projects after W.W. II which drastically changed the physical face of American cities, especially in downtown business districts. Social problems, best exemplified by racial tensions in the inner city, were also confronted by the Federal government with the adoption of massive social service programs that were initiated by Roosevelt's New Deal and expanded after 1950.

H 1355. McKELVEY, BLAKE. The Urbanization of America, 1860-1915. New Brunswick, N.J.: Rutgers University Press, 1963. 370 pp.
In the half century following the Civil War, the U.S. evolved into an urban nation. Four major forces characterized the urbanization process during this period. First, the dominance of New York City was felt throughout the country as it became the dominant financial and trade center. Second, cities competed for control over their regional provinces. This competition was fostered by the expansion of railroads as the U.S. engaged in Westward expansion. Third, the growth of new and varied communities was a product of mass immigration from Europe and the rural countryside of the U.S. The massive demographic transformation produced the fourth force, namely, the reorganization of economic, social, and political relationships in the city. The rise of political machines, boards of trade, trade unions, churches and synagogues, and reform organizations like the settlement house marked a change in urban life and the various institutions that exerted power in the city. The conflicts that resulted from these new relationships were frequently played out in problems centering upon public versus private control of city services and responsibilities.

H 1356. MELOSI, MARTIN V. Garbage in the Cities: Refuse, Reform, and the Environment, 1880-1980. College Station: Texas A&M Press, 1981. 268 pp.
The major physical consequence of the Industrial Revolution was an environmental crisis in cities. Until the transition from an agrarian to urban society in the 19th century, waste was not a serious problem. Refuse, then, is a uniquely urban problem. Modern cities have had a two-dimensional waste problem: first, the physical distress caused by overcrowding, poor sanitation, and primitive methods of disposal, and second, the rising affluence of the U.S. Before 1880, Melosi argues, there was little concern for the problem of refuse. From 1880 to 1920, reformers led by Col. George Waring in New York City resorted to a variety of solutions ranging from separate and combined sewerage systems to forming street cleaning leagues to get children involved in the issue. Sanitary reformers were split into two groups--a technical elite of sanitary engineers and citizen's organizations operating in the public realm. After 1920 the nature of the refuse problem changed as a result of suburbanization, the rise of a consumer culture, and the greater federal role in the management of cities. The refuse problem by the 1970s remained unsolved; it had only changed its form and magnitude. Thus, the rampant increase in solid waste

was a constant, central feature of American cities from 1880 to 1980.
Only the perception of it changed, from being treated as a nuisance to
recognizing it as a serious environmental danger.

H 1357. MILLER, ROBERTA BALSTAD. City and Hinterland: A Case Study of
         Urban Growth and Regional Development. Westport, Conn.: Green-
         wood Press, 1979. 179 pp.
In this case study the author examines the forces that shaped the development and relationships of Syracuse, New York, and its hinterland. Transportation was a key element. It influenced development even before the
Erie Canal reached the region. Miller finds that because of the extent
and importance of these links among city, hinterland, and nation, the
pattern of development resulted from a complex combination of efforts
and decisions made at the local, state, and national levels.

H 1358. MILLER, WILBUR R. Cops and Bobbies: Police Authority in New
         York and London, 1830-70. Chicago: University of Chicago Press,
         1977. 233 pp.
This exercise in comparative history examines the early years of professional police forces in 19th-century New York City and London. Miller
finds similar social conditions existing which encourged the adoption
of a preventive police system—rapid population growth, fear of riots
and street crime, and the rise of evangelical Protestantism and its urge
to regulate the morals and manners of the working-class. Despite these
similarities, two different police systems emerged. London's force prohibited patronage and political appointments. Police officers were not
permitted to vote and were detached from the community. The emphasis
on restraint, discipline, and limited personal discretion made the "bobby"
a model Englishman and subject to few charges of corruption. The New
York model was quite different. Highly political, "cops" were considered
part of the community and had social and personal ties to the neighborhood.
Lack of discipline led to a force characterized by corruption and arbitrary
law enforcement. The different approaches to crime were exemplified in
the use of guns which the New York police adopted for all its officers
in 1857, while London waited until the 20th century to do the same.

H 1359. MILLER, ZANE L. Boss Cox's Cincinnati: Urban Politics in the
         Progressive Era. New York: Oxford University Press, 1968.
         301 pp.
Boss Cox was an anomaly, a boss who was a Republican interested in moderate
reform. Tracing the rise and fall of Cox's machine from 1880 to 1920,
Miller describes the complex political situation in a city which was growing rapidly and which was in the process of becoming modernized. Bosses
tended to be concerned with inner-city problems, Miller notes, while
reformers emphasized the development of new residential neighborhoods.
The politics of Cincinnati suggest that residence rather than race,
religion, or ethnicity explain the urban social and political experience.

H 1360. MILLER, ZANE L. Suburb: Neighborhood and Community in Forest
         Park, Ohio, 1935-1976. Knoxville: University of Tennessee
         Press, 1981. 263 pp.
In his book, Miller traces the planning, development, settlement, and
growth of Forest Park, a suburb of Cincinnati. The author describes his
history as "symptomatic," that is, "as the consequence of a particular,
chronologically-bounded action." Miller defines three successive modes
of thought which structured the actions of the community: the "metropolitan," in which the "problems of [suburban] community was seen as a fundamentally metropolitan issue; the "community of limited liability," in
which residents make the distinction between city and suburb and demonstrate civil participation in attempts to better their community; and
the "community of advocacy," in which civic participation loses its motive

of community welfare, though it retains it for the individual's well-being. Miller believes these changing ideas of the suburb reflect more general attitudes toward urban society and help us understand the growth of the white-collar class.

H 1361. MOHL, RAYMOND A. Poverty in New York, 1783-1825. New York: Oxford University Press, 1971. 318 pp.
The problem of poverty has been a consistent theme in New York City history since the Colonial Period. Although the post-Revolution mercantile city expanded and grew, its upward curve was scarred with depressions, wars, embargoes, boycotts, and seasonal variations. The little-mentioned effect of this economic and social transformation was increasing poverty. Mohl employs newspapers, government records, and reform organization reports to show that poverty plagued the early Republican city. New York failed to adequately solve the problem because it adopted a haphazard succession of expedients and temporary solutions. Seeing poverty as the result of imperfect characters and personal defects, ameliorative institutions distinguished between "deserving" and "unworthy" poor. The former included temporarily unemployed workers, widows, the sick, and orphaned children, who usually received "outdoor" relief in the form of wood, food, clothing, and medicine. The unworthy poor lumped together prostitutes, beggars, and vagrants. During this period the municipal government assumed a greater role in helping the poor, best exemplified by the proliferation of newly constructed institutions like the almshouse and bridewell. Most poor relief, however, originated within private, philanthropic organizations, the most important being the Humane Society and the Society for the Prevention of Pauperism.

H 1362. MOLINE, NORMAN T. Mobility and the Small Town, 1900-1930: Transportation Change in Oregon, Illinois. Chicago: University of Chicago, Department of Geography, 1971. 169 pp.
The automobile introduced a new territorial scale of activity and changed the self-image of the small American town. Looking at the small town of Oregon, Illinois, Moline examines how this transformation took place. In 1900 trips to neighboring towns were infrequent, long, and travellers usually spent the night. The electrified urban interrailway system was the most popular means of quick transport, especially from 1900-1920. Still in an age of horse-drawn vehicles, roads were poorly constructed, very rough, and full of mud or dust. This situation changed with the automobile and the accompanying demand for better roads. The combination of the auto and paved roads induced drastic changes in the social behavior of Oregon's population. The auto replaced the horse for the Sunday drive. Individual travel became more popular. Youths went to other towns for entertainment, causing a reactionary "be-entertained-at-home" movement by parents. County fairs and high school athletics grew in importance. As shopping patterns changed, boosterism among neighboring towns grew more common, some even encouraging tourism and an expansion of hotel facilities. This pattern of technologically induced change continued throughout the century until 1960 when the auto was virtually the sole means of transport in Oregon.

H 1363. MONKKONEN, ERIC H. The Dangerous Class: Crime and Poverty in Columbus, Ohio, 1860-1886. Cambridge, Mass.: Harvard University Press, 1975. 186 pp.
Monkkonen questions whether urbanization and industrialization caused poverty and crime. He traces changes in the perception of "the dangerous class"--paupers, criminals, and children of the poor--in Columbus, Ohio. He concludes that cities and industry affected the quality of crime, but not the quantity. With change, the kinds and structure of crime changed, but very few paupers became criminals. In fact, the criminal class declined as Columbus grew and industrialized. Eventually, these changes affected the treatment of crime by law enforcement agencies in the city.

H 1364. MUMFORD, LEWIS. The Urban Prospect. New York: Harcourt, Brace,
& World, 1968. 255 pp.
Mumford has assembled a selection of essays written over the course of
more than half a century which deal with the nature of urban life. He
believes that the primary function of the modern city should be to bring
technology in line with human purposes. Too frequently planners fail
to include environmental and social factors in their concern for physical
change. Too much emphasis is placed on the automobile in American life
and this detracts from urban life. Building upon the work of Ebenezer
Howard, Mumford believes urban life has to achieve an equilibrium between
nature and megalopolis. The ideas of modern planners and architects,
especially Le Corbusier, have neglected the humane side of urban life.
By placing so much emphasis on the vertical city, the daily workings occurring in the horizontal city have been sadly ignored and undeveloped.
Mumford is not opposed to technological change, but criticizes the insensitive and de-humanizing manner in which it has often been employed.
Students and critics of the city should not focus solely upon the negative
results of urban life; rather, they must devise new strategies of development that would remedy these problems and prevent their repetition.

H 1365. MUSHKAT, JEROME. Tammany: The Evolution of a Political Machine,
1789-1865. Syracuse, N.Y.: Syracuse University Press, 1971.
476 pp.
Mushkat traces the development of the Tammany organization from its origins
as an open-ended, middle-class, anti-immigrant fraternal society to a
closed, Irish-dominated political machine in control of the New York Democratic Party. Tammany's success during this period is attributable to
its implementation of two major innovations: first, increased democracy
in politics, and second, the development of the party apparatus. In its
fluctuating back and forth between issues, individual politicians, and
different groups, Tammany was more interested in power than representing
a single constituency. Mushkat attributes Tammany's losses and weaknesses
to the organization's inability to shape or control progressive opposition
movements during the 19th century.

H 1366. PLATT, HAROLD L. City Building in the New South: The Growth
of Public Services in Houston, Texas, 1830-1910. Philadelphia:
Temple University Press, 1983. 252 pp.
The author examines political conflict over the acquisition and extension
of public services in a Southern city. He finds that concern gradually
shifted from questions of how to get public services to who should get
them first. Debate over such issues produced two political factions,
one calling for equitable distribution and the other ignoring this point
while suggesting public services be used to attract Northern investment.
The introduction of electric service began a new era in which the concern
for investment prevailed.

H 1367. PRED, ALLAN. Urban Growth and City Systems in the United States,
1840-1860. Cambridge, Mass.: Harvard University Press, 1980.
282 pp.
Identifying the period as one which saw the principal functions of major
cities changing, the author examines how urban interdependence "interacted
with the feedback process" of population growth. He finds that large
cities grew faster than small ones in this period because they enjoyed
the advantage of several "multipliers." These advantages of size--such
as more extensive economic ties and information sources--contributed to
"processual bridges" that linked the urban worlds of the early and late
19th century.

H 1368. PRESTON, HOWARD L. Automobile Age Atlanta: The Making of a Southern Metropolis, 1900-1935. Athens: University of Georgia Press, 1979. 203 pp.
Preston argues that the introduction of the car into Atlanta's economy transformed this Southern railroad center into a large city more like its Northern counterparts. After decribing Atlanta before the turn of the century, Preston outlines the conflict between the city's established public transit system, which was intent on preserving the urban demographic and economic concentration of the 19th-century city, and the automobile, which fostered suburbanization. Also discussed is the impact of the automobile on the economic structure, physical layout, and race relations of the city. Preston asserts that it was the early integration of the now predominant form of mass transport into the Atlantan community that assured its status as a regional political and economic power.

H 1369. QUANDT, JEAN B. From Small Town to the Great Community: The Social Thought of Progressive Intellectuals. New Brunswick, N.J.: Rutgers University Press, 1970. 260 pp.
In this intellectual history, Quandt identifies a group of Progressive thinkers who shared similar approaches to the problem of urbanization. These thinkers--Jane Addams, William Allen White, and John Dewey, among others--all believed that modern urban society should adopt the ethos of the small town, from which all these thinkers came: they "relied mainly on communication, moral suasion, and intimate local embodiment in institutions." Quandt outlines the general positions of the thinkers and demonstrates their relationship to contemporary European thought. Quandt concludes that a blindness to the new structure of urban society prevented these intellectuals from advocating the needed changes in the structure of national politics and culture.

H 1370. RAE, JOHN B. The Road and the Car in American Life. Cambridge, Mass.: MIT Press, 1971. 390 pp.
In this study of the economic and social impact of automotive highway transportation, Rae details the changes the introduction of the car has made on urban life. He places particular emphasis on the problems of traffic congestion, archaic street systems, and scarcity of urban land. Rae also discusses the growth of the suburbs in response to greater mobility, the decentralization of industry, and the greater links between city and country. In addition, the author treats the frequent failure of public transportation to initiate non-automotive movement of the city dweller.

H 1371. RAVITCH, DIANE. The Great School Wars: New York City, 1805-1973, A History of the Public Schools as a Battlefield of Social Change. New York: Basic Books, 1974. 449 pp.
Ravitch argues that there have been four important "school wars" in New York City's history. In each one, issues of centralized versus neighborhood control were preeminent themes. In the 1840s, conflict emerged between Catholic schools and the Protestant-supervised Free School Society over the issue of state funding. The dispute left both with no state aid and caused the creation of a ward-based, decentralized public school system. The second and third wars occurred during the Progressive era and called for efficiency and rationalization in the administration of schools. Eventually, control by local officials was removed and placed in a centralized board of education. In the 1960s, demands by the black leaders for community control of schools forced a conflict with teachers fearing a loss of job protection with the removal of centralized power. In each conflict, neither centralization nor local control ever solved the problem of the school system, and the education of lower-class children and church-state issues remain unresolved dilemmas.

H 1372. REPS, JOHN. Cities of the American West: A History of Frontier
Urban Planning. Princeton, N.J.: Princeton University Press,
1979. 827 pp.
Reps attempts to refute the Turner thesis that the frontier was the primary
factor in the development of the U.S. before 1900 and was the major influence in the creation of the American nation. According to Reps, Turner
failed to realize that towns preceded rural development or were established
at the same time that agricultural land was opened for farming and ranching.
The Western town was the vanguard of settlement and shaped the structure
of society rather than merely responding to it. Settlement patterns were
not random and irrational; selection of a good site was made by individuals,
groups, churches, railroad, or government agencies. Although planned,
many were not well designed and generally the West resisted all types
of centralized planning. Consequently, settlement was not a steady progression Westward. One unifying, physical theme emerged during the 19th
century, namely the prevailing use of the gridiron pattern in many Western
locations. Reps buttresses his argument with a wide variety of original
plans and 19th-century "birds' eye" views of cities.

H 1373. REPS, JOHN. The Making of Urban America: A History of City Planning in the U.S. Princeton, N.J.: Princeton University Press,
1965. 574 pp.
This comprehensive survey of the physical development of the American
city covers the Colonial period to the early 20th century. Relying upon
town plans, diagrams, and drawings, Reps shows how the Colonial city was
influenced by European designs from the Baroque and Renaissance Periods.
Spanish settlements in the South and Southwest best exemplify these more
ornate planning principles. English towns, in contrast, followed two
simpler models--the linear pattern where one street forms the spine of
the town, and the compact, square grid pattern. The most important of
the latter was Philadelphia, which set the pattern of grid development
in the U.S. By the early 19th century, demands by land developers and
speculators forced officials to adopt the grid as the basis of physical
development in New York City and many of the new, emerging Midwestern
towns. A later reaction against the grid produced the park movement and
efforts by early planners to integrate the natural environment with city
designs. Reps devotes space to a discussion of the company town and other
privately planned communities, and speculates as to why some worked and
others failed. He concludes with a discussion of the Chicago Exposition
of 1893 and its impact on the newly emerging planning profession of the
20th century.

H 1374. REPS, JOHN. Monumental Washington: The Planning and Development
of the Capital Center. Princeton, N.J.: Princeton University
Press, 1967. 221 pp.
Reps describes the physical transformation of Washington, D.C. from a
small Southern city full of creeks, canals, open sewers and dusty, dirty
streets to the modern, pristine, imperial city it is today. The precedents
for the creation of modern Washington were developed in the largely unrealized 19th-century plans of Pierre L'Enfant, Benjamin Latrobe, and
Andrew Jackson Downing. Yet not until the McMillan Commission Plan of
1902, the first modern city planning report in the U.S., were many of
these and other ideas implemented. Guided by Frederick Law Olmsted, Jr.,
Daniel Burnham, Charles Follen McKim, and Augustus Saint-Gaudens, the
Commission designed a capital city reflecting the Progressive antagonism
to corruption and the desire for civic beauty. Later in the century,
the imperial, anti-democratic, Beaux-Arts themes found in the plan would
be influential in the design of modern, Third World capital cities.

H 1375. RICE, BRADLEY R. Progressive Cities: The Commission Government
Movement in America, 1901-1920. Austin: University of Texas
Press, 1977. 160 pp.
The commission form of city government began in Galveston, Texas, in 1901,
following a hurricane and tidal wave which almost decimated the town.
The office of municipal commissioner became known as the Texas Idea and
was developed throughout the country. Outside of Texas, however, the
cities which adapted the commission form of government usually were smaller
and newer, places where machine politics had never had a strong hold.
Rice analyzes the success and failures of the commission form as well
as the reasons for its establishment in the 500 cities where it became
standard.

H 1376. RICHARDSON, JAMES F. The New York Police: Colonial Times to
1901. New York: Oxford University Press, 1970. 332 pp.
Richardson focuses upon the administration and politics of the law enforcement system in New York and spends less time discussing the daily functioning and duties of police officers. Prior to 1845, New York relied upon
a variety of appointed watches, constables, and marshalls to protect the
citizenry. With the rise of illegal saloons, commercialized vice, and
riots after 1830, a movement for a professionalized police force grew
in strength. The creation of such a force in 1845, however, did little
to solve these problems. From its inception, appointments to the force
were political, and native-born Protestants saw the Irish-controlled force
as a standing army against them. From 1857-1870 a state-controlled force
replaced the earlier local creation, only to revert back to the earlier
municipally-run approach after 1870. Much of the dissatisfaction with
the police during this time stemmed from middle-class fears of socially
related crimes such as illegal saloons, the Sunday law, prostitution,
and gambling.

H 1377. ROSENWAIKE, IRA. Population History of New York City. Syracuse,
N.Y.: Syracuse University Press, 1972. 224 pp.
This demographic history covers 300 years of New York City's population
changes. In a review of the city censuses, Rosenwaike traces the sources
of urban growth, analyzing migration patterns and the ethnic and religious
composition of the populace. The book chronicles the influx of foreigners
into the city and the subsequent expansion of suburbs around New York.

H 1378. ROSNER, DAVID. A Once Charitable Enterprise: Hospitals and Health
Care in Brooklyn and New York, 1885-1915. New York: Cambridge
University Press, 1982. 234 pp.
Rosner looks at the urban hospital during the Progressive era when it
was transformed from a group of idiosyncratic institutions to a modern
system of acute-care facilities. Nineteenth-century charity hospitals
were small, had few affiliated doctors, and attended to the primary care
needs of the working-class and ethnic communities in which they were usually located. After 1890, new hospital trustees introduced business techniques such as efficiency, bureaucracy, and cost accounting, seeing the
hospital as a business, not merely an institution of mercy and philanthropy.
In order to attract paying, middle-class patients, hospitals diminished
their charity functions and offered private rooms and special services
previously unavailable. The introduction of rationality and efficiency
in the health care system effectively moved control from the ward boss
and political machine to the professional administrator and physician.
The spatial and physical effect of this conflict emerged in New York Hospital's efforts to prevent immigrant and real estate interests from gaining
control of the development of Morningside Heights by selling the land
to another large, private, well-endowed institution--Columbia University.

H 1379. SCHIESL, MARTIN J. The Politics of Efficiency: Municipal Administration and Reform in America, 1880-1920. Berkeley: University
of California Press, 1977. 259 pp.
This book is a study of the drive to reform urban government during the
Progressive era. Schiesl examines such innovations as bureaus of municipal
research, first begun in New York in 1907; the city commission form of
government, first used in Galveston in 1901; and the city manager system
which Dayton pioneered in 1913. Schiesl argues that the driving force
behind these urban arrangements was most often businessmen determined to
remake government in the image of business.

H 1380. SCHNEIDER, JOHN C. Detroit and the Problem of Order, 1830-80:
A Geography of Crime, Riot, and Policing. Lincoln: University
of Nebraska Press, 1980. 171 pp.
The crisis of law and order that affected Detroit from 1830-80 was not
a problem that can be analyzed simply with a class-ethnic-political ideology interpretation. Schneider sees it as a spatial problem as well.
Greater fears existed of a "dangerous area" than of a "dangerous class."
This spatial interpretation reinforces Charles Tilly's thesis that in
the 19th century collective violence changed from a communal basis to
an associational one. As groups and functions became more segregated,
violence from daily social relations, common in the antebellum period,
changed to confrontations based on special-purpose associations like trade
unions. When collective violence occurred before the Civil War, it was
in ethnic neighborhoods and conducted by local groups, like Germans, trying
to oust offensive elements. Only when violent activity spilled over into
the "high rank" areas like the commercial and residential enclaves did
Detroit finally adopt a police force. Crime waves and the increase in crime
did not produce a professional police force; the appearance of crime in
the downtown central busines district did.

H 1381. SCOTT, MEL. American City Planning Since 1890. Berkeley: University of California Press, 1969. 745 pp.
Scott provides a chronological narrative of city planning in the U.S.
from its origins in the late 19th century. The early planning movement
in America grew out of the Progressive movement's war on poverty and the
numerous reform efforts affecting housing, education, sweatshops, and
unionism. City planning, with its specific interest in the aesthetic
environment, grew out of park planning and landscape architecture. The
Chicago Exposition of 1893 and the McMillan Plan for Washington, D.C.,
set the focus for urban planning until the Great Depression. Early planning was dominated by the engineering profession and was most concerned
with the physical city. After 1930, economic conditions forced this to
change and planners began to address social issues. The National Resources
Planning Board and the Green Belt Town program were among the earliest
Federal ventures into some form of national and urban planning. World
War II gave another boost to Federal intervention and during the following
decades the Federal government's role expanded into housing, highways,
and urban redevelopment. Many of the problems remained unsolved into
the 1960s as planners were continually split between those emphasizing
the physical city and others more concerned with social problems.

H 1382. SENNETT, RICHARD. Families Against the City: Middle-Class Homes
of Industrial Chicago, 1872-1890. Cambridge, Mass.: Harvard
University Press, 1974. 258 pp.
Informed by the theories of Erik Erikson, Sennett argues that the experience of life in Chicago had a pernicious effect on the attitudes of docile
middle-class husbands who retreated from the vigorous pluralism and perils
of the city into the refuge of the private family. Thereafter, the family
became the medium for interpersonal expression for the middle-class.
Marriage was not a transition to adulthood, but rather occurred within

adulthood. The retreat to the private family destroyed kinship bonds and weakened the father as an authority figure. Father and sons alike had greater mobility in large, extended families rather than small, nuclear ones. Sennett attributes this transformation to the bureaucratization of society.

H 1383. SPANN, EDWARD K. The New Metropolis: New York City, 1840-1857. New York: Columbia University Press, 1981. 346 pp.
Spann offers a study of New York City during the years 1840-57, a period of extraordinary economic growth in the city. Complementing his own research with a variety of secondary sources, Spann considers perennial urban problems such as poverty, inadequate streets and housing, rampant population growth, sanitation, and machine politics. Descriptions of the lifestyles of the wealthy during the period provide a contrast to these problems, demonstrating the extensive range of experience which characterizes urban living. Specific aspects of the city are considered in the context of city design and planning, urban space, the growth of suburbs, and the relationship between state and local governments.

H 1384. STAVE, BRUCE M. The New Deal and the Last Hurrah: Pittsburgh Machine Politics. Pittsburgh, Pa.: University of Pittsburgh Press, 1970. 262 pp.
Using Pittsburgh as a case study, Stave disputes the common assumption that the New Deal relief programs marked the end of the urban political machine; Pennsylvania Democrats simply used the new Federal funds as patronage, thereby gaining control of the previously Republican state. Stave discusses the internal dynamics of each political party, the voting patterns of Pittsburgh residents (both native and foreign born), the newfound political power of urban blacks, and various New Deal programs. He concludes that the post-Roosevelt machine is based not on the foreign-born immigrant, who had become established economically, but on the inner-city black, who is, in some measure, dependent on Federal programs for assistance.

H 1385. TEAFORD, JON C. City and Suburb: The Political Fragmentation of Metropolitan America, 1850-1970. Baltimore, Md.: Johns Hopkins University Press, 1979. 231 pp.
City and Suburb traces the struggle between the forces promoting decentralization of political power and those promoting centralization in urban America from the mid-19th century. Teaford begins with a historical account of the growth of suburbs to 1910, showing that suburbanites favored annexation if cities offered enough inducement in the way of services. Then he interrupts his narrative to discuss British policy of limiting city incorporation, a policy he finds more rational than the laissez-faire practices of American state legislatures. Teaford next describes how the suburbs won ascendancy from 1910 to W.W. II over a parallel movement to create a federative metropolis. The remainder of the book, except for a short chapter tracing urban developments from 1930 to 1970, is a study of the struggle of three cities--Cleveland, Pittsburgh, and St. Louis--to develop metropolitan government in the late 1920s and early 1930s.

H 1386. TEAFORD, JON C. The Municipal Revolution in America: Origins of Modern Urban Government, 1650-1825. Chicago: University of Chicago Press, 1975. 152 pp.
Teaford traces the changes which municipal government underwent in America between Colonial settlement and the early Republic. At first responsible for regulating and controlling all aspects of the urban marketplace, municipal governments lost this responsibility immediately before and during the Revolution as they became more democratic, and therefore weaker forces of social control. Following a discussion of the origins and nature of

this change, Teaford examines the effect it had on the development of American cities.

H 1387. **THERNSTROM, STEPHAN.** Poverty and Progress: Social Mobility in a 19th-Century City. Cambridge, Mass.: Harvard University Press, 1964. 286 pp.

America has long been seen as the land of opportunity for the common man. Thernstrom probes this belief by examining patterns of social mobility of the working-class families of Newburyport, Massachusetts, between 1850 and 1880. These years included the town's transformation to an industrial economy and its rapid demographic expansion. Thernstrom finds that despite the growth of economic opportunities, the substitution of a new and impersonal labor market for the direct, personal relations of the earlier 19th century meant greater insecurity of employment. Migration into the city, too, increased competition for jobs, as well as stimulating residential class segregation. In the thirty years covered by the study there was no trend toward greater accumulation of property by manual workers, and few such laborers moved into non-manual jobs. Nevertheless, Thernstrom discovers that throughout this period, most of those workers who stayed in the town accumulated moderate amounts of property and that they gradually improved their positions; hence the myth of mobility was sustained. Like other recent studies of the working class, this work offers evidence of great geographical mobility; moreover, this movement continued even after the town's total population had stabilized.

H 1388. **THERNSTROM, STEPHAN.** The Other Bostonians: Poverty and Progress in the American Metropolis, 1880-1970. Cambridge, Mass.: Harvard University Press, 1973. 345 pp.

Thernstrom studies the patterns of social and occupational mobility in urban America during the 19th and 20th centuries. His statistics are drawn from schedules of the census, marriage records, local birth records, the city directory, and other sources. On the basis of these figures, Thernstrom concludes that rising rates of occupational mobility from manual to non-manual jobs and from unskilled to skilled manual work were characteristic of Boston (as they were of the U.S. as a whole). Thernstrom also finds that a very high degree of transiency and migration was typical of American society long before the 20th century.

H 1389. **THERNSTROM, STEPHAN** and **RICHARD SENNETT**, eds. Nineteenth-Century Cities: Essays in the New Urban History. New Haven, Conn.: Yale University Press, 1969. 430 pp.

This book provides a collection of twelve papers with an afterword by Norman Birnbaum on the "new" urban history--history with a quantitative emphasis. According to the editors, the contributors all share three traits: an interest in linking sociological theory to historical data, the use of quantitative materials, and an emphasis on the social experience of unexceptional people. Employing a wide variety of methodologies, the articles fall loosely into groups on class and mobility patterns, residential patterns, elites and political control, and families.

H 1390. **TRACHTENBERG, ALAN.** Brooklyn Bridge: Fact and Symbol. Chicago: University of Chicago Press, 1979. 206 pp.

Merging poetry and technology, the Brooklyn Bridge emerges as one of the major symbols of America. Built at a time when the U.S. was becoming more urban, the bridge represented change and the conquering of nature. The U.S. had to become a technological power in order to survive and conquer the distances between its farflung regions. Thus, transportation acted as a unifying force in such a large nation. In focusing upon the Roeblings, the architects of the Bridge, the author covers the history and politics of its construction, arguing that much of the controversy about it is representative of this epoch of American history. John

Roebling saw the Bridge as a road for traffic below and a structure for poets above. Trachtenberg concludes with a discussion of the Bridge's importance to Hart Crane, Joseph Stella, and other American artists.

H 1391. WADE, RICHARD C. The Urban Frontier: The Rise of Western Cities, 1790-1830. Chicago: University of Chicago Press, 1959. 362 pp. Wade offers a study of five Western cities--Pittsburgh, Lexington, Cincinnati, Louisville, and St. Louis--and the manner in which they created regional spheres of influence. The first half of the book examines the founding of these cities in the latter half of the 18th century and their growth to 1815. Wade argues that although such factors as immigration and manufacturing helped produce growth, the major cause for the rise of these new urban centers was transportation advantages. This is why the book is divided at 1815 rather than at the depression of 1819; 1815 marked the successful use of the steamboat on the Ohio-Mississippi River system. The second half of the book covers up to 1830 and examines topics such as the growth of municipal services, the development of religious and educational institutions, and the beginnings of cultural institutions such as theaters and libraries.

H 1392. WALKER, SAMUEL. A Critical History of Police Reform: The Emergence of Professionalism. Lexington, Mass.: Heath, 1977. 206 pp. Walker provides an account of the development of the professional police force in urban America from 1830-1940. He describes the major schemes for reform of police administration, the use of police as an instrument for social reform, and the gradual growth of a Federal criminal justice policy. Walker also discusses the changing ethnic composition of the force, the rise and fall of police unionism, and the attitudes of the populace toward the police.

H 1393. WALLACE, ANTHONY F. C. Rockdale: The Growth of an American Village in the Early Industrial Revolution. New York: Knopf, 1978. 553 pp. Wallace, an anthropologist, examines how industrial Capitalism transformed life in an early 19th-century Pennsylvania village. He sees Rockdale as a self-sufficient community, much like a plantation, with individuals and families following well-defined, but changing roles. The impact of industrialization on the families of factory owners and workers alike, the role of evangelical Protestantism in the community, and the conflict over who should ultimately control the new technology are discussed and explained. During the 1820s and 1830s the U.S. grew more conservative, as was displayed by the expansion of slavery, the rise of machine politics and evangelical religions, and the denial of free blacks in the North to form economic and political rights. Wallace sees the failure of early industrial workers to control the industrialization process as part of this nation-wide shift to the right.

H 1394. WARD, DAVID. Cities and Immigrants: A Geography of Change in Nineteenth-Century America. New York: Oxford University Press, 1971. 164 pp. Written from a geographer's perspective, this study examines spatial relations in American cities during the period from 1790-1920, from the formation of the Republic to the emergence of a nation of cities. Ward destroys many myths about immigrant residential patterns in American cities: that the ghetto was a permanent residence for all who settled there; that all immigrants lived in crowded tenements; that tenement living connected to a high mortality rate. Furthermore, he asserts that the disorder in immigrant areas was partly the result of rapid population turnover.

H 1395. **WARE, CAROLINE F.** Greenwich Village, 1920-1930: A Comment on American Civilization in the Post-War Years. Boston: Houghton Mifflin, 1935. 496 pp.
Ware divides her study into three sections—Community, People, and Institutions—but the primary emphasis is on the people. She stresses that there was much more to Greenwich Village than the bohemian element. According to Ware, "Italian immigrants and their children, Irish longshoremen, truck-drivers, and politicians, Jewish shopkeepers, Spanish seamen, and a remnant of staid old American and German citizens made up the majority of the population and give the life of this community its social texture." She examines the lives of these people and chronicles the problems of those attempting to assimilate into American culture, where they were confronted by a social situation lacking in coherence, and a social reality that did not fit the traditional pattern of American culture they had learned in school.

H 1396. **WARNER, SAM BASS, Jr.** The Private City: Philadelphia in Three Periods of Its Growth. Philadelphia: University of Pennsylvania Press, 1968. 236 pp.
Warner provides a study of environmental change during three periods of Philadelphia's growth (1770-1780, 1830-1860, 1920-1930). The work focuses upon the physical city and ecological processes, and attempts to answer the question of how the physical structure of the city interacted with the lives of its inhabitants. Warner's thesis is that the crisis of the 20th-century American city can be explained as a consequence of the tradition of "privatism," a term he uses for the conjunction of individualism and materialism with problems requiring collective action and equitable distribution of scanty resources. Methodologically, the book exemplifies the use of quantified social statistics drawn from such sources as local tax lists and the U.S. Census.

H 1397. **WARNER, SAM BASS, Jr.** Streetcar Suburbs: The Process of Growth in Boston, 1870-1900. Cambridge, Mass.: Harvard University Press, 1962. 208 pp.
In a study of the expansion of Boston into affluent suburbs, which is based on the analysis of some 22,000 building permits issued for three suburbs, Warner offers important insights into the process of urban expansion during the last thirty years of the 19th century. Four major themes are developed: the structural patterns of the suburbs were largely determined by the extension of streetcars; the outward move of urbanites was animated by a revival of the rural ideal; the migrants from the city tended to group along economic rather than ethnic lines; and in spite of a lack of zoning laws, architectural styles and domestic practices achieved a strong degree of order and conformity. Warner includes seventy-seven maps and illustrations of houses as well as tables containing pertinent census data and other statistics.

H 1398. **WARNER, SAM BASS, Jr.** The Urban Wilderness: A History of the American City. New York: Harper & Row, 1972. 303 pp.
Warner contends that Americans, wracked by a traditional fear of the city, have no urban history, despite being an urban nation. He argues that there have been three critical periods of urban change. The first lasted from 1820-1870 and was dominated by commerce which was fostered by maritime trade and the expansion of canals. From 1870 to 1920 the segregated city evolved, typified by factories, railroads, and skyscrapers. The modern city, from 1920 to the present, is characterized by bureaucracy, the corporation, racism, and the automobile. The final portion of the book focuses on some of the ills of modern cities—housing, poverty, and health care— and concludes that class, racial, and sexual discrimination lie at the root of all urban problems.

H 1399. **WOLF, STEPHANIE.** Urban Village: Population, Community and Family Structure in Germantown, Pennsylvania, 1683-1800. Princeton, N.J.: Princeton University Press, 1976. 361 pp.
This demographic study deals primarily with the questions of population, property, and family structure in Germantown. Wolf's model is Philip Greven's study of Andover, Massachusetts. Like Greven, Wolf relies on the statistical techniques of the social sciences and uses these techniques to examine such topics as demographic details and the inequality of property distribution. Since Germantown is in the middle Colonies, her conclusions differ considerably from those of most New England community studies. Germantown emerges as a less structured village, with an emphasis on individual choice rather than community; thus mobility and economic advancement become more important than participation in church or government. Wolf argues that Germantown falls somewhere between the New England villages and the more formal legal structures of urban centers such as Philadelphia; hence the title, Urban Village.

H 1400. **WRIGHT, GWENDOLYN.** Building the Dream: A Social History of Housing in America. New York: Pantheon Books, 1981. 329 pp.
The American home has always reflected a desire by Americans to give tangible expression to their ideas and values. Beginning with the Puritans, Wright shows how these ideas and values have been expressed in the construction and design of many different modes of housing. The author looks at slave quarters, row houses, tenements, rural cottages, apartments, the company town, public housing, the planned community, the suburb, and the mobile home. Early American housing reflected a belief in a classless, homogeneous society in its uniform design and style. Eventually, as social divisions in American society became more acute, demands for a personalized dwelling space gained in popularity. Throughout this transition, ideas about the use of space reflected the aspirations of occupants and architects alike.

H 1401. **YOUNG, JAMES STERLING.** The Washington Community, 1800-1828. New York: Columbia University Press, 1966. 307 pp.
Young examines the governing group of the early national capitol and finds that the national rulers had an inner community life of their own and were influenced more by internal forces than external ones. Because the District was an isolated community, national public opinion was less important in policy-making. The physical design of the city had a two-purpose plan--to create a community with separate and discrete units, but also one accessible to and interactive with outside society. In its early years, Washington's settlement pattern was broken up into smaller subcommunities based on specific government branches, which reinforced the separation of powers. On the Hill, the boardinghouse was the basic social unit and at times acted as the foundation for a political structure in place of the party. The lack of institutional structures to alleviate conflict in Congress made that body increasingly unstable. In contrast, the White House community involved fewer boarding houses, was less transient, and was more stable than the Hill. What conflict there was occurred between diplomats, departments, and presidential candidates serving in the cabinet.

H 1402. **ZAUTZEVSKY, CYNTHIA.** Frederick Law Olmsted and the Boston Park System. Cambridge, Mass.: Harvard University Press, 1982. 262 pp.
This study is an account of the work of America's leading landscape architect, Frederick Law Olmsted, in one city during the 1880s and 1890s. Zautzevsky describes Olmsted's development of watercourse parks and Commonwealth Avenue to connect the Public Garden and Boston Common with large parks on the outer periphery of the city. It is a detailed case study of a planned urban design by the most famous 19th-century American planner.

H 1403. ZUNZ, OLIVIER. The Changing Face of Inequality: Urbanization, Industrial Development, and Immigrants in Detroit, 1880-1920. Chicago: University of Chicago Press, 1982. 482 pp.
Four major changes took place in Detroit from 1870 to 1920: it became larger and more dense; manufacturing increased; government and community organizations became more complex; and greater numbers of immigrants arrived. Detroit's economy in 1870 was still based on consumer goods like clothing, cigars, food, and furniture. By 1920 it was the fourth largest American city and the center of the auto manufacturing industry. Zunz finds that this economic transformation broke up ethnically homogeneous groups and made class a more important variable in the choice of marriage partners, size of families, and residential location. The weakening of ethnicity was imposed on all groups via the power of one group's (native whites) control of the industrialization process, not through the passage of time as traditional assimilation theory argues. The major exception to this process was the black population. Arriving last of all ethnic and racial groups, blacks experienced increasing segregation regardless of class. Thus, industrialization created a culturally homogeneous urban society in the case of whites and a divided invidious one for blacks.

XII.   REGIONAL HISTORY

H 1404. ABBOTT, SHIRLEY. Womenfolks, Growing Up Down South. New Haven, Conn.: Ticknor & Fields, 1983. 210 pp.
In writing about family members, other Southerners, and her own life, the author examines the emotions and experiences of girls growing up in the South. Faced with the fear that the Southern distinctiveness is passing, the author recounts those qualities, attitudes, and images which composed a uniquely Southern feminine culture. She concludes that while the South has changed, the fears of its cultural distinctiveness having vanished are unfounded.

H 1405. ABERNETHY, THOMAS PERKINS. Western Lands and the American Revolution. New York: Appleton-Century, 1937. 413 pp.
This history of 18th-century land speculation focuses on the role of Western land claims and ownership and their bearing on the American Revolution. The story begins with the early Virginia projects dating back to the middle of the 18th century, including the Ohio and Loyal land companies, and ends with the inauguration of the new government in 1789. These enterprises involved such prominent Virginians as George Washington and Patrick Henry. Abernethy also focuses on the conflict between Virginians and Northern promoters, such as Franklin and Samuel Wharton, and the extent to which common economic interests brought together men who took opposite sides in the political alignment.

H 1406. ALTSCHULER, GLENN C. and JAN M. SALTZGABER. Revivalism, Social Conscience, and Community in the Burned-Over District: The Trial of Rhoda Bement. Ithaca, N.Y.: Cornell University Press, 1983. 177 pp.
Divided into three sections, this book contains the annotated transcript of Rhoda Bement's 1843 church trial, an introduction by Altschuler on the cultural significance of revivalism in the area around Seneca Falls, New York, where the trial took place, and a concluding essay by Saltzgaber on religious activity and conflict within a community. Beyond a study of one woman's temperance, abolition, and women's rights activities which led to a religious trial, the authors examine the struggle between change and stability in a rural village.

H 1407. ANDREWS, CLARENCE A., ed. Growing Up in the Midwest. Ames: Iowa State University Press, 1981. 214 pp.
This anthology includes works of both fiction and non-fiction, by twenty-two authors of different ethnic and socio-economic backgrounds, that deal with growing up in the Midwest. The various works address the questions of how exactly does one define the "Midwest," and what did it mean for the respective writers to grow up there? The major theme throughout the essays is that the "Midwest" is as much a state of mind, or a feeling, as it is a geographic region. Contributors include Meridel Le Sueur, Edna Ferber, MacKinlay Kantor, Langston Hughes, and Gwendolyn Brooks.

H 1408. ARRINGTON, LEONARD J. Great Basin Kingdom: An Economic History of the Latter Day Saints, 1830-1900. Cambridge, Mass.: Harvard University Press, 1958. 534 pp.
This analysis of the role of the Mormon Church in the economic development of the Great Basin area (primarily Utah and Nevada) places the economic projects carried out by the Latter-Day Saints within the context of the values professed by the Church. Arrington finds a relationship between the Puritan notions of the role of the individual within the community and the Mormon concern for the economic well-being of Church members. The book concludes with the suggestion that the Mormons followed the demo-cratic ideals of America more closely than did the emerging industrial classes of the 19th century.

H 1409. ATHEARN, ROBERT G. William Tecumseh Sherman and the Settlement of the West. Norman: University of Oklahoma Press, 1956. 371 pp.
This work outlines General Sherman's plan for using a wedge of settlements to subdue the Indians in the West. Following the Civil War, Sherman was Military Commander for the entire area west of the Mississippi. The era from 1865 to 1885 saw a rush of settlers into both the Western plains and mountain areas, and Sherman's duty was to keep peace in the area. This work is primarily concerned with the evolution of his policy within a milieu of conflict and violence. Sherman's primary objective in protecting settlers from hostile tribes was made increasingly difficult by decreasing annual appropriations for the Army and the growth of a pacifist element in the East. He concentrated on giving military protection to railroad construction in the belief that this would provide comparative safety to the settlements in the area--a practice that proved effective.

H 1410. ATHERTON, LEWIS. The Cattle Kings. Bloomington: Indiana University Press, 1961. 308 pp.
This is an examination of cattlemen and their role in the settlement of the American West. Atherton depicts the ranchers and cattlemen as pioneer businessmen accepting the difficulties and hardships of life on the plains and providing a civilizing influence on the frontier. They characterized the mythical frontier American--rugged individualists, independent, self-reliant, enterprising, progressive, profane, and hard drinking. Finally, Atherton analyzes the relationship of the rancher with his famed employee, the cowboy, in both fact and fiction.

H 1411. BAKER, TOD A., ROBERT P. STEED, and LAURENCE W. MORELAND, eds. Religion and Politics in the South: Mass and Elite Perspectives. New York: Praeger, 1983. 191 pp.
The editors present nine analytical essays that grew out of the Citadel Symposium on Southern Politics in 1982. Four of the articles focus on the relationship between religion and politics among the general population, and the other essays deal with this phenomenon as it touched the lives of the elite. Evangelical Protestantism and the Democratic Party serve as common threads. The authors examine questions of how this symbiotic relationship between regional religion and politics has functioned in recent years.

H 1412. BANNON, JOHN FRANCIS. The Spanish Borderlands Frontier, 1513-
    1820. New York: Holt, Rinehart & Winston, 1970. 308 pp.
This book sets out in opposition to Frederic Jackson Turner's "frontier
hypothesis," arguing the case of the Spanish expansion in America. Bannon
suggests that although Anglo-Americans did settle much of the wilderness
in the Western frontier, there was also much territory that merely changed
sovereignty. New Mexico, Texas, Arizona, and California had already
largely been settled by the Spanish. Bannon then goes on to chronicle
the history of Spanish conquest and settlement starting with the conquis-
tadors until the Mexican independence from Spain and the signing of the
Adams-Onis agreement. The author focuses primarily on the Western frontier,
the conditions for its settlement, and the relations between Indians,
French, and Euro-Americans.

H 1413. BARTLETT, RICHARD A. The New Country: A Social History of the
    American Frontier, 1776-1890. New York: Oxford University Press,
    1974. 487 pp.
This broad social history, which refutes many standard myths of the West,
argues that settlers on the frontier experienced a greater degree of freedom
than had ever been known. Bartlett also relates the history of the West
to the development of the family, education, religion, occupations, transportation, and urbanization. He begins with a narrative of Western settlement from the opening of the Appalachians to the 1890 consensus; and he
then analyzes the people who participated in the Western movement, the
basic frontier occupation of farming, and the development of transportation.
Bartlett also examines the family, the role of women, and the level of
health among the settlers, transients, and fraternal orders. The study
concludes with the process of urbanization in the West.

H 1414. BATEMAN, FRED, ed. Business in the New South: A Historical Per-
    spective; Papers Presented at the First Annual Sewanee Economics
    Symposium, April 3-5, 1980. Sewanee, Tenn.: University of the
    South, 1981. 158 pp.
These papers attempt to repudiate the old view of the South as the one
section of the country not devoted to individual pursuit of economic gain.
The authors evaluate more recent interpretations that depict the South
as the last bastion of the traditional American virtues of the entrepreneurship, economic drive, and business acumen. Essays include introductory
statements on long-term trends in the Southern economy. Also included
are essays on Southern agriculture by Stanley L. Engerman, Gavin Wright,
and Harold D. Woodman. Finally, Bernard Weinstein and others discuss
the post-W.W. II Southern economy.

H 1415. BERWANGER, EUGENE H. The West and Reconstruction. Urbana: Uni-
    versity of Illinois Press, 1981. 294 pp.
Berwanger examines the role of the West and its reaction and relationship
to changes brought about by Reconstruction. The West was not isolated
and introspective. At this time, he argues, moved by the widespread spirit
of "national supremacy" after the Civil War, Westerners were concerned
with and active in national as well as regional issues. Berwanger notes
the contradictory tendencies of those Westerners who desired black political participation for the South, yet denied political power to their own
indigenous black populations.

H 1416. BIDWELL, PERCY W. and JOHN I. FALCONER. History of Agriculture
    in the Northern United States, 1620-1860. Washington, D.C.:
    Carnegie Institution, 1925. 512 pp.
While the authors concentrate mainly on New England, New York, and Pennsylvania, they also cover 19th-century developments in Maryland, Kentucky,
and Missouri. The volume covers the development of subsistence farming
in the earliest settlements, the achievement of self-sufficiency, the

production of small surpluses in the 18th century, and the transition to specialization accompanying expansion Westward after 1800. The authors characterize the period between 1800 and 1840 as one of expansion and progress, but they point out that even more rapid growth would take place in the next two decades.

H 1417. BILLINGTON, RAY ALLEN. America's Frontier Heritage. New York: Holt, Rinehart, & Winston, 1966. 302 pp.
In a series of essays, this book analyzes the influence of the frontier experience on American culture. Billington asserts that the Western settlers emphasized traits already unique to the American character, and that the frontier exposed the qualities of individualism, democracy, and nationalism which distinguished American life. Thus the frontier did not generate new traits so much as it deepened old ones. In this interpretation of the role of the frontier in shaping the American mind, Billington clarifies and supports the Turner thesis on the West's influence upon the national development.

H 1418. BILLINGTON, RAY ALLEN. The Far Western Frontier. New York: Harper, 1956. 324 pp.
Billington traces the history of the movement of settlers to the American West between 1830 and 1860, and he examines their objectives, motives, and expectations. He concentrates on the settlers themselves, and minimizes national politics and the manner in which the Western lands were acquired. Billington implicitly tests the "Frontier Thesis" of Frederick Jackson Turner. And in a slight modification he argues that there was not a monolithic "West," but rather that the region encompassed several disparate "empires." These regions, as divergent as Texas, Utah, Oregon, and California, all possessed different characteristics which effected the settlers differently.

H 1419. BILLINGTON, RAY ALLEN and JAMES BLAINE HEDGES. Westward Expansion: A History of the American Frontier. 1949; Rev. ed. New York: Macmillan, 1982. 892 pp.
This work supports Turner's thesis that the frontier experience shaped the American character; and one of the features of the latest edition is to make adjustments for the growing criticism directed against Turner. The book is organized around three regions, which are discussed chronologically and stress economic aspects: the Colonial frontier, the Trans-Appalachian frontier, and the Trans-Mississippi frontier. The latest edition also contains an added chapter on the cultures of Native Americans, improved maps, and discussions of the role of blacks and Mexican-Americans in frontier development.

H 1420. BOGUE, ALLEN G. Money at Interest: The Farm Mortgage on the Middle Border. Ithaca, N.Y.: Cornell University Press, 1955. 293 pp.
This study of the economic underpinnings of Populism calls into question the stereotype of the downtrodden Western farmer exploited by Eastern investors. Bogue examines the operation of the mortgage business in four states--Illinois, Iowa, Nebraska, and Kansas--between 1873 and 1895. He emphasizes the experiences of two frontier townships, one in Kansas and one in Nebraska. Farmers, he finds, did not pay monopoly prices on borrowed capital; by the late 1870s the supply of capital seeking sound mortgages exceeded demand. Investors generally avoided foreclosure, seeking not ownership of land but returns on their capital. Bogue notes that the local mortgage companies set up by brokers seeking to channel Eastern capital into Western mortgages were often run in an opportunistic fashion. This, he concludes, contributed in the late 1880s to the widespread failures which damaged Western farmers and Eastern investors alike.

H 1421. BOGUE, ALLAN G. _From Prairie to Corn Belt: Farming on the Illinois and Iowa Prairies in the 19th Century_. Chicago: University of Chicago Press, 1963. 310 pp.
In the 19th century, America's corn belt was concentrated in the Upper Mississippi Valley. Bogue examines the development of commercial agriculture in this area, focusing on the evolution of the individual farm. He explains that the first settlers moved into Iowa and Illinois from New York, Ohio, and Pennsylvania, and from Northern Europe--primarily Germany and Britain. Their early economic activity typically centered on lumbering rather than on farming, and land values remained low throughout the 1840s. By the early 1850s, however, transportation improvements had begun to open up distant markets, particularly in the South, and farmers had begun to concentrate on corn and livestock. By the 1870s, corn had replaced wheat as the region's main staple. Mechanization increased the productivity of land and labor, and Bogue describes the growing use of farm machinery before and after the Civil War. The author shows that technical and organizational innovations enabled many commercial farmers to prosper in the 1870s and 1880s, despite the hard times caused by declining prices.

H 1422. BRADEN, WALDO W. _The Oral Tradition in the South_. Baton Rouge: Louisiana State University Press, 1983. 131 pp.
This collection of essays traces the development of the myth of Southern oratory and its role in the region's culture. The tradition of distinctly Southern oratory began before the Civil War, when school books began inculcating an expansive, grandiloquent, persuasive form of public speaking. It was this oral tradition that became the "beau ideal of the southern way of life." Southern demagogues subverted this style, however, in attempts to use it to gain power for their own ends.

H 1423. BRANDFON, ROBERT L. _Cotton Kingdom of the New South: A History of the Yazoo Mississippi Delta from Reconstruction to the Twentieth Century_. Cambridge, Mass.: Harvard University Press, 1967. 227 pp.
Brandfon examines the experience of the Yazoo Mississippi Delta after Reconstruction. He argues that the New South potential for economic development was at last realized, but was assailed by anti-corporation hostility directed toward the Illinois Central Railroad, the principal element in uplifting the region. He discusses the postwar problems of taxation, land forfeiture, speculation, railroad development, immigration, pest infestation, convict labor, and high prices; and he concludes that speculation, railroad development, and immigration were necessary to reform cotton growing in the region.

H 1424. BRAY, ROBERT C. _Rediscoveries: Literature and Place in Illinois_. Urbana: University of Illinois Press, 1982. 167 pp.
Bray explores the issue of the "cultural wholeness" of a region by examining neglected literary works of the late 19th and early 20th centuries which were set in Illinois. The clash between the rural down-state and the big city up-state lives, and the transition involved in moving to the city, were central themes in this literature. The author suggests there is no Illinois school of writing but that these works illustrate a sense of place, the Midwest, which is dying.

H 1425. BROWN, RALPH H. _Historical Geography of the United States_. New York: Harcourt, Brace, 1948. 596 pp.
Brown surveys the varied character of American regions from the beginning of European settlement to the 1870s. He focuses on the physical geography of each region and its development by white settlers. The development and geographical transformation of different regions was frequently the result of specific economic developments: trade and travel on the Ohio

River; mining; farming; the fur trade in the upper Midwest; cattle and farming in the Plains States; and gold in parts of the Rocky Mountains. Examining climate, topography, natural resources, trade and travel routes, Brown describes and explains the settlement of each major region of the U.S.

H 1426. BRUCE, DICKSON D., Jr. The Rhetoric of Conservatism: The Virginia Convention of 1829-1830 and the Conservative Tradition of the South. San Marino, Calif.: Huntington Library, 1982. 218 pp.
Although focusing on a single incident, the author presents this as a study of "how political language and political beliefs work." Masked by more apparent differences with the North, Virginians also faced a multitude of internal divisions. Forced to deal with these differences by the Convention of 1829, they turned to principles rooted in the period before the Revolution as the framework for agreement. This conservative tradition emphasized political stability, the primacy of social obligations, and human limitations.

H 1427. BRUCE, DICKSON D., Jr. Violence and Culture in the Antebellum South. Austin: University of Texas Press, 1979. 322 pp.
The author examines the predilection, meaning, and sources of violence in Southern culture. Southerners, particularly the elite, have earned a reputation for violence as represented in the duel. In analyzing Southern folk moralities he finds that "tradition and experience conspired to dispose Southerners to pessimism." When this pessimism was combined with a view of passion as the uncontrollable "wellspring of human action," the result was acceptance of emotional outbursts of violence as a natural part of life.

H 1428. BULEY, R. CARLYLE. The Old Northwest: Pioneer Period, 1815-1840. 2 vols. Indianapolis: Indiana Historical Society, 1950. 1318 pp.
Buley offers a broad and comprehensive survey of the "Old Northwest" from 1815, the beginning of the "Great Migration," to 1840, approximately when the pioneer period closed. His primary concern is with the "way of life" of the first settlers: their physical and material culture, and their beliefs, attitudes, and values. He describes their farming methods, trade, and transportation, as well as their education, literature, and religion. Buley attempts to provide insight into the character of the original frontiersmen, and to discern their general hopes, objectives, and apprehensions. He also examines, to a lesser extent, the political developments concerning the growth and development of the region.

H 1429. CAUDILL, HARRY M. Theirs Be the Power: The Moguls of Eastern Kentucky. Urbana: University of Illinois Press, 1983. 189 pp.
Since the 19th century, a group of little-known, rich, and powerful men have dominated the economy and politics of eastern Kentucky through their manipulation of the region's natural resources. While the first generation of moguls may have died with the Great Depression, a new group has taken their place who, "steadfastly following the example of their predecessors, bestow few or no benefits on the region." Caudill examines the acquisition of power and its use to exploit and destroy the environment of a region.

H 1430. CHOATE, J. ERNEST, Jr. and JOE B. FRANTZ. The American Cowboy: The Myth and the Reality. Norman: University of Oklahoma Press, 1955. 232 pp.
Choate and Frantz assess both the image and the reality of the legendary American "Cowboy." First, they examine the cowboy within the context of the frontier environment, and trace the economic and social factors

which affected the cowboys: how they made a livelihood, how they lived, ate, dressed, and entertained themselves. In the second part of the work, Choate and Frantz critique the literature and lore surrounding the American cowboy, and determine to what degree these views were consistent with reality. They conclude that cowboy life was at best onerous, and that almost all writers, even some historians, tend to exaggerate and over-romanticize its positive aspects.

H 1431. COLTON, RAY C. The Civil War in the Western Territories: Arizona, Colorado, New Mexico, and Utah. Norman: University of Oklahoma Press, 1959. 230 pp.
This account of military activities in the Far West during the Civil War is primarily concerned with the major engagement in the West--the invasion of New Mexico and its aftermath. This section of the book chronicles the experiences of Confederate Colonel John R. Baylor and his Texas troops, their invasion of New Mexico and ultimate defeat by Union General Canby at Glorieta Pass. Also included are accounts of skirmishes with the Indians, as well as territory by territory catalogues of "home front" events.

H 1432. COWDREY, ALBERT E. This Land, This South: An Environmental History. Lexington: University Press of Kentucky, 1983. 236 pp.
In relating some of the ways that man and land have shaped each other, the author paints a picture of a fragile, changing landscape. From the prehistoric epoch to the present, the environment of the South has endured not because of man, but in spite of him. Knowledge of the relationship between this distinct environment and man, as in the case of particular diseases found in the region, adds another dimension to an understanding of the South.

H 1433. CURRENT, RICHARD N. Northernizing the South. Athens: University of Georgia Press, 1983. 147 pp.
Current's work consists of a series of essays focusing on the question of Southern distinctiveness. He states that a cultural gap existed at the founding of the Republic. This gap widened during the middle of the 19th century, as Northerners called for the "regeneration" of the South. The South, in turn, resisted militantly to defend its peculiarities. By 1861, two different civilizations existed in the U.S., hence the Civil War. By the 1880s, however, the North conceded defeat in its struggle to change the South, and reconciliation--predicated on the abandonment of the Negro--was begun. Current believes, although recognizing the intense disagreement over the issue, that the South today is no different from the North.

H 1434. CURTI, MERLE. The Making of an American Community: A Case Study of Democracy in a Frontier Community. Stanford, Calif.: Stanford University Press, 1939. 483 pp.
Studying Trempealeau County, Wisconsin, from 1850-80, Curti supplies objective, quantitative tests to the Turner thesis which argues that the frontier promoted American democracy. Curti finds that the accessibility of free or almost free land promoted economic equality and later produced political equality. A decade-by-decade analysis found higher percentages of foreign-born in the professions over time. Although there was little participation in politics, social activities, and intermarriage by the foreign-born in the early frontier decades, these activities increased over time, reflecting the Americanization process which Turner believed occurred on the frontier. Farmers especially made phenomenal economic gains in each decade. The gains for low-property groups were even greater than high-property ones, indicating that the rich became a little richer and the poor less poor. Similar results could have occurred in an area undergoing rapid democratic industrialization or where full employment followed a depression. In Trempealeau County, however, as in much of

frontier America, the stimulus for opportunity was provided by frontier conditions.

H 1435. **DALE, EDWARD E.** The Range Cattle Industry: Ranching on the Great Plains from 1865 to 1925. Norman: University of Oklahoma Press, 1930. 207 pp.
Dale examines the evolution of the Western cattle industry during the late 19th and early 20th centuries, discussing in sequence Texas, trail drives and ranching in the central and northern plains, and finally the old Southwest. Dale employs much quantitative data, rather than pure narrative, and relies heavily on census reports and Federal and state documents. He examines geographical factors, the relations of the cattle industry with both the government and Indians, and the competing frontiers of the Indians, the cattlemen, and the settlers.

H 1436. **DANIELS, BRUCE C.** Dissent and Conformity on Narragansett Bay: The Colonial Rhode Island Town. Middletown, Conn.: Wesleyan University Press, 1983. 137 pp.
Daniels examines Colonial Rhode Island towns to discern the degree to which the colony conformed to the rest of New England and the degree to which it differed. Rhode Island had been founded on the principle of religious and political dissent, whereas the rest of New England adhered to stability through rigid conformity. Rhode Island, according to Daniels, also tended to be more politically democratic than the rest of the region. Nevertheless, despite these and other important differences, Daniels concludes, the towns and townspeople of Rhode Island shared basic New England values and followed practices of other New England towns.

H 1437. **DAVIS, RONALD L. F.** Good and Faithful Labor: From Slavery to Sharecropping in the Natchez District, 1860-1890. Westport, Conn.: Greenwood Press, 1982. 225 pp.
Probing the origins of sharecropping in the region around Natchez after the Civil War, the author finds that black laborers, not white land owners, were responsible for the introduction of the system. Freedmen convinced land owners to adopt sharecropping as an alternative to the wage-labor, gang system of supervision that recalled the days of slavery. Even though sharecropping became associated with perpetual poverty, the author points out, "it was never able to reduce blacks to the state of dependency known in slavery."

H 1438. **DAY, CLARENCE A.** A History of Maine Agriculture, 1604-1860. Orono: University of Maine Press, 1954. 318 pp.
From the earliest Colonial days to the period immediately prior to the Civil War, Maine's agriculture developed in accordance with American agriculture as a whole. Day examines the spread of self-sufficient agriculture in the 17th century, paying particular attention to the influence of Indian practices on the early settlers. In the 18th century, the appearance of local markets along New England's Eastern seaboard encouraged farmers in Eastern Maine to produce a small commercial surplus and to begin diversifying into lumbering. Although markets for foodstuffs, particularly livestock, developed in Eastern Canada, these markets were not large enough to sustain more than spotty commercial development in Maine. During the 1820s and 1830s, the industrialization of Southern New England created a large urban market which attracted farm products from Maine and from the newly settled Western lands.

H 1439. DeCANIO, STEPHEN J. Agriculture in the Post-Bellum South: The Economics of Production and Supply. Cambridge, Mass.: MIT Press, 1974. 335 pp.

DeCanio tests the argument that postbellum economic institutions were responsible for the inability of the Southern economy to recover after the Civil War. He offers an econometric analysis of the contribution of labor to output and of the returns labor received. DeCanio concludes that specialization in cotton culture was a rational response to the economic conditions of that time. Postbellum markets, including the labor market, were competitive; blacks were not subject to economic exploitation in the labor market. Thus, Southern poverty cannot be explained by monopolistic institutions created after the Civil War. DeCanio points instead to the previous distribution of land and capital as the source of the region's agricultural problems.

H 1440. DEGLER, CARL N. Place Over Time: The Continuity of Southern Distinctiveness. Baton Rouge: Louisiana State University Press, 1977. 138 pp.

In this analysis of the unique Southern character, Degler argues that the region is still fundamentally shaped by Old South traditions. In support of this thesis, he examines the Old South's class and race systems and its political and economic doctrines. A concluding chapter on the 20th-century South finds many of the 19th-century traditions relatively unchanged; the region's homogeneity, its religious beliefs, political values, agricultural dependence, and—ironically—its recent struggles toward racial harmony still mark the South as a distinct region.

H 1441. DeVOTO, BERNARD. Across the Wide Missouri. Boston: Houghton Mifflin, 1947. 483 pp.

This book on the American West is a novelistic account of the life of the mountain man based on the Rocky Mountain excursions of Sir William Drummond Stewart, a British sportsman and officer. The narrative covers primarily the years 1832 to 1838. DeVoto describes the fur trade as both business and way of life for the mountain man. He delineates the characteristic experiences of the mountain man, the conditions that governed him, and the shape he gave to the American heritage; special concerns are how these experiences related to Western expansion, and how the mountain man lived.

H 1442. DICK, EVERETT. The Sod-House Frontier, 1854-1890: Social History of the Northern Plains from the Creation of Kansas and Nebraska to the Admission of the Dakotas. New York: Appleton-Century, 1937. 550 pp.

Dick offers a social history of immigrant farming in the Northern Midwest during the latter half of the 19th century, a period which immediately preceded the final settling of the frontier and the emergence of Populism. He examines the elements of daily life on the "sod-house frontier," and he describes the day-to-day activities of the settlers. Dick minimizes the role of politics and governmental institutions, and instead offers a wealth of details on a wide range of aspects of frontier life, such as boom towns, railroad and prairie trail settlements, sports and leisure, natural disasters, medicine, education, and the role of women and children on the frontier farm.

H 1443. DICKINSON, ROBERT E. Regional Concept: The Anglo-American Leaders. Boston: Routledge & Kegan Paul, 1976. 408 pp.

Dickinson traces the historical development of the "regional" concept in geography over the last fifty years through an examination of its leading proponents in Britain and America. The first half of the work is devoted to English regionalists and the second half concerns those in the U.S. The regional concept, according to Dickinson, "seeks to characterize and explain the uniqueness of terrestrial areas, viewed as associations of earthbound phenomena, physical, biotic, and human." Dickinson combines other authors' previously published biographical sketches with his own comments and conclusions.

H 1444. EATON, CLEMENT. The Growth of Southern Civilization, 1790-1860. New York: Harper & Row, 1961. 357 pp.
The work is a collection of the most important writings of Clement Eaton, whose contribution to the writing of Southern history has been immeasurable. The essays touch upon all aspects of antebellum Southern society--social, political, economic, and ideological--from the founding of the Republic up until the Civil War. Eaton examines not only the planter class, but also considers the profound influence which Afro-Americans and the white yeomanry had on the development of Southern civilization. He also recognizes the importance which the development of social and economic classes had on the antebellum South. Also included are chapters on creole civilization, Southern religion, John C. Calhoun, and the Southern mind.

H 1445. ELLER, RONALD D. Miners, Millhands, and Mountaineers: Industrialization of the Appalachian South, 1880-1930. Knoxville: University of Tennessee Press, 1982. 272 pp.
Eller examines the impact of industrial progress on Appalachian America. His focus is upon kin relations and self-sufficient farming techniques prior to the modernization that invaded the area. By 1930 the highlanders lived in a new environment characterized by rigid class distinctions, absentee landownership, and control by coal interests. The author argues that outsiders had a false understanding of mountain life. With a conception of the Appalachians as a backward people, reformers and industrialists could argue that they were bringing civilization to the mountains when in fact they were disrupting a traditional, preindustrial way of life.

H 1446. ELLIS, DAVID M. Landlords and Farmers in the Hudson-Mohawk Region, 1790-1850. Ithaca, N.Y.: Cornell University Press, 1946. 347 pp.
Ellis surveys farming in Eastern New York from the late 18th through the first half of the 19th century. In Colonial New York, agriculture was primarily self-sufficient, although it produced a small surplus of wheat. Continued migration Westward brought competition from Western grain, a problem that was felt in full after the Erie canal opened in 1825. Farmers of the Hudson-Mohawk region had to adjust their activities to meet the new competition by exploiting the growing urban markets of the Eastern seaboard. Some turned to sheep rearing and the wool trade, but the majority chose dairying. By 1850, the transportation revolution had blotted out completely the old pattern of self-sufficiency, and the farmers of Eastern New York had completely adjusted to a new type of intensive agriculture linked closely to the urban markets of the East.

H 1447. ELLIS, DAVID M. New York: City and State. Ithaca, N.Y.: Cornell University Press, 1979. 256 pp.
This book is a survey of how the city and state of New York achieved respective positions of national prominence. Faced with tremendous ethnic, religious, regional, political, and class differences, New York managed to bring "about a considerable measure of social peace and justice in a setting of relentless change and unequaled diversity." Because of this diversity, Ellis concludes, New York possesses the human material with which to excel in so many areas of national activity.

H 1448. FEHRENBACHER, DON E. The South and Three Sectional Crises. Baton
        Rouge: Louisiana State University Press, 1980. 81 pp.
Fehrenbacher investigates the causes of the Civil War by examining three
sectional crises during the 19th century. He focuses particular attention
on the voting behavior of the Southern representatives in Congress. He
argues that during the Missouri debate of 1819-1821 the South defined
for the first time the principle of the permanence of slavery as a Southern
institution. During the crisis of 1846-1850, triggered by the Wilmot
Proviso, Southerners embraced the principle of secession in order to defend
slavery. And during the final crisis of 1854-1861--which originated the
Kansas-Nebraska Act--the Southern states resorted to secession and the
military action necessary to carry it out.

H 1449. FRASER, WALTER J., Jr. and WINFRED B. MOORE, Jr., eds. From the
        Old South to the New: Essays on the Transitional South. Westport,
        Conn.: Greenwood Press, 1981. 286 pp.
This collection of nineteen essays traces the transformation of the South
from about 1850 to the present. The various topics addressed include:
the origins of the Jim Crow laws; change and continuity in Southern leadership and in the social history of the region; race relations; and the
main currents in Southern thought. The contributors include David Brion
Davis, Michael P. Johnson, Bertram Wyatt-Brown, Steven A. Channing, and
Lawrence Goodwyn.

H 1450. FRASER, WALTER J., Jr. and WINFRED B. MOORE, Jr., eds. The South-
        ern Enigma: Essays on Race, Class, and Folk Culture. Westport,
        Conn.: Greenwood Press, 1983. 240 pp.
The editors present a collection of essays originally presented at the
Citadel Conference on the South in 1981. Dividing the book into three
parts, they have included essays dealing with racial issues, essays focusing on questions regarding class, and a concluding group of essays examining folk culture and historiography. Historians Leon Litwack, George
Fredrickson, and Emory Thomas are among the contributors.

H 1451. FRAZER, ROBERT W. Forts and Supplies: The Role of the Army in
        the Economy of the Southwest, 1846-1861. Albuquerque: Univer-
        sity of New Mexico Press, 1983. 253 pp.
This book deals with the military contribution to a particular region
in the Southwest: making it safe for settlement and playing a crucial
role in the area's economic growth. The influx of army money in the form
of purchases of supplies and soldiers' pay stimulated local businesses
and attracted new ones. The security and profit potential afforded by
the army began a cycle of prosperity for the region.

H 1452. GATES, PAUL W. Fifty Million Acres: Conflicts Over Kansas Land
        Policy, 1854-1890. Ithaca, N.Y.: Cornell University Press,
        1954. 311 pp.
Throughout the second half of the 19th century, Kansas was beset by outbursts of civil strife and agrarian revolt. Gates argues that at the
root of these conflicts lay government policies on Indian lands and the
distribution of the public domain. The former were of particular importance because Indian reserves constituted a large part of the region's
land. Gates examines the scramble to control the distribution of Kansas
land and the subsequent competition between settlers and speculators for
the land itself. In the latter struggle, particularly in the case of
Indian land, railroads and speculators were favored over settlers and much
of the hostility between settlers and railroads was related to this initial
dispute. All of this contributed to the high incidence of Populist sentiments among farmers in the state in the early 1890s.

H 1453. GIBSON, ARRELL MORGAN. The Santa Fe and Taos Colonies: Age of the Muses, 1900-1942. Norman: University of Oklahoma Press, 1983. 308 pp.
Turning to natural surroundings and the exclusiveness of the region, artists moved to these two towns at the turn of the century. Eventually the most influential group in town affairs, the artists tried to preserve these qualities that had attracted them by protecting the region from progress. A rift grew between the local residents and the artists which—combined with the depression, W.W. II, and declining public interest in art—destroyed the region as an artist colony.

H 1454. GOETZMANN, WILLIAM H. Army Exploration in the American West, 1803-1863. New Haven, Conn.: Yale University Press, 1959. 309 pp.
This study of America's most significant period of discovery emphasizes the role of the U.S. Army Corps of Topographical Engineers in exploring and developing the West. Led by such heroic figures as John C. Fremont, the Army explorers surveyed the uncharted frontiers during the crucial period from 1838 to 1863, when the Corps was dissolved. The major undertakings of the Pacific railroad surveys, the Mexican boundary surveys, and the exploration of the Grand Canyon are included. Goetzmann recaptures a chapter in American history and at the same time charts the active role played by the Federal government in the development of the West.

H 1455. GOETZMANN, WILLIAM H. Exploration and Empire: The Explorer and the Scientist in the Winning of the American West. New York: Knopf, 1966. 656 pp.
Arguing that the West was explored over and over again by different generations of explorers schooled in Eastern sensibilities, Goetzmann delineates three distinct periods of Western exploration. Beginning with Lewis and Clark, American explorers spearheaded an imperial competition in the West that lasted until 1845. In the following period, which ended around 1860, military explorers, civilian scientists, and railroad scouts conducted a sweeping reconnaissance of the West inspired by a belief in Manifest Destiny. Finally, the sophisticated scientific surveys of the latter half of the century culminated in the formation of the U.S. Geological Survey and the Bureau of American Ethnology. In this narrative the explorer-scientist emerges as a major Western figure, as the author portrays the significance of such important figures as John Wesley Powell, Clarence King, Josiah Dwight Whitney, George M. Wheeler,

H 1456. GOLDMAN, MARK. High Hopes: The Rise and Decline of Buffalo, New York. Albany: State University of New York Press, 1983. 324 pp.
This book probes those "historical phenomena" that shaped one of the leading cities of western New York. At the turn of the century, Buffalo seemed to face a bright future as represented by its hosting of the Pan American exposition. The author determines that a combination of events, such as a decline in immigration, the opening of the St. Lawrence Seaway, and flight to the suburbs, brought unavoidable change and decline to the once promising city.

H 1457. GRANTHAM, DEWEY W. The Regional Imagination: The South and Recent American History. Nashville, Tenn.: Vanderbilt University Press, 1979. 269 pp.
In this collection of fourteen essays, most of them previously published, Grantham explores the respective roles which myth and reality play in shaping popular thought in and about the South. One major theme throughout is the continuity of Southern distinctiveness, which Grantham maintains is as strong as ever. On the other hand, he assesses general developments which have tended to "Americanize" the South: a national business system,

transportation, the media and communications, migration, and the emergence of the modern welfare state. Finally, Grantham discusses the politics of the South, where, he maintains, distinctiveness has remained most conspicuous.

H 1458. GRANTHAM, DEWEY W. Southern Progressivism: The Reconciliation of Progress and Tradition. Knoxville: University of Tennessee Press, 1983. 468 pp.
This comparison of Southern Progressivism with that in other areas of the nation points out that reform in the South was offered as "preventive social work." Motivated by a conservative tradition, the majority of Southern reformers were attempting to insure the continuation of a stable society rather than pursuing meaningful social and economic changes. In spite of their failure, Southern reformers, the author concludes, deserve credit for recognizing the problems that grew out of urbanization and industrialization.

H 1459. HAHN, STEVEN. The Roots of Southern Populism: Yeoman Farmers and the Transformation of the Georgia Upcountry, 1850-1890. New York: Oxford University Press, 1983. 340 pp.
Hahn attempts to explain the Southern Populist revolt of the 1890s by examining as a case study the transformation of the economy of the Georgia upcountry during the latter half of the 19th century. Before the Civil War, the Southern yeomenry had maintained a stable, autonomous, and subsistence-oriented economy, with minimal intrusion by or need for the marketplace. The social upheaval of the Civil War and Reconstruction, however, and the consequent development of sharecropping in the South, destroyed the stable world of the yeomenry, and led to the emergence of commercial agriculture and the resultant dependence on the marketplace. According to Hahn, the Georgian yeomen resisted this development and tried to preserve their traditional way of life. Hence, the Populist movement was the result of the yeomen's opposition to the emergence of capitalist agriculture and its attendant profit-oriented values.

H 1460. HOBSON, FRED, ed. South-Watching: Selected Essays by Gerald W. Johnson. Chapel Hill: University of North Carolina Press, 1983. 207 pp.
The work is a collection of twenty-two essays in which Gerald W. Johnson reflects on his life-long observations of the South and the profound changes which have occurred in the region in the 20th century. He touches upon many aspects of the South and upon the image of the region in the nation's mind. The work is divided into five sections: the first deals with negative aspects of the South, such as the Ku Klux Klan; the second part focuses on labor and economic strife; the third section looks at the popular images of the South; the fourth part discusses race and Southern politics; and the final section deals with North Carolina in particular, Johnson's native state.

H 1461. HOLLON, W. EUGENE. The Great American Desert Then and Now. New York: Oxford University Press, 1966. 284 pp.
This book updates the ideas of Walter P. Webb, a geographical-determinist historian. Hollon describes both the geography and climate of the region with an emphasis on its aridity. He examines the animals and Indians of the area and their adaptations to the ecological characteristics of the desert. Relating the story of European infiltration and exploitation, he focuses on the Spanish, the trappers and miners, the Mormons, the cattlemen, as well as efforts to turn the desert into a garden by irrigation and dry-farming. The remainder of the work is a contemporary description and appraisal of the region.

H 1462. **JACKSON, GREGORY, GEORGE MASNICK, ROGER BOLTON, SUSAN BARTLETT,**
and JOHN PITKIN. Regional Diversity: Growth in the United States,
1960-1990. Boston: Auburn House, 1981. 198 pp.
The projections in this Outlook Report indicate that the dispersion in
regional growth rates observed during the 1970s will widen during the
1980s. The fast-growing South Central and Mountain regions held less
than one-fourth of the nation's population in 1980, yet are projected to
account for more than 60% of U.S. population growth to 1990. The Mountain
region alone is expected to account for 17% of the national growth. In
sharp contrast, the urban industrial states in the Mid-Atlantic and East-
North Central regions are expected to suffer population losses as young
persons move to the "Sunbelt" seeking jobs, older persons retire there,
and low immigration fails to offset those losses. The overall picture
emerging from this Report is thus one of considerable diversity, both
in the rate of regional development and in its composition.

H 1463. **JAKLE, JOHN A.** The American Small Town: Twentieth Century Place
Images. Hamden, Conn.: Archon Books, 1982. 194 pp.
This study examines small-town iconography in fiction and photography
between 1900 and 1960. Jakle's survey, which concentrates on towns with
populations up to 10,000, focuses on small-town businesses, the layout
of city streets, ethnic neighborhoods, and areas on "the wrong side of
the tracks." Towns are viewed against backdrops of changing seasons and
changing historical and cultural contexts. Contending that the physical
landscape can act as a barometer of American values, Jakle charts the
evolution of the town from isolated "mecca" to its position in the world
of the automobile and the highway. The small-town mythos is analyzed
and discussed in this way through the medium of literature and print.

H 1464. **JENSEN, MERRILL,** ed. Regionalism in America. Madison: University
of Wisconsin Press, 1952. 425 pp.
Originally presented before a symposium at the University of Wisconsin
in 1949, the fifteen essays in this collection examine various aspects
of regionalism in America. They are divided into five parts which individually focus on the development and use of the regional concept, accounts
of historic regions, regionalism in a cultural context, government application of the regional principle as an administrative tool, and the value
of the regional concept.

H 1465. **JORDAN, TERRY G.** Trails to Texas: Southern Roots of Western
Cattle Ranching. Lincoln: University of Nebraska Press, 1981.
220 pp.
Jordan traces the origins of the Texas cattle ranch, which served as a
model for the open-range cattle ranching system of the 19th-century American West. The author describes the growth of 18th-century South Carolina's
cattle industry, and details its gradual expansion into Louisiana and
Texas. Jordan discusses the transformation of an essentially English
method of production to that suitable for Western geography, outlining
the accompanying changes in the ethnic make-up, political structure, and
culture of the West.

H 1466. **KIRWAN, ALBERT D.** Revolt of the Rednecks, Mississippi Politics:
1876-1925. Lexington: University of Kentucky Press, 1951.
328 pp.
This discussion of Mississippi focuses on the state's political leaders
and factions, their methods of gaining power, and their various achievements. Kirwan analyzes tensions between economic classes as the primary
force behind Mississippi politics, and he explores the role of racism
in political strategy. Portraits of the state's leaders are presented
with an analysis of the social climate in which they rose to power.

H 1467. KLINGAMAN, DAVID C. and RICHARD K. VEDDER. Essays in 19th-Century
Economic History: The Old Northwest. Athens: Ohio University
Press, 1975. 356 pp.
The focus of this book is on the East North Central states of the Old
Northwest, a region that showed the highest rate of growth in per capita
income in the U.S. during the second half of the 19th century. Several
essays deal with the sources, both quantitative and qualitative, of 19th-
century growth. The introduction offers an overview of the region's economic life. It is followed by three essays on land use: Gallman's "Agriculture and the Pace of 19th-Century Economic Growth," an essay by Richard
Esterlin dealing with regional patterns of agricultural production and
income, and an essay by Edward Rastatter on the land speculator in Ohio's
agricultural development. Subsequent sets of essays focus on the supply
and use of human resources, the formation of social overhead capital,
and the contribution such innovations as the canals and railroads made
to the region's growth.

H 1468. KOUSSER, J. MORGAN and JAMES M. McPHERSON, eds. Region, Race,
and Reconstruction: Essays in Honor of C. Vann Woodward. New
York: Oxford University Press, 1982. 463 pp.
This collection of essays includes works by Woodward's colleagues and
former students on issues of race and Reconstruction in the South. These
essays demonstrate the influence Woodward has had on the writing of Southern history. The various authors in general de-emphasize the role of
racism and concentrate on class and ideology as the key elements which
shaped the region. The authors include, among others, Bertram Wyatt-Brown,
Willie Lee Rose, Louis Harlan, Steven Hahn, Barbara Fields, and J. Mills
Thornton III. There is also a bibliography of the writings of Woodward
published before 1981 and a separate bibliography of books about Woodward.

H 1469. LAMAR, HOWARD R. The Far Southwest, 1846-1912: A Territorial
History. New Haven, Conn.: Yale University Press, 1966.
560 pp.
This study of Utah, Arizona, New Mexico, and Colorado during the late
19th century focuses on the supremacy of political power over geographic
or economic determinism in the process of regional development. Lamar
concentrates on political experiences rather than the social history shared
by all four territories. These include the development of political
parties, the roles played by Federally-appointed officials, territorial
assemblies, and probate judges. He also discusses topics that relate
the territories to the nation, such as public schools and education, monogamy, trial by jury and law enforcement, and land tenure.

H 1470. LAMPARD, ERIC E. The Rise of the Dairy Industry in Wisconsin:
A Study in Agricultural Change, 1820-1920. Madison: State Historical Society of Wisconsin, 1963. 466 pp.
As settlement in the third quarter of the 19th century spread to the Mississippi and to the new lands beyond, farmers in the old Northwest faced
growing competition from the new Western farmers. Lampard shows how this
crisis forced Wisconsin farmers to foresake wheat production and go into
animal husbandry and, in particular, into the dairy production. This
type of farming was organized predominantly on a small unit basis, although
it was the largest single industry in the state. Processing cooperatives
experienced rapid expansion, and eventually the corporate form of organization appeared within the farming industry.

H 1471. LAVENDER, DAVID. Bent's Fort. Garden City, N.Y.: Doubleday,
1954. 450 pp.
Lavender examines the origins and development of Fort Bent, which was
a key trading post on the Santa Fe Trail in what was Colorado during the
later 19th century. As an outpost of Western civilization in the midst

of a vast prairie wilderness, Fort Bent was a crucial factor in American expansion westward. Lavender explores the lives of the Bent family, founders of the trading post, and details their efforts to establish the post. He concentrates in particular on Charles Bent, who became the first governor of the State of New Mexico.

H 1472. LEMON, JAMES T. The Best Poor Man's Country: A Geographical Study of Early Southeastern Pennsylvania. Baltimore, Md.: Johns Hopkins University Press, 1972. 295 pp.
Lemon gives an analysis of the development of commercial agriculture in Southeastern Pennsylvania between the 1680s and the end of the 18th century. Migrants to this region were drawn predominantly from Europe's "middle orders" and they brought with them a familiarity with, and commitment to, commercial agriculture. Their economic individualism stimulated the growth of a market economy based on extensive, mixed farming, with an emphasis upon wheat production for export. Lemon analyzes agriculture's ties to the Atlantic commercial system and its links with the regional network of towns. He also studies the factors influencing decisions on settlement, land use, and cropping techniques; he concludes that climate, soil, and markets were generally of more influence than religious and ethnic considerations. Lemon finds that the settlers in this region lived well and achieved prosperity in the farm country of Pennsylvania.

H 1473. LINGEMAN, RICHARD. Small Town America: A Narrative History 1620 to the Present. New York: Putnam, 1980. 495 pp.
Drawing on county histories, literature, and numerous secondary sources, Lingeman chronicles the evolution of the American small town over three centuries. This socio-historical survey treats daily routines, religion, education, local government, architecture, leisure, social stratification and ethnicity, economics, sex roles, and other aspects of everyday life within a geographical and cultural context. Largely concerned with the Middle West, Lingeman also describes Puritan New England, mining towns, and prairie settlements. Changing attitudes toward towns are seen through the literature of Sherwood Anderson, Sinclair Lewis, Edgar Lee Masters, and others. The effects of urbanization and industrialism are evinced through dramatic social and demographic change.

H 1474. MADSON, JOHN. Where the Sky Began: Land of the Tallgrass Prairie. Boston: Houghton Mifflin, 1982. 321 pp.
Stretching Westward from isolated spots to Nebraska, and South from North Dakota to Oklahoma, the tallgrass prairie is a dying region. The author follows its history from before the arrival of Europeans to the present, examining the interaction between man and environment. He suggests that each has shaped the other to a significant degree, but that the introduction of extensive farming began a pattern of destruction from which the land will not recover.

H 1475. MAGDOL, EDWARD and JON L. WAKELYN, eds. The Southern Common People: Studies in Nineteenth-Century Social History. Westport, Conn.: Greenwood Press, 1980. 386 pp.
The editors bring together a collection of essays that focus on the lives and labors of white, middle-class Southerners. Although exploring a wide variety of topics, the contributors share an interest in the "nature of Southern society" and in defining those who were the "common people." Historian Ira Berlin points out in an afterword, that while sweeping conclusions are few, the essays serve as a foundation for the work that remains.

H 1476. MAIZLISH, STEPHEN E. The Triumph of Sectionalism: The Transfor-
mation of Ohio Politics, 1844-1856. Kent, Ohio: Kent State
University Press, 1983. 310 pp.
Through this case study of Ohio politics the author delves into the transformation of Jacksonian values and practices into a new political system.
The second party system had died in Ohio by the time of the Kansas-Nebraska
Act. Slavery was a concern, but the central issues were questions about
the state's economic development. Debate over the proper course split
Ohio into two camps, Hards and Softs, around which complex political fac-
tions grew. Regional alliances with these groups in the state produced
a political system based on sectionalism.

H 1477. MALONE, MICHAEL P., ed. Historians and the American West. Lincoln
University of Nebraska Press, 1983. 449 pp.
The work is a collection of eighteen historiographical essays critiquing
the treatment of various topics concerning the West, such as politics,
cities, ethnicity, women, industrialization, and violence. The contributors include, among others, Rodman Paul, Richard Maxwell Brown, W.
Turrentine Jackson, Charles C. Spence, and Herbert T. Hoover. The authors
attempt to come to grips with the role of the "West," both in the development of the U.S., and in American history. They also attempt to assess
why the West--both as a region and as an idea--no longer dominates American
historical writing, as it did during the heyday of Frederick Jackson Turner
in the early 20th century.

H 1478. McCARDELL, JOHN. The Idea of a Southern Nation: Southern Nationalists and Southern Nationalism, 1830-1860. New York: Norton,
1979. 394 pp.
McCardell sees the Nullification Crisis as the spark for ideas of Southern
nationalism, with South Carolinians playing the most prominent roles.
He shows the development of the idea in the writings of such Southerners
as James DeBow, Edmund Ruffin, and William Gilmore Simms. The idea spread
and became linked with the defense of slavery, although most Southerners
remained sectionalists, continuing, until 1861, to seek a place for the
South within the Union. Southern sectionalism saw itself as the true
heir of American freedom and justice. Consequently, the drive for Southern
independence grew out of the growing sectionalism, which portrayed the
South as threatened by an increasingly powerful and oppressive North--
at which point, sectionalism became nationalism.

H 1479. McDONALD, MICHAEL J. and WILLIAM BRUCE WHEELER. Knoxville, Tennessee: Continuity and Change in an Appalachian City. Knoxville:
University of Tennessee Press, 1983. 192 pp.
The authors examine the relationship between Appalachia and the New South
in a case study of a city in which the two meet. Industrialization came
to Knoxville after W.W. II and attracted nearby rural Appalachians to
new jobs. The city's old leaders allowed these newcomers and blacks to
participate because they shared a commitment to stability. A third group,
"preoccupied with development, economic growth, and progress," challenged
the city's tranquility with grand plans for a bright future which have
since become tarnished.

H 1480. McDOWELL, JOHN PATRICK. The Social Gospel in the South: The
Women's Home Mission Movement in the Methodist Episcopal Church,
South, 1886-1939. Baton Rouge: Louisiana State University Press,
1982. 167 pp.
This study attacks the myth that Southern churches had little interest
in social reform. A "progressive and constructive" concern for changing
the conditions in the South motivated this particular denomination's female
home mission leaders. Although they initially looked upon blacks and

immigrants with condescension, the home mission workers gradually extended their efforts to include all Southerners as they gradually realized all "creatures of God possessed inherent worth and deserved new respect."

H 1481. MEINIG, D. W. Imperial Texas: An Interpretive Essay in Cultural Geography. Austin: University of Texas Press, 1969. 145 pp.
Meinig presents a broad historical and geographic survey of Texas, not as a political unit, but as a "human region." He traces the settlement and development of the area, from an early simple framework to its modern complexities, assessing the extent to which Texas evolved as a distinctive cultural area and an autonomous functional region. Meinig examines the cultural patterns of the various peoples of Texas: who they are, where they came from, where they settled, and how they affected each other. Meinig also assesses the interrelationship between the population and its environment, and examines the networks of communication and transportation that tie the region together, in both the past and the present.

H 1482. MERK, FREDERICK. History of the Western Movement. New York: Knopf, 1978. 660 pp.
This work details the development of the area encompassed by the continental U.S. from the Pre-Columbian era to the mid-1970s. Merk concentrates on topics such as sectionalism and slavery, and the manner in which the political, economic, and geographic development of the sections shaped the U.S. The author also presents a detailed discussion of the ways Native Americans have helped to shape American development. The final section of the book examines current problems such as soil conservation, strip mining, water rights, land-use, and migratory farm workers.

H 1483. MIMS, EDWIN. The Advancing South: Stories of Progress and Reaction. Garden City, N.Y.: Doubleday, Page, 1926. 319 pp.
Mims presents an account of Southern liberalism in its struggle after the Civil War to succeed as an "important and significant intellectual renaissance." The adversary, to Mims, is the "Southern conservative," who is "a demagogue and a reactionary." This book focuses on progress in intellectual, literary, educational, social, and religious matters. Mims attempts to advance the liberal elements of traditional Southern culture, to overcome the scattered and regional nature of the liberal critique, and to reassert its power. He tries to reconcile the best elements of the traditional culture with its liberal and progressive elements.

H 1484. MORELAND, LAURENCE, TOD A. BAKER, and ROBERT P. STEED, eds. Contemporary Southern Political Attitudes and Behavior, Studies and Essays. New York: Praeger, 1982. 296 pp.
The editors offer a collection of fourteen analytic essays in three sections which collectively examine the basis of distinctive political patterns in the South. Focusing on the role of ideology in Southern politics, the authors of the essays in the first section probe the relation between political conservatism and the region's "traditional character." Contributors to the second section discuss the new patterns of party competition in the region. Relations between the "mass public," both black and white, and public officials serve as the topic of the third group of essays.

H 1485. O'CONNOR, CAROL A. A Sort of Utopia: Scarsdale, 1891-1981. Albany: State University of New York Press, 1983. 283 pp.
Beginning with the purchase of farmland for the creation of a suburb in the 1890s Scarsdale represented "an island of exclusivity" for wealthy urbanites seeking to escape the city. The opening of a rail link to Manhattan allowed wealthy New Yorkers to work in the city while living in an idealized community of the countryside. This case study demonstrates that concepts of class and culture have exercised considerable influence over the form and image of urban and suburban life.

H 1486. OSTERWEIS, ROLLIN G. The Myth of the Lost Cause. Hamden, Conn.:
         Archon Books, 1973. 188 pp.
This study examines the persistence of the romantic "lost cause" myth
in the South and its acceptance by northerners, the origins of the myth
after the Southern defeat in 1865, and the organizations that continued
to fight for the lost cause, such as the Ku Klux Klan and the United Confederate Veterans. The book analyzes the emergence of the myth in Southern
literature and in Northern as well as post-Civil War Southern culture.

H 1487. OSTERWEIS, ROLLIN G. Romanticism and Nationalism in the Old South.
         New Haven, Conn.: Yale University Press, 1949. 273 pp.
Osterweis analyzes the role of symbol and myth in providing cultural coherence. He examines the Old South's "cult of chivalry" and the numerous
manifestations of Romanticism in the region from the aristocratic traditions of Virginia to the camp-meetings and revivalism on the Southern
frontier. Looking primarily at literature, Osterweis discusses the role
of the chivalric tradition in creating Southern nationalism.

H 1488. PAUL, RODMAN WILSON. Mining Frontiers of the Far West, 1848-1880.
         New York: Holt, Rinehart, & Winston, 1963. 236 pp.
Paul offers a broad survey of mining in the American West during the later
half of the 19th century. He examines the mining frontier as an important
factor in the settling of the region and in the social order which
developed there. Paul also describes the close interrelationship between
widely scattered and disparate mining frontiers, comparing and contrasting
regions as divergent as California, Colorado, and the Black Hills of South
Dakota. Paul describes the technological factors of Western mining, and
examines the interplay between technology and the environment, emphasizing
the enduring features and innovations of Western mining and settlement.

H 1489. PEIRCE, NEAL R. The Border States. New York: Norton, 1975.
         415 pp.; The Deep South States of America. New York: Norton,
         1974. 584 pp.; The Great Plains States of America. New York:
         Norton, 1973. 402 pp.; The Mid-Atlantic States of America.
         New York: Norton, 1977. 416 pp.; The Mountain States of America.
         New York: Norton, 1972. 317 pp.; The New England States of
         America. New York: Norton, 1976. 447 pp.; The Pacific States
         of America. New York: Norton, 1972. 387 pp.
This series of surveys of America's regional cultures adopts a historical
framework to discover how particular regional characteristics have
developed. The studies concentrate on the politics and economics of each
region as well as major cities and ethnic groups. Among other topics
covered are the "livability" of the regions; pollution; the power bases
among the regions; the role of corporations, unions, universities, and
newspapers; and the development and influence of various ethnic cultures.
The work is primarily a chronicle of the diversity of peoples and lifestyles, geographic habitats, and political behavior in the U.S.

H 1490. PHILLIPS, ULRICH BONNELL. Life and Labor in the Old South. Boston:
         Little, Brown, 1929. 373 pp.
Phillips's volume is divided into four distinct parts, each devoted to
a different aspect of the Southern economy and society. The author provides background and development information on the economics of the antebellum period and analyzes its most important features. While Phillips
devotes some attention to patterns of commerce, his primary focus is on
the Southern labor system. Phillips describes slavery in all its aspects,
institutional, economic, and social. In general, he argues that slavery
was not economically efficient, its contribution being to civilize the
slaves rather than to enrich the masters. He stresses the benevolent
aspects of plantation slavery--a viewpoint which for years found general
acceptance among scholars.

H 1491. POMEROY, EARL S. The Pacific Slope: A History of California, Oregon, Washington, Idaho, Utah, and Nevada. New York: Knopf, 1965. 421 pp.
Pomeroy's history of this six-state region covers both the "Eastern" quality of the region and the dominance of cities rather than farms in the area. Pomeroy analyzes the politics of the region, especially in the 20th century, and provides an extensive examination of its economics. A treatment of the importance of railroads is also included.

H 1492. POMEROY, EARL S. In Search of the Golden West: The Tourist in Western America. New York: Knopf, 1957. 239 pp.
Pomeroy charts the development of tourism from the earliest aristocratic travelers in the 19th century to the vacationers of the 1950s. The attempt of Western states to lure tourists with gambling, entertainment, and sports is analyzed. Pomeroy discusses the ecological and economic effects of such industries as 19th-century railroad industrialists and 20th-century casino operators who enticed sightseers to the "golden" West.

H 1493. POMEROY, EARL S. The Territories and the United States, 1861-1890: Studies in Colonial Administration. Philadelphia: University of Pennsylvania Press, 1947. 163 pp.
Focusing on the relationship of frontier political institutions to the Federal government, Pomeroy provides a descriptive account of the territorial system of government. During the thirty years of Pomeroy's study there was a shift in public interest in the territories from slavery and public lands to Indian wars, mining, and Federal politics. The territorial belt became relatively stable politically and had certain common social and physiographic characteristics. Among the topics Pomeroy treats are territorial finances, the supervisory activities of the Departments of State and of the Interior, territorial justice, patronage, and representation in Congress.

H 1494. POSTON, DUDLEY, Jr. and ROBERT H. WELLER, eds. The Population of the South: Structure and Change in Social Demographic Context. Austin: University of Texas Press, 1981. 307 pp.
The ten essays in this collection assess recent changes in the demography of the South. The authors address such topics as fertility, mortality, migration, industrialization, and urbanization. Central themes to the works are: the changing nature of the Southern population, especially concerning race; the convergence of these changes with patterns found in the North; and the enduring legacy of Southern distinctiveness, especially concerning its economy. Contributors include: George Myers, William J. Serow, Susan E. Clarke, and Ronald R. Rindfuss.

H 1495. PRASSEL, FRANK R. The Western Peace Officer: A Legacy of Law and Order. Norman: University of Oklahoma Press, 1972. 330 pp.
This is a treatment of the reality behind one of America's most closely held hero myths, that of the sheriff of the old West. Prassel uses such sources as newspaper reports, court records, and police dockets to reconstruct a clear picture of Western lawmen and their problems. He discovers that it was not only the town marshalls and sheriffs who maintained order but also vigilante groups, private detective agencies, Indian police, and ranger companies. Prassel argues that these lawmen faced problems similar to those of contemporary urban police and that urban growth, rather than a "frontier tradition," is responsible for the region's crime pattern. He also argues, as do other recent Western historians, that the West's reputation for lawlessness has been exaggerated.

H 1496. REEVE, KAY AIKEN. Sante Fe and Taos, 1898-1942: An American
         Cultural Center. El Paso: Texas Western Press, 1982. 56 pp.
During the first half of the 20th century the unlikely, remote region
around Sante Fe and Taos became a productive, successful artist community
and then died. The author points to several factors that caused this
phenomenon. Initially artists were attracted by the region's environment
and Western character. Changes in the attitudes of locals and artists
combined with the coming of W.W. II contributed to the demise of the region
as an artist colony.

H 1497. ROBBINS, WILLIAM G., ROBERT J. FRANK, and RICHARD E. ROSS, eds.
         Regionalism and the Pacific Northwest. Corvallis: Oregon State
         University Press, 1983. 246 pp.
The essays in this volume examine the basis of the distinctive "entity"
of the Pacific Northwest. Although the authors explore a variety of topics
from the prehistoric period to the recent past, the emphasis is on the
region as "a state of mind." Two sets of attitudes, an optimistic view
of development held by older inhabitants and a critical pessimism of a
younger group, emerge as characteristic of this state of mind in recent
years.

H 1498. ROHRBOUGH, MALCOLM J. The Trans-Appalachian Frontier: People,
         Societies, and Institutions, 1775-1850. New York: Oxford Uni-
         versity Press, 1978. 444 pp.
The author describes, analyzes, and compares the several societies that
emerged on "the first frontier of the new American nation" across the
Appalachian Mountains. Life on this frontier that stretched from Michigan
to Florida was often difficult, but the natural abundance created an
optimism that, in turn, shaped the kinds of institutions created. Although
it is a "story of repeated success," the complexity of life on the frontier
"belied the simple picture of individual against the wilderness."

H 1499. ROSENBERG, BRUCE A. The Code of the West. Bloomington: Indiana
         University Press, 1982. 213 pp.
Through folklore and popular legends, the author examines what life was
like for inhabitants of the old West. Recurrent themes of mobility, survival, and hyperactivity appear throughout the glimpses of tales the author
includes. In comparing the stories of the old West to those of other
regions and cultures he determines the roots of many Western stories are
to be found not in the narratives of New England but in much older European
legends.

H 1500. RUSSELL, HOWARD S. A Long, Deep Furrow: Three Centuries of Farm-
         ing in New England. Hanover, N.H.: University Press of New
         England, 1976. 672 pp.
Russell describes the growth and development of New England farming from
settlement through the 20th century. The author details advances in agricultural method, including Yankee innovations of the plow and introduction
of Native American agriculture. Russell outlines the impact of a growing
national economy on the farming industry, forcing changes in crop choice
and farm life. Accounts of the establishment of agricultural colleges
and organizations as well as the growth of agribusiness in the 20th century
are also given.

H 1501. SALOUTOS, THEODORE and JOHN D. HICKS. Twentieth-Century Populism:
         Agricultural Discontent in the Middle West, 1900-1939. Lincoln:
         University of Nebraska Press, 1951. 581 pp.
Saloutos and Hicks contend that there was a strong radical wing in the
agrarian movement between 1900 and 1939. They describe farmers' discontent
during these years and the several organizations that represented the
Midwestern farmers. They also look at the American Society of Equity

and the Nonpartisan League, as well as more conservative groups such as the American Farm Bureau Federation. The book concludes with a discussion of the New Deal farm programs of the 1930s.

H 1502. SHARE, ALLEN J. Cities in the Commonwealth: Two Centuries of Urban Life in Kentucky. Lexington: University Press of Kentucky, 1982. 150 pp.
By focusing on Kentucky's leading cities of Lexington and Louisville, the author locates a number of themes central to the process of urbanization. Tracing the development of these cities from the 1770s through the 1970s, he demonstrates the ways in which phenomena such as boosterism, urban rivalries, and racial issues have shaped the form and function of the state's cities.

H 1503. SHIFFLETT, CRANDALL A. Patronage and Poverty in the Tobacco South: Louisa County, Virginia, 1860-1900. Knoxville: University of Tennessee Press, 1982. 159 pp.
Through this case study of one county in Virginia, the author "attempts to provide a general theory of continuity and change in the South with poverty at center stage." He finds in Louisa County that the traditional elite maintained their positions after the Civil War by adopting a system of "patronage capitalism." By controlling both production and distribution, the county's economic leaders prevented the creation of a free labor market. As a weapon to resist change, this system also perpetuated racism and poverty.

H 1504. SITTERSON, JOSEPH CARLYLE. Sugar Country: The Cane Sugar Industry in the South. Lexington: University of Kentucky Press, 1953. 414 pp.
Cane sugar was basic to the economic development of much of Louisiana and part of Texas, an area responsible for virtually the entire national output of sugar during the 19th century. Sugar was introduced to Louisiana in the 1750s but was cultivated only sporadically until the end of the century. The inadequate labor supply, which was the major constraint on expansion of the industry, was greatly increased when Louisiana was incorporated into the U.S. and was opened to the internal slave trade. Thereafter, the only limiting factors on the industry's success were the climate and the condition of the market. Sitterson supplements his account of the antebellum sugar economy with details of plantation life and labor. The second half of the book is devoted to a description of the transition to free labor and the reorganization of the industry after the Civil War.

H 1505. SMITH, ALFRED G. Economic Readjustment of an Old Cotton State: South Carolina, 1820-1860. Columbia: University of South Carolina Press, 1958. 239 pp.
Smith examines the reaction of South Carolina's established agricultural economy to competition in the form of cotton produced in newly settled areas. Those parts of the Old South which were dependent on production of cotton, such as South Carolina, were pressed by the growing competition from new farm lands in the West. Land exhaustion and the price depression of the 1820s encouraged heavy migration of capital and labor, further complicating the state's adjustment to the new situation. Despite these problems, cotton remained the state's primary crop. South Carolina's marketing facilities, experienced labor, capital, and transportation systems were all tied to cotton. Moreover, no local markets existed in which to sell commodities other than cotton.

H 1506. SMITH, PAGE. As a City upon a Hill: The Town in American History.
New York: Knopf, 1966. 332 pp.
In his history of the small town in the North and West U.S., Smith finds
that many of the town's institutions and much of its ideology can be traced
to the "covenanted community" of Puritan New England. The author notes
that the town defended its ties to the country through the 19th century
by idealizing the "wise and virtuous farmer," but adopted the individualism
of the city as the pace of American urbanization increased. In addition
to exploring the reasons why many towns were founded, Smith analyzes the
political, social, and economic changes the small town community underwent
in response to national issues.

H 1507. STEGNER, WALLACE and RICHARD W. ETULAIN. Conversations with
Wallace Stegner on Western History and Literature. Salt Lake
City: University of Utah Press, 1983. 207 pp.
This is a series of ten interviews with Pulitzer Prize winning historian-
author Wallace Stegner conducted by historian Richard W. Etulain in 1980
and 1981. Each interview is devoted to specific subjects such as Stegner's
early works, his book The Big Rock Candy Mountain, Mormons, or various
aspects of the American West and Western literature.

H 1508. STREET, JAMES H. The New Revolution in the Cotton Economy:
Mechanization and Its Consequences. Chapel Hill: University
of North Carolina Press, 1957. 294 pp.
By 1955, about one fourth of America's cotton crop was harvested by machine,
and the author concludes that at this point a revolution in cotton farming
was launched. Technical as well as economic factors explain why the cotton
industry lagged so far behind the mechanization of other farm industries.
The author analyzes the eventual displacement of men by machines. He
notes that mechanical harvesting altered tenure arrangements and encouraged
the creation of larger farm units. He predicts that land-use patterns
will continue to change and that farms, on the average, will grow larger.
The standard of living in the rural South will increase, he says, although
the farm population will continue to be displaced by the new machine.

H 1509. TINDALL, GEORGE BROWN. The Ethnic Southerners. Baton Rouge:
Louisiana State University Press, 1976. 251 pp.
In a collection of previously published essays, Tindall presents a broad
overview of the South and the dramatic changes which occurred there between
1930 and 1960. He examines such divergent topics as Southern ethnicity,
images of the South in the national psyche, race relations, politics,
20th-century Populism, and economic development. Tindall argues that
the South has maintained, and will continue to maintain, a distinctiveness
from the rest of the nation, yet the same forces of continuity and change
which have affected the nation have likewise influenced the South. Finally,
Tindall repudiates the notion of the "static" nature of Southern society,
and asserts that the New South will continue to rise and play an integral
role in national development.

H 1510. TURNER, FREDERICK JACKSON. The Frontier in American History.
New York: Holt, 1920. 375 pp.
This collection of essays elucidates Turner's famed "Frontier Thesis,"
in which he argues that the Western frontier explained American development
up until 1890. According to Turner, the frontier was the source of American democracy. It provided equality and economic opportunity, and was
a "safety-valve," which lured potentially discontented or radical elements
of the Eastern population to the West. Most important, however, the frontier rejuvenated American institutions and prevented them from developing
as had those of Europe, where, it was believed, social institutions
restricted human freedom and initiative. The work includes Turner's essay,
"The Significance of the Frontier in American History."

H 1511. UTLEY, ROBERT M. Frontiersmen in Blue: The United States Army and the Indian, 1848-1865. New York: Macmillan, 1967. 384 pp.
In this work, Utley examines the Army's role in the development and settlement of pre-Civil War America west of the Mississippi. He focuses on the campaigns the Army directed toward the Indians and its attempt to manage the Native American population in a way that "balanced the requirements of national expansion against those of humanity to an alien minority destined for subjugation." Although Utley blames Congress for the major failings of the Army in this period, he also points out areas in which the Army itself was at fault.

H 1512. WEBB, WALTER P. The Great Frontier. Austin: University of Texas Press, 1951. 434 pp.
Webb argues that the "Great Frontier" explains not only American development, but the development of Western civilization for the last 400 years. Indeed, he maintains that the frontier is one of the primary factors of modern history. The sudden acquisition of land and other forms of wealth by the people of Europe--made possible by the existence of the frontier-- precipitated a boom in the West. This boom, he asserts, lasted as long as the frontier was open, a period of four centuries. The ultimate result, Webb argues, was that modern Western institutions developed and matured during a boom--as opposed to medieval institutions, which did not--and were adapted to boom conditions.

H 1513. WEBB, WALTER P. The Great Plains. Boston: Ginn, 1931. 345 pp.
In this study of the Great Plains of America, Webb demosntrates how geographical limitations were overcome by technological ingenuity. The region examined is one where scant rainfall, level country, and a lack of trees create an environment sharply contrasted to the woodland areas of the East; thus the area was a natural interruption to Western expansion. Webb details technological improvements that made settlement of this region possible, such as the Colt revolver, barbed wire, windmills, and power machinery. The Industrial Revolution was full partner in the final occupation of the Continent. The book's chapters cover the physical region; native Indians; the Spanish frontier; the cattle kingdom; the search for transportation, fencing, and water; and finally, the effect of the Plains upon national law, American literature, and the American imagination.

H 1514. WHISNANT, DAVID E. All That Is Native & Fine: The Politics of Culture in an American Region. Chapel Hill: University of North Carolina Press, 1983. 340 pp.
Through three case studies the author examines the efforts of middle and upper-class, liberal "cultural workers" to understand, manipulate, and assist rural, poor, lower-class Southerners. These liberal reformers attempted to implement social change "cloaked in a mantle of romantic cultural revitalization." Characterized as the politics of culture, this intervention legitimized the region's culture at a time of social and economic upheaval.

H 1515. WHISNANT, DAVID E. Modernizing the Mountaineer: People, Power, and Planning in Appalachia. Boone, N.C.: Appalachian Consortium Press, 1980. 296 pp.
A perception of Appalachia as economically and culturally backward produced several attempts in the 20th century to redirect the region's development. From the Council of Southern Mountains to the more recent Appalachian Regional Commission, the power to plan the region's future has been given to or appropriated by a variety of extra-regional groups. In spite of the apparent success of some projects, most such efforts have failed.

Cultural values and assumptions, the author concludes, have been the key determinants of the region's development.

H 1516. WISHART, DAVID J. The Fur Trade of the American West, 1807-1840: A Geographical Synthesis. Lincoln: University of Nebraska Press, 1979. 237 pp.
Employing an interdisciplinary approach, the author examines the "relationships between the biological, physical, and cultural environments of the fur trade." Within the region of the Rocky Mountains and the Missouri River, the fur trade followed a cyclical pattern tied to the seasons. Fur trading changed by the 1820s, when a period of successful production replaced one of experimentation. It was, the author concludes, an early example of the destruction of an American environment.

H 1517. WOODWARD, C. VANN. The Burden of Southern History. Baton Rouge: Louisiana State University Press, 1968. 250 pp.
The essays collected in this book attempt to place Southern history within the context of the American experience, searching out the origins of the South's unique heritage. Two essays discuss distinct Southern culture: "The Search for Southern Identity" and "The Irony of Southern History." Both offer interpretations of the region's character and its pervasive sense of guilt. The unique Southern experience with poverty, racism, and military defeat created regional myths that stand in opposition to the national images of abundance, opportunity, and innocence.

H 1518. WOODWARD, C. VANN. Origins of the New South: 1877-1913. 1951; Rev. ed. Baton Rouge: Louisiana State University Press, 1972. 654 pp.
Woodward examines the South from the end of Reconstruction to 1913, the middle of the Progressive era and the inauguration of a Southerner as President. Woodward argues that the "New South" was dominated by a new class of industrialists and men of commerce who were thoroughly imbued with bourgeois values of profit, as opposed to the antebellum planters who had rejected these values. Woodward examines the disputed Hayes-Tilden election of 1876, and describes it as a political compromise between Northern and Southern conservatives who had similar economic and ideological interests. It was against these new dominant classes, claims Woodward, that the tenant-farmer and sharecropper voiced Populist protest. To obstruct this resistance, the "New Order" urged the re-commitment to "White Supremacy." The consequences of this move, was the destruction of the radical agrarianism of poor whites and set in motion the machinery, perfected in the Progressive Era, for the institutionalization of racism. This was achieved through the elimination of the suffrage and the legal establishment of segregation. According to Woodward, Woodrow Wilson epitomized this combination of Progressivism and racism.

H 1519. WRIGHT, LOUIS. Culture on the Moving Frontier. Bloomington: Indiana University Press, 1955. 273 pp.
Examining central ideas in six areas of the continually moving American frontier, Wright argues that the fundamental qualities of American culture were inherited from the British and repeated on successive frontiers. By demonstrating that conservative institutions prevailed on each of the geographical frontiers, Wright presents a counter-argument to Frederick Jackson Turner's thesis that the frontier produced innovation and liberal democracy, and supports the view that as a people Americans have remained astonishingly homogeneous in culture, despite ethnically diverse origins. Much of the book is also concerned with the transplantation and repetition of cultural experiences on successive geographical frontiers.

H 1520. WYATT-BROWN, BERTRAM. Southern Honor: Ethics and Behavior in the Old South. New York: Oxford University Press, 1982. 597 pp.
Searching for the foundations of the South, the author determines that honor rather than conscious shame or guilt were "the psychological and social underpinnings of Southern culture." After discussing the origins and meaning of honor, he demonstrates that it was a moral code that governed behavior in the South ranging from family relations to attitudes toward government while legitimizing racial and class injustice. The Civil War, for example, was in part the result of divergent understandings of this concept of honor.

XIII. LABOR HISTORY

H 1521. BALLACE, JANICE R. and ALAN D. BERKOWITZ. The Landrum-Griffin Act: Twenty Years of Federal Protection of Union Members' Rights. Philadelphia: Wharton School Industrial Research Unit, University of Pennsylvania, 1979. 363 pp.
This work, which is primarily a judicial history, examines the Labor-Management Reporting and Disclosure Act, or the Landrum-Griffin Act, of 1957. The authors analyze the ambiguities in the wording of the legislation and the loopholes and omissions that have compromised the effectiveness of the law. The authors are especially critical of the manner in which successive Secretaries of Labor have weakened the legislation through lax enforcement. They conclude, however, that the act as written by Congress has "withstood the test of time remarkably well," and has, when enforced, favorably affected the rights of unions and their members.

H 1522. BARNARD, JOHN. Walter Reuther and the Rise of the Auto Workers. Boston: Little, Brown, 1983. 236 pp.
Barnard outlines the career of American labor leader Walter Reuther and his role in the organization of the United Auto Workers, for which he served as president from 1946 until his death in 1970. Under Reuther's leadership the UAW developed a productive working relationship with the Democratic party in an attempt to bring about political changes within society. As a result of Reuther's political strategy the UAW's influence increased significantly. After Philip Murray's death, Reuther became the most important labor leader in the country, and the UAW was to become, upon the AFL-CIO merger in 1955, the leadership of the social unionist wing of that labor confederation.

H 1523. BECNEL, THOMAS. Labor, Church, and the Sugar Establishment: Louisiana, 1887-1976. Baton Rouge: Louisiana State University Press, 1980. 222 pp.
Becnel examines the history of union activities in Louisiana's sugar cane country. Centering on the activities of H. L. Mitchell, co-founder of the Southern Tenant Farmers' Union in 1934, this book attempts to explain the failure of unionism in the agricultural South. Becnel explores the effect of McCarthyism on the union movement as well as opposition from Senator Allen Ellender of Louisiana as sources of Mitchell's failure. Becnel focuses on the actions of the Catholic Church, specifically those of Archbishop Joseph Francis Rummell of New Orleans, which supported unionism. Rummell's mediation between the sugar growers and the union in order to avert strikes and violence is discussed. In addition, the author describes opposition of business to social action by priests, and its attempt to neutralize the political influence of the Catholic Church. The failure of the farmer's union in Louisiana is seen as a microcosm of union organizing throughout the rural South.

H 1524. BERNSTEIN, IRVING. The Lean Years: A History of the American
         Worker, 1920-1933. Boston: Houghton Mifflin, 1960. 577 pp.
Blending cultural and institutional labor history, Bernstein discussed
the social and economic conditions of both organized and unorganized
workers during the 1920s and the early years of the Great Depression.
Bernstein devotes particular attention to the decline of the labor movement
and the growing unemployment during this seemingly prosperous period.
He also examines the influence on workers and their unions of such trends
in the American economy as rationalization, technological innovation,
and changes in the composition of the labor force owing to immigration
quotas established earlier in that decade.

H 1525. BERNSTEIN, IRVING. Turbulent Years: A History of the American
         Worker, 1933-1941. Boston: Houghton Mifflin, 1970. 873 pp.
Bernstein examines the emergence of a national labor policy within the
context of the Great Depression of the 1930s and the worker militancy
that characterized that decade. Bernstein concentrates on the growth
and development of the labor movement during these years, particularly
the rise of the CIO, its break with the AFL, and the organization of mass
production workers. This organization was achieved and consolidated on
the basis of the enactment of the National Recovery Act section 7A and
spontaneous action of workers which included the use of sit-down strikes.

H 1526. BETTEN, NEIL. Catholic Activism and the Industrial Worker. Gaines-
         ville: University Presses of Florida, 1976. 191 pp.
Betten concentrates on Catholic support for unions from the late 19th
century through the early 1950s. He includes chapters on such labor
priests as Charles Owen Rice of Pittsburgh and John Boland of Buffalo,
as well as the "radio priest," Father Charles Coughlin. Betten also examines the relationship between the Association of Catholic Trade Unionists
and the Congress of Industrial Organizations. He argues that the ACTU
was a nucleus around which progressive anti-Communists gathered, and that
it contributed to the merger of the AFL and the CIO by separating the
CIO from Communist activists.

H 1527. BLUM, ALBERT A. A History of the American Labor Movement. 1963;
         Rev. ed. Washington, D.C.: American Historical Association,
         1972. 39 pp.
The author offers an outline of major trends in the development of the
American labor movement. Until the 1930s labor's most widely used tool
was collective bargaining, but after the legislation of the New Deal it
became equally acceptable to pursue goals through the political system.
At the same time the scope of union activity was expanded in an attempt
to bring about social and economic conditions that would benefit society
as a whole.

H 1528. BODNAR, JOHN. Anthracite People: Families, Unions and Work,
         1900-1940. Harrisburg: Pennsylvania Historical and Museum Com-
         mission, 1983. 100 pp.
Through a series of personal interviews, Bodnar explores the lives of
coal miners in the Wyoming Valley in the Northeastern corner of Pennsylvania. He finds that the miners and their families survived personal
disasters and economic hardship by adopting a communal spirit that led
individuals to turn to family, community, and the union in times of need.
Those interviewed discussed topics ranging from family life to tensions
between rival unions and strikes. Bodnar pays close attention to the
ethnic composition of mine workers and focuses on how traditional subcultures and values provide the basic element for solidarity and resistance.

H 1529. BODNAR, JOHN. Workers' World: Kinship, Community, and Protest in an Industrial Society, 1900-1940. Baltimore, Md.: Johns Hopkins University Press, 1982. 200 pp.
Bodnar presents an oral history of workers in Pennsylvania's major industries between 1900 and 1940. He argues that the rapid industrialization of the late 19th and early 20th centuries had caused significant social disorientation, and that workers lacked government-sponsored security programs or large-scale unions to fall back on. The workers' response was to seek security and survival through an "intricate network of kinship ties, job structures, and community relationships." These old kinship and ethnic ties not only served in the place of an institutional structure before 1930, Bodnar argues, but they also formed the basis of the major unionization movements of the 1930s and early 1940s.

H 1530. BORYCZKA, RAYMOND and LORIN LEE CARY. No Strength Without Union: An Illustrated History of Ohio Workers, 1803-1980. Columbus: Ohio Historical Society, 1982. 328 pp.
This monograph provides a history of Ohio's labor movement from the early 19th century to the present. Nineteenth-century topics include the impact of the canal boom of the 1830s, the rise of urbanization, the peculiar fusion of agricultural and industrial economies in Ohio pork houses, and the influx of immigrants in the late 1800s and consequent ethnic tensions. Also discussed is the rise of organized labor, the impact of the two World Wars and the New Deal, and the institutionalization of unions in the second half of the 20th century. The authors stress the development of a working-class culture, presenting letters, song lyrics, and oral histories. The book contains numerous illustrations and photographs of workers.

H 1531. BOTSCH, ROBERT EMIL. We Shall Not Overcome: Populism and Southern Blue-Collar Workers. Chapel Hill: University of North Carolina Press, 1980. 237 pp.
Botsch bases his findings on interviews with more than a dozen men working in a small Southern company town. He contends that Southern regionalism and Protestant fundamentalism are strong at least among white males. However, Botsch argues that particular issues, especially political and economic ones, can be taken in liberal and sometimes relatively radical directions. The conclusion is that a social and cultural conservatism must be tolerated if not respected.

H 1532. BRAVERMAN, HARRY. Labor and Monopoly Capital: The Degradation of Work in the Twentieth Century. New York: Monthly Review Press, 1974. 450 pp.
Braverman's critique of capitalist labor practices throughout the 20th century is written from a Marxist perspective. He suggests that division of labor was a function of economic efficiency; thus, it was the natural product of capital's efforts to maximize profits. Degradation of work, therefore, is viewed as a necessary consequence of technology and efficiency. In an effort to maximize production, capital sought to gain complete control of the work process. This "rationalization" of labor furthered the alienation of the worker and created a highly manipulative social order.

H 1533. BRODY, DAVID. The Butcher Workmen: A Study of Unionization. Cambridge, Mass.: Harvard University Press, 1964. 320 pp.
Brody describes the pattern of union growth and structural change within the packing industry and in the retail meat trade since the 1890s. The Meat Cutters' Union was organized in the late 19th century and was formed of local retail butchers. At that time the union adopted a decentralized structure suited to the nature of the industry. This structure helped the union adjust to the rise of the chain store, a major organizational innovation in retail food marketing during the 1920s and 1930s. Although

the Meat Cutters Union established a strong position in the meat packing industry, it was eventually supplanted by the United Packinghouse Workers' union.

H 1534. BRODY, DAVID. Steelworkers in America: The Nonunion Era. Cambridge, Mass.: Harvard University Press, 1960. 303 pp.
Brody's monograph examines the history of American steelworkers from the turn of the century until the eve of the Great Depression. The loss of shop floor power by skilled workers is seen to be the result of technological improvements (i.e., scientific management) which reduced management's dependency upon the workers' knowledge and experience. Tasks which previously demanded certain craft skills became increasingly performed by unskilled labor, at lower wages and with greater efficiency. As automation increased the productivity of the steel mills, workers' wages declined. As a result, both labor and management became engaged in conflict over control of the workplace. Management proved successful in controlling the workplace through the promotion of welfare Capitalism. The Great Steel Strike of 1919 is also discussed.

H 1535. BRODY, DAVID. Workers in Industrial America: Essays on the 20th Century Struggle. New York: Oxford University Press, 1980. 257 pp.
Brody's five essays examine the "changing nature of work and the changing character of the work force," the growth of unions during the early 1900s, and union opposition to certain political and industrial positions. The author examines the development of welfare Capitalism as a corporate response to unionism during the 1920s. The rise of the CIO and its impact on the AFL are also examined. Brody's book encompasses the struggle of the workers to control the workplace, and their eventual defeat as a result of the acceptance of collective bargaining, which improved the collective lot of the labor movement while decreasing the control of individual workers over the work place and processes itself.

H 1536. BROWNE, HENRY J. The Catholic Church and the Knights of Labor. Washington, D.C.: Catholic University of America Press, 1949. 415 pp.
This is a study of the relationship between the Knights of Labor and the Catholic Church from 1879 to 1891. Initial tensions between the two institutions resulted from the Knights' desire for secrecy, which they saw as a necessary defense against anti-labor and anti-Irish efforts in the 1870s. But because an oath was required, the Church opposed the secret nature of the organization. The leader of the Knights, Terence V. Powderly, the mayor of Scranton, Pennsylvania and son of Irish immigrants, spent much of his career working to show that secrecy was not dangerous to either ecclesiastical or civil society. As Powderly attempted to satisfy the Church, he rejected his earlier Socialism, condemning the use of violence, revolution, and strikes, and pleading conservatism. Eventually the defense of the Knights became personified in the Henry George mayoral campaign in New York in 1886. With the aid of such liberal prelates as James Cardinal Gibbons and Fr. Edward McGlynn, the Knights were finally sanctioned by the Church.

H 1537. BUDER, STANLEY. Pullman: An Experiment in Industrial Order and Community Planning, 1880-1930. New York: Oxford University Press, 1967. 263 pp.
Founded in the suburbs of Chicago in 1880, the model town of Pullman embodied its namesake's desire to demonstrate how business systems could serve the ends of public welfare as well as profit. The Pullman experiment provides a case-study of the transformation of labor-management relations as a result of the rapid industrialization occurring during these decades. In the case of Pullman, the experiment ultimately failed as order broke

down under the pressure of industrial conflict. But the founder's concern for order, and his emphasis on social engineering as the means whereby order might be achieved, remain instructive.

H 1538. BYRKIT, JAMES W. Forging the Copper Collar: Arizona's Labor-Management War of 1901-1920. Tucson: University of Arizona Press, 1982. 435 pp.
Byrkit describes the conflict between capital and labor in Arizona at the time of that state's transformation from rural frontier to industrial center. After discussing the development and initial successes of mine unionism in Arizona, the author describes the consolidation of power by the mine managers, particularly by the Phelps Dodge Corporation, owner of the Bisbee, Arizona copper mines. Byrkit recounts the events leading up to the corporation's decision to arrest and deport over a thousand unionized strikers at Bisbee in 1917, and details the corporation's propaganda campaign to justify its actions to the public. Byrkit argues that the country's acceptance of the deportation demonstrated a new corporate dominance over American political culture.

H 1539. CANTOR, MILTON, ed. American Workingclass Culture: Explorations in American Labor and Social History. Westport, Conn.: Greenwood Press, 1979. 444 pp.
In his introduction Cantor examines the attitudes and factors that influenced working class culture, and provides a historical overview of cultural development in industrial America during the 19th century. In the essays that follow, sixteen scholars discuss the specifics of working class culture. They deal with such topics as immigrant experiences, labor boycotts and strikes, the development of the female work force, and the resistance to industrial Capitalism. Also included are local studies of the working classes of New York City, Philadelphia, the mill towns of Massachusetts, and the mining towns of California.

H 1540. CARLSON, PETER. Roughneck, the Life and Times of Big Bill Haywood. New York: Norton, 1983. 352 pp.
Haywood is portrayed as a poor, desperate youth attracted to radicalism early in his life, eventually becoming the leading spokesman for both the Western Federation of Miners, and later the Industrial Workers of the World. Influenced by Eugene Debs, Haywood became a Socialist while still a member of the WFM. In his attempt to unite unskilled workers in their struggle against the employing class, Haywood advocated direct economic actions over political action, as he considered the latter ineffective for solving the problems of labor and believed that politicians were merely the tools of the owning class.

H 1541. CHRISTIE, ROBERT A. Empire in Wood: A History of the Carpenter's Union. Ithaca, N.Y.: Cornell University Press, 1956. 356 pp.
Christie's volume provides an economic explanation for the rise of business unionism. He centers on the development of one or the most powerful of the American Federation of Labor's constituent unions: the Carpenter's Union. In fact, Matthew Hutchinson, the Carpenter's Union president, was to play a major role in the AFL following the death of Samuel Gompers. Christie describes how the union aggressively expanded its jurisdiction to include workers less skilled than its original membership of master craftsmen. He then discusses the manner in which developments within the industry brought about changes in both the union's structure and policies.

H 1542. CLARK, PAUL F. The Miners' Fight for Democracy: Arnold Miller
and the Reform of the United Mine Workers. Ithaca, N.Y.: Cornell
University Press, 1981. 190 pp.
The purpose of this book is to document the "progress, problems and
dynamics" of the struggle by Arnold Miller and the Miners for Democracy
to reform the United Mine Workers Union. While much was accomplished
by the end of Miller's tenure as president of the UMW, the late 1970s
saw the reform movement grind to a halt as a result of developments in
the coal industry. Nevertheless, some of the reforms such as direct vote
by membership on the contract and no contract, no work rule, were instituted and remained. The reform spirit of Arnold Miller served as an inspiration for other labor groups within the Teamsters and Steelworkers unions.

H 1543. CLETUS, DANIEL E. Bitter Harvest: A History of California Farm-
workers, 1870-1941. Ithaca, N.Y.: Cornell University Press,
1981. 348 pp.
Cletus traces the history of California's agricultural workers. Composed
of a "captive peasantry" and ignored by the AFL, California's agricultural
labor force found radical labor organizations like the IWW and the Communist Party's trade unions attractive. Cletus's analysis revolves around
a historical three-way struggle between unionists, government officials,
and the California growers. The author suggests that internal conflict
and paternalism, which accompanied grass-root efforts to ameliorate the
conditions of the farm workers and redress the existing balance of power,
limited the effectiveness of any such efforts. While ignored by New Deal
legislation which had effected industrial workers, the farm workers
received support from the CIO's Cannery, Agricultural, Packing and Allied
Workers of America, but this effort proved far less productive than was
expected.

H 1544. COMMONS, JOHN R., et al. History of Labour in the United States.
4 vols. New York: Macmillan, 1918-1935. 2654 pp.
This collective work of the Wisconsin School of Labor History examines
the institutional relationships that shaped industrial relations in the
U.S. through the 19th and early 20th centuries. Volume I tells the story
of the Colonial and early national origins of the American labor movement,
of the first attempts at trade unionism in the 1830s, and of the humanitarian reform movements which frequently preoccupied labor leaders prior
to the Civil War. Volume II concentrates on the beginnings of national
trade unions and their eventual emergence as the dominant form of labor
organization. Volume III provides studies of wages, hours, and working
conditions between 1900 and 1930, and the last volume, authored by Selig
Perlman and Philip Taft, examines unions and their activities in the years
following W.W. II.

H 1545. CONLIN, JOSEPH R., ed. At the Point of Production: The Local
History of the I.W.W. Westport, Conn.: Greenwood Press, 1981.
349 pp.
Arguing that there were "many IWWs," this ten-essay collection illustrates
the diversity and wide range of activities of the Industrial Workers of
the World. The authors study the Wobblies in industrial cities such as
Akron, Ohio, Paterson, N.J., and Wichita, Kansas in the years before 1917.
Several essays also study the IWW after their sedition trials and the
flight of Bill Haywood to Russia in the 1920s. Conlin suggests that
because the Wobblies were frequently perceived as outsiders in communities
they tried to organize, they were easy targets for local government repression.

H 1546. COOPER, JERRY M. The Army and Civil Disorder: Federal Military
Intervention in Labor Disputes, 1887-1900. Westport, Conn.:
Greenwood Press, 1980. 284 pp.
Cooper examines the role of the U.S. Army in the major industrial conflicts
of the late 19th century. Included in this treatment are the railroad
strikes of 1877, the Homestead Strike of 1892, the Pullman Strike of 1894,
and the Coeur d'Alene strike of the 1890s. The author examines the transformation of the Army's role after 1877 from that of civil law enforcer
in labor disputes to that of military opposition to labor. The army was
used by employers to protect private property, maintain law and order,
and repress labor unrest.

H 1547. CORBIN, DAVID A. Life, Work, and Rebellion in the Coal Fields:
Southern West Virginia Coal Miners, 1880-1922. Urbana: University of Illinois Press, 1981. 282 pp.
Corbin examines a coal mining community of West Virginia, composed primarily of immigrants, blacks, and Appalachian farmers who had come to
the region attracted by the prospects of cash wages. Oppressed by a "company" town environment where dissent was brutally put down, the eventual
success of the miners under the auspices of the UMW, seen after the Cabin
Creek Strike of 1912, is chronicled by the author. Corbin maintains that
the southern West Virginia coal fields witnessed some of the bloodiest
labor strife ever to occur in the U.S. He argues that the strikes and
violence were neither primitive nor sporadic occurrences, but were rather
manifestations of a clear and coherent class consciousness. Miner militancy was the response of "fully sane and industrialized workers to conditions they understood and hated and wanted to change."

H 1548. CUMBLER, JOHN. Working Class Community in Industrial America:
Work, Leisure, and Struggle in Two Industrial Cities, 1880-1930.
Westport, Conn.: Greenwood Press, 1979. 283 pp.
This social history of two 19th-century Massachusetts towns, Lynn and
Fall River, examines the structure and conditions of labor and the rise
of a working class consciousness and communal solidarity. Whereas new
ethnic groups in Lynn became rapidly integrated into the centralized shoe-
making districts where residents lived nearby, immigrants in Fall River
clustered into various ethnic ghettos along the river, separated by conflict and suspicion. Social portraits of the working class communities
in these two cities provide a perspective on the diverse social manifestations of the workers' community and life.

H 1549. DAWLEY, ALAN. Class and Community: The Industrial Revolution
in Lynn. Cambridge, Mass.: Harvard University Press, 1976.
301 pp.
Dawley investigates the social effects of economic development in Lynn,
Massachusetts. Lynn was the center of shoe manufacturing during the middle
of the 19th century in the U.S. The majority of the shoeworkers were
young women. Dawley traces the growth of the shoe industry from artisanal
shop to shoe factory. Dawley also discusses the ideology behind the labor
protest of these women workers and calls its Republicanism. Reaching
back to touch the past, the women saw themselves as daughters of the American Revolution. Their struggles culminated in the greatest strike before
the Civil War, the Strike of 1860. After the war, with Irish immigrant
women replacing native Yankees, the ideology behind them changed but the
struggle continued within a precursor of the Knights of Labor, the Knights
of St. Crispin.

H 1550. **DUBOFSKY, MELVYN.** We Shall Be All: A History of the Industrial
Workers of the World. Chicago: Quadrangle Books, 1969. 557 pp.
Dubofsky's book covers the historical evolution of the Industrial Workers
of the World from its inception in 1905 until its eventual collapse in
the mid-1920s. Dubofsky suggests that IWW radicalism should be understood
as a product of what he terms "American exceptionalism." Conflict, violence, and radicalism, particularly within the mining communities, were
the direct result of the rapid economic growth of the West and the attempts
by corporate interests to exploit the natural resources of the land.
Dubofsky suggests that the failure of the IWW can be traced to three principal causes: (1) economic changes that occurred as a result of America's
entry into W.W. I; (2) government repression; and (3) internal inadequacies
that plagued the IWW throughout its history.

H 1551. **DUCKER, JAMES H.** Men of the Steel Rails: Workers on the Atchison,
Topeka & Santa Fe Railroad, 1869-1900. Lincoln: University
of Nebraska Press, 1983. 220 pp.
The author probes the "rules, rhythms and remuneration" that guided the
lives of workers on one railroad. Because of the class structure of small
company towns, unions were important socially and economically. Community
pressure could also influence the lives of the workers. In the case of
strikes, Ducker notes, the "working class backed the strikers as members
of their working class community, but the dominant economic and political
leaders insured that the town as a whole gave no substantive assistance
to rebellious employees."

H 1552. **EDWARDS, P. K.** Strikes in the United States: 1881-1974. New
York: St. Martin's Press, 1981. 336 pp.
Edwards offers a statistical survey of strikes between 1881 and 1974,
as 1880 was the first year in which the U.S. census attempted to record
strikes. Reversing the emphasis of the "Sombart thesis," Edwards asks
not why American workers tended to be less politically sophisticated than
their European counterparts, but rather why European workers were less
militant economically than the Americans. Edwards bases his economic
analysis on the quantitative method, but not on the conclusions of Edward
Shorter and Charles Tilly, who hold that European workers, especially
the French, consistently struck when political crises occurred, so that
the impact of their struggle would be magnified. Edwards sees no great
change in the intensity of strikes during the past century within the U.S.,
however, and explains this by stating that control of the workplace remains
the socio-economic reason for violent struggle between employer and employee.

H 1553. **EDWARDS, RICHARD.** Contested Terrain: The Transformation of the
Workplace in the Twentieth Century. New York: Basic Books,
1979. 261 pp.
Edwards examines the development of changing relations of production in
the workplace and the struggle for workshop control. Evolving out of
a 19th-century paternalistic owner control structure, relations of production during the early 20th century were dominated by the systematic
control of management. Two types of "structural" control evolved during
the 20th century: technical control, characterized by an impersonal rule
of production technology, and bureaucratic control, characterized by the
impersonal rule of law, wherein management's law is built into the social
and organizational structure of the company itself.

H 1554. **EDWARDS, RICHARD C., MICHAEL REICH,** and **DAVID M. GORDON,** eds.
Labor Market Segmentation. Lexington, Mass.: Heath, 1975.
297 pp.
This collection of essays, presented at the Conference on Labor Market
Segmentation held at Harvard University in 1973, focuses on the divisions
in the American working class. The editors' introduction outlines their

theory of segmentation, and the articles describe the labor process and the various labor markets in the U.S. Included among the articles are statistical analyses on women's wages by Mary Stevenson and on clerical occupations by Francine D. Blau. Alice Kessler-Harris provides a historical overview.

H 1555. EGGERT, GERALD. Steelmasters and Labor Reform, 1886-1923. Pittsburgh, Pa.: University of Pittsburgh Press, 1981. 212 pp.
Eggert examines the influence of American business leaders upon labor reforms during the Progressive era. At the center of Eggert's study is William Brown Dickson, an official from U.S. Steel and Midvale Steel and Ordinance. Dickson worked to promote employee representation and reduction of working hours. His reform efforts are a case study of managerial projects to bring about industrial reform through corporate planning. These attempts have since been called Welfare Capitalism.

H 1556. ERICKSON, CHARLOTTE. American Industry and the European Immigrant, 1860-1885. Cambridge, Mass.: Harvard University Press, 1959. 269 pp.
In the late 19th century, American labor organizations tried to eliminate job competition among immigrants by restricting their entry. In 1885, the Knights of Labor was victorious, through legislation, in stemming the flood of low-wage European immigrants. But, Erickson contends, the controversy absorbed the energies of the labor movement and forced craft groups into racist campaigns favoring immigration restrictions. Thus the organized craft groups ignored the problems of the unskilled workers and opposed attempts to create a public employment service. This, in turn, increased the divisions within the American working class, weakening the positions of both immigration workers and native craftsmen.

H 1557. EWEN, LYNDA ANN. Which Side Are You On? The Brookside Mine Strike in Harlan County. Chicago: Vanguard Books, 1979. 139 pp.
This book examines the struggle of a local chapter of the United Mine Workers of America in Mongolia County, West Virginia, against the Duke Power Company. Following a refusal from Duke's Brookside plant to negotiate with the UMWA in 1973, a strike began. Supported reluctantly by UMWA President Arnold Miller, the Harlan County local won a decisive victory against the power company. The author stresses the important role of the women of Harlan county in the mobilization of the striking miners.

H 1558. FALER, PAUL G. Mechanics and Manufacturers in the Early Industrial Revolution: Lynn, Massachusetts, 1780-1860. Albany: State University of New York Press, 1981. 267 pp.
This book focuses upon the transition from the "handicraft stage" to the "factory stage" of industrialization among the shoemakers of Lynn, Massachusetts. The author's thesis is that contrary to conventional interpretation, the appearance of the factory and even of mechanization was a late, not early, aspect of the industrial revolution. Faler shows that the unified community of 1800 had been divided as early as 1830 by the continuing decline of social and economic circumstances for wage workers, and their increasing reliance upon wages rather than property for their livelihood. As the result of the capitalists' concentration of property and the division of labor, class consciousness occurred well before a factory system or mechanization was introduced.

H 1559. FINE, SIDNEY. Sit-Down: The General Motors Strike of 1934-1937. Ann Arbor: University of Michigan Press, 1969. 448 pp.
In this work, Fine examines one of the most important labor conflicts of the 1930s--important because it fostered the organization of the auto industry and insured the growth of the CIO as a massive labor organization within the mass production industries. As a result of General Motors

"speed-up" efforts to cut costs, the auto workers, already overworked and outraged by their working environment, declared a massive "sit-down" strike. Much of Fine's book is devoted to an examination of the "sit-down community" which established a system of self-government and discipline, that included sanitation measures, postal services, and educational and recreational activities.

H 1560. FINK, GARY M. Labor's Search for Political Order: The Political Behavior of the Missouri Labor Movement, 1890-1940. Columbia: University of Missouri Press, 1973. 228 pp.
This work is a case study of the Missouri American Federation of Labor from its foundation till the end of the New Deal. Fink argues that the national AFL under Samuel Gompers generally opposed government intervention in labor disputes. The organization also held an apolitical attitude toward the state and took a non-partisan position on political parties. The AFL at lower levels, however, was not "volunteerist," and was quite political and very partisan on the issues that affected labor. By the end of the New Deal, the national AFL had also adopted these methods. The key to the institutionalization of this partnership between labor and the Democratic Party in Missouri was political patronage.

H 1561. FINK, LEON. Workingmen's Democracy: The Knights of Labor and American Politics. Urbana: University of Illinois Press, 1983. 249 pp.
Five cities (Rutland, Vermont; Rochester, New Hampshire; Kansas City, Missouri; Richmond, Virginia; and Milwaukee, Wisconsin) are analyzed as case studies of the political success achieved by the Knights of Labor during the critical year of 1886. Refuting the view that the Knights were strictly a manifestation of economic discontent, Fink points to their involvement in municipal politics as opposed to national politics. He challenges the theories of the Perlman-Commons school which argued that politics and trade unionism were diametrically opposed to one another and that this led to the Knights' fall. Fink demonstrates that the Knights of Labor was quite successful at local level politics. Its complementary status as labor union, cultural community and local political party gained it widespread if temporary success.

H 1562. FONER, PHILIP S. History of the Labor Movement in the United States. 6 volumes. New York: International, 1947-1982. 2688 pp.
Foner's multi-volume history chronicles the American labor movement from Colonial times until the entrance of the U.S. into W.W. I. Volume 1 covers the period of American labor from Colonial times to the establishment of the AFL in 1881. Volume 2 continues labor's story from 1881 until the close of the century. In Volume 3, Foner covers the policies and practices of the AFL during the period 1900-1909. Volume 4 is devoted entirely to the IWW. In Volume 5, the author examines the significance of organized labor during the Progressive era, particularly at state and municipal levels. Finally, in Volume 6, Foner looks at labor struggles on the eve of W.W. I.

H 1563. FONER, PHILIP S. Organized Labor and the Black Worker, 1619-1971. 1974; Rev. ed. New York: International, 1982. 492 pp.
Foner's book centers on the theme of racial discrimination in the American labor movement and the efforts of both blacks and whites to overcome it. He suggests that while many union leaders attempted to maintain racial solidarity--particularly within the Knights of Labor and the IWW--by the early 20th century, unions had succumbed to a racism institutionalized by organized labor and industrial mangement. However, Foner concludes, the CIO has contributed to the furtherance of interracial understanding.

600

H 1564. FUSFELD, DANIEL R. The Rise and Repression of Radical Labor
USA--1877-1918. Chicago: Charles H. Kerr, 1980. 46 pp.
Fusfeld chronicles the repression of labor militancy during the Populist
and Progressive periods. He contends that a rising militant and class-
conscious working class was beaten into submission by the dual powers
of state and industry. He argues that a coalition of corporate liberal
reformers and conservative labor leaders, by misleading and disarming
workers, ensured that repression would work. The feverish pitch of
patriotism which followed W.W. I and the popular hysteria brought about
by the Bolshevik Revolution provided the national atmosphere conducive
to the destruction of the labor movement in America.

H 1565. GALENSON, WALTER. The CIO Challenge to the AFL: A History of
the American Labor Movement, 1935-1941. Cambridge, Mass.:
Harvard University Press, 1960. 732 pp.
In this acocunt of the CIO challenge during the 1930s, Galenson examines
the course of union growth and policies in seventeen different industries.
Galenson concludes that the rise of the CIO profoundly altered the course
of American trade union history, resulting in the unionization of mass
production industries and altering the organizational and ideological
forms which had dominated American labor since the late 19th century.
However, Galenson argues, the AFL not only met the CIO challenge but
thrived during the W.W. II period. By the end of W.W. II, AFL membership
outnumbered that of the CIO.

H 1566. GARNEL, DONALD. The Rise of Teamster Power in the West. Berkeley:
University of California Press, 1972. 363 pp.
Until the 1920s, the local unions of the Teamsters operated within limited
labor markets and retained considerable autonomy. The technological transformation of motor transportation in the 1920s enlarged the dimensions
of those markets and brought about changes in the union's organizing and
administrative policies. Garnel's history of the unionization of the
Pacific Coast Highway trucking industry in the 1930s and 1940s describes
the Teamster's response to these new conditions by creating new area-wide
bodies to accommodate the highway drivers. This process was completed
by 1937 when the local union joined with the area-wide Highway Drivers'
Council to form a regional Teamsters' conference, the Western Conference
of Teamsters.

H 1567. GLABERMAN, MARTIN. Wartime Strikes: The Struggle Against the
No-Strike Pledge in the UAW During World War II. Detroit, Mich.:
Bewick, 1980. 158 pp.
Focusing on the wildcat strikes of 1944, Glaberman examines the growth
of radicalism in the UAW during W.W. II in response to the union's increasingly conservative leadership. The UAW's "no-strike pledge" became the
battleground between union leaders and left-wing critics. Wildcat strikes,
according to Glaberman, emerged spontaneously from a leaderless, unorganized rank and file, disillusioned with union bureaucratization and unwilling to allow its union's no-strike pledge to stand in the way of its own
best interests.

H 1568. GORDON, DAVID M., RICHARD EDWARDS, and MICHAEL REICH. Segmented
Work, Divided Workers: The Historical Transformation of Labor
in the United States. New York: Cambridge University Press,
1982. 288 pp.
The authors suggest that "three major structural transformations have
shaped the labor process and labor markets in the United States." "Pro-
letarianization" from 1820 to 1890 created a work force of wage laborers.
Crisis compounded by new technology distinguished the years from 1870
to W.W. II as a period of "homogenization" of workers. This development,
in turn, allowed employers to advance new tactics in their confrontation

601

with labor which resulted in a third period of "segmentation" that attempted to neutralize activist conflict.

H 1569. GREEN, JAMES R. The World of the Worker: Labor in Twentieth Century America. New York: Hill & Wang, 1980. 274 pp.
Green offers a broad overview of labor history in the U.S. from about 1880 to the present. His main concern is not with union leaders, but with the rank and file, the everyday worker. Green's primary theme is that of the workers' struggle for "control"--not necessarily meaning ownership of the means of production, but rather having the "freedom to determine certain activities at the workplace," that is, for workers' autonomy. Drawing on the most recent innovations and research of the new "social history," Green examines the fundamental changes wrought by the introduction of women and blacks into the industrial workforce. Finally, through a dialectical approach encompassing the political, social, and economic forces which affected and were affected by workers, Green sees as a central dynamic the struggle for power between workers and the established institutions of authority.

H 1570. GREEN, JAMES R., ed. Workers' Struggles, Past and Present: A "Radical America" Reader. Philadelphia: Temple University Press, 1983. 410 pp.
This work is a collection of twenty-one essays, by such authors as David Montgomery, Staughton Lynd, Nelson Lichtenstein, and others which appeared in Radical America between 1967 and 1982. The articles cover various topics dealing with working people's struggles against both employers for workers' control on the shop floor and against labor leaders for rank and file independence in the union hall. The various articles examine specific unions such as the Teamsters; certain industries such as steel; various individuals such as A. Philip Randolph; and particular groups such as blacks in Detroit.

H 1571. GREENE, VICTOR R. The Slavic Community on Strike: Immigrant Labor in Pennsylvania Anthracite. Notre Dame, Ind.: University of Notre Dame Press, 1968. 260 pp.
Greene investigates the connection of the Slavic community with labor unrest, attempts to offer an explanation for that behavior, and analyzes the effect of the activities of Slavic workers on industrial relations prior to 1903. Although Greene asserts that labor leaders in northeast Pennsylvania received Slavic immigrants with little enthusiasm, in reality the Slavic workers, families, and organizations supported labor protest more than other groups and were essential in the establishment of unions in the coal mining areas. Sources include Slavic accounts from parish histories as well as Slavic and English language newspapers.

H 1572. GREER, EDWARD. Big Steel: Black Politics and Corporate Power in Gary, Indiana. New York: Monthly Review Press, 1979. 287 pp.
Greer traces the history of blacks in Gary, Indiana, during the 20th century. According to the author, the rise of a black political power structure in Gary made no noticeable changes for the average city dweller. Greer examines the relationship between Gary's black power politics and its corporate power structure as well as U.S. Steel's exploitation of black workers and immigrants. According to Greer, the small business interests of Gary seldom acted to prevent U.S. Steel's exploitive practices, and seldom functioned as anything but a tool of corporate interests.

H 1573. GROB, GERALD. Workers and Utopia: A Study of Ideological Conflict in the American Labor Movement, 1865-1900. Evanston, Ill.: Northwestern University Press, 1961. 220 pp.
Grob sketches the development of workingmen's organizations during the late 19th century and describes labor's ideological responses to the changes in industry which had accompanied America's rapid economic growth. The author suggests that the early workingmen's groups were essentially reform-oriented political organizations. By the middle of the 19th century, however, the spread of the factory system gave rise to a new type of organization, the first of the trade unions that defined their goals in relatively narrow, economic terms. When growing economic and social conflict resulted in a serious organizational struggle, the Knights of Labor was destroyed and the trade unions created their own federation, the American Federation of Labor, which shortly became the dominant force in the American labor movement.

H 1574. GUTMAN, HERBERT G. Work, Culture, and Society in Industrializing America: Essays in American Working-Class and Social History. New York: Knopf, 1976. 343 pp.
In line with E. P. Thompson's analysis of the formation of the English working class, Gutman examines the creation of the American working class during the 19th century. The first essay deals with the challenges faced by people from preindustrial and immigrant cultures to the demands made by the factory discipline of the whistle and the clock. Gutman's other essays deal with various aspects of 19th-century working-class life and culture in America. One essay examines the importance of blacks in the United Mine Workers at the turn of the century. And another essay examines the social origins and mobility of the industrial elite in Paterson, New Jersey during the middle of the 19th century.

H 1575. HANLAN, J. P. The Working Population of Manchester, New Hampshire, 1840-1886. Ann Arbor, Mich.: UMI Research Press, 1981. 237 pp.
Hanlan uses company records, census manuscripts, town records, and newspapers to reconstruct the history of Manchester during the later half of the 19th century. He juxtaposes the town's social relations prior to the coming of the Amoskeag mills with that of the conflict which emerged after their arrival, and finds that "workers were not entirely victims of the industrialization process." Hanlan discerns a considerable degree of cultural continuity and ethnic cohesion from preindustrial to industrial Manchester, and argues that these preindustrial cultural values were a major factor in shaping the community which eventually emerged around the factories.

H 1576. HAREVEN, TAMARA and RANDOLPH LAUGENBACH. Amoskeag: Life and Work in an American Factory-City. New York: Pantheon Books, 1978. 395 pp.
Hareven and Laugenbach present an oral history of the workers at the Amoskeag Manufacturing Company in Manchester, New Hampshire, which was established as an example of the "new industrial order" by Boston entrepreneurs in the 1830s. Examined are first-generation immigrant workers as well as workers of second and third generations, owners of the corporation, families of workers, and the eventual strike and shut down of the factory in 1936. Contrary to the idea that large factories caused individual anomie and social fragmentation, Hareven and Laugenbach conclude that most of the workers had a highly developed sense of place and formed tightly knit societies around their family and ethnic association.

H 1577. HARRIS, HOWELL JOHN. The Right to Manage: Industrial Relations
          Policies of American Business in the 1940s. Madison: University
          of Wisconsin Press, 1982. 296 pp.
Concentrating on "central firms," Harris finds that the American business
community was the dynamic force in shaping the pattern of industrial relations in the 1940s. Labor, according to Harris, was merely reactive.
Business leaders helped shape public policy toward labor and stabilized
the shop. In addition, the leaders engineered acceptable contracts, and
confined unions to previously organized sectors, all of which are presented
as "valuable" gains.

H 1578. HENDERSON, JOHN P. Changes in the Industrial Distribution of
          Employment, 1919-1959. Urbana: University of Illinois Press,
          1961. 104 pp.
Henderson's study surveys annual employment data in all of America's major
industrial divisions. He tests the applicability of Petty's Law, which
states that the distribution of employment over time is characterized
by two basic shifts: a move from agriculture to manufacturing; and a
move from manufacturing into service industries. While Henderson discovers
that both shifts took place, only a small part of the increase in employment in the service sector (1919-59) was a result of a decline in the
goods-producing industries. Henderson finds that among goods-producing
industries, both mining and agriculture show an absolute decline in total
employment, while manufacturing and construction employment were steady
or rising.

H 1579. HEVENER, JOHN W. Which Side Are You On?: The Harlan County Coal
          Miners, 1931-39. Urbana: University of Illinois Press, 1978.
          216 pp.
Hevener documents the labor relations and social conditions of the Harlan
County miners during the 1930s. The book addresses a number of issues,
including union organizing campaigns and strikes and political corruption,
the successes and failures of New Deal labor policies, the social and
cultural attributes of the depressed Appalachian people, and the myth and
reality of American labor history. The author concludes that "more than
just a simple economic struggle to raise wages, shorten hours, and gain
job security, the union movement of the 1930s was a power struggle to
curb the operators' authoritarian control of the county's economic, political, and social life."

H 1580. HIRSCH, SUSAN E. Roots of the American Working Class: The Indus-
          trialization of Crafts in Newark, 1800-1860. Philadelphia:
          University of Pennsylvania Press, 1978. 170 pp.
Hirsch offers an analysis of the class structure of merchants, artisans,
and laborers in Newark in the first half of the 19th century. She suggests
that this class structure was broken down by industrialization, and was
replaced by a new structure of employers and workers, which emphasized
the relationship of people to the means of production. Politics are analyzed by Hirsch in terms of the development of status-ethnic competition
as the basis for party loyalty.

H 1581. HOERDER, DIRK, ed. American Labor and Immigration History, 1877-
          1920s: Recent European Research. Urbana: University of Illinois
          Press, 1983. 286 pp.
This volume is a collection of essays by thirteen European scholars on
American working class history during the late 19th and early 20th centuries, a period which witnessed both a rapid increase in industrialization
and in immigration. Hoerder has divided the essays into three parts:
one dealing with workers, intellectuals, and militancy; another focusing
on organization; and the last exploring immigration history from the perspective of European scholarship. The articles focus on the relationship

between the immigration of specific nationalities such as the Irish or the Finns to the U.S. and their subsequent activities in the labor market and in the labor movement. In addition, there are articles which examine the motivation for immigration and its impact on the homelands.

H 1582. HOWE, LOUISE KAPP. Pink Collar Workers: Inside the World of Women's Work. New York: Putnam, 1977. 301 pp.
Through primary research, statistical analysis, and personal interviews Howe examines jobs which society and the U.S. government have categorized as menial, low-paying women's work. Jobs such as beautician, sales worker, and waitress are characterized as "pink collar" jobs. The author concludes that while women entering positions dominated by men have received much attention, women's work is still a world apart. The majority of women workers remain relegated to positions of little respect and low pay.

H 1583. HUTCHINSON, JOHN. The Imperfect Union: A History of Corruption in American Trade Unions. New York: Dutton, 1970. 477 pp.
Hutchinson examines corruption in the American trade unions and the response of Congress to it. He also attempts to delineate labor's own efforts to overcome trade union corruption. Hutchinson suggests that while the labor movement did very little at first, George Meany did initiate a serious effort to rid the movement of crime after the AFL-CIO merger in 1955. Hutchinson argues that although corruption has continued to plague trade unions, both Meany's efforts and Congressional legislation combined to reduce the amount of corruption in the unions.

H 1584. JERNEGAN, MARCUS W. Laboring and Dependent Classes in Colonial America: 1607-1783. Chicago: University of Chicago Press, 1931. 256 pp.
These essays, first published during the 1920s, examine several previously neglected facets of the socio-economic conditions of the lower classes during the Colonial era. The author concentrates on the Southern and Northern Colonies. He examines aspects of slavery in Virginia and South Carolina, with particular reference to the slave as artisan rather than field laborer. He also discusses slave religious life. Jernegan compares indentured servitude in Virginia and New England, and examines some aspects of race relations between indentured servants and slaves. Finally, he considers the social and economic life of the white laboring classes of the Colonies, describing apprenticeship, public education, crime, and poor relief.

H 1585. KEERAN, ROGER. The Communist Party and the Auto Workers Unions. Bloomington: Indiana University Press, 1980. 340 pp.
Keeran argues that the Communist Party was the main expression of working-class radicalism in the U.S. from 1919 to 1949. During that period, the party had a dual character, a "blend" of national and international radicalism. In their emphasis on industrial unions during the 1930s, the Party worked extensively in organizing auto workers in Michigan. In organizing the first unemployment protests and sit-down strikes, the Party provides a base for the creation of the United Auto Workers union. During the period of cooperation and the Popular Front (1935-45), the party's influence among auto workers was significant. Eventually, however, the Left-Right division within the UAW that existed during W.W. II could not be bridged. The election of Walter Reuther as president in 1946 was a critical transition point in the union, which finally culminated in the ouster of the Party in 1949.

H 1586. KENNEALLY, JAMES J. Women and American Trade Unions. St. Albans, Vt.: Eden Press, 1978. 240 pp.
In this study of prominent women in the labor movement a history emerges of unions thwarting the efforts of women to gain representation. Male-dominated unions viewed working females as an "anomaly" which, they believed, pointed to the inadequacy of the male in the household. As a result, women had to fight a two-front war against sexism in the unions, which allowed them less than full partnership, and against their exploitation by management.

H 1587. KERN, ROBERT, ed. Labor in New Mexico: Unions Strikes, and Social History since 1881. Albuquerque: University of New Mexico Press, 1983. 349 pp.
This collection of eight essays by scholars in diverse fields explores a wide variety of topics relating to the lives of workers in New Mexico. The Knights of Labor, labor legislation, strikes, and women workers are among the topics explored. The editor offers the collection as a gauge against which to test national generalizations and as an attempt to relate the story of working class life in New Mexico.

H 1588. LASLETT, JOHN H. M. Labor and the Left: A Study of Socialist and Radical Influences in the American Labor Movement, 1881-1924. New York: Basic Books, 1970. 326 pp.
Laslett examines the relationship between organized labor and the political Left. Stressing the role of the affiliate unions of the AFL in terms of their actual locus of control within the labor movement, the author suggests that the success and failure of Socialism in the U.S. should be viewed as a product of what Laslett calls "American exceptionalism." He attributes the failure of Socialism within the unions to high wage levels, political pluralism, union pragmatism, and lack of class consciousness.

H 1589. LAURIE, BRUCE. Working People of Philadelphia, 1800-1850. Philadelphia: Temple University Press, 1980. 273 pp.
Laurie examines the many facets of working-class life in Philadelphia in the first half of the 19th century. He suggests the existence of three distinct forms of working-class culture in the early part of the century—the "revivalists" who accepted the new industrial discipline, the "traditionalists" who did not, and the "radicals" or free thinkers who retained a labor theory of value. Of these, Laurie suggests that radicalism failed because of the heterogeneity of Philadelphia's working-class culture and the weakness of the radical's producer ideology.

H 1590. LEVENSTEIN, HARVEY A. Communism, Anti-Communism, and the CIO. Westport, Conn.: Greenwood Press, 1981. 364 pp.
This is an account of relations between organized labor and the Left during the Roosevelt-Truman years. Levenstein details a multitude of splits between Communist political leaders and trade unionists and concludes that the Communists might have remained in their positions had it not been for the unrealistic demands of the Communist party leadership. Contrary to the notion that the 1930s was a period of general tolerance toward radicals, the author suggests that both government and the CIO were engaged in a continuing effort to undermine the Communists within the labor movement even before W.W. II.

H 1591. LEWIS, HAROLD G. Unionism and Relative Wages in the United States: An Empirical Enquiry. Chicago: University of Chicago Press, 1963. 308 pp.
Lewis examines the impact of labor unions on wage differentials among groups of workers. The issues covered include: the extent to which unions increased the wages of organized labor relative to the average wages of

all labor; the effect of unionism on the average wages of different industries; and to what extent the discernible impact of unions varied over
time as well as the reasons for that variation. The statistics, Lewis
contends, support his hypothesis that unions are more effective in maintaining wages in depressions than in raising them above levels set by the
market in times of near-full or full employment.

H 1592. LICHT, WALTER. Working for the Railroad: The Organization of
Work in the Nineteenth Century. Princeton, N.J.: Princeton
University Press, 1983. 328 pp.
This investigation of the daily lives of workers reveals that conflict
between workers and supervisors over conditions in the workplace often
sparked violent outbursts. In response to the violence which grew out
of arbitrary supervision and irregularly applied regulations, the railroads
replaced the traditional supervisors with the new standards and management
practices of the embryonic modern bureaucratic corporation. It was this
pattern of conflict and reparations, not a progressive search for efficiency, that produced change.

H 1593. LICHTENSTEIN, NELSON. Labor's War at Home: The CIO in World
War II. New York: Cambridge University Press, 1982. 319 pp.
Lichtenstein examines American political and labor history from the outbreak of W.W. II in Europe through the wave of major industrial strikes
which followed the War. He focuses on the internal organization of the
labor movement and on the relationship between the CIO, the AFL and the
Roosevelt Administration. Lichtenstein examines the transformation of
the CIO affiliates from unstructured, democratic, socially progressive
groups to a structured, centralized, conservative bureaucracy. He notes
how, under the leadership of Philip Murray and Walter Reuther, patriotism
and the fear of losing jobs to dissidents led to the CIO's cooperation
with the U.S. government.

H 1594. LINGENFELTER, RICHARD E. The Hardrock Miners: A History of the
Mining Labor Movement in the American West, 1863-1893. Berkeley:
University of California Press, 1974. 278 pp.
In response to the rapid mechanization of the mining industry, the hard
rock miners of the West turned to business unionism with some success
until the collapse of the silver market in 1893. The move to open pit
mining and the blurring of the distinctions between skilled and unskilled
positions "widened the breach between workers and owners." From this
perspective, violence was not the product of the rough frontier, but the
last resort of workers struggling against owners who had grown strong
enough to manipulate the law as "a tool of repression."

H 1595. LONDON, JOAN and HENRY ANDERSON. So Shall Ye Reap. New York:
Crowell, 1970. 208 pp.
This work is a history of the long struggle by the predominently Chicano
agricultural workers of California to organize themselves into unions.
The authors view this effort as one part of a world-wide movement for
social justice. After a brief survey of the agricultural industry in
California in the late 19th and early 20th centuries, and of the social
conditions of the workers, London and Anderson concentrate on the leaders
of the union movement: Father Thomas McCullough, Fred Van Dyke, Ernesto
Galarza and Cesar Chavez. They argue that the leaders, though important
organizers, must be seen within their social context. The leaders, the
authors note, were the focal point of a broadly based social movement,
which, they predict, will eventually succeed in gaining agricultural
laborers their rights.

H 1596. LONG, CLARENCE D. Wages and Earnings in the United States, 1860-
1890. Princeton, N.J.: Princeton University Press, 1960.
169 pp.
Long maintains that wages kept pace with productivity in the second half
of the 19th century. In analyzing daily wages and annual earnings, Long
finds they increased by approximately 50%. The decline in the cost of
living beginning in 1865 restored the dollar's buying power, so that the
real increase was also 50%. In addition, the author discovers that earnings were lowest in the South and highest on the Pacific coast. Differences were least pronounced among the Central, Mid-Atlantic, and New
England regions. He attributes approximately 20% of the overall wage
increase to shifts in the labor force from low to high paying industries.
Wages kept pace with productivity. And the greatest rises in wages and
productivity were concentrated in the 1880s, when capital-output ratios
also underwent a rapid increase.

H 1597. LUNT, RICHARD D. Law and Order Vs. the Miners: West Virginia,
1907-1933. Hamden, Conn.: Archon Books, 1979. 223 pp.
Following the U.S. Supreme Court's validation of individual employment
contracts (yellow dog contracts) in the famous case of Hitchman Coal Company v. Mitchell, Lunt explains how "law and order" worked against the
unionization of West Virginia miners during the first three decades of
the 20th century. The author then examines the way in which the Norris-
LaGuardia Act of 1932 and the National Industrial Recovery Act of 1933
reversed that precedent.

H 1598. MARSHALL, F. RAY. Labor in the South. Cambridge, Mass.: Harvard
University Press, 1967. 406 pp.
Stressing the South's historical uniqueness, Marshall examines the impact
of economics, demographics, geographics, and politics on the growth of
organized labor in the South. In his examination of major unions, trades,
and industries of the region, he discusses the union membership trends,
growth, and the impact of legislation. However, Marshall rejects the
notion that legislation had any significant impact on union growth; he
finds that economics far outweighed ideological, social, and political
factors in regard to union growth in the South.

H 1599. McKELVEY, JEAN TREPP. AFL Attitudes Toward Production, 1900-1932.
Ithaca, N.Y.: Cornell University Press, 1952. 148 pp.
McKelvey surveys the evolution of organized labor's attitude toward AFL
management and worker control of production. Prior to W.W. I, leaders
had resisted scientific management, convinced of a fundamental conflict
of interests between labor and capital. Labor's experiences during the
War, however, convinced many labor leaders that cooperation rather than
competition provided the best opportunities for labor, both organized and
unorganized. As a consequence, by 1932 organized labor had largely abandoned its earlier opposition to scientific management and the increased
productivity and reorganization of jobs and production techniques inspired
by it.

H 1600. McLAURIN, MELTON ALONZA. The Knights of Labor in the South.
Westport, Conn.: Greenwood Press, 1978. 232 pp.
Broad support for the Knights of Labor in the South suggests that Southerners were neither too docile nor too individualistic to organize. Initially strongest among white urban workers, the rise of the American Federation of Labor and the subsequent decision by the Knights to cooperate
with agrarian reformers changed the composition of the organization.
By the 1880s supporters were generally limited to the rural poor. The
Knights' appeal became limited by its inability to achieve results and
by the rise of the Colored Farmers' National Alliance.

H 1601. McWILLIAMS, CAREY. Factories in the Field: The Story of Migratory
         Farm Labor in California. Boston: Little, Brown, 1939. 334 pp.
McWilliams presents a general survey of California's first industry, agriculture, and of the workers who contributed to its development. The growth
of large-scale, intensive, and mechanized commercial agriculture in the
state was fast and furious, and represented a tremendous victory of technology over the arid environment. But these achievements did not occur
without profound and intense social conflict. McWilliams traces the history of racial and class exploitation of the migrant farm laborers, based
on an archaic system of land ownership dating, in some cases, back to Spanish rule. The oppression of Chinese, Japanese, Mexican, as well as native
laborers constitutes one of the "ugliest" chapters in the history of American industry, McWilliams maintains. And in spite of efforts on the part
of some organizers, the poor progress of the labor movement can be traced
to the relentless onslaught of capital, as well as the conservative nature
of the existing trade unions.

H 1602. McWILLIAMS, CAREY. Ill Fares the Land: Migrants and Migratory
         Labor in the United States. Boston: Little, Brown, 1944.
         419 pp.
In this study of two groups of migrant workers in American agriculture--
those who are depression and removal migrants and those who are habitual
migrant workers following an established migratory route--McWilliams calls
attention to the effect of technological displacement following the industrialization of American farms. In Book I, the author considers changes
in California agriculture, a typical way station for migrant workers,
and one family's attempt to make a place for themselves as farmers in California. Book II argues that the processes and problems described in Book
I are typical of the country. In Book III, McWilliams studies habitual
migrant labor and changes in migrant labor patterns due to industrialization. Finally, Book IV describes and analyzes general aspects of change
in agriculture, agricultural migration, and migrant worker life.

H 1603. MEIER, AUGUST and ELLIOTT RUDWICK. Black Detroit and the Rise
         of the UAW. New York: Oxford University Press, 1979. 289 pp.
The focus of this book is the role of black workers in the rise of the
United Auto Workers during the period 1935-45. Meier and Rudwick examine
the successful formation of a coalition between black rights organizations
and trade union leaders in the auto industry. Further, the authors explore
the changing activity of black workers' involvement in the auto unions
of the late 1930s, as well as the increasing visibility of a dissident
element within the black community of Detroit beginning with the Ford
organizing campaign of 1941.

H 1604. MEYER, STEPHEN III. The Five Dollar Day: Labor Management and
         Social Control in the Ford Motor Company, 1908-1921. Albany:
         State University Press of New York, 1981. 249 pp.
Meyer examines the development of the Ford Motor Company in its early
days, from 1908 to about 1921. His main concern is with the workers--
especially the impact of technology on the work process and management's
conscious effort to control labor--but he also examines the evolution
of the Ford Company's management. Meyer explores the development of
new industrial technology, the workers' reactions to the changes it caused,
and managerial efforts to overcome worker resistance to the new process
of production. While the "Five Dollar Day" has traditionally been viewed
as an example of Henry Ford's benevolence, Meyer argues that it was actually a means by which the company was able to establish greater control
over the work force at the workplace as well as the employees' personal
lives. Labor resisted these controls throughout the turbulent 1910s and
W.W. I, the result being greater union militancy. Meyer concludes with
the political repression of labor activists which followed the war, and

maintains that the Five Dollar Day was a failure as a long-term policy objective to control labor.

H 1605. **MILTON, DAVID.** The Politics of U.S. Labor: From the Great Depression to the New Deal. New York: Monthly Review Press, 1982. 182 pp.
Milton suggests that the price paid for the CIO's success was the workers' loss of control of the workplace. This trade-off which occurred during the 1930s, whereby the workers gave up their historic working class vision, was brought about as a direct consequence of Franklin Roosevelt's political maneuvering. In an effort to gain the support of the working class, Roosevelt convinced workers to trade off "political independence for economic rights" through the practice of collective bargaining. This, Milton contends, brought workers into the mainstream of the capitalist structure.

H 1606. **MONTGOMERY, DAVID.** Beyond Equality: Labor and the Radical Republicans: 1862-1872. New York: Knopf, 1967. 508 pp.
Montgomery analyzes the composition, ideology, and program of the American labor movement during the Civil War and Reconstruction. He argues that Radical Republicanism was an ideology consisting of different strands which represented different social forces. He sees manufacturers, workers and others marching under this banner during the war. After the war the bands were loosened as the national emergency had ended and nationalism was no longer sufficient to hold conflicting groups together. The concrete example he gives is the struggle for the eight-hour day which began in earnest around 1866. Radical Republicans, Montgomery argues, felt that labor was becoming too radical and attempting to go beyond political equality and toward economic equality. Since these Republicans would not work toward that end, labor sought political independence in a third party. With this rupture the Radicals lost their leadership within the broader party ranks.

H 1607. **MONTGOMERY, DAVID.** Workers' Control in America: Studies in the History of Work, Technology and Labor Struggles. New York: Cambridge University Press, 1979. 189 pp.
In this series of essays, Montgomery argues that industry's move toward scientific management and assembly line production in the first quarter of the 20th century was accompanied by a movement by workers to maintain traditional work patterns. The author traces "workers' control" from the late 19th-century craftsmen trying to protest their skills to the failure of the New Deal to supply workers with more control of the productive process. Montgomery contends that although management had gained the edge in the struggle to control the workplace during the 1920s, workers' control struggles reemerged in the 1930s, and forced state intervention to curb the worst excesses of management authority.

H 1608. **MORRIS, RICHARD B.**, ed. A History of the American Worker. Princeton, N.J.: Princeton University Press, 1983. 271 pp.
This collection of essays by leading labor historians represents a broad survey of American labor history from the Colonial period to the present. Essay topics include labor-capital struggles in the period of industrialization, the American labor movement from 1900 to the Great Depression, the changing role of organized labor in the 1930s and 1940s, and the future of collective bargaining. Contributors include, among others, Richard Morris, David Montgomery, Philip Taft, and Irving Bernstein. Morris includes a comprehensive bibliography, a glossary of labor terms, and a chronology of important dates in America working-class history.

H 1609. NADWORNY, MILTON J. Scientific Management and the Unions, 1900-
1932: A Historical Analysis. Cambridge, Mass.: Harvard University Press, 1955. 187 pp.
Nadworny provides an account of the development and operation of the Taylor
system of scientific management. He also examines the attitudes of union
leaders toward the practice and philosophy of scientific management.
Nadworny contends that an initial period of union hostility was succeeded,
after 1920, by years of cautious accommodation between scientific managers
and unions. Initially, both had sought unilateral power to determine
the organization of industrial production. The experiences of W.W. I,
however, encouraged greater union interest in production, leading toward
a more cordial relationship between unions and industrial engineers.

H 1610. NASH, MICHAEL. Conflict and Accommodation: Coal Miners, Steel
Workers, and Socialism, 1890-1920. Westport, Conn.: Greenwood
Press, 1982. 197 pp.
This study explores the relation between class conflict and class consciousness as reflected in electoral politics. Nash first traces labor relations
in the coal and steel industries during the 1880s and 1890s, and then
investigates the bituminous--or soft coal--strike of 1894, the anthracite
strike of 1902, the Bethlehem steel strike of 1915, and the Green Steel
Strike of 1919. Nash finds that violent class conflicts resulted in radicalization at the polls, of which the Populists and the Socialists were
the main beneficiaries. However, Nash finds that these changes were
extremely temporary, and that most unions and workers would later return
their votes to the two major parties.

H 1611. NELSON, DANIEL. Managers and Workers: Origins of the New Factory
System in the United States, 1880-1920. Madison: University
of Wisconsin Press, 1975. 234 pp.
Nelson describes the transformation of the factory in America between 1880
and 1920, and the rise of the "new factory system" which became the foundation of modern industrial administration. The dominant themes of this
new system were the substitution of formal, centralized controls for ad
hoc, decentralized controls, and the increasing influence of management
over the factory and its labor force. Nelson argues that there were three
essential dynamics at work in this process: the technological dynamic--
in which technological innovation transformed the factory design and
environment; the managerial dynamic--in which management attempted to impose
order and system on the manufacturing organization; and the personnel
dynamic--whereby management made deliberate efforts to organize and control
the factory labor force. This process had its greatest effect in large
manufacturing plants, such as textile, or iron and steel production.
Nelson sees industrial management based on scientific management principles
as a 20th-century innovation.

H 1612. NIELSON, GEORGIA PANTER. From Sky Girl to Flight Attendant:
Women and the Making of a Union. Ithaca, N.Y.: Industrial and
Labor Relations Press, 1982. 160 pp.
Nielson's book traces the "feminization of an occupation" from its beginning
in the 1920s through the emergence of the nation's only female-dominated
union in the 1970s. In an effort to achieve recognition as a group, attendants battled companies who saw women as cheap labor and marketing attractions and male-dominated locals that offered to include the attendants
only as a means of controlling them. Attendants encountered further resistance from the AFL-CIO, which refused to unify them as a single union,
and a Federal government which only reluctantly recognized their unionization.

H 1613. OZANNE, ROBERT. A Century of Labor Management Relations at
          McCormick and International Harvester. Madison: University of
          Wisconsin Press, 1967. 300 pp.
Emphasizing the impact of unionism, Ozanne examines the evolution of labor
management relations in a large corporation during the hundred years that
followed the Civil War. The early unions, Ozanne suggests, were flexible;
their failure was due to superior managerial power. Indeed, anti-union
attitudes shaped many management policies at McCormick and International
Harvester. Later, management invested in a series of welfare measures
and in 1903 created a personnel department to coordinate its welfare activities. Ozanne concludes that the major goal of these activities was to
prevent unionization. Not until government pressure was brought to bear
on the corporation during W.W. II did it reluctantly agree to bargain
with independent unions.

H 1614. OZANNE, ROBERT. Wages in Practice and Theory: McCormick and
          International Harvester, 1860-1960. Madison: University of Wis-
          consin Press, 1968. 181 pp.
Ozanne analyzes the factors shaping the wage movements of McCormick and
International Harvester. He finds that unionism had a pronounced effect
on the changing pattern of wages. For example, periods of rapid increase
in real wages are characterized by increases in union strength. Investigating the influence of other variables, Ozanne discovers that low demand
for labor has brought wage cuts during depressions, but that periods of
prosperity have not witnessed comparable increases. Nor is there a correlation between rising productivity and rising wages. Further, Ozanne
finds there is no correlation between profit and wage levels at International Harvester.

H 1615. PARMET, ROBERT D. Labor and Immigration in Industrial America.
          Boston: Twayne, 1981. 268 pp.
Parmet examines labor's restrictionist attitude toward new immigrants
in the late 19th century. His account begins with a discussion of the
anti-Chinese movement and organized labor's support for the enactment
of Chinese exclusion laws. Parmet then focuses on labor's response to
Southern and Eastern European immigrants. He suggests that prejudice
in the labor movement stemmed from labor's struggle to survive in a society dominated by industrial Capitalism. The book closes with a discussion
of the 1917 Literacy Act and the refugee crisis of the 1930s and W.W.
II.

H 1616. PERLMAN, SELIG. A Theory of the Labor Movement. New York:
          Macmillan, 1928. 321 pp.
In contrasting the American labor movement to those in other industrialized
nations, Perlman argues that the American Federation of Labor was largely
successful because its leadership understood the necessity of a united
economic front. The AFL leaders, Perlman maintains, recognized and indeed
believed in the importance of private property and personal initiative
in economic life, and eschewed more radical notions of working for fundamental changes in the American economic system. This "conservative" outlook was more acceptable to American workers than were the more radical
ideologies of the Socialists, Communists, or syndicalists.

H 1617. PERRY, LOUIS B. and RICHARD S. PERRY. A History of the Los Angeles
          Labor Movement, 1911-1941. Berkeley: University of California
          Press, 1963. 622 pp.
The Perrys examine the Los Angeles labor movement between 1911 and 1941
as a unique study of the labor movement in a major urban area. They claim
that the Los Angeles labor experience was unique because of its organization, leadership, union composition, and basic philosophy. In addition,
aside from San Francisco, no other American city had as powerful a group

of employers protecting their interests as Los Angeles. The work deals
with "urban" Los Angeles, and the authors admittedly neglect the agricultural labor movement in the area. The years between 1911 and 1941 witnessed a fundamental change regarding the conditions of, and the prevailing
attitudes toward, organized labor. This change was a result of the New
Deal, W.W. II, infiltration of Los Angeles by national industries accustomed to dealing with unions, and also of the establishment of Los Angeles
itself as a large, modern metropolis.

H 1618. **PESSEN, EDWARD.** Most Uncommon Jacksonians: The Radical Leaders
of the Early Labor Movement. Albany: State University of New
York Press, 1967. 208 pp.
In this historical analysis, Pessen suggests that the ideas of Jacksonian
labor leaders regarding the ills of American society were the direct offshoot of English radical thought of the Enlightenment. These men were
legitimate radicals, highly critical of an American society governed by
a self-seeking elite. Pessen first examines the Workingmen's party and
the trade union movement during the Jacksonian era. He then discusses
the careers and beliefs of a number of notable Jacksonian labor leaders,
including Thomas Skidmore, Robert Dale Owen, and William English.

H 1619. **PROSPER, PETER ANTHONY, Jr.** Concentration and the Rate of Change
of Wages in the United States, 1950-1962. New York: Arno Press,
1977. 144 pp.
After examining the rate at which wages changed over a twelve-year period,
the author concludes that "wages in more highly concentrated industries
rose relatively faster" than wages in other industries. Because of the
importance of the concentrated industries, this pattern of continual wage
increases helped to explain the phenomenon of rising wages in periods
of economic recession. In addition, Prosper finds considerable interdependence among wage changes, productivity changes, price changes, and
concentration.

H 1620. **RADOSH, RONALD.** American Labor and United States Foreign Policy.
New York: Random House, 1969. 463 pp.
As a consequence of its commitment to American Capitalism, organized labor
has officially supported U.S. foreign policy in the hope of gaining more
benefits for the working class. Where differences have occurred between
labor and government, they have been over style and tactics and not over
fundamental issues. In an effort to support Capitalism, labor's programs
have become anti-revolutionary, interventionist, and supportive of American
Cold War policies. This has led to the support of right-wing governments
in an effort to curb radicalism abroad. Radosh suggests that contrary
to their leaders' efforts, American workers have not benefited from these
expansionist practices.

H 1621. **RAMIREZ, BRUNO.** When Workers Fight: The Politics of Industrial
Relations in the Progressive Era, 1898-1916. Westport, Conn.:
Greenwood Press, 1978. 241 pp.
Ramirez attempts to analyze the relationship between collective bargaining
and the struggle for control of the workplace between labor and capital.
He suggests that collective bargaining appealed to management because
it represented a means for containing labor, and it appealed to labor
because it facilitated the institutional recognition of labor's new bargaining power. It also appealed to the political structure because it
represented a means by which to control the conflict between labor and
capital.

H 1622. RAYBACK, JOSEPH G. A History of American Labor. 1959; Rev. ed. New York: Macmillan, 1966. 459 pp.
Rayback's history of the American labor movement focuses on the modern era of trade union organization. The rise of the trade union is placed in the context of the rapid spread of mechanization in industry. Rayback describes the AFL's early growth, internal debates over structure, the attitudes of employers and government toward the attempts of trade unions to increase union influence, and the impact of radical ideas on the labor movement. In dealing with the preindustrial era, Rayback discusses free labor in Colonial times and in the years during the first half of the 19th century.

H 1623. REED, MERL E., LESLIE S. HOUGH, and GARY M. FINK, eds. Southern Workers and Their Unions, 1880-1875: Selected Papers, the Second Southern Labor History Conference, 1978. Westport, Conn.: Greenwood Press, 1981. 249 pp.
This collection of nine essays were first delivered at the Southern Labor History Conference in 1978. Authors and topics include, among others, Mark Wetherington on the strike of black workers in Savannah in 1891; Robert Ingalls on the 1931 strike of Tampa cigar workers; George Hopkins on Appalachian coal miners and union insurgency during the 1960s; and Robert McElvaine on organized labor and the Civil Rights movement in Mississippi from 1959 to 1966. The editors point to the activism of Southern workers and the changing fortunes of labor as central themes in many of the essays.

H 1624. REES, ALBERT. Real Wages in Manufacturing, 1890-1914. Princeton, N.J.: Princeton University Press, 1961. 163 pp.
Rees examines real wages between 1890 and 1914 and concludes that the previous estimates of the cost of living during this period have been upwardly biased. By using retail price data and by constructing an index of rents, Rees shows that the cost of living for these years was significantly below previously estimated levels. On the other hand, he finds that the available money wage estimates were largely correct. Thus real wages actually rose. The annual average rate of increase, 1.3%, was slightly lower than that estimated for 1860-90, and appreciably lower than the rate of increase since 1914. Rees shows that the rate of real wage growth equalled the rate of productivity increase.

H 1625. RODGERS, DANIEL T. The Work Ethic in Industrial America, 1850-1920. Chicago: University of Chicago Press, 1978. 300 pp.
This is a study of ideas about work; in particular, "it is a study of those threads of ideas that came together to affirm work as the core of the moral life." In preindustrial America, there was an unequaled commitment to the moral primacy of work. But the Industrial Revolution, Rodgers argues, left in tatters the network of economics and values that had given it birth. Northerners so radically transformed work that the old moral expectations would no longer hold. The triumph of industrialization thus was an ironic one, and throughout this volume Rodgers pursues one basic question: "What happened to work values when work itself was radically remade?"

H 1626. SCHATZ, RONALD W. The Electrical Workers: A History of Labor at General Electric and Westinghouse, 1923-1960. Urbana: University of Illinois Press, 1983. 279 pp.
Schatz examines the rationale and consequences of the CIO's unionization efforts within two electronic manufacturing companies and traces the decline of the union movement in both. Central to the study is the United Electrical, Radio and Machine Workers of America, the largest Communist-dominated union of the 1940s, and a leading labor voice in the technological fields. The author concludes that the resolution of political con-

614

flicts among union members and organizers was as important as resolving the struggles between workers and employers.

H 1627. SCHWANTES, CARLOS A. Radical Heritage: Labor Socialism, and Reform in Washington and British Columbia, 1885-1917. Seattle: University of Washington Press, 1979. 288 pp.
This book attempts to answer two questions: why political radicalism, industrial unionism, and dual unionism became so significant in the Pacific Northwest labor movement prior to W.W. I; and why the workers of British Columbia were able to build a strong Socialist Labor Party while their fellow workers to the South failed to do so. Schwantes suggests that a few highly developed urban centers, and a class of ruthless, exploitive entrepreneurs created an environment conducive to the formation of class consciousness and radical unionism. The failure to achieve a strong Socialist Labor Party is said to be the result of the ideology of individualism unique to America.

H 1628. SCHWIEDER, DOROTHY. Black Diamonds: Life and Work in Iowa's Coal Mining Communities, 1895-1925. Ames: Iowa State University Press, 1983. 203 pp.
Schwider examines the evolution of Iowa's coal mining communities from the late 19th century to 1925. Because the deposits of coal were relatively limited in Iowa, mining there was originally considered to be a "short-term" industry. Before it declined, however, the industry managed to attract workers whose presence changed the ethnic composition of the state, and who initiated the process of unionization. Schweider examines this union movement in the Iowa coal mines, and gauges the effect unionism had on the workplace, on women and the family, and on the ethnic community.

H 1629. SEATON, DOUGLAS P. Catholics and Radicals: The Association of Catholic Trade Unionists and the American Labor Movement, from Depression to Cold War. Lewisburg, Pa.: Bucknell University Press, 1981. 269 pp.
Seaton's book covers the influential Association of Catholic Trade Unionists from its conception in 1937, until the purge of the left from the CIO in 1949. The author contends that the Catholic Church has kept the American labor movement on a conservative path and that the ACTU was the organization that accomplished this during the latter half of the Great Depression, W.W. II and the early part of the Cold War. Seaton argues that tensions existed within the organization over whether to make anti-Communism or social justice the primary focus. Although anti-Communism especially after 1945 became the principal aim, the ACTU itself was accused by those who were anti-labor as being communistic. Although officially sanctioned by the Church, the ACTU was viewed suspiciously by many in the Catholic hierarchy and many among the laity. After 1949, like the Communist Party, it too was isolated from the labor movement mainstream.

H 1630. SHERGOLD, PETER R. Working-Class Life: The "American Standard" in Comparative Perspective, 1899-1913. Pittsburgh, Pa.: University of Pittsburgh Press, 1982. 306 pp.
Shergold examines the standard of living of industrial workers in Pittsburgh and Birmingham, England. He details wage structures, family incomes, food prices, and rents. Shergold argues that American workers were not substantially better off than their British counterparts. However, he maintains that class unity was less evident in Pittsburgh because of an inegalitarian income structure, ethnic heterogeneity, and racial prejudice. These factors, and not higher wages, fostered the growth of business unionism, rather than the class-oriented union movement which developed in Britain.

615

H 1631. SIRACUSA, CARL. A Mechanical People: Perceptions of the Industrial Order in Massachusetts, 1815-1880. Middletown, Conn.:
Wesleyan University Press, 1979. 313 pp.
Siracusa focuses on the working class response to industrialization.
Through an analysis of the speeches and published writings of leading
political figures, mainly Whigs, Democrats, and Republicans, he concludes
they generally praised the diversification of economic activity resulting
from industrialization. He then proceeds to examine why the process of
industrialization, with its accompanying social and economic changes,
gained significant support among the people of Massachusetts during this
period.

H 1632. STEIN, LEON. The Triangle Fire. Philadelphia: Lippincott, 1962.
224 pp.
Relying on the testimony of survivors and contemporary reporters, Stein
tells the story of the March 25, 1911 Triangle Shirtwaist Company fire
in which 146 people died. In the first part of the book he describes
the fire itself, the futile attempts of the workers to escape, and the
scene in the morgue. The second part of the book deals with the aftermath
of the tragedy, including chapters on the offers of help to the families
of the victims, the cries of protest, and the fight for protective legislation. Stein ends the book with the story of another tragic fire occurring forty-seven years later not far from the scene of the initial tragedy.

H 1633. STEINBERG, RONNIE. Wages and Hours: Labor and Reform in Twentieth-
Century America. New Brunswick, N.J.: Rutgers University Press,
1982. 274 pp.
This quantitative study examines the development of protective labor laws
as social reform. State and Federal laws are dealt within separate sections. Early laws applied to specific workers in limited areas. Protection was extended in the 1930s and 1940s as new legislation emerged and
old laws were modified and updated. The author examines the conditions
which prompted these laws, and discusses several theories concerning the
process of social legislation.

H 1634. SUGAR, MAURICE. The Ford Hunger March. Berkeley: Meiklejohn
Civil Liberties Institute, 1980. 146 pp.
Sugar's book examines Detroit's Ford Hunger March which occurred on March
7, 1932. Organized by the Unemployed Council and the Auto Workers Union
of the Trade Union Unity League (TUUL), this action resulted in the death
of four marchers and the wounding of two dozen others by police. Sugar's
account includes the resulting investigation and an examination of the
American Communist Party's considerable involvement in the event.

H 1635. SUTHERLAND, DANIEL E. Americans and Their Servants: Domestic
Service in the United States from 1800 to 1920. Baton Rouge:
Louisiana State University Press, 1981. 229 pp.
Sutherland draws a portrait of household and hotel laborers in the 19th
and early 20th centuries. He describes the servant shortage, the
employer's definition of a good servant, the household duties of servants,
and servant relationships and wages. The author also examines the mechanization of the home, which resulted in the decline of the domestic service
system in 20th-century America.

H 1636. TAFT, PHILIP. The A.F. of L. in the Time of Gompers. New York:
Harper, 1957. 508 pp.; The A.F. of L. from the Death of Gompers
to the Merger. New York: Harper, 1959. 499 pp.
In the first volume of her history of the American Federation of Labor,
Taft discusses the founding and early formative years of the AFL during
which the Federation developed its economic and political policies, including the rejection of Socialism and industrial unionism. The second volume

616

covers the dramatic appearance of the Congress of Industrial Organizations, the increase of political activism, and the labor movement's response to such events as the Cold War, the Civil Rights movement, and the emergence of the welfare state.

H 1637. **TAFT, PHILIP.** Organizing Dixie: Alabama Workers in the Industrial Era. 1980; Revised and edited by Gary M. Fink. Westport, Conn.: Greenwood Press, 1981. 228 pp.

In analyzing the trade union movement in Alabama in the late 19th and early 20th centuries, Taft rejects the assumption that Southern workers were unusually docile and willing to work for substandard wages. Examining the mining, textile, steel, and rubber industries, Taft discovers that Southern workers were neither ignorant of their exploitation nor uncritical of the paternalistic Southern economic elite. The formation of trade unions, however, forced workers to oppose the established order and racial conventions, action that risked social ostracism and sometimes death. Although by the 1960s, organized labor was a political force in Alabama, it was still fragmented by the inbred racism of many of its members.

H 1638. **ULMAN, LLOYD.** The Rise of the National Trade Union: The Development and Significance of Its Structure, Governing Institutions and Economic Policies. Cambridge, Mass.: Harvard University Press, 1955. 639 pp.

Ulman describes and analyzes the emergence of national labor unions from initial stages through national expansion. Workers originally banded together in local organizations, but as a result of changes in production methods and the development of a national market, worker organizations expanded to national membership. Thereafter the personal character of labor-management relations became increasingly impersonal, while the political and social functions stressed by early labor societies were being replaced by the wage-bargaining system.

H. 1639. **URBAN, WAYNE J.** Why Teachers Organized. Detroit, Mich.: Wayne State University Press, 1982. 202 pp.

Urban's monograph traces the history of teacher unionism during the period 1890-1930. Arguing along economic lines, the author cites salary schedules, equal pay, and tenure as the major issues around which the teachers united. Three major cities—Atlanta, Chicago, and New York—are used as case studies in this investigation. Two national associations, the American Federation of Teachers and the National Educational Association, are the key organizations around which the movement revolved. Urban stresses the usurpation of power from teachers by superintendents as a consequence of the "reform movement of the period."

H 1640. **VAN TINE, WARREN R.** The Making of a Labor Bureaucrat: Union Leadership in the United States, 1870-1920. Amherst: University of Massachusetts Press, 1973. 230 pp.

To explain the rise of trade union bureaucracy from 1870 to 1920, Van Tine focuses on the varying social backgrounds of labor leaders, the changing ideology of unionism, and the development of labor-management relations. He stresses the reorientation of union aims under the AFL, which unlike earlier organizations, accepted the existence of industrial Capitalism. This fostered the development of the "business unionist," who emphasized "bread-and-butter" issues rather than an overhaul of the economic system. Van Tine argues that the evolution of union structure and changes in rank-and-file attitudes also reflect the increased bureaucratization of American life at the turn of the century.

H 1641. WALKOWITZ, DANIEL J. Worker City, Company Town: Iron and Cotton
Worker Protest in Troy and Cohoes, New York, 1855-84. Urbana:
University of Illinois Press, 1978. 292 pp.
Walkowitz contrasts the development of labor protest in two cities with
different industrial and social histories. Troy was an iron city with
a long tradition of skilled male labor. Cohoes was a textile town with
women and children composing a large part of the work force. The textile
industry had undergone early mechanization, and technological innovations
continued to intervene in working-class lives throughout the period of
this study. The author compares the two cities, looking at ethnicity,
the disparate labor experiences, and the formation of working-class culture,
to understand the factors that contributed to working-class protest.

H 1642. WALSHOK, MARY LINDENSTEIN. Blue-Collar Women: Pioneers on the
Male Frontier. Garden City, N.Y.: Anchor Press, 1981.
310 pp.
Walshok seeks to shed light on the processes by which women break into
traditionally male dominated blue-collar jobs, and the relationship between
the women and their new roles. The book has three parts. In the first
part Walshok examines the various motives behind women's decisions to
seek employment in non-traditional work situations, and concentrates on
the role of the family and upbringing in contributing to these decisions.
In Part Two she treats blue-collar women on the job, focusing on job experiences, work relationships, and factors which contribute to job success.
Part Three looks at the reaction of the family to the women's new roles,
and also examines policies related to recruitment, training and retention
of blue-collar women in non-traditional employment. Walshok concentrates
on the experiences of California women during the 1970s, and includes
an appendix which addresses the issue of sociological research methods,
which include the interviewing of various groups of women over a number
of years.

H 1643. WARE, NORMAN J. The Labor Movement in the United States, 1860-
1895. New York: Appleton, 1929. 409 pp.
Ware's historical chronicle focuses on the Knights of Labor and on the
personality of Terence Powderly. Powderly's private letters, which had
become available in 1917, serve as one of the author's primary sources.
Ware details the Knights of Labor's internal dissents and jealousies.
He suggests that the Knights' failure to live up to the ideals which they
espoused should be seen as the product of human foolishness. He also
argues that in order to understand the labor movement during this period
one must consider Powderly's ineffectiveness and Samuel Gompers's unscrupulous nature as having been detrimental to the success of the Labor movement.

H 1644. YEARLEY, CLIFTON K., Jr. Britons in American Labor: A History
of the Influence of the United Kingdom Immigrants on American
Labor, 1820-1914. Baltimore, Md.: Johns Hopkins University
Press, 1957. 332 pp.
This volume examines how immigrants and ideas from the United Kingdom
influenced the early modern labor movements in the U.S. Yearley's survey
is a broad one, spanning the influx of English, Scottish, Welsh, and Irish
organizers to the U.S. between 1860 and 1914, as well as their leadership
roles in the early American miner, metalworker, and textile worker unions.
The author also examines the influence of the moderate amalgamated unions
in Britain on U.S. labor, and the spread of cooperative movement throughout
post-Civil War America.

H 1645.   ZIEGER, ROBERT H.   Republicans and Labor, 1919-1929.   Lexington:
          University of Kentucky Press, 1969.   303 pp.
Zieger's book concerns the methods by which the Republican administration
of Harding and Coolidge had successfully resolved the country's post-W.W.
I labor conflicts.   The author suggests that during the Harding Presidency,
Secretary of Commerce Herbert Hoover promoted industrial peace through
measures which were not favored by business interests.   Through his support
of immigration restrictions and of the three eight-hour shift day as
opposed to the standard two twelve-hour shift day maintained by the steel
industry, the Republican administration was favored by labor.   Zieger
suggests that both Harding and Coolidge supported a policy of neutralizing
the labor question by remaining out of the disputes as much as possible.
Consequently, the government's once traditional pro-management position
was soon replaced by a more neutral policy which allowed conflict situations to resolve themselves.

XIV.   BUSINESS HISTORY

H 1646.   ADAMS, DONALD R., Jr.   Finance and Enterprise in Early America:
          A Study of Stephen Girard's Bank, 1812-1831.   Philadelphia:
          University of Pennsylvania Press, 1978.   163 pp.
Adams argues that the enterprises of Stephen Girard provide a significant
link between the commercial-agrarian economy of the 18th century and the
dynamic economic system of the 19th.   Girard's decision to establish a
bank in 1812 typifies the early 19th-century trend in which mercantile
capital shifted into new types of investments; his bank developed strong
ties with internal improvement projects and became an important mechanism
for easing the flow of capital into developmental ventures.   Noting its
close involvement in government finance, Adams describes the operations
of Girard's bank from its foundation to its transformation into a chartered
bank four years after Girard's death in 1831.   Paying particular attention
to the bank's profitability, he finds that it compared favorably with
the non-bank enterprises that were the more usual recipients of mercantile
capital during this period.   Girard's bank was unique in enjoying considerable success at a time when private banks were generally being displaced
by chartered institutions.

H 1647.   ADLER, DOROTHY R.   British Investment in American Railroads, 1834-
          1898.   Charlottesville: University of Virginia Press, 1970.
          253 pp.
Adler points out that the American economy in the 19th century was accompanied by a marked increase in the volume of private capital flowing into
the country from abroad, and these funds played an important role in American economic development in general and in the growth of the railroad
industry in particular.   Adler charts the flow of British capital and
describes its origins, the different forms it took, and the uses to which
it was put.   After the Civil War, rentier investment became more common,
and the British market for high-yield American railroad bonds became much
wider.   In the third of Adler's periods (1879-1898), the flow of capital
for investment in income-producing rather than speculative ventures continued.   The London market grew, and during these years there was an
increase in active British participation in the direction and management
of the affairs of American railroad companies, a development motivated
at least in part by a desire to protect income-producing investments which
by 1890 amounted to 20% of the railroad industry's total capitalization.

H 1648. **ALBION, ROBERT G.** The Rise of New York Port, 1815-1860. New
York: Scribner, 1939. 485 pp.
Albion describes the process by which New York obtained and maintained
its position as America's leading seaport, stressing its importance to
import trade. In the decade of the 1820s, crucial innovations in transportation technology and in access to the interior ensured that New York
would maintain its position as America's leading port. Of these innovations, the opening of the Erie Canal in 1825 was clearly the most dramatic.
But the preoccupation of historians with the growing flood of goods from
the interior, Albion argues, has obscured New York's importance in importing. Even before the canal opened, the sailing and later steam packet
services established after the end of the War of 1812 had already confirmed
New York's premier position in transatlantic trade. As important was
New York's growing domination of the cotton trade. Hegemony in the European and Southern trading routes gave New York an unmatchable position
as an entrepot, a position reinforced by the opening of the interior
route to the West and sustained by continued innovations such as the introduction of steam power. By 1860, New York was handling two-thirds of
the nation's imports as well as one-third of its exports and was exceeded
only by London and Liverpool in total volume of shipping.

H 1649. **ALLEN, FREDERICK LEWIS.** The Great Pierpont Morgan. New York:
Harper, 1949. 306 pp.
One of the earliest "revisionist" studies of leading American capitalists,
Allen's biography of J. P. Morgan attempts to assess the financier's
general impact upon the American economy. Allen stresses Morgan's central
position in the nation's rapidly expanding industrial economy and argues
that he should be remembered as a rationalizing and disciplining force.
In this view, J. P. Morgan brought peace and cooperation through reorganization of railroads plagued by destructive competition; Morgan constantly
intervened to reform and strengthen businesses and to encourage their
growth. Without minimizing the great private power accumulated by Morgan,
Allen says that promotion of order in place of cutthroat competition in
transportation and manufacturing benefited the public. Indeed, he concludes, Morgan was motivated throughout his career less by an ambition
to accumulate personal wealth and power than by a commitment to serve
the public.

H 1650. **BABCOCK, GLENN D.** History of the United States Rubber Company:
A Case Study in Corporate Management. Bloomington: Bureau of
Business Research, Indiana University, 1966. 477 pp.
As a retired manager of the United States Rubber Company, Babcock surveys
the 20th-century history of the firm, which was founded in 1896 and which
brought together a number of rubber boot and shoe manufacturers into one
corporation. He narrates the development of corporation policy on such
subjects as accounting and finance, marketing, personnel and organization,
production management, product development, industrial engineering, public
relations, business law, international operations, and other similar topics.
The narrative ends with the early years of W.W. II, a time when the corporation was well established as one of America's largest manufacturing concerns.

H 1651. **BACHMAN, VAN CLEAF.** Peltries or Plantations: The Economic Policies of the Dutch West India Company in New Netherland, 1623-
1639. Baltimore, Md.: Johns Hopkins University Press, 1969.
183 pp.
Bachman argues against the traditional explanation for New Netherland's
lack of economic development in the late 1620s—that the Dutch West India
Company simply neglected the colony. According to him, the early history
of the Dutch colony of New Netherland was shaped instead by the inability
of the Company to decide between a policy of extracting maximum short-

run profits from the regional fur trade and a policy involving longer-term commitment to colonization and the production of agricultural staples. The first alternative would bring quick returns on a small investment but would almost certainly entail the loss of the unpopulated territory to a rival European power; the second would improve the Company's chances of retaining control of its investment but would add to the Company's costs, while disrupting the fur trade. In large part the Company's indecision reflected the extent of its commitment to other, more important commercial ventures in the Western hemisphere.

H 1652. BARGER, HAROLD. The Transportation Industries 1889-1946: A Study of Output, Employment, and Productivity. New York: National Bureau of Economic Research, 1951. 288 pp.
Analyzing the sixty years after 1890, Barger finds that the transportation industries experienced substantial overall growth in employment, productivity, and the volume of passenger and freight services supplied. Although the industries' relative contribution to national income declined from one-twelfth to one-fifteenth, productivity grew at an average annual rate of 2.2%, a performance not matched by any other sector of the economy. The author offers a detailed treatment of the performance of the transportation industries, separately and as a whole. He notes the resiliency of coastwise water transportation, the relative decline of steam and electric railroads, and the rapid growth of the new industries—pipelines and air travel. The most significant overall movement has been from rails to highways, and the only interruption in this secular trend occurred as a result of W.W. II.

H 1653. BARGER, HAROLD and HANS H. LANDSBERG. American Agriculture, 1890-1939: A Study of Output, Employment and Productivity. New York: National Bureau of Economic Research, 1942. 440 pp.
Barger and Landsberg examine agriculture at the point when the amount of land used for farming ceased to expand. They compile output figures for commodities such as grains, cotton, sugar, and livestock. The authors seek to determine how efficient U.S. farms were in utilizing their labor supply. Agriculture, they conclude, improved its output per worker at an annual rate of 1% to 1.5% between 1900 and 1930. In the Great Depression productivity declined; during W.W. II it increased dramatically.

H 1654. BARGER, HAROLD and SAM H. SCHURR. The Mining Industries, 1899-1939: A Study of Output, Employment and Productivity. New York: National Bureau of Economic Research, 1944. 452 pp.
This volume focuses on long-term trends in mining industries. The authors determine and index the output of the various sub-industries in mining (fuels, metals, miscellaneous other materials). They also provide data on employment and on the productivity of labor, technological changes in mining, and the relationship between technology and increases in productivity. While mining as a whole experienced dramatic increases in output per man per day, most of these advances took place in one part of the industry—petroleum mining.

H 1655. BAXTER, WILLIAM T. The House of Hancock: Business in Boston, 1724-1775. Cambridge, Mass.: Harvard University Press, 1945. 321 pp.
Baxter examines the mercantile careers of Thomas and John Hancock of Boston, concentrating especially on the former. The author describes the form and content of their commercial activities and business methods, showing that the Hancocks's operations were plagued by bad communications and by the lack of a reliable medium of exchange. They dealt—mostly on a small scale—in a wide range of products at wholesale and retail; they bought and sold ships as well as produce, doing business wherever immediate opportunities (legal or otherwise) arose. Profiting from the unique oppor-

tunities generated by wars and by government contracts, Thomas Hancock
became one of the wealthiest men in the Colonies by the end of his career.
John Hancock, on the other hand, Baxter explains, was more patriot than
businessman.

H 1656. BAYLEY, STEPHEN. In Good Taste: Style in Industrial Products
         1900 to 1960. New York: Van Nostrand, 1979. 255 pp.
Both the text and the photographs in this volume show how ideas about
the look of machines developed over a crucial sixty-year period. American-
made products and firms represented in this British study of international
trends include the Edison Home Model-A phonograph (1898), the Zippo cigar-
ette lighter (1932), the Parker arrow pen (1954), and the IBM golfball
electric typewriter (1961). Capsule statements about top industrial
designers and their clients appear at the end of the book.

H 1657. BERNSTEIN, MARVER H. Regulating Business by Independent Commission
         Princeton, N.J.: Princeton University Press, 1955. 306 pp.
Bernstein analyzes the commission form of regulations and argues that
commissions have been unsatisfactory instruments of government. After
describing the origins of the regulatory movements in the years 1877 to
1920, when America's modern administrative state was beginning to take
shape, Bernstein traces the intellectual currents that have characterized
the movement since 1920, pointing out that the supporters of this political
innovation have maintained throughout a faith in rational solutions by
experts. The author, however, is highly critical of the results of regulation in America. The commissions go through a regular life cycle of
four phases: gestation; youth; maturity, which is accompanied by devitali-
zation; and old age, which is characterized by debility and decline.
In the end, only the regulated parties normally want to keep the independent regulatory commission in operation, and they do so because they have
captured the commission and shaped it to their own--and not the public's--
ends.

H 1658. BLACKFORD, MANSEL G. The Politics of Business in California,
         1890-1920. Columbus: Ohio State University Press, 1977.
         221 pp.
This study examines the relationship between business groups and the process of politico-economic reform in California. Blackford concentrates
on three of the state's most important productive industries--agriculture,
oil, and lumber--and three supportive industries--banking, investment
banking, and insurance. He also examines the coalitions that formed around
two major issues: tax reform and railroad and public utility regulation.
He finds that business groups reacted to rapid industrial development
by mobilizing behind a broad spectrum of private and public issues.
Despite intense activity, they achieved only partial success in their political agendas. Blackford attributes this outcome to inadequate conceptualization of the problems they confronted, to political opposition from non-
business elements, and to dissension within their own ranks over such
questions as the effect of conservation measures on profitability. In
most cases, Blackford says, political compromises emerged which served
to reinforce pluralist rather than elitist strains within American politics.

H 1659. BRINGHURST, BRUCE. Antitrust and the Oil Monopoly: The Standard
         Oil Cases, 1890-1911. Westport, Conn.: Greenwood Press, 1979.
         296 pp.
This book is an attempt to uncover the reasons behind the failure of antitrust legislation to preserve competition and limit corporate power.
The author focuses on state and Federal efforts to control the Standard
Oil Corporation and concludes that despite the genuine concerns of lawmakers over the spread of monopoly, antitrust legislation has primarily
served as a mechanism for coping with public hostility toward big business.

H 1660. BRUCHEY, STUART W. Robert Oliver, Merchant of Baltimore, 1783-1819. Baltimore, Md.: Johns Hopkins University Press, 1957. 411 pp.
Bruchey treats Robert Oliver, one of the most prominent American merchants of the early national period, as representative of the resident merchants typical of that era of commercial Capitalism, in that his interests were wide and his business was marked by diversity rather than by specialization. The structure of his business—a family partnership—was also typical, and Bruchey describes the firm's day-to-day operations, including its relations with overseas agents, its internal administrative practices, and its general commercial policies. Bruchey stresses the high degree of flexibility Oliver displayed in adapting to changes in commercial conditions due to the international struggles of these years.

H 1661. BRUCHEY, STUART W., ed. Small Business in American Life. New York: Columbia University Press, 1980. 391 pp.
This collection of seventeen essays explores the impact of industrialization on small business from the late 18th century to the present. Leading economic, social, and labor historians have contributed selections on artisans, mechanics, small manufacturers, bankers, and retail shopkeepers; on "the rise of little business" in a period of increasing consolidation; and on the reciprocal influence of small business on other areas of economic, social, and cultural life. James Soltow, Harold Vatter, and Susan Hirsch take up the reasons for technological inventiveness in small manufacturing and electronics firms; Stuart Blumin explores the emergence of white-collar occupations; Eli Ginzberg and others draw on the behavioral sciences to shed light on small-scale entrepreneurship as a cultural phenomenon.

H 1662. BULEY, R. CARLYLE. The Equitable Life Assurance Society of the United States, 1859-1964. 2 vols. New York: Appleton-Century-Crofts, 1967. 1475 pp.
Buley's history of The Equitable charts the progress of the company which, almost from its inception, has dominated American life insurance and that by 1855 had become the largest insurance company in the world. Throughout its first forty years, the company was tightly controlled by its founder and major stockholder, Henry Baldwin Hyde, who guided its rapid early expansion by basing the company's business primarily on the promotion of tontine (or deferred dividend) life insurance. Following Hyde's death in 1899, there was a struggle over his successor, a conflict that helped precipitate the Armstrong Insurance Investigation of 1905. Buley describes the investigation and also chronicles the successful reorganization of the company in these years. Thereafter, he analyzes its investment policies, which ranged from cautious conservatism in the 1930s to renewed expansion after W.W. II.

H 1663. CAROSSO, VINCENT P. Investment Banking in America: A History. Cambridge, Mass.: Harvard University Press, 1970. 569 pp.
Carosso describes the specialized investment banks that arose during the late 19th century when the rapid development of an industrial economy in the U.S. had begun to generate demands for capital far in excess of the volume that could be supplied through the existing unspecialized middlemen (such as merchants) or through commercial banks. Carosso follows the development of investment banks through the 1950s, concentrating on the techniques and institutions of investment banking in New York. Dealing in special depth with the merchandizing of securities and the provision of services to issuers by the banks, Carosso finds that political and economic changes in the 20th century have altered the methods bankers employ to accumulate and direct the movement of capital funds. On balance, however, the economic function of the investment banks—the channeling of savings into longterm investments—has not changed in this century.

H 1664. CARROLL, CHARLES F. The Timber Economy of Puritan New England.
Providence, R.I.: Brown University Press, 1973. 221 pp.
Carroll gives a detailed assessment of the manner in which the early settlers used the vast timber resources of New England, and he explains the
forest industries' impact on 17th-century New England commercial economy.
In exploiting timber resources, the settlers initially concentrated on
developing wooden products for domestic use and for sale to new arrivals.
With the passing of the great migration in the early 1640s, however, the
money supply used to purchase English manufactures dried up, and the settlers had to find new ways to finance their purchases of English imports.
This led to the commercial exploitation of the forests; over the second
half of the 17th century, lumbering became the major industry of Northern
New England. The products of forest industries were of great importance
in trade, at first with the wine islands and Southern Europe, later with
England, the other mainland Colonies, and the West Indies.

H 1665. CHANDLER, ALFRED D., Jr. Strategy and Structure: Chapters in
the History of the Industrial Enterprise. Cambridge, Mass.:
MIT Press, 1962. 463 pp.
This book details the origins of the 20th-century American firm that is
characterized by decentralized organization and diversified operations.
In order to demonstrate that organizational innovations in corporate structure followed strategic entrepreneurial decisions about a firm's markets
and technological capabilities, Chandler concentrates on four pioneering
corporations--DuPont, General Motors, Standard Oil of New Jersey, and
Sears, Roebuck--all of which experienced substantial alterations in administrative and managerial structure following initial entrepreneurial
responses to important market changes. The book offers both a general treatment of these changing patterns of business behavior and a detailed description of how and why particular businessmen in these firms went about the
task of improving their corporations' structure.

H 1666. CHANDLER, ALFRED D., Jr. The Visible Hand: The Managerial Revolution in American Business. Cambridge, Mass.: Harvard University Press, 1977. 608 pp.
Chandler's synthesis of business history describes the development of
modern business enterprise in America; he shows how the "visible hand"
of management gradually replaced the "invisible hand" of the market mechanism in coordinating the distribution of goods and services with demand.
Chandler traces a complex causal chain in which market and transportation
developments led to innovations in production and distribution, which
in turn led to organizational innovations that enabled a new breed of
managers to coordinate the process of production. Finally, mass production
and mass distribution were combined within the same enterprises, setting
the scene for the emergence of the modern industrial corporation. The
author emphasizes that the growth of modern corporate enterprise in America
is a story of entrepreneurial response to changes in demand and to technological innovations in the process of production and distribution.

H 1667. CHANDLER, ALFRED D., Jr. and STEPHEN SALSBURY (with the assistance
of Adeline Cook Strange). Pierre S. DuPont and the Making of
the Modern Corporation. New York: Harper & Row, 1971. 722 pp.
Chandler and Salsbury trace the business career of DuPont, who was the
leading organizational architect of the giant General Motors Company at
a time when that firm was on the brink of collapse in the early 1920s.
They explain that after DuPont became an executive in the corporation
in 1902, the company experienced the tremendous growth that made it one
of America's leading firms by the 1920s. One of DuPont's major accomplishments was to preside over the 1920 decentralization that enabled the corporation to diversify efficiently and to manage widespread operations with
success. Later DuPont helped GMC adopt the same decentralized structure,

a new bureaucratic form that enabled GMC to seize the leading position in the automobile industry. The authors argue that as an organizational innovator, DuPont was exemplary because he managed to reorganize the firm and at the same time to keep the family's position intact.

H 1668. CLARK, VICTOR S. History of Manufactures in the United States.
3 vols. Washington, D.C.: Carnegie Institution, 1924.
1640 pp.
These volumes, which are based on documentary sources, describe the origin and development of manufacturing in the U.S. Commencing his account with the earliest settlements rather than focusing on the shorter period usually identified with "industrialization," Clark studies the factors which encouraged the growth of productive capacity in the manufacturing sector of the economy. His narrative stresses the particular aspects of specific industries, but Clark also offers a few generalized conclusions. He asserts, for example, that manufacturing has been the most important single factor in the transformation of American society and culture, exerting its influence by generating an abundance which during the early 19th century was already breaking down class distinctions and multiplying opportunities throughout society. He also attributes the enormous growth in manufacturing output to technical progress rather than to America's abundant natural resources or to the entrepreneurial skills of the country's citizens.

H 1669. COCHRAN, THOMAS C. American Business in the Twentieth Century.
Cambridge, Mass.: Harvard University Press, 1972. 259 pp.
Treating business as a social rather than a merely economic institution, Cochran places 20th-century business in a broad historical context that reaches backward into the Colonial era and outward to encompass cultural factors and political movements. He describes developments in small firms as well as those in the giant corporations that usually dominate our histories of the modern era. According technology a primary role in 20th-century business development, the author briefly reviews some of the major new technological industries and describes changes in older ones, and he also discusses the transformation of the political environment for business. In addition to the increasingly important role of government, Cochran also finds that organized labor and research and development have played crucial roles in the progress of business and the entire economy. Reviewing these and related changes, he concludes that business has actually strengthened its position in the American social order, in part because of diminishing differences between businessmen and institutions on the one hand, and the rest of society on the other.

H 1670. COCHRAN, THOMAS C. Business in American Life: A History. New York: McGraw-Hill, 1972. 402 pp.
Cochran maintains that throughout 300 years of American history, business has been more important than any other social institution in shaping American life. Beginning in the Colonial period, the author explores the dynamic interactions between business and businessmen and other American institutions, including the family as well as educational, religious, legal, and political institutions. While acknowledging that at times these relationships have been antagonistic, Cochran's survey stresses the positive manner in which business has influenced society.

H 1671. COCHRAN, THOMAS C. Frontiers of Change: Early Industrialism in America. New York: Oxford University Press, 1981. 179 pp.
According to Cochran, progress is a product of geography and culture. In comparing the early industrializing process of Britain and America, he suggests that although the two nations were somewhat similar geographically, America has a unique culture that allowed it to industrialize at an accelerated rate, a rate perhaps even greater than that of Britain.

America's immigrant-based, emerging culture emphasized craftsmanship, innovation and problem-solving; it encouraged risk-taking and openness to change; and it placed a premium on multi-skilled artisans as opposed to specialized workers. Cochran discusses the process of industrialization, as well as the achievements of America's industrializing culture and the effects of these achievements in 18th- and 19th-century American life.

H 1672. COCHRAN, THOMAS C. The Pabst Brewing Company: The History of an American Business. New York: New York University Press, 1948. 451 pp.

Cochran's history of the Pabst Brewing Company discusses all aspects of the company's institutional development, with particular emphasis on the period of rapid growth and rising profitability from the time of its incorporation in 1873 until the advent of Prohibition in 1919. During these years Pabst became a national enterprise, serving widespread markets and striving to dislodge smaller but well-entrenched local producers. Cochran considers the strategies of competition in the industry. He shows how breweries competed by soliciting the favors of the independent saloon-keepers who controlled the retail outlets, and how the brewers ultimately sought to integrate production with distribution by acquiring direct control of the retail trade. This proved a successful strategy and Cochran explains that in this regard Pabst followed a course similar to that adopted by many large firms in America's modern corporate economy.

H 1673. COCHRAN, THOMAS C. Railroad Leaders, 1845-90: The Business Mind in Action. Cambridge, Mass.: Harvard University Press, 1953. 564 pp.

Cochran explores the nature of the business culture, which, he holds, has had a decisive impact on American society. Analyzing the correspondence of the top managing executives of all Class I railroads throughout the later half of the 19th century, he describes, compares, and evaluates their expressed views on a wide range of business, political, and social topics. Cochran establishes profiles of the major social roles played by businessmen and shows how these roles influenced their ideas and actions. Finally, the study explains how these railroad leaders thought about subjects ranging from competition to labor relations, from their general social responsibilities to their necessary involvement in the day-to-day affairs of politics.

H 1674. CREAMER, DANIEL, SERGEI P. DOBROVOLSKY, and ISRAEL BORENSTEIN. Capital in Manufacturing and Mining: Its Formation and Financing. Princeton, N.J.: Princeton University Press, 1960. 344 pp.

This volume focuses on secular changes in capital stocks, capital-output ratios, and sources of investment. In Part I, Creamer and Borenstein present an analysis of capital and output in manufacturing and mining. Their findings indicate a long-term retardation in the rates of growth of both capital formation and output, which suggests that the industries had life-cycles that were reflected in their capital-output ratios and that ratio-raising factors, such as technological innovations, dominated an industry's early development, but not its maturity. This concept bears on Part II of the volume, in which Dobrovolsky discusses sources of capital financing. He concludes that internal funds have always outweighed external sources in importance and that the proportion of internally generated funds in total capital formation is increasing. Resorting to external funds is associated with bursts of rapid growth of the sort that usually occur in the early years of an industry's life cycle. This in turn indicates that as an industry matures, the contribution of depreciation charges to gross capital formation becomes of greater importance.

H 1675. DAVIS, PEARCE. The Development of the American Glass Industry. Cambridge, Mass.: Harvard University Press, 1949. 316 pp. According to Davis, the history of American glass manufacture is one of long-run expansion against the competition of European products; after the American Revolution, however, the French Revolution relieved this competitive pressure and stimulated the domestic industry's growth. By 1820, glass production was firmly established in the U.S. and total output continued to grow in the years that followed. The most significant changes came, however, in the period after 1890, with the introduction of new and more efficient machinery and the transformation of the industry's organization and productive relationships. By 1925, glass manufacture had become a typical large-scale, mass-production industry characterized by heavy capital investments. In the course of describing this industry's history, Davis analyzes the relationships between the growth of the industry and the government's tariff policy. He also examines the rise of organized labor after the Civil War to assess its impact on the industry's performance.

H 1676. DU BOFF, RICHARD B. Electric Power in American Manufacturing, 1889-1958. New York: Arno Press, 1979. 249 pp. This book explains how power production became centralized in one industry, supplying its output to a wide range of consumers who had formerly produced their own. The research shows that the most rapid power transformation in the manufacturing sector took place in the decade between 1909 and 1919. The author emphasizes the economics of power production and its impact on the output-capital ratio in manufacturing.

H 1677. EARLE, CARVILLE V. The Evolution of a Tidewater Settlement System: All Hallows' Parish, Maryland, 1650-1783. Chicago: University of Chicago, Department of Geography, 1975. 239 pp. This treatise in economic and cultural geography exposes the early development of a staple economy in Maryland. Earle describes the pervasive tobacco culture of the 17th- and 18th-century Chesapeake area, analyzing the complex relationships between tobacco production and marketing, and the patterns of settlement, land use, and transportation. Placing these developments in a context provided by the physical characteristics of the area and by the North Atlantic commercial system in which tobacco was traded, he shows that population gradually increased until the parish had an unfavorable man/land ratio; by that time, tenancy had become common and out-migration was on the rise. Earle shows how individual plantations, as well as the parish, responded to these changes, as well as to short-term fluctuations in the tobacco market.

H 1678. EAST, ROBERT A. Business Enterprise in the American Revolutionary Era. New York: Columbia University Press, 1938. 387 pp. East examines the Colonial background of corporate enterprises that were organized in the years after the American Revolution. He finds that although pre-Revolutionary business was expansive in character and responsible for numerous private commercial fortunes, it did not result in any major innovations in the organization of business. Few mechanisms for group investment existed, little such investment was undertaken, and the basic unit of non-agricultural economic organization was the individual merchant-capitalist using his own funds. However, the Revolution rearranged the pattern of commerce, stimulated domestic manufactures, and kindled an enterprising and associative spirit. Business interests began to band together for collective survival, creating new sorts of capitalist enterprise, such as commercial banks. Commercial interests sought public policies favorable to their enterprises. Their victory was confirmed with the adoption of the Constitution, which set a seal of national approval on the ascendancy of business interests over agrarian provincialism

H 1679. EICHNER, ALFRED S. The Emergence of Oligopoly: Sugar Refining
as a Case Study. Baltimore, Md.: Johns Hopkins University Press,
1969. 388 pp.
Noting that historians and economists have long been concerned with the
causes and results of the great merger movement of 1895-1907, Eichner
identifies the major source of the movement toward consolidation as being
an entrepreneurial desire to eliminate the price competition that was
threatening profits. In the 19th century, technological advances had
progressively rendered products more homogeneous and had lowered unit
costs. Furthermore, the rapid expansion of the domestic market through
transportation innovations had also led to the creation of new enterprises
that proliferated in an economic setting approaching that of perfect competition. Price-cutting led businessmen to experiment with informal agreements to limit output and maintain prices, but these understandings collapsed, and alternate forms of cooperation, such as trusts, were rendered
illegal. Entrepreneurs in sugar and other industries thus turned to corporate consolidation. At first their goal was monopoly, but the government's
antitrust policy forced them to accept oligopoly. As the leading firms
in the sugar refining industry improved their internal administrations
and their relations with one another, however, they settled into stable
patterns of economic behavior. In his analysis, Eichner emphasizes the
role that public policies played in shaping business behavior.

H 1680. EMMET, BORIS and JOHN E. JEUCK. Catalogues and Counters: A History of Sears, Roebuck and Company. Chicago: University of
Chicago Press, 1950. 788 pp.
This volume traces the evolution of the mail order catalogue as an institution and as a piece of Americana. The book places Sears in the larger
context of mass merchandising, the expansion of distribution and mail
networks, and the growth of rural consumer markets. Later sections deal
with corporate reorganizations under Robert Wood, who guided the company's
shift into department store retailing in the 1920s.

H 1681. ENGELBOURG, SAUL. Power and Morality: American Business Ethics
1840-1914. Westport, Conn.: Greenwood Press, 1980. 181 pp.
The author contends that during the period covered, business ethics fundamentally changed as a result of the increasing size and impersonality
of the American firm. Pools, for instance, had no legal standing and
businessmen either joined, adhered to, circumvented, or withdrew from
them as their interests seemed to dictate, even though they accepted pooling as a general principle. According to the author, such developments
represented a basic shift away from the controls that had regulated the
small, family-run enterprise.

H 1682. FABRICANT, SOLOMON. The Output of Manufacturing Industries, 1899-
1937. New York: National Bureau of Economic Research, 1940.
685 pp.
While providing statistics on the output of the nation's manufacturing
industries, Fabricant places the manufacturing sector in the context of
the entire national economy, discusses changes in productivity, and looks
at the growth of manufactures as an aspect of the more general process
of modern economic growth. The study includes detailed figures on the
output of various industries and major groups of industries. Fabricant
also offers an index for the total output of all manufacturing industries
in the U.S.

H 1683. FELL, JAMES E., Jr. Ores to Metals: The Rocky Mountain Smelting
Industry. Lincoln: University of Nebraska Press, 1980. 341 pp.
Much of Fell's study focuses on Colorado, where smelters appeared as early
as the 1860s in response to the miners' need for technologies that could
recover gold, silver, and other metals from ores resistant to better-known

methods of reduction. The discussion explains these processes and examines how the industry evolved from one composed of some thousand isolated enterprises into one dominated by several integrated firms.

H 1684. FENSTERMAKER, J. VAN. The Development of American Commercial Banking: 1782-1837. Kent, Ohio: Kent State University Press, 1965. 247 pp.
Fenstermaker studies both the national and regional aspects of the expansion of commercial banking. He explains that such banks first appeared in America in the late 18th century and began to spread early in the 19th century, when domestic and overseas markets grew and producers sought credit to expand production. The requirements of state governments for funds to finance internal government projects added to this growing demand for both long- and short-term capital. During the 1820s and 1830s, commercial banking thus enjoyed a rapid expansion. Fenstermaker finds that the spread of commercial banking materially aided the growth of the American economy, promoting the exchange of goods and services by providing a usable circulating medium to supplement the scarce supplies of specie and making funds available to both public and private borrowers.

H 1685. FISHLOW, ALBERT. American Railroads and the Transformation of the Antebellum Economy. Cambridge, Mass.: Harvard University Press, 1965. 452 pp.
Fishlow offers statistical evidence for his contention that railroads made an important and direct contribution to the growth of national income during the thirty years before the Civil War. He measures the railroads' direct contribution—through the extended transportation network and reduced transportation costs--to the growth of Gross National Product, estimating this at 4% of GNP by 1859. Placing the railroads in the context of the antebellum economy, he also determines their indirect economic effects, concluding that their impact was felt primarily in the agricultural sector. Fishlow stresses the role that the railroads played in hastening the expansion of commercial agriculture and Westward movement of settlers: in industry, the railroads' demand for rails stimulated technological advances in the manufacture of iron; commercially, the rails reinforced the already established East-West trading pattern. Fishlow finds that the railroads attracted large amounts of investment capital, helped quicken the pace of agricultural development, and created the foundation for the national market that would develop after the Civil War.

H 1686. FOGEL, ROBERT W. Railroads and American Economic Growth: Essays in Econometric History. Baltimore, Md.: Johns Hopkins University Press, 1964. 296 pp.
Fogel evaluates the contribution of railroad development to the overall growth of the American economy in the 19th century. Critical of previous historians' impressionistic emphases upon the "revolutionary" impact of the railroad, Fogel measures the direct and indirect benefits of railroad expansion. He uses econometric techniques as well as a counterfactual model and claims that railroad development had little effect on the costs of long-haul, bulk transport. The rails had a greater effect on short-haul costs, but the total social saving attributable to railroad use (compared with the alternative of a hypothetical canal-road system) amounted to only 4% of the Gross National Product in 1890. This figure, he says, is too small to justify the conclusion that the rails were an indispensable element in American economic development in the 19th century. Fogel argues that indirect effects were also insignificant; the stimulus felt by other parts of the economy as a result of railroad construction and the related demand for goods were not of any great importance. He concludes that no single innovation was absolutely essential to the nation's 19th-century growth.

H 1687. FRESE, JOSEPH R. and JACOB JUDDS, eds. Business Enterprise in Early New York. Tarrytown, N.Y.: Sleepy Hollow Press, 1979. 210 pp.

This collection of seven essays illuminates the development of business enterprise in New York before 1815. Thomas Cochran's opening remarks comment upon the rapid movement toward industrialization in the newly created U.S. Other contributors include Lawrence Leder on "Military Victualing in Colonial New York"; William Chazanof on "Land Speculation in Eighteenth-Century Colonial New York"; Barbara A. Chernow on "Robert Morris and Alexander Hamilton: Two Financiers in New York"; David L. Sterling on "William Duer, John Pintard, and the Panic of 1792"; Irene D. Neu on "Hudson Valley Extractive Industries before 1815"; and Milton M. Klein on "From Community to Status: The Development of the Legal Profession in Colonial New York." Government support of business is a dominant theme in these considerations, which also stress the high failure rate of business in this period.

H 1688. FRESE, JOSEPH R. and JACOB JUDD, eds. An Emerging Independent American Economy, 1815-1875. Tarrytown, N.Y.: Sleepy Hollow Press, 1980. 207 pp.

This volume includes seven papers on American enterprise. The authors emphasize aspects of the following topics that are particularly relevant today: Glenn Porter, "Technology and Business in the American Economy"; Dolores Greenberg, "Energy Flow in a Changing Economy, 1815-1880"; John F. Stover, "Canals and Turnpikes: America's Early Nineteenth-Century Transportation Network"; Ann M. Scanlon, "The Building of the New York Central: A Study in the Development of the International Iron Trade"; Harry H. Pierce, "Anglo-American Investors and Investment in the New York Central Railroad"; Edward Pessen, "The Business Elite of Antebellum New York City: Diversity, Continuity, Standing"; and Robert Lekachman, "American Business--Then and Now."

H 1689. FREYER, TONY ALLAN. Forms of Order: The Federal Courts and Business in American History. Greenwich, Conn.: JAI Press, 1979. 187 pp.

Freyer examines the interaction of law and business, combining research from his doctoral dissertation on Swift v. Tyson (1842)--a leading decision by the U.S. Supreme Court involving Federal jurisdiction over disputes arising out of interstate commercial activity--with new material presenting a more general analysis of the private law evolved by Federal judges in response to the growth of national business. Although emphasizing the antebellum period, he notes that confusion arising from the Federal pattern of shared sovereignty between state and national government persisted until the appearance of national regulatory agencies and uniform state codes in the early 20th century.

H 1690. FRIEDLAND, WILLIAM H., AMY E. BARTON, and ROBERT J. THOMAS. Manufacturing Green Gold: Capital, Labor and Technology in the Lettuce Industry. New York: Cambridge University Press, 1981. 159 pp.

This study examines the production of iceberg lettuce in America and focuses, in particular, on the development of a mechanical lettuce harvester and the consequences which resulted from harvester mechanization. The authors make three assertions: labor supply and control are critical, independent variables in the examination of work organization in all production systems and have been especially important in agriculture; the range of choices of new technologies will be greatly influenced by the economic organization of the industry and the relative power of the individual firms in the industry; differential outcomes, in terms of technological change, that result from change in the labor supply, control variable, will also be influenced by the interaction between the economic organization and the labor supply, control variables.

H 1691. **GALAMBOS, LOUIS P.** American Business History. Washington, D.C.:
Service Center for Teachers of History, 1967. 32 pp.
This essay reviews the origins and development of business history as
an academic discipline. The author sheds light on the evolution of this
discipline, which initially concentrated on institutional histories of
individual enterprises and profiles of particular businesses, and later
investigated the structure of business organizations and various business
strategies.

H 1692. **GALAMBOS, LOUIS P.** Competition and Cooperation: The Emergence
of a National Trade Association. Baltimore, Md.: Johns Hopkins
University Press, 1966. 329 pp.
In this study of the emergence and functioning of trade associations in
the cotton textile industry after the Civil War, Galambos describes three
distinct stages in the organization's evolution. Before 1900, regional
associations in New England and the Southeast developed out of social
gatherings at which businessmen met to exchange information. Between
1900 and 1925, the regional associations were transformed from rudimentary,
ad hoc organizations into so-called "service" organizations which had
permanent staffs and a broad range of economic and political programs.
However, full cooperation awaited the emergence of a national association
capable of planning for the industry as a whole. In cotton textiles,
this third stage was reached in 1926, with the creation of the Cotton
Textile Institute as a policy-making association having as its central
goal the overcoming of the industry's problems of overproduction and
destructive competition. The Cotton Textile Institute, with the support
of the government, tried unsuccessfully to control output and administer
prices. From 1932 through 1935 the Institute was a prime mover in the
search for political means of controlling competition, but after the demise
of the National Recovery Administration, the Institute reverted to the
status of a service organization.

H 1693. **GALAMBOS, LOUIS P.** (with the assistance of Barbara Barrow Spence).
The Public Image of Big Business in America, 1880-1940: A Quantitative Study in Social Change. Baltimore, Md.: Johns Hopkins
University Press, 1975. 324 pp.
The author assesses antitrust sentiment by examining information on and
evaluations of big business that appeared in various publications from
the years 1880-1940. In particular, he examines journals addressed to
farmers, professionals, and organized laborers. He concludes that there
were several major cycles of antitrust sentiment--in the 1890s, during
the progressive years, to the early 1920s, and in the 1930s. Galambos
finds that over the long run, middle-class Americans harbored less hostility toward giant corporations; while not particularly fond of large
firms, Americans learned to tolerate them by the late 1930s.

H 1694. **GALLMAN, ROBERT E.**, ed. Recent Developments in the Study of Business and Economic History: Essays in Memory of Herman E. Krooss.
Greenwich, Conn.: JAI Press, 1977. 305 pp.
This commissioned collection primarily contains critical surveys of recent
work on broadly defined topics in business and economic history. Of the
essays that deal specifically with topics in American history, several
are in essence bibliographical: Paul Uselding's survey of reseach on
technology in the 19th century; Michael D. Bordo and Anna J. Schwarz's
description of recent developments in the field of monetary economics;
and Ralph Hidy's comprehensive survey of recent publications in business
history. Two others meld bibliography with a critique of some concepts
and methodologies employed in recent work: Richard Easterlin's essay
on population in economic history, and Richard Sylla's article on the
role of financial intermediaries in industrialization.

H 1695. GIBB, GEORGE S. The Saco-Lowell Shops: Textile Machinery Building
in New England, 1813-1949. Cambridge, Mass.: Harvard University
Press, 1950. 835 pp.
Gibb's volume traces the evolution of a group of related textile and textile machinery companies, which originated in the early 19th century as
suppliers of textile machinery to their parent companies such as the Boston
Manufacturing Company at Waltham. Gibb shows that the machinery shops
eventually became separate companies that came to dominate the entire
textile machinery industry. Gibb's study includes descriptions of the
changing technology of textile machinery, and of developments in work,
working conditions, and labor relations in the companies. He places his
study in the general social and political context of 19th-century America,
but his main interest is trends in the industry--the appearance of a specialized capital-goods industry, diversification, growing competition,
and eventual merger.

H 1696. GIDDENS, PAUL H. Standard Oil Company (Indiana): Oil Pioneer
of the Middle West. New York: Appleton-Century-Crofts, 1955.
741 pp.
Giddens describes the history of Standard Oil of Indiana from its organization in 1889 to 1951. He concentrates on the company's growth, the
nature of its basic operations, and the changes in its business policies.
Standard Oil of Indiana was formed by the Standard Oil Trust to handle
the refining and marketing of crude oil from Indiana's Lima field. The
company overcame a major early obstacle, the high sulphur content of Lima
oil, and by the early 20th century it had built a highly successful refining and marketing organization that was capable of dominating the Midwestern market. After the epochal anti-trust dissolution had separated
the Indiana business from the supplies of crude and from the pipelines
controlled by the other Standard companies, Standard Oil of Indiana (Stano-
lind) gradually developed independent policies. It integrated backward
by adding oil properties and pipelines while expanding its investment
in refining and marketing. By the 1920s it had become the country's leading marketer of refined petroleum products.

H 1697. GIEBELHAUS, AUGUST W. Business and Government in the Oil Industry:
A Case Study of Sun Oil, 1876-1945. Greenwich, Conn.: JAI Press,
1980. 332 pp.
A study in the relations between business and government in the 20th century, this book uses the corporate history of Sun Oil as a representative
case in the evolutionary relationship between the petroleum industry and
government. Borrowing frameworks suggested by Norman Nordhause and Gabriel
Kolko, the author finds a growing consensus between industry and government
on petroleum policy--a consensus well-established by the end of W.W. II.

H 1698. GILBERT, GORMAN and ROBERT E. SAMUELS. The Taxicab: An Urban
Transportation Survivor. Chapel Hill: University of North Carolina Press, 1983. 200 pp.
The authors have made an effort to upgrade the image of taxi owners and
drivers in their socio-economic account of this indispensable form of small
business enterprise. In most large cities, the industry is subject to
extensive regulation and competition among numerous operators (they totaled
more than 5,300 across the country in 1975). These operators range from
franchises such as Yellow Cab to local concerns. The study includes data
on revenues, fares, and usage.

H 1699. GOLDSTEIN, JONATHAN. Philadelphia and the China Trade, 1682-1846: Commercial, Cultural, and Attitudinal Effects. University Park: Pennsylvania State University Press, 1978. 121 pp.
Goldstein discusses the establishment of direct trade links between Philadelphia and China after 1784 and evaluates what this interaction reveals about American attitudes toward the Chinese. The account deals with the questions of cultural diffusion posed by trade and uses photographs of silk, porcelain, and other decorative goods to explain how these items were emulated in the U.S. He also cites examples of Philadelphians' adaptation of household design, furnishings, and landscaping to demonstrate their positive regard for Chinese culture.

H 1700. GOSPEL, HOWARD F. and CRAIG P. LITTLER, eds. Managerial Strategies and Industrial Relations: An Historical and Comparative Study. London: Heinemann Educational Books, 1982. 201 pp.
This collection includes essays by eight authors who employ ideas suggested by Alfred Chandler, Harry Braverman, and other recent students of labor-management relations. An attempt to bridge the boundaries between business and labor history, the book proposes new approaches that probe the impact of workers and workplace relationships on the formulation of corporate strategies and structures. The articles focus on British cases; the rise of bureaucratic management in the U.S.; the use of Taylorism in a German electrical engineering firm; labor policy in a Japanese engineering company; and a comparative analysis of labor management in the four countries represented in the collection.

H 1701. GRANT, H. ROGER. Insurance Reform: Consumer Action in the Progressive Era. Ames: Iowa State University Press, 1979. 202 pp.
Grant examines the origins, development, and overall impact of the consumer crusade to reform the fire and life insurance industries. Focusing on New York, Wisconsin, Missouri, Kansas, and Texas, where the movement was most active between 1885 and 1915, he finds that this attack on dishonest and insolvent companies was promoted by policy holders and underwriters as well as by certain industry officials. His findings support the arguments of Gabriel Kolko and Robert Wiebe that insurance personnel echoed sentiments of other corporate leaders who endorsed order and efficiency through benevolent legislation, but when a flood of "unfriendly" laws seemed inevitable, they found Federal meddling less objectionable than state and local actions.

H 1702. GREEN, GEORGE D. Finance and Economic Development in the Old South: Louisiana Banking, 1804-1861. Palo Alto, Calif.: Stanford University Press, 1972. 268 pp.
Green uses Louisiana as a case study to analyze the connection between finance and economic development in general and between banking and antebellum economy in particular. Political and economic historians alike, he says, have condemned the rapid expansion of financial institutions in the 1830s and their sponsorship of a credit boom; these policies, the critics say, caused the Panic of 1837 and the severe recession which followed. Green argues to the contrary, maintaining that credit expansion encouraged not only speculation but also rapid and genuine economic growth by stimulating spending in the form of investment rather than consumption. The banks' intermediation greatly increased the available supplies of savings and allocated them efficiently among the competing demands for agricultural and commercial credit and for capital-intensive social overhead projects such as those in transportation. Although credit expanded faster than the rate of growth of the economy, Green says it was the "hard money" reaction which deepened the ensuing recession and delayed recovery.

H 1703. GREGORY, FRANCES W. Nathan Appleton: Merchant and Entrepreneur, 1779-1861. Charlottesville: University Press of Virginia, 1975. 358 pp.
Appleton's career, according to Gregory, exemplifies New England's transition from a commercial to an industrial economy. By 1800, Appleton had become a partner in his family's trading firm. He exhibited considerable mercantile skills during the fluctuations in commerce which accompanied the Anglo-French wars, the subsequent Embargo period, and the War of 1812. The commercial uncertainties of these years made New England merchants receptive to the idea of investing in industry, notably cotton-textile manufacturing, and in 1813 Appleton joined other merchants, among them Francis C. Lowell, in founding the Boston Manufacturing Company at Waltham. Appleton, who became one of the premier entrepreneurs in this fast-growing industry, was involved in marketing, banking, and insurance. Later, he was a leader in efforts to develop new transportation systems to serve the region's factory sites and to open up routes along which New England's goods could travel to Western markets.

H 1704. GRODINSKY, JULIUS. Jay Gould: His Business Career, 1867-1892. Philadelphia: University of Pennsylvania Press, 1957. 627 pp.
Grodinsky refutes the traditional assessment of Gould as one of the top-ranking predatory capitalists of the 19th century. Focusing on Gould as a manipulator of capital, Grodinsky assigns secondary importance to his contribution to railroad expansion and competition and places primary importance on Gould's stock market operations. A study of the mechanics of financial speculation shows that Gould was less than adept; he was a poor judge both of the market and of economic trends, and he failed to show great acumen in corporate affairs. Yet, Grodinsky concludes, Gould's contribution to American economic development had important positive elements. Gould's policies encouraged the construction of new railroad mileage and thus extended service; his rate wars benefited the shippers; and his financial manipulations brought large volumes of capital into productive enterprise.

H 1705. HAEGER, JOHN DENIS. The Investment Frontier: New York Businessmen and the Economic Development of the Old Northwest. Albany: State University of New York Press, 1981. 311 pp.
This revisionist interpretation of frontier economic development stresses the role of Eastern capitalists in providing Western communities with essential funds and financial expertise; thus Haeger acknowledges the frontier speculator's role in building an integrated national economy. He focuses on three representative financiers--Isaac Bronson, Arthur Bronson, and Charles Butler--who formed the New York Life Insurance and Trust Company in 1833 for the purpose of investing in the Old Northwest. The concerns that guided this partnership were exemplary of Eastern involvement, and these financiers' later independent speculation reflects divergent styles of Eastern investment: Arthur Bronson adhered to a conservative approach while Charles Butler was a risk-taking promoter.

H 1706. HAITES, ERIK F., JAMES MAK, and GARY M. WALTON. Western River Transportation: The Era of Early Internal Development. Baltimore, Md.: Johns Hopkins University Press, 1975. 209 pp.
The authors discuss the contribution of the steamboat to Western economic development, to the growth of markets, and to the spread of commercial agriculture. They point out that because the spread of a market economy was a fundamental aspect of economic growth in 19th-century America, and because market size depended largely on the cost, availability, and efficiency of transportation, the role of the steamboat deserves more attention than it has hitherto received. The authors decribe the transport savings achieved by the steamboat; its contribution to a competitive transportation

market; its continued benefits to the consumer; and the organizational improvements that increased the boat's efficiency.

H 1707. HAMMOND, BRAY. Banks and Politics in America: From the Revolution to the Civil War. Princeton, N.J.: Princeton University Press, 1957. 771 pp.
The period covered by Hammond's study of the political economy of banking was dominated by rapid growth, by severe economic fluctuations, and by the transition from a predominantly agrarian-commercial system to an increasingly industrial economic one. Placing his subject in this economic setting, the author describes the early search for adequate banking institutions and the pressures felt by entrepreneurs who needed scarce capital in order to take advantage of the nation's abundant natural resources. Hammond emphasizes the constructive role played by credit in financing the expansion of all forms of enterprise in the first half of the 19th century; banking institutions were, he says, necessarily unstable during these years. He interprets the Jacksonian battle over the Second Bank of the U.S. as an important phase in the ongoing struggle between different types of capitalists. Rather than the victory of agrarian democracy over the "money power," the bank war was a triumph of new enterprisers demanding looser controls on credit over an older, entrenched elite of Eastern capitalists.

H 1708. HEDGES, JAMES B. The Browns of Providence Plantations: Colonial Years. Cambridge, Mass.: Harvard University Press, 1952. 379 pp.
The author treats the history of this Rhode Island merchant-capitalist family as a history in microcosm of early American business development. Using the extensive Brown manuscripts, he describes the family's commercial operations from their beginnings in the early 18th century to 1790, from an initial concentration on maritime trade to extensive involvement in domestic manufacturing ventures financed by capital accumulated in the family's commercial operations. By the late 18th century, domestic manufacturing interests had largely eclipsed the family's interest in commerce, and in subsequent years the Browns continued to widen their operations. While he is concerned throughout with political aspects of his subject, the author provides a detailed account of the Browns's business techniques and activities, both legal and illegal.

H 1709. HEDGES, JAMES B. The Browns of Providence Plantations: The Nineteenth Century. Providence, R.I.: Brown University Press, 1968. 379 pp.
This volume extends Hedges's case history of the Brown family's variegated economic enterprises. The author describes the manner in which the Browns expanded their investments outside commerce, a development which had begun toward the end of the Colonial era. They placed their capital in a wide variety of businesses, but after 1820 their commercial activities were marked by indifferent success, and by 1840 they had largely ceased. In contrast, the family's investments in cotton manufacturing were extremely successful. The Browns, one of the region's older mercantile families, had pioneered power spinning in New England and had been engaged in cotton manufacturing since 1790. However, even during the years after 1815, when the textile industry was experiencing high profits and rapid growth, the Browns did not become completely specialized. Over the course of the 19th century, they entered such fields as banking, insurance, transportation, and land speculation.

H 1710. **HESKETT, JOHN.** Industrial Design. New York: Oxford University
Press, 1981. 216 pp.
This study describes the contributions of individual industrial designers
as well as the social pressures which have influenced their work. Heskett
discusses the material and institutional frameworks that developed as
production expanded beyond traditional crafts and made design an industrial
art. The major American contribution emphasized by the authors is Ford's
system for quantity production of a standard design with interchangeable
parts.

H 1711. **HIDY, RALPH W.** The House of Baring in American Trade and Finance:
English Merchant Bankers at Work, 1763-1861. Cambridge, Mass.:
Harvard University Press, 1949. 631 pp.
Hidy describes the role of a significant Anglo-American banking firm in
the marketing of American securities in London, and he thereby exposes
one mechanism for bringing British capital to America. In Part One of
the study, he follows the firm through the transition from mercantile
to industrial Capitalism and examines its accumulation of economic
resources and political influence, its investment in real property, and its
role in Anglo-American trade. In the 1830s, as Part Two shows, the firm
immersed itself completely in American affairs, becoming the leading intermediary between British capitalists and American entrepreneurs. Part
Three describes the end of the investment boom of the 1830s, when the
American economy was overtaken by recession and repudiation. The firm
then substantially curtailed its American operations, and thereafter the
U.S. was just one aspect in the Baring's highly diversified financial
operations.

H 1712. **HIDY, RALPH W.** and **MURIEL E. HIDY.** Pioneering in Big Business,
1882-1911: History of Standard Oil Company (New Jersey). New
York: Harper, 1955. 839 pp.
This book traces the history of the Standard Oil Company from its early
formation through the 1911 anti-trust suit that resulted in the combination's dismemberment. The authors were given full access to the company's
records, and their research has led them to criticize the so-called "Robber
Baron" approach to the study of big business and its leaders; instead,
they emphasize the chaos and destructive competition of the early years
of the industry, pointing out that the Standard Oil combination created
order and stability. The depression of the 1870s gave rise to the combination, and Standard Oil dealt with this problem by merging competing firms
and by stressing efficient, large-scale operations. The firm thus contributed to the development of both planned production and regularized distribution and marketing in oil and oil products. Rather than the machinations
of a group of conspirators bent on driving the "little man" out of business,
Standard Oil's policies are seen as normal competitive responses to a
rapidly changing economic environment.

H 1713. **HILDEBRAND, GRANT.** Designing for Industry: The Architecture
of Albert Kahn. Cambridge, Mass.: MIT Press, 1974. 232 pp.
The study evaluates the work of Albert Kahn, who maintained an architectural practice in Detroit, and who was the foremost industrial architect
of the early 20th century. From 1896 to 1942 Kahn designed more than
2,000 factories, including the Ford River Rouge complex in the 1920s.
Hildebrand places Kahn's work in the broader context of architectural
history by analyzing Kahn's evolving conception of the factory as an aesthetic, architectural form--a theme, Hildebrand argues, which has hitherto
been slighted in the history of architecture. The work also deals with
Kahn's relationship with business clients, and analyzes his non-industrial
architecture in separate chapters. Numerous illustrations of Kahn's work
complement the study.

H 1714. **HILL, FOREST G.** Roads, Rails, and Waterways: The Army Engineers and Early Transportation. Norman: University of Oklahoma Press, 1957. 248 pp.
Hill treats the Army Corps of Engineers as an important example of direct government participation in development activities in the first half of the 19th century. The Corps, Hill argues, was the only source of engineering knowledge available in the early Republic. This alone made national planning of a system of internal improvements seem realistic. Sectionalism was ultimately to block such schemes, but the government nonetheless provided engineering aid to all major transportation projects. In particular, Hill stresses the role of the army engineers in aiding the early railroads. Thereafter, the Corps was mainly involved in the surveying and mapping of Western lands, an undertaking that culminated in the Pacific Railroad surveys of the 1850s. Hill concludes that the activities of the Army Engineers illustrate why the extent of government participation in early American economic development cannot be measured merely in terms of direct financial aid.

H 1715. **HOLLANDER, SAMUEL.** The Sources of Increased Efficiency: A Study of DuPont Rayon Plants. Cambridge, Mass.: MIT Press, 1965. 228 pp.
By analyzing production cost data at five DuPont plants between 1929 and 1961, Hollander confirms the conclusions of a number of macro-economic studies that indicate that "technological change" accounts for most of the increased output per worker in the U.S. in the 20th century. The author considers as technological change any alterations in the techniques of production designed to reduce unit production costs. Of the net reductions in unit factory costs achieved by the five plants over the period under examination, Hollander says "technological change" accounted for 100% of the reduction in one plant and 85% and 95% at three others. At the fifth its contribution was only 35%, but this was due to the fact that it was a newly established plant which already embodied many of the improvements introduced in the others. The author suggests that technological change may be stimulated more often by a need to produce in larger volume than by a need to lower the costs of existing levels of output. Hollander characterizes most of this change as "minor" or incremental, meaning that it does not require extensive development and is simple to adopt with a minimum of organizational adaptation.

H 1716. **HUTCHINSON, WILLIAM H.** Oil, Land, and Politics: The California Career of Thomas Robert Bard. 2 vols. Norman: University of Oklahoma Press, 1965. 743 pp.
Hutchinson considers the major role Bard played in the development of the petroleum industry in California during the second half of the 19th century. Arriving in California in 1865 as a representative of the majority owner of the Philadelphia and California Petroleum Company, Bard oversaw the early exploration of the Ojai field and was responsible for California's first gusher in 1867. Major oil production began with the development of Ojai and with Bard's organization of the Union Oil Company in 1890. Bard also engaged in land speculation and became involved in local politics. Hutchinson describes Bard's business operations and the political campaigns that eventually led to his entry in the U.S. Senate in 1900 as the first member of that body to be chosen from Southern California.

H 1717. **INGHAM, JOHN N.** The Iron Barons: A Social Analysis of an American Urban Elite 1874-1965. Westport, Conn.: Greenwood Press, 1978. 242 pp.
Ingham attempts to uncover the social and cultural institutions that have conditioned America's entrepreneurial leaders. His study, which focuses on the social lives of forty-three core families who made their fortunes in Pittsburgh's iron industry, reveals a well-developed interactional

network of intermarriage, associational involvement, and residential clus-
tering that defined the levels of the city's upper crust. Similar findings
appear in comparative data on Philadelphia, Cleveland, Youngstown, Wheeling,
and Bethlehem.

H 1718. JENKINS, REESE V. Images and Enterprise: Technology and the
American Photographic Industry, 1839 to 1925. Baltimore, Md.:
Johns Hopkins University Press, 1976. 371 pp.
Reese documents the transformation of photography from a small, technically-
oriented craft industry that began with the commercial introduction of
the daguerreotype in 1839 to a complex business that developed in the
early 20th century. While recognizing the role of market factors and
marketing strategies, the author ties corporate development to a sequence
of stages characterized by distinctive product technologies; the emphasis
is more on the production of photographs and photographic equipment than
on the social and artistic dimensions of photography. As the chapters
on the silent cinematography and other topics show, the industry was
extremely diverse and included hundreds of firms, many of which have since
consolidated to form the corporate giants of today.

H 1719. JEREMY, DAVID J. Transatlantic Industrial Revolution: The Diffusion of Textile Technologies between Britain and America, 1790-
1830s. Cambridge, Mass.: MIT Press, 1981. 384 pp.
Jeremy examines the transfer of four technologies--cotton spinning, powerloom weaving, calico printing, and woolen manufacturing--in this analysis
of the respective contributions of and interactions between British and
American innovators during the early years of the Industrial Revolution.
Using data from company records, the U.S. 1820 Census of Manufactures,
and other sources, he develops a profile of American textile expansion
which he relates to a wide spectrum of social and technical factors, including the arrival of experienced British artisans and textile-mill workers;
the diffusion of published literature on British inventions; and the incentives and barriers to mechanization in both countries. Jeremy refutes
the notion of a one-way flow of personnel and ideas from the mother country
and argues that technical information moved back and forth across the
Atlantic, and at an earlier date than most historians have assumed.

H 1720. JOHNSON, ARTHUR M. The Challenge of Change: The Sun Oil Company
1945-1977. Columbus: Ohio State University Press, 1983.
481 pp.
Based in part on the papers of Sun's former president and chairman, Robert
G. Dunlop, this study seeks to provide an objective view of strategies
and decisions made in the face of rising public controversy surrounding
the oil industry. Johnson's analysis of managerial changes and issues
of social accountability broadens the scope beyond the usual limits of
corporate histories and sheds light on oil's impact on contemporary foreign
policy.

H 1721. JOHNSON, ARTHUR M. Petroleum Pipelines and Public Policy, 1906-
1959. Cambridge, Mass.: Harvard University Press, 1967.
555 pp.
Johnson argues that public policy did not result primarily from a struggle
between reformers and business interests; instead, both Federal and state
policies were largely shaped by intra-industry conflicts in which the
small producers and refiners used political power to resist the Standard
Oil combine. The major issue involved was whether the pipelines of the
integrated oil firms could be required to serve the public as common carriers. Drawing upon company records as well as public documents, the
author finds that although the technology and economics of pipelining
remained relatively constant, as did the amount of attention lavished
on the oil industry by government, the particular policies adopted changed
over the years. There were significant episodes of antitrust activity,

and in 1941 the industry negotiated a consent decree in a case that finally
brought to an end a decade of intense conflict over pipeline policy.
The decree and other government measures in the 1930s helped bring a new
measure of stability to the pipelines and the rest of the oil industry.

H 1722. JOHNSON, ARTHUR M. Winthrop Aldrich: Lawyer, Banker, Diplomat.
         Boston: Division of Research, Graduate School of Business Adminis-
         tration, Harvard University, 1968. 536 pp.
Johnson examines the major segments of Aldrich's career; Aldrich was suc-
cessively a youthful member of a New York law firm, President of the Equitable Trust and Chase National banks of New York City, Chairman of President
Truman's Advisory Committee for Financing Foreign Trade, and President
Eisenhower's Ambassador to Great Britain (1952-57). He was also active
in New York Republican politics and performed numerous public and quasi-
public functions, ranging from support for black education to sponsorship of the American Heritage Foundation. As a leader in the New York
banking community, Aldrich supported the separation of investment from
commercial banking carried out by the Banking Act of 1933, but he was
in general deeply opposed to Roosevelt's monetary policy, an antipathy
rooted in his aversion to direct governmental intervention in the economy.
As a spokesman for the banking community, he was active in pressing his
opinions on the public and the government throughout the 1930s. Johnson
concludes that Aldrich was a man who functioned as a liaison, providing
a "vital link" between different "groups, causes, and even governments."

H 1723. JOHNSON, ARTHUR M. and BARRY E. SUPPLE. Boston Capitalists and
         Western Railroads: A Study in the 19th Century Railroad Invest-
         ment Process. Cambridge, Mass.: Harvard University Press, 1967.
         392 pp.
Johnson and Supple maintain that business history is in essence the study
of individuals who seek new ways of making their capital productive in
an economic environment that constantly changes. In keeping with this
perspective, they study the expectations, policies, and rewards of those
Boston-based capitalists who invested in the expanding railroad industry
west of the Alleghenies. Their volume covers the period from 1820-90,
concentrating on the years after 1840. During these years the investors
in question began to redirect the capital they had previously invested
in the China trade. The authors find that the capitalists can be divided
into two types of investor—opportunistic (speculative) and developmental
(growth-oriented). By studying the histories of a number of recipient
railroads, Johnson and Supple show that the developmental investors frequently sought to protect their capital by taking an active part in the
management of the enterprise. By 1890, however, these powerful individuals
had been eclipsed by investment bankers and by the railroads' own managers.

H 1724. JOHNSON, JAMES P. The Politics of Soft Coal: The Bituminous
         Industry from World War I Through the New Deal. Urbana: Uni-
         versity of Illinois Press, 1979. 258 pp.
Johnson offers a history of the politics of the soft coal industry from
W.W. I through the New Deal era. He argues, firstly, that the war experience did not provide the New Dealers regulating coal with a usable past;
that the Fuel Administration of the Progressive Era proved hopeless in
dealing with the exigencies of the Depression. Secondly, industrial self-
government also failed in both war and depression, despite general support
and cooperation on the part of John Lewis and the United Mine Workers.
Lastly, Johnson claims that the coal industry was wrecked by fierce competition which prevented it from uniting and manipulating governmental
agencies for its own advantage. Hence the politics of soft coal are best
understood through a "structural approach," rather than in terms of government regulating business in the "public interest."

H 1725. JOSEPHSON, MATTHEW. The Robber Barons: The Great American Capitalists, 1861-1901. New York: Harcourt, Brace, 1934. 474 pp.
Josephson portrays the Civil War as a significant turning point when the
dominance of industrial Capitalism was established. He concentrates on
that small class of men--Jay Cooke, Jay Gould, Andrew Carnegie, J. P.
Morgan, John D. Rockefeller--whose relentless reorganization of American
economic life brought them social, political, and economic preeminence.
While tracing their careers, he stresses the corrupt and corrupting manner
in which the modern robber barons acquired their wealth. For Josephson,
the whole period is symbolized in the paradox that the nation achieved
its greatest economic progress in an era that brought to power a small
group of predators who reserved for themselves and their families the
greater share of America's new-found wealth.

H 1726. KARAMANSKI, THEODORE J. Fur Trade and Exploration: Opening the
Far Northwest 1821-1852. Norman: University of Oklahoma Press,
1983. 330 pp.
This is an account of early exploration in the Far Northwest. It contains
material on the role of the fur trade in the region; the political and
economic factors that influenced the policies of the Hudson Bay Company;
and the cultural differences that affected trade between the various groups
of Indian middlemen who inhabited the interior of British Columbia, the
western-most Northwest Territories, the Yukon, and Eastern Alaska.

H 1727. KELLER, MORTON. The Life Insurance Enterprise, 1885-1910: A
Study of the Limits of Corporate Power. Cambridge, Mass.:
Harvard University Press, 1963. 338 pp.
Noting that among the large corporations emerging in late 19th-century
America few equaled the power of the large insurance companies, Keller
analyzes the use of power in five of the greatest New York companies:
Equitable, Mutual Life, New York Life, Metropolitan, and Prudential.
The five companies, Keller says, were distinguished by a common set of
business practices that differentiated them from the rest of the industry.
Moreover, they were distinguished by a common set of business practices
that differentiated them from the American mainstream. Exercising power
decisively, the companies' chief executives ruthlessly pursued growth
in both domestic and foreign markets and sought complete control over
both the companies in which they invested and the governmental bodies
that were supposed to be regulating them. Keller suggests that prior
to governmental investigation and intervention, internal restraint on
the use of power had already evolved as a part of the corporate ideology
developing within this sub-society of companies. Voluntary self-restraint
by large corporations, he concludes, is as important an element in our
history as government regulation.

H 1728. KERR, K. AUSTIN. American Railroad Politics, 1914-1920: Rates,
Wages, and Efficiency. Pittsburgh, Pa.: University of Pittsburgh
Press, 1968. 250 pp.
Kerr explains that the outcome of Federal regulatory measures was once
assumed to reflect the stated intentions of those promoting and drafting
the nation's laws. In recent years, however, historians have become more
skeptical about the regulatory process, and many have concluded that the
regulatees have dominated the government agencies, rather than the other
way around. Examining railroad politics in the years following the passage
of the Mann-Eakins Act of 1910, Kerr claims that the shippers, and not
the railroad companies, gained most from control by the Interstate Commerce
Commission. Nor was the struggle limited to these three parties. Organized labor made its voice heard, as did advocates and scientific management
and other policies. Kerr carries his study through W.W. I to the passage
of the Transportation Act of 1920 and thereby illustrates the high degree
of continuity between the pre-War and post-War eras in the U.S. This

analysis of interest-group politics stresses the complexity of business-
government relations in the early decades of this century when the foundations were being laid for America's administrative state.

H 1729. KIM, SUNG BOK. Landlord and Tenant in Colonial New York: Manorial
Society, 1664-1775. Chapel Hill: University of North Carolina
Press, 1978. 456 pp.
Kim examines the origins, the economic and governmental structures, and
the functions of the four largest landed estates of 18th-century New York.
He concentrates on the political economy of landlordism and tenantry,
noting that great New York estates relied on the labor of agricultural
tenants which gave New York the largest tenant population of all the Colonies. In contrast to earlier historians, Kim portrays tenancy as a well-
functioning, equitable system, not an exploitive or feudal arrangement.
Many of the great landlords are more aptly described as merchants than
as landed gentry, for they had important commercial interests and had
a specific economic goal in promoting the development of their land so
as to stimulate the flow of agricultural produce--particularly wheat--
to be used in trade. These landowners actively competed for tenants,
offering leases and providing fixed capital; often the tenants gained
a financial stake in the land when they improved it. Tenancy thus ensured
the productive utilization of the land and helped the immigrant with little
capital to earn a livelihood.

H 1730. KIRKLAND, EDWARD C. Charles Francis Adams, Jr., 1835-1915: The
Patrician at Bay. Cambridge, Mass.: Harvard University Press,
1965. 256 pp.
Kirkland illustrates some of the contradictions in the life of Adams,
an atypical entrepreneur who was a member of one of America's most famous
families, a pioneer of railroad regulation in New England, an unexceptional
businessman, and a patrician opponent of the burgeoning industrial and
financial Capitalism of the late 19th century. Adams, Kirkland shows,
was an early proponent of "conservative" regulation of railroads because
he did not trust natural competitive forces to protect the public interest.
Adams's distrust of the depredations of capitalist enterprise remained
with him all his life, although it did not prevent him from making his
fortune through conventional speculative channels. His distrust, however,
was not that of the radical reformer, but that of the patrician confronting
the inexorable development of a new society and culture profoundly different from any that had gone before. As such, Adams stands as an articulate and influential spokesman for a current of opinion of considerable
importance in industrializing America, a current which criticized the
new order simply because it preferred the old.

H 1731. KIRKLAND, EDWARD C. Industry Comes of Age: Business, Labor,
and Public Policy. New York: Holt, Rinehart & Winston, 1961.
445 pp.
Kirkland's volume constitutes a history of the development of American
industry in the later half of the 19th century. Disinterested in isolating the determinants or measuring the dimensions of economic growth,
he refuses to impose any particular theoretical framework on the materials
covered and instead surveys a great variety of topics, including government
monetary policy, railroad construction and operation, the growth of new
industries such as steel and electrical power, the systematization of
factory production, the corporate revolution, urban growth, and the rise
of organized labor.

H 1732. KIRKLAND, EDWARD C. Men, Cities, and Transportation: A Study
        in New England History. 2 vols. Cambridge, Mass.: Harvard
        University Press, 1948. 1027 pp.
Kirkland's study of regional transportation in New England towns touches
upon the development of turnpikes and canals, but it is devoted mainly
to the growth of railroads. He examines the origins, financing, and construction of the railroads; the continuous process of consolidation which
occurred throughout the industry's history; managerial and organizational
structures; relations with the government and with workers; and rate fluctuations. In New England, he says, the railroad was first conceived as
a solution to Boston's declining commercial position relative to New York.
Gradually, however, the desire for the favorable commercial position which
railroad development would bring spread to other towns in the region,
notably Portland, Maine. As a consequence, the region was swept first
by a wave of enthusiasm for railroad building and subsequently by a wave
of disappointment at the returns realized. Throughout, the government
played an important role, first as a source of financial aid and later
as an agency of regulation. The railroads themselves sought solutions
to competitive pressures in informal cooperation and in consolidation.
By 1900, two major companies had emerged in the region, each of which
had also developed important links to the national railroad network.
These larger systems transcended the regional boundaries and interests
that had previously played the decisive role in determining the course
of New England's railroad development.

H 1733. KLEIN, MAURY. The Great Richmond Terminal: A Study in Businessmen
        and Business Strategy. Charlottesville: University Press of
        Virginia, 1970. 323 pp.
At the heart of the "New South," Klein says, lie concepts of economic
development and diversification that require historians to pay closer
attention to the nature of post-Civil War economic activity and to the
entrepreneurs who organized it. Klein focuses on the railroads of the
South in general and the Great Richmond Terminal in particular. The antebellum Southern railroads were developed by local entrepreneurs as discrete
enterprises to serve the particular needs of a limited territory. Following the Civil War, fierce competition developed between the lines,
giving rise to new construction and consolidation movements seeking to
develop viable regional systems. The Great Richmond Terminal--a holding
company--was the most ambitious of the organizational innovations created
in these years to bring order to this situation. In its heyday the
Terminal controlled over 9,000 miles of Southern tracks and brought into
one organization the railroads that dominated the key interterritorial
routes. In 1893, however, the company collapsed and was taken over by
J. P. Morgan, to whom fell the task of creating a unified regional rail
transport system.

H 1734. KOLKO, GABRIEL. Railroads and Regulation, 1877-1916. Princeton,
        N.J.: Princeton University Press, 1965. 273 pp.
Addressing the question of the relationship between government and the
emerging corporations of the late 19th and early 20th centuries, Kolko
disputes the idea that the central feature of this relationship was conflict engendered by public demands for the regulation of powerful monopolistic economic groups. Rather, he says, his case study of the railroads
shows that corporations actually sought the creation of regulatory bodies
as a source of order within their own industries. Throughout the 1870s
and 1880s, competing railroads had attempted to cartelize the industry
by adopting a uniform rate structure and by making a series of rate agreements. These understandings had repeatedly broken because the cooperating
parties were unable to force the rates either on railroads outside the
cartel or on each other. The railroads turned eventually to the Federal
government and actively sought the creation of a regulatory commission

which would enforce the rates upon which they agreed. Despite passage of the Interstate Commerce Act of 1887, it was not until the eve of W.W. I, Kolko says, that the railroads had achieved what they set out to create in 1887: a regulatory commission with effective powers to promote the industry's cartelization.

H 1735. KOSKOFF, DAVID E. The Mellons: The Chronicle of America's Richest Family. New York: Crowell, 1978. 602 pp.
Koskoff offers a collective biography of the family that founded Gulf Oil Corporation, the key bank in western Pennsylvania, and the National Gallery of Art in Washington. A family of Scotch-Irish descent, the Mellons settled in Pittsburgh in the 1830s where they made their first fortune in banking. By the 1890s they had invested in aluminum (Alcoa), carborundum, and an oil drilling venture that led to the founding of Gulf. The book also discusses the philanthropic interests of the Mellons, including the institution that grew into Carnegie-Mellon University; their work in government (Andrew Mellon served as Secretary of the Treasury under Harding); and the diverse business involvements of the third generation.

H 1736. KROOSS, HERMAN E. and CHARLES GILBERT. American Business History. Englewood Cliffs, N.J.: Prentice-Hall, 1972. 358 pp.
The authors survey business history from Colonial times to the present. They emphasize that in America private business enterprise has been the only mechanism by which the factors of production are combined to produce goods and stimulate economic growth, and they accordingly emphasize the role of the entrepreneurs who have performed this important function. However, they do not confine themselves simply to an examination of businessmen, business strategies, and business enterprises; they integrate the study of particular businessmen and firms with an analysis of long-term trends in business development and in business relations with other important elements in the economy—for example, government and labor.

H 1737. LARSON, HENRIETTA M. Jay Cooke, Private Banker. Cambridge, Mass.: Harvard University Press, 1936. 512 pp.
Larson's volume is both a study of investment banking in the middle decades of the 19th century and a detailed biography of a unique businessman; the book describes both the operations of a private banking firm in the years immediately preceding the era of finance Capitalism and focuses on the circumstances that led to Cooke's early and impressive success. His talent, according to Larson, lay in his ability to combine patriotism and salesmanship in his ventures and to sell war bonds during the Civil War. In his later career, Cooke was less successful, and his decline stemmed in part from important changes taking place in investment banking. Formerly a passive middleman between investor and user of capital, the investment banker was becoming by the 1870s more of an active participant in the affairs of those borrowers on whose behalf he acted as financial agent. Thus Cooke became deeply involved in the policies of the Northern Pacific Railroad, and when the company failed, so did Cooke and his firm.

H 1738. LARSON, HENRIETTA M. and KENNETH W. PORTER. History of Humble Oil and Refining Company: A Study in Industrial Growth. New York: Harper & Row, 1959. 769 pp.
This book covers the entire history of Humble Oil, one of the leading oil producers in America. The authors describe its formation by a number of small, independent producers in Texas in 1917, its formal affiliation with the Standard Oil Company of New Jersey in 1919, and its growth through the 1920s and 1930s. They emphasize the central role of top management and its ability to make good entrepreneurial decisions for the firm, explaining that the period of Humble's rise was characterized both by dynamism and by instability in the industry, thus indicating the company's need for strong and flexible administration. Larson and Porter discuss

the original move to affiliate with Jersey Standard, a policy that gave
Humble an important market and access to the extensive capital resources
needed to finance further expansion. They emphasize the company's willingness to use and finance the development of relevant technologies and its
increasing resort to science-based operations in its search for oil in
the 1920s. Throughout, the authors stress Humble's realization of the
need to reduce competition and to rationalize the oil-producing industry;
they describe the firm's support for private initiatives and public policies designed to achieve these ends.

H 1739. LARSON, HENRIETTA M., EVELYN H. KNOWLTON, and CHARLES S. POPPLE.
New Horizons, 1927-1950: History of Standard Oil Company (New
Jersey). New York: Harper & Row, 1971. 945 pp.
This volume carries forward the investigation of the Standard firm launched
by Ralph and Muriel Hidy. The authors detail the evolution of the company's major policies, viewing these programs from the board-room level
of top management and emphasizing the contributions of the business's
leaders. The study stresses three periods in Standard's development:
1927-39; 1939-45; and 1945-50. Standard's major problems during these
years were first to acquire adequate sources of oil over the long run,
and then to reorganize the firm to facilitate the performance of the entrepreneurial function--long term planning. Later, W.W. II shifted the nature
of Standard's problems entirely, as maximum production became the overriding goal. In the immediate postwar years, Standard had to achieve
a successful reconversion to postwar conditions, just as the entire nation
did. By 1950, the authors conclude, the firm had successfully made the
transition to multinational operations and had adopted an administration
appropriate to its new and complex tasks.

H 1740. LEWIS, W. DAVID and WESLEY PHILLIPS NEWTON. Delta: The History
of an Airline. Athens: University of Georgia Press, 1979.
503 pp.
Lewis and Newton stress the paternalistic approach of Delta's founder,
Collett Everman Woolman, in this attempt to write a scholarly history
of an airline that offered him full access to its business records, correspondence, and personnel. The account places Delta within the context
of the nation's expanding airline industry and explains the factors that
influenced many of its decisions in areas ranging from aircraft design
to marketing methods.

H 1741. LIVESAY, HAROLD C. Andrew Carnegie and the Rise of Big Business.
Boston: Little, Brown, 1975. 202 pp.
Livesay places Carnegie's career in the context of America's spectacular
economic growth in the second half of the 19th century. Working first
in one of America's major industries, textiles, Carnegie was subsequently
employed in two of the most important growth industries of the period--
telegraph and railroads. After a brief experience as a speculator-
financier, however, Carnegie concentrated on the steel industry, the most
important capital goods industry of the late 19th century. Livesay uses
the symmetry between Carnegie's career and the development of the American
economy to explore the factors responsible for the rapid growth of American
capital goods industries, where Carnegie made his most important and original contributions. From his earlier experience, Livesay says, Carnegie
learned management techniques that he subsequently applied to steel production, thereby introducing both innovations and accompanying technological changes that were widely imitated.

H 1742. LUBOVE, ROY. The Professional Altruist: The Emergence of Social
Work as a Career, 1880-1930. Cambridge, Mass.: Harvard University Press, 1965. 291 pp.
Lubove's history of social work in America emphasizes the development
of social work as an occupational subculture. The profession, according
to Lubove, developed from the tradition of "friendly visiting," prevalent
in the late 19th century, to the cultivation and use of new "scientific"
modes of analysis and therapy that occurred in the early 20th century.
This development culminated in the crystallization of a professional subculture whose members erected barriers to entry, agreed upon the possession
of credentials, identified a client population and sources of patronage
and support.

H 1743. LUNDBERG, DONALD E. The Tourist Business. Chicago: Institutions/
Volume Feeding Management Magazine, 1972. 276 pp.
Lundberg adopts an interdisciplinary approach in this introduction to
the travel business in America, citing pertinent developments in economics,
business, ecology, government, law, psychology, sociology, and anthropology.
Tourism in America is an increasingly complex field with numerous components and secondary businesses. In the introduction, the author traces
the origin and histories of the tourists. He analyzes why tourist travel
(education, culture, change, beauty, wonder, power, and challenge); devotes
attention to the economic and social impact of tourism; and provides information on current tourism research, marketing analysis, and the tourist-
destination development. This study contains twenty-two pages of illustrations and fifty-one pages of charts and maps.

H 1744. MacAVOY, PAUL W. The Economic Effects of Regulation: The Trunk-
Line Railroad Cartels and the Interstate Commerce Commission
before 1900. Cambridge, Mass.: MIT Press, 1965. 275 pp.
Blending history and econometrics, MacAvoy analyzes the effects of cartel
agreements among the major railroads east of the Mississippi and north
of the Ohio prior to 1900. He focuses on changes in the pattern of rates,
tonnage, and profits. He finds repeated attempts among the railroads
to stabilize freight rates, traffic, and profits, but the agreements were
unstable and rates fluctuated around a downward secular trend. After
the passage of the Interstate Commerce Act in 1887, however, the trunk
lines were able to create a far more solid cartel structure. Federal
regulation established the cartel's rate as the regulated rate and eliminated cheating by prohibiting rate discrimination. The prohibition worked
in favor of the previously disadvantaged short-haul customers and against
long-distance shippers. The cartel control backed by Federal regulation
remained intact until the late 1890s, by which time the lower courts had
weakened the authority of the ICC. Finally, in 1898, the Supreme Court
held that the railroads were conspiring to set rates in violation of the
Sherman Act. This effectively ended the government-sponsored cartel in
the railroad industry.

H 1745. MANGELS, WILLIAM F. The Outdoor Amusement Industry: From Earliest
Times to the Present. New York: Vintage Books, 1952. 206 pp.
This work, which was sponsored by the National Association of Amusement
Parks, Pools, and Beaches, and was written for potential managers, examines
the European origin of the amusement park and its adaptation to American
society in the mid-19th century. Mangels observes that recreation has
become a major factor in the American experience, and he focuses on the
significant parks and innovative amusement devices that have contributed
to the growth of the modern amusement park industry. Illustrated with
twenty-seven black-and-white photos and drawings, this study also includes
an appendix listing outdoor amusement associations and publications.

H 1746. MARTIN, ALBRO. Enterprise Denied: Origins of the Decline of
         American Railroads, 1897-1917. New York: Columbia University
         Press, 1971. 402 pp.
Martin locates the roots of America's railroad problem in the government
regulations that thwarted the industry's entrepreneurs. Until the regulatory system was strengthened in the progressive era by the Hepburn Act
(1906) and the Mann-Elkins Act (1910), the railroads were improving their
productivity and making a satisfactory adjustment to the nation's demands
for efficient rail transportation. The new regulatory environment, however,
made it impossible for the railroads to obtain the capital they needed
to finance improvements. The final showdown came in W.W. I when the warn-
ings of the railroad leaders were vindicated and the government was forced
to take over and operate the nation's rail system. Martin concludes that
the public policies of the Progressive era--those opposed to the trusts,
in favor of labor unions, and against rate increases--fatally weakened
one of America's most important industries.

H 1747. MASON, EDWARD S., ed. The Corporation in Modern Society. Cam-
         bridge, Mass.: Harvard University Press, 1959. 335 pp.
In addition to an introduction by Mason, readers of this collection will
find Carl Kaysen's article "The Corporation: How Much Power? What Scope?"
and W. Lloyd Warner's discussion of "The Corporation Man." In the latter
piece, the author argues that the rise of the large corporation has actually improved access to top business positions for those from lower social
and economic levels; education, he says, is the key to this form of upward
mobility. A less optimistic note is sounded in Jacob Schmookler's "Technological Progress and the Modern American Corporation," in which the
author concludes that the weaknesses in the private corporate sector of
the economy must largely be corrected by changes in public policy (including patent policy). Other contributions are Neil W. Chamberlain's "The
Corporation and the Trade Union"; John Litner's essay on corporate financial policies; and Raymond Vernon's "The American Corporation in Under-
developed Areas."

H 1748. McCONNELL, GRANT. The Decline of Agrarian Democracy. Berkeley:
         University of California Press, 1953. 226 pp.
Agricultural organizations in America have greatly increased their political influence in the 20th century, and McConnell is critical of the manner
in which they have acquired this power. Focusing primarily on the Farm
Bureau, he shows how this organization functioned as an interest group,
eschewing the third-party, Democratic politics that had characterized
the agrarian movement in the later part of the 19th century. McConnell
discusses the origins of the Farm Bureau, its relations with other, more
radical farm groups, and its legislative successes--particularly during
the 1930s. The Farm Bureau was largely responsible for drafting the legislation that granted Federal aid to agriculture. McConnell shows that
production controls and price supports were developed by and for the most
organized farmers. His account of agricultural organization includes
discussion of the post-W.W. II period.

H 1749. McGOULDRICK, PAUL F. New England Textiles in the Nineteenth Cen-
         tury: Profits and Investment. Cambridge, Mass.: Harvard Uni-
         versity Press, 1968. 307 pp.
This investigation of the economic behavior of a sample of New England
cotton textile firms focuses on specific questions involving their profitability, dividends, retention of earnings, output, borrowing, and investment policies over a fifty-year period between 1830 and 1885. McGouldrick
reconstructs each firm's annual balance sheets to determine how profits
and investment behavior changed over time. He finds little variation
in rates of profit but notes a decline in the ratio of profits to sales,
and he suggests that investment varied with profits rather than with sales

646

or capacity. He also finds that dividend pay-out rates were high and
that there was little lag in adjusting dividend rates to changes in profit
rates. McGouldrick concludes that investment in the New England textile
industry in particular and in manufacturing in general probably had a
stabilizing effect on the 19th-century economy. Investment lagged changes
in demand enough to avoid excessively rapid fluctuations in output. Output
fell short during upswings and exceeded it during recessions (causing
fluctuations in prices), but these cycles occurred around a steady upward
trend in output resulting from the increasing productivity of labor and
capital—thus the cycles were dampened. The main responsibility for down-
turns, McGouldrick suggests, rested with monetary and credit conditions.

H 1750. McGREGOR, ALEXANDER CAMPBELL. Counting Sheep: From Open Range
        to Agribusiness on the Columbia Plateau. Seattle: University
        of Washington Press, 1982. 482 pp.
This is a study of three generations of the McGregors, a Scottish-Canadian
family who created a ranching and farming business in the interior of
the Pacific Northwest. The family history provides a record of management
of 19th- and 20th-century land-extensive agriculture in the Northwest.
The author focuses on the work of wheat growers and livestock raisers,
and the transformation of remote, semi-arid lands into farmland.

H 1751. MEIKLE, JEFFREY L. Twentieth Century Limited: Industrial Design
        in America, 1925-1939. Philadelphia: Temple University Press,
        1979. 249 pp.
Meikle contrasts the present state of industrial design and its "limited
goal of providing individual businesses and their products with public
images conducive to profit," with the visions of those who established
industrial design as a profession in the 1930s. Seeing the movement's
leaders as self-conscious pioneers attempting to create a coherent environment for the Machine Age, he uses photographs, catalogs, and written
accounts to explain how business, technology, and ideology combined to
create new idioms for mass-produced goods. While some product innovations
were inspired by French decorative art of the 1920s, Meikle traces the
real roots of the industrial design profession to the needs of businesses
that, during the depression, believed products redesigned in the new styles
would stimulate the economy by attracting customers.

H 1752. MILLER, NATHAN. The Enterprise of a Free People: Aspects of
        Economic Development in New York State During the Canal Period,
        1792-1838. Ithaca, N.Y.: Cornell University Press, 1962.
        293 pp.
Miller claims that the construction of the Erie Canal offers perhaps the
best single example of the role played by government in promoting the
economic development of America in the early 19th century. Although the
government of New York State had begun to advance small-scale aid to manufacturers and farmers in the late 18th century, the creation of the canal
fund and the construction of the canal marked a departure from a relatively
passive to an extremely active role in advancing the state's economic
development. Miller also analyzes the financing of the Erie and Champlain
Canals and describes how and to what effect the canal revenues were used.

H 1753. MOSLEY, LEONARD. Blood Relations: The Rise and Fall of the
        du Ponts of Delaware. New York: Atheneum, 1980. 426 pp.
The work is a history of the du Pont family and its monolithic business,
starting with P. S. du Pont's arrival in America in 1800 and continuing
to the present day. Mosley intertwines the sordid aspects of the family's
history with its great achievements and contributions to mankind. He
recounts stories of intra-family rivalries and struggles; encouraging
war for the sake of profit; exploitation, cruelty, and murder; as well
as the family's dominance of Delaware politics. He balances this picture

with the achievements of the Du Pont corporation, including its great discovery—nylon. Finally, though the family remains one of America's wealthiest, Mosley tells of its decline as the dominating force in American society. Mosley was given access to all of the du Pont letters and papers—which had never before been granted to researchers.

H 1754. MYERS, MARGARET C. The New York Money Market: Origins and Develop ment. New York: Columbia University Press, 1931. 476 pp.
Meyers's history surveys New York's rise to a status of near equality with the leading financial centers of Europe. Focusing on the years between 1809 and 1913, Myers concentrates on the growth of a series of interrelated but specialized markets which, by the late 19th century, collectively comprised a sophisticated money market. New York's development as America's major financial center followed the city's commercial expansion in the first quarter of the 19th century; it was then that the city outstripped its East coast rivals, Baltimore, Philadelphia, and Boston. Before the Civil War, commerce was funded to an important extent by direct loans in foreign exchange and by European purchase of American securities, and New York became the primary American market for both types of dealings. Its commercial and financial status also attracted country bankers whose balances led to the development of a call loan market and a growing demand for commercial paper. In the late 19th century, a full-fledged commercial credit market arose, and the market in securities matured. Throughout this history, Myers stresses the fact that the lack of a central banking system posed great difficulties for the money market. Thus, New York's international position was not assured until the creation of the Federal Research System.

H 1755. NASH, GERALD D. United States Oil Policy, 1890-1964: Business and Government in 20th Century America. Pittsburgh, Pa.: University of Pittsburgh Press, 1968. 280 pp.
According to Nash, the American oil industry's contact with the government gradually forged a consensus that stressed the need for cooperation between business and government. President Theodore Roosevelt first articulated the central concept of this consensus when he insisted that government, previously a passive promoter and regulator of economic life, must enter into active cooperation with business and supervise the conduct of American private enterprise. Consequently, Roosevelt's New Nationalism shifted public policy away from negative programs (such as antitrust), which attempted to prevent undue concentrations of economic power. The Wilson administration, in its responses to W.W. I, created an institutional framework which facilitated collaboration between government and the oil industry; Coolidge pursued cooperation intelligently rather than slavishly; Hoover did not. Later, Franklin D. Roosevelt helped warring factions within the industry compromise their differences and established a public-private system of controls that stabilized domestic production and prices. This system—which combined the authority of a state agency in Texas with Federal power over interstate shipments—was crucial to the consensus that developed after W.W. II. Throughout the study, Nash describes the conflicts and compromises that had to be resolved and engineered before America could create this new system and adopt the ideology of cooperation.

H 1756. NELSON, DANIEL. Frederick Taylor and the Rise of Scientific Management. Madison: University of Wisconsin Press, 1980. 259 pp.
Nelson calls Taylor the "single most important contributor to the rise of a 'new factory system,' and of an aristocracy based on technical knowledge, educational and organizational skills rather than on inherited wealth, social and familial ties, or business acumen." This biography probes two themes: the ways in which Taylor's views were shaped by business and managerial developments, particularly his consulting assignments; and his conservatism and disdain for innovations in the labor-management and personnel fields.

648

H 1757. NELSON, RALPH. Merger Movements in American Industry, 1895-1956. Princeton, N.J.: Princeton University Press, 1959. 177 pp. Nelson points out that there have been three major waves of mergers: the first and largest at the turn of the century; the second during the late 1920s; and the third following W.W. II. In addition to providing the statistics on these long-run aspects of the phenomenon, the author lists the specific firms involved in mergers, with detailed breakdowns by industry. He analyzes the wave of mergers that peaked between 1899 and 1901, and he also discusses the relationships between merger activity and the business cycle.

H 1758. NEU, IRENE D. Erastus Corning: Merchant and Financier, 1794-1872. Ithaca, N.Y.: Cornell University Press, 1960. 212 pp. For Neu, Corning exemplifies the merchant-capitalist who dominated economic enterprise in antebellum America. Neu characterizes Corning as a self-made man who gained experience at an early age in iron and hardware retailing and wholesaling, and in general merchandizing. He expanded his operations after 1814, when he moved from Troy, New York, to the commercial center Albany, which allowed for his greater involvement in Western trade. Corning diversified his interests and ultimately invested in transportation. This involvement with the railroads of western New York ensured that his iron products, particularly iron rails, would be accessible to the expanding Western markets as well as other railroad companies. Corning became president of the Albany City Bank in 1834 and later used his knowledge of finance and railroads to engineer a series of railroad consolidations, the most famous of which produced the New York Central in 1854.

H 1759. NEVINS, ALAN. Study in Power: John D. Rockefeller, Industrialist and Philanthropist. 2 vols. New York: Scribner, 1953. 942 pp. Originally published in 1940 under the title John D. Rockefeller: The Heroic Age of American Enterprise, Nevins's work places Rockefeller against the background of a rapidly industrializing and relatively chaotic economy. Stressing the confusion and anarchic competition rampant in the oil industry during its initial phase of rapid growth, Nevins contends that Rockefeller was an organizing genius who created order and efficiency out of turmoil. Thus, according to Nevins, Rockefeller's position in Standard Oil was that of a benevolent despot. While acknowledging the enormous power that Rockefeller exercised over the oil industry, Nevins says that his actions were not those of the ruthless and sinister caricature created by contemporaries and progressive historians. While some of Rockefeller's policies were morally questionable, even these activities were typical of contemporary business practice. Consequently, the businessman is portrayed as an industrial statesman and prime mover of the nation's economic progress.

H 1760. NORRIS, JAMES D. R. G. Dun & Co., 1841-1900: The Development of Credit-Reporting in the Nineteenth Century. Westport, Conn.: Greenwood Press, 1978. 206 pp. Norris traces the transformation of the credit-reporting business in 19th-century America by focusing on the primary role of R. G. Dun & Co. and its innovative owner, Robert Graham Dun. Before the Civil War, credit had been based on the archaic principle of personal knowledge. But the rapid economic expansion of the early 19th century and the crisis of 1837 made clear the need for an efficient system for rating credit. Norris shows how after taking over the Mercantile Agency in 1858, Dun transformed it into a modern business providing information on firms throughout the world. Norris describes Dun's major innovations—his reliance on quantifiable data rather than personal acquaintance, and the creation of a systematic, reasonable, and accountable management system—to argue that Dun possessed one of the great business minds of the period. He further argues, however, that although Dun adopted the life-style of the "robber

barons," he did not share their social philosophy, nor did he embrace
their entrepreneurial characteristics.

H 1761. OLMSTEAD, ALLAN L. New York Savings Banks in the Ante-Bellum
Years, 1819-1861. Chapel Hill: University of North Carolina
Press, 1976. 236 pp.

Olmstead observes that the New York mutual savings banks of the 19th century were unique organizations; while they were philanthropic institutions
founded early in the century specifically to serve small depositors and
to encourage thrift among the working classes, they flourished during
a period of rapid economic growth better known for the accomplishments
of its capitalists than for its disinterest in profit. Olmstead's major
interest lies in examining the extent to which the philanthropic aspect
of the mutuals was an accurate expression of reality. He focuses on the
approximately twenty banks founded in the New York City area in the period
between 1820 and the Civil War, concentrating in particular on the Bank
for Savings in New York City, the major financial institution of its time.
Olmstead finds that the mutuals were not operated for profit; their behavior, as reflected in their administration and their investment choices,
predominately reflected their professed objectives. Deviations from this
pattern took place among the newer mutuals which sought out larger
depositors and invested in private projects. The legal limitations on their
investments greatly aided the state's pursuit of economic development,
as the mutuals were an important source of capital for New York's internal
improvement projects.

H 1762. OVERTON, RICHARD C. Burlington Route: A History of the Burlington
Lines. New York: Knopf, 1965. 623 pp.

Overton describes the expansion of the Chicago, Burlington and Quincy
Railroad from its foundation at the mid-point of the 19th century through
the problems encountered by the firm in the middle of the 20th century.
He chronicles the railroad's expansion, emphasizing the contribution made
to the nation's economic growth. Highlighted throughout the study are
Burlington's distinctive technological and organizational contributions,
including, for example, the pioneering diesel-electric locomotives in
the 1930s. Overton discusses the company's labor policies and the problems
encountered by the firm in the 20th century. The latter, he says, resulted
largely from the conditions created by powerful labor unions, by the competition of other forms of transportation, and by government regulation.

H 1763. PAPENFUSE, EDWARD C. In Pursuit of Profit: The Annapolis Merchants in the Era of the American Revolution, 1763-1805. Baltimore, Md.: Johns Hopkins University Press, 1975. 288 pp.

Papenfuse analyzes the commercial activities of approximately thirty prominent Annapolis tobacco merchants. He describes their business operations,
their successful challenge to the hegemony which the London-based system
held over the Maryland tobacco trade, their alliances with Baltimore merchants, and their role in encouraging urban development and agricultural
diversification. Papenfuse says these merchants were the first Americans
to employ domestically accumulated capital to achieve a prominent position
in the tobacco trade, a position they strengthened in the 1780s as they
reinvested money made in wartime profiteering. Although their economic
influence declined in the 1790s, the members of this elite continued to
wield considerable local power on the basis of their investments in agriculture.

H 1764. PARKER, WILLIAN N., ed. The Structure of the Cotton Economy of the Antebellum South. Washington, D.C.: Agricultural History Society, 1970. 169 pp.
This volume presents four major studies of self-sufficiency, profitability, and wealth concentration based on a cotton farm sample drawn from the 1860 census. James D. Foust and Dale E. Swan examine slave productivity and profitability. Robert E. Gallman focuses on farm and plantation self-sufficiency. Diane L. Lindstrom analyzes West-South grain flows after 1840. The collection also includes an essay by Parker tracing the hypothetical course of development of a free labor economy in the South after 1789, and it concludes with critiques of the Gallman and Parker essays by Stanley L. Engerman and Eugene D. Genovese, and with Morton Rothstein's survey of the literature of antebellum Southern economic development.

H 1765. PASKOFF, PAUL E. Industrial Evolution: Organization, Structure, and Growth of the Pennsylvania Iron Industry, 1750-1860. Baltimore, Md.: Johns Hopkins University Press, 1983. 208 pp.
Paskoff probes important aspects of the early iron industry by examining both the business practices of individual firms and the interplay of iron producers, markets, and the economy. He argues that the growth of the pre-Civil War iron industry was the result of gradual evolution and not sudden revolutionary change, as other scholars have claimed. The study relates the development of business organization to the adoption of new technologies and the impact of market pressures.

H 1766. PASSER, HAROLD C. The Electrical Manufacturers, 1875-1900. Cambridge, Mass.: Harvard University Press, 1953. 412 pp.
Passer studies competition, entrepreneurship, technological change, and economic growth in the infant electrical equipment manufacturing industry of the late 19th century. He focuses on the developments in the manufacture of arc lighting, incandescent lighting, electric power equipment, and traction systems. Describing the organizational changes that took place in the industry, he considers their impact on patterns of competition and discusses technological trends and their influence on the industry's pattern of growth. Passer also concentrates on the process of innovation in a new industry based on a new technology; he shows how technological innovations were translated into business operations. He stresses the fact that the industry's first leaders were engineer-entrepreneurs who possessed both the technological knowledge to design and develop a product and the business acumen needed to organize its production and marketing. Passer implies that engineer-entrepreneurship characterizes the early stages of development in highly technical industries, and he concludes that during later phases in an industry's life cycle, the large enterprises that control most of the production are less innovative than their small counterparts.

H 1767. PERKINS, EDWIN J. Financing Anglo-American Trade: The House of Brown, 1800-1880. Cambridge, Mass.: Harvard University Press, 1975. 323 pp.
Perkins analyzes the complex business and financial operations of the premier American merchant-banking firm active in Anglo-American trade of the 19th century. He first presents a chronological account of the firm's development, describing its trend toward specialization in particular fields of commercial activity and its reactions to the changes wrought by steam transportation and the telegraph. The second part of the book treats the firm's various functional activities, from dealing in advances and merchandise to handling letters of credit and foreign exchange. On the basis of research in manuscript collections, Perkins considers the manner in which trends in the firm's commercial strategy were related to its managerial decisions and its administrative structure.

H 1768. PETERSON, TRUDY HUSKAMP. Agricultural Exports, Farm Income, and
the Eisenhower Administration. Lincoln: University of Nebraska
Press, 1980. 222 pp.
Peterson examines the Eisenhower administration's attempt to maintain
agricultural income by expanding foreign markets. He discusses the formulation of the Agricultural Trade Development and Assistance Act of 1954
(later known as the Food for Peace Act), which allowed the President of
the U.S. to dispose of surplus farm commodities through such means as
seeking new markets, bartering for strategic materials, and making dona-
tions as part of foreign aid. Peterson also examines the implications
of holding back U.S. products from the Communist bloc.

H 1769. PETERSON, TRUDY HUSKAMP, ed. Farmers, Bureaucrats, and Middlemen:
Historical Perspectives on American Agriculture. Washington,
D.C.: Howard University Press, 1980. 357 pp.
These papers and proceedings of the National Archives Conference on American Agriculture, 1977, emphasize 20th-century themes and topics. Topics
include the social and political aspects of American agriculture; organizational and labor activism; the role of understudied groups including
tenants, sharecroppers, women, and migrants; agricultural research and
development; crop marketing; the relationship between agriculture and
the Federal government; and resources for studying agricultural history
in the National Archives. Several of the presentations also deal directly
with policy questions such as the controversies over agricultural chemicals
or the effectiveness of agricultural experiment stations in promoting
research.

H 1770. PHILLIPS, PAUL C. The Fur Trade. 2 vols. Norman: University
of Oklahoma Press, 1961. 1382 pp.
Phillips's volumes attend less to the romantic conception of the role
played by the American fur trade in the politics and economics of Western
nations between the 16th and 19th centuries. Instead, he examines this
important business as a stimulus to exploration and colonization, as an
influence on foreign and domestic policies, and as an actor in the development of Capitalism and imperialism. His study is based on a large body
of personal, business, and government records, both American and foreign.
Phillips did not quite complete this work; the concluding chapters are
by J. W. Smurr.

H 1771. POPE, DANIEL. The Making of Modern Advertising. New York: Basic
Books, 1983. 340 pp.
Pope takes issue with critics of the so-called persuasion industry in
this account of advertising practitioners who, in his view, were in business "to sell their clients' products, not to peddle ideology." He
describes how technological changes such as improved printing methods contributed to the formation of the oligopolistic corporations of today's
advertising world. He discusses how the modern industry began with the
first major national advertising campaigns launched by manufacturers of
patent medicines, and provides several chapters on the rise of the "truth
in advertising" movement by the 1920s.

H 1772. PORTER, GLENN. The Rise of Big Business, 1860-1910. New York:
Crowell, 1973. 119 pp.
Porter's book surveys the changes that occurred in America's corporate
economy in the late 19th century. The author, who criticizes the moral
approach to corporations and businessmen adopted by earlier historians,
embraces the type of institutional analysis pioneered by Alfred D. Chandler,
Jr. Big business, Porter says, developed as a consequence of improved
transportation and communications, technological advances in the processes
of production and distribution, political limitations on alternate forms
of organization, imitation of the most successful early combines, and

the availability of capital due to changes in the markets for securities. Porter describes the manner in which various entrepreneurs adopted the corporate form in order to ensure predictability in economic behavior and stability of returns.

H 1773. PORTER, GLENN and HAROLD C. LIVESAY. Merchants and Manufacturers: Studies in the Changing Structure of 19th Century Marketing. Baltimore, Md.: Johns Hopkins University Press, 1971. 257 pp. Porter and Livesay maintain that previous historians of the 19th century have concentrated too much on changes in the technology and organization of production and have given too little attention to distribution. In their view, marketing and distribution in America continued to be dominated by all-purpose merchants as late as 1815. In the years following 1815, the expansion of the volume of commerce led to increasing specialization, but merchants nevertheless remained the key figures in marketing. Producers began to displace merchants as distributors of manufactured goods only in the last decades of the century, when market density and technological complexity made it profitable for manufacturers to take over the function of distribution, especially at the wholesale level.

H 1774. PRATT, JOSEPH A. The Growth of a Refining Region. Greenwich, Conn.: JAI Press, 1980. 297 pp. Pratt analyzes the connections between institutions and economic growth in this study of the petroleum refining companies and their role in the development of the upper Texas Gulf Coast which began with the introduction of the first Gulf and Texaco plants in the early 20th century. The first chapter describes forces of regional economic development that were set in motion before 1900, and later sections trace the diversification and expansion of an oil-related complex of industries beginning around W.W. II. The book also provides an overview of the region's role in the national economy, which emerged early on because Houston provided a substantial share of the refined goods demanded by the urban-industrial centers in the Northeast as well as by the industrialized Southwest. The author applies various theories to describe the dramatic shifts brought about by the rapid construction of numerous large refineries in the region, but he finds no one explanation completely adequate.

H 1775. PREVITS, GARY JOHN and BARBARA DUBIS MERINO. A History of Accounting in America: An Historical Interpretation of the Cultural Significance of Accounting. New York: Wiley, 1979. 378 pp. The work examines the history of the practice (as opposed to the profession) of accounting in America, literally from 1492--by discussing the pecuniary practices of the first explorers and settlers--to the present day. Previts and Merino offer a general, chronological survey: each chapter explores the broader social, political, economic, and personal aspects of accounting in each particular period. Previts and Merino focus on the important persons, institutions, and events, but also devote much attention to the important theories concerning accounting. On its contemporary status and role, Previts and Merino suggest that accounting has become a means of political and economic control in American society.

H 1776. PRICE, JACOB M. France and the Chesapeake: A History of the French Tobacco Monopoly, 1674-1791, and of Its Relationship to the British and American Tobacco Trades. 2 vols. Ann Arbor: University of Michigan Press, 1973. 1239 pp. In this work, Price describes and analyzes the structure and operations of the French Tobacco Monopoly from its inception in 1674 to its destruction in 1791. The study is divided into three parts. The first is a business history of the monopoly itself, concentrating on its administrative structure and its purchasing, marketing, and distribution systems. The second describes the process of purchasing by French agents in Britain

and analyzes the impact of their activities on the tobacco trade. Part
Three is a history of the monopoly's last years of operation. In examining
the tobacco market, Price treats both formal administrative structures
and informal interpersonal networks such as kin networks.

H 1777. REDLICH, FRITZ. The Molding of American Banking: Men and Ideas.
2 vols. New York: Hafner, 1947, 1951. 517 pp.
Redlich uses a case study of banking to illustrate his Schumpterian theory
of the role of innovators in the development of economic institutions.
He concentrates on the particular functions that people wanted banks to
perform and on the innovations that bankers introduced in response to
changing economic circumstances. He examines in this manner the emergence
of American banking and the development of the banking system through
1840, touching upon Southern banks, savings banks, the Suffolk Bank System,
and treating the Second Bank of the United States in considerable detail.
The second volume carries this same theme through 1910 and discusses--
among other topics--the beginnings of clearing houses, investment banking,
and cooperation among banks.

H 1778. REED, MERL. New Orleans and the Railroad: The Struggle for Commercial Empire, 1830-1860. Baton Rouge: Louisiana State University Press, 1966. 172 pp.
Reed argues that antebellum railroad development in Louisiana was chaotic
and only partially successful. For many years New Orleans's water routes
seemed a more than adequate guarantee of commercial prosperity, and this
discouraged interest in railroads. The construction which did occur in
the 1830s and 1840s was hampered by a lack of capital and was confined
to short lines that either fed the waterways or were intended to serve
the city's growing urban and suburban populations. Not until the 1850s,
when the loss of trade galvanized both private economic interests and
the government, did the state begin to channel sufficient capital to the
railroads to permit real growth. By this time, however, New Orleans had
already lost its hold on much of the Western commerce; the city could
only hope for continued control over the trade of the South. This was
a more realistic prospect, Reed concludes, but this strategy was stymied
by the Civil War and the resulting fifteen-year hiatus in railroad construction.

H 1779. RUMELT, RICHARD P. Strategy, Structure, and Economic Performance.
Boston: Division of Research, Graduate School of Business Administration, Harvard University, 1974. 235 pp.
Rumelt studies the evolution of economic strategy and corporate structure
after W.W. II and argues that diversification has become the accepted
economic strategy among large corporations, most of which have now adopted
the decentralized product-division structure. The notable exceptions,
Rumelt shows, are the large vertically integrated firms in industries
such as steel and oil. Using data drawn from a sample of firms in "Fortune's 500," Rumelt claims that diversification and decentralization are
responsible for the improvement in economic performance of modern corporations. He thereby challenges those theories which stress that the key
factors in modern corporate growth have been integration and a high level
of technological development. Rumelt says, moreover, that the profit-
maximizing manager has not been replaced by a technocratic elite within
the modern corporation; in fact, adoption of the product-division structure
has required the participation of managers in ever-increasing numbers.

H 1780. **SALSBURY, STEPHEN.** The State, the Investor, and the Railroad:
The Boston and Albany, 1825-1867. Cambridge, Mass.: Harvard
University Press, 1967. 404 pp.
In this history of the railroad development in antebellum Massachusetts,
Salsbury shows how the appearance of differing interests precluded the
state's direct participation in the construction of railroads. Thus,
Salsbury argues, the Massachusetts experience qualifies the recent emphasis
on the role of government in 19th-century economic development. Although
laissez-faire was a prevailing myth, the state could in this instance
command neither the route of the railroad nor the timing of the decision
to build. Because of the variety of interests to which it had to answer,
the state's role was confined largely to passive assistance. These years
constituted an important turning point in Massachusetts's economic development. The desire to recapture the trade lost when the Erie Canal was
built did not encourage enough investment to build a competing rail system;
capitalists did not become interested in investing in a railroad until
the continued spread of textile manufacturing created new needs for a
system of transportation within the state. Nevertheless, the conflict
between commercial interests stressing long-haul commerce and manufacturers
seeking cheap local transportation continued and was reflected in the
railroad's rate structures.

H 1781. **SAUNDERS, RICHARD.** The Railroad Mergers and the Coming of Conrail.
Westport, Conn.: Greenwood Press, 1978. 389 pp.
Saunders cites various reasons for the failure of railroad mergers between
1950 and 1970: the sluggish ICC regulator system; difficulties in project
savings and benefits; capital shortages; and reactions from labor and
public interest groups protesting budgetary service cuts. This history
and study of public policy emphasizes Congressional inertia and public
subsidies of other forms of transportation as chief causes of the impasse
that triggered the merger movement.

H 1782. **SCHEIBER, HARRY N.** Ohio Canal Era: A Case Study of Government
and the Economy, 1820-61. Athens: Ohio University Press, 1969.
430 pp.
This volume describes the Ohio state government's role in promoting, planning, and developing the state's canal system. Scheiber discusses the
creation of the state's canal commission and its financial management
and administration of canal construction and operation. The author analyzes the impact of the canal system, and thus of state planning, on the
regional economy. He finds that the canal system influenced the pattern
of economic development in the state, a pattern that was altered in important respects by the coming of the railroad. Scheiber's study contradicts
the traditional view of 19th-century governments as laissez-faire, establishing that at least until mid-century, Ohio's political leaders consciously pursued the state's economic advancement.

H 1783. **SCHROEDER, GERTRUDE G.** The Growth of the Major Steel Companies,
1900-1950. Baltimore, Md.: Johns Hopkins University Press,
1952. 244 pp.
Schroeder first studies the formation of United States Steel, and then
examines the growth of this combine and of the other leading firms in
the industry. She finds that the major combine has lost a significant
part of its market share over the years, while the smaller independents
have gradually increased their shares of the market, and business failures
have been as rare as the birth of new firms. While the author does not
credit the smaller firms with more aggressive leadership or more innovative
techniques, the data do imply that the largest firms may have been less
oriented to growth and change than they might have been.

H 1784. SCHURR, SAM H., BRUCE C. NETSCHERT, et al. Energy in the American Economy, 1850-1975: An Economic Study of Its History and Prospects. Baltimore, Md.: Johns Hopkins University Press, 1960. 774 pp.

The authors describe the changing composition of America's energy base between 1850 and 1950, supplementing their survey with estimates of energy supply and demand through 1975. Their historical analysis focuses on the massive substitutions in energy sources over the last 100 years. Until the late 19th century, wood was still America's major energy source. By the early 20th century, however, coal had replaced wood, only to be replaced itself by oil and gas following W.W. II. The authors demonstrate that the rate of growth of America's energy supply has consistently outstripped that of consumption. They also provide data relating energy consumption to the Gross National Product, demonstrating that since 1920 the consumption of energy per unit of output has actually declined.

H 1785. SCHWARZ, JORDAN A. The Speculator: Bernard M. Baruch in Washington, 1917-1965. Chapel Hill: University of North Carolina Press, 1981. 679 pp.

This is a biography of the industrial statesman who emerged from a successful career as a Wall Street speculator to manage Wilson's war government. Baruch was an early spokesman for stabilization of business and promoted national economic policies intended to achieve market stabilization and social order. He first ventured onto the national scene in 1915 as a champion of American preparedness for involvement in W.W. I. Baruch went on to head the raw materials section of the War Industries Board until he became its chairman in 1918; he subsequently served as a source of economic advice and campaign contributions for Democrats in the Senate.

H 1786. SEDLAK, MICHAEL W. and HAROLD F. WILLIAMSON. The Evolution of Management Education: A History of the Northwestern University J. L. Kellogg Graduate School of Management 1908-1983. Urbana: University of Illinois Press, 1983. 202 pp.

Sedlak (a historian of education and social policy) and Williamson (author of many works in economic history) have joined in producing this account of one of the oldest collegiate business schools in the U.S. The collaborators have looked beyond institutional confines to find reasons for its success. Initially intended to facilitate the training of clerks and bookkeepers, Northwestern's program expanded in response to the changing structure of business and the efforts of deans who sought to develop a training course geared to the expressed needs of prospective employers of the school's students.

H 1787. SHEPHERD, JAMES F. and GARY M. WALTON. Shipping, Maritime Trade and the Development of Colonial America. New York: Cambridge University Press, 1972. 255 pp.

Shepherd and Walton analyze the role of export trade in the economic development of the American Colonies during the 18th century. Within a context set by their assessment of longterm trends in the growth of output, commerce, and population, the authors demonstrate that the proportion of Colonial economic activity devoted to supplying overseas markets was of primary importance and that overseas trade stimulated the growth of production for markets. They identify variations in the distribution of each colony's overseas markets and a high degree of regional specialization in production. By way of contrast, however, they also find an important invisible earnings component (commercial services) in the Colonial balance of payments—a component which, together with ship sales and the slave trade, tends to balance the visible trade in Southern commodities and to leave the Colonial balance of payments almost untouched by deficit. The authors thus conclude that American capital accumulation in the 18th century was due almost entirely to domestic saving, not to foreign borrowing.

H 1788. SOBEL, ROBERT. The Age of Giant Corporations: A Microeconomic
          History of American Business, 1914-1970. Westport, Conn.: Green-
          wood Press, 1972. 257 pp.
Sobel addresses America's transformation from a nation in which large
corporations were the exception to one in which they were the rule. He
regards this revolution in business organization as the primary force
in the remarkable growth of the American economy in the 20th century;
consequently, he examines the industries, corporations, and businessmen
that have played major roles in this transformation. Approaching his
subject chronologically, Sobel argues that the intertwining of business
and political power during W.W. I paved the way for a form of post-war
collaboration that effectively removed restraints on the expansion of
industrial enterprise. In the 1920s, the new consumer industries, such
as motion pictures and automobiles, came to be dominated by giant firms,
just as the steel, oil, and other industries had been at an earlier date.
All of these oligopolies experienced difficulties during the Great Depression, but as early as 1933, they experienced improved conditions and continued to strengthen their positions throughout the 1930s. Mobilization
in W.W. II again brought government and business into a close partnership,
a situation which presaged the post-war appearance of monopolies fed by
the increase in government expenditures. This condition in the modern
market, Sobel observes, has been accompanied by a new business structure--
the conglomerate, a company operating a group of units in unrelated markets.

H 1789. SOBEL, ROBERT. I.T.T.: The Management of Opportunity. New York:
          Times Books, 1982. 421 pp.
Written with the cooperation of I.T.T., this history of the corporation
concentrates on central management and strategy, rather than on the details
of its numerous subsidiaries. Smith recounts specific internal crises
such as the matter of succession, as well as larger political entanglements
such as the Nixon/Chile episodes. He describes the dramatic events leading
to consolidation, and illustrates the diversity that is I.T.T.'s hallmark,
especially as the overlapping visions of Behn, Geneen, and Araskog held
the corporation together. He concludes with a description of the giant
conglomerate's latest venture into telecommunications and information-
sharing.

H 1790. STOVER, JOHN F. The Railroads of the South, 1865-1900: A Study
          in Finance and Control. Chapel Hill: University of North Caro-
          lina Press, 1955. 310 pp.
Stover describes the growth of Northern financial influence over Southern
railroads during the Reconstruction period. He examines all the South's
major railroads, emphasizing the four major systems whose history illustrates the pattern of Northern encroachment. As Stover shows, Northern
entrepreneurs attempted to take over numerous railroads during the years
immediately following the war. The first major Northern takeover was
not mounted, however, until the early 1870s when the Pennsylvania Railroad
attempted to build up a Southern empire. More enduring success was
achieved by the Illinois Central during the late 1870s, and by 1890 the
Louisville and Nashville Railroad was firmly in Northern control. Thereafter, the conquest was carried on by J. P. Morgan, whose Southern Railway
came to include 6,000 miles of Southern lines.

H 1791. SUTTON, FRANCIS X., SEYMOUR E. HARRIS, CARL KAYSEN, and JAMES
          TOBIN. The American Business Creed. Cambridge, Mass.: Harvard
          University Press, 1956. 414 pp.
Based upon the public statements of business leaders and organizations,
this account describes the ideology characteristic of business in the
20th century. Defining ideology as a verbal-symbolic means of resolving
a group's major conflicts, the authors trace changes in the businessman's
ideology, which helps him cope with conflicts and anxieties that are gene-

657

rated by his particular occupation, especially conflicts in employer-
employee relations. The classical ideology of an earlier day stressed
the contractual dimension of these relationships--for instance the right
of the employee to strike the best possible bargain--but the authors find
that in the modern firm this sort of ideology would not suffice. They
discover a shift from classical ideology to managerial ideology, which
stresses the human relations aspect--that is, the social system aspect--
of employer-employee interaction. Stressing this shift in ideologies,
the authors find that while much from the 19th century is preserved in
the current belief system, the business creed has not ossified in this
century but has continued to develop in response to the new conflicts
arising in the business world.

H 1792. SWANN, LEONARD A., Jr. John Roach, Maritime Entrepreneur: The
Years as Naval Contractor, 1862-1886. Annapolis, Md.: United
States Naval Institute, 1965. 301 pp.
Swann reevaluates the business operations of John Roach, who was a pioneer
of iron and steel shipbuilding in America and a leader of the maritime
industry in the years after the Civil War. Questioning the conclusions
of earlier historians, Swann denies that Roach was a corrupt and incompetent shipbuilder deservedly brought to task during the Cleveland administration for shady dealings with the outgoing Republicans. Rather, Swann
explains Roach's business difficulties in terms of the enterprise which
he created. Roach's firm was a formidable achievement, integrating ship
construction with the production of iron plates and fittings and of marine
engines and machinery. Despite this, however, Roach was not an accomplished businessman; the rule-of-thumb methods he followed in ship construction were also used in the administration of his business. Consequently, Swann concludes, the difficulties which led to Roach's bankruptcy
in 1887 resulted from an outdated system of ad hoc management, a system
of the sort that would eventually be replaced in most large enterprises
by bureaucratic controls.

H 1793. SWIERENGA, ROBERT P. Pioneers and Profits: Land Speculation
on the Iowa Frontier. Ames: Iowa State University Press, 1968.
260 pp.
This study of land buying in Iowa prior to the Civil War revises the negative stereotype of the frontier land speculator. Speculators, Swierenga
finds, were in fact investors who performed many important services for
the settlers moving into Western areas. While more than half of Iowa's
land passed through the hands of speculators dealing in large acreages,
they neither retarded settlement by holding land off the market nor sold
at excessive prices. Indeed, Swierenga argues that speculators realized
returns on their investments not by restricting supply but by maintaining
a high rate of turnover; they frequently sold land below the market price
to maintain a high volume of transactions. As nonresident investors,
the speculators were an important source of credit for settlers and also
of tax revenue. They were instrumental in the process of locating, surveying, and parcelling land, and their expenditures in pursuit of profit
bolstered the local economy. Land speculators, Swierenga concludes, helped
stimulate the process of pioneer settlement and accelerated the economic
development of the Western frontier by bringing cultivable land onto the
market.

H 1794. SYLLA, RICHARD E. The American Capital Market, 1846-1914: A
Study of Effects on Public Policy and Economic Development.
New York: Arno Press, 1975. 306 pp.
Sylla contends that in the last forty years of the 19th century there
emerged a national capital market which became a powerful force in promoting industrialization and economic growth. This market was created
through the forging of direct links between its two hitherto separate

components: the money market, consisting of the various individual banking markets; and the open market, consisting of all of the more centralized, quasi-national markets for stocks, bonds, and commercial paper. These links were created as a direct consequence of policy decisions about commercial banking made during the Civil War period.

H 1795. TAYLOR, GEORGE R. and IRENE D. NEU. The American Railroad Network, 1861-1890. Cambridge, Mass.: Harvard University Press, 1956. 113 pp.
Taylor and Neu argue that the American railroad system did not reach maturity until after the Civil War. Although by that time the system had already undergone twenty-five years of rapid development that spread railroad lines over a great deal of territory, the authors argue that this extent is neither a sufficient nor a necessary indication of maturity. By paying attention to such matters as gauge difference, the authors construct a "more meaningful map" of the American railroad system, one that shows that before the Civil War neither the U.S. nor Canada had a physically integrated network. In the three decades following the Civil War, however, the national system was coordinated. The authors trace the process of physical integration and also show how integration was encouraged by breaks through bridges and ferries, and by the organizational consolidation of the railroad companies. By 1890, the railroad system no longer served specialized functions within particular areas but had expanded to become the chief means of transport in a market economy now grown to nationwide proportions.

H 1796. TEDLOW, RICHARD S. Keeping the Corporate Image: Public Relations and Business, 1900-1950. Greenwich, Conn.: JAI Press, 1979. 233 pp.
Tedlow examines planned, organized efforts on the part of business to control news through informing and cultivating the press, and to encourage corporations to alter their policies in accordance with perceived public desires. The study focuses on the role of corporate press liaisons, their impact on government and business policy, and the cultural implications of businessmen's attempts to emphasize image more than reality. By tracing the distinction between public relations and advertising as it has evolved since the 1920s, the author presents his subject as a healthy sign of business's need to defend itself in a democracy. As he notes, public relations have also been highly self-serving, for admissions of the unvarnished truth would probably contribute to a disorder that businessmen and other managers of today's large organizations would prefer to avoid.

H 1797. TEMIN, PETER. Iron and Steel in 19th Century America: An Economic Inquiry. Cambridge, Mass.: MIT Press, 1964. 304 pp.
Temin claims that between 1830 and 1900 the American iron and steel industry experienced rapid growth accompanied by significant changes in methods of production, raw material use, and industrial organization. He analyzes these developments by isolating those factors that influenced supply and demand. On the supply side, the impact of technological development was most significant. On the demand side, Temin shows how the high rate of national economic growth accelerated the expansion of the industry's output; in particular, rapid growth encouraged sustained expansion of the nation's transportation network, which, in turn, produced a rising demand for more and better rails. These demand-side factors encouraged the adoption of the Bessemer process and pushed the industry toward steel and away from cast and wrought iron production. Temin also explains how the Bessemer process influenced the nature of the firms in the industry.

H 1798. THORELLI, HANS B. The Federal Antitrust Policy: Origination
of an American Tradition. Baltimore, Md.: Johns Hopkins University Press, 1955. 658 pp.
Thorelli traces the origins of the Sherman Act to its roots in English
and American common law and constitutional theory, and he describes the
industrial changes and accompanying social and economic conflicts that
were the immediate cause of its passage. He also analyzes the legislative
evolution of the Act itself. On these foundations he builds a history
of the policy's implementation from 1890 until the creation of the Bureau
of Corporations in 1903. He says that while the Act was not simply a
nationalization of the common law, it nevertheless reflected the common
law's hostility toward restraints on competition. Thus the rule of reason
was a departure from the Act's true purpose. He does not, however, hold
the courts responsible for impeding the creation of an effective antitrust policy. Thorelli finds this to have been the result of a general
administrative apathy surrounding a fairly wide interpretation of "commerce" onto the Act, making it a potent threat to those business interests
whose economic behavior it was intended to regulate.

H 1799. TOLLES, FREDERICK B. Meeting House and Counting House: The Quaker
Merchants of Colonial Philadelphia, 1682-1763. Chapel Hill:
University of North Carolina Press, 1948. 292 pp.
Tolles describes the development of commerce in Philadelphia within the
context of the tension between that dimension of the Quaker ethic that
sanctioned economic individualism and the accumulation of wealth and that
which emphasized corporatism and was critical of the acquisitive spirit.
Quaker advocacy of social order and regularity in day-to-day life redounded
to the benefit of a rationalized capitalist economy; yet, at the same
time, their religion prevented the development of a completely individualistic brand of Capitalism. Within this general context, the author
describes the development of Philadelphia's commerce, underlining the importance of personal, religious, and familial contacts in integrating Philadelphia's trade with that of the North Atlantic system. He also discusses
other elements in Quaker economic life, including the economic role of
the Monthly Meeting and the contribution made by Quaker merchants to the
development of Pennsylvania's manufactures and mining.

H 1800. TOSTLEBE, ALVIN S. Capital in Agriculture: Its Formation and
Financing Since 1870. Princeton, N.J.: Princeton University
Press, 1957. 232 pp.
Tostlebe, who measures the growth of physical farm capital between 1870
and 1950, finds that a substantial increase in farm productivity occurred
during the first half of the 20th century. Between 1870 and 1910 the
capital stock, agricultural labor force, and gross farm output all doubled
in size. In the succeeding forty-year period, gross farm output doubled
once again. The number of persons engaged in agriculture, however, underwent an absolute decline, and the rate of growth of the stock of physical
capital slowed significantly. Tostlebe suggests that technical and institutional factors played a substantial role in the growth in farm productivity after 1910. Agriculture's gross capital formation was financed, the
author concludes, largely out of gross farm income. External financial
institutions may have helped to ease the flow of funds into and out of
the agricultural sector but, on balance, their contribution remained quite
small.

H 1801. TRESCOTT, PAUL B. Financing American Enterprise: The Story of
Commercial Banking. New York: Harper & Row, 1963. 304 pp.
In this volume, Trescott explores the contributions of commercial banks
to American economic growth. He points out that commercial banks financed
at least 10% of America's gross domestic capital formation between 1830
and 1930, a contribution exceeded only by retained business earnings and

by the personal wealth of individual capitalists. This made commercial banks the most important among the institutional sources of capital for financing American economic growth. Trescott surveys these institutions, paying particular attention to the period after 1863. He considers the role of the National Banking System and the commercial banks in America's smaller towns. The author shows how agriculture, commerce, industry, and transportation all benefited from the development of commercial bank credit. In particular, he discusses the active part the banks played in financing the growth of railroads after 1863 and the expansion of the automobile industry in the first thirty years of the 20th century.

H 1802. ULMER, MELVILLE J. Capital Transformation, Communications, and
        Public Utilities: Its Formation and Financing. Princeton, N.J.:
        Princeton University Press, 1960. 548 pp.
This study, which covers the years 1870-1950, focuses on the capital-intensive regulated industries--steam railroads, street and electric railways, bus lines, electric light and power, telephones, and other communications media. Ulmer finds that these industries shared certain characteristics that led them to behave in a distinctive manner when it came to capital formation. All were high technology industries, demanding high initial capital outlays that led to very high capital-output ratios. Each industry's initial growth was rapid, usually in excess of national output trends, due to the strong demand for the new service; technical improvements encouraged each industry's further extension and raised its productivity, stimulating a high rate of growth. This rapid expansion satisfied the original need, and once "the system" was completed, retardation set in both in capital formation and in capital-output ratios. Then the industry assumed a rate of growth at, or even below, the national average. This pattern is clearest in the case of the railroads. Ulmer explains these patterns and also demonstrates that the regulated industries shared a tendency to depend on internal sources of finance. Following the high initial rate of capital investment, financed largely from external sources, plant and equipment were used more intensively and capital-saving innovations were introduced, leading to a growing emphasis on financing.

H 1803. VOGELER, INGOLF. The Myth of the Family Farm: Agribusiness
        Dominance of U.S. Agriculture. Boulder, Colo.: Westview Press,
        1981. 352 pp.
Vogeler's study of agribusiness in U.S. agriculture focuses on the struggle between land interests in the public and private sectors. Vogeler argues that the predominance of the American family farm is a myth that obscures the nature of the role of agribusiness in U.S. farming. Through an analysis of Federal land legislation in the 19th and early 20th centuries, he traces the development of agribusiness, and demonstrates its impact on rural America. In the 20th century, the rapid disappearance of the family farm has been accompanied by new Federal farm legislation; Vogeler examines the effect of such legislation on the growth of large-scale farming interests. In the concluding section, he discusses the history of farmers' challenges to agribusiness, argues against an agrarian Capitalism in favor of an agrarian democracy, and calls for progressive rural change.

H 1804. WAGONER, HARLESS D. The U.S. Machine Tool Industry, from 1900
        to 1950. Cambridge, Mass.: MIT Press, 1968. 421 pp.
Noting that the machine tool industry plays a key role in modern industrial development by supplying goods to other industries, Wagoner surveys the industry's history from the beginning of the century to the Korean War, a period dominated by marked fluctuations in demand. Wagoner organizes his study topically within chronological periods and focuses primarily on the production, marketing, and organizational problems of the machine tool builders. From 1900 on, the greatest problem faced by producers in this industry was one of demand instability arising from the highly

exaggerated multiplier effects of cyclical fluctuations in business activity; while the rapid expansion of a major machine tool user could produce an excess of order, machine tool demand was normally below capacity because it consisted purely of demand for replacements. Although machine tool builders have collectively attempted to solve this problem, they have met with little success. They have been more successful in spreading good cost-accounting techniques and in promoting price stability. In 1933, for instance, they were able to achieve both ends through an NRA code, an agreement which was itself based on the voluntary code of ethics which the industry had developed five years previously.

H 1805. WALKER, DAVID A. Iron Frontier: The Discovery and Early Development of Minnesota's Three Ranges. St. Paul: Minnesota Historical Society Press, 1979. 315 pp.
Walker chronicles the development of iron mining on the extremely rich Vermilion, Mesabi, and Cuyana ranges of northeastern Minnesota. His intention is not to examine the social history of the region, but, instead, to focus on the "economic decision makers," including John D. Rockefeller, Andrew Carnegie, and the Merritt family, who developed these reserves so important to an industrial nation. Described are the opening of the ranges in the late 19th and early 20th centuries, the development of means to transport and market ore, entrepreneurial competition, and the corporate concentration and combination that became increasingly significant after the Panic of 1893.

H 1806. WALKER, DON D. Clio's Cowboys: Studies in the Historiography of the Cattle Trade. Lincoln: University of Nebraska Press, 1981. 210 pp.
Walker has collected essays concerning the lore of cowboys and the cattle trade. Focusing mostly on the 19th century, he states that he wishes to flesh out understanding of the culture and personality of the cowboy—a figure who in his opinion has become an empty abstraction in the popular American imagination. Walker has not attempted to produce a scholarly history, nor is his work a comprehensive view of frontier life. Rather, this work constitutes a loosely structured collection of Walker's responses to selected essays on cowboy lore. The topics are diverse, ranging from "Theodore Roosevelt's Sketches of the Cattle Trade," to "Prose and Poetry of the Cattle Industry," to "A Marxist View of the Cowboy." An annotated bibliography is included.

H 1807. WALSH, MARGARET. The Rise of the Midwestern Meat Packing Industry. Lexington: University Press of Kentucky, 1982. 182 pp.
Walsh traces the origins and evolution of Midwestern pork packing in areas not generally thought to have industrialized before the Civil War. Concentrating on the years between 1840 and 1870, the study focuses on the transformation of meatpacking from a rural pioneer activity, frequently financed by general storekeepers, into a genuine manufacturing enterprise made possible by the introduction of ice packing and a year-round production cycle. The account sheds light on processes of regional development, improvements in transportation, and other factors that accompanied the movement of the industry Westward from Cincinnati and into the new railroad centers of Chicago, St. Louis, and Milwaukee.

H 1808. WARE, CAROLINE F. The Early New England Cotton Manufacture: A Study in Industrial Beginnings. Boston: Houghton Mifflin, 1931. 349 pp.
Ware explains why the cotton industry developed in New England rather than elsewhere and discusses the factors influencing its evolution. She first describes the rapid expansion and technological change which the industry experienced between the Revolution and the establishment of the factory system. She then examines innovations in production and marketing

and changes in the social and economic conditions of the workers, concluding that the availability of labor, of water power, and of mercantile
capital especially favored New England's nascent manufactures. Very important, however, was New England's spirit of enterprise and its willingness
to produce large quantities of goods as cheaply as possible. Population
growth and Westward expansion then enlarged the market for domestic production. Mercantile capital financed a new form of industrial organization—the Waltham type of corporation—a vertically integrated firm using
the powerloom to manufacture large quantities of relatively inexpensive
cloth. This type of corporation dominated the industry during the antebellum years.

H 1809. WARREN, JAMES BELASCO. Americans on the Road: From Autocamp
to Motel, 1910-1945. Cambridge, Mass.: MIT Press, 1979.
212 pp.
A study of the social and economic impact of automobile touring, Warren's
study traces the transformation of an inexpensive, individualistic activity
of autocamping, which had anti-modernistic implications, into the nationally standardized motel business of the 1940s. The motel business crystallized in the mid-1920s as a response to the disorganization implied by
casual, unregulated autocamping of the last dozen years. In this way
hoboes and "gypsies" gave way as consumers to middle class tourists.
There is a discussion of the influence of various business and industry
interest groups upon the evolution of this industry.

H 1810. WELLS, MURRAY C. Accounting for Common Costs. Urbana: Center
for International Education and Research in Accounting, University
of Illinois, 1978. 179 pp.
In this and his companion monograph, A Bibliography of Cost Accounting:
Its Origins and Development to 1914, Wells has sought to dispel the confusion surrounding the various cost allocation techniques employed by
today's businesses. By focusing on the arguments supporting or rejecting
these methods, the author has developed a case study of the interaction
between current needs and past precedents in the business firm. He finds
that the greatest divergence in accounting practices occurred after 1900.
The author draws upon Thomas Kuhn's concept of scientific revolutions
to describe the alternatives presented by Frederick Taylor and others
to calculate unit costs of production.

H 1811. WHITE, GERALD T. A History of the Massachusetts Hospital Life
Insurance Company. Cambridge, Mass.: Harvard University Press,
1955. 229 pp.
White stresses that this company's significance lies less in its role
in the development of hospitals or life insurance than in its position
as a forerunner of the modern investment company. Founded in 1818 to
help support the newly established Massachusetts General Hospital by selling insurance, the company almost immediately undertook to manage the
investment of deposits in trust. Thus, it was the only institution of
its time offering a service normally performed by private trustees. Its
investment practices were innovative. The company placed all of its
resources in one general fund that it invested at first in mortgages and
later in manufacturing and railroad companies. It became the most important single source of intermediate credit for the New England textile
industry during the industry's phase of rapid expansion. The members
of the company's guiding body, the Committee of Finance, were among the
area's business leaders, and White documents their influence on the company's investment policies. As late as 1900, the company was still one
of the area's largest financial institutions, even though it was in decline.

H 1812. WHITE, PHILIP L. The Beekmans of New York in Politics and Commerce
         1648-1877. New York: New York Historical Society, 1956. 705 pp.
White's book is divided into three sections, the second of which concentrates on the mercantile careers of Gerard G. and James Beekman in Colonial
New York during the 18th century. The author, who bases his generalizations on an examination of the extensive Beekman family papers, emphasizes
the polygonal character of Colonial commerce. He suggests that by the
mid-18th century New York commerce was characterized by a relatively pronounced specialization of function in the merchant community.

H 1813. WILKINS, MIRA. The Emergence of Multinational Enterprise: Ameri-
         can Business Abroad from the Colonial Era to 1914. Cambridge,
         Mass.: Harvard University Press, 1970. 310 pp.
This work surveys the growth of direct American investment in and the
establishment of business operations overseas. Wilkins traces the origins
of such activity to those merchants who during the Colonial and Early
Republic periods established trading houses abroad which habitually reinvested commercial profits in local economies. Such operations were supplemented by the activities of individual entrepreneurs who emigrated
from the U.S. and built up enterprises while retaining their American
contacts. By the 19th century, some American companies began to enhance
their growth rates by expanding into other countries. The author describes
the rapid growth of business investment overseas after the Civil War and
shows how the development of efficient, international communities and
transportation networks was a crucial prerequisite for large scale investment overseas. By 1914, American companies had important interests throughout the Western hemisphere and in Western Europe.

H 1814. WILKINS, MIRA. The Maturing of Multinational Enterprise: American
         Business Abroad from 1914 to 1970. Cambridge, Mass.: Harvard
         University Press, 1974. 590 pp.
Wilkins argues that W.W. I stimulated large-scale American corporate investment beyond the Western hemisphere while weakening European competition.
The prosperity of the 1920s sustained this drive, which, despite the Depression of the 1930s, laid the basis for America's strong economic position
in world markets and sources of supply after W.W. II. While Wilkins
stresses the role played by the American government in the overseas expansion of American capital, her main goal, apart from describing the struggle
between American and European interests, is to explain the process of
direct foreign investment and the rise of the multinational corporation.
Wilkins argues that this process was a natural culmination of the corporate
growth and structural change that took place in the domestic market.
For American business, she states, integration, diversification, and direct
foreign investment were all parts of the same process. Wilkins thus
locates the American multinational corporation within the context of the
historical development of American business interests.

H 1815. WILLIAMSON, HAROLD F., ARNOLD R. DAUM, et al. The American
         Petroleum Industry. 2 vols. Evanston, Ill.: Northwestern Uni-
         versity Press, 1959, 1963. 1792 pp.
This study traces the history of the oil industry in America from its
beginnings in the mid-19th century through 1959. Volume 1, The Age of
Illumination: 1859-1899, describes the industry's early development and
the chaotic style of competition resulting from its atomistic organization.
This volume treats the rise of Standard Oil, whose innovative entrepreneurs
attempted to solve their problems by combining the competing refiners;
the authors describe the firm's successful efforts to coordinate production
and rationalize marketing and distribution. Volume II, The Age of Energy,
1899-1959, shows how the structure of the industry was influenced by the
growth of the gasoline market and by new discoveries in the West and Southwest. The appearance of new markets and new sources of supply stimulated

the entry and growth of new firms; the renewed competition resulted in a marked erosion of Standard Oil's once dominant position. By the 1930s, the industry had undergone a complete transition from near monopoly to oligopoly—a transition which, the authors emphasize, owed much to market forces and little to the famous antitrust decision of 1911.

H 1816. WOOD, CHARLES L. The Kansas Beef Industry. Lawrence: Regents
Press of Kansas, 1980. 352 pp.
Wood provides an account of the rise of the Kansas beef industry from the late 19th century to 1940. Major issues under consideration include the specialization of livestock production by region; the uses for which the cattle were being raised; and the transition from open range to ranch which resulted from the upgrading of livestock. Wood also discusses the rise of the Kansas City packing industry, which was contemporary with an expanding market structure, and the impact of the railroad on beef production and transport. The author stresses the growth of Federal aid to the industry in the 1930s as particularly important for an understanding of the current cattle business.

H 1817. WOODMAN, HAROLD D. King Cotton and His Retainers: Financing
and Marketing the Cotton Crop of the South, 1800-1925. Lexington:
University Press of Kentucky, 1968. 386 pp.
Woodman analyzes the changes in the marketing of cotton during the 19th century and rejects the characterization of middlemen as predators on the cotton trade. During the antebellum period, he argues, the varied supply and credit needs of the planters and farmers, the different sizes of the individual producer's crops, and the inefficiencies of transportation all made middlemen a crucial lynch-pin in the Southern economy; they played a vital role in getting the commercial staple to the world market. Nevertheless, the factor-planter system was an appropriate symbol of the imperfections in the South's quasi-capitalist, commercial economy. This system retarded the development of specialized commercial and credit institutions; its atomized and decentralized character delayed the growth of urban and inland communication centers. While enabling the South to benefit from its comparative market advantage in cotton production, the marketing and credit system inhibited the development of alternative economic activities. In the years following the Civil War, improved transportation and communication systems finally undermined the factors, which gave way to more specialized businesses. For the regional economy, however, this new commercial system brought no relief: the South remained a dependent, almost Colonial, region.

H 1818. WRIGHT, CALVIN. The Political Economy of the Cotton South: House-
holds, Markets, and Wealth in the Nineteenth Century. New York:
Norton, 1978. 205 pp.
Wright contends that the reexamination of traditional questions in Southern economic history by scholars employing econometric techniques largely supports the qualitative judgments of earlier historians. According to them, slavery retarded the development of an urban-industrial economy and discouraged European migration, thus tending to prevent diversification and mechanization. Moreover, in their view, the South's economic perpetuation of monoculture by sharecropping and crop liens, and the Civil War itself, was a result of the economics of slavery. Choosing to stress the decisive influence of slavery and its development during the 19th century, Wright argues that slavery removed from the Southern economy the crucial constraint which inhibited the expansion of family farming and specialization in staple production. The fate of the Southern economy became tied to the world market. When the international demand for cotton dropped after the Civil War, however, the South developed a surplus of labor which had no economic alternative except migration.

H 1819. YAEGER, MARY. Competition and Regulation: The Development of
Oligopoly in the Meat Packing Industry. Greenwich, Conn.: JAI
Press, 1981. 296 pp.
Yaeger's study is the first scholarly history of the modern meatpacking
industry. Adopting Chandler's strategy-structure model of analysis, she
finds that the meatpackers arrived at oligopoly through a strategy of
vertical integration designed to solve the problems of marketing a perish-
able product. The account explains how the pools formed by the meatpackers
in the 1890s created incentives for mergers that were simultaneously forestalled by government antitrust legislation.

XV. ECONOMIC HISTORY

H 1820. AITKEN, HUGH G. J., ed. Explorations in Enterprise. Cambridge,
Mass.: Harvard University Press, 1965. 420 pp.
These essays consider the "entrepreneurial school" of economic history
that flourished in the U.S. during the 1940s and 1950s and that focused
most of its attention on the businessmen and on their social, political,
and economic contexts. The editor brings together a series of articles
dealing with four different facets of entrepreneurial history: methodologies; discussions of social and cultural influences on entrepreneurial
behavior; portraits of individual entrepreneurs; and historical examinations of different varieties of entrepreneurship. The introductory essay
on the evolution of entrepreneurial history as an academic sub-discipline
is followed by five articles which outline various approaches to entrepreneurship: Arthur H. Cole, Joseph A. Schumpter, and W. T. Easterbrook
offer alternative definitions of entrepreneurship and of entrepreneurial
behavior; Leland Jenks and Thomas C. Cochran respectively analyze the entrepreneurial role and wider themes in American culture. Other essays by
Harold C. Passer and Bernard Bailyn are also included.

H 1821. ALDCROFT, DEREK H. From Versailles to Wall Street, 1919-29.
Berkeley: University of California Press, 1977. 372 pp.
Aldcroft surveys the period's key economic developments, concentrating
especially on those that he believes contributed most to the international
crisis of 1929 and the subsequent depression. He examines in some detail
the economic aftermath of W.W. I, the problems created by war debts and
reparations, and the period of international recovery from 1921 to 1925.
He shows how unsuitable were the efforts to achieve currency stabilization
and why the gold standard failed. Aldcroft finds the prosperity of the
late 1920s to have been built on a weak foundation, and after 1929, the
European nations and the U.S. suffered as a result of the failure over
the long term to solve the problems that had first arisen during the war.
A final chapter is devoted to a review of the secular trends (e.g., in
exports and productivity) in the world economy.

H 1822. ANDERSON, TERRY LEE. The Economic Growth of Seventeenth Century
New England: A Measurement of Regional Income. New York: Arno
Press, 1975. 160 pp.
In the course of making the first systematic quantification of 17th-century
Colonial growth, Anderson revises previous estimates of the performance
of the early American economy. The author finds evidence of rapid growth,
intensive as well as extensive, in the second half of the 17th century;
the rate of growth compares with the performance of the English economy
over the same period. Moreover, productivity increased substantially--
a result primarily of improvements in transportation and in the efficiency
of economic and governmental institutions. Throughout the period, Anderson

estimates, the region had a sustained per capita rate of growth of about 1.6%; this suggests that 17th-century growth rates equalled, and may even have exceeded, those of the 18th century. Anderson's figures indicate that there was far greater continuity in Colonial patterns of economic growth than historians have hitherto maintained.

H 1823. ANDREANO, RALPH L., ed. The Economic Impact of the American Civil War. Cambridge, Mass.: Schenkman Press, 1962. 203 pp.
This collection introduces the on-going debate over the consequences of the Civil War for American economic development. Parts one and two, which cover economic behavior and developments during the war, include essays by Wesley C. Mitchell and Eugene M. Lerner on currency inflation in the North and South, essays by Victor S. Clark and Emerson D. Fite on manufacturing and agricultural development, and essays by Lerner and James L. Sellers on the war and the Southern economy. Part three highlights the controversy over the relationship between Radical Reconstruction and Northeastern economic interests and includes essays by Howard K. Beale and Stanley Coben. Part four focuses on the war's effects on national, as opposed to sectional, economic development: Stephen Salsbury argues that the Civil War accelerated American economic growth; Thomas C. Cochran contends that growth was retarded by the war. The volume also includes a compendium of statistics on the American economy, 1850-1880.

H 1824. ANDREANO, RALPH L., ed. The New Economic History: Recent Papers on Methodology. New York: Wiley Press, 1970. 434 pp.
This collection consists of articles which appeared in Explorations in Entrepreneurial History between 1965 and 1968; all discuss the ideas and methodologies of that brand of economic history which employs advanced quantitative techniques and uses economic theory in solving historical problems. The first group of essays focuses on the impact of econometrics on traditional historical methods. Essays by Lance Davis and George G. Murphy analyze the conceptual and methodological differences between the "new" history and the "old"; J. R. T. Hughes's article concentrates on one element of the debate between the new and the old--the role of theory in historical investigation. Fritz Redlich concludes this discussion in a piece that recommends reconciliation; he argues that neither "scientific," quantitative approaches nor "humanistic," qualitative methods are without their problems. A second group of essays by R. L. Basmann, G. N. von Tunselmann, and Alfred Conrad focuses on the practical benefits to be realized by applying econometric techniques to historical materials and the problems encountered in that effort.

H 1825. AVERITT, ROBERT. The Dual Economy: The Dynamics of American Industry Structure. New York: Norton, 1968. 208 pp.
According to Averitt, the American economy consists of two types of economic units. The dominant form is the center firm, which is a giant multinational corporation in a technologically advanced industry; arrayed around these great corporations are smaller units, the peripheral firms. Averitt shows that the fate of the economy is increasingly linked to the success of the center firm, and he demonstrates how this economic structure affects both labor and the government. He concludes that this new dual system does and will work as long as the economy is experiencing a satisfactory rate of growth over the long run.

H 1826. BARGER, HAROLD. Distribution's Place in the American Economy Since 1869. Princeton, N.J.: Princeton University Press, 1955. 222 pp.
The growth of America's national market during the 19th century was accompanied by the development of an increasingly elaborate network of service industries. Among these, the industries handling the distribution of finished goods to retail sales outlets were of particular importance.

In this volume, Barger charts the increasingly elaborate network of service industries that developed in America between 1869 and 1949. He reaches three major conclusions: since the Civil War, employment in distribution--here defined as wholesaling and retailing of finished goods destined for retail outlets--has increased over the long run relative to employment in the rest of the economy; productivity in distribution has increased less rapidly than in commodity-producing industries; and the contribution of distribution costs to the retail price of finished goods increased through the first half of the period but has remained constant.

H 1827. **BATEMAN, FRED** and **THOMAS WEISS**. A Deplorable Society: The Failure of Industrialization in the Slave Economy. Chapel Hill: University of North Carolina Press, 1981. 237 pp.
Bateman and Weiss broaden the traditional focus of economic-historical study of the antebellum South, and criticize the work of Robert Fogel and Stanley Engerman, Time on the Cross (H 1031), and other cliometrical studies for concentrating on agriculture. The authors' survey of U.S. manufacturing census for 1850, 1860, and 1870 shows that while the South was indeed more heavily agricultural than other regions, it did have an industrial sector that was less "backward" than is generally assumed. Research in an extensive sample set reveals emerging agricultural, processing, textile, and iron manufacturing firms, some of which used slave labor. Bateman and Weiss conclude that non-economic factors, such as the inferior status of manufacturers in a planter society, were more important deterrents to industrial investment than any lack of raw materials and markets.

H 1828. **BEARD, CHARLES A.** An Economic Interpretation of the Constitution of the United States. New York: Macmillan, 1913. 330 pp.
Beard first reviews the property "safeguards" that guaranteed that all members of the Constitutional Convention would be men of substantial wealth. Next, he considers whether the delegates of the Convention represented distinct groups whose economic interests they understood and acted upon, and concludes that they did indeed possess a sense of solidarity. After examining the political doctrines of those who wrote the document, and the process of ratification, Beard concludes that "the Constitution was basically an economic document based upon the concept that the fundamental private rights of property are anterior to government and morally beyond the reach of popular majorities."

H 1829. **BECKER, WILLIAM H.** The Dynamics of Business-Government Relations: Industry and Exports, 1893-1921. Chicago: University of Chicago Press, 1982. 240 pp.
Becker argues that many of the important works by William Appleman Williams, Walter LeFeber, and other revisionist scholars pay insufficient attention to the economic basis of business decisions in their conclusions about the role of government in foreign economic matters. He stresses that major industrial exporters of the Progressive era often had more to lose from government intervention than smaller firms that were the main supporters of government assistance in the development of foreign markets.

H 1830. **BECKHARDT, BENJAMIN H.** The Federal Reserve System. New York: Columbia University Press, 1972. 584 pp.
Beckhardt discusses the operations of the Federal Reserve System since its foundation. After describing the historical circumstances leading to the 1913 Act and analyzing the system's administrative structure, he examines the Fed's policies during W.W. I and W.W. II and discusses its attempts to limit post-war inflation, its contributions to the maintenance of economic stability, its reactions to changes in the international gold standard and to the international crisis of the late 1920s, and its role in the development of new international monetary institutions after 1945.

Beckhardt also treats the problems of the 1960s—including America's persistent balance of payments deficit and the increase in short-term liabilities owed overseas—and describes the manner in which the system responded to these difficulties.

H 1831. BRANDES, STUART. American Welfare Capitalism, 1880-1940. Chicago: University of Chicago Press, 1976. 210 pp.
Welfare Capitalism, Brandes says, constituted one of the solutions offered by American businessmen to the crisis of modern labor-management relations. This solution accompanied and was a consequence of the rise of large organizations in business, and it has survived to the present in the guise of personal management. Brandes concentrates on those aspects which most affected blue-collar workers. He surveys housing, education, and recreation programs, the propagation of religion, profit sharing and pensions, medical aid and social work. He examines welfare Capitalism's direct substitute for independent trade unions—the employee representation plans and other forms of company unions. All such schemes, Brandes argues, were temporary expedients; the extent of the human problems created by industrialization required that solutions ultimately be implemented in public policy rather than in atomized private programs. The proponents of welfare Capitalism recognized that the problems they confronted required large-scale bureaucratic solutions, but the question they left unanswered was whether the resulting bureaucracies should be administered under private or public auspices. The New Deal settled that question, and Brandes says the history of welfare programs since the 1930s shows that the public approach has been greatly to the workers' benefit.

H 1832. BROCK, LESLIE V. The Currency of the American Colonies, 1700-1764: A Study in Colonial Finance and Imperial Relations. New York: Arno Press, 1975. 601 pp.
In this Colonial economic history, Brock criticizes those earlier historians who discussed money solely as a standard of deferred payments and who attacked Colonial paper currency as a debtor conspiracy to cheat creditors; he finds no evidence that Colonial interests divided conveniently into debtor and creditor groups. Further, the author contends that the other roles of paper money have been ignored. He emphasizes the necessity of having an acceptable medium of exchange to encourage the expansion of the Colonial economy and argues that specie was in far too limited supply to be able to play that role. Brock also stresses paper currency's function as an instrument of government finance.

H 1833. BRUCHEY, STUART W. The Roots of American Economic Growth, 1607-1861: An Essay in Social Causation. New York: Harper & Row, 1965. 234 pp.
Bruchey surveys the growth of the economy before the Civil War and locates the primary sources of economic growth in America's social and institutional context. He discusses the impact of the Protestant ethic on economic behavior and the manner in which mercantilism shaped the development of the Colonies. The author finds that the American economy experienced a slow but steady expansion from the late 18th century on and that this rate of growth began to accelerate in the 1830s when the domestic market became more integrated and truly national in scope. He concludes that social values and government policies were the prime movers of the rapid growth that took place after the 1820s. The government, at all levels, invested heavily in the vital transportation industries and extended new protections to private property. These policies (and the values that inspired them) launched the country on an extended phase of industrialization and economic growth.

H 1834. BURNS, ARTHUR R. The Decline of Competition: A Study of the
Evolution of American Industry. New York: McGraw-Hill, 1936.
619 pp.
Burns grounds his analysis in the theory of imperfect competition. He
reviews the basic outlines of the theory and surveys the emerging structure
and practices in American industry, with an eye to elements that reflect
the shift from a competitive system. Thus he discusses the trade association movement, emphasizing developments between 1912 and 1933, and
he considers the forms of behavior usually associated with oligopolistic
industries, including price leadership, sharing the market, price discrimination, and non-price competition. Burns reviews the evidence that prices
have indeed been stabilized as a result of practices such as these and
also looks at various patterns of integration (e.g., vertical and horizontal) in light of their effect on competition. Chapters are devoted
to the National Recovery Administration (1933-1935) and to the ends and
means of achieving social control in the American economy. Burns concludes
that the policy of enforcing competition has failed and that state intervention in some form is absolutely necessary.

H 1835. BURT, RONALD S. Corporate Profits and Cooption: Networks of
Market Constraints and Directorate Ties in the American Economy.
New York: Academic Press, 1983. 331 pp.
Burt considers the manner in which relations constrain the freedom to
act and how other relations are created to circumvent those constraints.
More specifically, the study examines the manner in which patterns of
buying and selling among sectors of the American economy constrain the
ability to make profits in manufacturing industries and the way firms
in those industries use their boards of directors to create cooptive relations through which the constraints can be circumvented. The author takes
a network model of structural autonomy, adopts it to the substantive area
of organizations and markets, and systematically traces the empirical
implications of the model for corporate profits and cooptive directorate
ties in the American economy.

H 1836. CAIN, LOUIS P. and PAUL J. USELDING, eds. Business Enterpise
and Economic Change: Essays in Honor of Harold F. Williamson.
Kent, Ohio: Kent State University Press, 1973. 323 pp.
These essays range through the broad fields of American business and economic history, both summarizing the state of the disciplines and indicating
some of the approaches employed by their major practitioners. Part one
surveys the discipline and assesses the contributions of particular schools
of inquiry--the institutional, the entrepreneurial, and the econometric.
The essays in part two show that behind the abstract processes and strategies suggested by the "rationalization" of business enterprise lies a
world of human managers experimenting in business practice and structure
as they respond to competitive pressure. Part three focuses more explicitly on the role of entrepreneurship in industrial development. Part
four presents two essays on the rarely studied topic of 19th- and 20th-
century black-owned life insurance enterprises. A critical commentary
by J. R. T. Hughes draws together the themes of each of the essays.

H 1837. CAMERON, RONDO, ed. Banking and Economic Development: Some Lessons of History. New York: Oxford University Press, 1972.
267 pp.
Cameron claims that the relative affluence of some nations can be understood by studying the interaction between four major variables: population,
resources, technology, and social institutions. While technological change
has primarily motivated economic development over the last 200 years,
the resulting growth was mediated through particular social institutions,
including the banking system. This observation provides a hypothesis
for this collection: the more backward an economy is, the more important

will be the role of intermediary institutions in mobilizing and allocating capital. Four of the case studies examine European countries--Serbia, Spain, Austria, and Italy--whose industrialization prior to 1914 was incomplete. These essays show that the ability of a banking system to pursue its role successfully depended upon the financial and political order and upon the absence of governmental proclivities for unproductive expenditures or ad hoc interference in the capital market. These optimal conditions did exist in the U.S. and are explored in essays on banking in antebellum Louisiana and on the national banking system. The essays show that when banks are not subject to interference, they can play a very effective role in promoting economic growth.

H 1838. CARTER, ANNE P. Structural Change in the American Economy. Cambridge, Mass.: Harvard University Press, 1970. 292 pp.
In her analysis of the American economy's intermediate industries between 1939 and 1961, Carter uses the input-output mode of analysis, which enables one to describe the structure of an economy at any given time by summing the inter-industry buying and selling of goods and services. Carter concentrates on detailed analysis of developments in all three major areas: those general sectors consisting primarily of services, energy, and transportation; materials producers; and metal working. She finds that over time the relative importance of different intermediate sectors has changed considerably. Firms in the energy and producers' services sectors, for example, have become more important to total intermediate output, indicating that growing specialization has accompanied technological development. Examining structural change in terms of total primary factor requirements, the author discovers that the amounts of labor and capital needed to produce a given output have fallen and that both labor and capital productivity have improved. Structural change for labor-saving purposes was the most significant development during these years.

H 1839. CHANDLER, ALFRED, Jr. and HERMAN DAEMS, eds. Managerial Hierarchies: Comparative Perspectives on the Rise of the Modern Industrial Empire. Cambridge, Mass.: Harvard University Press, 1980. 237 pp.
This volume explores the rise of big business as an international phenomenon and compares the development of the modern firm in the U.S., Great Britain, France, and Germany. Essays by seven contributors show that entrepreneurs in the different countries relied on various types of institutional arrangements: U.S. businessmen relied more heavily on the legal, financial, and administrative structures of the incorporated enterprise; Germans made more frequent use of the cartel; and the British and French used holding companies. The editors urge comparative studies of the impact of cultural attitudes, ideologies, political systems, and social structures on corporate enterprise.

H 1840. CLEMENS, PAUL G. E. The Atlantic Economy and Colonial Maryland's Eastern Shore: From Tobacco to Grain. Ithaca, N.Y.: Cornell University Press, 1980. 249 pp.
Clemens analyzes the way the Atlantic market economy shaped the development of the Eastern shore of Colonial Maryland. The study examines the interaction between internal and external factors as demonstrated in the changing nature of the agricultural base and the evolution of distinct social order. Clemens finds that market factors exerted a powerful influence on the early history of the region, which he divides into three phases: a boom period, which lasted up to the 1680s and resulted from a strong demand for tobacco in Europe; four decades of stagnation (1680-1720) brought about by falling tobacco prices; and a period of renewed growth as planters diversified through the production of agricultural staples, especially grain, in response to rising demand from overseas.

H 1841. CLOWSE, CONVERSE D. Economic Beginnings in Colonial South Carolina 1670-1730. Columbia: University of South Carolina Press, 1971. 283 pp.

Clowse's study of the settlement and economic development of Colonial South Carolina describes a pattern of growth that reappears in the experience of other plantation colonies. The pattern began with a struggle for subsistence and a search for exportable commodities (deerskins and naval stores) and continued through the discovery both of a staple (rice) and of a solution to the colony's inadequate labor supply (slavery). Consequently, staple agriculture expanded—following the investment of commercial and other capital in farming—and marginal producers were eventually eliminated. When this happened, the class of large planters became dominant in a colony committed to the commercial cultivation of a staple crop on large slave plantations.

H 1842. COCHRANE, WILLARD W. The Development of American Agriculture: A Historical Analysis. Minneapolis: University of Minnesota Press, 1979. 464 pp.

Cochrane analyzes the role agriculture played in the economic development of America. The study includes a concise chronology of American agriculture from Colonial times to the present; a summary of the forces of developmental and structural change including abundant land, farm mechanization, transportation, education, research, and government involvement; and a conceptual model of agricultural development between 1950 and 1977. The model suggests a pattern in which technological advancements worked in conjunction with price and income supports to speed a process of farm enlargement, or "cannibalism," in which strong producers consumed the weak. Cochrane concludes by incorporating these themes into a general argument for the use of historical analysis in policy planning.

H 1843. CODDINGTON, ALAN. Keynesian Economics: The Search for First Principles. London: George Allen & Unwin, 1983. 129 pp.

This book grew out of a series of papers, most of them published in the Journal of Economic Literature and the American Economic Review, which sought to explain the roots of Keynesian economics. Although the essays focus more on the theoretical problems presented by Keynesian theory, Keynes's fellow economist, Sir John Hicks, and the impact of Keynesian theory in the U.S., the book does focus on one aspect of intellectual life in America after the 1930s. Coddington treats Keynesian theory as an evolving world view and explores how economists have assimilated, developed and refined Keynesian ideas about how an economy might be managed so as to counteract a particular kind of malfunction to which it would otherwise be prone.

H 1844. CONFERENCES ON RESEARCH IN INCOME AND WEALTH. Output, Employment, and Productivity in the United States after 1800. New York: National Bureau of Economic Research, 1978. 860 pp.

In these fourteen essays, students of 19th-century American economic growth analyze a wide range of topics, including the performance of the entire economy, the experiences of particular industries, and the influence on productivity of changes in the technology of production. Two essays examine the growth of GNP and the changing deployment of the labor force in the 19th century. Three papers chart the growth experiences of the textile and construction industries, and another section is devoted to the development of large-scale extractive industries—coal and metal mining and petroleum. The two final sections are devoted to studies of productivity. The first of these includes papers on the impact of mechanization on manufacturing after 1840; on factors influencing the production of machine tools; and on the relative impact of different innovations on railroad productivity, 1840-1910. Another essay stresses the substantial improvement in agricultural productivity that occurred during the 19th century.

H 1845. DARBY, MICHAEL R. The Effects of Social Security on Income and
the Capital Stock. Washington, D.C.: American Enterprise Institute for Public Policy Research, 1979. 90 pp.
Darby focuses on the economic effects of the social security program,
and particularly on its effects on income and the capital stock. He first
finds that the zero-order-bequest life-cycle model, which was developed
to explain aggregate saving and capital holdings, had serious limitations.
He then maintains that, because the U.S. capital market is relatively
open internationally, the capital stock owned by U.S. residents wherever
located should be distinguished from that used in the nation by any owner.
Similarly, the income of U.S. residents (NNP) should, according to Darby,
be distinguished from the output of the U.S. (NDP).

H 1846. DAVIS, LANCE E. and DOUGLASS C. NORTH. Institutional Change and
American Economic Growth. New York: Cambridge University Press,
1971. 282 pp.
Davis and North develop an explicit, predictive theory of institutional
change and apply it to American history. They build on neo-classical
economics, developing a model that specifies the process by which an
"action group" perceives that some new form of institutional arrangement
will yield a stream of benefits that makes it profitable to undergo the
costs of innovating. The first part of the book presents the foundation
of this model of political and social behavior. The second part applies
the model to a number of important areas of American economic history,
such as land policy, the development of agriculture, transportation, and
communications, and the evolution of new forms of business organization.
In the final section, the authors critique their own model and their
results, pointing econometricians to the problems that still need to be
solved in developing this type of theory.

H 1847. DAVIS, LANCE E., RICHARD A. EASTERLIN, WILLIAM N. PARKER, et al.
American Economic Growth: An Economist's History of the United
States. New York: Harper & Row, 1972. 683 pp.
This work is co-authored by twelve exponents of the "new" economic history.
The book is divided into three major sections. The first, which is devoted
to the study of growth, includes an essay by Robert A. Gallman in which
he analyzes the growth of national income and gives primary responsibility
for America's extraordinary 19th-century expansion to quantitative
increases in the supply of various factors of production. He further
explains that during the 20th century, qualitative improvements in the
employment of those factors through technological development became far
more important. The second major section of the book discusses the four
factors of production--land, labor, capital, and technology--and the particular manner in which they were used in America. The third section
concentrates on the performance of particular industries and sectors of
the economy.

H 1848. DENISON, EDWARD F. Accounting for United States Economic Growth,
1929-1969. Washington, D.C.: Brookings Institution, 1974.
355 pp.
In this volume Denison expands and refines the analyses offered in his
previous studies of U.S. economic growth and introduces the idea of potential output. The latter concept enables the author to estimate what the
output of the economy would have been if demand had been at a standardized
level. Over the period studied, output grew at an annual rate of 3.33%--
as compared to a potential rate of growth of 3.41%. The author provides
detailed breakdowns of the sources of this growth and publishes all of
his estimates in the appendices that make up half of the book. In each
case, he is able to compare the impact of the factor contributing to growth
with its potential contribution. Thus, he is able to show that the labor
input contributed .57 percentage points (1929-1969) to growth but could

have added .86 percentage points if there had been no changes in working hours or in employment compensation. Similar estimates are offered for each source of growth, including advances in knowledge, economies of scale, and improved resource allocation.

H 1849. DENISON, EDWARD F. The Sources of Economic Growth in the United States and the Alternatives Before Us. New York: Committee for Economic Development, 1962. 297 pp.
Written in the context of a growing concern about the slow growth rate of the American economy, this study seeks to understand the sources of growth in the 20th century. The author examines the period between 1909 and 1960, focusing on the contribution to growth of new inputs (labor, land, and capital) and of increases in productivity; in each case, he looks also to the future with an eye to the prospects for improving the growth rate. The author also discusses other incentives and obstacles to growth, including government policies, monopolization, and research programs; he concludes by reviewing the nation's "menu of choices available to increase the growth rate."

H 1850. DETHLOFF, HENRY C. Americans and Free Enterprise. Englewood Cliffs, N.J.: Prentice-Hall, 1979. 336 pp.
This is an economic history of the American experience with Capitalism. Dethloff explores the concept of free enterprise in America, commenting on the theories of Adam Smith and Joseph Schumpter, and the effects of Calvinism, Nationalism, and Social Darwinism. He traces the growth of the American economy from the age of mercantilism and Colonial growth to the creation of a national economy under the guidance of the Supreme Court and the Constitution. He highlights the development of the American banking system in the 19th century, the Civil War, and Reconstruction. Moving into the early 20th century, the study draws attention to the role of the entrepreneur, the rise of Social Darwinism, and the labor unrest of the early decades. Urban development, the advent of the automobile industry, the origins of the Great Depression, the New Deal, the post-war period, and the concern with welfare are all surveyed. Dethloff also addresses the problems with the modern American economy, in particular the role of the multi-national corporation today.

H 1851. DORFMAN, JOSEPH. The Economic Mind in American Civilization, 1606-1933. 5 vols. New York: Viking Press, 1946-59. 2257 pp.
In five volumes Dorfman analyzes the role of economic ideas in American history from the earliest days of settlement to the inauguration of Franklin D. Roosevelt. His study raises the broad issue of the relationship between culture and economics. Volumes I and II span the period from 1606 to 1865; Volume III covers the end of the Civil War to 1918; and the final two volumes analyze economic history from 1918 to 1933.

H 1852. EASTERLIN, RICHARD A. Population, Labor Force, and Long Swings in Economic Growth: The American Experience. New York: Columbia University Press, 1968. 298 pp.
Easterlin maintains that since at least the early 19th century, American population growth has moved in waves lasting between fifteen and twenty-five years. Concentrating on the more complete data available for the period since 1870, he describes and analyzes this phenomenon, seeking to identify the precise manner in which demographic movements interacted with the economy. Easterlin finds that the demographic waves tended to arise in non-farm areas and were related to independent long swings in the growth of output and capital stocks. He argues that the demographic movements were induced by the impact of changes in economic conditions on the labor market. The demographic developments in turn had economic effects, stimulating demand for housing and consumer durables and creating

needs for substantial social overhead investment. Easterlin examines
the demographic movements in terms of the population, the labor force,
and the number of households and finds that since 1940, migration has
ceased to play a central role, and changes in the three categories have
begun to vary widely. In Parts Two and Three, Easterlin disaggregates
the data with reference to population and labor force growth and examines
changes in fertility and in labor force participation rates.

H 1853. FAULKNER, HAROLD U. The Decline of Laissez-Faire, 1897-1917.
         New York: Holt, Rinehart, & Winston, 1951. 433 pp.
Faulkner's volume places in a liberal or progressive context the unprecedented prosperity that America witnessed at the turn of the century, when
a series of institutional changes significantly altered the nation's capitalist system. He considers the rise of finance Capitalism and the advent
of economic Imperialism, and concentrates on the political reforms and
organizational responses related to the problems created by the nation's
economic transformation. He discusses antitrust, railroad regulation,
unionization, immigration restriction, agricultural measures, and a variety
of other policies that epitomized the spirit of reform. Throughout, he
directs the reader's attention to the next wave of reform on the horizon--
that is, the New Deal era that would fulfill the promise of Progressivism.

H 1854. FELDSTEIN, MARTIN, ed. The American Economy in Transition. Chi-
         cago: University of Chicago Press, 1980. 696 pp.
This collection of essays offers the general reader a broad yet critical
overview of changes in the American economy from 1945 to 1979. The book
combines background statements by leading scholars with personal reflections by individuals who have participated in the formation of government
policies and in directing the private economy. Topics include financial
markets; postwar macroeconomic thought and planning; international trade;
population and labor market trends; income distribution; technology and
productivity; and the role of government taxes, transfers, and spending.
It concludes with comments by Paul Samuelson. Each section includes a
guide to additional readings.

H 1855. FOGEL, ROBERT W. and STANLEY L. ENGERMAN, eds. The Reinterpre-
         tation of American Economic History. New York: Harper & Row,
         1971. 494 pp.
This collection of essays does not intend to develop a central theme around
which American economic history can be organized; rather, the editors
have collected examples of the "new" economic history. The essays are
grouped into categories by topic: the pattern and benefits of economic
growth; the sources of industrialization; the diffusion of new technology;
and American capital markets. There are also a number of essays on slavery,
immigration, and the investment in human capital through education.
Together, the essays provide perspective on the process of reevaluation
prompted by the use of economic theory, quantitative data, and econometric
techniques.

H 1856. FRICKEY, EDWIN. Production in the United States, 1860-1914.
         Cambridge, Mass.: Harvard University Press, 1947. 265 pp.
This study offers annual series for forty commodities produced or consumed
in the manufacturing sector and supplementary series for railroad operations and other forms of transportation and communication in the U.S.
Frickey uses these data to analyze trends in industrial and commercial
production. He constructs indexes for twelve industries--food products,
textiles and textile products, lumber, paper and printing, liquors and
beverages, chemicals, tobacco products, and land transportation vehicles--
as well as indexes for the products of these industries aggregated and
divided into durable and non-durable goods, and for total manufacturing.
Finally, he constructs a total manufacturing and commercial index, which

indicates that the American economy during these years experienced an average annual rate of growth of over 5% (with some slight retardation in the growth rate over time).

H 1857. FRIEDMAN, MILTON and ANNA J. SCHWARTZ. A Monetary History of the United States, 1869-1960. Princeton, N.J.: Princeton University Press, 1963. 860 pp.

Friedman and Schwartz analyze the role of monetary factors in the development of the modern American economy. The authors trace the changes that took place in the stock of money, explain those changes, and examine the implications for the national economy of these factors of the money supply and its related institutions. While they begin their study in the 1860s and discuss the politics and economics of the greenback and silver eras, Friedman and Schwartz direct more attention to the operations of the Federal Reserve System—particularly in the 1920s and the Great Depression of the 1930s. They also analyze the inflation that took place during W.W. II, the role of monetary policy in the post-war years, and the marked increase in the velocity of money since 1945. The volume includes Friedman's and Schwartz's data on the stock of money and places these statistics in a broad historical context.

H 1858. FRIEDMAN, MILTON and ANNA J. SCHWARTZ. Monetary Statistics of the United States: Estimates, Sources, Methods. New York: Columbia University Press, 1970. 629 pp.

The authors present their estimates of the quantity of money in the U.S. for the period 1867-1968. They explain the means of arriving at these figures and provide data on the various elements (such as currency held by the public) that made up the aggregate measures. Friedman and Schwartz also review the evidence available for the period before 1867.

H 1859. GALBRAITH, JOHN KENNETH. The Affluent Society. 1958; Rev. ed. Boston: Houghton Mifflin, 1976. 287 pp.

Long an opponent of free-market conservatism, Galbraith turned in 1958 against his production-oriented, Keynesian, former allies to argue that "increased production is not the final test of social achievement, the solvent for all social ills." Rampant production contains the engine of its own amplification, creating an ever-increasing spiral of desires, output, and consumption and promoting inflation and social imbalance. More importantly, it involves leaving a certain segment of the population mired in poverty, while consumption among other segments is steadily exacerbated. Galbraith argues in favor of an economic policy founded on efficiency and income security. His solution involves greater unemployment compensation, alternative sources of income for the unskilled and uneducated (hence chronically unemployed), and controls on wages and prices. Production and economic security thus unyoked, public funds could be supplemented through sales tax on all consumer goods. With funds diverted to alleviating the educational, physical, or emotional deficiencies of the underclasses, rather than being pumped back into the producing apparatus which represses them, these marginal people might begin to achieve economic and social stability.

H 1860. GALBRAITH, JOHN KENNETH. The Great Crash: 1929. Boston: Houghton Mifflin, 1954. 212 pp.

Galbraith describes and analyzes the great fall in stock market prices in America in 1929. He sets the stage for the Crash by highlighting the optimism of the late 1920s, looking in particular at the leaders who encouraged the boom rather than trying to control it. He shows that from Black Thursday through the end of the year, the nation's financial and political leaders tried to pump up the public's confidence, but to no avail. The American economy slid into its greatest depression, dragging with it the rest of the industrial nations. While Galbraith's subject is the Crash

and not the Great Depression, he analyzes the latter phenomenon as well
as the impact of the panic on embezzlement in the U.S.

H 1861. GALBRAITH, JOHN KENNETH. The New Industrial State. 1967; Rev.
        ed. Boston: Houghton Mifflin, 1972. 427 pp.
Galbraith contends that the market has ceased to be the controlling force
in the modern, industrial economy. The power of the market has been eroded
by the rise of giant bureaucratic corporations, which have replaced short-
run, market-oriented decision-making with long-run planning. The corporate
planning system is overseen by a technocratic leadership—the techno-
structure—whose quest for control leads it to transcend not only the market
but also the boundaries between the economy and the state. Modern technology calls for a type of planning that is antithetical to sudden shifts
in process and demand. The corporation has thus attempted to become independent of the consumer market by manipulating consumer demand, of the
labor market by substituting capital for labor, and of the capital market
by relying on its own retained earnings. The corporation, Galbraith says,
has achieved a large measure of independence from market restraints, but
only the government can now ensure that total demand will remain high
enough to keep the new system running. This goal has been achieved by
way of high military expenditure, a recourse that Galbraith criticizes
on several grounds.

H 1862. GALLMAN, ROBERT E. Developing the American Colonies, 1607-1783.
        Chicago: Scott, Foresman, 1964. 64 pp.
This survey touches upon the main features of Colonial economic history,
including mercantilism and the interplay of political and economic factors,
the accumulation of commercial capital and its domestic investment, and
the genesis of the domestic market. Gallman offers an analysis of the
manner in which the availability of different factors of production shaped
the patterns of development in the different colonies.

H 1863. GEORGE, PETER J. The Emergence of Industrial America: Strategic
        Factors in American Economic Growth since 1870. Albany: State
        University of New York Press, 1982. 242 pp.
George has gathered a series of nine papers which he originally delivered
at the University of Cambridge, England, in 1974. Aimed at students of
American economic and social history as well as a general reader, the
essays focus on technological and organizational changes in agriculture
and manufacturing, 1870-1930. The material is organized topically under
such broad themes as technological development, the coming of government
regulation, and the problems of America's mixed economy since W.W. II.
A chapter on the American entrepreneur focuses on the careers of Edison,
Carnegie, Ford, and J. P. Morgan.

H 1864. GOLDSMITH, RAYMOND W. Financial Intermediaries in the American
        Economy Since 1900. Princeton, N.J.: Princeton University Press,
        1958. 415 pp.
This volume examines the increasingly important role of intermediary institutions such as banks, insurance companies, government lending organizations, and mortgage companies that channel funds from savers to economic
units in need of outside capital. As Goldsmith demonstrates, the role
of these institutions has become more significant over the long run, and
the relative contribution of different types of organizations has changed
dramatically. Public sector institutions had by the 1950s come to handle
a significant percentage of these assets, and within the private sector,
banks had lost ground to insurance companies. These intermediaries continued to supply about two-thirds of the external funds that corporations
needed, about half of such funds to agriculture, and an increasing amount
of the capital needed for home mortgages. They played a greater role
over the years in financing state, local, and Federal government; between
1933 and 1952, they held over two-thirds of the Federal debt.

H 1865. GOLDSMITH, RAYMOND W. A Study of Saving in the United States.
3 vols. Princeton, N.J.: Princeton University Press, 1955.
2246 pp.
Goldsmith provides estimates of national income, wealth, and savings for
the years 1897-1949. The information is organized according to the membership of savers in one of seven classes: non-agricultural households; agricultural households; unincorporated busineses; corporations; the Federal
government; state governments; and local governments. These classes are
also combined in different groups to create data describing seven different
categories of saving: national saving (all saving); collective (government) saving; non-government saving; private saving; personal saving;
business saving; and saving by individuals. Drawing upon these figures,
Goldsmith describes a number of long-term trends in saving. The annual
"real" increase in per capita saving, adjusted for inflation, was about
1.8% over the period under examination; when population growth is taken
into account, this rate appears consistent with the rates of preceding
decades. Goldsmith also finds long-term stability in the saving-income
ratio. While he finds no particular trends in the distribution of savings
among the seven major groups, the forms of their saving have undergone
important transformations, and this alteration in form has had the important
effect of increasing the volume of personal savings handled by financial
intermediaries. Volume II treats the "Nature and Derivation of Annual
Estimates of Saving, 1897 to 1949." Volume III includes, among other "Special Studies," an account of family saving, 1888-1950, by Dorothy S. Brady,
and Horst Mendershausen's treatment of changes in estate tax wealth.

H 1866. GOODRICH, CARTER. Government Promotion of American Canals and
Railroads, 1800-1890. New York: Columbia University Press,
1960. 382 pp.
Goodrich synthesizes the research on the role played by government in
the development of the transportation systems that facilitated the rapid
enlargement of a market economy in 19th-century America. He finds that
government aid, whether direct or indirect, whether at state or Federal
levels, played a central role. Goodrich argues that the contributions
of all levels of government amounted to 70% of total investment in canals
and 30% of all investment in railroad building prior to the Civil War.
Thereafter, the balance between public and private investment shifted
as the financial contribution of public authorities declined to a negligible fraction of total railroad investment. Returns on government investment, Goodrich says, should be--and were--conceived in terms of the broad
public benefits accruing rather than in direct financial terms; indeed,
projects which promised high rates of return were almost universally left
to private enterprise. Goodrich concludes that the involvement of the
government at whatever level and in whatever amount was a pragmatic
response to a task--and to pressures from private interests--rather than
a matter of commitment to an ideological principle.

H 1867. GOODRICH, CARTER, et al. Canals and American Economic Development.
New York: Columbia University Press, 1961. 303 pp.
This collection suggests answers to two questions: what factors influenced
the decisions to undertake particular canal projects in antebellum America;
and what impact did the canals have on American economic growth? For
answers to the first question, the authors examine the financing and construction of the Erie, the Pennsylvania Mainline, and the New Jersey canals.
These case studies indicate that the decisions to construct canals grew,
in the first instance, out of the competition among Eastern seaboard cities
for the expanding Western market. In answer to the second question, the
book argues that the greatest relative reduction in the 19th-century transportation costs was made by canals replacing wagon haulage, not by the
railroads that first supplemented and later supplanted the canals. Further,
the reduction by canals was decisive in opening up the all-important East-

West commerce in bulky agricultural goods. The book thus underscores the importance to American economic growth of pre-railroad innovations in transportation and of the state governments that financed and controlled canal projects.

H 1868. **GRANT, H. ROGER.** Self-Help in the 1890s Depression. Ames: Iowa State University Press, 1983. 163 pp.
The author applauds the old-fashioned American bootstrap in these five case studies of efforts by ordinary citizens to counteract the effects of prolonged economic stress. During the 1890s their projects included community gardens, labor exchanges, cooperative stores, farmers' railroads, and intentional communities ("pragmatic utopias") of many kinds. Examples emphasize activity in the Midwest and Plains states and suggest that several approaches to social planning developed by the Populists were subsequently embraced by the Progressives.

H 1869. **GRESSLEY, GENE M.** Bankers and Cattlemen. New York: Knopf, 1966. 320 pp.
Gressley contends that Eastern and European investment in Western enterprise was a major factor in the development of that region in the years after the Civil War. Concentrating on the domestic capital provided by a core group of ninety-three investors, Gressley describes the process whereby private Eastern funds were mixed with Western enterprise to establish the open-range, stock-rearing industry. At first, Eastern investors normally became partners with local ranchers who directed the business. However, as the industry grew and investors multiplied, competition developed for land and water rights, and participants in the industry sought to protect their investments by accumulating these resources, gradually forcing out local ranchers. Beginning in the early 1880s, investors began to form corporations to help raise capital and to limit their liability. Gressley concludes that despite this change in organization, the industry was still not very profitable, especially during the lean years of the mid-1980s.

H 1870. **HANDLIN, OSCAR and MARY FLUG HANDLIN.** Commonwealth, a Study of the Role of Government in the American Economy: Massachusetts, 1774-1861. Cambridge, Mass.: Harvard University Press, 1969. 314 pp.
The Handlins contend that the history of government involvement in the economy of antebellum Massachusetts is the history of a transition from mercantilism to liberalism, from government direction of economic development to government regulation of the consequences of economic change. Originally, the state was conceived of as an expression of the common interest and because the development of a strong economy was central to the common interest, the state was held responsible for stimulating production. However, since there was public opposition to activities calling for state expenditures, the government granted the privilege of incorporation to groups embarking on such enterprises as the construction of bridges or roads, and the corporate form of business gradually acquired a private and autonomous character. As the mercantilist state of the early 19th century faded and private economic activity proliferated, Massachusetts developed a regulatory state that protected the public sphere by acting directly in areas such as education and by setting rules for private behavior in most areas of the economy. This transition, the Handlins find, was complete by 1860.

H 1871. **HARRINGTON, MICHAEL.** The Other America: Poverty in the United States. New York: Macmillan, 1962. 191 pp.
Harrington argues that the prosperity of America's modern industrial economy does not extend throughout American society. There exists another America, inhabited by 50 million people who live in a self-perpetuating

culture of poverty. The boundaries of this other America embrace the poorest paid urban and rural workers, the nation's dropouts and alcoholics, the vast majority of blacks, and many of the aged. In a series of impressionistic case studies, Harrington describes the economic underworld in which these people live, analyzes their problems and suggests possible solutions. Ultimately, Harrington concludes, the solution must be political, for economic growth does not of itself guarantee relief. The continuous process of technological innovation to achieve higher productivity is central to American economic growth in the 20th century, but this very process has erected a barrier between industry's well-paid jobs and the ill-educated and poor. The articulation of a clear set of social priorities by a vast new social and political movement, Harrington concludes, is the only possible means to eradicate poverty by countering the influence of powerful groups that dominate decision-making in contemporary America.

H 1872. HAWLEY, ELLIS W. The New Deal and the Problem of Monopoly: A
          Study in Economic Ambivalence. Princeton, N.J.: Princeton Uni-
          versity Press, 1966. 525 pp.
Hawley's study analyzes the different ideas and coalitions influencing the Federal government's policy toward economic planning in the 1930s. The author says that three distinct strains of thought were current throughout the decade. Business interests sought a fully cartelized economy with government blessing but without government participation. Government planners sought a similar "rationalization" of the economic structure but preferred to locate final control in the government while seeking to involve a wide range of economic interests in the decision-making process. Finally, Brandeisian liberals favored a policy of trust-busting and a return to free competition. Hawley's major conclusion is that no single view ever became completely dominant, even temporarily; rather than shifting decisively as one approach or another mustered temporary majority support, the government vacillated throughout the decade. Government policy was thus marked by improvisation and attempts to compromise the differences between these three alternate lines of policy rather than by the bold "experimentation" so often attributed to the New Deal by liberal historians.

H 1873. HEATH, MILTON S. Constructive Liberalism: The Role of the State
          in Economic Development in Georgia to 1860. Cambridge, Mass.:
          Harvard University Press, 1954. 448 pp.
Heath examines the Georgia government's active role in the state's antebellum economic development. Georgia's Colonial status as a social and consequently as a commercial experiment had involved a relatively high degree of centralized guidance, and government-directed social experimentation continued in the late 18th and early 19th centuries. Georgia's land policy stimulated a rate of settlement that far outran the capacity of existing services, leading to government involvement in the promotion and construction of essential transportation services. To develop railroads after 1833, it was necessary to coordinate a cooperative effort combining the resources of private groups, cooperation, and local and state governments in a common enterprise. Heath points out that the government was not looked upon as an entity separate from private groups and representing a distinct "public" interest, but was regarded more as one group among the many whose cooperation was needed if economic success was to be achieved.

H 1874. HICKMAN, BERT G. Growth and Stability of the Postwar Economy.
          Washington, D.C.: Brookings Institution, 1960. 426 pp.
Hickman examines the national economy for the years 1946-1958, stressing the degree to which stability was achieved along with a satisfactory rate of growth and a low average level of unemployment. He focuses on the major business cycles of these years and on the economy's ability to avoid a severe depression, analyzing in particular the contractions of 1948-

49, 1953-54, and 1957-58. The author dissects each of the postwar cycles, isolating the sources of the downturn and subsequent recovery. He then provides a general profile of the national economy, with detailed descriptions of development in Federal spending, in consumer demand, in industrial investments, and residential construction. He concludes with an appraisal of our monetary and fiscal policies, noting ominously that "the economy's bias toward price inflation has been largely a by-product of properties . . . which most persons would agree were desirable."

H 1875. HOFFMAN, CHARLES. The Depression of the Nineties: An Economic
          History. Westport, Conn.: Greenwood Press, 1970. 326 pp.
The depression of the 1890s, Hoffman says, was a sharp cyclical contraction occurring during an era characterized by very rapid economic growth. To account for the timing of the depression, the author reconstructs the major components of Gross National Product—domestic and foreign investment, domestic consumption, and Federal expenditure—so that he can trace the precise patterns of economic activity throughout the period. He also takes fluctuations in factor prices and the money supply into account, but relegates them to a secondary role. According to his estimates, a contraction in economic activity began after a peak had been reached in January 1893; the downturn was caused, he argues, by declining investment opportunities in railroads and building construction and was heralded by an earlier drop in the production of agricultural, electrical, and industrial machinery. The 1893 contraction lasted until mid-1894, when the first trough was reached. The economy then expanded until December 1895, when contraction again took place, and a second capacity was severely under-utilized, and unemployment approached 20% of the labor force. The depression lasted five years, and steady growth did not begin again until late 1897.

H 1876. HUGHES, JONATHAN R. T. Social Control in the Colonial Economy.
          Charlottesville: University Press of Virginia, 1976. 178 pp.
Examining nonmarket economic controls in America's formative years, Hughes traces the background of social control powers over economic life in Anglo-American law and custom. Written to explain direct measures of government intervention in the economy in the early 1970s, the book attempts to show the enduring impact of the Colonial experience on the American economy. The study is based on an analysis of four areas of economic life over which society has variously changed the mix of social control: regulations of numbers of participants; conditions of eligibility for participation; the prices charged by participants for services or production; and the quality of sevices or products allowed.

H 1877. HUGHES, JONATHAN R. T. The Vital Few: American Economic Progress
          and Its Protagonists. Boston: Houghton Mifflin, 1966. 504 pp.
Hughes identifies "the vital few" as eight leading figures in America's economic history—men who, by dint of their idealism (William Penn and Brigham Young), their inventiveness (Eli Whitney and Thomas Edison), their innovative spirit (Andrew Carnegie and Henry Ford), or their organizing skills (Edward Harriman and J. Pierpont Morgan) personify the characteristics that made the most telling contributions to America's economic success. Although he presents these figures in chronological order, Hughes argues that the four vital characteristics have no particular significance as a sequence; each is a "conceptual category," and together they form a taxonomy that can be used to understand the character of the American economic experience at any particular point in its development. The eight men are discussed in separate biographical essays, each of which treats the relationships between the leading character and his environment. A fifth category, stagnation and decline, has no surrogate, although Hughes considers it an essential element in his taxonomy.

H 1878. JAMES, JOHN A. Money and Capital Markets in Postbellum America.
         Princeton, N.J.: Princeton University Press, 1978. 283 pp.
James studies the structure and operation of the postbellum banking system
and the forces responsible for the narrowing of interregional interest
rate differentials. The book gives an overview of the banking system
as a whole; of the characteristics of the individual bank portfolio; and
of the mechanisms for interregional transfer of funds. The findings are
based on a reconstruction of interest rates and average rates of return
on lean and discount portfolios of country national banks and of reserve
city national banks. This information is drawn from annual reports of
the U.S. Comptroller of the Currency, 1888-1911.

H 1879. JENKS, LELAND H. The Migration of British Capital to 1875. New
         York: Knopf, 1927. 442 pp.
In his account of British capital exports during the first three quarters
of the 19th century, Jenks pays attention to changes in the direction
of the flow; the different mechanisms of transmittal provided by the British money market; and the uses to which investments were put. British
capital, he says, created an invisible empire, an extension of the British
economic system overseas. Although the boundaries of this domain conformed
loosely to those of the visible British Empire, much British investment
took place in Europe, South America, Mexico, and North America. British
willingness to invest in America originated with the desire to finance
American purchases of British exports. The flow of British capital accelerated when "country" investors (rentiers) turned away from European and
domestic opportunities and sought investments in America. This trend
accelerated during the 1830s as British funds flowed into state bonds.
The sheer volume of funds flowing into the U.S., Jenks concludes, was
responsible for the speculative boom of the mid-1930s, the panic of 1837,
and the subsequent recession. Inevitably, the rate of British investment
dropped sharply in the 1840s; thereafter British capitalists were cautious
about sending their funds to America.

H 1880. JONES, ALICE HANSON. The Wealth of a Nation to Be: The American
         Colonies on the Eve of the Revolution. New York: Columbia Uni-
         versity Press, 1980. 494 pp.
This volume is a statistical analysis of the economic condition of the
American Colonies at the time of the Revolution. Primarily using county
probate records, Jones measures the amount and type of wealth Americans
possessed, concluding that the colonists were materially better off per
capita than their European counterparts. She also analyzes the distribution of wealth in America (studying the upper, middle, and lower Colonies
separately), and then compares the distribution found in America with
that of other places and periods.

H 1881. KATZ, MICHAEL B., MICHAEL J. DOUCET, and MARK J. STERN. The Social
         Organization of Early Industrial Capitalism. Cambridge, Mass.:
         Harvard University Press, 1982. 444 pp.
The authors explore the social structure of industrial North America in
the third quarter of the 19th century through quantitative examinations
of Hamilton, Ontario, and Buffalo, New York. They seek through their
accumulated evidence to demonstrate that transciency and inequality were
central to social experience and, further, they contend that these were
inevitable consequences and necessary ingredients of a capitalist order.
Despite its apparent complexity, the social organization was basically
structured by the class relationships perpetuated by Capitalism. The
authors also consider ideology, education, and social mobility, particularly in terms of their role in the legitimization of the reigning system.
Their work is based on manuscript census reports, tax rolls, marriage
and school records, and the like.

H 1882. KEELER, THEODORE E. Railroads, Freight, and Public Policy. Washington, D.C.: Brookings Institution, 1983. 180 pp.
Although this study mainly focuses on the impact of the sweeping legislative reforms of 1976 and 1980, by which Congress relaxed Interstate Commerce Commission controls over railroad service rates, it also contains an analysis of the economic effects of government regulation before the 1976 reforms. Chapter Two provides a summary of the major developments in rail freight regulations beginning with the first state laws of the 1870s and 1880s and the Federal Interstate Commerce Act of 1887. Other sections examine detailed accounting data to argue that a large share of the nation's rail service is currently being provided at an economic loss.

H 1883. KENDRICK, JOHN W. Productivity Trends in the United States. Princeton, N.J.: Princeton University Press, 1961. 23 pp.
Using input-output analysis, Kendrick estimates the increases in productivity that characterized the entire economy in the years 1889-1957; various sectors of the economy (e.g., agriculture, mining, and contract construction); and thirty-three major industry groups. He provides separate data in manufacturing, for example, on foods, textiles, and chemicals. The productivity gains are given as annual rates of change for the ten-year intervals; the data upon which the estimates are based appear in the appendices. Kendrick concludes that American productivity in the private sector increased over a seventy-year period at an annual rate of about 1.7% and that physical output per manhour grew at about 2.4% per annum.

H 1884. KINDLEBERGER, CHARLES P. The World in Depression, 1929-30. Berkeley: University of California Press, 1973. 336 pp.
In this volume Kindleberger concludes that American policy decisions materially deepened the initial economic crisis and thereafter hindered efforts to alleviate the depression. After reviewing the various explanations of the depression, Kindleberger argues that America should have responded to the crisis of the late 1920s by taking over world economic leadership from Britain, by maintaining counter-cyclical, long-term lending, and by providing both a market of last resort for unwanted commodities and the discounting facilities needed by nations with balance of payment problems. Instead, the U.S. abdicated its responsibilities and the world's leading industrial nations then behaved like rival firms in an unstable oligopolistic industry lacking the constraints of a leading firm. After examining different countries' domestic policies designed to revive their economies and international efforts to bring about world recovery, he concludes that the lack of American leadership prevented the reestablishment of a general equilibrium in world markets and perpetuated the effects of the unstable conditions that had characterized the world economy since W.W. I.

H 1885. KUZNETS, SIMON. Capital in the American Economy: Its Formation and Financing. Princeton, N.J.: Princeton University Press, 1961. 664 pp.
Kuznets uses the results of five sector studies and three treatments of intermediate institutions to develop a general picture of the long-term trends in capital formation and financing in different areas of the American economy. He identifies long swings in the rate of growth of capital formation, each of about twenty years duration, and he examines the underlying secular trends between 1869 and 1955. Gross capital formation measured at current prices accounted for a fairly constant proportion of GNP. Measured in constant prices, the long-term gross capital formation trend declined slightly. The rate of consumption of durable capital—which Kuznets regards as a measure of economic obsolescence rather than of physical wear and tear—grew faster than the rate of gross capital formation. Consequently, the proportion of the net capital formation in net national product declined. Within gross capital formation, the

shares of construction and of inventories declined, while that of producer
durables grew. Within net domestic capital formation, the share accounted
for by government use rose, while that of households (nonfarm residential
construction) declined; the share of business, measured in constant prices,
rose slightly. Among the major divisions of the business sector, the
shares of mining and manufacturing industries rose while that of public
utilities fell. Agriculture, however, showed no discernible trend. In
the economy as a whole, most capital funds (about 60%) continued to originate in retained earnings. At the sectoral level, however, the ratio
of internal to external financing declined for the household and the government while it increased for business.

H 1886. KUZNETS, SIMON S. Modern Economic Growth: Rate, Structure and
         Spread. New Haven, Conn.: Yale University Press, 1966.
         529 pp.
Kuznets analyzes the phenomenon of modern economic growth, which he defines
as a sustained rise in population that takes place without any perceptible
fall in per capita output. In the modern epoch, however, growth has actually been accompanied by rising per capita production due to the growing
influence of science-based technology. Innovations have stimulated enormous increases in the aggregate volume of production and in productivity.
Tracing the uneven spread of modern economic growth through the world,
Kuznets notes the recurrence in different economies of the same changes
in the sectoral origin of output--the decline of agriculture and the rise
of manufacturing--and of the same changes within sectors, for example
the shift within manufacturing toward durable goods. Placing the American
experience in an international perspective, the author concludes that
American economic growth differs primarily because the volume of aggregate
production was so large. The per capita rate of growth of American output
and the evolution of the economy's structure were similar to developments
in other industrializing nations.

H 1887. KUZNETS, SIMON, ed. Income and Wealth of the United States:
         Trends and Structure. Baltimore, Md.: Johns Hopkins University
         Press, 1952. 328 pp.
This volume consists of two long essays, one by Simon Kuznets on income
trends and economic development since 1870 and the other by Raymond W.
Goldsmith on the growth of reproducible wealth in the 19th and 20th centuries. The essays contribute to the accumulation of statistical data
on American economic growth, and offer measured conclusions about the
analysis of aggregates and of long-term trends in the growth process.
Goldsmith concentrates on the measurement of per capita wealth, finding
an average rate of increase for 1800-1959 of 2% per annum, and analyzing
fluctuations in growth rate before and after the war years. Kuznets examines broader trends in the size, rate of growth, structure, and performance
of the American economy since the Civil War. Kuznets's introduction outlines the historical and philosophical reasons for the post-W.W. II revival
of interest in the idea of growth as a central concept of economic history.

H 1888. KUZNETS, SIMON and DOROTHY S. THOMAS. Population Redistribution
         and Economic Growth: United States, 1870-1950. 3 vols. Phila-
         delphia: American Philosophical Society, 1959-64. 1416 pp.
Drawing upon the U.S. census, 1870 to 1950, and upon the census of manufacturers and similar sources, the authors establish the relationships
between trends in the population and changes in the structure and intensity
of economic activity in the U.S. The volumes concentrate on population
redistribution (changes in the proportionate share of the country's population in fixed area units) and on economic growth (a long-term sustained
increase in the total population and in total and per capita economic
product). This study proposes that in the present epoch of technologically
induced growth, population redistribution (both through natural increase

and migration) is primarily a function of economic growth. The distribution of the country's population adjusts over time to the distribution
of economic opportunities. Changes in the latter have been unusually
rapid in the modern era, and migration, rather than birth and death rates,
has been the major mechanism of population redistribution.

H 1889. LEBERGOTT, STANLEY. The American Economy: Income, Wealth, and
Want. Princeton, N.J.: Princeton University Press, 1976.
382 pp.
In the first part of this volume, Lebergott analyzes the relationship
between poverty and our advanced industrial economy. Poverty, he points
out, is a relative phenomenon that cannot be abolished by economic growth
or by increases in the standard of living. Lebergott probes various policies that might be adopted in an effort to alter our distribution of income
in favor of the poor or otherwise to solve the problems of the poor.
In general he stresses the complexity of these tasks. He examines the
premises upon which America's public policies involving income and wealth
rest and the relative effects of demographic change and race in the distribution of poverty. In part two, the author develops five new sets
of data: on white and non-white income distribution between 1900 and
1970; on trends in the standard of living since 1900; and on expenditures
on services since 1900.

H 1890. LEBERGOTT, STANLEY. Manpower in Economic Growth: The American
Record Since 1800. New York: McGraw-Hill, 1974. 561 pp.
Lebergott studies the allocation of American labor among the different
sectors and industries of the economy during the 19th and 20th centuries.
To explain how labor was used and rewarded, he develops a new body of
statistical data on wages and prices, on employment and unemployment,
and on the general profile of the labor force—including age, sex, ethnicity, race, and regional distribution. Based on these statistics he
makes comparisons by industry, occupation, and skill. Moreover, Lebergott
places these quantitative findings in a broad historical context that
stresses the relationship between labor and economic growth. He emphasizes
the mobility of American labor, pointing out that American society as
a whole was characterized by a high degree of social and economic mobility,
and showing that labor was highly responsive to ecoomic rewards. Over
the long run, this responsiveness ensured that distortions in the nation's
labor markets would be minimized during the process of industrialization.

H 1891. LEE, SUSAN PREVIANT and PETER PASSELL. A New Economic View of
American History. New York: Norton, 1979. 410 pp.
Lee and Passell synthesize the major recent research on and interpretations
of American economic history from Colonial times to the Great Depression.
They offer a problem-oriented approach focused on data and techniques.
The book begins with an essay on the background and methodology of the
New Economic History, and subsequent chapters address themes of growth
and development, emphasizing the 19th century (eleven of the sixteen chap-
ters deal with the period before the Civil War).

H 1892. LEWIS, EUGENE. Public Entrepreneurship: Toward a Theory of Bureaucratic Political Power. Bloomington: Indiana University Press,
1980. 274 pp.
To illuminate the bureaucratic presence in modern American political life,
Lewis examines the public lives of three extremely powerful businessmen:
Admiral Hyman George Rickover, J. Edgar Hoover, and Robert Moses. He
analyzes the respective administrative styles of the three and their relationships with public and private opinion leaders. Lewis argues that
public bureaucracies and bureaucrats can, indeed must, be viewed as subjects of political theory since they have come to accumulate so much power,
and constitute the most important instruments for social, political and

economic change in 20th-century America. He further claims that this development belies the original designs for public bureaucracies, and hence has profound implications for American democracy.

H 1893. LIVESAY, HAROLD C. American Made: Men Who Shaped the American Economy. Boston: Little, Brown, 1979. 310 pp.
Livesay examines the lives of nine men who became great manufacturers and who were key contributors to the growth and development of American business: Eli Whitney, Cyrus McCormick, Andrew Carnegie, Thomas Edison, Henry Ford, Pierre S. du Pont, Alfred Sloan, Henry Ford II, and Edwin Land. Themes running throughout the work are: manufacturers, as a group, played perhaps the most important role in transforming America from a Colonial dependent into a world power; the development and triumph of the ideas of mass production and mass consumption as central to American business and life; and the interrelationship between American manufacturing and industry, the rugged American environment, and American culture and society.

H 1894. LURIE, JONATHAN. The Chicago Board of Trade 1859-1905: The Dynamics of Self-Regulation. Urbana: University of Illinois Press, 1979. 234 pp.
This analysis of the Chicago Board of Trade offers insights into the role of the exchange as a quasi-public regulatory agency whose emergence coincided with the growth of American administrative law. Much of the text focuses on the Board's battle against bucket shops as an affront to the Board's efforts to maintain an open market responsive to the competitive laws of supply and demand.

H 1895. MARTIN, EDGAR W. The Standard of Living in 1860: American Consumption Levels on the Eve of the Civil War. Chicago: University of Chicago Press, 1942. 451 pp.
Martin compiles statistics, facts, and opinions on how the average American lived during an important period of American development and provides a variegated catalog of the goods and services Americans possessed in 1860, grouped under the broad categories of food, housing, clothing, medical care, education, religion, and recreational facilities. He points out that by 1860 Americans had already achieved a higher standard of living than Europeans, consuming more food, living in more comfortable houses, and wearing better clothing.

H 1896. McCLELLAND, PETER D. Causal Explanation and Model Building in History, Economics, and the New Economic History. Ithaca, N.Y.: Cornell University Press, 1975. 290 pp.
McClelland, a practitioner of the "New Economic History," probes the fundamental nature of explanation in economic history. He reviews the several approaches that scholars have developed for dealing with this problem—historicism and the covering-law theory, for example—and he advances his own distinctive, moderate solution. He criticizes economic theory but nonetheless concludes that the use of theory and of new modes of statistical analysis have improved our understanding of economic history. He includes a description of various cliometric tools and of the art of counterfactual speculation.

H 1897. McCRAW, THOMAS K., ed. Regulation in Perspective: Historical Essays. Boston: Division of Research, Graduate School of Business Administration, Harvard University, 1981. 246 pp.
Five historians and one political scientist have contributed to this collection of essays on American governmental regulation in historical perspective. They often employ the comparative method—both temporal and geographical—and tend toward institutional and interpretive approaches, rather than quantitative ones. The essays use governmental regulation

to encompass other themes inherent in the study of industrial society: the cultural and ideological tension between individualism and communitarianism; the trade-off between efficiency and equity; and the contest between economic growth and environmental quality. The work also explores the broader questions of the advantages and disadvantages of adversarial versus cooperative relations between government and business.

H 1898. MERCER, LLOYD. Railroads and Land Grant Policy: A Study in Goverr
ment Intervention. New York: Academic Press, 1982. 268 pp.
This volume is a study of the economic efficiency of the railroad land grant system, based on a detailed cliometrical analysis of the economic rationality of government grants made available to six major North American transcontinental railroad systems. Mercer concludes that the government's policies were beneficial for society in terms of economic efficiency even though several of the railroads probably could have been constructed without Federal land subsidies.

H 1899. MEYERS, MARGARET G. A Financial History of the United States.
New York: Columbia University Press, 1970. 451 pp.
This volume offers a broad, non-technical introduction to America's financial history from Colonial times through the 1960s. Although organized chronologically, the narrative frequently turns aside to evaluate long-term developments or particular institutions. Meyers describes the major developments in public finance and also investigates the evolution of private institutions (particularly after the Revolution) and related topics such as changes in public attitudes toward personal debt in the 20th century.

H 1900. MITCHELL, BROADUS. Depression Decade: From New Era through New
Deal, 1929-1941. New York: Holt, Rinehart & Winston, 1947.
462 pp.
Mitchell reviews the origins of the Great Depression, which he traces to long-run trends in the world economy, to particular disequilibria resulting from W.W. I and to monetary policies here and abroad. He charts President Hoover's ill-fated responses to the crises, and argues that President Franklin D. Roosevelt benefited from Hoover's mistakes, from a willingness to experiment with new public policies, and from his confidence in the American people and their political institutions. The author describes several sets of policies the Roosevelt Administration developed in an effort to spur recovery and to provide relief. There are chapters on banking reform, the new price and production controls in agriculture, the National Recovery Administration, labor policies, public works, the Tennessee Valley Authority, and the reciprocal trade agreements with other countries.

H 1901. MULHOLLAND, JAMES A. A History of Metals in Colonial America.
University: University of Alabama Press, 1981. 215 pp.
This account of the introduction and early development of metals technology in America through 1800 emphasizes the growth of iron manufacture as an essential aspect of colonization. Only one other metal (copper) received significant attention from explorers and settlers in the Colonial period, whereas the Schuylkill River and its tributaries became the center of the greatest concentration of Colonial ironworks by the end of the 17th century.

H 1902. NASH, GERALD D. State Government and Economic Development: A
History of Administrative Policies in California, 1849-1933.
Berkeley: University of California Press, 1964. 379 pp.
Nash breaks with the tradition of studying public policy in terms of ideological statements and legislative enactments; instead, he emphasizes the administration of policy. He finds that in California there was a

remarkable continuity in the goals of state-level, political economy. The state promoted economic development, regulation, and research, and occasionally owned and operated enterprises. These activities were undertaken at the prompting of private interest groups that judged their resources inadequate to solve their economic problems. This type of intervention, Nash concludes, characterized the institutional relationships between government and economy from the Colonial era to the Great Depression. However, continuity in the ends of government action was accompanied by important changes in the means employed. Until the late 19th century, policy makers in California relied on the pressure of public opinion, on formal action in the courts, and on voluntarism; thereafter, they relied increasingly on coercive administrative action.

H 1903. **NETTELS, CURTIS P.** The Emergence of National Economy, 1775-1815. New York: Holt, Rinehart & Winston, 1962. 424 pp.
Nettels describes America's economic development in the four decades that followed the break with England. The study stresses the role of political institutions as factors shaping the pace and the direction of America's economic growth. He discusses the national economy that emerged as a result of the creation, in the Constitutional settlement, of a new institutional and legal framework. He emphasizes the formative effects of the destruction of barriers to domestic trade, of the prevalence of common laws, and of the existence of a common currency. In his view, the Revolution produced a decisive break with the trends that had characterized the Colonial period.

H 1904. **NETTELS, CURTIS P.** The Money Supply of the American Colonies Before 1720. Madison: University of Wisconsin Studies in the Social Sciences and History, 1934. 300 pp.
Nettels examines the money supply factors in the American Colonies that led to estrangement from Britain. He explains that throughout their early history, the American Colonies were beset by monetary problems. To maintain a rising standard of living the settlers depended on the importation of manufactured goods from Britain. British commercial policy, however, was predicated on mercantilist aspirations to maintain a favorable balance of payments. Moreover, the Colonies were confronted with increasingly adverse terms of trade as their production of agricultural staples grew faster than their British markets. Colonial trade deficits meant that specie accumulated in trade with other markets--Spanish America, the West Indies, Southern Europe--was drained off by payments for English imports, depriving the Colonies of a domestic medium of exchange. Colonial attempts to offset the disadvantages accruing from British policy led to precisely those developments which the policy was designed to prevent. The Northern Colonies extended their involvement in trade outside the Empire and embarked on local manufacturing. Thus began the estrangement which culminated in the Revolution.

H 1905. **NORTH, DOUGLASS C.** Structure and Change in Economic History. New York: Norton, 1981. 228 pp.
In attempting to develop a new framework for analyzing the economic past, North explores both political organizations and ideology as essential ingredients in an explanation of institutional change. He maintains that the institutional framework, or "structure," is the means by which human beings interact. Hence, it is of primary importance to develop a theory of institutional change. In Part I North suggests a theoretical recasting of much of economic history into new molds and does so in Part II by examining a thousand years of Western economic history. He presents a neoclassical model of a market economy, isolates factors which the model does not account for, proposes hypotheses to deal with these factors, and finally, outlines areas in which a satisfactory theoretical framework does not exist.

H 1906. PALMER, BRUCE. "Man Over Money": The Southern Populist Critique of American Capitalism. Chapel Hill: University of North Carolina Press, 1980. 311 pp.
Palmer believes that a study of Southern Populism is relevant to any contemporary critique of capitalism, and he consequently provides an account of the rise and fall of the Populist party in the 1890s. He is especially concerned with the role played by Southern ideas about society and the world in the formulation of specific aspects of Populist theory, and he devotes a large part of his study to the description and analysis of those ideas. He concludes that the grave and ultimately fatal contradictions embodied in Populist theory result from a brave attempt to synthesize the Southern historical experience and its intellectual heritage and to adapt this synthesis to economic and political realities.

H 1907. PORTER, GLENN, ed. Encyclopedia of American Economic History: Studies of the Principle Movements and Ideas. 3 vols. New York: Scribner, 1980. 1286 pp.
Porter and his five-member advisory board have sought to break down the barriers between economic history and other disciplines by making accessible the views of many specialists on a number of aspects of the collective economic experience as it is presently understood. The contributors have written essays on a wide range of subjects that are divided into the following categories: the historiography of American economic history; chronological overviews since the Colonial period; aspects of economic growth; and the business and social institutions that provided the framework for America's economic development. Bibliographical essays appear at the end of each section.

H 1908. PRICE, JACOB M. Capital and Credit in British Overseas Trade: The Trade from the Chesapeake, 1700-1776. Cambridge, Mass.: Harvard University Press, 1980. 233 pp.
The tobacco colonies of Virginia and Maryland depended on British importers, and Price investigates how these overseas merchants acquired the capital and credit to finance trade with America. He finds that many were textile manufacturers possessing a great ability to mobilize resources in a variety of ways: through their own capital; by reinvesting their earnings; through long-term borrowing on bonds; through short-term borrowing from banks; and by making full use of commercial credit from their suppliers.

H 1909. PRIMM, JAMES N. Economic Policy in the Development of a Western State: Missouri, 1820-1860. Cambridge, Mass.: Harvard University Press, 1954. 174 pp.
Primm finds that the state played a very active role in the economic affairs of the developing West. State intervention in Missouri was not generated by some new ideological stance about the public interest; instead, it was a result of a pragmatic concern for the promotion and financing of economic development in a region where scarcity of capital and a widely dispersed population hindered private initiatives. The state's first role was as a promoter. Subsequently, the state provided capital for international improvements such as railroads. Throughout, the government also engaged in important regulatory activities, particularly in the field of banking and finance.

H 1910. RAINBOLT, JOHN C. From Prescription to Persuasion: Manipulation of the Eighteenth Century Virginia Economy. Port Washington, N.Y.: Kennikat Press, 1974. 218 pp.
Rainbolt describes and analyzes the complex of motives behind leading 18th-century Virginians' efforts to promote the development of the colony's economy through diversification. Originally aimed at promoting English commercial prosperity by providing a wide range of needed products, diversification also came to be regarded as a solution to persistent over-

supply and price depression in the tobacco market. Virginia elites associated a diversified economic base with their ideal of an orderly colony of compact settlement which would sustain a hierarchical social and political structure. Rainbolt concludes, however, that the diversification schemes actually disrupted Virginia's economic growth--more cause than consequence of the disorder feared by the elites.

H 1911. RANSOM, ROGER L., RICHARD SUTCH, and GARY M. WALTON, eds. Explorations in the New Economic History: Essays in Honor of Douglass C. North. New York: Academic Press, 1981. 308 pp.
More than a dozen scholars contributed essays to this collection honoring one of the deans of American economic history. The essays are organized around the major themes in North's work: the effort to bring explicit scientific theory (mostly recent neoclassical economic theory) to the study of history; the examination of the relationship between growth and welfare; the analysis of property rights and institutional change; and the belief that economic specialization by region was the key to American antebellum growth.

H 1912. RATNER, SIDNEY, JAMES H. SOLTOW, and RICHARD SYLLA. The Revolution of the American Economy: Growth, Welfare, and Decision-Making. New York: Basic Books, 1980. 548 pp.
The authors combine old and new themes and methodologies in this account of the development of the American economy from its roots in the indigenous economies of the North American Indians to the super-industrial economy of today. Chapters on such topics as labor and welfare reflect an attempt to broaden the traditional conception of economic history through research on disadvantaged or oppressed groups.

H 1913. ROSTOW, WALT W. The Stages of Economic Growth: A Non-Communist Manifesto. New York: Cambridge University Press, 1960. 178 pp.
Rostow provides a comparative stage theory of modern economic growth. He argues that every nation's economic development--including that of the U.S.--can be evaluated by comparing its progress to a set of universal stages. Growth takes most nations out of the "traditional" stage into the stage of "preconditions" (where the U.S. actually began); if the progress continues, a dramatic "take-off" occurs. During a surge of technological development, the economy establishes leading sectors into which entrepreneurial groups channel investment capital (1843-1860 in the U.S.). Take-off is characterized by doubling the percentage of national income devoted to investment. The period after take-off, "Drive to Maturity," is characterized by rising productivity, by a high rate of investment, and by the spread of rapid growth to many new sectors of the economy. The concluding stage (after 1900 in the U.S.) is the age of "High Mass Consumption."

H 1914. SCHUMPETER, JOSEPH A. Capitalism, Socialism and Democracy. New York: Harper & Row, 1942. 381 pp.
Schumpeter's theory of economic growth emphasizes the role of the creative entrepreneur as a source of those vital innovations that lead to expansion. In this volume, he adds to this economic theory an analysis of the long-run socio-political ramifications of growth. He says that innovation and the process of creative destruction that it brings about necessarily breed political movements that seek to provide security for the masses. The resulting regulations--as well as the bureaucratization of management and the breakdown of the 19th-century family--dull the entrepreneurial spirit. The results include an inevitable drift toward Socialism--an outcome that does not necessarily bode ill for democracy, according to Schumpeter. While the author emphasizes European developments, he draws examples from the U.S. and clearly sees his theory as applicable to America's history.

H 1915. SCRANTON, PHILIP. Proprietary Capitalism: The Textile Manufacture at Philadelphia 1800-1885. New York: Cambridge University Press, 1983. 431 pp.
Scranton shifts the traditional geographical focus of U.S. textile history from New England to Philadelphia and finds a mix of small, separate, specialized firms whose organization contrasted sharply with that of the mass-producing corporate giants of Massachusetts. The author argues against the dominant tendency to use the evolving corporation as the unifying thread in American business history and makes cultural factors such as family and community structures a major focus of his own interpretation.

H 1916. SHARKEY, ROBERT P. Money, Class, and Party: An Economic Study of the Civil War and Reconstruction. Baltimore, Md.: Johns Hopkins University Press, 1959. 346 pp.
In this volume Sharkey examines the financial history of the Union, seeking answers to three questions: could the Civil War have been financed without resorting to paper money; were the progressive historians correct in arguing that sentiments on the paper money question reflected general party and class divisions within society; were the economic changes of the period sufficient to confirm Charles A. Beard's theory that the Civil War era marked the triumph of business and the dawning of a new machine age? Sharkey concludes that the greenback issue could not have been avoided, and after analyzing the motivations of the Radical Republicans and of four different Northern interest groups (manufacturers, farmers, bankers, and laborers), he finds that there were no significant cleavages along class or party lines on the paper money question. This conclusion, supplemented by an investigation of the cleavages over economic policy within Northeastern business groups, leads him to claim that Beard and other progressive historians overstated their arguments. The politics of the period are best understood, Sharkey suggests, in terms of the accommodations achieved by divergent interests in the North rather than in terms of the triumph of one group and the imposition of its economic and political will on all elements in the Union.

H 1917. SHARLIN, HAROLD ISSADORE, ed. Business and Its Environment: Essays for Thomas Cochran. Westport, Conn.: Greenwood Press, 1983. 228 pp.
As the originator and promoter of such concepts as the centrality of business in American society, the distinctiveness of the entrepreneur, role theory, and the use of the social sciences in history, Thomas Cochran has encouraged a wide range of approaches to problems of present concern. These eight essays by Cochran's students explore the relationship between the American government and private enterprise and emphasize business as a key to understanding American history and current public policy. They include two case studies of the union of business and government by James Flink and Bernard Mergen; two contrasting views of entrepreneurship by James Soltow and Harold Sharlin; essays by Stanley Bailis and Ronald Bayor on the role of businessmen in the diffusion of social change; and two studies of the formation of business communities (Michael Zuckerman analyzes the "casual conviviality" of planters in Colonial Virginia and Robert Walker explores the anatomy of American reform).

H 1918. SMITH, WALTER B. Economic Aspects of the Second Bank of the United States. Cambridge, Mass.: Harvard University Press, 1953. 314 pp.
This study focuses on the Second Bank from its foundation in 1816 to its demise in 1841. The author relates the bank to the major changes taking place in the American economy between the end of the Revolution and the recession of the 1840s, a period notable for a remarkable upsurge in domestic production and commercial activity. Throughout these years, Smith argues, the bank aimed at moderating fluctuations in economic activity

by exerting influence on state banks. The bank's pursuit of stability, according to Smith, was largely successful. Had its development been allowed to continue, he argues, the U.S. would early have gained an effective banking system. For political reasons, however, its powers were exaggerated and the Second Bank was destroyed. As a result, the U.S. was transformed from one of the most financially inventive nations into one of the most backward, with its currency and financial administration at the mercy of the states.

H 1919. SOLTOW, LEE. Men and Wealth in the United States, 1850-1970. New Haven, Conn.: Yale University Press, 1975. 206 pp. Soltow presents and analyzes census data on the distribution of wealth in America in the middle decades of the 19th century. Drawing data from census manuscripts of 1850, 1860, and 1870, the study includes breakdowns of real and personal property by age, region, place of birth (domestic or foreign), and occupation. Saltow examines the extent and concentration of property ownership, the average value of estates, and the extent and nature of inequality in wealth. He treats long-run trends by comparing his findings to data for the early 19th century and for the 20th century. Soltow's statistics indicate widespread inequality, with the greatest incidence of poverty among immigrants, city dwellers, and blacks. At the same time, men could expect their wealth to increase over time, and the average man at mid-century was relatively well off in terms of dollar amounts of wealth. Soltow thus presents a picture of opportunity existing amid inequality--conditions which, he says, remained remarkably stable during the next century.

H 1920. SOLTOW, LEE. Patterns of Wealthholding in Wisconsin Since 1850. Madison: University of Wisconsin Press, 1971. 168 pp. Soltow draws on materials taken from the censuses of 1850, 1860, and 1870 to determine whether an era of agrarian homogeneity was followed in the second half of the 19th century by a trend toward greater inequality in the distribution of wealth. Contrary to the widely accepted thesis of "growing inequality," he finds that Wisconsin wealth was already highly concentrated at mid-century. This basic situation remained unchanged in 1860 and 1870. Estimates based on post-1870 data indicate no apparent alteration in these distributions in the decades that followed. Wisconsin residents thus did not experience a golden era that was destroyed by industrialization and immigration. Rather, the high demand for farm labor and the migration of poor foreign-born into the area meant that Wisconsin was from the first marked by extensive inequality of wealth. This situation was tolerable, Soltow observes, because the state's rapid economic development continued to generate many opportunities for the accumulation of wealth by citizens at all levels of society.

H 1921. SOULE, GEORGE H. Prosperity Decade: From War to Depression, 1917-1929. New York: Holt, Rinehart & Winston, 1947. 365 pp. This volume provides a descriptive survey of the major features of American economic development during W.W. I and the 1920s. Introducing the period with an extensive account of wartime mobilization and related economic policies, Soule then discusses the increases in productivity that characterized the 1920s, as well as the international monetary and commercial instability that inevitably influenced American firms and farms. The book treats the agricultural depression, the government's farm policies, and the changes that took place in the economic position of the working class. Soule also seeks to explain why the decade ended in depression despite an impressive increase in productivity. Regarding the 1929 Stock Market Crash as symptom not cause, Soule argues that the major weakness of the American economy stemmed from a marked maldistribution of income, which, he suggests, had its roots deep in the structure of the modern American economy of large, technologically advanced firms that had an inordinate amount of power.

H 1922. STONE, ALAN. Economic Regulation and the Public Interest: The Federal Trade Commission in Theory and Practice. Ithaca, N.Y.: Cornell University Press, 1977. 314 pp.

Stone's analysis of the impact of the Federal Trade Commission on the structure and practices of American business concludes that the agency's influence has been slight. According to Stone, the FTC's problem was grounded in a fundamental paradox of modern Capitalism: the same enterprises that want to compete to improve their position at the expense of their rivals also want that position protected from competition. The legislation giving birth to the FTC and subsequently defining its goals has reflected these contradictory goals, and Stone establishes this point by surveying the legislative history of the agency. Even the Sherman Antitrust Act of 1890, apparently the embodiment of the principle of competition, was, according to Stone, intentionally limited by Congress to weaken its impact on the structure of business enterprise. Thereafter, Congressional statutes progressively limited the competitive principle even further. In most cases, he concludes, the appearance that the principle of competition has been protected is belied by the reality that particular competitors are being protected; the desire for industrial stability has consistently overridden the interest in competition.

H 1923. STUDENSKI, PAUL and HERMAN E. KROOSS. Financial History of the United States. 1952; Rev. ed. New York: McGraw-Hill, 1963. 605 pp.

This survey of American financial history traces the development of the fiscal, monetary, banking, and tariff policies of governments at all levels from the earliest Colonial years through the end of W.W. II. The authors focus on administrative as well as legislative developments, and on the theory of financial policy as well as its practice. They show how the goals of public policy have changed as the economy has grown and as new interest groups have succeeded each other in the enjoyment of political power. The authors describe the expansion of state and local activity in the first half of the 19th century, when there was a relative decline in action at the Federal level. After the Civil War these trends were reversed. With the continued growth of industrial Capitalism in the 20th century, and the added responsibilities of financing wars and alleviating depressions, Federal activity continued at a high level and the older orthodoxies governing public finance were abandoned. By the end of the 1930s, monetary and fiscal policies had become the central government's most important instruments for economic management.

H 1924. TAYLOR, GEORGE R. The Transportation Revolution, 1815-1860. New York: Holt, Rineholt & Winston, 1951. 490 pp.

Taylor treats the major developments in domestic and foreign commerce, the evolution of financial institutions, and the growth of manufacturing in the years before the Civil War. He concentrates on developments in the means of transportation and communication that cheapened and facilitated the movement of goods and persons, providing an important stimulus to the growth of an integrated national economy. This "transportation revolution," Taylor holds, is the key to understanding the American economy in the early 19th century. He surveys the construction, financing, and technological improvements in the three main forms of domestic transportation—roads, canals and waterways, and railroads—describing how each had to establish itself in direct competition with the existing systems. The book shows that bilateral East-West trade was established early in the canal era and that the railroads followed existing lines of communication and channels of trade, rather than initiating entirely new patterns.

H 1925. TAYLOR, GEORGE ROGERS and LUCIUS F. ELLSWORTH, eds. Approaches
to American Economic History. Charlottesville: University Press
of Virginia, 1971. 135 pp.
These essays introduce some of the major methodologies and approaches
currently used by economic and business historians. Hugh G. J. Aitken
and Alfred D. Chandler, Jr. deal with business history from an entrepreneurial and an institutional perspective; George Rogers Taylor evaluates
stage theories of economic growth; and Stephen Salsbury critiques Marx,
Beard, and the economic interpretation of history. Other essays deal
with the changes in the discipline of economic history resulting from
a heightened awareness of the techniques of other social sciences. Thomas
C. Cochran suggests how sociological models can be used in analyzing economic development; Robert Gallman considers the use and limitations of
econometric tools; and Dorothy S. Brady explains the input-output model
of economic analysis. The volume closes with Lance Davis's general
appraisal of the "new" economic history.

H 1926. TEMIN, PETER. Causal Factors in American Economic Growth in the
Nineteenth Century. New York: Macmillan, 1975. 88 pp.
This volume surveys the recent literature dealing with American economic
growth. Temin concentrates on those areas of investigation where the
use of economic models and the formulation of explicit hypotheses have
had the greatest impact in the last two decades. He looks at the measurement of growth; the effect of abundant natural resources, notably land;
the course of technological change; and the roles of a specific innovation
(the railroad), a specific financial institution (banking), and a specific
labor system (slavery). In each case he recounts the major points in
the recent debates, guiding the reader toward the appropriate body of
literature. Temin uses these discussions to make a general point: if
economic historians are going to improve their understanding of the growth
process, they must carefully distinguish those factors important for political or moral reasons from those important to the economy.

H 1927. TEMIN, PETER. Did Monetary Factors Cause the Great Depression?
New York: Norton, 1976. 201 pp.
Temin surveys the major, competing explanations of the causes of the Great
Depression. He examines the monetary explanations that stress the roles
played by the stock of money and, in turn, by the public policies that
influence money. He then considers the opposing hypothesis and its variations which identify spending as the culprit and are grounded in Keynesian
theory. Approaching his subject skeptically, Temin seeks in each part
of this discussion to identify the assumptions upon which the theories
are based. The spending hypothesis, he discovers, is useful but incomplete;
the monetary hypothesis inadequately explains the Great Depression and
is, in fact, less convincing than the spending theory.

H 1928. TEMIN, PETER. The Jacksonian Economy. New York: Norton, 1969.
208 pp.
Temin examines President Andrew Jackson's economic policies, probing the
interaction of economic and political factors in assessing the causes
and efforts of the Jacksonian programs. Evaluating the extent to which
the booms and crises of the 1830s were products of national policies, he
argues that Jackson's measures actually had little to do with the major
economic fluctuations of this period. The bank war had far greater significance as a political, rather than economic, event; and the destruction
of the Second Bank did not initiate a phase of unstable bank expansion.
Rather, demand for cotton and British eagerness to invest in America stimulated the economy, causing an expansion of the money suppply and inflation.
The general increase in prices was brought to an end by British efforts
to contract exports of investment capital and by a fall in cotton prices.
The result was the panic of 1837, a downturn which was neither severe

nor long lasting. In 1838 the economy recovered but during the following year falling cotton prices and constraints on British specie exports led to a more severe depression. Temin, who uses the neoclassical economic model as his primary tool of analysis, concludes that these fluctuations in economic activity were a product of forces beyond Jackson's control.

H 1929. UNGER, IRWIN. The Greenback Era: A Social and Political History of American Finance, 1865-1897. Princeton, N.J.: Princeton University Press, 1964. 467 pp.
In reevaluating the progressive interpretation of America's post-Civil War history, Unger takes issue with a dualist interpretation of the conflicts over monetary policy. He argues that businessmen were not all united behind deflation, nor were farmers uniformly in favor of soft money; rather, the debates were characterized by a multitude of conflicting opinions with contradictory expressions of interest often emanating from the same general quarters. Unger finds that religious background has more power than occupational orientation or economic activity as a variable predicting attitudes on the money question; hard money proponents had in common a Puritan-Calvinist religious orientation. The post-war monetary debates did not, therefore, reflect a struggle between the old agrarian America and the new industrial nation. Positions varied with alterations in business conditions, and no single economic interest adopted a unanimous and consistent position.

H 1930. VATTER, HAROLD G. The Drive to Industrial Maturity: The United States' Economy, 1860-1914. Westport, Conn.: Greenwood Press, 1976. 368 pp.
Vatter surveys America's economic growth between the Civil War and W.W. I, maintaining that America's growth in the 19th century was distinguished by its reliance on quantitative increases in inputs rather than qualitative improvements in productivity. He assigns to government policy a major role in easing access to these inputs and therefore in stimulating the economy. During the 20th century, furthermore, the economy's growth became increasingly dependent on qualitative improvements that brought about greater productivity. Within this general context, Vatter describes in topical chapters the changes that took place in manufacturing and agriculture, in the structures and policies of business enterprises, and in the social and political activities of agrarian and labor groups.

H 1931. VATTER, HAROLD G. The United States Economy in the 1950's. New York: Norton, 1963. 308 pp.
Vatter first surveys the national economy's performance during the late 1940s and the 1950s. He then analyzes the several business cycles of these years, explaining how the Korean War and general defense-related expenditures influenced the level of national income, unemployment, and prices. From these macro-considerations the author turns to various sectors of the economy, considering the slow- and fast-growing industries, changes in corporate financing and industrial organization, the roles of labor and agriculture, and the nation's international economic relations in the 1950s. While concerned about the decline in investment in plant and equipment that characterized the American economy, Vatter's treatment of the decade is positive, stressing the economic accomplishments of the Eisenhower era.

H 1932. WALTON, GARY M. and JAMES F. SHEPHERD. The Economic Rise of Early America. New York: Cambridge University Press, 1979. 226 pp.
The authors stress foreign trade as the key to understanding the growth of Colonial America. Their analytical framework emphasizes characteristics of an economy rich in land and natural resources but poor in labor and capital. The authors then turn to the effects of an expanding international economy on regional development. The study argues that given the

generally static nature of a rural frontier economy characterized by a
high degree of self-sufficiency and by small and scattered domestic markets,
any significant economic stimulation must have depended on the formation
of external commercial ties. In the Colonial case, development of cash
crops for export and the establishment of viable trade routes hastened
regional specialization and division of labor, which raised incomes and
propelled economic progress.

H 1933. WALTON, GARY M. and JAMES F. SHEPHERD, eds. Market Institutions
and Economic Progress in the New South, 1865-1900: Essays Stimulated by One Kind of Freedom: The Economic Consequences of Emancipation. New York: Academic Press, 1981. 162 pp.
This book is a collection of seven cliometric essays published in response
to One Kind of Freedom (H 1074) by Roger Ransom and Richard Sutch. As these
critiques show, the most controversial aspect of the work by Ransom and
Sutch was their "institutional" explanation of the methods used to coerce
Southern blacks into economic subjugation and of the micro-effects on
the postbellum economy. The papers include Claudia Goldin's "Credit Merchandising in the New South: The Role of Competition and Risk"; Peter
Temin's "Freedom and Coercion: Notes on the Analysis of Debt Peonage in
One Kind of Freedom"; Joseph D. Reid, Jr.'s "White Land, Black Labor,
and Agricultural Stagnation: The Causes and Effects of Sharecropping
in the Postbellum South"; Robert Ransom's and Richard Sutch's "Credit Merchandising in the Post-Emancipation South: Structure, Conduct, and Performance"; Gavin Wright's "Economic Freedom and Economic Progress in the New
South"; Stephen J. DeCanio's "Accumulation and Discrimination in the Post-
bellum South"; and Ransom's and Sutch's "Growth and Welfare in the American
South in the Nineteenth Century."

H 1934. WARKEN, PHILIP W. A History of the National Resources Planning
Board, 1933-1943. New York: Garland, 1979. 294 pp.
Warken traces the history of a government planning agency which, under
a variety of names, functioned from the early days of the New Deal through
the early years of W.W. II. Established to aid in the formulation of
public construction projects, the agency soon broadened its activities.
It collected information on, and inventoried, the nation's resources and
advised as to their use. With the onset of the World War, the agency
undertook to study such things as available energy sources, social welfare
programs, and industrial problems, and to coordinate planning for the
postwar period. Warken works from manuscript collections in the Franklin
D. Roosevelt Library and the National Archives, personal interviews, agency
publications, and secondary sources.

H 1935. WEINSTEIN, ALLEN. Prelude to Populism: Origins of the Silver
Issue, 1867-78. New Haven, Conn.: Yale University Press, 1970.
433 pp.
By examining the formative years of the silver movement, from the "Crime
of 1873" through the Bland-Allison Silver Purchase Act of 1878, Weinstein
refutes the conclusions reached by the "progressive" school. These historians, he says, viewed the events of the 1870s in light of the Populist
revolt of the 1890s and assumed a connection between the two movements.
But Weinstein finds that the coalition that fought for bimetallism in
the 1890s had not yet emerged in the early years of the silver movement.
Southern and Western agrarians were by no means committed to inflation
in the 1876s; Jacksonian hard-money sentiments persisted. Nor were the
Western silver producers particularly involved in the remonetization drive
of 1876-78. Support for bimetallism first arose among predominantly Eastern hard-money forces and later flourished as a partisan political issue.
Not until silver became identified exclusively with inflation in the 1880s,
however, could it contribute to the sharp political cleavage which was
to take place in the tumultuous decade of the 1890s.

H 1936. WHITE, EUGENE NELSON. The Regulation and Reform of the American
Banking System, 1900-1929. Princeton, N.J.: Princeton University
Press, 1983. 251 pp.
White studies both Federal and state attempts to regulate and reform American banking early in the century. He describes how essentially competing
state and Federal banking law created, late in the 19th century, a "dual
banking system" of state and national banks. White then details the fate
of this system in the decade and a half after the Federal Reserve Act
of 1913, as well as the progress of state banking reform. He finds state
and national banking reform to have failed in this period to initiate significant change--its achievements were, thus, limited. He believes the
resistance to branch banking, in particular, to have only compounded weaknesses in the banking system.

H 1937. WICKER, ELMUS R. Federal Reserve Monetary Policy, 1917-1933.
New York: Random House, 1966. 221 pp.
Wicker's history focuses on those top officials in the Fed and the U.S.
Treasury who shaped the nation's monetary policies from W.W. I to the beginning of the New Deal. Research in manuscript materials, including the
official files of the Board of Governors of the System, convinces the
author that these officials failed to meet the challenge of forging effective policies. Attached to specific and often outdated goals, unable
to understand fully the monetary tools (e.g., open market operations)
at their beck and call, and uncertain how the System could influence
national economy, these officers failed most significantly in the immediate
post-war years and in the period just before and after the Stock Market
collapse of 1929. Wicker recounts the policy debates of each successive
episode in the war and post-war eras, separating the myths of monetary
history from the realities that he finds etched in the archival record.

H 1938. WILLIAMSON, JEFFREY G. American Growth and the Balance Payments,
1820-1913. Chapel Hill: University of North Carolina Press,
1963. 198 pp.
By examining movements in goods, gold, and capital across America's borders
from 1820 to 1913, Williamson seeks to identify the long swings ("Kuznets
Cycles") in the American balance of payments and to explain how they were
connected with domestic growth and with international economic adjustments.
From about 1820, Williamson discovers, long swings existed in the importation of goods as a result of similar swings in domestic development.
Increasing deficits on current accounts reflected increasing American
demand for goods during the upswing of a long cycle in domestic development.
Improvements in the trade balances coincided with periods of stagnation
in domestic development. As Williamson notes, domestic cycles were also
associated with swings in specie and net capital movements. While he
analyzes these specie flows, the author concludes that they cannot explain
the rhythm of current account movements. For that explanation, he directs
attention to the long swings in the pace of domestic development, fluctuations that dominated changes in the trade balance, and capital flows.

H 1939. WILLIAMSON, JEFFREY G. Late Nineteenth Century American Economic
Development: A General Equilibrium History. New York: Cambridge
University Press, 1974. 350 pp.
Williamson uses a general equilibrium model to simulate the behavior of
the economy between the Civil War and the end of the 19th century. Employing a counter-factual analysis to identify the major sources of economic
growth, he considers, for instance, how the course of American development
would have been different had factors traditionally identified as crucial
been missing. He considers the impact of an elastic land supply; rapid
technical progress in agriculture; European integration; regional transportation improvement; changes in capital markets; and the deteriorating
world market conditions for American grains. He concludes that retardation

in the growth rate after 1885 can be traced to changes in the rate of capital formation rather than to the closure of the frontier or falling rates of increase in total factor productivity. The growing efficiency of financial intermediaries had little effect on post-war economic growth, but variations in world market demand and reductions in inter-regional transportation costs through railroad improvements did have significant impacts on the growth of GNP in America.

H 1940. WILLIAMSON, JEFFREY G. and PETER H. LINDERS. American Inequality: A Macroeconomic History. New York: Academic Press, 1980. 362 pp.
This book addresses the question of why American earnings, income, and wealth have seemed to be more unequal in some eras than others. Part I synthesizes research on the period before 1929, suggesting that inequality among free Americans before the Revolution was not too different from the levels we experience today. But inequality was not stable for the period in between: the main epoch of income inequality was the last four decades before the Civil War. Parts II and III examine some of the variables with which inequality has been correlated over American history, such as technology, demography, and capital accumulation. The evidence appears to refute the equality/growth trade-off suggested by Kuznets as being a necessary part of the process of economic development in currently advanced countries.

XVI. LEGAL HISTORY

H 1941. BASCH, NORMA. In the Eyes of the Law: Women, Marriage and Property in Nineteenth-Century New York. Ithaca, N.Y.: Cornell University Press, 1982. 255 pp.
Basch argues that the New York Married Women's Property Acts of 1848-49 grew out of the general codification movement rather than out of pressures put on the New York Legislature by antebellum Feminists. The merging of law and equity and the problem of debtor relief played major roles in the adoption of the legislation. The resulting expansions of women's rights in these bills, however, proved to be so limited that succeeding Feminists were forced to lobby for further legislation which came in 1860.

H 1942. BLOOMFIELD, MAXWELL. American Lawyers in a Changing Society, 1776-1876. Cambridge, Mass.: Harvard University Press, 1976. 397 pp.
This collection of essays offers biographical studies of nine significant American lawyers as well as topical articles on a disparate group of subjects such as "The Family in Antebellum Law," "Up-grading the Professional Image," "Riot Control in Philadelphia," and "Anti-lawyer Sentiment in the Early Republic." All of the biographical studies deal in some way with the development of the American bar.

H 1943. BOURGUIGNON, HENRY J. The First Federal Court: The Federal Appellate Prize Court of the American Revolution, 1775-1787. Philadelphia: American Philosophical Society, 1977. 362 pp.
The influence of the appellate prize court of the Revolutionary era upon the founders of the American judiciary system is the subject of this book. Appellate prize courts ruled on the taking of enemy ships by privateers during wartime, a practice which the Declaration of Paris abolished in 1856. Bourguignon traces the historical context of America's first Federal court and its impact on the judiciary system operating after the Revolution.

H 1944. BUGBEE, BRUCE W. The Genesis of American Patent and Copyright
Law. Washington, D.C.: Public Affairs Press, 1967. 208 pp.
This book traces the origins of laws protecting the rights of inventors
and authors to their earliest roots in the Renaissance. The focus of
the book is on the development of American patent and copyright laws,
from the first patent in 1641 through 20th-century legislation. Bugbee
augments his discussions with an examination of the philosophy underlying
patent and copyright legislation; in particular, he focuses on the position
that ideas themselves are property.

H 1945. CHASE, WILLIAM C. The American Law School and the Rise of Administrative Government. Madison: University of Wisconsin Press,
1982. 182 pp.
This study of the changing curriculum in American law schools at the turn
of the last century stresses the case method and its relationship to the
contemporary establishment of state and Federal regulatory commissions.
Influential law professors examined adjudication in the new administrative
commissions and regulatory agencies, and focused more on procedural issues
in instances when the decisions of such bodies were appealed to the appropriate courts. Consequently, the important policy-making roles of the
commissions tended to remain uninvestigated, Ernst Freund being the most
significant exception. Chase includes internal law school documents among
the sources of his study as well as a bibliographical essay.

H 1946. COOK, CHARLES M. The American Codification Movement: A Study
of Antebellum Legal Reform. Westport, Conn.: Greenwood Press,
1981. 234 pp.
Cook's volume on the history of American codification centers on the post-
Civil War as that time which best exemplifies the legal reform movement
in the U.S. The movement, writes Cook, "is best understood as an attempt
to deal with the problems of Antebellum legal development that occurred
with an already well-established legal tradition." This tradition was
a modified version of English common law, and was not ideally suited to
the rapid growth of the American legal system. Tracing codification back
to 1776, Cook then emphasizes the intellectual notions and debates behind
the movement. Cook closes with an examination of codification in New
York during the 1840s, where it continuted to thrive after national interest had waned.

H 1947. FAULKNER, ROBERT KENNETH. The Jurisprudence of John Marshall.
Princeton, N.J.: Princeton University Press, 1968. 307 pp.
Faulkner traces the development of Chief Justice Marshall's thought and
explores its underlying philosophy. Arranged topically, the book discusses,
among other things, Marshall's Lockean conception of "life, liberty, and
property," his insistence on a strong central government (including a
strong judiciary), and his belief in the future of the U.S. as a "legitimate empire." To Faulkner, Marshall's thought is not an attempt at a universal political theory, but is concerned primarily with the practical
problems of governance in the emerging American nation and is influenced
by the experience of an active political career. Faulkner also emphasizes
Marshall's role in establishing the authority of the U.S. Constitution
and the power of the Supreme Court.

H 1948. FEHRENBACHER, DON EDWARD. The Dred Scott Case: Its Significance
in American Law and Politics. New York: Oxford University Press,
1978. 741 pp.
This book examines the historical impact of the 1857 Supreme Court decision
on Dred Scott, which maintained that blacks could not claim citizenship.
Beginning with a detailed survey of slave law from 1619 until 1857, the
author proceeds to give his analysis of the Dred Scott decision: Fehrenbacher argues that the Court's ruling prefigured that of the Warren Court;

both resolved political and social crises by ruling major Federal legislation unconstitutional. The author gives little credence to the interpretation which sees the Dred Scott decision as one of the causes of the
Civil War.

H 1949. FINKELMAN, PAUL. An Imperfect Union: Slavery, Federalism, and
         Comity. Chapel Hill: University of North Carolina Press, 1981.
         378 pp.
Finkelman analyzes hundreds of appellate court cases in an effort to understand antebellum laws regarding slavery. He especially focuses on what
happened in Northern courts when judges faced slavery laws from the South
with which they disagreed. He argues that from the late 18th century
until the 1830s there was an attempt by both Northern and Southern judges
to accommodate the others' laws, but that Northern judges increasingly
argued for the freedom and rights of the slaves who were brought North
after 1830. The author places his legal history within the context of
the growing anti-slavery movement.

H 1950. FRIEDMAN, LAWRENCE M. A History of American Law. New York:
         Simon & Schuster, 1973. 655 pp.
Friedman details the colonial beginnings of the American legal system,
traces its development to 1850, and then carries the story forward to
1900. The author documents the history of various legal areas, including
state as well as Federal laws, and examines the manner in which society
and its power structures are embedded in the law. Finally, he analyzes
the interrelationship between social change and the legal system.

H 1951. GATES, PAUL WALLACE and ROBERT W. SWENSON. History of Public
         Land Law Development. Washington, D.C.: U.S. Government Printing
         Office, 1968. 828 pp.
This work surveys the way that the land system "affected those seeking
land ownership, whether farmers, speculators, lumbermen, livestock men,
or town promoters." About three-quarters of the work deals with the origin
and history of the public domain prior to the 20th century; the remainder
examines such topics as hydroelectric power, reclamation, forests, grazing,
and mineral lands. Gates also addresses subjects that have been the focus
of heated academic debate such as the significance of the Homestead Act,
the safety valve effect of public lands, slavery and the public lands,
the controversy of speculators and settlers, cheap land and Jacksonian
democracy, railroad land grants, and the choice between conservation or
preservation.

H 1952. GEWALT, GERARD W. The Promise of Power: The Legal Profession
         in Massachusetts 1760-1840. Westport, Conn.: Greenwood Press,
         1979. 254 pp.
Gewalt sees the tremendous increase in the power of the legal profession
as part of the general movement toward professionalization between 1760
and 1840. The first significant development for this profession occurred
in the post-Revolutionary period when law became linked with politics:
men began studying law as a means of entering the field of politics.
The Jacksonian era saw the emergence of what Gewalt calls the "modern
legal profession" in Massachusetts. At this time, law began to replace
religion as the primary force in Massachusetts society and lawyers secured
their place in the professional elite. Gewalt examines such things as
the role and growth of the Bar Association and the relationship between
radical reform movements and the rise of the legal profession.

H 1953. GILMORE, GRANT. The Ages of American Law. New Haven, Conn.:
Yale University Press, 1977. 154 pp.
In his review of America's legal past from 1800 to 1940, Gilmore isolates
three "ages" of American law. The first, 1800 to the Civil War, was the
high point, an age of great legal minds like John Marshall and Lemuel
Shaw, who retooled the Federal system and whose only failure was not coming
to terms with slavery. The second age, from the Civil War to W.W. I,
was "law's black night," an era dominated by the harsh example of Oliver
Wendell Holmes and by lawyers and judges confident in their ability to
find truth through law. The last age, the modern era, has seen the
reversal of this attitude and the rise of legal realism.

H 1954. GRAGLIA, LINO A. Disaster by Decree: The Supreme Court Decisions
on Race and the Schools. Ithaca, N.Y.: Cornell University Press,
1976. 351 pp.
Graglia argues that the 1954 Supreme Court case of Brown v. Board of Education of Topeka had a critical impact on the future of the Supreme Court
and on future race relations in the U.S. The decision was an impetus
to what Graglia sees as the "revolution" in race relations. And it was
through this issue of race and the schools that the Court first began to
expand its power. Prior to this case, the Court had acted as a conservative force, impeding the implementation of social change; subsequent to
Brown v. Board of Education, however, the Court became an instrument of
social progress.

H 1955. HALL, KERMIT L. The Politics of Justice: Lower Federal Judicial
Selection and the Second Party System, 1829-61. Lincoln: University of Nebraska Press, 1979. 268 pp.
Hall's study of the Federal judiciary spans the years 1829-61; he draws
on manuscripts, newspapers, and legal archives for his account of the
members of the judiciary, how they were selected, and how they functioned
in office. He presents a narrative account of the selection of approximately 200 men from Andrew Jackson to James Buchanan. Hall demonstrates
that the selection process was affected by both the slavery question and
issues concerning territorial expansion. He observed that as the political
structure modernized, it moved toward party-selection criteria rather
than personal-selection criteria for choosing members of the judiciary.

H 1956. HASKINS, GEORGE LEE and HERBERT A. JOHNSON. Foundations of Power:
John Marshall, 1801-15. New York: Macmillan, 1981. 687 pp.
This work, Volume II of The Oliver Wendell Holmes Devise: History of
the Supreme Court of the United States, provides an account of the early
years of the Marshall Court. It includes a discussion of the Court's interaction with politicians and politics, its business methods, and the socio-
economic background of American society which influenced its decisions.
Haskins and Johnson contend that the Marshall Court's principal long-range
achievement was the divorce of law from politics, thus creating an independent realm for the exercise of the legal mind free from outside influences.

H 1957. HIBBARD, BENJAMIN H. A History of the Public Land Policies.
Madison: University of Wisconsin Press, 1965. 579 pp.
Hibbard surveys the legislative history and the implementation of the
Federal land laws. For Hibbard, the story of the Westward movement is
bound up with the conflict between two very different views of land:
a source of immediate income, or as the key to national development.
The early Westward movement was marked by waves of speculation. Not until
1841 were positive steps taken which favored settlers over speculators.
The Homestead Act of 1862 was the culmination of the trend toward free
land for settlement. As Hibbard notes the small-farm homesteading which
was institutionalized by the Homestead Act was poorly administered and
inappropriate in the semi-arid regions of the West. Throughout the book,

Hibbard's sympathies are with the settlers and the Jeffersonian policies
that favored them.

H 1958. HINDUS, MICHAEL STEPHEN. Prison and Plantation: Crime, Justice,
and Authority in Massachusetts and South Carolina, 1767-1878.
Chapel Hill: University of North Carolina Press, 1980. 285 pp.
Hindus contrasts the development of criminal justice systems in Massachusetts and in South Carolina, attributing their differences to divergent
traditions and, most importantly, to the presence of slavery in South
Carolina and its absence in Massachusetts. Patterns of criminal prosecution and movements for reform are discussed. South Carolina plantations
and Massachusetts penitentiaries are compared as systems of production
and social control. Production in Massachusetts prisons is compared to
that of factories.

H 1959. HORWITZ, MORTON J. The Transformation of American Law, 1780-1860.
Cambridge, Mass.: Harvard University Press, 1977. 356 pp.
This book examines the formative years of American law, tracing its development from 18th-century common law systems to the sophisticated legal system
which facilitated industrialization and economic growth in the 19th century.
Horwitz argues that legal immunities for business entrepreneurs and changing interpretations of property rights helped create an inequitable economic system. He considers a broad range of material, taking into account
the changing economy and value systems operating between the Revolutionary
and Civil Wars.

H 1960. HURST, JAMES WILLARD. The Growth of American Law: The Law Makers.
Boston: Little, Brown, 1950. 502 pp.
This book is a study of lawmakers and lawyers in American social, political,
and governmental history. Rather than describing the history and progress
of substantive law, the author focuses on the growth of the functions
of the governmental legal bodies in American society. Hurst presents
five lawmaking agencies in detail—national and state legislatures, state
and Federal courts, state and national constitutions, the bar and bar
associations, and finally the executive power—and examines the changes
wrought by time in the functions and organization of each of these agencies.

H 1961. HURST, JAMES WILLARD. Law and the Conditions of Freedom in the
19th Century United States. Madison: University of Wisconsin
Press, 1956. 139 pp.
Hurst analyzes the role of law in the economic and social development
of the U.S., rejecting the notion that legal policy in the 19th century
was resolutely laissez-faire. He argues that the law and legal institutions played an important and positive role in the economic growth of the
U.S. According to Hurst, the law provided the principal means whereby
individuals and groups could make use of the positive power of the state
to maximize their own energies and to improve their ability to mobilize
the community's resources. The development of contract law was particularly important, Hurst argues, because it accelerated the process of mobilizing property for business ventures. By the end of the century, the law
had taken on additional administrative, regulatory, and planning functions
that were exercised both by new government agencies and by the pre-existing
legal institutions.

H 1962. HURST, JAMES WILLARD. Law and Economic Growth: The Legal History
of the Lumber Industry in Wisconsin, 1836-1915. Cambridge, Mass.:
Harvard University Press, 1964. 946 pp.
Hurst studies the growth of the lumber industry in Wisconsin. The author
analyzes the manner in which the legal decisions made between 1836-1915
facilitated and shaped the industry's development. The law had an unusually significant impact in this case because the public domain (and thus

the timber supply) was under the government's direct control. In addition, lumbermen looked to the government for aid. In this setting, the law of contract came to dominate the 19th-century legal order. Not until the 1890s, when the period of rapid expansion ended, did the state begin to play a role in actively directing the industry's long-term development.

H 1963. HYMAN, HAROLD M. and WILLIAM M. WIECEK. Equal Justice Under Law: Constitutional Development, 1835-1875. New York: Harper & Row, 1982. 571 pp.
Hyman's and Wiecek's volume is a synthesis of recent work on constitutional development in the U.S. in the middle four decades of the 19th century. The authors emphasize the states' role in encouraging private enterprise; employers, for instance, were protected from liability for industrial accidents through such judicial doctrines as "contributory negligence." State regulation of the economy was minimal; Federal regulation was even more so. The authors also discuss major cases involving slavery, especially Dred Scott, the wartime curtailment of civil liberties, and the interpretations of the post-Civil War amendments to the Constitution.

H 1964. IRONS, PETER. The New Deal Lawyers. Princeton, N.J.: Princeton University Press, 1982. 351 pp.
Irons focuses on the litigation strategies of Roosevelt administration lawyers assigned to the task of defending various controversial New Deal programs, including AAA, NIRA, and the National Labor Relations Act. He also presents a group portrait of some of the other lawyers who worked in the Federal government, and discusses the conflicts that the lawyers of the various and competing Federal agencies found themselves involved in.

H 1965. JAMES, JOSEPH BLISS. The Framing of the Fourteenth Amendment. Urbana: University of Illinois Press, 1956. 220 pp.
James has researched the origins of the Fourteenth Amendment. He discovers that conflict within the Republican Party was responsible for the vague, confusing wording of the amendment. Discussing the motives and goals of the framers of this important legislation, James clarifies the policies of Republicans toward both freedmen and Southern rebels. His research indicates that the amendment's authors intended to grant blacks the vote as well as full civil rights upon which individual states could not intrude.

H 1966. JOHNSON, JOHN W. American Legal Culture, 1908-1940. Westport, Conn.: Greenwood Press, 1981. 185 pp.
Johnson argues that the recourse to common law in 19th-century judicial decisions was supplanted at the turn of the century by an appeal to extra-legal information. The author notes the revolutionary impact of Louis Brandeis and analyzes Brandeis's use of labor statistics and other non-legal sources in the brief for Muller v. Oregon (1908). Jackson then traces the increased role of legislative history in court decisions which also complemented the demise of common law. Much of this change, he argues, was a result of the universalization of formal legal training during this period. In addition, Johnson describes the growth of "legal realism" in the 1930s and concludes the book with a discussion of the decline of the judicial "penchant for information" after 1940.

H 1967. KETTNER, JAMES H. The Development of American Citizenship, 1608-1870. Chapel Hill: University of North Carolina Press, 1978. 391 pp.
Kettner traces the growth of the legal ideal of equal citizenship. Beginning with the 17th-century English notion of "perpetual allegiance," he demonstrates that Colonial experiences with immigration and the debates over the legitimacy of the Revolution led Americans to adopt an ideal of "volitional allegiance" (which allowed for both naturalization and

expatriation). At the same time, the articulation of volitional allegiance
led to the ideal of equal citizenship, at least in a legal sense.

H 1968. KONIG, DAVID THOMAS. Law and Society in Puritan Massachusetts:
Essex County, 1629-1692. Chapel Hill: University of North Carolina Press, 1979. 215 pp.
This book discusses the origins of a legal system in early American society,
and its development according to the needs of the Puritan community.
At a time when the greatest source of authority for Puritans was the Church,
the issues of property, of balance of power, and of behavior within the
group required guidance and regulation outside of religion. The Puritans'
first model for a legal system was English common law, and thus it "closely
resembled the oligarchical patterns of English county or borough government." As property gained in importance, litigation began to replace
communalism. Property, and the economic and ministerial reliance of the
Church upon the State for support and maintenance combined to produce
a judicial and legal system that would assure the rights of citizens.
Konig closes with a discussion of the law's role in the witchcraft trials
at Salem.

H 1969. KUTLER, STANLEY I. Judicial Power and Reconstruction Politics.
Chicago: University of Chicago Press, 1968. 178 pp.
This book is a reassessment of the U.S. Supreme Court during the era of
Reconstruction. Traditionally, the Court of this period has been seen
as a spineless institution at the nadir of its power. Examining three
cases, Kutler argues that a tough, independent Court actually enlarged
its powers. In spite of continual congressional threats to curb the power
of the Court, the Court functioned as an ally of the Republicans, who
recognized the usefulness of the Court in its role as the final spokesman
on the Federal Constitution.

H 1970. KUTLER, STANLEY I. Privilege and Creative Destruction: The
Charles River Bridge Case. New York: Norton, 1971. 195 pp.
Kutler describes the controversy and ensuing litigation concerning the
Charles River Bridge from its construction in 1786 to the final Supreme
Court decision of 1837. He outlines the major arguments used by those
interested in maintaining a one-bridge monopoly in Boston and by those
who constructed a second, free bridge, and relates the case to the conflict
between privilege and progress in the burgeoning society of early 19th-
century America. Kutler also discusses the contemporary change in the
membership of the Supreme Court under Jackson and the subsequent shift
in the interpretation of corporate rights, and describes the impact of
the 1837 decision on later technological developments, including the introduction of the railroad.

H 1971. LEVY, LEONARD. Origins of the Fifth Amendment. New York: Oxford
University Press, 1968. 561 pp.
Levy analyzes the legal roots of the Constitution's Fifth Amendment—which
asserts the right of the accused to refuse to incriminate himself—and
finds its origins in the Restoration's common-law courts, which granted
defendants the right against self-incrimination. The analysis is largely
devoted to the legal processes developed in London. However, Levy examines
the adoption of the Fifth Amendment concept in America in the final three
chapters of the book.

H 1972. MURPHY, PAUL L. The Constitution in Crisis Times 1918-1968.
New York: Harper & Row, 1972. 570 pp.
Murphy traces the interpretation and understanding of the Constitution
from post-W.W. I America through the Warren Court. According to the author,
in the 1920s, the Court saw itself as a protector of private property;
however, by the 1960s, it had become a protector of those without private

property, and those who were in danger of being oppressed by the wealthy, powerful, and potentially tyrannical government. Murphy explores the origins of this change, whether or not it was a direct reaction to the growth of a powerful Federal government, and whether or not this changed function of the Court allowed America's democracy to run more smoothly.

H 1973. NELSON, WILLIAM E. Americanization of the Common Law: The Impact of Legal Change on Massachusetts Society, 1760-1830. Cambridge, Mass.: Harvard University Press, 1975. 269 pp.
Nelson argues that in the pre-Revolutionary legal system, juries had the power to determine law and used this prerogative to uphold local power and community-wide ethical standards. The Revolutionary era, however, witnessed the breakdown of the social and ethical consensus which underlaid jury-made law. Thus, the courts became arenas of conflict between interest groups. In particular, the wealthy and powerful used the courts to impose their beliefs and interests on the community as a whole.

H 1974. NELSON, WILLIAM E. Dispute and Conflict Resolution in Plymouth County, Massachusetts, 1725-1825. Chapel Hill: University of North Carolina Press, 1981. 212 pp.
In this analysis of the role of litigation in 18th- and early 19th-century Plymouth County, Nelson suggests that the intrusion of political and religious outsiders, and the expansion of commercial contacts, broke down the uniformity of Plymouth's communities. Although this transformation occurred throughout the 18th century, Nelson argues that it accelerated in the 1790s with the development of the first party system, the growth of religious diversity, and the spread of commerce. Consequently, whereas in the 18th century Plymouth residents settled their disputes communally (in church or town assemblies), by the early 19th century they turned to the legal system to resolve their conflicts.

H 1975. NIEMAN, DONALD G. To Set the Law in Motion: The Freedmen's Bureau and the Legal Rights of Blacks, 1865-1868. Millwood, N.Y.: K.T.O., 1979. 250 pp.
Nieman's book is a study of the Freedmen's Bureau's most important function--enforcing the legal rights of the newly freed slaves. The failure of the Bureau's creators to provide adequate means to carry out this mission quickly doomed it to failure. Although the revised legal codes of the Southern states granted equal legal status to blacks and whites, the return of the Southern courts to whites resulted in unequal administration of the law. Nieman suggests that the legal and constitutional structures which harbored the failures of the Freedmen's Bureau were never reformed.

H 1976. ROEBER, A. G. Faithful Magistrates and Republican Lawyers: Creators of Virginia Legal Culture, 1680-1810. Chapel Hill: University of North Carolina Press, 1981. 292 pp.
Roeber traces the emergence of a professional legal culture in Virginia which displaced the rituals and practices of the law that had served to reinforce the authority of the gentry. During the 18th century, emerging legal professionals sought to reform the administration of justice and to bring the standards and practices of English law to Virginia. Roeber traces the conflicts between the approaches to justice during the Revolutionary era and the Jeffersonian reform of Virginia's legal system. He concludes with reflections on the conservative nature of the Revolution in Virginia and the role of "country" notions of justice in Southern law.

H 1977. ROHRBOUGH, MALCOLM. The Land Office Business: The Settlement and Administration of American Public Lands, 1789-1837. New York: Oxford University Press, 1968. 331 pp.
This history of public land policies discusses the rise of the Land Office as a bureaucracy during the Jacksonian era, and the competition over the public territory which the Land Office handled. A portrait of political corruption and inefficiency emerges as Rohrbough examines the leading bureaucratic officials and the tenuous relations between the Federal organization and the local offices. Speculation over public land created a situation ripe for corruption and mismanagement until the Panic of 1837, which brought a halt to the frenetic sale of land.

H 1978. ROSENBERG, CHARLES E. The Trial of the Assassin Guiteau. Chicago: University of Chicago Press, 1968. 289 pp.
Rosenberg narrates the events leading to the assassination of President Garfield in 1881 and the famous trial which followed. He addresses several important themes pertinent to late 19th-century American society, law, and psychiatry. The volume deals with the trial of Charles Guiteau and the moral, legal, and medical issues which surrounded it, including the problem of defining criminal responsibility, the problem of whether or not an "insane" person could be held responsible for his acts, and the question of who can be considered an expert witness.

H 1979. RUSSELL, FRANCIS. Tragedy in Dedham: The Story of the Sacco-Vanzetti Case. New York: McGraw-Hill, 1962. 478 pp.
Russell's study is an attempt to reconstruct the attitudes and events surrounding the controversial Sacco-Vanzetti trial. Approaching the story as an interested reporter rather than as a historiographer, Russell describes the case as "one of those events that divide a society." Specifically, he focuses on the emotionally charged anti-Communist climate of the 1920s which came to bear on the trial, and the anti-immigration tensions which fed that climate. Russell's overall assessment is not without opinion, however, as he observes that "by and large one's view of the case depended on one's status in the community."

H 1980. TUSHNET, MARK V. The American Law of Slavery, 1810-1860: Considerations of Humanity and Interest. Princeton, N.J.: Princeton University Press, 1981. 262 pp.
Tushnet's study focuses on a number of cases involving slave criminals. He stresses the ironic contradictions inherent in these cases: Southern judges were forced to treat slaves as responsible individuals, though they simultaneously designated the slaves as legal chattel. Due to this anomaly, Southern justices ignored precedents and relaxed old procedures in order to deal with the situations which arose.

H 1981. WHITE, G. EDWARD. The American Judicial Tradition: Profiles of Leading American Judges. New York: Oxford University Press, 1976. 441 pp.
In his collection of studies on leading American judges and courts, White describes the interplay of changing social norms and intellectual assumptions with the institutional continuity of the judiciary. White argues that John Marshall was largely responsible for creating a coherent judiciary tradition, in which the main elements were a sensitive relation to politics, a balance between judiciary freedom and constraints, and a tension between independence and accountability of the individual judge. Within this continuity, White discerns a shift from the "oracular" tradition of the 19th century, in which judges "discovered" fixed legal principles and applied them to cases, to the 20th-century preference to making law, rather than to discovering it.

H 1982. WHITE, G. EDWARD. Tort Law in America: An Intellectual History.
New York: Oxford University Press, 1980. 283 pp.
White's study focuses on the professional ideology of legal thinkers and
elite jurists in the development of tort law in the U.S. Beginning in
the late 19th century, especially at Harvard Law School, separate tort
courses and studies appeared and soon became standard. White sees this
as an example of the trend toward rationalization and specialization evident in both intellectual and economic life in modern America.

LITERATURE

PREFACE

The study of our nation's literary works was accorded professional status in 1929, when the first journal to be devoted exclusively to the field, American Literature, was founded at Duke University. Americanists in the 1930s and early 1940s could "know the field" without too much difficulty, but in the years immediately following W.W. II critical literature about our own literature became a nearly overwhelming torrent and no abatement seems likely. Pending the further development of data banks which will allow a user seated at a terminal to punch in keywords and receive a printout of works dealing only with a chosen area of interest, the scholar must still laboriously compile information by consulting guides such as those listed below. Obviously the research problem is twofold: the student must endeavor to determine what studies of past years are worth the task of seeking out and he or she must try to keep up with the mass of information and commentary currently appearing in books and periodicals now issued around the globe. Though none is without its limitations, the reference works cited here at least provide basic assistance.

A starting point for knowledge about studies printed in the past (here arbitrarily defined as "before 1975") is Robert E. Spiller, et al., Literary History of the United States: Bibliography, 4th ed. (New York: Macmillan, 1974). Covering both general topics and individual authors, this volume conflates earlier bibliographies published in 1948, 1959, and 1972 and adds new material. Three volumes compiled by Lewis Leary (the third with the aid of John Auchard) supply fuller listings of periodical material: Articles on American Literature, 1900-1950 (1954); Articles on American Literature, 1950-1967 (1970); and Articles on American Literature, 1968-1975 (1979). (All three are published in Durham, N.C., by Duke University Press.) Other guides covering the pre-1975 period are Charles H. Nilon, Bibliography of Bibliographies in American Literature

(New York: Bowker, 1970) and Robert C. Schweik and Dieter Riesner, Reference Sources in English and American Literature (New York: Norton, 1977).

Numerous handbooks and companions have been published, including The Cambridge Handbook of American Literature, edited by Jack Salzman (New York: Cambridge University Press, 1986), The Oxford Companion to American Literature, edited by James D. Hart, 5th ed. (New York: Oxford University Press, 1985), and The Penguin Companion to American Literature, edited by Malcolm Bradbury, et al. (New York: McGraw-Hill, 1971).

Handbooks aimed principally at college students doing research papers are: Lewis Leary (with John Auchard), American Literature: A Study and Research Guide (New York: St. Martin's Press, 1976) and Harold H. Kolb, Jr., A Field Guide to the Study of American Literature (Charlottesville: University Press of Virginia, 1976). The most ambitious guide of this type, first published in 1959, is now available in a recent update: Clarence Gohdes and Sanford E. Marovitz, Bibliographical Guide to the Study of the Literature of the U.S.A., 5th ed. (Durham, N.C.: Duke University Press, 1984).

The major tool for keeping up with recent scholarship is the annual Modern Language Association International Bibliography (New York: Modern Language Association). Listings include both general works and individual author entries. Since 1981 a computer program has greatly expanded the usefulness of this basic volume. Items under an author's name are now classified according to content and are briefly annotated. A new Subject Index, which occupies about half the volume, is described as providing "access to names of persons, languages, groups, genres, stylistic and structural features, themes, sources, influences, processes, methodological approaches, theories, and other related topics."

A second primary guide to recent work is American Literary Scholarship (Durham, N.C.: Duke University Press), published annually since 1963. Based on the materials collected yearly in the Modern Language Association International Bibliography, it is a selective and critical

712

overview of the best (and often, for pedagogical purposes, of the worst) of a given year's production. Evaluative essays are devoted to a number of major authors; other topics are literature before 1800, 19th-century literature, 20th-century fiction, and poetry to the present. Further chapters cover drama, black literature, themes, topics, criticism, and foreign scholarship. A recent addition is an entry on general reference works. The volume is also invaluable for students who wish to check on changing currents in critical methodology. To supplement this overview readers of the journal American Literature can find an even more condensed update in each issue: "A Select, Annotated List of Current Articles on American Literature."

Those interested in wider coverage of criticism about regions of the U.S. will benefit from a number of specialized bibliographies. The South is well served by Louis D. Rubin, ed., A Bibliographical Guide to the Study of Southern Literature (Baton Rouge: Louisiana State University Press, 1969). This volume is continued by Jerry T. Williams, ed., Southern Literature, 1968-1975 (Boston: G. K. Hall, 1978). A yearly update is published in Mississippi Quarterly. Material on the Midwest is to be found in Gerald Nemanic's A Bibliographical Guide to Midwestern Literature (Iowa City: University of Iowa Press, 1981) and annually in Midamerica. The literature of the West is surveyed annually in Western American Literature.

Scholars researching an individual author should be aware of further sources: (1) book-length bibliographies (available for most of our major writers); (2) single-figure journals or newsletters (e.g., Poe Studies, Walt Whitman Review); (3) checklists and bibliographies in such journals as American Literary Realism, Modern Fiction Studies, Resources for American Literary Study, Twentieth Century Literature; and (4) Alan R. Weiner and Spencer Means, eds., Literary Criticism Index (Metuchen, N.J.: Scarecrow, 1984). Older bibliographical essays, still useful, include: James Woodress, ed., Eight American Authors, Rev. ed. (New York: Norton, 1972) and Jackson R. Bryer, ed., Sixteen Modern American Authors (New York: Norton, 1973). Earl N. Harbert and Robert H. Rees, eds., Fifteen American Authors Before 1900 (Madison: University of Wisconsin Press, 1984) is a revision of a work first published in 1971. The proliferation of women's studies and studies in black literature has also warranted specialized bibliographies. Representative are: Maurice Duke, Jackson R. Bryer, and M. Thomas Inge, eds., American Women Writers: Bibliographical Essays (Westport, Conn.: Greenwood Press, 1983) and M. Thomas Inge, Maurice Duke, and Jackson R. Bryer, eds., Black American Writers: Bibliographical Essays, 2 vols. (New York: St. Martin's Press, 1978).

Finally, dissertations should not be overlooked, since many excellent studies, owing to burgeoning publication costs, never make it into print. Consult James Woodress, Dissertations in American Literature, 1891-1966 (Durham, N.C.: Duke University Press, 1968). It may be updated with the serial volumes of Dissertation Abstracts International (Ann Arbor, Mich.: University Microfilms International).

Joseph V. Ridgely
Columbia University

I. GENERAL SURVEYS

L 1. **BLAIR, WALTER** and **HAMLIN HILL**. America's Humor: From Poor Richard to Doonesbury. New York: Oxford University Press, 1978. 559 pp.
A history of American humor from Colonial times to the present, this work examines various types of "jokelore," ranging from the literary comic tradition to popular and underground humor. The volume is divided into five sections. The first part, titled "Starters," discusses Colonial satire and the establishment of typically American stereotypes in the humor of Benjamin Franklin, John Wesley Jarvis, Mike Fink, and Davy Crockett. The second section, "The Golden Age of American Humor," focuses on the development and differentiation of regional characteristics in the work of antebellum humorists. In "And the War Came," Blair and Hill examine the "changes in folklore" effected by the Civil War, as reflected in the work of such local colorists as Artemus Ward, Josh Billings, Petroleum V. Nasby, and Bill Arp. The fourth section is devoted entirely to Mark Twain. The volume concludes with an examination of 20th-century urban, underground, and black humor, as well as the social satire of such writers as Robert Benchley, S. J. Perelman, E. B. White, and James Thurber.

L 2. **BLANKENSHIP, RUSSELL**. American Literature as an Expression of the National Mind. 1931; Rev. ed. New York: Holt, Rinehart & Winston, 1949. 776 pp.
In this work, Blankenship surveys American literature from John Winthrop to James T. Farrell. He assumes that a literary work is the product of culture and so expresses the values of a particular time and nation. Thus he begins with an overview of the physical, racial, and intellectual background of primary and secondary writers, grouped chronologically and, roughly, geographically. The work provides a historical introduction to some 150 writers.

L 3. **CHASE, RICHARD**. The American Novel and Its Tradition. Garden City, N.Y.: Doubleday, 1957. 266 pp.
In distinguishing between the "novel" and the "romance," Chase tries to define the American novel's achievements and failures. His thesis--derived in part from the writings of such novelists as Hawthorne and James--is that the American novel from earliest times incorporated a greater element of romance than did the English novel. Chase believes that the romance frees the author from some of the usual fictional requirements of verisimilitude, plot development, continuity, and realistic social morality so that he can focus on more intellectual and abstract concerns. The two major sources of the American prose-romance are the dramatic Puritan dichotomy between good and evil, and nostalgia for a rural past. Apart from this theoretical analysis, Chase studies in detail works by a number of authors, including Brockden Brown, Cooper, Hawthorne, Melville, James, Mark Twain, Fitzgerald, Norris, and Faulkner.

L 4. **COWIE, ALEXANDER**. The Rise of the American Novel. New York: American Book, 1948. 877 pp.
Cowie's work is a critical history of the American novel's evolution from William Hill Brown's The Power of Sympathy (1789), generally considered the first American novel, to Henry James's works in the 1880s and 1890s. A final chapter briefly assesses the new directions of American fiction from 1890 to 1940. Cowie synthesizes both major and minor authors by viewing their progression or retrogression comparatively: for example, in a single chapter he discusses Charles Brockden Brown's works alongside two lesser novels by Brown's contemporaries George Watterston and Samuel Woodworth. To assess the development of American fiction more fully, Cowie considers authors' economic, political, and religious backgrounds.

This approach also suggests his interest in individual contributions rather than strained divisions into "movements" and "schools" (e.g., the realistic novel, the Gothic school).

L 5. CUNLIFFE, MARCUS. The Literature of the United States. 1954; Rev.
    ed. Baltimore, Md.: Penguin Books, 1967. 409 pp.
This work spans American literature from the 17th to the 20th centuries.
It combines general introductory comments with specific allusions and
quotations. Chapter organization is varied: according to period (e.g.,
"Colonial America"), genre (e.g., "The American Theatre"), movement (e.g.,
"Realism in American Prose"), or complementary authors (e.g., "Melville
and Whitman"). Necessarily, Cunliffe spends most of his time on major
authors and works within these chapters, although he also alludes to a
number of minor figures and works. The emphasis is on 19th- and 20th-
century literature.

L 6. GRIMSTED, DAVID. Melodrama Unveiled: American Theater and Culture
    1800-1950. Chicago: University of Chicago Press, 1968. 285 pp.
Grimsted's goal is "to explain the popularity of that most banal of dramatic forms, the melodrama, and to glimpse that most devious of historical
objects, the popular mind of an age." In America, the melodrama was influenced by drama critics, religious leaders, and native writers, many of
whom called for a national theater. Shakespeare's plays (accompanied
by farces and musical numbers) were the standard fare of the age; however,
Shakespeare lacked "morality." The melodrama, on the other hand, functioned as a parable in which Virtue triumphed over obvious villains, thus
providing American audiences with examples of national ideals. Grimsted
describes the form of the melodrama, theater conditions, and theatrical
conventions, and provides a list of the most popular plays, afterpieces,
and types of play, as well as an extensive bibliography.

L 7. HOWARD, LEON. Literature and the American Tradition. Garden City,
    N.Y.: Doubleday, 1960. 354 pp.
Howard states that American Puritanism, which sought to restore the Church
to its primitive form, was grounded in a stable system of ethical values
stressing a trust in law and a willingness to accept judicial interpretation as a way of maintaining stability. All Puritan writing made this
commitment. But during the 18th century reason replaced revelation.
Unlike the English Romantic conceptions of Nature, the American idea of
Nature offered no stable psychological values; as a result, progress,
not the past, became part of the American consciousness. There were two
strains of American Romanticism: one, represented by Cooper, stressed
the positive role of intuition and individuality; the second, represented
by Poe, depicted the darker, grimmer workings of the mind. In works like
Emerson's "Nature" the American consciousness attends to man's relation
to external reality, including complex social organizations. In the
literature of the early 20th century this relationship predominates.
Howard's study thus traces the American philosophical tradition in literary
works.

L 8. HUGHES, GLENN. A History of the American Theatre, 1700-1950. New
    York: Samuel French, 1951. 562 pp.
Hughes's book is most useful as a reference source, for he attempts to
cover an immense subject in relatively few pages. He examines various
aspects of theatrical history, from the building of theaters to the fates
of individual actors. Almost half the book is devoted to the 20th century,
and gives a year-by-year account of the New York theater for that period.
Hughes includes chapters which focus on such special topics as: "The
Professional Appears: 1750-1775"; "Managers and Old Stars: 1870-1900";
and "Art vs. Commercialism: 1910-1920."

L 9. **JONES, HOWARD MUMFORD.** The Theory of American Literature. 1948;
Rev. ed. Ithaca, N.Y.: Cornell University Press, 1965. 225 pp.
Jones traces the development of literary history as a discipline in the
U.S. with a view toward reestablishing the discipline as an integral part
of any approach to the study of literature. He shows the influence of
domestic and foreign historical forces on the progress of the art and
describes the influence that works of literary history have had on the
organization of American education and on the development of a national
literary taste. He concludes that American scholars, unlike their European
counterparts, have only seldom approached the history of literature as
a philosophical problem, treating it more often as a sociological problem.
The 1965 reissue contains a new concluding chapter and a revised bibliography.

L 10. **LEHMANN-HAUPT, HELLMUT**, et al. The Book in America: A History
of the Making and Selling of Books in the United States. 1939;
Rev. ed. New York: Bowker, 1951. 493 pp.
This work forms a comprehensive account of the development of printing,
allied crafts and industries, bookselling, publishing, book collecting,
and the growth of libraries from Colonial times to the mid-20th century.
The establishment of the press in New England responded to the Colonists'
isolation, religious contentions, business interests, and reactions to
English thought and politics. However, to understand the development
of the book from 1860 to the present, one must examine technical and industrial
innovations in printing. In 20th-century America the newspaper
and the magazine appear to be more important than the book.

L 11. **LEWISOHN, LUDWIG.** The Story of American Literature. 1932; Rev.
ed. New York: Random House, 1939. 652 pp.
Discovering conventional literary history and adopting methods from
Freudian psychology, Lewisohn presents "a portrait of the American spirit
seen and delineated, as the human spirit itself is best seen, in and
through its mood of articulateness, of creative expression." Thus he
praises writers according to their psychological profile and selects works
according to their appeal to a modern audience. Lewisohn dismisses most
early American literature and the work of Brockden Brown, Cooper, Poe,
Melville, and the modern "neo-naturalists" (a rather unusual group, which
includes Morley Callaghan, Nathan Asch, and William Faulkner). The
work was originally published as Expressionism in America.

L 12. **LLOYD, JAMES B.**, ed. Lives of Mississippi Authors, 1817-1967.
Jackson: University Press of Mississippi, 1981. 489 pp.
This compilation of the lives of Mississippi authors includes entries
on approximately fifteen hundred writers who were born or lived in Mississippi,
and who published at least one work between 1817 and 1967. The
biographies and bibliographies are current to 1979. Major individuals
receive extensive treatment beyond the ordinary retelling of career.
Taken as a whole, this work is intended to be a "more comprehensive and
a more incisive view of Mississippi's culture than has before been possible."

L 13. **MACY, JOHN.** The Spirit of American Literature. New York: Doubleday,
Page, 1913. 347 pp.
Macy offers a series of essays reviewing many 19th-century writers. He
devotes a chapter to each of sixteen authors, endeavoring to present appreciative
discussions of the writers' works during their careers. These
chapters are neither strict literary histories nor bibliographic manuals;
Macy's aim is to provide a comprehensive view of each writer, introducing
such writers as Thoreau, Howells, Longfellow, Mark Twain, and Whittier
both to the student and to those with a general interest in literature.

L 14. MEYER, ROY W. The Middle Western Farm Novel in the Twentieth Century
Lincoln: University of Nebraska Press, 1965. 265 pp.
Meyer surveys Middle Western farm fiction of the late 19th and 20th centuries. He first attempts to define the characteristics of the farm novel
as a distinct literary genre, then discusses the farm in 19th-century
fiction. Primarily concerned with images of farm life in novels published
between 1891 and 1962, Meyer devotes separate chapters to various historical, social, economic, and psychological issues raised by the litrature.
An appendix briefly treats 140 representative works of this subgenre.

L 15. PARRINGTON, VERNON LOUIS. Main Currents in American Thought: An
Interpretation of American Literature from the Beginnings to 1920.
3 vols. New York: Harcourt, Brace & World, 1927-30. 1335 pp.
According to Parrington, literature reflects the genesis, development,
and conflict of political and economic ideas. Derived from pessimistic
Calvinism, 17th-century Puritan literature was generally anti-democratic
and conservative. With Jeffersonian economic ideas, which flourished
in the 19th century, came political liberalism. American Romanticism
and Transcendentalism, a kind of mystical Jeffersonianism, reflected
economic individualism. However, economic industrialism and the growth
of cities signaled the decay of Romanticism and of humane liberalism.
Mechanistic science gave rise to literary Realism. Since Parrington died
before he could complete his study, the third volume consists largely
of fragmentary notes and lectures.

L 16. PATTEE, FRED LEWIS. The Development of the American Short Story:
An Historical Survey. New York: Harper, 1923. 388 pp.
Pattee chronologically treats biography, literary history, literary influence, and criticism. He also discusses the effect of the rise of literary
journals and magazines on the development of the short story. Starting
with Washington Irving and ending with O. Henry, he emphasizes the short
story's development during the 19th century. Pattee acknowledges the
existence of short fiction before Irving but feels that the form of what
we now call the short story did not develop until Irving. The book offers
a consideration of minor 19th-century short story writers, as well as
detailed bibliographies at the end of each chapter.

L 17. PATTEE, FRED LEWIS. The First Century of American Literature.
New York: Appleton-Century, 1935. 614 pp.
In this third volume of his literary history of America (see also L 18
and L 19), Pattee maintains his belief that American literature "has been
an emanation from American life and American conditions." He focuses
on what he considers to be particularly American forms of literary expression: humor, essays, newspaper columns, and short stories.

L. 18. PATTEE, FRED LEWIS. A History of American Literature since 1870.
New York: Century, 1915. 449 pp.
The first of Pattee's three-part history of American literature (see also
L 17 and L 19), this work is concerned with the period beginning shortly
after the close of the Civil War. Pattee deals only with those authors
who did their first distinctive work before 1892, and centers his attention
on poetry, fiction, and the essay. The study is dominated by Pattee's
conviction that the great mass of writing of the post-Civil-War period
"could have been produced nowhere else but in the United States. They
are redolent of the new spirit of America: they are American literature."

L 19. PATTEE, FRED LEWIS. The New American Literature 1890-1930. New
York: Century, 1930. 507 pp.
Pattee asserts that American literature from 1890 to 1930 "departed so
widely from all that had gone before that it stands alone and unique."
The second volume of a three-part history of American literature (see

also L 17 and L 18), this study examines those aspects of literature of this period which the author identifies as being distinctly American.

L 20. QUINN, ARTHUR HOBSON. A History of American Drama. 2 parts. From the Beginning to the Civil War. 1923; Rev. ed. New York: Crofts, 1946. 530 pp. From the Civil War to the Present Day. 1927; Rev. ed. New York: Appleton-Century-Crofts, 1936. 432 pp.
Quinn's study was one of the first histories of American drama; as such, it has formed the basis for most subsequent studies. Part One begins with early theatrical performances in Colonial Virginia, New York, Charleston, and Philadelphia, and concludes with an examination of the influence of Dion Boucicault in the mid-1860s. Part Two moves from the work of Augustin Daly to the social comedy of Clyde Fitch in the first decade of the 20th century and, in the second volume, to the early work of Eugene O'Neill. The revised one-volume edition, which was issued in 1936, preserves the text of the original two volumes but also includes a new chapter entitled "The New Decade--1927-1936." Quinn provides an 80-page "Bibliography and Play List."

L 21. QUINN, ARTHUR HOBSON, ed. The Literature of the American People: An Historical and Critical Survey. New York: Appleton-Century-Crofts, 1951. 1172 pp.
This narrative of the literature and thought of the U.S., is divided into four parts: "The Colonial and Revolutionary Period" (Kenneth B. Murdock), "The Establishment of National Literature" (Arthur H. Quinn), "The Later Nineteenth Century" (Clarence Gohdes), and "The Twentieth Century" (George F. Whicher). Its aim is primarily pedagogical; its range extends from the intellectual sources and economic conditions of the Colonial writers to the conditions of authorship and audience under which the Modernists labored. Not simply contextual history, however, the study offers analysis as well. Topics discussed include Puritan poets, historians, theologians, and travellers; the 18th century's Colonial culture, and its main exemplars, Jonathan Edwards and Benjamin Franklin; the Revolutionary sensibility and its earliest fiction and poetry; the romances of the frontier, independence, and idealism; political battles and the slavery issue; the 19th-century historians; the growth of the monthly magazines; the emergence of Realism (for the middle class); the challenge of new social problems and science; impressionists and experimenters; the proletarian eruption; and new forms and new pressures.

L 22. RATHBUN, JOHN W., et al. American Literary Criticism 1800-1965. 3 vols. Vol. I [John Rathbun]: 1800-1860; Vol. II [John Rathbun and Harry H. Clark]: 1860-1905; Vol. III [Arnold L. Goldsmith]: 1905-1965. Boston: Twayne, 1979. 574 pp.
This is an introductory survey of the rise of criticism and the authors who practiced it. Volume I discusses the growth of a national literature and critics' attempts, under the influences of European Romanticism, historical scholarship, and judicial criticism, to define it. The volume concludes with an essay on the critical practice of Emerson and Poe. Volume II takes up the issues of Realism, Naturalism, and Aestheticism, examining the work of Henry James and George Santayana, among others. The final volume provides an account of the various critical approaches developed in the 20th century: New Humanism, Marxism, New Criticism, myth criticism, and Neo-Aristotelianism.

L 23. SEILHAMER, GEORGE O. History of the American Theatre. 3 vols. Philadelphia: Globe Printing House, 1888-91. 1184 pp.
Seilhamer's work explores American drama of the later half of the 18th century. Seilhamer concentrates on leading actors, acting companies, and productions, and publishes previously lost theater bills, casts, announcements, and records. The three volumes treat American theater before,

during, and after the Revolution, and examine the "New Foundations" of the Boston, Philadelphia, and Rhode Island companies of the 1790s.

L 24. SMITH, BERNARD. Forces in American Criticism: A Study in the History of American Literary Thought. New York: Harcourt, Brace, 1939. 401 pp.

Smith provides an introductory Marxist approach to the problems of the history of criticism. He emphasizes the ideological and social elements of American critical writings, sketching major figures and currents of thought by way of what Smith himself calls "scientific methods" rather than by subjective evaluations. His study focuses on such movements as Puritanism, Romanticism, Realism, and Expressionism, and on such writers as Charles Brockden Brown, Ralph Waldo Emerson, Henry James, and Floyd Dell.

L 25. SPILLER, ROBERT E. The Cycle of American Literature: An Essay in Historical Criticism. 1955; New York: Macmillan, 1967. 243 pp.

Following an organic theory of history, Spiller searches for broad patterns of inception, development, and decline in the major themes of America's literature. His major "cycle" traces American authors' initial acceptance of European conventions, their abandonment of those conventions, and their gradual, still incomplete struggle to develop a truly American literature. Within this cycle two minor cycles furnish structural organization for the book: the earlier Eastern American writers adopted and then rejected Europe's cultural values in order to create American Idealism; after about 1870, however, Western and Southern American writers rejected the conventional values of the East to produce American Realism. Spiller supplies brief surveys of most major literary figures from Jonathan Edwards to William Faulkner, placing each in a historical and geographical context. The 1967 edition adds an epilogue "which attempts to round out the story already told rather than to venture into the alluring morass of prophecy."

L 26. SPILLER, ROBERT E. et al., eds. Literary History of the United States. 3 vols. 1948; Rev. ed. 2 vols. New York: Macmillan, 1974. 1824 pp.

Updated and revised in 1974, this work is an account of America's literary past and the rise of American civilization. Fifty-seven scholars trace the development of American literature (in all its genres) from its Colonial roots to its position in the 1960s. The fourth edition leaves the main text of the previous editions unaltered. But a wholly new chapter on Emily Dickinson has been added; the chapter on the "End of an Era" has been virtually rewritten; and the "Postscript" section of the third edition has been dropped and new chapters by Ihab Hassan, Daniel Hoffman, and Gerald Weales added.

L 27. STAUFFER, DONALD BARLOW. A Short History of American Poetry. New York: Dutton, 1974. 459 pp.

Stauffer offers a "historical and critical survey of poetry written in America during the past three hundred and fifty years." He begins with the early Puritan and Dutch poets in the first chapter; by the twelfth he is discussing the generation of poets born in the 1920s and early 1930s. Stauffer has attempted to do several things: provide biographical and historical information where necessary; make connections between various poets and periods; give a sense of the range of a poet's work. He also makes two "large generalizations" which he tries to support throughout the study--namely, that American poetry is heterogeneous and that "American poets are in the main anti-traditional, or at least forward-looking."

L 28. STOVALL, FLOYD, ed. The Development of American Literary Criticism.
        Chapel Hill: University of North Carolina Press, 1955. 262 pp.
In this collection of essays, which were originally papers delivered at
a convention of the Modern Language Association, American literary criticism is examined from three perspectives: expository, taxonomic, and
evaluative. Aesthetic assertions are drawn from both critical and literary
works. The overall organization is chronological, dating from 1800 to
the 1930s. Critics such as Harry H. Clark and C. Hugh Holman discuss
various topics, ranging from "Changing Attitudes in Early American Literary
Criticism: 1800-1840" to "The Defense of Art: Criticism since 1930."

L 29. TAUBMAN, HOWARD. The Making of the American Theatre. 1965; Rev.
        ed. New York: Coward-McCann, 1967. 402 pp.
Taubman, a former daily drama critic for The New York Times, has written
a somewhat informal, anecdotal history of the American theater. Although
his survey begins with the Colonial period, more than two-thirds of the
discussion deals with post-1920 drama. Taubman does not limit his study
to serious drama; he also deals with musical productions, cultural milieu,
and the financial situations of the American theater throughout its history.
In addition, he deals with the roles played by specific individuals, like
Eugene O'Neill, in the development of the American theater.

L 30. TAYLOR, WALTER FULLER. The Economic Novel in America. Chapel Hill:
        University of North Carolina Press, 1942. 378 pp.
Taylor's aim is "to show how, between the Civil War and the turn of the
century, certain democratic and middle-class ideals, which had hitherto
been applied chiefly to politics, were so extended as to apply to economics
as well; how that democratic ideology found voice in our published fiction;
and how, consequently, there developed within that fiction a coherent
and incisive critique of capitalistic industrialism." These ideas were
formulated by economist Henry George and expressed in the fiction of Mark
Twain, Edward Bellamy, Hamlin Garland, William Dean Howells, and Frank
Norris. These writers, the author concludes, objected not to industrialism but to its capitalistic administration.

L 31. TAYLOR, WALTER FULLER. The Story of American Letters. Chicago:
        Regnery, 1956. 504 pp.
This volume, a reworking of Taylor's A History of American Letters (1936),
surveys American literary activity from 17th-century Virginia travel literature to the novels of Thomas Wolfe and William Faulkner. Taylor focuses
on the works of major writers in American history and, through introductory
essays, supplies background and general trends for each of his five chronological divisions: travel literature and the Puritan theology of the
17th century; the religious, political, and professional ideas of the
18th century; the Romantic and Realist impulses of the 19th century; and
the vestigial 19th-century traditions carried over into the 20th, with
their attendant reactions and revolts.

L 32. TRENT, WILLIAM PETERFIELD, et al., eds. The Cambridge History of
        American Literature. New York: Macmillan, 1917. 1488 pp.
This lengthy literary history, compiled by more than sixty scholars, deals
with the literature, literary figures, genres, philosophy, politics, social
situation, language, religion, and general history of America. Major
figures discussed include Brown, Bryant, Cooper, Edwards, Emerson, Franklin,
Hawthorne, Irving, James, Lincoln, Longfellow, Lowell, Poe, Thoreau, Twain,
Webster, Whitman, and Whittier. This work also deals with a number of
important subjects both in their influence on the literature and as events
themselves; some of these are Puritanism, Transcendentalism, the Civil
War, the emergence of American philosophy, the evolution of the English
language in America, and American politics.

L 33. VAN DOREN, CARL. The American Novel 1789–1939. 1921; Rev. ed.
New York: Macmillan, 1946. 406 pp.
This work traces the history of the American novel from its beginnings
to 1939. It is meant to record "the national imagination as exhibited
in the progress of native fiction." Although Van Doren takes poems, plays,
short stories, myths, and legends into account, his prime interest lies
with full-length fiction. Arranged chronologically, the book proceeds
from such early authors as Cooper and Brown to classic 19th-century writers
(Hawthorne, Melville, Twain, Howells, and James), exponents of Naturalism
(Crane and Garland), and 20th-century novelists (Wharton, Cather, and
Lewis).

L 34. VAUGHN, JACK A. Early American Dramatists: From the Beginnings
to 1900. New York: Ungar, 1981. 200 pp.
Vaughn surveys the careers and works of important American dramatists
from the Colonial period through the 19th century, with attention both
to the drama's development as an American form (use of American historical
and cultural subjects, exploitation of patriotic themes) and to elements
of stagecraft and American theatrical history (activities of theatrical
companies, emergence of the actor-dramatist, collaborations). He treats
such figures as Royall Tyler, William Dunlap, and Dion Boucicault, and
such movements as Romanticism and Realism.

L 35. VOSS, ARTHUR. The American Short Story: A Critical Survey. Norman:
University of Oklahoma Press, 1973. 399 pp.
Voss surveys the American short story from its early-19th-century begin-
nings (Washington Irving) to its mid-20th-century development (e.g., Eudora
Welty, Bernard Malamud, and Flannery O'Connor). He proceeds by chronology
and movement, sometimes covering a single major author (e.g., "Terror,
Mystery and Imagination: Edgar Allan Poe") and sometimes looking at a
number of writers (e.g., "The Short Story in Transition: Stephen Crane,
Jack London, Edith Wharton, Willa Cather, and Theodore Dreiser") within
one chapter. Voss combines background information, critical opinion,
and literary influences, and discusses the narrative technique of the
stories.

L 36. WAGENKNECHT, EDWARD. Cavalcade of the American Novel: From the
Birth of the Nation to the Middle of the Twentieth Century. New
York: Holt, 1952. 575 pp.
Wagenknecht's study is a history of the American novel from its beginnings
to the 1930s. He espouses historical criticism and attempts to present
novelists "upon their own terms," or to approach their experience as nearly
as possible in order to elucidate their meaning. The work of each writer
is presented in a separate section. Wagenknecht begins with a brief discussion of the early American novel, then examines both major and minor
authors, including Cooper, Hawthorne, Melville, Stowe, Twain, Howells,
James, Crane, London, Tarkington, Wharton, Glasgow, Dreiser, Cather, Cabell,
Lewis, Hemingway, and Dos Passos. Although this history focuses on the
novelists, it also deals with such movements as Naturalism, Realism, Modernism, and the beginnings of the Southern literary renaissance.

L 37. WAGGONER, HYATT H. American Poets from the Puritans to the Present.
1968; Rev. ed. Baton Rouge: Louisiana State University Press,
1984. 735 pp.
Starting with the assumption that Ralph Waldo Emerson is the central figure
in the American poetic tradition, Waggoner illuminates this poetic development by treating its most representative poets. Necessarily, as Waggoner
himself admits, a number of significant poets have been omitted, especially
contemporary poets. However, he believes that concentrating on Emerson's
influence and thought genuinely clarifies what is "American" about American
poetry from 1650 to 1970. Some elements discussed are the American poet's

concern with nature rather than society or culture, and his concern with
the eternal rather than the temporal. American poets have tended to turn
conventional poetic forms and traditional genres to their own purposes
(e.g., Emily Dickinson) or have abandoned them entirely (e.g., Walt
Whitman).

L 38. WILSON, EDMUND, ed. The Shock of Recognition: The Development
        of Literature in the United States, Recorded by the Men Who Made
        It. Garden City, N.Y.: Doublday, Doran, 1943. 1,290 pp.
Wilson gathers into this collection a representative selection of critical
pieces dealing with important American men of letters, written by important
American men of letters between about 1840 and 1930. These pieces, such
as Melville's review of Hawthorne and Emerson's famous letter to Whitman,
reveal in their juxtaposition the tone and temper of American literary
thought. Some of the authors, like H. L. Mencken, are primarily critics;
most are poets and novelists. Almost all of the pieces deal with the
work of a single author since Wilson excludes general discussions of literary theory. He prefaces each author's section with a brief introduction
and gives the full text of every document.

II.   COLONIAL PERIOD

L 39. ALDRIDGE, ALFRED OWEN. Early American Literature: A Comparatist
        Approach. Princeton, N.J.: Princeton University Press, 1982.
        322 pp.
Arguing that early American literature was neither narrowly parochial
nor confined to merely reproducing the formal and thematic qualities of
English letters, Aldridge examines that literature together with contemporary literature from the continent and Latin America. By tracing parallel developments and patterns of intercontinental influence and reception,
Aldridge shows how such texts as Benjamin Franklin's "Speech of Polly
Baker" and Joel Barlow's The Columbiad both partook of and actively contributed to the establishment of certain literary conventions and themes
important in European literary history. He finds comparisons with early
literature from the Ibero-American Colonies mutually illuminating because
of parallels in the two regions' histories of colonization and quests
for independence as well as parallels (and some instances of direct influence) in their development of Enlightenment thought and Revolutionary
ideology.

L 40. AMACHER, RICHARD E. American Political Writers, 1588-1800. Boston:
        Twayne, 1979. 250 pp.
Amacher examines the principal themes of non-fiction written in New England
during the 17th and 18th centuries. While the political discourse between
1588 and 1660 centers on the questions of freedom of conscience and ministerial control of government, the writing between 1660 and 1728 is concerned almost exclusively with the relation of church and state and dominated by the power struggle between Puritan orthodoxy and proponents of
the Enlightenment. Amacher traces the growth of anti-slavery sentiment
throughout the period and presents a catalogue of the theological, moral,
scientific, economic, and political objections. Alongside this account
of opposition to domestic slavery, the study examines the debates over
the Colonial right to resist economic and political servitude. A concluding chapter characterizes the debate between Federalists and Republicans
as one between political and economic interests competing for power in
the new Republic.

L 41. BERCOVITCH, SACVAN. The American Jeremiad. Madison: University
of Wisconsin Press, 1978. 239 pp.
Bercovitch argues that the Puritan notion of the elect nation, which guaranteed a glorious future to America, runs through American public rhetoric
starting with the Puritan jeremiads and continuing through 18th-century
millennial writings and Revolutionary rhetoric, which infused the institutions of the new nation with that status of chosenness. By means of
"rituals of consensus," repeated through Fourth of July speeches and other
public occasions, American rhetoric in the early Republic continued to
recapitulate the jeremiad structure, affirming a belief in America's destiny even while reciting its failings (of necessity temporary). Even
writers of the American Renaissance, including Emerson, Whitman, and
Melville, though they were critical of American society, finally reproduced this essentially affirmative rhetoric in their writings.

L 42. BERCOVITCH, SACVAN. The Puritan Origins of the American Self.
New Haven, Conn.: Yale University Press, 1975. 250 pp.
Bercovitch argues that Puritan language fused notions of community and
personal identity so as to make New England itself one of the elect, justified in its chosen status and protected from the possibility of even secular failure. Using the biography of John Winthrop, "Nehemias Americanus,"
from Cotton Mather's Magnalia Christi Americana, Bercovitch demonstrates
how the traditions of typology and the imitatio Christi combined with
the Puritans' feelings about the migration experience to produce this
imaginative rendering of redemptive American identity. This mythic meaning,
somewhat transformed, continued to be expressed through the 19th century,
and can be seen, as Bercovitch concludes, in the language of Hawthorne
and Emerson.

L 43. BERCOVITCH, SACVAN, ed. The American Puritan Imagination: Essays
in Revaluation. New York: Cambridge University Press, 1974.
265 pp.
Bercovitch's introduction explains how Puritan scholarship has come to
emphasize the way the Puritans' imagination structured their world. The
volume reprints essays by Norman S. Grabo, Larzer Ziff, David Minter,
and Cecilia Tichi on approaches, themes, and genres; by Jesper Rosenmeier,
Robert D. Richardson, Jr., Karl Keller, and David Levin on individual
writers; and by Daniel Shea, John Lynen, and Ursula Brumm on Puritan continuities into the 18th century and beyond.

L 44. BERCOVITCH, SACVAN, ed. Typology and Early American Literature.
Amherst: University of Massachusetts Press, 1972. 340 pp.
This collection reflects the importance to Puritan studies of typology,
both in delineating foreign influences on American literary and intellectual history and in clarifying the nature of the Puritan imagination.
The volume includes essays by Thomas Davis and Stephen Manning on traditions of scriptural exegesis; by Jesper Rosenmeier on William Bradford;
by Richard Reinitz on Roger Williams; by Mason Lowance on Cotton Mather
and Jonathan Edwards; and by Robert Reiter, Karl Keller, and Ursula Brumm
on Edward Taylor. Bercovitch has appended an extensive annotated bibliography on typology.

L 45. BIGELOW, GORDON E. Rhetoric and American Poetry of the Early
National Period. Gainesville: University of Florida Press, 1960.
77 pp.
This work analyzes a little-examined area: the relationship of rhetoric
to American poetry from 1775 to 1815. First Bigelow distinguishes poetry
and rhetoric as modes of discourse. Then he shows how verse of the early
national period conforms to rules of rhetoric, not poetry, and how it
therefore emphasizes declamation, didacticism, propaganda, and oratorical
structure. The work focuses on those poets most valued by contemporary

society and by posterity: Philip Freneau, Joel Barlow, David Humphreys, Timothy Dwight, John Trumbull, Francis Hopkinson, and Robert Treat Paine.

L 46. BOST, JAMES S. <u>Monarchs of the Mimic World or the American Theatre of the Eighteenth Century through the Managers—The Men Who Make It</u>. Orono: University of Maine at Orono Press, 1977. 194 pp.
This book is essentially a narrative cultural history of the world of early American theater. The plays themselves are backdrops to accounts of the various people who produced the plays: managers, actors, stagehands, and others. The focus is usually on the manager's role concerning actors, the audience, and the age, showing how the managers were able to keep theater alive in 18th-century America. Special note is made of David Douglass, Lewis Hallam Jr., Lewis Hallam Sr., Thomas Wignell, John Henry, William Dunlap, and John Hodgkinson because they were exemplary in fulfilling the duties of the manager.

L 47. CALDWELL, PATRICIA. <u>The Puritan Conversion Narrative: The Beginnings of American Expression</u>. New York: Cambridge University Press, 1983. 210 pp.
After discussing the origins of and controversies surrounding the early American practice of requiring "spiritual relations" for church membership, Caldwell locates in these narratives of religious conversion a peculiarly American literary form. Drawing largely on the narratives collected by Thomas Shepard from his Cambridge, Massachusetts, congregation between 1637 and 1645, she argues that these first-generation American documents can be distinguished from the writings of non-American Puritans by their obsession with but ambivalence about the land and the migration experience (thus differing too from the later writings of the more assured and prominent Cotton Mather and Edward Johnson); by their special anxieties about putting religious experience into language; and by their symbolic rather than allegorical mode of perceiving the world and incorporating it into the narrative of religious experience.

L 48. COOK, ELIZABETH C. <u>Literary Influences in Colonial Newspapers, 1704-1750</u>. New York: Columbia University Press, 1912. 279 pp.
Cook investigates the belletristic literature published in such Colonial newspapers as <u>The New England Courant</u>, <u>The American Mercury</u>, <u>The New York Gazette</u>, <u>The Virginia Gazette</u>, and <u>The South Carolina Gazette</u>. The belletristic pieces were derived in many cases from English essays, especially Joseph Addison's. Of the various genres appearing in the newspapers, the most common was satire directed against political figures and contemporary fashions. This study focuses on the influence of English secular literature on the philosophical-moral positions taken in the belletristic pieces. Although Colonial newspapers frequently published excerpts from English classics, they also included, as Cook shows, original poetry and prose which appealed to the common 18th-century reader.

L 49. DALY, ROBERT. <u>God's Altar: The World and the Flesh in Puritan Poetry</u>. Berkeley: University of California Press, 1978. 253 pp.
Daly shows that the Puritans, far from being hostile to poetry or the natural world, used earthly images as figures to help them understand and express religious truths. He discusses explicit statements about figural language by such Puritan writers as Samuel Willard and Richard Baxter, as well as the significance for Puritan poetry of the Ramist and Ignatian traditions. The works of Anne Bradstreet, Edward Taylor, Michael Wigglesworth, Philip Pain, Samuel Danforth, Richard Steere, Urian Oakes, Roger Williams, and others show the variety of ways in which Puritan poets mediated the relationship between the natural and the spiritual worlds.

725

L 50. DAVIS, RICHARD BEALE. Intellectual Life in the Colonial South,
       1585-1763. 3 vols. Knoxville: University of Tennessee Press,
       1978. 1810 pp.
These volumes offer an extended analysis and record of the intellectual
life of the Southeastern British Colonies in America and indicate the
nature, as well as the complexity, of the early Southern mind. Volume
I focuses on promotion, discovery, history, the Indian, and aspects of
education; Volume II on books and reading, religion and religious writing,
and science, technology, and agriculture; Volume III on the fine arts,
literature, politics and economics, and law and oratory.

L 51. DAVIS, RICHARD BEALE. Intellectual Life in Jefferson's Virginia,
       1790-1830. Chapel Hill: University of North Carolina Press, 1964.
       507 pp.
This study attempts to trace the genesis of the Virginian mind, which,
rooted in an agrarian economy, believed in the virtue of rural living.
Jefferson envisioned a secular university emphasizing rural values. In
various ways Virginia was also indebted to Scottish Presbyterianism.
Virginia's libraries, science, and literature are based on a particular
set of moral values which Jefferson embodied. These values are noticeable
in Virginia's law and politics, especially the concept of States' Rights.
Davis's study makes clear how the Virginian mind can be reconstructed
out of economic, social, and belletristic materials.

L 52. ELLIOTT, EMORY. Power and the Pulpit in Puritan New England. Prince-
       ton, N.J.: Princeton University Press, 1975. 240 pp.
Elliott argues that first-generation New Englanders, reluctant to pass
property and power on to their children, constructed a myth of declension
and a religious rhetoric of filial inadequacy and estrangement. In
response to the problems that this created for the children and grandchildren of the original emigrants, late 17th-century ministers like Samuel
Willard and Cotton Mather adopted a New Testament emphasis, valorizing
Christ's sonship. In support of this argument, Elliott discusses developments in 17th-century Massachusetts church and secular policies and Puritan
child-rearing practices, as well as ministerial language, especially the
images employed in sermons.

L 53. ELLIOTT, EMORY. Revolutionary Writers: Literature and Authority
       in the New Republic, 1725-1810. New York: Oxford University Press,
       1982. 324 pp.
In the face of emerging political and economic forces, the writers of
the New Republic sought a language and a rhetorical strategy to maintain
their social influence. Drawing from the Puritan legacy, the Enlightenment,
and Scottish Common Sense Philosophy, they hoped to reach a wider audience
and validate their position as artists and moral guardians. The lives,
work, and historical situation of Timothy Dwight, Joel Barlow, Philip
Freneau, Hugh Henry Brackenridge, and Charles Brockden Brown are central
to Elliott's analysis of this important phase of American literary history.

L 54. ELLIOTT, EMORY, ed. Puritan Influences in American Literature.
       Urbana: University of Illinois Press, 1979. 212 pp.
A recent trend in American scholarship has been to discover the Puritan
roots for much of our later culture; this collection of nine essays serves
to confirm the sense of that assertion. These essays (collected in honor
of the scholar Edward H. Davidson) are divided almost equally between
analyses of the obvious Puritans--Roger Williams, Anne Bradstreet, Edward
Taylor, and Jonathan Edwards--and the debts owed to them by their descendants (from Revolutionary War rhetoric to Hawthorne, Thoreau, Melville,
and Dickinson).

L 55. ELLIS, JOSEPH J. After the Revolution: Profiles of Early American
       Culture. New York: Norton, 1979. 256 pp.
Artists and others in the post-Revolutionary generation expected that
the freedom of the new political order would not only promote a thriving
and prosperous marketplace but would support a productive art world as
well. However, Ellis's surveys of the careers of Charles Willson Peale,
Hugh Henry Brackenridge, William Dunlap, and Noah Webster show that these
men found that artistic and economic successes were not always compatible.
In addition to having a heritage of hostility to the arts, the early capitalist society, rather than being hospitable to the arts, simply did not
always provide, economically or otherwise, for its artists. Their careers
and works often exemplify the ambivalence engendered by their disappointed
expectations: loyalty both to forward-looking liberal notions of a fluid
society and to a more conservative and stable Republicanism; desires to
offer their artistic talents in the service of Republican society combined
with feelings of guilt or cynicism about that enterprise. These artists,
however, stand at the beginning of a long American artistic tradition,
which is largely characterized by such ambivalences and unresolved contradictions.

L 56. EMERSON, EVERETT, ed. Major Writers of Early American Literature.
       Madison: University of Wisconsin Press, 1972. 302 pp.
This anthology of critical essays "provides a solid foundation for an
intelligent appreciation of the beginnings of American literature." From
all the essays, the editor isolates three themes in the literature: intellectualism, originality, and concern for America. Among the individual
essayists are such scholars as Richard Beale Davis, Lewis Leary, Donald
Stanford, and Sacvan Bercovitch. The collection includes a brief bibliography of editions and scholarship for each author: William Bradford,
Anne Bradstreet, Edward Taylor, Cotton Mather, William Byrd, Jonathan
Edwards, Benjamin Franklin, Philip Freneau, and Charles Brockden Brown.

L 57. GILMORE, MICHAEL T., ed. Early American Literature: A Collection
       of Critical Essays. Englewood Cliffs, N.J.: Prentice-Hall, 1980.
       184 pp.
These thirteen essays deal with various writings produced in America
between the founding of Jamestown (1607) and the end of the 18th century.
Noting the recent resurgence of interest in early American literature,
the editor identifies two developments in recent scholarship: the rediscovery of millennialism as a central component of Puritan thought and
the reassessment of 18th-century Republicanism which recognizes the controversy in Anglo-American political thought. Individual writers treated
in the essays include John Smith, Jonathan Edwards, Benjamin Franklin,
Thomas Jefferson, Thomas Paine, Robert Beverley, William Byrd II, and
Charles Brockden Brown. Other essays discuss Puritans and their influences
on later American writing, captivity narratives, Whig sentimentalism,
and the Colonial experience as a tradition. Contributors include Michael
Bell, Sacvan Bercovitch, Ursula Brumm, Robert Daly, Eric Foner, Perry
Miller, Kenneth Murdock, Edwin Rozwenc, Robert Sayre, Kenneth Silverman,
Lewis Simpson, Richard Slotkin, and Garry Wills.

L 58. GRANGER, BRUCE. American Essay Serials from Franklin to Irving.
       Knoxville: University of Tennessee Press, 1978. 277 pp.
This is an analysis of the form, style, structure, tone, and content of
the American periodical essay. Granger bases his study on fifty-one literary serials which were published in newspapers, magazines, and pamphlets
between 1722 and 1811 by such writers as Benjamin Franklin, John Trumbull,
Philip Freneau, Joseph Dennie, Judith Sargent Murray, William Wirt, James
Kirk Paulding, and Washington Irving, who used as models the essays of
Addison and Steele, Defoe, Pope, Swift, Johnson, and Goldsmith, among
others. The periodical essay in America is seen to have developed in

two general directions: "the essay which purported to be 'elegant, instructive, and diverting' [and] the essay which formally dealt with immediate problems of social, economic, political, and educational importance." Granger's book focuses on essay serials of the former—that is to say, literary—group.

L 59. GRANGER, BRUCE INGHAM. Political Satire in the American Revolution, 1763-1783. Ithaca, N.Y.: Cornell University Press, 1960. 314 pp.
Granger surveys over 500 satiric pieces in American newspapers, magazines, broadsides, pamphlets, and manuscripts for this study. He focuses on both recurrent subjects (the Stamp Act, the British Government, the British Army, the Continental Congress, the Continental Army, Patriots, Loyalists) and the most prominent satirists (e.g., Franklin, Freneau, Francis Hopkinson, Mercy Warren, John Witherspoon). "The grand American rebellion," as it was called, made the moment ripe for satire. "In the struggle toward the declaration and finally the fact of independence," Granger writes, "the American press, which had been unanimous in its opposition to stamped paper, proved as powerful a lever to revolution as did legislative action and party organization."

L 60. GUMMERE, RICHARD MOTT. The American Colonial Mind and the Classical Tradition: Essays in Comparative Culture. Cambridge, Mass.: Harvard University Press, 1963. 228 pp.
This work treats the impact of Greek and Roman ideas on the lives and thoughts of Americans from 1607 to 1789. Specifically, Gummere aims "to make clear the various ways in which the colonists used classical sources for illustration of their own lives and problems." However, Colonial Americans were generally not concerned with classical theory, politics, or philosophy, as much as pragmatic applications. The work shows how "their treatment of this heritage was informal."

L 61. HOWARD, LEON. The Connecticut Wits. Chicago: University of Chicago Press, 1943. 453 pp.
"The Connecticut Wits" comprised some of America's foremost 18th-century poets: John Trumbull, Timothy Dwight, David Humphreys, and Joel Barlow. Howard first examines the Yale curriculum's influence on the "Wits." Then he treats each poet individually, focusing on both biography and poetry. According to Howard, Trumbull showed his genius for personalized satire in The Progress of Dulness (1772) and M'Fingal (1773). Dwight unsuccessfully attempted an epic in The Conquest of Canaan (1785) but successfully tried pastoral poetry in Greenfield Hill (1794). Humphreys exploited nationalism for recognition and advancement. His verse, to Howard, is thus artificial and pretentious (e.g., "A Poem on the Happiness of America," 1786); like Dwight, Barlow failed in his attempt at epic (Vision of Columbus, 1782). His mock-heroic "The Hasty Pudding" is more satisfactory. Though reliant on English models, the "Wits" significantly contributed to formulating an American literary tradition.

L 62. JANTZ, HAROLD S. The First Century of New England Verse. Worcester, Mass.: American Antiquarian Society, 1944. 292 pp.
Nearly two-thirds of Jantz's work is a selection of newly discovered verse (e.g., by Charles Chauncey, John Fiske, Benjamin Tompson) and a bibliography, arranged by authors of 17th-century New England poetry. In the critical and historical survey which precedes these two sections, Jantz divides Colonial poets into seven chronologically arranged groups, from "The Patriarchs" (e.g., Thomas Dudley, Nathaniel Ward) to "The Third Native-Born Group" (e.g., John Danforth, Cotton Mather, Sarah Kemble Knight).

L 63. JONES, HOWARD MUMFORD. The Literature of Virginia in the Seventeenth
       Century. Charlottesville: University Press of Virginia, 1968.
       124 pp.
Jones asserts that although 17th-century Virginia produced no literary
masters, the literary life of the colony was active and in many instances,
first-rate. This aristocratic, secular literature provides both a sharp
contrast to the religious literature of New England and a basis for the
understanding of Southern culture. In this century Colonial prose transformed itself from Elizabethan mannerism (George Percy) to soberer styles
(the Berry-Moryson True Narrative and later legislative records). "In
the next [18th] century," Jones writes, "the prose style of William Byrd
II will bridge the gap between this literature and the Augustan manner
of Washington and Thomas Jefferson."

L 64. KAGLE, STEVEN K. American Diary Literature, 1620-1799. Boston:
       Twayne, 1979. 203 pp.
Kagle distinguishes diaries from other sorts of personal writing by their
periodic (rather than retrospective) production, which replicates the
life experience of gradual acquisition of knowledge. The most successful
diary, he says, is that sustained for the time of its production by some
tension in the writer's life that gives the diary some unity of subject,
style, and perspective. Kagle describes in detail many early American
diaries, categorizing them under the following headings: the spiritual
journal, travel diaries, diaries of romance and courtship, war diaries,
life diaries. He examines the more famliar writings--those of Michael
Wigglesworth, David Brainerd, John Woolman, Sarah Kemble Knight, John
Winthrop, Samuel Sewall, William Byrd, Cotton Mather, John Adams--as well
as those by lesser known authors.

L 65. LEMAY, J. A. LEO. Men of Letters in Colonial Maryland. Knoxville:
       University of Tennessee Press, 1972. 407 pp.
Each of the American Colonies, Lemay asserts, went through five major
stages in its literary history, represented by distinctive kinds of literature: tracts promoting the new settlements; chronicles of exploration;
reports of wars; poems and essays written by frontier citizens; and a
more refined and urbane literature, stimulated by the introduction of
the printing press. Lemay accepts Moses Tyler's thesis that the individual
colonies developed their characters independently from one another. Finding that Maryland's literary character has been somewhat neglected by
previous literary histories of the period, he delineates that character
with the biographies of ten prominent Maryland writers whose works typify
the five stages.

L 66. LEMAY, J. A. LEO, ed. Essays in Early Virginia Literature. New
       York: Burt Franklin, 1979. 282 pp.
Lemay's collection presents a composite of life and thought in Colonial
Virginia. Throughout the 17th century, Virginians hammered out an identity:
they viewed themselves both as Anglican Royalists and as manufacturers
of tobacco. This sense of self prompted the colonists to value aristocracy,
the pastoral tradition, and the Great Chain of Being. In turn, these
values coupled with economic prosperity generated a vehement nationalism
which fueled the Revolution. The factors contributing to this historical
development are studied in essays about such prominent Virginians as Thomas
Hariot, John White, John Smith, Samuel Purchas, Henry Norwood, John Cotton
of Queen's Creek, Robert Beverley, William Byrd, Samuel Davies, John Camm,
Arthur Lee, Thomas Jefferson, and St. George Tucker.

L 67. LEVERENZ, DAVID. The Language of Puritan Feeling: An Exploration in Literature, Psychology and Social History. New Brunswick, N.J.: Rutgers University Press, 1980. 346 pp.
Leverenz's psycho-social analysis of Puritan language produces another theory of declension. In the language of first-generation sermons and autobiographies lie the psychological components of an effective cultural "fantasy": stern paternal discipline and gentle maternal nurturing. On balance, these forces maintain the fantasy's power to dictate a social order and regulate behavior. However, the predominence of paternal chastisement and exclusion of maternal encouragement, evidenced in the jeremiads of the second and third generations, bring about the deterioration of Puritan orthodoxy in New England. Leverenz concludes his argument with the contention that American literature never recovers a language of sexual equilibrium.

L 68. LOWANCE, MASON I. The Language of Canaan: Metaphor and Symbol in New England from the Puritans to the Transcendentalists. Cambridge, Mass.: Harvard University Press, 1980. 335 pp.
Lowance asserts that two conflicting modes of Biblical exegesis—and of imaginative thinking—were available to 17th-century Puritan preachers and commentators. Typological readings found exact correspondences between prophetic Biblical types and their fulfillments in later historical events; the more literal allegorical readings identified resemblances between Biblical and other phenomena. Using the works of John Cotton, Samuel Mather, Edward Taylor, Cotton Mather, Jonathan Edwards, Joel Barlow, Ralph Waldo Emerson, and Henry David Thoreau, Lowance discusses the uses that early New England writers made of these two traditions, and their consequences for millennial thought and epistemological inquiry in later writers.

L 69. MORISON, SAMUEL ELIOT. The Intellectual Life of Colonial New England. 1936; Rev. ed. Ithaca, N.Y.: Cornell University Press, 1960. 288 pp.
First published as The Puritan Pronaos: Studies in the Intellectual Life of New England in the Seventeenth Century, Morison's study sets out to disprove the once prevalent notion that New England intellectual life between 1640 and 1740 was a "glacial period." Morison illustrates how intellectual life in the Colonies flourished during this time. For instance, elementary and grammar schools, as well as Harvard College, were established quickly. In addition, many settlers had impressive personal and public libraries, and printing and bookselling boomed. Certain literary genres—sermons, histories, political pamphlets, and devotional verse—prospered under Puritanism. The religious life of the Colonies definitely stimulated scientific inquiry. Morison's work forms an introduction to the effect of Puritanism on intellectual endeavor.

L 70. MURDOCK, KENNETH. Literature and Theology in Colonial New England. Cambridge, Mass.: Harvard University Press, 1949. 235 pp.
Murdock suggests a fundamental relationship between Puritan theology and literary theory and practice, claiming that contemporary literary theory uniquely conjoined intellect and audience by its Biblical emphasis, bare diction, and homely imagery ("the plain style"). Applying this theory first to the histories, Murdock shows their dual importance in spreading religion and documenting real events. More than any other genre, histories epitomized the Puritan attitude toward literature. "Personal literature" (diaries, autobiographies, journals, and biographies) best displayed the Puritan conviction that religious progress lay in each individual. Puritan poetry, claims Murdock, also fulfilled both literary and didactic criteria.

L 71. NYE, RUSSEL B. American Literary History: 1607-1830. New York: Knopf, 1970. 271 pp.
To follow the development of literary genres in American literature, Nye divides his work into three sections: from 1607 to 1730, Americans wrote as transplanted provincials who reflected European interests, issues, and models; from 1730 to 1790, Americans slowly developed their own identity within a Revolutionary society; and from 1790 to 1830, authors created a distinctively American literature.

L 72. PETTER, HENRI. The Early American Novel. Columbus: Ohio State University Press, 1971. 500 pp.
The work provides a descriptive and critical survey of the American novel up to 1820, updating and synthesizing previous work. Part I discusses the question of English influence, looks at a stereotypical early American romantic novelist (Susanna Haswell Rowson), and then considers one satirist of such romantic novels (Tabitha Tenney). Part II, in contrast, surveys didactic and satirical fiction. Part III comments on many of the 18th-century novels according to prevailing theme (e.g., "Illegitimate Love," "Seduction," "Cruel Parents"), while Part IV concentrates on adventure novels. In appendices, Petter provides plot synopses of many of the novels discussed and a bibliography of primary, complementary, and secondary works.

L 73. PIERCY, JOSEPHINE K. Studies in Literary Types in Seventeenth-Century America (1607-1710). 1939; Rev. ed. Hamden, Conn.: Archon Books, 1969. 368 pp.
Piercy analyzes prose writings to determine what literary forms were established in America before 1710 and to trace background influences on them. Part One covers such generic types as the almanac, the scientific essay, personal records, satire, meditations, the sermon, and biography. Part Two deals more generally with 17th-century literary forms, prose style, and the classical inheritance. The work does not treat each genre in detail, but provides an introduction to prose genres in early American literature.

L 74. RANKIN, HUGH F. The Theater in Colonial America. 1960; Chapel Hill: University of North Carolina Press, 1965. 239 pp.
This study approaches the theater's impact on Colonial culture from the historian's viewpoint rather than the dramatist's. It moves from the first theater in English America (Williamsburg, 1716), through the early struggling years, to the playing groups' height of popularity between 1770 and 1774. Using playbills, newspaper advertisements, and court records, Rankin unearths a mass of information on the early American theater: 18th-century acting practices, playhouse construction, scenery, opposition to professional drama in certain communities, and audience.

L 75. REYNOLDS, DAVID S. Faith in Fiction: The Emergence of Religious Literature in America. Cambridge, Mass.: Harvard University Press, 1981. 269 pp.
Reynolds's analysis of religious fiction written in America between 1785 and 1850 not only identifies a "popular religious aesthetic," but also illuminates one way American religion became identified with "secular morality, romantic ideality or heroic action." The fiction divides into three categories. The oriental tale, prevalent in magazines published between 1780 and 1820, presented heavenly visions, religious pilgrimages, and moral examples in benign contrast to a stern Puritanism. A second group, illustrative fiction, is composed of four schools: Calvinist; liberal; Biblical; Roman Catholic. Reynolds shows each contributing to the secularization of American religion, as, for example, the Biblical school did in its retelling of Biblical stories in human terms. Although the study lastly considers a fiction which violently satirizes various

forms of Calvinism, it emphasizes the ultimate popularity of post-Civil War religious fiction.

L 76. RICHARDSON, LYON N. A History of Early American Magazines 1741-
1789. New York: Thomas Nelson, 1931. 414 pp.
When Richardson published this work in 1931, little specific attention had been paid to the 18th-century American magazine except in general surveys. Here defined as "a general miscellany or repository of instruction and amusement," the early magazine forms the basis of Richardson's detailed study from the beginnings of periodical literature in America to the year of Washington's election as President. This work includes content analysis of thirty-seven periodicals, biographical information on their publishers, the general condition of 18th-century publishing, and the prevailing literary and historical trends.

L 77. SEELYE, JOHN. Prophetic Waters: The River in Early American Life
and Literature. New York: Oxford University Press, 1977.
423 pp.
Seelye approaches the first 150 years of the English in America through literary, psychological, and historical myth. Because rivers are so important in exploration and settlement, says Seelye, they possess literal and figurative force as symbols of the past (what is behind) and of the future (what is beyond). Interpreting the symbol of the river in contemporary narratives, histories, maps, and poetry, Seelye shows how the colonists' attitude toward the landscape accommodated their shifting attitude toward their "errand into the wilderness." Works by the Virginians (e.g., John Smith, William Byrd) and the Puritans (e.g., William Bradford, Cotton Mather) form components of a single literary continuum--the American epic-- which begins optimistically but ends pessimistically.

L 78. SHAW, PETER. American Patriots and the Rituals of Revolution.
Cambridge, Mass.: Harvard University Press, 1981. 279 pp.
Shaw argues that subversive activities in the years leading up to the American Revolution were often enacted in ritualized ways which, though typically regressive and extralogical, strengthened and directed the revolutionary energies of incipient American patriots. Analyzing both crowd behavior and the crises of conscience experienced by prominent patriot politicians (James Otis, John Adams, Joseph Hawley, and Josiah Quincy), Shaw discusses the roles of scapegoating, popular iconography, and the language and symbols of filial relations in allowing Americans to conduct their pre-revolutionary protests in expressive yet contained ways; these ritual rehearsals of the revolution figured the drive toward independence as a collective adolescent rite of passage toward maturity, but until 1776 displaced hostility away from the father/king and on to other, substitute figures, notably Massachusetts Governor Thomas Hutchinson. Shaw draws on a variety of materials and disciplines, including folk culture, psychohistory, and literary criticism.

L 79. SHEA, DANIEL B. Spiritual Autobiography in Early America. Princeton,
N.J.: Princeton University Press, 1968. 280 pp.
Shea's work analyzes twenty representative early Quaker and Puritan spiritual autobiographies. Their authors were primarily concerned with documenting their newfound grace, although the Puritans tended to assemble evidence to show their "election," while the Quakers recounted their long search for the "Truth." Shea locates each individual author's principle of selection and finds greater variety than scholars usually realize. He covers such authors as Elizabeth Ashbridge, John Woolman, Edward Taylor, Roger Clapp, Increase and Cotton Mather, Elizabeth White, and Jonathan Edwards. A bibliographical essay at the end suggests sources for primary works, historical background, and criticism.

L 80. SHURR, WILLIAM H. Rappaccini's Children: American Writers in a
Calvinist World. Lexington: University Press of Kentucky, 1981.
165 pp.
The Synod of Dort (1618-1619) canonized Calvinism and laid the foundation
of American culture. To develop this thesis, Shurr first identifies the
persistence in American thought of Dort's five points: total depravity,
unconditional election, limited atonement, irresistible grace, and per-
severance of the saints. The study then divides into two camps the varied
expressions of and responses to this Calvinism. The Transcendentalists,
on the one hand, attempt to free America from Calvinism; on the other
hand, a tradition represented by Wigglesworth, Edwards, Melville, and
Frost probes the nature of life and death in a cosmos controlled by
Calvin's angry, "diabolic" deity. In the context of this dichotomy, Shurr
considers the paradox of a democratic political system emerging in a culture which denies free will and insists on the total depravity of humanity.
The study funnels into an analysis of sexuality and tragedy and concludes
that Calvinism has circumscribed American notions of evil.

L 81. SILVERMAN, KENNETH. A Cultural History of the American Revolution:
Painting, Music, Literature, and the Theatre in the Colonies and
the United States from the Treaty of Paris to the Inauguration
of George Washington, 1763-1789. New York: Crowell, 1976.
699 pp.
Silverman argues that the Revolutionary period saw the establishment of
a vital and indigenous high cultural life in America. Dividing his study
into three parts, Silverman details the interrelationships among social
and aesthetic movements, military and political developments, and the
biographies and works of artists in the pre-war, wartime, and post-war
periods. Treating many figures and cultural artifacts, he discusses a
diversity of topics, such as artistic production in military camps, the
international art scene, the significance to the American-British cultural
conflict of the song "Yankee Doodle," and the development of urban high
culture.

L 82. TYLER, MOSES COIT. A History of American Literature: 1607-1765.
2 vols. New York: Putnam, 1878. 551 pp.
This work gave to 19th-century America a picture of its Colonial culture
richer and more varied than any had given before. Using documents of
all kinds, Tyler first presents each of the English Colonies as developing an individual character from 1607 to 1676. Then, using "Bacon's Rebellion" as a pivot, he presents the progress of Colonial thought toward
the national consciousness that emerged around 1765. Although he did
not undertake to "give an indiscriminate dictionary of all Americans who
ever wrote anything," Tyler did attempt "to make an appropriate mention
of every one of our early authors whose writings, whether many or few,
have any appreciable literary merit, or throw any helpful light upon the
evolution of thought and of style in America, during those flourishing
and indispensable days."

L 83. TYLER, MOSES COIT. The Literary History of the American Revolution
1763-1783. 2 vols. New York: Putnam, 1897. 1048 pp.
Tyler's study narrates the development of America's revolutionary spirit,
which necessarily conflicted with loyalist ideas. "The entire body of
American writings, from 1763 to 1783, whether serious or mirthful, in
prose or in verse, is here delineated in its most characteristic examples,"
Tyler writes, "for the purpose of exhibiting the several stages of thought
and emotion through which the American people passed during the two decades
of the struggle which resulted in our national Independence."

L 84. WRIGHT, LUELLA. The Literary Life of the Early Friends 1650-1725.
    New York: Columbia University Press, 1932. 309 pp.
In the 17th and early 18th centuries, the Quakers aggressively propagated
their religion in essays, sermons, histories, and, most typically, in
personal literature. Wright suggests that many of these documents have
little literary value, but the journals, diaries, autobiographies, and
confessions often give moving expression of Quaker beliefs: practical
(and often mystical) Christianity, social principles, and the power of
the "Inner Light."

L 85. WRIGHT, THOMAS GODDARD. Literary Culture in Early New England 1620-
    1730. New Haven, Conn.: Yale University Press, 1920. 322 pp.
Wright's study attempts to determine the culture of early New Englanders
by studying their education, their libraries, their ability to obtain
books, their use and appreciation of books, their relations with political
and literary life in England, and their literature. It corrects certain
errors regarding the so-called inadequacy of Colonial culture (e.g., that
more people were illiterate in New England than in Old England). Limited
to approximately the first 100 years of Colonial life, the book centers
on the New England Colonies and their hub, Boston.

L 86. WROTH, LAWRENCE C. The Colonial Printer. 1931; Rev. ed. Portland,
    Maine: Southworth-Antheonsen Press, 1938. 368 pp.
While the Colonial printer was not distinguished for typographical quality,
Wroth asks that we remember the difficulties under which he labored. The firs
sections of Wroth's work cover the Colonial printer's activities and the
tools and materials of his trade: press, type, ink, and paper. Subsequent
sections discuss shop procedure, labor conditions, the final product,
and remuneration. Considering the limitations on materials and equipment
in Colonial America, Wroth admires the tasks of which the Colonial printer
was capable (for instance, producing the Eliot Indian Bible or the Ephrata
Martyr Book). The second edition of this study of early American printing
is enlarged and revised to include more information about printing outside
New England.

L 87. ZIFF, LARZER. Puritanism in America: New Culture in a New World.
    New York: Viking Press, 1973. 338 pp.
To understand its effect on American life and letters, Ziff examines Puritanism as a political, social, and religious culture. As the author claims,
". . . this is the first book that attempts to synthesize the special
concerns of intellectual, social, and economic history into a single
account of the American Puritans." He shows how Puritans reacted to living
conditions in 16th-century England and to the daily problems they faced
in the Colonies in the 17th century. He also reexamines the roles of
notable political and literary figures like Roger Williams, Cotton and
Increase Mather, Edward Taylor, Samuel Sewall, Anne Hutchinson, and John
Winthrop. Ziff considers the Great Awakening in the 18th century and
concludes by demonstrating how Puritanism continues to affect 19th- and
20th-century American life.

III.   NINETEENTH CENTURY

L 88. AARON, DANIEL. The Unwritten War: American Writers and the Civil
    War. New York: Knopf, 1973. 385 pp.
Aaron tries to make sense of the strange inability of Americans to work
out a meaning for the Civil War. The War is the great and terrible event
of American history, and its enormity has never been comprehended, even

by the most gifted of American writers, although its tragic consequences for the consciousness of the succeeding generations have been embodied in Faulkner's fiction. Aaron seeks to understand this failure of the American imagination by reconstructing a series of divergent points of view as they were recorded before, during, and after the war. Early on, this failure was ascribed simply to the sterility of the American literary imagination. It was also attributed to the "spiritual censorship" of genteel literary culture. Aaron argues implicitly throughout that race relations—the fact of slavery—have contributed to an "emotional resistance" to writing about the war that blurred literary insight. The central issue of the war, the oppression of blacks, has appeared only peripherally in Civil War literature.

L 89. AHNEBRINK, LARS. The Beginning of Naturalism in American Fiction: A Study of the Works of Hamlin Garland, Stephen Crane, and Frank Norris with Special Reference to Some European Influences 1891- 1903. Uppsala, Sweden: American Institute in the University of Uppsala, 1950. 505 pp.
In an attempt to define the writers' positions in the emergence of American Naturalism, Ahnebrink pays particular attention "to relevant social, philosophical, and literary aspects of life in the United States during this period between the Civil War and the turn of the century." He is also particularly concerned with foreign influences—French, Russian, and Scandinavian—which have been limited mainly to related ideas, characters, episodes, and particulars. James, Howells, Crane, Norris, and Garland are the American writers most carefully studied; Zola, Turgenev, and Ibsen are considered in terms of their influence on American naturalists.

L 90. ANDERSON, QUENTIN. The Imperial Self: An Essay in American Literary and Cultural History. New York: Knopf, 1971. 274 pp.
Anderson's historical inquiry examines the individualism of Emerson, Whitman, and Henry James, three writers with "a profound extrasocial commitment." His thesis is "that the American flight from culture, from the institutions and emotional dispositions of associated life, took on form in the work of Emerson, Whitman and Henry James, and that it came to a culminating confrontation with what it claimed to supersede—the cosmic comedy of The Golden Bowl." Hawthorne's confidence in social forms is thus contrasted with Emerson's, Whitman's, and James's emphasis on the individual consciousness; the shift is from communal to psychic modes of self-reliance.

L 91. ARAC, JONATHAN. Commissioned Spirits: The Shaping of Social Motion in Dickens, Carlyle, Melville, and Hawthorne. New Brunswick, N.J.: Rutgers University Press, 1979. 190 pp.
Arac's study is focused on the way in which his four principal authors, "commissioned spirits," partook of "an imaginative mission to reveal and transform . . . the brute circumstances of the changing world in which they and their readers lived." Representative texts are seen to be grappling with "social motion" in their original use of plotmaking and linguistic organization. They indicate an alliance with the discourses of social theory, journalism, history, and polemic—an alliance engaged with a public soon to be expelled from fiction's purview. Arac describes this stance as an "overview," which had to be fashioned by these writers and was not "ready to hand."

L 92. ARVIN, NEWTON. American Pantheon. Edited by Daniel Aaron and Sylvan Schendler, with a memoir by Louis Kronenberger. New York: Delacorte Press, 1966. 251 pp.
This collection of Arvin's essays on 19th-century literature ranges from brief discussions of minor writers to full essays on Hawthorne and Melville, to whom Arvin devoted most of his scholarship. Many of the twenty-nine

pieces were originally reviews of contemporary books on 19th-century literary figures. Among the writers treated in this volume are Alcott, Beecher, Cable, Emerson, Hawthorne, Howells, James, Melville, Thoreau, Twain, Whitman, and Whittier.

L 93. BARNETT, LOUISE K. The Ignoble Savage: American Literary Racism, 1790-1890. Westport, Conn.: Greenwood Press, 1975. 220 pp.
Early captivity narratives and the Indian wars fixed the role of the Indian in white American literature: "the Puritan image of the devilish heathen sent to plague the settlement of the new world." Barnett studies variations of this figure in two main sections: "The White Fantasy World of the Frontier Romance" (featuring authors such as Cooper, James Kirke Paulding, Emerson Bennett, and William Gilmore Simms), and "The Subversive Periphery of the Frontier Romance" (in which Hawthorne and Melville undercut the optimism of white domination).

L 94. BAYM, NINA. Woman's Fiction: A Guide to Novels by and about Women in America, 1820-1870. Ithaca, N.Y.: Cornell University Press, 1978. 320 pp.
In discussing the writings of Susan Warner, E.D.E.N. Southworth, Maria Cummins, Caroline Lee Hentz, Catherine Sedgewick, Augusta Evans, and other, less well-known authors of the era, Baym seeks to counter the genteel and sentimental stereotype created by a tradition of predominantly male critics. She touches on the bestseller, the slavery novel, the temperance novel, the pious tract, the city novel, and other "types," demonstrating the way in which such novels organized the common concerns of their readers, with varying consequences.

L 95. BERTHOFF, WARNER. The Ferment of Realism: American Literature, 1884-1919. New York: Free Press, 1965. 330 pp.
In Berthoff's terms, literary history is "coextensive with social history, cultural history, intellectual history but is not identical with any of them"; and it has for its special province the works of men who have transcended everyday life. Thus Berthoff does not attempt a definition of realism as a coherent movement, although he finds common traits among American writers of this era; rather, he evaluates individual performances by placing each author in his milieu. He discusses the work of William Dean Howells, Frank Norris, and Stephen Crane, among others, and emphasizes the literary achievement of writers such as Thorstein Veblen and William James. Berthoff has not changed the original text for the reissue but has added a preface in which he reaffirms the usefulness of talking about individual authors and works, takes note of certain omissions from the original, and catalogues the notable scholarship about the era that has appeared since 1965.

L 96. BEWLEY, MARIUS. The Complex Fate: Hawthorne, Henry James and Some Other American Writers. Introduction and two Interpolations by F. R. Leavis. London: Chatto & Windus, 1952. 248 pp.
"During the nineteenth century," says Bewley, "the United States produced a line of novelists who represent her greatest achievement in art." This line runs from Cooper to Melville, Hawthorne, and James (Bewley's chief concern here). Modern American literature largely departs from this tradition and reflects contemporary social values, both positive (in Wallace Stevens) and negative (in H. L. Mencken and Kenneth Burke). Although Leavis criticizes some particular interpretations, he generally agrees with Bewley's method and estimation of modern society and literature.

L 97. BEWLEY, MARIUS. The Eccentric Design: Form in the Classic American Novel. New York: Columbia University Press, 1959. 327 pp.
Bewley hypothesizes that the American novel has its basis in the interplay of ideas, not, as in the English novel, in the actions of society. The origins of a national literature are traced to the earliest days of the Republic and the conflict between the English bias of Alexander Hamilton and the democratic spirit of Jefferson. James Fenimore Cooper, Bewley argues, presents the results of the failure to reconcile these tensions in the form of his novels: European economics and politics clash with American morality, and physical action is intimately linked with moral purpose. This tradition, the author contends, continues in the work of Hawthorne, Melville, James, and finally Fitzgerald.

L 98. BICKMAN, MARTIN. The Unsounded Centre: Jungian Studies in American Romanticism. Chapel Hill: University of North Carolina Press, 1980. 182 pp.
Bickman uses Jungian psychology to examine the writings of the major American Romantics. He shows how Jung's conceptualizations share many of the assumptions, especially about the nature of symbols, held by the Romantics. He then applies his heuristic model to representative texts (Poe, Dickinson, Emerson, Whitman) to explain how "American Romanticism can be viewed as part of the progressive self-discovery of the psyche."

L 99. BODE, CARL. The American Lyceum: Town Meeting of the Mind. New York: Oxford University Press, 1956. 275 pp.
The institution of the lyceum, imported from England in 1826, was rapidly Americanized. Bode traces this institution from its beginnings as a form of practical education through its greatest popularity as a lecture system throughout the U.S. in the 1850s. It died shortly after the Civil War, but its influence was felt in the universities which were founded in the late 19th century.

L 100. BOYNTON, PERCY H. The Rediscovery of the Frontier. Chicago: University of Chicago Press, 1931. 185 pp.
Using Frederick Jackson Turner's The Significance of the Frontier in American History (H 1510), Boynton analyzes the influence of the frontier and the pioneer on American literature. This influence was felt in literary criticism as critics called for native American subjects, particularly historical fiction of the West. Late 19th-century writers thus depicted pioneer life (especially native and immigrant farmers) and their own tours of the frontier. Boynton believes the energetic and optimistic spirit of the frontier will continue to influence American literature.

L 101. BRODHEAD, RICHARD H. Hawthorne, Melville, and the Novel. Chicago: University of Chicago Press, 1976. 212 pp.
Although he discusses only the works produced by these two novelists between 1850 and 1852 (The Scarlet Letter, The House of Seven Gables, Moby-Dick, The Blithedale Romance, and Pierre; or, The Ambiguities), Brodhead claims that Hawthorne and Melville created new formal possibilities for the novel; helped to domesticate the novel in America; and served as precursors to the later realists--Henry James, Mark Twain, and William Dean Howells. He notes a parallel development in their works: their art is, he claims, "in the fullest sense an experimental art." The vision provided by their works, according to Brodhead, belongs to a larger 19th-century phenomenon--the shift from seeing the world as governed from above to seeing it as governed by inherent laws and internal forces.

L 102. BROOKS, VAN WYCK. The Confident Years: 1885-1915. New York:
        Dutton, 1952. 627 pp.
This study concludes Brooks's series of literary histories bearing the
general title Makers and Finders: A History of the Writer in America
1800-1915. It assesses the literary milieux of writers outside New England
from Agnes Repplier in Philadelphia to Ambrose Bierce in San Francisco
and O. Henry in New York. The latter end of this period receives the
most attention, however, with discussions of the emerging trend in criticism, Mencken's reign in Baltimore, the Greenwich Village flowering of
Radicalism, and the nascence of Modernism.

L 103. BROOKS, VAN WYCK. The Dream of Arcadia: American Writers and
        Artists in Italy, 1760-1915. New York: Dutton, 1958. 272 pp.
Brooks notes that writers and artists traveled to Italy for rest and inspiration, but unlike the Europeans they had little contact with other
national cultures. Among the first Americans to make the pilgrimage were
the painters Benjamin West and John Copley. Other artists (e.g., Horatio
Greenough, W. W. Story) followed in the 19th century. Italy also provided
materials for American writers: Irving, Cooper, Hawthorne, Longfellow,
Fuller, Howells, James, and Wharton all incorporated observations about
the country into their work. Brooks has no real thesis to prove, but
does make clear the continuing influence and attraction of Italy for American writers and artists.

L 104. BROOKS, VAN WYCK. The Flowering of New England. New York: Dutton,
        1936. 550 pp.
This work is the second in Brooks's comprehensive literary history Makers
and Finders. Here he examines such writers and thinkers as Longfellow,
Emerson, Hawthorne, Thoreau, Bronson Alcott, and Margaret Fuller, who
contributed to the literary flowering of New England. The volume focuses
especially on the Transcendentalists, showing (in D. H. Lawrence's words)
how they belonged "to a living, organic, believing community." Brooks
defines this community as what Spengler called a "culture-city," in which
there is "a moment of equipoise, a widespread flowering of the imagination
in which the thoughts and feelings of the people, with all their faiths
and hopes, find expression."

L 105. BROOKS, VAN WYCK. New England: Indian Summer 1865-1914. New
        York: Dutton, 1940. 557 pp.
This work is the fourth of Brooks's five literary histories under the
overall title Makers and Finders. In this particular volume, the author
centers on New England, and especially Boston and Harvard, as the literary
milieu which produced or attracted such varied literary talents as Francis
Parkman, W. D. Howells, Henry Adams, and Emily Dickinson. In a phase
of literary history "so confused and complex and marked by such multifarious comings and goings," Brooks attempts to provide, through his regional
emphasis, a "unity of place" to ground his discussion.

L 106. BROOKS, VAN WYCK. The Times of Melville and Whitman. New York:
        Dutton, 1947. 489 pp.
This work is the third in Brooks's literary history titled Makers and
Finders. Brooks establishes how, in the wake of Irving, Cooper, and the
New England poets, a distinctively American culture appeared all over
the country. As Brooks concludes: "Mark Twain, for one, writing of Europe,
had cut the umbilical cord that united the still infant nation to the
mother-culture, and in Melville and Whitman, with two or three others
of comparable weight, America as a whole had found its voices." Although
the book focuses on Melville and Whitman, some of the other voices it
discusses are Bret Harte, Sidney Lanier, Joel Chandler Harris, Mary Murfree,
and George W. Cable.

L 107. BROOKS, VAN WYCK. The World of Washington Irving. 1944; Rev.
ed. New York: Dutton, 1950. 495 pp.
The earliest of Brooks's five literary histories with the overall title
Makers and Finders: A History of the Writer in America 1800-1915, this
volume covers early literature in various regions of the country and such
figures as Thomas Jefferson, Washington Irving, James Fenimore Cooper,
William Cullen Bryant, William Dunlap, and Edgar Allan Poe. This introduction to the Republic's first literature (it does not cover Colonial
works) ranges in methodology from biographical criticism to discussions
of literary milieu.

L 108. BUELL, LAWRENCE. Literary Transcendentalism: Style and Vision
in the American Renaissance. Ithaca, N.Y.: Cornell University
Press, 1973. 336 pp.
Calling his work a "combination of intellectual history, critical explication, and genre study," Buell sets out to survey Transcendentalist literature. He concentrates on the era before the Civil War when Transcendentalism was at its peak and discusses such literary figures as Emerson,
Thoreau, Ellery Channing, Jones Very, and Whitman. Noting that Transcendentalist literature has too often been judged by modern literary standards,
Buell attempts to define the Transcendentalists' aesthetic by examining
three of their major concerns (spirit, nature, and man) and the inherited
forms (conversation, sermon, scripture, religious self-examination, moral
essay) they used in dealing with these concerns.

L 109. CADY, EDWIN H. The Gentleman in America: A Literary Study in
American Culture. Syracuse, N.Y.: Syracuse University Press,
1949. 232 pp.
In his conclusion, Cady proposes his definition of the gentleman: "a
man whose inner balance of sensibility, good-will, and integrity issues
in moral dependability (the instinct to act rightly in a crisis); in cour-
tesy (the instinct to serve other people's physical and psychological
needs); and in the excellent performance of some good social function."
In literature, Cady finds this figure in the works of Puritan theologians,
Royall Tyler, John Adams, Thomas Jefferson, James Fenimore Cooper, Oliver
Wendell Holmes, William Dean Howells, and, most vividly, Ralph Waldo
Emerson.

L 110. CADY, EDWIN H. The Light of Common Day: Realism in American Fiction. Bloomington: Indiana University Press, 1971. 224 pp.
Cady defines realism as "a theory of Common Vision" which exhibits certain
major characteristics: literary revolution, critical view of the past,
emphasis on character rather than plot, democratic themes, moral reform,
and psychological interests. The ten "inter-connected" essays presented
here refine this definition, apply it to individual authors (Hawthorne,
Mark Twain, Howells, Crane, Owen Wister), and examine the significance
of this mode for the teacher of American literature.

L 111. CALLOW, JAMES T. Kindred Spirits: Knickerbocker Writers and American Artists, 1807-1855. Chapel Hill: University of North Carolina
Press, 1967. 287 pp.
Asserting that the relationship between visual and literary arts was especially close in the U.S. during the first half of the 19th century, Callow
focuses on the Knickerbockers--the artists of New York City and its
environs. He argues that the Knickerbocker writers, becoming popular earlier
than the visual artists, were able to help those artists by enhancing
Americans' appreciation of art. Unlike most earlier scholars, Callow
explores numerous lesser-known Knickerbockers (Gulian Verplanck, James
Kirk Paulding, John Howard Payne, Nathaniel Parker Willis, and others)
as well as the major figures (Irving, Bryant, and Cooper). He examines
literary and visual artists' lives, friendships, collaborations, and rela-

tionships developed around literary magazines. Callow discusses not only
landscape painting but also architecture, city planning, and genre painting.

L 112. CANBY, HENRY SEIDEL. Classic Americans: A Study of Eminent Ameri-
        can Writers from Irving to Whitman with an Introductory Survey
        of the Colonial Background of Our National Literature. New York:
        Harcourt, Brace, 1931. 371 pp.
Canby focuses on seven "classic Americans" of the 19th century: Irving,
Cooper, Emerson, Thoreau, Hawthorne (elucidated in part by a brief study
of Melville), Poe, and Whitman. He adds no new biographical data, but
he does consider each artist as an American writing in a particular setting;
his authors are "better understood when the environmental forces that
make the men that make the literature are not neglected." American literary history is seen as "the adjustment of a European, and generally British,
culture by new men to a new environment." This serves to explain several
peculiarities in American culture: the political precocity amid our apparent lag behind English models; "perplexing time relationship between American and European literatures, by which the really original American author
is usually both in advance of and behind his contemporaries overseas";
and the failure of "the first-rate literary mind" to express popular
opinion in a sprawling democracy.

L 113. CARSON, WILLIAM G. B. The Theatre on the Frontier: The Early
        Years of the St. Louis Stage. 1932; Rev. ed. New York: Benjamin
        Blom, 1965. 361 pp.
Carson first provides an introduction to the history of theater in America
and then focuses on the St. Louis stage from its beginnings in 1815 until
its full establishment by 1839. According to Carson, drama in St. Louis
began late due to the Catholic clergy's influence, the early settlers'
cultural dullness, and the town's geographical remoteness. However, as
immigration and accessibility improved, so did the theater until St. Louis
established the first professional theater west of the Mississippi in
1837 (the New St. Louis Theatre). By nature this work is specialized
but what it reveals of St. Louis drama accords with the larger historical
pattern of American drama.

L 114. CARTER, EVERETT. The American Idea: The Literary Response to
        American Optimism. Chapel Hill: University of North Carolina
        Press, 1977. 276 pp.
Carter argues that many American writers "were products of a controlling
social consciousness, a common idea, . . . and that the forms of these
writers were metaphors of their affirmation or rejection of that idea."
Against the prevailing tone of optimism in the 19th century, Carter
assesses the significance of "the writers of rejection"--Melville,
Hawthorne, and James--"the major affirmative writers"--Emerson, Thoreau,
Whitman, and Mark Twain--and "the minor worthy voices"--Lowell, Holmes,
and Longfellow. Although Carter emphasizes 19th-century authors, he begins
with 17th- and 18th-century writers to show the early responses to the
growing faith in goodness and progress.

L 115. CARTER, EVERETT. Howells and the Age of Realism. Philadelphia:
        Lippincott, 1954. 307 pp.
Carter's study of the "Age of Realism" in American literature--from the
end of the Civil War to about the turn of the century--presents William
Dean Howells as the period's representative figure, but it also considers
such men as Mark Twain, John DeForest, Edward Eggleston, and Albion Tourgee.
Realism began as a reaction against sentimentalism, taking over Romanticism's optimism and love of the commonplace, but discarding its metaphysics
for the Positivism of Comte and Taine. Later in the period, about 1876,
"critical Realism" emerged when certain events, especially the Haymarket
Affair, forced the Realists to curtail their enthusiastic optimism and
begin to consider the novel as a tool for social reform.

L 116. CHARVAT, WILLIAM. Literary Publishing in America 1790-1850. Phila-
      delphia: University of Pennsylvania Press, 1959. 94 pp.
Charvat's work treats those authors from 1790 to 1850 who were concerned
with both art and income and whose work, therefore, reveals the conflicting
pressures between the pure creative impulse and economic expediency.
The time span of Charvat's book covers the early success in the 1820s
and 1830s of the pioneering American publishers Cary and Lea, the disastrous coincidence of America's severe economic depression in the early
1840s and the competition in reprinting British books, and finally the
reconstruction of American literary publishing in the late 1840s. The
book covers publishing centers, the relationship between author and publisher (especially the problems of distribution and publishing capital),
and the status of literary genres and artifacts.

L 117. CHARVAT, WILLIAM. The Origins of American Critical Thought: 1810-
      1835. Philadelphia: University of Pennsylvania Press, 1936.
      218 pp.
Charvat outlines the basic critical principles of the early 19th century;
he isolates the critical issues of each major genre as they were seen
at the time, discussing controversies and tracing their origins; and he
gives brief histories of the various critical schools and journals, paying
special attention to the more important critics. The study also includes
a chapter on the influence of the Scottish "Common Sense" school of philosophy and rhetoric on American criticism.

L 118. COOLEY, THOMAS. Educated Lives: The Rise of Modern Autobiography
      in America. Columbus: Ohio State University Press, 1976.
      190 pp.
Cooley examines the "modern" autobiographies of Henry Adams, Mark Twain,
William Dean Howells, and Henry James. He argues that a radical innovation
in psychology, which occurred around 1865--the shift from viewing human
character as an essence that grows but does not change to viewing it as
the accumulation of adaptations to an environment--accounts for a shift
in autobiography: "cultivation" autobiographies (like Franklin's and
Thoreau's) are replaced by "education" autobiographies. Cooley prefaces
his discussion of the four major figures with an essay cataloguing the
types of autobiography present in the U.S. before 1865 and concludes with
brief treatments of three more recent autobiographies: Lincoln Steffens's,
Sherwood Anderson's, and Gertrude Stein's.

L 119. DAVIS, DAVID BRION. Homicide in American Fiction, 1798-1860:
      A Study in Social Values. Ithaca, N.Y.: Cornell University Press,
      1957. 346 pp.
Davis's purpose here is not literary criticism but "a historical analysis
of certain ideas associated with homicide" and of "the imaginative reaction
of writers to a growing awareness of violence in American life" between
1798 and 1860. The book is a social and intellectual history which uses
popular fiction for purposes of its own. Among the many novels examined
are those by Brown, Simms, and Cooper, as well as lesser-known works by
George Lippard, E. Z. C. Judson, and Joseph Holt Ingraham. Davis discovers
that, in much of this fiction, it is "implied that the victim was guilty
and deserving of punishment."

L 120. DORMON, JAMES H., Jr. Theater in the Ante Bellum South, 1815-1861.
      Chapel Hill: University of North Carolina Press, 1967. 322 pp.
This is both a theatrical history dealing with the origins and development
of "theatrical activity in the South," as well as a cultural history which
defines the nature of the theater. The work includes a history of what
was popular and a discussion of what this reveals about a changing South.
Dormon emphasizes that theater in the South was not "regional" or "provincial," but simply had a separate development.

741

L 121. DOUGLAS, ANN. The Feminization of American Culture. New York:
        Knopf, 1977. 403 pp.
Douglas examines the way in which the disestablishment of an older and
sterner religious tradition dovetailed with the rise of feminine self-
consciousness in best-selling novels and magazines of the 19th century.
Both women and the clergy, she claims, were pushed to the margins of the
culture and became narcissistic apologists for genteel "femininity"; this
feminine image was idealized by the very women that were exploited by
it. The larger result was a social preoccupation with glamor, banal melodrama, and the constant consumption of superfluous commodities, which
effectively neutralized all possibility of challenge to the male-dominated
sphere of aggressive industry.

L 122. EAKIN, PAUL JOHN. The New England Girl: Cultural Ideals in
        Hawthorne, Stowe, Howells and James. Athens: University of Georgia
        Press, 1976. 252 pp.
Eakin aims to outline the history of 19th-century New England culture
by analyzing heroines in the literature of Hawthorne, Stowe, Howells,
and James. For these writers, women functioned as an all-inclusive symbol
of cultural ideals and as a repository of the acknowledged moral code.
The first section documents the existence of this tradition in the works
of Stowe and Hawthorne and shows their heroines as "puritan maidens."
The second section, on Howells, illustrates the heroine's move to "romantic
rebel"; later chapters on James show her final evolution into the "all-
American girl."

L 123. ELLINGER, ESTHER PARKER. Southern War Poetry of the Civil War.
        Philadelphia: n.p., 1918. 192 pp.
This book contains poetry written in the Confederate States during the
Civil War. It begins with an introductory essay which stresses the different writing conditions of the Southern poets who, unlike the Northern
poets, wrote in a context of actual conflict. A following chapter outlines
the publishing history of Southern war poetry. Ellinger then divides
the poetry into three distinct periods: "poems of rebellion against oppression," "poetry of actual conflict," and finally poems of "disappointment,
discouragement and actual defeat." The remainder of the book consists
of a short reference bibliography; a bibliography of collections, anthologies, and Confederate imprints; and an extensive index of Southern war
poems of the Civil War.

L 124. FALK, ROBERT. The Victorian Mode in American Fiction 1865-1885.
        East Lansing: Michigan State University Press, 1964. 188 pp.
Falk's subject is Victorian Realism—the fiction of the "Gilded Age" by
John W. DeForest, Howells, James, and Twain; his method is "narrative
portraiture"—a literary and social history of the novelists' concepts
of reality; and his thesis is that after the shock of the Civil War,
America underwent a period of "recovery, re-orientation, and re-dedication."
Falk argues that the novelists grew from youthful experimentation and
uneasiness to a mature and confident depiction of the individual in society,
a commitment reflecting the like dedication of their countrymen.

L 125. FINE, DAVID M. The City, the Immigrant, and American Fiction,
        1880-1920. Metuchen, N.J.: Scarecrow Press, 1977. 182 pp.
Fine's first two chapters provide background material on the changing
ethnic make-up of American cities, from 1880 to 1920. Chapter three treats
the "tenement tale," chapter four the immigrant ghetto in American fiction,
and chapters five and six the immigrant labor novel. Chapter seven focuses
on Abraham Cahan. There is much material throughout on little-known works
about immigrants. A bibliography of immigrant fiction, critical materials,
and reviews concludes the work.

L 126. FINHOLT, RICHARD. American Visionary Fiction: Mad Metaphysics
as Salvation Psychology. Port Washington, N.Y.: Kennikat Press,
1978. 147 pp.
This book deals chiefly with the fiction of Melville, Poe, Mailer, Ellison,
and Dickey. Using Freud, Jung, Levi-Strauss, and Northrop Frye, Finholt
treats these writers as "subterranean miners" of the unconscious. He
argues that these authors fit Mailer's definition of writers whose works
"always have a touch of the grandiose, even the megalomaniacal: the reason
may be that the writings are part of a continuing and more or less comprehensive vision of existence into which everything must fit." Finholt
claims to identify an intellectual tradition in American fiction, "a tradition that takes the inner self as subject because the deeply thinking
mind is naturally drawn to its mysteries and the vision that arises from
them."

L 127. FRANKLIN, H. BRUCE. Future Perfect: American Science Fiction
of the Nineteenth Century. 1966; Rev. ed. New York: Oxford
University Press, 1978. 404 pp.
Although this work is in large part an anthology of 19th-century short
fiction, the critical introductions to each author provide, as Franklin
suggests of the works themselves, "insights into 19th-century America,
into the history of science and its relations to society, into the predictions, expectations, and fantasies of the present, and into the nature
of science fiction, and, thereby, of all fiction." Authors represented
include Nathaniel Hawthorne, Edgar Allan Poe, Herman Melville, Mark Twain,
Ambrose Bierce, and Edward Bellamy.

L 128. FREDERICK, JOHN T. The Darkened Sky: Nineteenth-Century American
Novelists and Religion. Notre Dame, Ind.: University of Notre
Dame Press, 1969. 276 pp.
The "religious tensions" of the 19th century, caused by several discrete
historical developments, are reflected in the six major novelists whom
Frederick examines here: James Fenimore Cooper, Nathaniel Hawthorne,
Herman Melville, Mark Twain, William Dean Howells, and Henry James. His
study suggests the extraordinary variety of their response to those ten-
sions in their experience and in their fiction.

L 129. FRYER, JUDITH. The Faces of Eve: Women in the Nineteenth-Century
American Novel. New York: Oxford University Press, 1976.
294 pp.
Fryer's basic assumption is that the dominant myth of American culture
is America as New World Garden of Eden. Attention by intellectual historians and literary critics has made the "American Adam" a stock figure
of American cultural interpretations. The "American Eve" is still largely
ignored, although she was an important figure to 19th-century thinkers,
especially novelists. Fryer's book forms a study of the American Eve
and her many faces. The first chapter analyzes the myth of America as
Eden. Succeeding chapters draw on Jungian criticism to establish the
following categories for fictional women: the Temptress, the American
Princess, the Great Mother, and the New Woman. A bibliography of books
and articles is appended.

L 130. FUSSELL, EDWIN. Frontier: American Literature and the American
West. Princeton, N.J.: Princeton University Press, 1965.
450 pp.
Drawing on Frederick Jackson Turner's theory of the significance of the
frontier, Fussell explains how religion and politics contributed to the
development of the frontier myth. In Fussell's hands the frontier metaphor
becomes the leading formal principle of early American literature. In
James Fenimore Cooper's Leatherstocking novels the West has moral and
aesthetic qualities. The Scarlet Letter takes place at the frontier where

the Old World meets the New. Hawthorne's frontier, like Cooper's, is indeterminate and pluralistic. Walden is the record of a pioneer on the frontier. While Moby-Dick reveals the heroism in the Westward Movement, The Confidence-Man shows the folly of that movement. The Civil War destroyed the vestiges of the American frontier. In Whitman's poetry the frontier themes are carried to their logical conclusion.

L 131. GILMORE, MICHAEL T. The Middle Way: Puritanism and Ideology in American Romantic Fiction. New Brunswick, N.J.: Rutgers University Press, 1977. 220 pp.
American Puritan culture directed much of its energy to working out a resolution between the opposing impulses of legalistic conformity and anarchic antinomianism; it is this legacy of the middle way that the Calvinists left to American literature. Gilmore examines the writings and careers of Cotton Mather and Benjamin Franklin to show how both were proponents of the "middle way." The fictions of Hawthorne, Melville, and James adopt the middle way as a moral term to explore the problem of reconciling material and spiritual experience, or maintaining principles while living in the world. Gilmore includes discussions of The Scarlet Letter, The House of the Seven Gables, Moby-Dick, Israel Potter, "Benito Cereno," Billy Budd, and The Golden Bowl.

L 132. GODDARD, HAROLD CLARKE. Studies in New England Transcendentalism. New York: Columbia University Press, 1908. 217 pp.
Goddard seeks to describe all original American contributions to the worldwide Transcendental movement. He asserts that most of the New England Transcendentalists held the same philosophy "in its large outlines" and that the philosophy itself was not particularly novel: its real contribution lay in "the blending of an idealistic, Platonistic metaphysics and the Puritan spirit, the fusion—at a high revolutionary temperature—of a philosophy and a character."

L 133. GOHDES, CLARENCE L. F. The Periodicals of American Transcendentalism. Durham, N.C.: Duke University Press, 1931. 264 pp.
This work studies the periodicals conducted or controlled by people like Orestes Brownson, Ralph Waldo Emerson, Ellery Channing, and Elizabeth Peabody who were known as, and considered themselves to be, Transcendentalists. Among these journals are The Boston Quarterly Review (1838-1842), The Dial (1840-1844), and The Massachusetts Quarterly Review (1847-1850). Gohdes also includes The Index (1870-1886) which, although it was not controlled by Transcendentalists, illuminates the movement's later history. The author believes the periodical literature is especially significant since it contains the information that the Transcendentalists wished to present to the public.

L 134. GURA, PHILIP F. The Wisdom of Words: Language, Theology, and Literature in the New England Renaissance. Middletown, Conn.: Wesleyan University Press, 1981. 203 pp.
Gura suggests that the flowering of symbolism among American Renaissance writers was made possible in part by the intense concern for language engendered by the theological controversies of the early 19th century. The Unitarians, rooted in 18th-century Lockean epistemology, maintained that scripture could be explicated fully by historical and contextual study. Trinitarians and such ministers as James Marsh and Horace Bushnell, influenced by Kantian idealism, argued that Biblical language, like religious truth itself, was inherently ambiguous and had to be approached imaginatively. Emerson, Thoreau, Hawthorne, and Melville worked within the bounds of aesthetics that were conditioned in some way by this notion of the ambiguity of language and the multiple significances of words.

L 135. GURA, PHILIP F. and JOEL MYERSON. Critical Essays on American
        Transcendentalism. Boston: G. K. Hall, 1982. 624 pp.
This work contains fifty-two essays or excerpts on the subject of Transcen-
dentalism--some by Transcendentalists, most by 19th- or 20th-century
scholars. It includes selections from the writings of Theodore Parker,
Edgar Allan Poe, Louisa May Alcott, Orestes Brownson, Oliver Wendell Holmes,
George Santayana, Rene Wellek, Perry Miller, Lawrence Buell, and Joel
Porte. In their introduction, the editors point out that Transcendentalism
affirmed the importance of faith and intuition within the context of an
increasingly materialistic America and that early criticism of Transcendentalism by conservative religious leaders was based on matters of doctrine. Such criticism later gave way to the recognition that Transcendentalism could be an ally in the struggle against Darwinian and Spencerian
philosophies. According to Gura and Myerson, the literary dimension of
the movement was largely ignored until 1926; it became the subject of
particularized study in the 1930s and 1940s; and only after W.W. II was
Transcendentalism studied in relation to American intellectual development
as a whole.

L 136. HABEGGER, ALFRED. Gender, Fantasy and Realism in American Litera-
        ture. New York: Columbia University Press, 1982. 378 pp.
Habegger argues that the form and concerns of American literary Realism,
far from developing from the work of European Realists, actually grew
out of the prolific and at the time immensely popular novels of American
female domestic writers of the 1850s. Beginning with an examination of
these domestic novels, Habegger interprets them as fantasies of a happy
marriage animated by deep cultural anxieties about sexual roles and marriage. Habegger goes on to explicate the difference between male and
female humor in the American novels, a difference which he believes challenges even as it reveals the conflicting "fantasies" at the core of male-
and female-authored realistic novels. Habegger's concluding chapters,
"W. D. Howells and American Masculinity" and "The Gentleman of Shalott:
Henry James and American Masculinity," examine Howells and James as peculiarly American realistic novelists who "were born to, and then established
themselves against, the maternal tradition of Anglo-American women's fiction."

L 137. HAMPSTEN, ELIZABETH. Read This Only to Yourself: The Private
        Writings of Midwestern Women, 1880-1910. Bloomington: Indiana
        University Press, 1982. 242 pp.
Hampsten examines the private writings--letters and diaries--of women
who lived in the Midwest, specifically in the Dakota Territory, during
the late 19th and early 20th centuries. She also looks at some published
writings by Willa Cather, Tillie Olson, Laura Ingalls Wilder, and Fannie
Dunn Quain (a doctor who also wrote newspaper articles). Hampsten begins
by reviewing some of the scholarly work that has been done on women's
private writing and on the collective experience of Western expansion,
claiming that the latter omits the woman's perspective on that experience.
Reading these private writings critically, she finds their repetitions
and omissions significant. Hampsten also asserts that these writings
are not "regional," since they give little attention to geographical place;
that they deal often, sometimes frankly, with life, death, and sexuality;
that these women wrote in a conversational, not artificial, style; and
that their friendships with other women were very important to these female
pioneers.

L 138. HARDING, BRIAN. American Literature in Context, II: 1830-1865.
        New York: Methuen, 1982. 247 pp.
Part of a series which emphasizes the cultural and historical context
of American literature (see L 351), this volume consists of twelve essays
on individual writers, each of which is introduced by an extract from

745

a primary source. Literary figures discussed are Ralph Waldo Emerson, Edgar Allan Poe, Nathaniel Hawthorne, Henry David Thoreau, Henry Wadsworth Longfellow, Herman Melville, and Walt Whitman. Harding focuses in particular on such themes as American conceptions of freedom; the religious heritage of New England Transcendentalism; the idea of national destiny; and the growing sense of disunity and sectional rivalry. Non-literary figures considered are William Ellery Channing, George Bancroft, Orestes A. Brownson, Francis Parkman, and Abraham Lincoln.

L 139. HAVENS, DANIEL F. The Columbian Muse of Comedy: The Development of a Native Tradition in Early American Social Comedy, 1787-1845. Carbondale: Southern Illinois University Press, 1973. 181 pp. From the appearance of Royall Tyler's The Contrast (1787) to Anna Cora Mowatt's Fashion (1845), American social comedy developed as a genre distinct from the British comedy of manners and sentimental comedy. Havens studies this development by focusing on The Contrast, William Dunlap's The Father (1789), James Nelson Barker's Tears and Smiles (1808), Robert Montgomery Bird's The City Looking Glass (1828), nine minor comic dramas, and Mowatt's Fashion. Social comedy is seen to be broader in scope than English comedy of manners; the former views folly with more seriousness, and has at its heart a "moral seriousness" and "reforming spirit." The author argues that a belief in the perfectibility of human beings is endemic to post-Restoration comedy, and appears in American social comedy vis-a-vis "certain real problems in mid-19th century American society: parvenu values, heiress-hunting foreigners, and filial obedience."

L 140. HERZOG, KRISTIN. Women, Ethnics, and Exotics: Images of Power in Mid-Nineteenth-Century American Fiction. Knoxville: University of Tennessee Press, 1983. 254 pp. Herzog begins by noting that most American literature of the early and mid-19th century had a narrow, masculine, and ethnocentric focus. But, she continues, some writers overcame this narrowness and included women, ethnics (blacks, Indians, immigrants), and exotics (characters "excitingly strange") in their fictions. Women and ethnics were, she claims, considered to be closer to nature, more primitive, than white males—the representatives of reason and civilization. By including sympathetic portraits of women and primitives in their novels, these writers sought to heal the split between "mind and body, reason and emotion, white and nonwhite, civilized and primitive, man and woman." Herzog discusses works by canonical figures (Hawthorne and Melville), a woman (Stowe), and two black writers (William Wells Brown and Martin R. Delany). She also discusses a Native American narrative—the epic of Dekanawida.

L 141. HIRSCH, DAVID H. Reality and Idea in the Early American Novel. The Hague: Mouton, 1971. 221 pp. Hirsch's opening theoretical chapter casts doubt on the assumption that the novel is an outgrowth of the stable world view of British empirical philosophers such as Locke. Next, he questions the assumption that the novel (which belongs to England) is "realistic" while the romance (primarily American) is "non-realistic." According to Hirsch, "reality" actually encompasses both the unknown, that is, the world of dreams, and the known, or material world. An examination of Hugh Henry Brackenridge, Charles Brockden Brown, and James Fenimore Cooper shows their attempts to convey ideas as well as to tell a story, although the dichotomy between instruction and pleasure sometimes strained the novel's form. Ultimately, such novelists as Hawthorne and Melville succeeded in combining morality, philosophy, and fictional craft.

L 142. HODGE, FRANCIS. Yankee Theatre: The Image of America on the Stage,
1825-1850. Austin: University of Texas Press, 1964. 320 pp.
Hodge examines the theater activities of four native comedians--James
H. Hackett, George H. Hill, Dan Marble, and Joshua Silsbee--to show how
"the Yankee character" was developed. The "country Jonathan," a figure
often both unsophisticated and shrewd, was at the center of a native American drama for about one hundred years. Thus the study earns its title,
for although it focuses on only four practitioners, it uses them to show
what was happening generally in the American theater.

L 143. HOFFMAN, DANIEL G. Form and Fable in American Fiction. New York:
Oxford University Press, 1961. 368 pp.
Hoffman's work identifies the themes ("fables") that most influenced the
early 19th-century fiction writers Washington Irving, Nathaniel Hawthorne,
Herman Melville, and Mark Twain: the isolation of the individual, his
rebellion against authority and tradition, his lone confrontation with
certain fundamental ("primal") forces, and his need to rediscover or
redefine his identity. Hoffman believes certain archetypal patterns from
myth, folklore, and ritual provided structures ("forms") for exploring
these themes. The "romance," says the author, proved particularly adaptable in form and content to the different needs of the four writers and
was the culmination of the previous allegorical, Gothic, and Transcendental
tradition. This book's opening section traces the major themes the four
authors found in folk traditions; subsequent sections closely analyze
Hawthorne's best tales, Melville's Moby-Dick and The Confidence-Man, and
Mark Twain's Adventures of Huckleberry Finn. A final chapter summarizes
the book's findings and conclusions.

L 144. IRWIN, JOHN T. American Hieroglyphics: The Symbol of the Egyptian
Hieroglyphics in the American Renaissance. New Haven, Conn.:
Yale University Press, 1980. 371 pp.
Jean-Francois Champollion deciphered Egyptian hieroglyphics. Irwin
attempts to "decipher" not only the impact of Champollion's work, but also
the symbolic nature of the writings of Emerson, Thoreau, Whitman, Melville,
Hawthorne, and especially Poe. This book should not be mistaken as a
mere continuation of Charles Feidelson's work; Irwin's special interest
is the relation of "the image of the hieroglyphics to the larger reciprocal
questions of the origin and limits of symbolization and the symbolization
of origins and ends." To this end, Irwin employs both practical and speculative criticism, revealing the many ways that a text can be considered
the author's "inscribed shadow self, a hieroglyphic double."

L 145. KAPLAN, HAROLD. Democratic Humanism and American Literature.
Chicago: University of Chicago Press, 1972. 298 pp.
Kaplan is searching for "the ethical intelligence in American democracy
in the work of its classic writers." When he examines the works of the
19th-century masters (Emerson, Thoreau, Cooper, Poe, Hawthorne, Melville,
Whitman, Twain, and James), he finds "a markedly subtle dialectic, its
chief terms opposing cultural nostalgia, or the claim for order, against
the idealization of nature and freedom." In this study of recurring political myths in American literature, Kaplan combines the political theories
of Alexis de Tocqueville with the literary criticism of D. H. Lawrence.

L 146. KAPLAN, HAROLD. Power and Order: Henry Adams and the Naturalist
Tradition in American Fiction. Chicago: University of Chicago
Press, 1981. 142 pp.
Kaplan explores how "neoscientific premises" and "neopolitical conclusions" produced a system of thought embodied in turn-of-the-century Naturalist fiction. Henry Adams, who was preoccupied with the concept of Force,
is the central subject of this work. Naturalist fiction, Kaplan argues,
expresses apocalyptically the "myth of power and conflict"--the belief

that forces, not individuals, determine history and human character. The other writers whose work he examines are Dreiser, Norris, Crane, and, to a lesser degree, Dos Passos. Recognizing forces as the effective causes of history, the Naturalists yet had the alternative of choosing, as Adams did, an "acceptable" force to worship.

L 147. **KAUL, A. N.** The American Vision: Actual and Ideal Society in Nineteenth-Century Fiction. New Haven, Conn.: Yale University Press, 1963. 340 pp.
Kaul's task is two-fold. He first provides a broad historical study of 19th-century American society, concentrating especially on the surviving remnants of Puritan culture. He then analyzes the responses of Cooper, Hawthorne, Melville, and Mark Twain to this society and how these responses influenced their fictional strategies. Intensely involved with the question of "society," they were less concerned with social realism than with moral values. "Exploration of existing society," Kaul argues, "led them repeatedly to the theme of ideal community life."

L 148. **KERR, HOWARD.** Mediums, and Spirit Rappers, and Roaring Radicals: Spiritualism in American Literature, 1850-1900. Urbana: University of Illinois Press, 1972. 262 pp.
Kerr asserts that American spiritualism began in 1848 with the mysterious and fraudulent spirit rappings near Rochester, New York. The movement combined elements of physical phenomena, such as poltergeists, with psychical phenomena, mainly versions of mesmerism. Literary reactions to spiritualism included the humorous (e.g., those by James Russell Lowell and Melville), the occult (Hawthorne and Fitz-James O'Brien), and the satiric (Orestes Brownson and Bayard Taylor). After 1860, spiritualism no longer retained popular support, although writers such as Howells, Twain, and James recalled the effects of the movement in their fiction.

L 149. **KIENIEWICZ, TERESA.** Men, Women, and the Novelist: Fact and Fiction in the American Novel of the 1870s and 1880s. Washington, D.C.: University Press of America, 1982. 171 pp.
In this study of the impact of social history on the novel, the author examines selected works by Mark Twain, Horatio Alger, William Dean Howells, Henry James, and Edith Wharton, as well as popular novels, which are not well-known today, and magazine fiction. These writers, she says, both reflect the social currents and tensions of their culture and influence them, through a controlling didactic moral purpose. Kieniewicz argues that much of the fiction of these decades was an attempt to come to terms with (partly by denying the effect of) rapid and far-reaching changes in American society, such as the rise of the individual entrepreneur as cultural hero, tensions between capitalists and workers, the formation and then gradual breakdown of the cult of ideal womanhood, and the ideology of men's and women's separate spheres.

L 150. **KINDILLIEN, CARLIN T.** American Poetry in the Eighteen Nineties. Providence, R.I.: Brown University Press, 1956. 223 pp.
This book is an attempt to survey virtually all of the poetry published in the U.S. in the 1890s in "original volumes of poetry." Summaries of the literary scene and the poetic techniques of the decade frame four chapters which consider the poetry topically. Kindillien offers more literary history than literary criticism, and makes no strong attempt to separate what we now consider the enduring poetry of the decade from the fashionable, which is consistent with the author's purpose to identify the contribution of the minor poets to the literary scene. Regional concerns are examined, including the traditions those regions discarded or upheld; subjects and themes—especially the encroachment of the modern city and its influence on the country—are also studied for the variety of ways in which they were represented.

L 151. KNIGHT, GRANT C. The Critical Period in American Literature.
        Chapel Hill: University of North Carolina Press, 1951. 208 pp.
Knight discusses what he believes is the victory of the Realists over
the Romanticists in the literary "battle" of the 1890s in the U.S. The
battle was precipitated by the unresolved issues of the Civil War and
the disparity between Americans' ideals, which were still romantic, and
their behavior, which was governed by the requirements of post-war industry
and business. Using a "historio-sociological approach," Knight discusses
texts in their historical contexts.

L 152. KOLB, HAROLD H., Jr. The Illusion of Life: American Realism as
        a Literary Form. Charlottesville: University Press of Virginia,
        1969. 180 pp.
Kolb resists definitions of literary movements but does find a style characteristic of Realism. He notes seven traits common to James, Twain,
and Howells, the developers of American Realism: "their rejection of
omniscient narration, their experimentation with point of view and a language appropriate to humor and satire, their condemnation of American
materialism . . ., and their ultimate faith in style and art." These
writers also shared a "nontranscendental" or "unidealized" philosophy,
everyday subject matter, and a relativistic morality. Kolb analyzes the
contribution of the three authors, places Realism in a historical context,
and concludes with a twenty-six page bibliography of primary and secondary
sources.

L 153. KRAMER, AARON. The Prophetic Tradition in American Poetry, 1835-
        1900. Rutherford, N.J.: Fairleigh Dickinson University Press,
        1968. 416 pp.
This book examines specific poetic responses to episodes of anti-democratic
feelings in the 19th century, namely, racism (in relation to Indians as
well as slaves), imperialism, and mobbism. Kramer concludes that our
greatest poets "were most desirous of rising above partisan issues," and
yet were the speakers for the right cause in bad times, "surmounting personal limitations and hesitations in order to serve as the inspired instruments of truth."

L 154. LEASE, BENJAMIN. Anglo-American Encounters: England and the Rise
        of American Literature. New York: Cambridge University Press,
        1981. 299 pp.
Lease considers ten major American writers of the early 19th century.
Seeking to comprehend what England meant to them (and to a lesser degree
what they meant to England), he explores the biographies and writings
for interesting anecdotes and reflections concerning Britain. Emerson,
Thoreau, Whitman, and Stowe are distinguished for having carried on friendships with English men or women of letters. Those who had no such advantage, Lease argues, tended to feel alienated from England. Nevertheless,
his compilation of historical accounts and plot synopses gives the impression that by the 1850s the Anglo-American literary relation had been
further developed.

L 155. LEVIN, HARRY. The Power of Blackness: Hawthorne, Poe, Melville.
        New York: Knopf, 1958. 263 pp.
Interested in understanding a writer's creative imagination, Levin examines
the archetypal imagery and subjects in Hawthorne, Poe, and Melville.
Their themes suggest a darker, more ominous side to 19th-century American
literature. In different ways each writer has a vision of evil: Hawthorne
employs an historical consciousness; Poe an analytic rigor; and Melville
an archetypal imagery. Although focusing on three writers, Levin alludes
to many others.

L 156. LEWIS, R. W. B. The American Adam: Innocence, Tragedy and Tra-
        dition in the Nineteenth Century. Chicago: University of Chicago
        Press, 1959. 205 pp.
Lewis discovers in American literature between 1820 and 1860 the beginnings
of a "native American mythology" whose central image is "the authentic
American as a figure of heroic innocence and vast potentialities, poised
at the start of a new history." Lewis's history takes the form of a dialogue among three opposing fundamental attitudes: a yearning for a lost
sense of history, an enthusiastic optimism looking toward the future,
and an ironic acknowledgment of both man's tragic suffering and the heights
of dignity that suffering allows him to achieve.

L 157. LIVELY, ROBERT A. Fiction Fights the Civil War: An Unfinished
        Chapter in the Literary History of the American People. Chapel
        Hill: University of North Carolina Press, 1957. 230 pp.
Over five hundred novels written about the Civil War are scrutinized here.
Lively begins with the phenomenon of the mass outpouring of such fiction
which has continued unabated from 1863 to the present. He then focuses
on the relation between the fiction and history, and concludes by examining
some of the best of that fiction--including works by John W. DeForest,
James Lane Allen, Stephen Crane, Ellen Glasgow, William Faulkner, and
Allen Tate.

L 158. LOSHE, LILLIE D. The Early American Novel. New York: Columbia
        University Press, 1907. 131 pp.
Loshe divides the early American novel (1789-1830) into three categories:
sentimental, Gothic, and historical. The works of some of the earlier
novelists like Sarah Wentworth Morton, H. H. Brackenridge, and Susanna
Rowson exhibit concern with the romantic, didactic, and satiric intents
of the sentimental novel tradition as established by the works of
Richardson, Fielding, and Sterne. Loshe considers the fiction of the
Englishman William Godwin to be the foundation of the psychological Gothic
tradition of which Charles Brockden Brown is the greatest early American
exponent. The historical tradition of the early American novel is evidenced primarily in the Indian stories of Ann Elizabeth Bleecker, Gilbert
Imlay, John Davis, Samuel Woodworth, and Brown. The last chapter of
Loshe's study examines the fiction of James Fenimore Cooper in the light
of these three traditions.

L 159. LYNN, KENNETH S. Mark Twain and Southwestern Humor. Boston:
        Little, Brown, 1959. 300 pp.
Lynn's study illuminates the connection between cultural-political history
and literary criticism. He contrasts William Byrd's conception of Virginia
as a new version of aristocratic London with the Western American frontier
and its violence. On to the frontier came a self-controlled Gentleman
modelled on Whig ideals who was the hero of Southwestern humorists. But
out of the frontier came the native American vernacular, and with the
rise of Jacksonian democracy the gentlemanly style virtually disappears.
Drawing on earlier literary types and techniques, like the frame tale,
Twain's writings fuse the Gentleman and the Clown, giving rise to the
naive American democrat. No longer is the stress on frontier violence;
rather, Twain emphasizes the hero's reaction to the violence. Twain's
greatest contribution is his vernacular honesty, which destroyed the Southern myth. Toward the end, however, Twain depicts a hero alienated from
society by his knowledge.

L 160. MANI, LAKSHMI. The Apocalyptic Vision in Nineteenth-Century Ameri-
        can Fiction: A Study of Cooper, Hawthorne, and Melville. Washing-
        ton, D.C.: University Press of America, 1981. 334 pp.
Mani argues that although the 17th-century Puritans tempered their millennial expectations with an awareness of the catastrophe that would accompany
the apocalypse and of the obligations incumbent upon them because of their
expectations, that dark side of apocalyptic thinking was gradually lost,
until, by the 19th century, American millennial thought was unmitigatedly
optimistic and served to justify cultural expansion and to obscure social
problems. In order to expose the shallowness of that optimistic vision,
Cooper, Hawthorne, and Melville invoked apocalyptic structures and notions
of perfectionism in their works, often imaging some ideal of social perfection which is ultimately shown to be hollow or marred by some recalci-
trant human failing.

L 161. MARTIN, JAY. Harvests of Change: American Literature 1865-1914.
        Englewood Cliffs, N.J.: Prentice-Hall, 1967. 382 pp.
Martin's thesis is that amid the vast and rapid cultural changes between
the Civil War and the W.W. I American writers attempted both to preserve
traditional culture and to alert their readers to the meanings of the
changes. He briefly treats many major figures (e.g., Crane, Howells,
Norris, Frost) and minor figures (e.g., Sidney Lanier, Edward Eggleston,
Hamlin Garland, Sarah Orne Jewett) and devotes entire chapters to Mark
Twain and Henry James. Martin adopts a sociological approach to literature
and assumes a familiarity with the various texts.

L 162. MARTIN, RONALD E. American Literature and the Universe of Force.
        Durham, N.C.: Duke University Press, 1981. 277 pp.
Martin argues that the late 19th-century concept of reality as a system
of forces--which he calls the "universe of force"--profoundly affected
America's culture and literature of the turn of the century. This concept
of the universe was radically new in being neither anthropomorphic nor
theological. Martin discusses the development of 19th-century science,
in particular, the discovery of the Law of Conservation of Force. He
then devotes a chapter to Spencer, whose cosmic system based on the concept
of force influenced American thought, and another to the Americanization
of Spencer's thought. He examines four authors and their responses to
the universe of force: Henry Adams, highly intellectual and aesthetically
sophisticated; and Norris, London, and Dreiser--who according to Martin
received their ideas about a deterministic universe of force at second
or third hand.

L 163. MATTHIESSEN, FRANCIS OTTO. American Renaissance: Art and Expres-
        sion in the Age of Emerson and Whitman. New York: Oxford Uni-
        versity Press, 1941. 678 pp.
Matthiessen's study focuses on the fruitful period of 1850-1855 and
explores the literary and cultural climate in which Emerson, Hawthorne,
Melville, Thoreau, and Whitman wrote. Each author and his work are set
within a contemporary context. All five were committed to democracy and
shared certain tastes and sensibilities. Some--Thoreau and Whitman--
advocated a functional style. Most importantly, their works show a recurrent concern for the confrontation of individual and society, the nature
of good and evil, and the use of symbolism to fuse appearance and reality.

L 164. MILLER, PERRY. The Raven and the Whale: The War of Words and
        Wits in the Era of Poe and Melville. New York: Harcourt, Brace,
        1956. 370 pp.
As Miller's subtitle suggests, his work is not solely about Poe and
Melville but is also about the conscious "war of words and wits" during
their times. Miller's study calls for a closer examination of Poe and
Melville in relation to their social and historical context and literary

751

milieu. The book treats New York literary society; its journals (the North American Review, the Knickerbocker); editors (Evert Duyckinck, Lewis Gaylord Clark); clubs (the Tetractys Club); reviewers (Rufus Griswold); and their interaction with Poe and Melville.

L 165. MILLER, TICE L. Bohemians and Critics: American Theatre Criticism in the Nineteenth Century. Metuchen, N.J.: Scarecrow Press, 1981. 190 pp.
Miller's study concentrates on five major theater critics of the mid-Victorian period in America: Henry Clapp, Jr., Edward G. P. Wilkins, William Winter, Stephen Ryder Fiske, and Andrew C. Wheeler. The case studies attempt to assess the education and talent of each critic, to measure the influence on each of French culture and aesthetics, and to consider the impact each had on American theater. While the opening chapter establishes a historical context in which to place the individual studies, the concluding chapter draws them together and makes suggestions about the state of theater criticism in Victorian America.

L 166. MITCHELL, LEE CLARK. Witnesses to a Vanishing America: The Nineteenth-Century Response. Princeton, N.J.: Princeton University Press, 1981. 320 pp.
Mitchell shows that even in the midst of Western expansion, some 19th-century Americans had ambivalent or regretful feelings about the concomitant destruction of both the wilderness and Native American cultures. In small but significant numbers, they evinced impulses to preserve records of that fast-vanishing part of America in the form of nature preserves, archives, historical accounts, paintings, photographs, and writings. Moreover, this consciousness among an active minority of Americans eventually gave way to the development of anthropological study as a rigorous academic discipline, governed by notions of cultural relativism, as well as to critical reexaminations of that supplanting white culture, with its technology and "progress." Mitchell has examined a variety of cultural figures and texts, including, among many others, painters Thomas Cole, George Catlin, and Seth Eastman; photographer Edward Curtis; historians Francis Parkman and William Prescott; anthropologist Franz Boas; and writers James Fenimore Cooper, Washington Irving, Herman Melville, Mark Twain, and Willa Cather.

L 167. MIXON, WAYNE. Southern Writers and the New South Movement, 1865–1913. Chapel Hill: University of North Carolina Press, 1980. 169 pp.
Mixon's work classifies the complex reactions of twelve Southern writers to the controversy of the New South Movement. He begins each chapter with a brief biography and then examines the themes of nostalgia, romance, materialism, the arcadian ideal, and anti-Northern sentiment found in each author's work. John Esten Cooke is examined in relation to the work ethic and the pastoral ideal; Sidney Lanier in relation to the place of trade in the New South; Joel Chandler Harris in relation to the "yeoman tradition"; and other writers such as Mark Twain, George W. Cable, and Charles Chesnutt in relation to other issues central to the New South Movement.

L 168. MORGAN, HOWARD WAYNE. American Writers in Rebellion: From Mark Twain to Dreiser. New York: Hill & Wang, 1965. 206 pp.
Morgan discusses the lives and literary careers of five major American authors of the two generations after the Civil War: Mark Twain, William Dean Howells, Hamlin Garland, Frank Norris, and Theodore Dreiser. He examines the authors' responses to the changing political, social, and economic conditions of their times and the manners in which these authors expressed their criticisms and rebellions through the various literary techniques, subjects, and attitudes associated with the traditions of Romanticism, Realism, and Naturalism.

L 169. MUMFORD, LEWIS. The Golden Day: A Study in American Literature and Culture. 1926; Rev. ed. Boston: Beacon Press, 1957. 144 pp.
American culture, says Mumford, was shaped by "the breakdown of the medi-eval synthesis" and by the transference of a Protestant "abstract and fragmentary culture" to a new world. These forces united in the mid-19th century to produce the "Golden Day" of American literature: the era of Emerson, Thoreau, Whitman, Hawthorne, and Melville. Mumford focuses on this period, and argues that after the Civil War pragmatism created new attitudes and ideas in literature. In his introduction to the 1957 edition, Mumford points out what he sees to be the importance of Romanticism and rebellion in forming the "New World man" and his literature. He also reevaluates his critical judgments of both the post-Civil War writers and such popular 19th-century authors as Longfellow and Holmes, acknowl-edging their role in the historical development of American literature.

L 170. MYERSON, JOEL. The New England Transcendentalists and the Dial. Madison, N.J.: Fairleigh Dickinson University Press, 1980. 345 pp.
Myerson tells the history of the Dial, a periodical under the editorship of The Transcendental Club, Ralph Waldo Emerson, and Margaret Fuller. Identifying the editorial and financial problems which accompanied the publication of each volume, Myerson also records the critical and popular response to the Dial. The study concludes with a catalogue of brief bio-graphies of the contributors and a table of contents for each edition which lists both contributors and the names of their publications. Myerson has also appended an extensive bibliography of primary and secondary mater-ials.

L 171. NOLAN, CHARLES J., Jr. Aaron Burr and the American Literary Imagi-nation. Westport, Conn.: Greenwood Press, 1980. 210 pp.
Divided into four sections, this book provides, first, a sketch of the historical Aaron Burr; second, a treatment of the legendary Burr as he emerges from press accounts and personal writings of contemporaries; third, an account of Burr as he appears in drama and fiction--how various authors, frequently influenced by legend, depicted Colonel Burr and how their views of him shifted over the years; and fourth, some conclusions about what Burr has meant and continues to mean to American culture.

L 172. PAPASHVILY, HELEN WAITE. All the Happy Endings: A Study of the Domestic Novel in America, the Women Who Wrote It, the Women Who Read It, in the Nineteenth Century. New York: Harper, 1956. 231 pp.
Papashvily studies the enormous popularity of 19th-century American domes-tic novels, which she defines as sentimental tales of contemporary domestic life, usually written by and for women. The center of interest in this fiction was the home and the housewife, both of which the novelists glori-fied and idealized. Middle-class, young, and penurious, the "scribbling women" (Hawthorne's phrase) usually possessed another trait in common: that some man close to them had betrayed their trust. This male villain found his way into their fiction where he reinforced the stereotype of the unscrupulous male victimizing the innocent female. Paradoxically, these depictions also helped subtly to foment a social rebellion as women reacted against such dominance.

L 173. PARKS, EDD WINFIELD. Ante-Bellum Southern Literary Critics. Athens: University of Georgia Press, 1962. 358 pp.
Parks's purpose in this book is to discuss the intellectual literary his-tory of the south from 1785 to 1861. After two brief chapters summarizing the "intent" of the humorists and the novelists Parks devotes separate chapters to Thomas Jefferson, Hugh Swinton Legare, Richard Henry Wilde,

William Gilmore Simms, Philip Pendleton Cooke, Thomas Holley Chivers, William J. Grayson, Henry Timrod, and Paul Hamilton Hayne.

L 174. **PIZER, DONALD.** Realism and Naturalism in Nineteenth-Century American Literature. Carbondale: Southern Illinois University Press, 1966. 176 pp.

Pizer here gathers essays on two related subjects: a definition of Realism and of Naturalism, and a description of the relationship between 19th-century criticism and these two movements. The work of Howells, James, and Twain suggests that Realism included more diverse subjects than most critics would acknowledge and that it was "ethically idealistic." The Naturalists (e.g., Dreiser, Norris, and Stephen Crane) attempted "to represent the intermingling in life of controlling force and individual worth." In criticism, the age saw the influence of evolutionary theory (in the writing of Thomas Sergeant Perry), Pragmatism (in Hamlin Garland), and Primitivism (in Frank Norris). Pizer argues strenuously for the importance of these concepts in both 19th- and 20th-century American literature.

L 175. **PORTE, JOEL.** The Romance in America: Studies in Cooper, Poe, Hawthorne, Melville, and James. Middletown, Conn.: Wesleyan University Press, 1969. 235 pp.

Porte devotes one chapter to each of the authors whom he sees as forming "a fictional tradition running throughout the nineteenth century." Despite the considerable differences among these five writers, they share a flexible and variable "theory of stylized art" which they employ "in order to explore large questions . . . about race, history, nature, human motivation, and art." Porte explains that "romance is characterized by a need self-consciously to define its own aims." It thus provides the theme as well as the form of many of these authors' works. Each of the authors sought to fulfill the role of romancer by "reflexively questioning" his own assumptions within the form and theme of his work.

L 176. **PRITCHARD, JOHN PAUL.** Return to the Fountains: Some Classical Sources of American Criticism. Durham, N.C.: Duke University Press, 1942. 271 pp.

Pritchard examines the influence of Aristotle and Horace on American critics from William Cullen Bryant to the New Humanists (Irving Babbitt and Paul Elmer More) and Stuart Pratt Sherman in the early 20th century. Included are individual chapters on the poetics of Poe, Emerson, Thoreau, Hawthorne, Longfellow, and others, with concluding remarks on mimesis, plot, and character in American literary criticism.

L 177. **RICHARDSON, ROBERT D., Jr.** Myth and Literature in the American Renaissance. Bloomington: Indiana University Press, 1978. 309 pp.

Richardson examines the ways in which 19th-century writers dealt with the "problem of myth." He asserts that the subjects to which authors were drawn during this era "invited comparison with the same traditional myths they were trying to supersede." Richardson divides the process of myth-making into two traditions: the rationalist or skeptical version modelled after Paine and Voltaire, and the Romantic or affirmative version. After examining one "pure" advocate of each version (Theodore Parker and Bronson Alcott), he moves on to the complex syntheses in the works of Emerson, Thoreau, Whitman, Hawthorne, and Melville.

L 178. **RIDGELY, J. V.** Nineteenth-Century Southern Literature. Lexington: University Press of Kentucky, 1980. 128 pp.

After a discussion of Colonial Southern literature, Ridgely surveys the major works of such 19th-century authors as John Pendleton Kennedy, William Gilmore Simms, Joel Chandler Harris, Thomas Nelson Page, George Washington Cable, and Mark Twain. He argues that as the Civil War approached, South-

ern writers grew gradually more unified in their defense of the South
and of slavery, and that this felt necessity to demonstrate loyalty to
all aspects of Southern civilization inhibited literary creativity.
Despite some dissenting voices, Southern letters after the war were dominated by the local colorists, who nostalgically elaborated on and solidified the myth of the old South.

L 179. **RINGE, DONALD A.** The Pictorial Mode: Space and Time in the Art
of Bryant, Irving and Cooper. Lexington: University Press of
Kentucky, 1971. 244 pp.
Ringe suggests that critics of 19th-century art can gloss literary works
of that period because writers and painters expressed in common the epistemology of the age. In particular, the Hudson River School of painting
clarifies the art of those writers who occasionally wrote about the Hudson
River area. Art critics and philosophers of the 19th century, especially
those of the Scottish Common Sense School, identified the mutual interests
and analogous techniques of art and literature as painters and writers
depicted their natural and moral subjects. The authors and painters considered include William Cullen Bryant, Thomas Cole, James Fenimore Cooper,
Asher Durand, and Washington Irving.

L 180. **ROSE, ANNE C.** Transcendentalism as a Social Movement, 1830-1850.
New Haven, Conn.: Yale University Press, 1981. 269 pp.
Rose proposes that the Transcendentalists, though ultimately ineffectual
as social reformers, were much more socially active and radical than they
are usually pictured. She explains the origins of Transcendentalism as
a religious reform faction within Unitarianism, which developed with a
sensitivity to economic issues, and engendered such negative reactions
from conservative Boston Unitarians along the way that it evolved as a
truly radical, alternative social vision. Rose discusses the thought
and lives of six major Transcendentalist figures (Orestes Brownson, George
Ripley, Elizabeth Peabody, Margaret Fuller, Bronson Alcott, and Ralph
Waldo Emerson); the Transcendentalist "come-outer" communities, Fruitlands
and Brook Farm; and the connections and tensions between Transcendentalist
ideas on social reform and family life.

L 181. **ROURKE, CONSTANCE.** Trumpets of Jubilee. New York: Harcourt,
Brace, 1927. 445 pp.
Rourke studies five "successful leaders" of the 19th century: Henry Ward
Beecher, Harriet Beecher Stowe, Lyman Beecher, Horace Greeley, and P. T.
Barnum. She is interested in their "sense of wonder" and their belief
in "magnitude," and implies that there is something perennially and char-
acteristically American in their "pursuit of liberty, laughter, composure,
or even power."

L 182. **ROWE, ANNE E.** The Enchanted Country: Northern Writers in the
South, 1865-1910. Baton Rouge: Louisiana State University Press,
1978. 155 pp.
This study defines, through the "writings of selected non-southerners,"
Northern attitudes toward the South during Reconstruction and its after-
math. The writers whose work is specifically studied include Harriet
Beecher Stowe, Albion Tourgee, John W. DeForest, Constance Fenimore Woolson,
Lafcadio Hearn, Owen Wister, and Henry James. Rowe concludes that the
later writers are guilty of an "overt idealization of the escapist, faraway
country."

L 183. ROWE, JOHN CARLOS. Through the Custom-House: Nineteenth-Century American Fiction and Modern Theory. Baltimore, Md.: Johns Hopkins University Press, 1982. 214 pp.
Describing his work as "an experiment in intertextual criticism," Rowe examines six 19th-century American literary texts that are traditionally considered marginal in relation to philosophical "pretexts" written by six 20th-century thinkers: Thoreau's A Week is discussed in relation to Heidegger; Hawthorne's Blithedale Romance to Sartre; Poe's Narrative of A. Gordon Pym to Freud; Melville's "Bartleby" to Derrida; Twain's Pudd'nhead Wilson to Nietzsche; and James's Sacred Fount to Saussure and Benveniste. Rowe argues that these texts exhibit modernity but are not simply a historical anticipation of 20th-century modernity; rather, they are modern in that they are intertextual--metaliterary--each the result of the author's interpreting a literary tradition, his own oeuvre, and the "linguistic sign" itself.

L 184. RUSK, RALPH LESLIE. The Literature of the Middle Western Frontier. 2 vols. New York: Columbia University Press, 1925. 876 pp.
Rusk covers all forms of writing published in and about the frontier of the Midwest until 1841, including travel and observation, newspapers and magazines, controversial writings, scholarly writings and school books, fiction, poetry, and drama. Most of the second volume is a bibliography divided into similar categories. The work is a reference guide governed by the premise that the "literature of the West which is most significant as a memorial of that era is the mediocre work of men whose chief usefulness was their part in that humble mission."

L 185. SAUM, LEWIS O. The Popular Mood of Pre-Civil War America. Westport, Conn.: Greenwood Press, 1980. 336 pp.
To identify the main lines of popular, antebellum thought, Saum has studied approximately two thousand diaries and autobiographies written between 1830 and 1860. He generalizes that, while common people adhered to a religious perspective which granted the inscrutability of providence, they capitalized upon opportunities for social, economic, and occasionally political advancement. His account of popular political and social theory challenges more traditional assumptions about democracy. Moreover, an analysis of notions of the frontier and the relation between nature and society argues that modern scholars have misunderstood the "mood" of antebellum America. To strengthen that argument, Saum throughout sets elite culture against popular culture, Emerson, Hawthorne, and Melville against the common people.

L 186. SCHEICK, WILLIAM J. The Half-Blood: A Cultural Symbol in 19th-Century American Fiction. Lexington: University Press of Kentucky, 1979. 106 pp.
Scheick explains how the fictional half-blood provided American authors with a means of embodying the universal conflict within the human self between nature and civilization. Although he touches on some earlier and some later writers, Scheick focuses on 19th-century prose writers who depicted half-bloods. In general, the attitude toward the half-blood was, like the attitude toward the frontier, ambivalent. But Southern writers more often showed hostility toward the half-blood, depicting him or her as evil and grotesque, while Northern writers seemingly could not decide whether the half-blood was a threat or a promise for American society. Scheick notes that the half-blood was a "safer" topic than the mulatto. He also observes that, perhaps because of a fear of miscegenation, the half-blood in spirit (Natty Bumppo, for instance) often replaced the half-blood in fact within these fictions.

L 187. SMITH, ALLAN GARDNER. The Analysis of Motives: Early American
        Psychology and Motives. Amsterdam: Rodolpi, 1980. 195 pp.
Smith inspects the psychological theory operative in the fiction of Charles
Brockden Brown, Edgar Allan Poe, and Nathaniel Hawthorne. In separate
chapters, the study gauges the extent to which 19th-century psychological
method and theory influenced each author's analysis of human behavior.
An appendix which catalogues and describes the prevailing psychological
theories of the 19th century concludes the work.

L 188. SMITH, FRANCES FOSTER. Witnessing Slavery: The Development of
        Ante-Bellum Slave Narratives. Westport, Conn.: Greenwood Press,
        1979. 187 pp.
Smith dates the earliest American slave narratives in the 18th century,
and her study examines those written through the end of the Civil War.
While identifying stylistic and thematic differences, Smith concentrates
on defining a pattern which unites the disparate narratives into a canon.
Moreover, the literary and cultural analyses not only explain the political,
economic, and technological causes which account for the pattern's emergence, but also firmly root the literature in its cultural context.

L 189. SMITH, HENRY NASH. Democracy and the Novel: Popular Resistance
        to Classic American Writers. New York: Oxford University Press,
        1978. 204 pp.
Smith has grouped together essays about five major American writers who
depended upon writing for their livelihood--Hawthorne, Melville, Howells,
Twain, and James--into a book in which he argues that all but Howells
were "in collision" with the "secular faith" upon which popular American
culture rested. They sought to escape the conventions, ideological and
formal, of middle-brow literature, even though they relied upon some degree
of popular reception and may have made some use of those conventions.
Smith also includes a treatment of Henry Ward Beecher's Norwood, a novel
which sets forth the values of the post-War era when the genteel tradition
dominated the aesthetic realm. He wishes to trace the connections between
pre-Civil War Romanticism and post-Civil War Realism--connections he says
most critics have overlooked.

L 190. SMITH, HENRY NASH. Virgin Land: The American West as Symbol and
        Myth. Cambridge, Mass.: Harvard University Press, 1950.
        305 pp.
Smith notes that the impact of the Western frontier on the American consciousness has had great consequences for American literature. The Westward expansion of the early 19th century was expressed not only in economic
and political programs but also in literature. The central figure in
this literature, the frontiersman, was ambivalent or hostile toward civilization. In the late 19th century the American West was cultivated by
the yeoman, who replaced the frontiersman and cowboy as the central literary figure. But this free farmer was not truly heroic. The fact of the
Industrial Revolution clashed with the myth of the frontier, resulting
in a late 19th-century disillusionment with the agrarian utopia. In his
study Smith examines diaries, newspapers, legal documents, and literary
works, both major and minor.

L 191. SPENCER, BENJAMIN T. The Quest for Nationality: An American
        Literary Campaign. Syracuse, N.Y.: Syracuse University Press,
        1957. 389 pp.
Spencer's study charts the growth and definition of a national literature
during the three centuries after the first Colonists. He traces the almost
indigenous preoccupation with the relationship of literature and nationality, and shows how, once "possessed" by America, writers attempted to
"possess," comprehend, define, and enlarge it in turn. In chapters on
the early literature, Transcendentalism, regional literature, Walt Whitman,

and the rise of Realism, Spencer documents how "the quest for nationality was a concern for literary integrity—for delivering American writers from the sterile obligation to express what their own experience had not nurtured and what their own society did not require." Spencer believes that the quest terminated in 1892, by which time the deaths of Whitman, Lowell, Whittier, and others had put an end to a generation. "The importance of the conscious pursuit of nationality," he argues, "is in a measure suggested by the fact that scarcely a native author of any importance before 1900 failed to engage in the inquiry and to declare himself publicly on its issues."

L 192. STARR, KEVIN. Americans and the California Dream 1850-1915. New York: Oxford University Press, 1973. 479 pp.
Starr chronicles the development of California's regional culture by examining both historical facts and the interpretations of those facts formulated by Californians and other Americans. He notes the "utopian imperative" under which the area developed—its regional version of the American dream of creating a perfect society in the wilderness. Starr's discussion is chronological, beginning with the period just before California's annexation and ending with the San Francisco Fair (1915). The intellectuals, authors, and artists he treats include Richard Henry Dana, Jr., Walter Colton, Bret Harte, Henry George, Josiah Royce, Clarence King, John Muir, Frank Norris, Jack London, Ambrose Bierce, Joaquin Miller, Gertrude Atherton, John and Jessie Fremont, and Isadora Duncan.

L 193. SUNDQUIST, ERIC J. Home as Found: Authority and Genealogy in Nineteenth-Century American Literature. Baltimore, Md.: Johns Hopkins University Press, 1979. 209 pp.
The four authors studied by Sundquist—Cooper, Hawthorne, Thoreau, and Melville—while rebellious and experimental, also felt a loss and a desire to either return to the past or to repeat their own experiments, turning them into "sacraments." The critic's model for the conflict between rebellion and tradition is the sacrificial totem meal that "Freud finds so strikingly fused with the Oedipal situation." Thus Sundquist explores not only themes of authority and authorship but also of incest (Cooper and Melville), "the paradox-riddled cultivation of Nature (Thoreau), and the sexual transgression against ancestral law (Hawthorne)." Interested in Freud the cultural historian rather than the clinician, Sundquist enlarges his study by examining how these authors looked to their own families for "a model for the social and political constructs still so much in question for a recently conceived nation."

L 194. SUNDQUIST, ERIC J., ed. American Realism: New Essays. Baltimore, Md.: Johns Hopkins University Press, 1982. 298 pp.
Stating that American Realism is particularly difficult to define since it "has no school" and refuses to abandon the complex vision of pre-Civil War "romance," Sundquist proceeds to define the movement historically, at least for the purposes of this collection of essays: literary Realism begins in America with those writers who appeared on the scene after the Civil War and ends (although, as Sundquist notes, some may argue that it has not yet ended) in the first decades of the 20th century. He further notes that "the romance of money," which pervaded the culture and was contemporaneous with Realism, altered both human values and the sense of the self, thus affecting novelists' depictions of "reality." Authors whose works are discussed include Hawthorne, Howells, Twain, James, Stephen Crane, Jewett, Freeman, Gilman, Norris, Wharton, and Dreiser. Among the contributors to this volume are Richard Brodhead, Eric Cheyfitz, Laurence Holland, Walter Benn Michaels, Donald Pease, Sundquist, and Alan Trachtenberg.

L 195. TAYLOR, GORDON O. The Passages of Thought: Psychological Representation in the American Novel 1870-1900. New York: Oxford
University Press, 1969. 172 pp.
Taylor studies selected works of James, Howells, Crane, Norris, and Dreiser
not to evaluate these works but to define the shifts in "fictive psychology" in late 19th-century American fiction. He includes two topics in
this "fictive psychology": "the author's premises concerning the nature
of the mind, and his embodiment of these premises in fictive art." The
movement in such psychological representation is from a moral to an environmental frame of reference and from consideration of "static, discrete
mental states" to "a concept of organically linked mental states." Thus,
at the beginning of the 20th century, the American novel derives its organizing principle from physiological and psychological, rather than moral
or romantic, plots.

L 196. THOMPSON, G. R. and VIRGIL L. LOKKE, eds. Ruined Eden of the Present: Hawthorne, Melville and Poe. West Lafayette, Ind.: Purdue
University Press, 1981. 371 pp.
Sixteen essays of widely varying method and argument are assembled in
this book to honor Darrel Abel. The variety of approaches presented in
the volume is intended to reflect Abel's notions of the fragmented age
of Hawthorne, Melville, and Poe. Nina Baym, Richard Fogle, Hershel Parker,
Patrick F. Quinn, and G. R. Thompson are among the critics contributing
to this festschrift.

L 197. WALKER, ROBERT H. The Poet and the Gilded Age: Social Themes
in Late 19th Century American Verse. Philadelphia: University
of Pennsylvania Press, 1963. 387 pp.
Walker's subject is, almost equally, the poet and the age; he sets out
"to re-examine the Gilded Age in the light of the verse produced by its
citizens." Rarely citing the best known poetry of the time--by Whitman
or James Russell Lowell, for instance--Walker examines a host of lesser-
known poets and their responses to particular subjects. Chapters are
devoted to attitudes toward expansionism, urbanism, economic progress,
politics, suffrage for women, temperance, immigration, and science.

L 198. WILLIAMS, BENJAMIN BUFORD. A Literary History of Alabama: The
Nineteenth Century. Rutherford, N.J.: Fairleigh Dickinson Uni-
versity Press, 1979. 258 pp.
This literary history treats authors active from the establishment of
the first printing press in Alabama in 1807 to the close of the century.
Bringing to light forgotten and undervalued work, Williams studies numerous
genres: the novel, poetry, drama, biography, autobiography, journal,
memoir, history, and journalism. He argues that such writers as Anne
Newport Royall, a journalist and America's first female editor; Joseph
Glover Baldwin, whose humor influenced Mark Twain's; the best-selling
author Caroline Lee Hentz; and the popular Augusta Evans Wilson not only
establish the importance of this body of writing, but ultimately prove
more representative of the South as a whole than more canonical figures.

L 199. WILLIAMS, KENNY J. Prairie Voices: A Literary History of Chicago
from the Frontier to 1893. Nashville, Tenn.: Townsend Press,
1980. 487 pp.
Wishing to avoid the period of Chicago's literary history that has already
received a great deal of attention--the late 19th and early 20th centuries--
Williams limits his discussion to Chicago's 19th century, because, he
argues, the story of Chicago's literature, like the story of its architecture, is rooted in the earlier era. He also claims that Chicago, "as
a place, an idea, or an image," typified the expansionism of 19th-century
America--that its popular image has become an "integral part of American
civilization." He examines the historical romance of Chicago in its fur-

trading, Indian-warfare days; the development of journalism in the city (inextricably bound up with its early literature); the history of Chicago's publishing companies; the amassing of fortunes in Chicago that led to a desire for culture; and the effects on culture of the Great Fire. The late 19th century, Williams states, heralded the end of the genteel tradition in Chicago, which was replaced by a more realistic artistic mode, one that acknowledged Chicago as a commercial giant. The result was the "Chicago novel," a type of novel containing an "urban sense of history," and answering, in a way, the call for a Western literature.

L 200. WILSON, EDMUND. Patriotic Gore: Studies in the Literature of the American Civil War. New York: Oxford University Press, 1962. 816 pp.
Wilson focuses on 19th-century novels, diaries, memoirs, letters, and speeches which take the Civil War as their subject. In sixteen essays he examines the historical and psychological conditions that yielded these compositions and shows the value of literature to understanding a historical event--even when such literature demonstrates our irrationality. Wilson's discussion takes into consideration the various literary genres used, and the particular views of each writer. Among the literary figures examined are Harriet Beecher Stowe, Sidney Lanier, Albion W. Tourgee, George W. Cable, Kate Chopin, Ambrose Bierce, John W. DeForest, and Oliver Wendell Holmes.

L 201. ZIFF, LARZER. The American 1890s: Life and Times of a Lost Generation. New York: Viking Press, 1966. 376 pp.
Claiming that the artists of the 1890s were truly a "lost" generation "cut off before its time and revivified only . . . when history had made room for it," Ziff depicts the culture of the era as one of contrasts. He argues that, although romance--nostalgic, escapist yearning for ideal stasis--dominated the scene, another, more dynamic and socially unsettling tendency also existed in the 1890s. Artists representing this latter tendency were, he states, the "true precursors" of 20th-century American literature and art. He examines individual writers (Howells, Twain, James, Crane, Norris, Garland, Robinson, Dreiser, and others) and groups of writers (journalists, women writers, Midwestern writers, and poets who produced ornamental poetry). Ziff concludes that the social Realism of the early 1890s, fostered by immense social disturbance, gave way, in the wake of boom times and a successful war, to muckraking and "formulations of the new nationalism."

L 202. ZIFF, LARZER. Literary Democracy: The Declaration of Cultural Independence in America. New York: Viking Press, 1981. 333 pp.
Ziff argues that the writers of the American Renaissance established a truly American literature, which used indigenous materials and developed unique formal characteristics. The works he surveys, by Emerson, Poe, Thoreau, Hawthorne, Whitman, Melville, George Lippard, Stowe, George Washington Harris, and others, all show an interest in working out the problem of that new American form of social organization, democracy, and its implications for individual, and especially writerly, activity. These writers' ability to so analyze the culture was often enhanced by their being in some way alienated from or dispossessed by it.

IV. TWENTIETH CENTURY

L 203. AARON, DANIEL. Writers on the Left: Episodes in American Literary
        Communism. New York: Harcourt Brace & World, 1961. 460 pp.
Aaron focuses on individual writers and events from 1912 to 1940 in order
to analyze the alienation of artists and writers, the appeal of the idea
of Communism and of the image of Russia, and the final rejection of Communism. After W.W. I, literary radicals (e.g., Floyd Dell, Max Eastman)
gathered in Greenwich Village and later in Paris. During the Depression
and the rise of Nazism, many prominent writers, such as Malcolm Cowley,
Theodore Dreiser, John Dos Passos, Kenneth Burke, Edmund Wilson, and
Richard Wright, sympathized with the Communist Party. Most split with
the Party, however, over the German-Russian alliance and the pressures
for artistic conformity.

L 204. ABRAMSON, DORIS E. Negro Playwrights in the American Theater 1925-
        1959. New York: Columbia University Press, 1969. 335 pp.
Abramson first presents an introductory study of two early plays by black
authors: William Wells Brown's The Escape (1858) and Joseph S. Cotten's
Caleb the Degenerate (1903). Her prime concern is the drama of the 20th
century, from Garland Anderson's Appearances and Wallace Thurman's Harlem
in the twenties, to Harlem and Off-Broadway writers (William Branch, Alice
Childress, Loften Mitchell) and Broadway playwrights (Louis Peterson,
Lorraine Hansberry) of the 1950s, as well as the works of Amiri Baraka
(LeRoi Jones), Ossie Davis, and James Baldwin. Discussions of the plays
consider "the Negro's position in the political-economic-social scene"
and the theater in which the plays were produced. The focus, however,
is on the developing tradition of black theater; the plays are examined
for "their reflection of Negro problems." The predominantly white audiences on Broadway are examined for the way in which they affect the plays,
as is the problem of separatist messages to Harlem audiences who wish
to be assimilated into white middle-class culture.

L 205. ADAMS, J. DONALD. The Shape of Books to Come. New York: Viking
        Press, 1944. 202 pp.
Adams writes that "this book derives from the profound conviction that
literature, during the years immediately ahead, will seek above all else
to restore the dignity of the human spirit." With that moral purpose
firmly stated, the author begins his assessment of American literature
of the first half of the 20th century. He decries the "mood of negation"
and "spiritual poverty" in the works of such writers as Dreiser, Faulkner,
and Anderson. He praises the "positive spirit" (a "commitment to belief"
which nourishes the inner life) of John Steinbeck and Sinclair Lewis,
and he notes the "affirmative tone" and "courage" of many of the female
writers of the period, most notably Glasgow, Cather, and Elizabeth Madox
Roberts. Adams's work is an index to the critical and cultural temper
of the 1940s and a re-statement of the need for a moral purpose in art.

L 206. ALDRIDGE, JOHN W. After the Lost Generation: A Critical Study
        of the Writers of Two Wars. New York: McGraw-Hill, 1951.
        263 pp.
According to Aldridge, the Lost Generation (Hemingway, Dos Passos, and
Fitzgerald) shared a sense of "disillusionment and denial released by
the broken promises of the first war." These writers, however, were able
to convert that sense of social failure into artistic success; the writers
who followed them have no such common experience or shared values. Their
failures, Aldridge asserts, are due to the lack of critical attention
to fiction, the moral confusion in contemporary society, and a decline
in artistic talent. Part I is devoted to a discussion of the writers

of the Lost Generation. Part II, titled "The New Writers of the Forties,"
examines the work of Irwin Shaw, Norman Mailer, Truman Capote, Paul Bowles,
Gore Vidal, and others.

L 207. ALDRIDGE, JOHN W. The Devil in the Fire: Retrospective Essays
        on American Literature and Culture, 1951-1971. New York: Harper's
        Magazine Press, 1972. 364 pp.
This volume collects Aldridge's essays in literary and cultural commentary,
originally printed in other collections and magazines over a twenty-year
period. Included are essays on the postwar literary scene; pre-war writers,
such as Hemingway, Fitzgerald, and Dos Passos; and contemporary writers,
such as Mailer, Updike, Styron, Bellow, Barthelme, and Kosinski.

L 208. ALDRIDGE, JOHN W. In Search of Heresy: American Literature in
        an Age of Conformity. New York: McGraw-Hill, 1956. 210 pp.
Aldridge assumes that in modern society "will" has lost "supremacy as
an instrument of moral choice" and has been replaced by law. "Heresy,"
which etymologically "means a taking or choice," is thus no longer an
alternative to "conformism." The result is a tension in American fiction
between "the forces of dogma and heresy, conformity and dissent, hate
and love, guilt and innocence, sin and redemption." Aldridge applies
this hypothesis to the works of such writers as Ernest Hemingway, J. D.
Salinger, Saul Bellow, Herman Wouk, Malcolm Cowley, and Ira Wolfert.

L 209. ALDRIDGE, JOHN W. Time to Murder and Create: The Contemporary
        Novel in Crisis. New York: McKay, 1966. 264 pp.
These varied essays—each "written at a different time and for a different
occasion"—focus generally on the post-1945 American novel. Among the
more general essays are specific assessments of writers as different as
O'Hara, Styron, McCarthy, Bellow, Mailer, Updike, and Cheever, as well
as retrospective glances at Fitzgerald and Lewis. Aldridge says that
he works from no governing idea or thesis in this collection of essays;
however, he does suggest that these essays are sometimes tied together
by his interest in imagination in the novel and the failure of the novel
to hold the attention of the contemporary audience.

L 210. ALVAREZ, A. Stewards of Excellence: Studies on Modern English
        and American Poets. New York: Scribner, 1958. 191 pp.
Published in England as The Shaping Spirit, these essays attempt to answer
two questions: What are the essential differences between English and
American poetic traditions, and why has modern poetry been so unimpressive?
Unlike English poets, American poets had to create their own poetic tradition. Generally avoiding detailed analysis and evaluation of particular
poems, Alvarez discusses the typical qualities of Ezra Pound, Hart Crane,
and Wallace Stevens, in whose poems he sees an American poetic language
evolving.

L 211. BALAKIAN, NONA and CHARLES SIMMONS, eds. The Creative Present:
        Notes on Contemporary American Fiction. 1963; Rev. ed. New York:
        Gordian Press, 1973. 269 pp.
This collection of essays tries to place contemporary American fiction
in a critical perspective. The editors believe that a number of promising
writers were ignored while those two "literary giants" Faulkner and
Hemingway were alive. The Creative Present focuses on writers who possess
both "accomplishment and potentiality," including Baldwin, Mailer, Salinger,
Nabokov, McCullers, Kerouac, and Updike. Among their collective characteristics are awareness of style as a technical (not necessarily experimental)
tool, emphasis in their work on complete synthesis rather than a single
psychological state, and preoccupation with the nature and limits of
reality. In each essay, covering a maximum of three writers, the critic
evaluates the novelists and provides his own personal interpretations.

L 212. **BALDWIN, CHARLES C.** The Men Who Make Our Novels. 1919; Rev.
ed. New York: Dodd, Mead, 1924. 612 pp.
This work contains eighty-eight biographies of American male novelists
(no women are included). The author interviewed many of the writers before
writing the biographical sketches in which he describes such things as
the writer's physical appearance and habits. Although he mentions the
novels each has published, Baldwin's comments are mostly descriptive rather
than evaluative. Treated more or less as equals in this work, the majority
of the writers discussed do not now receive much critical attention.

L 213. **BARTLETT, LEE,** ed. The Beats: Essays in Criticism. Jefferson,
N.C.: McFarland, 1981. 237 pp.
Bartlett has selected fourteen essays to serve as a modest extension of
Thomas Parkinson's Casebook on the Beat (see L 369). The essays were
chosen as modern, positive analyses of the Beats as writers, not as men
or political figures. Bartlett, William Everson, and Albert Gelpi attempt
to identify "a certain stylistic and thematic cohesion to the Beat Generation." Geoffrey Thurley and John Clellon Holmes focus on the poets;
William L. Stull and R. G. Peterson on Burroughs; James Breslin and Thomas
Merrill on Ginsberg; Parkinson and Robert Kern on Snyder; George Dardess
on Kerouac; Barbara Christian on Kaufman; and L. A. Ianni on Ferlinghetti.

L 214. **BAUMGARTEN, MURRAY.** City Scriptures: Modern Jewish Writing.
Cambridge, Mass.: Harvard University Press, 1982. 179 pp.
Baumgarten proposes an "interlinguistic reading of texts, in which inter-
ference is to be understood as interreference." He traces the way in
which Yiddish lurks behind the English used by modern Jewish writers.
He discusses works by Saul Bellow, Bernard Malamud, Henry and Philip Roth,
Johanna Kaplan, Alfred Kazin, Cynthia Ozick, Isaac Babel, Isaac Bashevis
Singer, E. L. Doctorow, and others. Although modern Jewish writing is,
as Baumgarten points out, an urban phenomenon, he draws several parallels
between these writers and the writers of the New England Renaissance,
particularly Melville and Hawthorne. Both groups, he argues, emerge from
a religious culture and attempt, through language, to establish the basis
for selfhood in relation to that traditional culture.

L 215. **BEACH, JOSEPH WARREN.** American Fiction 1920-1940. New York:
Macmillan, 1941. 371 pp.
Beach's study is devoted to eight modern novelists: Dos Passos, Hemingway,
Faulkner, Wolfe, Farrell, Caldwell, Marquand, and Steinbeck. These authors,
says Beach, wrote in the shadow of two wars, and consequently shared an
unsettled tone, social concern, and a "negative idealism"--implicit standards and optimism in opposition to the worlds they depict.

L 216. **BEACH, JOSEPH WARREN.** Obsessive Images: Symbolism in Poetry of
the 1930's and 1940's. Edited by William Van O'Connor. Minneapolis: University of Minnesota Press, 1960. 396 pp.
This unfinished work offers a detailed analysis of rhetoric in American
poetry of the 1930s and 1940s. At the beginning, Beach speculates on
why certain words and images (terror, geography, travel, and the hero)
appear and examines their occurrence. His work is based on the overwhelming influence of such poets as Eliot, Yeats, Crane, and Stevens. Later
chapters move away from "obsessive images" toward poets' themes and social
attitudes; here Beach reveals his own "secular humanism." Finally, he
explains his brief treatment of Robinson, Pound, Frost, Sandburg, and
the Imagists.

L 217. BEIDLER, PHILIP. American Literature and the Experience of Vietnam.
         Athens: University of Georgia Press, 1982. 220 pp.
Analyzing fiction and non-fiction alike, Beidler defines ways authors
have contributed to the collective myth of Vietnam. He examines the work
of Tim O'Brien, Philip Caputo, Ron Kovic, Norman Mailer, William Eastlake,
and others. These authors share a concern both with detailing exactly
how an event felt and with an event's potential mythical signification.
This mythology of Vietnam offers its own unique images, but one can locate
its antecedents in American classical literature and in recent popular
culture. Beidler briefly defines the connections between the writings
of Mather, Cooper, Melville, and Mark Twain and the writings of the Vietnam authors. He then traces the development of "new modes of sense-making"
through three time periods—1958-1970, 1970-1975, and 1975-1981.

L 218. BENTLEY, ERIC. The Dramatic Event: An American Chronicle. New
         York: Horizon Press, 1954. 278 pp.
Bentley views the theater of the early 1950s from a drama critic's viewpoint: the critic "tells you what the show is, argues the pros and cons
of it in a series of observations and counter-observations, and announces
if, in his opinion, the whole thing is any good." The critic assumes
this stance as he reviews over fifty American productions of English,
European, and American plays—including works by Eugene O'Neill, Truman
Capote, Lillian Hellman, Tennessee Williams, and T. S. Eliot. Bentley
adds an estimation of the state of contemporary theater and observations
on the means of production.

L 219. BERNSTEIN, MICHAEL ANDRE. The Tale of the Tribe: Ezra Pound and
         the Modern Verse Epic. Princeton, N.J.: Princeton University
         Press, 1980. 320 pp.
Bernstein starts with Pound's challenge to the seeming impossibility of
reconciling the three terms of the subtitle, "modern," "verse," and "epic,"
by attempting in the Cantos to write "a long poem including history,"
which would, after the manner of classical epic, articulate solutions,
through moral exempla, to the historical and social needs of an entire
"tribe" or polis. Bernstein then explicates and evaluates Pound's Cantos,
William Carlos Williams's Paterson, and Charles Olson's Maximus Poems
as expressions of this explicitly epic intention, and elucidates the paradox of the modern epic bard, attentive to both material and ideal history,
both the larger archetype and the particular local reality.

L 220. BERNSTEIN, SAMUEL J. The Strands Entwined: A New Direction in
         American Drama. Boston: Northeastern University Press, 1980.
         158 pp.
The "strands" of the title are American Naturalistic/Realistic and European
Absurdist theater, as they figure in plays of the late 1960s and early
1970s. Rabe's Sticks and Bones, Guare's The House of Blue Leaves, Bullin's
The Taking of Miss Janie, Anderson's Double-Solitaire, and Albee's Seascape
each receive a chapter which begins with a review of the criticism of
that play, then locates it within the body of the author's work. Next,
each discussion centers on the play in performance, and considers its
Absurdist and Naturalistic elements. The initial and final chapters give
an overview of modern American drama and argue for the value and interrelatedness of these works.

L 221. BERTHOFF, WARNER. A Literature Without Qualities: American Writing
         Since 1945. Berkeley: University of California Press, 1979.
         204 pp.
Berthoff studies the writing of Thomas Pynchon, John Barth, Joseph Heller,
Wallace Stevens, and Henry Miller to identify the historical character
of American writing since the 1940s and to highlight the elusive nature
of creativity in modern American culture. Literature readily recreates

a multitude of shared human experiences and values. American literature thus expresses the collective representations and shared ideas of American society. Berthoff pursues the "mythic promise no rising generation has failed to assert." He searches for more than writings destined to stand the test of time, seeking to discover the logic and imaginative strength through which new literary creations emerge.

L 222. BIGSBY, C. W. E. Confrontation and Commitment: A Study of Con-
temporary American Drama, 1959-1966. Columbia: University of
Missouri Press, 1968. 187 pp.
In his introduction, Bigsby establishes the difference between the theater of the absurd (which views man as "impotent and despairing") and the theater of confrontation (which holds that martyrdom and redemption are possible, and that man's impotence and despair are of his own making). In addition, he argues that American theater from 1959 to 1966 may be divided into two categories: the drama of confrontation and the drama of social and racial commitment. Bigsby first examines the work of dramatists of confrontation such as Arthur Miller, Jack Gelber, and Edward Albee; he then discusses dramatists of commitment, including Lorraine Hansberry, LeRoi Jones, and James Baldwin. This work both synthesizes contemporary drama and criticizes the work of individual playwrights.

L 223. BIGSBY, C. W. E. A Critical Introduction to Twentieth Century
American Drama: Volume 1: 1900-1940. New York: Cambridge Uni-
versity Press, 1982. 342 pp.
Bigsby asserts that the 20th century marks the beginning of American drama as a serious art form. The emergence of the playwright and director as the dominant forces of the drama, as opposed to the actor, is a 20th-century phenomenon. Bigsby studies the themes as well as the theater groups and playwrights of the early 1900s in a series of essays. Included in this collection are studies of the Provincetown Players, Eugene O'Neill, The Theatre Guild, Clifford Odets and the Group Theatre, Left-wing Theater, The Federal Theatre and the Living Newspaper, Black Drama, Thornton Wilder, and Lillian Hellman.

L 224. BILIK, DOROTHY SEIDMAN. Immigrant-Survivors: Post-Holocaust Con-
sciousness in Recent Jewish American Fiction. Middletown, Conn.:
Wesleyan University Press, 1981. 207 pp.
Bilik argues against the assertions of critics--Robert Alter, Leslie Fiedler, Allen Guttmann--who look only at the Jewish American novels of assimilation written by and about second- or third-generation Jews and claim that Jewish American fiction is on its way to extinction. She points to the reappearance of immigrants in works that represent "the delayed expression by Jewish American writers of a post-Holocaust consciousness." Arguing that these immigrant-survivor novels form a "recognizable subgenre of Jewish American literature," Bilik examines closely the work of six writers: Bernard Malamud, Edward Wallant, Susan Fromberg Schaeffer, I. B. Singer, Saul Bellow, and Arthur Cohen. The protagonists she discusses are, according to her, in America not of America--philosophical "loners" who are more concerned with the tragic past of Jews than with present success and assimilation.

L 225. BLACKMUR, R. P. The Double Agent: Essays in Craft and Elucidation.
New York: Arrow, 1935. 302 pp.
In his criticism Blackmur focuses on the relation between content and form, or what he calls "the establishment and appreciation of human or moral values." This value lies in the artist's formal, arranged presentation of meaning in life. In this collection of essays, all but two previously published, he applies these principles to the work of e. e. cummings, Ezra Pound, Wallace Stevens, Hart Crane, Marianne Moore, T. S. Eliot, and Henry James; and to the criticism of Granville Hicks, Kenneth Burke, and I. A. Richards.

L 226. BLACKMUR, R. P. Language as Gesture: Essays in Poetry. New York:
        Harcourt, Brace, 1952. 440 pp.
Blackmur asserts that all arts presume gesture; thus analogies to painting
and dance help to illuminate language, that is, poetry. Verbal analysis
can show how poetic language incorporates physical or emotional actions.
While some gestures condense poetic meaning, others expand it. From the
view of poetic art, Blackmur explains and defends some modern poets:
Eliot, Pound, and Stevens. But some moderns, like Dickinson and Hart
Crane, are difficult because the poets have exercised no rational art.
Although much of his criticism depends on close verbal analyses, Blackmur
occasionally discusses the moral values underlying modern poetry.

L 227. BLACKMUR, R. P. The Lion and the Honeycomb: Essays in Solicitude
        and Critique. New York: Harcourt, Brace, 1955. 309 pp.
Blackmur gathers here seventeen essays written between 1935 and 1955.
His subjects include Herman Melville, Henry Adams, and Henry James; modern
criticism and aesthetic theory; contemporary culture and the humanities.
Blackmur emphasizes the importance of aesthetic form and moral value,
and his essays therefore often combine literary analysis with criticism
of modern American life.

L 228. BLAKE, NELSON MANFRED. Novelists' America: Fiction as History,
        1910-1940. Syracuse, N.Y.: Syracuse University Press, 1969.
        271 pp.
Noting that the historian can turn to documents written by articulate
people for "official" history, Blake proposes that turning to works of
the imagination enables the social historian to learn something of the
history of the inarticulate people, and he justifies turning to fiction
by arguing that the "disciplined creations" of novelists contain substantial "components of reality." He discusses works by eight authors who
came to maturity during the period 1910-1940: Wolfe, Lewis, Fitzgerald,
Faulkner, Steinbeck, Dos Passos, Farrell, and Wright. This period, Blake
explains, forms a distinct epoch during which American innocence came
to an end and a new "urbanized, sophisticated, yet troubled" society arose.
In his discussion of these authors' lives and works, he claims to provide
neither literary criticism nor history, but merely the "material for history."

L 229. BLOTNER, JOSEPH. The Modern American Political Novel, 1900-1960.
        Austin: University of Texas Press, 1966. 424 pp.
Blotner's goal is "to discover the image of American politics presented
in American novels of the sixty-year span from 1900 through 1960" and
to evaluate the aesthetic quality of those novels. He employs Jungian
psychology, particularly the archetype of the hero, to connect these many
different works. The book includes discussions of a formidable number
(138) of overlooked novels and traces the parallels between American politics and literature. It attempts to examine the complex relationship
between the different realms of experience, both cultural and aesthetic.
"The reader may find in the novelist's work another conception of truth
in this area of human experience," Blotner writes, "a view which—Aristotle
claimed—goes beyond the particular to the universal . . . the best of
these distillations will offer some further understanding of the American
political experience."

L 230. BOGAN, LOUISE. Achievement in American Poetry, 1900-1950. Chicago:
        Regnery, 1951. 157 pp.
Bogan feels that by 1900 American poetry was dominated by genteel morality
and bourgeois craving for comfort and entertainment. Artists thus had
to attack traditional taste and technique before they could write. Early
in the century poets could survive by living in Bohemian or academic isolation. Later developments—such as George Santayana's Harvard classes,

the little magazines (Mencken's Smart Set, Harriet Monroe's Poetry, The Little Review, and The Dial), and European influences (Serge Diaghilev's Ballet Russe, Ibsen's drama, and the prose of Joyce, Proust, and Mann)-- enabled American poets to flourish. The growth of informed criticism and the further incorporation of European standards solidified the triumph over hypocrisy in American poetry.

L 231. BOGARDUS, RALPH F. and FRED HOBSON, eds. Literature at the Barricades: The American Writer in the 1930's. University: University of Alabama Press, 1982. 227 pp.
This book of essays had its beginning in a symposium on "The American Writer in the 1930's" held in Alabama in October 1978. The 1930s, according to the editors, caused Americans to question the American Dream more seriously than ever before. Artists became politically conscious; literary Naturalism experienced a rebirth. Yet Modernist experimentation did not cease altogether. The essays in this collection focus, to varying degrees, on the dilemma faced by intellectuals in the 1930s: how to reconcile Modernism and the realities of the Depression. Contributors include Daniel Aaron, James T. Farrell, Josephine Herbst, Irving Howe, Hugh Kenner, Townsend Ludington, Donald Pizer, and Louis D. Rubin, Jr. Farrell's and Herbst's pieces (written earlier, not for the symposium), as well as Howe's, deal with the era as a whole. Major figures discussed in the other essays include Dos Passos, John Howard Lawson, Farrell, Steinbeck, Wright, Agee, Harriette Arnow, Oppen, Zukofsky, Edmund Wilson, intellectuals associated with the Partisan Review, and Southern, Depression-era writers.

L 232. BOYNTON, PERCY H. America in Contemporary Fiction. Chicago: University of Chicago Press, 1940. 274 pp.
In an opening chapter entitled, "Changing Values," Boynton writes: "Up to now the people have always had something to believe in, and from time to time some one to look to as an embodiment of that belief: the power of faith, the power of social efficiency, the power of manifest destiny, the power of a righteous existing order. A reading of representative American novelists reveals at length the quandary in which America finds itself." The novelists Boynton then considers include Hergesheimer, Cabell, Anderson, Dreiser, Cather, Lewis, Dos Passos, Wolfe, Rolvaag, and Steinbeck. Although several of the essays originally appeared in other volumes, seven are here printed for the first time.

L 233. BRADBURY, JOHN M. The Fugitives: A Critical Account. Chapel Hill: University of North Carolina Press, 1958. 300 pp.
Bradbury's study, which avoids biographical hypotheses and attempts rather to adhere to "organic" aesthetic criteria, is "an attempt to set the Fugitive group as a whole in its proper historical place, and to indicate the nature of the contributions which each has made thus far to our literary heritage." He thus supplies an overview of the group's work through 1956 and an individual assessment of the achievements in poetry, fiction, and criticism of John Crowe Ransom, Allen Tate, and Robert Penn Warren. Bradbury's work is particularly useful as a literary history; he analyzes the philosophical and cultural genesis of the Fugitives and follows their influence on modern aesthetic formalism.

L 234. BRADBURY, MALCOLM. The Modern American Novel. New York: Oxford University Press, 1983. 186 pp.
A survey of the American novel from the 1890s to the present, this study treats the novel as a product of the culture and distinct history out of which it is created, and offers a comparative examination of the genre itself, emphasizing the important changes and "recoveries" it has undergone in "American hands." Bradbury attempts to define and trace the major movements in American fiction. He pays particular attention to the cultural, social, and intellectual factors that influenced the rise of the

novel in the U.S., and outlines the relation of the American novel to its European counterpart.

L 235. BRUSS, PAUL. Victims: Textual Strategies in Recent American Fiction. Lewisburg, Pa.: Bucknell University Press, 1981. 238 pp.
Bruss treats the responses of Vladimir Nabokov, Donald Barthelme, and Jerzy Kosinski to what he defines as the problems of modern fiction: chief among these problems are the victimization of the author, reader, or text by language; and repression by the conventions of fiction. Bruss stresses the importance of murder, or language as a kind of murder, in Kosinski's and Nabokov's fiction. Nabokov's interest in authorial problems, Barthelme's meditation on problems of text, and Kosinski's focus on the dilemmas of the perceiver, especially the reader as perceiver, dominate Bruss's discussion. Nabokov's Lolita, Pale Fire, and Ada, and Kosinski's Steps, Cockpit, and Blind Date are test cases, but the chapters he devotes to the authors begin with a general discussion of their whole corpus.

L 236. BUTTITTA, TONY and BARRY WITHAM. Uncle Sam Presents: A Memoir of the Federal Theatre, 1935-1939. Philadelphia: University of Pennsylvania Press, 1982. 249 pp.
Buttitta and Witham offer a personal account of the Works Progress Administration's (WPA) Federal Theatre Project. Buttitta, who worked as press agent, writer, and historian for the first Federally subsidized American theater, reflects upon the four years of the project's existence. Both he and Witham quote heavily from Arena, Hallie Flannigan's 1940 memoir of her life as director of the project. The volume contains a foreword by Malcolm Cowley and an introduction by Harold Clurman.

L 237. CAMBON, GLAUCO. The Inclusive Flame: Studies in American Poetry. Bloomington: Indiana University Press, 1963. 248 pp.
Cambon's work explores "the recurrent American endeavor to grasp a totality of experience through poetry." He sees American poets as being paradoxically free from, though also fettered to, European culture. Nineteenth-century American poets, especially Whitman and Dickinson, conveyed the sense of "virgin space and virgin time." American poets, having rejected the cultural burden of the past, were then obligated to make something of that seemingly unlimited potential. Chapter one covers the 19th-century poetic heritage, focusing on Whitman and Dickinson, while subsequent chapters individually discuss Edward Arlington Robinson, Wallace Stevens, Hart Crane, William Carlos Williams, and Robert Lowell as they reappropriated this cultural space.

L 238. CARGILL, OSCAR. Intellectual America: Ideas on the March. New York: Macmillan, 1941. 766 pp.
This volume provides an account of the European ideologies--"the invading forces"--that arrived in America during modern times (defined by Cargill as the period 1890-1940). Declaring the triumph of modern criticism to be the recognition of the difference between ideologies (culturally pervasive) and philosophies (personal), Cargill proposes a new discipline--ideodynamics, or the study of ideology. Ideodynamics, he claims, will avoid the oversimplifications of the history-of-ideas approach and will serve as a "disciplinarian to criticism." He then proceeds to identify and analyze the ideologies interacting in the American culture of his time: French Naturalism and Decadence, German Absolutism, English Liberalism, Primitivism, Intelligentsia movements, and Freudianism. Cargill claims that these ideologies helped to eliminate complacency and to prepare society for change.

L 239. CASEY, DANIEL J. and ROBERT E. RHODES, eds. Irish-American Fiction:
        Essays in Criticism. New York: AMS Press, 1979. 172 pp.
The editors have sought to compile a comprehensive study of Irish-American
writing by selecting essays on a diverse array of representative writers.
The only editorial stipulation is that the writer show awareness of his
or her Irish identity (hence the concentration on Irish-Catholic authors).
Finley Peter Dunne, F. Scott Fitzgerald, and James T. Farrell are perhaps
the best known. The eight other essays include an overview of Irish
stereotypes and an examination of women writers in Irish-American fiction.
The book also features a 170-page bibliography of over fifty authors,
with selected criticism included.

L 240. CHARNEY, MAURICE. Sexual Fiction. New York: Methuen, 1981.
        180 pp.
Charney attempts to answer the question of how and why sexual fiction
succeeds by focusing on the conventions and innovations of thirteen novels
commonly labeled pornographic. Pornography, as Charney defines it, is
"all narrative material that makes important and open use of sexual activity as its subject matter." It is a fictional genre, or subgenre, similar
to science fiction, whose primary concerns were established by the Marquis
de Sade and then elaborated by such authors as Pauline Reage, Jean de
Berg, "Walter," Erica Jong, Philip Roth, D. H. Lawrence, Vladimir Nabokov,
Henry Miller, Gael Greene, Terry Southern, and John Cleland.

L 241. CHRISTIAN, BARBARA. Black Women Novelists: The Development of
        a Tradition, 1892-1976. Westport, Conn.: Greenwood Press, 1980.
        268 pp.
Christian's book is divided into two parts. In the first, she presents
a brief history of the image of the black woman in literature from 1892,
through the years of the Harlem Renaissance, to the 1940s and 1950s, when
the element of protest entered into black women's writing—when these
writers began to create characters who were ordinary women. In the second
part of the book, she examines closely the novels of three contemporary
black women: Paule Marshall, Toni Morrison, and Alice Walker. Christian
argues that contemporary black women novelists respond to stereotypes
of the black woman (the mammy, the loose woman, the tragic mulatta) by
attempting their own definition of woman rather than creating countertypes
as earlier writers did, and that the theme of the black woman's frustrated
creative self informs these contemporary novels.

L 242. CLURMAN, HAROLD. The Fervent Years: The Story of the Group Theatre
        and the Thirties. New York: Knopf, 1945. 298 pp.
Clurman asserts that the Group Theatre, actively producing plays from
1931 to 1941, was an enormously important social and intellectual experiment as well as the source of some of the best dramatic productions in
American theatrical history. He tells the history of this experiment—
in which he participated as a founder, director, and producer—and shows
the idealism which perhaps doomed it from the start but which explains
the nostalgia with which it is still remembered by the participants.

L 243. COFFMAN, STANLEY K., Jr. Imagism: A Chapter for the History of
        Modern Poetry. Norman: University of Oklahoma Press, 1951.
        235 pp.
Imagism is a study of the theory and practice of that group of American
and British poets "who, between 1912 and 1917, joined in reaction against
the careless technique and extra-poetic values of much nineteenth-century
verse." The central figures—F. S. Flint, Ezra Pound, Amy Lowell, H.
D., John Gould Fletcher, and Richard Aldington—are discussed in terms
of their own work and their relation to affiliated movements like Futurism,
Impressionism, and Vorticism. This literary history suggests, too, how
other poets (especially Frost, Williams, and Eliot) found Imagism useful
then finally confining.

L 244. COHEN, SARAH B., ed. Comic Relief: Humor in Contemporary American
       Literature. Urbana: University of Illinois Press, 1978. 339 pp.
This volume contains sixteen essays by various critics on literary humor
of the 1950s, 1960s, and 1970s in the writings of John Barth, Mary McCarthy,
Ralph Ellison, Edward Albee, Thomas Pynchon, and others; on humor of the
South in Flannery O'Connor, William Faulkner, and Erskine Caldwell; on
Jewish humor in Saul Bellow and Philip Roth; on humor in the poetry of
John Berryman, John Crowe Ransom, Karl Shapiro, Richard Wilbur, and others;
and on cosmic irony in the science fiction of William Tenn, Robert Sheckley,
Frederick Pohl, C. M. Kornbluth, and Kurt Vonnegut, Jr.

L 245. COHN, RUBY. Dialogue in American Drama. Bloomington: Indiana
       University Press, 1971. 340 pp.
Cohn's point of departure is the "pervasive mistrust of language" which
she finds in contemporary theater; it leads her to a close examination
of language in the plays of Eugene O'Neill, Arthur Miller, Tennessee
Williams, and Edward Albee--"the few American playwrights who seem to me
to have written original and distinctive dramatic dialogue." Two long
later chapters are devoted to dramatic experiments of 20th-century fiction
writers and poets.

L 246. CONN, PETER. The Divided Mind: Ideology and Imagination in America,
       1898-1917. New York: Cambridge University Press, 1983. 358 pp.
In this study of American culture from the turn of the century to W.W.
I, Conn stresses the divided consciousness which makes up the temper of
the times: "A revolution was occurring, but one that provoked and met
a counterrevolutionary reply." His examination of this dialectic takes
the form of chapters not only on the literary works of Henry James, Jack
London, Kate Chopin, W. E. B. Du Bois, Ellen Glasgow, and Edith Wharton,
but also on nonliterary figures such as Booker T. Washington, Frank Lloyd
Wright, Charles Ives, Alfred Stieglitz, and Emma Goldman.

L 247. CONNOLLY, CYRIL. Previous Convictions. New York: Harper & Row,
       1963. 414 pp.
Of the four sections into which the essays of this collection are divided,
only one--entitled "The Modern Movement"--deals extensively with American
writers. The essays are brief, written in response to the publication
of letters or essays (Ezra Pound's essays, Yeats's letters); biographies
(Edel's of Henry James, Brinnin's of Gertrude Stein, Mizener's and
Turnbull's of F. Scott Fitzgerald); critical works (Hugh Kenner's book on
Eliot); novels (Ernest Hemingway's Across the River and Into the Trees,
Budd Schulberg's The Disenchanted); and one memoir (Sylvia Beach's).
Connolly also includes pieces written about Hemingway and e. e. cummings
at the time of their deaths.

L 248. CONRAD, PETER. Imagining America. New York: Oxford University
       Press, 1980. 319 pp.
Conrad believes that America is so diverse and accommodating that it is
like a vessel whose contents are first imagined and then found and placed
inside. To substantiate this thesis, the author examines the lives of
twelve Englishmen in America and shows how each discovered "truths to
sustain any fiction." He begins with Victorian imaginative constructs
of landscape and society, and concludes with analyses of how Lawrence,
Huxley, Auden, and Isherwood created private, spiritual worlds for themselves. The continual rediscoveries of America increasingly became discoveries of the self.

L 249. COOK, BRUCE. The Beat Generation. New York: Scribner, 1971.
248 pp.
This chronicle of the phenomenon of the Beats begins with the meeting
of Jack Kerouac and Allen Ginsberg in 1945 and ends with the Woodstock
rock festival in 1969. Part memoir, part cultural history, The Beat Generation claims a vast significance for the Beats as it deals in particular
with the life and work of Ginsberg, Kerouac, Gregory Corso, William
Burroughs, John Clellon Holmes, Michael McClure, Gary Snyder, and Robert
Duncan. Buttressed by evidence of the Beats' public antics and various
reactions to them--Diana Trilling's, for example, amid the Columbia milieu--
Cook assesses their significance in terms of a long tradition of American
cultural dissent.

L 250. COOK, SYLVIA JENKINS. From Tobacco Road to Route 66: The Southern
Poor White in Fiction. Chapel Hill: University of North Carolina
Press, 1976. 208 pp.
Cook tells the history of a prominent folk figure and examines its use
by 20th-century American writers. The "poor white" tradition, whose
development begins in the 18th century, produces a stereotype which novel-
ists of the 1930s adopt to make political, economic, and social statements.
Thus, the "poor white" figures centrally in indictments of the modern
South and American culture made by William Faulkner, James Agee, and John
Steinbeck. Cook also argues that this folk tradition was widely used
by writers of proletarian fiction, such as Mary Heaton Vorse, Fielding
Burke, Myra Page, Grace Lumpkin, Sherwood Anderson, and William Rollins.

L 251. COOPERMAN, STANLEY. World War I and the American Novel. Baltimore,
Md.: Johns Hopkins University Press, 1967. 271 pp.
Cooperman's book "represents an attempt to view literature as a dynamic
'echo of meaning' within and part of a cultural process." For the writers
of the 1920s, the cultural process of the war became an adventurous Great
Crusade against reactionary society. The failure of that Crusade produced
the cultural alienation of the heroes and anti-heroes of Dos Passos,
Hemingway, Faulkner, and e. e. cummings. Cooperman discusses numerous
writers and critics, including Willa Cather, James Stevens, Granville
Hicks, and Archibald MacLeish.

L 252. COWAN, LOUISE. The Fugitive Group: A Literary History. Baton
Rouge: Louisiana State University Press, 1959. 277 pp.
The Fugitives, a group of sixteen poets living and publishing in Nashville
in the 1920s, developed a body of poetry expressing the literary ideals
of their Southern society. The leading members (John Crowe Ransom, Robert
Penn Warren, Allen Tate, and Donald Davidson) valued classical learning,
"a code of manners and morals, with its underlying gentilesse," oral traditions, and poetic form (particularly allegory). Cowan's study chronologically traces the group from their initial discussions at Vanderbilt
University in 1903 to the final issue of the Fugitive magazine in 1925
and the appearance of their anthology in 1928. The work, based on Cowan's
doctoral dissertation, is extensively annotated and includes an appendix
listing the contents of the magazine.

L 253. COWLEY, MALCOLM. The Dream of the Golden Mountains: Remembering
the 30's. New York: Viking Press, 1980. 317 pp.
Cowley takes up the thread of Exile's Return (see L 254), but in this
volume is more interested in social events and the desire of many 1930s
writers to form a revolutionary brotherhood, the "dream" of the title.
In following the changes at The New Republic, Cowley also attempts to
trace the changes in national mood. His discussions include a consideration of the rise and waning of the Communist Party, labor strikes, the
Bonus Army, Roosevelt's early days as President, The New Masses, Partisan
Review, proletarian literature, and Marxist criticism. He examines the

work of such authors as Theodore Dreiser, Hart Crane, Clifford Odets, John Cheever, Mary McCarthy, Muriel Rukeyser, and Eleanor Clark.

L 254. COWLEY, MALCOLM. Exile's Return: A Literary Odyssey of the Nineteen Twenties. New York: Norton, 1934. 322 pp.
Cowley asserts that the "Lost Generation" (Hemingway, Fitzgerald, Dos Passos, et al.) shared a detachment from native values as a result of years at college and in the war, travel in foreign lands, adventures abroad and at home, and the return to America. After the war the aesthetic rebels returned to New York City but shared little with the political radicals there. Traveling to Paris, they encountered Eliot, Joyce, Proust, and the French symbolists, who were briefly intriguing but finally unsatisfactory models. So the Americans returned to New York, where they edited magazines and fought the literary establishment. Most eventually became disenchanted with city life and sought to isolate themselves by moving from commercial society on to farms. Hart Crane and Harry Crosby, both of whom committed suicide, best represent this sense of isolation and alienation.

L 255. COWLEY, MALCOLM. The Literary Situation. 1954; Rev. ed. New York: Viking Press, 1966. 259 pp.
Cowley conceives of his book as "a social history of the literature of our times." As such, it takes a general look at whole categories of books—war novels, the "new" fiction, and the new criticism—and at the common qualities of each group. In addition, it surveys the writing profession, the publishing business in its present transitional period, and the effect of publishing changes on fictional and poetic types. Cowley's final chapter describes changes in American life that are likely to produce a different literature from a new generation of writers in the future.

L 256. COWLEY, MALCOLM. A Second Flowering: Works and Days of the Lost Generation. New York: Viking Press, 1973. 276 pp.
Born between 1894 and 1900, eight writers—Fitzgerald, Hemingway, Dos Passos, Cummings, Wilder, Faulkner, Wolfe, and Hart Crane—shared similar experiences produced by the horror of W.W. I and its aftermath. Cowley notes that, though profoundly moral writers, they did not respond in similar ways to their frantic world. Some left America for France. Some, like Cummings, revolted against the literary establishment; others, like Crane, suffered personal anguish. Moving between personal reminiscence and stylistic analysis, Cowley's essays demonstrate the cultural coherence of eight major writers of the Lost Generation.

L 257. COWLEY, MALCOLM. Think Back on Us: A Contemporary Chronicle of the 1930's by Malcolm Cowley. Edited by Henry Dan Piper. Carbondale: Southern Illinois University Press, 1967. 400 pp.
The volume gathers Cowley's essays written in the 1930s when he was literary editor of The New Republic. The two sections—"The Social Record" and "The Literary Record"—are arranged chronologically and include Cowley's remarks on the Bonus Army, Communism, and the Writers' Congress, as well as his literary evaluations of e. e. cummings, Dos Passos, Fitzgerald, Faulkner, Richard Wright, and others.

L 258. COWLEY, MALCOLM, ed. After the Genteel Tradition: American Writers Since 1910. New York: Norton, 1937. 270 pp.
Cowley identifies a turning point between the genteel generation of Howells, Richard Gilder, and Henry Van Dyke, and the more turbulent generation of Dreiser, O'Neill, Cather, et al. Fourteen essays on fifteen different writers attempt to place each author in a historical context. Dos Passos, Hemingway, and Thomas Wolfe are the latest to be considered. The postscript defines and describes the general tendencies of the post-Howells writers: populism, realism, a cosmopolitan sophistication, and what Cowley terms "carnal mysticism."

L 259. CRAIG, E. QUINTA. Black Drama and the Federal Theatre Era: Beyond the Formal Horizons. Amherst: University of Massachusetts Press, 1980. 239 pp.
In 1935, the Federal Theatre Project was launched by the Works Project Administration. Craig asserts that in 1974 a wealth of new material on the Federal Theatre Project was uncovered, revealing a great deal concerning the Negro Units of The Federal Theatre. This new documentation forms the basis of her study, which also involves analysis of the unknown contributions of many black playwrights, directors, actors, and productions.

L 260. DARDIS, TOM. Some Time in the Sun. 1976; Rev. ed. New York: Penguin Books, 1981. 297 pp.
Dardis accounts for the portions of their lives that F. Scott Fitzgerald, William Faulkner, Nathanael West, Aldous Huxley, and James Agee spent in Hollywood writing filmscripts. He begins by claiming that biographers—of Fitzgerald and Faulkner, in particular—have glossed over, in embarrassment, these writers' Hollywood years. Granting that the money attracted and kept them there, Dardis nevertheless argues that these writers were unfairly accused of having become "hacks." He asserts that their filmwriting (some of which he discusses in the biographical essays) is, with the exception of West's routine genre films, of "lasting interest."

L 261. DAVIDSON, DONALD. Still Rebels, Still Yankees and Other Essays. Baton Rouge: Louisiana State University Press, 1957. 284 pp.
The seventeen occasional essays gathered here "are mostly concerned with the impact of the modern regime" and "the response of tradition to that impact, in the arts and in society," especially in the South. Founder of The Fugitive, and contributor to I'll Take My Stand (see L 318), Davidson continues with some of the preoccupations of his earlier The Attack on Leviathan (1938), and represents the often conservative and agrarian traditions which flowered at Vanderbilt University in the 1920s and 1930s.

L 262. DEMBO, L. S. Conceptions of Reality in Modern American Poetry. Berkeley: University of California Press, 1966. 248 pp.
Certain 20th-century poets, like Eliot, Pound, Stevens, and Hart Crane, assumed that the artist possesses not only a unique mode of perception but a special knowledge of reality. Dembo argues that, because their poetry is analogous to aesthetics and epistemology, their poems can be illuminated by the philosophical work of Hulme and Bergson. These poets believe in a transcendent reality, which conventional reasoning cannot apprehend. By internalizing objective reality through myth and language, they express their faith in and the beauty of an ultimate reality.

L 263. DICKEY, JAMES. Babel to Byzantium: Poets and Poetry Now. New York: Farrar, Straus, & Giroux, 1968. 296 pp.
Dickey, a contemporary American poet, here gathers his analyses and evaluations of sixty-eight modern poets and, under the heading "The Poet Turns on Himself," offers a consideration of five poems and three essays. These pieces are brief, personal evaluations, guided by what Dickey calls "some intuitive, mysterious, and perhaps subliminal" consistency of judgment.

L 264. DOWNER, ALAN S. Fifty Years of American Drama, 1900-1950. Chicago: Regnery, 1951. 158 pp.
Downer writes not about the literature of the theater but about plays and their performances. He is interested in the play as product: "where it came from, how it developed, and where it arrived." This study discusses theatrical production; popular plays which have faded in reputation; significant producers, directors, and companies; and the merging of various forms in the shaping of the modern American theater.

L 265. DUFFEY, BERNARD. The Chicago Renaissance in American Letters:
        A Critical History. East Lansing: Michigan State University
        Press, 1954. 286 pp.
The rise of Chicago as a literary center began in the 1880s with the newspaper writings of Eugene Field and Finley Peter Dunne and with the fiction
of Henry Blake Fuller. Two strains then emerged: the genteel tradition
of the Dial magazine and "The Little Room" meetings; and the realism of
Hamlin Garland, Joseph Kirkland, Will Payne, and William Vaughan Moody.
Duffey also studies later writers such as Robert Herrick, Edgar Lee Masters,
Sherwood Anderson, Carl Sandburg, and Vachel Lindsay, all of whom wrote
in, and often of, Chicago before the city lost much of its literary
eminence in the mid-1920s.

L 266. EARNEST, ERNEST. The Single Vision: The Alienation of American
        Intellectuals. New York: New York University Press, 1970.
        241 pp.
Earnest's subject is the American literary renaissance of 1910 to 1930;
his thesis is that "certain limitations of vision shared by writers between
1910 and 1930 produced distortions in our literature for a long time."
According to Earnest, these novelists (Dreiser, Hemingway, Faulkner),
dramatists (O'Neill), and poets (Eliot, Frost, Stevens) expressed a common
theme which has overwhelmed American literature: the alienation of the
sensitive intellectual from the cultural wasteland of modern America.

L 267. EBERHART, RICHARD. Of Poetry and Poets. Urbana: University of
        Illinois Press, 1979. 312 pp.
This volume is made up of previously published pieces--essays on poetry
in general or on particular poets, various interviews in which Eberhart
was the interviewee, and speeches. The essays, though not a systematic
study, give us one poet's reflections upon the place of poetry within
our culture ("Poetry is in the center of life.") and upon poets (mostly
Americans) of the 20th century. Eberhart was acquainted personally with
most of the poets about whom he writes: Stevens, Auden, Frost, Roethke,
Jarrell, Cummings, and others. Stating in one essay that "Poetry may
not change the fate of nations," Eberhart writes in another, "What we
need now is a poetry of the people, a poetry to represent the wilderness
of new feelings we have in this turbulent time [post-Watergate]." James
Dickey has written a foreword for the book.

L 268. EISINGER, CHESTER E. Fiction of the Forties. Chicago: University
        of Chicago Press, 1963. 392 pp.
Eisinger claims that "fiction, during the forties, was the chief and best
way to achieve" self-knowledge, and spends much of his introductory chapter
defining the characteristic moral and ethical searches of the decade as
displayed in fiction. The book is divided into chapters titled "The War
Novel"; "Naturalism: The Tactics of Survival"; "Fiction and the Liberal
Reassessment"; "The Conservative Imagination"; "The New Fiction"; and
"In Search of Man and Americans," in which Eisinger discusses the "existential crisis" in the fiction of the period.

L 269. FABRE, GENEVIEVE. Drumbeats, Masks, and Metaphor: Contemporary
        Afro-American Theatre. Translated by Melvin Dixon. Cambridge,
        Mass.: Harvard University Press, 1983. 274 pp.
Fabre's basic assumption is that black drama since 1945 must be examined
as a socio-cultural phenomenon. In the first section, she outlines the
historical precedents and theoretical foundations of the New Black Theater,
placing special emphasis on the social and cultural context of its creation.
She divides contemporary black drama into two categories: the militant
theater of protest and the ethnic theater of black experience. The second
section of this volume defines and discusses the militant theater which,
according to Fabre, is didactic in nature and rejects the authority of

white images, metaphors, or "masks" as definitions of black ethnic identity. Militant playwrights discussed include Amiri Baraka, Douglas Turner Ward, Ted Shine, Ben Caldwell, and Sonia Sanchez. The theater of experience is characterized here as a celebration of separate and rich black culture, and is usually presented as "a dialogue in the language of blacks about their own experiences." Playwrights in this category are James Baldwin, Ed Bullins, Melvin Van Peebles, Edgar White, and Ernest J. Gaines. Fabre concludes with a more general discussion of the relation between theater and culture.

L 270. FISCH, HAROLD. The Dual Image: The Figure of the Jew in English and American Literature. New York: KTAV Publishing House, 1971. 149 pp.
Using Coleridge's dual image of the Jew as both Isaiah and Levi of Holywell Street--"both noble and ignoble, black and white"--Fisch surveys the literary archetype of the Jew from the medieval period to contemporary America and Israel. Although many of the authors he examines are not American (e.g., Shakespeare, George Eliot, Joyce), that work provides the necessary background for a study of Jewish characters and authors in America (Saul Bellow, Henry Roth, Bernard Malamud, Karl Shapiro). "The Jew," according to the author, "is inevitably a figure of polarity, of radical ambiguity." As a result, the author argues that the contradictions of this archetype have become "paradigms for a universal reality" in a modern world--whose characteristic literary mode is tragicomedy.

L 271. FRENCH, WARREN. The Social Novel at the End of an Era. Carbondale: Southern Illinois University Press, 1966. 212 pp.
French defines the social novel as "a work that is so related to some specific historic phenomena that a detailed knowledge of the historical situations is essential to a full understanding of the novel at the same time that the artist's manipulation of his materials provides an understanding of why the historical events involved occurred." His central texts are Faulkner's The Hamlet, Steinbeck's The Grapes of Wrath, and Hemingway's For Whom the Bell Tolls. He also discusses work by Dalton Trumbo, Elgin Groseclose, Richard Wright, Pietro di Donato, and Robert Penn Warren.

L 272. FRENCH, WARREN, ed. The Fifties: Fiction, Poetry, Drama. De Land, Fla.: Everett/Edwards, 1970. 316 pp.
This collection of original papers is organized around three long essays: the editor's "The Age of Salinger," Kingsley Widmer's "The Beat in the Rise of Populist Culture," and C. W. E. Bigsby's "From Protest to Paradox: The Black Writer at Mid-Century." This structure reflects the editor's belief that in the 1950s "'movements' mattered more than genres"; in this context the twenty-one critics study such authors as Bernard Malamud, Norman Mailer, Flannery O'Connor, Richard Eberhart, and Richard Wilbur.

L 273. FRENCH, WARREN, ed. The Forties: Fiction, Poetry, Drama. De Land, Fla.: Everett/Edwards, 1969. 330 pp.
These twenty-four essays (with an eight-page bibliographic survey) by twenty-one different critics examine the effect of the war on the art of the period, general literary trends, "Highlights of the Decade," and individual authors such as Theodore Dreiser, Eudora Welty, Wallace Stevens, Eugene O'Neill, Rodgers and Hammerstein, Carson McCullers, Truman Capote, Tennessee Williams, and Robert Penn Warren.

L 274. FRENCH, WARREN, ed. The Thirties: Fiction, Poetry, Drama. De Land, Fla.: Everett/Edwards, 1967. 253 pp.
"This book," says the editor, "is an unsystematic introduction to the generally exciting American literature of a generally depressing decade." Opening with the stock market collapse in 1929 and closing with Hitler's

invasion of Poland, the decade produced "a triumphant literature" which
included novels by Hemingway, Wolfe, Steinbeck, West, and Faulkner; drama
by Maxwell Anderson and Odets; poetry by Pound, Stevens, and MacLeish.
Twenty-eight essays by twenty-three critics cover these and other topics.

L 275. FRIEDMAN, ALAN WARREN. Multivalence: The Moral Quality of Form
        in the Modern Novel. Baton Rouge: Louisiana State University
        Press, 1978. 215 pp.
"Multivalence" is Friedman's term for the elaborate and often complex
narrative strategies characteristic of modern fiction. He first establishes the primacy of multivalence in modern literature--discussing in
detail Henry Miller, William Faulkner, and four other modern masters--
and then moves on to his central concern, to defend multivalence from
the charge of ethical sloppiness. He insists that, in the hands of a
great writer, multivalence leads to "a multimoral, pluralistic flux in
which disparate and irreconcilable voices all claim (with varying degrees
of legitimacy) to speak with the rights and perquisites of authorial
privilege."

L 276. FROHOCK, W. M. The Novel of Violence in America: 1920-1950.
        1950; Rev. ed. Dallas, Tex.: Southern Methodist University Press,
        1957. 238 pp.
The novel of violence of Frohock's title is really the violent novel in
two manifestations. In the "novel of erosion," time is repetitive, weary-
ing, and defeating. In the "novel of destiny," time imposes a sense of
urgency where violence is "the characteristic mark of the human, and the
acts of violence are performed with great lucidity." Frohock studies
these two types in the fiction of Dos Passos, Wolfe, Farrell, Warren,
Caldwell, Steinbeck, Faulkner, Hemingway, and Agee.

L 277. FROHOCK, W. M. Strangers to This Ground: Cultural Diversity in
        Contemporary American Writing. Dallas, Tex.: Southern Methodist
        University Press, 1961. 180 pp.
Frohock's thesis has been sharpened by European complaints about American
sameness; he discovers "variety amid monotony" within our recent fiction
and advances his central thesis that "the image of the American hero of
our time is the image of a D.P. (displaced person)." "The experience
of moving from culture to culture" is a central American experience, as
is the inability of recent fictional characters to fit into the new culture.
In individual chapters, Frohock examines the poetry and fiction of Lionel
Trilling, F. Scott Fitzgerald, James Gould Cozzens, Edna St. Vincent Millay,
Emily Dickinson, Ezra Pound, and Jack Kerouac.

L 278. FULLER, EDMUND. Man in Modern Fiction: Some Minority Opinions
        on Contemporary American Writing. New York: Random House, 1958.
        171 pp.
The occasion for this book is Fuller's fear "that a corrupted and debased
image of man has become current and become influential through the per-
suasiveness and literary skills of some of its projectors." He is interested in "that image of man found in the Judeo-Christian tradition."
This view of man and the values which attend this view are "no guarantee
of literary merit," according to the author; but he is more interested
in this view's influence in the world. In response to his critics, the
author contends that his position is not a repressive one, and that "Jesus
Himself" rejected conventional morality and respectability; he champions
a "view of man," not a moral code.

L 279. GAGE, JOHN T. In the Arresting Eye: The Rhetoric of Imagism.
Baton Rouge: Louisiana State University Press, 1981. 188 pp.
Gage takes the poems published in Imagist anthologies from 1914 to 1917
as his primary sources, along with selected later anthologies in order
to represent Imagism's lesser figures and lesser known works. His discussion of their rhetoric accounts first for their manifestos and polemical
writings and extends that discussion to make general remarks about contemporary poetry. Gage refutes some attackers of Imagism, such as Yvor
Winters, and also criticizes the Imagists' own theory, which he feels
has hampered the reputation of their verse. Gage shows that despite their
hostility to "rhetoric" as they defined it, they made successful use of
its techniques.

L 280. GALLOWAY, DAVID D. The Absurd Hero in American Fiction: Updike,
Styron, Bellow, and Salinger. 1966; Rev. ed. Austin: University
of Texas Press, 1981. 265 pp.
Absurd literature in any form shares "the belief that human experience
is fragmented, irritating, apparently unredeemable." After defining the
absurd hero and how he is different in fiction than he is in drama,
Galloway turns to discussions of the Absurd Man in the fiction of four
writers: John Updike, William Styron, Saul Bellow, and J. D. Salinger.
The author's emphasis is on these writers who "can express despair without
succumbing to it," who identify absurdity in order to suggest paths of
integrity to help us through it. "Recognizing the discontinuity of much
modern experience," the writers under discussion "have seen man's plight
in terms of a continuous humanistic tradition" and so "can question and
deny the validity of traditional consolations without denying the traditions of the human spirit."

L 281. GARDINER, HAROLD C., ed. Fifty Years of the American Novel: A
Christian Appraisal. New York: Scribner, 1951. 304 pp.
This collection of essays brings together sixteen Catholic critics who
approach literature with a demand that the novelist face "man on his own
level." "It is only when the novelist approaches human nature on a sub-
human level," says the editor, "that the critic will protest that the
novel has become unhuman—and therefore, in a profound sense, irreligious."
The critics apply this standard to the works of Wharton, Dreiser, Glasgow,
Cather, Lewis, Marquand, Fitzgerald, Dos Passos, Faulkner, Hemingway,
Wolfe, Steinbeck, Farrell, Warren, and the novelists of W.W. II.

L 282. GARDNER, JOHN. On Moral Fiction. New York: Basic Books, 1978.
214 pp.
Gardner insists that "true art is by its nature moral. . . . It is not
didactic because, instead of teaching by authority and force, it explores,
open-mindedly, to learn what it should teach." He therefore indicts many
contemporary novelists (most notably Thomas Pynchon, John Updike, and
John Barth) for cynicism and amorality. Gardner argues strenuously for
clear moral purpose in fiction—that is, fiction which is life-affirming;
his work is a restatement of classic aesthetic principles in contemporary
American society. He argues that fiction writers must take note of audience and write more than self-reflexively; novels, he asserts, must affirm
the value of human life and provide models of how to live.

L 283. GASSNER, JOHN. Dramatic Soundings: Evaluations and Retractions
Culled from 30 Years of Dramatic Criticism. Edited by Glenn Loney.
New York: Crown, 1968. 716 pp.
Many of the pieces collected in this volume are New York Times reviews
by Gassner of individual productions (ranging from Broadway musicals to
plays by Tennessee Williams and Edward Albee); some are essays on world
theater (Shakespeare, Shaw, Ibsen, Strindberg) or dramatic theory and
practice and the state of modern theater. The essays date from 1935 to

1966. Gassner calls his volume "history more than criticism," subjective documentation more than objective evaluation.

L 284. GASSNER, JOHN. Theatre at the Crossroads: Plays and Playwrights of the Mid-Century American Stage. New York: Holt, Rinehart, 1960. 327 pp.
Gassner offers "an assessment of the mid-century theatre as viewed from the vantage point of Broadway and off-Broadway stage production since World War II." The book is divided between general essays which trace current "situations" back to the end of the 19th century in some instances, and specific "chronicle-criticism" of some sixty-odd productions of the period. The avant-garde is seen to be less radical than commonly assumed, harking back to Jarry, Apollinaire, and Strindberg; and the author concludes that there is a "crisis" in modern drama—a "crossroads"—beyond which the "continuing tension between naturalism and a variety of alternatives of dramatic stylization will in some form be resolved."

L 285. GEISMAR, MAXWELL. American Moderns: From Rebellion to Conformity. New York: Hill & Wang, 1958. 265 pp.
The last of Geismar's four books on the American novel since the Civil War, American Moderns is an "informal daybook or journal of the times." His subject is the fiction of about 1945-1955. The usually short essays are divided into three parts: general essays on the state of fiction, earlier major figures in decline (Dreiser, Hemingway, Dos Passos, Faulkner, Lewis, Wolfe, Cozzens, Steinbeck, and Marquand), and the rise of the post-war generation (Mailer, Hersey, Algren, Salinger, Bellow, Jones, Styron, and Griffin).

L 286. GEISMAR, MAXWELL. The Last of the Provincials: The American Novel, 1915-1925: H. L. Mencken, Sinclair Lewis, Willa Cather, Sherwood Anderson, F. Scott Fitzgerald. Boston: Houghton Mifflin, 1947. 404 pp.
As in Geismar's Rebels and Ancestors (see L 287), the present volume provides "individual studies of the novelists who reflect and also help to form our changing cultural scene" (in this case, the authors of the title). Mencken is presented as "a dominant literary voice of the American twenties," one of the literary temperaments who reacted to the change from an "agrarian and provincial society ('the States') to an industrialized urban power." Although varied and complex, the writers discussed all "present the particular historical motif of the period: the final conquest of the American town, and the values of an older rural life, by the New Economic Order of the industrialized cities."

L 287. GEISMAR, MAXWELL. Rebels and Ancestors: The American Novel, 1890-1915: Frank Norris, Stephen Crane, Jack London, Ellen Glasgow, Theodore Dreiser. Boston: Houghton Mifflin, 1953. 435 pp.
Geismar represents his book as a series of "biographies of inner conviction as well as an informal record of social events in the nineteen hundreds"; it contains chapters on the life and work of his titular authors and an additional chapter on Naturalism and its social implications for the next generation. Geismar is most anxious "to describe these literary figures in their own terms above all," revealing the ways in which "the much abused term 'Naturalism' was not only converted to local usage and idiom by each of the novelists but adapted to the wants and needs of particular spirits."

L 288. GEISMAR, MAXWELL. Writers in Crisis: The American Novel, 1925-1940. Boston: Houghton Mifflin, 1942. 308 pp.
Assuming that "a writer's technique reveals his inner personality, or that his personality makes his technique," Geismar analyzes the "literary personalities" of Lardner, Hemingway, Dos Passos, Faulkner, Wolfe, and Steinbeck. Each of these writers experienced a crisis of American culture

between the wars whereby society and the artist were set hopelessly in conflict. Although the later fiction of Hemingway and Faulkner suggests a reconciliation, Geismar believes that these works lack the technical brilliance and youthful enthusiasm which characterized the literature of the 1920s and 1930s.

L 289. **GIRGUS, SAM B.** The Law of the Heart: Individualism and the Modern Self in American Literature. Austin: University of Texas Press, 1979. 192 pp.
Girgus's central assumption is that the concerns of Modernism mesh perfectly with any attempt to define the American self because "both the attempt to find authentic selfhood and the attempt to override and escape the chains of history are concepts intrinsic to the American experience." On the one hand, Edgar Allan Poe, James Fenimore Cooper, and Charles Ives embody an escaping and inward-turning self. Emerson, Whitman, Henry and William James, Howells, Fitzgerald, Dewey, and Bellow, however, seek to engage in a pragmatic and humanistic way an "open, pluralistic, and changing" reality and culture as totalitarian or "imperial" selves. The ever-present danger, argues Girgus, is that as the American defines his self and its relation to his culture, he may end up following what Hegel calls "the Law of the Heart," the tendency to locate the universal within self-consciousness. By perverting liberty, there is no hope of self-actualization or of meaningful interaction within society.

L 290. **GOLDEN, JOSEPH.** The Death of Tinker Bell: The American Theatre in the Twentieth Century. Syracuse, N.Y.: Syracuse University Press, 1967. 181 pp.
Tinker Bell symbolizes "sustained dramatic vision, viable imagination, and national character," Golden explains to his readers, the playgoing public. This impetus, he claims, is dead in modern drama. Echoing the critic Joseph Wood Krutch, Golden says that even O'Neill's poetic diction is not commensurate with his considerable dramatic power. The author explores American drama's historical tendency to use bombastic verse and idealized (often European) settings, which compound the problem of producing good poetry and good drama. Writing poetic drama in America is further complicated by modern notions of the non-hero and the anti-hero. Golden sees such playwrights as Thornton Wilder, Tennessee Williams, and Arthur Miller as "modern medievalists" primarily interested in allegory and symbolism. Tinker Bell may be "an abortive myth," but Golden hopes that the 20th century still might be conducive to her birth.

L 291. **GOLDSMITH, ARNOLD L.** American Literary Criticism: 1905-1965. Boston: G. K. Hall, 1979. 198 pp.
Goldsmith emphasizes the differences between competing and overlapping schools of criticism. Each movement is defined, in large part, by its reaction to previous critics. The New Humanists criticized the writers championed by the Impressionists. The Formalists were attacked by the Chicago School who were, in turn, found wanting by the Myth Critics. Individual critics, usually quoted at length, are analyzed in terms of both their own achievement and their contribution to one or more schools.

L 292. **GOLDSTEIN, MALCOLM.** The Political Stage: American Drama and Theater of the Great Depression. New York: Oxford University Press, 1974. 482 pp.
Goldstein's history ignores no part of the American stage of the 1930s. He treats the independent and Broadway theaters in separate chapters—also the background of the 1920s, and the intellectual and political currents of the times—but his major emphasis is on the group projects. Thus the Theatre Union, the Group Theatre, the Theatre Guild, the Federal Theatre, and the Mercury Theatre are all treated. Goldstein divides his

subject into two halves at 1935, the watershed year. In short, the work is a "close-focused look at the writers, producers, directors, and actors who helped to give the cultural life of the Great Depression its own special tang."

L 293. GOSSETT, LOUISE Y. Violence in Recent Southern Fiction. Durham, N.C.: Duke University Press, 1965. 207 pp.
Gossett's subject is the "grotesqueness and violence" in Southern fiction between 1930 and the early 1960s. The violence depicted is both physical and psychological; both violence and the grotesque are "dramatizations of disorder." Gossett traces these matters in a prefatory chapter on Wolfe, Caldwell, and Faulkner, and in individual chapters on Robert Penn Warren, Flannery O'Connor, Eudora Welty, William Styron, William Goyen, Truman Capote, Carson McCullers, and Shirley Ann Grau.

L 294. GOTTFRIED, MARTIN. A Theater Divided: The Postwar American Stage. Boston: Little, Brown, 1967. 330 pp.
The division alluded to in the title is between what Gottfried calls the theater's "right wing" and "left wing," between the established and the experimental, between most of Broadway and most of off-Broadway. Gottfried writes about the history of this division since 1945 in a combative voice which does not favor one wing over the other, but yearns for a resolution.

L 295. GOULD, JEAN. American Women Poets: Pioneers of Modern Poetry. New York: Dodd, Mead, 1980. 301 pp.
To demonstrate more clearly the contribution of American women poets, Gould amplifies existing work on the biographies and poetry of ten poets. Her emphasis is on the obstacles to writing poetry and living as poets encountered by her subjects, and on the steps to the creation and dissemination of their work. Gould treats each poet in a separate chapter, in chronological order: Dickinson, Lowell, Stein, Teasdale, Wylie, Doolittle, Moore, Millay, Bogan, and Deutsch.

L 296. GRAY, RICHARD. The Literature of Memory: Modern Writers of the American South. Baltimore, Md.: Johns Hopkins University Press, 1977. 377 pp.
Gray's focus is on "the relationship between literature, history, and historiography." The work covers the field from the 1930s to the 1970s and includes detailed documentation and a 46-page bibliography. He devotes chapters to the historical context; the Agrarians (Robert Penn Warren, Allen Tate, John Crowe Ranson); writers on the "good farmer" (Elizabeth Madox Roberts, Erskine Caldwell, Thomas Wolfe); writers of the "fine planter" (Caroline Gordon, Eudora Welty, Katherine Anne Porter); Faulkner; and contemporary authors (William Styron, Flannery O'Connor, Carson McCullers).

L 297. GREGORY, HORACE and MARYA ZATURENSKA. A History of American Poetry, 1900-1940. New York: Harcourt, Brace, 1946. 524 pp.
Gregory and Zaturenska believe that "there has been a tendency to overrate the importance of literary movements in poetry"; thus the history of poetry offered here is the history of individual poets. Certainly no important poet of the forty years (1900-1940) has been ignored; the focus of attention, then, is judging the accomplishment of each poet. This history was one of the first attempts to assess American poetic accomplishments of the 20th century.

L 298. HARPER, HOWARD M., Jr. Desperate Faith: A Study of Bellow,
       Salinger, Mailer, Baldwin, and Updike. Chapel Hill: University
       of North Carolina Press, 1967. 200 pp.
Harper's subject is the response of these five writers to "universal
problems"--the basic questions of the human condition. Although each writer
poses the question in different terms, all share a tragic perspective.
Man is "beset by doubts and destined to die, yet full of significance
and capable of salvation," hence his "desperate faith" in the face of
what Paul Tillich called the "ultimate questions." "Although the writer
may oppose popular, institutionalized values," Harper suggests, "he must
still respond to them and to the universal problems which he, simply as
a human being, shares with the men of his time. The artist's response
to these problems, the problems involved in what Malraux has called la
condition humaine, give his work its most enduring interest."

L 299. HARTWICK, HARRY. The Foreground of American Fiction. New York:
       American Book, 1934. 447 pp.
Hartwick's purpose is to explain the American novel from 1890 to 1930
not as the product of any one cultural force, but in relation to its social,
economic, religious, philosophic, and literary environment. The novel
is seen as both an index of the American mind and as the product of the
numerous forces and ideas which are that mind. To show just how the American novel reflects the American mind, Hartwick organizes his study "with
reference to four general philosophic tendencies": "The Noble Savage,"
"Beyond Life," "New Worlds for Old," and "Laws as Wings." The writers
considered include Crane, Dreiser, Cabell, Hergesheimer, Dos Passos,
Wharton, and Cather.

L 300. HASSAN, IHAB. Radical Innocence: Studies in the Contemporary
       American Novel. Princeton, N.J.: Princeton University Press,
       1961. 362 pp.
Hassan's work analyzes the image of the hero in contemporary American
literature. According to the author, because the modern world continually
affronts man, he often responds either as rebel or victim. Both responses
indicate an existential affirmation that Hassan calls "radical innocence."
The work divides into three sections: "The Hero and the World"; "The
Forms of Fiction" (Styron, Swados, Mailer, Buechner, Malamud, Ellison,
Gold, Cheever, and Dunleavy); and "The Individual Talent" (McCullers,
Capote, Salinger, and Bellow). This structure parallels the fictional
shift from hypothesis to example, from general to specific. The work
attempts to impose thematic order on recent novelists and their works.

L 301. HASSAN, IHAB. The Right Promethean Fire: Imagination, Science,
       and Cultural Change. Urbana: University of Illinois Press, 1980.
       207 pp.
Declaring that we find ourselves in a "postmodernist, posthumanist" world--
"between history and hope"--Hassan urges breaking down the boundaries
between disciplines and proceeds to discuss not just literature and criticism but also science and its connection to imagination. The "chapters"
of the book (four essays and the final masque "Prometheus as Performer:
Toward a Posthumanist Culture?") are separated by passages from Hassan's
journals. The prose sections of the essays themselves are supplemented
with quotations or drawings in the margins and sometimes interrupted with
typographically distinct asides to the reader. In the essays, Hassan
recognizes criticism as ineluctably arbitrary, discusses changing conceptions of literature and language as well as our (in)ability to determine
what either means, and links science, "a powerful agent of change," to
imagination. Hassan argues that indeterminacy is not synonymous with
anarchy; rather, it awaits a new organizing principle. "Humanists," if
they will adopt the spirit of change, as science has, may be able to mediate between "history and hope."

L 302. **HATCHER, HARLAN**. Creating the Modern American Novel. New York: Farrar & Rinehart, 1935. 307 pp.

Hatcher's work is essentially a survey of American novels from the late 19th century to the mid-1930s in which he treats individual works and authors briefly. He groups these novels into six (roughly chronological) categories: realistic novels; satire and social protest; psychological novels (about sex); romances in a realistic age; novels by the war generation; and novelistic modes of the 1930s (hard-boiled, proletarian, and romantic fiction). In addition to figures now considered major—James, Crane, Howells, Norris, Dreiser, Cather, Lewis, Dos Passos, Toomer, DuBois, Hughes, Anderson, Hemingway, Stein, and Faulkner—Hatcher writes about numerous writers who are now less well-known. He appends a list of those novelists awarded the Pulitzer Prize between 1918 and 1934.

L 303. **HELLMAN, JOHN**. Fables of Fact: The New Journalism as New Fiction. Urbana: University of Illinois Press, 1981. 141 pp.

Hellman's thesis is that Norman Mailer, Tom Wolfe, Hunter S. Thompson, and Michael Herr created a merger of what Scholes terms "fabulist" fiction, journalism, and realistic fictional technique, into a new genre of fiction in order to transform events and surpass the powers of conventional journalism. Wolfe's Kandy-Kolored Tangerine-Flake Streamlined Baby and Capote's In Cold Blood are Hellman's starting point, and Wolfe's essay "The New Journalism," and Mas'ud Zavarzadeh's The Mythopoeic Reality (see L 436) are two theoretical bases for Hellman's observations. Works by Kesey, Pynchon, and Nabokov are treated as they relate to New Journalism.

L 304. **HICKS, JACK**. In the Singer's Temple: Prose Fictions of Barthelme, Gaines, Brautigan, Piercy, Kesey, and Kosinski. Chapel Hill: University of North Carolina Press, 1981. 293 pp.

Hicks begins by setting forth his basic premises: Realism has been the dominant mode in American fiction, with fiction serving as a "modified recording instrument," especially in times of national crisis; during the past two decades young writers have not, even though it has been a period of crisis, used social and political reality as material in their fictions. Rather, he argues, they take these "sterner realities" and treat them metaphorically. Hicks concentrates upon six writers who, he claims, represent the major tendencies in American fiction of the 1960s and 1970s. Donald Barthelme's writing serves as Hicks's example of metafiction; Ernest Gaines serves as an example of the Afro-American writer creating "fiction of social and historical imagination." Single works by Marge Piercy, Richard Brautigan, and Ken Kesey are discussed as countercultural fiction. Hicks also discusses Jerzy Kosinski's fiction as "romance of terror."

L 305. **HILFER, ANTHONY CHANNELL**. The Revolt from the Village 1915-1930. Chapel Hill: University of North Carolina Press, 1969. 271 pp.

Hilfer points out that the "revolt from the village" (a phrase originally used by Carl Van Doren in 1921) involved writers who attacked the myth of the small town's being a place of innocence—a "rural paradise." The village, he claims, was for them a synecdoche standing for middle-class American civilization in general. He identifies two revolts: one in the late 19th century, which involved such writers as Garland, Frederic, Crane, and Twain; and the revolt that began with Masters's Spoon River Anthology (1915) and peaked with Lewis's Main Street (1920). Other writers involved in this second revolt—Hilfer's main focus—include Willa Cather, Van Wyck Brooks, H. L. Mencken, Sherwood Anderson, T. S. Stribling, and Thomas Wolfe. After 1930, he claims, many writers returned to a nostalgic, idealized view of the village.

L 306. HIMELSTEIN, MORGAN Y. Drama Was a Weapon: The Left-Wing Theatre in New York, 1929-1941. New Brunswick, N.J.: Rutgers University Press, 1963. 300 pp.

Himelstein's history of this theatrical period goes beyond the plays produced and the groups producing them to examine the social forces at work and to explain the final failure of what the author terms the Communist Party's hope to control the theater. He examines the ways in which the "social" theater of the Depression was "beset" by the Communist Party. "Armed with the slogan, 'Drama is a weapon,' the Communist Party attempted to infiltrate and control the American stage during the Great Depression of the nineteen-thirties," the author argues. The Federal Theatre, the Mercury Theatre, Broadway, and the Group Theatre are among those examined for Communist infiltration.

L 307. HOEVELER, J. DAVID, Jr. The New Humanism: A Critique of Modern America, 1900-1940. Charlottesville: University Press of Virginia, 1977. 207 pp.

The New Humanists "were cultural traditionalists, defensive of classical principles of art, deeply skeptical about human nature, and neo-Burkean in their political and social views." Hoeveler wishes "to present a comprehensive intellectual portrait of this group." Along with a definition of New Humanism, Hoeveler gives us much information about the founders of the movement (Irving Babbitt and Paul Elmer More) and their most influential students (Stuart Pratt Sherman and Norman Foerster).

L 308. HOFFMAN, DANIEL, ed. Harvard Guide to Contemporary American Writing. Cambridge, Mass.: Harvard University Press, 1979. 618 pp.

Not a guide in the usual sense, this volume contains original essays by Alan Trachtenberg on the "Intellectual Background"; A. Walton Litz on "Literary Criticism"; Leo Braudy on "Realists, Naturalists, and Novelists of Manners"; Lewis Simpson on "Southern Fiction"; Mark Schechner on "Jewish Writers"; Josephine Hendin on "Experimental Fiction"; Nathan A. Scott, Jr., on "Black Literature"; Elizabeth Janeway on "Women's Literature"; Gerald Weales on "Drama"; and Daniel Hoffman on "Poetry: After Modernism," "Poetry: Schools of Dissidents," and "Poetry: Dissidents from Schools." The overall focus is on American writing after 1945.

L 309. HOFFMAN, FREDERICK J. The Art of Southern Fiction: A Study of Some Modern Novelists. Carbondale: Southern Illinois University Press, 1967. 198 pp.

Certain interests, themes, and characteristics are common to Southern writers like Eudora Welty, Carson McCullers, James Agee, Flannery O'Connor, Robert Penn Warren, and William Styron. Their writings, Hoffman argues, are informed by a tradition which emphasizes "place." Because this is a conquered place, the tradition is characterized by a sense of limitation and guilt. Thus place carries moral values. Hoffman defines two extremes in the writings themselves: the extreme of oratory and the extreme of the restricted image. Despite varieties of place, time, and fantasy in the writings, the imaginative significance of the Civil War unifies Southern fiction.

L 310. HOFFMAN, FREDERICK J. Freudianism and the Literary Mind. 1945; Rev. ed. Baton Rouge: Louisiana State University Press, 1957. 350 pp.

Hoffman's study summarizes Freud's theory of psychoanalysis, evaluates the impact of the theory on literature and criticism in the first half of the 20th century, and explains the nature of several important writers' debts to the theory. This study includes a theoretical chapter on influence, an account of Greenwich Village's reception of Freud's ideas, and various discussions of the Freudianism of such American writers as Sherwood Anderson, Waldo Frank, F. Scott Fitzgerald, James Huneker, Conrad Aiken, and Ludwig Lewisohn.

L 311. HOFFMAN, FREDERICK J. The Modern Novel in America 1900-1950.
        1951; Rev. ed. Chicago: Regnery, 1956. 224 pp.
Hoffman addresses two central issues in the modern novel: Henry James's
technical and theoretical concerns, and the naturalists' questioning of
the novelist's social responsibility. He then examines the implications
of these concerns in the works of Cather, Glasgow, Stein, Fitzgerald,
Hemingway, and novelists of the 1930s and 1940s. The author's major concern is to study the effect of "the novelist's attitude toward his materials (his aesthetic and his social views) upon the formal method used
and its consequence for the realization of character, narrative sequence
and pace, and setting." The focus is upon the success of these formal
results that occur from the work on the artist's materials.

L 312. HOFFMAN, FREDERICK J. The Twenties: American Writing in the Post-
        war Decade. New York: Viking Press, 1955. 466 pp.
Hoffman presents the 1920s "from the perspective of its literature"; each
of the eight chapters uses a literary text which he feels "would serve
best to present in a sharp and meaningful way the issues, concerns, and
points of view discussed in it." Thus, for example, the chapter on "Forms
of Experiment and Improvisation" uses as its text Hart Crane's The Bridge.
Other central texts are The Waste Land, The Great Gatsby, The Sun Also
Rises, Babbitt, Hugh Selwyn Mauberley, and the work of Willa Cather.
The Twenties offers social, cultural, and intellectual history as well
as literary analyses.

L 313. HOFFMAN, FREDERICK J., CHARLES ALLEN, and CAROLYN F. ULRICH. The
        Little Magazine: A History and a Bibliography. Princeton, N.J.:
        Princeton University Press, 1947. 450 pp.
The "little magazine" as defined here is a 20th-century American phenomenon:
small journals of intellectual importance "which have lived a kind of
private life of their own on the margins of culture" and which, for various
reasons, began to proliferate around 1910. The authors follow them through
W.W. II, discussing the range of the preoccupations of the little magazines
and their part in the formulations of literary history and culture. The
latter half of this book is an annotated bibliography of the little magazines founded between 1891 and 1945.

L 314. HOLDEN, JONATHAN. The Rhetoric of the Contemporary Lyric. Blooming-
        ton: Indiana University Press, 1980. 136 pp.
Seven independently conceived essays make up this volume in which Holden
attempts to define an approach to American poetry of the 1970s. He begins
with a look at poetic styles in recent history: pre-Modernist (poetry
of sensibility); Modernist; and the "studied artlessness" and "affected
naturalness" (reactions to Modernism) of poetry in the 1970s. He discusses
"found" poetry, which consists of prose passages written as verse to constitute poems (he offers Williams's poetry as an example). Both Stephen
Dunn (who, according to Holden, translates urban banalities into poetic
art) and John Ashbery (whose architectonic poetry, he claims, is analogous
to Abstract Expressionist painting) get chapters of their own. The book
ends with an essay in which Holden challenges Marjorie Perloff's suggestion
that American poetry of the 1970s--like nearly everything else during
that decade--became more conservative.

L 315. HOLDER, ALAN. The Imagined Past: Portrayals of Our History in
        Modern American Literature. Lewisburg, Pa.: Bucknell University
        Press, 1980. 283 pp.
In his introduction, Holder discusses how various 19th-century American
writers--Irving, Cooper, Longfellow, Hawthorne, Simms, and Cable--dealt
with the "thinness" of American history. He attributes a "critical consciousness" (the ability to see the flaws as well as the picturesqueness
of the past) to Hawthorne and Cable. In the body of his work, Holder

turns to 20th-century producers of "historical literature" who, he claims, were able to take the past for granted in a way that the earlier writers were not. These writers include Williams, Faulkner, Tate, Welty, Warren, Styron, Barth, Berryman, Charles Olson, and Robert Lowell. Needing something "greater than their present," they look critically at the past, and yet are entranced by it.

L 316. HOWARD, RICHARD. Alone with America: Essays on the Art of Poetry in the United States Since 1950. 1969; Rev. ed. New York: Atheneum, 1980. 678 pp.
In 1969, Howard offered forty-one studies of American poets who had come into maturity since the Korean War. He described his project as a "reconnaissance": to find out who is there and what is to be known about them. In the 1980 enlarged edition, Howard has not altered the number or the names of the poets discussed. Instead, he has extended the discussion to account for recent activity (or inactivity) of those forty-one. That number excludes the older "masters"—Berryman, Bishop, Jarrell, Lowell, Roethke, and Wilbur—but includes essays on poets as disparate as Snyder, Hecht, Ginsberg, and Wright.

L 317. HYMAN, STANLEY EDGAR. The Armed Vision: A Study in the Methods of Modern Literary Criticism. 1948; Rev. ed. New York: Vintage Books, 1955. 402 pp.
The dominant characteristic of modern criticism, says Hyman, is "the organized use of non-literary techniques and bodies of knowledge to obtain insights into literature." The critics and "non-literary techniques" he examines are: Yvor Winters (evaluation in criticism), T. S. Eliot (tradition), Van Wyck Brooks (biography), Constance Rourke (folklore), Maud Bodkin (psychology), R. P. Blackmur (exegesis), and—his favorites—William Empson, I. A. Richards, and Kenneth Burke. Hyman's work provides an introduction to modern critical methods.

L 318. I'll Take My Stand: The South and the Agrarian Tradition. By Twelve Southerners. New York: Harper, 1930. 359 pp.
The twelve contributors to this Agrarian manifesto include many of the leading literary figures of the modern South, including John Crowe Ransom, Allen Tate, Robert Penn Warren, Stark Young, and Donald Davidson. They share a firm opposition to industrialism ("a system that has so little regard for individual wants") and a commitment to Agrarianism ("a form of labor that is pursued with intelligence and leisure"). "The modern man has lost his sense of vocation," argue the authors. "The theory of agrarianism is that the culture of the soil is the best and most sensitive of vocations, and that therefore it should have the economic preference and enlist the maximum number of workers." The authors assert that the right relation of "man to man," "man to nature," and "man to religion" will follow from Agrarianism.

L 319. JOHNSON, ABBY and RONALD JOHNSON. Propaganda and Aesthetics: The Literary Politics of Afro-American Magazines in the Twentieth Century. Amherst: University of Massachusetts Press, 1979. 249 pp.
The history of Afro-American magazines in the 20th century provides insight into the ongoing debate among black artists and intellectuals as to whether Afro-American literature should have as its primary goal the aesthetic needs of the individual artist or the collective interests of Afro-American, minority culture. The project of this book is to analyze this debate as it surfaces in and shapes the Afro-American periodical literature of the 20th century.

L 320. KALSTONE, DAVID. Five Temperaments. New York: Oxford University
        Press, 1977. 212 pp.
Kalstone has written a book about "the ways some contemporary American
poets have chosen to describe and dramatize their lives." The poets he
discusses came "of age in the 1950s and early 1960s"; they have gone
through remarkable changes in their poetic careers and in the ways they
have used their own experience. One chapter each is devoted to Elizabeth
Bishop, Robert Lowell, James Merrill, Adrienne Rich, and John Ashbery.

L 321. KARL, FREDERICK. American Fictions, 1940-1980: A Comprehensive
        History and Critical Evaluation. New York: Harper & Row, 1983.
        637 pp.
Karl proposes that his work, which deals in succession with the fictions
of numerous American writers of the past four decades, will be both "an
interpretation of key fiction" and a "reading of the culture." He notes
that American fiction of this era relies on the modern movement (particularly in its emphasis on inventiveness--a vital quality) and further
asserts that American writers are still learning the lessons of modernism,
which is exhausted in Europe. Chapters about each of the four decades
are arranged chronologically and supplemented with chapters about particular categories of fiction (the broadly defined "political" novel, novels
about the female experience, minimalism in fiction, nonfiction novels)
and about continuing concerns in American literature (themes, preoccupation
with spatiality, the pastoral). Although he states that American fiction
is no longer simply American (Europe is an important factor), Karl also
argues that no novel has "illuminated more a country, a people, a direction" than the American novel of the past four decades.

L 322. KAZIN, ALFRED. Bright Book of Life: American Novelists and Story-
        tellers from Hemingway to Mailer. Boston: Little, Brown, 1973.
        334 pp.
Kazin's first two essays mourn the passing of two modern writers, Ernest
Hemingway and William Faulkner, for whom literary style was a moral and
meaningful way of shaping reality. The last seven essays classify and
evaluate a substantial number of post-modern writers. Although Kazin
classifies storytellers as Southern, women, Jewish, war, factual, and
absurdist writers, he details the differences among writers in the same
class.

L 323. KAZIN, ALFRED. The Inmost Leaf: A Selection of Essays. New York:
        Noonday Press, 1955. 273 pp.
Although several of the essays in this collection are book reviews, Kazin
does not restrict himself to a literary look at America; nor does he dis-
cuss only American authors, even though American topics predominate.
Among the authors whose work Kazin discusses are William and Henry James,
Edmund Wilson, Paul Rosenfeld, Henry David Thoreau, F. Scott Fitzgerald,
Ellen Glasgow, Scribner's editor Maxwell Perkins, e. e. cummings, Herman
Melville, Sherwood Anderson, Theodore Dreiser, and William Faulkner.
Kazin also includes excerpts from a journal he kept while in Italy (June-
December 1947), an essay on how Frederick Jackson Turner's frontier thesis
has provided historians with the "American equation," observations on
the increasing number of writers working within academia, and a piece
on attending Broadway performances in which he champions the old-fashioned
largesse of musicals as opposed to the pretentious high-brow introspection
of some modern plays.

L 324. KAZIN, ALFRED. On Native Grounds: An Interpretation of American
        Prose Literature. New York: Reynal & Hitchcock, 1942. 541 pp.
A "moral history" of the diverse forces which combined to produce the
concerns of American men of letters from 1890 to 1940, Kazin's book
describes prose literature as a product of the social reality from which

it arises. He characterizes American literature as being, typically, a reaction against that reality. Kazin's method is almost impressionistic; he sets vignettes of major and minor figures against the prevailing tone of political and economic history, evoking both the confusions and the enthusiasms of the period. A postscript was added by Kazin to the 1956 abridged paperback edition.

L 325. KENNER, HUGH. A Homemade World: The American Modernist Writers. New York: Knopf, 1975. 221 pp.
"A fifty year reshaping of the American language," says Kenner, "is the topic of this book." American Modernism is defined as the cultivation of an aesthetic point of view by both poets (Moore, Williams, Stevens) and novelists (Hemingway, Faulkner, Fitzgerald). In many ways a companion to Kenner's The Pound Era (see L 326), the work studies those 20th-century writers who remained in America, a group which has a variety of motives and purposes but which "hangs together" in spite of itself. Its writers "shared hidden sources of craftsmanship, hidden incentives to rewrite a page, which we can trace to a doctrine of perception--the work valued both in itself and in its power to denote." Language, in short, "confines what we can perceive, what think, what discuss."

L 326. KENNER, HUGH. The Pound Era. Berkeley: University of California Press, 1971. 606 pp.
Pound provides the focus for Kenner's meditation on Modernism both in America and abroad. Kenner's method moves from biography to formal analysis to examination of cultural forms and traditions. He elucidates Pound's debt to and belief in ancient Greek and Chinese traditions, Imagism, and Vorticism, and their ability to revivify post-fin de siecle art. Kenner argues that Eliot, Wyndham Lewis, and Pound invented a language, subjects, and poetic forms which enabled them to shake off the influence of 19th-century rhetoric.

L 327. KING, RICHARD H. A Southern Renaissance: The Cultural Awakening of the American South, 1930-1955. New York: Oxford University Press, 1980. 350 pp.
Armed with psychoanalytic theory as a critical tool, King sets forth a literary and intellectual history of the Southern Renaissance. He calls his work "psychohistory"--"cultural anthropology in the broadest sense of the term." The Southern Renaissance, he claims, started in the 1930s when Southern writers and intellectuals began the attempt to come to terms not only with Southern tradition but also with historical consciousness itself--in brief, to come to terms with "Southern family romance." This movement was not, according to King, exclusively literary or exclusively led by conservatives such as the Agrarians. Faulkner and his lifelong "fictional exploration of the Southern family romance" are discussed at relative length. Other writers discussed include Will Percy, Allen Tate, Lillian Smith, Robert Penn Warren, Thomas Wolfe, and James Agee, as well as historians C. Vann Woodward and W. J. Cash, and social scientists V. O. Key, Howard Odum, and Rupert Vance.

L 328. KLEIN, MARCUS. After Alienation: American Novels in Mid-Century. New York: World, 1962. 307 pp.
Klein argues that, since about 1950, our best new novelists have not written from a stance of "alienation" from American life, but rather of "accommodation." He illustrates his argument with individual chapters on Saul Bellow, Ralph Ellison, James Baldwin, Wright Morris, and Bernard Malamud. These novelists share the notion "that at this point in history things must be salvaged," and their fiction "is shaped by the social and political pressures of an age that is the most desperate in all history." Their novels share acts of "adjustment to the social fact" when rebellion exhausts itself as a kind of certainty in regard to society. "Accommodation

for Klein suggests the "simultaneous engagement and disengagement" which arises out of the need to eliminate the distance between self and society and the realization that such distance requires continual readjustment.

L 329. KLEIN, MARCUS. Foreigners: The Making of American Literature 1900-1940. Chicago: University of Chicago Press, 1981. 332 pp.

Klein opens his work with the observation that American writers of this century, unlike American writers of the mid-19th century who could declare their independence from a cultural tradition because that tradition (English) was readily identifiable, face the problem of discovering a tradition. Those struggling to create a cultural tradition divide into two groups: those writers from "established American families who imagine themselves to be marginal (an elite), who are participants in modernism and self-appointed conservators of Western culture; and those who are by birth marginal (immigrants, Blacks, the proletariat), who tend to be participants in socialism and inventors of 'America'—its language and literature." The book is divided into three parts. In the first, Klein distinguishes between the two groups mentioned; in the second, he examines Southern, Western, proletarian, and urban ghetto literatures. The third part consists of biographical essays about three authors: Michael Gold, Nathanael West, and Richard Wright.

L 330. KLINKOWITZ, JEROME. The American 1960's: Imaginative Acts in a Decade of Change. Ames: Iowa State University Press, 1980. 119 pp.

Klinkowitz first justifies the study of the 1960s as a legitimately isolable decade. Then, by treating presidential images, popular music, fiction, and art, he shows how the American collective imagination of the time expressed a "new idea." This idea became an aesthetic which celebrated the artist, the act of creation, and the principle of "authenticity." Artists realized the aesthetic by ridding themselves of inherited ways of perception and by learning how to create their own authentic world. Klinkowitz details these new acts of creation and briefly explores the causes behind the explosions of the 1960s.

L 331. KLINKOWITZ, JEROME. Literary Disruptions: The Making of a Post-Contemporary American Fiction. 1975; Rev. ed. Urbana: University of Illinois Press, 1980. 296 pp.

The "post-contemporary" authors (including Vonnegut, Barthelme, Kosinski, Baraka, Gilbert Sorrentino) form one school of today's American fiction quite distinct from the more publicized "regressive parodists" (Barth and Pynchon). Vonnegut, Barthelme, and Kosinski are "literary disruptives" whose commitments to "formal experimentation, a thematic interest in the imaginative transformation of reality," and self-conscious artistry signal the rebirth of the novel. The writers under discussion are seen to have disrupted the novelistic tradition at a point most crucial, when the "death of the novel" was proclaimed to be imminent. Their "disruptive" fictions spurn mimesis and instead present a vision in which "physical, social, and political conditions" are in disorder: to have imposed a rational order on them would have amounted to an "aesthetic mess," according to the author.

L 332. KLINKOWITZ, JEROME. The Practice of Fiction in America: Writers from Hawthorne to the Present. Ames: Iowa State University Press, 1980. 128 pp.

Klinkowitz describes an ongoing battle between the cultural demand for realism and the writer's own literary subjectivity. Favoring the latter quality, he traces the ascendancy of experimental self-reflective texts in American fiction. Hawthorne, Howells, Chopin, Fitzgerald, and Faulkner set the stage. Updike, Vonnegut, Barthelme, Ronald Sukenick, Clarence

Major, and Gerald Rosen are among the contemporary writers discussed. In particular, Klinkowitz presents Willard Motley as a type of "tragic hero" who was defeated by his publisher's demand for conventional fiction.

L 333. KNIGHT, GRANT C. The Strenuous Age in American Literature. Chapel
       Hill: University of North Carolina Press, 1954. 270 pp.
In this sequel to The Critical Period in American Literature (see L 151), Knight discusses the literature of the first decade of the 20th century within the context of the historical events and social forces of the time. He defines the "strenuous age" in terms of a conflict in American morality between "Americanismus," a confusion of monetary with moral values, and "Americanism," a brand of individualism exemplified in the public life of Theodore Roosevelt and characterized in literature by the "Strong Man" archetype.

L 334. KRAMER, DALE. Chicago Renaissance: The Literary Life in the Mid-
       west, 1900-1930. New York: Appleton-Century, 1966. 369 pp.
Kramer begins with a brief history of Chicago in the late 19th century, then provides introductory biographical sketches of six major figures of the Chicago Renaissance: Floyd Dell, Theodore Dreiser, Sherwood Anderson, Carl Sandburg, Edgar Lee Masters, and Vachel Lindsay. He returns to these figures periodically throughout the remaining, more or less chrono- logical, treatment of the Chicago Renaissance. Other important persons or institutions he discusses include the Friday Literary Review, Maurice Browne and his Little Theatre, Hamlin Garland, Henry Fuller, W. M. Reedy, Harriet Monroe and Poetry, and Margaret Anderson and the Little Review. Pointing out that the Chicago Renaissance peaked in 1915-1916, Kramer also notes that the lack of activity during the war years and the 1920s was followed by an upsurge in the 1930s (Farrell, Levin, Wright, Algren, and Halper).

L 335. KRUTCH, JOSEPH WOOD. The American Drama Since 1918: An Informal
       History. 1939; Rev. ed. New York: Braziller, 1957. 344 pp.
In this examination of the progress of American drama, Krutch claims that American plays are less concerned with intellectual pioneering and social reform than European plays. He discusses "realistic" dramatists (Elmer Rice, Maxwell Anderson); assesses Eugene O'Neill's achievement, especially his success in combining contemporary drama with tragedy; details the success of comic dramatists such as George Kaufman and S. N. Behrman; and shows the rise of "social criticism" drama at the hands of such authors as Elmer Rice and Clifford Odets. Krutch claims that only Maxwell Anderson succeeded in writing good verse drama in the 1930s. For the 1940s he names two dominant playwrights: Arthur Miller, following the "social criticism" tradition; and Tennessee Williams, following the poetic tradi- tion of Anderson.

L 336. LANGFORD, RICHARD E., ed. Essays in Modern American Literature.
       De Land, Fla.: Stetson University Press, 1963. 122 pp.
Langford's collection addresses an audience of students and general readers. The essays, written almost exclusively by teachers of American literature, introduce the key texts, themes, concerns and techniques of authors writing during the late 19th and 20th centuries: Herman Melville, Henry James, Stephen Crane, F. Scott Fitzgerald, William Faulkner, Eugene O'Neill, John Steinbeck, Tennessee Williams, Jack Kerouac, James Gould Cozzens, and James Purdy.

L 337. LEVIN, HARRY. Memories of the Moderns. New York: New Directions, 1980. 257 pp.
This work is a collection of essays, speeches, and letters which Levin composed, for the most part, during the 1970s. Although the critic does not present these essays as a systematic examination of the modern movement, the collection includes retrospective treatments of many of the most important figures within that movement, with many of whom Levin was personally acquainted: Eliot, Pound, Joyce, Heinrich and Thomas Mann, Hesse, Hemingway, Dos Passos, William Carlos Williams, Aiken, Sartre, Auden, Delmor Schwartz, Jarrell, I. A. Richards, Edmund Wilson, Nabokov, and F. O. Matthiessen. Suggesting that 20th-century (especially Modernist) literature relies on "intercultural communication," Levin notes that the "American scene has never been complete without its European horizon."

L 338. LIPTON, LAWRENCE. The Holy Barbarians. New York: Messner, 1959. 318 pp.
The Beat Generation of the 1950s, which Lipton states began in the 1920s, has received slight notice from literary critics or historians despite the talented writers (e.g., Kenneth Rexroth, Henry Miller, Allen Ginsberg, Lawrence Ferlinghetti) who are included in this group. Lipton presents an account of the movement as "a kind of evolutionary, historical process" through a series of vignettes of life at Venice, California, and through essays on the life style, philosophy, and literary antecedents of the Beats.

L 339. LODGE, DAVID. Working with Structuralism: Essays and Reviews on Nineteenth- and Twentieth-Century Literature. Boston: Routledge & Kegan Paul, 1981. 207 pp.
Lodge applies to concrete critical tasks the concepts and methods of anti-empirical classical Structuralism exemplified in the work of Jakobson and Levi-Strauss, and more recently by Todorov and Genette. Refining Jakobson's metaphoric-metonymic polarity as a key to all discourse, the opening chapter explains the terminology and procedures which are later employed in analyses of texts by Hemingway, Dickens, and Hardy, and Tom Wolfe's anthology of New Journalism. Working through particular instances Lodge explores how Structuralist description may render evaluative criticism more precise.

L 340. LOVE, GLEN A. New Americans: The Westerner and the Modern Experience in the American Novel. Lewisburg, Pa.: Bucknell University Press, 1982. 265 pp.
Love begins by discussing the 1893 World's Fair and how it symbolized the disappearance of the frontier in America, a disappearance noted by Frederick Jackson Turner in the same year. America was becoming urban; a class of professionals—architects, inventors, scientists, and engineers—was rising, replacing the frontiersman, yeoman farmer, and robber baron. Granting that some writers (Twain and James) exhibited hostility toward the city and machines, Love identifies a "frontier-inspired progress-oriented tradition" in which writers attempt (not without some ambivalence) to unite pastoral and urban elements. The authors he places in this tradition are Norris, Garland, Cather, Anderson, and Sinclair Lewis.

L 341. LOWITT, RICHARD and MAURINE BEASLEY. One Third of a Nation: Lorena Hickock Reports on the Great Depression. Urbana: University of Illinois Press, 1981. 378 pp.
Lorena Hickock, one of the first great newspaperwomen, was hired by Harry L. Hopkins, FDR's Federal relief administrator, to report on how Americans in 1933 and 1934 were reacting to the programs he was supervising. This collection of ninety-three of her lengthy and detailed reports from every state except those in the Northwest stems from her in-depth interviews with a full range of people. The authors write: "Indeed, possibly the

only reporting to rival Hickock's on the human side of the Great Depression would be some of the periodical pieces that Edmund Wilson wrote in 1930 and 1931."

L 342. LUCCOCK, HALFORD E. Contemporary American Literature and Religion. Chicago: Willett, Clark, 1934. 300 pp.
Luccock examines literature of the previous fifteen years to ascertain its "spiritual and moral significance." He declares that American literature has reached the end of an era--that cynicism, rebellion for its own sake, and revelry have become exhausted. Luccock justifies looking at the realistic literature in relation to religion, even though it has no overt relationship to religion; for it tries to tell things as they are. Religion, he argues, cannot afford to be blind to contemporary reality or to ignore the literature that tries to capture that reality. Among the authors whose work he discusses are Dreiser, Anderson, Lewis, Masters, Cather, Glasgow, Herrick, Ferber, Hemingway, Dos Passos, and Cabell.

L 343. LUTWACK, LEONARD. Heroic Fiction: The Epic Tradition and American Novels of the Twentieth Century. Carbondale: Southern Illinois University Press, 1971. 174 pp.
Lutwack's claim is that "novels drawing upon the epic have been written in America and deserve identification as a minority tradition, if nothing else." This tradition is essentially 20th-century in formulation (Cooper and Melville lack sufficient consistency). Lutwack discusses The Octopus, The Grapes of Wrath, For Whom the Bell Tolls, Bellow's novels, and Invisible Man, concluding that the tradition is alive. "The cyclical renewal of life is the grand theme of American epic novels"; accordingly, Lutwack studies his texts by fixing the relations of traditional materials and influences to "a broad and varied stream of narrative art in which the heroic, the mythic, and the transcendent are the chief ingredients and of which the epic is the definitive expression."

L 344. LYNN, KENNETH S. The Dream of Success: A Study of the Modern American Imagination. Boston: Atlantic/Little, Brown, 1955. 269 pp.
The fullest mythic expression of the American dream of success comes in the popular fiction of Horatio Alger, Jr., to whom Lynn devotes an introductory chapter. Lynn then focuses on five novelists who responded in various ways to this dream during the first two decades of this century: Dreiser, London, David Graham Phillips, Frank Norris, and Robert Herrick. According to Lynn, what they all have in common is their attempt to struggle with "the disparity between myth and reality" in those decades.

L 345. LYON, JAMES K. Bertolt Brecht in America. Princeton, N.J.: Princeton University Press, 1980. 408 pp.
This work is an account of the dramatist and poet's "American exile" (1941-1947) based on extensive interviews with those who knew Brecht and consultation of unpublished manuscript sources. Topics discussed include the young Brecht's idealistic vision of America; his largely unsuccessful struggles to find recognition and work in Hollywood and on Broadway without losing artistic control of his productions; his aesthetic and ideological collaborations and disagreements with other emigres and Americans in the theater, screen, and literary worlds; his reputation as a "difficult" individual; his refusal of Americanization; his anti-fascist political activities; and his relation to Stalinism and to the American left, ending with his testimony to the House Un-American Activities Committee.

L 346. MADDEN, DAVID, ed. Proletarian Writers of the Thirties. Carbondale Southern Illinois University Press, 1968. 278 pp.
Labeling proletarian literature "the most visible and identifiable of genres in the Thirties," Madden has assembled fifteen essays which, from a variety of perspectives, analyze this Depression-era phenomenon. The collection opens with two general essays by Leslie Fiedler and Gerald Green, and proceeds with a series of essays on specific writers such as John Dos Passos, Edward Dahlberg, Robert Cantwell, and Jack Conroy (by such critics as Leo Gurko, Irving Howe, and Conroy himself). Marcus Klein and Chester Eisinger assess, respectively, the "conflict between the litera-ture of revolt and literary modernism," and the treatment of the individual in leftist fiction, while Frederick Hoffman explores proletarian aesthetics. The volume closes with an essay by Allen Guttmann on proletarian poetry.

L 347. MAGNY, CLAUDE-EDMONDE. The Age of the American Novel: The Film Aesthetic of Fiction Between the Two Wars. 1948; Translated by Eleanor Hochman. New York: Ungar, 1972. 232 pp.
The author defines the "age of the American novel" as the era between the wars and notes the "aridity" of post-W.W. II American novels. Claiming that both films and novels answer our need to be taken out of ourselves and provide an individual, not a group, artistic experience, Magny shows how the novels of Dos Passos, Hemingway, Steinbeck, Faulkner, and others imitated such film techniques as objective presentation, ellipsis, and cutting (inserting close-ups to break linear narrative). She discusses how imitating film techniques enabled these writers to treat time in radi-cally new ways. She also argues that Faulkner's works, unlike those of his contemporaries, belong "beyond time and period."

L 348. MALIN, IRVING. Jews and Americans. Carbondale: Southern Illinois University Press, 1965. 193 pp.
Malin explains both why Jewish writing of the present has a particular appeal in America and ways in which a Jew and an American--"often in the same person"--look at each other. The seven writers he discusses in some detail are Karl Shapiro, Delmore Schwartz, Isaac Rosenfeld, Leslie Fiedler, Saul Bellow, Bernard Malamud, and Philip Roth. Malin argues that "there is an American-Jewish context," a "community of feeling" which transcends individual style and different genres. Yet each of his writers he sees as consciously having faced his Jewishness. The writers, because they rebel against the God of their ancestors, and because they flee from ortho-dox commitments, "belong to a 'deceptive' community," but in an ironic way they also mirror the concerns of their ancestors.

L 349. MANLY, JOHN MATTHEWS and EDITH RICKERT. Contemporary American Literature. New York: Harcourt, Brace, 1922. 188 pp.
In compiling their list of contemporary American authors ("contemporary" defined as those writing since 1914), the authors state that they had two guiding principles: first, to include experimental work; and second, to represent various tendencies within literature. They preface the author entries with lists of indexes and critical periodicals, reference works, anthologies, and bibliographies. The entries, arranged alphabetically by author, include biographical information, information about the author's publications, and—for the more important writers--suggestions for reading those works and lists of critical studies or reviews of his or her work. The volume concludes with lists in which the authors are categorized accord-ing to the genre in which they write, their places of birth, and the sub-jects treated in their writings.

L 350. MARGOLIES, EDWARD. Native Sons: A Critical Study of Twentieth-
Century Negro American Authors. Philadelphia: Lippincott, 1968.
210 pp.
In two brief introductory chapters Margolies establishes a historical
context for black writing, including a brief literary history of black
writers from 1900 to 1940. He then devotes separate chapters to major
writers since 1940: William Attaway, Richard Wright, Chester Himes, James
Baldwin, Ralph Ellison, Malcolm X, William Demby, and LeRoi Jones. "The
central concern of this book," writes the author, "is the Negro's evaluation of his historical and cultural experience in this century." The
novels under discussion document the variety of responses in this century
to racial oppression; fear and self-hatred as well as pride and defiance
inform this tradition of novel writing whose tutelary spirit is Richard
Wright.

L 351. MASSA, ANN. American Literature in Context, IV: 1900-1930. New
York: Methuen, 1982. 205 pp.
Massa's book is part of a series designed to examine "the peculiarly American cultural context out of which the nation's literature has developed"
(see also L 138). Divided into fourteen chapters on individual authors,
this study focuses on topics which clarify both a writer's contribution
to American letters and the attention to such issues as internationalism
and expatriatism (Henry James, Gertrude Stein, Ezra Pound, and Ernest
Hemingway); autobiography (Henry Adams); science and religion (H. L.
Mencken); society and manners (Edith Wharton, Sinclair Lewis, Jean Toomer,
and F. Scott Fitzgerald); and the nature of the creative imagination
(Sherwood Anderson, William Faulkner, Wallace Stevens, and Eugene O'Neill).

L 352. MATERER, TIMOTHY. Vortex: Pound, Eliot, and Lewis. Ithaca, N.Y.:
Cornell University Press, 1979. 231 pp.
Examining the crosscurrents in the careers of the Vorticist movement's
major artistic figures, Materer employs Pound's metaphor of the "vortex"
as a key description of the convergence of a modernist aesthetic with
historical forces. Materer investigates the aesthetic, social, and philosophical principles which run through the decades of collaboration and
controversy to form a definite pattern in literary history. The early
history traces Vorticism's efforts to revolutionize the arts in England
through the journal Blast and in the sculpture of Gaudier-Brzeska. The
later history concerns the movement's struggle to rekindle its pre-war
energy, including Pound's unsuccessful attempt to bring Joyce into the
Vorticists' orbit.

L 353. MATHEWS, JANE DE HART. The Federal Theatre, 1935-1939: Plays,
Relief, and Politics. Princeton, N.J.: Princeton University Press,
1967. 342 pp.
The Federal Theatre, sponsored by the Works Progress Administration of
Franklin Roosevelt's New Deal, was designed to provide work for thousands
of theater personnel and to entertain millions of Americans. According
to Mathews, the project succeeded largely because it was "shaped by individuals committed to the creation of a theatre with regional roots and
socially relevant plays." It did not, however, become the basis for a
national theater, as many people desired, and after four years Congress
refused to continue its funding. Mathews's work is neither a detailed
account of regional theater nor an analysis of individual works but a
research study (with a fifteen-page bibliography) of American theater
and culture in the Depression.

L 354. **MAZZARO, JEROME**. Postmodern American Poetry. Urbana: University
of Illinois Press, 1980. 203 pp.
In this work Mazzaro offers a study of W. H. Auden, Randall Jarrell,
Theodore Roethke, David Ignatow, John Berryman, Sylvia Plath, and Elizabeth
Bishop. He traces the break with the Modernist aesthetic of fragmentation
and withdrawal of the self to Auden and Jarrell's embrace of Marx, Freud,
and Darwin, and to later writers' preoccupation with a historically determined and (sometimes) politically activist self, defined through language
and through involvement with the particularity of experience. Rather
than offering readings of poems, Mazzaro quotes extensively from poets'
statements about their own intentions and influences, and from other
critics.

L 355. **McCOLE, C. JOHN**. Lucifer at Large. London: Longmans, Green,
1937. 337 pp.
McCole insists that "the values of art should be transcending values."
He argues against most 20th-century American literature—the Naturalists,
Sherwood Anderson, Hemingway, Dos Passos, Faulkner, and many others—on
the basis of its betrayal, as he sees it, of his belief "that men live
by a definite system of values, and that these values are absolute and
objective."

L 356. **McCORMICK, JOHN**. The Middle Distance: A Comparative History of
American Imaginative Literature: 1919-1932. New York: Free
Press, 1971. 256 pp.
This literary history distances itself from both the nostalgic definition
of the 1920s as "roaring" and the pragmatic and patriotic view of the
period's writers as "irresponsible." The study seeks to account for the
1920s' enormous burst of literary activity by examining the new intensity of the question history posed to these writers—that of their relation
to literary tradition. Systems of belief and ideas are examined in order
to describe the shape of the post-W.W. I world as well as the (mostly
canonical) writers' responses to it. Post-war writers, while not Romantics,
are seen to have been confronted with a world similar to the one the Romantics faced—and therefore needed a new philosophy upon which to found
their view of it.

L 357. **McFADDEN, GEORGE**. Discovering the Comic. Princeton, N.J.: Princeton University Press, 1982. 254 pp.
Husserl, Ingarden, Nietzsche, Bergson, Schiller, and Plato ground this
historical exploration of comedy, in which James, Barthelme, Patchen,
Roth, and Pynchon are among the authors considered. McFadden's thesis
is that in the 18th century a new ethos of comedy emerged, which unites
upper and lower classes in a single plot and reverses hierarchical order.
McFadden asserts that the theories of Aristotle and Freud on the comic
are both inadequate to describe this new comedy. Classical, romantic,
and modern comedy—the type which receives the bulk of attention—are
discussed in separate chapters. A chapter on the theory of comedy considers Bergson, Freud, Mauron, Concord, and Frye. Nietzsche, as the father
of black comedy, receives separate treatment along with Barthes, and
Barthelme's Snow White serves as a test of Barthes's theories. A concluding
chapter treats James's "The Pupil" and suggests directions for further
research.

L 358. **MELLARD, JAMES M**. The Exploded Form: The Modernist Novel in
America. Urbana: University of Illinois Press, 1980. 208 pp.
Mellard identifies three stages in the history of the modern novel—naive,
critical, and sophisticated—in order to narrate what has happened to
novelistic form. At the same time, he sets up a "'proto-metaphoric' paradigm" to explain authors' attitudes toward form. This paradigm pictures
modern authors exploding the novel-as-genre into different modes. Mellard

794

discusses the scientific and philosophic backgrounds of each stage and then turns to a representative text. He concludes that while we have yet to enter a post-modern stage, the successor to The Sound and the Fury, Catch-22, and Trout Fishing in America will resemble Tim O'Brien's Going After Cacciato.

L 359. MICKELSON, ANNE Z. Reaching Out: Sensitivity and Order in Recent American Fiction by Women. Metuchen, N.J.: Scarecrow Press, 1979. 241 pp.
Mickelson examines works published in the last two decades by twelve American women (Joyce Carol Oates, Erica Jong, Lois Gould, Gail Godwin, Joan Didion, Sarah E. Wright, Toni Morrison, Alice Walker, Marge Piercy, Sara Davidson, Marilyn French, and Grace Paley). She prefaces this discussion with a brief examination of how recent American fiction by males has depicted women and of the position women currently occupy in this culture. She characterizes their writing as exhibiting three characteristically American traits: "the search for identity, the plea for egalitarianism, and the revolutionary zeal to create new modes of expression." Whereas male writers fear and struggle with a sense of dissolution, these female writers, Mickelson argues, occupy themselves with the dissolution that will make way for a more "relevant and organic" order.

L 360. MILLGATE, MICHAEL. American Social Fiction: James to Cozzens. New York: Barnes & Noble, 1964. 217 pp.
American novelists, says Millgate, "have lacked assurance in their treatment of society." They have been "worried, confused, or angered—rarely amused—by the irreconcilability of American ideals and American experience." Such reactions have rarely resulted in aesthetically successful novels dealing with American society. Millgate derives this thesis from a study of James, Howells, Norris, Dreiser, Anderson, Lewis, Dos Passos, Cozzens, and the two writers who possessed a sense of history and so wrote significant social fiction: Edith Wharton and F. Scott Fitzgerald.

L 361. MILLS, RALPH J., Jr. Contemporary American Poetry. New York: Random House, 1965. 262 pp.
This book serves as an introduction to the work of twelve poets who have gained substantial reputations since W.W. II: Eberhart, Kunitz, Roethke, Bishop, Brother Antoninus, Shapiro, Gardner, Lowell, Wilbur, Levertov, Wright, and Sexton. The study examines the work of these poets through 1965.

L 362. NADEAU, ROBERT L. Readings from the New Book on Nature: Physics and Metaphysics in the Modern Novel. Amherst: University of Massachusetts Press, 1981. 213 pp.
Nadeau argues that scientific thought has greatly influenced literature, in part because metaphysical assumptions are as important to the work of scientists as they are to humanists. He outlines first the development in Greek culture of ideas implicit to Newtonian science, and then explores the influence of the new physics on the metaphysics of such modern novelists as John Fowles, John Barth, John Updike, Kurt Vonnegut, Jr., Thomas Pynchon, Tom Robbins, and Don DeLillo.

L 363. NELSON, CARY. Our Last First Poets: Vision and History in Contemporary American Poetry. Urbana: University of Illinois Press, 1981. 215 pp.
Nelson discusses a group of poets whose careers were established by the early 1960s: Theodore Roethke, Galway Kinnell, Robert Duncan, Adrienne Rich, and W. S. Merwin. These poets wrote open-form poetry which, according to Nelson, is envisioned as a "communal" kind of poetry, required almost by definition to be "democratically responsive," involved with history. He focuses on the tension between personal, poetic vision and

national, historical actuality--a tension which he says was always present
in American poetry but was certainly exacerbated by the Vietnam war.
Nelson, in fact, prefaces his chapters on individual poets with a chapter
on Vietnam War poetry because he feels this poetry serves as a "telling
introduction" to the tension pervasive in American poetry.

L 364. O'CONNOR, WILLIAM VAN. An Age of Criticism: 1900-1950. Chicago:
Regnery, 1952. 182 pp.
This history of American critical thought in the first half of the 20th
century is written from an analytical critic's point of view and represents
the beliefs and tenets of several critical schools and individual critics
of the period. In successive chapters it treats the "genteel," impressionist, realist, organicist, historical, "new humanist," social, psychological,
mythic, and analytical critics. Although the book pays some attention
to historical and social influences, it is primarily concerned with
classifying the types of theories and with distinguishing the individual
approaches.

L 365. O'CONNOR, WILLIAM VAN. Sense and Sensibility in Modern Poetry.
Chicago: University of Chicago Press, 1948. 279 pp.
O'Connor's subject is "the dichotomy of thought and sensibility" in modern
(i.e., 20th-century) British and American poetry. He cites a great range
of poets writing in English, and in chapters devoted, for instance, to
"The Break with Verism," "The Influence of the Metaphysicals," and "Forms
of Obscurity," he tries to isolate the phenomena which characterize the
modern. This is an attempt to grapple with the issues of emerging Modernism up to 1948.

L 366. OHASHI, KENZABURO, ed. The Traditional and the Anti-Traditional:
Studies in Contemporary American Literature. Tokyo: Tokyo
Chapter of the American Literature Society of Japan, 1980.
370 pp.
This work is a collection of essays about a three-year American studies
project by Japanese scholars. The scope of the project extends from W.W.
II to the present decade, but most attention has been paid to the 1960s.
The Tokyo critics are generally interested in establishing a comprehensive
historical overview. Particularly attentive to development within genres,
the book is divided into sections on poetry, fiction, and drama. Also
included are an overview of American literature's reception in post-war
Japan and a transcription of a 1978 symposium.

L 367. OLDERMAN, RAYMOND M. Beyond the Wasteland: A Study of the American
Novel in the Nineteen-Sixties. New Haven, Conn.: Yale University
Press, 1972. 258 pp.
Olderman's subject is the "essential vision" of the novelists of the 1960s.
"In the sixties," he says, "the form of romance has veered toward the
fable; it employs the comedy known as black humor, and it is defined by
the individual's encounter with a fabulous world--a world made a mystery
by the extraordinary nature of fact, and made a wasteland by an extraordinary sense of impotence." Contemporary American writers like John Barth,
Thomas Pynchon, and Kurt Vonnegut, Jr. have united existential philosophy
with The Waste Land's myth of the wounded Fisher King and the quest of
the Grail Knight.

L 368. OTTEN, TERRY. After Innocence: Visions of the Fall in Modern
Literature. Pittsburgh, Penn.: University of Pittsburgh Press,
1982. 224 pp.
Claiming that the myth of the Fall is an appropriate metaphor for what
it means to be human--a story irreducible in its richness--Otten examines
how the Fall figures in a few, carefully selected modern texts. He begins
by discussing the Romantics, for whom the Fall was psychological, rather

than historical or theological, because--Otten believes--Romanticism was
the beginning of the modern temperament. Although he does consider non-
American authors, five of the ten works he discusses are by Americans:
Henry James's The Turn of the Screw, Arthur Miller's After the Fall, Edward
Albee's Who's Afraid of Virginia Woolf?, James Dickey's Deliverance, and
Stanley Kubrick and Arthur C. Clarke's 2001: A Space Odyssey. Religion
remains a part of human culture, Otten believes, even though it is as
much the artist's as the priest's province.

L 369. PARKINSON, THOMAS, ed. A Casebook on the Beat. New York: Crowell,
         1961. 326 pp.
The aim of this volume is to present a comprehensive view of the writings
of the Beat generation. The material selected is intended to indicate
the "pros and cons" of the movement and to clarify the motives of individual writers. The first section of the book, entitled "Some Writers
of the Beat Generation," consists of poetry, fiction, and essays written
by Allen Ginsberg, Jack Kerouac, Gregory Corso, William S. Burroughs,
Lawrence Ferlinghetti, Gary Snyder, and others. The second section,
"Criticism and Commentary," presents various critical views of the movement
and its literature. Essayists include Kenneth Rexroth, Norman Podhoretz,
Herbert Gold, and John Ciardi.

L 370. PAUL, SHERMAN. The Lost America of Love: Rereading Robert Creeley,
         Edward Dorn, and Robert Duncan. Baton Rouge: Louisiana State
         University Press, 1981. 276 pp.
Paul employs an "open, serial, meditative form" for his treatment of the
verse of these three poets. The work consists not of a scholarly argument with scholarly apparatus, but of Paul's first responses (arranged
like journal entries) upon rereading their poems. It constitutes "open
criticism"--a criticism that waives judgment and is, Paul argues, appropriate in a time when art has become more deeply personal. Love--"the
outstanding debt we owe Whitman"--is a major theme in this work. Paul
includes biographical information about the poets (where they were, who
they knew, what they read) and establishes connections between their works
and the verse of other poets: Pound, Williams, H. D., Crane, Olson,
and Whitman. Paul also takes note of how their poetry reflects or makes
use of American history, geography, and politics.

L 371. PEDEN, WILLIAM. The American Short Story: Front Line in the
         National Defence of Literature. 1964; Rev. ed. with new title,
         The American Short Story: Continuity and Change, 1940-1975.
         Boston: Houghton Mifflin, 1975. 215 pp.
Peden indicates the major directions and achievements of the American
short story since 1940, claiming that it has become the dominant, characteristic American literary form. Its qualities, he says, are "vigor,
variety, and high artistic achievement." Thematically arranged, the chapters cover the authors of loneliness and alienation (Eudora Welty, John
Cheever), reality and illusion (Truman Capote, Carson McCullers), sanity
and insanity (Jean Stafford, Tennessee Williams), war (John Horne Burns),
social conscience (Bernard Malamud, I. B. Singer), regionality (Katherine
Anne Porter, Eudora Welty), and science fiction (Isaac Asimov, Ray
Bradbury). This organization encourages analysis of an author's general
characteristics rather than a close reading of individual stories. An
appendix contains a checklist of notable American modern short story
writers.

L 372. PERLOFF, MARJORIE. The Poetics of Indeterminacy: Rimbaud to
Cage. Princeton, N.J.: Princeton University Press, 1981.
339 pp.
Rimbaud, in Perloff's argument, is more important to American poets than
any other French poet because of his mastery of disassociated language
and a perspective from which ideas and things become indeterminate. She
demonstrates Rimbaud's influence on Stein, Williams, Pound, Ashbery, Antin,
Cage, and Beckett. Perloff explores the relation of American artists
to French poetry and visual art. Her topics include Stein's construction
of word-systems and use of visual art; Williams's debt to Apollinaire
in Spring and All and Kora in Hell; Pound's use of fragmentary structure
in the Cantos; Ashbery's use of puzzles, dream and parody; and Cage and
Antin's emphasis on performance.

L 373. PETRIE, DENNIS W. Ultimately Fiction: Design in Modern American
Literary Biography. West Lafayette, Ind.: Purdue University
Press, 1981. 232 pp.
Petrie limits his discussion to literary biography, arguing that these
biographies--always "ultimately fiction"--should not only supply information but also exploit their "potential value as aesthetic objects."
After a brief history of the subgenre, Petrie presents a theory of literary
biography: the biographer, after getting all the facts, should develop
a personal vision of his or her subject and then transmit it with style.
He identifies three kinds of literary biography: those that focus on
the subject as a famous writer, not as an artist; portraits that lack
any treatment of the subject's writings; and those written by one artist
in search of another, in which both the life and art of the subject are
discussed. Petrie focuses on the following recent biographies of American
authors: Blotner's Faulkner, Turnbull's Scott Fitzgerald, Swanberg's
Dreiser, and Edel's Henry James.

L 374. PEYER, BERND. Hyemeyohsts Storm's "Seven Arrows": Fiction and
Anthropology in the Native American Novel. Wiesbaden: Franz
Steiner Verlag, 1979. 220 pp.
Peyer points out that those who think of Native American art and culture
as something vanished or degenerating are wrong. After giving a brief
history of Native American written literature and of the Cheyenne tribe,
Peyer turns to Hyemeyohsts Storm's novel Seven Arrows (1972), the first
novel published under Harper & Row's Native American Publishing Program.
He explains that he chose Seven Arrows because (1) it deals with the history of the Plains from mid-19th century to the present; (2) it consciously
incorporates traditional elements resulting in innovative content, style,
and structure; (3) it sold a relatively large number of copies (183,000);
and (4) it was controversial (Cheyenne elders and some anthropologists
objected to its alleged inaccuracies). Peyer approaches the novel mainly
by examining the traditional religious elements within it and discusses
its actual style and structure briefly at the end. He asserts that the
book is, as it claims to be, universal--about all peoples and all religions.

L 375. PHILLIPS, ROBERT. The Confessional Poets. Carbondale: Southern
Illinois University Press, 1973. 173 pp.
Since M. L. Rosenthal labeled certain contemporary poets "confessional"
in The New Poets (see L 385), studies of those poets have proliferated.
Phillips brings together a great deal of the theory and practice of those
poets who may--or may not--be partaking of what is here called "autobiographical frenzy." The poets treated in some detail, after an opening
chapter of definition, are Robert Lowell, W. D. Snodgrass, Anne Sexton,
John Berryman, Theodore Roethke, and Sylvia Plath. "All confessional
art," the author argues, "whether poetry or not, is a means of killing
the beasts within us, those dreadful dragons of dreams and experiences
that must be hunted down, cornered, and exposed in order to be destroyed."

This is "poetry written in opposition to, or reaction from, the Eliotic aesthetic which influenced several generations of poets."

L 376. PIKE, BURTON. The Image of the City in Modern Literature. Princeton, N.J.: Princeton University Press, 1981. 162 pp.
Claiming that he intends not to write literary criticism but to "show how literature can contribute to the understanding of culture," Pike examines the "word-cities" (literary or mythical archetypes of cities) as they have appeared in European as well as American literature. He begins by noting that as long as there has been literature there have been cities and ambivalence toward cities in literature (the Bible, the Iliad, etc.). The city has five models: ancient, medieval, Renaissance, industrial (19th century), and post-industrial. For 19th-century writers, the city meant the isolation of the individual from community: it was, for Hawthorne, a "paved solitude." In 20th-century literature, the city represents "fragmentation of the very concept of community." Pike does not discuss the relationship between country and city, saying that it has been treated sufficiently already.

L 377. PINSKER, SANFORD. Between Two Worlds: The American Novel in the 1960's. Troy, N.Y.: Whitson, 1980. 139 pp.
Pinsker identifies the 1960s as a Post-Modernist era and examines the strategies of novelists writing in that era. Some, he writes, head in a tentative direction; others are certain, definitely "American." In his opening chapter, he provides an overview of the shift from Modernism to Post-Modernism, noting the influence of Hemingway and the introspection of fiction (notably Salinger's) during the "stifling" 1950s. In subsequent chapters, he discusses Black Humorists and how they reveal the absurdity of the world; American-Jewish writing; Styron's and Malamud's "historical" writing; Barth; Vonnegut; David Madden; and I. B. Singer and Joyce Carol Oates, who, rather than trying to "out antiart" other writers, turn to some old-fashioned angles as a response to Modernism.

L 378. PODHORETZ, NORMAN. Doings and Undoings: The Fifties and After in American Writing. New York: Farrar, Straus, 1964. 371 pp.
In this book, the longtime editor of Commentary magazine offers twenty-seven occasional essays, each of which "was written in hot response to a particular event and out of a highly specific context." The subjects range from individual books (e.g., Arendt's Eichmann in Jerusalem), to general appraisals of authors (e.g., Faulkner, Edmund Wilson, Mailer, Bellow, Roth), to matters of social policy and history (e.g., "The World of TV Drama" and "My Negro Problem—And Ours"). The book is a reflection of the concerns of intellectuals in America from about 1954 to 1963.

L 379. PROFFER, CARL R., ed. and trans. Soviet Criticism of American Literature in the Sixties: An Anthology. Ann Arbor, Mich.: Ardis, 1972. 213 pp.
Proffer's collection attempts to assess the state of American literary studies in the Soviet Union. The book reviews, critical essays, and short monographs grouped in Section One study 20th-century writers and texts: J. D. Salinger, Mary McCarthy, Henry Miller, John Cheever, Saul Bellow, John Updike, William Styron, Lionel Trilling, Norman Mailer, Carson McCullers, F. Scott Fitzgerald, Ernest Hemingway, and William Faulkner. Section Two surveys Russian criticism and translations of American literature.

L 380. PUTZ, MANFRED. The Story of Identity: American Fiction of the Sixties. Stuttgart: Metzler, 1979. 293 pp.
Using structuralist methodology, Putz defines what he calls a new genre: the fable of identity. He finds in the work of six representative authors—Barth, Brautigan, Pynchon, Rhinehart, Sukenick, and Nabokov—a preoccupa-

tion with the dichotomy of self and world and the attempt, and typical
failure, by the hero to imaginatively transcend alienation. He takes
his study a step further and uses sociological and psychological models
to identify and explain deep structures which the novels under consideration share in common. Finally, he examines American culture of the 1960s
to discover why the problem of identity arose so compellingly in that
decade. The development of this "new fiction," Putz argues, can be defined
as a shift from thematic concerns to the problems of fiction itself, "and
from there to problems of the reader's attitude towards and participation
in the act of fictional communication."

L 381. RAHV, PHILIP. Essays on Literature & Politics, 1932-1972. Edited
         by Arabel J. Porter and Andrew J. Duosin. Boston: Houghton
         Mifflin, 1978. 366 pp.
The editors have arranged this collection of Rahv's essays in three sections: "American Writers and Writing"; "Russian and European Literature";
and "Politics, Religion, and Culture." The result is a diverse anthology
that includes "Paleface and Redskin," Rahv's well-known formulation of
American literature, five essays examining Dostoyevsky that nearly constitute a small monograph on that author, and evaluations of such writers
as Nathaniel Hawthorne, Henry James, Franz Kafka, Leo Tolstoy, and Saul
Bellow, as well as reflections on political and cultural issues ranging
from proletarian literature to the New Left. A brief memoir by Mary
McCarthy introduces the volume.

L 382. REVELL, PETER. Quest in Modern American Poetry. Totowa, N.J.:
         Barnes & Noble, 1981. 245 pp.
Revell charts the Modernist epistemological voyage to understanding in
Conrad Aiken's The Divine Pilgrim, Ezra Pound's Cantos, T. S. Eliot's
Four Quartets, H. D.'s Trilogy, and William Carlos Williams's Paterson.
He sees this quest "to reclaim for spiritual use the realm of matter laid
waste by empiricism" as lying at the heart of the Modernist enterprise,
and finds its roots in Whitman and Emerson as well as Bergson and Freud.
Introductory biographical material, particularly concerning the interrela-
tionships among this group of poets, is provided.

L 383. RIDEOUT, WALTER B. The Radical Novel in the United States, 1900-
         1954: Some Interrelations of Literature and Society. Cambridge,
         Mass.: Harvard University Press, 1956. 339 pp.
Rideout's work is an attempt to define the place of radical fiction within
our literature. According to Rideout, "The full story of the radical
novel in the United States must show that, although it has been confined
to the twentieth century, it has come in two waves rather than one."
The first wave consisted of a sizeable body of fiction which was produced
by writers responding positively to Socialism. The second wave, the literature of the 1930s, was produced primarily by writers influenced by Communism. If the writers in this latter group deliberately cut themselves
off from their predecessors, both groups shared in common "an attempt
to express through the literary form of the novel a predominantly Marxist
point of view toward society."

L 384. ROSENTHAL, M. L. The Modern Poets: A Critical Introduction.
         New York: Oxford University Press, 1960. 288 pp.
Rosenthal sets himself the task of making modern poetry accessible to
the general reader. He believes that the difficulty of modern poetry
lies not in an inherent obscurity of meaning but in the privacy of the
poet's perspective; and, beginning with three long chapters devoted,
respectively, to Yeats, Pound, and Eliot, he endeavors to orient the reader
to the sensibility and world-view of these modern poets as well as to
their work. Subsequent chapters cover all the major poets of the modern
period, from Edwin Arlington Robinson to W. H. Auden, and the book ends

with a look at the work of later poets such as Dylan Thomas, Robert Lowell, and Charles Olson.

L 385. ROSENTHAL, M. L. The New Poets: American and British Poetry Since World War II. New York: Oxford University Press, 1967. 350 pp. In a sequel to his The Modern Poets: A Critical Introduction (see L 384), Rosenthal surveys the post-war poetry scene in the U.S. and Great Britain. The conviction underlying his analysis is that the poetry being written since the period of the great moderns has a distinctive character of its own; and, as he did in The Modern Poets, Rosenthal frames his examination of the post-war poets with an outline of the new sensibility--alienated, fragmented, and displaced--that informs their work. A long chapter on "Robert Lowell and 'Confessional' Poetry" sets the tone for the survey, and the work of all the major post-war poets is discussed, with separate chapters devoted to contemporary British and contemporary Irish poetry.

L 386. RUBIN, LOUIS D., Jr. The Faraway Country: Writers of the Modern South. Seattle: University of Washington Press, 1963. 256 pp. Rubin's nine essays collected here "represent an attempt to use literature in order to understand Southern life." Mark Twain is the prototype for modern Southern authors; "he grew up in a small, contained community, and . . . was propelled by his art and his times far beyond that community." When such authors returned to their homes, they found the intrusions of modern society, and so the "real South" they remembered became the faraway country of their imaginations. To demonstrate this thesis, Rubin examines works of George W. Cable, William Faulkner, Thomas Wolfe, Robert Penn Warren, Eudora Welty, the Agrarians (Warren, Donald Davidson, John Crowe Ransom, and Allen Tate), and William Styron.

L 387. RUBIN, LOUIS D., Jr. The Wary Fugitives: Four Poets and the South. Baton Rouge: Louisiana State University Press, 1978. 384 pp. Examining the work of John Crowe Ransom, Allen Tate, Donald Davidson, and Robert Penn Warren, Rubin analyzes "the relationship between modern southern literature and southern life." These four poets began their careers at Vanderbilt University in the 1920s and later published their own magazine, The Fugitive. In 1930, they expressed their Agrarian commitment to Southern rural tradition in I'll Take My Stand (see L 318), "a book written by young men who came later to modernism, and came to it out of a community experience that was historically apprehended." Rubin uses this work as his focal point, tracing its genesis and its consequences in the careers of the four poets.

L 388. RUBIN, LOUIS D., Jr. and ROBERT D. JACOBS, eds. Southern Renascence: The Literature of the Modern South. Baltimore, Md.: Johns Hopkins University Press, 1953. 450 pp. This collection of essays was one of the first works to survey and analyze the literature of the modern South. The essays are arranged in four main sections: "The Mind of the South," "The Themes of Southern Literature," "The Novelists of the South," and "The Poetry of the South." A forum of different views, this book contains specific and comparative essays representing different critical approaches. The work attempts to view Southern writers within their geographical and cultural milieu. Some of the writers and critics covered are William Faulkner, Allen Tate, Robert Penn Warren, Ellen Glasgow, James Branch Cabell, Katherine Anne Porter, John Crowe Ransom, Donald Davidson, and Cleanth Brooks.

L 389. RULAND, RICHARD. The Rediscovery of American Literature: Premises of Critical Taste, 1900-1940. Cambridge, Mass.: Harvard University Press, 1967. 329 pp.
In separate essays Ruland examines the values of a group of foremost early 20th-century American critics, including Van Wyck Brooks, H. L. Mencken, Irving Babbitt, and F. O. Matthiessen. As a whole, the work considers the influence of belief on literary criticism from W.W. I to the 1930s, when widespread interest in literature's social and political implications raised the question of "cultural nationalism." In Ruland's words, "again the role of the national literature in shaping the nation's identity became a subject for debate."

L 390. SCHOLES, ROBERT. The Fabulators. New York: Oxford University Press, 1967. 180 pp.
Scholes wishes us to believe that "fabulators" are a particular kind of fiction writer, to be distinguished from the novelist or the satirist. Fabulators have a special "delight in design" and a necessary "didactic quality"; hence the modern fabulator "tends away from the representation of reality but returns toward actual human life by way of ethically controlled fantasy." The modern fabulists discussed include Durrell and Murdoch from England; and Vonnegut, Southern, Hawkes, and Barth from America.

L 391. SCHORER, MARK. The World We Imagine: Selected Essays. New York: Farrar, Straus & Giroux, 1968. 402 pp.
The essays collected in this volume treat a range of authors and issues. Opening with a theoretical discussion, "Technique as Discovery," Schorer looks at 20th-century American fiction to argue that technique distinguishes art from reality. Parts III and IV, devoted almost exclusively to D. H. Lawrence and Sinclair Lewis, includes discussions of Women in Love, Lady Chatterley's Lover, Elmer Gantry, the Lawrence-Lewis relationship, and Lewis's biography. Studies of Hamlin Garland, Conrad Aiken, Katherine Anne Porter, Carson McCullers, and Truman Capote constitute Part V. Part VI, "Some Relationships," examines the personal and professional interaction among Gertrude Stein, Sherwood Anderson, F. Scott Fitzgerald, and Ernest Hemingway.

L 392. SIENICKA, MARTA, ed. Traditions in the Twentieth Century American Literature. Poznan, Poland: Adam Mickiewicz University Press, 1981. 288 pp.
This work consists of the proceedings of the second symposium on American literature which was held at Kiekrz, Poland, in December 1979. The conference was organized by the Institute of English at Poznan. The twenty-one papers presented in this volume, although widely varying in subject matter, all were meant to explore "the nature and varieties of the traditions which were formative for American literature in this century." Contributors include Teresa Balazy, C. W. E. Bigsby, Marc Chenetier, Josef Jarab, Teresa Kieniewicz, and Richard Martin.

L 393. SINGAL, DANIEL JOSEPH. The War Within: From Victorian to Modernist Thought in the South, 1919-1945. Chapel Hill: University of North Carolina Press, 1982. 442 pp.
Singal begins by arguing that Allen Tate's contention that the Southern Renaissance was fueled by a marked social change—the shift from an agrarian to an industrial society and the tensions created by that shift—does not accurately or adequately account for the phenomenon. Nor, Siegal notes, does any change within the realm of thought alone explain the shift from Victorianism to Modernism that occurred during the Southern Renaissance. Claiming that one must look at the sensibilities and circumstances of the intellectuals whose works embodied that shift, Singal employs a biographical approach. He identifies three stages within this shift and

discusses representative figures associated with each: Post-Victorians--
those who tried to break with Victorianism but ultimately remained loyal
to 19th-century ideals (Ulrich B. Phillips, Ellen Glasgow, Broadus
Mitchell); and transitional figures (Howard W. Odum, William Faulkner,
the Agrarians); and those who were unquestionably Modernists (William
Terry Couch, Rupert B. Vance, Guy B. Johnson, Arthur F. Raper, and Robert
Penn Warren).

L 394. SINGH, AMRITJIT. The Novels of the Harlem Renaissance: Twelve
        Black Writers 1923-1933. University Park: Pennsylvania State
        University Press, 1976. 175 pp.
This study examines twenty-one novels by twelve black writers of the Harlem
Renaissance. In order to clarify the "aesthetic and sociocultural
impulses" that lie behind the production of these works of art, Singh focuses
on several key issues: self-definition, class, caste, and color. In
the first chapter, he outlines the social, political, and cultural context,
and explores the concept of the Harlem Renaissance itself, with all of
its contradictions and controversies. He then proceeds in thematically
organized chapters to discuss novels by Arna Bontemps, Countee Cullen,
W. E. B. DuBois, Jessie Redmon Fauset, Rudolph Fisher, Langston Hughes,
Nella Larsen, Claude McKay, George S. Schuyler, Wallace Thurman, Jean
Toomer, and Walter F. White.

L 395. SMITH, STAN. Inviolable Voice: History and Twentieth-Century
        Poetry. Atlantic Highlands, N.J.: Humanities Press, 1982.
        243 pp.
This study examines the presence of history in modern British and American
poems, and focuses on two main themes: the embeddedness of any poet in
his or her particular historical context, and the unavoidable complicity
of poetry's individual "inviolable voice" with the forces of history extrin-
sic to the self. Smith begins with T. S. Eliot, and discusses in turn
Thomas Hardy, Edward Thomas, Eliot, Ezra Pound, W. H. Auden, Thom Gunn
and Ted Hughes, Philip Larkin, D. J. Enright and Brian Patten, Sylvia
Plath, and Robert Lowell. Each poet is placed in the context of biography,
cultural surroundings, and literary history, and Smith reads particular
poems and parts of poems upon which the struggle between poetic voice
and the march of history are inscribed.

L 396. SPENCER, BENJAMIN T. Patterns of Nationality: Twentieth-Century
        Literary Versions of America. New York: Burt Franklin, 1981.
        243 pp.
In this book, which is a supplement to the earlier The Quest for Nationality (see L 191), Spencer examines how eight 20th-century American writers
have envisioned America. He purposely leaves the notion of nationality
pluralistic, because he finds 20th-century American nationality to be
still in the making. In the early chapters, he discusses how there has
been an almost continuous attempt to break with the English tradition,
how American writers have always been self-conscious about the connection
between the national character and their own styles, and how Whitman and
Mark Twain became central figures for early 20th-century American writers.
The eight writers he discusses (in separate chapters) are Stein, Pound,
Williams, Anderson, Fitzgerald, Hart Crane, Dahlberg, and Mailer.

L 397. SPIVEY, TED R. The Journey Beyond Tragedy: A Study of Myth and
        Modern Fiction. Orlando: University Presses of Florida, 1980.
        190 pp.
Relying on the work of Carl Jung, Joseph Campbell, and Mircea Eliade,
Spivey examines selected fiction and poetry by George Eliot, Thomas Hardy,
Oscar Wilde, Ernest Hemingway, Hermann Hesse, James Joyce, William Faulkner,
D. H. Lawrence, Flannery O'Connor, Romain Gary, Walker Percy, T. S. Eliot,
and Thomas Mann as representatives of the Modernist era. A mythic vision,

according to Spivey, allows an author to transcend pessimism and guilt and give to the reader a hopeful substitute.

L 398. STEVICK, PHILLIP. Alternative Pleasures: Post-Realist Fiction and the Tradition. Urbana: University of Illinois Press, 1981. 150 pp.
This appreciation of post-Realist fiction—primarily of the 1970s—groups texts by theme and features obscure authors along with major figures. Concerned with defining a tradition, Stevick considers such topics as metaphors for the novel, verbal collage, sentimentality, naive narration, satire, and fictional "dreck." A concluding chapter explains that the approaches to this literature which depend on a study of "schools," major figures, an aesthetic credo, an ideology, a mediating critic or man of letters, or a current critical vocabulary are fundamentally inadequate.

L 399. STRAUMANN, HEINRICH. American Literature in the Twentieth Century. 1951; Rev. ed. New York: Harper Torchbooks, 1965. 224 pp.
The original 1951 edition has been updated to include new notes on contemporary writers. Both a reference guide and a survey study, Straumann's book provides a series of brief discussions on a broad number of major writers and literary movements of this century. While keeping biography and critical interpretation to a minimum, Straumann addresses himself to each author's general concerns and beliefs as expressed in their works. Over seventy such discussions (some of which cover several authors) are presented.

L 400. SUTTON, WALTER. Modern American Criticism. Englewood Cliffs, N.J.: Prentice-Hall, 1963. 298 pp.
Sutton's work provides a survey of 20th-century American literary criticism and its aesthetic and social context. He divides modern criticism into six major schools (early psychological criticism, new humanism, liberal and Marxist criticism, New Criticism, neo-Aristotelian criticism, psychological and myth criticism) and supplies chapters on the history of criticism and "Criticism as a Social Act."

L 401. TANNER, TONY. City of Words: American Fiction 1950-1970. New York: Harper & Row, 1971. 463 pp.
Tanner analyzes the American imagination as it expresses itself in selected novels from 1950 to 1970. These novels share a fundamental tension: an "abiding dread" that life is patterned by others. Tanner not only draws on literary criticism but also on modern social anthropology (people have no direct contact with experience but react according to an intervening set of patterns), behavioral psychology (people are always dominated by situational context), and linguistics (people's thoughts are determined by unconscious, individualized language patterns). This synthetic work analyzes such novelists as Vladimir Nabokov, Ralph Ellison, Saul Bellow, Joseph Heller, William Burroughs, Thomas Pynchon, Kurt Vonnegut, Jr., John Barth, Sylvia Plath, Bernard Malamud, Norman Mailer, and Ken Kesey.

L 402. TASHJIAN, DICKRAN. William Carlos Williams and the American Scene, 1920-1940. Berkeley: University of California Press, 1978. 168 pp.
Tashjian's focus is the avant-garde between the 1913 Armory Show and W.W. II. The representative figure is Williams, the painter/poet who stood at the edge as both an observer and as a revolutionary. Relying on cultural studies by Michael Kammen and Victor Turner, Tashjian examines the roles of photographers, painters, and poets in society as they sought to develop a new "cultural design." This book combines the photographs of Man Ray and Alfred Steiglitz, the paintings of the Social Realists, the poetry of Williams, and a variety of contributions by others in order to "regain contact" with "those varied groupings of artists who wanted to create a distinctive and authentic American Art."

L 403. TATE, ALLEN. Reactionary Essays on Poetry and Ideas. New York: Scribner, 1936. 240 pp.

These fifteen occasional essays, sometimes expanded from their earlier publication in journals, reveal many of the preoccupations of the Fugitive and Agrarian movements and some of the methods of the New Criticism, with which Tate is also associated. Included are an enlarged version of the essay "Religion and the Old South" from I'll Take My Stand (see L 318); essays on the American poets, Dickinson, Hart Crane, Pound, E. A. Robinson, Eliot, and Cummings; and several more general essays on poetry and philosophy.

L 404. THORP, WILLARD. American Writing in the Twentieth Century. Cambridge, Mass.: Harvard University Press, 1960. 353 pp.

For Thorp, American literature between 1900 and 1950 constitutes a second "Renaissance," perhaps greater than the first (1840-1850) in its scope. Chapters One, Four, and Five examine American fiction and the vogue for Realism and Naturalism; Chapters Two and Six consider American poetry; Chapter Three analyzes American drama up to 1940; Chapter Seven looks at the most influential of the regional movements, the "Southern Renaissance"; and Chapter Eight deals chronologically with the critical reception of American literature. Although this work is general, Thorp concludes each chapter with a detailed consideration of one representative author.

L 405. TOMLINSON, CHARLES. Some Americans: A Personal Record. Berkeley: University of California Press, 1981. 134 pp.

Tomlinson chronicles through his friendships with American poets and scholars during the 1950s his exposure as a poet to American poetics, especially the "objectivists." Through anecdotes and recollections he writes the autobiography of his poetic assimilation of the divergent American reactions to the Poundian-Eliotic aesthetic. His chapters include descriptions of meetings with William Carlos Williams, Marianne Moore, Robert Lowell, and Yvor Winters, and an introduction to the radical objectivism of Louis Zukofsky and George Oppen.

L 406. VENDLER, HELEN. Part of Nature, Part of Us: Modern American Poets. Cambridge, Mass.: Harvard University Press, 1980. 376 pp.

This work is a collection of book reviews and short essays previously published separately between 1968 and 1979. Vendler's stance is that of an appreciative reader introducing often difficult poetry to a general audience. She takes each poet as an individual, asking: what is his moral vision? what are his touchstones from the literary past? and what is the shape of his career? Individual essays deal with such poets as Stevens, Lowell, Moore, Warren, Auden, Bishop, Jarrell, Berryman, O'Hara, Ginsberg, Rich, and Plath, as well as the facsimile edition of The Waste Land and three groups of new books.

L 407. VOS, NELVIN. The Great Pendulum of Becoming: Images in Modern Drama. Grand Rapids, Mich.: Christian University Press, 1980. 135 pp.

According to Vos, the great chain of being (ordered, harmonious, and locating man between the angels and animals) is replaced in modern drama with a cosmos in which man's place is sometimes shared with animals and machines, and in which chaos and change are powerful forces. Vos groups the authors he discusses in terms of the pre-eminent images in their work: chaos, creation, and becoming. He further uses the organization of the Divine Comedy to group themes he considers infernal, paradisiacal, or purgatorial: the bestial, impotence, the American dream, alcohol, recovering an ideal world, performing, waiting, and dying. Authors treated are O'Neill, Saroyan, Williams, Jason Miller, Arthur Miller, George O'Neil, Osborne, Pinter, and Kaiser.

L 408. WAGGONER, HYATT H. The Heel of Elohim: Science and Values in
Modern American Poetry. Norman: University of Oklahoma Press,
1950. 235 pp.
Waggoner desires "to throw some light on the nature of modern American
poetry by viewing it against a backdrop of science and scientific philosophy." He notes a "tension between the facts of science and the facts
of poetry," and shows how this tension has affected and been dealt with
by six American poets: Robinson, Frost, Eliot, Jeffers, MacLeish, and
Hart Crane. The book is an "essay in philosophical criticism," and in
some ways a reaction against "positivistic materialism."

L 409. WAGNER, LINDA W. American Modern: Essays in Fiction and Poetry.
Port Washington, N.Y.: Kennikat Press, 1980. 263 pp.
In this collection of previously published essays--some about the Modernist
era as a whole, some about individual works, most about individual writers--
Wagner examines not just major American Modernists but also later writers
whose work has been influenced by Modernists. Early in the book she lists
four assumptions about modern American literature: (1) writers after
1900 were struggling toward a new nationalism; (2) they rebelled against
the "rhetoric of ameliorization" that betrayed beliefs; (3) they had an
obsession with innovation and techniques; (4) they had a belief in human
capacity--in the heroism of daring. She asserts that the aesthetic dominating 19th- and 20th-century American literature--a peculiarly American
egocentricity--is "the creation through language of the individual."
Writers discussed by Wagner include Hemingway, Dos Passos, Faulkner, Stein,
Anderson, Pynchon, Williams, Berryman, Levertov, and Rich.

L 410. WALLACE, RONALD. The Last Laugh: Form and Affirmation in the
Contemporary American Comic Novel. Columbia: University of Missouri Press, 1979. 159 pp.
In an effort to place the work of Barth, Hawkes, Nabokov, Kesey, and Coover
in a comic tradition, and to formulate the generic and recurring aspects
of the comic form, Wallace rejects the idea that "black humor" is either
new or a purely American phenomenon. Using generic categories derived
from Aristotle and Frye, Wallace analyzes how recent comic novels incorporate the violence and chaos of modern life by combining the conventional
character types, plot patterns, and stylistic devices of an earlier comedy.

L 411. WALSH, JEFFREY. American War Literature 1914 to Vietnam. New
York: St. Martin's Press, 1982. 218 pp.
Walsh analyzes both fiction and poetry in his account of the war literature
produced during the 20th century in America. He details the traditions
developed in each genre as they emerge from various experiences of war,
primarily W.W. I, W.W. II, and the Vietnam conflict. In his discussion
of war fiction, Walsh takes e. e. cummings's novel The Enormous Room and
Ernest Hemingway's A Farewell to Arms as the major examples of modernist
war novels. He addresses war poetry in separate chapters with a particular
focus on the poetry produced following W.W. II. For his discussion of
war poetry, Walsh concentrates on the works of Randall Jarrell, Louis
Simpson, and Richard Eberhart. The volume concludes with a chapter devoted
to the portrayals of the Vietnam conflict and its ramifications in the
works of such writers as Norman Mailer, Joseph Heller, and Kurt Vonnegut,
Jr.

L 412. WEALES, GERALD. American Drama Since World War II. New York:
Harcourt, Brace & World, 1962. 246 pp.
Weales's book is a critical description of American plays produced between
1945 and 1961. Weales devotes separate chapters to Arthur Miller and
Tennessee Williams and discusses such groups as "The New Pineros" (e.g.,
William Inge), "The Video Boys" (e.g., Paddy Chayefsky, Rod Serling),
and "The Playwrights of the Twenties and Thirties" (e.g., Elmer Rice, George
S. Kaufman). He also studies musical comedy, off-Broadway plays, adap-
tations, and comedy--in all, a great number of plays and playwrights.

L 413. **WEBER, RONALD.** The Literature of Fact: Literary Nonfiction in American Writing. Athens: Ohio University Press, 1980. 181 pp.
Rejecting the term "New Journalism" as too broad, Weber assigns the label "literary nonfiction" to works based on documentation but informed by the intent to narrate a theme: "the writer tries to draw together the conflicting roles of observer and maker, journalist and artist." Keeping in mind the historical interaction between journalism and fiction, he analyzes the work of Capote, Mailer, Wolfe, Agee, C. D. B. Bryan, and others writing between 1960 and 1980. As far as these works are history, Weber demands from them credibility and an account of research methods. As far as they are art, he demands "the meaningful resonance of fiction" and the avoidance of the narcissism of self-revelation. Unlike some critics, Weber believes that literary nonfiction attempted neither to replace the novel nor to erase the distinction between fact and fiction.

L 414. **WEBSTER, GRANT.** The Republic of Letters: A History of Postwar American Literary Opinion. Baltimore, Md.: Johns Hopkins University Press, 1979. 381 pp.
Webster's purpose in this work is to do for American criticism what Thomas Kuhn did for science in The Structure of Scientific Revolutions—to describe how literary ideologies or paradigms (which he calls "charters") come into being or disappear and to discuss two particular charters at length. The two he discusses—the Formalists and the New York Intellectuals—were the dominant critical schools in America during the 1940s and 1950s. Key figures among the Formalists were Eliot, Brooks, Wellek, Wimsatt, and Krieger; among the New York group were Trilling, Rahv, Howe, Kazin, and Wilson. Webster urges his theory of charters because, he claims, it yields a science of criticism and improves our understanding of critical works by taking into account their social and ideological contexts.

L 415. **WEINBERG, HELEN.** The New Novel in America: The Kafkan Mode in Contemporary Fiction. Ithaca, N.Y.: Cornell University Press, 1970. 248 pp.
Weinberg uses "Kafka's novels as an index to the ways that the modernist sensibility may yet write for the sake of life, not the sake of art"; Kafka is presented as "the spiritual pioneer" for some contemporary American novelists who have rebelled against "aestheticism and whose heroes are "spiritual activists." Kafka is examined first, and then Bellow, Mailer, Salinger, Malamud, Roth, Gold, Baldwin, Ellison, and Cassill.

L 416. **WERNER, CRAIG HANSEN.** Paradoxical Resolutions: American Fiction Since James Joyce. Urbana: University of Illinois Press, 1982. 225 pp.
Speaking of 20th-century American fiction and Joyce's influence upon it, Werner claims that Joyce has "helped us to understand our tradition, our direction, our rhythm, and our flow." He argues that throughout the 19th century, there was no resolution between the Realistic and Romantic traditions of American literature—no resolution of the ambiguous relationship between the hero and the community—and that Joyce (who saw the role of the writer as that of mediator between dream and reality) provided American writers with a model for creating that resolution. Among those Werner sees as influenced by Joyce are Faulkner, Gaddis, Wright, and Pynchon.

L 417. **WEST, RAY B., Jr.** The Short Story in America 1900-1950. Chicago: Regnery, 1952. 147 pp.
In this work, West combines critical and synthetic comments, sketching plot only when necessary. The book begins with a definition of the short story and an assessment of the 19th-century tales of Hawthorne, Poe, Melville, and James. It then moves to short works by "Naturalist" authors

(e.g., Crane, Anderson) and "Traditionalists" (e.g., Fitzgerald, Warren). A separate chapter considers two "masters of the modern short story," Ernest Hemingway and William Faulkner, and the concluding chapter analyzes short fiction of the 1940s by Eudora Welty, Truman Capote, and others.

L 418. WEST, THOMAS REED. Flesh of Steel: Literature and the Machine in American Culture. Nashville, Tenn.: Vanderbilt University Press, 1967. 155 pp.
The subject of West's book is "the machine, and machine civilization, in the two characters of discipline and energy." Authors considered-- Sherwood Anderson, Waldo Frank, John Dos Passos, Thorstein Veblen, Carl Sandburg, Harold Stearns, Lewis Mumford, and Sinclair Lewis--are all contemporary but cover no single genre, literary movement, or intellectual school. West relates modern views of the machine to a historical background, briefly indicates some authors who have viewed the machine favorably, and acknowledges the inadequacy of the term "machine." Appended are a bibliography and a list of additional references.

L 419. WHIPPLE, THOMAS KING. Spokesmen. New York: Appleton, 1928. 276 pp.
Basing his work on the criticism of Max Eastman and Van Wyck Brooks, Whipple examines individual authors and American culture. He feels that 20th-century American writers were confined by their surroundings and temperaments to themes of spiritual frustration. The critic asserts that some (Vachel Lindsay, Theodore Dreiser, Sinclair Lewis) were literary adolescents unable to express social complaints. Others (Henry Adams, E. A. Robinson) pessimistically wrote of the individual's struggle amid national chaos. Occasionally writers triumphed over the limitations of their backgrounds; Robert Frost, Carl Sandburg and Willa Cather successfully used American materials, and Sherwood Anderson and Eugene O'Neill penetrated the surface of American life in their tragedies. The American situation, Whipple concludes, exalts the practical, or acquisitive, nature. The poetic temper, which seeks to experience rather than exploit life, cannot flourish in such an environment.

L 420. WICKES, GEORGE. Americans in Paris. Garden City, N.Y.: Doubleday, 1969. 290 pp.
Wickes discusses the lives led and art created by six American artists who chose to live and work in Paris at some point during the first four decades of the 20th century: Gertrude Stein, e. e. cummings, Man Ray, Ernest Hemingway, Virgil Thomson, and Henry Miller. Noting that many Americans expatriated to Paris during this period, Wickes states that he has chosen these six because they stayed in Paris an "appreciable length of time" and produced significant work there. They went abroad, he insists, for "positive rather than negative reasons"--to work seriously in a setting where arts and letters were respected and where the pressure to conform was less. Wickes includes a chronology of important "art" events of the era and several photographs.

L 421. WILDER, AMOS N. Theology and Modern Literature. Cambridge, Mass.: Harvard University Press, 1958. 145 pp.
Wilder examines the interdependence of religion and aesthetics. He is primarily interested in how the present religious crisis in our culture has affected modern literature, how an understanding of theology can inform aesthetic judgment, and how authentic literary art can embody theological problems in a way that is denied to more discursive approaches. In the final chapter on Faulkner's The Sound and the Fury, Wilder comments more generally on the American literary tradition.

L 422. WILSON, EDMUND. The American Earthquake: A Documentary of the
     Twenties and Thirties. New York: Doubleday, 1958. 576 pp.
Wilson intends this "selection" from his "non-literary articles written
during the twenties and thirties" to run "parallel to the literary material
collected" in The Shores of Light (see L 426). Most of the ninety-odd
selections were first published in The New Republic; they reflect both
the giddiness of the twenties and the sense of looming disaster of the
1930s. Wilson examines the excesses of both decades, analyzing a range
of social and cultural events and upheavals.

L 423. WILSON, EDMUND. The Bit Between My Teeth: A Literary Chronicle
     of 1950-1965. New York: Farrar, Straus, 1965. 694 pp.
Wilson's march through the literary occasions of his lifetime continues
in this "chronicle," made up of his contributions to magazines and journals
(especially The New Yorker) during a fifteen-year period. The subjects
of these forty-three essays include the correspondence of Justice Holmes
with Harold Laski, John Peale Bishop, Max Beerbohm, James Branch Cabell,
and other literary memoirs.

L 424. WILSON, EDMUND. Classics and Commercials: A Literary Chronicle
     of the Forties. New York: Farrar, Straus, 1950. 534 pp.
Subtitled "A Literary Chronicle of the Forties," this collection brings
together much of Wilson's literary journalism of the period. Most pieces
originally appeared in The New Yorker, The New Republic, or The Nation.
The occasion of each essay is usually a new book, but subjects include
James Joyce, the American Civil War, and "George Grosz in the United
States." The collection more generally treats the practice of letters
during and after W.W. II.

L 425. WILSON, EDMUND. The Devils and Canon Barham: Ten Essays on Poets,
     Novelists and Monsters. New York: Farrar, Straus, 1973. 219 pp.
This is the last collection of Wilson's occasional pieces, brought out
after his death in 1972. Among the essays are assessments of Hemingway's
posthumously published Islands in the Stream, The Waste Land, H. L. Mencken,
and two neglected American novelists, Henry Blake Fuller and Harold
Frederic.

L 426. WILSON, EDMUND. The Forties. Edited by Leon Edel. New York:
     Farrar, Straus & Giroux, 1983. 356 pp.
Unlike Wilson's previous volumes, The Twenties (see L 429) and The Thirties
(see L 428), which he began to prepare for publication himself, this is
a wholly posthumous volume. It consists of selections from Wilson's notebooks and journals, including notes for The Wound and the Bow, a critical
work, and for a never-completed autobiographical novel. It also includes
journal entries Wilson made after visits with people--George Santayana,
the Zuni of New Mexico, John Dos Passos, Edna St. Vincent Millay--or to
places--Italy, London, Greece, Nevada, the West Coast, Haiti, and elsewhere.
Edel provides an introduction, a chronology of Wilson's life during this
time, and brief notes on background information.

L 427. WILSON, EDMUND. The Shores of Light: A Literary Chronicle of
     the Twenties and Thirties. New York: Farrar, Straus & Young,
     1952. 814 pp.
This is the first of Wilson's "chronicles" covering his literary work
in particular periods. Here he has revised much of his periodical publication (seventy-three of the ninety-seven pieces "first appeared in
the New Republic"); draws on the personal reminiscences he later published
in The Twenties (see L 429); and discusses major American writers of the
period.

L 428. WILSON, EDMUND. The Thirties. Edited by Leon Edel. New York:
Farrar, Straus & Giroux, 1980. 730 pp.
Edel reconstructed this volume from Wilson's notebooks, manuscripts, and
diaries. Wilson's texts comment on the economic, social, and literary
issues of the 1930s and take in much of the wide range of artists,
scholars, and literary journalists Wilson encountered. Travels throughout
America and to Russia are chronicled as they relate to Wilson's search
for political and social answers to that era's problems. Wilson's day-
to-day life and reflections are left intact: Edel fills in gaps in the
narrative with summaries of Wilson's intervening activities and provides
historical notation on names and events mentioned in Wilson's text.

L 429. WILSON, EDMUND. The Twenties: From Notebooks and Diaries of the
Period. Edited by Leon Edel. New York: Farrar, Straus & Giroux,
1975. 557 pp.
Wilson was working on this book when he died in 1972; for it, the editor
writes, he "had assembled the greater part out of old notebooks of the
time and inserted certain passages of memory which gave the book an autobiographical cast." Wilson writes about people and places as well as
about his physical and intellectual experiences. The work is divided
chronologically into two parts, 1919-1925 and 1926-1930, with general
commentary by the editor preceding each section.

L 430. WINTERS, YVOR. Primitivism and Decadence: A Study of American
Experimental Poetry. New York: Arrow, 1937. 146 pp.
This study is an attempt to elucidate the methods of the "Experimental
school" in American poetry. Among the poets considered are Hart Crane,
Robinson Jeffers, T. S. Eliot, Ezra Pound, William Carlos Williams,
Marianne Moore, Wallace Stevens, and Archibald MacLeish. Winters concludes
with the judgment that experimental poetry is incomplete insofar as it
does not make full use of the possibilities of language.

L 431. WOODWARD, KATHLEEN. At Last, the Real Distinguished Thing: The
Late Poems of Eliot, Pound, Stevens, and Williams. Columbus:
Ohio State University Press, 1980. 175 pp.
Admitting that this work grows out of her interest in two seemingly disparate problems--the distinction between Modernism and Postmodernism and
the problems of aging and the elderly in our culture--Woodward examines
the later poetry of four major poets. She concentrates on one long poem
by each: Eliot's Four Quartets, Pound's Pisan Cantos, Stevens's The Rock,
and Williams's Paterson V. In our culture, she notes, we value action
or change (which are both associated with youth) over stasis (associated
with age), but only a certain stasis (achieved through balancing) yields
wisdom. She claims the late poems of these four poets embody something
our culture lacks--"the pursuit of the eternal."

L 432. WYATT, DAVID M. Prodigal Sons: A Study in Authorship and Authority.
Baltimore, Md.: Johns Hopkins University Press, 1980. 172 pp.
A crucial point in an author's life, argues Wyatt, is the moment he reconciles himself to an authority he has returned to after a fall and a period
of wandering. Wyatt locates this moment in the careers of James, Yeats,
Synge, Hemingway, Faulkner, Agee, Warren, and Davies. He then describes
this moment as part of the author's development to discover an authoritative stance. As a "critic of careers," Wyatt adopts as his primary
critical principle the importance of the effects of the outside world
upon the generation of a text. Wyatt writes, "criticism of careers thus
presumes a consonance of form and meaning, but the form and the meaning
arise out of the 'before' and 'after' of a personal history, rather than
from the balanced stress of forces in a timeless work of art."

L 433. YOUNG, THOMAS DANIEL. The Past in the Present: A Thematic Study of Modern Southern Fiction. Baton Rouge: Louisiana State University Press, 1981. 189 pp.

Young discusses seven works by as many writers, to support his thesis that the classical-Christian tradition does not constitute the matrix of thought in modern Southern fiction. Young asserts that these writers believed in a tradition of ritual, ceremony, and manners, but nevertheless a tradition without God. Works by William Faulkner, Allen Tate, Robert Penn Warren, Eudora Welty, Flannery O'Connor, Walker Percy, and John Barth are examined for their various alternatives to religious belief.

L 434. YOUNG, THOMAS DANIEL. Tennessee Writers. Knoxville: University of Tennessee Press, 1981. 121 pp.

Three overlapping groups of influential literary men lived and wrote in 20th-century Tennessee: The Fugitives, the Agrarians, and the Southern New Critics. Young traces the careers and intentions of these writers, focusing on John Crowe Ransom, Allen Tate, Robert Penn Warren, and Donald Davidson. He frames his discussion of the Southern Renaissance with a brief description of Southern humorists and local colorists--G. W. Harris, Mary N. Murfree--and an examination of four contemporary writers--Mildred Haun, James Agee, Peter Taylor, Cormac McCarthy.

L 435. YOUNG, THOMAS DANIEL. Waking Their Neighbors Up: The Nashville Agrarians Rediscovered. Athens: University of Georgia Press, 1982. 86 pp.

This work comes out of the 1980 Lamar Memorial Lectures at Mercer University which commemorated the fiftieth anniversary of the publication of I'll Take My Stand (see L 318)--the foundational document of the Agrarian movement. Noting that I'll Take My Stand was a misunderstood document, Young argues that the Agrarians did not urge a retreat into the past; rather, they sought to warn society, as Thoreau had warned his society in the previous century, about the destructive tendencies in its development: material acquisitiveness, spiritual disorder, purposelessness, and destruction of individual integrity. He accounts for the variety of rhetorical approaches by noting that the contributors had widely divergent training, talent, and perspectives. Young devotes his final chapter to discussing some subsequent publications by the contributors.

L 436. ZAVARZADEH, MAS'UD. The Mythopoeic Reality: The Postwar American Nonfiction Novel. Urbana: University of Illinois Press, 1976. 262 pp.

Zavarzadeh describes his theory of what is the proper fictive response to "the multifarious pressures of contemporary America which render all interpretations of 'reality' arbitrary and therefore at the same time both accurate and absurd." The nonfictional novel exists because authorial interpretation is impossible; the chaos refuses to be ordered. Zavarzadeh first reconstructs the cultural and scientific forces which rendered the epistemological basis for the traditional novel useless. He then analyzes the generic structure of the nonfiction novel, using original terms to replace the traditional critical vocabulary. In Part II he discusses various kinds of nonfiction novels, using Hiroshima, In Cold Blood, The Electric Kool-Aid Acid Test, Armies of the Night, a, and La Vida as examples. He asserts that these works have replaced the traditional novel and have arisen out of the need to unify fact and fiction.

V.   THEMES

L 437. **ALLEN, WALTER.** The Urgent West: The American Dream and Modern
        Man. New York: Dutton, 1969. 240 pp.
Allen singles out the American Dream as the shaping force which, while
it does not necessarily make American literature better than that of different nations, certainly sets it apart. The first of the three sections
of this work provides a brief history of America—its progress and
population—and includes brief references to literary works. The second
section combines biography with literary discussion to deal with the following figures: Cooper, Hawthorne, Melville, Emerson, Thoreau, Whitman,
Poe, Twain, Dickinson and, to a lesser extent, Farrell, Cather, Hemingway,
Wolfe, Dos Passos, Hart Crane, and Henry Roth. The short third section
discusses the contemporary political and cultural "Americanization" of
the world.

L 438. **ANDREWS, WILLIAM L.,** ed. Literary Romanticism in America. Baton
        Rouge: Louisiana State University Press, 1981. 136 pp.
Romanticism, defined by Robert Spiller as "the ability to wonder and
reflect," figures in each of the essays collected in this volume. All
the people treated here in some way both idealized and questioned their
society. Included are essays by Clarence Gohdes on Emerson; Arlin Turner
on Hawthorne; William L. Andrews on black writers of the 1850s; Louis
D. Rubin, Jr. on Thomas Wolfe; C. Hugh Holman on Allen Tate; Panthea Reid
Broughton on Walker Percy; and John Seelye on Richard Nixon and the Self-
Made Man.

L 439. **ASSELINEAU, ROGER.** The Transcendentalist Constant in American
        Literature. New York: Gotham Library of New York University
        Press, 1980. 181 pp.
Asselineau has gathered several essays (conceived and written independently
of one another) in which he discusses Transcendentalism—not in a pure
but in a general form—in the work of several 19th- and 20th-century American writers. His emphasis is not, as one might expect, on Emerson:
instead, five of twelve chapters are devoted to Whitman. The 20th-century
writers that Asselineau treats at length, some of whom are more often
thought of as Realists or Naturalists than as Transcendentalists, are
Dreiser, O'Neill, Anderson, Hemingway, Tennessee Williams, and the
neglected poet Walter Lowenfels (whom Asselineau calls "the Whitman of the
twentieth century"). According to Asselineau, a fundamental belief in
the mystery and beauty of life and a tendency to "sing themselves" (in
the guise of characters) make these writers transcendentalists. The essays
combine biographical material with literary analysis.

L 440. **AUCHINCLOSS, LOUIS.** Pioneers and Caretakers: A Study of 9 American
        Women Novelists. Minneapolis: University of Minnesota Press,
        1961. 202 pp.
Auchincloss bases his account of the works of nine women novelists—Sarah
Orne Jewett, Edith Wharton, Ellen Glasgow, Willa Cather, Elizabeth Madox
Roberts, Katherine Anne Porter, Jean Stafford, Carson McCullers, and Mary
McCarthy—on a "common American denominator" that "runs through" their
fiction. For Auchincloss these authors do not possess the dark vision
of America which characterizes the works of Theodore Dreiser, Sinclair
Lewis, and William Faulkner. The author maintains that the critique of
America embodied in the novels he discusses stems from a conservative
sensibility which seeks to preserve rather than to undermine American
traditions. Auchincloss's theme originates in his readings of Jewett's
The Country of the Pointed Firs, Wharton's The Age of Innocence, Glasgow's
Barren Ground, Cather's My Antonia, and Roberts's The Time of Man. There

is a particular emphasis on the literary and cultural traditions of New
England and the South.

L 441. BAKER, HOUSTON A., Jr. The Journey Back: Issues in Black Litera-
        ture and Criticism. Chicago: University of Chicago Press, 1980.
        198 pp.
Baker argues that black American literature is particularly complex because
of the dynamic conflict in these works between the meanings available
to a white audience and the separate semantic and structural meanings
unique to black culture and language. Black literature not only partakes
of its own idiom, which is deceptively similar to that of "white" culture,
but also is frequently structured, both thematically and linguistically,
by that very tension or opposition between the two systems of meaning.
Baker asserts that the critic of black literature must be especially sensitive to black culture in order to interpret that tension adequately.
He suggests the variety of ways in which black writers have worked with
this tension by discussing works by Jupiter Hammon, Phillis Wheatley,
Gustavus Vassa, Frederick Douglass, Booker T. Washington, W. E. B. DuBois,
Richard Wright, James Baldwin, Ralph Ellison, Amiri Baraka, Gwendolyn
Brooks, and others; and by considering the "Black Aesthetic" movement,
and the history of critical evaluation of black American literature.

L 442. BANTA, MARTHA. Failure and Success in America: A Literary Debate.
        Princeton, N.J.: Princeton University Press, 1978. 568 pp.
The obsession with success has long been perceived as peculiarly American,
and part of Banta's purpose here is to understand the relation of that
obsession, in personal terms, to an American's sense of his country.
"The focus is upon the varying effects which ideas about success and failure have had upon that personal and national narrative developed by any
mind which asks, . . . 'Are we together--self and nation--succeeding or
have we already failed?'" The study examines such themes as the different
ways of facing failure, the several types of successful American, and
the variety of apocalyptic visions "which American imaginations have
offered as a way out of personal and national failure by forcing a conclusion to all human action." The writers most often cited and examined
are Ralph Waldo Emerson, Mark Twain, Henry Adams, William James, Gertrude
Stein, Henry David Thoreau, Henry James, and Norman Mailer.

L 443. BARTHOLD, BONNIE J. Black Time: Fiction of Africa, the Caribbean,
        and the United States. New Haven, Conn.: Yale University Press,
        1981. 209 pp.
Barthold's intent is "to see black fiction whole, as a phenomenon that
transcends geographic and national boundaries and in which structure is
inseparable from substance." Her primary assumption is that blacks have
suffered from a greatly accelerated sense of time, the loss of pre-history
occurring nearly simultaneously with the gain of modern industrialization.
She first examines the historicity of this phenomenon, and then traces
time-related themes and concurrent forms in a variety of texts. Finally,
she moves to close readings of seven representative novels: Arrow of
God by Chinua Achebe, In the Castle of My Skin by George Lamming, Cane
by Jean Toomer, Blood on the Forge by William Attaway, Why Are We So Blest?
by Ayi Kwei Armah, Song of Solomon by Toni Morrison, and Season of Anomy
by Wole Soyinka.

L 444. BASLER, ROY P. The Lincoln Legend: A Study in Changing Conceptions.
        Boston: Houghton Mifflin, 1935. 336 pp.
Basler, editor of the Lincoln papers, here gives a study of how various
artists--in sculpture, painting, poetry, fiction, drama, and biographical
prose--have "created about Lincoln a national legend or myth which in
conception is much like the hero-myths of other nations." He traces particular versions of the legendary Lincoln as prophet, emancipator, martyr,

and savior, among others. Basler neither accepts nor denies the mythical
Lincoln, but shows how that figure has been created and modified in the
course of American literature and art. He includes a nineteen-page bibliography of poetry, fiction, and drama dealing with Lincoln.

L 445. BECKER, GEORGE J. Realism in Modern Literature. New York: Ungar,
1980. 227 pp.
Becker maps the social and economic conditions which enabled Realism to
become the dominant mode of perception throughout the 19th century and
up to W.W. I. Although he sees "genuine Realism" as a matter of
convention, determined by the limitations of a relative aesthetic, he
still insists that the movement is able to be located in time and is not
universally applicable to the history of Western art. The opening chapter
reviews the new scientific and philosophical ideas which conditioned the
"realist" aesthetic; the remaining chapters outline Realism's many manifestations, from romantic Realism through socialist Realism.

L 446. BERRYMAN, CHARLES. From Wilderness to Wasteland: The Trial of
the Puritan God in the American Imagination. Port Washington,
N.Y.: Kennikat Press, 1979. 214 pp.
Berryman's interdisciplinary study examines responses to the Puritan conception of God. The analysis begins with the first generation of Puritans
and moves on to Cotton Mather, Jonathan Edwards and the Great Awakening,
Benjamin Franklin, Thomas Jefferson, Ralph Waldo Emerson, Nathaniel
Hawthorne, Herman Melville, and T. S. Eliot. Offering another version of
the declension argument, Berryman claims that the Puritan God, as conceived
in 1630, gradually changed face and lost power due to the challenges of
Colonial expansion, Enlightenment philosophy, Transcendental alternatives
to Christianity, and economic and political developments in the 19th and
20th centuries.

L 447. BERZON, JUDITH R. Neither White Nor Black: The Mulatto Character
in American Fiction. New York: New York University Press, 1978.
280 pp.
America, says Berzon, is a two-caste society: white and black. Mulattoes
have always occupied a marginal position in this culture, though in fact
they have been treated as members of the oppressed black race. Many fiction writers have chosen the mulatto for a subject: Mark Twain, William
Faulkner, Robert Penn Warren, Gertrude Stein, Sinclair Lewis, and Willa
Cather. Through the use of the mulatto character, these writers "present
a bleak picture of the ways in which our particular American reality has
fostered social, political, and economic inequality between the races
and almost overwhelming obstacles to a healthy adjustment for full- and
mixed-blood American blacks."

L 448. BIER, JESSE. The Rise and Fall of American Humor. New York:
Holt, Rinehart & Winston, 1968. 506 pp.
"American comedy," says Bier, "is voracious, deflationary, skeptical,
cynical, pessimistic, blasphemous, and black." The rise of this American
humor was intimately linked to the development of literary Realism, particularly in the work of the frontier humorists of the Jacksonian period
(c. 1830-1840) and of the post-Civil War years. Comedy flourished again
in the 1930s, but subsequently declined as it offered only a hysterical
response to conventional values. Bier discusses humor in both the acknowledged masters of comedy (e.g., A. B. Longstreet, Mark Twain, James Thurber)
and the "serious" writers (e.g., Cooper, Melville, Faulkner).

L 449. BIGSBY, C. W. E. The Second Black Renaissance: Essays in Black
       Literature. Westport, Conn.: Greenwood Press, 1980. 321 pp.
Bigsby identifies a second Black Renaissance (the first being the Harlem
Renaissance of the 1920s and 1930s) which began with Richard Wright's
Native Son and blossomed in the 1950s and 1960s. Drawing upon Lionel
Trilling's definition of liberalism as sentiment rather than statement,
Bigsby argues that the writing produced by this Renaissance is essentially
liberal; it holds on to moral values rather than succumbing to an absurdist
attitude. He discusses two elements in the writing he examines: the
attempt to define self within society, and the attempt to maintain a balance between language as liberating force and language as that which
seduces a writer into denying reality. Wright, Ellison, and Baldwin are
treated in three separate chapters. In other chapters Bigsby discusses
how black and Jewish writers have revived a liberal tradition generally
abandoned by "Wasp" writers; he traces how blacks, in the 1960s, embraced
and then later retreated from an apocalyptic tone; and he devotes one
chapter each to black autobiography, drama, and poetry.

L 450. BIGSBY, C. W. E., ed. The Black American Writer. 2 vols. De
       Land, Fla.: Everett/Edwards, 1969. 526 pp.
The Black American Writer, a two-volume collection of essays on black
literary achievement, examines the major writers from the 18th century
onward, assesses the difficulties facing them, and analyzes the critical problems in a field fraught with cultural, social, political, and
racial prejudice. The essays present the controversy over the white man's
motives and qualifications as a critic of black literature. Volume one
covers fiction and includes contributions by James Baldwin, Ralph Ellison,
and Langston Hughes. Volume two covers poetry and drama and includes
discussions of Gwendolyn Brooks, Lorraine Hansberry, and Amiri Baraka.

L 451. BLAIR, WALTER. Horse Sense in American Humor, from Benjamin
       Franklin to Ogden Nash. Chicago: University of Chicago Press,
       1942. 341 pp.
"Horse sense" perhaps could be defined as common sense in a pithy form;
to say that someone has it is a form of American praise. Blair traces
the use of horse sense in American humor from Benjamin Franklin to Ogden
Nash "to explore changes in the form of what has been . . . the most efficient kind of appeal to the American mind." The central figures for Blair
include Lincoln, Benchley, Twain, Thurber, Will Rogers, Finley Peter Dunne,
James Russell Lowell, and the group of humorists who worked the lecture
circuits and wrote for newspapers in the 19th century.

L 452. BLASING, MUTLU KONUK. The Art of Life: Studies in American Auto-
       biographical Literature. Austin: University of Texas Press,
       1977. 193 pp.
In her discussion, Blasing focuses on Walden, Song of Myself, James's
"Prefaces," The Education of Henry Adams, Paterson, and some of Frank
O'Hara's poetry. She is not interested in historical treatments, but
in the occasions when the "interaction of personality and collective life
that the autobiography embodies is reflected in the author's personal
appropriation of the language of the times." Thus each autobiographer
takes on a cultural role in the very act of writing.

L 453. BLOOM, HAROLD. Poetry and Repression: Revisionism from Blake
       to Stevens. New Haven, Conn.: Yale University Press, 1976.
       293 pp.
Bloom offers a highly theoretical and schematic treatment—by way of Vico,
Freud, Nietzche, Gnosticism, and the Kabbalah—of the Romantic tradition
of the Sublime in the works of Blake, Wordsworth, Shelley, Keats, Tennyson,
Browning, Yeats, Emerson, Whitman, and Wallace Stevens. Poems, according
to Bloom, are stagings of the poet's Oedipal struggle with his poetic

precursors; the later poet triumphs by deforming or misreading the tropes of the earlier one. This chapter of Bloom's theory might be classified as philosophy of literature, for it is more concerned with abstract and absolute categories than with illuminating individual poems or poets.

L 454. BLOOM, HAROLD. Wallace Stevens: The Poems of Our Climate. Ithaca
N.Y.: Cornell University Press, 1976. 413 pp.
In Bloom's view a poem begins with an absence. The poet's task is seen as a threefold process: (1) to recognize the "First Idea," (2) to recognize the inhumanity of the "First Idea" itself, and (3) to reimagine the "First Idea." Stevens's poetry, from its exposure of the "First Idea" in Harmonium (1923) to its reimagining in the later works, stands as the philosophical and poetic outcome of modern American Romanticism. In his consideration of Stevens's poetry and poetics, Bloom locates the function of absence in the development of an American Romantic poetics. He notes the continuity between the Romantic dialectic of Wordsworth, Shelley, and Keats (ethos, logos, and pathos) and its transformation, via Emerson, into an American dialectic (Fate, Freedom, and Power). Although this volume depends on and extends Bloom's meta-criticism, it is explicitly concerned with detailed readings of Stevens's poetry. Bloom demonstrates Stevens's fundamental adherence to an Emersonian dialectic through his poetic kinship with Walt Whitman.

L 455. BLUESTEIN, GENE. The Voice of the Folk: Folklore and American
Literary Theory. Amherst: University of Massachusetts Press,
1972. 170 pp.
Bluestein examines, first, the interest of Emerson and Whitman in the writings of Johann Gottfried von Herder; second, the work of Constance Rourke in American Studies; third, the black folklore studies of John and Alan Lomax; and finally, contemporary "rock" music. "What binds these figures together," says the author, "is the belief that the highest cultural values can be derived from what cultivated classes often describe condescendingly as the vulgar, lowest levels of society." Such belief was articulated by Herder, and its exponents include contemporary black artists who make this argument on behalf of a culture usually excluded from the American mainstream. Folk art is seen here as a "major source of materials which sophisticated society uses to fashion its literary expression." Bluestein also touches incidentally on such authors as Faulkner and Ellison, and such topics as jazz and ideology.

L 456. BODE, CARL, ed. The Great Experiment in American Literature:
Six Lectures. New York: Praeger, 1961. 152 pp.
This collection of six essays is organized around the theme that American literature can be characterized by "its many different forms, its searching of language, its attempt to push meaning to the utmost . . ., [its] constant experimentation with words." The contributors explore this notion in essays on Poe (by Robert Spiller), Whitman (by Norman Jeffares), Emily Dickinson (by Dennis Welland), Wallace Stevens (by Geoffrey Moore), and Hemingway (by Arthur Mizener). The volume originated in a series of public lectures sponsored by the American embassy in Great Britain and attempts to provide an introduction to readers not familiar with the field.

L 457. BODE, CARL, ed. The Young Rebel in American Literature: Seven
Lectures. London: William Heinemann, 1959. 172 pp.
The seven lectures, presented in Britain, were sponsored by the American Embassy in London. Although the seven critics differ in style and focus, they share a concern for the individuality of the author as expressed in his writings. The theme of the young rebel draws attention to the personal characteristics of the writers discussed: Thoreau, Whitman, Sinclair Lewis, Fitzgerald, Mencken, and Steinbeck. The one exception is the lecture on Faulkner, which exclusively attends to Faulkner's rebellious characters.

L 458. BOLLER, PAUL F., Jr. Freedom and Fate in American Thought from
        Edwards to Dewey. Dallas, Tex.: Southern Methodist University
        Press, 1978. 300 pp.
Boller studies the thought of nine American writer-philosophers in regard
to the issue of freedom and necessity. He considers the complex responses
to this issue by Jonathan Edwards, Thomas Paine, Ralph Waldo Emerson,
John C. Calhoun, Frederick Douglass, Edward Bellamy, William James, Mark
Twain, and John Dewey. The authors are examined in relation to three
main definitions of freedom (or liberty): self-realization, the absence
of constraints to personal fulfillment; self-perfection, the bringing
of passions and prejudices into harmony with reason or moral law; and
self-determination, the freedom from a certain amount of antecedent determining conditions to act in accord with the individual will.

L 459. BONE, ROBERT. The Negro Novel in America. 1958; Rev. ed. New
        Haven, Conn.: Yale University Press, 1965. 289 pp.
Bone suggests that to understand novels by black authors readers must
acknowledge a distinct black culture in America and the opposing forces
which have shaped that culture: assimilation into the white middle class,
and black nationalism. Bone begins by urging the importance of social
analysis, but he is not primarily a social historian. As he moves from
the early writers (e.g., Paul Laurence Dunbar, W. E. B. Dubois) to the
Harlem Renaissance (e.g., Langston Hughes, Countee Cullen) and contemporary writers (e.g., Richard Wright, James Baldwin), his attention shifts
from social analysis to formal analysis, aesthetic evaluation, and a consideration of the tension between art and racial propaganda in contemporary
literature.

L 460. BOWDEN, EDWIN T. The Dungeon of the Heart: Human Isolation and
        the American Novel. New York: Macmillan, 1961. 175 pp.
This work is not primarily intended for the scholar; the author says it
is for "anyone interested in the American novel or in the patterns of
American life." To illustrate the relationship between life and literature,
Bowden examines the problem of human isolation in twelve 19th- and 20th-
century American novels. Most of these novels are major works (e.g.,
Huckleberry Finn, The Scarlet Letter, Light in August), although some
lesser known works are also included. Bowden begins with the Puritan
history Of Plymouth Plantation to show how isolation is present in American
literature from the earliest times, and then continues with sections on
frontier isolation, individualism, and Realism.

L 461. BRAUN, SIDNEY and SEYMOUR LAINOFF, eds. Transatlantic Mirrors:
        Essays in Franco-American Literary Relations. Boston: Twayne,
        1978. 271 pp.
This volume collects various essays, prefaces, and reviews written by
American authors on French novelists and poets as well as the critical
reception and evaluation of American writers by their French counterparts.
Beginning with Crevecoeur's 1782 essay "What Is an American?," Transatlantic Mirrors contains thirty-two selections from both French and American
writers of the 19th and 20th centuries, including Balzac on Cooper, Emerson
on Montaigne, and Andre Malraux on Faulkner. It concludes with Henry
Miller's 1959 essay on Blaise Cendrars.

L 462. BRAWLEY, BENJAMIN. The Negro in Literature and Art in the United
        States. 1918; Rev. ed. New York: Duffield, 1929. 231 pp.
This book is a general survey of black American literature and art from
their beginnings to the early 20th century. Literature predominates as
Brawley writes separate chapters on such key figures as Phillis Wheatley,
Frederick Douglass, Charles W. Chesnutt, and James W. Johnson. Four chapters sketch contributions by black artists to the stage, painting, sculpture, and music. Appendices deal more generally with American fiction

and contemporary literature, and a bibliography lists primary and secondary works.

L 463. **BRIDGMAN, RICHARD.** The Colloquial Style in America. New York: Oxford University Press, 1966. 254 pp.
Bridgman traces the development of a national prose style, which was rooted in the American vernacular, first expressed in Huckleberry Finn, refined by Henry James, and passed on to Hemingway through Gertrude Stein. Bridgman claims that "American prose style changed significantly between 1825 and 1925." The change "was toward greater concreteness of diction and simplicity of syntax," and "was initiated primarily in dialect pieces and in fictional dialogue." In the late 1800s, according to Bridgman, "writers became increasingly conscious of the techniques of colloquial writing" and their techniques, which emphasized the "individual verb unit," caused a "fragmentation of syntax" and "the use of repetition to bind and unify."

L 464. **BROOKS, PAUL.** Speaking for Nature: How Literary Naturalists from Henry Thoreau to Rachel Carson Have Shaped America. Boston: Houghton Mifflin, 1980. 286 pp.
Brooks discusses the American journalists, essayists, and scientists who, since Thoreau, have written on American nature. He covers the histories of these figures—their meetings, influences, accomplishments—touching upon the more anecdotal moments. Brooks, known best as a conservationist, is especially concerned with biographical sources, but attempts to characterize the related literature.

L 465. **BROWN, JANET.** Feminist Drama: Definition and Critical Analysis. Metuchen, N.J.: Scarecrow Press, 1979. 161 pp.
Brown applies to a number of recent plays Kenneth Burke's literary theory that works of art are shaped by "rhetorical strategizing." Four of the plays, she finds, fit her definition of a Feminist drama as "one in which the agent, a woman, seeks autonomy within an unjust socio-sexual hierarchy." The works discussed are The Bed Was Full by Rosalyn Drexler; In the Boom Boom Room by David Rabe; Wine in the Wilderness by Alice Childress; Birth and After Birth by Tina Howe (Brown finds this play not to be Feminist); a group of short plays created by various Feminist theater collectives; and for colored girls who have considered suicide/when the rainbow is enuf by Ntozake Shange.

L 466. **BROWN, STERLING A.** The Negro in American Fiction. Washington, D.C.: Associates in Negro Folk Education, 1937. 209 pp; and Negro Poetry and Drama. Washington, D.C.: Associates in Negro Folk Education, 1937. 142 pp.
Brown's two works are "comprehensive surveys in the field of iconography, tracing through American fiction, poetry, and drama the changing image of the Negro." When first published in 1937, they sought to destroy the stereotypes of blacks to which society still clung. These studies also indicate that the American literary imagination has been obsessed with racist attitudes. Brown stresses literature portraying blacks realistically and uses folk material as well as more "conventional" literature. The two volumes were published as one in 1969 under the title Negro Poetry and Drama and the Negro in American Fiction.

L 467. **BRUCE-NOVOA, JUAN D.** Chicano Authors: Inquiry by Interview. Austin: University of Texas Press, 1980. 292 pp.
This is a collection of responses of fourteen Chicano authors to a mail survey conducted by Bruce-Novoa. The writers answer questions about their families, their careers, their language(s), their art, and their politics. In addition to the interviews, Bruce-Novoa provides a long essay describing

the themes of Chicano poetry, theater, and fiction, which serves as an introduction to what is defined as interlingual, revolutionary, and subversive literature.

L 468. BRYAN, WILLIAM ALFRED. George Washington in American Literature
1775-1865. New York: Columbia University Press, 1952. 280 pp.
After a brief portrait of Washington as seen by his contemporaries, Bryan examines the image of Washington in oratory, biography, verse, drama, and fiction. Among the authors whom Bryan cites are Hugh Henry Brackenridge, Irving, Freneau, Cooper, and Thackeray. Although the image of Washington varied somewhat, especially during and after the Civil War, one figure dominates the literature: "the type of man the new nation could produce . . . the ideal American."

L 469. BUDD, LOUIS J., EDWIN H. CADY, and CARL L. ANDERSON, eds. Toward
a New American Literary History: Essays in Honor of Arlin Turner.
Durham, N.C.: Duke University Press, 1980. 279 pp.
This collection of seventeen essays includes treatments of cultural and historical issues, literary movements as well as studies of individual writers. Among the topics discussed are Puritan literature and culture, the American Renaissance period, the works of American Modernism, and the Harlem Renaissance. The volume also contains essays specifically devoted to Benjamin Franklin, Davy Crockett, Nathaniel Hawthorne, Ellen Glasgow, Upton Sinclair, Ezra Pound, and Carl Van Vechten. Contributors to this festschrift include Robert Spiller, Sacvan Bercovitch, John Seelye, Gay Wilson Allen, Darwin T. Turner, Donald Pizer, and Russel B. Nye.

L 470. BUTCHER, MARGARET JUST. The Negro in American Culture: Based
on Materials Left by Alain Locke. 1956; Rev. ed. New York:
Knopf, 1972. 313 pp.
The purpose of this book is "to trace in historical sequence . . . both the folk and the formal contributions of the American Negro to American culture as a whole." Individual chapters are devoted to music, dance, folklore, and formal poetry, and to more general considerations such as the "figure of the Negro" in modern American fiction and drama—artifacts with blacks as subjects, written either by whites or blacks.

L 471. CALVERTON, V. F. The Liberation of American Literature. New
York: Scribner, 1932. 500 pp.
Calverton's book, he suggests, is not so much literary criticism as it is social history. Adopting a Marxist stance, he finds the sources of American culture and literature in economic and social conflict. American literature, says Calverton, has been dominated by the "colonial complex" ("intellectual inferiority, artistic imitativeness, and cultural retardation") and by "petty bourgeois individualism and idealism." The history of American literature is thus the story of movement through four stages: determined adaptation, self-conscious nationalism, struggle for freedom, and liberation.

L 472. CARPENTER, FREDERIC I. American Literature and the Dream. New
York: Philosophical Library, 1955. 220 pp.
Carpenter's thesis is that American literature is distinctive because of the pervasive concept of the "American dream." Although this is difficult to define, it influences plot in fiction and the imagination in poetry. American literature assumes a new pattern, structured by authorial attitudes toward the American dream: the Transcendentalists are philosophers of the dream; the Genteel Traditionalists, its opponents; the Romantics, its emotional enthusiasts; and the Realists, its sympathetic critics. Before analysing the literature, Carpenter provides a partial definition of the American dream by recalling some of its elements, such as "freedom," "progress," and "democracy." He then looks at the traditional categories

of American literature and suggests new definitions. Finally, he reinter-
prets the literature of individual 19th- and 20th-century authors.

L 473. CHASE, RICHARD. The Democratic Vista: A Dialogue on Life and
        Letters in Contemporary America. Garden City, N.Y.: Doubleday,
        1958. 180 pp.
The point of Chase's book is to radically reconsider American culture,
especially its politics and literature. To do so, he adopts the structure
of a dialogue among several characters, predominantly "George" and "Ralph"
(who generally stands for the author). Ralph believes this is a transitional period in the development of American culture, a time of "revision
and retrenchment" between two creative eras. He also holds that despite
material advances, the quality of intellectual, moral, and aesthetic life
is unsatisfactory. George, on the other hand, argues that this is a period
of success and maturity in its own right. The debate is inconclusive.

L 474. CLARK, HARRY HAYDEN, ed. Transitions in American Literary History.
        Durham, N.C.: Duke University Press, 1954. 479 pp.
This work stresses why American literary history developed as it did and
why emphases changed from one period to the next. The work assumes four
main periods of American literature up to 1891--Puritanism, Neoclassicism,
Romanticism, and Realism--and focuses on the transitions between them.
This general structure is divided into a series of rises and falls: "The
Decline of Puritanism," "The Decline of Neoclassicism (1801-1848)," "The
Rise of Romanticism (1805-1855)," "The Rise of Transcendentalism (1815-
1860)," "The Decline of Romantic Idealism (1855-1871)," and "The Rise
of Realism."

L 475. COHEN, HENNIG, ed. The American Culture: Approaches to the Study
        of the United States. Boston: Houghton Mifflin, 1968. 416 pp.
These essays, reprinted from the American Quarterly, display the range
of work done in American Studies. The five sections ("Images and Myths,"
"Ideas," "Machines," "Mass Society," and "Varieties of Cultural Evidence")
include several essays directly dealing with literary topics (e.g., Irving
Howe's "The Southern Myth and Faulkner" and Howard Mumford Jones's "Literature and Orthodoxy in Boston after the Civil War"), and many pieces examining the cultural context of American literature.

L 476. COHN, JAN. The Palace or the Poorhouse: The American House as
        Cultural Symbol. East Lansing: Michigan State University Press,
        1979. 267 pp.
This book explores the continuing existence of the house as a dominant
symbol in American culture. American attitudes toward the house range,
however, from anti-materialist scorn to the idealization of the family
homestead and the simple cottage. Since the complexities and contradictions in the symbol of the house are endemic to American culture, Cohn
describes the attitudes developed in fiction, but also ranges widely
through the extra-literary writings of politicians, reformers, anarchists,
Feminists, social utopianists, and hucksters, from the 17th century to
the present. Figures discussed include William Dean Howells, Hamlin
Garland, Frank Lloyd Wright, Alfred A. Wright, and Edith Wharton.

L 477. COOLEY, JOHN R. Savages and Naturals: Black Portraits by White
        Writers in Modern American Literature. Newark: University of
        Delaware Press, 1982. 203 pp.
Cooley notes that the white imagination tends to impose primitivism as
a characteristic onto black fictional characters. This tendency continues
Western civilization's preoccupation with the primitive but is shaped
by peculiarities of the American situation. Cooley identifies two modes
of this tendency: seeing blacks as "savages" (evil, threats to civilization) and seeing them as "naturals" (good, free of the unnatural com-

plexity of modern life). He limits his discussion to 20th-century and
a single late 19th-century American writer: Crane, Lindsay, O'Neill,
and Waldo Frank (who depict blacks as savages); and Faulkner, Welty, Mailer,
and Vonnegut (who depict them as naturals). Even well-meaning white
writers, he argues, typically fail to create successful black characters,
and the result is one of the two modes of primitivist stereotyping.

L 478. COPE, JACKSON I. and GEOFFREY GREEN, eds. Novel vs. Fiction:
The Contemporary Reformation. Norman, Okla.: Pilgrim Books,
1981. 166 pp.
Cope, considering the recent outpouring of excellent fictions, argues
that critical theories of genre interact symbiotically with writers to
work "both as validation and challenge to the enterprise of turning fantasy
into new forms of fiction." Green adds "that the pervasive modern insight
. . . that our lives are composed of relativistic contingencies, deprived
of any ultimate coherence," also accounts for our "contemporary reformation." Thus this collection serves as an example of a symbiotic relationship between writer and critic. Cope's two essays on genre are juxtaposed
with interviews with Robert Coover and Leslie Fiedler. Christine Brooke-
Rose, Raymond Federman, Geoffrey Green, and Peter Bailey seek to define
the directions and intentions of contemporary fictions. Robert Alter,
Max F. Schulz, and Donald R. Wineke focus on Fowles, Barth, and Hawkes,
respectively.

L 479. CORNILLON, SUSAN KOPPELMAN. Images of Women in Fiction: Feminist
Perspectives. 1972; Rev. ed. Bowling Green, Ohio: Bowling Green
University Press, 1973. 399 pp.
The essays in this collection illustrate the recent application of Feminist
consciousness to literary analyses of American and European fiction.
The book is divided into four parts depicting women's social roles, past
and present. The first section, "Woman as Heroine," considers traditional
views of women; the second division, "The Invisible Woman," covers the
roles women are forced to play in fiction; the third part, called "The
Woman as Hero," investigates fiction in which women are portrayed as whole
people; and the last section, "Feminist Aesthetics," includes essays
on the modern woman's manifesto and details her goals and desires.
Cornillon's book attempts to see literature in "feminist perspectives" by
including both theory and practice.

L 480. COUSER, G. THOMAS. American Autobiography: The Prophetic Mode.
Amherst: University of Massachusetts Press, 1979. 222 pp.
Couser claims that from the outset there has been a "prophetic mode" in
American autobiographies. He studies about twenty works in particular,
from Increase Mather to Norman Mailer, and asserts that it is a native
American form influenced as much by the Puritan experience as by the prophetic books of the Bible. It "must be read as religious literature,"
as the writer tries to respond to some general crisis as well as deal
with the question of what it means to be an American.

L 481. DATHORNE, O. R. Dark Ancestor: The Literature of the Black Man
in the Caribbean. Baton Rouge: Louisiana State University Press,
1981. 278 pp.
Dathorne examines "Afro-New World" literature to discover the nature of
black identity in the Americas. Though his discussion focuses mainly
on Caribbean literature, Dathorne also considers literature of the U.S.,
and Canada, and Central and South America. He discusses black literary
movements—the Harlem Renaissance, Negritude (in France), and Negrista (in
Cuba and Puerto Rico)—and mentions some 20th-century white artists who
have experimented with African cultural forms. He writes of two syntheses
of African and European cultures within the New World: in primary synthesis, both black Africans and white Europeans leave behind "tribal"

allegiances to become New World blacks and New World whites; in secondary synthesis (yet to be achieved), black and white cease to exist as subcategories of the category "New World persons."

L 482. DAVENPORT, GUY. The Geography of the Imagination. San Francisco: North Point Press, 1981. 384 pp.
Davenport's forty essays presented here range over a wide field of interest—from finding arrowheads in Georgia fields as a child to finding the American lyric voice in Whitman's poems as a scholar. His twin concerns with the art of "seeing" and the sense of place, especially the places where the imagination is rooted, unify the collection. "The imagination," Davenport argues, "is like the drunk man who lost his watch, and must get drunk to find it. It is as intimate as speech and custom, and to trace its ways we need to reeducate our eyes." This volume includes essays on Louis Agassiz, Charles Ives, Herman Melville, Marianne Moore, Charles Olson, Wallace Stevens, Eudora Welty, and Louis Zukofsky.

L 483. DAVIDSON, CATHY N. and E. M. BRONER, eds. The Lost Tradition: Mothers and Daughters in Literature. New York: Ungar, 1980. 327 pp.
The twenty-four essays in this collection trace "forty centuries of a literature of mothers and daughters." Although the discussion is not limited to American literature, numerous works by American authors are discussed. Some of those writing on American literature note how fictional daughters, often motherless, lack a strong or satisfactory model for motherhood. But more recent literary endeavors by American women have, according to these essayists, been attempts to explore the bond between mother and daughter, to overcome antagonism between them—an antagonism engendered by patriarchal society—and to re-establish a sense of matrilineage. Writers or topics discussed include the following: fiction of the new Republic; Emily Dickinson; Ellen Glasgow; Edith Wharton; Sylvia Plath; Tillie Olsen; minority writers such as Alice Walker, Toni Morrison, Cynthia Ozick, Margaret Walker, Anzia Yezierska; Southwestern Native American literature; and autobiographical works by Maya Angelou, Nikki Giovanni, Jane Howard, Maxine Hong Kingston, and Margaret Mead.

L 484. DEEGAN, DOROTHY YOST. The Stereotype of the Single Woman in American Novels: A Social Study with Implications for the Education of Women. New York: King's Crown, 1951. 252 pp.
Deegan's "pioneer venture" examines the American novel's socio-psychological content rather than its literary merit. On the assumption that literature both creates and reflects social attitudes, Deegan's work, patterned on educational research, studies the stereotype of the single woman that writers have perpetuated. Sections one and two cover procedure, outlining the problem and its setting, defining terms, and describing the sampling. Section three offers case studies of seven fictional women and establishes an emerging pattern of stereotyping which lags far behind the social reality of single women. In section four, these findings are corroborated by information from a wider selection of novels. Finally, Deegan suggests that society should not educate women to view marriage as heaven and the single life as hell; rather, society should educate women for either possibility. Authors examined include Louisa May Alcott, Willa Cather, Ellen Glasgow, William Dean Howells, and Nathaniel Hawthorne.

L 485. DeMOTT, ROBERT J. and SANFORD E. MAROVITZ. Artful Thunder: Visions of the Romantic Tradition in American Literature in Honor of Howard P. Vincent. Kent, Ohio: Kent State University Press, 1975. 312 pp.

This festschrift includes three brief essays in which the authors reminisce about Howard Vincent and several essays on topics in 19th- and 20th-century American literature written by former students or colleagues. Authors discussed include Brockden Brown, Poe, Hawthorne, Thoreau, Melville (five essays), Dickinson, Hart Crane, Emerson, Nemerov, Shelley, Stevens, and Duncan. There is also a poem (Orca, Part Two) by Paul Metcalf. Contributors include Thomas M. Davis, Harrison Hayford, Sydney J. Krause, Eric Mottram, Nathalia Wright, and Donald J. Yannella.

L 486. DENNY, MARGARET and WILLIAM H. GILMAN, eds. The American Writer and the European Tradition. Minneapolis: University of Minnesota Press, 1950. 192 pp.

The twelve essays, written for a conference on the title subject and reprinted here, range in subject from "The Renaissance Tradition in America" to "Some European Views of Contemporary American Literature." They illustrate the shifting relationship between Europe and America, and the mutual influences that have been exercised. Among the contributors are Louis B. Wright, Henry Nash Smith, Leon Howard, Alfred Kazin, Lionel Trilling, and Harry Levin.

L 487. DETWEILER, ROBERT. Four Spiritual Crises in Mid-Century American Fiction. Gainesville: University of Florida Press, 1964. 53 pp.

Detweiler's study deals specifically with four single works by William Styron, Philip Roth, J. D. Salinger, and John Updike. Each work is examined for affinities with certain religious philosophies. Stryon's Set This House on Fire is set against the writings of Paul Tillich, Updike's Rabbit, Run against the writings of Reinhold Niebuhr, Roth's Letting Go against the writings of Martin Buber, and Salinger's Franny and Zooey is read within the framework of a "weak amalgamation" of Christianity, Zen Buddhism, existential terminology, and Jewish tradition. Detweiler is particularly interested in the "accommodation" themes of modern American novelists.

L 488. DIAMOND, ARLYN and LEE R. EDWARDS, eds. The Authority of Experience: Essays in Feminist Criticism. Amherst: University of Massachusetts Press, 1977. 304 pp.

This work divides into three parts: essays dealing theoretically with Feminist criticism, those applying this criticism to English literature, and those applying it to American literature. Although diverse in content, these essays share Feminism as a basic assumption and argue for an understanding of literature in terms of its wider social and moral context. They seek to "measure literary reality on the one side against historical and personally felt reality on the other." The focus is less on the inadequacy of literature's representation of work than on the misconceptions of past critics, "the received evaluations about literature which, rooted in bias, have far too long passed for disinterested impartiality." Thus a wide range of traditionally defined classics—Chaucer, Shakespeare, Defoe—are examined alongside newer, more specifically Feminist, authors— Woolf, Lessing, Chopin, and Porter.

L 489. DOBIE, J. FRANK. Guide to Life and Literature of the Southwest. 1943; Rev. ed. Dallas, Tex.: Southern Methodist University Press, 1952. 222 pp.

Dobie emphasizes that this book is a guide and not a bibliography, but it "includes most of the books about the Southwest that people in general would agree on as making good reading." It is composed of short bibliographical chapters with commentaries on subjects as disparate as Indian culture, the Texas Rangers, the Pony Express, the Bad Man tradition, birds and wildflowers, fiction, and poetry and drama.

L 490. DONDORE, DOROTHY ANNE. The Prairie and the Making of Middle America: Four Centuries of Description. Cedar Rapids, Iowa: Torch, 1926. 472 pp.
Dondore has written both a narrative and an informal descriptive bibliography of the enormous range of recorded responses to the American Midwest from the early 1520s through the early 1920s, from the early Spanish explorers through Sinclair Lewis. She includes all forms of writing—history, official reports, informal correspondence, fiction and poetry—and surveys them for evidence of the changes in the region from wilderness to frontier to modern civilization.

L 491. DOODY, TERRENCE. Confession and Community in the Novel. Baton Rouge: Louisiana State University Press, 1980. 200 pp.
Doody distinguishes confessional novels from other first-person novels by the "speaker's intention to realize himself in community." As an act of community, confessional narrative has a special attitude toward its audience. Doody first examines the rhetoric of confession in classic texts: The Confessions of Jean-Jacques Rousseau and St. Augustine. A comparison of the idea of community in the confessional narrators of Moll Flanders, Notes from Underground and Moby-Dick composes the following section. In the second part of the book Doody looks at the way in which confessional fiction defines both self and audience in An American Tragedy, The Great Gatsby, Lord Jim, and Absalom, Absalom!

L 492. DRINNON, RICHARD. Facing West: The Metaphysics of Indian-Hating and Empire-Building. Minneapolis: University of Minnesota Press, 1980. 552 pp.
Although he does not take them up in chronological order, Drinnon discusses figures who oppose or represent mainstream attitudes toward natives—from John Endicott (1620s) to Jefferson to Henry Adams to Robert Lowell (1960s). He discusses historical phenomena as well—from the Pequot War (1636) to "Manifest Destiny" to the War in the Philippines to Viet Nam (1960s). Acknowledging his debt to Freud's Civilization and Its Discontents, Drinnon argues that the "metaphysics of Indian-hating" (a phrase he takes from Melville) is the philosophical basis of the Euro-centric attempt to eradicate native flora, fauna, and peoples from the U.S. For Europeans and their descendants, native peoples—whether Indians or Filipinos or Vietnamese—are the "dark others" and represent a freedom of sensuality that must be repressed. But the repression is not always successful: the Ishmaels (figures such as Thomas Morton, Henry David Thoreau, George Catlin, and Melville) constitute a "perennially reborn countertradition" of those seeking truly to understand and belong to the land. The book includes reproductions of drawings and photographs.

L 493. DUFFEY, BERNARD. Poetry in America: Expression and Its Values in the Times of Bryant, Whitman, and Pound. Durham, N.C.: Duke University Press, 1978. 358 pp.
This work combines literary criticism and cultural history to study four generally distinctive periods of expression: the first beginning with the post-Romantic work of Bryant and running through Emerson, Poe, and Thoreau, in which poetic assumptions are dominated by ideas of coherence; the second comprising the Civil War poetry which reflects the uncertainties and dualities of society; the third period marked by insecurity and a sense of contradiction which are pronounced in Robinson, Frost, and Jeffers; and the fourth in which the functions of poetry as illustrated by Ezra Pound, William Carlos Williams, and their contemporaries are rooted in the consciousness of poets themselves.

L 494. DUNLAP, GEORGE ARTHUR. The City in the American Novel, 1789-1900:
A Study of American Novels Portraying Contemporary Conditions
in New York, Philadelphia, and Boston. Philadelphia: University
of Pennsylvania Press, 1934. 187 pp.
Dunlap defines two goals for his study: "(1) to trace chronologically
the facts about the various phases of life in the city which the contemporary novels record; and (2) to determine whether the same novels have
qualities that make them of permanent literary value." He does this by
studying the struggle for success in the city, disasters of city life,
and the religious, social, literary, and political life of the city as
reflected in novels by Charles Brockden Brown, F. Marion Crawford, Edgar
Fawcett, William Dean Howells, Catherine Sedgwick, Charles Dudley Warner,
and others.

L 495. DUSENBURY, WINIFRED L. The Theme of Loneliness in Modern American
Drama. Gainesville: University of Florida Press, 1960. 231 pp.
The theme of loneliness illustrates how the primarily "realistic" contemporary American playwright takes material from the world around him.
Dusenbury groups individual plays according to the dramatist's presentation
of the basic cause of loneliness ("a suffering self-awareness of separation"). These categories encompass personal failure, homelessness, an
unhappy family, a love affair's failure, socioeconomic forces, the tensions
of the spiritual and the material, and the lonely hero. Of the twenty-
six plays examined, six are by Eugene O'Neill; playwrights considered
also include Clifford Odets, Arthur Miller, Elmer Rice, and Tennessee
Williams. To explore fully the theme of loneliness, these playwrights
have used the various dramatic techniques of Realism, Naturalism, Expressionism, Impressionism, Surrealism, and Symbolism.

L 496. EARNEST, ERNEST. The American Eve in Fact and Fiction, 1775-1914.
Urbana: University of Illinois Press, 1974. 280 pp.
From the late 18th century, the "American girl" impressed novelists and
European travellers as a unique type set apart by up-bringing, freedom,
grace, beauty, and innocence. Earnest's study is concerned with the authenticity of this view. Although he treats characters in novels by James,
Howells, and others, he focuses on actual girls as revealed in diaries,
memoirs, and biographies. He discovers first that the real girls were
far different from their fictional counterparts, and that these "new"
girls grew into "new" women. Not a history of American Feminism, Earnest's
work combines history and literature to answer the question: "What were
American girls and women really like between the Revolution and World
War I?"

L 497. EDEL, LEON. Stuff of Sleep and Dreams: Experiments in Literary
Psychoanalysis. New York: Harper & Row, 1982. 254 pp.
Reminiscences of literary settings, such as Thoreau's Walden Pond, combine
with literary psychoanalysis, autobiography, and literary history to structure this work. Edel's concern is with the psychology and biography of
his authors, and his insights are drawn chiefly from Freud and Adler,
although he cites Coleridge, Yeats, and other artists. The first two
chapters define and explain Edel's approach, and discuss various historical
problems of the 1920s and 1930s as Edel experienced them in Paris and
Vienna. The James family receives the most detailed and lengthy analysis. Other literary figures examined include Henry David Thoreau, W.
H. Auden, Willa Cather, Edmund Wilson, and T. S. Eliot.

L 498. ELLMANN, MARY. Thinking about Women. New York: Harcourt, Brace
& World, 1968. 240 pp.
Ellmann's work examines and classifies the "reiteration" of female stereotypes in literature. She suggests a correlation betwen authority (male)
and curiosity, and points out that the traditional analogies between the

male and strength and the female and weakness are ironically reinforced
by both sexes. The author identifies a dozen or so feminine stereotypes--
e.g., passivity, piety, spirituality--then analyzes differences in tone
among various authors such as Jane Austen, Norman Mailer, Sigmund Freud,
and Mary McCarthy.

L 499. FALK, ROBERT, ed. Literature and Ideas in America: Essays in
Memory of Harry Hayden Clark. Athens: Ohio University Press,
1975. 243 pp.
These eleven essays treat individual authors in the context of the ideas
and intellectual movements of their time (e.g., Emerson and science, Twain
and scientific investigations). The volume also contains essays on Freneau,
fiction in the North American Review, Emerson and literary ethics,
Thoreau's religious thought, Hawthorne's The Blithedale Romance, the novels
of Oliver Wendell Holmes, James's The Sacred Fount, Frank Norris's The
Octopus, and Gertrude Stein.

L 500. FEIDELSON, CHARLES, Jr. Symbolism and American Literature. Chicago:
University of Chicago Press, 1953. 355 pp.
Feidelson considers the common bond of the 19th-century American Romantics
(Emerson, Hawthorne, Melville, Poe, and Whitman) in specifically aesthetic
terms: "their devotion to the possibilities of symbolism." Symbolism
is not only a key to their literature but also a link between their literature and ours. Thus Feidelson's aims are synthetic: first he discusses
Hawthorne, Whitman, Melville, and Poe individually; next he analyzes the
Symbolistic imagination; then, he shows the native historical roots of
American Symbolism; and finally he relates 19th-century American Symbolism
to modern literature. The book provides both critiques of individual
works and a theoretical framework for studying 19th-century American Romanticism.

L 501. FEIDELSON, CHARLES, Jr. and PAUL BRODTKORB, Jr., eds. Interpre-
tations of American Literature. New York: Oxford University
Press, 1959. 386 pp.
This collection includes interpretive essays about canonical figures--
Hawthorne, Poe, Melville, Emerson, Thoreau, Whitman, Dickinson, Twain,
James, Hemingway, and Faulkner--or about individual works by these writers.
In addition, it includes an essay by Lionel Trilling, who examines V.
L. Parrington's evaluation of American literature, and an essay by Roy
Harvey Pearce about poets who give "primary devotion to personality" (in
particular, Stevens, Williams, and Cummings). Contributors include Hyatt
Waggoner, Q. D. Leavis, Darrel Abel, Edward H. Davidson, John Parke, R.
W. Short, Perry Miller, Richard P. Adams, Stephen E. Whicher, Sherman
Paul, Richard Chase, Calvin S. Brown, Allen Tate, Leo Marx, James M. Cox,
Dorothy Van Ghent, Dorothea Krook, E. M. Halliday, Frederick J. Hoffman,
R. W. B. Lewis, and Alfred Kazin.

L 502. FETTERLY, JUDITH. The Resisting Reader: A Feminist Approach to
American Fiction. Bloomington: Indiana University Press, 1978.
198 pp.
Fetterly here attempts to re-evaluate a series of major American literary
texts by reading them with a Feminist perspective. Her method resists
traditional critical, mostly male, responses to female characters. She
discusses in detail four short stories and four novels, including "The
Birthmark," "Rip Van Winkle," The Great Gatsby, A Farewell to Arms, and
The Bostonians.

L 503. FIEDLER, LESLIE A. Love and Death in the American Novel. 1960;
Rev. ed. New York: Stein & Day, 1966. 512 pp.
Fiedler would have the reader approach his work "not as a conventional
scholarly book—or an eccentric one—but a kind of gothic novel (complete
with touches of black humor) whose subject is the American experience
as recorded in our classic fiction." His psychoanalytic discussion of
Brockden Brown, Cooper, Hawthorne, Melville, Twain, Faulkner, and numerous
minor figures leads him to the archetype of American fiction and culture:
"its implacable nostalgia for the infantile." Fiedler identifies the
retreat from heterosexuality—indeed, from any healthy sexuality—as peculiarly American, and recounts the way in which this retreat has informed
the American novel since its inception: Natty Bumppo and Chingachgook,
Huck Finn and Jim, Ishmael and Ahab all testify to the repression of sexuality from this literature, save for its interstices, which are filled
in with male projections of women—the Dark Lady on the one hand, and
the sexless innocent on the other.

L 504. FIEDLER, LESLIE A. The Return of the Vanishing American. New
York: Stein & Day, 1968. 192 pp.
Fiedler intends his three books—Love and Death in the American Novel
(L 503), Waiting for the End (L 505), and The Return of the Vanishing
American—as a single work defining "the myths which gave a special character to art and life in America." In this third study, Fiedler concerns
himself with the Indian and the myths he has engendered among white Americans. Fiedler explores two fundamental questions: (1) the nature of
the Western in its classic or traditional form, and (2) the elements that
make the 20th-century Western new. This work attempts to give an overview
of the white man's capacity to mythologize from his dealings with Indians.

L 505. FIEDLER, LESLIE A. Waiting for the End. New York: Stein & Day,
1964. 256 pp.
The second in Fiedler's informal trilogy, this work discusses American
literature since the demise of Hemingway and Faulkner. Characteristically,
Fiedler continues his "mythic" approach to literature. He deals with
the themes of war, exile, depression, heaven, and hell, as well as the
figures of the Jew and Indian. Paradoxically, what confronts the modern
artist is not the predicted Armageddon but "a long slow decadence in which
the arts will continue to thrive."

L 506. FISHER, DEXTER and ROBERT STEPTO, eds. Afro-American Literature:
The Reconstruction of Instruction. New York: Modern Language
Association of America, 1978. 255 pp.
A 1977 seminar entitled "The Reconstruction of Instruction" gave rise
to this collection of thirteen essays, which focuses primarily on how
Afro-American literature should be taught. The revisionary approach,
suggested by the title, is applied mostly to expanding the borders of
the subject. Folklore, blues lyric, and dialect all come under considera-
tion. The collection as a whole challenges narrower definitions of the
Afro-American literary canon and how the study of it should be conducted.

L 507. FLUCK, WINIFRIED, ed. Forms and Functions of History in American
Literature: Essays in Honor of Ursula Brumm. Berlin: Erich
Schmidt Verlag, 1981. 205 pp.
These twelve essays deal with the many complex connections between imagina-
tion and history, the hallmark of Ursula Brumm's work in American studies.
Nine essays discuss individual authors, including Thomas Morton, de
Crevecoeur, Jefferson, Hawthorne, Emerson, Twain, Hemingway, and McLuhan.
Three essays, broader in scope—"The Ideological Context of the American
Renaissance," "The Long Withdrawing Roar: 80 Years of the Ocean's Message
in American Poetry," and "Fortune's Wheel and Revolution: On the Pica-
resque View of History"—conclude the festschrift.

L 508. FOERSTER, NORMAN. Nature in American Literature: Studies in the
        Modern View of Nature. New York: Macmillan, 1923. 324 pp.
America presented a rich natural setting for artists, yet not until the
work of Cooper and Bryant did American writers look closely at their
natural surroundings rather than at classical and Christian traditions.
Since then, however, according to Foerster, American writers have exhibited
"striking curiosity" about and "ardent emotional devotion" to nature.
Foerster's juxtaposition of naturalists John Muir and John Burroughs with
such 19th-century literary figures as Bryant, Whittier, Emerson, Thoreau,
Lowell, Whitman, and Lanier reveals the continuing and widely shared interest in nature and natural phenomena.

L 509. FOERSTER, NORMAN. Toward Standards: A Study of the Present Criti-
        cal Movement in American Letters. New York: Farrar & Rinehart,
        1928. 224 pp.
Writing at the end of the 1920s, Foerster predicted the demise of Naturalism and the rise of Humanism, especially in literary criticism. This
book examines what he feels are the three critical points of view: the
personal (impressionist), the historical, and the real (humanist). The
humanists, say Foerster, "seek to transcend not only the personal but
also the historical estimate and to attain a judgment in terms of permanently human values." Foerster devotes chapters to a study of "Humanism
in the Renaissance," "Impressionism," "History: Journalism," "History:
Prophecy," and "Humanism in the Twentieth Century," with "A Note on Humanism and Religion."

L 510. FRANKLIN, H. BRUCE. The Victim as Criminal and Artist: Literature
        from the American Prison. New York: Oxford University Press,
        1978. 337 pp.
"My subject," says Franklin, "is literature created by those members of
the oppressed classes who have become artists with words through their
experience of being defined by the state as criminals." The critic notes
that predominantly white male literary critics have too long neglected
or misunderstood the works of Native Americans, Chicanos, and Afro-
Americans, and especially those works written in slavery or prison. Franklin
includes chapters on slave narratives, prison literature, individual
authors (Malcolm Braly, Chester Himes), and a thirty-three page "Annotated
Bibliography of Literature by Convicts: 1800-1977."

L 511. FREDMAN, STEPHEN. Poet's Prose: The Crisis in American Verse.
        New York: Cambridge University Press, 1983. 173 pp.
Fredman argues that American poetics is currently shifting from a concern
with meter and matter to the question of whether poetry is possible at
all. Fredman discusses the American prose poem beginning with William
Carlos Williams and continuing through to contemporary poets such as John
Ashbery. He isolates the sentence as the basic unit of meaning and finds
the origins of the American prose poem in the two separate but interdependent American genres, oratory and meditation. Fredman demonstrates,
referring to Emerson's attempts to unite these genres, a model and rationale for the 20th-century prose poems.

L 512. FUSSELL, EDWIN S. Lucifer in Harness: American Meter, Metaphor,
        and Diction. Princeton, N.J.: Princeton University Press, 1973.
        182 pp.
Fussell's thesis is that the American poet has felt "harnessed" by the
literature and literary tradition of England, the mother country. His
work investigates the dilemma of 19th- and 20th-century American poetry
in terms of meter, metaphor, and diction--areas scholars have neglected,
but which poets have not. Poets discussed include Poe, Whitman, Hart
Crane, Stevens, Dickinson, Frost, and Robinson.

L 513. GAYLE, ADDISON, Jr., ed. The Black Aesthetic. New York: Doubleday
        1971. 432 pp.
The thirty-three essays in this collection all try to illuminate a central
question: is art by blacks informed by a sense of beauty which can be
understood only by a special aesthetic? The answer of most of the essayists is "yes." The essays are gathered under the headings of theory,
music, poetry, drama, and fiction, with contributors such as Hoyt W. Fuller,
Larry Neal, Langston Hughes, Richard Wright, and Ishmael Reed. Various
aspects of a black aesthetic are addressed by these writers and find their
unifying theme in the idea of this aesthetic as a corrective--"a means
of helping black people out of the polluted mainstream of Americanism."
Uniquely black as opposed to "universal" cultural experiences result in
an art which logically demands unique critical tools (in the form of this
aesthetic) for evaluation.

L 514. GELFANT, BLANCHE HOUSMAN. The American City Novel. Norman: Uni-
        versity of Oklahoma Press, 1954. 289 pp.
Gelfant argues that in the 20th century the American city novel has become
a separate literary genre, which she has "sought to define . . . by its
intention, materials, and motifs." The city is seen as an agent in this
fiction, "a key actor in a human drama" which shapes character and plot
to a greater degree than in works that the author describes as "urban
local color fiction." Alienation--characters who are "self-divided"--
is the main theme of this genre. After establishing her definition, the
author discusses the work of Dreiser, Anderson, Wharton, Wolfe, Dos Passos,
and Farrell, and concludes with a view of the mid-century experiments
of Willard Motley and Nelson Algren, among others.

L 515. GELPI, ALBERT. The Tenth Muse: The Psyche of the American Poet.
        Cambridge, Mass.: Harvard University Press, 1975. 327 pp.
Gelpi here is less interested in the poet's conscious "thought process"
than in his "psyche." He wants "to discern the elusive connections between
the cultural situation and the psychological situation of the poets as
those connections contributed to poetic theory and practice during the
formative period of American literature." After an initial chapter defining terms, Gelpi turns to a number of major poets before 1900: Taylor,
Emerson, Poe, Whitman, and Dickinson.

L 516. GIBSON, DONALD B. Politics of Literary Expression: A Study of
        Major Black Writers. Westport, Conn.: Greenwood Press, 1981.
        225 pp.
Suggesting that modes of criticism that remove literature from the realm
of time and history lead to misinterpretation of black literature, Gibson
proposes a theoretical base for practical criticism. He theorizes that
literary value emerges as a function of social value, grounded in time
and history. Literature functions both to sustain currently existing
values and standards, and to criticize these values and standards as a
means to change. Gibson applies his definition in essays on the works
of Richard Wright, Ralph Ellison, James Baldwin, Charles W. Chesnutt,
and Jean Toomer. Focusing on the role of creative literature as a political instrument, these essays address, as well, each author's sensitivity
to the social situation of his particular time.

L 517. GLOSTER, HUGH M. Negro Voices in American Fiction. Chapel Hill:
        University of North Carolina Press, 1948. 295 pp.
Gloster's work attempts to present "the Negro as his own interpreter."
He gleans information from 20th-century American fiction--novels and short
stories reflecting black psychology, interests, achievements, aspirations,
and racial awareness. Because racial factors motivate much of fiction,
black authors, according to Gloster, chiefly write about their status
as a "segregated, oppressed, ridiculed, and exploited minority." Gloster

treats themes, attitudes, and backgrounds, and includes both well and
lesser known writers. The book provides an account of black social history
and literature from approximately 1900 to 1940.

L 518. GREEN, MARTIN. Re-Appraisals: Some Commonsense Readings in Ameri-
        can Literature. London: Evelyn, 1963. 252 pp.
Green believes that literary scholarship is guilty of much of the "alienation" current in America, and wishes to change "the ideas about literature,
about the imagination as a whole, which scholarly studies now promote."
He attempts to do so with essays on many major American authors—among
them Emerson, Hawthorne, Melville, Twain, Whitman, James, Faulkner,
Salinger, and Nabokov. He strives to reevaluate these writers, and American
literature in general, to force us to move away from "a theory of American
literature which distorts our response to what is there."

L 519. GUNN, GILES. The Interpretation of Otherness: Literature, Religion,
        and the American Imagination. New York: Oxford University Press,
        1979. 250 pp.
Gunn argues that a religious, or transcendent, view of human experience
exerts enormous force on American literature. His specific illustrations
come from readings of Melville, Dickinson, Twain, Frost, Fitzgerald, and
William Carlos Williams. The author begins with a cautionary chapter
on the "religious use and abuse of literature," before moving to a discussion of our literature up to W.W. II. He attempts to formulate "the
connections between the literary and the cultural on the one side and
the religious and theological on the other by exploring the putative common
ground between them." Culture and "cultural material, namely symbols"
comprise that common ground. Literature is seen to test the validity
of cultural symbols, and religion to construct them, and both do this
in order to map the shape of American experience.

L 520. GUNN, JANET VARNER. Autobiography: Toward a Poetics of Experience.
        Philadelphia: University of Pennsylvania Press, 1982. 151 pp.
Gunn begins by noting the recent critical interest in autobiography and
the recognition that autobiography is literary and not just historical.
Although willing to grant that autobiography may have more significance
in its anthropological than in its literary function, Gunn urges that
the literary elements of autobiography not be overlooked. She approaches
the problem of defining autobiography as a genre by discussing autobiography in relation to hermeneutics, narrative theory, and current debate
about the determinacy of meaning in texts. She posits three interrelated
moments in the autobiographical situation: autobiographical impulse (to
make sense of experience), autobiographical perspective (putting experience
into language), and autobiographical response (reader's relation to text).
The texts she examines include Walden and Black Elk Speaks.

L 521. GUTTMANN, ALLEN. The Conservative Tradition in America. New York:
        Oxford University Press, 1967. 214 pp.
The conservative tradition in America, with its roots in Edmund Burke,
has been a minority tradition. Guttmann defines it most simply as a "dream
of an orderly, disciplined, hierarchical society inwardly formed by a
sense of the past." He traces images of that dream from pre-Revolutionary
America through some 19th-century writers, including Cooper, Hawthorne,
and James, and on into the present, and examines the continuing debate
that conservatives have engaged in with liberals.

L 522. **GUTTMANN, ALLEN.** The Jewish Writer in America: Assimilation and
the Crisis of Identity. New York: Oxford University Press, 1971.
256 pp.
After defining the complex question of the Jewish relation to and assimilation into American life, Guttmann devotes three chapters to literary
history, one to Saul Bellow, and one to the topic, "The End of the Jewish
People?" While interested in the issue of tradition and continuity,
Guttmann also emphasizes the "ways in which the Jews in America have come
to differ from their ancestors," and discusses the resulting "crisis of
identity." The range of authors examined includes Abraham Cahan, Meyer
Levin, Daniel Fuchs, Alfred Kazin, Ludwig Lewisohn, Philip Roth, Henry
Roth, Paul Goodman, and Allen Ginsberg.

L 523. **HARAP, LOUIS.** The Image of the Jew in American Literature from
Early Republic to Mass Immigration. Philadelphia: Jewish Pub-
lication Society of America, 1974. 586 pp.
Harap is "mainly interested in discovering the image of the Jew as a social
phenomenon and as an indicator of the real status of the Jew in the United
States throughout history." To do this, he examines major writers
(Longfellow, Whittier, Hawthorne, Melville, Whitman, Twain, Howells, James),
minor authors (Albert Aiken, Henry Harland, Joseph Ingram), Jewish authors
(Abraham Cahan, Emma Lazarus, Mordecai Noah), and many "subliterary"
writers. Harap asserts that "The present study shows that the Jew was
a minor, if not peripheral, element in the work of most major American
writers before our century." Themes discussed include those of the Wandering Jew (in both secular and religious literature), the self-image of
the Jew in the 19th century, and the Jew in the earliest beginnings of
the American Jewish novel.

L 524. **HARPER, MICHAEL S.** and **ROBERT B. STEPTO**, eds. Chant of Saints:
A Gathering of Afro-American Literature, Art, and Scholarship.
Urbana: University of Illinois Press, 1979. 490 pp.
The editors have included substantial selections from each artist/critic,
whether it be fiction, photographs, poetry, paintings, or non-fiction.
The selections are accompanied by either interviews with the authors or
critical pieces on their works, and are loosely grouped according to shared
cultural or historical concerns. Contributors of fiction and poetry
include Toni Morrison, Alice Walker, Ernest J. Gaines, Derek Walcott, and
Robert Hayden. Critics and essayists include Ralph Ellison, Albert Murray,
Robert Farris Thompson, and Charles T. Davis.

L 525. **HARRIS, TRUDIER.** From Mammies to Militants: Domestics in Black
American Literature. Philadelphia: Temple University Press,
1982. 203 pp.
Harris examines the portrayal of black female domestics in the fiction
of Charles W. Chesnutt, Kristin Hunter, Toni Morrison, Richard Wright,
Ann Petry, William Melvin Kelley, Alice Childress, John A. Williams,
Douglas Turner Ward, Barbara Woods, Ted Shine, and Ed Bullins. Largely
concerned with power relationships between black maids and their white
employers, her interdisciplinary analysis focuses on the influences geography and folk culture have on the portrayal of black women; the reasons
why an author stereotypes or draws three-dimensional characters; and the
relation between politics and art.

L 526. **HAUCK, RICHARD BOYD.** A Cheerful Nihilism: Confidence and "The
Absurd" in American Humorous Fiction. Bloomington: Indiana University Press, 1971. 269 pp.
American writers have variously responded to the absurd--"a sense of meaninglessness in nature and lack of moral direction in people." Jonathan
Edwards proposed a reliance on faith, and Benjamin Franklin offered an
alogical confidence in natural phenomena. According to Hauck, Melville

presents the most complete grappling with the problems of meaninglessness, but it is Mark Twain--with his predecessors, the frontier storytellers-- who supplies the comic response. In the 20th century, William Faulkner and John Barth continue this tradition.

L 527. **HENDERSON, HARRY B., III.** Versions of the Past: The Historical Imagination in American Fiction. New York: Oxford University Press, 1974. 344 pp.
Against the persistent view that American literature lacks "a sense of history," Henderson sets the view that a number of American classics-- including Hawthorne's The Scarlet Letter, Melville's Billy Budd, and Faulkner's Absalom, Absalom!--do show a real sense of the past. The authors manifest this awareness of history by responding to a particular past and to a present dilemma. The work analyzes major 19th-century historians and reconstructs two major frames of reference which are keys for the whole book: the "progressive," according to which society moves toward fulfilling such ideals as freedom and justice; and the "holist," where such ideals play no decisive role in history.

L 528. **HERRON, IMA HONAKER.** The Small Town in American Literature. Durham, N.C.: Duke University Press, 1939. 477 pp.
Herron traces "the literary evolution of the American village and small town" through three stages: "slavish imitation of English village tradi- tion" in New England and the Middle Atlantic Colonies; changes brought on by Westward expansion; and standardization as a result of urban develop- ment. After a brief discussion of actual American towns, Herron proceeds geographically through the Northeast, Middle West, Far West, and Southern representations of village life and concludes with a look at modern "Cru- saders and Skeptics" (e.g., Sherwood Anderson, Sinclair Lewis, William Faulkner, and Thomas Wolfe), and "A Glance Backward."

L 529. **HICKS, GRANVILLE.** The Great Tradition: An Interpretation of Ameri- can Literature Since the Civil War. 1933; Rev. ed. New York: Macmillan, 1935. 341 pp.
Hicks's study is a Marxist interpretation of American literature from the era of industrialism after the Civil War (James Russell Lowell and Walt Whitman) to the "younger generation" of authors active in the 1930s (John Dos Passos, James Farrell, and others). Hicks's original aim was to present "a history of bourgeois literature." In the 1935 edition, he added a chapter entitled "Direction" which is devoted entirely to the achievements of contemporary revolutionary writers. In 1969, this volume appeared with a new foreword and afterword by the author, in which he disavows many of his critical judgments. For example, his earlier politi- cal reservations about the work of Mark Twain, Henry James, Robert Frost, William Faulkner, and T. S. Eliot are replaced by aesthetic praise, and his enthusiasm for the novels of Sinclair Lewis is qualified.

L 530. **HIGGS, ROBERT J.** Laurel and Thorn: The Athlete in American Litera- ture. Lexington: University Press of Kentucky, 1981. 182 pp.
Campbell, Huizinga, and Veblen provide a theoretical basis for Higgs's examination of the athlete as a symbol and mythical figure that reveals America's social self-image. Authors treated include Edward Albee, F. Scott Fitzgerald, Ernest Hemingway, Sinclair Lewis, Sherwood Anderson, Jack London, Walker Percy, Philip Roth, and John Updike. Athletes are classed by broad divisions, as Apollo, Dionysus, and Adonis, with subtopics under those headings--for example: "the dumb athlete," "the sporting gentleman," "the muscular Christian," and "brave new men" under the Apollo category.

L 531. **HILFER, ANTHONY CHANNEL.** The Ethics of Intensity in American Fiction. Austin: University of Texas Press, 1981. 165 pp.
Hilfer follows Aristotle's definition of ethos and pathos, and argues
that pathos has displaced ethos as a principle of characterization in
American fiction. In conjunction with this he considers Peirce's and
William James's contributions to Pragmatism to be intimately related to
the realistic fiction of Henry James, William Dean Howells, and selected
work of Theodore Dreiser and Gertrude Stein. Hilfer uses his definition
of the self as portrayed in Victorian fiction as a point of contrast to
those American authors. In developing his thesis he also discusses imagery
and pathos in Whitman's work, James's "The Beast in the Jungle" and The
Wings of the Dove, Dreiser's Sister Carrie and An American Tragedy, and
Stein's Melanctha.

L 532. **HINTZ, HOWARD W.** The Quaker Influence in American Literature.
New York: Revell, 1940. 96 pp.
Hintz includes a variety of authors in his study: famous Quakers (William
Penn, John Woolman, John Greenleaf Whittier), writers of Quaker descent
(Thomas Paine, Charles Brockden Brown, James Fenimore Cooper, Walt Whitman),
and one "neither a Friend nor a descendant of Friends" (Ralph Waldo
Emerson). This brief study of Quaker writers, themes, and subjects intro-
duces several areas for further research.

L 533. **HOLMAN, C. HUGH.** Windows on the World: Essays on American Social
Fiction. Knoxville: University of Tennessee Press, 1979.
205 pp.
This volume presents eleven essays on American realism as a literary mode,
on satiric humor in American social fiction, and on individual authors
(John Marquand, Ellen Glasgow, William Faulkner, and Thomas Wolfe).
Holman's thesis is that the Bildungsroman—or novel of education—is a
basic type in American fiction and that the novel's central action displays
an essentially American attitude of "pragmatic acceptance" to the violent
events of the social world.

L 534. **HOLROYD, STUART.** Emergence from Chaos. Boston: Houghton Mifflin,
1957. 224 pp.
Holroyd's subject is "how a number of poets have reacted to the modern
predicament," to "the spiritual chaos" which "manifests itself equally
in indifference to religion on the one hand and fanatical embracing of
substitute religions on the other." He discusses six poets in detail:
Whitman, Eliot, Dylan Thomas, Yeats, Rimbaud, and Rilke. Eliot, the last
discussed, is found to be the most valuable, although his "critical criteria have been religious and ethical rather than literary." This is
entirely consistent with the "propagandistic aspect" of the book's "attack
on humanism and . . . plea for the rediscovery of a religious standard
of values." The "chaos" of the title is not only that of a chaotic world,
but that also of the unconscious, and it is in "man's endeavor to overcome
this chaos within himself that all religion has its origin."

L 535. **HORTON, ROD W.** and **HERBERT W. EDWARDS.** Backgrounds of American
Literary Thought. 1952; Rev. ed. New York: Appleton-Century-
Crofts, 1967. 538 pp.
The authors provide "in compact and relatively simplified form certain
historical and intellectual materials necessary to a fuller understanding
of the leading American authors." Chapters are devoted to such particular
subjects as Puritanism, Unitarianism and Transcendentalism, Marxism, Imperialism and Isolation, Freudianism, the South, and Postwar Science. As
the book's title suggests, the focus is on the intellectual history which
formed the American writer; "even the facts of literary history are
omitted."

L 536. HOWARD, HELEN ADDISON. American Indian Poetry. Boston: Twayne,
         1979. 157 pp.
Acknowledging the barriers that divide Indian and English expression,
Howard approaches Indian poetry through the work of eight American literati
who sought to merge the two literatures and cultures through "translation"
or "interpretation." He concludes that the "interpreters," who try to
capture the spirit of Indian poetry in their own writing, tend to lose
the authenticity of the linguistic forms. Alternatively, the "translators"
are more faithful to the original verse, but are less accessible to the
untrained Euro-American reader. While reaching these conclusions, Howard
attempts to make the verse more critically accessible by building familiarity with the American Indian poetic tradition.

L 537. HUBBELL, JAY B. The South in American Literature: 1607-1900.
         Durham, N.C.: Duke University Press, 1954. 987 pp.
Hubbell divides the literary history of the American South into five periods and adds an epilogue covering the first half of the 20th century.
The section for each period begins with chapters on historical background,
education, literary climate, and related topics; chapters on individual
authors and on topics of importance to the period follow. The chapters
on individual authors, many of whom do not have established reputations,
contain primarily biography, canon, contemporary reception, and description
of representative work. Hubbell's intent is to recover for the South
a literary tradition which he feels has been lost or neglected.

L 538. HUBBELL, JAY B. Southern Life in Fiction. Athens: University
         of Georgia Press, 1960. 99 pp.
Hubbell suggests that the reading of regional fiction, including "subliterary fiction," will, if one is not too restrictive about quality and chronology, give "a comprehensive picture" of life. The first of the three
lectures printed here deals with this observation generally; the latter
two deal respectively with the fiction of Virginia and Georgia, especially
during the 19th century.

L 539. HUBBELL, JAY B. Who Are the Major American Writers? A Study of
         the Changing Literary Canon. Durham, N.C.: Duke University Press,
         1972. 344 pp.
Hubbell charts the changing reputations of American writers of the last
160 years. Working as a literary historian, he gathers information from
numerous sources: literary histories, anthologies, book reviews, popular
magazines, scholarly journals and monographs, and archives of the Hall
of Fame for Great Americans and the American Academy of Arts and Letters.
The study insists on the temporary relativity of literary judgment, labels
great that literature which withstands the test of time, and suggests
that Americans have trouble identifying greatness in artists, educators,
scientists, and statesmen.

L 540. HUF, LINDA. A Portrait of the Artist as a Young Woman: The Writer
         as Heroine in American Literature. New York: Ungar, 1983.
         196 pp.
Huf examines six novels, Ruth Hall by Fanny Fern, The Story of Avis by
Elizabeth Stuart Phelps, The Awakening by Kate Chopin, The Song of the
Lark by Willa Cather, The Heart Is a Lonely Hunter by Carson McCullers,
and The Bell Jar by Sylvia Plath, as examples of a rare genre, the female
Kunstlerroman. She explains the rarity of such books by pointing to the
hostility of critics and readers to books which depicted a woman choosing
the vocation of an artist and rejecting selfless devotion to wifehood
and motherhood; contrasts this with the widespread tolerance of the egotism
of heroes of the male Kunstlerroman; and traces a characteristic but
developing plot pattern followed by such novels.

L 541. HUGHES, CARL MILTON. The Negro Novelist: A Discussion of the
Writings of American Negro Novelists 1940-1950. 1953; Rev. ed.
New York: Citadel Press, 1970. 288 pp.
Hughes claims to continue and update Vernon Loggins's The Negro Author
(see L 563) by examining black fiction between 1940 and 1950. In the
early 20th century, black writers focused on racial themes and black life;
however, in the mid-20th century, they broadened their perspectives to
include American social problems in general. Black fiction thus moves
from "Portrayals of Bitterness" to "Limited Perspective" and finally to
"Common Denominator: Man"—the titles of chapters two, three, and five.
Expanding their material, black writers of the 1940s and 1950s moved beyond
the mechanistic and deterministic (i.e., Naturalistic) elements earlier
writers favored. Hughes's last chapter discusses the reputations of such
novelists as Richard Wright, Chester Himes, Carl Offord, and Willard Motley,
who finally have been acknowledged by critics as "serious writers."

L 542. ISAACS, EDITH J. R. The Negro in the American Theatre. New York:
Theatre Arts Books, 1947. 143 pp.
This short book gives an introduction to black performers in American
theater, opera, drama, and music hall up to the mid-1940s. Isaacs deals
briefly with the history before 1890 when performers such as Billy Kersands
and James Bland sang, played the banjo, acted, or danced. She focuses
most of her attention, however, on the 20th century and covers performers
(Bert Williams), composers (W. C. Handy), actors (Charles Gilpin and Paul
Robeson), tap dancers (Bill Robinson), musicians (Louis Armstrong), and
opera singers (Camilla Williams).

L 543. JACKSON, BLYDEN and LOUIS D. RUBIN, Jr. Black Poetry in America:
Two Essays in Historical Interpretation. Baton Rouge: Louisiana
State University Press, 1974. 119 pp.
The authors hope to encourage the recent interest in black poetry by offering, "within a brief compass, an interpretation, basically along historical
lines, of certain of the main currents and principal directions of black
American poetry." Rubin's essay, covering the years 1746-1923, is about
"the search for a language" in which to write; Jackson's essay, beginning
with the Harlem Renaissance and continuing to the present, suggests that
modern black poets have found one. A substantial bibliography on the
subject is appended.

L 544. JARRELL, RANDALL. Kipling, Auden & Co.: Essays and Reviews 1935-
1964. New York: Farrar, Straus, 1980. 381 pp.
The essays and reviews collected here in chronological order make available
"virtually all of Jarrell's previously uncollected criticism." This collection follows Jarrell's earlier critical assemblages, Poetry and the
Age (L 545), A Sad Heart at the Supermarket (L 546), and The Third Book
of Criticism (L 547). These pieces, originally published in popular magazines, in scholarly journals, and as introductions, show Jarrell's range
of interest and judgment—from Aristotle and Shakespeare to contemporary
writing and painting. Most of the collection, despite the title, is on
modern American poetry, fiction, and criticism.

L 545. JARRELL, RANDALL. Poetry and the Age. New York: Knopf, 1953.
271 pp.
Although not explicitly linked, Jarrell's essays fall into two classes:
criticism of modern American culture, and detailed analysis of poems by
Walt Whitman, Wallace Stevens, Robert Frost, and Marianne Moore. Generally,
these essays sympathize with modern poets who face an audience made hostile
by the poets' apparent obscurity. The analytic essays, in particular,
attempt to demonstrate how an experienced, sympathetic reader should understand modern poetry.

L 546. JARRELL, RANDALL. A Sad Heart at the Supermarket. New York:
        Atheneum, 1962. 211 pp.
Unlike Jarrell's other books of criticism (Poetry and the Age, The Third
Book of Criticism, and Kipling, Auden & Co.), this volume is made up of
more general essays on such subjects as "The Intellectual in America"
and "The Taste of the Age." The essays are detailed analyses of our culture and its comic and serious predicaments.

L 547. JARRELL, RANDALL. The Third Book of Criticism. New York: Farrar,
        Straus, 1969. 334 pp.
The nine essays gathered in this posthumous collection are concerned with
various topics, including Christina Stead's The Man Who Loved Children,
Wallace Stevens, Robert Graves, W. H. Auden, Robert Frost's "Home Burial,"
Russian short novels, and Rudyard Kipling. The volume concludes with
a general examination of American poetry of the last fifty years.

L 548. JAYE, MICHAEL C. and ANN CHALMERS WATTS, eds. Literature & the
        Urban Experience: Essays on the City and Literature. New Bruns-
        wick, N.J.: Rutgers University Press, 1981. 256 pp.
This collection of one poem and twenty essays grew out of a conference
held at Rutgers University in April 1980. The essays are divided into
two categories. The first category represents traditional literary criticism and includes essays by Oates, Morrison, Spender, Vendler, Leo Marx,
Kazin, Hassan, Fiedler, and Richard Eder on a variety of writers (Crane,
Dreiser, Bellow, Updike, Lowell, Ellison, Baldwin, Fitzgerald, Malamud,
Melville, Mailer, Pynchon, Barthelme, and others). The second category
includes informal essays by James Baldwin, Amiri Baraka, Jerre Mangione,
Pedro Juan Soto, David Ignatow, Marge Piercy, Joan Burstyn, M. Jerry Weiss,
and John Holt. Several of these essays include autobiographical elements,
but they also discuss the relationship between literature and society.
The last four discuss the shortcomings of literature available to inner-
city dwellers--children, in particular. According to the editors, all
the writers represented in this collection exhibit an "ambiguous attitude"
toward the city.

L 549. JONES, ANNE GOODWYN. Tomorrow Is Another Day: The Woman Writer
        in the South, 1859-1936. Baton Rouge: Louisiana State University
        Press, 1981. 401 pp.
Jones combines biography and literary analysis to examine works by seven
Southern women writers of the late 19th and early 20th centuries--Augusta
Jane Evans, Grace King, Kate Chopin, Mary Johnston, Ellen Glasgow, Frances
Newman, and Margaret Mitchell--all of whom were raised to be "Southern
ladies," and wrote before the Southern Literary Renaissance. Jones has
chosen to discuss only the works that address the question of Southern
womanhood. She begins with a history of the "sources, ideological use,
and persistence of the image of the Southern lady" and describes the conditions in which the Southern woman writer found herself. She then devotes
a chapter to each author, concluding that these authors, simultaneously
romanticists and realists, all exhibit a certain ambivalence toward the
inherited image of the Southern woman.

L 550. KARANIKAS, ALEXANDER. Hellenes and Hellions: Modern Greek Char-
        acters in American Literature. Urbana: University of Illinois
        Press, 1981. 511 pp.
Karanikas here studies the nature of Greek characters in a broad range
of American literature. He began the project in order to determine whether
or not the Greek characters have been stereotyped in America, and he concludes that they have not. In the process, he provides a complex, if
not conclusive, sociology of Greeks in American culture. Topics considered
include assimilation by Greek immigrants, stereotypes used by both Greek
and non-Greek authors, and the influence of classical Greece upon modern
American writings by and about Greeks.

L 551. KELLMAN, STEVEN G. The Self-Begetting Novel. New York: Columbia
University Press, 1980. 154 pp.
Kellman identifies a kind of novel he calls "self-begetting," a novel
which is supremely self-reflexive and permits its author to allude frequently and at length to other literary works. Self-begetting novels,
whose heroes are often without parents, satisfy the authors' self-creative
urges. Although Kellman deals first with French and English novels, he
devotes an entire chapter to American self-begetting art. He notes that
introspection has been a mania in American literature, as exhibited in
the work of Adams, Thoreau, James, Miller, and others. Some writers create
"selves" by creating art (Whitman, Kerouac, Mailer, et al.), and this
tendency is as noticeable, he claims, in writers such as Whitman as it
is in Proust.

L 552. KEYSSAR, HELENE. The Curtain and the Veil: Strategies in Black
Drama. New York: Burt Franklin, 1981. 298 pp.
Keyssar draws upon the critical approaches of Kenneth Burke, Stanley Cavell,
J. L. Styan, and Stanley Fish in her examination of eight plays by seven
black American dramatists: Langston Hughes, Theodore Ward, Lorraine
Hansberry, Willis Richardson, Imamu Amiri Baraka, Ed Bullins, and Ntozake
Shange. She notes that playwrights, especially black playwrights, must
choose between instructing and entertaining their audiences, between presenting what they think those audiences ought to see and presenting what
they will pay to see. Quoting DuBois, Keyssar establishes that there
are two "classes" of dramatic situations: "inner life" situations,
depicted for black audiences; and "contact of black and white" situations,
depicted for mixed audiences. She discusses the eight plays in relation
to these categories. The appendices consist of an essay on the "strategic
approach," a brief survey of black drama criticism, and a previously published bibliography of black drama and scholarship on the subject.

L 553. KING, JOHN OWEN. The Iron of Melancholy: Structures of Spiritual
Conversion in America from the Puritan Conscience to Victorian
Neurosis. Middletown, Conn.: Wesleyan University Press, 1983.
457 pp.
King believes that the dominating myth of America as a garden of Eden
should be replaced by a myth of spiritual crisis and regeneration, of
wilderness and the path out of wilderness. In chapters that examine the
spiritual travails of representative Americans, from Cotton Mather and
Jonathan Edwards to the elder Henry James and William James, Josiah Royce,
and James Jackson Putnam, King argues that the American character has
been one that is tormented by a penitential obsession and is alienated
by the landscape it inhabits. Toward the end of the book, in a chapter
entitled "American Apocalypse: Max Weber," King summarizes his thesis
by showing how the Puritan conscience became the Victorian neurological
"case," and how both the Puritan concept of salvation through work and
the Victorian obsessive-compulsive personality crystallized into Weber's
Protestant ethic.

L 554. KOLODNY, ANNETTE. The Lay of the Land: Metaphor as Experience
and History in American Life and Letters. Chapel Hill: University
of North Carolina Press, 1975. 185 pp.
Kolodny examines "what is probably America's oldest and most cherished
fantasy: a daily reality of harmony between man and nature based on an
experience of the land as essentially feminine—that is, not simply the
land as mother, but the land as woman, the total female principle of gra-
tification—enclosing the individual in an environment of receptivity,
repose, and painless and integral satisfaction." She traces 200 years
of American literary history in less than 200 pages, using the critical
tools of Freudian scholarship. She concentrates on six representative
figures: Freneau, Crevecoeur, Audubon, Cooper, Simms, and Faulkner.

L 555. KRAPP, GEORGE PHILLIP. The English Language in America. 2 vols.
New York: Century, 1925. 732 pp.
This book is a descriptive history of the English language in America,
which Krapp traces not only through observation and scholarship but also
through literature. His chapters on literary dialects and vocabulary
attempt to contribute to an understanding of the development of general
"dialects" and vocabulary. Regional writers often employed phonetic representations of dialect; some of these became frozen in the orthography
and as a result were incorporated more broadly and readily. Volume two
is a contribution to the field of pronunciation. Various theories regarding the development of dialects, primarily based on climate and geographical setting, are discussed.

L 556. KRAUSE, SYDNEY J. Essays on Determinism in American Literature.
Kent, Ohio: Kent State University Press, 1964. 116 pp.
The eight essays collected here relate determinism to the reading of American literature and seek "to broaden the reference of determinism from
within and without the framework of naturalism." While some of the authors
discussed seem to fall naturally within the range of determinism (Farrell
and Dos Passos especially), others do not (e.g., Melville, Faulkner,
William James, and Mark Twain). Determinism is assumed to be a philosophical force that motivates the desire for freedom; that desire is explored
as it informs the writers under discussion.

L 557. LAWRENCE, DAVID HERBERT. Studies in Classic American Literature.
New York: Seltzer, 1923. 264 pp.
Lawrence's main assumption is that the Pilgrims first came to America
to escape Europe. From this he constructs a "national psychology," claiming that American writers display two overriding concerns: first, the
disintegration and removal of the old (European) tradition; and second,
the formation of a new (American) tradition. Franklin and Crevecoeur
still depended too much on European tradition to develop a wholly national
identity. Cooper came closer to achieving it; Poe, however, was obsessed
by the death and disintegration of the European psyche. Hawthorne and
Melville moved nearer to an American identity, but only Whitman conveyed
American nationalism as a native tradition. Lawrence thus sees American
literature in an organic, developing process.

L 558. LEE, A. ROBERT, ed. Black Fiction: New Studies in the Afro-
American Novel Since 1945. New York: Harper & Row, 1980.
245 pp.
This collection of essays offers eleven different approaches to modern
black fiction. Individual novelists such as Richard Wright, Langston
Hughes, Ann Petry, Ralph Ellison, James Baldwin, Imamu Amiri Baraka, and
Ishmael Reed are treated at length. The last essays deal with larger
topics: political apocalypticism, Feminism, and new narrative modes.
Each essay defines how black writers have gone beyond realism, aspiring
to portray the black experience "in its most ruthless identity."

L 559. LEE, L. E. and MERRILL LEWIS. Women, Women Writers, and the West.
Troy, N.Y.: Whitston, 1980. 252 pp.
A collection of eighteen articles by various authors, dealing with women's
interpretation of "the western experience"; "changing images of men and
women" in works by Western writers of both sexes; the Western woman as
writer; and writing about frontier experience by women from Canada and
Australia. This collection seeks to amplify our largely mythologized
understanding of the literature of the West by including examination of
women's perspectives on the frontier, and includes discussions of major
figures (Willa Cather, Hamlin Garland, and Wallace Stegner), as well as
material about largely unknown women diarists, historians, novelists,
and poets.

L 560. LEE, ROBERT EDSON. From West to East: Studies in the Literature of the American West. Urbana: University of Illinois Press, 1966. 172 pp.
This book complements Edwin Fussell's Frontier (see L 130). Lee examines a group of writers from the early 19th century into the present who went West and responded to that experience, "but who were unable, for a variety of reasons, to transform the first-hand experience of history into a literature of their own." Lee examines particularly the work of Lewis and Clark, Timothy Flint, James Hall, Washington Irving, Francis Parkman, Mark Twain, Willa Cather, and Bernard DeVoto.

L 561. LIEBER, TODD M. Endless Experiments: Essays on the Heroic Experience in American Romanticism. Columbus: Ohio State University Press, 1973. 277 pp.
Lieber examines "the dramatic experience of the Romantic hero" in some key American texts, in which "the drama of self . . . furnishes the material for the central 'action' and thus becomes the heroic experience of the literature." He begins with the "Romantic vision" as formulated by Emerson, then deals with Thoreau, Whitman, Melville, Poe, William Carlos Williams (a close reading of selective texts), and concludes with Wallace Stevens in order to show "the posture of the Romantic Sensibility in the modern age."

L 562. LINDBERG, GARY. The Confidence Man in American Literature. New York: Oxford University Press, 1982. 319 pp.
Lindberg asserts that the figure of the confidence man is central to the American imagination, and finds versions thereof in many writers, including Melville, Poe, Franklin, Brockden Brown, Howells, Dreiser, Jefferson, Whitman, William James, Emerson, Thoreau, Hawthorne, Mark Twain, P. T. Barnum, Faulkner, Heller, Ellison, Bellow, Kesey, the Beats, and Barth. The confidence man's interest in the techniques of self-creation rather than in their result or identity per se makes him an ebullient, exciting figure—one which clarifies the distance between the culture's stated values and its practices and which embodies the promissory tone that characterizes American ideology.

L 563. LOGGINS, VERNON. The Negro Author: His Development in America. New York: Columbia University Press, 1931. 480 pp.
This is a work on black literature in America up to 1900. Loggins provides a general survey of "consciously produced" literature by black authors, and covers such areas as early authorship (1760-1790), writings of the pioneer racial leaders (1790-1840), writings of the leading antislavery agents and the racial leaders (1840-1865), and fiction and poetry (1865-1900). The volume provides a bibliography of primary works.

L 564. LUDWIG, RICHARD M., ed. Aspects of American Poetry: Essays Presented to Howard Mumford Jones. Columbus: Ohio State University Press, 1962. 335 pp.
This collection of essays on American poetry is a tribute to the scholar Howard Mumford Jones. Two of the essayists write about American poetry in general: Edwin Fussell, in an essay on metrics; and G. Ferris Cronkhite, on beliefs about poetic inspiration. Other essays deal with individual poets: Poe, Whitman, Pound, Frost, Sherwood Anderson, Hart Crane, Stevens, Auden, and Tate. Wallace Douglas's essay is a discussion of the Agrarians, the culture out of which they came, and New Criticism. Other contributors are Marvin Felheim, Richard Ludwig, Claude Simpson, Walter Rideout, Albert Van Nostrand, Richard Ellmann, Frederick McDowell, and Radcliffe Squires. Appended to the essays is a bibliography of works by Howard Mumford Jones.

L 565. LYNEN, JOHN F. The Design of the Present: Essays on Time and
        Form in American Literature. New Haven, Conn.: Yale University
        Press, 1969. 441 pp.
Lynen examines the irreconcilable duality of present, finite, particular
experience and infinite, universal transcendence; he claims that American
authors are always trying to reconcile this opposition. The source of
this duality is the sense of time bequeathed by Puritanism—a sense in
which all varieties of time are reduced to the sharply contrasting present
and eternity. According to Lynen, Anne Bradstreet was the first American
writer to realize that making the present an emblem of all times would
require a new poetic form; seeming opposites, Edwards and Franklin both
sought to unite the duality in images of perfect harmony; Irving and Cooper
found a transcendent present in the merging of consciousness and landscape;
and Poe, Whitman, and Eliot, unable to feel that history unites the present
and eternity, made "a history of metaphysics."

L 566. LYNN, KENNETH S. Visions of America: Eleven Literary Historical
        Essays. Westport, Conn.: Greenwood Press, 1973. 206 pp.
The eleven essays reprinted here provide introductions to major literary
works and figures and serve, as the author suggests, to "justify the interdisciplinary methods of American studies." Whitman's theme of "the creative singular and the receptive plural, the lonely conscience and the
collective needs, the individual versus the democracy" unites Lynn's
studies of Thoreau, Uncle Tom's Cabin, Huckleberry Finn, William Dean
Howells, Frank Norris's The Octopus, Dreiser's Sister Carrie, Emma Goldman,
Constance Rourke, Edmund Wilson, John Dos Passos, and "Violence in American
Literature and Folklore." Also examined is the related theme of protest
and reform—"the degree of social involvement pursued by the writer."

L 567. LYONS, JOHN O. The College Novel in America. Carbondale: Southern
        Illinois University Press, 1962. 208 pp.
In Lyons's work the subgenre known as the "academic novel" appears also
as the "novel of academic life" or the "college novel" or the "university
novel." Although Lyons omits what he calls the "comic novel of academic
life," he does discuss briefly what in his opinion is the greatest such
novel, Randall Jarrell's Pictures from an Institution (1954). The loose
structure of the discussion gives Lyons room to mention a plethora of
novels, from Hawthorne's Fanshawe (1828) to Nabokov's Pnin (1957). A
bibliography of academic novels to the time of publication is included.

L 568. LYTTLE, DAVID. Studies in Religion in Early American Literature:
        Edwards, Poe, Channing, Emerson, Some Minor Transcendentalists,
        Hawthorne, and Thoreau. Lanham, Md.: University Press of America,
        1983. 247 pp.
Lyttle studies the theological and philosophical thought of various Ameri-
can writers from Jonathan Edwards to Henry David Thoreau, and is especially
concerned with their changing perceptions of "the nature of God and man."
The book opens with a discussion of Edwards's Calvinist doctrine of the
"Supernatural Light," then examines the work of Edgar Allan Poe, William
Ellery Channing, Sr., Ralph Waldo Emerson, some of the minor Transcendentalists, Nathaniel Hawthorne, and Henry David Thoreau. In his introduction,
Lyttle identifies an underlying ideological progression in the literature,
from the Puritan stance that the source of life and revelation is "supernatural conscious intelligence external to man" to the Romantic belief
that "this source is within man . . . and 'unconscious.'" Also included
in the volume is a previously unpublished sermon by Channing entitled
"Father of Spirits."

L 569. MacKETHAN, LUCINDA HARDWICK. The Dream of Arcady: Place and Time
in Southern Literature. Baton Rouge: Louisiana State University
Press, 1980. 229 pp.
MacKethan argues that for the hundred years following the Civil War, Southern literature partook significantly of the conventions of the pastoral
mode. In confronting the modernization of their society, Southern writers
of this period tended to posit, by way of contrast, a prewar society that
was rural, naturally hierarchical and stable, neighborly--and emphatically
past. The late 19th-century writers she treats, Sidney Lanier, Thomas
Nelson Page, Joel Chandler Harris, and Charles Chesnutt, were, in their
invocations of the plantation and Jeffersonian agrarian myths, primarily
interested in bemoaning the passing of this Arcadian world; still, their
works demonstrate greater or lesser degrees of awareness of the limitations
of the facticity and even of the mythic value of that world, which was
ultimately based on slavery. Twentieth-century writers—Jean Toomer,
the Fugitive-Agrarians, William Faulkner, and Eudora Welty--show greater
ironic detachment from this myth but still invoke the pastoral dichotomies
in order to express ambivalence about Southern history and about its passing or modernization.

L 570. MacLEAN, ROBERT M. Narcissus and the Voyeur: Three Books and
Two Films. The Hague: Mouton, 1979. 239 pp.
MacLean chooses five rather disparate works (Melville's Moby-Dick, Agee's
Let Us Now Praise Famous Men, Burrough's Naked Lunch, Antonioni's film
The Passenger, and Godard's film Alphaville) and gives each a fairly close
reading, cross-referencing the parallels and similarities among them.
What they have in common, he claims, is that they are all five reports
and "self-reflexive comments on the nature of reporting"--all evidently
influenced by empirical epistemology. In a separate chapter, MacLean
explains the empirical epistemologies of Locke (identified as an influence
on Melville and Antonioni), of early I. A. Richards (influence on Agee),
and of Wittgenstein (influence on Burroughs and Godard). He also discusses
Hawthorne's Chillingworth and Melville's Tommo (Typee) as empirical eyes.

L 571. MALE, ROY R. Enter, Mysterious Stranger: American Cloistral Fiction. Norman: University of Oklahoma Press, 1979. 128 pp.
Not all American fiction, argues Male, involves a man on the road in search
of identity. The pattern of another strain, that of the genre of cloistral fiction, "dramatizes in one form or another the decision to stand
firm and confront invasion." The typical story involves a mysterious
stranger who intrudes upon another's fixed world, tests or transforms
the insider, and then leaves the insider to work out the significance
of the experience. Male discusses the conventions, variations, and themes
of a wide diversity of stories, and then concludes with an essay on how
the issues raised by this genre mirror the issues of the relationship
between the intruder-author and the stay-at-home reader. Writers under
discussion include Herman Melville, Stephen Crane, Robert Penn Warren,
Flannery O'Connor, William Faulkner, Ken Kesey, and Mark Twain.

L 572. MALE, ROY R., ed. Money Talks: Language and Lucre in American
Fiction. Norman: University of Oklahoma Press, 1980. 149 pp.
There is a special identity between language and money: "each is a medium
to represent value that comes to be valuable in itself." The possible
corruption both may instill comes from their illusory existence as being
nothing more than means of exchange; easily manipulated, money and language
may mask a vacuum of trust. In their essays, Leslie Fiedler, Mark Harris,
and Herbert Gold confess and explain their relations with money and fiction.
Six other essayists analyze the same relationships in the fiction of Poe,
James, Hemingway, Doctorow, Gaddis, and Bellow.

L 573. MARTIN, ROBERT K. The Homosexual Tradition in American Poetry.
         Austin: University of Texas Press, 1979. 259 pp.
Martin asserts that critics have misread major poems because they minimize
or dismiss the extent to which an author's homosexuality influences poetic
production and intention. Walt Whitman, Hart Crane, Allen Ginsberg, Robert
Duncan, Thom Gunn, Edward Field, Richard Howard, James Merrill, and Alfred
Carn deliberately identify themselves as homosexuals--Martin's principle
of selection. Each author, following Whitman's lead, uses poetry as a
forum for sexual proclamation and definition. A canon thus emerges in
which a "sense of shared sexuality" allows gay poets to communicate, to
work out the problems of sexual oppression, and to compensate for their
exclusion from a literary tradition dominated by heterosexual men.

L 574. MARX, LEO. The Machine in the Garden: Technology and the Pastoral
         Ideal. New York: Oxford University Press, 1964. 392 pp.
Marx traces the pastoral ideal in American literature, with its emphasis
on an idealized landscape and a withdrawal from civilization, back to
Virgil and Shakespeare. In 18th-century American writings the image of
the edenic garden and the myth of the Golden Age predominate. But in
the 19th century, urban technology, symbolized by the machine, rose to
challenge the rural myth associated with Jefferson. Three versions of
the pastoral ideal appeared: the transcendental version of Emerson and
Thoreau, the tragic version of Hawthorne and Melville, and the vernacular
version of Mark Twain. The contradiction between the rural myth and technological facts persists in 20th-century American literature. Marx examines the imagery of the garden and the machine in both major and minor
works.

L 575. MAXWELL, D. E. S. American Fiction: The Intellectual Background.
         New York: Columbia University Press, 1963. 306 pp.
Maxwell regards literature not as works of art which can be better understood when perceived against the background of intellectual history, but
as documents which exemplify stages in the history of ideas. Cooper's
achievement, from this perspective, lies not in his characterization but
in "the clashes of principles" which the characters represent--the political, ethical, and sociological principles at issue in society. Maxwell
presents literary history as the product of intellectual determinism.
He attributes actual creativity to discursive thought and relegates literature to accommodating the ideas of philosophy to a particular historical
situation.

L 576. McCARTHY, MARY. Ideas and the Novel. New York: Harcourt Brace
         Jovanovich, 1980. 121 pp.
McCarthy reflects upon the relationship between ideas and novels, starting
with a discussion of Henry James, who excluded both ideas and "common
factuality" from his novels. Modernists, she notes, regarded James as
the Master and fostered the assumption that the novel of ideas is inferior
to the art novel. McCarthy points out that 19th-century novels were "idea-
carriers." In conclusion, she states that, although the novel of ideas
is "dated," Jewish novelists in the U. S. (Bellow, Malamud, Philip Roth)
seem to have a special license to include ideas. She argues that strategies for including ideas must be devised if the novel is to be revitalized.

L 577. McCLAVE, HEATHER, ed. Women Writers of the Short Story. Englewood
         Cliffs, N.J.: Prentice-Hall, 1980. 171 pp.
This collection of essays begins with a lengthy introduction by the editor,
which explains her approach and describes previous work in this field,
as well as the grounds for selecting essays by both practitioners of the
short story and literary critics. The contributors to the collection
include Warner Berthoff, R. W. B. Lewis, Eudora Welty, Joyce Carol Oates,
and Lionel Trilling, writing on such authors as Katherine Anne Porter,

Edith Wharton, Eudora Welty, and Flannery O'Conner (about whom there are four essays).

L 578. McNALL, SALLY ALLEN. Who Is in the House? A Psychological Study of Two Centuries of Women's Fiction in America, 1795 to the Present. New York: Elsevier-North Holland, 1981. 153 pp.
This work is a Feminist approach, via Jungian and Kleinian theories of ego development, to popular romantic, domestic, and gothic fiction written by, about, and for women. This fiction, McNall argues, replicates the socialization of women by which they are rendered unable to separate fully from their mothers, achieve ego individuation, and relate properly and independently to love objects. While historical changes cause this pattern to be revealed in different ways—the 19th-century heroine must become her saintly, childlike, yet nurturing mother, while the 20th-century hero-ine must surpass and do away with a cold, rejecting or independent mother—the transference of total dependence on the mother to total dependence on the husband remains consistent.

L 579. MERRILL, DANA K. American Biography: Its Theory and Practice. Portland, Maine: Bowker, 1957. 266 pp.
The book is divided into two parts: a theoretical section followed by a practical section. In the theoretical part, Merrill explains the nature of biography and the reasons for its appeal to both writers and readers; he describes the principles and methods American biographers have inherited from various sources as far back as Petrarch; and he traces the steps in writing a biography, classifying and illustrating the different types of biographical work. In the practical part, he makes a historical and critical survey of biography from the 17th to the mid-20th century. His appendices include a selective list of biographies from 1920-1925, a note on campaign biographies, and a note on criminal biographies.

L 580. MESSENGER, CHRISTIAN K. Sport and the Spirit of Play in American Fiction: Hawthorne to Faulkner. New York: Columbia University Press, 1981. 359 pp.
Claiming that sport and play are central to the American social pattern, Messenger examines depictions primarily of sport (but also, to some degree, of play) in American fiction. He first establishes how sport and play as depicted in writings by Hawthorne, Irving, Cooper, and Thoreau define American communal and personal responsibilities. Messenger then introduces three categories of sports heroes: the Popular Sports Hero (democratic, strong, he has his origins in the frontier and becomes the team player in other roles), the School Sports Hero (plays to prepare himself for other roles), and the Ritual Sports Hero (who seeks self-knowledge through sport). The writers who receive major emphasis in the main portion of the book are Hemingway, Faulkner, Fitzgerald, and Lardner.

L 581. MILLER, JAMES E., Jr. The American Quest for a Supreme Fiction: Whitman's Legacy in the Personal Epic. Chicago: University of Chicago Press, 1979. 332 pp.
Miller here explores "the interrelationships among America's 'classic' long poems." He is interested in tracing an American tradition: "the placement of the self in the center" of an extended narrative poem. He considers longer poems by Lowell, Berryman, Stevens, Pound, Eliot, Williams, Crane, Olson, and Ginsberg in order to define this tradition of epic. The first three chapters examine the impact of Whitman and the Beats on Berryman and Lowell; establish the characteristics of "personal epic"; and follow the genre from Joel Barlow to the present. Miller then applies his findings to each of the major figures listed above.

L 582. MILLER, R. BAXTER, ed. Black American Literature and Humanism.
Lexington: University Press of Kentucky, 1981. 114 pp.
Seven essayists define the work of black writers as humanistic, and discuss
the nature of Humanism itself. This latter concern is part of the general
trend to create a Black Aesthetic. Richard Barksdale, George Kent, and
R. Baxter Miller write on Hughes and Brooks; Chester J. Fontenot, Jr.
attempts to write cultural and formal criticism; Trudier Harris writes
on Sarah Wright, Alice Walker, and Paule Marshall; and Alice Childress
and Michael S. Harper contribute a manifesto and a "fictional" reminiscence,
respectively.

L 583. MILLER, WAYNE CHARLES. An Armed America, Its Face in Fiction:
A History of the American Military Novel. New York: New York
University Press, 1970. 294 pp.
Miller's study ranges from the novels of Cooper and Melville to the fiction
of John Marquand, James Gould Cozzens, and Joseph Heller. Although dis-
avowing overt politics, Miller resents the influence of the military and
of conservative politicians in the U.S. and warns of the danger that influence presents. Not all of his novelists condemn the military. The author
attempts to understand American culture and the relation of its products
to a "military definition of reality"—i.e., what kind of cultural history
these products reflect and influence.

L 584. MILNE, GORDON. The American Political Novel. Norman: University
of Oklahoma Press, 1966. 212 pp.
Milne finds the origins of the modern political novel in the political
allegories of the late 18th century and in the novels of Hugh Henry
Brackenbridge and James Fenimore Cooper. The genre flourished after the
Civil War, particularly in the works of Mark Twain, John De Forest, and
Henry Adams, and even more dramatically in the first decades of the 20th
century. The spirit of protest and reform enlivened the novels of the
muckrakers (e.g., Winston Churchill, David Graham Phillips). Since 1920,
political novels have continued to urge reform while also endorsing doctrines such as Marxism or Fascism. Milne argues that the best of modern
political novelists include Robert Penn Warren, Edwin O'Connor, and Allen
Drury.

L 585. MILNE, GORDON. The Sense of Society: A History of the American
Novel of Manners. Rutherford, N.J.: Fairleigh Dickinson University Press, 1977. 305 pp.
This book summarizes the ongoing debate about the importance of the novel
of manners in America, and treats in detail the authors most identified
with this genre, or subgenre: Henry James, William Dean Howells, Edith
Wharton, Ellen Glasgow, John P. Marquand, and Louis Auchincloss. The
author also surveys the work of the prime theorists of the novel of manners,
including Lionel Trilling, James Tuttleton, and Michael Millgate.

L 586. MINTER, DAVID L. The Interpreted Design as a Structural Principle
in American Prose. New Haven, Conn.: Yale University Press,
1969. 246 pp.
The "interpreted design" of Minter's title is a metaphor for the works
his study discusses: those structured by the juxtaposition of two
characters—one a man of firm design, the other a man of interpretation whose
mind and voice convey the man of design's story. The first section shows
the anticipation in early American literature of the themes and structures
of the autobiographies discussed in the second part of the study and the
novels discussed in the third. Sections two and three selectively analyze
18th- through 20th-century American literary works by Edwards, Franklin,
Thoreau, Hawthorne, James, Fitzgerald, and Faulkner. Minter's study is
especially concerned with theme and genre.

844

L 587. MIZENER, ARTHUR. The Sense of Life in the Modern Novel. Boston:
    Houghton Mifflin, 1963. 291 pp.
What Mizener claims to be a modest subject is, in fact, massive--"the
relation of the represented life in the novel to 'nature,' and the effects
this relation has on the novel's expression of values." The "sense of
life" in any novel, according to Mizener, lies in its "representation
of nature." He discusses in detail many 19th- and 20th-century British
and American novels (the majority are 20th-century American), and focuses
on five different kinds of 20th-century American heroes: Faulkner's Gavin
Stevens, Fitzgerald's Monroe Stahr, Hemingway's Nick Adams, Salinger's
Seymour Glass, and Updike's Peter Caldwell. These writers deal in various
ways with the "peculiarly troubled relationship between the representation
of nature and the expression of values in the American novel." The final
chapter finds a solution to this conflict in Allen Tate's The Fathers.

L 588. MIZENER, ARTHUR. Twelve Great American Novels. New York: New
    American Library, 1967. 198 pp.
Mizener intends this work as a "practical" introduction for the intelligent
but uninitiated reader of American novels. His discussions of twelve
"representative" novels, he states, have no unifying thesis and exhibit
no "novelties of interpretation." He does say, however, that American
novels divide into two groups: those in which outer reality is more important, and those in which inner reality takes precedence. The novels discussed, in chronological order, are Cooper's The Deerslayer, Hawthorne's
The Scarlet Letter, Melville's Moby-Dick, Twain's Huckleberry Finn,
Wharton's The Age of Innocence, Dos Passos's The Big Money, Fitzgerald's
Tender Is the Night, Hemingway's The Sun Also Rises, Faulkner's The Sound
and the Fury, Cozzens's Guard of Honor, and Warren's All the King's Men.

L 589. MOLLINGER, ROBERT N. Psychoanalysis and Literature: An Introduc-
    tion. Chicago: Nelson-Hall, 1981. 178 pp.
Mollinger's warrant for this study is that "psychoanalysis and literature
have found in each other compatible and comparable humanistic endeavors."
He first examines psychoanalytic literary criticism from Freud to Holland,
quoting the major critics and their opponents. Then he explains the basics
of psychoanalytic theory. Finally he applies both Freudian and Jungian
theory to symbol, character, text, oeuvre, author, and reader. Both the
work and the lives of Stevens, Poe, Melville, and Plath serve as examples
covered individually in each of the last nine chapters.

L 590. MORRIS, WESLEY. Toward a New Historicism. Princeton, N.J.: Prince-
    ton University Press, 1972. 265 pp.
This is a thematic study of the last 100 years of literary theory, primarily American, with regard to the question of the relationship between
literature and history. It starts with the assumption that aesthetics
and literary history should be united in criticism, and that the "new
historicist must argue that the individual work stands free of its historical context while it simultaneously draws its audience toward that
context." With this relationship for his focus, and this goal for his
criterion, Morris describes, analyzes, and evaluates critical theories.

L 591. MORRIS, WRIGHT. The Territory Ahead: Critical Interpretations
    in American Literature. New York: Harcourt, Brace, 1961.
    247 pp.
Morris's central theme is "the prevailing tendency of the American mind
to take to the woods," of which Huck Finn's "lighting out for the territory" is only the most conspicuous example. Morris looks at some of our
best writers--among them Thoreau, Whitman, Melville, Twain, Hemingway,
Wolfe, Fitzgerald, and Faulkner--in this light, and in one passage contrasts Henry James's use of the past with that of the artist Norman
Rockwell.

L 592. MOSES, MONTROSE J. The American Dramatist. 1911; Rev. ed. Boston:
Little, Brown, 1925. 474 pp.
Moses presents an account of American theater from its colonial beginnings
to the early 20th century. He principally discusses the works and biographies of the dramatists, but he also considers actors, stage managers,
designers, producers, theater programs, and playhouses. Despite finding
America's productions to be nearly all imitative of European work, especially during the early periods, he is sympathetic to the problems of American dramatists and attempts to explain the causes of their failure to
produce "truly original" work.

L 593. MOSES, WILSON JEREMIAH. Black Messiahs and Uncle Toms. University
Park: Pennsylvania State University Press, 1982. 279 pp.
Moses's book is both a sociological and literary critical study of trends
in black culture as they are crystallized in leadership and, more specifically, messianic myths. When he examines black messianism as an individual
phenomenon, Moses turns to the careers of Booker T. Washington, Marcus
Garvey, Joe Louis, and Martin Luther King, Jr. When he examines black
messianism as a group phenomenon, he explicates the various permutations
of the Uncle Tom myth and, in general, how "black messianism reconciles
the sense of separateness that black people feel and their fundamental
belief that they are truly American." Moses explores black messianism's
African roots, its intimate relationship with white messianism (from the
Massachusetts Bay Colony to "manifest destiny"), and its effect on recent
political matters. Two authors--W. E. B. DuBois and Ralph Ellison--are
accorded particularly close scrutiny.

L 594. MOSSBERG, CHRISTER LENNART. Scandinavian Immigrant Literature.
Boise, Idaho: Boise State University Press, 1981. 52 pp.
Mossberg narrates the history of the literature of those who had lived
between the two worlds of Scandinavia and America in the years 1850-1925.
Tracing the development from travel guides and letters of anonymous immigrants to the novels of Kristofer Janson, Peer Strømme, Carl Hansen, Simon
Johnson, Ole Rølvaag, and Sophus Winther, Mossberg isolates and explicates
common themes and characters. He argues that immigrant literature offers
a challenge to mainstream American literature. The immigrant perspective, "contrary to the Adamic myth of Americans at the dawn of a new history," takes into account the redemptive quality of Old World spiritualism
in the face of the corruption of New World materialism.

L 595. NAGEL, JAMES, ed. American Fiction: Historical and Critical Essays.
Boston: Twayne, 1977. 208 pp.
This work commemorating the American Bicentennial contains essays by Daniel
Aaron on the "Occasional Novel"; John Cawelti on "The Writer as Celebrity";
Melvin Friedman on American fiction since 1950; Joseph Katz on American
Realism; Harrison T. Meserole on early American Fiction; Donald Pizer
on Theodore Dreiser; Milton Stern on Romantic Fiction; Ronald Sukenick
on fiction of the 1970s; Darwin Turner on Black Fiction; Linda Wagner
on fiction of the era 1915-1940; and Viola H. Winner on "The Pictorial
Vision in American Fiction." It concludes with a "Conversation" recording
a dialogue among the participants.

L 596. NAGEL, JAMES and RICHARD ASTRO, eds. American Literature: The
New England Heritage. New York: Garland, 1981. 181 pp.
The ten essays by ten critics which comprise this volume were presented
at Northeastern University at a 1980 conference of the same title as the
book. Ordered chronologically, the book opens with "A Kind of Burr:
Colonial New England's Heritage of Wit" and extends to "Recent New England
Fiction: Outsiders and Insiders." True to the regional topic, most of
the essays examine the broader New England literary climate during a par-
ticular period. Critics who focus upon individual writers include Hershel
Parker (on Melville) and Samuel F. Morse (on Frost).

L 597. NOBLE, DAVID W. The Eternal Adam and the New World Garden: The
Central Myth in the American Novel Since 1830. New York:
Braziller, 1968. 226 pp.
Noble approaches American fiction as a historian of ideas, in particular
the idea of "the transcendence of time." Europeans, claims Noble, "firmly
defined the meaning of the New World as the Garden in which men of the
Old World would be redeemed." He finds this theme in six groups of writers:
the Jeremiahs (Cooper, Hawthorne, Melville); the Realists (Twain, Howells,
James); the Naturalists (Norris, Crane, Dreiser); the lost generation
(Winston Churchill, Hemingway, Fitzgerald); after the lost generation
(Faulkner, Warren, Cozzens); and the present (Mailer, Baldwin, Bellow).

L 598. OSTENDORF, BERNDT. Black Literature in White America. Totowa,
N.J.: Barnes & Noble, 1982. 166 pp.
Observing that interest in Black Studies began in Europe, Ostendorf--a
German--sets out to examine black literature (which stems from an oral
tradition) in white America (where a literate culture has generally dominated). Since he sees black culture as an oral culture, Ostendorf discusses not just black writers but also black musicians, especially jazz
musicians. He asserts that American black culture has a "conflict-ridden
nature and [an] ambivalent interpretability." He examines how black
writers have dealt with the problem of a double audience (whites and blacks),
beginning with Phillis Wheatley--who identified with her oppressors--and
ending with Ellison, who, Ostendorf claims, explores the richness of black
oral tradition and is a forerunner of the cultural nationalism that rejects
Ellison as an Uncle Tom. Ostendorf ends by discussing the 1960s and 1970s--
a time when America discovered the affirmative and celebratory richness
of the black tradition.

L 599. OSWALD, JOHN CLYDE. Printing in the Americas. New York: Gregg,
1937. 565 pp.
Oswald claims that "the story of printing in America is almost the story
of America itself." He charts the history of printing in North, Central,
and South America, as well as Canada. The work provides an overview of
the subject, proceeding state by state (country by country in the case
of South America, and province by province in Canada), describing in large
part the founders and maintainers of the first presses in each case.
The chronicle is not exhaustive in its reference to the printers in any
single area; instead, it traces histories which "have stretched through
long periods and those who are at present prominent because of their scale
of operations."

L 600. PAYNE, LADELL. Black Novelists and the Southern Literary Tradition.
Athens: University of Georgia Press, 1981. 101 pp.
Payne argues that black literature's ties to the Southern literary tradition are as strong a cohesive force as the "blackness" of the literature.
Southern literature, as characterized here, emphasizes a sense of place,
family, and history and focuses on the individual in time of chaos and
the individual in search of identity. Separate chapters are devoted to
the work of Charles Waddell Chesnutt, James Weldon Johnson, Jean Toomer,
Richard Wright, and Ralph Ellison. The study concludes with a reappraisal
of the terms "Southern," "black," and "literary tradition."

L 601. PEARCE, ROY HARVEY. The Continuity of American Poetry. 1961;
Rev. ed. Princeton, N.J.: Princeton University Press, 1969.
442 pp.
Assuming a relationship between the development of American poetry and
that of American culture, Pearce traces the continuity of two traditions
in the poetry: Adamic and mythic. In general, the American poet, refusing
to accept his culture's values, tries to justify his own existence. The
Colonial poets sought to uncover God's plan, while later poets made a

world through the imagination; thus 19th- and early 20th-century poets share an impulse toward antinomianism. This study ranges from Puritan poets to 19th-century popular poets; from the epic tradition (The Columbiad, Song of Myself, The Bridge) to the individualist tradition (Emerson, Dickinson); and from Robinson and Frost to Eliot and Stevens.

L 602. PEARCE, ROY HARVEY. The Savages of America: A Study of the Indian and the Idea of Civilization. 1953; Rev. ed. published as: Savagism and Civilization: A Study of the Indian and the American Mind. Baltimore, Md.: Johns Hopkins University Press, 1965. 260 pp.
From earliest times, Americans have been obsessed by civilization and savagism, contends Pearce. To illuminate this ironic and developing relationship, he draws on history and literature from 1609 to 1851 to show how Americans saw "civilizing" the Indians as a triumph over the past and a symbol of progress. Pearce traces this attitude to the 17th-century Puritans, who believed in their divine right to Indian lands and considered Indians devils when they resisted occupation. Although Puritans tried to convert Indians, this contact with "civilization" ironically introduced disease, drunkenness, and immorality. Despite a theoretical belief in "the noble savage," 18th-century Americans viewed Indians as remnants of a savage past they had outgrown. This attitude culminated in the 19th century's justification of destroying Indians in the name of civilization and Christianity.

L 603. PERSONS, STOW. The Decline of American Gentility. New York: Columbia University Press, 1973. 336 pp.
The aim of this book is to examine the causes for "the final disappearance of a social type that had flourished throughout the Western world for three centuries or more": the gentleman. Persons argues that during the 19th century the "theory and practice of gentility" suffered a process of "diffusion and attenuation," and that by the end of W.W. I the gentry bore no particular distinction from the common people. The first four chapters describe the characteristics of the 19th-century gentry, and those remaining describe the gentry's alienation and then decline amid "mass society." The author concludes that "the successor to the 19th-century gentleman is the alienated intellectual."

L 604. PHELAN, JAMES. Worlds from Words: A Theory of Language in Fiction. Chicago: University of Chicago Press, 1981. 259 pp.
Though Phelan presents a general theory of the relation between language and fiction, he equally emphasizes a close analysis of five works, two of which are The Ambassadors and Sister Carrie. Phelan tests his own theory by pairing competing theories with challenging texts. His hypothesis is that the role of language changes from one novel to the next and even within the same novel. He concludes that language is subordinate to essentially non-linguistic elements such as plot and character, yet he finally allows that the flexibility of critical pluralism is a far better stance to take than the rigidity of critical monism.

L 605. PILKINGTON, WILLIAM T., ed. Critical Essays on the Western American Novel. Boston: G. K. Hall, 1980. 275 pp.
This collection of twenty-four previously published essays is devoted to both "serious" and "popular" novels set west of the Mississippi. The introduction presents a brief history of scholarship in Western American literature. The volume is divided into two main sections: general criticism and essays on individual novelists. Authors discussed include Vardis Fisher, A. B. Guthrie, Louis L'Amour, Walter Van Tilburg Clark, and Frederick Manfred.

L 606. **POIRIER, RICHARD.** The Performing Self: Compositions and Decompo-
sitions in the Languages of Contemporary Life. New York: Oxford
University Press, 1971. 203 pp.
Poirier's ambitious effort here, in nine essays on a wide range of literary
and cultural subjects, is to suggest how "literature and the ways of reading it . . . can be an object lesson for other more distinctly political
or social performances." Thus he often shifts ground, from British and
American "classic" writers (Joyce, Eliot, James, Frost), to contemporary
writers (Mailer, Nabokov, Borges), to rock music and rock music festivals,
to the modern university curriculum. The Performing Self is an attempt
to use a mind trained in literary criticism for an analysis of wider cultural attitudes and problems.

L 607. **POIRIER, RICHARD.** A World Elsewhere: The Place of Style in American Literature. New York: Oxford University Press, 1966.
257 pp.
The works of our major authors, according to Poirier, "are alive with
the effort to stabilize certain feelings and attitudes that have, as it
were, no place in the world, no place at all except where a writer's style
can give them one." Thus Poirier's reading of central American texts
is intensely focused on the nature of the expression, "the sounds, identities, and presences shaped by these technical aspects of expression."
Poirier deals in detail with major works by Hawthorne, Cooper, Emerson,
Thoreau, Twain, James, Wharton, Dreiser, Faulkner, and Fitzgerald.

L 608. **PORTER, CAROLYN.** Seeing and Being: The Plight of the Participant
Observer in Emerson, James, Adams, and Faulkner. Middletown,
Conn.: Wesleyan University Press, 1981. 339 pp.
To dispute the claim that American literature is basically ahistorical
and asocial, Porter writes that some major writers attempted not a flight
from culture, but a critical examination of and protest against American
capitalist society. Adopting the terminology of Marxist critical theory,
Porter argues that Emerson's "Nature," James's The Golden Bowl, Adams's
Education, and Faulkner's Absalom, Absalom! dramatize the tendency in
capitalist society to reify social relations—that is, to pretend to be
merely contemplating an objective reality rather than to acknowledge one's
own complicity in constructing that reality, both imaginatively and materially. Porter shows how each of these writers attempts to expose and
resist that tendency; she concludes, though, that each finally demonstrates
the effects of reification himself and implicates the reader in that process as well.

L 609. **PRATT, ANNIS.** Archetypal Patterns of Women's Fiction. Bloomington:
Indiana University Press, 1981. 211 pp.
In her investigation of women's fiction, Pratt discusses a body of material
that displays some degree of continuity and a uniformity of concern.
She explores the literary forms of women's fiction that share commonalities
with specific, primitive, and prehistoric myths and tales. Following
the pattern of human development, she examines novels concerning women's
initiation into adulthood and maturity, entry into marriage and social
involvement, and quest for sexuality and human transformation. Each section explores the interplay between a woman's power and powerlessness
and the rebellion against social norms and prescribed roles in a male-
dominated society. Authors discussed include Margaret Drabble, Josephine
Herbst, Sarah Orne Jewett, and May Sarton.

L 610. PRYSE, MARJORIE. The Mark and the Knowledge: Social Stigma in
Classic American Literature. Columbus: Ohio State University
Press, 1979. 179 pp.
Pryse suggests that the American-ness of all American fiction may be understood through an analysis of Hester Prynne (The Scarlet Letter), Ishmael
(Moby Dick), Joe Christmas (Light in August), and the title character
of Invisible Man, each of whom is "marked" in his or her struggle to regain
identity after falling from different sorts of grace: "The fiction of
social and metaphysical isolation . . . provides the context within which
American literature becomes 'American.'" The "mark" of social difference,
that is a given community's way of affirming its own identity by defining
its outcasts, is a peculiarly American trait; and the "recurrent focus
on marked characters," in the terms of this study, can be seen as "both
the method and the consequence of the American transcendental imagination,"
whose exemplars are the four novels under discussion.

L 611. QUILLIGAN, MAUREEN. The Language of Allegory: Defining the Genre.
Ithaca, N.Y.: Cornell University Press, 1979. 299 pp.
Asserting that "narrative allegory has its source in a culture's attitude
toward language," Quilligan further argues that allegory is legitimately
its own genre—a class of literature "hung up on words." Supporting her
arguments with discussions of texts ranging from Le roman de la rose to
Gravity's Rainbow, Quilligan examines texts in relation to their pretexts
(previous works in the genre), contexts (historical setting), and the
reader (who is the ultimate "producer of meaning"). She mentions that
there have been few true allegories since the 17th century except for
those that have appeared as a result of Emersonian developments in American
epistemology and literature. The American writers whose works she discusses are Hawthorne, Melville, Nabokov, and Pynchon.

L 612. RAHV, PHILIP. Image and Idea: Twenty Essays on Literary Themes.
1949; Rev. ed. Norfolk, Conn.: New Directions, 1957. 241 pp.
Rahv has revised fourteen previously published articles for inclusion
in this volume. Essays with American subjects include "Paleface and Redskin," which identifies a dissociation between "energy" or experience
and sensibility or consciousness in American literature, and "The Cult
of Experience in American Writing," which explores uniquely American attitudes toward experience in the art of Henry James, Walt Whitman, and Ernest
Hemingway, among others. Rahv also offers various critical sketches of
the work of individual authors, including pieces on Nathaniel Hawthorne,
Henry James, Henry Miller, and William Carlos Williams.

L 613. RAHV, PHILIP. Literature and the Sixth Sense. Boston: Houghton
Mifflin, 1969. 445 pp.
The forty-four essays collected in this volume are in some instances
reprinted from Rahv's earlier collections Image and Idea (see L 612) and
The Myth and the Powerhouse (see L 615), and include more than a dozen
pieces which were previously unpublished in book form. By publishing
a representative selection of essays written through the years, the author
hopes to "restore a proper perspective on what has transpired in American
literary culture during the past thirty years." More than half of these
essays are on 19th- and 20th-century American writers, including Nathaniel
Hawthorne, Henry James, Herman Melville, T. S. Eliot, Ernest Hemingway,
Arthur Miller, Saul Bellow, and Bernard Malamud. Rahv's approach is
informed by a sense of political significance, which began with his early
training in Marxism.

L 614. RAHV, PHILIP. Literature in America. New York: Meridian Books,
        1957. 452 pp.
In compiling this anthology of American literary criticism, Rahv selected
pieces that observe and analyze American "writing in which the emphasis
. . . is on national characteristics in relation to the national experience." He notes that he had an abundance of material to choose from insofar as much American literary criticism constitutes a "search for America"--
an attempt to define American. One of the earliest tasks of American
criticism, Rahv points out, was identifying--and insisting upon--the differences between European and American literature. The forty selections
are arranged in roughly chronological order, beginning with an essay by
Tocqueville (1835) and ending with one by Henry Bamford Parkes (1956).
A substantial number of major American literary figures are represented
in this anthology.

L 615. RAHV, PHILIP. The Myth and the Powerhouse. New York: Farrar,
        Straus & Giroux, 1965. 243 pp.
The sixteen pieces collected in this volume were all published previously
in journals; they consist of nine full-length essays and seven critical
sketches. The title piece, "The Myth and the Powerhouse," attacks the
critical trend which Rahv perceives as faddish "myth-and-symbol hunting."
In other essays, he examines the growth of religiosity among American
intellectuals; discusses various aspects of the "New Criticism"; and in
"The Native Bias" meditates on the meaning of the phrase "characteristically American" when it is applied to literary texts. Rahv's critical
sketches include pieces on Henry James, T. S. Eliot, Ernest Hemingway,
Saul Bellow, Arthur Miller, and Norman Mailer.

L 616. REDDING, J. SAUNDERS. To Make a Poet Black. Chapel Hill: Uni-
        versity of North Carolina Press, 1938. 142 pp.
Redding's work combines factual material and criticism of black American
literature to highlight the relationship of black history and letters.
The 18th-century black literary forerunners, Jupiter Hammon, Phillis
Wheatley, and George Moses Horton, had to satisfy black and white audiences,
which, Redding asserts, explains the schizophrenic quality of their work.
From 1830 to 1895, black literature was dominated by the spoken prose
of protest, whose most representative writers were Charles Remond, William
Wells Brown, and Frederick Douglass. After the Civil War, dialect became
a key medium of expression, though it settled into stereotype and caricature. The 1920s saw the emergence of "the masculine literature of the
'New Negro'" in works by Claude McKay and Jean Toomer, then later, Countee
Cullen and Langston Hughes, whose dominant themes are futility, pessimism,
and atavism.

L 617. ROBINSON, CECIL. With the Ears of Strangers: The Mexican in Ameri-
        can Literature. Tucson: University of Arizona Press, 1963.
        338 pp.
Robinson argues that "because it not only borders upon the United States
but makes a deep cultural penetration northward from the boundary, Mexico's
influence upon American literature has been unlike any other foreign influence." He traces that influence in separate sections, the first roughly
through the American Civil War, the second since that time. Early Americans were repelled by the Mexican influence; but "toward the end of the
nineteenth century when the pace of American life had become increasingly
harassing . . . Americans felt the impulse to portray and to read about
Mexican culture in quite a different light." Indeed, later writers have
tended to find "intriguing and salutary" the aspects of Mexican society
that earlier Americans had distrusted. Topics discussed include Catholicism, courtesy, cowardice, and sexuality.

L 618. ROEMER, KENNETH M., ed. America as Utopia. New York: Burt
         Franklin, 1981. 410 pp.
Roemer includes an array of essays representing four general approaches
to the documentation and understanding of utopian literature in America.
Often placed in an international context, this literature is examined
by the authors themselves, by critics explicating both individual works
and general trends and themes, and by literary historians and biblio-
graphers. Roemer's introduction defines at length the term "utopia";
an extract from Ursula Le Guin's The Dispossessed concludes the collection.
The contributors discuss such authors as Jack London, William Morris,
and Mark Twain and topics such as Feminist utopias and utopias of nature.

L 619. ROSENBLATT, ROGER. Black Fiction. Cambridge, Mass.: Harvard
         University Press, 1974. 211 pp.
"Black fiction," says Rosenblatt, "is a literature both American and anti-
or extra-American, modern and anti-modern, in sum, a body of writing not
usefully classifiable except by the kind and number of things it is not."
He first attempts to identify what it is not (not completely modern, not
entirely American, not wholly fiction), then discusses the nature of "cyclical patterns" in Richard Wright's Native Son, James Baldwin's Go Tell
It on the Mountain, and Jean Toomer's Cane. Other topics addressed include
humor in black fiction, and the visions of white America presented in
Paul Dunbar's The Uncalled, Ann Petry's Country Place, William Kelley's
dem, and James Baldwin's Another Country. Rosenblatt concludes this volume
with a more general look at heroism and tragedy in black fiction.

L 620. ROSS, ISHBEL. The Expatriates. New York: Crowell, 1970.
         339 pp.
Ross traces the "expatriate tradition"--a tradition of Americans living
abroad which flowered in the 1920s but had its roots in the era of the
American revolution. The first expatriates, he notes, were diplomats
such as John Adams, Benjamin Franklin, and Thomas Jefferson. But artists,
he claims, have consistently made up a substantial part of the expatriate
contingent. Among these artists were painters (Benjamin West, John Copley,
John Sargent, James Whistler, Mary Cassatt), writers (Irving, James,
Wharton, Stein, Pound, Hemingway, Fitzgerald), and performing artists such
as Josephine Baker. Contemporary expatriates, he notes, are mostly abroad
in an official capacity--as members of the armed forces, government
employees, or Peace Corps volunteers. The time these Americans spent abroad,
Ross suggests, shaped not just their personal developments but also the
American civilization which even those who did not return to America helped
to change.

L 621. ROURKE, CONSTANCE. American Humor: A Study of the National Char-
         acter. New York: Harcourt, Brace, 1931. 324 pp.
By examining stories, plays, and periodicals, Rourke traces American humor
as it appears in literary themes and techniques. Certain typical figures,
like the Yankee and the Backwoodsman, show the comic aspect of the American
character. Rourke discusses black songs and other kinds of works not
usually considered literary. Occasionally her argument results in viewing
as humorous some writers who are traditionally seen as serious writers.
This work is especially concerned with the relationship between American
humorists and their culture.

L 622. ROURKE, CONSTANCE. The Roots of American Culture and Other Essays.
         Edited by Van Wyck Brooks. New York: Harcourt, Brace, 1942.
         305 pp.
Rourke's unfulfilled intention was to write a full-length history of American culture; this posthumously published volume contains a series of essays
on related aspects of the nation's culture, which she sees as self-
sufficient and independent from European forms, as many scholars in her time

did not. This argument is proposed in the title piece and further
developed in essays on subjects as various as early theatricals and music,
the Shakers, folklore, black literature, and American art.

L 623. RUBIN, JOAN. Constance Rourke and American Culture. Chapel Hill:
University of North Carolina Press, 1980. 244 pp.
Rubin's critique (a one-chapter biography is included) examines not only
Rourke's contribution to folklore and humor, but also her position as
a major figure in American intellectual history. Rubin proceeds thematically, providing the context which defined the problems Rourke faced.
Each chapter is based on one of the issues to which Rourke devoted herself—
"the adequacy of American traditions, the definition of culture, the character of myth, the effects of popular prose style, and the connection
between politics and criticism." The assumptions underlying Rourke's
work require excavation, according to the author, and "this study establishes the context for Rourke's defense of American culture—the controversies that engaged her, the books that influenced her thinking, the
premises that lay underneath her vocabulary."

L 624. RUBIN, LOUIS D., Jr. The Curious Death of the Novel. Baton Rouge:
Louisiana State University Press, 1967. 302 pp.
Rubin gathers here fifteen essays on a variety of topics unified by the
theme of "difference." He writes: "The experience of difference of a
Jew in a Christian society, a Roman Catholic in the Protestant, rural
South, a Southerner in an industrial society, even the experience of an
Edgar Poe in an optimistic progress-worshipping civilization—the awareness
of difference, the consciousness that one is not fully a member in good
standing, gives form to a writer's insights into his experience." Rubin
discusses Poe's heroism, Mencken's public letters, and Flannery O'Connor's
Southern Catholicism. He denies the "death of the novel" while asserting
the failure of any one contemporary novelist to attain the stature of
Faulkner or Hemingway.

L 625. RUBIN, LOUIS D., Jr., ed. The Comic Imagination in American Literature. New Brunswick, N.J.: Rutgers University Press, 1973.
430 pp.
The thirty-two essays collected here were originally prepared for broadcast
overseas by the Voice of America. Although they are introductory lectures
designed for an audience not intimately familiar with American literature,
the essays attempt to offer scholarly discussions of individual writers
(e.g., Franklin, Irving, Twain, Faulkner), regional humor (New England,
the South, the Southwest), comic modes (satire, the tall tale, black humor),
and special topics such as Jewish humor, light verse, and minstrel shows.

L 626. RUDICH, NORMAN, ed. Weapons of Criticism: Marxism in America
and the Literary Tradition. Palo Alto, Calif.: Ramparts Press,
1976. 377 pp.
This collection of essays, which grew out of the discussion group of the
American Institute for Marxist Studies (1968-70) and the forum sponsored
by the Radical Caucus held at the 1972 Modern Language Association Convention, marks an era in literary criticism Rudich calls the "Marxist
Renaissance." The collection has two parts: essays that are theoretical,
discussing in general terms relations between Marxism and literature,
other philosophies, political groups, or art; and examples of practical
criticism. Among the works examined from a Marxist perspective are texts
by Melville, Poe, James, and Fitzgerald. The essays have been chosen,
the editor states, to represent as many of the tendencies in Marxist literary thought as possible, but he also claims that on one point all are
agreed: the distinction between intellectual and physical labor—inherent
in a class society—should be made to disappear.

L 627. **SANTAYANA, GEORGE**. The Genteel Tradition: Nine Essays. Edited
by Douglas L. Wilson. Cambridge, Mass.: Harvard University Press,
1967. 201 pp.
In the essay which supplies the title for this collection, "The Genteel
Tradition in American Philosophy" (1911), Santayana defines the basic
dichotomy in American culture: "America is not simply . . . a young country with an old mentality; it is a country with two mentalities, one a
survival of the beliefs and standards of the fathers, the other an expression of the instincts, practice, and discoveries of the younger generations." Santayana's phrase and his examination of 19th- and early 20th-
century American literature, philosophy, and culture have become standard
concepts in American Studies. The essays gathered here include his study
of "Genteel American Poetry" (1915), "Philosophical Opinion in America"
(1918), and "Materialism and Idealism in America" (1919).

L 628. **SAROTTE, GEORGES-MICHEL**. Like a Brother, Like a Lover: Male Homosexuality in the American Novel and Theatre from Herman Melville
to James Baldwin. Translated by Richard Miller. Garden City,
N.Y.: Anchor Press, 1978. 305 pp.
This work was originally a dissertation in French. Sarotte deliberately
avoids sexual politics while testifying to the sheer existence of covert
and overt homosexuality in American literature. Rife with examples, the
books spends most of its time categorizing these instances of literary
homosexuality into situational types (i.e., relations between Adolescents,
Teacher and Pupil, White and Black). Later, Sarotte examines homosexual
themes in the work of individual authors, including Tennessee Williams,
Edward Albee, Henry James, Jack London, Ernest Hemingway, and Norman Mailer.

L 629. **SAYRE, ROBERT F.** The Examined Self: Benjamin Franklin, Henry
Adams, Henry James. Princeton, N.J.: Princeton University Press,
1964. 212 pp.
This work is a study of the autobiographies of Benjamin Franklin, Henry
Adams, and Henry James in relation to one another and, more widely, in
relation to their literary and cultural backgrounds. Sayre chooses these
three autobiographies for distinct reasons. Admired by both Adams and
James, Franklin's Autobiography prepared the way for the two later works
and is essential for any discussion of American autobiography. Adams
and James, historian and novelist respectively, approached autobiography
from different directions, yet as friends they also shared many values.
Sayre's analysis covers specific and comparative criticism for each work.

L 630. **SCHULZ, MAX F.** Black Humor Fiction of the Sixties. Athens: Ohio
University Press, 1973. 156 pp.
Schulz defines the genre "black humor fiction" and uses the work of John
Barth, Kurt Vonnegut, Jr., Jorge Luis Borges, Thomas Berger, Thomas Pynchon,
Robert Coover, Bruce Jay Friedman, and Charles Wright as examples. Each
chapter is devoted to a single aspect of his definition. Schulz argues
that black humor is neither sick, absurd, nor comic. It is, instead,
a cultural product of the 1960s, "whose anxieties proceeding from pluralism, conformity, and an irresolute value system give it both its method
and its subject."

L 631. **SCHULZ, MAX F.** Radical Sophistication: Studies in Contemporary
Jewish-American Novelists. Athens: Ohio University Press, 1969.
224 pp.
The writers who are Schulz's subject all deal with "the humanistic exploration of man's place in society," and thus form "a fictional movement of
their own," neither traditional nor despairing. An introductory chapter
on the nature of this "radical sophistication" is followed by chapters
on Nathanael West, Bernard Malamud, Norman Mailer, Saul Bellow, Leslie
Fiedler, Edward Lewis Wallant, Bruce Jay Friedman, and J. D. Salinger.

L 632. **SIMPSON, LEWIS P.** The Brazen Face of History: Studies in the
Literary Consciousness in America. Baton Rouge: Louisiana State
University Press, 1980. 276 pp.
Modern American history, according to Simpson, can be defined by the ascend-
ancy of the mind and its transference of all that surrounds it into itself.
In this wide-ranging collection of revised, previously published essays,
Simpson is "particularly concerned with the agency of transference, the
Third Realm, or the Republic of letters; and with the major consequence
of the transference: loss of transcendent reference for being and a ten-
dency . . . toward the closure of history in the self of the writer."
Part I concerns post-Revolutionary War writers, particularly Franklin
and Hawthorne; Part II focuses on postbellum America, and writers such
as Kate Chopin, Malcom Cowley, and Allen Tate.

L 633. **SIMPSON, LEWIS P.** The Man of Letters in New England and the South:
Essays on the History of the Literary Vocation in America. Baton
Rouge: Louisiana State University Press, 1973. 256 pp.
Simpson organizes these ten previously published essays into two sections.
The first part, entitled "The New England Ideal," treats the early 19th-
century Boston minister Joseph Stevens Buckminster, the New England mer-
chant Fredric Tudor and his brother William, Ralph Waldo Emerson, and
William Dean Howells. The second section, "The Southern Quest for Literary
Authority," contains essays on Edgar Allan Poe, Mark Twain, William Faulkner,
George Marion O'Donnell and modern Southern literary criticism, Southern
novelists, and the Agrarians. Of these authors, Simpson writes "about
their possession of letters—in some cases about their being possessed
by letters."

L 634. **SKAGGS, MERRILL MAGUIRE.** The Folk of Southern Fiction. Athens:
University of Georgia Press, 1972. 280 pp.
Skaggs's purpose is to discuss a specific part of "southern American local
color fiction"—the literary use of "the plain folk." The tradition began
with the Southwestern humorists of the 1830s. After discussing them,
Skaggs goes on to examine the social and economic bases for such characters,
the nature of their lives, and the various stereotypes made of them, and
concludes with the 20th-century masters of the tradition: William Faulkner,
Eudora Welty, and Flannery O'Connor.

L 635. **SKARDAL, DOROTHY BURTON.** The Divided Heart: Scandinavian Immigrant
Experience through Literary Sources. Lincoln: University of
Nebraska Press, 1974. 394 pp.
This book proposes "to use literary works as historical documents, in
an attempt to preserve the depth, vividness, and complexity of individual
human lives within the broad generalizations of history." The literature
of the Scandinavian immigrant experience began in the 1870s and was mostly
exhausted, through assimilation, by the 1940s. Skardal studies virtually
every literary genre, and concludes that, with the addition of necessary
historical analysis, the work tells a complete "inside story" of immigrant
experience.

L 636. **SLOTKIN, RICHARD.** Regeneration through Violence: The Mythology
of the American Frontier, 1600-1860. Middletown, Conn.: Wesleyan
University Press, 1973. 670 pp.
According to Slotkin, a country's mythology is the key to approaching
its national character. He believes the early colonists saw in America
a way to regenerate themselves economically, spiritually, and nationally,
but that the means to regeneration came to include violence. At this
point, the myth of regeneration through violence became the structuring
metaphor of the American experience. By examining relevant literature,
Slotkin shows how this myth evolved and how it gained credence and power.
The author traces his thesis over two and a half centuries. He focuses

on many works of early American literature concerned with the Indian and
the frontier.

L 637. **SPENDER, STEPHEN.** Love-Hate Relations: English and American Sen-
        sibilities. New York: Random House, 1974. 318 pp.
Spender examines both the common literature, language, and tradition of
England and America and the "revolutionary break" of America from European
history. Throughout the first 150 years of American culture, American
writers formed their ideas of their own country by comparing it to England,
and they created a literature which both accepted and rejected European
conventions. Spender studies this ambivalence in such American writers
as Emerson, Whitman, James, and Pound, as well as the reaction of English
writers such as E. M. Forster and D. H. Lawrence, whose Studies in Classic
American Literature is one of Spender's prime texts.

L 638. **SPENGEMANN, WILLIAM C.** The Adventurous Muse: The Poetics of Ameri-
        can Fiction, 1789-1900. New Haven, Conn.: Yale University Press,
        1977. 290 pp.
Spengemann focuses on a natural contrast in American writing between works
of travel and adventure and works of domestic existence. Travel is a
way of testing and forming the self, however dangerously; the hearth is
a place to be, in virtue and safety. Both have consequences for fiction,
as we are shown especially in such works as Modern Chivalry, Charlotte
Temple, The Narrative of Arthur Gordon Pym, The Deerslayer, "Roger Malvin's
Burial," Moby-Dick, and Huckleberry Finn.

L 639. **SPER, FELIX.** From Native Roots: A Panorama of Our Regional Drama.
        Caldwell, Idaho: Caxton, 1948. 342 pp.
Sper finds the origins of regional drama in tales of folk heroes. These
figures came to drama in the late 19th century through realistic fiction
and anthropological studies of folk culture. Earlier, only caricatures
of Indians, Negroes, and Yankees had provided indigenous American elements
to local theater. In the 20th century regional drama has developed fully
in thirteen areas from Yankee New England to the white South and the
Pacific Northwest. Sper's descriptive study surveys the field and provides
an extensive bibliography.

L 640. **SPILLER, ROBERT E.** Late Harvest: Essays and Addresses in American
        Literature and Culture. Westport, Conn.: Greenwood Press, 1981.
        280 pp.
This collection of essays by one of the first scholars of the American
Studies movement is framed by autobiographical commentary; Spiller introduces each essay by placing it in the context of his career. The first
three essays deal with the central ideas which gave form to his scholarly
work. The next seven essays are concerned with the "philosophical and
architectural aspects" of American literary history, and the last four
provide a succinct history of the formation and growth of American Studies.

L 641. **SPILLER, ROBERT E.** Milestones in American Literary History. West-
        port, Conn.: Greenwood Press, 1977. 152 pp.
Thirty-two reviews (1922-1960) of key books in American literature and
thought are listed in this volume, with two prefaces--one to Spiller's
The Cycle of American Literature and one to the Literary History of the
United States--and "A Letter to American Literary Historians." Taken
together, these constitute Spiller's response to major interpretations
of American literature over approximately four decades. Reviews of such
books as Matthiessen's American Renaissance (see L 163), Parrington's
Main Currents in American Thought (see L 15), and Cowley's Exile's Return
(see L 254) reflect Spiller's concern with the cultural contexts of American literary study.

L 642. SPILLER, ROBERT E. The Oblique Light: Studies in Literary History
and Biography. New York: Macmillan, 1968. 280 pp.
Spiller has collected here previously published essays "which focus on
individual writers and seem to have contributed to important reinterpre-
tations by setting the artist back into what can be reconstructed of his
own physical, emotional, and intellectual environments." He divides the
work into four sections: "The Discoverers" (Franklin, Cooper, W. E.
Channing, Emerson); "The Shapers" (Hawthorne, Lanier, Henry Adams, Edmund
Wilson); "Trans-Atlantic Perspectives" ("The English Literary Horizon:
1815-35" and "The American in Europe"); and a "Postscript" ("Those Early
Days: A Personal Memoir").

L 643. SPRINGER, MARLENE, ed. What Manner of Woman: Essays on English
and American Life and Literature. New York: New York University
Press, 1977. 357 pp.
The essays collected here, which cover British and American literature
and history from medieval to modern times, contrast literary women to
real women; their functions as symbols rather than persons in literature
and often in society; their actual and imagined sexuality; and their legal,
economic, and intellectual status. The work proceeds chronologically,
examining first the major periods of English literature and then the main
movements in American literature. Its purpose, however, is not to offer
an original perspective on literature but to provide scholars with a compendium and overview of women as characters and authors.

L 644. STANFORD, CHARLES L. The Quest for Paradise: Europe and the American Moral Imagination. Urbana: University of Illinois Press,
1961. 282 pp.
Stanford defines "the dominant American mode of apprehending reality" as
the never-ending search for an earthly paradise. He traces this search
from the American beginnings through the 19th century in various imaginative and religious forms, paying particular attention to Thomas Jefferson
and Henry James. He concludes with chapters on 20th-century diplomacy
(seen in the light of this quest) and literature, the main theme of which
"has been the dispossession from paradise." Nevertheless, "the myth of
Eden continues to dominate the American imagination."

L 645. STEPTO, ROBERT. From Behind the Veil: A Study of Afro-American
Narrative. Urbana: University of Illinois Press, 1979.
203 pp.
Stepto has assembled a "history of the historical consciousness" of Afro-
American written narrative. The work divides into two sections entitled
"The Call" and "The Response." "The Call" investigates the formal char-
acteristics of four slave narratives. Stepto presents the various forms
of narrative through the works of Henry Bibb, Solomon Northrup, Frederick
Douglass, and William Wells Brown. An examination of Booker T. Washington's
and W. E. B. DuBois's revision and revoicing of these narrative types
completes the first section. "The Response" focuses on three works:
The Autobiography of an Ex-Colored Man, Black Boy, and Invisible Man.
These works of the modern era echo the themes of immersion and ascent
of earlier writings and point to the new forms of narrative in Afro-
American literature.

L 646. STEWART, GRACE. A New Mythos: The Novel of the Artist as Heroine,
1877-1977. St. Alban's, Vt.: Eden Press Women's Publications,
1979. 200 pp.
Past work on myth by Levi-Strauss, Campbell, Jung, and others suffers
from a patriarchal bias, Stewart argues. Her response is to focus on
female authors' use of mythic patterns. Central to her discussion are
the Faust and Persephone myths, and the Kuntstlerroman, which she considers
a subcategory of quest literature. She discusses Sylvia Plath, Willa

Cather, Natalie Petesch, Muriel Spark, Mary Austin, Zelda Fitzgerald, Erica Jong, May Sarton, and Elizabeth Stuart Phelps in terms of their relation to those myths, tracing the pattern of the interior journey to the underworld or through a labyrinth. In discussing authors, Stewart emphasizes their literary work, though she draws on biographical, psychoanalytic, and anthropological scholarship.

L 647. STEWART, RANDALL. American Literature and Christian Doctrine.
        Baton Rouge: Louisiana State University Press, 1958. 154 pp.
Calling his book "an exploration, tentative and fragmentary," Stewart warns that he will "approach the subject of literature and religion from the literary side." He is particularly interested in the relation to Christian doctrine of Franklin, Emerson, Hawthorne, Melville, James, Crane, Dreiser, Wolfe, Eliot, Hemingway, Faulkner, and Warren. His conclusion is that most of our best writers, however heterodox, are concerned with "eternal moral welfare."

L 648. STOUT, JANIS P. The Journey Narrative in American Literature:
        Patterns and Departures. Westport, Conn.: Greenwood Press, 1983.
        272 pp.
The purpose of this volume is to explore the less obvious functions of "the journey" as theme and symbolic action in American literature. After a prefatory chapter which generally treats the relation of the journey to American aspirations, Stout identifies and defines the basic, recurrent "patterns of journey narrative" in a broad range of literature, from James Fenimore Cooper to Jack Kerouac. She then examines various "departures" or variations from these patterns, in which the journey serves a more complex and "multidimensional" function. Authors discussed in this section include Herman Melville, William Faulkner, Hart Crane, Wallace Stevens, Saul Bellow, and Philip Roth.

L 649. STROUT, CUSHING. The Veracious Imagination: Essays on American
        History, Literature, and Biography. Middletown, Conn.: Wesleyan
        University Press, 1981. 290 pp.
In this collection of essays (most of them previously published), Strout opposes the assumption that only scientific laws embody truth and champions the ability of narrative "to provide genuine explanation." He investigates the related fields of history, fiction, biography, and psychoanalysis—all of which rely, at least traditionally, on narrative (chronological ordering). Structuralists, he argues, allow their "voracious imaginations" to fictionalize history—reduce it to rhetoric—but society needs the "veracious imagination" (a term borrowed from George Eliot) that will historicize fiction. Strout also attempts to counter the tendency in criticism to overemphasize the mythological element of American literature, examines the recent revival of the documentary, and discusses the use and abuse by historians of other methodologies (notably psychoanalysis). He cites or analyzes numerous critical, literary, and intellectual works of both the 19th and 20th centuries.

L 650. SUTTON, WALTER. American Free Verse: The Modern Revolution in
        Poetry. New York: New Directions, 1973. 230 pp.
"Emphasizing both theory and practice," the author states in his foreword, "the following chapters discuss representative figures and groups of poets from the beginning of the 19th century, through the revolutionary modern period, in which free verse was established as a dominant mode, to the contemporary post-war years, which have produced a rich variety of poetic interests and achievements." American poets (e.g., Whitman, Pound, Cummings, Williams) have dominated modern free verse: of late, the attention of their successors has turned from aesthetic to social concerns.

L 651. TANNER, TONY. The Reign of Wonder: Naivety and Reality in American
        Literature. New York: Cambridge University Press, 1965. 388 pp.
Tanner asserts that American writers inherited from Wordsworth and the
Romantics a regard for wonder--the child's passive admiration rather than
judgment. In the 19th century, Americans adopted this "wondering vision"
to deal with their new world; in contemporary literature they still prefer
this stance. Tanner makes four major divisions: the Transcendentalists
(Thoreau, Whitman, and particularly Emerson); Mark Twain; the 20th century
(Stein, Anderson, Hemingway); and Henry James. He concludes with a contrast between J. D. Salinger's "mystic" horror and Walker Percy's "naive"
wonder at society. Tanner identifies a recurring problem with form, noting
the existence of "some prior notion of shaping intent, some initial focus
which directs vision without determining results."

L 652. TAYLOR, WILLIAM R. Cavalier and Yankee: The Old South and American
        National Character. New York: Braziller, 1961. 384 pp.
This study of the history of ideas sets out to "isolate the conditions
in America" which led, by 1860, to the "idea of a divided culture"--the
widespread notion that characteristic differences existed between North-
erner and Southerner. Theoretical and practical discussions, conducted
by various writers and thinkers from the beginnings of the Republic, tended
to provoke "this kind of introspection and myth-making, especially in
the South." Taylor tells much about the national mind when he examines
the longevity of the American belief in the "Old South."

L 653. TICHI, CECELIA. New World, New Earth: Environmental Reform in
        American Literature from the Puritans Through Whitman. New Haven,
        Conn.: Yale University Press, 1979. 290 pp.
Tichi's central thesis is that American writers before and including
Whitman considered environmental reform inseparable from America's moral
regeneration. Land reform, she argues, has strong ties to millennialist
history and the American desire to construct a Utopian new earth. In
addition to familiar texts by major figures, Tichi uses magazine articles,
letters, speeches, and diaries to support her view. Whole chapters are
devoted to Puritan land reform; Edward Johnson; the dogma of the "engineered earth" of the Revolutionary period; Joel Barlow; Thoreau; Cooper
and Bancroft as skeptical assessors of the New Millenium; and Whitman
as an environmental reformer.

L 654. TRILLING, LIONEL. The Liberal Imagination: Essays on Literature
        and Society. New York: Viking Press, 1950. 303 pp.
This collection of essays, some of which appeared in literary journals,
opposes V. L. Parrington's idea of culture as a "flowing stream." Trilling
suggests that culture is dialectical, with liberalism forming one element
in that dialectic. Liberal criticism should convey the variousness, the
possibilities, and complexities of society. Thus Henry James is superior
to Theodore Dreiser because James's way of thinking involves not only
material but moral realities. Certain books--Huckleberry Finn and, to
a lesser degree, Winesburg, Ohio--render the truth and reality of moral
passion. Several essays explore the complex relationship between art
and Freudian psychology. Trilling's discussion ranges from the novels
of James and Fitzgerald, to the little literary magazines, to the Kinsey
Report on American sexual habits.

L 655. TURNER, LORENZO DOW. Anti-Slavery Sentiment in American Literature
        Prior to 1865. Washington, D.C.: Association for the Study of
        Negro Life and History, 1929. 188 pp.
The five main chapters of Dow's study are arranged around natural eras
in the history of slavery in the United States from 1641 to 1865. During
these eras the grounds for resisting slavery shifted according to moral,
religious, social, economic, political, and sentimental factors. Early

in American history, the basis was chiefly didactic and religious, according to the literary practices and cultural concerns of the time; by the mid-19th century the grounds of opposition were mainly moral and sentimental—Uncle Tom's Cabin being its chief exemplar. A wide range of literature—including social, economic, and religious texts—is consulted throughout the course of the study.

L 656. TUTTLETON, JAMES W. The Novel of Manners in America. Chapel Hill: University of North Carolina Press, 1972. 304 pp.
Tuttleton's opening chapter defines the novel of manners, discusses the typical ways in which authors have generated the illusion of society, and explains the difficulties American authors have had finding materials suitable to the genre in their country's unusually young and homogeneous culture. Succeeding chapters present the achievements of ten important American novelists of manners: Cooper, James, Howells, Wharton, Lewis, Fitzgerald, O'Hara, Marquand, Cozzens, and Auchincloss. Tuttleton tries to provide a broad base of evidence for his generalizations by covering many novels, instead of exploring the more subtle variations of the genre.

L 657. UMPHLETT, WILEY LEE. The Sporting Myth and the American Experience. Cranbury, N.J.: Associated University Presses, 1975. 205 pp.
Umphlett contends that the American sporting experience "has provided the American writer with a rich source of subject matter, which . . . can and often does have profound meaning." Treating the work of Cooper, Hemingway, and Updike, among others, Umphlett argues that many American writers have used the dynamics of sport as mythological coordinates upon which they plot the search for psychological and moral meaning. The emblematic American hero is often embodied in an athlete or sportsman, and his archetypal movement from innocence to experience—a movement generally predicated upon a moment or moments of encounter between the hero and nature, society, or the self—has taken a variety of sporting forms, ranging from Natty Bumppo living on the frontier to Santiago struggling to reel the great marlin to Roy Hobbs's decision to throw the world series.

L 658. WADLINGTON, WARWICK. The Confidence Game in American Literature. Princeton, N.J.: Princeton University Press, 1975. 321 pp.
Wadlington examines works by three American authors: Herman Melville, Mark Twain, and Nathanael West. He chooses the Trickster archetype, which stands for a protean force of continuing origination, to describe not only the world imagined by these authors but also the relationship between them and their readers. Confidence, according to Wadlington, depends upon fixed boundaries and mutual belief, but the Trickster "dissolves boundaries" and "creates new alignments." Wadlington argues that Americans have always been "confidence men"—dispensers of assurance—but that the current "existential failure of confidence" has caused us to place a greater value on the works he discusses—works in which the characters, and to some degree, the authors are tricksters. He also argues that the writings of Melville, Mark Twain, and West resist resolution and are not, as some critics have argued, apocalyptic.

L 659. WAGGONER, HYATT H. American Visionary Poetry. Baton Rouge: Louisiana State University Press, 1982. 226 pp.
Noting that "visionary" is a word often applied imprecisely to poetry, Waggoner tries to establish a definition. Visionary poetry—"a cultural symptom destined to disappear as culture changes"—is created by poets who, according to Waggoner, perceive "what is 'out there,' beyond the conscious mind and the self, . . . using the senses and imaginative intelligence as a means of discovery." He begins his discussion of poets with Whitman, whom he calls "our greatest poet." Other poets he identifies as visionary poets and discusses are Crane, Williams, Roethke, Ammons, and David Wagoner. (Dickinson, Frost, Eliot, and Stevens—not visionaries—

are discussed in an appendix.) Positing that visionary poetry can survive
with uncertainty but not with skepticism, Waggoner expresses optimism
(drawing on writings by the philosophers William Barrett and Gregory
Bateson) that visionary poems may become less--not more--rare in the near
future.

L 660. WALCUTT, CHARLES CHILD. American Literary Naturalism: A Divided
Stream. Minneapolis: University of Minnesota Press, 1956.
332 pp.
Walcutt's first chapter defines Naturalism as a philosophical attitude,
shared by a number of American novelists who wrote between 1890 and 1940,
which accepted the premises of materialistic determinism. The work of
these novelists often suffers from "a never-resolved tension between the
ideal of perfect unity and the brutal facts of existence"--a tension
between Transcendentalism and scientific positivism, between determinism's
exclusion of free will and the novelists' desires for social reform.
Because Naturalism was a philosophical orientation--not a stylistic movement like Romanticism or Realism--its history can be seen as a continual
search for an appropriate form. The later chapters of Walcutt's work
follow this search in the works of Zola and ten American Naturalistic
authors.

L 661. WALKER, CHERYL. The Nightingale's Burden: Women Poets and American
Culture Before 1900. Bloomington: Indiana University Press,
1982. 189 pp.
The Nightingale's Burden takes up the question of an American women's
poetic tradition. Walker uses the recurring figure of Philomela, the
mythological violated woman who became a nightingale, to frame her discussion of women's conformity and resistance to male culture and conventional strictures on women's roles, and women poets' ambivalence toward
power and self-sacrifice. Major figures such as Anne Bradstreet and Emily
Dickinson are discussed along with poets of the sentimental and post-
sentimental traditions; the final chapter discusses their legacy to 20th-
century women poets. Some biographical information is provided, but more
emphasis is placed on overall historical and cultural context.

L 662. WATTS, EMILY STIPES. The Poetry of American Women from 1632 to
1945. Austin: University of Texas Press, 1977. 218 pp.
The poetry written by American women before 1945, says Watt, has been
unfairly neglected, in part because it has not "expressed the essentially
male image of the transcendent hero or American Adam." To correct this
oversight, she examines six periods in American history, focusing on such
poets as Anne Bradstreet, Emily Dickinson, and Gertrude Stein, as well
as such lesser-known authors as Mercy Otis Warren, Ann Bleecker, Elizabeth
Oakes Smith, Lydia Huntley Sigourney, and Elinor Wylie. "Feminist realism,"
according to Watts, is perhaps the characteristic of the poetry.

L 663. WEIMER, DAVID. The City as Metaphor. New York: Random House,
1966. 151 pp.
How have American writers responded to American cities? Weimer sets out
to answer this question by describing how our cities have been overhauled,
appropriated, and sometimes even invented by our best literary imaginations.
The nature of the process is shown in individual chapters on Whitman,
James, Crane, Dreiser, Cummings, Fitzgerald, William Carlos Williams,
and Auden.

L 664. WESTBROOK, PERRY D. Free Will and Determinism in American Litera-
     ture. Cranbury, N.J.: Associated Universities Press, 1979.
     275 pp.
Westbrook argues that American literature alternates between Naturalist
and Humanist tendencies, or refinements and syntheses of those doctrines.
He discusses Zola, Marx, Freud, Spencer, and other writers, grounding
his argument with an examination of the writings of Calvin and Augustine.
Arminianism, Deism, Transcendentalism, and Pragmatism are chief among
the movements touched upon in this study. Authors such as Wigglesworth,
Taylor, Hawthorne, Melville, Freeman, Dickinson, Brown, Holmes, Stowe,
Twain, Crane, Norris, London, Dreiser, Glasgow, Faulkner, Howells, James,
Wharton, Cather, and Hemingway are discussed in chronological order, and
grouped as Westbrook interprets their stand in relation to his key concepts.

L 665. WESTBROOK, WAYNE W. Wall Street in the American Novel. New York:
     New York University Press, 1980. 213 pp.
Westbrook surveys novels which in some way are concerned with the stock
market and speculation. The symbolic significance of Wall Street to
authors from Melville to Bellow, argues Westbrook, can be traced back to
what the Puritans of the Bay Colony said about gambling: "a sinful violation of the laws of honesty." Thus every Wall Street novel is about
the Fall, and not about the psyches of businessmen. Westbrook's book
progresses chronologically, intertwining discussions of American economic
history with such fictional themes as money and lust, guilt, and diabolical
pacts.

L 666. WILSON, EDMUND. Axel's Castle: A Study in the Imaginative Litera-
     ture of 1870-1930. New York: Scribner, 1931. 319 pp.
Wilson's purpose in the first of his extended literary studies is to demonstrate that "W. B. Yeats, James Joyce, T. S. Eliot, Gertrude Stein, Marcel
Proust and Paul Valery represent the culmination of a self-conscious and
very important literary movement." That movement, a "counterpart" to
Romanticism, is Symbolism. Wilson traces the movement through its modern
masters, defining the nature of this phenomenon and its relation to modern
literary culture.

L 667. WINTERS, YVOR. In Defense of Reason. 1947; Rev. ed. Denver:
     Swallow Press, 1960. 611 pp.
Most of the essays in this volume are reprinted form earlier books by
Winters: Primitivism and Decadence (see L 429), Maule's Curse (see L
668), and The Anatomy of Nonsense (1943). Throughout these essays
Winters's criticism rests upon his central criterion that the best literature
is that which most efficiently communicates a statement about human experience by utilizing both the denotative and connotative powers of words.
He believes that poetry is more efficient, and therefore more highly
developed, than prose because it also takes advantage of the conventions
of rhythmic and formal organization. Moreover, Winters judges poems according to their moral stance. He believes in the existence of "absolute
truths" and holds that most poetry suffers from having faulty moral
premises.

L 668. WINTERS, YVOR. Maule's Curse: Seven Studies in the History of
     American Obscurantism: Hawthorne--Cooper--Melville--Poe--Emerson--
     Jones Very--Emily Dickinson--Henry James. Norfolk, Conn.: New
     Directions, 1938. 240 pp.
This work is an extension of Winters's earlier critical volume on 20th-
century American experimental poetry, Primitivism and Decadence (see L
429). The present volume also studies the forms of conscious or unconscious obscurantism which, the author claims, are the ultimate development
of Romantic aesthetic principles qualified by American history. Essentially, Winters tries to assess the intellectual or moral significance
of literary forms by examining the individual 19th-century authors mentioned in the subtitle.

L 669. WRIGHT, AUSTIN M. The Formal Principle in the Novel. Ithaca,
        N.Y.: Cornell University Press, 1982. 308 pp.
An examination of the theoretical principle of unity in the novel is the
focus of Wright's study. He first redefines the principle by considering
the assumptions on which it rests, its function as a descriptive tool,
and its use as a practical device. In particular, "plot," the relation
of the novel to novellas, short stories, and non-literary art find new
definitions. Wright then defends them through an analysis of The Portrait
of a Lady, The Sound and the Fury, Ironside Man, and Pale Fire. The book
closes with a discussion of Wright's own novelistic practices.

L 670. WRIGHT, NATHALIA. American Novelists in Italy: The Discoverers:
        Allston to James. Philadelphia: University of Pennsylvania Press,
        1965. 288 pp.
This work is "concerned with the influence of their experiences in Italy
on the fiction of the first group of American writers to be notably
affected by travel in that country." After two early chapters on the literary explorers of Italy--including Washington Allston, Irving, Tuckerman,
and Harriet Beecher Stowe--the study devotes one chapter each to Cooper,
Hawthorne, Howells, and James. A concluding chapter suggests that, from
Allston on, the American novels based in Italy have a characteristic pattern, and that their writers found in Italy both inspiration and restraint.

L 671. YOUNG, PHILIP. Three Bags Full: Essays in American Fiction.
        New York: Harcourt Brace Jovanovich, 1972. 231 pp.
Young's collection of essays falls into three sections (the three "bags"
of his title). He devotes his first section to four essays on Hemingway.
The second "bag" contains pieces on Hawthorne criticism, The House of
the Seven Gables, Typee, Huckleberry Finn, and the reaction of the American
novel to American life. Finally, the third "bag" comprises two seminal
essays on Pocahontas and Rip Van Winkle.

L 672. YU, BEONGCHEON. The Great Circle: American Writers and the Orient.
        Detroit, Mich.: Wayne State University Press, 1983. 266 pp.
Yu focuses on the influence of "orientalism" in American literature; he
is especially concerned with those writers who responded directly to Indian,
Chinese, and Japanese culture, and who thereby helped develop a tradition
of "American literary orientalism." Part One examines the influence of
the Orient, particularly Indian religion and philosophy, on the thought
of Ralph Waldo Emerson, Henry David Thoreau, and Walt Whitman. In Part
Two, Yu looks at how the literary careers of Henry Adams, John La Farge,
Percival Lowell, Ernest Fenollosa, and Lafcadio Hearn were affected by
the authors' travels or "pilgrimages" to Japan. Part Three follows the
development of American orientalism into the 20th century, devoting a
chapter each to Irving Babbitt, Eugene O'Neill, T. S. Eliot, and Ezra
Pound. The epilogue briefly traces the impact of the Orient on the postwar
Beat generation, with special attention given to J. D. Salinger, Jack
Kerouac, and Gary Snyder.

L 673. ZLOTNICK, JOAN. Portrait of an American City: The Novelists'
        New York. Port Washington, N.Y.: Kennikat Press, 1982.
        250 pp.
Zlotkin considers fictional depictions of New York City. Ranging through
an extensive bibliography of primary materials, the study examines the
positive and negative images of New York presented in American literature.
Thus, Zlotkin surveys major periods in American literary history: Colonial
America and the New Republic; Antebellum North; The Gay Nineties; The
Early Twentieth Century; Post-World War Two; and Contemporary America.